MW00784692

The Complete Plays of George Bernard Shaw (1893-1921)

By

George Bernard Shaw

ISBN: 978-1-78139-348-2

Contents

WIDOWERS' HOUSES

ACT I ... 9
ACT II ... 17
ACT III ... 28

THE PHILANDERER

ACT I ... 37
ACT II ... 47
ACT III ... 54
ACT IV ... 62

MRS WARREN'S PROFESSION

THE AUTHOR'S APOLOGY ... 71
ACT I ... 82
ACT II ... 89
ACT III ... 98
ACT IV ... 104

ARMS AND THE MAN

INTRODUCTION ... 113
ACT I ... 115
ACT II ... 122
ACT III ... 132

CANDIDA

ACT I ... 145
ACT II ... 156
ACT III ... 165

THE MAN OF DESTINY

THE MAN OF DESTINY ... 175

YOU NEVER CAN TELL

ACT I ... 195
ACT II ... 206
ACT III ... 221
ACT IV ... 230

THE DEVIL'S DISCIPLE

ACT I ... 241
ACT II ... 251
ACT III ... 260
NOTES TO THE DEVIL'S DISCIPLE ... 272
BURGOYNE ... 272
BRUDENELL ... 275

CAESAR AND CLEOPATRA

ACT I ... 277
ACT II ... 286
ACT III ... 296
ACT IV ... 305
ACT V ... 317
NOTES TO CAESAR AND CLEOPATRA ... 320
CLEOPATRA'S CURE FOR BALDNESS ... 320

CAPTAIN BRASSBOUND'S CONVERSION

ACT I 325

ACT II 335

ACT III 347

NOTES TO CAPTAIN BRASSBOUND'S CONVERSION 359

SOURCES OF THE PLAY 359

MAN AND SUPERMAN

EPISTLE DEDICATORY TO ARTHUR BINGHAM WALKLEY 363

ACT I 376

ACT II 394

ACT III 403

ACT IV 432

PASSION, POISON, AND PETRIFACTION

PASSION, POISON, AND PETRIFACTION 447

JOHN BULL'S OTHER ISLAND

ACT I 455

ACT II 465

ACT III 473

ACT IV 485

HOW HE LIED TO HER HUSBAND

PREFACE 501

HOW HE LIED TO HER HUSBAND 503

MAJOR BARBARA

ACT I 513

ACT II 522

ACT III 538

THE INTERLUDE AT THE PLAYHOUSE

THE INTERLUDE AT THE PLAYHOUSE 555

THE ADMIRABLE BASHVILLE

PREFACE 559

ACT I 562

ACT II 564

ACT III 572

NOTE ON MODERN PRIZEFIGHTING 575

PRESS CUTTINGS

PRESS CUTTINGS 583

THE DOCTOR'S DILEMMA:

ACT I 601

ACT II 615

ACT III 621
ACT IV 631
ACT V 638

GETTING MARRIED

GETTING MARRIED 643

THE SHEWING-UP OF BLANCO POSNET

THE SHEWING-UP OF BLANCO POSNET 685

MISALLIANCE

MISALLIANCE 698

THE DARK LADY OF THE SONNETS

THE DARK LADY OF THE SONNETS 739

FANNY'S FIRST PLAY

PREFACE TO FANNY'S FIRST PLAY 747
INDUCTION 748
ACT I 754
ACT II 759
ACT III 764
EPILOGUE 776

ANDROCLES AND THE LION

PROLOGUE 781
ACT I 783
ACT II 790
EXPLANATION 799

PYGMALION

PREFACE TO PYGMALION 803
A Professor of Phonetics. 803
ACT I 805
ACT II 809
ACT III 820
ACT IV 827
ACT V 830

OVERRULED

PREFACE TO OVERRULED. 845
THE ALLEVIATIONS OF MONOGAMY. 845
INACCESSIBILITY OF THE FACTS. 845
THE CONVENTION OF JEALOUSY 846
THE MISSING DATA OF A SCIENTIFIC NATURAL HISTORY OF MARRIAGE. 846
ARTIFICIAL RETRIBUTION. 847
THE FAVORITE SUBJECT OF FARCICAL COMEDY. 847
THE PSEUDO SEX PLAY. 848
ART AND MORALITY 848
THE LIMITS OF STAGE PRESENTATION. 848
PRUDERIES OF THE FRENCH STAGE 849
OUR DISILLUSIVE SCENERY. 849

HOLDING THE MIRROR UP TO NATURE................ 850
FARCICAL COMEDY SHIRKING ITS SUBJECT............................ 850
OVERRULED................................... 851

GREAT CATHERINE (WHOM GLORY STILL ADORES)

THE AUTHOR'S APOLOGY FOR GREAT CATHERINE 863
THE FIRST SCENE 866
THE SECOND SCENE 871
THE THIRD SCENE 875
THE FOURTH SCENE 876

THE INCA OF PERUSALEM

PROLOGUE....................................... 883
THE PLAY....................................... 884

AUGUSTUS DOES HIS BIT

AUGUSTUS DOES HIS BIT 895

ANNAJANSKA, THE BOLSHEVIK EMPRESS

ANNAJANSKA, THE BOLSHEVIK EMPRESS 905

HEARTBREAK HOUSE

ACT I... 913
ACT II 930
ACT III 948

O'FLAHERTY V.C.

A RECRUITING PAMPHLET.......... 957
O'FLAHERTY V.C. 958

BACK TO METHUSELAH

PART I 969
ACT I 969
ACT II 976
PART II 982
PART III... 1003
PART IV... 1022
ACT I 1022
ACT II..................................... 1036
ACT III.................................... 1044
PART V. 1047

WIDOWERS' HOUSES

ACT I

In the garden restaurant of a hotel at Remagen on the Rhine, on a fine afternoon in August in the eighteen-eighties. Looking down the Rhine towards Bonn, the gate leading from the garden to the riverside is seen on the right. The hotel is on the left. It has a wooden annexe with an entrance marked Table d'Hote. A waiter is in attendance.

A couple of English tourists come out of the hotel. The younger, Dr Harry Trench, is about 24, stoutly built, thick in the neck, close-cropped and black in the hair, with undignified medical-student manners, frank, hasty, rather boyish. The other, Mr William de Burgh Cokane, is older probably over 40, possibly 50 an ill-nourished, scanty-haired gentleman, with affected manners ; fidgety, touchy, and constitutionally ridiculous in uncompassionate eyes.

COKANE [*on the threshold of the hotel, calling peremptorily to the waiter*] Two beers for us out here. [*The waiter goes for the beer. Cokane comes into the garden*]. We have got the room with the best view in the hotel, Harry, thanks to my tact. We'll leave in the morning and do Mainz and Frankfurt. There is a very graceful female statue in the private house of a nobleman in Frankfurt. Also a zoo. Next day, Nuremberg ! finest collection of instruments of torture in the world.

TRENCH. All right. You look out the trains, will you ? [*He takes out a Continental Brads haw, and tosses it on one of the tables*].

COKANE [*baulking himself in the act of sitting down*] Pah ! the seat is all dusty. These foreigners are deplorably unclean in their habits.

TRENCH [*buoyantly*] Never mind : it dont matter, old chappie. Buck up, Billy, buck up. Enjoy yourself. [*He throws Cokane into the chair, and sits down opposite him, taking out his pipe, and singing noisily*]

Pour out the Rhine wine : let it flow Like a free and bounding river

COKANE [*scandalized*] In the name of common decency, Harry, will you remember that you are a gentleman and not a coster on Hampstead Heath on Bank Holiday ? Would you dream of behaving like this in London ?

TRENCH. Oh, rot ! Ive come abroad to enjoy myself. So would you if youd just passed an examination after four years in the medical school and walking the hospital. [*He again bursts into song*].

COKANE [*rising*] Trench : either you travel as a gentleman, or you travel alone. This is what makes Englishmen unpopular on the Continent. It may not matter before the natives ; but the people who came on board the steamer at Bonn are English. I have been uneasy all the afternoon about what they must think of us. Look at our appearance.

TRENCH. Whats wrong with our appearance ?

COKANE. Neglige, my dear fellow, neglige. On the steamboat a little neglige was quite en regie ; but here, in this hotel, some of them are sure to dress for dinner ; and you have nothing but that Norfolk jacket. How are they to know that you are well connected if you do not shew it by your manners ?

TRENCH. Pooh ! the steamboat people were the scum of the earth Americans and all sorts. They may go hang themselves, Billy. I shall not bother about them. [*He strikes a match, and proceeds to light his pipe*].

COKANE. Do drop calling me Billy in public, Trench. My name is Cokane. I am sure they were persons of consequence : you were struck with the distinguished appearance of the father yourself.

TRENCH [*sobered at once*] What ! those people ? [*He blows out the match and puts up his pipe*].

COKANE [*following up his advantage triumphantly*] Here, Harry, here: at this hotel. I recognized the father's umbrella in the hall.

TRENCH [*with a touch of genuine shame*] I suppose I ought to have brought a change. But a lot of luggage is such a nuisance ; and [*rising abruptly*] at all events we can go and have a wash. [*He turns to go into the hotel, but stops in consternation, seeing some people coming up to the riverside gate*]. Oh, I say ! Here they are.

[*A lady and gentleman, followed by a porter with some light parcels, not luggage, but shop purchases, come into the garden. They are apparently father and daughter. The gentleman is 50, tall, well preserved, and of upright carriage. His incisive, domineering utterance and imposing style, with his strong aquiline nose and resolute clean-shaven mouth, give him an air of importance. He wears a light grey frock-coat with silk linings, a white hat, and a field-glass slung in a new leather case. A self-made man, formidable to servants, not easily accessible to anyone. His daughter is a well-dressed, well-fed, good-looking, strong-minded young woman, presentably ladylike, but still her father's daughter. Nevertheless fresh and attractive, and none the worse for being vital and energetic rather than delicate and refined*].

COKANE [*quickly taking the arm of Trench, who is staring as if transfixed*] Recollect yourself, Harry : presence of mind, presence of mind ! [*He strolls with him towards the hotel. The waiter comes out with the beer*]. Kellner: ceci-la est notre table. Est ce que vous comprenez Francais ?

WAITER. Yes, zare. Oil right, zare.

THE GENTLEMAN [*to his porter*] Place those things on that table. [*The porter does not understand*],

WAITER [*interposing*] Zese zhentellmen are using zis table, zare. Vould you mind

THE GENTLEMAN [*severely*] You should have told me so before. [*To Cokane, with fierce condescension*] I regret the mistake, sir.

COKANE. Dont mention it, my dear sir : dont mention it. Retain the place, I beg.

THE GENTLEMAN [*coldly turning his back on him*] Thank you. [*To the porter*] Place them on that table. [*The porter makes no movement until the gentleman points to the parcels and peremptorily raps on another table, nearer the gate*].

PORTER. Ja wohl, gnad'g' Herr. [*He puts down the parcels*].

THE GENTLEMAN [*taking out a handful of money*] Waiter.

WAITER [*awestruck*] Yes, zare.

THE GENTLEMAN. Tea. For two. Out here.

WAITER. Yes, zare. [*He goes into the hotel*].

[*The gentleman selects a small coin from his handful of money, and gives it to the porter, who receives it with a submissive touch to his cap, and goes out, not daring to speak. His daughter sits down and opens a parcel of photographs. The gentleman takes out a Baedeker; places a chair for himself; and then, before sitting down, looks truculently at Cokane, as if waiting for him to take himself off. Cokane, not at all abashed, resumes his place at the other table with an air of modest good breeding, and calls to Trench, who is prowling irresolutely in the background*].

COKANE. Trench, my dear fellow : your beer is waiting for you. [*He drinks*].

TRENCH [*glad of the excuse to come back to his chair*] Thank you, Cokane. [*He also drinks*].

COKANE. By the way, Harry, I have often meant to ask you : is Lady Roxdale your mother's sister or your father's ? [*This shot tells immediately. The gentleman is perceptibly interested*].

TRENCH. My mother's, of course. What put that into your head?

COKANE. Nothing. I was just thinking hm ! She will expect you to marry, Harry : a doctor ought to marry.

TRENCH. What has she got to do with it ?

COKANE. A great deal, dear boy. She looks forward to floating your wife in society in London.

TRENCH. What rot !

COKANE. Ah, you are young, dear boy : you dont know the importance of these things apparently idle ceremonial trifles, really the springs and wheels of a great aristocratic system. [*The waiter comes back with the tea things, which he brings to the gentleman's table. Cokane rises and addresses the gentleman*]. My dear sir, excuse my addressing you ; but I cannot help feeling that you prefer this table and that we are in your way.

THE GENTLEMAN [*graciously*] Thank you. Blanche : this gentleman very kindly offers us his table, if you would prefer it.

BLANCHE. Oh, thanks : it makes no difference.

THE GENTLEMAN [*to Cokane*] We are fellow travellers, I believe, sir.

COKANE. Fellow travellers and fellow countrymen. Ah, we rarely feel the charm of our own tongue until it reaches our ears under a foreign sky. You have no doubt noticed that ?

THE GENTLEMAN [*a little puzzled*] Hm ! From a romantic point of view, possibly, very possibly. As a matter of fact, the sound of English makes me feel at home ; and I dislike feeling at home when I am abroad. It is not precisely what one goes to the expense for. [*He looks at Trench"*]. I think this gentle-gentleman travelled with us also.

COKANE [*acting as master of the ceremonies*] My valued friend, Dr Trench. [*The gentleman and Trench rise*]. Trench, my dear fellow, allow me to introduce you to er ? [*He looks enquiringly at the gentleman, waiting for the name*]

THE GENTLEMAN. Permit me to shake your hand, Dr Trench. My name is Sartorius ; and I have the honor of being known to Lady Roxdale, who is, I believe, a near relative of yours. Blanche. [*Six looks up*]. Dr Trench. [*They bow*].

TRENCH. Perhaps I should introduce my friend Cokane to you, Mr Sartorius : Mr William de Burgh Cokane. [*Cokane makes an elaborate bow. Sartorius accepts it with dignity. The waiter meanwhile returns with teapot, hot water, etc.*].

SARTORIUS [*to the waiter*] Two more cups.

WAITER. Yes, zare. [*He goes into the hotel*].

BLANCHE. Do you take sugar, Mr Cokane ?

COKANE. Thank you. [*To Sartorius*] This is really too kind. Harry : bring your chair round.

SARTORIUS. You are very welcome. [*Trench brings his chair to the tea table ; and they all sit round it. The waiter returns with two more cups*].

WAITER. Table d'hote at 'alf past zix, zhentellmenn. Ahnyzing else now, zare ?

SARTORIUS. No. You can go. [*The waiter goes*].

COKANE [*very agreeably*] Do you contemplate a long stay here, Miss Sartorius ?

BLANCHE. We were thinking of going on to Rolandseck. Is it as nice as this place ?

COKANE. Harry : the Baedeker. Thank you. [*He consults the index, and looks out Rolandseck*].

BLANCHE. Sugar, Dr Trench ?

TRENCH. Thanks. [*She hands him the cup, and looks meaningly at Lim for an instant. He looks down hastily, and glances apprehensively at Sartorius, who is preoccupied with a piece of bread and butter*].

COKANE. Rolandseck appears to be an extremely interesting place. [*Rereads*] "It is one of the most beautiful and frequented spots on the river, and is surrounded with numerous villas and pleasant gardens, chiefly belonging to wealthy merchants from the Lower Rhine, and extending along the wooded slopes at the back of the village."

BLANCHE. That sounds civilized and comfortable. I vote we go there.

SARTORIUS. Quite like our place at Surbiton, my dear.

BLANCHE. Quite.

COKANE. You have a place down the river ? Ah, I envy you.

SARTORIUS. No : I have merely taken a furnished villa at Surbiton for the summer. I live in Bedford Square. I am a vestryman and must reside in the parish.

BLANCHE. Another cup, Mr Cokane ?

COKANE. Thank you, no. [*To Sartorius*] I presume you have been round this little place. Not much to see here, except the Apollinaris Church.

SARTORIUS [*scandalized*] The what !

COKANE. The Apollinaris Church.

SARTORIUS. A strange name to give a church. Very continental, I must say.

COKANE. Ah, yes, yes, yes. That is where our neighbors fall short sometimes, Mr Sartorius : taste taste is what they occasionally fail in. But in this instance they are not to blame. The water is called after the church, not the church after the water.

SARTORIUS [*as if this were an extenuating circumstance, but not a complete excuse*] I am glad to hear it. Is the church a celebrated one ?

COKANE. Baedeker stars it.

SARTORIUS [*respectfully*] Oh, in that case I should like to see it.

COKANE [*reading*] " erected in 1839 by Zwirner, the late eminent architect of the cathedral of Cologne, at the expense of Count Fiirstenberg-Stammheim."

SARTORIUS [*much impressed*] We must certainly see that, Mr Cokane. I had no idea that the architect of Cologne cathedral lived so recently.

BLANCHE. Dont let us bother about any more churches, papa. Theyre all the same ; and I'm tired to death of them.

SARTORIUS. Well, my dear, if you think it sensible to take a long and expensive journey to see what there is to be seen, and then go away without seeing it

BLANCHE. Not this afternoon, papa, please.

SARTORIUS. My dear : I should like you to see everything. It is part of your education

BLANCHE [*rising, with a petulant sigh*] Oh, my education ! Very well, very well : I suppose I must go through with it. Are you coming, Dr Trench I

[*With a grimace"*] I'm sure the Johannis Church will be a treat for you.

COKANE [*laughing softly and archly*] Ah, excellent, excellent : very good, indeed. [*Seriously*] But do you know, Miss Sartorius, there actually are Johannis churches here several of them as well as Apollinaris ones ?

SARTORIUS [*sententiously, taking out his fold-glass and leading the way to the gate*] There is many a true word spoken in jest, Mr Cokane.

COKANE [*accompanying him*] How true ! How true ! [*They go out together, ruminating profoundly. Blanche makes no movement to follow them. She watches until they are safely out of sight, and then posts herself before Trench, looking at him with an enigmatic smile, which he returns with a half sheepish, half conceited grin*] .

BLANCHE. Well ! So you have done it at last.

TRENCH. Yes. At least Cokane's done it. I told you he'd manage it. He's rather an ass in some ways ; but lie has tremendous tact.

BLANCHE [*contemptuously*] Tact ! Thats not tact : thats inquisitiveness. Inquisitive people always have a lot of practice in getting into conversation with strangers. Why didnt you speak to my father yourself on the boat ? You were ready enough to speak to me without any introduction,

TRENCH. I didnt particularly want to talk to him.

BLANCHE. It didnt occur to you, I suppose, that you put me in a false position by that.

TRENCH. Oh, I dont see that, exactly. Besides, your father isnt an easy man to tackle. Of course, now that I know him, I see that he's pleasant enough ; but then youve got to know him first, havnt you ?

BLANCHE [*impatiently*] Everybody is afraid of papa : I'm sure I dont know why. [*She sits down again, pouting a little*].

TRENCH [*tenderly*] However, it's all right now : isnt it ? [*He sits near her*].

BLANCHE [*sharply*] I dont know. How should I ? You had no right to speak to me that day on board the steamer. You thought I was alone, because [*with false pathos*] I had no mother with me.

TRENCH [*protesting*] Oh, I say ! Come ! It was you who spoke to me. Of course I was only too glad of the chance ; but on my word I shouldnt have moved an eyelid if you hadnt given me a lead.

BLANCHE. I only asked you the name of a castle. There was nothing unladylike in that.

TRENCH. Of course not. Why shouldnt you ? [*With renewed tenderness*] But it's all right now : isnt it ?

BLANCHE [*softly, looking subtly at him*] Is it ?

TRENCH [*suddenly becoming shy*] I I suppose so. By the way, what about the Apollinaris Church ? Your father expects us to follow him, doesnt he ?

BLANCHE [*with suppressed resentment*] Dont let me detain you if you wish to see it.

TRENCH. Wont you come ?

BLANCHE. No. [*She turns her face away moodily*].

TRENCH [*alarmed*] I say : youre not offended, are you ? [*She looks round at him for a moment with a reproachful film on her eyes*]. Blanche. [*She bristles instantly ; overdoes it ; and frightens him*], I beg your pardon for calling you by your name ; but I er [*She corrects her mistake by softening her expression eloquently. He responds with a gush*] You dont mind, do you ? I felt sure you wouldnt, somehow. Well, look here. I have no idea how you will

1 receive this : it must seem horribly abrupt ; but the circumstances do not admit of the fact is, my utter want of tact [*he founders more and more, unable to see that she can hardly contain her eagerness*]. Now, if it were Cokane

BLANCHE [*impatiently*] Cokane !

TRENCH [*terrified*] No, not Cokane. Though I assure you I was only going to say about him that

BLANCHE. That he will be back presently with papa.

TRENCH [*stupidly*] Yes : they cant be very long now. I hope I'm not detaining you.

BLANCHE. I thought you were detaining me because you had something to say.

TRENCH [*totally unnerved*] Not at all. At least, nothing very particular. That is, I'm afraid you wouldnt think it very particular. Another time, perhaps

BLANCHE. What other time ? How do you know that we shall ever meet again ? [*Desperately*] Tell me now. I want you to tell me now.

TRENCH. Well, I was thinking that if we could make up our minds to or not to at least er [*His nervousness deprives him of the power of speech*],

BLANCHE [*giving him up as hopeless*] I dont think theres much danger of your making up your mind, Dr Trench.

TRENCH [*stammering*] I only thought [*He stops and looks at her piteously. She hesitates a moment , and then puts her hands into his with calculated impulsiveness. He catches her in his arms with a cry of relief*]. Dear Blanche ! - I thought I should never have said it. I believe I should have stood stuttering here all day if you hadnt helped me out with it.

BLANCHE [*trying to get away from him*] I didnt help you out with it.

TRENCH [*holding her*] I dont mean that you did it on purpose, of course. Only instinctively.

BLANCHE [*still a little anxious*] But you havnt said anything.

TRENCH. What more can I say than this ? [*He kisses her again*].

BLANCHE [*overcome by the kiss, but holding on to her point*] But Harry

TRENCH [*delighted at the name*] Yes.

BLANCHE. When shall we be married ?

TRENCH. At the first church we meet : the Apollinaris Church, if you like.

BLANCHE. No, but seriously. This is serious, Harry : you musnt joke about it.

TRENCH [*looking suddenly round to the riverside gate and quickly releasing her*]. Sh ! Here they are back again.

BLANCHE. Oh, d [*The word is drowned by the clangor of a bell from within the hotel. The waiter appears on the steps, ringing it. Cokane and Sartorius are seen returning by the river gate*].

WAITER. Table d'hote in dwendy minutes, ladies and zhentellmenn. [*He goes into the hotel*].

SARTORIUS [*gravely*] I intended you to accompany us, Blanche.

BLANCHE. Yes, papa. We were just about to start.

SARTORIUS. We are rather dusty : we must make ourselves presentable at the table d'hote. I think you. had better come in with me, my child. Come. [*He offers Blanche his arm. The gravity of his manner overawes them all. Blanche silently takes his arm and goes into the hotel with him. Cokane, hardly less momentous than Sartorius himself, contemplates Trench with the severity of a judge*],

COKANE [*with reprobation*] No, my dear boy. No, no. Never. I blush for you was never so ashamed in my life. You have been taking advantage of that unprotected girl.

TRENCH [*hotly*] Cokane !

COKANE [*inexorable*] Her father seems to be a perfect gentleman. I obtained the privilege of his acquaintance : I introduced you : I allowed him to believe that he might leave his daughter in your charge with absolute confidence.

And what did I see on our return ? what did her father see ? Oh, Trench, Trench ! No, my dear fellow, no, no. Bad taste, Harry, bad form !

TRENCH. Stuff! There was nothing to see.

COKANE. Nothing to see ! She, a perfect lady, a person of the highest breeding, actually in your arms ; and you say there was nothing to see ! with a waiter there actually ringing a heavy bell to call attention to his presence. [*Lecturing him with redoubled severity*] Have you no principles, Trench ? Have you no religious convictions ? Have you no acquaintance with the usages of society ? You actually kissed

TRENCH. You didnt see me kiss her.

COKANE. We not only saw but heard it: the report positively reverberated down the Rhine. Dont condescend to subterfuge, Trench.

TRENCH. Nonsense, my dear Billy. You

COKANE. There you go again. Dont use that low abbreviation. How am I to preserve the respect of fellow travellers of position and wealth, if I am to be Billied at every turn ? My name is William : William de Burgh Cokane.

TRENCH. Oh, bother ! There : dont be offended, old chap. Whats the use of putting your back up at every trifle ? It comes natural to me to call you Billy : it suits you, somehow.

COKANE [*mortified*] You have no delicacy of feeling, Trench no tact. I never mention it to anyone ; but nothing, I am afraid, will ever make a true gentleman of you. [*Sartorius appears on the threshold of the hotel*]. Here is my friend Sartorius, coming, no doubt, to ask you for an explanation of your conduct. I really should not have been surprised to see him bring a horsewhip with him. I shall not intrude on the painful scene.

TRENCH. Dont go, confound it. I dont want to meet him alone just now.

COKANE [*shaking his head*] Delicacy, Harry, delicacy !

Good taste ! Savoir faire ! [*He walks away. Trench tries to escape in the opposite direction by strolling off towards the garden entrance*].

SARTORIUS [*mesmerically*] Dr Trench.

TRENCH [*stopping and fuming*] Oh, is that you, Mr Sartorius ? How did you find the church ?

[*Sartorius, without a word, points to a seat. Trench, half hypnotized by his own nervousness and the impressiveness of Sartorius, sits down helplessly*].

SARTORIUS [*also seating himself*] You have been speaking to my daughter, Dr Trench.

TRENCH [*with an attempt at ease of manner*] Yes : we had a conversation quite a chat, in fact whilst you were at the church with Cokane. How did you get on with Cokane, Mr Sartorius ? I always think he has such wonderful tact.

SARTORIUS [*ignoring the digression*] I have just had a word with my daughter, Dr Trench ; and I find her under the impression that something has passed between you which it is my duty as a father the father of a motherless girl to inquire into at once. My daughter, perhaps foolishly, has taken you quite seriously ; and

TRENCH. But

SARTORIUS. One moment, if you will be so good. I have been a young man myself younger, perhaps, than you would suppose from my present appearance. I mean, of course, in character. If you were not serious

TRENCH [*ingenuously*] But I was perfectly serious. I want to marry your daughter, Mr Sartorius. I hope you dont object.

SARTORIUS [*condescending to Trench's humility from the mere instinct to seize an advantage, and yet deferring to Lady Roxdale 1 s relative*] So far, no. I may say that your proposal seems to be an honorable and straightforward one, and that it is very gratifying to me personally.

TRENCH [*agreeably surprised*] Then I suppose we may consider the affair as settled. It's really very good of you.

1 SARTORIUS. Gently, Dr Trench, gently. Such a transaction as this cannot be settled off-hand.

TRENCH. Not off-hand, no. There are settlements and things, of course. But it may be regarded as settled between ourselves, maynt it ?

SARTORIUS. Hm ! Have you nothing further to mention ?

TRENCH. Only that that No : I dont know that I have, except that I love

SARTORIUS [*interrupting*] Anything about your family, for example ? You do not anticipate any objection on their part, do you ?

TRENCH. Oh, they have nothing to do with it.

SARTORIUS [*warmly*] Excuse me, sir : they have a great deal to do with it. [*Trench is abashed*], I am resolved that my daughter shall approach no circle in which she will not be received with the full consideration to which her education and her breeding [*here his self-control slips a little ; and he repeats, as if Trench had contradicted him*] I say, her breeding entitle her.

TRENCH [*bewildered*] Of course not. But what makes you think my family wont like Blanche ? Of course my father was a younger son ; and Ive had to take to a profession and all that ; so my people wont expect us to entertain them : theyll know we cant afford it. But theyll entertain us : they always ask me.

SARTORIUS. That wont do for me, sir. Families often think it due to themselves to turn their backs on newcomers whom they may not think quite good enough for them.

TRENCH. But I assure you my people arnt a bit snobbish. Blanche is a lady : thatll be good enough for them.

SARTORIUS [*moved*] I am glad you think so. [*He offers his hand. Trench, astonished, takes if*]. I think so myself. [*He presses Trenchs hand gratefully and releases it*]. And now, Dr Trench, since you have acted handsomely, you shall have no cause to complain of me. There shall be no difficulty about money : you shall entertain as much as you please : I will guarantee all that. But I must have a guarantee on my side that she will be received on equal terms by your family.

TRENCH. Guarantee !

SARTORIUS. Yes, a reasonable guarantee. I shall expect you to write to your relatives explaining your intention, and adding what you think proper as to my daughter's fitness for the best society. When you can shew me a few letters from the principal members of your family, congratulating you in a fairly cordial way, I shall be satisfied. Can I say more ?

TRENCH [*much puzzled, but grateful*] No indeed. You are really very good. Many thanks. Since you wish it, I'll write to my people. But I assure you youll find them as jolly as possible over it. I'll make them write by return.

SARTORIUS. Thank you. In the meantime, I must ask you not to regard the matter as settled.

TRENCH. Oh ! Not to regard the I see. You mean between Blanche and

SARTORIUS. I mean between you and Miss Sartorius. When I interrupted your conversation here some time ago, you and she were evidently regarding it as settled. In case difficulties arise, and the match you see I call it a match be broken off, I should not wish Blanche to think that she had allowed a gentleman to to [*Trench nods sympathetically*] Quite so. May I depend on you to keep a fair distance, and so spare me the necessity of having to restrain an intercourse which promises to be very pleasant to us all ?

TRENCH. Certainly; since you prefer it. [*They shake hands on it*].

SARTORIUS [*rising*] You will write to-day, I think you said ?

TRENCH [*eagerly*] I'll write now, before I leave here straight off.

SARTORIUS. I will leave you to yourself then. [*He hesitates, the conversation having made him self-conscious and embarrassed; then recovers himself with an effort and adds with dignity, as he turns to go*] I am pleased to have come to an understanding with you. [*He goes into the hotel; and Cokane, who has been hanging about inquisitively , emerges from the shrubbery*].

TRENCH [*excitedly*] Billy, old chap : youre just in time to do me a favour. I want you to draft a letter for me to copy out.

COKANE. I came with you on this tour as a friend, Trench : not as a secretary.

TRENCH. Well, youll write as a friend. It's to my Aunt Maria, about Blanche and me. To tell her, you know.

COKANE. Tell her about Blanche and you ! Tell her about your conduct ! Betray you, my friend ; and forget that I am writing to a lady ? Never !

TRENCH. Bosh, Billy : dont pretend you dont understand. We're engaged engaged, my boy: what do you think of that ? I must write by to-night's post. You are the man to tell me what to say. Come, old chap [*coaxing him to sit down at one of the tables*] : here's a pencil. Have you a bit of oh, here : thisll do : write it on the back of the map. [*He tears the map out of his Baedeker and spreads it face downwards on the table. Cokane takes the pencil and prepares to write*]. Thats right. Thanks awfully, old chap ! Now fire away. [*Anxiously*] Be careful how you word it, though, Cokane.

COKANE [*putting down the pencil*] If you doubt my ability to express myself becomingly to Lady Roxdale

TRENCH [*propitiating him*] All right, old fellow, all right : theres not a man alive who could do it half so well as you. I only wanted to explain. You see, Sartorius has got it into his head, somehow, that my people will snub Blanche ; and he wont consent unless they send letters and invitations and congratulations and the deuce knows what not. So just put it in such a way that Aunt Maria will write by return saying she is delighted, and asking us Blanche and me, you know to stay with her, and so forth. You know what I mean. Just tell her all about it in a chatty way ; and

COKANE [*crushingly*] If you will tell me all about it in a chatty way, I daresay I can communicate it to Lady Roxdale with proper delicacy. What is Sartorius ?

TRENCH [*taken aback*] I dont know : I didnt ask. It's a sort of question you cant very well put to a man at least a man like him. Do you think you could word the letter so as to pass all that over ? I really dont like to ask him.

COKANE. I can pass it over if you wish. Nothing easier. But if you think Lady Roxdale will pass it over, I differ from you. I may be wrong : no doubt I am. I generally am wrong, I believe ; but that is my opinion.

TRENCH [*much perplexed*] Oh, confound it ! What the deuce am I to do ? Cant you say he's a gentleman : that wont commit us to anything. If you dwell on his being well off, and Blanche an only child, Aunt Maria will be satisfied.

COKANE. Henry Trench : when will you begin to get a little sense ? This is a serious business. Act responsibly, Harry : act responsibly.

TRENCH. Bosh ! Dont be moral !

COKANE. I am not moral, Trench. At least I am not a moralist : that is the expression I should have used moral, but not a moralist. If you are going to get money with your wife, doesnt it concern your family to know how that money was made ? Doesnt it concern you, Harry ? [*Trench looks at him helplessly, twisting his fingers nervously. Cokane throws down the pencil and leans back with ostentatious indifference*]. Of course it is no business of mine : I only throw out the suggestion. Sartorius may be a retired burglar for all I know. [*Sartorius and Blanche, ready for dinner, come from the hotel*].

TRENCH. Sh ! Here they come. Get the letter finished before dinner, like a good old chappie : I shall be awfully obliged to you.

COKANE [*impatiently*] Leave me, leave me : you disturb me. [*He waves him off and begins to write*].

TRENCH [*humbly and gratefully*] Yes, old chap. Thanks awfully.

[*By this time Blanche has left her father and is strolling of towards the riverside. Sartorius comes down the garden, Baedeker in hand, and sits near Cokane, reading. Trench addresses him*]. You wont mind my taking Blanche in to dinner, I hope, sir ?

SARTORIUS. By all means, Dr Trench. Pray do so. [*He graciously waves him off to join Blanche. Trench hurries after her through the gate. The light reddens as the Rhenish sunset begins. Cokane, making wry faces in the agonies of composition, is disconcerted to find Sartorius' s eye upon him*].

SARTORIUS. I do not disturb you, I hope, Mr Cokane.

COKANE. By no means. Our friend Trench has entrusted me with a difficult and delicate task. He has requested me, as a friend of the family, to write to them on a subject that concerns you.

SARTORIUS. Indeed, Mr Cokane. Well, the communication could not be in better hands.

COKANE [*with an air of modesty*] Ah, that is going too far, my dear sir, too far. Still, you see what Trench is. A capital fellow in his way, Mr Sartorius, an excellent young fellow. But family communications like these require good manners. They require tact ; and tact is Trench's weak point. He has an excellent heart, but no tact none whatever. Everything depends on the way the matter is put to Lady Roxdale. But as to that, you may rely on me. I understand the sex.

SARTORIUS. Well, however she may receive it and I care as little as any man, Mr Cokane, how people may choose to receive me I trust I may at least have the pleasure of seeing you sometimes at my house when we return to England.

COKANE [*overwhelmed*] My dear sir! You express yourself in the true spirit of an English gentleman.

SARTORIUS. Not at all. You will always be most welcome. But I fear I have disturbed you in the composition of your letter. Pray resume it. I shall leave you to yourself. [*He pretends to rise, but checks himself to add*] Unless indeed I can assist you in any way ? by clearing up any point on which you are not informed, for instance ; or even, if I may so far presume on my years, giving you the benefit of my experience as to the best way of wording the matter. [*Cokane looks a little surprised at this. Sartorius looks hard at him, and continues deliberately and meaningly*] I shall always be happy to help any friend of Dr Trench's, in any way, to the best of my ability and of my means.

COKANE. My dear sir : you are really very good. Trench and I were putting our heads together over the letter just now ; and there certainly were one or two points on which we were a little in the dark. [*Scrupulously*] But I would not permit Harry to question you. No. I pointed out to him that, as a matter of taste, it would be more delicate to wait until you volunteered the necessary information.

SARTORIUS. Hm ! May I ask what you have said, so far ?

COKANE. " My dear Aunt Maria." That is, Trench's dear Aunt Maria, my friend Lady Roxdale. You understand that I am only drafting a letter for Trench to copy.

SARTORIUS. Quite so. Will you proceed ; or would it help you if I were to suggest a word or two ?

COKANE [*effusively*] Your suggestions will be most valuable, my dear sir, most welcome.

SARTORIUS. I think I should begin in some such way as this. " In travelling with my friend Mr Cokane up the Rhine"

COKANE [*murmuring as he -writes*] Invaluable, invaluable. The very thing. " my friend Mr Cokane up the Rhine"

SARTORIUS. "I have made the acquaintance of" or you may say "picked up," or "come across," if you think that would suit your friend's style better. We must not be too formal.

COKANE. " Picked up " ! oh no : too degage, Mr Sartorius, too degage. I should say "had the privilege of becoming acquainted with."

SARTORIUS [*quickly*] By no means : Lady Roxdale must judge of that for herself. Let it stand as I said. " I have made the acquaintance of a young lady, the daughter of " [*He hesitates*].

COKANE [*writing*] "acquaintance of a young lady, the daughter of" yes ?

SARTORIUS. "of" you had better say "a gentleman."

COKANE [*surprised*] Of course.

SARTORIUS [*with sudden passion*] It is not of course, sir, [*Cokane, startled, looks at him with dawning suspicion. Sartorius recovers himself somewhat shamefacedly*]. Hm ! " of a gentleman of considerable wealth and position "

COKANE [*echoing him with a new note of coldness in his voice as he writes the last words*] " and position "

SARTORIUS. "which, however, he has made entirely for himself." [*Cokane, now fully enlightened, stares at him instead of writing*]. Have you written that ?

COKANE [*expanding into an attitude of patronage and encouragement*] Ah, indeed. Quite so, quite so. [*He writes*] " entirely for himself." Just so. Proceed, Mr Sartorius, proceed. Very clearly expressed.

SARTORIUS. "The young lady will inherit the bulk of her father's fortune, and will be liberally treated on her marriage. Her education has been of the most expensive and complete kind obtainable ; and her surroundings have been characterized by the strictest refinement. She is in every essential particular "

COKANE [*interrupting*] Excuse the remark ; but dont you think this is rather too much in the style of a prospectus of the young lady ? I throw out the suggestion as a matter of taste.

SARTORIUS [*troubled*] Perhaps you are right. I am of course not dictating the exact words ;

COKANE. Of course not : of course not.

SARTORIUS. but I desire that there may be no wrong impression as to my daughter's er breeding. As to myself

COKANE. Oh, it will be sufficient to mention your profession, or pursuits, or [*He pauses; and they look pretty hard at one another*].

SARTORIUS [*very deliberately*] My income, sir, is derived from the rental of a very extensive real estate in London. Lady Roxdale is one of the head landlords ; and Dr Trench holds a mortgage from which, if I mistake not, his entire income is derived. The truth is, Mr Cokane, I am quite well acquainted with Dr Trench's position and affairs ; and I have long desired to know him personally.

COKANE [*again obsequious, but still inquisitive*] What a remarkable coincidence ! In what quarter is the estate situated, did you say ?

SARTORIUS. In London, sir. Its management occupies as much of my time as is not devoted to the ordinary pursuits of a gentleman. [*He rises and takes out his card case*]. The rest I leave to your discretion. [*He leaves a card on the table*]. That is my address at Surbiton. If it should unfortunately happen, Mr Cokane, that this leads to nothing but a disappointment for Blanche, probably she would rather not see you afterwards. But if all turns out as we hope, Dr Trench's best friends will then be our best friends.

COKANE [*rising and confronting Sartorius confidently, pencil and paper in hand*] Rely on me, Mr Sartorius. The letter is already finished here [*pointing to his brain*]. In five minutes it will be finished there [*He points to the paper ; nods to emphasize the assertion ; and begins to pace up and down the garden, writing, and tapping his forehead from time to time as he goes, with every appearance of severe intellectual exertion*].

SARTORIUS [*falling through the gate after a glance at his watch*] Blanche.

BLANCHE [*replying in the distance*] Yes ?

SARTORIUS. Time, my dear. [*He goes into the table d'hote*].

BLANCHE [*nearer*] Coming. [*She comes back through the gate, followed by Trench*],

TRENCH [*in a half whisper, as Blanche goes towards the table d'hote*] Blanche : stop one moment. [*She stops*]. We must be careful when your father is by. I had to promise him not to regard anything as settled until I hear from my people at home.

BLANCHE [*chilled*] Oh, I see. Your family may object to me ; and then it will be all over between us. They are almost sure to.

TRENCH [*anxiously*] Dont say that, Blanche : it sounds as if you didnt care. I hope you regard it as settled. You havnt made any promise, you know.

BLANCHE [*earnestly*] Yes, I have : I promised papa too. But I have broken my promise for your sake. I suppose I am not so conscientious as you. And if the matter is not to be regarded as settled, family or no family, promise or no promise, let us break it off here and now.

TRENCH [*intoxicated with affection*] Blanche : on my most sacred honor, family or no family, promise or no promise [*The waiter reappears at the table d'hote entrance, ringing his bell loudly*]. Damn that noise !

COKANE [*as he comes to them, flourishing the letter*] Finished, dear boy, finished. Done to a turn, punctually to the second. C'est fini, mon cher garcon, c'est fini. [*Sartorius returns*].

SARTORIUS. Will you take Blanche in, Dr Trench ? [*Trench takes Blanche into the table d'hote*]. Is the letter finished, Mr Cokane ?

COKANE [*with an author's pride, handing his draft to Sartorius*] There ! [*Sartorius reads it, nodding gravely over it with complete approval*].

SARTORIUS [*returning the draft*] Thank you, Mr Cokane. You have the pen of a ready writer.

COKANE [*as they go in together*] Not at all, not at all. A little tact, Mr Sartorius ; a little knowledge of the world ; a little experience of women [*They disappear into the annexe*].

ACT II

In the library of a handsomely appointed villa at Surbiton on a sunny forenoon in September. Sartorius is busy at a writing table, littered with business letters. The fireplace, decorated for summer, is close behind him : the window is in the opposite wall. Between the table and the window Blanche, in her prettiest frock, sits reading The Queen. The door, painted, like all the woodwork, in the blackest shade of red, with brass fittings and moulded posts and pediment, is in the middle. All the walls are lined with shelves of smartly tooled books, fitting into their places like bricks. A library ladder stands in the corner.

SARTORIUS. Blanche.

BLANCHE. Yes, papa.

SARTORIUS. I have some news here.

BLANCHE. What is it ?

SARTORIUS. I mean news for you from Trench.

BLANCHE [*with affected indifference*] Indeed ?

SARTORIUS. "Indeed?" ! Is that all you have to say to me ? Oh, very well. [*He resumes his work. Silence*].

BLANCHE. What do his people say, papa ?

SARTORIUS. His people ! I dont know. [*Still busy. Another pause*].

BLANCHE. What does he say?

SARTORIUS. He ! He says nothing. [*He folds a letter leisurely and looks for the envelope*]. He prefers to communicate the result of his where did I put oh, here. Yes : he prefers to communicate the result in person.

BLANCHE [*springing up*] Oh, papa ! When is he coming ?

SARTORIUS. If he walks from the station, he may arrive in the course of the next half-hour. If he drives, he may be here at any moment.

BLANCHE [*making hastily for the door*] Oh !

SARTORIUS. Blanche.

BLANCHE. Yes, papa.

SARTORIUS. You will of course not meet him until he has spoken to me.

BLANCHE [*hypocritically*] Of course not, papa. I shouldnt have thought of such a thing.

SARTORIUS. That is all. [*She is going, when he puts out his hand, and says with fatherly emotion*] My dear child. [*She responds by going over to kiss him. A tap at the door*]. Come in. [*Lickcheese enters, carrying a black handbag. He is a shabby, needy man, with dirty face and linen, scrubby beard and whiskers, going bald. A nervous, wiry, pertinacious sort of human terrier, judged by his mouth and eyes, but miserably apprehensive and servile before Sartorius. He bids Blanche " Good morning, miss " and she passes out with a slight and contemptuous recognition of him*].

LICKCHEESE. Good morning, sir.

SARTORIUS [*harsh and peremptory*] Good morning.

LICKCHEESE [*taking a little sack of money from his bag*] Not much this morning, sir. I have just had the honor of making Dr Trench's acquaintance, sir.

SARTORIUS [*looking up from his writing, displeased*] Indeed ?

LICKCHEESE. Yes, sir. Dr Trench asked his way of me, and was kind enough to drive me from the station.

SARTORIUS. Where is he, then ?

LICKCHEESE. I left him in the hall, with his friend, sir. I should think he is speaking to Miss Sartorius.

SARTORIUS. Hm ! What do you mean by his friend ?

LICKCHEESE. There is a Mr Cokane with him, sir. SARTORIUS. I see you have been talking to him, eh ? LICKCHEESE. As we drove along : yes, sir. SARTORIUS [*sharply*] Why did you not come by the nine o'clock train ?

LICKCHEESE. I thought

SARTORIUS. It cannot be helped now ; so never mind what you thought. But do not put off my business again to the last moment. Has there been any further trouble about the St Giles property ?

LICKCHEESE. The Sanitary Inspector has been complaining again about No. 13 Robbins's Row. He says he'll bring it before the vestry.

SARTORIUS. Did you tell him that I am on the vestry ?

LICKCHEESE. Yes, Sir.

SARTORIUS. What did he say to that ?

LICKCHEESE. Said he supposed so, or you wouldnt dare to break the law so scand'lous. I only tell you what he said.

SARTORIUS. Hm ! Do you know his name !

LICKCHEESE. Yes, sir. Speakman.

SARTORIUS. Write it down in the diary for the day of the next meeting of the Health Committee. I will teach Mr Speakman his duty to members of the vestry.

LICKCHEESE [*doubtfully*] The vestry cant hurt him, sir. He's under the Local Government Board.

SARTORIUS. I did not ask you that. Let me see the books. [*Lickcheese produces the rent book, and hands it- to Sartorius ; then makes the desired entry in the diary on the table, watching Sartorius with misgiving as the rent book is examined. Sartorius rises, frowning*] 1 14.5. for repairs to No. 13. What does this mean ?

LICKCHEESE. Well, sir, it was the staircase on the third floor. It was downright dangerous : there werent but three whole steps in it, and no handrail. I thought it best to have a few boards put in.

SARTORIUS. Boards ! Firewood, sir, firewood ! They will burn every stick of it. You have spent twenty-four shillings of my money on firewood for them.

LICKCHEESE. There ought to be stone stairs, sir : it would be a saving in the long run. The clergyman says

SARTORIUS. What! who says?

LICKCHEESE. The clergyman, sir, only the clergyman. Not that I make much account of him ; but if you knew how he has worried me over that staircase

SARTORIUS. I am an Englishman ; and I will suffer no priest to interfere in my business. [*He turns suddenly on Lickcheese*]. Now look here, Mr Lickcheese ! This is the third time this year that you have brought me a bill of over a pound for repairs. I have warned you repeatedly against dealing with these tenement houses as if they were mansions in a West-End square. I have had occasion to warn you too against discussing my affairs with strangers. You have chosen to disregard my wishes. You are discharged.

LICKCHEESE [*dismayed*] Oh, sir, dont say that.

SARTORIUS [*fiercely*] You are discharged.

LICKCHEESE. Well, Mr Sartorius, it is hard, so it is. No man alive could have screwed more out of them poor destitute devils for you than I have, or spent less in doing it. I have dirtied my hands at it until theyre not fit for clean work hardly ; and now you turn me

SARTORIUS [*interrupting him menacingly*] What do you mean by dirtying your hands ? If I find that you have stepped an inch outside the letter of the law, Mr Lickcheese, I will prosecute you myself. The way to keep your hands clean is to gain the confidence of your employers. You will do well to bear that in mind in your next situation.

THE PARLOR MAID [*opening the door*] Mr Trench and Mr Cokane. [*Cokane and Trench come in: Trench festively dressed and in buoyant spirits, Cokane highly self-satisfied*].

SARTORIUS. How do you do, Dr Trench ? Good morning,

Mr Cokane. I am pleased to see you here. Mr Lickcheese : you will place your accounts and money on the table : I will examine them and settle with you presently. [*Lickcheese retires to the table, and begins to arrange his accounts, greatly depressed*].

TRENCH [*glancing at Lickcheese*] I hope we're not in the way.

SARTORIUS. By no means. Sit down, pray. I fear you have been kept waiting.

TRENCH [*taking Blanche's chair*] Not at all. Weve only just come in. [*He takes out a packet of letters and begins untying them*].

COKANE [*going to a chair nearer the window, but stopping to look admiringly round before sitting down*] You must be happy here with all these books, Mr Sartorius. A literary atmosphere.

SARTORIUS [*resuming his seat*] I have not looked into them. They are pleasant for Blanche occasionally when she wishes to read. I chose the house because it is on gravel. The death-rate is very low.

TRENCH [*triumphantly*] I have any amount of letters for you. All my people are delighted that I am going to settle. Aunt Maria wants Blanche to be married from her house. [*He hands Sartorius a letter*].

SARTORIUS. Aunt Maria ?

COKANE. Lady Roxdale, my dear sir : he means Lady Roxdale. Do express yourself with a little more tact, my dear fellow.

TRENCH. Lady Roxdale, of course. Uncle Harry

COKANE. Sir Harry Trench. His godfather, my dear sir, his godfather.

TRENCH. Just so. The pleasantest fellow for his age you ever met. He offers us his house at St Andrews for a couple of months, if we care to pass our honeymoon there. [*He hands Sartorius another letter*]. It's the sort of house nobody can live in, you know ; but it's a nice thing for him to offer. Dont you think so ?

SARTORIUS [*dissembling a thrill at the titles*] No doubt. These seem very gratifying, Dr Trench.

TRENCH. Yes, arnt they ? Aunt Maria has really behaved like a brick. If you read the postscript youll see she spotted Cokane's hand in my letter. [*Chuckling*] He wrote it for me.

SARTORIUS [*glancing at Cokane*] Indeed ! Mr Cokane evidently did it with great tact.

COKANE [*returning the glance*] Dont mention it.

TRENCH [*gleefully*] Well, what do you say now, Mr Sartorius ? May we regard the matter as settled at last ?

SARTORIUS. Quite settled. [*He rises and offers his hand. Trench, glowing with gratitude, rises and shakes it vehemently, unable to find words for his feelings*].

COKANE [*coming between them*]. Allow me to congratulate you both. [*He shakes hands with the two at the same time*].

SARTORIUS. And now, gentlemen, I have a word to say to my daughter. Dr Trench : you will not, I hope, grudge me the pleasure of breaking this news to her : I have had to disappoint her more than once since I last saw you. Will you excuse me for ten minutes ?

COKANE [*in a flush of friendly protest*] My dear sir : can you ask?

TRENCH. Certainly.

SARTORIUS. Thank you. [*He goes out*].

TRENCH [*chuckling again*] He wont have any news to break, poor old boy : she's seen all the letters already.

COKANE. I must say your behavior has been far from straightforward, Harry. You have been carrying on a clandestine correspondence.

LICKCHEESE [*stealthily*] Gentlemen

TRENCH }

COKANE } [*Turning. They had forgotten his presence*] Hallo!

LICKCHEESE [*coming between them very humbly, but in mortal anxiety and haste*] Look here, gentlemen. [*To Trench*] You, sir, I address myself to more particlar. Will you say a word in my favor to the guvnor ? He's just given me the sack ; and I have four children looking to me for their bread. A word from you, sir, on this happy day, might get him to take me on again.

TRENCH [*embarrassed*] Well, you see, Mr Lickcheese, I dont see how I can interfere. I'm very sorry, of course.

COKANE. Certainly you cannot interfere. It would be in the most execrable taste.

LICKCHEESE. Oh, gentlemen, youre young ; and you dont know what loss of employment means to the like of me. What harm would it do you to help a poor man ? Just listen to the circumstances, sir. I only

TRENCH [*moved, but snatching at an excuse for taking a high tone in avoiding the unpleasantness of helping him*] No : I had rather not. Excuse my saying plainly that I think Mr Sartorius is not a man to act hastily or harshly. I have always found him very fair and generous ; and I believe he is a better judge of the circumstances than I am.

COKANE [*inquisitive*] I think you ought to hear the circumstances, Harry. It can do no harm. Hear the circumstances by all means.

LICKCHEESE. Never mind, sir : it aint any use. When I hear that man called generous and fair ! well, never mind.

TRENCH [*severely*] If you wish me to do anything for you, Mr Lickcheese, let me tell you that you are not going the right way about it in speaking ill of Mr Sartorius.

LICKCHEESE. Have I said one word against him, sir ? I leave it to your friend : have I said a word ?

COKANE. True : true. Quite true. Harry: be just.

LICKCHEESE. Mark my words, gentlemen : he'll find what a man he's lost the very first week's rents the new man'll bring him. Youll find the difference yourself, Dr Trench, if you or your children come into the property. Ive took money there when no other collector alive would have wrung it out. And this is the thanks I get for it ! Why, see here, gentlemen ! Look at that bag of money on the table. Hardly a penny of that but there was a hungry child crying for the bread it would have bought. But I got it for him screwed and worried and bullied it out of them. I look here, gentlemen : I'm pretty seasoned to the work ; but theres money there that I couldnt have taken if it hadnt been for the thought of my own children depending on me for giving him satisfaction. And because I charged him four-and-twenty shillin' to mend a staircase that three women have been hurt on, and that would have got him prosecuted for manslaughter if it had been let go much longer, he gives me the sack. Wouldnt listen to a word, though I would have offered to make up the money out of my own pocket aye, and am willing to do it still if you will only put in a word for me.

TRENCH [*aghast*] You took money that ought to have fed starving children ! Serve you right ! If I had been the father of one of those children, I'd have given you something worse than the sack. I wouldnt say a word to save your soul, if you have such a thing. Mr Sartorius was quite right.

LICKCHEESE [*staring at him, surprised into contemptuous amusement in the midst of his anxiety*] Just listen to this ! Well, you are an innocent young gentleman. Do you suppose he sacked me because I was too hard ? Not a bit on it : it was because I wasnt hard enough. I never heard him say he was satisfied yet : no, nor he wouldnt, not if I skinned em alive, I dont say he's the worst landlord in London : he couldnt be worse than some ; but he's no better than the worst I ever had to do with. And, though I say it, I'm better than the best collector he ever done business with. Ive screwed more and spent less on his properties than anyone would believe that knows what such properties are. I know my merits, Dr Trench, and will speak for myself if no one else will.

COKANE. What description of properties ? Houses ?

LICKCHEESE. Tenement houses, let from week to week by the room or half room aye, or quarter room. It pays when you know how to work it, sir. Nothing like it. It's been calculated on the cubic foot of space, sir, that you can get higher rents letting by the room than you can for a mansion in Park Lane.

TRENCH. I hope Mr Sartorius hasnt much of that sort of property, however it may pay.

LICKCHEESE. He has nothing else, sir ; and he shews his sense in it, too. Every few hundred pounds he could scrape together he bought old houses with houses that you wouldnt hardly look at without holding your nose. He has em in St Giles's : he has em in Marylebone : he has em in Bethnal Green. Just look how he lives himself, and youll see the good of it to him. He likes a low death-rate and a gravel soil for himself, he does. You come down with me to Robbins's Row ; and I'll shew you a soil and a death-rate, so I will ! And, mind you, it's me that makes it pay him so well. Catch him going down to collect his own rents ! Not likely !

TRENCH. Do you mean to say that all his property all his means come from this sort of thing ?

LICKCHEESE. Every penny of it, sir. [*Trench, overwhelmed, has to sit down*].

COKANE [*looking compassionately at him*] Ah, my dear fellow, the love of money is the root of all evil.

LICKCHEESE. Yes, sir ; and we'd all like to have the tree growing in our garden.

COKANE [*revolted*] Mr Lickcheese : I did not address myself to you. I do not wish to be severe with you ; but there is something peculiarly repugnant to my feelings in the calling of a rent collector.

LICKCHEESE. It's no worse than many another. I have my children looking to me.

COKANE. True : I admit it. So has our friend Sartorius. His affection for his daughter is a redeeming point a redeeming point, certainly.

LICKCHEESE. She's a lucky daughter, sir. Many another daughter has been turned out upon the streets to gratify his affection for her. Thats what business is, sir, you see. Come, sir : I think your friend will say a word for me now he knows I'm not in fault.

TRENCH [*rising angrily*] I will not. It's a damnable business from beginning to end ; and you deserve no better luck for helping in it. Ive seen it all among the outpatients at the hospital ; and it used to make my blood boil to think that such things couldnt be prevented.

LICKCHEESE [*his suppressed spleen breaking out*] Oh indeed, sir. But I suppose youll take your share when you marry Miss Blanche, all the same. [*Furiously*] Which of us is the worse, I should like to know me that wrings the money out to keep a home over my children, or you that spend it and try to shove the blame on to me ?

COKANE. A most improper observation to address to a gentleman, Mr Lickcheese ! A most revolutionary sentiment !

LICKCHEESE. Perhaps so. But then Robbins's Row aint a school for manners. You collect a week or two there youre welcome to my place if I cant keep it for myself and youll hear a little plain speaking, so you will.

COKANE [*with dignity*] Do you know to whom you are speaking, my good man ?

LICKCHEESE [*recklessly*] I know well enough who I'm speaking to. What do I care for you, or a thousand such ? I'm poor : thats enough to make a rascal of me. No consideration for me nothing to be got by saying a word for me ! [*Suddenly cringing to Trench*] Just a word, sir. It would cost you nothing. [*Sartorius appears at the door, unobserved*]. Have some feeling for the poor.

TRENCH. I'm afraid you have shewn very little, by your own confession.

LICKCHEESE [*breaking out again*] More than your precious father-in-law, anyhow. I [*Sartorius's voice, striking in with deadly coldness, paralyzes him*].

SARTORIUS. You will come here to-morrow not later than ten, Mr Lickcheese, to conclude our business. I shall trouble you no further to-day. [*Lickcheese, cowed, goes out amid dead silence. Sartorius continues, after an awkward pause*] He is one of my agents, or rather was ; for I have unfortunately had to dismiss him for repeatedly disregarding my instructions. [*Trench says nothing. Sartorius throws of his embarrassment, and assumes a jocose, rallying air, unbecoming to him under any circumstances, and just now almost unbearably jarring*], Blanche will be down presently, Harry [*Trench recoils*] I suppose I must call you Harry now. What do you say to a stroll through the garden, Mr Cokane ? We are celebrated here for our flowers.

COKANE. Charmed, my dear sir, charmed. Life here is an idyll a perfect idyll. We were just dwelling on it.

SARTORIUS [*slyly*] Harry can follow with Blanche. She will be down directly.

TRENCH [*hastily*] No. I cant face her just now.

SARTORIUS [*rallying him*] Indeed ! Ha, ha ! [*The laugh, the first they have heard from him', sets Trench's teeth on edge. Cokane is taken aback, but instantly recovers himself*].

COKANE. Ha ! ha ! ha ! Ho ! ho !

TRENCH. But you dont understand.

SARTORIUS. Oh, I think we do, I think we do. Eh, Mr Cokane? Ha! ha!

COKANE. I should think we do. Ha ! ha ! ha !

[*They go out together, laughing at him. He collapses into a chair, shuddering in every nerve. Blanche appears at the door. Her face lights up when she sees that he is alone. She trips noiselessly to the back of his chair and clasps her hands over his eyes. With a convulsive start and exclamation he springs up and breaks away from her*].

BLANCHE [*astonished*] Harry !

TRENCH [*with distracted politeness*] I beg your pardon. I was thinking wont you sit down ?

BLANCHE [*looking suspiciously at him*] Is anything the matter? [*She sits down slowly near the writing table. He takes Cokane's chair*].

TRENCH. No. Oh no.

BLANCHE. Papa has not been disagreeable, I hope.

TRENCH. No : I have hardly spoken to him since I was with you. [*He rises; takes up his chair; and plants it beside hers. This pleases her better. She looks at him with her most winning smile. A sort of sob breaks from him ; and he catches her hands and kisses them passionately. Then, looking into her eyes with intense earnestness, he says*] Blanche : are you fond of money ?

BLANCHE [*gaily*] Very. Are you going to give me any ?

TRENCH [*wincing*] Dont make a joke of it : I'm serious. Do you know that we shall be very poor ?

BLANCHE. Is that what made you look as if you had neuralgia ?

TRENCH [*pleadingly*] My dear : it's no laughing matter. Do you know that I have a bare seven hundred a year to live on ?

BLANCHE. How dreadful !

TRENCH. Blanche : it's very serious indeed : I assure you it is.

BLANCHE. It would keep me rather short in my housekeeping, dearest boy, if I had nothing of my own. But papa has promised me that I shall be richer than ever when we are married.

TRENCH. We must do the best we can with seven hundred. I think we ought to be self-supporting.

BLANCHE. Thats just what I mean to be, Harry. If I were to eat up half your £700, I should be making you twice as poor ; but I'm going to make you twice as rich instead. [*He shakes his head*]. Has papa made any difficulty ?

TRENCH [*rising with a sigh and taking his chair back to its former place*] No, none at all. [*He sits down dejectedly. When Blanche speaks again her face and voice betray the beginning of a struggle with her temper*].

BLANCHE. Harry : are you too proud to take money from my father ?

TRENCH. Yes, Blanche : I am too proud.

BLANCHE [*after a pause*] That is not nice to me, Harry.

TRENCH. You must bear with me, Blanche. I I cant explain. After all, it's very natural.

BLANCHE. Has it occurred to you that I may be proud, too?

TRENCH. Oh, thats nonsense. No one will accuse you of marrying for money.

BLANCHE. No one would think the worse of me if I did, or of you either. [*She rises and begins to walk restlessly about*]. We really cannot live on seven hundred a year, Harry ; and I dont think it quite fair of you to ask me merely because youre afraid of people talking.

TRENCH. It's not that alone, Blanche.

BLANCHE. What else is it, then ?

TRENCH. Nothing. I

BLANCHE [*getting behind him, and speaking with forced playfulness as she bends over him, her hands on his shoulders*] Of course it's nothing. Now dont be absurd, Harry : be good ; and listen to me : I know how to settle it. You are too proud to owe anything to me ; and I am too proud to owe anything to you. You have seven hundred a year. Well, I will take just seven hundred a year from papa at first ; and then we shall be quits. Now, now, Harry, you know youve not a word to say against that.

TRENCH. It's impossible.

BLANCHE. Impossible !

TRENCH. Yes, impossible. I have resolved not to take any money from your father.

BLANCHE. But he'll give the money to me, not to you.

TRENCH. It's the same thing. [*With an effort to be sentimental*] I love you too well to see any distinction. [*He puts up his hand half-heartedly : she takes it over his shoulder with equal indecision. They are both trying hard to conciliate one another*].

BLANCHE. Thats a very nice way of putting it, Harry ; but I'm sure theres something I ought to know. Has papa been disagreeable ?

TRENCH. No : he has been very kind to me, at least. It's not that. It's nothing you can guess, Blanche. It would only pain you perhaps offend you.

I dont mean, of course, that we shall live always on seven hundred a year. I intend to go at my profession in earnest, and work my fingers to the bone.

BLANCHE [*playing with his fingers, still over his shoulder*] But I shouldnt like you with your fingers worked to the bone, Harry. I must be told what the matter is. [*He takes his hand quickly away : she flushes angrily ; and her voice is no longer even an imitation of the voice of a lady as she exclaims*] I hate secrets ; and I dont like to be treated as if I were a child.

TRENCH [*annoyed by her tone*] Theres nothing to tell. I dont choose to trespass on your father's generosity : thats all.

BLANCHE. You had no objection half an hour ago, when you met me in the hall, and shewed me all the letters. Your family doesnt object. Do you object?

TRENCH [*earnestly*] I do not indeed. It's only a question of money.

BLANCHE [*imploringly, the voice softening and refining for the last time*] Harry : theres no use in our fencing in this way. Papa will never consent to my being absolutely dependent on you ; and I dont like the idea of it myself. If you even mention such a thing to him you will break off the match : you will indeed.

TRENCH [*obstinately*] I cant help that.

BLANCHE [*white with rage*] You cant help ! Oh, I'm beginning to understand. I will save you the trouble. You can tell papa that I have broken off the match ; and then there will be no further difficulty.

TRENCH [*taken aback*] What do you mean, Blanche ? Are you offended ?

BLANCHE. Offended ! How dare you ask me ?

TRENCH. Dare !

BLANCHE. How much more manly it would have been to confess that you were trifling with me that time on the Rhine ! Why did you come here today ? Why did you write to your people ?

TRENCH. Well, Blanche, if you are going to lose your temper

BLANCHE. Thats no answer. You depended on your family to get you out of your engagement ; and they did not object : they were only too glad to be rid of you. You were not mean enough to stay away, and not manly enough to tell the truth. You thought you could provoke me to break the engagement: thats so like a man to try to put the woman in the wrong. Well, you have your way : I release you. I wish youd opened my eyes by downright brutality by striking me by anything rather than shuffling as you have done.

TRENCH [*hotly*] Shuffle ! If I'd thought you capable of turning on me like this, I'd never have spoken to you. Ive a good mind never to speak to you again.

BLANCHE. You shall not not ever. I will take care of that [*going to the door*].

TRENCH [*alarmed*] What are you going to do ?

BLANCHE. To get your letters your false letters, and your presents your hateful presents, to return them to you. I'm very glad it's all broken off; and if [*as she puts her hand to the door it is opened from without by Sartorius, who enters and shuts it behind him*].

SARTORIUS [*interrupting her severely*] Hush, pray, Blanche : you are forgetting yourself: you can be heard all over the house. What is the matter ?

BLANCHE [*too angry to care whether she is overheard or not*] You had better ask him. He has some excuse about money.

SARTORIUS. Excuse ! Excuse for what ?

BLANCHE. For throwing me over.

TRENCH [*vehemently*] I declare I never

BLANCHE [*interrupting him still more vehemently"*] You did. You did. You are doing nothing else [*Trench begins repeating his contradiction and she her assertion ; so that they both speak angrily together*].

SARTORIUS [*in desperation at the noise*] Silence. [*Still more formidably*] Silence. [*They obey. He proceeds firmly*] Blanche : you must control your temper : I will not have these repeated scenes within hearing of the servants. Dr Trench will answer for himself to me. You had better leave us. [*He opens the door, and calls*] Mr Cokane : will you kindly join us here.

COKANE [*in the conservatory*] Coming, my dear sir, coming. [*He appears at the door*].

BLANCHE. I'm sure I have no wish to stay. I hope I shall find you alone when I come back. [*An inarticulate exclamation bursts from Trench. She goes out, passing Cokane resentfully. He looks after her in surprise ; then looks questioningly at the two men. Sartorius shuts the door with an angry stroke, and turns to Trench*].

SARTORIUS [*aggressively*] Sir

TRENCH [*interrupting him more aggressively*] Well, sir ?

COKANE [*getting between them*] Gently, dear boy, gently. Suavity, Harry, suavity.

SARTORIUS [*mastering himself*] If you have anything to say to me, Dr Trench, I will listen to you patiently. You will then allow me to say what I have to say on my part.

TRENCH [*ashamed*] I beg your pardon. Of course, yes. Fire away.

SARTORIUS. May I take it that you have refused to fulfil your engagement with my daughter ?

TRENCH. Certainly not : your daughter has refused to fulfil her engagement with me. But the match is broken off, if thats what you mean.

SARTORIUS. Dr Trench : I will be plain with you. I know that Blanche has a quick temper. It is part of her strong character and her physical courage, which is greater than that of most men, I can assure you. You must be prepared for that. If this quarrel is only Blanche's temper, you may take my word for it that it will be over before to-morrow. But I understood from what she said just now that you have made some difficulty on the score of money.

TRENCH [*with renewed excitement*] It was Miss Sartorius who made the difficulty. I shouldnt have minded that so much, if it hadnt been for the things she said. She shewed that she doesnt care that [*snapping his fingers*] for me.

COKANE [*soothingly*] Dear boy

TRENCH. Hold your tongue, Billy : it's enough to make a man wish he'd never seen a woman. Look here, Mr Sartorius : I put the matter to her as delicately and considerately as possible, never mentioning a word of my reasons, but just asking her to be content to live on my own little income ; and yet she turned on me as if I'd behaved like a savage.

SARTORIUS. Live on your income ! Impossible : my daughter is accustomed to a proper establishment. Did I not expressly undertake to provide for that ? Did she not tell you I promised her to do so ?

TRENCH. Yes, I know all about that, Mr Sartorius ; and I'm greatly obliged to you ; but I'd rather not take anything from you except Blanche herself.

SARTORIUS. And why did you not say so before ?

TRENCH. No matter why. Let us drop the subject.

SARTORIUS. No matter ! But it does matter, sir. I insist on an answer. Why did you not say so before ?

TRENCH. I didnt know before.

SARTORIUS [*provoked*] Then you ought to have known your own mind before entering into such a very serious engagement. [*He flings angrily away across the room and back*].

TRENCH [*much injured*] I ought to have known ! Cokane : is this reasonable ? [*Cokane's features are contorted by an air of judicial consideration ; but he ?says nothing ; and Trench again addresses Sartorius, this time with a marked diminution of respect*]. How the deuce could I have known ? You didnt tell me.

SARTORIUS. You are trifling with me, sir. You say that you did not know your own mind before.

TRENCH. I say nothing of the sort. I say that I did not know where your money came from before.

SARTORIUS. That is not true, sir. I

COKANE. Gently, my dear sir. Gently, Harry, dear boy. Suaviter in modo : fort

TRENCH. Let him begin, then. What does he mean by attacking me in this fashion ?

SARTORIUS. Mr Cokane : you will bear me out. I was explicit on the point. I said I was a self-made man ; and I am not ashamed of it.

TRENCH. You are nothing of the sort. I found out this morning from your man Lickcheese, or whatever his confounded name is that your fortune has been made out of a parcel of unfortunate creatures that have hardly enough to keep body and soul together made by screwing, and bullying, and driving, and all sorts of pettifogging tyranny.

SARTORIUS [*outraged*] Sir ! [*They confront one another threateningly*] .

COKANE [*softly*] Rent must be paid, dear boy. It is inevitable, Harry, inevitable. [*Trench turns away petulantly. Sartorius looks after him reflectively for a moment ; then resumes his former deliberate and dignified manner, and addresses Trench with studied consideration, but with a perceptible condescension to his youth and folly*].

SARTORIUS. I am afraid, Dr Trench, that you are a very young hand at business ; and I am sorry I forgot that for a moment or so. May I ask you to suspend your judgment until we have a little quiet discussion of this sentimental notion of yours ? if you will excuse me for calling it so. [*He takes a chair, and motions Trench to another on his right*],

COKANE. Very nicely put, my dear sir. Come, Harry : sit down and listen ; and consider the matter calmly and judicially. Dont be headstrong.

TRENCH. I have no objection to sit down and listen ; but I dont see how that can make black white ; and I am tired of being turned on as if I were in the wrong. [*He sits down. Cokane sits at his elbow, on his right. They compose themselves for a conference*].

SARTORIUS. I assume, to begin with, Dr Trench, that you are not a Socialist, or anything of that sort.

TRENCH. Certainly not. I'm a Conservative at least, if I ever took the trouble to vote, I should vote for the Conservative and against the other fellow.

COKANE. True blue, Harry, true blue !

SARTORIUS. I am glad to find that so far we are in perfect sympathy. I am, of course, a Conservative ; not a narrow or prejudiced one, I hope, nor at all opposed to true progress, but still a sound Conservative. As to Lickcheese, I need say no more about him than that I have dismissed him from my service this morning for a breach of trust ; and you will hardly accept his testimony as friendly or disinterested. As to my business, it is simply to provide homes suited to the small means of very poor people, who require roofs to shelter them just like other people. Do you suppose I can keep up those roofs for nothing ?

TRENCH. Yes : thats all very fine ; but the point is, what sort of homes do you give them for their money ? People must live somewhere, or else go to jail. Advantage is taken of that to make them pay for houses that are not fit for dogs. Why dont you build proper dwellings, and give fair value for the money you take ?

SARTORIUS [*pitying his innocence*] My young friend: these poor people do not know how to live in proper dwellings : they would wreck them in a week. You doubt me : try it for yourself. You are welcome to replace all the missing bannisters, handrails, cistern lids and dusthole tops at your own expense ; and you will find them missing again in less than three days burnt, sir, every stick of them. I do not blame the poor creatures : they need fires, and often have no other way of getting them. But I really cannot spend pound after pound in repairs for them to pull down, when I can barely get them to pay me four and sixpence a week for a room, which is the recognized fair London rent. No, gentlemen : when people are very poor, you cannot help them, no matter how much you may sympathize with them. It does them more harm than good in the long run. I prefer to save my money in order to provide additional houses for the homeless, and to lay by a little for Blanche. [*He looks at them. They are silent: Trench unconvinced, but talked down; Cokane humanely perplexed. Sartorius bends his brows ; comes forward in his chair as if gathering himself together for a spring; and addresses himself, with impressive significance, to Trench*]. And now, Dr Trench, may I ask what your income is derived from !

TRENCH [*defiantly*] From interest not from houses. M y hands are clean as far as that goes. Interest on a mortgage.

SARTORIUS [*forcibly*] Yes: a mortgage on my property. When I, to use your own words, screw, and bully, and drive these people to pay what they have freely undertaken to pay me, I cannot touch one penny of the money they give me until I have first paid you your £700 out of it. What Lickcheese did for me, I do for you. He and I are alike intermediaries : you are the principal. It is because of the risks I run through the poverty of my tenants that you exact interest from me at the monstrous and exorbitant rate of seven per cent, forcing me to exact the uttermost farthing in my turn from the tenants. And yet, Dr Trench, you have not hesitated to speak contemptuously of me because I have applied my industry and forethought to the management of our property, and am maintaining it by the same honorable means.

COKANE [*greatly relieved*] Admirable, my dear sir, excellent ! I felt instinctively that Trench was talking unpractical nonsense. Let us drop the subject, my dear boy : you only make an ass of yourself when you meddle in business matters. I told you it was inevitable.

TRENCH [*dazed*] Do you mean to say that I am just as bad as you are ?

COKANE. Shame, Harry, shame ! Grossly bad taste ! Be a gentleman. Apologize.

SARTORIUS. Allow me, Mr Cokane. [*To Trench*] If, when you say you are just as bad as I am, you mean that you are just as powerless to alter the state of society, then you are unfortunately quite right. [*Trench does not at once reply. He stares at S art onus, and then hangs his head and gazes stupidly at the floor, morally beggared, with his clasped knuckles between his knees, a living picture of disillusion. Cokane comes sympathetically to him and puts an encouraging hand on his shoulder*].

COKANE [*gently*] Come, Harry, come ! Pull yourself together. You owe a word to Mr Sartorius.

TRENCH [*still stupefied, slowly unlaces his fingers ; puts his hands on his knees, and lifts himself upright ; pulls his waistcoat straight with a tug; and tries to take his disenchantment philosophically as he turns to Sartorius*]. Well, people who live in glass houses have no right to throw stones. But, on my honor, I never knew that my house was a glass one until you pointed it out. I beg your pardon. [*He offers his hand*].

SARTORIUS. Say no more, Harry : your feelings do you credit : I assure you I feel exactly as you do, myself. Every man who has a heart must wish that a better state of things was practicable. But unhappily it is not.

TRENCH [*a little consoled*] I suppose not.

COKANE. Not a doubt of it, my dear sir : not a doubt of it. The increase of the population is at the bottom of it all.

SARTORIUS [*to Trench*] I trust I have convinced you that you need no more object to Blanche sharing my fortune, than I need object to her sharing yours.

TRENCH [*with dull wistfulness*] It seems so. We're all in the same swim, it appears. I hope youll excuse my making such a fuss.

SARTORIUS. Not another word. In fact, I thank you for refraining from explaining the nature of your scruples to Blanche : I admire that in you, Harry. Perhaps it will be as well to leave her in ignorance.

TRENCH [*anxiously*] But I must explain now. You saw how angry she was.

SARTORIUS. You had better leave that to me. [*He looks at his watch, and rings the bell*]. Lunch is nearly due : while you are getting ready for it I can see Blanche ; and I hope the result will be quite satisfactory to us all. [*The parlor maid answers the bell: he addresses her with his habitual peremptoriness*] Tell Miss Blanche I want her.

THE PARLOR MAID [*her face falling expressively*] Yes, sir. [*She turns reluctantly to go*].

SARTORIUS [*on second thoughts*] Stop. [*She stops*]. My love to Miss Blanche ; and I am alone here and would like to see her for a moment if she is not busy.

THE PARLOR MAID [*relieved*] Yes, sir. [*She goes out*].

SARTORIUS. I will shew you your room, Harry. I hope you will soon be perfectly at home in it. You also, Mr Cokane, must learn your way about here. Let us go before Blanche comes. [*He leads the way to the door*].

COKANE [*cheerily, following him*] Our little discussion has given me quite an appetite.

TRENCH [*moodily*] It's taken mine away. [*They go out, Sartorius holding the door for them. He is following when the parlor maid reappears. She is a snivelling, sympathetic creature, and is on the verge of tears*].

SARTORIUS. Well : is Miss Blanche coming ?

THE PARLOR MAID. Yes, sir. I think so, sir.

SARTORIUS. Wait here until she comes ; and tell her that I will be back in a moment.

THE PARLOR MAID. Yes, SIT. [*She comes into the room. Sartorius looks suspiciously at her as she passes him. He half closes the door and follows her*].

SARTORIUS [*lowering his voice*] Whats the matter with you ?

THE PARLOR MAID [*whimpering*] Nothing, sir.

SARTORIUS [*at the same pitch, more menacingly*] Take care how you behave yourself when there are visitors present. Do you hear ?

THE PARLOR MAID. Yes, sir. [*Sartorius goes out*].

SARTORIUS [*outside*] Excuse me : I had a word to say to the servant. [*Trench is heard replying " Not at all" Cokane " Dont mention it, my dear sir." The murmur of their voices passes out of hearing. The parlor maid sniffs ; dries her eyes ; goes to one of the bookcases ; and takes some brown paper and a ball of string from a drawer. 8 he puts them on the table and wrestles with another sob. Blanche comes in, with a jewel box in her hands. Her expression is that of a strong and determined woman in an intense passion. The maid looks at her with a mixture of abject wounded affection and bodily terror*].

BLANCHE [*looking round*] Where's my father ?

THE PARLOR MAID [*tremulously propitiatory*] He left word he'd be back directly, miss. I'm sure he wont be long. Here's the paper and string all ready, miss. [*She spreads the paper on the table*] Can I do the parcel for you, miss ?

BLANCHE. No. Mind your own business. [*She empties the box on the sheet of brown paper. It contains a packet of letters and some jewellery. She plucks a ring from her finger and throws it down on the heap so angrily that it rolls away and falls on the carpet. The maid submissively picks it up and puts it on the table, again sniffing and drying her eyes*], What are you crying for ?

THE PARLOR MAID [*plaintively*] You speak so brutal to me, Miss Blanche ; and I do love you so. I'm sure no one else would stay and put up with what I have to put up with.

BLANCHE. Then go. I dont want you. Do you hear. Go.

THE PARLOR MAID [*piteously, falling on her knees*] Oh no, Miss Blanche. Dont send me away from you : dont

BLANCHE [*with fierce disgust*] Agh ! I hate the sight of you. [*The maid, wounded to the heart, cries bitterly*]. Hold your tongue. Are those two gentlemen gone ?

THE PARLOR MAID [*weeping*] Oh, how could you say such a thing to me, Miss Blanche : me that

BLANCHE [*seizing her by the hair and throat*] Stop that noise, I tell you, unless you want me to kill you.

THE PARLOR MAID [*protesting and imploring, but in a carefully subdued voice*] Let me go, Miss Blanche : you know youll be sorry : you always are. Remember how dreadfully my head was cut last time.

BLANCHE [*raging*] Answer me, will you. Have they gone ?

THE PARLOR MAID. Lickcheese has gone, looking dreadf [*she breaks off with a stifled cry as Blanche's fingers tighten furiously on her*].

BLANCHE. Did I ask you about Lickcheese ? You beast : you know who I mean : youre doing it on purpose.

THE PARLOR MAID [*in a gasp*] *Theyre staying to lunch.*

BLANCHE [*looking intently into her face*] He ?

THE PARLOR MAID [*whispering with a sympathetic nod*] Yes, miss. [*Blanche slowly releases her and stands upright with clenched fists and set face. The parlor maid, recognizing the passing of the crisis of passion, and fearing no further violence, sits discomfitedly on her heels, and tries to arrange her hair and cap, whimpering a little with exhaustion and soreness*]. Now youve set my hands all trembling ; and I shall jingle the things on the tray at lunch so that everybody will notice me. It's too bad of you, Miss Bl [*Sartorius coughs outside*].

BLANCHE [*quickly*] Sh ! Get up. [*The parlor maid hastily gets up, and goes out as demurely as she can, passing Sartorius on her way to the door. He glances sternly at her and comes to Blanche. The parlor maid shuts the door softly behind her*].

SARTORIUS [*mournfully*] My dear : can you not make a little better fight with your temper ?

BLANCHE [*panting with the subsidence of her fit*] No I cant. I wont. I do my best. Nobody who really cares for me gives me up because of my temper. I never shew my temper to any of the servants but that girl ; and she is the only one that will stay with us.

SARTORIUS. But, my dear, remember that we have to meet our visitors at luncheon presently. I have run down before them to say that I have arranged that little difficulty with Trench. It was only a piece of mischief made by Lickcheese. Trench is a young fool ; but it is all right now.

BLANCHE. I dont want to marry a fool.

SARTORIUS. Then you will have to take a husband over thirty, Blanche. You must not expect too much, my child. You will be richer than your husband, and, I think, cleverer too. I am better pleased that it should be so.

BLANCHE [*seizing his arm*] *Papa.*

SARTORIUS. Yes, my dear.

BLANCHE. May I do as I like about this marriage ; or must I do as you like ?

SARTORIUS [*uneasily*] Blanche

BLANCHE. No, papa : you must answer me.

SARTORIUS [*abandoning his self-control, and giving way recklessly to his affection for her*] You shall do as you like now and always, my beloved child. I only wish to do as my own darling pleases.

BLANCHE. Then I will not marry him. He has played fast and loose with me. He thinks us beneath him : he is ashamed of us : he dared to object to being benefited by you as if it were not natural for him to owe you everything ; and yet the money tempted him after all. [*She throws her arms hysterically about his neck*] Papa : I dont want to marry : I only want to stay with you and be happy as we have always been. I hate the thought of being married : I dont care for him : I dont want to leave you. [*Trench and Cokane come in; but she can hear nothing but her own voice and does not notice them*]. Only send him away : promise me that you will send him away and keep me here with you as we have always [*seeing Trench*] Oh ! [*She hides her face on her father's breast*].

TRENCH [*nervously*] I hope we are not intruding.

SARTORIUS [*formidably*] Dr Trench : my daughter has changed her mind.

TRENCH [*disconcerted*] Am I to understand

COKANE [*striking in in his most vinegary manner*] I think, Harry, under the circumstances, we have no alternative but to seek luncheon elsewhere.

TRENCH. But, Mr Sartorius, have you explained ?

SARTORIUS [*straight in Trench's face*] I have explained, sir. Good morning. [*Trench, outraged, advances a step. Blanche sinks away from her father into a chair. Sartorius stands his ground rigidly*]

TRENCH [*turning away indignantly*] Come on, Cokane.

COKANE. Certainly, Harry, certainly. [*Trench goes out, very angry. The parlor maid, with a tray jingling in her hands, passes outside*] You have disappointed me, sir, very acutely. Good morning. [*He follows Trench*],

ACT III

The drawing-room in Sartorius's house in Bedford Square. Winter evening: fire burning, curtains drawn and lamps lighted. Sartorius and Blanche are sitting glumly near the fire. The parlor maid, who has just brought in coffee, is placing it on a small table between them. There is a large table in the middle of the room. Looking from it towards the two windows, the pianoforte, a grand, is on the right, with a photographic portrait of Blanche on a miniature easel on the top. There are two doors, one on the left, further forward than the fireplace, leading to the study ; the other by the corner nearest the right hand window, leading to the lobby. Blanche has her work basket at hand, and is knitting. Sartorius, closer to the fire, has a newspaper. The parlor maid goes out.

SARTORIUS. Blanche, my love.

BLANCHE. Yes.

SARTORIUS. I had a long talk to the doctor today about our going abroad.

BLANCHE [*impatiently*] I am quite well ; and I will not go abroad. I loathe the very thought of the Continent. Why will you bother me so about my health ?

SARTORIUS. It was not about your health, Blanche, but about my own.

BLANCHE [*rising"*] Yours ! [*She goes anxiously to him*]. Oh, papa, theres nothing the matter with you, I hope ?

SARTORIUS. There will be there must be, Blanche, long before you begin to consider yourself an old woman.

BLANCHE. But theres nothing the matter now ?

SARTORIUS. Well, my dear, the doctor says I need change, travel, excitement

BLANCHE. Excitement! You need excitement ! [*She laughs joylessly, and sits down on the rug at his feet*]. How is it, papa, that you, who are so clever with everybody else, are not a bit clever with me ? Do you think I cant see through your little plan to take me abroad ? Since I will not be the invalid and allow you to be the nurse, you are to be the invalid and I am to be the nurse.

SARTORIUS. Well, Blanche, if you will have it that you are well and have nothing preying on your spirits, I must insist on being ill and have something preying on mine. And indeed, my girl, there is no use in our going on as we have for the last four months. You have not been happy ; and I have been far from comfortable. [*Blanche's face clouds : she turns away from him and sits dumb and brooding. He waits in vain for some reply ; then adds in a lower tone*] Need you be so inflexible, Blanche ?

BLANCHE. I thought you admired inflexibility: you have always prided yourself on it.

SARTORIUS. Nonsense, my dear, nonsense. I have had to give in often enough. And I could shew you plenty of soft fellows who have done as well as I, and enjoyed themselves more, perhaps. If it is only for the sake of inflexibility that you are standing out

BLANCHE. I am not standing out. I dont know what you mean. [*She tries to rise and go away*].

SARTORIUS [*catching her arm and arresting her on her knees*] Come, my child : you must not trifle with me as if I were a stranger. You are fretting because

BLANCHE [*violently twisting herself free and speaking as she rises*] If you say it, papa, I will kill myself. It is not true. If he were here on his knees tonight, I would walk out of the house sooner than endure it. [*She goes out excitedly. Sartorius, greatly troubled, turns again to the fire with a heavy sigh*].

SARTORIUS [*gazing gloomily into the glow*] Now if I fight it out with her, no more comfort for months ! I might as well live with my clerk or my servant. And if I give in now, I shall have to give in always. Well ! I cant help it. I have stuck to having my own way all my life ; but there must be an end to that drudgery some day. She is young : let her have her turn at it. [*the parlor maid comes in*].

THE PARLOR MAID. Please, sir, Mr Lickcheese wants to see you very particlar. On important business your business, he told me to say.

SARTORIUS. Mr Lickcheese ! Do you mean Lickcheese who used to come here on my business ?

THE PARLOR MAID. Yes, sir. But indeed, sir, youd scarcely know him.

SARTORIUS [*frowning*] Hm ! Starving, I suppose. Come to beg ?

THE PARLOR MAID [*intensely repudiating the idea*] O-o-o-o-h NO, sir. Quite the gentleman, sir ! Sealskin overcoat, sir ! Come in a hansom, all shaved and clean ! I'm sure he's come into a fortune, sir.

SARTORIUS. Hm ! Shew him up.

[*Lickcheese, who has been waiting at the door, instantly comes in. The change in his appearance is dazzling. He is in evening dress, with an overcoat lined throughout with furs presenting all the hues of the tiger. His shirt is fastened at the breast with a single diamond stud. His silk hat is of the glossiest black ; a handsome gold watch-chain hangs like a garland on his jilled-out waistcoat ; he has shaved his whiskers and grown a moustache, the ends of which are waxed and pointed. As Sartorius stares speechless at him, he stands, smiling, to be admired, intensely enjoying the effect he is producing. The parlor maid, hardly less pleased with her own share in this coup-de-theatre, goes out beaming, full of the news for the kitchen. Lickcheese clinches the situation by a triumphant nod at Sartorius*].

SARTORIUS [*bracing himself hostile*] Well ?

LICKCHEESE. Quite well, Sartorius, thankee.

SARTORIUS. I was not asking after your health, sir, as you know, I think, as well as I do. What is your business ?

LICKCHEESE. Business that I can take elsewhere if I meet with less civility than I please to put up with, Sartorius. You and me is man and man now. It was money that used to be my master, and not you : dont think it. Now that I'm independent in respect of money

SARTORIUS [*crossing determinedly to the door, and holding it open*] You can take your independence out of my house, then. I wont have it here.

LICKCHEESE [*indulgently*] Come, Sartorius : dont be stiffnecked. I come here as a friend to put money in your pocket. No use in your lettin on to me that youre above money. Eh ?

SARTORIUS [*hesitates, and at last shuts the door, saying guardedly*] How much money ?

LICKCHEESE [*victorious, going to Blanche' s chair and taking off his overcoat*] Ah ! there you speak like yourself, Sartorius. Now suppose you ask me to sit down and make myself comfortable.

SARTORIUS [*coming from the door*] I have a mind to put you downstairs by the back of your neck, you infernal blackguard.

LICKCHEESE [*not a bit ruffled, hangs his overcoat on the back of Blanche's chair, pulling a cigar case out of one of the pockets as he does so*]. You and me is too much of a pair for me to take anything you say in bad part, Sartorius. 'Ave a cigar.

SARTORIUS. No smoking here : this is my daughter's room. However, sit down, sit down. [*They sit*].

LICKCHEESE. I' bin gittin on a little since I saw you last.

SARTORIUS. So I see.

LICKCHEESE. I owe it partly to you, you know. Does that surprise you ?

SARTORIUS. It doesnt concern me.

LICKCHEESE. So you think, Sartorius ; because it never did concern you how I got on, so long as I got you on by bringin in the rents. But I picked up something for myself down at Robbins's Row.

SARTORIUS. I always thought so. Have you come to make restitution ?

LICKCHEESE. You wouldnt take it if I offered it to you, Sartorius. It wasnt money : it was knowledge knowledge of the great public question of the Housing of the Working Classes. You know theres a Royal Commission on it, dont you ?

SARTORIUS. Oh, I see. Youve been giving evidence.

LICKCHEESE. Giving evidence ! Not me. What good would that do me ? Only my expenses ; and that not on the professional scale, neither. No : I gev no evidence. But I'll tell you what I did. I kep it back, jest to oblige one or two people whose feelins would a bin urt by seein their names in a bluebook as keepin a fever den. Their Agent got so friendly with me over it that he put his name on a bill of mine to the tune of well, no matter : it gev me a start ; and a start was all I ever wanted to get on my feet. Ive got a copy of the first report of the Commission in the pocket of my overcoat. [*He rises and gets at his overcoat, from a pocket of which he takes a bluebook*]. I turned down the page to shew you : I thought youd like to see it. [*He doubles the book back at the place indicated, and hands it to Sartorius*].

SARTORIUS. So blackmail is the game, eh ? [*He puts the book on the table without looking at it, and strikes it emphatically with his fist*]. I dont care that for my name being in bluebooks. My friends dont read them ; and I'm neither a Cabinet Minister nor a candidate for Parliament. Theres nothing to be got out of me on that lay.

LICKCHEESE [*shocked*] *Blackmail ! Oh, Mr Sartorius, do you think I would let out a word about your premises ? Round on an old pal ! no : that aint Lickcheese's way. Besides, they know all about you already. Them stairs that you and me quarrelled about, they was a whole arternoon examinin the clergyman that made such a fuss you remember ? about the women that was urt on it. He made the worst he could of it, in an ungentlemanly, unchristian spirit. I wouldnt have that clergyman's disposition for worlds. Oh no : thats not what was in my thoughts.*

SARTORIUS. Come, come, man : what was in your thoughts ? Out with it.

LICKCHEESE [*with provoking deliberation, smiling and looking mysteriously at him*] You aint spent a few hundreds in repairs since we parted, ave you ? [*Sartorius, losing patience, makes a threatening movement*]. Now dont fly out at me. I know a landlord that owned as beastly a slum as you could find in London, down there by the Tower. By my advice that man put half the houses into first-class repair, and let the other half to a new Company : the North Thames Iced Mutton Depot Company, of which I hold a few shares promoters' shares. And what was the end of it, do you think ?

SARTORIUS. Smash, I suppose.

LICKCHEESE. Smash ! not a bit of it. Compensation, Mr Sartorius, compensation. Do you understand that ?

SARTORIUS. Compensation for what ?

LICKCHEESE. Why, the land was wanted for an extension of the Mint ; and the Company had to be bought out, and the buildings compensated for. Somebody has to know these things beforehand, you know, no matter how dark theyre kept.

SARTORIUS [*interested, but cautious*] Well ?

LICKCHEESE. Is that all you have to say to me, Mr Sartorius ? " Well " ! as if I was next door's dog ! Suppose I'd got wind of a new street that would knock down Robbins's Row and turn Burke's Walk into a frontage worth thirty pound a foot ! would you say no more to me than [*mimicking*] "Well " ? [*Sartorius hesitates, looking at him in great doubt : Lickcheese rises and exhibits himself*] *Come : look at my get-up, Mr Sartorius. Look at this watchchain ! Look at the corporation Ive got on me ! Do you think all that came from keeping my mouth shut ? No: it came from keeping my ears and eyes open.* [*Blanche comes in, followed by the parlor maid, who has a silver tray on which she collects the coffee cups. Sartorius, impatient at the interruption, rises and motions Lickcheese to the door of the study*].

SARTORIUS. Sh ! We must talk this over in the study. There is a good fire there ; and you can smoke. Blanche : an old friend of ours.

LICKCHEESE. And a kind one to me. I hope I see you well, Miss Blanche.

BLANCHE. Why, it's Mr Lickcheese ! I hardly knew you.

LICKCHEESE. I find you a little changed yourself, miss.

BLANCHE [*hastily*] Oh, I am the same as ever. How are Mrs Lickcheese and the chil

SARTORIUS [*impatiently*] We have business to transact, Blanche. You can talk to Mr Lickcheese afterwards. Come on. [*Sartorius and Lickcheese go into the study. Blanche, surprised at her father's abruptness, looks after them for a moment. Then, see-seeing Lickcheese' 's overcoat on her chair, she takes it up, amused, and looks at the fur*],

THE PARLOR MAID. Oh, we are fine, aint we, Miss Blanche ? I think Mr Lickcheese must have come into a legacy. [*Confidentially*] I wonder what he can want with the master, Miss Blanche ! He brought him this big book. [*8 he shews the bluebook to Blanche*].

BLANCHE [*her curiosity roused*] Let me see. [*She takes the book and looks at it*]. Theres something about papa in it. [*She sits down and begins to read*].

THE PARLOR MAID [*folding the tea-table and putting it out of the way*] He looks ever s'much younger, Miss Blanche, dont he ? I couldnt help laughing when I saw him with his whiskers shaved off : it do look so silly when youre not accustomed to it. [*No answer from Blanche*]. You havnt finished your coffee, miss : I suppose I may take it away ? [*No answer*]. Oh, you are interested in Mr Lickcheese's book, miss. [*Blanche springs up. The parlor maid looks at her face, and instantly hurries out of the room on tiptoe with her fray*].

BLANCHE. So that was why he would not touch the money. [*She tries to tear the book across ; but that is impossible ; so she throws it violently into the fireplace. It falls into the fender*]. Oh, if only a girl could have no father, no family, just as I have no mother ! Clergyman ! beast ! " The worst slum landlord in London." " Slum landlord." Oh ! [*She covers her face with her hands and sinks shuddering into the chair on which the overcoat lies. The study door opens*].

LICKCHEESE [*in the study*] You just wait five minutes : I'll fetch him. [*Blanche snatches a piece of work from her basket and sits erect and quiet, stitching at it. Lickcheese comes back, speaking to Sartorius, who follows him*]. He lodges round the corner in Gower Street ; and my private ansom's at the door. By your leave, Miss Blanche [*pulling gently at his overcoat*],

BLANCHE [*rising*] I beg your pardon. I hope I havnt crushed it.

LICKCHEESE [*gallantly, as he gets into the coat*] Youre welcome to crush it again now, Miss Blanche. Dont say good evenin to me, miss : I'm comin back presently me and a friend or two. Ta ta, Sartorius: I shant be long. [*He goes out. Sartorius looks about for the blue book*].

BLANCHE. I thought we were done with Lickcheese.

SARTORIUS. Not quite yet, I think. He left a book here for me to look over, a large book in a blue paper cover. Has the girl put it away? [*He sees it in the fender ; looks at Blanche; and adds*] Have you seen it ?

BLANCHE. No. Yes. [*Angrily*] No : I have not seen it. What have I to do with it ? [*Sartorius picks the book up and dusts it; then sits down quietly to read. After a glance up and down the columns, he nods assentingly, as if he found there exactly what he expected*].

SARTORIUS. It's a curious thing, Blanche, that the Parliamentary gentlemen who write such books as these should be so ignorant of practical business. One would suppose, to read this, that we are the most grasping, grinding, heartless pair in the world, you and I.

BLANCHE. .Is it not true about the state of the houses, I mean ?

SARTORIUS [*calmly*] Oh, quite true.

BLANCHE. Then it is not our fault ?

SARTORIUS. My dear : if we made the houses any better, the rents would have to be raised so much that the poor people would be unable to pay, and would be thrown homeless on the streets.

BLANCHE. Well, turn them out and get in a respectable class of people. Why should we have the disgrace of harbouring such wretches?

SARTORIUS [*opening his eyes*] That sounds a little hard on them, doesnt it, my child ?

BLANCHE. Oh, I hate the poor. At least, I hate those dirty, drunken, disreputable people who live like pigs. If they must be provided for, let other people look after them. How can you expect anyone to think well of us when such things are written about us in that infamous book ?

SARTORIUS [*coldly and a little wistfully*] I see I have made a real lady of you, Blanche.

BLANCHE [*defiantly*] Well, are you sorry for that ?

SARTORIUS. No, my dear : of course not. But do you know, Blanche, that my mother was a very poor woman, and that her poverty was not her fault ?

BLANCHE. I suppose not ; but the people we want to mix with now dont know that. And it was not my fault ; so I dont see why I should be made to suffer for it.

SARTORIUS [*enraged*] Who makes you suffer for it, miss ? What would you be now but for what your grandmother did for me when she stood at her wash-tub for thirteen hours a day and thought herself rich when she made fifteen shillings a week ?

BLANCHE [*angrily*] I suppose I should have been down on her level instead of being raised above it, as I am now. Would you like us to go and live in that place in the book for the sake of grandmamma ? I hate the idea of such things. I dont want to know about them. I love you because you brought me up to something better. [*Half aside, as she turns away from him*] I should hate you if you had not.

SARTORIUS [*giving in*] Well, my child, I suppose it is natural for you to feel that way, after your bringing up. It is the ladylike view of the matter. So dont let us quarrel, my girl. You shall not be made to suffer any more. I have made up my mind to improve the property, and get in quite a new class of tenants. There ! does that satisfy you ? I am only waiting for the consent of the ground landlord, Lady Roxdale.

BLANCHE. Lady Roxdale !

SARTORIUS. Yes. But I shall expect the mortgagee to take his share of the risk.

BLANCHE. The mortgagee ! Do you mean [*She cannot finish the sentence : Sartorius does it for her*].

SARTORIUS. Harry Trench. Yes. And remember, Blanche : if he consents to join me in the scheme, I shall have to be friends with him.

BLANCHE. And to ask him to the house ?

SARTORIUS. Only on business. You need not meet him unless you like.

BLANCHE [*overwhelmed*] *When is he coming ?*

SARTORIUS. There is no time to be lost. Lickcheese has gone to ask him to come round.

BLANCHE [*in dismay*] Then he will be here in a few minutes ! What shall I do ?

SARTORIUS. I advise you to receive him as if nothing had happened, and then go out and leave us to our business. You are not afraid to meet him ?

BLANCHE. Afraid ! No, most certainly not. But [*Lickcheese y s voice is heard without*] Here they are. Dont say I'm here, papa. [*She rushes away into the study. Lickcheese comes in with Trench and Cokane. Cokane shakes hands effusively with Sartorius. Trench, who is coarsened and sullen, and has evidently not been making the best of his disappointment, bows shortly and resentfully. Lickcheese covers the general embarrassment by talking cheerfully until they are all seated round the large table : Trench nearest the fireplace ; Cokane nearest the piano ; and the other two between them, with Lickcheese next Cokane*].

LICKCHEESE. Here we are, all friends round St Paul's. You remember Mr Cokane : he does a little business for me now as a friend, and gives me a help with my correspondence sekketerry we call it. Ive no litery style, and thats the truth ; so Mr Cokane kindly puts it into my letters and draft prospectuses and advertisements and the like. Dont you, Cokane ? Of course you do : why shouldnt you ? He's been helping me to-night to persuade his old friend, Dr Trench, about the matter we were speaking of.

COKANE [*austerely"*] No, Mr Lickcheese, not trying to persuade him. No : this is a matter of principle with me. I say it is your duty, Henry your duty to put those abominable buildings into proper and habitable repair. As a man of science you owe it to the community to perfect the sanitary arrangements. In questions of duty there is no room for persuasion, even from the oldest friend.

SARTORIUS [*to Trench*] I certainly feel, as Mr Cokane puts it, that it is our duty : one which I have perhaps too long neglected out of regard for the poorest class of tenants.

LICKCHEESE. Not a doubt of it, gents, a dooty. I can be as sharp as any man when it's a question of business ; but dooty's another thing.

TRENCH. Well, I dont see that it's any more my duty now than it was four months ago. I look at it simply as a question of so much money.

COKANE. Shame, Harry, shame ! Shame !

TRENCH. Oh, shut up, you fool. [*Cokane springs up. Lickcheese catches his coat and holds him*]

LICKCHEESE. Steady, steady, Mr Sekketerry. Dr Trench is only joking.

COKANE. I insist on the withdrawal of that expression. I have been called a fool.

TRENCH [*morosely*] So you are a fool.

COKANE. Then you are a damned fool. Now, sir !

TRENCH. All right. Now weve settled that. [*Cokane, with a snort, sits down*]. What I mean is this. Dont lets have any nonsense about this job. As I understand it, Robbins's Row is to be pulled down to make way for the new street into the Strand ; and the straight tip now is to go for compensation.

LICKCHEESE [*chuckling*] That'so, Dr Trench. Thats it.

TRENCH [*continuing*] Well, it appears that the dirtier a place is the more rent you get ; and the decenter it is, the more compensation you get. So we're to give up dirt and go in for decency.

SARTORIUS. I should not put it exactly in that way ; but

COKANE. Quite right, Mr Sartorius, quite right. The case could not have been stated in worse taste or with less tact.

LICKCHEESE. Sh-sh-sh-sh !

SARTORIUS. I do not quite go with you there, Mr Cokane. Dr Trench puts the case frankly as a man of business. I take the wider view of a public man. We live in a progressive age ; and humanitarian ideas are advancing and must be taken into account. But my practical conclusion is the same as his. I should hardly feel justified in making a large claim for compensation under existing circumstances.

LICKCHEESE. Of course not ; and you wouldnt get it if you did. You see, it's like this, Dr Trench. Theres no doubt that the Vestries has legal powers to play old Harry with slum properties, and spoil the houseknacking game if they please. That didnt matter in the good old times, because the Vestries used to be us ourselves. Nobody ever knew a word about the election ; and we used to get ten of us into a room and elect one another, and do what we liked. Well, that cock wont fight any longer ; and, to put it short, the game is up for men in the position of you and Mr Sartorius. My advice to you is, take the present chance of getting out of it. Spend a little money on the block at the Cribbs Market end enough to make it look like a model dwelling ; and let the other block to me on fair terms for a depot of the North Thames Iced Mutton Company. Theyll be knocked down inside of two year to make room for the new north and south main thoroughfare ; and youll be compensated to the tune of double the present valuation, with the cost of the improvements thrown in. Leave things as they are ; and you stand a good chance of being fined, or condemned, or pulled down before long. Now's your time.

COKANE. Hear, hear ! Hear, hear ! Hear, hear ! Admirably put from the business point of view ! I recognize the uselessness of putting the moral point of view to you, Trench ; but even you must feel the cogency of Mr Lickcheese's business statement.

TRENCH. But why cant you act without me ? What have I got to do with it ? I'm only a mortgagee.

SARTORIUS. There is a certain risk in this compensation investment, Dr Trench. The County Council may alter the line of the new street. If that happens, the money spent in improving the houses will be thrown away simply thrown away. Worse than thrown away, in fact ; for the new buildings may stand unlet or half let for years. But you will expect your seven per cent as usual.

TRENCH. A man must live.

COCKANE. Je n'en vois pas la necessite.

TRENCH. Shut up, Billy ; or else speak some language you understand. No, Mr Sartorius : I should be very glad to stand in with you if I could afford it ; but I cant ; so theres an end of that.

LICKCHEESE. Well, all I can say is that youre a very foolish young man.

COKANE. What did I tell you, Harry ?

TRENCH. I dont see that it's any business of yours, Mr Lickcheese.

LICKCHEESE. It's a free country : every man has a right to his opinion. [*Cokane cries "Hear, hear!"*] Come: wheres your feelins for them poor people, Dr Trench ? Remember how it went to your heart when I first told you about them. What ! are you going to turn hard?

TRENCH. No : it wont do : you cant get over me that way. You proved to me before that there was no use in being sentimental over that slum shop of ours ; and it's no good your turning round on the philanthropic tack now that you want me to put my capital into your speculation. Ive had my lesson ; and I'm going to stick to my present income. It's little enough for me as it is.

SARTORIUS. It really matters nothing to me, Dr Trench, how you decide. I can easily raise the money elsewhere and pay you off. Then, since you are resolved to run no risks, you can invest your £10,000 in Consols and get 250 a year for it instead of 700. [*Trench, completely outwitted, stares at them in consternation. Cokane breaks the silence*].

COKANE. This is what comes of being avaricious, Harry. Two thirds of your income gone at one blow. And I must say it serves you right.

TRENCH. Thats all very fine ; but I dont understand it. If you can do this to me, why didnt you do it long ago ?

SARTORIUS. Because, as I should probably have had to borrow at the same rate, I should have saved nothing ; whereas you would have lost over .400 a very serious matter for you. I had no desire to be unfriendly ; and even now I should be glad to let the mortgage stand, were it not that the circumstances mentioned by Mr Lickcheese force my hand. Besides, Dr Trench, I hoped for some time that our interests might be joined by closer ties even than those of friendship.

LICKCHEESE [*jumping up, relieved*] There ! Now the murder's out. Excuse me, Dr Trench. Excuse me, Mr Sartorius : excuse my freedom. Why not Dr Trench marry Miss Blanche, and settle the whole affair that way ? [*Sensation. Lickcheese sits down triumphant*].

COKANE. You forget, Mr Lickcheese, that the young lady, whose taste has to be considered, decisively objected to him.

TRENCH. Oh ! Perhaps you think she was struck with you.

COKANE. I do not say so, Trench. No man of any delicacy would suggest such a thing. You have an untutored mind, Trench, an untutored mind.

TRENCH. Well, Cokane : Ive told you my opinion of you already.

COKANE [*rising wildly*] And I have told you my opinion of you. I will repeat it if you wish. I am ready to repeat it.

LICKCHEESE. Come, Mr Sekketerry : you and me, as married men, is out of the unt as far as young ladies is concerned. I know Miss Blanche : she has her father's eye for business. Explain this job to her ; and she'll make it up with Dr Trench. Why not have a bit of romance in business when it costs nothing ? We all have our feelins : we aint mere calculatin machines.

SARTORIUS [*revolted*] Do you think, Lickcheese, that my daughter is to be made part of a money bargain between you and these gentlemen ?

LICKCHEESE. Oh come, Sartorius : dont talk as if you was the only father in the world. I have a daughter too ; and my feelins in that matter is just as fine as yours. I propose nothing but what is for Miss Blanche's advantage and Dr Trench's.

COKANE. Lickcheese expresses himself roughly, Mr Sartorius ; but his is a sterling nature ; and what he says is to the point. If Miss Sartorius can really bring herself to care for Harry, I am far from desiring to stand in the way of such an arrangement.

TRENCH. Why, what have you got to do with it ?

LICKCHEESE. Easy, Dr Trench, easy. We want your opinion. Are you still on for marrying Miss Blanche if she's agreeable ?

TRENCH [*shortly"*] I dont know that I am. [*Sartorius rises indignantly*].

LICKCHEESE. Easy one moment, Mr Sartorius. [*To Trench*] Come, Dr Trench : you say you dont know that you are. But do you know that you aint ? thats what we want to know.

TRENCH [*sulkily*] I wont have the relations between Miss Sartorius and myself made part of a bargain. [*He rises to leave the table*].

LICKCHEESE [*rising*] Thats enough : a gentleman could say no less. [*Insinuatingly*] Now, would you mind me and Cokane and the guvnor steppin into the study to arrange about the lease to the North Thames Iced Mutton Company ?

TRENCH. Oh, I dont mind. I'm going home. Theres nothing else to say.

LICKCHEESE. No, dont go. Only just a minute : me and Cokane will be back in no time to see you home. Youll wait for us, wont you ? theres a good fellow !

TRENCH. Well, if you wish, yes.

LICKCHEESE [*cheerily*] Didnt I know you would !

SARTORIUS [*at the study door, to Cokane*] After you, sir. [*Cokane bows formally and goes into the study*].

LICKCHEESE [*at the door, aside to Sartorius*] You never ad such a managin man as me, Sartorius. [*He goes into the study chuckling, followed by Sartorius*].

[*Trench, left alone, looks round carefully and listens a moment. Then he goes on tiptoe to the piano and leans upon it with folded arms, gazing at Blanche's portrait. Blanche herself appears presently at the study door. When she sees how he is occupied, she closes it softly and steals over to him, watching him intently. He rises from his leaning attitude, and takes the portrait from the easel, holding it out before him at arms length ; then, taking a second look round to reassure himself that nobody is watching him, finds Blanche close upon him. He drops the portrait and stares at her without the least presence of mind*].

BLANCHE [*shrewishly*] Well ? So you have come back here. You have had the meanness to come into this house again. [*He flushes and retreats a step. 8 he follows him up remorselessly*]. What a poor spirited creature you must be ! Why dont you go ? [*Red and wincing, he starts huffily to get his hat from the table ; but when he turns to the door with it she deliberately gets in his way, so that he has to stop*]. I dont want you to stay. [*For a moment they stand face to face ', quite close to one another, she provocative, taunting, half defying, half inviting him to advance, in a flush of undisguised animal excitement. It suddenly flashes on him that all this ferocity is erotic that she is making love to him. His eye lights up: a cunning expression comes into the corners of his mouth : with a heavy assumption of indifference he walks straight back to his chair, and plants himself in it with his arms folded. She comes down the room after him*]. But I forgot : you have found that there is some money to be made here. Lickcheese told you. You, who were so disinterested, so independent, that you could not accept anything from my father ! [*At the end of every sentence she waits to see what execution she has done*]. I suppose you will try to perpersuade me that you have come down here on a great philanthropic enterprise to befriend the poor by having those houses rebuilt, eh ? [*Trench maintains his attitude and makes no sign*]. Yes : when my father makes you do -it. And when Lickcheese has discovered some way of making it profitable. Oh, I know papa ; and I know you. And for the sake of that, you come back here into the house where you were refused ordered out. [*Trench's face darkens : her eyes gleam as she sees it*]. Aha ! you remember that. You know it's true : you cant deny it. [*She sits down, and softens her tone a little as she affects to pity him*]. Ah, let me tell you that you cut a poor figure, a very, very poor figure, Harry. [*At the word "Harry" he relaxes the fold of his arms ; and a faint grin of anticipated victory appears on his face*]. And you, too, a gentleman ! so highly connected ! with such distinguished relations ! so particular as to where your money comes from ! I wonder at you. I really wonder at you. I should have thought that if your family brought you nothing else, it might at least have brought you some sense of personal dignity. Perhaps you think you look dignified at present, eh ? [*No reply*]. Well, I can assure you that you dont : you look most ridiculous as foolish as a man could look you dont know what to say ; and you dont know what to do. But after all, I really dont see what anyone could say in defence of such conduct. [*He looks straight in front of him, and purses up his lips as if whistling. This annoys her ; and she becomes affectedly polite*]. I am afraid I am in your way, Dr Trench. [*She rises*]. I shall not intrude on you any longer. You seem so perfectly at home that I need make no apology for leaving you to yourself. [*She makes a feint of going to the door ; but he does not budge ; and she returns and comes behind his chair*]. Harry. [*He does not turn. She comes a step nearer*]. Harry : I want you to answer me a question. [*Earnestly, stooping over him*] Look me in the face. [*No reply*]. Do you hear ? [*Putting her hand on his shoulder*] Look me in the face. [*He still stares straight in front of him. She suddenly kneels down beside him with her breast against his right shoulder, and, taking his face in her hands, twists it sharply towards her*]. Harry : what were you doing with my photograph just now, when you thought you were alone ? [*His face writhes as he tries hard not to smile. She flings her arms round him, and crushes him in an ecstatic embrace as she adds, with furious tenderness*] How dare you touch anything belonging to me? [*The study door opens and voices are heard*].

TRENCH. I hear some one coming. [*She regains her chair with a bound, and pushes it back as far as possible. Cokane, Lickcheese and Sartorius come from the study. Sartorius and Lickcheese come to Trench. Cokane crosses to Blanche in his most killing manner"*].

COKANE. How do you do, Miss Sartorius ? Nice weather for the return of l'enfant prodigue, eh ?

BLANCHE. Capital, Mr Cokane. So glad to see you. [*She gives him her hand, which he kisses with gallantry*].

LICKCHEESE [*on Trench's left, in a low voice*] Any noos for us, Mr Trench?

TRENCH [*to Sartorius, on his right*] I'll stand in, compensation or no compensation. [*He shakes Sartorius' s hand. The parlor maid has just appeared at the door*].

BLANCHE. Supper is ready, papa.

COKANE. Allow me.

[*Exeunt omnes : Blanche on Cokane's arm ; Lickcheese jocosely taking Sartorius on one arm, and Trench on the other*].

THE PHILANDERER

ACT I

A lady and gentleman are making love to one another in the drawing-room of a flat in Ashly Gardens in the Victoria district of London. It is past ten at night. The walls are hung with theatrical engravings and photographs—Kemble as Hamlet, Mrs. Siddons as Queen Katharine pleading in court, Macready as Werner (after Maclise), Sir Henry Irving as Richard III (after Long), Miss Ellen Terry, Mrs. Kendal, Miss Ada Rehan, Madame Sarah Bernhardt, Mr. Henry Arthur Jones, Mr. A. W. Pinero, Mr. Sydney Grundy, and so on, but not the Signora Duse or anyone connected with Ibsen. The room is not a perfect square, the right hand corner at the back being cut off diagonally by the doorway, and the opposite corner rounded by a turret window filled up with a stand of flowers surrounding a statue of Shakespear. The fireplace is on the right, with an armchair near it. A small round table, further forward on the same side, with a chair beside it, has a yellow-backed French novel lying open on it. The piano, a grand, is on the left, open, with the keyboard in full view at right angles to the wall. The piece of music on the desk is "When other lips." Incandescent lights, well shaded, are on the piano and mantelpiece. Near the piano is a sofa, on which the lady and gentleman are seated affectionately side by side, in one another's arms.

The lady, Grace Tranfield, is about 32, slight of build, delicate of feature, and sensitive in expression. She is just now given up to the emotion of the moment; but her well closed mouth, proudly set brows, firm chin, and elegant carriage show plenty of determination and self respect. She is in evening dress.

The gentleman, Leonard Charteris, a few years older, is unconventionally but smartly dressed in a velvet jacket and cashmere trousers. His collar, dyed Wotan blue, is part of his shirt, and turns over a garnet coloured scarf of Indian silk, secured by a turquoise ring. He wears blue socks and leather sandals. The arrangement of his tawny hair, and of his moustaches and short beard, is apparently left to Nature; but he has taken care that Nature shall do him the fullest justice. His amative enthusiasm, at which he is himself laughing, and his clever, imaginative, humorous ways, contrast strongly with the sincere tenderness and dignified quietness of the woman.

CHARTERIS (impulsively clasping Grace). My dearest love.

GRACE (responding affectionately). My darling. Are you happy?

CHARTERIS. In Heaven.

GRACE. My own.

CHARTERIS. My heart's love. (He sighs happily, and takes her hands in his, looking quaintly at her.) That must positively be my last kiss, Grace, or I shall become downright silly. Let us talk. (Releases her and sits a little apart from her.) Grace: is this your first love affair?

GRACE. Have you forgotten that I am a widow? Do you think I married Tranfield for money?

CHARTERIS. How do I know? Besides, you might have married him not because you loved him, but because you didn't love anybody else. When one is young, one marries out of mere curiosity, just to see what it's like.

GRACE. Well, since you ask me, I never was in love with Tranfield, though I only found that out when I fell in love with you. But I used to like him for being in love with me. It brought out all the good in him so much that I have wanted to be in love with some one ever since. I hope, now that I am in love with you, you will like me for it just as I liked Tranfield.

CHARTERIS. My dear, it is because I like you that I want to marry you. I could love anybody—any pretty woman, that is.

GRACE. Do you really mean that, Leonard?

CHARTERIS. Of course. Why not?

GRACE (reflecting). Never mind why. Now tell me, is this your first love affair?

CHARTERIS (amazed at the simplicity of the question). No, bless my soul. No—nor my second, nor my third.

GRACE. But I mean your first serious one.

CHARTERIS (with a certain hesitation). Yes. (There is a pause. She is not convinced. He adds, with a very perceptible load on his conscience.) It is the first in which *I* have been serious.

GRACE (searchingly). I see. The other parties were always serious.

CHARTERIS. No, not always—heaven forbid!

GRACE. How often?

CHARTERIS. Well, once.

GRACE. Julia Craven?

CHARTERIS (recoiling). Who told you that? (She shakes her head mysteriously, and he turns away from her moodily and adds) You had much better not have asked.

GRACE (gently). I'm sorry, dear. (She puts out her hand and pulls softly at him to bring him near her again.)

CHARTERIS (yielding mechanically to the pull, and allowing her hand to rest on his arm, but sitting squarely without the least attempt to return the caress). Do I feel harder to the touch than I did five minutes ago?

GRACE. What nonsense!

CHARTERIS. I feel as if my body had turned into the toughest of hickory. That is what comes of reminding me of Julia Craven.

(Brooding, with his chin on his right hand and his elbow on his knee.)

I have sat alone with her just as I am sitting with you—

GRACE (shrinking from him). Just!

CHARTERIS (sitting upright and facing her steadily). Just exactly. She has put her hands in mine, and laid her cheek against mine, and listened to me saying all sorts of silly things. (Grace, chilled to the soul, rises from the sofa and sits down on the piano stool, with her back to the keyboard.) Ah, you don't want to hear any more of the story. So much the better.

GRACE (deeply hurt, but controlling herself). When did you break it off?

CHARTERIS (guiltily). Break it off?

GRACE (firmly). Yes, break it off.

CHARTERIS. Well, let me see. When did I fall in love with you?

GRACE. Did you break it off then?

CHARTERIS (mischievously, making it plainer and plainer that it has not been broken off). It was clear then, of course, that it must be broken off.

GRACE. And did you break it off?

CHARTERIS. Oh, yes: *I* broke it off,

GRACE. But did she break it off?

CHARTERIS (rising). As a favour to me, dearest, change the subject. Come away from the piano: I want you to sit here with me. (Takes a step towards her.)

GRACE. No. I also have grown hard to the touch—much harder than hickory for the present. Did she break it off?

CHARTERIS. My dear, be reasonable. It was fully explained to her that it was to be broken off.

GRACE. Did she accept the explanation?

CHARTERIS. She did what a woman like Julia always does. When I explained personally, she said it was not my better self that was speaking, and that she knew I still really loved her. When I wrote it to her with brutal explicitness, she read the letter carefully and then sent it back to me with a note to say that she had not had the courage to open it, and that I ought to be ashamed of having written it. (Comes beside Grace, and puts his left hand caressingly round her neck.) You see, dearie, she won't look the situation in the face.

GRACE. (shaking off his hand and turning a little away on the stool). I am afraid, from the light way in which you speak of it, you did not sound the right chord.

CHARTERIS. My dear, when you are doing what a woman calls breaking her heart, you may sound the very prettiest chords you can find on the piano; but to her ears it is just like this—(Sits down on the bass end of the keyboard. Grace puts her fingers in her ears. He rises and moves away from the piano, saying) No, my dear: I've been kind; I've been frank; I've been everything that a goodnatured man could be: she only takes it as the making up of a lover's quarrel. (Grace winces.) Frankness and kindness: one is as the other—especially frankness. I've tried both. (He crosses to the fireplace, and stands facing the fire, looking at the ornaments on the mantelpiece and warming his hands.)

GRACE (Her voice a little strained). What are you going to try now?

CHARTERIS (on the hearthrug, turning to face her). Action, my dear! Marriage!! In that she must believe. She won't be convinced by anything short of it, because, you see, I have had some tremendous philanderings before and have gone back to her after them.

GRACE. And so that is why you want to marry me?

CHARTERIS. I cannot deny it, my love. Yes: it is your mission to rescue me from Julia.

GRACE (rising). Then, if you please, I decline to be made use of for any such purpose. I will not steal you from another woman. (She begins to walk up and down the room with ominous disquiet.)

CHARTERIS. Steal me! (Comes towards her.) Grace: I have a question to put to you as an advanced woman. Mind! as an advanced woman. Does Julia belong to me? Am I her owner—her master?

GRACE. Certainly not. No woman is the property of a man. A woman belongs to herself and to nobody else.

CHARTERIS. Quite right. Ibsen for ever! That's exactly my opinion. Now tell me, do I belong to Julia; or have I a right to belong to myself?

GRACE (puzzled). Of course you have; but—

CHARTERIS (interrupting her triumphantly). Then how can you steal me from Julia if I don't belong to her? (Catching her by the shoulders and holding her out at arm's length in front of him.) Eh, little philosopher? No, my dear: if Ibsen sauce is good for the goose, it's good for the gander as well. Besides (coaxing her) it was nothing but a philander with Julia—nothing else in the world, I assure you.

GRACE (breaking away from him). So much the worse! I hate your philanderings: they make me ashamed of you and of myself. (Goes to the sofa and sits in the right hand corner of it, leaning gloomily on her elbow with her face averted.)

CHARTERIS. Grace: you utterly misunderstand the origin of my philanderings. (Sits down beside her.) Listen to me: am I a particularly handsome man?

GRACE (turning to him as if astonished at his conceit). No!

CHARTERIS (triumphantly). You admit it. Am I a well dressed man?

GRACE. Not particularly.

CHARTERIS. Of course not. Have I a romantic mysterious charm about me?—do I look as if a secret sorrow preyed on me?—am I gallant to women?

GRACE. Not in the least.

CHARTERIS. Certainly not. No one can accuse me of it. Then whose fault is it that half the women I speak to fall in love with me? Not mine: I hate it: it bores me to distraction. At first it flattered me—delighted me—that was how Julia got me, because she was the first woman who had the pluck to make me a declaration. But I soon had enough of it; and at no time have I taken the initiative and persecuted women with my advances as women have persecuted me. Never. Except, of course, in your case.

GRACE. Oh, you need not make any exception. I had a good deal of trouble to induce you to come and see us. You were very coy.

CHARTERIS (fondly, taking her hand). With you, dearest, the coyness was sheer coquetry. I loved you from the first, and fled only that you might pursue. But come! let us talk about something really interesting. (Takes her in his arms.) Do you love me better than anyone else in the world?

GRACE. I don't think you like to be loved too much.

CHARTERIS. That depends on who the person is. You (pressing her to his heart) cannot love me too much: you cannot love me half enough. I reproach you every day for your coldness—your— (Violent double knock heard without. They start and listen, still in one another's arms, hardly daring to breathe.) Who the deuce is calling at this hour?

GRACE. I can't imagine. (They listen guiltily. The door of the flat is opened without. They hastily get away from one another.)

A WOMAN'S VOICE OUTSIDE. Is Mr. Charteris here?

CHARTERIS (springing up). Julia! The devil! (Stands at the left of the sofa with his hands on it, bending forward with his eyes fixed on the door.)

GRACE (rising also). What can she want?

THE VOICE. Never mind: I will announce myself. (A beautiful, dark, tragic looking woman, in mantle and bonnet, appears at the door, raging furiously.) Oh, this is charming. I have interrupted a pretty tete-a-tete. Oh, you villain! (She comes straight at Grace. Charteris runs across behind the sofa and stops her. She struggles furiously with him. Grace preserves her self possession, but retreats quietly to the piano. Julia, finding Charteris too strong for her, gives up her attempt to get at Grace, but strikes him in the face as she frees herself.)

CHARTERIS (shocked). Oh, Julia, Julia! This is too bad.

JULIA. Is it, indeed, too bad? What are you doing up here with that woman? You scoundrel! But now listen to me; Leonard: you have driven me to desperation; and I don't care what I do, or who hears me. I'll not bear it. She shall not have my place with you—

CHARTERIS. Sh-sh!

JULIA. No, no: I don't care: I will expose her true character before everybody. You belong to me: you have no right to be here; and she knows it.

CHARTERIS. I think you had better let me take you home, Julia.

JULIA. I will not. I am not going home: I am going to stay here—here—until I have made you give her up.

CHARTERIS. My dear, you must be reasonable. You really cannot stay in Mrs. Tranfield's house if she objects. She can ring the bell and have us both put out.

JULIA. Let her do it then. Let her ring the bell if she dares. Let us see how this pure virtuous creature will face the scandal of what I will declare about her. Let us see how you will face it. I have nothing to lose. Everybody knows how you have treated me: you have boasted of your conquests, you poor pitiful, vain creature—I am the common talk of your acquaintances and hers. Oh, I have calculated my advantage (tearing off her mantle): I am a most unhappy and injured woman; but I am not the fool you take me to be. I am going to stay—see! (She flings the mantle on the round table; puts her bonnet on it, and sits down.) Now, Mrs. Tranfield: there is the bell: (pointing to the button beside the fireplace) why don't you ring? (Grace, looking attentively at Charteris, does not move.) Ha! ha! I thought so.

CHARTERIS (quietly, without relaxing his watch on Julia). Mrs. Tranfield: I think you had better go into another room. (Grace makes a movement towards the door, but stops and looks inquiringly at Charteris as Julia springs up. He advances a step so as to prevent her from getting to the door.)

JULIA. She shall not. She shall stay here. She shall know what you are, and how you have been in love with me—how it is not two days since you kissed me and told me that the future would be as happy as the past. (Screaming at him) You did: deny it if you dare.

CHARTERIS (to Grace in a low voice). Go!

GRACE (with nonchalant disgust—going). Get her away as soon as you can, Leonard.

(Julia, with a stifled cry of rage, rushes at Grace, who is crossing behind the sofa towards door. Charteris seizes her and prevents her from getting past the sofa. Grace goes out. Charteris, holding Julia fast, looks around to the door to see whether Grace is safely out of the room.)

JULIA (suddenly ceasing to struggle and speaking with the most pathetic dignity). Oh, there is no need to be violent. (He passes her across to the left end of the sofa, and leans against the right end, panting and mopping his forehead). That is worthy of you!—to use brute force—to humiliate me before her! (She breaks down and bursts into tears.)

CHARTERIS (to himself with melancholy conviction). This is going to be a cheerful evening. Now patience, patience, patience! (Sits on a chair near the round table.)

JULIA (in anguish). Leonard, have you no feeling for me?

CHARTERIS. Only an intense desire to get you safely out of this.

JULIA (fiercely). I am not going to stir.

CHARTERIS (wearily). Well, well. (Heaves a long sigh. They sit silent for awhile, Julia struggling, not to regain her self control, but to maintain her rage at boiling point.)

JULIA (rising suddenly). I am going to speak to that woman.

CHARTERIS (jumping up). No, no. Hang it, Julia, don't let's have another wrestling match. I have the strength, but not the wind: you're too young for me. Sit down or else let me take you home. Suppose her father comes in.

JULIA. I don't care. It rests with you. I am ready to go if she will give you up: until then I stay. Those are my terms: you owe me that, (She sits down determinedly. Charteris looks at her for a moment; then, making up his mind, goes resolutely to the couch, sits down near the right hand end of it, she being at the left; and says with biting emphasis)—

CHARTERIS. I owe you just exactly nothing.

JULIA (reproachfully). Nothing! You can look me in the face and say that? Oh, Leonard!

CHARTERIS. Let me remind you, Julia, that when first we became acquainted, the position you took up was that of a woman of advanced views.

JULIA. That should have made you respect me the more.

CHARTERIS (placably). So it did, my dear. But that is not the point. As a woman of advanced views, you were determined to be free. You regarded marriage as a degrading bargain, by which a woman sold herself to a man for the social status of a wife and the right to be supported and pensioned in old age out of his income. That's the advanced view—our view. Besides, if you had married me, I might have turned out a drunkard, a criminal, an imbecile, a horror to you; and you couldn't have released yourself. Too big a risk, you see. That's the rational view—our view. Accordingly, you reserved the right to leave me at any time if you found our companionship incompatible with—what was the expression you used?—with your full development as a human being: I think that was how you put the Ibsenist view—our view. So I had to be content with a charming philander, which taught me a great deal, and brought me some hours of exquisite happiness.

JULIA. Leonard: you confess then that you owe me something?

CHARTERIS (haughtily). No: what I received, I paid. Did you learn nothing from me?—was there no delight for you in our friendship?

JULIA (vehemently and movingly; for she is now sincere). No. You made me pay dearly for every moment of happiness. You revenged yourself on me for the humiliation of being the slave of your passion for me. I was never sure of you for a moment. I trembled whenever a letter came from you, lest it should contain some stab for me. I dreaded your visits almost as much as I longed for them. I was your plaything, not your companion. (She rises, exclaiming) Oh, there was such suffering in my happiness that I hardly knew joy from pain. (She sinks on the piano stool, and adds, as she buries her face in her hands and turns away from him) Better for me if I had never met you!

CHARTERIS (rising indignantly). You ungenerous wretch! Is this your gratitude for the way I have just been flattering you? What have I not endured from you—endured with angelic patience? Did I not find out, before our friendship was a fortnight old, that all your advanced views were merely a fashion picked up and followed like any other fashion, without understanding or meaning a word of them? Did you not, in spite of your care for your own liberty, set up claims on me compared to which the claims of the most jealous wife would have been trifles. Have I a single woman friend whom you have not abused as old, ugly, vicious—

JULIA (quickly looking up). So they are.

CHARTERIS. Well, then, I'll come to grievances that even you can understand. I accuse you of habitual and intolerable jealousy and ill temper; of insulting me on imaginary provocation: of positively beating me; of stealing letters of mine—

JULIA (rising). Yes, nice letters.

CHARTERIS. —of breaking your solemn promises not to do it again; of spending hours—aye, days! piecing together the contents of my waste paper basket in your search for more letters; and then representing yourself as an ill used saint and martyr wantonly betrayed and deserted by a selfish monster of a man.

JULIA. I was justified in reading your letters. Our perfect confidence in one another gave me the right to do it.

CHARTERIS. Thank you. Then I hasten to break off a confidence which gives such rights. (Sits down sulkily on sofa.)

JULIA (with her right hand on the back of the sofa, bending over him threateningly). You have no right to break it off.

CHARTERIS. I have. You refused to marry me because—

JULIA. I did not. You never asked me. If we were married, you would never dare treat me as you are doing now.

CHARTERIS (laboriously going back to his argument). It was understood between us as people of advanced views that we were not to marry because, as the law stands, I might have become a drunkard, a—

JULIA. —a criminal, an imbecile or a horror. You said that before.

(Sits down beside him with a fling.)

CHARTERIS (politely). I beg your pardon, my dear. I know I have a habit of repeating myself. The point is that you reserved your freedom to give me up when you pleased.

JULIA. Well, what of that? I do not please to give you up; and I will not. You have not become a drunkard or a criminal.

CHARTERIS. You don't see the point yet, Julia. You seem to forget that in reserving your freedom to leave me in case I should turn out badly, you also reserved my freedom to leave you in case you should turn out badly.

JULIA. Very ingenious. And pray, have *I* become a drunkard, or a criminal, or an imbecile?

CHARTERIS (rising). You have become what is infinitely worse than all three together—a jealous termagant.

JULIA (shaking her head bitterly). Yes, abuse me—call me names.

CHARTERIS. I now assert the right I reserved—the right of breaking with you when I please. Advanced views, Julia, involve advanced duties: you cannot be an advanced woman when you want to bring a man to your feet, and a conventional woman when you want to hold him there against his will.

Advanced people form charming friendships: conventional people marry. Marriage suits a good deal of people; and its first duty is fidelity. Friendship suits some people; and its first duty is unhesitating, uncomplaining acceptance of a notice of a change of feeling from either side. You chose friendship instead of marriage. Now do your duty, and accept your notice.

JULIA. Never! We are engaged in the eye of—the eye of—

CHARTERIS (sitting down quickly beside her). Yes, Julia. Can't you get it out? In the eye of something that advanced women don't believe in, en?

JULIA (throwing herself at his feet). O Leonard, don't be cruel. I am too miserable to argue—to think. I only know I love you. You reproach me with not wanting to marry you. I would have married you at any time after I came to love you, if you had asked me. I will marry you now if you will.

CHARTERIS. I won't, my dear. That's flat. We're intellectually incompatible.

JULIA. But why? We could be so happy. You love me—I know you love me—I feel it. You say "My dear" to me: you have said it several times this evening. I know I have been wicked, odious, bad. I say nothing in defence of myself. But don't be hard on me. I was distracted by the thought of losing you. I can't face life without you Leonard. I was happy when I met you: I had never loved anyone; and if you had only let me alone I could have gone on contentedly by myself. But I can't now. I must have you with me. Don't cast me off without a thought of all I have at stake. I could be a friend to you if you would only let me—if you would only tell me your plans—give me a share in your work—treat me as something more than the amusement of an idle hour. Oh Leonard, Leonard, you've never given me a chance: indeed you haven't. I'll take pains; I'll read; I'll try to think; I'll conquer my jealousy; I'll— (She breaks down, rocking her head desperately on his knee and writhing.) Oh, I'm mad: I'm mad: you'll kill me if you desert me.

CHARTERIS (petting her). My dear love, don't cry—don't go on in this way. You know I can't help it.

JULIA (sobbing as he rises and coaxingly lifts her with him). Oh, you can, you can. One word from you will make us happy for ever.

CHARTERIS (diplomatically). Come, my dear: we really must go. We can't stay until Cuthbertson comes. (Releases her gently and takes her mantle from the table.) Here is your mantle: put it on and be good. You have given me a terrible evening: you must have some consideration for me.

JULIA (dangerous again). Then I am to be cast off.

CHARTERIS (coaxingly). You are to put on your bonnet, dearest. (He puts the mantle on her shoulders.)

JULIA (with a bitter half laugh, half sob). Well, I suppose I must do what I am told. (She goes to the table, and looks for her bonnet. She sees the yellow-backed French novel.) Ah, look at that! (holds it out to him.) Look—look at what the creature reads—filthy, vile French stuff that no decent woman would touch. And you—you have been reading it with her.

CHARTERIS. You recommended that book to me yourself.

JULIA. Faugh! (Dashes it on the floor.)

CHARTERIS (running anxiously to the book). Don't damage property,

Julia. (He picks it up and dusts it.) Making scenes is an affair of sentiment: damaging property is serious. (Replaces it on the table.)

And now do pray come along.

JULIA (implacably). You can go: there is nothing to prevent you. I will not stir. (She sits down stubbornly on the sofa.)

CHARTERIS (losing patience). Oh come! I am not going to begin all this over again. There are limits even to my forbearance. Come on.

JULIA. I will not, I tell you.

CHARTERIS. Then good night. (He makes resolutely for the door. With a rush, she gets there before him, and bars his way.) I thought you wanted me to go.

JULIA (at the door). You shall not leave me here alone.

CHARTERIS. Then come with me.

JULIA. Not until you have sworn to me to give up that woman.

CHARTERIS. My dear, I will swear anything if you will only come away and put an end to this.

JULIA (perplexed—doubting him). You will swear?

CHARTERIS. Solemnly. Propose the oath. I have been on the point of swearing for the last half hour.

JULIA (despairingly). You are only making fun of me. I want no oaths.

I want your promise—your sacred word of honour.

CHARTERIS. Certainly—anything you demand, on condition that you come away immediately. On my sacred word of honour as a gentleman—as an

Englishman—as anything you like—I will never see her again, never speak to her, never think of her. Now come.

JULIA. But are you in earnest? Will you keep your word?

CHARTERIS (smiling subtly). Now you are getting unreasonable. Do come along without any more nonsense. At any rate, I am going. I am not strong enough to carry you home; but I am strong enough to make my way through that door in spite of you. You will then have a new grievance against me for my brutal violence. (He takes a step towards the door.)

JULIA (solemnly). If you do, I swear I will throw myself from that window, Leonard, as you pass out.

CHARTERIS (unimpressed). That window is at the back of the building. I shall pass out at the front; so you will not hurt me. Good night. (He approaches the door.)

JULIA. Leonard: have you no pity?

CHARTERIS. Not in the least. When you condescend to these antics you force me to despise you. How can a woman who behaves like a spoiled child and talks like a sentimental novel have the audacity to dream of being a companion for a man of any sort of sense or character? (She gives an inarticulate cry and throws herself sobbing on his breast.) Come, don't cry, my dear Julia: you don't look half so beautiful as when you're happy; and it takes all the starch out of my shirt front. Come along.

JULIA (affectionately). I'll come, dear, if you wish it. Give me one kiss.

CHARTERIS (exasperated). This is too much. No: I'm dashed if I will. Here, let me go, Julia. (She clings to him.) Will you come without another word if I give you a kiss?

JULIA. I will do anything you wish, darling.

CHARTERIS. Well, here. (He takes her in his arms and gives her an unceremonious kiss.) Now remember your promise. Come along.

JULIA. That was not a nice kiss, dearest. I want one of our old real kisses.

CHARTERIS (furious). Oh, go to the deuce. (He disengages himself impulsively; and she, as if he had flung her down, falls pathetically with a stifled moan. With an angry look at her, he strides out and slams the door. She raises herself on one hand, listening to his retreating footsteps. They stop. Her face lights up with eager, triumphant cunning. The steps return hastily. She throws herself down again as before. Charteris reappears, in the utmost dismay, exclaiming) Julia: we're done. Cuthbertson's coming upstairs with your father—(she sits up quickly) do you hear?—the two fathers.

JULIA (sitting on the floor). Impossible. They don't know one another.

CHARTERIS (desperately). I tell you they are coming up together like brothers. What on earth are we to do?

JULIA (scrambling up with the help of his hand). Quick, the lift: we can go down in that. (She rushes to the table for her bonnet.)

CHARTERIS. No, the man's gone home; and the lift's locked.

JULIA (putting on bonnet at express speed). Let's go up to the next floor.

CHARTERIS. There's no next floor. We're at the top of the house. No, no, you must invent some thumping lie. I can't think of one: you can, Julia. Exercise all your genius. I'll back you up.

JULIA. But———

CHARTERIS. Sh-sh! Here they are. Sit down and look at home. (Julia tears off her bonnet and mantle; throws them on the table; and darts to the piano at which she seats herself.)

JULIA. Come and sing. (She plays the symphony to "When other lips." He stands at the piano, as if about to sing. Two elderly gentlemen enter. Julia stops playing.)

The elder of the two gentlemen, Colonel Daniel Craven, affects the bluff, simple veteran, and carries it off pleasantly and well, having a fine upright figure, and being, in fact, a goodnaturedly impulsive, credulous person who, after an entirely thoughtless career as an officer and a gentleman, is now being startled into some sort of self-education by the surprising proceedings of his children.

His companion, Mr. Joseph Cuthbertson, Grace's father, has none of the Colonel's boyishness. He is a man of fervent idealistic sentiment, so frequently outraged by the facts of life, that he has acquired an habitually indignant manner, which unexpectedly becomes enthusiastic or affectionate when he speaks.

The two men differ greatly in expression. The Colonel's face is lined with weather, with age, with eating and drinking, and with the cumulative effects of many petty vexations, but not with thought: he is still fresh, and he has by no means full expectations of pleasure and novelty. Cuthbertson has the lines of sedentary London brain work, with its chronic fatigue and longing for rest and recreative emotion, and its disillusioned indifference to adventure and enjoyment, except as a means of recuperation.

They are both in evening dress; and Cuthbertson wears his fur collared overcoat, which, with his vigilant, irascible eye, piled up hair, and the honorable earnestness with which he takes himself, gives him an air of considerable consequence.

CUTHBERTSON (with a hospitable show of delight at finding visitors). Don't stop, Miss Craven. Go on, Charteris. (He comes down behind the sofa, and hangs his overcoat on it, after taking an opera glass and a theatre programme from the pockets, and putting them down on the piano. Craven meanwhile goes to the fire-place and stands on the hearthrug.)

CHARTERIS. No, thank you. Miss Craven has just been taking me through an old song; and I've had enough of it. (He takes the song off the piano desk and lays it aside; then closes the lid over the keyboard.)

JULIA (passing between the sofa and piano to shake hands with Cuthbertson). Why, you've brought Daddy! What a surprise! (Looking across to Craven.) So glad you've come, Dad. (She takes a chair near the window, and sits there.)

CUTHBERTSON. Craven: let me introduce you to Mr. Leonard Charteris, the famous Ibsenist philosopher.

CRAVEN. Oh, we know one another already. Charteris is quite at home at our house, Jo.

CUTHBERTSON. I beg both your pardons. (Charteris sits down on the piano stool.) He's quite at home here too. By the bye, where's Grace?

JULIA and CHARTERIS. Er— (They stop and look at one another.)

JULIA (politely). I beg your pardon, Mr. Charteris: I interrupted you.

CHARTERIS. Not at all, Miss Craven. (An awkward pause.)

CUTHBERTSON (to help them out). You were going to tell about Grace,

Charteris.

CHARTERIS. I was only going to say that I didn't know that you and

Craven were acquainted.

CRAVEN. Why, *I* didn't know it until to-night. It's a most extraordinary thing. We met by chance at the theatre; and he turns out to be my oldest friend.

CUTHBERTSON (energetically). Yes, Craven; and do you see how this proves what I was saying to you about the breaking up of family life? Here are all our young people—Grace and Miss Julia and the rest—bosom friends, inseparables; and yet we two, who knew each other before they were born, might never have met again if you hadn't popped into the stall next to mine to-night by pure chance. Come, sit down (bustling over to him affectionately and pushing him into the arm chair above the fire): there's your place, by my fireside, whenever you choose to fill it. (He posts himself at the right end of the sofa, leaning against it and admiring Craven.) Just imagine your being Dan Craven!

CRAVEN. Just imagine your being Jo Cuthbertson, though! That's a far more extraordinary coincidence, because I'd got it into my head that your name was Tranfield.

CUTHBERTSON. Oh, that's my daughter's name. She's a widow, you know.

How uncommonly well you look, Dan! The years haven't hurt you much.

CRAVEN (suddenly becoming unnaturally gloomy). I look well. I even feel well. But my days are numbered.

CUTHBERTSON (alarmed). Oh don't say that, my dear fellow. I hope not.

JULIA (with anguish in her voice). Daddy! (Cuthbertson looks inquiringly around at her.)

CRAVEN. There, there, my dear: I was wrong to talk of it. It's a sad subject. But it's better that Cuthbertson should know. We used to be very close friends, and are so still, I hope. (Cuthbertson goes to Craven and presses his hand silently; then returns to sofa and sits, pulling out his handkerchief and displaying some emotion.)

CHARTERIS (a little impatiently). The fact is, Cuthbertson, Craven's a devout believer in the department of witchcraft called medical science. He's celebrated in all the medical schools as an example of the newest sort of liver complaint. The doctors say he can't last another year; and he has fully made up his mind not to survive next Easter, just to oblige them.

CRAVEN (with military affectation). It's very kind of you to try to keep up my spirits by making light of it, Charteris. But I shall be ready when my time comes. I'm a soldier. (A sob from Julia.) Don't cry, Julia.

CUTHBERTSON (huskily). I hope you may long be spared, Dan.

CRAVEN. To oblige me, Jo, change the subject. (He gets up and again posts himself on the hearthrug with his back to the fire.)

CHARTERIS. Try and persuade him to join our club, Cuthbertson. He mopes.

JULIA. It's no use. Sylvia and I are always at him to join; but he won't.

CRAVEN. My child, I have my own club.

CHARTERIS (contemptuously). Yes, the Junior Army and Navy! Do you call that a club? Why, they daren't let a woman cross the doorstep!

CRAVEN (a little ruffled). Clubs are a matter of taste, Charteris. You like a cock and hen club: I don't. It's bad enough to have Julia and her sister—a girl under twenty—spending half their time at such a place. Besides, now really, such a name for a club! The Ibsen club! I should be laughed out of London. The Ibsen club! Come, Cuthbertson, back me up. I'm sure you agree with me.

CHARTERIS. Cuthbertson's a member.

CRAVEN (amazed). No! Why, he's been talking to me all the evening about the way in which everything is going to the dogs through advanced ideas in the younger generation.

CHARTERIS. Of course. He's been studying it in the club. He's always there.

CUTHBERTSON (warmly). Not always. Don't exaggerate, Charteris. You know very well that though I joined the club on Grace's account, thinking that her father's presence there would be a protection and a—a sort of sanction, as it were—I never approved of it.

CRAVEN (tactlessly harping on Cuthbertson's inconsistency). Well, you know, this is unexpected: now it's really very unexpected. I should never have thought it from hearing you talk, Jo. Why, you said the whole modern movement was abhorrent to you because your life had been passed in witnessing scenes of suffering nobly endured and sacrifice willingly rendered by womanly women and manly men and deuce knows what else. Is it at the Ibsen club that you see all this manliness and womanliness?

CHARTERIS. Certainly not: the rules of the club forbid anything of that sort. Every candidate for membership must be nominated by a man and a woman, who both guarantee that the candidate, if female, is not womanly, and if male, is not manly.

CRAVEN (chuckling cunningly and stooping to press his heated trousers against his legs, which are chilly). Won't do, Charteris. Can't take me in with so thin a story as that.

CUTHBERTSON (vehemently). It's true. It's monstrous, but it's true.

CRAVEN (with rising indignation, as he begins to draw the inevitable inferences). Do you mean to say that somebody had the audacity to guarantee that my Julia is not a womanly woman?

CHARTERIS (darkly). It sounds incredible; but a man was found ready to take that inconceivable lie on his conscience.

JULIA (firing up). If he has nothing worse than that on his conscience, he may sleep pretty well. In what way am I more womanly than any of the rest of them, I should like to know? They are always saying things like that behind my back—I hear of them from Sylvia. Only the other day a member of the committee said I ought never to have been elected—that you (to Charteris) had smuggled me in. I should like to see her say it to my face: that's all.

CRAVEN. But, my precious, I most sincerely hope she was right. She paid you the highest compliment. Why, the place must be a den of infamy.

CUTHBERTSON (emphatically). So it is, Craven, so it is.

CHARTERIS. Exactly. That's what keeps it so select: nobody but people whose reputations are above suspicion dare belong to it. If we once got a good name, we should become a mere whitewashing shop for all the shady characters in London. Better join us, Craven. Let me put you up.

CRAVEN. What! Join a club where there's some scoundrel who guaranteed my daughter to be an unwomanly woman! If I weren't an invalid, I'd kick him.

CHARTERIS. Oh don't say that. It was I who did it.

CRAVEN (reproachfully). You! Now upon my soul, Charteris, this is very vexing. Now how could you bring yourself to do such a thing?

CHARTERIS. She made me. Why, I had to guarantee Cuthbertson as unmanly; and he's the leading representative of manly sentiment in London.

CRAVEN. That didn't do Jo any harm: but it took away my Julia's character.

JULIA (outraged). Daddy!

CHARTERIS. Not at the Ibsen club, quite the contrary. After all, what can we do? You know what breaks up most clubs for men and women. There's a quarrel—a scandal—cherchez la femme—always a woman at the bottom of it. Well, we knew this when we founded the club; but we noticed that the woman at the bottom of it was always a womanly woman. The unwomanly women who work for their living and know how to take care of themselves never give any trouble. So we simply said we wouldn't have any womanly women; and when one gets smuggled in she has to take care not to behave in a womanly way. We get on all right. (He rises.) Come to lunch with me there tomorrow and see the place.

CUTHBERTSON (rising). No, he's engaged to me. But you can join us.

CHARTERIS. What hour?

CUTHBERTSON. Any time after twelve. (To Craven) It's at 90 Cork street, at the other end of the Burlington Arcade.

CRAVEN (making a note). 90, you say. After twelve. (He suddenly relapses into gloom.) By the bye, don't order anything special for me. I'm not allowed wine—only Apollinaris. No meat either—only a scrap of fish occasionally. I'm to have a short life, but not a merry one. (Sighing.) Well, well. (Bracing himself up.) Now, Julia, it's time for us to be off. (Julia rises.)

CUTHBERTSON. But where on earth is Grace? I must go and look for her.

(He turns to the door.)

JULIA (stopping him). Oh, pray don't disturb her, Mr. Cuthbertson.

She's so tired.

CUTHBERTSON. But just for a moment to say good night. (Julia and Charteris look at one another in dismay. Cuthbertson looks quickly at them, perceiving that something is wrong.)

CHARTERIS. We must make a clean breast of it, I see.

CUTHBERTSON. Clean breast?

CHARTERIS. The truth is, Cuthbertson, Mrs. Tranfield, who is, as you know, the most thoughtful of women, took it into her head that I—well, that I particularly wanted to speak to Miss Craven alone. So she said she was tired and wanted to go to bed.

CRAVEN (scandalized). Tut! tut!

CUTHBERTSON. Oho! is that it? Then it's all right. She never goes to bed as early as this. I'll fetch her in a moment. (He goes out confidently, leaving Charteris aghast.)

JULIA. Now you've done it. (She rushes to the round table and snatches up her mantle and bonnet.) I'm off. (She makes for the door.)

CRAVEN (horrified). What are you doing, Julia? You can't go until you've said good night to Mrs. Tranfield. It would be horribly rude.

JULIA. You can stay if you like, Daddy: I can't. I'll wait for you in the hall. (She hurries out.)

CRAVEN (following her). But what on earth am I to say? (Stopping as she disappears, and turning to Charteris grumbling) Now really you know, Charteris, this is devilish awkward, upon my life it is. That was a most indelicate thing of you to say plump out before us all—that about you and Julia.

CHARTERIS. I'll explain it all to-morrow. Just at present we'd really better follow Julia's example and bolt. (He starts for the door.)

CRAVEN (intercepting him). Stop! don't leave me like this: I shall look like a fool. Now I shall really take it in bad part if you run away, Charteris.

CHARTERIS (resignedly). All right. I'll stay. (Lifts himself on to the shoulder of the grand piano and sits there swinging his legs and contemplating Craven resignedly.)

CRAVEN (pacing up and down). I'm excessively vexed about Julia's conduct, I am indeed. She can't bear to be crossed in the slightest thing, poor child. I'll have to apologize for her you know: her going away is a downright slap in the face for these people here. Cuthbertson may be offended already for all I know.

CHARTERIS. Oh never mind about him. Mrs. Tranfield bosses this establishment.

CRAVEN (cunningly). Ah, that's it, is it? He's just the sort of fellow that would have no control over his daughter. (He goes back to his former place on the hearthrug with his back to the fire.) By the bye, what the dickens did he mean by all that about passing his life amid—what was it?—" scenes of suffering nobly endured and sacrifice willingly rendered by womanly women and manly men" and a lot more of the same sort? I suppose he's something in a hospital.

CHARTERIS. Hospital! Nonsense: he's a dramatic critic. Didn't you hear me say that he was the leading representative of manly sentiment in London?

CRAVEN. You don't say so. Now really, who'd have thought it! How jolly it must be to be able to go to the theatre for nothing! I must ask him to get me a few tickets occasionally. But isn't it ridiculous for a man to talk like that! I'm hanged if he don't take what he sees on the stage quite seriously.

CHARTERIS. Of course: that's why he's a good critic. Besides, if you take people seriously off the stage, why shouldn't you take them seriously on it, where they're under some sort of decent restraint? (He jumps down off piano and goes up to the window. Cuthbertson comes back.)

CUTHBERTSON (to Craven, rather sheepishly). The fact is, Grace has gone to bed. I must apologize to you and Miss— (He turns to Julia's seat, and stops on seeing it vacant.)

CRAVEN (embarrassed). It is I who have to apologize for Julia, Jo.

She—

CHARTERIS (interrupting). She said she was quite sure that if we didn't go, you'd persuade Mrs.

Tranfield to get up to say good night for the sake of politeness; so she went straight off.

CUTHBERTSON. Very kind of her indeed. I'm really ashamed—

CRAVEN. Don't mention it, Jo, don't mention it. She's waiting for me below. (Going.) Good night. Good night, Charteris.

CHARTERIS. Good night.

CUTHBERTSON (seeing Craven out). Good-night. Say good night and thanks to Miss Craven for me. To-morrow any time after twelve, remember. (They go out; and Charteris with a long sigh crosses to the fireplace, thoroughly tired out.)

CRAVEN (outside). All right.

CUTHBERTSON (outside). Take care of the stairs; they're rather steep. Good night. (The outside door shuts; and Cuthbertson returns. Instead of entering, he stands in the doorway with one hand in the breast of his waistcoat, eyeing Charteris sternly.)

CHARTERIS. What's the matter?

CUTHBERTSON (sternly). Charteris: what's been going on here? I insist on knowing. Grace has not gone to bed: I have seen and spoken with her. What is it all about?

CHARTERIS. Ask your theatrical experience, Cuthbertson. A man, of course.

CUTHBERTSON (coming forward and confronting him). Don't play the fool with me, Charteris: I'm too old a hand to be amused by it. I ask you, seriously, what's the matter?

CHARTERIS. I tell you, seriously, I'm the matter, Julia wants to marry me: I want to marry Grace. I came here to-night to sweetheart Grace.

Enter Julia. Alarums and excursions. Exit Grace. Enter you and Craven.

Subterfuges and excuses. Exeunt Craven and Julia. And here we are.

That's the whole story. Sleep over it. Good night. (He leaves.)

CUTHBERTSON (staring after him). Well I'll be—

(The act drop descends.)

END OF ACT I.

ACT II

Next day at noon, in the Library of the Ibsen club. A spacious room, with glass doors right and left. At the back, in the middle, is the fireplace, surmounted by a handsome mantelpiece, with a bust of Ibsen, and decorated inscriptions of the titles of his plays. There are circular recesses at each side of fireplace, with divan seats running round them, and windows at the top, the space between the divan and the window sills being lined with books. A long settee is placed before the fire. Along the back of the settee, and touching it, is a green table, littered with journals. A revolving bookcase stands in the foreground, a little to the left, with an easy chair close to it. On the right, between the door and the recess, is a light library stepladder. Placards inscribed "silence" are conspicuously exhibited here and there.

(Cuthbertson is seated in the easy chair at the revolving bookstand, reading the "Daily Graphic." Dr. Paramore is on the divan in the right hand recess, reading "The British Medical Journal." He is young as age is counted in the professions—barely forty. His hair is wearing bald on his forehead; and his dark arched eyebrows, coming rather close together, give him a conscientiously sinister appearance. He wears the frock coat and cultivates the "bedside manner" of the fashionable physician with scrupulous conventionality. Not at all a happy or frank man, but not consciously unhappy nor intentionally insincere, and highly self satisfied intellectually.

Sylvia Craven is sitting in the middle of the settee before the fire, only the back of her head being visible. She is reading a volume of Ibsen. She is a girl of eighteen, small and trim, wearing a smart tailor-made dress, rather short, and a Newmarket jacket, showing a white blouse with a light silk sash and a man's collar and watch chain so arranged as to look as like a man's waistcoat and shirt-front as possible without spoiling the prettiness of the effect. A Page Boy's voice, monotonously calling for Dr. Paramore, is heard approaching outside on the right.)

PAGE (outside). Dr. Paramore, Dr. Paramore, Dr. Paramore. (He enters carrying a salver with a card on it.) Dr. Par—

PARAMORE (sharply, sitting up). Here, boy. (The boy presents the salver. Paramore takes the card and looks at it.) All right: I'll come down to him. (The boy goes. Paramore rises, and comes from the recess, throwing his paper on the table.) Good morning, Mr. Cuthbertson (stopping to pull out his cuffs and shake his coat straight) Mrs. Tranfield quite well, I hope?

SYLVIA (turning her head indignantly). Sh—sh—sh! (Paramore turns, surprised. Cuthbertson rises energetically and looks across the bookstand to see who is the author of this impertinence.)

PARAMORE (to Sylvia—stiffly). I beg your pardon, Miss Craven: I did not mean to disturb you.

SYLVIA (flustered and self assertive). You may talk as much as you like if you will only have the common consideration to first ask whether the other people object. What I protest against is your assumption that my presence doesn't matter because I'm only a female member. That's all. Now go on, pray: you don't disturb me in the least. (She turns to the fire, and again buries herself in Ibsen.)

CUTHBERTSON (with emphatic dignity). No gentleman would have dreamt of objecting to our exchanging a few words, madam. (She takes no notice. He resumes angrily.) As a matter of fact I was about to say to Dr. Paramore that if he would care to bring his visitor up here, *I* should not object. The impudence! (Dashes his paper down on the chair.)

PARAMORE. Oh, many thanks; but it's only an instrument maker.

CUTHBERTSON. Any new medical discoveries, doctor?

PARAMORE. Well, since you ask me, yes—perhaps a most important one. I have discovered something that has hitherto been overlooked—a minute duct in the liver of the guinea pig. Miss Craven will forgive my mentioning it when I say that it may throw an important light on her father's case. The first thing, of course, is to find out what the duct is there for.

CUTHBERTSON (reverently—feeling that he is in the presence of science). Indeed. How will you do that?

PARAMORE. Oh, easily enough, by simply cutting the duct and seeing what will happen to the guinea pig. (Sylvia rises, horrified.) I shall require a knife specially made to get at it. The man who is waiting for me downstairs has brought me a few handles to try before fitting it and sending it to the laboratory. I am afraid it would not do to bring such weapons up here.

SYLVIA. If you attempt such a thing, Dr. Paramore, I will complain to the committee. The majority of the committee are anti-vivisectionists. You ought to be ashamed of yourself. (She flounces out at the right hand door.)

PARAMORE (with patient contempt). That's the sort of thing we scientific men have to put up with nowadays, Mr. Cuthbertson. Ignorance, superstition, sentimentality: they are all one. A guinea pig's convenience is set above the health and lives of the entire human race.

CUTHBERTSON (vehemently). It's not ignorance or superstition, Paramore: it's sheer downright Ibsenism: that's what it is. I've been wanting to sit comfortably at the fire the whole morning; but I've never had a chance with that girl there. I couldn't go and plump myself down on a seat beside her: goodness knows what she'd think I wanted. That's one of the delights of having women in the club: when they come in here they all want to sit at the fire and adore that bust. I sometimes feel that I should like to take the poker and fetch it a wipe across the nose—ugh!

PARAMORE. I must say I prefer the elder Miss Craven to her sister.

CUTHBERTSON (his eyes lighting up). Ah, Julia! I believe you. A splendid fine creature—every inch a woman. No Ibsenism about her!

PARAMORE. I quite agree with you there, Mr. Cuthbertson. Er—by the way, do you think is Miss Craven attached to Charteris at all?

CUTHBERTSON. What, that fellow! Not he. He hangs about after her; but he's not man enough for her. A woman of that sort likes a strong, manly, deep-throated, broad-chested man.

PARAMORE (anxiously). Hm, a sort of sporting character, you think?

CUTHBERTSON. Oh, no, no. A scientific man, perhaps, like yourself. But you know what I mean—a MAN. (Strikes himself a sounding blow on the chest.)

PARAMORE. Of course; but Charteris is a man.

CUTHBERTSON. Pah! you don't see what I mean. (The Page Boy returns with his salver.)

PAGE BOY (calling monotonously as before). Mr. Cuthbertson, Mr.
Cuthbertson, Mr. Cuth—

CUTHBERTSON. Here, boy. (He takes a card from the salver.) Bring the gentleman up here. (The boy goes out.) It's Craven. He's coming to lunch with me and Charteris. You might join us if you've nothing better to do, when you've finished with the instrument man. If Julia turns up I'll ask her too.

PARAMORE (flushing with pleasure). I shall be very happy. Thank you. (He is going out at the right hand door when Craven enters.) Good morning, Colonel Craven.

CRAVEN (at the door). Good morning—glad to see you. I'm looking for
Cuthbertson.

PARAMORE (smiling). There he is. (He goes out.)

CUTHBERTSON (greeting Craven effusively). Delighted to see you. Now will you come to the smoking room, or will you sit down here and have a chat while we're waiting for Charteris. If you like company, the smoking room is always full of women. Here we shall have it pretty well all to ourselves until about three o'clock.

CRAVEN. I don't like to see women smoking. I'll make myself comfortable here. (Sits in an easy chair on the right.)

CUTHBERTSON (taking a chair beside him, on his left). Neither do I. There's not a room in this club where I can enjoy a pipe quietly without a woman coming in and beginning to roll a cigarette. It's a disgusting habit in a woman: it's not natural to her sex.

CRAVEN (sighing). Ah, Jo, times have changed since we both courted Molly Ebden all those years ago. I took my defeat well, old chap, didn't I?

CUTHBERTSON (with earnest approval). You did, Dan. The thought of it has often helped me to behave well myself: it has, on my honour.

CRAVEN. Yes, you always believe in hearth and home, Jo—in a true

English wife and a happy wholesome fireside. How did Molly turn out?

CUTHBERTSON (trying to be fair to Molly). Well, not bad. She might have been worse. You see I couldn't stand her relations: all the men were roaring cads; and she couldn't get on with my mother. And then she hated being in town; and of course I couldn't live in the country on account of my work. But we hit it off as well as most people, until we separated.

CRAVEN (taken aback). Separated! (He is irresistibly amused.) Oh, that was the end of the hearth and home, Jo, was it?

CUTHBERTSON (warmly). It was not my fault, Dan. (Sentimentally.) Some day the world will know how I loved that woman. But she was incapable of valuing a true man's affection. Do you know, she often said she wished she'd married you instead.

CRAVEN (sobered by the suggestion). Dear me, dear me! Well, perhaps it was better as it was. You heard about my marriage, I suppose.

CUTHBERTSON. Oh yes: we all heard of it.

CRAVEN. Well, Jo, I may as well make a clean breast of it—everybody knew it. I married for money.

CUTHBERTSON (encouragingly). And why not, Dan, why not? We can't get on without it, you know.

CRAVEN (with sincere feeling). I got to be very fond of her, Jo. I had a home until she died. Now everything's changed. Julia's always here. Sylvia's of a different nature; but she's always here too.

CUTHBERTSON (sympathetically). I know. It's the same with Grace. She's always here.

CRAVEN. And now they want me to be always here. They're at me every day to join the club—to stop my grumbling, I suppose. That's what I want to consult you about. Do you think I ought to join?

CUTHBERTSON. Well, if you have no conscientious objection—

CRAVEN (testily interrupting him). I object to the existence of the place on principle; but what's the use of that? Here it is in spite of my objection, and I may as well have the benefit of any good that may be in it.

CUTHBERTSON (soothing him). Of course: that's the only reasonable view of the matter. Well, the fact is, it's not so inconvenient as you might think. When you're at home, you have the house more to yourself; and when you want to have your family about you, you can dine with them at the club.

CRAVEN (not much attracted by this). True.

CUTHBERTSON. Besides, if you don't want to dine with them, you needn't.

CRAVEN (convinced). True, very true. But don't they carry on here, rather?

CUTHBERTSON. Oh, no, they don't exactly carry on. Of course the usual tone of the club is low, because the women smoke and earn their own living and all that; but still there's nothing actually to complain of. And it's convenient, certainly. (Charteris comes in, looking round for them.)

CRAVEN (rising). Do you know, I've a great mind to join, just to see what it's like. Would you mind putting me up?

CUTHBERTSON. Delighted, Dan, delighted. (He grasps Craven's hand.)

CHARTERIS (putting one hand on Craven's shoulder and the other on Cuthbertson's). Bless you, my children! (Cuthbertson, a little wounded in his dignity, moves away. The Colonel takes the jest in the utmost good humor.)

CRAVEN (cordially). Hallo!

CHARTERIS (to Craven). Hope I haven't disturbed your chat by coming too soon.

CRAVEN. Not at all. Welcome, dear boy. (Shakes his hand.)

CHARTERIS. That's right. I'm earlier than I intended. The fact is, I have something rather pressing to say to Cuthbertson.

CRAVEN. Private!

CHARTERIS. Not particularly. (To Cuthbertson.) Only what we were speaking of last night.

CUTHBERTSON. Well, Charteris, I think that is private, or ought to be.

CRAVEN (going up towards the table). I'll just take a look at the

Times—

CHARTERIS (stopping him). Oh, it's no secret: everybody in the club guesses it. (To Cuthbertson.) Has Grace never mentioned to you that she wants to marry me?

CUTHBERTSON (indignantly). She has mentioned that you want to marry her.

CHARTERIS. Ah; but then it's not what I want, but what Grace wants, that will weigh with you.

CRAVEN (a little shocked). Excuse me Charteris: this is private. I'll leave you to yourselves. (Again moves towards the table.)

CHARTERIS. Wait a bit, Craven: you're concerned in this. Julia wants to marry me too.

CRAVEN (in a tone of the strongest remonstrance). Now really! Now upon my life and soul!

CHARTERIS. It's a fact, I assure you. Didn't it strike you as rather odd, our being up there last night and Mrs. Tranfield not with us?

CRAVEN. Well, yes it did. But you explained it. And now really, Charteris, I must say your explanation was in shocking bad taste before Julia.

CHARTERIS. Never mind. It was a good, fat, healthy, bouncing lie.

CRAVEN and CUTHBERTSON. Lie!

CHARTERIS. Didn't you suspect that?

CRAVEN. Certainly not. Did you, Jo?

CUTHBERTSON. No, most emphatically.

CRAVEN. What's more, I don't believe you. I'm sorry to have to say such a thing; but you forget that Julia was present and didn't contradict you.

CHARTERIS. She didn't want to.

CRAVEN. Do you mean to say that my daughter deceived me?

CHARTERIS. Delicacy towards me compelled her to, Craven.

CRAVEN (taking a very serious tone). Now look here, Charteris: have you any proper sense of the fact that you're standing between two fathers?

CUTHBERTSON. Quite right, Dan, quite right. I repeat the question on my own account.

CHARTERIS. Well, I'm a little dazed still by standing for so long between two daughters; but I think I grasp the situation. (Cuthbertson flings away with an exclamation of disgust.)

CRAVEN. Then I'm sorry for your manners, Charteris: that's all. (He turns away sulkily; then suddenly fires up and turns on Charteris.) How dare you tell me my daughter wants to marry you. Who are you, pray, that she should have any such ambition?

CHARTERIS. Just so; she couldn't have made a worse choice. But she won't listen to reason. I've talked to her like a father myself—I assure you, my dear Craven, I've said everything that you could have said; but it's no use: she won't give me up. And if she won't listen to me, what likelihood is there of her listening to you?

CRAVEN (in angry bewilderment). Cuthbertson: did you ever hear anything like this?

CUTHBERTSON. Never! Never!

CHARTERIS. Oh, bother? Come, don't behave like a couple of conventional old fathers: this is a serious affair. Look at these letters (producing a letter and a letter-card.) This (showing the card) is from Grace—by the way, Cuthbertson, I wish you'd ask her not to write on letter-cards: the blue colour makes it so easy for Julia to pick the bits out of my waste paper basket and piece them together. Now listen. "My dear Leonard: Nothing could make it worth my while to be exposed to such scenes as last night's. You had much better go back to Julia and forget me. Yours sincerely, Grace Tranfield."

CUTHBERTSON (infuriated). Damnation!

CHARTERIS (turning to Craven and preparing to read the letter). Now for Julia. (The Colonel turns away to hide his face from Charteris, anticipating a shock, and puts his hand on a chair to steady himself.) "My dearest boy. Nothing will make me believe that this odious woman can take my place in your heart. I send some of the letters you wrote me when we first met; and I ask you to read them. They will recall what you felt when you wrote them. You cannot have changed so much as to be indifferent to me: whoever may have struck your fancy for the moment, your heart is still mine"—and so on: you know the sort of thing—"Ever and always your loving Julia." (The Colonel sinks on the chair and covers his face with his hand.) You don't suppose she's serious, do you: that's the sort of thing she writes me three times a day. (To Cuthbertson) Grace is in earnest though, confound it. (He holds out Grace's letter.) A blue card as usual! This time I shall not trust the waste paper basket. (He goes to the fire, and throws the letters into it.)

CUTHBERTSON (facing him with folded arms as he comes down again). May

I ask, Mr. Charteris, is this the New Humour?

CHARTERIS (still too preoccupied with his own difficulty to have any sense of the effect he is producing on the others). Oh, stuff! Do you suppose it's a joke to be situated as I am? You've got your head so stuffed with the New Humour and the New Woman and the New This, That and the Other, all mixed up with your own old Adam, that you've lost your senses.

CUTHBERTSON (strenuously). Do you see that old man, grown grey in the honoured service of his country, whose last days you have blighted?

CHARTERIS (surprised, looking at Craven and realizing his distress with genuine concern). I'm very sorry. Come, Craven; don't take it to heart. (Craven shakes his head.) I assure you it means nothing: it happens to me constantly.

CUTHBERTSON. There is only one excuse for you. You are not fully responsible for your actions. Like all advanced people, you have got neurasthenia.

CHARTERIS (appalled). Great Heavens! what's that?

CUTHBERTSON. I decline to explain. You know as well as I do. I am going downstairs now to order lunch. I shall order it for three; but the third place is for Paramore, whom I have invited, not for you. (He goes out through the left hand door.)

CHARTERIS (putting his hand on Craven's shoulder). Come, Craven; advise me. You've been in this sort of fix yourself probably.

CRAVEN. Charteris: no woman writes such letters to a man unless he has made advances to her.

CHARTERIS (mournfully). How little you know the world, Colonel! The

New Woman is not like that.

CRAVEN. I can only give you very old fashioned advice, my boy; and that is that it's well to be off with the Old Woman before you're on with the New. I'm sorry you told me. You might have waited for my death: it's not far off now. (His head droops again. Julia and Paramore enter on the right. Julia stops as she catches sight of Charteris, her face clouding and her breast heaving. Paramore, seeing the Colonel apparently ill, hurries down to him with the bedside manner in full play.)

CHARTERIS (seeing Julia). Oh Lord! (He retreats under the lee of the revolving bookstand.)

PARAMORE (sympathetically to the Colonel). Allow me. (Takes his wrist and begins to count his pulse.)

CRAVEN (looking up). Eh? (Withdraws his hand and rises rather crossly.) No, Paramore: it's not my liver now: it's private business. (A chase now begins between Julia and Charteris, all the more exciting to them because the huntress and her prey must alike conceal the real object of their movements from the others. Charteris first makes for the right hand door. Julia immediately moves back to it, barring his path. He doubles back round the bookstand, setting it whirling as he makes for the left door, Julia crossing in pursuit of him. He is about to escape when he is cut off by the return of Cuthbertson. He turns back and sees Julia close upon him. There being nothing else for it, he bolts up into the recess to the left of the fireplace.)

CUTHBERTSON. Good morning, Miss Craven. (They shake hands.) Won't you join us at lunch? Paramore's coming too.

JULIA. Thanks: I shall be very pleased. (She goes up with affected purposelessness towards the recess. Charteris, almost trapped in it, crosses to the right hand recess by way of the fender, knocking down the fire irons with a crash as he does so.)

CRAVEN (who has crossed to the whirling bookcase and stopped it). What the dickens are you doing there, Charteris?

CHARTERIS. Nothing. It's such a confounded room to get about in.

JULIA (maliciously). Yes, isn't it. (She is moving back to guard the right hand door, when Cuthbertson appears at it.)

CUTHBERTSON. May I take you down? (He offers her his arm.)

JULIA. No, really: you know it's against the rules of the club to coddle women in any way. Whoever is nearest to the door goes first.

CUTHBERTSON. Oh well, if you insist. Come, gentlemen: let us go to lunch in the Ibsen fashion—the unsexed fashion. (He goes out on the left followed by Paramore, laughing. Craven goes last. He turns at the door to see whether Julia is coming, and stops when he sees she is not.)

CRAVEN. Come, Julia.

JULIA (with patronising affection). Yes, Daddy, dear, presently. (Charteris is meanwhile stealing to the right hand door.) Don't wait for me: I'll come in a moment. (The Colonel hesitates.) It's all right, Daddy.

CRAVEN (very gravely). Don't be long, my dear. (He goes out.)

CHARTERIS. I'm off. (Makes a dash for the right hand door.)

JULIA (darting at him and seizing his wrist). Aren't you coming?

CHARTERIS. No. Unhand me Julia. (He tries to get away: she holds him.)

If you don't let me go, I'll scream for help.

JULIA (reproachfully). Leonard! (He breaks away from her.) Oh, how can you be so rough with me, dear. Did you get my letter?

CHARTERIS. Burnt it—(she turns away, struck to the heart, and buries her face in her hands)—along with hers.

JULIA (quickly turning again). Hers! Has she written to you?

CHARTERIS. Yes, to break off with me on your account.

JULIA (her eyes gleaming). Ah!

CHARTERIS. You are pleased. Wretch! Now you have lost the last scrap of my regard. (He turns to go, but is stopped by the return of Sylvia. Julia turns away and stands pretending to read a paper which she picks up from the table.)

SYLVIA (offhandedly). Hallo, Charteris: how are you getting on? (She takes his arm familiarly and walks down the room with him.) Have you seen Grace Tranfield this morning? (Julia drops the paper and comes a step nearer to listen.) You generally know where she is to be found.

CHARTERIS. I shall never know any more, Sylvia. She's quarrelled with me.

SYLVIA. Sylvia! How often am I to tell you that I am not Sylvia at the club?

CHARTERIS. I forgot. I beg your pardon, Craven, old chap (slaps her on the shoulder).

SYLVIA. That's better—a little overdone, but better.

JULIA. Don't be a fool, Silly.

SYLVIA. Remember, Julia, if you please, that here we are members of the club, not sisters. I don't take liberties with you here on family grounds: don't you take any with me. (She goes to the settee and resumes her former place.)

CHARTERIS. Quite right, Craven. Down with the tyranny of the elder sister!

JULIA. You ought to know better than to encourage a child to make herself ridiculous, Leonard, even at my expense.

CHARTERIS (seating himself on the edge of the table). Your lunch will be cold, Julia. (Julia is about to retort furiously when she is checked by the reappearance of Cuthbertson at the left hand door.)

CUTHBERTSON. What has become of you, Miss Craven? Your father is getting quite uneasy. We're all waiting for you.

JULIA. So I have just been reminded, thank you. (She goes out angrily past him, Sylvia looking round to see.)

CUTHBERTSON (looking first after her, then at Charteris). More neurasthenia. (He follows her.)

SYLVIA (jumping up on her knees on the settee and speaking over the back of it). What's up, Charteris? Julia been making love to you?

CHARTERIS (speaking to her over his shoulder). No. Blowing me up for making love to Grace.

SYLVIA. Serve you right. You are an awful devil for philandering.

CHARTERIS (calmly). Do you consider it good club form to talk that way to a man who might nearly be your father?

SYLVIA (knowingly). Oh, I know you, my lad.

CHARTERIS. Then you know that I never pay any special attention to any woman.

SYLVIA (thoughtfully). Do you know, Leonard, I really believe you. I don't think you care a bit more for one woman than for another.

CHARTERIS. You mean I don't care a bit less for one woman than another.

SYLVIA. That makes it worse. But what I mean is that you never bother about their being only women: you talk to them just as you do to me or any other fellow. That's the secret of your success. You can't think how sick they get of being treated with the respect due to their sex.

CHARTERIS. Ah, if Julia only had your wisdom, Craven! (He gets off the table with a sigh and perches himself reflectively on the stepladder.)

SYLVIA. She can't take things easy, can she, old man? But don't you be afraid of breaking her heart: she gets over her little tragedies. We found that out at home when our great sorrow came.

CHARTERIS. What was that?

SYLVIA. I mean when we learned that poor papa had Paramore's disease. But it was too late to inoculate papa. All they could do was to prolong his life for two years more by putting him on a strict diet. Poor old boy! they cut off his liquor; and he's not allowed to eat meat.

CHARTERIS. Your father appears to me to be uncommonly well.

SYLVIA. Yes, you would think he was a great deal better. But the microbes are at work, slowly but surely. In another year it will be all over. Poor old Dad! it's unfeeling to talk about him in this attitude: I must sit down properly. (She comes down from the settee and takes the chair near the bookstand.) I should like papa to live for ever just to take the conceit out of Paramore. I believe he's in love with Julia.

CHARTERIS (starting up excitedly). In love with Julia! A ray of hope on the horizon! Do you really mean it?

SYLVIA. I should think I do. Why do you suppose he's hanging about the club to-day in a beautiful new coat and tie instead of attending to his patients? That lunch with Julia will finish him. He'll ask Daddy's consent before they come back—I'll bet you three to one he will, in anything you please.

CHARTERIS. Gloves?

SYLVIA. No: cigarettes.

CHARTERIS. Done! But what does she think about it? Does she give him any encouragement?

SYLVIA. Oh, the usual thing. Enough to keep any other woman from getting him.

CHARTERIS. Just so. I understand. Now listen to me: I am going to speak as a philosopher. Julia is jealous of everybody—everybody. If she saw you flirting with Paramore she'd begin to value him directly. You might play up a little, Craven, for my sake—eh?

SYLVIA (rising). You're too awful, Leonard. For shame? However, anything to oblige a fellow Ibsenite. I'll bear your affair in mind. But I think it would be more effective if you got Grace to do it.

CHARTERIS. Think so? Hm! perhaps you're right.

PAGE BOY (outside as before). Dr. Paramore, Dr. Paramore, Dr.

Paramore—

SYLVIA. They ought to get that boy's voice properly cultivated: it's a disgrace to the club. (She goes into the recess on Ibsen's left. The page enters carrying the British Medical Journal.)

CHARTERIS (calling to the page). Dr. Paramore is in the dining room.

PAGE BOY. Thank you, sir. (He is about to go into the dining room when

Sylvia swoops on him.)

SYLVIA. Here: where are you taking that paper? It belongs to this room.

PAGE BOY. It's Dr. Paramore's particular orders, miss. The British

Medical Journal has always to be brought to him dreckly it comes.

SYLVIA. What cheek? Charteris: oughtn't we to stop this on principle?

CHARTERIS. Certainly not. Principle's the poorest reason I know for making yourself nasty.

SYLVIA. Bosh! Ibsen!

CHARTERIS (to the page). Off with you, my boy: Dr. Paramore's waiting breathless with expectation.

PAGE BOY (seriously). Indeed, sir. (He hurries off.)

CHARTERIS. That boy will make his way in this country. He has no sense of humour. (Grace comes in. Her dress, very convenient and businesslike, is made to please herself and serve her own purposes without the slightest regard to fashion, though by no means without a careful concern for her personal elegance. She enters briskly, like an habitually busy woman.)

SYLVIA (running to her). Here you are at last Tranfield, old girl.

I've been waiting for you this last hour. I'm starving.

GRACE. All right, dear. (To Charteris.) Did you get my letter?

CHARTERIS. Yes. I wish you wouldn't write on those confounded blue letter cards.

SYLVIA (to Grace). Shall I go down first and secure a table?

CHARTERIS (taking the reply out of Grace's mouth). Do, old boy.

SYLVIA. Don't be too long. (She goes into the dining room.)

GRACE. Well?

CHARTERIS. I'm afraid to face you after last night. Can you imagine a more horrible scene? Don't you hate the very sight of me after it?

GRACE. Oh, no.

CHARTERIS. Then you ought to. Ugh! it was hideous—an insult—an outrage. A nice end to all my plans for making you happy—for making you an exception to all the women who swear I have made them miserable!

GRACE (sitting down placidly). I am not at all miserable. I'm sorry; but I shan't break my heart.

CHARTERIS. No: yours is a thoroughbred heart: you don't scream and cry every time it's pinched. That's why you are the only possible woman for me.

GRACE (shaking her head). Not now. Never any more.

CHARTERIS. Never! What do you mean?

GRACE. What I say, Leonard.

CHARTERIS. Jilted again! The fickleness of women I love is only equaled by the infernal constancy of the women who love me. Well, well! I see how it is, Grace: you can't get over that horrible scene last night. Imagine her saying I had kissed her within the last two days!

GRACE (rising eagerly). Was that not true?

CHARTERIS. True! No: a thumping lie.

GRACE. Oh, I'm so glad. That was the only thing that really hurt me.

CHARTERIS. Just why she said it. How adorable of you to care! My darling. (He seizes her hands and presses them to his breast.)

GRACE. Remember! it's all broken off.

CHARTERIS. Ah yes: you have my heart in your hands. Break it. Throw my happiness out of the window.

GRACE. Oh, Leonard, does your happiness really depend on me?

CHARTERIS (tenderly). Absolutely. (She beams with delight. A sudden revulsion comes to him at the sight: he recoils, dropping her hands and crying) Ah no: why should I lie to you? (He folds his arms and adds firmly) My happiness depends on nobody but myself. I can do without you.

GRACE (nerving herself). So you shall. Thank you for the truth. Now *I* will tell you the truth.

CHARTERIS (unfolding his arms and again recoiling). No, please. Don't. As a philosopher, it's my business to tell other people the truth; but it's not their business to tell it to me. I don't like it: it hurts.

GRACE (quietly). It's only that I love you.

CHARTERIS. Ah! that's not a philosophic truth. You may tell me that as often as you like. (He takes her in his arms.)

GRACE. Yes, Leonard; but I'm an advanced woman. (He checks himself and looks at her in some consternation.) I'm what my father calls a New Woman. (He lets her go and stares at her.) I quite agree with all your ideas.

CHARTERIS (scandalized). That's a nice thing for a respectable woman to say! You ought to be ashamed of yourself.

GRACE. I am quite in earnest about them too, though you are not; and I will never marry a man I love too much. It would give him a terrible advantage over me: I should be utterly in his power. That's what the New Woman is like. Isn't she right, Mr. Philosopher?

CHARTERIS. The struggle between the Philosopher and the Man is fearful, Grace. But the Philosopher says you are right.

GRACE. I know I am right. And so we must part.

CHARTERIS. Not at all. You must marry some one else; and then I'll come and philander with you. (Sylvia comes back.)

SYLVIA (holding the door open). Oh, I say: come along. I'm starving.

CHARTERIS. So am I. I'll lunch with you if I may.

SYLVIA. I thought you would. I've ordered soup for three. (Grace passes out. Sylvia continues, to Charteris) You can watch Paramore from our table: he's pretending to read the British Medical Journal; but he must be making up his mind for the plunge: he looks green with nervousness.

CHARTERIS. Good luck to him. (He goes out, followed by Sylvia.)

END OF ACT II.

ACT III

Still the library. Ten minutes later. Julia, angry and miserable, comes in from the dining room, followed by Craven. She crosses the room tormentedly, and throws herself into a chair.

CRAVEN (impatiently). What is the matter? Has everyone gone mad to-day? What do you mean by suddenly getting up from the table and tearing away like that? What does Paramore mean by reading his paper and not answering when he's spoken to? (Julia writhes impatiently.) Come, come (tenderly): won't my pet tell her own father what— (irritably) what the devil is wrong with everybody? Do pull yourself straight, Julia, before Cuthbertson comes. He's only paying the bill: he'll be here in a moment.

JULIA. I couldn't bear it any longer. Oh, to see them sitting there at lunch together, laughing, chatting, making game of me! I should have screamed out in another moment—I should have taken a knife and killed her—I should have—(Cuthbertson appears with the luncheon bill in his hand. He stuffs it into his waistcoat pocket as he comes to them. He begins speaking the moment he enters.)

CUTHBERTSON. I'm afraid you've had a very poor lunch, Dan. It's disheartening to see you picking at a few beans and drinking soda water. I wonder how you live!

JULIA. That's all he ever takes, Mr. Cuthbertson, I assure you. He hates to be bothered about it.

CRAVEN. Where's Paramore?

CUTHBERTSON. Reading his paper, I asked him wasn't he coming; but he didn't hear me. It's amazing how anything scientific absorbs him. Clever man! Monstrously clever man!

CRAVEN (pettishly). Oh yes, that's all very well, Jo; but it's not good manners at table: he should shut up the shop sometimes. Heaven knows I am only too anxious to forget his science, since it has pronounced my doom. (He sits down with a melancholy air.)

CUTHBERTSON (compassionately). You mustn't think about that, Craven: perhaps he was mistaken. (He sighs deeply and sits down.) But he is certainly a very clever fellow. He thinks twice before he commits himself. (They sit in silence, full of the gloomiest thoughts. Suddenly Paramore enters, pale and in the utmost disorder, with the British Medical Journal in his clenched hand. They rise in alarm. He tries to speak, but chokes, clutches at his throat, and staggers. Cuthbertson quickly takes his chair and places it behind Paramore, who sinks into it as they crowd about him, Craven at his right shoulder, Cuthbertson on his left, and Julia behind Craven.)

CRAVEN. What's the matter, Paramore?

JULIA. Are you ill?

CUTHBERTSON. No bad news, I hope?

PARAMORE (despairingly). The worst of news! Terrible news! Fatal news!

My disease—

CRAVEN (quickly). Do you mean my disease?

PARAMORE (fiercely). I mean my disease—Paramore's disease—the disease I discovered—the work of my life. Look here (pointing to the B. M. J. with a ghastly expression of horror.) If this is true, it was all a mistake: there is no such disease. (Cuthbertson and Julia look at one another, hardly daring to believe the good news.)

CRAVEN (in strong remonstrance). And you call this bad news! Now really, Paramore—

PARAMORE (cutting him short hoarsely). It's natural for you to think only of yourself. I don't blame you: all invalids are selfish. Only a scientific man can feel what I feel now. (Writhing under a sense of intolerable injustice.) It's the fault of the wickedly sentimental laws of this country. I was not able to make experiments enough—only three dogs and a monkey. Think of that, with all Europe full of my professional rivals—men burning to prove me wrong! There is freedom in France—enlightened republican France. One Frenchman experiments on two hundred monkeys to disprove my theory. Another sacrifices 36 pounds—three hundred dogs at three francs apiece—to upset the monkey experiments. A third proves them to be both wrong by a single experiment in which he gets the temperature of a camel's liver 60 degrees below zero. And now comes this cursed Italian who has ruined me. He has a government grant to buy animals with, besides the run of the largest hospital in Italy. (With desperate resolution) But I won't be beaten by any Italian. I'll go to Italy myself. I'll re-discover my disease: I know it exists; I feel it; and I'll prove it if I have to experiment on every mortal animal that's got a liver at all. (He folds his arms and breathes hard at them.)

CRAVEN (his sense of injury growing upon him). Am I to understand, Paramore, that you took it on yourself to pass sentence of death—yes, of Death—on me, on the strength of three dogs and an infernal monkey?

PARAMORE (utterly contemptuous of Craven's narrow personal view of the matter). Yes. That was all I could get a license for.

CRAVEN. Now upon my soul, Paramore, I'm vexed at this. I don't wish to be unfriendly; but I'm extremely vexed, really. Why, confound it, do you realize what you've done? You've cut off my meat and drink for a year—made me an object of public scorn—a miserable vegetarian and a teetotaller.

PARAMORE (rising). Well, you can make up for lost time now. (Bitterly, shewing Craven the Journal) There! you can read for yourself. The camel was fed on beef dissolved in alcohol; and he gained weight under it. Eat and drink as much as you please. (Still unable to stand without support, he makes his way past Cuthbertson to the revolving bookcase and stands there with his back to them, leaning on it with his head on his hand.)

CRAVEN (grumbling). Oh yes, it's very easy for you to talk, Paramore. But what am I to say to the Humanitarian societies and the Vegetarian societies that have made me a Vice President?

CUTHBERTSON (chuckling). Aha! You made a virtue of it, did you, Dan?

CRAVEN (warmly). I made a virtue of necessity, Jo. No one can blame me.

JULIA (soothing him). Well, never mind, Daddy. Come back to the dining room and have a good beefsteak.

CRAVEN (shuddering). Ugh! (Plaintively) No: I've lost my old manly taste for it. My very nature's been corrupted by living on pap. (To Paramore.) That's what comes of all this vivisection. You go experimenting on horses; and of course the result is that you try to get me into condition by feeding me on beans.

PARAMORE (curtly, without changing his position). Well, if they've done you good, so much the better for you.

CRAVEN (querulously). That's all very well; but it's very vexing. You don't half see how serious it is to make a man believe that he has only another year to live: you really don't, Paramore: I can't help saying it. I've made my will, which was altogether unnecessary; and I've been reconciled to a lot of people I'd quarrelled with—people I can't stand under ordinary circumstances. Then I've let the girls get round me at home to an extent I should never have done if I'd had my life before me. I've done a lot of serious thinking and reading and extra church going. And now it turns out simple waste of time. On my soul, it's too disgusting: I'd far rather die like a man when I said I would.

PARAMORE (as before). Perhaps you may. Your heart's shaky, if that's any satisfaction to you.

CRAVEN (offended). You must excuse me, Paramore, if I say that I no longer feel any confidence in your opinion as a medical man. (Paramore's eye flashes: he straightens himself and listens.) I paid you a pretty stiff fee for that consultation when you condemned me; and I can't say I think you gave me value for it.

PARAMORE (turning and facing Craven with dignity). That's unanswerable, Colonel Craven. I shall return the fee.

CRAVEN. Oh, it's not the money; but I think you ought to realize your position. (Paramore turns stiffly away. Craven follows him impulsively, exclaiming remorsefully) Well, perhaps it was a nasty thing of me to allude to it. (He offers Paramore his hand.)

PARAMORE (conscientiously taking it). Not at all. You are quite in the right, Colonel Craven. My diagnosis was wrong; and I must take the consequences.

CRAVEN (holding his hand). No, don't say that. It was natural enough: my liver is enough to set any man's diagnosis wrong. (A long handshake, very trying to Paramore's nerves. Paramore then retires to the recess on Ibsen's left, and throws himself on the divan with a half suppressed sob, bending over the British Medical Journal with his head on his hands and his elbows on his knees.)

CUTHBERTSON (who has been rejoicing with Julia at the other side of the room). Well, let's say no more about it. I congratulate you, Craven, and hope you may long be spared. (Craven offers his hand.) No, Dan: your daughter first. (He takes Julia's hand gently and hands her across to Craven, into whose arms she flies with a gush of feeling.)

JULIA. Dear old Daddy!

CRAVEN. Ah, is Julia glad that the old Dad is let off for a few years more?

JULIA (almost crying). Oh, so glad: so glad! (Cuthbertson sobs audibly. The Colonel is affected. Sylvia, entering from the dining room, stops abruptly at the door on seeing the three. Paramore, in the recess, escapes her notice.)

SYLVIA. Hallo!

CRAVEN. Tell her the news, Julia: it would sound ridiculous from me. (He goes to the weeping Cuthbertson, and pats him consolingly on the shoulder.)

JULIA. Silly: only think! Dad's not ill at all. It was only a mistake of Dr. Paramore's. Oh, dear! (She catches Craven's left hand and stoops to kiss it, his right hand being still on Cuthbertson's shoulder.)

SYLVIA (contemptuously). I knew it. Of course it was nothing but eating too much. I always said Paramore was an ass. (Sensation. Cuthbertson, Craven and Julia turn in consternation.)

PARAMORE (without malice). Never mind, Miss Craven. That is what is being said all over Europe now. Never mind.

SYLVIA (a little abashed). I'm so sorry, Dr. Paramore. You must excuse a daughter's feelings.

CRAVEN (huffed). It evidently doesn't make much difference to you,

Sylvia.

SYLVIA. I'm not going to be sentimental over it, Dad, you may bet. (Coming to Craven.) Besides, I knew it was nonsense all along. (Petting him.) Poor dear old Dad! why should your days be numbered any more than any one else's? (He pats her cheek, mollified. Julia impatiently turns away from them.) Come to the smoking room, and let's see what you can do after teetotalling for a year.

CRAVEN (playfully). Vulgar little girl! (He pinches her ear.) Shall we come, Jo! You'll be the better for a pick-me-up after all this emotion.

CUTHBERTSON. I'm not ashamed of it, Dan. It has done me good. (He goes up to the table and shakes his fist at the bust over the mantelpiece.) It would do you good too if you had eyes and ears to take it in.

CRAVEN (astonished). Who?

SYLVIA. Why, good old Henrik, of course.

CRAVEN (puzzled). Henrik?

CUTHBERTSON (impatiently). Ibsen, man: Ibsen. (He goes out by the staircase door followed by Sylvia, who kisses her hand to the bust as she passes. Craven stares blankly after her, and then up at the bust. Giving the problem up as insoluble, he shakes his head and follows them. Near the door he checks himself and comes back.)

CRAVEN (softly). By the way, Paramore?—

PARAMORE (rousing himself with an effort). Yes?

CRAVEN. You weren't in earnest that time about my heart, were you?

PARAMORE. Oh, nothing, nothing. There's a slight murmur—mitral valves a little worn, perhaps; but they'll last your time if you're careful. Don't smoke too much.

CRAVEN. What! More privations! Now really, Paramore, really—

PARAMORE (rising distractedly). Excuse me: I can't pursue the subject.

I—I—

JULIA. Don't worry him now, Daddy.

CRAVEN. Well, well: I won't. (He comes to Paramore, who is pacing restlessly up and down the middle of the room.) Come, Paramore, I'm not selfish, believe me: I can feel for your disappointment. But you must face it like a man. And after all, now really, doesn't this shew that there's a lot of rot about modern science? Between ourselves, you know, it's horribly cruel: you must admit that it's a deuced nasty thing to go ripping up and crucifying camels and monkeys. It must blunt all the finer feelings sooner or later.

PARAMORE (turning on him). How many camels and horses and men were ripped up in that Soudan campaign where you won your Victoria Cross, Colonel Craven?

CRAVEN (firing up). That was fair fighting—a very different thing,

Paramore.

PARAMORE. Yes, Martinis and machine guns against naked spearmen.

CRAVEN (hotly). I took my chance with the rest, Dr. Paramore. I risked my own life: don't forget that.

PARAMORE (with equal spirit). And I have risked mine, as all doctors do, oftener than any soldier.

CRAVEN. That's true. I didn't think of that. I beg your pardon, Paramore: I'll never say another word against your profession. But I hope you'll let me stick to the good old-fashioned shaking up treatment for my liver—a clinking run across country with the hounds.

PARAMORE (with bitter irony). Isn't that rather cruel—a pack of dogs ripping up a fox?

JULIA (coming coaxingly between them). Oh, please don't begin arguing again. Do go to the smoking room, Daddy: Mr. Cuthbertson will wonder what has become of you.

CRAVEN. Very well, very well: I'll go. But you're really not reasonable to-day, Paramore, to talk that way of fair sport—

JULIA. Sh—sh (coaxing him toward the door).

CRAVEN. Well, well, I'm off. (He goes good-humoredly, pushed out by

Julia.)

JULIA (turning at the door with her utmost witchery of manner). Don't look so disappointed, Dr. Paramore. Cheer up. You've been most kind to us; and you've done papa a lot of good.

PARAMORE (delighted, rushing over to her). How beautiful it is of you to say that to me, Miss Craven!

JULIA. I hate to see any one unhappy. I can't bear unhappiness. (She runs out, casting a Parthian glance at him as she flies. Paramore stands enraptured, gazing after her through the glass door. Whilst he is thus absorbed Charteris comes in from the dining room and touches him on the arm.)

PARAMORE (starting). Eh! What's the matter?

CHARTERIS (significantly). Charming woman, isn't she, Paramore?

(Looking admiringly at him.) How have you managed to fascinate her?

PARAMORE. I! Do you really mean— (He looks at him; then recovers himself and adds coldly.) Excuse me: this is a subject I do not care to jest about. (He walks away from Charteris down the side of the room, and sits down in an easy chair reading his Journal to intimate that he does not wish to pursue the conversation.)

CHARTERIS (ignoring the hint and coolly taking a chair beside him). Why don't you get married, Paramore? You know it's a scandalous thing for a man in your profession to be single.

PARAMORE (shortly, still pretending to read). That's my own business, not yours.

CHARTERIS. Not at all: it's pre-eminently a social question. You're going to get married, aren't you?

PARAMORE. Not that I am aware of.

CHARTERIS (alarmed). No! Don't say that. Why?

PARAMORE (rising angrily and rapping one of the SILENCE placards). Allow me to call your attention to that. (He crosses to the easy chair near the revolving bookstand, and flings himself into it with determined hostility.)

CHARTERIS (following him, too deeply concerned to mind the rebuff). Paramore: you alarm me more than I can say. You've been and muffed this business somehow. I know perfectly well what you've been up to; and I fully expected to find you a joyful accepted suitor.

PARAMORE (angrily). Yes, you have been watching me because you admire Miss Craven yourself. Well, you may go in and win now. You will be pleased to hear that I am a ruined man.

CHARTERIS. You! Ruined! How? The turf?

PARAMORE (contemptuously). The turf!! Certainly not.

CHARTERIS. Paramore: if the loan of all I possess will help you over this difficulty, you're welcome to it.

PARAMORE (rising in surprise). Charteris! I—(suspiciously.) Are you joking?

CHARTERIS. Why on earth do you always suspect me of joking? I never was more serious in my life.

PARAMORE (shamed by Charteris's generosity). Then I beg your pardon. I thought the news would please you.

CHARTERIS (deprecating this injustice to his good feeling). My dear fellow—!

PARAMORE. I see I was wrong. I am really very sorry. (They shake hands.) And now you may as well learn the truth. I had rather you heard it from me than from the gossip of the club. My liver discovery has been—er—er—(he cannot bring himself to say it).

CHARTERIS (helping him out). Confirmed? (Sadly.) I see: the poor

Colonel's doomed.

PARAMORE. No: on the contrary, it has been—er—called in question. The Colonel now believes himself to be in perfectly good health; and my friendly relations with the Cravens are entirely spoiled.

CHARTERIS. Who told him about it?

PARAMORE. I did, of course, the moment I read the news in this. (He shews the Journal and puts it down on the bookstand.)

CHARTERIS. Why, man, you've been a messenger of glad tidings! Didn't you congratulate him?

PARAMORE (scandalised). Congratulate him! Congratulate a man on the worst blow pathological science has received for the last three hundred years!

CHARTERIS. No, no, no. Congratulate him on having his life saved. Congratulate Julia on having her father spared. Swear that your discovery and your reputation are as nothing to you compared with the pleasure of restoring happiness to the household in which the best hopes of your life are centred. Confound it, man, you'll never get married if you can't turn things to account with a woman in these little ways.

PARAMORE (gravely). Excuse me; but my self-respect is dearer to me even than Miss Craven. I cannot trifle with scientific questions for the sake of a personal advantage. (He turns away coldly and goes toward the table.)

CHARTERIS. Well, this beats me! The nonconformist conscience is bad enough; but the scientific conscience is the very devil. (He follows Paramore and puts his arm familiarly round his shoulder, bringing him back again whilst he speaks.) Now look here, Paramore: I've got no conscience in that sense at all: I loathe it as I loathe all the snares of idealism; but I have some common humanity and common sense. (He replaces him in the easy chair and sits down opposite him.) Come: what is a really scientific theory?—a true theory, isn't it?

PARAMORE. No doubt.

CHARTERIS. For instance, you have a theory about Craven's liver, eh?

PARAMORE. I still believe that to be a true theory, though it has been upset for the moment.

CHARTERIS. And you have a theory that it would be pleasant to be married to Julia?

PARAMORE. I suppose so—in a sense.

CHARTERIS. That theory also will be upset, probably, before you're a year older.

PARAMORE. Always cynical, Charteris.

CHARTERIS. Never mind that. Now it's a perfectly damnable thing for you to hope that your liver theory is true, because it amounts to hoping that Craven will die an agonizing death. (This strikes Paramore as paradoxical; but it startles him.) But it's amiable and human to hope that your theory about Julia is right, because it amounts to hoping that she may live happily ever after.

PARAMORE. I do hope that with all my soul—(correcting himself) I mean with all my function of hoping.

CHARTERIS. Then, since both theories are equally scientific, why not devote yourself, as a humane man, to proving the amiable theory rather than the damnable one?

PARAMORE. But how?

CHARTERIS. I'll tell you. You think I'm fond of Julia myself. So I am; but then I'm fond of everybody; so I don't count. Besides, if you try the scientific experiment of asking her whether she loves me, she'll tell you that she hates and despises me. So I'm out of the running. Nevertheless, like you, I hope that she may be happy with all my—what did you call your soul?

PARAMORE (impatiently). Oh, go on, go on: finish what you were going to say.

CHARTERIS (suddenly affecting complete indifference, and rising carelessly). I don't know that I have anything more to say. If I were you I should invite the Cravens to tea in honor of the Colonel's escape from a horrible doom. By the way, if you've done with that British Medical Journal, I should like to see how they've smashed your theory up.

PARAMORE (wincing as he also rises). Oh, certainly, if you wish it. I have no objection. (He takes the Journal from the bookstand.) I admit that the Italian experiments apparently upset my theory. But please remember that it is doubtful—extremely doubtful—whether anything can be proved by experiments on animals. (He hands Charteris the Journal.)

CHARTERIS (taking it). It doesn't matter: I don't intend to make any. (He retires to the recess on Ibsen's right, picking up the step ladder as he passes and placing it so that he is able to use it for a leg rest as he settles himself to read on the divan with his back to the corner of the mantelpiece. Paramore goes to the left hand door, and is about to leave the library when he meets Grace entering.)

GRACE. How do you do, Dr. Paramore. So glad to see you. (They shake hands.)

PARAMORE. Thanks. Quite well, I hope?

GRACE. Quite, thank you. You're looking overworked. We must take more care of you, Doctor.

PARAMORE. You are very kind.

GRACE. It is you who are too kind—to your patients. You sacrifice yourself. Have a little rest. Come and talk to me—tell me all about the latest scientific discoveries, and what I ought to read to keep myself up to date. But perhaps you're busy.

PARAMORE. No, not at all. Only too delighted. (They go into the recess on Ibsen's left, and sit there chatting in whispers, very confidentially.)

CHARTERIS. How they all love a doctor! They can say what they like to him! (Julia returns. He takes his feet down from the ladder and sits up.) Whew! (Julia wanders down his side of the room, apparently looking for someone. Charteris steals after her.)

CHARTERIS (in a low voice). Looking for me, Julia?

JULIA (starting violently). Oh! How you startled me!

CHARTERIS. Sh! I want to shew you something. Look! (He points to the pair in the recess.)

JULIA (jealously). That woman!

CHARTERIS. My young woman, carrying off your young man.

JULIA. What do you mean? Do you dare insinuate—

CHARTERIS. Sh—sh—sh! Don't disturb them. (Paramore rises; takes down a book; and sits on a footstool at Grace's feet.)

JULIA. Why are they whispering like that?

CHARTERIS. Because they don't want anyone to hear what they are saying to one another. (Paramore shews Grace a picture in the book. They both laugh heartily over it.)

JULIA. What is he shewing her?

CHARTERIS. Probably a diagram of the liver. (Julia, with an exclamation of disgust makes for the recess. Charteris catches her sleeve.) Stop: be careful, Julia. (She frees herself by giving him a push which upsets him into the easy chair; then crosses to the recess and stands looking down at Grace and Paramore from the corner next the fireplace.)

JULIA (with suppressed fury). You seem to have found a very interesting book, Dr. Paramore. (They look up, astonished.) May I ask what it is? (She stoops swiftly; snatches the book from Paramore; and comes down to the table quickly to look at it whilst they rise in amazement.) Good Words! (She flings it on the table and sweeps back past Charteris, exclaiming contemptuously) You fool! (Paramore and Grace, meanwhile, come from the recess; Paramore bewildered, Grace very determined.)

CHARTERIS (aside to Julia as he gets out of the easy chair). Idiot!

She'll have you turned out of the club for this.

JULIA (terrified). She can't—can she?

PARAMORE. What is the matter, Miss Craven?

CHARTERIS (hastily). Nothing—my fault—a stupid, practical joke. I beg your pardon and Mrs. Tranfield's.

GRACE (firmly). It is not your fault in the least, Mr. Charteris. Dr. Paramore: will you oblige me by finding Sylvia Craven for me, if you can?

PARAMORE (hesitating). But—

GRACE. I want you to go now, if you please.

PARAMORE (succumbing). Certainly. (He bows and goes out by the staircase door.)

GRACE. You are going with him, Charteris.

JULIA. You will not leave me here to be insulted by this woman, Mr.

Charteris. (She takes his arm as if to go with him.)

GRACE. When two ladies quarrel in this club, it is against the rules to settle it when there are gentlemen present—especially the gentleman they are quarrelling about. I presume you do not wish to break that rule, Miss Craven. (Julia sullenly drops Charteris's arm. Grace turns to Charteris and adds) Now! Trot off.

CHARTERIS. Certainly, certainly. (He follows Paramore ignominiously.)

GRACE (to Julia, with quiet peremptoriness). Now: what have you to say to me?

JULIA (suddenly throwing herself tragically on her knees at Grace's feet). Don't take him from me. Oh don't—don't be so cruel. Give him back to me. You don't know what you're doing—what our past has been—how I love him. You don't know—

GRACE. Get up; and don't be a fool. Suppose anyone comes in and sees you in that ridiculous attitude!

JULIA. I hardly know what I'm doing. I don't care what I'm doing: I'm too miserable. Oh, won't you listen to me?

GRACE. Do you suppose I am a man to be imposed on by this sort of rubbish?

JULIA (getting up and looking darkly at her). You intend to take him from me, then?

GRACE. Do you expect me to help you to keep him after the way you have behaved?

JULIA (trying her theatrical method in a milder form—reasonable and impulsively goodnatured instead of tragic). I know I was wrong to act as I did last night. I beg your pardon. I am sorry. I was mad.

GRACE. Not a bit mad. You calculated to an inch how far you could go. When he is present to stand between us and play out the scene with you, I count for nothing. When we are alone you fall back on your natural way of getting anything you want—crying for it like a baby until it is given to you.

JULIA (with unconcealed hatred). You learnt this from him.

GRACE. I learnt it from yourself, last night and now. How I hate to be a woman when I see, by you, what wretched childish creatures we are! Those two men would cut you dead and have you turned out of the club if you were a man and had behaved in such a way before them. But because you are only a woman, they are forbearing, sympathetic, gallant—Oh, if you had a scrap of self-respect, their indulgence would make you creep all over. I understand now why Charteris has no respect for women.

JULIA. How dare you say that?

GRACE. Dare! I love him. And I have refused his offer to marry me.

JULIA (incredulous but hopeful). You have refused!

GRACE. Yes: because I will not give myself to any man who has learnt how to treat women from you and your like. I can do without his love, but not without his respect; and it is your fault that I cannot have both. Take his love then; and much good may it do you! Run to him and beg him to have mercy on you and take you back.

JULIA. Oh, what a liar you are! He loved me before he ever saw you—before he ever dreamt of you, you pitiful thing. Do you think *I* need go down on my knees to men to make them come to me? That may be your experience, you creature with no figure: it is not mine. There are dozens of men who would give their souls for a look from me. I have only to lift my finger.

GRACE. Lift it then; and see whether he will come.

JULIA. How I should like to kill you! I don't know why I don't.

GRACE. Yes: you like to get out of your difficulties cheaply—at other people's expense. It is something to boast of, isn't it, that dozens of men would make love to you if you invited them?

JULIA (sullenly). I suppose it's better to be like you, with a cold heart and a serpent's tongue. Thank Heaven, I have a heart: that is why you can hurt me as I cannot hurt you. And you are a coward. You are giving him up to me without a struggle.

GRACE. Yes, it is for you to struggle. I wish you success. (She turns away contemptuously and is going to the dining-room door when Sylvia enters on the opposite side, followed by Cuthbertson and Craven, who come to Julia, whilst Sylvia crosses to Grace.)

SYLVIA. Here I am, sent by the faithful Paramore. He hinted that I'd better bring the elder members of the family too: here they are. What's the row?

GRACE (quietly). Nothing, dear. There's no row.

JULIA (hysterically, tottering and stretching out her arms to Craven).

Daddy!

CRAVEN (taking her in his arms). My precious! What's the matter?

JULIA (through her tears). She's going to have me expelled from the club; and we shall all be disgraced. Can she do it, Daddy?

CRAVEN. Well, really, the rules of this club are so extraordinary that I don't know. (To Grace.) May I ask, Mrs. Tranfield, whether you have any complaint to make of my daughter's conduct?

GRACE. Yes, Colonel Craven. I am going to complain to the committee.

SYLVIA. I knew you'd overdo it some day, Julia. (Craven, at a loss, looks at Cuthbertson.)

CUTHBERTSON. Don't look at me, Dan. Within these walls a father's influence counts for nothing.

CRAVEN. May I ask the ground of complaint, Mrs. Tranfield?

GRACE. Simply that Miss Craven is essentially a womanly woman, and, as such, not eligible for membership.

JULIA. It's false. I'm not a womanly woman. I was guaranteed when I joined just as you were.

GRACE. By Mr. Charteris, I think, at your own request. I shall call him as a witness to your thoroughly womanly conduct just now in his presence and Dr. Paramore's.

CRAVEN. Cuthbertson: are they joking; or am I dreaming?

CUTHBERTSON (grimly). It's real, Dan: you're awake.

SYLVIA (taking Craven's left arm and hugging it affectionately). Dear old Rip Van Winkle!

CRAVEN. Well, Mrs. Tranfield, all I can say is that I hope you will succeed in establishing your complaint, and that Julia may soon see the last of this most outrageous institution. (Sylvia, still caressing his arm, laughs at him; Charteris returns.)

CHARTERIS (at the door). May I come in?

SYLVIA (releasing the Colonel). Yes: you're wanted here as a witness.

(Charteris comes in.) It's a bad case of womanliness.

GRACE (half aside to him, significantly). You understand. (Julia, watching them jealously, leaves her father and gets close to Charteris. Grace adds aloud) I shall expect your support before the committee.

JULIA. If you have a scrap of manhood you will take my part.

CHARTERIS. But then I shall be expelled for being a manly man. Besides, I'm on the committee myself; I can't act as judge and witness, too. You must apply to Paramore: he saw it all.

GRACE. Where is Dr. Paramore?

CHARTERIS. Just gone home.

JULIA (with sudden resolution). What is Dr. Paramore's number in

Savile Row?

CHARTERIS. Seventy-nine. (Julia goes out quickly by the staircase door, to their astonishment. Charteris follows her to the door, which swings back in his face, leaving him staring after her through, the glass. Sylvia runs to Grace.)

SYLVIA. Grace: go after her. Don't let her get beforehand with Paramore. She'll tell him the most heartbreaking stories about how she's been treated, and get him round completely.

CRAVEN (floundering). Sylvia! Is that the way to speak of your sister, miss? (Grace squeezes Sylvia's hand to console her, and sits down calmly. Sylvia posts herself behind Grace's chair, leaning over the back to watch the ensuing colloquy between the three men.) I assure you, Mrs. Tranfield, Dr. Paramore has just invited us all to take afternoon tea with him; and if my daughter has gone to his house, she is simply taking advantage of his invitation to extricate herself from a very embarrassing scene here. We're all going there. Come, Sylvia. (He turns to go, followed by Cuthbertson.)

CHARTERIS (in consternation). Stop! (He gets between Craven and

Cuthbertson.) What hurry is there? Can't you give the man time?

CRAVEN. Time! What for?

CHARTERIS (talking foolishly in his agitation). Well, to get a little rest, you know—a busy professional man like that! He's not had a moment to himself all day.

CRAVEN. But Julia's with him.

CHARTERIS. Well, no matter: she's only one person. And she ought to have an opportunity of laying her case before him. As a member of the committee, I think that's only just. Be reasonable, Craven: give him half an hour.

CUTHBERTSON (sternly). What do you mean by this, Charteris?

CHARTERIS. Nothing, I assure you. Only common consideration for poor

Paramore.

CUTHBERTSON. You've some motive. Craven: I strongly advise that we go at once. (He grasps the door handle.)

CHARTERIS (coaxingly). No, no. (He puts his hand persuasively on Craven's arm, adding) It's not good for your liver, Craven, to rush about immediately after lunch.

CUTHBERTSON. His liver's cured. Come on. Craven. (He opens the door.)

CHARTERIS (catching Cuthbertson by the sleeve). Cuthbertson, you're mad. Paramore's going to propose to Julia. We must give him time: he's not the man to come to the point in three minutes as you or I would. (Turning to Craven) Don't you see?—that will get me out of the difficulty we were speaking of this morning—you and I and Cuthbertson. You remember?

CRAVEN. Now, is this a thing to say plump out before everybody,

Charteris? Confound it, have you no decency?

CUTHBERTSON (severely). None whatever.

CHARTERIS (turning to Cuthbertson). No—don't be unkind, Cuthbertson. Back me up. My future, her future, Mrs. Tranfield's future, Craven's future, everybody's future depends on our finding Julia Paramore's affianced bride when we go over to Savile Row. He's certain to propose if you'll only give him time. You know you're a kindly and sensible man as well as a deucedly clever one, Cuthbertson, in spite of all your nonsense. Say a word for me.

CRAVEN. I'm quite willing to leave the decision to Cuthbertson; and I have no doubt whatever as to what that decision will be. (Cuthbertson carefully shuts the door, and comes back into the room with an air of weighty reflection.)

CUTHBERTSON. I am now going to speak as a man of the world: that is, without moral responsibility.

CRAVEN. Quite so, Jo. Of course.

CUTHBERTSON. Therefore, though I have no sympathy whatever with Charteris's views, I think we can do no harm by waiting—say ten minutes or so. (He sits down.)

CHARTERIS (delighted). Ah, there's nobody like you after all,

Cuthbertson, when there's a difficult situation to be judged.

CRAVEN (deeply disappointed). Oh, well, Jo, if that is your decision, I must keep my word and abide by it. Better sit down and make ourselves comfortable, I suppose. (He sits also, under protest.)

CHARTERIS (fidgeting about). I can't sit down: I'm too restless. The fact is, Julia has made me so nervous that I can't answer for myself until I know her decision. Mrs. Tranfield will tell you what a time I've had lately. Julia's really a most determined woman, you know.

CRAVEN (starting up). Well, upon my life! Upon my honor and conscience!! Now really!!! I shall go this instant. Come on, Sylvia. Cuthbertson: I hope you'll mark your sense of this sort of thing by coming on to Paramore's with us at once. (He marches to the door.)

CHARTERIS (desperately). Craven: you're trifling with your daughter's happiness. I only ask five minutes more.

CRAVEN. Not five seconds, sir. Fie for shame, Charteris! (He goes out.)

CUTHBERTSON (to Charteris, as he passes him on his way to the door).

Bungler! (He follows Craven.)

SYLVIA. Serve you right, you duffer! (She follows Cuthbertson.)

CHARTERIS. Oh, these headstrong old men! (To Grace) Nothing to be done now but go with them and delay the Colonel as much as possible. So I'm afraid I must leave you.

GRACE (rising). Not at all. Paramore invited me, too, when we were talking over there.

CHARTERIS (aghast). You don't mean to say you're coming!

GRACE. Most certainly. Do you suppose I will let that woman think I am afraid to meet her? (Charteris sinks on a chair with a prolonged groan.) Come: don't be silly: you'll not overtake the Colonel if you delay any longer.

CHARTERIS. Why was I ever born, child of misfortune that I am! (He rises despairingly.) Well, if you must come, you must. (He offers his arm, which she takes.) By the way, what happened after I left you?

GRACE. I gave her a lecture on her behavior which she will remember to the last day of her life.

CHARTERIS (approvingly). That was right, darling. (He slips his arm round her waist.) Just one kiss—to soothe me.

GRACE (complacently offering her cheek). Foolish boy! (He kisses her.)

Now come along. (They go out together.)

END OF ACT III.

ACT IV

Sitting-room in Paramore's apartments in Savile Row. The darkly respectable furniture is, so to speak, en suite with Paramore's frock coat and cuffs. Viewing the room from the front windows, the door is seen in the opposite wall near the left hand corner.

Another door, a light, noiseless partition one covered with a green baize, is in the right hand wall toward the back, leading to Paramore's consulting room. The fireplace is on the left. At the nearest corner of it a couch is placed at right angles to the wall, settlewise. On the right the wall is occupied by a bookcase, further forward than the green baize door. Beyond the door is a cabinet of anatomical preparations, with a framed photograph of Rembrandt's School of Anatomy hanging on the wall above it. In front, a little to the right, a tea-table.

Paramore is seated in a round-backed chair, on castors, pouring out tea. Julia sits opposite him, with her back to the fire. He is in high spirits: she very downcast.

PARAMORE (handing her the cup he has just filled). There! Making tea is one of the few things I consider myself able to do thoroughly well. Cake?

JULIA. No, thank you. I don't like sweet things. (She sets down the cup untasted.)

PARAMORE. Anything wrong with the tea?

JULIA. No, it's very nice.

PARAMORE. I'm afraid I'm a very bad entertainer. The fact is, I'm too professional. I only shine in consultation. I almost wish you had something the matter with you; so that you might call out my knowledge and sympathy. As it is, I can only admire you, and feel how pleasant it is to have you here.

JULIA (bitterly). And pet me, and say pretty things to me! I wonder you don't offer me a saucer of milk at once?

PARAMORE (astonished). Why?

JULIA. Because you seem to regard me very much as if I were a Persian cat.

PARAMORE (in strong remonstrance). Miss Cra—

JULIA (cutting him short). Oh, you needn't protest. I'm used to it:

It's the only sort of attachment I seem always to inspire.

(Ironically) You can't think how flattering it is!

PARAMORE. My dear Miss Craven, what a cynical thing to say! You! who are loved at first sight by the people in the street as you pass. Why, in the club I can tell by the faces of the men whether you have been lately in the room or not.

JULIA (shrinking fiercely). Oh, I hate that look in their faces. Do you know that I have never had one human being care for me since I was born?

PARAMORE. That's not true, Miss Craven. Even if it were true of your father, and of Charteris, who loves you madly in spite of your dislike for him, it is not true of me.

JULIA (startled). Who told you that about Charteris?

PARAMORE. Why, he himself.

JULIA (with deep, poignant conviction). He cares for only one person in the world; and that is himself. There is not in his whole nature one unselfish spot. He would not spend one hour of his real life with—(a sob chokes her: she rises passionately, crying) You are all alike, every one of you. Even my father only makes a pet of me. (She goes away to the fireplace and stands with her back to him.)

PARAMORE (following her humbly). I don't deserve this from you: indeed

I do not.

JULIA (rating him). Then why do you talk about me with Charteris, behind my back?

PARAMORE. We said nothing disparaging of you. Nobody shall ever do that in my presence. We spoke of the subject nearest our hearts.

JULIA. His heart! Oh, God, his heart! (She sits down on the couch and hides her face.)

PARAMORE (sadly). I am afraid you love him, for all that, Miss Craven.

JULIA (raising her head instantly). If he says that, he lies. If ever you hear it said that I cared for him, contradict it: it is false.

PARAMORE (quickly advancing to her). Miss Craven: is the way clear for me then?

JULIA (pettishly—losing interest in the conversation and looking crossly into the fire). What do you mean?

PARAMORE (impetuously). You must see what I mean. Contradict the rumour of your attachment to Charteris, not by words—it has gone too far for that—but by becoming my wife. (Earnestly.) Believe me: it is not merely your beauty that attracts me: (Julia, interested, looks up at him quickly) I know other beautiful women. It is your heart, your sincerity, your sterling reality, (Julia rises and gazes at him, breathless with a new hope) your great gifts of character that are only half developed because you have never been understood by those about you.

JULIA (looking intently at him, and yet beginning to be derisively sceptical in spite of herself). Have you really seen all that in me?

PARAMORE. I have felt it. I have been alone in the world; and I need you, Julia. That is how I have divined that you, also, are alone in the world.

JULIA (with theatrical pathos). You are right there. I am indeed alone in the world.

PARAMORE (timidly approaching her). With you I should not be alone.

And you?—with me?

JULIA. You! (She gets quickly out of his reach, taking refuge at the tea-table.) No, no. I can't bring myself— (She breaks off, perplexed, and looks uneasily about her.) Oh, I don't know what to do. You will expect too much from me. (She sits down.)

PARAMORE. I have more faith in you than you have in yourself. Your nature is richer than you think.

JULIA (doubtfully). Do you really believe that I am not the shallow, jealous, devilish tempered creature they all pretend I am?

PARAMORE. I am ready to place my happiness in your hands. Does that prove what I think of you?

JULIA. Yes: I believe you really care for me. (He approaches her eagerly: she has a violent revulsion, and rises with her hand raised as if to beat him off, crying) No, no, no, no. I cannot. It's impossible. (She goes towards the door.)

PARAMORE (looking wistfully after her). Is it Charteris?

JULIA (stopping and turning). Ah, you think that! (She comes back.) Listen to me. If I say yes, will you promise not to touch me—to give me time to accustom myself to the idea of our new relations?

PARAMORE. I promise most faithfully. I would not press you for the world.

JULIA. Then—then—yes: I promise. (He is about to utter his rapture; she will not have it.) Now, not another word of it. Let us forget it. (She resumes her seat at the table.) Give me some more tea. (He hastens to his former seat. As he passes, she puts her left hand on his arm and says) Be good to me, Percy, I need it sorely.

PARAMORE (transported). You have called me Percy! Hurrah! (Charteris and Craven come in. Paramore hastens to meet them, beaming.) Delighted to see you here with me, Colonel Craven. And you, too, Charteris. Sit down. (The Colonel sits down on the end of the couch.) Where are the others?

CHARTERIS. Sylvia has dragged Cuthbertson off into the Burlington Arcade to buy some caramels. He likes to encourage her in eating caramels: he thinks it's a womanly taste. Besides, he likes them himself. They'll be here presently. (He strolls across to the cabinet and pretends to study the Rembrandt photograph, so as to be as far out of Julia's reach as possible.)

CRAVEN. Yes; and Charteris has been trying to persuade me that there's a short cut between Cork Street and Savile Row somewhere in Conduit Street. Now did you ever hear such nonsense? Then he said my coat was getting shabby, and wanted me to go into Poole's and order a new one. Paramore: is my coat shabby?

PARAMORE. Not that I can see.

CRAVEN. I should think not. Then he wanted to draw me into a dispute about the Egyptian war. We should have been here quarter of an hour ago only for his nonsense.

CHARTERIS (still contemplating Rembrandt). I did my best to keep him from disturbing you, Paramore.

PARAMORE (gratefully). You have come in the nick of time. Colonel

Craven: I have something very particular to say to you.

CRAVEN (springing up in alarm). In private, Paramore: now really it must be in private.

PARAMORE (surprised). Of course. I was about to suggest my consulting room: there's nobody there. Miss Craven: will you excuse me: Charteris will entertain you until I return. (He leads the way to the green baize door.)

CHARTERIS (aghast). Oh, I say, hadn't you better wait until the others come?

PARAMORE (exultant). No need for further delay now, my best friend.

(He wrings Charteris's hand.) Will you come, Colonel?

CRAVEN. At your service, Paramore: at your service. (Craven and Paramore go into the consulting room. Julia turns her head and stares insolently at Charteris. His nerves play him false: he is completely out of countenance in a moment. She rises suddenly. He starts, and comes hastily forward between the table and the bookcase. She crosses to that side behind the table; and he immediately crosses to the opposite side in front of it, dodging her.)

CHARTERIS (nervously). Don't, Julia. Now don't abuse your advantage. You've got me here at your mercy. Be good for once; and don't make a scene.

JULIA (contemptuously). Do you suppose I am going to touch you?

CHARTERIS. No. Of course not. (She comes forward on her side of the table. He retreats on his side of it. She looks at him with utter scorn; sweeps across to the couch; and sits down imperially. With a great sigh of relief he drops into Paramore's chair.)

JULIA. Come here. I have something to say to you.

CHARTERIS. Yes? (He rolls the chair a few inches towards her.)

JULIA. Come here, I say. I am not going to shout across the room at you. Are you afraid of me?

CHARTERIS. Horribly. (He moves the chair slowly, with great misgiving, to the end of the couch.)

JULIA (with studied insolence). Has that woman told you that she has given you up to me without an attempt to defend her conquest?

CHARTERIS (whispering persuasively). Shew that you are capable of the same sacrifice. Give me up, too.

JULIA. Sacrifice! And so you think I'm dying to marry you, do you?

CHARTERIS. I am afraid your intentions have been honourable, Julia.

JULIA. You cad!

CHARTERIS (with a sigh). I confess I am something either more or less than a gentleman, Julia. You once gave me the benefit of the doubt.

JULIA. Indeed! *I* never told you so. If you cannot behave like a gentleman, you had better go back to the society of the woman who has given you up—if such a cold-blooded, cowardly creature can be called a woman. (She rises majestically; he makes his chair fly back to the table.) I know you now, Leonard Charteris, through and through, in all your falseness, your petty spite, your cruelty and your vanity. The place you coveted has been won by a man more worthy of it.

CHARTERIS (springing up, and coming close to her, gasping with eagerness). What do you mean? Out with it. Have you accep—

JULIA. I am engaged to Dr. Paramore.

CHARTERIS (enraptured). My own Julia! (He attempts to embrace her.)

JULIA (recoiling—he catching her hands and holding them). How dare you! Are you mad? Do you wish me to call Dr. Paramore?

CHARTERIS. Call everybody, my darling—everybody in London. Now I shall no longer have to be brutal—to defend myself—to go in fear of you. How I have looked forward to this day! You know now that I don't want you to marry me or to love me: Paramore can have all that. I only want to look on and rejoice disinterestedly in the happiness of (kissing her hand) my dear Julia (kissing the other), my beautiful Julia. (She tears her hands away and raises them as if to strike him, as she did the night before at Cuthbertson's.) No use to threaten me now: I am not afraid of those hands—the loveliest hands in the world.

JULIA. How have you the face to turn round like this after insulting and torturing me!

CHARTERIS. Never mind, dearest: you never did understand me; and you never will. Our vivisecting friend has made a successful experiment at last.

JULIA (earnestly). It is you who are the vivisector—a far crueller, more wanton vivisector than he.

CHARTERIS. Yes; but then I learn so much more from my experiments than he does! And the victims learn as much as I do. That's where my moral superiority comes in.

JULIA (sitting down again on the couch with rueful humour). Well, you shall not experiment on me any more. Go to your Grace if you want a victim. She'll be a tough one.

CHARTERIS (reproachfully sitting down beside her). And you drove me to propose to her to escape from you! Suppose she had accepted me, where should I be now?

JULIA. Where *I* am, I suppose, now that I have accepted Paramore.

CHARTERIS. But I should have made Grace unhappy. (Julia sneers). However, now I come to think of it, you'll make Paramore unhappy. And yet if you refused him he would be in despair. Poor devil!

JULIA (her temper flashing up for a moment again). He is a better man than you.

CHARTERIS (humbly). I grant you that, my dear.

JULIA (impetuously). Don't call me your dear. And what do you mean by saying that I shall make him unhappy? Am I not good enough for him?

CHARTERIS (dubiously). Well, that depends on what you mean by good enough.

JULIA (earnestly). You might have made me good if you had chosen to. You had a great power over me. I was like a child in your hands; and you knew it.

CHARTERIS (with comic acquiescence). Yes, my dear. That means that whenever you got jealous and flew into a violent rage, I could always depend on it's ending happily if I only waited long enough, and petted you very hard all the time. When you had had your fling, and called the object of your jealousy every name you could lay your tongue to, and abused me to your heart's content for a couple of hours, then the reaction would come; and you would at last subside into a soothing rapture of affection which gave you a sensation of being angelically good and forgiving. Oh, I know that sort of goodness! You may have thought on these occasions that I was bringing out your latent amiability; but I thought you were bringing out mine, and using up rather more than your fair share of it.

JULIA. According to you, then, I have no good in me! I am an utterly vile, worthless woman. Is that it?

CHARTERIS. Yes, if you are to be judged as you judge others. From the conventional point of view, there's nothing to be said for you, Julia—nothing. That's why I have to find some other point of view to save my self-respect when I remember how I have loved you. Oh, what I have learnt from you!—from you, who could learn nothing from me! I made a fool of you; and you brought me wisdom: I broke your heart; and you brought me joy: I made you curse your womanhood; and you revealed my manhood to me. Blessings forever and ever on my Julia's name! (With genuine emotion, he takes her hand to kiss it again.)

JULIA (snatching her hand away in disgust). Oh, stop talking that nasty sneering stuff.

CHARTERIS (laughingly appealing to the heavens). She calls it nasty sneering stuff! Well, well: I'll never talk like that to you again, dearest. It only means that you are a beautiful woman, and that we all love you.

JULIA. Don't say that: I hate it. It sounds as if I were a mere animal.

CHARTERIS. Hm! A fine animal is a very wonderful thing. Don't let us disparage animals, Julia.

JULIA. That is what you really think me.

CHARTERIS. Come, Julia: you don't expect me to admire you for your moral qualities, do you? (She turns and looks hard at him. He starts up apprehensively and backs away from her. She rises and follows him up slowly and intently.)

JULIA (deliberately). I have seen you very much infatuated with this depraved creature who has no moral qualities.

CHARTERIS (retreating). Keep off, Julia. Remember your new obligations to Paramore.

JULIA (overtaking him in the middle of the room). Never mind Paramore: that is my business. (She grasps the lapels of his coat in her hands, and looks fixedly at him.) Oh, if the people you talk so cleverly to could only know you as I know you! Sometimes I wonder at myself for ever caring for you.

CHARTERIS (beaming at her). Only sometimes?

JULIA. You fraud! You humbug! You miserable little plaster saint! (He looks delighted.) Oh! (In a paroxysm half of rage, half of tenderness, she shakes him, growling over him like a tigress over her cub. Paramore and Craven at this moment return from the consulting room, and are thunderstruck at the spectacle.)

CRAVEN (shouting, utterly scandalized). Julia!! (Julia releases

Charteris, but stands her ground disdainfully as they come forward,

Craven on her left, Paramore on her right.)

PARAMORE. What's the matter?

CHARTERIS. Nothing, nothing. You'll soon get used to this, Paramore.

CRAVEN. Now really, Julia, this is a very extraordinary way to behave.

It's not fair to Paramore.

JULIA (coldly). If Dr. Paramore objects he can break off our engagement. (To Paramore) Pray don't hesitate.

PARAMORE (looking doubtfully and anxiously at her). Do you wish me to break it off?

CHARTERIS (alarmed). Nonsense! don't act so hastily. It was my fault. I annoyed Miss Craven—insulted her. Hang it all, don't go and spoil everything like this.

CRAVEN. This is most infernally perplexing. I can't believe that you insulted Julia, Charteris. I've no doubt you annoyed her—you'd annoy anybody; upon my soul you would—but insult!—now what do you mean by that?

PARAMORE (very earnestly). Miss Craven; delicacy and sincerity I ask you to be frank with me. What are the relations between you and Charteris?

JULIA. Ask him. (She goes to the fireplace, her back on them.)

CHARTERIS. Certainly: I'll confess. I'm in love with Miss Craven—always have been; and I've persecuted her with my addresses ever since I knew her. It's been no use: she utterly despises me. A moment ago the spectacle of a rival's happiness stung me to make a nasty, sneering speech; and she—well, she just shook me a little, as you saw.

PARAMORE (chivalrously). I shall never forget that you helped me to win her, Charteris. (Julia quickly, a spasm of fury in her face.)

CHARTERIS. Sh! For Heaven's sake don't mention it.

CRAVEN. This is a very different story to the one you told Cuthbertson and myself this morning. You'll excuse my saying that it sounds much more like the truth. Come: you were humbugging us, weren't you?

CHARTERIS. Ask Julia. (Paramore and Craven turn to Julia. Charteris remains doggedly looking straight before him.)

JULIA. It's quite true. He has been in love with me; he has persecuted me; and I utterly despise him.

GRAVEN. Don't rub it in, Julia: it's not kind. No man is quite himself when he's crossed in love. (To Charteris.) Now listen to me, Charteris. When I was a young fellow, Cuthbertson and I fell in love with the same woman. She preferred Cuthbertson. I was taken aback: I won't deny it. But I knew my duty; and I did it. I gave her up and wished Cuthbertson joy. He told me this morning, when we met after many years, that he has respected and liked me ever since for it. And I believe him and feel the better for it. (Impressively.) Now, Charteris, Paramore and you stand to-day where Cuthbertson and I stood on a certain July evening thirty-five years ago. How are you going to take it?

JULIA (indignantly). How is he going to take it, indeed! Really, papa, this is too much. If Mrs. Cuthbertson wouldn't have you, it may have been very noble of you to make a virtue of giving her up, just as you made a virtue of being a teetotaller when Percy cut off your wine. But he shan't be virtuous over me. I have refused him; and if he doesn't like it he can—he can—

CHARTERIS. I can lump it. Precisely. Craven: you can depend on me. I'll lump it. (He moves off nonchalantly, and leans against the bookcase with his hands in his pockets.)

CRAVEN (hurt). Julia: you don't treat me respectfully. I don't wish to complain; but that was not a becoming speech.

JULIA (bursting into tears and throwing herself into the large chair). Is there anyone in the world who has any feeling for me—who does not think me utterly vile? (Craven and Paramore hurry to her in the greatest consternation.)

CRAVEN (remorsefully). My pet: I didn't for a moment mean—

JULIA. Must I stand to be bargained for by two men—passed from one to the other like a slave in the market, and not say a word in my own defence?

CRAVEN. But, my love—

JULIA. Oh, go away, all of you. Leave me. I—oh— (She gives way to a passion of tears.)

PARAMORE (reproachfully to Craven). You've wounded her cruelly,

Colonel Craven—cruelly.

CRAVEN. But I didn't mean to: I said nothing. Charteris: was I harsh?

CHARTERIS. You forget the revolt of the daughters, Craven. And you certainly wouldn't have gone on like that to any grown up woman who was not your daughter.

CRAVEN. Do you mean to say that I am expected to treat my daughter the same as I would any other girl?

PARAMORE. I should say certainly, Colonel Craven.

CRAVEN. Well, dash me if I will. There!

PARAMORE. If you take that tone, I have nothing more to say. (He crosses the room with offended dignity and posts himself with his back to the bookcase beside Charteris.)

JULIA (with a sob). Daddy.

CRAVEN (turning solicitously to her). Yes, my love.

JULIA (looking up at him tearfully and kissing his hand). Don't mind them. You didn't mean it, Daddy, did you?

CRAVEN. No, no, my precious. Come: don't cry.

PARAMORE (to Charteris, looking at Julia with delight). How beautiful she is!

CHARTERIS (throwing up his hands). Oh, Lord help you, Paramore! (He leaves the bookcase and sits at the end of the couch farthest from the fire. Meanwhile Sylvia arrives.)

SYLVIA (contemplating Julia). Crying again! Well, you are a womanly one!

CRAVEN. Don't worry your sister, Sylvia. You know she can't bear it.

SYLVIA. I speak for her good, Dad. All the world can't be expected to know that she's the family baby.

JULIA. You will get your ears boxed presently, Silly.

CRAVEN. Now, now, now, my dear children, really now! Come, Julia: put up your handkerchief before Mrs. Tranfield sees you. She's coming along with Jo.

JULIA (rising). That woman again!

SYLVIA. Another row! Go it, Julia!

CRAVEN. Hold your tongue, Sylvia. (He turns commandingly to Julia.)

Now look here, Julia.

CHARTERIS. Hallo! A revolt of the fathers!

CRAVEN. Silence, Charteris. (To Julia, unanswerably.) The test of a man or woman's breeding is how they behave in a quarrel. Anybody can behave well when things are going smoothly. Now you said to-day, at that iniquitous club, that you were not a womanly woman. Very well: I don't mind. But if you are not going to behave like a lady when Mrs. Tranfield comes into this room, you've got to behave like a gentleman; or fond as I am of you, I'll cut you dead exactly as I would if you were my son.

PARAMORE (remonstrating). Colonel Craven—

CRAVEN (cutting him short). Don't be a fool, Paramore.

JULIA (tearfully excusing herself). I'm sure, Daddy—

CRAVEN. Stop snivelling. I'm not speaking as your Daddy now: I'm speaking as your commanding officer.

SYLVIA. Good old Victoria Cross! (Craven turns sharply on her; and she darts away behind Charteris, and presently seats herself on the couch, so that she and Charteris are shoulder to shoulder, facing opposite ways. Cuthbertson arrives with Grace, who remains near the door whilst her father joins the others.)

CRAVEN. Ah, Jo, here you are. Now, Paramore, tell 'em the news.

PARAMORE. Mrs. Tranfield—Cuthbertson—allow me to introduce you to my future wife.

CUTHBERTSON (coming forward to shake hands with Paramore). My heartiest congratulations! (Paramore goes to shake hands with Grace.)

Miss Craven: you will accept Grace's congratulations as well as mine,

I hope.

CRAVEN. She will, Jo. (In a tone of command.) Now, Julia. (Julia slowly rises.)

CUTHBERTSON. Now, Grace. (He conducts her to Julia's right; then posts himself on the hearthrug, with his back to the fire, watching them. The Colonel keeps guard on the other side.)

GRACE (speaking in a low voice to Julia alone). So you have shewn him that you can do without him! Now I take back everything I said. Will you shake hands with me? (Julia gives her hand painfully, with her face averted.) They think this a happy ending, Julia—these men—our lords and masters! (The two stand silent, hand in hand.)

SYLVIA (leaning back across the couch, aside to Charteris). Has she really chucked you? (He nods assent. She looks at him dubiously, and adds) I expect you chucked her.

CUTHBERTSON. And now, Paramore, mind you don't stand any chaff from Charteris about this. He's in the same predicament himself. He's engaged to Grace.

JULIA (dropping Grace's hand, and speaking with breathless anguish, but not violently). Again!

CHARTERIS (rising hastily). Don't be alarmed. It's all off.

SYLVIA (rising indignantly). What! You've chucked Grace too! What a shame! (She goes to the other side of the room, fuming.)

CHARTERIS (following her and putting his hand soothingly on her shoulder). She won't have me, old chap—that is (turning to the others) unless Mrs. Tranfield has changed her mind again.

GRACE. No: we shall remain very good friends, I hope; but nothing would induce me to marry you. (She goes to chair above the fireplace and sits down with perfect composure.)

JULIA. Ah! (She sits down with a great sigh of relief.)

SYLVIA (consoling Charteris). Poor old Leonard!

CHARTERIS. Yes: this is the doom of the philanderer. I shall have to go on philandering now all my life. No domesticity, no fireside, no little ones, nothing at all in Cuthbertson's line! Nobody will marry me—unless you, Sylvia—eh?

SYLVIA. Not if I know it, Charteris.

CHARTERIS (to them all). You see!

CRAVEN (coming between Charteris and Sylvia). Now you really shouldn't make a jest of these things: upon my life and soul you shouldn't, Charteris.

CUTHBERTSON (on the hearthrug). The only use he can find for sacred things is to make a jest of them. That's the New Order. Thank Heaven, we belong to the Old Order, Dan!

CHARTERIS. Cuthbertson: don't be symbolic.

CUTHBERTSON (outraged). Symbolic! That is an accusation of Ibsenism.

What do you mean?

CHARTERIS. Symbolic of the Old Order. Don't persuade yourself that you represent the Old Order. There never was any Old Order.

CRAVEN. There I flatly contradict you and stand up for Jo. I'd no more have behaved as you do when I was a young man than I'd have cheated at cards. *I* belong to the Old Order.

CHARTERIS. You're getting old, Craven; and you want to make a merit of it, as usual.

CRAVEN. Come, now, Charteris: you're not offended, I hope. (With a conciliatory outburst.) Well, perhaps I shouldn't have said that about cheating at cards. I withdraw it (offering his hand).

CHARTERIS (taking Craven's hand). No offence, my dear Craven: none in the world. I didn't mean to shew any temper. But (aside, after looking round to see whether the others are listening) only just consider!—the spectacle of a rival's happiness!

CRAVEN (aloud, decisively). Charteris: now you've got to behave like a man. Your duty's plain before you. (To Cuthbertson.) Am I right, Jo?

CUTHBERTSON (firmly). You are, Dan.

CRAVEN (to Charteris). Go straight up and congratulate Julia. And do it like a gentleman, smiling.

CHARTERIS. Colonel: I will. Not a muscle shall betray the conflict within.

CRAVEN. Julia: Charteris has not congratulated you yet. He's coming to do it. (Julia rises and fixes a dangerous look on Charteris.)

SYLVIA (whispering quickly behind Charteris as he is about to advance). Take care. She's going to hit you. I know her. (Charteris stops and looks cautiously at Julia, measuring the situation. They regard one another steadfastly for a moment. Grace softly rises and gets close to Julia.)

CHARTERIS (whispering over his shoulder to Sylvia). I'll chance it.

(He walks confidently up to Julia.) Julia? (He proffers his hand.)

JULIA (exhausted, allowing herself to take it). You are right. I am a worthless woman.

CHARTERIS (triumphant, and gaily remonstrating). Oh, why?

JULIA. Because I am not brave enough to kill you.

GRACE (taking her in her arms as she sinks, almost fainting, away from him). Oh, no. Never make a hero of a philanderer. (Charteris, amused and untouched, shakes his head laughingly. The rest look at Julia with concern, and even a little awe, feeling for the first time the presence of a keen sorrow.)

CURTAIN.

MRS WARREN'S PROFESSION

With The Author's Apology (1902)

THE AUTHOR'S APOLOGY

Mrs Warren's Profession has been performed at last, after a delay of only eight years; and I have once more shared with Ibsen the triumphant amusement of startling all but the strongest-headed of the London theatre critics clean out of the practice of their profession. No author who has ever known the exultation of sending the Press into an hysterical tumult of protest, of moral panic, of involuntary and frantic confession of sin, of a horror of conscience in which the power of distinguishing between the work of art on the stage and the real life of the spectator is confused and overwhelmed, will ever care for the stereotyped compliments which every successful farce or melodrama elicits from the newspapers. Give me that critic who rushed from my play to declare furiously that Sir George Crofts ought to be kicked. What a triumph for the actor, thus to reduce a jaded London journalist to the condition of the simple sailor in the Wapping gallery, who shouts execrations at Iago and warnings to Othello not to believe him! But dearer still than such simplicity is that sense of the sudden earthquake shock to the foundations of morality which sends a pallid crowd of critics into the street shrieking that the pillars of society are cracking and the ruin of the State is at hand. Even the Ibsen champions of ten years ago remonstrate with me just as the veterans of those brave days remonstrated with them. Mr Grein, the hardy iconoclast who first launched my plays on the stage alongside Ghosts and The Wild Duck, exclaimed that I have shattered his ideals. Actually his ideals! What would Dr Relling say? And Mr William Archer himself disowns me because I "cannot touch pitch without wallowing in it". Truly my play must be more needed than I knew; and yet I thought I knew how little the others know.

Do not suppose, however, that the consternation of the Press reflects any consternation among the general public. Anybody can upset the theatre critics, in a turn of the wrist, by substituting for the romantic commonplaces of the stage the moral commonplaces of the pulpit, platform, or the library. Play Mrs Warren's Profession to an audience of clerical members of the Christian Social Union and of women well experienced in Rescue, Temperance, and Girls' Club work, and no moral panic will arise; every man and woman present will know that as long as poverty makes virtue hideous and the spare pocket-money of rich bachelordom makes vice dazzling, their daily hand-to-hand fight against prostitution with prayer and persuasion, shelters and scanty alms, will be a losing one. There was a time when they were able to urge that though "the white-lead factory where Anne Jane was poisoned" may be a far more terrible place than Mrs Warren's house, yet hell is still more dreadful. Nowadays they no longer believe in hell; and the girls among whom they are working know that they do not believe in it, and would laugh at them if they did. So well have the rescuers learnt that Mrs Warren's defence of herself and indictment of society is the thing that most needs saying, that those who know me personally reproach me, not for writing this play, but for wasting my energies on "pleasant plays" for the amusement of frivolous people, when I can build up such excellent stage sermons on their own work. Mrs Warren's Profession is the one play of mine which I could submit to a censorship without doubt of the result; only, it must not be the censorship of the minor theatre critic, nor of an innocent court official like the Lord Chamberlain's Examiner, much less of people who consciously profit by Mrs Warren's profession, or who personally make use of it, or who hold the widely whispered view that it is an indispensable safety-valve for the protection of domestic virtue, or, above all, who are smitten with a sentimental affection for our fallen sister, and would "take her up tenderly, lift her with care, fashioned so slenderly, young, and SO fair." Nor am I prepared to accept the verdict of the medical gentlemen who would compulsorily sanitate and register Mrs Warren, whilst leaving Mrs Warren's patrons, especially her military patrons, free to destroy her health and anybody else's without fear of reprisals. But I should be quite content to have my play judged by, say, a joint committee of the Central Vigilance Society and the Salvation Army. And the sterner moralists the members of the committee were, the better.

Some of the journalists I have shocked reason so unripely that they will gather nothing from this but a confused notion that I am accusing the National Vigilance Association and the Salvation Army of complicity in my own scandalous immorality. It will seem to them that people who would stand this play would stand anything. They are quite mistaken. Such an audience as I have described would be revolted by many of our fashionable plays. They would leave the theatre convinced that the Plymouth Brother who still regards the playhouse as one of the gates of hell is perhaps the safest adviser on the subject of which he knows so little. If I do not draw the same conclusion, it is not because I am one of those who claim that art is exempt from moral obligations, and deny that the writing or performance of a play is a moral act, to be treated on exactly the same footing as theft or murder if it produces equally mischievous consequences. I am convinced that fine art is the subtlest, the most seductive, the most effective instrument of moral propaganda in the world, excepting only the example of personal conduct; and I waive even this exception in favor of the art of the stage, because it works by exhibiting examples of personal conduct made intelligible and moving to crowds of unobservant, unreflecting people to whom real life means nothing. I have pointed out again and again that the influence of the theatre in England is growing so great that whilst private conduct, religion, law, science, politics, and morals are becoming more and more theatrical, the theatre itself remains impervious to common sense, religion, science, politics, and morals. That is why I fight the theatre, not with pamphlets and sermons and treatises, but with plays; and so effective do I find the dramatic method that I have no doubt I shall at last persuade even London to take its conscience and its brains with it when it goes to the theatre, instead of leaving them at home with its prayer-book as it does at present. Consequently, I am the last man in the world to deny that if the net effect of performing Mrs Warren's Profession were an increase in the number of persons entering that profession, its performance should be dealt with accordingly.

Now let us consider how such recruiting can be encouraged by the theatre. Nothing is easier. Let the King's Reader of Plays, backed by the Press, make an unwritten but perfectly well understood regulation that members of Mrs Warren's profession shall be tolerated on the stage only when they are beautiful, exquisitely dressed, and sumptuously lodged and fed; also that they shall, at the end of the play, die of consumption to the sympathetic tears of the whole audience, or step into the next room to commit suicide, or at least be turned out by their protectors and passed on to be "redeemed" by old and faithful lovers who have adored them in spite of their levities. Naturally, the poorer girls in the gallery will believe in the beauty, in the exquisite dresses, and the luxurious living, and will see that there is no real necessity for the consumption, the suicide, or the ejectment: mere pious forms, all of them, to save the Censor's face. Even if these purely official catastrophes carried any conviction, the majority of English girls remain so poor, so dependent, so well aware that the drudgeries of such honest work as is within their reach are likely enough to lead them eventually to lung disease, premature death, and domestic desertion or brutality, that they would still see reason to prefer the primrose path to the strait path of virtue, since both, vice at worst and virtue at best, lead to the same end in poverty and overwork. It is true that the Board School mistress will tell you that only girls of a certain kind will reason in this way. But alas! that certain kind turns out on inquiry to be simply the pretty, dainty kind: that is, the only kind that gets the chance of acting on such reasoning. Read the first report of the Commission on the Housing of the Working Classes [*Bluebook C 4402, 8d., 1889*]; read the Report on Home Industries (sacred word, Home!) issued by the Women's Industrial Council [*Home Industries of Women in London, 1897, 1s., 12 Buckingham Street, W. C.*]; and ask yourself whether, if the lot in life therein described were your lot in life, you would not prefer the lot of Cleopatra, of Theodora, of the Lady of the Camellias, of Mrs Tanqueray, of Zaza, of Iris. If you can go deep enough into things to be able to say no, how many ignorant half-starved girls will believe you are speaking sincerely? To them the lot of Iris is heavenly in comparison with their own. Yet our King, like his predecessors, says to the dramatist, "Thus, and thus only, shall you present Mrs Warren's profession on the stage, or you shall starve. Witness Shaw, who told the untempting truth about it, and whom We, by the Grace of God, accordingly disallow and suppress, and do what in Us lies to silence." Fortunately, Shaw cannot be silenced. "The harlot's cry from street to street" is louder than the voices of all the kings. I am not dependent on the theatre, and cannot be starved into making my play a standing advertisement of the attractive side of Mrs Warren's business.

Here I must guard myself against a misunderstanding. It is not the fault of their authors that the long string of wanton's tragedies, from Antony and Cleopatra to Iris, are snares to poor girls, and are objected to on that account by many earnest men and women who consider Mrs Warren's Profession an excellent sermon. Mr Pinero is in no way bound to suppress the fact that his Iris is a person to be envied by millions of better women. If he made his play false to life by inventing fictitious disadvantages for her, he would be acting as unscrupulously as any tract writer. If society chooses to provide for its Irises better than for its working women, it must not expect honest playwrights to manufacture spurious evidence to save its credit. The mischief lies in the deliberate suppression of the other side of the case: the refusal to allow Mrs Warren to expose the drudgery and repulsiveness of plying for hire among coarse, tedious drunkards; the determination not to let the Parisian girl in Brieux's Les Avaries come on the stage and drive into people's minds what her diseases mean for her and for themselves. All that, says the King's Reader in effect, is horrifying, loathsome.

Precisely: what does he expect it to be? would he have us represent it as beautiful and gratifying? The answer to this question, I fear, must be a blunt Yes; for it seems impossible to root out of an Englishman's mind the notion that vice is delightful, and that abstention from it is privation. At all events, as long as the tempting side of it is kept towards the public, and softened by plenty of sentiment and sympathy, it is welcomed by our Censor, whereas the slightest attempt to place it in the light of the policeman's lantern or the Salvation Army shelter is checkmated at once as not merely disgusting, but, if you please, unnecessary.

Everybody will, I hope, admit that this state of things is intolerable; that the subject of Mrs Warren's profession must be either tapu altogether, or else exhibited with the warning side as freely displayed as the tempting side. But many persons will vote for a complete tapu, and an impartial sweep from the boards of Mrs Warren and Gretchen and the rest; in short, for banishing the sexual instincts from the stage altogether. Those who think this impossible can hardly have considered the number and importance of the subjects which are actually banished from the stage. Many plays, among them Lear, Hamlet, Macbeth, Coriolanus, Julius Caesar, have no sex complications: the thread of their action can be followed by children who could not understand a single scene of Mrs Warren's Profession or Iris. None of our plays rouse the sympathy of the audience by an exhibition of the pains of maternity, as Chinese plays constantly do. Each nation has its own particular set of tapus in addition to the common human stock; and though each of these tapus limits the scope of the dramatist, it does not make drama impossible. If the Examiner were to refuse to license plays with female characters in them, he would only be doing to the stage what our tribal customs already do to the pulpit and the bar. I have myself written a rather entertaining play with only one woman in it, and she is quite heartwhole; and I could just as easily write a play without a woman in it at all. I will even go so far as to promise the Mr Redford my support if he will introduce this limitation for part of the year, say during Lent, so as to make a close season for that dullest of stock dramatic subjects, adultery, and force our managers and authors to find out what all great dramatists find out spontaneously: to wit, that people who sacrifice every other consideration to love are as hopelessly unheroic on the stage as lunatics or dipsomaniacs. Hector is the world's hero; not Paris nor Antony.

But though I do not question the possibility of a drama in which love should be as effectively ignored as cholera is at present, there is not the slightest chance of that way out of the difficulty being taken by the Mr Redford. If he attempted it there would be a revolt in which he would be swept away in spite of my singlehanded efforts to defend him. A complete tapu is politically impossible. A complete toleration is equally impossible to Mr Redford, because his occupation would be gone if there were no tapu to enforce. He is therefore compelled to maintain the present compromise of a partial tapu, applied, to the best of his judgement, with a careful respect to persons and to public opinion. And a very sensible English solution of the difficulty, too, most readers will say. I should not dispute it if dramatic poets really were what English public opinion generally assumes them to be during their lifetime: that is, a licentiously irregular group to be kept in order in a rough and ready way by a magistrate who will stand no nonsense from them. But I cannot admit that the class represented by Eschylus, Sophocles, Aristophanes, Euripides, Shakespear, Goethe, Ibsen, and Tolstoy, not to mention our own contemporary playwrights, is as much in place in Mr Redford's office as a pickpocket is in Bow Street. Further, it is not true that the Censorship, though it certainly suppresses Ibsen and Tolstoy, and would suppress Shakespear but for the absurd rule that a play once licensed is always licensed (so that Wycherly is permitted and Shelley prohibited), also suppresses unscrupulous playwrights. I challenge Mr Redford to mention any extremity of sexual misconduct which any manager in his senses would risk presenting on the London stage that has not been presented under his license and that of his predecessor. The compromise, in fact, works out in practice in favor of loose plays as against earnest ones.

To carry conviction on this point, I will take the extreme course of narrating the plots of two plays witnessed within the last ten years by myself at London West End theatres, one licensed by the late Queen Victoria's Reader of Plays, the other by the present Reader to the King. Both plots conform to the strictest rules of the period when La Dame aux Camellias was still a forbidden play, and when The Second Mrs Tanqueray would have been tolerated only on condition that she carefully explained to the audience that when she met Captain Ardale she sinned "but in intention."

Play number one. A prince is compelled by his parents to marry the daughter of a neighboring king, but loves another maiden. The scene represents a hall in the king's palace at night. The wedding has taken place that day; and the closed door of the nuptial chamber is in view of the audience. Inside, the princess awaits her bridegroom. A duenna is in attendance. The bridegroom enters. His sole desire is to escape from a marriage which is hateful to him. An idea strikes him. He will assault the duenna, and get ignominiously expelled from the palace by his indignant father-in-law. To his horror, when he proceeds to carry out this stratagem, the duenna, far from raising an alarm, is flattered, delighted, and compliant. The assaulter becomes the assaulted. He flings her angrily to the ground, where she remains placidly. He flies. The father enters; dismisses the duenna; and listens at the keyhole of his daughter's nuptial chamber, uttering various pleasantries, and declaring, with a shiver, that a sound of kissing, which he supposes to proceed from within, makes him feel young again.

In deprecation of the scandalized astonishment with which such a story as this will be read, I can only say that it was not presented on the stage until its propriety had been certified by the chief officer of the Queen of England's household.

Story number two. A German officer finds himself in an inn with a French lady who has wounded his national vanity. He resolves to humble her by committing a rape upon her. He announces his purpose. She remonstrates, implores, flies to the doors and finds them locked, calls for help and finds none at hand, runs screaming from side to side, and, after a harrowing scene, is overpowered and faints. Nothing further being possible on the stage without actual felony, the officer then relents and leaves her. When she recovers, she believes that he has carried out his threat; and during the rest of the play she is represented as vainly vowing vengeance upon him, whilst she is really falling in love with him under the influence of his imaginary crime against her. Finally she consents to marry him; and the curtain falls on their happiness.

This story was certified by the present King's Reader, acting for the Lord Chamberlain, as void in its general tendency of "anything immoral or otherwise improper for the stage." But let nobody conclude therefore that Mr Redford is a monster, whose policy it is to deprave the theatre. As a matter of fact, both the above stories are strictly in order from the official point of view. The incidents of sex which they contain, though carried in both to the extreme point at which another step would be dealt with, not by the King's Reader, but by the police, do not involve adultery, nor any allusion to Mrs Warren's profession, nor to the fact that the children of any polyandrous group will, when they grow up, inevitably be confronted, as those of Mrs Warren's group are in my play, with the insoluble problem of their own possible consanguinity. In short, by depending wholly on the coarse humors and the physical fascination of sex, they comply with all the formulable requirements of the Censorship, whereas plays in which these humors and fascinations are discarded, and the social problems created by sex seriously faced and dealt with, inevitably ignore the official formula and are suppressed. If the old rule against the exhibition of illicit sex relations on stage were revived, and the subject absolutely barred, the only result would be that Antony and Cleopatra, Othello (because of the Bianca episode), Troilus and Cressida, Henry IV, Measure for Measure, Timon of Athens, La Dame aux Camellias, The Profligate, The Second Mrs Tanqueray, The Notorious Mrs Ebbsmith, The Gay Lord Quex, Mrs Dane's Defence, and Iris would be swept from the stage, and placed under the same ban as Tolstoy's Dominion of Darkness and Mrs Warren's Profession, whilst such plays as the two described above would have a monopoly of the theatre as far as sexual interest is concerned.

What is more, the repulsiveness of the worst of the certified plays would protect the Censorship against effective exposure and criticism. Not long ago an American Review of high standing asked me for an article on the Censorship of the English stage. I replied that such an article would involve passages too disagreeable for publication in a magazine for general family reading. The editor persisted nevertheless; but not until he had declared his readiness to face this, and had pledged himself to insert the article unaltered (the particularity of the pledge extending even to a specification of the exact number of words in the article) did I consent to the proposal. What was the result?

The editor, confronted with the two stories given above, threw his pledge to the winds, and, instead of returning the article, printed it with the illustrative examples omitted, and nothing left but the argument from political principles against the Censorship. In doing this he fired my broadside after withdrawing the cannon balls; for neither the Censor nor any other Englishman, except perhaps Mr Leslie Stephen and a few other veterans of the dwindling old guard of Benthamism, cares a dump about political principle. The ordinary Briton thinks that if every other Briton is not kept under some form of tutelage, the more childish the better, he will abuse his freedom viciously. As far as its principle is concerned, the Censorship is the most popular institution in England; and the playwright who criticizes it is slighted as a blackguard agitating for impunity. Consequently nothing can really shake the confidence of the public in the Lord Chamberlain's department except a remorseless and unbowdlerized narration of the licentious fictions which slip through its net, and are hallmarked by it with the approval of the Throne. But since these narrations cannot be made public without great difficulty, owing to the obligation an editor is under not to deal unexpectedly with matters that are not *virginibus puerisque*, the chances are heavily in favor of the Censor escaping all remonstrance. With the exception of such comments as I was able to make in my own critical articles in The World and The Saturday Review when the pieces I have described were first produced, and a few ignorant protests by churchmen against much better plays which they confessed they had not seen nor read, nothing has been said in the press that could seriously disturb the easygoing notion that the stage would be much worse than it admittedly is but for the vigilance of the King's Reader. The truth is, that no manager would dare produce on his own responsibility the pieces he can now get royal certificates for at two guineas per piece.

I hasten to add that I believe these evils to be inherent in the nature of all censorship, and not merely a consequence of the form the institution takes in London. No doubt there is a staggering absurdity in appointing an ordinary clerk to see that the leaders of European literature do not corrupt the morals of the nation, and to restrain Sir Henry Irving, as a rogue and a vagabond, from presuming to impersonate Samson or David on the stage, though any other sort of artist may daub these scriptural figures on a signboard or carve them on a tombstone without hindrance. If the General Medical Council, the Royal College of Physicians, the Royal Academy of Arts, the Incorporated Law Society, and Convocation were abolished, and their functions handed over to the Mr Redford, the Concert of Europe would presumably declare England mad, and treat her accordingly. Yet, though neither medicine nor painting nor law nor the

Church moulds the character of the nation as potently as the theatre does, nothing can come on the stage unless its dimensions admit of its passing through Mr Redford's mind! Pray do not think that I question Mr Redford's honesty. I am quite sure that he sincerely thinks me a blackguard, and my play a grossly improper one, because, like Tolstoy's Dominion of Darkness, it produces, as they are both meant to produce, a very strong and very painful impression of evil. I do not doubt for a moment that the rapine play which I have described, and which he licensed, was quite incapable in manuscript of producing any particular effect on his mind at all, and that when he was once satisfied that the ill-conducted hero was a German and not an English officer, he passed the play without studying its moral tendencies. Even if he had undertaken that study, there is no more reason to suppose that he is a competent moralist than there is to suppose that I am a competent mathematician. But truly it does not matter whether he is a moralist or not. Let nobody dream for a moment that what is wrong with the Censorship is the shortcoming of the gentleman who happens at any moment to be acting as Censor. Replace him to-morrow by an Academy of Letters and an Academy of Dramatic Poetry, and the new and enlarged filter will still exclude original and epoch-making work, whilst passing conventional, old-fashioned, and vulgar work without question. The conclave which compiles the index of the Roman Catholic Church is the most august, ancient, learned, famous, and authoritative censorship in Europe. Is it more enlightened, more liberal, more tolerant that the comparatively infinitesimal office of the Lord Chamberlain? On the contrary, it has reduced itself to a degree of absurdity which makes a Catholic university a contradiction in terms. All censorships exist to prevent anyone from challenging current conceptions and existing institutions. All progress is initiated by challenging current concepts, and executed by supplanting existing institutions. Consequently the first condition of progress is the removal of censorships. There is the whole case against censorships in a nutshell.

It will be asked whether theatrical managers are to be allowed to produce what they like, without regard to the public interest. But that is not the alternative. The managers of our London music-halls are not subject to any censorship. They produce their entertainments on their own responsibility, and have no two-guinea certificates to plead if their houses are conducted viciously. They know that if they lose their character, the County Council will simply refuse to renew their license at the end of the year; and nothing in the history of popular art is more amazing than the improvement in music-halls that this simple arrangement has produced within a few years. Place the theatres on the same footing, and we shall promptly have a similar revolution: a whole class of frankly blackguardly plays, in which unscrupulous low comedians attract crowds to gaze at bevies of girls who have nothing to exhibit but their prettiness, will vanish like the obscene songs which were supposed to enliven the squalid dulness, incredible to the younger generation, of the music-halls fifteen years ago. On the other hand, plays which treat sex questions as problems for thought instead of as aphrodisiacs will be freely performed. Gentlemen of Mr Redford's way of thinking will have plenty of opportunity of protesting against them in Council; but the result will be that the Mr Redford will find his natural level; Ibsen and Tolstoy theirs; so no harm will be done.

This question of the Censorship reminds me that I have to apologize to those who went to the recent performance of Mrs Warren's Profession expecting to find it what I have just called an aphrodisiac. That was not my fault; it was Mr Redford's. After the specimens I have given of the tolerance of his department, it was natural enough for thoughtless people to infer that a play which overstepped his indulgence must be a very exciting play indeed. Accordingly, I find one critic so explicit as to the nature of his disappointment as to say candidly that "such airy talk as there is upon the matter is utterly unworthy of acceptance as being a representation of what people with blood in them think or do on such occasions." Thus am I crushed between the upper millstone of the Mr Redford, who thinks me a libertine, and the nether popular critic, who thinks me a prude. Critics of all grades and ages, middle-aged fathers of families no less than ardent young enthusiasts, are equally indignant with me. They revile me as lacking in passion, in feeling, in manhood. Some of them even sum the matter up by denying me any dramatic power: a melancholy betrayal of what dramatic power has come to mean on our stage under the Censorship! Can I be expected to refrain from laughing at the spectacle of a number of respectable gentlemen lamenting because a playwright lures them to the theatre by a promise to excite their senses in a very special and sensational manner, and then, having successfully trapped them in exceptional numbers, proceeds to ignore their senses and ruthlessly improve their minds? But I protest again that the lure was not mine. The play had been in print for four years; and I have spared no pains to make known that my plays are built to induce, not voluptuous reverie but intellectual interest, not romantic rhapsody but humane concern. Accordingly, I do not find those critics who are gifted with intellectual appetite and political conscience complaining of want of dramatic power. Rather do they protest, not altogether unjustly, against a few relapses into staginess and caricature which betray the young playwright and the old playgoer in this early work of mine.

As to the voluptuaries, I can assure them that the playwright, whether he be myself or another, will always disappoint them. The drama can do little to delight the senses: all the apparent instances to the contrary are instances of the personal fascination of the performers. The drama of pure feeling is no longer in the hands of the playwright: it has been conquered by the musician, after whose enchantments all the verbal arts seem cold and tame. Romeo and Juliet with the loveliest Juliet is dry, tedious, and rhetorical in comparison with Wagner's Tristan, even though Isolde be both fourteen stone and forty, as she often is in Germany. Indeed, it needed no Wagner to convince the public of this. The voluptuous sentimentality of Gounod's Faust and Bizet's Carmen has captured the common playgoer; and there is, flatly, no future now for any drama without music except the drama of thought. The attempt to produce a genus of opera without music (and this absurdity is what our fashionable theatres have been driving at for a long time without knowing it) is far less hopeful than my own determination to accept problem as the normal materiel of the drama.

That this determination will throw me into a long conflict with our theatre critics, and with the few playgoers who go to the theatre as often as the critics, I well know; but I am too well equipped for the strife to be deterred by it, or to bear malice towards the losing side. In trying to produce the sensuous effects of opera, the fashionable drama has become so flaccid in its sentimentality, and the intellect of its frequenters so atrophied by disuse, that the reintroduction of problem, with its remorseless logic and iron framework of fact, inevitably produces at first an overwhelming impression of coldness and inhuman rationalism. But this will soon pass away. When the intellectual muscle and moral nerve of the critics has been developed in the struggle with modern problem plays, the pettish luxuriousness of the clever ones, and the sulky sense of disadvantaged weakness in the sentimental ones, will clear away; and it will be seen that only in the problem play is there any real drama, because drama is no mere setting up of the camera to nature: it is the presentation in parable of the conflict between Man's will and his environment: in a word, of problem. The vapidness of such drama as the pseudo-operatic plays contain lies in the fact that in them animal passion, sentimentally diluted, is shewn in conflict, not with real circumstances, but with a set of conventions and assumptions half of which do not exist off the stage, whilst the other half can either be evaded by a pretence of compliance or defied with complete impunity by any reasonably strong-minded person. Nobody can feel that such conventions are really compulsory; and consequently nobody can believe in the stage pathos that accepts them as an inexorable fate, or in the genuineness of the people who indulge in such pathos. Sitting at such plays, we do not believe: we make-believe. And the habit of make-believe becomes at last so rooted that criticism of the theatre insensibly ceases to be criticism at all, and becomes more and more a chronicle of the fashionable enterprises of the only realities left on the stage: that is, the performers in their own persons. In this phase the playwright who attempts to revive genuine drama produces the disagreeable impression of the pedant who attempts to start a serious discussion at a fashionable at-home. Later on, when he has driven the tea services out and made the people who had come to use the theatre as a drawing-room understand that it is they and not the dramatist who are the intruders, he has to face the accusation that his plays ignore human feeling, an illusion produced by that very resistance of fact and law to human feeling which creates drama. It is the *deus ex machina* who, by suspending that resistance, makes the fall of the curtain an immediate necessity, since drama ends exactly where resistance ends. Yet the introduction of this resistance produces so strong an impression of heartlessness nowadays that a distinguished critic has summed up the impression made on him by Mrs Warren's Profession, by declaring that "the difference between the spirit of Tolstoy and the spirit of Mr Shaw is the difference between the spirit of Christ and the spirit of Euclid." But the epigram would be as good if Tolstoy's name were put in place of mine and D'Annunzio's in place of Tolstoy. At the same time I accept the enormous compliment to my reasoning powers with sincere complacency; and I promise my flatterer that when he is sufficiently accustomed to and therefore undazzled by problem on the stage to be able to attend to the familiar factor of humanity in it as well as to the unfamiliar one of a real environment, he will both see and feel that Mrs Warren's Profession is no mere theorem, but a play of instincts and temperaments in conflict with each other and with a flinty social problem that never yields an inch to mere sentiment.

I go further than this. I declare that the real secret of the cynicism and inhumanity of which shallower critics accuse me is the unexpectedness with which my characters behave like human beings, instead of conforming to the romantic logic of the stage. The axioms and postulates of that dreary mimanthropometry are so well known that it is almost impossible for its slaves to write tolerable last acts to their plays, so conventionally do their conclusions follow from their premises. Because I have thrown this logic ruthlessly overboard, I am accused of ignoring, not stage logic, but, of all things, human feeling. People with completely theatrified imaginations tell me that no girl would treat her mother as Vivie Warren does, meaning that no stage heroine would in a popular sentimental play. They say this just as they might say that no two straight lines would enclose a space. They do not see how completely inverted their vision has become even when I throw its preposterousness in their faces, as I repeatedly do in this very play. Praed, the sentimental artist (fool that I was not to make him a theatre critic instead of an architect!) burlesques them by expecting all through the piece that the feelings of others will be logically deducible from their family relationships and from his "conventionally unconventional" social code. The sarcasm is lost on the critics: they, saturated with the same logic, only think him the sole sensible person on the stage. Thus it comes about that the more completely the dramatist is emancipated from the illusion that men and women are primarily reasonable beings, and the more powerfully he insists on the ruthless indifference of their great dramatic antagonist, the external world, to their whims and emotions, the surer he is to be denounced as blind to the very distinction on which his whole work is built. Far from ignoring idiosyncrasy, will, passion, impulse, whim, as factors in human action, I have placed them so nakedly on the stage that the elderly citizen, accustomed to see them clothed with the veil of manufactured logic about duty, and to disguise even his own impulses from himself in this way, finds the picture as unnatural as Carlyle's suggested painting of parliament sitting without its clothes.

I now come to those critics who, intellectually baffled by the problem in Mrs Warren's Profession, have made a virtue of running away from it. I will illustrate their method by quotation from Dickens, taken from the fifth chapter of Our Mutual Friend:

"Hem!" began Wegg. "This, Mr Boffin and Lady, is the first chapter of the first wollume of the Decline and Fall off——" here he looked hard at the book, and stopped.

"What's the matter, Wegg?"

"Why, it comes into my mind, do you know, sir," said Wegg with an air of insinuating frankness (having first again looked hard at the book), "that you made a little mistake this morning, which I had meant to set you right in; only something put it out of my head. I think you said Rooshan Empire, sir?"

"It is Rooshan; ain't it, Wegg?"

"No, sir. Roman. Roman."

"What's the difference, Wegg?"

"The difference, sir?" Mr Wegg was faltering and in danger of breaking down, when a bright thought flashed upon him. "The difference, sir? There you place me in a difficulty, Mr Boffin. Suffice it to observe, that the difference is best postponed to some other occasion when Mrs Boffin does not honor us with her company. In Mrs Boffin's presence, sir, we had better drop it."

Mr Wegg thus came out of his disadvantage with quite a chivalrous air, and not only that, but by dint of repeating with a manly delicacy, "In Mrs Boffin's presence, sir, we had better drop it!" turned the disadvantage on Boffin, who felt that he had committed himself in a very painful manner.

I am willing to let Mr Wegg drop it on these terms, provided I am allowed to mention here that Mrs Warren's Profession is a play for women; that it was written for women; that it has been performed and produced mainly through the determination of women that it should be performed and produced; that the enthusiasm of women made its first performance excitingly successful; and that not one of these women had any inducement to support it except their belief in the timeliness and the power of the lesson the play teaches. Those who were "surprised to see ladies present" were men; and when they proceeded to explain that the journals they represented could not possibly demoralize the public by describing such a play, their editors cruelly devoted the space saved by their delicacy to an elaborate and respectful account of the progress of a young lord's attempt to break the bank at Monte Carlo. A few days sooner Mrs Warren would have been crowded out of their papers by an exceptionally abominable police case. I do not suggest that the police case should have been suppressed; but neither do I believe that regard for public morality had anything to do with their failure to grapple with the performance by the Stage Society. And, after all, there was no need to fall back on Silas Wegg's subterfuge. Several critics saved the faces of their papers easily enough by the simple expedient of saying all they had to say in the tone of a shocked governess lecturing a naughty child. To them I might plead, in Mrs Warren's words, "Well, it's only good manners to be ashamed, dearie;" but it surprises me, recollecting as I do the effect produced by Miss Fanny Brough's delivery of that line, that gentlemen who shivered like violets in a zephyr as it swept through them, should so completely miss the full width of its application as to go home and straightway make a public exhibition of mock modesty.

My old Independent Theatre manager, Mr Grein, besides that reproach to me for shattering his ideals, complains that Mrs Warren is not wicked enough, and names several romancers who would have clothed her black soul with all the terrors of tragedy. I have no doubt they would; but if you please, my dear Grein, that is just what I did not want to do. Nothing would please our sanctimonious British public more than to throw the whole guilt of Mrs Warren's profession on Mrs Warren herself. Now the whole aim of my play is to throw that guilt on the British public itself. You may remember that when you produced my first play, Widowers' Houses, exactly the same misunderstanding arose. When the virtuous young gentleman rose up in wrath against the slum landlord, the slum landlord very effectively shewed him that slums are the product, not of individual Harpagons, but of the indifference of virtuous young gentlemen to the condition of the city they live in, provided they live at the west end of it on money earned by someone else's labor. The notion that prostitution is created by the wickedness of Mrs Warren is as silly as the notion—prevalent, nevertheless, to some extent in Temperance circles—that drunkenness is created by the wickedness of the publican. Mrs Warren is not a whit a worse woman than the reputable daughter who cannot endure her. Her indifference to the ultimate social consequences of her means of making money, and her discovery of that means by the ordinary method of taking the line of least resistance to getting it, are too common in English society to call for any special remark. Her vitality, her thrift, her energy, her outspokenness, her wise care of her daughter, and the managing capacity which has enabled her and her sister to climb from the fried fish shop down by the Mint to the establishments of which she boasts, are all high English social virtues. Her defence of herself is so overwhelming that it provokes the St James Gazette to declare that "the tendency of the play is wholly evil" because "it contains one of the boldest and most specious defences of an immoral life for poor women that has ever been penned." Happily the St James Gazette here speaks in its haste. Mrs Warren's defence of herself is not only bold and specious, but valid and unanswerable. But it is no defence at all of the vice which she organizes. It is no defence of an immoral life to say that the alternative offered by society collectively to poor women is a miserable life, starved, overworked, fetid, ailing, ugly. Though it is quite natural and RIGHT for Mrs Warren to choose what is, according to her lights, the least immoral alternative, it is none the less infamous of society to offer such alternatives. For the alternatives offered are not morality and immorality, but two sorts of immorality. The man who cannot see that starvation, overwork, dirt, and disease are as antisocial as prostitution—that they are the vices and crimes of a nation, and not merely its misfortunes—is (to put it as politely as possible) a hopelessly Private Person.

The notion that Mrs Warren must be a fiend is only an example of the violence and passion which the slightest reference to sex arouses in undisciplined minds, and which makes it seem natural for our lawgivers to punish silly and negligible indecencies with a ferocity unknown in dealing with, for example, ruinous financial swindling. Had my play been titled Mr Warren's Profession, and Mr Warren been a bookmaker, nobody would have expected me to make him a villain as well. Yet gambling is a vice, and bookmaking an institution, for which there is absolutely nothing to be said. The moral and economic evil done by trying to get other people's money without working for it (and this is the essence of gambling) is not only enormous but uncompensated. There are no two sides to the question of gambling, no circumstances which force us to tolerate it lest its suppression lead to worse things, no consensus of opinion among responsible classes, such as magistrates and military commanders, that it is a necessity, no Athenian records of gambling made splendid by the talents of its professors, no contention that instead of violating morals it only violates a legal institution which is in many respects oppressive and unnatural, no possible plea that the instinct on which it is founded is a vital one. Prostitution can confuse the issue with all these excuses: gambling has none of them. Consequently, if Mrs Warren must needs be a demon, a bookmaker must be a cacodemon. Well, does anybody who knows the sporting world really believe that bookmakers are worse than their neighbors? On the contrary, they have to be a good deal better; for in that world nearly everybody whose social rank does not exclude such an occupation would be a bookmaker if he could; but the strength of character for handling large sums of money and for strict settlements and unflinching payment of losses is so rare that successful bookmakers are rare too. It may seem that at least public spirit cannot be one of a bookmaker's virtues; but I can testify from personal experience that excellent public work is done with money subscribed by bookmakers. It is true that there are abysses in bookmaking: for example, welshing. Mr Grein hints that there are abysses in Mrs Warren's profession also. So there are in every profession: the error lies in supposing that every member of them sounds these depths. I sit on a public body which prosecutes Mrs Warren zealously; and I can assure Mr Grein that she is often leniently dealt with because she has conducted her business "respectably" and held herself above its vilest branches. The degrees in infamy are as numerous and as scrupulously observed as the degrees in the peerage: the moralist's notion that there are depths at which the moral atmosphere ceases is as delusive as the rich man's notion that there are no social jealousies or snobberies among the very poor. No: had I drawn Mrs Warren as a fiend in human form, the very people who now rebuke me for flattering her would probably be the first to deride me for deducing her character logically from occupation instead of observing it accurately in society.

One critic is so enslaved by this sort of logic that he calls my portraiture of the Reverend Samuel Gardner an attack on religion.

According to this view Subaltern Iago is an attack on the army, Sir John Falstaff an attack on knighthood, and King Claudius an attack on royalty. Here again the clamor for naturalness and human feeling, raised by so many critics when they are confronted by the real thing on the stage, is really a clamor for the most mechanical and superficial sort of logic. The dramatic reason for making the clergyman what Mrs Warren calls "an old stick-in-the-mud," whose son, in spite of much capacity and charm, is a cynically worthless member of society, is to set up a mordant contrast between him and the woman of infamous profession, with her well brought-up, straightforward, hardworking daughter. The critics who have missed the contrast have doubtless observed often enough that many clergymen are in the Church through no genuine calling, but simply because, in circles which can command preferment, it is the refuge of "the fool of the family"; and that clergymen's sons are often conspicuous reactionists against the restraints imposed on them in childhood by their father's profession. These critics must know, too, from history if not from experience, that women as unscrupulous as Mrs Warren have distinguished themselves as administrators and rulers, both commercially and politically. But both observation and knowledge are left behind when journalists go to the theatre. Once in their stalls, they assume that it is "natural" for clergymen to be saintly, for soldiers to be heroic, for lawyers to be hard-hearted, for sailors to be simple and generous, for doctors to perform miracles with little bottles, and for Mrs Warren to be a beast and a demon. All this is not only not natural, but not dramatic. A man's profession only enters into the drama of his life when it comes into conflict with his nature. The result of this conflict is tragic in Mrs Warren's case, and comic in the clergyman's case (at least we are savage enough to laugh at it); but in both cases it is illogical, and in both cases natural. I repeat, the critics who accuse me of sacrificing nature to logic are so sophisticated by their profession that to them logic is nature, and nature absurdity.

Many friendly critics are too little skilled in social questions and moral discussions to be able to conceive that respectable gentlemen like themselves, who would instantly call the police to remove Mrs Warren if she ventured to canvass them personally, could possibly be in any way responsible for her proceedings. They remonstrate sincerely, asking me what good such painful exposures can possibly do. They might as well ask what good Lord Shaftesbury did by devoting his life to the exposure of evils (by no means yet remedied) compared to which the worst things brought into view or even into surmise by this play are trifles. The good of mentioning them is that you make people so extremely uncomfortable about them that they finally stop blaming "human nature" for them, and begin to support measures for their reform.

Can anything be more absurd than the copy of The Echo which contains a notice of the performance of my play? It is edited by a gentleman who, having devoted his life to work of the Shaftesbury type, exposes social evils and clamors for their reform in every column except one; and that one is occupied by the declaration of the paper's kindly theatre critic, that the performance left him "wondering what useful purpose the play was intended to serve." The balance has to be redressed by the more fashionable papers, which usually combine capable art criticism with West-End solecism on politics and sociology. It is very noteworthy, however, on comparing the press explosion produced by Mrs Warren's Profession in 1902 with that produced by Widowers' Houses about ten years earlier, that whereas in 1892 the facts were frantically denied and the persons of the drama flouted as monsters of wickedness, in 1902 the facts are admitted and the characters recognized, though it is suggested that this is exactly why no gentleman should mention them in public. Only one writer has ventured to imply this time that the poverty mentioned by Mrs Warren has since been quietly relieved, and need not have been dragged back to the footlights. I compliment him on his splendid mendacity, in which he is unsupported, save by a little plea in a theatrical paper which is innocent enough to think that ten guineas a year with board and lodging is an impossibly low wage for a barmaid. It goes on to cite Mr Charles Booth as having testified that there are many laborers' wives who are happy and contented on eighteen shillings a week. But I can go further than that myself. I have seen an Oxford agricultural laborer's wife looking cheerful on eight shillings a week; but that does not console me for the fact that agriculture in England is a ruined industry. If poverty does not matter as long as it is contented, then crime does not matter as long as it is unscrupulous. The truth is that it is only then that it does matter most desperately. Many persons are more comfortable when they are dirty than when they are clean; but that does not recommend dirt as a national policy.

Here I must for the present break off my arduous work of educating the Press. We shall resume our studies later on; but just now I am tired of playing the preceptor; and the eager thirst of my pupils for improvement does not console me for the slowness of their progress. Besides, I must reserve space to gratify my own vanity and do justice to the six artists who acted my play, by placing on record the hitherto unchronicled success of the first representation. It is not often that an author, after a couple of hours of those rare alternations of excitement and intensely attentive silence which only occur in the theatre when actors and audience are reacting on one another to the utmost, is able to step on the stage and apply the strong word genius to the representation with the certainty of eliciting an instant and overwhelming assent from the audience. That was my good fortune on the afternoon of Sunday, the fifth of January last. I was certainly extremely fortunate in my interpreters in the enterprise, and that not alone in respect of their artistic talent; for had it not been for their superhuman patience, their imperturbable good humor and good fellowship, there could have been no performance. The terror of the Censor's power gave us trouble enough to break up any ordinary commercial enterprise. Managers promised and even engaged their theatres to us after the most explicit warnings that the play was unlicensed, and at the last moment suddenly realized that Mr Redford had their livelihoods in the hollow of his hand, and backed out. Over and over again the date and place were fixed and the tickets printed, only to be canceled, until at last the desperate and overworked manager of the Stage Society could only laugh, as criminals broken on the wheel used to laugh at the second stroke. We rehearsed under great difficulties. Christmas pieces and plays for the new year were being produced in all directions; and my six actor colleagues were busy people, with engagements in these pieces in addition to their current professional work every night. On several raw winter days stages for rehearsal were unattainable even by the most distinguished applicants; and we shared corridors and saloons with them whilst the stage was given over to children in training for Boxing night. At last we had to rehearse at an hour at which no actor or actress has been out of bed within the memory of man; and we sardonically congratulated one another every morning on our rosy matutinal looks and the improvement wrought by our early rising in our health and characters. And all this, please observe, for a society without treasury or commercial prestige, for a play which was being denounced in advance as unmentionable, for an author without influence at the fashionable theatres! I victoriously challenge the West End managers to get as much done for interested motives, if they can.

Three causes made the production the most notable that has fallen to my lot. First, the veto of the Censor, which put the supporters of the play on their mettle. Second, the chivalry of the Stage Society, which, in spite of my urgent advice to the contrary, and my demonstration of the difficulties, dangers, and expenses the enterprise would cost, put my discouragements to shame and resolved to give battle at all costs to the attempt of the Censorship to suppress the play. Third, the artistic spirit of the actors, who made the play their own and carried it through triumphantly in spite of a series of disappointments and annoyances much more trying to the dramatic temperament than mere difficulties.

The acting, too, required courage and character as well as skill and intelligence. The veto of the Censor introduced quite a novel element of moral responsibility into the undertaking. And the characters were very unusual on the English stage. The younger heroine is, like her mother, an Englishwoman to the backbone, and not, like the heroines of our fashionable drama, a prima donna of Italian origin. Consequently she was sure to be denounced as unnatural and undramatic by the critics. The most vicious man in the play is not in the least a stage villain; indeed, he regards his own moral character with the sincere complacency of a hero of melodrama. The amiable devotee of romance and beauty is shewn at an age which brings out the futilization which these worships are apt to produce if they are made the staple of life instead of the sauce. The attitude of the clever young people to their elders is faithfully represented as one of pitiless ridicule and unsympathetic criticism, and forms a spectacle incredible to those who, when young, were not cleverer than their nearest elders, and painful to those sentimental parents who shrink from the cruelty of youth, which pardons nothing because it knows nothing. In short, the characters and their relations are of a kind that the routineer critic has not yet learned to place; so that their misunderstanding was a foregone conclusion. Nevertheless, there was no hesitation behind the curtain. When it went up at last, a stage much too small for the company was revealed to an auditorium much too small for the audience. But the players, though it was impossible for them to forget their own discomfort, at once made the spectators forget theirs. It certainly was a model audience, responsive from the first line to the last; and it got no less than it deserved in return.

I grieve to add that the second performance, given for the edification of the London Press and of those members of the Stage Society who cannot attend the Sunday performances, was a less inspiriting one than the first. A solid phalanx of theatre-weary journalists in an afternoon humor, most of them committed to irreconcilable disparagement of problem plays, and all of them bound by etiquette to be as undemonstrative as possible, is not exactly the sort of audience that rises at the performers and cures them of the inevitable reaction after an excitingly successful first night. The artist nature is a sensitive and therefore a vindictive one; and masterful players have a way with recalcitrant audiences of rubbing a play into them instead of delighting them with it. I should describe the second performance of Mrs Warren's Profession, especially as to its earlier stages, as decidedly a rubbed-in one. The rubbing was no doubt salutary; but it must have hurt some of the thinner skins. The charm of the lighter passages fled; and the strong scenes, though they again carried everything before them, yet discharged that duty in a grim fashion, doing execution on the enemy rather than moving them to repentance and confession. Still, to those who had not seen the first performance, the effect was sufficiently impressive; and they had the advantage of witnessing a fresh development in Mrs Warren, who, artistically jealous, as I took it, of the overwhelming effect of the end of the second act on the previous day, threw herself into the fourth act in quite a new way, and achieved the apparently impossible feat of surpassing herself. The compliments paid to Miss Fanny Brough by the critics, eulogistic as they are, are the compliments of men three-fourths duped as Partridge was duped by Garrick. By much of her acting they were so completely taken in that they did not recognize it as acting at all. Indeed, none of the six players quite escaped this consequence of their own thoroughness. There was a distinct tendency among the less experienced critics to complain of their sentiments and behavior. Naturally, the author does not share that grievance.

PICCARD'S COTTAGE, JANUARY 1902.

[*Mrs Warren's Profession was performed for the first time in the theatre of the New Lyric Club, London, on the 5th and 6th January 1902, with Madge McIntosh as Vivie, Julius Knight as Praed, Fanny Brough as Mrs Warren, Charles Goodhart as Crofts, Harley Granville-Barker as Frank, and Cosmo Stuart as the Reverend Samuel Gardner.*]

ACT I

[*Summer afternoon in a cottage garden on the eastern slope of a hill a little south of Haslemere in Surrey. Looking up the hill, the cottage is seen in the left hand corner of the garden, with its thatched roof and porch, and a large latticed window to the left of the porch. A paling completely shuts in the garden, except for a gate on the right. The common rises uphill beyond the paling to the sky line. Some folded canvas garden chairs are leaning against the side bench in the porch. A lady's bicycle is propped against the wall, under the window. A little to the right of the porch a hammock is slung from two posts. A big canvas umbrella, stuck in the ground, keeps the sun off the hammock, in which a young lady is reading and making notes, her head towards the cottage and her feet towards the gate. In front of the hammock, and within reach of her hand, is a common kitchen chair, with a pile of serious-looking books and a supply of writing paper on it.*]

[*A gentleman walking on the common comes into sight from behind the cottage. He is hardly past middle age, with something of the artist about him, unconventionally but carefully dressed, and clean-shaven except for a moustache, with an eager susceptible face and very amiable and considerate manners. He has silky black hair, with waves of grey and white in it. His eyebrows are white, his moustache black. He seems not certain of his way. He looks over the palings; takes stock of the place; and sees the young lady.*]

THE GENTLEMAN [*taking off his hat*] I beg your pardon. Can you direct me to Hindhead View—Mrs Alison's?

THE YOUNG LADY [*glancing up from her book*] This is Mrs Alison's. [*She resumes her work*].

THE GENTLEMAN. Indeed! Perhaps—may I ask are you Miss Vivie Warren?

THE YOUNG LADY [*sharply, as she turns on her elbow to get a good look at him*] Yes.

THE GENTLEMAN [*daunted and conciliatory*] I'm afraid I appear intrusive. My name is Praed. [*Vivie at once throws her books upon the chair, and gets out of the hammock*]. Oh, pray don't let me disturb you.

VIVIE [*striding to the gate and opening it for him*] Come in, Mr Praed. [*He comes in*]. Glad to see you. [*She proffers her hand and takes his with a resolute and hearty grip. She is an attractive specimen of the sensible, able, highly-educated young middle-class Englishwoman. Age 22. Prompt, strong, confident, self-possessed. Plain business-like dress, but not dowdy. She wears a chatelaine at her belt, with a fountain pen and a paper knife among its pendants*].

PRAED. Very kind of you indeed, Miss Warren. [*She shuts the gate with a vigorous slam. He passes in to the middle of the garden, exercising his fingers, which are slightly numbed by her greeting*]. Has your mother arrived?

VIVIE [*quickly, evidently scenting aggression*] Is she coming?

PRAED [*surprised*] Didn't you expect us?

VIVIE. No.

PRAED. Now, goodness me, I hope I've not mistaken the day. That would be just like me, you know. Your mother arranged that she was to come down from London and that I was to come over from Horsham to be introduced to you.

VIVIE [*not at all pleased*] Did she? Hm! My mother has rather a trick of taking me by surprise—to see how I behave myself while she's away, I suppose. I fancy I shall take my mother very much by surprise one of these days, if she makes arrangements that concern me without consulting me beforehand. She hasnt come.

PRAED [*embarrassed*] I'm really very sorry.

VIVIE [*throwing off her displeasure*] It's not your fault, Mr Praed, is it? And I'm very glad you've come. You are the only one of my mother's friends I have ever asked her to bring to see me.

PRAED [*relieved and delighted*] Oh, now this is really very good of you, Miss Warren!

VIVIE. Will you come indoors; or would you rather sit out here and talk?

PRAED. It will be nicer out here, don't you think?

VIVIE. Then I'll go and get you a chair. [*She goes to the porch for a garden chair*].

PRAED [*following her*] Oh, pray, pray! Allow me. [*He lays hands on the chair*].

VIVIE [*letting him take it*] Take care of your fingers; theyre rather dodgy things, those chairs. [*She goes across to the chair with the books on it; pitches them into the hammock; and brings the chair forward with one swing*].

PRAED [*who has just unfolded his chair*] Oh, now do let me take that hard chair. I like hard chairs.

VIVIE. So do I. Sit down, Mr Praed. [*This invitation she gives with a genial peremptoriness, his anxiety to please her clearly striking her as a sign of weakness of character on his part. But he does not immediately obey*].

PRAED. By the way, though, hadnt we better go to the station to meet your mother?

VIVIE [*coolly*] Why? She knows the way.

PRAED [*disconcerted*] Er—I suppose she does [*he sits down*].

VIVIE. Do you know, you are just like what I expected. I hope you are disposed to be friends with me.

PRAED [*again beaming*] Thank you, my *dear* Miss Warren; thank you. Dear me! I'm so glad your mother hasnt spoilt you!

VIVIE. How?

PRAED. Well, in making you too conventional. You know, my dear Miss Warren, I am a born anarchist. I hate authority. It spoils the relations between parent and child; even between mother and daughter. Now I was always afraid that your mother would strain her authority to make you very conventional. It's such a relief to find that she hasnt.

VIVIE. Oh! have I been behaving unconventionally?

PRAED. Oh no: oh dear no. At least, not conventionally unconventionally, you understand. [*She nods and sits down. He goes on, with a cordial outburst*] But it was so charming of you to say that you were disposed to be friends with me! You modern young ladies are splendid: perfectly splendid!

VIVIE [*dubiously*] Eh? [*watching him with dawning disappointment as to the quality of his brains and character*].

PRAED. When I was your age, young men and women were afraid of each other: there was no good fellowship. Nothing real. Only gallantry copied out of novels, and as vulgar and affected as it could be. Maidenly reserve! gentlemanly chivalry! always saying no when you meant yes! simple purgatory for shy and sincere souls.

VIVIE. Yes, I imagine there must have been a frightful waste of time. Especially women's time.

PRAED. Oh, waste of life, waste of everything. But things are improving. Do you know, I have been in a positive state of excitement about meeting you ever since your magnificent achievements at Cambridge: a thing unheard of in my day. It was perfectly splendid, your tieing with the third wrangler. Just the right place, you know. The first wrangler is always a dreamy, morbid fellow, in whom the thing is pushed to the length of a disease.

VIVIE. It doesn't pay. I wouldn't do it again for the same money.

PRAED [*aghast*] The same money!

VIVIE. Yes. Fifty pounds. Perhaps you don't know how it was. Mrs Latham, my tutor at Newnham, told my mother that I could distinguish myself in the mathematical tripos if I went in for it in earnest. The papers were full just then of Phillipa Summers beating the senior wrangler. You remember about it, of course.

PRAED [*shakes his head energetically*] !!!

VIVIE. Well, anyhow, she did; and nothing would please my mother but that I should do the same thing. I said flatly that it was not worth my while to face the grind since I was not going in for teaching; but I offered to try for fourth wrangler or thereabouts for fifty pounds. She closed with me at that, after a little grumbling; and I was better than my bargain. But I wouldn't do it again for that. Two hundred pounds would have been nearer the mark.

PRAED [*much damped*] Lord bless me! Thats a very practical way of looking at it.

VIVIE. Did you expect to find me an unpractical person?

PRAED. But surely it's practical to consider not only the work these honors cost, but also the culture they bring.

VIVIE. Culture! My dear Mr Praed: do you know what the mathematical tripos means? It means grind, grind, grind for six to eight hours a day at mathematics, and nothing but mathematics.

I'm supposed to know something about science; but I know nothing except the mathematics it involves. I can make calculations for engineers, electricians, insurance companies, and so on; but I know next to nothing about engineering or electricity or insurance. I don't even know arithmetic well. Outside mathematics, lawn-tennis, eating, sleeping, cycling, and walking, I'm a more ignorant barbarian than any woman could possibly be who hadn't gone in for the tripos.

PRAED [*revolted*] What a monstrous, wicked, rascally system! I knew it! I felt at once that it meant destroying all that makes womanhood beautiful!

VIVIE. I don't object to it on that score in the least. I shall turn it to very good account, I assure you.

PRAED. Pooh! In what way?

VIVIE. I shall set up chambers in the City, and work at actuarial calculations and conveyancing. Under cover of that I shall do some law, with one eye on the Stock Exchange all the time. I've come down here by myself to read law: not for a holiday, as my mother imagines. I hate holidays.

PRAED. You make my blood run cold. Are you to have no romance, no beauty in your life?

VIVIE. I don't care for either, I assure you.

PRAED. You can't mean that.

VIVIE. Oh yes I do. I like working and getting paid for it. When I'm tired of working, I like a comfortable chair, a cigar, a little whisky, and a novel with a good detective story in it.

PRAED [*rising in a frenzy of repudiation*] I don't believe it. I am an artist; and I can't believe it: I refuse to believe it. It's only that you havn't discovered yet what a wonderful world art can open up to you.

VIVIE. Yes I have. Last May I spent six weeks in London with Honoria Fraser. Mamma thought we were doing a round of sightseeing together; but I was really at Honoria's chambers in Chancery Lane every day, working away at actuarial calculations for her, and helping her as well as a greenhorn could. In the evenings we smoked and talked, and never dreamt of going out except for exercise. And I never enjoyed myself more in my life.

I cleared all my expenses and got initiated into the business without a fee in the bargain.

PRAED. But bless my heart and soul, Miss Warren, do you call that discovering art?

VIVIE. Wait a bit. That wasn't the beginning. I went up to town on an invitation from some artistic people in Fitzjohn's Avenue: one of the girls was a Newnham chum. They took me to the National Gallery—

PRAED [*approving*] Ah!! [*He sits down, much relieved*].

VIVIE [*continuing*]—to the Opera—

PRAED [*still more pleased*] Good!

VIVIE.—and to a concert where the band played all the evening: Beethoven and Wagner and so on. I wouldn't go through that experience again for anything you could offer me. I held out for civility's sake until the third day; and then I said, plump out, that I couldn't stand any more of it, and went off to Chancery Lane. N o w you know the sort of perfectly splendid modern young lady I am. How do you think I shall get on with my mother?

PRAED [*startled*] Well, I hope—er—

VIVIE. It's not so much what you hope as what you believe, that I want to know.

PRAED. Well, frankly, I am afraid your mother will be a little disappointed. Not from any shortcoming on your part, you know: I don't mean that. But you are so different from her ideal.

VIVIE. Her what?!

PRAED. Her ideal.

VIVIE. Do you mean her ideal of ME?

PRAED. Yes.

VIVIE. What on earth is it like?

PRAED. Well, you must have observed, Miss Warren, that people who are dissatisfied with their own bringing-up generally think that the world would be all right if everybody were to be brought up quite differently. Now your mother's life has been—er—I suppose you know—

VIVIE. Don't suppose anything, Mr Praed. I hardly know my mother. Since I was a child I have lived in England, at school or at college, or with people paid to take charge of me. I have been boarded out all my life. My mother has lived in Brussels or Vienna and never let me go to her. I only see her when she visits England for a few days. I don't complain: it's been very pleasant; for people have been very good to me; and there has always been plenty of money to make things smooth. But don't imagine I know anything about my mother. I know far less than you do.

PRAED [*very ill at ease*] In that case—[*He stops, quite at a loss. Then, with a forced attempt at gaiety*] But what nonsense we are talking! Of course you and your mother will get on capitally. [*He rises, and looks abroad at the view*]. What a charming little place you have here!

VIVIE [*unmoved*] Rather a violent change of subject, Mr Praed. Why won't my mother's life bear being talked about?

PRAED. Oh, you mustn't say that. Isn't it natural that I should have a certain delicacy in talking to my old friend's daughter about her behind her back? You and she will have plenty of opportunity of talking about it when she comes.

VIVIE. No: she won't talk about it either. [*Rising*] However, I daresay you have good reasons for telling me nothing. Only, mind this, Mr Praed, I expect there will be a battle royal when my mother hears of my Chancery Lane project.

PRAED [*ruefully*] I'm afraid there will.

VIVIE. Well, I shall win because I want nothing but my fare to London to start there to-morrow earning my own living by devilling for Honoria. Besides, I have no mysteries to keep up; and it seems she has. I shall use that advantage over her if necessary.

PRAED [*greatly shocked*] Oh no! No, pray. Youd not do such a thing.

VIVIE. Then tell me why not.

PRAED. I really cannot. I appeal to your good feeling. [*She smiles at his sentimentality*]. Besides, you may be too bold. Your mother is not to be trifled with when she's angry.

VIVIE. You can't frighten me, Mr Praed. In that month at Chancery Lane I had opportunities of taking the measure of one or two women v e r y like my mother. You may back me to win. But if I hit harder in my ignorance than I need, remember it is you who refuse to enlighten me. Now, let us drop the subject. [*She takes her chair and replaces it near the hammock with the same vigorous swing as before*].

PRAED [*taking a desperate resolution*] One word, Miss Warren. I had better tell you. It's very difficult; but—

[*Mrs Warren and Sir George Crofts arrive at the gate. Mrs Warren is between 40 and 50, formerly pretty, showily dressed in a brilliant hat and a gay blouse fitting tightly over her bust and flanked by fashionable sleeves. Rather spoilt and domineering, and decidedly vulgar, but, on the whole, a genial and fairly presentable old blackguard of a woman.*]

[*Crofts is a tall powerfully-built man of about 50, fashionably dressed in the style of a young man. Nasal voice, reedier than might be expected from his strong frame. Clean-shaven bulldog jaws, large flat ears, and thick neck: gentlemanly combination of the most brutal types of city man, sporting man, and man about town.*]

VIVIE. Here they are. [*Coming to them as they enter the garden*] How do, mater? Mr Praed's been here this half hour, waiting for you.

MRS WARREN. Well, if you've been waiting, Praddy, it's your own fault: I thought youd have had the gumption to know I was coming by the 3.10 train. Vivie: put your hat on, dear: youll get sunburnt. Oh, I forgot to introduce you. Sir George Crofts: my little Vivie.

[*Crofts advances to Vivie with his most courtly manner. She nods, but makes no motion to shake hands.*]

CROFTS. May I shake hands with a young lady whom I have known by reputation very long as the daughter of one of my oldest friends?

VIVIE [*who has been looking him up and down sharply*] If you like.

[*She takes his tenderly proferred hand and gives it a squeeze that makes him open his eyes; then turns away, and says to her mother*] Will you come in, or shall I get a couple more chairs? [*She goes into the porch for the chairs*].

MRS WARREN. Well, George, what do you think of her?

CROFTS [*ruefully*] She has a powerful fist. Did you shake hands with her, Praed?

PRAED. Yes: it will pass off presently.

CROFTS. I hope so. [*Vivie reappears with two more chairs. He hurries to her assistance*]. Allow me.

MRS WARREN [*patronizingly*] Let Sir George help you with the chairs, dear.

VIVIE [*pitching them into his arms*] Here you are. [*She dusts her hands and turns to Mrs Warren*]. Youd like some tea, wouldn't you?

MRS WARREN [*sitting in Praed's chair and fanning herself*] I'm dying for a drop to drink.

VIVIE. I'll see about it. [*She goes into the cottage*].

[*Sir George has by this time managed to unfold a chair and plant it by Mrs Warren, on her left. He throws the other on the grass and sits down, looking dejected and rather foolish, with the handle of his stick in his mouth. Praed, still very uneasy, fidgets around the garden on their right.*]

MRS WARREN [*to Praed, looking at Crofts*] Just look at him, Praddy: he looks cheerful, don't he? He's been worrying my life out these three years to have that little girl of mine shewn to him; and now that Ive done it, he's quite out of countenance. [*Briskly*] Come! sit up, George; and take your stick out of your mouth. [*Crofts sulkily obeys*].

PRAED. I think, you know—if you don't mind my saying so—that we had better get out of the habit of thinking of her as a little girl. You see she has really distinguished herself; and I'm not sure, from what I have seen of her, that she is not older than any of us.

MRS WARREN [*greatly amused*] Only listen to him, George! Older than any of us! Well she *has* been stuffing you nicely with her importance.

PRAED. But young people are particularly sensitive about being treated in that way.

MRS WARREN. Yes; and young people have to get all that nonsense taken out of them, and good deal more besides. Don't you interfere, Praddy: I know how to treat my own child as well as you do. [*Praed, with a grave shake of his head, walks up the garden with his hands behind his back. Mrs Warren pretends to laugh, but looks after him with perceptible concern. Then, she whispers to Crofts*] Whats the matter with him? What does he take it like that for?

CROFTS [*morosely*] Youre afraid of Praed.

MRS WARREN. What! Me! Afraid of dear old Praddy! Why, a fly wouldn't be afraid of him.

CROFTS. *You're* afraid of him.

MRS WARREN [*angry*] I'll trouble you to mind your own business, and not try any of your sulks on me. I'm not afraid of y o u, anyhow. If you can't make yourself agreeable, youd better go home. [*She gets up, and, turning her back on him, finds herself face to face with Praed*]. Come, Praddy, I know it was only your tender-heartedness. Youre afraid I'll bully her.

PRAED. My dear Kitty: you think I'm offended. Don't imagine that: pray don't. But you know I often notice things that escape you; and though you never take my advice, you sometimes admit afterwards that you ought to have taken it.

MRS WARREN. Well, what do you notice now?

PRAED. Only that Vivie is a grown woman. Pray, Kitty, treat her with every respect.

MRS WARREN [*with genuine amazement*] Respect! Treat my own daughter with respect! What next, pray!

VIVIE [*appearing at the cottage door and calling to Mrs Warren*] Mother: will you come to my room before tea?

MRS WARREN. Yes, dearie. [*She laughs indulgently at Praed's gravity, and pats him on the cheek as she passes him on her way to the porch*]. Don't be cross, Praddy. [*She follows Vivie into the cottage*].

CROFTS [*furtively*] I say, Praed.

PRAED. Yes.

CROFTS. I want to ask you a rather particular question.

PRAED. Certainly. [*He takes Mrs Warren's chair and sits close to Crofts*].

CROFTS. Thats right: they might hear us from the window. Look here: did Kitty every tell you who that girl's father is?

PRAED. Never.

CROFTS. Have you any suspicion of who it might be?

PRAED. None.

CROFTS [*not believing him*] I know, of course, that you perhaps might feel bound not to tell if she had said anything to you. But it's very awkward to be uncertain about it now that we shall be meeting the girl every day. We don't exactly know how we ought to feel towards her.

PRAED. What difference can that make? We take her on her own merits. What does it matter who her father was?

CROFTS [*suspiciously*] Then you know who he was?

PRAED [*with a touch of temper*] I said no just now. Did you not hear me?

CROFTS. Look here, Praed. I ask you as a particular favor. If you *do* know [*movement of protest from Praed*]—I only say, if you know, you might at least set my mind at rest about her. The fact is, I fell attracted.

PRAED [*sternly*] What do you mean?

CROFTS. Oh, don't be alarmed: it's quite an innocent feeling. Thats what puzzles me about it. Why, for all I know, *I* might be her father.

PRAED. You! Impossible!

CROFTS [*catching him up cunningly*] You know for certain that I'm not?

PRAED. I know nothing about it, I tell you, any more than you. But really, Crofts—oh no, it's out of the question. Theres not the least resemblance.

CROFTS. As to that, theres no resemblance between her and her mother that I can see. I suppose she's not y o u r daughter, is she?

PRAED [*rising indignantly*] Really, Crofts—!

CROFTS. No offence, Praed. Quite allowable as between two men of the world.

PRAED [*recovering himself with an effort and speaking gently and gravely*] Now listen to me, my dear Crofts. [*He sits down again*].

I have nothing to do with that side of Mrs Warren's life, and never had. She has never spoken to me about it; and of course I have never spoken to her about it. Your delicacy will tell you that a handsome woman needs some friends who are not—well, not on that footing with her. The effect of her own beauty would become a torment to her if she could not escape from it occasionally. You are probably on much more confidential terms with Kitty than I am. Surely you can ask her the question yourself.

CROFTS. I h a v e asked her, often enough. But she's so determined to keep the child all to herself that she would deny that it ever had a father if she could. [*Rising*] I'm thoroughly uncomfortable about it, Praed.

PRAED [*rising also*] Well, as you are, at all events, old enough to be her father, I don't mind agreeing that we both regard Miss Vivie in a parental way, as a young girl who we are bound to protect and help. What do you say?

CROFTS [*aggressively*] I'm no older than you, if you come to that.

PRAED. Yes you are, my dear fellow: you were born old. I was born a boy: Ive never been able to feel the assurance of a grown-up man in my life. [*He folds his chair and carries it to the porch*].

MRS WARREN [*calling from within the cottage*] Prad-dee! George! Tea-ea-ea-ea!

CROFTS [*hastily*] She's calling us. [*He hurries in*].

[*Praed shakes his head bodingly, and is following Crofts when he is hailed by a young gentleman who has just appeared on the common, and is making for the gate. He is pleasant, pretty, smartly dressed, cleverly good-for-nothing, not long turned 20, with a charming voice and agreeably disrespectful manners. He carries a light sporting magazine rifle.*]

THE YOUNG GENTLEMAN. Hallo! Praed!

PRAED. Why, Frank Gardner! [*Frank comes in and shakes hands cordially*]. What on earth are you doing here?

FRANK. Staying with my father.

PRAED. The Roman father?

FRANK. He's rector here. I'm living with my people this autumn for the sake of economy. Things came to a crisis in July: the Roman father had to pay my debts. He's stony broke in consequence; and so am I. What are you up to in these parts? do you know the people here?

PRAED. Yes: I'm spending the day with a Miss Warren.

FRANK [*enthusiastically*] What! Do you know Vivie? Isn't she a jolly girl? I'm teaching her to shoot with this [*putting down the rifle*]. I'm so glad she knows you: youre just the sort of fellow she ought to know. [*He smiles, and raises the charming voice almost to a singing tone as he exclaims*] It's e v e r so jolly to find you here, Praed.

PRAED. I'm an old friend of her mother. Mrs Warren brought me over to make her daughter's acquaintance.

FRANK. The mother! Is *she* here?

PRAED. Yes: inside, at tea.

MRS WARREN [*calling from within*] Prad-dee-ee-ee-eee! The tea-cake'll be cold.

PRAED [*calling*] Yes, Mrs Warren. In a moment. I've just met a friend here.

MRS WARREN. A what?

PRAED [*louder*] A friend.

MRS WARREN. Bring him in.

PRAED. All right. [*To Frank*] Will you accept the invitation?

FRANK [*incredulous, but immensely amused*] Is that Vivie's mother?

PRAED. Yes.

FRANK. By Jove! What a lark! Do you think she'll like me?

PRAED. I've no doubt youll make yourself popular, as usual. Come in and try [*moving towards the house*].

FRANK. Stop a bit. [*Seriously*] I want to take you into my confidence.

PRAED. Pray don't. It's only some fresh folly, like the barmaid at Redhill.

FRANK. It's ever so much more serious than that. You say you've only just met Vivie for the first time?

PRAED. Yes.

FRANK [*rhapsodically*] Then you can have no idea what a girl she is. Such character! Such sense! And her cleverness! Oh, my eye, Praed, but I can tell you she is clever! And—need I add?—she loves me.

CROFTS [*putting his head out of the window*] I say, Praed: what are you about? Do come along. [*He disappears*].

FRANK. Hallo! Sort of chap that would take a prize at a dog show, ain't he? Who's he?

PRAED. Sir George Crofts, an old friend of Mrs Warren's. I think we had better come in.

[*On their way to the porch they are interrupted by a call from the gate. Turning, they see an elderly clergyman looking over it.*]

THE CLERGYMAN [*calling*] Frank!

FRANK. Hallo! [*To Praed*] The Roman father. [*To the clergyman*] Yes, gov'nor: all right: presently. [*To Praed*] Look here, Praed: youd better go in to tea. I'll join you directly.

PRAED. Very good. [*He goes into the cottage*].

[*The clergyman remains outside the gate, with his hands on the top of it. The Rev. Samuel Gardner, a beneficed clergyman of the Established Church, is over 50. Externally he is pretentious, booming, noisy, important. Really he is that obsolescent phenomenon the fool of the family dumped on the Church by his father the patron, clamorously asserting himself as father and clergyman without being able to command respect in either capacity.*]

REV. S. Well, sir. Who are your friends here, if I may ask?

FRANK. Oh, it's all right, gov'nor! Come in.

REV. S. No, sir; not until I know whose garden I am entering.

FRANK. It's all right. It's Miss Warren's.

REV. S. I have not seen her at church since she came.

FRANK. Of course not: she's a third wrangler. Ever so intellectual. Took a higher degree than you did; so why should she go to hear you preach?

REV. S. Don't be disrespectful, sir.

FRANK. Oh, it don't matter: nobody hears us. Come in. [*He opens the gate, unceremoniously pulling his father with it into the garden*]. I want to introduce you to her. Do you remember the advice you gave me last July, gov'nor?

REV. S. [*severely*] Yes. I advised you to conquer your idleness and flippancy, and to work your way into an honorable profession and live on it and not upon me.

FRANK. No: thats what you thought of afterwards. What you actually said was that since I had neither brains nor money, I'd better turn my good looks to account by marrying someone with both. Well, look here. Miss Warren has brains: you can't deny that.

REV. S. Brains are not everything.

FRANK. No, of course not: theres the money—

REV. S. [*interrupting him austerely*] I was not thinking of money, sir. I was speaking of higher things. Social position, for instance.

FRANK. I don't care a rap about that.

REV. S. But I do, sir.

FRANK. Well, nobody wants y o u to marry her. Anyhow, she has what amounts to a high Cambridge degree; and she seems to have as much money as she wants.

REV. S. [*sinking into a feeble vein of humor*] I greatly doubt whether she has as much money as y o u will want.

FRANK. Oh, come: I havn't been so very extravagant. I live ever so quietly; I don't drink; I don't bet much; and I never go regularly to the razzle-dazzle as you did when you were my age.

REV. S. [*booming hollowly*] Silence, sir.

FRANK. Well, you told me yourself, when I was making every such an ass of myself about the barmaid at Redhill, that you once offered a woman fifty pounds for the letters you wrote to her when—

REV. S. [*terrified*] Sh-sh-sh, Frank, for Heaven's sake! [*He looks round apprehensively Seeing no one within earshot he plucks up courage to boom again, but more subduedly*]. You are taking an ungentlemanly advantage of what I confided to you for your own good, to save you from an error you would have repented all your life long. Take warning by your father's follies, sir; and don't make them an excuse for your own.

FRANK. Did you ever hear the story of the Duke of Wellington and his letters?

REV. S. No, sir; and I don't want to hear it.

FRANK. The old Iron Duke didn't throw away fifty pounds: not he. He just wrote: "Dear Jenny: publish and be damned! Yours affectionately, Wellington." Thats what you should have done.

REV. S. [*piteously*] Frank, my boy: when I wrote those letters I put myself into that woman's power. When I told you about them I put myself, to some extent, I am sorry to say, in your power. She refused my money with these words, which I shall never forget. "Knowledge is power" she said; "and I never sell power."

Thats more than twenty years ago; and she has never made use of her power or caused me a moment's uneasiness. You are behaving worse to me than she did, Frank.

FRANK. Oh yes I dare say! Did you ever preach at her the way you preach at me every day?

REV. S. [*wounded almost to tears*] I leave you, sir. You are incorrigible. [*He turns towards the gate*].

FRANK [*utterly unmoved*] Tell them I shan't be home to tea, will you, gov'nor, like a good fellow? [*He moves towards the cottage door and is met by Praed and Vivie coming out*].

VIVIE [*to Frank*] Is that your father, Frank? I do so want to meet him.

FRANK. Certainly. [*Calling after his father*] Gov'nor. Youre wanted. [*The parson turns at the gate, fumbling nervously at his hat. Praed crosses the garden to the opposite side, beaming in anticipation of civilities*]. My father: Miss Warren.

VIVIE [*going to the clergyman and shaking his hand*] Very glad to see you here, Mr Gardner. [*Calling to the cottage*] Mother: come along: youre wanted.

[*Mrs Warren appears on the threshold, and is immediately transfixed, recognizing the clergyman.*]

VIVIE [*continuing*] Let me introduce—

MRS WARREN [*swooping on the Reverend Samuel*] Why it's Sam Gardner, gone into the Church! Well, I never! Don't you know us, Sam? This is George Crofts, as large as life and twice as natural. Don't you remember me?

REV. S. [*very red*] I really—er—

MRS WARREN. Of course you do. Why, I have a whole album of your letters still: I came across them only the other day.

REV. S. [*miserably confused*] Miss Vavasour, I believe.

MRS WARREN [*correcting him quickly in a loud whisper*] Tch! Nonsense! Mrs Warren: don't you see my daughter there?

ACT II

[*Inside the cottage after nightfall. Looking eastward from within instead of westward from without, the latticed window, with its curtains drawn, is now seen in the middle of the front wall of the cottage, with the porch door to the left of it. In the left-hand side wall is the door leading to the kitchen. Farther back against the same wall is a dresser with a candle and matches on it, and Frank's rifle standing beside them, with the barrel resting in the plate-rack. In the centre a table stands with a lighted lamp on it. Vivie's books and writing materials are on a table to the right of the window, against the wall. The fireplace is on the right, with a settle: there is no fire. Two of the chairs are set right and left of the table.*]

[*The cottage door opens, shewing a fine starlit night without; and Mrs Warren, her shoulders wrapped in a shawl borrowed from Vivie, enters, followed by Frank, who throws his cap on the window seat. She has had enough of walking, and gives a gasp of relief as she unpins her hat; takes it off; sticks the pin through the crown; and puts it on the table.*]

MRS WARREN. O Lord! I don't know which is the worst of the country, the walking or the sitting at home with nothing to do. I could do with a whisky and soda now very well, if only they had such a things in this place.

FRANK. Perhaps Vivie's got some.

MRS WARREN. Nonsense! What would a young girl like her be doing with such things! Never mind: it don't matter. I wonder how she passes her time here! I'd a good deal rather be in Vienna.

FRANK. Let me take you there. [*He helps her to take off her shawl, gallantly giving her shoulders a very perceptible squeeze as he does so*].

MRS WARREN. Ah! would you? I'm beginning to think youre a chip of the old block.

FRANK. Like the gov'nor, eh? [*He hangs the shawl on the nearest chair, and sits down*].

MRS WARREN. Never you mind. What do you know about such things?

Youre only a boy. [*She goes to the hearth to be farther from temptation*].

FRANK. Do come to Vienna with me? It'd be ever such larks.

MRS WARREN. No, thank you. Vienna is no place for you—at least not until youre a little older. [*She nods at him to emphasize this piece of advice. He makes a mock-piteous face, belied by his laughing eyes. She looks at him; then comes back to him*]. Now, look here, little boy [*taking his face in her hands and turning it up to her*]: I know you through and through by your likeness to your father, better than you know yourself. Don't you go taking any silly ideas into your head about me. Do you hear?

FRANK [*gallantly wooing her with his voice*] Can't help it, my dear Mrs Warren: it runs in the family.

[*She pretends to box his ears; then looks at the pretty laughing upturned face of a moment, tempted. At last she kisses him, and immediately turns away, out of patience with herself.*]

MRS WARREN. There! I shouldn't have done that. I *am* wicked. Never you mind, my dear: it's only a motherly kiss. Go and make love to Vivie.

FRANK. So I have.

MRS WARREN [*turning on him with a sharp note of alarm in her voice*] What!

FRANK. Vivie and I are ever such chums.

MRS WARREN. What do you mean? Now see here: I won't have any young scamp tampering with my little girl. Do you hear? I won't have it.

FRANK [*quite unabashed*] My dear Mrs Warren: don't you be alarmed. My intentions are honorable: ever so honorable; and your little girl is jolly well able to take care of herself. She don't need looking after half so much as her mother. She ain't so handsome, you know.

MRS WARREN [*taken aback by his assurance*] Well, you have got a nice healthy two inches of cheek all over you. I don't know where you got it. Not from your father, anyhow.

CROFTS [*in the garden*] The gipsies, I suppose?

REV. S. [*replying*] The broomsquires are far worse.

MRS WARREN [*to Frank*] S-sh! Remember! you've had your warning.

[*Crofts and the Reverend Samuel Gardner come in from the garden, the clergyman continuing his conversation as he enters.*]

REV. S. The perjury at the Winchester assizes is deplorable.

MRS WARREN. Well? what became of you two? And wheres Praddy and Vivie?

CROFTS [*putting his hat on the settle and his stick in the chimney corner*] They went up the hill. We went to the village. I wanted a drink. [*He sits down on the settle, putting his legs up along the seat*].

MRS WARREN. Well, she oughtn't to go off like that without telling me. [*To Frank*] Get your father a chair, Frank: where are your manners? [*Frank springs up and gracefully offers his father his chair; then takes another from the wall and sits down at the table, in the middle, with his father on his right and Mrs Warren on his left*]. George: where are you going to stay to-night? You can't stay here. And whats Praddy going to do?

CROFTS. Gardner'll put me up.

MRS WARREN. Oh, no doubt you've taken care of yourself! But what about Praddy?

CROFTS. Don't know. I suppose he can sleep at the inn.

MRS WARREN. Havn't you room for him, Sam?

REV. S. Well—er—you see, as rector here, I am not free to do as I like. Er—what is Mr Praed's social position?

MRS WARREN. Oh, he's all right: he's an architect. What an old stick-in-the-mud you are, Sam!

FRANK. Yes, it's all right, gov'nor. He built that place down in Wales for the Duke. Caernarvon Castle they call it. You must have heard of it. [*He winks with lightning smartness at Mrs Warren, and regards his father blandly*].

REV. S. Oh, in that case, of course we shall only be too happy. I suppose he knows the Duke personally.

FRANK. Oh, ever so intimately! We can stick him in Georgina's old room.

MRS WARREN. Well, thats settled. Now if those two would only come in and let us have supper. Theyve no right to stay out after dark like this.

CROFTS [*aggressively*] What harm are they doing you?

MRS WARREN. Well, harm or not, I don't like it.

FRANK. Better not wait for them, Mrs Warren. Praed will stay out as long as possible. He has never known before what it is to stray over the heath on a summer night with my Vivie.

CROFTS [*sitting up in some consternation*] I say, you know! Come!

REV. S. [*rising, startled out of his professional manner into real force and sincerity*] Frank, once and for all, it's out of the question. Mrs Warren will tell you that it's not to be thought of.

CROFTS. Of course not.

FRANK [*with enchanting placidity*] Is that so, Mrs Warren?

MRS WARREN [*reflectively*] Well, Sam, I don't know. If the girl wants to get married, no good can come of keeping her unmarried.

REV. S. [*astounded*] But married to *him!*—your daughter to my son! Only think: it's impossible.

CROFTS. Of course it's impossible. Don't be a fool, Kitty.

MRS WARREN [*nettled*] Why not? Isn't my daughter good enough for your son?

REV. S. But surely, my dear Mrs Warren, you know the reasons—

MRS WARREN [*defiantly*] I know no reasons. If you know any, you can tell them to the lad, or to the girl, or to your congregation, if you like.

REV. S. [*collapsing helplessly into his chair*] You know very well that I couldn't tell anyone the reasons. But my boy will believe me when I tell him there a r e reasons.

FRANK. Quite right, Dad: he will. But has your boy's conduct ever been influenced by your reasons?

CROFTS. You can't marry her; and thats all about it. [*He gets up and stands on the hearth, with his back to the fireplace, frowning determinedly*].

MRS WARREN [*turning on him sharply*] What have you got to do with it, pray?

FRANK [*with his prettiest lyrical cadence*] Precisely what I was going to ask, myself, in my own graceful fashion.

CROFTS [*to Mrs Warren*] I suppose you don't want to marry the girl to a man younger than herself and without either a profession or twopence to keep her on. Ask Sam, if you don't believe me. [*To the parson*] How much more money are you going to give him?

REV. S. Not another penny. He has had his patrimony; and he spent the last of it in July. [*Mrs Warren's face falls*].

CROFTS [*watching her*] There! I told you. [*He resumes his place on the settle and puts his legs on the seat again, as if the matter were finally disposed of*].

FRANK [*plaintively*] This is ever so mercenary. Do you suppose Miss Warren's going to marry for money? If we love one another—

MRS WARREN. Thank you. Your love's a pretty cheap commodity, my lad. If you have no means of keeping a wife, that settles it; you can't have Vivie.

FRANK [*much amused*] What do y o u say, gov'nor, eh?

REV. S. I agree with Mrs Warren.

FRANK. And good old Crofts has already expressed his opinion.

CROFTS [*turning angrily on his elbow*] Look here: I want none of your cheek.

FRANK [*pointedly*] I'm e v e r so sorry to surprise you, Crofts; but you allowed yourself the liberty of speaking to me like a father a moment ago. One father is enough, thank you.

CROFTS [*contemptuously*] Yah! [*He turns away again*].

FRANK [*rising*] Mrs Warren: I cannot give my Vivie up, even for your sake.

MRS WARREN [*muttering*] Young scamp!

FRANK [*continuing*] And as you no doubt intend to hold out other prospects to her, I shall lose no time in placing my case before her. [*They stare at him; and he begins to declaim gracefully*] He either fears his fate too much, Or his deserts are small, That dares not put it to the touch, To gain or lose it all.

[*The cottage doors open whilst he is reciting; and Vivie and Praed come in. He breaks off. Praed puts his hat on the dresser. There is an immediate im-*

provement in the company's behavior. Crofts takes down his legs from the settle and pulls himself together as Praed joins him at the fireplace. Mrs War-Warren loses her ease of manner and takes refuge in querulousness.]

MRS WARREN. Wherever have you been, Vivie?

VIVIE [*taking off her hat and throwing it carelessly on the table*] On the hill.

MRS WARREN. Well, you shouldn't go off like that without letting me know. How could I tell what had become of you? And night coming on too!

VIVIE [*going to the door of the kitchen and opening it, ignoring her mother*] Now, about supper? [*All rise except Mrs Warren*] We shall be rather crowded in here, I'm afraid.

MRS WARREN. Did you hear what I said, Vivie?

VIVIE [*quietly*] Yes, mother. [*Reverting to the supper difficulty*] How many are we? [*Counting*] One, two, three, four, five, six. Well, two will have to wait until the rest are done: Mrs Alison has only plates and knives for four.

PRAED. Oh, it doesn't matter about me. I—

VIVIE. You have had a long walk and are hungry, Mr Praed: you shall have your supper at once. I can wait myself. I want one person to wait with me. Frank: are you hungry?

FRANK. Not the least in the world. Completely off my peck, in fact.

MRS WARREN [*to Crofts*] Neither are you, George. You can wait.

CROFTS. Oh, hang it, I've eaten nothing since tea-time. Can't Sam do it?

FRANK. Would you starve my poor father?

REV. S. [*testily*] Allow me to speak for myself, sir. I am perfectly willing to wait.

VIVIE [*decisively*] There's no need. Only two are wanted. [*She opens the door of the kitchen*]. Will you take my mother in, Mr Gardner. [*The parson takes Mrs Warren; and they pass into the kitchen. Praed and Crofts follow. All except Praed clearly disapprove of the arrangement, but do not know how to resist it. Vivie stands at the door looking in at them*]. Can you squeeze past to that corner, Mr Praed: it's rather a tight fit. Take care of your coat against the white-wash: that right. Now, are you all comfortable?

PRAED [*within*] Quite, thank you.

MRS WARREN [*within*] Leave the door open, dearie. [*Vivie frowns; but Frank checks her with a gesture, and steals to the cottage door, which he softly sets wide open*]. Oh Lor, what a draught! Youd better shut it, dear.

[*Vivie shuts it with a slam, and then, noting with disgust that her mother's hat and shawl are lying about, takes them tidily to the window seat, whilst Frank noiselessly shuts the cottage door.*]

FRANK [*exulting*] Aha! Got rid of em. Well, Vivvums: what do you think of my governor?

VIVIE [*preoccupied and serious*] I've hardly spoken to him. He doesn't strike me as a particularly able person.

FRANK. Well, you know, the old man is not altogether such a fool as he looks. You see, he was shoved into the Church, rather; and in trying to live up to it he makes a much bigger ass of himself than he really is. I don't dislike him as much as you might expect. He means well. How do you think youll get on with him?

VIVIE [*rather grimly*] I don't think my future life will be much concerned with him, or with any of that old circle of my mother's, except perhaps Praed. [*She sits down on the settle*] What do you think of my mother?

FRANK. Really and truly?

VIVIE. Yes, really and truly.

FRANK. Well, she's ever so jolly. But she's rather a caution, isn't she? And Crofts! Oh, my eye, Crofts! [*He sits beside her*].

VIVIE. What a lot, Frank!

FRANK. What a crew!

VIVIE [*with intense contempt for them*] If I thought that *I* was like that—that I was going to be a waster, shifting along from one meal to another with no purpose, and no character, and no grit in me, I'd open an artery and bleed to death without one moment's hesitation.

FRANK. Oh no, you wouldn't. Why should they take any grind when they can afford not to? I wish I had their luck. No: what I object to is their form. It isn't the thing: it's slovenly, ever so slovenly.

VIVIE. Do you think your form will be any better when youre as old as Crofts, if you don't work?

FRANK. Of course I do. Ever so much better. Vivvums mustn't lecture: her little boy's incorrigible. [*He attempts to take her face caressingly in his hands*].

VIVIE [*striking his hands down sharply*] Off with you: Vivvums is not in a humor for petting her little boy this evening. [*She rises and comes forward to the other side of the room*].

FRANK [*following her*] How unkind!

VIVIE [*stamping at him*] Be serious. I'm serious.

FRANK. Good. Let us talk learnedly, Miss Warren: do you know that all the most advanced thinkers are agreed that half the diseases of modern civilization are due to starvation of the affections of the young. Now, *I*—

VIVIE [*cutting him short*] You are very tiresome. [*She opens the inner door*] Have you room for Frank there? He's complaining of starvation.

MRS WARREN [*within*] Of course there is [*clatter of knives and glasses as she moves the things on the table*]. Here! theres room now beside me. Come along, Mr Frank.

FRANK. Her little boy will be ever so even with his Vivvums for this. [*He passes into the kitchen*].

MRS WARREN [*within*] Here, Vivie: come on you too, child. You must be famished. [*She enters, followed by Crofts, who holds the door open with marked deference. She goes out without looking at him; and he shuts the door after her*]. Why George, you can't be done: you've eaten nothing. Is there anything wrong with you?

CROFTS. Oh, all I wanted was a drink. [*He thrusts his hands in his pockets, and begins prowling about the room, restless and sulky*].

MRS WARREN. Well, I like enough to eat. But a little of that cold beef and cheese and lettuce goes a long way. [*With a sigh of only half repletion she sits down lazily on the settle*].

CROFTS. What do you go encouraging that young pup for?

MRS WARREN [*on the alert at once*] Now see here, George: what are you up to about that girl? I've been watching your way of looking at her. Remember: I know you and what your looks mean.

CROFTS. Theres no harm in looking at her, is there?

MRS WARREN. I'd put you out and pack you back to London pretty soon if I saw any of your nonsense. My girl's little finger is more to me than your whole body and soul. [*Crofts receives this with a sneering grin. Mrs Warren, flushing a little at her failure to impose on him in the character of a theatrically devoted mother, adds in a lower key*] Make your mind easy: the young pup has no more chance than you have.

CROFTS. Mayn't a man take an interest in a girl?

MRS WARREN. Not a man like you.

CROFTS. How old is she?

MRS WARREN. Never you mind how old she is.

CROFTS. Why do you make such a secret of it?

MRS WARREN. Because I choose.

CROFTS. Well, I'm not fifty yet; and my property is as good as it ever was—

MRS [*interrupting him*] Yes; because youre as stingy as youre vicious.

CROFTS [*continuing*] And a baronet isn't to be picked up every day.

No other man in my position would put up with you for a mother-in-law. Why shouldn't she marry me?

MRS WARREN. You!

CROFTS. We three could live together quite comfortably. I'd die before her and leave her a bouncing widow with plenty of money. Why not? It's been growing in my mind all the time I've been walking with that fool inside there.

MRS WARREN [*revolted*] Yes; it's the sort of thing that *would* grow in your mind.

[*He halts in his prowling; and the two look at one another, she steadfastly, with a sort of awe behind her contemptuous disgust: he stealthily, with a carnal gleam in his eye and a loose grin.*]

CROFTS [*suddenly becoming anxious and urgent as he sees no sign of sympathy in her*] Look here, Kitty: youre a sensible woman: you needn't put on any moral airs. I'll ask no more questions; and you need answer none. I'll settle the whole property on her; and if you want a checque for yourself on the wedding day, you can name any figure you like—in reason.

MRS WARREN. So it's come to that with you, George, like all the other worn-out old creatures!

CROFTS [*savagely*] Damn you!

[*Before she can retort the door of the kitchen is opened; and the voices of the others are heard returning. Crofts, unable to recover his presence of mind, hurries out of the cottage. The clergyman appears at the kitchen door.*]

REV. S. [*looking round*] Where is Sir George?

MRS WARREN. Gone out to have a pipe. [*The clergyman takes his hat from the table, and joins Mrs Warren at the fireside. Meanwhile, Vivie comes in, followed by Frank, who collapses into the nearest chair with an air of extreme exhaustion. Mrs Warren looks round at Vivie and says, with her affectation of maternal patronage even more forced than usual*] Well, dearie: have you had a good supper?

VIVIE. You know what Mrs Alison's suppers are. [*She turns to Frank and pets him*] Poor Frank! was all the beef gone? did it get nothing but bread and cheese and ginger beer? [*Seriously, as if she had done quite enough trifling for one evening*] Her butter is really awful. I must get some down from the stores.

FRANK. Do, in Heaven's name!

[*Vivie goes to the writing-table and makes a memorandum to order the butter. Praed comes in from the kitchen, putting up his handkerchief, which he has been using as a napkin.*]

REV. S. Frank, my boy: it is time for us to be thinking of home.

Your mother does not know yet that we have visitors.

PRAED. I'm afraid we're giving trouble.

FRANK [*rising*] Not the least in the world: my mother will be delighted to see you. She's a genuinely intellectual artistic woman; and she sees nobody here from one year's end to another except the gov'nor; so you can imagine how jolly dull it pans out for her. [*To his father*] Y o u r e not intellectual or artistic: are you pater? So take Praed home at once; and I'll stay here and entertain Mrs Warren. Youll pick up Crofts in the garden. He'll be excellent company for the bull-pup.

PRAED [*taking his hat from the dresser, and coming close to Frank*] Come with us, Frank. Mrs Warren has not seen Miss Vivie for a long time; and we have prevented them from having a moment together yet.

FRANK [*quite softened, and looking at Praed with romantic admiration*] Of course. I forgot. Ever so thanks for reminding me. Perfect gentleman, Praddy. Always were. My ideal through life. [*He rises to go, but pauses a moment between the two older men, and puts his hand on Praed's shoulder*]. Ah, if you had only been my father instead of this unworthy old man! [*He puts his other hand on his father's shoulder*].

REV. S. [*blustering*] Silence, sir, silence: you are profane.

MRS WARREN [*laughing heartily*] You should keep him in better order, Sam. Good-night. Here: take George his hat and stick with my compliments.

REV. S. [*taking them*] Good-night. [*They shake hands. As he passes Vivie he shakes hands with her also and bids her good-night. Then, in booming command, to Frank*] Come along, sir, at once. [*He goes out*].

MRS WARREN. Byebye, Praddy.

PRAED. Byebye, Kitty.

[*They shake hands affectionately and go out together, she accompanying him to the garden gate.*]

FRANK [*to Vivie*] Kissums?

VIVIE [*fiercely*] No. I hate you. [*She takes a couple of books and some paper from the writing-table, and sits down with them at the middle table, at the end next the fireplace*].

FRANK [*grimacing*] Sorry. [*He goes for his cap and rifle. Mrs Warren returns. He takes her hand*] Good-night, dear Mrs Warren. [*He kisses her hand. She snatches it away, her lips tightening, and looks more than half disposed to box his ears. He laughs mischievously and runs off, clapping-to the door behind him*].

MRS WARREN [*resigning herself to an evening of boredom now that the men are gone*] Did you ever in your life hear anyone rattle on so? Isn't he a tease? [*She sits at the table*]. Now that I think of it, dearie, don't you go encouraging him. I'm sure he's a regular good-for-nothing.

VIVIE [*rising to fetch more books*] I'm afraid so. Poor Frank! I shall have to get rid of him; but I shall feel sorry for him, though he's not worth it. That man Crofts does not seem to me to be good for much either: is he? [*She throws the books on the table rather roughly*].

MRS WARREN [*galled by Vivie's indifference*] What do you know of men, child, to talk that way of them? Youll have to make up your mind to see a good deal of Sir George Crofts, as he's a friend of mine.

VIVIE [*quite unmoved*] Why? [*She sits down and opens a book*]. Do you expect that we shall be much together? You and I, I mean?

MRS WARREN [*staring at her*] Of course: until youre married. Youre not going back to college again.

VIVIE. Do you think my way of life would suit you? I doubt it.

MRS WARREN. Y o u r way of life! What do you mean?

VIVIE [*cutting a page of her book with the paper knife on her chatelaine*] Has it really never occurred to you, mother, that I have a way of life like other people?

MRS WARREN. What nonsense is this youre trying to talk? Do you want to shew your independence, now that youre a great little person at school? Don't be a fool, child.

VIVIE [*indulgently*] Thats all you have to say on the subject, is it, mother?

MRS WARREN [*puzzled, then angry*] Don't you keep on asking me questions like that. [*Violently*] Hold your tongue. [*Vivie works on, losing no time, and saying nothing*]. You and your way of life, indeed! What next? [*She looks at Vivie again. No reply*].

Your way of life will be what I please, so it will. [*Another pause*]. Ive been noticing these airs in you ever since you got that tripos or whatever you call it. If you think I'm going to put up with them, youre mistaken; and the sooner you find it out, the better. [*Muttering*] All I have to say on the subject, indeed! [*Again raising her voice angrily*] Do you know who youre speaking to, Miss?

VIVIE [*looking across at her without raising her head from her book*] No. Who are you? What are you?

MRS WARREN [*rising breathless*] You young imp!

VIVIE. Everybody knows my reputation, my social standing, and the profession I intend to pursue. I know nothing about you. What is that way of life which you invite me to share with you and Sir George Crofts, pray?

MRS WARREN. Take care. I shall do something I'll be sorry for after, and you too.

VIVIE [*putting aside her books with cool decision*] Well, let us drop the subject until you are better able to face it. [*Looking critically at her mother*] You want some good walks and a little lawn tennis to set you up. You are shockingly out of condition: you were not able to manage twenty yards uphill today without stopping to pant; and your wrists are mere rolls of fat. Look at mine. [*She holds out her wrists*].

MRS WARREN [*after looking at her helplessly, begins to whimper*] Vivie—

VIVIE [*springing up sharply*] Now pray don't begin to cry. Anything but that. I really cannot stand whimpering. I will go out of the room if you do.

MRS WARREN [*piteously*] Oh, my darling, how can you be so hard on me? Have I no rights over you as your mother?

VIVIE. A r e you my mother?

MRS WARREN. *Am* I your mother? Oh, Vivie!

VIVIE. Then where are our relatives? my father? our family friends? You claim the rights of a mother: the right to call me fool and child; to speak to me as no woman in authority over me at college dare speak to me; to dictate my way of life; and to force on me the acquaintance of a brute whom anyone can see to be the most vicious sort of London man about town. Before I give myself the trouble to resist such claims, I may as well find out whether they have any real existence.

MRS WARREN [*distracted, throwing herself on her knees*] Oh no, no.

Stop, stop. I *am* your mother: I swear it. Oh, you can't mean to turn on me—my own child! it's not natural. You believe me, don't you? Say you believe me.

VIVIE. Who was my father?

MRS WARREN. You don't know what youre asking. I can't tell you.

VIVIE [*determinedly*] Oh yes you can, if you like. I have a right to know; and you know very well that I have that right. You can refuse to tell me if you please; but if you do, you will see the last of me tomorrow morning.

MRS WARREN. Oh, it's too horrible to hear you talk like that. You wouldn't—you *couldn't* leave me.

VIVIE [*ruthlessly*] Yes, without a moment's hesitation, if you trifle with me about this. [*Shivering with disgust*] How can I feel sure that I may not have the contaminated blood of that brutal waster in my veins?

MRS WARREN. No, no. On my oath it's not he, nor any of the rest that you have ever met. I'm certain of that, at least.

[*Vivie's eyes fasten sternly on her mother as the significance of this flashes on her.*]

VIVIE [*slowly*] You are certain of that, at *least*. Ah! You mean that that is all you are certain of. [*Thoughtfully*] I see. [*Mrs Warren buries her face in her hands*]. Don't do that, mother: you know you don't feel it a bit. [*Mrs Warren takes down her hands and looks up deplorably at Vivie, who takes out her watch and says*] Well, that is enough for tonight. At what hour would you like breakfast? Is half-past eight too early for you?

MRS WARREN [*wildly*] My God, what sort of woman are you?

VIVIE [*coolly*] The sort the world is mostly made of, I should hope. Otherwise I don't understand how it gets its business done.

Come [*taking her mother by the wrist and pulling her up pretty resolutely*]: pull yourself together. Thats right.

MRS WARREN [*querulously*] Youre very rough with me, Vivie.

VIVIE. Nonsense. What about bed? It's past ten.

MRS WARREN [*passionately*] Whats the use of my going to bed? Do you think I could sleep?

VIVIE. Why not? I shall.

MRS WARREN. You! you've no heart. [*She suddenly breaks out vehemently in her natural tongue—the dialect of a woman of the people—with all her affectations of maternal authority and conventional manners gone, and an overwhelming inspiration of true conviction and scorn in her*] Oh, I wont bear it: I won't put up with the injustice of it. What right have you to set yourself up above me like this? You boast of what you are to me—to *me*, who gave you a chance of being what you are. What chance had I? Shame on you for a bad daughter and a stuck-up prude!

VIVIE [*sitting down with a shrug, no longer confident; for her replies, which have sounded sensible and strong to her so far, now begin to ring rather woodenly and even priggishly against the new tone of her mother*] Don't think for a moment I set myself above you in any way. You attacked me with the conventional authority of a mother: I defended myself with the conventional superiority of a respectable woman. Frankly, I am not going to stand any of your nonsense; and when you drop it I shall not expect you to stand any of mine. I shall always respect your right to your own opinions and your own way of life.

MRS WARREN. My own opinions and my own way of life! Listen to her talking! Do you think I was brought up like you? able to pick and choose my own way of life? Do you think I did what I did because I liked it, or thought it right, or wouldn't rather have gone to college and been a lady if I'd had the chance?

VIVIE. Everybody has some choice, mother. The poorest girl alive may not be able to choose between being Queen of England or Principal of Newnham; but she can choose between ragpicking and flowerselling, according to her taste. People are always blaming circumstances for what they are. I don't believe in circumstances. The people who get on in this world are the people who get up and look for the circumstances they want, and, if they can't find them, make them.

MRS WARREN. Oh, it's easy to talk, isn't it? Here! would you like to know what *my* circumstances were?

VIVIE. Yes: you had better tell me. Won't you sit down?

MRS WARREN. Oh, I'll sit down: don't you be afraid. [*She plants her chair farther forward with brazen energy, and sits down. Vivie is impressed in spite of herself*]. D'you know what your gran'mother was?

VIVIE. No.

MRS WARREN. No, you don't. I do. She called herself a widow and had a fried-fish shop down by the Mint, and kept herself and four daughters out of it. Two of us were sisters: that was me and Liz; and we were both good-looking and well made. I suppose our father was a well-fed man: mother pretended he was a gentleman; but I don't know. The other two were only half sisters: undersized, ugly, starved looking, hard working, honest poor creatures: Liz and I would have half-murdered them if mother hadn't half-murdered us to keep our hands off them. They were the respectable ones. Well, what did they get by their respectability? I'll tell you. One of them worked in a whitelead factory twelve hours a day for nine shillings a week until she died of lead poisoning. She only expected to get her hands a little paralyzed; but she died. The other was always held up to us as a model because she married a Government laborer in the Deptford victualling yard, and kept his room and the three children neat and tidy on eighteen shillings a week—until he took to drink. That was worth being respectable for, wasn't it?

VIVIE [*now thoughtfully attentive*] Did you and your sister think so?

MRS WARREN. Liz didn't, I can tell you: she had more spirit. We both went to a church school—that was part of the ladylike airs we gave ourselves to be superior to the children that knew nothing and went nowhere—and we stayed there until Liz went out one night and never came back. I know the schoolmistress thought I'd soon follow her example; for the clergyman was always warning me that Lizzie'd end by jumping off Waterloo Bridge. Poor fool: that was all he knew about it! But I was more afraid of the whitelead factory than I was of the river; and so would you have been in my place. That clergyman got me a situation as a scullery maid in a temperance restaurant where they sent out for anything you liked. Then I was a waitress; and then I went to the bar at Waterloo station: fourteen hours a day serving drinks and washing glasses for four shillings a week and my board. That was considered a great promotion for me. Well, one cold, wretched night, when I was so tired I could hardly keep myself awake, who should come up for a half of Scotch but Lizzie, in a long fur cloak, elegant and comfortable, with a lot of sovereigns in her purse.

VIVIE [*grimly*] My aunt Lizzie!

MRS WARREN. Yes; and a very good aunt to have, too. She's living down at Winchester now, close to the cathedral, one of the most respectable ladies there. Chaperones girls at the country ball, if you please. No river for Liz, thank you! You remind me of Liz a little: she was a first-rate business woman—saved money from the beginning—never let herself look too like what she was—never lost her head or threw away a chance. When she saw I'd grown up good-looking she said to me across the bar "What are you doing there, you little fool? wearing out your health and your appearance for other people's profit!" Liz was saving money then to take a house for herself in Brussels; and she thought we two could save faster than one. So she lent me some money and gave me a start; and I saved steadily and first paid her back, and then went into business with her as a partner. Why shouldn't I have done it? The house in Brussels was real high class: a much better place for a woman to be in than the factory where Anne Jane got poisoned. None of the girls were ever treated as I was treated in the scullery of that temperance place, or at the Waterloo bar, or at home. Would you have had me stay in them and become a worn out old drudge before I was forty?

VIVIE [*intensely interested by this time*] No; but why did you choose that business? Saving money and good management will succeed in any business.

MRS WARREN. Yes, saving money. But where can a woman get the money to save in any other business? Could y o u save out of four shillings a week and keep yourself dressed as well? Not you. Of course, if youre a plain woman and can't earn anything more; or if you have a turn for music, or the stage, or newspaper-writing: thats different. But neither Liz nor I had any turn for such things at all: all we had was our appearance and our turn for pleasing men. Do you think we were such fools as to let other people trade in our good looks by employing us as shopgirls, or barmaids, or waitresses, when we could trade in them ourselves and get all the profits instead of starvation wages? Not likely.

VIVIE. You were certainly quite justified—from the business point of view.

MRS WARREN. Yes; or any other point of view. What is any respectable girl brought up to do but to catch some rich man's fancy and get the benefit of his money by marrying him?—as if a marriage ceremony could make any difference in the right or wrong of the thing! Oh, the hypocrisy of the world makes me sick! Liz and I had to work and save and calculate just like other people; elseways we should be as poor as any good-for-nothing drunken waster of a woman that thinks her luck will last for ever. [*With great energy*] I despise such people: theyve no character; and if theres a thing I hate in a woman, it's want of character.

VIVIE. Come now, mother: frankly! Isn't it part of what you call character in a woman that she should greatly dislike such a way of making money?

MRS WARREN. Why, of course. Everybody dislikes having to work and make money; but they have to do it all the same. I'm sure I've often pitied a poor girl, tired out and in low spirits, having to try to please some man that she doesn't care two straws for—some half-drunken fool that thinks he's making himself agreeable when he's teasing and worrying and disgusting a woman so that hardly any money could pay her for putting up with it. But she has to bear with disagreeables and take the rough with the smooth, just like a nurse in a hospital or anyone else. It's not work that any woman would do for pleasure, goodness knows; though to hear the pious people talk you would suppose it was a bed of roses.

VIVIE. Still, you consider it worth while. It pays.

MRS WARREN. Of course it's worth while to a poor girl, if she can resist temptation and is good-looking and well conducted and sensible. It's far better than any other employment open to her.

I always thought that it oughtn't to be. It *can't* be right, Vivie, that there shouldn't be better opportunities for women. I stick to that: it's wrong. But it's so, right or wrong; and a girl must make the best of it. But of course it's not worth while for a lady. If you took to it youd be a fool; but I should have been a fool if I'd taken to anything else.

VIVIE [*more and more deeply moved*] Mother: suppose we were both as poor as you were in those wretched old days, are you quite sure that you wouldn't advise me to try the Waterloo bar, or marry a laborer, or even go into the factory?

MRS WARREN [*indignantly*] Of course not. What sort of mother do you take me for! How could you keep your self-respect in such starvation and slavery? And whats a woman worth? whats life worth? without self-respect! Why am I independent and able to give my daughter a first-rate education, when other women that had just as good opportunities are in the gutter? Because I always knew how to respect myself and control myself. Why is Liz looked up to in a cathedral town? The same reason. Where would we be now if we'd minded the clergyman's foolishness? Scrubbing floors for one and sixpence a day and nothing to look forward to but the workhouse infirmary. Don't you be led astray by people who don't know the world, my girl. The only way for a woman to provide for herself decently is for her to be good to some man that can afford to be good to her. If she's in his own station of life, let her make him marry her; but if she's far beneath him she can't expect it: why should she? it wouldn't be for her own happiness. Ask any lady in London society that has daughters; and she'll tell you the same, except that I tell you straight and she'll tell you crooked. Thats all the difference.

VIVIE [*fascinated, gazing at her*] My dear mother: you are a wonderful woman: you are stronger than all England. And are you really and truly not one wee bit doubtful—or—or—ashamed?

MRS WARREN. Well, of course, dearie, it's only good manners to be ashamed of it: it's expected from a woman. Women have to pretend to feel a great deal that they don't feel. Liz used to be angry with me for plumping out the truth about it. She used to say that when every woman could learn enough from what was going on in the world before her eyes, there was no need to talk about it to her. But then Liz was such a perfect lady! She had the true instinct of it; while I was always a bit of a vulgarian. I used to be so pleased when you sent me your photos to see that you were growing up like Liz: you've just her ladylike, determined way. But I can't stand saying one thing when everyone knows I mean another. Whats the use in such hypocrisy? If people arrange the world that way for women, theres no good pretending it's arranged the other way. No: I never was a bit ashamed really. I consider I had a right to be proud of how we managed everything so respectably, and never had a word against us, and how the girls were so well taken care of. Some of them did very well: one of them married an ambassador. But of course now I daren't talk about such things: whatever would they think of us! [*She yawns*]. Oh dear! I do believe I'm getting sleepy after all. [*She stretches herself lazily, thoroughly relieved by her explosion, and placidly ready for her night's rest*].

VIVIE. I believe it is I who will not be able to sleep now. [*She goes to the dresser and lights the candle. Then she extinguishes the lamp, darkening the room a good deal*]. Better let in some fresh air before locking up. [*She opens the cottage door, and finds that it is broad moonlight*]. What a beautiful night! Look! [*She draws the curtains of the window. The landscape is seen bathed in the radiance of the harvest moon rising over Blackdown*].

MRS WARREN [*with a perfunctory glance at the scene*] Yes, dear; but take care you don't catch your death of cold from the night air.

VIVIE [*contemptuously*] Nonsense.

MRS WARREN [*querulously*] Oh yes: everything I say is nonsense, according to you.

VIVIE [*turning to her quickly*] No: really that is not so, mother.

You have got completely the better of me tonight, though I intended it to be the other way. Let us be good friends now.

MRS WARREN [*shaking her head a little ruefully*] So it *has* been the other way. But I suppose I must give in to it. I always got the worst of it from Liz; and now I suppose it'll be the same with you.

VIVIE. Well, never mind. Come: good-night, dear old mother. [*She takes her mother in her arms*].

MRS WARREN [*fondly*] I brought you up well, didn't I, dearie?

VIVIE. You did.

MRS WARREN. And youll be good to your poor old mother for it, won't you?

VIVIE. I will, dear. [*Kissing her*] Good-night.

MRS WARREN [*with unction*] Blessings on my own dearie darling! a mother's blessing!

[*She embraces her daughter protectingly, instinctively looking upward for divine sanction.*]

ACT III

[*In the Rectory garden next morning, with the sun shining from a cloudless sky. The garden wall has a five-barred wooden gate, wide enough to admit a carriage, in the middle. Beside the gate hangs a bell on a coiled spring, communicating with a pull outside. The carriage drive comes down the middle of the garden and then swerves to its left, where it ends in a little gravelled circus opposite the Rectory porch. Beyond the gate is seen the dusty high road, parallel with the wall, bounded on the farther side by a strip of turf and an unfenced pine wood. On the lawn, between the house and the drive, is a clipped yew tree, with a garden bench in its shade. On the opposite side the garden is shut in by a box hedge; and there is a little sundial on the turf, with an iron chair near it. A little path leads through the box hedge, behind the sundial.*]

[*Frank, seated on the chair near the sundial, on which he has placed the morning paper, is reading The Standard. His father comes from the house, red-eyed and shivery, and meets Frank's eye with misgiving.*]

FRANK [*looking at his watch*] Half-past eleven. Nice hour for a rector to come down to breakfast!

REV. S. Don't mock, Frank: don't mock. I am a little—er—[*Shivering*]—

FRANK. Off color?

REV. S. [*repudiating the expression*] No, sir: *unwell* this morning. Where's your mother?

FRANK. Don't be alarmed: she's not here. Gone to town by the 11.13 with Bessie. She left several messages for you. Do you feel equal to receiving them now, or shall I wait til you've breakfasted?

REV. S. I h a v e breakfasted, sir. I am surprised at your mother going to town when we have people staying with us. They'll think it very strange.

FRANK. Possibly she has considered that. At all events, if Crofts is going to stay here, and you are going to sit up every night with him until four, recalling the incidents of your fiery youth, it is clearly my mother's duty, as a prudent housekeeper, to go up to the stores and order a barrel of whisky and a few hundred siphons.

REV. S. I did not observe that Sir George drank excessively.

FRANK. You were not in a condition to, gov'nor.

REV. S. Do you mean to say that *I*—?

FRANK [*calmly*] I never saw a beneficed clergyman less sober. The anecdotes you told about your past career were so awful that I really don't think Praed would have passed the night under your roof if it hadnt been for the way my mother and he took to one another.

REV. S. Nonsense, sir. I am Sir George Crofts' host. I must talk to him about something; and he has only one subject. Where is Mr Praed now?

FRANK. He is driving my mother and Bessie to the station.

REV. S. Is Crofts up yet?

FRANK. Oh, long ago. He hasn't turned a hair: he's in much better practice than you. Has kept it up ever since, probably. He's taken himself off somewhere to smoke.

[*Frank resumes his paper. The parson turns disconsolately towards the gate; then comes back irresolutely.*]

REV. S. Er—Frank.

FRANK. Yes.

REV. S. Do you think the Warrens will expect to be asked here after yesterday afternoon?

FRANK. Theyve been asked already.

REV. S. [*appalled*] What!!!

FRANK. Crofts informed us at breakfast that you told him to bring Mrs Warren and Vivie over here today, and to invite them to make this house their home. My mother then found she must go to town by the 11.13 train.

REV. S. [*with despairing vehemence*] I never gave any such invitation. I never thought of such a thing.

FRANK [*compassionately*] How do you know, gov'nor, what you said and thought last night?

PRAED [*coming in through the hedge*] Good morning.

REV. S. Good morning. I must apologize for not having met you at breakfast. I have a touch of—of—

FRANK. Clergyman's sore throat, Praed. Fortunately not chronic.

PRAED [*changing the subject*] Well I must say your house is in a charming spot here. Really most charming.

REV. S. Yes: it is indeed. Frank will take you for a walk, Mr Praed, if you like. I'll ask you to excuse me: I must take the opportunity to write my sermon while Mrs Gardner is away and you are all amusing yourselves. You won't mind, will you?

PRAED. Certainly not. Don't stand on the slightest ceremony with me.

REV. S. Thank you. I'll—er—er—[*He stammers his way to the porch and vanishes into the house*].

PRAED. Curious thing it must be writing a sermon every week.

FRANK. Ever so curious, if he did it. He buys em. He's gone for some soda water.

PRAED. My dear boy: I wish you would be more respectful to your father. You know you can be so nice when you like.

FRANK. My dear Praddy: you forget that I have to live with the governor. When two people live together—it don't matter whether theyre father and son or husband and wife or brother and sister—they can't keep up the polite humbug thats so easy for ten minutes on an afternoon call. Now the governor, who unites to many admirable domestic qualities the irresoluteness of a sheep and the pompousness and aggressiveness of a jackass—

PRAED. No, pray, pray, my dear Frank, remember! He is your father.

FRANK. I give him due credit for that. [*Rising and flinging down his paper*] But just imagine his telling Crofts to bring the Warrens over here! He must have been ever so drunk. You know, my dear Praddy, my mother wouldn't stand Mrs Warren for a moment. Vivie mustn't come here until she's gone back to town.

PRAED. But your mother doesn't know anything about Mrs Warren, does she? [*He picks up the paper and sits down to read it*].

FRANK. I don't know. Her journey to town looks as if she did. Not that my mother would mind in the ordinary way: she has stuck like a brick to lots of women who had got into trouble. But they were all nice women. Thats what makes the real difference. Mrs Warren, no doubt, has her merits; but she's ever so rowdy; and my mother simply wouldn't put up with her. So—hallo! [*This exclamation is provoked by the reappearance of the clergyman, who comes out of the house in haste and dismay*].

REV. S. Frank: Mrs Warren and her daughter are coming across the heath with Crofts: I saw them from the study windows. What *am* I to say about your mother?

FRANK. Stick on your hat and go out and say how delighted you are to see them; and that Frank's in the garden; and that mother and Bessie have been called to the bedside of a sick relative, and were ever so sorry they couldn't stop; and that you hope Mrs Warren slept well; and—and—say any blessed thing except the truth, and leave the rest to Providence.

REV. S. But how are we to get rid of them afterwards?

FRANK. Theres no time to think of that now. Here! [*He bounds into the house*].

REV. S. He's so impetuous. I don't know what to do with him, Mr Praed.

FRANK [*returning with a clerical felt hat, which he claps on his father's head*]. Now: off with you. [*Rushing him through the gate*]. Praed and I'll wait here, to give the thing an unpremeditated air. [*The clergyman, dazed but obedient, hurries off*].

FRANK. We must get the old girl back to town somehow, Praed. Come! Honestly, dear Praddy, do you like seeing them together?

PRAED. Oh, why not?

FRANK [*his teeth on edge*] Don't it make your flesh creep ever so little? that wicked old devil, up to every villainy under the sun, I'll swear, and Vivie—ugh!

PRAED. Hush, pray. Theyre coming.

[*The clergyman and Crofts are seen coming along the road, followed by Mrs Warren and Vivie walking affectionately together.*]

FRANK. Look: she actually has her arm round the old woman's waist. It's her right arm: she began it. She's gone sentimental, by God! Ugh! ugh! Now do you feel the creeps? [*The clergyman opens the gate: and Mrs Warren and Vivie pass him and stand in the middle of the garden looking at the house. Frank, in an ecstasy of dissimulation, turns gaily to Mrs Warren, exclaiming*] Ever so delighted to see you, Mrs Warren. This quiet old rectory garden becomes you perfectly.

MRS WARREN. Well, I never! Did you hear that, George? He says I look well in a quiet old rectory garden.

REV. S. [*still holding the gate for Crofts, who loafs through it, heavily bored*] You look well everywhere, Mrs Warren.

FRANK. Bravo, gov'nor! Now look here: lets have a treat before lunch. First lets see the church. Everyone has to do that. It's a regular old thirteenth century church, you know: the gov'nor's ever so fond of it, because he got up a restoration fund and had it completely rebuilt six years ago. Praed will be able to shew its points.

PRAED [*rising*] Certainly, if the restoration has left any to shew.

REV. S. [*mooning hospitably at them*] I shall be pleased, I'm sure, if Sir George and Mrs Warren really care about it.

MRS WARREN. Oh, come along and get it over.

CROFTS [*turning back toward the gate*] I've no objection.

REV. S. Not that way. We go through the fields, if you don't mind. Round here. [*He leads the way by the little path through the box hedge*].

CROFTS. Oh, all right. [*He goes with the parson*].

[*Praed follows with Mrs Warren. Vivie does not stir: she watches them until they have gone, with all the lines of purpose in her face marking it strongly.*]

FRANK. Ain't you coming?

VIVIE. No. I want to give you a warning, Frank. You were making fun of my mother just now when you said that about the rectory garden. That is barred in the future. Please treat my mother with as much respect as you treat your own.

FRANK. My dear Viv: she wouldn't appreciate it: the two cases require different treatment. But what on earth has happened to you? Last night we were perfectly agreed as to your mother and her set. This morning I find you attitudinizing sentimentally with your arm around your parent's waist.

VIVIE [*flushing*] Attitudinizing!

FRANK. That was how it struck me. First time I ever saw you do a second-rate thing.

VIVIE [*controlling herself*] Yes, Frank: there has been a change: but I don't think it a change for the worse. Yesterday I was a little prig.

FRANK. And today?

VIVIE [*wincing; then looking at him steadily*] Today I know my mother better than you do.

FRANK. Heaven forbid!

VIVIE. What do you mean?

FRANK. Viv: theres a freemasonry among thoroughly immoral people that you know nothing of. You've too much character. *That's* the bond between your mother and me: that's why I know her better than youll ever know her.

VIVIE. You are wrong: you know nothing about her. If you knew the circumstances against which my mother had to struggle—

FRANK [*adroitly finishing the sentence for her*] I should know why she is what she is, shouldn't I? What difference would that make?

Circumstances or no circumstances, Viv, you won't be able to stand your mother.

VIVIE [*very angry*] Why not?

FRANK. Because she's an old wretch, Viv. If you ever put your arm around her waist in my presence again, I'll shoot myself there and then as a protest against an exhibition which revolts me.

VIVIE. Must I choose between dropping your acquaintance and dropping my mother's?

FRANK [*gracefully*] That would put the old lady at ever such a disadvantage. No, Viv: your infatuated little boy will have to stick to you in any case. But he's all the more anxious that you shouldn't make mistakes. It's no use, Viv: your mother's impossible. She may be a good sort; but she's a bad lot, a very bad lot.

VIVIE [*hotly*] Frank—! [*He stands his ground. She turns away and sits down on the bench under the yew tree, struggling to recover her self-command. Then she says*] Is she to be deserted by the world because she's what you call a bad lot? Has she no right to live?

FRANK. No fear of that, Viv: *she* won't ever be deserted. [*He sits on the bench beside her*].

VIVIE. But I am to desert her, I suppose.

FRANK [*babyishly, lulling her and making love to her with his voice*] Mustn't go live with her. Little family group of mother and daughter wouldn't be a success. Spoil o u r little group.

VIVIE [*falling under the spell*] What little group?

FRANK. The babes in the wood: Vivie and little Frank. [*He nestles against her like a weary child*]. Lets go and get covered up with leaves.

VIVIE [*rhythmically, rocking him like a nurse*] Fast asleep, hand in hand, under the trees.

FRANK. The wise little girl with her silly little boy.

VIVIE. The dear little boy with his dowdy little girl.

FRANK. Ever so peaceful, and relieved from the imbecility of the little boy's father and the questionableness of the little girl's—

VIVIE [*smothering the word against her breast*] Sh-sh-sh-sh! little girl wants to forget all about her mother. [*They are silent for some moments, rocking one another. Then Vivie wakes up with a shock, exclaiming*] What a pair of fools we are! Come: sit up. Gracious! your hair. [*She smooths it*]. I wonder do all grown up people play in that childish way when nobody is looking.

I never did it when I was a child.

FRANK. Neither did I. You are my first playmate. [*He catches her hand to kiss it, but checks himself to look around first. Very unexpectedly, he sees Crofts emerging from the box hedge*]. Oh damn!

VIVIE. Why damn, dear?

FRANK [*whispering*] Sh! Here's this brute Crofts. [*He sits farther away from her with an unconcerned air*].

CROFTS. Could I have a few words with you, Miss Vivie?

VIVIE. Certainly.

CROFTS [*to Frank*] Youll excuse me, Gardner. Theyre waiting for you in the church, if you don't mind.

FRANK [*rising*] Anything to oblige you, Crofts—except church. If you should happen to want me, Vivvums, ring the gate bell. [*He goes into the house with unruffled suavity*].

CROFTS [*watching him with a crafty air as he disappears, and speaking to Vivie with an assumption of being on privileged terms with her*] Pleasant young fellow that, Miss Vivie. Pity he has no money, isn't it?

VIVIE. Do you think so?

CROFTS. Well, whats he to do? No profession. No property. Whats he good for?

VIVIE. I realize his disadvantages, Sir George.

CROFTS [*a little taken aback at being so precisely interpreted*] Oh, it's not that. But while we're in this world we're in it; and money's money. [*Vivie does not answer*]. Nice day, isn't it?

VIVIE [*with scarcely veiled contempt for this effort at conversation*] Very.

CROFTS [*with brutal good humor, as if he liked her pluck*] Well thats not what I came to say. [*Sitting down beside her*] Now listen, Miss Vivie. I'm quite aware that I'm not a young lady's man.

VIVIE. Indeed, Sir George?

CROFTS. No; and to tell you the honest truth I don't want to be either. But when I say a thing I mean it; and when I feel a sentiment I feel it in earnest; and what I value I pay hard money for. Thats the sort of man I am.

VIVIE. It does you great credit, I'm sure.

CROFTS. Oh, I don't mean to praise myself. I have my faults, Heaven knows: no man is more sensible of that than I am. I know I'm not perfect: thats one of the advantages of being a middle-aged man; for I'm not a young man, and I know it. But my code is a simple one, and, I think, a good one. Honor between man and man; fidelity between man and woman; and no can't about this religion or that religion, but an honest belief that things are making for good on the whole.

VIVIE [*with biting irony*] "A power, not ourselves, that makes for righteousness," eh?

CROFTS [*taking her seriously*] Oh certainly. Not ourselves, of course. Y o u understand what I mean. Well, now as to practical matters. You may have an idea that I've flung my money about; but I havn't: I'm richer today than when I first came into the property. I've used my knowledge of the world to invest my money in ways that other men have overlooked; and whatever else I may be, I'm a safe man from the money point of view.

VIVIE. It's very kind of you to tell me all this.

CROFTS. Oh well, come, Miss Vivie: you needn't pretend you don't see what I'm driving at. I want to settle down with a Lady Crofts. I suppose you think me very blunt, eh?

VIVIE. Not at all: I am very much obliged to you for being so definite and business-like. I quite appreciate the offer: the money, the position, *Lady Crofts*, and so on. But I think I will say no, if you don't mind, I'd rather not. [*She rises, and strolls across to the sundial to get out of his immediate neighborhood*].

CROFTS [*not at all discouraged, and taking advantage of the additional room left him on the seat to spread himself comfortably, as if a few preliminary refusals were part of the inevitable routine of courtship*] I'm in no hurry. It was only just to let you know in case young Gardner should try to trap you. Leave the question open.

VIVIE [*sharply*] My no is final. I won't go back from it.

[*Crofts is not impressed. He grins; leans forward with his elbows on his knees to prod with his stick at some unfortunate insect in the grass; and looks cunningly at her. She turns away impatiently.*]

CROFTS. I'm a good deal older than you. Twenty-five years: quarter of a century. I shan't live for ever; and I'll take care that you shall be well off when I'm gone.

VIVIE. I am proof against even that inducement, Sir George. Don't you think youd better take your answer? There is not the slightest chance of my altering it.

CROFTS [*rising, after a final slash at a daisy, and coming nearer to her*] Well, no matter. I could tell you some things that would change your mind fast enough; but I wont, because I'd rather win you by honest affection. I was a good friend to your mother: ask her whether I wasn't. She'd never have make the money that paid for your education if it hadnt been for my advice and help, not to mention the money I advanced her. There are not many men who would have stood by her as I have. I put not less than forty thousand pounds into it, from first to last.

VIVIE [*staring at him*] Do you mean to say that you were my mother's business partner?

CROFTS. Yes. Now just think of all the trouble and the explanations it would save if we were to keep the whole thing in the family, so to speak. Ask your mother whether she'd like to have to explain all her affairs to a perfect stranger.

VIVIE. I see no difficulty, since I understand that the business is wound up, and the money invested.

CROFTS [*stopping short, amazed*] Wound up! Wind up a business thats paying 35 per cent in the worst years! Not likely. Who told you that?

VIVIE [*her color quite gone*] Do you mean that it is still—? [*She stops abruptly, and puts her hand on the sundial to support herself. Then she gets quickly to the iron chair and sits down*].

What business are you talking about?

CROFTS. Well, the fact is it's not what would considered exactly a high-class business in my set—the country set, you know—o u r set it will be if you think better of my offer. Not that theres any mystery about it: don't think that. Of course you know by your mother's being in it that it's perfectly straight and honest. I've known her for many years; and I can say of her that she'd cut off her hands sooner than touch anything that was not what it ought to be. I'll tell you all about it if you like. I don't know whether you've found in travelling how hard it is to find a really comfortable private hotel.

VIVIE [*sickened, averting her face*] Yes: go on.

CROFTS. Well, thats all it is. Your mother has got a genius for managing such things. We've got two in Brussels, one in Ostend, one in Vienna, and two in Budapest. Of course there are others besides ourselves in it; but we hold most of the capital; and your mother's indispensable as managing director. You've noticed, I daresay, that she travels a good deal. But you see you can't mention such things in society. Once let out the word hotel and everybody thinks you keep a public-house. You wouldn't like people to say that of your mother, would you? Thats why we're so reserved about it. By the way, youll keep it to yourself, won't you? Since it's been a secret so long, it had better remain so.

VIVIE. And this is the business you invite me to join you in?

CROFTS. Oh no. My wife shan't be troubled with business. Youll not be in it more than you've always been.

VIVIE. *I* always been! What do you mean?

CROFTS. Only that you've always lived on it. It paid for your education and the dress you have on your back. Don't turn up your nose at business, Miss Vivie: where would your Newnhams and Girtons be without it?

VIVIE [*rising, almost beside herself*] Take care. I know what this business is.

CROFTS [*starting, with a suppressed oath*] Who told you?

VIVIE. Your partner. My mother.

CROFTS [*black with rage*] The old—

VIVIE. Just so.

[*He swallows the epithet and stands for a moment swearing and raging foully to himself. But he knows that his cue is to be sympathetic. He takes refuge in generous indignation.*]

CROFTS. She ought to have had more consideration for you. *I'd* never have told you.

VIVIE. I think you would probably have told me when we were married: it would have been a convenient weapon to break me in with.

CROFTS [*quite sincerely*] I never intended that. On my word as a gentleman I didn't.

[*Vivie wonders at him. Her sense of the irony of his protest cools and braces her. She replies with contemptuous self-possession.*]

VIVIE. It does not matter. I suppose you understand that when we leave here today our acquaintance ceases.

CROFTS. Why? Is it for helping your mother?

VIVIE. My mother was a very poor woman who had no reasonable choice but to do as she did. You were a rich gentleman; and you did the same for the sake of 35 per cent. You are a pretty common sort of scoundrel, I think. That is my opinion of you.

CROFTS [*after a stare: not at all displeased, and much more at his ease on these frank terms than on their former ceremonious ones*] Ha! ha! ha! ha! Go it, little missie, go it: it doesn't hurt me and it amuses you. Why the devil shouldn't I invest my money that way? I take the interest on my capital like other people: I hope you don't think I dirty my own hands with the work.

Come! you wouldn't refuse the acquaintance of my mother's cousin the Duke of Belgravia because some of the rents he gets are earned in queer ways. You wouldn't cut the Archbishop of Canterbury, I suppose, because the Ecclesiastical Commissioners have a few publicans and sinners among their tenants. Do you remember your Crofts scholarship at Newnham? Well, that was founded by my brother the M.P. He gets his 22 per cent out of a factory with 600 girls in it, and not one of them getting wages enough to live on. How d'ye suppose they manage when they have no family to fall back on? Ask your mother. And do you expect me to turn my back on 35 per cent when all the rest are pocketing what they can, like sensible men? No such fool! If youre going to pick and choose your acquaintances on moral principles, youd better clear out of this country, unless you want to cut yourself out of all decent society.

VIVIE [*conscience stricken*] You might go on to point out that I myself never asked where the money I spent came from. I believe I am just as bad as you.

CROFTS [*greatly reassured*] Of course you are; and a very good thing too! What harm does it do after all? [*Rallying her jocularly*] So you don't think me such a scoundrel now you come to think it over. Eh?

VIVIE. I have shared profits with you: and I admitted you just now to the familiarity of knowing what I think of you.

CROFTS [*with serious friendliness*] To be sure you did. You won't find me a bad sort: I don't go in for being superfine intellectually; but Ive plenty of honest human feeling; and the old Crofts breed comes out in a sort of instinctive hatred of anything low, in which I'm sure youll sympathize with me. Believe me, Miss Vivie, the world isn't such a bad place as the croakers make out. As long as you don't fly openly in the face of society, society doesn't ask any inconvenient questions; and it makes precious short work of the cads who do. There are no secrets better kept than the secrets everybody guesses. In the class of people I can introduce you to, no lady or gentleman would so far forget themselves as to discuss my business affairs or your mothers. No man can offer you a safer position.

VIVIE [*studying him curiously*] I suppose you really think youre getting on famously with me.

CROFTS. Well, I hope I may flatter myself that you think better of me than you did at first.

VIVIE [*quietly*] I hardly find you worth thinking about at all now. When I think of the society that tolerates you, and the laws that protect you! when I think of how helpless nine out of ten young girls would be in the hands of you and my mother! the unmentionable woman and her capitalist bully—

CROFTS [*livid*] Damn you!

VIVIE. You need not. I feel among the damned already.

[*She raises the latch of the gate to open it and go out. He follows her and puts his hand heavily on the top bar to prevent its opening.*]

CROFTS [*panting with fury*] Do you think I'll put up with this from you, you young devil?

VIVIE [*unmoved*] Be quiet. Some one will answer the bell. [*Without flinching a step she strikes the bell with the back of her hand. It clangs harshly; and he starts back involuntarily. Almost immediately Frank appears at the porch with his rifle*].

FRANK [*with cheerful politeness*] Will you have the rifle, Viv; or shall I operate?

VIVIE. Frank: have you been listening?

FRANK [*coming down into the garden*] Only for the bell, I assure you; so that you shouldn't have to wait. I think I shewed great insight into your character, Crofts.

CROFTS. For two pins I'd take that gun from you and break it across your head.

FRANK [*stalking him cautiously*] Pray don't. I'm ever so careless in handling firearms. Sure to be a fatal accident, with a reprimand from the coroner's jury for my negligence.

VIVIE. Put the rifle away, Frank: it's quite unnecessary.

FRANK. Quite right, Viv. Much more sportsmanlike to catch him in a trap. [*Crofts, understanding the insult, makes a threatening movement*]. Crofts: there are fifteen cartridges in the magazine here; and I am a dead shot at the present distance and at an object of your size.

CROFTS. Oh, you needn't be afraid. I'm not going to touch you.

FRANK. Ever so magnanimous of you under the circumstances! Thank you.

CROFTS. I'll just tell you this before I go. It may interest you, since youre so fond of one another. Allow me, Mister Frank, to introduce you to your half-sister, the eldest daughter of the Reverend Samuel Gardner. Miss Vivie: you half-brother. Good morning! [*He goes out through the gate and along the road*].

FRANK [*after a pause of stupefaction, raising the rifle*] Youll testify before the coroner that it's an accident, Viv. [*He takes aim at the retreating figure of Crofts. Vivie seizes the muzzle and pulls it round against her breast*].

VIVIE. Fire now. You may.

FRANK [*dropping his end of the rifle hastily*] Stop! take care. [*She lets it go. It falls on the turf*]. Oh, you've given your little boy such a turn. Suppose it had gone off! ugh! [*He sinks on the garden seat, overcome*].

VIVIE. Suppose it had: do you think it would not have been a relief to have some sharp physical pain tearing through me?

FRANK [*coaxingly*] Take it ever so easy, dear Viv. Remember: even if the rifle scared that fellow into telling the truth for the first time in his life, that only makes us the babes in the woods in earnest. [*He holds out his arms to her*]. Come and be covered up with leaves again.

VIVIE [*with a cry of disgust*] Ah, not that, not that. You make all my flesh creep.

FRANK. Why, whats the matter?

VIVIE. Goodbye. [*She makes for the gate*].

FRANK [*jumping up*] Hallo! Stop! Viv! Viv! [*She turns in the gateway*] Where are you going to? Where shall we find you?

VIVIE. At Honoria Fraser's chambers, 67 Chancery Lane, for the rest of my life. [*She goes off quickly in the opposite direction to that taken by Crofts*].

FRANK. But I say—wait—dash it! [*He runs after her*].

ACT IV

[*Honoria Fraser's chambers in Chancery Lane. An office at the top of New Stone Buildings, with a plate-glass window, distempered walls, electric light, and a patent stove. Saturday afternoon. The chimneys of Lincoln's Inn and the western sky beyond are seen through the window. There is a double writing table in the middle of the room, with a cigar box, ash pans, and a portable electric reading lamp almost snowed up in heaps of papers and books. This table has knee holes and chairs right and left and is very untidy. The clerk's desk, closed and tidy, with its high stool, is against the wall, near a door communicating with the inner rooms. In the opposite wall is the door leading to the public corridor. Its upper panel is of opaque glass, lettered in black on the outside, FRASER AND WARREN. A baize screen hides the corner between this door and the window.*]

[*Frank, in a fashionable light-colored coaching suit, with his stick, gloves, and white hat in his hands, is pacing up and down in the office. Somebody tries the door with a key.*]

FRANK [*calling*] Come in. It's not locked.

[*Vivie comes in, in her hat and jacket. She stops and stares at him.*]

VIVIE [*sternly*] What are you doing here?

FRANK. Waiting to see you. I've been here for hours. Is this the way you attend to your business? [*He puts his hat and stick on the table, and perches himself with a vault on the clerk's stool, looking at her with every appearance of being in a specially restless, teasing, flippant mood*].

VIVIE. I've been away exactly twenty minutes for a cup of tea. [*She takes off her hat and jacket and hangs them behind the screen*]. How did you get in?

FRANK. The staff had not left when I arrived. He's gone to play cricket on Primrose Hill. Why don't you employ a woman, and give your sex a chance?

VIVIE. What have you come for?

FRANK [*springing off the stool and coming close to her*] Viv: lets go and enjoy the Saturday half-holiday somewhere, like the staff.

What do you say to Richmond, and then a music hall, and a jolly supper?

VIVIE. Can't afford it. I shall put in another six hours work before I go to bed.

FRANK. Can't afford it, can't we? Aha! Look here. [*He takes out a handful of sovereigns and makes them chink*]. Gold, Viv: gold!

VIVIE. Where did you get it?

FRANK. Gambling, Viv: gambling. Poker.

VIVIE. Pah! It's meaner than stealing it. No: I'm not coming. [*She sits down to work at the table, with her back to the glass door, and begins turning over the papers*].

FRANK [*remonstrating piteously*] But, my dear Viv, I want to talk to you ever so seriously.

VIVIE. Very well: sit down in Honoria's chair and talk here. I like ten minutes chat after tea. [*He murmurs*]. No use groaning: I'm inexorable. [*He takes the opposite seat disconsolately*]. Pass that cigar box, will you?

FRANK [*pushing the cigar box across*] Nasty womanly habit. Nice men don't do it any longer.

VIVIE. Yes: they object to the smell in the office; and we've had to take to cigarets. See! [*She opens the box and takes out a cigaret, which she lights. She offers him one; but he shakes his head with a wry face. She settles herself comfortably in her chair, smoking*]. Go ahead.

FRANK. Well, I want to know what you've done—what arrangements you've made.

VIVIE. Everything was settled twenty minutes after I arrived here. Honoria has found the business too much for her this year; and she was on the point of sending for me and proposing a partnership when I walked in and told her I hadn't a farthing in the world. So I installed myself and packed her off for a fortnight's holiday. What happened at Haslemere when I left?

FRANK. Nothing at all. I said youd gone to town on particular business.

VIVIE. Well?

FRANK. Well, either they were too flabbergasted to say anything, or else Crofts had prepared your mother. Anyhow, she didn't say anything; and Crofts didn't say anything; and Praddy only stared. After tea they got up and went; and I've not seen them since.

VIVIE [*nodding placidly with one eye on a wreath of smoke*] Thats all right.

FRANK [*looking round disparagingly*] Do you intend to stick in this confounded place?

VIVIE [*blowing the wreath decisively away, and sitting straight up*] Yes. These two days have given me back all my strength and self-possession. I will never take a holiday again as long as I live.

FRANK [*with a very wry face*] Yes! You look quite happy. And as hard as nails.

VIVIE [*grimly*] Well for me that I am!

FRANK [*rising*] Look here, Viv: we must have an explanation. We parted the other day under a complete misunderstanding. [*He sits on the table, close to her*].

VIVIE [*putting away the cigaret*] Well: clear it up.

FRANK. You remember what Crofts said.

VIVIE. Yes.

FRANK. That revelation was supposed to bring about a complete change in the nature of our feeling for one another. It placed us on the footing of brother and sister.

VIVIE. Yes.

FRANK. Have you ever had a brother?

VIVIE. No.

FRANK. Then you don't know what being brother and sister feels like? Now I have lots of sisters; and the fraternal feeling is quite familiar to me. I assure you my feeling for you is not the least in the world like it. The girls will go *their* way; I will go mine; and we shan't care if we never see one another again. Thats brother and sister. But as to you, I can't be easy if I have to pass a week without seeing you. Thats not brother and sister. Its exactly what I felt an hour before Crofts made his revelation. In short, dear Viv, it's love's young dream.

VIVIE [*bitingly*] The same feeling, Frank, that brought your father to my mother's feet. Is that it?

FRANK [*so revolted that he slips off the table for a moment*] I very strongly object, Viv, to have my feelings compared to any which the Reverend Samuel is capable of harboring; and I object still more to a comparison of you to your mother. [*Resuming his perch*] Besides, I don't believe the story. I have taxed my father with it, and obtained from him what I consider tantamount to a denial.

VIVIE. What did he say?

FRANK. He said he was sure there must be some mistake.

VIVIE. Do you believe him?

FRANK. I am prepared to take his word against Crofts'.

VIVIE. Does it make any difference? I mean in your imagination or conscience; for of course it makes no real difference.

FRANK [*shaking his head*] None whatever to *me*.

VIVIE. Nor to me.

FRANK [*staring*] But this is ever so surprising! [*He goes back to his chair*]. I thought our whole relations were altered in your imagination and conscience, as you put it, the moment those words were out of that brute's muzzle.

VIVIE. No: it was not that. I didn't believe him. I only wish I could.

FRANK. Eh?

VIVIE. I think brother and sister would be a very suitable relation for us.

FRANK. You really mean that?

VIVIE. Yes. It's the only relation I care for, even if we could afford any other. I mean that.

FRANK [*raising his eyebrows like one on whom a new light has dawned, and rising with quite an effusion of chivalrous sentiment*] My dear Viv: why didn't you say so before? I am ever so sorry for persecuting you. I understand, of course.

VIVIE [*puzzled*] Understand what?

FRANK. Oh, I'm not a fool in the ordinary sense: only in the Scriptural sense of doing all the things the wise man declared to be folly, after trying them himself on the most extensive scale. I see I am no longer Vivvums's little boy. Don't be alarmed: I shall never call you Vivvums again—at least unless you get tired of your new little boy, whoever he may be.

VIVIE. My new little boy!

FRANK [*with conviction*] Must be a new little boy. Always happens that way. No other way, in fact.

VIVIE. None that you know of, fortunately for you.

[*Someone knocks at the door.*]

FRANK. My curse upon yon caller, whoe'er he be!

VIVIE. It's Praed. He's going to Italy and wants to say goodbye. I asked him to call this afternoon. Go and let him in.

FRANK. We can continue our conversation after his departure for Italy. I'll stay him out. [*He goes to the door and opens it*]. How are you, Praddy? Delighted to see you. Come in.

[*Praed, dressed for travelling, comes in, in high spirits.*]

PRAED. How do you do, Miss Warren? [*She presses his hand cordially, though a certain sentimentality in his high spirits jars upon her*]. I start in an hour from Holborn Viaduct. I wish I could persuade you to try Italy.

VIVIE. What for?

PRAED. Why, to saturate yourself with beauty and romance, of course.

[*Vivie, with a shudder, turns her chair to the table, as if the work waiting for her there were a support to her. Praed sits opposite to her. Frank places a chair near Vivie, and drops lazily and carelessly into it, talking at her over his shoulder.*]

FRANK. No use, Praddy. Viv is a little Philistine. She is indifferent to *my* romance, and insensible to *my* beauty.

VIVIE. Mr Praed: once for all, there is no beauty and no romance in life for me. Life is what it is; and I am prepared to take it as it is.

PRAED [*enthusiastically*] You will not say that if you come with me to Verona and on to Venice. You will cry with delight at living in such a beautiful world.

FRANK. This is most eloquent, Praddy. Keep it up.

PRAED. Oh, I assure you *I* have cried—I shall cry again, I hope—at fifty! At your age, Miss Warren, you would not need to go so far as Verona. Your spirits would absolutely fly up at the mere sight of Ostend. You would be charmed with the gaiety, the vivacity, the happy air of Brussels.

VIVIE [*springing up with an exclamation of loathing*] Agh!

PRAED [*rising*] Whats the matter?

FRANK [*rising*] Hallo, Viv!

VIVIE [*to Praed, with deep reproach*] Can you find no better example of your beauty and romance than Brussels to talk to me about?

PRAED [*puzzled*] Of course it's very different from Verona. I don't suggest for a moment that—

VIVIE [*bitterly*] Probably the beauty and romance come to much the same in both places.

PRAED [*completely sobered and much concerned*] My dear Miss Warren: I—[*looking enquiringly at Frank*] Is anything the matter?

FRANK. She thinks your enthusiasm frivolous, Praddy. She's had ever such a serious call.

VIVIE [*sharply*] Hold your tongue, Frank. Don't be silly.

FRANK [*sitting down*] Do you call this good manners, Praed?

PRAED [*anxious and considerate*] Shall I take him away, Miss Warren? I feel sure we have disturbed you at your work.

VIVIE. Sit down: I'm not ready to go back to work yet. [*Praed sits*]. You both think I have an attack of nerves. Not a bit of it. But there are two subjects I want dropped, if you don't mind.

One of them [*to Frank*] is love's young dream in any shape or form: the other [*to Praed*] is the romance and beauty of life, especially Ostend and the gaiety of Brussels. You are welcome to any illusions you may have left on these subjects: I have none. If we three are to remain friends, I must be treated as a woman of business, permanently single [*to Frank*] and permanently unromantic [*to Praed*].

FRANK. I also shall remain permanently single until you change your mind. Praddy: change the subject. Be eloquent about something else.

PRAED [*diffidently*] I'm afraid theres nothing else in the world that I *can* talk about. The Gospel of Art is the only one I can preach. I know Miss Warren is a great devotee of the Gospel of Getting On; but we can't discuss that without hurting your feelings, Frank, since you are determined not to get on.

FRANK. Oh, don't mind my feelings. Give me some improving advice by all means: it does me ever so much good. Have another try to make a successful man of me, Viv. Come: lets have it all: energy, thrift, foresight, self-respect, character. Don't you hate people who have no character, Viv?

VIVIE [*wincing*] Oh, stop, stop. Let us have no more of that horrible cant. Mr Praed: if there are really only those two gospels in the world, we had better all kill ourselves; for the same taint is in both, through and through.

FRANK [*looking critically at her*] There is a touch of poetry about you today, Viv, which has hitherto been lacking.

PRAED [*remonstrating*] My dear Frank: aren't you a little unsympathetic?

VIVIE [*merciless to herself*] No: it's good for me. It keeps me from being sentimental.

FRANK [*bantering her*] Checks your strong natural propensity that way, don't it?

VIVIE [*almost hysterically*] Oh yes: go on: don't spare me. I was sentimental for one moment in my life—beautifully sentimental—by moonlight; and now—

FRANK [*quickly*] I say, Viv: take care. Don't give yourself away.

VIVIE. Oh, do you think Mr Praed does not know all about my mother? [*Turning on Praed*] You had better have told me that morning, Mr Praed. You are very old fashioned in your delicacies, after all.

PRAED. Surely it is you who are a little old fashioned in your prejudices, Miss Warren. I feel bound to tell you, speaking as an artist, and believing that the most intimate human relationships are far beyond and above the scope of the law, that though I know that your mother is an unmarried woman, I do not respect her the less on that account. I respect her more.

FRANK [*airily*] Hear! hear!

VIVIE [*staring at him*] Is that *all* you know?

PRAED. Certainly that is all.

VIVIE. Then you neither of you know anything. Your guesses are innocence itself compared with the truth.

PRAED [*rising, startled and indignant, and preserving his politeness with an effort*] I hope not. [*More emphatically*] I hope not, Miss Warren.

FRANK [*whistles*] Whew!

VIVIE. You are not making it easy for me to tell you, Mr Praed.

PRAED [*his chivalry drooping before their conviction*] If there is anything worse—that is, anything else—are you sure you are right to tell us, Miss Warren?

VIVIE. I am sure that if I had the courage I should spend the rest of my life in telling everybody—stamping and branding it into them until they all felt their part in its abomination as I feel mine. There is nothing I despise more than the wicked convention that protects these things by forbidding a woman to mention them. And yet I can't tell you. The two infamous words that describe what my mother is are ringing in my ears and struggling on my tongue; but I can't utter them: the shame of them is too horrible for me. [*She buries her face in her hands. The two men, astonished, stare at one another and then at her. She raises her head again desperately and snatches a sheet of paper and a pen*]. Here: let me draft you a prospectus.

FRANK. Oh, she's mad. Do you hear, Viv? mad. Come! pull yourself together.

VIVIE. You shall see. [*She writes*]. "Paid up capital: not less than forty thousand pounds standing in the name of Sir George Crofts, Baronet, the chief shareholder. Premises at Brussels, Ostend, Vienna, and Budapest. Managing director: Mrs Warren"; and now don't let us forget h e r qualifications: the two words. [*She writes the words and pushes the paper to them*]. There! Oh no: don't read it: don't! [*She snatches it back and tears it to pieces; then seizes her head in her hands and hides her face on the table*].

[*Frank, who has watched the writing over her shoulder, and opened his eyes very widely at it, takes a card from his pocket; scribbles the two words on it; and silently hands it to Praed, who reads it with amazement, and hides it hastily in his pocket.*]

FRANK [*whispering tenderly*] Viv, dear: thats all right. I read what you wrote: so did Praddy. We understand. And we remain, as this leaves us at present, yours ever so devotedly.

PRAED. We do indeed, Miss Warren. I declare you are the most splendidly courageous woman I ever met.

[*This sentimental compliment braces Vivie. She throws it away from her with an impatient shake, and forces herself to stand up, though not without some support from the table.*]

FRANK. Don't stir, Viv, if you don't want to. Take it easy.

VIVIE. Thank you. You can always depend on me for two things: not to cry and not to faint. [*She moves a few steps towards the door of the inner room, and stops close to Praed to say*] I shall need much more courage than that when I tell my mother that we have come to a parting of the ways. Now I must go into the next room for a moment to make myself neat again, if you don't mind.

PRAED. Shall we go away?

VIVIE. No: I'll be back presently. Only for a moment. [*She goes into the other room, Praed opening the door for her*].

PRAED. What an amazing revelation! I'm extremely disappointed in Crofts: I am indeed.

FRANK. I'm not in the least. I feel he's perfectly accounted for at last. But what a facer for me, Praddy! I can't marry her now.

PRAED [*sternly*] Frank! [*The two look at one another, Frank unruffled, Praed deeply indignant*]. Let me tell you, Gardner, that if you desert her now you will behave very despicably.

FRANK. Good old Praddy! Ever chivalrous! But you mistake: it's not the moral aspect of the case: it's the money aspect. I really can't bring myself to touch the old woman's money now.

PRAED. And was that what you were going to marry on?

FRANK. What else? *I* havn't any money, nor the smallest turn for making it. If I married Viv now she would have to support me; and I should cost her more than I am worth.

PRAED. But surely a clever bright fellow like you can make something by your own brains.

FRANK. Oh yes, a little. [*He takes out his money again*]. I made all that yesterday in an hour and a half. But I made it in a highly speculative business. No, dear Praddy: even if Bessie and Georgina marry millionaires and the governor dies after cutting them off with a shilling, I shall have only four hundred a year. And he won't die until he's three score and ten: he hasn't originality enough. I shall be on short allowance for the next twenty years. No short allowance for Viv, if I can help it. I withdraw gracefully and leave the field to the gilded youth of England. So that settled. I shan't worry her about it: I'll just send her a little note after we're gone. She'll understand.

PRAED [*grasping his hand*] Good fellow, Frank! I heartily beg your pardon. But must you never see her again?

FRANK. Never see her again! Hang it all, be reasonable. I shall come along as often as possible, and be her brother. I can *not* understand the absurd consequences you romantic people expect from the most ordinary transactions. [*A knock at the door*]. I wonder who this is. Would you mind opening the door? If it's a client it will look more respectable than if I appeared.

PRAED. Certainly. [*He goes to the door and opens it. Frank sits down in Vivie's chair to scribble a note*]. My dear Kitty: come in: come in.

[*Mrs Warren comes in, looking apprehensively around for Vivie. She has done her best to make herself matronly and dignified. The brilliant hat is replaced by a sober bonnet, and the gay blouse covered by a costly black silk mantle. She is pitiably anxious and ill at ease: evidently panic-stricken.*]

MRS WARREN [*to Frank*] What! Y o u r e here, are you?

FRANK [*turning in his chair from his writing, but not rising*] Here, and charmed to see you. You come like a breath of spring.

MRS WARREN. Oh, get out with your nonsense. [*In a low voice*] Where's Vivie?

[*Frank points expressively to the door of the inner room, but says nothing.*]

MRS WARREN [*sitting down suddenly and almost beginning to cry*] Praddy: won't she see me, don't you think?

PRAED. My dear Kitty: don't distress yourself. Why should she not?

MRS WARREN. Oh, you never can see why not: youre too innocent. Mr Frank: did she say anything to you?

FRANK [*folding his note*] She *must* see you, if [*very expressively*] you wait til she comes in.

MRS WARREN [*frightened*] Why shouldn't I wait?

[*Frank looks quizzically at her; puts his note carefully on the ink-bottle, so that Vivie cannot fail to find it when next she dips her pen; then rises and devotes his attention entirely to her.*]

FRANK. My dear Mrs Warren: suppose you were a sparrow—ever so tiny and pretty a sparrow hopping in the roadway—and you saw a steam roller coming in your direction, would you wait for it?

MRS WARREN. Oh, don't bother me with your sparrows. What did she run away from Haslemere like that for?

FRANK. I'm afraid she'll tell you if you rashly await her return.

MRS WARREN. Do you want me to go away?

FRANK. No: I always want you to stay. But I *advise* you to go away.

MRS WARREN. What! And never see her again!

FRANK. Precisely.

MRS WARREN [*crying again*] Praddy: don't let him be cruel to me. [*She hastily checks her tears and wipes her eyes*]. She'll be so angry if she sees I've been crying.

FRANK [*with a touch of real compassion in his airy tenderness*] You know that Praddy is the soul of kindness, Mrs Warren. Praddy: what do you say? Go or stay?

PRAED [*to Mrs Warren*] I really should be very sorry to cause you unnecessary pain; but I think perhaps you had better not wait. The fact is—[*Vivie is heard at the inner door*].

FRANK. Sh! Too late. She's coming.

MRS WARREN. Don't tell her I was crying. [*Vivie comes in. She stops gravely on seeing Mrs Warren, who greets her with hysterical cheerfulness*]. Well, dearie. So here you are at last.

VIVIE. I am glad you have come: I want to speak to you. You said you were going, Frank, I think.

FRANK. Yes. Will you come with me, Mrs Warren? What do you say to a trip to Richmond, and the theatre in the evening? There is safety in Richmond. No steam roller there.

VIVIE. Nonsense, Frank. My mother will stay here.

MRS WARREN [*scared*] I don't know: perhaps I'd better go. We're disturbing you at your work.

VIVIE [*with quiet decision*] Mr Praed: please take Frank away. Sit down, mother. [*Mrs Warren obeys helplessly*].

PRAED. Come, Frank. Goodbye, Miss Vivie.

VIVIE [*shaking hands*] Goodbye. A pleasant trip.

PRAED. Thank you: thank you. I hope so.

FRANK [*to Mrs Warren*] Goodbye: youd ever so much better have taken my advice. [*He shakes hands with her. Then airily to Vivie*] Byebye, Viv.

VIVIE. Goodbye. [*He goes out gaily without shaking hands with her*].

PRAED [*sadly*] Goodbye, Kitty.

MRS WARREN [*snivelling*]—oobye!

[*Praed goes. Vivie, composed and extremely grave, sits down in Honoria's chair, and waits for her mother to speak. Mrs Warren, dreading a pause, loses no time in beginning.*]

MRS WARREN. Well, Vivie, what did you go away like that for without saying a word to me! How could you do such a thing! And what have you done to poor George? I wanted him to come with me; but he shuffled out of it. I could see that he was quite afraid of you. Only fancy: he wanted me not to come. As if [*trembling*] I should be afraid of you, dearie. [*Vivie's gravity deepens*]. But of course I told him it was all settled and comfortable between us, and that we were on the best of terms. [*She breaks down*]. Vivie: whats the meaning of this? [*She produces a commercial envelope, and fumbles at the enclosure with trembling fingers*]. I got it from the bank this morning.

VIVIE. It is my month's allowance. They sent it to me as usual the other day. I simply sent it back to be placed to your credit, and asked them to send you the lodgment receipt. In future I shall support myself.

MRS WARREN [*not daring to understand*] Wasn't it enough? Why didn't you tell me? [*With a cunning gleam in her eye*] I'll double it: I was intending to double it. Only let me know how much you want.

VIVIE. You know very well that that has nothing to do with it. From this time I go my own way in my own business and among my own friends. And you will go yours. [*She rises*]. Goodbye.

MRS WARREN [*rising, appalled*] Goodbye?

VIVIE. Yes: goodbye. Come: don't let us make a useless scene: you understand perfectly well. Sir George Crofts has told me the whole business.

MRS WARREN [*angrily*] Silly old—[*She swallows an epithet, and then turns white at the narrowness of her escape from uttering it*].

VIVIE. Just so.

MRS WARREN. He ought to have his tongue cut out. But I thought it was ended: you said you didn't mind.

VIVIE [*steadfastly*] Excuse me: I *do* mind.

MRS WARREN. But I explained—

VIVIE. You explained how it came about. You did not tell me that it is still going on [*She sits*].

[*Mrs Warren, silenced for a moment, looks forlornly at Vivie, who waits, secretly hoping that the combat is over. But the cunning expression comes back into Mrs Warren's face; and she bends across the table, sly and urgent, half whispering.*]

MRS WARREN. Vivie: do you know how rich I am?

VIVIE. I have no doubt you are very rich.

MRS WARREN. But you don't know all that that means; youre too young. It means a new dress every day; it means theatres and balls every night; it means having the pick of all the gentlemen in Europe at your feet; it means a lovely house and plenty of servants; it means the choicest of eating and drinking; it means everything you like, everything you want, everything you can think of. And what are you here? A mere drudge, toiling and moiling early and late for your bare living and two cheap dresses a year. Think over it. [*Soothingly*] Youre shocked, I know. I can enter into your feelings; and I think they do you credit; but trust me, nobody will blame you: you may take my word for that. I know what young girls are; and I know youll think better of it when you've turned it over in your mind.

VIVIE. So that's how it is done, is it? You must have said all that to many a woman, to have it so pat.

MRS WARREN [*passionately*] What harm am I asking you to do? [*Vivie turns away contemptuously. Mrs Warren continues desperately*] Vivie: listen to me: you don't understand: you were taught wrong on purpose: you don't know what the world is really like.

VIVIE [*arrested*] Taught wrong on purpose! What do you mean?

MRS WARREN. I mean that youre throwing away all your chances for nothing. You think that people are what they pretend to be: that the way you were taught at school and college to think right and proper is the way things really are. But it's not: it's all only a pretence, to keep the cowardly slavish common run of people quiet. Do you want to find that out, like other women, at forty, when you've thrown yourself away and lost your chances; or won't you take it in good time now from your own mother, that loves you and swears to you that it's truth: gospel truth? [*Urgently*] Vivie: the big people, the clever people, the managing people, all know it. They do as I do, and think what I think. I know plenty of them. I know them to speak to, to introduce you to, to make friends of for you. I don't mean anything wrong: thats what you don't understand: your head is full of ignorant ideas about me. What do the people that taught you know about life or about people like me? When did they ever meet me, or speak to me, or let anyone tell them about me? the fools! Would they ever have done anything for you if I hadn't paid them? Havn't I told you that I want you to be respectable? Havn't I brought you up to be respectable? And how can you keep it up without my money and my influence and Lizzie's friends? Can't you see that youre cutting your own throat as well as breaking my heart in turning your back on me?

VIVIE. I recognize the Crofts philosophy of life, mother. I heard it all from him that day at the Gardners'.

MRS WARREN. You think I want to force that played-out old sot on you! I don't, Vivie: on my oath I don't.

VIVIE. It would not matter if you did: you would not succeed. [*Mrs Warren winces, deeply hurt by the implied indifference towards her affectionate intention. Vivie, neither understanding this nor concerning herself about it, goes on calmly*] Mother: you don't at all know the sort of person I am. I don't object to Crofts more than to any other coarsely built man of his class. To tell you the truth, I rather admire him for being strongminded enough to enjoy himself in his own way and make plenty of money instead of living the usual shooting, hunting, dining-out, tailoring, loafing life of his set merely because all the rest do it. And I'm perfectly aware that if I'd been in the same circumstances as my aunt Liz, I'd have done exactly what she did.

I don't think I'm more prejudiced or straitlaced than you: I think I'm less. I'm certain I'm less sentimental. I know very well that fashionable morality is all a pretence, and that if I took your money and devoted the rest of my life to spending it fashionably, I might be as worthless and vicious as the silliest woman could possibly be without having a word said to me about it. But I don't want to be worthless. I shouldn't enjoy trotting about the park to advertize my dressmaker and carriage builder, or being bored at the opera to shew off a shopwindowful of diamonds.

MRS WARREN [*bewildered*] But—

VIVIE. Wait a moment: I've not done. Tell me why you continue your business now that you are independent of it. Your sister, you told me, has left all that behind her. Why don't you do the same?

MRS WARREN. Oh, it's all very easy for Liz: she likes good society, and has the air of being a lady. Imagine *me* in a cathedral town! Why, the very rooks in the trees would find me out even if I could stand the dulness of it. I must have work and excitement, or I should go melancholy mad. And what else is there for me to do? The life suits me: I'm fit for it and not for anything else. If I didn't do it somebody else would; so I don't do any real harm by it. And then it brings in money; and I like making money. No: it's no use: I can't give it up—not for anybody. But what need you know about it? I'll never mention it. I'll keep Crofts away. I'll not trouble you much: you see I have to be constantly running about from one place to another. Youll be quit of me altogether when I die.

VIVIE. No: I am my mother's daughter. I am like you: I must have work, and must make more money than I spend. But my work is not your work, and my way is not your way. We must part. It will not make much difference to us: instead of meeting one another for perhaps a few months in twenty years, we shall never meet: thats all.

MRS WARREN [*her voice stifled in tears*] Vivie: I meant to have been more with you: I did indeed.

VIVIE. It's no use, mother: I am not to be changed by a few cheap tears and entreaties any more than you are, I daresay.

MRS WARREN [*wildly*] Oh, you call a mother's tears cheap.

VIVIE. They cost you nothing; and you ask me to give you the peace and quietness of my whole life in exchange for them. What use would my company be to you if you could get it? What have we two in common that could make either of us happy together?

MRS WARREN [*lapsing recklessly into her dialect*] We're mother and daughter. I want my daughter. I've a right to you. Who is to care for me when I'm old? Plenty of girls have taken to me like daughters and cried at leaving me; but I let them all go because I had you to look forward to. I kept myself lonely for you. You've no right to turn on me now and refuse to do your duty as a daughter.

VIVIE [*jarred and antagonized by the echo of the slums in her mother's voice*] My duty as a daughter! I thought we should come to that presently. Now once for all, mother, you want a daughter and Frank wants a wife. I don't want a mother; and I don't want a husband. I have spared neither Frank nor myself in sending him about his business. Do you think I will spare you?

MRS WARREN [*violently*] Oh, I know the sort you are: no mercy for yourself or anyone else. *I* know. My experience has done that for me anyhow: I can tell the pious, canting, hard, selfish woman when I meet her. Well, keep yourself to yourself: *I* don't want you. But listen to this. Do you know what I would do with you if you were a baby again? aye, as sure as there's a Heaven above us.

VIVIE. Strangle me, perhaps.

MRS WARREN. No: I'd bring you up to be a real daughter to me, and not what you are now, with your pride and your prejudices and the college education you stole from me: yes, stole: deny it if you can: what was it but stealing? I'd bring you up in my own house, I would.

VIVIE [*quietly*] In one of your own houses.

MRS WARREN [*screaming*] Listen to her! listen to how she spits on her mother's grey hairs! Oh, may you live to have your own daughter tear and trample on you as you have trampled on me. And you will: you will. No woman ever had luck with a mother's curse on her.

VIVIE. I wish you wouldn't rant, mother. It only hardens me. Come: I suppose I am the only young woman you ever had in your power that you did good to. Don't spoil it all now.

MRS WARREN. Yes, Heaven forgive me, it's true; and you are the only one that ever turned on me. Oh, the injustice of it! the injustice! the injustice! I always wanted to be a good woman. I tried honest work; and I was slave-driven until I cursed the day I ever heard of honest work. I was a good mother; and because I made my daughter a good woman she turns me out as if I were a leper. Oh, if I only had my life to live over again! I'd talk to that lying clergyman in the school. From this time forth, so help me Heaven in my last hour, I'll do wrong and nothing but wrong. And I'll prosper on it.

VIVIE. Yes: it's better to choose your line and go through with it. If I had been you, mother, I might have done as you did; but I should not have lived one life and believed in another. You are a conventional woman at heart. That is why I am bidding you goodbye now. I am right, am I not?

MRS WARREN [*taken aback*] Right to throw away all my money!

VIVIE. No: right to get rid of you? I should be a fool not to. Isn't that so?

MRS WARREN [*sulkily*] Oh well, yes, if you come to that, I suppose you are. But Lord help the world if everybody took to doing the right thing! And now I'd better go than stay where I'm not wanted. [*She turns to the door*].

VIVIE [*kindly*] Won't you shake hands?

MRS WARREN [*after looking at her fiercely for a moment with a savage impulse to strike her*] No, thank you. Goodbye.

VIVIE [*matter-of-factly*] Goodbye. [*Mrs Warren goes out, slamming the door behind her. The strain on Vivie's face relaxes; her grave expression breaks up into one of joyous content; her breath goes out in a half sob, half laugh of intense relief. She goes buoyantly to her place at the writing table; pushes the electric lamp out of the way; pulls over a great sheaf of papers; and is in the act of dipping her pen in the ink when she finds Frank's note. She opens it unconcernedly and reads it quickly, giving a little laugh at some quaint turn of expression in it*]. And goodbye, Frank. [*She tears the note up and tosses the pieces into the wastepaper basket without a second thought. Then she goes at her work with a plunge, and soon becomes absorbed in its figures.*]

ARMS AND THE MAN

INTRODUCTION

To the irreverent—and which of us will claim entire exemption from that comfortable classification?—there is something very amusing in the attitude of the orthodox criticism toward Bernard Shaw. He so obviously disregards all the canons and unities and other things which every well-bred dramatist is bound to respect that his work is really unworthy of serious criticism (orthodox). Indeed he knows no more about the dramatic art than, according to his own story in "The Man of Destiny," Napoleon at Tavazzano knew of the Art of War. But both men were successes each in his way—the latter won victories and the former gained audiences, in the very teeth of the accepted theories of war and the theatre. Shaw does not know that it is unpardonable sin to have his characters make long speeches at one another, apparently thinking that this embargo applies only to long speeches which consist mainly of bombast and rhetoric. There never was an author who showed less predilection for a specific medium by which to accomplish his results. He recognized, early in his days, many things awry in the world and he assumed the task of mundane reformation with a confident spirit. It seems such a small job at twenty to set the times aright. He began as an Essayist, but who reads essays now-a-days?—he then turned novelist with no better success, for no one would read such preposterous stuff as he chose to emit. He only succeeded in proving that absolutely rational men and women—although he has created few of the latter—can be most extremely disagreeable to our conventional way of thinking.

As a last resort, he turned to the stage, not that he cared for the dramatic art, for no man seems to care less about "Art for Art's sake," being in this a perfect foil to his brilliant compatriot and contemporary, Wilde. He cast his theories in dramatic forms merely because no other course except silence or physical revolt was open to him. For a long time it seemed as if this resource too was doomed to fail him. But finally he has attained a hearing and now attempts at suppression merely serve to advertise their victim.

It will repay those who seek analogies in literature to compare Shaw with Cervantes. After a life of heroic endeavor, disappointment, slavery, and poverty, the author of "Don Quixote" gave the world a serious work which caused to be laughed off the world's stage forever the final vestiges of decadent chivalry.

The institution had long been outgrown, but its vernacular continued to be the speech and to express the thought "of the world and among the vulgar," as the quaint, old novelist puts it, just as to-day the novel intended for the consumption of the unenlightened must deal with peers and millionaires and be dressed in stilted language. Marvellously he succeeded, but in a way he least intended. We have not yet, after so many years, determined whether it is a work to laugh or cry over. "It is our joyfullest modern book," says Carlyle, while Landor thinks that "readers who see nothing more than a burlesque in 'Don Quixote' have but shallow appreciation of the work."

Shaw in like manner comes upon the scene when many of our social usages are outworn. He sees the fact, announces it, and we burst into guffaws. The continuous laughter which greets Shaw's plays arises from a real contrast in the point of view of the dramatist and his audiences. When Pinero or Jones describes a whimsical situation we never doubt for a moment that the author's point of view is our own and that the abnormal predicament of his characters appeals to him in the same light as to his audience. With Shaw this sense of community of feeling is wholly lacking. He describes things as he sees them, and the house is in a roar. Who is right? If we were really using our own senses and not gazing through the glasses of convention and romance and make-believe, should we see things as Shaw does?

Must it not cause Shaw to doubt his own or the public's sanity to hear audiences laughing boisterously over tragic situations? And yet, if they did not come to laugh, they would not come at all. Mockery is the price he must pay for a hearing. Or has he calculated to a nicety the power of reaction? Does he seek to drive us to aspiration by the portrayal of sordidness, to disinterestedness by the picture of selfishness, to illusion by disillusionment? It is impossible to believe that he is unconscious of the humor of his dramatic situations, yet he stoically gives no sign. He even dares the charge, terrible in proportion to its truth, which the most serious of us shrinks from—the lack of a sense of humor. Men would rather have their integrity impugned.

In "Arms and the Man" the subject which occupies the dramatist's attention is that survival of barbarity—militarism—which raises its horrid head from time to time to cast a doubt on the reality of our civilization. No more hoary superstition survives than that the donning of a uniform changes the nature of the wearer. This notion pervades society to such an extent that when we find some soldiers placed upon the stage acting rationally, our conventionalized senses are shocked. The only men who have no illusions about war are those who have recently been there, and, of course, Mr. Shaw, who has no illusions about anything.

It is hard to speak too highly of "Candida." No equally subtle and incisive study of domestic relations exists in the English drama. One has to turn to George Meredith's "The Egoist" to find such character dissection. The central note of the play is, that with the true woman, weakness which appeals to the maternal instinct is more powerful than strength which offers protection. Candida is quite unpoetic, as, indeed, with rare exceptions, women are prone to be. They have small delight in poetry, but are the stuff of which poems and dreams are made. The husband glorying in his strength but convicted of his weakness, the poet pitiful in his physical impotence but strong in his perception of truth, the hopelessly de-moralized manufacturer, the conventional and hence emotional typist make up a group which the drama of any language may be challenged to rival.

In "The Man of Destiny" the object of the dramatist is not so much the destruction as the explanation of the Napoleonic tradition, which has so powerfully influenced generation after generation for a century. However the man may be regarded, he was a miracle. Shaw shows that he achieved his extraordinary career by suspending, for himself, the pressure of the moral and conventional atmosphere, while leaving it operative for others. Those who study this play—extravaganza, that it is—will attain a clearer comprehension of Napoleon than they can get from all the biographies.

"You Never Can Tell" offers an amusing study of the play of social conventions. The "twins" illustrate the disconcerting effects of that perfect frankness which would make life intolerable. Gloria demonstrates the powerlessness of reason to overcome natural instincts. The idea that parental duties and functions can be fulfilled by the light of such knowledge as man and woman attain by intuition is brilliantly lampooned. Crampton, the father, typifies the common superstition that among the privileges of parenthood are inflexibility, tyranny, and respect, the last entirely regardless of whether it has been deserved.

The waiter, William, is the best illustration of the man "who knows his place" that the stage has seen. He is the most pathetic figure of the play. One touch of verisimilitude is lacking; none of the guests gives him a tip, yet he maintains his urbanity. As Mr. Shaw has not yet visited America he may be unaware of the improbability of this situation.

To those who regard literary men merely as purveyors of amusement for people who have not wit enough to entertain themselves, Ibsen and Shaw, Maeterlinck and Gorky must remain enigmas. It is so much pleasanter to ignore than to face unpleasant realities—to take Riverside Drive and not Mulberry Street as the exponent of our life and the expression of our civilization. These men are the sappers and miners of the advancing army of justice. The audience which demands the truth and despises the contemptible conventions that dominate alike our stage and our life is daily growing. Shaw and men like him—if indeed he is not absolutely unique—will not for the future lack a hearing.

M.

ACT I

Night. A lady's bedchamber in Bulgaria, in a small town near the Dragoman Pass. It is late in November in the year 1885, and through an open window with a little balcony on the left can be seen a peak of the Balkans, wonderfully white and beautiful in the starlit snow. The interior of the room is not like anything to be seen in the east of Europe. It is half rich Bulgarian, half cheap Viennese. The counterpane and hangings of the bed, the window curtains, the little carpet, and all the ornamental textile fabrics in the room are oriental and gorgeous: the paper on the walls is occidental and paltry. Above the head of the bed, which stands against a little wall cutting off the right hand corner of the room diagonally, is a painted wooden shrine, blue and gold, with an ivory image of Christ, and a light hanging before it in a pierced metal ball suspended by three chains. On the left, further forward, is an ottoman. The washstand, against the wall on the left, consists of an enamelled iron basin with a pail beneath it in a painted metal frame, and a single towel on the rail at the side. A chair near it is Austrian bent wood, with cane seat. The dressing table, between the bed and the window, is an ordinary pine table, covered with a cloth of many colors, but with an expensive toilet mirror on it. The door is on the right; and there is a chest of drawers between the door and the bed. This chest of drawers is also covered by a variegated native cloth, and on it there is a pile of paper backed novels, a box of chocolate creams, and a miniature easel, on which is a large photograph of an extremely handsome officer, whose lofty bearing and magnetic glance can be felt even from the portrait. The room is lighted by a candle on the chest of drawers, and another on the dressing table, with a box of matches beside it.

The window is hinged doorwise and stands wide open, folding back to the left. Outside a pair of wooden shutters, opening outwards, also stand open. On the balcony, a young lady, intensely conscious of the romantic beauty of the night, and of the fact that her own youth and beauty is a part of it, is on the balcony, gazing at the snowy Balkans. She is covered by a long mantle of furs, worth, on a moderate estimate, about three times the furniture of her room.

Her reverie is interrupted by her mother, Catherine Petkoff, a woman over forty, imperiously energetic, with magnificent black hair and eyes, who might be a very splendid specimen of the wife of a mountain farmer, but is determined to be a Viennese lady, and to that end wears a fashionable tea gown on all occasions.

CATHERINE (entering hastily, full of good news). Raina—(she pronounces it Rah-eena, with the stress on the ee) Raina—(she goes to the bed, expecting to find Raina there.) Why, where—(Raina looks into the room.) Heavens! child, are you out in the night air instead of in your bed? You'll catch your death. Louka told me you were asleep.

RAINA (coming in). I sent her away. I wanted to be alone. The stars are so beautiful! What is the matter?

CATHERINE. Such news. There has been a battle!

RAINA (her eyes dilating). Ah! (She throws the cloak on the ottoman, and comes eagerly to Catherine in her nightgown, a pretty garment, but evidently the only one she has on.)

CATHERINE. A great battle at Slivnitza! A victory! And it was won by Sergius.

RAINA (with a cry of delight). Ah! (Rapturously.) Oh, mother! (Then, with sudden anxiety) Is father safe?

CATHERINE. Of course: he sent me the news. Sergius is the hero of the hour, the idol of the regiment.

RAINA. Tell me, tell me. How was it! (Ecstatically) Oh, mother, mother, mother! (Raina pulls her mother down on the ottoman; and they kiss one another frantically.)

CATHERINE (with surging enthusiasm). You can't guess how splendid it is. A cavalry charge—think of that! He defied our Russian commanders—acted without orders—led a charge on his own responsibility—headed it himself—was the first man to sweep through their guns. Can't you see it, Raina; our gallant splendid Bulgarians with their swords and eyes flashing, thundering down like an avalanche and scattering the wretched Servian dandies like chaff. And you—you kept Sergius waiting a year before you would be betrothed to him. Oh, if you have a drop of Bulgarian blood in your veins, you will worship him when he comes back.

RAINA. What will he care for my poor little worship after the acclamations of a whole army of heroes? But no matter: I am so happy—so proud! (She rises and walks about excitedly.) It proves that all our ideas were real after all.

CATHERINE (indignantly). Our ideas real! What do you mean?

RAINA. Our ideas of what Sergius would do—our patriotism—our heroic ideals. Oh, what faithless little creatures girls are!—I sometimes used to doubt whether they were anything but dreams. When I buckled on Sergius's sword he looked so noble: it was treason to think of disillusion or humiliation or failure. And yet—and yet—(Quickly.) Promise me you'll never tell him.

CATHERINE. Don't ask me for promises until I know what I am promising.

RAINA. Well, it came into my head just as he was holding me in his arms and looking into my eyes, that perhaps we only had our heroic ideas because we are so fond of reading Byron and Pushkin, and because we were so delighted with the opera that season at Bucharest. Real life is so seldom like that—indeed never, as far as I knew it then. (Remorsefully.) Only think, mother, I doubted him: I wondered whether all his heroic qualities and his soldiership might not prove mere imagination when he went into a real battle. I had an uneasy fear that he might cut a poor figure there beside all those clever Russian officers.

CATHERINE. A poor figure! Shame on you! The Servians have Austrian officers who are just as clever as our Russians; but we have beaten them in every battle for all that.

RAINA (laughing and sitting down again). Yes, I was only a prosaic little coward. Oh, to think that it was all true—that Sergius is just as splendid and noble as he looks—that the world is really a glorious world for women who can see its glory and men who can act its romance! What happiness! what unspeakable fulfilment! Ah! (She throws herself on her knees beside her mother and flings her arms passionately round her. They are interrupted by the entry of Louka, a handsome, proud girl in a pretty Bulgarian peasant's dress with double apron, so defiant that her servility to Raina is almost insolent. She is afraid of Catherine, but even with her goes as far as she dares. She is just now excited like the others; but she has no sympathy for Raina's raptures and looks contemptuously at the ecstasies of the two before she addresses them.)

LOUKA. If you please, madam, all the windows are to be closed and the shutters made fast. They say there may be shooting in the streets. (Raina and Catherine rise together, alarmed.) The Servians are being chased right back through the pass; and they say they may run into the town. Our cavalry will be after them; and our people will be ready for them you may be sure, now that they are running away. (She goes out on the balcony and pulls the outside shutters to; then steps back into the room.)

RAINA. I wish our people were not so cruel. What glory is there in killing wretched fugitives?

CATHERINE (business-like, her housekeeping instincts aroused). I must see that everything is made safe downstairs.

RAINA (to Louka). Leave the shutters so that I can just close them if I hear any noise.

CATHERINE (authoritatively, turning on her way to the door). Oh, no, dear, you must keep them fastened. You would be sure to drop off to sleep and leave them open. Make them fast, Louka.

LOUKA. Yes, madam. (She fastens them.)

RAINA. Don't be anxious about me. The moment I hear a shot, I shall blow out the candles and roll myself up in bed with my ears well covered.

CATHERINE. Quite the wisest thing you can do, my love. Good-night.

RAINA. Good-night. (They kiss one another, and Raina's emotion comes back for a moment.) Wish me joy of the happiest night of my life—if only there are no fugitives.

CATHERINE. Go to bed, dear; and don't think of them. (She goes out.)

LOUKA (secretly, to Raina). If you would like the shutters open, just give them a push like this. (She pushes them: they open: she pulls them to again.) One of them ought to be bolted at the bottom; but the bolt's gone.

RAINA (with dignity, reproving her). Thanks, Louka; but we must do what we are told. (Louka makes a grimace.) Good-night.

LOUKA (carelessly). Good-night. (She goes out, swaggering.)

(Raina, left alone, goes to the chest of drawers, and adores the portrait there with feelings that are beyond all expression. She does not kiss it or press it to her breast, or shew it any mark of bodily affection; but she takes it in her hands and elevates it like a priestess.)

RAINA (looking up at the picture with worship.) Oh, I shall never be unworthy of you any more, my hero—never, never, never.

(She replaces it reverently, and selects a novel from the little pile of books. She turns over the leaves dreamily; finds her page; turns the book inside out at it; and then, with a happy sigh, gets into bed and prepares to read herself to sleep. But before abandoning herself to fiction, she raises her eyes once more, thinking of the blessed reality and murmurs)

My hero! my hero!

(A distant shot breaks the quiet of the night outside. She starts, listening; and two more shots, much nearer, follow, startling her so that she scrambles out of bed, and hastily blows out the candle on the chest of drawers. Then, putting her fingers in her ears, she runs to the dressing-table and blows out the light there, and hurries back to bed. The room is now in darkness: nothing is visible but the glimmer of the light in the pierced ball before the image, and the starlight seen through the slits at the top of the shutters. The firing breaks out again: there is a startling fusillade quite close at hand. Whilst it is still echoing, the shutters disappear, pulled open from without, and for an instant the rectangle of snowy starlight flashes out with the figure of a man in black upon it. The shutters close immediately and the room is dark again. But the silence is now broken by the sound of panting. Then there is a scrape; and the flame of a match is seen in the middle of the room.)

RAINA (crouching on the bed). Who's there? (The match is out instantly.) Who's there? Who is that?

A MAN'S VOICE (in the darkness, subduedly, but threateningly). Sh—sh! Don't call out or you'll be shot. Be good; and no harm will happen to you. (She is heard leaving her bed, and making for the door.) Take care, there's no use in trying to run away. Remember, if you raise your voice my pistol will go off. (Commandingly.) Strike a light and let me see you. Do you hear? (Another moment of silence and darkness. Then she is heard retreating to the dressing-table. She lights a candle, and the mystery is at an end. A man of about 35, in a deplorable plight, bespattered with mud and blood and snow, his belt and the strap of his revolver case keeping together the torn ruins of the blue coat of a Servian artillery officer. As far as the candlelight and his unwashed, unkempt condition make it possible to judge, he is a man of middling stature and undistinguished appearance, with strong neck and shoulders, a roundish, obstinate looking head covered with short crisp bronze curls, clear quick blue eyes and good brows and mouth, a hopelessly prosaic nose like that of a strong-minded baby, trim soldierlike carriage and energetic manner, and with all his wits about him in spite of his desperate predicament—even with a sense of humor of it, without, however, the least intention of trifling with it or throwing away a chance. He reckons up what he can guess about Raina—her age, her social position, her character, the extent to which she is frightened—at a glance, and continues, more politely but still most determinedly) Excuse my disturbing you; but you recognise my uniform—Servian. If I'm caught I shall be killed. (Determinedly.) Do you understand that?

RAINA. Yes.

MAN. Well, I don't intend to get killed if I can help it. (Still more determinedly.) Do you understand that? (He locks the door with a snap.)

RAINA (disdainfully). I suppose not. (She draws herself up superbly, and looks him straight in the face, saying with emphasis) Some soldiers, I know, are afraid of death.

MAN (with grim goodhumor). All of them, dear lady, all of them, believe me. It is our duty to live as long as we can, and kill as many of the enemy as we can. Now if you raise an alarm—

RAINA (cutting him short). You will shoot me. How do you know that I am afraid to die?

MAN (cunningly). Ah; but suppose I don't shoot you, what will happen then? Why, a lot of your cavalry—the greatest blackguards in your army—will burst into this pretty room of yours and slaughter me here like a pig; for I'll fight like a demon: they shan't get me into the street to amuse themselves with: I know what they are. Are you prepared to receive that sort of company in your present undress? (Raina, suddenly conscious of her nightgown, instinctively shrinks and gathers it more closely about her. He watches her, and adds, pitilessly) It's rather scanty, eh? (She turns to the ottoman. He raises his pistol instantly, and cries) Stop! (She stops.) Where are you going?

RAINA (with dignified patience). Only to get my cloak.

MAN (darting to the ottoman and snatching the cloak). A good idea. No: I'll keep the cloak: and you will take care that nobody comes in and sees you without it. This is a better weapon than the pistol. (He throws the pistol down on the ottoman.)

RAINA (revolted). It is not the weapon of a gentleman!

MAN. It's good enough for a man with only you to stand between him and death. (As they look at one another for a moment, Raina hardly able to believe that even a Servian officer can be so cynically and selfishly unchivalrous, they are startled by a sharp fusillade in the street. The chill of imminent death hushes the man's voice as he adds) Do you hear? If you are going to bring those scoundrels in on me you shall receive them as you are. (Raina meets his eye with unflinching scorn. Suddenly he starts, listening. There is a step outside. Someone tries the door, and then knocks hurriedly and urgently at it. Raina looks at the man, breathless. He throws up his head with the gesture of a man who sees that it is all over with him, and, dropping the manner which he has been assuming to intimidate her, flings the cloak to her, exclaiming, sincerely and kindly) No use: I'm done for. Quick! wrap yourself up: they're coming!

RAINA (catching the cloak eagerly). Oh, thank you. (She wraps herself up with great relief. He draws his sabre and turns to the door, waiting.)

LOUKA (outside, knocking). My lady, my lady! Get up, quick, and open the door.

RAINA (anxiously). What will you do?

MAN (grimly). Never mind. Keep out of the way. It will not last long.

RAINA (impulsively). I'll help you. Hide yourself, oh, hide yourself, quick, behind the curtain. (She seizes him by a torn strip of his sleeve, and pulls him towards the window.)

MAN (yielding to her). There is just half a chance, if you keep your head. Remember: nine soldiers out of ten are born fools. (He hides behind the curtain, looking out for a moment to say, finally) If they find me, I promise you a fight—a devil of a fight! (He disappears. Raina takes of the cloak and throws it across the foot of the bed. Then with a sleepy, disturbed air, she opens the door. Louka enters excitedly.)

LOUKA. A man has been seen climbing up the water-pipe to your balcony—a Servian. The soldiers want to search for him; and they are so wild and drunk and furious. My lady says you are to dress at once.

RAINA (as if annoyed at being disturbed). They shall not search here. Why have they been let in?

CATHERINE (coming in hastily). Raina, darling, are you safe? Have you seen anyone or heard anything?

RAINA. I heard the shooting. Surely the soldiers will not dare come in here?

CATHERINE. I have found a Russian officer, thank Heaven: he knows Sergius. (Speaking through the door to someone outside.) Sir, will you come in now! My daughter is ready.

(A young Russian officer, in Bulgarian uniform, enters, sword in hand.)

THE OFFICER. (with soft, feline politeness and stiff military carriage). Good evening, gracious lady; I am sorry to intrude, but there is a fugitive hiding on the balcony. Will you and the gracious lady your mother please to withdraw whilst we search?

RAINA (petulantly). Nonsense, sir, you can see that there is no one on the balcony. (She throws the shutters wide open and stands with her back to the curtain where the man is hidden, pointing to the moonlit balcony. A couple of shots are fired right under the window, and a bullet shatters the glass opposite Raina, who winks and gasps, but stands her ground, whilst Catherine screams, and the officer rushes to the balcony.)

THE OFFICER. (on the balcony, shouting savagely down to the street). Cease firing there, you fools: do you hear? Cease firing, damn you. (He glares down for a moment; then turns to Raina, trying to resume his polite manner.) Could anyone have got in without your knowledge? Were you asleep?

RAINA. No, I have not been to bed.

THE OFFICER. (impatiently, coming back into the room). Your neighbours have their heads so full of runaway Servians that they see them everywhere. (Politely.) Gracious lady, a thousand pardons. Goodnight. (Military bow, which Raina returns coldly. Another to Catherine, who follows him out. Raina closes the shutters. She turns and sees Louka, who has been watching the scene curiously.)

RAINA. Don't leave my mother, Louka, whilst the soldiers are here. (Louka glances at Raina, at the ottoman, at the curtain; then purses her lips secretively, laughs to herself, and goes out. Raina follows her to the door, shuts it behind her with a slam, and locks it violently. The man immediately steps out from behind the curtain, sheathing his sabre, and dismissing the danger from his mind in a businesslike way.)

MAN. A narrow shave; but a miss is as good as a mile. Dear young lady, your servant until death. I wish for your sake I had joined the Bulgarian army instead of the Servian. I am not a native Servian.

RAINA (haughtily). No, you are one of the Austrians who set the Servians on to rob us of our national liberty, and who officer their army for them. We hate them!

MAN. Austrian! not I. Don't hate me, dear young lady. I am only a Swiss, fighting merely as a professional soldier. I joined Servia because it was nearest to me. Be generous: you've beaten us hollow.

RAINA. Have I not been generous?

MAN. Noble!—heroic! But I'm not saved yet. This particular rush will soon pass through; but the pursuit will go on all night by fits and starts. I must take my chance to get off during a quiet interval. You don't mind my waiting just a minute or two, do you?

RAINA. Oh, no: I am sorry you will have to go into danger again. (Motioning towards ottoman.) Won't you sit—(She breaks off with an irrepressible cry of alarm as she catches sight of the pistol. The man, all nerves, shies like a frightened horse.)

MAN (irritably). Don't frighten me like that. What is it?

RAINA. Your pistol! It was staring that officer in the face all the time. What an escape!

MAN (vexed at being unnecessarily terrified). Oh, is that all?

RAINA (staring at him rather superciliously, conceiving a poorer and poorer opinion of him, and feeling proportionately more and more at her ease with him). I am sorry I frightened you. (She takes up the pistol and hands it to him.) Pray take it to protect yourself against me.

MAN (grinning wearily at the sarcasm as he takes the pistol). No use, dear young lady: there's nothing in it. It's not loaded. (He makes a grimace at it, and drops it disparagingly into his revolver case.)

RAINA. Load it by all means.

MAN. I've no ammunition. What use are cartridges in battle? I always carry chocolate instead; and I finished the last cake of that yesterday.

RAINA (outraged in her most cherished ideals of manhood). Chocolate! Do you stuff your pockets with sweets—like a schoolboy—even in the field?

MAN. Yes. Isn't it contemptible?

(Raina stares at him, unable to utter her feelings. Then she sails away scornfully to the chest of drawers, and returns with the box of confectionery in her hand.)

RAINA. Allow me. I am sorry I have eaten them all except these. (She offers him the box.)

MAN (ravenously). You're an angel! (He gobbles the comfits.) Creams! Delicious! (He looks anxiously to see whether there are any more. There are none. He accepts the inevitable with pathetic goodhumor, and says, with grateful emotion) Bless you, dear lady. You can always tell an old soldier by the inside of his holsters and cartridge boxes. The young ones carry pistols and cartridges; the old ones, grub. Thank you. (He hands back the box. She snatches it contemptuously from him and throws it away. This impatient action is so sudden that he shies again.) Ugh! Don't do things so suddenly, gracious lady. Don't revenge yourself because I frightened you just now.

RAINA (superbly). Frighten me! Do you know, sir, that though I am only a woman, I think I am at heart as brave as you.

MAN. I should think so. You haven't been under fire for three days as I have. I can stand two days without shewing it much; but no man can stand three days: I'm as nervous as a mouse. (He sits down on the ottoman, and takes his head in his hands.) Would you like to see me cry?

RAINA (quickly). No.

MAN. If you would, all you have to do is to scold me just as if I were a little boy and you my nurse. If I were in camp now they'd play all sorts of tricks on me.

RAINA (a little moved). I'm sorry. I won't scold you. (Touched by the sympathy in her tone, he raises his head and looks gratefully at her: she immediately draws hack and says stiffly) You must excuse me: our soldiers are not like that. (She moves away from the ottoman.)

MAN. Oh, yes, they are. There are only two sorts of soldiers: old ones and young ones. I've served fourteen years: half of your fellows never smelt powder before. Why, how is it that you've just beaten us? Sheer ignorance of the art of war, nothing else. (Indignantly.) I never saw anything so unprofessional.

RAINA (ironically). Oh, was it unprofessional to beat you?

MAN. Well, come, is it professional to throw a regiment of cavalry on a battery of machine guns, with the dead certainty that if the guns go off not a horse or man will ever get within fifty yards of the fire? I couldn't believe my eyes when I saw it.

RAINA (eagerly turning to him, as all her enthusiasm and her dream of glory rush back on her). Did you see the great cavalry charge? Oh, tell me about it. Describe it to me.

MAN. You never saw a cavalry charge, did you?

RAINA. How could I?

MAN. Ah, perhaps not—of course. Well, it's a funny sight. It's like slinging a handful of peas against a window pane: first one comes; then two or three close behind him; and then all the rest in a lump.

RAINA (her eyes dilating as she raises her clasped hands ecstatically). Yes, first One!—the bravest of the brave!

MAN (prosaically). Hm! you should see the poor devil pulling at his horse.

RAINA. Why should he pull at his horse?

MAN (impatient of so stupid a question). It's running away with him, of course: do you suppose the fellow wants to get there before the others and be killed? Then they all come. You can tell the young ones by their wildness and their slashing. The old ones come bunched up under the number one guard: they know that they are mere projectiles, and that it's no use trying to fight. The wounds are mostly broken knees, from the horses cannoning together.

RAINA. Ugh! But I don't believe the first man is a coward. I believe he is a hero!

MAN (goodhumoredly). That's what you'd have said if you'd seen the first man in the charge to-day.

RAINA (breathless). Ah, I knew it! Tell me—tell me about him.

MAN. He did it like an operatic tenor—a regular handsome fellow, with flashing eyes and lovely moustache, shouting a war-cry and charging like Don Quixote at the windmills. We nearly burst with laughter at him; but when the sergeant ran up as white as a sheet, and told us they'd sent us the wrong cartridges, and that we couldn't fire a shot for the next ten minutes, we laughed at the other side of our mouths. I never felt so sick in my life, though I've been in one or two very tight places. And I hadn't even a revolver cartridge—nothing but chocolate. We'd no bayonets—nothing. Of course, they just cut us to bits. And there was Don Quixote flourishing like a drum major, thinking he'd done the cleverest thing ever known, whereas he ought to be courtmartialled for it. Of all the fools ever let loose on a field of battle, that man must be the very maddest. He and his regiment simply committed suicide—only the pistol missed fire, that's all.

RAINA (deeply wounded, but steadfastly loyal to her ideals). Indeed! Would you know him again if you saw him?

MAN. Shall I ever forget him. (She again goes to the chest of drawers. He watches her with a vague hope that she may have something else for him to eat. She takes the portrait from its stand and brings it to him.)

RAINA. That is a photograph of the gentleman—the patriot and hero—to whom I am betrothed.

MAN (looking at it). I'm really very sorry. (Looking at her.) Was it fair to lead me on? (He looks at the portrait again.) Yes: that's him: not a doubt of it. (He stifles a laugh.)

RAINA (quickly). Why do you laugh?

MAN (shamefacedly, but still greatly tickled). I didn't laugh, I assure you. At least I didn't mean to. But when I think of him charging the windmills and thinking he was doing the finest thing—(chokes with suppressed laughter).

RAINA (sternly). Give me back the portrait, sir.

MAN (with sincere remorse). Of course. Certainly. I'm really very sorry. (She deliberately kisses it, and looks him straight in the face, before returning to the chest of drawers to replace it. He follows her, apologizing.) Perhaps I'm quite wrong, you know: no doubt I am. Most likely he had got wind of the cartridge business somehow, and knew it was a safe job.

RAINA. That is to say, he was a pretender and a coward! You did not dare say that before.

MAN (with a comic gesture of despair). It's no use, dear lady: I can't make you see it from the professional point of view. (As he turns away to get back to the ottoman, the firing begins again in the distance.)

RAINA (sternly, as she sees him listening to the shots). So much the better for you.

MAN (turning). How?

RAINA. You are my enemy; and you are at my mercy. What would I do if I were a professional soldier?

MAN. Ah, true, dear young lady: you're always right. I know how good you have been to me: to my last hour I shall remember those three chocolate creams. It was unsoldierly; but it was angelic.

RAINA (coldly). Thank you. And now I will do a soldierly thing. You cannot stay here after what you have just said about my future husband; but I will go out on the balcony and see whether it is safe for you to climb down into the street. (She turns to the window.)

MAN (changing countenance). Down that waterpipe! Stop! Wait! I can't! I daren't! The very thought of it makes me giddy. I came up it fast enough with death behind me. But to face it now in cold blood!—(He sinks on the ottoman.) It's no use: I give up: I'm beaten. Give the alarm. (He drops his head in his hands in the deepest dejection.)

RAINA (disarmed by pity). Come, don't be disheartened. (She stoops over him almost maternally: he shakes his head.) Oh, you are a very poor soldier—a chocolate cream soldier. Come, cheer up: it takes less courage to climb down than to face capture—remember that.

MAN (dreamily, lulled by her voice). No, capture only means death; and death is sleep—oh, sleep, sleep, sleep, undisturbed sleep! Climbing down the pipe means doing something—exerting myself—thinking! Death ten times over first.

RAINA (softly and wonderingly, catching the rhythm of his weariness). Are you so sleepy as that?

MAN. I've not had two hours' undisturbed sleep since the war began. I'm on the staff: you don't know what that means. I haven't closed my eyes for thirty-six hours.

RAINA (desperately). But what am I to do with you.

MAN (staggering up). Of course I must do something. (He shakes himself; pulls himself together; and speaks with rallied vigour and courage.) You see, sleep or no sleep, hunger or no hunger, tired or not tired, you can always do a thing when you know it must be done. Well, that pipe must be got down—(He hits himself on the chest, and adds)—Do you hear that, you chocolate cream soldier? (He turns to the window.)

RAINA (anxiously). But if you fall?

MAN. I shall sleep as if the stones were a feather bed. Good-bye. (He makes boldly for the window, and his hand is on the shutter when there is a terrible burst of firing in the street beneath.)

RAINA (rushing to him). Stop! (She catches him by the shoulder, and turns him quite round.) They'll kill you.

MAN (coolly, but attentively). Never mind: this sort of thing is all in my day's work. I'm bound to take my chance. (Decisively.) Now do what I tell you. Put out the candles, so that they shan't see the light when I open the shutters. And keep away from the window, whatever you do. If they see me, they're sure to have a shot at me.

RAINA (clinging to him). They're sure to see you: it's bright moonlight. I'll save you—oh, how can you be so indifferent? You want me to save you, don't you?

MAN. I really don't want to be troublesome. (She shakes him in her impatience.) I am not indifferent, dear young lady, I assure you. But how is it to be done?

RAINA. Come away from the window—please. (She coaxes him back to the middle of the room. He submits humbly. She releases him, and addresses him patronizingly.) Now listen. You must trust to our hospitality. You do not yet know in whose house you are. I am a Petkoff.

MAN. What's that?

RAINA (rather indignantly). I mean that I belong to the family of the Petkoffs, the richest and best known in our country.

MAN. Oh, yes, of course. I beg your pardon. The Petkoffs, to be sure. How stupid of me!

RAINA. You know you never heard of them until this minute. How can you stoop to pretend?

MAN. Forgive me: I'm too tired to think; and the change of subject was too much for me. Don't scold me.

RAINA. I forgot. It might make you cry. (He nods, quite seriously. She pouts and then resumes her patronizing tone.) I must tell you that my father holds the highest command of any Bulgarian in our army. He is (proudly) a Major.

MAN (pretending to be deeply impressed). A Major! Bless me! Think of that!

RAINA. You shewed great ignorance in thinking that it was necessary to climb up to the balcony, because ours is the only private house that has two rows of windows. There is a flight of stairs inside to get up and down by.

MAN. Stairs! How grand! You live in great luxury indeed, dear young lady.

RAINA. Do you know what a library is?

MAN. A library? A roomful of books.

RAINA. Yes, we have one, the only one in Bulgaria.

MAN. Actually a real library! I should like to see that.

RAINA (affectedly). I tell you these things to shew you that you are not in the house of ignorant country folk who would kill you the moment they saw your Servian uniform, but among civilized people. We go to Bucharest every year for the opera season; and I have spent a whole month in Vienna.

MAN. I saw that, dear young lady. I saw at once that you knew the world.

RAINA. Have you ever seen the opera of Ernani?

MAN. Is that the one with the devil in it in red velvet, and a soldier's chorus?

RAINA (contemptuously). No!

MAN (stifling a heavy sigh of weariness). Then I don't know it.

RAINA. I thought you might have remembered the great scene where Ernani, flying from his foes just as you are tonight, takes refuge in the castle of his bitterest enemy, an old Castilian noble. The noble refuses to give him up. His guest is sacred to him.

MAN (quickly waking up a little). Have your people got that notion?

RAINA (with dignity). My mother and I can understand that notion, as you call it. And if instead of threatening me with your pistol as you did, you had simply thrown yourself as a fugitive on our hospitality, you would have been as safe as in your father's house.

MAN. Quite sure?

RAINA (turning her back on him in disgust.) Oh, it is useless to try and make you understand.

MAN. Don't be angry: you see how awkward it would be for me if there was any mistake. My father is a very hospitable man: he keeps six hotels; but I couldn't trust him as far as that. What about YOUR father?

RAINA. He is away at Slivnitza fighting for his country. I answer for your safety. There is my hand in pledge of it. Will that reassure you? (She offers him her hand.)

MAN (looking dubiously at his own hand). Better not touch my hand, dear young lady. I must have a wash first.

RAINA (touched). That is very nice of you. I see that you are a gentleman.

MAN (puzzled). Eh?

RAINA. You must not think I am surprised. Bulgarians of really good standing—people in OUR position—wash their hands nearly every day. But I appreciate your delicacy. You may take my hand. (She offers it again.)

MAN (kissing it with his hands behind his back). Thanks, gracious young lady: I feel safe at last. And now would you mind breaking the news to your mother? I had better not stay here secretly longer than is necessary.

RAINA. If you will be so good as to keep perfectly still whilst I am away.

MAN. Certainly. (He sits down on the ottoman.)

(Raina goes to the bed and wraps herself in the fur cloak. His eyes close. She goes to the door, but on turning for a last look at him, sees that he is dropping off to sleep.)

RAINA (at the door). You are not going asleep, are you? (He murmurs inarticulately: she runs to him and shakes him.) Do you hear? Wake up: you are falling asleep.

MAN. Eh? Falling aslee—? Oh, no, not the least in the world: I was only thinking. It's all right: I'm wide awake.

RAINA (severely). Will you please stand up while I am away. (He rises reluctantly.) All the time, mind.

MAN (standing unsteadily). Certainly—certainly: you may depend on me.

(Raina looks doubtfully at him. He smiles foolishly. She goes reluctantly, turning again at the door, and almost catching him in the act of yawning. She goes out.)

MAN (drowsily). Sleep, sleep, sleep, sleep, slee—(The words trail off into a murmur. He wakes again with a shock on the point of falling.) Where am I? That's what I want to know: where am I? Must keep awake. Nothing keeps me awake except danger—remember that—(intently) danger, danger, danger, dan— Where's danger? Must find it. (He starts of vaguely around the room in search of it.) What am I looking for? Sleep—danger—don't know. (He stumbles against the bed.) Ah, yes: now I know. All right now. I'm to go to bed, but not to sleep—be sure not to sleep—because of danger. Not to lie down, either, only sit down. (He sits on the bed. A blissful expression comes into his face.) Ah! (With a happy sigh he sinks back at full length; lifts his boots into the bed with a final effort; and falls fast asleep instantly.)

(Catherine comes in, followed by Raina.)

RAINA (looking at the ottoman). He's gone! I left him here.

CATHERINE, Here! Then he must have climbed down from the—

RAINA (seeing him). Oh! (She points.)

CATHERINE (scandalized). Well! (She strides to the left side of the bed, Raina following and standing opposite her on the right.) He's fast asleep. The brute!

RAINA (anxiously). Sh!

CATHERINE (shaking him). Sir! (Shaking him again, harder.) Sir!! (Vehemently shaking very bard.) Sir!!!

RAINA (catching her arm). Don't, mamma: the poor dear is worn out. Let him sleep.

CATHERINE (letting him go and turning amazed to Raina). The poor dear! Raina!!! (She looks sternly at her daughter. The man sleeps profoundly.)

ACT II

The sixth of March, 1886. In the garden of major Petkoff's house. It is a fine spring morning; and the garden looks fresh and pretty. Beyond the paling the tops of a couple of minarets can be seen, shewing that there is a valley there, with the little town in it. A few miles further the Balkan mountains rise and shut in the view. Within the garden the side of the house is seen on the right, with a garden door reached by a little flight of steps. On the left the stable yard, with its gateway, encroaches on the garden. There are fruit bushes along the paling and house, covered with washing hung out to dry. A path runs by the house, and rises by two steps at the corner where it turns out of the right along the front. In the middle a small table, with two bent wood chairs at it, is laid for breakfast with Turkish coffee pot, cups, rolls, etc.; but the cups have been used and the bread broken. There is a wooden garden seat against the wall on the left.

Louka, smoking a cigaret, is standing between the table and the house, turning her back with angry disdain on a man-servant who is lecturing her. He is a middle-aged man of cool temperament and low but clear and keen intelligence, with the complacency of the servant who values himself on his rank in servility, and the imperturbability of the accurate calculator who has no illusions. He wears a white Bulgarian costume jacket with decorated harder, sash, wide knickerbockers, and decorated gaiters. His head is shaved up to the crown, giving him a high Japanese forehead. His name is Nicola.

NICOLA. Be warned in time, Louka: mend your manners. I know the mistress. She is so grand that she never dreams that any servant could dare to be disrespectful to her; but if she once suspects that you are defying her, out you go.

LOUKA. I do defy her. I will defy her. What do I care for her?

NICOLA. If you quarrel with the family, I never can marry you. It's the same as if you quarrelled with me!

LOUKA. You take her part against me, do you?

NICOLA (sedately). I shall always be dependent on the good will of the family. When I leave their service and start a shop in Sofia, their custom will be half my capital: their bad word would ruin me.

LOUKA. You have no spirit. I should like to see them dare say a word against me!

NICOLA (pityingly). I should have expected more sense from you, Louka. But you're young, you're young!

LOUKA. Yes; and you like me the better for it, don't you? But I know some family secrets they wouldn't care to have told, young as I am. Let them quarrel with me if they dare!

NICOLA (with compassionate superiority). Do you know what they would do if they heard you talk like that?

LOUKA. What could they do?

NICOLA. Discharge you for untruthfulness. Who would believe any stories you told after that? Who would give you another situation? Who in this house would dare be seen speaking to you ever again? How long would your father be left on his little farm? (She impatiently throws away the end of her cigaret, and stamps on it.) Child, you don't know the power such high people have over the like of you and me when we try to rise out of our poverty against them. (He goes close to her and lowers his voice.) Look at me, ten years in their service. Do you think I know no secrets? I know things about the mistress that she wouldn't have the master know for a thousand levas. I know things about him that she wouldn't let him hear the last of for six months if I blabbed them to her. I know things about Raina that would break off her match with Sergius if—

LOUKA (turning on him quickly). How do you know? I never told you!

NICOLA (opening his eyes cunningly). So that's your little secret, is it? I thought it might be something like that. Well, you take my advice, and be respectful; and make the mistress feel that no matter what you know or don't know, they can depend on you to hold your tongue and serve the family faithfully. That's what they like; and that's how you'll make most out of them.

LOUKA (with searching scorn). You have the soul of a servant, Nicola.

NICOLA (complacently). Yes: that's the secret of success in service.

(A loud knocking with a whip handle on a wooden door, outside on the left, is heard.)

MALE VOICE OUTSIDE. Hollo! Hollo there! Nicola!

LOUKA. Master! back from the war!

NICOLA (quickly). My word for it, Louka, the war's over. Off with you and get some fresh coffee. (He runs out into the stable yard.)

LOUKA (as she puts the coffee pot and the cups upon the tray, and carries it into the house). You'll never put the soul of a servant into me.

(Major Petkoff comes from the stable yard, followed by Nicola. He is a cheerful, excitable, insignificant, unpolished man of about 50, naturally unambitious except as to his income and his importance in local society, but just now greatly pleased with the military rank which the war has thrust on him as a man of consequence in his town. The fever of plucky patriotism which the Servian attack roused in all the Bulgarians has pulled him through the war; but he is obviously glad to be home again.)

PETKOFF (pointing to the table with his whip). Breakfast out here, eh?

NICOLA. Yes, sir. The mistress and Miss Raina have just gone in.

PETKOFF (fitting down and taking a roll). Go in and say I've come; and get me some fresh coffee.

NICOLA. It's coming, sir. (He goes to the house door. Louka, with fresh coffee, a clean cup, and a brandy bottle on her tray meets him.) Have you told the mistress?

LOUKA. Yes: she's coming.

(Nicola goes into the house. Louka brings the coffee to the table.)

PETKOFF. Well, the Servians haven't run away with you, have they?

LOUKA. No, sir.

PETKOFF. That's right. Have you brought me some cognac?

LOUKA (putting the bottle on the table). Here, sir.

PETKOFF. That's right. (He pours some into his coffee.)

(Catherine who has at this early hour made only a very perfunctory toilet, and wears a Bulgarian apron over a once brilliant, but now half worn out red dressing gown, and a colored handkerchief tied over her thick black hair, with Turkish slippers on her bare feet, comes from the house, looking astonishingly handsome and stately under all the circumstances. Louka goes into the house.)

CATHERINE. My dear Paul, what a surprise for us. (She stoops over the back of his chair to kiss him.) Have they brought you fresh coffee?

PETKOFF. Yes, Louka's been looking after me. The war's over. The treaty was signed three days ago at Bucharest; and the decree for our army to demobilize was issued yesterday.

CATHERINE (springing erect, with flashing eyes). The war over! Paul: have you let the Austrians force you to make peace?

PETKOFF (submissively). My dear: they didn't consult me. What could *I* do? (She sits down and turns away from him.) But of course we saw to it that the treaty was an honorable one. It declares peace—

CATHERINE (outraged). Peace!

PETKOFF (appeasing her).—but not friendly relations: remember that. They wanted to put that in; but I insisted on its being struck out. What more could I do?

CATHERINE. You could have annexed Servia and made Prince Alexander Emperor of the Balkans. That's what I would have done.

PETKOFF. I don't doubt it in the least, my dear. But I should have had to subdue the whole Austrian Empire first; and that would have kept me too long away from you. I missed you greatly.

CATHERINE (relenting). Ah! (Stretches her hand affectionately across the table to squeeze his.)

PETKOFF. And how have you been, my dear?

CATHERINE. Oh, my usual sore throats, that's all.

PETKOFF (with conviction). That comes from washing your neck every day. I've often told you so.

CATHERINE. Nonsense, Paul!

PETKOFF (over his coffee and cigaret). I don't believe in going too far with these modern customs. All this washing can't be good for the health: it's not natural. There was an Englishman at Phillipopolis who used to wet himself all over with cold water every morning when he got up. Disgusting! It all comes from the English: their climate makes them so dirty that they have to be perpetually washing themselves. Look at my father: he never had a bath in his life; and he lived to be ninety-eight, the healthiest man in Bulgaria. I don't mind a good wash once a week to keep up my position; but once a day is carrying the thing to a ridiculous extreme.

CATHERINE. You are a barbarian at heart still, Paul. I hope you behaved yourself before all those Russian officers.

PETKOFF. I did my best. I took care to let them know that we had a library.

CATHERINE. Ah; but you didn't tell them that we have an electric bell in it? I have had one put up.

PETKOFF. What's an electric bell?

CATHERINE. You touch a button; something tinkles in the kitchen; and then Nicola comes up.

PETKOFF. Why not shout for him?

CATHERINE. Civilized people never shout for their servants. I've learnt that while you were away.

PETKOFF. Well, I'll tell you something I've learnt, too. Civilized people don't hang out their washing to dry where visitors can see it; so you'd better have all that (indicating the clothes on the bushes) put somewhere else.

CATHERINE. Oh, that's absurd, Paul: I don't believe really refined people notice such things.

(Someone is heard knocking at the stable gates.)

PETKOFF. There's Sergius. (Shouting.) Hollo, Nicola!

CATHERINE. Oh, don't shout, Paul: it really isn't nice.

PETKOFF. Bosh! (He shouts louder than before.) Nicola!

NICOLA (appearing at the house door). Yes, sir.

PETKOFF. If that is Major Saranoff, bring him round this way. (He pronounces the name with the stress on the second syllable—Sarah-noff.)

NICOLA. Yes, sir. (He goes into the stable yard.)

PETKOFF. You must talk to him, my dear, until Raina takes him off our hands. He bores my life out about our not promoting him—over my head, mind you.

CATHERINE. He certainly ought to be promoted when he marries Raina. Besides, the country should insist on having at least one native general.

PETKOFF. Yes, so that he could throw away whole brigades instead of regiments. It's no use, my dear: he has not the slightest chance of promotion until we are quite sure that the peace will be a lasting one.

NICOLA (at the gate, announcing). Major Sergius Saranoff! (He goes into the house and returns presently with a third chair, which he places at the table. He then withdraws.)

(Major Sergius Saranoff, the original of the portrait in Raina's room, is a tall, romantically handsome man, with the physical hardihood, the high spirit, and the susceptible imagination of an untamed mountaineer chieftain. But his remarkable personal distinction is of a characteristically civilized type. The ridges of his eyebrows, curving with a ram's-horn twist round the marked projections at the outer corners, his jealously observant eye, his nose, thin, keen, and apprehensive in spite of the pugnacious high bridge and large nostril, his assertive chin, would not be out of place in a Paris salon. In short, the clever, imaginative barbarian has an acute critical faculty which has been thrown into intense activity by the arrival of western civilization in the Balkans; and the result is precisely what the advent of nineteenth-century thought first produced in England: to-wit, Byronism. By his brooding on the perpetual failure, not only of others, but of himself, to live up to his imaginative ideals, his consequent cynical scorn for humanity, the jejune credulity as to the absolute validity of his ideals and the unworthiness of the world in disregarding them, his wincings and mockeries under the sting of the petty disillusions which every hour spent among men brings to his infallibly quick observation, he has acquired the half tragic, half ironic air, the mysterious moodiness, the suggestion of a strange and terrible history that has left him nothing but undying remorse, by which Childe Harold fascinated the grandmothers of his English contemporaries. Altogether it is clear that here or nowhere is Raina's ideal hero. Catherine is hardly less enthusiastic, and much less reserved in shewing her enthusiasm. As he enters from the stable gate, she rises effusively to greet him. Petkoff is distinctly less disposed to make a fuss about him.)

PETKOFF. Here already, Sergius. Glad to see you!

CATHERINE. My dear Sergius!(She holds out both her hands.)

SERGIUS (kissing them with scrupulous gallantry). My dear mother, if I may call you so.

PETKOFF (drily). Mother-in-law, Sergius; mother-in-law! Sit down, and have some coffee.

SERGIUS. Thank you, none for me. (He gets away from the table with a certain distaste for Petkoff's enjoyment of it, and posts himself with conscious grace against the rail of the steps leading to the house.)

CATHERINE. You look superb—splendid. The campaign has improved you. Everybody here is mad about you. We were all wild with enthusiasm about that magnificent cavalry charge.

SERGIUS (with grave irony). Madam: it was the cradle and the grave of my military reputation.

CATHERINE. How so?

SERGIUS. I won the battle the wrong way when our worthy Russian generals were losing it the right way. That upset their plans, and wounded their self-esteem. Two of their colonels got their regiments driven back on the correct principles of scientific warfare. Two major-generals got killed strictly according to military etiquette. Those two colonels are now major-generals; and I am still a simple major.

CATHERINE. You shall not remain so, Sergius. The women are on your side; and they will see that justice is done you.

SERGIUS. It is too late. I have only waited for the peace to send in my resignation.

PETKOFF (dropping his cup in his amazement). Your resignation!

CATHERINE. Oh, you must withdraw it!

SERGIUS (with resolute, measured emphasis, folding his arms). I never withdraw!

PETKOFF (vexed). Now who could have supposed you were going to do such a thing?

SERGIUS (with fire). Everyone that knew me. But enough of myself and my affairs. How is Raina; and where is Raina?

RAINA (suddenly coming round the corner of the house and standing at the top of the steps in the path). Raina is here. (She makes a charming picture as they all turn to look at her. She wears an underdress of pale green silk, draped with an overdress of thin ecru canvas embroidered with gold. On her head she wears a pretty Phrygian cap of gold tinsel. Sergius, with an exclamation of pleasure, goes impulsively to meet her. She stretches out her hand: he drops chivalrously on one knee and kisses it.)

PETKOFF (aside to Catherine, beaming with parental pride). Pretty, isn't it? She always appears at the right moment.

CATHERINE (impatiently). Yes: she listens for it. It is an abominable habit.

(Sergius leads Raina forward with splendid gallantry, as if she were a queen. When they come to the table, she turns to him with a bend of the head; he bows; and thus they separate, he coming to his place, and she going behind her father's chair.)

RAINA (stooping and kissing her father). Dear father! Welcome home!

PETKOFF (patting her cheek). My little pet girl. (He kisses her; she goes to the chair left by Nicola for Sergius, and sits down.)

CATHERINE. And so you're no longer a soldier, Sergius.

SERGIUS. I am no longer a soldier. Soldiering, my dear madam, is the coward's art of attacking mercilessly when you are strong, and keeping out of harm's way when you are weak. That is the whole secret of successful fighting. Get your enemy at a disadvantage; and never, on any account, fight him on equal terms. Eh, Major!

PETKOFF. They wouldn't let us make a fair stand-up fight of it. However, I suppose soldiering has to be a trade like any other trade.

SERGIUS. Precisely. But I have no ambition to succeed as a tradesman; so I have taken the advice of that bagman of a captain that settled the exchange of prisoners with us at Peerot, and given it up.

PETKOFF. What, that Swiss fellow? Sergius: I've often thought of that exchange since. He over-reached us about those horses.

SERGIUS. Of course he over-reached us. His father was a hotel and livery stable keeper; and he owed his first step to his knowledge of horse-dealing. (With mock enthusiasm.) Ah, he was a soldier—every inch a soldier! If only I had bought the horses for my regiment instead of foolishly leading it into danger, I should have been a field-marshal now!

CATHERINE. A Swiss? What was he doing in the Servian army?

PETKOFF. A volunteer of course—keen on picking up his profession. (Chuckling.) We shouldn't have been able to begin fighting if these foreigners hadn't shewn us how to do it: we knew nothing about it; and neither did the Servians. Egad, there'd have been no war without them.

RAINA. Are there many Swiss officers in the Servian Army?

PETKOFF. No—all Austrians, just as our officers were all Russians. This was the only Swiss I came across. I'll never trust a Swiss again. He cheated us—humbugged us into giving him fifty able bodied men for two hundred confounded worn out chargers. They weren't even eatable!

SERGIUS. We were two children in the hands of that consummate soldier, Major: simply two innocent little children.

RAINA. What was he like?

CATHERINE. Oh, Raina, what a silly question!

SERGIUS. He was like a commercial traveller in uniform. Bourgeois to his boots.

PETKOFF (grinning). Sergius: tell Catherine that queer story his friend told us about him—how he escaped after Slivnitza. You remember?—about his being hid by two women.

SERGIUS (with bitter irony). Oh, yes, quite a romance. He was serving in the very battery I so unprofessionally charged. Being a thorough soldier, he ran away like the rest of them, with our cavalry at his heels. To escape their attentions, he had the good taste to take refuge in the chamber of some patriotic young Bulgarian lady. The young lady was enchanted by his persuasive commercial traveller's manners. She very modestly entertained him for an hour or so and then called in her mother lest her conduct should appear unmaidenly. The old lady was equally fascinated; and the fugitive was sent on his way in the morning, disguised in an old coat belonging to the master of the house, who was away at the war.

RAINA (rising with marked stateliness). Your life in the camp has made you coarse, Sergius. I did not think you would have repeated such a story before me. (She turns away coldly.)

CATHERINE (also rising). She is right, Sergius. If such women exist, we should be spared the knowledge of them.

PETKOFF. Pooh! nonsense! what does it matter?

SERGIUS (ashamed). No, Petkoff: I was wrong. (To Raina, with earnest humility.) I beg your pardon. I have behaved abominably. Forgive me, Raina. (She bows reservedly.) And you, too, madam. (Catherine bows graciously and sits down. He proceeds solemnly, again addressing Raina.) The glimpses I have had of the seamy side of life during the last few months have made me cynical; but I should not have brought my cynicism here—least of all into your presence, Raina. I—(Here, turning to the others, he is evidently about to begin a long speech when the Major interrupts him.)

PETKOFF. Stuff and nonsense, Sergius. That's quite enough fuss about nothing: a soldier's daughter should be able to stand up without flinching to a little strong conversation. (He rises.) Come: it's time for us to get to business. We have to make up our minds how those three regiments are to get back to Phillipopolis:—there's no forage for them on the Sofia route. (He goes towards the house.) Come along. (Sergius is about to follow him when Catherine rises and intervenes.)

CATHERINE. Oh, Paul, can't you spare Sergius for a few moments? Raina has hardly seen him yet. Perhaps I can help you to settle about the regiments.

SERGIUS (protesting). My dear madam, impossible: you—

CATHERINE (stopping him playfully). You stay here, my dear Sergius: there's no hurry. I have a word or two to say to Paul. (Sergius instantly bows and steps back.) Now, dear (taking Petkoff's arm), come and see the electric bell.

PETKOFF. Oh, very well, very well. (They go into the house together affectionately. Sergius, left alone with Raina, looks anxiously at her, fearing that she may be still offended. She smiles, and stretches out her arms to him.)

(Exit R. into house, followed by Catherine.)

SERGIUS (hastening to her, but refraining from touching her without express permission). Am I forgiven?

RAINA (placing her hands on his shoulder as she looks up at him with admiration and worship). My hero! My king.

SERGIUS. My queen! (He kisses her on the forehead with holy awe.)

RAINA. How I have envied you, Sergius! You have been out in the world, on the field of battle, able to prove yourself there worthy of any woman in the world; whilst I have had to sit at home inactive,—dreaming—useless—doing nothing that could give me the right to call myself worthy of any man.

SERGIUS. Dearest, all my deeds have been yours. You inspired me. I have gone through the war like a knight in a tournament with his lady looking on at him!

RAINA. And you have never been absent from my thoughts for a moment. (Very solemnly.) Sergius: I think we two have found the higher love. When I think of you, I feel that I could never do a base deed, or think an ignoble thought.

SERGIUS. My lady, and my saint! (Clasping her reverently.)

RAINA (returning his embrace). My lord and my g—

SERGIUS. Sh—sh! Let me be the worshipper, dear. You little know how unworthy even the best man is of a girl's pure passion!

RAINA. I trust you. I love you. You will never disappoint me, Sergius. (Louka is heard singing within the house. They quickly release each other.) Hush! I can't pretend to talk indifferently before her: my heart is too full. (Louka comes from the house with her tray. She goes to the table, and begins to clear it, with her back turned to them.) I will go and get my hat; and then we can go out until lunch time. Wouldn't you like that?

SERGIUS. Be quick. If you are away five minutes, it will seem five hours. (Raina runs to the top of the steps and turns there to exchange a look with him and wave him a kiss with both hands. He looks after her with emotion for a moment, then turns slowly away, his face radiant with the exultation of the scene which has just passed. The movement shifts his field of vision, into the corner of which there now comes the tail of Louka's double apron. His eye gleams at once. He takes a stealthy look at her, and begins to twirl his moustache nervously, with his left hand akimbo on his hip. Finally, striking the ground with his heels in something of a cavalry swagger, he strolls over to the left of the table, opposite her, and says) Louka: do you know what the higher love is?

LOUKA (astonished). No, sir.

SERGIUS. Very fatiguing thing to keep up for any length of time, Louka. One feels the need of some relief after it.

LOUKA (innocently). Perhaps you would like some coffee, sir? (She stretches her hand across the table for the coffee pot.)

SERGIUS (taking her hand). Thank you, Louka.

LOUKA (pretending to pull). Oh, sir, you know I didn't mean that. I'm surprised at you!

SERGIUS (coming clear of the table and drawing her with him). I am surprised at myself, Louka. What would Sergius, the hero of Slivnitza, say if he saw me now? What would Sergius, the apostle of the higher love, say if he saw me now? What would the half dozen Sergiuses who keep popping in and out of this handsome figure of mine say if they caught us here? (Letting go her hand and slipping his arm dexterously round her waist.) Do you consider my figure handsome, Louka?

LOUKA. Let me go, sir. I shall be disgraced. (She struggles: he holds her inexorably.) Oh, will you let go?

SERGIUS (looking straight into her eyes). No.

LOUKA. Then stand back where we can't be seen. Have you no common sense?

SERGIUS. Ah, that's reasonable. (He takes her into the stableyard gateway, where they are hidden from the house.)

LOUKA (complaining). I may have been seen from the windows: Miss Raina is sure to be spying about after you.

SERGIUS (stung—letting her go). Take care, Louka. I may be worthless enough to betray the higher love; but do not you insult it.

LOUKA (demurely). Not for the world, sir, I'm sure. May I go on with my work please, now?

SERGIUS (again putting his arm round her). You are a provoking little witch, Louka. If you were in love with me, would you spy out of windows on me?

LOUKA. Well, you see, sir, since you say you are half a dozen different gentlemen all at once, I should have a great deal to look after.

SERGIUS (charmed). Witty as well as pretty. (He tries to kiss her.)

LOUKA (avoiding him). No, I don't want your kisses. Gentlefolk are all alike—you making love to me behind Miss Raina's back, and she doing the same behind yours.

SERGIUS (recoiling a step). Louka!

LOUKA. It shews how little you really care!

SERGIUS (dropping his familiarity and speaking with freezing politeness). If our conversation is to continue, Louka, you will please remember that a gentleman does not discuss the conduct of the lady he is engaged to with her maid.

LOUKA. It's so hard to know what a gentleman considers right. I thought from your trying to kiss me that you had given up being so particular.

SERGIUS (turning from her and striking his forehead as he comes back into the garden from the gateway). Devil! devil!

LOUKA. Ha! ha! I expect one of the six of you is very like me, sir, though I am only Miss Raina's maid. (She goes back to her work at the table, taking no further notice of him.)

SERGIUS (speaking to himself). Which of the six is the real man?—that's the question that torments me. One of them is a hero, another a buffoon, another a humbug, another perhaps a bit of a blackguard. (He pauses and looks furtively at Louka, as he adds with deep bitterness) And one, at least, is a coward—jealous, like all cowards. (He goes to the table.) Louka.

LOUKA. Yes?

SERGIUS. Who is my rival?

LOUKA. You shall never get that out of me, for love or money.

SERGIUS. Why?

LOUKA. Never mind why. Besides, you would tell that I told you; and I should lose my place.

SERGIUS (holding out his right hand in affirmation). No; on the honor of a—(He checks himself, and his hand drops nerveless as he concludes, sardonically)—of a man capable of behaving as I have been behaving for the last five minutes. Who is he?

LOUKA. I don't know. I never saw him. I only heard his voice through the door of her room.

SERGIUS. Damnation! How dare you?

LOUKA (retreating). Oh, I mean no harm: you've no right to take up my words like that. The mistress knows all about it. And I tell you that if that gentleman ever comes here again, Miss Raina will marry him, whether he likes it or not. I know the difference between the sort of manner you and she put on before one another and the real manner. (Sergius shivers as if she had stabbed him. Then, setting his face like iron, he strides grimly to her, and grips her above the elbows with both bands.)

SERGIUS. Now listen you to me!

LOUKA (wincing). Not so tight: you're hurting me!

SERGIUS. That doesn't matter. You have stained my honor by making me a party to your eavesdropping. And you have betrayed your mistress—

LOUKA (writhing). Please—

SERGIUS. That shews that you are an abominable little clod of common clay, with the soul of a servant. (He lets her go as if she were an unclean thing, and turns away, dusting his hands of her, to the bench by the wall, where he sits down with averted head, meditating gloomily.)

LOUKA (whimpering angrily with her hands up her sleeves, feeling her bruised arms). You know how to hurt with your tongue as well as with your hands. But I don't care, now I've found out that whatever clay I'm made of, you're made of the same. As for her, she's a liar; and her fine airs are a cheat; and I'm worth six of her. (She shakes the pain off hardily; tosses her head; and sets to work to put the things on the tray. He looks doubtfully at her once or twice. She finishes packing the tray, and laps the cloth over the edges, so as to carry all out together. As she stoops to lift it, he rises.)

SERGIUS. Louka! (She stops and looks defiantly at him with the tray in her hands.) A gentleman has no right to hurt a woman under any circumstances. (With profound humility, uncovering his head.) I beg your pardon.

LOUKA. That sort of apology may satisfy a lady. Of what use is it to a servant?

SERGIUS (thus rudely crossed in his chivalry, throws it off with a bitter laugh and says slightingly). Oh, you wish to be paid for the hurt? (He puts on his shako, and takes some money from his pocket.)

LOUKA (her eyes filling with tears in spite of herself). No, I want my hurt made well.

SERGIUS (sobered by her tone). How?

(She rolls up her left sleeve; clasps her arm with the thumb and fingers of her right hand; and looks down at the bruise. Then she raises her head and looks straight at him. Finally, with a superb gesture she presents her arm to be kissed. Amazed, he looks at her; at the arm; at her again; hesitates; and then, with shuddering intensity, exclaims)

SERGIUS. Never! (and gets away as far as possible from her.)

(Her arm drops. Without a word, and with unaffected dignity, she takes her tray, and is approaching the house when Raina returns wearing a hat and jacket in the height of the Vienna fashion of the previous year, 1885. Louka makes way proudly for her, and then goes into the house.)

RAINA. I'm ready! What's the matter? (Gaily.) Have you been flirting with Louka?

SERGIUS (hastily). No, no. How can you think such a thing?

RAINA (ashamed of herself). Forgive me, dear: it was only a jest. I am so happy to-day.

(He goes quickly to her, and kisses her hand remorsefully. Catherine comes out and calls to them from the top of the steps.)

CATHERINE (coming down to them). I am sorry to disturb you, children; but Paul is distracted over those three regiments. He does not know how to get them to Phillipopolis; and he objects to every suggestion of mine. You must go and help him, Sergius. He is in the library.

RAINA (disappointed). But we are just going out for a walk.

SERGIUS. I shall not be long. Wait for me just five minutes. (He runs up the steps to the door.)

RAINA (following him to the foot of the steps and looking up at him with timid coquetry). I shall go round and wait in full view of the library windows. Be sure you draw father's attention to me. If you are a moment longer than five minutes, I shall go in and fetch you, regiments or no regiments.

SERGIUS (laughing). Very well. (He goes in. Raina watches him until he is out of her sight. Then, with a perceptible relaxation of manner, she begins to pace up and down about the garden in a brown study.)

CATHERINE. Imagine their meeting that Swiss and hearing the whole story! The very first thing your father asked for was the old coat we sent him off in. A nice mess you have got us into!

RAINA (gazing thoughtfully at the gravel as she walks). The little beast!

CATHERINE. Little beast! What little beast?

RAINA. To go and tell! Oh, if I had him here, I'd stuff him with chocolate creams till he couldn't ever speak again!

CATHERINE. Don't talk nonsense. Tell me the truth, Raina. How long was he in your room before you came to me?

RAINA (whisking round and recommencing her march in the opposite direction). Oh, I forget.

CATHERINE. You cannot forget! Did he really climb up after the soldiers were gone, or was he there when that officer searched the room?

RAINA. No. Yes, I think he must have been there then.

CATHERINE. You think! Oh, Raina, Raina! Will anything ever make you straightforward? If Sergius finds out, it is all over between you.

RAINA (with cool impertinence). Oh, I know Sergius is your pet. I sometimes wish you could marry him instead of me. You would just suit him. You would pet him, and spoil him, and mother him to perfection.

CATHERINE (opening her eyes very widely indeed). Well, upon my word!

RAINA (capriciously—half to herself). I always feel a longing to do or say something dreadful to him—to shock his propriety—to scandalize the five senses out of him! (To Catherine perversely.) I don't care whether he finds out about the chocolate cream soldier or not. I half hope he may. (She again turns flippantly away and strolls up the path to the corner of the house.)

CATHERINE. And what should I be able to say to your father, pray?

RAINA (over her shoulder, from the top of the two steps). Oh, poor father! As if he could help himself! (She turns the corner and passes out of sight.)

CATHERINE (looking after her, her fingers itching). Oh, if you were only ten years younger! (Louka comes from the house with a salver, which she carries hanging down by her side.) Well?

LOUKA. There's a gentleman just called, madam—a Servian officer—

CATHERINE (flaming). A Servian! How dare he—(Checking herself bitterly.) Oh, I forgot. We are at peace now. I suppose we shall have them calling every day to pay their compliments. Well, if he is an officer why don't you tell your master? He is in the library with Major Saranoff. Why do you come to me?

LOUKA. But he asks for you, madam. And I don't think he knows who you are: he said the lady of the house. He gave me this little ticket for you. (She takes a card out of her bosom; puts it on the salver and offers it to Catherine.)

CATHERINE (reading). "Captain Bluntschli!" That's a German name.

LOUKA. Swiss, madam, I think.

CATHERINE (with a bound that makes Louka jump back). Swiss! What is he like?

LOUKA (timidly). He has a big carpet bag, madam.

CATHERINE. Oh, Heavens, he's come to return the coat! Send him away—say we're not at home—ask him to leave his address and I'll write to him—Oh, stop: that will never do. Wait! (She throws herself into a chair to think it out. Louka waits.) The master and Major Saranoff are busy in the library, aren't they?

LOUKA. Yes, madam.

CATHERINE (decisively). Bring the gentleman out here at once. (Imperatively.) And be very polite to him. Don't delay. Here (impatiently snatching the salver from her): leave that here; and go straight back to him.

LOUKA. Yes, madam. (Going.)

CATHERINE. Louka!

LOUKA (stopping). Yes, madam.

CATHERINE. Is the library door shut?

LOUKA. I think so, madam.

CATHERINE. If not, shut it as you pass through.

LOUKA. Yes, madam. (Going.)

CATHERINE. Stop! (Louka stops.) He will have to go out that way (indicating the gate of the stable yard). Tell Nicola to bring his bag here after him. Don't forget.

LOUKA (surprised). His bag?

CATHERINE. Yes, here, as soon as possible. (Vehemently.) Be quick! (Louka runs into the house. Catherine snatches her apron off and throws it behind a bush. She then takes up the salver and uses it as a mirror, with the result that the handkerchief tied round her head follows the apron. A touch to her hair and a shake to her dressing gown makes her presentable.) Oh, how—how—how can a man be such a fool! Such a moment to select! (Louka appears at the door of the house, announcing "Captain Bluntschli;" and standing aside at the top of the steps to let him pass before she goes in again. He is the man of the adventure in Raina's room. He is now clean, well brushed, smartly uniformed, and out of trouble, but still unmistakably the same man. The moment Louka's back is turned, Catherine swoops on him with hurried, urgent, coaxing appeal.) Captain Bluntschli, I am very glad to see you; but you must leave this house at once. (He raises his eyebrows.) My husband has just returned, with my future son-in-law; and they know nothing. If they did, the consequences would be terrible. You are a foreigner: you do not feel our national animosities as we do. We still hate the Servians: the only effect of the peace on my husband is to make him feel like a lion baulked of his prey. If he discovered our secret, he would never forgive me; and my daughter's life would hardly be safe. Will you, like the chivalrous gentleman and soldier you are, leave at once before he finds you here?

BLUNTSCHLI (disappointed, but philosophical). At once, gracious lady. I only came to thank you and return the coat you lent me. If you will allow me to take it out of my bag and leave it with your servant as I pass out, I need detain you no further. (He turns to go into the house.)

CATHERINE (catching him by the sleeve). Oh, you must not think of going back that way. (Coaxing him across to the stable gates.) This is the shortest way out. Many thanks. So glad to have been of service to you. Good-bye.

BLUNTSCHLI. But my bag?

CATHERINE. It will be sent on. You will leave me your address.

BLUNTSCHLI. True. Allow me. (He takes out his card-case, and stops to write his address, keeping Catherine in an agony of impatience. As he hands her the card, Petkoff, hatless, rushes from the house in a fluster of hospitality, followed by Sergius.)

PETKOFF (as he hurries down the steps). My dear Captain Bluntschli—

CATHERINE. Oh Heavens! (She sinks on the seat against the wall.)

PETKOFF (too preoccupied to notice her as he shakes Bluntschli's hand heartily). Those stupid people of mine thought I was out here, instead of in the—haw!—library. (He cannot mention the library without betraying how proud he is of it.) I saw you through the window. I was wondering why you didn't come in. Saranoff is with me: you remember him, don't you?

SERGIUS (saluting humorously, and then offering his hand with great charm of manner). Welcome, our friend the enemy!

PETKOFF. No longer the enemy, happily. (Rather anxiously.) I hope you've come as a friend, and not on business.

CATHERINE. Oh, quite as a friend, Paul. I was just asking Captain Bluntschli to stay to lunch; but he declares he must go at once.

SERGIUS (sardonically). Impossible, Bluntschli. We want you here badly. We have to send on three cavalry regiments to Phillipopolis; and we don't in the least know how to do it.

BLUNTSCHLI (suddenly attentive and businesslike). Phillipopolis! The forage is the trouble, eh?

PETKOFF (eagerly). Yes, that's it. (To Sergius.) He sees the whole thing at once.

BLUNTSCHLI. I think I can shew you how to manage that.

SERGIUS. Invaluable man! Come along! (Towering over Bluntschli, he puts his hand on his shoulder and takes him to the steps, Petkoff following. As Bluntschli puts his foot on the first step, Raina comes out of the house.)

RAINA (completely losing her presence of mind). Oh, the chocolate cream soldier!

(Bluntschli stands rigid. Sergius, amazed, looks at Raina, then at Petkoff, who looks back at him and then at his wife.)

CATHERINE (with commanding presence of mind). My dear Raina, don't you see that we have a guest here—Captain Bluntschli, one of our new Servian friends?

(Raina bows; Bluntschli bows.)

RAINA. How silly of me! (She comes down into the centre of the group, between Bluntschli and Petkoff) I made a beautiful ornament this morning for the ice pudding; and that stupid Nicola has just put down a pile of plates on it and spoiled it. (To Bluntschli, winningly.) I hope you didn't think that you were the chocolate cream soldier, Captain Bluntschli.

BLUNTSCHLI (laughing). I assure you I did. (Stealing a whimsical glance at her.) Your explanation was a relief.

PETKOFF (suspiciously, to Raina). And since when, pray, have you taken to cooking?

CATHERINE. Oh, whilst you were away. It is her latest fancy.

PETKOFF (testily). And has Nicola taken to drinking? He used to be careful enough. First he shews Captain Bluntschli out here when he knew quite well I was in the—hum!—library; and then he goes downstairs and breaks Raina's chocolate soldier. He must—(At this moment Nicola appears at the top of the steps R., with a carpet bag. He descends; places it respectfully before Bluntschli; and waits for further orders. General amazement. Nicola, unconscious of the effect he is producing, looks perfectly satisfied with himself. When Petkoff recovers his power of speech, he breaks out at him with) Are you mad, Nicola?

NICOLA (taken aback). Sir?

PETKOFF. What have you brought that for?

NICOLA. My lady's orders, sir. Louka told me that—

CATHERINE (interrupting him). My orders! Why should I order you to bring Captain Bluntschli's luggage out here? What are you thinking of, Nicola?

NICOLA (after a moment's bewilderment, picking up the bag as he addresses Bluntschli with the very perfection of servile discretion). I beg your pardon, sir, I am sure. (To Catherine.) My fault, madam! I hope you'll overlook it! (He bows, and is going to the steps with the bag, when Petkoff addresses him angrily.)

PETKOFF. You'd better go and slam that bag, too, down on Miss Raina's ice pudding! (This is too much for Nicola. The bag drops from his hands on Petkoff's corns, eliciting a roar of anguish from him.) Begone, you butter-fingered donkey.

NICOLA (snatching up the bag, and escaping into the house). Yes, sir.

CATHERINE. Oh, never mind, Paul, don't be angry!

PETKOFF (muttering). Scoundrel. He's got out of hand while I was away. I'll teach him. (Recollecting his guest.) Oh, well, never mind. Come, Bluntschli, lets have no more nonsense about you having to go away. You know very well you're not going back to Switzerland yet. Until you do go back you'll stay with us.

RAINA. Oh, do, Captain Bluntschli.

PETKOFF (to Catherine). Now, Catherine, it's of you that he's afraid. Press him and he'll stay.

CATHERINE. Of course I shall be only too delighted if (appealingly) Captain Bluntschli really wishes to stay. He knows my wishes.

BLUNTSCHLI (in his driest military manner). I am at madame's orders.

SERGIUS (cordially). That settles it!

PETKOFF (heartily). Of course!

RAINA. You see, you must stay!

BLUNTSCHLI (smiling). Well, If I must, I must! (Gesture of despair from Catherine.)

ACT III

In the library after lunch. It is not much of a library, its literary equipment consisting of a single fixed shelf stocked with old paper-covered novels, broken backed, coffee stained, torn and thumbed, and a couple of little hanging shelves with a few gift books on them, the rest of the wall space being occupied by trophies of war and the chase. But it is a most comfortable sitting-room. A row of three large windows in the front of the house shew a mountain panorama, which is just now seen in one of its softest aspects in the mellowing afternoon light. In the left hand corner, a square earthenware stove, a perfect tower of colored pottery, rises nearly to the ceiling and guarantees plenty of warmth. The ottoman in the middle is a circular bank of decorated cushions, and the window seats are well upholstered divans. Little Turkish tables, one of them with an elaborate hookah on it, and a screen to match them, complete the handsome effect of the furnishing. There is one object, however, which is hopelessly out of keeping with its surroundings. This is a small kitchen table, much the worse for wear, fitted as a writing table with an old canister full of pens, an eggcup filled with ink, and a deplorable scrap of severely used pink blotting paper.

At the side of this table, which stands on the right, Bluntschli is hard at work, with a couple of maps before him, writing orders. At the head of it sits Sergius, who is also supposed to be at work, but who is actually gnawing the feather of a pen, and contemplating Bluntschli's quick, sure, businesslike progress with a mixture of envious irritation at his own incapacity, and awestruck wonder at an ability which seems to him almost miraculous, though its prosaic character forbids him to esteem it. The major is comfortably established on the ottoman, with a newspaper in his hand and the tube of the hookah within his reach. Catherine sits at the stove, with her back to them, embroidering. Raina, reclining on the divan under the left hand window, is gazing in a daydream out at the Balkan landscape, with a neglected novel in her lap.

The door is on the left. The button of the electric bell is between the door and the fireplace.

PETKOFF (looking up from his paper to watch how they are getting on at the table). Are you sure I can't help you in any way, Bluntschli?

BLUNTSCHLI (without interrupting his writing or looking up). Quite sure, thank you. Saranoff and I will manage it.

SERGIUS (grimly). Yes: we'll manage it. He finds out what to do; draws up the orders; and I sign 'em. Division of labour, Major. (Bluntschli passes him a paper.) Another one? Thank you. (He plants the papers squarely before him; sets his chair carefully parallel to them; and signs with the air of a man resolutely performing a difficult and dangerous feat.) This hand is more accustomed to the sword than to the pen.

PETKOFF. It's very good of you, Bluntschli, it is indeed, to let yourself be put upon in this way. Now are you quite sure I can do nothing?

CATHERINE (in a low, warning tone). You can stop interrupting, Paul.

PETKOFF (starting and looking round at her). Eh? Oh! Quite right, my love, quite right. (He takes his newspaper up, but lets it drop again.) Ah, you haven't been campaigning, Catherine: you don't know how pleasant it is for us to sit here, after a good lunch, with nothing to do but enjoy ourselves. There's only one thing I want to make me thoroughly comfortable.

CATHERINE. What is that?

PETKOFF. My old coat. I'm not at home in this one: I feel as if I were on parade.

CATHERINE. My dear Paul, how absurd you are about that old coat! It must be hanging in the blue closet where you left it.

PETKOFF. My dear Catherine, I tell you I've looked there. Am I to believe my own eyes or not? (Catherine quietly rises and presses the button of the electric bell by the fireplace.) What are you shewing off that bell for? (She looks at him majestically, and silently resumes her chair and her needlework.) My dear: if you think the obstinacy of your sex can make a coat out of two old dressing gowns of Raina's, your waterproof, and my mackintosh, you're mistaken. That's exactly what the blue closet contains at present. (Nicola presents himself.)

CATHERINE (unmoved by Petkoff's sally). Nicola: go to the blue closet and bring your master's old coat here—the braided one he usually wears in the house.

NICOLA. Yes, madam. (Nicola goes out.)

PETKOFF. Catherine.

CATHERINE. Yes, Paul?

PETKOFF. I bet you any piece of jewellery you like to order from Sofia against a week's housekeeping money, that the coat isn't there.

CATHERINE. Done, Paul.

PETKOFF (excited by the prospect of a gamble). Come: here's an opportunity for some sport. Who'll bet on it? Bluntschli: I'll give you six to one.

BLUNTSCHLI (imperturbably). It would be robbing you, Major. Madame is sure to be right. (Without looking up, he passes another batch of papers to Sergius.)

SERGIUS (also excited). Bravo, Switzerland! Major: I bet my best charger against an Arab mare for Raina that Nicola finds the coat in the blue closet.

PETKOFF (eagerly). Your best char—

CATHERINE (hastily interrupting him). Don't be foolish, Paul. An Arabian mare will cost you 50,000 levas.

RAINA (suddenly coming out of her picturesque revery). Really, mother, if you are going to take the jewellery, I don't see why you should grudge me my Arab.

(Nicola comes back with the coat and brings it to Petkoff, who can hardly believe his eyes.)

CATHERINE. Where was it, Nicola?

NICOLA. Hanging in the blue closet, madam.

PETKOFF. Well, I am d—

CATHERINE (stopping him). Paul!

PETKOFF. I could have sworn it wasn't there. Age is beginning to tell on me. I'm getting hallucinations. (To Nicola.) Here: help me to change. Excuse me, Bluntschli. (He begins changing coats, Nicola acting as valet.) Remember: I didn't take that bet of yours, Sergius. You'd better give Raina that Arab steed yourself, since you've roused her expectations. Eh, Raina? (He looks round at her; but she is again rapt in the landscape. With a little gush of paternal affection and pride, he points her out to them and says) She's dreaming, as usual.

SERGIUS. Assuredly she shall not be the loser.

PETKOFF. So much the better for her. I shan't come off so cheap, I expect. (The change is now complete. Nicola goes out with the discarded coat.) Ah, now I feel at home at last. (He sits down and takes his newspaper with a grunt of relief.)

BLUNTSCHLI (to Sergius, handing a paper). That's the last order.

PETKOFF (jumping up). What! finished?

BLUNTSCHLI. Finished. (Petkoff goes beside Sergius; looks curiously over his left shoulder as he signs; and says with childlike envy) Haven't you anything for me to sign?

BLUNTSCHLI. Not necessary. His signature will do.

PETKOFF. Ah, well, I think we've done a thundering good day's work. (He goes away from the table.) Can I do anything more?

BLUNTSCHLI. You had better both see the fellows that are to take these. (To Sergius.) Pack them off at once; and shew them that I've marked on the orders the time they should hand them in by. Tell them that if they stop to drink or tell stories—if they're five minutes late, they'll have the skin taken off their backs.

SERGIUS (rising indignantly). I'll say so. And if one of them is man enough to spit in my face for insulting him, I'll buy his discharge and give him a pension. (He strides out, his humanity deeply outraged.)

BLUNTSCHLI (confidentially). Just see that he talks to them properly, Major, will you?

PETKOFF (officiously). Quite right, Bluntschli, quite right. I'll see to it. (He goes to the door importantly, but hesitates on the threshold.) By the bye, Catherine, you may as well come, too. They'll be far more frightened of you than of me.

CATHERINE (putting down her embroidery). I daresay I had better. You will only splutter at them. (She goes out, Petkoff holding the door for her and following her.)

BLUNTSCHLI. What a country! They make cannons out of cherry trees; and the officers send for their wives to keep discipline! (He begins to fold and docket the papers. Raina, who has risen from the divan, strolls down the room with her hands clasped behind her, and looks mischievously at him.)

RAINA. You look ever so much nicer than when we last met. (He looks up, surprised.) What have you done to yourself?

BLUNTSCHLI. Washed; brushed; good night's sleep and breakfast. That's all.

RAINA. Did you get back safely that morning?

BLUNTSCHLI. Quite, thanks.

RAINA. Were they angry with you for running away from Sergius's charge?

BLUNTSCHLI. No, they were glad; because they'd all just run away themselves.

RAINA (going to the table, and leaning over it towards him). It must have made a lovely story for them—all that about me and my room.

BLUNTSCHLI. Capital story. But I only told it to one of them—a particular friend.

RAINA. On whose discretion you could absolutely rely?

BLUNTSCHLI. Absolutely.

RAINA. Hm! He told it all to my father and Sergius the day you exchanged the prisoners. (She turns away and strolls carelessly across to the other side of the room.)

BLUNTSCHLI (deeply concerned and half incredulous). No! you don't mean that, do you?

RAINA (turning, with sudden earnestness). I do indeed. But they don't know that it was in this house that you hid. If Sergius knew, he would challenge you and kill you in a duel.

BLUNTSCHLI. Bless me! then don't tell him.

RAINA (full of reproach for his levity). Can you realize what it is to me to deceive him? I want to be quite perfect with Sergius—no meanness, no smallness, no deceit. My relation to him is the one really beautiful and noble part of my life. I hope you can understand that.

BLUNTSCHLI (sceptically). You mean that you wouldn't like him to find out that the story about the ice pudding was a—a—a—You know.

RAINA (wincing). Ah, don't talk of it in that flippant way. I lied: I know it. But I did it to save your life. He would have killed you. That was the second time I ever uttered a falsehood. (Bluntschli rises quickly and looks doubtfully and somewhat severely at her.) Do you remember the first time?

BLUNTSCHLI. I! No. Was I present?

RAINA. Yes; and I told the officer who was searching for you that you were not present.

BLUNTSCHLI. True. I should have remembered it.

RAINA (greatly encouraged). Ah, it is natural that you should forget it first. It cost you nothing: it cost me a lie!—a lie!! (She sits down on the ottoman, looking straight before her with her hands clasped on her knee. Bluntschli, quite touched, goes to the ottoman with a particularly reassuring and considerate air, and sits down beside her.)

BLUNTSCHLI. My dear young lady, don't let this worry you. Remember: I'm a soldier. Now what are the two things that happen to a soldier so often that he comes to think nothing of them? One is hearing people tell lies (Raina recoils): the other is getting his life saved in all sorts of ways by all sorts of people.

RAINA (rising in indignant protest). And so he becomes a creature incapable of faith and of gratitude.

BLUNTSCHLI (making a wry face). Do you like gratitude? I don't. If pity is akin to love, gratitude is akin to the other thing.

RAINA. Gratitude! (Turning on him.) If you are incapable of gratitude you are incapable of any noble sentiment. Even animals are grateful. Oh, I see now exactly what you think of me! You were not surprised to hear me lie. To you it was something I probably did every day—every hour. That is how men think of women. (She walks up the room melodramatically.)

BLUNTSCHLI (dubiously). There's reason in everything. You said you'd told only two lies in your whole life. Dear young lady: isn't that rather a short allowance? I'm quite a straightforward man myself; but it wouldn't last me a whole morning.

RAINA (staring haughtily at him). Do you know, sir, that you are insulting me?

BLUNTSCHLI. I can't help it. When you get into that noble attitude and speak in that thrilling voice, I admire you; but I find it impossible to believe a single word you say.

RAINA (superbly). Captain Bluntschli!

BLUNTSCHLI (unmoved). Yes?

RAINA (coming a little towards him, as if she could not believe her senses). Do you mean what you said just now? Do you know what you said just now?

BLUNTSCHLI. I do.

RAINA (gasping). I! I!!! (She points to herself incredulously, meaning "I, Raina Petkoff, tell lies!" He meets her gaze unflinchingly. She suddenly sits down beside him, and adds, with a complete change of manner from the heroic to the familiar) How did you find me out?

BLUNTSCHLI (promptly). Instinct, dear young lady. Instinct, and experience of the world.

RAINA (wonderingly). Do you know, you are the first man I ever met who did not take me seriously?

BLUNTSCHLI. You mean, don't you, that I am the first man that has ever taken you quite seriously?

RAINA. Yes, I suppose I do mean that. (Cosily, quite at her ease with him.) How strange it is to be talked to in such a way! You know, I've always gone on like that—I mean the noble attitude and the thrilling voice. I did it when I was a tiny child to my nurse. She believed in it. I do it before my parents.

They believe in it. I do it before Sergius. He believes in it.

BLUNTSCHLI. Yes: he's a little in that line himself, isn't he?

RAINA (startled). Do you think so?

BLUNTSCHLI. You know him better than I do.

RAINA. I wonder—I wonder is he? If I thought that—! (Discouraged.) Ah, well, what does it matter? I suppose, now that you've found me out, you despise me.

BLUNTSCHLI (warmly, rising). No, my dear young lady, no, no, no a thousand times. It's part of your youth—part of your charm. I'm like all the rest of them—the nurse—your parents—Sergius: I'm your infatuated admirer.

RAINA (pleased). Really?

BLUNTSCHLI (slapping his breast smartly with his hand, German fashion). Hand aufs Herz! Really and truly.

RAINA (very happy). But what did you think of me for giving you my portrait?

BLUNTSCHLI (astonished). Your portrait! You never gave me your portrait.

RAINA (quickly). Do you mean to say you never got it?

BLUNTSCHLI. No. (He sits down beside her, with renewed interest, and says, with some complacency.) When did you send it to me?

RAINA (indignantly). I did not send it to you. (She turns her head away, and adds, reluctantly.) It was in the pocket of that coat.

BLUNTSCHLI (pursing his lips and rounding his eyes). Oh-o-oh! I never found it. It must be there still.

RAINA (springing up). There still!—for my father to find the first time he puts his hand in his pocket! Oh, how could you be so stupid?

BLUNTSCHLI (rising also). It doesn't matter: it's only a photograph: how can he tell who it was intended for? Tell him he put it there himself.

RAINA (impatiently). Yes, that is so clever—so clever! What shall I do?

BLUNTSCHLI. Ah, I see. You wrote something on it. That was rash!

RAINA (annoyed almost to tears). Oh, to have done such a thing for you, who care no more—except to laugh at me—oh! Are you sure nobody has touched it?

BLUNTSCHLI. Well, I can't be quite sure. You see I couldn't carry it about with me all the time: one can't take much luggage on active service.

RAINA. What did you do with it?

BLUNTSCHLI. When I got through to Peerot I had to put it in safe keeping somehow. I thought of the railway cloak room; but that's the surest place to get looted in modern warfare. So I pawned it.

RAINA. Pawned it!!!

BLUNTSCHLI. I know it doesn't sound nice; but it was much the safest plan. I redeemed it the day before yesterday. Heaven only knows whether the pawnbroker cleared out the pockets or not.

RAINA (furious—throwing the words right into his face). You have a low, shopkeeping mind. You think of things that would never come into a gentleman's head.

BLUNTSCHLI (phlegmatically). That's the Swiss national character, dear lady.

RAINA. Oh, I wish I had never met you. (She flounces away and sits at the window fuming.)

(Louka comes in with a heap of letters and telegrams on her salver, and crosses, with her bold, free gait, to the table. Her left sleeve is looped up to the shoulder with a brooch, shewing her naked arm, with a broad gilt bracelet covering the bruise.)

LOUKA (to Bluntschli). For you. (She empties the salver recklessly on the table.) The messenger is waiting. (She is determined not to be civil to a Servian, even if she must bring him his letters.)

BLUNTSCHLI (to Raina). Will you excuse me: the last postal delivery that reached me was three weeks ago. These are the subsequent accumulations. Four telegrams—a week old. (He opens one.) Oho! Bad news!

RAINA (rising and advancing a little remorsefully). Bad news?

BLUNTSCHLI. My father's dead. (He looks at the telegram with his lips pursed, musing on the unexpected change in his arrangements.)

RAINA. Oh, how very sad!

BLUNTSCHLI. Yes: I shall have to start for home in an hour. He has left a lot of big hotels behind him to be looked after. (Takes up a heavy letter in a long blue envelope.) Here's a whacking letter from the family solicitor. (He pulls out the enclosures and glances over them.) Great Heavens! Seventy! Two hundred! (In a crescendo of dismay.) Four hundred! Four thousand!! Nine thousand six hundred!!! What on earth shall I do with them all?

RAINA (timidly). Nine thousand hotels?

BLUNTSCHLI. Hotels! Nonsense. If you only knew!—oh, it's too ridiculous! Excuse me: I must give my fellow orders about starting. (He leaves the room hastily, with the documents in his hand.)

LOUKA (tauntingly). He has not much heart, that Swiss, though he is so fond of the Servians. He has not a word of grief for his poor father.

RAINA (bitterly). Grief!—a man who has been doing nothing but killing people for years! What does he care? What does any soldier care? (She goes to the door, evidently restraining her tears with difficulty.)

LOUKA. Major Saranoff has been fighting, too; and he has plenty of heart left. (Raina, at the door, looks haughtily at her and goes out.) Aha! I thought you wouldn't get much feeling out of your soldier. (She is following Raina when Nicola enters with an armful of logs for the fire.)

NICOLA (grinning amorously at her). I've been trying all the afternoon to get a minute alone with you, my girl. (His countenance changes as he notices her arm.) Why, what fashion is that of wearing your sleeve, child?

LOUKA (proudly). My own fashion.

NICOLA. Indeed! If the mistress catches you, she'll talk to you. (He throws the logs down on the ottoman, and sits comfortably beside them.)

LOUKA. Is that any reason why you should take it on yourself to talk to me?

NICOLA. Come: don't be so contrary with me. I've some good news for you. (He takes out some paper money. Louka, with an eager gleam in her eyes, comes close to look at it.) See, a twenty leva bill! Sergius gave me that out of pure swagger. A fool and his money are soon parted. There's ten levas more. The Swiss gave me that for backing up the mistress's and Raina's lies about him. He's no fool, he isn't. You should have heard old Catherine downstairs as polite as you please to me, telling me not to mind the Major being a little impatient; for they knew what a good servant I was—after making a fool and a liar of me before them all! The twenty will go to our savings; and you shall have the ten to spend if you'll only talk to me so as to remind me I'm a human being. I get tired of being a servant occasionally.

LOUKA (scornfully). Yes: sell your manhood for thirty levas, and buy me for ten! Keep your money. You were born to be a servant. I was not. When you set up your shop you will only be everybody's servant instead of somebody's servant.

NICOLA (picking up his logs, and going to the stove). Ah, wait till you see. We shall have our evenings to ourselves; and I shall be master in my own house, I promise you. (He throws the logs down and kneels at the stove.)

LOUKA. You shall never be master in mine. (She sits down on Sergius's chair.)

NICOLA (turning, still on his knees, and squatting down rather forlornly, on his calves, daunted by her implacable disdain). You have a great ambition in you, Louka. Remember: if any luck comes to you, it was I that made a woman of you.

LOUKA. You!

NICOLA (with dogged self-assertion). Yes, me. Who was it made you give up wearing a couple of pounds of false black hair on your head and reddening your lips and cheeks like any other Bulgarian girl? I did. Who taught you to trim your nails, and keep your hands clean, and be dainty about yourself, like a fine Russian lady? Me! do you hear that? me! (She tosses her head defiantly; and he rises, ill-humoredly, adding more coolly) I've often thought that if Raina were out of the way, and you just a little less of a fool and Sergius just a little more of one, you might come to be one of my grandest customers, instead of only being my wife and costing me money.

LOUKA. I believe you would rather be my servant than my husband. You would make more out of me. Oh, I know that soul of yours.

NICOLA (going up close to her for greater emphasis). Never you mind my soul; but just listen to my advice. If you want to be a lady, your present behaviour to me won't do at all, unless when we're alone. It's too sharp and imprudent; and impudence is a sort of familiarity: it shews affection for me. And don't you try being high and mighty with me either. You're like all country girls: you think it's genteel to treat a servant the way I treat a stable-boy. That's only your ignorance; and don't you forget it. And don't be so ready to defy everybody. Act as if you expected to have your own way, not as if you expected to be ordered about. The way to get on as a lady is the same as the way to get on as a servant: you've got to know your place; that's the secret of it. And you may depend on me to know my place if you get promoted. Think over it, my girl. I'll stand by you: one servant should always stand by another.

LOUKA (rising impatiently). Oh, I must behave in my own way. You take all the courage out of me with your cold-blooded wisdom. Go and put those logs on the fire: that's the sort of thing you understand. (Before Nicola can retort, Sergius comes in. He checks himself a moment on seeing Louka; then goes to the stove.)

SERGIUS (to Nicola). I am not in the way of your work, I hope.

NICOLA (in a smooth, elderly manner). Oh, no, sir, thank you kindly. I was only speaking to this foolish girl about her habit of running up here to the library whenever she gets a chance, to look at the books. That's the worst of her education, sir: it gives her habits above her station. (To Louka.) Make that table tidy, Louka, for the Major. (He goes out sedately.)

(Louka, without looking at Sergius, begins to arrange the papers on the table. He crosses slowly to her, and studies the arrangement of her sleeve reflectively.)

SERGIUS. Let me see: is there a mark there? (He turns up the bracelet and sees the bruise made by his grasp. She stands motionless, not looking at him: fascinated, but on her guard.) Ffff! Does it hurt?

LOUKA. Yes.

SERGIUS. Shall I cure it?

LOUKA (instantly withdrawing herself proudly, but still not looking at him). No. You cannot cure it now.

SERGIUS (masterfully). Quite sure? (He makes a movement as if to take her in his arms.)

LOUKA. Don't trifle with me, please. An officer should not trifle with a servant.

SERGIUS (touching the arm with a merciless stroke of his forefinger). That was no trifle, Louka.

LOUKA. No. (Looking at him for the first time.) Are you sorry?

SERGIUS (with measured emphasis, folding his arms). I am never sorry.

LOUKA (wistfully). I wish I could believe a man could be so unlike a woman as that. I wonder are you really a brave man?

SERGIUS (unaffectedly, relaxing his attitude). Yes: I am a brave man. My heart jumped like a woman's at the first shot; but in the charge I found that I was brave. Yes: that at least is real about me.

LOUKA. Did you find in the charge that the men whose fathers are poor like mine were any less brave than the men who are rich like you?

SERGIUS (with bitter levity.) Not a bit. They all slashed and cursed and yelled like heroes. Psha! the courage to rage and kill is cheap. I have an English bull terrier who has as much of that sort of courage as the whole Bulgarian nation, and the whole Russian nation at its back. But he lets my groom thrash him, all the same. That's your soldier all over! No, Louka, your poor men can cut throats; but they are afraid of their officers; they put up with insults and blows; they stand by and see one another punished like children—-aye, and help to do it when they are ordered. And the officers!—-well (with a short, bitter laugh) I am an officer. Oh, (fervently) give me the man who will defy to the death any power on earth or in heaven that sets itself up against his own will and conscience: he alone is the brave man.

LOUKA. How easy it is to talk! Men never seem to me to grow up: they all have schoolboy's ideas. You don't know what true courage is.

SERGIUS (ironically). Indeed! I am willing to be instructed.

LOUKA. Look at me! how much am I allowed to have my own will? I have to get your room ready for you—to sweep and dust, to fetch and carry. How could that degrade me if it did not degrade you to have it done for you? But (with subdued passion) if I were Empress of Russia, above everyone in the world, then—ah, then, though according to you I could shew no courage at all; you should see, you should see.

SERGIUS. What would you do, most noble Empress?

LOUKA. I would marry the man I loved, which no other queen in Europe has the courage to do. If I loved you, though you would be as far beneath me as I am beneath you, I would dare to be the equal of my inferior. Would you dare as much if you loved me? No: if you felt the beginnings of love for me you would not let it grow. You dare not: you would marry a rich man's daughter because you would be afraid of what other people would say of you.

SERGIUS (carried away). You lie: it is not so, by all the stars! If I loved you, and I were the Czar himself, I would set you on the throne by my side. You know that I love another woman, a woman as high above you as heaven is above earth. And you are jealous of her.

LOUKA. I have no reason to be. She will never marry you now. The man I told you of has come back. She will marry the Swiss.

SERGIUS (recoiling). The Swiss!

LOUKA. A man worth ten of you. Then you can come to me; and I will refuse you. You are not good enough for me. (She turns to the door.)

SERGIUS (springing after her and catching her fiercely in his arms). I will kill the Swiss; and afterwards I will do as I please with you.

LOUKA (in his arms, passive and steadfast). The Swiss will kill you, perhaps. He has beaten you in love. He may beat you in war.

SERGIUS (tormentedly). Do you think I believe that she—she! whose worst thoughts are higher than your best ones, is capable of trifling with another man behind my back?

LOUKA. Do you think she would believe the Swiss if he told her now that I am in your arms?

SERGIUS (releasing her in despair). Damnation! Oh, damnation! Mockery, mockery everywhere: everything I think is mocked by everything I do. (He strikes himself frantically on the breast.) Coward, liar, fool! Shall I kill myself like a man, or live and pretend to laugh at myself? (She again turns to go.) Louka! (She stops near the door.) Remember: you belong to me.

LOUKA (quietly). What does that mean—an insult?

SERGIUS (commandingly). It means that you love me, and that I have had you here in my arms, and will perhaps have you there again. Whether that is an insult I neither know nor care: take it as you please. But (vehemently) I will not be a coward and a trifler. If I choose to love you, I dare marry you, in spite of all Bulgaria. If these hands ever touch you again, they shall touch my affianced bride.

LOUKA. We shall see whether you dare keep your word. But take care. I will not wait long.

SERGIUS (again folding his arms and standing motionless in the middle of the room). Yes, we shall see. And you shall wait my pleasure.

(Bluntschli, much preoccupied, with his papers still in his hand, enters, leaving the door open for Louka to go out. He goes across to the table, glancing at her as he passes. Sergius, without altering his resolute attitude, watches him steadily. Louka goes out, leaving the door open.)

BLUNTSCHLI (absently, sitting at the table as before, and putting down his papers). That's a remarkable looking young woman.

SERGIUS (gravely, without moving). Captain Bluntschli.

BLUNTSCHLI. Eh?

SERGIUS. You have deceived me. You are my rival. I brook no rivals. At six o'clock I shall be in the drilling-ground on the Klissoura road, alone, on horseback, with my sabre. Do you understand?

BLUNTSCHLI (staring, but sitting quite at his ease). Oh, thank you: that's a cavalry man's proposal. I'm in the artillery; and I have the choice of weapons. If I go, I shall take a machine gun. And there shall be no mistake about the cartridges this time.

SERGIUS (flushing, but with deadly coldness). Take care, sir. It is not our custom in Bulgaria to allow invitations of that kind to be trifled with.

BLUNTSCHLI (warmly). Pooh! don't talk to me about Bulgaria. You don't know what fighting is. But have it your own way. Bring your sabre along. I'll meet you.

SERGIUS (fiercely delighted to find his opponent a man of spirit). Well said, Switzer. Shall I lend you my best horse?

BLUNTSCHLI. No: damn your horse!—-thank you all the same, my dear fellow. (Raina comes in, and hears the next sentence.) I shall fight you on foot. Horseback's too dangerous: I don't want to kill you if I can help it.

RAINA (hurrying forward anxiously). I have heard what Captain Bluntschli said, Sergius. You are going to fight. Why? (Sergius turns away in silence, and goes to the stove, where he stands watching her as she continues, to Bluntschli) What about?

BLUNTSCHLI. I don't know: he hasn't told me. Better not interfere, dear young lady. No harm will be done: I've often acted as sword instructor. He won't be able to touch me; and I'll not hurt him. It will save explanations. In the morning I shall be off home; and you'll never see me or hear of me again. You and he will then make it up and live happily ever after.

RAINA (turning away deeply hurt, almost with a sob in her voice). I never said I wanted to see you again.

SERGIUS (striding forward). Ha! That is a confession.

RAINA (haughtily). What do you mean?

SERGIUS. You love that man!

RAINA (scandalized). Sergius!

SERGIUS. You allow him to make love to you behind my back, just as you accept me as your affianced husband behind his. Bluntschli: you knew our relations; and you deceived me. It is for that that I call you to account, not for having received favours that I never enjoyed.

BLUNTSCHLI (jumping up indignantly). Stuff! Rubbish! I have received no favours. Why, the young lady doesn't even know whether I'm married or not.

RAINA (forgetting herself). Oh! (Collapsing on the ottoman.) Are you?

SERGIUS. You see the young lady's concern, Captain Bluntschli. Denial is useless. You have enjoyed the privilege of being received in her own room, late at night—

BLUNTSCHLI (interrupting him pepperily). Yes; you blockhead! She received me with a pistol at her head. Your cavalry were at my heels. I'd have blown out her brains if she'd uttered a cry.

SERGIUS (taken aback). Bluntschli! Raina: is this true?

RAINA (rising in wrathful majesty). Oh, how dare you, how dare you?

BLUNTSCHLI. Apologize, man, apologize! (He resumes his seat at the table.)

SERGIUS (with the old measured emphasis, folding his arms). I never apologize.

RAINA (passionately). This is the doing of that friend of yours, Captain Bluntschli. It is he who is spreading this horrible story about me. (She walks about excitedly.)

BLUNTSCHLI. No: he's dead—burnt alive.

RAINA (stopping, shocked). Burnt alive!

BLUNTSCHLI. Shot in the hip in a wood yard. Couldn't drag himself out. Your fellows' shells set the timber on fire and burnt him, with half a dozen other poor devils in the same predicament.

RAINA. How horrible!

SERGIUS. And how ridiculous! Oh, war! war! the dream of patriots and heroes! A fraud, Bluntschli, a hollow sham, like love.

RAINA (outraged). Like love! You say that before me.

BLUNTSCHLI. Come, Saranoff: that matter is explained.

SERGIUS. A hollow sham, I say. Would you have come back here if nothing had passed between you, except at the muzzle of your pistol? Raina is mistaken about our friend who was burnt. He was not my informant.

RAINA. Who then? (Suddenly guessing the truth.) Ah, Louka! my maid, my servant! You were with her this morning all that time after—-after—- Oh, what sort of god is this I have been worshipping! (He meets her gaze with sardonic enjoyment of her disenchantment. Angered all the more, she goes closer to him, and says, in a lower, intenser tone) Do you know that I looked out of the window as I went upstairs, to have another sight of my hero; and I saw something that I did not understand then. I know now that you were making love to her.

SERGIUS (with grim humor). You saw that?

RAINA. Only too well. (She turns away, and throws herself on the divan under the centre window, quite overcome.)

SERGIUS (cynically). Raina: our romance is shattered. Life's a farce.

BLUNTSCHLI (to Raina, goodhumoredly). You see: he's found himself out now.

SERGIUS. Bluntschli: I have allowed you to call me a blockhead. You may now call me a coward as well. I refuse to fight you. Do you know why?

BLUNTSCHLI. No; but it doesn't matter. I didn't ask the reason when you cried on; and I don't ask the reason now that you cry off. I'm a professional soldier. I fight when I have to, and am very glad to get out of it when I haven't to. You're only an amateur: you think fighting's an amusement.

SERGIUS. You shall hear the reason all the same, my professional. The reason is that it takes two men—real men—men of heart, blood and honor—to make a genuine combat. I could no more fight with you than I could make love to an ugly woman. You've no magnetism: you're not a man, you're a machine.

BLUNTSCHLI (apologetically). Quite true, quite true. I always was that sort of chap. I'm very sorry. But now that you've found that life isn't a farce, but something quite sensible and serious, what further obstacle is there to your happiness?

RAINA (riling). You are very solicitous about my happiness and his. Do you forget his new love—Louka? It is not you that he must fight now, but his rival, Nicola.

SERGIUS. Rival!! (Striking his forehead.)

RAINA. Did you not know that they are engaged?

SERGIUS. Nicola! Are fresh abysses opening! Nicola!!

RAINA (sarcastically). A shocking sacrifice, isn't it? Such beauty, such intellect, such modesty, wasted on a middle-aged servant man! Really, Sergius, you cannot stand by and allow such a thing. It would be unworthy of your chivalry.

SERGIUS (losing all self-control). Viper! Viper! (He rushes to and fro, raging.)

BLUNTSCHLI. Look here, Saranoff; you're getting the worst of this.

RAINA (getting angrier). Do you realize what he has done, Captain Bluntschli? He has set this girl as a spy on us; and her reward is that he makes love to her.

SERGIUS. False! Monstrous!

RAINA. Monstrous! (Confronting him.) Do you deny that she told you about Captain Bluntschli being in my room?

SERGIUS. No; but—

RAINA (interrupting). Do you deny that you were making love to her when she told you?

SERGIUS. No; but I tell you—

RAINA (cutting him short contemptuously). It is unnecessary to tell us anything more. That is quite enough for us. (She turns her back on him and sweeps majestically back to the window.)

BLUNTSCHLI (quietly, as Sergius, in an agony of mortification, rinks on the ottoman, clutching his averted head between his fists). I told you you were getting the worst of it, Saranoff.

SERGIUS. Tiger cat!

RAINA (running excitedly to Bluntschli). You hear this man calling me names, Captain Bluntschli?

BLUNTSCHLI. What else can he do, dear lady? He must defend himself somehow. Come (very persuasively), don't quarrel. What good does it do? (Raina, with a gasp, sits down on the ottoman, and after a vain effort to look vexedly at Bluntschli, she falls a victim to her sense of humor, and is attacked with a disposition to laugh.)

SERGIUS. Engaged to Nicola! (He rises.) Ha! ha! (Going to the stove and standing with his back to it.) Ah, well, Bluntschli, you are right to take this huge imposture of a world coolly.

RAINA (to Bluntschli with an intuitive guess at his state of mind). I daresay you think us a couple of grown up babies, don't you?

SERGIUS (grinning a little). He does, he does. Swiss civilization nursetending Bulgarian barbarism, eh?

BLUNTSCHLI (blushing). Not at all, I assure you. I'm only very glad to get you two quieted. There now, let's be pleasant and talk it over in a friendly way. Where is this other young lady?

RAINA. Listening at the door, probably.

SERGIUS (shivering as if a bullet had struck him, and speaking with quiet but deep indignation). I will prove that that, at least, is a calumny. (He goes with dignity to the door and opens it. A yell of fury bursts from him as he looks out. He darts into the passage, and returns dragging in Louka, whom he flings against the table, R., as he cries) Judge her, Bluntschli—you, the moderate, cautious man: judge the eavesdropper.

(Louka stands her ground, proud and silent.)

BLUNTSCHLI (shaking his head). I mustn't judge her. I once listened myself outside a tent when there was a mutiny brewing. It's all a question of the degree of provocation. My life was at stake.

LOUKA. My love was at stake. (Sergius flinches, ashamed of her in spite of himself.) I am not ashamed.

RAINA (contemptuously). Your love! Your curiosity, you mean.

LOUKA (facing her and retorting her contempt with interest). My love, stronger than anything you can feel, even for your chocolate cream soldier.

SERGIUS (with quick suspicion—to Louka). What does that mean?

LOUKA (fiercely). It means—

SERGIUS (interrupting her slightingly). Oh, I remember, the ice pudding. A paltry taunt, girl.

(Major Petkoff enters, in his shirtsleeves.)

PETKOFF. Excuse my shirtsleeves, gentlemen. Raina: somebody has been wearing that coat of mine: I'll swear it—somebody with bigger shoulders than mine. It's all burst open at the back. Your mother is mending it. I wish she'd make haste. I shall catch cold. (He looks more attentively at them.) Is anything the matter?

RAINA. No. (She sits down at the stove with a tranquil air.)

SERGIUS. Oh, no! (He sits down at the end of the table, as at first.)

BLUNTSCHLI (who is already seated). Nothing, nothing.

PETKOFF (sitting down on the ottoman in his old place). That's all right. (He notices Louka.) Anything the matter, Louka?

LOUKA. No, sir.

PETKOFF (genially). That's all right. (He sneezes.) Go and ask your mistress for my coat, like a good girl, will you? (She turns to obey; but Nicola enters with the coat; and she makes a pretence of having business in the room by taking the little table with the hookah away to the wall near the windows.)

RAINA (rising quickly, as she sees the coat on Nicola's arm). Here it is, papa. Give it to me, Nicola; and do you put some more wood on the fire. (She takes the coat, and brings it to the Major, who stands up to put it on. Nicola attends to the fire.)

PETKOFF (to Raina, teasing her affectionately). Aha! Going to be very good to poor old papa just for one day after his return from the wars, eh?

RAINA (with solemn reproach). Ah, how can you say that to me, father?

PETKOFF. Well, well, only a joke, little one. Come, give me a kiss. (She kisses him.) Now give me the coat.

RAINA. Now, I am going to put it on for you. Turn your back. (He turns his back and feels behind him with his arms for the sleeves. She dexterously takes the photograph from the pocket and throws it on the table before Bluntschli, who covers it with a sheet of paper under the very nose of Sergius, who looks on amazed, with his suspicions roused in the highest degree. She then helps Petkoff on with his coat.) There, dear! Now are you comfortable?

PETKOFF. Quite, little love. Thanks. (He sits down; and Raina returns to her seat near the stove.) Oh, by the bye, I've found something funny. What's the meaning of this? (He put his hand into the picked pocket.) Eh? Hallo! (He tries the other pocket.) Well, I could have sworn—(Much puzzled, he tries the breast pocket.) I wonder—(Tries the original pocket.) Where can it—(A light flashes on him; he rises, exclaiming) Your mother's taken it.

RAINA (very red). Taken what?

PETKOFF. Your photograph, with the inscription: "Raina, to her Chocolate Cream Soldier—a souvenir." Now you know there's something more in this than meets the eye; and I'm going to find it out. (Shouting) Nicola!

NICOLA (dropping a log, and turning). Sir!

PETKOFF. Did you spoil any pastry of Miss Raina's this morning?

NICOLA. You heard Miss Raina say that I did, sir.

PETKOFF. I know that, you idiot. Was it true?

NICOLA. I am sure Miss Raina is incapable of saying anything that is not true, sir.

PETKOFF. Are you? Then I'm not. (Turning to the others.) Come: do you think I don't see it all? (Goes to Sergius, and slaps him on the shoulder.) Sergius: you're the chocolate cream soldier, aren't you?

SERGIUS (starting up). I! a chocolate cream soldier! Certainly not.

PETKOFF. Not! (He looks at them. They are all very serious and very conscious.) Do you mean to tell me that Raina sends photographic souvenirs to other men?

SERGIUS (enigmatically). The world is not such an innocent place as we used to think, Petkoff.

BLUNTSCHLI (rising). It's all right, Major. I'm the chocolate cream soldier. (Petkoff and Sergius are equally astonished.) The gracious young lady saved my life by giving me chocolate creams when I was starving—shall I ever forget their flavour! My late friend Stolz told you the story at Peerot. I was the fugitive.

PETKOFF. You! (He gasps.) Sergius: do you remember how those two women went on this morning when we mentioned it? (Sergius smiles cynically. Petkoff confronts Raina severely.) You're a nice young woman, aren't you?

RAINA (bitterly). Major Saranoff has changed his mind. And when I wrote that on the photograph, I did not know that Captain Bluntschli was married.

BLUNTSCHLI (much startled protesting vehemently). I'm not married.

RAINA (with deep reproach). You said you were.

BLUNTSCHLI. I did not. I positively did not. I never was married in my life.

PETKOFF (exasperated). Raina: will you kindly inform me, if I am not asking too much, which gentleman you are engaged to?

RAINA. To neither of them. This young lady (introducing Louka, who faces them all proudly) is the object of Major Saranoff's affections at present.

PETKOFF. Louka! Are you mad, Sergius? Why, this girl's engaged to Nicola.

NICOLA (coming forward). I beg your pardon, sir. There is a mistake. Louka is not engaged to me.

PETKOFF. Not engaged to you, you scoundrel! Why, you had twenty-five levas from me on the day of your betrothal; and she had that gilt bracelet from Miss Raina.

NICOLA (with cool unction). We gave it out so, sir. But it was only to give Louka protection. She had a soul above her station; and I have been no more than her confidential servant. I intend, as you know, sir, to set up a shop later on in Sofia; and I look forward to her custom and recommendation should she marry into the nobility. (He goes out with impressive discretion, leaving them all staring after him.)

PETKOFF (breaking the silence). Well, I am—hm!

SERGIUS. This is either the finest heroism or the most crawling baseness. Which is it, Bluntschli?

BLUNTSCHLI. Never mind whether it's heroism or baseness. Nicola's the ablest man I've met in Bulgaria. I'll make him manager of a hotel if he can speak French and German.

LOUKA (suddenly breaking out at Sergius). I have been insulted by everyone here. You set them the example. You owe me an apology. (Sergius immediately, like a repeating clock of which the spring has been touched, begins to fold his arms.)

BLUNTSCHLI (before he can speak). It's no use. He never apologizes.

LOUKA. Not to you, his equal and his enemy. To me, his poor servant, he will not refuse to apologize.

SERGIUS (approvingly). You are right. (He bends his knee in his grandest manner.) Forgive me!

LOUKA. I forgive you. (She timidly gives him her hand, which he kisses.) That touch makes me your affianced wife.

SERGIUS (springing up). Ah, I forgot that!

LOUKA (coldly). You can withdraw if you like.

SERGIUS. Withdraw! Never! You belong to me! (He puts his arm about her and draws her to him.) (Catherine comes in and finds Louka in Sergius's arms, and all the rest gazing at them in bewildered astonishment.)

CATHERINE. What does this mean? (Sergius releases Louka.)

PETKOFF. Well, my dear, it appears that Sergius is going to marry Louka instead of Raina. (She is about to break out indignantly at him: he stops her by exclaiming testily.) Don't blame me: I've nothing to do with it. (He retreats to the stove.)

CATHERINE. Marry Louka! Sergius: you are bound by your word to us!

SERGIUS (folding his arms). Nothing binds me.

BLUNTSCHLI (much pleased by this piece of common sense). Saranoff: your hand. My congratulations. These heroics of yours have their practical side after all. (To Louka.) Gracious young lady: the best wishes of a good Republican! (He kisses her hand, to Raina's great disgust.)

CATHERINE (threateningly). Louka: you have been telling stories.

LOUKA. I have done Raina no harm.

CATHERINE (haughtily). Raina! (Raina is equally indignant at the liberty.)

LOUKA. I have a right to call her Raina: she calls me Louka. I told Major Saranoff she would never marry him if the Swiss gentleman came back.

BLUNTSCHLI (surprised). Hallo!

LOUKA (turning to Raina). I thought you were fonder of him than of Sergius. You know best whether I was right.

BLUNTSCHLI. What nonsense! I assure you, my dear Major, my dear Madame, the gracious young lady simply saved my life, nothing else. She never cared two straws for me. Why, bless my heart and soul, look at the young lady and look at me. She, rich, young, beautiful, with her imagination full of fairy princes and noble natures and cavalry charges and goodness knows what! And I, a common-place Swiss soldier who hardly knows what a decent life is after fifteen years of barracks and battles—a vagabond—a man who has spoiled all his chances in life through an incurably romantic disposition—a man—

SERGIUS (starting as if a needle had pricked him and interrupting Bluntschli in incredulous amazement). Excuse me, Bluntschli: what did you say had spoiled your chances in life?

BLUNTSCHLI (promptly). An incurably romantic disposition. I ran away from home twice when I was a boy. I went into the army instead of into my father's business. I climbed the balcony of this house when a man of sense would have dived into the nearest cellar. I came sneaking back here to have another look at the young lady when any other man of my age would have sent the coat back—

PETKOFF. My coat!

BLUNTSCHLI.—Yes: that's the coat I mean—would have sent it back and gone quietly home. Do you suppose I am the sort of fellow a young girl falls in love with? Why, look at our ages! I'm thirty-four: I don't suppose the young lady is much over seventeen. (This estimate produces a marked sensation, all the rest turning and staring at one another. He proceeds innocently.) All that adventure which was life or death to me, was only a schoolgirl's game to her—chocolate creams and hide and seek. Here's the proof! (He takes the photograph from the table.) Now, I ask you, would a woman who took the affair seriously have sent me this and written on it: "Raina, to her chocolate cream soldier—a souvenir"? (He exhibits the photograph triumphantly, as if it settled the matter beyond all possibility of refutation.)

PETKOFF. That's what I was looking for. How the deuce did it get there?

BLUNTSCHLI (to Raina complacently). I have put everything right, I hope, gracious young lady!

RAINA (in uncontrollable vexation). I quite agree with your account of yourself. You are a romantic idiot. (Bluntschli is unspeakably taken aback.) Next time I hope you will know the difference between a schoolgirl of seventeen and a woman of twenty-three.

BLUNTSCHLI (stupefied). Twenty-three! (She snaps the photograph contemptuously from his hand; tears it across; and throws the pieces at his feet.)

SERGIUS (with grim enjoyment of Bluntschli's discomfiture). Bluntschli: my one last belief is gone. Your sagacity is a fraud, like all the other things. You have less sense than even I have.

BLUNTSCHLI (overwhelmed). Twenty-three! Twenty-three!! (He considers.) Hm! (Swiftly making up his mind.) In that case, Major Petkoff, I beg to propose formally to become a suitor for your daughter's hand, in place of Major Saranoff retired.

RAINA. You dare!

BLUNTSCHLI. If you were twenty-three when you said those things to me this afternoon, I shall take them seriously.

CATHERINE (loftily polite). I doubt, sir, whether you quite realize either my daughter's position or that of Major Sergius Saranoff, whose place you propose to take. The Petkoffs and the Saranoffs are known as the richest and most important families in the country. Our position is almost historical: we can go back for nearly twenty years.

PETKOFF. Oh, never mind that, Catherine. (To Bluntschli.) We should be most happy, Bluntschli, if it were only a question of your position; but hang it, you know, Raina is accustomed to a very comfortable establishment. Sergius keeps twenty horses.

BLUNTSCHLI. But what on earth is the use of twenty horses? Why, it's a circus.

CATHERINE (severely). My daughter, sir, is accustomed to a first-rate stable.

RAINA. Hush, mother, you're making me ridiculous.

BLUNTSCHLI. Oh, well, if it comes to a question of an establishment, here goes! (He goes impetuously to the table and seizes the papers in the blue envelope.) How many horses did you say?

SERGIUS. Twenty, noble Switzer!

BLUNTSCHLI. I have two hundred horses. (They are amazed.) How many carriages?

SERGIUS. Three.

BLUNTSCHLI. I have seventy. Twenty-four of them will hold twelve inside, besides two on the box, without counting the driver and conductor. How many tablecloths have you?

SERGIUS. How the deuce do I know?

BLUNTSCHLI. Have you four thousand?

SERGIUS. NO.

BLUNTSCHLI. I have. I have nine thousand six hundred pairs of sheets and blankets, with two thousand four hundred eider-down quilts. I have ten thousand knives and forks, and the same quantity of dessert spoons. I have six hundred servants. I have six palatial establishments, besides two livery stables, a tea garden and a private house. I have four medals for distinguished services; I have the rank of an officer and the standing of a gentleman; and I have three native languages. Show me any man in Bulgaria that can offer as much.

PETKOFF (with childish awe). Are you Emperor of Switzerland?

BLUNTSCHLI. My rank is the highest known in Switzerland: I'm a free citizen.

CATHERINE. Then Captain Bluntschli, since you are my daughter's choice, I shall not stand in the way of her happiness. (Petkoff is about to speak.) That is Major Petkoff's feeling also.

PETKOFF. Oh, I shall be only too glad. Two hundred horses! Whew!

SERGIUS. What says the lady?

RAINA (pretending to sulk). The lady says that he can keep his tablecloths and his omnibuses. I am not here to be sold to the highest bidder.

BLUNTSCHLI. I won't take that answer. I appealed to you as a fugitive, a beggar, and a starving man. You accepted me. You gave me your hand to kiss, your bed to sleep in, and your roof to shelter me—

RAINA (interrupting him). I did not give them to the Emperor of Switzerland!

BLUNTSCHLI. That's just what I say. (He catches her hand quickly and looks her straight in the face as he adds, with confident mastery) Now tell us who you did give them to.

RAINA (succumbing with a shy smile). To my chocolate cream soldier!

BLUNTSCHLI (with a boyish laugh of delight). That'll do. Thank you. (Looks at his watch and suddenly becomes businesslike.) Time's up, Major. You've managed those regiments so well that you are sure to be asked to get rid of some of the Infantry of the Teemok division. Send them home by way of Lom Palanka. Saranoff: don't get married until I come back: I shall be here punctually at five in the evening on Tuesday fortnight. Gracious ladies—good evening. (He makes them a military bow, and goes.)

SERGIUS. What a man! What a man!

CANDIDA

ACT I

A fine October morning in the north east suburbs of London, a vast district many miles away from the London of Mayfair and St. James's, much less known there than the Paris of the Rue de Rivoli and the Champs Elysees, and much less narrow, squalid, fetid and airless in its slums; strong in comfortable, prosperous middle class life; wide-streeted, myriad-populated; well-served with ugly iron urinals, Radical clubs, tram lines, and a perpetual stream of yellow cars; enjoying in its main thoroughfares the luxury of grass-grown "front gardens," untrodden by the foot of man save as to the path from the gate to the hall door; but blighted by an intolerable monotony of miles and miles of graceless, characterless brick houses, black iron railings, stony pavements, slaty roofs, and respectably ill dressed or disreputably poorly dressed people, quite accustomed to the place, and mostly plodding about somebody else's work, which they would not do if they themselves could help it. The little energy and eagerness that crop up show themselves in cockney cupidity and business "push." Even the policemen and the chapels are not infrequent enough to break the monotony. The sun is shining cheerfully; there is no fog; and though the smoke effectually prevents anything, whether faces and hands or bricks and mortar, from looking fresh and clean, it is not hanging heavily enough to trouble a Londoner.

This desert of unattractiveness has its oasis. Near the outer end of the Hackney Road is a park of 217 acres, fenced in, not by railings, but by a wooden paling, and containing plenty of greensward, trees, a lake for bathers, flower beds with the flowers arranged carefully in patterns by the admired cockney art of carpet gardening and a sandpit, imported from the seaside for the delight of the children, but speedily deserted on its becoming a natural vermin preserve for all the petty fauna of Kingsland, Hackney and Hoxton. A bandstand, an unfinished forum for religious, anti-religious and political orators, cricket pitches, a gymnasium, and an old fashioned stone kiosk are among its attractions. Wherever the prospect is bounded by trees or rising green grounds, it is a pleasant place. Where the ground stretches far to the grey palings, with bricks and mortar, sky signs, crowded chimneys and smoke beyond, the prospect makes it desolate and sordid.

The best view of Victoria Park is from the front window of St. Dominic's Parsonage, from which not a single chimney is visible. The parsonage is a semi-detached villa with a front garden and a porch. Visitors go up the flight of steps to the porch: tradespeople and members of the family go down by a door under the steps to the basement, with a breakfast room, used for all meals, in front, and the kitchen at the back. Upstairs, on the level of the hall door, is the drawing-room, with its large plate glass window looking on the park. In this room, the only sitting-room that can be spared from the children and the family meals, the parson, the Reverend James Mavor Morell does his work. He is sitting in a strong round backed revolving chair at the right hand end of a long table, which stands across the window, so that he can cheer himself with the view of the park at his elbow. At the opposite end of the table, adjoining it, is a little table; only half the width of the other, with a typewriter on it. His typist is sitting at this machine, with her back to the window. The large table is littered with pamphlets, journals, letters, nests of drawers, an office diary, postage scales and the like. A spare chair for visitors having business with the parson is in the middle, turned to his end. Within reach of his hand is a stationery case, and a cabinet photograph in a frame. Behind him the right hand wall, recessed above the fireplace, is fitted with bookshelves, on which an adept eye can measure the parson's divinity and casuistry by a complete set of Browning's poems and Maurice's Theological Essays, and guess at his politics from a yellow backed Progress and Poverty, Fabian Essays, a Dream of John Ball, Marx's Capital, and half a dozen other literary landmarks in Socialism. Opposite him on the left, near the typewriter, is the door. Further down the room, opposite the fireplace, a bookcase stands on a cellaret, with a sofa near it. There is a generous fire burning; and the hearth, with a comfortable armchair and a japanned flower painted coal scuttle at one side, a miniature chair for a boy or girl on the other, a nicely varnished wooden mantelpiece, with neatly moulded shelves, tiny bits of mirror let into the panels, and a travelling clock in a leather case (the inevitable wedding present), and on the wall above a large autotype of the chief figure in Titian's Virgin of the Assumption, is very inviting. Altogether the room is the room of a good housekeeper, vanquished, as far as the table is concerned, by an untidy man, but elsewhere mistress of the situation. The furniture, in its ornamental aspect, betrays the style of the advertised "drawing-room suite" of the pushing suburban furniture dealer; but there is nothing useless or pretentious in the room. The paper and panelling are dark, throwing the big cheery window and the park outside into strong relief.

The Reverend James Mavor Morell is a Christian Socialist clergyman of the Church of England, and an active member of the Guild of St. Matthew and the Christian Social Union. A vigorous, genial, popular man of forty, robust and goodlooking, full of energy, with pleasant, hearty, considerate manners, and a sound, unaffected voice, which he uses with the clean, athletic articulation of a practised orator, and with a wide range and perfect command of expression. He is a first rate clergyman, able to say what he likes to whom he likes, to lecture people without setting himself up against them, to impose his authority on them without humiliating them, and to interfere in their business without impertinence. His well-spring of spiritual enthusiasm and sympathetic emotion has never run dry for a moment: he still eats and sleeps heartily enough to win the daily battle between exhaustion and recuperation triumphantly. Withal, a great baby, pardonably vain of his powers and unconsciously pleased with himself. He has a healthy complexion, a good forehead, with the brows somewhat blunt, and the eyes bright and eager, a mouth resolute, but not particularly well cut, and a substantial nose, with the mobile, spreading nostrils of the dramatic orator, but, like all his features, void of subtlety.

The typist, Miss Proserpine Garnett, is a brisk little woman of about 30, of the lower middle class, neatly but cheaply dressed in a black merino skirt and a blouse, rather pert and quick of speech, and not very civil in her manner, but sensitive and affectionate. She is clattering away busily at her machine whilst Morell opens the last of his morning's letters. He realizes its contents with a comic groan of despair.

PROSERPINE. Another lecture?

MORELL. Yes. The Hoxton Freedom Group want me to address them on Sunday morning (great emphasis on "Sunday," this being the unreasonable part of the business). What are they?

PROSERPINE. Communist Anarchists, I think.

MORELL. Just like Anarchists not to know that they can't have a parson on Sunday! Tell them to come to church if they want to hear me: it will do them good. Say I can only come on Mondays and Thursdays. Have you the diary there?

PROSERPINE (taking up the diary). Yes.

MORELL. Have I any lecture on for next Monday?

PROSERPINE (referring to diary). Tower Hamlets Radical Club.

MORELL. Well, Thursday then?

PROSERPINE. English Land Restoration League.

MORELL. What next?

PROSERPINE. Guild of St. Matthew on Monday. Independent Labor Party, Greenwich Branch, on Thursday. Monday, Social-Democratic Federation, Mile End Branch. Thursday, first Confirmation class— (Impatiently). Oh, I'd better tell them you can't come. They're only half a dozen ignorant and conceited costermongers without five shillings between them.

MORELL (amused). Ah; but you see they're near relatives of mine, Miss Garnett.

PROSERPINE (staring at him). Relatives of YOURS!

MORELL. Yes: we have the same father—in Heaven.

PROSERPINE (relieved). Oh, is that all?

MORELL (with a sadness which is a luxury to a man whose voice expresses it so finely). Ah, you don't believe it. Everybody says it: nobody believes it—nobody. (Briskly, getting back to business.) Well, well! Come, Miss Proserpine, can't you find a date for the costers? What about the 25th?: that was vacant the day before yesterday.

PROSERPINE (referring to diary). Engaged—the Fabian Society.

MORELL. Bother the Fabian Society! Is the 28th gone too?

PROSERPINE. City dinner. You're invited to dine with the Founder's Company.

MORELL. That'll do; I'll go to the Hoxton Group of Freedom instead. (She enters the engagement in silence, with implacable disparagement of the Hoxton Anarchists in every line of her face. Morell bursts open the cover of a copy of The Church Reformer, which has come by post, and glances through Mr. Stewart Hendlam's leader and the Guild of St. Matthew news. These proceedings are presently enlivened by the appearance of Morell's curate, the Reverend Alexander Mill, a young gentleman gathered by Morell from the nearest University settlement, whither he had come from Oxford to give the east end of London the benefit of his university training. He is a conceitedly well intentioned, enthusiastic, immature person, with nothing positively unbearable about him except a habit of speaking with his lips carefully closed for half an inch from each corner, a finicking arthulation, and a set of horribly corrupt vowels, notably ow for o, this being his chief means of bringing Oxford refinement to bear on Hackney vulgarity. Morell, whom he has won over by a doglike devotion, looks up indulgently from The Church Reformer as he enters, and remarks) Well, Lexy! Late again, as usual.

LEXY. I'm afraid so. I wish I could get up in the morning.

MORELL (exulting in his own energy). Ha! ha! (Whimsically.) Watch and pray, Lexy: watch and pray.

LEXY. I know. (Rising wittily to the occasion.) But how can I watch and pray when I am asleep? Isn't that so, Miss Prossy?

PROSERPINE (sharply). Miss Garnett, if you please.

LEXY. I beg your pardon—Miss Garnett.

PROSERPINE. You've got to do all the work today.

LEXY. Why?

PROSERPINE. Never mind why. It will do you good to earn your supper before you eat it, for once in a way, as I do. Come: don't dawdle. You should have been off on your rounds half an hour ago.

LEXY (perplexed). Is she in earnest, Morell?

MORELL (in the highest spirits—his eyes dancing). Yes. *I* am going to dawdle to-day.

LEXY. You! You don't know how.

MORELL (heartily). Ha! ha! Don't I? I'm going to have this day all to myself—or at least the forenoon. My wife's coming back: she's due here at 11.45.

LEXY (surprised). Coming back already—with the children? I thought they were to stay to the end of the month.

MORELL. So they are: she's only coming up for two days, to get some flannel things for Jimmy, and to see how we're getting on without her.

LEXY (anxiously). But, my dear Morell, if what Jimmy and Fluffy had was scarlatina, do you think it wise—

MORELL. Scarlatina!—rubbish, German measles. I brought it into the house myself from the Pycroft Street School. A parson is like a doctor, my boy: he must face infection as a soldier must face bullets. (He rises and claps Lexy on the shoulder.) Catch the measles if you can, Lexy: she'll nurse you; and what a piece of luck that will be for you!—eh?

LEXY (smiling uneasily). It's so hard to understand you about Mrs. Morell—

MORELL (tenderly). Ah, my boy, get married—get married to a good woman; and then you'll understand. That's a foretaste of what will be best in the Kingdom of Heaven we are trying to establish on earth. That will cure you of dawdling. An honest man feels that he must pay Heaven for every hour of happiness with a good spell of hard, unselfish work to make others happy. We have no more right to consume happiness without producing it than to consume wealth without producing it. Get a wife like my Candida; and you'll always be in arrear with your repayment. (He pats Lexy affectionately on the back, and is leaving the room when Lexy calls to him.)

LEXY. Oh, wait a bit: I forgot. (Morell halts and turns with the door knob in his hand.) Your father-in-law is coming round to see you. (Morell shuts the door again, with a complete change of manner.)

MORELL (surprised and not pleased). Mr. Burgess?

LEXY. Yes. I passed him in the park, arguing with somebody. He gave me good day and asked me to let you know that he was coming.

MORELL (half incredulous). But he hasn't called here for—I may almost say for years. Are you sure, Lexy? You're not joking, are you?

LEXY (earnestly). No, sir, really.

MORELL (thoughtfully). Hm! Time for him to take another look at Candida before she grows out of his knowledge. (He resigns himself to the inevitable, and goes out. Lexy looks after him with beaming, foolish worship.)

LEXY. What a good man! What a thorough, loving soul he is! (He takes Morell's place at the table, making himself very comfortable as he takes out a cigaret.)

PROSERPINE (impatiently, pulling the letter she has been working at off the typewriter and folding it.) Oh, a man ought to be able to be fond of his wife without making a fool of himself about her.

LEXY (shocked). Oh, Miss Prossy!

PROSERPINE (rising busily and coming to the stationery case to get an envelope, in which she encloses the letter as she speaks). Candida here, and Candida there, and Candida everywhere! (She licks the envelope.) It's enough to drive anyone out of their SENSES (thumping the envelope to make it stick) to hear a perfectly commonplace woman raved about in that absurd manner merely because she's got good hair, and a tolerable figure.

LEXY (with reproachful gravity). I think her extremely beautiful, Miss Garnett. (He takes the photograph up; looks at it; and adds, with even greater impressiveness) EXTREMELY beautiful. How fine her eyes are!

PROSERPINE. Her eyes are not a bit better than mine—now! (He puts down the photograph and stares austerely at her.) And you know very well that you think me dowdy and second rate enough.

LEXY (rising majestically). Heaven forbid that I should think of any of God's creatures in such a way! (He moves stiffly away from her across the room to the neighbourhood of the bookcase.)

PROSERPINE. Thank you. That's very nice and comforting.

LEXY (saddened by her depravity). I had no idea you had any feeling against Mrs. Morell.

PROSERPINE (indignantly). I have no feeling against her. She's very nice, very good-hearted: I'm very fond of her and can appreciate her real qualities far better than any man can. (He shakes his head sadly and turns to the bookcase, looking along the shelves for a volume. She follows him with intense pepperiness.) You don't believe me? (He turns and faces her. She pounces at him with spitfire energy.) You think I'm jealous. Oh, what a profound knowledge of the human heart you have, Mr. Lexy Mill! How well you know the weaknesses of Woman, don't you? It must be so nice to be a man and have a fine penetrating intellect instead of mere emotions like us, and to know that the reason we don't share your amorous delusions is that we're all jealous of one another! (She abandons him with a toss of her shoulders, and crosses to the fire to warm her hands.)

LEXY. Ah, if you women only had the same clue to Man's strength that you have to his weakness, Miss Prossy, there would be no Woman Question.

PROSERPINE (over her shoulder, as she stoops, holding her hands to the blaze). Where did you hear Morell say that? You didn't invent it yourself: you're not clever enough.

LEXY. That's quite true. I am not ashamed of owing him that, as I owe him so many other spiritual truths. He said it at the annual conference of the Women's Liberal Federation. Allow me to add that though they didn't appreciate it, I, a mere man, did. (He turns to the bookcase again, hoping that this may leave her crushed.)

PROSERPINE (putting her hair straight at the little panel of mirror in the mantelpiece). Well, when you talk to me, give me your own ideas, such as they are, and not his. You never cut a poorer figure than when you are trying to imitate him.

LEXY (stung). I try to follow his example, not to imitate him.

PROSERPINE (coming at him again on her way back to her work). Yes, you do: you IMITATE him. Why do you tuck your umbrella under your left arm instead of carrying it in your hand like anyone else? Why do you walk with your chin stuck out before you, hurrying along with that eager look in your eyes—you, who never get up before half past nine in the morning? Why do you say "knoaledge" in church, though you always say "knolledge" in private conversation! Bah! do you think I don't know? (She goes back to the typewriter.) Here, come and set about your work: we've wasted enough time for one morning. Here's a copy of the diary for to-day. (She hands him a memorandum.)

LEXY (deeply offended). Thank you. (He takes it and stands at the table with his back to her, reading it. She begins to transcribe her shorthand notes on the typewriter without troubling herself about his feelings. Mr. Burgess enters unannounced. He is a man of sixty, made coarse and sordid by the compulsory selfishness of petty commerce, and later on softened into sluggish bumptiousness by overfeeding and commercial success. A vulgar, ignorant, guzzling man, offensive and contemptuous to people whose labor is cheap, respectful to wealth and rank, and quite sincere and without rancour or envy in both attitudes. Finding him without talent, the world has offered him no decently paid work except ignoble work, and he has become in consequence, somewhat hoggish. But he has no suspicion of this himself, and honestly regards his commercial prosperity as the inevitable and socially wholesome triumph of the ability, industry, shrewdness and experience in business of a man who in private is easygoing, affectionate and humorously convivial to a fault. Corporeally, he is a podgy man, with a square, clean shaven face and a square beard under his chin; dust colored, with a patch of grey in the centre, and small watery blue eyes with a plaintively sentimental expression, which he transfers easily to his voice by his habit of pompously intoning his sentences.)

BURGESS (stopping on the threshold, and looking round). They told me Mr. Morell was here.

PROSERPINE (rising). He's upstairs. I'll fetch him for you.

BURGESS (staring boorishly at her). You're not the same young lady as used to typewrite for him?

PROSERPINE. No.

BURGESS (assenting). No: she was younger. (Miss Garnett stolidly stares at him; then goes out with great dignity. He receives this quite obtusely, and crosses to the hearth-rug, where he turns and spreads himself with his back to the fire.) Startin' on your rounds, Mr. Mill?

LEXY (folding his paper and pocketing it). Yes: I must be off presently.

BURGESS (momentously). Don't let me detain you, Mr. Mill. What I come about is private between me and Mr. Morell.

LEXY (huffily). I have no intention of intruding, I am sure, Mr. Burgess. Good morning.

BURGESS (patronizingly). Oh, good morning to you. (Morell returns as Lexy is making for the door.)

MORELL (to Lexy). Off to work?

LEXY. Yes, sir.

MORELL (patting him affectionately on the shoulder). Take my silk handkerchief and wrap your throat up. There's a cold wind. Away with you.

(Lexy brightens up, and goes out.)

BURGESS. Spoilin' your curates, as usu'l, James. Good mornin'. When I pay a man, an' 'is livin' depen's on me, I keep him in his place.

MORELL (rather shortly). I always keep my curates in their places as my helpers and comrades. If you get as much work out of your clerks and warehousemen as I do out of my curates, you must be getting rich pretty fast. Will you take your old chair?

(He points with curt authority to the arm chair beside the fireplace; then takes the spare chair from the table and sits down in front of Burgess.)

BURGESS (without moving). Just the same as hever, James!

MORELL. When you last called—it was about three years ago, I think—you said the same thing a little more frankly. Your exact words then were: "Just as big a fool as ever, James?"

BURGESS (soothingly). Well, perhaps I did; but (with conciliatory cheerfulness) I meant no offence by it. A clergyman is privileged to be a bit of a fool, you know: it's on'y becomin' in his profession that he should. Anyhow, I come here, not to rake up hold differences, but to let bygones be bygones. (Suddenly becoming very solemn, and approaching Morell.) James: three year ago, you done me a hill turn. You done me hout of a contrac'; an' when I gev you 'arsh words in my nat'ral disappointment, you turned my daughrter again me. Well, I've come to act the part of a Cherischin. (Offering his hand.) I forgive you, James.

MORELL (starting up). Confound your impudence!

BURGESS (retreating, with almost lachrymose deprecation of this treatment). Is that becomin' language for a clergyman, James?—and you so partic'lar, too?

MORELL (hotly). No, sir, it is not becoming language for a clergyman. I used the wrong word. I should have said damn your impudence: that's what St. Paul, or any honest priest would have said to you. Do you think I have forgotten that tender of yours for the contract to supply clothing to the workhouse?

BURGESS (in a paroxysm of public spirit). I acted in the interest of the ratepayers, James. It was the lowest tender: you can't deny that.

MORELL. Yes, the lowest, because you paid worse wages than any other employer—starvation wages—aye, worse than starvation wages—to the women who made the clothing. Your wages would have driven them to the streets to keep body and soul together. (Getting angrier and angrier.) Those women were my parishioners. I shamed the Guardians out of accepting your tender: I shamed the ratepayers out of letting them do it: I shamed everybody but you. (Boiling over.) How dare you, sir, come here and offer to forgive me, and talk about your daughter, and—

BURGESS. Easy, James, easy, easy. Don't git hinto a fluster about nothink. I've howned I was wrong.

MORELL (fuming about). Have you? I didn't hear you.

BURGESS. Of course I did. I hown it now. Come: I harsk your pardon for the letter I wrote you. Is that enough?

MORELL (snapping his fingers). That's nothing. Have you raised the wages?

BURGESS (triumphantly). Yes.

MORELL (stopping dead). What!

BURGESS (unctuously). I've turned a moddle hemployer. I don't hemploy no women now: they're all sacked; and the work is done by machinery. Not a man 'as less than sixpence a hour; and the skilled 'ands gits the Trade Union rate. (Proudly.) What 'ave you to say to me now?

MORELL (overwhelmed). Is it possible! Well, there's more joy in heaven over one sinner that repenteth— (Going to Burgess with an explosion of apologetic cordiality.) My dear Burgess, I most heartily beg your pardon for my hard thoughts of you. (Grasps his hand.) And now, don't you feel the better for the change? Come, confess, you're happier. You look happier.

BURGESS (ruefully). Well, p'raps I do. I s'pose I must, since you notice it. At all events, I git my contrax asseppit (accepted) by the County Council. (Savagely.) They dussent'ave nothink to do with me unless I paid fair wages—curse 'em for a parcel o' meddlin' fools!

MORELL (dropping his hand, utterly discouraged). So that was why you raised the wages! (He sits down moodily.)

BURGESS (severely, in spreading, mounting tones). Why else should I do it? What does it lead to but drink and huppishness in workin' men? (He seats himself magisterially in the easy chair.) It's hall very well for you, James: it gits you hinto the papers and makes a great man of you; but you never think of the 'arm you do, puttin' money into the pockets of workin' men that they don't know 'ow to spend, and takin' it from people that might be makin' a good huse on it.

MORELL (with a heavy sigh, speaking with cold politeness). What is your business with me this morning? I shall not pretend to believe that you are here merely out of family sentiment.

BURGESS (obstinately). Yes, I ham—just family sentiment and nothink else.

MORELL (with weary calm). I don't believe you!

BURGESS (rising threateningly). Don't say that to me again, James Mavor Morell.

MORELL (unmoved). I'll say it just as often as may be necessary to convince you that it's true. I don't believe you.

BURGESS (collapsing into an abyss of wounded feeling). Oh, well, if you're determined to be unfriendly, I s'pose I'd better go. (He moves reluctantly towards the door. Morell makes no sign. He lingers.) I didn't hexpect to find a hunforgivin' spirit in you, James. (Morell still not responding, he takes a few more reluctant steps doorwards. Then he comes back whining.) We huseter git on well enough, spite of our different opinions. Why are you so changed to me? I give you my word I come here in pyorr (pure) frenliness, not wishin' to be on bad terms with my hown daughrter's 'usban'. Come, James: be a Cherishin and shake 'ands. (He puts his hand sentimentally on Morell's shoulder.)

MORELL (looking up at him thoughtfully). Look here, Burgess. Do you want to be as welcome here as you were before you lost that contract?

BURGESS. I do, James. I do—honest.

MORELL. Then why don't you behave as you did then?

BURGESS (cautiously removing his hand). 'Ow d'y'mean?

MORELL. I'll tell you. You thought me a young fool then.

BURGESS (coaxingly). No, I didn't, James. I—

MORELL (cutting him short). Yes, you did. And I thought you an old scoundrel.

BURGESS (most vehemently deprecating this gross self-accusation on Morell's part). No, you didn't, James. Now you do yourself a hinjustice.

MORELL. Yes, I did. Well, that did not prevent our getting on very well together. God made you what I call a scoundrel as he made me what you call a fool. (The effect of this observation on Burgess is to remove the keystone of his moral arch. He becomes bodily weak, and, with his eyes fixed on Morell in a helpless stare, puts out his hand apprehensively to balance himself, as if the floor had suddenly sloped under him. Morell proceeds in the same tone of quiet conviction.) It was not for me to quarrel with his handiwork in the one case more than in the other. So long as you come here honestly as a self-respecting, thorough, convinced scoundrel, justifying your scoundrelism, and proud of it, you are welcome. But (and now Morell's tone becomes formidable; and he rises and strikes the back of the chair for greater emphasis) I won't have you here snivelling about being a model employer and a converted man when you're only an apostate with your coat turned for the sake of a County Council contract. (He nods at him to enforce the point; then goes to the hearth-rug, where he takes up a comfortably commanding position with his back to the fire, and continues) No: I like a man to be true to himself, even in wickedness. Come now: either take your hat and go; or else sit down and give me a good scoundrelly reason for wanting to be friends with me. (Burgess, whose emotions have subsided sufficiently to be expressed by a dazed grin, is relieved by this concrete proposition. He ponders it for a moment, and then, slowly and very modestly, sits down in the chair Morell has just left.) That's right. Now, out with it.

BURGESS (chuckling in spite of himself.) Well, you ARE a queer bird, James, and no mistake. But (almost enthusiastically) one carnt 'elp likin' you; besides, as I said afore, of course one don't take all a clorgyman says seriously, or the world couldn't go on. Could it now? (He composes himself for graver discourse, and turning his eyes on Morell proceeds with dull seriousness.) Well, I don't mind tellin' you, since it's your wish we should be free with one another, that I did think you a bit of a fool once; but I'm beginnin' to think that p'r'aps I was be'ind the times a bit.

MORELL (delighted). Aha! You're finding that out at last, are you?

BURGESS (portentously). Yes, times 'as changed mor'n I could a believed. Five yorr (year) ago, no sensible man would a thought o' takin' up with your ideas. I hused to wonder you was let preach at all. Why, I know a clorgyman that 'as bin kep' hout of his job for yorrs by the Bishop of London, although the pore feller's not a bit more religious than you are. But to-day, if henyone was to offer to bet me a thousan' poun' that you'll end by bein' a bishop yourself, I shouldn't venture to take the bet. You and yore crew are gettin' hinfluential: I can see that. They'll 'ave to give you something someday, if it's only to stop yore mouth. You 'ad the right instinc' arter all, James: the line you took is the payin' line in the long run fur a man o' your sort.

MORELL (decisively—offering his hand). Shake hands, Burgess. Now you're talking honestly. I don't think they'll make me a bishop; but if they do, I'll introduce you to the biggest jobbers I can get to come to my dinner parties.

BURGESS (who has risen with a sheepish grin and accepted the hand of friendship). You will 'ave your joke, James. Our quarrel's made up now, isn't it?

A WOMAN'S VOICE. Say yes, James.

Startled, they turn quickly and find that Candida has just come in, and is looking at them with an amused maternal indulgence which is her characteristic expression. She is a woman of 33, well built, well nourished, likely, one guesses, to become matronly later on, but now quite at her best, with the double charm of youth and motherhood. Her ways are those of a woman who has found that she can always manage people by engaging their affection, and who does so frankly and instinctively without the smallest scruple. So far, she is like any other pretty woman who is just clever enough to make the most of her sexual attractions for trivially selfish ends; but Candida's serene brow, courageous eyes, and well set mouth and chin signify largeness of mind and dignity of character to ennoble her cunning in the affections. A wisehearted observer, looking at her, would at once guess that whoever had placed the Virgin of the Assumption over her hearth did so because he fancied some spiritual resemblance between them, and yet would not suspect either her husband or herself of any such idea, or indeed of any concern with the art of Titian.

Just now she is in bonnet and mantle, laden with a strapped rug with her umbrella stuck through it, a handbag, and a supply of illustrated papers.

MORELL (shocked at his remissness). Candida! Why—(looks at his watch, and is horrified to find it so late.) My darling! (Hurrying to her and seizing the rug strap, pouring forth his remorseful regrets all the time.) I intended to meet you at the train. I let the time slip. (Flinging the rug on the sofa.) I was so engrossed by—(returning to her)—I forgot—oh! (He embraces her with penitent emotion.)

BURGESS (a little shamefaced and doubtful of his reception). How ors you, Candy? (She, still in Morell's arms, offers him her cheek, which he kisses.) James and me is come to a unnerstandin'—a honourable unnerstandin'. Ain' we, James?

MORELL (impetuously). Oh, bother your understanding! You've kept me late for Candida. (With compassionate fervor.) My poor love: how did you manage about the luggage?—how—

CANDIDA (stopping him and disengaging herself). There, there, there. I wasn't alone. Eugene came down yesterday; and we traveled up together.

MORELL (pleased). Eugene!

CANDIDA. Yes: he's struggling with my luggage, poor boy. Go out, dear, at once; or he will pay for the cab; and I don't want that. (Morell hurries out. Candida puts down her handbag; then takes off her mantle and bonnet and puts them on the sofa with the rug, chatting meanwhile.) Well, papa, how are you getting on at home?

BURGESS. The 'ouse ain't worth livin' in since you left it, Candy. I wish you'd come round and give the gurl a talkin' to. Who's this Eugene that's come with you?

CANDIDA. Oh, Eugene's one of James's discoveries. He found him sleeping on the Embankment last June. Haven't you noticed our new picture (pointing to the Virgin)? He gave us that.

BURGESS (incredulously). Garn! D'you mean to tell me—your hown father!—that cab touts or such like, orf the Embankment, buys pictur's like that? (Severely.) Don't deceive me, Candy: it's a 'Igh Church pictur; and James chose it hisself.

CANDIDA. Guess again. Eugene isn't a cab tout.

BURGESS. Then wot is he? (Sarcastically.) A nobleman, I 'spose.

CANDIDA (delighted—nodding). Yes. His uncle's a peer—a real live earl.

BURGESS (not daring to believe such good news). No!

CANDIDA. Yes. He had a seven day bill for 55 pounds in his pocket when James found him on the Embankment. He thought he couldn't get any money for it until the seven days were up; and he was too shy to ask for credit. Oh, he's a dear boy! We are very fond of him.

BURGESS (pretending to belittle the aristocracy, but with his eyes gleaming). Hm, I thort you wouldn't git a piorr's (peer's) nevvy visitin' in Victoria Park unless he were a bit of a flat. (Looking again at the picture.) Of course I don't 'old with that pictur, Candy; but still it's a 'igh class, fust rate work of art: I can see that. Be sure you hintroduce me to him, Candy. (He looks at his watch anxiously.) I can only stay about two minutes.

Morell comes back with Eugene, whom Burgess contemplates moist-eyed with enthusiasm. He is a strange, shy youth of eighteen, slight, effeminate, with a delicate childish voice, and a hunted, tormented expression and shrinking manner that show the painful sensitiveness that very swift and acute apprehensiveness produces in youth, before the character has grown to its full strength. Yet everything that his timidity and frailty suggests is contradicted by his face. He is miserably irresolute, does not know where to stand or what to do with his hands and feet, is afraid of Burgess, and would run away into solitude if he dared; but the very intensity with which he feels a perfectly commonplace position shows great nervous force, and his nostrils and mouth show a fiercely petulant wilfulness, as to the quality of which his great imaginative eyes and fine brow are reassuring. He is so entirely uncommon as to be almost unearthly; and to prosaic people there is something noxious in this unearthliness, just as to poetic people there is something angelic in it. His dress is anarchic. He wears an old blue serge jacket, unbuttoned over a woollen lawn tennis shirt, with a silk handkerchief for a cravat, trousers matching the jacket, and brown canvas shoes. In these garments he has apparently lain in the heather and waded through the waters; but there is no evidence of his having ever brushed them.

As he catches sight of a stranger on entering, he stops, and edges along the wall on the opposite side of the room.

MORELL (as he enters). Come along: you can spare us quarter of an hour, at all events. This is my father-in-law, Mr. Burgess—Mr. Marchbanks.

MARCHBANKS (nervously backing against the bookcase). Glad to meet you, sir.

BURGESS (crossing to him with great heartiness, whilst Morell joins Candida at the fire). Glad to meet YOU, I'm shore, Mr. Morchbanks. (Forcing him to shake hands.) 'Ow do you find yoreself this weather? 'Ope you ain't lettin' James put no foolish ideas into your 'ed?

MARCHBANKS. Foolish ideas! Oh, you mean Socialism. No.

BURGESS. That's right. (Again looking at his watch.) Well, I must go now: there's no 'elp for it. Yo're not comin' my way, are you, Mr. Morchbanks?

MARCHBANKS. Which way is that?

BURGESS. Victawriar Pork station. There's a city train at 12.25.

MORELL. Nonsense. Eugene will stay to lunch with us, I expect.

MARCHBANKS (anxiously excusing himself). No—I—I—

BURGESS. Well, well, I shan't press you: I bet you'd rather lunch with Candy. Some night, I 'ope, you'll come and dine with me at my club, the Freeman Founders in Nortn Folgit. Come, say you will.

MARCHBANKS. Thank you, Mr. Burgess. Where is Norton Folgate—down in Surrey, isn't it? (Burgess, inexpressibly tickled, begins to splutter with laughter.)

CANDIDA (coming to the rescue). You'll lose your train, papa, if you don't go at once. Come back in the afternoon and tell Mr. Marchbanks where to find the club.

BURGESS (roaring with glee). Down in Surrey—har, har! that's not a bad one. Well, I never met a man as didn't know Nortn Folgit before.(Abashed at his own noisiness.) Good-bye, Mr. Morchbanks: I know yo're too 'ighbred to take my pleasantry in bad part. (He again offers his hand.)

MARCHBANKS (taking it with a nervous jerk). Not at all.

BURGESS. Bye, bye, Candy. I'll look in again later on. So long, James.

MORELL. Must you go?

BURGESS. Don't stir. (He goes out with unabated heartiness.)

MORELL. Oh, I'll see you out. (He follows him out. Eugene stares after them apprehensively, holding his breath until Burgess disappears.)

CANDIDA (laughing). Well, Eugene. (He turns with a start and comes eagerly towards her, but stops irresolutely as he meets her amused look.) What do you think of my father?

MARCHBANKS. I—I hardly know him yet. He seems to be a very nice old gentleman.

CANDIDA (with gentle irony). And you'll go to the Freeman Founders to dine with him, won't you?

MARCHBANKS (miserably, taking it quite seriously). Yes, if it will please you.

CANDIDA (touched). Do you know, you are a very nice boy, Eugene, with all your queerness. If you had laughed at my father I shouldn't have minded; but I like you ever so much better for being nice to him.

MARCHBANKS. Ought I to have laughed? I noticed that he said something funny; but I am so ill at ease with strangers; and I never can see a joke! I'm very sorry. (He sits down on the sofa, his elbows on his knees and his temples between his fists, with an expression of hopeless suffering.)

CANDIDA (bustling him goodnaturedly). Oh, come! You great baby, you! You are worse than usual this morning. Why were you so melancholy as we came along in the cab?

MARCHBANKS. Oh, that was nothing. I was wondering how much I ought to give the cabman. I know it's utterly silly; but you don't know how dreadful such things are to me—how I shrink from having to deal with strange people. (Quickly and reassuringly.) But it's all right. He beamed all over and touched his hat when Morell gave him two shillings. I was on the point of offering him ten. (Candida laughs heartily. Morell comes back with a few letters and newspapers which have come by the midday post.)

CANDIDA. Oh, James, dear, he was going to give the cabman ten shillings—ten shillings for a three minutes' drive—oh, dear!

MORELL (at the table, glancing through the letters). Never mind her, Marchbanks. The overpaying instinct is a generous one: better than the underpaying instinct, and not so common.

MARCHBANKS (relapsing into dejection). No: cowardice, incompetence. Mrs. Morell's quite right.

CANDIDA. Of course she is. (She takes up her handbag.) And now I must leave you to James for the present. I suppose you are too much of a poet to know the state a woman finds her house in when she's been away for three weeks. Give me my rug. (Eugene takes the strapped rug from the couch, and gives it to her. She takes it in her left hand, having the bag in her right.) Now hang my cloak across my arm. (He obeys.) Now my hat. (He puts it into the hand which has the bag.) Now open the door for me. (He hurries up before her and opens the door.) Thanks. (She goes out; and Marchbanks shuts the door.)

MORELL (still busy at the table). You'll stay to lunch, Marchbanks, of course.

MARCHBANKS (scared). I mustn't. (He glances quickly at Morell, but at once avoids his frank look, and adds, with obvious disingenuousness) I can't.

MORELL (over his shoulder). You mean you won't.

MARCHBANKS (earnestly). No: I should like to, indeed. Thank you very much. But—but—

MORELL (breezily, finishing with the letters and coming close to him). But—but—but—but—bosh! If you'd like to stay, stay. You don't mean to persuade me you have anything else to do. If you're shy, go and take a turn in the park and write poetry until half past one; and then come in and have a good feed.

MARCHBANKS. Thank you, I should like that very much. But I really mustn't. The truth is, Mrs. Morell told me not to. She said she didn't think you'd ask me to stay to lunch, but that I was to remember, if you did, that you didn't really want me to. (Plaintively.) She said I'd understand; but I don't. Please don't tell her I told you.

MORELL (drolly). Oh, is that all? Won't my suggestion that you should take a turn in the park meet the difficulty?

MARCHBANKS. How?

MORELL (exploding good-humoredly). Why, you duffer—(But this boisterousness jars himself as well as Eugene. He checks himself, and resumes, with affectionate seriousness) No: I won't put it in that way. My dear lad: in a happy marriage like ours, there is something very sacred in the return of the wife to her home. (Marchbanks looks quickly at him, half anticipating his meaning.) An old friend or a truly noble and sympathetic soul is not in the way on such occasions; but a chance visitor is. (The hunted, horror-stricken expression comes out with sudden vividness in Eugene's face as he understands. Morell, occupied with his own thought, goes on without noticing it.) Candida thought I would rather not have you here; but she was wrong. I'm very fond of you, my boy, and I should like you to see for yourself what a happy thing it is to be married as I am.

MARCHBANKS, Happy!—YOUR marriage! You think that! You believe that!

MORELL (buoyantly). I know it, my lad. La Rochefoucauld said that there are convenient marriages, but no delightful ones. You don't know the comfort of seeing through and through a thundering liar and rotten cynic like that fellow. Ha, ha! Now off with you to the park, and write your poem. Half past one, sharp, mind: we never wait for anybody.

MARCHBANKS (wildly). No: stop: you shan't. I'll force it into the light.

MORELL (puzzled). Eh? Force what?

MARCHBANKS. I must speak to you. There is something that must be settled between us.

MORELL (with a whimsical glance at the clock). Now?

MARCHBANKS (passionately). Now. Before you leave this room. (He retreats a few steps, and stands as if to bar Morell's way to the door.)

MORELL (without moving, and gravely, perceiving now that there is something serious the matter). I'm not going to leave it, my dear boy: I thought YOU were. (Eugene, baffled by his firm tone, turns his back on him, writhing with anger. Morell goes to him and puts his hand on his shoulder strongly and kindly, disregarding his attempt to shake it off) Come: sit down quietly; and tell me what it is. And remember; we are friends, and need not fear that either of us will be anything but patient and kind to the other, whatever we may have to say.

MARCHBANKS (twisting himself round on him). Oh, I am not forgetting myself: I am only (covering his face desperately with his hands) full of horror. (Then, dropping his hands, and thrusting his face forward fiercely at Morell, he goes on threateningly.) You shall see whether this is a time for patience and kindness. (Morell, firm as a rock, looks indulgently at him.) Don't look at me in that self-complacent way. You think yourself stronger than I am; but I shall stagger you if you have a heart in your breast.

MORELL (powerfully confident). Stagger me, my boy. Out with it.

MARCHBANKS. First—

MORELL. First?

MARCHBANKS. I love your wife.

(Morell recoils, and, after staring at him for a moment in utter amazement, bursts into uncontrollable laughter. Eugene is taken aback, but not disconcerted; and he soon becomes indignant and contemptuous.)

MORELL (sitting down to have his laugh out). Why, my dear child, of course you do. Everybody loves her: they can't help it. I like it. But (looking up whimsically at him) I say, Eugene: do you think yours is a case to be talked about? You're under twenty: she's over thirty. Doesn't it look rather too like a case of calf love?

MARCHBANKS (vehemently). YOU dare say that of her! You think that way of the love she inspires! It is an insult to her!

MORELL (rising; quickly, in an altered tone). To her! Eugene: take care. I have been patient. I hope to remain patient. But there are some things I won't allow. Don't force me to show you the indulgence I should show to a child. Be a man.

MARCHBANKS (with a gesture as if sweeping something behind him). Oh, let us put aside all that cant. It horrifies me when I think of the doses of it she has had to endure in all the weary years during which you have selfishly and blindly sacrificed her to minister to your self-sufficiency—YOU (turning on him) who have not one thought—one sense—in common with her.

MORELL (philosophically). She seems to bear it pretty well. (Looking him straight in the face.) Eugene, my boy: you are making a fool of yourself—a very great fool of yourself. There's a piece of wholesome plain speaking for you.

MARCHBANKS. Oh, do you think I don't know all that? Do you think that the things people make fools of themselves about are any less real and true than the things they behave sensibly about? (Morell's gaze wavers for the first time. He instinctively averts his face and stands listening, startled and thoughtful.) They are more true: they are the only things that are true. You are very calm and sensible and moderate with me because you can see that I am a fool about your wife; just as no doubt that old man who was here just now is very wise over your socialism, because he sees that YOU are a fool about it. (Morell's perplexity deepens markedly. Eugene follows up his advantage, plying him fiercely with questions.) Does that prove you wrong? Does your complacent superiority to me prove that I am wrong?

MORELL (turning on Eugene, who stands his ground). Marchbanks: some devil is putting these words into your mouth. It is easy—terribly easy—to shake a man's faith in himself. To take advantage of that to break a man's spirit is devil's work. Take care of what you are doing. Take care.

MARCHBANKS (ruthlessly). I know. I'm doing it on purpose. I told you I should stagger you.

(They confront one another threateningly for a moment. Then Morell recovers his dignity.)

MORELL (with noble tenderness). Eugene: listen to me. Some day, I hope and trust, you will be a happy man like me. (Eugene chafes intolerantly, repudiating the worth of his happiness. Morell, deeply insulted, controls himself with fine forbearance, and continues steadily, with great artistic beauty of delivery) You will be married; and you will be working with all your might and valor to make every spot on earth as happy as your own home. You will be one of the makers of the Kingdom of Heaven on earth; and—who knows?—you may be a pioneer and master builder where I am only a humble journeyman; for don't think, my boy, that I cannot see in you, young as you are, promise of higher powers than I can ever pretend to. I well know that it is in the poet that the holy spirit of man—the god within him—is most godlike. It should make you tremble to think of that—to think that the heavy burthen and great gift of a poet may be laid upon you.

MARCHBANKS (unimpressed and remorseless, his boyish crudity of assertion telling sharply against Morell's oratory). It does not make me tremble. It is the want of it in others that makes me tremble.

MORELL (redoubling his force of style under the stimulus of his genuine feeling and Eugene's obduracy). Then help to kindle it in them—in ME—-not to extinguish it. In the future—when you are as happy as I am—I will be your true brother in the faith. I will help you to believe that God has given us a world that nothing but our own folly keeps from being a paradise. I will help you to believe that every stroke of your work is sowing happiness for the great harvest that all—even the humblest—shall one day reap. And last, but trust me, not least, I will help you to believe that your wife loves you and is happy in her home. We need such help, Marchbanks: we need it greatly and always. There are so many things to make us doubt, if once we let our understanding be troubled. Even at home, we sit as if in camp, encompassed by a hostile army of doubts. Will you play the traitor and let them in on me?

MARCHBANKS (looking round him). Is it like this for her here always? A woman, with a great soul, craving for reality, truth, freedom, and being fed on metaphors, sermons, stale perorations, mere rhetoric. Do you think a woman's soul can live on your talent for preaching?

MORELL (Stung). Marchbanks: you make it hard for me to control myself. My talent is like yours insofar as it has any real worth at all. It is the gift of finding words for divine truth.

MARCHBANKS (impetuously). It's the gift of the gab, nothing more and nothing less. What has your knack of fine talking to do with the truth, any more than playing the organ has? I've never been in your church; but I've been to your political meetings; and I've seen you do what's called rousing the meeting to enthusiasm: that is, you excited them until they behaved exactly as if they were drunk. And their wives looked on and saw clearly enough what fools they were. Oh, it's an old story: you'll find it in the Bible. I imagine King David, in his fits of enthusiasm, was very like you. (Stabbing him with the words.) "But his wife despised him in her heart."

MORELL (wrathfully). Leave my house. Do you hear? (He advances on him threateningly.)

MARCHBANKS (shrinking back against the couch). Let me alone. Don't touch me. (Morell grasps him powerfully by the lapel of his coat: he cowers down on the sofa and screams passionately.) Stop, Morell, if you strike me, I'll kill myself. I won't bear it. (Almost in hysterics.) Let me go. Take your hand away.

MORELL (with slow, emphatic scorn.) You little snivelling, cowardly whelp. (Releasing him.) Go, before you frighten yourself into a fit.

MARCHBANKS (on the sofa, gasping, but relieved by the withdrawal of Morell's hand). I'm not afraid of you: it's you who are afraid of me.

MORELL (quietly, as he stands over him). It looks like it, doesn't it?

MARCHBANKS (with petulant vehemence). Yes, it does. (Morell turns away contemptuously. Eugene scrambles to his feet and follows him.) You think because I shrink from being brutally handled—because (with tears in his voice) I can do nothing but cry with rage when I am met with violence—because I can't lift a heavy trunk down from the top of a cab like you—because I can't fight you for your wife as a navvy would: all that makes you think that I'm afraid of you. But you're wrong. If I haven't got what you call British pluck, I haven't British cowardice either: I'm not afraid of a clergyman's ideas. I'll fight your ideas. I'll rescue her from her slavery to them: I'll pit my own ideas against them. You are driving me out of the house because you daren't let her choose between your ideas and mine. You are afraid to let me see her again. (Morell, angered, turns suddenly on him. He flies to the door in involuntary dread.) Let me alone, I say. I'm going.

MORELL (with cold scorn). Wait a moment: I am not going to touch you: don't be afraid. When my wife comes back she will want to know why you have gone. And when she finds that you are never going to cross our threshold again, she will want to have that explained, too. Now I don't wish to distress her by telling her that you have behaved like a blackguard.

MARCHBANKS (Coming back with renewed vehemence). You shall—you must. If you give any explanation but the true one, you are a liar and a coward. Tell her what I said; and how you were strong and manly, and shook me as a terrier shakes a rat; and how I shrank and was terrified; and how you called me a snivelling little whelp and put me out of the house. If you don't tell her, I will: I'll write to her.

MORELL (taken aback.) Why do you want her to know this?

MARCHBANKS (with lyric rapture.) Because she will understand me, and know that I understand her. If you keep back one word of it from her—if you are not ready to lay the truth at her feet as I am—then you will know to the end of your days that she really belongs to me and not to you. Good-bye. (Going.)

MORELL (terribly disquieted). Stop: I will not tell her.

MARCHBANKS (turning near the door). Either the truth or a lie you MUST tell her, if I go.

MORELL (temporizing). Marchbanks: it is sometimes justifiable.

MARCHBANKS (cutting him short). I know—to lie. It will be useless. Good-bye, Mr. Clergyman.

(As he turns finally to the door, it opens and Candida enters in housekeeping attire.)

CANDIDA. Are you going, Eugene?(Looking more observantly at him.) Well, dear me, just look at you, going out into the street in that state! You ARE a poet, certainly. Look at him, James! (She takes him by the coat, and brings him forward to show him to Morell.) Look at his collar! look at his tie! look at his hair! One would think somebody had been throttling you. (The two men guard themselves against betraying their consciousness.) Here! Stand still. (She buttons his collar; ties his neckerchief in a bow; and arranges his hair.) There! Now you look so nice that I think you'd better stay to lunch after all, though I told you you mustn't. It will be ready in half an hour. (She puts a final touch to the bow. He kisses her hand.) Don't be silly.

MARCHBANKS. I want to stay, of course—unless the reverend gentleman, your husband, has anything to advance to the contrary.

CANDIDA. Shall he stay, James, if he promises to be a good boy and to help me to lay the table? (Marchbanks turns his head and looks steadfastly at Morell over his shoulder, challenging his answer.)

MORELL (shortly). Oh, yes, certainly: he had better. (He goes to the table and pretends to busy himself with his papers there.)

MARCHBANKS (offering his arm to Candida). Come and lay the table.(She takes it and they go to the door together. As they go out he adds) I am the happiest of men.

MORELL. So was I—an hour ago.

ACT II

The same day. The same room. Late in the afternoon. The spare chair for visitors has been replaced at the table, which is, if possible, more untidy than before. Marchbanks, alone and idle, is trying to find out how the typewriter works. Hearing someone at the door, he steals guiltily away to the window and pretends to be absorbed in the view. Miss Garnett, carrying the notebook in which she takes down Morell's letters in shorthand from his dictation, sits down at the typewriter and sets to work transcribing them, much too busy to notice Eugene. Unfortunately the first key she strikes sticks.

PROSERPINE. Bother! You've been meddling with my typewriter, Mr. Marchbanks; and there's not the least use in your trying to look as if you hadn't.

MARCHBANKS (timidly). I'm very sorry, Miss Garnett. I only tried to make it write.

PROSERPINE. Well, you've made this key stick.

MARCHBANKS (earnestly). I assure you I didn't touch the keys. I didn't, indeed. I only turned a little wheel. (He points irresolutely at the tension wheel.)

PROSERPINE. Oh, now I understand. (She sets the machine to rights, talking volubly all the time.) I suppose you thought it was a sort of barrel-organ. Nothing to do but turn the handle, and it would write a beautiful love letter for you straight off, eh?

MARCHBANKS (seriously). I suppose a machine could be made to write love-letters. They're all the same, aren't they!

PROSERPINE (somewhat indignantly: any such discussion, except by way of pleasantry, being outside her code of manners). How do I know? Why do you ask me?

MARCHBANKS. I beg your pardon. I thought clever people—people who can do business and write letters, and that sort of thing—always had love affairs.

PROSERPINE (rising, outraged). Mr. Marchbanks! (She looks severely at him, and marches with much dignity to the bookcase.)

MARCHBANKS (approaching her humbly). I hope I haven't offended you. Perhaps I shouldn't have alluded to your love affairs.

PROSERPINE (plucking a blue book from the shelf and turning sharply on him). I haven't any love affairs. How dare you say such a thing?

MARCHBANKS (simply). Really! Oh, then you are shy, like me. Isn't that so?

PROSERPINE. Certainly I am not shy. What do you mean?

MARCHBANKS (secretly). You must be: that is the reason there are so few love affairs in the world. We all go about longing for love: it is the first need of our natures, the loudest cry Of our hearts; but we dare not utter our longing: we are too shy. (Very earnestly.) Oh, Miss Garnett, what would you not give to be without fear, without shame—

PROSERPINE (scandalized), Well, upon my word!

MARCHBANKS (with petulant impatience). Ah, don't say those stupid things to me: they don't deceive me: what use are they? Why are you afraid to be your real self with me? I am just like you.

PROSERPINE. Like me! Pray, are you flattering me or flattering yourself? I don't feel quite sure which. (She turns to go back to the typewriter.)

MARCHBANKS (stopping her mysteriously). Hush! I go about in search of love; and I find it in unmeasured stores in the bosoms of others. But when I try to ask for it, this horrible shyness strangles me; and I stand dumb, or worse than dumb, saying meaningless things—foolish lies. And I see the affection I am longing for given to dogs and cats and pet birds, because they come and ask for it. (Almost whispering.) It must be asked for: it is like a ghost: it cannot speak unless it is first spoken to. (At his normal pitch, but with deep melancholy.) All the love in the world is longing to speak; only it dare not, because it is shy, shy, shy. That is the world's tragedy. (With a deep sigh he sits in the spare chair and buries his face in his hands.)

PROSERPINE (amazed, but keeping her wits about her—her point of honor in encounters with strange young men). Wicked people get over that shyness occasionally, don't they?

MARCHBANKS (scrambling up almost fiercely). Wicked people means people who have no love: therefore they have no shame. They have the power to ask love because they don't need it: they have the power to offer it because they have none to give. (He collapses into his seat, and adds, mournfully) But we, who have love, and long to mingle it with the love of others: we cannot utter a word. (Timidly.) You find that, don't you?

PROSERPINE. Look here: if you don't stop talking like this, I'll leave the room, Mr. Marchbanks: I really will. It's not proper. (She resumes her seat at the typewriter, opening the blue book and preparing to copy a passage from it.)

MARCHBANKS (hopelessly). Nothing that's worth saying IS proper. (He rises, and wanders about the room in his lost way, saying) I can't understand you, Miss Garnett. What am I to talk about?

PROSERPINE (snubbing him). Talk about indifferent things, talk about the weather.

MARCHBANKS. Would you stand and talk about indifferent things if a child were by, crying bitterly with hunger?

PROSERPINE. I suppose not.

MARCHBANKS. Well: I can't talk about indifferent things with my heart crying out bitterly in ITS hunger.

PROSERPINE. Then hold your tongue.

MARCHBANKS. Yes: that is what it always comes to. We hold our tongues. Does that stop the cry of your heart?—for it does cry: doesn't it? It must, if you have a heart.

PROSERPINE (suddenly rising with her hand pressed on her heart). Oh, it's no use trying to work while you talk like that. (She leaves her little table and sits on the sofa. Her feelings are evidently strongly worked on.) It's no business of yours, whether my heart cries or not; but I have a mind to tell you, for all that.

MARCHBANKS. You needn't. I know already that it must.

PROSERPINE. But mind: if you ever say I said so, I'll deny it.

MARCHBANKS (compassionately). Yes, I know. And so you haven't the courage to tell him?

PROSERPINE (bouncing up). HIM! Who?

MARCHBANKS. Whoever he is. The man you love. It might be anybody. The curate, Mr. Mill, perhaps.

PROSERPINE (with disdain). Mr. Mill!!! A fine man to break my heart about, indeed! I'd rather have you than Mr. Mill.

MARCHBANKS (recoiling). No, really—I'm very sorry; but you mustn't think of that. I—

PROSERPINE. (testily, crossing to the fire and standing at it with her back to him). Oh, don't be frightened: it's not you. It's not any one particular person.

MARCHBANKS. I know. You feel that you could love anybody that offered—

PROSERPINE (exasperated). Anybody that offered! No, I do not. What do you take me for?

MARCHBANKS (discouraged). No use. You won't make me REAL answers—only those things that everybody says. (He strays to the sofa and sits down disconsolately.)

PROSERPINE (nettled at what she takes to be a disparagement of her manners by an aristocrat). Oh, well, if you want original conversation, you'd better go and talk to yourself.

MARCHBANKS. That is what all poets do: they talk to themselves out loud; and the world overhears them. But it's horribly lonely not to hear someone else talk sometimes.

PROSERPINE. Wait until Mr. Morell comes. HE'LL talk to you. (Marchbanks shudders.) Oh, you needn't make wry faces over him: he can talk better than you. (With temper.) He'd talk your little head off. (She is going back angrily to her place, when, suddenly enlightened, he springs up and stops her.)

MARCHBANKS. Ah, I understand now!

PROSERPINE (reddening). What do you understand?

MARCHBANKS. Your secret. Tell me: is it really and truly possible for a woman to love him?

PROSERPINE (as if this were beyond all bounds). Well!!

MARCHBANKS (passionately). No, answer me. I want to know: I MUST know. I can't understand it. I can see nothing in him but words, pious resolutions, what people call goodness. You can't love that.

PROSERPINE (attempting to snub him by an air of cool propriety). I simply don't know what you're talking about. I don't understand you.

MARCHBANKS (vehemently). You do. You lie—

PROSERPINE. Oh!

MARCHBANKS. You DO understand; and you KNOW. (Determined to have an answer.) Is it possible for a woman to love him?

PROSERPINE (looking him straight in the face.) Yes. (He covers his face with his hands.) Whatever is the matter with you! (He takes down his hands and looks at her. Frightened at the tragic mask presented to her, she hurries past him at the utmost possible distance, keeping her eyes on his face until he turns from her and goes to the child's chair beside the hearth, where he sits in the deepest dejection. As she approaches the door, it opens and Burgess enters. On seeing him, she ejaculates) Praise heaven, here's somebody! (and sits down, reassured, at her table. She puts a fresh sheet of paper into the typewriter as Burgess crosses to Eugene.)

BURGESS (bent on taking care of the distinguished visitor). Well: so this is the way they leave you to yourself, Mr. Morchbanks. I've come to keep you company. (Marchbanks looks up at him in consternation, which is quite lost on him.) James is receivin' a deppitation in the dinin' room; and Candy is hupstairs educatin' of a young stitcher gurl she's hinterusted in. She's settin' there learnin' her to read out of the "'Ev'nly Twins." (Condolingly.) You must find it lonesome here with no one but the typist to talk to. (He pulls round the easy chair above fire, and sits down.)

PROSERPINE (highly incensed). He'll be all right now that he has the advantage of YOUR polished conversation: that's one comfort, anyhow. (She begins to typewrite with clattering asperity.)

BURGESS (amazed at her audacity). Hi was not addressin' myself to you, young woman, that I'm awerr of.

PROSERPINE (tartly, to Marchbanks). Did you ever see worse manners, Mr. Marchbanks?

BURGESS (with pompous severity). Mr. Morchbanks is a gentleman and knows his place, which is more than some people do.

PROSERPINE (fretfully). It's well you and I are not ladies and gentlemen: I'd talk to you pretty straight if Mr. Marchbanks wasn't here. (She pulls the letter out of the machine so crossly that it tears.) There, now I've spoiled this letter—have to be done all over again. Oh, I can't contain myself—silly old fathead!

BURGESS (rising, breathless with indignation). Ho! I'm a silly ole fathead, am I? Ho, indeed (gasping). Hall right, my gurl! Hall right. You just wait till I tell that to your employer. You'll see. I'll teach you: see if I don't.

PROSERPINE. I—

BURGESS (cutting her short). No, you've done it now. No huse a-talkin' to me. I'll let you know who I am. (Proserpine shifts her paper carriage with a defiant bang, and disdainfully goes on with her work.) Don't you take no notice of her, Mr. Morchbanks. She's beneath it. (He sits down again loftily.)

MARCHBANKS (miserably nervous and disconcerted). Hadn't we better change the subject. I—I don't think Miss Garnett meant anything.

PROSERPINE (with intense conviction). Oh, didn't I though, just!

BURGESS. I wouldn't demean myself to take notice on her.

(An electric bell rings twice.)

PROSERPINE (gathering up her note-book and papers). That's for me. (She hurries out.)

BURGESS (calling after her). Oh, we can spare you. (Somewhat relieved by the triumph of having the last word, and yet half inclined to try to improve on it, he looks after her for a moment; then subsides into his seat by Eugene, and addresses him very confidentially.) Now we're alone, Mr. Morchbanks, let me give you a friendly 'int that I wouldn't give to everybody. 'Ow long 'ave you known my son-in-law James here?

MARCHBANKS. I don't know. I never can remember dates. A few months, perhaps.

BURGESS. Ever notice anything queer about him?

MARCHBANKS. I don't think so.

BURGESS (impressively). No more you wouldn't. That's the danger in it. Well, he's mad.

MARCHBANKS. Mad!

BURGESS. Mad as a Morch 'are. You take notice on him and you'll see.

MARCHBANKS (beginning). But surely that is only because his opinions—

BURGESS (touching him with his forefinger on his knee, and pressing it as if to hold his attention with it). That's wot I used tee think, Mr. Morchbanks. Hi thought long enough that it was honly 'is hopinions; though, mind you, hopinions becomes vurry serious things when people takes to hactin on 'em as 'e does. But that's not wot I go on. (He looks round to make sure that they are alone, and bends over to Eugene's ear.) Wot do you think he says to me this mornin' in this very room?

MARCHBANKS. What?

BURGESS. He sez to me—this is as sure as we're settin' here now—he sez: "I'm a fool," he sez;—"and yore a scounderl"—as cool as possible. Me a scounderl, mind you! And then shook 'ands with me on it, as if it was to my credit! Do you mean to tell me that that man's sane?

MORELL. (outside, calling to Proserpine, holding the door open). Get all their names and addresses, Miss Garnett.

PROSERPINE (in the distance). Yes, Mr. Morell.

(Morell comes in, with the deputation's documents in his hands.)

BURGESS (aside to Marchbanks). Yorr he is. Just you keep your heye on him and see. (Rising momentously.) I'm sorry, James, to 'ave to make a complaint to you. I don't want to do it; but I feel I oughter, as a matter o' right and duty.

MORELL. What's the matter?

BURGESS. Mr. Morchbanks will bear me out: he was a witness. (Very solemnly.) Your young woman so far forgot herself as to call me a silly ole fat 'ead.

MORELL (delighted—with tremendous heartiness). Oh, now, isn't that EXACTLY like Prossy? She's so frank: she can't contain herself! Poor Prossy! Ha! Ha!

BURGESS (trembling with rage). And do you hexpec me to put up with it from the like of 'ER?

MORELL. Pooh, nonsense! you can't take any notice of it. Never mind. (He goes to the cellaret and puts the papers into one of the drawers.)

BURGESS. Oh, I don't mind. I'm above it. But is it RIGHT?—that's what I want to know. Is it right?

MORELL. That's a question for the Church, not for the laity. Has it done you any harm, that's the question for you, eh? Of course, it hasn't. Think no more of it. (He dismisses the subject by going to his place at the table and setting to work at his correspondence.)

BURGESS (aside to Marchbanks). What did I tell you? Mad as a 'atter. (He goes to the table and asks, with the sickly civility of a hungry man) When's dinner, James?

MORELL. Not for half an hour yet.

BURGESS (with plaintive resignation). Gimme a nice book to read over the fire, will you, James: thur's a good chap.

MORELL. What sort of book? A good one?

BURGESS (with almost a yell of remonstrance). Nah-oo! Summat pleasant, just to pass the time. (Morell takes an illustrated paper from the table and offers it. He accepts it humbly.) Thank yer, James. (He goes back to his easy chair at the fire, and sits there at his ease, reading.)

MORELL (as he writes). Candida will come to entertain you presently. She has got rid of her pupil. She is filling the lamps.

MARCHBANKS (starting up in the wildest consternation). But that will soil her hands. I can't bear that, Morell: it's a shame. I'll go and fill them. (He makes for the door.)

MORELL. You'd better not. (Marchbanks stops irresolutely.) She'd only set you to clean my boots, to save me the trouble of doing it myself in the morning.

BURGESS (with grave disapproval). Don't you keep a servant now, James?

MORELL. Yes; but she isn't a slave; and the house looks as if I kept three. That means that everyone has to lend a hand. It's not a bad plan: Prossy and I can talk business after breakfast whilst we're washing up. Washing up's no trouble when there are two people to do it.

MARCHBANKS (tormentedly). Do you think every woman is as coarse-grained as Miss Garnett?

BURGESS (emphatically). That's quite right, Mr. Morchbanks. That's quite right. She IS corse-grained.

MORELL (quietly and significantly). Marchbanks!

MARCHBANKS. Yes.

MORELL. How many servants does your father keep?

MARCHBANKS. Oh, I don't know. (He comes back uneasily to the sofa, as if to get as far as possible from Morell's questioning, and sits down in great agony of mind, thinking of the paraffin.)

MORELL. (very gravely). So many that you don't know. (More aggressively.) Anyhow, when there's anything coarse-grained to be done, you ring the bell and throw it on to somebody else, eh? That's one of the great facts in YOUR existence, isn't it?

MARCHBANKS. Oh, don't torture me. The one great fact now is that your wife's beautiful fingers are dabbling in paraffin oil, and that you are sitting here comfortably preaching about it—everlasting preaching, preaching, words, words, words.

BURGESS (intensely appreciating this retort). Ha, ha! Devil a better. (Radiantly.) 'Ad you there, James, straight.

(Candida comes in, well aproned, with a reading lamp trimmed, filled, and ready for lighting. She places it on the table near Morell, ready for use.)

CANDIDA (brushing her finger tips together with a slight twitch of her nose). If you stay with us, Eugene, I think I will hand over the lamps to you.

MARCHBANKS. I will stay on condition that you hand over all the rough work to me.

CANDIDA. That's very gallant; but I think I should like to see how you do it first. (Turning to Morell.) James: you've not been looking after the house properly.

MORELL. What have I done—or not done—my love?

CANDIDA (with serious vexation). My own particular pet scrubbing brush has been used for blackleading. (A heart-breaking wail bursts from Marchbanks. Burgess looks round, amazed. Candida hurries to the sofa.) What's the matter? Are you ill, Eugene?

MARCHBANKS. No, not ill. Only horror, horror, horror! (He bows his head on his hands.)

BURGESS (shocked). What! Got the 'orrors, Mr. Morchbanks! Oh, that's bad, at your age. You must leave it off grajally.

CANDIDA (reassured). Nonsense, papa. It's only poetic horror, isn't it, Eugene? (Petting him.)

BURGESS (abashed). Oh, poetic 'orror, is it? I beg your pordon, I'm shore. (He turns to the fire again, deprecating his hasty conclusion.)

CANDIDA. What is it, Eugene—the scrubbing brush? (He shudders.) Well, there! never mind. (She sits down beside him.) Wouldn't you like to present me with a nice new one, with an ivory back inlaid with mother-of-pearl?

MARCHBANKS (softly and musically, but sadly and longingly). No, not a scrubbing brush, but a boat—a tiny shallop to sail away in, far from the world, where the marble floors are washed by the rain and dried by the sun, where the south wind dusts the beautiful green and purple carpets. Or a chariot—to carry us up into the sky, where the lamps are stars, and don't need to be filled with paraffin oil every day.

MORELL (harshly). And where there is nothing to do but to be idle, selfish and useless.

CANDIDA (jarred). Oh, James, how could you spoil it all!

MARCHBANKS (firing up). Yes, to be idle, selfish and useless: that is to be beautiful and free and happy: hasn't every man desired that with all his soul for the woman he loves? That's my ideal: what's yours, and that of all the dreadful people who live in these hideous rows of houses? Sermons and scrubbing brushes! With you to preach the sermon and your wife to scrub.

CANDIDA (quaintly). He cleans the boots, Eugene. You will have to clean them to-morrow for saying that about him.

MARCHBANKS. Oh! don't talk about boots. Your feet should be beautiful on the mountains.

CANDIDA. My feet would not be beautiful on the Hackney Road without boots.

BURGESS (scandalized). Come, Candy, don't be vulgar. Mr. Morchbanks ain't accustomed to it. You're givin' him the 'orrors again. I mean the poetic ones.

(Morell is silent. Apparently he is busy with his letters: really he is puzzling with misgiving over his new and alarming experience that the surer he is of his moral thrusts, the more swiftly and effectively Eugene parries them. To find himself beginning to fear a man whom he does not respect affects him bitterly.)

(Miss Garnett comes in with a telegram.)

PROSERPINE (handing the telegram to Morell). Reply paid. The boy's waiting. (To Candida, coming back to her machine and sitting down.) Maria is ready for you now in the kitchen, Mrs. Morell. (Candida rises.) The onions have come.

MARCHBANKS (convulsively). Onions!

CANDIDA. Yes, onions. Not even Spanish ones—nasty little red onions. You shall help me to slice them. Come along.

(She catches him by the wrist and runs out, pulling him after her. Burgess rises in consternation, and stands aghast on the hearth-rug, staring after them.)

BURGESS. Candy didn't oughter 'andle a peer's nevvy like that. It's goin' too fur with it. Lookee 'ere, James: do 'e often git taken queer like that?

MORELL (shortly, writing a telegram). I don't know.

BURGESS (sentimentally). He talks very pretty. I allus had a turn for a bit of potery. Candy takes arter me that-a-way: huse ter make me tell her fairy stories when she was on'y a little kiddy not that 'igh (indicating a stature of two feet or thereabouts).

MORELL (preoccupied). Ah, indeed. (He blots the telegram, and goes out.)

PROSERPINE. Used you to make the fairy stories up out of your own head?

(Burgess, not deigning to reply, strikes an attitude of the haughtiest disdain on the hearth-rug.)

PROSERPINE (calmly). I should never have supposed you had it in you. By the way, I'd better warn you, since you've taken such a fancy to Mr. Marchbanks. He's mad.

BURGESS. Mad! Wot! 'Im too!!

PROSERPINE. Mad as a March hare. He did frighten me, I can tell you just before you came in that time. Haven't you noticed the queer things he says?

BURGESS. So that's wot the poetic 'orrors means. Blame me if it didn't come into my head once or twyst that he must be off his chump! (He crosses the room to the door, lifting up his voice as he goes.) Well, this is a pretty sort of asylum for a man to be in, with no one but you to take care of him!

PROSERPINE (as he passes her). Yes, what a dreadful thing it would be if anything happened to YOU!

BURGESS (loftily). Don't you address no remarks to me. Tell your hemployer that I've gone into the garden for a smoke.

PROSERPINE (mocking). Oh!

(Before Burgess can retort, Morell comes back.)

BURGESS (sentimentally). Goin' for a turn in the garden to smoke, James.

MORELL (brusquely). Oh, all right, all right. (Burgess goes out pathetically in the character of the weary old man. Morell stands at the table, turning over his papers, and adding, across to Proserpine, half humorously, half absently) Well, Miss Prossy, why have you been calling my father-in-law names?

PROSERPINE (blushing fiery red, and looking quickly up at him, half scared, half reproachful). I—(She bursts into tears.)

MORELL (with tender gaiety, leaning across the table towards her, and consoling her). Oh, come, come, come! Never mind, Pross: he IS a silly old fathead, isn't he?

(With an explosive sob, she makes a dash at the door, and vanishes, banging it. Morell, shaking his head resignedly, sighs, and goes wearily to his chair, where he sits down and sets to work, looking old and careworn.)

(Candida comes in. She has finished her household work and taken of the apron. She at once notices his dejected appearance, and posts herself quietly at the spare chair, looking down at him attentively; but she says nothing.)

MORELL (looking up, but with his pen raised ready to resume his work). Well? Where is Eugene?

CANDIDA. Washing his hands in the scullery—under the tap. He will make an excellent cook if he can only get over his dread of Maria.

MORELL (shortly). Ha! No doubt. (He begins writing again.)

CANDIDA (going nearer, and putting her hand down softly on his to stop him, as she says). Come here, dear. Let me look at you. (He drops his pen and yields himself at her disposal. She makes him rise and brings him a little away from the table, looking at him critically all the time.) Turn your face to the light. (She places him facing the window.) My boy is not looking well. Has he been overworking?

MORELL. Nothing more than usual.

CANDIDA. He looks very pale, and grey, and wrinkled, and old. (His melancholy deepens; and she attacks it with wilful gaiety.) Here (pulling him towards the easy chair) you've done enough writing for to-day. Leave Prossy to finish it and come and talk to me.

MORELL. But—

CANDIDA. Yes, I MUST be talked to sometimes. (She makes him sit down, and seats herself on the carpet beside his knee.) Now (patting his hand) you're beginning to look better already. Why don't you give up all this tiresome overworking—going out every night lecturing and talking? Of course what you say is all very true and very right; but it does no good: they don't mind what you say to them one little bit. Of course they agree with you; but what's the use of people agreeing with you if they go and do just the opposite of what you tell them the moment your back is turned? Look at our congregation at St. Dominic's! Why do they come to hear you talking about Christianity every Sunday? Why, just because they've been so full of business and money-making for six days that they want to forget all about it and have a rest on the seventh, so that they can go back fresh and make money harder than ever! You positively help them at it instead of hindering them.

MORELL (with energetic seriousness). You know very well, Candida, that I often blow them up soundly for that. But if there is nothing in their church-going but rest and diversion, why don't they try something more amusing—more self-indulgent? There must be some good in the fact that they prefer St. Dominic's to worse places on Sundays.

CANDIDA. Oh, the worst places aren't open; and even if they were, they daren't be seen going to them. Besides, James, dear, you preach so splendidly that it's as good as a play for them. Why do you think the women are so enthusiastic?

MORELL (shocked). Candida!

CANDIDA. Oh, *I* know. You silly boy: you think it's your Socialism and your religion; but if it was that, they'd do what you tell them instead of only coming to look at you. They all have Prossy's complaint.

MORELL. Prossy's complaint! What do you mean, Candida?

CANDIDA. Yes, Prossy, and all the other secretaries you ever had. Why does Prossy condescend to wash up the things, and to peel potatoes and abase herself in all manner of ways for six shillings a week less than she used to get in a city office? She's in love with you, James: that's the reason. They're all in love with you. And you are in love with preaching because you do it so beautifully. And you think it's all enthusiasm for the kingdom of Heaven on earth; and so do they. You dear silly!

MORELL. Candida: what dreadful, what soul-destroying cynicism! Are you jesting? Or—can it be?—are you jealous?

CANDIDA (with curious thoughtfulness). Yes, I feel a little jealous sometimes.

MORELL (incredulously). What! Of Prossy?

CANDIDA (laughing). No, no, no, no. Not jealous of anybody. Jealous for somebody else, who is not loved as he ought to be.

MORELL. Me!

CANDIDA. You! Why, you're spoiled with love and worship: you get far more than is good for you. No: I mean Eugene.

MORELL (startled). Eugene!

CANDIDA. It seems unfair that all the love should go to you, and none to him, although he needs it so much more than you do. (A convulsive movement shakes him in spite of himself.) What's the matter? Am I worrying you?

MORELL (hastily). Not at all. (Looking at her with troubled intensity.) You know that I have perfect confidence in you, Candida.

CANDIDA. You vain thing! Are you so sure of your irresistible attractions?

MORELL. Candida: you are shocking me. I never thought of my attractions. I thought of your goodness—your purity. That is what I confide in.

CANDIDA. What a nasty, uncomfortable thing to say to me! Oh, you ARE a clergyman, James—a thorough clergyman.

MORELL (turning away from her, heart-stricken). So Eugene says.

CANDIDA (with lively interest, leaning over to him with her arms on his knee). Eugene's always right. He's a wonderful boy: I have grown fonder and fonder of him all the time I was away. Do you know, James, that though he has not the least suspicion of it himself, he is ready to fall madly in love with me?

MORELL (grimly). Oh, he has no suspicion of it himself, hasn't he?

CANDIDA. Not a bit. (She takes her arms from his knee, and turns thoughtfully, sinking into a more restful attitude with her hands in her lap.) Some day he will know when he is grown up and experienced, like you. And he will know that I must have known. I wonder what he will think of me then.

MORELL. No evil, Candida. I hope and trust, no evil.

CANDIDA (dubiously). That will depend.

MORELL (bewildered). Depend!

CANDIDA (looking at him). Yes: it will depend on what happens to him. (He look vacantly at her.) Don't you see? It will depend on how he comes to learn what love really is. I mean on the sort of woman who will teach it to him.

MORELL (quite at a loss). Yes. No. I don't know what you mean.

CANDIDA (explaining). If he learns it from a good woman, then it will be all right: he will forgive me.

MORELL. Forgive!

CANDIDA. But suppose he learns it from a bad woman, as so many men do, especially poetic men, who imagine all women are angels! Suppose he only discovers the value of love when he has thrown it away and degraded himself in his ignorance. Will he forgive me then, do you think?

MORELL. Forgive you for what?

CANDIDA (realizing how stupid he is, and a little disappointed, though quite tenderly so). Don't you understand? (He shakes his head. She turns to him again, so as to explain with the fondest intimacy.) I mean, will he forgive me for not teaching him myself? For abandoning him to the bad women for the sake of my goodness—my purity, as you call it? Ah, James, how little you understand me, to talk of your confidence in my goodness and purity! I would give them both to poor Eugene as willingly as I would give my shawl to a beggar dying of cold, if there were nothing else to restrain me. Put your trust in my love for you, James, for if that went, I should care very little for your sermons—mere phrases that you cheat yourself and others with every day. (She is about to rise.)

MORELL. HIS words!

CANDIDA (checking herself quickly in the act of getting up, so that she is on her knees, but upright). Whose words?

MORELL. Eugene's.

CANDIDA (delighted). He is always right. He understands you; he understands me; he understands Prossy; and you, James—you understand nothing. (She laughs, and kisses him to console him. He recoils as if stung, and springs up.)

MORELL. How can you bear to do that when—oh, Candida (with anguish in his voice) I had rather you had plunged a grappling iron into my heart than given me that kiss.

CANDIDA (rising, alarmed). My dear: what's the matter?

MORELL (frantically waving her off). Don't touch me.

CANDIDA (amazed). James!

(They are interrupted by the entrance of Marchbanks, with Burgess, who stops near the door, staring, whilst Eugene hurries forward between them.)

MARCHBANKS. Is anything the matter?

MORELL (deadly white, putting an iron constraint on himself). Nothing but this: that either you were right this morning, or Candida is mad.

BURGESS (in loudest protest). Wot! Candy mad too! Oh, come, come, come! (He crosses the room to the fireplace, protesting as he goes, and knocks the ashes out of his pipe on the bars. Morell sits down desperately, leaning forward to hide his face, and interlacing his fingers rigidly to keep them steady.)

CANDIDA (to Morell, relieved and laughing). Oh, you're only shocked! Is that all? How conventional all you unconventional people are!

BURGESS. Come: be'ave yourself, Candy. What'll Mr. Morchbanks think of you?

CANDIDA. This comes of James teaching me to think for myself, and never to hold back out of fear of what other people may think of me. It works beautifully as long as I think the same things as he does. But now, because I have just thought something different!—look at him—just look!

(She points to Morell, greatly amused. Eugene looks, and instantly presses his band on his heart, as if some deadly pain had shot through it, and sits down on the sofa like a man witnessing a tragedy.)

BURGESS (on the hearth-rug). Well, James, you certainly ain't as himpressive lookin' as usu'l.

MORELL (with a laugh which is half a sob). I suppose not. I beg all your pardons: I was not conscious of making a fuss. (Pulling himself together.)

Well, well, well, well, well! (He goes back to his place at the table, setting to work at his papers again with resolute cheerfulness.)

CANDIDA (going to the sofa and sitting beside Marchbanks, still in a bantering humor). Well, Eugene, why are you so sad? Did the onions make you cry?

(Morell cannot prevent himself from watching them.)

MARCHBANKS (aside to her). It is your cruelty. I hate cruelty. It is a horrible thing to see one person make another suffer.

CANDIDA (petting him ironically). Poor boy, have I been cruel? Did I make it slice nasty little red onions?

MARCHBANKS (earnestly). Oh, stop, stop: I don't mean myself. You have made him suffer frightfully. I feel his pain in my own heart. I know that it is not your fault—it is something that must happen; but don't make light of it. I shudder when you torture him and laugh.

CANDIDA (incredulously). I torture James! Nonsense, Eugene: how you exaggerate! Silly! (She looks round at Morell, who hastily resumes his writing. She goes to him and stands behind his chair, bending over him.) Don't work any more, dear. Come and talk to us.

MORELL (affectionately but bitterly). Ah no: I can't talk. I can only preach.

CANDIDA (caressing him). Well, come and preach.

BURGESS (strongly remonstrating). Aw, no, Candy. 'Ang it all! (Lexy Mill comes in, looking anxious and important.)

LEXY (hastening to shake hands with Candida). How do you do, Mrs. Morell? So glad to see you back again.

CANDIDA. Thank you, Lexy. You know Eugene, don't you?

LEXY. Oh, yes. How do you do, Marchbanks?

MARCHBANKS. Quite well, thanks.

LEXY (to Morell). I've just come from the Guild of St. Matthew. They are in the greatest consternation about your telegram. There's nothing wrong, is there?

CANDIDA. What did you telegraph about, James?

LEXY (to Candida). He was to have spoken for them tonight. They've taken the large hall in Mare Street and spent a lot of money on posters. Morell's telegram was to say he couldn't come. It came on them like a thunderbolt.

CANDIDA (surprized, and beginning to suspect something wrong). Given up an engagement to speak!

BURGESS. First time in his life, I'll bet. Ain' it, Candy?

LEXY (to Morell). They decided to send an urgent telegram to you asking whether you could not change your mind. Have you received it?

MORELL (with restrained impatience). Yes, yes: I got it.

LEXY. It was reply paid.

MORELL. Yes, I know. I answered it. I can't go.

CANDIDA. But why, James?

MORELL (almost fiercely). Because I don't choose. These people forget that I am a man: they think I am a talking machine to be turned on for their pleasure every evening of my life. May I not have ONE night at home, with my wife, and my friends?

(They are all amazed at this outburst, except Eugene. His expression remains unchanged.)

CANDIDA. Oh, James, you know you'll have an attack of bad conscience to-morrow; and *I* shall have to suffer for that.

LEXY (intimidated, but urgent). I know, of course, that they make the most unreasonable demands on you. But they have been telegraphing all over the place for another speaker: and they can get nobody but the President of the Agnostic League.

MORELL (promptly). Well, an excellent man. What better do they want?

LEXY. But he always insists so powerfully on the divorce of Socialism from Christianity. He will undo all the good we have been doing. Of course you know best; but—(He hesitates.)

CANDIDA (coaxingly). Oh, DO go, James. We'll all go.

BURGESS (grumbling). Look 'ere, Candy! I say! Let's stay at home by the fire, comfortable. He won't need to be more'n a couple-o'-hour away.

CANDIDA. You'll be just as comfortable at the meeting. We'll all sit on the platform and be great people.

EUGENE (terrified). Oh, please don't let us go on the platform. No—everyone will stare at us—I couldn't. I'll sit at the back of the room.

CANDIDA. Don't be afraid. They'll be too busy looking at James to notice you.

MORELL (turning his head and looking meaningly at her over his shoulder). Prossy's complaint, Candida! Eh?

CANDIDA (gaily). Yes.

BURGESS (mystified). Prossy's complaint. Wot are you talking about, James?

MORELL (not heeding him, rises; goes to the door; and holds it open, shouting in a commanding voice). Miss Garnett.

PROSERPINE (in the distance). Yes, Mr. Morell. Coming. (They all wait, except Burgess, who goes stealthily to Lexy and draws him aside.)

BURGESS. Listen here, Mr. Mill. Wot's Prossy's complaint? Wot's wrong with 'er?

LEXY (confidentially). Well, I don't exactly know; but she spoke very strangely to me this morning. I'm afraid she's a little out of her mind sometimes.

BURGESS (overwhelmed). Why, it must be catchin'! Four in the same 'ouse! (He goes back to the hearth, quite lost before the instability of the human intellect in a clergyman's house.)

PROSERPINE (appearing on the threshold). What is it, Mr. Morell?

MORELL. Telegraph to the Guild of St. Matthew that I am coming.

PROSERPINE (surprised). Don't they expect you?

MORELL (peremptorily). Do as I tell you.

(Proserpine frightened, sits down at her typewriter, and obeys. Morell goes across to Burgess, Candida watching his movements all the time with growing wonder and misgiving.)

MORELL. Burgess: you don't want to come?

BURGESS (in deprecation). Oh, don't put it like that, James. It's only that it ain't Sunday, you know.

MORELL. I'm sorry. I thought you might like to be introduced to the chairman. He's on the Works Committee of the County Council and has some influence in the matter of contracts. (Burgess wakes up at once. Morell, expecting as much, waits a moment, and says) Will you come?

BURGESS (with enthusiasm). Course I'll come, James. Ain' it always a pleasure to 'ear you.

MORELL (turning from him). I shall want you to take some notes at the meeting, Miss Garnett, if you have no other engagement. (She nods, afraid to speak.) You are coming, Lexy, I suppose.

LEXY. Certainly.

CANDIDA. We are all coming, James.

MORELL. No: you are not coming; and Eugene is not coming. You will stay here and entertain him—to celebrate your return home. (Eugene rises, breathless.)

CANDIDA. But James—

MORELL (authoritatively). I insist. You do not want to come; and he does not want to come. (Candida is about to protest.) Oh, don't concern yourselves: I shall have plenty of people without you: your chairs will be wanted by unconverted people who have never heard me before.

CANDIDA (troubled). Eugene: wouldn't you like to come?

MORELL. I should be afraid to let myself go before Eugene: he is so critical of sermons. (Looking at him.) He knows I am afraid of him: he told me as much this morning. Well, I shall show him how much afraid I am by leaving him here in your custody, Candida.

MARCHBANKS (to himself, with vivid feeling). That's brave. That's beautiful. (He sits down again listening with parted lips.)

CANDIDA (with anxious misgiving). But—but—Is anything the matter, James? (Greatly troubled.) I can't understand—

MORELL. Ah, I thought it was I who couldn't understand, dear. (He takes her tenderly in his arms and kisses her on the forehead; then looks round quietly at Marchbanks.)

ACT III

Late in the evening. Past ten. The curtains are drawn, and the lamps lighted. The typewriter is in its case; the large table has been cleared and tidied; everything indicates that the day's work is done.

Candida and Marchbanks are seated at the fire. The reading lamp is on the mantelshelf above Marchbanks, who is sitting on the small chair reading aloud from a manuscript. A little pile of manuscripts and a couple of volumes of poetry are on the carpet beside him. Candida is in the easy chair with the poker, a light brass one, upright in her hand. She is leaning back and looking at the point of it curiously, with her feet stretched towards the blaze and her heels resting on the fender, profoundly unconscious of her appearance and surroundings.

MARCHBANKS (breaking off in his recitation): Every poet that ever lived has put that thought into a sonnet. He must: he can't help it. (He looks to her for assent, and notices her absorption in the poker.) Haven't you been listening? (No response.) Mrs. Morell!

CANDIDA (starting). Eh?

MARCHBANKS. Haven't you been listening?

CANDIDA (with a guilty excess of politeness). Oh, yes. It's very nice. Go on, Eugene. I'm longing to hear what happens to the angel.

MARCHBANKS (crushed—the manuscript dropping from his hand to the floor). I beg your pardon for boring you.

CANDIDA. But you are not boring me, I assure you. Please go on. Do, Eugene.

MARCHBANKS. I finished the poem about the angel quarter of an hour ago. I've read you several things since.

CANDIDA (remorsefully). I'm so sorry, Eugene. I think the poker must have fascinated me. (She puts it down.)

MARCHBANKS. It made me horribly uneasy.

CANDIDA. Why didn't you tell me? I'd have put it down at once.

MARCHBANKS. I was afraid of making you uneasy, too. It looked as if it were a weapon. If I were a hero of old, I should have laid my drawn sword between us. If Morell had come in he would have thought you had taken up the poker because there was no sword between us.

CANDIDA (wondering). What? (With a puzzled glance at him.) I can't quite follow that. Those sonnets of yours have perfectly addled me. Why should there be a sword between us?

MARCHBANKS (evasively). Oh, never mind. (He stoops to pick up the manuscript.)

CANDIDA. Put that down again, Eugene. There are limits to my appetite for poetry—even your poetry. You've been reading to me for more than two hours—ever since James went out. I want to talk.

MARCHBANKS (rising, scared). No: I mustn't talk. (He looks round him in his lost way, and adds, suddenly) I think I'll go out and take a walk in the park. (Making for the door.)

CANDIDA. Nonsense: it's shut long ago. Come and sit down on the hearth-rug, and talk moonshine as you usually do. I want to be amused. Don't you want to?

MARCHBANKS (in half terror, half rapture). Yes.

CANDIDA. Then come along. (She moves her chair back a little to make room. He hesitates; then timidly stretches himself on the hearth-rug, face upwards, and throws back his head across her knees, looking up at her.)

MARCHBANKS. Oh, I've been so miserable all the evening, because I was doing right. Now I'm doing wrong; and I'm happy.

CANDIDA (tenderly amused at him). Yes: I'm sure you feel a great grown up wicked deceiver—quite proud of yourself, aren't you?

MARCHBANKS (raising his head quickly and turning a little to look round at her). Take care. I'm ever so much older than you, if you only knew. (He turns quite over on his knees, with his hands clasped and his arms on her lap, and speaks with growing impulse, his blood beginning to stir.) May I say some wicked things to you?

CANDIDA (without the least fear or coldness, quite nobly, and with perfect respect for his passion, but with a touch of her wise-hearted maternal humor). No. But you may say anything you really and truly feel. Anything at all, no matter what it is. I am not afraid, so long as it is your real self that speaks, and not a mere attitude—a gallant attitude, or a wicked attitude, or even a poetic attitude. I put you on your honor and truth. Now say whatever you want to.

MARCHBANKS (the eager expression vanishing utterly from his lips and nostrils as his eyes light up with pathetic spirituality). Oh, now I can't say anything: all the words I know belong to some attitude or other—all except one.

CANDIDA. What one is that?

MARCHBANKS (softly, losing himself in the music of the name). Candida, Candida, Candida, Candida, Candida. I must say that now, because you have put me on my honor and truth; and I never think or feel Mrs. Morell: it is always Candida.

CANDIDA. Of course. And what have you to say to Candida?

MARCHBANKS. Nothing, but to repeat your name a thousand times. Don't you feel that every time is a prayer to you?

CANDIDA. Doesn't it make you happy to be able to pray?

MARCHBANKS. Yes, very happy.

CANDIDA. Well, that happiness is the answer to your prayer. Do you want anything more?

MARCHBANKS (in beatitude). No: I have come into heaven, where want is unknown.

(Morell comes in. He halts on the threshold, and takes in the scene at a glance.)

MORELL (grave and self-contained). I hope I don't disturb you. (Candida starts up violently, but without the smallest embarrassment, laughing at herself. Eugene, still kneeling, saves himself from falling by putting his hands on the seat of the chair, and remains there, staring open mouthed at Morell.)

CANDIDA (as she rises). Oh, James, how you startled me! I was so taken up with Eugene that I didn't hear your latch-key. How did the meeting go off? Did you speak well?

MORELL. I have never spoken better in my life.

CANDIDA. That was first rate! How much was the collection?

MORELL. I forgot to ask.

CANDIDA (to Eugene). He must have spoken splendidly, or he would never have forgotten that. (To Morell.) Where are all the others?

MORELL. They left long before I could get away: I thought I should never escape. I believe they are having supper somewhere.

CANDIDA (in her domestic business tone). Oh; in that case, Maria may go to bed. I'll tell her. (She goes out to the kitchen.)

MORELL (looking sternly down at Marchbanks). Well?

MARCHBANKS (squatting cross-legged on the hearth-rug, and actually at ease with Morell—even impishly humorous). Well?

MORELL. Have you anything to tell me?

MARCHBANKS. Only that I have been making a fool of myself here in private whilst you have been making a fool of yourself in public.

MORELL. Hardly in the same way, I think.

MARCHBANKS (scrambling up—eagerly). The very, very, VERY same way. I have been playing the good man just like you. When you began your heroics about leaving me here with Candida—

MORELL (involuntarily). Candida?

MARCHBANKS. Oh, yes: I've got that far. Heroics are infectious: I caught the disease from you. I swore not to say a word in your absence that I would not have said a month ago in your presence.

MORELL. Did you keep your oath?

MARCHBANKS. (suddenly perching himself grotesquely on the easy chair). I was ass enough to keep it until about ten minutes ago. Up to that moment I went on desperately reading to her—reading my own poems—anybody's poems—to stave off a conversation. I was standing outside the gate of Heaven, and refusing to go in. Oh, you can't think how heroic it was, and how uncomfortable! Then—

MORELL (steadily controlling his suspense). Then?

MARCHBANKS (prosaically slipping down into a quite ordinary attitude in the chair). Then she couldn't bear being read to any longer.

MORELL. And you approached the gate of Heaven at last?

MARCHBANKS. Yes.

MORELL. Well? (Fiercely.) Speak, man: have you no feeling for me?

MARCHBANKS (softly and musically). Then she became an angel; and there was a flaming sword that turned every way, so that I couldn't go in; for I saw that that gate was really the gate of Hell.

MORELL (triumphantly). She repulsed you!

MARCHBANKS (rising in wild scorn). No, you fool: if she had done that I should never have seen that I was in Heaven already. Repulsed me! You think that would have saved me—virtuous indignation! Oh, you are not worthy to live in the same world with her. (He turns away contemptuously to the other side of the room.)

MORELL (who has watched him quietly without changing his place). Do you think you make yourself more worthy by reviling me, Eugene?

MARCHBANKS. Here endeth the thousand and first lesson. Morell: I don't think much of your preaching after all: I believe I could do it better myself. The man I want to meet is the man that Candida married.

MORELL. The man that—? Do you mean me?

MARCHBANKS. I don't mean the Reverend James Mavor Morell, moralist and windbag. I mean the real man that the Reverend James must have hidden somewhere inside his black coat—the man that Candida loved. You can't make a woman like Candida love you by merely buttoning your collar at the back instead of in front.

MORELL (boldly and steadily). When Candida promised to marry me, I was the same moralist and windbag that you now see. I wore my black coat; and my collar was buttoned behind instead of in front. Do you think she would have loved me any the better for being insincere in my profession?

MARCHBANKS (on the sofa hugging his ankles). Oh, she forgave you, just as she forgives me for being a coward, and a weakling, and what you call a snivelling little whelp and all the rest of it. (Dreamily.) A woman like that has divine insight: she loves our souls, and not our follies and vanities and illusions, or our collars and coats, or any other of the rags and tatters we are rolled up in. (He reflects on this for an instant; then turns intently to question Morell.) What I want to know is how you got past the flaming sword that stopped me.

MORELL (meaningly). Perhaps because I was not interrupted at the end of ten minutes.

MARCHBANKS (taken aback). What!

MORELL. Man can climb to the highest summits; but he cannot dwell there long.

MARCHBANKS. It's false: there can he dwell for ever and there only. It's in the other moments that he can find no rest, no sense of the silent glory of life. Where would you have me spend my moments, if not on the summits?

MORELL. In the scullery, slicing onions and filling lamps.

MARCHBANKS. Or in the pulpit, scrubbing cheap earthenware souls?

MORELL. Yes, that, too. It was there that I earned my golden moment, and the right, in that moment, to ask her to love me. I did not take the moment on credit; nor did I use it to steal another man's happiness.

MARCHBANKS (rather disgustedly, trotting back towards the fireplace). I have no doubt you conducted the transaction as honestly as if you were buying a pound of cheese. (He stops on the brink of the hearth-rug and adds, thoughtfully, to himself, with his back turned to Morell) I could only go to her as a beggar.

MORELL (starting). A beggar dying of cold—asking for her shawl?

MARCHBANKS (turning, surprised). Thank you for touching up my poetry. Yes, if you like, a beggar dying of cold asking for her shawl.

MORELL (excitedly). And she refused. Shall I tell you why she refused? I CAN tell you, on her own authority. It was because of—

MARCHBANKS. She didn't refuse.

MORELL. Not!

MARCHBANKS. She offered me all I chose to ask for, her shawl, her wings, the wreath of stars on her head, the lilies in her hand, the crescent moon beneath her feet—

MORELL (seizing him). Out with the truth, man: my wife is my wife: I want no more of your poetic fripperies. I know well that if I have lost her love and you have gained it, no law will bind her.

MARCHBANKS (quaintly, without fear or resistance). Catch me by the shirt collar, Morell: she will arrange it for me afterwards as she did this morning. (With quiet rapture.) I shall feel her hands touch me.

MORELL. You young imp, do you know how dangerous it is to say that to me? Or (with a sudden misgiving) has something made you brave?

MARCHBANKS. I'm not afraid now. I disliked you before: that was why I shrank from your touch. But I saw to-day—when she tortured you—that you love her. Since then I have been your friend: you may strangle me if you like.

MORELL (releasing him). Eugene: if that is not a heartless lie—if you have a spark of human feeling left in you—will you tell me what has happened during my absence?

MARCHBANKS. What happened! Why, the flaming sword—(Morell stamps with impatience.) Well, in plain prose, I loved her so exquisitely that I wanted nothing more than the happiness of being in such love. And before I had time to come down from the highest summits, you came in.

MORELL (suffering deeply). So it is still unsettled—still the misery of doubt.

MARCHBANKS. Misery! I am the happiest of men. I desire nothing now but her happiness. (With dreamy enthusiasm.) Oh, Morell, let us both give her up. Why should she have to choose between a wretched little nervous disease like me, and a pig-headed parson like you? Let us go on a pilgrimage, you to the east and I to the west, in search of a worthy lover for her—some beautiful archangel with purple wings—

MORELL. Some fiddlestick. Oh, if she is mad enough to leave me for you, who will protect her? Who will help her? who will work for her? who will be a father to her children? (He sits down distractedly on the sofa, with his elbows on his knees and his head propped on his clenched fists.)

MARCHBANKS (snapping his fingers wildly). She does not ask those silly questions. It is she who wants somebody to protect, to help, to work for—somebody to give her children to protect, to help and to work for. Some grown up man who has become as a little child again. Oh, you fool, you fool, you triple fool! I am the man, Morell: I am the man. (He dances about excitedly, crying.) You don't understand what a woman is. Send for her, Morell: send for her and let her choose between—(The door opens and Candida enters. He stops as if petrified.)

CANDIDA (amazed, on the threshold). What on earth are you at, Eugene?

MARCHBANKS (oddly). James and I are having a preaching match; and he is getting the worst of it. (Candida looks quickly round at Morell. Seeing that he is distressed, she hurries down to him, greatly vexed, speaking with vigorous reproach to Marchbanks.)

CANDIDA. You have been annoying him. Now I won't have it, Eugene: do you hear? (Putting her hand on Morell's shoulder, and quite forgetting her wifely tact in her annoyance.) My boy shall not be worried: I will protect him.

MORELL (rising proudly). Protect!

CANDIDA (not heeding him—to Eugene). What have you been saying?

MARCHBANKS (appalled). Nothing—

CANDIDA. Eugene! Nothing?

MARCHBANKS (piteously). I mean—I—I'm very sorry. I won't do it again: indeed I won't. I'll let him alone.

MORELL (indignantly, with an aggressive movement towards Eugene). Let me alone! You young—

CANDIDA (Stopping him). Sh—no, let me deal with him, James.

MARCHBANKS. Oh, you're not angry with me, are you?

CANDIDA (severely). Yes, I am—very angry. I have a great mind to pack you out of the house.

MORELL (taken aback by Candida's vigor, and by no means relishing the sense of being rescued by her from another man). Gently, Candida, gently. I am able to take care of myself.

CANDIDA (petting him). Yes, dear: of course you are. But you mustn't be annoyed and made miserable.

MARCHBANKS (almost in tears, turning to the door). I'll go.

CANDIDA. Oh, you needn't go: I can't turn you out at this time of night. (Vehemently.) Shame on you! For shame!

MARCHBANKS (desperately). But what have I done?

CANDIDA. I know what you have done—as well as if I had been here all the time. Oh, it was unworthy! You are like a child: you cannot hold your tongue.

MARCHBANKS. I would die ten times over sooner than give you a moment's pain.

CANDIDA (with infinite contempt for this puerility). Much good your dying would do me!

MORELL. Candida, my dear: this altercation is hardly quite seemingly. It is a matter between two men; and I am the right person to settle it.

CANDIDA. Two MEN! Do you call that a man? (To Eugene.) You bad boy!

MARCHBANKS (gathering a whimsically affectionate courage from the scolding). If I am to be scolded like this, I must make a boy's excuse. He began it. And he's bigger than I am.

CANDIDA (losing confidence a little as her concern for Morell's dignity takes the alarm). That can't be true. (To Morell.) You didn't begin it, James, did you?

MORELL (contemptuously). No.

MARCHBANKS (indignant). Oh!

MORELL (to Eugene). YOU began it—this morning. (Candida, instantly connecting this with his mysterious allusion in the afternoon to something told him by Eugene in the morning, looks quickly at him, wrestling with the enigma. Morell proceeds with the emphasis of offended superiority.) But your other point is true. I am certainly the bigger of the two, and, I hope, the stronger, Candida. So you had better leave the matter in my hands.

CANDIDA (again soothing him). Yes, dear; but—(Troubled.) I don't understand about this morning.

MORELL (gently snubbing her). You need not understand, my dear.

CANDIDA. But, James, I—(The street bell rings.) Oh, bother! Here they all come. (She goes out to let them in.)

MARCHBANKS (running to Morell). Oh, Morell, isn't it dreadful? She's angry with us: she hates me. What shall I do?

MORELL (with quaint desperation, clutching himself by the hair). Eugene: my head is spinning round. I shall begin to laugh presently. (He walks up and down the middle of the room.)

MARCHBANKS (following him anxiously). No, no: she'll think I've thrown you into hysterics. Don't laugh. (Boisterous voices and laughter are heard approaching. Lexy Mill, his eyes sparkling, and his bearing denoting unwonted elevation of spirit, enters with Burgess, who is greasy and self-complacent, but has all his wits about him. Miss Garnett, with her smartest hat and jacket on, follows them; but though her eyes are brighter than before, she is evidently a prey to misgiving. She places herself with her back to her typewriting table, with one hand on it to rest herself, passes the other across her forehead as if she were a little tired and giddy. Marchbanks relapses into shyness and edges away into the corner near the window, where Morell's books are.)

MILL (exhilaratedly). Morell: I MUST congratulate you. (Grasping his hand.) What a noble, splendid, inspired address you gave us! You surpassed yourself.

BURGESS. So you did, James. It fair kep' me awake to the last word. Didn't it, Miss Garnett?

PROSERPINE (worriedly). Oh, I wasn't minding you: I was trying to make notes. (She takes out her note-book, and looks at her stenography, which nearly makes her cry.)

MORELL. Did I go too fast, Pross?

PROSERPINE. Much too fast. You know I can't do more than a hundred words a minute. (She relieves her feelings by throwing her note-book angrily beside her machine, ready for use next morning.)

MORELL (soothingly). Oh, well, well, never mind, never mind, never mind. Have you all had supper?

LEXY. Mr. Burgess has been kind enough to give us a really splendid supper at the Belgrave.

BURGESS (with effusive magnanimity). Don't mention it, Mr. Mill. (Modestly.) You're 'arty welcome to my little treat.

PROSERPINE. We had champagne! I never tasted it before. I feel quite giddy.

MORELL (surprised). A champagne supper! That was very handsome. Was it my eloquence that produced all this extravagance?

MILL (rhetorically). Your eloquence, and Mr. Burgess's goodness of heart. (With a fresh burst of exhilaration.) And what a very fine fellow the chairman is, Morell! He came to supper with us.

MORELL (with long drawn significance, looking at Burgess). O-o-o-h, the chairman. NOW I understand.

(Burgess, covering a lively satisfaction in his diplomatic cunning with a deprecatory cough, retires to the hearth. Lexy folds his arms and leans against the cellaret in a high-spirited attitude. Candida comes in with glasses, lemons, and a jug of hot water on a tray.)

CANDIDA. Who will have some lemonade? You know our rules: total abstinence. (She puts the tray on the table, and takes up the lemon squeezers, looking enquiringly round at them.)

MORELL. No use, dear. They've all had champagne. Pross has broken her pledge.

CANDIDA (to Proserpine). You don't mean to say you've been drinking champagne!

PROSERPINE (stubbornly). Yes, I do. I'm only a beer teetotaller, not a champagne teetotaller. I don't like beer. Are there any letters for me to answer, Mr. Morell?

MORELL. No more to-night.

PROSERPINE. Very well. Good-night, everybody.

LEXY (gallantly). Had I not better see you home, Miss Garnett?

PROSERPINE. No, thank you. I shan't trust myself with anybody to-night. I wish I hadn't taken any of that stuff. (She walks straight out.)

BURGESS (indignantly). Stuff, indeed! That gurl dunno wot champagne is! Pommery and Greeno at twelve and six a bottle. She took two glasses a'most straight hoff.

MORELL (a little anxious about her). Go and look after her, Lexy.

LEXY (alarmed). But if she should really be— Suppose she began to sing in the street, or anything of that sort.

MORELL. Just so: she may. That's why you'd better see her safely home.

CANDIDA. Do, Lexy: there's a good fellow. (She shakes his hand and pushes him gently to the door.)

LEXY. It's evidently my duty to go. I hope it may not be necessary. Good-night, Mrs. Morell. (To the rest.) Good-night. (He goes. Candida shuts the door.)

BURGESS. He was gushin' with hextra piety hisself arter two sips. People carn't drink like they huseter. (Dismissing the subject and bustling away from the hearth.) Well, James: it's time to lock up. Mr. Morchbanks: shall I 'ave the pleasure of your company for a bit of the way home?

MARCHBANKS (affrightedly). Yes: I'd better go. .(He hurries across to the door; but Candida places herself before it, barring his way.)

CANDIDA (with quiet authority). You sit down. You're not going yet.

MARCHBANKS (quailing). No: I—I didn't mean to. (He comes back into the room and sits down abjectly on the sofa.)

CANDIDA. Mr. Marchbanks will stay the night with us, papa.

BURGESS. Oh, well, I'll say good-night. So long, James. (He shakes hands with Morell and goes on to Eugene.) Make 'em give you a night light by your bed, Mr. Morchbanks: it'll comfort you if you wake up in the night with a touch of that complaint of yores. Good-night.

MARCHBANKS. Thank you: I will. Good-night, Mr. Burgess. (They shake hands and Burgess goes to the door.)

CANDIDA (intercepting Morell, who is following Burgess). Stay here, dear: I'll put on papa's coat for him. (She goes out with Burgess.)

MARCHBANKS. Morell: there's going to be a terrible scene. Aren't you afraid?

MORELL. Not in the least.

MARCHBANKS. I never envied you your courage before. (He rises timidly and puts his hand appealingly on Morell's forearm.) Stand by me, won't you?

MORELL (casting him off gently, but resolutely). Each for himself, Eugene. She must choose between us now. (He goes to the other side of the room as Candida returns. Eugene sits down again on the sofa like a guilty schoolboy on his best behaviour.)

CANDIDA (between them, addressing Eugene). Are you sorry?

MARCHBANKS (earnestly). Yes, heartbroken.

CANDIDA. Well, then, you are forgiven. Now go off to bed like a good little boy: I want to talk to James about you.

MARCHBANKS (rising in great consternation). Oh, I can't do that, Morell. I must be here. I'll not go away. Tell her.

CANDIDA (with quick suspicion). Tell me what? (His eyes avoid hers furtively. She turns and mutely transfers the question to Morell.)

MORELL (bracing himself for the catastrophe). I have nothing to tell her, except (here his voice deepens to a measured and mournful tenderness) that she is my greatest treasure on earth—if she is really mine.

CANDIDA (coldly, offended by his yielding to his orator's instinct and treating her as if she were the audience at the Guild of St. Matthew). I am sure Eugene can say no less, if that is all.

MARCHBANKS (discouraged). Morell: she's laughing at us.

MORELL (with a quick touch of temper). There is nothing to laugh at. Are you laughing at us, Candida?

CANDIDA (with quiet anger). Eugene is very quick-witted, James. I hope I am going to laugh; but I am not sure that I am not going to be very angry. (She goes to the fireplace, and stands there leaning with her arm on the mantelpiece and her foot on the fender, whilst Eugene steals to Morell and plucks him by the sleeve.)

MARCHBANKS (whispering). Stop Morell. Don't let us say anything.

MORELL (pushing Eugene away without deigning to look at him). I hope you don't mean that as a threat, Candida.

CANDIDA (with emphatic warning). Take care, James. Eugene: I asked you to go. Are you going?

MORELL (putting his foot down). He shall not go. I wish him to remain.

MARCHBANKS. I'll go. I'll do whatever you want. (He turns to the door.)

CANDIDA. Stop! (He obeys.) Didn't you hear James say he wished you to stay? James is master here. Don't you know that?

MARCHBANKS (flushing with a young poet's rage against tyranny). By what right is he master?

CANDIDA (quietly). Tell him, James.

MORELL (taken aback). My dear: I don't know of any right that makes me master. I assert no such right.

CANDIDA (with infinite reproach). You don't know! Oh, James, James! (To Eugene, musingly.) I wonder do you understand, Eugene! No: you're too young. Well, I give you leave to stay—to stay and learn. (She comes away from the hearth and places herself between them.) Now, James: what's the matter? Come: tell me.

MARCHBANKS (whispering tremulously across to him). Don't.

CANDIDA. Come. Out with it!

MORELL (slowly). I meant to prepare your mind carefully, Candida, so as to prevent misunderstanding.

CANDIDA. Yes, dear: I am sure you did. But never mind: I shan't misunderstand.

MORELL. Well—er—(He hesitates, unable to find the long explanation which he supposed to be available.)

CANDIDA. Well?

MORELL (baldly). Eugene declares that you are in love with him.

MARCHBANKS (frantically). No, no, no, no, never. I did not, Mrs. Morell: it's not true. I said I loved you, and that he didn't. I said that I understood you, and that he couldn't. And it was not after what passed there before the fire that I spoke: it was not, on my word. It was this morning.

CANDIDA (enlightened). This morning!

MARCHBANKS. Yes. (He looks at her, pleading for credence, and then adds, simply) That was what was the matter with my collar.

CANDIDA (after a pause; for she does not take in his meaning at once). His collar! (She turns to Morell, shocked.) Oh, James: did you—(she stops)?

MORELL (ashamed). You know, Candida, that I have a temper to struggle with. And he said (shuddering) that you despised me in your heart.

CANDIDA (turning quickly on Eugene). Did you say that?

MARCHBANKS (terrified). No!

CANDIDA (severely). Then James has just told me a falsehood. Is that what you mean?

MARCHBANKS. No, no: I—I— (blurting out the explanation desperately) —it was David's wife. And it wasn't at home: it was when she saw him dancing before all the people.

MORELL (taking the cue with a debater's adroitness). Dancing before all the people, Candida; and thinking he was moving their hearts by his mission when they were only suffering from—Prossy's complaint. (She is about to protest: he raises his hand to silence her, exclaiming) Don't try to look indignant, Candida:—

CANDIDA (interjecting). Try!

MORELL (continuing). Eugene was right. As you told me a few hours after, he is always right. He said nothing that you did not say far better yourself. He is the poet, who sees everything; and I am the poor parson, who understands nothing.

CANDIDA (remorsefully). Do you mind what is said by a foolish boy, because I said something like it again in jest?

MORELL. That foolish boy can speak with the inspiration of a child and the cunning of a serpent. He has claimed that you belong to him and not to me; and, rightly or wrongly, I have come to fear that it may be true. I will not go about tortured with doubts and suspicions. I will not live with you and keep a secret from you. I will not suffer the intolerable degradation of jealousy. We have agreed—he and I—that you shall choose between us now. I await your decision.

CANDIDA (slowly recoiling a step, her heart hardened by his rhetoric in spite of the sincere feeling behind it). Oh! I am to choose, am I? I suppose it is quite settled that I must belong to one or the other.

MORELL (firmly). Quite. You must choose definitely.

MARCHBANKS (anxiously). Morell: you don't understand. She means that she belongs to herself.

CANDIDA (turning on him). I mean that and a good deal more, Master Eugene, as you will both find out presently. And pray, my lords and masters, what have you to offer for my choice? I am up for auction, it seems. What do you bid, James?

MORELL (reproachfully). Cand— (He breaks down: his eyes and throat fill with tears: the orator becomes the wounded animal.) I can't speak—

CANDIDA (impulsively going to him). Ah, dearest—

MARCHBANKS (in wild alarm). Stop: it's not fair. You mustn't show her that you suffer, Morell. I am on the rack, too; but I am not crying.

MORELL (rallying all his forces). Yes: you are right. It is not for pity that I am bidding. (He disengages himself from Candida.)

CANDIDA (retreating, chilled). I beg your pardon, James; I did not mean to touch you. I am waiting to hear your bid.

MORELL (with proud humility). I have nothing to offer you but my strength for your defence, my honesty of purpose for your surety, my ability and industry for your livelihood, and my authority and position for your dignity. That is all it becomes a man to offer to a woman.

CANDIDA (quite quietly). And you, Eugene? What do you offer?

MARCHBANKS. My weakness! my desolation! my heart's need!

CANDIDA (impressed). That's a good bid, Eugene. Now I know how to make my choice.

She pauses and looks curiously from one to the other, as if weighing them. Morell, whose lofty confidence has changed into heartbreaking dread at Eugene's bid, loses all power of concealing his anxiety. Eugene, strung to the highest tension, does not move a muscle.

MORELL (in a suffocated voice—the appeal bursting from the depths of his anguish). Candida!

MARCHBANKS (aside, in a flash of contempt). Coward!

CANDIDA (significantly). I give myself to the weaker of the two.

Eugene divines her meaning at once: his face whitens like steel in a furnace that cannot melt it.

MORELL (bowing his head with the calm of collapse). I accept your sentence, Candida.

CANDIDA. Do you understand, Eugene?

MARCHBANKS. Oh, I feel I'm lost. He cannot bear the burden.

MORELL (incredulously, raising his bead with prosaic abruptness). Do you mean, me, Candida?

CANDIDA (smiling a little). Let us sit and talk comfortably over it like three friends. (To Morell.) Sit down, dear. (Morell takes the chair from the fireside—the children's chair.) Bring me that chair, Eugene. (She indicates the easy chair. He fetches it silently, even with something like cold strength, and places it next Morell, a little behind him. She sits down. He goes to the sofa and sits there, still silent and inscrutable. When they are all settled she begins, throwing a spell of quietness on them by her calm, sane, tender tone.) You remember what you told me about yourself, Eugene: how nobody has cared for you since your old nurse died: how those clever, fashionable sisters and successful brothers of yours were your mother's and father's pets: how miserable you were at Eton: how your father is trying to starve you into returning to Oxford: how you have had to live without comfort or welcome or refuge, always lonely, and nearly always disliked and misunderstood, poor boy!

MARCHBANKS (faithful to the nobility of his lot). I had my books. I had Nature. And at last I met you.

CANDIDA. Never mind that just at present. Now I want you to look at this other boy here—MY boy—spoiled from his cradle. We go once a fortnight to see his parents. You should come with us, Eugene, and see the pictures of the hero of that household. James as a baby! the most wonderful of all babies. James holding his first school prize, won at the ripe age of eight! James as the captain of his eleven! James in his first frock coat! James under all sorts of glorious circumstances! You know how strong he is (I hope he didn't hurt you)—how clever he is—how happy! (With deepening gravity.) Ask James's mother and his three sisters what it cost to save James the trouble of doing anything but be strong and clever and happy. Ask ME what it costs to be James's mother and three sisters and wife and mother to his children all in one. Ask Prossy and Maria how troublesome the house is even when we have no visitors to help us to slice the onions. Ask the tradesmen who want to worry James and spoil his beautiful sermons who it is that puts them off. When there is money to give, he gives it: when there is money to refuse, I refuse it. I build a castle of comfort and indulgence and love for him, and stand sentinel always to keep little vulgar cares out. I make him master here, though he does not know it, and could not tell you a moment ago how it came to be so. (With sweet irony.) And when he thought I might go away with you, his only anxiety was what should become of ME! And to tempt me to stay he offered me (leaning forward to stroke his hair caressingly at each phrase) his strength for MY defence, his industry for my livelihood, his position for my dignity, his— (Relenting.) Ah, I am mixing up your beautiful sentences and spoiling them, am I not, darling? (She lays her cheek fondly against his.)

MORELL (quite overcome, kneeling beside her chair and embracing her with boyish ingenuousness). It's all true, every word. What I am you have made me with the labor of your hands and the love of your heart! You are my wife, my mother, my sisters: you are the sum of all loving care to me.

CANDIDA (in his arms, smiling, to Eugene). Am I YOUR mother and sisters to you, Eugene?

MARCHBANKS (rising with a fierce gesture of disgust). Ah, never. Out, then, into the night with me!

CANDIDA (rising quickly and intercepting him). You are not going like that, Eugene?

MARCHBANKS (with the ring of a man's voice—no longer a boy's—in the words). I know the hour when it strikes. I am impatient to do what must be done.

MORELL (rising from his knee, alarmed). Candida: don't let him do anything rash.

CANDIDA (confident, smiling at Eugene). Oh, there is no fear. He has learnt to live without happiness.

MARCHBANKS. I no longer desire happiness: life is nobler than that. Parson James: I give you my happiness with both hands: I love you because you have filled the heart of the woman I loved. Good-bye. (He goes towards the door.)

CANDIDA. One last word. (He stops, but without turning to her.) How old are you, Eugene?

MARCHBANKS. As old as the world now. This morning I was eighteen.

CANDIDA (going to him, and standing behind him with one hand caressingly on his shoulder). Eighteen! Will you, for my sake, make a little poem out of the two sentences I am going to say to you? And will you promise to repeat it to yourself whenever you think of me?

MARCHBANKS (without moving). Say the sentences.

CANDIDA. When I am thirty, she will be forty-five. When I am sixty, she will be seventy-five.

MARCHBANKS (turning to her). In a hundred years, we shall be the same age. But I have a better secret than that in my heart. Let me go now. The night outside grows impatient.

CANDIDA. Good-bye. (She takes his face in her hands; and as he divines her intention and bends his knee, she kisses his forehead. Then he flies out into the night. She turns to Morell, holding out her arms to him.) Ah, James! (They embrace. But they do not know the secret in the poet's heart.)

THE MAN OF DESTINY

THE MAN OF DESTINY

The twelfth of May, 1796, in north Italy, at Tavazzano, on the road from Lodi to Milan. The afternoon sun is blazing serenely over the plains of Lombardy, treating the Alps with respect and the anthills with indulgence, not incommoded by the basking of the swine and oxen in the villages nor hurt by its cool reception in the churches, but fiercely disdainful of two hordes of mischievous insects which are the French and Austrian armies. Two days before, at Lodi, the Austrians tried to prevent the French from crossing the river by the narrow bridge there; but the French, commanded by a general aged 27, Napoleon Bonaparte, who does not understand the art of war, rushed the fireswept bridge, supported by a tremendous cannonade in which the young general assisted with his own hands. Cannonading is his technical specialty; he has been trained in the artillery under the old regime, and made perfect in the military arts of shirking his duties, swindling the paymaster over travelling expenses, and dignifying war with the noise and smoke of cannon, as depicted in all military portraits. He is, however, an original observer, and has perceived, for the first time since the invention of gunpowder, that a cannon ball, if it strikes a man, will kill him. To a thorough grasp of this remarkable discovery, he adds a highly evolved faculty for physical geography and for the calculation of times and distances. He has prodigious powers of work, and a clear, realistic knowledge of human nature in public affairs, having seen it exhaustively tested in that department during the French Revolution. He is imaginative without illusions, and creative without religion, loyalty, patriotism or any of the common ideals. Not that he is incapable of these ideals: on the contrary, he has swallowed them all in his boyhood, and now, having a keen dramatic faculty, is extremely clever at playing upon them by the arts of the actor and stage manager. Withal, he is no spoiled child. Poverty, ill-luck, the shifts of impecunious shabby-gentility, repeated failure as a would-be author, humiliation as a rebuffed time server, reproof and punishment as an incompetent and dishonest officer, an escape from dismissal from the service so narrow that if the emigration of the nobles had not raised the value of even the most rascally lieutenant to the famine price of a general he would have been swept contemptuously from the army: these trials have ground the conceit out of him, and forced him to be self-sufficient and to understand that to such men as he is the world will give nothing that he cannot take from it by force. In this the world is not free from cowardice and folly; for Napoleon, as a merciless cannonader of political rubbish, is making himself useful. indeed, it is even now impossible to live in England without sometimes feeling how much that country lost in not being conquered by him as well as by Julius Caesar.

However, on this May afternoon in 1796, it is early days with him. He is only 26, and has but recently become a general, partly by using his wife to seduce the Directory (then governing France) partly by the scarcity of officers caused by the emigration as aforesaid; partly by his faculty of knowing a country, with all its roads, rivers, hills and valleys, as he knows the palm of his hand; and largely by that new faith of his in the efficacy of firing cannons at people. His army is, as to discipline, in a state which has so greatly shocked some modern writers before whom the following story has been enacted, that they, impressed with the later glory of "L'Empereur," have altogether refused to credit it. But Napoleon is not "L'Empereur" yet: he has only just been dubbed "Le Petit Caporal," and is in the stage of gaining influence over his men by displays of pluck. He is not in a position to force his will on them, in orthodox military fashion, by the cat o' nine tails. The French Revolution, which has escaped suppression solely through the monarchy's habit of being at least four years in arrear with its soldiers in the matter of pay, has substituted for that habit, as far as possible, the habit of not paying at all, except in promises and patriotic flatteries which are not compatible with martial law of the Prussian type. Napoleon has therefore approached the Alps in command of men without money, in rags, and consequently indisposed to stand much discipline, especially from upstart generals. This circumstance, which would have embarrassed an idealist soldier, has been worth a thousand cannon to Napoleon. He has said to his army, "You have patriotism and courage; but you have no money, no clothes, and deplorably indifferent food. In Italy there are all these things, and glory as well, to be gained by a devoted army led by a general who regards loot as the natural right of the soldier. I am such a general. En avant, mes enfants!" The result has entirely justified him. The army conquers Italy as the locusts conquered Cyprus. They fight all day and march all night, covering impossible distances and appearing in incredible places, not because every soldier carries a field marshal's baton in his knapsack, but because he hopes to carry at least half a dozen silver forks there next day.

It must be understood, by the way, that the French army does not make war on the Italians. It is there to rescue them from the tyranny of their Austrian conquerors, and confer republican institutions on them; so that in incidentally looting them, it merely makes free with the property of its friends, who ought to be grateful to it, and perhaps would be if ingratitude were not the proverbial failing of their country. The Austrians, whom it fights, are a thoroughly respectable regular army, well disciplined, commanded by gentlemen trained and versed in the art of war: at the head of them Beaulieu, practising the classic art of war under orders from Vienna, and getting horribly beaten by Napoleon, who acts on his own responsibility in defiance of professional precedents or orders from Paris. Even when the Austrians win a battle, all that is necessary is to wait until their routine obliges them to return to their quarters for afternoon tea, so to speak, and win it back again from them: a course pursued later on with brilliant success at Marengo. On the whole, with his foe handicapped by Austrian statesmanship, classic generalship, and the exigencies of the aristocratic social structure of Viennese society, Napoleon finds it possible to be irresistible without working heroic miracles. The world, however, likes miracles and heroes, and is quite incapable of conceiving the action of such forces as academic militarism or Viennese drawing-roomism. Hence it has already begun to manufacture "L'Empereur," and thus to make it difficult for the romanticists of a hundred years later to credit the little scene now in question at Tavazzano as aforesaid.

The best quarters at Tavazzano are at a little inn, the first house reached by travellers passing through the place from Milan to Lodi. It stands in a vineyard; and its principal room, a pleasant refuge from the summer heat, is open so widely at the back to this vineyard that it is almost a large veranda. The bolder children, much excited by the alarums and excursions of the past few days, and by an irruption of French troops at six o'clock, know that the French commander has quartered himself in this room, and are divided between a craving to peep in at the front windows and a mortal terror of the sentinel, a young gentleman-soldier, who, having no natural moustache, has had a most ferocious one painted on his face with boot blacking by his sergeant. As his heavy uniform, like all the uniforms of that day, is designed for parade without the least reference to his health or comfort, he perspires profusely in the sun; and his painted moustache has run in little streaks down his chin and round his neck except where it has dried in stiff japanned flakes, and had its sweeping outline chipped off in grotesque little bays and headlands, making him unspeakably ridiculous in the eye of History a hundred years later, but monstrous and horrible to the contemporary north Italian infant, to whom nothing would seem more natural than that he should relieve the monotony of his guard by pitchforking a stray child up on his bayonet, and eating it uncooked. Nevertheless one girl of bad character, in whom an instinct of privilege with soldiers is already dawning, does peep in at the safest window for a moment, before a glance and a clink from the sentinel sends her flying. Most of what she sees she has seen before: the vineyard at the back, with the old winepress and a cart among the vines; the door close down on her right leading to the inn entry; the landlord's best sideboard, now in full action for dinner, further back on the same side; the fireplace on the other side, with a couch near it, and another door, leading to the inner rooms, between it and the vineyard; and the table in the middle with its repast of

Milanese risotto, cheese, grapes, bread, olives, and a big wickered flask of red wine.

The landlord, Giuseppe Grandi, is also no novelty. He is a swarthy, vivacious, shrewdly cheerful, black-curled, bullet headed, grinning little man of 40. Naturally an excellent host, he is in quite special spirits this evening at his good fortune in having the French commander as his guest to protect him against the license of the troops, and actually sports a pair of gold earrings which he would otherwise have hidden carefully under the winepress with his little equipment of silver plate.

Napoleon, sitting facing her on the further side of the table, and Napoleon's hat, sword and riding whip lying on the couch, she sees for the first time. He is working hard, partly at his meal, which he has discovered how to dispatch, by attacking all the courses simultaneously, in ten minutes (this practice is the beginning of his downfall), and partly at a map which he is correcting from memory, occasionally marking the position of the forces by taking a grapeskin from his mouth and planting it on the map with his thumb like a wafer. He has a supply of writing materials before him mixed up in disorder with the dishes and cruets; and his long hair gets sometimes into the risotto gravy and sometimes into the ink.

GIUSEPPE. Will your excellency—

NAPOLEON (intent on his map, but cramming himself mechanically with his left hand). Don't talk. I'm busy.

GIUSEPPE (with perfect goodhumor). Excellency: I obey.

NAPOLEON. Some red ink.

GIUSEPPE. Alas! excellency, there is none.

NAPOLEON (with Corsican facetiousness). Kill something and bring me its blood.

GIUSEPPE (grinning). There is nothing but your excellency's horse, the sentinel, the lady upstairs, and my wife.

NAPOLEON. Kill your wife.

GIUSEPPE. Willingly, your excellency; but unhappily I am not strong enough. She would kill me.

NAPOLEON. That will do equally well.

GIUSEPPE. Your excellency does me too much honor. (Stretching his hand toward the flask.) Perhaps some wine will answer your excellency's purpose.

NAPOLEON (hastily protecting the flask, and becoming quite serious). Wine! No: that would be waste. You are all the same: waste! waste! waste! (He marks the map with gravy, using his fork as a pen.) Clear away. (He finishes his wine; pushes back his chair; and uses his napkin, stretching his legs and leaning back, but still frowning and thinking.)

GIUSEPPE (clearing the table and removing the things to a tray on the sideboard). Every man to his trade, excellency. We innkeepers have plenty of cheap wine: we think nothing of spilling it. You great generals have plenty of cheap blood: you think nothing of spilling it. Is it not so, excellency?

NAPOLEON. Blood costs nothing: wine costs money. (He rises and goes to the fireplace.)

GIUSEPPE. They say you are careful of everything except human life, excellency.

NAPOLEON. Human life, my friend, is the only thing that takes care of itself. (He throws himself at his ease on the couch.)

GIUSEPPE (admiring him). Ah, excellency, what fools we all are beside you! If I could only find out the secret of your success!

NAPOLEON. You would make yourself Emperor of Italy, eh?

GIUSEPPE. Too troublesome, excellency: I leave all that to you. Besides, what would become of my inn if I were Emperor? See how you enjoy looking on at me whilst I keep the inn for you and wait on you! Well, I shall enjoy looking on at you whilst you become Emperor of Europe, and govern the country for me. (Whilst he chatters, he takes the cloth off without removing the map and inkstand, and takes the corners in his hands and the middle of the edge in his mouth, to fold it up.)

NAPOLEON. Emperor of Europe, eh? Why only Europe?

GIUSEPPE. Why, indeed? Emperor of the world, excellency! Why not? (He folds and rolls up the cloth, emphasizing his phrases by the steps of the process.) One man is like another (fold): one country is like another (fold): one battle is like another. (At the last fold, he slaps the cloth on the table and deftly rolls it up, adding, by way of peroration) Conquer one: conquer all. (He takes the cloth to the sideboard, and puts it in a drawer.)

NAPOLEON. And govern for all; fight for all; be everybody's servant under cover of being everybody's master: Giuseppe.

GIUSEPPE (at the sideboard). Excellency.

NAPOLEON. I forbid you to talk to me about myself.

GIUSEPPE (coming to the foot of the couch). Pardon. Your excellency is so unlike other great men. It is the subject they like best.

NAPOLEON. Well, talk to me about the subject they like next best, whatever that may be.

GIUSEPPE (unabashed). Willingly, your excellency. Has your excellency by any chance caught a glimpse of the lady upstairs?

(Napoleon promptly sits up and looks at him with an interest which entirely justifies the implied epigram.)

NAPOLEON. How old is she?

GIUSEPPE. The right age, excellency.

NAPOLEON. Do you mean seventeen or thirty?

GIUSEPPE. Thirty, excellency.

NAPOLEON. Goodlooking?

GIUSEPPE. I cannot see with your excellency's eyes: every man must judge that for himself. In my opinion, excellency, a fine figure of a lady. (Slyly.) Shall I lay the table for her collation here?

NAPOLEON (brusquely, rising). No: lay nothing here until the officer for whom I am waiting comes back. (He looks at his watch, and takes to walking to and fro between the fireplace and the vineyard.)

GIUSEPPE (with conviction). Excellency: believe me, he has been captured by the accursed Austrians. He dare not keep you waiting if he were at liberty.

NAPOLEON (turning at the edge of the shadow of the veranda). Giuseppe: if that turns out to be true, it will put me into such a temper that nothing short of hanging you and your whole household, including the lady upstairs, will satisfy me.

GIUSEPPE. We are all cheerfully at your excellency's disposal, except the lady. I cannot answer for her; but no lady could resist you, General.

NAPOLEON (sourly, resuming his march). Hm! You will never be hanged. There is no satisfaction in hanging a man who does not object to it.

GIUSEPPE (sympathetically). Not the least in the world, excellency: is there? (Napoleon again looks at his watch, evidently growing anxious.) Ah, one can see that you are a great man, General: you know how to wait. If it were a corporal now, or a sub-lieutenant, at the end of three minutes he would be swearing, fuming, threatening, pulling the house about our ears.

NAPOLEON. Giuseppe: your flatteries are insufferable. Go and talk outside. (He sits down again at the table, with his jaws in his hands, and his elbows propped on the map, poring over it with a troubled expression.)

GIUSEPPE. Willingly, your excellency. You shall not be disturbed. (He takes up the tray and prepares to withdraw.)

NAPOLEON. The moment he comes back, send him to me.

GIUSEPPE. Instantaneously, your excellency.

A LADY'S VOICE (calling from some distant part of the inn). Giusep-pe! (The voice is very musical, and the two final notes make an ascending interval.)

NAPOLEON (startled). What's that? What's that?

GIUSEPPE (resting the end of his tray on the table and leaning over to speak the more confidentially). The lady, excellency.

NAPOLEON (absently). Yes. What lady? Whose lady?

GIUSEPPE. The strange lady, excellency.

NAPOLEON. What strange lady?

GIUSEPPE (with a shrug). Who knows? She arrived here half an hour before you in a hired carriage belonging to the Golden Eagle at Borghetto. Actually by herself, excellency. No servants. A dressing bag and a trunk: that is all. The postillion says she left a horse—a charger, with military trappings, at the Golden Eagle.

NAPOLEON. A woman with a charger! That's extraordinary.

THE LADY'S VOICE (the two final notes now making a peremptory descending interval). Giuseppe!

NAPOLEON (rising to listen). That's an interesting voice.

GIUSEPPE. She is an interesting lady, excellency. (Calling.) Coming, lady, coming. (He makes for the inner door.)

NAPOLEON (arresting him with a strong hand on his shoulder). Stop. Let her come.

VOICE. Giuseppe!! (Impatiently.)

GIUSEPPE (pleadingly). Let me go, excellency. It is my point of honor as an innkeeper to come when I am called. I appeal to you as a soldier.

A MAN's VOICE (outside, at the inn door, shouting). Here, someone. Hello! Landlord. Where are you? (Somebody raps vigorously with a whip handle on a bench in the passage.)

NAPOLEON (suddenly becoming the commanding officer again and throwing Giuseppe off). There he is at last. (Pointing to the inner door.) Go. Attend to your business: the lady is calling you. (He goes to the fireplace and stands with his back to it with a determined military air.)

GIUSEPPE (with bated breath, snatching up his tray). Certainly, excellency. (He hurries out by the inner door.)

THE MAN's VOICE (impatiently). Are you all asleep here? (The door opposite the fireplace is kicked rudely open; and a dusty sub-lieutenant bursts into the room. He is a chuckle-headed young man of 24, with the fair, delicate, clear skin of a man of rank, and a self-assurance on that ground which the French Revolution has failed to shake in the smallest degree. He has a thick silly lip, an eager credulous eye, an obstinate nose, and a loud confident voice. A young man without fear, without reverence, without imagination, without sense, hopelessly insusceptible to the Napoleonic or any other idea, stupendously egotistical, eminently qualified to rush in where angels fear to tread, yet of a vigorous babbling vitality which bustles him into the thick of things. He is just now boiling with vexation, attributable by a superficial observer to his impatience at not being promptly attended to by the staff of the inn, but in which a more discerning eye can perceive a certain moral depth, indicating a more permanent and momentous grievance. On seeing Napoleon, he is sufficiently taken aback to check himself and salute; but he does not betray by his manner any of that prophetic consciousness of Marengo and Austerlitz, Waterloo and St. Helena, or the Napoleonic pictures of Delaroche and Meissonier, which modern culture will instinctively expect from him.)

NAPOLEON (sharply). Well, sir, here you are at last. Your instructions were that I should arrive here at six, and that I was to find you waiting for me with my mail from Paris and with despatches. It is now twenty minutes to eight. You were sent on this service as a hard rider with the fastest horse in the camp. You arrive a hundred minutes late, on foot. Where is your horse!

THE LIEUTENANT (moodily pulling off his gloves and dashing them with his cap and whip on the table). Ah! where indeed? That's just what I should like to know, General. (With emotion.) You don't know how fond I was of that horse.

NAPOLEON (angrily sarcastic). Indeed! (With sudden misgiving.) Where are the letters and despatches?

THE LIEUTENANT (importantly, rather pleased than otherwise at having some remarkable news). I don't know.

NAPOLEON (unable to believe his ears). You don't know!

LIEUTENANT. No more than you do, General. Now I suppose I shall be court-martialled. Well, I don't mind being court-martialled; but (with solemn determination) I tell you, General, if ever I catch that innocent looking youth, I'll spoil his beauty, the slimy little liar! I'll make a picture of him. I'll—

NAPOLEON (advancing from the hearth to the table). What innocent looking youth? Pull yourself together, sir, will you; and give an account of yourself.

LIEUTENANT (facing him at the opposite side of the table, leaning on it with his fists). Oh, I'm all right, General: I'm perfectly ready to give an account of myself. I shall make the court-martial thoroughly understand that the fault was not mine. Advantage has been taken of the better side of my nature; and I'm not ashamed of it. But with all respect to you as my commanding officer, General, I say again that if ever I set eyes on that son of Satan, I'll—

NAPOLEON (angrily). So you said before.

LIEUTENANT (drawing himself upright). I say it again, just wait until I catch him. Just wait: that's all. (He folds his arms resolutely, and breathes hard, with compressed lips.)

NAPOLEON. I AM waiting, sir—for your explanation.

LIEUTENANT (confidently). You'll change your tone, General, when you hear what has happened to me.

NAPOLEON. Nothing has happened to you, sir: you are alive and not disabled. Where are the papers entrusted to you?

LIEUTENANT. Nothing! Nothing!! Oho! Well, we'll see. (Posing himself to overwhelm Napoleon with his news.) He swore eternal brotherhood with me. Was that nothing? He said my eyes reminded him of his sister's eyes. Was that nothing? He cried—actually cried—over the story of my separation from Angelica. Was that nothing? He paid for both bottles of wine, though he only ate bread and grapes himself. Perhaps you call that nothing! He gave me his pistols and his horse and his despatches—most important despatches—and let me go away with them. (Triumphantly, seeing that he has reduced Napoleon to blank stupefaction.) Was THAT nothing?

NAPOLEON (enfeebled by astonishment). What did he do that for?

LIEUTENANT (as if the reason were obvious). To show his confidence in me. (Napoleon's jaw does not exactly drop; but its hinges become nerveless. The Lieutenant proceeds with honest indignation.) And I was worthy of his confidence: I brought them all back honorably. But would you believe it?—when I trusted him with MY pistols, and MY horse, and MY despatches—

NAPOLEON (enraged). What the devil did you do that for?

LIEUTENANT. Why, to show my confidence in him, of course. And he betrayed it—abused it—never came back. The thief! the swindler! the heartless, treacherous little blackguard! You call that nothing, I suppose. But look here, General: (again resorting to the table with his fist for greater emphasis) YOU may put up with this outrage from the Austrians if you like; but speaking for myself personally, I tell you that if ever I catch—

NAPOLEON (turning on his heel in disgust and irritably resuming his march to and fro). Yes: you have said that more than once already.

LIEUTENANT (excitedly). More than once! I'll say it fifty times; and what's more, I'll do it. You'll see, General. I'll show my confidence in him, so I will. I'll—

NAPOLEON. Yes, yes, sir: no doubt you will. What kind of man was he?

LIEUTENANT. Well, I should think you ought to be able to tell from his conduct the sort of man he was.

NAPOLEON. Psh! What was he like?

LIEUTENANT. Like! He's like—well, you ought to have just seen the fellow: that will give you a notion of what he was like. He won't be like it five minutes after I catch him; for I tell you that if ever—

NAPOLEON (shouting furiously for the innkeeper). Giuseppe! (To the Lieutenant, out of all patience.) Hold your tongue, sir, if you can.

LIEUTENANT. I warn you it's no use to try to put the blame on me. (Plaintively.) How was I to know the sort of fellow he was? (He takes a chair from between the sideboard and the outer door; places it near the table; and sits down.) If you only knew how hungry and tired I am, you'd have more consideration.

GIUSEPPE (returning). What is it, excellency?

NAPOLEON (struggling with his temper). Take this—this officer. Feed him; and put him to bed, if necessary. When he is in his right mind again, find out what has happened to him and bring me word. (To the Lieutenant.) Consider yourself under arrest, sir.

LIEUTENANT (with sulky stiffness). I was prepared for that. It takes a gentleman to understand a gentleman. (He throws his sword on the table. Giuseppe takes it up and politely offers it to Napoleon, who throws it violently on the couch.)

GIUSEPPE (with sympathetic concern). Have you been attacked by the Austrians, lieutenant? Dear, dear, dear!

LIEUTENANT (contemptuously). Attacked! I could have broken his back between my finger and thumb. I wish I had, now. No: it was by appealing to the better side of my nature: that's what I can't get over. He said he'd never met a man he liked so much as me. He put his handkerchief round my neck because a gnat bit me, and my stock was chafing it. Look! (He pulls a handkerchief from his stock. Giuseppe takes it and examines it.)

GIUSEPPE (to Napoleon). A lady's handkerchief, excellency. (He smells it.) Perfumed!

NAPOLEON. Eh? (He takes it and looks at it attentively.) Hm! (He smells it.) Ha! (He walks thoughtfully across the room, looking at the handkerchief, which he finally sticks in the breast of his coat.)

LIEUTENANT. Good enough for him, anyhow. I noticed that he had a woman's hands when he touched my neck, with his coaxing, fawning ways, the mean, effeminate little hound. (Lowering his voice with thrilling intensity.) But mark my words, General. If ever—

THE LADY'S VOICE (outside, as before). Giuseppe!

LIEUTENANT (petrified). What was that?

GIUSEPPE. Only a lady upstairs, lieutenant, calling me.

LIEUTENANT. Lady!

VOICE. Giuseppe, Giuseppe: where ARE you?

LIEUTENANT (murderously). Give me that sword. (He strides to the couch; snatches the sword; and draws it.)

GIUSEPPE (rushing forward and seizing his right arm.) What are you thinking of, lieutenant? It's a lady: don't you hear that it's a woman's voice?

LIEUTENANT. It's HIS voice, I tell you. Let me go. (He breaks away, and rushes to the inner door. It opens in his face; and the Strange Lady steps in. She is a very attractive lady, tall and extraordinarily graceful, with a delicately intelligent, apprehensive, questioning face—perception in the brow, sensitiveness in the nostrils, character in the chin: all keen, refined, and original. She is very feminine, but by no means weak: the lithe, tender figure is hung on a strong frame: the hands and feet, neck and shoulders, are no fragile ornaments, but of full size in proportion to her stature, which considerably exceeds that of Napoleon and the innkeeper, and leaves her at no disadvantage with the lieutenant. Only her elegance and radiant charm keep the secret of her size and strength. She is not, judging by her dress, an admirer of the latest fashions of the Directory; or perhaps she uses up her old dresses for travelling. At all events she wears no jacket with extravagant lapels, no Greco-Tallien sham chiton, nothing, indeed, that the Princesse de Lamballe might not have worn. Her dress of flowered silk is long waisted, with a Watteau pleat behind, but with the paniers reduced to mere rudiments, as she is too tall for them. It is cut low in the neck, where it is eked out by a creamy fichu. She is fair, with golden brown hair and grey eyes.)

(She enters with the self-possession of a woman accustomed to the privileges of rank and beauty. The innkeeper, who has excellent natural manners, is highly appreciative of her. Napoleon, on whom her eyes first fall, is instantly smitten self-conscious. His color deepens: he becomes stiffer and less at ease than before. She perceives this instantly, and, not to embarrass him, turns in an infinitely well bred manner to pay the respect of a glance to the other gentleman, who is staring at her dress, as at the earth's final masterpiece of treacherous dissimulation, with feelings altogether inexpressible and indescribable. As she looks at him, she becomes deadly pale. There is no mistaking her expression: a revelation of some fatal error utterly unexpected, has suddenly appalled her in the midst of tranquillity, security and victory. The next moment a wave of color rushes up from beneath the creamy fichu and drowns her whole face. One can see that she is blushing all over her body. Even the lieutenant, ordinarily incapable of observation, and just now lost in the tumult of his wrath, can see a thing when it is painted red for him. Interpreting the blush as the involuntary confession of black deceit confronted with its victim, he points to it with a loud crow of retributive triumph, and then, seizing her by the wrist, pulls her past him into the room as he claps the door to, and plants himself with his back to it.)

LIEUTENANT. So I've got you, my lad. So you've disguised yourself, have you? (In a voice of thunder.) Take off that skirt.

GIUSEPPE (remonstrating). Oh, lieutenant!

LADY (affrighted, but highly indignant at his having dared to touch her). Gentlemen: I appeal to you. Giuseppe. (Making a movement as if to run to Giuseppe.)

LIEUTENANT (interposing, sword in hand). No you don't.

LADY (taking refuge with Napoleon). Ah, sir, you are an officer—a general. You will protect me, will you not?

LIEUTENANT. Never you mind him, General. Leave me to deal with him.

NAPOLEON. With him! With whom, sir? Why do you treat this lady in such a fashion?

LIEUTENANT. Lady! He's a man! the man I showed my confidence in. (Advancing threateningly.) Here you—

LADY (running behind Napoleon and in her agitation embracing the arm which he instinctively extends before her as a fortification). Oh, thank you, General. Keep him away.

NAPOLEON. Nonsense, sir. This is certainly a lady (she suddenly drops his arm and blushes again); and you are under arrest. Put down your sword, sir, instantly.

LIEUTENANT. General: I tell you he's an Austrian spy. He passed himself off on me as one of General Massena's staff this afternoon; and now he's passing himself off on you as a woman. Am I to believe my own eyes or not?

LADY. General: it must be my brother. He is on General Massena's staff. He is very like me.

LIEUTENANT (his mind giving way). Do you mean to say that you're not your brother, but your sister?—the sister who was so like me?—who had my beautiful blue eyes? It was a lie: your eyes are not like mine: they're exactly like your own. What perfidy!

NAPOLEON. Lieutenant: will you obey my orders and leave the room, since you are convinced at last that this is no gentleman?

LIEUTENANT. Gentleman! I should think not. No gentleman would have abused my confi—

NAPOLEON (out of all patience). Enough, sir, enough. Will you leave the room. I order you to leave the room.

LADY. Oh, pray let ME go instead.

NAPOLEON (drily). Excuse me, madame. With all respect to your brother, I do not yet understand what an officer on General Massena's staff wants with my letters. I have some questions to put to you.

GIUSEPPE (discreetly). Come, lieutenant. (He opens the door.)

LIEUTENANT. I'm off. General: take warning by me: be on your guard against the better side of your nature. (To the lady.) Madame: my apologies. I thought you were the same person, only of the opposite sex; and that naturally misled me.

LADY (sweetly). It was not your fault, was it? I'm so glad you're not angry with me any longer, lieutenant. (She offers her hand.)

LIEUTENANT (bending gallantly to kiss it). Oh, madam, not the lea— (Checking himself and looking at it.) You have your brother's hand. And the same sort of ring.

LADY (sweetly). We are twins.

LIEUTENANT. That accounts for it. (He kisses her hand.) A thousand pardons. I didn't mind about the despatches at all: that's more the General's affair than mine: it was the abuse of my confidence through the better side of my nature. (Taking his cap, gloves, and whip from the table and going.) You'll excuse my leaving you, General, I hope. Very sorry, I'm sure. (He talks himself out of the room. Giuseppe follows him and shuts the door.)

NAPOLEON (looking after them with concentrated irritation). Idiot! (The Strange Lady smiles sympathetically. He comes frowning down the room between the table and the fireplace, all his awkwardness gone now that he is alone with her.)

LADY. How can I thank you, General, for your protection?

NAPOLEON (turning on her suddenly). My despatches: come! (He puts out his hand for them.)

LADY. General! (She involuntarily puts her hands on her fichu as if to protect something there.)

NAPOLEON. You tricked that blockhead out of them. You disguised yourself as a man. I want my despatches. They are there in the bosom of your dress, under your hands.

LADY (quickly removing her hands). Oh, how unkindly you are speaking to me! (She takes her handkerchief from her fichu.) You frighten me. (She touches her eyes as if to wipe away a tear.)

NAPOLEON. I see you don't know me madam, or you would save yourself the trouble of pretending to cry.

LADY (producing an effect of smiling through her tears). Yes, I do know you. You are the famous General Buonaparte. (She gives the name a marked Italian pronunciation Bwaw-na-parr-te.)

NAPOLEON (angrily, with the French pronunciation). Bonaparte, madame, Bonaparte. The papers, if you please.

LADY. But I assure you— (He snatches the handkerchief rudely from her.) General! (Indignantly.)

NAPOLEON (taking the other handkerchief from his breast). You were good enough to lend one of your handkerchiefs to my lieutenant when you robbed him. (He looks at the two handkerchiefs.) They match one another. (He smells them.) The same scent. (He flings them down on the table.) I am waiting for the despatches. I shall take them, if necessary, with as little ceremony as the handkerchief. (This historical incident was used eighty years later, by M. Victorien Sardou, in his drama entitled "Dora.")

LADY (in dignified reproof). General: do you threaten women?

NAPOLEON (bluntly). Yes.

LADY (disconcerted, trying to gain time). But I don't understand. I—

NAPOLEON. You understand perfectly. You came here because your Austrian employers calculated that I was six leagues away. I am always to be found where my enemies don't expect me. You have walked into the lion's den. Come: you are a brave woman. Be a sensible one: I have no time to waste. The papers. (He advances a step ominously).

LADY (breaking down in the childish rage of impotence, and throwing herself in tears on the chair left beside the table by the lieutenant). I brave! How little you know! I have spent the day in an agony of fear. I have a pain here from the tightening of my heart at every suspicious look, every threatening movement. Do you think every one is as brave as you? Oh, why will not you brave people do the brave things? Why do you leave them to us, who have no courage at all? I'm not brave: I shrink from violence: danger makes me miserable.

NAPOLEON (interested). Then why have you thrust yourself into danger?

LADY. Because there is no other way: I can trust nobody else. And now it is all useless—all because of you, who have no fear, because you have no heart, no feeling, no— (She breaks off, and throws herself on her knees.) Ah, General, let me go: let me go without asking any questions. You shall have your despatches and letters: I swear it.

NAPOLEON (holding out his hand). Yes: I am waiting for them. (She gasps, daunted by his ruthless promptitude into despair of moving him by cajolery; but as she looks up perplexedly at him, it is plain that she is racking her brains for some device to outwit him. He meets her regard inflexibly.)

LADY (rising at last with a quiet little sigh). I will get them for you. They are in my room. (She turns to the door.)

NAPOLEON. I shall accompany you, madame.

LADY (drawing herself up with a noble air of offended delicacy).I cannot permit you, General, to enter my chamber.

NAPOLEON. Then you shall stay here, madame, whilst I have your chamber searched for my papers.

LADY (spitefully, openly giving up her plan). You may save yourself the trouble. They are not there.

NAPOLEON. No: I have already told you where they are. (Pointing to her breast.)

LADY (with pretty piteousness). General: I only want to keep one little private letter. Only one. Let me have it.

NAPOLEON (cold and stern). Is that a reasonable demand, madam?

LADY (encouraged by his not refusing point blank). No; but that is why you must grant it. Are your own demands reasonable? thousands of lives for the sake of your victories, your ambitions, your destiny! And what I ask is such a little thing. And I am only a weak woman, and you a brave man. (She looks at him with her eyes full of tender pleading and is about to kneel to him again.)

NAPOLEON (brusquely). Get up, get up. (He turns moodily away and takes a turn across the room, pausing for a moment to say, over his shoulder) You're talking nonsense; and you know it. (She gets up and sits down in almost listless despair on the couch. When he turns and sees her there, he feels that his victory is complete, and that he may now indulge in a little play with his victim. He comes back and sits beside her. She looks alarmed and moves a little away from him; but a ray of rallying hope beams from her eye. He begins like a man enjoying some secret joke.) How do you know I am a brave man?

LADY (amazed). You! General Buonaparte. (Italian pronunciation.)

NAPOLEON. Yes, I, General Bonaparte (emphasizing the French pronunciation).

LADY. Oh, how can you ask such a question? you! who stood only two days ago at the bridge at Lodi, with the air full of death, fighting a duel with cannons across the river! (Shuddering.) Oh, you DO brave things.

NAPOLEON. So do you.

LADY. I! (With a sudden odd thought.) Oh! Are you a coward?

NAPOLEON (laughing grimly and pinching her cheek). That is the one question you must never ask a soldier. The sergeant asks after the recruit's height, his age, his wind, his limb, but never after his courage. (He gets up and walks about with his hands behind him and his head bowed, chuckling to himself.)

LADY (as if she had found it no laughing matter). Ah, you can laugh at fear. Then you don't know what fear is.

NAPOLEON (coming behind the couch). Tell me this. Suppose you could have got that letter by coming to me over the bridge at Lodi the day before yesyesterday! Suppose there had been no other way, and that this was a sure way—if only you escaped the cannon! (She shudders and covers her eyes for a moment with her hands.) Would you have been afraid?

LADY. Oh, horribly afraid, agonizingly afraid. (She presses her hands on her heart.) It hurts only to imagine it.

NAPOLEON (inflexibly). Would you have come for the despatches?

LADY (overcome by the imagined horror). Don't ask me. I must have come.

NAPOLEON. Why?

LADY. Because I must. Because there would have been no other way.

NAPOLEON (with conviction). Because you would have wanted my letter enough to bear your fear. There is only one universal passion: fear. Of all the thousand qualities a man may have, the only one you will find as certainly in the youngest drummer boy in my army as in me, is fear. It is fear that makes men fight: it is indifference that makes them run away: fear is the mainspring of war. Fear! I know fear well, better than you, better than any woman. I once saw a regiment of good Swiss soldiers massacred by a mob in Paris because I was afraid to interfere: I felt myself a coward to the tips of my toes as I looked on at it. Seven months ago I revenged my shame by pounding that mob to death with cannon balls. Well, what of that? Has fear ever held a man back from anything he really wanted—or a woman either? Never. Come with me; and I will show you twenty thousand cowards who will risk death every day for the price of a glass of brandy. And do you think there are no women in the army, braver than the men, because their lives are worth less? Psha! I think nothing of your fear or your bravery. If you had had to come across to me at Lodi, you would not have been afraid: once on the bridge, every other feeling would have gone down before the necessity—the necessity—for making your way to my side and getting what you wanted.

And now, suppose you had done all this—suppose you had come safely out with that letter in your hand, knowing that when the hour came, your fear had tightened, not your heart, but your grip of your own purpose—that it had ceased to be fear, and had become strength, penetration, vigilance, iron resolution—how would you answer then if you were asked whether you were a coward?

LADY (rising). Ah, you are a hero, a real hero.

NAPOLEON. Pooh! there's no such thing as a real hero. (He strolls down the room, making light of her enthusiasm, but by no means displeased with himself for having evoked it.)

LADY. Ah, yes, there is. There is a difference between what you call my bravery and yours. You wanted to win the battle of Lodi for yourself and not for anyone else, didn't you?

NAPOLEON. Of course. (Suddenly recollecting himself.) Stop: no. (He pulls himself piously together, and says, like a man conducting a religious service) I am only the servant of the French republic, following humbly in the footsteps of the heroes of classical antiquity. I win battles for humanity—for my country, not for myself.

LADY (disappointed). Oh, then you are only a womanish hero, after all. (She sits down again, all her enthusiasm gone, her elbow on the end of the couch, and her cheek propped on her hand.)

NAPOLEON (greatly astonished). Womanish!

LADY (listlessly). Yes, like me. (With deep melancholy.) Do you think that if I only wanted those despatches for myself, I dare venture into a battle for them? No: if that were all, I should not have the courage to ask to see you at your hotel, even. My courage is mere slavishness: it is of no use to me for my own purposes. It is only through love, through pity, through the instinct to save and protect someone else, that I can do the things that terrify me.

NAPOLEON (contemptuously). Pshaw! (He turns slightingly away from her.)

LADY. Aha! now you see that I'm not really brave. (Relapsing into petulant listlessness.) But what right have you to despise me if you only win your battles for others? for your country! through patriotism! That is what I call womanish: it is so like a Frenchman!

NAPOLEON (furiously). I am no Frenchman.

LADY (innocently). I thought you said you won the battle of Lodi for your country, General Bu—shall I pronounce it in Italian or French?

NAPOLEON. You are presuming on my patience, madam. I was born a French subject, but not in France.

LADY (folding her arms on the end of the couch, and leaning on them with a marked access of interest in him). You were not born a subject at all, I think.

NAPOLEON (greatly pleased, starting on a fresh march). Eh? Eh? You think not.

LADY. I am sure of it.

NAPOLEON. Well, well, perhaps not. (The self-complacency of his assent catches his own ear. He stops short, reddening. Then, composing himself into a solemn attitude, modelled on the heroes of classical antiquity, he takes a high moral tone.) But we must not live for ourselves alone, little one. Never forget that we should always think of others, and work for others, and lead and govern them for their own good. Self-sacrifice is the foundation of all true nobility of character.

LADY (again relaxing her attitude with a sigh). Ah, it is easy to see that you have never tried it, General.

NAPOLEON (indignantly, forgetting all about Brutus and Scipio). What do you mean by that speech, madam?

LADY. Haven't you noticed that people always exaggerate the value of the things they haven't got? The poor think they only need riches to be quite happy and good. Everybody worships truth, purity, unselfishness, for the same reason—because they have no experience of them. Oh, if they only knew!

NAPOLEON (with angry derision). If they only knew! Pray, do you know?

LADY (with her arms stretched down and her hands clasped on her knees, looking straight before her). Yes. I had the misfortune to be born good. (Glancing up at him for a moment.) And it is a misfortune, I can tell you, General. I really am truthful and unselfish and all the rest of it; and it's nothing but cowardice; want of character; want of being really, strongly, positively oneself.

NAPOLEON. Ha? (Turning to her quickly with a flash of strong interest.)

LADY (earnestly, with rising enthusiasm). What is the secret of your power? Only that you believe in yourself. You can fight and conquer for yourself and for nobody else. You are not afraid of your own destiny. You teach us what we all might be if we had the will and courage; and that (suddenly sinking on her knees before him) is why we all begin to worship you. (She kisses his hands.)

NAPOLEON (embarrassed). Tut, tut! Pray rise, madam.

LADY. Do not refuse my homage: it is your right. You will be emperor of France.

NAPOLEON (hurriedly). Take care. Treason!

LADY (insisting). Yes, emperor of France; then of Europe; perhaps of the world. I am only the first subject to swear allegiance. (Again kissing his hand.) My Emperor!

NAPOLEON (overcome, raising her). Pray, pray. No, no, little one: this is folly. Come: be calm, be calm. (Petting her.) There, there, my girl.

LADY (struggling with happy tears). Yes, I know it is an impertinence in me to tell you what you must know far better than I do. But you are not angry with me, are you?

NAPOLEON. Angry! No, no: not a bit, not a bit. Come: you are a very clever and sensible and interesting little woman. (He pats her on the cheek.) Shall we be friends?

LADY (enraptured). Your friend! You will let me be your friend! Oh! (She offers him both her hands with a radiant smile.) You see: I show my confidence in you.

NAPOLEON (with a yell of rage, his eyes flashing). What!

LADY. What's the matter?

NAPOLEON. Show your confidence in me! So that I may show my confidence in you in return by letting you give me the slip with the despatches, eh? Ah, Dalila, Dalila, you have been trying your tricks on me; and I have been as great a gull as my jackass of a lieutenant. (He advances threateningly on her.) Come: the despatches. Quick: I am not to be trifled with now.

LADY (flying round the couch). General—

NAPOLEON. Quick, I tell you. (He passes swiftly up the middle of the room and intercepts her as she makes for the vineyard.)

LADY (at bay, confronting him). You dare address me in that tone.

NAPOLEON. Dare!

LADY. Yes, dare. Who are you that you should presume to speak to me in that coarse way? Oh, the vile, vulgar Corsican adventurer comes out in you very easily.

NAPOLEON (beside himself). You she devil! (Savagely.) Once more, and only once, will you give me those papers or shall I tear them from you—by force?

LADY (letting her hands fall). Tear them from me—by force! (As he glares at her like a tiger about to spring, she crosses her arms on her breast in the attitude of a martyr. The gesture and pose instantly awaken his theatrical instinct: he forgets his rage in the desire to show her that in acting, too, she has met her match. He keeps her a moment in suspense; then suddenly clears up his countenance; puts his hands behind him with provoking coolness; looks at her up and down a couple of times; takes a pinch of snuff; wipes his fingers carefully and puts up his handkerchief, her heroic pose becoming more and more ridiculous all the time.)

NAPOLEON (at last). Well?

LADY (disconcerted, but with her arms still crossed devotedly). Well: what are you going to do?

NAPOLEON. Spoil your attitude.

LADY. You brute! (abandoning the attitude, she comes to the end of the couch, where she turns with her back to it, leaning against it and facing him with her hands behind her.)

NAPOLEON. Ah, that's better. Now listen to me. I like you. What's more, I value your respect.

LADY. You value what you have not got, then.

NAPOLEON. I shall have it presently. Now attend to me. Suppose I were to allow myself to be abashed by the respect due to your sex, your beauty, your heroism and all the rest of it? Suppose I, with nothing but such sentimental stuff to stand between these muscles of mine and those papers which you have about you, and which I want and mean to have: suppose I, with the prize within my grasp, were to falter and sneak away with my hands empty; or, what would be worse, cover up my weakness by playing the magnanimous hero, and sparing you the violence I dared not use, would you not despise me from the depths of your woman's soul? Would any woman be such a fool? Well, Bonaparte can rise to the situation and act like a woman when it is necessary. Do you understand?

The lady, without speaking, stands upright, and takes a packet of papers from her bosom. For a moment she has an intense impulse to dash them in his face. But her good breeding cuts her off from any vulgar method of relief. She hands them to him politely, only averting her head. The moment he takes them, she hurries across to the other side of the room; covers her face with her hands; and sits down, with her body turned away to the back of the chair.

NAPOLEON (gloating over the papers). Aha! That's right. That's right. (Before opening them he looks at her and says) Excuse me. (He sees that she is hiding her face.) Very angry with me, eh? (He unties the packet, the seal of which is already broken, and puts it on the table to examine its contents.)

LADY (quietly, taking down her hands and showing that she is not crying, but only thinking). No. You were right. But I am sorry for you.

NAPOLEON (pausing in the act of taking the uppermost paper from the packet). Sorry for me! Why?

LADY. I am going to see you lose your honor.

NAPOLEON. Hm! Nothing worse than that? (He takes up the paper.)

LADY. And your happiness.

NAPOLEON. Happiness, little woman, is the most tedious thing in the world to me. Should I be what I am if I cared for happiness? Anything else?

LADY. Nothing— (He interrupts her with an exclamation of satisfaction. She proceeds quietly) except that you will cut a very foolish figure in the eyes of France.

NAPOLEON (quickly). What? (The hand holding the paper involuntarily drops. The lady looks at him enigmatically in tranquil silence. He throws the letter down and breaks out into a torrent of scolding.) What do you mean? Eh? Are you at your tricks again? Do you think I don't know what these papers contain? I'll tell you. First, my information as to Beaulieu's retreat. There are only two things he can do—leatherbrained idiot that he is!—shut himself up in Mantua or violate the neutrality of Venice by taking Peschiera. You are one of old Leatherbrain's spies: he has discovered that he has been betrayed, and has sent you to intercept the information at all hazards—as if that could save him from ME, the old fool! The other papers are only my usual correspondence from Paris, of which you know nothing.

LADY (prompt and businesslike). General: let us make a fair division. Take the information your spies have sent you about the Austrian army; and give me the Paris correspondence. That will content me.

NAPOLEON (his breath taken away by the coolness of the proposal). A fair di— (He gasps.) It seems to me, madame, that you have come to regard my letters as your own property, of which I am trying to rob you.

LADY (earnestly). No: on my honor I ask for no letter of yours—not a word that has been written by you or to you. That packet contains a stolen letter: a letter written by a woman to a man—a man not her husband—a letter that means disgrace, infamy—

NAPOLEON. A love letter?

LADY (bitter-sweetly). What else but a love letter could stir up so much hate?

NAPOLEON. Why is it sent to me? To put the husband in my power, eh?

LADY. No, no: it can be of no use to you: I swear that it will cost you nothing to give it to me. It has been sent to you out of sheer malice—solely to injure the woman who wrote it.

NAPOLEON. Then why not send it to her husband instead of to me?

LADY (completely taken aback). Oh! (Sinking back into the chair.) I—I don't know. (She breaks down.)

NAPOLEON. Aha! I thought so: a little romance to get the papers back. (He throws the packet on the table and confronts her with cynical goodhumor.) Per Bacco, little woman, I can't help admiring you. If I could lie like that, it would save me a great deal of trouble.

LADY (wringing her hands). Oh, how I wish I really had told you some lie! You would have believed me then. The truth is the one thing that nobody will believe.

NAPOLEON (with coarse familiarity, treating her as if she were a vivandiere). Capital! Capital! (He puts his hands behind him on the table, and lifts himself on to it, sitting with his arms akimbo and his legs wide apart.) Come: I am a true Corsican in my love for stories. But I could tell them better than you if I set my mind to it. Next time you are asked why a letter compromising a wife should not be sent to her husband, answer simply that the husband would not read it. Do you suppose, little innocent, that a man wants to be compelled by public opinion to make a scene, to fight a duel, to break up his household, to injure his career by a scandal, when he can avoid it all by taking care not to know?

LADY (revolted). Suppose that packet contained a letter about your own wife?

NAPOLEON (offended, coming off the table). You are impertinent, madame.

LADY (humbly). I beg your above suspicion.

NAPOLEON (with a deliberate assumption of superiority). You have committed an indiscretion. I pardon you. In future, do not permit yourself to introduce real persons in your romances.

LADY (politely ignoring a speech which is to her only a breach of good manners, and rising to move towards the table). General: there really is a woman's letter there. (Pointing to the packet.) Give it to me.

NAPOLEON (with brute conciseness, moving so as to prevent her getting too near the letters). Why?

LADY. She is an old friend: we were at school together. She has written to me imploring me to prevent the letter falling into your hands.

NAPOLEON. Why has it been sent to me?

LADY. Because it compromises the director Barras.

NAPOLEON (frowning, evidently startled). Barras! (Haughtily.) Take care, madame. The director Barras is my attached personal friend.

LADY (nodding placidly). Yes. You became friends through your wife.

NAPOLEON. Again! Have I not forbidden you to speak of my wife? (She keeps looking curiously at him, taking no account of the rebuke. More and more irritated, he drops his haughty manner, of which he is himself somewhat impatient, and says suspiciously, lowering his voice) Who is this woman with whom you sympathize so deeply?

LADY. Oh, General! How could I tell you that?

NAPOLEON (ill-humoredly, beginning to walk about again in angry perplexity). Ay, ay: stand by one another. You are all the same, you women.

LADY (indignantly). We are not all the same, any more than you are. Do you think that if *I* loved another man, I should pretend to go on loving my husband, or be afraid to tell him or all the world? But this woman is not made that way. She governs men by cheating them; and (with disdain) they like it, and let her govern them. (She sits down again, with her back to him.)

NAPOLEON (not attending to her). Barras, Barras I— (Turning very threateningly to her, his face darkening.) Take care, take care: do you hear? You may go too far.

LADY (innocently turning her face to him). What's the matter?

NAPOLEON. What are you hinting at? Who is this woman?

LADY (meeting his angry searching gaze with tranquil indifference as she sits looking up at him with her right arm resting lightly along the back of her chair, and one knee crossed over the other). A vain, silly, extravagant creature, with a very able and ambitious husband who knows her through and through—knows that she has lied to him about her age, her income, her social position, about everything that silly women lie about—knows that she is incapable of fidelity to any principle or any person; and yet could not help loving her—could not help his man's instinct to make use of her for his own advancement with Barras.

NAPOLEON (in a stealthy, coldly furious whisper). This is your revenge, you she cat, for having had to give me the letters.

LADY. Nonsense! Or do you mean that YOU are that sort of man?

NAPOLEON (exasperated, clasps his hands behind him, his fingers twitching, and says, as he walks irritably away from her to the fireplace). This woman will drive me out of my senses. (To her.) Begone.

LADY (seated immovably). Not without that letter.

NAPOLEON. Begone, I tell you. (Walking from the fireplace to the vineyard and back to the table.) You shall have no letter. I don't like you. You're a detestable woman, and as ugly as Satan. I don't choose to be pestered by strange women. Be off. (He turns his back on her. In quiet amusement, she leans her cheek on her hand and laughs at him. He turns again, angrily mocking her.) Ha! ha! ha! What are you laughing at?

LADY. At you, General. I have often seen persons of your sex getting into a pet and behaving like children; but I never saw a really great man do it before.

NAPOLEON (brutally, flinging the words in her face). Pooh: flattery! flattery! coarse, impudent flattery!

LADY (springing up with a bright flush in her cheeks). Oh, you are too bad. Keep your letters. Read the story of your own dishonor in them; and much good may they do you. Good-bye. (She goes indignantly towards the inner door.)

NAPOLEON. My own—! Stop. Come back. Come back, I order you. (She proudly disregards his savagely peremptory tone and continues on her way to the door. He rushes at her; seizes her by the wrist; and drags her back.) Now, what do you mean? Explain. Explain, I tell you, or—(Threatening her. She looks at him with unflinching defiance.) Rrrr! you obstinate devil, you. Why can't you answer a civil question?

LADY (deeply offended by his violence). Why do you ask me? You have the explanation.

NAPOLEON. Where?

LADY (pointing to the letters on the table). There. You have only to read it. (He snatches the packet up, hesitates; looks at her suspiciously; and throws it down again.)

NAPOLEON. You seem to have forgotten your solicitude for the honor of your old friend.

LADY. She runs no risk now: she does not quite understand her husband.

NAPOLEON. I am to read the letter, then? (He stretches out his hand as if to take up the packet again, with his eye on her.)

LADY. I do not see how you can very well avoid doing so now. (He instantly withdraws his hand.) Oh, don't be afraid. You will find many interesting things in it.

NAPOLEON. For instance?

LADY. For instance, a duel—with Barras, a domestic scene, a broken household, a public scandal, a checked career, all sorts of things.

NAPOLEON. Hm! (He looks at her, takes up the packet and looks at it, pursing his lips and balancing it in his hand; looks at her again; passes the packet into his left hand and puts it behind his back, raising his right to scratch the back of his head as he turns and goes up to the edge of the vineyard, where he stands for a moment looking out into the vines, deep in thought. The Lady watches him in silence, somewhat slightingly. Suddenly he turns and comes back again, full of force and decision.) I grant your request, madame. Your courage and resolution deserve to succeed. Take the letters for which you have fought so well; and remember henceforth that you found the vile, vulgar Corsican adventurer as generous to the vanquished after the battle as he was resolute in the face of the enemy before it. (He offers her the packet.)

LADY (without taking it, looking hard at him). What are you at now, I wonder? (He dashes the packet furiously to the floor.) Aha! I've spoiled that attitude, I think. (She makes him a pretty mocking curtsey.)

NAPOLEON (snatching it up again). Will you take the letters and begone (advancing and thrusting them upon her)?

LADY (escaping round the table). No: I don't want letters.

NAPOLEON. Ten minutes ago, nothing else would satisfy you.

LADY (keeping the table carefully between them). Ten minutes ago you had not insulted me past all bearing.

NAPOLEON. I— (swallowing his spleen) I apologize.

LADY (coolly). Thanks. (With forced politeness he offers her the packet across the table. She retreats a step out of its reach and says) But don't you want to know whether the Austrians are at Mantua or Peschiera?

NAPOLEON. I have already told you that I can conquer my enemies without the aid of spies, madame.

LADY. And the letter! don't you want to read that?

NAPOLEON. You have said that it is not addressed to me. I am not in the habit of reading other people's letters. (He again offers the packet.)

LADY. In that case there can be no objection to your keeping it. All I wanted was to prevent your reading it. (Cheerfully.) Good afternoon, General. (She turns coolly towards the inner door.)

NAPOLEON (furiously flinging the packet on the couch). Heaven grant me patience! (He goes up determinedly and places himself before the door.) Have you any sense of personal danger? Or are you one of those women who like to be beaten black and blue?

LADY. Thank you, General: I have no doubt the sensation is very voluptuous; but I had rather not. I simply want to go home: that's all. I was wicked enough to steal your despatches; but you have got them back; and you have forgiven me, because (delicately reproducing his rhetorical cadence) you are as generous to the vanquished after the battle as you are resolute in the face of the enemy before it. Won't you say good-bye to me? (She offers her hand sweetly.)

NAPOLEON (repulsing the advance with a gesture of concentrated rage, and opening the door to call fiercely). Giuseppe! (Louder.) Giuseppe! (He bangs the door to, and comes to the middle of the room. The lady goes a little way into the vineyard to avoid him.)

GIUSEPPE (appearing at the door). Excellency?

NAPOLEON. Where is that fool?

GIUSEPPE. He has had a good dinner, according to your instructions, excellency, and is now doing me the honor to gamble with me to pass the time.

NAPOLEON. Send him here. Bring him here. Come with him. (Giuseppe, with unruffled readiness, hurries off. Napoleon turns curtly to the lady, saying) I must trouble you to remain some moments longer, madame. (He comes to the couch. She comes from the vineyard down the opposite side of the room to the sideboard, and posts herself there, leaning against it, watching him. He takes the packet from the couch and deliberately buttons it carefully into his breast pocket, looking at her meanwhile with an expression which suggests that she will soon find out the meaning of his proceedings, and will not like it. Nothing more is said until the lieutenant arrives followed by Giuseppe, who stands modestly in attendance at the table. The lieutenant, without cap, sword or gloves, and much improved in temper and spirits by his meal, chooses the Lady's side of the room, and waits, much at his ease, for Napoleon to begin.)

NAPOLEON. Lieutenant.

LIEUTENANT (encouragingly). General.

NAPOLEON. I cannot persuade this lady to give me much information; but there can be no doubt that the man who tricked you out of your charge was, as she admitted to you, her brother.

LIEUTENANT (triumphantly). What did I tell you, General! What did I tell you!

NAPOLEON. You must find that man. Your honor is at stake; and the fate of the campaign, the destiny of France, of Europe, of humanity, perhaps, may depend on the information those despatches contain.

LIEUTENANT. Yes, I suppose they really are rather serious (as if this had hardly occurred to him before).

NAPOLEON (energetically). They are so serious, sir, that if you do not recover them, you will be degraded in the presence of your regiment.

LIEUTENANT. Whew! The regiment won't like that, I can tell you.

NAPOLEON. Personally, I am sorry for you. I would willingly conceal the affair if it were possible. But I shall be called to account for not acting on the despatches. I shall have to prove to all the world that I never received them, no matter what the consequences may be to you. I am sorry; but you see that I cannot help myself.

LIEUTENANT (goodnaturedly). Oh, don't take it to heart, General: it's really very good of you. Never mind what happens to me: I shall scrape through somehow; and we'll beat the Austrians for you, despatches or no despatches. I hope you won't insist on my starting off on a wild goose chase after the fellow now. I haven't a notion where to look for him.

GIUSEPPE (deferentially). You forget, Lieutenant: he has your horse.

LIEUTENANT (starting). I forgot that. (Resolutely.) I'll go after him, General: I'll find that horse if it's alive anywhere in Italy. And I shan't forget the despatches: never fear. Giuseppe: go and saddle one of those mangy old posthorses of yours, while I get my cap and sword and things. Quick march. Off with you (bustling him).

GIUSEPPE. Instantly, Lieutenant, instantly. (He disappears in the vineyard, where the light is now reddening with the sunset.)

LIEUTENANT (looking about him on his way to the inner door). By the way, General, did I give you my sword or did I not? Oh, I remember now. (Fretfully.) It's all that nonsense about putting a man under arrest: one never knows where to find— (Talks himself out of the room.)

LADY (still at the sideboard). What does all this mean, General?

NAPOLEON. He will not find your brother.

LADY. Of course not. There's no such person.

NAPOLEON. The despatches will be irrecoverably lost.

LADY. Nonsense! They are inside your coat.

NAPOLEON. You will find it hard, I think, to prove that wild statement. (The Lady starts. He adds, with clinching emphasis) Those papers are lost.

LADY (anxiously, advancing to the corner of the table). And that unfortunate young man's career will be sacrificed.

NAPOLEON. HIS career! The fellow is not worth the gunpowder it would cost to have him shot. (He turns contemptuously and goes to the hearth, where he stands with his back to her.)

LADY (wistfully). You are very hard. Men and women are nothing to you but things to be used, even if they are broken in the use.

NAPOLEON (turning on her). Which of us has broken this fellow—I or you? Who tricked him out of the despatches? Did you think of his career then?

LADY (naively concerned about him). Oh, I never thought of that. It was brutal of me; but I couldn't help it, could I? How else could I have got the papers? (Supplicating.) General: you will save him from disgrace.

NAPOLEON (laughing sourly). Save him yourself, since you are so clever: it was you who ruined him. (With savage intensity.) I HATE a bad soldier.

He goes out determinedly through the vineyard. She follows him a few steps with an appealing gesture, but is interrupted by the return of the lieutenant, gloved and capped, with his sword on, ready for the road. He is crossing to the outer door when she intercepts him.

LADY. Lieutenant.

LIEUTENANT (importantly). You mustn't delay me, you know. Duty, madame, duty.

LADY (imploringly). Oh, sir, what are you going to do to my poor brother?

LIEUTENANT. Are you very fond of him?

LADY. I should die if anything happened to him. You must spare him. (The lieutenant shakes his head gloomily.) Yes, yes: you must: you shall: he is not fit to die. Listen to me. If I tell you where to find him—if I undertake to place him in your hands a prisoner, to be delivered up by you to General Bonaparte—will you promise me on your honor as an officer and a gentleman not to fight with him or treat him unkindly in any way?

LIEUTENANT. But suppose he attacks me. He has my pistols.

LADY. He is too great a coward.

LIEUTENANT. I don't feel so sure about that. He's capable of anything.

LADY. If he attacks you, or resists you in any way, I release you from your promise.

LIEUTENANT. My promise! I didn't mean to promise. Look here: you're as bad as he is: you've taken an advantage of me through the better side of my nature. What about my horse?

LADY. It is part of the bargain that you are to have your horse and pistols back.

LIEUTENANT. Honor bright?

LADY. Honor bright. (She offers her hand.)

LIEUTENANT (taking it and holding it). All right: I'll be as gentle as a lamb with him. His sister's a very pretty woman. (He attempts to kiss her.)

LADY (slipping away from him). Oh, Lieutenant! You forget: your career is at stake—the destiny of Europe—of humanity.

LIEUTENANT. Oh, bother the destiny of humanity (Making for her.) Only a kiss.

LADY (retreating round the table). Not until you have regained your honor as an officer. Remember: you have not captured my brother yet.

LIEUTENANT (seductively). You'll tell me where he is, won't you?

LADY. I have only to send him a certain signal; and he will be here in quarter of an hour.

LIEUTENANT. He's not far off, then.

LADY. No: quite close. Wait here for him: when he gets my message he will come here at once and surrender himself to you. You understand?

LIEUTENANT (intellectually overtaxed). Well, it's a little complicated; but I daresay it will be all right.

LADY. And now, whilst you're waiting, don't you think you had better make terms with the General?

LIEUTENANT. Oh, look here, this is getting frightfully complicated. What terms?

LADY. Make him promise that if you catch my brother he will consider that you have cleared your character as a soldier. He will promise anything you ask on that condition.

LIEUTENANT. That's not a bad idea. Thank you: I think I'll try it.

LADY. Do. And mind, above all things, don't let him see how clever you are.

LIEUTENANT. I understand. He'd be jealous.

LADY. Don't tell him anything except that you are resolved to capture my brother or perish in the attempt. He won't believe you. Then you will produce my brother—

LIEUTENANT (interrupting as he masters the plot). And have the laugh at him! I say: what a clever little woman you are! (Shouting.) Giuseppe!

LADY. Sh! Not a word to Giuseppe about me. (She puts her finger on her lips. He does the same. They look at one another warningly. Then, with a ravishing smile, she changes the gesture into wafting him a kiss, and runs out through the inner door. Electrified, he bursts into a volley of chuckles. Giuseppe comes back by the outer door.)

GIUSEPPE. The horse is ready, Lieutenant.

LIEUTENANT. I'm not going just yet. Go and find the General, and tell him I want to speak to him.

GIUSEPPE (shaking his head). That will never do, Lieutenant.

LIEUTENANT. Why not?

GIUSEPPE. In this wicked world a general may send for a lieutenant; but a lieutenant must not send for a general.

LIEUTENANT. Oh, you think he wouldn't like it. Well, perhaps you're right: one has to be awfully particular about that sort of thing now we've got a republic.

Napoleon reappears, advancing from the vineyard, buttoning the breast of his coat, pale and full of gnawing thoughts.

GIUSEPPE (unconscious of Napoleon's approach). Quite true, Lieutenant, quite true. You are all like innkeepers now in France: you have to be polite to everybody.

NAPOLEON (putting his hand on Giuseppe's shoulder). And that destroys the whole value of politeness, eh?

LIEUTENANT. The very man I wanted! See here, General: suppose I catch that fellow for you!

NAPOLEON (with ironical gravity). You will not catch him, my friend.

LIEUTENANT. Aha! you think so; but you'll see. Just wait. Only, if I do catch him and hand him over to you, will you cry quits? Will you drop all this about degrading me in the presence of my regiment? Not that I mind, you know; but still no regiment likes to have all the other regiments laughing at it.

NAPOLEON. (a cold ray of humor striking pallidly across his gloom). What shall we do with this officer, Giuseppe? Everything he says is wrong.

GIUSEPPE (promptly). Make him a general, excellency; and then everything he says will be right.

LIEUTENANT (crowing). Haw-aw! (He throws himself ecstatically on the couch to enjoy the joke.)

NAPOLEON (laughing and pinching Giuseppe's ear). You are thrown away in this inn, Giuseppe. (He sits down and places Giuseppe before him like a schoolmaster with a pupil.) Shall I take you away with me and make a man of you?

GIUSEPPE (shaking his head rapidly and repeatedly). No, thank you, General. All my life long people have wanted to make a man of me. When I was a boy, our good priest wanted to make a man of me by teaching me to read and write. Then the organist at Melegnano wanted to make a man of me by teaching me to read music. The recruiting sergeant would have made a man of me if I had been a few inches taller. But it always meant making me work; and I am too lazy for that, thank Heaven! So I taught myself to cook and became an innkeeper; and now I keep servants to do the work, and have nothing to do myself except talk, which suits me perfectly.

NAPOLEON (looking at him thoughtfully). You are satisfied?

GIUSEPPE (with cheerful conviction). Quite, excellency.

NAPOLEON. And you have no devouring devil inside you who must be fed with action and victory—gorged with them night and day—who makes you pay, with the sweat of your brain and body, weeks of Herculean toil for ten minutes of enjoyment—who is at once your slave and your tyrant, your genius and your doom—who brings you a crown in one hand and the oar of a galley slave in the other—who shows you all the kingdoms of the earth and offers to make you their master on condition that you become their servant!—have you nothing of that in you?

GIUSEPPE. Nothing of it! Oh, I assure you, excellency, MY devouring devil is far worse than that. He offers me no crowns and kingdoms: he expects to get everything for nothing—sausages, omelettes, grapes, cheese, polenta, wine—three times a day, excellency: nothing less will content him.

LIEUTENANT. Come, drop it, Giuseppe: you're making me feel hungry again.

(Giuseppe, with an apologetic shrug, retires from the conversation, and busies himself at the table, dusting it, setting the map straight, and replacing Napoleon's chair, which the lady has pushed back.)

NAPOLEON (turning to the lieutenant with sardonic ceremony). I hope *I* have not been making you feel ambitious.

LIEUTENANT. Not at all: I don't fly so high. Besides: I'm better as I am: men like me are wanted in the army just now. The fact is, the Revolution was all very well for civilians; but it won't work in the army. You know what soldiers are, General: they WILL have men of family for their officers. A subaltern must be a gentleman, because he's so much in contact with the men. But a general, or even a colonel, may be any sort of riff-raff if he understands the shop well enough. A lieutenant is a gentleman: all the rest is chance. Why, who do you suppose won the battle of Lodi? I'll tell you. My horse did.

NAPOLEON (rising) Your folly is carrying you too far, sir. Take care.

LIEUTENANT. Not a bit of it. You remember all that red-hot cannonade across the river: the Austrians blazing away at you to keep you from crossing, and you blazing away at them to keep them from setting the bridge on fire? Did you notice where I was then?

NAPOLEON (with menacing politeness). I am sorry. I am afraid I was rather occupied at the moment.

GIUSEPPE (with eager admiration). They say you jumped off your horse and worked the big guns with your own hands, General.

LIEUTENANT. That was a mistake: an officer should never let himself down to the level of his men. (Napoleon looks at him dangerously, and begins to walk tigerishly to and fro.) But you might have been firing away at the Austrians still, if we cavalry fellows hadn't found the ford and got across and turned old Beaulieu's flank for you. You know you daren't have given the order to charge the bridge if you hadn't seen us on the other side. Consequently, I say that whoever found that ford won the battle of Lodi. Well, who found it? I was the first man to cross: and I know. It was my horse that found it. (With conviction, as he rises from the couch.) That horse is the true conqueror of the Austrians.

NAPOLEON (passionately). You idiot: I'll have you shot for losing those despatches: I'll have you blown from the mouth of a cannon: nothing less could make any impression on you. (Baying at him.) Do you hear? Do you understand?

A French officer enters unobserved, carrying his sheathed sabre in his hand.

LIEUTENANT (unabashed). IF I don't capture him, General. Remember the if.

NAPOLEON. If! If!! Ass: there is no such man.

THE OFFICER (suddenly stepping between them and speaking in the unmistakable voice of the Strange Lady). Lieutenant: I am your prisoner. (She offers him her sabre. They are amazed. Napoleon gazes at her for a moment thunderstruck; then seizes her by the wrist and drags her roughly to him, looking closely and fiercely at her to satisfy himself as to her identity; for it now begins to darken rapidly into night, the red glow over the vineyard giving way to clear starlight.)

NAPOLEON. Pah! (He flings her hand away with an exclamation of disgust, and turns his back on her with his hand in his breast and his brow lowering.)

LIEUTENANT (triumphantly, taking the sabre). No such man: eh, General? (To the Lady.) I say: where's my horse?

LADY. Safe at Borghetto, waiting for you, Lieutenant.

NAPOLEON (turning on them). Where are the despatches?

LADY. You would never guess. They are in the most unlikely place in the world. Did you meet my sister here, any of you?

LIEUTENANT. Yes. Very nice woman. She's wonderfully like you; but of course she's better looking.

LADY (mysteriously). Well, do you know that she is a witch?

GIUSEPPE (running down to them in terror, crossing himself). Oh, no, no, no. It is not safe to jest about such things. I cannot have it in my house, excellency.

LIEUTENANT. Yes, drop it. You're my prisoner, you know. Of course I don't believe in any such rubbish; but still it's not a proper subject for joking.

LADY. But this is very serious. My sister has bewitched the General. (Giuseppe and the Lieutenant recoil from Napoleon.) General: open your coat: you will find the despatches in the breast of it. (She puts her hand quickly on his breast.) Yes: there they are: I can feel them. Eh? (She looks up into his face half coaxingly, half mockingly.) Will you allow me, General? (She takes a button as if to unbutton his coat, and pauses for permission.)

NAPOLEON (inscrutably). If you dare.

LADY. Thank you. (She opens his coat and takes out the despatches.) There! (To Giuseppe, showing him the despatches.) See!

GIUSEPPE (flying to the outer door). No, in heaven's name! They're bewitched.

LADY (turning to the Lieutenant). Here, Lieutenant: YOU'RE not afraid of them.

LIEUTENANT (retreating). Keep off. (Seizing the hilt of the sabre.) Keep off, I tell you.

LADY (to Napoleon). They belong to you, General. Take them.

GIUSEPPE. Don't touch them, excellency. Have nothing to do with them.

LIEUTENANT. Be careful, General: be careful.

GIUSEPPE. Burn them. And burn the witch, too.

LADY (to Napoleon). Shall I burn them?

NAPOLEON (thoughtfully). Yes, burn them. Giuseppe: go and fetch a light.

GIUSEPPE (trembling and stammering). Do you mean go alone—in the dark—with a witch in the house?

NAPOLEON. Psha! You're a poltroon. (To the Lieutenant.) Oblige me by going, Lieutenant.

LIEUTENANT (remonstrating). Oh, I say, General! No, look here, you know: nobody can say I'm a coward after Lodi. But to ask me to go into the dark by myself without a candle after such an awful conversation is a little too much. How would you like to do it yourself?

NAPOLEON (irritably). You refuse to obey my order?

LIEUTENANT (resolutely). Yes, I do. It's not reasonable. But I'll tell you what I'll do. If Giuseppe goes, I'll go with him and protect him.

NAPOLEON (to Giuseppe). There! will that satisfy you? Be off, both of you.

GIUSEPPE (humbly, his lips trembling). W—willingly, your excellency. (He goes reluctantly towards the inner door.) Heaven protect me! (To the lieutenant.) After you, Lieutenant.

LIEUTENANT. You'd better go first: I don't know the way.

GIUSEPPE. You can't miss it. Besides (imploringly, laying his hand on his sleeve), I am only a poor innkeeper; and you are a man of family.

LIEUTENANT. There's something in that. Here: you needn't be in such a fright. Take my arm. (Giuseppe does so.) That's the way.(They go out, arm in arm. It is now starry night. The lady throws the packet on the table and seats herself at her ease on the couch enjoying the sensation of freedom from petticoats.)

LADY. Well, General: I've beaten you.

NAPOLEON (walking about). You have been guilty of indelicacy—of unwomanliness. Do you consider that costume a proper one to wear?

LADY. It seems to me much the same as yours.

NAPOLEON. Psha! I blush for you.

LADY (naively). Yes: soldiers blush so easily! (He growls and turns away. She looks mischievously at him, balancing the despatches in her hand.) Wouldn't you like to read these before they're burnt, General? You must be dying with curiosity. Take a peep. (She throws the packet on the table, and turns her face away from it.) I won't look.

NAPOLEON. I have no curiosity whatever, madame. But since you are evidently burning to read them, I give you leave to do so.

LADY. Oh, I've read them already.

NAPOLEON (starting). What!

LADY. I read them the first thing after I rode away on that poor lieutenant's horse. So you see I know what's in them; and you don't.

NAPOLEON. Excuse me: I read them there in the vineyard ten minutes ago.

LADY. Oh! (Jumping up.) Oh, General I've not beaten you. I do admire you so. (He laughs and pats her cheek.) This time really and truly without shamming, I do you homage (kissing his hand).

NAPOLEON (quickly withdrawing it). Brr! Don't do that. No more witchcraft.

LADY. I want to say something to you—only you would misunderstand it.

NAPOLEON. Need that stop you?

LADY. Well, it is this. I adore a man who is not afraid to be mean and selfish.

NAPOLEON (indignantly). I am neither mean nor selfish.

LADY. Oh, you don't appreciate yourself. Besides, I don't really mean meanness and selfishness.

NAPOLEON. Thank you. I thought perhaps you did.

LADY. Well, of course I do. But what I mean is a certain strong simplicity about you.

NAPOLEON. That's better.

LADY. You didn't want to read the letters; but you were curious about what was in them. So you went into the garden and read them when no one was looking, and then came back and pretended you hadn't. That's the meanest thing I ever knew any man do; but it exactly fulfilled your purpose; and so you weren't a bit afraid or ashamed to do it.

NAPOLEON (abruptly). Where did you pick up all these vulgar scruples—this (with contemptuous emphasis) conscience of yours? I took you for a lady—an aristocrat. Was your grandfather a shopkeeper, pray?

LADY. No: he was an Englishman.

NAPOLEON. That accounts for it. The English are a nation of shopkeepers. Now I understand why you've beaten me.

LADY. Oh, I haven't beaten you. And I'm not English.

NAPOLEON. Yes, you are—English to the backbone. Listen to me: I will explain the English to you.

LADY (eagerly). Do. (With a lively air of anticipating an intellectual treat, she sits down on the couch and composes herself to listen to him. Secure of his audience, he at once nerves himself for a performance. He considers a little before he begins; so as to fix her attention by a moment of suspense. His style is at first modelled on Talma's in Corneille's "Cinna;" but it is somewhat lost in the darkness, and Talma presently gives way to Napoleon, the voice coming through the gloom with startling intensity.)

NAPOLEON. There are three sorts of people in the world, the low people, the middle people, and the high people. The low people and the high people are alike in one thing: they have no scruples, no morality. The low are beneath morality, the high above it. I am not afraid of either of them: for the low are unscrupulous without knowledge, so that they make an idol of me; whilst the high are unscrupulous without purpose, so that they go down before my will. Look you: I shall go over all the mobs and all the courts of Europe as a plough goes over a field. It is the middle people who are dangerous: they have both knowledge and purpose. But they, too, have their weak point. They are full of scruples—chained hand and foot by their morality and respectability.

LADY. Then you will beat the English; for all shopkeepers are middle people.

NAPOLEON. No, because the English are a race apart. No Englishman is too low to have scruples: no Englishman is high enough to be free from their tyranny. But every Englishman is born with a certain miraculous power that makes him master of the world. When he wants a thing, he never tells himself that he wants it. He waits patiently until there comes into his mind, no one knows how, a burning conviction that it is his moral and religious duty to conquer those who have got the thing he wants. Then he becomes irresistible. Like the aristocrat, he does what pleases him and grabs what he wants: like the shopkeeper, he pursues his purpose with the industry and steadfastness that come from strong religious conviction and deep sense of moral responsibility. He is never at a loss for an effective moral attitude. As the great champion of freedom and national independence, he conquers and annexes half the world, and calls it Colonization. When he wants a new market for his adulterated Manchester goods, he sends a missionary to teach the natives the gospel of peace. The natives kill the missionary: he flies to arms in defence of Christianity; fights for it; conquers for it; and takes the market as a reward from heaven. In defence of his island shores, he puts a chaplain on board his ship; nails a flag with a cross on it to his top-gallant mast; and sails to the ends of the earth, sinking, burning and destroying all who dispute the empire of the seas with him. He boasts that a slave is free the moment his foot touches British soil; and he sells the children of his poor at six years of age to work under the lash in his factories for sixteen hours a day. He makes two revolutions, and then declares war on our one in the name of law and order. There is nothing so bad or so good that you will not find Englishmen doing it; but you will never find an Englishman in the wrong. He does everything on principle. He fights you on patriotic principles; he robs you on business principles; he enslaves you on imperial principles; he bullies you on manly principles; he supports his king on loyal principles, and cuts off his king's head on republican principles. His watchword is always duty; and he never forgets that the nation which lets its duty get on the opposite side to its interest is lost. He—

LADY. W-w-w-w-w-wh! Do stop a moment. I want to know how you make me out to be English at this rate.

NAPOLEON (dropping his rhetorical style). It's plain enough. You wanted some letters that belonged to me. You have spent the morning in stealing them—yes, stealing them, by highway robbery. And you have spent the afternoon in putting me in the wrong about them—in assuming that it was I who wanted to steal YOUR letters—in explaining that it all came about through my meanness and selfishness, and your goodness, your devotion, your self-sacrifice. That's English.

LADY. Nonsense. I am sure I am not a bit English. The English are a very stupid people.

NAPOLEON. Yes, too stupid sometimes to know when they're beaten. But I grant that your brains are not English. You see, though your grandfather was an Englishman, your grandmother was—what? A Frenchwoman?

LADY. Oh, no. An Irishwoman.

NAPOLEON (quickly). Irish! (Thoughtfully.) Yes: I forgot the Irish. An English army led by an Irish general: that might be a match for a French army led by an Italian general. (He pauses, and adds, half jestingly, half moodily) At all events, YOU have beaten me; and what beats a man first will beat him last. (He goes meditatively into the moonlit vineyard and looks up. She steals out after him. She ventures to rest her hand on his shoulder, overcome by the beauty of the night and emboldened by its obscurity.)

LADY (softly). What are you looking at?

NAPOLEON (pointing up). My star.

LADY. You believe in that?

NAPOLEON. I do. (They look at it for a moment, she leaning a little on his shoulder.)

LADY. Do you know that the English say that a man's star is not complete without a woman's garter?

NAPOLEON (scandalized—abruptly shaking her off and coming back into the room). Pah! The hypocrites! If the French said that, how they would hold up their hands in pious horror! (He goes to the inner door and holds it open, shouting) Hallo! Giuseppe. Where's that light, man. (He comes between the table and the sideboard, and moves the chair to the table, beside his own.) We have still to burn the letter. (He takes up the packet. Giuseppe comes back, pale and still trembling, carrying a branched candlestick with a couple of candles alight, in one hand, and a broad snuffers tray in the other.)

GIUSEPPE (piteously, as he places the light on the table). Excellency: what were you looking up at just now—out there? (He points across his shoulder to the vineyard, but is afraid to look round.)

NAPOLEON (unfolding the packet). What is that to you?

GIUSEPPE (stammering). Because the witch is gone—vanished; and no one saw her go out.

LADY (coming behind him from the vineyard). We were watching her riding up to the moon on your broomstick, Giuseppe. You will never see her again.

GIUSEPPE. Gesu Maria! (He crosses himself and hurries out.)

NAPOLEON (throwing down the letters in a heap on the table). Now. (He sits down at the table in the chair which he has just placed.)

LADY. Yes; but you know you have THE letter in your pocket. (He smiles; takes a letter from his pocket; and tosses it on the top of the heap. She holds it up and looks at him, saying) About Caesar's wife.

NAPOLEON. Caesar's wife is above suspicion. Burn it.

LADY (taking up the snuffers and holding the letter to the candle flame with it). I wonder would Caesar's wife be above suspicion if she saw us here together!

NAPOLEON (echoing her, with his elbows on the table and his cheeks on his hands, looking at the letter). I wonder! (The Strange Lady puts the letter down alight on the snuffers tray, and sits down beside Napoleon, in the same attitude, elbows on table, cheeks on hands, watching it burn. When it is burnt, they simultaneously turn their eyes and look at one another. The curtain steals down and hides them.)

YOU NEVER CAN TELL

ACT I

In a dentist's operating room on a fine August morning in 1896. Not the usual tiny London den, but the best sitting room of a furnished lodging in a terrace on the sea front at a fashionable watering place. The operating chair, with a gas pump and cylinder beside it, is half way between the centre of the room and one of the corners. If you look into the room through the window which lights it, you will see the fireplace in the middle of the wall opposite you, with the door beside it to your left; an M.R.C.S. diploma in a frame hung on the chimneypiece; an easy chair covered in black leather on the hearth; a neat stool and bench, with vice, tools, and a mortar and pestle in the corner to the right. Near this bench stands a slender machine like a whip provided with a stand, a pedal, and an exaggerated winch. Recognising this as a dental drill, you shudder and look away to your left, where you can see another window, underneath which stands a writing table, with a blotter and a diary on it, and a chair. Next the writing table, towards the door, is a leather covered sofa. The opposite wall, close on your right, is occupied mostly by a bookcase. The operating chair is under your nose, facing you, with the cabinet of instruments handy to it on your left. You observe that the professional furniture and apparatus are new, and that the wall paper, designed, with the taste of an undertaker, in festoons and urns, the carpet with its symmetrical plans of rich, cabbagy nosegays, the glass gasalier with lustres; the ornamental gilt rimmed blue candlesticks on the ends of the mantelshelf, also glass draped with lustres, and the ormolu clock under a glass-cover in the middle between them, its uselessness emphasized by a cheap American clock disrespectfully placed beside it and now indicating 12 o'clock noon, all combine with the black marble which gives the fireplace the air of a miniature family vault, to suggest early Victorian commercial respectability, belief in money, Bible fetichism, fear of hell always at war with fear of poverty, instinctive horror of the passionate character of art, love and Roman Catholic religion, and all the first fruits of plutocracy in the early generations of the industrial revolution.

There is no shadow of this on the two persons who are occupying the room just now. One of them, a very pretty woman in miniature, her tiny figure dressed with the daintiest gaiety, is of a later generation, being hardly eighteen yet. This darling little creature clearly does not belong to the room, or even to the country; for her complexion, though very delicate, has been burnt biscuit color by some warmer sun than England's; and yet there is, for a very subtle observer, a link between them. For she has a glass of water in her hand, and a rapidly clearing cloud of Spartan obstinacy on her tiny firm set mouth and quaintly squared eyebrows. If the least line of conscience could be traced between those eyebrows, an Evangelical might cherish some faint hope of finding her a sheep in wolf's clothing—for her frock is recklessly pretty—but as the cloud vanishes it leaves her frontal sinus as smoothly free from conviction of sin as a kitten's.

The dentist, contemplating her with the self-satisfaction of a successful operator, is a young man of thirty or thereabouts. He does not give the impression of being much of a workman: his professional manner evidently strikes him as being a joke, and is underlain by a thoughtless pleasantry which betrays the young gentleman still unsettled and in search of amusing adventures, behind the newly set-up dentist in search of patients. He is not without gravity of demeanor; but the strained nostrils stamp it as the gravity of the humorist. His eyes are clear, alert, of sceptically moderate size, and yet a little rash; his forehead is an excellent one, with plenty of room behind it; his nose and chin cavalierly handsome. On the whole, an attractive, noticeable beginner, of whose prospects a man of business might form a tolerably favorable estimate.

THE YOUNG LADY (handing him the glass). Thank you. (In spite of the biscuit complexion she has not the slightest foreign accent.)

THE DENTIST (putting it down on the ledge of his cabinet of instruments). That was my first tooth.

THE YOUNG LADY (aghast). Your first! Do you mean to say that you began practising on me?

THE DENTIST. Every dentist has to begin on somebody.

THE YOUNG LADY. Yes: somebody in a hospital, not people who pay.

THE DENTIST (laughing). Oh, the hospital doesn't count. I only meant my first tooth in private practice. Why didn't you let me give you gas?

THE YOUNG LADY. Because you said it would be five shillings extra.

THE DENTIST (shocked). Oh, don't say that. It makes me feel as if I had hurt you for the sake of five shillings.

THE YOUNG LADY (with cool insolence). Well, so you have! (She gets up.) Why shouldn't you? it's your business to hurt people. (It amuses him to be treated in this fashion: he chuckles secretly as he proceeds to clean and replace his instruments. She shakes her dress into order; looks inquisitively about her; and goes to the window.) You have a good view of the sea from these rooms! Are they expensive?

THE DENTIST. Yes.

THE YOUNG LADY. You don't own the whole house, do you?

THE DENTIST. No.

THE YOUNG LADY (taking the chair which stands at the writing-table and looking critically at it as she spins it round on one leg.) Your furniture isn't quite the latest thing, is it?

THE DENTIST. It's my landlord's.

THE YOUNG LADY. Does he own that nice comfortable Bath chair? (pointing to the operating chair.)

THE DENTIST. No: I have that on the hire-purchase system.

THE YOUNG LADY (disparagingly). I thought so. (Looking about her again in search of further conclusions.) I suppose you haven't been here long?

THE DENTIST. Six weeks. Is there anything else you would like to know?

THE YOUNG LADY (the hint quite lost on her). Any family?

THE DENTIST. I am not married.

THE YOUNG LADY. Of course not: anybody can see that. I meant sisters and mother and that sort of thing.

THE DENTIST. Not on the premises.

THE YOUNG LADY. Hm! If you've been here six weeks, and mine was your first tooth, the practice can't be very large, can it?

THE DENTIST. Not as yet. (He shuts the cabinet, having tidied up everything.)

THE YOUNG LADY. Well, good luck! (She takes our her purse.) Five shillings, you said it would be?

THE DENTIST. Five shillings.

THE YOUNG LADY (producing a crown piece). Do you charge five shillings for everything?

THE DENTIST. Yes.

THE YOUNG LADY. Why?

THE DENTIST. It's my system. I'm what's called a five shilling dentist.

THE YOUNG LADY. How nice! Well, here! (holding up the crown piece) a nice new five shilling piece! your first fee! Make a hole in it with the thing you drill people's teeth with and wear it on your watch-chain.

THE DENTIST. Thank you.

THE PARLOR MAID (appearing at the door). The young lady's brother, sir.

A handsome man in miniature, obviously the young lady's twin, comes in eagerly. He wears a suit of terra-cotta cashmere, the elegantly cut frock coat lined in brown silk, and carries in his hand a brown tall hat and tan gloves to match. He has his sister's delicate biscuit complexion, and is built on the same small scale; but he is elastic and strong in muscle, decisive in movement, unexpectedly deeptoned and trenchant in speech, and with perfect manners and a finished personal style which might be envied by a man twice his age. Suavity and self-possession are points of honor with him; and though this, rightly considered, is only the modern mode of boyish self-consciousness, its effect is none the less staggering to his elders, and would be insufferable in a less prepossessing youth. He is promptitude itself, and has a question ready the moment he enters.

THE YOUNG GENTLEMAN. Am I on time?

THE YOUNG LADY. No: it's all over.

THE YOUNG GENTLEMAN. Did you howl?

THE YOUNG LADY. Oh, something awful. Mr. Valentine: this is my brother Phil. Phil: this is Mr.

Valentine, our new dentist. (Valentine and Phil bow to one another. She proceeds, all in one breath.) He's only been here six weeks; and he's a bachelor. The house isn't his; and the furniture is the landlord's; but the professional plant is hired. He got my tooth out beautifully at the first go; and he and I are great friends.

PHILIP. Been asking a lot of questions?

THE YOUNG LADY (as if incapable of doing such a thing). Oh, no.

PHILIP. Glad to hear it. (To Valentine.) So good of you not to mind us, Mr. Valentine. The fact is, we've never been in England before; and our mother tells us that the people here simply won't stand us. Come and lunch with us. (Valentine, bewildered by the leaps and bounds with which their acquaintanceship is proceeding, gasps; but he has no opportunity of speaking, as the conversation of the twins is swift and continuous.)

THE YOUNG LADY. Oh, do, Mr. Valentine.

PHILIP. At the Marine Hotel—half past one.

THE YOUNG LADY. We shall be able to tell mamma that a respectable Englishman has promised to lunch with us.

PHILIP. Say no more, Mr. Valentine: you'll come.

VALENTINE. Say no more! I haven't said anything. May I ask whom I have the pleasure of entertaining? It's really quite impossible for me to lunch at the Marine Hotel with two perfect strangers.

THE YOUNG LADY (flippantly). Ooooh! what bosh! One patient in six weeks! What difference does it make to you?

PHILIP (maturely). No, Dolly: my knowledge of human nature confirms Mr. Valentine's judgment. He is right. Let me introduce Miss Dorothy Clandon, commonly called Dolly. (Valentine bows to Dolly. She nods to him.) I'm Philip Clandon. We're from Madeira, but perfectly respectable, so far.

VALENTINE. Clandon! Are you related to—

DOLLY (unexpectedly crying out in despair). Yes, we are.

VALENTINE (astonished). I beg your pardon?

DOLLY. Oh, we are, we are. It's all over, Phil: they know all about us in England. (To Valentine.) Oh, you can't think how maddening it is to be related to a celebrated person, and never be valued anywhere for our own sakes.

VALENTINE. But excuse me: the gentleman I was thinking of is not celebrated.

DOLLY (staring at him). Gentleman! (Phil is also puzzled.)

VALENTINE. Yes. I was going to ask whether you were by any chance a daughter of Mr. Densmore Clandon of Newbury Hall.

DOLLY (vacantly). No.

PHILIP. Well come, Dolly: how do you know you're not?

DOLLY (cheered). Oh, I forgot. Of course. Perhaps I am.

VALENTINE. Don't you know?

PHILIP. Not in the least.

DOLLY. It's a wise child—

PHILIP (cutting her short). Sh! (Valentine starts nervously; for the sound made by Philip, though but momentary, is like cutting a sheet of silk in two with a flash of lightning. It is the result of long practice in checking Dolly's indiscretions.) The fact is, Mr. Valentine, we are the children of the celebrated Mrs. Lanfrey Clandon, an authoress of great repute—in Madeira. No household is complete without her works. We came to England to get away from them. They are called the Twentieth Century Treatises.

DOLLY. Twentieth Century Cooking.

PHILIP. Twentieth Century Creeds.

DOLLY. Twentieth Century Clothing.

PHILIP. Twentieth Century Conduct.

DOLLY. Twentieth Century Children.

PHILIP. Twentieth Century Parents.

DOLLY. Cloth limp, half a dollar.

PHILIP. Or mounted on linen for hard family use, two dollars. No family should be without them. Read them, Mr. Valentine: they'll improve your mind.

DOLLY. But not till we've gone, please.

PHILIP. Quite so: we prefer people with unimproved minds. Our own minds are in that fresh and unspoiled condition.

VALENTINE (dubiously). Hm!

DOLLY (echoing him inquiringly). Hm? Phil: he prefers people whose minds are improved.

PHILIP. In that case we shall have to introduce him to the other member of the family: the Woman of the Twentieth Century; our sister Gloria!

DOLLY (dithyrambically). Nature's masterpiece!

PHILIP. Learning's daughter!

DOLLY. Madeira's pride!

PHILIP. Beauty's paragon!

DOLLY (suddenly descending to prose). Bosh! No complexion.

VALENTINE (desperately). May I have a word?

PHILIP (politely). Excuse us. Go ahead.

DOLLY (very nicely). So sorry.

VALENTINE (attempting to take them paternally). I really must give a hint to you young people—

DOLLY (breaking out again). Oh, come: I like that. How old are you?

PHILIP. Over thirty.

DOLLY. He's not.

PHILIP (confidently). He is.

DOLLY (emphatically). Twenty-seven.

PHILIP (imperturbably). Thirty-three.

DOLLY. Stuff!

PHILIP (to Valentine). I appeal to you, Mr. Valentine.

VALENTINE (remonstrating). Well, really— (resigning himself.) Thirty-one.

PHILIP (to Dolly). You were wrong.

DOLLY. So were you.

PHILIP (suddenly conscientious). We're forgetting our manners, Dolly.

DOLLY (remorseful). Yes, so we are.

PHILIP (apologetic). We interrupted you, Mr. Valentine.

DOLLY. You were going to improve our minds, I think.

VALENTINE. The fact is, your—

PHILIP (anticipating him). Our appearance?

DOLLY. Our manners?

VALENTINE (ad misericordiam). Oh, do let me speak.

DOLLY. The old story. We talk too much.

PHILIP. We do. Shut up, both. (He seats himself on the arm of the opposing chair.)

DOLLY. Mum! (She sits down in the writing-table chair, and closes her lips tight with the tips of her fingers.)

VALENTINE. Thank you. (He brings the stool from the bench in the corner; places it between them; and sits down with a judicial air. They attend to him with extreme gravity. He addresses himself first to Dolly.) Now may I ask, to begin with, have you ever been in an English seaside resort before? (She shakes her head slowly and solemnly. He turns to Phil, who shakes his head quickly and expressively.) I thought so. Well, Mr. Clandon, our acquaintance has been short; but it has been voluble; and I have gathered enough to convince me that you are neither of you capable of conceiving what life in an English seaside resort is. Believe me, it's not a question of manners and appearance. In those respects we enjoy a freedom unknown in Madeira. (Dolly shakes her head vehemently.) Oh, yes, I assure you. Lord de Cresci's sister bicycles in knickerbockers; and the rector's wife advocates dress reform and wears hygienic boots. (Dolly furtively looks at her own shoe: Valentine catches her in the act, and deftly adds) No, that's not the sort of boot I mean. (Dolly's shoe vanishes.) We don't bother much about dress and manners in England, because, as a nation we don't dress well and we've no manners. But—and now will you excuse my frankness? (They nod.) Thank you. Well, in a seaside resort there's one thing you must have before anybody can afford to be seen going about with you; and that's a father, alive or dead. (He looks at them alternately, with emphasis. They meet his gaze like martyrs.) Am I to infer that you have omitted that indispensable part of your social equipment? (They confirm him by melancholy nods.) Them I'm sorry to say that if you are going to stay here for any length of time, it will be impossible for me to accept your kind invitation to lunch. (He rises with an air of finality, and replaces the stool by the bench.)

PHILIP (rising with grave politeness). Come, Dolly. (He gives her his arm.)

DOLLY. Good morning. (They go together to the door with perfect dignity.)

VALENTINE (overwhelmed with remorse). Oh, stop, stop. (They halt and turn, arm in arm.) You make me feel a perfect beast.

DOLLY. That's your conscience: not us.

VALENTINE (energetically, throwing off all pretence of a professional manner). My conscience! My conscience has been my ruin. Listen to me. Twice before I have set up as a respectable medical practitioner in various parts of England. On both occasions I acted conscientiously, and told my patients the brute truth instead of what they wanted to be told. Result, ruin. Now I've set up as a dentist, a five shilling dentist; and I've done with conscience forever. This is my last chance. I spent my last sovereign on moving in; and I haven't paid a shilling of rent yet. I'm eating and drinking on credit; my landlord is as rich as a Jew and as hard as nails; and I've made five shillings in six weeks. If I swerve by a hair's breadth from the straight line of the most rigid respectability, I'm done for. Under such a circumstance, is it fair to ask me to lunch with you when you don't know your own father?

DOLLY. After all, our grandfather is a canon of Lincoln Cathedral.

VALENTINE (like a castaway mariner who sees a sail on the horizon). What! Have you a grandfather?

DOLLY. Only one.

VALENTINE. My dear, good young friends, why on earth didn't you tell me that before? A cannon of Lincoln! That makes it all right, of course. Just excuse me while I change my coat. (He reaches the door in a bound and vanishes. Dolly and Phil stare after him, and then stare at one another. Missing their audience, they droop and become commonplace at once.)

PHILIP (throwing away Dolly's arm and coming ill-humoredly towards the operating chair). That wretched bankrupt ivory snatcher makes a compliment of allowing us to stand him a lunch—probably the first square meal he has had for months. (He gives the chair a kick, as if it were Valentine.)

DOLLY. It's too beastly. I won't stand it any longer, Phil. Here in England everybody asks whether you have a father the very first thing.

PHILIP. I won't stand it either. Mamma must tell us who he was.

DOLLY. Or who he is. He may be alive.

PHILIP. I hope not. No man alive shall father me.

DOLLY. He might have a lot of money, though.

PHILIP. I doubt it. My knowledge of human nature leads me to believe that if he had a lot of money he wouldn't have got rid of his affectionate family so easily. Anyhow, let's look at the bright side of things. Depend on it, he's dead. (He goes to the hearth and stands with his back to the fireplace, spreading himself. The parlor maid appears. The twins, under observation, instantly shine out again with their former brilliancy.)

THE PARLOR MAID. Two ladies for you, miss. Your mother and sister, miss, I think.

Mrs. Clandon and Gloria come in. Mrs. Clandon is between forty and fifty, with a slight tendency to soft, sedentary fat, and a fair remainder of good looks, none the worse preserved because she has evidently followed the old tribal matronly fashion of making no pretension in that direction after her marriage, and might almost be suspected of wearing a cap at home. She carries herself artificially well, as women were taught to do as a part of good manners by dancing masters and reclining boards before these were superseded by the modern artistic cult of beauty and health. Her hair, a flaxen hazel fading into white, is crimped, and parted in the middle with the ends plaited and made into a knot, from which observant people of a certain age infer that Mrs. Clandon had sufficient individuality and good taste to stand out resolutely against the now forgotten chignon in her girlhood. In short, she is distinctly old fashioned for her age in dress and manners. But she belongs to the forefront of her own period (say 1860-80) in a jealously assertive attitude of character and intellect, and in being a woman of cultivated interests rather than passionately developed personal affections. Her voice and ways are entirely kindly and humane; and she lends herself conscientiously to the occasional demonstrations of fondness by which her children mark their esteem for her; but displays of personal sentiment secretly embarrass her: passion in her is humanitarian rather than human: she feels strongly about social questions and principles, not about persons. Only, one observes that this reasonableness and intense personal privacy, which leaves her relations with Gloria and Phil much as they might be between her and the children of any other woman, breaks down in the case of Dolly. Though almost every word she addresses to her is necessarily in the nature of a remonstrance for some breach of decorum, the tenderness in her voice is unmistakable; and it is not surprising that years of such remonstrance have left Dolly hopelessly spoiled.

Gloria, who is hardly past twenty, is a much more formidable person than her mother. She is the incarnation of haughty highmindedness, raging with the impatience of an impetuous, dominative character paralyzed by the impotence of her youth, and unwillingly disciplined by the constant danger of ridicule from her lighter-handed juniors. Unlike her mother, she is all passion; and the conflict of her passion with her obstinate pride and intense fastidiousness results in a freezing coldness of manner. In an ugly woman all this would be repulsive; but Gloria is an attractive woman. Her deep chestnut hair, olive brown skin, long eyelashes, shaded grey eyes that often flash like stars, delicately turned full lips, and compact and supple, but muscularly plump figure appeal with disdainful frankness to the senses and imagination. A very dangerous girl, one would say, if the moral passions were not also marked, and even nobly marked, in a fine brow. Her tailor-made skirt-and-jacket dress of saffron brown cloth, seems conventional when her back is turned; but it displays in front a blouse of sea-green silk which upsets its conventionality with one stroke, and sets her apart as effectually as the twins from the ordinary run of fashionable seaside humanity.

Mrs. Clandon comes a little way into the room, looking round to see who is present. Gloria, who studiously avoids encouraging the twins by betraying any interest in them, wanders to the window and looks out with her thoughts far away. The parlor maid, instead of withdrawing, shuts the door and waits at it.

MRS. CLANDON. Well, children? How is the toothache, Dolly?

DOLLY. Cured, thank Heaven. I've had it out. (She sits down on the step of the operating chair. Mrs. Clandon takes the writing-table chair.)

PHILIP (striking in gravely from the hearth). And the dentist, a first-rate professional man of the highest standing, is coming to lunch with us.

MRS. CLANDON (looking round apprehensively at the servant). Phil!

THE PARLOR MAID. Beg pardon, ma'am. I'm waiting for Mr. Valentine. I have a message for him.

DOLLY. Who from?

MRS. CLANDON (shocked). Dolly! (Dolly catches her lips with her finger tips, suppressing a little splutter of mirth.)

THE PARLOR MAID. Only the landlord, ma'am.

Valentine, in a blue serge suit, with a straw hat in his hand, comes back in high spirits, out of breath with the haste he has made. Gloria turns from the window and studies him with freezing attention.

PHILIP. Let me introduce you, Mr. Valentine. My mother, Mrs. Lanfrey Clandon. (Mrs. Clandon bows. Valentine bows, self-possessed and quite equal to the occasion.) My sister Gloria. (Gloria bows with cold dignity and sits down on the sofa. Valentine falls in love at first sight and is miserably confused. He fingers his hat nervously, and makes her a sneaking bow.)

MRS. CLANDON. I understand that we are to have the pleasure of seeing you at luncheon to-day, Mr. Valentine.

VALENTINE. Thank you—er—if you don't mind—I mean if you will be so kind—(to the parlor maid testily) What is it?

THE PARLOR MAID. The landlord, sir, wishes to speak to you before you go out.

VALENTINE. Oh, tell him I have four patients here. (The Clandons look surprised, except Phil, who is imperturbable.) If he wouldn't mind waiting just two minutes, I—I'll slip down and see him for a moment. (Throwing himself confidentially on her sense of the position.) Say I'm busy, but that I want to see him.

THE PARLOR MAID (reassuringly). Yes, sir. (She goes.)

MRS. CLANDON (on the point of rising). We are detaining you, I am afraid.

VALENTINE. Not at all, not at all. Your presence here will be the greatest help to me. The fact is, I owe six week's rent; and I've had no patients until to-day. My interview with my landlord will be considerably smoothed by the apparent boom in my business.

DOLLY (vexed). Oh, how tiresome of you to let it all out! And we've just been pretending that you were a respectable professional man in a first-rate position.

MRS. CLANDON (horrified). Oh, Dolly, Dolly! My dearest, how can you be so rude? (To Valentine.) Will you excuse these barbarian children of mine, Mr. Valentine?

VALENTINE. Thank you, I'm used to them. Would it be too much to ask you to wait five minutes while I get rid of my landlord downstairs?

DOLLY. Don't be long. We're hungry.

MRS. CLANDON (again remonstrating). Dolly, dear!

VALENTINE (to Dolly). All right. (To Mrs. Clandon.) Thank you: I shan't be long. (He steals a look at Gloria as he turns to go. She is looking gravely at him. He falls into confusion.) I—er—er—yes—thank you (he succeeds at last in blundering himself out of the room; but the exhibition is a pitiful one).

PHILIP. Did you observe? (Pointing to Gloria.) Love at first sight. You can add his scalp to your collection, Gloria.

MRS. CLANDON. Sh—sh, pray, Phil. He may have heard you.

PHILIP. Not he. (Bracing himself for a scene.) And now look here, mamma. (He takes the stool from the bench; and seats himself majestically in the middle of the room, taking a leaf out of Valentine's book. Dolly, feeling that her position on the step of the operating chair is unworthy of the dignity of the occasion, rises, looking important and determined; crosses to the window; and stands with her back to the end of the writing-table, her hands behind her and on the table. Mrs. Clandon looks at them, wondering what is coming. Gloria becomes attentive. Philip straightens his back; places his knuckles symmetrically on his knees; and opens his case.) Dolly and I have been talking over things a good deal lately; and I don't think, judging from my knowledge of human nature—we don't think that you (speaking very staccato, with the words detached) quite appreciate the fact—

DOLLY (seating herself on the end of the table with a spring). That we've grown up.

MRS. CLANDON. Indeed? In what way have I given you any reason to complain?

PHILIP. Well, there are certain matters upon which we are beginning to feel that you might take us a little more into your confidence.

MRS. CLANDON (rising, with all the placidity of her age suddenly broken up; and a curious hard excitement, dignified but dogged, ladylike but implacable—the manner of the Old Guard of the Women's Rights movement—coming upon her). Phil: take care. Remember what I have always taught you. There are two sorts of family life, Phil; and your experience of human nature only extends, so far, to one of them. (Rhetorically.) The sort you know is based on mutual respect, on recognition of the right of every member of the household to independence and privacy (her emphasis on "privacy" is intense) in their personal concerns. And because you have always enjoyed that, it seems such a matter of course to you that you don't value it. But (with biting acrimony) there is another sort of family life: a life in which husbands open their wives' letters, and call on them to account for every farthing of their expenditure and every moment of their time; in which women do the same to their children; in which no room is private and no hour sacred; in which duty, obedience, affection, home, morality and religion are detestable tyrannies, and life is a vulgar round of punishments and lies, coercion and rebellion, jealousy, suspicion, recrimination—Oh! I cannot describe it to you: fortunately for you, you know nothing about it. (She sits down, panting. Gloria has listened to her with flashing eyes, sharing all her indignation.)

DOLLY (inaccessible to rhetoric). See Twentieth Century Parents, chapter on Liberty, passim.

MRS. CLANDON (touching her shoulder affectionately, soothed even by a gibe from her). My dear Dolly: if you only knew how glad I am that it is nothing but a joke to you, though it is such bitter earnest to me. (More resolutely, turning to Philip.) Phil, I never ask you questions about your private concerns. You are not going to question me, are you?

PHILIP. I think it due to ourselves to say that the question we wanted to ask is as much our business as yours.

DOLLY. Besides, it can't be good to keep a lot of questions bottled up inside you. You did it, mamma; but see how awfully it's broken out again in me.

MRS. CLANDON. I see you want to ask your question. Ask it.

DOLLY AND PHILIP (beginning simultaneously). Who— (They stop.)

PHILIP. Now look here, Dolly: am I going to conduct this business or are you?

DOLLY. You.

PHILIP. Then hold your mouth. (Dolly does so literally.) The question is a simple one. When the ivory snatcher—

MRS. CLANDON (remonstrating). Phil!

PHILIP. Dentist is an ugly word. The man of ivory and gold asked us whether we were the children of Mr. Densmore Clandon of Newbury Hall. In pursuance of the precepts in your treatise on Twentieth Century Conduct, and your repeated personal exhortations to us to curtail the number of unnecessary lies we tell, we replied truthfully the we didn't know.

DOLLY. Neither did we.

PHILIP. Sh! The result was that the gum architect made considerable difficulties about accepting our invitation to lunch, although I doubt if he has had anything but tea and bread and butter for a fortnight past. Now my knowledge of human nature leads me to believe that we had a father, and that you probably know who he was.

MRS. CLANDON (her agitation returning). Stop, Phil. Your father is nothing to you, nor to me (vehemently). That is enough. (The twins are silenced, but not satisfied. Their faces fall. But Gloria, who has been following the altercation attentively, suddenly intervenes.)

GLORIA (advancing). Mother: we have a right to know.

MRS. CLANDON (rising and facing her). Gloria! "We!" Who is "we"?

GLORIA (steadfastly). We three. (Her tone is unmistakable: she is pitting her strength against her mother for the first time. The twins instantly go over to the enemy.)

MRS. CLANDON (wounded). In your mouth "we" used to mean you and I, Gloria.

PHILIP (rising decisively and putting away the stool). We're hurting you: let's drop it. We didn't think you'd mind. I don't want to know.

DOLLY (coming off the table). I'm sure I don't. Oh, don't look like that, mamma. (She looks angrily at Gloria.)

MRS. CLANDON (touching her eyes hastily with her handkerchief and sitting down again). Thank you, my dear. Thanks, Phil.

GLORIA (inexorably). We have a right to know, mother.

MRS. CLANDON (indignantly). Ah! You insist.

GLORIA. Do you intend that we shall never know?

DOLLY. Oh, Gloria, don't. It's barbarous.

GLORIA (with quiet scorn). What is the use of being weak? You see what has happened with this gentleman here, mother. The same thing has happened to me.

MRS. CLANDON { What do you mean?

DOLLY. { Oh, tell us.
PHILIP {What happened to you?

GLORIA. Oh, nothing of any consequence. (She turns away from them and goes up to the easy chair at the fireplace, where she sits down, almost with her back to them. As they wait expectantly, she adds, over her shoulder, with studied indifference.) On board the steamer the first officer did me the honor to propose to me.

DOLLY. No, it was to me.

MRS. CLANDON. The first officer! Are you serious, Gloria? What did you say to him? (correcting herself) Excuse me: I have no right to ask that.

GLORIA. The answer is pretty obvious. A woman who does not know who her father was cannot accept such an offer.

MRS. CLANDON. Surely you did not want to accept it?

GLORIA (turning a little and raising her voice). No; but suppose I had wanted to!

PHILIP. Did that difficulty strike you, Dolly?

DOLLY. No, I accepted him.

GLORIA [*all crying*] { Accepted him!
MRS. CLANDON [*out*] { Dolly!
PHILIP [*together*] { Oh, I say!

DOLLY [*naively*]. He did look such a fool!

MRS. CLANDON. But why did you do such a thing, Dolly?

DOLLY. For fun, I suppose. He had to measure my finger for a ring. You'd have done the same thing yourself.

MRS. CLANDON. No, Dolly, I would not. As a matter of fact the first officer did propose to me; and I told him to keep that sort of thing for women were young enough to be amused by it. He appears to have acted on my advice. (She rises and goes to the hearth.) Gloria: I am sorry you think me weak; but I cannot tell you what you want. You are all too young.

PHILIP. This is rather a startling departure from Twentieth Century principles.

DOLLY (quoting). "Answer all your children's questions, and answer them truthfully, as soon as they are old enough to ask them." See Twentieth Century Motherhood—

PHILIP. Page one—

DOLLY. Chapter one—

PHILIP. Sentence one.

MRS. CLANDON. My dears: I did not say that you were too young to know. I said you were too young to be taken into my confidence. You are very bright children, all of you; but I am glad for your sakes that you are still very inexperienced and consequently very unsympathetic. There are some experiences of mine that I cannot bear to speak of except to those who have gone through what I have gone through. I hope you will never be qualified for such confidences. But I will take care that you shall learn all you want to know. Will that satisfy you?

PHILIP. Another grievance, Dolly.

DOLLY. We're not sympathetic.

GLORIA (leaning forward in her chair and looking earnestly up at her mother). Mother: I did not mean to be unsympathetic.

MRS. CLANDON (affectionately). Of course not, dear. Do you think I don't understand?

GLORIA (rising). But, mother—

MRS. CLANDON (drawing back a little). Yes?

GLORIA (obstinately). It is nonsense to tell us that our father is nothing to us.

MRS. CLANDON (provoked to sudden resolution). Do you remember your father?

GLORIA (meditatively, as if the recollection were a tender one). I am not quite sure. I think so.

MRS. CLANDON (grimly). You are not sure?

GLORIA. No.

MRS. CLANDON (with quiet force). Gloria: if I had ever struck you— (Gloria recoils: Philip and Dolly are disagreeably shocked; all three start at her, revolted as she continues)—struck you purposely, deliberately, with the intention of hurting you, with a whip bought for the purpose! Would you remember that, do you think? (Gloria utters an exclamation of indignant repulsion.) That would have been your last recollection of your father, Gloria, if I had not taken you away from him. I have kept him out of your life: keep him now out of mine by never mentioning him to me again. (Gloria, with a shudder, covers her face with her hands, until, hearing someone at the door, she turns away and pretends to occupy herself looking at the names of the books in the bookcase. Mrs. Clandon sits down on the sofa. Valentine returns.).

VALENTINE. I hope I've not kept you waiting. That landlord of mine is really an extraordinary old character.

DOLLY (eagerly). Oh, tell us. How long has he given you to pay?

MRS. CLANDON (distracted by her child's bad manners). Dolly, Dolly, Dolly dear! You must not ask questions.

DOLLY (demurely). So sorry. You'll tell us, won't you, Mr. Valentine?

VALENTINE. He doesn't want his rent at all. He's broken his tooth on a Brazil nut; and he wants me to look at it and to lunch with him afterwards.

DOLLY. Then have him up and pull his tooth out at once; and we'll bring him to lunch, too. Tell the maid to fetch him along. (She runs to the bell and rings it vigorously. Then, with a sudden doubt she turns to Valentine and adds) I suppose he's respectable—really respectable.

VALENTINE. Perfectly. Not like me.

DOLLY. Honest Injun? (Mrs. Clandon gasps faintly; but her powers of remonstrance are exhausted.)

VALENTINE. Honest Injun!

DOLLY. Then off with you and bring him up.

VALENTINE (looking dubiously at Mrs. Clandon). I daresay he'd be delighted if—er—?

MRS. CLANDON (rising and looking at her watch). I shall be happy to see your friend at lunch, if you can persuade him to come; but I can't wait to see him now: I have an appointment at the hotel at a quarter to one with an old friend whom I have not seen since I left England eighteen years ago. Will you excuse me?

VALENTINE. Certainly, Mrs. Clandon.

GLORIA. Shall I come?

MRS. CLANDON. No, dear. I want to be alone. (She goes out, evidently still a good deal troubled. Valentine opens the door for her and follows her out.)

PHILIP (significantly—to Dolly). Hmhm!

DOLLY (significantly to Philip). Ahah! (The parlor maid answers the bell.)

DOLLY. Show the old gentleman up.

THE PARLOR MAID (puzzled). Madam?

DOLLY. The old gentleman with the toothache.

PHILIP. The landlord.

THE PARLOR MAID. Mr. Crampton, Sir?

PHILIP. Is his name Crampton?

DOLLY (to Philip). Sounds rheumaticky, doesn't it?

PHILIP. Chalkstones, probably.

DOLLY (over her shoulder, to the parlor maid). Show Mr. Crampstones up. (Goes R. to writing-table chair).

THE PARLOR MAID (correcting her). Mr. Crampton, miss. (She goes.)

DOLLY (repeating it to herself like a lesson). Crampton, Crampton, Crampton, Crampton, Crampton. (She sits down studiously at the writing-table.) I must get that name right, or Heaven knows what I shall call him.

GLORIA. Phil: can you believe such a horrible thing as that about our father—what mother said just now?

PHILIP. Oh, there are lots of people of that kind. Old Chalice used to thrash his wife and daughters with a cartwhip.

DOLLY (contemptuously). Yes, a Portuguese!

PHILIP. When you come to men who are brutes, there is much in common between the Portuguese and the English variety, Doll. Trust my knowledge of human nature. (He resumes his position on the hearthrug with an elderly and responsible air.)

GLORIA (with angered remorse). I don't think we shall ever play again at our old game of guessing what our father was to be like. Dolly: are you sorry for your father—the father with lots of money?

DOLLY. Oh, come! What about your father—the lonely old man with the tender aching heart? He's pretty well burst up, I think.

PHILIP. There can be no doubt that the governor is an exploded superstition. (Valentine is heard talking to somebody outside the door.) But hark: he comes.

GLORIA (nervously). Who?

DOLLY. Chalkstones.

PHILIP. Sh! Attention. (They put on their best manners. Philip adds in a lower voice to Gloria) If he's good enough for the lunch, I'll nod to Dolly; and if she nods to you, invite him straight away.

(Valentine comes back with his landlord. Mr. Fergus Crampton is a man of about sixty, tall, hard and stringy, with an atrociously obstinate, ill tempered, grasping mouth, and a querulously dogmatic voice. Withal he is highly nervous and sensitive, judging by his thin transparent skin marked with multitudinous lines, and his slender fingers. His consequent capacity for suffering acutely from all the dislike that his temper and obstinacy can bring upon him is proved by his wistful, wounded eyes, by a plaintive note in his voice, a painful want of confidence in his welcome, and a constant but indifferently successful effort to correct his natural incivility of manner and proneness to take offence. By his keen brows and forehead he is clearly a shrewd man; and there is no sign of straitened means or commercial diffidence about him: he is well dressed, and would be classed at a guess as a prosperous master manufacturer in a business inherited from an old family in the aristocracy of trade. His navy blue coat is not of the usual fashionable pattern. It is not exactly a pilot's coat; but it is cut that way, double breasted, and with stout buttons and broad lapels, a coat for a shipyard rather than a counting house. He has taken a fancy to Valentine, who cares nothing for his crossness of grain and treats him with a sort of disrespectful humanity, for which he is secretly grateful.)

VALENTINE. May I introduce—this is Mr. Crampton—Miss Dorothy Clandon, Mr. Philip Clandon, Miss Clandon. (Crampton stands nervously bowing. They all bow.) Sit down, Mr. Crampton.

DOLLY (pointing to the operating chair). That is the most comfortable chair, Mr. Ch—crampton.

CRAMPTON. Thank you; but won't this young lady—(indicating Gloria, who is close to the chair)?

GLORIA. Thank you, Mr. Crampton: we are just going.

VALENTINE (bustling him across to the chair with good-humored peremptoriness). Sit down, sit down. You're tired.

CRAMPTON. Well, perhaps as I am considerably the oldest person present, I— (He finishes the sentence by sitting down a little rheumatically in the operating chair. Meanwhile, Philip, having studied him critically during his passage across the room, nods to Dolly; and Dolly nods to Gloria.)

GLORIA. Mr. Crampton: we understand that we are preventing Mr. Valentine from lunching with you by taking him away ourselves. My mother would be very glad, indeed, if you would come too.

CRAMPTON (gratefully, after looking at her earnestly for a moment). Thank you. I will come with pleasure.

GLORIA [*politely*] { Thank you very much—er—

DOLLY [*murmuring*].{ So glad—er—

PHILIP { Delighted, I'm sure—er—

(The conversation drops. Gloria and Dolly look at one another; then at Valentine and Philip. Valentine and Philip, unequal to the occasion, look away from them at one another, and are instantly so disconcerted by catching one another's eye, that they look back again and catch the eyes of Gloria and Dolly. Thus, catching one another all round, they all look at nothing and are quite at a loss. Crampton looks about him, waiting for them to begin. The silence becomes unbearable.)

DOLLY (suddenly, to keep things going). How old are you, Mr. Crampton?

GLORIA (hastily). I am afraid we must be going, Mr. Valentine. It is understood, then, that we meet at half past one. (She makes for the door. Philip goes with her. Valentine retreats to the bell.)

VALENTINE. Half past one. (He rings the bell.) Many thanks. (He follows Gloria and Philip to the door, and goes out with them.)

DOLLY (who has meanwhile stolen across to Crampton). Make him give you gas. It's five shillings extra: but it's worth it.

CRAMPTON (amused). Very well. (Looking more earnestly at her.) So you want to know my age, do you? I'm fifty-seven.

DOLLY (with conviction). You look it.

CRAMPTON (grimly). I dare say I do.

DOLLY. What are you looking at me so hard for? Anything wrong? (She feels whether her hat is right.)

CRAMPTON. You're like somebody.

DOLLY. Who?

CRAMPTON. Well, you have a curious look of my mother.

DOLLY (incredulously). Your mother!!! Quite sure you don't mean your daughter?

CRAMPTON (suddenly blackening with hate). Yes: I'm quite sure I don't mean my daughter.

DOLLY (sympathetically). Tooth bad?

CRAMPTON. No, no: nothing. A twinge of memory, Miss Clandon, not of toothache.

DOLLY. Have it out. "Pluck from the memory a rooted sorrow:" with gas, five shillings extra.

CRAMPTON (vindictively). No, not a sorrow. An injury that was done me once: that's all. I don't forget injuries; and I don't want to forget them. (His features settle into an implacable frown.)

(re-enter Philip: to look for Dolly. He comes down behind her unobserved.)

DOLLY (looking critically at Crampton's expression). I don't think we shall like you when you are brooding over your sorrows.

PHILIP (who has entered the room unobserved, and stolen behind her). My sister means well, Mr. Crampton: but she is indiscreet. Now Dolly, outside! (He takes her towards the door.)

DOLLY (in a perfectly audible undertone). He says he's only fifty-seven; and he thinks me the image of his mother; and he hates his daughter; and—(She is interrupted by the return of Valentine.)

VALENTINE. Miss Clandon has gone on.

PHILIP. Don't forget half past one.

DOLLY. Mind you leave Mr. Crampton with enough teeth to eat with. (They go out. Valentine comes down to his cabinet, and opens it.)

CRAMPTON. That's a spoiled child, Mr. Valentine. That's one of your modern products. When I was her age, I had many a good hiding fresh in my memory to teach me manners.

VALENTINE (taking up his dental mirror and probe from the shelf in front of the cabinet). What did you think of her sister?

CRAMPTON. You liked her better, eh?

VALENTINE (rhapsodically). She struck me as being— (He checks himself, and adds, prosaically) However, that's not business. (He places himself behind Crampton's right shoulder and assumes his professional tone.) Open, please. (Crampton opens his mouth. Valentine puts the mirror in, and examines his teeth.) Hm! You have broken that one. What a pity to spoil such a splendid set of teeth! Why do you crack nuts with them? (He withdraws the mirror, and comes forward to converse with Crampton.)

CRAMPTON. I've always cracked nuts with them: what else are they for? (Dogmatically.) The proper way to keep teeth good is to give them plenty of use on bones and nuts, and wash them every day with soap— plain yellow soap.

VALENTINE. Soap! Why soap?

CRAMPTON. I began using it as a boy because I was made to; and I've used it ever since. And I never had toothache in my life.

VALENTINE. Don't you find it rather nasty?

CRAMPTON. I found that most things that were good for me were nasty. But I was taught to put up with them, and made to put up with them. I'm used to it now: in fact, I like the taste when the soap is really good.

VALENTINE (making a wry face in spite of himself). You seem to have been very carefully educated, Mr. Crampton.

CRAMPTON (grimly). I wasn't spoiled, at all events.

VALENTINE (smiling a little to himself). Are you quite sure?

CRAMPTON. What d'y' mean?

VALENTINE. Well, your teeth are good, I admit. But I've seen just as good in very self-indulgent mouths. (He goes to the ledge of cabinet and changes the probe for another one.)

CRAMPTON. It's not the effect on the teeth: it's the effect on the character.

VALENTINE (placably). Oh, the character, I see. (He recommences operations.) A little wider, please. Hm! That one will have to come out: it's past saving. (He withdraws the probe and again comes to the side of the chair to converse.) Don't be alarmed: you shan't feel anything. I'll give you gas.

CRAMPTON. Rubbish, man: I want none of your gas. Out with it. People were taught to bear necessary pain in my day.

VALENTINE. Oh, if you like being hurt, all right. I'll hurt you as much as you like, without any extra charge for the beneficial effect on your character.

CRAMPTON (rising and glaring at him). Young man: you owe me six weeks' rent.

VALENTINE. I do.

CRAMPTON. Can you pay me?

VALENTINE. No.

CRAMPTON (satisfied with his advantage). I thought not. How soon d'y' think you'll be able to pay me if you have no better manners than to make game of your patients? (He sits down again.)

VALENTINE. My good sir: my patients haven't all formed their characters on kitchen soap.

CRAMPTON (suddenly gripping him by the arm as he turns away again to the cabinet). So much the worse for them. I tell you you don't understand my character. If I could spare all my teeth, I'd make you pull them all out one after another to shew you what a properly hardened man can go through with when he's made up his mind to do it. (He nods at him to enforce the effect of this declaration, and releases him.)

VALENTINE (his careless pleasantry quite unruffled). And you want to be more hardened, do you?

CRAMPTON. Yes.

VALENTINE (strolling away to the bell). Well, you're quite hard enough for me already—as a landlord. (Crampton receives this with a growl of grim humor. Valentine rings the bell, and remarks in a cheerful, casual way, whilst waiting for it to be answered.) Why did you never get married, Mr. Crampton? A wife and children would have taken some of the hardness out of you.

CRAMPTON (with unexpected ferocity). What the devil is that to you? (The parlor maid appears at the door.)

VALENTINE (politely). Some warm water, please. (She retires: and Valentine comes back to the cabinet, not at all put out by Crampton's rudeness, and carries on the conversation whilst he selects a forceps and places it ready to his hand with a gag and a drinking glass.) You were asking me what the devil that was to me. Well, I have an idea of getting married myself.

CRAMPTON (with grumbling irony). Naturally, sir, naturally. When a young man has come to his last farthing, and is within twenty-four hours of having his furniture distrained upon by his landlord, he marries. I've noticed that before. Well, marry; and be miserable.

VALENTINE. Oh, come, what do you know about it?

CRAMPTON. I'm not a bachelor.

VALENTINE. Then there is a Mrs. Crampton?

CRAMPTON (wincing with a pang of resentment). Yes—damn her!

VALENTINE (unperturbed). Hm! A father, too, perhaps, as well as a husband, Mr. Crampton?

CRAMPTON. Three children.

VALENTINE (politely). Damn them?—eh?

CRAMPTON (jealously). No, sir: the children are as much mine as hers. (The parlor maid brings in a jug of hot water.)

VALENTINE. Thank you. (He takes the jug from her, and brings it to the cabinet, continuing in the same idle strain) I really should like to know your family, Mr. Crampton. (The parlor maid goes out: and he pours some hot water into the drinking glass.)

CRAMPTON. Sorry I can't introduce you, sir. I'm happy to say that I don't know where they are, and don't care, so long as they keep out of my way. (Valentine, with a hitch of his eyebrows and shoulders, drops the forceps with a clink into the glass of hot water.) You needn't warm that thing to use on me. I'm not afraid of the cold steel. (Valentine stoops to arrange the gas pump and cylinder beside the chair.) What's that heavy thing?

VALENTINE. Oh, never mind. Something to put my foot on, to get the necessary purchase for a good pull. (Crampton looks alarmed in spite of himself. Valentine stands upright and places the glass with the forceps in it ready to his hand, chatting on with provoking indifference.) And so you advise me not to get married, Mr. Crampton? (He stoops to fit the handle on the apparatus by which the chair is raised and lowered.)

CRAMPTON (irritably). I advise you to get my tooth out and have done reminding me of my wife. Come along, man. (He grips the arms of the chair and braces himself.)

VALENTINE (pausing, with his hand on the lever, to look up at him and say). What do you bet that I don't get that tooth out without your feeling it?

CRAMPTON. Your six week's rent, young man. Don't you gammon me.

VALENTINE (jumping at the bet and winding him aloft vigorously). Done! Are you ready? (Crampton, who has lost his grip of the chair in his alarm at its sudden ascent, folds his arms: sits stiffly upright: and prepares for the worst. Valentine lets down the back of the chair to an obtuse angle.)

CRAMPTON (clutching at the arms of the chair as he falls back). Take care man. I'm quite helpless in this po—-

VALENTINE (deftly stopping him with the gag, and snatching up the mouthpiece of the gas machine). You'll be more helpless presently. (He presses the mouthpiece over Crampton's mouth and nose, leaning over his chest so as to hold his head and shoulders well down on the chair. Crampton makes an inarticulate sound in the mouthpiece and tries to lay hands on Valentine, whom he supposes to be in front of him. After a moment his arms wave aimlessly, then subside and drop. He is quite insensible. Valentine, with an exclamation of somewhat preoccupied triumph, throws aside the mouthpiece quickly: picks up the forceps adroitly from the glass: and—the curtain falls.)

END OF ACT I.

ACT II

On the terrace at the Marine Hotel. It is a square flagged platform, with a parapet of heavy oil jar pilasters supporting a broad stone coping on the outer edge, which stands up over the sea like a cliff. The head waiter of the establishment, busy laying napkins on a luncheon table with his back to the sea, has the hotel on his right, and on his left, in the corner nearest the sea, the flight of steps leading down to the beach.

When he looks down the terrace in front of him he sees a little to his left a solitary guest, a middle-aged gentleman sitting on a chair of iron laths at a little iron table with a bowl of lump sugar and three wasps on it, reading the Standard, with his umbrella up to defend him from the sun, which, in August and at less than an hour after noon, is toasting his protended insteps. Just opposite him, at the hotel side of the terrace, there is a garden seat of the ordinary esplanade pattern. Access to the hotel for visitors is by an entrance in the middle of its facade, reached by a couple of steps on a broad square of raised pavement. Nearer the parapet there lurks a way to the kitchen, masked by a little trellis porch. The table at which the waiter is occupied is a long one, set across the terrace with covers and chairs for five, two at each side and one at the end next the hotel. Against the parapet another table is prepared as a buffet to serve from.

The waiter is a remarkable person in his way. A silky old man, white-haired and delicate looking, but so cheerful and contented that in his encouraging presence ambition stands rebuked as vulgarity, and imagination as treason to the abounding sufficiency and interest of the actual. He has a certain expression peculiar to men who have been extraordinarily successful in their calling, and who, whilst aware of the vanity of success, are untouched by envy.

The gentleman at the iron table is not dressed for the seaside. He wears his London frock coat and gloves; and his tall silk hat is on the table beside the sugar bowl. The excellent condition and quality of these garments, the gold-rimmed folding spectacles through which he is reading the Standard, and the Times at his elbow overlaying the local paper, all testify to his respectability. He is about fifty, clean shaven, and close-cropped, with the corners of his mouth turned down purposely, as if he suspected them of wanting to turn up, and was determined not to let them have their way. He has large expansive ears, cod colored eyes, and a brow kept resolutely wide open, as if, again, he had resolved in his youth to be truthful, magnanimous, and incorruptible, but had never succeeded in making that habit of mind automatic and unconscious. Still, he is by no means to be laughed at. There is no sign of stupidity or infirmity of will about him: on the contrary, he would pass anywhere at sight as a man of more than average professional capacity and responsibility. Just at present he is enjoying the weather and the sea too much to be out of patience; but he has exhausted all the news in his papers and is at present reduced to the advertisements, which are not sufficiently succulent to induce him to persevere with them.

THE GENTLEMAN (yawning and giving up the paper as a bad job). Waiter!

WAITER. Sir? (coming down C.)

THE GENTLEMAN. Are you quite sure Mrs. Clandon is coming back before lunch?

WAITER. Quite sure, sir. She expects you at a quarter to one, sir. (The gentleman, soothed at once by the waiter's voice, looks at him with a lazy smile. It is a quiet voice, with a gentle melody in it that gives sympathetic interest to his most commonplace remark; and he speaks with the sweetest propriety, neither dropping his aitches nor misplacing them, nor committing any other vulgarism. He looks at his watch as he continues) Not that yet, sir, is it? 12:43, sir. Only two minutes more to wait, sir. Nice morning, sir?

THE GENTLEMAN. Yes: very fresh after London.

WAITER. Yes, sir: so all our visitors say, sir. Very nice family, Mrs. Clandon's, sir.

THE GENTLEMAN. You like them, do you?

WAITER. Yes, sir. They have a free way with them that is very taking, sir, very taking indeed, sir: especially the young lady and gentleman.

THE GENTLEMAN. Miss Dorothea and Mr. Philip, I suppose.

WAITER. Yes, sir. The young lady, in giving an order, or the like of that, will say, "Remember, William, we came to this hotel on your account, having heard what a perfect waiter you are." The young gentleman will tell me that I remind him strongly of his father (the gentleman starts at this) and that he expects me to act by him as such. (Soothing, sunny cadence.) Oh, very peasant, sir, very affable and pleasant indeed!

THE GENTLEMAN. You like his father! (He laughs at the notion.)

WAITER. Oh, we must not take what they say too seriously, sir. Of course, sir, if it were true, the young lady would have seen the resemblance, too, sir.

THE GENTLEMAN. Did she?

WAITER. No, sir. She thought me like the bust of Shakespear in Stratford Church, sir. That is why she calls me William, sir. My real name is Walter, sir. (He turns to go back to the table, and sees Mrs. Clandon coming up to the terrace from the beach by the steps.) Here is Mrs. Clandon, sir. (To Mrs. Clandon, in an unobtrusively confidential tone) Gentleman for you, ma'am.

MRS. CLANDON. We shall have two more gentlemen at lunch, William.

WAITER. Right, ma'am. Thank you, ma'am. (He withdraws into the hotel. Mrs. Clandon comes forward looking round for her visitor, but passes over the gentleman without any sign of recognition.)

THE GENTLEMAN (peering at her quaintly from under the umbrella). Don't you know me?

MRS. CLANDON (incredulously, looking hard at him) Are you Finch McComas?

McCOMAS. Can't you guess? (He shuts the umbrella; puts it aside; and jocularly plants himself with his hands on his hips to be inspected.)

MRS. CLANDON. I believe you are. (She gives him her hand. The shake that ensues is that of old friends after a long separation.) Where's your beard?

McCOMAS (with humorous solemnity). Would you employ a solicitor with a beard?

MRS. CLANDON (pointing to the silk hat on the table). Is that your hat?

McCOMAS. Would you employ a solicitor with a sombrero?

MRS. CLANDON. I have thought of you all these eighteen years with the beard and the sombrero. (She sits down on the garden seat. McComas takes his chair again.) Do you go to the meetings of the Dialectical Society still?

McCOMAS (gravely). I do not frequent meetings now.

MRS. CLANDON. Finch: I see what has happened. You have become respectable.

McCOMAS. Haven't you?

MRS. CLANDON. Not a bit.

McCOMAS. You hold to your old opinions still?

MRS. CLANDON. As firmly as ever.

McCOMAS. Bless me! And you are still ready to make speeches in public, in spite of your sex (Mrs. Clandon nods); to insist on a married woman's right to her own separate property (she nods again); to champion Darwin's view of the origin of species and John Stuart Mill's essay on Liberty (nod); to read Huxley, Tyndall and George Eliot (three nods); and to demand University degrees, the opening of the professions, and the parliamentary franchise for women as well as men?

MRS. CLANDON (resolutely). Yes: I have not gone back one inch; and I have educated Gloria to take up my work where I left it. That is what has brought me back to England: I felt that I had no right to bury her alive in Madeira—my St. Helena, Finch. I suppose she will be howled at as I was; but she is prepared for that.

McCOMAS. Howled at! My dear good lady: there is nothing in any of those views now-a-days to prevent her from marrying a bishop. You reproached me just now for having become respectable. You were wrong: I hold to our old opinions as strongly as ever. I don't go to church; and I don't pretend I do. I call myself what I am: a Philosophic Radical, standing for liberty and the rights of the individual, as I learnt to do from my master Herbert Spencer. Am I howled at? No: I'm indulged as an old fogey. I'm out of everything, because I've refused to bow the knee to Socialism.

MRS. CLANDON (shocked). Socialism.

McCOMAS. Yes, Socialism. That's what Miss Gloria will be up to her ears in before the end of the month if you let her loose here.

MRS. CLANDON (emphatically). But I can prove to her that Socialism is a fallacy.

McCOMAS (touchingly). It is by proving that, Mrs. Clandon, that I have lost all my young disciples. Be careful what you do: let her go her own way. (With some bitterness.) We're old-fashioned: the world thinks it has left us behind. There is only one place in all England where your opinions would still pass as advanced.

MRS. CLANDON (scornfully unconvinced). The Church, perhaps?

McCOMAS. No, the theatre. And now to business! Why have you made me come down here?

MRS. CLANDON. Well, partly because I wanted to see you—

McCOMAS (with good-humored irony). Thanks.

MRS. CLANDON. —and partly because I want you to explain everything to the children. They know nothing; and now that we have come back to England, it is impossible to leave them in ignorance any longer. (Agitated.) Finch: I cannot bring myself to tell them. I— (She is interrupted by the twins and Gloria. Dolly comes tearing up the steps, racing Philip, who combines a terrific speed with unhurried propriety of bearing which, however, costs him the race, as Dolly reaches her mother first and almost upsets the garden seat by the precipitancy of her arrival.)

DOLLY (breathless). It's all right, mamma. The dentist is coming; and he's bringing his old man.

MRS. CLANDON. Dolly, dear: don't you see Mr. McComas? (Mr. McComas rises, smilingly.)

DOLLY (her face falling with the most disparagingly obvious disappointment). This! Where are the flowing locks?

PHILIP (seconding her warmly). Where the beard?—the cloak?—the poetic exterior?

DOLLY. Oh, Mr. McComas, you've gone and spoiled yourself. Why didn't you wait till we'd seen you?

McCOMAS (taken aback, but rallying his humor to meet the emergency). Because eighteen years is too long for a solicitor to go without having his hair cut.

GLORIA (at the other side of McComas). How do you do, Mr. McComas? (He turns; and she takes his hand and presses it, with a frank straight look into his eyes.) We are glad to meet you at last.

McCOMAS. Miss Gloria, I presume? (Gloria smiles assent, and releases his hand after a final pressure. She then retires behind the garden seat, leaning over the back beside Mrs. Clandon.) And this young gentleman?

PHILIP. I was christened in a comparatively prosaic mood. My name is—

DOLLY (completing his sentence for him declamatorily). "Norval. On the Grampian hills"—

PHILIP (declaiming gravely). "My father feeds his flock, a frugal swain"—

MRS. CLANDON (remonstrating). Dear, dear children: don't be silly. Everything is so new to them here, Finch, that they are in the wildest spirits. They think every Englishman they meet is a joke.

DOLLY. Well, so he is: it's not our fault.

PHILIP. My knowledge of human nature is fairly extensive, Mr. McComas; but I find it impossible to take the inhabitants of this island seriously.

McCOMAS. I presume, sir, you are Master Philip (offering his hand)?

PHILIP (taking McComas's hand and looking solemnly at him). I was Master Philip—was so for many years; just as you were once Master Finch. (He gives his hand a single shake and drops it; then turns away, exclaiming meditatively) How strange it is to look back on our boyhood! (McComas stares after him, not at all pleased.)

DOLLY (to Mrs. Clandon). Has Finch had a drink?

MRS. CLANDON (remonstrating). Dearest: Mr. McComas will lunch with us.

DOLLY. Have you ordered for seven? Don't forget the old gentleman.

MRS. CLANDON. I have not forgotten him, dear. What is his name?

DOLLY. Chalkstones. He'll be here at half past one. (To McComas.) Are we like what you expected?

MRS. CLANDON (changing her tone to a more earnest one). Dolly: Mr. McComas has something more serious than that to tell you. Children: I have asked my old friend to answer the question you asked this morning. He is your father's friend as well as mine: and he will tell you the story more fairly than I could. (Turning her head from them to Gloria.) Gloria: are you satisfied?

GLORIA (gravely attentive). Mr. McComas is very kind.

McCOMAS (nervously). Not at all, my dear young lady: not at all. At the same time, this is rather sudden. I was hardly prepared—er—

DOLLY (suspiciously). Oh, we don't want anything prepared.

PHILIP (exhorting him). Tell us the truth.

DOLLY (emphatically). Bald headed.

McCOMAS (nettled). I hope you intend to take what I have to say seriously.

PHILIP (with profound mock gravity). I hope it will deserve it, Mr. McComas. My knowledge of human nature teaches me not to expect too much.

MRS. CLANDON (remonstrating). Phil—

PHILIP. Yes, mother, all right. I beg your pardon, Mr. McComas: don't mind us.

DOLLY (in conciliation). We mean well.

PHILIP. Shut up, both.

(Dolly holds her lips. McComas takes a chair from the luncheon table; places it between the little table and the garden seat with Dolly on his right and Philip on his left; and settles himself in it with the air of a man about to begin a long communication. The Clandons match him expectantly.)

McCOMAS. Ahem! Your father—

DOLLY (interrupting). How old is he?

PHILIP. Sh!

MRS. CLANDON (softly). Dear Dolly: don't let us interrupt Mr. McComas.

McCOMAS (emphatically). Thank you, Mrs. Clandon. Thank you. (To Dolly.) Your father is fifty-seven.

DOLLY (with a bound, startled and excited). Fifty-seven! Where does he live?

MRS. CLANDON (remonstrating). Dolly, Dolly!

McCOMAS (stopping her). Let me answer that, Mrs. Clandon. The answer will surprise you considerably. He lives in this town. (Mrs. Clandon rises. She and Gloria look at one another in the greatest consternation.)

DOLLY (with conviction). I knew it! Phil: Chalkstones is our father.

McCOMAS. Chalkstones!

DOLLY. Oh, Crampstones, or whatever it is. He said I was like his mother. I knew he must mean his daughter.

PHILIP (very seriously). Mr. McComas: I desire to consider your feelings in every possible way: but I warn you that if you stretch the long arm of coincidence to the length of telling me that Mr. Crampton of this town is my father, I shall decline to entertain the information for a moment.

McCOMAS. And pray why?

PHILIP. Because I have seen the gentleman; and he is entirely unfit to be my father, or Dolly's father, or Gloria's father, or my mother's husband.

McCOMAS. Oh, indeed! Well, sir, let me tell you that whether you like it or not, he is your father, and your sister' father, and Mrs. Clandon's husband. Now! What have you to say to that!

DOLLY (whimpering). You needn't be so cross. Crampton isn't your father.

PHILIP. Mr. McComas: your conduct is heartless. Here you find a family enjoying the unspeakable peace and freedom of being orphans. We have never seen the face of a relative—never known a claim except the claim of freely chosen friendship. And now you wish to thrust into the most intimate relationship with us a man whom we don't know—

DOLLY (vehemently). An awful old man! (reproachfully) And you began as if you had quite a nice father for us.

McCOMAS (angrily). How do you know that he is not nice? And what right have you to choose your own father? (raising his voice.) Let me tell you, Miss Clandon, that you are too young to—

DOLLY (interrupting him suddenly and eagerly). Stop, I forgot! Has he any money?

McCOMAS. He has a great deal of money.

DOLLY (delighted). Oh, what did I always say, Phil?

PHILIP. Dolly: we have perhaps been condemning the old man too hastily. Proceed, Mr. McComas.

McCOMAS. I shall not proceed, sir. I am too hurt, too shocked, to proceed.

MRS. CLANDON (urgently). Finch: do you realize what is happening? Do you understand that my children have invited that man to lunch, and that he will be here in a few moments?

McCOMAS (completely upset). What! do you mean—am I to understand—is it—

PHILIP (impressively). Steady, Finch. Think it out slowly and carefully. He's coming—coming to lunch.

GLORIA. Which of us is to tell him the truth? Have you thought of that?

MRS. CLANDON. Finch: you must tell him.

DOLLY Oh, Finch is no good at telling things. Look at the mess he has made of telling us.

McCOMAS. I have not been allowed to speak. I protest against this.

DOLLY (taking his arm coaxingly). Dear Finch: don't be cross.

MRS. CLANDON. Gloria: let us go in. He may arrive at any moment.

GLORIA (proudly). Do not stir, mother. I shall not stir. We must not run away.

MRS. CLANDON (delicately rebuking her). My dear: we cannot sit down to lunch just as we are. We shall come back again. We must have no bravado. (Gloria winces, and goes into the hotel without a word.) Come, Dolly. (As she goes into the hotel door, the waiter comes out with plates, etc., for two additional covers on a tray.)

WAITER. Gentlemen come yet, ma'am?

MRS. CLANDON. Two more to come yet, thank you. They will be here, immediately. (She goes into the hotel. The waiter takes his tray to the service table.)

PHILIP. I have an idea. Mr. McComas: this communication should be made, should it not, by a man of infinite tact?

McCOMAS. It will require tact, certainly.

PHILIP Good! Dolly: whose tact were you noticing only this morning?

DOLLY (seizing the idea with rapture). Oh, yes, I declare! William!

PHILIP. The very man! (Calling) William!

WAITER. Coming, sir.

McCOMAS (horrified). The waiter! Stop, stop! I will not permit this. I—

WAITER (presenting himself between Philip and McComas). Yes, sir. (McComas's complexion fades into stone grey; and all movement and expression desert his eyes. He sits down stupefied.)

PHILIP. William: you remember my request to you to regard me as your son?

WAITER (with respectful indulgence). Yes, sir. Anything you please, sir.

PHILIP. William: at the very outset of your career as my father, a rival has appeared on the scene.

WAITER. Your real father, sir? Well, that was to be expected, sooner or later, sir, wasn't it? (Turning with a happy smile to McComas.) Is it you, sir?

McCOMAS (renerved by indignation). Certainly not. My children know how to behave themselves.

PHILIP. No, William: this gentleman was very nearly my father: he wooed my mother, but wooed her in vain.

McCOMAS (outraged). Well, of all the—

PHILIP. Sh! Consequently, he is only our solicitor. Do you know one Crampton, of this town?

WAITER. Cock-eyed Crampton, sir, of the Crooked Billet, is it?

PHILIP. I don't know. Finch: does he keep a public house?

McCOMAS (rising scandalized). No, no, no. Your father, sir, is a well-known yacht builder, an eminent man here.

WAITER (impressed). Oh, beg pardon, sir, I'm sure. A son of Mr. Crampton's! Dear me!

PHILIP. Mr. Crampton is coming to lunch with us.

WAITER (puzzled). Yes, sir. (Diplomatically.) Don't usually lunch with his family, perhaps, sir?

PHILIP (impressively). William: he does not know that we are his family. He has not seen us for eighteen years. He won't know us. (To emphasize the communication he seats himself on the iron table with a spring, and looks at the waiter with his lips compressed and his legs swinging.)

DOLLY. We want you to break the news to him, William.

WAITER. But I should think he'd guess when he sees your mother, miss. (Philip's legs become motionless at this elucidation. He contemplates the waiter raptly.)

DOLLY (dazzled). I never thought of that.

PHILIP. Nor I. (Coming off the table and turning reproachfully on McComas.) Nor you.

DOLLY. And you a solicitor!

PHILIP. Finch: Your professional incompetence is appalling. William: your sagacity puts us all to shame.

DOLLY You really are like Shakespear, William.

WAITER. Not at all, sir. Don't mention it, miss. Most happy, I'm sure, sir. (Goes back modestly to the luncheon table and lays the two additional covers, one at the end next the steps, and the other so as to make a third on the side furthest from the balustrade.)

PHILIP (abruptly). Finch: come and wash your hands. (Seizes his arm and leads him toward the hotel.)

McCOMAS. I am thoroughly vexed and hurt, Mr. Clandon—

PHILIP (interrupting him). You will get used to us. Come, Dolly. (McComas shakes him off and marches into the hotel. Philip follows with unruffled composure.)

DOLLY (turning for a moment on the steps as she follows them). Keep your wits about you, William. There will be fire-works.

WAITER. Right, miss. You may depend on me, miss. (She goes into the hotel.)

(Valentine comes lightly up the steps from the beach, followed doggedly by Crampton. Valentine carries a walking stick. Crampton, either because he is old and chilly, or with some idea of extenuating the unfashionableness of his reefer jacket, wears a light overcoat. He stops at the chair left by McComas in the middle of the terrace, and steadies himself for a moment by placing his hand on the back of it.)

CRAMPTON. Those steps make me giddy. (He passes his hand over his forehead.) I have not got over that infernal gas yet.

(He goes to the iron chair, so that he can lean his elbows on the little table to prop his head as he sits. He soon recovers, and begins to unbutton his overcoat. Meanwhile Valentine interviews the waiter.)

VALENTINE. Waiter!

WAITER (coming forward between them). Yes, sir.

VALENTINE. Mrs. Lanfrey Clandon.

WAITER (with a sweet smile of welcome). Yes, sir. We're expecting you, sir. That is your table, sir. Mrs. Clandon will be down presently, sir. The young lady and young gentleman were just talking about your friend, sir.

VALENTINE. Indeed!

WAITER (smoothly melodious). Yes, sire. Great flow of spirits, sir. A vein of pleasantry, as you might say, sir. (Quickly, to Crampton, who has risen to get the overcoat off.) Beg pardon, sir, but if you'll allow me (helping him to get the overcoat off and taking it from him). Thank you, sir. (Crampton sits down again; and the waiter resumes the broken melody.) The young gentleman's latest is that you're his father, sir.

CRAMPTON. What!

WAITER. Only his joke, sir, his favourite joke. Yesterday, I was to be his father. To-day, as soon as he knew you were coming, sir, he tried to put it up on me that you were his father, his long lost father—not seen you for eighteen years, he said.

CRAMPTON (startled). Eighteen years!

WAITER. Yes, sir. (With gentle archness.) But I was up to his tricks, sir. I saw the idea coming into his head as he stood there, thinking what new joke he'd have with me. Yes, sir: that's the sort he is: very pleasant, ve—ry off hand and affable indeed, sir. (Again changing his tempo to say to Valentine, who is putting his stick down against the corner of the garden seat) If you'll allow me, sir? (Taking Valentine's stick.) Thank you, sir. (Valentine strolls up to the luncheon table and looks at the menu. The waiter turns to Crampton and resumes his lay.) Even the solicitor took up the joke, although he was in a manner of speaking in my confidence about the young gentleman, sir. Yes, sir, I assure you, sir. You would never imagine what respectable professional gentlemen from London will do on an outing, when the sea air takes them, sir.

CRAMPTON. Oh, there's a solicitor with them, is there?

WAITER. The family solicitor, sir—yes, sir. Name of McComas, sir. (He goes towards hotel entrance with coat and stick, happily unconscious of the bomblike effect the name has produced on Crampton.)

CRAMPTON (rising in angry alarm). McComas! (Calls to Valentine.) Valentine! (Again, fiercely.) Valentine!! (Valentine turns.) This is a plant, a conspiracy. This is my family—my children—my infernal wife.

VALENTINE (coolly). On, indeed! Interesting meeting! (He resumes his study of the menu.)

CRAMPTON. Meeting! Not for me. Let me out of this. (Calling to the waiter.) Give me that coat.

WAITER. Yes, sir. (He comes back, puts Valentine's stick carefully down against the luncheon table; and delicately shakes the coat out and holds it for Crampton to put on.) I seem to have done the young gentleman an injustice, sir, haven't I, sir.

CRAMPTON. Rrrh! (He stops on the point of putting his arms into the sleeves, and turns to Valentine with sudden suspicion.) Valentine: you are in this. You made this plot. You—

VALENTINE (decisively). Bosh! (He throws the menu down and goes round the table to look out unconcernedly over the parapet.)

CRAMPTON (angrily). What d'ye— (McComas, followed by Philip and Dolly, comes out. He vacillates for a moment on seeing Crampton.)

WAITER (softly—interrupting Crampton). Steady, sir. Here they come, sir. (He takes up the stick and makes for the hotel, throwing the coat across his arm. McComas turns the corners of his mouth resolutely down and crosses to Crampton, who draws back and glares, with his hands behind him. McComas, with his brow opener than ever, confronts him in the majesty of a spotless conscience.)

WAITER (aside, as he passes Philip on his way out). I've broke it to him, sir.

PHILIP. Invaluable William! (He passes on to the table.)

DOLLY (aside to the waiter). How did he take it?

WAITER (aside to her). Startled at first, miss; but resigned—very resigned, indeed, miss. (He takes the stick and coat into the hotel.)

McCOMAS (having stared Crampton out of countenance). So here you are, Mr. Crampton.

CRAMPTON. Yes, here—caught in a trap—a mean trap. Are those my children?

PHILIP (with deadly politeness). Is this our father, Mr. McComas?

McCOMAS. Yes—er— (He loses countenance himself and stops.)

DOLLY (conventionally). Pleased to meet you again. (She wanders idly round the table, exchanging a smile and a word of greeting with Valentine on the way.)

PHILIP. Allow me to discharge my first duty as host by ordering your wine. (He takes the wine list from the table. His polite attention, and Dolly's unconcerned indifference, leave Crampton on the footing of the casual acquaintance picked up that morning at the dentist's. The consciousness of it goes through the father with so keen a pang that he trembles all over; his brow becomes wet; and he stares dumbly at his son, who, just conscious enough of his own callousness to intensely enjoy the humor and adroitness of it, proceeds pleasantly.) Finch: some crusted old port for you, as a respectable family solicitor, eh?

McCOMAS (firmly). Apollinaris only. I prefer to take nothing heating. (He walks away to the side of the terrace, like a man putting temptation behind him.)

PHILIP. Valentine—?

VALENTINE. Would Lager be considered vulgar?

PHILIP. Probably. We'll order some. Dolly takes it. (Turning to Crampton with cheerful politeness.) And now, Mr. Crampton, what can we do for you?

CRAMPTON. What d'ye mean, boy?

PHILIP. Boy! (Very solemnly.) Whose fault is it that I am a boy?

(Crampton snatches the wine list rudely from him and irresolutely pretends to read it. Philip abandons it to him with perfect politeness.)

DOLLY (looking over Crampton's right shoulder). The whisky's on the last page but one.

CRAMPTON. Let me alone, child.

DOLLY. Child! No, no: you may call me Dolly if you like; but you mustn't call me child. (She slips her arm through Philip's; and the two stand looking at Crampton as if he were some eccentric stranger.)

CRAMPTON (mopping his brow in rage and agony, and yet relieved even by their playing with him). McComas: we are—ha!—going to have a pleasant meal.

McCOMAS (pusillanimously). There is no reason why it should not be pleasant. (He looks abjectly gloomy.)

PHILIP. Finch's face is a feast in itself. (Mrs. Clandon and Gloria come from the hotel. Mrs. Clandon advances with courageous self-possession and marked dignity of manner. She stops at the foot of the steps to address Valentine, who is in her path. Gloria also stops, looking at Crampton with a certain repulsion.)

MRS. CLANDON. Glad to see you again, Mr. Valentine. (He smiles. She passes on and confronts Crampton, intending to address him with perfect composure; but his aspect shakes her. She stops suddenly and says anxiously, with a touch of remorse.) Fergus: you are greatly changed.

CRAMPTON (grimly). I daresay. A man does change in eighteen years.

MRS. CLANDON (troubled). I—I did not mean that. I hope your health is good.

CRAMPTON. Thank you. No: it's not my health. It's my happiness: that's the change you meant, I think. (Breaking out suddenly.) Look at her, McComas! Look at her; and look at me! (He utters a half laugh, half sob.)

PHILIP. Sh! (Pointing to the hotel entrance, where the waiter has just appeared.) Order before William!

DOLLY (touching Crampton's arm warningly with her finger). Ahem! (The waiter goes to the service table and beckons to the kitchen entrance, whence issue a young waiter with soup plates, and a cook, in white apron and cap, with the soup tureen. The young waiter remains and serves: the cook goes out, and reappears from time to time bringing in the courses. He carves, but does not serve. The waiter comes to the end of the luncheon table next the steps.)

MRS. CLANDON (as they all assemble about the table). I think you have all met one another already to-day. Oh, no, excuse me. (Introducing) Mr. Valentine: Mr. McComas. (She goes to the end of the table nearest the hotel.) Fergus: will you take the head of the table, please.

CRAMPTON. Ha! (Bitterly.) The head of the table!

WAITER (holding the chair for him with inoffensive encouragement). This end, sir. (Crampton submits, and takes his seat.) Thank you, sir.

MRS. CLANDON. Mr. Valentine: will you take that side (indicating the side nearest the parapet) with Gloria? (Valentine and Gloria take their places, Gloria next Crampton and Valentine next Mrs. Clandon.) Finch: I must put you on this side, between Dolly and Phil. You must protect yourself as best you can. (The three take the remaining side of the table, Dolly next her mother, Phil next his father, and McComas between them. Soup is served.)

WAITER (to Crampton). Thick or clear, sir?

CRAMPTON (to Mrs. Clandon). Does nobody ask a blessing in this household?

PHILIP (interposing smartly). Let us first settle what we are about to receive. William!

WAITER. Yes, sir. (He glides swiftly round the table to Phil's left elbow. On his way he whispers to the young waiter) Thick.

PHILIP. Two small Lagers for the children as usual, William; and one large for this gentleman (indicating Valentine). Large Apollinaris for Mr. McComas.

WAITER. Yes, sir.

DOLLY. Have a six of Irish in it, Finch?

McCOMAS (scandalized). No—no, thank you.

PHILIP. Number 413 for my mother and Miss Gloria as before; and— (turning enquiringly to Crampton) Eh?

CRAMPTON (scowling and about to reply offensively). I—

WAITER (striking in mellifluously). All right, sir. We know what Mr. Crampton likes here, sir. (He goes into the hotel.)

PHILIP (looking gravely at his father). You frequent bars. Bad habit! (The cook, accompanied by a waiter with a supply of hot plates, brings in the fish from the kitchen to the service table, and begins slicing it.)

CRAMPTON. You have learnt your lesson from your mother, I see.

MRS. CLANDON. Phil: will you please remember that your jokes are apt to irritate people who are not accustomed to us, and that your father is our guest to-day.

CRAMPTON (bitterly). Yes, a guest at the head of my own table. (The soup plates are removed.)

DOLLY (sympathetically). Yes: it's embarrassing, isn't it? It's just as bad for us, you know.

PHILIP. Sh! Dolly: we are both wanting in tact. (To Crampton.) We mean well, Mr. Crampton; but we are not yet strong in the filial line. (The waiter returns from the hotel with the drinks.) William: come and restore good feeling.

WAITER (cheerfully). Yes, sir. Certainly, sir. Small Lager for you, sir. (To Crampton.) Seltzer and Irish, sir. (To McComas.) Apollinaris, sir. (To Dolly.) Small Lager, miss. (To Mrs. Clandon, pouring out wine.) 413, madam. (To Valentine.) Large Lager for you, sir. (To Gloria.) 413, miss.

DOLLY (drinking). To the family!

PHILIP. (drinking). Hearth and Home! (Fish is served.)

McCOMAS (with an obviously forced attempt at cheerful domesticity). We are getting on very nicely after all.

DOLLY (critically). After all! After all what, Finch?

CRAMPTON (sarcastically). He means that you are getting on very nicely in spite of the presence of your father. Do I take your point rightly, Mr. McComas?

McCOMAS (disconcerted). No, no. I only said "after all" to round off the sentence. I—er—er—er—-

WAITER (tactfully). Turbot, sir?

McCOMAS (intensely grateful for the interruption). Thank you, waiter: thank you.

WAITER (sotto voce). Don't mention it, sir. (He returns to the service table.)

CRAMPTON (to Phil). Have you thought of choosing a profession yet?

PHILIP. I am keeping my mind open on that subject. William!

WAITER. Yes, sir.

PHILIP. How long do you think it would take me to learn to be a really smart waiter?

WAITER. Can't be learnt, sir. It's in the character, sir. (Confidentially to Valentine, who is looking about for something.) Bread for the lady, sir? yes, sir. (He serves bread to Gloria, and resumes at his former pitch.) Very few are born to it, sir.

PHILIP. You don't happen to have such a thing as a son, yourself, have you?

WAITER. Yes, sir: oh, yes, sir. (To Gloria, again dropping his voice.) A little more fish, miss? you won't care for the joint in the middle of the day.

GLORIA. No, thank you. (The fish plates are removed.)

DOLLY. Is your son a waiter, too, William?

WAITER (serving Gloria with fowl). Oh, no, miss, he's too impetuous. He's at the Bar.

McCOMAS (patronizingly). A potman, eh?

WAITER (with a touch of melancholy, as if recalling a disappointment softened by time). No, sir: the other bar—your profession, sir. A Q.C., sir.

McCOMAS (embarrassed). I'm sure I beg your pardon.

WAITER. Not at all, sir. Very natural mistake, I'm sure, sir. I've often wished he was a potman, sir. Would have been off my hands ever so much sooner, sir. (Aside to Valentine, who is again in difficulties.) Salt at your elbow, sir. (Resuming.) Yes, sir: had to support him until he was thirty-seven, sir. But doing well now, sir: very satisfactory indeed, sir. Nothing less than fifty guineas, sir.

McCOMAS. Democracy, Crampton!—modern democracy!

WAITER (calmly). No, sir, not democracy: only education, sir. Scholarships, sir. Cambridge Local, sir. Sidney Sussex College, sir. (Dolly plucks his sleeve and whispers as he bends down.) Stone ginger, miss? Right, miss. (To McComas.) Very good thing for him, sir: he never had any turn for real work, sir. (He goes into the hotel, leaving the company somewhat overwhelmed by his son's eminence.)

VALENTINE. Which of us dare give that man an order again!

DOLLY. I hope he won't mind my sending him for ginger-beer.

CRAMPTON (doggedly). While he's a waiter it's his business to wait. If you had treated him as a waiter ought to be treated, he'd have held his tongue.

DOLLY. What a loss that would have been! Perhaps he'll give us an introduction to his son and get us into London society. (The waiter reappears with the ginger-beer.)

CRAMPTON (growling contemptuously). London society! London society!! You're not fit for any society, child.

DOLLY (losing her temper). Now look here, Mr. Crampton. If you think—

WAITER (softly, at her elbow). Stone ginger, miss.

DOLLY (taken aback, recovers her good humor after a long breath and says sweetly). Thank you, dear William. You were just in time. (She drinks.)

McCOMAS (making a fresh effort to lead the conversation into dispassionate regions). If I may be allowed to change the subject, Miss Clandon, what is the established religion in Madeira?

GLORIA. I suppose the Portuguese religion. I never inquired.

DOLLY. The servants come in Lent and kneel down before you and confess all the things they've done: and you have to pretend to forgive them. Do they do that in England, William?

WAITER. Not usually, miss. They may in some parts: but it has not come under my notice, miss. (Catching Mrs. Clandon's eye as the young waiter offers her the salad bowl.) You like it without dressing, ma'am: yes, ma'am, I have some for you. (To his young colleague, motioning him to serve Gloria.) This side, Jo. (He takes a special portion of salad from the service table and puts it beside Mrs. Clandon's plate. In doing so he observes that Dolly is making a wry face.) Only a bit of watercress, miss, got in by mistake. (He takes her salad away.) Thank you, miss. (To the young waiter, admonishing him to serve Dolly afresh.) Jo. (Resuming.) Mostly members of the Church of England, miss.

DOLLY. Members of the Church of England! What's the subscription?

CRAMPTON (rising violently amid general consternation). You see how my children have been brought up, McComas. You see it; you hear it. I call all of you to witness— (He becomes inarticulate, and is about to strike his fist recklessly on the table when the waiter considerately takes away his plate.)

MRS. CLANDON (firmly). Sit down, Fergus. There is no occasion at all for this outburst. You must remember that Dolly is just like a foreigner here. Pray sit down.

CRAMPTON (subsiding unwillingly). I doubt whether I ought to sit here and countenance all this. I doubt it.

WAITER. Cheese, sir; or would you like a cold sweet?

CRAMPTON (take aback). What? Oh!—cheese, cheese.

DOLLY. Bring a box of cigarettes, William.

WAITER. All ready, miss. (He takes a box of cigarettes from the service table and places them before Dolly, who selects one and prepares to smoke. He then returns to his table for a box of vestas.)

CRAMPTON (staring aghast at Dolly). Does she smoke?

DOLLY (out of patience). Really, Mr. Crampton, I'm afraid I'm spoiling your lunch. I'll go and have my cigarette on the beach. (She leaves the table with petulant suddenness and goes down the steps. The waiter attempts to give her the matches; but she is gone before he can reach her.)

CRAMPTON (furiously). Margaret: call that girl back. Call her back, I say.

McCOMAS (trying to make peace). Come, Crampton: never mind. She's her father's daughter: that's all.

MRS. CLANDON (with deep resentment). I hope not, Finch. (She rises: they all rise a little.) Mr. Valentine: will you excuse me: I am afraid Dolly is hurt and put out by what has passed. I must go to her.

CRAMPTON. To take her part against me, you mean.

MRS. CLANDON (ignoring him). Gloria: will you take my place whilst I am away, dear. (She crosses to the steps. Crampton's eyes follow her with bitter hatred. The rest watch her in embarrassed silence, feeling the incident to be a very painful one.)

WAITER (intercepting her at the top of the steps and offering her a box of vestas). Young lady forgot the matches, ma'am. If you would be so good, ma'am.

MRS. CLANDON (surprised into grateful politeness by the witchery of his sweet and cheerful tones). Thank you very much. (She takes the matches and goes down to the beach. The waiter shepherds his assistant along with him into the hotel by the kitchen entrance, leaving the luncheon party to themselves.)

CRAMPTON (throwing himself back in his chair). There's a mother for you, McComas! There's a mother for you!

GLORIA (steadfastly). Yes: a good mother.

CRAMPTON. And a bad father? That's what you mean, eh?

VALENTINE (rising indignantly and addressing Gloria). Miss Clandon: I—

CRAMPTON (turning on him). That girl's name is Crampton, Mr. Valentine, not Clandon. Do you wish to join them in insulting me?

VALENTINE (ignoring him). I'm overwhelmed, Miss Clandon. It's all my fault: I brought him here: I'm responsible for him. And I'm ashamed of him.

CRAMPTON. What d'y' mean?

GLORIA (rising coldly). No harm has been done, Mr. Valentine. We have all been a little childish, I am afraid. Our party has been a failure: let us break it up and have done with it. (She puts her chair aside and turns to the steps, adding, with slighting composure, as she passes Crampton.) Good-bye, father.

(She descends the steps with cold, disgusted indifference. They all look after her, and so do not notice the return of the waiter from the hotel, laden with Crampton's coat, Valentine's stick, a couple of shawls and parasols, a white canvas umbrella, and some camp stools.)

CRAMPTON (to himself, staring after Gloria with a ghastly expression). Father! Father!! (He strikes his fist violently on the table.) Now—

WAITER (offering the coat). This is yours, sir, I think, sir. (Crampton glares at him; then snatches it rudely and comes down the terrace towards the garden seat, struggling with the coat in his angry efforts to put it on. McComas rises and goes to his assistance; then takes his hat and umbrella from the little iron table, and turns towards the steps. Meanwhile the waiter, after thanking Crampton with unruffled sweetness for taking the coat, offers some of his burden to Phil.) The ladies' sunshades, sir. Nasty glare off the sea to-day, sir: very trying to the complexion, sir. I shall carry down the camp stools myself, sir.

PHILIP. You are old, Father William; but you are the most considerate of men. No: keep the sunshades and give me the camp stools (taking them).

WAITER (with flattering gratitude). Thank you, sir.

PHILIP. Finch: share with me (giving him a couple). Come along. (They go down the steps together.)

VALENTINE (to the waiter). Leave me something to bring down—one of these. (Offering to take a sunshade.)

WAITER (discreetly). That's the younger lady's, sir. (Valentine lets it go.) Thank you, sir. If you'll allow me, sir, I think you had better have this. (He puts down the sunshades on Crampton's chair, and produces from the tail pocket of his dress coat, a book with a lady's handkerchief between the leaves, marking the page.) The eldest young lady is reading it at present. (Valentine takes it eagerly.) Thank you, sir. Schopenhauer, sir, you see. (He takes up the sunshades again.) Very interesting author, sir: especially on the subject of ladies, sir. (He goes down the steps. Valentine, about to follow him, recollects Crampton and changes his mind.)

VALENTINE (coming rather excitedly to Crampton). Now look here, Crampton: are you at all ashamed of yourself?

CRAMPTON (pugnaciously). Ashamed of myself! What for?

VALENTINE. For behaving like a bear. What will your daughter think of me for having brought you here?

CRAMPTON. I was not thinking of what my daughter was thinking of you.

VALENTINE. No, you were thinking of yourself. You're a perfect maniac.

CRAMPTON (heartrent). She told you what I am—a father—a father robbed of his children. What are the hearts of this generation like? Am I to come here after all these years—to see what my children are for the first time! to hear their voices!—and carry it all off like a fashionable visitor; drop in to lunch; be Mr. Crampton—M i s t e r Crampton! What right have they to talk to me like that? I'm their father: do they deny that? I'm a man, with the feelings of our common humanity: have I no rights, no claims? In all these years who have I had round me? Servants, clerks, business acquaintances. I've had respect from them—aye, kindness. Would one of them have spoken to me as that girl spoke?—would one of them have laughed at me as that boy was laughing at me all the time? (Frantically.) My own children! M i s t e r Crampton! My—

VALENTINE. Come, come: they're only children. The only one of them that's worth anything called you father.

CRAMPTON (wildly). Yes: "good-bye, father." Oh, yes: she got at my feelings—with a stab!

VALENTINE (taking this in very bad part). Now look here, Crampton: you just let her alone: she's treated you very well. I had a much worse time of it at lunch than you.

CRAMPTON. You!

VALENTINE (with growing impetuosity). Yes: I. I sat next to her; and I never said a single thing to her the whole time—couldn't think of a blessed word. And not a word did she say to me.

CRAMPTON. Well?

VALENTINE. Well? Well??? (Tackling him very seriously and talking faster and faster.) Crampton: do you know what's been the matter with me to-day? You don't suppose, do you, that I'm in the habit of playing such tricks on my patients as I played on you?

CRAMPTON. I hope not.

VALENTINE. The explanation is that I'm stark mad, or rather that I've never been in my real senses before. I'm capable of anything: I've grown up at last: I'm a Man; and it's your daughter that's made a man of me.

CRAMPTON (incredulously). Are you in love with my daughter?

VALENTINE (his words now coming in a perfect torrent). Love! Nonsense: it's something far above and beyond that. It's life, it's faith, it's strength, certainty, paradise—

CRAMPTON (interrupting him with acrid contempt). Rubbish, man! What have you to keep a wife on? You can't marry her.

VALENTINE. Who wants to marry her? I'll kiss her hands; I'll kneel at her feet; I'll live for her; I'll die for her; and that'll be enough for me. Look at her book! See! (He kisses the handkerchief.) If you offered me all your money for this excuse for going down to the beach and speaking to her again, I'd only laugh at you. (He rushes buoyantly off to the steps, where he bounces right into the arms of the waiter, who is coming up form the beach. The two save themselves from falling by clutching one another tightly round the waist and whirling one another around.)

WAITER (delicately). Steady, sir, steady.

VALENTINE (shocked at his own violence). I beg your pardon.

WAITER. Not at all, sir, not at all. Very natural, sir, I'm sure, sir, at your age. The lady has sent me for her book, sir. Might I take the liberty of asking you to let her have it at once, sir?

VALENTINE. With pleasure. And if you will allow me to present you with a professional man's earnings for six weeks— (offering him Dolly's crown piece.)

WAITER (as if the sum were beyond his utmost expectations). Thank you, sir: much obliged. (Valentine dashes down the steps.) Very high-spirited young gentleman, sir: very manly and straight set up.

CRAMPTON (in grumbling disparagement). And making his fortune in a hurry, no doubt. I know what his six weeks' earnings come to. (He crosses the terrace to the iron table, and sits down.)

WAITER (philosophically). Well, sir, you never can tell. That's a principle in life with me, sir, if you'll excuse my having such a thing, sir. (Delicately sinking the philosopher in the waiter for a moment.) Perhaps you haven't noticed that you hadn't touched that seltzer and Irish, sir, when the party broke up. (He takes the tumbler from the luncheon table, and sets if before Crampton.) Yes, sir, you never can tell. There was my son, sir! who ever thought that he would rise to wear a silk gown, sir? And yet to-day, sir, nothing less than fifty guineas, sir. What a lesson, sir!

CRAMPTON. Well, I hope he is grateful to you, and recognizes what he owes you.

WAITER. We get on together very well, very well indeed, sir, considering the difference in our stations. (With another of his irresistible transitions.) A small lump of sugar, sir, will take the flatness out of the seltzer without noticeably sweetening the drink, sir. Allow me, sir. (He drops a lump of sugar into the tumbler.) But as I say to him, where's the difference after all? If I must put on a dress coat to show what I am, sir, he must put on a wig and gown to show what he is. If my income is mostly tips, and there's a pretence that I don't get them, why, his income is mostly fees, sir; and I understand there's a pretence that he don't get them! If he likes society, and his profession brings him into contact with all ranks, so does mine, too, sir. If it's a little against a barrister to have a waiter for his father, sir, it's a little against a waiter to have a barrister for a son: many people consider it a great liberty, sir, I assure you, sir. Can I get you anything else, sir?

CRAMPTON. No, thank you. (With bitter humility.) I suppose that's no objection to my sitting here for a while: I can't disturb the party on the beach here.

WAITER (with emotion). Very kind of you, sir, to put it as if it was not a compliment and an honour to us, Mr. Crampton, very kind indeed. The more you are at home here, sir, the better for us.

CRAMPTON (in poignant irony). Home!

WAITER (reflectively). Well, yes, sir: that's a way of looking at it, too, sir. I have always said that the great advantage of a hotel is that it's a refuge from home life, sir.

CRAMPTON. I missed that advantage to-day, I think.

WAITER. You did, sir, you did. Dear me! It's the unexpected that always happens, isn't it? (Shaking his head.) You never can tell, sir: you never can tell. (He goes into the hotel.)

CRAMPTON (his eyes shining hardly as he props his drawn, miserable face on his hands). Home! Home!! (He drops his arms on the table and bows his head on them, but presently hears someone approaching and hastily sits bolt upright. It is Gloria, who has come up the steps alone, with her sunshade and her book in her hands. He looks defiantly at her, with the brutal obstinacy of his mouth and the wistfulness of his eyes contradicting each other pathetically. She comes to the corner of the garden seat and stands with her back to it, leaning against the end of it, and looking down at him as if wondering at his weakness: too curious about him to be cold, but supremely indifferent to their kinship.) Well?

GLORIA. I want to speak with you for a moment.

CRAMPTON (looking steadily at her). Indeed? That's surprising. You meet your father after eighteen years; and you actually want to speak to him for a moment! That's touching: isn't it? (He rests his head on his hands, and looks down and away from her, in gloomy reflection.)

GLORIA. All that is what seems to me so nonsensical, so uncalled for. What do you expect us to feel for you—to do for you? What is it you want? Why are you less civil to us than other people are? You are evidently not very fond of us—why should you be? But surely we can meet without quarrelling.

CRAMPTON (a dreadful grey shade passing over his face). Do you realize that I am your father?

GLORIA. Perfectly.

CRAMPTON. Do you know what is due to me as your father?

GLORIA. For instance—-?

CRAMPTON (rising as if to combat a monster). For instance! For instance!! For instance, duty, affection, respect, obedience—

GLORIA (quitting her careless leaning attitude and confronting him promptly and proudly). I obey nothing but my sense of what is right. I respect nothing that is not noble. That is my duty. (She adds, less firmly) As to affection, it is not within my control. I am not sure that I quite know what affection means. (She turns away with an evident distaste for that part of the subject, and goes to the luncheon table for a comfortable chair, putting down her book and sunshade.)

CRAMPTON (following her with his eyes). Do you really mean what you are saying?

GLORIA (turning on him quickly and severely). Excuse me: that is an uncivil question. I am speaking seriously to you; and I expect you to take me seriously. (She takes one of the luncheon chairs; turns it away from the table; and sits down a little wearily, saying) Can you not discuss this matter coolly and rationally?

CRAMPTON. Coolly and rationally! No, I can't. Do you understand that? I can't.

GLORIA (emphatically). No. That I c a n n o t understand. I have no sympathy with—

CRAMPTON (shrinking nervously). Stop! Don't say anything more yet; you don't know what you're doing. Do you want to drive me mad? (She frowns, finding such petulance intolerable. He adds hastily) No: I'm not angry: indeed I'm not. Wait, wait: give me a little time to think. (He stands for a moment, screwing and clinching his brows and hands in his perplexity; then takes the end chair from the luncheon table and sits down beside her, saying, with a touching effort to be gentle and patient) Now, I think I have it. At least I'll try.

GLORIA (firmly). You see! Everything comes right if we only think it resolutely out.

CRAMPTON (in sudden dread). No: don't think. I want you to feel: that's the only thing that can help us. Listen! Do you—but first—I forgot. What's your name? I mean you pet name. They can't very well call you Sophronia.

GLORIA (with astonished disgust). Sophronia! My name is Gloria. I am always called by it.

CRAMPTON (his temper rising again). Your name is Sophronia, girl: you were called after your aunt Sophronia, my sister: she gave you your first Bible with your name written in it.

GLORIA. Then my mother gave me a new name.

CRAMPTON (angrily). She had no right to do it. I will not allow this.

GLORIA. You had no right to give me your sister's name. I don't know her.

CRAMPTON. You're talking nonsense. There are bounds to what I will put up with. I will not have it. Do you hear that?

GLORIA (rising warningly). Are you resolved to quarrel?

CRAMPTON (terrified, pleading). No, no: sit down. Sit down, won't you? (She looks at him, keeping him in suspense. He forces himself to utter the obnoxious name.) Gloria. (She marks her satisfaction with a slight tightening of the lips, and sits down.) There! You see I only want to shew you that I am your father, my—my dear child. (The endearment is so plaintively inept that she smiles in spite of herself, and resigns herself to indulge him a little.) Listen now. What I want to ask you is this. Don't you remember me at all? You were only a tiny child when you were taken away from me; but you took plenty of notice of things. Can't you remember someone whom you loved, or (shyly) at least liked in a childish way? Come! someone who let you stay in his study and look at his toy boats, as you thought them? (He looks anxiously into her face for some response, and continues less hopefully and more urgently) Someone who let you do as you liked there and never said a word to you except to tell you that you must sit still and not speak? Someone who was something that no one else was to you—who was your father.

GLORIA (unmoved). If you describe things to me, no doubt I shall presently imagine that I remember them. But I really remember nothing.

CRAMPTON (wistfully). Has your mother never told you anything about me?

GLORIA. She has never mentioned your name to me. (He groans involuntarily. She looks at him rather contemptuously and continues) Except once; and then she did remind me of something I had forgotten.

CRAMPTON (looking up hopefully). What was that?

GLORIA (mercilessly). The whip you bought to beat me with.

CRAMPTON (gnashing his teeth). Oh! To bring that up against me! To turn from me! When you need never have known. (Under a grinding, agonized breath.) Curse her!

GLORIA (springing up). You wretch! (With intense emphasis.) You wretch!! You dare curse my mother!

CRAMPTON. Stop; or you'll be sorry afterwards. I'm your father.

GLORIA. How I hate the name! How I love the name of mother! You had better go.

CRAMPTON. I—I'm choking. You want to kill me. Some—I— (His voice stifles: he is almost in a fit.)

GLORIA (going up to the balustrade with cool, quick resourcefulness, and calling over to the beach). Mr. Valentine!

VALENTINE (answering from below). Yes.

GLORIA. Come here a moment, please. Mr. Crampton wants you. (She returns to the table and pours out a glass of water.)

CRAMPTON (recovering his speech). No: let me alone. I don't want him. I'm all right, I tell you. I need neither his help nor yours. (He rises and pulls himself together.) As you say, I had better go. (He puts on his hat.) Is that your last word?

GLORIA. I hope so. (He looks stubbornly at her for a moment; nods grimly, as if he agreed to that; and goes into the hotel. She looks at him with equal steadiness until he disappears, when she makes a gesture of relief, and turns to speak to Valentine, who comes running up the steps.)

VALENTINE (panting). What's the matter? (Looking round.) Where's Crampton?

GLORIA. Gone. (Valentine's face lights up with sudden joy, dread, and mischief. He has just realized that he is alone with Gloria. She continues indifferently) I thought he was ill; but he recovered himself. He wouldn't wait for you. I am sorry. (She goes for her book and parasol.)

VALENTINE. So much the better. He gets on my nerves after a while. (Pretending to forget himself.) How could that man have so beautiful a daughter!

GLORIA (taken aback for a moment; then answering him with polite but intentional contempt). That seems to be an attempt at what is called a pretty speech. Let me say at once, Mr. Valentine, that pretty speeches make very sickly conversation. Pray let us be friends, if we are to be friends, in a sensible and wholesome way. I have no intention of getting married; and unless you are content to accept that state of things, we had much better not cultivate each other's acquaintance.

VALENTINE (cautiously). I see. May I ask just this one question? Is your objection an objection to marriage as an institution, or merely an objection to marrying me personally?

GLORIA. I do not know you well enough, Mr. Valentine, to have any opinion on the subject of your personal merits. (She turns away from him with infinite indifference, and sits down with her book on the garden seat.) I do not think the conditions of marriage at present are such as any self-respecting woman can accept.

VALENTINE (instantly changing his tone for one of cordial sincerity, as if he frankly accepted her terms and was delighted and reassured by her principles). Oh, then that's a point of sympathy between us already. I quite agree with you: the conditions are most unfair. (He takes off his hat and throws it gaily on the iron table.) No: what I want is to get rid of all that nonsense. (He sits down beside her, so naturally that she does not think of objecting, and proceeds, with enthusiasm) Don't you think it a horrible thing that a man and a woman can hardly know one another without being supposed to have designs of that kind? As if there were no other interests—no other subjects of conversation—as if women were capable of nothing better!

GLORIA (interested). Ah, now you are beginning to talk humanly and sensibly, Mr. Valentine.

VALENTINE (with a gleam in his eye at the success of his hunter's guile). Of course!—two intelligent people like us. Isn't it pleasant, in this stupid, convention-ridden world, to meet with someone on the same plane—someone with an unprejudiced, enlightened mind?

GLORIA (earnestly). I hope to meet many such people in England.

VALENTINE (dubiously). Hm! There are a good many people here— nearly forty millions. They're not all consumptive members of the highly educated classes like the people in Madeira.

GLORIA (now full of her subject). Oh, everybody is stupid and prejudiced in Madeira—weak, sentimental creatures! I hate weakness; and I hate sentiment.

VALENTINE. That's what makes you so inspiring.

GLORIA (with a slight laugh). Am I inspiring?

VALENTINE Yes. Strength's infectious.

GLORIA. Weakness is, I know.

VALENTINE (with conviction). Y o u're strong. Do you know that you changed the world for me this morning? I was in the dumps, thinking of my unpaid rent, frightened about the future. When you came in, I was dazzled. (Her brow clouds a little. He goes on quickly.) That was silly, of course; but really and truly something happened to me. Explain it how you will, my blood got— (he hesitates, trying to think of a sufficiently unimpassioned word) —oxygenated:

my muscles braced; my mind cleared; my courage rose. That's odd, isn't it? considering that I am not at all a sentimental man.

GLORIA (uneasily, rising). Let us go back to the beach.

VALENTINE (darkly—looking up at her). What! you feel it, too?

GLORIA. Feel what?

VALENTINE. Dread.

GLORIA. Dread!

VALENTINE. As if something were going to happen. It came over me suddenly just before you proposed that we should run away to the others.

GLORIA (amazed). That's strange—very strange! I had the same presentiment.

VALENTINE. How extraordinary! (Rising.) Well: shall we run away?

GLORIA. Run away! Oh, no: that would be childish. (She sits down again. He resumes his seat beside her, and watches her with a gravely sympathetic air. She is thoughtful and a little troubled as she adds) I wonder what is the scientific explanation of those fancies that cross us occasionally!

VALENTINE. Ah, I wonder! It's a curiously helpless sensation: isn't it?

GLORIA (rebelling against the word). Helpless?

VALENTINE. Yes. As if Nature, after allowing us to belong to ourselves and do what we judged right and reasonable for all these years, were suddenly lifting her great hand to take us—her two little children—by the scruff's of our little necks, and use us, in spite of ourselves, for her own purposes, in her own way.

GLORIA. Isn't that rather fanciful?

VALENTINE (with a new and startling transition to a tone of utter recklessness). I don't know. I don't care. (Bursting out reproachfully.) Oh, Miss Clandon, Miss Clandon: how could you?

GLORIA. What have I done?

VALENTINE. Thrown this enchantment on me. I'm honestly trying to be sensible—scientific—everything that you wish me to be. But—but— oh, don't you see what you have set to work in my imagination?

GLORIA (with indignant, scornful sternness). I hope you are not going to be so foolish—so vulgar—as to say love.

VALENTINE (with ironical haste to disclaim such a weakness). No, no, no. Not love: we know better than that. Let's call it chemistry. You can't deny that there is such a thing as chemical action, chemical affinity, chemical combination—the most irresistible of all natural forces. Well, you're attracting me irresistibly—chemically.

GLORIA (contemptuously). Nonsense!

VALENTINE. Of course it's nonsense, you stupid girl. (Gloria recoils in outraged surprise.) Yes, stupid girl: t h a t's a scientific fact, anyhow. You're a prig—a feminine prig: that's what you are. (Rising.) Now I suppose you've done with me for ever. (He goes to the iron table and takes up his hat.)

GLORIA (with elaborate calm, sitting up like a High-school-mistress posing to be photographed). That shows how very little you understand my real character. I am not in the least offended. (He pauses and puts his hat down again.) I am always willing to be told of my own defects, Mr. Valentine, by my friends, even when they are as absurdly mistaken about me as you are. I have many faults—very serious faults—of character and temper; but if there is one thing that I am not, it is what you call a prig. (She closes her lips trimly and looks steadily and challengingly at him as she sits more collectedly than ever.)

VALENTINE (returning to the end of the garden seat to confront her more emphatically). Oh, yes, you are. My reason tells me so: my knowledge tells me so: my experience tells me so.

GLORIA. Excuse my reminding you that your reason and your knowledge and your experience are not infallible. At least I hope not.

VALENTINE. I must believe them. Unless you wish me to believe my eyes, my heart, my instincts, my imagination, which are all telling me the most monstrous lies about you.

GLORIA (the collectedness beginning to relax). Lies!

VALENTINE (obstinately). Yes, lies. (He sits down again beside her.) Do you expect me to believe that you are the most beautiful woman in the world?

GLORIA. That is ridiculous, and rather personal.

VALENTINE. Of course it's ridiculous. Well, that's what my eyes tell me. (Gloria makes a movement of contemptuous protest.) No: I'm not flattering. I tell you I don't believe it. (She is ashamed to find that this does not quite please her either.) Do you think that if you were to turn away in disgust from my weakness, I should sit down here and cry like a child?

GLORIA (beginning to find that she must speak shortly and pointedly to keep her voice steady). Why should you, pray?

VALENTINE (with a stir of feeling beginning to agitate his voice). Of course not: I'm not such an idiot. And yet my heart tells me I should—my fool of a heart. But I'll argue with my heart and bring it to reason. If I loved you a thousand times, I'll force myself to look the truth steadily in the face. After all, it's easy to be sensible: the facts are the facts. What's this place? it's not heaven: it's the Marine Hotel. What's the time? it's not eternity: it's about half past one in the afternoon. What am I? a dentist—a five shilling dentist!

GLORIA. And I am a feminine prig.

VALENTINE. (passionately). No, no: I can't face that: I must have one illusion left—the illusion about you. I love you. (He turns towards her as if the impulse to touch her were ungovernable: she rises and stands on her guard wrathfully. He springs up impatiently and retreats a step.) Oh, what a fool I am!—an idiot! You don't understand: I might as well talk to the stones on the beach. (He turns away, discouraged.)

GLORIA (reassured by his withdrawal, and a little remorseful). I am sorry. I do not mean to be unsympathetic, Mr. Valentine; but what can I say?

VALENTINE (returning to her with all his recklessness of manner replaced by an engaging and chivalrous respect). You can say nothing, Miss Clandon. I beg your pardon: it was my own fault, or rather my own bad luck. You see, it all depended on your naturally liking me. (She is about to speak: he stops her deprecatingly.) Oh, I know you mustn't tell me whether you like me or not; but—

GLORIA (her principles up in arms at once). Must not! Why not? I am a free woman: why should I not tell you?

VALENTINE (pleading in terror, and retreating). Don't. I'm afraid to hear.

GLORIA (no longer scornful). You need not be afraid. I think you are sentimental, and a little foolish; but I like you.

VALENTINE (dropping into the iron chair as if crushed). Then it's all over. (He becomes the picture of despair.)

GLORIA (puzzled, approaching him). But why?

VALENTINE. Because liking is not enough. Now that I think down into it seriously, I don't know whether I like you or not.

GLORIA (looking down at him with wondering concern). I'm sorry.

VALENTINE (in an agony of restrained passion). Oh, don't pity me. Your voice is tearing my heart to pieces. Let me alone, Gloria. You go down into the very depths of me, troubling and stirring me—I can't struggle with it—I can't tell you—

GLORIA (breaking down suddenly). Oh, stop telling me what you feel: I can't bear it.

VALENTINE (springing up triumphantly, the agonized voice now solid, ringing, and jubilant). Ah, it's come at last—my moment of courage. (He seizes her hands: she looks at him in terror.) Our moment of courage! (He draws her to him; kisses her with impetuous strength; and laughs boyishly.) Now you've done it, Gloria. It's all over: we're in love with one another. (She can only gasp at him.) But what a dragon you were! And how hideously afraid I was!

PHILIP'S VOICE (calling from the beach). Valentine!

DOLLY'S VOICE. Mr. Valentine!

VALENTINE. Good-bye. Forgive me. (He rapidly kisses her hands, and runs away to the steps, where he meets Mrs. Clandon, ascending. Gloria, quite lost, can only start after him.)

MRS. CLANDON. The children want you, Mr. Valentine. (She looks anxiously around.) Is he gone?

VALENTINE (puzzled). He? (Recollecting.) Oh, Crampton. Gone this long time, Mrs. Clandon. (He runs off buoyantly down the steps.)

GLORIA (sinking upon the seat). Mother!

MRS. CLANDON (hurrying to her in alarm). What is it, dear?

GLORIA (with heartfelt, appealing reproach). Why didn't you educate me properly?

MRS. CLANDON (amazed). My child: I did my best.

GLORIA. Oh, you taught me nothing—nothing.

MRS. CLANDON. What is the matter with you?

GLORIA (with the most intense expression). Only shame—shame— shame. (Blushing unendurably, she covers her face with her hands and turns away from her mother.)

END OF ACT II.

ACT III

The Clandon's sitting room in the hotel. An expensive apartment on the ground floor, with a French window leading to the gardens. In the centre of the room is a substantial table, surrounded by chairs, and draped with a maroon cloth on which opulently bound hotel and railway guides are displayed. A visitor entering through the window and coming down to this central table would have the fireplace on his left, and a writing table against the wall on his right, next the door, which is further down. He would, if his taste lay that way, admire the wall decoration of Lincrusta Walton in plum color and bronze lacquer, with dado and cornice; the ormolu consoles in the corners; the vases on pillar pedestals of veined marble with bases of polished black wood, one on each side of the window; the ornamental cabinet next the vase on the side nearest the fireplace, its centre compartment closed by an inlaid door, and its corners rounded off with curved panes of glass protecting shelves of cheap blue and white pottery; the bamboo tea table, with folding shelves, in the corresponding space on the other side of the window; the pictures of ocean steamers and Landseer's dogs; the saddlebag ottoman in line with the door but on the other side of the room; the two comfortable seats of the same pattern on the hearthrug; and finally, on turning round and looking up, the massive brass pole above the window, sustaining a pair of maroon rep curtains with decorated borders of staid green. Altogether, a room well arranged to flatter the occupant's sense of importance, and reconcile him to a charge of a pound a day for its use.

Mrs. Clandon sits at the writing table, correcting proofs. Gloria is standing at the window, looking out in a tormented revery.

The clock on the mantelpiece strikes five with a sickly clink, the bell being unable to bear up against the black marble cenotaph in which it is immured.

MRS. CLANDON. Five! I don't think we need wait any longer for the children. They are sure to get tea somewhere.

GLORIA (wearily). Shall I ring?

MRS. CLANDON. Do, my dear. (Gloria goes to the hearth and rings.) I have finished these proofs at last, thank goodness!

GLORIA (strolling listlessly across the room and coming behind her mother's chair). What proofs?

MRS. CLANDON The new edition of Twentieth Century Women.

GLORIA (with a bitter smile). There's a chapter missing.

MRS. CLANDON (beginning to hunt among her proofs). Is there? Surely not.

GLORIA. I mean an unwritten one. Perhaps I shall write it for you—when I know the end of it. (She goes back to the window.)

MRS. CLANDON. Gloria! More enigmas!

GLORIA. Oh, no. The same enigma.

MRS. CLANDON (puzzled and rather troubled; after watching her for a moment). My dear.

GLORIA (returning). Yes.

MRS. CLANDON. You know I never ask questions.

GLORIA (kneeling beside her chair). I know, I know. (She suddenly throws her arms about her mother and embraces her almost passionately.)

MRS. CLANDON. (gently, smiling but embarrassed). My dear: you are getting quite sentimental.

GLORIA (recoiling). Ah, no, no. Oh, don't say that. Oh! (She rises and turns away with a gesture as if tearing herself.)

MRS. CLANDON (mildly). My dear: what is the matter? What— (The waiter enters with the tea tray.)

WAITER (balmily). This was what you rang for, ma'am, I hope?

MRS. CLANDON. Thank you, yes. (She turns her chair away from the writing table, and sits down again. Gloria crosses to the hearth and sits crouching there with her face averted.)

WAITER (placing the tray temporarily on the centre table). I thought so, ma'am. Curious how the nerves seem to give out in the afternoon without a cup of tea. (He fetches the tea table and places it in front of Mrs. Cladon, conversing meanwhile.) the young lady and gentleman have just come back, ma'am: they have been out in a boat, ma'am. Very pleasant on a fine afternoon like this—very pleasant and invigorating indeed. (He takes the tray from the centre table and puts it on the tea table.) Mr. McComas will not come to tea, ma'am: he has gone to call upon Mr. Crampton. (He takes a couple of chairs and sets one at each end of the tea table.)

GLORIA (looking round with an impulse of terror). And the other gentleman?

WAITER (reassuringly, as he unconsciously drops for a moment into the measure of "I've been roaming," which he sang as a boy.) Oh, he's coming, miss, he's coming. He has been rowing the boat, miss, and has just run down the road to the chemist's for something to put on the blisters. But he will be here directly, miss—directly. (Gloria, in ungovernable apprehension, rises and hurries towards the door.)

MRS. CLANDON. (half rising). Glo— (Gloria goes out. Mrs. Clandon looks perplexedly at the waiter, whose composure is unruffled.)

WAITER (cheerfully). Anything more, ma'am?

MRS. CLANDON. Nothing, thank you.

WAITER. Thank you, ma'am. (As he withdraws, Phil and Dolly, in the highest spirits, come tearing in. He holds the door open for them; then goes out and closes it.)

DOLLY (ravenously). Oh, give me some tea. (Mrs. Clandon pours out a cup for her.) We've been out in a boat. Valentine will be here presently.

PHILIP. He is unaccustomed to navigation. Where's Gloria?

MRS. CLANDON (anxiously, as she pours out his tea). Phil: there is something the matter with Gloria. Has anything happened? (Phil and Dolly look at one another and stifle a laugh.) What is it?

PHILIP (sitting down on her left). Romeo—

DOLLY (sitting down on her right). —and Juliet.

PHILIP (taking his cup of tea from Mrs. Clandon). Yes, my dear mother: the old, old story. Dolly: don't take all the milk. (He deftly takes the jug from her.) Yes: in the spring—

DOLLY. —a young man's fancy—

PHILIP. —lightly turns to—thank you (to Mrs. Clandon, who has passed the biscuits) —thoughts of love. It also occurs in the autumn. The young man in this case is—

DOLLY. Valentine.

PHILIP. And his fancy has turned to Gloria to the extent of—

DOLLY. —kissing her—

PHILIP. —on the terrace—

DOLLY (correcting him). —on the lips, before everybody.

MRS. CLANDON (incredulously). Phil! Dolly! Are you joking? (They shake their heads.) Did she allow it?

PHILIP. We waited to see him struck to earth by the lightning of her scorn;—

DOLLY. —but he wasn't.

PHILIP. She appeared to like it.

DOLLY. As far as we could judge. (Stopping Phil, who is about to pour out another cup.) No: you've sworn off two cups.

MRS. CLANDON (much troubled). Children: you must not be here when Mr. Valentine comes. I must speak very seriously to him about this.

PHILIP. To ask him his intentions? What a violation of Twentieth Century principles!

DOLLY. Quite right, mamma: bring him to book. Make the most of the nineteenth century while it lasts.

PHILIP. Sh! Here he is. (Valentine comes in.)

VALENTINE Very sorry to be late for tea, Mrs. Clandon. (She takes up the tea-pot.) No, thank you: I never take any. No doubt Miss Dolly and Phil have explained what happened to me.

PHILIP (momentously rising). Yes, Valentine: we have explained.

DOLLY (significantly, also rising). We have explained very thoroughly.

PHILIP. It was our duty. (Very seriously.) Come, Dolly. (He offers Dolly his arm, which she takes. They look sadly at him, and go out gravely, arm in arm. Valentine stares after them, puzzled; then looks at Mrs. Clandon for an explanation.)

MRS. CLANDON (rising and leaving the tea table). Will you sit down, Mr. Valentine. I want to speak to you a little, if you will allow me. (Valentine sits down slowly on the ottoman, his conscience presaging a bad quarter of an hour. Mrs. Clandon takes Phil's chair, and seats herself deliberately at a convenient distance from him.) I must begin by throwing myself somewhat at your consideration. I am going to speak of a subject of which I know very little—perhaps nothing. I mean love.

VALENTINE. Love!

MRS. CLANDON. Yes, love. Oh, you need not look so alarmed as that, Mr. Valentine: I am not in love with you.

VALENTINE (overwhelmed). Oh, really, Mrs.— (Recovering himself.) I should be only too proud if you were.

MRS. CLANDON. Thank you, Mr. Valentine. But I am too old to begin.

VALENTINE. Begin! Have you never—?

MRS. CLANDON. Never. My case is a very common one, Mr. Valentine. I married before I was old enough to know what I was doing. As you have seen for yourself, the result was a bitter disappointment for both my husband and myself. So you see, though I am a married woman, I have never been in love; I have never had a love affair; and to be quite frank with you, Mr. Valentine, what I have seen of the love affairs of other people has not led me to regret that deficiency in my experience. (Valentine, looking very glum, glances sceptically at her, and says nothing. Her color rises a little; and she adds, with restrained anger) You do not believe me?

VALENTINE (confused at having his thought read). Oh, why not? Why not?

MRS. CLANDON. Let me tell you, Mr. Valentine, that a life devoted to the Cause of Humanity has enthusiasms and passions to offer which far transcend the selfish personal infatuations and sentimentalities of romance. Those are not your enthusiasms and passions, I take it? (Valentine, quite aware that she despises him for it, answers in the negative with a melancholy shake of the head.) I thought not. Well, I am equally at a disadvantage in discussing those so-called affairs of the heart in which you appear to be an expert.

VALENTINE (restlessly). What are you driving at, Mrs. Clandon?

MRS. CLANDON. I think you know.

VALENTINE. Gloria?

MRS. CLANDON. Yes. Gloria.

VALENTINE (surrendering). Well, yes: I'm in love with Gloria. (Interposing as she is about to speak.) I know what you're going to say: I've no money.

MRS. CLANDON. I care very little about money, Mr. Valentine.

VALENTINE. Then you're very different to all the other mothers who have interviewed me.

MRS. CLANDON. Ah, now we are coming to it, Mr. Valentine. You are an old hand at this. (He opens his mouth to protest: she cuts him short with some indignation.) Oh, do you think, little as I understand these matters, that I have not common sense enough to know that a man who could make as much way in one interview with such a woman as my daughter, can hardly be a novice!

VALENTINE. I assure you—

MRS. CLANDON (stopping him). I am not blaming you, Mr. Valentine. It is Gloria's business to take care of herself; and you have a right to amuse yourself as you please. But—

VALENTINE (protesting). Amuse myself! Oh, Mrs. Clandon!

MRS. CLANDON (relentlessly). On your honor, Mr. Valentine, are you in earnest?

VALENTINE (desperately). On my honor I am in earnest. (She looks searchingly at him. His sense of humor gets the better of him; and he adds quaintly) Only, I always have been in earnest; and yet—here I am, you see!

MRS. CLANDON. This is just what I suspected. (Severely.) Mr. Valentine: you are one of those men who play with women's affections.

VALENTINE. Well, why not, if the Cause of Humanity is the only thing worth being serious about? However, I understand. (Rising and taking his hat with formal politeness.) You wish me to discontinue my visits.

MRS. CLANDON. No: I am sensible enough to be well aware that Gloria's best chance of escape from you now is to become better acquainted with you.

VALENTINE (unaffectedly alarmed). Oh, don't say that, Mrs. Clandon. You don't think that, do you?

MRS. CLANDON. I have great faith, Mr. Valentine, in the sound training Gloria's mind has had since she was a child.

VALENTINE (amazingly relieved). O-oh! Oh, that's all right. (He sits down again and throws his hat flippantly aside with the air of a man who has no longer anything to fear.)

MRS. CLANDON (indignant at his assurance). What do you mean?

VALENTINE (turning confidentially to her). Come: shall I teach you something, Mrs. Clandon?

MRS. CLANDON (stiffly). I am always willing to learn.

VALENTINE. Have you ever studied the subject of gunnery—artillery—cannons and war-ships and so on?

MRS. CLANDON. Has gunnery anything to do with Gloria?

VALENTINE. A great deal—by way of illustration. During this whole century, my dear Mrs. Clandon, the progress of artillery has been a duel between the maker of cannons and the maker of armor plates to keep the cannon balls out. You build a ship proof against the best gun known: somebody makes a better gun and sinks your ship. You build a heavier ship, proof against that gun: somebody makes a heavier gun and sinks you again. And so on. Well, the duel of sex is just like that.

MRS. CLANDON. The duel of sex!

VALENTINE. Yes: you've heard of the duel of sex, haven't you? Oh, I forgot: you've been in Madeira: the expression has come up since your time. Need I explain it?

MRS. CLANDON (contemptuously). No.

VALENTINE. Of course not. Now what happens in the duel of sex? The old fashioned mother received an old fashioned education to protect her against the wiles of man. Well, you know the result: the old fashioned man got round her. The old fashioned woman resolved to protect her daughter more effectually—to find some armor too strong for the old fashioned man. So she gave her daughter a scientific education—your plan. That was a corker for the old fashioned man: he said it wasn't fair—unwomanly and all the rest of it. But that didn't do him any good. So he had to give up his old fashioned plan of attack—you know—going down on his knees and swearing to love, honor and obey, and so on.

MRS. CLANDON. Excuse me: that was what the woman swore.

VALENTINE. Was it? Ah, perhaps you're right—yes: of course it was. Well, what did the man do?

Just what the artillery man does— went one better than the woman—educated himself scientifically and beat her at that game just as he had beaten her at the old game. I learnt how to circumvent the Women's Rights woman before I was twenty- three: it's all been found out long ago. You see, my methods are thoroughly modern.

MRS. CLANDON (with quiet disgust). No doubt.

VALENTINE. But for that very reason there's one sort of girl against whom they are of no use.

MRS. CLANDON. Pray which sort?

VALENTINE. The thoroughly old fashioned girl. If you had brought up Gloria in the old way, it would have taken me eighteen months to get to the point I got to this afternoon in eighteen minutes. Yes, Mrs. Clandon: the Higher Education of Women delivered Gloria into my hands; and it was you who taught her to believe in the Higher Education of Women.

MRS. CLANDON (rising). Mr. Valentine: you are very clever.

VALENTINE (rising also). Oh, Mrs. Clandon!

MRS. CLANDON And you have taught me n o t h i n g. Good-bye.

VALENTINE (horrified). Good-bye! Oh, mayn't I see her before I go?

MRS. CLANDON. I am afraid she will not return until you have gone Mr. Valentine. She left the room expressly to avoid you.

VALENTINE (thoughtfully). That's a good sign. Good-bye. (He bows and makes for the door, apparently well satisfied.)

MRS. CLANDON (alarmed). Why do you think it a good sign?

VALENTINE (turning near the door). Because I am mortally afraid of her; and it looks as if she were mortally afraid of me. (He turns to go and finds himself face to face with Gloria, who has just entered. She looks steadfastly at him. He stares helplessly at her; then round at Mrs. Clandon; then at Gloria again, completely at a loss.)

GLORIA (white, and controlling herself with difficulty). Mother: is what Dolly told me true?

MRS. CLANDON. What did she tell you, dear?

GLORIA. That you have been speaking about me to this gentleman.

VALENTINE (murmuring). This gentleman! Oh!

MRS. CLANDON (sharply). Mr. Valentine: can you hold your tongue for a moment? (He looks piteously at them; then, with a despairing shrug, goes back to the ottoman and throws his hat on it.)

GLORIA (confronting her mother, with deep reproach). Mother: what right had you to do it?

MRS. CLANDON. I don't think I have said anything I have no right to say, Gloria.

VALENTINE (confirming her officiously). Nothing. Nothing whatever. (Gloria looks at him with unspeakable indignation.) I beg your pardon. (He sits down ignominiously on the ottoman.)

GLORIA. I cannot believe that any one has any right even to think about things that concern me only. (She turns away from them to conceal a painful struggle with her emotion.)

MRS. CLANDON. My dear, if I have wounded your pride—

GLORIA (turning on them for a moment). My p r i d e! My pride!! Oh, it's gone: I have learnt now that I have no strength to be proud of. (Turning away again.) But if a woman cannot protect herself, no one can protect her. No one has any right to try—not even her mother. I know I have lost your confidence, just as I have lost this man's respect;— (She stops to master a sob.)

VALENTINE (under his breath). This man! (Murmuring again.) Oh!

MRS. CLANDON (in an undertone). Pray be silent, sir.

GLORIA (continuing). —but I have at least the right to be left alone in my disgrace. I am one of those weak creatures born to be mastered by the first man whose eye is caught by them; and I must fulfill my destiny, I suppose. At least spare me the humiliation of trying to save me. (She sits down, with her handkerchief to her eyes, at the farther end of the table.)

VALENTINE (jumping up). Look here—

MRS. CLANDON. Mr. Va—

VALENTINE (recklessly). No: I will speak: I've been silent for nearly thirty seconds. (He goes up to Gloria.) Miss Clandon—

GLORIA (bitterly). Oh, not Miss Clandon: you have found that it is quite safe to call me Gloria.

VALENTINE. No, I won't: you'll throw it in my teeth afterwards and accuse me of disrespect. I say it's a heartbreaking falsehood that I don't respect you. It's true that I didn't respect your old pride: why should I? It was nothing but cowardice. I didn't respect your intellect: I've a better one myself: it's a masculine specialty. But when the depths stirred!—when my moment came!—when you made me brave!—ah, then, then, t h e n!

GLORIA. Then you respected me, I suppose.

VALENTINE. No, I didn't: I adored you. (She rises quickly and turns her back on him.) And you can never take that moment away from me. So now I don't care what happens. (He comes down the room addressing a cheerful explanation to nobody in particular.) I'm perfectly aware that I'm talking nonsense. I can't help it. (To Mrs. Clandon.) I love Gloria; and there's an end of it.

MRS. CLANDON (emphatically). Mr. Valentine: you are a most dangerous man. Gloria: come here. (Gloria, wondering a little at the command, obeys, and stands, with drooping head, on her mother's right hand, Valentine being on the opposite side. Mrs. Clandon then begins, with intense scorn.) Ask this man whom you have inspired and made brave, how many women have inspired him before (Gloria looks up suddenly with a flash of jealous anger and amazement); how many times he has laid the trap in which he has caught you; how often he has baited it with the same speeches; how much practice it has taken to make him perfect in his chosen part in life as the Duellist of Sex.

VALENTINE. This isn't fair. You're abusing my confidence, Mrs. Clandon.

MRS. CLANDON. Ask him, Gloria.

GLORIA (in a flush of rage, going over to him with her fists clenched). Is that true?

VALENTINE. Don't be angry—

GLORIA (interrupting him implacably). Is it true? Did you ever say that before? Did you ever feel that before—for another woman?

VALENTINE (bluntly). Yes. (Gloria raises her clenched hands.)

MRS. CLANDON (horrified, springing to her side and catching her uplifted arm). Gloria!! My dear! You're forgetting yourself. (Gloria, with a deep expiration, slowly relaxes her threatening attitude.)

VALENTINE. Remember: a man's power of love and admiration is like any other of his powers: he has to throw it away many times before he learns what is really worthy of it.

MRS. CLANDON. Another of the old speeches, Gloria. Take care.

VALENTINE (remonstrating). Oh!

GLORIA (to Mrs. Clandon, with contemptuous self-possession). Do you think I need to be warned now? (To Valentine.) You have tried to make me love you.

VALENTINE. I have.

GLORIA. Well, you have succeeded in making me hate you— passionately.

VALENTINE (philosophically). It's surprising how little difference there is between the two. (Gloria turns indignantly away from him. He continues, to Mrs. Clandon) I know men whose wives love them; and they go on exactly like that.

MRS. CLANDON. Excuse me, Mr. Valentine; but had you not better go?

GLORIA. You need not send him away on my account, mother. He is nothing to me now; and he will amuse Dolly and Phil. (She sits down with slighting indifference, at the end of the table nearest the window.)

VALENTINE (gaily). Of course: that's the sensible way of looking at it. Come, Mrs. Clandon: you can't quarrel with a mere butterfly like me.

MRS. CLANDON. I very greatly mistrust you, Mr. Valentine. But I do not like to think that your unfortunate levity of disposition is mere shamelessness and worthlessness;—

GLORIA (to herself, but aloud). It is shameless; and it is worthless.

MRS. CLANDON. —so perhaps we had better send for Phil and Dolly and allow you to end your visit in the ordinary way.

VALENTINE (as if she had paid him the highest compliment). You overwhelm me, Mrs. Clandon. Thank you. (The waiter enters.)

WAITER. Mr. McComas, ma'am.

MRS. CLANDON. Oh, certainly. Bring him in.

WAITER. He wishes to see you in the reception-room, ma'am.

MRS. CLANDON. Why not here?

WAITER. Well, if you will excuse my mentioning it, ma'am, I think Mr. McComas feels that he would get fairer play if he could speak to you away from the younger members of your family, ma'am.

MRS. CLANDON. Tell him they are not here.

WAITER. They are within sight of the door, ma'am; and very watchful, for some reason or other.

MRS. CLANDON (going). Oh, very well: I'll go to him.

WAITER (holding the door open for her). Thank you, ma'am. (She goes out. He comes back into the room, and meets the eye of Valentine, who wants him to go.) All right, sir. Only the tea-things, sir. (Taking the tray.) Excuse me, sir. Thank you sir. (He goes out.)

VALENTINE (to Gloria). Look here. You will forgive me, sooner or later. Forgive me now.

GLORIA (rising to level the declaration more intensely at him). Never! While grass grows or water runs, never, never, never!!!

VALENTINE (unabashed). Well, I don't care. I can't be unhappy about anything. I shall never be unhappy again, never, never, never, while grass grows or water runs. The thought of you will always make me wild with joy. (Some quick taunt is on her lips: he interposes swiftly.) No: I never said that before: that's new.

GLORIA. It will not be new when you say it to the next woman.

VALENTINE. Oh, don't, Gloria, don't. (He kneels at her feet.)

GLORIA. Get up. Get up! How dare you? (Phil and Dolly, racing, as usual, for first place, burst into the room. They check themselves on seeing what is passing. Valentine springs up.)

PHILIP (discreetly). I beg your pardon. Come, Dolly. (He turns to go.)

GLORIA (annoyed). Mother will be back in a moment, Phil. (Severely.) Please wait here for her. (She turns away to the window, where she stands looking out with her back to them.)

PHILIP (significantly). Oh, indeed. Hmhm!

DOLLY. Ahah!

PHILIP. You seem in excellent spirits, Valentine.

VALENTINE. I am. (Comes between them.) Now look here. You both know what's going on, don't you? (Gloria turns quickly, as if anticipating some fresh outrage.)

DOLLY. Perfectly.

VALENTINE. Well, it's all over. I've been refused—scorned. I'm only here on sufferance. You understand: it's all over. Your sister is in no sense entertaining my addresses, or condescending to interest herself in me in any way. (Gloria, satisfied, turns back contemptuously to the window.) Is that clear?

DOLLY. Serve you right. You were in too great a hurry.

PHILIP (patting him on the shoulder). Never mind: you'd never have been able to call your soul your own if she'd married you. You can now begin a new chapter in your life.

DOLLY. Chapter seventeen or thereabouts, I should imagine.

VALENTINE (much put out by this pleasantry). No: don't say things like that. That's just the sort of thoughtless remark that makes a lot of mischief.

DOLLY. Oh, indeed. Hmhm!

PHILIP. Ahah! (He goes to the hearth and plants himself there in his best head-of-the-family attitude.)

McComas, looking very serious, comes in quickly with Mrs. Clandon, whose first anxiety is about Gloria. She looks round to see where she is, and is going to join her at the window when Gloria comes down to meet her with a marked air of trust and affection. Finally, Mrs. Clandon takes her former seat, and Gloria posts herself behind it. McComas, on his way to the ottoman, is hailed by Dolly.

DOLLY. What cheer, Finch?

McCOMAS (sternly). Very serious news from your father, Miss Clandon. Very serious news indeed. (He crosses to the ottoman, and sits down. Dolly, looking deeply impressed, follows him and sits beside him on his right.)

VALENTINE. Perhaps I had better go.

McCOMAS. By no means, Mr. Valentine. You are deeply concerned in this. (Valentine takes a chair from the table and sits astride of it, leaning over the back, near the ottoman.) Mrs. Clandon: your husband demands the custody of his two younger children, who are not of age. (Mrs. Clandon, in quick alarm, looks instinctively to see if Dolly is safe.)

DOLLY (touched). Oh, how nice of him! He likes us, mamma.

McCOMAS. I am sorry to have to disabuse you of any such idea, Miss Dorothea.

DOLLY (cooing ecstatically). Dorothee-ee-ee-a! (Nestling against his shoulder, quite overcome.) Oh, Finch!

McCOMAS (nervously, moving away). No, no, no, no!

MRS. CLANDON (remonstrating). D e a r e s t Dolly! (To McComas.) The deed of separation gives me the custody of the children.

McCOMAS. It also contains a covenant that you are not to approach or molest him in any way.

MRS. CLANDON. Well, have I done so?

McCOMAS. Whether the behavior of your younger children amounts to legal molestation is a question on which it may be necessary to take counsel's opinion. At all events, Mr. Crampton not only claims to have been molested; but he believes that he was brought here by a plot in which Mr. Valentine acted as your agent.

VALENTINE. What's that? Eh?

McCOMAS. He alleges that you drugged him, Mr. Valentine.

VALENTINE. So I did. (They are astonished.)

McCOMAS. But what did you do that for?

DOLLY. Five shillings extra.

McCOMAS (to Dolly, short-temperedly). I must really ask you, Miss Clandon, not to interrupt this very serious conversation with irrelevant interjections. (Vehemently.) I insist on having earnest matters earnestly and reverently discussed. (This outburst produces an apologetic silence, and puts McComas himself out of countenance. He coughs, and starts afresh, addressing himself to Gloria.) Miss Clandon: it is my duty to tell you that your father has also persuaded himself that Mr. Valentine wishes to marry you—

VALENTINE (interposing adroitly). I do.

McCOMAS (offended). In that case, sir, you must not be surprised to find yourself regarded by the young lady's father as a fortune hunter.

VALENTINE. So I am. Do you expect my wife to live on what I earn? ten-pence a week!

McCOMAS (revolted). I have nothing more to say, sir. I shall return and tell Mr. Crampton that this family is no place for a father. (He makes for the door.)

MRS. CLANDON (with quiet authority). Finch! (He halts.) If Mr. Valentine cannot be serious, you can. Sit down. (McComas, after a brief struggle between his dignity and his friendship, succumbs, seating himself this time midway between Dolly and Mrs. Clandon.) You know that all this is a made up case—that Fergus does not believe in it any more than you do. Now give me your real advice—your sincere, friendly advice: you know I have always trusted your judgment. I promise you the children will be quiet.

McCOMAS (resigning himself). Well, well! What I want to say is this. In the old arrangement with your husband, Mrs. Clandon, you had him at a terrible disadvantage.

MRS. CLANDON. How so, pray?

McCOMAS. Well, you were an advanced woman, accustomed to defy public opinion, and with no regard for what the world might say of you.

MRS. CLANDON (proud of it). Yes: that is true. (Gloria, behind the chair, stoops and kisses her mother's hair, a demonstration which disconcerts her extremely.)

McCOMAS. On the other hand, Mrs. Clandon, your husband had a great horror of anything getting into the papers. There was his business to be considered, as well as the prejudices of an old-fashioned family.

MRS. CLANDON. Not to mention his own prejudices.

McCOMAS. Now no doubt he behaved badly, Mrs. Clandon—

MRS. CLANDON (scornfully). No doubt.

McCOMAS. But was it altogether his fault?

MRS. CLANDON. Was it mine?

McCOMAS (hastily). No. Of course not.

GLORIA (observing him attentively). You do not mean that, Mr. McComas.

McCOMAS. My dear young lady, you pick me up very sharply. But let me just put this to you. When a man makes an unsuitable marriage (nobody's fault, you know, but purely accidental incompatibility of tastes); when he is deprived by that misfortune of the domestic sympathy which, I take it, is what a man marries for; when in short, his wife is rather worse than no wife at all (through no fault of his own, of course), is it to be wondered at if he makes matters worse at first by blaming her, and even, in his desperation, by occasionally drinking himself into a violent condition or seeking sympathy elsewhere?

MRS. CLANDON. I did not blame him: I simply rescued myself and the children from him.

McCOMAS. Yes: but you made hard terms, Mrs. Clandon. You had him at your mercy: you brought him to his knees when you threatened to make the matter public by applying to the Courts for a judicial separation. Suppose he had had that power over you, and used it to take your children away from you and bring them up in ignorance of your very name, how would you feel? what would you do? Well, won't you make some allowance for his feelings?—in common humanity.

MRS. CLANDON. I never discovered his feelings. I discovered his temper, and his— (she shivers) the rest of his common humanity.

McCOMAS (wistfully). Women can be very hard, Mrs. Clandon.

VALENTINE. That's true.

GLORIA (angrily). Be silent. (He subsides.)

McCOMAS (rallying all his forces). Let me make one last appeal. Mrs. Clandon: believe me, there are men who have a good deal of feeling, and kind feeling, too, which they are not able to express. What you miss in Crampton is that mere veneer of civilization, the art of shewing worthless attentions and paying insincere compliments in a kindly, charming way. If you lived in London, where the whole system is one of false good-fellowship, and you may know a man for twenty years without finding out that he hates you like poison, you would soon have your eyes opened. There we do unkind things in a kind way: we say bitter things in a sweet voice: we always give our friends chloroform when we tear them to pieces. But think of the other side of it! Think of the people who do kind things in an unkind way—people whose touch hurts, whose voices jar, whose tempers play them false, who wound and worry the people they love in the very act of trying to conciliate them, and yet who need affection as much as the rest of us. Crampton has an abominable temper, I admit. He has no manners, no tact, no grace. He'll never be able to gain anyone's affection unless they will take his desire for it on trust. Is he to have none—not even pity—from his own flesh and blood?

DOLLY (quite melted). Oh, how beautiful, Finch! How nice of you!

PHILIP (with conviction). Finch: this is eloquence—positive eloquence.

DOLLY. Oh, mamma, let us give him another chance. Let us have him to dinner.

MRS. CLANDON (unmoved). No, Dolly: I hardly got any lunch. My dear Finch: there is not the least use in talking to me about Fergus. You have never been married to him: I have.

McCOMAS (to Gloria). Miss Clandon: I have hitherto refrained from appealing to you, because, if what Mr. Crampton told me to be true, you have been more merciless even than your mother.

GLORIA (defiantly). You appeal from her strength to my weakness!

McCOMAS. Not your weakness, Miss Clandon. I appeal from her intellect to your heart.

GLORIA. I have learnt to mistrust my heart. (With an angry glance at Valentine.) I would tear my heart and throw it away if I could. My answer to you is my mother's answer. (She goes to Mrs. Clandon, and stands with her arm about her; but Mrs. Clandon, unable to endure this sort of demonstrativeness, disengages herself as soon as she can without hurting Gloria's feelings.)

McCOMAS (defeated). Well, I am very sorry—very sorry. I have done my best. (He rises and prepares to go, deeply dissatisfied.)

MRS. CLANDON. But what did you expect, Finch? What do you want us to do?

McCOMAS. The first step for both you and Crampton is to obtain counsel's opinion as to whether he is bound by the deed of separation or not. Now why not obtain this opinion at once, and have a friendly meeting (her face hardens)—or shall we say a neutral meeting?—to settle the difficulty—here—in this hotel—to-night? What do you say?

MRS. CLANDON. But where is the counsel's opinion to come from?

McCOMAS. It has dropped down on us out of the clouds. On my way back here from Crampton's I met a most eminent Q.C., a man whom I briefed in the case that made his name for him. He has come down here from Saturday to Monday for the sea air, and to visit a relative of his who lives here. He has been good enough to say that if I can arrange a meeting of the parties he will come and help us with his opinion. Now do let us seize this chance of a quiet friendly family adjustment. Let me bring my friend here and try to persuade Crampton to come, too. Come: consent.

MRS. CLANDON (rather ominously, after a moment's consideration). Finch: I don't want counsel's opinion, because I intend to be guided by my own opinion. I don't want to meet Fergus again, because I don't like him, and don't believe the meeting will do any good. However (rising), you have persuaded the children that he is not quite hopeless. Do as you please.

McCOMAS (taking her hand and shaking it). Thank you, Mrs. Clandon. Will nine o'clock suit you?

MRS. CLANDON. Perfectly. Phil: will you ring, please. (Phil rings the bell.) But if I am to be accused of conspiring with Mr. Valentine, I think he had better be present.

VALENTINE (rising). I quite agree with you. I think it's most important.

McCOMAS. There can be no objection to that, I think. I have the greatest hopes of a happy settlement. Good-bye for the present. (He goes out, meeting the waiter; who holds the door for him to pass through.)

MRS. CLANDON. We expect some visitors at nine, William. Can we have dinner at seven instead of half-past?

WAITER (at the door). Seven, ma'am? Certainly, ma'am. It will be a convenience to us this busy evening, ma'am. There will be the band and the arranging of the fairy lights and one thing or another, ma'am.

DOLLY. The fairy lights!

PHILIP. The band! William: what mean you?

WAITER. The fancy ball, miss—

DOLLY and PHILIP (simultaneously rushing to him). Fancy ball!

WAITER. Oh, yes, sir. Given by the regatta committee for the benefit of the Life-boat, sir. (To Mrs. Clandon.) We often have them, ma'am: Chinese lanterns in the garden, ma'am: very bright and pleasant, very gay and innocent indeed. (To Phil.) Tickets downstairs at the office, sir, five shillings: ladies half price if accompanied by a gentleman.

PHILIP (seizing his arm to drag him off). To the office, William!

DOLLY (breathlessly, seizing his other arm). Quick, before they're all sold. (They rush him out of the room between them.)

MRS. CLANDON. What on earth are they going to do? (Going out.) I really must go and stop this— (She follows them, speaking as she disappears. Gloria stares coolly at Valentine, and then deliberately looks at her watch.)

VALENTINE. I understand. I've stayed too long. I'm going.

GLORIA (with disdainful punctiliousness). I owe you some apology, Mr. Valentine. I am conscious of having spoken somewhat sharply— perhaps rudely—to you.

VALENTINE. Not at all.

GLORIA. My only excuse is that it is very difficult to give consideration and respect when there is no dignity of character on the other side to command it.

VALENTINE (prosaically). How is a man to look dignified when he's infatuated?

GLORIA (effectually unstilted). Don't say those things to me. I forbid you. They are insults.

VALENTINE. No: they're only follies. I can't help them.

GLORIA. If you were really in love, it would not make you foolish: it would give you dignity—earnestness—even beauty.

VALENTINE. Do you really think it would make me beautiful? (She turns her back on him with the coldest contempt.) Ah, you see you're not in earnest. Love can't give any man new gifts. It can only heighten the gifts he was born with.

GLORIA (sweeping round at him again). What gifts were you born with, pray?

VALENTINE. Lightness of heart.

GLORIA. And lightness of head, and lightness of faith, and lightness of everything that makes a man.

VALENTINE. Yes, the whole world is like a feather dancing in the light now; and Gloria is the sun. (She rears her head angrily.) I beg your pardon: I'm off. Back at nine. Good-bye. (He runs off gaily, leaving her standing in the middle of the room staring after him.)

END OF ACT III

ACT IV

The same room. Nine o'clock. Nobody present. The lamps are lighted; but the curtains are not drawn. The window stands wide open; and strings of Chinese lanterns are glowing among the trees outside, with the starry sky beyond. The band is playing dance-music in the garden, drowning the sound of the sea.

The waiter enters, shewing in Crampton and McComas. Crampton looks cowed and anxious. He sits down wearily and timidly on the ottoman.

WAITER. The ladies have gone for a turn through the grounds to see the fancy dresses, sir. If you will be so good as to take seats, gentlemen, I shall tell them. (He is about to go into the garden through the window when McComas stops him.)

McCOMAS. One moment. If another gentleman comes, shew him in without any delay: we are expecting him.

WAITER. Right, sir. What name, sir?

McCOMAS. Boon. Mr. Boon. He is a stranger to Mrs. Clandon; so he may give you a card. If so, the name is spelt B.O.H.U.N. You will not forget.

WAITER (smiling). You may depend on me for that, sir. My own name is Boon, sir, though I am best known down here as Balmy Walters, sir. By rights I should spell it with the aitch you, sir; but I think it best not to take that liberty, sir. There is Norman blood in it, sir; and Norman blood is not a recommendation to a waiter.

McCOMAS. Well, well: "True hearts are more than coronets, and simple faith than Norman blood."

WAITER. That depends a good deal on one's station in life, sir. If you were a waiter, sir, you'd find that simple faith would leave you just as short as Norman blood. I find it best to spell myself B. double-O.N., and to keep my wits pretty sharp about me. But I'm taking up your time, sir. You'll excuse me, sir: your own fault for being so affable, sir. I'll tell the ladies you're here, sir. (He goes out into the garden through the window.)

McCOMAS. Crampton: I can depend on you, can't I?

CRAMPTON. Yes, yes. I'll be quiet. I'll be patient. I'll do my best.

McCOMAS. Remember: I've not given you away. I've told them it was all their fault.

CRAMPTON. You told me that it was all my fault.

McCOMAS. I told you the truth.

CRAMPTON (plaintively). If they will only be fair to me!

McCOMAS. My dear Crampton, they won't be fair to you: it's not to be expected from them at their age. If you're going to make impossible conditions of this kind, we may as well go back home at once.

CRAMPTON. But surely I have a right—

McCOMAS (intolerantly). You won't get your rights. Now, once for all, Crampton, did your promises of good behavior only mean that you won't complain if there's nothing to complain of? Because, if so— (He moves as if to go.)

CRAMPTON (miserably). No, no: let me alone, can't you? I've been bullied enough: I've been tormented enough. I tell you I'll do my best. But if that girl begins to talk to me like that and to look at me like— (He breaks off and buries his head in his hands.)

McCOMAS (relenting). There, there: it'll be all right, if you will only bear and forbear. Come, pull yourself together: there's someone coming. (Crampton, too dejected to care much, hardly changes his attitude. Gloria enters from the garden; McComas goes to meet her at the window; so that he can speak to her without being heard by Crampton.) There he is, Miss Clandon. Be kind to him. I'll leave you with him for a moment. (He goes into the garden. Gloria comes in and strolls coolly down the middle of the room.)

CRAMPTON (looking round in alarm). Where's McComas?

GLORIA (listlessly, but not unsympathetically). Gone out—to leave us together. Delicacy on his part, I suppose. (She stops beside him and looks quaintly down at him.) Well, father?

CRAMPTON (a quaint jocosity breaking through his forlornness). Well, daughter? (They look at one another for a moment, with a melancholy sense of humor.)

GLORIA. Shake hands. (They shake hands.)

CRAMPTON (holding her hand). My dear: I'm afraid I spoke very improperly of your mother this afternoon.

GLORIA. Oh, don't apologize. I was very high and mighty myself; but I've come down since: oh, yes: I've been brought down. (She sits on the floor beside his chair.)

CRAMPTON. What has happened to you, my child?

GLORIA. Oh, never mind. I was playing the part of my mother's daughter then; but I'm not: I'm my father's daughter. (Looking at him funnily.) That's a come down, isn't it?

CRAMPTON (angry). What! (Her odd expression does not alter. He surrenders.) Well, yes, my dear: I suppose it is, I suppose it is. (She nods sympathetically.) I'm afraid I'm sometimes a little irritable; but I know what's right and reasonable all the time, even when I don't act on it. Can you believe that?

GLORIA. Believe it! Why, that's myself—myself all over. I know what's right and dignified and strong and noble, just as well as she does; but oh, the things I do! the things I do! the things I let other people do!!

CRAMPTON (a little grudgingly in spite of himself). As well as she does? You mean your mother?

GLORIA (quickly). Yes, mother. (She turns to him on her knees and seizes his hands.) Now listen. No treason to her: no word, no thought against her. She is our superior—yours and mine—high heavens above us. Is that agreed?

CRAMPTON. Yes, yes. Just as you please, my dear.

GLORIA (not satisfied, letting go his hands and drawing back from him). You don't like her?

CRAMPTON. My child: you haven't been married to her. I have. (She raises herself slowly to her feet, looking at him with growing coldness.) She did me a great wrong in marrying me without really caring for me. But after that, the wrong was all on my side, I dare say. (He offers her his hand again.)

GLORIA (taking it firmly and warningly). Take care. That's a dangerous subject. My feelings—my miserable, cowardly, womanly feelings—may be on your side; but my conscience is on hers.

CRAMPTON. I'm very well content with that division, my dear. Thank you. (Valentine arrives. Gloria immediately becomes deliberately haughty.)

VALENTINE. Excuse me; but it's impossible to find a servant to announce one: even the never failing William seems to be at the ball. I should have gone myself; only I haven't five shillings to buy a ticket. How are you getting on, Crampton? Better, eh?

CRAMPTON. I am myself again, Mr. Valentine, no thanks to you.

VALENTINE. Look at this ungrateful parent of yours, Miss Clandon! I saved him from an excruciating pang; and he reviles me!

GLORIA (coldly). I am sorry my mother is not here to receive you, Mr. Valentine. It is not quite nine o'clock; and the gentleman of whom Mr. McComas spoke, the lawyer, is not yet come.

VALENTINE. Oh, yes, he is. I've met him and talked to him. (With gay malice.) You'll like him, Miss Clandon: he's the very incarnation of intellect. You can hear his mind working.

GLORIA (ignoring the jibe). Where is he?

VALENTINE. Bought a false nose and gone into the fancy ball.

CRAMPTON (crustily, looking at his watch). It seems that everybody has gone to this fancy ball instead of keeping to our appointment here.

VALENTINE. Oh, he'll come all right enough: that was half an hour ago. I didn't like to borrow five shillings from him and go in with him; so I joined the mob and looked through the railings until Miss Clandon disappeared into the hotel through the window.

GLORIA. So it has come to this, that you follow me about in public to stare at me.

VALENTINE. Yes: somebody ought to chain me up.

Gloria turns her back on him and goes to the fireplace. He takes the snub very philosophically, and goes to the opposite side of the room. The waiter appears at the window, ushering in Mrs. Clandon and McComas.

MRS. CLANDON (hurrying in). I am so sorry to have kept you waiting.

A grotesquely majestic stranger, in a domino and false nose, with goggles, appears at the window.

WAITER (to the stranger). Beg pardon, sir; but this is a private apartment, sir. If you will allow me, sir, I will shew you to the American bar and supper rooms, sir. This way, sir.

He goes into the gardens, leading the way under the impression that the stranger is following him. The majestic one, however, comes straight into the room to the end of the table, where, with impressive deliberation, he takes off the false nose and then the domino, rolling up the nose into the domino and throwing the bundle on the table like a champion throwing down his glove. He is now seen to be a stout, tall man between forty and fifty, clean shaven, with a midnight oil pallor emphasized by stiff black hair, cropped short and oiled, and eyebrows like early Victorian horsehair upholstery. Physically and spiritually, a coarsened man: in cunning and logic, a ruthlessly sharpened one. His bearing as he enters is sufficiently imposing and disquieting; but when he speaks, his powerful, menacing voice, impressively articulated speech, strong inexorable manner, and a terrifying power of intensely critical listening raise the impression produced by him to absolute tremendousness.

THE STRANGER. My name is Bohun. (General awe.) Have I the honor of addressing Mrs. Clandon? (Mrs. Clandon bows. Bohun bows.) Miss Clandon? (Gloria bows. Bohun bows.) Mr. Clandon?

CRAMPTON (insisting on his rightful name as angrily as he dares). My name is Crampton, sir.

BOHUN. Oh, indeed. (Passing him over without further notice and turning to Valentine.) Are you Mr. Clandon?

VALENTINE (making it a point of honor not to be impressed by him). Do I look like it? My name is Valentine. I did the drugging.

BOHUN. Ah, quite so. Then Mr. Clandon has not yet arrived?

WAITER (entering anxiously through the window). Beg pardon, ma'am; but can you tell me what became of that— (He recognizes Bohun, and loses all his self-possession. Bohun waits rigidly for him to pull himself together. After a pathetic exhibition of confusion, he recovers himself sufficiently to address Bohun weakly but coherently.) Beg pardon, sir, I'm sure, sir. Was—was it you, sir?

BOHUN (ruthlessly). It was I.

WAITER (brokenly). Yes, sir. (Unable to restrain his tears.) You in a false nose, Walter! (He sinks faintly into a chair at the table.) I beg pardon, ma'am, I'm sure. A little giddiness—

BOHUN (commandingly). You will excuse him, Mrs. Clandon, when I inform you that he is my father.

WAITER (heartbroken). Oh, no, no, Walter. A waiter for your father on the top of a false nose! What will they think of you?

MRS. CLANDON (going to the waiter's chair in her kindest manner). I am delighted to hear it, Mr. Bohun. Your father has been an excellent friend to us since we came here. (Bohun bows gravely.)

WAITER (shaking his head). Oh, no, ma'am. It's very kind of you— very ladylike and affable indeed, ma'am; but I should feel at a great disadvantage off my own proper footing. Never mind my being the gentleman's father, ma'am: it is only the accident of birth after all, ma'am. (He gets up feebly.) You'll all excuse me, I'm sure, having interrupted your business. (He begins to make his way along the table, supporting himself from chair to chair, with his eye on the door.)

BOHUN. One moment. (The waiter stops, with a sinking heart.) My father was a witness of what passed to-day, was he not, Mrs. Clandon?

MRS. CLANDON. Yes, most of it, I think.

BOHUN. In that case we shall want him.

WAITER (pleading). I hope it may not be necessary, sir. Busy evening for me, sir, with that ball: very busy evening indeed, sir.

BOHUN (inexorably). We shall want you.

MRS. CLANDON (politely). Sit down, won't you?

WAITER (earnestly). Oh, if you please, ma'am, I really must draw the line at sitting down. I couldn't let myself be seen doing such a thing, ma'am: thank you, I am sure, all the same. (He looks round from face to face wretchedly, with an expression that would melt a heart of stone.)

GLORIA. Don't let us waste time. William only wants to go on taking care of us. I should like a cup of coffee.

WAITER (brightening perceptibly). Coffee, miss? (He gives a little gasp of hope.) Certainly, miss. Thank you, miss: very timely, miss, very thoughtful and considerate indeed. (To Mrs. Clandon, timidly but expectantly.) Anything for you, ma'am?

MRS. CLANDON Er—oh, yes: it's so hot, I think we might have a jug of claret cup.

WAITER (beaming). Claret cup, ma'am! Certainly, ma'am.

GLORIA Oh, well I'll have a claret cup instead of coffee. Put some cucumber in it.

WAITER (delighted). Cucumber, miss! yes, miss. (To Bohun.) Anything special for you, sir? You don't like cucumber, sir.

BOHUN. If Mrs. Clandon will allow me—syphon—Scotch.

WAITER. Right, sir. (To Crampton.) Irish for you, sir, I think, sir? (Crampton assents with a grunt. The waiter looks enquiringly at Valentine.)

VALENTINE. I like the cucumber.

WAITER. Right, sir. (Summing up.) Claret cup, syphon, one Scotch and one Irish?

MRS. CLANDON. I think that's right.

WAITER (perfectly happy). Right, ma'am. Directly, ma'am. Thank you. (He ambles off through the window, having sounded the whole gamut of human happiness, from the bottom to the top, in a little over two minutes.)

McCOMAS. We can begin now, I suppose?

BOHUN. We had better wait until Mrs. Clandon's husband arrives.

CRAMPTON. What d'y' mean? I'm her husband.

BOHUN (instantly pouncing on the inconsistency between this and his previous statement). You said just now your name was Crampton.

CRAMPTON. So it is.

MRS. CLANDON	[*all four*]	{ I—
GLORIA	[*speaking*]	{ My—
McCOMAS	[*simul-*]	{ Mrs.—
VALENTINE	[*taneously*].	{ You—

BOHUN (drowning them in two thunderous words). One moment. (Dead silence.) Pray allow me. Sit down everybody. (They obey humbly. Gloria takes the saddle-bag chair on the hearth. Valentine slips around to her side of the room and sits on the ottoman facing the window, so that he can look at her. Crampton sits on the ottoman with his back to Valentine's. Mrs. Clandon, who has all along kept at the opposite side of the room in order to avoid Crampton as much as possible, sits near the door, with McComas beside her on her left. Bohun places himself magisterially in the centre of the group, near the corner of the table on Mrs. Clandon's side. When they are settled, he fixes Crampton with his eye, and begins.) In this family, it appears, the husband's name is Crampton: the wife's Clandon. Thus we have on the very threshold of the case an element of confusion.

VALENTINE (getting up and speaking across to him with one knee on the ottoman). But it's perfectly simple.

BOHUN (annihilating him with a vocal thunderbolt). It is. Mrs. Clandon has adopted another name. That is the obvious explanation which you feared I could not find out for myself. You mistrust my intelligence, Mr. Valentine— (Stopping him as he is about to protest.) No: I don't want you to answer that: I want you to think over it when you feel your next impulse to interrupt me.

VALENTINE (dazed). This is simply breaking a butterfly on a wheel. What does it matter? (He sits down again.)

BOHUN. I will tell you what it matters, sir. It matters that if this family difference is to be smoothed over as we all hope it may be, Mrs. Clandon, as a matter of social convenience and decency, will have to resume her husband's name. (Mrs. Clandon assumes an expression of the most determined obstinacy.) Or else Mr. Crampton will have to call himself Mr. Clandon. (Crampton looks indomitably resolved to do nothing of the sort.) No doubt you think that an easy matter, Mr. Valentine. (He looks pointedly at Mrs. Clandon, then at Crampton.) I differ from you. (He throws himself back in his chair, frowning heavily.)

McCOMAS (timidly). I think, Bohun, we had perhaps better dispose of the important questions first.

BOHUN. McComas: there will be no difficulty about the important questions. There never is. It is the trifles that will wreck you at the harbor mouth. (McComas looks as if he considered this a paradox.) You don't agree with me, eh?

McCOMAS (flatteringly). If I did—

BOHUN (interrupting him). If you did, you would be me, instead of being what you are.

McCOMAS (fawning on him). Of course, Bohun, your specialty—

BOHUN (again interrupting him). My specialty is being right when other people are wrong. If you agreed with me I should be of no use here. (He nods at him to drive the point home; then turns suddenly and forcibly on Crampton.) Now you, Mr. Crampton: what point in this business have you most at heart?

CRAMPTON (beginning slowly). I wish to put all considerations of self aside in this matter—

BOHUN (interrupting him). So do we all, Mr. Crampton. (To Mrs. Clandon.) Y o u wish to put self aside, Mrs. Clandon?

MRS. CLANDON. Yes: I am not consulting my own feelings in being here.

BOHUN. So do you, Miss Clandon?

GLORIA. Yes.

BOHUN. I thought so. We all do.

VALENTINE. Except me. My aims are selfish.

BOHUN. That's because you think an impression of sincerity will produce a better effect on Miss Clandon than an impression of disinterestedness. (Valentine, utterly dismantled and destroyed by this just remark, takes refuge in a feeble, speechless smile. Bohun, satisfied at having now effectually crushed all rebellion, throws himself back in his chair, with an air of being prepared to listen tolerantly to their grievances.) Now, Mr. Crampton, go on. It's understood that self is put aside. Human nature always begins by saying that.

CRAMPTON. But I mean it, sir.

BOHUN. Quite so. Now for your point.

CRAMPTON. Every reasonable person will admit that it's an unselfish one—the children.

BOHUN. Well? What about the children?

CRAMPTON (with emotion). They have—

BOHUN (pouncing forward again). Stop. You're going to tell me about your feelings, Mr. Crampton. Don't: I sympathize with them; but they're not my business. Tell us exactly what you want: that's what we have to get at.

CRAMPTON (uneasily). It's a very difficult question to answer, Mr. Bohun.

BOHUN. Come: I'll help you out. What do you object to in the present circumstances of the children?

CRAMPTON. I object to the way they have been brought up.

BOHUN. How do you propose to alter that now?

CRAMPTON. I think they ought to dress more quietly.

VALENTINE. Nonsense.

BOHUN (instantly flinging himself back in his chair, outraged by the interruption). When you are done, Mr. Valentine—when you are quite done.

VALENTINE. What's wrong with Miss Clandon's dress?

CRAMPTON (hotly to Valentine). My opinion is as good as yours.

GLORIA (warningly). Father!

CRAMPTON (subsiding piteously). I didn't mean you, my dear. (Pleading earnestly to Bohun.) But the two younger ones! you have not seen them, Mr. Bohun; and indeed I think you would agree with me that there is something very noticeable, something almost gay and frivolous in their style of dressing.

MRS. CLANDON (impatiently). Do you suppose I choose their clothes for them? Really this is childish.

CRAMPTON (furious, rising). Childish! (Mrs. Clandon rises indignantly.)

McCOMAS [*all ris-*] } Crampton, you promised—

VALENTINE [*ing and*] } Ridiculous. They dress charmingly.

[*speaking*] }

GLORIA [*together*]. } Pray let us behave reasonably.

Tumult. Suddenly they hear a chime of glasses in the room behind them. They turn in silent surprise and find that the waiter has just come back from the bar in the garden, and is jingling his tray warningly as he comes softly to the table with it.

WAITER (to Crampton, setting a tumbler apart on the table). Irish for you, sir. (Crampton sits down a little shamefacedly. The waiter sets another tumbler and a syphon apart, saying to Bohun) Scotch and syphon for you, sir. (Bohun waves his hand impatiently. The waiter places a large glass jug in the middle.) And claret cup. (All subside into their seats. Peace reigns.)

MRS. CLANDON (humbly to Bohun). I am afraid we interrupted you, Mr. Bohun.

BOHUN (calmly). You did. (To the waiter, who is going out.) Just wait a bit.

WAITER. Yes, sir. Certainly, sir. (He takes his stand behind Bohun's chair.)

MRS. CLANDON (to the waiter). You don't mind our detaining you, I hope. Mr. Bohun wishes it.

WAITER (now quite at his ease). Oh, no, ma'am, not at all, ma'am. It is a pleasure to me to watch the working of his trained and powerful mind—very stimulating, very entertaining and instructive indeed, ma'am.

BOHUN (resuming command of the proceedings). Now, Mr. Crampton: we are waiting for you. Do you give up your objection to the dressing, or do you stick to it?

CRAMPTON (pleading). Mr. Bohun: consider my position for a moment. I haven't got myself alone to consider: there's my sister Sophronia and my brother-in-law and all their circle. They have a great horror of anything that is at all—at all—well—

BOHUN. Out with it. Fast? Loud? Gay?

CRAMPTON. Not in any unprincipled sense of course; but—but— (blurting it out desperately) those two children would shock them. They're not fit to mix with their own people. That's what I complain of.

MRS. CLANDON (with suppressed impatience). Mr. Valentine: do you think there is anything fast or loud about Phil and Dolly?

VALENTINE. Certainly not. It's utter bosh. Nothing can be in better taste.

CRAMPTON. Oh, yes: of course you say so.

MRS. CLANDON. William: you see a great deal of good English society. Are my children overdressed?

WAITER (reassuringly). Oh, dear, no, ma'am. (Persuasively.) Oh, no, sir, not at all. A little pretty and tasty no doubt; but very choice and classy—very genteel and high toned indeed. Might be the son and daughter of a Dean, sir, I assure you, sir. You have only to look at them, sir, to— (At this moment a harlequin and columbine, dancing to the music of the band in the garden, which has just reached the coda of a waltz, whirl one another into the room. The harlequin's dress is made of lozenges, an inch square, of turquoise blue silk and gold alternately. His hat is gilt and his mask turned up. The columbine's petticoats are the epitome of a harvest field, golden orange and poppy crimson, with a tiny velvet jacket for the poppy stamens. They pass, an exquisite and dazzling apparition, between McComas and Bohun, and then back in a circle to the end of the table, where, as the final chord of the waltz is struck, they make a tableau in the middle of the company, the harlequin down on his left knee, and the columbine standing on his right knee, with her arms curved over her head. Unlike their dancing, which is charmingly graceful, their attitudinizing is hardly a success, and threatens to end in a catastrophe.)

THE COLUMBINE (screaming). Lift me down, somebody: I'm going to fall. Papa: lift me down.

CRAMPTON (anxiously running to her and taking her hands). My child!

DOLLY (jumping down with his help). Thanks: so nice of you. (Phil, putting his hat into his belt, sits on the side of the table and pours out some claret cup. Crampton returns to his place on the ottoman in great perplexity.) Oh, what fun! Oh, dear. (She seats herself with a vault on the front edge of the table, panting.) Oh, claret cup! (She drinks.)

BOHUN (in powerful tones). This is the younger lady, is it?

DOLLY (slipping down off the table in alarm at his formidable voice and manner). Yes, sir. Please, who are you?

MRS. CLANDON. This is Mr. Bohun, Dolly, who has very kindly come to help us this evening.

DOLLY. Oh, then he comes as a boon and a blessing—

PHILIP. Sh!

CRAMPTON. Mr. Bohun—McComas: I appeal to you. Is this right? Would you blame my sister's family for objecting to this?

DOLLY (flushing ominously). Have you begun again?

CRAMPTON (propitiating her). No, no. It's perhaps natural at your age.

DOLLY (obstinately). Never mind my age. Is it pretty?

CRAMPTON. Yes, dear, yes. (He sits down in token of submission.)

DOLLY (following him insistently). Do you like it?

CRAMPTON. My child: how can you expect me to like it or to approve of it?

DOLLY (determined not to let him off). How can you think it pretty and not like it?

McCOMAS (rising, angry and scandalized). Really I must say— (Bohun, who has listened to Dolly with the highest approval, is down on him instantly.)

BOHUN. No: don't interrupt, McComas. The young lady's method is right. (To Dolly, with tremendous emphasis.) Press your questions, Miss Clandon: press your questions.

DOLLY (rising). Oh, dear, you are a regular overwhelmer! Do you always go on like this?

BOHUN (rising). Yes. Don't you try to put me out of countenance, young lady: you're too young to do it. (He takes McComas's chair from beside Mrs. Clandon's and sets it beside his own.) Sit down. (Dolly, fascinated, obeys; and Bohun sits down again. McComas, robbed of his seat, takes a chair on the other side between the table and the ottoman.) Now, Mr. Crampton, the facts are before you—both of them. You think you'd like to have your two youngest children to live with you. Well, you wouldn't— (Crampton tries to protest; but Bohun will not have it on any terms.) No, you wouldn't: you think you would; but I know better than you. You'd want this young lady here to give up dressing like a stage columbine in the evening and like a fashionable columbine in the morning. Well, she won't—never. She thinks she will; but—

DOLLY (interrupting him). No I don't. (Resolutely.) I'll n e v e r give up dressing prettily. Never. As Gloria said to that man in Madeira, never, never, never while grass grows or water runs.

VALENTINE (rising in the wildest agitation). What! What! (Beginning to speak very fast.) When did she say that? Who did she say that to?

BOHUN (throwing himself back with massive, pitying remonstrance). Mr. Valentine—

VALENTINE (pepperily). Don't you interrupt me, sir: this is something really serious. I i n s i s t on knowing who Miss Clandon said that to.

DOLLY. Perhaps Phil remembers. Which was it, Phil? number three or number five?

VALENTINE. Number five!!!

PHILIP. Courage, Valentine. It wasn't number five: it was only a tame naval lieutenant that was always on hand—the most patient and harmless of mortals.

GLORIA (coldly). What are we discussing now, pray?

VALENTINE (very red). Excuse me: I am sorry I interrupted. I shall intrude no further, Mrs. Clandon. (He bows to Mrs. Clandon and marches away into the garden, boiling with suppressed rage.)

DOLLY. Hmhm!

PHILIP. Ahah!

GLORIA. Please go on, Mr. Bohun.

DOLLY (striking in as Bohun, frowning formidably, collects himself for a fresh grapple with the case). You're going to bully us, Mr. Bohun.

BOHUN. I—

DOLLY (interrupting him). Oh, yes, you are: you think you're not; but you are. I know by your eyebrows.

BOHUN (capitulating). Mrs. Clandon: these are clever children— clear headed, well brought up children. I make that admission deliberately. Can you, in return, point out to me any way of inducting them to hold their tongues?

MRS. CLANDON. Dolly, dearest—!

PHILIP. Our old failing, Dolly. Silence! (Dolly holds her mouth.)

MRS. CLANDON. Now, Mr. Bohun, before they begin again—

WAITER (softer). Be quick, sir: be quick.

DOLLY (beaming at him). Dear William!

PHILIP. Sh!

BOHUN (unexpectedly beginning by hurling a question straight at Dolly). Have you any intention of getting married?

DOLLY. I! Well, Finch calls me by my Christian name.

McCOMAS. I will not have this. Mr. Bohun: I use the young lady's Christian name naturally as an old friend of her mother's.

DOLLY. Yes, you call me Dolly as an old friend of my mother's. But what about Dorothee-ee-a? (McComas rises indignantly.)

CRAMPTON (anxiously, rising to restrain him). Keep your temper, McComas. Don't let us quarrel. Be patient.

McCOMAS. I will not be patient. You are shewing the most wretched weakness of character, Crampton. I say this is monstrous.

DOLLY. Mr. Bohun: please bully Finch for us.

BOHUN. I will. McComas: you're making yourself ridiculous. Sit down.

McCOMAS. I—

BOHUN (waving him down imperiously). No: sit down, sit down. (McComas sits down sulkily; and Crampton, much relieved, follows his example.)

DOLLY (to Bohun, meekly). Thank you.

BOHUN. Now, listen to me, all of you. I give no opinion, McComas, as to how far you may or may not have committed yourself in the direction indicated by this young lady. (McComas is about to protest.) No: don't interrupt me: if she doesn't marry you she will marry somebody else. That is the solution of the difficulty as to her not bearing her father's name. The other lady intends to get married.

GLORIA (flushing). Mr. Bohun!

BOHUN. Oh, yes, you do: you don't know it; but you do.

GLORIA (rising). Stop. I warn you, Mr. Bohun, not to answer for my intentions.

BOHUN (rising). It's no use, Miss Clandon: you can't put me down. I tell you your name will soon be neither Clandon nor Crampton; and I could tell you what it will be if I chose. (He goes to the other end of the table, where he unrolls his domino, and puts the false nose on the table. When he moves they all rise;

and Phil goes to the window. Bohun, with a gesture, summons the waiter to help him in robing.) Mr. Crampton: your notion of going to law is all nonsense: your children will be of age before you could get the point decided. (Allowing the waiter to put the domino on his shoulders.) You can do nothing but make a friendly arrangement. If you want your family more than they want you, you'll get the worse of the arrangement: if they want you more than you want them, you'll get the better of it. (He shakes the domino into becoming folds and takes up the false nose. Dolly gazes admiringly at him.) The strength of their position lies in their being very agreeable people personally. The strength of your position lies in your income. (He claps on the false nose, and is again grotesquely transfigured.)

DOLLY (running to him). Oh, now you look quite like a human being. Mayn't I have just one dance with you? C a n you dance? (Phil, resuming his part of harlequin, waves his hat as if casting a spell on them.)

BOHUN (thunderously). Yes: you think I can't; but I can. Come along. (He seizes her and dances off with her through the window in a most powerful manner, but with studied propriety and grace. The waiter is meanwhile busy putting the chairs back in their customary places.)

PHILIP. "On with the dance: let joy be unconfined." William!

WAITER. Yes, sir.

PHILIP. Can you procure a couple of dominos and false noses for my father and Mr. McComas?

McCOMAS. Most certainly not. I protest—

CRAMPTON. No, no. What harm will it do, just for once, McComas? Don't let us be spoil-sports.

McCOMAS. Crampton: you are not the man I took you for. (Pointedly.) Bullies are always cowards. (He goes disgustedly towards the window.)

CRAMPTON (following him). Well, never mind. We must indulge them a little. Can you get us something to wear, waiter?

WAITER. Certainly, sir. (He precedes them to the window, and stands aside there to let them pass out before him.) This way, sir. Dominos and noses, sir?

McCOMAS (angrily, on his way out). I shall wear my own nose.

WAITER (suavely). Oh, dear, yes, sir: the false one will fit over it quite easily, sir: plenty of room, sir, plenty of room. (He goes out after McComas.)

CRAMPTON (turning at the window to Phil with an attempt at genial fatherliness). Come along, my boy, come along. (He goes.)

PHILIP (cheerily, following him). Coming, dad, coming. (On the window threshold, he stops; looking after Crampton; then turns fantastically with his bat bent into a halo round his head, and says with a lowered voice to Mrs. Clandon and Gloria) Did you feel the pathos of that? (He vanishes.)

MRS. CLANDON (left alone with Gloria). Why did Mr. Valentine go away so suddenly, I wonder?

GLORIA (petulantly). I don't know. Yes, I d o know. Let us go and see the dancing. (They go towards the window, and are met by Valentine, who comes in from the garden walking quickly, with his face set and sulky.)

VALENTINE (stiffly). Excuse me. I thought the party had quite broken up.

GLORIA (nagging). Then why did you come back?

VALENTINE. I came back because I am penniless. I can't get out that way without a five shilling ticket.

MRS. CLANDON. Has anything annoyed you, Mr. Valentine?

GLORIA. Never mind him, mother. This is a fresh insult to me: that is all.

MRS. CLANDON (hardly able to realize that Gloria is deliberately provoking an altercation). Gloria!

VALENTINE. Mrs. Clandon: have I said anything insulting? Have I done anything insulting?

GLORIA. you have implied that my past has been like yours. That is the worst of insults.

VALENTINE. I imply nothing of the sort. I declare that my past has been blameless in comparison with yours.

MRS. CLANDON (most indignantly). Mr. Valentine!

VALENTINE. Well, what am I to think when I learn that Miss Clandon has made exactly the same speeches to other men that she has made to me—when I hear of at least five former lovers, with a tame naval lieutenant thrown in? Oh, it's too bad.

MRS. CLANDON. But you surely do not believe that these affairs— mere jokes of the children's—were serious, Mr. Valentine?

VALENTINE. Not to you—not to her, perhaps. But I know what the men felt. (With ludicrously genuine earnestness.) Have you ever thought of the wrecked lives, the marriages contracted in the recklessness of despair, the suicides, the—the—the—

GLORIA (interrupting him contemptuously). Mother: this man is a sentimental idiot. (She sweeps away to the fireplace.)

MRS. CLANDON (shocked). Oh, my d e a r e s t Gloria, Mr. Valentine will think that rude.

VALENTINE. I am not a sentimental idiot. I am cured of sentiment for ever. (He sits down in dudgeon.)

MRS. CLANDON. Mr. Valentine: you must excuse us all. Women have to unlearn the false good manners of their slavery before they acquire the genuine good manners of their freedom. Don't think Gloria vulgar (Gloria turns, astonished): she is not really so.

GLORIA. Mother! You apologize for me to h i m!

MRS. CLANDON. My dear: you have some of the faults of youth as well as its qualities; and Mr. Valentine seems rather too old fashioned in his ideas about his own sex to like being called an idiot. And now had we not better go and see what Dolly is doing? (She goes towards the window. Valentine rises.)

GLORIA. Do you go, mother. I wish to speak to Mr. Valentine alone.

MRS. CLANDON (startled into a remonstrance). My dear! (Recollecting herself.) I beg your pardon, Gloria. Certainly, if you wish. (She bows to Valentine and goes out.)

VALENTINE. Oh, if your mother were only a widow! She's worth six of you.

GLORIA. That is the first thing I have heard you say that does you honor.

VALENTINE. Stuff! Come: say what you want to say and let me go.

GLORIA. I have only this to say. You dragged me down to your level for a moment this afternoon. Do you think, if that had ever happened before, that I should not have been on my guard—that I should not have known what was coming, and known my own miserable weakness?

VALENTINE (scolding at her passionately). Don't talk of it in that way. What do I care for anything in you but your weakness, as you call it? You thought yourself very safe, didn't you, behind your advanced ideas! I amused myself by upsetting t h e m pretty easily.

GLORIA (insolently, feeling that now she can do as she likes with him). Indeed!

VALENTINE. But why did I do it? Because I was being tempted to awaken your heart—to stir the depths in you. Why was I tempted? Because Nature was in deadly earnest with me when I was in jest with her. When the great moment came, who was awakened? who was stirred? in whom did the depths break up? In myself—m y s e l f: I was transported: you were only offended—shocked. You were only an ordinary young lady, too ordinary to allow tame lieutenants to go as far as I went. That's all. I shall not trouble you with conventional apologies. Good-bye. (He makes resolutely for the door.)

GLORIA. Stop. (He hesitates.) Oh, will you understand, if I tell you the truth, that I am not making an advance to you?

VALENTINE. Pooh! I know what you're going to say. You think you're not ordinary—that I was right—that you really have those depths in your nature. It flatters you to believe it. (She recoils.) Well, I grant that you are not ordinary in some ways: you are a clever girl (Gloria stifles an exclamation of rage, and takes a threatening step towards him); but you've not been awakened yet. You didn't care: you don't care. It was my tragedy, not yours. Good-bye. (He turns to the door. She watches him, appalled to see him slipping from her grasp. As he turns the handle, he pauses; then turns again to her, offering his hand.) Let us part kindly.

GLORIA (enormously relieved, and immediately turning her back on him deliberately.) Good-bye. I trust you will soon recover from the wound.

VALENTINE (brightening up as it flashes on him that he is master of the situation after all). I shall recover: such wounds heal more than they harm. After all, I still have my own Gloria.

GLORIA (facing him quickly). What do you mean?

VALENTINE. The Gloria of my imagination.

GLORIA (proudly). Keep your own Gloria—the Gloria of your imagination. (Her emotion begins to break through her pride.) The real Gloria—the Gloria who was shocked, offended, horrified—oh, yes, quite truly—who was driven almost mad with shame by the feeling that all her power over herself had been broken down at her first real encounter with—with— (The color rushes over her face again. She covers it with her left hand, and puts her right on his left arm to support herself.)

VALENTINE. Take care. I'm losing my senses again. (Summoning all her courage, she takes away her hand from her face and puts it on his right shoulder, turning him towards her and looking him straight in the eyes. He begins to protest agitatedly.) Gloria: be sensible: it's no use: I haven't a penny in the world.

GLORIA. Can't you earn one? Other people do.

VALENTINE (half delighted, half frightened). I never could—you'd be unhappy— My dearest love: I should be the merest fortune-hunting adventurer if—

(Her grip on his arms tightens; and she kisses him.) Oh, Lord! (Breathless.) Oh, I— (He gasps.) I don't know anything about women: twelve years' experience is not enough. (In a gust of jealousy she throws him away from her; and he reels her back into the chair like a leaf before the wind, as Dolly dances in, waltzing with the waiter, followed by Mrs. Clandon and Finch, also waltzing, and Phil pirouetting by himself.)

DOLLY (sinking on the chair at the writing-table). Oh, I'm out of breath. How beautifully you waltz, William!

MRS. CLANDON (sinking on the saddlebag seat on the hearth). Oh, how could you make me do such a silly thing, Finch! I haven't danced since the soiree at South Place twenty years ago.

GLORIA (peremptorily at Valentine). Get up. (Valentine gets up abjectly.) Now let us have no false delicacy. Tell my mother that we have agreed to marry one another. (A silence of stupefaction ensues. Valentine, dumb with panic, looks at them with an obvious impulse to run away.)

DOLLY (breaking the silence). Number Six!

PHILIP. Sh!

DOLLY (tumultuously). Oh, my feelings! I want to kiss somebody; and we bar it in the family. Where's Finch?

McCOMAS (starting violently). No, positively— (Crampton appears in the window.)

DOLLY (running to Crampton). Oh, you're just in time. (She kisses him.) Now (leading him forward) bless them.

GLORIA. No. I will have no such thing, even in jest. When I need a blessing, I shall ask my mother's.

CRAMPTON (to Gloria, with deep disappointment). Am I to understand that you have engaged yourself to this young gentleman?

GLORIA (resolutely). Yes. Do you intend to be our friend or—

DOLLY (interposing). —or our father?

CRAMPTON. I should like to be both, my child. But surely—! Mr. Valentine: I appeal to your sense of honor.

VALENTINE. You're quite right. It's perfect madness. If we go out to dance together I shall have to borrow five shillings from her for a ticket. Gloria: don't be rash: you're throwing yourself away. I'd much better clear straight out of this, and never see any of you again. I shan't commit suicide: I shan't even be unhappy. It'll be a relief to me: I—I'm frightened, I'm positively frightened; and that's the plain truth.

GLORIA (determinedly). You shall not go.

VALENTINE (quailing). No, dearest: of course not. But—oh, will somebody only talk sense for a moment and bring us all to reason! I can't. Where's Bohun? Bohun's the man. Phil: go and summon Bohun—

PHILIP. From the vastly deep. I go. (He makes his bat quiver in the air and darts away through the window.)

WAITER (harmoniously to Valentine). If you will excuse my putting in a word, sir, do not let a matter of five shillings stand between you and your happiness, sir. We shall be only too pleased to put the ticket down to you: and you can settle at your convenience. Very glad to meet you in any way, very happy and pleased indeed, sir.

PHILIP (re-appearing). He comes. (He waves his bat over the window. Bohun comes in, taking off his false nose and throwing it on the table in passing as he comes between Gloria and Valentine.)

VALENTINE. The point is, Mr. Bohun—

McCOMAS (interrupting from the hearthrug). Excuse me, sir: the point must be put to him by a solicitor. The question is one of an engagement between these two young people. The lady has some property, and (looking at Crampton) will probably have a good deal more.

CRAMPTON. Possibly. I hope so.

VALENTINE. And the gentleman hasn't a rap.

BOHUN (nailing Valentine to the point instantly). Then insist on a settlement. That shocks your delicacy: most sensible precautions do. But you ask my advice; and I give it to you. Have a settlement.

GLORIA (proudly). He shall have a settlement.

VALENTINE. My good sir, I don't want advice for myself. Give h e r some advice.

BOHUN. She won't take it. When you're married, she won't take yours either— (turning suddenly on Gloria) oh, no, you won't: you think you will; but you won't. He'll set to work and earn his living— (turning suddenly to Valentine) oh, yes, you will: you think you won't; but you will. She'll make you.

CRAMPTON (only half persuaded). Then, Mr. Bohun, you don't think this match an unwise one?

BOHUN. Yes, I do: all matches are unwise. It's unwise to be born; it's unwise to be married; it's unwise to live; and it's unwise to die.

WAITER (insinuating himself between Crampton and Valentine). Then, if I may respectfully put in a word in, sir, so much the worse for wisdom! (To Valentine, benignly.) Cheer up, sir, cheer up: every man is frightened of marriage when it comes to the point; but it often turns out very comfortable, very enjoyable and happy indeed, sir—from time to time. I never was master in my own house, sir: my wife was like your young lady: she was of a commanding and masterful disposition, which my son has inherited. But if I had my life to live twice over, I'd do it again, I'd do it again, I assure you. You never can tell, sir: you never can tell.

PHILIP. Allow me to remark that if Gloria has made up her mind—

DOLLY. The matter's settled and Valentine's done for. And we're missing all the dances.

VALENTINE (to Gloria, gallantly making the best of it). May I have a dance—

BOHUN (interposing in his grandest diapason). Excuse me: I claim that privilege as counsel's fee. May I have the honor—thank you. (He dances away with Gloria and disappears among the lanterns, leaving Valentine gasping.)

VALENTINE (recovering his breath). Dolly: may I— (offering himself as her partner)?

DOLLY. Nonsense! (Eluding him and running round the table to the fireplace.) Finch—my Finch! (She pounces on McComas and makes him dance.)

McCOMAS (protesting). Pray restrain—really— (He is borne off dancing through the window.)

VALENTINE (making a last effort). Mrs. Clandon: may I—

PHILIP (forestalling him). Come, mother. (He seizes his mother and whirls her away.)

MRS. CLANDON (remonstrating). Phil, Phil— (She shares McComas's fate.)

CRAMPTON (following them with senile glee). Ho! ho! He! he! he! (He goes into the garden chuckling at the fun.)

VALENTINE (collapsing on the ottoman and staring at the waiter). I might as well be a married man already. (The waiter contemplates the captured Duellist of Sex with affectionate commiseration, shaking his head slowly.)

CURTAIN.

THE DEVIL'S DISCIPLE

ACT I

At the most wretched hour between a black night and a wintry morning in the year 1777, Mrs. Dudgeon, of New Hampshire, is sitting up in the kitchen and general dwelling room of her farm house on the outskirts of the town of Websterbridge. She is not a prepossessing woman. No woman looks her best after sitting up all night; and Mrs. Dudgeon's face, even at its best, is grimly trenched by the channels into which the barren forms and observances of a dead Puritanism can pen a bitter temper and a fierce pride. She is an elderly matron who has worked hard and got nothing by it except dominion and detestation in her sordid home, and an unquestioned reputation for piety and respectability among her neighbors, to whom drink and debauchery are still so much more tempting than religion and rectitude, that they conceive goodness simply as self-denial. This conception is easily extended to others—denial, and finally generalized as covering anything disagreeable. So Mrs. Dudgeon, being exceedingly disagreeable, is held to be exceedingly good. Short of flat felony, she enjoys complete license except for amiable weaknesses of any sort, and is consequently, without knowing it, the most licentious woman in the parish on the strength of never having broken the seventh commandment or missed a Sunday at the Presbyterian church.

The year 1777 is the one in which the passions roused of the breaking off of the American colonies from England, more by their own weight than their own will, boiled up to shooting point, the shooting being idealized to the English mind as suppression of rebellion and maintenance of British dominion, and to the American as defence of liberty, resistance to tyranny, and selfsacrifice on the altar of the Rights of Man. Into the merits of these idealizations it is not here necessary to inquire: suffice it to say, without prejudice, that they have convinced both Americans and English that the most high minded course for them to pursue is to kill as many of one another as possible, and that military operations to that end are in full swing, morally supported by confident requests from the clergy of both sides for the blessing of God on their arms.

Under such circumstances many other women besides this disagreeable Mrs. Dudgeon find themselves sitting up all night waiting for news. Like her, too, they fall asleep towards morning at the risk of nodding themselves into the kitchen fire. Mrs. Dudgeon sleeps with a shawl over her head, and her feet on a broad fender of iron laths, the step of the domestic altar of the fireplace, with its huge hobs and boiler, and its hinged arm above the smoky mantel-shelf for roasting. The plain kitchen table is opposite the fire, at her elbow, with a candle on it in a tin sconce. Her chair, like all the others in the room, is uncushioned and unpainted; but as it has a round railed back and a seat conventionally moulded to the sitter's curves, it is comparatively a chair of state. The room has three doors, one on the same side as the fireplace, near the corner, leading to the best bedroom; one, at the opposite end of the opposite wall, leading to the scullery and washhouse; and the house door, with its latch, heavy lock, and clumsy wooden bar, in the front wall, between the window in its middle and the corner next the bedroom door. Between the door and the window a rack of pegs suggests to the deductive observer that the men of the house are all away, as there are no hats or coats on them. On the other side of the window the clock hangs on a nail, with its white wooden dial, black iron weights, and brass pendulum. Between the clock and the corner, a big cupboard, locked, stands on a dwarf dresser full of common crockery.

On the side opposite the fireplace, between the door and the corner, a shamelessly ugly black horsehair sofa stands against the wall. An inspection of its stridulous surface shows that Mrs. Dudgeon is not alone. A girl of sixteen or seventeen has fallen asleep on it. She is a wild, timid looking creature with black hair and tanned skin. Her frock, a scanty garment, is rent, weatherstained, berrystained, and by no means scrupulously clean. It hangs on her with a freedom which, taken with her brown legs and bare feet, suggests no great stock of underclothing.

Suddenly there comes a tapping at the door, not loud enough to wake the sleepers. Then knocking, which disturbs Mrs. Dudgeon a little. Finally the latch is tried, whereupon she springs up at once.

MRS. DUDGEON (threateningly). Well, why don't you open the door? (She sees that the girl is asleep and immediately raises a clamor of heartfelt vexation.) Well, dear, dear me! Now this is— (shaking her) wake up, wake up: do you hear?

THE GIRL (sitting up). What is it?

MRS. DUDGEON. Wake up; and be ashamed of yourself, you unfeeling sinful girl, falling asleep like that, and your father hardly cold in his grave.

THE GIRL (half asleep still). I didn't mean to. I dropped off—

MRS. DUDGEON (cutting her short). Oh yes, you've plenty of excuses, I daresay. Dropped off! (Fiercely, as the knocking recommences.) Why don't you get up and let your uncle in? after me waiting up all night for him! (She pushes her rudely off the sofa.) There: I'll open the door: much good you are to wait up. Go and mend that fire a bit.

The girl, cowed and wretched, goes to the fire and puts a log on. Mrs. Dudgeon unbars the door and opens it, letting into the stuffy kitchen a little of the freshness and a great deal of the chill of the dawn, also her second son Christy, a fattish, stupid, fair-haired, round-faced man of about 22, muffled in a plaid shawl and grey overcoat. He hurries, shivering, to the fire, leaving Mrs. Dudgeon to shut the door.

CHRISTY (at the fire). F—f—f! but it is cold. (Seeing the girl, and staring lumpishly at her.) Why, who are you?

THE GIRL (shyly). Essie.

MRS. DUDGEON. Oh you may well ask. (To Essie.) Go to your room, child, and lie down since you haven't feeling enough to keep you awake. Your history isn't fit for your own ears to hear.

ESSIE. I—

MRS. DUDGEON (peremptorily). Don't answer me, Miss; but show your obedience by doing what I tell you. (Essie, almost in tears, crosses the room to the door near the sofa.) And don't forget your prayers. (Essie goes out.) She'd have gone to bed last night just as if nothing had happened if I'd let her.

CHRISTY (phlegmatically). Well, she can't be expected to feel Uncle Peter's death like one of the family.

MRS. DUDGEON. What are you talking about, child? Isn't she his daughter—the punishment of his wickedness and shame? (She assaults her chair by sitting down.)

CHRISTY (staring). Uncle Peter's daughter!

MRS. DUDGEON. Why else should she be here? D'ye think I've not had enough trouble and care put upon me bringing up my own girls, let alone you and your good-for-nothing brother, without having your uncle's bastards—

CHRISTY (interrupting her with an apprehensive glance at the door by which Essie went out). Sh! She may hear you.

MRS. DUDGEON (raising her voice). Let her hear me. People who fear God don't fear to give the devil's work its right name. (Christy, soullessly indifferent to the strife of Good and Evil, stares at the fire, warming himself.) Well, how long are you going to stare there like a stuck pig? What news have you for me?

CHRISTY (taking off his hat and shawl and going to the rack to hang them up). The minister is to break the news to you. He'll be here presently.

MRS. DUDGEON. Break what news?

CHRISTY (standing on tiptoe, from boyish habit, to hang his hat up, though he is quite tall enough to reach the peg, and speaking with callous placidity, considering the nature of the announcement). Father's dead too.

MRS. DUDGEON (stupent). Your father!

CHRISTY (sulkily, coming back to the fire and warming himself again, attending much more to the fire than to his mother). Well, it's not my fault. When we got to Nevinstown we found him ill in bed. He didn't know us at first. The minister sat up with him and sent me away. He died in the night.

MRS. DUDGEON (bursting into dry angry tears). Well, I do think this is hard on me—very hard on me. His brother, that was a disgrace to us all his life, gets hanged on the public gallows as a rebel; and your father, instead of staying at home where his duty was, with his own family, goes after him and dies, leaving everything on my shoulders. After sending this girl to me to take care of, too! (She plucks her shawl vexedly over her ears.) It's sinful, so it is; downright sinful.

CHRISTY (with a slow, bovine cheerfulness, after a pause). I think it's going to be a fine morning, after all.

MRS. DUDGEON (railing at him). A fine morning! And your father newly dead! Where's your feelings, child?

CHRISTY (obstinately). Well, I didn't mean any harm. I suppose a man may make a remark about the weather even if his father's dead.

MRS. DUDGEON (bitterly). A nice comfort my children are to me! One son a fool, and the other a lost sinner that's left his home to live with smugglers and gypsies and villains, the scum of the earth!

Someone knocks.

CHRISTY (without moving). That's the minister.

MRS. DUDGEON (sharply). Well, aren't you going to let Mr. Anderson in?

Christy goes sheepishly to the door. Mrs. Dudgeon buries her face in her hands, as it is her duty as a widow to be overcome with grief. Christy opens the door, and admits the minister, Anthony Anderson, a shrewd, genial, ready Presbyterian divine of about 50, with something of the authority of his profession in his bearing. But it is an altogether secular authority, sweetened by a conciliatory, sensible manner not at all suggestive of a quite thoroughgoing otherworldliness. He is a strong, healthy man, too, with a thick, sanguine neck; and his keen, cheerful mouth cuts into somewhat fleshy corners. No doubt an excellent parson, but still a man capable of making the most of this world, and perhaps a little apologetically conscious of getting on better with it than a sound Presbyterian ought.

ANDERSON (to Christy, at the door, looking at Mrs. Dudgeon whilst he takes off his cloak). Have you told her?

CHRISTY. She made me. (He shuts the door; yawns; and loafs across to the sofa where he sits down and presently drops off to sleep.)

Anderson looks compassionately at Mrs. Dudgeon. Then he hangs his cloak and hat on the rack. Mrs. Dudgeon dries her eyes and looks up at him.

ANDERSON. Sister: the Lord has laid his hand very heavily upon you.

MRS. DUDGEON (with intensely recalcitrant resignation). It's His will, I suppose; and I must bow to it. But I do think it hard. What call had Timothy to go to Springtown, and remind everybody that he belonged to a man that was being hanged?—and (spitefully) that deserved it, if ever a man did.

ANDERSON (gently). They were brothers, Mrs. Dudgeon.

MRS. DUDGEON. Timothy never acknowledged him as his brother after we were married: he had too much respect for me to insult me with such a brother. Would such a selfish wretch as Peter have come thirty miles to see Timothy hanged, do you think? Not thirty yards, not he. However, I must bear my cross as best I may: least said is soonest mended.

ANDERSON (very grave, coming down to the fire to stand with his back to it). Your eldest son was present at the execution, Mrs. Dudgeon.

MRS. DUDGEON (disagreeably surprised). Richard?

ANDERSON (nodding). Yes.

MRS. DUDGEON (vindictively). Let it be a warning to him. He may end that way himself, the wicked, dissolute, godless— (she suddenly stops; her voice fails; and she asks, with evident dread) Did Timothy see him?

ANDERSON. Yes.

MRS. DUDGEON (holding her breath). Well?

ANDERSON. He only saw him in the crowd: they did not speak. (Mrs. Dudgeon, greatly relieved, exhales the pent up breath and sits at her ease again.) Your husband was greatly touched and impressed by his brother's awful death. (Mrs. Dudgeon sneers. Anderson breaks off to demand with some indignation) Well, wasn't it only natural, Mrs. Dudgeon? He softened towards his prodigal son in that moment. He sent for him to come to see him.

MRS. DUDGEON (her alarm renewed). Sent for Richard!

ANDERSON. Yes; but Richard would not come. He sent his father a message; but I'm sorry to say it was a wicked message—an awful message.

MRS. DUDGEON. What was it?

ANDERSON. That he would stand by his wicked uncle, and stand against his good parents, in this world and the next.

MRS. DUDGEON (implacably). He will be punished for it. He will be punished for it—in both worlds.

ANDERSON. That is not in our hands, Mrs. Dudgeon.

MRS. DUDGEON. Did I say it was, Mr. Anderson. We are told that the wicked shall be punished. Why should we do our duty and keep God's law if there is to be no difference made between us and those who follow their own likings and dislikings, and make a jest of us and of their Maker's word?

ANDERSON. Well, Richard's earthly father has been merciful and his heavenly judge is the father of us all.

MRS. DUDGEON (forgetting herself). Richard's earthly father was a softheaded—

ANDERSON (shocked). Oh!

MRS. DUDGEON (with a touch of shame). Well, I am Richard's mother. If I am against him who has any right to be for him? (Trying to conciliate him.) Won't you sit down, Mr. Anderson? I should have asked you before; but I'm so troubled.

ANDERSON. Thank you— (He takes a chair from beside the fireplace, and turns it so that he can sit comfortably at the fire. When he is seated he adds, in the tone of a man who knows that he is opening a difficult subject.) Has Christy told you about the new will?

MRS. DUDGEON (all her fears returning). The new will! Did Timothy—? (She breaks off, gasping, unable to complete the question.)

ANDERSON. Yes. In his last hours he changed his mind.

MRS. DUDGEON (white with intense rage). And you let him rob me?

ANDERSON. I had no power to prevent him giving what was his to his own son.

MRS. DUDGEON. He had nothing of his own. His money was the money I brought him as my marriage portion. It was for me to deal with my own money and my own son. He dare not have done it if I had been with him; and well he knew it. That was why he stole away like a thief to take advantage of the law to rob me by making a new will behind my back. The more shame on you, Mr. Anderson,—you, a minister of the gospel—to act as his accomplice in such a crime.

ANDERSON (rising). I will take no offence at what you say in the first bitterness of your grief.

MRS. DUDGEON (contemptuously). Grief!

ANDERSON. Well, of your disappointment, if you can find it in your heart to think that the better word.

MRS. DUDGEON. My heart! My heart! And since when, pray, have you begun to hold up our hearts as trustworthy guides for us?

ANDERSON (rather guiltily). I—er—

MRS. DUDGEON (vehemently). Don't lie, Mr. Anderson. We are told that the heart of man is deceitful above all things, and desperately wicked. My heart belonged, not to Timothy, but to that poor wretched brother of his that has just ended his days with a rope round his neck—aye, to Peter Dudgeon. You know it: old Eli Hawkins, the man to whose pulpit you succeeded, though you are not worthy to loose his shoe latchet, told it you when he gave over our souls into your charge. He warned me and strengthened me against my heart, and made me marry a Godfearing man—as he thought. What else but that discipline has made me the woman I am? And you, you who followed your heart in your marriage, you talk to me of what I find in my heart. Go home to your pretty wife, man; and leave me to my prayers. (She turns from him and leans with her elbows on the table, brooding over her wrongs and taking no further notice of him.)

ANDERSON (willing enough to escape). The Lord forbid that I should come between you and the source of all comfort! (He goes to the rack for his coat and hat.)

MRS. DUDGEON (without looking at him). The Lord will know what to forbid and what to allow without your help.

ANDERSON. And whom to forgive, I hope—Eli Hawkins and myself, if we have ever set up our preaching against His law. (He fastens his cloak, and is now ready to go.) Just one word—on necessary business, Mrs. Dudgeon. There is the reading of the will to be gone through; and Richard has a right to be present. He is in the town; but he has the grace to say that he does not want to force himself in here.

MRS. DUDGEON. He shall come here. Does he expect us to leave his father's house for his convenience? Let them all come, and come quickly, and go quickly. They shall not make the will an excuse to shirk half their day's work. I shall be ready, never fear.

ANDERSON (coming back a step or two). Mrs. Dudgeon: I used to have some little influence with you. When did I lose it?

MRS. DUDGEON (still without turning to him). When you married for love. Now you're answered.

ANDERSON. Yes: I am answered. (He goes out, musing.)

MRS. DUDGEON (to herself, thinking of her husband). Thief! Thief!! (She shakes herself angrily out of the chair; throws back the shawl from her head; and sets to work to prepare the room for the reading of the will, beginning by replacing Anderson's chair against the wall, and pushing back her own to the window. Then she calls, in her hard, driving, wrathful way) Christy. (No answer: he is fast asleep.) Christy. (She shakes him roughly.) Get up out of that; and be ashamed of yourself—sleeping, and your father dead! (She returns to the table; puts the candle on the mantelshelf; and takes from the table drawer a red table cloth which she spreads.)

CHRISTY (rising reluctantly). Well, do you suppose we are never going to sleep until we are out of mourning?

MRS. DUDGEON. I want none of your sulks. Here: help me to set this table. (They place the table in the middle of the room, with Christy's end towards the fireplace and Mrs. Dudgeon's towards the sofa. Christy drops the table as soon as possible, and goes to the fire, leaving his mother to make the final adjustments of its position.) We shall have the minister back here with the lawyer and all the family to read the will before you have done toasting yourself. Go and wake that girl; and then light the stove in the shed: you can't have your breakfast here. And mind you wash yourself, and make yourself fit to receive the company. (She punctuates these orders by going to the cupboard; unlocking it; and producing a decanter of wine, which has no doubt stood there untouched since the last state occasion in the family, and some glasses, which she sets on the table. Also two green ware plates, on one of which she puts a barmbrack with a knife beside it. On the other she shakes some biscuits out of a tin, putting back one or two, and counting the rest.) Now mind: there are ten biscuits there: let there be ten there when I come back after dressing myself. And keep your fingers off the raisins in that cake. And tell Essie the same. I suppose I can trust you to bring in the case of stuffed birds without breaking the glass? (She replaces the tin in the cupboard, which she locks, pocketing the key carefully.)

CHRISTY (lingering at the fire). You'd better put the inkstand instead, for the lawyer.

MRS. DUDGEON. That's no answer to make to me, sir. Go and do as you're told. (Christy turns sullenly to obey.) Stop: take down that shutter before you go, and let the daylight in: you can't expect me to do all the heavy work of the house with a great heavy lout like you idling about.

Christy takes the window bar out of its damps, and puts it aside; then opens the shutter, showing the grey morning. Mrs. Dudgeon takes the sconce from the mantelshelf; blows out the candle; extinguishes the snuff by pinching it with her fingers, first licking them for the purpose; and replaces the sconce on the shelf.

CHRISTY (looking through the window). Here's the minister's wife.

MRS. DUDGEON (displeased). What! Is she coming here?

CHRISTY. Yes.

MRS. DUDGEON. What does she want troubling me at this hour, before I'm properly dressed to receive people?

CHRISTY. You'd better ask her.

MRS. DUDGEON (threateningly). You'd better keep a civil tongue in your head. (He goes sulkily towards the door. She comes after him, plying him with instructions.) Tell that girl to come to me as soon as she's had her breakfast. And tell her to make herself fit to be seen before the people. (Christy goes out and slams the door in her face.) Nice manners, that! (Someone knocks at the house door: she turns and cries inhospitably.) Come in. (Judith Anderson, the minister's wife, comes in. Judith is more than twenty years younger than her husband, though she will never be as young as he in vitality. She is pretty and proper and ladylike, and has been admired and petted into an opinion of herself sufficiently favorable to give her a self-assurance which serves her instead of strength. She has a pretty taste in dress, and in her face the pretty lines of a sentimental character formed by dreams. Even her little self-complacency is pretty, like a child's vanity. Rather a pathetic creature to any sympathetic observer who knows how rough a place the world is. One feels, on the whole, that Anderson might have chosen worse, and that she, needing protection, could not have chosen better.) Oh, it's you, is it, Mrs. Anderson?

JUDITH (very politely—almost patronizingly). Yes. Can I do anything for you, Mrs. Dudgeon? Can I help to get the place ready before they come to read the will?

MRS. DUDGEON (stiffly). Thank you, Mrs. Anderson, my house is always ready for anyone to come into.

MRS. ANDERSON (with complacent amiability). Yes, indeed it is. Perhaps you had rather I did not intrude on you just now.

MRS. DUDGEON. Oh, one more or less will make no difference this morning, Mrs. Anderson. Now that you're here, you'd better stay. If you wouldn't mind shutting the door! (Judith smiles, implying "How stupid of me" and shuts it with an exasperating air of doing something pretty and becoming.) That's better. I must go and tidy myself a bit. I suppose you don't mind stopping here to receive anyone that comes until I'm ready.

JUDITH (graciously giving her leave). Oh yes, certainly. Leave them to me, Mrs. Dudgeon; and take your time. (She hangs her cloak and bonnet on the rack.)

MRS. DUDGEON (half sneering). I thought that would be more in your way than getting the house ready. (Essie comes back.) Oh, here you are! (Severely) Come here: let me see you. (Essie timidly goes to her. Mrs. Dudgeon takes her roughly by the arm and pulls her round to inspect the results of her attempt to clean and tidy herself—results which show little practice and less conviction.) Mm! That's what you call doing your hair properly, I suppose. It's easy to see what you are, and how you were brought up. (She throws her arms away, and goes on, peremptorily.) Now you listen to me and do as you're told. You sit down there in the corner by the fire; and when the company comes don't dare to speak until you're spoken to. (Essie creeps away to the fireplace.) Your father's people had better see you and know you're there: they're as much bound to keep you from starvation as I am. At any rate they might help. But let me have no chattering and making free with them, as if you were their equal. Do you hear?

ESSIE. Yes.

MRS. DUDGEON. Well, then go and do as you're told.

(Essie sits down miserably on the corner of the fender furthest from the door.) Never mind her, Mrs. Anderson: you know who she is and what she is. If she gives you any trouble, just tell me; and I'll settle accounts with her. (Mrs. Dudgeon goes into the bedroom, shutting the door sharply behind her as if even it had to be made to do its duty with a ruthless hand.)

JUDITH (patronizing Essie, and arranging the cake and wine on the table more becomingly). You must not mind if your aunt is strict with you. She is a very good woman, and desires your good too.

ESSIE (in listless misery). Yes.

JUDITH (annoyed with Essie for her failure to be consoled and edified, and to appreciate the kindly condescension of the remark). You are not going to be sullen, I hope, Essie.

ESSIE. No.

JUDITH. That's a good girl! (She places a couple of chairs at the table with their backs to the window, with a pleasant sense of being a more thoughtful housekeeper than Mrs. Dudgeon.) Do you know any of your father's relatives?

ESSIE. No. They wouldn't have anything to do with him: they were too religious. Father used to talk about Dick Dudgeon; but I never saw him.

JUDITH (ostentatiously shocked). Dick Dudgeon! Essie: do you wish to be a really respectable and grateful girl, and to make a place for yourself here by steady good conduct?

ESSIE (very half-heartedly). Yes.

JUDITH. Then you must never mention the name of Richard Dudgeon—never even think about him. He is a bad man.

ESSIE. What has he done?

JUDITH. You must not ask questions about him, Essie. You are too young to know what it is to be a bad man. But he is a smuggler; and he lives with gypsies; and he has no love for his mother and his family; and he wrestles and plays games on Sunday instead of going to church. Never let him into your presence, if you can help it, Essie; and try to keep yourself and all womanhood unspotted by contact with such men.

ESSIE. Yes.

JUDITH (again displeased). I am afraid you say Yes and No without thinking very deeply.

ESSIE. Yes. At least I mean—

JUDITH (severely). What do you mean?

ESSIE (almost crying). Only—my father was a smuggler; and— (Someone knocks.)

JUDITH. They are beginning to come. Now remember your aunt's directions, Essie; and be a good girl. (Christy comes back with the stand of stuffed birds under a glass case, and an inkstand, which he places on the table.) Good morning, Mr. Dudgeon. Will you open the door, please: the people have come.

CHRISTY. Good morning. (He opens the house door.)

The morning is now fairly bright and warm; and Anderson, who is the first to enter, has left his cloak at home. He is accompanied by Lawyer Hawkins, a brisk, middleaged man in brown riding gaiters and yellow breeches, looking as much squire as solicitor. He and Anderson are allowed precedence as representing the learned professions. After them comes the family, headed by the senior uncle, William Dudgeon, a large, shapeless man, bottle-nosed and evidently no ascetic at table. His clothes are not the clothes, nor his anxious wife the wife, of a prosperous man. The junior uncle, Titus Dudgeon, is a wiry little terrier of a man, with an immense and visibly purse-proud wife, both free from the cares of the William household.

Hawkins at once goes briskly to the table and takes the chair nearest the sofa, Christy having left the inkstand there. He puts his hat on the floor beside him, and produces the will. Uncle William comes to the fire and stands on the hearth warming his coat tails, leaving Mrs. William derelict near the door. Uncle Titus, who is the lady's man of the family, rescues her by giving her his disengaged arm and bringing her to the sofa, where he sits down warmly between his own lady and his brother's. Anderson hangs up his hat and waits for a word with Judith.

JUDITH. She will be here in a moment. Ask them to wait. (She taps at the bedroom door. Receiving an answer from within, she opens it and passes through.)

ANDERSON (taking his place at the table at the opposite end to Hawkins). Our poor afflicted sister will be with us in a moment. Are we all here?

CHRISTY (at the house door, which he has just shut). All except Dick.

The callousness with which Christy names the reprobate jars on the moral sense of the family. Uncle William shakes his head slowly and repeatedly. Mrs. Titus catches her breath convulsively through her nose. Her husband speaks.

UNCLE TITUS. Well, I hope he will have the grace not to come. I hope so.

The Dudgeons all murmur assent, except Christy, who goes to the window and posts himself there, looking out. Hawkins smiles secretively as if he knew something that would change their tune if they knew it. Anderson is uneasy: the love of solemn family councils, especially funereal ones, is not in his nature. Judith appears at the bedroom door.

JUDITH (with gentle impressiveness). Friends, Mrs. Dudgeon. (She takes the chair from beside the fireplace; and places it for Mrs. Dudgeon, who comes from the bedroom in black, with a clean handkerchief to her eyes. All rise, except Essie. Mrs. Titus and Mrs. William produce equally clean handkerchiefs and weep. It is an affecting moment.)

UNCLE WILLIAM. Would it comfort you, sister, if we were to offer up a prayer?

UNCLE TITUS. Or sing a hymn?

ANDERSON (rather hastily). I have been with our sister this morning already, friends. In our hearts we ask a blessing.

ALL (except Essie). Amen.

They all sit down, except Judith, who stands behind Mrs. Dudgeon's chair.

JUDITH (to Essie). Essie: did you say Amen?

ESSIE (scaredly). No.

JUDITH. Then say it, like a good girl.

ESSIE. Amen.

UNCLE WILLIAM (encouragingly). That's right: that's right. We know who you are; but we are willing to be kind to you if you are a good girl and deserve it. We are all equal before the Throne.

This republican sentiment does not please the women, who are convinced that the Throne is precisely the place where their superiority, often questioned in this world, will be recognized and rewarded.

CHRISTY (at the window). Here's Dick.

Anderson and Hawkins look round sociably. Essie, with a gleam of interest breaking through her misery, looks up. Christy grins and gapes expectantly at the door. The rest are petrified with the intensity of their sense of Virtue menaced with outrage by the approach of flaunting Vice. The reprobate appears in the doorway, graced beyond his alleged merits by the morning sunlight. He is certainly the best looking member of the family; but his expression is reckless and sardonic, his manner defiant and satirical, his dress picturesquely careless. Only his forehead and mouth betray an extraordinary steadfastness, and his eyes are the eyes of a fanatic.

RICHARD (on the threshold, taking off his hat). Ladies and gentlemen: your servant, your very humble servant. (With this comprehensive insult, he throws his hat to Christy with a suddenness that makes him jump like a negligent wicket keeper, and comes into the middle of the room, where he turns and deliberately surveys the company.) How happy you all look! how glad to see me! (He turns towards Mrs. Dudgeon's chair; and his lip rolls up horribly from his dog tooth as he meets her look of undisguised hatred.) Well, mother: keeping up appearances as usual? that's right, that's right. (Judith pointedly moves away from his neighborhood to the other side of the kitchen, holding her skirt instinctively as if to save it from contamination. Uncle Titus promptly marks his approval of her action by rising from the sofa, and placing a chair for her to sit down upon.) What! Uncle William! I haven't seen you since you gave up drinking. (Poor Uncle William, shamed, would protest; but Richard claps him heartily on his shoulder, adding) you have given it up, haven't you? (releasing him with a playful push) of course you have: quite right too; you overdid it. (He turns away from Uncle William and makes for the sofa.) And now, where is that upright horsedealer Uncle Titus? Uncle Titus: come forth. (He comes upon him holding the chair as Judith sits down.) As usual, looking after the ladies.

UNCLE TITUS (indignantly). Be ashamed of yourself, sir—

RICHARD (interrupting him and shaking his hand in spite of him). I am: I am; but I am proud of my uncle—proud of all my relatives (again surveying them) who could look at them and not be proud and joyful? (Uncle Titus, overborne, resumes his seat on the sofa. Richard turns to the table.) Ah, Mr. Anderson, still at the good work, still shepherding them. Keep them up to the mark, minister, keep them up to the mark. Come! (with a spring he seats himself on the table and takes up the decanter) clink a glass with me, Pastor, for the sake of old times.

ANDERSON. You know, I think, Mr. Dudgeon, that I do not drink before dinner.

RICHARD. You will, some day, Pastor: Uncle William used to drink before breakfast. Come: it will give your sermons unction. (He smells the wine and makes a wry face.) But do not begin on my mother's company sherry. I stole some when I was six years old; and I have been a temperate man ever since. (He puts the decanter down and changes the subject.) So I hear you are married, Pastor, and that your wife has a most ungodly allowance of good looks.

ANDERSON (quietly indicating Judith). Sir: you are in the presence of my wife. (Judith rises and stands with stony propriety.)

RICHARD (quickly slipping down from the table with instinctive good manners). Your servant, madam: no offence. (He looks at her earnestly.) You deserve your reputation; but I'm sorry to see by your expression that you're a good woman.

(She looks shocked, and sits down amid a murmur of indignant sympathy from his relatives. Anderson, sensible enough to know that these demonstrations can only gratify and encourage a man who is deliberately trying to provoke them, remains perfectly goodhumored.) All the same, Pastor, I respect you more than I did before. By the way, did I hear, or did I not, that our late lamented Uncle Peter, though unmarried, was a father?

UNCLE TITUS. He had only one irregular child, sir.

RICHARD. Only one! He thinks one a mere trifle! I blush for you, Uncle Titus.

ANDERSON. Mr. Dudgeon you are in the presence of your mother and her grief.

RICHARD. It touches me profoundly, Pastor. By the way, what has become of the irregular child?

ANDERSON (pointing to Essie). There, sir, listening to you.

RICHARD (shocked into sincerity). What! Why the devil didn't you tell me that before? Children suffer enough in this house without— (He hurries remorsefully to Essie.) Come, little cousin! never mind me: it was not meant to hurt you. (She looks up gratefully at him. Her tearstained face affects him violently, and he bursts out, in a transport of wrath) Who has been making her cry? Who has been ill-treating her? By God—

MRS. DUDGEON (rising and confronting him). Silence your blasphemous tongue. I will hear no more of this. Leave my house.

RICHARD. How do you know it's your house until the will is read? (They look at one another for a moment with intense hatred; and then she sinks, checkmated, into her chair. Richard goes boldly up past Anderson to the window, where he takes the railed chair in his hand.) Ladies and gentlemen: as the eldest son of my late father, and the unworthy head of this household, I bid you welcome. By your leave, Minister Anderson: by your leave, Lawyer Hawkins. The head of the table for the head of the family. (He places the chair at the table between the minister and the attorney; sits down between them; and addresses the assembly with a presidential air.) We meet on a melancholy occasion: a father dead! an uncle actually hanged, and probably damned. (He shakes his head deploringly. The relatives freeze with horror.) That's right: pull your longest faces (his voice suddenly sweetens gravely as his glance lights on Essie) provided only there is hope in the eyes of the child. (Briskly.) Now then, Lawyer Hawkins: business, business. Get on with the will, man.

TITUS. Do not let yourself be ordered or hurried, Mr. Hawkins.

HAWKINS (very politely and willingly). Mr. Dudgeon means no offence, I feel sure. I will not keep you one second, Mr. Dudgeon. Just while I get my glasses— (he fumbles for them. The Dudgeons look at one another with misgiving).

RICHARD. Aha! They notice your civility, Mr. Hawkins. They are prepared for the worst. A glass of wine to clear your voice before you begin. (He pours out one for him and hands it; then pours one for himself.)

HAWKINS. Thank you, Mr. Dudgeon. Your good health, sir.

RICHARD. Yours, sir. (With the glass half way to his lips, he checks himself, giving a dubious glance at the wine, and adds, with quaint intensity.) Will anyone oblige me with a glass of water?

Essie, who has been hanging on his every word and movement, rises stealthily and slips out behind Mrs. Dudgeon through the bedroom door, returning presently with a jug and going out of the house as quietly as possible.

HAWKINS. The will is not exactly in proper legal phraseology.

RICHARD. No: my father died without the consolations of the law.

HAWKINS. Good again, Mr. Dudgeon, good again. (Preparing to read) Are you ready, sir?

RICHARD. Ready, aye ready. For what we are about to receive, may the Lord make us truly thankful. Go ahead.

HAWKINS (reading). "This is the last will and testament of me Timothy Dudgeon on my deathbed at Nevinstown on the road from Springtown to Websterbridge on this twenty-fourth day of September, one thousand seven hundred and seventy seven. I hereby revoke all former wills made by me and declare that I am of sound mind and know well what I am doing and that this is my real will according to my own wish and affections."

RICHARD (glancing at his mother). Aha!

HAWKINS (shaking his head). Bad phraseology, sir, wrong phraseology. "I give and bequeath a hundred pounds to my younger son Christopher Dudgeon, fifty pounds to be paid to him on the day of his marriage to Sarah Wilkins if she will have him, and ten pounds on the birth of each of his children up to the number of five."

RICHARD. How if she won't have him?

CHRISTY. She will if I have fifty pounds.

RICHARD. Good, my brother. Proceed.

HAWKINS. "I give and bequeath to my wife Annie Dudgeon, born Annie Primrose"—you see he did not know the law, Mr. Dudgeon: your mother was not born Annie: she was christened so—"an annuity of fifty-two pounds a year for life (Mrs. Dudgeon, with all eyes on her, holds herself convulsively rigid) to be paid out of the interest on her own money"—there's a way to put it, Mr. Dudgeon! Her own money!

MRS. DUDGEON. A very good way to put God's truth. It was every penny my own. Fifty-two pounds a year!

HAWKINS. "And I recommend her for her goodness and piety to the forgiving care of her children, having stood between them and her as far as I could to the best of my ability."

MRS. DUDGEON. And this is my reward! (raging inwardly) You know what I think, Mr. Anderson you know the word I gave to it.

ANDERSON. It cannot be helped, Mrs. Dudgeon. We must take what comes to us. (To Hawkins.) Go on, sir.

HAWKINS. "I give and bequeath my house at Websterbridge with the land belonging to it and all the rest of my property soever to my eldest son and heir, Richard Dudgeon."

RICHARD. Oho! The fatted calf, Minister, the fatted calf.

HAWKINS. "On these conditions—"

RICHARD. The devil! Are there conditions?

HAWKINS. "To wit: first, that he shall not let my brother Peter's natural child starve or be driven by want to an evil life."

RICHARD (emphatically, striking his fist on the table). Agreed.

Mrs. Dudgeon, turning to look malignantly at Essie, misses her and looks quickly round to see where she has moved to; then, seeing that she has left the room without leave, closes her lips vengefully.

HAWKINS. "Second, that he shall be a good friend to my old horse Jim"— (again slacking his head) he should have written James, sir.

RICHARD. James shall live in clover. Go on.

HAWKINS. "—and keep my deaf farm laborer Prodger Feston in his service."

RICHARD. Prodger Feston shall get drunk every Saturday.

HAWKINS. "Third, that he make Christy a present on his marriage out of the ornaments in the best room."

RICHARD (holding up the stuffed birds). Here you are, Christy.

CHRISTY (disappointed). I'd rather have the China peacocks.

RICHARD. You shall have both. (Christy is greatly pleased.) Go on.

HAWKINS. "Fourthly and lastly, that he try to live at peace with his mother as far as she will consent to it."

RICHARD (dubiously). Hm! Anything more, Mr. Hawkins?

HAWKINS (solemnly). "Finally I gave and bequeath my soul into my Maker's hands, humbly asking forgiveness for all my sins and mistakes, and hoping that he will so guide my son that it may not be said that I have done wrong in trusting to him rather than to others in the perplexity of my last hour in this strange place."

ANDERSON. Amen.

THE UNCLES AND AUNTS. Amen.

RICHARD. My mother does not say Amen.

MRS. DUDGEON (rising, unable to give up her property without a struggle). Mr. Hawkins: is that a proper will? Remember, I have his rightful, legal will, drawn up by yourself, leaving all to me.

HAWKINS. This is a very wrongly and irregularly worded will, Mrs. Dudgeon; though (turning politely to Richard) it contains in my judgment an excellent disposal of his property.

ANDERSON (interposing before Mrs. Dudgeon can retort). That is not what you are asked, Mr. Hawkins. Is it a legal will?

HAWKINS. The courts will sustain it against the other.

ANDERSON. But why, if the other is more lawfully worded?

HAWKING. Because, sir, the courts will sustain the claim of a man—and that man the eldest son—against any woman, if they can. I warned you, Mrs. Dudgeon, when you got me to draw that other will, that it was not a wise will, and that though you might make him sign it, he would never be easy until he revoked it. But you wouldn't take advice; and now Mr. Richard is cock of the walk. (He takes his hat from the floor; rises; and begins pocketing his papers and spectacles.)

This is the signal for the breaking-up of the party. Anderson takes his hat from the rack and joins Uncle William at the fire. Uncle Titus fetches Judith her things from the rack. The three on the sofa rise and chat with Hawkins. Mrs. Dudgeon, now an intruder in her own house, stands erect, crushed by the weight of the law on women, accepting it, as she has been trained to accept all monstrous calamities, as proofs of the greatness of the power that inflicts them, and of her own wormlike insignificance. For at this time, remember, Mary Wollstonecraft is as yet only a girl of eighteen, and her Vindication of the Rights of Women is still fourteen years off. Mrs. Dudgeon is rescued from her apathy by Essie, who comes back with the jug full of water. She is taking it to Richard when Mrs. Dudgeon stops her.

MRS. DUDGEON (threatening her). Where have you been? (Essie, appalled, tries to answer, but cannot.) How dare you go out by yourself after the orders I gave you?

ESSIE. He asked for a drink— (she stops, her tongue cleaving to her palate with terror).

JUDITH (with gentler severity). Who asked for a drink? (Essie, speechless, points to Richard.)

RICHARD. What! I!

JUDITH (shocked). Oh Essie, Essie!

RICHARD. I believe I did. (He takes a glass and holds it to Essie to be filled. Her hand shakes.) What! afraid of me?

ESSIE (quickly). No. I— (She pours out the water.)

RICHARD (tasting it). Ah, you've been up the street to the market gate spring to get that. (He takes a draught.) Delicious! Thank you. (Unfortunately, at this moment he chances to catch sight of Judith's face, which expresses the most prudish disapproval of his evident attraction for Essie, who is devouring him with her grateful eyes. His mocking expression returns instantly. He puts down the glass; deliberately winds his arm round Essie's shoulders; and brings her into the middle of the company. Mrs. Dudgeon being in Essie's way as they come past the table, he says) By your leave, mother (and compels her to make way for them). What do they call you? Bessie?

ESSIE. Essie.

RICHARD. Essie, to be sure. Are you a good girl, Essie?

ESSIE (greatly disappointed that he, of all people should begin at her in this way) Yes. (She looks doubtfully at Judith.) I think so. I mean I—I hope so.

RICHARD. Essie: did you ever hear of a person called the devil?

ANDERSON (revolted). Shame on you, sir, with a mere child—

RICHARD. By your leave, Minister: I do not interfere with your sermons: do not you interrupt mine. (To Essie.) Do you know what they call me, Essie?

ESSIE. Dick.

RICHARD (amused: patting her on the shoulder). Yes, Dick; but something else too. They call me the Devil's Disciple.

ESSIE. Why do you let them?

RICHARD (seriously). Because it's true. I was brought up in the other service; but I knew from the first that the Devil was my natural master and captain and friend. I saw that he was in the right, and that the world cringed to his conqueror only through fear. I prayed secretly to him; and he comforted me, and saved me from having my spirit broken in this house of children's tears. I promised him my soul, and swore an oath that I would stand up for him in this world and stand by him in the next. (Solemnly) That promise and that oath made a man of me. From this day this house is his home; and no child shall cry in it: this hearth is his altar; and no soul shall ever cower over it in the dark evenings and be afraid. Now (turning forcibly on the rest) which of you good men will take this child and rescue her from the house of the devil?

JUDITH (coming to Essie and throwing a protecting arm about her). I will. You should be burnt alive.

ESSIE. But I don't want to. (She shrinks back, leaving Richard and Judith face to face.)

RICHARD (to Judith). Actually doesn't want to, most virtuous lady!

UNCLE TITUS. Have a care, Richard Dudgeon. The law—

RICHARD (turning threateningly on him). Have a care, you. In an hour from this there will be no law here but martial law. I passed the soldiers within six miles on my way here: before noon Major Swindon's gallows for rebels will be up in the market place.

ANDERSON (calmly). What have we to fear from that, sir?

RICHARD. More than you think. He hanged the wrong man at Springtown: he thought Uncle Peter was respectable, because the Dudgeons had a good name. But his next example will be the best man in the town to whom he can bring home a rebellious word. Well, we're all rebels; and you know it.

ALL THE MEN (except Anderson). No, no, no!

RICHARD. Yes, you are. You haven't damned King George up hill and down dale as I have; but you've prayed for his defeat; and you, Anthony Anderson, have conducted the service, and sold your family bible to buy a pair of pistols. They mayn't hang me, perhaps; because the moral effect of the Devil's Disciple dancing on nothing wouldn't help them. But a Minister! (Judith, dismayed, clings to Anderson) or a lawyer! (Hawkins smiles like a man able to take care of himself) or an upright horsedealer! (Uncle Titus snarls at him in rags and terror) or a reformed drunkard (Uncle William, utterly unnerved, moans and wobbles with fear) eh? Would that show that King George meant business—ha?

ANDERSON (perfectly self-possessed). Come, my dear: he is only trying to frighten you. There is no danger. (He takes her out of the house. The rest crowd to the door to follow him, except Essie, who remains near Richard.)

RICHARD (boisterously derisive). Now then: how many of you will stay with me; run up the American flag on the devil's house; and make a fight for freedom? (They scramble out, Christy among them, hustling one another in their haste.) Ha ha! Long live the devil! (To Mrs. Dudgeon, who is following them) What mother! are you off too?

MRS. DUDGEON (deadly pale, with her hand on her heart as if she had received a deathblow). My curse on you! My dying curse! (She goes out.)

RICHARD (calling after her). It will bring me luck. Ha ha ha!

ESSIE (anxiously). Mayn't I stay?

RICHARD (turning to her). What! Have they forgotten to save your soul in their anxiety about their own bodies? Oh yes: you may stay. (He turns excitedly away again and shakes his fist after them. His left fist, also clenched, hangs down. Essie seizes it and kisses it, her tears falling on it. He starts and looks at it.) Tears! The devil's baptism! (She falls on her knees, sobbing. He stoops goodnaturedly to raise her, saying) Oh yes, you may cry that way, Essie, if you like.

ACT II

Minister Anderson's house is in the main street of Websterbridge, not far from the town hall. To the eye of the eighteenth century New Englander, it is much grander than the plain farmhouse of the Dudgeons; but it is so plain itself that a modern house agent would let both at about the same rent. The chief dwelling room has the same sort of kitchen fireplace, with boiler, toaster hanging on the bars, movable iron griddle socketed to the hob, hook above for roasting, and broad fender, on which stand a kettle and a plate of buttered toast. The door, between the fireplace and the corner, has neither panels, fingerplates nor handles: it is made of plain boards, and fastens with a latch. The table is a kitchen table, with a treacle colored cover of American cloth, chapped at the corners by draping. The tea service on it consists of two thick cups and saucers of the plainest ware, with milk jug and bowl to match, each large enough to contain nearly a quart, on a black japanned tray, and, in the middle of the table, a wooden trencher with a big loaf upon it, and a square half pound block of butter in a crock. The big oak press facing the fire from the opposite side of the room, is for use and storage, not for ornament; and the minister's house coat hangs on a peg from its door, showing that he is out; for when he is in it is his best coat that hangs there. His big riding boots stand beside the press, evidently in their usual place, and rather proud of themselves. In fact, the evolution of the minister's kitchen, dining room and drawing room into three separate apartments has not yet taken place; and so, from the point of view of our pampered period, he is no better off than the Dudgeons.

But there is a difference, for all that. To begin with, Mrs. Anderson is a pleasanter person to live with than Mrs. Dudgeon. To which Mrs. Dudgeon would at once reply, with reason, that Mrs. Anderson has no children to look after; no poultry, pigs nor cattle; a steady and sufficient income not directly dependent on harvests and prices at fairs; an affectionate husband who is a tower of strength to her: in short, that life is as easy at the minister's house as it is hard at the farm. This is true; but to explain a fact is not to alter it; and however little credit Mrs. Anderson may deserve for making her home happier, she has certainly succeeded in doing it. The outward and visible signs of her superior social pretensions are a drugget on the floor, a plaster ceiling between the timbers and chairs which, though not upholstered, are stained and polished. The fine arts are represented by a mezzotint portrait of some Presbyterian divine, a copperplate of Raphael's St. Paul preaching at Athens, a rococo presentation clock on the mantelshelf, flanked by a couple of miniatures, a pair of crockery dogs with baskets in their mouths, and, at the corners, two large cowrie shells. A pretty feature of the room is the low wide latticed window, nearly its whole width, with little red curtains running on a rod half way up it to serve as a blind. There is no sofa; but one of the seats, standing near the press, has a railed back and is long enough to accommodate two people easily. On the whole, it is rather the sort of room that the nineteenth century has ended in struggling to get back to under the leadership of Mr. Philip Webb and his disciples in domestic architecture, though no genteel clergyman would have tolerated it fifty years ago.

The evening has closed in; and the room is dark except for the cosy firelight and the dim oil lamps seen through the window in the wet street, where there is a quiet, steady, warm, windless downpour of rain. As the town clock strikes the quarter, Judith comes in with a couple of candles in earthenware candlesticks, and sets them on the table. Her self-conscious airs of the morning are gone: she is anxious and frightened. She goes to the window and peers into the street. The first thing she sees there is her husband, hurrying here through the rain. She gives a little gasp of relief, not very far removed from a sob, and turns to the door. Anderson comes in, wrapped in a very wet cloak.

JUDITH (running to him). Oh, here you are at last, at last! (She attempts to embrace him.)

ANDERSON (keeping her off). Take care, my love: I'm wet. Wait till I get my cloak off. (He places a chair with its back to the fire; hangs his cloak on it to dry; shakes the rain from his hat and puts it on the fender; and at last turns with his hands outstretched to Judith.) Now! (She flies into his arms.) I am not late, am I? The town clock struck the quarter as I came in at the front door. And the town clock is always fast.

JUDITH. I'm sure it's slow this evening. I'm so glad you're back.

ANDERSON (taking her more closely in his arms). Anxious, my dear?

JUDITH. A little.

ANDERSON. Why, you've been crying.

JUDITH. Only a little. Never mind: it's all over now. (A bugle call is heard in the distance. She starts in terror and retreats to the long seat, listening.) What's that?

ANDERSON (following her tenderly to the seat and making her sit down with him). Only King George, my dear. He's returning to barracks, or having his roll called, or getting ready for tea, or booting or saddling or something. Soldiers don't ring the bell or call over the banisters when they want anything: they send a boy out with a bugle to disturb the whole town.

JUDITH. Do you think there is really any danger?

ANDERSON. Not the least in the world.

JUDITH. You say that to comfort me, not because you believe it.

ANDERSON. My dear: in this world there is always danger for those who are afraid of it. There's a danger that the house will catch fire in the night; but we shan't sleep any the less soundly for that.

JUDITH. Yes, I know what you always say; and you're quite right. Oh, quite right: I know it. But—I suppose I'm not brave: that's all. My heart shrinks every time I think of the soldiers.

ANDERSON. Never mind that, dear: bravery is none the worse for costing a little pain.

JUDITH. Yes, I suppose so. (Embracing him again.) Oh how brave you are, my dear! (With tears in her eyes.) Well, I'll be brave too: you shan't be ashamed of your wife.

ANDERSON. That's right. Now you make me happy. Well, well! (He rises and goes cheerily to the fire to dry his shoes.) I called on Richard Dudgeon on my way back; but he wasn't in.

JUDITH (rising in consternation). You called on that man!

ANDERSON (reassuring her). Oh, nothing happened, dearie. He was out.

JUDITH (almost in tears, as if the visit were a personal humiliation to her). But why did you go there?

ANDERSON (gravely). Well, it is all the talk that Major Swindon is going to do what he did in Springtown—make an example of some notorious rebel, as he calls us. He pounced on Peter Dudgeon as the worst character there; and it is the general belief that he will pounce on Richard as the worst here.

JUDITH. But Richard said—

ANDERSON (goodhumoredly cutting her short). Pooh! Richard said! He said what he thought would frighten you and frighten me, my dear. He said what perhaps (God forgive him!) he would like to believe. It's a terrible thing to think of what death must mean for a man like that. I felt that I must warn him. I left a message for him.

JUDITH (querulously). What message?

ANDERSON. Only that I should be glad to see him for a moment on a matter of importance to himself; and that if he would look in here when he was passing he would be welcome.

JUDITH (aghast). You asked that man to come here!

ANDERSON. I did.

JUDITH (sinking on the seat and clasping her hands). I hope he won't come! Oh, I pray that he may not come!

ANDERSON. Why? Don't you want him to be warned?

JUDITH. He must know his danger. Oh, Tony, is it wrong to hate a blasphemer and a villain? I do hate him! I can't get him out of my mind: I know he will bring harm with him. He insulted you: he insulted me: he insulted his mother.

ANDERSON (quaintly). Well, dear, let's forgive him; and then it won't matter.

JUDITH. Oh, I know it's wrong to hate anybody; but—

ANDERSON (going over to her with humorous tenderness). Come, dear, you're not so wicked as you think. The worst sin towards our fellow creatures is not to hate them, but to be indifferent to them: that's the essence of inhumanity. After all, my dear, if you watch people carefully, you'll be surprised to find how like hate is to love. (She starts, strangely touched—even appalled. He is amused at her.) Yes: I'm quite in earnest. Think of how some of our married friends worry one another, tax one another, are jealous of one another, can't bear to let one another out of sight for a day, are more like jailers and slave-owners than lovers. Think of those very same people with their enemies, scrupulous, lofty, self-respecting, determined to be independent of one another, careful of how they speak of one another—pooh! haven't you often thought that if they only knew it, they were better friends to their enemies than to their own husbands and wives? Come: depend on it, my dear, you are really fonder of Richard than you are of me, if you only knew it. Eh?

JUDITH. Oh, don't say that: don't say that, Tony, even in jest. You don't know what a horrible feeling it gives me.

ANDERSON (Laughing). Well, well: never mind, pet. He's a bad man; and you hate him as he deserves. And you're going to make the tea, aren't you?

JUDITH (remorsefully). Oh yes, I forgot. I've been keeping you waiting all this time. (She goes to the fire and puts on the kettle.)

ANDERSON (going to the press and taking his coat off). Have you stitched up the shoulder of my old coat?

JUDITH. Yes, dear. (She goes to the table, and sets about putting the tea into the teapot from the caddy.)

ANDERSON (as he changes his coat for the older one hanging on the press, and replaces it by the one he has just taken off). Did anyone call when I was out?

JUDITH. No, only— (someone knocks at the door. With a start which betrays her intense nervousness, she retreats to the further end of the table with the tea caddy and spoon, in her hands, exclaiming) Who's that?

ANDERSON (going to her and patting her encouragingly on the shoulder). All right, pet, all right. He won't eat you, whoever he is. (She tries to smile, and nearly makes herself cry. He goes to the door and opens it. Richard is there, without overcoat or cloak.) You might have raised the latch and come in, Mr. Dudgeon. Nobody stands on much ceremony with us. (Hospitably.) Come in. (Richard comes in carelessly and stands at the table, looking round the room with a slight pucker of his nose at the mezzotinted divine on the wall. Judith keeps her eyes on the tea caddy.) Is it still raining? (He shuts the door.)

RICHARD. Raining like the very (his eye catches Judith's as she looks quickly and haughtily up)—I beg your pardon; but (showing that his coat is wet) you see—!

ANDERSON. Take it off, sir; and let it hang before the fire a while: my wife will excuse your shirtsleeves. Judith: put in another spoonful of tea for Mr. Dudgeon.

RICHARD (eyeing him cynically). The magic of property, Pastor! Are even YOU civil to me now that I have succeeded to my father's estate?

Judith throws down the spoon indignantly.

ANDERSON (quite unruffled, and helping Richard off with his coat). I think, sir, that since you accept my hospitality, you cannot have so bad an opinion of it. Sit down. (With the coat in his hand, he points to the railed seat. Richard, in his shirtsleeves, looks at him half quarrelsomely for a moment; then, with a nod, acknowledges that the minister has got the better of him, and sits down on the seat. Anderson pushes his cloak into a heap on the seat of the chair at the fire, and hangs Richard's coat on the back in its place.)

RICHARD. I come, sir, on your own invitation. You left word you had something important to tell me.

ANDERSON. I have a warning which it is my duty to give you.

RICHARD (quickly rising). You want to preach to me. Excuse me: I prefer a walk in the rain. (He makes for his coat.)

ANDERSON (stopping him). Don't be alarmed, sir; I am no great preacher. You are quite safe. (Richard smiles in spite of himself. His glance softens: he even makes a gesture of excuse. Anderson, seeing that he has tamed him, now addresses him earnestly.) Mr. Dudgeon: you are in danger in this town.

RICHARD. What danger?

ANDERSON. Your uncle's danger. Major Swindon's gallows.

RICHARD. It is you who are in danger. I warned you—

ANDERSON (interrupting him goodhumoredly but authoritatively). Yes, yes, Mr. Dudgeon; but they do not think so in the town. And even if I were in danger, I have duties here I must not forsake. But you are a free man. Why should you run any risk?

RICHARD. Do you think I should be any great loss, Minister?

ANDERSON. I think that a man's life is worth saving, whoever it belongs to. (Richard makes him an ironical bow. Anderson returns the bow humorously.) Come: you'll have a cup of tea, to prevent you catching cold?

RICHARD. I observe that Mrs. Anderson is not quite so pressing as you are, Pastor.

JUDITH (almost stifled with resentment, which she has been expecting her husband to share and express for her at every insult of Richard's). You are welcome for my husband's sake. (She brings the teapot to the fireplace and sets it on the hob.)

RICHARD. I know I am not welcome for my own, madam. (He rises.) But I think I will not break bread here, Minister.

ANDERSON (cheerily). Give me a good reason for that.

RICHARD. Because there is something in you that I respect, and that makes me desire to have you for my enemy.

ANDERSON. That's well said. On those terms, sir, I will accept your enmity or any man's. Judith: Mr. Dudgeon will stay to tea. Sit down: it will take a few minutes to draw by the fire. (Richard glances at him with a troubled face; then sits down with his head bent, to hide a convulsive swelling of his throat.) I was just saying to my wife, Mr. Dudgeon, that enmity— (she grasps his hand and looks imploringly at him, doing both with an intensity that checks him at once) Well, well, I mustn't tell you, I see; but it was nothing that need leave us worse friend—enemies, I mean. Judith is a great enemy of yours.

RICHARD. If all my enemies were like Mrs. Anderson I should be the best Christian in America.

ANDERSON (gratified, patting her hand). You hear that, Judith? Mr. Dudgeon knows how to turn a compliment.

The latch is lifted from without.

JUDITH (starting). Who is that?

Christy comes in.

CHRISTY (stopping and staring at Richard). Oh, are YOU here?

RICHARD. Yes. Begone, you fool: Mrs. Anderson doesn't want the whole family to tea at once.

CHRISTY (coming further in). Mother's very ill.

RICHARD. Well, does she want to see ME?

CHRISTY. No.

RICHARD. I thought not.

CHRISTY. She wants to see the minister—at once.

JUDITH (to Anderson). Oh, not before you've had some tea.

ANDERSON. I shall enjoy it more when I come back, dear. (He is about to take up his cloak.)

CHRISTY. The rain's over.

ANDERSON (dropping the cloak and picking up his hat from the fender). Where is your mother, Christy?

CHRISTY. At Uncle Titus's.

ANDERSON. Have you fetched the doctor?

CHRISTY. No: she didn't tell me to.

ANDERSON. Go on there at once: I'll overtake you on his doorstep. (Christy turns to go.) Wait a moment. Your brother must be anxious to know the particulars.

RICHARD. Psha! not I: he doesn't know; and I don't care. (Violently.) Be off, you oaf. (Christy runs out. Richard adds, a little shamefacedly) We shall know soon enough.

ANDERSON. Well, perhaps you will let me bring you the news myself. Judith: will you give Mr. Dudgeon his tea, and keep him here until I return?

JUDITH (white and trembling). Must I—

ANDERSON (taking her hands and interrupting her to cover her agitation). My dear: I can depend on you?

JUDITH (with a piteous effort to be worthy of his trust). Yes.

ANDERSON (pressing her hand against his cheek). You will not mind two old people like us, Mr. Dudgeon. (Going.) I shall not say good evening: you will be here when I come back. (He goes out.)

They watch him pass the window, and then look at each other dumbly, quite disconcerted. Richard, noting the quiver of her lips, is the first to pull himself together.

RICHARD. Mrs. Anderson: I am perfectly aware of the nature of your sentiments towards me. I shall not intrude on you. Good evening. (Again he starts for the fireplace to get his coat.)

JUDITH (getting between him and the coat). No, no. Don't go: please don't go.

RICHARD (roughly). Why? You don't want me here.

JUDITH. Yes, I— (wringing her hands in despair) Oh, if I tell you the truth, you will use it to torment me.

RICHARD (indignantly). Torment! What right have you to say that? Do you expect me to stay after that?

JUDITH. I want you to stay; but (suddenly raging at him like an angry child) it is not because I like you.

RICHARD. Indeed!

JUDITH. Yes: I had rather you did go than mistake me about that. I hate and dread you; and my husband knows it. If you are not here when he comes back, he will believe that I disobeyed him and drove you away.

RICHARD (ironically). Whereas, of course, you have really been so kind and hospitable and charming to me that I only want to go away out of mere contrariness, eh?

Judith, unable to bear it, sinks on the chair and bursts into tears.

RICHARD. Stop, stop, stop, I tell you. Don't do that. (Putting his hand to his breast as if to a wound.) He wrung my heart by being a man. Need you tear it by being a woman? Has he not raised you above my insults, like himself? (She stops crying, and recovers herself somewhat, looking at him with a scared curiosity.) There: that's right. (Sympathetically.) You're better now, aren't you? (He puts his hand encouragingly on her shoulder. She instantly rises haughtily, and stares at him defiantly. He at once drops into his usual sardonic tone.) Ah, that's better. You are yourself again: so is Richard. Well, shall we go to tea like a quiet respectable couple, and wait for your husband's return?

JUDITH (rather ashamed of herself). If you please. I—I am sorry to have been so foolish. (She stoops to take up the plate of toast from the fender.)

RICHARD. I am sorry, for your sake, that I am—what I am. Allow me. (He takes the plate from her and goes with it to the table.)

JUDITH (following with the teapot). Will you sit down? (He sits down at the end of the table nearest the press. There is a plate and knife laid there. The other plate is laid near it; but Judith stays at the opposite end of the table, next the fire, and takes her place there, drawing the tray towards her.) Do you take sugar?

RICHARD. No; but plenty of milk. Let me give you some toast. (He puts some on the second plate, and hands it to her, with the knife. The action shows quietly how well he knows that she has avoided her usual place so as to be as far from him as possible.)

JUDITH (consciously). Thanks. (She gives him his tea.) Won't you help yourself?

RICHARD. Thanks. (He puts a piece of toast on his own plate; and she pours out tea for herself.)

JUDITH (observing that he tastes nothing). Don't you like it? You are not eating anything.

RICHARD. Neither are you.

JUDITH (nervously). I never care much for my tea. Please don't mind me.

RICHARD (Looking dreamily round). I am thinking. It is all so strange to me. I can see the beauty and peace of this home: I think I have never been more at rest in my life than at this moment; and yet I know quite well I could never live here. It's not in my nature, I suppose, to be domesticated. But it's very beautiful: it's almost holy. (He muses a moment, and then laughs softly.)

JUDITH (quickly). Why do you laugh?

RICHARD. I was thinking that if any stranger came in here now, he would take us for man and wife.

JUDITH (taking offence). You mean, I suppose, that you are more my age than he is.

RICHARD (staring at this unexpected turn). I never thought of such a thing. (Sardonic again.) I see there is another side to domestic joy.

JUDITH (angrily). I would rather have a husband whom everybody respects than—than—

RICHARD. Than the devil's disciple. You are right; but I daresay your love helps him to be a good man, just as your hate helps me to be a bad one.

JUDITH. My husband has been very good to you. He has forgiven you for insulting him, and is trying to save you. Can you not forgive him for being so much better than you are? How dare you belittle him by putting yourself in his place?

RICHARD. Did I?

JUDITH. Yes, you did. You said that if anybody came in they would take us for man and— (she stops, terror-stricken, as a squad of soldiers tramps past the window) The English soldiers! Oh, what do they—

RICHARD (listening). Sh!

A VOICE (outside). Halt! Four outside: two in with me.

Judith half rises, listening and looking with dilated eyes at Richard, who takes up his cup prosaically, and is drinking his tea when the latch goes up with a sharp click, and an English sergeant walks into the room with two privates, who post themselves at the door. He comes promptly to the table between them.

THE SERGEANT. Sorry to disturb you, mum! duty! Anthony Anderson: I arrest you in King George's name as a rebel.

JUDITH (pointing at Richard). But that is not— (He looks up quickly at her, with a face of iron. She stops her mouth hastily with the hand she has raised to indicate him, and stands staring affrightedly.)

THE SERGEANT. Come, Parson; put your coat on and come along.

RICHARD. Yes: I'll come. (He rises and takes a step towards his own coat; then recollects himself, and, with his back to the sergeant, moves his gaze slowly round the room without turning his head until he sees Anderson's black coat hanging up on the press. He goes composedly to it; takes it down; and puts it on. The idea of himself as a parson tickles him: he looks down at the black sleeve on his arm, and then smiles slyly at Judith, whose white face shows him that what she is painfully struggling to grasp is not the humor of the situation but its horror. He turns to the sergeant, who is approaching him with a pair of handcuffs hidden behind him, and says lightly) Did you ever arrest a man of my cloth before, Sergeant?

THE SERGEANT (instinctively respectful, half to the black coat, half to Richard's good breeding). Well, no sir. At least, only an army chaplain. (Showing the handcuffs.) I'm sorry, air; but duty—

RICHARD. Just so, Sergeant. Well, I'm not ashamed of them: thank you kindly for the apology. (He holds out his hands.)

SERGEANT (not availing himself of the offer). One gentleman to another, sir. Wouldn't you like to say a word to your missis, sir, before you go?

RICHARD (smiling). Oh, we shall meet again before—eh? (Meaning "before you hang me.")

SERGEANT (loudly, with ostentatious cheerfulness). Oh, of course, of course. No call for the lady to distress herself. Still— (in a lower voice, intended for Richard alone) your last chance, sir.

They look at one another significantly for a moment. Than Richard exhales a deep breath and turns towards Judith.

RICHARD (very distinctly). My love. (She looks at him, pitiably pale, and tries to answer, but cannot—tries also to come to him, but cannot trust herself to stand without the support of the table.) This gallant gentleman is good enough to allow us a moment of leavetaking. (The sergeant retires delicately and joins his men near the door.) He is trying to spare you the truth; but you had better know it. Are you listening to me? (She signifies assent.) Do you understand that I am going to my death? (She signifies that she understands.) Remember, you must find our friend who was with us just now. Do you understand? (She signifies yes.) See that you get him safely out of harm's way. Don't for your life let him know of my danger; but if he finds it out, tell him that he cannot save me: they would hang him; and they would not spare me. And tell him that I am steadfast in my religion as he is in his, and that he may depend on me to the death. (He turns to go, and meets the eye of the sergeant, who looks a little suspicious. He considers a moment, and then, turning roguishly to Judith with something of a smile breaking through his earnestness, says) And now, my dear, I am afraid the sergeant will not believe that you love me like a wife unless you give one kiss before I go.

He approaches her and holds out his arms. She quits the table and almost falls into them.

JUDITH (the words choking her). I ought to—it's murder—

RICHARD. No: only a kiss (softly to her) for his sake.

JUDITH. I can't. You must—

RICHARD (folding her in his arms with an impulse of compassion for her distress). My poor girl!

Judith, with a sudden effort, throws her arms round him; kisses him; and swoons away, dropping from his arms to the ground as if the kiss had killed her.

RICHARD (going quickly to the sergeant). Now, Sergeant: quick, before she comes to. The handcuffs. (He puts out his hands.)

SERGEANT (pocketing them). Never mind, sir: I'll trust you. You're a game one. You ought to a bin a soldier, sir. Between them two, please. (The soldiers place themselves one before Richard and one behind him. The sergeant opens the door.)

RICHARD (taking a last look round him). Goodbye, wife: goodbye, home. Muffle the drums, and quick march!

The sergeant signs to the leading soldier to march. They file out quickly.

When Anderson returns from Mrs. Dudgeon's he is astonished to find the room apparently empty and almost in darkness except for the glow from the fire; for one of the candles has burnt out, and the other is at its last flicker.

ANDERSON. Why, what on earth—? (Calling) Judith, Judith! (He listens: there is no answer.) Hm! (He goes to the cupboard; takes a candle from the drawer; lights it at the flicker of the expiring one on the table; and looks wonderingly at the untasted meal by its light. Then he sticks it in the candlestick; takes off his hat; and scratches his head, much puzzled. This action causes him to look at the floor for the first time; and there he sees Judith lying motionless with her eyes closed. He runs to her and stoops beside her, lifting her head.) Judith.

JUDITH (waking; for her swoon has passed into the sleep of exhaustion after suffering). Yes. Did you call? What's the matter?

ANDERSON. I've just come in and found you lying here with the candles burnt out and the tea poured out and cold. What has happened?

JUDITH (still astray). I don't know. Have I been asleep? I suppose— (she stops blankly) I don't know.

ANDERSON (groaning). Heaven forgive me, I left you alone with that scoundrel. (Judith remembers. With an agonized cry, she clutches his shoulders and drags herself to her feet as he rises with her. He clasps her tenderly in his arms.) My poor pet!

JUDITH (frantically clinging to him). What shall I do? Oh my God, what shall I do?

ANDERSON. Never mind, never mind, my dearest dear: it was my fault. Come: you're safe now; and you're not hurt, are you? (He takes his arms from her to see whether she can stand.) There: that's right, that's right. If only you are not hurt, nothing else matters.

JUDITH. No, no, no: I'm not hurt.

ANDERSON. Thank Heaven for that! Come now: (leading her to the railed seat and making her sit down beside him) sit down and rest: you can tell me about it to-morrow. Or, (misunderstanding her distress) you shall not tell me at all if it worries you. There, there! (Cheerfully.) I'll make you some fresh tea: that will set you up again. (He goes to the table, and empties the teapot into the slop bowl.)

JUDITH (in a strained tone). Tony.

ANDERSON. Yes, dear?

JUDITH. Do you think we are only in a dream now?

ANDERSON (glancing round at her for a moment with a pang of anxiety, though he goes on steadily and cheerfully putting fresh tea into the pot). Perhaps so, pet. But you may as well dream a cup of tea when you're about it.

JUDITH. Oh, stop, stop. You don't know— (Distracted she buries her face in her knotted hands.)

ANDERSON (breaking down and coming to her). My dear, what is it? I can't bear it any longer: you must tell me. It was all my fault: I was mad to trust him.

JUDITH. No: don't say that. You mustn't say that. He—oh no, no: I can't. Tony: don't speak to me. Take my hands—both my hands. (He takes them, wondering.) Make me think of you, not of him. There's danger, frightful danger; but it is your danger; and I can't keep thinking of it: I can't, I can't: my mind goes back to his danger. He must be saved—no: you must be saved: you, you, you. (She springs up as if to do something or go somewhere, exclaiming) Oh, Heaven help me!

ANDERSON (keeping his seat and holding her hands with resolute composure). Calmly, calmly, my pet. You're quite distracted.

JUDITH. I may well be. I don't know what to do. I don't know what to do. (Tearing her hands away.) I must save him. (Anderson rises in alarm as she runs wildly to the door. It is opened in her face by Essie, who hurries in, full of anxiety. The surprise is so disagreeable to Judith that it brings her to her senses. Her tone is sharp and angry as she demands) What do you want?

ESSIE. I was to come to you.

ANDERSON. Who told you to?

ESSIE (staring at him, as if his presence astonished her). Are you here?

JUDITH. Of course. Don't be foolish, child.

ANDERSON. Gently, dearest: you'll frighten her. (Going between them.) Come here, Essie. (She comes to him.) Who sent you?

ESSIE. Dick. He sent me word by a soldier. I was to come here at once and do whatever Mrs. Anderson told me.

ANDERSON (enlightened). A soldier! Ah, I see it all now! They have arrested Richard. (Judith makes a gesture of despair.)

ESSIE. No. I asked the soldier. Dick's safe. But the soldier said you had been taken—

ANDERSON. I! (Bewildered, he turns to Judith for an explanation.)

JUDITH (coaxingly) All right, dear: I understand. (To Essie.) Thank you, Essie, for coming; but I don't need you now. You may go home.

ESSIE (suspicious) Are you sure Dick has not been touched? Perhaps he told the soldier to say it was the minister. (Anxiously.) Mrs. Anderson: do you think it can have been that?

ANDERSON. Tell her the truth if it is so, Judith. She will learn it from the first neighbor she meets in the street. (Judith turns away and covers her eyes with her hands.)

ESSIE (wailing). But what will they do to him? Oh, what will they do to him? Will they hang him? (Judith shudders convulsively, and throws herself into the chair in which Richard sat at the tea table.)

ANDERSON (patting Essie's shoulder and trying to comfort her). I hope not. I hope not. Perhaps if you're very quiet and patient, we may be able to help him in some way.

ESSIE. Yes—help him—yes, yes, yes. I'll be good.

ANDERSON. I must go to him at once, Judith.

JUDITH (springing up). Oh no. You must go away—far away, to some place of safety.

ANDERSON. Pooh!

JUDITH (passionately). Do you want to kill me? Do you think I can bear to live for days and days with every knock at the door—every footstep—giving me a spasm of terror? to lie awake for nights and nights in an agony of dread, listening for them to come and arrest you?

ANDERSON. Do you think it would be better to know that I had run away from my post at the first sign of danger?

JUDITH (bitterly). Oh, you won't go. I know it. You'll stay; and I shall go mad.

ANDERSON. My dear, your duty—

JUDITH (fiercely). What do I care about my duty?

ANDERSON (shocked). Judith!

JUDITH. I am doing my duty. I am clinging to my duty. My duty is to get you away, to save you, to leave him to his fate. (Essie utters a cry of distress and sinks on the chair at the fire, sobbing silently.) My instinct is the same as hers—to save him above all things, though it would be so much better for him to die! so much greater! But I know you will take your own way as he took it. I have no power. (She sits down sullenly on the railed seat.) I'm only a woman: I can do nothing but sit here and suffer. Only, tell him I tried to save you—that I did my best to save you.

ANDERSON. My dear, I am afraid he will be thinking more of his own danger than of mine.

JUDITH. Stop; or I shall hate you.

ANDERSON (remonstrating). Come, am I to leave you if you talk like this! your senses. (He turns to Essie.) Essie.

ESSIE (eagerly rising and drying her eyes). Yes?

ANDERSON. Just wait outside a moment, like a good girl: Mrs. Anderson is not well. (Essie looks doubtful.) Never fear: I'll come to you presently; and I'll go to Dick.

ESSIE. You are sure you will go to him? (Whispering.) You won't let her prevent you?

ANDERSON (smiling). No, no: it's all right. All right. (She goes.) That's a good girl. (He closes the door, and returns to Judith.)

JUDITH (seated—rigid). You are going to your death.

ANDERSON (quaintly). Then I shall go in my best coat, dear. (He turns to the press, beginning to take off his coat.) Where—? (He stares at the empty nail for a moment; then looks quickly round to the fire; strides across to it; and lifts Richard's coat.) Why, my dear, it seems that he has gone in my best coat.

JUDITH (still motionless). Yes.

ANDERSON. Did the soldiers make a mistake?

JUDITH. Yes: they made a mistake.

ANDERSON. He might have told them. Poor fellow, he was too upset, I suppose.

JUDITH. Yes: he might have told them. So might I.

ANDERSON. Well, it's all very puzzling—almost funny. It's curious how these little things strike us even in the most— (he breaks off and begins putting on Richard's coat) I'd better take him his own coat. I know what he'll say— (imitating Richard's sardonic manner) "Anxious about my soul, Pastor, and also about your best coat." Eh?

JUDITH. Yes, that is just what he will say to you. (Vacantly.) It doesn't matter: I shall never see either of you again.

ANDERSON (rallying her). Oh pooh, pooh, pooh! (He sits down beside her.) Is this how you keep your promise that I shan't be ashamed of my brave wife?

JUDITH. No: this is how I break it. I cannot keep my promises to him: why should I keep my promises to you?

ANDERSON. Don't speak so strangely, my love. It sounds insincere to me. (She looks unutterable reproach at him.) Yes, dear, nonsense is always insincere; and my dearest is talking nonsense. Just nonsense. (Her face darkens into dumb obstinacy. She stares straight before her, and does not look at him again, absorbed in Richard's fate. He scans her face; sees that his rallying has produced no effect; and gives it up, making no further effort to conceal his anxiety.) I wish I knew what has frightened you so. Was there a struggle? Did he fight?

JUDITH. No. He smiled.

ANDERSON. Did he realise his danger, do you think?

JUDITH. He realised yours.

ANDERSON. Mine!

JUDITH (monotonously). He said, "See that you get him safely out of harm's way." I promised: I can't keep my promise. He said, "Don't for your life let him know of my danger." I've told you of it. He said that if you found it out, you could not save him—that they will hang him and not spare you.

ANDERSON (rising in generous indignation). And you think that I will let a man with that much good in him die like a dog, when a few words might make him die like a Christian? I'm ashamed of you, Judith.

JUDITH. He will be steadfast in his religion as you are in yours; and you may depend on him to the death. He said so.

ANDERSON. God forgive him! What else did he say?

JUDITH. He said goodbye.

ANDERSON (fidgeting nervously to and fro in great concern). Poor fellow, poor fellow! You said goodbye to him in all kindness and charity, Judith, I hope.

JUDITH. I kissed him.

ANDERSON. What! Judith!

JUDITH. Are you angry?

ANDERSON. No, no. You were right: you were right. Poor fellow, poor fellow! (Greatly distressed.) To be hanged like that at his age! And then did they take him away?

JUDITH (wearily). Then you were here: that's the next thing I remember. I suppose I fainted. Now bid me goodbye, Tony. Perhaps I shall faint again. I wish I could die.

ANDERSON. No, no, my dear: you must pull yourself together and be sensible. I am in no danger—not the least in the world.

JUDITH (solemnly). You are going to your death, Tony—your sure death, if God will let innocent men be murdered. They will not let you see him: they will arrest you the moment you give your name. It was for you the soldiers came.

ANDERSON (thunderstruck). For me!!! (His fists clinch; his neck thickens; his face reddens; the fleshy purses under his eyes become injected with hot blood; the man of peace vanishes, transfigured into a choleric and formidable man of war. Still, she does not come out of her absorption to look at him: her eyes are steadfast with a mechanical reflection of Richard's stead-fastness.)

JUDITH. He took your place: he is dying to save you. That is why he went in your coat. That is why I kissed him.

ANDERSON (exploding). Blood an' owns! (His voice is rough and dominant, his gesture full of brute energy.) Here! Essie, Essie!

ESSIE (running in). Yes.

ANDERSON (impetuously). Off with you as hard as you can run, to the inn. Tell them to saddle the fastest and strongest horse they have (Judith rises breathless, and stares at him incredulously)—the chestnut mare, if she's fresh—without a moment's delay. Go into the stable yard and tell the black man there that I'll give him a silver dollar if the horse is waiting for me when I come, and that I am close on your heels. Away with you. (His energy sends Essie flying from the room. He pounces on his riding boots; rushes with them to the chair at the fire; and begins pulling them on.)

JUDITH (unable to believe such a thing of him). You are not going to him!

ANDERSON (busy with the boots). Going to him! What good would that do? (Growling to himself as he gets the first boot on with a wrench) I'll go to them, so I will. (To Judith peremptorily) Get me the pistols: I want them. And money, money: I want money—all the money in the house. (He stoops over the other boot, grumbling) A great satisfaction it would be to him to have my company on the gallows. (He pulls on the boot.)

JUDITH. You are deserting him, then?

ANDERSON. Hold your tongue, woman; and get me the pistols. (She goes to the press and takes from it a leather belt with two pistols, a powder horn, and a bag of bullets attached to it. She throws it on the table. Then she unlocks a drawer in the press and takes out a purse. Anderson grabs the belt and buckles it on, saying) If they took him for me in my coat, perhaps they'll take me for him in his. (Hitching the belt into its place) Do I look like him?

JUDITH (turning with the purse in her hand). Horribly unlike him.

ANDERSON (snatching the purse from her and emptying it on the table). Hm! We shall see.

JUDITH (sitting down helplessly). Is it of any use to pray, do you think, Tony?

ANDERSON (counting the money). Pray! Can we pray Swindon's rope off Richard's neck?

JUDITH. God may soften Major Swindon's heart.

ANDERSON (contemptuously—pocketing a handful of money). Let him, then. I am not God; and I must go to work another way. (Judith gasps at the blasphemy. He throws the purse on the table.) Keep that. I've taken 25 dollars.

JUDITH. Have you forgotten even that you are a minister?

ANDERSON. Minister be—faugh! My hat: where's my hat? (He snatches up hat and cloak, and puts both on in hot haste.) Now listen, you. If you can get a word with him by pretending you're his wife, tell him to hold his tongue until morning: that will give me all the start I need.

JUDITH (solemnly). You may depend on him to the death.

ANDERSON. You're a fool, a fool, Judith (for a moment checking the torrent of his haste, and speaking with something of his old quiet and impressive conviction). You don't know the man you're married to. (Essie returns. He swoops at her at once.) Well: is the horse ready?

ESSIE (breathless). It will be ready when you come.

ANDERSON. Good. (He makes for the door.)

JUDITH (rising and stretching out her arms after him involuntarily). Won't you say goodbye?

ANDERSON. And waste another half minute! Psha! (He rushes out like an avalanche.)

ESSIE (hurrying to Judith). He has gone to save Richard, hasn't he?

JUDITH. To save Richard! No: Richard has saved him. He has gone to save himself. Richard must die.

Essie screams with terror and falls on her knees, hiding her face. Judith, without heeding her, looks rigidly straight in front of her, at the vision of Richard, dying.

ACT III

Early next morning the sergeant, at the British headquarters in the Town Hall, unlocks the door of a little empty panelled waiting room, and invites Judith to enter. She has had a bad night, probably a rather delirious one; for even in the reality of the raw morning, her fixed gaze comes back at moments when her attention is not strongly held.

The sergeant considers that her feelings do her credit, and is sympathetic in an encouraging military way. Being a fine figure of a man, vain of his uniform and of his rank, he feels specially qualified, in a respectful way, to console her.

SERGEANT. You can have a quiet word with him here, mum.

JUDITH. Shall I have long to wait?

SERGEANT. No, mum, not a minute. We kep him in the Bridewell for the night; and he's just been brought over here for the court martial. Don't fret, mum: he slep like a child, and has made a rare good breakfast.

JUDITH (incredulously). He is in good spirits!

SERGEANT. Tip top, mum. The chaplain looked in to see him last night; and he won seventeen shillings off him at spoil five. He spent it among us like the gentleman he is. Duty's duty, mum, of course; but you're among friends here. (The tramp of a couple of soldiers is heard approaching.) There: I think he's coming. (Richard comes in, without a sign of care or captivity in his bearing. The sergeant nods to the two soldiers, and shows them the key of the room in his hand. They withdraw.) Your good lady, sir.

RICHARD (going to her). What! My wife. My adored one. (He takes her hand and kisses it with a perverse, raffish gallantry.) How long do you allow a brokenhearted husband for leave-taking, Sergeant?

SERGEANT. As long as we can, sir. We shall not disturb you till the court sits.

RICHARD. But it has struck the hour.

SERGEANT. So it has, sir; but there's a delay. General Burgoyne's just arrived—Gentlemanly Johnny we call him, sir—and he won't have done finding fault with everything this side of half past. I know him, sir: I served with him in Portugal. You may count on twenty minutes, sir; and by your leave I won't waste any more of them. (He goes out, locking the door. Richard immediately drops his raffish manner and turns to Judith with considerate sincerity.)

RICHARD. Mrs. Anderson: this visit is very kind of you. And how are you after last night? I had to leave you before you recovered; but I sent word to Essie to go and look after you. Did she understand the message?

JUDITH (breathless and urgent). Oh, don't think of me: I haven't come here to talk about myself. Are they going to—to— (meaning "to hang you")?

RICHARD (whimsically). At noon, punctually. At least, that was when they disposed of Uncle Peter. (She shudders.) Is your husband safe? Is he on the wing?

JUDITH. He is no longer my husband.

RICHARD (opening his eyes wide). Eh!

JUDITH. I disobeyed you. I told him everything. I expected him to come here and save you. I wanted him to come here and save you. He ran away instead.

RICHARD. Well, that's what I meant him to do. What good would his staying have done? They'd only have hanged us both.

JUDITH (with reproachful earnestness). Richard Dudgeon: on your honour, what would you have done in his place?

RICHARD. Exactly what he has done, of course.

JUDITH. Oh, why will you not be simple with me—honest and straightforward? If you are so selfish as that, why did you let them take you last night?

RICHARD (gaily). Upon my life, Mrs. Anderson, I don't know. I've been asking myself that question ever since; and I can find no manner of reason for acting as I did.

JUDITH. You know you did it for his sake, believing he was a more worthy man than yourself.

RICHARD (laughing). Oho! No: that's a very pretty reason, I must say; but I'm not so modest as that. No: it wasn't for his sake.

JUDITH (after a pause, during which she looks shamefacedly at him, blushing painfully). Was it for my sake?

RICHARD (gallantly). Well, you had a hand in it. It must have been a little for your sake. You let them take me, at all events.

JUDITH. Oh, do you think I have not been telling myself that all night? Your death will be at my door. (Impulsively, she gives him her hand, and adds, with intense earnestness) If I could save you as you saved him, I would do it, no matter how cruel the death was.

RICHARD (holding her hand and smiling, but keeping her almost at arm's length). I am very sure I shouldn't let you.

JUDITH. Don't you see that I can save you?

RICHARD. How? By changing clothes with me, eh?

JUDITH (disengaging her hand to touch his lips with it). Don't (meaning "Don't jest"). No: by telling the Court who you really are.

RICHARD (frowning). No use: they wouldn't spare me; and it would spoil half of his chance of escaping. They are determined to cow us by making an example of somebody on that gallows to-day. Well, let us cow them by showing that we can stand by one another to the death. That is the only force that can send Burgoyne back across the Atlantic and make America a nation.

JUDITH (impatiently). Oh, what does all that matter?

RICHARD (laughing). True: what does it matter? what does anything matter? You see, men have these strange notions, Mrs. Anderson; and women see the folly of them.

JUDITH. Women have to lose those they love through them.

RICHARD. They can easily get fresh lovers.

JUDITH (revolted). Oh! (Vehemently) Do you realise that you are going to kill yourself?

RICHARD. The only man I have any right to kill, Mrs. Anderson. Don't be concerned: no woman will lose her lover through my death. (Smiling) Bless you, nobody cares for me. Have you heard that my mother is dead?

JUDITH. Dead!

RICHARD. Of heart disease—in the night. Her last word to me was her curse: I don't think I could have borne her blessing. My other relatives will not grieve much on my account. Essie will cry for a day or two; but I have provided for her: I made my own will last night.

JUDITH (stonily, after a moment's silence). And I!

RICHARD (surprised). You?

JUDITH. Yes, I. Am I not to care at all?

RICHARD (gaily and bluntly). Not a scrap. Oh, you expressed your feelings towards me very frankly yesterday. What happened may have softened you for the moment; but believe me, Mrs. Anderson, you don't like a bone in my skin or a hair on my head. I shall be as good a riddance at 12 today as I should have been at 12 yesterday.

JUDITH (her voice trembling). What can I do to show you that you are mistaken?

RICHARD. Don't trouble. I'll give you credit for liking me a little better than you did. All I say is that my death will not break your heart.

JUDITH (almost in a whisper). How do you know? (She puts her hands on his shoulders and looks intently at him.)

RICHARD (amazed—divining the truth). Mrs. Anderson!!! (The bell of the town clock strikes the quarter. He collects himself, and removes her hands, saying rather coldly) Excuse me: they will be here for me presently. It is too late.

JUDITH. It is not too late. Call me as witness: they will never kill you when they know how heroically you have acted.

RICHARD (with some scorn). Indeed! But if I don't go through with it, where will the heroism be? I shall simply have tricked them; and they'll hang me for that like a dog. Serve me right too!

JUDITH (wildly). Oh, I believe you WANT to die.

RICHARD (obstinately). No I don't.

JUDITH. Then why not try to save yourself? I implore you—listen. You said just now that you saved him for my sake—yes (clutching him as he recoils with a gesture of denial) a little for my sake. Well, save yourself for my sake. And I will go with you to the end of the world.

RICHARD (taking her by the wrists and holding her a little way from him, looking steadily at her). Judith.

JUDITH (breathless—delighted at the name). Yes.

RICHARD. If I said—to please you—that I did what I did ever so little for your sake, I lied as men always lie to women. You know how much I have lived with worthless men—aye, and worthless women too. Well, they could all rise to some sort of goodness and kindness when they were in love. (The word love comes from him with true Puritan scorn.) That has taught me to set very little store by the goodness that only comes out red hot. What I did last night, I did in cold blood, caring not half so much for your husband, or (ruthlessly) for you (she droops, stricken) as I do for myself. I had no motive and no interest: all I can tell you is that when it came to the point whether I would take my neck out of the noose and put another man's into it, I could not do it. I don't know why not: I see myself as a fool for my pains; but I could not and I cannot. I have been brought up standing by the law of my own nature; and I may not go against it, gallows or no gallows. (She has slowly raised her head and is now looking full at him.) I should have done the same for any other man in the town, or any other man's wife. (Releasing her.) Do you understand that?

JUDITH. Yes: you mean that you do not love me.

RICHARD (revolted—with fierce contempt). Is that all it means to you?

JUDITH. What more—what worse—can it mean to me?

(The sergeant knocks. The blow on the door jars on her heart.) Oh, one moment more. (She throws herself on her knees.) I pray to you—

RICHARD. Hush! (Calling) Come in. (The sergeant unlocks the door and opens it. The guard is with him.)

SERGEANT (coming in). Time's up, sir.

RICHARD. Quite ready, Sergeant. Now, my dear. (He attempts to raise her.)

JUDITH (clinging to him). Only one thing more—I entreat, I implore you. Let me be present in the court. I have seen Major Swindon: he said I should be allowed if you asked it. You will ask it. It is my last request: I shall never ask you anything again. (She clasps his knee.) I beg and pray it of you.

RICHARD. If I do, will you be silent?

JUDITH. Yes.

RICHARD. You will keep faith?

JUDITH. I will keep— (She breaks down, sobbing.)

RICHARD (taking her arm to lift her). Just—her other arm, Sergeant.

They go out, she sobbing convulsively, supported by the two men.

Meanwhile, the Council Chamber is ready for the court martial. It is a large, lofty room, with a chair of state in the middle under a tall canopy with a gilt crown, and maroon curtains with the royal monogram G. R. In front of the chair is a table, also draped in maroon, with a bell, a heavy inkstand, and writing materials on it. Several chairs are set at the table. The door is at the right hand of the occupant of the chair of state when it has an occupant: at present it is empty. Major Swindon, a pale, sandy-haired, very conscientious looking man of about 45, sits at the end of the table with his back to the door, writing. He is alone until the sergeant announces the General in a subdued manner which suggests that Gentlemanly Johnny has been making his presence felt rather heavily.

SERGEANT. The General, sir.

Swindon rises hastily. The General comes in, the sergeant goes out. General Burgoyne is 55, and very well preserved. He is a man of fashion, gallant enough to have made a distinguished marriage by an elopement, witty enough to write successful comedies, aristocratically-connected enough to have had opportunities of high military distinction. His eyes, large, brilliant, apprehensive, and intelligent, are his most remarkable feature: without them his fine nose and small mouth would suggest rather more fastidiousness and less force than go to the making of a first rate general. Just now the eyes are angry and tragic, and the mouth and nostrils tense.

BURGOYNE. Major Swindon, I presume.

SWINDON. Yes. General Burgoyne, if I mistake not. (They bow to one another ceremoniously.) I am glad to have the support of your presence this morning. It is not particularly lively business, hanging this poor devil of a minister.

BURGOYNE (throwing himself onto Swindon's chair). No, sir, it is not. It is making too much of the fellow to execute him: what more could you have done if he had been a member of the Church of England? Martyrdom, sir, is what these people like: it is the only way in which a man can become famous without ability. However, you have committed us to hanging him: and the sooner he is hanged the better.

SWINDON. We have arranged it for 12 o'clock. Nothing remains to be done except to try him.

BURGOYNE (looking at him with suppressed anger). Nothing—except to save our own necks, perhaps. Have you heard the news from Springtown?

SWINDON. Nothing special. The latest reports are satisfactory.

BURGOYNE (rising in amazement). Satisfactory, sir! Satisfactory!! (He stares at him for a moment, and then adds, with grim intensity) I am glad you take that view of them.

SWINDON (puzzled). Do I understand that in your opinion—

BURGOYNE. I do not express my opinion. I never stoop to that habit of profane language which unfortunately coarsens our profession. If I did, sir, perhaps I should be able to express my opinion of the news from Springtown—the news which YOU (severely) have apparently not heard. How soon do you get news from your supports here?—in the course of a month eh?

SWINDON (turning sulky). I suppose the reports have been taken to you, sir, instead of to me. Is there anything serious?

BURGOYNE (taking a report from his pocket and holding it up). Springtown's in the hands of the rebels. (He throws the report on the table.)

SWINDON (aghast). Since yesterday!

BURGOYNE. Since two o'clock this morning. Perhaps WE shall be in their hands before two o'clock to-morrow morning. Have you thought of that?

SWINDON (confidently). As to that, General, the British soldier will give a good account of himself.

BURGOYNE (bitterly). And therefore, I suppose, sir, the British officer need not know his business: the British soldier will get him out of all his blunders with the bayonet. In future, sir, I must ask you to be a little less generous with the blood of your men, and a little more generous with your own brains.

SWINDON. I am sorry I cannot pretend to your intellectual eminence, sir. I can only do my best, and rely on the devotion of my countrymen.

BURGOYNE (suddenly becoming suavely sarcastic). May I ask are you writing a melodrama, Major Swindon?

SWINDON (flushing). No, sir.

BURGOYNE. What a pity! WHAT a pity! (Dropping his sarcastic tone and facing him suddenly and seriously) Do you at all realize, sir, that we have nothing standing between us and destruction but our own bluff and the sheepishness of these colonists? They are men of the same English stock as ourselves: six to one of us (repeating it emphatically), six to one, sir; and nearly half our troops are Hessians, Brunswickers, German dragoons, and Indians with scalping knives. These are the countrymen on whose devotion you rely! Suppose the colonists find a leader! Suppose the news from Springtown should turn out to mean that they have already found a leader! What shall we do then? Eh?

SWINDON (sullenly). Our duty, sir, I presume.

BURGOYNE (again sarcastic—giving him up as a fool). Quite so, quite so. Thank you, Major Swindon, thank you. Now you've settled the question, sir—thrown a flood of light on the situation. What a comfort to me to feel that I have at my side so devoted and able an officer to support me in this emergency! I think, sir, it will probably relieve both our feelings if we proceed to hang this dissenter without further delay (he strikes the bell), especially as I am debarred by my principles from the customary military vent for my feelings. (The sergeant appears.) Bring your man in.

SERGEANT. Yes, sir.

BURGOYNE. And mention to any officer you may meet that the court cannot wait any longer for him.

SWINDON (keeping his temper with difficulty). The staff is perfectly ready, sir. They have been waiting your convenience for fully half an hour. PERFECTLY ready, sir.

BURGOYNE (blandly). So am I. (Several officers come in and take their seats. One of them sits at the end of the table furthest from the door, and acts throughout as clerk to the court, making notes of the proceedings. The uniforms are those of the 9th, 20th, 21st, 24th, 47th, 53rd, and 62nd British Infantry. One officer is a Major General of the Royal Artillery. There are also German officers of the Hessian Rifles, and of German dragoon and Brunswicker regiments.) Oh, good morning, gentlemen. Sorry to disturb you, I am sure. Very good of you to spare us a few moments.

SWINDON. Will you preside, sir?

BURGOYNE (becoming additionally, polished, lofty, sarcastic and urbane now that he is in public). No, sir: I feel my own deficiencies too keenly to presume so far. If you will kindly allow me, I will sit at the feet of Gamaliel. (He takes the chair at the end of the table next the door, and motions Swindon to the chair of state, waiting for him to be seated before sitting himself.)

SWINDON (greatly annoyed). As you please, sir. I am only trying to do my duty under excessively trying circumstances. (He takes his place in the chair of state.)

Burgoyne, relaxing his studied demeanor for the moment, sits down and begins to read the report with knitted brows and careworn looks, reflecting on his desperate situation and Swindon's uselessness. Richard is brought in. Judith walks beside him. Two soldiers precede and two follow him, with the sergeant in command. They cross the room to the wall opposite the door; but when Richard has just passed before the chair of state the sergeant stops him with a touch on the arm, and posts himself behind him, at his elbow. Judith stands timidly at the wall. The four soldiers place themselves in a squad near her.

BURGOYNE (looking up and seeing Judith). Who is that woman?

SERGEANT. Prisoner's wife, sir.

SWINDON (nervously). She begged me to allow her to be present; and I thought—

BURGOYNE (completing the sentence for him ironically). You thought it would be a pleasure for her. Quite so, quite so. (Blandly) Give the lady a chair; and make her thoroughly comfortable.

The sergeant fetches a chair and places it near Richard.

JUDITH. Thank you, sir. (She sits down after an awe-stricken curtsy to Burgoyne, which he acknowledges by a dignified bend of his head.)

SWINDON (to Richard, sharply). Your name, sir?

RICHARD (affable, but obstinate). Come: you don't mean to say that you've brought me here without knowing who I am?

SWINDON. As a matter of form, sir, give your name.

RICHARD. As a matter of form then, my name is Anthony Anderson, Presbyterian minister in this town.

BURGOYNE (interested). Indeed! Pray, Mr. Anderson, what do you gentlemen believe?

RICHARD. I shall be happy to explain if time is allowed me. I cannot undertake to complete your conversion in less than a fortnight.

SWINDON (snubbing him). We are not here to discuss your views.

BURGOYNE (with an elaborate bow to the unfortunate Swindon). I stand rebuked.

SWINDON (embarrassed). Oh, not you, I as—

BURGOYNE. Don't mention it. (To Richard, very politely) Any political views, Mr. Anderson?

RICHARD. I understand that that is just what we are here to find out.

SWINDON (severely). Do you mean to deny that you are a rebel?

RICHARD. I am an American, sir.

SWINDON. What do you expect me to think of that speech, Mr. Anderson?

RICHARD. I never expect a soldier to think, sir.

Burgoyne is boundlessly delighted by this retort, which almost reconciles him to the loss of America.

SWINDON (whitening with anger). I advise you not to be insolent, prisoner.

RICHARD. You can't help yourself, General. When you make up your mind to hang a man, you put yourself at a disadvantage with him. Why should I be civil to you? I may as well be hanged for a sheep as a lamb.

SWINDON. You have no right to assume that the court has made up its mind without a fair trial. And you will please not address me as General. I am Major Swindon.

RICHARD. A thousand pardons. I thought I had the honor of addressing Gentlemanly Johnny.

Sensation among the officers. The sergeant has a narrow escape from a guffaw.

BURGOYNE (with extreme suavity). I believe I am Gentlemanly Johnny, sir, at your service. My more intimate friends call me General Burgoyne. (Richard bows with perfect politeness.) You will understand, sir, I hope, since you seem to be a gentleman and a man of some spirit in spite of your calling, that if we should have the misfortune to hang you, we shall do so as a mere matter of political necessity and military duty, without any personal ill-feeling.

RICHARD. Oh, quite so. That makes all the difference in the world, of course.

They all smile in spite of themselves: and some of the younger officers burst out laughing.

JUDITH (her dread and horror deepening at every one of these jests and compliments). How CAN you?

RICHARD. You promised to be silent.

BURGOYNE (to Judith, with studied courtesy). Believe me, madam, your husband is placing us under the greatest obligation by taking this very disagreeable business so thoroughly in the spirit of a gentleman. Sergeant: give Mr. Anderson a chair. (The sergeant does so. Richard sits down.) Now, Major Swindon: we are waiting for you.

SWINDON. You are aware, I presume, Mr. Anderson, of your obligations as a subject of His Majesty King George the Third.

RICHARD. I am aware, sir, that His Majesty King George the Third is about to hang me because I object to Lord North's robbing me.

SWINDON. That is a treasonable speech, sir.

RICHARD (briefly). Yes. I meant it to be.

BURGOYNE (strongly deprecating this line of defence, but still polite). Don't you think, Mr. Anderson, that this is rather—if you will excuse the word—a vulgar line to take? Why should you cry out robbery because of a stamp duty and a tea duty and so forth? After all, it is the essence of your position as a gentleman that you pay with a good grace.

RICHARD. It is not the money, General. But to be swindled by a pig-headed lunatic like King George.

SWINDON (scandalised). Chut, sir—silence!

SERGEANT (in stentorian tones, greatly shocked). Silence!

BURGOYNE (unruffled). Ah, that is another point of view. My position does not allow of my going into that, except in private. But (shrugging his shoulders) of course, Mr. Anderson, if you are determined to be hanged (Judith flinches), there's nothing more to be said. An unusual taste! however (with a final shrug)—!

SWINDON (to Burgoyne). Shall we call witnesses?

RICHARD. What need is there of witnesses? If the townspeople here had listened to me, you would have found the streets barricaded, the houses loopholed, and the people in arms to hold the town against you to the last man. But you arrived, unfortunately, before we had got out of the talking stage; and then it was too late.

SWINDON (severely). Well, sir, we shall teach you and your townspeople a lesson they will not forget. Have you anything more to say?

RICHARD. I think you might have the decency to treat me as a prisoner of war, and shoot me like a man instead of hanging me like a dog.

BURGOYNE (sympathetically). Now there, Mr. Anderson, you talk like a civilian, if you will excuse my saying so. Have you any idea of the average marksmanship of the army of His Majesty King George the Third? If we make you up a firing party, what will happen? Half of them will miss you: the rest will make a mess of the business and leave you to the provo-marshal's pistol. Whereas we can hang you in a perfectly workmanlike and agreeable way. (Kindly) Let me persuade you to be hanged, Mr. Anderson?

JUDITH (sick with horror). My God!

RICHARD (to Judith). Your promise! (To Burgoyne) Thank you, General: that view of the case did not occur to me before. To oblige you, I withdraw my objection to the rope. Hang me, by all means.

BURGOYNE (smoothly). Will 12 o'clock suit you, Mr. Anderson?

RICHARD. I shall be at your disposal then, General.

BURGOYNE (rising). Nothing more to be said, gentlemen. (They all rise.)

JUDITH (rushing to the table). Oh, you are not going to murder a man like that, without a proper trial—without thinking of what you are doing—without— (She cannot find words.)

RICHARD. Is this how you keep your promise?

JUDITH. If I am not to speak, you must. Defend yourself: save yourself: tell them the truth.

RICHARD (worriedly). I have told them truth enough to hang me ten times over. If you say another word you will risk other lives; but you will not save mine.

BURGOYNE. My good lady, our only desire is to save unpleasantness. What satisfaction would it give you to have a solemn fuss made, with my friend Swindon in a black cap and so forth? I am sure we are greatly indebted to the admirable tact and gentlemanly feeling shown by your husband.

JUDITH (throwing the words in his face). Oh, you are mad. Is it nothing to you what wicked thing you do if only you do it like a gentleman? Is it nothing to you whether you are a murderer or not, if only you murder in a red coat? (Desperately) You shall not hang him: that man is not my husband.

The officers look at one another, and whisper: some of the Germans asking their neighbors to explain what the woman has said. Burgoyne, who has been visibly shaken by Judith's reproach, recovers himself promptly at this new development. Richard meanwhile raises his voice above the buzz.

RICHARD. I appeal to you, gentlemen, to put an end to this. She will not believe that she cannot save me. Break up the court.

BURGOYNE (in a voice so quiet and firm that it restores silence at once). One moment, Mr. Anderson. One moment, gentlemen. (He resumes his seat. Swindon and the officers follow his example.) Let me understand you clearly, madam. Do you mean that this gentleman is not your husband, or merely—I wish to put this with all delicacy—that you are not his wife?

JUDITH. I don't know what you mean. I say that he is not my husband—that my husband has escaped. This man took his place to save him. Ask anyone in the town—send out into the street for the first person you find there, and bring him in as a witness. He will tell you that the prisoner is not Anthony Anderson.

BURGOYNE (quietly, as before). Sergeant.

SERGEANT. Yes sir.

BURGOYNE. Go out into the street and bring in the first townsman you see there.

SERGEANT (making for the door). Yes sir.

BURGOYNE (as the sergeant passes). The first clean, sober townsman you see.

SERGEANT. Yes Sir. (He goes out.)

BURGOYNE. Sit down, Mr. Anderson—if I may call you so for the present. (Richard sits down.) Sit down, madam, whilst we wait. Give the lady a newspaper.

RICHARD (indignantly). Shame!

BURGOYNE (keenly, with a half smile). If you are not her husband, sir, the case is not a serious one—for her. (Richard bites his lip silenced.)

JUDITH (to Richard, as she returns to her seat). I couldn't help it. (He shakes his head. She sits down.)

BURGOYNE. You will understand of course, Mr. Anderson, that you must not build on this little incident. We are bound to make an example of somebody.

RICHARD. I quite understand. I suppose there's no use in my explaining.

BURGOYNE. I think we should prefer independent testimony, if you don't mind.

The sergeant, with a packet of papers in his hand, returns conducting Christy, who is much scared.

SERGEANT (giving Burgoyne the packet). Dispatches, Sir. Delivered by a corporal of the 53rd. Dead beat with hard riding, sir.

Burgoyne opens the dispatches, and presently becomes absorbed in them. They are so serious as to take his attention completely from the court martial.

SERGEANT (to Christy). Now then. Attention; and take your hat off. (He posts himself in charge of Christy, who stands on Burgoyne's side of the court.)

RICHARD (in his usual bullying tone to Christy). Don't be frightened, you fool: you're only wanted as a witness. They're not going to hang YOU.

SWINDON. What's your name?

CHRISTY. Christy.

RICHARD (impatiently). Christopher Dudgeon, you blatant idiot. Give your full name.

SWINDON. Be silent, prisoner. You must not prompt the witness.

RICHARD. Very well. But I warn you you'll get nothing out of him unless you shake it out of him. He has been too well brought up by a pious mother to have any sense or manhood left in him.

BURGOYNE (springing up and speaking to the sergeant in a startling voice). Where is the man who brought these?

SERGEANT. In the guard-room, sir.

Burgoyne goes out with a haste that sets the officers exchanging looks.

SWINDON (to Christy). Do you know Anthony Anderson, the Presbyterian minister?

CHRISTY. Of course I do. (Implying that Swindon must be an ass not to know it.)

SWINDON. Is he here?

CHRISTY (staring round). I don't know.

SWINDON. Do you see him?

CHRISTY. No.

SWINDON. You seem to know the prisoner?

CHRISTY. Do you mean Dick?

SWINDON. Which is Dick?

CHRISTY (pointing to Richard). Him.

SWINDON. What is his name?

CHRISTY. Dick.

RICHARD. Answer properly, you jumping jackass. What do they know about Dick?

CHRISTY. Well, you are Dick, ain't you? What am I to say?

SWINDON. Address me, sir; and do you, prisoner, be silent. Tell us who the prisoner is.

CHRISTY. He's my brother Dudgeon.

SWINDON. Your brother!

CHRISTY. Yes.

SWINDON. You are sure he is not Anderson.

CHRISTY. Who?

RICHARD (exasperatedly). Me, me, me, you—

SWINDON. Silence, sir.

SERGEANT (shouting). Silence.

RICHARD (impatiently). Yah! (To Christy) He wants to know am I Minister Anderson. Tell him, and stop grinning like a zany.

CHRISTY (grinning more than ever). YOU Pastor Anderson! (To Swindon) Why, Mr. Anderson's a minister—-a very good man; and Dick's a bad character: the respectable people won't speak to him. He's the bad brother: I'm the good one, (The officers laugh outright. The soldiers grin.)

SWINDON. Who arrested this man?

SERGEANT. I did, sir. I found him in the minister's house, sitting at tea with the lady with his coat off, quite at home. If he isn't married to her, he ought to be.

SWINDON. Did he answer to the minister's name?

SERGEANT. Yes sir, but not to a minister's nature. You ask the chaplain, sir.

SWINDON (to Richard, threateningly). So, sir, you have attempted to cheat us. And your name is Richard Dudgeon?

RICHARD. You've found it out at last, have you?

SWINDON. Dudgeon is a name well known to us, eh?

RICHARD. Yes: Peter Dudgeon, whom you murdered, was my uncle.

SWINDON. Hm! (He compresses his lips and looks at Richard with vindictive gravity.)

CHRISTY. Are they going to hang you, Dick?

RICHARD. Yes. Get out: they've done with you.

CHRISTY. And I may keep the china peacocks?

RICHARD (jumping up). Get out. Get out, you blithering baboon, you. (Christy flies, panicstricken.)

SWINDON (rising—all rise). Since you have taken the minister's place, Richard Dudgeon, you shall go through with it. The execution will take place at 12 o'clock as arranged; and unless Anderson surrenders before then you shall take his place on the gallows. Sergeant: take your man out.

JUDITH (distracted). No, no—

SWINDON (fiercely, dreading a renewal of her entreaties). Take that woman away.

RICHARD (springing across the table with a tiger-like bound, and seizing Swindon by the throat). You infernal scoundrel.

The sergeant rushes to the rescue from one side, the soldiers from the other. They seize Richard and drag him back to his place. Swindon, who has been thrown supine on the table, rises, arranging his stock. He is about to speak, when he is anticipated by Burgoyne, who has just appeared at the door with two papers in his hand: a white letter and a blue dispatch.

BURGOYNE (advancing to the table, elaborately cool). What is this? What's happening? Mr. Anderson: I'm astonished at you.

RICHARD. I am sorry I disturbed you, General. I merely wanted to strangle your understrapper there. (Breaking out violently at Swindon) Why do you raise the devil in me by bullying the woman like that? You oatmeal faced dog, I'd twist your cursed head off with the greatest satisfaction. (He puts out his hands to the sergeant) Here: handcuff me, will you; or I'll not undertake to keep my fingers off him.

The sergeant takes out a pair of handcuffs and looks to Burgoyne for instructions.

BURGOYNE. Have you addressed profane language to the lady, Major Swindon?

SWINDON (very angry). No, sir, certainly not. That question should not have been put to me. I ordered the woman to be removed, as she was disorderly; and the fellow sprang at me. Put away those handcuffs. I am perfectly able to take care of myself.

RICHARD. Now you talk like a man, I have no quarrel with you.

BURGOYNE. Mr. Anderson—

SWINDON. His name is Dudgeon, sir, Richard Dudgeon. He is an impostor.

BURGOYNE (brusquely). Nonsense, sir; you hanged Dudgeon at Springtown.

RICHARD. It was my uncle, General.

BURGOYNE. Oh, your uncle. (To Swindon, handsomely) I beg your pardon, Major Swindon. (Swindon acknowledges the apology stiffly. Burgoyne turns to Richard) We are somewhat unfortunate in our relations with your family. Well, Mr. Dudgeon, what I wanted to ask you is this: Who is (reading the name from the letter) William Maindeck Parshotter?

RICHARD. He is the Mayor of Springtown.

BURGOYNE. Is William—Maindeck and so on—a man of his word?

RICHARD. Is he selling you anything?

BURGOYNE. No.

RICHARD. Then you may depend on him.

BURGOYNE. Thank you, Mr.—'m Dudgeon. By the way, since you are not Mr. Anderson, do we still—eh, Major Swindon? (meaning "do we still hang him?")

RICHARD. The arrangements are unaltered, General.

BURGOYNE. Ah, indeed. I am sorry. Good morning, Mr. Dudgeon. Good morning, madam.

RICHARD (interrupting Judith almost fiercely as she is about to make some wild appeal, and taking her arm resolutely). Not one word more. Come.

She looks imploringly at him, but is overborne by his determination. They are marched out by the four soldiers: the sergeant, very sulky, walking between Swindon and Richard, whom he watches as if he were a dangerous animal.

BURGOYNE. Gentlemen: we need not detain you. Major Swindon: a word with you. (The officers go out. Burgoyne waits with unruffled serenity until the last of them disappears. Then he becomes very grave, and addresses Swindon for the first time without his title.) Swindon: do you know what this is (showing him the letter)?

SWINDON. What?

BURGOYNE. A demand for a safe-conduct for an officer of their militia to come here and arrange terms with us.

SWINDON. Oh, they are giving in.

BURGOYNE. They add that they are sending the man who raised Springtown last night and drove us out; so that we may know that we are dealing with an officer of importance.

SWINDON. Pooh!

BURGOYNE. He will be fully empowered to arrange the terms of—guess what.

SWINDON. Their surrender, I hope.

BURGOYNE. No: our evacuation of the town. They offer us just six hours to clear out.

SWINDON. What monstrous impudence!

BURGOYNE. What shall we do, eh?

SWINDON. March on Springtown and strike a decisive blow at once.

BURGOYNE (quietly). Hm! (Turning to the door) Come to the adjutant's office.

SWINDON. What for?

BURGOYNE. To write out that safe-conduct. (He puts his hand to the door knob to open it.)

SWINDON (who has not budged). General Burgoyne.

BURGOYNE (returning). Sir?

SWINDON. It is my duty to tell you, sir, that I do not consider the threats of a mob of rebellious tradesmen a sufficient reason for our giving way.

BURGOYNE (imperturbable). Suppose I resign my command to you, what will you do?

SWINDON. I will undertake to do what we have marched south from Boston to do, and what General Howe has marched north from New York to do: effect a junction at Albany and wipe out the rebel army with our united forces.

BURGOYNE (enigmatically). And will you wipe out our enemies in London, too?

SWINDON. In London! What enemies?

BURGOYNE (forcibly). Jobbery and snobbery, incompetence and Red Tape. (He holds up the dispatch and adds, with despair in his face and voice) I have just learnt, sir, that General Howe is still in New York.

SWINDON (thunderstruck). Good God! He has disobeyed orders!

BURGOYNE (with sardonic calm). He has received no orders, sir. Some gentleman in London forgot to dispatch them: he was leaving town for his holiday, I believe. To avoid upsetting his arrangements, England will lose her American colonies; and in a few days you and I will be at Saratoga with 5,000 men to face 16,000 rebels in an impregnable position.

SWINDON (appalled). Impossible!

BURGOYNE (coldly). I beg your pardon!

SWINDON. I can't believe it! What will History say?

BURGOYNE. History, sir, will tell lies, as usual. Come: we must send the safe-conduct. (He goes out.)

SWINDON (following distractedly). My God, my God! We shall be wiped out.

As noon approaches there is excitement in the market place. The gallows which hangs there permanently for the terror of evildoers, with such minor advertizers and examples of crime as the pillory, the whipping post, and the stocks, has a new rope attached, with the noose hitched up to one of the uprights, out of reach of the boys. Its ladder, too, has been brought out and placed in position by the town beadle, who stands by to guard it from unauthorized climbing. The Websterbridge townsfolk are present in force, and in high spirits; for the news has spread that it is the devil's disciple and not the minister that the Continentals (so they call Burgoyne's forces) are about to hang: consequently the execution can be enjoyed without any misgiving as to its righteousness, or to the cowardice of allowing it to take place without a struggle. There is even some fear of a disappointment as midday approaches and the arrival of the beadle with the ladder remains the only sign of preparation. But at last reassuring shouts of Here they come: Here they are, are heard; and a company of soldiers with fixed bayonets, half British infantry, half Hessians, tramp quickly into the middle of the market place, driving the crowd to the sides.

SERGEANT. Halt. Front. Dress. (The soldiers change their column into a square enclosing the gallows, their petty officers, energetically led by the sergeant, hustling the persons who find themselves inside the square out at the corners.) Now then! Out of it with you: out of it. Some o' you'll get strung up yourselves presently. Form that square there, will you, you damned Hoosians. No use talkin' German to them: talk to their toes with the butt ends of your muskets: they'll understand that. GET out of it, will you? (He comes upon Judith, standing near the gallows.) Now then: YOU'VE no call here.

JUDITH. May I not stay? What harm am I doing?

SERGEANT. I want none of your argufying. You ought to be ashamed of yourself, running to see a man hanged that's not your husband. And he's no better than yourself. I told my major he was a gentleman; and then he goes and tries to strangle him, and calls his blessed Majesty a lunatic. So out of it with you, double quick.

JUDITH. Will you take these two silver dollars and let me stay?

The sergeant, without an instant's hesitation, looks quickly and furtively round as he shoots the money dexterously into his pocket. Then he raises his voice in virtuous indignation.

SERGEANT. ME take money in the execution of my duty! Certainly not. Now I'll tell you what I'll do, to teach you to corrupt the King's officer. I'll put you under arrest until the execution's over. You just stand there; and don't let me see you as much as move from that spot until you're let. (With a swift wink at her he points to the corner of the square behind the gallows on his right, and turns noisily away, shouting) Now then dress up and keep 'em back, will you?

Cries of Hush and Silence are heard among the townsfolk; and the sound of a military band, playing the Dead March from Saul, is heard. The crowd becomes quiet at once; and the sergeant and petty officers, hurrying to the back of the square, with a few whispered orders and some stealthy hustling cause it to open and admit the funeral procession, which is protected from the crowd by a double file of soldiers. First come Burgoyne and Swindon, who, on entering the square, glance with distaste at the gallows, and avoid passing under it by wheeling a little to the right and stationing themselves on that side. Then Mr. Brudenell, the chaplain, in his surplice, with his prayer book open in his hand, walking beside Richard, who is moody and disorderly. He walks doggedly through the gallows framework, and posts himself a little in front of it. Behind him comes the executioner, a stalwart soldier in his shirtsleeves. Following him, two soldiers haul a light military waggon. Finally comes the band, which posts itself at the back of the square, and finishes the Dead March. Judith, watching Richard painfully, steals down to the gallows, and stands leaning against its right post. During the conversation which follows, the two soldiers place the cart under the gallows, and stand by the shafts, which point backwards. The executioner takes a set of steps from the cart and places it ready for the prisoner to mount. Then he climbs the tall ladder which stands against the gallows, and cuts the string by which the rope is hitched up; so that the noose drops dangling over the cart, into which he steps as he descends.

RICHARD (with suppressed impatience, to Brudenell). Look here, sir: this is no place for a man of your profession. Hadn't you better go away?

SWINDON. I appeal to you, prisoner, if you have any sense of decency left, to listen to the ministrations of the chaplain, and pay due heed to the solemnity of the occasion.

THE CHAPLAIN (gently reproving Richard). Try to control yourself, and submit to the divine will. (He lifts his book to proceed with the service.)

RICHARD. Answer for your own will, sir, and those of your accomplices here (indicating Burgoyne and Swindon): I see little divinity about them or you. You talk to me of Christianity when you are in the act of hanging your enemies. Was there ever such blasphemous nonsense! (To Swindon, more rudely) You've got up the solemnity of the occasion, as you call it, to impress the people with your own dignity—Handel's music and a clergyman to make murder look like piety! Do you suppose I am going to help you? You've asked me to choose the rope because you don't know your own trade well enough to shoot me properly. Well, hang away and have done with it.

SWINDON (to the chaplain). Can you do nothing with him, Mr. Brudenell?

CHAPLAIN. I will try, sir. (Beginning to read) Man that is born of woman hath—

RICHARD (fixing his eyes on him). "Thou shalt not kill."

The book drops in Brudenell's hands.

CHAPLAIN (confessing his embarrassment). What am I to say, Mr. Dudgeon?

RICHARD. Let me alone, man, can't you?

BURGOYNE (with extreme urbanity). I think, Mr. Brudenell, that as the usual professional observations seem to strike Mr. Dudgeon as incongruous under the circumstances, you had better omit them until—er—until Mr. Dudgeon can no longer be inconvenienced by them. (Brudenell, with a shrug, shuts his book and retires behind the gallows.) YOU seem in a hurry, Mr. Dudgeon.

RICHARD (with the horror of death upon him). Do you think this is a pleasant sort of thing to be kept waiting for? You've made up your mind to commit murder: well, do it and have done with it.

BURGOYNE. Mr. Dudgeon: we are only doing this—

RICHARD. Because you're paid to do it.

SWINDON. You insolent— (He swallows his rage.)

BURGOYNE (with much charm of manner). Ah, I am really sorry that you should think that, Mr. Dudgeon. If you knew what my commission cost me, and what my pay is, you would think better of me. I should be glad to part from you on friendly terms.

RICHARD. Hark ye, General Burgoyne. If you think that I like being hanged, you're mistaken. I don't like it; and I don't mean to pretend that I do. And if you think I'm obliged to you for hanging me in a gentlemanly way, you're wrong there too. I take the whole business in devilish bad part; and the only satisfaction I have in it is that you'll feel a good deal meaner than I'll look when it's over. (He turns away, and is striding to the cart when Judith advances and interposes with her arms stretched out to him. Richard, feeling that a very little will upset his self-possession, shrinks from her, crying) What are you doing here? This is no place for you. (She makes a gesture as if to touch him. He recoils impatiently.) No: go away, go away; you'll unnerve me. Take her away, will you?

JUDITH. Won't you bid me good-bye?

RICHARD (allowing her to take his hand). Oh good-bye, good-bye. Now go—go—quickly. (She clings to his hand—will not be put off with so cold a last farewell—at last, as he tries to disengage himself, throws herself on his breast in agony.)

SWINDON (angrily to the sergeant, who, alarmed at Judith's movement, has come from the back of the square to pull her back, and stopped irresolutely on finding that he is too late). How is this? Why is she inside the lines?

SERGEANT (guiltily). I dunno, sir. She's that artful can't keep her away.

BURGOYNE. You were bribed.

SERGEANT (protesting). No, Sir—

SWINDON (severely). Fall back. (He obeys.)

RICHARD (imploringly to those around him, and finally to Burgoyne, as the least stolid of them). Take her away. Do you think I want a woman near me now?

BURGOYNE (going to Judith and taking her hand). Here, madam: you had better keep inside the lines; but stand here behind us; and don't look.

Richard, with a great sobbing sigh of relief as she releases him and turns to Burgoyne, flies for refuge to the cart and mounts into it. The executioner takes off his coat and pinions him.

JUDITH (resisting Burgoyne quietly and drawing her hand away). No: I must stay. I won't look. (She goes to the right of the gallows. She tries to look at Richard, but turns away with a frightful shudder, and falls on her knees in prayer. Brudenell comes towards her from the back of the square.)

BURGOYNE (nodding approvingly as she kneels). Ah, quite so. Do not disturb her, Mr. Brudenell: that will do very nicely. (Brudenell nods also, and withdraws a little, watching her sympathetically. Burgoyne resumes his former position, and takes out a handsome gold chronometer.) Now then, are those preparations made? We must not detain Mr. Dudgeon.

By this time Richard's hands are bound behind him; and the noose is round his neck. The two soldiers take the shaft of the wagon, ready to pull it away. The executioner, standing in the cart behind Richard, makes a sign to the sergeant.

SERGEANT (to Burgoyne). Ready, sir.

BURGOYNE. Have you anything more to say, Mr. Dudgeon? It wants two minutes of twelve still.

RICHARD (in the strong voice of a man who has conquered the bitterness of death). Your watch is two minutes slow by the town clock, which I can see from here, General. (The town clock strikes the first stroke of twelve. Involuntarily the people flinch at the sound, and a subdued groan breaks from them.) Amen! my life for the world's future!

ANDERSON (shouting as he rushes into the market place). Amen; and stop the execution. (He bursts through the line of soldiers opposite Burgoyne, and rushes, panting, to the gallows.) I am Anthony Anderson, the man you want.

The crowd, intensely excited, listens with all its ears. Judith, half rising, stares at him; then lifts her hands like one whose dearest prayer has been granted.

SWINDON. Indeed. Then you are just in time to take your place on the gallows. Arrest him.

At a sign from the sergeant, two soldiers come forward to seize Anderson.

ANDERSON (thrusting a paper under Swindon's nose). There's my safe-conduct, sir.

SWINDON (taken aback). Safe-conduct! Are you—!

ANDERSON (emphatically). I am. (The two soldiers take him by the elbows.) Tell these men to take their hands off me.

SWINDON (to the men). Let him go.

SERGEANT. Fall back.

The two men return to their places. The townsfolk raise a cheer; and begin to exchange exultant looks, with a presentiment of triumph as they see their Pastor speaking with their enemies in the gate.

ANDERSON (exhaling a deep breath of relief, and dabbing his perspiring brow with his handkerchief). Thank God, I was in time!

BURGOYNE (calm as ever, and still watch in hand). Ample time, sir. Plenty of time. I should never dream of hanging any gentleman by an American clock. (He puts up his watch.)

ANDERSON. Yes: we are some minutes ahead of you already, General. Now tell them to take the rope from the neck of that American citizen.

BURGOYNE (to the executioner in the cart—very politely). Kindly undo Mr. Dudgeon.

The executioner takes the rope from Richard's neck, unties his hands, and helps him on with his coat.

JUDITH (stealing timidly to Anderson). Tony.

ANDERSON (putting his arm round her shoulders and bantering her affectionately). Well what do you think of you husband, NOW, eh?—eh??—eh???

JUDITH. I am ashamed— (She hides her face against his breast.)

BURGOYNE (to Swindon). You look disappointed, Major Swindon.

SWINDON. You look defeated, General Burgoyne.

BURGOYNE. I am, sir; and I am humane enough to be glad of it. (Richard jumps down from the cart, Brudenell offering his hand to help him, and runs to Anderson, whose left hand he shakes heartily, the right being occupied by Judith.) By the way, Mr. Anderson, I do not quite understand. The safe-conduct was for a commander of the militia. I understand you are a— (he looks as pointedly as his good manners permit at the riding boots, the pistols, and Richard's coat, and adds) a clergyman.

ANDERSON (between Judith and Richard). Sir: it is in the hour of trial that a man finds his true profession. This foolish young man (placing his hand on Richard's shoulder) boasted himself the Devil's Disciple; but when the hour of trial came to him, he found that it was his destiny to suffer and be faithful to the death. I thought myself a decent minister of the gospel of peace; but when the hour of trial came to me, I found that it was my destiny to be a man of action and that my place was amid the thunder of the captains and the shouting. So I am starting life at fifty as Captain Anthony Anderson of the Springtown militia; and the Devil's Disciple here will start presently as the Reverend Richard Dudgeon, and wag his pow in my old pulpit, and give good advice to this silly sentimental little wife of mine (putting his other hand on her shoulder. She steals a glance at Richard to see how the prospect pleases him). Your mother told me, Richard, that I should never have chosen Judith if I'd been born for the ministry. I am afraid she was right; so, by your leave, you may keep my coat and I'll keep yours.

RICHARD. Minister—I should say Captain. I have behaved like a fool.

JUDITH. Like a hero.

RICHARD. Much the same thing, perhaps. (With some bitterness towards himself) But no: if I had been any good, I should have done for you what you did for me, instead of making a vain sacrifice.

ANDERSON. Not vain, my boy. It takes all sorts to make a world—saints as well as soldiers. (Turning to Burgoyne) And now, General, time presses; and America is in a hurry. Have you realized that though you may occupy towns and win battles, you cannot conquer a nation?

BURGOYNE. My good sir, without a Conquest you cannot have an aristocracy. Come and settle the matter at my quarters.

ANDERSON. At your service, sir. (To Richard) See Judith home for me, will you, my boy? (He hands her over to him.) Now General. (He goes busily up the market place towards the Town Hall, Leaving Judith and Richard together. Burgoyne follows him a step or two; then checks himself and turns to Richard.)

BURGOYNE. Oh, by the way, Mr. Dudgeon, I shall be glad to see you at lunch at half-past one. (He pauses a moment, and adds, with politely veiled slyness) Bring Mrs. Anderson, if she will be so good. (To Swindon, who is fuming) Take it quietly, Major Swindon: your friend the British soldier can stand up to anything except the British War Office. (He follows Anderson.)

SERGEANT (to Swindon). What orders, sir?

SWINDON (savagely). Orders! What use are orders now? There's no army. Back to quarters; and be d— (He turns on his heel and goes.)

SERGEANT (pugnacious and patriotic, repudiating the idea of defeat). 'Tention. Now then: cock up your chins, and show 'em you don't care a damn for 'em. Slope arms! Fours! Wheel! Quick march!

The drum marks time with a tremendous bang; the band strikes up British Grenadiers; and the sergeant, Brudenell, and the English troops march off defiantly to their quarters. The townsfolk press in behind, and follow them up the market, jeering at them; and the town band, a very primitive affair, brings up the rear, playing Yankee Doodle. Essie, who comes in with them, runs to Richard.

ESSIE. Oh, Dick!

RICHARD (good-humoredly, but wilfully). Now, now: come, come! I don't mind being hanged; but I will not be cried over.

ESSIE. No, I promise. I'll be good. (She tries to restrain her tears, but cannot.) I—I want to see where the soldiers are going to. (She goes a little way up the market, pretending to look after the crowd.)

JUDITH. Promise me you will never tell him.

RICHARD. Don't be afraid.

They shake hands on it.

ESSIE (calling to them). They're coming back. They want you.

Jubilation in the market. The townsfolk surge back again in wild enthusiasm with their band, and hoist Richard on their shoulders, cheering him.

CURTAIN.

NOTES TO THE DEVIL'S DISCIPLE

BURGOYNE

General John Burgoyne, who is presented in this play for the first time (as far as I am aware) on the English stage, is not a conventional stage soldier, but as faithful a portrait as it is in the nature of stage portraits to be. His objection to profane swearing is not borrowed from Mr. Gilbert's H. M. S. Pinafore: it is taken from the Code of Instructions drawn up by himself for his officers when he introduced Light Horse into the English army. His opinion that English soldiers should be treated as thinking beings was no doubt as unwelcome to the military authorities of his time, when nothing was thought of ordering a soldier a thousand lashes, as it will be to those modern victims of the flagellation neurosis who are so anxious to revive that discredited sport. His military reports are very clever as criticisms, and are humane and enlightened within certain aristocratic limits, best illustrated perhaps by his declaration, which now sounds so curious, that he should blush to ask for promotion on any other ground than that of family influence. As a parliamentary candidate, Burgoyne took our common expression "fighting an election" so very literally that he led his supporters to the poll at Preston in 1768 with a loaded pistol in each hand, and won the seat, though he was fined 1,000 pounds, and denounced by Junius, for the pistols.

It is only within quite recent years that any general recognition has become possible for the feeling that led Burgoyne, a professed enemy of oppression in India and elsewhere, to accept his American command when so many other officers threw up their commissions rather than serve in a civil war against the Colonies. His biographer De Fonblanque, writing in 1876, evidently regarded his position as indefensible. Nowadays, it is sufficient to say that Burgoyne was an Imperialist. He sympathized with the colonists; but when they proposed as a remedy the disruption of the Empire, he regarded that as a step backward in civilization. As he put it to the House of Commons, "while we remember that we are contending against brothers and fellow subjects, we must also remember that we are contending in this crisis for the fate of the British Empire." Eighty-four years after his defeat, his republican conquerors themselves engaged in a civil war for the integrity of their Union. In 1886 the Whigs who represented the anti-Burgoyne tradition of American Independence in English politics, abandoned Gladstone and made common cause with their political opponents in defence of the Union between England and Ireland. Only the other day England sent 200,000 men into the field south of the equator to fight out the question whether South Africa should develop as a Federation of British Colonies or as an independent Afrikander United States. In all these cases the Unionists who were detached from their parties were called renegades, as Burgoyne was. That, of course, is only one of the unfortunate consequences of the fact that mankind, being for the most part incapable of politics, accepts vituperation as an easy and congenial substitute. Whether Burgoyne or Washington, Lincoln or Davis, Gladstone or Bright, Mr. Chamberlain or Mr. Leonard Courtney was in the right will never be settled, because it will never be possible to prove that the government of the victor has been better for mankind than the government of the vanquished would have been. It is true that the victors have no doubt on the point; but to the dramatist, that certainty of theirs is only part of the human comedy. The American Unionist is often a Separatist as to Ireland; the English Unionist often sympathizes with the Polish Home Ruler; and both English and American Unionists are apt to be Disruptionists as regards that Imperial Ancient of Days, the Empire of China. Both are Unionists concerning Canada, but with a difference as to the precise application to it of the Monroe doctrine. As for me, the dramatist, I smile, and lead the conversation back to Burgoyne.

Burgoyne's surrender at Saratoga made him that occasionally necessary part of our British system, a scapegoat. The explanation of his defeat given in the play is founded on a passage quoted by De Fonblanque from Fitzmaurice's Life of Lord Shelburne, as follows: "Lord George Germain, having among other peculiarities a particular dislike to be put out of his way on any occasion, had arranged to call at his office on his way to the country to sign the dispatches; but as those addressed to Howe had not been faircopied, and he was not disposed to be balked of his projected visit to Kent, they were not signed then and were forgotten on his return home." These were the dispatches instructing Sir William Howe, who was in New York, to effect a junction at Albany with Burgoyne, who had marched from Boston for that purpose. Burgoyne got as far as Saratoga, where, failing the expected reinforcement, he was hopelessly outnumbered, and his officers picked off, Boer fashion, by the American farmer-sharpshooters. His own collar was pierced by a bullet. The publicity of his defeat, however, was more than compensated at home by the fact that Lord George's trip to Kent had not been interfered with, and that nobody knew about the oversight of the dispatch. The policy of the English Government and Court for the next two years was simply concealment of Germain's neglect. Burgoyne's demand for an inquiry was defeated in the House of Commons by the court party; and when he at last obtained a committee, the king got rid of it by a prorogation. When Burgoyne realized what had happened about the instructions to Howe (the scene in which I have represented him as learning it before Saratoga is not historical: the truth did not dawn on him until many months afterwards) the king actually took advantage of his being a prisoner of war in England on parole, and ordered him to return to America into captivity. Burgoyne immediately resigned all his appointments; and this practically closed his military career, though he was afterwards made Commander of the Forces in Ireland for the purpose of banishing him from parliament.

The episode illustrates the curious perversion of the English sense of honor when the privileges and prestige of the aristocracy are at stake. Mr. Frank Harris said, after the disastrous battle of Modder River, that the English, having lost America a century ago because they preferred George III, were quite prepared to lose South Africa to-day because they preferred aristocratic commanders to successful ones. Horace Walpole, when the parliamentary recess came at a critical period of the War of Independence, said that the Lords could not be expected to lose their pheasant shooting for the sake of America. In the working class, which, like all classes, has its own official aristocracy, there is the same reluctance to discredit an institution or to "do a man out of his job." At bottom, of course, this apparently shameless sacrifice of great public interests to petty personal ones, is simply the preference of the ordinary man for the things he can feel and understand to the things that are beyond his capacity. It is stupidity, not dishonesty.

Burgoyne fell a victim to this stupidity in two ways. Not only was he thrown over, in spite of his high character and distinguished services, to screen a court favorite who had actually been cashiered for cowardice and misconduct in the field fifteen years before; but his peculiar critical temperament and talent, artistic, satirical, rather histrionic, and his fastidious delicacy of sentiment, his fine spirit and humanity, were just the qualities to make him disliked by stupid people because of their dread of ironic criticism. Long after his death, Thackeray, who had an intense sense of human character, but was typically stupid in valuing and interpreting it, instinctively sneered at him and exulted in his defeat. That sneer represents the common English attitude towards the Burgoyne type. Every instance in which the critical genius is defeated, and the stupid genius (for both temperaments have their genius) "muddles through all right," is popular in England. But Burgoyne's failure was not the work of his own temperament, but of the stupid temperament. What man could do under the circumstances he did, and did handsomely and loftily. He fell, and his ideal empire was dismembered, not through his own misconduct, but because Sir George Germain overestimated the importance of his Kentish holiday, and underestimated the difficulty of conquering those remote and inferior creatures, the colonists. And King George and the rest of the nation agreed, on the whole, with Germain. It is a significant point that in America, where Burgoyne was an enemy and an invader, he was admired and praised. The climate there is no doubt more favorable to intellectual vivacity.

I have described Burgoyne's temperament as rather histrionic; and the reader will have observed that the Burgoyne of the Devil's Disciple is a man who plays his part in life, and makes all its points, in the manner of a born high comedian. If he had been killed at Saratoga, with all his comedies unwritten, and his plan for turning As You Like It into a Beggar's Opera unconceived, I should still have painted the same picture of him on the strength of his reply to the articles of capitulation proposed to him by his American conqueror General Gates. Here they are:

PROPOSITION.

1. General Burgoyne's army being reduced by repeated defeats, by desertion, sickness, etc., their provisions exhausted, their military horses, tents and baggage taken or destroyed, their retreat cut off, and their camp invested, they can only be allowed to surrender as prisoners of war.

ANSWER.

1. Lieut.-General Burgoyne's army, however reduced, will never admit that their retreat is cut off while they have arms in their hands.

PROPOSITION.

2. The officers and soldiers may keep the baggage belonging to them. The generals of the United States never permit individuals to be pillaged.

ANSWER.

2. Noted.

PROPOSITION.

3. The troops under his Excellency General Burgoyne will be conducted by the most convenient route to New England, marching by easy marches, and sufficiently provided for by the way.

ANSWER.

3. Agreed.

PROPOSITION.

4. The officers will be admitted on parole and will be treated with the liberality customary in such cases, so long as they, by proper behaviour, continue to deserve it; but those who are apprehended having broke their parole, as some British officers have done, must expect to be close confined.

ANSWER.

4. There being no officer in this army, under, or capable of being under, the description of breaking parole, this article needs no answer.

PROPOSITION.

5. All public stores, artillery, arms, ammunition, carriages, horses, etc., etc., must be delivered to commissaries appointed to receive them.

ANSWER.

5. All public stores may be delivered, arms excepted.

PROPOSITION.

6. These terms being agreed to and signed, the troops under his Excellency's, General Burgoyne's command, may be drawn up in their encampments, where they will be ordered to ground their arms, and may thereupon be marched to the river-side on their way to Bennington.

ANSWER.

6. This article is inadmissible in any extremity. Sooner than this army will consent to ground their arms in their encampments, they will rush on the enemy determined to take no quarter.

And, later on, "If General Gates does not mean to recede from the 6th article, the treaty ends at once: the army will to a man proceed to any act of desperation sooner than submit to that article."

Here you have the man at his Burgoynest. Need I add that he had his own way; and that when the actual ceremony of surrender came, he would have played poor General Gates off the stage, had not that commander risen to the occasion by handing him back his sword.

In connection with the reference to Indians with scalping knives, who, with the troops hired from Germany, made up about half Burgoyne's force, I may mention that Burgoyne offered two of them a reward to guide a Miss McCrea, betrothed to one of the English officers, into the English lines.

The two braves quarrelled about the reward; and the more sensitive of them, as a protest against the unfairness of the other, tomahawked the young lady. The usual retaliations were proposed under the popular titles of justice and so forth; but as the tribe of the slayer would certainly have followed suit by a massacre of whites on the Canadian frontier, Burgoyne was compelled to forgive the crime, to the intense disgust of indignant Christendom.

BRUDENELL

Brudenell is also a real person. At least an artillery chaplain of that name distinguished himself at Saratoga by reading the burial service over Major Fraser under fire, and by a quite readable adventure, chronicled by Burgoyne, with Lady Harriet Ackland. Lady Harriet's husband achieved the remarkable feat of killing himself, instead of his adversary, in a duel. He overbalanced himself in the heat of his swordsmanship, and fell with his head against a pebble. La-Lady Harriet then married the warrior chaplain, who, like Anthony Anderson in the play, seems to have mistaken his natural profession.

The rest of the Devil's Disciple may have actually occurred, like most stories invented by dramatists; but I cannot produce any documents. Major Swindon's name is invented; but the man, of course, is real. There are dozens of him extant to this day.

CAESAR AND CLEOPATRA

ACT I

An October night on the Syrian border of Egypt towards the end of the XXXIII Dynasty, in the year 706 by Roman computation, afterwards reckoned by Christian computation as 48 B.C. A great radiance of silver fire, the dawn of a moonlit night, is rising in the east. The stars and the cloudless sky are our own contemporaries, nineteen and a half centuries younger than we know them; but you would not guess that from their appearance. Below them are two notable drawbacks of civilization: a palace, and soldiers. The palace, an old, low, Syrian building of whitened mud, is not so ugly as Buckingham Palace; and the officers in the courtyard are more highly civilized than modern English officers: for example, they do not dig up the corpses of their dead enemies and mutilate them, as we dug up Cromwell and the Mahdi. They are in two groups: one intent on the gambling of their captain Belzanor, a warrior of fifty, who, with his spear on the ground beside his knee, is stooping to throw dice with a sly-looking young Persian recruit; the other gathered about a guardsman who has just finished telling a naughty story (still current in English barracks) at which they are laughing uproariously. They are about a dozen in number, all highly aristocratic young Egyptian guardsmen, handsomely equipped with weapons and armor, very unEnglish in point of not being ashamed of and uncomfortable in their professional dress; on the contrary, rather ostentatiously and arrogantly warlike, as valuing themselves on their military caste.

Belzanor is a typical veteran, tough and wilful; prompt, capable and crafty where brute force will serve; helpless and boyish when it will not: an effective sergeant, an incompetent general, a deplorable dictator. Would, if influentially connected, be employed in the two last capacities by a modern European State on the strength of his success in the first. Is rather to be pitied just now in view of the fact that Julius Caesar is invading his country. Not knowing this, is intent on his game with the Persian, whom, as a foreigner, he considers quite capable of cheating him.

His subalterns are mostly handsome young fellows whose interest in the game and the story symbolizes with tolerable completeness the main interests in life of which they are conscious. Their spears are leaning against the walls, or lying on the ground ready to their hands. The corner of the courtyard forms a triangle of which one side is the front of the palace, with a doorway, the other a wall with a gateway. The storytellers are on the palace side: the gamblers, on the gateway side. Close to the gateway, against the wall, is a stone block high enough to enable a Nubian sentinel, standing on it, to look over the wall. The yard is lighted by a torch stuck in the wall. As the laughter from the group round the storyteller dies away, the kneeling Persian, winning the throw, snatches up the stake from the ground.

BELZANOR. By Apis, Persian, thy gods are good to thee.

THE PERSIAN. Try yet again, O captain. Double or quits!

BELZANOR. No more. I am not in the vein.

THE SENTINEL (poising his javelin as he peers over the wall). Stand. Who goes there?

They all start, listening. A strange voice replies from without.

VOICE. The bearer of evil tidings.

BELZANOR (calling to the sentry). Pass him.

THE SENTINEL. (grounding his javelin). Draw near, O bearer of evil tidings.

BELZANOR (pocketing the dice and picking up his spear). Let us receive this man with honor. He bears evil tidings.

The guardsmen seize their spears and gather about the gate, leaving a way through for the new comer.

PERSIAN (rising from his knee). Are evil tidings, then, honorable?

BELZANOR. O barbarous Persian, hear my instruction. In Egypt the bearer of good tidings is sacrificed to the gods as a thank offering but no god will accept the blood of the messenger of evil. When we have good tidings, we are careful to send them in the mouth of the cheapest slave we can find. Evil tidings are borne by young noblemen who desire to bring themselves into notice. (They join the rest at the gate.)

THE SENTINEL. Pass, O young captain; and bow the head in the House of the Queen.

VOICE. Go anoint thy javelin with fat of swine, O Blackamoor; for before morning the Romans will make thee eat it to the very butt.

The owner of the voice, a fairhaired dandy, dressed in a different fashion to that affected by the guardsmen, but no less extravagantly, comes through the gateway laughing. He is somewhat battle-stained; and his left forearm, bandaged, comes through a torn sleeve. In his right hand he carries a Roman sword in its sheath. He swaggers down the courtyard, the Persian on his right, Belzanor on his left, and the guardsmen crowding down behind him.

BELZANOR. Who art thou that laughest in the House of Cleopatra the Queen, and in the teeth of Belzanor, the captain of her guard?

THE NEW COMER. I am Bel Affris, descended from the gods.

BELZANOR (ceremoniously). Hail, cousin!

ALL (except the Persian). Hail, cousin!

PERSIAN. All the Queen's guards are descended from the gods, O stranger, save myself. I am Persian, and descended from many kings.

BEL AFFRIS (to the guardsmen). Hail, cousins! (To the Persian, condescendingly) Hail, mortal!

BELZANOR. You have been in battle, Bel Affris; and you are a soldier among soldiers. You will not let the Queen's women have the first of your tidings.

BEL AFFRIS. I have no tidings, except that we shall have our throats cut presently, women, soldiers, and all.

PERSIAN (to Belzanor). I told you so.

THE SENTINEL (who has been listening). Woe, alas!

BEL AFFRIS (calling to him). Peace, peace, poor Ethiop: destiny is with the gods who painted thee black. (To Belzanor) What has this mortal (indicating the Persian) told you?

BELZANOR. He says that the Roman Julius Caesar, who has landed on our shores with a handful of followers, will make himself master of Egypt. He is afraid of the Roman soldiers. (The guardsmen laugh with boisterous scorn.) Peasants, brought up to scare crows and follow the plough. Sons of smiths and millers and tanners! And we nobles, consecrated to arms, descended from the gods!

PERSIAN. Belzanor: the gods are not always good to their poor relations.

BELZANOR (hotly, to the Persian). Man to man, are we worse than the slaves of Caesar?

BEL AFFRIS (stepping between them). Listen, cousin. Man to man, we Egyptians are as gods above the Romans.

THE GUARDSMEN (exultingly). Aha!

BEL AFFRIS. But this Caesar does not pit man against man: he throws a legion at you where you are weakest as he throws a stone from a catapult; and that legion is as a man with one head, a thousand arms, and no religion. I have fought against them; and I know.

BELZANOR (derisively). Were you frightened, cousin?

The guardsmen roar with laughter, their eyes sparkling at the wit of their captain.

BEL AFFRIS. No, cousin; but I was beaten. They were frightened (perhaps); but they scattered us like chaff.

The guardsmen, much damped, utter a growl of contemptuous disgust.

BELZANOR. Could you not die?

BEL AFFRIS. No: that was too easy to be worthy of a descendant of the gods. Besides, there was no time: all was over in a moment. The attack came just where we least expected it.

BELZANOR. That shows that the Romans are cowards.

BEL AFFRIS. They care nothing about cowardice, these Romans: they fight to win. The pride and honor of war are nothing to them.

PERSIAN. Tell us the tale of the battle. What befell?

THE GUARDSMEN (gathering eagerly round Bel Afris). Ay: the tale of the battle.

BEL AFFRIS. Know then, that I am a novice in the guard of the temple of Ra in Memphis, serving neither Cleopatra nor her brother Ptolemy, but only the high gods. We went a journey to inquire of Ptolemy why he had driven Cleopatra into Syria, and how we of Egypt should deal with the Roman Pompey, newly come to our shores after his defeat by Caesar at Pharsalia. What, think ye, did we learn? Even that Caesar is coming also in hot pursuit of his foe, and that Ptolemy has slain Pompey, whose severed head he holds in readiness to present to the conqueror. (Sensation among the guardsmen.) Nay, more: we found that Caesar is already come; for we had not made half a day's journey on our way back when we came upon a city rabble flying from his legions, whose landing they had gone out to withstand.

BELZANOR. And ye, the temple guard! Did you not withstand these legions?

BEL AFFRIS. What man could, that we did. But there came the sound of a trumpet whose voice was as the cursing of a black mountain. Then saw we a moving wall of shields coming towards us. You know how the heart burns when you charge a fortified wall; but how if the fortified wall were to charge YOU?

THE PERSIAN (exulting in having told them so). Did I not say it?

BEL AFFRIS. When the wall came nigh, it changed into a line of men—common fellows enough, with helmets, leather tunics, and breastplates. Every man of them flung his javelin: the one that came my way drove through my shield as through a papyrus—lo there! (he points to the bandage on his left arm) and would have gone through my neck had I not stooped. They were charging at the double then, and were upon us with short swords almost as soon as their javelins. When a man is close to you with such a sword, you can do nothing with our weapons: they are all too long.

THE PERSIAN. What did you do?

BEL AFFRIS. Doubled my fist and smote my Roman on the sharpness of his jaw. He was but mortal after all: he lay down in a stupor; and I took his sword and laid it on. (Drawing the sword) Lo! a Roman sword with Roman blood on it!

THE GUARDSMEN (approvingly). Good! (They take the sword and hand it round, examining it curiously.)

THE PERSIAN. And your men?

BEL AFFRIS. Fled. Scattered like sheep.

BELZANOR (furiously). The cowardly slaves! Leaving the descendants of the gods to be butchered!

BEL AFFRIS (with acid coolness). The descendants of the gods did not stay to be butchered, cousin. The battle was not to the strong; but the race was to the swift. The Romans, who have no chariots, sent a cloud of horsemen in pursuit, and slew multitudes. Then our high priest's captain rallied a dozen descendants of the gods and exhorted us to die fighting. I said to myself: surely it is safer to stand than to lose my breath and be stabbed in the back; so I joined our captain and stood. Then the Romans treated us with respect; for no man attacks a lion when the field is full of sheep, except for the pride and honor of war, of which these Romans know nothing. So we escaped with our lives; and I am come to warn you that you must open your gates to Caesar; for his advance guard is scarce an hour behind me; and not an Egyptian warrior is left standing between you and his legions.

THE SENTINEL. Woe, alas! (He throws down his javelin and flies into the palace.)

BELZANOR. Nail him to the door, quick! (The guardsmen rush for him with their spears; but he is too quick for them.) Now this news will run through the palace like fire through stubble.

BEL AFFRIS. What shall we do to save the women from the Romans?

BELZANOR. Why not kill them?

PERSIAN. Because we should have to pay blood money for some of them. Better let the Romans kill them: it is cheaper.

BELZANOR (awestruck at his brain power). O subtle one! O serpent!

BEL AFFRIS. But your Queen?

BELZANOR. True: we must carry off Cleopatra.

BEL AFFRIS. Will ye not await her command?

BELZANOR. Command! A girl of sixteen! Not we. At Memphis ye deem her a Queen: here we know better. I will take her on the crupper of my horse. When we soldiers have carried her out of Caesar's reach, then the priests and the nurses and the rest of them can pretend she is a queen again, and put their commands into her mouth.

PERSIAN. Listen to me, Belzanor.

BELZANOR. Speak, O subtle beyond thy years.

THE PERSIAN. Cleopatra's brother Ptolemy is at war with her. Let us sell her to him.

THE GUARDSMEN. O subtle one! O serpent!

BELZANOR. We dare not. We are descended from the gods; but Cleopatra is descended from the river Nile; and the lands of our fathers will grow no grain if the Nile rises not to water them. Without our father's gifts we should live the lives of dogs.

PERSIAN. It is true: the Queen's guard cannot live on its pay. But hear me further, O ye kinsmen of Osiris.

THE GUARDSMEN. Speak, O subtle one. Hear the serpent begotten!

PERSIAN. Have I heretofore spoken truly to you of Caesar, when you thought I mocked you?

GUARDSMEN. Truly, truly.

BELZANOR (reluctantly admitting it). So Bel Affris says.

PERSIAN. Hear more of him, then. This Caesar is a great lover of women: he makes them his friends and counselors.

BELZANOR. Faugh! This rule of women will be the ruin of Egypt.

THE PERSIAN. Let it rather be the ruin of Rome! Caesar grows old now: he is past fifty and full of labors and battles. He is too old for the young women; and the old women are too wise to worship him.

BEL AFFRIS. Take heed, Persian. Caesar is by this time almost within earshot.

PERSIAN. Cleopatra is not yet a woman: neither is she wise. But she already troubles men's wisdom.

BELZANOR. Ay: that is because she is descended from the river Nile and a black kitten of the sacred White Cat. What then?

PERSIAN. Why, sell her secretly to Ptolemy, and then offer ourselves to Caesar as volunteers to fight for the overthrow of her brother and the rescue of our Queen, the Great Granddaughter of the Nile.

THE GUARDSMEN. O serpent!

PERSIAN. He will listen to us if we come with her picture in our mouths. He will conquer and kill her brother, and reign in Egypt with Cleopatra for his Queen. And we shall be her guard.

GUARDSMEN. O subtlest of all the serpents! O admiration! O wisdom!

BEL AFFRIS. He will also have arrived before you have done talking, O word spinner.

BELZANOR. That is true. (An affrighted uproar in the palace interrupts him.) Quick: the flight has begun: guard the door. (They rush to the door and form a cordon before it with their spears. A mob of women-servants and nurses surges out. Those in front recoil from the spears, screaming to those behind to keep back. Belzanor's voice dominates the disturbance as he shouts) Back there. In again, unprofitable cattle.

THE GUARDSMEN. Back, unprofitable cattle.

BELZANOR. Send us out Ftatateeta, the Queen's chief nurse.

THE WOMEN (calling into the palace). Ftatateeta, Ftatateeta. Come, come. Speak to Belzanor.

A WOMAN. Oh, keep back. You are thrusting me on the spearheads.

A huge grim woman, her face covered with a network of tiny wrinkles, and her eyes old, large, and wise; sinewy handed, very tall, very strong; with the mouth of a bloodhound and the jaws of a bulldog, appears on the threshold. She is dressed like a person of consequence in the palace, and confronts the guardsmen insolently.

FTATATEETA. Make way for the Queen's chief nurse.

BELZANOR. (with solemn arrogance). Ftatateeta: I am Belzanor, the captain of the Queen's guard, descended from the gods.

FTATATEETA. (retorting his arrogance with interest). Belzanor: I am Ftatateeta, the Queen's chief nurse; and your divine ancestors were proud to be painted on the wall in the pyramids of the kings whom my fathers served.

The women laugh triumphantly.

BELZANOR (with grim humor) Ftatateeta: daughter of a long-tongued, swivel-eyed chameleon, the Romans are at hand. (A cry of terror from the women: they would fly but for the spears.) Not even the descendants of the gods can resist them; for they have each man seven arms, each carrying seven spears. The blood in their veins is boiling quicksilver; and their wives become mothers in three hours, and are slain and eaten the next day.

A shudder of horror from the women. Ftatateeta, despising them and scorning the soldiers, pushes her way through the crowd and confronts the spear points undismayed.

FTATATEETA. Then fly and save yourselves, O cowardly sons of the cheap clay gods that are sold to fish porters; and leave us to shift for ourselves.

BELZANOR. Not until you have first done our bidding, O terror of manhood. Bring out Cleopatra the Queen to us and then go whither you will.

FTATATEETA (with a derisive laugh). Now I know why the gods have taken her out of our hands. (The guardsmen start and look at one another). Know, thou foolish soldier, that the Queen has been missing since an hour past sun down.

BELZANOR (furiously). Hag: you have hidden her to sell to Caesar or her brother. (He grasps her by the left wrist, and drags her, helped by a few of the guard, to the middle of the courtyard, where, as they fling her on her knees, he draws a murderous looking knife.) Where is she? Where is she? or—(He threatens to cut her throat.)

FTATATEETA (savagely). Touch me, dog; and the Nile will not rise on your fields for seven times seven years of famine.

BELZANOR (frightened, but desperate). I will sacrifice: I will pay. Or stay. (To the Persian) You, O subtle one: your father's lands lie far from the Nile. Slay her.

PERSIAN (threatening her with his knife). Persia has but one god; yet he loves the blood of old women. Where is Cleopatra?

FTATATEETA. Persian: as Osiris lives, I do not know. I chide her for bringing evil days upon us by talking to the sacred cats of the priests, and carrying them in her arms. I told her she would be left alone here when the Romans came as a punishment for her disobedience. And now she is gone—run away—hidden. I speak the truth. I call Osiris to witness.

THE WOMEN (protesting officiously). She speaks the truth, Belzanor.

BELZANOR. You have frightened the child: she is hiding. Search—quick—into the palace—search every corner.

The guards, led by Belzanor, shoulder their way into the palace through the flying crowd of women, who escape through the courtyard gate.

FTATATEETA (screaming). Sacrilege! Men in the Queen's chambers! Sa— (Her voice dies away as the Persian puts his knife to her throat.)

BEL AFFRIS (laying a hand on Ftatateeta's left shoulder). Forbear her yet a moment, Persian. (To Ftatateeta, very significantly) Mother: your gods are asleep or away hunting; and the sword is at your throat. Bring us to where the Queen is hid, and you shall live.

FTATATEETA (contemptuously). Who shall stay the sword in the hand of a fool, if the high gods put it there? Listen to me, ye young men without understanding. Cleopatra fears me; but she fears the Romans more. There is but one power greater in her eyes than the wrath of the Queen's nurse and the cruelty of Caesar; and that is the power of the Sphinx that sits in the desert watching the way to the sea. What she would have it know, she tells into the ears of the sacred cats; and on her birthday she sacrifices to it and decks it with poppies. Go ye therefore into the desert and seek Cleopatra in the shadow of the Sphinx; and on your heads see to it that no harm comes to her.

BEL AFFRIS (to the Persian). May we believe this, O subtle one?

PERSIAN. Which way come the Romans?

BEL AFFRIS. Over the desert, from the sea, by this very Sphinx.

PERSIAN (to Ftatateeta). O mother of guile! O aspic's tongue! You have made up this tale so that we two may go into the desert and perish on the spears of the Romans. (Lifting his knife) Taste death.

FTATATEETA. Not from thee, baby. (She snatches his ankle from under him and flies stooping along the palace wall vanishing in the darkness within its precinct. Bel Affris roars with laughter as the Persian tumbles. The guardsmen rush out of the palace with Belzanor and a mob of fugitives, mostly carrying bundles.)

PERSIAN. Have you found Cleopatra?

BELZANOR. She is gone. We have searched every corner.

THE NUBIAN SENTINEL (appearing at the door of the palace). Woe! Alas! Fly, fly!

BELZANOR. What is the matter now?

THE NUBIAN SENTINEL. The sacred white cat has been stolen. Woe! Woe! (General panic. They all fly with cries of consternation. The torch is thrown down and extinguished in the rush. Darkness. The noise of the fugitives dies away. Dead silence. Suspense. Then the blackness and stillness breaks softly into silver mist and strange airs as the windswept harp of Memnon plays at the dawning of the moon. It rises full over the desert; and a vast horizon comes into relief, broken by a huge shape which soon reveals itself in the spreading radiance as a Sphinx pedestalled on the sands. The light still clears, until the upraised eyes of the image are distinguished looking straight forward and upward in infinite fearless vigil, and a mass of color between its great paws defines itself as a heap of red poppies on which a girl lies motionless, her silken vest heaving gently and regularly with the breathing of a dreamless sleeper, and her braided hair glittering in a shaft of moonlight like a bird's wing.

Suddenly there comes from afar a vaguely fearful sound [*it might be the bellow of a Minotaur softened by great distance*] and Memnon's music stops. Silence: then a few faint high-ringing trumpet notes. Then silence again. Then a man comes from the south with stealing steps, ravished by the mystery of the night, all wonder, and halts, lost in contemplation, opposite the left flank of the Sphinx, whose bosom, with its burden, is hidden from him by its massive shoulder.)

THE MAN. Hail, Sphinx: salutation from Julius Caesar! I have wandered in many lands, seeking the lost regions from which my birth into this world exiled me, and the company of creatures such as I myself. I have found flocks and pastures, men and cities, but no other Caesar, no air native to me, no man kindred to me, none who can do my day's deed, and think my night's thought. In the little world yonder, Sphinx, my place is as high as yours in this great desert; only I wander, and you sit still; I conquer, and you endure; I work and wonder, you watch and wait; I look up and am dazzled, look down and am darkened, look round and am puzzled, whilst your eyes never turn from looking out—out of the world—to the lost region—the home from which we have strayed. Sphinx, you and I, strangers to the race of men, are no strangers to one another: have I not been conscious of you and of this place since I was born? Rome is a madman's dream: this is my Reality. These starry lamps of yours I have seen from afar in Gaul, in Britain, in Spain, in Thessaly, signalling great secrets to some eternal sentinel below, whose post I never could find. And here at last is their sentinel—an image of the constant and immortal part of my life, silent, full of thoughts, alone in the silver desert. Sphinx, Sphinx: I have climbed mountains at night to hear in the distance the stealthy footfall of the winds that chase your sands in forbidden play—our invisible children, O Sphinx, laughing in whispers. My way hither was the way of destiny; for I am he of whose genius you are the symbol: part brute, part woman, and part God—nothing of man in me at all. Have I read your riddle, Sphinx?

THE GIRL (who has wakened, and peeped cautiously from her nest to see who is speaking). Old gentleman.

CAESAR (starting violently, and clutching his sword). Immortal gods!

THE GIRL. Old gentleman: don't run away.

CAESAR (stupefied). "Old gentleman: don't run away!!!" This! To Julius Caesar!

THE GIRL (urgently). Old gentleman.

CAESAR. Sphinx: you presume on your centuries. I am younger than you, though your voice is but a girl's voice as yet.

THE GIRL. Climb up here, quickly; or the Romans will come and eat you.

CAESAR (running forward past the Sphinx's shoulder, and seeing her). A child at its breast! A divine child!

THE GIRL. Come up quickly. You must get up at its side and creep round.

CAESAR (amazed). Who are you?

THE GIRL. Cleopatra, Queen of Egypt.

CAESAR. Queen of the Gypsies, you mean.

CLEOPATRA. You must not be disrespectful to me, or the Sphinx will let the Romans eat you. Come up. It is quite cosy here.

CAESAR (to himself). What a dream! What a magnificent dream! Only let me not wake, and I will conquer ten continents to pay for dreaming it out to the end. (He climbs to the Sphinx's flank, and presently reappears to her on the pedestal, stepping round its right shoulder.)

CLEOPATRA. Take care. That's right. Now sit down: you may have its other paw. (She seats herself comfortably on its left paw.) It is very powerful and will protect us; but (shivering, and with plaintive loneliness) it would not take any notice of me or keep me company. I am glad you have come: I was very lonely. Did you happen to see a white cat anywhere?

CAESAR (sitting slowly down on the right paw in extreme wonderment). Have you lost one?

CLEOPATRA. Yes: the sacred white cat: is it not dreadful? I brought him here to sacrifice him to the Sphinx; but when we got a little way from the city a black cat called him, and he jumped out of my arms and ran away to it. Do you think that the black cat can have been my great-great-great-grandmother?

CAESAR (staring at her). Your great-great-great-grandmother! Well, why not? Nothing would surprise me on this night of nights.

CLEOPATRA. I think it must have been. My great-grandmother's great-grandmother was a black kitten of the sacred white cat; and the river Nile made her his seventh wife. That is why my hair is so wavy. And I always want to be let do as I like, no matter whether it is the will of the gods or not: that is because my blood is made with Nile water.

CAESAR. What are you doing here at this time of night? Do you live here?

CLEOPATRA. Of course not: I am the Queen; and I shall live in the palace at Alexandria when I have killed my brother, who drove me out of it. When I am old enough I shall do just what I like. I shall be able to poison the slaves and see them wriggle, and pretend to Ftatateeta that she is going to be put into the fiery furnace.

CAESAR. Hm! Meanwhile why are you not at home and in bed?

CLEOPATRA. Because the Romans are coming to eat us all. YOU are not at home and in bed either.

CAESAR (with conviction). Yes I am. I live in a tent; and I am now in that tent, fast asleep and dreaming. Do you suppose that I believe you are real, you impossible little dream witch?

CLEOPATRA (giggling and leaning trustfully towards him). You are a funny old gentleman. I like you.

CAESAR. Ah, that spoils the dream. Why don't you dream that I am young?

CLEOPATRA. I wish you were; only I think I should be more afraid of you. I like men, especially young men with round strong arms; but I am afraid of them. You are old and rather thin and stringy; but you have a nice voice; and I like to have somebody to talk to, though I think you are a little mad. It is the moon that makes you talk to yourself in that silly way.

CAESAR. What! you heard that, did you? I was saying my prayers to the great Sphinx.

CLEOPATRA. But this isn't the great Sphinx.

CAESAR (much disappointed, looking up at the statue). What!

CLEOPATRA. This is only a dear little kitten of the Sphinx. Why, the great Sphinx is so big that it has a temple between its paws. This is my pet Sphinx. Tell me: do you think the Romans have any sorcerers who could take us away from the Sphinx by magic?

CAESAR. Why? Are you afraid of the Romans?

CLEOPATRA (very seriously). Oh, they would eat us if they caught us. They are barbarians. Their chief is called Julius Caesar. His father was a tiger and his mother a burning mountain; and his nose is like an elephant's trunk. (Caesar involuntarily rubs his nose.) They all have long noses, and ivory tusks, and little tails, and seven arms with a hundred arrows in each; and they live on human flesh.

CAESAR. Would you like me to show you a real Roman?

CLEOPATRA (terrified). No. You are frightening me.

CAESAR. No matter: this is only a dream—

CLEOPATRA (excitedly). It is not a dream: it is not a dream. See, see. (She plucks a pin from her hair and jabs it repeatedly into his arm.)

CAESAR. Ffff—Stop. (Wrathfully) How dare you?

CLEOPATRA (abashed). You said you were dreaming. (Whimpering) I only wanted to show you—

CAESAR (gently). Come, come: don't cry. A queen mustn't cry. (He rubs his arm, wondering at the reality of the smart.) Am I awake? (He strikes his hand against the Sphinx to test its solidity. It feels so real that he begins to be alarmed, and says perplexedly) Yes, I—(quite panic-stricken) no: impossible: madness, madness! (Desperately) Back to camp—to camp. (He rises to spring down from the pedestal.)

CLEOPATRA (flinging her arms in terror round him). No: you shan't leave me. No, no, no: don't go. I'm afraid—afraid of the Romans.

CAESAR (as the conviction that he is really awake forces itself on him). Cleopatra: can you see my face well?

CLEOPATRA. Yes. It is so white in the moonlight.

CAESAR. Are you sure it is the moonlight that makes me look whiter than an Egyptian? (Grimly) Do you notice that I have a rather long nose?

CLEOPATRA (recoiling, paralyzed by a terrible suspicion). Oh!

CAESAR. It is a Roman nose, Cleopatra.

CLEOPATRA. Ah! (With a piercing scream she springs up; darts round the left shoulder of the Sphinx; scrambles down to the sand; and falls on her knees in frantic supplication, shrieking) Bite him in two, Sphinx: bite him in two. I meant to sacrifice the white cat—I did indeed—I (Caesar, who has slipped down from the pedestal, touches her on the shoulder) Ah! (She buries her head in her arms.)

CAESAR. Cleopatra: shall I teach you a way to prevent Caesar from eating you?

CLEOPATRA (clinging to him piteously). Oh do, do, do. I will steal Ftatateeta's jewels and give them to you. I will make the river Nile water your lands twice a year.

CAESAR. Peace, peace, my child. Your gods are afraid of the Romans: you see the Sphinx dare not bite me, nor prevent me carrying you off to Julius Caesar.

CLEOPATRA (in pleading murmurings). You won't, you won't. You said you wouldn't.

CAESAR. Caesar never eats women.

CLEOPATRA (springing up full of hope). What!

CAESAR (impressively). But he eats girls (she relapses) and cats. Now you are a silly little girl; and you are descended from the black kitten. You are both a girl and a cat.

CLEOPATRA (trembling). And will he eat me?

CAESAR. Yes; unless you make him believe that you are a woman.

CLEOPATRA. Oh, you must get a sorcerer to make a woman of me. Are you a sorcerer?

CAESAR. Perhaps. But it will take a long time; and this very night you must stand face to face with Caesar in the palace of your fathers.

CLEOPATRA. No, no. I daren't.

CAESAR. Whatever dread may be in your soul—however terrible Caesar may be to you—you must confront him as a brave woman and a great queen; and you must feel no fear. If your hand shakes: if your voice quavers; then—night and death! (She moans.) But if he thinks you worthy to rule, he will set you on the throne by his side and make you the real ruler of Egypt.

CLEOPATRA (despairingly). No: he will find me out: he will find me out.

CAESAR (rather mournfully). He is easily deceived by women. Their eyes dazzle him; and he sees them not as they are, but as he wishes them to appear to him.

CLEOPATRA (hopefully). Then we will cheat him. I will put on Ftatateeta's head-dress; and he will think me quite an old woman.

CAESAR. If you do that he will eat you at one mouthful.

CLEOPATRA. But I will give him a cake with my magic opal and seven hairs of the white cat baked in it; and—

CAESAR (abruptly). Pah! you are a little fool. He will eat your cake and you too. (He turns contemptuously from her.)

CLEOPATRA (running after him and clinging to him). Oh, please, PLEASE! I will do whatever you tell me. I will be good! I will be your slave. (Again the terrible bellowing note sounds across the desert, now closer at hand. It is the bucina, the Roman war trumpet.)

CAESAR. Hark!

CLEOPATRA (trembling). What was that?

CAESAR. Caesar's voice.

CLEOPATRA (pulling at his hand). Let us run away. Come. Oh, come.

CAESAR. You are safe with me until you stand on your throne to receive Caesar. Now lead me thither.

CLEOPATRA (only too glad to get away). I will, I will. (Again the bucina.) Oh, come, come, come: the gods are angry. Do you feel the earth shaking?

CAESAR. It is the tread of Caesar's legions.

CLEOPATRA (drawing him away). This way, quickly. And let us look for the white cat as we go. It is he that has turned you into a Roman.

CAESAR. Incorrigible, oh, incorrigible! Away! (He follows her, the bucina sounding louder as they steal across the desert. The moonlight wanes: the horizon again shows black against the sky, broken only by the fantastic silhouette of the Sphinx. The sky itself vanishes in darkness, from which there is no relief until the gleam of a distant torch falls on great Egyptian pillars supporting the roof of a majestic corridor. At the further end of this corridor a Nubian slave appears carrying the torch. Caesar, still led by Cleopatra, follows him. They come down the corridor, Caesar peering keenly about at the strange architecture, and at the pillar shadows between which, as the passing torch makes them hurry noiselessly backwards, figures of men with wings and hawks' heads, and vast black marble cats, seem to flit in and out of ambush. Further along, the wall turns a corner and makes a spacious transept in which Caesar sees, on his right, a throne, and behind the throne a door. On each side of the throne is a slender pillar with a lamp on it.)

CAESAR. What place is this?

CLEOPATRA. This is where I sit on the throne when I am allowed to wear my crown and robes. (The slave holds his torch to show the throne.)

CAESAR. Order the slave to light the lamps.

CLEOPATRA (shyly). Do you think I may?

CAESAR. Of course. You are the Queen. (She hesitates.) Go on.

CLEOPATRA (timidly, to the slave). Light all the lamps.

FTATATEETA (suddenly coming from behind the throne). Stop. (The slave stops. She turns sternly to Cleopatra, who quails like a naughty child.) Who is this you have with you; and how dare you order the lamps to be lighted without my permission? (Cleopatra is dumb with apprehension.)

CAESAR. Who is she?

CLEOPATRA. Ftatateeta.

FTATATEETA (arrogantly). Chief nurse to—

CAESAR (cutting her short). I speak to the Queen. Be silent. (To Cleopatra) Is this how your servants know their places? Send her away; and you (to the slave) do as the Queen has bidden. (The slave lights the lamps. Meanwhile Cleopatra stands hesitating, afraid of Ftatateeta.) You are the Queen: send her away.

CLEOPATRA (cajoling). Ftatateeta, dear: you must go away—just for a little.

CAESAR. You are not commanding her to go away: you are begging her. You are no Queen. You will be eaten. Farewell. (He turns to go.)

CLEOPATRA (clutching him). No, no, no. Don't leave me.

CAESAR. A Roman does not stay with queens who are afraid of their slaves.

CLEOPATRA. I am not afraid. Indeed I am not afraid.

FTATATEETA. We shall see who is afraid here. (Menacingly) Cleopatra—

CAESAR. On your knees, woman: am I also a child that you dare trifle with me? (He points to the floor at Cleopatra's feet. Ftatateeta, half cowed, half savage, hesitates. Caesar calls to the Nubian) Slave. (The Nubian comes to him.) Can you cut off a head? (The Nubian nods and grins ecstatically, showing all his teeth. Caesar takes his sword by the scabbard, ready to offer the hilt to the Nubian, and turns again to Ftatateeta, repeating his gesture.) Have you remembered yourself, mistress?

Ftatateeta, crushed, kneels before Cleopatra, who can hardly believe her eyes.

FTATATEETA (hoarsely). O Queen, forget not thy servant in the days of thy greatness.

CLEOPATRA (blazing with excitement). Go. Begone. Go away. (Ftatateeta rises with stooped head, and moves backwards towards the door. Cleopatra watches her submission eagerly, almost clapping her hands, which are trembling. Suddenly she cries) Give me something to beat her with. (She snatches a snake-skin from the throne and dashes after Ftatateeta, whirling it like a scourge in the air. Caesar makes a bound and manages to catch her and hold her while Ftatateeta escapes.)

CAESAR. You scratch, kitten, do you?

CLEOPATRA (breaking from him). I will beat somebody. I will beat him. (She attacks the slave.) There, there, there! (The slave flies for his life up the corridor and vanishes. She throws the snake-skin away and jumps on the step of the throne with her arms waving, crying) I am a real Queen at last—a real, real Queen! Cleopatra the Queen! (Caesar shakes his head dubiously, the advantage of the change seeming open to question from the point of view of the general welfare of Egypt. She turns and looks at him exultantly. Then she jumps down from the step, runs to him, and flings her arms round him rapturously, crying) Oh, I love you for making me a Queen.

CAESAR. But queens love only kings.

CLEOPATRA. I will make all the men I love kings. I will make you a king. I will have many young kings, with round, strong arms; and when I am tired of them I will whip them to death; but you shall always be my king: my nice, kind, wise, proud old king.

CAESAR. Oh, my wrinkles, my wrinkles! And my child's heart! You will be the most dangerous of all Caesar's conquests.

CLEOPATRA (appalled). Caesar! I forgot Caesar. (Anxiously) You will tell him that I am a Queen, will you not? a real Queen. Listen! (stealthily coaxing him) let us run away and hide until Caesar is gone.

CAESAR. If you fear Caesar, you are no true Queen; and though you were to hide beneath a pyramid, he would go straight to it and lift it with one hand. And then—! (He chops his teeth together.)

CLEOPATRA (trembling). Oh!

CAESAR. Be afraid if you dare. (The note of the bucina resounds again in the distance. She moans with fear. Caesar exalts in it, exclaiming) Aha! Caesar approaches the throne of Cleopatra. Come: take your place. (He takes her hand and leads her to the throne. She is too downcast to speak.) Ho, there, Teetatota. How do you call your slaves?

CLEOPATRA (spiritlessly, as she sinks on the throne and cowers there, shaking). Clap your hands.

He claps his hands. Ftatateeta returns.

CAESAR. Bring the Queen's robes, and her crown, and her women; and prepare her.

CLEOPATRA (eagerly—recovering herself a little). Yes, the Crown, Ftatateeta: I shall wear the crown.

FTATATEETA. For whom must the Queen put on her state?

CAESAR. For a citizen of Rome. A king of kings, Totateeta.

CLEOPATRA (stamping at her). How dare you ask questions? Go and do as you are told. (Ftatateeta goes out with a grim smile. Cleopatra goes on eagerly, to Caesar) Caesar will know that I am a Queen when he sees my crown and robes, will he not?

CAESAR. No. How shall he know that you are not a slave dressed up in the Queen's ornaments?

CLEOPATRA. You must tell him.

CAESAR. He will not ask me. He will know Cleopatra by her pride, her courage, her majesty, and her beauty. (She looks very doubtful.) Are you trembling?

CLEOPATRA (shivering with dread). No, I—I— (in a very sickly voice) No.

Ftatateeta and three women come in with the regalia.

FTATATEETA. Of all the Queen's women, these three alone are left. The rest are fled. (They begin to deck Cleopatra, who submits, pale and motionless.)

CAESAR. Good, good. Three are enough. Poor Caesar generally has to dress himself.

FTATATEETA (contemptuously). The Queen of Egypt is not a Roman barbarian. (To Cleopatra) Be brave, my nursling. Hold up your head before this stranger.

CAESAR (admiring Cleopatra, and placing the crown on her head). Is it sweet or bitter to be a Queen, Cleopatra?

CLEOPATRA. Bitter.

CAESAR. Cast out fear; and you will conquer Caesar. Tota: are the Romans at hand?

FTATATEETA. They are at hand; and the guard has fled.

THE WOMEN (wailing subduedly). Woe to us!

The Nubian comes running down the hall.

NUBIAN. The Romans are in the courtyard. (He bolts through the door. With a shriek, the women fly after him. Ftatateeta's jaw expresses savage resolution: she does not budge. Cleopatra can hardly restrain herself from following them. Caesar grips her wrist, and looks steadfastly at her. She stands like a martyr.)

CAESAR. The Queen must face Caesar alone. Answer "So be it."

CLEOPATRA (white). So be it.

CAESAR (releasing her). Good.

A tramp and tumult of armed men is heard. Cleopatra's terror increases. The bucina sounds close at hand, followed by a formidable clangor of trumpets. This is too much for Cleopatra: she utters a cry and darts towards the door. Ftatateeta stops her ruthlessly.

FTATATEETA. You are my nursling. You have said "So be it"; and if you die for it, you must make the Queen's word good. (She hands Cleopatra to Caesar, who takes her back, almost beside herself with apprehension, to the throne.)

CAESAR. Now, if you quail—! (He seats himself on the throne.)

She stands on the step, all but unconscious, waiting for death. The Roman soldiers troop in tumultuously through the corridor, headed by their ensign with his eagle, and their bucinator, a burly fellow with his instrument coiled round his body, its brazen bell shaped like the head of a howling wolf. When they reach the transept, they stare in amazement at the throne; dress into ordered rank opposite it; draw their swords and lift them in the air with a shout of HAIL CAESAR. Cleopatra turns and stares wildly at Caesar; grasps the situation; and, with a great sob of relief, falls into his arms.

ACT II

Alexandria. A hall on the first floor of the Palace, ending in a loggia approached by two steps. Through the arches of the loggia the Mediterranean can be seen, bright in the morning sun. The clean lofty walls, painted with a procession of the Egyptian theocracy, presented in profile as flat ornament, and the absence of mirrors, sham perspectives, stuffy upholstery and textiles, make the place handsome, wholesome, simple and cool, or, as a rich English manufacturer would express it, poor, bare, ridiculous and unhomely. For Tottenham Court Road civilization is to this Egyptian civilization as glass bead and tattoo civilization is to Tottenham Court Road.

The young king Ptolemy Dionysus (aged ten) is at the top of the steps, on his way in through the loggia, led by his guardian Pothinus, who has him by the hand. The court is assembled to receive him. It is made up of men and women (some of the women being officials) of various complexions and races, mostly Egyptian; some of them, comparatively fair, from lower Egypt; some, much darker, from upper Egypt; with a few Greeks and Jews. Prominent in a group on Ptolemy's right hand is Theodotus, Ptolemy's tutor. Another group, on Ptolemy's left, is headed by Achillas, the general of Ptolemy's troops. Theodotus is a little old man, whose features are as cramped and wizened as his limbs, except his tall straight forehead, which occupies more space than all the rest of his face. He maintains an air of magpie keenness and profundity, listening to what the others say with the sarcastic vigilance of a philosopher listening to the exercises of his disciples. Achillas is a tall handsome man of thirty-five, with a fine black beard curled like the coat of a poodle. Apparently not a clever man, but distinguished and dignified. Pothinus is a vigorous man of fifty, a eunuch, passionate, energetic and quick witted, but of common mind and character; impatient and unable to control his temper. He has fine tawny hair, like fur. Ptolemy, the King, looks much older than an English boy of ten; but he has the childish air, the habit of being in leading strings, the mixture of impotence and petulance, the appearance of being excessively washed, combed and dressed by other hands, which is exhibited by court-bred princes of all ages.

All receive the King with reverences. He comes down the steps to a chair of state which stands a little to his right, the only seat in the hall. Taking his place before it, he looks nervously for instructions to Pothinus, who places himself at his left hand.

POTHINUS. The King of Egypt has a word to speak.

THEODOTUS (in a squeak which he makes impressive by sheer self-opinionativeness). Peace for the King's word!

PTOLEMY (without any vocal inflexions: he is evidently repeating a lesson). Take notice of this all of you. I am the firstborn son of Auletes the Flute Blower who was your King. My sister Berenice drove him from his throne and reigned in his stead but—but (he hesitates)—

POTHINUS (stealthily prompting).—but the gods would not suffer—

PTOLEMY. Yes—the gods would not suffer—not suffer (he stops; then, crestfallen) I forget what the gods would not suffer.

THEODOTUS. Let Pothinus, the King's guardian, speak for the King.

POTHINUS (suppressing his impatience with difficulty). The King wished to say that the gods would not suffer the impiety of his sister to go unpunished.

PTOLEMY (hastily). Yes: I remember the rest of it. (He resumes his monotone). Therefore the gods sent a stranger, one Mark Antony, a Roman captain of horsemen, across the sands of the desert and he set my father again upon the throne. And my father took Berenice my sister and struck her head off. And now that my father is dead yet another of his daughters, my sister Cleopatra, would snatch the kingdom from me and reign in my place. But the gods would not suffer (Pothinus coughs admonitorily)—the gods—the gods would not suffer—

POTHINUS (prompting).—will not maintain—

PTOLEMY. Oh yes—will not maintain such iniquity, they will give her head to the axe even as her sister's. But with the help of the witch Ftatateeta she hath cast a spell on the Roman Julius Caesar to make him uphold her false pretence to rule in Egypt. Take notice then that I will not suffer—that I will not suffer—(pettishly, to Pothinus)—What is it that I will not suffer?

POTHINUS (suddenly exploding with all the force and emphasis of political passion). The King will not suffer a foreigner to take from him the throne of our Egypt. (A shout of applause.) Tell the King, Achillas, how many soldiers and horsemen follow the Roman?

THEODOTUS. Let the King's general speak!

ACHILLAS. But two Roman legions, O King. Three thousand soldiers and scarce a thousand horsemen.

The court breaks into derisive laughter; and a great chattering begins, amid which Rufio, a Roman officer, appears in the loggia. He is a burly, black-bearded man of middle age, very blunt, prompt and rough, with small clear eyes, and plump nose and cheeks, which, however, like the rest of his flesh, are in ironhard condition.

RUFIO (from the steps). Peace, ho! (The laughter and chatter cease abruptly.) Caesar approaches.

THEODOTUS (with much presence of mind). The King permits the Roman commander to enter!

Caesar, plainly dressed, but, wearing an oak wreath to conceal his baldness, enters from, the loggia, attended by Britannus, his secretary, a Briton, about forty, tall, solemn, and already slightly bald, with a heavy, drooping, hazel-colored moustache trained so as to lose its ends in a pair of trim whiskers. He is carefully dressed in blue, with portfolio, inkhorn, and reed pen at his girdle. His serious air and sense of the importance of the business in hand is in marked contrast to the kindly interest of Caesar, who looks at the scene, which is new to him, with the frank curiosity of a child, and then turns to the King's chair: Britannus and Rufio posting themselves near the steps at the other side.

CAESAR (looking at Pothinus and Ptolemy). Which is the King? The man or the boy?

POTHINUS. I am Pothinus, the guardian of my lord the King.

Caesar (patting Ptolemy kindly on the shoulder). So you are the King. Dull work at your age, eh? (To Pothinus) your servant, Pothinus. (He turns away unconcernedly and comes slowly along the middle of the hall, looking from side to side at the courtiers until he reaches Achillas.) And this gentleman?

THEODOTUS. Achillas, the King's general.

CAESAR (to Achillas, very friendly). A general, eh? I am a general myself. But I began too old, too old. Health and many victories, Achillas!

ACHILLAS. As the gods will, Caesar.

CAESAR (turning to Theodotus). And you, sir, are—?

THEODOTUS. Theodotus, the King's tutor.

CAESAR. You teach men how to be kings, Theodotus. That is very clever of you. (Looking at the gods on the walls as he turns away from Theodotus and goes up again to Pothinus.) And this place?

POTHINUS. The council chamber of the chancellors of the King's treasury, Caesar.

CAESAR. Ah! That reminds me. I want some money.

POTHINUS. The King's treasury is poor, Caesar.

CAESAR. Yes: I notice that there is but one chair in it.

RUFIO (shouting gruffly). Bring a chair there, some of you, for Caesar.

PTOLEMY (rising shyly to offer his chair). Caesar—

CAESAR (kindly). No, no, my boy: that is your chair of state. Sit down.

He makes Ptolemy sit down again. Meanwhile Rufio, looking about him, sees in the nearest corner an image of the god Ra, represented as a seated man with the head of a hawk. Before the image is a bronze tripod, about as large as a three-legged stool, with a stick of incense burning on it. Rufio, with Roman resourcefulness and indifference to foreign superstitions, promptly seizes the tripod; shakes off the incense; blows away the ash; and dumps it down behind Caesar, nearly in the middle of the hall.

RUFIO. Sit on that, Caesar.

A shiver runs through the court, followed by a hissing whisper of Sacrilege!

CAESAR (seating himself). Now, Pothinus, to business. I am badly in want of money.

BRITANNUS (disapproving of these informal expressions). My master would say that there is a lawful debt due to Rome by Egypt, contracted by the King's deceased father to the Triumvirate; and that it is Caesar's duty to his country to require immediate payment.

CAESAR (blandly). Ah, I forgot. I have not made my companions known here. Pothinus: this is Britannus, my secretary. He is an islander from the western end of the world, a day's voyage from Gaul. (Britannus bows stiffly.) This gentleman is Rufio, my comrade in arms. (Rufio nods.) Pothinus: I want 1,600 talents.

The courtiers, appalled, murmur loudly, and Theodotus and Achillas appeal mutely to one another against so monstrous a demand.

POTHINUS (aghast). Forty million sesterces! Impossible. There is not so much money in the King's treasury.

CAESAR (encouragingly). ONLY sixteen hundred talents, Pothinus. Why count it in sesterces? A sestertius is only worth a loaf of bread.

POTHINUS. And a talent is worth a racehorse. I say it is impossible. We have been at strife here, because the King's sister Cleopatra falsely claims his throne. The King's taxes have not been collected for a whole year.

CAESAR. Yes they have, Pothinus. My officers have been collecting them all the morning. (Renewed whisper and sensation, not without some stifled laughter, among the courtiers.)

RUFIO (bluntly). You must pay, Pothinus. Why waste words? You are getting off cheaply enough.

POTHINUS (bitterly). Is it possible that Caesar, the conqueror of the world, has time to occupy himself with such a trifle as our taxes?

CAESAR. My friend: taxes are the chief business of a conqueror of the world.

POTHINUS. Then take warning, Caesar. This day, the treasures of the temples and the gold of the King's treasury will be sent to the mint to be melted down for our ransom in the sight of the people. They shall see us sitting under bare walls and drinking from wooden cups. And their wrath be on your head, Caesar, if you force us to this sacrilege!

CAESAR. Do not fear, Pothinus: the people know how well wine tastes in wooden cups. In return for your bounty, I will settle this dispute about the throne for you, if you will. What say you?

POTHINUS. If I say no, will that hinder you?

RUFIO (defiantly). No.

CAESAR. You say the matter has been at issue for a year, Pothinus. May I have ten minutes at it?

POTHINUS. You will do your pleasure, doubtless.

CAESAR. Good! But first, let us have Cleopatra here.

THEODOTUS. She is not in Alexandria: she is fled into Syria.

CAESAR. I think not. (To Rufio) Call Totateeta.

RUFIO (calling). Ho there, Teetatota.

Ftatateeta enters the loggia, and stands arrogantly at the top of the steps.

FTATATEETA. Who pronounces the name of Ftatateeta, the Queen's chief nurse?

CAESAR. Nobody can pronounce it, Tota, except yourself. Where is your mistress?

Cleopatra, who is hiding behind Ftafateeta, peeps out at them, laughing. Caesar rises.

CAESAR. Will the Queen favor us with her presence for a moment?

CLEOPATRA (pushing Ftatateeta aside and standing haughtily on the brink of the steps). Am I to behave like a Queen?

CAESAR. Yes.

Cleopatra immediately comes down to the chair of state; seizes Ptolemy and drags him out of his seat; then takes his place in the chair. Ftatateeta seats herself on the step of the loggia, and sits there, watching the scene with sybilline intensity.

PTOLEMY (mortified, and struggling with his tears). Caesar: this is how she treats me always. If I am a King why is she allowed to take everything from me?

CLEOPATRA. You are not to be King, you little cry-baby. You are to be eaten by the Romans.

CAESAR (touched by Ptolemy's distress). Come here, my boy, and stand by me.

Ptolemy goes over to Caesar, who, resuming his seat on the tripod, takes the boy's hand to encourage him. Cleopatra, furiously jealous, rises and glares at them.

CLEOPATRA (with flaming cheeks). Take your throne: I don't want it. (She flings away from the chair, and approaches Ptolemy, who shrinks from her.) Go this instant and sit down in your place.

CAESAR. Go, Ptolemy. Always take a throne when it is offered to you.

RUFIO. I hope you will have the good sense to follow your own advice when we return to Rome, Caesar.

Ptolemy slowly goes back to the throne, giving Cleopatra a wide berth, in evident fear of her hands. She takes his place beside Caesar.

CAESAR. Pothinus—

CLEOPATRA (interrupting him). Are you not going to speak to me?

CAESAR. Be quiet. Open your mouth again before I give you leave; and you shall be eaten.

CLEOPATRA. I am not afraid. A queen must not be afraid. Eat my husband there, if you like: he is afraid.

CAESAR (starting). Your husband! What do you mean?

CLEOPATRA (pointing to Ptolemy). That little thing.

The two Romans and the Briton stare at one another in amazement.

THEODOTUS. Caesar: you are a stranger here, and not conversant with our laws. The kings and queens of Egypt may not marry except with their own royal blood. Ptolemy and Cleopatra are born king and consort just as they are born brother and sister.

BRITANNUS (shocked). Caesar: this is not proper.

THEODOTUS (outraged). How!

CAESAR (recovering his self-possession). Pardon him. Theodotus: he is a barbarian, and thinks that the customs of his tribe and island are the laws of nature.

BRITANNUS. On the contrary, Caesar, it is these Egyptians who are barbarians; and you do wrong to encourage them. I say it is a scandal.

CAESAR. Scandal or not, my friend, it opens the gate of peace. (He rises and addresses Pothinus seriously.) Pothiuus: hear what I propose.

RUFIO. Hear Caesar there.

CAESAR. Ptolemy and Cleopatra shall reign jointly in Egypt.

ACHILLAS. What of the King's younger brother and Cleopatra's younger sister?

RUFIO (explaining). There is another little Ptolemy, Caesar: so they tell me.

CAESAR. Well, the little Ptolemy can marry the other sister; and we will make them both a present of Cyprus.

POTHINUS (impatiently). Cyprus is of no use to anybody.

CAESAR. No matter: you shall have it for the sake of peace.

BRITANNUS (unconsciously anticipating a later statesman). Peace with honor, Pothinus.

POTHINUS (mutinously). Caesar: be honest. The money you demand is the price of our freedom. Take it; and leave us to settle our own affairs.

THE BOLDER COURTIERS (encouraged by Pothinus's tone and Caesar's quietness). Yes, yes. Egypt for the Egyptians!

The conference now becomes an altercation, the Egyptians becoming more and more heated. Caesar remains unruffled; but Rufio grows fiercer and doggeder, and Britannus haughtily indignant.

RUFIO (contemptuously). Egypt for the Egyptians! Do you forget that there is a Roman army of occupation here, left by Aulus Gabinius when he set up your toy king for you?

ACHILLAS (suddenly asserting himself). And now under my command. I am the Roman general here, Caesar.

CAESAR (tickled by the humor of the situation). And also the Egyptian general, eh?

POTHINUS (triumphantly). That is so, Caesar.

CAESAR (to Achillas). So you can make war on the Egyptians in the name of Rome and on the Romans—on me, if necessary—in the name of Egypt?

ACHILLAS. That is so, Caesar.

CAESAR. And which side are you on at present, if I may presume to ask, general?

ACHILLAS. On the side of the right and of the gods.

CAESAR. Hm! How many men have you?

ACHILLAS. That will appear when I take the field.

RUFIO (truculently). Are your men Romans? If not, it matters not how many there are, provided you are no stronger than 500 to ten.

POTHINUS. It is useless to try to bluff us, Rufio. Caesar has been defeated before and may be defeated again. A few weeks ago Caesar was flying for his life before Pompey: a few months hence he may be flying for his life before Cato and Juba of Numidia, the African King.

ACHILLAS (following up Pothinus's speech menacingly). What can you do with 4,000 men?

THEODOTUS (following up Achillas's speech with a raucous squeak). And without money? Away with you.

ALL THE COURTIERS (shouting fiercely and crowding towards Caesar). Away with you. Egypt for the Egyptians! Begone.

Rufio bites his beard, too angry to speak. Caesar sits on comfortably as if he were at breakfast, and the cat were clamoring for a piece of Finnan-haddie.

CLEOPATRA. Why do you let them talk to you like that Caesar? Are you afraid?

CAESAR. Why, my dear, what they say is quite true.

CLEOPATRA. But if you go away, I shall not be Queen.

CAESAR. I shall not go away until you are Queen.

POTHINUS. Achillas: if you are not a fool, you will take that girl whilst she is under your hand.

RUFIO (daring them). Why not take Caesar as well, Achillas?

POTHINUS (retorting the defiance with interest). Well said, Rufio. Why not?

RUFIO. Try, Achillas. (Calling) Guard there.

The loggia immediately fills with Caesar's soldiers, who stand, sword in hand, at the top of the steps, waiting the word to charge from their centurion, who carries a cudgel. For a moment the Egyptians face them proudly: then they retire sullenly to their former places.

BRITANNUS. You are Caesar's prisoners, all of you.

CAESAR (benevolently). Oh no, no, no. By no means. Caesar's guests, gentlemen.

CLEOPATRA. Won't you cut their heads off?

CAESAR. What! Cut off your brother's head?

CLEOPATRA. Why not? He would cut off mine, if he got the chance. Wouldn't you, Ptolemy?

PTOLEMY (pale and obstinate). I would. I will, too, when I grow up.

Cleopatra is rent by a struggle between her newly-acquired dignity as a queen, and a strong impulse to put out her tongue at him. She takes no part in the scene which follows, but watches it with curiosity and wonder, fidgeting with the restlessness of a child, and sitting down on Caesar's tripod when he rises.

POTHINUS. Caesar: if you attempt to detain us—

RUFIO. He will succeed, Egyptian: make up your mind to that. We hold the palace, the beach, and the eastern harbor. The road to Rome is open; and you shall travel it if Caesar chooses.

CAESAR (courteously). I could do no less, Pothinus, to secure the retreat of my own soldiers. I am accountable for every life among them. But you are free to go. So are all here, and in the palace.

RUFIO (aghast at this clemency). What! Renegades and all?

CAESAR (softening the expression). Roman army of occupation and all, Rufio.

POTHINUS (desperately). Then I make a last appeal to Caesar's justice. I shall call a witness to prove that but for us, the Roman army of occupation, led by the greatest soldier in the world, would now have Caesar at its mercy. (Calling through the loggia) Ho, there, Lucius Septimius (Caesar starts, deeply moved): if my voice can reach you, come forth and testify before Caesar.

CAESAR (shrinking). No, no.

THEODOTUS. Yes, I say. Let the military tribune bear witness.

Lucius Septimius, a clean shaven, trim athlete of about 40, with symmetrical features, resolute mouth, and handsome, thin Roman nose, in the dress of a Roman officer, comes in through the loggia and confronts Caesar, who hides his face with his robe for a moment; then, mastering himself, drops it, and confronts the tribune with dignity.

POTHINUS. Bear witness, Lucius Septimius. Caesar came hither in pursuit of his foe. Did we shelter his foe?

LUCIUS. As Pompey's foot touched the Egyptian shore, his head fell by the stroke of my sword.

THEODOTUS (with viperish relish). Under the eyes of his wife and child! Remember that, Caesar! They saw it from the ship he had just left. We have given you a full and sweet measure of vengeance.

CAESAR (with horror). Vengeance!

POTHINUS. Our first gift to you, as your galley came into the roadstead, was the head of your rival for the empire of the world. Bear witness, Lucius Septimius: is it not so?

LUCIUS. It is so. With this hand, that slew Pompey, I placed his head at the feet of Caesar.

CAESAR. Murderer! So would you have slain Caesar, had Pompey been victorious at Pharsalia.

LUCIUS. Woe to the vanquished, Caesar! When I served Pompey, I slew as good men as he, only because he conquered them. His turn came at last.

THEODOTUS (flatteringly). The deed was not yours, Caesar, but ours—nay, mine; for it was done by my counsel. Thanks to us, you keep your reputation for clemency, and have your vengeance too.

CAESAR. Vengeance! Vengeance!! Oh, if I could stoop to vengeance, what would I not exact from you as the price of this murdered man's blood. (They shrink back, appalled and disconcerted.) Was he not my son-in-law, my ancient friend, for 20 years the master of great Rome, for 30 years the compeller of victory? Did not I, as a Roman, share his glory? Was the Fate that forced us to fight for the mastery of the world, of our making? Am I Julius Caesar, or am I a wolf, that you fling to me the grey head of the old soldier, the laurelled conqueror, the mighty Roman, treacherously struck down by this callous ruffian, and then claim my gratitude for it! (To Lucius Septimius) Begone: you fill me with horror.

LUCIUS (cold and undaunted). Pshaw! You have seen severed heads before, Caesar, and severed right hands too, I think; some thousands of them, in Gaul, after you vanquished Vercingetorix. Did you spare him, with all your clemency? Was that vengeance?

CAESAR. No, by the gods! Would that it had been! Vengeance at least is human. No, I say: those severed right hands, and the brave Vercingetorix basely strangled in a vault beneath the Capitol, were (with shuddering satire) a wise severity, a necessary protection to the commonwealth, a duty of statesmanship—follies and fictions ten times bloodier than honest vengeance! What a fool was I then! To think that men's lives should be at the mercy of such fools! (Humbly) Lucius Septimius, pardon me: why should the slayer of Vercingetorix rebuke the slayer of Pompey? You are free to go with the rest. Or stay if you will: I will find a place for you in my service.

LUCIUS. The odds are against you, Caesar. I go. (He turns to go out through the loggia.)

RUFIO (full of wrath at seeing his prey escaping). That means that he is a Republican.

LUCIUS (turning defiantly on the loggia steps). And what are you?

RUFIO. A Caesarian, like all Caesar's soldiers.

CAESAR (courteously). Lucius: believe me, Caesar is no Caesarian. Were Rome a true republic, then were Caesar the first of Republicans. But you have made your choice. Farewell.

LUCIUS. Farewell. Come, Achillas, whilst there is yet time.

Caesar, seeing that Rufio's temper threatens to get the worse of him, puts his hand on his shoulder and brings him down the hall out of harm's way, Britannus accompanying them and posting himself on Caesar's right hand. This movement brings the three in a little group to the place occupied by Achillas, who moves haughtily away and joins Theodotus on the other side. Lucius Septimius goes out through the soldiers in the loggia. Pothinus, Theodotus and Achillas follow him with the courtiers, very mistrustful of the soldiers, who close up in their rear and go out after them, keeping them moving without much ceremony. The King is left in his chair, piteous, obstinate, with twitching face and fingers. During these movements Rufio maintains an energetic grumbling, as follows:—

RUFIO (as Lucius departs). Do you suppose he would let us go if he had our heads in his hands?

CAESAR. I have no right to suppose that his ways are any baser than mine.

RUFIO. Psha!

CAESAR. Rufio: if I take Lucius Septimius for my model, and become exactly like him, ceasing to be Caesar, will you serve me still?

BRITANNUS. Caesar: this is not good sense. Your duty to Rome demands that her enemies should be prevented from doing further mischief. (Caesar, whose delight in the moral eye-to-business of his British secretary is inexhaustible, smiles intelligently.)

RUFIO. It is no use talking to him, Britannus: you may save your breath to cool your porridge. But mark this, Caesar. Clemency is very well for you; but what is it for your soldiers, who have to fight tomorrow the men you spared yesterday? You may give what orders you please; but I tell you that your next victory will be a massacre, thanks to your clemency. I, for one, will take no prisoners. I will kill my enemies in the field; and then you can preach as much clemency as you please: I shall never have to fight them again. And now, with your leave, I will see these gentry off the premises. (He turns to go.)

CAESAR (turning also and seeing Ptolemy). What! Have they left the boy alone! Oh shame, shame!

RUFIO (taking Ptolemy's hand and making him rise). Come, your majesty!

PTOLEMY (to Caesar, drawing away his hand from Rufio). Is he turning me out of my palace?

RUFIO (grimly). You are welcome to stay if you wish.

CAESAR (kindly). Go, my boy. I will not harm you; but you will be safer away, among your friends. Here you are in the lion's mouth.

PTOLEMY (turning to go). It is not the lion I fear, but (looking at Rufio) the jackal. (He goes out through the loggia.)

CAESAR (laughing approvingly). Brave boy!

CLEOPATRA (jealous of Caesar's approbation, calling after Ptolemy). Little silly. You think that very clever.

CAESAR. Britannus: Attend the King. Give him in charge to that Pothinus fellow. (Britannus goes out after Ptolemy.)

RUFIO (pointing to Cleopatra). And this piece of goods? What is to be done with HER? However, I suppose I may leave that to you. (He goes out through the loggia.)

CLEOPATRA (flushing suddenly and turning on Caesar). Did you mean me to go with the rest?

CAESAR (a little preoccupied, goes with a sigh to Ptolemy's chair, whilst she waits for his answer with red cheeks and clenched fists). You are free to do just as you please, Cleopatra.

CLEOPATRA. Then you do not care whether I stay or not?

CAESAR (smiling). Of course I had rather you stayed.

CLEOPATRA. Much, MUCH rather?

CAESAR (nodding). Much, much rather.

CLEOPATRA. Then I consent to stay, because I am asked. But I do not want to, mind.

CAESAR. That is quite understood. (Calling) Totateeta.

Ftatateeta, still seated, turns her eyes on him with a sinister expression, but does not move.

CLEOPATRA (with a splutter of laughter). Her name is not Totateeta: it is Ftatateeta. (Calling) Ftatateeta. (Ftatateeta instantly rises and comes to Cleopatra.)

CAESAR (stumbling over the name). Ftatafeeta will forgive the erring tongue of a Roman. Tota: the Queen will hold her state here in Alexandria. Engage women to attend upon her; and do all that is needful.

FTATATEETA. Am I then the mistress of the Queen's household?

CLEOPATRA (sharply). No: I am the mistress of the Queen's household. Go and do as you are told, or I will have you thrown into the Nile this very afternoon, to poison the poor crocodiles.

CAESAR (shocked). Oh no, no.

CLEOPATRA. Oh yes, yes. You are very sentimental, Caesar; but you are clever; and if you do as I tell you, you will soon learn to govern.

Caesar, quite dumbfounded by this impertinence, turns in his chair and stares at her.

Ftatateeta, smiling grimly, and showing a splendid set of teeth, goes, leaving them alone together.

CAESAR. Cleopatra: I really think I must eat you, after all.

CLEOPATRA (kneeling beside him and looking at him with eager interest, half real, half affected to show how intelligent she is). You must not talk to me now as if I were a child.

CAESAR. You have been growing up since the Sphinx introduced us the other night; and you think you know more than I do already.

CLFOPATRA (taken down, and anxious to justify herself). No: that would be very silly of me: of course I know that. But, (suddenly) are you angry with me?

CAESAR. No.

CLEOPATRA (only half believing him). Then why are you so thoughtful?

CAESAR (rising). I have work to do, Cleopatra.

CLEOPATRA (drawing back). Work! (Offended) You are tired of talking to me; and that is your excuse to get away from me.

CAESAR (sitting down again to appease her). Well, well: another minute. But then—work!

CLFOPATRA. Work! What nonsense! You must remember that you are a King now: I have made you one. Kings don't work.

CAESAR. Oh! Who told you that, little kitten? Eh?

CLEOPATRA. My father was King of Egypt; and he never worked. But he was a great King, and cut off my sister's head because she rebelled against him and took the throne from him.

CAESAR. Well; and how did he get his throne back again?

CLEOPATRA (eagerly, her eyes lighting up). I will tell you. A beautiful young man, with strong round arms, came over the desert with many horsemen, and slew my sister's husband and gave my father back his throne. (Wistfully) I was only twelve then. Oh, I wish he would come again, now that I am a Queen. I would make him my husband.

CAESAR. It might be managed, perhaps; for it was I who sent that beautiful young man to help your father.

CLEOPATRA (enraptured). You know him!

CAESAR (nodding). I do.

CLEOPATRA. Has he come with you? (Caesar shakes his head: she is cruelly disappointed.) Oh, I wish he had, I wish he had. If only I were a little older; so that he might not think me a mere kitten, as you do! But perhaps that is because YOU are old. He is many, MANY years younger than you, is he not?

CAESAR (as if swallowing a pill). He is somewhat younger.

CLEOPATRA. Would he be my husband, do you think, if I asked him?

CAESAR. Very likely.

CLEOPATRA. But I should not like to ask him. Could you not persuade him to ask me—without knowing that I wanted him to?

CAESAR (touched by her innocence of the beautiful young man's character). My poor child!

CLEOPATRA. Why do you say that as if you were sorry for me? Does he love anyone else?

CAESAR. I am afraid so.

CLEOPATRA (tearfully). Then I shall not be his first love.

CAESAR. Not quite the first. He is greatly admired by women.

CLEOPATRA. I wish I could be the first. But if he loves me, I will make him kill all the rest. Tell me: is he still beautiful? Do his strong round arms shine in the sun like marble?

CAESAR. He is in excellent condition—considering how much he eats and drinks.

CLEOPATRA. Oh, you must not say common, earthly things about him; for I love him. He is a god.

CAESAR. He is a great captain of horsemen, and swifter of foot than any other Roman.

CLEOPATRA. What is his real name?

CAESAR (puzzled). His REAL name?

CLEOPATRA. Yes. I always call him Horus, because Horus is the most beautiful of our gods. But I want to know his real name.

CAESAR. His name is Mark Antony.

CLEOPATRA (musically). Mark Antony, Mark Antony, Mark Antony! What a beautiful name! (She throws her arms round Caesar's neck.) Oh, how I love you for sending him to help my father! Did you love my father very much?

CAESAR. No, my child; but your father, as you say, never worked. I always work. So when he lost his crown he had to promise me 16,000 talents to get it back for him.

CLEOPATRA. Did he ever pay you?

CAESAR. Not in full.

CLEOPATRA. He was quite right: it was too dear. The whole world is not worth 16,000 talents.

CAESAR. That is perhaps true, Cleopatra. Those Egyptians who work paid as much of it as he could drag from them. The rest is still due. But as I most likely shall not get it, I must go back to my work. So you must run away for a little and send my secretary to me.

CLEOPATRA (coaxing). No: I want to stay and hear you talk about Mark Antony.

CAESAR. But if I do not get to work, Pothinus and the rest of them will cut us off from the harbor; and then the way from Rome will be blocked.

CLEOPATRA. No matter: I don't want you to go back to Rome.

CAESAR. But you want Mark Antony to come from it.

CLEOPATRA (springing up). Oh yes, yes, yes: I forgot. Go quickly and work, Caesar; and keep the way over the sea open for my Mark Antony. (She runs out through the loggia, kissing her hand to Mark Antony across the sea.)

CAESAR (going briskly up the middle of the hall to the loggia steps). Ho, Britannus. (He is startled by the entry of a wounded Roman soldier, who confronts him from the upper step.) What now?

SOLDIER (pointing to his bandaged head). This, Caesar; and two of my comrades killed in the market place.

CAESAR (quiet but attending). Ay. Why?

SOLDIER. There is an army come to Alexandria, calling itself the Roman army.

CAESAR. The Roman army of occupation. Ay?

SOLDIER. Commanded by one Achillas.

CAESAR. Well?

SOLDIER. The citizens rose against us when the army entered the gates. I was with two others in the market place when the news came. They set upon us. I cut my way out; and here I am.

CAESAR. Good. I am glad to see you alive. (Rufio enters the loggia hastily, passing behind the soldier to look out through one of the arches at the quay beneath.) Rufio, we are besieged.

RUFIO. What! Already?

CAESAR. Now or tomorrow: what does it matter? We SHALL be besieged.

Britannus runs in.

BRITANNUS. Caesar—

CAESAR (anticipating him). Yes: I know. (Rufio and Britannus come down the hall from the loggia at opposite sides, past Caesar, who waits for a moment near the step to say to the soldier.) Comrade: give the word to turn out on the beach and stand by the boats. Get your wound attended to. Go. (The soldier hurries out. Caesar comes down the hall between Rufio and Britannus) Rufio: we have some ships in the west harbor. Burn them.

RUFIO (staring). Burn them!!

CAESAR. Take every boat we have in the east harbor, and seize the Pharos—that island with the lighthouse. Leave half our men behind to hold the beach and the quay outside this palace: that is the way home.

RUFIO (disapproving strongly). Are we to give up the city?

CAESAR. We have not got it, Rufio. This palace we have; and—what is that building next door?

RUFIO. The theatre.

CAESAR. We will have that too: it commands the strand, for the rest, Egypt for the Egyptians!

RUFIO. Well, you know best, I suppose. Is that all?

CAESAR. That is all. Are those ships burnt yet?

RUFIO. Be easy: I shall waste no more time. (He runs out.)

BRITANNUS. Caesar: Pothinus demands speech of you. It's my opinion he needs a lesson. His manner is most insolent.

CAESAR. Where is he?

BRITANNUS. He waits without.

CAESAR. Ho there! Admit Pothinus.

Pothinus appears in the loggia, and comes down the hall very haughtily to Caesar's left hand.

CAESAR. Well, Pothinus?

POTHINUS. I have brought you our ultimatum, Caesar.

CAESAR. Ultimatum! The door was open: you should have gone out through it before you declared war. You are my prisoner now. (He goes to the chair and loosens his toga.)

POTHINUS (scornfully). I YOUR prisoner! Do you know that you are in Alexandria, and that King Ptolemy, with an army outnumbering your little troop a hundred to one, is in possession of Alexandria?

CAESAR (unconcernedly taking off his toga and throwing it on the chair). Well, my friend, get out if you can. And tell your friends not to kill any more Romans in the market place. Otherwise my soldiers, who do not share my celebrated clemency, will probably kill you. Britannus: Pass the word to the guard; and fetch my armor. (Britannus runs out. Rufio returns.) Well?

RUFIO (pointing from the loggia to a cloud of smoke drifting over the harbor). See there! (Pothinus runs eagerly up the steps to look out.)

CAESAR. What, ablaze already! Impossible!

RUFIO. Yes, five good ships, and a barge laden with oil grappled to each. But it is not my doing: the Egyptians have saved me the trouble. They have captured the west harbor.

CAESAR (anxiously). And the east harbor? The lighthouse, Rufio?

RUFIO (with a sudden splutter of raging ill usage, coming down to Caesar and scolding him). Can I embark a legion in five minutes? The first cohort is already on the beach. We can do no more. If you want faster work, come and do it yourself?

CAESAR (soothing him). Good, good. Patience, Rufio, patience.

RUFIO. Patience! Who is impatient here, you or I? Would I be here, if I could not oversee them from that balcony?

CAESAR. Forgive me, Rufio; and (anxiously) hurry them as much as—

He is interrupted by an outcry as of an old man in the extremity of misfortune. It draws near rapidly; and Theodotus rushes in, tearing his hair, and squeaking the most lamentable exclamations. Rufio steps back to stare at him, amazed at his frantic condition. Pothinus turns to listen.

THEODOTUS (on the steps, with uplifted arms). Horror unspeakable! Woe, alas! Help!

RUFIO. What now?

CAESAR (frowning). Who is slain?

THEODOTUS. Slain! Oh, worse than the death of ten thousand men! Loss irreparable to mankind!

RUFIO. What has happened, man?

THEODOTUS (rushing down the hall between them). The fire has spread from your ships. The first of the seven wonders of the world perishes. The library of Alexandria is in flames.

RUFIO. Psha! (Quite relieved, he goes up to the loggia and watches the preparations of the troops on the beach.)

CAESAR. Is that all?

THEODOTUS (unable to believe his senses). All! Caesar: will you go down to posterity as a barbarous soldier too ignorant to know the value of books?

CAESAR. Theodotus: I am an author myself; and I tell you it is better that the Egyptians should live their lives than dream them away with the help of books.

THEODOTUS (kneeling, with genuine literary emotion: the passion of the pedant). Caesar: once in ten generations of men, the world gains an immortal book.

CAESAR (inflexible). If it did not flatter mankind, the common executioner would burn it.

THEODOTUS. Without history, death would lay you beside your meanest soldier.

CAESAR. Death will do that in any case. I ask no better grave.

THEODOTUS. What is burning there is the memory of mankind.

CAESAR. A shameful memory. Let it burn.

THEODOTUS (wildly). Will you destroy the past?

CAESAR. Ay, and build the future with its ruins. (Theodotus, in despair, strikes himself on the temples with his fists.) But harken, Theodotus, teacher of kings: you who valued Pompey's head no more than a shepherd values an onion, and who now kneel to me, with tears in your old eyes, to plead for a few sheepskins scrawled with errors. I cannot spare you a man or a bucket of water just now; but you shall pass freely out of the palace. Now, away with you to Achillas; and borrow his legions to put out the fire. (He hurries him to the steps.)

POTHINUS (significantly). You understand, Theodotus: I remain a prisoner.

THEODOTUS. A prisoner!

CAESAR. Will you stay to talk whilst the memory of mankind is burning? (Calling through the loggia) Ho there! Pass Theodotus out. (To Theodotus) Away with you.

THEODOTUS (to Pothinus). I must go to save the library. (He hurries out.)

CAESAR. Follow him to the gate, Pothinus. Bid him urge your people to kill no more of my soldiers, for your sake.

POTHINUS. My life will cost you dear if you take it, Caesar. (He goes out after Theodotus.)

Rufio, absorbed in watching the embarkation, does not notice the departure of the two Egyptians.

RUFIO (shouting from the loggia to the beach). All ready, there?

A CENTURION (from below). All ready. We wait for Caesar.

CAESAR. Tell them Caesar is coming—the rogues! (Calling) Britannicus. (This magniloquent version of his secretary's name is one of Caesar's jokes. In later years it would have meant, quite seriously and officially, Conqueror of Britain.)

RUFIO (calling down). Push off, all except the longboat. Stand by it to embark, Caesar's guard there. (He leaves the balcony and comes down into the hall.) Where are those Egyptians? Is this more clemency? Have you let them go?

CAESAR (chuckling). I have let Theodotus go to save the library. We must respect literature, Rufio.

RUFIO (raging). Folly on folly's head! I believe if you could bring back all the dead of Spain, Gaul and Thessaly to life, you would do it that we might have the trouble of fighting them over again.

CAESAR. Might not the gods destroy the world if their only thought were to be at peace next year? (Rufio, out of all patience, turns away in anger. Caesar suddenly grips his sleeve, and adds slyly in his ear.) Besides, my friend: every Egyptian we imprison means imprisoning two Roman soldiers to guard him. Eh?

RUFIO. Agh! I might have known there was some fox's trick behind your fine talking. (He gets away from Caesar with an ill-humored shrug, and goes to the balcony for another look at the preparations; finally goes out.)

CAESAR. Is Britannus asleep? I sent him for my armor an hour ago. (Calling) Britannicus, thou British islander. Britannicus!

Cleopatra, runs in through the loggia with Caesar's helmet and sword, snatched from Britannus, who follows her with a cuirass and greaves. They come down to Caesar, she to his left hand, Britannus to his right.

CLEOPATRA. I am going to dress you, Caesar. Sit down. (He obeys.) These Roman helmets are so becoming! (She takes off his wreath.) Oh! (She bursts out laughing at him.)

CAESAR. What are you laughing at?

CLEOPATRA. You're bald (beginning with a big B, and ending with a splutter).

CAESAR (almost annoyed). Cleopatra! (He rises, for the convenience of Britannus, who puts the cuirass on him.)

CLEOPATRA. So that is why you wear the wreath—to hide it.

BRITANNUS. Peace, Egyptian: they are the bays of the conqueror. (He buckles the cuirass.)

CLEOPATRA. Peace, thou: islander! (To Caesar) You should rub your head with strong spirits of sugar, Caesar. That will make it grow.

CAESAR (with a wry face). Cleopatra: do you like to be reminded that you are very young?

CLEOPATRA (pouting). No.

CAESAR (sitting down again, and setting out his leg for Britannus, who kneels to put on his greaves). Neither do I like to be reminded that I am—middle aged. Let me give you ten of my superfluous years. That will make you 26 and leave me only—no matter. Is it a bargain?

CLEOPATRA. Agreed. 26, mind. (She puts the helmet on him.) Oh! How nice! You look only about 50 in it!

BRITANNUS (Looking up severely at Cleopatra). You must not speak in this manner to Caesar.

CLEOPATRA. Is it true that when Caesar caught you on that island, you were painted all over blue?

BRITANNUS. Blue is the color worn by all Britons of good standing. In war we stain our bodies blue; so that though our enemies may strip us of our clothes and our lives, they cannot strip us of our respectability. (He rises.)

CLEOPATRA (with Caesar's sword). Let me hang this on. Now you look splendid. Have they made any statues of you in Rome?

CAESAR. Yes, many statues.

CLEOPATRA. You must send for one and give it to me.

RUFIO (coming back into the loggia, more impatient than ever). Now Caesar: have you done talking? The moment your foot is aboard there will be no holding our men back: the boats will race one another for the lighthouse.

CAESAR (drawing his sword and trying the edge). Is this well set to-day, Britannicus? At Pharsalia it was as blunt as a barrel-hoop.

BRITANNUS. It will split one of the Egyptian's hairs to-day, Caesar. I have set it myself.

CLEOPATRA (suddenly throwing her arms in terror round Caesar). Oh, you are not really going into battle to be killed?

CAESAR. No, Cleopatra. No man goes to battle to be killed.

CLEOPATRA. But they DO get killed. My sister's husband was killed in battle. You must not go. Let HIM go (pointing to Rufio. They all laugh at her). Oh please, PLEASE don't go. What will happen to ME if you never come back?

CAESAR (gravely). Are you afraid?

CLEOPATRA (shrinking). No.

CAESAR (with quiet authority). Go to the balcony; and you shall see us take the Pharos. You must learn to look on battles. Go. (She goes, downcast, and looks out from the balcony.) That is well. Now, Rufio. March.

CLEOPATRA (suddenly clapping her hands). Oh, you will not be able to go!

CAESAR. Why? What now?

CLEOPATRA. They are drying up the harbor with buckets—a multitude of soldiers—over there (pointing out across the sea to her left)—they are dipping up the water.

RUFIO (hastening to look). It is true. The Egyptian army! Crawling over the edge of the west harbor like locusts. (With sudden anger he strides down to Caesar.) This is your accursed clemency, Caesar. Theodotus has brought them.

CAESAR (delighted at his own cleverness). I meant him to, Rufio. They have come to put out the fire. The library will keep them busy whilst we seize the lighthouse. Eh? (He rushes out buoyantly through the loggia, followed by Britannus.)

RUFIO (disgustedly). More foxing! Agh! (He rushes off. A shout from the soldiers announces the appearance of Caesar below).

CENTURION (below). All aboard. Give way there. (Another shout.)

CLEOPATRA (waving her scarf through the loggia arch). Goodbye, goodbye, dear Caesar. Come back safe. Goodbye!

ACT III

The edge of the quay in front of the palace, looking out west over the east harbor of Alexandria to Pharos island, just off the end of which, and connected with it by a narrow mole, is the famous lighthouse, a gigantic square tower of white marble diminishing in size storey by storey to the top, on which stands a cresset beacon. The island is joined to the main land by the Heptastadium, a great mole or causeway five miles long bounding the harbor on the south.

In the middle of the quay a Roman sentinel stands on guard, pilum in hand, looking out to the lighthouse with strained attention, his left hand shading his eyes. The pilum is a stout wooden shaft 41 feet long, with an iron spit about three feet long fixed in it. The sentinel is so absorbed that he does not notice the approach from the north end of the quay of four Egyptian market porters carrying rolls of carpet, preceded by Ftatateeta and Apollodorus the Sicilian.

Apollodorus is a dashing young man of about 24, handsome and debonair, dressed with deliberate astheticism in the most delicate purples and dove greys, with ornaments of bronze, oxydized silver, and stones of jade and agate. His sword, designed as carefully as a medieval cross, has a blued blade showing through an openwork scabbard of purple leather and filagree. The porters, conducted by Ftatateeta, pass along the quay behind the sentinel to the steps of the palace, where they put down their bales and squat on the ground. Apollodorus does not pass along with them: he halts, amused by the preoccupation of the sentinel.

APOLLODORUS (calling to the sentinel). Who goes there, eh?

SENTINEL (starting violently and turning with his pilum at the charge, revealing himself as a small, wiry, sandy-haired, conscientious young man with an elderly face). What's this? Stand. Who are you?

APOLLODORUS. I am Apollodorus the Sicilian. Why, man, what are you dreaming of? Since I came through the lines beyond the theatre there, I have brought my caravan past three sentinels, all so busy staring at the lighthouse that not one of them challenged me. Is this Roman discipline?

SENTINEL. We are not here to watch the land but the water. Caesar has just landed on the Pharos. (Looking at Ftatateeta) What have you here? Who is this piece of Egyptian crockery?

FTATATEETA. Apollodorus: rebuke this Roman dog; and bid him bridle his tongue in the presence of Ftatateeta, the mistress of the Queen's household.

APOLLODORUS. My friend: this is a great lady, who stands high with Caesar.

SENTINEL (not at all impressed, pointing to the carpets). And what is all this truck?

APOLLODORUS. Carpets for the furnishing of the Queen's apartments in the palace. I have picked them from the best carpets in the world; and the Queen shall choose the best of my choosing.

SENTINEL. So you are the carpet merchant?

APOLLODORUS (hurt). My friend: I am a patrician.

SENTINEL. A patrician! A patrician keeping a shop instead of following arms!

APOLLODORUS. I do not keep a shop. Mine is a temple of the arts. I am a worshipper of beauty. My calling is to choose beautiful things for beautiful Queens. My motto is Art for Art's sake.

SENTINEL. That is not the password.

APOLLODORUS. It is a universal password.

SENTINEL. I know nothing about universal passwords. Either give me the password for the day or get back to your shop.

Ftatateeta, roused by his hostile tone, steals towards the edge of the quay with the step of a panther, and gets behind him.

APOLLODORUS. How if I do neither?

SENTINEL. Then I will drive this pilum through you.

APOLLODORUS. At your service, my friend. (He draws his sword, and springs to his guard with unruffled grace.)

FTATATEETA (suddenly seizing the sentinel's arms from behind). Thrust your knife into the dog's throat, Apollodorus. (The chivalrous Apollodorus laughingly shakes his head; breaks ground away from the sentinel towards the palace; and lowers his point.)

SENTINEL (struggling vainly). Curse on you! Let me go. Help ho!

FTATATEETA (lifting him from the ground). Stab the little Roman reptile. Spit him on your sword.

A couple of Roman soldiers, with a centurion, come running along the edge of the quay from the north end. They rescue their comrade, and throw off Ftatateeta, who is sent reeling away on the left hand of the sentinel.

CENTURION (an unattractive man of fifty, short in his speech and manners, with a vine wood cudgel in his hand). How now? What is all this?

FTATATEETA (to Apollodorus). Why did you not stab him? There was time!

APOLLODORUS. Centurion: I am here by order of the Queen to—

CENTURION (interrupting him). The Queen! Yes, yes: (to the sentinel) pass him in. Pass all these bazaar people in to the Queen, with their goods. But mind you pass no one out that you have not passed in—not even the Queen herself.

SENTINEL. This old woman is dangerous: she is as strong as three men. She wanted the merchant to stab me.

APOLLODORUS. Centurion: I am not a merchant. I am a patrician and a votary of art.

CENTURION. Is the woman your wife?

APOLLODORUS (horrified). No, no! (Correcting himself politely) Not that the lady is not a striking figure in her own way. But (emphatically) she is NOT my wife.

FTATATEETA (to the Centurion). Roman: I am Ftatateeta, the mistress of the Queen's household.

CENTURION. Keep your hands off our men, mistress; or I will have you pitched into the harbor, though you were as strong as ten men. (To his men) To your posts: march! (He returns with his men the way they came.)

FTATATEETA (looking malignantly after him). We shall see whom Isis loves best: her servant Ftatateeta or a dog of a Roman.

SENTINEL (to Apollodorus, with a wave of his pilum towards the palace). Pass in there; and keep your distance. (Turning to Ftatateeta) Come within a yard of me, you old crocodile; and I will give you this (the pilum) in your jaws.

CLEOPATRA (calling from the palace). Ftatateeta, Ftatateeta.

FTATATEETA (Looking up, scandalized). Go from the window, go from the window. There are men here.

CLEOPATRA. I am coming down.

FTATATEETA (distracted). No, no. What are you dreaming of? O ye gods, ye gods! Apollodorus: bid your men pick up your bales; and in with me quickly.

APOLLODORUS. Obey the mistress of the Queen's household.

FTATATEETA (impatiently, as the porters stoop to lift the bales). Quick, quick: she will be out upon us. (Cleopatra comes from the palace and runs across the quay to Ftatateeta.) Oh that ever I was born!

CLEOPATRA (eagerly). Ftatateeta: I have thought of something. I want a boat—at once.

FTATATEETA. A boat! No, no: you cannot. Apollodorus: speak to the Queen.

APOLLODORUS (gallantly). Beautiful Queen: I am Apollodorus the Sicilian, your servant, from the bazaar. I have brought you the three most beautiful Persian carpets in the world to choose from.

CLEOPATRA. I have no time for carpets to-day. Get me a boat.

FTATATEETA. What whim is this? You cannot go on the water except in the royal barge.

APOLLODORUS. Royalty, Ftatateeta, lies not in the barge but in the Queen. (To Cleopatra) The touch of your majesty's foot on the gunwale of the meanest boat in the harbor will make it royal. (He turns to the harbor and calls seaward) Ho there, boatman! Pull in to the steps.

CLEOPATRA. Apollodorus: you are my perfect knight; and I will always buy my carpets through you. (Apollodorus bows joyously. An oar appears above the quay; and the boatman, a bullet-headed, vivacious, grinning fellow, burnt almost black by the sun, comes up a flight of steps from the water on the sentinel's right, oar in hand, and waits at the top.) Can you row, Apollodorus?

APOLLODORUS. My oars shall be your majesty's wings. Whither shall I row my Queen? To the lighthouse. Come. (She makes for the steps.)

SENTINEL (opposing her with his pilum at the charge). Stand. You cannot pass.

CLEOPATRA (flushing angrily). How dare you? Do you know that I am the Queen?

SENTINEL. I have my orders. You cannot pass.

CLEOPATRA. I will make Caesar have you killed if you do not obey me.

SENTINEL. He will do worse to me if I disobey my officer. Stand back.

CLEOPATRA. Ftatateeta: strangle him.

SENTINEL (alarmed—looking apprehensively at Ftatateeta, and brandishing his pilum). Keep off there.

CLEOPATRA (running to Apollodorus). Apollodorus: make your slaves help us.

APOLLODORUS. I shall not need their help, lady. (He draws his sword.) Now soldier: choose which weapon you will defend yourself with. Shall it be sword against pilum, or sword against sword?

SENTINEL. Roman against Sicilian, curse you. Take that. (He hurls his pilum at Apollodorus, who drops expertly on one knee. The pilum passes whizzing over his head and falls harmless. Apollodorus, with a cry of triumph, springs up and attacks the sentinel, who draws his sword and defends himself, crying) Ho there, guard. Help!

Cleopatra, half frightened, half delighted, takes refuge near the palace, where the porters are squatting among the bales. The boatman, alarmed, hurries down the steps out of harm's way, but stops, with his head just visible above the edge of the quay, to watch the fight. The sentinel is handicapped by his fear of an attack in the rear from Ftatateeta. His swordsmanship, which is of a rough and ready sort, is heavily taxed, as he has occasionally to strike at her to keep her off between a blow and a guard with Apollodorus. The Centurion returns with several soldiers. Apollodorus springs back towards Cleopatra as this reinforcement confronts him.

CENTURION (coming to the sentinel's right hand). What is this? What now?

SENTINEL (panting). I could do well enough for myself if it weren't for the old woman. Keep her off me: that is all the help I need.

CENTURION. Make your report, soldier. What has happened?

FTATATEETA. Centurion: he would have slain the Queen.

SENTINEL (bluntly). I would, sooner than let her pass. She wanted to take boat, and go—so she said—to the lighthouse. I stopped her, as I was ordered to; and she set this fellow on me. (He goes to pick up his pilum and returns to his place with it.)

CENTURION (turning to Cleopatra). Cleopatra: I am loath to offend you; but without Caesar's express order we dare not let you pass beyond the Roman lines.

APOLLODORUS. Well, Centurion; and has not the lighthouse been within the Roman lines since Caesar landed there?

CLEOPATRA. Yes, yes. Answer that, if you can.

CENTURION (to Apollodorus). As for you, Apollodorus, you may thank the gods that you are not nailed to the palace door with a pilum for your meddling.

APOLLODORUS (urbanely). My military friend, I was not born to be slain by so ugly a weapon. When I fall, it will be (holding up his sword) by this white queen of arms, the only weapon fit for an artist. And now that you are convinced that we do not want to go beyond the lines, let me finish killing your sentinel and depart with the Queen.

CENTURION (as the sentinel makes an angry demonstration). Peace there. Cleopatra. I must abide by my orders, and not by the subtleties of this Sicilian. You must withdraw into the palace and examine your carpets there.

CLEOPATRA (pouting). I will not: I am the Queen. Caesar does not speak to me as you do. Have Caesar's centurions changed manners with his scullions?

CENTURION (sulkily). I do my duty. That is enough for me.

APOLLODORUS. Majesty: when a stupid man is doing something he is ashamed of, he always declares that it is his duty.

CENTURION (angry). Apollodorus—

APOLLODORUS (interrupting him with defiant elegance). I will make amends for that insult with my sword at fitting time and place. Who says artist, says duelist. (To Cleopatra) Hear my counsel, star of the east. Until word comes to these soldiers from Caesar himself, you are a prisoner. Let me go to him with a message from you, and a present; and before the sun has stooped half way to the arms of the sea, I will bring you back Caesar's order of release.

CENTURION (sneering at him), And you will sell the Queen the present, no doubt.

APOLLODORUS. Centurion: the Queen shall have from me, without payment, as the unforced tribute of Sicilian taste to Egyptian beauty, the richest of these carpets for her present to Caesar.

CLEOPATRA (exultantly, to the Centurion). Now you see what an ignorant common creature you are!

CENTURION (curtly). Well, a fool and his wares are soon parted (He turns to his men). Two more men to this post here; and see that no one leaves the palace but this man and his merchandize. If he draws his sword again inside the lines, kill him. To your posts. March.

He goes out, leaving two auxiliary sentinels with the other.

APOLLODORUS (with polite goodfellowship). My friends: will you not enter the palace and bury our quarrel in a bowl of wine? (He takes out his purse, jingling the coins in it.) The Queen has presents for you all.

SENTINEL (very sulky). You heard our orders. Get about your business.

FIRST AUXILIARY. Yes: you ought to know better. Off with you.

SECOND AUXILIARY (looking longingly at the purse—this sentinel is a hooknosed man, unlike his comrade, who is squab faced). Do not tantalize a poor man.

APOLLODORUS (to Cleopatra). Pearl of Queens: the Centurion is at hand; and the Roman soldier is incorruptible when his officer is looking. I must carry your word to Caesar.

CLEOPATRA (who has been meditating among the carpets). Are these carpets very heavy?

APOLLODORUS. It matters not how heavy. There are plenty of porters.

CLEOPATRA. How do they put the carpets into boats? Do they throw them down?

APOLLODORUS. Not into small boats, majesty. It would sink them.

CLEOPATRA. Not into that man's boat, for instance? (Pointing to the boatman.)

APOLLODORUS. No. Too small.

CLEOPATRA. But you can take a carpet to Caesar in it if I send one?

APOLLODORUS. Assuredly.

CLEOPATRA. And you will have it carried gently down the steps and take great care of it?

APOLLODORUS. Depend on me.

CLEOPATRA. Great, GREAT care?

APOLLODORUS. More than of my own body.

CLEOPATRA. You will promise me not to let the porters drop it or throw it about?

APOLLODORUS. Place the most delicate glass goblet in the palace in the heart of the roll, Queen; and if it be broken, my head shall pay for it.

CLEOPATRA. Good. Come, Ftatateeta. (Ftatateeta comes to her. Apollodorus offers to squire them into the palace.) No, Apollodorus, you must not come. I will choose a carpet for myself. You must wait here. (She runs into the palace.)

APOLLODORUS (to the porters). Follow this lady (indicating Ftatateeta); and obey her.

The porters rise and take up their bales.

FTATATEETA (addressing the porters as if they were vermin). This way. And take your shoes off before you put your feet on those stairs.

She goes in, followed by the porters with the carpets. Meanwhile Apollodorus goes to the edge of the quay and looks out over the harbor. The sentinels keep their eyes on him malignantly.

APOLLODORUS (addressing the sentinel). My friend—

SENTINEL (rudely). Silence there.

FIRST AUXILIARY. Shut your muzzle, you.

SECOND AUXILIARY (in a half whisper, glancing apprehensively towards the north end of the quay). Can't you wait a bit?

APOLLODORUS. Patience, worthy three-headed donkey. (They mutter ferociously; but he is not at all intimidated.) Listen: were you set here to watch me, or to watch the Egyptians?

SENTINEL. We know our duty.

APOLLODORUS. Then why don't you do it? There's something going on over there. (Pointing southwestward to the mole.)

SENTINEL (sulkily). I do not need to be told what to do by the like of you.

APOLLODORUS. Blockhead. (He begins shouting) Ho there, Centurion. Hoiho!

SENTINEL. Curse your meddling. (Shouting) Hoiho! Alarm! Alarm!

FIRST AND SECOND AUXILIARIES. Alarm! alarm! Hoiho!

The Centurion comes running in with his guard.

CENTURION. What now? Has the old woman attacked you again? (Seeing Apollodorus) Are YOU here still?

APOLLODORUS (pointing as before). See there. The Egyptians are moving. They are going to recapture the Pharos. They will attack by sea and land: by land along the great mole; by sea from the west harbor. Stir yourselves, my military friends: the hunt is up. (A clangor of trumpets from several points along the quay.) Aha! I told you so.

CENTURION (quickly). The two extra men pass the alarm to the south posts. One man keep guard here. The rest with me—quick.

The two auxiliary sentinels run off to the south. The Centurion and his guard run of northward; and immediately afterwards the bucina sounds. The four porters come from the palace carrying a carpet, followed by Ftatateeta.

SENTINEL (handling his pilum apprehensively). You again! (The porters stop.)

FTATATEETA. Peace, Roman fellow: you are now single-handed. Apollodorus: this carpet is Cleopatra's present to Caesar. It has rolled up in it ten precious goblets of the thinnest Iberian crystal, and a hundred eggs of the sacred blue pigeon. On your honor, let not one of them be broken.

APOLLODORUS. On my head be it. (To the porters) Into the boat with them carefully.

The porters carry the carpet to the steps.

FIRST PORTER (looking down at the boat). Beware what you do, sir. Those eggs of which the lady speaks must weigh more than a pound apiece. This boat is too small for such a load.

BOATMAN (excitedly rushing up the steps). Oh thou injurious porter! Oh thou unnatural son of a she-camel! (To Apollodorus) My boat, sir, hath often carried five men. Shall it not carry your lordship and a bale of pigeons' eggs? (To the porter) Thou mangey dromedary, the gods shall punish thee for this envious wickedness.

FIRST PORTER (stolidly). I cannot quit this bale now to beat thee; but another day I will lie in wait for thee.

APPOLODORUS (going between them). Peace there. If the boat were but a single plank, I would get to Caesar on it.

FTATATEETA (anxiously). In the name of the gods, Apollodorus, run no risks with that bale.

APOLLODORUS. Fear not, thou venerable grotesque: I guess its great worth. (To the porters) Down with it, I say; and gently; or ye shall eat nothing but stick for ten days.

The boatman goes down the steps, followed by the porters with the bale: Ftatateeta and Apollodorus watching from the edge.

APOLLODORUS. Gently, my sons, my children—(with sudden alarm) gently, ye dogs. Lay it level in the stern—so—'tis well.

FTATATEETA (screaming down at one of the porters). Do not step on it, do not step on it. Oh thou brute beast!

FIRST PORTER (ascending). Be not excited, mistress: all is well.

FTATATEETA (panting). All well! Oh, thou hast given my heart a turn! (She clutches her side, gasping.)

The four porters have now come up and are waiting at the stairhead to be paid.

APOLLODORUS. Here, ye hungry ones. (He gives money to the first porter, who holds it in his hand to show to the others. They crowd greedily to see how much it is, quite prepared, after the Eastern fashion, to protest to heaven against their patron's stinginess. But his liberality overpowers them.)

FIRST PORTER. O bounteous prince!

SECOND PORTER. O lord of the bazaar!

THIRD PORTER. O favored of the gods!

FOURTH PORTER. O father to all the porters of the market!

SENTINEL (enviously, threatening them fiercely with his pilum). Hence, dogs: off. Out of this. (They fly before him northward along the quay.)

APOLLODORUS. Farewell, Ftatateeta. I shall be at the lighthouse before the Egyptians. (He descends the steps.)

FTATATEETA. The gods speed thee and protect my nursling!

The sentry returns from chasing the porters and looks down at the boat, standing near the stairhead lest Ftatateeta should attempt to escape.

APOLLODORUS (from beneath, as the boat moves off). Farewell, valiant pilum pitcher.

SENTINEL. Farewell shopkeeper.

APOLLODORUS. Ha, ha! Pull, thou brave boatman, pull. So Ho-o-o-o-o! (He begins to sing in barcarolle measure to the rhythm of the oars)

My heart, my heart, spread out thy wings: Shake off thy heavy load of love—

Give me the oars, O son of a snail.

SENTINEL (threatening Ftatateeta). Now mistress: back to your henhouse. In with you.

FTATATEETA (falling on her knees and stretching her hands over the waters). Gods of the seas, bear her safely to the shore!

SENTINEL. Bear WHO safely? What do you mean?

FTATATEETA (looking darkly at him). Gods of Egypt and of Vengeance, let this Roman fool be beaten like a dog by his captain for suffering her to be taken over the waters.

SENTINEL. Accursed one: is she then in the boat? (He calls over the sea) Hoiho, there, boatman! Hoiho!

APOLLODORUS (singing in the distance). My heart, my heart, be whole and free: Love is thine only enemy.

Meanwhile Rufio, the morning's fighting done, sits munching dates on a faggot of brushwood outside the door of the lighthouse, which towers gigantic to the clouds on his left. His helmet, full of dates, is between his knees; and a leathern bottle of wine is by his side. Behind him the great stone pedestal of the lighthouse is shut in from the open sea by a low stone parapet, with a couple of steps in the middle to the broad coping. A huge chain with a hook hangs down from the lighthouse crane above his head. Faggots like the one he sits on lie beneath it ready to be drawn up to feed the beacon.

Caesar is standing on the step at the parapet looking out anxiously, evidently ill at ease. Britannus comes out of the lighthouse door.

RUFIO. Well, my British islander. Have you been up to the top?

BRITANNUS. I have. I reckon it at 200 feet high.

RUFIO. Anybody up there?

BRITANNUS. One elderly Tyrian to work the crane; and his son, a well conducted youth of 14.

RUFIO (looking at the chain). What! An old man and a boy work that! Twenty men, you mean.

BRITANNUS. Two only, I assure you. They have counterweights, and a machine with boiling water in it which I do not understand: it is not of British design. They use it to haul up barrels of oil and faggots to burn in the brazier on the roof.

RUFIO. But—

BRITANNUS. Excuse me: I came down because there are messengers coming along the mole to us from the island. I must see what their business is. (He hurries out past the lighthouse.)

CAESAR (coming away from the parapet, shivering and out of sorts). Rufio: this has been a mad expedition. We shall be beaten. I wish I knew how our men are getting on with that barricade across the great mole.

RUFIO (angrily). Must I leave my food and go starving to bring you a report?

CAESAR (soothing him nervously). No, Rufio, no. Eat, my son. Eat. (He takes another turn, Rufio chewing dates meanwhile.) The Egyptians cannot be such fools as not to storm the barricade and swoop down on us here before it is finished. It is the first time I have ever run an avoidable risk. I should not have come to Egypt.

RUFIO. An hour ago you were all for victory.

CAESAR (apologetically). Yes: I was a fool—rash, Rufio—boyish.

RUFIO. Boyish! Not a bit of it. Here. (Offering him a handful of dates.)

CAESAR. What are these for?

RUFIO. To eat. That's what's the matter with you. When a man comes to your age, he runs down before his midday meal. Eat and drink; and then have another look at our chances.

CAESAR (taking the dates). My age! (He shakes his head and bites a date.) Yes, Rufio: I am an old man—worn out now—true, quite true. (He gives way to melancholy contemplation, and eats another date.) Achillas is still in his prime: Ptolemy is a boy. (He eats another date, and plucks up a little.) Well, every dog has his day; and I have had mine: I cannot complain. (With sudden cheerfulness) These dates are not bad, Rufio. (Britannus returns, greatly excited, with a leathern bag. Caesar is himself again in a moment.) What now?

BRITANNUS (triumphantly). Our brave Rhodian mariners have captured a treasure. There! (He throws the bag down at Caesar's feet.) Our enemies are delivered into our hands.

CAESAR. In that bag?

BRITANNUS. Wait till you hear, Caesar. This bag contains all the letters which have passed between Pompey's party and the army of occupation here.

CAESAR. Well?

BRITANNUS (impatient of Caesar's slowness to grasp the situation). Well, we shall now know who your foes are. The name of every man who has plotted against you since you crossed the Rubicon may be in these papers, for all we know.

CAESAR. Put them in the fire.

BRITANNUS. Put them—(he gasps)!!!!

CAESAR. In the fire. Would you have me waste the next three years of my life in proscribing and condemning men who will be my friends when I have proved that my friendship is worth more than Pompey's was—than Cato's is. O incorrigible British islander: am I a bull dog, to seek quarrels merely to show how stubborn my jaws are?

BRITANNUS. But your honor—the honor of Rome—

CAESAR. I do not make human sacrifices to my honor, as your Druids do. Since you will not burn these, at least I can drown them. (He picks up the bag and throws it over the parapet into the sea.)

BRITANNUS. Caesar: this is mere eccentricity. Are traitors to be allowed to go free for the sake of a paradox?

RUFIO (rising). Caesar: when the islander has finished preaching, call me again. I am going to have a look at the boiling water machine. (He goes into the lighthouse.)

BRITANNUS (with genuine feeling). O Caesar, my great master, if I could but persuade you to regard life seriously, as men do in my country!

CAESAR. Do they truly do so, Britannus?

BRITANNUS. Have you not been there? Have you not seen them? What Briton speaks as you do in your moments of levity? What Briton neglects to attend the services at the sacred grove? What Briton wears clothes of many colors as you do, instead of plain blue, as all solid, well esteemed men should? These are moral questions with us. CAESAR. Well, well, my friend: some day I shall settle down and have a blue toga, perhaps. Meanwhile, I must get on as best I can in my flippant Roman way. (Apollodorus comes past the lighthouse.) What now?

BRITANNUS (turning quickly, and challenging the stranger with official haughtiness). What is this? Who are you? How did you come here?

APOLLODORUS. Calm yourself, my friend: I am not going to eat you. I have come by boat, from Alexandria, with precious gifts for Caesar.

CAESAR. From Alexandria!

BRITANNUS (severely). That is Caesar, sir.

RUFIO (appearing at the lighthouse door). What's the matter now?

APOLLODORUS. Hail, great Caesar! I am Apollodorus the Sicilian, an artist.

BRITANNUS. An artist! Why have they admitted this vagabond?

CAESAR. Peace, man. Apollodorus is a famous patrician amateur.

BRITANNUS (disconcerted). I crave the gentleman's pardon. (To Caesar) I understood him to say that he was a professional. (Somewhat out of countenance, he allows Apollodorus to approach Caesar, changing places with him. Rufio, after looking Apollodorus up and down with marked disparagement, goes to the other side of the platform.)

CAESAR. You are welcome, Apollodorus. What is your business?

APOLLODORUS. First, to deliver to you a present from the Queen of Queens.

CAESAR. Who is that?

APOLLODORUS. Cleopatra of Egypt.

CAESAR (taking him into his confidence in his most winning manner). Apollodorus: this is no time for playing with presents. Pray you, go back to the Queen, and tell her that if all goes well I shall return to the palace this evening.

APOLLODORUS. Caesar: I cannot return. As I approached the lighthouse, some fool threw a great leathern bag into the sea. It broke the nose of my boat; and I had hardly time to get myself and my charge to the shore before the poor little cockleshell sank.

CAESAR. I am sorry, Apollodorus. The fool shall be rebuked. Well, well: what have you brought me? The Queen will be hurt if I do not look at it.

RUFIO. Have we time to waste on this trumpery? The Queen is only a child.

CAESAR. Just so: that is why we must not disappoint her. What is the present, Apollodorus?

APOLLODORUS. Caesar: it is a Persian carpet—a beauty! And in it are—so I am told—pigeons' eggs and crystal goblets and fragile precious things. I dare not for my head have it carried up that narrow ladder from the causeway.

RUFIO. Swing it up by the crane, then. We will send the eggs to the cook; drink our wine from the goblets; and the carpet will make a bed for Caesar.

APOLLODORUS. The crane! Caesar: I have sworn to tender this bale of carpet as I tender my own life.

CAESAR (cheerfully). Then let them swing you up at the same time; and if the chain breaks, you and the pigeons' eggs will perish together. (He goes to the chairs and looks up along it, examining it curiously.)

APOLLODORUS (to Britannus). Is Caesar serious?

BRITANNUS. His manner is frivolous because he is an Italian; but he means what he says.

APOLLODORUS. Serious or not, he spoke well. Give me a squad of soldiers to work the crane.

BRITANNUS. Leave the crane to me. Go and await the descent of the chain.

APOLLODORUS. Good. You will presently see me there (turning to them all and pointing with an eloquent gesture to the sky above the parapet) rising like the sun with my treasure.

He goes back the way he came. Britannus goes into the lighthouse.

RUFIO (ill-humoredly). Are you really going to wait here for this foolery, Caesar?

CAESAR (backing away from the crane as it gives signs of working). Why not?

RUFIO. The Egyptians will let you know why not if they have the sense to make a rush from the shore end of the mole before our barricade is finished. And here we are waiting like children to see a carpet full of pigeons' eggs.

The chain rattles, and is drawn up high enough to clear the parapet. It then swings round out of sight behind the lighthouse.

CAESAR. Fear not, my son Rufio. When the first Egyptian takes his first step along the mole, the alarm will sound; and we two will reach the barricade from our end before the Egyptians reach it from their end—we two, Rufio: I, the old man, and you, his biggest boy. And the old man will be there first. So peace; and give me some more dates.

APOLLODORUS (from the causeway below). So-ho, haul away. So-ho-o-o-o! (The chain is drawn up and comes round again from behind the lighthouse. Apollodorus is swinging in the air with his bale of carpet at the end of it. He breaks into song as he soars above the parapet.)

Aloft, aloft, behold the blue That never shone in woman's eyes

Easy there: stop her. (He ceases to rise.) Further round! (The chain comes forward above the platform.)

RUFIO (calling up). Lower away there. (The chain and its load begin to descend.)

APOLLODORUS (calling up). Gently—slowly—mind the eggs.

RUFIO (calling up). Easy there—slowly—slowly.

Apollodorus and the bale are deposited safely on the flags in the middle of the platform. Rufio and Caesar help Apollodorus to cast off the chain from the bale.

RUFIO. Haul up.

The chain rises clear of their heads with a rattle. Britannus comes from the lighthouse and helps them to uncord the carpet.

APOLLODORUS (when the cords are loose). Stand off, my friends: let Caesar see. (He throws the carpet open.)

RUFIO. Nothing but a heap of shawls. Where are the pigeons' eggs?

APOLLODORUS. Approach, Caesar; and search for them among the shawls.

RUFIO (drawing his sword). Ha, treachery! Keep back, Caesar: I saw the shawl move: there is something alive there.

BRITANNUS (drawing his sword). It is a serpent.

APOLLODORUS. Dares Caesar thrust his hand into the sack where the serpent moves?

RUFIO (turning on him). Treacherous dog—

CAESAR. Peace. Put up your swords. Apollodorus: your serpent seems to breathe very regularly. (He thrusts his hand under the shawls and draws out a bare arm.) This is a pretty little snake.

RUFIO (drawing out the other arm). Let us have the rest of you.

They pull Cleopatra up by the wrists into a sitting position. Britannus, scandalized, sheathes his sword with a drive of protest.

CLEOPATRA (gasping). Oh, I'm smothered. Oh, Caesar; a man stood on me in the boat; and a great sack of something fell upon me out of the sky; and then the boat sank, and then I was swung up into the air and bumped down.

CAESAR (petting her as she rises and takes refuge on his breast). Well, never mind: here you are safe and sound at last.

RUFIO. Ay; and now that she is here, what are we to do with her?

BRITANNUS. She cannot stay here, Caesar, without the companionship of some matron.

CLEOPATRA (jealously, to Caesar, who is obviously perplexed). Aren't you glad to see me?

CAESAR. Yes, yes; I am very glad. But Rufio is very angry; and Britannus is shocked.

CLEOPATRA (contemptuously). You can have their heads cut off, can you not?

CAESAR. They would not be so useful with their heads cut off as they are now, my sea bird.

RUFIO (to Cleopatra). We shall have to go away presently and cut some of your Egyptians' heads off. How will you like being left here with the chance of being captured by that little brother of yours if we are beaten?

CLEOPATRA. But you mustn't leave me alone. Caesar you will not leave me alone, will you?

RUFIO. What! Not when the trumpet sounds and all our lives depend on Caesar's being at the barricade before the Egyptians reach it? Eh?

CLEOPATRA. Let them lose their lives: they are only soldiers.

CAESAR (gravely). Cleopatra: when that trumpet sounds, we must take every man his life in his hand, and throw it in the face of Death. And of my soldiers who have trusted me there is not one whose hand I shall not hold more sacred than your head. (Cleopatra is overwhelmed. Her eyes fill with tears.) Apollodorus: you must take her back to the palace.

APOLLODORUS. Am I a dolphin, Caesar, to cross the seas with young ladies on my back? My boat is sunk: all yours are either at the barricade or have returned to the city. I will hail one if I can: that is all I can do. (He goes back to the causeway.)

CLEOPATRA (struggling with her tears). It does not matter. I will not go back. Nobody cares for me.

CAESAR. Cleopatra—

CLEOPATRA. You want me to be killed.

CAESAR (still more gravely). My poor child: your life matters little here to anyone but yourself. (She gives way altogether at this, casting herself down on the faggots weeping. Suddenly a great tumult is heard in the distance, bucinas and trumpets sounding through a storm of shouting. Britannus rushes to the parapet and looks along the mole. Caesar and Rufio turn to one another with quick intelligence.)

CAESAR. Come, Rufio.

CLEOPATRA (scrambling to her knees and clinging to him). No, no. Do not leave me, Caesar. (He snatches his skirt from her clutch.) Oh!

BRITANNUS (from the parapet). Caesar: we are cut off. The Egyptians have landed from the west harbor between us and the barricade!!!

RUFIO (running to see). Curses! It is true. We are caught like rats in a trap.

CAESAR (ruthfully). Rufio, Rufio: my men at the barricade are between the sea party and the shore party. I have murdered them.

RUFIO (coming back from the parapet to Caesar's right hand). Ay: that comes of fooling with this girl here.

APOLLODORUS (coming up quickly from the causeway). Look over the parapet, Caesar.

CAESAR. We have looked, my friend. We must defend ourselves here.

APOLLODORUS. I have thrown the ladder into the sea. They cannot get in without it.

RUFIO. Ay; and we cannot get out. Have you thought of that?

APOLLODORUS. Not get out! Why not? You have ships in the east harbor.

BRITANNUS (hopefully, at the parapet). The Rhodian galleys are standing in towards us already. (Caesar quickly joins Britannus at the parapet.)

RUFIO (to Apollodorus, impatiently). And by what road are we to walk to the galleys, pray?

APOLLODORUS (with gay, defiant rhetoric). By the road that leads everywhere—the diamond path of the sun and moon. Have you never seen the child's shadow play of The Broken Bridge? "Ducks and geese with ease get over"—eh? (He throws away his cloak and cap, and binds his sword on his back.)

RUFIO. What are you talking about?

APOLLODORUS. I will show you. (Calling to Britannus) How far off is the nearest galley?

BRITANNUS. Fifty fathom.

CAESAR. No, no: they are further off than they seem in this clear air to your British eyes. Nearly quarter of a mile, Apollodorus.

APOLLODORUS. Good. Defend yourselves here until I send you a boat from that galley.

RUFIO. Have you wings, perhaps?

APOLLODORUS. Water wings, soldier. Behold!

He runs up the steps between Caesar and Britannus to the coping of the parapet; springs into the air; and plunges head foremost into the sea.

CAESAR (like a schoolboy—wildly excited). Bravo, bravo! (Throwing off his cloak) By Jupiter, I will do that too.

RUFIO (seizing him). You are mad. You shall not.

CAESAR. Why not? Can I not swim as well as he?

RUFIO (frantic). Can an old fool dive and swim like a young one? He is twenty-five and you are fifty.

CAESAR (breaking loose from Rufio). Old!!!

BRITANNUS (shocked). Rufio: you forget yourself.

CAESAR. I will race you to the galley for a week's pay, father Rufio.

CLEOPATRA. But me! Me!! Me!!! What is to become of me?

CAESAR. I will carry you on my back to the galley like a dolphin. Rufio: when you see me rise to the surface, throw her in: I will answer for her. And then in with you after her, both of you.

CLEOPATRA. No, no, NO. I shall be drowned.

BRITANNUS. Caesar: I am a man and a Briton, not a fish. I must have a boat. I cannot swim.

CLEOPATRA. Neither can I.

CAESAR (to Britannus). Stay here, then, alone, until I recapture the lighthouse: I will not forget you. Now, Rufio.

RUFIO. You have made up your mind to this folly?

CAESAR. The Egyptians have made it up for me. What else is there to do? And mind where you jump: I do not want to get your fourteen stone in the small of my back as I come up. (He runs up the steps and stands on the coping.)

BRITANNUS (anxiously). One last word, Caesar. Do not let yourself be seen in the fashionable part of Alexandria until you have changed your clothes.

CAESAR (calling over the sea). Ho, Apollodorus: (he points skyward and quotes the barcarolle)

The white upon the blue above—

APOLLODORUS (swimming in the distance)

Is purple on the green below—

CAESAR (exultantly). Aha! (He plunges into the sea.)

CLEOPATRA (running excitedly to the steps). Oh, let me see. He will be drowned. (Rufio seizes her.) Ah—ah—ah—ah! (He pitches her screaming into the sea. Rufio and Britannus roar with laughter.)

RUFIO (looking down after her). He has got her. (To Britannus) Hold the fort, Briton. Caesar will not forget you. (He springs off.)

BRITANNUS (running to the steps to watch them as they swim). All safe, Rufio?

RUFIO (swimming). All safe.

CAESAR (swimming further of). Take refuge up there by the beacon; and pile the fuel on the trap door, Britannus.

BRITANNUS (calling in reply). I will first do so, and then commend myself to my country's gods. (A sound of cheering from the sea. Britannus gives full vent to his excitement) The boat has reached him: Hip, hip, hip, hurrah!

ACT IV

Cleopatra's sousing in the east harbor of Alexandria was in October 48 B. C. In March 47 she is passing the afternoon in her boudoir in the palace, among a bevy of her ladies, listening to a slave girl who is playing the harp in the middle of the room. The harpist's master, an old musician, with a lined face, prominent brows, white beard, moustache and eyebrows twisted and horned at the ends, and a consciously keen and pretentious expression, is squatting on the floor close to her on her right, watching her performance. Ftatateeta is in attendance near the door, in front of a group of female slaves. Except the harp player all are seated: Cleopatra in a chair opposite the door on the other side of the room; the rest on the ground. Cleopatra's ladies are all young, the most conspicuous being Charmian and Iras, her favorites. Charmian is a hatchet faced, terra cotta colored little goblin, swift in her movements, and neatly finished at the hands and feet. Iras is a plump, goodnatured creature, rather fatuous, with a profusion of red hair, and a tendency to giggle on the slightest provocation.

CLEOPATRA. Can I—

FTATATEETA (insolently, to the player). Peace, thou! The Queen speaks. (The player stops.)

CLEOPATRA (to the old musician). I want to learn to play the harp with my own hands. Caesar loves music. Can you teach me?

MUSICIAN. Assuredly I and no one else can teach the Queen. Have I not discovered the lost method of the ancient Egyptians, who could make a pyramid tremble by touching a bass string? All the other teachers are quacks: I have exposed them repeatedly.

CLEOPATRA. Good: you shall teach me. How long will it take?

MUSICIAN. Not very long: only four years. Your Majesty must first become proficient in the philosophy of Pythagoras.

CLEOPATRA. Has she (indicating the slave) become proficient in the philosophy of Pythagoras?

MUSICIAN. Oh, she is but a slave. She learns as a dog learns.

CLEOPATRA. Well, then, I will learn as a dog learns; for she plays better than you. You shall give me a lesson every day for a fortnight. (The musician hastily scrambles to his feet and bows profoundly.) After that, whenever I strike a false note you shall be flogged; and if I strike so many that there is not time to flog you, you shall be thrown into the Nile to feed the crocodiles. Give the girl a piece of gold; and send them away.

MUSICIAN (much taken aback). But true art will not be thus forced.

FTATATEETA (pushing him out). What is this? Answering the Queen, forsooth. Out with you.

He is pushed out by Ftatateeta, the girl following with her harp, amid the laughter of the ladies and slaves.

CLEOPATRA. Now, can any of you amuse me? Have you any stories or any news?

IRAS. Ftatateeta—

CLEOPATRA. Oh, Ftatateeta, Ftatateeta, always Ftatateeta. Some new tale to set me against her.

IRAS. No: this time Ftatateeta has been virtuous. (All the ladies laugh—not the slaves.) Pothinus has been trying to bribe her to let him speak with you.

CLEOPATRA (wrathfully). Ha! You all sell audiences with me, as if I saw whom you please, and not whom I please. I should like to know how much of her gold piece that harp girl will have to give up before she leaves the palace.

IRAS. We can easily find out that for you.

The ladies laugh.

CLEOPATRA (frowning). You laugh; but take care, take care. I will find out some day how to make myself served as Caesar is served.

CHARMIAN. Old hooknose! (They laugh again.)

CLEOPATRA (revolted). Silence. Charmian: do not you be a silly little Egyptian fool. Do you know why I allow you all to chatter impertinently just as you please, instead of treating you as Ftatateeta would treat you if she were Queen?

CHARMIAN. Because you try to imitate Caesar in everything; and he lets everybody say what they please to him.

CLEOPATRA. No; but because I asked him one day why he did so; and he said "Let your women talk; and you will learn something from them." What have I to learn from them? I said. "What they ARE," said he; and oh! you should have seen his eye as he said it. You would have curled up, you shallow things. (They laugh. She turns fiercely on Iras) At whom are you laughing—at me or at Caesar?

IRAS. At Caesar.

CLEOPATRA. If you were not a fool, you would laugh at me; and if you were not a coward you would not be afraid to tell me so. (Ftatateeta returns.) Ftatateeta: they tell me that Pothinus has offered you a bribe to admit him to my presence.

FTATATEETA (protesting). Now by my father's gods—

CLEOPATRA (cutting her short despotically). Have I not told you not to deny things? You would spend the day calling your father's gods to witness to your virtues if I let you. Go take the bribe; and bring in Pothinus. (Ftatateeta is about to reply.) Don't answer me. Go.

Ftatateeta goes out; and Cleopatra rises and begins to prowl to and fro between her chair and the door, meditating. All rise and stand.

IRAS (as she reluctantly rises). Heigho! I wish Caesar were back in Rome.

CLEOPATRA (threateningly). It will be a bad day for you all when he goes. Oh, if I were not ashamed to let him see that I am as cruel at heart as my father, I would make you repent that speech! Why do you wish him away?

CHARMIAN. He makes you so terribly prosy and serious and learned and philosophical. It is worse than being religious, at OUR ages. (The ladies laugh.)

CLEOPATRA. Cease that endless cackling, will you. Hold your tongues.

CHARMIAN (with mock resignation). Well, well: we must try to live up to Caesar.

They laugh again. Cleopatra rages silently as she continues to prowl to and fro. Ftatateeta comes back with Pothinus, who halts on the threshold.

FTATATEETA (at the door). Pothinus craves the ear of the—

CLEOPATRA. There, there: that will do: let him come in.

(She resumes her seat. All sit down except Pothinus, who advances to the middle of the room. Ftatateeta takes her former place.) Well, Pothinus: what is the latest news from your rebel friends?

POTHINUS (haughtily). I am no friend of rebellion. And a prisoner does not receive news.

CLEOPATRA. You are no more a prisoner than I am—than Caesar is. These six months we have been besieged in this palace by my subjects. You are allowed to walk on the beach among the soldiers. Can I go further myself, or can Caesar?

POTHINUS. You are but a child, Cleopatra, and do not understand these matters.

The ladies laugh. Cleopatra looks inscrutably at him.

CHARMIAN. I see you do not know the latest news, Pothinus.

POTHINUS. What is that?

CHARMIAN. That Cleopatra is no longer a child. Shall I tell you how to grow much older, and much, MUCH wiser in one day?

POTHINUS. I should prefer to grow wiser without growing older.

CHARMIAN. Well, go up to the top of the lighthouse; and get somebody to take you by the hair and throw you into the sea. (The ladies laugh.)

CLEOPATRA. She is right, Pothinus: you will come to the shore with much conceit washed out of you. (The ladies laugh. Cleopatra rises impatiently.) Begone, all of you. I will speak with Pothinus alone. Drive them out, Ftatateeta. (They run out laughing. Ftatateeta shuts the door on them.) What are YOU waiting for?

FTATATEETA. It is not meet that the Queen remain alone with—

CLEOPATRA (interrupting her). Ftatateeta: must I sacrifice you to your father's gods to teach you that I am Queen of Egypt, and not you?

FTATATEETA (indignantly). You are like the rest of them. You want to be what these Romans call a New Woman. (She goes out, banging the door.)

CLEOPATRA (sitting down again). Now, Pothinus: why did you bribe Ftatateeta to bring you hither?

POTHINUS (studying her gravely). Cleopatra: what they tell me is true. You are changed.

CLEOPATRA. Do you speak with Caesar every day for six months: and YOU will be changed.

POTHINUS. It is the common talk that you are infatuated with this old man.

CLEOPATRA. Infatuated? What does that mean? Made foolish, is it not? Oh no: I wish I were.

POTHINUS. You wish you were made foolish! How so?

CLEOPATRA. When I was foolish, I did what I liked, except when Ftatateeta beat me; and even then I cheated her and did it by stealth. Now that Caesar has made me wise, it is no use my liking or disliking; I do what must be done, and have no time to attend to myself. That is not happiness; but it is greatness. If Caesar were gone, I think I could govern the Egyptians; for what Caesar is to me, I am to the fools around me.

POTHINUS (looking hard at her). Cleopatra: this may be the vanity of youth.

CLEOPATRA. No, no: it is not that I am so clever, but that the others are so stupid.

POTHINUS (musingly). Truly, that is the great secret.

CLEOPATRA. Well, now tell me what you came to say?

POTHINUS (embarrassed). I! Nothing.

CLEOPATRA. Nothing!

POTHINUS. At least—to beg for my liberty: that is all.

CLEOPATRA. For that you would have knelt to Caesar. No, Pothinus: you came with some plan that depended on Cleopatra being a little nursery kitten. Now that Cleopatra is a Queen, the plan is upset.

POTHINUS (bowing his head submissively). It is so.

CLEOPATRA (exultant). Aha!

POTHINUS (raising his eyes keenly to hers). Is Cleopatra then indeed a Queen, and no longer Caesar's prisoner and slave?

CLEOPATRA. Pothinus: we are all Caesar's slaves—all we in this land of Egypt—whether we will or no. And she who is wise enough to know this will reign when Caesar departs.

POTHINUS. You harp on Caesar's departure.

CLEOPATRA. What if I do?

POTHINUS. Does he not love you?

CLEOPATRA. Love me! Pothinus: Caesar loves no one. Who are those we love? Only those whom we do not hate: all people are strangers and enemies to us except those we love. But it is not so with Caesar. He has no hatred in him: he makes friends with everyone as he does with dogs and children. His kindness to me is a wonder: neither mother, father, nor nurse have ever taken so much care for me, or thrown open their thoughts to me so freely.

POTHINUS. Well: is not this love?

CLEOPATRA. What! When he will do as much for the first girl he meets on his way back to Rome? Ask his slave, Britannus: he has been just as good to him. Nay, ask his very horse! His kindness is not for anything in ME: it is in his own nature.

POTHINUS. But how can you be sure that he does not love you as men love women?

CLEOPATRA. Because I cannot make him jealous. I have tried.

POTHINUS. Hm! Perhaps I should have asked, then, do you love him?

CLEOPATRA. Can one love a god? Besides, I love another Roman: one whom I saw long before Caesar—no god, but a man—one who can love and hate—one whom I can hurt and who would hurt me.

POTHINUS. Does Caesar know this?

CLEOPATRA. Yes

POTHINUS. And he is not angry.

CLEOPATRA. He promises to send him to Egypt to please me!

POTHINUS. I do not understand this man?

CLEOPATRA (with superb contempt). YOU understand Caesar! How could you? (Proudly) I do—by instinct.

POTHINUS (deferentially, after a moment's thought). Your Majesty caused me to be admitted today. What message has the Queen for me?

CLEOPATRA. This. You think that by making my brother king, you will rule in Egypt, because you are his guardian and he is a little silly.

POTHINUB. The Queen is pleased to say so.

CLEOPATRA. The Queen is pleased to say this also. That Caesar will eat up you, and Achillas, and my brother, as a cat eats up mice; and that he will put on this land of Egypt as a shepherd puts on his garment. And when he has done that, he will return to Rome, and leave Cleopatra here as his viceroy.

POTHINUS (breaking out wrathfully). That he will never do. We have a thousand men to his ten; and we will drive him and his beggarly legions into the sea.

CLEOPATRA (with scorn, getting up to go). You rant like any common fellow. Go, then, and marshal your thousands; and make haste; for Mithridates of Pergamos is at hand with reinforcements for Caesar. Caesar has held you at bay with two legions: we shall see what he will do with twenty.

POTHINUS. Cleopatra—

CLEOPATRA. Enough, enough: Caesar has spoiled me for talking to weak things like you. (She goes out. Pothinus, with a gesture of rage, is following, when Ftatateeta enters and stops him.)

POTHINUS. Let me go forth from this hateful place.

FTATATEETA. What angers you?

POTHINUS. The curse of all the gods of Egypt be upon her! She has sold her country to the Roman, that she may buy it back from him with her kisses.

FTATATEETA. Fool: did she not tell you that she would have Caesar gone?

POTHINUS. You listened?

FTATATEETA. I took care that some honest woman should be at hand whilst you were with her.

POTHINUS. Now by the gods—

FTATATEETA. Enough of your gods! Caesar's gods are all powerful here. It is no use YOU coming to Cleopatra: you are only an Egyptian. She will not listen to any of her own race: she treats us all as children.

POTHINUS. May she perish for it!

FTATATEETA (balefully). May your tongue wither for that wish! Go! send for Lucius Septimius, the slayer of Pompey. He is a Roman: may be she will listen to him. Begone!

POTHINUS (darkly). I know to whom I must go now.

FTATATEETA (suspiciously). To whom, then?

POTHINUS. To a greater Roman than Lucius. And mark this, mistress. You thought, before Caesar came, that Egypt should presently be ruled by you and your crew in the name of Cleopatra. I set myself against it.

FTATATEETA (interrupting him—wrangling). Ay; that it might be ruled by you and YOUR crew in the name of Ptolemy.

POTHINUS. Better me, or even you, than a woman with a Roman heart; and that is what Cleopatra is now become. Whilst I live, she shall never rule. So guide yourself accordingly. (He goes out.)

It is by this time drawing on to dinner time. The table is laid on the roof of the palace; and thither Rufio is now climbing, ushered by a majestic palace official, wand of office in hand, and followed by a slave carrying an inlaid stool. After many stairs they emerge at last into a massive colonnade on the roof. Light curtains are drawn between the columns on the north and east to soften the westering sun. The official leads Rufio to one of these shaded sections. A cord for pulling the curtains apart hangs down between the pillars.

THE OFFICIAL (bowing). The Roman commander will await Caesar here.

The slave sets down the stool near the southernmost column, and slips out through the curtains.

RUFIO (sitting down, a little blown). Pouf! That was a climb. How high have we come?

THE OFFICIAL. We are on the palace roof, O Beloved of Victory!

RUFIO. Good! the Beloved of Victory has no more stairs to get up.

A second official enters from the opposite end, walking backwards.

THE SECOND OFFICIAL. Caesar approaches.

Caesar, fresh from the bath, clad in a new tunic of purple silk, comes in, beaming and festive, followed by two slaves carrying a light couch, which is hardly more than an elaborately designed bench. They place it near the northmost of the two curtained columns. When this is done they slip out through the curtains; and the two officials, formally bowing, follow them. Rufio rises to receive Caesar.

CAESAR (coming over to him). Why, Rufio! (Surveying his dress with an air of admiring astonishment) A new baldrick! A new golden pommel to your sword! And you have had your hair cut! But not your beard—? Impossible! (He sniffs at Rufio's beard.) Yes, perfumed, by Jupiter Olympus!

RUFIO (growling). Well: is it to please myself?

CAESAR (affectionately). No, my son Rufio, but to please me—to celebrate my birthday.

RUFIO (contemptuously). Your birthday! You always have a birthday when there is a pretty girl to be flattered or an ambassador to be conciliated. We had seven of them in ten months last year.

CAESAR (contritely). It is true, Rufio! I shall never break myself of these petty deceits.

RUFIO. Who is to dine with us—besides Cleopatra?

CAESAR. Apollodorus the Sicilian.

RUFIO. That popinjay!

CAESAR. Come! the popinjay is an amusing dog—tells a story; sings a song; and saves us the trouble of flattering the Queen. What does she care for old politicians and campfed bears like us? No: Apollodorus is good company, Rufio, good company.

RUFIO. Well, he can swim a bit and fence a bit: he might be worse, if he only knew how to hold his tongue.

CAESAR. The gods forbid he should ever learn! Oh, this military life! this tedious, brutal life of action! That is the worst of us Romans: we are mere doers and drudgers: a swarm of bees turned into men. Give me a good talker—one with wit and imagination enough to live without continually doing something!

RUFIO. Ay! a nice time he would have of it with you when dinner was over! Have you noticed that I am before my time?

CAESAR. Aha! I thought that meant something. What is it?

RUFIO. Can we be overheard here?

CAESAR. Our privacy invites eavesdropping. I can remedy that. (He claps his hands twice. The curtains are drawn, revealing the roof garden with a banqueting table set across in the middle for four persons, one at each end, and two side by side. The side next Caesar and Rufio is blocked with golden wine vessels and basins. A gorgeous major-domo is superintending the laying of the table by a staff of slaves. The colonnade goes round the garden at both sides to the further end, where a gap in it, like a great gateway, leaves the view open to the sky beyond the western edge of the roof, except in the middle, where a life size image of Ra, seated on a huge plinth, towers up, with hawk head and crown of asp and disk. His altar, which stands at his feet, is a single white stone.) Now everybody can see us, nobody will think of listening to us. (He sits down on the bench left by the two slaves.)

RUFIO (sitting down on his stool). Pothinus wants to speak to you. I advise you to see him: there is some plotting going on here among the women.

CAESAR. Who is Pothinus?

RUFIO. The fellow with hair like squirrel's fur—the little King's bear leader, whom you kept prisoner.

CAESAR (annoyed). And has he not escaped?

RUFIO. No.

CAESAR (rising imperiously). Why not? You have been guarding this man instead of watching the enemy. Have I not told you always to let prisoners escape unless there are special orders to the contrary? Are there not enough mouths to be fed without him?

RUFIO. Yes; and if you would have a little sense and let me cut his throat, you would save his rations. Anyhow, he WON'T escape. Three sentries have told him they would put a pilum through him if they saw him again. What more can they do? He prefers to stay and spy on us. So would I if I had to do with generals subject to fits of clemency.

CAESAR (resuming his seat, argued down). Hm! And so he wants to see me.

RUFIO. Ay. I have brought him with me. He is waiting there (jerking his thumb over his shoulder) under guard.

CAESAR. And you want me to see him?

RUFIO (obstinately). I don't want anything. I daresay you will do what you like. Don't put it on to me.

CAESAR (with an air of doing it expressly to indulge Rufio). Well, well: let us have him.

RUFIO (calling). Ho there, guard! Release your man and send him up. (Beckoning) Come along!

Pothinus enters and stops mistrustfully between the two, looking from one to the other.

CAESAR (graciously). Ah, Pothinus! You are welcome. And what is the news this afternoon?

POTHINUS. Caesar: I come to warn you of a danger, and to make you an offer.

CAESAR. Never mind the danger. Make the offer.

RUFIO. Never mind the offer. What's the danger?

POTHINUS. Caesar: you think that Cleopatra is devoted to you.

CAESAR (gravely). My friend: I already know what I think. Come to your offer.

POTHINUS. I will deal plainly. I know not by what strange gods you have been enabled to defend a palace and a few yards of beach against a city and an army. Since we cut you off from Lake Mareotis, and you dug wells in the salt sea sand and brought up buckets of fresh water from them, we have known that your gods are irresistible, and that you are a worker of miracles. I no longer threaten you.

RUFIO (sarcastically). Very handsome of you, indeed.

POTHINUS. So be it: you are the master. Our gods sent the north west winds to keep you in our hands; but you have been too strong for them.

CAESAR (gently urging him to come to the point). Yes, yes, my friend. But what then?

RUFIO. Spit it out, man. What have you to say?

POTHINUS. I have to say that you have a traitress in your camp. Cleopatra.

THE MAJOR-DOMO (at the table, announcing). The Queen! (Caesar and Rufio rise.)

RUFIO (aside to Pothinus). You should have spat it out sooner, you fool. Now it is too late.

Cleopatra, in gorgeous raiment, enters in state through the gap in the colonnade, and comes down past the image of Ra and past the table to Caesar. Her retinue, headed by Ftatateeta, joins the staff at the table. Caesar gives Cleopatra his seat, which she takes.

CLEOPATRA (quickly, seeing Pothinus). What is HE doing here?

CAESAR (seating himself beside her, in the most amiable of tempers). Just going to tell me something about you. You shall hear it. Proceed, Pothinus.

POTHINUS (disconcerted). Caesar— (He stammers.)

CAESAR. Well, out with it.

POTHINUS. What I have to say is for your ear, not for the Queen's.

CLEOPATRA (with subdued ferocity). There are means of making you speak. Take care.

POTHINUS (defiantly). Caesar does not employ those means.

CAESAR. My friend: when a man has anything to tell in this world, the difficulty is not to make him tell it, but to prevent him from telling it too often. Let me celebrate my birthday by setting you free. Farewell: we'll not meet again.

CLEOPATRA (angrily). Caesar: this mercy is foolish.

POTHINUS (to Caesar). Will you not give me a private audience? Your life may depend on it. (Caesar rises loftily.)

RUFIO (aside to Pothinus). Ass! Now we shall have some heroics.

CAESAR (oratorically). Pothinus—

RUFIO (interrupting him). Caesar: the dinner will spoil if you begin preaching your favourite sermon about life and death.

CLEOPATRA (priggishly). Peace, Rufio. I desire to hear Caesar.

RUFIO (bluntly). Your Majesty has heard it before. You repeated it to Apollodorus last week; and he thought it was all your own. (Caesar's dignity collapses. Much tickled, he sits down again and looks roguishly at Cleopatra, who is furious. Rufio calls as before) Ho there, guard! Pass the prisoner out. He is released. (To Pothinus) Now off with you. You have lost your chance.

POTHINUS (his temper overcoming his prudence). I WILL speak.

CAESAR (to Cleopatra). You see. Torture would not have wrung a word from him.

POTHINUS. Caesar: you have taught Cleopatra the arts by which the Romans govern the world.

CAESAR. Alas! They cannot even govern themselves. What then?

POTHINUS. What then? Are you so besotted with her beauty that you do not see that she is impatient to reign in Egypt alone, and that her heart is set on your departure?

CLEOPATRA (rising). Liar!

CAESAR (shocked). What! Protestations! Contradictions!

CLEOPATRA (ashamed, but trembling with suppressed rage). No. I do not deign to contradict. Let him talk. (She sits down again.)

POTHINUS. From her own lips I have heard it. You are to be her catspaw: you are to tear the crown from her brother's head and set it on her own, delivering us all into her hand—delivering yourself also. And then Caesar can return to Rome, or depart through the gate of death, which is nearer and surer.

CAESAR (calmly). Well, my friend; and is not this very natural?

POTHINUS (astonished). Natural! Then you do not resent treachery?

CAESAR. Resent! O thou foolish Egyptian, what have I to do with resentment? Do I resent the wind when it chills me, or the night when it makes me stumble in the darkness? Shall I resent youth when it turns from age, and ambition when it turns from servitude? To tell me such a story as this is but to tell me that the sun will rise to-morrow.

CLEOPATRA (unable to contain herself). But it is false—false. I swear it.

CAESAR. It is true, though you swore it a thousand times, and believed all you swore. (She is convulsed with emotion. To screen her, he rises and takes Pothinus to Rufio, saying) Come, Rufio: let us see Pothinus past the guard. I have a word to say to him. (Aside to them) We must give the Queen a moment to recover herself. (Aloud) Come. (He takes Pothinus and Rufio out with him, conversing with them meanwhile.) Tell your friends, Pothinus, that they must not think I am opposed to a reasonable settlement of the country's affairs— (They pass out of hearing.)

CLEOPATRA (in a stifled whisper). Ftatateeta, Ftatateeta.

FTATATEETA (hurrying to her from the table and petting her). Peace, child: be comforted—

CLEOPATRA (interrupting her). Can they hear us?

FTATATEETA. No, dear heart, no.

CLEOPATRA. Listen to me. If he leaves the Palace alive, never see my face again.

FTATATEETA. He? Poth—

CLEOPATRA (striking her on the mouth). Strike his life out as I strike his name from your lips. Dash him down from the wall. Break him on the stones. Kill, kill, KILL him.

FTATATEETA (showing all her teeth). The dog shall perish.

CLEOPATRA. Fail in this, and you go out from before me forever.

FTATATEETA (resolutely). So be it. You shall not see my face until his eyes are darkened.

Caesar comes back, with Apollodorus, exquisitely dressed, and Rufio.

CLEOPATRA (to Ftatateeta). Come soon—soon. (Ftatateeta turns her meaning eyes for a moment on her mistress; then goes grimly away past Ra and out. Cleopatra runs like a gazelle to Caesar.) So you have come back to me, Caesar. (Caressingly) I thought you were angry. Welcome, Apollodorus. (She gives him her hand to kiss, with her other arm about Caesar.)

APOLLODORUS. Cleopatra grows more womanly beautiful from week to week.

CLEOPATRA. Truth, Apollodorus?

APOLLODORUS. Far, far short of the truth! Friend Rufio threw a pearl into the sea: Caesar fished up a diamond.

CAESAR. Caesar fished up a touch of rheumatism, my friend. Come: to dinner! To dinner! (They move towards the table.)

CLEOPATRA (skipping like a young fawn). Yes, to dinner. I have ordered SUCH a dinner for you, Caesar!

CAESAR. Ay? What are we to have?

CLEOPATRA. Peacocks' brains.

CAESAR (as if his mouth watered). Peacocks' brains, Apollodorus!

APOLLODORUS. Not for me. I prefer nightingales' tongues. (He goes to one of the two covers set side by side.)

CLEOPATRA. Roast boar, Rufio!

RUFIO (gluttonously). Good! (He goes to the seat next Apollodorus, on his left.)

CAESAR (looking at his seat, which is at the end of the table, to Ra's left hand). What has become of my leathern cushion?

CLEOPATRA (at the opposite end). I have got new ones for you.

THE MAJOR-DOMO. These cushions, Caesar, are of Maltese gauze, stuffed with rose leaves.

CAESAR. Rose leaves! Am I a caterpillar? (He throws the cushions away and seats himself on the leather mattress underneath.)

CLEOPATRA. What a shame! My new cushions!

THE MAJOR-DOMO (at Caesar's elbow). What shall we serve to whet Caesar's appetite?

CAESAR. What have you got?

THE MAJOR-DOMO. Sea hedgehogs, black and white sea acorns, sea nettles, beccaficoes, purple shellfish—

CAESAR. Any oysters?

THE MAJOR-DOMO. Assuredly.

CAESAR. BRITISH oysters?

THE MAJOR-DOMO (assenting). British oysters, Caesar.

CAESAR. Oysters, then. (The Major-Domo signs to a slave at each order; and the slave goes out to execute it.) I have been in Britain—that western land of romance—the last piece of earth on the edge of the ocean that surrounds the world. I went there in search of its famous pearls. The British pearl was a fable; but in searching for it I found the British oyster.

APOLLODORUS. All posterity will bless you for it. (To the Major-Domo) Sea hedgehogs for me.

RUFIO. Is there nothing solid to begin with?

THE MAJOR-DOMO. Fieldfares with asparagus—

CLEOPATRA (interrupting). Fattened fowls! Have some fattened fowls, Rufio.

RUFIO. Ay, that will do.

CLEOPATRA (greedily). Fieldfares for me.

THE MAJOR-DOMO. Caesar will deign to choose his wine? Sicilian, Lesbian, Chian—

RUFIO (contemptuously). All Greek.

APOLLODORUS. Who would drink Roman wine when he could get Greek? Try the Lesbian, Caesar.

CAESAR. Bring me my barley water.

RUFIO (with intense disgust). Ugh! Bring ME my Falernian. (The Falernian is presently brought to him.)

CLEOPATRA (pouting). It is waste of time giving you dinners, Caesar. My scullions would not condescend to your diet.

CAESAR (relenting). Well, well: let us try the Lesbian. (The Major-Domo fills Caesar's goblet; then Cleopatra's and Apollodorus's.) But when I return to Rome, I will make laws against these extravagances. I will even get the laws carried out.

CLEOPATRA (coaxingly). Never mind. To-day you are to be like other people: idle, luxurious, and kind. (She stretches her hand to him along the table.)

CAESAR. Well, for once I will sacrifice my comfort (kissing her hand) there! (He takes a draught of wine.) Now are you satisfied?

CLEOPATRA. And you no longer believe that I long for your departure for Rome?

CAESAR. I no longer believe anything. My brains are asleep. Besides, who knows whether I shall return to Rome?

RUFIO (alarmed). How? Eh? What?

CAESAR. What has Rome to show me that I have not seen already? One year of Rome is like another, except that I grow older, whilst the crowd in the Appian Way is always the same age.

APOLLODORUS. It is no better here in Egypt. The old men, when they are tired of life, say "We have seen everything except the source of the Nile."

CAESAR (his imagination catching fire). And why not see that? Cleopatra: will you come with me and track the flood to its cradle in the heart of the regions of mystery? Shall we leave Rome behind us—Rome, that has achieved greatness only to learn how greatness destroys nations of men who are not great! Shall I make you a new kingdom, and build you a holy city there in the great unknown?

CLEOPATRA (rapturously). Yes, Yes. You shall.

RUFIO. Ay: now he will conquer Africa with two legions before we come to the roast boar.

APOLLODORUS. Come: no scoffing, this is a noble scheme: in it Caesar is no longer merely the conquering soldier, but the creative poet-artist. Let us name the holy city, and consecrate it with Lesbian Wine—and Cleopatra shall name it herself.

CLEOPATRA. It shall be called Caesar's Gift to his Beloved.

APOLLODORUS. No, no. Something vaster than that—something universal, like the starry firmament.

CAESAR (prosaically). Why not simply The Cradle of the Nile?

CLEOPATRA. No: the Nile is my ancestor; and he is a god. Oh! I have thought of something. The Nile shall name it himself. Let us call upon him. (To the Major-Domo) Send for him. (The three men stare at one another; but the Major-Domo goes out as if he had received the most matter-of-fact order.) And (to the retinue) away with you all.

The retinue withdraws, making obeisance.

A priest enters, carrying a miniature sphinx with a tiny tripod before it. A morsel of incense is smoking in the tripod. The priest comes to the table and places the image in the middle of it. The light begins to change to the magenta purple of the Egyptian sunset, as if the god had brought a strange colored shadow with him. The three men are determined not to be impressed; but they feel curious in spite of themselves.

CAESAR. What hocus-pocus is this?

CLEOPATRA. You shall see. And it is NOT hocus-pocus. To do it properly, we should kill something to please him; but perhaps he will answer Caesar without that if we spill some wine to him.

APOLLODORUS (turning his head to look up over his shoulder at Ra). Why not appeal to our hawkheaded friend here?

CLEOPATRA (nervously). Sh! He will hear you and be angry.

RUFIO (phlegmatically). The source of the Nile is out of his district, I expect.

CLEOPATRA. No: I will have my city named by nobody but my dear little sphinx, because it was in its arms that Caesar found me asleep. (She languishes at Caesar; then turns curtly to the priest.) Go, I am a priestess, and have power to take your charge from you. (The priest makes a reverence and goes out.) Now let us call on the Nile all together. Perhaps he will rap on the table.

CAESAR. What! Table rapping! Are such superstitions still believed in this year 707 of the Republic?

CLEOPATRA. It is no superstition: our priests learn lots of things from the tables. Is it not so, Apollodorus?

APOLLODORUS. Yes: I profess myself a converted man. When Cleopatra is priestess, Apollodorus is devotee. Propose the conjuration.

CLEOPATRA. You must say with me "Send us thy voice, Father Nile."

ALL FOUR (holding their glasses together before the idol). Send us thy voice, Father Nile.

The death cry of a man in mortal terror and agony answers them. Appalled, the men set down their glasses, and listen. Silence. The purple deepens in the sky. Caesar, glancing at Cleopatra, catches her pouring out her wine before the god, with gleaming eyes, and mute assurances of gratitude and worship. Apollodorus springs up and runs to the edge of the roof to peer down and listen.

CAESAR (looking piercingly at Cleopatra). What was that?

CLEOPATRA (petulantly). Nothing. They are beating some slave.

CAESAR. Nothing!

RUFIO. A man with a knife in him, I'll swear.

CAESAR (rising). A murder!

APOLLODORUS (at the back, waving his hand for silence). S-sh! Silence. Did you hear that?

CAESAR. Another cry?

APOLLODORUS (returning to the table). No, a thud. Something fell on the beach, I think.

RUFIO (grimly, as he rises). Something with bones in it, eh?

CAESAR (shuddering). Hush, hush, Rufio. (He leaves the table and returns to the colonnade: Rufio following at his left elbow, and Apollodorus at the other side.)

CLEOPATRA (still in her place at the table). Will you leave me, Caesar? Apollodorus: are you going?

APOLLODORUS. Faith, dearest Queen, my appetite is gone.

CAESAR. Go down to the courtyard, Apollodorus; and find out what has happened.

Apollodorus nods and goes out, making for the staircase by which Rufio ascended.

CLEOPATRA. Your soldiers have killed somebody, perhaps. What does it matter?

The murmur of a crowd rises from the beach below. Caesar and Rufio look at one another.

CAESAR. This must be seen to. (He is about to follow Apollodorus when Rufio stops him with a hand on his arm as Ftatateeta comes back by the far end of the roof, with dragging steps, a drowsy satiety in her eyes and in the corners of the bloodhound lips. For a moment Caesar suspects that she is drunk with wine. Not so Rufio: he knows well the red vintage that has inebriated her.)

RUFIO (in a low tone). There is some mischief between those two.

FTATATEETA. The Queen looks again on the face of her servant.

Cleopatra looks at her for a moment with an exultant reflection of her murderous expression. Then she flings her arms round her; kisses her repeatedly and savagely; and tears off her jewels and heaps them on her. The two men turn from the spectacle to look at one another. Ftatateeta drags herself sleepily to the altar; kneels before Ra; and remains there in prayer. Caesar goes to Cleopatra, leaving Rufio in the colonnade.

CAESAR (with searching earnestness). Cleopatra: what has happened?

CLEOPATRA (in mortal dread of him, but with her utmost cajolery). Nothing, dearest Caesar. (With sickly sweetness, her voice almost failing) Nothing. I am innocent. (She approaches him affectionately)

Dear Caesar: are you angry with me? Why do you look at me so? I have been here with you all the time. How can I know what has happened?

CAESAR (reflectively). That is true.

CLEOPATRA (greatly relieved, trying to caress him). Of course it is true. (He does not respond to the caress.) You know it is true, Rufio.

The murmur without suddenly swells to a roar and subsides.

RUFIO. I shall know presently. (He makes for the altar in the burly trot that serves him for a stride, and touches Ftatateeta on the shoulder.) Now, mistress: I shall want you. (He orders her, with a gesture, to go before him.)

FTATATEETA (rising and glowering at him). My place is with the Queen.

CLEOPATRA. She has done no harm, Rufio.

CAESAR (to Rufio). Let her stay.

RUFIO (sitting down on the altar). Very well. Then my place is here too; and you can see what is the matter for yourself. The city is in a pretty uproar, it seems.

CAESAR (with grave displeasure). Rufio: there is a time for obedience.

RUFIO. And there is a time for obstinacy. (He folds his arms doggedly.)

CAESAR (to Cleopatra). Send her away.

CLEOPATRA (whining in her eagerness to propitiate him). Yes, I will. I will do whatever you ask me, Caesar, always, because I love you. Ftatateeta: go away.

FTATATEETA. The Queen's word is my will. I shall be at hand for the Queen's call. (She goes out past Ra, as she came.)

RUFIO (following her). Remember, Caesar, YOUR bodyguard also is within call. (He follows her out.)

Cleopatra, presuming upon Caesar's submission to Rufio, leaves the table and sits down on the bench in the colonnade.

CLEOPATRA. Why do you allow Rufio to treat you so? You should teach him his place.

CAESAR. Teach him to be my enemy, and to hide his thoughts from me as you are now hiding yours.

CLEOPATRA (her fears returning). Why do you say that, Caesar? Indeed, indeed, I am not hiding anything. You are wrong to treat me like this. (She stifles a sob.) I am only a child; and you turn into stone because you think some one has been killed. I cannot bear it. (She purposely breaks down and weeps. He looks at her with profound sadness and complete coldness. She looks up to see what effect she is producing. Seeing that he is unmoved, she sits up, pretending to struggle with her emotion and to put it bravely away.) But there: I know you hate tears: you shall not be troubled with them. I know you are not angry, but only sad; only I am so silly, I cannot help being hurt when you speak coldly. Of course you are quite right: it is dreadful to think of anyone being killed or even hurt; and I hope nothing really serious has— (Her voice dies away under his contemptuous penetration.)

CAESAR. What has frightened you into this? What have you done? (A trumpet sounds on the beach below.) Aha! That sounds like the answer.

CLEOPATRA (sinking back trembling on the bench and covering her face with her hands). I have not betrayed you, Caesar: I swear it.

CAESAR. I know that. I have not trusted you. (He turns from her, and is about to go out when Apollodorus and Britannus drag in Lucius Septimius to him. Rufio follows. Caesar shudders.) Again, Pompey's murderer!

RUFIO. The town has gone mad, I think. They are for tearing the palace down and driving us into the sea straight away. We laid hold of this renegade in clearing them out of the courtyard.

CAESAR. Release him. (They let go his arms.) What has offended the citizens, Lucius Septimius?

LUCIUS. What did you expect, Caesar? Pothinus was a favorite of theirs.

CAESAR. What has happened to Pothinus? I set him free, here, not half an hour ago. Did they not pass him out?

LUCIUS. Ay, through the gallery arch sixty feet above ground, with three inches of steel in his ribs. He is as dead as Pompey. We are quits now, as to killing—you and I.

CAESAR. (shocked). Assassinated!—our prisoner, our guest! (He turns reproachfully on Rufio) Rufio—

RUFIO (emphatically—anticipating the question). Whoever did it was a wise man and a friend of yours (Cleopatra is greatly emboldened); but none of US had a hand in it. So it is no use to frown at me. (Caesar turns and looks at Cleopatra.)

CLEOPATRA (violently—rising). He was slain by order of the Queen of Egypt. I am not Julius Caesar the dreamer, who allows every slave to insult him. Rufio has said I did well: now the others shall judge me too. (She turns to the others.) This Pothinus sought to make me conspire with him to betray Caesar to Achillas and Ptolemy. I refused; and he cursed me and came privily to Caesar to accuse me of his own treachery. I caught him in the act; and he insulted me—ME, the Queen! To my face. Caesar would not revenge me: he spoke him fair and set him free. Was I right to avenge myself? Speak, Lucius.

LUCIUS. I do not gainsay it. But you will get little thanks from Caesar for it.

CLEOPATRA. Speak, Apollodorus. Was I wrong?

APOLLODORUS. I have only one word of blame, most beautiful. You should have called upon me, your knight; and in fair duel I should have slain the slanderer.

CLEOPATRA (passionately). I will be judged by your very slave, Caesar. Britannus: speak. Was I wrong?

BRITANNUS. Were treachery, falsehood, and disloyalty left unpunished, society must become like an arena full of wild beasts, tearing one another to pieces. Caesar is in the wrong.

CAESAR (with quiet bitterness). And so the verdict is against me, it seems.

CLEOPATRA (vehemently). Listen to me, Caesar. If one man in all Alexandria can be found to say that I did wrong, I swear to have myself crucified on the door of the palace by my own slaves.

CAESAR. If one man in all the world can be found, now or forever, to know that you did wrong, that man will have either to conquer the world as I have, or be crucified by it. (The uproar in the streets again reaches them.) Do you hear? These knockers at your gate are also believers in vengeance and in stabbing. You have slain their leader: it is right that they shall slay you. If you doubt it, ask your four counselors here. And then in the name of that RIGHT (He emphasizes the word with great scorn.) shall I not slay them for murdering their Queen, and be slain in my turn by their countrymen as the invader of their fatherland? Can Rome do less then than slay these slayers too, to show the world how Rome avenges her sons and her honor? And so, to the end of history, murder shall breed murder, always in the name of right and honor and peace, until the gods are tired of blood and create a race that can understand. (Fierce uproar. Cleopatra becomes white with terror.) Hearken, you who must not be insulted. Go near enough to catch their words: you will find them bitterer than the tongue of Pothinus. (Loftily wrapping himself up in an impenetrable dignity.) Let the Queen of Egypt now give her orders for vengeance, and take her measures for defense; for she has renounced Caesar. (He turns to go.)

CLEOPATRA (terrified, running to him and falling on her knees). You will not desert me, Caesar. You will defend the palace.

CAESAR. You have taken the powers of life and death upon you. I am only a dreamer.

CLEOPATRA. But they will kill me.

CAESAR. And why not?

CLEOPATRA. In pity—

CAESAR. Pity! What! Has it come to this so suddenly, that nothing can save you now but pity? Did it save Pothinus?

She rises, wringing her hands, and goes back to the bench in despair. Apollodorus shows his sympathy with her by quietly posting himself behind the bench. The sky has by this time become the most vivid purple, and soon begins to change to a glowing pale orange, against which the colonnade and the great image show darklier and darklier.

RUFIO. Caesar: enough of preaching. The enemy is at the gate.

CAESAR (turning on him and giving way to his wrath). Ay; and what has held him baffled at the gate all these months? Was it my folly, as you deem it, or your wisdom? In this Egyptian Red Sea of blood, whose hand has held all your heads above the waves? (Turning on Cleopatra) And yet, When Caesar says to such an one, "Friend, go free," you, clinging for your little life to my sword, dare steal out and stab him in the back? And you, soldiers and gentlemen, and honest servants as you forget that you are, applaud this assassination, and say "Caesar is in the wrong." By the gods, I am tempted to open my hand and let you all sink into the flood.

CLEOPATRA (with a ray of cunning hope). But, Caesar, if you do, you will perish yourself.

Caesar's eyes blaze.

RUFIO (greatly alarmed). Now, by great Jove, you filthy little Egyptian rat, that is the very word to make him walk out alone into the city and leave us here to be cut to pieces. (Desperately, to Caesar) Will you desert us because we are a parcel of fools? I mean no harm by killing: I do it as a dog kills a cat, by instinct. We are all dogs at your heels; but we have served you faithfully.

CAESAR (relenting). Alas, Rufio, my son, my son: as dogs we are like to perish now in the streets.

APOLLODORUS (at his post behind Cleopatra's seat). Caesar, what you say has an Olympian ring in it: it must be right; for it is fine art. But I am still on the side of Cleopatra. If we must die, she shall not want the devotion of a man's heart nor the strength of a man's arm.

CLEOPATRA (sobbing). But I don't want to die.

CAESAR (sadly). Oh, ignoble, ignoble!

LUCIUS (coming forward between Caesar and Cleopatra). Hearken to me, Caesar. It may be ignoble; but I also mean to live as long as I can.

CAESAR. Well, my friend, you are likely to outlive Caesar. Is it any magic of mine, think you, that has kept your army and this whole city at bay for so long? Yesterday, what quarrel had they with me that they should risk their lives against me? But to-day we have flung them down their hero, murdered; and now every man of them is set upon clearing out this nest of assassins—for such we are and no more. Take courage then; and sharpen your sword. Pompey's head has fallen; and Caesar's head is ripe.

APOLLODORUS. Does Caesar despair?

CAESAR (with infinite pride). He who has never hoped can never despair. Caesar, in good or bad fortune, looks his fate in the face.

LUCIUS. Look it in the face, then; and it will smile as it always has on Caesar.

CAESAR (with involuntary haughtiness). Do you presume to encourage me?

LUCIUS. I offer you my services. I will change sides if you will have me.

CAESAR (suddenly coming down to earth again, and looking sharply at him, divining that there is something behind the offer). What! At this point?

LUCIUS (firmly). At this point.

RUFIO. Do you suppose Caesar is mad, to trust you?

LUCIUS. I do not ask him to trust me until he is victorious. I ask for my life, and for a command in Caesar's army. And since Caesar is a fair dealer, I will pay in advance.

CAESAR. Pay! How?

LUCIUS. With a piece of good news for you.

Caesar divines the news in a flash.

RUFIO. What news?

CAESAR (with an elate and buoyant energy which makes Cleopatra sit up and stare). What news! What news, did you say, my son Rufio? The relief has arrived: what other news remains for us? Is it not so, Lucius Septimius? Mithridates of Pergamos is on the march.

LUCIUS. He has taken Pelusium.

CAESAR (delighted). Lucius Septimius: you are henceforth my officer. Rufio: the Egyptians must have sent every soldier from the city to prevent Mithridates crossing the Nile. There is nothing in the streets now but mob—mob!

LUCIUS. It is so. Mithridates is marching by the great road to Memphis to cross above the Delta. Achillas will fight him there.

CAESAR (all audacity). Achillas shall fight Caesar there. See, Rufio. (He runs to the table; snatches a napkin; and draws a plan on it with his finger dipped in wine, whilst Rufio and Lucius Septimius crowd about him to watch, all looking closely, for the light is now almost gone.) Here is the palace (pointing to his plan): here is the theatre. You (to Rufio) take twenty men and pretend to go by THAT street (pointing it out); and whilst they are stoning you, out go the cohorts by this and this. My streets are right, are they, Lucius?

LUCIUS. Ay, that is the fig market—

CAESAR (too much excited to listen to him). I saw them the day we arrived. Good! (He throws the napkin on the table and comes down again into the colonnade.) Away, Britannus: tell Petronius that within an hour half our forces must take ship for the western lake. See to my horse and armor. (Britannus runs out.) With the rest I shall march round the lake and up the Nile to meet Mithridates. Away, Lucius; and give the word.

Lucius hurries out after Britannus.

RUFIO. Come: this is something like business.

CAESAR (buoyantly). Is it not, my only son? (He claps his hands. The slaves hurry in to the table.) No more of this mawkish reveling: away with all this stuff: shut it out of my sight and be off with you. (The slaves begin to remove the table; and the curtains are drawn, shutting in the colonnade.) You understand about the streets, Rufio?

RUFIO. Ay, I think I do. I will get through them, at all events.

The bucina sounds busily in the courtyard beneath.

CAESAR. Come, then: we must talk to the troops and hearten them. You down to the beach: I to the courtyard. (He makes for the staircase.)

CLEOPATRA (rising from her seat, where she has been quite neglected all this time, and stretching out her hands timidly to him). Caesar.

CAESAR (turning). Eh?

CLEOPATRA. Have you forgotten me?

CAESAR. (indulgently). I am busy now, my child, busy. When I return your affairs shall be settled. Farewell; and be good and patient.

He goes, preoccupied and quite indifferent. She stands with clenched fists, in speechless rage and humiliation.

RUFIO. That game is played and lost, Cleopatra. The woman always gets the worst of it.

CLEOPATRA (haughtily). Go. Follow your master.

RUFIO (in her ear, with rough familiarity). A word first. Tell your executioner that if Pothinus had been properly killed—IN THE THROAT—he would not have called out. Your man bungled his work.

CLEOPATRA (enigmatically). How do you know it was a man?

RUFIO (startled, and puzzled). It was not you: you were with us when it happened. (She turns her back scornfully on him. He shakes his head, and draws the curtains to go out. It is now a magnificent moonlit night. The table has been removed. Ftatateeta is seen in the light of the moon and stars, again in prayer before the white altar-stone of Ra. Rufio starts; closes the curtains again softly; and says in a low voice to Cleopatra) Was it she? With her own hand?

CLEOPATRA (threateningly). Whoever it was, let my enemies beware of her. Look to it, Rufio, you who dare make the Queen of Egypt a fool before Caesar.

RUFIO (looking grimly at her). I will look to it, Cleopatra. (He nods in confirmation of the promise, and slips out through the curtains, loosening his sword in its sheath as he goes.)

ROMAN SOLDIERS (in the courtyard below). Hail, Caesar! Hail, hail!

Cleopatra listens. The bucina sounds again, followed by several trumpets.

CLEOPATRA (wringing her hands and calling). Ftatateeta. Ftatateeta. It is dark; and I am alone. Come to me. (Silence.) Ftatateeta. (Louder.) Ftatateeta. (Silence. In a panic she snatches the cord and pulls the curtains apart.)

Ftatateeta is lying dead on the altar of Ra, with her throat cut. Her blood deluges the white stone.

ACT V

High noon. Festival and military pageant on the esplanade before the palace. In the east harbor Caesar's galley, so gorgeously decorated that it seems to be rigged with flowers, is along-side the quay, close to the steps Apollodorus descended when he embarked with the carpet. A Roman guard is posted there in charge of a gangway, whence a red floorcloth is laid down the middle of the esplanade, turning off to the north opposite the central gate in the palace front, which shuts in the esplanade on the south side. The broad steps of the gate, crowded with Cleopatra's ladies, all in their gayest attire, are like a flower garden. The facade is lined by her guard, officered by the same gallants to whom Bel Affris announced the coming of Caesar six months before in the old palace on the Syrian border. The north side is lined by Roman soldiers, with the townsfolk on tiptoe behind them, peering over their heads at the cleared esplanade, in which the officers stroll about, chatting. Among these are Belzanor and the Persian; also the Centurion, vinewood cudgel in hand, battle worn, thick-booted, and much outshone, both socially and decoratively, by the Egyptian officers.

Apollodorus makes his way through the townsfolk and calls to the officers from behind the Roman line.

APOLLODORUS. Hullo! May I pass?

CENTURION. Pass Apollodorus the Sicilian there! (The soldiers let him through.)

BELZANOR. Is Caesar at hand?

APOLLODORUS. Not yet. He is still in the market place. I could not stand any more of the roaring of the soldiers! After half an hour of the enthusiasm of an army, one feels the need of a little sea air.

PERSIAN. Tell us the news. Hath he slain the priests?

APOLLODORUS. Not he. They met him in the market place with ashes on their heads and their gods in their hands. They placed the gods at his feet. The only one that was worth looking at was Apis: a miracle of gold and ivory work. By my advice he offered the chief priest two talents for it.

BELZANOR (appalled). Apis the all-knowing for two talents! What said the chief priest?

APOLLODORUS. He invoked the mercy of Apis, and asked for five.

BELZANOR. There will be famine and tempest in the land for this.

PERSIAN. Pooh! Why did not Apis cause Caesar to be vanquished by Achillas? Any fresh news from the war, Apollodorus?

APOLLODORUS. The little King Ptolemy was drowned.

BELZANOR. Drowned! How?

APOLLODORUS. With the rest of them. Caesar attacked them from three sides at once and swept them into the Nile. Ptolemy's barge sank.

BELZANOR. A marvelous man, this Caesar! Will he come soon, think you?

APOLLODORUS. He was settling the Jewish question when I left.

A flourish of trumpets from the north, and commotion among the townsfolk, announces the approach of Caesar.

PERSIAN. He has made short work of them. Here he comes. (He hurries to his post in front of the Egyptian lines.)

BELZANOR (following him). Ho there! Caesar comes.

The soldiers stand at attention, and dress their lines. Apollodorus goes to the Egyptian line.

CENTURION (hurrying to the gangway guard). Attention there! Caesar comes.

Caesar arrives in state with Rufio: Britannus following. The soldiers receive him with enthusiastic shouting.

RUFIO (at his left hand). You have not yet appointed a Roman governor for this province.

CAESAR (Looking whimsically at him, but speaking with perfect gravity). What say you to Mithridates of Pergamos, my reliever and rescuer, the great son of Eupator?

RUFIO. Why, that you will want him elsewhere. Do you forget that you have some three or four armies to conquer on your way home?

CAESAR. Indeed! Well, what say you to yourself?

RUFIO (incredulously). I! I a governor! What are you dreaming of? Do you not know that I am only the son of a freedman?

CAESAR (affectionately). Has not Caesar called you his son? (Calling to the whole assembly) Peace awhile there; and hear me.

THE ROMAN SOLDIERS. Hear Caesar.

CAESAR. Hear the service, quality, rank and name of the Roman governor. By service, Caesar's shield; by quality, Caesar's friend; by rank, a Roman soldier. (The Roman soldiers give a triumphant shout.) By name, Rufio. (They shout again.)

RUFIO (kissing Caesar's hand). Ay: I am Caesar's shield; but of what use shall I be when I am no longer on Caesar's arm? Well, no matter— (He becomes husky, and turns away to recover himself.)

CAESAR. Where is that British Islander of mine?

BRITANNUS (coming forward on Caesar's right hand). Here, Caesar.

CAESAR. Who bade you, pray, thrust yourself into the battle of the Delta, uttering the barbarous cries of your native land, and affirming yourself a match for any four of the Egyptians, to whom you applied unseemly epithets?

BRITANNUS. Caesar: I ask you to excuse the language that escaped me in the heat of the moment.

CAESAR. And how did you, who cannot swim, cross the canal with us when we stormed the camp?

BRITANNUS. Caesar: I clung to the tail of your horse.

CAESAR. These are not the deeds of a slave, Britannicus, but of a free man.

BRITANNUS. Caesar: I was born free.

CAESAR. But they call you Caesar's slave.

BRITANNUS. Only as Caesar's slave have I found real freedom.

CAESAR (moved). Well said. Ungrateful that I am, I was about to set you free; but now I will not part from you for a million talents. (He claps him friendly on the shoulder. Britannus, gratified, but a trifle shamefaced, takes his hand and kisses it sheepishly.)

BELZANOR (to the Persian). This Roman knows how to make men serve him.

PERSIAN. Ay: men too humble to become dangerous rivals to him.

BELZANOR. O subtle one! O cynic!

CAESAR (seeing Apollodorus in the Egyptian corner and calling to him). Apollodorus: I leave the art of Egypt in your charge. Remember: Rome loves art and will encourage it ungrudgingly.

APOLLODORUS. I understand, Caesar. Rome will produce no art itself; but it will buy up and take away whatever the other nations produce.

CAESAR. What! Rome produces no art! Is peace not an art? Is war not an art? Is government not an art? Is civilization not an art? All these we give you in exchange for a few ornaments. You will have the best of the bargain. (Turning to Rufio) And now, what else have I to do before I embark? (Trying to recollect) There is something I cannot remember: what CAN it be? Well, well: it must remain undone: we must not waste this favorable wind. Farewell, Rufio.

RUFIO. Caesar: I am loath to let you go to Rome without your shield. There are too many daggers there.

CAESAR. It matters not: I shall finish my life's work on my way back; and then I shall have lived long enough. Besides: I have always disliked the idea of dying: I had rather be killed. Farewell.

RUFIO (with a sigh, raising his hands and giving Caesar up as incorrigible). Farewell. (They shake hands.)

CAESAR (waving his hand to Apollodorus). Farewell, Apollodorus, and my friends, all of you. Aboard!

The gangway is run out from the quay to the ship. As Caesar moves towards it, Cleopatra, cold and tragic, cunningly dressed in black, without ornaments or decoration of any kind, and thus making a striking figure among the brilliantly dressed bevy of ladies as she passes through it, comes from the palace and stands on the steps. Caesar does not see her until she speaks.

CLEOPATRA. Has Cleopatra no part in this leave taking?

CAESAR (enlightened). Ah, I KNEW there was something. (To Rufio) How could you let me forget her, Rufio? (Hastening to her) Had I gone without seeing you, I should never have forgiven myself. (He takes her hands, and brings her into the middle of the esplanade. She submits stonily.) Is this mourning for me?

CLEOPATRA. NO.

CAESAR (remorsefully). Ah, that was thoughtless of me! It is for your brother.

CLEOPATRA. No.

CAESAR. For whom, then?

CLEOPATRA. Ask the Roman governor whom you have left us.

CAESAR. Rufio?

CLEOPATRA. Yes: Rufio. (She points at him with deadly scorn.) He who is to rule here in Caesar's name, in Caesar's way, according to Caesar's boasted laws of life.

CAESAR (dubiously). He is to rule as he can, Cleopatra. He has taken the work upon him, and will do it in his own way.

CLEOPATRA. Not in your way, then?

CAESAR (puzzled). What do you mean by my way?

CLEOPATRA. Without punishment. Without revenge. Without judgment.

CAESAR (approvingly). Ay: that is the right way, the great way, the only possible way in the end. (To Rufio) Believe it, Rufio, if you can.

RUFIO. Why, I believe it, Caesar. You have convinced me of it long ago. But look you. You are sailing for Numidia to-day. Now tell me: if you meet a hungry lion you will not punish it for wanting to eat you?

CAESAR (wondering what he is driving at). No.

RUFIO. Nor revenge upon it the blood of those it has already eaten.

CAESAR. No.

RUFIO. Nor judge it for its guiltiness.

CAESAR. No.

RUFIO. What, then, will you do to save your life from it?

CAESAR (promptly). Kill it, man, without malice, just as it would kill me. What does this parable of the lion mean?

RUFIO. Why, Cleopatra had a tigress that killed men at bidding. I thought she might bid it kill you some day. Well, had I not been Caesar's pupil, what pious things might I not have done to that tigress? I might have punished it. I might have revenged Pothinus on it.

CAESAR (interjects). Pothinus!

RUFIO (continuing). I might have judged it. But I put all these follies behind me; and, without malice, only cut its throat. And that is why Cleopatra comes to you in mourning.

CLEOPATRA (vehemently). He has shed the blood of my servant Ftatateeta. On your head be it as upon his, Caesar, if you hold him free of it.

CAESAR (energetically). On my head be it, then; for it was well done. Rufio: had you set yourself in the seat of the judge, and with hateful ceremonies and appeals to the gods handed that woman over to some hired executioner to be slain before the people in the name of justice, never again would I have touched your hand without a shudder. But this was natural slaying: I feel no horror at it.

Rufio, satisfied, nods at Cleopatra, mutely inviting her to mark that.

CLEOPATRA (pettish and childish in her impotence). No: not when a Roman slays an Egyptian. All the world will now see how unjust and corrupt Caesar is.

CAESAR (taking her handy coaxingly). Come: do not be angry with me. I am sorry for that poor Totateeta. (She laughs in spite of herself.) Aha! You are laughing. Does that mean reconciliation?

CLEOPATRA (angry with herself for laughing). No, no, NO!! But it is so ridiculous to hear you call her Totateeta.

CAESAR. What! As much a child as ever, Cleopatra! Have I not made a woman of you after all?

CLEOPATRA. Oh, it is you, who are a great baby: you make me seem silly because you will not behave seriously. But you have treated me badly; and I do not forgive you.

CAESAR. Bid me farewell.

CLEOPATRA. I will not.

CAESAR (coaxing). I will send you a beautiful present from Rome.

CLEOPATRA (proudly). Beauty from Rome to Egypt indeed! What can Rome give ME that Egypt cannot give me?

APOLLODORUS. That is true, Caesar. If the present is to be really beautiful, I shall have to buy it for you in Alexandria.

CAESAR. You are forgetting the treasures for which Rome is most famous, my friend. You cannot buy THEM in Alexandria.

APOLLODORUS. What are they, Caesar?

CAESAR. Her sons. Come, Cleopatra: forgive me and bid me farewell; and I will send you a man, Roman from head to heel and Roman of the noblest; not old and ripe for the knife; not lean in the arms and cold in the heart; not hiding a bald head under his conqueror's laurels; not stooped with the weight of the world on his shoulders; but brisk and fresh, strong and young, hoping in the morning, fighting in the day, and reveling in the evening. Will you take such an one in exchange for Caesar?

CLEOPATRA (palpitating). His name, his name?

CAESAR. Shall it be Mark Antony? (She throws herself in his arms.)

RUFIO. You are a bad hand at a bargain, mistress, if you will swap Caesar for Antony.

CAESAR. So now you are satisfied.

CLEOPATRA. You will not forget.

CAESAR. I will not forget. Farewell: I do not think we shall meet again. Farewell. (He kisses her on the forehead. She is much affected and begins to sniff. He embarks.)

THE ROMAN SOLDIERS (as he sets his foot on the gangway). Hail, Caesar; and farewell!

He reaches the ship and returns Rufio's wave of the hand.

APOLLODORUS (to Cleopatra). No tears, dearest Queen: they stab your servant to the heart. He will return some day.

CLEOPATRA. I hope not. But I can't help crying, all the same. (She waves her handkerchief to Caesar; and the ship begins to move.)

THE ROMAN SOLDIERS (drawing their swords and raising them in the air). Hail, Caesar!

NOTES TO CAESAR AND CLEOPATRA

CLEOPATRA'S CURE FOR BALDNESS

For the sake of conciseness in a hurried situation I have made Cleopatra recommend rum. This, I am afraid, is an anachronism: the only real one in the play. To balance it, I give a couple of the remedies she actually believed in. They are quoted by Galen from Cleopatra's book on Cosmetic.

"For bald patches, powder red sulphuret of arsenic and take it up with oak gum, as much as it will bear. Put on a rag and apply, having soaped the place well first. I have mixed the above with a foam of nitre, and it worked well."

Several other receipts follow, ending with: "The following is the best of all, acting for fallen hairs, when applied with oil or pomatum; acts also for falling off of eyelashes or for people getting bald all over. It is wonderful. Of domestic mice burnt, one part; of vine rag burnt, one part; of horse's teeth burnt, one part; of bear's grease one; of deer's marrow one; of reed bark one. To be pounded when dry, and mixed with plenty of honey til it gets the consistency of honey; then the bear's grease and marrow to be mixed (when melted), the medicine to be put in a brass flask, and the bald part rubbed til it sprouts."

Concerning these ingredients, my fellow-dramatist, Gilbert Murray, who, as a Professor of Greek, has applied to classical antiquity the methods of high scholarship (my own method is pure divination), writes to me as follows: "Some of this I don't understand, and possibly Galen did not, as he quotes your heroine's own language. Foam of nitre is, I think, something like soapsuds. Reed bark is an odd expression. It might mean the outside membrane of a reed: I do not know what it ought to be called. In the burnt mice receipt I take that you first mixed the solid powders with honey, and then added the grease. I expect Cleopatra preferred it because in most of the others you have to lacerate the skin, prick it, or rub it till it bleeds. I do not know what vine rag is. I translate literally."

APPARENT ANACHRONISMS

The only way to write a play which shall convey to the general public an impression of antiquity is to make the characters speak blank verse and abstain from reference to steam, telegraphy, or any of the material conditions of their existence. The more ignorant men are, the more convinced are they that their little parish and their little chapel is an apex which civilization and philosophy have painfully struggled up the pyramid of time from a desert of savagery. Savagery, they think, became barbarism; barbarism became ancient civilization; ancient civilization became Pauline Christianity; Pauline Christianity became Roman Catholicism; Roman Catholicism became the Dark Ages; and the Dark Ages were finally enlightened by the Protestant instincts of the English race. The whole process is summed up as Progress with a capital P. And any elderly gentleman of Progressive temperament will testify that the improvement since he was a boy is enormous.

Now if we count the generations of Progressive elderly gentlemen since, say, Plato, and add together the successive enormous improvements to which each of them has testified, it will strike us at once as an unaccountable fact that the world, instead of having been improved in 67 generations out all recognition, presents, on the whole, a rather less dignified appearance in Ibsen's Enemy of the People than in Plato's Republic. And in truth, the period of time covered by history is far too short to allow of any perceptible progress in the popular sense of Evolution of the Human Species. The notion that there has been any such Progress since Caesar's time (less than 20 centuries) is too absurd for discussion. All the savagery, barbarism, dark ages and the rest of it of which we have any record as existing in the past, exists at the present moment. A British carpenter or stonemason may point out that he gets twice as much money for his labor as his father did in the same trade, and that his suburban house, with its bath, its cottage piano, its drawingroom suite, and its album of photographs, would have shamed the plainness of his grandmother's. But the descendants of feudal barons, living in squalid lodgings on a salary of fifteen shillings a week instead of in castles on princely revenues, do not congratulate the world on the change. Such changes, in fact, are not to the point. It has been known, as far back as our records go, that man running wild in the woods is different to man kennelled in a city slum; that a dog seems to understand a shepherd better than a hewer of wood and drawer of water can understand an astronomer; and that breeding, gentle nurture and luxurious food and shelter will produce a kind of man with whom the common laborer is socially incompatible. The same thing is true of horses and dogs. Now there is clearly room for great changes in the world by increasing the percentage of individuals who are carefully bred and gently nurtured even to finally making the most of every man and woman born. But that possibility existed in the days of the Hittites as much as it does today. It does not give the slightest real support to the common assumption that the civilized contemporaries of the Hittites were unlike their civilized descendants to-day.

This would appear the truest commonplace if it were not that the ordinary citizen's ignorance of the past combines with his idealization of the present to mislead and flatter him. Our latest book on the new railway across Asia describes the dulness of the Siberian farmer and the vulgar pursepride of the Siberian man of business without the least consciousness that the sting of contemptuous instances given might have been saved by writing simply "Farmers and provincial plutocrats in Siberia are exactly what they are in England." The latest professor descanting on the civilization of the Western Empire in the fifth century feels bound to assume, in the teeth of his own researches, that the Christian was one sort of animal and the Pagan another. It might as well be assumed, as indeed it generally is assumed by implication, that a murder committed with a poisoned arrow is different to a murder committed with a Mauser rifle. All such notions are illusions. Go back to the first syllable of recorded time, and there you will find your Christian and your Pagan, your yokel and your poet, helot and hero, Don Quixote and Sancho, Tamino and Papageno, Newton and bushman unable to count eleven, all alive and contemporaneous, and all convinced that they are heirs of all the ages and the privileged recipients of THE truth (all others damnable heresies), just as you have them to-day, flourishing in countries each of which is the bravest and best that ever sprang at Heaven's command from out of the azure main.

Again, there is the illusion of "increased command over Nature," meaning that cotton is cheap and that ten miles of country road on a bicycle have replaced four on foot. But even if man's increased command over Nature included any increased command over himself (the only sort of command relevant to his evolution into a higher being), the fact remains that it is only by running away from the increased command over Nature to country places where Nature is still in primitive command over Man that he can recover from the effects of the smoke, the stench, the foul air, the overcrowding, the racket, the ugliness, the dirt which the cheap cotton costs us. If manufacturing activity means Progress, the town must be more advanced than the country; and the field laborers and village artizans of to-day must be much less changed from the servants of Job than the proletariat of modern London from the proletariat of Caesar's Rome. Yet the cockney proletarian is so inferior to the village laborer that it is only by steady recruiting from the country that London is kept alive. This does not seem as if the change since Job's time were Progress in the popular sense: quite the reverse. The common stock of discoveries in physics has accumulated a little: that is all.

One more illustration. Is the Englishman prepared to admit that the American is his superior as a human being? I ask this question because the scarcity of labor in America relatively to the demand for it has led to a development of machinery there, and a consequent "increase of command over Nature" which makes many of our English methods appear almost medieval to the up-to-date Chicagoan. This means that the American has an advantage over the Englishman of exactly the same nature that the Englishman has over the contemporaries of Cicero. Is the Englishman prepared to draw the same conclusion in both cases? I think not. The American, of course, will draw it cheerfully; but I must then ask him whether, since a modern negro has a greater "command over Nature" than Washington had, we are also to accept the conclusion, involved in his former one, that humanity has progressed from Washington to the fin de siecle negro.

Finally, I would point out that if life is crowned by its success and devotion in industrial organization and ingenuity, we had better worship the ant and the bee (as moralists urge us to do in our childhood), and humble ourselves before the arrogance of the birds of Aristophanes.

My reason then for ignoring the popular conception of Progress in Caesar and Cleopatra is that there is no reason to suppose that any Progress has taken place since their time. But even if I shared the popular delusion, I do not see that I could have made any essential difference in the play. I can only imitate humanity as I know it. Nobody knows whether Shakespeare thought that ancient Athenian joiners, weavers, or bellows menders were any different from Elizabethan ones; but it is quite certain that one could not have made them so, unless, indeed, he had played the literary man and made Quince say, not "Is all our company here?" but "Bottom: was not that Socrates that passed us at the Piraeus with Glaucon and Polemarchus on his way to the house of Kephalus." And so on.

CLEOPATRA

Cleopatra was only sixteen when Caesar went to Egypt; but in Egypt sixteen is a riper age than it is in England. The childishness I have ascribed to her, as far as it is childishness of character and not lack of experience, is not a matter of years. It may be observed in our own climate at the present day in many women of fifty. It is a mistake to suppose that the difference between wisdom and folly has anything to do with the difference between physical age and physical youth. Some women are younger at seventy than most women at seventeen.

It must be borne in mind, too, that Cleopatra was a queen, and was therefore not the typical Greek-cultured, educated Egyptian lady of her time. To represent her by any such type would be as absurd as to represent George IV by a type founded on the attainments of Sir Isaac Newton. It is true that an ordinarily well educated Alexandrian girl of her time would no more have believed bogey stories about the Romans than the daughter of a modern Oxford professor would believe them about the Germans (though, by the way, it is possible to talk great nonsense at Oxford about foreigners when we are at war with them). But I do not feel bound to believe that Cleopatra was well educated. Her father, the illustrious Flute Blower, was not at all a parent of the Oxford professor type. And Cleopatra was a chip of the old block.

BRITANNUS

I find among those who have read this play in manuscript a strong conviction that an ancient Briton could not possibly have been like a modern one. I see no reason to adopt this curious view. It is true that the Roman and Norman conquests must have for a time disturbed the normal British type produced by the climate. But Britannus, born before these events, represents the unadulterated Briton who fought Caesar and impressed Roman observers much as we should expect the ancestors of Mr. Podsnap to impress the cultivated Italians of their time.

I am told that it is not scientific to treat national character as a product of climate. This only shows the wide difference between common knowledge and the intellectual game called science. We have men of exactly the same stock, and speaking the same language, growing in Great Britain, in Ireland, and in America. The result is three of the most distinctly marked nationalities under the sun. Racial characteristics are quite another matter. The difference between a Jew and a Gentile has nothing to do with the difference between an Englishman and a German. The characteristics of Britannus are local characteristics, not race characteristics. In an ancient Briton they would, I take it, be exaggerated, since modern Britain, disforested, drained, urbanified and consequently cosmopolized, is presumably less characteristically British than Caesar's Britain.

And again I ask does anyone who, in the light of a competent knowledge of his own age, has studied history from contemporary documents, believe that 67 generations of promiscuous marriage have made any appreciable difference in the human fauna of these isles? Certainly I do not.

JULIUS CAESAR

As to Caesar himself, I have purposely avoided the usual anachronism of going to Caesar's books, and concluding that the style is the man. That is only true of authors who have the specific literary genius, and have practised long enough to attain complete self-expression in letters. It is not true even on these conditions in an age when literature is conceived as a game of style, and not as a vehicle of self-expression by the author. Now Caesar was an amateur stylist writing books of travel and campaign histories in a style so impersonal that the authenticity of the later volumes is disputed. They reveal some of his qualities just as the Voyage of a Naturalist Round the World reveals some of Darwin's, without expressing his private personality. An Englishman reading them would say that Caesar was a man of great common sense and good taste, meaning thereby a man without originality or moral courage.

In exhibiting Caesar as a much more various person than the historian of the Gallic wars, I hope I have not succumbed unconsciously to the dramatic illusion to which all great men owe part of their reputation and some the whole of it. I admit that reputations gained in war are specially questionable. Able civilians taking up the profession of arms, like Caesar and Cromwell, in middle age, have snatched all its laurels from opponent commanders bred to it, apparently because capable persons engaged in military pursuits are so scarce that the existence of two of them at the same time in the same hemisphere is extremely rare. The capacity of any conqueror is therefore more likely than not to be an illusion produced by the incapacity of his adversary. At all events, Caesar might have won his battles without being wiser than Charles XII or Nelson or Joan of Arc, who were, like most modern "self-made" millionaires, half-witted geniuses, enjoying the worship accorded by all races to certain forms of insanity. But Caesar's victories were only advertisements for an eminence that would never have become popular without them. Caesar is greater off the battle field than on it. Nelson off his quarterdeck was so quaintly out of the question that when his head was injured at the battle of the Nile, and his conduct became for some years openly scandalous, the difference was not important enough to be noticed. It may, however, be said that peace hath her illusory reputations no less than war. And it is certainly true that in civil life mere capacity for work—the power of killing a dozen secretaries under you, so to speak, as a life-or-death courier kills horses—enables men with common ideas and superstitions to distance all competitors in the strife of political ambition. It was this power of work that astonished Cicero as the most prodigious of Caesar's gifts, as it astonished later observers in Napoleon before it wore him out. How if Caesar were nothing but a Nelson and a Gladstone combined! A prodigy of vitality without any special quality of mind! Nay, with ideas that were worn out before he was born, as Nelson's and Gladstone's were! I have considered that possibility too, and rejected it. I cannot cite all the stories about Caesar which seem to me to show that he was genuinely original; but let me at least point out that I have been careful to attribute nothing but originality to him. Originality gives a man an air of frankness, generosity, and magnanimity by enabling him to estimate the value of truth, money, or success in any particular instance quite independently of convention and moral generalization. He therefore will not, in the ordinary Treasury bench fashion, tell a lie which everybody knows to be a lie (and consequently expects him as a matter of good taste to tell). His lies are not found out: they pass for candors. He understands the paradox of money, and gives it away when he can get most for it: in other words, when its value is least, which is just when a common man tries hardest to get it. He knows that the real moment of success is not the moment apparent to the crowd. Hence, in order to produce an impression of complete disinterestedness and magnanimity, he has only to act with entire selfishness; and this is perhaps the only sense in which a man can be said to be naturally great. It is in this sense that I have represented Caesar as great. Having virtue, he has no need of goodness. He is neither forgiving, frank, nor generous, because a man who is too great to resent has nothing to forgive; a man who says things that other people are afraid to say need be no more frank than

Bismarck was; and there is no generosity in giving things you do not want to people of whom you intend to make use. This distinction between virtue and goodness is not understood in England: hence the poverty of our drama in heroes. Our stage attempts at them are mere goody-goodies. Goodness, in its popular British sense of self-denial, implies that man is vicious by nature, and that supreme goodness is supreme martyrdom. Not sharing that pious opinion, I have not given countenance to it in any of my plays. In this I follow the precedent of the ancient myths, which represent the hero as vanquishing his enemies, not in fair fight, but with enchanted sword, superequine horse and magical invulnerability, the possession of which, from the vulgar moralistic point of view, robs his exploits of any merit whatever.

As to Caesar's sense of humor, there is no more reason to assume that he lacked it than to assume that he was deaf or blind. It is said that on the occasion of his assassination by a conspiracy of moralists (it is always your moralist who makes assassination a duty, on the scaffold or off it), he defended himself until the good Brutes struck him, when he exclaimed "What! you too, Brutes!" and disdained further fight. If this be true, he must have been an incorrigible comedian. But even if we waive this story, or accept the traditional sentimental interpretation of it, there is still abundant evidence of his lightheartedness and adventurousness. Indeed it is clear from his whole history that what has been called his ambition was an instinct for exploration. He had much more of Columbus and Franklin in him than of Henry V.

However, nobody need deny Caesar a share, at least, of the qualities I have attributed to him. All men, much more Julius Caesars, possess all qualities in some degree. The really interesting question is whether I am right in assuming that the way to produce an impression of greatness is by exhibiting a man, not as mortifying his nature by doing his duty, in the manner which our system of putting little men into great positions (not having enough great men in our influential families to go round) forces us to inculcate, but by simply doing what he naturally wants to do. For this raises the question whether our world has not been wrong in its moral theory for the last 2,500 years or so. It must be a constant puzzle to many of us that the Christian era, so excellent in its intentions, should have been practically such a very discreditable episode in the history of the race. I doubt if this is altogether due to the vulgar and sanguinary sensationalism of our religious legends, with their substitution of gross physical torments and public executions for the passion of humanity. Islam, substituting voluptuousness for torment (a merely superficial difference, it is true) has done no better. It may have been the failure of Christianity to emancipate itself from expiatory theories of moral responsibility, guilt, innocence, reward, punishment, and the rest of it, that baffled its intention of changing the world. But these are bound up in all philosophies of creation as opposed to cosmism. They may therefore be regarded as the price we pay for popular religion.

CAPTAIN BRASSBOUND'S CONVERSION

ACT I

On the heights overlooking the harbor of Mogador, a seaport on the west coast of Morocco, the missionary, in the coolness of the late afternoon, is following the precept of Voltaire by cultivating his garden. He is an elderly Scotchman, spiritually a little weatherbeaten, as having to navigate his creed in strange waters crowded with other craft but still a convinced son of the Free Church and the North African Mission, with a faithful brown eye, and a peaceful soul. Physically a wiry small-knit man, well tanned, clean shaven, with delicate resolute features and a twinkle of mild humor. He wears the sun helmet and pagri, the neutral-tinted spectacles, and the white canvas Spanish sand shoes of the modern Scotch missionary: but instead of a cheap tourist's suit from Glasgow, a grey flannel shirt with white collar, a green sailor knot tie with a cheap pin in it, he wears a suit of clean white linen, acceptable in color, if not in cut, to the Moorish mind.

The view from the garden includes much Atlantic Ocean and a long stretch of sandy coast to the south, swept by the north east trade wind, and scantily nourishing a few stunted pepper trees, mangy palms, and tamarisks. The prospect ends, as far as the land is concerned, in little hills that come nearly to the sea: rudiments, these, of the Atlas Mountains. The missionary, having had daily opportunities of looking at this seascape for thirty years or so, pays no heed to it, being absorbed in trimming a huge red geranium bush, to English eyes unnaturally big, which, with a dusty smilax or two, is the sole product of his pet flower-bed. He is sitting to his work on a Moorish stool. In the middle of the garden there is a pleasant seat in the shade of a tamarisk tree. The house is in the south west corner of the garden, and the geranium bush in the north east corner.

At the garden-door of the house there appears presently a man who is clearly no barbarian, being in fact a less agreeable product peculiar to modern commercial civilization. His frame and flesh are those of an ill-nourished lad of seventeen; but his age is inscrutable: only the absence of any sign of grey in his mud colored hair suggests that he is at all events probably under forty, without prejudice to the possibility of his being under twenty. A Londoner would recognize him at once as an extreme but hardy specimen of the abortion produced by nature in a city slum. His utterance, affectedly pumped and hearty, and naturally vulgar and nasal, is ready and fluent: nature, a Board School education, and some kerbstone practice having made him a bit of an orator. His dialect, apart from its base nasal delivery, is not unlike that of smart London society in its tendency to replace diphthongs by vowels (sometimes rather prettily) and to shuffle all the traditional vowel pronunciations. He pronounces ow as ah, and i as aw, using the ordinary ow for o, i for a, a for u, and e for a, with this reservation, that when any vowel is followed by an r he signifies its presence, not by pronouncing the r, which he never does under these circumstances, but by prolonging and modifying the vowel, sometimes even to the extreme degree of pronouncing it properly. As to his yol for l (a compendious delivery of the provincial eh-al), and other metropolitan refinements, amazing to all but cockneys, they cannot be indicated, save in the above imperfect manner, without the aid of a phonetic alphabet. He is dressed in somebody else's very second best as a coast-guardsman, and gives himself the airs of a stage tar with sufficient success to pass as a possible fish porter of bad character in casual employment during busy times at Billingsgate. His manner shows an earnest disposition to ingratiate himself with the missionary, probably for some dishonest purpose.

THE MAN. Awtenoon, Mr. Renkin. (The missionary sits up quickly, and turns, resigning himself dutifully to the interruption.) Yr honor's eolth.

RANKIN (reservedly). Good afternoon, Mr. Drinkwotter.

DRINKWATER. You're not best pleased to be hinterrupted in yr bit o gawdnin bow the lawk o me, gavner.

RANKIN. A missionary knows nothing of leks of that soart, or of disleks either, Mr. Drinkwotter. What can I do for ye?

DRINKWATER (heartily). Nathink, gavner. Awve brort noos fer yer.

RANKIN. Well, sit ye doon.

DRINKWATER. Aw thenk yr honor. (He sits down on the seat under the tree and composes himself for conversation.) Hever ear o Jadge Ellam?

RANKIN. Sir Howrrd Hallam?

DRINKWATER. Thet's im-enginest jadge in Hingland!—awlus gives the ket wen it's robbry with voylence, bless is awt. Aw sy nathink agin im: awm all fer lor mawseolf, AW em.

RANKIN. Well?

DRINKWATER. Hever ear of is sist-in-lor: Lidy Sisly Winefleet?

RANKIN. Do ye mean the celebrated Leddy—the traveller?

DRINKWATER. Yuss: should think aw doo. Walked acrost Harfricar with nathink but a little dawg, and wrowt abaht it in the Dily Mile (the Daily Mail, a popular London newspaper), she did.

RANKIN. Is she Sir Howrrd Hallam's sister-in-law?

DRINKWATER. Deeceased wawfe's sister: yuss: thet's wot SHE is.

RANKIN. Well, what about them?

DRINKWATER. Wot abaht them! Waw, they're EAH. Lannid aht of a steam yacht in Mogador awber not twenty minnits agow. Gorn to the British cornsl's. E'll send em orn to you: e ynt got naowheres to put em. Sor em awr (hire) a Harab an two Krooboys to kerry their laggige. Thort awd cam an teoll yer.

RANKIN. Thank you. It's verra kind of you, Mr. Drinkwotter.

DRINKWATER. Down't mention it, gavner. Lor bless yer, wawn't it you as converted me? Wot was aw wen aw cam eah but a pore lorst sinner? Down't aw ow y'a turn fer thet? Besawds, gavner, this Lidy Sisly Winefleet mawt wor't to tike a walk crost Morocker—a rawd inter the mahntns or sech lawk. Weoll, as you knaow, gavner, thet cawn't be done eah withaht a hescort.

RANKIN. It's impoassible: th' would oall b' murrdered. Morocco is not lek the rest of Africa.

DRINKWATER. No, gavner: these eah Moors ez their religion; an it mikes em dinegerous. Hever convert a Moor, gavner?

RANKIN (with a rueful smile). No.

DRINKWATER (solemnly). Nor never will, gavner.

RANKIN. I have been at work here for twenty-five years, Mr. Drinkwotter; and you are my first and only convert.

DRINKWATER. Down't seem naow good, do it, gavner?

RANKIN. I don't say that. I hope I have done some good. They come to me for medicine when they are ill; and they call me the Christian who is not a thief. THAT is something.

DRINKWATER. Their mawnds kennot rawse to Christiennity lawk hahrs ken, gavner: thet's ah it is. Weoll, ez haw was syin, if a hescort is wornted, there's maw friend and commawnder Kepn Brarsbahnd of the schooner Thenksgivin, an is crew, incloodin mawseolf, will see the lidy an Jadge Ellam through henny little excursion in reason. Yr honor mawt mention it.

RANKIN. I will certainly not propose anything so dangerous as an excursion.

DRINKWATER (virtuously). Naow, gavner, nor would I awst you to. (Shaking his head.) Naow, naow: it IS dinegerous. But hall the more call for a hescort if they should ev it hin their mawnds to gow.

RANKIN. I hope they won't.

DRINKWATER. An sow aw do too, gavner.

RANKIN (pondering). 'Tis strange that they should come to Mogador, of all places; and to my house! I once met Sir Howrrd Hallam, years ago.

DRINKWATER (amazed). Naow! didger? Think o thet, gavner! Waw, sow aw did too. But it were a misunnerstedin, thet wors. Lef the court withaht a stine on maw kerrickter, aw did.

RANKIN (with some indignation). I hope you don't think I met Sir Howrrd in that way.

DRINKWATER. Mawt yeppn to the honestest, best meanin pusson, aw do assure yer, gavner.

RANKIN. I would have you to know that I met him privately, Mr. Drinkwotter. His brother was a dear friend of mine. Years ago. He went out to the West Indies.

DRINKWATER. The Wust Hindies! Jist acrost there, tather sawd thet howcean (pointing seaward)! Dear me! We cams hin with vennity, an we deepawts in dawkness. Down't we, gavner?

RANKIN (pricking up his ears). Eh? Have you been reading that little book I gave you?

DRINKWATER. Aw hev, et odd tawms. Very camfitn, gavner. (He rises, apprehensive lest further catechism should find him unprepared.) Awll sy good awtenoon, gavner: you're busy hexpectin o Sr Ahrd an Lidy Sisly, ynt yer? (About to go.)

RANKIN (stopping him). No, stop: we're oalways ready for travellers here. I have something else to say—a question to ask you.

DRINKWATER (with a misgiving, which he masks by exaggerating his hearty sailor manner). An weollcome, yr honor.

RANKIN. Who is this Captain Brassbound?

DRINKWATER (guiltily). Kepn Brarsbahnd! E's-weoll, e's maw Kepn, gavner.

RANKIN. Yes. Well?

DRINKWATER (feebly). Kepn of the schooner Thenksgivin, gavner.

RANKIN (searchingly). Have ye ever haird of a bad character in these seas called Black Paquito?

DRINKWATER (with a sudden radiance of complete enlightenment). Aoh, nar aw tikes yer wiv me, yr honor. Nah sammun es bin a teolln you thet Kepn Brarsbahnd an Bleck Pakeetow is hawdentically the sime pussn. Ynt thet sow?

RANKIN. That is so. (Drinkwater slaps his knee triumphantly. The missionary proceeds determinedly) And the someone was a verra honest, straightforward man, as far as I could judge.

DRINKWATER (embracing the implication). Course a wors, gavner: Ev aw said a word agin him? Ev aw nah?

RANKIN. But is Captain Brassbound Black Paquito then?

DRINKWATER. Waw, it's the nime is blessed mather give im at er knee, bless is little awt! Ther ynt naow awm in it. She ware a Wust Hinjin—howver there agin, yer see (pointing seaward)—leastwaws, naow she worn't: she were a Brazilian, aw think; an Pakeetow's Brazilian for a bloomin little perrit—awskin yr pawdn for the word. (Sentimentally) Lawk as a Hinglish lidy mawt call er little boy Birdie.

RANKIN (not quite convinced). But why BLACK Paquito?

DRINKWATER (artlessly). Waw, the bird in its netral stite bein green, an e evin bleck air, y' knaow—

RANKIN (cutting him short). I see. And now I will put ye another question. WHAT is Captain Brassbound, or Paquito, or whatever he calls himself?

DRINKWATER (officiously). Brarsbahnd, gavner. Awlus calls isseolf Brarsbahnd.

RANKIN. Well. Brassbound, then. What is he?

DRINKWATER (fervently). You awsks me wot e is, gavner?

RANKIN (firmly). I do.

DRINKWATER (with rising enthusiasm). An shll aw teoll yer wot e is, yr honor?

RANKIN (not at all impressed). If ye will be so good, Mr. Drinkwotter.

DRINKWATER (with overwhelming conviction). Then awll teoll you, gavner, wot he is. Ee's a Paffick Genlmn: thet's wot e is.

RANKIN (gravely). Mr. Drinkwotter: pairfection is an attribute, not of West Coast captains, but of thr Maaker. And there are gentlemen and gentlemen in the world, espaecially in these latitudes. Which sort of gentleman is he?

DRINKWATER. Hinglish genlmn, gavner. Hinglish speakin; Hinglish fawther; West Hinjin plawnter; Hinglish true blue breed. (Reflectively) Tech o brahn from the mather, preps, she bein Brazilian.

RANKIN. Now on your faith as a Christian, Felix Drinkwotter, is Captain Brassbound a slaver or not?

DRINKWATER (surprised into his natural cockney pertness). Naow e ynt.

RANKIN. Are ye SURE?

DRINKWATER. Waw, a sliver is abaht the wanne thing in the wy of a genlmn o fortn thet e YNT.

RANKIN. I've haird that expression "gentleman of fortune" before, Mr. Drinkwotter. It means pirate. Do ye know that?

DRINKWATER. Bless y'r awt, y' cawnt be a pawrit naradys. Waw, the aw seas is wuss pleest nor Piccadilly Suckus. If aw was to do orn thet there Hetlentic Howcean the things aw did as a bwoy in the Worterleoo Rowd, awd ev maw air cat afore aw could turn maw ed. Pawrit be blaowed!—awskink yr pawdn, gavner. Nah, jest to shaow you ah little thet there striteforard man y' mide mention on knaowed wot e was atorkin abaht: oo would you spowse was the marster to wich Kepn Brarsbahnd served apprentice, as yr mawt sy?

RANKIN. I don't know.

DRINKWATER. Gawdn, gavner, Gawdn. Gawdn o Kawtoom—stetcher stends in Trifawlgr Square to this dy. Trined Bleck Pakeetow in smawshin hap the slive riders, e did. Promist Gawdn e wouldn't never smaggle slives nor gin, an (with suppressed aggravation) WOWN'T, gavner, not if we gows dahn on ahr bloomin bended knees to im to do it.

RANKIN (drily). And DO ye go down on your bended knees to him to do it?

DRINKWATER (somewhat abashed). Some of huz is hanconverted men, gavner; an they sy: You smaggles wanne thing, Kepn; waw not hanather?

RANKIN. We've come to it at last. I thought so. Captain Brassbound is a smuggler.

DRINKWATER. Weoll, waw not? Waw not, gavner? Ahrs is a Free Tride nition. It gows agin us as Hinglishmen to see these bloomin furriners settin ap their Castoms Ahses and spheres o hinfluence and sich lawk hall owver Arfricar. Daown't Harfricar belong as much to huz as to them? thet's wot we sy. Ennywys, there ynt naow awm in ahr business. All we daz is hescort, tourist HOR commercial. Cook's hexcursions to the Hatlas Mahntns: thet's hall it is. Waw, it's spreadin civlawzytion, it is. Ynt it nah?

RANKIN. You think Captain Brassbound's crew sufficiently equipped for that, do you?

DRINKWATER. Hee-quipped! Haw should think sow. Lawtnin rawfles, twelve shots in the meggezine! Oo's to storp us?

RANKIN. The most dangerous chieftain in these parts, the Sheikh Sidi el Assif, has a new American machine pistol which fires ten bullets without loadin; and his rifle has sixteen shots in the magazine.

DRINKWATER (indignantly). Yuss; an the people that sells sich things into the ends o' them eathen bleck niggers calls theirseolves Christians! It's a crool shime, sow it is.

RANKIN. If a man has the heart to pull the trigger, it matters little what color his hand is, Mr. Drinkwotter. Have ye anything else to say to me this afternoon?

DRINKWATER (rising). Nathink, gavner, cept to wishyer the bust o yolth, and a many cornverts. Awtenoon, gavner.

RANKIN. Good afternoon to ye, Mr. Drinkwotter.

As Drinkwater turns to go, a Moorish porter comes from the house with two Krooboys.

THE PORTER (at the door, addressing Rankin). Bikouros (Moroccan for Epicurus, a general Moorish name for the missionaries, who are supposed by the Moors to have chosen their calling through a love of luxurious idleness): I have brought to your house a Christian dog and his woman.

DRINKWATER. There's eathen menners fer yer! Calls Sr Ahrd Ellam an Lidy Winefleet a Christian dorg and is woman! If ee ed you in the dorck et the Centl Crimnal, you'd fawnd aht oo was the dorg and oo was is marster, pretty quick, you would.

RANKIN. Have you broat their boxes?

THE PORTER. By Allah, two camel loads!

RANKIN. Have you been paid?

THE PORTER. Only one miserable dollar, Bikouros. I have brought them to your house. They will pay you. Give me something for bringing gold to your door.

DRINKWATER. Yah! You oughter bin bawn a Christian, you ought. You knaow too mach.

RANKIN. You have broat onnly trouble and expense to my door, Hassan; and you know it. Have I ever charged your wife and children for my medicines?

HASSAN (philosophically). It is always permitted by the Prophet to ask, Bikouros. (He goes cheerfully into the house with the Krooboys.)

DRINKWATER. Jist thort eed trah it orn, a did. Hooman nitre is the sime everywheres. Them eathens is jast lawk you an' me, gavner.

A lady and gentleman, both English, come into the garden. The gentleman, more than elderly, is facing old age on compulsion, not resignedly. He is clean shaven, and has a brainy rectangular forehead, a resolute nose with strongly governed nostrils, and a tightly fastened down mouth which has evidently shut in much temper and anger in its time. He has a habit of deliberately assumed authority and dignity, but is trying to take life more genially and easily in his character of tourist, which is further borne out by his white hat and summery racecourse attire.

The lady is between thirty and forty, tall, very goodlooking, sympathetic, intelligent, tender and humorous, dressed with cunning simplicity not as a businesslike, tailor made, gaitered tourist, but as if she lived at the next cottage and had dropped in for tea in blouse and flowered straw hat. A woman of great vitality and humanity, who begins a casual acquaintance at the point usually attained by English people after thirty years acquaintance when they are capable of reaching it at all. She pounces genially on Drinkwater, who is smirking at her, hat in hand, with an air of hearty welcome. The gentleman, on the other hand, comes down the side of the garden next the house, instinctively maintaining a distance between himself and the others.

THE LADY (to Drinkwater). How dye do? Are you the missionary?

DRINKWATER (modestly). Naow, lidy, aw will not deceive you, thow the mistike his but netral. Awm wanne of the missionary's good works, lidy—is first cornvert, a umble British seaman—countrymen o yours, lidy, and of is lawdship's. This eah is Mr. Renkin, the bust worker in the wust cowst vawnyawd. (Introducing the judge) Mr. Renkin: is lawdship Sr Ahrd Ellam. (He withdraws discreetly into the house.)

SIR HOWARD (to Rankin). I am sorry to intrude on you, Mr. Rankin; but in the absence of a hotel there seems to be no alternative.

LADY CICELY (beaming on him). Besides, we would so much RATHER stay with you, if you will have us, Mr. Rankin.

SIR HOWARD (introducing her). My sister-in-law, Lady Cicely Waynflete, Mr. Rankin.

RANKIN. I am glad to be of service to your leddyship. You will be wishing to have some tea after your journey, I'm thinking.

LADY CICELY. Thoughtful man that you are, Mr. Rankin! But we've had some already on board the yacht. And I've arranged everything with your servants; so you must go on gardening just as if we were not here.

SIR HOWARD. I am sorry to have to warn you, Mr. Rankin, that Lady Cicely, from travelling in Africa, has acquired a habit of walking into people's houses and behaving as if she were in her own.

LADY CICELY. But, my dear Howard, I assure you the natives like it.

RANKIN (gallantly). So do I.

LADY CICELY (delighted). Oh, that is so nice of you, Mr. Rankin. This is a delicious country! And the people seem so good! They have such nice faces! We had such a handsome Moor to carry our luggage up! And two perfect pets of Krooboys! Did you notice their faces, Howard?

SIR HOWARD. I did; and I can confidently say, after a long experience of faces of the worst type looking at me from the dock, that I have never seen so entirely villainous a trio as that Moor and the two Krooboys, to whom you gave five dollars when they would have been perfectly satisfied with one.

RANKIN (throwing up his hands). Five dollars! 'Tis easy to see you are not Scotch, my leddy.

LADY CICELY. Oh, poor things, they must want it more than we do; and you know, Howard, that Mahometans never spend money in drink.

RANKIN. Excuse me a moment, my leddy. I have a word in season to say to that same Moor. (He goes into the house.)

LADY CICELY (walking about the garden, looking at the view and at the flowers). I think this is a perfectly heavenly place.

Drinkwater returns from the house with a chair.

DRINKWATER (placing the chair for Sir Howard). Awskink yr pawdn for the libbety, Sr Ahrd.

SIR HOWARD (looking a him). I have seen you before somewhere.

DRINKWATER. You ev, Sr Ahrd. But aw do assure yer it were hall a mistike.

SIR HOWARD. As usual. (He sits down.) Wrongfully convicted, of course.

DRINKWATER (with sly delight). Naow, gavner. (Half whispering, with an ineffable grin) Wrorngfully hacquittid!

SIR HOWARD. Indeed! That's the first case of the kind I have ever met.

DRINKWATER. Lawd, Sr Ahrd, wot jagginses them jurymen was! You an me knaowed it too, didn't we?

SIR HOWARD. I daresay we did. I am sorry to say I forget the exact nature of the difficulty you were in. Can you refresh my memory?

DRINKWATER. Owny the aw sperrits o youth, y' lawdship. Worterleoo Rowd kice. Wot they calls Ooliganism.

SIR HOWARD. Oh! You were a Hooligan, were you?

LADY CICELY (puzzled). A Hooligan!

DRINKWATER (deprecatingly). Nime giv huz pore thortless leds baw a gent on the Dily Chrornicle, lidy. (Rankin returns. Drinkwater immediately withdraws, stopping the missionary for a moment near the threshold to say, touching his forelock) Awll eng abaht within ile, gavner, hin kice aw should be wornted. (He goes into the house with soft steps.)

Lady Cicely sits down on the bench under the tamarisk. Rankin takes his stool from the flowerbed and sits down on her left, Sir Howard being on her right.

LADY CICELY. What a pleasant face your sailor friend has, Mr. Rankin! He has been so frank and truthful with us. You know I don't think anybody can pay me a greater compliment than to be quite sincere with me at first sight. It's the perfection of natural good manners.

SIR HOWARD. You must not suppose, Mr. Rankin, that my sister-in-law talks nonsense on purpose. She will continue to believe in your friend until he steals her watch; and even then she will find excuses for him.

RANKIN (drily changing the subject). And how have ye been, Sir Howrrd, since our last meeting that morning nigh forty year ago down at the docks in London?

SIR HOWARD (greatly surprised, pulling himself together) Our last meeting! Mr. Rankin: have I been unfortunate enough to forget an old acquaintance?

RANKIN. Well, perhaps hardly an acquaintance, Sir Howrrd. But I was a close friend of your brother Miles: and when he sailed for Brazil I was one of the little party that saw him off. You were one of the party also, if I'm not mistaken. I took particular notice of you because you were Miles's brother and I had never seen ye before. But ye had no call to take notice of me.

SIR HOWARD (reflecting). Yes: there was a young friend of my brother's who might well be you. But the name, as I recollect it, was Leslie.

RANKIN. That was me, sir. My name is Leslie Rankin; and your brother and I were always Miles and Leslie to one another.

SIR HOWARD (pluming himself a little). Ah! that explains it. I can trust my memory still, Mr. Rankin; though some people do complain that I am growing old.

RANKIN. And where may Miles be now, Sir Howard?

SIR HOWARD (abruptly). Don't you know that he is dead?

RANKIN (much shocked). Never haird of it. Dear, dear: I shall never see him again; and I can scarcely bring his face to mind after all these years. (With moistening eyes, which at once touch Lady Cicely's sympathy) I'm right sorry—right sorry.

SIR HOWARD (decorously subduing his voice). Yes: he did not live long: indeed, he never came back to England. It must be nearly thirty years ago now that he died in the West Indies on his property there.

RANKIN (surprised). His proaperty! Miles with a proaperty!

SIR HOWARD. Yes: he became a planter, and did well out there, Mr. Rankin. The history of that property is a very curious and interesting one—at least it is so to a lawyer like myself.

RANKIN. I should be glad to hear it for Miles's sake, though I am no lawyer, Sir Howrrd.

LADY CICELY. I never knew you had a brother, Howard.

SIR HOWARD (not pleased by this remark). Perhaps because you never asked me. (Turning more blandly to Rankin) I will tell you the story, Mr. Rankin. When Miles died, he left an estate in one of the West Indian islands. It was in charge of an agent who was a sharpish fellow, with all his wits about him. Now, sir, that man did a thing which probably could hardly be done with impunity even here in Morocco, under the most barbarous of surviving civilizations. He quite simply took the estate for himself and kept it.

RANKIN. But how about the law?

SIR HOWARD. The law, sir, in that island, consisted practically of the Attorney General and the Solicitor General; and these gentlemen were both retained by the agent. Consequently there was no solicitor in the island to take up the case against him.

RANKIN. Is such a thing possible to-day in the British Empire?

SIR HOWARD (calmly). Oh, quite. Quite.

LADY CICELY. But could not a firstrate solicitor have been sent out from London?

SIR HOWARD. No doubt, by paying him enough to compensate him for giving up his London practice: that is, rather more than there was any reasonable likelihood of the estate proving worth.

RANKIN. Then the estate was lost?

SIR HOWARD. Not permanently. It is in my hands at present.

RANKIN. Then how did ye get it back?

SIR HOWARD (with crafty enjoyment of his own cunning). By hoisting the rogue with his own petard. I had to leave matters as they were for many years; for I had my own position in the world to make. But at last I made it. In the course of a holiday trip to the West Indies, I found that this dishonest agent had left the island, and placed the estate in the hands of an agent of his own, whom he was foolish enough to pay very badly. I put the case before that agent; and he decided to treat the estate as my property. The robber now found himself in exactly the same position he had formerly forced me into. Nobody in the island would act against me, least of all the Attorney and Solicitor General, who appreciated my influence at the Colonial Office. And so I got the estate back. "The mills of the gods grind slowly," Mr. Rankin; "but they grind exceeding small."

LADY CICELY. Now I suppose if I'd done such a clever thing in England, you'd have sent me to prison.

SIR HOWARD. Probably, unless you had taken care to keep outside the law against conspiracy. Whenever you wish to do anything against the law, Cicely, always consult a good solicitor first.

LADY CICELY. So I do. But suppose your agent takes it into his head to give the estate back to his wicked old employer!

SIR HOWARD. I heartily wish he would.

RANKIN (openeyed). You wish he WOULD!!

SIR HOWARD. Yes. A few years ago the collapse of the West Indian sugar industry converted the income of the estate into an annual loss of about 150 pounds a year. If I can't sell it soon, I shall simply abandon it—unless you, Mr. Rankin, would like to take it as a present.

RANKIN (laughing). I thank your lordship: we have estates enough of that sort in Scotland. You're setting with your back to the sun, Leddy Ceecily, and losing something worth looking at. See there. (He rises and points seaward, where the rapid twilight of the latitude has begun.)

LADY CICELY (getting up to look and uttering a cry of admiration). Oh, how lovely!

SIR HOWARD (also rising). What are those hills over there to the southeast?

RANKIN. They are the outposts, so to speak, of the Atlas Mountains.

LADY CICELY. The Atlas Mountains! Where Shelley's witch lived! We'll make an excursion to them to-morrow, Howard.

RANKIN. That's impoassible, my leddy. The natives are verra dangerous.

LADY CICELY. Why? Has any explorer been shooting them?

RANKIN. No. But every man of them believes he will go to heaven if he kills an unbeliever.

LADY CICELY. Bless you, dear Mr. Rankin, the people in England believe that they will go to heaven if they give all their property to the poor. But they don't do it. I'm not a bit afraid of that.

RANKIN. But they are not accustomed to see women going about unveiled.

LADY CICELY. I always get on best with people when they can see my face.

SIR HOWARD. Cicely: you are talking great nonsense and you know it. These people have no laws to restrain them, which means, in plain English, that they are habitual thieves and murderers.

RANKIN. Nay, nay: not exactly that.

LADY CICELY (indignantly). Of course not. You always think, Howard, that nothing prevents people killing each other but the fear of your hanging them for it. But what nonsense that is! And how wicked! If these people weren't here for some good purpose, they wouldn't have been made, would they, Mr. Rankin?

RANKIN. That is a point, certainly, Leddy Ceecily.

SIR HOWARD. Oh, if you are going to talk theology—

LADY CICELY. Well, why not? theology is as respectable as law, I should think. Besides, I'm only talking commonsense. Why do people get killed by savages? Because instead of being polite to them, and saying Howdyedo? like me, people aim pistols at them. I've been among savages—cannibals and all sorts. Everybody said they'd kill me. But when I met them, I said Howdyedo? and they were quite nice. The kings always wanted to marry me.

SIR HOWARD. That does not seem to me to make you any safer here, Cicely. You shall certainly not stir a step beyond the protection of the consul, if I can help it, without a strong escort.

LADY CICELY. I don't want an escort.

SIR HOWARD. I do. And I suppose you will expect me to accompany you.

RANKIN. 'Tis not safe, Leddy Ceecily. Really and truly, 'tis not safe. The tribes are verra fierce; and there are cities here that no Christian has ever set foot in. If you go without being well protected, the first chief you meet well seize you and send you back again to prevent his followers murdering you.

LADY CICELY. Oh, how nice of him, Mr. Rankin!

RANKIN. He would not do it for your sake, Leddy Ceecily, but for his own. The Sultan would get into trouble with England if you were killed; and the Sultan would kill the chief to pacify the English government.

LADY CICELY. But I always go everywhere. I KNOW the people here won't touch me. They have such nice faces and such pretty scenery.

SIR HOWARD (to Rankin, sitting down again resignedly). You can imagine how much use there is in talking to a woman who admires the faces of the ruffians who infest these ports, Mr. Rankin. Can anything be done in the way of an escort?

RANKIN. There is a certain Captain Brassbound here who trades along the coast, and occasionally escorts parties of merchants on journeys into the interior. I understand that he served under Gordon in the Soudan.

SIR HOWARD. That sounds promising. But I should like to know a little more about him before I trust myself in his hands.

RANKIN. I quite agree with you, Sir Howrrd. I'll send Felix Drinkwotter for him. (He claps his hands. An Arab boy appears at the house door.) Muley: is sailor man here? (Muley nods.) Tell sailor man bring captain. (Muley nods and goes.)

SIR HOWARD. Who is Drinkwater?

RANKIN. His agent, or mate: I don't rightly know which.

LADY CICELY. Oh, if he has a mate named Felix Drinkwater, it must be quite a respectable crew. It is such a nice name.

RANKIN. You saw him here just now. He is a convert of mine.

LADY CICELY (delighted). That nice truthful sailor!

SIR HOWARD (horrified). What! The Hooligan!

RANKIN (puzzled). Hooligan? No, my lord: he is an Englishman.

SIR HOWARD. My dear Mr. Rankin, this man was tried before me on a charge of street ruffianism.

RANKIN. So he told me. He was badly broat up, I am afraid. But he is now a converted man.

LADY CICELY. Of course he is. His telling you so frankly proves it. You know, really, Howard, all those poor people whom you try are more sinned against than sinning. If you would only talk to them in a friendly way instead of passing cruel sentences on them, you would find them quite nice to you. (Indignantly) I won't have this poor man trampled on merely because his mother brought him up as a Hooligan. I am sure nobody could be nicer than he was when he spoke to us.

SIR HOWARD. In short, we are to have an escort of Hooligans commanded by a filibuster. Very well, very well. You will most likely admire all their faces; and I have no doubt at all that they will admire yours.

Drinkwater comes from the house with an Italian dressed in a much worn suit of blue serge, a dilapidated Alpine hat, and boots laced with scraps of twine. He remains near the door, whilst Drinkwater comes forward between Sir Howard and Lady Cicely.

DRINKWATER. Yr honor's servant. (To the Italian) Mawtzow: is lawdship Sr Ahrd Ellam. (Marzo touches his hat.) Er Lidyship Lidy Winefleet. (Marzo touches his hat.) Hawtellian shipmite, lidy. Hahr chef.

LADY CICELY (nodding affably to Marzo). Howdyedo? I love Italy. What part of it were you born in?

DRINKWATER. Worn't bawn in Hitly at all, lidy. Bawn in Ettn Gawdn (Hatton Garden). Hawce barrer an street pianner Hawtellian, lidy: thet's wot e is. Kepn Brarsbahnd's respects to yr honors; an e awites yr commawnds.

RANKIN. Shall we go indoors to see him?

SIR HOWARD. I think we had better have a look at him by daylight.

RANKIN. Then we must lose no time: the dark is soon down in this latitude. (To Drinkwater) Will ye ask him to step out here to us, Mr. Drinkwotter?

DRINKWATER. Rawt you aw, gavner. (He goes officiously into the house.)

Lady Cicely and Rankin sit down as before to receive the Captain. The light is by this time waning rapidly, the darkness creeping west into the orange crimson.

LADY CICELY (whispering). Don't you feel rather creepy, Mr. Rankin? I wonder what he'll be like.

RANKIN. I misdoubt me he will not answer, your leddyship.

There is a scuffling noise in the house; and Drinkwater shoots out through the doorway across the garden with every appearance of having been violently kicked. Marzo immediately hurries down the garden on Sir Howard's right out of the neighborhood of the doorway.

DRINKWATER (trying to put a cheerful air on much mortification and bodily anguish). Narsty step to thet ere door tripped me hap, it did. (Raising his voice and narrowly escaping a squeak of pain) Kepn Brarsbahnd. (He gets as far from the house as possible, on Rankin's left. Rankin rises to receive his guest.)

An olive complexioned man with dark southern eyes and hair comes from the house. Age about 36. Handsome features, but joyless; dark eyebrows drawn towards one another; mouth set grimly; nostrils large and strained: a face set to one tragic purpose. A man of few words, fewer gestures, and much significance. On the whole, interesting, and even attractive, but not friendly. He stands for a moment, saturnine in the ruddy light, to see who is present, looking in a singular and rather deadly way at Sir Howard; then with some surprise and uneasiness at Lady Cicely. Finally he comes down into the middle of the garden, and confronts Rankin, who has been glaring at him in consternation from the moment of his entrance, and continues to do so in so marked a way that the glow in Brassbound's eyes deepens as he begins to take offence.

BRASSBOUND. Well, sir, have you stared your fill at me?

RANKIN (recovering himself with a start). I ask your pardon for my bad manners, Captain Brassbound. Ye are extraordinair lek an auld college friend of mine, whose face I said not ten minutes gone that I could no longer bring to mind. It was as if he had come from the grave to remind me of it.

BRASSBOUND. Why have you sent for me?

RANKIN. We have a matter of business with ye, Captain.

BRASSBOUND. Who are "we"?

RANKIN. This is Sir Howrrd Hallam, who will be well known to ye as one of Her Majesty's judges.

BRASSBOUND (turning the singular look again on Sir Howard). The friend of the widow! the protector of the fatherless!

SIR HOWARD (startled). I did not know I was so favorably spoken of in these parts, Captain Brassbound. We want an escort for a trip into the mountains.

BRASSBOUND (ignoring this announcement). Who is the lady?

RANKIN. Lady Ceecily Waynflete, his lordship's sister-in-law.

LADY CICELY. Howdyedo, Captain Brassbound? (He bows gravely.)

SIR HOWARD (a little impatient of these questions, which strike him as somewhat impertinent). Let us come to business, if you please. We are thinking of making a short excursion to see the country about here. Can you provide us with an escort of respectable, trustworthy men?

BRASSBOUND. No.

DRINKWATER (in strong remonstrance). Nah, nah, nah! Nah look eah, Kepn, y'knaow—

BRASSBOUND (between his teeth). Hold your tongue.

DRINKWATER (abjectly). Yuss, Kepn.

RANKIN. I understood it was your business to provide escorts, Captain Brassbound.

BRASSBOUND. You were rightly informed. That IS my business.

LADY CICELY. Then why won't you do it for us?

BRASSBOUND. You are not content with an escort. You want respectable, trustworthy men. You should have brought a division of London policemen with you. My men are neither respectable nor trustworthy.

DRINKWATER (unable to contain himself). Nah, nah, look eah, Kepn. If you want to be moddist, be moddist on your aown accahnt, nort on mawn.

BRASSBOUND. You see what my men are like. That rascal (indicating Marzo) would cut a throat for a dollar if he had courage enough.

MARZO. I not understand. I no spik Englis.

BRASSBOUND. This thing (pointing to Drinkwater) is the greatest liar, thief, drunkard, and rapscallion on the west coast.

DRINKWATER (affecting an ironic indifference). Gow orn, Gow orn. Sr Ahrd ez erd witnesses to maw kerrickter afoah. E knaows ah mech to believe of em.

LADY CICELY. Captain Brassbound: I have heard all that before about the blacks; and I found them very nice people when they were properly treated.

DRINKWATER (chuckling: the Italian is also grinning). Nah, Kepn, nah! Owp yr prahd o y'seolf nah.

BRASSBOUND. I quite understand the proper treatment for him, madam. If he opens his mouth again without my leave, I will break every bone in his skin.

LADY CICELY (in her most sunnily matter-of-fact way). Does Captain Brassbound always treat you like this, Mr. Drinkwater?

Drinkwater hesitates, and looks apprehensively at the Captain.

BRASSBOUND. Answer, you dog, when the lady orders you. (To Lady Cicely) Do not address him as Mr. Drinkwater, madam: he is accustomed to be called Brandyfaced Jack.

DRINKWATER (indignantly). Eah, aw sy! nah look eah, Kepn: maw nime is Drinkworter. You awsk em et Sin Jorn's in the Worterleoo Rowd. Orn maw grenfawther's tombstown, it is.

BRASSBOUND. It will be on your own tombstone, presently, if you cannot hold your tongue. (Turning to the others) Let us understand one another, if you please. An escort here, or anywhere where there are no regular disciplined forces, is what its captain makes it. If I undertake this business, I shall be your escort. I may require a dozen men, just as I may require a dozen horses. Some of the horses will be vicious; so will all the men. If either horse or man tries any of his viciousness on me, so much the worse for him; but it will make no difference to you. I will order my men to behave themselves before the lady; and they shall obey their orders. But the lady will please understand that I take my own way with them and suffer no interference.

LADY CICELY. Captain Brassbound: I don't want an escort at all. It will simply get us all into danger; and I shall have the trouble of getting it out again. That's what escorts always do. But since Sir Howard prefers an escort, I think you had better stay at home and let me take charge of it. I know your men will get on perfectly well if they're properly treated.

DRINKWATER (with enthusiasm). Feed aht o yr and, lidy, we would.

BRASSBOUND (with sardonic assent). Good. I agree. (To Drinkwater) You shall go without me.

DRINKWATER. (terrified). Eah! Wot are you a syin orn? We cawn't gow withaht yer. (To Lady Cicely) Naow, lidy: it wouldn't be for yr hown good. Yer cawn't hexpect a lot o poor honeddikited men lawk huz to ran ahrseolvs into dineger withaht naow Kepn to teoll us wot to do. Naow, lidy: hoonawted we stend: deevawdid we fall.

LADY CICELY. Oh, if you prefer your captain, have him by all means. Do you LIKE to be treated as he treats you?

DRINKWATER (with a smile of vanity). Weoll, lidy: y cawn't deenaw that e's a Paffick Genlmn. Bit hawbitrairy, preps; but hin a genlmn you looks for sich. It tikes a hawbitrairy wanne to knock aht them eathen Shikes, aw teoll yer.

BRASSBOUND. That's enough. Go.

DRINKWATER. Weoll, aw was hownly a teolln the lidy thet— (A threatening movement from Brassbound cuts him short. He flies for his life into the house, followed by the Italian.)

BRASSBOUND. Your ladyship sees. These men serve me by their own free choice. If they are dissatisfied, they go. If I am dissatisfied, they go. They take care that I am not dissatisfied.

SIR HOWARD (who has listened with approval and growing confidence). Captain Brassbound: you are the man I want. If your terms are at all reasonable, I will accept your services if we decide to make an excursion. You do not object, Cicely, I hope.

LADY CICELY. Oh no. After all, those men must really like you, Captain Brassbound. I feel sure you have a kind heart. You have such nice eyes.

SIR HOWARD (scandalized). My DEAR Cicely: you really must restrain your expressions of confidence in people's eyes and faces. (To Brassbound) Now, about terms, Captain?

BRASSBOUND. Where do you propose to go?

SIR HOWARD. I hardly know. Where CAN we go, Mr. Rankin?

RANKIN. Take my advice, Sir Howrrd. Don't go far.

BRASSBOUND. I can take you to Meskala, from which you can see the Atlas Mountains. From Meskala I can take you to an ancient castle in the hills, where you can put up as long as you please. The customary charge is half a dollar a man per day and his food. I charge double.

SIR HOWARD. I suppose you answer for your men being sturdy fellows, who will stand to their guns if necessary.

BRASSBOUND. I can answer for their being more afraid of me than of the Moors.

LADY CICELY. That doesn't matter in the least, Howard. The important thing, Captain Brassbound, is: first, that we should have as few men as possible, because men give such a lot of trouble travelling. And then, they must have good lungs and not be always catching cold. Above all, their clothes must be of good wearing material. Otherwise I shall be nursing and stitching and mending all the way; and it will be trouble enough, I assure you, to keep them washed and fed without that.

BRASSBOUND (haughtily). My men, madam, are not children in the nursery.

LADY CICELY (with unanswerable conviction). Captain Brassbound: all men are children in the nursery. I see that you don't notice things. That poor Italian had only one proper bootlace: the other was a bit of string. And I am sure from Mr. Drinkwater's complexion that he ought to have some medicine.

BRASSBOUND (outwardly determined not to be trifled with: inwardly puzzled and rather daunted). Madam: if you want an escort, I can provide you with an escort. If you want a Sunday School treat, I can NOT provide it.

LADY CICELY (with sweet melancholy). Ah, don't you wish you could, Captain? Oh, if I could only show you my children from Waynflete Sunday School! The darlings would love this place, with all the camels and black men. I'm sure you would enjoy having them here, Captain Brassbound; and it would be such an education for your men! (Brassbound stares at her with drying lips.)

SIR HOWARD. Cicely: when you have quite done talking nonsense to Captain Brassbound, we can proceed to make some definite arrangement with him.

LADY CICELY. But it's arranged already. We'll start at eight o'clock to-morrow morning, if you please, Captain. Never mind about the Italian: I have a big box of clothes with me for my brother in Rome; and there are some bootlaces in it. Now go home to bed and don't fuss yourself. All you have to do is to bring your men round; and I'll see to the rest. Men are always so nervous about moving. Goodnight. (She offers him her hand. Surprised, he pulls off his cap for the first time. Some scruple prevents him from taking her hand at once. He hesitates; then turns to Sir Howard and addresses him with warning earnestness.)

BRASSBOUND. Sir Howard Hallam: I advise you not to attempt this expedition.

SIR HOWARD. Indeed! Why?

BRASSBOUND. You are safe here. I warn you, in those hills there is a justice that is not the justice of your courts in England. If you have wronged a man, you may meet that man there. If you have wronged a woman, you may meet her son there. The justice of those hills is the justice of vengeance.

SIR HOWARD (faintly amused). You are superstitious, Captain. Most sailors are, I notice. However, I have complete confidence in your escort.

BRASSBOUND (almost threateningly). Take care. The avenger may be one of the escort.

SIR HOWARD. I have already met the only member of your escort who might have borne a grudge against me, Captain; and he was acquitted.

BRASSBOUND. You are fated to come, then?

SIR HOWARD (smiling). It seems so.

BRASSBOUND. On your head be it! (To Lady Cicely, accepting her hand at last) Goodnight.

He goes. It is by this time starry night.

ACT II

Midday. A roam in a Moorish castle. A divan seat runs round the dilapidated adobe walls, which are partly painted, partly faced with white tiles patterned in green and yellow. The ceiling is made up of little squares, painted in bright colors, with gilded edges, and ornamented with gilt knobs. On the cement floor are mattings, sheepskins, and leathern cushions with geometrical patterns on them. There is a tiny Moorish table in the middle; and at it a huge saddle, with saddle cloths of various colors, showing that the room is used by foreigners accustomed to chairs. Anyone sitting at the table in this seat would have the chief entrance, a large horseshoe arch, on his left, and another saddle seat between him and the arch; whilst, if susceptible to draughts, he would probably catch cold from a little Moorish door in the wall behind him to his right.

Two or three of Brassbound's men, overcome by the midday heat, sprawl supine on the floor, with their reefer coats under their heads, their knees uplifted, and their calves laid comfortably on the divan. Those who wear shirts have them open at the throat for greater coolness. Some have jerseys. All wear boots and belts, and have guns ready to their hands. One of them, lying with his head against the second saddle seat, wears what was once a fashionable white English yachting suit. He is evidently a pleasantly worthless young English gentleman gone to the bad, but retaining sufficient self-respect to shave carefully and brush his hair, which is wearing thin, and does not seem to have been luxuriant even in its best days.

The silence is broken only by the snores of the young gentleman, whose mouth has fallen open, until a few distant shots half waken him. He shuts his mouth convulsively, and opens his eyes sleepily. A door is violently kicked outside; and the voice of Drinkwater is heard raising urgent alarm.

DRINKWATER. Wot ow! Wike ap there, will yr. Wike ap. (He rushes in through the horseshoe arch, hot and excited, and runs round, kicking the sleepers) Nah then. Git ap. Git ap, will yr, Kiddy Redbrook. (He gives the young qentleman a rude shove.)

REDBOOK (sitting up). Stow that, will you. What's amiss?

DRINKWATER (disgusted). Wot's amiss! Didn't eah naow fawrin, I spowse.

REDBROOK. No.

DRINKWATER (sneering). Naow. Thort it sifer nort, didn't yr?

REDBROOK (with crisp intelligence). What! You're running away, are you? (He springs up, crying) Look alive, Johnnies: there's danger. Brandyfaced Jack's on the run. (They spring up hastily, grasping their guns.)

DRINKWATER. Dineger! Yuss: should think there wors dineger. It's howver, thow, as it mowstly his baw the tawm YOU'RE awike. (They relapse into lassitude.) Waw wasn't you on the look-aht to give us a end? Bin hattecked baw the Benny Seeras (Beni Siras), we ev, an ed to rawd for it pretty strite, too, aw teoll yr. Mawtzow is it: the bullet glawnst all rahnd is bloomin brisket. Brarsbahnd e dropt the Shike's oss at six unnern fifty yawds. (Bustling them about) Nah then: git the plice ready for the British herristoracy, Lawd Ellam and Lidy Wineflete.

REDBOOK. Lady faint, eh?

DRINKWATER. Fynt! Not lawkly. Wornted to gow an talk, to the Benny Seeras: blaow me if she didn't! huz wot we was frahtnd of. Tyin up Mawtzow's wound, she is, like a bloomin orspittle nass. (Sir Howard, with a copious pagri on his white hat, enters through the horseshoe arch, followed by a couple of men supporting the wounded Marzo, who, weeping and terrorstricken by the prospect of death and of subsequent torments for which he is conscious of having eminently qualified himself, has his coat off and a bandage round his chest. One of his supporters is a blackbearded, thickset, slow, middleaged man with an air of damaged respectability, named—as it afterwards appears—Johnson. Lady Cicely walks beside Marzo. Redbrook, a little shamefaced, crosses the room to the opposite wall as far away as possible from the visitors. Drinkwater turns and receives them with jocular ceremony.) Weolcome to Brarsbahnd Cawstl, Sr Ahrd an lidy. This eah is the corfee and commercial room.

Sir Howard goes to the table and sits on the saddle, rather exhausted. Lady Cicely comes to Drinkwater.

LADY CICELY. Where is Marzo's bed?

DRINKWATER. Is bed, lidy? Weoll: e ynt petickler, lidy. E ez is chawce of henny flegstown agin thet wall.

They deposit Marzo on the flags against the wall close to the little door. He groans. Johnson phlegmatically leaves him and joins Redbrook.

LADY CICELY. But you can't leave him there in that state.

DRINKWATER. Ow: e's hall rawt. (Strolling up callously to Marzo) You're hall rawt, ynt yer, Mawtzow? (Marzo whimpers.) Corse y'aw.

LADY CICELY (to Sir Howard). Did you ever see such a helpless lot of poor creatures? (She makes for the little door.)

DRINKWATER. Eah! (He runs to the door and places himself before it.) Where mawt yr lidyship be gowin?

LADY CICELY. I'm going through every room in this castle to find a proper place to put that man. And now I'll tell you where YOU'RE going. You're going to get some water for Marzo, who is very thirsty. And then, when I've chosen a room for him, you're going to make a bed for him there.

DRINKWATER (sarcastically). Ow! Henny ather little suvvice? Mike yrseolf at owm, y' knaow, lidy.

LADY CICELY (considerately). Don't go if you'd rather not, Mr. Drinkwater. Perhaps you're too tired. (Turning to the archway) I'll ask Captain Brassbound: he won't mind.

DRINKWATER (terrified, running after her and getting between her and the arch). Naow, naow! Naow, lidy: doesn't you goes disturbin the Kepn. Awll see to it.

LADY CICELY (gravely). I was sure you would, Mr. Drinkwater. You have such a kind face. (She turns back and goes out through the small door.)

DRINKWATER (looking after her). Garn!

SIR HOWARD (to Drinkwater). Will you ask one of your friends to show me to my room whilst you are getting the water?

DRINKWATER (insolently). Yr room! Ow: this ynt good enaf fr yr, ynt it? (Ferociously) Oo a you orderin abaht, ih?

SIR HOWARD (rising quietly, and taking refuge between Redbrook and Johnson, whom he addresses). Can you find me a more private room than this?

JOHNSON (shaking his head). I've no orders. You must wait til the capn comes, sir.

DRINKWATER (following Sir Howard). Yuss; an whawl you're witin, yll tike your horders from me: see?

JOHNSON (with slow severity, to Drinkwater). Look here: do you see three genlmen talkin to one another here, civil and private, eh?

DRINKWATER (chapfallen). No offence, Miste Jornsn—

JOHNSON (ominously). Ay; but there is offence. Where's your manners, you guttersnipe? (Turning to Sir Howard) That's the curse o this kind o life, sir: you got to associate with all sorts. My father, sir, was Capn Johnson o Hull—owned his own schooner, sir. We're mostly gentlemen here, sir, as you'll find, except the poor ignorant foreigner and that there scum of the submerged tenth. (Contemptuously looking at Drinkwater) HE ain't nobody's son: he's only a offspring o coster folk or such.

DRINKWATER (bursting into tears). Clawss feelin! thet's wot it is: clawss feelin! Wot are yer, arter all, bat a bloomin gang o west cowst cazhls (casual ward paupers)? (Johnson is scandalized; and there is a general thrill of indignation.) Better ev naow fembly, an rawse aht of it, lawk me, than ev a specble one and disgrice it, lawk you.

JOHNSON. Brandyfaced Jack: I name you for conduct and language unbecoming to a gentleman.

Those who agree will signify the same in the usual manner.

ALL (vehemently). Aye.

DRINKWATER (wildly). Naow.

JOHNSON. Felix Drinkwater: are you goin out, or are you goin to wait til you're chucked out? You can cry in the passage. If you give any trouble, you'll have something to cry for.

They make a threatenng movement towards Drinkwater.

DRINKWATER (whimpering). You lee me alown: awm gowin. There's n'maw true demmecrettick feelin eah than there is in the owl bloomin M division of Noontn Corzwy coppers (Newington Causeway policemen).

As he slinks away in tears towards the arch, Brassbound enters. Drinkwater promptly shelters himself on the captain's left hand, the others retreating to the opposite side as Brassbound advances to the middle of the room. Sir Howard retires behind them and seats himself on the divan, much fatigued.

BRASSBOUND (to Drinkwater). What are you snivelling at?

DRINKWATER. You awsk the wust cowst herristorcracy. They fawnds maw cornduck hanbecammin to a genlmn.

Brassbound is about to ask Johnson for an explanation, when Lady Cicely returns through the little door, and comes between Brassbound and Drinkwater.

LADY CICELY (to Drinkwater). Have you fetched the water?

DRINKWATER. Yuss: nah YOU begin orn me. (He weeps afresh.)

LADY CICELY (surprised). Oh! This won't do, Mr. Drinkwater. If you cry, I can't let you nurse your friend.

DRINKWATER (frantic). Thet'll brike maw awt, wown't it nah? (With a lamentable sob, he throws himself down on the divan, raging like an angry child.)

LADY CICELY (after contemplating him in astonishment for a moment). Captain Brassbound: are there any charwomen in the Atlas Mountains?

BRASSBOUND. There are people here who will work if you pay them, as there are elsewhere.

LADY CICELY. This castle is very romantic, Captain; but it hasn't had a spring cleaning since the Prophet lived in it. There's only one room I can put that wounded man into. It's the only one that has a bed in it: the second room on the right out of that passage.

BRASSBOUND (haughtily). That is my room, madam.

LADY CICELY (relieved). Oh, that's all right. It would have been so awkward if I had had to ask one of your men to turn out. You won't mind, I know. (All the men stare at her. Even Drinkwater forgets his sorrows in his stupefaction.)

BRASSBOUND. Pray, madam, have you made any arrangements for my accommodation?

LADY CICELY (reassuringly). Yes: you can have my room instead wherever it may be: I'm sure you chose me a nice one. I must be near my patient; and I don't mind roughing it. Now I must have Marzo moved very carefully. Where is that truly gentlemanly Mr. Johnson?—oh, there you are, Mr. Johnson. (She runs to Johnson, past Brassbound, who has to step back hastily out of her way with every expression frozen out of his face except one of extreme and indignant dumbfoundedness). Will you ask your strong friend to help you with Marzo: strong people are always so gentle.

JOHNSON. Let me introdooce Mr. Redbrook. Your ladyship may know his father, the very Rev. Dean Redbrook. (He goes to Marzo.)

REDBROOK. Happy to oblige you, Lady Cicely.

LADY CICELY (shaking hands). Howdyedo? Of course I knew your father—Dunham, wasn't it? Were you ever called—

REDBROOK. The kid? Yes.

LADY CICELY. But why—

REDBROOK (anticipating the rest of the question). Cards and drink, Lady Sis. (He follows Johnson to the patient. Lady Cicely goes too.) Now, Count Marzo. (Marzo groans as Johnson and Redbrook raise him.)

LADY CICELY. Now they're NOT hurting you, Marzo. They couldn't be more gentle.

MARZO. Drink.

LADY CICELY. I'll get you some water myself. Your friend Mr. Drinkwater was too overcome—take care of the corner—that's it—the second door on the right. (She goes out with Marzo and his bearers through the little door.)

BRASSBOUND (still staring). Well, I AM damned—!

DRINKWATER (getting up). Weoll, blimey!

BRASSBOUND (turning irritably on him). What did you say?

DRINKWATER. Weoll, wot did yer sy yrseolf, kepn? Fust tawm aw yever see y' afride of ennybody. (The others laugh.)

BRASSBOUND. Afraid!

DRINKWATER (maliciously). She's took y' bed from hander yr for a bloomin penny hawcemen. If y' ynt afride, let's eah yer speak ap to er wen she cams bawck agin.

BRASSBOUND (to Sir Howard). I wish you to understand, Sir Howard, that in this castle, it is I who give orders, and no one else. Will you be good enough to let Lady Cicely Waynflete know that.

SIR HOWARD (sitting up on the divan and pulling himself together). You will have ample opportunity for speaking to Lady Cicely yourself when she returns. (Drinkwater chuckles: and the rest grin.)

BRASSBOUND. My manners are rough, Sir Howard. I have no wish to frighten the lady.

SIR HOWARD. Captain Brassbound: if you can frighten Lady Cicely, you will confer a great obligation on her family. If she had any sense of danger, perhaps she would keep out of it.

BRASSBOUND. Well, sir, if she were ten Lady Cicelys, she must consult me while she is here.

DRINKWATER. Thet's rawt, kepn. Let's eah you steblish yr hawthority. (Brassbound turns impatiently on him: He retreats remonstrating) Nah, nah, nah!

SIR HOWARD. If you feel at all nervous, Captain Brassbound, I will mention the matter with pleasure.

BRASSBOUND. Nervous, sir! no. Nervousness is not in my line. You will find me perfectly capable of saying what I want to say—with considerable emphasis, if necessary. (Sir Howard assents with a polite but incredulous nod.)

DRINKWATER. Eah, eah!

Lady Cicely returns with Johnson and Redbrook. She carries a jar.

LADY CICELY (stopping between the door and the arch). Now for the water. Where is it?

REDBROOK. There's a well in the courtyard. I'll come and work the bucket.

LADY CICELY. So good of you, Mr. Redbrook. (She makes for the horseshoe arch, followed by Redbrook.)

DRINKWATER. Nah, Kepn Brassbound: you got sathink to sy to the lidy, ynt yr?

LADY CICELY (stopping). I'll come back to hear it presently, Captain. And oh, while I remember it (coming forward between Brassbound and Drinkwater), do please tell me Captain, if I interfere with your arrangements in any way. It I disturb you the least bit in the world, stop me at once. You have all the responsibility; and your comfort and your authority must be the first thing. You'll tell me, won't you?

BRASSBOUND (awkwardly, quite beaten). Pray do as you please, madam.

LADY CICELY. Thank you. That's so like you, Captain. Thank you. Now, Mr. Redbrook! Show me the way to the well. (She follows Redbrook out through the arch.)

DRINKWATER. Yah! Yah! Shime! Beat baw a woman!

JOHNSON (coming forward on Brassbound's right). What's wrong now?

DRINKWATER (with an air of disappointment and disillusion). Down't awsk me, Miste Jornsn. The kepn's naow clawss arter all.

BRASSBOUND (a little shamefacedly). What has she been fixing up in there, Johnson?

JOHNSON. Well: Marzo's in your bed. Lady wants to make a kitchen of the Sheikh's audience chamber, and to put me and the Kid handy in his bedroom in case Marzo gets erysipelas and breaks out violent. From what I can make out, she means to make herself matron of this institution. I spose it's all right, isn't it?

DRINKWATER. Yuss, an horder huz abaht as if we was keb tahts! An the kepn afride to talk bawck at er!

Lady Cicely returns with Redbrook. She carries the jar full of water.

LADY CICELY (putting down the jar, and coming between Brassbound and Drinkwater as before). And now, Captain, before I go to poor Marzo, what have you to say to me?

BRASSBOUND. I! Nothing.

DRINKWATER. Down't fank it, gavner. Be a men!

LADY CICELY (looking at Drinkwater, puzzled). Mr. Drinkwater said you had.

BRASSBOUND (recovering himself). It was only this. That fellow there (pointing to Drinkwater) is subject to fits of insolence. If he is impertinent to your ladyship, or disobedient, you have my authority to order him as many kicks as you think good for him; and I will see that he gets them.

DRINKWATER (lifting up his voice in protest). Nah, nah—

LADY CICELY. Oh, I couldn't think of such a thing, Captain Brassbound. I am sure it would hurt Mr. Drinkwater.

DRINKWATER (lachrymosely). Lidy's hinkyp'ble o sich bawbrous usage.

LADY CICELY. But there's one thing I SHOULD like, if Mr. Drinkwater won't mind my mentioning it. It's so important if he's to attend on Marzo.

BRASSBOUND. What is that?

LADY CICELY. Well—you WON'T mind, Mr. Drinkwater, will you?

DRINKWATER (suspiciously). Wot is it?

LADY CICELY. There would be so much less danger of erysipelas if you would be so good as to take a bath.

DRINKWATER (aghast). A bawth!

BRASSBOUND (in tones of command). Stand by, all hands. (They stand by.) Take that man and wash him. (With a roar of laughter they seize him.)

DRINKWATER (in an agony of protest). Naow, naow. Look eah—

BRASSBOUND (ruthlessly). In COLD water.

DRINKWATER (shrieking). Na-a-a-a-ow. Aw eawn't, aw toel yer. Naow. Aw sy, look eah. Naow, naow, naow, naow, naow, NAOW!!!

He is dragged away through the arch in a whirlwind of laughter, protests and tears.

LADY CICELY. I'm afraid he isn't used to it, poor fellow; but REALLY it will do him good, Captain Brassbound. Now I must be off to my patient. (She takes up her jar and goes out by the little door, leaving Brassbound and Sir Howard alone together.)

SIR HOWARD (rising). And now, Captain Brass—

BRASSBOUND (cutting him short with a fierce contempt that astonishes him). I will attend to you presently. (Calling) Johnson. Send me Johnson there. And Osman. (He pulls off his coat and throws it on the table, standing at his ease in his blue jersey.)

SIR HOWARD (after a momentary flush of anger, with a controlled force that compels Brassbound's attention in spite of himself). You seem to be in a strong position with reference to these men of yours.

BRASSBOUND. I am in a strong position with reference to everyone in this castle.

SIR HOWARD (politely but threateningly). I have just been noticing that you think so. I do not agree with you. Her Majesty's Government, Captain Brassbound, has a strong arm and a long arm. If anything disagreeable happens to me or to my sister-in-law, that arm will be stretched out. If that happens you will not be in a strong position. Excuse my reminding you of it.

BRASSBOUND (grimly). Much good may it do you! (Johnson comes in through the arch.) Where is Osman, the Sheikh's messenger? I want him too.

JOHNSON. Coming, Captain. He had a prayer to finish.

Osman, a tall, skinny, whiteclad, elderly Moor, appears in the archway.

BRASSBOUND. Osman Ali (Osman comes forward between Brassbound and Johnson): you have seen this unbeliever (indicating Sir Howard) come in with us?

OSMAN. Yea, and the shameless one with the naked face, who flattered my countenance and offered me her hand.

JOHNSON. Yes; and you took it too, Johnny, didn't you?

BRASSBOUND. Take horse, then; and ride fast to your master the Sheikh Sidi el Assif.

OSMAN (proudly). Kinsman to the Prophet.

BRASSBOUND. Tell him what you have seen here. That is all. Johnson: give him a dollar; and note the hour of his going, that his master may know how fast he rides.

OSMAN. The believer's word shall prevail with Allah and his servant Sidi el Assif.

BRASSBOUND. Off with you.

OSMAN. Make good thy master's word ere I go out from his presence, O Johnson el Hull.

JOHNSON. He wants the dollar.

Brassbound gives Osman a coin.

OSMAN (bowing). Allah will make hell easy for the friend of Sidi el Assif and his servant. (He goes out through the arch.)

BRASSBOUND (to Johnson). Keep the men out of this until the Sheikh comes. I have business to talk over. When he does come, we must keep together all: Sidi el Assif's natural instinct will be to cut every Christian throat here.

JOHNSON. We look to you, Captain, to square him, since you invited him over.

BRASSBOUND. You can depend on me; and you know it, I think.

JOHNSON (phlegmatically). Yes: we know it. (He is going out when Sir Howard speaks.)

SIR HOWARD. You know also, Mr. Johnson, I hope, that you can depend on ME.

JOHNSON (turning). On YOU, sir?

SIR HOWARD. Yes: on me. If my throat is cut, the Sultan of Morocco may send Sidi's head with a hundred thousand dollars blood-money to the Colonial Office; but it will not be enough to save his kingdom—any more than it would saw your life, if your Captain here did the same thing.

JOHNSON (struck). Is that so, Captain?

BRASSBOUND. I know the gentleman's value—better perhaps than he knows it himself. I shall not lose sight of it.

Johnson nods gravely, and is going out when Lady Cicely returns softly by the little door and calls to him in a whisper. She has taken off her travelling things and put on an apron. At her chatelaine is a case of sewing materials.

LADY CICELY. Mr. Johnson. (He turns.) I've got Marzo to sleep. Would you mind asking the gentlemen not to make a noise under his window in the courtyard.

JOHNSON. Right, maam. (He goes out.)

Lady Cicely sits down at the tiny table, and begins stitching at a sling bandage for Marzo's arm. Brassbound walks up and down on her right, muttering to himself so ominously that Sir Howard quietly gets out of his way by crossing to the other side and sitting down on the second saddle seat.

SIR HOWARD. Are you yet able to attend to me for a moment, Captain Brassbound?

BRASSBOUND (still walking about). What do you want?

SIR HOWARD. Well, I am afraid I want a little privacy, and, if you will allow me to say so, a little civility. I am greatly obliged to you for bringing us safely off to-day when we were attacked. So far, you have carried out your contract. But since we have been your guests here, your tone and that of the worst of your men has changed—intentionally changed, I think.

BRASSBOUND (stopping abruptly and flinging the announcement at him). You are not my guest: you are my prisoner.

SIR HOWARD. Prisoner!

Lady Cicely, after a single glance up, continues stitching, apparently quite unconcerned.

BRASSBOUND. I warned you. You should have taken my warning.

SIR HOWARD (immediately taking the tone of cold disgust for moral delinquency). Am I to understand, then, that you are a brigand? Is this a matter of ransom?

BRASSBOUND (with unaccountable intensity). All the wealth of England shall not ransom you.

SIR HOWARD. Then what do you expect to gain by this?

BRASSBOUND. Justice on a thief and a murderer.

Lady Cicely lays down her work and looks up anxiously.

SIR HOWARD (deeply outraged, rising with venerable dignity). Sir: do you apply those terms to me?

BRASSBOUND. I do. (He turns to Lady Cicely, and adds, pointing contemptuously to Sir Howard) Look at him. You would not take this virtuously indignant gentleman for the uncle of a brigand, would you?

Sir Howard starts. The shock is too much for him: he sits down again, looking very old; and his hands tremble; but his eyes and mouth are intrepid, resolute, and angry.

LADY CICELY. Uncle! What do you mean?

BRASSBOUND. Has he never told you about my mother? this fellow who puts on ermine and scarlet and calls himself Justice.

SIR HOWARD (almost voiceless). You are the son of that woman!

BRASSBOUND (fiercely). "That woman!" (He makes a movement as if to rush at Sir Howard.)

LADY CICELY (rising quickly and putting her hand on his arm). Take care. You mustn't strike an old man.

BRASSBOUND (raging). He did not spare my mother—"that woman," he calls her—because of her sex. I will not spare him because of his age. (Lowering his tone to one of sullen vindictiveness) But I am not going to strike him. (Lady Cicely releases him, and sits down, much perplexed. Brassbound continues, with an evil glance at Sir Howard) I shall do no more than justice.

SIR HOWARD (recovering his voice and vigor). Justice! I think you mean vengeance, disguised as justice by your passions.

BRASSBOUND. To many and many a poor wretch in the dock YOU have brought vengeance in that disguise—the vengeance of society, disguised as justice by ITS passions. Now the justice you have outraged meets you disguised as vengeance. How do you like it?

SIR HOWARD. I shall meet it, I trust, as becomes an innocent man and an upright judge. What do you charge against me?

BRASSBOUND. I charge you with the death of my mother and the theft of my inheritance.

SIR HOWARD. As to your inheritance, sir, it was yours whenever you came forward to claim it. Three minutes ago I did not know of your existence. I affirm that most solemnly. I never knew—never dreamt—that my brother Miles left a son. As to your mother, her case was a hard one—perhaps the hardest that has come within even my experience. I mentioned it, as such, to Mr. Rankin, the missionary, the evening we met you. As to her death, you know—you MUST know—that she died in her native country, years after our last meeting. Perhaps you were too young to know that she could hardly have expected to live long.

BRASSBOUND. You mean that she drank.

SIR HOWARD. I did not say so. I do not think she was always accountable for what she did.

BRASSBOUND. Yes: she was mad too; and whether drink drove her to madness or madness drove her to drink matters little. The question is, who drove her to both?

SIR HOWARD. I presume the dishonest agent who seized her estate did. I repeat, it was a hard case—a frightful injustice. But it could not be remedied.

BRASSBOUND. You told her so. When she would not take that false answer you drove her from your doors. When she exposed you in the street and threatened to take with her own hands the redress the law denied her, you had her imprisoned, and forced her to write you an apology and leave the country to regain her liberty and save herself from a lunatic asylum. And when she was gone, and dead, and forgotten, you found for yourself the remedy you could not find for her. You recovered the estate easily enough then, robber and rascal that you are. Did he tell the missionary that, Lady Cicely, eh?

LADY CICELY (sympathetically). Poor woman! (To Sir Howard) Couldn't you have helped her, Howard?

SIR HOWARD. No. This man may be ignorant enough to suppose that when I was a struggling barrister I could do everything I did when I was Attorney General. You know better. There is some excuse for his mother. She was an uneducated Brazilian, knowing nothing of English society, and driven mad by injustice.

BRASSBOUND. Your defence—

SIR HOWARD (interrupting him determinedly). I do not defend myself. I call on you to obey the law.

BRASSBOUND. I intend to do so. The law of the Atlas Mountains is administered by the Sheikh Sidi el Assif. He will be here within an hour. He is a judge like yourself. You can talk law to him. He will give you both the law and the prophets.

SIR HOWARD. Does he know what the power of England is?

BRASSBOUND. He knows that the Mahdi killed my master Gordon, and that the Mahdi died in his bed and went to paradise.

SIR HOWARD. Then he knows also that England's vengeance was on the Mahdi's track.

BRASSBOUND. Ay, on the track of the railway from the Cape to Cairo. Who are you, that a nation should go to war for you? If you are missing, what will your newspapers say? A foolhardy tourist. What will your learned friends at the bar say? That it was time for you to make room for younger and better men. YOU a national hero! You had better find a goldfield in the Atlas Mountains. Then all the governments of Europe will rush to your rescue. Until then, take care of yourself; for you are going to see at last the hypocrisy in the sanctimonious speech of the judge who is sentencing you, instead of the despair in the white face of the wretch you are recommending to the mercy of your God.

SIR HOWARD (deeply and personally offended by this slight to his profession, and for the first time throwing away his assumed dignity and rising to approach Brassbound with his fists clenched; so that Lady Cicely lifts one eye from her work to assure herself that the table is between them). I have no more to say to you, sir. I am not afraid of you, nor of any bandit with whom you may be in league. As to your property, it is ready for you as soon as you come to your senses and claim it as your father's heir. Commit a crime, and you will become an outlaw, and not only lose the property, but shut the doors of civilization against yourself for ever.

BRASSBOUND. I will not sell my mother's revenge for ten properties.

LADY CICELY (placidly). Besides, really, Howard, as the property now costs 150 pounds a year to keep up instead of bringing in anything, I am afraid it would not be of much use to him. (Brassbound stands amazed at this revelation.)

SIR HOWARD (taken aback). I must say, Cicely, I think you might have chosen a more suitable moment to mention that fact.

BRASSBOUND (with disgust). Agh! Trickster! Lawyer! Even the price you offer for your life is to be paid in false coin. (Calling) Hallo there! Johnson! Redbrook! Some of you there! (To Sir Howard) You ask for a little privacy: you shall have it. I will not endure the company of such a fellow—

SIR HOWARD (very angry, and full of the crustiest pluck). You insult me, sir. You are a rascal. You are a rascal.

Johnson, Redbrook, and a few others come in through the arch.

BRASSBOUND. Take this man away.

JOHNSON. Where are we to put him?

BRASSBOUND. Put him where you please so long as you can find him when he is wanted.

SIR HOWARD. You will be laid by the heels yet, my friend.

REDBROOK (with cheerful tact). Tut tut, Sir Howard: what's the use of talking back? Come along: we'll make you comfortable.

Sir Howard goes out through the arch between Johnson and Redbrook, muttering wrathfully. The rest, except Brassbound and Lady Cicely, follow.

Brassbound walks up and down the room, nursing his indignation. In doing so he unconsciously enters upon an unequal contest with Lady Cicely, who sits quietly stitching. It soon becomes clear that a tranquil woman can go on sewing longer than an angry man can go on fuming. Further, it begins to dawn on Brassbound's wrath-blurred perception that Lady Cicely has at some unnoticed stage in the proceedings finished Marzo's bandage, and is now stitching a coat. He stops; glances at his shirtsleeves; finally realizes the situation.

BRASSBOUND. What are you doing there, madam?

LADY CICELY. Mending your coat, Captain Brassbound.

BRASSBOUND. I have no recollection of asking you to take that trouble.

LADY CICELY. No: I don't suppose you even knew it was torn. Some men are BORN untidy. You cannot very well receive Sidi el—what's his name?—with your sleeve half out.

BRASSBOUND (disconcerted). I—I don't know how it got torn.

LADY CICELY. You should not get virtuously indignant with people. It bursts clothes more than anything else, Mr. Hallam.

BRASSBOUND (flushing, quickly). I beg you will not call me Mr. Hallam. I hate the name.

LADY CICELY. Black Paquito is your pet name, isn't it?

BRASSBOUND (huffily). I am not usually called so to my face.

LADY CICELY (turning the coat a little). I'm so sorry. (She takes another piece of thread and puts it into her needle, looking placidly and reflectively upward meanwhile.) Do you know, You are wonderfully like your uncle.

BRASSBOUND. Damnation!

LADY CICELY. Eh?

BRASSBOUND. If I thought my veins contained a drop of his black blood, I would drain them empty with my knife. I have no relations. I had a mother: that was all.

LADY CICELY (unconvinced) I daresay you have your mother's complexion. But didn't you notice Sir Howard's temper, his doggedness, his high spirit: above all, his belief in ruling people by force, as you rule your men; and in revenge and punishment, just as you want to revenge your mother? Didn't you recognize yourself in that?

BRASSBOUND (startled). Myself!—in that!

LADY CECILY (returning to the tailoring question as if her last remark were of no consequence whatever). Did this sleeve catch you at all under the arm? Perhaps I had better make it a little easier for you.

BRASSBOUND (irritably). Let my coat alone. It will do very well as it is. Put it down.

LADY CICILY. Oh, don't ask me to sit doing nothing. It bores me so.

BRASSBOUND. In Heaven's name then, do what you like! Only don't worry me with it.

LADY CICELY. I'm so sorry. All the Hallams are irritable.

BRASSBOUND (penning up his fury with difficulty). As I have already said, that remark has no application to me.

LADY CICELY (resuming her stitching). That's so funny! They all hate to be told that they are like one another.

BRASSBOUND (with the beginnings of despair in his voice). Why did you come here? My trap was laid for him, not for you. Do you know the danger you are in?

LADY CICELY. There's always a danger of something or other. Do you think it's worth bothering about?

BRASSBOUND (scolding her). Do I THINK! Do you think my coat's worth mending?

LADY CICELY (prosaically). Oh yes: it's not so far gone as that.

BRASSBOUND. Have you any feeling? Or are you a fool?

LADY CICELY. I'm afraid I'm a dreadful fool. But I can't help it. I was made so, I suppose.

BRASSBOUND. Perhaps you don't realize that your friend my good uncle will be pretty fortunate if he is allowed to live out his life as a slave with a set of chains on him?

LADY CICELY. Oh, I don't know about that, Mr. H—I mean Captain Brassbound. Men are always thinking that they are going to do something grandly wicked to their enemies; but when it comes to the point, really bad men are just as rare as really good ones.

BRASSBOUND. You forget that I am like my uncle, according to you. Have you any doubt as to the reality of HIS badness?

LADY CICELY. Bless me! your uncle Howard is one of the most harmless of men—much nicer than most professional people. Of course he does dreadful things as a judge; but then if you take a man and pay him 5,000 pounds a year to be wicked, and praise him for it, and have policemen and courts and laws and juries to drive him into it so that he can't help doing it, what can you expect? Sir Howard's all right when he's left to himself. We caught a burglar one night at Waynflete when he was staying with us; and I insisted on his locking the poor man up until the police came, in a room with a window opening on the lawn. The man came back next day and said he must return to a life of crime unless I gave him a job in the garden; and I did. It was much more sensible than giving him ten years penal servitude: Howard admitted it. So you see he's not a bit bad really.

BRASSBOUND. He had a fellow feeling for a thief, knowing he was a thief himself. Do you forget that he sent my mother to prison?

LADY CICELY (softly). Were you very fond of your poor mother, and always very good to her?

BRASSBOUND (rather taken aback). I was not worse than other sons, I suppose.

LADY CICELY (opening her eyes very widely). Oh! Was THAT all?

BRASSBOUND (exculpating himself, full of gloomy remembrances). You don't understand. It was not always possible to be very tender with my mother. She had unfortunately a very violent temper; and she—she—

LADY CICELY. Yes: so you told Howard. (With genuine pity for him) You must have had a very unhappy childhood.

BRASSBOUND (grimily). Hell. That was what my childhood was. Hell.

LADY CICELY. Do you think she would really have killed Howard, as she threatened, if he hadn't sent her to prison?

BRASSBOUND (breaking out again, with a growing sense of being morally trapped). What if she did? Why did he rob her? Why did he not help her to get the estate, as he got it for himself afterwards?

LADY CICELY. He says he couldn't, you know. But perhaps the real reason was that he didn't like her. You know, don't you, that if you don't like people you think of all the reasons for not helping them, and if you like them you think of all the opposite reasons.

BRASSBOUND. But his duty as a brother!

LADY CICELY. Are you going to do your duty as a nephew?

BRASSBOUND. Don't quibble with me. I am going to do my duty as a son; and you know it.

LADY CICELY. But I should have thought that the time for that was in your mother's lifetime, when you could have been kind and forbearing with her. Hurting your uncle won't do her any good, you know.

BRASSBOUND. It will teach other scoundrels to respect widows and orphans. Do you forget that there is such a thing as justice?

LADY CICELY (gaily shaking out the finished coat). Oh, if you are going to dress yourself in ermine and call yourself Justice, I give you up. You are just your uncle over again; only he gets £5,000 a year for it, and you do it for nothing.

(She holds the coat up to see whether any further repairs are needed.)

BRASSBOUND (sulkily). You twist my words very cleverly. But no man or woman has ever changed me.

LADY CICELY. Dear me! That must be very nice for the people you deal with, because they can always depend on you; but isn't it rather inconvenient for yourself when you change your mind?

BRASSBOUND. I never change my mind.

LADY CICELY (rising with the coat in her hands). Oh! Oh!! Nothing will ever persuade me that you are as pigheaded as that.

BRASSBOUND (offended). Pigheaded!

LADY CICELY (with quick, caressing apology). No, no, no. I didn't mean that. Firm! Unalterable! Resolute! Ironwilled! Stonewall Jackson! That's the idea, isn't it?

BRASSBOUND (hopelessly). You are laughing at me.

LADY CICELY. No: trembling, I assure you. Now will you try this on for me: I'm SO afraid I have made it too tight under the arm. (She holds it behind him.)

BRASSBOUND (obeying mechanically). You take me for a fool I think. (He misses the sleeve.)

LADY CICELY. No: all men look foolish when they are feeling for their sleeves.

BRASSBOUND. Agh! (He turns and snatches the coat from her; then puts it on himself and buttons the lowest button.)

LADY CICELY (horrified). Stop. No. You must NEVER pull a coat at the skirts, Captain Brassbound: it spoils the sit of it. Allow me. (She pulls the lappels of his coat vigorously forward) Put back your shoulders. (He frowns, but obeys.) That's better. (She buttons the top button.) Now button the rest from the top down. DOES it catch you at all under the arm?

BRASSBOUND (miserably—all resistance beaten out of him). No.

LADY CICELY. That's right. Now before I go back to poor Marzo, say thank you to me for mending your jacket, like a nice polite sailor.

BRASSBOUND (sitting down at the table in great agitation). Damn you! you have belittled my whole life to me. (He bows his head on his hands, convulsed.)

LADY CICELY (quite understanding, and putting her hand kindly on his shoulder). Oh no. I am sure you have done lots of kind things and brave things, if you could only recollect them. With Gordon for instance? Nobody can belittle that.

He looks up at her for a moment; then kisses her hand. She presses his and turns away with her eyes so wet that she sees Drinkwater, coming in through the arch just then, with a prismatic halo round him. Even when she sees him clearly, she hardly recognizes him; for he is ludicrously clean and smoothly brushed; and his hair, formerly mud color, is now a lively red.

DRINKWATER. Look eah, kepn. (Brassbound springs up and recovers himself quickly.) Eahs the bloomin Shike jest appeahd on the orawzn wiv abaht fifty men. Thy'll be eah insawd o ten minnits, they will.

LADY CICELY. The Sheikh!

BRASSBOUND. Sidi el Assif and fifty men! (To Lady Cicely) You were too late: I gave you up my vengeance when it was no longer in my hand. (To Drinkwater) Call all hands to stand by and shut the gates. Then all here to me for orders; and bring the prisoner.

DRINKWATER. Rawt, kepn. (He runs out.)

LADY CICELY. Is there really any danger for Howard?

BRASSBOUND. Yes. Danger for all of us unless I keep to my bargain with this fanatic.

LADY CICELY. What bargain?

BRASSBOUND. I pay him so much a head for every party I escort through to the interior. In return he protects me and lets my caravans alone. But I have sworn an oath to him to take only Jews and true believers—no Christians, you understand.

LADY CICELY. Then why did you take us?

BRASSBOUND. I took my uncle on purpose—and sent word to Sidi that he was here.

LADY CICELY. Well, that's a pretty kettle of fish, isn't it?

BRASSBOUND. I will do what I can to save him—and you. But I fear my repentance has come too late, as repentance usually does.

LADY CICELY (cheerfully). Well, I must go and look after Marzo, at all events. (She goes out through the little door. Johnson, Redbrook and the rest come in through the arch, with Sir Howard, still very crusty and determined. He keeps close to Johnson, who comes to Brassbound's right, Redbrook taking the other side.)

BRASSBOUND. Where's Drinkwater?

JOHNSON. On the lookout. Look here, Capn: we don't half like this job. The gentleman has been talking to us a bit; and we think that he IS a gentleman, and talks straight sense.

REDBROOK. Righto, Brother Johnson. (To Brassbound) Won't do, governor. Not good enough.

BRASSBOUND (fiercely). Mutiny, eh?

REDBROOK. Not at all, governor. Don't talk Tommy rot with Brother Sidi only five minutes gallop off. Can't hand over an Englishman to a nigger to have his throat cut.

BRASSBOUND (unexpectedly acquiescing). Very good. You know, I suppose, that if you break my bargain with Sidi, you'll have to defend this place and fight for your lives in five minutes. That can't be done without discipline: you know that too. I'll take my part with the rest under whatever leader you are willing to obey. So choose your captain and look sharp about it. (Murmurs of surprise and discontent.)

VOICES. No, no. Brassbound must command.

BRASSBOUND. You're wasting your five minutes. Try Johnson.

JOHNSON. No. I haven't the head for it.

BRASSBOUND. Well, Redbrook.

REDBROOK. Not this Johnny, thank you. Haven't character enough.

BRASSBOUND. Well, there's Sir Howard Hallam for You! HE has character enough.

A VOICE. He's too old.

ALL. No, no. Brassbound, Brassbound.

JOHNSON. There's nobody but you, Captain.

REDRROOK. The mutiny's over, governor. You win, hands down.

BRASSBOUND (turning on them). Now listen, you, all of you. If I am to command here, I am going to do what I like, not what you like. I'll give this gentleman here to Sidi or to the devil if I choose. I'll not be intimidated or talked back to. Is that understood?

REDBROOK (diplomatically). He's offered a present of five hundred quid if he gets safe back to Mogador, governor. Excuse my mentioning it.

SIR HOWARD. Myself AND Lady Cicely.

BRASSBOUND. What! A judge compound a felony! You greenhorns, he is more likely to send you all to penal servitude if you are fools enough to give him the chance.

VOICES. So he would. Whew! (Murmurs of conviction.)

REDBROOK. Righto, governor. That's the ace of trumps.

BRASSBOUND (to Sir Howard). Now, have you any other card to play? Any other bribe? Any other threat? Quick. Time presses.

SIR HOWARD. My life is in the hands of Providence. Do your worst.

BRASSBOUND. Or my best. I still have that choice.

DRINKWATER (running in). Look eah, kepn. Eah's anather lot cammin from the sahth heast. Hunnerds of em, this tawm. The owl dezzit is lawk a bloomin Awd Pawk demonstrition. Aw blieve it's the Kidy from Kintorfy. (General alarm. All look to Brassbound.)

BRASSBOUND (eagerly). The Cadi! How far off?

DRINKWATER. Matter o two mawl.

BRASSBOUND. We're saved. Open the gates to the Sheikh.

DRINKWATER (appalled, almost in tears). Naow, naow. Lissn, kepn (Pointing to Sir Howard): e'll give huz fawv unnerd red uns. (To the others) Ynt yer spowk to im, Miste Jornsn—Miste Redbrook—

BRASSBOUND (cutting him short). Now then, do you understand plain English? Johnson and Redbrook: take what men you want and open the gates to the Sheikh. Let him come straight to me. Look alive, will you.

JOHNSON. Ay ay, sir.

REDBROOK. Righto, governor.

They hurry out, with a few others. Drinkwater stares after them, dumbfounded by their obedience.

BRASSBOUND (taking out a pistol). You wanted to sell me to my prisoner, did you, you dog.

DRINKWATER (falling on his knees with a yell). Naow! (Brassbound turns on him as if to kick him. He scrambles away and takes refuge behind Sir Howard.)

BRASSBOUND. Sir Howard Hallam: you have one chance left. The Cadi of Kintafi stands superior to the Sheikh as the responsible governor of the whole province. It is the Cadi who will be sacrificed by the Sultan if England demands satisfaction for any injury to you. If we can hold the Sheikh in parley until the Cadi arrives, you may frighten the Cadi into forcing the Sheikh to release you. The Cadi's coming is a lucky chance for YOU.

SIR HOWARD. If it were a real chance, you would not tell me of it. Don't try to play cat and mouse with me, man.

DRINKWATER (aside to Sir Howard, as Brassbound turns contemptuously away to the other side of the room). It ynt mach of a chawnst, Sr Ahrd. But if there was a ganbowt in Mogador Awbr, awd put a bit on it, aw would.

Johnson, Redbrook, and the others return, rather mistrustfully ushering in Sidi el Assif, attended by Osman and a troop of Arabs. Brassbound's men keep together on the archway side, backing their captain. Sidi's followers cross the room behind the table and assemble near Sir Howard, who stands his ground. Drinkwater runs across to Brassbound and stands at his elbow as he turns to face Sidi.

Sidi el Aasif, clad in spotless white, is a nobly handsome Arab, hardly thirty, with fine eyes, bronzed complexion, and instinctively dignified carriage. He places himself between the two groups, with Osman in attendance at his right hand.

OSMAN (pointing out Sir Howard). This is the infidel Cadi. (Sir Howard bows to Sidi, but, being an infidel, receives only the haughtiest stare in acknowledgement.) This (pointing to Brassbound) is Brassbound the Franguestani captain, the servant of Sidi.

DRINKWATER (not to be outdone, points out the Sheikh and Osman to Brassbound). This eah is the Commawnder of the Fythful an is Vizzeer Rosman.

SIDI. Where is the woman?

OSMAN. The shameless one is not here.

BRASSBOUND. Sidi el Assif, kinsman of the Prophet: you are welcome.

REDBROOK (with much aplomb). There is no majesty and no might save in Allah, the Glorious, the Great!

DRINKWATER. Eah, eah!

OSMAN (to Sidi). The servant of the captain makes his profession of faith as a true believer.

SIDI. It is well.

BRASSBOUND (aside to Redbrook). Where did you pick that up?

REDRROOK (aside to Brassbound). Captain Burton's Arabian Nights—copy in the library of the National Liberal Club.

LADY CICELY (calling without). Mr. Drinkwater. Come and help me with Marzo. (The Sheikh pricks up his ears. His nostrils and eyes expand.)

OSMAN. The shameless one!

BRASSBOUND (to Drinkwater, seizing him by the collar and slinging him towards the door). Off with you.

Drinkwater goes out through the little door.

OSMAN. Shall we hide her face before she enters?

SIDI. NO.

Lady Cicely, who has resumed her travelling equipment, and has her hat slung across her arm, comes through the little door supporting Marzo, who is very white, but able to get about. Drinkwater has his other arm. Redbrook hastens to relieve Lady Cicely of Marzo, taking him into the group behind Brassbound. Lady Cicely comes forward between Brassbound and the Sheikh, to whom she turns affably.

LADY CICELY (proffering her hand). Sidi el Assif, isn't it? How dye do? (He recoils, blushing somewhat.)

OSMAN (scandalized). Woman; touch not the kinsman of the Prophet.

LADY CICELY. Oh, I see. I'm being presented at court. Very good. (She makes a presentation curtsey.)

REDBROOK. Sidi el Assif: this is one of the mighty women Sheikhs of Franguestan. She goes unveiled among Kings; and only princes may touch her hand.

LADY CICELY. Allah upon thee, Sidi el Assif! Be a good little Sheikh, and shake hands.

SIDI (timidly touching her hand). Now this is a wonderful thing, and worthy to be chronicled with the story of Solomon and the Queen of Sheba. Is it not so, Osman Ali?

OSMAN. Allah upon thee, master! it is so.

SIDI. Brassbound Ali: the oath of a just man fulfils itself without many words. The infidel Cadi, thy captive, falls to my share.

BRASSBOUND (firmly). It cannot be, Sidi el Assif. (Sidi's brows contract gravely.) The price of his blood will be required of our lord the Sultan. I will take him to Morocco and deliver him up there.

SIDI (impressively). Brassbound: I am in mine own house and amid mine own people. I am the Sultan here. Consider what you say; for when my word goes forth for life or death, it may not be recalled.

BRASSBOUND. Sidi el Assif: I will buy the man from you at what price you choose to name; and if I do not pay faithfully, you shall take my head for his.

SIDI. It is well. You shall keep the man, and give me the woman in payment.

SIR HOWARD AND BRASSBOUND (with the same impulse). No, no.

LADY CICELY (eagerly). Yes, yes. Certainly, Mr. Sidi. Certainly.

Sidi smiles gravely.

SIR HOWARD. Impossible.

BRASSBOUND. You don't know what you're doing.

LADY CICELY. Oh, don't I? I've not crossed Africa and stayed with six cannibal chiefs for nothing. (To the Sheikh) It's all right, Mr. Sidi: I shall be delighted.

SIR HOWARD. You are mad. Do you suppose this man will treat you as a European gentleman would?

LADY CICELY. No: he'll treat me like one of Nature's gentlemen: look at his perfectly splendid face! (Addressing Osman as if he were her oldest and most attached retainer.) Osman: be sure you choose me a good horse; and get a nice strong camel for my luggage.

Osman, after a moment of stupefaction, hurries out. Lady Cicely puts on her hat and pins it to her hair, the Sheikh gazing at her during the process with timid admiration.

DRINKWATER (chuckling). She'll mawch em all to church next Sunder lawk a bloomin lot o' cherrity kids: you see if she doesn't.

LADY CICELY (busily). Goodbye, Howard: don't be anxious about me; and above all, don't bring a parcel of men with guns to rescue me. I shall be all right now that I am getting away from the escort. Captain Brassbound: I rely on you to see that Sir Howard gets safe to Mogador. (Whispering) Take your hand off that pistol. (He takes his hand out of his pocket, reluctantly.) Goodbye.

A tumult without. They all turn apprehensively to the arch. Osman rushes in.

OSMAN. The Cadi, the Cadi. He is in anger. His men are upon us. Defend—

The Cadi, a vigorous, fatfeatured, choleric, whitehaired and bearded elder, rushes in, cudgel in hand, with an overwhelming retinue, and silences

Osman with a sounding thwack. In a moment the back of the room is crowded with his followers. The Sheikh retreats a little towards his men; and the Cadi comes impetuously forward between him and Lady Cicely.

THE CADI. Now woe upon thee, Sidi el Assif, thou child of mischief!

SIDI (sternly). Am I a dog, Muley Othman, that thou speakest thus to me?

THE CADI. Wilt thou destroy thy country, and give us all into the hands of them that set the sea on fire but yesterday with their ships of war? Where are the Franguestani captives?

LADY CICELY. Here we are, Cadi. How dye do?

THE CADI. Allah upon thee, thou moon at the full! Where is thy kinsman, the Cadi of Franguestan? I am his friend, his servant. I come on behalf of my master the Sultan to do him honor, and to cast down his enemies.

SIR HOWARD. You are very good, I am sure.

SIDI (graver than ever). Muley Othman—

TAE CADI (fumbling in his breast). Peace, peace, thou inconsiderate one. (He takes out a letter.)

BRASSBOUND. Cadi—

THE CADI. Oh thou dog, thou, thou accursed Brassbound, son of a wanton: it is thou hast led Sidi el Assif into this wrongdoing. Read this writing that thou hast brought upon me from the commander of the warship.

BRASSBOUND. Warship! (He takes the letter and opens it, his men whispering to one another very low-spiritedly meanwhile.)

REDBROOK. Warship! Whew!

JOHNSON. Gunboat, praps.

DRINKWATER. Lawk bloomin Worterleoo buses, they are, on this cowst.

Brassbound folds up the letter, looking glum.

SIR HOWARD (sharply). Well, sir, are we not to have the benefit of that letter? Your men are waiting to hear it, I think.

BRASSBOUND. It is not a British ship. (Sir Howard's face falls.)

LADY CICELY. What is it, then?

BRASSBOUND. An American cruiser. The Santiago.

THE CADI (tearing his beard). Woe! alas! it is where they set the sea on fire.

SIDI. Peace, Muley Othman: Allah is still above us.

JOHNSON. Would you mind readin it to us, capn?

BRASSBOUND (grimly). Oh, I'll read it to you. "Mogador Harbor. 26 Sept. 1899. Captain Hamlin Kearney, of the cruiser Santiago, presents the compliments of the United States to the Cadi Muley Othman el Kintafi, and announces that he is coming to look for the two British travellers Sir Howard Hallam and Lady Cicely Waynflete, in the Cadi's jurisdiction. As the search will be conducted with machine guns, the prompt return of the travellers to Mogador Harbor will save much trouble to all parties."

THE CADI. As I live, O Cadi, and thou, moon of loveliness, ye shall be led back to Mogador with honor. And thou, accursed Brassbound, shall go thither a prisoner in chains, thou and thy people. (Brassbound and his men make a movement to defend themselves.) Seize them.

LADY CICELY. Oh, please don't fight. (Brassbound, seeing that his men are hopelessly outnumbered, makes no resistance. They are made prisoners by the Cadi's followers.)

SIDI (attempting to draw his scimitar). The woman is mine: I will not forego her. (He is seized and overpowered after a Homeric struggle.)

SIR HOWARD (drily). I told you you were not in a strong position, Captain Brassbound. (Looking implacably at him.) You are laid by the heels, my friend, as I said you would be.

LADY CICELY. But I assure you—

BRASSBOUND (interrupting her). What have you to assure him of? You persuaded me to spare him. Look at his face. Will you be able to persuade him to spare me?

ACT III

Torrid forenoon filtered through small Moorish windows high up in the adobe walls of the largest room in Leslie Rankin's house. A clean cool room, with the table (a Christian article) set in the middle, a presidentially elbowed chair behind it, and an inkstand and paper ready for the sitter. A couple of cheap American chairs right and left of the table, facing the same way as the presidential chair, give a judicial aspect to the arrangement. Rankin is placing a little tray with a jug and some glasses near the inkstand when Lady Cicely's voice is heard at the door, which is behind him in the corner to his right.

LADE CICELY. Good morning. May I come in?

RANKIN. Certainly. (She comes in, to the nearest end of the table. She has discarded all travelling equipment, and is dressed exactly as she might be in Surrey on a very hot day.) Sit ye doon, Leddy Ceecily.

LADY CICELY (sitting down). How nice you've made the room for the inquiry!

RANKIN (doubtfully). I could wish there were more chairs. Yon American captain will preside in this; and that leaves but one for Sir Howrrd and one for your leddyship. I could almost be tempted to call it a maircy that your friend that owns the yacht has sprained his ankle and cannot come. I misdoubt me it will not look judeecial to have Captain Kearney's officers squatting on the floor.

LADY CICELY. Oh, they won't mind. What about the prisoners?

RANKIN. They are to be broat here from the town gaol presently.

LADY CICELY. And where is that silly old Cadi, and my handsome Sheikh Sidi? I must see them before the inquiry,or they'll give Captain Kearney quite a false impression of what happened.

RANKIN. But ye cannot see them. They decamped last night, back to their castles in the Atlas.

LADY CICELY (delighted). No!

RANKIN. Indeed and they did. The poor Cadi is so terrified by all he has haird of the destruction of the Spanish fleet, that he daren't trust himself in the captain's hands. (Looking reproachfully at her) On your journey back here, ye seem to have frightened the poor man yourself, Leddy Ceecily, by talking to him about the fanatical Chreestianity of the Americans. Ye have largely yourself to thank if he's gone.

LADY CICELY. Allah be praised! WHAT a weight off our minds, Mr. Rankin!

RANKIN (puzzled). And why? Do ye not understand how necessary their evidence is?

LADY CICELY. THEIR evidence! It would spoil everything. They would perjure themselves out of pure spite against poor Captain Brassbound.

RANKIN (amazed). Do ye call him POOR Captain Brassbound! Does not your leddyship know that this Brasshound is—Heaven forgive me for judging him!—a precious scoundrel? Did ye not hear what Sir Howrrd told me on the yacht last night?

LADY CICELY. All a mistake, Mr. Rankin: all a mistake, I assure you. You said just now, Heaven forgive you for judging him! Well, that's just what the whole quarrel is about. Captain Brassbound is just like you: he thinks we have no right to judge one another; and its Sir Howard gets £5,000 a year for doing nothing else but judging people, he thinks poor Captain Brassbound a regular Anarchist. They quarreled dreadfully at the castle. You mustn't mind what Sir Howard says about him: you really mustn't.

RANKIN. But his conduct—

LADY CICELY. Perfectly saintly, Mr. Rankin. Worthy of yourself in your best moments. He forgave Sir Howard, and did all he could to save him.

RANKIN. Ye astoanish me, Leddy Ceecily.

LADY CICELY. And think of the temptation to behave badly when he had us all there helpless!

RANKIN. The temptation! ay: that's true. Ye're ower bonny to be cast away among a parcel o lone, lawless men, my leddy.

LADY CICELY (naively). Bless me, that's quite true; and I never thought of it! Oh, after that you really must do all you can to help Captain Brassbound.

RANKIN (reservedly). No: I cannot say that, Leddy Ceecily. I doubt he has imposed on your good nature and sweet disposeetion. I had a crack with the Cadi as well as with Sir Howrrd; and there is little question in my mind but that Captain Brassbound is no better than a breegand.

LADY CICELY (apparently deeply impressed). I wonder whether he can be, Mr. Rankin. If you think so, that's heavily against him in my opinion, because you have more knowledge of men than anyone else here. Perhaps I'm mistaken. I only thought you might like to help him as the son of your old friend.

RANKIN (startled). The son of my old friend! What d'ye mean?

LADY CICELY. Oh! Didn't Sir Howard tell you that? Why, Captain Brassbound turns out to be Sir Howard's nephew, the son of the brother you knew.

RANKIN (overwhelmed). I saw the likeness the night he came here! It's true: it's true. Uncle and nephew!

LADY CICELY. Yes: that's why they quarrelled so.

RANKIN (with a momentary sense of ill usage). I think Sir Howrrd might have told me that.

LADY CICELY. Of course he OUGHT to have told you. You see he only tells one side of the story. That comes from his training as a barrister. You mustn't think he's naturally deceitful: if he'd been brought up as a clergyman, he'd have told you the whole truth as a matter of course.

RANKIN (too much perturbed to dwell on his grievance). Leddy Ceecily: I must go to the prison and see the lad. He may have been a bit wild; but I can't leave poor Miles's son unbefriended in a foreign gaol.

LADY CICELY (rising, radiant). Oh, how good of you! You have a real kind heart of gold, Mr. Rankin. Now, before you go, shall we just put our heads together, and consider how to give Miles's son every chance—I mean of course every chance that he ought to have.

RANKIN (rather addled). I am so confused by this astoanishing news—

LADY CICELY. Yes, yes: of course you are. But don't you think he would make a better impression on the American captain if he were a little more respectably dressed?

RANKIN. Mebbe. But how can that be remedied here in Mogador?

LADY CICELY. Oh, I've thought of that. You know I'm going back to England by way of Rome, Mr. Rankin; and I'm bringing a portmanteau full of clothes for my brother there: he's ambassador, you know, and has to be VERY particular as to what he wears. I had the portmanteau brought here this morning. Now WOULD you mind taking it to the prison, and smartening up Captain Brassbound a little. Tell him he ought to do it to show his respect for me; and he will. It will be quite easy: there are two Krooboys waiting to carry the portmanteau. You will: I know you will. (She edges him to the door.) And do you think there is time to get him shaved?

RANKIN (succumbing, half bewildered). I'll do my best.

LADY CICELY. I know you will. (As he is going out) Oh! one word, Mr. Rankin. (He comes back.) The Cadi didn't know that Captain Brassbound was Sir Howard's nephew, did he?

RANKIN. No.

LADY CICELY. Then he must have misunderstood everything quite dreadfully. I'm afraid, Mr. Rankin—though you know best, of course—that we are bound not to repeat anything at the inquiry that the Cadi said. He didn't know, you see.

RANKIN (cannily). I take your point, Leddy Ceecily. It alters the case. I shall certainly make no allusion to it.

LADY CICELY (magnanimously). Well, then, I won't either. There! They shake hands on it. Sir Howard comes in.

SIR HOWARD. Good morning Mr. Rankin. I hope you got home safely from the yacht last night.

RANKIN. Quite safe, thank ye, Sir Howrrd.

LADY CICELY. Howard, he's in a hurry. Don't make him stop to talk.

SIR HOWARD. Very good, very good. (He comes to the table and takes Lady Cicely's chair.)

RANKIN. Oo revoir, Leddy Ceecily.

LADY CICELY. Bless you, Mr. Rankin. (Rankin goes out. She comes to the other end of the table, looking at Sir Howard with a troubled, sorrowfully sympathetic air, but unconsciously making her right hand stalk about the table on the tips of its fingers in a tentative stealthy way which would put Sir Howard on his guard if he were in a suspicious frame of mind, which, as it happens, he is not.) I'm so sorry for you, Howard, about this unfortunate inquiry.

SIR HOWARD (swinging round on his chair, astonished). Sorry for ME! Why?

LADY CICELY. It will look so dreadful. Your own nephew, you know.

SIR HOWARD. Cicely: an English judge has no nephews, no sons even, when he has to carry out the law.

LADY CICELY. But then he oughtn't to have any property either. People will never understand about the West Indian Estate. They'll think you're the wicked uncle out of the Babes in the Wood. (With a fresh gush of compassion) I'm so SO sorry for you.

SIR HOWARD (rather stiffly). I really do not see how I need your commiseration, Cicely. The woman was an impossible person, half mad, half drunk. Do you understand what such a creature is when she has a grievance, and imagines some innocent person to be the author of it?

LADY CICELY (with a touch of impatience). Oh, quite. THAT'll be made clear enough. I can see it all in the papers already: our half mad, half drunk sister-in-law, making scenes with you in the street, with the police called in, and prison and all the rest of it. The family will be furious. (Sir Howard quails. She instantly follows up her advantage with) Think of papa!

SIR HOWARD. I shall expect Lord Waynflete to look at the matter as a reasonable man.

LADY CICELY. Do you think he's so greatly changed as that, Howard?

SIR HOWARD (falling back on the fatalism of the depersonalized public man). My dear Cicely: there is no use discussing the matter. It cannot be helped, however disagreeable it may be.

LADY CICELY. Of course not. That's what's so dreadful. Do you think people will understand?

SIR HOWARD. I really cannot say. Whether they do or not, I cannot help it.

LADY CICELY. If you were anybody but a judge, it wouldn't matter so much. But a judge mustn't even be misunderstood. (Despairingly) Oh, it's dreadful, Howard: it's terrible! What would poor Mary say if she were alive now?

SIR HOWARD (with emotion). I don't think, Cicely, that my dear wife would misunderstand me.

LADY CICELY. No: SHE'D know you mean well. And when you came home and said, "Mary: I've just told all the world that your sister-in-law was a police court criminal, and that I sent her to prison; and your nephew is a brigand, and I'm sending HIM to prison." she'd have thought it must be all right because you did it. But you don't think she would have LIKED it, any more than papa and the rest of us, do you?

SIR HOWARD (appalled). But what am I to do? Do you ask me to compound a felony?

LADY CICELY (sternly). Certainly not. I would not allow such a thing, even if you were wicked enough to attempt it. No. What I say is, that you ought not to tell the story yourself

SIR HOWARD. Why?

LADY CICELY. Because everybody would say you are such a clever lawyer you could make a poor simple sailor like Captain Kearney believe anything. The proper thing for you to do, Howard, is to let ME tell the exact truth. Then you can simply say that you are bound to confirm me. Nobody can blame you for that.

SIR HOWARD (looking suspiciously at her). Cicely: you are up to some devilment.

LADY CICELY (promptly washing her hands of his interests). Oh, very well. Tell the story yourself, in your own clever way. I only proposed to tell the exact truth. You call that devilment. So it is, I daresay, from a lawyer's point of view.

SIR HOWARD. I hope you're not offended.

LADY CICELY (with the utmost goodhumor). My dear Howard, not a bit. Of course you're right: you know how these things ought to be done. I'll do exactly what you tell me, and confirm everything you say.

SIR HOWARD (alarmed by the completeness of his victory). Oh, my dear, you mustn't act in MY interest. You must give your evidence with absolute impartiality. (She nods, as if thoroughly impressed and reproved, and gazes at him with the steadfast candor peculiar to liars who read novels. His eyes turn to the ground; and his brow clouds perplexedly. He rises; rubs his chin nervously with his forefinger; and adds) I think, perhaps, on reflection, that there is something to be said for your proposal to relieve me of the very painful duty of telling what has occurred.

LADI CICELY (holding off). But you'd do it so very much better.

SIR HOWARD. For that very reason, perhaps, it had better come from you.

LADY CICELY (reluctantly). Well, if you'd rather.

SIR HOWARD. But mind, Cicely, the exact truth.

LADY CICELY (with conviction). The exact truth. (They shake hands on it.)

SIR HOWARD (holding her hand). Fiat justitia: ruat coelum!

LADY CICELY. Let Justice be done, though the ceiling fall.

An American bluejacket appears at the door.

BLUEJACKET. Captain Kearney's cawmpliments to Lady Waynflete; and may he come in?

LADY CICELY. Yes. By all means. Where are the prisoners?

BLUEJACKET. Party gawn to the jail to fetch em, marm.

LADY CICELY. Thank you. I should like to be told when they are coming, if I might.

BLUEJACKET. You shall so, marm. (He stands aside, saluting, to admit his captain, and goes out.)

Captain Hamlin Kearney is a robustly built western American, with the keen, squeezed, wind beaten eyes and obstinately enduring mouth of his profession. A curious ethnological specimen, with all the nations of the old world at war in his veins, he is developing artificially in the direction of sleekness and culture under the restraints of an overwhelming dread of European criticism, and climatically in the direction of the indiginous North American, who is already in possession of his hair, his cheekbones, and the manlier instincts in him, which the sea has rescued from civilization. The world, pondering on the great part of its own future which is in his hands, contemplates him with wonder as to what the devil he will evolve into in another century or two. Meanwhile he presents himself to Lady Cicely as a blunt sailor who has something to say to her concerning her conduct which he wishes to put politely, as becomes an officer addressing a lady, but also with an emphatically implied rebuke, as an American addressing an English person who has taken a liberty.

LADY CICELY (as he enters). So glad you've come, Captain Kearney.

KEARNEY (coming between Sir Howard and Lady Cicely). When we parted yesterday ahfternoon, Lady Waynflete, I was unaware that in the course of your visit to my ship you had entirely altered the sleeping arrangements of my stokers. I thahnk you.

As captain of the ship, I am customairily cawnsulted before the orders of English visitors are carried out; but as your alterations appear to cawndooce to the comfort of the men, I have not interfered with them.

LADY CICELY. How clever of you to find out! I believe you know every bolt in that ship.

Kearney softens perceptibly.

SIR HOWARD. I am really very sorry that my sister-in-law has taken so serious a liberty, Captain Kearney. It is a mania of hers—simply a mania. Why did your men pay any attention to her?

KEARNEY (with gravely dissembled humor). Well, I ahsked that question too. I said, Why did you obey that lady's orders instead of waiting for mine? They said they didn't see exactly how they could refuse. I ahsked whether they cawnsidered that discipline. They said, Well, sir, will you talk to the lady yourself next time?

LADY CICELY. I'm so sorry. But you know, Captain, the one thing that one misses on board a man-of-war is a woman.

KEARNEY. We often feel that deprivation verry keenly, Lady Waynflete.

LADY CICELY. My uncle is first Lord of the Admiralty; and I am always telling him what a scandal it is that an English captain should be forbidden to take his wife on board to look after the ship.

KEARNEY. Stranger still, Lady Waynflete, he is not forbidden to take any other lady. Yours is an extraordinairy country—to an Amerrican.

LADY CICELY. But it's most serious, Captain. The poor men go melancholy mad, and ram each other's ships and do all sorts of things.

SIR HOWARD. Cicely: I beg you will not talk nonsense to Captain Kearney. Your ideas on some subjects are really hardly decorous.

LADY CICELY (to Kearney). That's what English people are like, Captain Kearney. They won't hear of anything concerning you poor sailors except Nelson and Trafalgar. YOU understand me, don't you?

KEARNEY (gallantly). I cawnsider that you have more sense in your wedding ring finger than the British Ahdmiralty has in its whole cawnstitootion, Lady Waynflete.

LADY CICELY. Of course I have. Sailors always understand things.

The bluejacket reappears.

BLUEJACKET (to Lady Cicely). Prisoners coming up the hill, marm.

KEARNEY (turning sharply on him). Who sent you in to say that?

BLUEJACKET (calmly). British lady's orders, sir. (He goes out, unruffled, leaving Kearney dumbfounded.)

SIR HOWARD (contemplating Kearney's expression with dismay). I am really very sorry, Captain Kearney. I am quite aware that Lady Cicely has no right whatever to give orders to your men.

LADY CICELY. I didn't give orders: I just asked him. He has such a nice face! Don't you think so, Captain Kearney? (He gasps, speechless.) And now will you excuse me a moment. I want to speak to somebody before the inquiry begins. (She hurries out.)

KEARNEY. There is sertnly a wonderful chahrn about the British aristocracy, Sir Howard Hallam. Are they all like that? (He takes the presidential chair.)

SIR HOWARD (resuming his seat on Kearney's right). Fortunately not, Captain Kearney. Half a dozen such women would make an end of law in England in six months.

The bluejacket comes to the door again.

BLUEJACKET. All ready, sir.

KEARNEY. Verry good. I'm waiting.

The bluejacket turns and intimates this to those without.

The officers of the Santiago enter.

SIR HOWARD (rising and bobbing to them in a judicial manner). Good morning, gentlemen.

They acknowledge the greeting rather shyly, bowing or touching their caps, and stand in a group behind Kearney.

KEARNEY (to Sir Howard). You will be glahd to hear that I have a verry good account of one of our prisoners from our chahplain, who visited them in the gaol. He has expressed a wish to be cawnverted to Episcopalianism.

SIR HOWARD (drily). Yes, I think I know him.

KEARNEY. Bring in the prisoners.

BLUEJACKET (at the door). They are engaged with the British lady, sir. Shall I ask her—

KEARNEY (jumping up and exploding in storm piercing tones). Bring in the prisoners. Tell the lady those are my orders. Do you hear? Tell her so. (The bluejacket goes out dubiously. The officers look at one another in mute comment on the unaccountable pepperiness of their commander.)

SIR HOWARD (suavely). Mr. Rankin will be present, I presume.

KEARNEY (angrily). Rahnkin! Who is Rahnkin?

SIR HOWARD. Our host the missionary.

KEARNEY (subsiding unwillingly). Oh! Rahnkin, is he? He'd better look sharp or he'll be late. (Again exploding.) What are they doing with those prisoners?

Rankin hurries in, and takes his place near Sir Howard.

SIR HOWARD. This is Mr. Rankin, Captain Kearney.

RANKIN. Excuse my delay, Captain Kearney. The leddy sent me on an errand. (Kearney grunts.) I thought I should be late. But the first thing I heard when I arrived was your officer giving your compliments to Leddy Ceecily, and would she kindly allow the prisoners to come in, as you were anxious to see her again. Then I knew I was in time.

KEARNEY. Oh, that was it, was it? May I ask, sir, did you notice any sign on Lady Waynflete's part of cawmplying with that verry moderate request?

LADY CICELY (outside). Coming, coming.

The prisoners are brought in by a guard of armed bluejackets.

Drinkwater first, again elaborately clean, and conveying by a virtuous and steadfast smirk a cheerful confidence in his innocence. Johnson solid and inexpressive, Redbrook unconcerned and debonair, Marzo uneasy. These four form a little group together on the captain's left. The rest wait unintelligently on Providence in a row against the wall on the same side, shepherded by the bluejackets. The first bluejacket, a petty officer, posts himself on the captain's right, behind Rankin and Sir Howard. Finally Brassbound appears with Lady Cicely on his arm. He is in fashionable frock coat and trousers, spotless collar and cuffs, and elegant boots. He carries a glossy tall hat in his hand. To an unsophisticated eye, the change is monstrous and appalling; and its effect on himself is so unmanning that he is quite out of countenance—a shaven Samson. Lady Cicely, however, is greatly pleased with it; and the rest regard it as an unquestionable improvement. The officers fall back gallantly to allow her to pass. Kearney rises to receive her, and stares with some surprise at Brassbound as he stops at the table on his left. Sir Howard rises punctiliously when Kearney rises and sits when he sits.

KEARNEY. Is this another gentleman of your party, Lady Waynflete? I presume I met you lahst night, sir, on board the yacht.

BRASSBOUND. No. I am your prisoner. My name is Brassbound.

DRINKWATER (officiously). Kepn Brarsbahnd, of the schooner Thenksgiv—

REDBROOK (hastily). Shut up, you fool. (He elbows Drinkwater into the background.)

KEARNEY (surprised and rather suspicious). Well, I hardly understahnd this. However, if you are Captain Brassbound, you can take your place with the rest. (Brassbound joins Redbrook and Johnson. Kearney sits down again, after inviting Lady Cicely, with a solemn gesture, to take the vacant chair.) Now let me see. You are a man of experience in these matters, Sir Howard Hallam. If you had to conduct this business, how would you start?

LADY CICELY. He'd call on the counsel for the prosecution, wouldn't you, Howard?

SIR HOWARD. But there is no counsel for the prosecution, Cicely.

LADY CICELY. Oh yes there is. I'm counsel for the prosecution. You mustn't let Sir Howard make a speech, Captain Kearney: his doctors have positively forbidden anything of that sort. Will you begin with me?

KEARNEY. By your leave, Lady Waynfiete, I think I will just begin with myself. Sailor fashion will do as well here as lawyer fashion.

LADY CICELY. Ever so much better, dear Captain Kearney. (Silence. Kearney composes himself to speak. She breaks out again). You look so nice as a judge!

A general smile. Drinkwater splutters into a half suppressed laugh.

REDBROOK (in a fierce whisper). Shut up, you fool, will you? (Again he pushes him back with a furtive kick.)

SIR HOWARD (remonstrating). Cicely!

KEARNEY (grimly keeping his countenance). Your ladyship's cawmpliments will be in order at a later stage. Captain Brassbound: the position is this. My ship, the United States cruiser Santiago, was spoken off Mogador latest Thursday by the yacht Redgauntlet. The owner of the aforesaid yacht, who is not present through having sprained his ankle, gave me sertn information. In cawnsequence of that information the Santiago made the twenty knots to Mogador Harbor inside of fifty-seven minutes. Before noon next day a messenger of mine gave the Cadi of the district sertn information. In cawnsequence of that information the Cadi stimulated himself to some ten knots an hour, and lodged you and your men in Mogador jail at my disposal. The Cadi then went back to his mountain fahstnesses; so we shall not have the pleasure of his company here to-day. Do you follow me so far?

BRASSBOUND. Yes. I know what you did and what the Cadi did. The point is, why did you do it?

KEARNEY. With doo patience we shall come to that presently. Mr. Rahnkin: will you kindly take up the parable?

RANKIN. On the very day that Sir Howrrd and Lady Cicely started on their excursion I was applied to for medicine by a follower of the Sheikh Sidi el Assif. He told me I should never see Sir Howrrd again, because his master knew he was a Christian and would take him out of the hands of Captain Brassbound. I hurried on board the yacht and told the owner to scour the coast for a gunboat or cruiser to come into the harbor and put persuasion on the authorities. (Sir Howard turns and looks at Rankin with a sudden doubt of his integrity as a witness.)

KEARNEY. But I understood from our chahplain that you reported Captain Brassbound as in league with the Sheikh to deliver Sir Howard up to him.

RANKIN. That was my first hasty conclusion, Captain Kearney. But it appears that the compact between them was that Captain Brassbound should escort travellers under the Sheikh's protection at a certain payment per head, provided none of them were Christians. As I understand it, he tried to smuggle Sir Howrrd through under this compact, and the Sheikh found him out.

DRINKWATER. Rawt, gavner. Thet's jest ah it wors. The Kepn—

REDBROOK (again suppressing him). Shut up, you fool, I tell you.

SIR HOWARD (to Rankin). May I ask have you had any conversation with Lady Cicely on this subject?

RANKIN (naively). Yes. (Sir Howard qrunts emphatically, as who should say "I thought so." Rankin continues, addressing the court) May I say how sorry I am that there are so few chairs, Captain and gentlemen.

KEARNEY (with genial American courtesy). Oh, THAT's all right, Mr. Rahnkin. Well, I see no harm so far: it's human fawlly, but not human crime. Now the counsel for the prosecution can proceed to prosecute. The floor is yours, Lady Waynflete.

LADY CICELY (rising). I can only tell you the exact truth—

DRINKWATER (involuntarily). Naow, down't do thet, lidy—

REDBROOK (as before). SHUT up, you fool, will you?

LADY CICELY. We had a most delightful trip in the hills; and Captain Brassbound's men could not have been nicer—I must say that for them—until we saw a tribe of Arabs—such nice looking men!—and then the poor things were frightened.

KEARNEY. The Arabs?

LADY CICELY. No: Arabs are never frightened. The escort, of course: escorts are always frightened. I wanted to speak to the Arab chief; but Captain Brassbound cruelly shot his horse; and the chief shot the Count; and then—

KEARNEY. The Count! What Count?

LADY CICELY. Marzo. That's Marzo (pointing to Marzo, who grins and touches his forehead).

KEARNEY (slightly overwhelmed by the unexpected profusion of incident and character in her story). Well, what happened then?

LADY CICELY. Then the escort ran away—all escorts do—and dragged me into the castle, which you really ought to make them clean and whitewash thoroughly, Captain Kearney. Then Captain Brassbound and Sir Howard turned out to be related to one another (sensation); and then of course, there was a quarrel. The Hallams always quarrel.

SIR HOWARD (rising to protest). Cicely! Captain Kearney: this man told me—

LADY CICELY (swiftly interrupting him). You mustn't say what people told you: it's not evidence. (Sir Howard chokes with indignation.)

KEARNEY (calmly). Allow the lady to proceed, Sir Howard Hallam.

SIR HOWARD (recovering his self-control with a gulp, and resuming his seat). I beg your pardon, Captain Kearney.

LADY CICELY. Then Sidi came.

KEARNEY. Sidney! Who was Sidney?

LADY CICELY. No, Sidi. The Sheikh. Sidi el Assif. A noble creature, with such a fine face! He fell in love with me at first sight—

SIR HOWARD (remonstrating). Cicely!

LADY CICELY. He did: you know he did. You told me to tell the exact truth.

KEARNEY. I can readily believe it, madam. Proceed.

LADY CICELY. Well, that put the poor fellow into a most cruel dilemma. You see, he could claim to carry off Sir Howard, because Sir Howard is a Christian. But as I am only a woman, he had no claim to me.

KEARNEY (somewhat sternly, suspecting Lady Cicely of aristocratic atheism). But you are a Christian woman.

LADY CICELY. No: the Arabs don't count women. They don't believe we have any souls.

RANKIN. That is true, Captain: the poor benighted creatures!

LADY CICELY. Well, what was he to do? He wasn't in love with Sir Howard; and he WAS in love with me. So he naturally offered to swop Sir Howard for me. Don't you think that was nice of him, Captain Kearney?

KEARNEY. I should have done the same myself, Lady Waynflete. Proceed.

LADY CICELY. Captain Brassbound, I must say, was nobleness itself, in spite of the quarrel between himself and Sir Howard. He refused to give up either of us, and was on the point of fighting for us when in came the Cadi with your most amusing and delightful letter, captain, and bundled us all back to Mogador after calling my poor Sidi the most dreadful names, and putting all the blame on Captain Brassbound. So here we are. Now, Howard, isn't that the exact truth, every word of it?

SIR HOWARD. It is the truth, Cicely, and nothing but the truth. But the English law requires a witness to tell the WHOLE truth.

LADY CICELY. What nonsense! As if anybody ever knew the whole truth about anything! (Sitting down, much hurt and discouraged.) I'm sorry you wish Captain Kearney to understand that I am an untruthful witness.

SIR HOWARD. No: but—

LADY CICELY. Very well, then: please don't say things that convey that impression.

KEARNEY. But Sir Howard told me yesterday that Captain Brassbound threatened to sell him into slavery.

LADY CICELY (springing up again). Did Sir Howard tell you the things he said about Captain Brassbound's mother? (Renewed sensation.) I told you they quarrelled, Captain Kearney. I said so, didn't I?

REDBROOK (crisply). Distinctly. (Drinkwater opens his mouth to corroborate.) Shut up, you fool.

LADY CICELY. Of course I did. Now, Captain Kearney, do YOU want me—does Sir Howard want me—does ANYBODY want me to go into the details of that shocking family quarrel? Am I to stand here in the absence of any individual of my own sex and repeat the language of two angry men?

KEARNEY (rising impressively). The United States navy will have no hahnd in offering any violence to the pure instincts of womanhood. Lady Waynflete: I thahnk you for the delicacy with which you have given your evidence. (Lady Cicely beams on him gratefully and sits down triumphant.) Captain Brassbound: I shall not hold you respawnsible for what you may have said when the English bench addressed you in the language of the English forecas-forecastle— (Sir Howard is about to protest.) No, Sir Howard Hallam: excuse ME. In moments of pahssion I have called a man that myself. We are glahd to find real flesh and blood beneath the ermine of the judge. We will all now drop a subject that should never have been broached in a lady's presence. (He resumes his seat, and adds, in a businesslike tone) Is there anything further before we release these men?

BLUEJACKET. There are some dawcuments handed over by the Cadi, sir. He reckoned they were sort of magic spells. The chahplain ordered them to be reported to you and burnt, with your leave, sir.

KEARNEY. What are they?

BLUEJACKET (reading from a list). Four books, torn and dirty, made up of separate numbers, value each wawn penny, and entitled Sweeny Todd, the Demon Barber of London; The Skeleton Horseman—

DRINKWATER (rushing forward in painful alarm, and anxiety). It's maw lawbrary, gavner. Down't burn em.

KEARNEY. You'll be better without that sort of reading, my man.

DRINKWATER (in intense distress, appealing to Lady Cicely) Down't let em burn em, Lidy. They dasn't if you horder them not to. (With desperate eloquence) Yer dunno wot them books is to me. They took me aht of the sawdid reeyellities of the Worterleoo Rowd. They formed maw mawnd: they shaowed me sathink awgher than the squalor of a corster's lawf—

REDBROOK (collaring him). Oh shut up, you fool. Get out. Hold your ton—

DRINKWATER (frantically breaking from him). Lidy, lidy: sy a word for me. Ev a feelin awt. (His tears choke him: he clasps his hands in dumb entreaty.)

LADY CICELY (touched). Don't burn his books. Captain. Let me give them back to him.

KEARNEY. The books will be handed over to the lady.

DRINKWATER (in a small voice). Thenkyer, Lidy. (He retires among his comrades, snivelling subduedly.)

REDBROOK (aside to him as he passes). You silly ass, you. (Drinkwater sniffs and does not reply.)

KEARNEY. I suppose you and your men accept this lady's account of what passed, Captain Brassbound.

BRASSBOUND (gloomily). Yes. It is true—as far as it goes.

KEARNEY (impatiently). Do you wawnt it to go any further?

MARZO. She leave out something. Arab shoot me. She nurse me. She cure me.

KEARNEY. And who are you, pray?

MARZO (seized with a sanctimonious desire to demonstrate his higher nature). Only dam thief. Dam liar. Dam rascal. She no lady.

JOHNSON (revolted by the seeming insult to the English peerage from a low Italian). What? What's that you say?

MARZO. No lady nurse dam rascal. Only saint. She saint. She get me to heaven—get us all to heaven. We do what we like now.

LADY CICELY. Indeed you will do nothing of the sort Marzo, unless you like to behave yourself very nicely indeed. What hour did you say we were to lunch at, Captain Kearney?

KEARNEY. You recall me to my dooty, Lady Waynflete. My barge will be ready to take off you and Sir Howard to the Santiago at one o'clawk. (He rises.) Captain Brassbound: this innquery has elicited no reason why I should detain you or your men. I advise you to ahct as escort in future to heathens exclusively. Mr. Rahnkin: I thahnk you in the name of the United States for the hospitahlity you have extended to us today; and I invite you to accompany me bahck to my ship with a view to lunch at half-past one. Gentlemen: we will wait on the governor of the gaol on our way to the harbor (He goes out, following his officers, and followed by the bluejackets and the petty officer.)

SIR HOWARD (to Lady Cicely). Cicely: in the course of my professional career I have met with unscrupulous witnesses, and, I am sorry to say, unscrupulous counsel also. But the combination of unscrupulous witness and unscrupulous counsel I have met to-day has taken away my breath You have made me your accomplice in defeating justice.

LADY CICELY. Yes: aren't you glad it's been defeated for once? (She takes his arm to go out with him.) Captain Brassbound: I will come back to say goodbye before I go. (He nods gloomily. She goes out with Sir Howard, following the Captain and his staff.)

RANKIN (running to Brassbound and taking both his hands). I'm right glad ye're cleared. I'll come back and have a crack with ye when yon lunch is over. God bless ye. (Hs goes out quickly.)

Brassbound and his men, left by themselves in the room, free and unobserved, go straight out of their senses. They laugh; they dance; they embrace one another; they set to partners and waltz clumsily; they shake hands repeatedly and maudlinly. Three only retain some sort of self-possession. Marzo, proud of having successfully thrust himself into a leading part in the recent proceedings and made a dramatic speech, inflates his chest, curls his scanty moustache, and throws himself into a swaggering pose, chin up and right foot forward, despising the emotional English barbarians around him. Brassbound's eyes and the working of his mouth show that he is infected with the general excitement; but he bridles himself savagely. Redbrook, trained to affect indifference, grins cynically; winks at Brassbound; and finally relieves himself by assuming the character of a circus ringmaster, flourishing an imaginary whip and egging on the rest to wilder exertions. A climax is reached when Drinkwater, let loose without a stain on his character for the second time, is rapt by belief in his star into an ecstasy in which, scorning all partnership, he becomes as it were a whirling dervish, and executes so miraculous a clog dance that the others gradually cease their slower antics to stare at him.

BRASSBOUND (tearing off his hat and striding forward as Drinkwater collapses, exhausted, and is picked up by Redbrook). Now to get rid of this respectable clobber and feel like a man again. Stand by, all hands, to jump on the captain's tall hat. (He puts the hat down and prepares to jump on it. The effect is startling, and takes him completely aback. His followers, far from appreciating his iconoclasm, are shocked into scandalized sobriety, except Redbrook, who is immensely tickled by their prudery.)

DRINKWATER. Naow, look eah, kepn: that ynt rawt. Dror a lawn somewhere.

JOHNSON. I say nothin agen a bit of fun, Capn, but let's be gentlemen.

REDBROOK. I suggest to you, Brassbound, that the clobber belongs to Lady Sis. Ain't you going to give it back to her?

BRASSBOUND (picking up the hat and brushing the dust off it anxiously). That's true. I'm a fool. All the same, she shall not see me again like this. (He pulls off the coat and waistcoat together.) Does any man here know how to fold up this sort of thing properly?

REDBROOK. Allow me, governor. (He takes the coat and waistcoat to the table, and folds them up.)

BRASSBOUND (loosening his collar and the front of his shirt). Brandyfaced Jack: you're looking at these studs. I know what's in your mind.

DRINKWATER (indignantly). Naow yer down't: nort a bit on it. Wot's in maw mawnd is secrifawce, seolf-secrifawce.

BRASSBOUND. If one brass pin of that lady's property is missing, I'll hang you with my own hands at the gaff of the Thanksgiving—and would, if she were lying under the guns of all the fleets in Europe. (He pulls off the shirt and stands in his blue jersey, with his hair ruffled. He passes his hand through it and exclaims) Now I am half a man, at any rate.

REDBROOK. A horrible combination, governor: churchwarden from the waist down, and the rest pirate. Lady Sis won't speak to you in it.

BRASSBOUND. I'll change altogether. (He leaves the room to get his own trousers.)

REDBROOK (softly). Look here, Johnson, and gents generally. (They gather about him.) Spose she takes him back to England!

MARZO (trying to repeat his success). Im! Im only dam pirate. She saint, I tell you—no take any man nowhere.

JOHNSON (severely). Don't you be a ignorant and immoral foreigner. (The rebuke is well received; and Marzo is hustled into the background and extinguished.) She won't take him for harm; but she might take him for good. And then where should we be?

DRINKWATER. Brarsbahnd ynt the ownly kepn in the world. Wot mikes a kepn is brines an knollidge o lawf. It ynt thet ther's naow sitch pusson: it's thet you dunno where to look fr im. (The implication that he is such a person is so intolerable that they receive it with a prolonged burst of booing.)

BRASSBOUND (returning in his own clothes, getting into his jacket as he comes). Stand by, all. (They start asunder guiltily, and wait for orders.) Redbrook: you pack that clobber in the lady's portmanteau, and put it aboard the yacht for her. Johnson: you take all hands aboard the Thanksgiving; look through the stores: weigh anchor; and make all ready for sea. Then send Jack to wait for me at the slip with a boat; and give me a gunfire for a signal. Lose no time.

JOHNSON. Ay, ay, air. All aboard, mates.

ALL. Ay, ay. (They rush out tumultuously.)

When they are gone, Brassbound sits down at the end of the table, with his elbows on it and his head on his fists, gloomily thinking. Then he takes from the breast pocket of his jacket a leather case, from which he extracts a scrappy packet of dirty letters and newspaper cuttings. These he throws on the table. Next comes a photograph in a cheap frame. He throws it down untenderly beside the papers; then folds his arms, and is looking at it with grim distaste when Lady Cicely enters. His back is towards her; and he does not hear her. Perceiving this, she shuts the door loudly enough to attract his attention. He starts up.

LADY CICELY (coming to the opposite end of the table). So you've taken off all my beautiful clothes!

BRASSBOUND. Your brother's, you mean. A man should wear his own clothes; and a man should tell his own lies. I'm sorry you had to tell mine for me to-day.

LADY CICELY. Oh, women spend half their lives telling little lies for men, and sometimes big ones. We're used to it. But mind! I don't admit that I told any to-day.

BRASSBOUND. How did you square my uncle?

LADY CICELY. I don't understand the expression.

BRASSBOUND. I mean—

LADY CICELY. I'm afraid we haven't time to go into what you mean before lunch. I want to speak to you about your future. May I?

BRASSBOUND (darkening a little, but politely). Sit down. (She sits down. So does he.)

LADY CICELY. What are your plans?

BRASSBOUND. I have no plans. You will hear a gun fired in the harbor presently. That will mean that the Thanksgiving's anchor's weighed and that she is waiting for her captain to put out to sea. And her captain doesn't know now whether to turn her head north or south.

LADY CICELY. Why not north for England?

BRASSBOUND. Why not south for the Pole?

LADY CICELY. But you must do something with yourself.

BRASSBOUND (settling himself with his fists and elbows weightily on the table and looking straight and powerfully at her). Look you: when you and I first met, I was a man with a purpose. I stood alone: I saddled no friend, woman or man, with that purpose, because it was against law, against religion, against my own credit and safety. But I believed in it; and I stood alone for it, as a man should stand for his belief, against law and religion as much as against wickedness and selfishness. Whatever I may be, I am none of your fairweather sailors that'll do nothing for their creed but go to Heaven for it. I was ready to go to hell for mine. Perhaps you don't understand that.

LADY CICELY. Oh bless you, yes. It's so very like a certain sort of man.

BRASSBOUND. I daresay but I've not met many of that sort. Anyhow, that was what I was like. I don't say I was happy in it; but I wasn't unhappy, because I wasn't drifting. I was steering a course and had work in hand. Give a man health and a course to steer; and he'll never stop to trouble about whether he's happy or not.

LADY CICELY. Sometimes he won't even stop to trouble about whether other people are happy or not.

BRASSBOUND. I don't deny that: nothing makes a man so selfish as work. But I was not self-seeking: it seemed to me that I had put justice above self. I tell you life meant something to me then. Do you see that dirty little bundle of scraps of paper?

LADY CICELY. What are they?

BRASSBOUND. Accounts cut out of newspapers. Speeches made by my uncle at charitable dinners, or sentencing men to death—pious, high-minded speeches by a man who was to me a thief and a murderer! To my mind they were more weighty, more momentous, better revelations of the wickedness of law and respectability than the book of the prophet Amos. What are they now? (He quietly tears the newspaper cuttings into little fragments and throws them away, looking fixedly at her meanwhile.)

LADY CICELY. Well, that's a comfort, at all events.

BRASSBOUND. Yes; but it's a part of my life gone: YOUR doing, remember. What have I left? See here! (He take up the letters) the letters my uncle wrote to my mother, with her comments on their cold drawn insolence, their treachery and cruelty. And the piteous letters she wrote to him later on, returned unopened. Must they go too?

LADY CICELY (uneasily). I can't ask you to destroy your mother's letters.

BRASSBOUND. Why not, now that you have taken the meaning out of them? (He tears them.) Is that a comfort too?

LADY CICELY. It's a little sad; but perhaps it is best so.

BRASSBOUND. That leaves one relic: her portrait. (He plucks the photograph out of its cheap case.)

LADY CICELY (with vivid curiosity). Oh, let me see. (He hands it to her. Before she can control herself, her expression changes to one of unmistakable disappointment and repulsion.)

BRASSBOUND (with a single sardonic cachination). Ha! You expected something better than that. Well, you're right. Her face does not look well opposite yours.

LADY CICELY (distressed). I said nothing.

BRASSBOUND. What could you say? (He takes back the portrait: she relinquishes it without a word. He looks at it; shakes his head; and takes it quietly between his finger and thumb to tear it.)

LADY CICELY (staying his hand). Oh, not your mother's picture!

BRASSBOUND. If that were your picture, would you like your son to keep it for younger and better women to see?

LADY CICELY (releasing his hand). Oh, you are dreadful! Tear it, tear it. (She covers her eyes for a moment to shut out the sight.)

BRASSBOUND (tearing it quietly). You killed her for me that day in the castle; and I am better without her. (He throws away the fragments.) Now everything is gone. You have taken the old meaning out of my life; but you have put no new meaning into it. I can see that you have some clue to the world that makes all its difficulties easy for you; but I'm not clever enough to seize it. You've lamed me by showing me that I take life the wrong way when I'm left to myself.

LADY CICELY. Oh no. Why do you say that?

BRASSBOUND. What else can I say? See what I've done! My uncle is no worse a man than myself—better, most likely; for he has a better head and a higher place. Well, I took him for a villain out of a storybook. My mother would have opened anybody else's eyes: she shut mine. I'm a stupider man than Brandyfaced Jack even; for he got his romantic nonsense out of his penny numbers and such like trash; but I got just the same nonsense out of life and experience. (Shaking his head) It was vulgar—VULGAR. I see that now; for you've opened my eyes to the past; but what good is that for the future? What am I to do? Where am I to go?

LADY CICELY. It's quite simple. Do whatever you like. That's what I always do.

BRASSBOUND. That answer is no good to me. What I like is to have something to do; and I have nothing. You might as well talk like the missionary and tell me to do my duty.

LADY CICELY (quickly). Oh no thank you. I've had quite enough of your duty, and Howard's duty. Where would you both be now if I'd let you do it?

BRASSBOUND. We'd have been somewhere, at all events. It seems to me that now I am nowhere.

LADY CICELY. But aren't you coming back to England with us?

BRASSBOUND. What for?

LADY CICELY. Why, to make the most of your opportunities.

BRASSBOUND. What opportunities?

LADY CICELY. Don't you understand that when you are the nephew of a great bigwig, and have influential connexions, and good friends among them, lots of things can be done for you that are never done for ordinary ship captains?

BRASSBOUND. Ah; but I'm not an aristocrat, you see. And like most poor men, I'm proud. I don't like being patronized.

LADY CICELY. What is the use of saying that? In my world, which is now your world—OUR world—getting patronage is the whole art of life. A man can't have a career without it.

BRASSBOUND. In my world a man can navigate a ship and get his living by it.

LADY CICELY. Oh, I see you're one of the Idealists—the Impossibilists! We have them, too, occasionally, in our world. There's only one thing to be done with them.

BRASSBOUND. What's that?

LADY CICELY. Marry them straight off to some girl with enough money for them, and plenty of sentiment. That's their fate.

BRASSBOUND. You've spoiled even that chance for me. Do you think I could look at any ordinary woman after you? You seem to be able to make me do pretty well what you like; but you can't make me marry anybody but yourself.

LADY CICELY. Do you know, Captain Paquito, that I've married no less than seventeen men (Brassbound stares) to other women. And they all opened the subject by saying that they would never marry anybody but me.

BRASSBOUND. Then I shall be the first man you ever found to stand to his word.

LADY CICELY (part pleased, part amused, part sympathetic). Do you really want a wife?

BRASSBOUND. I want a commander. Don't undervalue me: I am a good man when I have a good leader. I have courage: I have determination: I'm not a drinker: I can command a schooner and a shore party if I can't command a ship or an army. When work is put upon me, I turn neither to save my life nor to fill my pocket. Gordon trusted me; and he never regretted it. If you trust me, you shan't regret it. All the same, there's something wanting in me: I suppose I'm stupid.

LADY CICELY. Oh, you're not stupid.

BRASSBOUND. Yes I am. Since you saw me for the first time in that garden, you've heard me say nothing clever. And I've heard you say nothing that didn't make me laugh, or make me feel friendly, as well as telling me what to think and what to do. That's what I mean by real cleverness. Well, I haven't got it. I can give an order when I know what order to give. I can make men obey it, willing or unwilling. But I'm stupid, I tell you: stupid. When there's no Gordon to command me, I can't think of what to do. Left to myself, I've become half a brigand. I can kick that little gutterscrub Drinkwater; but I find myself doing what he puts into my head because I can't think of anything else. When you came, I took your orders as naturally as I took Gordon's, though I little thought my next commander would be a woman. I want to take service under you. And there's no way in which that can be done except marrying you. Will you let me do it?

LADY CICELY. I'm afraid you don't quite know how odd a match it would be for me according to the ideas of English society.

BRASSBOUND. I care nothing about English society: let it mind its own business.

LADY CICELY (rising, a little alarmed). Captain Paquito: I am not in love with you.

BRASSBOUND (also rising, with his gaze still steadfastly on her). I didn't suppose you were: the commander is not usually in love with his subordinate.

LADY CICELY. Nor the subordinate with the commander.

BRASSBOUND (assenting firmly). Nor the subordinate with the commander.

LADY CICELY (learning for the first time in her life what terror is, as she finds that he is unconsciously mesmerizing her). Oh, you are dangerous!

BRASSBOUND. Come: are you in love with anybody else? That's the question.

LADY CICELY (shaking her head). I have never been in love with any real person; and I never shall. How could I manage people if I had that mad little bit of self left in me? That's my secret.

BRASSBOUND. Then throw away the last bit of self. Marry me.

LADY CICELY (vainly struggling to recall her wandering will). Must I?

BRASSBOUND. There is no must. You CAN. I ask you to. My fate depends on it.

LADY CICELY. It's frightful; for I don't mean to—don't wish to.

BRASSBOUND. But you will.

LADY CICELY (quite lost, slowly stretches out her hand to give it to him). I— (Gunfire from the Thanksgiving. His eyes dilate. It wakes her from her trance) What is that?

BRASSBOUND. It is farewell. Rescue for you—safety, freedom! You were made to be something better than the wife of Black Paquito. (He kneels and takes her hands) You can do no more for me now: I have blundered somehow on the secret of command at last (he kisses her hands): thanks for that, and for a man's power and purpose restored and righted. And farewell, farewell, farewell.

LADY CICELY (in a strange ecstasy, holding his hands as he rises). Oh, farewell. With my heart's deepest feeling, farewell, farewell.

BRASSBOUND. With my heart's noblest honor and triumph, farewell. (He turns and flies.)

LADY CICELY. How glorious! how glorious! And what an escape!

CURTAIN

NOTES TO CAPTAIN BRASSBOUND'S CONVERSION

SOURCES OF THE PLAY

I claim as a notable merit in the authorship of this play that I have been intelligent enough to steal its scenery, its surroundings, its atmosphere, its geography, its knowledge of the east, its fascinating Cadis and Kearneys and Sheikhs and mud castles from an excellent book of philosophic travel and vivid adventure entitled Mogreb-el-Acksa (Morocco the Most Holy) by Cunninghame Graham. My own first hand knowledge of Morocco is based on a morning's walk through Tangier, and a cursory observation of the coast through a binocular from the deck of an Orient steamer, both later in date than the writing of the play.

Cunninghame Graham is the hero of his own book; but I have not made him the hero of my play, because so incredible a personage must have destroyed its likelihood—such as it is. There are moments when I do not myself believe in his existence. And yet he must be real; for I have seen him with these eyes; and I am one of the few men living who can decipher the curious alphabet in which he writes his private letters. The man is on public record too. The battle of Trafalgar Square, in which he personally and bodily assailed civilization as represented by the concentrated military and constabular forces of the capital of the world, can scarcely be forgotten by the more discreet spectators, of whom I was one. On that occasion civilization, qualitatively his inferior, was quantitatively so hugely in excess of him that it put him in prison, but had not sense enough to keep him there. Yet his getting out of prison was as nothing compared to his getting into the House of Commons. How he did it I know not; but the thing certainly happened, somehow. That he made pregnant utterances as a legislator may be taken as proved by the keen philosophy of the travels and tales he has since tossed to us; but the House, strong in stupidity, did not understand him until in an inspired moment he voiced a universal impulse by bluntly damning its hypocrisy. Of all the eloquence of that silly parliament, there remains only one single damn. It has survived the front bench speeches of the eighties as the word of Cervantes survives the oraculations of the Dons and Deys who put him, too, in prison. The shocked House demanded that he should withdraw his cruel word. "I never withdraw," said he; and I promptly stole the potent phrase for the sake of its perfect style, and used it as a cockade for the Bulgarian hero of Arms and the Man. The theft prospered; and I naturally take the first opportunity of repeating it. In what other Lepantos besides Trafalgar Square Cunninghame Graham has fought, I cannot tell. He is a fascinating mystery to a sedentary person like myself. The horse, a dangerous animal whom, when I cannot avoid, I propitiate with apples and sugar, he bestrides and dominates fearlessly, yet with a true republican sense of the rights of the four-legged fellowcreature whose martyrdom, and man's shame therein, he has told most powerfully in his Calvary, a tale with an edge that will cut the soft cruel hearts and strike fire from the hard kind ones. He handles the other lethal weapons as familiarly as the pen: medieval sword and modern Mauser are to him as umbrellas and kodaks are to me. His tales of adventure have the true Cervantes touch of the man who has been there—so refreshingly different from the scenes imagined by bloody-minded clerks who escape from their servitude into literature to tell us how men and cities are conceived in the counting house and the volunteer corps. He is, I understand, a Spanish hidalgo: hence the superbity of his portrait by Lavery (Velasquez being no longer available). He is, I know, a Scotch laird. How he contrives to be authentically the two things at the same time is no more intelligible to me than the fact that everything that has ever happened to him seems to have happened in Paraguay or Texas instead of in Spain or Scotland. He is, I regret to add, an impenitent and unashamed dandy: such boots, such a hat, would have dazzled D'Orsay himself. With that hat he once saluted me in Regent St. when I was walking with my mother. Her interest was instantly kindled; and the following conversation ensued. "Who is that?" "Cunninghame Graham." "Nonsense! Cunninghame Graham is one of your Socialists: that man is a gentleman." This is the punishment of vanity, a fault I have myself always avoided, as I find conceit less troublesome and much less expensive. Later on somebody told him of Tarudant, a city in Morocco in which no Christian had ever set foot. Concluding at once that it must be an exceptionally desirable place to live in, he took ship and horse: changed the hat for a turban; and made straight for the sacred city, via Mogador. How he fared, and how he fell into the hands of the Cadi of Kintafi, who rightly held that there was more danger to Islam in one Cunninghame Graham than in a thousand Christians, may be learnt from his account of it in Mogreb-el-Acksa, without which Captain Brassbound's Conversion would never have been written.

I am equally guiltless of any exercise of invention concerning the story of the West Indian estate which so very nearly serves as a peg to hang Captain Brassbound. To Mr. Frederick Jackson of Hindhead, who, against all his principles, encourages and abets me in my career as a dramatist, I owe my knowledge of those main facts of the case which became public through an attempt to make the House of Commons act on them. This being so, I must add that the character of Captain Brassbound's mother, like the recovery of the estate by the next heir, is an interpolation of my own. It is not, however, an invention. One of the evils of the pretence that our institutions represent abstract principles of justice instead of being mere social scaffolding is that persons of a certain temperament take the pretence seriously, and when the law is on the side of injustice, will not accept the situation, and are driven mad by their vain struggle against it. Dickens has drawn the type in his Man from Shropshire in Bleak House. Most public men and all lawyers have been appealed to by victims of this sense of injustice—the most unhelpable of afflictions in a society like ours.

ENGLISH AND AMERICAN DIALECTS

The fact that English is spelt conventionally and not phonetically makes the art of recording speech almost impossible. What is more, it places the modern dramatist, who writes for America as well as England, in a most trying position. Take for example my American captain and my English lady. I have spelt the word conduce, as uttered by the American captain, as cawndooce, to suggest (very roughly) the American pronunciation to English readers. Then why not spell the same word, when uttered by Lady Cicely, as kerndewce, to suggest the English pronunciation to American readers? To this I have absolutely no defence: I can only plead that an author who lives in England necessarily loses his consciousness of the peculiarities of English speech, and sharpens his consciousness of the points in which American speech differs from it; so that it is more convenient to leave English peculiarities to be recorded by American authors. I must, however, most vehemently disclaim any intention of suggesting that English pronunciation is authoritative and correct. My own tongue is neither American English nor English English, but Irish English; so I am as nearly impartial in the matter as it is in human nature to be. Besides, there is no standard English pronunciation any more than there is an American one: in England every county has its catchwords, just as no doubt every state in the Union has. I cannot believe that the pioneer American, for example, can spare time to learn that last refinement of modern speech, the exquisite diphthong, a farfetched combination of the French eu and the English e, with which a New Yorker pronounces such words as world, bird &c. I have spent months without success in trying to achieve glibness with it.

To Felix Drinkwater also I owe some apology for implying that all his vowel pronunciations are unfashionable. They are very far from being so. As far as my social experience goes (and I have kept very mixed company) there is no class in English society in which a good deal of Drinkwater pronunciation does not pass unchallenged save by the expert phonetician. This is no mere rash and ignorant jibe of my own at the expense of my English neighbors. Academic authority in the matter of English speech is represented at present by Mr. Henry Sweet, of the University of Oxford, whose Elementarbuch des gesprochenen Engliach, translated into his native language for the use of British islanders as a Primer of Spoken English, is the most accessible standard work on the subject. In such words as plum, come, humbug, up, gum, etc., Mr. Sweet's evidence is conclusive. Ladies and gentlemen in Southern England pronounce them as plam, kam, hambag, ap, gan, etc., exactly as Felix Drinkwater does. I could not claim Mr. Sweet's authority if I dared to whisper that such coster English as the rather pretty dahn tahn for down town, or the decidedly ugly cowcow for cocoa is current in very polite circles. The entire nation, costers and all, would undoubtedly repudiate any such pronunciation as vulgar. All the same, if I were to attempt to represent current "smart" cockney speech as I have attempted to represent Drinkwater's, without the niceties of Mr. Sweet's Romic alphabets, I am afraid I should often have to write dahn tahn and cowcow as being at least nearer to the actual sound than down town and cocoa. And this would give such offence that I should have to leave the country; for nothing annoys a native speaker of English more than a faithful setting down in phonetic spelling of the sounds he utters. He imagines that a departure from conventional spelling indicates a departure from the correct standard English of good society. Alas! this correct standard English of good society is unknown to phoneticians. It is only one of the many figments that bewilder our poor snobbish brains. No such thing exists; but what does that matter to people trained from infancy to make a point of honor of belief in abstractions and incredibilities? And so I am compelled to hide Lady Cicely's speech under the veil of conventional orthography.

I need not shield Drinkwater, because he will never read my book. So I have taken the liberty of making a special example of him, as far as that can be done without a phonetic alphabet, for the benefit of the mass of readers outside London who still form their notions of cockney dialect on Sam Weller. When I came to London in 1876, the Sam Weller dialect had passed away so completely that I should have given it up as a literary fiction if I had not discovered it surviving in a Middlesex village, and heard of it from an Essex one. Some time in the eighties the late Andrew Tuer called attention in the Pall Mall Gazette to several peculiarities of modern cockney, and to the obsolescence of the Dickens dialect that was still being copied from book to book by authors who never dreamt of using their ears, much less of training them to listen. Then came Mr. Anstey's cockney dialogues in Punch, a great advance, and Mr. Chevalier's coster songs and patter. The Tompkins verses contributed by Mr. Barry Pain to the London Daily Chronicle have also done something to bring the literary convention for cockney English up to date. But Tompkins sometimes perpetrates horrible solecisms. He will pronounce face as fits, accurately enough; but he will rhyme it quite impossibly to nice, which Tompkins would pronounce as newts: for example Mawl Enn Rowd for Mile End Road. This aw for i, which I have made Drinkwater use, is the latest stage of the old diphthongal oi, which Mr. Chevalier still uses. Irish, Scotch and north country readers must remember that Drinkwater's rs are absolutely unpronounced when they follow a vowel, though they modify the vowel very considerably. Thus, luggage is pronounced by him as laggige, but turn is not pronounced as tern, but as teun with the eu sounded as in French. The London r seems thoroughly understood in America, with the result, however, that the use of the r by Artemus Ward and other American dialect writers causes Irish people to misread them grotesquely. I once saw the pronunciation of malheureux represented in a cockney handbook by mal-err-err: not at all a bad makeshift to instruct a Londoner, but out of the question elsewhere in the British Isles. In America, representations of English speech dwell too derisively on the dropped or interpolated h. American writers have apparently not noticed the fact that the south English h is not the same as the never-dropped Irish and American h, and that to ridicule an Englishman for dropping it is as absurd as to ridicule the whole French and Italian nation for doing the same. The American h, helped out by a general agreement to pronounce wh as hw, is tempestuously audible, and cannot be dropped without being immediately missed. The London h is so comparatively quiet at all times, and so completely inaudible in wh, that it probably fell out of use simply by escaping the ears of children learning to speak. However that may be, it is kept alive only by the literate classes who are reminded constantly of its existence by seeing it on paper.

Roughly speaking, I should say that in England he who bothers about his hs is a fool, and he who ridicules a dropped h a snob. As to the interpolated h, my experience as a London vestryman has convinced me that it is often effective as a means of emphasis, and that the London language would be poorer without it. The objection to it is no more respectable than the objection of a street boy to a black man or to a lady in knickerbockers.

I have made only the most perfunctory attempt to represent the dialect of the missionary. There is no literary notation for the grave music of good Scotch.

BLACKDOWN, August 1900

MAN AND SUPERMAN

A COMEDY AND A PHILOSOPHY

EPISTLE DEDICATORY TO ARTHUR BINGHAM WALKLEY

My dear Walkley:

You once asked me why I did not write a Don Juan play. The levity with which you assumed this frightful responsibility has probably by this time enabled you to forget it; but the day of reckoning has arrived: here is your play! I say your play, because qui facit per alium facit per se. Its profits, like its labor, belong to me: its morals, its manners, its philosophy, its influence on the young, are for you to justify. You were of mature age when you made the suggestion; and you knew your man. It is hardly fifteen years since, as twin pioneers of the New Journalism of that time, we two, cradled in the same new sheets, made an epoch in the criticism of the theatre and the opera house by making it a pretext for a propaganda of our own views of life. So you cannot plead ignorance of the character of the force you set in motion. You meant me to epater le bourgeois; and if he protests, I hereby refer him to you as the accountable party.

I warn you that if you attempt to repudiate your responsibility, I shall suspect you of finding the play too decorous for your taste. The fifteen years have made me older and graver. In you I can detect no such becoming change. Your levities and audacities are like the loves and comforts prayed for by Desdemona: they increase, even as your days do grow. No mere pioneering journal dares meddle with them now: the stately Times itself is alone sufficiently above suspicion to act as your chaperone; and even the Times must sometimes thank its stars that new plays are not produced every day, since after each such event its gravity is compromised, its platitude turned to epigram, its portentousness to wit, its propriety to elegance, and even its decorum into naughtiness by criticisms which the traditions of the paper do not allow you to sign at the end, but which you take care to sign with the most extravagant flourishes between the lines. I am not sure that this is not a portent of Revolution. In eighteenth century France the end was at hand when men bought the Encyclopedia and found Diderot there. When I buy the Times and find you there, my prophetic ear catches a rattle of twentieth century tumbrils.

However, that is not my present anxiety. The question is, will you not be disappointed with a Don Juan play in which not one of that hero's mille e tre adventures is brought upon the stage? To propitiate you, let me explain myself. You will retort that I never do anything else: it is your favorite jibe at me that what I call drama is nothing but explanation. But you must not expect me to adopt your inexplicable, fantastic, petulant, fastidious ways: you must take me as I am, a reasonable, patient, consistent, apologetic, laborious person, with the temperament of a schoolmaster and the pursuits of a vestryman. No doubt that literary knack of mine which happens to amuse the British public distracts attention from my character; but the character is there none the less, solid as bricks. I have a conscience; and conscience is always anxiously explanatory. You, on the contrary, feel that a man who discusses his conscience is much like a woman who discusses her modesty. The only moral force you condescend to parade is the force of your wit: the only demand you make in public is the demand of your artistic temperament for symmetry, elegance, style, grace, refinement, and the cleanliness which comes next to godliness if not before it. But my conscience is the genuine pulpit article: it annoys me to see people comfortable when they ought to be uncomfortable; and I insist on making them think in order to bring them to conviction of sin. If you don't like my preaching you must lump it. I really cannot help it.

In the preface to my Plays for Puritans I explained the predicament of our contemporary English drama, forced to deal almost exclusively with cases of sexual attraction, and yet forbidden to exhibit the incidents of that attraction or even to discuss its nature. Your suggestion that I should write a Don Juan play was virtually a challenge to me to treat this subject myself dramatically. The challenge was difficult enough to be worth accepting, because, when you come to think of it, though we have plenty of dramas with heroes and heroines who are in love and must accordingly marry or perish at the end of the play, or about people whose relations with one another have been complicated by the marriage laws, not to mention the looser sort of plays which trade on the tradition that illicit love affairs are at once vicious and delightful, we have no modern English plays in which the natural attraction of the sexes for one another is made the mainspring of the action. That is why we insist on beauty in our performers, differing herein from the countries our friend William Archer holds up as examples of seriousness to our childish theatres. There the Juliets and Isoldes, the Romeos and Tristans, might be our mothers and fathers. Not so the English actress. The heroine she impersonates is not allowed to discuss the elemental relations of men and women: all her romantic twaddle about novelet-made love, all her purely legal dilemmas as to whether she was married or "betrayed," quite miss our hearts and worry our minds. To console ourselves we must just look at her. We do so; and her beauty feeds our starving emotions. Sometimes we grumble ungallantly at the lady because she does not act as well as she looks. But in a drama which, with all its preoccupation with sex, is really void of sexual interest, good looks are more desired than histrionic skill.

Let me press this point on you, since you are too clever to raise the fool's cry of paradox whenever I take hold of a stick by the right instead of the wrong end. Why are our occasional attempts to deal with the sex problem on the stage so repulsive and dreary that even those who are most determined that sex questions shall be held open and their discussion kept free, cannot pretend to relish these joyless attempts at social sanitation? Is it not because at bottom they are utterly sexless? What is the usual formula for such plays? A woman has, on some past occasion, been brought into conflict with the law which regulates the relations of the sexes. A man, by falling in love with her, or marrying her, is brought into conflict with the social convention which discountenances the woman. Now the conflicts of individuals with law and convention can be dramatized like all other human conflicts; but they are purely judicial; and the fact that we are much more curious about the suppressed relations between the man and the woman than about the relations between both and our courts of law and private juries of matrons, produces that sensation of evasion, of dissatisfaction, of fundamental irrelevance, of shallowness, of useless disagreeableness, of total failure to edify and partial failure to interest, which is as familiar to you in the theatres as it was to me when I, too, frequented those uncomfortable buildings, and found our popular playwrights in the mind to (as they thought) emulate Ibsen.

I take it that when you asked me for a Don Juan play you did not want that sort of thing. Nobody does: the successes such plays sometimes obtain are due to the incidental conventional melodrama with which the experienced popular author instinctively saves himself from failure. But what did you want? Owing to your unfortunate habit—you now, I hope, feel its inconvenience—of not explaining yourself, I have had to discover this for myself. First, then, I have had to ask myself, what is a Don Juan? Vulgarly, a libertine. But your dislike of vulgarity is pushed to the length of a defect (universality of character is impossible without a share of vulgarity); and even if you could acquire the taste, you would find yourself overfed from ordinary sources without troubling me. So I took it that you demanded a Don Juan in the philosophic sense.

Philosophically, Don Juan is a man who, though gifted enough to be exceptionally capable of distinguishing between good and evil, follows his own instincts without regard to the common statute, or canon law; and therefore, whilst gaining the ardent sympathy of our rebellious instincts (which are flattered by the brilliancies with which Don Juan associates them) finds himself in mortal conflict with existing institutions, and defends himself by fraud and farce as unscrupulously as a farmer defends his crops by the same means against vermin. The prototypic Don Juan, invented early in the XVI century by a Spanish monk, was presented, according to the ideas of that time, as the enemy of God, the approach of whose vengeance is felt throughout the drama, growing in menace from minute to minute. No anxiety is caused on Don Juan's account by any minor antagonist: he easily eludes the police, temporal and spiritual; and when an indignant father seeks private redress with the sword, Don Juan kills him without an effort. Not until the slain father returns from heaven as the agent of God, in the form of his own statue, does he prevail against his slayer and cast him into hell. The moral is a monkish one: repent and reform now; for to-morrow it may be too late. This is really the only point on which Don Juan is sceptical; for he is a devout believer in an ultimate hell, and risks damnation only because, as he is young, it seems so far off that repentance can be postponed until he has amused himself to his heart's content.

But the lesson intended by an author is hardly ever the lesson the world chooses to learn from his book. What attracts and impresses us in El Burlador de Sevilla is not the immediate urgency of repentance, but the heroism of daring to be the enemy of God. From Prometheus to my own Devil's Disciple, such enemies have always been popular. Don Juan became such a pet that the world could not bear his damnation. It reconciled him sentimentally to God in a second version, and clamored for his canonization for a whole century, thus treating him as English journalism has treated that comic foe of the gods, Punch. Moliere's Don Juan casts back to the original in point of impenitence; but in piety he falls off greatly. True, he also proposes to repent; but in what terms? "Oui, ma foi! il faut s'amender. Encore vingt ou trente ans de cette vie-ci, et puis nous songerons a nous." After Moliere comes the artist-enchanter, the master of masters, Mozart, who reveals the hero's spirit in magical harmonies, elfin tones, and elate darting rhythms as of summer lightning made audible. Here you have freedom in love and in morality mocking exquisitely at slavery to them, and interesting you, attracting you, tempting you, inexplicably forcing you to range the hero with his enemy the statue on a transcendant plane, leaving the prudish daughter and her priggish lover on a crockery shelf below to live piously ever after.

After these completed works Byron's fragment does not count for much philosophically. Our vagabond libertines are no more interesting from that point of view than the sailor who has a wife in every port, and Byron's hero is, after all, only a vagabond libertine. And he is dumb: he does not discuss himself with a Sganarelle-Leporello or with the fathers or brothers of his mistresses: he does not even, like Casanova, tell his own story. In fact he is not a true Don Juan at all; for he is no more an enemy of God than any romantic and adventurous young sower of wild oats. Had you and I been in his place at his age, who knows whether we might not have done as he did, unless indeed your fastidiousness had saved you from the empress Catherine. Byron was as little of a philosopher as Peter the Great: both were instances of that rare and useful, but unedifying variation, an energetic genius born without the prejudices or superstitions of his contemporaries. The resultant unscrupulous freedom of thought made Byron a greater poet than Wordsworth just as it made Peter a greater king than George III; but as it was, after all, only a negative qualification, it did not prevent Peter from being an appalling blackguard and an arrant poltroon, nor did it enable Byron to become a religious force like Shelley. Let us, then, leave Byron's Don Juan out of account. Mozart's is the last of the true Don Juans; for by the time he was of age, his cousin Faust had, in the hands of Goethe, taken his place and carried both his warfare and his reconciliation with the gods far beyond mere lovemaking into politics, high art, schemes for reclaiming new continents from the ocean, and recognition of an eternal womanly principle in the universe. Goethe's Faust and Mozart's Don Juan were the last words of the XVIII century on the subject; and by the time the polite critics of the XIX century, ignoring William Blake as superficially as the XVIII had ignored Hogarth or the XVII Bunyan, had got past the Dickens-Macaulay Dumas-Guizot stage and the Stendhal-Meredith-Turgenieff stage, and were confronted with philosophic fiction by such pens as Ibsen's and Tolstoy's, Don Juan had changed his sex and become Dona Juana, breaking out of the Doll's House and asserting herself as an individual instead of a mere item in a moral pageant.

Now it is all very well for you at the beginning of the XX century to ask me for a Don Juan play; but you will see from the foregoing survey that Don Juan is a full century out of date for you and for me; and if there are millions of less literate people who are still in the eighteenth century, have they not Moliere and Mozart, upon whose art no human hand can improve? You would laugh at me if at this time of day I dealt in duels and ghosts and "womanly" women. As to mere libertinism, you would be the first to remind me that the Festin de Pierre of Moliere is not a play for amorists, and that one bar of the voluptuous sentimentality of Gounod or Bizet would appear as a licentious stain on the score of Don Giovanni. Even the more abstract parts of the Don Juan play are dilapidated past use: for instance, Don Juan's supernatural antagonist hurled those who refuse to repent into lakes of burning brimstone, there to be tormented by devils with horns and tails. Of that antagonist, and of that conception of repentance, how much is left that could be used in a play by me dedicated to you? On the other hand, those forces of middle class public opinion which hardly existed for a Spanish nobleman in the days of the first Don Juan, are now triumphant everywhere. Civilized society is one huge bourgeoisie: no nobleman dares now shock his greengrocer. The women, "marchesane, principesse, cameriere, cittadine" and all, are become equally dangerous: the sex is aggressive, powerful: when women are wronged they do not group themselves pathetically to sing "Protegga il giusto cielo": they grasp formidable legal and social weapons, and retaliate. Political parties are wrecked and public careers undone by a single indiscretion. A man had better have all the statues in London to supper with him, ugly as they are, than be brought to the bar of the Nonconformist Conscience by Donna Elvira. Excommunication has become almost as serious a business as it was in the X century.

As a result, Man is no longer, like Don Juan, victor in the duel of sex. Whether he has ever really been may be doubted: at all events the enormous superiority of Woman's natural position in this matter is telling with greater and greater force. As to pulling the Nonconformist Conscience by the beard as Don Juan plucked the beard of the Commandant's statue in the convent of San Francisco, that is out of the question nowadays: prudence and good manners alike forbid it to a hero with any mind. Besides, it is Don Juan's own beard that is in danger of plucking. Far from relapsing into hypocrisy, as Sganarelle feared, he has unexpectedly discovered a moral in his immorality. The growing recognition of his new point of view is heaping responsibility on him. His former jests he has had to take as seriously as I have had to take some of the jests of Mr W. S. Gilbert. His scepticism, once his least tolerated quality, has now triumphed so completely that he can no longer assert himself by witty negations, and must, to save himself from cipherdom, find an affirmative position. His thousand and three affairs of gallantry, after becoming, at most, two immature intrigues leading to sordid and prolonged complications and humiliations, have been discarded altogether as unworthy of his philosophic dignity and compromising to his newly acknowledged position as the founder of a school. Instead of pretending to read Ovid he does actually read Schopenhaur and Nietzsche, studies Westermarck, and is concerned for the future of the race instead of for the freedom of his own instincts. Thus his profligacy and his dare-devil airs have gone the way of his sword and mandoline into the rag shop of anachronisms and superstitions. In fact, he is now more Hamlet than Don Juan; for though the lines put into the actor's mouth to indicate to the pit that Hamlet is a philosopher are for the most part mere harmonious platitude which, with a little debasement of the word-music, would be properer to Pecksniff, yet if you separate the real hero, inarticulate and unintelligible to himself except in flashes of inspiration, from the performer who has to talk at any cost through five acts; and if you also do what you must always do in Shakespear's tragedies: that is, dissect out the absurd sensational incidents and physical violences of the borrowed story from the genuine Shakespearian tissue, you will get a true Promethean foe of the gods, whose instinctive attitude towards women much resembles that to which Don Juan is now driven. From this point of view Hamlet was a developed Don Juan whom Shakespear palmed off as a reputable man just as he palmed poor Macbeth off as a murderer. To-day the palming off is no longer necessary (at least on your plane and mine) because Don Juanism is no longer misunderstood as mere Casanovism. Don Juan himself is almost ascetic in his desire to avoid that misunderstanding; and so my attempt to bring him up to date by launching him as a modern Englishman into a modern English environment has produced a figure superficially quite unlike the hero of Mozart.

And yet I have not the heart to disappoint you wholly of another glimpse of the Mozartian dissoluto punito and his antagonist the statue. I feel sure you would like to know more of that statue—to draw him out when he is off duty, so to speak. To gratify you, I have resorted to the trick of the strolling theatrical manager who advertizes the pantomime of Sinbad the Sailor with a stock of second-hand picture posters designed for Ali Baba. He simply thrusts a few oil jars into the valley of diamonds, and so fulfils the promise held out by the hoardings to the public eye. I have adapted this simple device to our occasion by thrusting into my perfectly modern three-act play a totally extraneous act in which my hero, enchanted by the air of the Sierra, has a dream in which his Mozartian ancestor appears and philosophizes at great length in a Shavio-Socratic dialogue with the lady, the statue, and the devil.

But this pleasantry is not the essence of the play. Over this essence I have no control. You propound a certain social substance, sexual attraction to wit, for dramatic distillation; and I distil it for you. I do not adulterate the product with aphrodisiacs nor dilute it with romance and water; for I am merely executing your commission, not producing a popular play for the market. You must therefore (unless, like most wise men, you read the play first and the preface afterwards) prepare yourself to face a trumpery story of modern London life, a life in which, as you know, the ordinary man's main business is to get means to keep up the position and habits of a gentleman, and the ordinary woman's business is to get married. In 9,999 cases out of 10,000, you can count on their doing nothing, whether noble or base, that conflicts with these ends; and that assurance is what you rely on as their religion, their morality, their principles, their patriotism, their reputation, their honor and so forth.

On the whole, this is a sensible and satisfactory foundation for society. Money means nourishment and marriage means children; and that men should put nourishment first and women children first is, broadly speaking, the law of Nature and not the dictate of personal ambition. The secret of the prosaic man's success, such as it is, is the simplicity with which he pursues these ends: the secret of the artistic man's failure, such as that is, is the versatility with which he strays in all directions after secondary ideals. The artist is either a poet or a scallawag: as poet, he cannot see, as the prosaic man does, that chivalry is at bottom only romantic suicide: as scallawag, he cannot see that it does not pay to spunge and beg and lie and brag and neglect his person. Therefore do not misunderstand my plain statement of the fundamental constitution of London society as an Irishman's reproach to your nation. From the day I first set foot on this foreign soil I knew the value of the prosaic qualities of which Irishmen teach Englishmen to be ashamed as well as I knew the vanity of the poetic qualities of which Englishmen teach Irishmen to be proud. For the Irishman instinctively disparages the quality which makes the Englishman dangerous to him; and the Englishman instinctively flatters the fault that makes the Irishman harmless and amusing to him. What is wrong with the prosaic Englishman is what is wrong with the prosaic men of all countries: stupidity. The vitality which places nourishment and children first, heaven and hell a somewhat remote second, and the health of society as an organic whole nowhere, may muddle successfully through the comparatively tribal stages of gregariousness; but in nineteenth century nations and twentieth century empires the determination of every man to be rich at all costs, and of every woman to be married at all costs, must, without a highly scientific social organization, produce a ruinous development of poverty, celibacy, prostitution, infant mortality, adult degeneracy, and everything that wise men most dread. In short, there is no future for men, however brimming with crude vitality, who are neither intelligent nor politically educated enough to be Socialists. So do not misunderstand me in the other direction either: if I appreciate the vital qualities of the Englishman as I appreciate the vital qualities of the bee, I do not guarantee the Englishman against being, like the bee (or the Canaanite) smoked out and unloaded of his honey by beings inferior to himself in simple acquisitiveness, combativeness, and fecundity, but superior to him in imagination and cunning.

The Don Juan play, however, is to deal with sexual attraction, and not with nutrition, and to deal with it in a society in which the serious business of sex is left by men to women, as the serious business of nutrition is left by women to men. That the men, to protect themselves against a too aggressive prosecution of the women's business, have set up a feeble romantic convention that the initiative in sex business must always come from the man, is true; but the pretence is so shallow that even in the theatre, that last sanctuary of unreality, it imposes only on the inexperienced. In Shakespear's plays the woman always takes the initiative. In his problem plays and his popular plays alike the love interest is the interest of seeing the woman hunt the man down. She may do it by blandishment, like Rosalind, or by stratagem, like Mariana; but in every case the relation between the woman and the man is the same: she is the pursuer and contriver, he the pursued and disposed of. When she is baffled, like Ophelia, she goes mad and commits suicide; and the man goes straight from her funeral to a fencing match. No doubt Nature, with very young creatures, may save the woman the trouble of scheming: Prospero knows that he has only to throw Ferdinand and Miranda together and they will mate like a pair of doves; and there is no need for Perdita to capture Florizel as the lady doctor in All's Well That Ends Well (an early Ibsenite heroine) captures Bertram. But the mature cases all illustrate the Shakespearian law. The one apparent exception, Petruchio, is not a real one: he is most carefully characterized as a purely commercial matrimonial adventurer. Once he is assured that Katharine has money, he undertakes to marry her before he has seen her. In real life we find not only Petruchios, but Mantalinis and Dobbins who pursue women with appeals to their pity or jealousy or vanity, or cling to them in a romantically infatuated way. Such effeminates do not count in the world scheme: even Bunsby dropping like a fascinated bird into the jaws of Mrs MacStinger is by comparison a true tragic object of pity and terror. I find in my own plays that Woman, projecting herself dramatically by my hands (a process over which I assure you I have no more real control than I have over my wife), behaves just as Woman did in the plays of Shakespear.

And so your Don Juan has come to birth as a stage projection of the tragi-comic love chase of the man by the woman; and my Don Juan is the quarry instead of the huntsman. Yet he is a true Don Juan, with a sense of reality that disables convention, defying to the last the fate which finally overtakes him. The woman's need of him to enable her to carry on Nature's most urgent work, does not prevail against him until his resistance gathers her energy to a climax at which she dares to throw away her customary exploitations of the conventional affectionate and dutiful poses, and claim him by natural right for a purpose that far transcends their mortal personal purposes.

Among the friends to whom I have read this play in manuscript are some of our own sex who are shocked at the "unscrupulousness," meaning the total disregard of masculine fastidiousness, with which the woman pursues her purpose. It does not occur to them that if women were as fastidious as men, morally or physically, there would be an end of the race. Is there anything meaner then to throw necessary work upon other people and then disparage it as unworthy and indelicate. We laugh at the haughty American nation because it makes the negro clean its boots and then proves the moral and physical inferiority of the negro by the fact that he is a shoeblack; but we ourselves throw the whole drudgery of creation on one sex, and then imply that no female of any womanliness or delicacy would initiate any effort in that direction. There are no limits to male hypocrisy in this matter. No doubt there are moments when man's sexual immunities are made acutely humiliating to him. When the terrible moment of birth arrives, its supreme importance and its superhuman effort and peril, in which the father has no part, dwarf him into the meanest insignificance: he slinks out of the way of the humblest petticoat, happy if he be poor enough to be pushed out of the house to outface his ignominy by drunken rejoicings. But when the crisis is over he takes his revenge, swaggering as the breadwinner, and speaking of Woman's "sphere" with condescension, even with chivalry, as if the kitchen and the nursery were less important than the office in the city. When his swagger is exhausted he drivels into erotic poetry or sentimental uxoriousness; and the Tennysonian King Arthur posing as Guinevere becomes Don Quixote grovelling before Dulcinea. You must admit that here Nature beats Comedy out of the field: the wildest hominist or feminist farce is insipid after the most commonplace "slice of life." The pretence that women do not take the initiative is part of the farce. Why, the whole world is strewn with snares, traps, gins and pitfalls for the capture of men by women. Give women the vote, and in five years there will be a crushing tax on bachelors. Men, on the other hand, attach penalties to marriage, depriving women of property, of the franchise, of the free use of their limbs, of that ancient symbol of immortality, the right to make oneself at home in the house of God by taking off the hat, of everything that he can force Woman to dispense with without compelling himself to dispense with her. All in vain. Woman must marry because the race must perish without her travail: if the risk of death and the certainty of pain, danger and unutterable discomforts cannot deter her, slavery and swaddled ankles will not. And yet we assume that the force that carries women through all these perils and hardships, stops abashed before the primnesses of our behavior for young ladies. It is assumed that the woman must wait, motionless, until she is wooed. Nay, she often does wait motionless. That is how the spider waits for the fly. But the spider spins her web. And if the fly, like my hero, shows a strength that promises to extricate him, how swiftly does she abandon her pretence of passiveness, and openly fling coil after coil about him until he is secured for ever!

If the really impressive books and other art-works of the world were produced by ordinary men, they would express more fear of women's pursuit than love of their illusory beauty. But ordinary men cannot produce really impressive art-works. Those who can are men of genius: that is, men selected by Nature to carry on the work of building up an intellectual consciousness of her own instinctive purpose. Accordingly, we observe in the man of genius all the unscrupulousness and all the "self-sacrifice" (the two things are the same) of Woman. He will risk the stake and the cross; starve, when necessary, in a garret all his life; study women and live on their work and care as Darwin studied worms and lived upon sheep; work his nerves into rags without payment, a sublime altruist in his disregard of himself, an atrocious egotist in his disregard of others. Here Woman meets a purpose as impersonal, as irresistible as her own; and the clash is sometimes tragic. When it is complicated by the genius being a woman, then the game is one for a king of critics: your George Sand becomes a mother to gain experience for the novelist and to develop her, and gobbles up men of genius, Chopins, Mussets and the like, as mere hors d'oeuvres.

I state the extreme case, of course; but what is true of the great man who incarnates the philosophic consciousness of Life and the woman who incarnates its fecundity, is true in some degree of all geniuses and all women. Hence it is that the world's books get written, its pictures painted, its statues modelled, its symphonies composed, by people who are free of the otherwise universal dominion of the tyranny of sex. Which leads us to the conclusion, astonishing to the vulgar, that art, instead of being before all things the expression of the normal sexual situation, is really the only department in which sex is a superseded and secondary power, with its consciousness so confused and its purpose so perverted, that its ideas are mere fantasy to common men. Whether the artist becomes poet or philosopher, moralist or founder of a religion, his sexual doctrine is nothing but a barren special pleading for pleasure, excitement, and knowledge when he is young, and for contemplative tranquillity when he is old and satiated. Romance and Asceticism, Amorism and Puritanism are equally unreal in the great Philistine world. The world shown us in books, whether the books be confessed epics or professed gospels, or in codes, or in political orations, or in philosophic systems, is not the main world at all: it is only the self-consciousness of certain abnormal people who have the specific artistic talent and temperament. A serious matter this for you and me, because the man whose consciousness does not correspond to that of the majority is a madman; and the old habit of worshipping madmen is giving way to the new habit of locking them up. And since what we call education and culture is for the most part nothing but the substitution of reading for experience, of literature for life, of the obsolete fictitious for the contemporary real, education, as you no doubt observed at Oxford, destroys, by supplantation, every mind that is not strong enough to see through the imposture and to use the great Masters of Arts as what they really are and no more: that is, patentees of highly questionable methods of thinking, and manufacturers of highly questionable, and for the majority but half valid representations of life. The schoolboy who uses his Homer to throw at his fellow's head makes perhaps the safest and most rational use of him; and I observe with reassurance that you occasionally do the same, in your prime, with your Aristotle.

Fortunately for us, whose minds have been so overwhelmingly sophisticated by literature, what produces all these treatises and poems and scriptures of one sort or another is the struggle of Life to become divinely conscious of itself instead of blindly stumbling hither and thither in the line of least resistance. Hence there is a driving towards truth in all books on matters where the writer, though exceptionally gifted is normally constituted, and has no private axe to grind. Copernicus had no motive for misleading his fellowmen as to the place of the sun in the solar system: he looked for it as honestly as a shepherd seeks his path in a mist. But Copernicus would not have written love stories scientifically. When it comes to sex relations, the man of genius does not share the common man's danger of capture, nor the woman of genius the common woman's overwhelming specialization. And that is why our scriptures and other art works, when they deal with love, turn from honest attempts at science in physics to romantic nonsense, erotic ecstasy, or the stern asceticism of satiety ("the road of excess leads to the palace of wisdom" said William Blake; for "you never know what is enough unless you know what is more than enough").

There is a political aspect of this sex question which is too big for my comedy, and too momentous to be passed over without culpable frivolity. It is impossible to demonstrate that the initiative in sex transactions remains with Woman, and has been confirmed to her, so far, more and more by the suppression of rapine and discouragement of importunity, without being driven to very serious reflections on the fact that this initiative is politically the most important of all the initiatives, because our political experiment of democracy, the last refuge of cheap misgovernment, will ruin us if our citizens are ill bred.

When we two were born, this country was still dominated by a selected class bred by political marriages. The commercial class had not then completed the first twenty-five years of its new share of political power; and it was itself selected by money qualification, and bred, if not by political marriage, at least by a pretty rigorous class marriage. Aristocracy and plutocracy still furnish the figureheads of politics; but they are now dependent on the votes of the promiscuously bred masses. And this, if you please, at the very moment when the political problem, having suddenly ceased to mean a very limited and occasional interference, mostly by way of jobbing public appointments, in the mismanagement of a tight but parochial little island, with occasional meaningless prosecution of dynastic wars, has become the industrial reorganization of Britain, the construction of a practically international Commonwealth, and the partition of the whole of Africa and perhaps the whole of Asia by the civilized Powers. Can you believe that the people whose conceptions of society and conduct, whose power of attention and scope of interest, are measured by the British theatre as you know it to-day, can either handle this colossal task themselves, or understand and support the sort of mind and character that is (at least comparatively) capable of handling it? For remember: what our voters are in the pit and gallery they are also in the polling booth. We are all now under what Burke called "the hoofs of the swinish multitude." Burke's language gave great offence because the implied exceptions to its universal application made it a class insult; and it certainly was not for the pot to call the kettle black. The aristocracy he defended, in spite of the political marriages by which it tried to secure breeding for itself, had its mind undertrained by silly schoolmasters and governesses, its character corrupted by gratuitous luxury, its self-respect adulterated to complete spuriousness by flattery and flunkeyism. It is no better to-day and never will be any better: our very peasants have something morally hardier in them that culminates occasionally in a Bunyan, a Burns, or a Carlyle. But observe, this aristocracy, which was overpowered from 1832 to 1885 by the middle class, has come back to power by the votes of "the swinish multitude." Tom Paine has triumphed over Edmund Burke; and the swine are now courted electors. How many of their own class have these electors sent to parliament? Hardly a dozen out of 670, and these only under the persuasion of conspicuous personal qualifications and popular eloquence. The multitude thus pronounces judgment on its own units: it admits itself unfit to govern, and will vote only for a man morphologically and generically transfigured by palatial residence and equipage, by transcendent tailoring, by the glamor of aristocratic kinship. Well, we two know these transfigured persons, these college passmen, these well groomed monocular Algys and Bobbies, these cricketers to whom age brings golf instead of wisdom, these plutocratic products of "the nail and sarspan business as he got his money by." Do you know whether to laugh or cry at the notion that they, poor devils! will drive a team of continents as they drive a four-in-hand; turn a jostling anarchy of casual trade and speculation into an ordered productivity; and federate our colonies into a world-Power of the first magnitude? Give these people the most perfect political constitution and the soundest political program that benevolent omniscience can devise for them, and they will interpret it into mere fashionable folly or canting charity as infallibly as a savage converts the philosophical theology of a Scotch missionary into crude African idolatry.

I do not know whether you have any illusions left on the subject of education, progress, and so forth. I have none. Any pamphleteer can show the way to better things; but when there is no will there is no way. My nurse was fond of remarking that you cannot make a silk purse out of a sow's ear, and the more I see of the efforts of our churches and universities and literary sages to raise the mass above its own level, the more convinced I am that my nurse was right. Progress can do nothing but make the most of us all as we are, and that most would clearly not be enough even if those who are already raised out of the lowest abysses would allow the others a chance. The bubble of Heredity has been pricked: the certainty that acquirements are negligible as elements in practical heredity has demolished the hopes of the educationists as well as the terrors of the degeneracy mongers; and we know now that there is no hereditary "governing class" any more than a hereditary hooliganism. We must either breed political capacity or be ruined by Democracy, which was forced on us by the failure of the older alternatives. Yet if Despotism failed only for want of a capable benevolent despot, what chance has Democracy, which requires a whole population of capable voters: that is, of political critics who, if they cannot govern in person for lack of spare energy or specific talent for administration, can at least recognize and appreciate capacity and benevolence in others, and so govern through capably benevolent representatives? Where are such voters to be found to-day? Nowhere. Promiscuous breeding has produced a weakness of character that is too timid to face the full stringency of a thoroughly competitive struggle for existence and too lazy and petty to organize the commonwealth cooperatively. Being cowards, we defeat natural selection under cover of philanthropy: being sluggards, we neglect artificial selection under cover of delicacy and morality.

Yet we must get an electorate of capable critics or collapse as Rome and Egypt collapsed. At this moment the Roman decadent phase of panem et circenses is being inaugurated under our eyes. Our newspapers and melodramas are blustering about our imperial destiny; but our eyes and hearts turn eagerly to the American millionaire. As his hand goes down to his pocket, our fingers go up to the brims of our hats by instinct. Our ideal prosperity is not the prosperity of the industrial north, but the prosperity of the Isle of Wight, of Folkestone and Ramsgate, of Nice and Monte Carlo. That is the only prosperity you see on the stage, where the workers are all footmen, parlourmaids, comic lodging-letters and fashionable professional men, whilst the heroes and heroines are miraculously provided with unlimited dividends, and eat gratuitously, like the knights in Don Quixote's books of chivalry.

The city papers prate of the competition of Bombay with Manchester and the like. The real competition is the competition of Regent Street with the Rue de Rivoli, of Brighton and the south coast with the Riviera, for the spending money of the American Trusts. What is all this growing love of pageantry, this effusive loyalty, this officious rising and uncovering at a wave from a flag or a blast from a brass band? Imperialism: Not a bit of it. Obsequiousness, servility, cupidity roused by the prevailing smell of money. When Mr Carnegie rattled his millions in his pockets all England became one rapacious cringe. Only, when Rhodes (who had probably been reading my Socialism for Millionaires) left word that no idler was to inherit his estate, the bent backs straightened mistrustfully for a moment. Could it be that the Diamond King was no gentleman after all? However, it was easy to ignore a rich man's solecism. The ungentlemanly clause was not mentioned again; and the backs soon bowed themselves back into their natural shape.

But I hear you asking me in alarm whether I have actually put all this tub thumping into a Don Juan comedy. I have not. I have only made my Don Juan a political pamphleteer, and given you his pamphlet in full by way of appendix. You will find it at the end of the book. I am sorry to say that it is a common practice with romancers to announce their hero as a man of extraordinary genius, and to leave his works entirely to the reader's imagination; so that at the end of the book you whisper to yourself ruefully that but for the author's solemn preliminary assurance you should hardly have given the gentleman credit for ordinary good sense. You cannot accuse me of this pitiable barrenness, this feeble evasion. I not only tell you that my hero wrote a revolutionists' handbook: I give you the handbook at full length for your edification if you care to read it. And in that handbook you will find the politics of the sex question as I conceive Don Juan's descendant to understand them. Not that I disclaim the fullest responsibility for his opinions and for those of all my characters, pleasant and unpleasant. They are all right from their several points of view; and their points of view are, for the dramatic moment, mine also. This may puzzle the people who believe that there is such a thing as an absolutely right point of view, usually their own. It may seem to them that nobody who doubts this can be in a state of grace. However that may be, it is certainly true that nobody who agrees with them can possibly be a dramatist, or indeed anything else that turns upon a knowledge of mankind. Hence it has been pointed out that Shakespear had no conscience. Neither have I, in that sense.

You may, however, remind me that this digression of mine into politics was preceded by a very convincing demonstration that the artist never catches the point of view of the common man on the question of sex, because he is not in the same predicament. I first prove that anything I write on the relation of the sexes is sure to be misleading; and then I proceed to write a Don Juan play. Well, if you insist on asking me why I behave in this absurd way, I can only reply that you asked me to, and that in any case my treatment of the subject may be valid for the artist, amusing to the amateur, and at least intelligible and therefore possibly suggestive to the Philistine. Every man who records his illusions is providing data for the genuinely scientific psychology which the world still waits for. I plank down my view of the existing relations of men to women in the most highly civilized society for what it is worth. It is a view like any other view and no more, neither true nor false, but, I hope, a way of looking at the subject which throws into the familiar order of cause and effect a sufficient body of fact and experience to be interesting to you, if not to the play-going public of London. I have certainly shown little consideration for that public in this enterprise; but I know that it has the friendliest disposition towards you and me as far as it has any consciousness of our existence, and quite understands that what I write for you must pass at a considerable height over its simple romantic head. It will take my books as read and my genius for granted, trusting me to put forth work of such quality as shall bear out its verdict. So we may disport ourselves on our own plane to the top of our bent; and if any gentleman points out that neither this epistle dedicatory nor the dream of Don Juan in the third act of the ensuing comedy is suitable for immediate production at a popular theatre we need not contradict him. Napoleon provided Talma with a pit of kings, with what effect on Talma's acting is not recorded. As for me, what I have always wanted is a pit of philosophers; and this is a play for such a pit.

I should make formal acknowledgment to the authors whom I have pillaged in the following pages if I could recollect them all. The theft of the brigand-poetaster from Sir Arthur Conan Doyle is deliberate; and the metamorphosis of Leporello into Enry Straker, motor engineer and New Man, is an intentional dramatic sketch for the contemporary embryo of Mr H. G. Wells's anticipation of the efficient engineering class which will, he hopes, finally sweep the jabberers out of the way of civilization. Mr Barrio has also, whilst I am correcting my proofs, delighted London with a servant who knows more than his masters. The conception of Mendoza Limited I trace back to a certain West Indian colonial secretary, who, at a period when he and I and Mr Sidney Webb were sowing our political wild oats as a sort of Fabian Three Musketeers, without any prevision of the surprising respectability of the crop that followed, recommended Webb, the encyclopedic and inexhaustible, to form himself into a company for the benefit of the shareholders. Octavius I take over unaltered from Mozart; and I hereby authorize any actor who impersonates him, to sing "Dalla sua pace" (if he can) at any convenient moment during the representation. Ann was suggested to me by the fifteenth century Dutch morality called Everyman, which Mr William Poel has lately resuscitated so triumphantly. I trust he will work that vein further, and recognize that Elizabethan Renascence fustian is no more bearable after medieval poesy than Scribe after Ibsen. As I sat watching Everyman at the Charterhouse, I said to myself Why not Everywoman? Ann was the result: every woman is not Ann; but Ann is Everywoman.

That the author of Everyman was no mere artist, but an artist-philosopher, and that the artist-philosophers are the only sort of artists I take quite seriously, will be no news to you. Even Plato and Boswell, as the dramatists who invented Socrates and Dr Johnson, impress me more deeply than the romantic playwrights. Ever since, as a boy, I first breathed the air of the transcendental regions at a performance of Mozart's Zauberflote, I have been proof against the garish splendors and alcoholic excitements of the ordinary stage combinations of Tappertitian romance with the police intelligence. Bunyan, Blake, Hogarth and Turner (these four apart and above all the English Classics), Goethe, Shelley, Schopenhaur, Wagner, Ibsen, Morris, Tolstoy, and Nietzsche are among the writers whose peculiar sense of the world I recognize as more or less akin to my own. Mark the word peculiar. I read Dickens and Shakespear without shame or stint; but their pregnant observations and demonstrations of life are not co-ordinated into any philosophy or religion: on the contrary, Dickens's sentimental assumptions are violently contradicted by his observations; and Shakespear's pessimism is only his wounded humanity. Both have the specific genius of the fictionist and the common sympathies of human feeling and thought in pre-eminent degree. They are often saner and shrewder than the philosophers just as Sancho-Panza was often saner and shrewder than Don Quixote. They clear away vast masses of oppressive gravity by their sense of the ridiculous, which is at bottom a combination of sound moral judgment with lighthearted good humor. But they are concerned with the diversities of the world instead of with its unities: they are so irreligious that they exploit popular religion for professional purposes without delicacy or scruple (for example, Sydney Carton and the ghost in Hamlet!): they are anarchical, and cannot balance their exposures of Angelo and Dogberry, Sir Leicester Dedlock and Mr Tite Barnacle, with any portrait of a prophet or a worthy leader: they have no constructive ideas: they regard those who have them as dangerous fanatics: in all their fictions there is no leading thought or inspiration for which any man could conceivably risk the spoiling of his hat in a shower, much less his life. Both are alike forced to borrow motives for the more strenuous actions of their personages from the common stockpot of melodramatic plots; so that Hamlet has to be stimulated by the prejudices of a policeman and Macbeth by the cupidities of a bushranger. Dickens, without the excuse of having to manufacture motives for Hamlets and Macbeths, superfluously punt his crew down the stream of his monthly parts by mechanical devices which I leave you to describe, my own memory being quite baffled by the simplest question as to Monks in Oliver Twist, or the long lost parentage of Smike, or the relations between the Dorrit and Clennam families so inopportunely discovered by Monsieur Rigaud Blandois. The truth is, the world was to Shakespear a great "stage of fools" on which he was utterly bewildered. He could see no sort of sense in living at all; and Dickens saved himself from the despair of the dream in The Chimes by taking the world for granted and busying himself with its details. Neither of them could do anything with a serious positive character: they could place a human figure before you with perfect verisimilitude; but when the moment came for making it live and move, they found, unless it made them laugh, that they had a puppet on their hands, and had to invent some artificial external stimulus to make it work. This is what is the matter with Hamlet all through: he has no will except in his bursts of temper. Foolish Bardolaters make a virtue of this after their fashion: they declare that the play is the tragedy of irresolution; but all Shakespear's projections of the deepest humanity he knew have the same defect: their characters and manners are lifelike; but their actions are forced on them from without, and the external force is grotesquely inappropriate except when it is quite conventional, as in the case of Henry V. Falstaff is more vivid than any of these serious reflective characters, because he is self-acting: his motives are his own appetites and instincts and humors. Richard III, too, is delightful as the whimsical comedian who stops a funeral to make love to the corpse's widow; but when, in the next act, he is replaced by a stage villain who smothers babies and offs with people's heads, we are revolted at the imposture and repudiate the changeling. Faulconbridge, Coriolanus, Leontes are admirable descriptions of instinctive temperaments: indeed the play of Coriolanus is the greatest of Shakespear's comedies; but description is not philosophy; and comedy neither compromises the author nor reveals him. He must be judged by those characters into which he puts what he knows of himself, his Hamlets and Macbeths and Lears and Prosperos. If these characters are agonizing in a void about factitious melodramatic murders and revenges and the like, whilst the comic characters walk with their feet on solid ground, vivid and amusing, you know that the author has much to show and nothing to teach. The comparison between Falstaff and Prospero is like the comparison between Micawber and David Copperfield. At the end of the book you know Micawber, whereas you only know what has happened to David, and are not interested enough in him to wonder what his politics or religion might be if anything so stupendous as a religious or political idea, or a general idea of any sort, were to occur to him. He is tolerable as a child; but he never becomes a man, and might be left out of his own biography altogether but for his usefulness as a stage confidant, a Horatio or "Charles his friend" what they call on the stage a feeder.

Now you cannot say this of the works of the artist-philosophers. You cannot say it, for instance, of The Pilgrim's Progress. Put your Shakespearian hero and coward, Henry V and Pistol or Parolles, beside Mr Valiant and Mr Fearing, and you have a sudden revelation of the abyss that lies between the fashionable author who could see nothing in the world but personal aims and the tragedy of their disappointment or the comedy of their incongruity, and the field preacher who achieved virtue and courage by identifying himself with the purpose of the world as he understood it. The contrast is enormous: Bunyan's coward stirs your blood more than Shakespear's hero, who actually leaves you cold and secretly hostile. You suddenly see that Shakespear, with all his flashes and divinations, never understood virtue and courage, never conceived how any man who was not a fool could, like Bunyan's hero, look back from the brink of the river of death over the strife and labor of his pilgrimage, and say "yet do I not repent me"; or, with the panache of a millionaire, bequeath "my sword to him that shall succeed me in my pilgrimage, and my courage and skill to him that can get it." This is the true joy in life, the being used for a purpose recognized by yourself as a mighty one; the being thoroughly worn out before you are thrown on the scrap heap; the being a force of Nature instead of a feverish selfish little clod of ailments and grievances complaining that the world will not devote itself to making you happy. And also the only real tragedy in life is the being used by personally minded men for purposes which you recognize to be base. All the rest is at worst mere misfortune or mortality: this alone is misery, slavery, hell on earth; and the revolt against it is the only force that offers a man's work to the poor artist, whom our personally minded rich people would so willingly employ as pandar, buffoon, beauty monger, sentimentalizer and the like.

It may seem a long step from Bunyan to Nietzsche; but the difference between their conclusions is purely formal. Bunyan's perception that righteousness is filthy rags, his scorn for Mr Legality in the village of Morality, his defiance of the Church as the supplanter of religion, his insistence on courage as the virtue of virtues, his estimate of the career of the conventionally respectable and sensible Worldly Wiseman as no better at bottom than the life and death of Mr Badman: all this, expressed by Bunyan in the terms of a tinker's theology, is what Nietzsche has expressed in terms of post-Darwinian, post-Schopenhaurian philosophy; Wagner in terms of polytheistic mythology; and Ibsen in terms of mid-XIX century Parisian dramaturgy. Nothing is new in these matters except their novelties: for instance, it is a novelty to call Justification by Faith "Wille," and Justification by Works "Vorstellung." The sole use of the novelty is that you and I buy and read Schopenhaur's treatise on Will and Representation when we should not dream of buying a set of sermons on Faith versus Works. At bottom the controversy is the same, and the dramatic results are the same. Bunyan makes no attempt to present his pilgrims as more sensible or better conducted than Mr Worldly Wiseman. Mr W. W.'s worst enemies, as Mr Embezzler, Mr Never-go-to-Church-on-Sunday, Mr Bad Form, Mr Murderer, Mr Burglar, Mr Co-respondent, Mr Blackmailer, Mr Cad, Mr Drunkard, Mr Labor Agitator and so forth, can read the Pilgrim's Progress without finding a word said against them; whereas the respectable people who snub them and put them in prison, such as Mr W.W. himself and his young friend Civility; Formalist and Hypocrisy; Wildhead, Inconsiderate, and Pragmatick (who were clearly young university men of good family and high feeding); that brisk lad Ignorance, Talkative, By-Ends of Fairspeech and his mother-in-law Lady Feigning, and other reputable gentlemen and citizens, catch it very severely. Even Little Faith, though he gets to heaven at last, is given to understand that it served him right to be mobbed by the brothers Faint Heart, Mistrust, and Guilt, all three recognized members of respectable society and veritable pillars of the law. The whole allegory is a consistent attack on morality and respectability, without a word that one can remember against vice and crime. Exactly what is complained of in Nietzsche and Ibsen, is it not? And also exactly what would be complained of in all the literature which is great enough and old enough to have attained canonical rank, officially or unofficially, were it not that books are admitted to the canon by a compact which confesses their greatness in consideration of abrogating their meaning; so that the reverend rector can agree with the prophet Micah as to his inspired style without being committed to any complicity in Micah's furiously Radical opinions. Why, even I, as I force myself; pen in hand, into recognition and civility, find all the force of my onslaught destroyed by a simple policy of non-resistance. In vain do I redouble the violence of the language in which I proclaim my heterodoxies. I rail at the theistic credulity of Voltaire, the amoristic superstition of Shelley, the revival of tribal soothsaying and idolatrous rites which Huxley called Science and mistook for an advance on the Pentateuch, no less than at the welter of ecclesiastical and professional humbug which saves the face of the stupid system of violence and robbery which we call Law and Industry. Even atheists reproach me with infidelity and anarchists with nihilism because I cannot endure their moral tirades. And yet, instead of exclaiming "Send this inconceivable Satanist to the stake," the respectable newspapers pith me by announcing "another book by this brilliant and thoughtful writer." And the ordinary citizen, knowing that an author who is well spoken of by a respectable newspaper must be all right, reads me, as he reads Micah, with undisturbed edification from his own point of view. It is narrated that in the eighteen-seventies an old lady, a very devout Methodist, moved from Colchester to a house in the neighborhood of the City Road, in London, where, mistaking the Hall of Science for a chapel, she sat at the feet of Charles Bradlaugh for many years, entranced by his eloquence, without questioning his orthodoxy or moulting a feather of her faith. I fear I small be defrauded of my just martyrdom in the same way.

However, I am digressing, as a man with a grievance always does. And after all, the main thing in determining the artistic quality of a book is not the opinions it propagates, but the fact that the writer has opinions. The old lady from Colchester was right to sun her simple soul in the energetic radiance of Bradlaugh's genuine beliefs and disbeliefs rather than in the chill of such mere painting of light and heat as elocution and convention can achieve. My contempt for belles lettres, and for amateurs who become the heroes of the fanciers of literary virtuosity, is not founded on any illusion of mind as to the permanence of those forms of thought (call them opinions) by which I strive to communicate my bent to my fellows. To younger men they are already outmoded; for though they have no more lost their logic than an eighteenth century pastel has lost its drawing or its color, yet, like the pastel, they grow indefinably shabby, and will grow shabbier until they cease to count at all, when my books will either perish, or, if the world is still poor enough to want them, will have to stand, with Bunyan's, by quite amorphous qualities of temper and energy. With this conviction I cannot be a bellettrist. No doubt I must recognize, as even the Ancient Mariner did, that I must tell my story entertainingly if I am to hold the wedding guest spellbound in spite of the siren sounds of the loud bassoon. But "for art's sake" alone I would not face the toil of writing a single sentence. I know that there are men who, having nothing to say and nothing to write, are nevertheless so in love with oratory and with literature that they keep desperately repeating as much as they can understand of what others have said or written aforetime. I know that the leisurely tricks which their want of conviction leaves them free to play with the diluted and misapprehended message supply them with a pleasant parlor game which they call style. I can pity their dotage and even sympathize with their fancy. But a true original style is never achieved for its own sake: a man may pay from a shilling to a guinea, according to his means, to see, hear, or read another man's act of genius; but he will not pay with his whole life and soul to become a mere virtuoso in literature, exhibiting an accomplishment which will not even make money for him, like fiddle playing. Effectiveness of assertion is the Alpha and Omega of style. He who has nothing to assert has no style and can have none: he who has something to assert will go as far in power of style as its momentousness and his conviction will carry him. Disprove his assertion after it is made, yet its style remains. Darwin has no more destroyed the style of Job nor of Handel than Martin Luther destroyed the style of Giotto. All the assertions get disproved sooner or later; and so we find the world full of a magnificent debris of artistic fossils, with the matter-of-fact credibility gone clean out of them, but the form still splendid. And that is why the old masters play the deuce with our mere susceptibles. Your Royal Academician thinks he can get the style of Giotto without Giotto's beliefs, and correct his perspective into the bargain. Your man of letters thinks he can get Bunyan's or Shakespear's style without Bunyan's conviction or Shakespear's apprehension, especially if he takes care not to split his infinitives. And so with your Doctors of Music, who, with their collections of discords duly prepared and resolved or retarded or anticipated in the manner of the great composers, think they can learn the art of Palestrina from Cherubim's treatise. All this academic art is far worse than the trade in sham antique furniture; for the man who sells me an oaken chest which he swears was made in the XIII century, though as a matter of fact he made it himself only yesterday, at least does not pretend that there are any modern ideas in it, whereas your academic copier of fossils offers them to you as the latest outpouring of the human spirit, and, worst of all, kidnaps young people as pupils and persuades them that his limitations are rules, his observances dexterities, his timidities good taste, and his emptinesses purities. And when he declares that art should not be didactic, all the people who have nothing to teach and all the people who don't want to learn agree with him emphatically.

I pride myself on not being one of these susceptible: If you study the electric light with which I supply you in that Bumbledonian public capacity of mine over which you make merry from time to time, you will find that your house contains a great quantity of highly susceptible copper wire which gorges itself with electricity and gives you no light whatever. But here and there occurs a scrap of intensely insusceptible, intensely resistant material; and that stubborn scrap grapples with the current and will not let it through until it has made itself useful to you as those two vital qualities of literature, light and heat. Now if I am to be no mere copper wire amateur but a luminous author, I must also be a most intensely refractory person, liable to go out and to go wrong at inconvenient moments, and with incendiary possibilities. These are the faults of my qualities; and I assure you that I sometimes dislike myself so much that when some irritable reviewer chances at that moment to pitch into me with zest, I feel unspeakably relieved and obliged. But I never dream of reforming, knowing that I must take myself as I am and get what work I can out of myself. All this you will understand; for there is community of material between us: we are both critics of life as well as of art; and you have perhaps said to yourself when I have passed your windows, "There, but for the grace of God, go I." An awful and chastening reflection, which shall be the closing cadence of this immoderately long letter from yours faithfully,

G. BERNARD SHAW. WOKING, 1903

ACT I

Roebuck Ramsden is in his study, opening the morning letters. The study, handsomely and solidly furnished, proclaims the man of means. Not a speck of dust is visible: it is clear that there are at least two housemaids and a parlormaid downstairs, and a housekeeper upstairs who does not let them spare elbow-grease. Even the top of Roebuck's head is polished: on a sunshiny day he could heliograph his orders to distant camps by merely nodding. In no other respect, however, does he suggest the military man. It is in active civil life that men get his broad air of importance, his dignified expectation of deference, his determinate mouth disarmed and refined since the hour of his success by the withdrawal of opposition and the concession of comfort and precedence and power. He is more than a highly respectable man: he is marked out as a president of highly respectable men, a chairman among directors, an alderman among councillors, a mayor among aldermen. Four tufts of iron-grey hair, which will soon be as white as isinglass, and are in other respects not at all unlike it, grow in two symmetrical pairs above his ears and at the angles of his spreading jaws. He wears a black frock coat, a white waistcoat (it is bright spring weather), and trousers, neither black nor perceptibly blue, of one of those indefinitely mixed hues which the modern clothier has produced to harmonize with the religions of respectable men. He has not been out of doors yet to-day; so he still wears his slippers, his boots being ready for him on the hearthrug. Surmising that he has no valet, and seeing that he has no secretary with a shorthand notebook and a typewriter, one meditates on how little our great burgess domesticity has been disturbed by new fashions and methods, or by the enterprise of the railway and hotel companies which sell you a Saturday to Monday of life at Folkestone as a real gentleman for two guineas, first class fares both ways included.

How old is Roebuck? The question is important on the threshold of a drama of ideas; for under such circumstances everything depends on whether his adolescence belonged to the sixties or to the eighties. He was born, as a matter of fact, in 1839, and was a Unitarian and Free Trader from his boyhood, and an Evolutionist from the publication of the Origin of Species. Consequently he has always classed himself as an advanced thinker and fearlessly outspoken reformer.

Sitting at his writing table, he has on his right the windows giving on Portland Place. Through these, as through a proscenium, the curious spectator may contemplate his profile as well as the blinds will permit. On his left is the inner wall, with a stately bookcase, and the door not quite in the middle, but somewhat further from him. Against the wall opposite him are two busts on pillars: one, to his left, of John Bright; the other, to his right, of Mr Herbert Spencer. Between them hang an engraved portrait of Richard Cobden; enlarged photographs of Martineau, Huxley, and George Eliot; autotypes of allegories by Mr G.F. Watts (for Roebuck believed in the fine arts with all the earnestness of a man who does not understand them), and an impression of Dupont's engraving of Delaroche's Beaux Artes hemicycle, representing the great men of all ages. On the wall behind him, above the mantelshelf, is a family portrait of impenetrable obscurity.

A chair stands near the writing table for the convenience of business visitors. Two other chairs are against the wall between the busts.

A parlormaid enters with a visitor's card. Roebuck takes it, and nods, pleased. Evidently a welcome caller.

RAMSDEN. Show him up.

The parlormaid goes out and returns with the visitor.

THE MAID. Mr Robinson.

Mr Robinson is really an uncommonly nice looking young fellow. He must, one thinks, be the jeune premier; for it is not in reason to suppose that a second such attractive male figure should appear in one story. The slim shapely frame, the elegant suit of new mourning, the small head and regular features, the pretty little moustache, the frank clear eyes, the wholesome bloom and the youthful complexion, the well brushed glossy hair, not curly, but of fine texture and good dark color, the arch of good nature in the eyebrows, the erect forehead and neatly pointed chin, all announce the man who will love and suffer later on. And that he will not do so without sympathy is guaranteed by an engaging sincerity and eager modest serviceableness which stamp him as a man of amiable nature. The moment he appears, Ramsden's face expands into fatherly liking and welcome, an expression which drops into one of decorous grief as the young man approaches him with sorrow in his face as well as in his black clothes. Ramsden seems to know the nature of the bereavement. As the visitor advances silently to the writing table, the old man rises and shakes his hand across it without a word: a long, affectionate shake which tells the story of a recent sorrow common to both.

RAMSDEN. [*concluding the handshake and cheering up*] Well, well, Octavius, it's the common lot. We must all face it someday. Sit down.

Octavius takes the visitor's chair. Ramsden replaces himself in his own.

OCTAVIUS. Yes: we must face it, Mr Ramsden. But I owed him a great deal. He did everything for me that my father could have done if he had lived.

RAMSDEN. He had no son of his own, you see.

OCTAVIUS. But he had daughters; and yet he was as good to my sister as to me. And his death was so sudden! I always intended to thank him—to let him know that I had not taken all his care of me as a matter of course, as any boy takes his father's care. But I waited for an opportunity and now he is dead—dropped without a moment's warning. He will never know what I felt. [*He takes out his handkerchief and cries unaffectedly*].

RAMSDEN. How do we know that, Octavius? He may know it: we cannot tell. Come! Don't grieve. [*Octavius masters himself and puts up his handkerchief*]. That's right. Now let me tell you something to console you. The last time I saw him—it was in this very room—he said to me: "Tavy is a generous lad and the soul of honor; and when I see how little consideration other men get from their sons, I realize how much better than a son he's been to me." There! Doesn't that do you good?

OCTAVIUS. Mr Ramsden: he used to say to me that he had met only one man in the world who was the soul of honor, and that was Roebuck Ramsden.

RAMSDEN. Oh, that was his partiality: we were very old friends, you know. But there was something else he used to say about you. I wonder whether I ought to tell you or not!

OCTAVIUS. You know best.

RAMSDEN. It was something about his daughter.

OCTAVIUS. [*eagerly*] About Ann! Oh, do tell me that, Mr Ramsden.

RAMSDEN. Well, he said he was glad, after all, you were not his son, because he thought that someday Annie and you—[*Octavius blushes vividly*]. Well, perhaps I shouldn't have told you. But he was in earnest.

OCTAVIUS. Oh, if only I thought I had a chance! You know, Mr Ramsden, I don't care about money or about what people call position; and I can't bring myself to take an interest in the business of struggling for them. Well, Ann has a most exquisite nature; but she is so accustomed to be in the thick of that sort of thing that she thinks a man's character incomplete if he is not ambitious. She knows that if she married me she would have to reason herself out of being ashamed of me for not being a big success of some kind.

RAMSDEN. [*Getting up and planting himself with his back to the fireplace*] Nonsense, my boy, nonsense! You're too modest. What does she know about the real value of men at her age? [*More seriously*] Besides, she's a wonderfully dutiful girl. Her father's wish would be sacred to her. Do you know that since she grew up to years of discretion, I don't believe she has ever once given her own wish as a reason for doing anything or not doing it. It's always "Father wishes me to," or "Mother wouldn't like it." It's really almost a fault in her. I have often told her she must learn to think for herself.

OCTAVIUS. [*shaking his head*] I couldn't ask her to marry me because her father wished it, Mr Ramsden.

RAMSDEN. Well, perhaps not. No: of course not. I see that. No: you certainly couldn't. But when you win her on your own merits, it will be a great happiness to her to fulfil her father's desire as well as her own. Eh? Come! you'll ask her, won't you?

OCTAVIUS. [*with sad gaiety*] At all events I promise you I shall never ask anyone else.

RAMSDEN. Oh, you shan't need to. She'll accept you, my boy—although [*here he suddenly becomes very serious indeed*] you have one great drawback.

OCTAVIUS. [*anxiously*] What drawback is that, Mr Ramsden? I should rather say which of my many drawbacks?

RAMSDEN. I'll tell you, Octavius. [*He takes from the table a book bound in red cloth*]. I have in my hand a copy of the most infamous, the most scandalous, the most mischievous, the most blackguardly book that ever escaped burning at the hands of the common hangman. I have not read it: I would not soil my mind with such filth; but I have read what the papers say of it. The title is quite enough for me. [*He reads it*]. The Revolutionist's Handbook and Pocket Companion by John Tanner, M.I.R.C., Member of the Idle Rich Class.

OCTAVIUS. [*smiling*] But Jack—

RAMSDEN. [*testily*] For goodness' sake, don't call him Jack under my roof [*he throws the book violently down on the table, Then, somewhat relieved, he comes past the table to Octavius, and addresses him at close quarters with impressive gravity*]. Now,

Octavius, I know that my dead friend was right when he said you were a generous lad. I know that this man was your schoolfellow, and that you feel bound to stand by him because there was a boyish friendship between you. But I ask you to consider the altered circumstances. You were treated as a son in my friend's house. You lived there; and your friends could not be turned from the door. This Tanner was in and out there on your account almost from his childhood. He addresses Annie by her Christian name as freely as you do. Well, while her father was alive, that was her father's business, not mine. This man Tanner was only a boy to him: his opinions were something to be laughed at, like a man's hat on a child's head. But now Tanner is a grown man and Annie a grown woman. And her father is gone. We don't as yet know the exact terms of his will; but he often talked it over with me; and I have no more doubt than I have that you're sitting there that the will appoints me Annie's trustee and guardian. [*Forcibly*] Now I tell you, once for all, I can't and I won't have Annie placed in such a position that she must, out of regard for you, suffer the intimacy of this fellow Tanner. It's not fair: it's not right: it's not kind. What are you going to do about it?

OCTAVIUS. But Ann herself has told Jack that whatever his opinions are, he will always be welcome because he knew her dear father.

RAMSDEN. [*out of patience*] That girl's mad about her duty to her parents. [*He starts off like a goaded ox in the direction of John Bright, in whose expression there is no sympathy for him. As he speaks, he fumes down to Herbert Spencer, who receives him still more coldly*] Excuse me, Octavius; but there are limits to social toleration. You know that I am not a bigoted or prejudiced man. You know that I am plain Roebuck Ramsden when other men who have done less have got handles to their names, because I have stood for equality and liberty of conscience while they were truckling to the Church and to the aristocracy. Whitefield and I lost chance after chance through our advanced opinions. But I draw the line at Anarchism and Free Love and that sort of thing. If I am to be Annie's guardian, she will have to learn that she has a duty to me. I won't have it: I will not have it. She must forbid John Tanner the house; and so must you.

The parlormaid returns.

OCTAVIUS. But—

RAMSDEN. [*calling his attention to the servant*] Ssh! Well?

THE MAID. Mr Tanner wishes to see you, sir.

RAMSDEN. Mr Tanner!

OCTAVIUS. Jack!

RAMSDEN. How dare Mr Tanner call on me! Say I cannot see him.

OCTAVIUS. [*hurt*] I am sorry you are turning my friend from your door like that.

THE MAID. [*calmly*] He's not at the door, sir. He's upstairs in the drawingroom with Miss Ramsden. He came with Mrs Whitefield and Miss Ann and Miss Robinson, sir.

Ramsden's feelings are beyond words.

OCTAVIUS. [*grinning*] That's very like Jack, Mr Ramsden. You must see him, even if it's only to turn him out.

RAMSDEN. [*hammering out his words with suppressed fury*] Go upstairs and ask Mr Tanner to be good enough to step down here. [*The parlormaid goes out; and Ramsden returns to the fireplace, as to a fortified position*]. I must say that of all the confounded pieces of impertinence—well, if these are Anarchist manners I hope you like them. And Annie with him! Annie! A— [*he chokes*].

OCTAVIUS. Yes: that's what surprises me. He's so desperately afraid of Ann. There must be something the matter.

Mr John Tanner suddenly opens the door and enters. He is too young to be described simply as a big man with a beard. But it is already plain that middle life will find him in that category. He has still some of the slimness of youth; but youthfulness is not the effect he aims at: his frock coat would befit a prime minister; and a certain high chested carriage of the shoulders, a lofty pose of the head, and the Olympian majesty with which a mane, or rather a huge wisp, of hazel colored hair is thrown back from an imposing brow, suggest Jupiter rather than Apollo. He is prodigiously fluent of speech, restless, excitable (mark the snorting nostril and the restless blue eye, just the thirty-secondth of an inch too wide open), possibly a little mad. He is carefully dressed, not from the vanity that cannot resist finery, but from a sense of the importance of everything he does which leads him to make as much of paying a call as other men do of getting married or laying a foundation stone. A sensitive, susceptible, exaggerative, earnest man: a megalomaniac, who would be lost without a sense of humor.

Just at present the sense of humor is in abeyance. To say that he is excited is nothing: all his moods are phases of excitement. He is now in the panic-stricken phase; and he walks straight up to Ramsden as if with the fixed intention of shooting him on his own hearthrug. But what he pulls from his breast pocket is not a pistol, but a foolscap document which he thrusts under the indignant nose of Ramsden as he exclaims—

TANNER. Ramsden: do you know what that is?

RAMSDEN. [*loftily*] No, Sir.

TANNER. It's a copy of Whitefield's will. Ann got it this morning.

RAMSDEN. When you say Ann, you mean, I presume, Miss Whitefield.

TANNER. I mean our Ann, your Ann, Tavy's Ann, and now, Heaven help me, my Ann!

OCTAVIUS. [*rising, very pale*] What do you mean?

TANNER. Mean! [*He holds up the will*]. Do you know who is appointed Ann's guardian by this will?

RAMSDEN. [*coolly*] I believe I am.

TANNER. You! You and I, man. I! I!! I!!! Both of us! [*He flings the will down on the writing table*].

RAMSDEN. You! Impossible.

TANNER. It's only too hideously true. [*He throws himself into Octavius's chair*]. Ramsden: get me out of it somehow. You don't know Ann as well as I do. She'll commit every crime a respectable woman can; and she'll justify every one of them by saying that it was the wish of her guardians. She'll put everything on us; and we shall have no more control over her than a couple of mice over a cat.

OCTAVIUS. Jack: I wish you wouldn't talk like that about Ann.

TANNER. This chap's in love with her: that's another complication. Well, she'll either jilt him and say I didn't approve of him, or marry him and say you ordered her to. I tell you, this is the most staggering blow that has ever fallen on a man of my age and temperament.

RAMSDEN. Let me see that will, sir. [*He goes to the writing table and picks it up*]. I cannot believe that my old friend Whitefield would have shown such a want of confidence in me as to associate me with— [*His countenance falls as he reads*].

TANNER. It's all my own doing: that's the horrible irony of it. He told me one day that you were to be Ann's guardian; and like a fool I began arguing with him about the folly of leaving a young woman under the control of an old man with obsolete ideas.

RAMSDEN. [*stupended*] My ideas obsolete!!!!!

TANNER. Totally. I had just finished an essay called Down with Government by the Greyhaired; and I was full of arguments and illustrations. I said the proper thing was to combine the experience of an old hand with the vitality of a young one. Hang me if he didn't take me at my word and alter his will—it's dated only a fortnight after that conversation—appointing me as joint guardian with you!

RAMSDEN. [*pale and determined*] I shall refuse to act.

TANNER. What's the good of that? I've been refusing all the way from Richmond; but Ann keeps on saying that of course she's only an orphan; and that she can't expect the people who were glad to come to the house in her father's time to trouble much about her now. That's the latest game. An orphan! It's like hearing an ironclad talk about being at the mercy of the winds and waves.

OCTAVIUS. This is not fair, Jack. She is an orphan. And you ought to stand by her.

TANNER. Stand by her! What danger is she in? She has the law on her side; she has popular sentiment on her side; she has plenty of money and no conscience. All she wants with me is to load up all her moral responsibilities on me, and do as she likes at the expense of my character. I can't control her; and she can compromise me as much as she likes. I might as well be her husband.

RAMSDEN. You can refuse to accept the guardianship. I shall certainly refuse to hold it jointly with you.

TANNER. Yes; and what will she say to that? what does she say to it? Just that her father's wishes are sacred to her, and that she shall always look up to me as her guardian whether I care to face the responsibility or not. Refuse! You might as well refuse to accept the embraces of a boa constrictor when once it gets round your neck.

OCTAVIUS. This sort of talk is not kind to me, Jack.

TANNER. [*rising and going to Octavius to console him, but still lamenting*] If he wanted a young guardian, why didn't he appoint Tavy?

RAMSDEN. Ah! why indeed?

OCTAVIUS. I will tell you. He sounded me about it; but I refused the trust because I loved her. I had no right to let myself be forced on her as a guardian by her father. He spoke to her about it; and she said I was right. You know I love her, Mr Ramsden; and Jack knows it too. If Jack loved a woman, I would not compare her to a boa constrictor in his presence, however much I might dislike her [*he sits down between the busts and turns his face to the wall*].

RAMSDEN. I do not believe that Whitefield was in his right senses when he made that will. You have admitted that he made it under your influence.

TANNER. You ought to be pretty well obliged to me for my influence. He leaves you two thousand five hundred for your trouble. He leaves Tavy a dowry for his sister and five thousand for himself.

OCTAVIUS. [*his tears flowing afresh*] Oh, I can't take it. He was too good to us.

TANNER. You won't get it, my boy, if Ramsden upsets the will.

RAMSDEN. Ha! I see. You have got me in a cleft stick.

TANNER. He leaves me nothing but the charge of Ann's morals, on the ground that I have already more money than is good for me. That shows that he had his wits about him, doesn't it?

RAMSDEN. [*grimly*] I admit that.

OCTAVIUS. [*rising and coming from his refuge by the wall*] Mr Ramsden: I think you are prejudiced against Jack. He is a man of honor, and incapable of abusing—

TANNER. Don't, Tavy: you'll make me ill. I am not a man of honor: I am a man struck down by a dead hand. Tavy: you must marry her after all and take her off my hands. And I had set my heart on saving you from her!

OCTAVIUS. Oh, Jack, you talk of saving me from my highest happiness.

TANNER. Yes, a lifetime of happiness. If it were only the first half hour's happiness, Tavy, I would buy it for you with my last penny. But a lifetime of happiness! No man alive could bear it: it would be hell on earth.

RAMSDEN. [*violently*] Stuff, sir. Talk sense; or else go and waste someone else's time: I have something better to do than listen to your fooleries [*he positively kicks his way to his table and resumes his seat*].

TANNER. You hear him, Tavy! Not an idea in his head later than eighteen-sixty. We can't leave Ann with no other guardian to turn to.

RAMSDEN. I am proud of your contempt for my character and opinions, sir. Your own are set forth in that book, I believe.

TANNER. [*eagerly going to the table*] What! You've got my book! What do you think of it?

RAMSDEN. Do you suppose I would read such a book, sir?

TANNER. Then why did you buy it?

RAMSDEN. I did not buy it, sir. It has been sent me by some foolish lady who seems to admire your views. I was about to dispose of it when Octavius interrupted me. I shall do so now, with your permission. [*He throws the book into the waste paper basket with such vehemence that Tanner recoils under the impression that it is being thrown at his head*].

TANNER. You have no more manners than I have myself. However, that saves ceremony between us. [*He sits down again*]. What do you intend to do about this will?

OCTAVIUS. May I make a suggestion?

RAMSDEN. Certainly, Octavius.

OCTAVIUS. Aren't we forgetting that Ann herself may have some wishes in this matter?

RAMSDEN. I quite intend that Annie's wishes shall be consulted in every reasonable way. But she is only a woman, and a young and inexperienced woman at that.

TANNER. Ramsden: I begin to pity you.

RAMSDEN. [*hotly*] I don't want to know how you feel towards me, Mr Tanner.

TANNER. Ann will do just exactly what she likes. And what's more, she'll force us to advise her to do it; and she'll put the blame on us if it turns out badly. So, as Tavy is longing to see her—

OCTAVIUS. [*shyly*] I am not, Jack.

TANNER. You lie, Tavy: you are. So let's have her down from the drawing-room and ask her what she intends us to do. Off with you, Tavy, and fetch her. [*Tavy turns to go*]. And don't be long for the strained relations between myself and Ramsden will make the interval rather painful [*Ramsden compresses his lips, but says nothing—*].

OCTAVIUS. Never mind him, Mr Ramsden. He's not serious. [*He goes out*].

RAMSDEN [*very deliberately*] Mr Tanner: you are the most impudent person I have ever met.

TANNER. [*seriously*] I know it, Ramsden. Yet even I cannot wholly conquer shame. We live in an atmosphere of shame. We are ashamed of everything that is real about us; ashamed of ourselves, of our relatives, of our incomes, of our accents, of our opinions, of our experience, just as we are ashamed of our naked skins. Good Lord, my dear Ramsden, we are ashamed to walk, ashamed to ride in an omnibus, ashamed to hire a hansom instead of keeping a carriage, ashamed of keeping one horse instead of two and a groom-gardener instead of a coachman and footman. The more things a man is ashamed of, the more respectable he is. Why, you're ashamed to buy my book, ashamed to read it: the only thing you're not ashamed of is to judge me for it without having read it; and even that only means that you're ashamed to have heterodox opinions. Look at the effect I produce because my fairy godmother withheld from me this gift of shame. I have every possible virtue that a man can have except—

RAMSDEN. I am glad you think so well of yourself.

TANNER. All you mean by that is that you think I ought to be ashamed of talking about my virtues. You don't mean that I haven't got them: you know perfectly well that I am as sober and honest a citizen as yourself, as truthful personally, and much more truthful politically and morally.

RAMSDEN. [*touched on his most sensitive point*] I deny that. I will not allow you or any man to treat me as if I were a mere member of the British public. I detest its prejudices; I scorn its narrowness; I demand the right to think for myself. You pose as an advanced man. Let me tell you that I was an advanced man before you were born.

TANNER. I knew it was a long time ago.

RAMSDEN. I am as advanced as ever I was. I defy you to prove that I have ever hauled down the flag. I am more advanced than ever I was. I grow more advanced every day.

TANNER. More advanced in years, Polonius.

RAMSDEN. Polonius! So you are Hamlet, I suppose.

TANNER. No: I am only the most impudent person you've ever met. That's your notion of a thoroughly bad character. When you want to give me a piece of your mind, you ask yourself, as a just and upright man, what is the worst you can fairly say of me. Thief, liar, forger, adulterer, perjurer, glutton, drunkard? Not one of these names fit me. You have to fall back on my deficiency in shame. Well, I admit it. I even congratulate myself; for if I were ashamed of my real self, I should cut as stupid a figure as any of the rest of you. Cultivate a little impudence, Ramsden; and you will become quite a remarkable man.

RAMSDEN. I have no—

TANNER. You have no desire for that sort of notoriety. Bless you, I knew that answer would come as well as I know that a box of matches will come out of an automatic machine when I put a penny in the slot: you would be ashamed to say anything else.

The crushing retort for which Ramsden has been visibly collecting his forces is lost for ever; for at this point Octavius returns with Miss Ann Whitefield and her mother; and Ramsden springs up and hurries to the door to receive them. Whether Ann is good-looking or not depends upon your taste; also and perhaps chiefly on your age and sex. To Octavius she is an enchantingly beautiful woman, in whose presence the world becomes transfigured, and the puny limits of individual consciousness are suddenly made infinite by a mystic memory of the whole life of the race to its beginnings in the east, or even back to the paradise from which it fell. She is to him the reality of romance, the leaner good sense of nonsense, the unveiling of his eyes, the freeing of his soul, the abolition of time, place and circumstance, the etherealization of his blood into rapturous rivers of the very water of life itself, the revelation of all the mysteries and the sanctification of all the dogmas. To her mother she is, to put it as moderately as possible, nothing whatever of the kind. Not that Octavius's admiration is in any way ridiculous or discreditable. Ann is a well formed creature, as far as that goes; and she is perfectly ladylike, graceful, and comely, with ensnaring eyes and hair. Besides, instead of making herself an eyesore, like her mother, she has devised a mourning costume of black and violet silk which does honor to her late father and reveals the family tradition of brave unconventionality by which Ramsden sets such store.

But all this is beside the point as an explanation of Ann's charm. Turn up her nose, give a cast to her eye, replace her black and violet confection by the apron and feathers of a flower girl, strike all the aitches out of her speech, and Ann would still make men dream. Vitality is as common as humanity; but, like humanity, it sometimes rises to genius; and Ann is one of the vital geniuses. Not at all, if you please, an oversexed person: that is a vital defect, not a true excess. She is a perfectly respectable, perfectly self-controlled woman, and looks it; though her pose is fashionably frank and impulsive. She inspires confidence as a person who will do nothing she does not mean to do; also some fear, perhaps, as a woman who will probably do everything she means to do without taking more account of other people than may be necessary and what she calls right. In short, what the weaker of her own sex sometimes call a cat.

Nothing can be more decorous than her entry and her reception by Ramsden, whom she kisses. The late Mr Whitefield would be gratified almost to impatience by the long faces of the men (except Tanner, who is fidgety), the silent handgrasps, the sympathetic placing of chairs, the sniffing of the widow, and the liquid eye of the daughter, whose heart, apparently, will not let her control her tongue to speech. Ramsden and Octavius take the two chairs from the wall, and place them for the two ladies; but Ann comes to Tanner and takes his chair, which he offers with a brusque gesture, subsequently relieving his irritation by sitting down on the corner of the writing table with studied indecorum. Octavius gives Mrs Whitefield a chair next Ann, and himself takes the vacant one which Ramsden has placed under the nose of the effigy of Mr Herbert Spencer.

Mrs Whitefield, by the way, is a little woman, whose faded flaxen hair looks like straw on an egg. She has an expression of muddled shrewdness, a squeak of protest in her voice, and an odd air of continually elbowing away some larger person who is crushing her into a corner. One guesses her as one of those women who are conscious of being treated as silly and negligible, and who, without having strength enough to assert themselves effectually, at any rate never submit to their fate. There is a touch of chivalry in Octavius's scrupulous attention to her, even whilst his whole soul is absorbed by Ann.

Ramsden goes solemnly back to his magisterial seat at the writing table, ignoring Tanner, and opens the proceedings.

RAMSDEN. I am sorry, Annie, to force business on you at a sad time like the present. But your poor dear father's will has raised a very serious question. You have read it, I believe?

[*Ann assents with a nod and a catch of her breath, too much affected to speak*].

I must say I am surprised to find Mr Tanner named as joint guardian and trustee with myself of you and Rhoda. [*A pause. They all look portentous; but they have nothing to say. Ramsden, a little ruffled by the lack of any response, continues*] I don't know that I can consent to act under such conditions. Mr Tanner has, I understand, some objection also; but I do not profess to understand its nature: he will no doubt speak for himself. But we are agreed that we can decide nothing until we know your views. I am afraid I shall have to ask you to choose between my sole guardianship and that of Mr Tanner; for I fear it is impossible for us to undertake a joint arrangement.

ANN. [*in a low musical voice*] Mamma—

MRS WHITEFIELD. [*hastily*] Now, Ann, I do beg you not to put it on me. I have no opinion on the subject; and if I had, it would probably not be attended to. I am quite with whatever you three think best.

Tanner turns his head and looks fixedly at Ramsden, who angrily refuses to receive this mute communication.

ANN. [*resuming in the same gentle voice, ignoring her mother's bad taste*] Mamma knows that she is not strong enough to bear the whole responsibility for me and Rhoda without some help and advice. Rhoda must have a guardian; and though I am older, I do not think any young unmarried woman should be left quite to her own guidance. I hope you agree with me, Granny?

TANNER. [*starting*] Granny! Do you intend to call your guardians Granny?

ANN. Don't be foolish, Jack. Mr Ramsden has always been Grandpapa Roebuck to me: I am Granny's Annie; and he is Annie's Granny. I christened him so when I first learned to speak.

RAMSDEN. [*sarcastically*] I hope you are satisfied, Mr Tanner. Go on, Annie: I quite agree with you.

ANN. Well, if I am to have a guardian, CAN I set aside anybody whom my dear father appointed for me?

RAMSDEN. [*biting his lip*] You approve of your father's choice, then?

ANN. It is not for me to approve or disapprove. I accept it. My father loved me and knew best what was good for me.

RAMSDEN. Of course I understand your feeling, Annie. It is what I should have expected of you; and it does you credit. But it does not settle the question so completely as you think. Let me put a case to you. Suppose you were to discover that I had been guilty of some disgraceful action—that I was not the man your poor dear father took me for. Would you still consider it right that I should be Rhoda's guardian?

ANN. I can't imagine you doing anything disgraceful, Granny.

TANNER. [*to Ramsden*] You haven't done anything of the sort, have you?

RAMSDEN. [*indignantly*] No sir.

MRS. WHITEFIELD. [*placidly*] Well, then, why suppose it?

ANN. You see, Granny, Mamma would not like me to suppose it.

RAMSDEN. [*much perplexed*] You are both so full of natural and affectionate feeling in these family matters that it is very hard to put the situation fairly before you.

TANNER. Besides, my friend, you are not putting the situation fairly before them.

RAMSDEN. [*sulkily*] Put it yourself, then.

TANNER. I will. Ann: Ramsden thinks I am not fit be your guardian; and I quite agree with him. He considers that if your father had read my book, he wouldn't have appointed me. That book is the disgraceful action he has been talking about. He thinks it's your duty for Rhoda's sake to ask him to act alone and to make me withdraw. Say the word and I will.

ANN. But I haven't read your book, Jack.

TANNER. [*diving at the waste-paper basket and fishing the book out for her*] Then read it at once and decide.

RAMSDEN. If I am to be your guardian, I positively forbid you to read that book, Annie. [*He smites the table with his fist and rises*].

ANN. Of course, if you don't wish it. [*She puts the book on the table*].

TANNER. If one guardian is to forbid you to read the other guardian's book, how are we to settle it? Suppose I order you to read it! What about your duty to me?

ANN. [*gently*] I am sure you would never purposely force me into a painful dilemma, Jack.

RAMSDEN. [*irritably*] Yes, yes, Annie: this is all very well, and, as I said, quite natural and becoming. But you must make a choice one way or the other. We are as much in a dilemma as you.

ANN. I feel that I am too young, too inexperienced, to decide. My father's wishes are sacred to me.

MRS WHITEFIELD. If you two men won't carry them out I must say it is rather hard that you should put the responsibility on Ann. It seems to me that people are always putting things on other people in this world.

RAMSDEN. I am sorry you take it that way.

ANN. [*touchingly*] Do you refuse to accept me as your ward, Granny?

RAMSDEN. No: I never said that. I greatly object to act with Mr Tanner: that's all.

MRS. WHITEFIELD. Why? What's the matter with poor Jack?

TANNER. My views are too advanced for him.

RAMSDEN. [*indignantly*] They are not. I deny it.

ANN. Of course not. What nonsense! Nobody is more advanced than Granny. I am sure it is Jack himself who has made all the difficulty. Come, Jack! Be kind to me in my sorrow. You don't refuse to accept me as your ward, do you?

TANNER. [*gloomily*] No. I let myself in for it; so I suppose I must face it. [*He turns away to the bookcase, and stands there, moodily studying the titles of the volumes*].

ANN. [*rising and expanding with subdued but gushing delight*] Then we are all agreed; and my dear father's will is to be carried out. You don't know what a joy that is to me and to my mother! [*She goes to Ramsden and presses both his hands, saying*] And I shall have my dear Granny to help and advise me. [*She casts a glance at Tanner over her shoulder*]. And Jack the Giant Killer. [*She goes past her mother to Octavius*]. And Jack's inseparable friend Ricky-ticky-tavy [*he blushes and looks inexpressibly foolish*].

MRS WHITEFIELD. [*rising and shaking her widow's weeds straight*] Now that you are Ann's guardian, Mr Ramsden, I wish you would speak to her about her habit of giving people nicknames. They can't be expected to like it. [*She moves towards the door*].

ANN. How can you say such a thing, Mamma! [*Glowing with affectionate remorse*] Oh, I wonder can you be right! Have I been inconsiderate? [*She turns to Octavius, who is sitting astride his chair with his elbows on the back of it. Putting her hand on his forehead the turns his face up suddenly*]. Do you want to be treated like a grown up man? Must I call you Mr Robinson in future?

OCTAVIUS. [*earnestly*] Oh please call me Ricky-ticky—tavy, "Mr Robinson" would hurt me cruelly. [*She laughs and pats his cheek with her finger; then comes back to Ramsden*]. You know I'm beginning to think that Granny is rather a piece of impertinence. But I never dreamt of its hurting you.

RAMSDEN. [*breezily, as he pats her affectionately on the back*] My dear Annie, nonsense. I insist on Granny. I won't answer to any other name than Annie's Granny.

ANN. [*gratefully*] You all spoil me, except Jack.

TANNER. [*over his shoulder, from the bookcase*] I think you ought to call me Mr Tanner.

ANN. [*gently*] No you don't, Jack. That's like the things you say on purpose to shock people: those who know you pay no attention to them. But, if you like, I'll call you after your famous ancestor Don Juan.

RAMSDEN. Don Juan!

ANN. [*innocently*] Oh, is there any harm in it? I didn't know. Then I certainly won't call you that. May I call you Jack until I can think of something else?

TANKER. Oh, for Heaven's sake don't try to invent anything worse. I capitulate. I consent to Jack. I embrace Jack. Here endeth my first and last attempt to assert my authority.

ANN. You see, Mamma, they all really like to have pet names.

MRS WHITEFIELD. Well, I think you might at least drop them until we are out of mourning.

ANN. [*reproachfully, stricken to the soul*] Oh, how could you remind me, mother? [*She hastily leaves the room to conceal her emotion*].

MRS WHITEFIELD. Of course. My fault as usual! [*She follows Ann*].

TANNER. [*coming from the bookcase*] Ramsden: we're beaten—smashed—nonentitized, like her mother.

RAMSDEN. Stuff, Sir. [*He follows Mrs Whitefield out of the room*].

TANNER. [*left alone with Octavius, stares whimsically at him*] Tavy: do you want to count for something in the world?

OCTAVIUS. I want to count for something as a poet: I want to write a great play.

TANNER. With Ann as the heroine?

OCTAVIUS. Yes: I confess it.

TANNER. Take care, Tavy. The play with Ann as the heroine is all right; but if you're not very careful, by Heaven she'll marry you.

OCTAVIUS. [*sighing*] No such luck, Jack!

TANNER. Why, man, your head is in the lioness's mouth: you are half swallowed already—in three bites—Bite One, Ricky; Bite Two, Ticky; Bite Three, Tavy; and down you go.

OCTAVIUS. She is the same to everybody, Jack: you know her ways.

TANNER. Yes: she breaks everybody's back with the stroke of her paw; but the question is, which of us will she eat? My own opinion is that she means to eat you.

OCTAVIUS. [*rising, pettishly*] It's horrible to talk like that about her when she is upstairs crying for her father. But I do so want her to eat me that I can bear your brutalities because they give me hope.

TANNER. Tavy; that's the devilish side of a woman's fascination: she makes you will your own destruction.

OCTAVIUS. But it's not destruction: it's fulfilment.

TANNER. Yes, of HER purpose; and that purpose is neither her happiness nor yours, but Nature's. Vitality in a woman is a blind fury of creation. She sacrifices herself to it: do you think she will hesitate to sacrifice you?

OCTAVIUS. Why, it is just because she is self-sacrificing that she will not sacrifice those she loves.

TANNER. That is the profoundest of mistakes, Tavy. It is the self-sacrificing women that sacrifice others most recklessly. Because they are unselfish, they are kind in little things. Because they have a purpose which is not their own purpose, but that of the whole universe, a man is nothing to them but an instrument of that purpose.

OCTAVIUS. Don't be ungenerous, Jack. They take the tenderest care of us.

TANNER. Yes, as a soldier takes care of his rifle or a musician of his violin. But do they allow us any purpose or freedom of our own? Will they lend us to one another? Can the strongest man escape from them when once he is appropriated? They tremble when we are in danger, and weep when we die; but the tears are not for us, but for a father wasted, a son's breeding thrown away. They accuse us of treating them as a mere means to our pleasure; but how can so feeble and transient a folly as a man's selfish pleasure enslave a woman as the whole purpose of Nature embodied in a woman can enslave a man?

OCTAVIUS. What matter, if the slavery makes us happy?

TANNER. No matter at all if you have no purpose of your own, and are, like most men, a mere breadwinner. But you, Tavy, are an artist: that is, you have a purpose as absorbing and as unscrupulous as a woman's purpose.

OCTAVIUS. Not unscrupulous.

TANNER. Quite unscrupulous. The true artist will let his wife starve, his children go barefoot, his mother drudge for his living at seventy, sooner than work at anything but his art. To women he is half vivisector, half vampire. He gets into intimate relations with them to study them, to strip the mask of convention from them, to surprise their inmost secrets, knowing that they have the power to rouse his deepest creative energies, to rescue him from his cold reason, to make him see visions and dream dreams, to inspire him, as he calls it. He persuades women that they may do this for their own purpose whilst he really means them to do it for his. He steals the mother's milk and blackens it to make printer's ink to scoff at her and glorify ideal women with. He pretends to spare her the pangs of childbearing so that he may have for himself the tenderness and fostering that belong of right to her children. Since marriage began, the great artist has been known as a bad husband. But he is worse: he is a child-robber, a bloodsucker, a hypocrite and a cheat. Perish the race and wither a thousand women if only the sacrifice of them enable him to act Hamlet better, to paint a finer picture, to write a deeper poem, a greater play, a profounder philosophy! For mark you, Tavy, the artist's work is to show us ourselves as we really are. Our minds are nothing but this knowledge of ourselves; and he who adds a jot to such knowledge creates new mind as surely as any woman creates new men. In the rage of that creation he is as ruthless as the woman, as dangerous to her as she to him, and as horribly fascinating. Of all human struggles there is none so treacherous and remorseless as the struggle between the artist man and the mother woman. Which shall use up the other? that is the issue between them. And it is all the deadlier because, in your romanticist cant, they love one another.

OCTAVIUS. Even if it were so—and I don't admit it for a moment—it is out of the deadliest struggles that we get the noblest characters.

TANNER. Remember that the next time you meet a grizzly bear or a Bengal tiger, Tavy.

OCTAVIUS. I meant where there is love, Jack.

TANNER. Oh, the tiger will love you. There is no love sincerer than the love of food. I think Ann loves you that way: she patted your cheek as if it were a nicely underdone chop.

OCTAVIUS. You know, Jack, I should have to run away from you if I did not make it a fixed rule not to mind anything you say. You come out with perfectly revolting things sometimes.

Ramsden returns, followed by Ann. They come in quickly, with their former leisurely air of decorous grief changed to one of genuine concern, and, on Ramsden's part, of worry. He comes between the two men, intending to address Octavius, but pulls himself up abruptly as he sees Tanner.

RAMSDEN. I hardly expected to find you still here, Mr Tanner.

TANNER. Am I in the way? Good morning, fellow guardian [*he goes towards the door*].

ANN. Stop, Jack. Granny: he must know, sooner or later.

RAMSDEN. Octavius: I have a very serious piece of news for you. It is of the most private and delicate nature—of the most painful nature too, I am sorry to say. Do you wish Mr Tanner to be present whilst I explain?

OCTAVIUS. [*turning pale*] I have no secrets from Jack.

RAMSDEN. Before you decide that finally, let me say that the news concerns your sister, and that it is terrible news.

OCTAVIUS. Violet! What has happened? Is she—dead?

RAMSDEN. I am not sure that it is not even worse than that.

OCTAVIUS. Is she badly hurt? Has there been an accident?

RAMSDEN. No: nothing of that sort.

TANNER. Ann: will you have the common humanity to tell us what the matter is?

ANN. [*half whispering*] I can't. Violet has done something dreadful. We shall have to get her away somewhere. [*She flutters to the writing table and sits in Ramsden's chair, leaving the three men to fight it out between them*].

OCTAVIUS. [*enlightened*] Is that what you meant, Mr Ramsden?

RAMSDEN. Yes. [*Octavius sinks upon a chair, crushed*]. I am afraid there is no doubt that Violet did not really go to Eastbourne three weeks ago when we thought she was with the Parry Whitefields. And she called on a strange doctor yesterday with a wedding ring on her finger. Mrs. Parry Whitefield met her there by chance; and so the whole thing came out.

OCTAVIUS. [*rising with his fists clenched*] Who is the scoundrel?

ANN. She won't tell us.

OCTAVIUS. [*collapsing upon his chair again*] What a frightful thing!

TANNER. [*with angry sarcasm*] Dreadful. Appalling. Worse than death, as Ramsden says. [*He comes to Octavius*]. What would you not give, Tavy, to turn it into a railway accident, with all her bones broken or something equally respectable and deserving of sympathy?

OCTAVIUS. Don't be brutal, Jack.

TANNER. Brutal! Good Heavens, man, what are you crying for? Here is a woman whom we all supposed to be making bad water color sketches, practising Grieg and Brahms, gadding about to concerts and parties, wasting her life and her money. We suddenly learn that she has turned from these sillinesses to the fulfilment of her highest purpose and greatest function—to increase, multiply and replenish the earth. And instead of admiring her courage and rejoicing in her instinct; instead of crowning the completed womanhood and raising the triumphal strain of "Unto us a child is born: unto us a son is given," here you are—you who have been as merry as Brigs in your mourning for the dead—all pulling long faces and looking as ashamed and disgraced as if the girl had committed the vilest of crimes.

RAMSDEN. [*roaring with rage*] I will not have these abominations uttered in my house [*he smites the writing table with his fist*].

TANNER. Look here: if you insult me again I'll take you at your word and leave your house. Ann: where is Violet now?

ANN. Why? Are you going to her?

TANNER. Of course I am going to her. She wants help; she wants money; she wants respect and congratulation. She wants every chance for her child.

She does not seem likely to get it from you: she shall from me. Where is she?

ANN. Don't be so headstrong, Jack. She's upstairs.

TANNER. What! Under Ramsden's sacred roof! Go and do your miserable duty, Ramsden. Hunt her out into the street. Cleanse your threshold from her contamination. Vindicate the purity of your English home. I'll go for a cab.

ANN. [*alarmed*] Oh, Granny, you mustn't do that.

OCTAVIUS. [*broken-heartedly, rising*] I'll take her away, Mr Ramsden. She had no right to come to your house.

RAMSDEN. [*indignantly*] But I am only too anxious to help her. [*turning on Tanner*] How dare you, sir, impute such monstrous intentions to me? I protest against it. I am ready to put down my last penny to save her from being driven to run to you for protection.

TANNER. [*subsiding*] It's all right, then. He's not going to act up to his principles. It's agreed that we all stand by Violet.

OCTAVIUS. But who is the man? He can make reparation by marrying her; and he shall, or he shall answer for it to me.

RAMSDEN. He shall, Octavius. There you speak like a man.

TANNER. Then you don't think him a scoundrel, after all?

OCTAVIUS. Not a scoundrel! He is a heartless scoundrel.

RAMSDEN. A damned scoundrel. I beg your pardon, Annie; but I can say no less.

TANNER. So we are to marry your sister to a damned scoundrel by way of reforming her character! On my soul, I think you are all mad.

ANN. Don't be absurd, Jack. Of course you are quite right, Tavy; but we don't know who he is: Violet won't tell us.

TANNER. What on earth does it matter who he is? He's done his part; and Violet must do the rest.

RAMSDEN. [*beside himself*] Stuff! lunacy! There is a rascal in our midst, a libertine, a villain worse than a murderer; and we are not to learn who he is! In our ignorance we are to shake him by the hand; to introduce him into our homes; to trust our daughters with him; to—to—

ANN. [*coaxingly*] There, Granny, don't talk so loud. It's most shocking: we must all admit that; but if Violet won't tell us, what can we do? Nothing. Simply nothing.

RAMSDEN. Hmph! I'm not so sure of that. If any man has paid Violet any special attention, we can easily find that out. If there is any man of notoriously loose principles among us—

TANNER. Ahem!

RAMSDEN. [*raising his voice*] Yes sir, I repeat, if there is any man of notoriously loose principles among us—

TANNER. Or any man notoriously lacking in self-control.

RAMSDEN. [*aghast*] Do you dare to suggest that I am capable of such an act?

TANNER. My dear Ramsden, this is an act of which every man is capable. That is what comes of getting at cross purposes with Nature. The suspicion you have just flung at me clings to us all. It's a sort of mud that sticks to the judge's ermine or the cardinal's robe as fast as to the rags of the tramp. Come, Tavy: don't look so bewildered: it might have been me: it might have been Ramsden; just as it might have been anybody. If it had, what could we do but lie and protest as Ramsden is going to protest.

RAMSDEN. [*choking*] I—I—I—

TANNER. Guilt itself could not stammer more confusedly, And yet you know perfectly well he's innocent, Tavy.

RAMSDEN. [*exhausted*] I am glad you admit that, sir. I admit, myself, that there is an element of truth in what you say, grossly as you may distort it to gratify your malicious humor. I hope, Octavius, no suspicion of me is possible in your mind.

OCTAVIUS. Of you! No, not for a moment.

TANNER. [*drily*] I think he suspects me just a little.

OCTAVIUS. Jack: you couldn't—you wouldn't—

TANNER. Why not?

OCTAVIUS. [*appalled*] Why not!

TANNER. Oh, well, I'll tell you why not. First, you would feel bound to quarrel with me. Second, Violet doesn't like me. Third, if I had the honor of being the father of Violet's child, I should boast of it instead of denying it. So be easy: our Friendship is not in danger.

OCTAVIUS. I should have put away the suspicion with horror if only you would think and feel naturally about it. I beg your pardon.

TANNER. MY pardon! nonsense! And now let's sit down and have a family council. [*He sits down. The rest follow his example, more or less under protest*]. Violet is going to do the State a service; consequently she must be packed abroad like a criminal until it's over. What's happening upstairs?

ANN. Violet is in the housekeeper's room—by herself, of course.

TANNER. Why not in the drawingroom?

ANN. Don't be absurd, Jack. Miss Ramsden is in the drawingroom with my mother, considering what to do.

TANNER. Oh! the housekeeper's room is the penitentiary, I suppose; and the prisoner is waiting to be brought before her judges. The old cats!

ANN. Oh, Jack!

RAMSDEN. You are at present a guest beneath the roof of one of the old cats, sir. My sister is the mistress of this house.

TANNER. She would put me in the housekeeper's room, too, if she dared, Ramsden. However, I withdraw cats. Cats would have more sense. Ann: as your guardian, I order you to go to Violet at once and be particularly kind to her.

ANN. I have seen her, Jack. And I am sorry to say I am afraid she is going to be rather obstinate about going abroad. I think Tavy ought to speak to her about it.

OCTAVIUS. How can I speak to her about such a thing [*he breaks down*]?

ANN. Don't break down, Ricky. Try to bear it for all our sakes.

RAMSDEN. Life is not all plays and poems, Octavius. Come! face it like a man.

TANNER. [*chafing again*] Poor dear brother! Poor dear friends of the family! Poor dear Tabbies and Grimalkins. Poor dear everybody except the woman who is going to risk her life to create another life! Tavy: don't you be a selfish ass. Away with you and talk to Violet; and bring her down here if she cares to come. [*Octavius rises*]. Tell her we'll stand by her.

RAMSDEN. [*rising*] No, sir—

TANNER. [*rising also and interrupting him*] Oh, we understand: it's against your conscience; but still you'll do it.

OCTAVIUS. I assure you all, on my word, I never meant to be selfish. It's so hard to know what to do when one wishes earnestly to do right.

TANNER. My dear Tavy, your pious English habit of regarding the world as a moral gymnasium built expressly to strengthen your character in, occasionally leads you to think about your own confounded principles when you should be thinking about other people's necessities. The need of the present hour is a happy mother and a healthy baby. Bend your energies on that; and you will see your way clearly enough.

Octavius, much perplexed, goes out.

RAMSDEN. [*facing Tanner impressively*] And Morality, sir? What is to become of that?

TANNER. Meaning a weeping Magdalen and an innocent child branded with her shame. Not in our circle, thank you. Morality can go to its father the devil.

RAMSDEN. I thought so, sir. Morality sent to the devil to please our libertines, male and female. That is to be the future of England, is it?

TANNER. Oh, England will survive your disapproval. Meanwhile, I understand that you agree with me as to the practical course we are to take?

RAMSDEN. Not in your spirit sir. Not for your reasons.

TANNER. You can explain that if anybody calls you to account, here or hereafter. [*He turns away, and plants himself in front of Mr Herbert Spencer, at whom he stares gloomily*].

ANN. [*rising and coming to Ramsden*] Granny: hadn't you better go up to the drawingroom and tell them what we intend to do?

RAMSDEN. [*looking pointedly at Tanner*] I hardly like to leave you alone with this gentleman. Will you not come with me?

ANN. Miss Ramsden would not like to speak about it before me, Granny. I ought not to be present.

RAMSDEN. You are right: I should have thought of that. You are a good girl, Annie.

He pats her on the shoulder. She looks up at him with beaming eyes and he goes out, much moved. Having disposed of him, she looks at Tanner. His back being turned to her, she gives a moment's attention to her personal appearance, then softly goes to him and speaks almost into his ear.

ANN. Jack [*he turns with a start*]: are you glad that you are my guardian? You don't mind being made responsible for me, I hope.

TANNER. The latest addition to your collection of scapegoats, eh?

ANN. Oh, that stupid old joke of yours about me! Do please drop it. Why do you say things that you know must pain me? I do my best to please you, Jack: I suppose I may tell you so now that you are my guardian. You will make me so unhappy if you refuse to be friends with me.

TANNER. [*studying her as gloomily as he studied the dust*] You need not go begging for my regard. How unreal our moral judgments are! You seem to me to have absolutely no conscience—only hypocrisy; and you can't see the difference—yet there is a sort of fascination about you. I always attend to you, somehow. I should miss you if I lost you.

ANN. [*tranquilly slipping her arm into his and walking about with him*] But isn't that only natural, Jack? We have known each other since we were children. Do you remember?

TANNER. [*abruptly breaking loose*] Stop! I remember EVERYTHING.

ANN. Oh, I daresay we were often very silly; but—

TANNER. I won't have it, Ann. I am no more that schoolboy now than I am the dotard of ninety I shall grow into if I live long enough. It is over: let me forget it.

ANN. Wasn't it a happy time? [*She attempts to take his arm again*].

TANNER. Sit down and behave yourself. [*He makes her sit down in the chair next the writing table*]. No doubt it was a happy time for you. You were a good girl and never compromised yourself. And yet the wickedest child that ever was slapped could hardly have had a better time. I can understand the success with which you bullied the other girls: your virtue imposed on them. But tell me this: did you ever know a good boy?

ANN. Of course. All boys are foolish sometimes; but Tavy was always a really good boy.

TANNER. [*struck by this*] Yes: you're right. For some reason you never tempted Tavy.

ANN. Tempted! Jack!

TANNER. Yes, my dear Lady Mephistopheles, tempted. You were insatiably curious as to what a boy might be capable of, and diabolically clever at getting through his guard and surprising his inmost secrets.

ANN. What nonsense! All because you used to tell me long stories of the wicked things you had done—silly boys tricks! And you call such things inmost secrets: Boys' secrets are just like men's; and you know what they are!

TANNER. [*obstinately*] No I don't. What are they, pray?

ANN. Why, the things they tell everybody, of course.

TANNER. Now I swear I told you things I told no one else. You lured me into a compact by which we were to have no secrets from one another. We were to tell one another everything, I didn't notice that you never told me anything.

ANN. You didn't want to talk about me, Jack. You wanted to talk about yourself.

TANNER. Ah, true, horribly true. But what a devil of a child you must have been to know that weakness and to play on it for the satisfaction of your own curiosity! I wanted to brag to you, to make myself interesting. And I found myself doing all sorts of mischievous things simply to have something to tell you about. I fought with boys I didn't hate; I lied about things I might just as well have told the truth about; I stole things I didn't want; I kissed little girls I didn't care for. It was all bravado: passionless and therefore unreal.

ANN. I never told of you, Jack.

TANNER. No; but if you had wanted to stop me you would have told of me. You wanted me to go on.

ANN. [*flashing out*] Oh, that's not true: it's NOT true, Jack. I never wanted you to do those dull, disappointing, brutal, stupid, vulgar things. I always hoped that it would be something really heroic at last. [*Recovering herself*] Excuse me, Jack; but the things you did were never a bit like the things I wanted you to do. They often gave me great uneasiness; but I could not tell on you and get you into trouble. And you were only a boy. I knew you would grow out of them. Perhaps I was wrong.

TANNER. [*sardonically*] Do not give way to remorse, Ann. At least nineteen twentieths of the exploits I confessed to you were pure lies. I soon noticed that you didn't like the true stories.

ANN. Of course I knew that some of the things couldn't have happened. But—

TANNER. You are going to remind me that some of the most disgraceful ones did.

ANN. [*fondly, to his great terror*] I don't want to remind you of anything. But I knew the people they happened to, and heard about them.

TANNER. Yes; but even the true stories were touched up for telling. A sensitive boy's humiliations may be very good fun for ordinary thickskinned grown-ups; but to the boy himself they are so acute, so ignominious, that he cannot confess them—cannot but deny them passionately. However, perhaps it was as well for me that I romanced a bit; for, on the one occasion when I told you the truth, you threatened to tell of me.

ANN. Oh, never. Never once.

TANNER. Yes, you did. Do you remember a dark-eyed girl named Rachel Rosetree? [*Ann's brows contract for an instant involuntarily*]. I got up a love affair with her; and we met one night in the garden and walked about very uncomfortably with our arms round one another, and kissed at parting, and were most conscientiously romantic. If that love affair had gone on, it would have bored me to death; but it didn't go on; for the next thing that happened was that Rachel cut me because she found out that I had told you. How did she find it out? From you. You went to her and held the guilty secret over her head, leading her a life of abject terror and humiliation by threatening to tell on her.

ANN. And a very good thing for her, too. It was my duty to stop her misconduct; and she is thankful to me for it now.

TANNER. Is she?

ANN. She ought to be, at all events.

TANNER. It was not your duty to stop my misconduct, I suppose.

ANN. I did stop it by stopping her.

TANNER. Are you sure of that? You stopped my telling you about my adventures; but how do you know that you stopped the adventures?

ANN. Do you mean to say that you went on in the same way with other girls?

TANNER. No. I had enough of that sort of romantic tomfoolery with Rachel.

ANN. [*unconvinced*] Then why did you break off our confidences and become quite strange to me?

TANNER. [*enigmatically*] It happened just then that I got something that I wanted to keep all to myself instead of sharing it with you.

ANN. I am sure I shouldn't have asked for any of it if you had grudged it.

TANNER. It wasn't a box of sweets, Ann. It was something you'd never have let me call my own.

ANN. [*incredulously*] What?

TANNER. My soul.

ANN. Oh, do be sensible, Jack. You know you're talking nonsense.

TANNER. The most solemn earnest, Ann. You didn't notice at that time that you were getting a soul too. But you were. It was not for nothing that you suddenly found you had a moral duty to chastise and reform Rachel. Up to that time you had traded pretty extensively in being a good child; but you had never set up a sense of duty to others. Well, I set one up too. Up to that time I had played the boy buccaneer with no more conscience than a fox in a poultry farm. But now I began to have scruples, to feel obligations, to find that veracity and honor were no longer goody-goody expressions in the mouths of grown up people, but compelling principles in myself.

ANN. [*quietly*] Yes, I suppose you're right. You were beginning to be a man, and I to be a woman.

TANNER. Are you sure it was not that we were beginning to be something more? What does the beginning of manhood and womanhood mean in most people's mouths? You know: it means the beginning of love. But love began long before that for me. Love played its part in the earliest dreams and follies and romances I can remember—may I say the earliest follies and romances we can remember?—though we did not understand it at the time. No: the change that came to me was the birth in me of moral passion; and I declare that according to my experience moral passion is the only real passion.

ANN. All passions ought to be moral, Jack.

TANNER. Ought! Do you think that anything is strong enough to impose oughts on a passion except a stronger passion still?

ANN. Our moral sense controls passion, Jack. Don't be stupid.

TANNER. Our moral sense! And is that not a passion? Is the devil to have all the passions as well as all the good times? If it were not a passion—if it were not the mightiest of the passions, all the other passions would sweep it away like a leaf before a hurricane. It is the birth of that passion that turns a child into a man.

ANN. There are other passions, Jack. Very strong ones.

TANNER. All the other passions were in me before; but they were idle and aimless—mere childish greedinesses and cruelties, curiosities and fancies, habits and superstitions, grotesque and ridiculous to the mature intelligence. When they suddenly began to shine like newly lit flames it was by no light of their own, but by the radiance of the dawning moral passion. That passion dignified them, gave them conscience and meaning, found them a mob of appetites and organized them into an army of purposes and principles. My soul was born of that passion.

ANN. I noticed that you got more sense. You were a dreadfully destructive boy before that.

TANNER. Destructive! Stuff! I was only mischievous.

ANN. Oh Jack, you were very destructive. You ruined all the young fir trees by chopping off their leaders with a wooden sword. You broke all the cucumber frames with your catapult. You set fire to the common: the police arrested Tavy for it because he ran away when he couldn't stop you. You—

TANNER. Pooh! pooh! pooh! these were battles, bombardments, stratagems to save our scalps from the red Indians. You have no imagination, Ann. I am ten times more destructive now than I was then. The moral passion has taken my destructiveness in hand and directed it to moral ends. I have become a reformer, and, like all reformers, an iconoclast. I no longer break cucumber frames and burn gorse bushes: I shatter creeds and demolish idols.

ANN. [*bored*] I am afraid I am too feminine to see any sense in destruction. Destruction can only destroy.

TANNER. Yes. That is why it is so useful. Construction cumbers the ground with institutions made by busybodies. Destruction clears it and gives us breathing space and liberty.

ANN. It's no use, Jack. No woman will agree with you there.

TANNER. That's because you confuse construction and destruction with creation and murder. They're quite different: I adore creation and abhor murder. Yes: I adore it in tree and flower, in bird and beast, even in you. [*A flush of interest and delight suddenly clears the growing perplexity and boredom from her face*]. It was the creative instinct that led you to attach me to you by bonds that have left their mark on me to this day. Yes, Ann: the old childish compact between us was an unconscious love compact.

ANN. Jack!

TANNER. Oh, don't be alarmed—

ANN. I am not alarmed.

TANNER. [*whimsically*] Then you ought to be: where are your principles?

ANN. Jack: are you serious or are you not?

TANNER. Do you mean about the moral passion?

ANN. No, no; the other one. [*Confused*] Oh! you are so silly; one never knows how to take you.

TANNER. You must take me quite seriously. I am your guardian; and it is my duty to improve your mind.

ANN. The love compact is over, then, is it? I suppose you grew tired of me?

TANNER. No; but the moral passion made our childish relations impossible. A jealous sense of my new individuality arose in me.

ANN. You hated to be treated as a boy any longer. Poor Jack!

TANNER. Yes, because to be treated as a boy was to be taken on the old footing. I had become a new person; and those who knew the old person laughed at me. The only man who behaved sensibly was my tailor: he took my measure anew every time he saw me, whilst all the rest went on with their old measurements and expected them to fit me.

ANN. You became frightfully self-conscious.

TANNER. When you go to heaven, Ann, you will be frightfully conscious of your wings for the first year or so. When you meet your relatives there, and they persist in treating you as if you were still a mortal, you will not be able to bear them. You will try to get into a circle which has never known you except as an angel.

ANN. So it was only your vanity that made you run away from us after all?

TANNER. Yes, only my vanity, as you call it.

ANN. You need not have kept away from ME on that account.

TANNER. From you above all others. You fought harder than anybody against my emancipation.

ANN. [*earnestly*] Oh, how wrong you are! I would have done anything for you.

TANNER. Anything except let me get loose from you. Even then you had acquired by instinct that damnable woman's trick of heaping obligations on a man, of placing yourself so entirely and helplessly at his mercy that at last he dare not take a step without running to you for leave. I know a poor wretch whose one desire in life is to run away from his wife. She prevents him by threatening to throw herself in front of the engine of the train he leaves her in. That is what all women do. If we try to go where you do not want us to go there is no law to prevent us, but when we take the first step your breasts are under our foot as it descends: your bodies are under our wheels as we start. No woman shall ever enslave me in that way.

ANN. But, Jack, you cannot get through life without considering other people a little.

TANNER. Ay; but what other people? It is this consideration of other people or rather this cowardly fear of them which we call consideration that makes us the sentimental slaves we are. To consider you, as you call it, is to substitute your will for my own. How if it be a baser will than mine? Are women taught better than men or worse? Are mobs of voters taught better than statesmen or worse? Worse, of course, in both cases. And then what sort of world are you going to get, with its public men considering its voting mobs, and its private men considering their wives? What does Church and State mean nowadays? The Woman and the Ratepayer.

ANN. [*placidly*] I am so glad you understand politics, Jack: it will be most useful to you if you go into parliament [*he collapses like a pricked bladder*]. But I am sorry you thought my influence a bad one.

TANNER. I don't say it was a bad one. But bad or good, I didn't choose to be cut to your measure. And I won't be cut to it.

ANN. Nobody wants you to, Jack. I assure you—really on my word—I don't mind your queer opinions one little bit. You know we have all been brought up to have advanced opinions. Why do you persist in thinking me so narrow minded?

TANNER. That's the danger of it. I know you don't mind, because you've found out that it doesn't matter. The boa constrictor doesn't mind the opinions of a stag one little bit when once she has got her coils round it.

ANN. [*rising in sudden enlightenment*] O-o-o-o-oh! NOW I understand why you warned Tavy that I am a boa constrictor. Granny told me. [*She laughs and throws her boa around her neck*]. Doesn't it feel nice and soft, Jack?

TANNER. [*in the toils*] You scandalous woman, will you throw away even your hypocrisy?

ANN. I am never hypocritical with you, Jack. Are you angry? [*She withdraws the boa and throws it on a chair*]. Perhaps I shouldn't have done that.

TANNER. [*contemptuously*] Pooh, prudery! Why should you not, if it amuses you?

ANN. [*Shyly*] Well, because—because I suppose what you really meant by the boa constrictor was THIS [*she puts her arms round his neck*].

TANNER. [*Staring at her*] Magnificent audacity! [*She laughs and pats his cheeks*]. Now just to think that if I mentioned this episode not a soul would believe me except the people who would cut me for telling, whilst if you accused me of it nobody would believe my denial.

ANN. [*taking her arms away with perfect dignity*] You are incorrigible, Jack. But you should not jest about our affection for one another. Nobody could possibly misunderstand it. YOU do not misunderstand it, I hope.

TANNER. My blood interprets for me, Ann. Poor Ricky Tiky Tavy!

ANN. [*looking quickly at him as if this were a new light*] Surely you are not so absurd as to be jealous of Tavy.

TANNER. Jealous! Why should I be? But I don't wonder at your grip of him. I feel the coils tightening round my very self, though you are only playing with me.

ANN. Do you think I have designs on Tavy?

TANNER. I know you have.

ANN. [*earnestly*] Take care, Jack. You may make Tavy very happy if you mislead him about me.

TANNER. Never fear: he will not escape you.

ANN. I wonder are you really a clever man!

TANNER. Why this sudden misgiving on the subject?

ANN. You seem to understand all the things I don't understand; but you are a perfect baby in the things I do understand.

TANNER. I understand how Tavy feels for you, Ann; you may depend on that, at all events.

ANN. And you think you understand how I feel for Tavy, don't you?

TANNER. I know only too well what is going to happen to poor Tavy.

ANN. I should laugh at you, Jack, if it were not for poor papa's death. Mind! Tavy will be very unhappy.

TANNER. Yes; but he won't know it, poor devil. He is a thousand times too good for you. That's why he is going to make the mistake of his life about you.

ANN. I think men make more mistakes by being too clever than by being too good [*she sits down, with a trace of contempt for the whole male sex in the elegant carriage of her shoulders*].

TANNER. Oh, I know you don't care very much about Tavy. But there is always one who kisses and one who only allows the kiss. Tavy will kiss; and you will only turn the cheek. And you will throw him over if anybody better turns up.

ANN. [*offended*] You have no right to say such things, Jack. They are not true, and not delicate. If you and Tavy choose to be stupid about me, that is not my fault.

TANNER. [*remorsefully*] Forgive my brutalities, Ann. They are levelled at this wicked world, not at you. [*She looks up at him, pleased and forgiving. He becomes cautious at once*]. All the same, I wish Ramsden would come back. I never feel safe with you: there is a devilish charm—or no: not a charm, a subtle interest [*she laughs*]. Just so: you know it; and you triumph in it. Openly and shamelessly triumph in it!

ANN. What a shocking flirt you are, Jack!

TANNER. A flirt!! I!!

ANN. Yes, a flirt. You are always abusing and offending people, but you never really mean to let go your hold of them.

TANNER. I will ring the bell. This conversation has already gone further than I intended.

Ramsden and Octavius come back with Miss Ramsden, a hardheaded old maiden lady in a plain brown silk gown, with enough rings, chains and brooches to show that her plainness of dress is a matter of principle, not of poverty. She comes into the room very determinedly: the two men, perplexed and downcast, following her. Ann rises and goes eagerly to meet her. Tanner retreats to the wall between the busts and pretends to study the pictures. Ramsden goes to his table as usual; and Octavius clings to the neighborhood of Tanner.

MISS RAMSDEN. [*almost pushing Ann aside as she comes to Mr. Whitefield's chair and plants herself there resolutely*] I wash my hands of the whole affair.

OCTAVIUS. [*very wretched*] I know you wish me to take Violet away, Miss Ramsden. I will. [*He turns irresolutely to the door*].

RAMSDEN. No no—

MISS RAMSDEN. What is the use of saying no, Roebuck? Octavius knows that I would not turn any truly contrite and repentant woman from your doors. But when a woman is not only wicked, but intends to go on being wicked, she and I part company.

ANN. Oh, Miss Ramsden, what do you mean? What has Violet said?

RAMSDEN. Violet is certainly very obstinate. She won't leave London. I don't understand her.

MISS RAMSDEN. I do. It's as plain as the nose on your face, Roebuck, that she won't go because she doesn't want to be separated from this man, whoever he is.

ANN. Oh, surely, surely! Octavius: did you speak to her?

OCTAVIUS. She won't tell us anything. She won't make any arrangement until she has consulted somebody. It can't be anybody else than the scoundrel who has betrayed her.

TANNER. [*to Octavius*] Well, let her consult him. He will be glad enough to have her sent abroad. Where is the difficulty?

MISS RAMSDEN. [*Taking the answer out of Octavius's mouth*]. The difficulty, Mr Jack, is that when he offered to help her I didn't offer to become her accomplice in her wickedness. She either pledges her word never to see that man again, or else she finds some new friends; and the sooner the better.

[*The parlormaid appears at the door. Ann hastily resumes her seat, and looks as unconcerned as possible. Octavius instinctively imitates her*].

THE MAID. The cab is at the door, ma'am.

MISS RAMSDEN. What cab?

THE MAID. For Miss Robinson.

MISS RAMSDEN. Oh! [*Recovering herself*] All right. [*The maid withdraws*]. She has sent for a cab.

TANNER. I wanted to send for that cab half an hour ago.

MISS RAMSDEN. I am glad she understands the position she has placed herself in.

RAMSDEN. I don't like her going away in this fashion, Susan. We had better not do anything harsh.

OCTAVIUS. No: thank you again and again; but Miss Ramsden is quite right. Violet cannot expect to stay.

ANN. Hadn't you better go with her, Tavy?

OCTAVIUS. She won't have me.

MISS RAMSDEN. Of course she won't. She's going straight to that man.

TANNER. As a natural result of her virtuous reception here.

RAMSDEN. [*much troubled*] There, Susan! You hear! and there's some truth in it. I wish you could reconcile it with your principles to be a little patient with this poor girl. She's very young; and there's a time for everything.

MISS RAMSDEN. Oh, she will get all the sympathy she wants from the men. I'm surprised at you, Roebuck.

TANNER. So am I, Ramsden, most favorably.

Violet appears at the door. She is as impenitent and self-assured a young lady as one would desire to see among the best behaved of her sex. Her small head and tiny resolute mouth and chin; her haughty crispness of speech and trimness of carriage; the ruthless elegance of her equipment, which includes a very smart hat with a dead bird in it, mark a personality which is as formidable as it is exquisitely pretty. She is not a siren, like Ann: admiration comes to her without any compulsion or even interest on her part; besides, there is some fun in Ann, but in this woman none, perhaps no mercy either: if anything restrains her, it is intelligence and pride, not compassion. Her voice might be the voice of a schoolmistress addressing a class of girls who had disgraced themselves, as she proceeds with complete composure and some disgust to say what she has come to say.

VIOLET. I have only looked in to tell Miss Ramsden that she will find her birthday present to me, the filagree bracelet, in the housekeeper's room.

TANNER. Do come in, Violet, and talk to us sensibly.

VIOLET. Thank you: I have had quite enough of the family conversation this morning. So has your mother, Ann: she has gone home crying. But at all events, I have found out what some of my pretended friends are worth. Good bye.

TANNER. No, no: one moment. I have something to say which I beg you to hear. [*She looks at him without the slightest curiosity, but waits, apparently as much to finish getting her glove on as to hear what he has to say*]. I am altogether on your side in this matter. I congratulate you, with the sincerest respect, on having the courage to do what you have done. You are entirely in the right; and the family is entirely in the wrong.

Sensation. Ann and Miss Ramsden rise and turn toward the two. Violet, more surprised than any of the others, forgets her glove, and comes forward into the middle of the room, both puzzled and displeased. Octavius alone does not move or raise his head; he is overwhelmed with shame.

ANN. [*pleading to Tanner to be sensible*] Jack!

MISS RAMSDEN. [*outraged*] Well, I must say!

VIOLET. [*sharply to Tanner*] Who told you?

TANNER. Why, Ramsden and Tavy of course. Why should they not?

VIOLET. But they don't know.

TANNER. Don't know what?

VIOLET. They don't know that I am in the right, I mean.

TANNER. Oh, they know it in their hearts, though they think themselves bound to blame you by their silly superstitions about morality and propriety and so forth. But I know, and the whole world really knows, though it dare not say so, that you were right to follow your instinct; that vitality and bravery are the greatest qualities a woman can have, and motherhood her solemn initiation into womanhood; and that the fact of your not being legally married matters not one scrap either to your own worth or to our real regard for you.

VIOLET. [*flushing with indignation*] Oh! You think me a wicked woman, like the rest. You think I have not only been vile, but that I share your abominable opinions. Miss Ramsden: I have borne your hard words because I knew you would be sorry for them when you found out the truth. But I won't bear such a horrible insult as to be complimented by Jack on being one of the wretches of whom he approves. I have kept my marriage a secret for my husband's sake. But now I claim my right as a married woman not to be insulted.

OCTAVIUS. [*raising his head with inexpressible relief*] You are married!

VIOLET. Yes; and I think you might have guessed it. What business had you all to take it for granted that I had no right to wear my wedding ring? Not one of you even asked me: I cannot forget that.

TANNER. [*in ruins*] I am utterly crushed. I meant well—I apologize—abjectly apologize.

VIOLET. I hope you will be more careful in future about the things you say. Of course one does not take them seriously. But they are very disagreeable, and rather in bad taste.

TANNER. [*bowing to the storm*] I have no defence: I shall know better in future than to take any woman's part. We have all disgraced ourselves in your eyes, I am afraid, except Ann, SHE befriended you. For Ann's sake, forgive us.

VIOLET. Yes: Ann has been very kind; but then Ann knew.

TANNER. Oh!

MISS RAMSDEN. [*stiffly*] And who, pray, is the gentleman who does not acknowledge his wife?

VIOLET. [*promptly*] That is my business, Miss Ramsden, and not yours. I have my reasons for keeping my marriage a secret for the present.

RAMSDEN. All I can say is that we are extremely sorry, Violet. I am shocked to think of how we have treated you.

OCTAVIUS. [*awkwardly*] I beg your pardon, Violet. I can say no more.

MISS RAMSDEN. [*still loth to surrender*] Of course what you say puts a very different complexion on the matter. All the same, I owe it to myself—

VIOLET. [*cutting her short*] You owe me an apology, Miss Ramsden: that's what you owe both to yourself and to me. If you were a married woman you would not like sitting in the housekeeper's room and being treated like a naughty child by young girls and old ladies without any serious duties and responsibilities.

TANNER. Don't hit us when we're down, Violet. We seem to have made fools of ourselves; but really it was you who made fools of us.

VIOLET. It was no business of yours, Jack, in any case.

TANNER. No business of mine! Why, Ramsden as good as accused me of being the unknown gentleman.

Ramsden makes a frantic demonstration; but Violet's cool keen anger extinguishes it.

VIOLET. You! Oh, how infamous! how abominable! How disgracefully you have all been talking about me! If my husband knew it he would never let me speak to any of you again. [*To Ramsden*] I think you might have spared me, at least.

RAMSDEN. But I assure you I never—at least it is a monstrous perversion of something I said that—

MISS RAMSDEN. You needn't apologize, Roebuck. She brought it all on herself. It is for her to apologize for having deceived us.

VIOLET. I can make allowances for you, Miss Ramsden: you cannot understand how I feel on this subject though I should have expected rather better taste from people of greater experience. However, I quite feel that you have all placed yourselves in a very painful position; and the most truly considerate thing for me to do is to go at once. Good morning.

She goes, leaving them staring.

Miss RAMSDEN. Well, I must say—!

RAMSDEN. [*plaintively*] I don't think she is quite fair to us.

TANNER. You must cower before the wedding ring like the rest of us, Ramsden. The cup of our ignominy is full.

ACT II

On the carriage drive in the park of a country house near Richmond a motor car has broken down. It stands in front of a clump of trees round which the drive sweeps to the house, which is partly visible through them: indeed Tanner, standing in the drive with the car on his right hand, could get an unobstructed view of the west corner of the house on his left were he not far too much interested in a pair of supine legs in blue serge trousers which protrude from beneath the machine. He is watching them intently with bent back and hands supported on his knees. His leathern overcoat and peaked cap proclaim him one of the dismounted passengers.

THE LEGS. Aha! I got him.

TANNER. All right now?

THE LEGS. All right now.

Tanner stoops and takes the legs by the ankles, drawing their owner forth like a wheelbarrow, walking on his hands, with a hammer in his mouth. He is a young man in a neat suit of blue serge, clean shaven, dark eyed, square fingered, with short well brushed black hair and rather irregular sceptically turned eyebrows. When he is manipulating the car his movements are swift and sudden, yet attentive and deliberate. With Tanner and Tanner's friends his manner is not in the least deferential, but cool and reticent, keeping them quite effectually at a distance whilst giving them no excuse for complaining of him. Nevertheless he has a vigilant eye on them always, and that, too, rather cynically, like a man who knows the world well from its seamy side. He speaks slowly and with a touch of sarcasm; and as he does not at all affect the gentleman in his speech, it may be inferred that his smart appearance is a mark of respect to himself and his own class, not to that which employs him.

He now gets into the car to test his machinery and put his cap and overcoat on again. Tanner takes off his leather overcoat and pitches it into the car. The chauffeur (or automobilist or motoreer or whatever England may presently decide to call him) looks round inquiringly in the act of stowing away his hammer.

THE CHAUFFEUR. Had enough of it, eh?

TANNER. I may as well walk to the house and stretch my legs and calm my nerves a little. [*Looking at his watch*] I suppose you know that we have come from Hyde Park Corner to Richmond in twenty-one minutes.

THE CHAUFFEUR. I'd have done it under fifteen if I'd had a clear road all the way.

TANNER. Why do you do it? Is it for love of sport or for the fun of terrifying your unfortunate employer?

THE CHAUFFEUR. What are you afraid of?

TANNER. The police, and breaking my neck.

THE CHAUFFEUR. Well, if you like easy going, you can take a bus, you know. It's cheaper. You pay me to save your time and give you the value of your thousand pound car. [*He sits down calmly*].

TANNER. I am the slave of that car and of you too. I dream of the accursed thing at night.

THE CHAUFFEUR. You'll get over that. If you're going up to the house, may I ask how long you're goin to stay there? Because if you mean to put in the whole morning talkin to the ladies, I'll put the car in the stables and make myself comfortable. If not, I'll keep the car on the go about here til you come.

TANNER. Better wait here. We shan't be long. There's a young American gentleman, a Mr Malone, who is driving Mr Robinson down in his new American steam car.

THE CHAUFFEUR. [*springing up and coming hastily out of the car to Tanner*] American steam car! Wot! racin us down from London!

TANNER. Perhaps they're here already.

THE CHAUFFEUR. If I'd known it! [*with deep reproach*] Why didn't you tell me, Mr Tanner?

TANNER. Because I've been told that this car is capable of 84 miles an hour; and I already know what YOU are capable of when there is a rival car on the road. No, Henry: there are things it is not good for you to know; and this was one of them. However, cheer up: we are going to have a day after your own heart. The American is to take Mr Robinson and his sister and Miss Whitefield. We are to take Miss Rhoda.

THE CHAUFFEUR. [*consoled, and musing on another matter*] That's Miss Whitefield's sister, isn't it?

TANNER. Yes.

THE CHAUFFEUR. And Miss Whitefield herself is goin in the other car? Not with you?

TANNER. Why the devil should she come with me? Mr Robinson will be in the other car. [*The Chauffeur looks at Tanner with cool incredulity, and turns to the car, whistling a popular air softly to himself. Tanner, a little annoyed, is about to pursue the subject when he hears the footsteps of Octavius on the gravel. Octavius is coming from the house, dressed for motoring, but without his overcoat*]. We've lost the race, thank Heaven: here's Mr Robinson. Well, Tavy, is the steam car a success?

OCTAVIUS. I think so. We came from Hyde Park Corner here in seventeen minutes. [*The Chauffeur, furious, kicks the car with a groan of vexation*]. How long were you?

TANNER. Oh, about three quarters of an hour or so.

THE CHAUFFEUR. [*remonstrating*] Now, now, Mr Tanner, come now! We could ha done it easy under fifteen.

TANNER. By the way, let me introduce you. Mr Octavius Robinson: Mr Enry Straker.

STRAKER. Pleased to meet you, sir. Mr Tanner is gittin at you with his Enry Straker, you know. You call it Henery. But I don't mind, bless you.

TANNER. You think it's simply bad taste in me to chaff him, Tavy. But you're wrong. This man takes more trouble to drop his aiches than ever his father did to pick them up. It's a mark of caste to him. I have never met anybody more swollen with the pride of class than Enry is.

STRAKER. Easy, easy! A little moderation, Mr Tanner.

TANNER. A little moderation, Tavy, you observe. You would tell me to draw it mild, But this chap has been educated. What's more, he knows that we haven't. What was that board school of yours, Straker?

STRAKER. Sherbrooke Road.

TANNER. Sherbrooke Road! Would any of us say Rugby! Harrow! Eton! in that tone of intellectual snobbery? Sherbrooke Road is a place where boys learn something; Eton is a boy farm where we are sent because we are nuisances at home, and because in after life, whenever a Duke is mentioned, we can claim him as an old schoolfellow.

STRAKER. You don't know nothing about it, Mr. Tanner. It's not the Board School that does it: it's the Polytechnic.

TANNER. His university, Octavius. Not Oxford, Cambridge, Durham, Dublin or Glasgow. Not even those Nonconformist holes in Wales. No, Tavy. Regent Street, Chelsea, the Borough—I don't know half their confounded names: these are his universities, not mere shops for selling class limitations like ours. You despise Oxford, Enry, don't you?

STRAKER. No, I don't. Very nice sort of place, Oxford, I should think, for people that like that sort of place. They teach you to be a gentleman there. In the Polytechnic they teach you to be an engineer or such like. See?

TANNER. Sarcasm, Tavy, sarcasm! Oh, if you could only see into Enry's soul, the depth of his contempt for a gentleman, the arrogance of his pride in being an engineer, would appal you. He positively likes the car to break down because it brings out my gentlemanly helplessness and his workmanlike skill and resource.

STRAKER. Never you mind him, Mr Robinson. He likes to talk. We know him, don't we?

OCTAVIUS. [*earnestly*] But there's a great truth at the bottom of what he says. I believe most intensely in the dignity of labor.

STRAKER. [*unimpressed*] That's because you never done any Mr Robinson. My business is to do away with labor. You'll get more out of me and a machine than you will out of twenty laborers, and not so much to drink either.

TANNER. For Heaven's sake, Tavy, don't start him on political economy. He knows all about it; and we don't. You're only a poetic Socialist, Tavy: he's a scientific one.

STRAKER. [*unperturbed*] Yes. Well, this conversation is very improvin; but I've got to look after the car; and you two want to talk about your ladies. I know. [*He retires to busy himself about the car; and presently saunters off towards the house*].

TANNER. That's a very momentous social phenomenon.

OCTAVIUS. What is?

TANNER. Straker is. Here have we literary and cultured persons been for years setting up a cry of the New Woman whenever some unusually old fashioned female came along; and never noticing the advent of the New Man. Straker's the New Man.

OCTAVIUS. I see nothing new about him, except your way of chaffing him. But I don't want to talk about him just now. I want to speak to you about Ann.

TANNER. Straker knew even that. He learnt it at the Polytechnic, probably. Well, what about Ann? Have you proposed to her?

OCTAVIUS. [*self-reproachfully*] I was brute enough to do so last night.

TANNER. Brute enough! What do you mean?

OCTAVIUS. [*dithyrambically*] Jack: we men are all coarse. We never understand how exquisite a woman's sensibilities are. How could I have done such a thing!

TANNER. Done what, you maudlin idiot?

OCTAVIUS. Yes, I am an idiot. Jack: if you had heard her voice! if you had seen her tears! I have lain awake all night thinking of them. If she had reproached me, I could have borne it better.

TANNER. Tears! that's dangerous. What did she say?

OCTAVIUS. She asked me how she could think of anything now but her dear father. She stifled a sob—[*he breaks down*].

TANNER. [*patting him on the back*] Bear it like a man, Tavy, even if you feel it like an ass. It's the old game: she's not tired of playing with you yet.

OCTAVIUS. [*impatiently*] Oh, don't be a fool, Jack. Do you suppose this eternal shallow cynicism of yours has any real bearing on a nature like hers?

TANNER. Hm! Did she say anything else?

OCTAVIUS. Yes; and that is why I expose myself and her to your ridicule by telling you what passed.

TANNER. [*remorsefully*] No, dear Tavy, not ridicule, on my honor! However, no matter. Go on.

OCTAVIUS. Her sense of duty is so devout, so perfect, so—

TANNER. Yes: I know. Go on.

OCTAVIUS. You see, under this new arrangement, you and Ramsden are her guardians; and she considers that all her duty to her father is now transferred to you. She said she thought I ought to have spoken to you both in the first instance. Of course she is right; but somehow it seems rather absurd that I am to come to you and formally ask to be received as a suitor for your ward's hand.

TANNER. I am glad that love has not totally extinguished your sense of humor, Tavy.

OCTAVIUS. That answer won't satisfy her.

TANNER. My official answer is, obviously, Bless you, my children: may you be happy!

OCTAVIUS. I wish you would stop playing the fool about this. If it is not serious to you, it is to me, and to her.

TANNER. You know very well that she is as free to choose as you. She does not think so.

TANNER. Oh, doesn't she! just! However, say what you want me to do.

OCTAVIUS. I want you to tell her sincerely and earnestly what you think about me. I want you to tell her that you can trust her to me—that is, if you feel you can.

TANNER. I have no doubt that I can trust her to you. What worries me is the idea of trusting you to her. Have you read Maeterlinck's book about the bee?

OCTAVIUS. [*keeping his temper with difficulty*] I am not discussing literature at present.

TANNER. Be just a little patient with me. I am not discussing literature: the book about the bee is natural history. It's an awful lesson to mankind. You think that you are Ann's suitor; that you are the pursuer and she the pursued; that it is your part to woo, to persuade, to prevail, to overcome. Fool: it is you who are the pursued, the marked down quarry, the destined prey. You need not sit looking longingly at the bait through the wires of the trap: the door is open, and will remain so until it shuts behind you for ever.

OCTAVIUS. I wish I could believe that, vilely as you put it.

TANNER. Why, man, what other work has she in life but to get a husband? It is a woman's business to get married as soon as possible, and a man's to keep unmarried as long as he can. You have your poems and your tragedies to work at: Ann has nothing.

OCTAVIUS. I cannot write without inspiration. And nobody can give me that except Ann.

TANNER. Well, hadn't you better get it from her at a safe distance? Petrarch didn't see half as much of Laura, nor Dante of Beatrice, as you see of Ann now; and yet they wrote first-rate poetry—at least so I'm told. They never exposed their idolatry to the test of domestic familiarity; and it lasted them to their graves. Marry Ann and at the end of a week you'll find no more inspiration than in a plate of muffins.

OCTAVIUS. You think I shall tire of her.

TANNER. Not at all: you don't get tired of muffins. But you don't find inspiration in them; and you won't in her when she ceases to be a poet's dream and becomes a solid eleven stone wife. You'll be forced to dream about somebody else; and then there will be a row.

OCTAVIUS. This sort of talk is no use, Jack. You don't understand. You have never been in love.

TANNER. I! I have never been out of it. Why, I am in love even with Ann. But I am neither the slave of love nor its dupe. Go to the bee, thou poet: consider her ways and be wise. By Heaven, Tavy, if women could do without our work, and we ate their children's bread instead of making it, they would kill us as the spider kills her mate or as the bees kill the drone. And they would be right if we were good for nothing but love.

OCTAVIUS. Ah, if we were only good enough for Love! There is nothing like Love: there is nothing else but Love: without it the world would be a dream of sordid horror.

TANNER. And this—this is the man who asks me to give him the hand of my ward! Tavy: I believe we were changed in our cradles, and that you are the real descendant of Don Juan.

OCTAVIUS. I beg you not to say anything like that to Ann.

TANNER. Don't be afraid. She has marked you for her own; and nothing will stop her now. You are doomed. [*Straker comes back with a newspaper*]. Here comes the New Man, demoralizing himself with a halfpenny paper as usual.

STRAKER. Now, would you believe it: Mr Robinson, when we're out motoring we take in two papers, the Times for him, the Leader or the Echo for me. And do you think I ever see my paper? Not much. He grabs the Leader and leaves me to stodge myself with his Times.

OCTAVIUS. Are there no winners in the Times?

TANNER. Enry don't old with bettin, Tavy. Motor records are his weakness. What's the latest?

STRAKER. Paris to Biskra at forty mile an hour average, not countin the Mediterranean.

TANNER. How many killed?

STRAKER. Two silly sheep. What does it matter? Sheep don't cost such a lot: they were glad to ave the price without the trouble o sellin em to the butcher. All the same, d'y'see, there'll be a clamor agin it presently; and then the French Government'll stop it; an our chance will be gone see? That what makes me fairly mad: Mr Tanner won't do a good run while he can.

TANNER. Tavy: do you remember my uncle James?

OCTAVIUS. Yes. Why?

TANNER. Uncle James had a first rate cook: he couldn't digest anything except what she cooked. Well, the poor man was shy and hated society. But his cook was proud of her skill, and wanted to serve up dinners to princes and ambassadors. To prevent her from leaving him, that poor old man had to give a big dinner twice a month, and suffer agonies of awkwardness. Now here am I; and here is this chap Enry Straker, the New Man. I loathe travelling; but I rather like Enry. He cares for nothing but tearing along in a leather coat and goggles, with two inches of dust all over him, at sixty miles an hour and the risk of his life and mine. Except, of course, when he is lying on his back in the mud under the machine trying to find out where it has given way. Well, if I don't give him a thousand mile run at least once a fortnight I shall lose him. He will give me the sack and go to some American millionaire; and I shall have to put up with a nice respectful groom-gardener-amateur, who will touch his hat and know his place. I am Enry's slave, just as Uncle James was his cook's slave.

STRAKER. [*exasperated*] Garn! I wish I had a car that would go as fast as you can talk, Mr Tanner. What I say is that you lose money by a motor car unless you keep it workin. Might as well ave a pram and a nussmaid to wheel you in it as that car and me if you don't git the last inch out of us both.

TANNER. [*soothingly*] All right, Henry, all right. We'll go out for half an hour presently.

STRAKER. [*in disgust*] Arf an ahr! [*He returns to his machine; seats himself in it; and turns up a fresh page of his paper in search of more news*].

OCTAVIUS. Oh, that reminds me. I have a note for you from Rhoda. [*He gives Tanner a note*].

TANNER. [*opening it*] I rather think Rhoda is heading for a row with Ann. As a rule there is only one person an English girl hates more than she hates her mother; and that's her eldest sister. But Rhoda positively prefers her mother to Ann. She—[*indignantly*] Oh, I say!

OCTAVIUS. What's the matter?

TANNER. Rhoda was to have come with me for a ride in the motor car. She says Ann has forbidden her to go out with me.

Straker suddenly begins whistling his favorite air with remarkable deliberation. Surprised by this burst of larklike melody, and jarred by a sardonic note in its cheerfulness, they turn and look inquiringly at him. But he is busy with his paper; and nothing comes of their movement.

OCTAVIUS. [*recovering himself*] Does she give any reason?

TANNER. Reason! An insult is not a reason. Ann forbids her to be alone with me on any occasion. Says I am not a fit person for a young girl to be with. What do you think of your paragon now?

OCTAVIUS. You must remember that she has a very heavy responsibility now that her father is dead. Mrs Whitefield is too weak to control Rhoda.

TANNER. [*staring at him*] In short, you agree with Ann.

OCTAVIUS. No; but I think I understand her. You must admit that your views are hardly suited for the formation of a young girl's mind and character.

TANNER. I admit nothing of the sort. I admit that the formation of a young lady's mind and character usually consists in telling her lies; but I object to the particular lie that I am in the habit of abusing the confidence of girls.

OCTAVIUS. Ann doesn't say that, Jack.

TANNER. What else does she mean?

STRAKER. [*catching sight of Ann coming from the house*] Miss Whitefield, gentlemen. [*He dismounts and strolls away down the avenue with the air of a man who knows he is no longer wanted*].

ANN. [*coming between Octavius and Tanner*]. Good morning, Jack. I have come to tell you that poor Rhoda has got one of her headaches and cannot go out with you to-day in the car. It is a cruel disappointment to her, poor child!

TANNER. What do you say now, Tavy.

OCTAVIUS. Surely you cannot misunderstand, Jack. Ann is showing you the kindest consideration, even at the cost of deceiving you.

ANN. What do you mean?

TANNER. Would you like to cure Rhoda's headache, Ann?

ANN. Of course.

TANNER. Then tell her what you said just now; and add that you arrived about two minutes after I had received her letter and read it.

ANN. Rhoda has written to you!

TANNER. With full particulars.

OCTAVIUS. Never mind him, Ann. You were right, quite right. Ann was only doing her duty, Jack; and you know it. Doing it in the kindest way, too.

ANN. [*going to Octavius*] How kind you are, Tavy! How helpful! How well you understand!

Octavius beams.

TANNER. Ay: tighten the coils. You love her, Tavy, don't you?

OCTAVIUS. She knows I do.

ANN. Hush. For shame, Tavy!

TANNER. Oh, I give you leave. I am your guardian; and I commit you to Tavy's care for the next hour.

ANN. No, Jack. I must speak to you about Rhoda. Ricky: will you go back to the house and entertain your American friend? He's rather on Mamma's hands so early in the morning. She wants to finish her housekeeping.

OCTAVIUS. I fly, dearest Ann [*he kisses her hand*].

ANN. [*tenderly*] Ricky Ticky Tavy!

He looks at her with an eloquent blush, and runs off.

TANNER. [*bluntly*] Now look here, Ann. This time you've landed yourself; and if Tavy were not in love with you past all salvation he'd have found out what an incorrigible liar you are.

ANN. You misunderstand, Jack. I didn't dare tell Tavy the truth.

TANNER. No: your daring is generally in the opposite direction. What the devil do you mean by telling Rhoda that I am too vicious to associate with her? How can I ever have any human or decent relations with her again, now that you have poisoned her mind in that abominable way?

ANN. I know you are incapable of behaving badly.

TANNER. Then why did you lie to her?

ANN. I had to.

TANNER. Had to!

ANN. Mother made me.

TANNER. [*his eye flashing*] Ha! I might have known it. The mother! Always the mother!

ANN. It was that dreadful book of yours. You know how timid mother is. All timid women are conventional: we must be conventional, Jack, or we are so cruelly, so vilely misunderstood. Even you, who are a man, cannot say what you think without being misunderstood and vilified—yes: I admit it: I have had to vilify you. Do you want to have poor Rhoda misunderstood and vilified to the same way? Would it be right for mother to let her expose herself to such treatment before she is old enough to judge for herself?

TANNER. In short, the way to avoid misunderstanding is for everybody to lie and slander and insinuate and pretend as hard as they can. That is what obeying your mother comes to.

ANN. I love my mother, Jack.

TANNER. [*working himself up into a sociological rage*] Is that any reason why you are not to call your soul your own? Oh, I protest against this vile abjection of youth to age! look at fashionable society as you know it. What does it pretend to be? An exquisite dance of nymphs. What is it? A horrible procession of wretched girls, each in the claws of a cynical, cunning, avaricious, disillusioned, ignorantly experienced, foul-minded old woman whom she calls mother, and whose duty it is to corrupt her mind and sell her to the highest bidder. Why do these unhappy slaves marry anybody, however old and vile, sooner than not marry at all? Because marriage is their only means of escape from these decrepit fiends who hide their selfish ambitions, their jealous hatreds of the young rivals who have supplanted them, under the mask of maternal duty and family affection. Such things are abominable: the voice of nature proclaims for the daughter a father's care and for the son a mother's. The law for father and son and mother and daughter is not the law of love: it is the law of revolution, of emancipation, of final supersession of the old and worn-out by the young and capable. I tell you, the first duty of manhood and womanhood is a Declaration of Independence: the man who pleads his father's authority is no man: the woman who pleads her mother's authority is unfit to bear citizens to a free people.

ANN. [*watching him with quiet curiosity*] I suppose you will go in seriously for politics some day, Jack.

TANNER. [*heavily let down*] Eh? What? Wh—? [*Collecting his scattered wits*] What has that got to do with what I have been saying?

ANN. You talk so well.

TANNER. Talk! Talk! It means nothing to you but talk. Well, go back to your mother, and help her to poison Rhoda's imagination as she has poisoned yours. It is the tame elephants who enjoy capturing the wild ones.

ANN. I am getting on. Yesterday I was a boa constrictor: to-day I am an elephant.

TANNER. Yes. So pack your trunk and begone; I have no more to say to you.

ANN. You are so utterly unreasonable and impracticable. What can I do?

TANNER. Do! Break your chains. Go your way according to your own conscience and not according to your mother's. Get your mind clean and vigorous; and learn to enjoy a fast ride in a motor car instead of seeing nothing in it but an excuse for a detestable intrigue. Come with me to Marseilles and across to Algiers and to Biskra, at sixty miles an hour. Come right down to the Cape if you like. That will be a Declaration of Independence with a vengeance. You can write a book about it afterwards. That will finish your mother and make a woman of you.

ANN. [*thoughtfully*] I don't think there would be any harm in that, Jack. You are my guardian: you stand in my father's place, by his own wish. Nobody could say a word against our travelling together. It would be delightful: thank you a thousand times, Jack. I'll come.

TANNER. [*aghast*] You'll come!!!

ANN. Of course.

TANNER. But— [*he stops, utterly appalled; then resumes feebly*] No: look here, Ann: if there's no harm in it there's no point in doing it.

ANN. How absurd you are! You don't want to compromise me, do you?

TANNER. Yes: that's the whole sense of my proposal.

ANN. You are talking the greatest nonsense; and you know it. You would never do anything to hurt me.

TANNER. Well, if you don't want to be compromised, don't come.

ANN. [*with simple earnestness*] Yes, I will come, Jack, since you wish it. You are my guardian; and think we ought to see more of one another and come to know one another better. [*Gratefully*] It's very thoughtful and very kind of you, Jack, to offer me this lovely holiday, especially after what I said about Rhoda. You really are good—much better than you think. When do we start?

TANNER. But—

The conversation is interrupted by the arrival of Mrs Whitefield from the house. She is accompanied by the American gentleman, and followed by Ramsden and Octavius.

Hector Malone is an Eastern American; but he is not at all ashamed of his nationality. This makes English people of fashion think well of him, as of a young fellow who is manly enough to confess to an obvious disadvantage without any attempt to conceal or extenuate it. They feel that he ought not to be made to suffer for what is clearly not his fault, and make a point of being specially kind to him. His chivalrous manners to women, and his elevated moral sentiments, being both gratuitous and unusual, strike them as being a little unfortunate; and though they find his vein of easy humor rather amusing when it has ceased to puzzle them (as it does at first), they have had to make him understand that he really must not tell anecdotes unless they are strictly personal and scandalous, and also that oratory is an accomplishment which belongs to a cruder stage of civilization than that in which his migration has landed him. On these points Hector is not quite convinced: he still thinks that the British are apt to make merits of their stupidities, and to represent their various incapacities as points of good breeding. English life seems to him to suffer from a lack of edifying rhetoric (which he calls moral tone); English behavior to show a want of respect for womanhood; English pronunciation to fail very vulgarly in tackling such words as world, girl, bird, etc.; English society to be plain spoken to an extent which stretches occasionally to intolerable coarseness; and English intercourse to need enlivening by games and stories and other pastimes; so he does not feel called upon to acquire these defects after taking great paths to cultivate himself in a first rate manner before venturing across the Atlantic. To this culture he finds English people either totally indifferent as they very commonly are to all culture, or else politely evasive, the truth being that Hector's culture is nothing but a state of saturation with our literary exports of thirty years ago, reimported by him to be unpacked at a moment's notice and hurled at the head of English literature, science and art, at every conversational opportunity. The dismay set up by these sallies encourages him in his belief that he is helping to educate England. When he finds people chattering harmlessly about Anatole France and Nietzsche, he devastates them with Matthew Arnold, the Autocrat of the Breakfast Table, and even Macaulay; and as he is devoutly religious at bottom, he first leads the unwary, by humorous irreverences, to wave popular theology out of account in discussing moral questions with him, and then scatters them in confusion by demanding whether the carrying out of his ideals of conduct was not the manifest object of God Almighty in creating honest men and pure women. The engaging freshness of his personality and the dumbfoundering staleness of his culture make it extremely difficult to decide whether he is worth knowing; for whilst his company is undeniably pleasant and enlivening, there is intellectually nothing new to be got out of him, especially as he despises politics, and is careful not to talk commercial shop, in which department he is probably much in advance of his English capitalist friends. He gets on best with romantic Christians of the amoristic sect: hence the friendship which has sprung up between him and Octavius.

In appearance Hector is a neatly built young man of twenty-four, with a short, smartly trimmed black beard, clear, well shaped eyes, and an ingratiating vivacity of expression. He is, from the fashionable point of view, faultlessly dressed. As he comes along the drive from the house with Mrs Whitefield he is sedulously making himself agreeable and entertaining, and thereby placing on her slender wit a burden it is unable to bear. An Englishman would let her alone, accepting boredom and indifference of their common lot; and the poor lady wants to be either let alone or let prattle about the things that interest her.

Ramsden strolls over to inspect the motor car. Octavius joins Hector.

ANN. [*pouncing on her mother joyously*] Oh, mamma, what do you think! Jack is going to take me to Nice in his motor car. Isn't it lovely? I am the happiest person in London.

TANNER. [*desperately*] Mrs Whitefield objects. I am sure she objects. Doesn't she, Ramsden?

RAMSDEN. I should think it very likely indeed.

ANN. You don't object, do you, mother?

MRS WHITEFIELD. I object! Why should I? I think it will do you good, Ann. [*Trotting over to Tanner*] I meant to ask you to take Rhoda out for a run occasionally: she is too much in the house; but it will do when you come back.

TANNER. Abyss beneath abyss of perfidy!

ANN. [*hastily, to distract attention from this outburst*] Oh, I forgot: you have not met Mr Malone. Mr Tanner, my guardian: Mr Hector Malone.

HECTOR. Pleased to meet you, Mr Tanner. I should like to suggest an extension of the travelling party to Nice, if I may.

ANN. Oh, we're all coming. That's understood, isn't it?

HECTOR. I also am the modest possessor of a motor car. If Miss Robinson will allow me the privilege of taking her, my car is at her service.

OCTAVIUS. Violet!

General constraint.

ANN. [*subduedly*] Come, mother: we must leave them to talk over the arrangements. I must see to my travelling kit.

Mrs Whitefield looks bewildered; but Ann draws her discreetly away; and they disappear round the corner towards the house.

HECTOR. I think I may go so far as to say that I can depend on Miss Robinson's consent.

Continued embarrassment.

OCTAVIUS. I'm afraid we must leave Violet behind, There are circumstances which make it impossible for her to come on such an expedition.

HECTOR. [*amused and not at all convinced*] Too American, eh? Must the young lady have a chaperone?

OCTAVIUS. It's not that, Malone—at least not altogether.

HECTOR. Indeed! May I ask what other objection applies?

TANNER. [*impatiently*] Oh, tell him, tell him. We shall never be able to keep the secret unless everybody knows what it is. Mr Malone: if you go to Nice with Violet, you go with another man's wife. She is married.

HECTOR. [*thunderstruck*] You don't tell me so!

TANNER. We do. In confidence.

RAMSDEN. [*with an air of importance, lest Malone should suspect a misalliance*] Her marriage has not yet been made known: she desires that it shall not be mentioned for the present.

HECTOR. I shall respect the lady's wishes. Would it be indiscreet to ask who her husband is, in case I should have an opportunity of consulting him about this trip?

TANNER. We don't know who he is.

HECTOR. [*retiring into his shell in a very marked manner*] In that case, I have no more to say.

They become more embarrassed than ever.

OCTAVIUS. You must think this very strange.

HECTOR. A little singular. Pardon me for saving so.

RAMSDEN. [*half apologetic, half huffy*] The young lady was married secretly; and her husband has forbidden her, it seems, to declare his name. It is only right to tell you, since you are interested in Miss—er—in Violet.

OCTAVIUS. [*sympathetically*] I hope this is not a disappointment to you.

HECTOR. [*softened, coming out of his shell again*] Well it is a blow. I can hardly understand how a man can leave a wife in such a position. Surely it's not customary. It's not manly. It's not considerate.

OCTAVIUS. We feel that, as you may imagine, pretty deeply.

RAMSDEN. [*testily*] It is some young fool who has not enough experience to know what mystifications of this kind lead to.

HECTOR. [*with strong symptoms of moral repugnance*] I hope so. A man need be very young and pretty foolish too to be excused for such conduct. You take a very lenient view, Mr Ramsden. Too lenient to my mind. Surely marriage should ennoble a man.

TANNER. [*sardonically*] Ha!

HECTOR. Am I to gather from that cacchination that you don't agree with me, Mr Tanner?

TANNER. [*drily*] Get married and try. You may find it delightful for a while: you certainly won't find it ennobling. The greatest common measure of a man and a woman is not necessarily greater than the man's single measure.

HECTOR. Well, we think in America that a woman's moral number is higher than a man's, and that the purer nature of a woman lifts a man right out of himself, and makes him better than he was.

OCTAVIUS. [*with conviction*] So it does.

TANNER. No wonder American women prefer to live in Europe! It's more comfortable than standing all their lives on an altar to be worshipped. Anyhow, Violet's husband has not been ennobled. So what's to be done?

HECTOR. [*shaking his head*] I can't dismiss that man's conduct as lightly as you do, Mr Tanner. However, I'll say no more. Whoever he is, he's Miss Robinson's husband; and I should be glad for her sake to think better of him.

OCTAVIUS. [*touched; for he divines a secret sorrow*] I'm very sorry, Malone. Very sorry.

HECTOR. [*gratefully*] You're a good fellow, Robinson, Thank you.

TANNER. Talk about something else. Violet's coming from the house.

HECTOR. I should esteem it a very great favor, men, if you would take the opportunity to let me have a few words with the lady alone. I shall have to cry off this trip; and it's rather a delicate—

RAMSDEN. [*glad to escape*] Say no more. Come Tanner, Come, Tavy. [*He strolls away into the park with Octavius and Tanner, past the motor car*].

Violet comes down the avenue to Hector.

VIOLET. Are they looking?

HECTOR. No.

She kisses him.

VIOLET. Have you been telling lies for my sake?

HECTOR. Lying! Lying hardly describes it. I overdo it. I get carried away in an ecstasy of mendacity. Violet: I wish you'd let me own up.

VIOLET. [*instantly becoming serious and resolute*] No, no. Hector: you promised me not to.

HECTOR. I'll keep my promise until you release me from it. But I feel mean, lying to those men, and denying my wife. Just dastardly.

VIOLET. I wish your father were not so unreasonable.

HECTOR. He's not unreasonable. He's right from his point of view. He has a prejudice against the English middle class.

VIOLET. It's too ridiculous. You know how I dislike saying such things to you, Hector; but if I were to—oh, well, no matter.

HECTOR. I know. If you were to marry the son of an English manufacturer of office furniture, your friends would consider it a misalliance. And here's my silly old dad, who is the biggest office furniture man in the world, would show me the door for marrying the most perfect lady in England merely because she has no handle to her name. Of course it's just absurd. But I tell you, Violet, I don't like deceiving him. I feel as if I was stealing his money. Why won't you let me own up?

VIOLET. We can't afford it. You can be as romantic as you please about love, Hector; but you mustn't be romantic about money.

HECTOR. [*divided between his uxoriousness and his habitual elevation of moral sentiment*] That's very English. [*Appealing to her impulsively*] Violet: Dad's bound to find us out some day.

VIOLET. Oh yes, later on of course. But don't let's go over this every time we meet, dear. You promised—

HECTOR. All right, all right, I—

VIOLET. [*not to be silenced*] It is I and not you who suffer by this concealment; and as to facing a struggle and poverty and all that sort of thing I simply will not do it. It's too silly.

HECTOR. You shall not. I'll sort of borrow the money from my dad until I get on my own feet; and then I can own up and pay up at the same time.

VIOLET. [*alarmed and indignant*] Do you mean to work? Do you want to spoil our marriage?

HECTOR. Well, I don't mean to let marriage spoil my character. Your friend Mr Tanner has got the laugh on me a bit already about that; and—

VIOLET. The beast! I hate Jack Tanner.

HECTOR. [*magnanimously*] Oh, he's all right: he only needs the love of a good woman to ennoble him. Besides, he's proposed a motoring trip to Nice; and I'm going to take you.

VIOLET. How jolly!

HECTOR. Yes; but how are we going to manage? You see, they've warned me off going with you, so to speak. They've told me in confidence that you're married. That's just the most overwhelming confidence I've ever been honored with.

Tanner returns with Straker, who goes to his car.

TANNER. Your car is a great success, Mr Malone. Your engineer is showing it off to Mr Ramsden.

HECTOR. [*eagerly—forgetting himself*] Let's come, Vi.

VIOLET. [*coldly, warning him with her eyes*] I beg your pardon, Mr Malone, I did not quite catch—

HECTOR. [*recollecting himself*] I ask to be allowed the pleasure of showing you my little American steam car, Miss Robinson.

VIOLET. I shall be very pleased. [*They go off together down the avenue*].

TANNER. About this trip, Straker.

STRAKER. [*preoccupied with the car*] Yes?

TANNER. Miss Whitefield is supposed to be coming with me.

STRAKER. So I gather.

TANNER. Mr Robinson is to be one of the party.

STRAKER. Yes.

TANNER. Well, if you can manage so as to be a good deal occupied with me, and leave Mr Robinson a good deal occupied with Miss Whitefield, he will be deeply grateful to you.

STRAKER. [*looking round at him*] Evidently.

TANNER. "Evidently!" Your grandfather would have simply winked.

STRAKER. My grandfather would have touched his at.

TANNER. And I should have given your good nice respectful grandfather a sovereign.

STRAKER. Five shillins, more likely. [*He leaves the car and approaches Tanner*]. What about the lady's views?

TANNER. She is just as willing to be left to Mr Robinson as Mr Robinson is to be left to her. [*Straker looks at his principal with cool scepticism; then turns to the car whistling his favorite air*]. Stop that aggravating noise. What do you mean by it? [*Straker calmly resumes the melody and finishes it. Tanner politely hears it out before he again addresses Straker, this time with elaborate seriousness*]. Enry: I have ever been a warm advocate of the spread of music among the masses; but I object to your obliging the company whenever Miss Whitefield's name is mentioned. You did it this morning, too.

STRAKER. [*obstinately*] It's not a bit o use. Mr Robinson may as well give it up first as last.

TANNER. Why?

STRAKER. Garn! You know why. Course it's not my business; but you needn't start kiddin me about it.

TANNER. I am not kidding. I don't know why.

STRAKER. [*Cheerfully sulky*] Oh, very well. All right. It ain't my business.

TANNER. [*impressively*] I trust, Enry, that, as between employer and engineer, I shall always know how to keep my proper distance, and not intrude my private affairs on you. Even our business arrangements are subject to the approval of your Trade Union. But don't abuse your advantages. Let me remind you that Voltaire said that what was too silly to be said could be sung.

STRAKER. It wasn't Voltaire: it was Bow Mar Shay.

TANNER. I stand corrected: Beaumarchais of course. Now you seem to think that what is too delicate to be said can be whistled. Unfortunately your whistling, though melodious, is unintelligible. Come! there's nobody listening: neither my genteel relatives nor the secretary of your confounded Union. As man to man, Enry, why do you think that my friend has no chance with Miss Whitefield?

STRAKER. Cause she's arter summun else.

TANNER. Bosh! who else?

STRAKER. You.

TANNER. Me!!!

STRAKER. Mean to tell me you didn't know? Oh, come, Mr Tanner!

TANNER. [*in fierce earnest*] Are you playing the fool, or do you mean it?

STRAKER. [*with a flash of temper*] I'm not playin no fool. [*More coolly*] Why, it's as plain as the nose on your face. If you ain't spotted that, you don't know much about these sort of things. [*Serene again*] Ex-cuse me, you know, Mr Tanner; but you asked me as man to man; and I told you as man to man.

TANNER. [*wildly appealing to the heavens*] Then I—I am the bee, the spider, the marked down victim, the destined prey.

STRAKER. I dunno about the bee and the spider. But the marked down victim, that's what you are and no mistake; and a jolly good job for you, too, I should say.

TANNER. [*momentously*] Henry Straker: the moment of your life has arrived.

STRAKER. What d'y'mean?

TANNER. That record to Biskra.

STRAKER. [*eagerly*] Yes?

TANNER. Break it.

STRAKER. [*rising to the height of his destiny*] D'y'mean it?

TANNER. I do.

STRAKER. When?

TANNER. Now. Is that machine ready to start?

STRAKER. [*quailing*] But you can't—

TANNER. [*cutting him short by getting into the car*] Off we go. First to the bank for money; then to my rooms for my kit; then to your rooms for your kit; then break the record from London to Dover or Folkestone; then across the channel and away like mad to Marseilles, Gibraltar, Genoa, any port from which we can sail to a Mahometan country where men are protected from women.

STRAKER. Garn! you're kiddin.

TANNER. [*resolutely*] Stay behind then. If you won't come I'll do it alone. [*He starts the motor*].

STRAKER. [*running after him*] Here! Mister! arf a mo! steady on! [*he scrambles in as the car plunges forward*].

ACT III

Evening in the Sierra Nevada. Rolling slopes of brown, with olive trees instead of apple trees in the cultivated patches, and occasional prickly pears instead of gorse and bracken in the wilds. Higher up, tall stone peaks and precipices, all handsome and distinguished. No wild nature here: rather a most aristocratic mountain landscape made by a fastidious artist-creator. No vulgar profusion of vegetation: even a touch of aridity in the frequent patches of stones: Spanish magnificence and Spanish economy everywhere.

Not very far north of a spot at which the high road over one of the passes crosses a tunnel on the railway from Malaga to Granada, is one of the mountain amphitheatres of the Sierra. Looking at it from the wide end of the horse-shoe, one sees, a little to the right, in the face of the cliff, a romantic cave which is really an abandoned quarry, and towards the left a little hill, commanding a view of the road, which skirts the amphitheatre on the left, maintaining its higher level on embankments and on an occasional stone arch. On the hill, watching the road, is a man who is either a Spaniard or a Scotchman. Probably a Spaniard, since he wears the dress of a Spanish goatherd and seems at home in the Sierra Nevada, but very like a Scotchman for all that. In the hollow, on the slope leading to the quarry-cave, are about a dozen men who, as they recline at their cave round a heap of smouldering white ashes of dead leaf and brushwood, have an air of being conscious of themselves as picturesque scoundrels honoring the Sierra by using it as an effective pictorial background. As a matter of artistic fact they are not picturesque; and the mountains tolerate them as lions tolerate lice. An English policeman or Poor Law Guardian would recognize them as a selected band of tramps and ablebodied paupers.

This description of them is not wholly contemptuous. Whoever has intelligently observed the tramp, or visited the ablebodied ward of a workhouse, will admit that our social failures are not all drunkards and weaklings. Some of them are men who do not fit the class they were born into. Precisely the same qualities that make the educated gentleman an artist may make an uneducated manual laborer an ablebodied pauper. There are men who fall helplessly into the workhouse because they are good far nothing; but there are also men who are there because they are strongminded enough to disregard the social convention (obviously not a disinterested one on the part of the ratepayer) which bids a man live by heavy and badly paid drudgery when he has the alternative of walking into the workhouse, announcing himself as a destitute person, and legally compelling the Guardians to feed, clothe and house him better than he could feed, clothe and house himself without great exertion. When a man who is born a poet refuses a stool in a stockbroker's office, and starves in a garret, spunging on a poor landlady or on his friends and relatives rather than work against his grain; or when a lady, because she is a lady, will face any extremity of parasitic dependence rather than take a situation as cook or parlormaid, we make large allowances for them. To such allowances the ablebodied pauper and his nomadic variant the tramp are equally entitled.

Further, the imaginative man, if his life is to be tolerable to him, must have leisure to tell himself stories, and a position which lends itself to imaginative decoration. The ranks of unskilled labor offer no such positions. We misuse our laborers horribly; and when a man refuses to be misused, we have no right to say that he is refusing honest work. Let us be frank in this matter before we go on with our play; so that we may enjoy it without hypocrisy. If we were reasoning, farsighted people, four fifths of us would go straight to the Guardians for relief, and knock the whole social system to pieces with most beneficial reconstructive results. The reason we do got do this is because we work like bees or ants, by instinct or habit, not reasoning about the matter at all. Therefore when a man comes along who can and does reason, and who, applying the Kantian test to his conduct, can truly say to us, If everybody did as I do, the world would be compelled to reform itself industrially, and abolish slavery and squalor, which exist only because everybody does as you do, let us honor that man and seriously consider the advisability of following his example. Such a man is the able-bodied, able-minded pauper. Were he a gentleman doing his best to get a pension or a sinecure instead of sweeping a crossing, nobody would blame him; for deciding that so long as the alternative lies between living mainly at the expense of the community and allowing the community to live mainly at his, it would be folly to accept what is to him personally the greater of the two evils.

We may therefore contemplate the tramps of the Sierra without prejudice, admitting cheerfully that our objects—briefly, to be gentlemen of fortune—are much the same as theirs, and the difference in our position and methods merely accidental. One or two of them, perhaps, it would be wiser to kill without malice in a friendly and frank manner; for there are bipeds, just as there are quadrupeds, who are too dangerous to be left unchained and unmuzzled; and these cannot fairly expect to have other men's lives wasted in the work of watching them. But as society has not the courage to kill them, and, when it catches them, simply wreaks on them some superstitious expiatory rites of torture and degradation, and than lets them loose with heightened qualifications for mischief; it is just as well that they are at large in the Sierra, and in the hands of a chief who looks as if he might possibly, on provocation, order them to be shot.

This chief, seated in the centre of the group on a squared block of stone from the quarry, is a tall strong man, with a striking cockatoo nose, glossy black hair, pointed beard, upturned moustache, and a Mephistophelean affectation which is fairly imposing, perhaps because the scenery admits of a larger swagger than Piccadilly, perhaps because of a certain sentimentality in the man which gives him that touch of grace which alone can excuse deliberate picturesqueness. His eyes and mouth are by no means rascally; he has a fine voice and a ready wit; and whether he is really the strongest man in the party, or not, he looks it. He is certainly, the best fed, the best dressed, and the best trained. The fact that he speaks English is not unexpected in spite of the Spanish landscape; for with the exception of one man who might be guessed as a bullfighter ruined by drink and one unmistakable Frenchman, they are all cockney or American; therefore, in a land of cloaks and sombreros, they mostly wear seedy overcoats, woollen mufflers, hard hemispherical hats, and dirty brown gloves. Only a very few dress after their leader, whose broad sombrero with a cock's feather in the band, and voluminous cloak descending to his high boots, are as un-English as possible. None of them are armed; and the ungloved ones keep their hands in their pockets because it is their national belief that it must be dangerously cold in the open air with the night coming on. (It is as warm an evening as any reasonable man could desire).

Except the bullfighting inebriate there is only one person in the company who looks more than, say, thirty-three. He is a small man with reddish whiskers, weak eyes, and the anxious look of a small tradesman in difficulties. He wears the only tall hat visible: it shines in the sunset with the sticky glow of some sixpenny patent hat reviver, often applied and constantly tending to produce a worse state of the original surface than the ruin it was applied to remedy. He has a collar and cuff of celluloid; and his brown Chesterfield overcoat, with velvet collar, is still presentable. He is pre-eminently the respectable man of the party, and is certainly over forty, possibly over fifty. He is the corner man on the leader's right, opposite three men in scarlet ties on his left. One of these three is the Frenchman. Of the remaining two, who are both English, one is argumentative, solemn, and obstinate; the other rowdy and mischievous.

The chief, with a magnificent fling of the end of his cloak across his left shoulder, rises to address them. The applause which greets him shows that he is a favorite orator.

THE CHIEF. Friends and fellow brigands. I have a proposal to make to this meeting. We have now spent three evenings in discussing the question Have Anarchists or Social-Democrats the most personal courage? We have gone into the principles of Anarchism and Social-Democracy at great length. The cause of Anarchy has been ably represented by our one Anarchist, who doesn't know what Anarchism means [*laughter*]—

THE ANARCHIST. [*rising*] A point of order, Mendoza—

MENDOZA. [*forcibly*] No, by thunder: your last point of order took half an hour. Besides, Anarchists don't believe in order.

THE ANARCHIST. [*mild, polite but persistent: he is, in fact, the respectable looking elderly man in the celluloid collar and cuffs*] That is a vulgar error. I can prove—

MENDOZA. Order, order.

THE OTHERS [*shouting*] Order, order. Sit down. Chair! Shut up.

The Anarchist is suppressed.

MENDOZA. On the other hand we have three Social-Democrats among us. They are not on speaking terms; and they have put before us three distinct and incompatible views of Social-Democracy.

THE MAJORITY. [*shouting assent*] Hear, hear! So we are. Right.

THE ROWDY SOCIAL-DEMOCRAT. [*smarting under oppression*] You ain't no Christian. You're a Sheeny, you are.

MENDOZA. [*with crushing magnanimity*] My friend; I am an exception to all rules. It is true that I have the honor to be a Jew; and, when the Zionists need a leader to reassemble our race on its historic soil of Palestine, Mendoza will not be the last to volunteer [*sympathetic applause—hear, hear, etc.*]. But I am not a slave to any superstition. I have swallowed all the formulas, even that of Socialism; though, in a sense, once a Socialist, always a Socialist.

THE SOCIAL-DEMOCRATS. Hear, hear!

MENDOZA. But I am well aware that the ordinary man—even the ordinary brigand, who can scarcely be called an ordinary man [*Hear, hear!*]—is not a philosopher. Common sense is good enough for him; and in our business affairs common sense is good enough for me. Well, what is our business here in the Sierra Nevada, chosen by the Moors as the fairest spot in Spain? Is it to discuss abstruse questions of political economy? No: it is to hold up motor cars and secure a more equitable distribution of wealth.

THE SULKY SOCIAL-DEMOCRAT. All made by labor, mind you.

MENDOZA. [*urbanely*] Undoubtedly. All made by labor, and on its way to be squandered by wealthy vagabonds in the dens of vice that disfigure the sunny shores of the Mediterranean. We intercept that wealth. We restore it to circulation among the class that produced it and that chiefly needs it—the working class. We do this at the risk of our lives and liberties, by the exercise of the virtues of courage, endurance, foresight, and abstinence—especially abstinence. I myself have eaten nothing but prickly pears and broiled rabbit for three days.

THE SULKY SOCIAL-DEMOCRAT. [*Stubbornly*] No more ain't we.

MENDOZA. [*indignantly*] Have I taken more than my share?

THE SULKY SOCIAL-DEMOCRAT. [*unmoved*] Why should you?

THE ANARCHIST. Why should he not? To each according to his needs: from each according to his means.

THE FRENCHMAN. [*shaking his fist at the anarchist*] Fumiste!

MENDOZA. [*diplomatically*] I agree with both of you.

THE GENUINELY ENGLISH BRIGANDS. Hear, hear! Bravo, Mendoza!

MENDOZA. What I say is, let us treat one another as gentlemen, and strive to excel in personal courage only when we take the field.

THE ROWDY SOCIAL-DEMOCRAT. [*derisively*] Shikespear.

A whistle comes from the goatherd on the hill. He springs up and points excitedly forward along the road to the north.

THE GOATHERD. Automobile! Automobile! [*He rushes down the hill and joins the rest, who all scramble to their feet*].

MENDOZA. [*in ringing tones*] To arms! Who has the gun?

THE SULKY SOCIAL-DEMOCRAT. [*handing a rifle to Mendoza*] Here.

MENDOZA. Have the nails been strewn in the road?

THE ROWDY SOCIAL-DEMOCRAT. Two ahnces of em.

MENDOZA. Good! [*To the Frenchman*] With me, Duval. If the nails fail, puncture their tires with a bullet. [*He gives the rifle to Duval, who follows him up the hill. Mendoza produces an opera glass. The others hurry across to the road and disappear to the north*].

MENDOZA. [*on the hill, using his glass*] Two only, a capitalist and his chauffeur. They look English.

DUVAL. Angliche! Aoh yess. Cochons! [*Handling the rifle*] Faut tire, n'est-ce-pas?

MENDOZA. No: the nails have gone home. Their tire is down: they stop.

DUVAL. [*shouting to the others*] Fondez sur eux, nom de Dieu!

MENDOZA. [*rebuking his excitement*] Du calme, Duval: keep your hair on. They take it quietly. Let us descend and receive them.

Mendoza descends, passing behind the fire and coming forward, whilst Tanner and Straker, in their motoring goggles, leather coats, and caps, are led in from the road by brigands.

TANNER. Is this the gentleman you describe as your boss? Does he speak English?

THE ROWDY SOCIAL-DEMOCRAT. Course he does. Y'don't suppowz we Hinglishmen lets ahrselves be bossed by a bloomin Spenniard, do you?

MENDOZA. [*with dignity*] Allow me to introduce myself: Mendoza, President of the League of the Sierra! [*Posing loftily*] I am a brigand: I live by robbing the rich.

TANNER. [*promptly*] I am a gentleman: I live by robbing the poor. Shake hands.

THE ENGLISH SOCIAL-DEMOCRATS. Hear, hear!

General laughter and good humor. Tanner and Mendoza shake hands. The Brigands drop into their former places.

STRAKER. Ere! where do I come in?

TANNER. [*introducing*] My friend and chauffeur.

THE SULKY SOCIAL-DEMOCRAT. [*suspiciously*] Well, which is he? friend or show-foor? It makes all the difference you know.

MENDOZA. [*explaining*] We should expect ransom for a friend. A professional chauffeur is free of the mountains. He even takes a trifling percentage of his princpal's ransom if he will honor us by accepting it.

STRAKER. I see. Just to encourage me to come this way again. Well, I'll think about it.

DUVAL. [*impulsively rushing across to Straker*] Mon frere! [*He embraces him rapturously and kisses him on both cheeks*].

STRAKER. [*disgusted*] Ere, git out: don't be silly. Who are you, pray?

DUVAL. Duval: Social-Democrat.

STRAKER. Oh, you're a Social-Democrat, are you?

THE ANARCHIST. He means that he has sold out to the parliamentary humbugs and the bourgeoisie. Compromise! that is his faith.

DUVAL. [*furiously*] I understand what he say. He say Bourgeois. He say Compromise. Jamais de la vie! Miserable menteur—

STRAKER. See here, Captain Mendoza, ow much o this sort o thing do you put up with here? Are we avin a pleasure trip in the mountains, or are we at a Socialist meetin?

THE MAJORITY. Hear, hear! Shut up. Chuck it. Sit down, etc. etc. [*The Social-Democrats and the Anarchist are hurtled into the background. Straker, after superintending this proceeding with satisfac-*

tion, places himself on Mendoza's left, Tanner being on his right].

MENDOZA. Can we offer you anything? Broiled rabbit and prickly pears—

TANNER. Thank you: we have dined.

MENDOZA. [*to his followers*] Gentlemen: business is over for the day. Go as you please until morning.

The Brigands disperse into groups lazily. Some go into the cave. Others sit down or lie down to sleep in the open. A few produce a pack of cards and move off towards the road; for it is now starlight; and they know that motor cars have lamps which can be turned to account for lighting a card party.

STRAKER. [*calling after them*] Don't none of you go fooling with that car, d'ye hear?

MENDOZA. No fear, Monsieur le Chauffeur. The first one we captured cured us of that.

STRAKER. [*interested*] What did it do?

MENDOZA. It carried three brave comrades of ours, who did not know how to stop it, into Granada, and capsized them opposite the police station. Since then we never touch one without sending for the chauffeur. Shall we chat at our ease?

TANNER. By all means.

Tanner, Mendoza, and Straker sit down on the turf by the fire. Mendoza delicately waives his presidential dignity, of which the right to sit on the squared stone block is the appanage, by sitting on the ground like his guests, and using the stone only as a support for his back.

MENDOZA. It is the custom in Spain always to put off business until to-morrow. In fact, you have arrived out of office hours. However, if you would prefer to settle the question of ransom at once, I am at your service.

TANNER. To-morrow will do for me. I am rich enough to pay anything in reason.

MENDOZA. [*respectfully, much struck by this admission*] You are a remarkable man, sir. Our guests usually describe themselves as miserably poor.

TANNER. Pooh! Miserably poor people don't own motor cars.

MENDOZA. Precisely what we say to them.

TANNER. Treat us well: we shall not prove ungrateful.

STRAKER. No prickly pears and broiled rabbits, you know. Don't tell me you can't do us a bit better than that if you like.

MENDOZA. Wine, kids, milk, cheese and bread can be procured for ready money.

STRAKER. [*graciously*] Now you're talking.

TANNER. Are you all Socialists here, may I ask?

MENDOZA. [*repudiating this humiliating misconception*] Oh no, no, no: nothing of the kind, I assure you. We naturally have modern views as to the justice of the existing distribution of wealth: otherwise we should lose our self-respect. But nothing that you could take exception to, except two or three faddists.

TANNER. I had no intention of suggesting anything discreditable. In fact, I am a bit of a Socialist myself.

STRAKER. [*drily*] Most rich men are, I notice.

MENDOZA. Quite so. It has reached us, I admit. It is in the air of the century.

STRAKER. Socialism must be looking up a bit if your chaps are taking to it.

MENDOZA. That is true, sir. A movement which is confined to philosophers and honest men can never exercise any real political influence: there are too few of them. Until a movement shows itself capable of spreading among brigands, it can never hope for a political majority.

TANNER. But are your brigands any less honest than ordinary citizens?

MENDOZA. Sir: I will be frank with you. Brigandage is abnormal. Abnormal professions attract two classes: those who are not good enough for ordinary bourgeois life and those who are too good for it. We are dregs and scum, sir: the dregs very filthy, the scum very superior.

STRAKER. Take care! some o the dregs'll hear you.

MENDOZA. It does not matter: each brigand thinks himself scum, and likes to hear the others called dregs.

TANNER. Come! you are a wit. [*Mendoza inclines his head, flattered*]. May one ask you a blunt question?

MENDOZA. As blunt as you please.

TANNER. How does it pay a man of your talent to shepherd such a flock as this on broiled rabbit and prickly pears? I have seen men less gifted, and I'll swear less honest, supping at the Savoy on foie gras and champagne.

MENDOZA. Pooh! they have all had their turn at the broiled rabbit, just as I shall have my turn at the Savoy. Indeed, I have had a turn there already—as waiter.

TANNER. A waiter! You astonish me!

MENDOZA. [*reflectively*] Yes: I, Mendoza of the Sierra, was a waiter. Hence, perhaps, my cosmopolitanism. [*With sudden intensity*] Shall I tell you the story of my life?

STRAKER. [*apprehensively*] If it ain't too long, old chap—

TANNER. [*interrupting him*] Tsh-sh: you are a Philistine, Henry: you have no romance in you. [*To Mendoza*] You interest me extremely, President. Never mind Henry: he can go to sleep.

MENDOZA. The woman I loved—

STRAKER. Oh, this is a love story, is it? Right you are. Go on: I was only afraid you were going to talk about yourself.

MENDOZA. Myself! I have thrown myself away for her sake: that is why I am here. No matter: I count the world well lost for her. She had, I pledge you my word, the most magnificent head of hair I ever saw. She had humor; she had intellect; she could cook to perfection; and her highly strung temperament made her uncertain, incalculable, variable, capricious, cruel, in a word, enchanting.

STRAKER. A six shillin novel sort o woman, all but the cookin. Er name was Lady Gladys Plantagenet, wasn't it?

MENDOZA. No, sir: she was not an earl's daughter. Photography, reproduced by the half-tone process, has made me familiar with the appearance of the daughters of the English peerage; and I can honestly say that I would have sold the lot, faces, dowries, clothes, titles, and all, for a smile from this woman. Yet she was a woman of the people, a worker: otherwise—let me reciprocate your bluntness—I should have scorned her.

TANNER. Very properly. And did she respond to your love?

MENDOZA. Should I be here if she did? She objected to marry a Jew.

TANNER. On religious grounds?

MENDOZA. No: she was a freethinker. She said that every Jew considers in his heart that English people are dirty in their habits.

TANNER. [*surprised*] Dirty!

MENDOZA. It showed her extraordinary knowledge of the world; for it is undoubtedly true. Our elaborate sanitary code makes us unduly contemptuous of the Gentile.

TANNER. Did you ever hear that, Henry?

STRAKER. I've heard my sister say so. She was cook in a Jewish family once.

MENDOZA. I could not deny it; neither could I eradicate the impression it made on her mind. I could have got round any other objection; but no woman can stand a suspicion of indelicacy as to her person. My entreaties were in vain: she always retorted that she wasn't good enough for me, and recommended me to marry an accursed barmaid named Rebecca Lazarus, whom I loathed. I talked of suicide: she offered me a packet of beetle poison to do it with. I hinted at murder: she went into hysterics; and as I am a living man I went to America so that she might sleep without dreaming that I was stealing upstairs to cut her throat. In America I went out west and fell in with a man who was wanted by the police for holding trains. It was he who had the idea of holding up motors cars—in the South of Europe: a welcome idea to a desperate and disappointed man. He gave me some valuable introductions to capitalists of the right sort. I formed a syndicate; and the present enterprise is the result. I became leader, as the Jew always becomes leader, by his brains and imagination. But with all my pride of race I would give everything I possess to be an Englishman. I am like a boy: I cut her name on the trees and her initials on the sod. When I am alone I lie down and tear my wretched hair and cry Louisa—

STRAKER. [*startled*] Louisa!

MENDOZA. It is her name—Louisa—Louisa Straker—

TANNER. Straker!

STRAKER. [*scrambling up on his knees most indignantly*] Look here: Louisa Straker is my sister, see? Wot do you mean by gassin about her like this? Wot she got to do with you?

MENDOZA. A dramatic coincidence! You are Enry, her favorite brother!

STRAKER. Oo are you callin Enry? What call have you to take a liberty with my name or with hers? For two pins I'd punch your fat ed, so I would.

MENDOZA. [*with grandiose calm*] If I let you do it, will you promise to brag of it afterwards to her? She will be reminded of her Mendoza: that is all I desire.

TANNER. This is genuine devotion, Henry. You should respect it.

STRAKER. [*fiercely*] Funk, more likely.

MENDOZA. [*springing to his feet*] Funk! Young man: I come of a famous family of fighters; and as your sister well knows, you would have as much chance against me as a perambulator against your motor car.

STRAKER. [*secretly daunted, but rising from his knees with an air of reckless pugnacity*] I ain't afraid of you. With your Louisa! Louisa! Miss Straker is good enough for you, I should think.

MENDOZA. I wish you could persuade her to think so.

STRAKER. [*exasperated*] Here—

TANNER. [*rising quickly and interposing*] Oh come, Henry: even if you could fight the President you can't fight the whole League of the Sierra. Sit down again and be friendly. A cat may look at a king; and even a President of brigands may look at your sister. All this family pride is really very old fashioned.

STRAKER. [*subdued, but grumbling*] Let him look at her. But wot does he mean by makin out that she ever looked at im? [*Reluctantly resuming his couch on the turf*] Ear him talk, one ud think she was keepin company with him. [*He turns his back on them and composes himself to sleep*].

MENDOZA. [*to Tanner, becoming more confidential as he finds himself virtually alone with a sympathetic listener in the still starlight of the mountains; for all the rest are asleep by this time*] It was just so with her, sir. Her intellect reached forward into the twentieth century: her social prejudices and family affections reached back into the dark ages. Ah, sir, how the words of Shakespear seem to fit every crisis in our emotions!

I loved Louisa: 40,000 brothers Could not with all their quantity of love Make up my sum.

And so on. I forget the rest. Call it madness if you will—infatuation. I am an able man, a strong man: in ten years I should have owned a first-class hotel. I met her; and you see! I am a brigand, an outcast. Even Shakespear cannot do justice to what I feel for Louisa. Let me read you some lines that I have written about her myself. However slight their literary merit may be, they express what I feel better than any casual words can. [*He produces a packet of hotel bills scrawled with manuscript, and kneels at the fire to decipher them, poking it with a stick to make it glow*].

TANNER. [*clapping him rudely on the shoulder*] Put them in the fire, President.

MENDOZA. [*startled*] Eh?

TANNER. You are sacrificing your career to a monomania.

MENDOZA. I know it.

TANNER. No you don't. No man would commit such a crime against himself if he really knew what he was doing. How can you look round at these august hills, look up at this divine sky, taste this finely tempered air, and then talk like a literary hack on a second floor in Bloomsbury?

MENDOZA. [*shaking his head*] The Sierra is no better than Bloomsbury when once the novelty has worn off. Besides, these mountains make you dream of women—of women with magnificent hair.

TANNER. Of Louisa, in short. They will not make me dream of women, my friend: I am heart-whole.

MENDOZA. Do not boast until morning, sir. This is a strange country for dreams.

TANNER. Well, we shall see. Goodnight. [*He lies down and composes himself to sleep*].

Mendoza, with a sigh, follows his example; and for a few moments there is peace in the Sierra. Then Mendoza sits up suddenly and says pleadingly to Tanner—

MENDOZA. Just allow me to read a few lines before you go to sleep. I should really like your opinion of them.

TANNER. [*drowsily*] Go on. I am listening.

MENDOZA. I saw thee first in Whitsun week Louisa, Louisa—

TANNER. [*roaring himself*] My dear President, Louisa is a very pretty name; but it really doesn't rhyme well to Whitsun week.

MENDOZA. Of course not. Louisa is not the rhyme, but the refrain.

TANNER. [*subsiding*] Ah, the refrain. I beg your pardon. Go on.

MENDOZA. Perhaps you do not care for that one: I think you will like this better. [*He recites, in rich soft tones, and to slow time*]

> Louisa, I love thee. I love thee, Louisa. Louisa, Louisa, Louisa, I love thee. One name and one phrase make my music, Louisa. Louisa, Louisa, Louisa, I love thee.
>
> Mendoza thy lover, Thy lover, Mendoza, Mendoza adoringly lives for Louisa. There's nothing but that in the world for Mendoza. Louisa, Louisa, Mendoza adores thee.

[*Affected*] There is no merit in producing beautiful lines upon such a name. Louisa is an exquisite name, is it not?

TANNER. [*all but asleep, responds with a faint groan*].

MENDOZA.

> O wert thou, Louisa, The wife of Mendoza, Mendoza's Louisa, Louisa Mendoza, How blest were the life of

Louisa's Mendoza! How painless his
longing of love for Louisa!

That is real poetry—from the heart—from the heart of hearts. Don't you think it will move her?

No answer.

[*Resignedly*] Asleep, as usual. Doggrel to all the world; heavenly music to me! Idiot that I am to wear my heart on my sleeve! [*He composes himself to sleep, murmuring*] Louisa, I love thee; I love thee, Louisa; Louisa, Louisa, Louisa, I—

Straker snores; rolls over on his side; and relapses into sleep. Stillness settles on the Sierra; and the darkness deepens. The fire has again buried itself in white ash and ceased to glow. The peaks show unfathomably dark against the starry firmament; but now the stars dim and vanish; and the sky seems to steal away out of the universe. Instead of the Sierra there is nothing; omnipresent nothing. No sky, no peaks, no light, no sound, no time nor space, utter void. Then somewhere the beginning of a pallor, and with it a faint throbbing buzz as of a ghostly violoncello palpitating on the same note endlessly. A couple of ghostly violins presently take advantage of this bass

and therewith the pallor reveals a man in the void, an incorporeal but visible man, seated, absurdly enough, on nothing. For a moment he raises his head as the music passes him by. Then, with a heavy sigh, he droops in utter dejection; and the violins, discouraged, retrace their melody in despair and at last give it up, extinguished by wailings from uncanny wind instruments, thus:—

It is all very odd. One recognizes the Mozartian strain; and on this hint, and by the aid of certain sparkles of violet light in the pallor, the man's costume explains itself as that of a Spanish nobleman of the XV-XVI century. Don Juan, of course; but where? why? how? Besides, in the brief lifting of his face, now hidden by his hat brim, there was a curious suggestion of Tanner. A more critical, fastidious, handsome face, paler and colder, without Tanner's impetuous credulity and enthusiasm, and without a touch of his modern plutocratic vulgarity, but still a resemblance, even an identity. The name too: Don Juan Tenorio, John Tanner. Where on earth—or elsewhere—have we got to from the XX century and the Sierra?

Another pallor in the void, this time not violet, but a disagreeable smoky yellow. With it, the whisper of a ghostly clarionet turning this tune into infinite sadness:

The yellowish pallor moves: there is an old crone wandering in the void, bent and toothless; draped, as well as one can guess, in the coarse brown frock of some religious order. She wanders and wanders in her slow hopeless way, much as a wasp flies in its rapid busy way, until she blunders against the thing she seeks: companionship. With a sob of relief the poor old creature clutches at the presence of the man and addresses him in her dry unlovely voice, which can still express pride and resolution as well as suffering.

THE OLD WOMAN. Excuse me; but I am so lonely; and this place is so awful.

DON JUAN. A new comer?

THE OLD WOMAN. Yes: I suppose I died this morning. I confessed; I had extreme unction; I was in bed with my family about me and my eyes fixed on the cross. Then it grew dark; and when the light came back it was this light by which I walk seeing nothing. I have wandered for hours in horrible loneliness.

DON JUAN. [*sighing*] Ah! you have not yet lost the sense of time. One soon does, in eternity.

THE OLD WOMAN. Where are we?

DON JUAN. In hell.

THE OLD WOMAN [*proudly*] Hell! I in hell! How dare you?

DON JUAN. [*unimpressed*] Why not, Senora?

THE OLD WOMAN. You do not know to whom you are speaking. I am a lady, and a faithful daughter of the Church.

DON JUAN. I do not doubt it.

THE OLD WOMAN. But how then can I be in hell? Purgatory, perhaps: I have not been perfect: who has? But hell! oh, you are lying.

DON JUAN. Hell, Senora, I assure you; hell at its best that is, its most solitary—though perhaps you would prefer company.

THE OLD WOMAN. But I have sincerely repented; I have confessed.

DON JUAN. How much?

THE OLD WOMAN. More sins than I really committed. I loved confession.

DON JUAN. Ah, that is perhaps as bad as confessing too little. At all events, Senora, whether by oversight or intention, you are certainly damned, like myself; and there is nothing for it now but to make the best of it.

THE OLD WOMAN [*indignantly*] Oh! and I might have been so much wickeder! All my good deeds wasted! It is unjust.

DON JUAN. No: you were fully and clearly warned. For your bad deeds, vicarious atonement, mercy without justice. For your good deeds, justice without mercy. We have many good people here.

THE OLD WOMAN. Were you a good man?

DON JUAN. I was a murderer.

THE OLD WOMAN. A murderer! Oh, how dare they send me to herd with murderers! I was not as bad as that: I was a good woman. There is some mistake: where can I have it set right?

DON JUAN. I do not know whether mistakes can be corrected here. Probably they will not admit a mistake even if they have made one.

THE OLD WOMAN. But whom can I ask?

DON JUAN. I should ask the Devil, Senora: he understands the ways of this place, which is more than I ever could.

THE OLD WOMAN. The Devil! I speak to the Devil!

DON JUAN. In hell, Senora, the Devil is the leader of the best society.

THE OLD WOMAN. I tell you, wretch, I know I am not in hell.

DON JUAN. How do you know?

THE OLD WOMAN. Because I feel no pain.

DON JUAN. Oh, then there is no mistake: you are intentionally damned.

THE OLD WOMAN. Why do you say that?

DON JUAN. Because hell, Senora, is a place for the wicked. The wicked are quite comfortable in it: it was made for them. You tell me you feel no pain. I conclude you are one of those for whom Hell exists.

THE OLD WOMAN. Do you feel no pain?

DON JUAN. I am not one of the wicked, Senora; therefore it bores me, bores me beyond description, beyond belief.

THE OLD WOMAN. Not one of the wicked! You said you were a murderer.

DON JUAN. Only a duel. I ran my sword through an old man who was trying to run his through me.

THE OLD WOMAN. If you were a gentleman, that was not a murder.

DON JUAN. The old man called it murder, because he was, he said, defending his daughter's honor. By this he meant that because I foolishly fell in love with her and told her so, she screamed; and he tried to assassinate me after calling me insulting names.

THE OLD WOMAN. You were like all men. Libertines and murderers all, all, all!

DON JUAN. And yet we meet here, dear lady.

THE OLD WOMAN. Listen to me. My father was slain by just such a wretch as you, in just such a duel, for just such a cause. I screamed: it was my duty. My father drew on my assailant: his honor demanded it. He fell: that was the reward of honor. I am here: in hell, you tell me that is the reward of duty. Is there justice in heaven?

DON JUAN. No; but there is justice in hell: heaven is far above such idle human personalities. You will be welcome in hell, Senora. Hell is the home of honor, duty, justice, and the rest of the seven deadly virtues. All the wickedness on earth is done in their name: where else but in hell should they have their reward? Have I not told you that the truly damned are those who are happy in hell?

THE OLD WOMAN. And are you happy here?

DON JUAN. [*Springing to his feet*] No; and that is the enigma on which I ponder in darkness. Why am I here? I, who repudiated all duty, trampled honor underfoot, and laughed at justice!

THE OLD WOMAN. Oh, what do I care why you are here? Why am I here? I, who sacrificed all my inclinations to womanly virtue and propriety!

DON JUAN. Patience, lady: you will be perfectly happy and at home here. As with the poet, "Hell is a city much like Seville."

THE OLD WOMAN. Happy! here! where I am nothing! where I am nobody!

DON JUAN. Not at all: you are a lady; and wherever ladies are is hell. Do not be surprised or terrified: you will find everything here that a lady can desire, including devils who will serve you from sheer love of servitude, and magnify your importance for the sake of dignifying their service—the best of servants.

THE OLD WOMAN. My servants will be devils.

DON JUAN. Have you ever had servants who were not devils?

THE OLD WOMAN. Never: they were devils, perfect devils, all of them. But that is only a manner of speaking. I thought you meant that my servants here would be real devils.

DON JUAN. No more real devils than you will be a real lady. Nothing is real here. That is the horror of damnation.

THE OLD WOMAN. Oh, this is all madness. This is worse than fire and the worm.

DON JUAN. For you, perhaps, there are consolations. For instance: how old were you when you changed from time to eternity?

THE OLD WOMAN. Do not ask me how old I was as if I were a thing of the past. I am 77.

DON JUAN. A ripe age, Senora. But in hell old age is not tolerated. It is too real. Here we worship Love and Beauty. Our souls being entirely damned, we cultivate our hearts. As a lady of 77, you would not have a single acquaintance in hell.

THE OLD WOMAN. How can I help my age, man?

DON JUAN. You forget that you have left your age behind you in the realm of time. You are no more 77 than you are 7 or 17 or 27.

THE OLD WOMAN. Nonsense!

DON JUAN. Consider, Senora: was not this true even when you lived on earth? When you were 70, were you really older underneath your wrinkles and your grey hams than when you were 30?

THE OLD WOMAN. No, younger: at 30 I was a fool. But of what use is it to feel younger and look older?

DON JUAN. You see, Senora, the look was only an illusion. Your wrinkles lied, just as the plump smooth skin of many a stupid girl of 17, with heavy spirits and decrepit ideas, lies about her age? Well, here we have no bodies: we see each other as bodies only because we learnt to think about one another under that aspect when we were alive; and we still think in that way, knowing no other. But we can appear to one another at what age we choose. You have but to will any of your old looks back, and back they will come.

THE OLD WOMAN. It cannot be true.

DON JUAN. Try.

THE OLD WOMAN. Seventeen!

DON JUAN. Stop. Before you decide, I had better tell you that these things are a matter of fashion. Occasionally we have a rage for 17; but it does not last long. Just at present the fashionable age is 40—or say 37; but there are signs of a change. If you were at all good-looking at 27, I should suggest your trying that, and setting a new fashion.

THE OLD WOMAN. I do not believe a word you are saying. However, 27 be it. [*Whisk! the old woman becomes a young one, and so handsome that in the radiance into which her dull yellow halo has suddenly lightened one might almost mistake her for Ann Whitefield*].

DON JUAN. Dona Ana de Ulloa!

ANA. What? You know me!

DON JUAN. And you forget me!

ANA. I cannot see your face. [*He raises his hat*]. Don Juan Tenorio! Monster! You who slew my father! even here you pursue me.

DON JUAN. I protest I do not pursue you. Allow me to withdraw [*going*].

ANA. [*reining his arm*] You shall not leave me alone in this dreadful place.

DON JUAN. Provided my staying be not interpreted as pursuit.

ANA. [*releasing him*] You may well wonder how I can endure your presence. My dear, dear father!

DON JUAN. Would you like to see him?

ANA. My father HERE!!!

DON JUAN. No: he is in heaven.

ANA. I knew it. My noble father! He is looking down on us now. What must he feel to see his daughter in this place, and in conversation with his murderer!

DON JUAN. By the way, if we should meet him—

ANA. How can we meet him? He is in heaven.

DON JUAN. He condescends to look in upon us here from time to time. Heaven bores him. So let me warn you that if you meet him he will be mortally offended if you speak of me as his murderer! He maintains that he was a much better swordsman than I, and that if his foot had not slipped he would have killed me. No doubt he is right: I was not a good fencer. I never dispute the point; so we are excellent friends.

ANA. It is no dishonor to a soldier to be proud of his skill in arms.

DON JUAN. You would rather not meet him, probably.

ANA. How dare you say that?

DON JUAN. Oh, that is the usual feeling here. You may remember that on earth—though of course we never confessed it—the death of anyone we knew, even those we liked best, was always mingled with a certain satisfaction at being finally done with them.

ANA. Monster! Never, never.

DON JUAN. [*placidly*] I see you recognize the feeling. Yes: a funeral was always a festivity in black, especially the funeral of a relative. At all events, family ties are rarely kept up here. Your father is quite accustomed to this: he will not expect any devotion from you.

ANA. Wretch: I wore mourning for him all my life.

DON JUAN. Yes: it became you. But a life of mourning is one thing: an eternity of it quite another. Besides, here you are as dead as he. Can anything be more ridiculous than one dead person mourning for another? Do not look shocked, my dear Ana; and do not be alarmed: there is plenty of humbug in hell (indeed there is hardly anything else); but the humbug of death and age and change is dropped because here WE are all dead and all eternal. You will pick up our ways soon.

ANA. And will all the men call me their dear Ana?

DON JUAN. No. That was a slip of the tongue. I beg your pardon.

ANA. [*almost tenderly*] Juan: did you really love me when you behaved so disgracefully to me?

DON JUAN. [*impatiently*] Oh, I beg you not to begin talking about love. Here they talk of nothing else but love—its beauty, its holiness, its spirituality, its devil knows what!—excuse me; but it does so bore me. They don't know what they're talking about. I do. They think they have achieved the perfection of love because they have no bodies. Sheer imaginative debauchery! Faugh!

ANA. Has even death failed to refine your soul, Juan? Has the terrible judgment of which my father's statue was the minister taught you no reverence?

DON JUAN. How is that very flattering statue, by the way? Does it still come to supper with naughty people and cast them into this bottomless pit?

ANA. It has been a great expense to me. The boys in the monastery school would not let it alone: the mischievous ones broke it; and the studious ones wrote their names on it. Three new noses in two years, and fingers without end. I had to leave it to its fate at last; and now I fear it is shockingly mutilated. My poor father!

DON JUAN. Hush! Listen! [*Two great chords rolling on syncopated waves of sound break forth: D minor and its dominant: a round of dreadful joy to all musicians*]. Ha! Mozart's statue music. It is your father. You had better disappear until I prepare him. [*She vanishes*].

From the void comes a living statue of white marble, designed to represent a majestic old man. But he waives his majesty with infinite grace; walks with a feather-like step; and makes every wrinkle in his war worn visage brim over with holiday joyousness. To his sculptor he owes a perfectly trained figure, which he carries erect and trim; and the ends of his moustache curl up, elastic as watchsprings, giving him an air which, but for its Spanish dignity, would be called jaunty. He is on the pleasantest terms with Don Juan. His voice, save for a much more distinguished intonation, is so like the voice of Roebuck Ramsden that it calls attention to the fact that they are not unlike one another in spite of their very different fashion of shaving.

DON JUAN. Ah, here you are, my friend. Why don't you learn to sing the splendid music Mozart has written for you?

THE STATUE. Unluckily he has written it for a bass voice. Mine is a counter tenor. Well: have you repented yet?

DON JUAN. I have too much consideration for you to repent, Don Gonzalo. If I did, you would have no excuse for coming from Heaven to argue with me.

THE STATUE. True. Remain obdurate, my boy. I wish I had killed you, as I should have done but for an accident. Then I should have come here; and you would have had a statue and a reputation for piety to live up to. Any news?

DON JUAN. Yes: your daughter is dead.

THE STATUE. [*puzzled*] My daughter? [*Recollecting*] Oh! the one you were taken with. Let me see: what was her name?

DON JUAN. Ana.

THE STATUE. To be sure: Ana. A goodlooking girl, if I recollect aright. Have you warned Whatshisname—her husband?

DON JUAN. My friend Ottavio? No: I have not seen him since Ana arrived.

Ana comes indignantly to light.

ANA. What does this mean? Ottavio here and YOUR friend! And you, father, have forgotten my name. You are indeed turned to stone.

THE STATUE. My dear: I am so much more admired in marble than I ever was in my own person that I have retained the shape the sculptor gave me. He was one of the first men of his day: you must acknowledge that.

ANA. Father! Vanity! personal vanity! from you!

THE STATUE. Ah, you outlived that weakness, my daughter: you must be nearly 80 by this time. I was cut off (by an accident) in my 64th year, and am considerably your junior in consequence. Besides, my child, in this place, what our libertine friend here would call the farce of parental wisdom is dropped. Regard me, I beg, as a fellow creature, not as a father.

ANA. You speak as this villain speaks.

THE STATUE. Juan is a sound thinker, Ana. A bad fencer, but a sound thinker.

ANA. [*horror creeping upon her*] I begin to understand. These are devils, mocking me. I had better pray.

THE STATUE. [*consoling her*] No, no, no, my child: do not pray. If you do, you will throw away the main advantage of this place. Written over the gate here are the words "Leave every hope behind, ye who enter." Only think what a relief that is! For what is hope? A form of moral responsibility. Here there is no hope, and consequently no duty, no work, nothing to be gained by praying, nothing to be lost by doing what you like. Hell, in short, is a place where you have nothing to do but amuse yourself. [*Don Juan sighs deeply*]. You sigh, friend Juan; but if you dwelt in heaven, as I do, you would realize your advantages.

DON JUAN. You are in good spirits to-day, Commander. You are positively brilliant. What is the matter?

THE STATUE. I have come to a momentous decision, my boy. But first, where is our friend the Devil? I must consult him in the matter. And Ana would like to make his acquaintance, no doubt.

ANA. You are preparing some torment for me.

DON JUAN. All that is superstition, Ana. Reassure yourself. Remember: the devil is not so black as he is painted.

THE STATUE. Let us give him a call.

At the wave of the statue's hand the great chords roll out again but this time Mozart's music gets grotesquely adulterated with Gounod's. A scarlet halo begins to glow; and into it the Devil rises, very Mephistophelean, and not at all unlike Mendoza, though not so interesting. He looks older; is getting prematurely bald; and, in spite of an effusion of goodnature and friendliness, is peevish and sensitive when his advances are not reciprocated. He does not inspire much confidence in his powers of hard work or endurance, and is, on the whole, a disagreeably self-indulgent looking person; but he is clever and plausible, though perceptibly less well bred than the two other men, and enormously less vital than the woman.

THE DEVIL. [*heartily*] Have I the pleasure of again receiving a visit from the illustrious Commander of Calatrava? [*Coldly*] Don Juan, your servant. [*Politely*] And a strange lady? My respects, Senora.

ANA. Are you—

THE DEVIL. [*bowing*] Lucifer, at your service.

ANA. I shall go mad.

THE DEVIL. [*gallantly*] Ah, Senora, do not be anxious. You come to us from earth, full of the prejudices and terrors of that priest-ridden place. You have heard me ill spoken of; and yet, believe me, I have hosts of friends there.

ANA. Yes: you reign in their hearts.

THE DEVIL. [*shaking his head*] You flatter me, Senora; but you are mistaken. It is true that the world cannot get on without me; but it never gives me credit for that: in its heart it mistrusts and hates me. Its sympathies are all with misery, with poverty, with starvation of the body and of the heart. I call on it to sympathize with joy, with love, with happiness, with beauty.

DON JUAN. [*nauseated*] Excuse me: I am going. You know I cannot stand this.

THE DEVIL. [*angrily*] Yes: I know that you are no friend of mine.

THE STATUE. What harm is he doing you, Juan? It seems to me that he was talking excellent sense when you interrupted him.

THE DEVIL. [*warmly shaking the statue's hand*] Thank you, my friend: thank you. You have always understood me: he has always disparaged and avoided me.

DON JUAN. I have treated you with perfect courtesy.

THE DEVIL. Courtesy! What is courtesy? I care nothing for mere courtesy. Give me warmth of heart, true sincerity, the bond of sympathy with love and joy—

DON JUAN. You are making me ill.

THE DEVIL. There! [*Appealing to the statue*] You hear, sir! Oh, by what irony of fate was this cold selfish egotist sent to my kingdom, and you taken to the icy mansions of the sky!

THE STATUE. I can't complain. I was a hypocrite; and it served me right to be sent to heaven.

THE DEVIL. Why, sir, do you not join us, and leave a sphere for which your temperament is too sympathetic, your heart too warm, your capacity for enjoyment too generous?

THE STATUE. I have this day resolved to do so. In future, excellent Son of the Morning, I am yours. I have left Heaven for ever.

THE DEVIL. [*again grasping his hand*] Ah, what an honor for me! What a triumph for our cause! Thank you, thank you. And now, my friend—I may call you so at last—could you not persuade HIM to take the place you have left vacant above?

THE STATUE. [*shaking his head*] I cannot conscientiously recommend anybody with whom I am on friendly terms to deliberately make himself dull and uncomfortable.

THE DEVIL. Of course not; but are you sure HE would be uncomfortable? Of course you know best: you brought him here originally; and we had the greatest hopes of him. His sentiments were in the best taste of our best people. You remember how he sang? [*He begins to sing in a nasal operatic baritone, tremulous from an eternity of misuse in the French manner*].

Vivan le femmine! Viva il buon vino!

THE STATUE. [*taking up the tune an octave higher in his counter tenor*]

Sostegno a gloria D'umanita.

THE DEVIL. Precisely. Well, he never sings for us now.

DON JUAN. Do you complain of that? Hell is full of musical amateurs: music is the brandy of the damned. May not one lost soul be permitted to abstain?

THE DEVIL. You dare blaspheme against the sublimest of the arts!

DON JUAN. [*with cold disgust*] You talk like a hysterical woman fawning on a fiddler.

THE DEVIL. I am not angry. I merely pity you. You have no soul; and you are unconscious of all that you lose. Now you, Senor Commander, are a born musician. How well you sing! Mozart would be delighted if he were still here; but he moped and went to heaven. Curious how these clever men, whom you would have supposed born to be popular here, have turned out social failures, like Don Juan!

DON JUAN. I am really very sorry to be a social failure.

THE DEVIL. Not that we don't admire your intellect, you know. We do. But I look at the matter from your own point of view. You don't get on with us. The place doesn't suit you. The truth is, you have—I won't say no heart; for we know that beneath all your affected cynicism you have a warm one.

DON JUAN. [*shrinking*] Don't, please don't.

THE DEVIL. [*nettled*] Well, you've no capacity for enjoyment. Will that satisfy you?

DON JUAN. It is a somewhat less insufferable form of cant than the other. But if you'll allow me, I'll take refuge, as usual, in solitude.

THE DEVIL. Why not take refuge in Heaven? That's the proper place for you. [*To Ana*] Come, Senora! could you not persuade him for his own good to try a change of air?

ANA. But can he go to Heaven if he wants to?

THE DEVIL. What's to prevent him?

ANA. Can anybody—can I go to Heaven if I want to?

THE DEVIL. [*rather contemptuously*] Certainly, if your taste lies that way.

ANA. But why doesn't everybody go to Heaven, then?

THE STATUE. [*chuckling*] I can tell you that, my dear. It's because heaven is the most angelically dull place in all creation: that's why.

THE DEVIL. His excellency the Commander puts it with military bluntness; but the strain of living in Heaven is intolerable. There is a notion that I was turned out of it; but as a matter of fact nothing could have induced me to stay there. I simply left it and organized this place.

THE STATUE. I don't wonder at it. Nobody could stand an eternity of heaven.

THE DEVIL. Oh, it suits some people. Let us be just, Commander: it is a question of temperament. I don't admire the heavenly temperament: I don't understand it: I don't know that I particularly want to understand it; but it takes all sorts to make a universe. There is no accounting for tastes: there are people who like it. I think Don Juan would like it.

DON JUAN. But—pardon my frankness—could you really go back there if you desired to; or are the grapes sour?

THE DEVIL. Back there! I often go back there. Have you never read the book of Job? Have you any canonical authority for assuming that there is any barrier between our circle and the other one?

ANA. But surely there is a great gulf fixed.

THE DEVIL. Dear lady: a parable must not be taken literally. The gulf is the difference between the angelic and the diabolic temperament. What more impassable gulf could you have? Think of what you have seen on earth. There is no physical gulf between the philosopher's class room and the bull ring; but the bull fighters do not come to the class room for all that. Have you ever been in the country where I have the largest following—England? There they have great racecourses, and also concert rooms where they play the classical compositions of his Excellency's friend Mozart. Those who go to the racecourses can stay away from them and go to the classical concerts instead if they like: there is no law against it; for Englishmen never will be slaves: they are free to do whatever the Government and public opinion allows them to do. And the classical concert is admitted to be a higher, more cultivated, poetic, intellectual, ennobling place than the racecourse. But do the lovers of racing desert their sport and flock to the concert room? Not they. They would suffer there all the weariness the Commander has suffered in heaven. There is the great gulf of the parable between the two places. A mere physical gulf they could bridge; or at least I could bridge it for them (the earth is full of Devil's Bridges); but the gulf of dislike is impassable and eternal. And that is the only gulf that separates my friends here from those who are invidiously called the blest.

ANA. I shall go to heaven at once.

THE STATUE. My child; one word of warning first. Let me complete my friend Lucifer's similitude of the classical concert. At every one of those concerts in England you will find rows of weary people who are there, not because they really like classical music, but because they think they ought to like it. Well, there is the same thing in heaven. A number of people sit there in glory, not because they are happy, but because they think they owe it to their position to be in heaven. They are almost all English.

THE DEVIL. Yes: the Southerners give it up and join me just as you have done. But the English really do not seem to know when they are thoroughly miserable. An Englishman thinks he is moral when he is only uncomfortable.

THE STATUE. In short, my daughter, if you go to Heaven without being naturally qualified for it, you will not enjoy yourself there.

ANA. And who dares say that I am not naturally qualified for it? The most distinguished princes of the Church have never questioned it. I owe it to myself to leave this place at once.

THE DEVIL. [*offended*] As you please, Senora. I should have expected better taste from you.

ANA. Father: I shall expect you to come with me. You cannot stay here. What will people say?

THE STATUE. People! Why, the best people are here—princes of the church and all. So few go to Heaven, and so many come here, that the blest, once called a heavenly host, are a continually dwindling minority. The saints, the fathers, the elect of long ago are the cranks, the faddists, the outsiders of to-day.

THE DEVIL. It is true. From the beginning of my career I knew that I should win in the long run by sheer weight of public opinion, in spite of the long campaign of misrepresentation and calumny against me. At bottom the universe is a constitutional one; and with such a majority as mine I cannot be kept permanently out of office.

DON JUAN. I think, Ana, you had better stay here.

ANA. [*jealously*] You do not want me to go with you.

DON JUAN. Surely you do not want to enter Heaven in the company of a reprobate like me.

ANA. All souls are equally precious. You repent, do you not?

DON JUAN. My dear Ana, you are silly. Do you suppose heaven is like earth, where people persuade themselves that what is done can be undone by repentance; that what is spoken can be unspoken by withdrawing it; that what is true can be annihilated by a general agreement to give it the lie? No: heaven is the home of the masters of reality: that is why I am going thither.

ANA. Thank you: I am going to heaven for happiness. I have had quite enough of reality on earth.

DON JUAN. Then you must stay here; for hell is the home of the unreal and of the seekers for happiness. It is the only refuge from heaven, which is, as I tell you, the home of the masters of reality, and from earth, which is the home of the slaves of reality. The earth is a nursery in which men and women play at being heros and heroines, saints and sinners; but they are dragged down from their fool's paradise by their bodies: hunger and cold and thirst, age and decay and disease, death above all, make them slaves of reality: thrice a day meals must be eaten and digested: thrice a century a new generation must be engendered: ages of faith, of romance, and of science are all driven at last to have but one prayer, "Make me a healthy animal." But here you escape the tyranny of the flesh; for here you are not an animal at all: you are a ghost, an appearance, an illusion, a convention, deathless, ageless: in a word, bodiless. There are no social questions here, no political questions, no religious questions, best of all, perhaps, no sanitary questions. Here you call your appearance beauty, your emotions love, your sentiments heroism, your aspirations virtue, just as you did on earth; but here there are no hard facts to contradict you, no ironic contrast of your needs with your pretensions, no human comedy, nothing but a perpetual romance, a universal melodrama. As our German friend put it in his poem, "the poetically nonsensical here is good sense; and the Eternal Feminine draws us ever upward and on"—without getting us a step farther. And yet you want to leave this paradise!

ANA. But if Hell be so beautiful as this, how glorious must heaven be!

The Devil, the Statue, and Don Juan all begin to speak at once in violent protest; then stop, abashed.

DON JUAN. I beg your pardon.

THE DEVIL. Not at all. I interrupted you.

THE STATUE. You were going to say something.

DON JUAN. After you, gentlemen.

THE DEVIL. [*to Don Juan*] You have been so eloquent on the advantages of my dominions that I leave you to do equal justice to the drawbacks of the alternative establishment.

DON JUAN. In Heaven, as I picture it, dear lady, you live and work instead of playing and pretending. You face things as they are; you escape nothing but glamor; and your steadfastness and your peril are your glory. If the play still goes on here and on earth, and all the world is a stage, Heaven is at least behind the scenes. But Heaven cannot be described by metaphor. Thither I shall go presently, because there I hope to escape at last from lies and from the tedious, vulgar pursuit of happiness, to spend my eons in contemplation—

THE STATUE. Ugh!

DON JUAN. Senor Commander: I do not blame your disgust: a picture gallery is a dull place for a blind man. But even as you enjoy the contemplation of such romantic mirages as beauty and pleasure; so would I enjoy the contemplation of that which interests me above all things namely, Life: the force that ever strives to attain greater power of contemplating itself. What made this brain of mine, do you think? Not the need to move my limbs; for a rat with half my brains moves as well as I. Not merely the need to do, but the need to know what I do, lest in my blind efforts to live I should be slaying myself.

THE STATUE. You would have slain yourself in your blind efforts to fence but for my foot slipping, my friend.

DON JUAN. Audacious ribald: your laughter will finish in hideous boredom before morning.

THE STATUE. Ha ha! Do you remember how I frightened you when I said something like that to you from my pedestal in Seville? It sounds rather flat without my trombones.

DON JUAN. They tell me it generally sounds flat with them, Commander.

ANA. Oh, do not interrupt with these frivolities, father. Is there nothing in Heaven but contemplation, Juan?

DON JUAN. In the Heaven I seek, no other joy. But there is the work of helping Life in its struggle upward. Think of how it wastes and scatters itself, how it raises up obstacles to itself and destroys itself in its ignorance and blindness. It needs a brain, this irresistible force, lest in its ignorance it should resist itself. What a piece of work is man! says the poet. Yes: but what a blunderer! Here is the highest miracle of organization yet attained by life, the most intensely alive thing that exists, the most conscious of all the organisms; and yet, how wretched are his brains! Stupidity made sordid and cruel by the realities learnt from toil and poverty: Imagination resolved to starve sooner than face these realities, piling up illusions to hide them, and calling itself cleverness, genius! And each accusing the other of its own defect: Stupidity accusing Imagination of folly, and Imagination accusing Stupidity of ignorance: whereas, alas! Stupidity has all the knowledge, and Imagination all the intelligence.

THE DEVIL. And a pretty kettle of fish they make of it between them. Did I not say, when I was arranging that affair of Faust's, that all Man's reason has done for him is to make him beastlier than any beast. One splendid body is worth the brains of a hundred dyspeptic, flatulent philosophers.

DON JUAN. You forget that brainless magnificence of body has been tried. Things immeasurably greater than man in every respect but brain have existed and perished. The megatherium, the icthyosaurus have paced the earth with seven-league steps and hidden the day with cloud vast wings. Where are they now? Fossils in museums, and so few and imperfect at that, that a knuckle bone or a tooth of one of them is prized beyond the lives of a thousand soldiers. These things lived and wanted to live; but for lack of brains they did not know how to carry out their purpose, and so destroyed themselves.

THE DEVIL. And is Man any the less destroying himself for all this boasted brain of his? Have you walked up and down upon the earth lately? I have; and I have examined Man's wonderful inventions. And I tell you that in the arts of life man invents nothing; but in the arts of death he outdoes Nature herself, and produces by chemistry and machinery all the slaughter of plague, pestilence and famine. The peasant I tempt to-day eats and drinks what was eaten and drunk by the peasants of ten thousand years ago; and the house he lives in has not altered as much in a thousand centuries as the fashion of a lady's bonnet in a score of weeks. But when he goes out to slay, he carries a marvel of mechanism that lets loose at the touch of his finger all the hidden molecular energies, and leaves the javelin, the arrow, the blowpipe of his fathers far behind. In the arts of peace Man is a bungler. I have seen his cotton factories and the like, with machinery that a greedy dog could have invented if it had wanted money instead of food. I know his clumsy typewriters and bungling locomotives and tedious bicycles: they are toys compared to the Maxim gun, the submarine torpedo boat. There is nothing in Man's industrial machinery but his greed and sloth: his heart is in his weapons. This marvellous force of Life of which you boast is a force of Death: Man measures his strength by his destructiveness. What is his religion? An excuse for hating ME. What is his law? An excuse for hanging YOU. What is his morality? Gentility! an excuse for consuming without producing. What is his art? An excuse for gloating over pictures of slaughter. What are his politics? Either the worship of a despot because a despot can kill, or parliamentary cockfighting. I spent an evening lately in a certain celebrated legislature, and heard the pot lecturing the kettle for its blackness, and ministers answering questions. When I left I chalked up on the door the old nursery saying—"Ask no questions and you will be told no lies." I bought a sixpenny family magazine, and found it full of pictures of young men shooting and stabbing one another. I saw a man die: he was a London bricklayer's laborer with seven children. He left seventeen pounds club money; and his wife spent it all on his funeral and went into the workhouse with the children next day. She would not have spent sevenpence on her children's schooling: the law had to force her to let them be taught gratuitously; but on death she spent all she had. Their imagination glows, their energies rise up at the idea of death, these people: they love it; and the more horrible it is the more they enjoy it. Hell is a place far above their comprehension: they derive their notion of it from two of the greatest fools that ever lived, an Italian and an Englishman. The Italian described it as a place of mud, frost, filth, fire, and venomous serpents: all torture. This ass, when he was not lying about me, was maundering about some woman whom he saw once in the street. The Englishman described me as being expelled from Heaven by cannons and gunpowder; and to this day every Briton believes that the whole of his silly story is in the Bible. What else he says I do not know; for it is all in a long poem which neither I nor anyone else ever succeeded in wading through. It is the same in everything. The highest form of literature is the tragedy, a play in which everybody is murdered at the end. In the old chronicles you read of earthquakes and pestilences, and are told that these showed the power and majesty of God and the littleness of Man. Nowadays the chronicles describe battles. In a battle two bodies of men shoot at one another with bullets and explosive shells until one body runs away, when the others chase the fugitives on horseback and cut them to pieces as they fly. And this, the chronicle concludes, shows the greatness and majesty of empires, and the littleness of the vanquished. Over such battles the people run about the streets yelling with delight, and egg their Governments on to spend hundreds of millions of money in the slaughter, whilst the strongest Ministers dare not spend an extra penny in the pound against the poverty and pestilence through which they themselves daily walk. I could give you a thousand instances; but they all come to the same thing: the power that governs the earth is not the power of Life but of Death; and the inner need that has nerved Life to the effort of organizing itself into the human being is not the need for higher life but for a more efficient engine of destruction. The plague, the famine, the earthquake, the tempest were too spasmodic in their action; the tiger and crocodile were too easily satiated and not cruel enough: something more constantly, more ruthlessly, more ingeniously destructive was needed; and that something was Man, the inventor of the rack, the stake, the gallows, and the electrocutor; of the sword and gun; above all, of justice, duty, patriotism and all the other isms by which even those who are clever enough to be humanely disposed are persuaded to become the most destructive of all the destroyers.

DON JUAN. Pshaw! all this is old. Your weak side, my diabolic friend, is that you have always been a gull: you take Man at his own valuation. Nothing would flatter him more than your opinion of him. He loves to think of himself as bold and bad. He is neither one nor the other: he is only a coward. Call him tyrant, murderer, pirate, bully; and he will adore you, and swagger about with the consciousness of having the blood of the old sea kings in his veins. Call him liar and thief; and he will only take an action against you for libel. But call him coward; and he will go mad with rage: he will face death to outface that stinging truth. Man gives every reason for his conduct save one, every excuse for his crimes save one, every plea for his safety save one; and that one is his cowardice. Yet all his civilization is founded on his cowardice, on his abject tameness, which he calls his respectability. There are limits to what a mule or an ass will stand; but Man will suffer himself to be degraded until his vileness becomes so loathsome to his oppressors that they themselves are forced to reform it.

THE DEVIL. Precisely. And these are the creatures in whom you discover what you call a Life Force!

DON JUAN. Yes; for now comes the most surprising part of the whole business.

THE STATUE. What's that?

DON JUAN. Why, that you can make any of these cowards brave by simply putting an idea into his head.

THE STATUE. Stuff! As an old soldier I admit the cowardice: it's as universal as sea sickness, and matters just as little. But that about putting an idea into a man's head is stuff and nonsense. In a battle all you need to make you fight is a little hot blood and the knowledge that it's more dangerous to lose than to win.

DON JUAN. That is perhaps why battles are so useless. But men never really overcome fear until they imagine they are fighting to further a universal purpose—fighting for an idea, as they call it. Why was the Crusader braver than the pirate? Because he fought, not for himself, but for the Cross. What force was it that met him with a valor as reckless as his own? The force of men who fought, not for themselves, but for Islam. They took Spain from us, though we were fighting for our very hearths and homes; but when we, too, fought for that mighty idea, a Catholic Church, we swept them back to Africa.

THE DEVIL. [*ironically*] What! you a Catholic, Senor Don Juan! A devotee! My congratulations.

THE STATUE. [*seriously*] Come come! as a soldier, I can listen to nothing against the Church.

DON JUAN. Have no fear, Commander: this idea of a Catholic Church will survive Islam, will survive the Cross, will survive even that vulgar pageant of incompetent schoolboyish gladiators which you call the Army.

THE STATUE. Juan: you will force me to call you to account for this.

DON JUAN. Useless: I cannot fence. Every idea for which Man will die will be a Catholic idea. When the Spaniard learns at last that he is no better than the Saracen, and his prophet no better than Mahomet, he will arise, more Catholic than ever, and die on a barricade across the filthy slum he starves in, for universal liberty and equality.

THE STATUE. Bosh!

DON JUAN. What you call bosh is the only thing men dare die for. Later on, Liberty will not be Catholic enough: men will die for human perfection, to which they will sacrifice all their liberty gladly.

THE DEVIL. Ay: they will never be at a loss for an excuse for killing one another.

DON JUAN. What of that? It is not death that matters, but the fear of death. It is not killing and dying that degrade us, but base living, and accepting the wages and profits of degradation. Better ten dead men than one live slave or his master. Men shall yet rise up, father against son and brother against brother, and kill one another for the great Catholic idea of abolishing slavery.

THE DEVIL. Yes, when the Liberty and Equality of which you prate shall have made free white Christians cheaper in the labor market than by auction at the block.

DON JUAN. Never fear! the white laborer shall have his turn too. But I am not now defending the illusory forms the great ideas take. I am giving you examples of the fact that this creature Man, who in his own selfish affairs is a coward to the backbone, will fight for an idea like a hero. He may be abject as a citizen; but he is dangerous as a fanatic. He can only be enslaved whilst he is spiritually weak enough to listen to reason. I tell you, gentlemen, if you can show a man a piece of what he now calls God's work to do, and what he will later on call by many new names, you can make him entirely reckless of the consequences to himself personally.

ANA. Yes: he shirks all his responsibilities, and leaves his wife to grapple with them.

THE STATUE. Well said, daughter. Do not let him talk you out of your common sense.

THE DEVIL. Alas! Senor Commander, now that we have got on to the subject of Woman, he will talk more than ever. However, I confess it is for me the one supremely interesting subject.

DON JUAN. To a woman, Senora, man's duties and responsibilities begin and end with the task of getting bread for her children. To her, Man is only a means to the end of getting children and rearing them.

ANA. Is that your idea of a woman's mind? I call it cynical and disgusting materialism.

DON JUAN. Pardon me, Ana: I said nothing about a woman's whole mind. I spoke of her view of Man as a separate sex. It is no more cynical than her view of herself as above all things a Mother. Sexually, Woman is Nature's contrivance for perpetuating its highest achievement. Sexually, Man is Woman's contrivance for fulfilling Nature's behest in the most economical way. She knows by instinct that far back in the evolutional process she invented him, differentiated him, created him in order to produce something better than the single-sexed process can produce. Whilst he fulfils the purpose for which she made him, he is welcome to his dreams, his follies, his ideals, his heroisms, provided that the keystone of them all is the worship of woman, of motherhood, of the family, of the hearth. But how rash and dangerous it was to invent a separate creature whose sole function was her own impregnation! For mark what has happened. First, Man has multiplied on her hands until there are as many men as women; so that she has been unable to employ for her purposes more than a fraction of the immense energy she has left at his disposal by saving him the exhausting labor of gestation. This superfluous energy has gone to his brain and to his muscle. He has become too strong to be controlled by her bodily, and too imaginative and mentally vigorous to be content with mere self-reproduction. He has created civilization without consulting her, taking her domestic labor for granted as the foundation of it.

ANA. THAT is true, at all events.

THE DEVIL. Yes; and this civilization! what is it, after all?

DON JUAN. After all, an excellent peg to hang your cynical commonplaces on; but BEFORE all, it is an attempt on Man's part to make himself something more than the mere instrument of Woman's purpose. So far, the result of Life's continual effort not only to maintain itself, but to achieve higher and higher organization and completer self-consciousness, is only, at best, a doubtful campaign between its forces and those of Death and Degeneration. The battles in this campaign are mere blunders, mostly won, like actual military battles, in spite of the commanders.

THE STATUE. That is a dig at me. No matter: go on, go on.

DON JUAN. It is a dig at a much higher power than you, Commander. Still, you must have noticed in your profession that even a stupid general can win battles when the enemy's general is a little stupider.

THE STATUE. [*very seriously*] Most true, Juan, most true. Some donkeys have amazing luck.

DON JUAN. Well, the Life Force is stupid; but it is not so stupid as the forces of Death and Degeneration. Besides, these are in its pay all the time. And so Life wins, after a fashion. What mere copiousness of fecundity can supply and mere greed preserve, we possess. The survival of whatever form of civilization can produce the best rifle and the best fed rifle-riflemen is assured.

THE DEVIL. Exactly! the survival, not of the most effective means of Life but of the most effective means of Death. You always come back to my point, in spite of your wrigglings and evasions and sophistries, not to mention the intolerable length of your speeches.

DON JUAN. Oh come! who began making long speeches? However, if I overtax your intellect, you can leave us and seek the society of love and beauty and the rest of your favorite boredoms.

THE DEVIL. [*much offended*] This is not fair, Don Juan, and not civil. I am also on the intellectual plane. Nobody can appreciate it more than I do. I am arguing fairly with you, and, I think, utterly refuting you. Let us go on for another hour if you like.

DON JUAN. Good: let us.

THE STATUE. Not that I see any prospect of your coming to any point in particular, Juan. Still, since in this place, instead of merely killing time we have to kill eternity, go ahead by all means.

DON JUAN. [*somewhat impatiently*] My point, you marbleheaded old masterpiece, is only a step ahead of you. Are we agreed that Life is a force which has made innumerable experiments in organizing itself; that the mammoth and the man, the mouse and the megatherium, the flies and the fleas and the Fathers of the Church, are all more or less successful attempts to build up that raw force into higher and higher individuals, the ideal individual being omnipotent, omniscient, infallible, and withal completely, unilludedly self-conscious: in short, a god?

THE DEVIL. I agree, for the sake of argument.

THE STATUE. I agree, for the sake of avoiding argument.

ANA. I most emphatically disagree as regards the Fathers of the Church; and I must beg you not to drag them into the argument.

DON JUAN. I did so purely for the sake of alliteration, Ana; and I shall make no further allusion to them. And now, since we are, with that exception, agreed so far, will you not agree with me further that Life has not measured the success of its attempts at godhead by the beauty or bodily perfection of the result, since in both these respects the birds, as our friend Aristophanes long ago pointed out, are so extraordinarily superior, with their power of flight and their lovely plumage, and, may I add, the touching poetry of their loves and nestings, that it is inconceivable that Life, having once produced them, should, if love and beauty were her object, start off on another line and labor at the clumsy elephant and the hideous ape, whose grandchildren we are?

ANA. Aristophanes was a heathen; and you, Juan, I am afraid, are very little better.

THE DEVIL. You conclude, then, that Life was driving at clumsiness and ugliness?

DON JUAN. No, perverse devil that you are, a thousand times no. Life was driving at brains—at its darling object: an organ by which it can attain not only self-consciousness but self-understanding.

THE STATUE. This is metaphysics, Juan. Why the devil should—[*to the Devil*] I BEG your pardon.

THE DEVIL. Pray don't mention it. I have always regarded the use of my name to secure additional emphasis as a high compliment to me. It is quite at your service, Commander.

THE STATUE. Thank you: that's very good of you. Even in heaven, I never quite got out of my old military habits of speech. What I was going to ask Juan was why Life should bother itself about getting a brain. Why should it want to understand itself? Why not be content to enjoy itself?

DON JUAN. Without a brain, Commander, you would enjoy yourself without knowing it, and so lose all the fun.

THE STATUE. True, most true. But I am quite content with brain enough to know that I'm enjoying myself. I don't want to understand why. In fact, I'd rather not. My experience is that one's pleasures don't bear thinking about.

DON JUAN. That is why intellect is so unpopular. But to Life, the force behind the Man, intellect is a necessity, because without it he blunders into death. Just as Life, after ages of struggle, evolved that wonderful bodily organ the eye, so that the living organism could see where it was going and what was coming to help or threaten it, and thus avoid a thousand dangers that formerly slew it, so it is evolving to-day a mind's eye that shall see, not the physical world, but the purpose of Life, and thereby enable the individual to work for that purpose instead of thwarting and baffling it by setting up shortsighted personal aims as at present. Even as it is, only one sort of man has ever been happy, has ever been universally respected among all the conflicts of interests and illusions.

THE STATUE. You mean the military man.

DON JUAN. Commander: I do not mean the military man. When the military man approaches, the world locks up its spoons and packs off its womankind. No: I sing, not arms and the hero, but the philosophic man: he who seeks in contemplation to discover the inner will of the world, in invention to discover the means of fulfilling that will, and in action to do that will by the so-discovered means. Of all other sorts of men I declare myself tired. They're tedious failures. When I was on earth, professors of all sorts prowled round me feeling for an unhealthy spot in me on which they could fasten. The doctors of medicine bade me consider what I must do to save my body, and offered me quack cures for imaginary diseases. I replied that I was not a hypochondriac; so they called me Ignoramus and went their way. The doctors of divinity bade me consider what I must do to save my soul; but I was not a spiritual hypochondriac any more than a bodily one, and would not trouble myself about that either; so they called me Atheist and went their way. After them came the politician, who said there was only one purpose in Nature, and that was to get him into parliament. I told him I did not care whether he got into parliament or not; so he called me Mugwump and went his way. Then came the romantic man, the Artist, with his love songs and his paintings and his poems; and with him I had great delight for many years, and some profit; for I cultivated my senses for his sake; and his songs taught me to hear better, his paintings to see better, and his poems to feel more deeply. But he led me at last into the worship of Woman.

ANA. Juan!

DON JUAN. Yes: I came to believe that in her voice was all the music of the song, in her face all the beauty of the painting, and in her soul all the emotion of the poem.

ANA. And you were disappointed, I suppose. Well, was it her fault that you attributed all these perfections to her?

DON JUAN. Yes, partly. For with a wonderful instinctive cunning, she kept silent and allowed me to glorify her; to mistake my own visions, thoughts, and feelings for hers. Now my friend the romantic man was often too poor or too timid to approach those women who were beautiful or refined enough to seem to realize his ideal; and so he went to his grave believing in his dream. But I was more favored by nature and circumstance. I was of noble birth and rich; and when my person did not please, my conversation flattered, though I generally found myself fortunate in both.

THE STATUE. Coxcomb!

DON JUAN. Yes; but even my coxcombry pleased. Well, I found that when I had touched a woman's imagination, she would allow me to persuade myself that she loved me; but when my suit was granted she never said "I am happy: my love is satisfied": she always said, first, "At last, the barriers are down," and second, "When will you come again?"

ANA. That is exactly what men say.

DON JUAN. I protest I never said it. But all women say it. Well, these two speeches always alarmed me; for the first meant that the lady's impulse had been solely to throw down my fortifications and gain my citadel; and the second openly announced that henceforth she regarded me as her property, and counted my time as already wholly at her disposal.

THE DEVIL. That is where your want of heart came in.

THE STATUE. [*shaking his head*] You shouldn't repeat what a woman says, Juan.

ANA. [*severely*] It should be sacred to you.

THE STATUE. Still, they certainly do always say it. I never minded the barriers; but there was always a slight shock about the other, unless one was very hard hit indeed.

DON JUAN. Then the lady, who had been happy and idle enough before, became anxious, preoccupied with me, always intriguing, conspiring, pursuing, watching, waiting, bent wholly on making sure of her prey—I being the prey, you understand. Now this was not what I had bargained for. It may have been very proper and very natural; but it was not music, painting, poetry and joy incarnated in a beautiful woman. I ran away from it. I ran away from it very often: in fact I became famous for running away from it.

ANA. Infamous, you mean.

DON JUAN. I did not run away from you. Do you blame me for running away from the others?

ANA. Nonsense, man. You are talking to a woman of 77 now. If you had had the chance, you would have run away from me too—if I had let you. You would not have found it so easy with me as with some of the others. If men will not be faithful to their home and their duties, they must be made to be. I daresay you all want to marry lovely incarnations of music and painting and poetry. Well, you can't have them, because they don't exist. If flesh and blood is not good enough for you you must go without: that's all. Women have to put up with flesh-and-blood husbands—and little enough of that too, sometimes; and you will have to put up with flesh-and-blood wives. The Devil looks dubious. The Statue makes a wry face. I see you don't like that, any of you; but it's true, for all that; so if you don't like it you can lump it.

DON JUAN. My dear lady, you have put my whole case against romance into a few sentences. That is just why I turned my back on the romantic man with the artist nature, as he called his infatuation. I thanked him for teaching me to use my eyes and ears; but I told him that his beauty worshipping and happiness hunting and woman idealizing was not worth a dump as a philosophy of life; so he called me Philistine and went his way.

ANA. It seems that Woman taught you something, too, with all her defects.

DON JUAN. She did more: she interpreted all the other teaching for me. Ah, my friends, when the barriers were down for the first time, what an astounding illumination! I had been prepared for infatuation, for intoxication, for all the illusions of love's young dream; and lo! never was my perception clearer, nor my criticism more ruthless. The most jealous rival of my mistress never saw every blemish in her more keenly than I. I was not duped: I took her without chloroform.

ANA. But you did take her.

DON JUAN. That was the revelation. Up to that moment I had never lost the sense of being my own master; never consciously taken a single step until my reason had examined and approved it. I had come to believe that I was a purely rational creature: a thinker! I said, with the foolish philosopher, "I think; therefore I am." It was Woman who taught me to say "I am; therefore I think." And also "I would think more; therefore I must be more."

THE STATUE. This is extremely abstract and metaphysical, Juan. If you would stick to the concrete, and put your discoveries in the form of entertaining anecdotes about your adventures with women, your conversation would be easier to follow.

DON JUAN. Bah! what need I add? Do you not understand that when I stood face to face with Woman, every fibre in my clear critical brain warned me to spare her and save myself. My morals said No. My conscience said No. My chivalry and pity for her said No. My prudent regard for myself said No. My ear, practised on a thousand songs and symphonies; my eye, exercised on a thousand paintings; tore her voice, her features, her color to shreds. I caught all those tell-tale resemblances to her father and mother by which I knew what she would be like in thirty years time. I noted the gleam of gold from a dead tooth in the laughing mouth: I made curious observations of the strange odors of the chemistry of the nerves. The visions of my romantic reveries, in which I had trod the plains of heaven with a deathless, ageless creature of coral and ivory, deserted me in that supreme hour. I remembered them and desperately strove to recover their illusion; but they now seemed the emptiest of inventions: my judgment was not to be corrupted: my brain still said No on every issue. And whilst I was in the act of framing my excuse to the lady, Life seized me and threw me into her arms as a sailor throws a scrap of fish into the mouth of a seabird.

THE STATUE. You might as well have gone without thinking such a lot about it, Juan. You are like all the clever men: you have more brains than is good for you.

THE DEVIL. And were you not the happier for the experience, Senor Don Juan?

DON JUAN. The happier, no: the wiser, yes. That moment introduced me for the first time to myself, and, through myself, to the world. I saw then how useless it is to attempt to impose conditions on the irresistible force of Life; to preach prudence, careful selection, virtue, honor, chastity—

ANA. Don Juan: a word against chastity is an insult to me.

DON JUAN. I say nothing against your chastity, Senora, since it took the form of a husband and twelve children. What more could you have done had you been the most abandoned of women?

ANA. I could have had twelve husbands and no children that's what I could have done, Juan. And let me tell you that that would have made all the difference to the earth which I replenished.

THE STATUE. Bravo Ana! Juan: you are floored, quelled, annihilated.

DON JUAN. No; for though that difference is the true essential difference—Dona Ana has, I admit, gone straight to the real point—yet it is not a difference of love or chastity, or even constancy; for twelve children by twelve different husbands would have replenished the earth perhaps more effectively. Suppose my friend Ottavio had died when you were thirty, you would never have remained a widow: you were too beautiful. Suppose the successor of Ottavio had died when you were forty, you would still have been irresistible; and a woman who marries twice marries three times if she becomes free to do so. Twelve lawful children borne by one highly respectable lady to three different fathers is not impossible nor condemned by public opinion. That such a lady may be more law abiding than the poor girl whom we used to spurn into the gutter for bearing one unlawful infant is no doubt true; but dare you say she is less self-indulgent?

ANA. She is less virtuous: that is enough for me.

DON JUAN. In that case, what is virtue but the Trade Unionism of the married? Let us face the facts, dear Ana. The Life Force respects marriage only because marriage is a contrivance of its own to secure the greatest number of children and the closest care of them. For honor, chastity and all the rest of your moral figments it cares not a rap. Marriage is the most licentious of human institutions—

ANA. Juan!

THE STATUE. [*protesting*] Really!—

DON JUAN. [*determinedly*] I say the most licentious of human institutions: that is the secret of its popularity. And a woman seeking a husband is the most unscrupulous of all the beasts of prey. The confusion of marriage with morality has done more to destroy the conscience of the human race than any other single error. Come, Ana! do not look shocked: you know better than any of us that marriage is a mantrap baited with simulated accomplishments and delusive idealizations. When your sainted mother, by dint of scoldings and punishments, forced you to learn how to play half a dozen pieces on the spinet which she hated as much as you did—had she any other purpose than to delude your suitors into the belief that your husband would have in his home an angel who would fill it with melody, or at least play him to sleep after dinner? You married my friend Ottavio: well, did you ever open the spinet from the hour when the Church united him to you?

ANA. You are a fool, Juan. A young married woman has something else to do than sit at the spinet without any support for her back; so she gets out of the habit of playing.

DON JUAN. Not if she loves music. No: believe me, she only throws away the bait when the bird is in the net.

ANA. [*bitterly*] And men, I suppose, never throw off the mask when their bird is in the net. The husband never becomes negligent, selfish, brutal—oh never!

DON JUAN. What do these recriminations prove, Ana? Only that the hero is as gross an imposture as the heroine.

ANA. It is all nonsense: most marriages are perfectly comfortable.

DON JUAN. "Perfectly" is a strong expression, Ana. What you mean is that sensible people make the best of one another. Send me to the galleys and chain me to the felon whose number happens to be next before mine; and I must accept the inevitable and make the best of the companionship. Many such companionships, they tell me, are touchingly affectionate; and most are at least tolerably friendly. But that does not make a chain a desirable ornament nor the galleys an abode of bliss. Those who talk most about the blessings of marriage and the constancy of its vows are the very people who declare that if the chain were broken and the prisoners left free to choose, the whole social fabric would fly asunder. You cannot have the argument both ways. If the prisoner is happy, why lock him in? If he is not, why pretend that he is?

ANA. At all events, let me take an old woman's privilege again, and tell you flatly that marriage peoples the world and debauchery does not.

DON JUAN. How if a time comes when this shall cease to be true? Do you not know that where there is a will there is a way—that whatever Man really wishes to do he will finally discover a means of doing? Well, you have done your best, you virtuous ladies, and others of your way of thinking, to bend Man's mind wholly towards honorable love as the highest good, and to understand by honorable love romance and beauty and happiness in the possession of beautiful, refined, delicate, affectionate women. You have taught women to value their own youth, health, shapeliness, and refinement above all things. Well, what place have squalling babies and household cares in this exquisite paradise of the senses and emotions? Is it not the inevitable end of it all that the human will shall say to the human brain: Invent me a means by which I can have love, beauty, romance, emotion, passion without their wretched penalties, their expenses, their worries, their trials, their illnesses and agonies and risks of death, their retinue of servants and nurses and doctors and schoolmasters.

THE DEVIL. All this, Senor Don Juan, is realized here in my realm.

DON JUAN. Yes, at the cost of death. Man will not take it at that price: he demands the romantic delights of your hell whilst he is still on earth. Well, the means will be found: the brain will not fail when the will is in earnest. The day is coming when great nations will find their numbers dwindling from census to census; when the six roomed villa will rise in price above the family mansion; when the viciously reckless poor and the stupidly pious rich will delay the extinction of the race only by degrading it; whilst the boldly prudent, the thriftily selfish and ambitious, the imaginative and poetic, the lovers of money and solid comfort, the worshippers of success, art, and of love, will all oppose to the Force of Life the device of sterility.

THE STATUE. That is all very eloquent, my young friend; but if you had lived to Ana's age, or even to mine, you would have learned that the people who get rid of the fear of poverty and children and all the other family troubles, and devote themselves to having a good time of it, only leave their minds free for the fear of old age and ugliness and impotence and death. The childless laborer is more tormented by his wife's idleness and her constant demands for amusement and distraction than he could be by twenty children; and his wife is more wretched than he. I have had my share of vanity; for as a young man I was admired by women; and as a statue I am praised by art critics. But I confess that had I found nothing to do in the world but wallow in these delights I should have cut my throat. When I married Ana's mother—or perhaps, to be strictly correct, I should rather say when I at last gave in and allowed Ana's mother to marry me—I knew that I was planting thorns in my pillow, and that marriage for me, a swaggering young officer thitherto unvanquished, meant defeat and capture.

ANA. [*scandalized*] Father!

THE STATUE. I am sorry to shock you, my love; but since Juan has stripped every rag of decency from the discussion I may as well tell the frozen truth.

ANA. Hmf! I suppose I was one of the thorns.

THE STATUE. By no means: you were often a rose. You see, your mother had most of the trouble you gave.

DON JUAN. Then may I ask, Commander, why you have left Heaven to come here and wallow, as you express it, in sentimental beatitudes which you confess would once have driven you to cut your throat?

THE STATUE. [*struck by this*] Egad, that's true.

THE DEVIL. [*alarmed*] What! You are going back from your word. [*To Don Juan*] And all your philosophizing has been nothing but a mask for proselytizing! [*To the Statue*] Have you forgotten already the hideous dulness from which I am offering you a refuge here? [*To Don Juan*] And does your demonstration of the approaching sterilization and extinction of mankind lead to anything better than making the most of those pleasures of art and love which you yourself admit refined you, elevated you, developed you?

DON JUAN. I never demonstrated the extinction of mankind. Life cannot will its own extinction either in its blind amorphous state or in any of the forms into which it has organized itself. I had not finished when His Excellency interrupted me.

THE STATUE. I begin to doubt whether you ever will finish, my friend. You are extremely fond of hearing yourself talk.

DON JUAN. True; but since you have endured so much you may as well endure to the end. Long before this sterilization which I described becomes more than a clearly foreseen possibility, the reaction will begin. The great central purpose of breeding the race, ay, breeding it to heights now deemed superhuman: that purpose which is now hidden in a mephitic cloud of love and romance and prudery and fastidiousness, will break through into clear sunlight as a purpose no longer to be confused with the gratification of personal fancies, the impossible realization of boys' and girls' dreams of bliss, or the need of older people for companionship or money. The plain-spoken marriage services of the vernacular Churches will no longer be abbreviated and half suppressed as indelicate. The sober decency, earnestness and authority of their declaration of the real purpose of marriage will be honored and accepted, whilst their romantic vowings and pledgings and until-death-do-us-partings and the like will be expunged as unbearable frivolities. Do my sex the justice to admit, Senora, that we have always recognized that the sex relation is not a personal or friendly relation at all.

ANA. Not a personal or friendly relation! What relation is more personal? more sacred? more holy?

DON JUAN. Sacred and holy, if you like, Ana, but not personally friendly. Your relation to God is sacred and holy: dare you call it personally friendly? In the sex relation the universal creative energy, of which the parties are both the helpless agents, overrides and sweeps away all personal considerations and dispenses with all personal relations. The pair may be utter strangers to one another, speaking different languages, differing in race and color, in age and disposition, with no bond between them but a possibility of that fecundity for the sake of which the Life Force throws them into one another's arms at the exchange of a glance. Do we not recognize this by allowing marriages to be made by parents without consulting the woman? Have you not often expressed your disgust at the immorality of the English nation, in which women and men of noble birth become acquainted and court each other like peasants? And how much does even the peasant know of his bride or she of him before he engages himself? Why, you would not make a man your lawyer or your family doctor on so slight an acquaintance as you would fall in love with and marry him!

ANA. Yes, Juan: we know the libertine's philosophy. Always ignore the consequences to the woman.

DON JUAN. The consequences, yes: they justify her fierce grip of the man. But surely you do not call that attachment a sentimental one. As well call the policeman's attachment to his prisoner a love relation.

ANA. You see you have to confess that marriage is necessary, though, according to you, love is the slightest of all the relations.

DON JUAN. How do you know that it is not the greatest of all the relations? far too great to be a personal matter. Could your father have served his country if he had refused to kill any enemy of Spain unless he personally hated him? Can a woman serve her country if she refuses to marry any man she does not personally love? You know it is not so: the woman of noble birth marries as the man of noble birth fights, on political and family grounds, not on personal ones.

THE STATUE. [*impressed*] A very clever point that, Juan: I must think it over. You are really full of ideas. How did you come to think of this one?

DON JUAN. I learnt it by experience. When I was on earth, and made those proposals to ladies which, though universally condemned, have made me so interesting a hero of legend, I was not infrequently met in some such way as this. The lady would say that she would countenance my advances, provided they were honorable. On inquiring what that proviso meant, I found that it meant that I proposed to get possession of her property if she had any, or to undertake her support for life if she had not; that I desired her continual companionship, counsel and conversation to the end of my days, and would bind myself under penalties to be always enraptured by them; and, above all, that I would turn my back on all other women for ever for her sake. I did not object to these conditions because they were exorbitant and inhuman: it was their extraordinary irrelevance that prostrated me. I invariably replied with perfect frankness that I had never dreamt of any of these things; that unless the lady's character and intellect were equal or superior to my own, her conversation must degrade and her counsel mislead me; tha t her constant companionship might, for all I knew, become intolerably tedious to me; that I could not answer for my feelings for a week in advance, much less to the end of my life; that to cut me off from all natural and unconstrained relations with the rest of my fellow creatures would narrow and warp me if I submitted to it, and, if not, would bring me under the curse of clandestinity; that, finally, my proposals to her were wholly unconnected with any of these matters, and were the outcome of a perfectly simple impulse of my manhood towards her womanhood.

ANA. You mean that it was an immoral impulse.

DON JUAN. Nature, my dear lady, is what you call immoral. I blush for it; but I cannot help it. Nature is a pandar, Time a wrecker, and Death a murderer. I have always preferred to stand up to those facts and build institutions on their recognition. You prefer to propitiate the three devils by proclaiming their chastity, their thrift, and their loving kindness; and to base your institutions on these flatteries. Is it any wonder that the institutions do not work smoothly?

THE STATUE. What used the ladies to say, Juan?

DON JUAN. Oh, come! Confidence for confidence. First tell me what you used to say to the ladies.

THE STATUE. I! Oh, I swore that I would be faithful to the death; that I should die if they refused me; that no woman could ever be to me what she was—

ANA. She? Who?

THE STATUE. Whoever it happened to be at the time, my dear. I had certain things I always said. One of them was that even when I was eighty, one white hair of the woman I loved would make me tremble more than the thickest gold tress from the most beautiful young head. Another was that I could not bear the thought of anyone else being the mother of my children.

DON JUAN. [*revolted*] You old rascal!

THE STATUE. [*Stoutly*] Not a bit; for I really believed it with all my soul at the moment. I had a heart: not like you. And it was this sincerity that made me successful.

DON JUAN. Sincerity! To be fool enough to believe a ramping, stamping, thumping lie: that is what you call sincerity! To be so greedy for a woman that you deceive yourself in your eagerness to deceive her: sincerity, you call it!

THE STATUE. Oh, damn your sophistries! I was a man in love, not a lawyer. And the women loved me for it, bless them!

DON JUAN. They made you think so. What will you say when I tell you that though I played the lawyer so callously, they made me think so too? I also had my moments of infatuation in which I gushed nonsense and believed it. Sometimes the desire to give pleasure by saying beautiful things so rose in me on the flood of emotion that I said them recklessly. At other times I argued against myself with a devilish coldness that drew tears. But I found it just as hard to escape in the one case as in the others. When the lady's instinct was set on me, there was nothing for it but lifelong servitude or flight.

ANA. You dare boast, before me and my father, that every woman found you irresistible.

DON JUAN. Am I boasting? It seems to me that I cut the most pitiable of figures. Besides, I said "when the lady's instinct was set on me." It was not always so; and then, heavens! what transports of virtuous indignation! what overwhelming defiance to the dastardly seducer! what scenes of Imogen and Iachimo!

ANA. I made no scenes. I simply called my father.

DON JUAN. And he came, sword in hand, to vindicate outraged honor and morality by murdering me.

THE STATUE. Murdering! What do you mean? Did I kill you or did you kill me?

DON JUAN. Which of us was the better fencer?

THE STATUE. I was.

DON JUAN. Of course you were. And yet you, the hero of those scandalous adventures you have just been relating to us, you had the effrontery to pose as the avenger of outraged morality and condemn me to death! You would have slain me but for an accident.

THE STATUE. I was expected to, Juan. That is how things were arranged on earth. I was not a social reformer; and I always did what it was customary for a gentleman to do.

DON JUAN. That may account for your attacking me, but not for the revolting hypocrisy of your subsequent proceedings as a statue.

THE STATUE. That all came of my going to Heaven.

THE DEVIL. I still fail to see, Senor Don Juan, that these episodes in your earthly career and in that of the Senor Commander in any way discredit my view of life. Here, I repeat, you have all that you sought without anything that you shrank from.

DON JUAN. On the contrary, here I have everything that disappointed me without anything that I have not already tried and found wanting. I tell you that as long as I can conceive something better than myself I cannot be easy unless I am striving to bring it into existence or clearing the way for it. That is the law of my life. That is the working within me of Life's incessant aspiration to higher organization, wider, deeper, intenser self-consciousness, and clearer self-understanding. It was the supremacy of this purpose that reduced love for me to the mere pleasure of a moment, art for me to the mere schooling of my faculties, religion for me to a mere excuse for laziness, since it had set up a God who looked at the world and saw that it was good, against the instinct in me that looked through my eyes at the world and saw that it could be improved. I tell you that in the pursuit of my own pleasure, my own health, my own fortune, I have never known happiness. It was not love for Woman that delivered me into her hands: it was fatigue, exhaustion. When I was a child, and bruised my head against a stone, I ran to the nearest woman and cried away my pain against her apron. When I grew up, and bruised my soul against the brutalities and stupidities with which I had to strive, I did again just what I had done as a child. I have enjoyed, too, my rests, my recuperations, my breathing times, my very prostrations after strife; but rather would I be dragged through all the circles of the foolish Italian's Inferno than through the pleasures of Europe. That is what has made this place of eternal pleasures so deadly to me. It is the absence of this instinct in you that makes you that strange monster called a Devil. It is the success with which you have diverted the attention of men from their real purpose, which in one degree or another is the same as mine, to yours, that has earned you the name of The Tempter. It is the fact that they are doing your will, or rather drifting with your want of will, instead of doing their own, that makes them the uncomfortable, false, restless, artificial, petulant, wretched creatures they are.

THE DEVIL. [*mortified*] Senor Don Juan: you are uncivil to my friends.

DON JUAN. Pooh! why should I be civil to them or to you? In this Palace of Lies a truth or two will not hurt you. Your friends are all the dullest dogs I know. They are not beautiful: they are only decorated. They are not clean: they are only shaved and starched. They are not dignified: they are only fashionably dressed. They are not educated they are only college passmen. They are not religious: they are only pewrenters. They are not moral: they are only conventional. They are not virtuous: they are only cowardly. They are not even vicious: they are only "frail." They are not artistic: they are only lascivious. They are not prosperous: they are only rich. They are not loyal, they are only servile; not dutiful, only sheepish; not public spirited, only patriotic; not courageous, only quarrelsome; not determined, only obstinate; not masterful, only domineering; not self-controlled, only obtuse; not self-respecting, only vain; not kind, only sentimental; not social, only gregarious; not considerate, only polite; not intelligent, only opinionated; not progressive, only factious; not imaginative, only superstitious; not just, only vindictive; not generous, only propitiatory; not disciplined, only cowed; and not truthful at all—liars every one of them, to the very backbone of their souls.

THE STATUE. Your flow of words is simply amazing, Juan. How I wish I could have talked like that to my soldiers.

THE DEVIL. It is mere talk, though. It has all been said before; but what change has it ever made? What notice has the world ever taken of it?

DON JUAN. Yes, it is mere talk. But why is it mere talk? Because, my friend, beauty, purity, respectability, religion, morality, art, patriotism, bravery and the rest are nothing but words which I or anyone else can turn inside out like a glove. Were they realities, you would have to plead guilty to my indictment; but fortunately for your self-respect, my diabolical friend, they are not realities. As you say, they are mere words, useful for duping barbarians into adopting civilization, or the civilized poor into submitting to be robbed and enslaved. That is the family secret of the governing caste; and if we who are of that caste aimed at more Life for the world instead of at more power and luxury for our miserable selves, that secret would make us great. Now, since I, being a nobleman, am in the secret too, think how tedious to me must be your unending cant about all these moralistic figments, and how squalidly disastrous your sacrifice of your lives to them! If you even believed in your moral game enough to play it fairly, it would be interesting to watch; but you don't: you cheat at every trick; and if your opponent outcheats you, you upset the table and try to murder him.

THE DEVIL. On earth there may be some truth in this, because the people are uneducated and cannot appreciate my religion of love and beauty; but here—

DON JUAN. Oh yes: I know. Here there is nothing but love and beauty. Ugh! it is like sitting for all eternity at the first act of a fashionable play, before the complications begin. Never in my worst moments of superstitious terror on earth did I dream that Hell was so horrible. I live, like a hairdresser, in the continual contemplation of beauty, toying with silken tresses. I breathe an atmosphere of sweetness, like a confectioner's shopboy. Commander: are there any beautiful women in Heaven?

THE STATUE. None. Absolutely none. All dowdies. Not two pennorth of jewellery among a dozen of them. They might be men of fifty.

DON JUAN. I am impatient to get there. Is the word beauty ever mentioned; and are there any artistic people?

THE STATUE. I give you my word they won't admire a fine statue even when it walks past them.

DON JUAN. I go.

THE DEVIL. Don Juan: shall I be frank with you?

DON JUAN. Were you not so before?

THE DEVIL. As far as I went, yes. But I will now go further, and confess to you that men get tired of everything, of heaven no less than of hell; and that all history is nothing but a record of the oscillations of the world between these two extremes. An epoch is but a swing of the pendulum; and each generation thinks the world is progressing because it is always moving. But when you are as old as I am; when you have a thousand times wearied of heaven, like myself and the Commander, and a thousand times wearied of hell, as you are wearied now, you will no longer imagine that every swing from heaven to hell is an emancipation, every swing from hell to heaven an evolution. Where you now see reform, progress, fulfilment of upward tendency, continual ascent by Man on the stepping stones of his dead selves to higher things, you will see nothing but an infinite comedy of illusion. You will discover the profound truth of the saying of my friend Koheleth, that there is nothing new under the sun. Vanitas vanitatum—

DON JUAN. [*out of all patience*] By Heaven, this is worse than your cant about love and beauty. Clever dolt that you are, is a man no better than a worm, or a dog than a wolf, because he gets tired of everything? Shall he give up eating because he destroys his appetite in the act of gratifying it? Is a field idle when it is fallow? Can the Commander expend his hellish energy here without accumulating heavenly energy for his next term of blessedness? Granted that the great Life Force has hit on the device of the clockmaker's pendulum, and uses the earth for its bob; that the history of each oscillation, which seems so novel to us the actors, is but the history of the last oscillation repeated; nay more, that in the unthinkable infinitude of time the sun throws off the earth and catches it again a thousand times as a circus rider throws up a ball, and that the total of all our epochs is but the moment between the toss and the catch, has the colossal mechanism no purpose?

THE DEVIL. None, my friend. You think, because you have a purpose, Nature must have one. You might as well expect it to have fingers and toes because you have them.

DON JUAN. But I should not have them if they served no purpose. And I, my friend, am as much a part of Nature as my own finger is a part of me. If my finger is the organ by which I grasp the sword and the mandoline, my brain is the organ by which Nature strives to understand itself. My dog's brain serves only my dog's purposes; but my brain labors at a knowledge which does nothing for me personally but make my body bitter to me and my decay and death a calamity. Were I not possessed with a purpose beyond my own I had better be a ploughman than a philosopher; for the ploughman lives as long as the philosopher, eats more, sleeps better, and rejoices in the wife of his bosom with less misgiving. This is because the philosopher is in the grip of the Life Force. This Life Force says to him "I have done a thousand wonderful things unconsciously by merely willing to live and following the line of least resistance: now I want to know myself and my destination, and choose my path; so I have made a special brain—a philosopher's brain—to grasp this knowledge for me as the husbandman's hand grasps the plough for me. And this" says the Life Force to the philosopher "must thou strive to do for me until thou diest, when I will make another brain and another philosopher to carry on the work."

THE DEVIL. What is the use of knowing?

DON JUAN. Why, to be able to choose the line of greatest advantage instead of yielding in the direction of the least resistance. Does a ship sail to its destination no better than a log drifts nowhither? The philosopher is Nature's pilot. And there you have our difference: to be in hell is to drift: to be in heaven is to steer.

THE DEVIL. On the rocks, most likely.

DON JUAN. Pooh! which ship goes oftenest on the rocks or to the bottom—the drifting ship or the ship with a pilot on board?

THE DEVIL. Well, well, go your way, Senor Don Juan. I prefer to be my own master and not the tool of any blundering universal force. I know that beauty is good to look at; that music is good to hear; that love is good to feel; and that they are all good to think about and talk about. I know that to be well exercised in these sensations, emotions, and studies is to be a refined and cultivated being. Whatever they may say of me in churches on earth, I know that it is universally admitted in good society that the prince of Darkness is a gentleman; and that is enough for me. As to your Life Force, which you think irresistible, it is the most resistible thing in the world for a person of any character. But if you are naturally vulgar and credulous, as all reformers are, it will thrust you first into religion, where you will sprinkle water on babies to save their souls from me; then it will drive you from religion into science, where you will snatch the babies from the water sprinkling and inoculate them with disease to save them from catching it accidentally; then you will take to politics, where you will become the catspaw of corrupt functionaries and the henchman of ambitious humbugs; and the end will be despair and decrepitude, broken nerve and shattered hopes, vain regrets for that worst and silliest of wastes and sacrifices, the waste and sacrifice of the power of enjoyment: in a word, the punishment of the fool who pursues the better before he has secured the good.

DON JUAN. But at least I shall not be bored. The service of the Life Force has that advantage, at all events. So fare you well, Senor Satan.

THE DEVIL. [*amiably*] Fare you well, Don Juan. I shall often think of our interesting chats about things in general. I wish you every happiness: Heaven, as I said before, suits some people. But if you should change your mind, do not forget that the gates are always open here to the repentant prodigal. If you feel at any time that warmth of heart, sincere unforced affection, innocent enjoyment, and warm, breathing, palpitating reality—

DON JUAN. Why not say flesh and blood at once, though we have left those two greasy commonplaces behind us?

THE DEVIL. [*angrily*] You throw my friendly farewell back in my teeth, then, Don Juan?

DON JUAN. By no means. But though there is much to be learnt from a cynical devil, I really cannot stand a sentimental one. Senor Commander: you know the way to the frontier of hell and heaven. Be good enough to direct me.

THE STATUE. Oh, the frontier is only the difference between two ways of looking at things. Any road will take you across it if you really want to get there.

DON JUAN. Good. [*saluting Dona Ana*] Senora: your servant.

ANA. But I am going with you.

DON JUAN. I can find my own way to heaven, Ana; but I cannot find yours [*he vanishes*].

ANA. How annoying!

THE STATUE. [*calling after him*] Bon voyage, Juan! [*He wafts a final blast of his great rolling chords after him as a parting salute. A faint echo of the first ghostly melody comes back in acknowledgment*]. Ah! there he goes. [*Puffing a long breath out through his lips*] Whew! How he does talk! They'll never stand it in heaven.

THE DEVIL. [*gloomily*] His going is a political defeat. I cannot keep these Life Worshippers: they all go. This is the greatest loss I have had since that Dutch painter went—a fellow who would paint a hag of 70 with as much enjoyment as a Venus of 20.

THE STATUE. I remember: he came to heaven. Rembrandt.

THE DEVIL. Ay, Rembrandt. There a something unnatural about these fellows. Do not listen to their gospel, Senor Commander: it is dangerous. Beware of the pursuit of the Superhuman: it leads to an indiscriminate contempt for the Human. To a man, horses and dogs and cats are mere species, outside the moral world. Well, to the Superman, men and women are a mere species too, also outside the moral world. This Don Juan was kind to women and courteous to men as your daughter here was kind to her pet cats and dogs; but such kindness is a denial of the exclusively human character of the soul.

THE STATUE. And who the deuce is the Superman?

THE DEVIL. Oh, the latest fashion among the Life Force fanatics. Did you not meet in Heaven, among the new arrivals, that German Polish madman—what was his name? Nietzsche?

THE STATUE. Never heard of him.

THE DEVIL. Well, he came here first, before he recovered his wits. I had some hopes of him; but he was a confirmed Life Force worshipper. It was he who raked up the Superman, who is as old as Prometheus; and the 20th century will run after this newest of the old crazes when it gets tired of the world, the flesh, and your humble servant.

THE STATUE. Superman is a good cry; and a good cry is half the battle. I should like to see this Nietzsche.

THE DEVIL. Unfortunately he met Wagner here, and had a quarrel with him.

THE STATUE. Quite right, too. Mozart for me!

THE DEVIL. Oh, it was not about music. Wagner once drifted into Life Force worship, and invented a

Superman called Siegfried. But he came to his senses afterwards. So when they met here, Nietzsche denounced him as a renegade; and Wagner wrote a pamphlet to prove that Nietzsche was a Jew; and it ended in Nietzsche's going to heaven in a huff. And a good riddance too. And now, my friend, let us hasten to my palace and celebrate your arrival with a grand musical service.

THE STATUE. With pleasure: you're most kind.

THE DEVIL. This way, Commander. We go down the old trap [*he places himself on the grave trap*].

THE STATUE. Good. [*Reflectively*] All the same, the Superman is a fine conception. There is something statuesque about it. [*He places himself on the grave trap beside The Devil. It begins to descend slowly. Red glow from the abyss*]. Ah, this reminds me of old times.

THE DEVIL. And me also.

ANA. Stop! [*The trap stops*].

THE DEVIL. You, Senora, cannot come this way. You will have an apotheosis. But you will be at the palace before us.

ANA. That is not what I stopped you for. Tell me where can I find the Superman?

THE DEVIL. He is not yet created, Senora.

THE STATUE. And never will be, probably. Let us proceed: the red fire will make me sneeze. [*They descend*].

ANA. Not yet created! Then my work is not yet done. [*Crossing herself devoutly*] I believe in the Life to Come. [*Crying to the universe*] A father—a father for the Superman!

She vanishes into the void; and again there is nothing: all existence seems suspended infinitely. Then, vaguely, there is a live human voice crying somewhere. One sees, with a shock, a mountain peak showing faintly against a lighter background. The sky has returned from afar; and we suddenly remember where we were. The cry becomes distinct and urgent: it says Automobile, Automobile. The complete reality comes back with a rush: in a moment it is full morning in the Sierra; and the brigands are scrambling to their feet and making for the road as the goatherd runs down from the hill, warning them of the approach of another motor. Tanner and Mendoza rise amazedly and stare at one another with scattered wits. Straker sits up to yawn for a moment before he gets on his feet, making it a point of honor not to show any undue interest in the excitement of the bandits. Mendoza gives a quick look to see that his followers are attending to the alarm; then exchanges a private word with Tanner.

MENDOZA. Did you dream?

TANNER. Damnably. Did you?

MENDOZA. Yes. I forget what. You were in it.

TANNER. So were you. Amazing

MENDOZA. I warned you. [*a shot is heard from the road*]. Dolts! they will play with that gun. [*The brigands come running back scared*]. Who fired that shot? [*to Duval*] Was it you?

DUVAL. [*breathless*] I have not shoot. Dey shoot first.

ANARCHIST. I told you to begin by abolishing the State. Now we are all lost.

THE ROWDY SOCIAL-DEMOCRAT. [*stampeding across the amphitheatre*] Run, everybody.

MENDOZA. [*collaring him; throwing him on his back; and drawing a knife*] I stab the man who stirs. [*He blocks the way. The stampede it checked*]. What has happened?

THE SULKY SOCIAL-DEMOCRAT, A motor—

THE ANARCHIST. Three men—

DUVAL. Deux femmes—

MENDOZA. Three men and two women! Why have you not brought them here? Are you afraid of them?

THE ROWDY ONE. [*getting up*] Thyve a hescort. Ow, de-ooh lut's ook it, Mendowza.

THE SULKY ONE. Two armored cars full o soldiers at the end o the valley.

ANARCHIST. The shot was fired in the air. It was a signal.

Straker whistles his favorite air, which falls on the ears of the brigands like a funeral march.

TANNER. It is not an escort, but an expedition to capture you. We were advised to wait for it; but I was in a hurry.

THE ROWDY ONE. [*in an agony of apprehension*] And Ow my good Lord, ere we are, wytin for em! Lut's tike to the mahntns.

MENDOZA. Idiot, what do you know about the mountains? Are you a Spaniard? You would be given up by the first shepherd you met. Besides, we are already within range of their rifles.

THE ROWDY ONE. Bat—

MENDOZA. Silence. Leave this to me. [*To Tanner*] Comrade: you will not betray us.

STRAKER. Oo are you callin comrade?

MENDOZA. Last night the advantage was with me. The robber of the poor was at the mercy of the robber of the rich. You offered your hand: I took it.

TANNER. I bring no charge against you, comrade. We have spent a pleasant evening with you: that is all.

STRAKER. I gev my and to nobody, see?

MENDOZA. [*turning on him impressively*] Young man, if I am tried, I shall plead guilty, and explain what drove me from England, home and duty. Do you wish to have the respectable name of Straker dragged through the mud of a Spanish criminal court? The police will search me. They will find Louisa's portrait. It will be published in the illustrated papers. You blench. It will be your doing, remember.

STRAKER. [*with baffled rage*] I don't care about the court. It's avin our name mixed up with yours that I object to, you blackmailin swine, you.

MENDOZA. Language unworthy of Louisa's brother! But no matter: you are muzzled: that is enough for us. [*He turns to face his own men, who back uneasily across the amphitheatre towards the cave to take refuge behind him, as a fresh party, muffled for motoring, comes from the road in riotous spirits. Ann, who makes straight for Tanner, comes first; then Violet, helped over the rough ground by Hector holding her right hand and Ramsden her left. Mendoza goes to his presidential block and seats himself calmly with his rank and file grouped behind him, and his Staff, consisting of Duval and the Anarchist on his right and the two Social-Democrats on his left, supporting him in flank*].

ANN. It's Jack!

TANNER. Caught!

HECTOR. Why, certainly it is. I said it was you, Tanner, We've just been stopped by a puncture: the road is full of nails.

VIOLET. What are you doing here with all these men?

ANN. Why did you leave us without a word of warning?

HECTOR. I want that bunch of roses, Miss Whitefield. [*To Tanner*] When we found you were gone, Miss Whitefield bet me a bunch of roses my car would not overtake yours before you reached Monte Carlo.

TANNER. But this is not the road to Monte Carlo.

HECTOR. No matter. Miss Whitefield tracked you at every stopping place: she is a regular Sherlock Holmes.

TANNER. The Life Force! I am lost.

OCTAVIUS. [*Bounding gaily down from the road into the amphitheatre, and coming between Tanner and Straker*] I am so glad you are safe, old chap. We were afraid you had been captured by brigands.

RAMSDEN. [*who has been staring at Mendoza*] I seem to remember the face of your friend here. [*Mendoza rises politely and advances with a smile between Ann and Ramsden*].

HECTOR. Why, so do I.

OCTAVIUS. I know you perfectly well, Sir; but I can't think where I have met you.

MENDOZA. [*to Violet*] Do YOU remember me, madam?

VIOLET. Oh, quite well; but I am so stupid about names.

MENDOZA. It was at the Savoy Hotel. [*To Hector*] You, sir, used to come with this lady [*Violet*] to lunch. [*To Octavius*] You, sir, often brought this lady [*Ann*] and her mother to dinner on your way to the Lyceum Theatre. [*To Ramsden*] You, sir, used to come to supper, with [*dropping his voice to a confidential but perfectly audible whisper*] several different ladies.

RAMSDEN. [*angrily*] Well, what is that to you, pray?

OCTAVIUS. Why, Violet, I thought you hardly knew one another before this trip, you and Malone!

VIOLET. [*vexed*] I suppose this person was the manager.

MENDOZA. The waiter, madam. I have a grateful recollection of you all. I gathered from the bountiful way in which you treated me that you all enjoyed your visits very much.

VIOLET. What impertinence! [*She turns her back on him, and goes up the hill with Hector*].

RAMSDEN. That will do, my friend. You do not expect these ladies to treat you as an acquaintance, I suppose, because you have waited on them at table.

MENDOZA. Pardon me: it was you who claimed my acquaintance. The ladies followed your example. However, this display of the unfortunate manners of your class closes the incident. For the future, you will please address me with the respect due to a stranger and fellow traveller. [*He turns haughtily away and resumes his presidential seat*].

TANNER. There! I have found one man on my journey capable of reasonable conversation; and you all instinctively insult him. Even the New Man is as bad as any of you. Enry: you have behaved just like a miserable gentleman.

STRAKER. Gentleman! Not me.

RAMSDEN. Really, Tanner, this tone—

ANN. Don't mind him, Granny: you ought to know him by this time [*she takes his arm and coaxes him away to the hill to join Violet and Hector. Octavius follows her, doglike*].

VIOLET. [*calling from the hill*] Here are the soldiers. They are getting out of their motors.

DUVAL. [*panicstricken*] Oh, nom de Dieu!

THE ANARCHIST. Fools: the State is about to crush you because you spared it at the prompting of the political hangers-on of the bourgeoisie.

THE SULKY SOCIAL-DEMOCRAT. [*argumentative to the last*] On the contrary, only by capturing the State machine—

THE ANARCHIST. It is going to capture you.

THE ROWDY SOCIAL-DEMOCRAT. [*his anguish culminating*] Ow, chock it. Wot are we ere for? WOT are we wytin for?

MENDOZA. [*between his teeth*] Goon. Talk politics, you idiots: nothing sounds more respectable. Keep it up, I tell you.

The soldiers line the road, commanding the amphitheatre with their rifles. The brigands, struggling with an over-whelming impulse to hide behind one another, look as unconcerned as they can. Mendoza rises superbly, with undaunted front. The officer in command steps down from the road in to the amphitheatre; looks hard at the brigands; and then inquiringly at Tanner.

THE OFFICER. Who are these men, Senor Ingles?

TANNER. My escort.

Mendoza, with a Mephistophelean smile, bows profoundly. An irrepressible grin runs from face to face among the brigands. They touch their hats, except the Anarchist, who defies the State with folded arms.

ACT IV

The garden of a villa in Granada. Whoever wishes to know what it is like must go to Granada and see. One may prosaically specify a group of hills dotted with villas, the Alhambra on the top of one of the hills, and a considerable town in the valley, approached by dusty white roads in which the children, no matter what they are doing or thinking about, automatically whine for halfpence and reach out little clutching brown palms for them; but there is nothing in this description except the Alhambra, the begging, and the color of the roads, that does not fit Surrey as well as Spain. The difference is that the Surrey hills are comparatively small and ugly, and should properly be called the Surrey Protuberances; but these Spanish hills are of mountain stock: the amenity which conceals their size does not compromise their dignity.

This particular garden is on a hill opposite the Alhambra; and the villa is as expensive and pretentious as a villa must be if it is to be let furnished by the week to opulent American and English visitors. If we stand on the lawn at the foot of the garden and look uphill, our horizon is the stone balustrade of a flagged platform on the edge of infinite space at the top of the hill. Between us and this platform is a flower garden with a circular basin and fountain in the centre, surrounded by geometrical flower beds, gravel paths, and clipped yew trees in the genteelest order. The garden is higher than our lawn; so we reach it by a few steps in the middle of its embankment. The platform is higher again than the garden, from which we mount a couple more steps to look over the balustrade at a fine view of the town up the valley and of the hills that stretch away beyond it to where, in the remotest distance, they become mountains. On our left is the villa, accessible by steps from the left hand corner of the garden. Returning from the platform through the garden and down again to the lawn (a movement which leaves the villa behind us on our right) we find evidence of literary interests on the part of the tenants in the fact that there is no tennis net nor set of croquet hoops, but, on our left, a little iron garden table with books on it, mostly yellow-backed, and a chair beside it. A chair on the right has also a couple of open books upon it. There are no newspapers, a circumstance which, with the absence of games, might lead an intelligent spectator to the most far reaching conclusions as to the sort of people who live in the villa. Such speculations are checked, however, on this delightfully fine afternoon, by the appearance at a little gate in a paling an our left, of Henry Straker in his professional costume. He opens the gate for an elderly gentleman, and follows him on to the lawn.

This elderly gentleman defies the Spanish sun in a black frock coat, tall silk bat, trousers in which narrow stripes of dark grey and lilac blend into a highly respectable color, and a black necktie tied into a bow over spotless linen. Probably therefore a man whose social position needs constant and scrupulous affirmation without regard to climate: one who would dress thus for the middle of the Sahara or the top of

Mont Blanc. And since he has not the stamp of the class which accepts as its life-mission the advertizing and maintenance of first rate tailoring and millinery, he looks vulgar in his finery, though in a working dress of any kind he would look dignified enough. He is a bullet cheeked man with a red complexion, stubbly hair, smallish eyes, a hard mouth that folds down at the corners, and a dogged chin. The looseness of skin that comes with age has attacked his throat and the laps of his cheeks; but he is still hard as an apple above the mouth; so that the upper half of his face looks younger than the lower. He has the self-confidence of one who has made money, and something of the truculence of one who has made it in a brutalizing struggle, his civility having under it a perceptible menace that he has other methods in reserve if necessary. Withal, a man to be rather pitied when he is not to be feared; for there is something pathetic about him at times, as if the huge commercial machine which has worked him into his frock coat had allowed him very little of his own way and left his affections hungry and baffled. At the first word that falls from him it is clear that he is an Irishman whose native intonation has clung to him through many changes of place and rank. One can only guess that the original material of his speech was perhaps the surly Kerry brogue; but the degradation of speech that occurs in London, Glasgow, Dublin and big cities generally has been at work on it so long that nobody but an arrant cockney would dream of calling it a brogue now; for its music is almost gone, though its surliness is still perceptible. Straker, as a very obvious cockney, inspires him with implacable contempt, as a stupid Englishman who cannot even speak his own language properly. Straker, on the other hand, regards the old gentleman's accent as a joke thoughtfully provided by Providence expressly for the amusement of the British race, and treats him normally with the indulgence due to an inferior and unlucky species, but occasionally with indignant alarm when the old gentleman shows signs of intending his Irish nonsense to be taken seriously.

STRAKER. I'll go tell the young lady. She said you'd prefer to stay here [*he turns to go up through the garden to the villa*].

MALONE. [*who has been looking round him with lively curiosity*] The young lady? That's Miss Violet, eh?

STRAKER. [*stopping on the steps with sudden suspicion*] Well, you know, don't you?

MALONE. Do I?

STRAKER. [*his temper rising*] Well, do you or don't you?

MALONE. What business is that of yours?

Straker, now highly indignant, comes back from the steps and confronts the visitor.

STRAKER. I'll tell you what business it is of mine. Miss Robinson—

MALONE. [*interrupting*] Oh, her name is Robinson, is it? Thank you.

STRAKER. Why, you don't know even her name?

MALONE. Yes I do, now that you've told me.

STRAKER. [*after a moment of stupefaction at the old man's readiness in repartee*] Look here: what do you mean by gittin into my car and lettin me bring you here if you're not the person I took that note to?

MALONE. Who else did you take it to, pray?

STRAKER. I took it to Mr Ector Malone, at Miss Robinson's request, see? Miss Robinson is not my principal: I took it to oblige her. I know Mr Malone; and he ain't you, not by a long chalk. At the hotel they told me that your name is Ector Malone.

MALONE. Hector Malone.

STRAKER. [*with calm superiority*] Hector in your own country: that's what comes o livin in provincial places like Ireland and America. Over here you're Ector: if you avn't noticed it before you soon will.

The growing strain of the conversation is here relieved by Violet, who has sallied from the villa and through the garden to the steps, which she now descends, coming very opportunely between Malone and Straker.

VIOLET. [*to Straker*] Did you take my message?

STRAKER. Yes, miss. I took it to the hotel and sent it up, expecting to see young Mr Malone. Then out walks this gent, and says it's all right and he'll come with me. So as the hotel people said he was Mr Ector Malone, I fetched him. And now he goes back on what he said. But if he isn't the gentleman you meant, say the word: it's easy enough to fetch him back again.

MALONE. I should esteem it a great favor if I might have a short conversation with you, madam. I am Hector's father, as this bright Britisher would have guessed in the course of another hour or so.

STRAKER. [*coolly defiant*] No, not in another year or so. When we've ad you as long to polish up as we've ad im, perhaps you'll begin to look a little bit up to is mark. At present you fall a long way short. You've got too many aitches, for one thing. [*To Violet, amiably*] All right, Miss: you want to talk to him: I shan't intrude. [*He nods affably to Malone and goes out through the little gate in the paling*].

VIOLET. [*very civilly*] I am so sorry, Mr Malone, if that man has been rude to you. But what can we do? He is our chauffeur.

MALONE. Your what?

VIOLET. The driver of our automobile. He can drive a motor car at seventy miles an hour, and mend it when it breaks down. We are dependent on our motor cars; and our motor cars are dependent on him; so of course we are dependent on him.

MALONE. I've noticed, madam, that every thousand dollars an Englishman gets seems to add one to the number of people he's dependent on. However, you needn't apologize for your man: I made him talk on purpose. By doing so I learnt that you're staying here in Grannida with a party of English, including my son Hector.

VIOLET. [*conversationally*] Yes. We intended to go to Nice; but we had to follow a rather eccentric member of our party who started first and came here. Won't you sit down? [*She clears the nearest chair of the two books on it*].

MALONE. [*impressed by this attention*] Thank you. [*He sits down, examining her curiously as she goes to the iron table to put down the books. When she turns to him again, he says*] Miss Robinson, I believe?

VIOLET. [*sitting down*] Yes.

MALONE. [*Taking a letter from his pocket*] Your note to Hector runs as follows [*Violet is unable to repress a start. He pauses quietly to take out and put on his spectacles, which have gold rims*]: "Dearest: they have all gone to the Alhambra for the afternoon. I have shammed headache and have the garden all to myself. Jump into Jack's motor: Straker will rattle you here in a jiffy. Quick, quick, quick. Your loving Violet." [*He looks at her; but by this time she has recovered herself, and meets his spectacles with perfect composure. He continues slowly*] Now I don't know on what terms young people associate in English society; but in America that note would be considered to imply a very considerable degree of affectionate intimacy between the parties.

VIOLET. Yes: I know your son very well, Mr Malone. Have you any objection?

MALONE. [*somewhat taken aback*] No, no objection exactly. Provided it is understood that my son is altogether dependent on me, and that I have to be consulted in any important step he may propose to take.

VIOLET. I am sure you would not be unreasonable with him, Mr Malone.

MALONE. I hope not, Miss Robinson; but at your age you might think many things unreasonable that don't seem so to me.

VIOLET. [*with a little shrug*] Oh well, I suppose there's no use our playing at cross purposes, Mr Malone. Hector wants to marry me.

MALONE. I inferred from your note that he might. Well, Miss Robinson, he is his own master; but if he marries you he shall not have a rap from me. [*He takes off his spectacles and pockets them with the note*].

VIOLET. [*with some severity*] That is not very complimentary to me, Mr Malone.

MALONE. I say nothing against you, Miss Robinson: I daresay you are an amiable and excellent young lady. But I have other views for Hector.

VIOLET. Hector may not have other views for himself, Mr Malone.

MALONE. Possibly not. Then he does without me: that's all. I daresay you are prepared for that. When a young lady writes to a young man to come to her quick, quick, quick, money seems nothing and love seems everything.

VIOLET. [*sharply*] I beg your pardon, Mr Malone: I do not think anything so foolish. Hector must have money.

MALONE. [*staggered*] Oh, very well, very well. No doubt he can work for it.

VIOLET. What is the use of having money if you have to work for it? [*She rises impatiently*]. It's all nonsense, Mr Malone: you must enable your son to keep up his position. It is his right.

MALONE. [*grimly*] I should not advise you to marry him on the strength of that right, Miss Robinson.

Violet, who has almost lost her temper, controls herself with an effort; unclenches her fingers; and resumes her seat with studied tranquillity and reasonableness.

VIOLET. What objection have you to me, pray? My social position is as good as Hector's, to say the least. He admits it.

MALONE. [*shrewdly*] You tell him so from time to time, eh? Hector's social position in England, Miss Robinson, is just what I choose to buy for him. I have made him a fair offer. Let him pick out the most historic house, castle or abbey that England contains. The day that he tells me he wants it for a wife worthy of its traditions, I buy it for him, and give him the means of keeping it up.

VIOLET. What do you mean by a wife worthy of its traditions? Cannot any well bred woman keep such a house for him?

MALONE. No: she must be born to it.

VIOLET. Hector was not born to it, was he?

MALONE. His granmother was a barefooted Irish girl that nursed me by a turf fire. Let him marry another such, and I will not stint her marriage portion. Let him raise himself socially with my money or raise somebody else so long as there is a social profit somewhere, I'll regard my expenditure as justified. But there must be a profit for someone. A marriage with you would leave things just where they are.

VIOLET. Many of my relations would object very much to my marrying the grandson of a common woman, Mr Malone. That may be prejudice; but so is your desire to have him marry a title prejudice.

MALONE. [*rising, and approaching her with a scrutiny in which there is a good deal of reluctant respect*] You seem a pretty straightforward downright sort of a young woman.

VIOLET. I do not see why I should be made miserably poor because I cannot make profits for you. Why do you want to make Hector unhappy?

MALONE. He will get over it all right enough. Men thrive better on disappointments in love than on disappointments in money. I daresay you think that sordid; but I know what I'm talking about. My father died of starvation in Ireland in the black 47, Maybe you've heard of it.

VIOLET. The Famine?

MALONE. [*with smouldering passion*] No, the starvation. When a country is full of food, and exporting it, there can be no famine. My father was starved dead; and I was starved out to America in my mother's arms. English rule drove me and mine out of Ireland. Well, you can keep Ireland. I and my like are coming back to buy England; and we'll buy the best of it. I want no middle class properties and no middle class women for Hector. That's straightforward isn't it, like yourself?

VIOLET. [*icily pitying his sentimentality*] Really, Mr Malone, I am astonished to hear a man of your age and good sense talking in that romantic way. Do you suppose English noblemen will sell their places to you for the asking?

MALONE. I have the refusal of two of the oldest family mansions in England. One historic owner can't afford to keep all the rooms dusted: the other can't afford the death duties. What do you say now?

VIOLET. Of course it is very scandalous; but surely you know that the Government will sooner or later put a stop to all these Socialistic attacks on property.

MALONE. [*grinning*] D'y' think they'll be able to get that done before I buy the house—or rather the abbey? They're both abbeys.

VIOLET. [*putting that aside rather impatiently*] Oh, well, let us talk sense, Mr Malone. You must feel that we haven't been talking sense so far.

MALONE. I can't say I do. I mean all I say.

VIOLET. Then you don't know Hector as I do. He is romantic and faddy—he gets it from you, I fancy—and he wants a certain sort of wife to take care of him. Not a faddy sort of person, you know.

MALONE. Somebody like you, perhaps?

VIOLET. [*quietly*] Well, yes. But you cannot very well ask me to undertake this with absolutely no means of keeping up his position.

MALONE. [*alarmed*] Stop a bit, stop a bit. Where are we getting to? I'm not aware that I'm asking you to undertake anything.

VIOLET. Of course, Mr Malone, you can make it very difficult for me to speak to you if you choose to misunderstand me.

MALONE. [*half bewildered*] I don't wish to take any unfair advantage; but we seem to have got off the straight track somehow.

Straker, with the air of a man who has been making haste, opens the little gate, and admits Hector, who, snorting with indignation, comes upon the lawn, and is making for his father when Violet, greatly dismayed, springs up and intercepts him. Straker doer not wait; at least he does not remain visibly within earshot.

VIOLET. Oh, how unlucky! Now please, Hector, say nothing. Go away until I have finished speaking to your father.

HECTOR. [*inexorably*] No, Violet: I mean to have this thing out, right away. [*He puts her aside; passes her by; and faces his father, whose cheeks darken as his Irish blood begins to simmer*]. Dad: you've not played this hand straight.

MALONE. Hwat d'y'mean?

HECTOR. You've opened a letter addressed to me. You've impersonated me and stolen a march on this lady. That's dishonorable.

MALONE. [*threateningly*] Now you take care what you're saying, Hector. Take care, I tell you.

HECTOR. I have taken care. I am taking care. I'm taking care of my honor and my position in English society.

MALONE. [*hotly*] Your position has been got by my money: do you know that?

HECTOR. Well, you've just spoiled it all by opening that letter. A letter from an English lady, not addressed to you—a confidential letter! a delicate letter! a private letter opened by my father! That's a sort of thing a man can't struggle against in England. The sooner we go back together the better. [*He appeals mutely to the heavens to witness the shame and anguish of two outcasts*].

VIOLET. [*snubbing him with an instinctive dislike for scene making*] Don't be unreasonable, Hector. It was quite natural of Mr Malone to open my letter: his name was on the envelope.

MALONE. There! You've no common sense, Hector. I thank you, Miss Robinson.

HECTOR. I thank you, too. It's very kind of you. My father knows no better.

MALONE. [*furiously clenching his fists*] Hector—

HECTOR. [*with undaunted moral force*] Oh, it's no use hectoring me. A private letter's a private letter, dad: you can't get over that.

MALONE [*raising his voice*] I won't be talked back to by you, d'y' hear?

VIOLET. Ssh! please, please. Here they all come.

Father and son, checked, glare mutely at one another as Tanner comes in through the little gate with Ramsden, followed by Octavius and Ann.

VIOLET. Back already!

TANNER. The Alhambra is not open this afternoon.

VIOLET. What a sell!

Tanner passes on, and presently finds himself between Hector and a strange elder, both apparently on the verge of personal combat. He looks from one to the other for an explanation. They sulkily avoid his eye, and nurse their wrath in silence.

RAMSDEN. Is it wise for you to be out in the sunshine with such a headache, Violet?

TANNER. Have you recovered too, Malone?

VIOLET. Oh, I forgot. We have not all met before. Mr Malone: won't you introduce your father?

HECTOR. [*with Roman firmness*] No, I will not. He is no father of mine.

MALONE. [*very angry*] You disown your dad before your English friends, do you?

VIOLET. Oh please don't make a scene.

Ann and Octavius, lingering near the gate, exchange an astonished glance, and discreetly withdraw up the steps to the garden, where they can enjoy the disturbance without intruding. On their way to the steps Ann sends a little grimace of mute sympathy to Violet, who is standing with her back to the little table, looking on in helpless annoyance as her husband soars to higher and higher moral eminences without the least regard to the old man's mil-millions.

HECTOR. I'm very sorry, Miss Robinson; but I'm contending for a principle. I am a son, and, I hope, a dutiful one; but before everything I'm a Man!!! And when dad treats my private letters as his own, and takes it on himself to say that I shan't marry you if I am happy and fortunate enough to gain your consent, then I just snap my fingers and go my own way.

TANNER. Marry Violet!

RAMSDEN. Are you in your senses?

TANNER. Do you forget what we told you?

HECTOR. [*recklessly*] I don't care what you told me.

RAMSDEN. [*scandalized*] Tut tut, sir! Monstrous! [*he flings away towards the gate, his elbows quivering with indignation*]

TANNER. Another madman! These men in love should be locked up. [*He gives Hector up as hopeless, and turns away towards the garden, but Malone, taking offence in a new direction, follows him and compels him, by the aggressivenes of his tone, to stop*].

MALONE. I don't understand this. Is Hector not good enough for this lady, pray?

TANNER. My dear sir, the lady is married already. Hector knows it; and yet he persists in his infatuation. Take him home and lock him up.

MALONE. [*bitterly*] So this is the high-born social tone I've spoilt by my ignorant, uncultivated behavior! Makin love to a married woman! [*He comes angrily between Hector and Violet, and almost bawls into Hector's left ear*] You've picked up that habit of the British aristocracy, have you?

HECTOR. That's all right. Don't you trouble yourself about that. I'll answer for the morality of what I'm doing.

TANNER. [*coming forward to Hector's right hand with flashing eyes*] Well said, Malone! You also see that mere marriage laws are not morality! I agree with you; but unfortunately Violet does not.

MALONE. I take leave to doubt that, sir. [*Turning on Violet*] Let me tell you, Mrs Robinson, or whatever your right name is, you had no right to send that letter to my son when you were the wife of another man.

HECTOR. [*outraged*] This is the last straw. Dad: you have insulted my wife.

MALONE. YOUR wife!

TANNER. YOU the missing husband! Another moral impostor! [*He smites his brow, and collapses into Malone's chair*].

MALONE. You've married without my consent!

RAMSDEN. You have deliberately humbugged us, sir!

HECTOR. Here: I have had just about enough of being badgered. Violet and I are married: that's the long and the short of it. Now what have you got to say—any of you?

MALONE. I know what I've got to say. She's married a beggar.

HECTOR. No; she's married a Worker [*his American pronunciation imparts an overwhelming intensity to this simple and unpopular word*]. I start to earn my own living this very afternoon.

MALONE. [*sneering angrily*] Yes: you're very plucky now, because you got your remittance from me yesterday or this morning, I reckon. Wait til it's spent. You won't be so full of cheek then.

HECTOR. [*producing a letter from his pocket-book*] Here it is [*thrusting it on his father*]. Now you just take your remittance and yourself out of my life. I'm done with remittances; and I'm done with you. I don't sell the privilege of insulting my wife for a thousand dollars.

MALONE. [*deeply wounded and full of concern*] Hector: you don't know what poverty is.

HECTOR. [*fervidly*] Well, I want to know what it is. I want'be a Man. Violet: you come along with me, to your own home: I'll see you through.

OCTAVIUS. [*jumping down from the garden to the lawn and running to Hector's left hand*] I hope you'll shake hands with me before you go, Hector. I admire and respect you more than I can say. [*He is affected almost to tears as they shake hands*].

VIOLET. [*also almost in tears, but of vexation*] Oh don't be an idiot, Tavy. Hector's about as fit to become a workman as you are.

TANNER. [*rising from his chair on the other ride of Hector*] Never fear: there's no question of his becoming a navvy, Mrs Malone. [*To Hector*] There's really no difficulty about capital to start with. Treat me as a friend: draw on me.

OCTAVIUS. [*impulsively*] Or on me.

MALONE. [*with fierce jealousy*] Who wants your dirty money? Who should he draw on but his own father? [*Tanner and Octavius recoil, Octavius rather hurt, Tanner consoled by the solution of the money difficulty. Violet looks up hopefully*]. Hector: don't be rash, my boy. I'm sorry for what I said: I never meant to insult Violet: I take it all back. She's just the wife you want: there!

HECTOR. [*Patting him on the shoulder*] Well, that's all right, dad. Say no more: we're friends again. Only, I take no money from anybody.

MALONE. [*pleading abjectly*] Don't be hard on me, Hector. I'd rather you quarrelled and took the money than made friends and starved. You don't know what the world is: I do.

HECTOR. No, no, NO. That's fixed: that's not going to change. [*He passes his father inexorably by, and goes to Violet*]. Come, Mrs Malone: you've got to move to the hotel with me, and take your proper place before the world.

VIOLET. But I must go in, dear, and tell Davis to pack. Won't you go on and make them give you a room overlooking the garden for me? I'll join you in half an hour.

HECTOR. Very well. You'll dine with us, Dad, won't you?

MALONE. [*eager to conciliate him*] Yes, yes.

HECTOR. See you all later. [*He waves his hand to Ann, who has now been joined by Tanner, Octavius, and Ramsden in the garden, and goes out through the little gate, leaving his father and Violet together on the lawn*].

MALONE. You'll try to bring him to his senses, Violet: I know you will.

VIOLET. I had no idea he could be so headstrong. If he goes on like that, what can I do?

MALONE. Don't be discurridged: domestic pressure may be slow; but it's sure. You'll wear him down. Promise me you will.

VIOLET. I will do my best. Of course I think it's the greatest nonsense deliberately making us poor like that.

MALONE. Of course it is.

VIOLET. [*after a moment's reflection*] You had better give me the remittance. He will want it for his hotel bill. I'll see whether I can induce him to accept it. Not now, of course, but presently.

MALONE. [*eagerly*] Yes, yes, yes: that's just the thing [*he hands her the thousand dollar bill, and adds cunningly*] Y'understand that this is only a bachelor allowance.

VIOLET. [*Coolly*] Oh, quite. [*She takes it*]. Thank you. By the way, Mr Malone, those two houses you mentioned—the abbeys.

MALONE. Yes?

VIOLET. Don't take one of them until I've seen it. One never knows what may be wrong with these places.

MALONE. I won't. I'll do nothing without consulting you, never fear.

VIOLET. [*politely, but without a ray of gratitude*] Thanks: that will be much the best way. [*She goes calmly back to the villa, escorted obsequiously by Malone to the upper end of the garden*].

TANNER. [*drawing Ramsden's attention to Malone's cringing attitude as he takes leave of Violet*] And that poor devil is a billionaire! one of the master spirits of the age! Led on a string like a pug dog by the first girl who takes the trouble to despise him. I wonder will it ever come to that with me. [*He comes down to the lawn.*]

RAMSDEN. [*following him*] The sooner the better for you.

MALONE. [*clapping his hands as he returns through the garden*] That'll be a grand woman for Hector. I wouldn't exchange her for ten duchesses. [*He descends to the lawn and comes between Tanner and Ramsden*].

RAMSDEN. [*very civil to the billionaire*] It's an unexpected pleasure to find you in this corner of the world, Mr Malone. Have you come to buy up the Alhambra?

MALONE. Well, I don't say I mightn't. I think I could do better with it than the Spanish government. But that's not what I came about. To tell you the truth, about a month ago I overheard a deal between two men over a bundle of shares. They differed about the price: they were young and greedy, and didn't know that if the shares were worth what was bid for them they must be worth what was asked, the margin being too small to be of any account, you see. To amuse meself, I cut in and bought the shares. Well, to this day I haven't found out what the business is. The office is in this town; and the name is Mendoza, Limited. Now whether Mendoza's a mine, or a steamboat line, or a bank, or a patent article—

TANNER. He's a man. I know him: his principles are thoroughly commercial. Let us take you round the town in our motor, Mr Malone, and call on him on the way.

MALONE. If you'll be so kind, yes. And may I ask who—

TANNER. Mr Roebuck Ramsden, a very old friend of your daughter-in-law.

MALONE. Happy to meet you, Mr Ramsden.

RAMSDEN. Thank you. Mr Tanner is also one of our circle.

MALONE. Glad to know you also, Mr Tanner.

TANNER. Thanks. [*Malone and Ramsden go out very amicably through the little gate. Tanner calls to Octavius, who is wandering in the garden with Ann*] Tavy! [*Tavy comes to the steps, Tanner whispers loudly to him*] Violet has married a financier of brigands. [*Tanner hurries away to overtake Malone and Ramsden. Ann strolls to the steps with an idle impulse to torment Octavius*].

ANN. Won't you go with them, Tavy?

OCTAVIUS. [*tears suddenly flushing his eyes*] You cut me to the heart, Ann, by wanting me to go [*he comes down on the lawn to hide his face from her. She follows him caressingly*].

ANN. Poor Ricky Ticky Tavy! Poor heart!

OCTAVIUS. It belongs to you, Ann. Forgive me: I must speak of it. I love you. You know I love you.

ANN. What's the good, Tavy? You know that my mother is determined that I shall marry Jack.

OCTAVIUS. [*amazed*] Jack!

ANN. It seems absurd, doesn't it?

OCTAVIUS. [*with growing resentment*] Do you mean to say that Jack has been playing with me all this time? That he has been urging me not to marry you because he intends to marry you himself?

ANN. [*alarmed*] No no: you mustn't lead him to believe that I said that: I don't for a moment think that Jack knows his own mind. But it's clear from my father's will that he wished me to marry Jack. And my mother is set on it.

OCTAVIUS. But you are not bound to sacrifice yourself always to the wishes of your parents.

ANN. My father loved me. My mother loves me. Surely their wishes are a better guide than my own selfishness.

OCTAVIUS. Oh, I know how unselfish you are, Ann. But believe me—though I know I am speaking in my own interest—there is another side to this question. Is it fair to Jack to marry him if you do not love him? Is it fair to destroy my happiness as well as your own if you can bring yourself to love me?

ANN. [*looking at him with a faint impulse of pity*] Tavy, my dear, you are a nice creature—a good boy.

OCTAVIUS. [*humiliated*] Is that all?

ANN. [*mischievously in spite of her pity*] That's a great deal, I assure you. You would always worship the ground I trod on, wouldn't you?

OCTAVIUS. I do. It sounds ridiculous; but it's no exaggeration. I do; and I always shall.

ANN. Always is a long word, Tavy. You see, I shall have to live up always to your idea of my divinity; and I don't think I could do that if we were married. But if I marry Jack, you'll never be disillusioned—at least not until I grow too old.

OCTAVIUS. I too shall grow old, Ann. And when I am eighty, one white hair of the woman I love will make me tremble more than the thickest gold tress from the most beautiful young head.

ANN. [*quite touched*] Oh, that's poetry, Tavy, real poetry. It gives me that strange sudden sense of an echo from a former existence which always seems to me such a striking proof that we have immortal souls.

OCTAVIUS. Do you believe that is true?

ANN. Tavy, if it is to become true you must lose me as well as love me.

OCTAVIUS. Oh! [*he hastily sits down at the little table and covers his face with his hands*].

ANN. [*with conviction*] Tavy: I wouldn't for worlds destroy your illusions. I can neither take you nor let you go. I can see exactly what will suit you. You must be a sentimental old bachelor for my sake.

OCTAVIUS. [*desperately*] Ann: I'll kill myself.

ANN. Oh no you won't: that wouldn't be kind. You won't have a bad time. You will be very nice to women; and you will go a good deal to the opera. A broken heart is a very pleasant complaint for a man in London if he has a comfortable income.

OCTAVIUS. [*considerably cooled, but believing that he is only recovering his self-control*] I know you mean to be kind, Ann. Jack has persuaded you that cynicism is a good tonic for me. [*He rises with quiet dignity*].

ANN. [*studying him slyly*] You see, I'm disillusionizing you already. That's what I dread.

OCTAVIUS. You do not dread disillusionizing Jack.

ANN. [*her face lighting up with mischievous ecstasy—whispering*] I can't: he has no illusions about me. I shall surprise Jack the other way. Getting over an unfavorable impression is ever so much easier than living up to an ideal. Oh, I shall enrapture Jack sometimes!

OCTAVIUS. [*resuming the calm phase of despair, and beginning to enjoy his broken heart and delicate attitude without knowing it*] I don't doubt that. You will enrapture him always. And he—the fool!—thinks you would make him wretched.

ANN. Yes: that's the difficulty, so far.

OCTAVIUS. [*heroically*] Shall I tell him that you love?

ANN. [*quickly*] Oh no: he'd run away again.

OCTAVIUS. [*shocked*] Ann: would you marry an unwilling man?

ANN. What a queer creature you are, Tavy! There's no such thing as a willing man when you really go for him. [*She laughs naughtily*]. I'm shocking you, I suppose. But you know you are really getting a sort of satisfaction already in being out of danger yourself.

OCTAVIUS [*startled*] Satisfaction! [*Reproachfully*] You say that to me!

ANN. Well, if it were really agony, would you ask for more of it?

OCTAVIUS. Have I asked for more of it?

ANN. You have offered to tell Jack that I love him. That's self-sacrifice, I suppose; but there must be some satisfaction in it. Perhaps it's because you're a poet. You are like the bird that presses its breast against the sharp thorn to make itself sing.

OCTAVIUS. It's quite simple. I love you; and I want you to be happy. You don't love me; so I can't make you happy myself; but I can help another man to do it.

ANN. Yes: it seems quite simple. But I doubt if we ever know why we do things. The only really simple thing is to go straight for what you want and grab it. I suppose I don't love you, Tavy; but sometimes I feel as if I should like to make a man of you somehow. You are very foolish about women.

OCTAVIUS. [*almost coldly*] I am content to be what I am in that respect.

ANN. Then you must keep away from them, and only dream about them. I wouldn't marry you for worlds, Tavy.

OCTAVIUS. I have no hope, Ann: I accept my ill luck. But I don't think you quite know how much it hurts.

ANN. You are so softhearted! It's queer that you should be so different from Violet. Violet's as hard as nails.

OCTAVIUS. Oh no. I am sure Violet is thoroughly womanly at heart.

ANN. [*with some impatience*] Why do you say that? Is it unwomanly to be thoughtful and businesslike and sensible? Do you want Violet to be an idiot—or something worse, like me?

OCTAVIUS. Something worse—like you! What do you mean, Ann?

ANN. Oh well, I don't mean that, of course. But I have a great respect for Violet. She gets her own way always.

OCTAVIUS. [*sighing*] So do you.

ANN. Yes; but somehow she gets it without coaxing—without having to make people sentimental about her.

OCTAVIUS. [*with brotherly callousness*] Nobody could get very sentimental about Violet, I think, pretty as she is.

ANN. Oh yes they could, if she made them.

OCTAVIUS. But surely no really nice woman would deliberately practise on men's instincts in that way.

ANN. [*throwing up her hands*] Oh Tavy, Tavy, Ricky Ticky Tavy, heaven help the woman who marries you!

OCTAVIUS. [*his passion reviving at the name*] Oh why, why, why do you say that? Don't torment me. I don't understand.

ANN. Suppose she were to tell fibs, and lay snares for men?

OCTAVIUS. Do you think I could marry such a woman—I, who have known and loved you?

ANN. Hm! Well, at all events, she wouldn't let you if she were wise. So that's settled. And now I can't talk any more. Say you forgive me, and that the subject is closed.

OCTAVIUS. I have nothing to forgive; and the subject is closed. And if the wound is open, at least you shall never see it bleed.

ANN. Poetic to the last, Tavy. Goodbye, dear. [*She pats his check; has an impulse to kiss him and then another impulse of distaste which prevents her; finally runs away through the garden and into the villa*].

Octavius again takes refuge at the table, bowing his head on his arms and sobbing softly. Mrs Whitefield, who has been pottering round the Granada shops, and has a net full of little parcels in her hand, comes in through the gate and sees him.

MRS WHITEFIELD. [*running to him and lifting his head*] What's the matter, Tavy? Are you ill?

OCTAVIUS. No, nothing, nothing.

MRS WHITEFIELD. [*still holding his head, anxiously*] But you're crying. Is it about Violet's marriage?

OCTAVIUS. No, no. Who told you about Violet?

MRS WHITEFIELD. [*restoring the head to its owner*] I met Roebuck and that awful old Irishman. Are you sure you're not ill? What's the matter?

OCTAVIUS. [*affectionately*] It's nothing—only a man's broken heart. Doesn't that sound ridiculous?

MRS WHITEFIELD. But what is it all about? Has Ann been doing anything to you?

OCTAVIUS. It's not Ann's fault. And don't think for a moment that I blame you.

MRS WHITEFIELD. [*startled*] For what?

OCTAVIUS. [*pressing her hand consolingly*] For nothing. I said I didn't blame you.

MRS WHITEFIELD. But I haven't done anything. What's the matter?

OCTAVIUS. [*smiling sadly*] Can't you guess? I daresay you are right to prefer Jack to me as a husband for Ann; but I love Ann; and it hurts rather. [*He rises and moves away from her towards the middle of the lawn*].

MRS WHITEFIELD. [*following him hastily*] Does Ann say that I want her to marry Jack?

OCTAVIUS. Yes: she has told me.

MRS WHITEFIELD. [*thoughtfully*] Then I'm very sorry for you, Tavy. It's only her way of saying SHE wants to marry Jack. Little she cares what I say or what I want!

OCTAVIUS. But she would not say it unless she believed it. Surely you don't suspect Ann of—of DECEIT!!

MRS WHITEFIELD. Well, never mind, Tavy. I don't know which is best for a young man: to know too little, like you, or too much, like Jack.

Tanner returns.

TANNER. Well, I've disposed of old Malone. I've introduced him to Mendoza, Limited; and left the two brigands together to talk it out. Hullo, Tavy! anything wrong?

OCTAVIUS. I must go wash my face, I see. [*To Mrs Whitefield*] Tell him what you wish. [*To Tanner*] You may take it from me, Jack, that Ann approves of it.

TANNER. [*puzzled by his manner*] Approves of what?

OCTAVIUS. Of what Mrs Whitefield wishes. [*He goes his way with sad dignity to the villa*].

TANNER. [*to Mrs Whitefield*] This is very mysterious. What is it you wish? It shall be done, whatever it is.

MRS WHITEFIELD. [*with snivelling gratitude*] Thank you, Jack. [*She sits down. Tanner brings the other chair from the table and sits close to her with his elbows on his knees, giving her his whole attention*]. I don't know why it is that other people's children are so nice to me, and that my own have so little consideration for me. It's no wonder I don't seem able to care for Ann and Rhoda as I do for you and Tavy and Violet. It's a very queer world. It used to be so straightforward and simple; and now nobody seems to think and feel as they ought. Nothing has been right since that speech that Professor Tyndall made at Belfast.

TANNER. Yes: life is more complicated than we used to think. But what am I to do for you?

MRS WHITEFIELD. That's just what I want to tell you. Of course you'll marry Ann whether I like it myself or not—

TANNER. [*starting*] It seems to me that I shall presently be married to Ann whether I like it myself or not.

MRS WHITEFIELD. [*peacefully*] Oh, very likely you will: you know what she is when she has set her mind on anything. But don't put it on me: that's all I ask. Tavy has just let out that she's been saying that I am making her marry you; and the poor boy is breaking his heart about it; for he is in love with her himself, though what he sees in her so wonderful, goodness knows: I don't. It's no use telling Tavy that Ann puts things into people's heads by telling them that I want them when the thought of them never crossed my mind. It only sets Tavy against me. But you know better than that. So if you marry her, don't put the blame on me.

TANNER. [*emphatically*] I haven't the slightest intention of marrying her.

MRS WHITEFIELD. [*slyly*] She'd suit you better than Tavy. She'd meet her match in you, Jack. I'd like to see her meet her match.

TANNER. No man is a match for a woman, except with a poker and a pair of hobnailed boots. Not always even then. Anyhow, I can't take the poker to her. I should be a mere slave.

MRS WHITEFIELD. No: she's afraid of you. At all events, you would tell her the truth about herself. She wouldn't be able to slip out of it as she does with me.

TANNER. Everybody would call me a brute if I told Ann the truth about herself in terms of her own moral code. To begin with, Ann says things that are not strictly true.

MRS WHITEFIELD. I'm glad somebody sees she is not an angel.

TANNER. In short—to put it as a husband would put it when exasperated to the point of speaking out—she is a liar. And since she has plunged Tavy head over ears in love with her without any intention of marrying him, she is a coquette, according to the standard definition of a coquette as a woman who rouses passions she has no intention of gratifying. And as she has now reduced you to the point of being willing to sacrifice me at the altar for the mere satisfaction of getting me to call her a liar to her face, I may conclude that she is a bully as well. She can't bully men as she bullies women; so she habitually and unscrupulously uses her personal fascination to make men give her whatever she wants. That makes her almost something for which I know no polite name.

MRS WHITEFIELD. [*in mild expostulation*] Well, you can't expect perfection, Jack.

TANNER. I don't. But what annoys me is that Ann does. I know perfectly well that all this about her being a liar and a bully and a coquette and so forth is a trumped-up moral indictment which might be brought against anybody. We all lie; we all bully as much as we dare; we all bid for admiration without the least intention of earning it; we all get as much rent as we can out of our powers of fascination. If Ann would admit this I shouldn't quarrel with her. But she won't. If she has children she'll take advantage of their telling lies to amuse herself by whacking them. If another woman makes eyes at me, she'll refuse to know a coquette. She will do just what she likes herself whilst insisting on everybody else doing what the conventional code prescribes. In short, I can stand everything except her confounded hypocrisy. That's what beats me.

MRS WHITEFIELD. [*carried away by the relief of hearing her own opinion so eloquently expressed*] Oh, she is a hypocrite. She is: she is. Isn't she?

TANNER. Then why do you want to marry me to her?

MRS WHITEFIELD. [*querulously*] There now! put it on me, of course. I never thought of it until Tavy told me she said I did. But, you know, I'm very fond of Tavy: he's a sort of son to me; and I don't want him to be trampled on and made wretched.

TANNER. Whereas I don't matter, I suppose.

MRS WHITEFIELD. Oh, you are different, somehow: you are able to take care of yourself. You'd serve her out. And anyhow, she must marry somebody.

TANNER. Aha! there speaks the life instinct. You detest her; but you feel that you must get her married.

MRS WHITEFIELD. [*rising, shocked*] Do you mean that I detest my own daughter! Surely you don't believe me to be so wicked and unnatural as that, merely because I see her faults.

TANNER. [*cynically*] You love her, then?

MRS WHITEFIELD. Why, of course I do. What queer things you say, Jack! We can't help loving our own blood relations.

TANNER. Well, perhaps it saves unpleasantness to say so. But for my part, I suspect that the tables of consanguinity have a natural basis in a natural repugnance [*he rises*].

MRS WHITEFIELD. You shouldn't say things like that, Jack. I hope you won't tell Ann that I have been speaking to you. I only wanted to set myself right with you and Tavy. I couldn't sit mumchance and have everything put on me.

TANNER. [*politely*] Quite so.

MRS WHITEFIELD. [*dissatisfied*] And now I've only made matters worse. Tavy's angry with me because I don't worship Ann. And when it's been put into my head that Ann ought to marry you, what can I say except that it would serve her right?

TANNER. Thank you.

MRS WHITEFIELD. Now don't be silly and twist what I say into something I don't mean. I ought to have fair play—

Ann comes from the villa, followed presently by Violet, who is dressed for driving.

ANN. [*coming to her mother's right hand with threatening suavity*] Well, mamma darling, you seem to be having a delightful chat with Jack. We can hear you all over the place.

MRS WHITEFIELD. [*appalled*] Have you overheard—

TANNER. Never fear: Ann is only—well, we were discussing that habit of hers just now. She hasn't heard a word.

MRS WHITEFIELD. [*stoutly*] I don't care whether she has or not: I have a right to say what I please.

VIOLET. [*arriving on the lawn and coming between Mrs Whitefield and Tanner*] I've come to say goodbye. I'm off for my honeymoon.

MRS WHITEFIELD. [*crying*] Oh don't say that, Violet. And no wedding, no breakfast, no clothes, nor anything.

VIOLET. [*petting her*] It won't be for long.

MRS WHITEFIELD. Don't let him take you to America. Promise me that you won't.

VIOLET. [*very decidedly*] I should think not, indeed. Don't cry, dear: I'm only going to the hotel.

MRS WHITEFIELD. But going in that dress, with your luggage, makes one realize—[*she chokes, and then breaks out again*] How I wish you were my daughter, Violet!

VIOLET. [*soothing her*] There, there: so I am. Ann will be jealous.

MRS WHITEFIELD. Ann doesn't care a bit for me.

ANN. Fie, mother! Come, now: you mustn't cry any more: you know Violet doesn't like it [*Mrs Whitefzeld dries her eyes, and subsides*].

VIOLET. Goodbye, Jack.

TANNER. Goodbye, Violet.

VIOLET. The sooner you get married too, the better. You will be much less misunderstood.

TANNER. [*restively*] I quite expect to get married in the course of the afternoon. You all seem to have set your minds on it.

VIOLET. You might do worse. [*To Mrs Whitefield: putting her arm round her*] Let me take you to the hotel with me: the drive will do you good. Come in and get a wrap. [*She takes her towards the villa*].

MRS WHITEFIELD. [*as they go up through the garden*] I don't know what I shall do when you are gone, with no one but Ann in the house; and she always occupied with the men! It's not to be expected that your husband will care to be bothered with an old woman like me. Oh, you needn't tell me: politeness is all very well; but I know what people think—[*She talks herself and Violet out of sight and hearing*].

Ann, musing on Violet's opportune advice, approaches Tanner; examines him humorously for a moment from toe to top; and finally delivers her opinion.

ANN. Violet is quite right. You ought to get married.

TANNER. [*explosively*] Ann: I will not marry you. Do you hear? I won't, won't, won't, won't, WON'T marry you.

ANN. [*placidly*] Well, nobody axd you, sir she said, sir she said, sir she said. So that's settled.

TANNER. Yes, nobody has asked me; but everybody treats the thing as settled. It's in the air. When we meet, the others go away on absurd pretexts to leave us alone together. Ramsden no longer scowls at me: his eye beams, as if he were already giving you away to me in church. Tavy refers me to your mother and gives me his blessing. Straker openly treats you as his future employer: it was he who first told me of it.

ANN. Was that why you ran away?

TANNER. Yes, only to be stopped by a lovesick brigand and run down like a truant schoolboy.

ANN. Well, if you don't want to be married, you needn't be [*she turns away from him and sits down, much at her ease*].

TANNER. [*following her*] Does any man want to be hanged? Yet men let themselves be hanged without a struggle for life, though they could at least give the chaplain a black eye. We do the world's will, not our own. I have a frightful feeling that I shall let myself be married because it is the world's will that you should have a husband.

ANN. I daresay I shall, someday.

TANNER. But why me—me of all men? Marriage is to me apostasy, profanation of the sanctuary of my soul, violation of my manhood, sale of my birthright, shameful surrender, ignominious capitulation, acceptance of defeat. I shall decay like a thing that has served its purpose and is done with; I shall change from a man with a future to a man with a past; I shall see in the greasy eyes of all the other husbands their relief at the arrival of a new prisoner to share their ignominy. The young men will scorn me as one who has sold out: to the young women I, who have always been an enigma and a possibility, shall be merely somebody else's property—and damaged goods at that: a secondhand man at best.

ANN. Well, your wife can put on a cap and make herself ugly to keep you in countenance, like my grandmother.

TANNER. So that she may make her triumph more insolent by publicly throwing away the bait the moment the trap snaps on the victim!

ANN. After all, though, what difference would it make? Beauty is all very well at first sight; but who ever looks at it when it has been in the house three days? I thought our pictures very lovely when papa bought them; but I haven't looked at them for years. You never bother about my looks: you are too well used to me. I might be the umbrella stand.

TANNER. You lie, you vampire: you lie.

ANN. Flatterer. Why are you trying to fascinate me, Jack, if you don't want to marry me?

TANNER. The Life Force. I am in the grip of the Life Force.

ANN. I don't understand in the least: it sounds like the Life Guards.

TANNER. Why don't you marry Tavy? He is willing. Can you not be satisfied unless your prey struggles?

ANN. [*turning to him as if to let him into a secret*] Tavy will never marry. Haven't you noticed that that sort of man never marries?

TANNER. What! a man who idolizes women who sees nothing in nature but romantic scenery for love duets! Tavy, the chivalrous, the faithful, the tenderhearted and true! Tavy never marry! Why, he was born to be swept up by the first pair of blue eyes he meets in the street.

ANN. Yes, I know. All the same, Jack, men like that always live in comfortable bachelor lodgings with broken hearts, and are adored by their landladies, and never get married. Men like you always get married.

TANNER. [*Smiting his brow*] How frightfully, horribly true! It has been staring me in the face all my life; and I never saw it before.

ANN. Oh, it's the same with women. The poetic temperament's a very nice temperament, very amiable, very harmless and poetic, I daresay; but it's an old maid's temperament.

TANNER. Barren. The Life Force passes it by.

ANN. If that's what you mean by the Life Force, yes.

TANNER. You don't care for Tavy?

ANN. [*looking round carefully to make sure that Tavy is not within earshot*] No.

TANNER. And you do care for me?

ANN. [*rising quietly and shaking her finger at him*] Now Jack! Behave yourself.

TANNER. Infamous, abandoned woman! Devil!

ANN. Boa-constrictor! Elephant!

TANNER. Hypocrite!

ANN. [*Softly*] I must be, for my future husband's sake.

TANNER. For mine! [*Correcting himself savagely*] I mean for his.

ANN.[*ignoring the correction*] Yes, for yours. You had better marry what you call a hypocrite, Jack. Women who are not hypocrites go about in rational dress and are insulted and get into all sorts of hot water. And then their husbands get dragged in too, and live in continual dread of fresh complications. Wouldn't you prefer a wife you could depend on?

TANNER. No, a thousand times no: hot water is the revolutionist's element. You clean men as you clean milkpails, by scalding them.

ANN. Cold water has its uses too. It's healthy.

TANNER. [*despairingly*] Oh, you are witty: at the supreme moment the Life Force endows you with every quality. Well, I too can be a hypocrite. Your father's will appointed me your guardian, not your suitor. I shall be faithful to my trust.

ANN. [*in low siren tones*] He asked me who would I have as my guardian before he made that will. I chose you!

TANNER. The will is yours then! The trap was laid from the beginning.

ANN. [*concentrating all her magic*] From the beginning from our childhood—for both of us—by the Life Force.

TANNER. I will not marry you. I will not marry you.

ANN. Oh; you will, you will.

TANNER. I tell you, no, no, no.

ANN. I tell you, yes, yes, yes.

TANNER. NO.

ANN. [*coaxing—imploring—almost exhausted*] Yes. Before it is too late for repentance. Yes.

TANNER. [*struck by the echo from the past*] When did all this happen to me before? Are we two dreaming?

ANN. [*suddenly losing her courage, with an anguish that she does not conceal*] No. We are awake; and you have said no: that is all.

TANNER. [*brutally*] Well?

ANN. Well, I made a mistake: you do not love me.

TANNER. [*seizing her in his arms*] It is false: I love you. The Life Force enchants me: I have the whole world in my arms when I clasp you. But I am fighting for my freedom, for my honor, for myself, one and indivisible.

ANN. Your happiness will be worth them all.

TANNER. You would sell freedom and honor and self for happiness?

ANN. It will not be all happiness for me. Perhaps death.

TANNER. [*groaning*] Oh, that clutch holds and hurts. What have you grasped in me? Is there a father's heart as well as a mother's?

ANN. Take care, Jack: if anyone comes while we are like this, you will have to marry me.

TANNER. If we two stood now on the edge of a precipice, I would hold you tight and jump.

ANN. [*panting, failing more and more under the strain*] Jack: let me go. I have dared so frightfully—it is lasting longer than I thought. Let me go: I can't bear it.

TANNER. Nor I. Let it kill us.

ANN. Yes: I don't care. I am at the end of my forces. I don't care. I think I am going to faint.

At this moment Violet and Octavius come from the villa with Mrs Whitefield, who is wrapped up for driving. Simultaneously Malone and Ramsden, followed by Mendoza and Straker, come in through the little gate in the paling. Tanner shamefacedly releases Ann, who raises her hand giddily to her forehead.

MALONE. Take care. Something's the matter with the lady.

RAMSDEN. What does this mean?

VIOLET. [*running between Ann and Tanner*] Are you ill?

ANN. [*reeling, with a supreme effort*] I have promised to marry Jack. [*She swoons. Violet kneels by her and chafes her band. Tanner runs round to her other hand, and tries to lift her bead. Octavius goes to Violet's assistance, but does not know what to do. Mrs Whitefield hurries back into the villa. Octavius, Malone and Ramsden run to Ann and crowd round her, stooping to assist. Straker coolly comes to Ann's feet, and Mendoza to her head, both upright and self-possessed*].

STRAKER. Now then, ladies and gentlemen: she don't want a crowd round her: she wants air—all the air she can git. If you please, gents— [*Malone and Ramsden allow him to drive them gently past Ann and up the lawn towards the garden, where Octavius, who has already become conscious of his uselessness, joins them. Straker, following them up, pauses for a moment to instruct Tanner*]. Don't lift er ed, Mr Tanner: let it go flat so's the blood can run back into it.

MENDOZA. He is right, Mr Tanner. Trust to the air of the Sierra. [*He withdraws delicately to the garden steps*].

TANNER. [*rising*] I yield to your superior knowledge of physiology, Henry. [*He withdraws to the corner of the lawn; and Octavius immediately hurries down to him*].

TAVY. [*aside to Tanner, grasping his hand*] Jack: be very happy.

TANNER. [*aside to Tavy*] I never asked her. It is a trap for me. [*He goes up the lawn towards the garden. Octavius remains petrified*].

MENDOZA. [*intercepting Mrs Whitefield, who comes from the villa with a glass of brandy*] What is this, madam [*he takes it from her*]?

MRS WHITEFIELD. A little brandy.

MENDOZA. The worst thing you could give her. Allow me. [*He swallows it*]. Trust to the air of the Sierra, madam.

For a moment the men all forget Ann and stare at Mendoza.

ANN. [*in Violet's ear, clutching her round the neck*] Violet, did Jack say anything when I fainted?

VIOLET. No.

ANN. Ah! [*with a sigh of intense relief she relapses*].

MRS WHITEFIELD. Oh, she's fainted again.

They are about to rush back to her; but Mendoza stops them with a warning gesture.

ANN. [*supine*] No I haven't. I'm quite happy.

TANNER. [*suddenly walking determinedly to her, and snatching her hand from Violet to feel her pulse*] Why, her pulse is positively bounding. Come, getup. What nonsense! Up with you. [*He gets her up summarily*].

ANN. Yes: I feel strong enough now. But you very nearly killed me, Jack, for all that.

MALONE. A rough wooer, eh? They're the best sort, Miss Whitefield. I congratulate Mr Tanner; and I hope to meet you and him as frequent guests at the Abbey.

ANN. Thank you. [*She goes past Malone to Octavius*] Ricky Ticky Tavy: congratulate me. [*Aside to him*] I want to make you cry for the last time.

TAVY. [*steadfastly*] No more tears. I am happy in your happiness. And I believe in you in spite of everything.

RAMSDEN. [*coming between Malone and Tanner*] You are a happy man, Jack Tanner. I envy you.

MENDOZA. [*advancing between Violet and Tanner*] Sir: there are two tragedies in life. One is not to get your heart's desire. The other is to get it. Mine and yours, sir.

TANNER. Mr Mendoza: I have no heart's desires. Ramsden: it is very easy for you to call me a happy man: you are only a spectator. I am one of the principals; and I know better. Ann: stop tempting Tavy, and come back to me.

ANN. [*complying*] You are absurd, Jack. [*She takes his proffered arm*].

TANNER. [*continuing*] I solemnly say that I am not a happy man. Ann looks happy; but she is only triumphant, successful, victorious. That is not happiness, but the price for which the strong sell their happiness. What we have both done this afternoon is to renounce tranquillity, above all renounce the romantic possibilities of an unknown future, for the cares of a household and a family. I beg that no man may seize the occasion to get half drunk and utter imbecile speeches and coarse pleasantries at my expense. We propose to furnish our own house according to our own taste; and I hereby give notice that the seven or eight travelling clocks, the four or five dressing cases, the salad bowls, the carvers and fish slices, the copy of Tennyson in extra morocco, and all the other articles you are preparing to heap upon us, will be instantly sold, and the proceeds devoted to circulating free copies of the Revolutionist's Handbook. The wedding will take place three days after our return to England, by special license, at the office of the district superintendent registrar, in the presence of my solicitor and his clerk, who, like his clients, will be in ordinary walking dress.

VIOLET. [*with intense conviction*] You are a brute, Jack.

ANN. [*looking at him with fond pride and caressing his arm*] Never mind her, dear. Go on talking.

TANNER. Talking!

Universal laughter.

PASSION, POISON, AND PETRIFACTION

or
THE FATAL GAZOGENE

PASSION, POISON, AND PETRIFACTION

This tragedy was written at the request of Mr Cyril Maude, under whose direction it was performed repeatedly, with colossal: success, in a booth in Regent's Park, for the benefit of The Actors' Orphanage, on the 14th July 1905, by Miss Irene Vanbrugh, Miss Nancy Price, Mr G. P. Hundey, Mr Cyril Maude, Mr Eric Lewis, Mr Arthur Williams, and Mr Lerinox Pawle.

As it is extremely difficult to find an actor capable of eating a real ceiling, it will be found convenient in performance to substitute the tops of old wedding cakes for bits of plaster. There is but little difference in material between the two substances; but the taste of the wedding cake is considered more agreeable by many people.

The orchestra should consist of at least a harp, a drum, and a pair of cymbals, these instruments being the most useful in enhancing the stage effect.

The landlord may with equal propriety be a landlady, if that arrangement be better suited to the resources of the company.

As the Bill Bailey song has not proved immortal, any equally appropriate ditty of the moment may be substituted.

In a bed-sitting room in a fashionable quarter of London a lady sits at her dressing-table, with her maid combing her hair. It is late. and the electric lamps are glowing. Apparently the room is bedless, but there stands against the opposite wall to that at which the dressing-table is placed a piece of furniture that suggests a bookcase without carrying con-conviction. On the same side is a chest of drawers of that disastrous kind which, recalcitrant to the opener until she is provoked to violence, then suddenly come wholly out and defy all her efforts to fit them in again. Opposite this chest of drawers, on the lady's side of the room, is a cupboard. The presence of a row of gentleman's boots beside the chest of drawers proclaims that the lady is married. Her own boots are beside the cupboard. The third wall is pierced midway by the door, above which is a cuckoo clock. Near the door a pedestal bears a portrait bust of the lady in plaster. There is a fan on the dressing-table, a hatbox and rug strap on the chest of drawers, an umbrella and a bootjack against the wall near the bed. The general impression is one of brightness, beauty, and social ambition, damped by somewhat inadequate means. A certain air of theatricality is produced by the fact that though the room is rectangular it has only three walls. Not a sound is heard except the overture and the crackling of the lady's hair as the maid's brush draws electric sparks from it in the dry air of the London midsummer. The cuckoo clock strikes sixteen.

THE LADY. How much did the clock strike, Phyllis?

PHYLLIS. Sixteen, my lady.

THB LADY. That means eleven o'clock, does it not?

PHYLLIS. Eleven at night, my lady. In the morning it means half-past two; so if you hear it strike sixteen during your slumbers, do not rise.

THE LADY. I will not, Phyllis. Phyllis: I am weary. I will go to bed. Prepare my couch.

Phyllis crosses the room to the bookcase and touches a button. The front of the bookcase falls out with a crash and becomes a bed. A roll of distant thunder echoes the crash.

PHYLLIS [*shuddering*] It is a terrible night Heaven help all poor mariners at sea! My master is late. I trust nothing has happened to him. Your bed is ready, my lady.

THE LADY. Thank you, Phyllis. [*She rises and approaches the bed.*] Goodnight.

PHYLLIS. Will your ladyship not undress?

THE LADY. Not tonight, Phyllis. [*Glancing through where the fourth wall is missing*] Not under the circumstances.

PHYLLIS [*impulsively throwing herself on her knees by her mistress's side, and clasping her round the waist*] *Oh, my beloved mistress, I know not why or how; but I feel that I shall* never see you alive again. There is murder in the air. [*Thunder.*] Hark!

THE LADY. Strange! As I sat there methought I heard angels singing. "Oh, wont you come home. Bill Bailey?" Why should angels call me Bill Bailey? My name is Magnesia Fitztollemache.

PHYLLIS [*emphasizing the title*] Lady Magnesia Fitztollemache.

LADY MAGNESIA. In case we should never again meet in this world, let us take a last farewell.

PHYLLIS [*embracing her with tears*] My poor murdered angel mistress!

LADY MAGNESIA. In case we should meet again, call me at half-past eleven.

PHYLLIS. I will, I will.

Phyllis withdraws, overcome by emotion. Lady Magnesia switches off the electric light, and immediately hears the angels quite distinctly. They sing Bill Bailey so sweetly that she can attend to nothing else and forgets to remove even her boots as she draws the coverlet over herself and sinks to sleep, lulled by celestial harmony. A white radiance plays on her pillow, and lights up her beautiful face. But the thunder growls again, and a lurid red glow concentrates itself on the door, which is presently flung open, revealing a saturnine figure in evening dress, partially concealed by a crimson cloak. As he steals towards the bed the unnatural glare in his eyes and the broad-bladed dagger nervously gripped in his right hand bode ill for the sleeping lady. Providentially she sneezes on the very brink of eternity, and the tension of the murderer's nerves is such that he bolts precipitately under the bed at the sudden and startling ***Atscha!*** *A dull, heavy, rhythmic thumping—the beating of his heart—betrays his whereabouts. Soon he emerges cautiously and raises his head above the bed coverlet level.*

THE MURDERER. I can no longer cower here listening to the agonized thumpings of my own heart She but snoze in her sleep. I'll do't. [*He again raises the dagger. The angels sing again. He cowers*] What is this? Has that tune reached Heaven?

LADY MAGNESIA. [*waking and sitting up*] My husband! [*All the colors of the rainbow chase one another up his face with ghastly brilliancy.*] Why do you change color? And what on earth are you doing with that dagger?

FITZ [*affecting unconcern, hut unhinged*] It is a present for you: a present from mother. Pretty. Isnt it? [*he displays it fatuously*].

LADY MAGNESIA. But she promised me a fish slice.

FITZ. This is a combination fish slice and dagger. One day you have salmon for dinner. The next you have a murder to commit. See?

LADY MAGNESIA. My sweet mother-in-law! [*Someone knocks at the door.*] That is Adolphus's knock. [*Fitz's face turns a dazzling green.*] What has happened to your complexion? You have turned green. Now I think of it, you always do when Adolphus is mentioned. Arnt you going to let him in?

FITZ. Certainly not. [*He goes to the door.*] Adolphus: you cannot enter. My wife is undressed and in bed.

LADY MAGNESIA. [*rising*] I am not Come in, Adolphus. [*she switches on the electric light.*]

ADOLPHUS. [*without*] Something most important has happened. I must come in for a moment.

FITZ. [*calling to Adolphus*] Something important happened? What is it?

ADOLPHUS [*without*] My new clothes have come home.

FITZ. He says his new clothes have come home.

LADY MAGNESIA [*running to the door and opening it*] Oh, come in, come in. Let me see.

Adolphus Bastable enters. He is in evening dress, made in the latest fashion, with the right half of the coat and the left half of the trousers yellow and the other halves black. His silver-spangled waistcoat has a crimson handkerchief stuck between it and his shirt front.

ADOLPHUS. What do you think of it?

LADY MAGNESIA. It is a dream! a creation! [*she turns him about to admire him.*]

ADOLPHUS [*proudly*] I shall never be mistaken for a waiter again.

FITZ. A drink, Adolphus?

ADOLPHUS. Thanks.

[*Fitztollemache goes to the cupboard and takes out a tray with tumblers and a bottle of whisky. He puts them on the dressing-table.*]

FITZ. Is the gazogene full?

LADY MAGNESIA. Yes: you put in the powders yourself today.

FITZ. [*sardonically*] So I did. The special powders! Hal ha! ha! ha! ha! [*His face Is again strangely variegated.*]

LADY MAGNESIA. Your complexion is really going to pieces. Why do you laugh in that silly way at nothing?

FITZ. Nothing! Ha, ha! Nothing! Ha, ha, ha!

ADOLPHUS. I hope, Mr Fitztollemache, you are not laughing at my clothes. I warn you that I am an Englishman. You may laugh at my manners, at my brains, at my national institutions; but if you laugh at my clothes, one of us must die.

Thunder.

FITZ. I laughed but at the irony of Fate. [*He takes a gazogene from the cupboard.*]

ADOLPHUS. [*satisfied*] Oh, that! Oh, yes, of course!

FITZ. Let us drown all unkindness in a loving cup. [*He puts the gazogene on the floor in the middle of the room.*] Pardon the absence of a table: we found it in the way and pawned it. [*He takes the whisky bottle from the dressing-table.*]

LADY MAGNESIA. We picnic at home now. It is delightful. [*She takes three tumblers from the dressing-table and sits on the floor, presiding over the gazogene, with Fitz and Adolphus squatting on her left and right respectively. Fitz pours whisky into the tumblers.*]

FITZ. [*as Magnesia is about to squirt soda into his tumbler*] Stay! No soda for me. Let Adolphus have it all—all. I will take mine neat.

LADY MAGNESIA [*proffering tumbler to Adolphus*] Pledge me, Adolphus.

FITZ. Kiss the cup, Magnesia. Pledge her, man. Drink deep.

ADOLPHUS. To Magnesia!

FITZ. To Magnesia! [*The two men drink.*] It is done. [*Scrambling to his feet*] Adolphus: you have but ten minutes to live—if so long.

ADOLPHUS. What mean you?

MAGNESIA. [*rising*] My mind misgives me. I have a strange feeling here. [*touching her heart*]

ADOLPHUS. So have I, but lower down. [*touching his stomach*] That gazogene is disagreeing with me.

FITZ. It was poisoned!

Sensation.

ADOLPHUS [*rising*] Help! Police!

FITZ. Dastard! you would appeal to the law! Can you not die like a gentleman?

ADOLPHUS. But so young! when I have only worn my new clothes once.

MAGNESIA. It is too horrible. [*To Fitz*] Fiend! what drove you to this wicked deed?

FITZ. Jealousy. You admired his clothes: you did not admire mine.

ADOLPHUS. My clothes [*his face lights up with heavenly radiance*] Have I indeed been found worthy to be the first clothes-martyr? Welcome, death! Hark! angels call me. [*The celestial choir again raises its favorite chant. He listens with a rapt expression. Suddenly the angels sing out of tune, and the radiance on the poisoned man's face turns a sickly green*] Yah—ah! Oh—ahoo! The gazogene is disagreeing extremely. Oh! [*he throws himself on the bed,writhing.*]

MAGNESIA. [*to Fitz*] Monster: what have you done? [*She points to the distorted figure on the bed.*] That was once a Man, beautiful and glorious. What have you made of it? A writhing, agonized,miserable, moribund worm.

ADOLPHUS. [*in a tone of the strongest remonstrance*] Oh, I say! Oh, come! No: look here. Magnesia! Really!

MAGNESIA. Oh, is this a time for petty vanity? Think of your misspent life—

ADOLPHUS [*much injured*] Whose misspent life?

MAGNESIA [*continuing relentlessly*] Look into your conscience: look into your stomach. [*Adolphus collapses in hideous spasms. She turns to Fitz.*] And this is your handiwork!

FITZ. Mine is a passionate nature. Magnesia. I must have your undivided love. I must have your love: do you hear? LOVE! LOVE!! LOVE!!! LOVE!!!! LOVE!!!!! [*He raves, accompanied by a fresh paroxysm from the victim on the bed.*]

MAGNESIA. [*with sudden resolution*] You shall have it.

FITZ [*enraptured*] Magnesia! I have recovered your love! Oh, how slight appears the sacrifice of this man compared to so glorious a reward! I would poison ten men without a thought of self to gain one smile from you.

ADOLPHUS. [*in a broken voice*] Farewell, Magnesia: my last hour is at hand. Farewell, farewell, farewell!

MAGNESIA. At this supreme moment, George Fitztollemache, I solemnly dedicate to you all that I formerly dedicated to poor Adolphus.

ADOLPHUS. Oh, please not poor Adolphus yet. I still live, you know.

MAGNESIA. The vital spark but flashes before it vanishes. [*Adolphus groans.*] And now, Adolphus, take this last comfort from the unhappy Magnesia Fitztollemache. As I have dedicated to George all that I gave to you, so I will bury in your grave—or in your urn if you are cremated—all that I gave to him.

FITZ. I hardly follow this.

MAGNESIA. I will explain. George: hitherto I have given Adolphus all the romance of my nature—all my love—all my dreams—all my caresses. Henceforth they are yours!

FITZ. Angel!

MAGNESIA. Adolphus: forgive me if this pains you.

ADOLPHUS. Dont mention it I hardly feel it The gazogene is so much worse. [*Taken bad again*] Oh!

MAGNESIA. Peace, poor sufferer: there is still some balm. You are about to hear what I am going to dedicate to you.

ADOLPHUS. All I ask is a peppermint lozenge, for mercy's sake.

MAGNESIA. I have something far better than any lozenge: the devotion of a lifetime. Formerly it was George's. I kept his house, or rather, his lodgings. I mended his clothes. I darned his socks. I bought his food. I interviewed his creditors. I stood between him and the servants. I administered his domestic finances. When his hair needed cutting or his countenance was imperfectly washed, I pointed it out to him. The trouble that all this gave me made him prosaic in my eyes. Familiarity bred contempt Now all that shall end. My husband shall be my hero, my lover, my perfect knight He shall shield me from all care and trouble. He shall ask nothing in return but love—boundless, priceless, rapturous, soul-enthralling love. Love! LOVE! LOVE! [*she raves and flings her arms about Fitz.*] And the duties I formerly discharged shall be replaced by the one supreme duty of duties: the duty of weeping at Adolphus's tomb.

FITZ.[*reflectively*] My ownest, this sacrifice makes me feel that I have perhaps been a little selfish. I cannot help feeling that there is much to be said for the old arrangement Why should Adolphus die for my sake?

ADOLPHUS. I am not dying for your sake, Fitz. I am dying because you poisoned me.

MAGNESIA. You do not fear to die, Adolphus, do you?

ADOLPHUS. N-n-no, I dont exactly fear to die. Still—

FITZ. Still, if an antidote—

ADOLPHUS. [*bounding from the bed*] Antidote!

MAGNESIA. [*with wild hope*] Antidote!

FITZ. If an antidote would not be too much of an anti-climax.

ADOLPHUS. Anti-climax be blowed! Do you think I am going to die to please the critics? Out with your antidote. Quick!

FITZ. The best antidote to the poison I have given you is lime, plenty of lime.

ADOLPHUS. Lime! You mock me! Do you think I carry lime about in my pockets?

FITZ. There is the plaster ceiling.

MAGNESIA. Yes, the ceiling. Saved, saved, saved!

All three frantically shy boots at the ceiling. Flakes of plaster rain down which Adolphus devours, at first ravenously, then with a marked falling off in relish.

MAGNESIA. [*picking up a huge slice*] Take this, Adolphus: it is the largest. [*she crams it into his mouth.*]

FITZ. Ha! a lump off the cornice! Try this.

ADOLPHUS. [*desperately*] Stop! stop!

MAGNESIA. Do not stop. You will die. [*She tries to stuff him again.*]

ADOLPHUS [*resolutely*] I prefer death.

MAGNESIA and FITZ. [*throwing themselves on their knees on either side of him*] For our sakes, Adolphus, persevere.

ADOLPHUS. No: unless you can supply lime in liquid form, I must perish. Finish that ceiling I cannot and will not.

MAGNESIA. I have a thought—an inspiration. My bust [*She snatches it from its pedestal and brings it to him.*]

ADOLPHUS [*gazing fondly at it*] Can I resist it?

FITZ. Try the bun.

ADOLPHUS. [*gnawing the knot of hair at the back of the bust's head: it makes him ill.*] Yah, I cannot. I cannot. Not even your bust, Magnesia. Do not ask me. Let me die.

FITZ. [*pressing the bust on him*] Force yourself to take a mouthful. Down with it, Adolphus!

ADOLPHUS. Useless. It would not stay down. Water! Some fluid! Ring for something to drink [*He chokes.*] MAGNESIA. I will save you [*She rushes to the bell and rings.*]

Phyllis, in her night-gown, with her hair prettify made up into a chevaux defrise *of crocuses with pink and yellow curlpapers, rushes in straight to Magnesia.*

PHYLLIS. [*hysterically*] My beloved mistress, once more we meet [*She sees Fitztollemache and screams.*] Ah! ah! ah! A man! [*She sees Adolphus*] Men!! [*She flies, but Fitztollemache seizes her by the night-gown just as she is escaping.*] Unhand me, villain!

FITZ. This is no time for prudery, girl. Mr Bastable is dying.

PHYLLIS. [*with concern*] Indeed, sir? I hope he will not think it unfeeling of me to appear at his deathbed in curl papers.

MAGNESIA. We know you have a good heart, Phyllis. Take this [*giving her the bust*]; dissolve it in a jug of hot water; and bring it back instantly. Mr Bastable's life depends on your haste.

PHYLLIS. [*hesitating*] It do seem a pity, dont it, my lady, to spoil your lovely bust?

ADOLPHUS. Tush! This craze for fine art is beyond alt bounds. Off with you [*he pushes her out*]. Drink, drink, drink! My entrails are parched. Drink! [*he rushes deliriously to the gazogene.*]

FITZ. [*rushing after him*] Madman, you forget! It is poisoned!

ADOLPHUS. I dont care. Drink, drink! [*They wrestle madly for the gazogene. In the struggle they squirt all its contents away, mostly into one another's face. Adolphus at last flings Fitztollemache to the floor, and puts the spout into his mouth.*] *Empty! empty!* [*with a shriek of despair he collapses on the bed, clasping the gazogene like a baby, and weeping over it.*]

FITZ. [*aside to Magnesia*] Magnesia: I have always pretended not to notice it; but you keep a siphon for your private use in my hatbox.

MAGNESIA. I use it for washing old lace; but no matter: he shall have it [*she produces a siphon from the hat-box, and offers a tumbler of soda-water to Adolphus.*]

ADOLPHUS. Thanks, thanks, oh, thanks! [*He drinks. A terrific fizzing is heard. He starts up screaming*] *Help! help! The ceiling is effervescing! I am BURSTING!* [*He wallows convulsively on the bed.*]

FITZ. Quick! the rug strap! [*They pack him with blankets and strap him.*] Is that tight enough?

MAGNESIA. [*anxiously*] Will you hold, do you think?

ADOLPHUS. The peril is past The soda-water has gone flat.

MAGNESIA and FITZ Thank heaven!

Phyllis returns with a washstand ewer, in which she has dissolved the bust.

MAGNESIA [*snatching it*] At last!

FITZ. You are saved. Drain it to the dregs.

Fitztollemache holds the lip of the ewer to Adolphus's mouth and gradually raises it until it stands upside down. Adolphus's efforts to swallow it are fearful, Phyllis thumping his back when he chokes and Magnesia loosening the straps when he moans. At last, with a sigh of relief, he sinks tack in the women's arms. Fitz shakes the empty ewer upside down like a potman shaking the froth out of a flagon.

ADOLPHUS. How inexpressibly soothing to the chest! A delicious numbness steals through all my members. I would sleep.

MAGNESIA–
FITZ ——> [*whispering together*] Let him sleep.
PHYLLIS–

He sleeps. Celestial harps are heard, but their chords cease on the abrupt entrance of the landlord, a vulgar person in pyjamas.

THE LANDLORD. Eah! Eah! Wots this? Wots all this noise? Ah kin ennybody sleep through it? [*Looking at the floor and ceiling*] Ellow! wot you bin doin te maw ceilin?

FITZ. Silence, or leave the room. If you wake that man he dies.

THE LANDLORD. If e kin sleep through the noise you three mikes e kin sleep through ennythink.

MAGNESIA. Detestable vulgarian: your pronunciation jars on the finest chords of my nature. Begone!

THE LANDLORD. [*looking at Adolphus*] Aw downt blieve eze esleep. Aw blieve eze dead. [*Calling*] Pleece! Pleecel Merder! [*A blue halo plays mysteriously on the door,which opens and reveals a policeman. Thunder*] Eah, pleecmin: these three's bin an murdered this gent between em, an naw tore moy ahse dahn.

THE POLICEMAN. [*offended*] Policeman, indeed! Wheres your manners?

FITZ. Officer—

THE POLICEMAN. [*with distinguished consideration*] Sir?

FITZ. As between gentlemen—

THE POLICEMAN. [*bowing*] Sir. to you.

FITZ. [*bowing*] I may inform you that my friend had an acute attack of indigestion. No carbonate of soda being available, he swallowed a portion of this man's ceiling. [*Pointing to Adolphus*] Behold the result!

THE POLICEMAN. The ceiling was poisoned! Well, of all the artful— [*he collars the landlord.*] *I arrest you for wilful murder.*

THE LANDLORD. [*appealing to the heavens*] Ow, is this jestice? Ah could aw tell e wiz gowin te eat moy ceilin?

THE POLICEMAN. [*releasing him*] True. The case is more complicated than I thought [*He tries to lift Adolphus's arm but cannot.*] Stiff already.

THE LANDLORD [*trying to lift Adolphus's leg*] An' precious evvy.[*Feeling the calf*] Woy, eze gorn ez awd ez niles.

FITZ [*rushing to the bed*] What is this?

MAGNESIA. Oh, say not he is dead. Phyllis: fetch a doctor. [*Phyllis runs out. They all try to lift Adolphus, but he is perfectly stiff, and as heavy as lead.*] Rouse him. Shake him.

THE POLICEMAN. [*exhausted*] Whew! Is he a man or a statue? [*Magnesia utters a piercing scream.*] Whats wrong, Miss?

MAGNESIA. [*to Fitz*] Do you not see what has happened?

FITZ. [*striking his forehead*] Horror on horror's head!

THE LANDLORD. Wotjemean?

MAGNESIA The plaster has set inside him. The officer was right: he is indeed a living statue.

[*Magnesia flings herself on the stony breast of Adolphus. Fitztollemache buries his head in his hands, and his chest heaves convulsively. The policeman takes a small volume from his pocket and consults it.*]

THE POLICEMAN. This case is not provided for in my book of instructions. It dont seem no use trying artificial respiration, do it? [*To the landlord*] Here! lend a hand, you. We'd best take him and set him up in Trafalgar Square.

THE LANDLORD. Aushd pat im in the cestern an worsh it aht of im.

Phyllis comes back with a Doctor.

PHYLLIS. The medical man, my lady.

THE POLICEMAN. A poison case, sir.

THE DOCTOR. Do you mean to say that an unqualified person! a layman! has dared to administer poison in my district?

THE POLICEMAN. [*raising Magnesia tenderly*] It looks like it. Hold up, my lady.

THE DOCTOR Not a moment must be lost The patient must be kept awake at all costs. Constant and violent motion is necessary. [*He snatches Magnesia from the policeman, and rushes her about the room.*]

FITZ. Stop! That is not the poisoned person!

THE DOCTOR. It is you, then. Why did you not say so before?[*He seizes Fitztollemache and rushes him about.*]

THE LANDLORD. Naow, naow, thet ynt im.

THE DOCTOR. What, you! [*He pounces on the landlord and rushes him round.*]

THE LANDLORD. Eah! chack it [*He trips the doctor up. Both fall.*] Jest owld this leoonatic, will you. Mister Horficer?

THE POLICEMAN. [*dragging both of them to their feet*] Come out of it, will you. You must all come with me to me station.

Thunder.

MAGNESIA What! In this frightful storm!

The hail patters noisily on the window.

PHYLLIS. I think it's raining.

The wind howls.

THE LANDLORD. It's thanderin and lawtnin.

FITZ. It's dangerous.

THE POLICEMAN [*drawing his baton and whistle*] If you wont come quietly, then—

He whistles. A fearful flash is followed by an appalling explosion of heaven's artillery. A thunderbolt enters the room, and strikes the helmet of the devoted constable, whence it is attracted to the waistcoat of the doctor by the lancet in his pocket. Finally it leaps with fearful force on the landlord, who, being of a gross and spongy nature, absorbs the electric fluid at the cost of his life. The others look on horrorstricken as the three victims, after reeling, jostling, cannon-

ing through a ghastly quadrille, at last sink inanimate on the carpet.

MAGNESIA [*listening at the doctor's chest*] Dead!

FITZ. [*kneeling by the landlord, and raising his hand, which drops with a thud*] Dead!

PHYLLIS [*seizing the looking-glass and holding it to the Policeman's lips*] Dead!

FITZ [*solemnly rising*] The copper attracted the lightning.

MAGNESIA [*rising*] After life's fitful fever they sleep well. Phyllis: sweep them up.

Phyllis replaces the looking-glass on the dressing-table, takes up the fan, and fans the policeman, who rolls away like a leaf before the wind, to the wall. She disposes similarly of the landlord and doctor.

PHYLLIS Will they be in your way if I leave them there until morning, my lady? Or shall I bring up the ashpan and take them away?

MAGNESIA. They will not disturb us. Goodnight, Phyllis.

PHYLLIS. Goodnight, my lady. Goodnight, sir. [*She retires.*]

MAGNESIA. And now, husband, let us perform our last sad duty to our friend. He has become his own monument. Let us erect him. He is heavy; but love can do much.

FITZ. A little leverage will get him on his feet Give me my umbrella.

MAGNESIA. True.

She hands him the umbrella, and takes up the bootjack. They get them under Adolphus's back, and prize him up on his feet.

FITZ. Thats done it! Whew!

MAGNESIA. [*kneeling at the left hand of the statue*] For ever and for ever, Adolphus.

FITZ.[*kneeling at the right hand of the statue*] The rest is silence.

The Angels sing Bill Bailey. The statue raises its hands in an attitude of blessing, and turns its limelit face to heaven as the curtain falls. National Anthem.

ATTENDANTS [*in front*] All out for the next performance. Pass along, please, ladies and gentlemen: pass along.

JOHN BULL'S OTHER ISLAND

ACT I

Great George Street, Westminster, is the address of Doyle and Broadbent, civil engineers. On the threshold one reads that the firm consists of Mr Lawrence Doyle and Mr Thomas Broadbent, and that their rooms are on the first floor. Most of their rooms are private; for the partners, being bachelors and bosom friends, live there; and the door marked Private, next the clerks' office, is their domestic sitting room as well as their reception room for clients. Let me describe it briefly from the point of view of a sparrow on the window sill. The outer door is in the opposite wall, close to the right hand corner. Between this door and the left hand corner is a hatstand and a table consisting of large drawing boards on trestles, with plans, rolls of tracing paper, mathematical instruments and other draughtsman's accessories on it. In the left hand wall is the fireplace, and the door of an inner room between the fireplace and our observant sparrow. Against the right hand wall is a filing cabinet, with a cupboard on it, and, nearer, a tall office desk and stool for one person. In the middle of the room a large double writing table is set across, with a chair at each end for the two partners. It is a room which no woman would tolerate, smelling of tobacco, and much in need of repapering, repainting, and recarpeting; but this is the effect of bachelor untidiness and indifference, not want of means; for nothing that Doyle and Broadbent themselves have purchased is cheap; nor is anything they want lacking. On the walls hang a large map of South America, a pictorial advertisement of a steamship company, an impressive portrait of Gladstone, and several caricatures of Mr Balfour as a rabbit and Mr Chamberlain as a fox by Francis Carruthers Gould.

At twenty minutes to five o'clock on a summer afternoon in 1904, the room is empty. Presently the outer door is opened, and a valet comes in laden with a large Gladstone bag, and a strap of rugs. He carries them into the inner room. He is a respectable valet, old enough to have lost all alacrity, and acquired an air of putting up patiently with a great deal of trouble and indifferent health. The luggage belongs to Broadbent, who enters after the valet. He pulls off his overcoat and hangs it with his hat on the stand. Then he comes to the writing table and looks through the letters which are waiting for him. He is a robust, full-blooded, energetic man in the prime of life, sometimes eager and credulous, sometimes shrewd and roguish, sometimes portentously solemn, sometimes jolly and impetuous, always buoyant and irresistible, mostly likeable, and enormously absurd in his most earnest moments. He bursts open his letters with his thumb, and glances through them, flinging the envelopes about the floor with reckless untidiness whilst he talks to the valet.

BROADBENT [*calling*] Hodson.

HODSON [*in the bedroom*] Yes sir.

BROADBENT. Don't unpack. Just take out the things I've worn; and put in clean things.

HODSON [*appearing at the bedroom door*] Yes sir. [*He turns to go back into the bedroom*].

BROADBENT. And look here! [*Hodson turns again*]. Do you remember where I put my revolver?

HODSON. Revolver, sir? Yes sir. Mr Doyle uses it as a paper-weight, sir, when he's drawing.

BROADBENT. Well, I want it packed. There's a packet of cartridges somewhere, I think. Find it and pack it as well.

HODSON. Yes sir.

BROADBENT. By the way, pack your own traps too. I shall take you with me this time.

HODSON [*hesitant*]. Is it a dangerous part you're going to, sir? Should I be expected to carry a revolver, sir?

BROADBENT. Perhaps it might be as well. I'm going to Ireland.

HODSON [*reassured*]. Yes sir.

BROADBENT. You don't feel nervous about it, I suppose?

HODSON. Not at all, sir. I'll risk it, sir.

BROADBENT. Have you ever been in Ireland?

HODSON. No sir. I understand it's a very wet climate, sir. I'd better pack your india-rubber overalls.

BROADBENT. Do. Where's Mr Doyle?

HODSON. I'm expecting him at five, sir. He went out after lunch.

BROADBENT. Anybody been looking for me?

HODSON. A person giving the name of Haffigan has called twice to-day, sir.

BROADBENT. Oh, I'm sorry. Why didn't he wait? I told him to wait if I wasn't in.

HODSON. Well Sir, I didn't know you expected him; so I thought it best to—to—not to encourage him, sir.

BROADBENT. Oh, he's all right. He's an Irishman, and not very particular about his appearance.

HODSON. Yes sir, I noticed that he was rather Irish....

BROADBENT. If he calls again let him come up.

HODSON. I think I saw him waiting about, sir, when you drove up. Shall I fetch him, sir?

BROADBENT. Do, Hodson.

HODSON. Yes sir [*He makes for the outer door*].

BROADBENT. He'll want tea. Let us have some.

HODSON [*stopping*]. I shouldn't think he drank tea, sir.

BROADBENT. Well, bring whatever you think he'd like.

HODSON. Yes sir [*An electric bell rings*]. Here he is, sir. Saw you arrive, sir.

BROADBENT. Right. Show him in. [*Hodson goes out. Broadbent gets through the rest of his letters before Hodson returns with the visitor*].

HODSON. Mr Affigan.

Haffigan is a stunted, shortnecked, smallheaded, redhaired man of about 30, with reddened nose and furtive eyes. He is dressed in seedy black, almost clerically, and might be a tenth-rate schoolmaster ruined by drink. He hastens to shake Broadbent's hand with a show of reckless geniality and high spirits, helped out by a rollicking stage brogue. This is perhaps a comfort to himself, as he is secretly pursued by the horrors of incipient delirium tremens.

HAFFIGAN. Tim Haffigan, sir, at your service. The top o the mornin to you, Misther Broadbent.

BROADBENT [*delighted with his Irish visitor*]. Good afternoon, Mr Haffigan.

TIM. An is it the afthernoon it is already? Begorra, what I call the mornin is all the time a man fasts afther breakfast.

BROADBENT. Haven't you lunched?

TIM. Divil a lunch!

BROADBENT. I'm sorry I couldn't get back from Brighton in time to offer you some; but—

TIM. Not a word, sir, not a word. Sure it'll do tomorrow. Besides, I'm Irish, sir: a poor ather, but a powerful dhrinker.

BROADBENT. I was just about to ring for tea when you came. Sit down, Mr Haffigan.

TIM. Tay is a good dhrink if your nerves can stand it. Mine can't.

Haffigan sits down at the writing table, with his back to the filing cabinet. Broadbent sits opposite him. Hodson enters emptyhanded; takes two glasses, a siphon, and a tantalus from the cupboard; places them before Broadbent on the writing table; looks ruthlessly at Haffigan, who cannot meet his eye; and retires.

BROADBENT. Try a whisky and soda.

TIM [*sobered*]. There you touch the national wakeness, sir. [*Piously*] Not that I share it meself. I've seen too much of the mischief of it.

BROADBENT [*pouring the whisky*]. Say when.

TIM. Not too sthrong. [*Broadbent stops and looks enquiringly at him*]. Say half-an-half. [*Broadbent, somewhat startled by this demand, pours a little more, and again stops and looks*]. Just a dhrain more: the lower half o the tumbler doesn't hold a fair half. Thankya.

BROADBENT [*laughing*]. You Irishmen certainly do know how to drink. [*Pouring some whisky for himself*] Now that's my poor English idea of a whisky and soda.

TIM. An a very good idea it is too. Dhrink is the curse o me unhappy counthry. I take it meself because I've a wake heart and a poor digestion; but in principle I'm a teetoatler.

BROADBENT [*suddenly solemn and strenuous*]. So am I, of course. I'm a Local Optionist to the backbone. You have no idea, Mr Haffigan, of the ruin that is wrought in this country by the unholy alliance of the publicans, the bishops, the Tories, and The Times. We must close the public-houses at all costs [*he drinks*].

TIM. Sure I know. It's awful [*he drinks*]. I see you're a good Liberal like meself, sir.

BROADBENT. I am a lover of liberty, like every true Englishman, Mr Haffigan. My name is Broadbent. If my name were Breitstein, and I had a hooked nose and a house in Park Lane, I should carry a Union Jack handkerchief and a penny trumpet, and tax the food of the people to support the Navy League, and clamor for the destruction of the last remnants of national liberty—

TIM. Not another word. Shake hands.

BROADBENT. But I should like to explain—

TIM. Sure I know every word you're goin to say before yev said it. I know the sort o man yar. An so you're thinkin o comin to Ireland for a bit?

BROADBENT. Where else can I go? I am an Englishman and a Liberal; and now that South Africa has been enslaved and destroyed, there is no country left to me to take an interest in but Ireland. Mind: I don't say that an Englishman has not other duties. He has a duty to Finland and a duty to Macedonia. But what sane man can deny that an Englishman's first duty is his duty to Ireland? Unfortunately, we have politicians here more unscrupulous than Bobrikoff, more bloodthirsty than Abdul the Damned; and it is under their heel that Ireland is now writhing.

TIM. Faith, they've reckoned up with poor oul Bobrikoff anyhow.

BROADBENT. Not that I defend assassination: God forbid! However strongly we may feel that the unfortunate and patriotic young man who avenged the wrongs of Finland on the Russian tyrant was perfectly right from his own point of view, yet every civilized man must regard murder with abhorrence. Not even in defence of Free Trade would I lift my hand against a political opponent, however richly he might deserve it.

TIM. I'm sure you wouldn't; and I honor you for it. You're goin to Ireland, then, out o sympithy: is it?

BROADBENT. I'm going to develop an estate there for the Land Development Syndicate, in which I am interested. I am convinced that all it needs to make it pay is to handle it properly, as estates are handled in England. You know the English plan, Mr Haffigan, don't you?

TIM. Bedad I do, sir. Take all you can out of Ireland and spend it in England: that's it.

BROADBENT [*not quite liking this*]. My plan, sir, will be to take a little money out of England and spend it in Ireland.

TIM. More power to your elbow! an may your shadda never be less! for you're the broth of a boy intirely. An how can I help you? Command me to the last dhrop o me blood.

BROADBENT. Have you ever heard of Garden City?

TIM [*doubtfully*]. D'ye mane Heavn?

BROADBENT. Heaven! No: it's near Hitchin. If you can spare half an hour I'll go into it with you.

TIM. I tell you hwat. Gimme a prospectus. Lemme take it home and reflect on it.

BROADBENT. You're quite right: I will. [*He gives him a copy of Mr Ebenezer Howard's book, and several pamphlets*]. You understand that the map of the city—the circular construction—is only a suggestion.

TIM. I'll make a careful note o that [*looking dazedly at the map*].

BROADBENT. What I say is, why not start a Garden City in Ireland?

TIM [*with enthusiasm*]. That's just what was on the tip o me tongue to ask you. Why not? [*Defiantly*] Tell me why not.

BROADBENT. There are difficulties. I shall overcome them; but there are difficulties. When I first arrive in Ireland I shall be hated as an Englishman. As a Protestant, I shall be denounced from every altar. My life may be in danger. Well, I am prepared to face that.

TIM. Never fear, sir. We know how to respict a brave innimy.

BROADBENT. What I really dread is misunderstanding. I think you could help me to avoid that. When I heard you speak the other evening in Bermondsey at the meeting of the National League, I saw at once that you were—You won't mind my speaking frankly?

TIM. Tell me all me faults as man to man. I can stand anything but flatthery.

BROADBENT. May I put it in this way?—that I saw at once that you were a thorough Irishman, with all the faults and all, the qualities of your race: rash and improvident but brave and goodnatured; not likely to succeed in business on your own account perhaps, but eloquent, humorous, a lover of freedom, and a true follower of that great Englishman Gladstone.

TIM. Spare me blushes. I mustn't sit here to be praised to me face. But I confess to the goodnature: it's an Irish wakeness. I'd share me last shillin with a friend.

BROADBENT. I feel sure you would, Mr Haffigan.

TIM [*impulsively*]. Damn it! call me Tim. A man that talks about Ireland as you do may call me anything. Gimme a howlt o that whisky bottle [*he replenishes*].

BROADBENT [*smiling indulgently*]. Well, Tim, will you come with me and help to break the ice between me and your warmhearted, impulsive countrymen?

TIM. Will I come to Madagascar or Cochin China wid you? Bedad I'll come to the North Pole wid you if yll pay me fare; for the divil a shillin I have to buy a third class ticket.

BROADBENT. I've not forgotten that, Tim. We must put that little matter on a solid English footing, though the rest can be as Irish as you please. You must come as my—my—well, I hardly know what to call it. If we call you my agent, they'll shoot you. If we call you a bailiff, they'll duck you in the horsepond. I have a secretary already; and—

TIM. Then we'll call him the Home Secretary and me the Irish Secretary. Eh?

BROADBENT [*laughing industriously*]. Capital. Your Irish wit has settled the first difficulty. Now about your salary—

TIM. A salary, is it? Sure I'd do it for nothin, only me cloes ud disgrace you; and I'd be dhriven to borra money from your friends: a thing that's agin me nacher. But I won't take a penny more than a hundherd a year. [*He looks with restless cunning at Broadbent, trying to guess how far he may go*].

BROADBENT. If that will satisfy you—

TIM [*more than reassured*]. Why shouldn't it satisfy me? A hundherd a year is twelve-pound a month, isn't it?

BROADBENT. No. Eight pound six and eightpence.

TIM. Oh murdher! An I'll have to sind five timme poor oul mother in Ireland. But no matther: I said a hundherd; and what I said I'll stick to, if I have to starve for it.

BROADBENT [*with business caution*]. Well, let us say twelve pounds for the first month. Afterwards, we shall see how we get on.

TIM. You're a gentleman, sir. Whin me mother turns up her toes, you shall take the five pounds off; for your expinses must be kep down wid a sthrong hand; an—[*He is interrupted by the arrival of Broadbent's partner.*]

Mr Laurence Doyle is a man of 36, with cold grey eyes, strained nose, fine fastidious lips, critical brown, clever head, rather refined and goodlooking on the whole, but with a suggestion of thinskinedness and dissatisfaction that contrasts strongly with Broadbent's eupeptic jollity.

He comes in as a man at home there, but on seeing the stranger shrinks at once, and is about to withdraw when Broadbent reassures him. He then comes forward to the table, between the two others.

DOYLE [*retreating*]. You're engaged.

BROADBENT. Not at all, not at all. Come in. [*To Tim*] This gentleman is a friend who lives with me here: my partner, Mr Doyle. [*To Doyle*] This is a new Irish friend of mine, Mr Tim Haffigan.

TIM [*rising with effusion*]. Sure it's meself that's proud to meet any friend o Misther Broadbent's. The top o the mornin to you, sir! Me heart goes out teeye both. It's not often I meet two such splendid speciments iv the Anglo-Saxon race.

BROADBENT [*chuckling*] Wrong for once, Tim. My friend Mr Doyle is a countryman of yours.

Tim is noticeably dashed by this announcement. He draws in his horns at once, and scowls suspiciously at Doyle under a vanishing mark of goodfellowship: cringing a little, too, in mere nerveless fear of him.

DOYLE [*with cool disgust*]. Good evening. [*He retires to the fireplace, and says to Broadbent in a tone which conveys the strongest possible hint to Haffigan that he is unwelcome*] Will you soon be disengaged?

TIM [*his brogue decaying into a common would-be genteel accent with an unexpected strain of Glasgow in it*]. I must be going. Ivnmportnt engeegement in the west end.

BROADBENT [*rising*]. It's settled, then, that you come with me.

TIM. Ish'll be verra pleased to accompany ye, sir.

BROADBENT. But how soon? Can you start tonight—from Paddington? We go by Milford Haven.

TIM [*hesitating*]. Well—I'm afreed—I [*Doyle goes abruptly into the bedroom, slamming the door and shattering the last remnant of Tim's nerve. The poor wretch saves himself from bursting into tears by plunging again into his role of daredevil Irishman. He rushes to Broadbent; plucks at his sleeve with trembling fingers; and pours forth his entreaty with all the brogue be can muster, subduing his voice lest Doyle should hear and return*]. Misther Broadbent: don't humiliate me before a fella counthryman. Look here: me cloes is up the spout. Gimme a fypounnote—I'll pay ya nex choosda whin me ship comes home—or you can stop it out o me month's sallery. I'll be on the platform at Paddnton punctial an ready. Gimme it quick, before he comes back. You won't mind me axin, will ye?

BROADBENT. Not at all. I was about to offer you an advance for travelling expenses. [*He gives him a bank note*].

TIM [*pocketing it*]. Thank you. I'll be there half an hour before the thrain starts. [*Larry is heard at the bedroom door, returning*]. Whisht: he's comin back. Goodbye an God bless ye. [*He hurries out almost crying, the 5 pound note and all the drink it means to him being too much for his empty stomach and over-strained nerves*].

DOYLE [*returning*]. Where the devil did you pick up that seedy swindler? What was he doing here? [*He goes up to the table where the plans are, and makes a note on one of them, referring to his pocket book as he does so*].

BROADBENT. There you go! Why are you so down on every Irishman you meet, especially if he's a bit shabby? poor devil! Surely a fellow-countryman may pass you the top of the morning without offence, even if his coat is a bit shiny at the seams.

DOYLE [*contemptuously*]. The top of the morning! Did he call you the broth of a boy? [*He comes to the writing table*].

BROADBENT [*triumphantly*]. Yes.

DOYLE. And wished you more power to your elbow?

BROADBENT. He did.

DOYLE. And that your shadow might never be less?

BROADBENT. Certainly.

DOYLE [*taking up the depleted whisky bottle and shaking his head at it*]. And he got about half a pint of whisky out of you.

BROADBENT. It did him no harm. He never turned a hair.

DOYLE. How much money did he borrow?

BROADBENT. It was not borrowing exactly. He showed a very honorable spirit about money. I believe he would share his last shilling with a friend.

DOYLE. No doubt he would share his friend's last shilling if his friend was fool enough to let him. How much did he touch you for?

BROADBENT. Oh, nothing. An advance on his salary—for travelling expenses.

DOYLE. Salary! In Heaven's name, what for?

BROADBENT. For being my Home Secretary, as he very wittily called it.

DOYLE. I don't see the joke.

BROADBENT. You can spoil any joke by being cold blooded about it. I saw it all right when he said it. It was something—something really very amusing—about the Home Secretary and the Irish Secretary. At all events, he's evidently the very man to take with me to Ireland to break the ice for me. He can gain the confidence of the people there, and make them friendly to me. Eh? [*He seats himself on the office stool, and tilts it back so that the edge of the standing desk supports his back and prevents his toppling over*].

DOYLE. A nice introduction, by George! Do you suppose the whole population of Ireland consists of drunken begging letter writers, or that even if it did, they would accept one another as references?

BROADBENT. Pooh! nonsense! He's only an Irishman. Besides, you don't seriously suppose that Haffigan can humbug me, do you?

DOYLE. No: he's too lazy to take the trouble. All he has to do is to sit there and drink your whisky while you humbug yourself. However, we needn't argue about Haffigan, for two reasons. First, with your money in his pocket he will never reach Paddington: there are too many public houses on the way. Second, he's not an Irishman at all.

BROADBENT. Not an Irishman! [*He is so amazed by the statement that he straightens himself and brings the stool bolt upright*].

DOYLE. Born in Glasgow. Never was in Ireland in his life. I know all about him.

BROADBENT. But he spoke—he behaved just like an Irishman.

DOYLE. Like an Irishman!! Is it possible that you don't know that all this top-o-the-morning and broth-of-a-boy and more-power-to-your-elbow business is as peculiar to England as the Albert Hall concerts of Irish music are? No Irishman ever talks like that in Ireland, or ever did, or ever will. But when a thoroughly worthless Irishman comes to England, and finds the whole place full of romantic duffers like you, who will let him loaf and drink and sponge and brag as long as he flatters your sense of moral superiority by playing the fool and degrading himself and his country, he soon learns the antics that take you in. He picks them up at the theatre or the music hall. Haffigan learnt the rudiments from his father, who came from my part of Ireland. I knew his uncles, Matt and Andy Haffigan of Rosscullen.

BROADBENT [*still incredulous*]. But his brogue!

DOYLE. His brogue! A fat lot you know about brogues! I've heard you call a Dublin accent that you could hang your hat on, a brogue. Heaven help you! you don't know the difference between Connemara and Rathmines. [*With violent irritation*] Oh, damn Tim Haffigan! Let's drop the subject: he's not worth wrangling about.

BROADBENT. What's wrong with you today, Larry? Why are you so bitter?

Doyle looks at him perplexedly; comes slowly to the writing table; and sits down at the end next the fireplace before replying.

DOYLE. Well: your letter completely upset me, for one thing.

BROADBENT. Why?

LARRY. Your foreclosing this Rosscullen mortgage and turning poor Nick Lestrange out of house and home has rather taken me aback; for I liked the old rascal when I was a boy and had the run of his park to play in. I was brought up on the property.

BROADBENT. But he wouldn't pay the interest. I had to foreclose on behalf of the Syndicate. So now I'm off to Rosscullen to look after the property myself. [*He sits down at the writing table opposite Larry, and adds, casually, but with an anxious glance at his partner*] You're coming with me, of course?

DOYLE [*rising nervously and recommencing his restless movements*]. That's it. That's what I dread. That's what has upset me.

BROADBENT. But don't you want to see your country again after 18 years absence? to see your people, to be in the old home again? To—

DOYLE [*interrupting him very impatiently*]. Yes, yes: I know all that as well as you do.

BROADBENT. Oh well, of course [*with a shrug*] if you take it in that way, I'm sorry.

DOYLE. Never you mind my temper: it's not meant for you, as you ought to know by this time. [*He sits down again, a little ashamed of his petulance; reflects a moment bitterly; then bursts out*] I have an instinct against going back to Ireland: an instinct so strong that I'd rather go with you to the South Pole than to Rosscullen.

BROADBENT. What! Here you are, belonging to a nation with the strongest patriotism! the most inveterate homing instinct in the world! and you pretend you'd rather go anywhere than back to Ireland. You don't suppose I believe you, do you? In your heart—

DOYLE. Never mind my heart: an Irishman's heart is nothing but his imagination. How many of all those millions that have left Ireland have ever come back or wanted to come back? But what's the use of talking to you? Three verses of twaddle about the Irish emigrant "sitting on the stile, Mary," or three hours of Irish patriotism in Bermondsey or the Scotland Division of Liverpool, go further with you than all the facts that stare you in the face. Why, man alive, look at me! You know the way I nag, and worry, and carp, and cavil, and disparage, and am never satisfied and never quiet, and try the patience of my best friends.

BROADBENT. Oh, come, Larry! do yourself justice. You're very amusing and agreeable to strangers.

DOYLE. Yes, to strangers. Perhaps if I was a bit stiffer to strangers, and a bit easier at home, like an Englishman, I'd be better company for you.

BROADBENT. We get on well enough. Of course you have the melancholy of the Celtic race—

DOYLE [*bounding out of his chair*] Good God!!!

BROADBENT [*slyly*]—and also its habit of using strong language when there's nothing the matter.

DOYLE. Nothing the matter! When people talk about the Celtic race, I feel as if I could burn down London. That sort of rot does more harm than ten Coercion Acts. Do you suppose a man need be a Celt to feel melancholy in Rosscullen? Why, man, Ireland was peopled just as England was; and its breed was crossed by just the same invaders.

BROADBENT. True. All the capable people in Ireland are of English extraction. It has often struck me as a most remarkable circumstance that the only party in parliament which shows the genuine old English character and spirit is the Irish party. Look at its independence, its determination, its defiance of bad Governments, its sympathy with oppressed nationalities all the world over! How English!

DOYLE. Not to mention the solemnity with which it talks old-fashioned nonsense which it knows perfectly well to be a century behind the times. That's English, if you like.

BROADBENT. No, Larry, no. You are thinking of the modern hybrids that now monopolize England. Hypocrites, humbugs, Germans, Jews, Yankees, foreigners, Park Laners, cosmopolitan riffraff. Don't call them English. They don't belong to the dear old island, but to their confounded new empire; and by George! they're worthy of it; and I wish them joy of it.

DOYLE [*unmoved by this outburst*]. There! You feel better now, don't you?

BROADBENT [*defiantly*]. I do. Much better.

DOYLE. My dear Tom, you only need a touch of the Irish climate to be as big a fool as I am myself. If all my Irish blood were poured into your veins, you wouldn't turn a hair of your constitution and character. Go and marry the most English Englishwoman you can find, and then bring up your son in Rosscullen; and that son's character will be so like mine and so unlike yours that everybody will accuse me of being his father. [*With sudden anguish*] Rosscullen! oh, good Lord, Rosscullen! The dullness! the hopelessness! the ignorance! the bigotry!

BROADBENT [*matter-of-factly*]. The usual thing in the country, Larry. Just the same here.

DOYLE [*hastily*]. No, no: the climate is different. Here, if the life is dull, you can be dull too, and no great harm done. [*Going off into a passionate dream*] But your wits can't thicken in that soft moist air, on those white springy roads, in those misty rushes and brown bogs, on those hillsides of granite rocks and magenta heather. You've no such colors in the sky, no such lure in the distances, no such sadness in the evenings. Oh, the dreaming! the dreaming! the torturing, heartscalding, never satisfying dreaming, dreaming, dreaming, dreaming! [*Savagely*] No debauchery that ever coarsened and brutalized an Englishman can take the worth and usefulness out of him like that dreaming. An Irishman's imagination never lets him alone, never convinces him, never satisfies him; but it makes him that he can't face reality nor deal with it nor handle it nor conquer it: he can only sneer at them that do, and [*bitterly, at Broadbent*] be "agreeable to strangers," like a good-for-nothing woman on the streets. [*Gabbling at Broadbent across the table*] It's all dreaming, all imagination. He can't be religious. The inspired Churchman that teaches him the sanctity of life and the importance of conduct is sent away empty; while the poor village priest that gives him a miracle or a sentimental story of a saint, has cathedrals built for him out of the pennies of the poor. He can't be intelligently political, he dreams of what the Shan Van Vocht said in ninety-eight. If you want to interest him in Ireland you've got to call the unfortunate island Kathleen ni Hoolihan and pretend she's a little old woman. It saves thinking. It saves working. It saves everything except imagination, imagination, imagination; and imagination's such a torture that you can't bear it without whisky. [*With fierce shivering self-contempt*] At last you get that you can bear nothing real at all: you'd rather starve than cook a meal; you'd rather go shabby and dirty than set your mind to take care of your clothes and wash yourself; you nag and squabble at home because your wife isn't an angel, and she despises you because you're not a hero; and you hate the whole lot round you because they're only poor slovenly useless devils like yourself. [*Dropping his voice like a man making some shameful confidence*] And all the while there goes on a horrible, senseless, mischievous laughter. When you're young, you exchange drinks with other young men; and you exchange vile stories with them; and as you're too futile to be able to help or cheer them, you chaff and sneer and taunt them for not doing the things you daren't do yourself. And all the time you laugh, laugh, laugh! eternal derision, eternal envy, eternal folly, eternal fouling and staining and degrading, until, when you come at last to a country where men take a question seriously and give a serious answer to it, you deride them for having no sense of humor, and plume yourself on your own worthlessness as if it made you better than them.

BROADBENT [*roused to intense earnestness by Doyle's eloquence*]. Never despair, Larry. There are great possibilities for Ireland. Home Rule will work wonders under English guidance.

DOYLE [*pulled up short, his face twitching with a reluctant smile*]. Tom: why do you select my most tragic moments for your most irresistible strokes of humor?

BROADBENT. Humor! I was perfectly serious. What do you mean? Do you doubt my seriousness about Home Rule?

DOYLE. I am sure you are serious, Tom, about the English guidance.

BROADBENT [*quite reassured*]. Of course I am. Our guidance is the important thing. We English must place our capacity for government without stint at the service of nations who are less fortunately endowed in that respect; so as to allow them to develop in perfect freedom to the English level of self-government, you know. You understand me?

DOYLE. Perfectly. And Rosscullen will understand you too.

BROADBENT [*cheerfully*]. Of course it will. So that's all right. [*He pulls up his chair and settles himself comfortably to lecture Doyle*]. Now, Larry, I've listened carefully to all you've said about Ireland; and I can see nothing whatever to prevent your coming with me. What does it all come to? Simply that you were only a young fellow when you were in Ireland. You'll find all that chaffing and drinking and not knowing what to be at in Peckham just the same as in Donnybrook. You looked at Ireland with a boy's eyes and saw only boyish things. Come back with me and look at it with a man's, and get a better opinion of your country.

DOYLE. I daresay you're partly right in that: at all events I know very well that if I had been the son of a laborer instead of the son of a country landagent, I should have struck more grit than I did. Unfortunately I'm not going back to visit the Irish nation, but to visit my father and Aunt Judy and Nora Reilly and Father Dempsey and the rest of them.

BROADBENT. Well, why not? They'll be delighted to see you, now that England has made a man of you.

DOYLE [*struck by this*]. Ah! you hit the mark there, Tom, with true British inspiration.

BROADBENT. Common sense, you mean.

DOYLE [*quickly*]. No I don't: you've no more common sense than a gander. No Englishman has any common sense, or ever had, or ever will have. You're going on a sentimental expedition for perfectly ridiculous reasons, with your head full of political nonsense that would not take in any ordinarily intelligent donkey; but you can hit me in the eye with the simple truth about myself and my father.

BROADBENT [*amazed*]. I never mentioned your father.

DOYLE [*not heeding the interruption*]. There he is in Rosscullen, a landagent who's always been in a small way because he's a Catholic, and the landlords are mostly Protestants. What with land courts reducing rents and Land Acts turning big estates into little holdings, he'd be a beggar this day if he hadn't bought his own little farm under the Land Purchase Act. I doubt if he's been further from home than Athenmullet for the last twenty years. And here am I, made a man of, as you say, by England.

BROADBENT [*apologetically*]. I assure you I never meant—

DOYLE. Oh, don't apologize: it's quite true. I daresay I've learnt something in America and a few other remote and inferior spots; but in the main it is by living with you and working in double harness with you that I have learnt to live in a real world and not in an imaginary one. I owe more to you than to any Irishman.

BROADBENT [*shaking his head with a twinkle in his eye*]. Very friendly of you, Larry, old man, but all blarney. I like blarney; but it's rot, all the same.

DOYLE. No it's not. I should never have done anything without you; although I never stop wondering at that blessed old head of yours with all its ideas in watertight compartments, and all the compartments warranted impervious to anything that it doesn't suit you to understand.

BROADBENT [*invincible*]. Unmitigated rot, Larry, I assure you.

DOYLE. Well, at any rate you will admit that all my friends are either Englishmen or men of the big world that belongs to the big Powers. All the serious part of my life has been lived in that atmosphere: all the serious part of my work has been done with men of that sort. Just think of me as I am now going back to Rosscullen! to that hell of littleness and monotony! How am I to get on with a little country landagent that ekes out his 5 per cent with a little farming and a scrap of house property in the nearest country town? What am I to say to him? What is he to say to me?

BROADBFNT [*scandalized*]. But you're father and son, man!

DOYLE. What difference does that make? What would you say if I proposed a visit to YOUR father?

BROADBENT [*with filial rectitude*]. I always made a point of going to see my father regularly until his mind gave way.

DOYLE [*concerned*]. Has he gone mad? You never told me.

BROADBENT. He has joined the Tariff Reform League. He would never have done that if his mind had not been weakened. [*Beginning to declaim*] He has fallen a victim to the arts of a political charlatan who—

DOYLE [*interrupting him*]. You mean that you keep clear of your father because he differs from you about Free Trade, and you don't want to quarrel with him. Well, think of me and my father! He's a Nationalist and a Separatist. I'm a metallurgical chemist turned civil engineer. Now whatever else metallurgical chemistry may be, it's not national. It's international. And my business and yours as civil engineers is to join countries, not to separate them. The one real political conviction that our business has rubbed into us is that frontiers are hindrances and flags confounded nuisances.

BROADBENT [*still smarting under Mr Chamberlain's economic heresy*]. Only when there is a protective tariff—

DOYLE [*firmly*] Now look here, Tom: you want to get in a speech on Free Trade; and you're not going to do it: I won't stand it. My father wants to make

St George's Channel a frontier and hoist a green flag on College Green; and I want to bring Galway within 3 hours of Colchester and 24 of New York. I want Ireland to be the brains and imagination of a big Commonwealth, not a Robinson Crusoe island. Then there's the religious difficulty. My Catholicism is the Catholicism of Charlemagne or Dante, qualified by a great deal of modern science and folklore which Father Dempsey would call the ravings of an Atheist. Well, my father's Catholicism is the Catholicism of Father Dempsey.

BROADBENT [*shrewdly*]. I don't want to interrupt you, Larry; but you know this is all gammon. These differences exist in all families; but the members rub on together all right. [*Suddenly relapsing into portentousness*] Of course there are some questions which touch the very foundations of morals; and on these I grant you even the closest relationships cannot excuse any compromise or laxity. For instance—

DOYLE [*impatiently springing up and walking about*]. For instance, Home Rule, South Africa, Free Trade, and the Education Rate. Well, I should differ from my father on every one of them, probably, just as I differ from you about them.

BROADBENT. Yes; but you are an Irishman; and these things are not serious to you as they are to an Englishman.

DOYLE. What! not even Home Rule!

BROADBENT [*steadfastly*]. Not even Home Rule. We owe Home Rule not to the Irish, but to our English Gladstone. No, Larry: I can't help thinking that there's something behind all this.

DOYLE [*hotly*]. What is there behind it? Do you think I'm humbugging you?

BROADBENT. Don't fly out at me, old chap. I only thought—

DOYLE. What did you think?

BROADBENT. Well, a moment ago I caught a name which is new to me: a Miss Nora Reilly, I think. [*Doyle stops dead and stares at him with something like awe*]. I don't wish to be impertinent, as you know, Larry; but are you sure she has nothing to do with your reluctance to come to Ireland with me?

DOYLE [*sitting down again, vanquished*]. Thomas Broadbent: I surrender. The poor silly-clever Irishman takes off his hat to God's Englishman. The man who could in all seriousness make that recent remark of yours about Home Rule and Gladstone must be simply the champion idiot of all the world. Yet the man who could in the very next sentence sweep away all my special pleading and go straight to the heart of my motives must be a man of genius. But that the idiot and the genius should be the same man! how is that possible? [*Springing to his feet*] By Jove, I see it all now. I'll write an article about it, and send it to Nature.

BROADBENT [*staring at him*]. What on earth—

DOYLE. It's quite simple. You know that a caterpillar—

BROADBENT. A caterpillar!!!

DOYLE. Yes, a caterpillar. Now give your mind to what I am going to say; for it's a new and important scientific theory of the English national character. A caterpillar—

BROADBENT. Look here, Larry: don't be an ass.

DOYLE [*insisting*]. I say a caterpillar and I mean a caterpillar. You'll understand presently. A caterpillar [*Broadbent mutters a slight protest, but does not press it*] when it gets into a tree, instinctively makes itself look exactly like a leaf; so that both its enemies and its prey may mistake it for one and think it not worth bothering about.

BROADBENT. What's that got to do with our English national character?

DOYLE. I'll tell you. The world is as full of fools as a tree is full of leaves. Well, the Englishman does what the caterpillar does. He instinctively makes himself look like a fool, and eats up all the real fools at his ease while his enemies let him alone and laugh at him for being a fool like the rest. Oh, nature is cunning, cunning! [*He sits down, lost in contemplation of his word-picture*].

BROADBENT [*with hearty admiration*]. Now you know, Larry, that would never have occurred to me. You Irish people are amazingly clever. Of course it's all tommy rot; but it's so brilliant, you know! How the dickens do you think of such things! You really must write an article about it: they'll pay you something for it. If Nature won't have it, I can get it into Engineering for you: I know the editor.

DOYLE. Let's get back to business. I'd better tell you about Nora Reilly.

BROADBENT. No: never mind. I shouldn't have alluded to her.

DOYLE. I'd rather. Nora has a fortune.

BROADBENT [*keenly interested*]. Eh? How much?

DOYLE. Forty per annum.

BROADBENT. Forty thousand?

DOYLE. No, forty. Forty pounds.

BROADBENT [*much dashed.*] That's what you call a fortune in Rosscullen, is it?

DOYLE. A girl with a dowry of five pounds calls it a fortune in Rosscullen. What's more 40 pounds a year IS a fortune there; and Nora Reilly enjoys a good deal of social consideration as an heiress on the strength of it. It has helped my father's household through many a tight place. My father was her father's agent. She came on a visit to us when he died, and has lived with us ever since.

BROADBENT [*attentively, beginning to suspect Larry of misconduct with Nora, and resolving to get to the bottom of it*]. Since when? I mean how old were you when she came?

DOYLE. I was seventeen. So was she: if she'd been older she'd have had more sense than to stay with us. We were together for 18 months before I went up to Dublin to study. When I went home for Christmas and Easter, she was there: I suppose it used to be something of an event for her, though of course I never thought of that then.

BROADBENT. Were you at all hard hit?

DOYLE. Not really. I had only two ideas at that time, first, to learn to do something; and then to get out of Ireland and have a chance of doing it. She didn't count. I was romantic about her, just as I was romantic about Byron's heroines or the old Round Tower of Rosscullen; but she didn't count any more than they did. I've never crossed St George's Channel since for her sake—never even landed at Queenstown and come back to London through Ireland.

BROADBENT. But did you ever say anything that would justify her in waiting for you?

DOYLE. No, never. But she IS waiting for me.

BROADBENT. How do you know?

DOYLE. She writes to me—on her birthday. She used to write on mine, and send me little things as presents; but I stopped that by pretending that it was no use when I was travelling, as they got lost in the foreign post-offices. [*He pronounces post-offices with the stress on offices, instead of on post*].

BROADBENT. You answer the letters?

DOYLE. Not very punctually. But they get acknowledged at one time or another.

BROADBENT. How do you feel when you see her handwriting?

DOYLE. Uneasy. I'd give 50 pounds to escape a letter.

BROADBENT [*looking grave, and throwing himself back in his chair to intimate that the cross-examination is over, and the result very damaging to the witness*] Hm!

DOYLE. What d'ye mean by Hm!?

BROADBENT. Of course I know that the moral code is different in Ireland. But in England it's not considered fair to trifle with a woman's affections.

DOYLE. You mean that an Englishman would get engaged to another woman and return Nora her letters and presents with a letter to say he was unworthy of her and wished her every happiness?

BROADBENT. Well, even that would set the poor girl's mind at rest.

DOYLE. Would it? I wonder! One thing I can tell you; and that is that Nora would wait until she died of old age sooner than ask my intentions or condescend to hint at the possibility of my having any. You don't know what Irish pride is. England may have knocked a good deal of it out of me; but she's never been in England; and if I had to choose between wounding that delicacy in her and hitting her in the face, I'd hit her in the face without a moment's hesitation.

BROADBENT [*who has been nursing his knee and reflecting, apparently rather agreeably*]. You know, all this sounds rather interesting. There's the Irish charm about it. That's the worst of you: the Irish charm doesn't exist for you.

DOYLE. Oh yes it does. But it's the charm of a dream. Live in contact with dreams and you will get something of their charm: live in contact with facts and you will get something of their brutality. I wish I could find a country to live in where the facts were not brutal and the dreams not unreal.

BROADBENT [*changing his attitude and responding to Doyle's earnestness with deep conviction: his elbows on the table and his hands clenched*]. Don't despair, Larry, old boy: things may look black; but there will be a great change after the next election.

DOYLE [*jumping up*]. Oh get out, you idiot!

BROADBENT [*rising also, not a bit snubbed*]. Ha! ha! you may laugh; but we shall see. However, don't let us argue about that. Come now! you ask my advice about Miss Reilly?

DOYLE [*reddening*]. No I don't. Damn your advice! [*Softening*] Let's have it, all the same.

BROADBENT. Well, everything you tell me about her impresses me favorably. She seems to have the feelings of a lady; and though we must face the fact that in England her income would hardly maintain her in the lower middle class—

DOYLE [*interrupting*]. Now look here, Tom. That reminds me. When you go to Ireland, just drop talking about the middle class and bragging of belonging to it. In Ireland you're either a gentleman or you're not. If you want to be particularly offensive to Nora, you can call her a Papist; but if you call her a middle-class woman, Heaven help you!

BROADBENT [*irrepressible*]. Never fear. You're all descended from the ancient kings: I know that. [*Complacently*] I'm not so tactless as you think, my boy. [*Earnest again*] I expect to find Miss Reilly a perfect lady; and I strongly advise you to come and have another look at her before you make up your mind about her. By the way, have you a photograph of her?

DOYLE. Her photographs stopped at twenty-five.

BROADBENT [*saddened*]. Ah yes, I suppose so. [*With feeling, severely*] Larry: you've treated that poor girl disgracefully.

DOYLE. By George, if she only knew that two men were talking about her like this—!

BROADBENT. She wouldn't like it, would she? Of course not. We ought to be ashamed of ourselves, Larry. [*More and more carried away by his new fancy*]. You know, I have a sort of presentiment that Miss Really is a very superior woman.

DOYLE [*staring hard at him*]. Oh you have, have you?

BROADBENT. Yes I have. There is something very touching about the history of this beautiful girl.

DOYLE. Beau—! Oho! Here's a chance for Nora! and for me! [*Calling*] Hodson.

HODSON [*appearing at the bedroom door*]. Did you call, sir?

DOYLE. Pack for me too. I'm going to Ireland with Mr Broadbent.

HODSON. Right, sir. [*He retires into the bedroom.*]

BROADBENT [*clapping Doyle on the shoulder*]. Thank you, old chap. Thank you.

ACT II

Rosscullen. Westward a hillside of granite rock and heather slopes upward across the prospect from south to north, a huge stone stands on it in a naturally impossible place, as if it had been tossed up there by a giant. Over the brow, in the desolate valley beyond, is a round tower. A lonely white high road trending away westward past the tower loses itself at the foot of the far mountains. It is evening; and there are great breadths of silken green in the Irish sky. The sun is setting.

A man with the face of a young saint, yet with white hair and perhaps 50 years on his back, is standing near the stone in a trance of intense melancholy, looking over the hills as if by mere intensity of gaze he could pierce the glories of the sunset and see into the streets of heaven. He is dressed in black, and is rather more clerical in appearance than most English curates are nowadays; but he does not wear the collar and waistcoat of a parish priest. He is roused from his trance by the chirp of an insect from a tuft of grass in a crevice of the stone. His face relaxes: he turns quietly, and gravely takes off his hat to the tuft, addressing the insect in a brogue which is the jocular assumption of a gentleman and not the natural speech of a peasant.

THE MAN. An is that yourself, Misther Grasshopper? I hope I see you well this fine evenin.

THE GRASSHOPPER [*prompt and shrill in answer*]. X.X.

THE MAN [*encouragingly*]. That's right. I suppose now you've come out to make yourself miserable by admyerin the sunset?

THE GRASSHOPPER [*sadly*]. X.X.

THE MAN. Aye, you're a thrue Irish grasshopper.

THE GRASSHOPPER [*loudly*]. X.X.X.

THE MAN. Three cheers for ould Ireland, is it? That helps you to face out the misery and the poverty and the torment, doesn't it?

THE GRASSHOPPER [*plaintively*]. X.X.

THE MAN. Ah, it's no use, me poor little friend. If you could jump as far as a kangaroo you couldn't jump away from your own heart an its punishment. You can only look at Heaven from here: you can't reach it. There! [*pointing with his stick to the sunset*] that's the gate o glory, isn't it?

THE GRASSHOPPER [*assenting*]. X.X.

THE MAN. Sure it's the wise grasshopper yar to know that! But tell me this, Misther Unworldly Wiseman: why does the sight of Heaven wring your heart an mine as the sight of holy wather wrings the heart o the divil? What wickedness have you done to bring that curse on you? Here! where are you jumpin to? Where's your manners to go skyrocketin like that out o the box in the middle o your confession [*he threatens it with his stick*]?

THE GRASSHOPPER [*penitently*]. X.

THE MAN [*lowering the stick*]. I accept your apology; but don't do it again. And now tell me one thing before I let you go home to bed. Which would you say this counthry was: hell or purgatory?

THE GRASSHOPPER. X.

THE MAN. Hell! Faith I'm afraid you're right. I wondher what you and me did when we were alive to get sent here.

THE GRASSHOPPER [*shrilly*]. X.X.

THE MAN [*nodding*]. Well, as you say, it's a delicate subject; and I won't press it on you. Now off widja.

THE GRASSHOPPER. X.X. [*It springs away*].

THE MAN [*waving his stick*] God speed you! [*He walks away past the stone towards the brow of the hill. Immediately a young laborer, his face distorted with terror, slips round from behind the stone.*]

THE LABORER [*crossing himself repeatedly*]. Oh glory be to God! glory be to God! Oh Holy Mother an all the saints! Oh murdher! murdher! [*Beside himself, calling Fadher Keegan! Fadher Keegan*]!

THE MAN [*turning*]. Who's there? What's that? [*He comes back and finds the laborer, who clasps his knees*] Patsy Farrell! What are you doing here?

PATSY. O for the love o God don't lave me here wi dhe grasshopper. I hard it spakin to you. Don't let it do me any harm, Father darlint.

KEEGAN. Get up, you foolish man, get up. Are you afraid of a poor insect because I pretended it was talking to me?

PATSY. Oh, it was no pretending, Fadher dear. Didn't it give three cheers n say it was a divil out o hell? Oh say you'll see me safe home, Fadher; n put a blessin on me or somethin [*he moans with terror*].

KEEGAN. What were you doin there, Patsy, listnin? Were you spyin on me?

PATSY. No, Fadher: on me oath an soul I wasn't: I was waitn to meet Masther Larry n carry his luggage from the car; n I fell asleep on the grass; n you woke me talkin to the grasshopper; n I hard its wicked little voice. Oh, d'ye think I'll die before the year's out, Fadher?

KEEGAN. For shame, Patsy! Is that your religion, to be afraid of a little deeshy grasshopper? Suppose it was a divil, what call have you to fear it? If I could ketch it, I'd make you take it home widja in your hat for a penance.

PATSY. Sure, if you won't let it harm me, I'm not afraid, your riverence. [*He gets up, a little reassured. He is a callow, flaxen polled, smoothfaced, downy chinned lad, fully grown but not yet fully filled out, with blue eyes and an instinctively acquired air of helplessness and silliness, indicating, not his real character, but a cunning developed by his constant dread of a hostile dominance, which he habitually tries to disarm and tempt into unmasking by pretending to be a much greater fool than he really is. Englishmen think him half-witted, which is exactly what he intends them to think. He is clad in corduroy trousers, unbuttoned waistcoat, and coarse blue striped shirt*].

KEEGAN [*admonitorily*]. Patsy: what did I tell you about callin me Father Keegan an your reverence? What did Father Dempsey tell you about it?

PATSY. Yis, Fadher.

KEEGAN. Father!

PATSY [*desperately*]. Arra, hwat am I to call you? Fadher Dempsey sez you're not a priest; n we all know you're not a man; n how do we know what ud happen to us if we showed any disrespect to you? N sure they say wanse a priest always a priest.

KEEGAN [*sternly*]. It's not for the like of you, Patsy, to go behind the instruction of your parish priest and set yourself up to judge whether your Church is right or wrong.

PATSY. Sure I know that, sir.

KEEGAN. The Church let me be its priest as long as it thought me fit for its work. When it took away my papers it meant you to know that I was only a poor madman, unfit and unworthy to take charge of the souls of the people.

PATSY. But wasn't it only because you knew more Latn than Father Dempsey that he was jealous of you?

KEEGAN [*scolding him to keep himself from smiling*]. How dar you, Patsy Farrell, put your own wicked little spites and foolishnesses into the heart of your priest? For two pins I'd tell him what you just said.

PATSY [*coaxing*] Sure you wouldn't—

KEEGAN. Wouldn't I? God forgive you! You're little better than a heathen.

PATSY. Deedn I am, Fadher: it's me bruddher the tinsmith in Dublin you're thinkin of. Sure he had to be a freethinker when he larnt a thrade and went to live in the town.

KEEGAN. Well, he'll get to Heaven before you if you're not careful, Patsy. And now you listen to me, once and for all. You'll talk to me and pray for me by the name of Pether Keegan, so you will. And when you're angry and tempted to lift your hand agen the donkey or stamp your foot on the little grasshopper, remember that the donkey's Pether Keegan's brother, and the grasshopper Pether Keegan's friend. And when you're tempted to throw a stone at a sinner or a curse at a beggar, remember that Pether Keegan is a worse sinner and a worse beggar, and keep the stone and the curse for him the next time you meet him. Now say God bless you, Pether, to me before I go, just to practise you a bit.

PATSY. Sure it wouldn't be right, Fadher. I can't—

KEEGAN. Yes you can. Now out with it; or I'll put this stick into your hand an make you hit me with it.

PATSY [*throwing himself on his knees in an ecstasy of adoration*]. Sure it's your blessin I want, Fadher Keegan. I'll have no luck widhout it.

KEEGAN [*shocked*]. Get up out o that, man. Don't kneel to me: I'm not a saint.

PATSY [*with intense conviction*]. Oh in throth yar, sir. [*The grasshopper chirps. Patsy, terrified, clutches at Keegan's hands*] Don't set it on me, Fadher: I'll do anythin you bid me.

KEEGAN [*pulling him up*]. You bosthoon, you! Don't you see that it only whistled to tell me Miss Reilly's comin? There! Look at her and pull yourself together for shame. Off widja to the road: you'll be late for the car if you don't make haste [*bustling him down the hill*]. I can see the dust of it in the gap already.

PATSY. The Lord save us! [*He goes down the hill towards the road like a haunted man*].

Nora Reilly comes down the hill. A slight weak woman in a pretty muslin print gown [*her best*], she is a figure commonplace enough to Irish eyes; but on the inhabitants of fatter-fed, crowded, hustling and bustling modern countries she makes a very different impression. The absence of any symptoms of coarseness or hardness or appetite in her, her comparative delicacy of manner and sensibility of apprehension, her thin hands and slender figure, her travel accent, with the caressing plaintive Irish melody of her speech, give her a charm which is all the more effective because, being untravelled, she is unconscious of it, and never dreams of deliberately dramatizing and exploiting it, as the Irishwoman in England does. For Tom Broadbent therefore, an attractive woman, whom he would even call ethereal. To Larry Doyle, an everyday woman fit only for the eighteenth century, helpless, useless, almost sexless, an invalid without the excuse of disease, an incarnation of everything in Ireland that drove him out of it. These judgments have little value and no finality; but they are the judgments on which her fate hangs just at present. Keegan touches his hat to her: he does not take it off.

NORA. Mr Keegan: I want to speak to you a minute if you don't mind.

KEEGAN [*dropping the broad Irish vernacular of his speech to Patsy*]. An hour if you like, Miss Reilly: you're always welcome. Shall we sit down?

NORA. Thank you. [*They sit on the heather. She is shy and anxious; but she comes to the point promptly because she can think of nothing else*]. They say you did a gradle o travelling at one time.

KEEGAN. Well you see I'm not a Mnooth man [*he means that he was not a student at Maynooth College*]. When I was young I admired the older generation of priests that had been educated in Salamanca. So when I felt sure of my vocation I went to Salamanca. Then I walked from Salamanca to Rome, an sted in a monastery there for a year. My pilgrimage to Rome taught me that walking is a better way of travelling than the train; so I walked from Rome to the Sorbonne in Paris; and I wish I could have walked from Paris to Oxford; for I was very sick on the sea. After a year of Oxford I had to walk to Jerusalem to walk the Oxford feeling off me. From Jerusalem I came back to Patmos, and spent six months at the monastery of Mount Athos. From that I came to Ireland and settled down as a parish priest until I went mad.

NORA [*startled*]. Oh dons say that.

KEEGAN. Why not? Don't you know the story? how I confessed a black man and gave him absolution; and how he put a spell on me and drove me mad.

NORA. How can you talk such nonsense about yourself? For shame!

KEEGAN. It's not nonsense at all: it's true—in a way. But never mind the black man. Now that you know what a travelled man I am, what can I do for you? [*She hesitates and plucks nervously at the heather. He stays her hand gently*]. Dear Miss Nora: don't pluck the little flower. If it was a pretty baby you wouldn't want to pull its head off and stick it in a vawse o water to look at. [*The grasshopper chirps: Keegan turns his head and addresses it in the vernacular*]. Be aisy, me son: she won't spoil the swing-swong in your little three. [*To Nora, resuming his urbane style*] You see I'm quite cracked; but never mind: I'm harmless. Now what is it?

NORA [*embarrassed*]. Oh, only idle curiosity. I wanted to know whether you found Ireland—I mean the country part of Ireland, of course—very small and backwardlike when you came back to it from Rome and Oxford and all the great cities.

KEEGAN. When I went to those great cities I saw wonders I had never seen in Ireland. But when I came back to Ireland I found all the wonders there waiting for me. You see they had been there all the time; but my eyes had never been opened to them. I did not know what my own house was like, because I had never been outside it.

NORA. D'ye think that's the same with everybody?

KEEGAN. With everybody who has eyes in his soul as well as in his head.

NORA. But really and truly now, weren't the people rather disappointing? I should think the girls must have seemed rather coarse and dowdy after the foreign princesses and people? But I suppose a priest wouldn't notice that.

KEEGAN. It's a priest's business to notice everything. I won't tell you all I noticed about women; but I'll tell you this. The more a man knows, and the farther he travels, the more likely he is to marry a country girl afterwards.

NORA [*blushing with delight*]. You're joking, Mr Keegan: I'm sure yar.

KEEGAN. My way of joking is to tell the truth. It's the funniest joke in the world.

NORA [*incredulous*]. Galong with you!

KEEGAN [*springing up actively*]. Shall we go down to the road and meet the car? [*She gives him her hand and he helps her up*]. Patsy Farrell told me you were expecting young Doyle.

NORA [*tossing her chin up at once*]. Oh, I'm not expecting him particularly. It's a wonder he's come back at all. After staying away eighteen years he can harly expect us to be very anxious to see him, can he now?

KEEGAN. Well, not anxious perhaps; but you will be curious to see how much he has changed in all these years.

NORA [*with a sudden bitter flush*]. I suppose that's all that brings him back to look at us, just to see how much WE'VE changed. Well, he can wait and see me be candlelight: I didn't come out to meet him: I'm going to walk to the Round Tower [*going west across the hill*].

KEEGAN. You couldn't do better this fine evening. [*Gravely*] I'll tell him where you've gone. [*She turns as if to forbid him; but the deep understanding in his eyes makes that impossible; and she only looks at him earnestly and goes. He watches her disappear on the other side of the hill; then says*] Aye, he's come to torment you; and you're driven already to torment him. [*He shakes his head, and goes slowly away across the hill in the opposite direction, lost in thought*].

By this time the car has arrived, and dropped three of its passengers on the high road at the foot of the hill. It is a monster jaunting car, black and dilapidated, one of the last survivors of the public vehicles known to earlier generations as Beeyankiny cars, the Irish having laid violent tongues on the name of their projector, one Bianconi, an enterprising Italian. The three passengers are the parish priest, Father Dempsey; Cornelius Doyle, Larry's father; and Broadbent, all in overcoats and as stiff as only an Irish car could make them.

The priest, stout and fatherly, falls far short of that finest type of countryside pastor which represents the genius of priesthood; but he is equally far above the base type in which a strongminded and unscrupulous peasant uses the Church to extort money, power, and privilege. He is a priest neither by vocation nor ambition, but because the life suits him. He has boundless authority over his flock, and taxes them stiffly enough to be a rich man. The old Protestant ascendency is now too broken to gall him. On the whole, an easygoing, amiable, even modest man as long as his dues are paid and his authority and dignity fully admitted.

Cornelius Doyle is an elder of the small wiry type, with a hardskinned, rather worried face, clean shaven except for sandy whiskers blanching into a lustreless pale yellow and quite white at the roots. His dress is that of a country-town titan of business: that is, an oldish shooting suit, and elastic sided boots quite unconnected with shooting. Feeling shy with Broadbent, he is hasty, which is his way of trying to appear genial.

Broadbent, for reasons which will appear later, has no luggage except a field glass and a guide book. The other two have left theirs to the unfortunate Patsy Farrell, who struggles up the hill after them, loaded with a sack of potatoes, a hamper, a fat goose, a colossal salmon, and several paper parcels.

Cornelius leads the way up the hill, with Broadbent at his heels. The priest follows; and Patsy lags laboriously behind.

CORNELIUS. This is a bit of a climb, Mr. Broadbent; but it's shorter than goin round be the road.

BROADBENT [*stopping to examine the great stone*]. Just a moment, Mr Doyle: I want to look at this stone. It must be Finian's die-cast.

CORNELIUS [*in blank bewilderment*]. Hwat?

BROADBENT. Murray describes it. One of your great national heroes—I can't pronounce the name—Finian Somebody, I think.

FATHER DEMPSEY [*also perplexed, and rather scandalized*]. Is it Fin McCool you mean?

BROADBENT. I daresay it is. [*Referring to the guide book*]. Murray says that a huge stone, probably of Druidic origin, is still pointed out as the die cast by Fin in his celebrated match with the devil.

CORNELIUS [*dubiously*]. Jeuce a word I ever heard of it!

FATHER DEMPSEY [*very seriously indeed, and even a little severely*]. Don't believe any such nonsense, sir. There never was any such thing. When people talk to you about Fin McCool and the like, take no notice of them. It's all idle stories and superstition.

BROADBENT [*somewhat indignantly; for to be rebuked by an Irish priest for superstition is more than he can stand*]. You don't suppose I believe it, do you?

FATHER DEMPSEY. Oh, I thought you did. D'ye see the top o the Roun Tower there? That's an antiquity worth lookin at.

BROADBENT [*deeply interested*]. Have you any theory as to what the Round Towers were for?

FATHER DEMPSEY [*a little offended*]. A theory? Me! [*Theories are connected in his mind with the late Professor Tyndall, and with scientific scepticism generally: also perhaps with the view that the Round Towers are phallic symbols*].

CORNELIUS [*remonstrating*]. Father Dempsey is the priest of the parish, Mr Broadbent. What would he be doing with a theory?

FATHER DEMPSEY [*with gentle emphasis*]. I have a KNOWLEDGE of what the Roun Towers were, if that's what you mean. They are the forefingers of the early Church, pointing us all to God.

Patsy, intolerably overburdened, loses his balance, and sits down involuntarily. His burdens are scattered over the hillside. Cornelius and Father Dempsey turn furiously on him, leaving Broadbent beaming at the stone and the tower with fatuous interest.

CORNELIUS. Oh, be the hokey, the sammin's broke in two! You schoopid ass, what d'ye mean?

FATHER DEMPSEY. Are you drunk, Patsy Farrell? Did I tell you to carry that hamper carefully or did I not?

PATSY [*rubbing the back of his head, which has almost dented a slab of granite*] Sure me fut slpt. Howkn I carry three men's luggage at wanst?

FATHER DEMPSEY. You were told to leave behind what you couldn't carry, an go back for it.

PATSY. An whose things was I to lave behind? Hwat would your reverence think if I left your hamper behind in the wet grass; n hwat would the masther say if I left the sammin and the goose be the side o the road for annywan to pick up?

CORNELIUS. Oh, you've a dale to say for yourself, you, butther-fingered omadhaun. Wait'll Ant Judy sees the state o that sammin: SHE'LL talk to you. Here! gimme that birdn that fish there; an take Father Dempsey's hamper to his house for him; n then come back for the rest.

FATHER DEMPSEY. Do, Patsy. And mind you don't fall down again.

PATSY. Sure I—

CORNELIUS [*bustling him up the bill*] Whisht! heres Ant Judy. [*Patsy goes grumbling in disgrace, with Father Dempsey's hamper*].

Aunt Judy comes down the hill, a woman of 50, in no way remarkable, lively and busy without energy or grip, placid without tranquillity, kindly without concern for others: indeed without much concern for herself: a contented product of a narrow, strainless life. She wears her hair parted in the middle and quite smooth, with a fattened bun at the back. Her dress is a plain brown frock, with a woollen pelerine of black and aniline mauve over her shoulders, all very trim in honor of the occasion. She looks round for Larry; is puzzled; then stares incredulously at Broadbent.

AUNT JUDY. Surely to goodness that's not you, Larry!

CORNELIUS. Arra how could he be Larry, woman alive? Larry's in no hurry home, it seems. I haven't set eyes on him. This is his friend, Mr Broadbent. Mr Broadbent, me sister Judy.

AUNT JUDY [*hospitably: going to Broadbent and shaking hands heartily*]. Mr. Broadbent! Fancy me takin you for Larry! Sure we haven't seen a sight of him for eighteen years, n he only a lad when he left us.

BROADBENT. It's not Larry's fault: he was to have been here before me. He started in our motor an hour before Mr Doyle arrived, to meet us at Athenmullet, intending to get here long before me.

AUNT JUDY. Lord save us! do you think he's had n axidnt?

BROADBENT. No: he's wired to say he's had a breakdown and will come on as soon as he can. He expects to be here at about ten.

AUNT JUDY. There now! Fancy him trustn himself in a motor and we all expectn him! Just like him! he'd never do anything like anybody else. Well, what can't be cured must be injoored. Come on in, all of you. You must be dyin for your tea, Mr Broadbent.

BROADBENT [*with a slight start*]. Oh, I'm afraid it's too late for tea [*he looks at his watch*].

AUNT JUDY. Not a bit: we never have it airlier than this. I hope they gave you a good dinner at Athenmullet.

BROADBENT [*trying to conceal his consternation as he realizes that he is not going to get any dinner after his drive*] Oh—er—excellent, excellent. By the way, hadn't I better see about a room at the hotel? [*They stare at him*].

CORNELIUS. The hotel!

FATHER DEMPSEY. Hwat hotel?

AUNT JUDY. Indeedn you'e not goin to a hotel. You'll stay with us. I'd have put you into Larry's room, only the boy's pallyass is too short for you; but we'll make a comfortable bed for you on the sofa in the parlor.

BROADBENT. You're very kind, Miss Doyle; but really I'm ashamed to give you so much trouble unnecessarily. I shan't mind the hotel in the least.

FATHER DEMPSEY. Man alive! There's no hotel in Rosscullen.

BROADBENT. No hotel! Why, the driver told me there was the finest hotel in Ireland here. [*They regard him joylessly*].

AUNT JUDY. Arra would you mind what the like of him would tell you? Sure he'd say hwatever was the least trouble to himself and the pleasantest to you, thinkin you might give him a thruppeny bit for himself or the like.

BROADBENT. Perhaps there's a public house.

FATHER DEMPSEY [*grimly.*] There's seventeen.

AUNT JUDY. Ah then, how could you stay at a public house? They'd have no place to put you even if it was a right place for you to go. Come! is it the sofa you're afraid of? If it is, you can have me own bed. I can sleep with Nora.

BROADBENT. Not at all, not at all: I should be only too delighted. But to upset your arrangements in this way—

CORNELIUS [*anxious to cut short the discussion, which makes him ashamed of his house; for he guesses Broadbent's standard of comfort a little more accurately than his sister does*] That's all right: it'll be no trouble at all. Hweres Nora?

AUNT JUDY. Oh, how do I know? She slipped out a little while ago: I thought she was goin to meet the car.

CORNELIUS [*dissatisfied*] It's a queer thing of her to run out o the way at such a time.

AUNT JUDY. Sure she's a queer girl altogether. Come. Come in, come in.

FATHER DEMPSEY. I'll say good-night, Mr Broadbent. If there's anything I can do for you in this parish, let me know. [*He shakes hands with Broadbent*].

BROADBENT [*effusively cordial*]. Thank you, Father Dempsey. Delighted to have met you, sir.

FATHER DEMPSEY [*passing on to Aunt Judy*]. Good-night, Miss Doyle.

AUNT JUDY. Won't you stay to tea?

FATHER DEMPSEY. Not to-night, thank you kindly: I have business to do at home. [*He turns to go, and meets Patsy Farrell returning unloaded*]. Have you left that hamper for me?

PATSY. Yis, your reverence.

FATHER DEMPSEY. That's a good lad [*going*].

PATSY [*to Aunt Judy*] Fadher Keegan sez—

FATHER DEMPSEY [*turning sharply on him*]. What's that you say?

PATSY [*frightened*]. Fadher Keegan—

FATHER DEMPSEY. How often have you heard me bid you call Mister Keegan in his proper name, the same as I do? Father Keegan indeed! Can't you tell the difference between your priest and any ole madman in a black coat?

PATSY. Sure I'm afraid he might put a spell on me.

FATHER DEMPSEY [*wrathfully*]. You mind what I tell you or I'll put a spell on you that'll make you lep. D'ye mind that now? [*He goes home*].

Patsy goes down the hill to retrieve the fish, the bird, and the sack.

AUNT JUDY. Ah, hwy can't you hold your tongue, Patsy, before Father Dempsey?

PATSY. Well, what was I to do? Father Keegan bid me tell you Miss Nora was gone to the Roun Tower.

AUNT JUDY. An hwy couldn't you wait to tell us until Father Dempsey was gone?

PATSY. I was afeerd o forgetn it; and then maybe he'd a sent the grasshopper or the little dark looker into me at night to remind me of it. [*The dark looker is the common grey lizard, which is supposed to walk down the throats of incautious sleepers and cause them to perish in a slow decline*].

CORNELIUS. Yah, you great gaum, you! Widjer grasshoppers and dark lookers! Here: take up them things and let me hear no more o your foolish lip.

[*Patsy obeys*]. You can take the sammin under your oxther. [*He wedges the salmon into Patsy's axilla*].

PATSY. I can take the goose too, sir. Put it on me back and gimme the neck of it in me mouth. [*Cornelius is about to comply thoughtlessly*].

AUNT JUDY [*feeling that Broadbent's presence demands special punctiliousness*]. For shame, Patsy! to offer to take the goose in your mouth that we have to eat after you! The master'll bring it in for you. [*Patsy, abashed, yet irritated by this ridiculous fastidiousness, takes his load up the hill*].

CORNELIUS. What the jeuce does Nora want to go to the Roun Tower for?

AUNT JUDY. Oh, the Lord knows! Romancin, I suppose. Props she thinks Larry would go there to look for her and see her safe home.

BROADBENT. I'm afraid it's all the fault of my motor. Miss Reilly must not be left to wait and walk home alone at night. Shall I go for her?

AUNT JUDY [*contemptuously*]. Arra hwat ud happen to her? Hurry in now, Corny. Come, Mr Broadbent. I left the tea on the hob to draw; and it'll be black if we don't go in an drink it.

They go up the hill. It is dark by this time.

Broadbent does not fare so badly after all at Aunt Judy's board. He gets not only tea and bread-and-butter, but more mutton chops than he has ever conceived it possible to eat at one sitting. There is also a most filling substance called potato cake. Hardly have his fears of being starved been replaced by his first misgiving that he is eating too much and will be sorry for it tomorrow, when his appetite is revived by the production of a bottle of illicitly distilled whisky, called pocheen, which he has read and dreamed of [*he calls it pottine*] and is now at last to taste. His good humor rises almost to excitement before Cornelius shows signs of sleepiness. The contrast between Aunt Judy's table service and that of the south and east coast hotels at which he spends his Fridays-to-Tuesdays when he is in London, seems to him delightfully Irish. The almost total atrophy of any sense of enjoyment in Cornelius, or even any desire for it or toleration of the possibility of life being something better than a round of sordid worries, relieved by tobacco, punch, fine mornings, and petty successes in buying and selling, passes with his guest as the whimsical affectation of a shrewd Irish humorist and incorrigible spendthrift. Aunt Judy seems to him an incarnate joke. The likelihood that the joke will pall after a month or so, and is probably not apparent at any time to born Rossculleners, or that he himself unconsciously entertains Aunt Judy by his fantastic English personality and English mispronunciations, does not occur to him for a moment. In the end he is so charmed, and so loth to go to bed and perhaps dream of prosaic England, that he insists on going out to smoke a cigar and look for Nora Reilly at the Round Tower. Not that any special insistence is needed; for the English inhibitive instinct does not seem to exist in Rosscullen. Just as Nora's liking to miss a meal and stay out at the Round Tower is accepted as a sufficient reason for her doing it, and for the family going to bed and leaving the door open for her, so Broadbent's whim to go out for a late stroll provokes neither hospitable remonstrance nor surprise. Indeed Aunt Judy wants to get rid of him whilst she makes a bed for him on the sofa. So off he goes, full fed, happy and enthusiastic, to explore the valley by moonlight.

The Round Tower stands about half an Irish mile from Rosscullen, some fifty yards south of the road on a knoll with a circle of wild greensward on it. The road once ran over this knoll; but modern engineering has tempered the level to the Beeyankiny car by carrying the road partly round the knoll and partly through a cutting; so that the way from the road to the tower is a footpath up the embankment through furze and brambles.

On the edge of this slope, at the top of the path, Nora is straining her eyes in the moonlight, watching for Larry. At last she gives it up with a sob of impatience, and retreats to the hoary foot of the tower, where she sits down discouraged and cries a little. Then she settles herself resignedly to wait, and hums a song—not an Irish melody, but a hackneyed English drawing-room ballad of the season before last—until some slight noise suggests a footstep, when she springs up eagerly and runs to the edge of the slope again. Some moments of silence and suspense follow, broken by unmistakable footsteps. She gives a little gasp as she sees a man approaching.

NORA. Is that you, Larry? [*Frightened a little*] Who's that?

[*BROADBENT's voice from below on the path*]. Don't be alarmed.

NORA. Oh, what an English accent you've got!

BROADBENT [*rising into view*] I must introduce myself—

NORA [*violently startled, retreating*]. It's not you! Who are you? What do you want?

BROADBENT [*advancing*]. I'm really so sorry to have alarmed you, Miss Reilly. My name is Broadbent. Larry's friend, you know.

NORA [*chilled*]. And has Mr Doyle not come with you?

BROADBENT. No. I've come instead. I hope I am not unwelcome.

NORA [*deeply mortified*]. I'm sorry Mr Doyle should have given you the trouble, I'm sure.

BROADBENT. You see, as a stranger and an Englishman, I thought it would be interesting to see the Round Tower by moonlight.

NORA. Oh, you came to see the tower. I thought—[*confused, trying to recover her manners*] Oh, of course. I was so startled—It's a beautiful night, isn't it?

BROADBENT. Lovely. I must explain why Larry has not come himself.

NORA. Why should he come? He's seen the tower often enough: it's no attraction to him. [*Genteelly*] An what do you think of Ireland, Mr Broadbent? Have you ever been here before?

BROADBENT. Never.

NORA. An how do you like it?

BROADBENT [*suddenly betraying a condition of extreme sentimentality*]. I can hardly trust myself to say how much I like it. The magic of this Irish scene, and—I really don't want to be personal, Miss Reilly; but the charm of your Irish voice—

NORA [*quite accustomed to gallantry, and attaching no seriousness whatever to it*]. Oh, get along with you, Mr Broadbent! You're breaking your heart about me already, I daresay, after seeing me for two minutes in the dark.

BROADBENT. The voice is just as beautiful in the dark, you know. Besides, I've heard a great deal about you from Larry.

NORA [*with bitter indifference*]. Have you now? Well, that's a great honor, I'm sure.

BROADBENT. I have looked forward to meeting you more than to anything else in Ireland.

NORA [*ironically*]. Dear me! did you now?

BROADBENT. I did really. I wish you had taken half as much interest in me.

NORA. Oh, I was dying to see you, of course. I daresay you can imagine the sensation an Englishman like you would make among us poor Irish people.

BROADBENT. Ah, now you're chaffing me, Miss Reilly: you know you are. You mustn't chaff me. I'm very much in earnest about Ireland and everything Irish. I'm very much in earnest about you and about Larry.

NORA. Larry has nothing to do with me, Mr Broadbent.

BROADBENT. If I really thought that, Miss Reilly, I should—well, I should let myself feel that charm of which I spoke just now more deeply than I—than I—

NORA. Is it making love to me you are?

BROADBENT [*scared and much upset*]. On my word I believe I am, Miss Reilly. If you say that to me again I shan't answer for myself: all the harps of Ireland are in your voice. [*She laughs at him. He suddenly loses his head and seizes her arms, to her great indignation*]. Stop laughing: do you hear? I am in earnest—in English earnest. When I say a thing like that to a woman, I mean it. [*Releasing her and trying to recover his ordinary manner in spite of his bewildering emotion*] I beg your pardon.

NORA. How dare you touch me?

BROADBENT. There are not many things I would not dare for you. That does not sound right perhaps; but I really—[*he stops and passes his hand over his forehead, rather lost*].

NORA. I think you ought to be ashamed. I think if you were a gentleman, and me alone with you in this place at night, you would die rather than do such a thing.

BROADBENT. You mean that it's an act of treachery to Larry?

NORA. Deed I don't. What has Larry to do with it? It's an act of disrespect and rudeness to me: it shows what you take me for. You can go your way now; and I'll go mine. Goodnight, Mr Broadbent.

BROADBENT. No, please, Miss Reilly. One moment. Listen to me. I'm serious: I'm desperately serious. Tell me that I'm interfering with Larry; and I'll go straight from this spot back to London and never see you again. That's on my honor: I will. Am I interfering with him?

NORA [*answering in spite of herself in a sudden spring of bitterness*]. I should think you ought to know better than me whether you're interfering with him. You've seen him oftener than I have. You know him better than I do, by this time. You've come to me quicker than he has, haven't you?

BROADBENT. I'm bound to tell you, Miss Reilly, that Larry has not arrived in Rosscullen yet. He meant to get here before me; but his car broke down; and he may not arrive until to-morrow.

NORA [*her face lighting up*]. Is that the truth?

BROADBENT. Yes: that's the truth. [*She gives a sigh of relief*]. You're glad of that?

NORA [*up in arms at once*]. Glad indeed! Why should I be glad? As we've waited eighteen years for him we can afford to wait a day longer, I should think.

BROADBENT. If you really feel like that about him, there may be a chance for another man yet. Eh?

NORA [*deeply offended*]. I suppose people are different in England, Mr Broadbent; so perhaps you don't mean any harm. In Ireland nobody'd mind what a man'd say in fun, nor take advantage of what a woman might say in answer to it. If a woman couldn't talk to a man for two minutes at their first meeting without being treated the way you're treating me, no decent woman would ever talk to a man at all.

BROADBENT. I don't understand that. I don't admit that. I am sincere; and my intentions are perfectly honorable. I think you will accept the fact that I'm an Englishman as a guarantee that I am not a man to act hastily or romantically, though I confess that your voice had such an extraordinary effect on me just now when you asked me so quaintly whether I was making love to you—

NORA [*flushing*] I never thought—

BROADHHNT [*quickly*]. Of course you didn't. I'm not so stupid as that. But I couldn't bear your laughing at the feeling it gave me. You—[*again struggling with a surge of emotion*] you don't know what I— [*he chokes for a moment and then blurts out with unnatural steadiness*] Will you be my wife?

NORA [*promptly*]. Deed I won't. The idea! [*Looking at him more carefully*] Arra, come home, Mr Broadbent; and get your senses back again. I think you're not accustomed to potcheen punch in the evening after your tea.

BROADBENT [*horrified*]. Do you mean to say that I—I—I—my God! that I appear drunk to you, Miss Reilly?

NORA [*compassionately*]. How many tumblers had you?

BROADBENT [*helplessly*]. Two.

NORA. The flavor of the turf prevented you noticing the strength of it. You'd better come home to bed.

BROADBENT [*fearfully agitated*]. But this is such a horrible doubt to put into my mind—to—to— For Heaven's sake, Miss Reilly, am I really drunk?

NORA [*soothingly*]. You'll be able to judge better in the morning. Come on now back with me, an think no more about it. [*She takes his arm with motherly solicitude and urges him gently toward the path*].

BROADBENT [*yielding in despair*]. I must be drunk—frightfully drunk; for your voice drove me out of my senses [*he stumbles over a stone*]. No: on my word, on my most sacred word of honor, Miss Reilly, I tripped over that stone. It was an accident; it was indeed.

NORA. Yes, of course it was. Just take my arm, Mr Broadbent, while we're goin down the path to the road. You'll be all right then.

BROADBENT [*submissively taking it*]. I can't sufficiently apologize, Miss Reilly, or express my sense of your kindness when I am in such a disgusting state. How could I be such a bea— [*he trips again*] damn the heather! my foot caught in it.

NORA. Steady now, steady. Come along: come. [*He is led down to the road in the character of a convicted drunkard. To him there it something divine in the sympathetic indulgence she substitutes for the angry disgust with which one of his own countrywomen would resent his supposed condition. And he has no suspicion of the fact, or of her ignorance of it, that when an Englishman is sentimental he behaves very much as an Irishman does when he is drunk*].

ACT III

Next morning Broadbent and Larry are sitting at the ends of a breakfast table in the middle of a small grass plot before Cornelius Doyle's house. They have finished their meal, and are buried in newspapers. Most of the crockery is crowded upon a large square black tray of japanned metal. The teapot is of brown delft ware. There is no silver; and the butter, on a dinner plate, is en bloc. The background to this breakfast is the house, a small white slated building, accessible by a half-glazed door. A person coming out into the garden by this door would find the table straight in front of him, and a gate leading to the road half way down the garden on his right; or, if he turned sharp to his left, he could pass round the end of the house through an unkempt shrubbery. The mutilated remnant of a huge planter statue, nearly dissolved by the rains of a century, and vaguely resembling a majestic female in Roman draperies, with a wreath in her hand, stands neglected amid the laurels. Such statues, though apparently works of art, grow naturally in Irish gardens. Their germination is a mystery to the oldest inhabitants, to whose means and taste they are totally foreign.

There is a rustic bench, much roiled by the birds, and decorticated and split by the weather, near the little gate. At the opposite side, a basket lies unmolested because it might as well be there as anywhere else. An empty chair at the table was lately occupied by Cornelius, who has finished his breakfast and gone in to the room in which he receives rents and keeps his books and cash, known in the household as "the office." This chair, like the two occupied by Larry and Broadbent, has a mahogany frame and is upholstered in black horsehair.

Larry rises and goes off through the shrubbery with his newspaper. Hodson comes in through the garden gate, disconsolate. Broadbent, who sits facing the gate, augurs the worst from his expression.

BROADBENT. Have you been to the village?

HODSON. No use, sir. We'll have to get everything from London by parcel post.

BROADBENT. I hope they made you comfortable last night.

HODSON. I was no worse than you were on that sofa, sir. One expects to rough it here, sir.

BROADBENT. We shall have to look out for some other arrangement. [*Cheering up irrepressibly*] Still, it's no end of a joke. How do you like the Irish, Hodson?

HODSON. Well, sir, they're all right anywhere but in their own country. I've known lots of em in England, and generally liked em. But here, sir, I seem simply to hate em. The feeling come over me the moment we landed at Cork, sir. It's no use my pretendin, sir: I can't bear em. My mind rises up agin their ways, somehow: they rub me the wrong way all over.

BROADBENT. Oh, their faults are on the surface: at heart they are one of the finest races on earth. [*Hodson turns away, without affecting to respond to his enthusiasm*]. By the way, Hodson—

HODSON [*turning*]. Yes, sir.

BROADBENT. Did you notice anything about me last night when I came in with that lady?

HODSON [*surprised*]. No, sir.

BROADBENT. Not any—er—? You may speak frankly.

HODSON. I didn't notice nothing, sir. What sort of thing ded you mean, sir?

BROADBENT. Well—er—er—well, to put it plainly, was I drunk?

HODSON [*amazed*]. No, sir.

BROADBENT. Quite sure?

HODSON. Well, I should a said rather the opposite, sir. Usually when you've been enjoying yourself, you're a bit hearty like. Last night you seemed rather low, if anything.

BROADBENT. I certainly have no headache. Did you try the pottine, Hodson?

HODSON. I just took a mouthful, sir. It tasted of peat: oh! something horrid, sir. The people here call peat turf. Potcheen and strong porter is what they like, sir. I'm sure I don't know how they can stand it. Give me beer, I say.

BROADBENT. By the way, you told me I couldn't have porridge for breakfast; but Mr Doyle had some.

HODSON. Yes, sir. Very sorry, sir. They call it stirabout, sir: that's how it was. They know no better, sir.

BROADBENT. All right: I'll have some tomorrow.

Hodson goes to the house. When he opens the door he finds Nora and Aunt Judy on the threshold. He stands aside to let them pass, with the air of a well trained servant oppressed by heavy trials. Then he goes in. Broadbent rises. Aunt Judy goes to the table and collects the plates and cups on the tray. Nora goes to the back of the rustic seat and looks out at the gate with the air of a woman accustomed to have nothing to do. Larry returns from the shrubbery.

BROADBENT. Good morning, Miss Doyle.

AUNT JUDY [*thinking it absurdly late in the day for such a salutation*]. Oh, good morning. [*Before moving his plate*] Have you done?

BROADBENT. Quite, thank you. You must excuse us for not waiting for you. The country air tempted us to get up early.

AUNT JUDY. N d'ye call this airly, God help you?

LARRY. Aunt Judy probably breakfasted about half past six.

AUNT JUDY. Whisht, you!—draggin the parlor chairs out into the gardn n givin Mr Broadbent his death over his meals out here in the cold air. [*To Broadbent*] Why d'ye put up with his foolishness, Mr Broadbent?

BROADBENT. I assure you I like the open air.

AUNT JUDY. Ah galong! How can you like what's not natural? I hope you slept well.

NORA. Did anything wake yup with a thump at three o'clock? I thought the house was falling. But then I'm a very light sleeper.

LARRY. I seem to recollect that one of the legs of the sofa in the parlor had a way of coming out unexpectedly eighteen years ago. Was that it, Tom?

BROADBENT [*hastily*]. Oh, it doesn't matter: I was not hurt—at least—er—

AUNT JUDY. Oh now what a shame! An I told Patsy Farrll to put a nail in it.

BROADBENT. He did, Miss Doyle. There was a nail, certainly.

AUNT JUDY. Dear oh dear!

An oldish peasant farmer, small, leathery, peat faced, with a deep voice and a surliness that is meant to be aggressive, and is in effect pathetic—the voice of a man of hard life and many sorrows—comes in at the gate. He is old enough to have perhaps worn a long tailed frieze coat and knee breeches in his time; but now he is dressed respectably in a black frock coat, tall hat, and pollard colored trousers; and his face is as clean as washing can make it, though that is not saying much, as the habit is recently acquired and not yet congenial.

THE NEW-COMER [*at the gate*]. God save all here! [*He comes a little way into the garden*].

LARRY [*patronizingly, speaking across the garden to him*]. Is that yourself, Mat Haffigan? Do you remember me?

MATTHEW [*intentionally rude and blunt*]. No. Who are you?

NORA. Oh, I'm sure you remember him, Mr Haffigan.

MATTHEW [*grudgingly admitting it*]. I suppose he'll be young Larry Doyle that was.

LARRY. Yes.

MATTHEW [*to Larry*]. I hear you done well in America.

LARRY. Fairly well.

MATTHEW. I suppose you saw me brother Andy out dhere.

LARRY. No. It's such a big place that looking for a man there is like looking for a needle in a bundle of hay. They tell me he's a great man out there.

MATTHEW. So he is, God be praised. Where's your father?

AUNT JUDY. He's inside, in the office, Mr Haffigan, with Barney Doarn n Father Dempsey.

Matthew, without wasting further words on the company, goes curtly into the house.

LARRY [*staring after him*]. Is anything wrong with old Mat?

NORA. No. He's the same as ever. Why?

LARRY. He's not the same to me. He used to be very civil to Master Larry: a deal too civil, I used to think. Now he's as surly and stand-off as a bear.

AUNT JUDY. Oh sure he's bought his farm in the Land Purchase. He's independent now.

NORA. It's made a great change, Larry. You'd harly know the old tenants now. You'd think it was a liberty to speak t'dhem—some o dhem. [*She goes to the table, and helps to take off the cloth, which she and Aunt Judy fold up between them*].

AUNT JUDY. I wonder what he wants to see Corny for. He hasn't been here since he paid the last of his old rent; and then he as good as threw it in Corny's face, I thought.

LARRY. No wonder! Of course they all hated us like the devil. Ugh! [*Moodily*] I've seen them in that office, telling my father what a fine boy I was, and plastering him with compliments, with your honor here and your honor there, when all the time their fingers were itching to beat his throat.

AUNT JUDY. Deedn why should they want to hurt poor Corny? It was he that got Mat the lease of his farm, and stood up for him as an industrious decent man.

BROADBENT. Was he industrious? That's remarkable, you know, in an Irishman.

LARRY. Industrious! That man's industry used to make me sick, even as a boy. I tell you, an Irish peasant's industry is not human: it's worse than the industry of a coral insect. An Englishman has some sense about working: he never does more than he can help—and hard enough to get him to do that without scamping it; but an Irishman will work as if he'd die the moment he stopped. That man Matthew Haffigan and his brother Andy made a farm out of a patch of stones on the hillside—cleared it and dug it with their own naked hands and bought their first spade out of their first crop of potatoes. Talk of making two blades of wheat grow where one grew before! those two men made a whole field of wheat grow where not even a furze bush had ever got its head up between the stones.

BROADBENT. That was magnificent, you know. Only a great race is capable of producing such men.

LARRY. Such fools, you mean! What good was it to them? The moment they'd done it, the landlord put a rent of 5 pounds a year on them, and turned them out because they couldn't pay it.

AUNT JUDY. Why couldn't they pay as well as Billy Byrne that took it after them?

LARRY [*angrily*]. You know very well that Billy Byrne never paid it. He only offered it to get possession. He never paid it.

AUNT JUDY. That was because Andy Haffigan hurt him with a brick so that he was never the same again. Andy had to run away to America for it.

BROADBENT [*glowing with indignation*]. Who can blame him, Miss Doyle? Who can blame him?

LARRY [*impatiently*]. Oh, rubbish! What's the good of the man that's starved out of a farm murdering the man that's starved into it? Would you have done such a thing?

BROADBENT. Yes. I—I—I—I—[*stammering with fury*] I should have shot the confounded landlord, and wrung the neck of the damned agent, and blown the farm up with dynamite, and Dublin Castle along with it.

LARRY. Oh yes: you'd have done great things; and a fat lot of good you'd have got out of it, too! That's an Englishman all over! make bad laws and give away all the land, and then, when your economic incompetence produces its natural and inevitable results, get virtuously indignant and kill the people that carry out your laws.

AUNT JUDY. Sure never mind him, Mr Broadbent. It doesn't matter, anyhow, because there's harly any landlords left; and ther'll soon be none at all.

LARRY. On the contrary, ther'll soon be nothing else; and the Lord help Ireland then!

AUNT JUDY. Ah, you're never satisfied, Larry. [*To Nora*] Come on, alanna, an make the paste for the pie. We can leave them to their talk. They don't want us [*she takes up the tray and goes into the house*].

BROADBENT [*rising and gallantly protesting*] Oh, Miss Doyle! Really, really—

Nora, following Aunt Judy with the rolled-up cloth in her hands, looks at him and strikes him dumb. He watches her until she disappears; then comes to Larry and addresses him with sudden intensity.

BROADBENT. Larry.

LARRY. What is it?

BROADBENT. I got drunk last night, and proposed to Miss Reilly.

LARRY. You HWAT??? [*He screams with laughter in the falsetto Irish register unused for that purpose in England*].

BROADBENT. What are you laughing at?

LARRY [*stopping dead*]. I don't know. That's the sort of thing an Irishman laughs at. Has she accepted you?

BROADBENT. I shall never forget that with the chivalry of her nation, though I was utterly at her mercy, she refused me.

LARRY. That was extremely improvident of her. [*Beginning to reflect*] But look here: when were you drunk? You were sober enough when you came back from the Round Tower with her.

BROADBENT. No, Larry, I was drunk, I am sorry to say. I had two tumblers of punch. She had to lead me home. You must have noticed it.

LARRY. I did not.

BROADBENT. She did.

LARRY. May I ask how long it took you to come to business? You can hardly have known her for more than a couple of hours.

BROADBENT. I am afraid it was hardly a couple of minutes. She was not here when I arrived; and I saw her for the first time at the tower.

LARRY. Well, you are a nice infant to be let loose in this country! Fancy the potcheen going to your head like that!

BROADBENT. Not to my head, I think. I have no headache; and I could speak distinctly. No: potcheen goes to the heart, not to the head. What ought I to do?

LARRY. Nothing. What need you do?

BROADBENT. There is rather a delicate moral question involved. The point is, was I drunk enough not to be morally responsible for my proposal? Or was I sober enough to be bound to repeat it now that I am undoubtedly sober?

LARRY. I should see a little more of her before deciding.

BROADBENT. No, no. That would not be right. That would not be fair. I am either under a moral obligation or I am not. I wish I knew how drunk I was.

LARRY. Well, you were evidently in a state of blithering sentimentality, anyhow.

BROADBENT. That is true, Larry: I admit it. Her voice has a most extraordinary effect on me. That Irish voice!

LARRY [*sympathetically*]. Yes, I know. When I first went to London I very nearly proposed to walk out with a waitress in an Aerated Bread shop because her Whitechapel accent was so distinguished, so quaintly touching, so pretty—

BROADBENT [*angrily*]. Miss Reilly is not a waitress, is she?

LARRY. Oh, come! The waitress was a very nice girl.

BROADBENT. You think every Englishwoman an angel. You really have coarse tastes in that way, Larry. Miss Reilly is one of the finer types: a type rare in England, except perhaps in the best of the aristocracy.

LARRY. Aristocracy be blowed! Do you know what Nora eats?

BROADBENT. Eats! what do you mean?

LARRY. Breakfast: tea and bread-and-butter, with an occasional rasher, and an egg on special occasions: say on her birthday. Dinner in the middle of the day, one course and nothing else. In the evening, tea and bread-and-butter again. You compare her with your Englishwomen who wolf down from three to five meat meals a day; and naturally you find her a sylph. The difference is not a difference of type: it's the difference between the woman who eats not wisely but too well, and the woman who eats not wisely but too little.

BROADBENT [*furious*]. Larry: you—you—you disgust me. You are a damned fool. [*He sits down angrily on the rustic seat, which sustains the shock with difficulty*].

LARRY. Steady! stead-eee! [*He laughs and seats himself on the table*].

Cornelius Doyle, Father Dempsey, Barney Doran, and Matthew Haffigan come from the house. Doran is a stout bodied, short armed, roundheaded, red-haired man on the verge of middle age, of sanguine temperament, with an enormous capacity for derisive, obscene, blasphemous, or merely cruel and senseless fun, and a violent and impetuous intolerance of other temperaments and other opinions, all this representing energy and capacity wasted and demoralized by want of sufficient training and social pressure to force it into beneficent activity and build a character with it; for Barney is by no means either stupid or weak. He is recklessly untidy as to his person; but the worst effects of his neglect are mitigated by a powdering of flour and mill dust; and his unbrushed clothes, made of a fashionable tailor's sackcloth, were evidently chosen regardless of expense for the sake of their appearance.

Matthew Haffigan, ill at ease, coasts the garden shyly on the shrubbery side until he anchors near the basket, where he feels least in the way. The priest comes to the table and slaps Larry on the shoulder. Larry, turning quickly, and recognizing Father Dempsey, alights from the table and shakes the priest's hand warmly. Doran comes down the garden between Father Dempsey and Matt; and Cornelius, on the other side of the table, turns to Broadbent, who rises genially.

CORNELIUS. I think we all met las night.

DORAN. I hadn't that pleasure.

CORNELIUS. To be sure, Barney: I forgot. [*To Broadbent, introducing Barney*] Mr Doran. He owns that fine mill you noticed from the car.

BROADBENT [*delighted with them all*]. Most happy, Mr Doran. Very pleased indeed.

Doran, not quite sure whether he is being courted or patronized, nods independently.

DORAN. How's yourself, Larry?

LARRY. Finely, thank you. No need to ask you. [*Doran grins; and they shake hands*].

CORNELIUS. Give Father Dempsey a chair, Larry.

Matthew Haffigan runs to the nearest end of the table and takes the chair from it, placing it near the basket; but Larry has already taken the chair from the other end and placed it in front of the table. Father Dempsey accepts that more central position.

CORNELIUS. Sit down, Barney, will you; and you, Mat.

Doran takes the chair Mat is still offering to the priest; and poor Matthew, outfaced by the miller, humbly turns the basket upside down and sits on it. Cornelius brings his own breakfast chair from the table and sits down on Father Dempsey's right. Broadbent resumes his seat on the rustic bench. Larry crosses to the bench and is about to sit down beside him when Broadbent holds him off nervously.

BROADBENT. Do you think it will bear two, Larry?

LARRY. Perhaps not. Don't move. I'll stand. [*He posts himself behind the bench*].

They are all now seated, except Larry; and the session assumes a portentous air, as if something important were coming.

CORNELIUS. Props you'll explain, Father Dempsey.

FATHER DEMPSEY. No, no: go on, you: the Church has no politics.

CORNELIUS. Were yever thinkin o goin into parliament at all, Larry?

LARRY. Me!

FATHER DEMPSEY [*encouragingly*] Yes, you. Hwy not?

LARRY. I'm afraid my ideas would not be popular enough.

CORNELIUS. I don't know that. Do you, Barney?

DORAN. There's too much blatherumskite in Irish politics a dale too much.

LARRY. But what about your present member? Is he going to retire?

CORNELIUS. No: I don't know that he is.

LARRY [*interrogatively*]. Well? then?

MATTHEW [*breaking out with surly bitterness*]. We've had enough of his foolish talk agen lanlords. Hwat call has he to talk about the lan, that never was outside of a city office in his life?

CORNELIUS. We're tired of him. He doesn't know hwere to stop. Every man can't own land; and some men must own it to employ them. It was all very well when solid men like Doran and me and Mat were kep from ownin land. But hwat man in his senses ever wanted to give land to Patsy Farrll an dhe like o him?

BROADBENT. But surely Irish landlordism was accountable for what Mr Haffigan suffered.

MATTHEW. Never mind hwat I suffered. I know what I suffered adhout you tellin me. But did I ever ask for more dhan the farm I made wid me own hans: tell me that, Corny Doyle, and you that knows. Was I fit for the responsibility or was I not? [*Snarling angrily at Cornelius*] Am I to be compared to Patsy Farrll, that doesn't harly know his right hand from his left? What did he ever suffer, I'd like to know?

CORNELIUS. That's just what I say. I wasn't comparin you to your disadvantage.

MATTHEW [*implacable*]. Then hwat did you mane be talkin about givin him lan?

DORAN. Aisy, Mat, aisy. You're like a bear with a sore back.

MATTHEW [*trembling with rage*]. An who are you, to offer to taitch me manners?

FATHER DEMPSEY [*admonitorily*]. Now, now, now, Mat none o dhat. How often have I told you you're too ready to take offence where none is meant? You don't understand: Corny Doyle is saying just what you want to have said. [*To Cornelius*] Go on, Mr Doyle; and never mind him.

MATTHEW [*rising*]. Well, if me lan is to be given to Patsy and his like, I'm goin oura dhis. I—

DORAN [*with violent impatience*] Arra who's goin to give your lan to Patsy, yowl fool ye?

FATHER DEMPSEY. Aisy, Barney, aisy. [*Sternly, to Mat*] I told you, Matthew Haffigan, that Corny Doyle was sayin nothin against you. I'm sorry your priest's word is not good enough for you. I'll go, sooner than stay to make you commit a sin against the Church. Good morning, gentlemen. [*He rises. They all rise, except Broadbent*].

DORAN [*to Mat*]. There! Sarve you dam well right, you cantankerous oul noodle.

MATTHEW [*appalled*]. Don't say dhat, Fadher Dempsey. I never had a thought agen you or the Holy Church. I know I'm a bit hasty when I think about the lan. I ax your pardn for it.

FATHER DEMPSEY [*resuming his seat with dignified reserve*]. Very well: I'll overlook it this time. [*He sits down. The others sit down, except Matthew. Father Dempsey, about to ask Corny to proceed, remembers Matthew and turns to him, giving him just a crumb of graciousness*]. Sit down, Mat. [*Matthew, crushed, sits down in disgrace, and is silent, his eyes shifting piteously from one speaker to another in an intensely mistrustful effort to understand them*]. Go on, Mr Doyle. We can make allowallowances. Go on.

CORNELIUS. Well, you see how it is, Larry. Round about here, we've got the land at last; and we want no more Goverment meddlin. We want a new class o man in parliament: one dhat knows dhat the farmer's the real backbone o the country, n doesn't care a snap of his fingers for the shoutn o the riff-raff in the towns, or for the foolishness of the laborers.

DORAN. Aye; an dhat can afford to live in London and pay his own way until Home Rule comes, instead o wantin subscriptions and the like.

FATHER DEMPSEY. Yes: that's a good point, Barney. When too much money goes to politics, it's the Church that has to starve for it. A member of parliament ought to be a help to the Church instead of a burden on it.

LARRY. Here's a chance for you, Tom. What do you say?

BROADBENT [*deprecatory, but important and smiling*]. Oh, I have no claim whatever to the seat. Besides, I'm a Saxon.

DORAN. A hwat?

BROADBENT. A Saxon. An Englishman.

DORAN. An Englishman. Bedad I never heard it called dhat before.

MATTHEW [*cunningly*]. If I might make so bould, Fadher, I wouldn't say but an English Prodestn mightn't have a more indepindent mind about the lan, an be less afeerd to spake out about it, dhan an Irish Catholic.

CORNELIUS. But sure Larry's as good as English: aren't you, Larry?

LARRY. You may put me out of your head, father, once for all.

CORNELIUS. Arra why?

LARRY. I have strong opinions which wouldn't suit you.

DORAN [*rallying him blatantly*]. Is it still Larry the bould Fenian?

LARRY. No: the bold Fenian is now an older and possibly foolisher man.

CORNELIUS. Hwat does it matter to us hwat your opinions are? You know that your father's bought his farm, just the same as Mat here n Barney's mill. All we ask now is to be let alone. You've nothin against that, have you?

LARRY. Certainly I have. I don't believe in letting anybody or anything alone.

CORNELIUS [*losing his temper*]. Arra what d'ye mean, you young fool? Here I've got you the offer of a good seat in parliament; n you think yourself mighty smart to stand there and talk foolishness to me. Will you take it or leave it?

LARRY. Very well: I'll take it with pleasure if you'll give it to me.

CORNELIUS [*subsiding sulkily*]. Well, why couldn't you say so at once? It's a good job you've made up your mind at last.

DORAN [*suspiciously*]. Stop a bit, stop a bit.

MATTHEW [*writhing between his dissatisfaction and his fear of the priest*]. It's not because he's your son that he's to get the sate. Fadher Dempsey: wouldn't you think well to ask him what he manes about the lan?

LARRY [*coming down on Mat promptly*]. I'll tell you, Mat. I always thought it was a stupid, lazy, good-for-nothing sort of thing to leave the land in the hands of the old landlords without calling them to a strict account for the use they made of it, and the condition of the people on it. I could see for myself that they thought of nothing but what they could get out of it to spend in England; and that they mortgaged and mortgaged until hardly one of them owned his own property or could have afforded to keep it up decently if he'd wanted to. But I tell you plump and plain, Mat, that if anybody thinks things will be any better now that the land is handed over to a lot of little men like you, without calling you to account either, they're mistaken.

MATTHEW [*sullenly*]. What call have you to look down on me? I suppose you think you're everybody because your father was a land agent.

LARRY. What call have you to look down on Patsy Farrell? I suppose you think you're everybody because you own a few fields.

MATTHEW. Was Patsy Farrll ever ill used as I was ill used? tell me dhat.

LARRY. He will be, if ever he gets into your power as you were in the power of your old landlord. Do you think, because you're poor and ignorant and half-crazy with toiling and moiling morning noon and night, that you'll be any less greedy and oppressive to them that have no land at all than old Nick Lestrange, who was an educated travelled gentleman that would not have been tempted as hard by a hundred pounds as you'd be by five shillings? Nick was too high above Patsy Farrell to be jealous of him; but you, that are only one little step above him, would die sooner than let him come up that step; and well you know it.

MATTHEW [*black with rage, in a low growl*]. Lemme oura this. [*He tries to rise; but Doran catches his coat and drags him down again*] I'm goin, I say. [*Raising his voice*] Leggo me coat, Barney Doran.

DORAN. Sit down, yowl omadhaun, you. [*Whispering*] Don't you want to stay an vote against him?

FATHER DEMPSEY [*holding up his finger*] Mat! [*Mat subsides*]. Now, now, now! come, come! Hwats all dhis about Patsy Farrll? Hwy need you fall out about HIM?

LARRY. Because it was by using Patsy's poverty to undersell England in the markets of the world that we drove England to ruin Ireland. And she'll ruin us again the moment we lift our heads from the dust if we trade in cheap labor; and serve us right too! If I get into parliament, I'll try to get an Act to prevent any of you from giving Patsy less than a pound a week [*they all start, hardly able to believe their ears*] or working him harder than you'd work a horse that cost you fifty guineas.

DORAN. Hwat!!!

CORNELIUS [*aghast*]. A pound a—God save us! the boy's mad.

Matthew, feeling that here is something quite beyond his powers, turns openmouthed to the priest, as if looking for nothing less than the summary excommunication of Larry.

LARRY. How is the man to marry and live a decent life on less?

FATHER DEMPSEY. Man alive, hwere have you been living all these years? and hwat have you been dreaming of? Why, some o dhese honest men here can't make that much out o the land for themselves, much less give it to a laborer.

LARRY [*now thoroughly roused*]. Then let them make room for those who can. Is Ireland never to have a chance? First she was given to the rich; and now that they have gorged on her flesh, her bones are to be flung to the poor, that can do nothing but suck the marrow out of her. If we can't have men of honor own the land, lets have men of ability. If we can't have men with ability, let us at least have men with capital. Anybody's better than Mat, who has neither honor, nor ability, nor capital, nor anything but mere brute labor and greed in him, Heaven help him!

DORAN. Well, we're not all foostherin oul doddherers like Mat. [*Pleasantly, to the subject of this description*] Are we, Mat?

LARRY. For modern industrial purposes you might just as well be, Barney. You're all children: the big world that I belong to has gone past you and left you. Anyhow, we Irishmen were never made to be farmers; and we'll never do any good at it. We're like the Jews: the Almighty gave us brains, and bid us farm them, and leave the clay and the worms alone.

FATHER DEMPSEY [*with gentle irony*]. Oh! is it Jews you want to make of us? I must catechize you a bit meself, I think. The next thing you'll be proposing is to repeal the disestablishment of the so-called Irish Church.

LARRY. Yes: why not? [*Sensation*].

MATTHEW [*rancorously*]. He's a turncoat.

LARRY. St Peter, the rock on which our Church was built, was crucified head downwards for being a turncoat.

FATHER DEMPSEY [*with a quiet authoritative dignity which checks Doran, who is on the point of breaking out*]. That's true. You hold your tongue as befits your ignorance, Matthew Haffigan; and trust your priest to deal with this young man. Now, Larry Doyle, whatever the blessed St Peter was crucified for, it was not for being a Prodestan. Are you one?

LARRY. No. I am a Catholic intelligent enough to see that the Protestants are never more dangerous to us than when they are free from all alliances with the State. The so-called Irish Church is stronger today than ever it was.

MATTHEW. Fadher Dempsey: will you tell him dhat me mother's ant was shot and kilt dead in the sthreet o Rosscullen be a soljer in the tithe war? [*Frantically*] He wants to put the tithes on us again. He—

LARRY [*interrupting him with overbearing contempt*]. Put the tithes on you again! Did the tithes ever come off you? Was your land any dearer when you paid the tithe to the parson than it was when you paid the same money to Nick Lestrange as rent, and he handed it over to the Church Sustentation Fund? Will you always be duped by Acts of Parliament that change nothing but the necktie of the man that picks your pocket? I'll tell you what I'd do with you, Mat Haffigan: I'd make you pay tithes to your own Church. I want the Catholic Church established in Ireland: that's what I want. Do you think that I, brought up to regard myself as the son of a great and holy Church, can bear to see her begging her bread from the ignorance and superstition of men like you? I would have her as high above worldly want as I would have her above worldly pride or ambition. Aye; and I would have Ireland compete with Rome itself for the chair of St Peter and the citadel of the Church; for Rome, in spite of all the blood of the martyrs, is pagan at heart to this day, while in Ireland the people is the Church and the Church the people.

FATHER DEMPSEY [*startled, but not at all displeased*]. Whisht, man! You're worse than mad Pether Keegan himself.

BROADBENT [*who has listened in the greatest astonishment*]. You amaze me, Larry. Who would have thought of your coming out like this! [*Solemnly*] But much as I appreciate your really brilliant eloquence, I implore you not to desert the great Liberal principle of Disestablishment.

LARRY. I am not a Liberal: Heaven forbid! A disestablished Church is the worst tyranny a nation can groan under.

BROADBENT [*making a wry face*]. DON'T be paradoxical, Larry. It really gives me a pain in my stomach.

LARRY. You'll soon find out the truth of it here. Look at Father Dempsey! he is disestablished: he has nothing to hope or fear from the State; and the result is that he's the most powerful man in Rosscullen. The member for Rosscullen would shake in his shoes if Father Dempsey looked crooked at him. [*Father Dempsey smiles, by no means averse to this acknowledgment of his authority*]. Look at yourself! you would defy the established Archbishop of Canterbury ten times a day; but catch you daring to say a word that would shock a Nonconformist! not you. The Conservative party today is the only one that's not priestridden—excuse the expression, Father [*Father Dempsey nods tolerantly*]—cause it's the only one that has established its Church and can prevent a clergyman becoming a bishop if he's not a Statesman as well as a Churchman.

He stops. They stare at him dumbfounded, and leave it to the priest to answer him.

FATHER DEMPSEY [*judicially*]. Young man: you'll not be the member for Rosscullen; but there's more in your head than the comb will take out.

LARRY. I'm sorry to disappoint you, father; but I told you it would be no use. And now I think the candidate had better retire and leave you to discuss his successor. [*He takes a newspaper from the table and goes away through the shrubbery amid dead silence, all turning to watch him until he passes out of sight round the corner of the house*].

DORAN [*dazed*]. Hwat sort of a fella is he at all at all?

FATHER DEMPSEY. He's a clever lad: there's the making of a man in him yet.

MATTHEW [*in consternation*]. D'ye mane to say dhat yll put him into parliament to bring back Nick

Lesthrange on me, and to put tithes on me, and to rob me for the like o Patsy Farrll, because he's Corny Doyle's only son?

DORAN [*brutally*]. Arra hould your whisht: who's goin to send him into parliament? Maybe you'd like us to send you dhere to thrate them to a little o your anxiety about dhat dirty little podato patch o yours.

MATTHEW [*plaintively*]. Am I to be towld dhis afther all me sufferins?

DORAN. Och, I'm tired o your sufferins. We've been hearin nothin else ever since we was childher but sufferins. Haven it wasn't yours it was somebody else's; and haven it was nobody else's it was ould Irelan's. How the divil are we to live on wan anodher's sufferins?

FATHER DEMPSEY. That's a thrue word, Barney Doarn; only your tongue's a little too familiar wi dhe devil. [*To Mat*] If you'd think a little more o the sufferins of the blessed saints, Mat, an a little less o your own, you'd find the way shorter from your farm to heaven. [*Mat is about to reply*] Dhere now! Dhat's enough! we know you mean well; an I'm not angry with you.

BROADBENT. Surely, Mr Haffigan, you can see the simple explanation of all this. My friend Larry Doyle is a most brilliant speaker; but he's a Tory: an ingrained oldfashioned Tory.

CORNELIUS. N how d'ye make dhat out, if I might ask you, Mr Broadbent?

BROADBENT [*collecting himself for a political deliverance*]. Well, you know, Mr Doyle, there's a strong dash of Toryism in the Irish character. Larry himself says that the great Duke of Wellington was the most typical Irishman that ever lived. Of course that's an absurd paradox; but still there's a great deal of truth in it. Now I am a Liberal. You know the great principles of the Liberal party. Peace—

FATHER DEMPSEY [*piously*]. Hear! hear!

BROADBENT [*encouraged*]. Thank you. Retrenchment—[*he waits for further applause*].

MATTHEW [*timidly*]. What might rethrenchment mane now?

BROADBENT. It means an immense reduction in the burden of the rates and taxes.

MATTHEW [*respectfully approving*]. Dhats right. Dhats right, sir.

BROADBENT [*perfunctorily*]. And, of course, Reform.

CORNELIUS }
FATHER DEMPSEY [*conventionally*]. Of course.
DORAN {

MATTHEW [*still suspicious*]. Hwat does Reform mane, sir? Does it mane altherin annythin dhats as it is now?

BROADBENT [*impressively*]. It means, Mr Haffigan, maintaining those reforms which have already been conferred on humanity by the Liberal Party, and trusting for future developments to the free activity of a free people on the basis of those reforms.

DORAN. Dhat's right. No more meddlin. We're all right now: all we want is to be let alone.

CORNELIUS. Hwat about Home Rule?

BROADBENT [*rising so as to address them more imposingly*]. I really cannot tell you what I feel about Home Rule without using the language of hyperbole.

DORAN. Savin Fadher Dempsey's presence, eh?

BROADBENT [*not understanding him*] Quite so—er—oh yes. All I can say is that as an Englishman I blush for the Union. It is the blackest stain on our national history. I look forward to the time-and it cannot be far distant, gentlemen, because Humanity is looking forward to it too, and insisting on it with no uncertain voice—I look forward to the time when an Irish legislature shall arise once more on the emerald pasture of College Green, and the Union Jack—that detestable symbol of a decadent Imperialism—be replaced by a flag as green as the island over which it waves—a flag on which we shall ask for England only a modest quartering in memory of our great party and of the immortal name of our grand old leader.

DORAN [*enthusiastically*]. Dhat's the style, begob! [*He smites his knee, and winks at Mat*].

MATTHEW. More power to you, Sir!

BROADBENT. I shall leave you now, gentlemen, to your deliberations. I should like to have enlarged on the services rendered by the Liberal Party to the religious faith of the great majority of the people of Ireland; but I shall content myself with saying that in my opinion you should choose no representative who—no matter what his personal creed may be—is not an ardent supporter of freedom of conscience, and is not prepared to prove it by contributions, as lavish as his means will allow, to the great and beneficent work which you, Father Dempsey [*Father Dempsey bows*], are doing for the people of Rosscullen. Nor should the lighter, but still most important question of the sports of the people be forgotten. The local cricket club—

CORNELIUS. The hwat!

DORAN. Nobody plays bats ball here, if dhat's what you mean.

BROADBENT. Well, let us say quoits. I saw two men, I think, last night—but after all, these are questions of detail. The main thing is that your candidate, whoever he may be, shall be a man of some means, able to help the locality instead of burdening it. And if he were a countryman of my own, the moral effect on the House of Commons would be immense! tremendous! Pardon my saying these few words: nobody feels their impertinence more than I do. Good morning, gentlemen.

He turns impressively to the gate, and trots away, congratulating himself, with a little twist of his head and cock of his eye, on having done a good stroke of political business.

HAFFIGAN [*awestruck*]. Good morning, sir.

THE REST. Good morning. [*They watch him vacantly until he is out of earshot*].

CORNELIUS. Hwat d'ye think, Father Dempsey?

FATHER DEMPSEY [*indulgently*] Well, he hasn't much sense, God help him; but for the matter o that, neither has our present member.

DORAN. Arra musha he's good enough for parliament what is there to do there but gas a bit, an chivy the Goverment, an vote wi dh Irish party?

CORNELIUS [*ruminatively*]. He's the queerest Englishman I ever met. When he opened the paper dhis mornin the first thing he saw was that an English expedition had been bet in a battle in Inja somewhere; an he was as pleased as Punch! Larry told him that if he'd been alive when the news o Waterloo came, he'd a died o grief over it. Bedad I don't think he's quite right in his head.

DORAN. Divil a matther if he has plenty o money. He'll do for us right enough.

MATTHEW [*deeply impressed by Broadbent, and unable to understand their levity concerning him*]. Did you mind what he said about rethrenchment? That was very good, I thought.

FATHER DEMPSEY. You might find out from Larry, Corny, what his means are. God forgive us all! it's poor work spoiling the Egyptians, though we have good warrant for it; so I'd like to know how much spoil there is before I commit meself. [*He rises. They all rise respectfully*].

CORNELIUS [*ruefully*]. I'd set me mind on Larry himself for the seat; but I suppose it can't be helped.

FATHER DEMPSEY [*consoling him*]. Well, the boy's young yet; an he has a head on him. Goodbye, all. [*He goes out through the gate*].

DORAN. I must be goin, too. [*He directs Cornelius's attention to what is passing in the road*]. Look at me bould Englishman shakin hans wid Fadher Dempsey for all the world like a candidate on election day. And look at Fadher Dempsey givin him a squeeze an a wink as much as to say It's all right, me boy. You watch him shakin hans with me too: he's waitn for me. I'll tell him he's as good as elected. [*He goes, chuckling mischievously*].

CORNELIUS. Come in with me, Mat. I think I'll sell you the pig after all. Come in an wet the bargain.

MATTHEW [*instantly dropping into the old whine of the tenant*]. I'm afeerd I can't afford the price, sir. [*He follows Cornelius into the house*].

Larry, newspaper still in hand, comes back through the shrubbery. Broadbent returns through the gate.

LARRY. Well? What has happened.

BROADBENT [*hugely self-satisfied*]. I think I've done the trick this time. I just gave them a bit of straight talk; and it went home. They were greatly impressed: everyone of those men believes in me and will vote for me when the question of selecting a candidate comes up. After all, whatever you say, Larry, they like an Englishman. They feel they can trust him, I suppose.

LARRY. Oh! they've transferred the honor to you, have they?

BROADBENT [*complacently*]. Well, it was a pretty obvious move, I should think. You know, these fellows have plenty of shrewdness in spite of their Irish oddity. [*Hodson comes from the house. Larry sits in Doran's chair and reads*]. Oh, by the way, Hodson—

HODSON [*coming between Broadbent and Larry*]. Yes, sir?

BROADBENT. I want you to be rather particular as to how you treat the people here.

HODSON. I haven't treated any of em yet, sir. If I was to accept all the treats they offer me I shouldn't be able to stand at this present moment, sir.

BROADBENT. Oh well, don't be too standoffish, you know, Hodson. I should like you to be popular. If it costs anything I'll make it up to you. It doesn't matter if you get a bit upset at first: they'll like you all the better for it.

HODSON. I'm sure you're very kind, sir; but it don't seem to matter to me whether they like me or not. I'm not going to stand for parliament here, sir.

BROADBENT. Well, I am. Now do you understand?

HODSON [*waking up at once*]. Oh, I beg your pardon, sir, I'm sure. I understand, sir.

CORNELIUS [*appearing at the house door with Mat*]. Patsy'll drive the pig over this evenin, Mat. Goodbye. [*He goes back into the house. Mat makes for the gate. Broadbent stops him. Hodson, pained by the derelict basket, picks it up and carries it away behind the house*].

BROADBENT [*beaming candidatorially*]. I must thank you very particularly, Mr Haffigan, for your support this morning. I value it because I know that the real heart of a nation is the class you represent, the yeomanry.

MATTHEW [*aghast*] The yeomanry!!!

LARRY [*looking up from his paper*]. Take care, Tom! In Rosscullen a yeoman means a sort of Orange Bashi-Bazouk. In England, Mat, they call a freehold farmer a yeoman.

MATTHEW [*huffily*]. I don't need to be insthructed be you, Larry Doyle. Some people think no one knows anythin but dhemselves. [*To Broadbent, deferentially*] Of course I know a gentleman like you would not compare me to the yeomanry. Me own granfather was flogged in the sthreets of Athenmullet be them when they put a gun in the thatch of his house an then went and found it there, bad cess to them!

BROADBENT [*with sympathetic interest*]. Then you are not the first martyr of your family, Mr Haffigan?

MATTHEW. They turned me out o the farm I made out of the stones o Little Rosscullen hill wid me own hans.

BROADBENT. I have heard about it; and my blood still boils at the thought. [*Calling*] Hodson—

HODSON [*behind the corner of the house*] Yes, sir. [*He hurries forward*].

BROADBENT. Hodson: this gentleman's sufferings should make every Englishman think. It is want of thought rather than want of heart that allows such iniquities to disgrace society.

HODSON [*prosaically*]. Yes sir.

MATTHEW. Well, I'll be goin. Good mornin to you kindly, sir.

BROADBENT. You have some distance to go, Mr Haffigan: will you allow me to drive you home?

MATTHEW. Oh sure it'd be throublin your honor.

BROADBENT. I insist: it will give me the greatest pleasure, I assure you. My car is in the stable: I can get it round in five minutes.

MATTHEW. Well, sir, if you wouldn't mind, we could bring the pig I've just bought from Corny.

BROADBENT [*with enthusiasm*]. Certainly, Mr Haffigan: it will be quite delightful to drive with a pig in the car: I shall feel quite like an Irishman. Hodson: stay with Mr Haffigan; and give him a hand with the pig if necessary. Come, Larry; and help me. [*He rushes away through the shrubbery*].

LARRY [*throwing the paper ill-humoredly on the chair*]. Look here, Tom! here, I say! confound it! [*he runs after him*].

MATTHEW [*glowering disdainfully at Hodson, and sitting down on Cornelius's chair as an act of social self-assertion*] N are you the valley?

HODSON. The valley? Oh, I follow you: yes: I'm Mr Broadbent's valet.

MATTHEW. Ye have an aisy time of it: you look purty sleek. [*With suppressed ferocity*] Look at me! Do I look sleek?

HODSON [*sadly*]. I wish I ad your ealth: you look as hard as nails. I suffer from an excess of uric acid.

MATTHEW. Musha what sort o disease is zhouragassid? Didjever suffer from injustice and starvation? Dhat's the Irish disease. It's aisy for you to talk o sufferin, an you livin on the fat o the land wid money wrung from us.

HODSON [*Coolly*]. Wots wrong with you, old chap? Has ennybody been doin ennything to you?

MATTHEW. Anythin timme! Didn't your English masther say that the blood biled in him to hear the way they put a rint on me for the farm I made wid me own hans, and turned me out of it to give it to Billy Byrne?

HODSON. Ow, Tom Broadbent's blood boils pretty easy over ennything that appens out of his own country. Don't you be taken in by my ole man, Paddy.

MATTHEW [*indignantly*]. Paddy yourself! How dar you call me Paddy?

HODSON [*unmoved*]. You just keep your hair on and listen to me. You Irish people are too well off: that's what's the matter with you. [*With sudden passion*] You talk of your rotten little farm because you made it by chuckin a few stownes dahn a hill! Well, wot price my grenfawther, I should like to know, that fitted up a fuss clawss shop and built up a fuss clawss drapery business in London by sixty years work, and then was chucked aht of it on is ed at the end of is lease withaht a penny for his goodwill. You talk of evictions! you that cawn't be moved until you've run up eighteen months rent. I once ran up four weeks in Lambeth when I was aht of a job in winter. They took the door off its inges and the winder aht of its sashes on me, and gave my wife pnoomownia. I'm a widower now. [*Between his teeth*] Gawd! when I think of the things we Englishmen av to put up with, and hear you Irish hahlin abaht your silly little grievances, and see the way you makes it worse for us by the rotten wages you'll come over and take and the rotten places you'll sleep in, I jast feel that I could take the oul bloomin British awland and make you a present of it, jast to let you find out wot real ardship's like.

MATTHEW [*starting up, more in scandalized incredulity than in anger*]. D'ye have the face to set up England agen Ireland for injustices an wrongs an disthress an sufferin?

HODSON [*with intense disgust and contempt, but with Cockney coolness*]. Ow, chuck it, Paddy. Cheese it. You danno wot ardship is over ere: all you know is ah to ahl abaht it. You take the biscuit at that, you do. I'm a Owm Ruler, I am. Do you know why?

MATTHEW [*equally contemptuous*]. D'ye know, yourself?

HODSON. Yes I do. It's because I want a little attention paid to my own country; and thet'll never be as long as your chaps are ollerin at Wesminister as if nowbody mettered but your own bloomin selves. Send em back to hell or C'naught, as good oul English Cromwell said. I'm jast sick of Ireland. Let it gow. Cut the cable. Make it a present to Germany to keep the oul Kyzer busy for a while; and give poor owld England a chawnce: thets wot I say.

MATTHEW [*full of scorn for a man so ignorant as to be unable to pronounce the word Connaught, which practically rhymes with bonnet in Ireland, though in Hodson's dialect it rhymes with untaught*]. Take care we don't cut the cable ourselves some day, bad scran to you! An tell me dhis: have yanny Coercion Acs in England? Have yanny removables? Have you Dublin Castle to suppress every newspaper dhat takes the part o your own counthry?

HODSON. We can beyave ahrselves withaht sich things.

MATTHEW. Bedad you're right. It'd only be waste o time to muzzle a sheep. Here! where's me pig? God forgimme for talkin to a poor ignorant craycher like you.

HODSON [*grinning with good-humored malice, too convinced of his own superiority to feel his withers wrung*]. Your pig'll ave a rare doin in that car, Paddy. Forty miles an ahr dahn that rocky lane will strike it pretty pink, you bet.

MATTHEW [*scornfully*]. Hwy can't you tell a raisonable lie when you're about it? What horse can go forty mile an hour?

HODSON. Orse! Wy, you silly oul rotten it's not a orse it's a mowtor. Do you suppose Tom Broadbent would gow off himself to arness a orse?

MATTHEW [*in consternation*]. Holy Moses! Don't tell me it's the ingine he wants to take me on.

HODSON. Wot else?

MATTHEW. Your sowl to Morris Kelly! why didn't you tell me that before? The divil an ingine he'll get me on this day. [*His ear catches an approaching teuf-teuf*] Oh murdher! it's comin afther me: I hear the puff puff of it. [*He runs away through the gate, much to Hodson's amusement. The noise of the motor ceases; and Hodson, anticipating Broadbent's return, throws off the politician and recomposes himself as a valet. Broadbent and Larry come through the shrubbery. Hodson moves aside to the gate*].

BROADBENT. Where is Mr Haffigan? Has he gone for the pig?

HODSON. Bolted, sir! Afraid of the motor, sir.

BROADBENT [*much disappointed*]. Oh, that's very tiresome. Did he leave any message?

HODSON. He was in too great a hurry, sir. Started to run home, sir, and left his pig behind him.

BROADBENT [*eagerly*]. Left the pig! Then it's all right. The pig's the thing: the pig will win over every Irish heart to me. We'll take the pig home to Haffigan's farm in the motor: it will have a tremendous effect. Hodson!

HODSON. Yes sir?

BROADBENT. Do you think you could collect a crowd to see the motor?

HODSON. Well, I'll try, sir.

BROADBENT. Thank you, Hodson: do.

Hodson goes out through the gate.

LARRY [*desperately*]. Once more, Tom, will you listen to me?

BROADBENT. Rubbish! I tell you it will be all right.

LARRY. Only this morning you confessed how surprised you were to find that the people here showed no sense of humor.

BROADBENT [*suddenly very solemn*]. Yes: their sense of humor is in abeyance: I noticed it the moment we landed. Think of that in a country where every man is a born humorist! Think of what it means! [*Impressively*] Larry we are in the presence of a great national grief.

LARRY. What's to grieve them?

BROADBENT. I divined it, Larry: I saw it in their faces. Ireland has never smiled since her hopes were buried in the grave of Gladstone.

LARRY. Oh, what's the use of talking to such a man? Now look here, Tom. Be serious for a moment if you can.

BROADBENT [*stupent*] Serious! I!!!

LARRY. Yes, you. You say the Irish sense of humor is in abeyance. Well, if you drive through Rosscullen in a motor car with Haffigan's pig, it won't stay in abeyance. Now I warn you.

BROADBENT [*breezily*]. Why, so much the better! I shall enjoy the joke myself more than any of them. [*Shouting*] Hallo, Patsy Farrell, where are you?

PATSY [*appearing in the shrubbery*]. Here I am, your honor.

BROADBENT. Go and catch the pig and put it into the car—we're going to take it to Mr Haffigan's. [*He gives Larry a slap on the shoulders that sends him staggering off through the gate, and follows him buoyantly, exclaiming*] Come on, you old croaker! I'll show you how to win an Irish seat.

PATSY [*meditatively*]. Bedad, if dhat pig gets a howlt o the handle o the machine— [*He shakes his head ominously and drifts away to the pigsty*].

ACT IV

The parlor in Cornelius Doyle's house. It communicates with the garden by a half glazed door. The fireplace is at the other side of the room, opposite the door and windows, the architect not having been sensitive to draughts. The table, rescued from the garden, is in the middle; and at it sits Keegan, the central figure in a rather crowded apartment.

Nora, sitting with her back to the fire at the end of the table, is playing backgammon across its corner with him, on his left hand. Aunt Judy, a little further back, sits facing the fire knitting, with her feet on the fender. A little to Keegan's right, in front of the table, and almost sitting on it, is Barney Doran. Half a dozen friends of his, all men, are between him and the open door, supported by others outside. In the corner behind them is the sofa, of mahogany and horsehair, made up as a bed for Broadbent. Against the wall behind Keegan stands a mahogany sideboard. A door leading to the interior of the house is near the fireplace, behind Aunt Judy. There are chairs against the wall, one at each end of the sideboard. Keegan's hat is on the one nearest the inner door; and his stick is leaning against it. A third chair, also against the wall, is near the garden door.

There is a strong contrast of emotional atmosphere between the two sides of the room. Keegan is extraordinarily stern: no game of backgammon could possibly make a man's face so grim. Aunt Judy is quietly busy. Nora it trying to ignore Doran and attend to her game.

On the other hand Doran is reeling in an ecstasy of mischievous mirth which has infected all his friends. They are screaming with laughter, doubled up, leaning on the furniture and against the walls, shouting, screeching, crying.

AUNT JUDY [*as the noise lulls for a moment*]. Arra hold your noise, Barney. What is there to laugh at?

DORAN. It got its fut into the little hweel—[*he is overcome afresh; and the rest collapse again*].

AUNT JUDY. Ah, have some sense: you're like a parcel o childher. Nora, hit him a thump on the back: he'll have a fit.

DORAN [*with squeezed eyes, exsuflicate with cachinnation*] Frens, he sez to dhem outside Doolan's: I'm takin the gintleman that pays the rint for a dhrive.

AUNT JUDY. Who did he mean be that?

DORAN. They call a pig that in England. That's their notion of a joke.

AUNT JUDY. Musha God help them if they can joke no better than that!

DORAN [*with renewed symptoms*]. Thin—

AUNT JUDY. Ah now don't be tellin it all over and settin yourself off again, Barney.

NORA. You've told us three times, Mr Doran.

DORAN. Well but whin I think of it—!

AUNT JUDY. Then don't think of it, alanna.

DORAN. There was Patsy Farrll in the back sate wi dhe pig between his knees, n me bould English boyoh in front at the machinery, n Larry Doyle in the road startin the injine wid a bed winch. At the first puff of it the pig lep out of its skin and bled Patsy's nose wi dhe ring in its snout. [*Roars of laughter: Keegan glares at them*]. Before Broadbint knew hwere he was, the pig was up his back and over into his lap; and bedad the poor baste did credit to Corny's thrainin of it; for it put in the fourth speed wid its right crubeen as if it was enthered for the Gordn Bennett.

NORA [*reproachfully*]. And Larry in front of it and all! It's nothn to laugh at, Mr Doran.

DORAN. Bedad, Miss Reilly, Larry cleared six yards backwards at wan jump if he cleared an inch; and he'd a cleared seven if Doolan's granmother hadn't cotch him in her apern widhout intindin to. [*Immense merriment*].

AUNT JUDY, Ah, for shame, Barney! the poor old woman! An she was hurt before, too, when she slipped on the stairs.

DORAN. Bedad, ma'am, she's hurt behind now; for Larry bouled her over like a skittle. [*General delight at this typical stroke of Irish Rabelaisianism*].

NORA. It's well the lad wasn't killed.

DORAN. Faith it wasn't o Larry we were thinkin jus dhen, wi dhe pig takin the main sthreet o Rosscullen on market day at a mile a minnit. Dh ony thing Broadbint could get at wi dhe pig in front of him was a fut brake; n the pig's tail was undher dhat; so that whin he thought he was putn non the brake he was ony squeezin the life out o the pig's tail. The more he put the brake on the more the pig squealed n the fasther he dhruv.

AUNT JUDY. Why couldn't he throw the pig out into the road?

DORAN. Sure he couldn't stand up to it, because he was spanchelled-like between his seat and dhat thing like a wheel on top of a stick between his knees.

AUNT JUDY. Lord have mercy on us!

NORA. I don't know how you can laugh. Do you, Mr Keegan?

KEEGAN [*grimly*]. Why not? There is danger, destruction, torment! What more do we want to make us merry? Go on, Barney: the last drops of joy are not squeezed from the story yet. Tell us again how our brother was torn asunder.

DORAN [*puzzled*]. Whose bruddher?

KEEGAN. Mine.

NORA. He means the pig, Mr Doran. You know his way.

DORAN [*rising gallantly to the occasion*]. Bedad I'm sorry for your poor bruddher, Misther Keegan; but I recommend you to thry him wid a couple o fried eggs for your breakfast tomorrow. It was a case of Excelsior wi dhat ambitious baste; for not content wid jumpin from the back seat into the front wan, he jumped from the front wan into the road in front of the car. And—

KEEGAN. And everybody laughed!

NORA. Don't go over that again, please, Mr Doran.

DORAN. Faith be the time the car went over the poor pig dhere was little left for me or anywan else to go over except wid a knife an fork.

AUNT JUDY. Why didn't Mr Broadbent stop the car when the pig was gone?

DORAN. Stop the car! He might as well ha thried to stop a mad bull. First it went wan way an made fireworks o Molly Ryan's crockery stall; an dhen it slewed round an ripped ten fut o wall out o the corner o the pound. [*With enormous enjoyment*] Begob, it just tore the town in two and sent the whole dam market to blazes. [*Nora offended, rises*].

KEEGAN [*indignantly*]. Sir!

DORAN [*quickly*]. Savin your presence, Miss Reilly, and Misther Keegan's. Dhere! I won't say anuddher word.

NORA. I'm surprised at you, Mr Doran. [*She sits down again*].

DORAN [*refectively*]. He has the divil's own luck, that Englishman, annyway; for when they picked him up he hadn't a scratch on him, barrn hwat the pig did to his cloes. Patsy had two fingers out o jynt; but the smith pulled them sthraight for him. Oh, you never heard such a hullaballoo as there was. There was Molly, cryin Me chaney, me beautyful chaney! n oul Mat shoutin Me pig, me pig! n the polus takin the number o the car, n not a man in the town able to speak for laughin—

KEEGAN [*with intense emphasis*]. It is hell: it is hell. Nowhere else could such a scene be a burst of happiness for the people.

Cornelius comes in hastily from the garden, pushing his way through the little crowd.

CORNELIUS. Whisht your laughin, boys! Here he is. [*He puts his hat on the sideboard, and goes to the fireplace, where he posts himself with his back to the chimneypiece*].

AUNT JUDY. Remember your behavior, now.

Everybody becomes silent, solemn, concerned, sympathetic. Broadbent enters, roiled and disordered as to his motoring coat: immensely important and serious as to himself. He makes his way to the end of the table nearest the garden door, whilst Larry, who accompanies him, throws his motoring coat on the sofa bed, and sits down, watching the proceedings.

BROADBENT [*taking off his leather cap with dignity and placing it on the table*]. I hope you have not been anxious about me.

AUNT JUDY. Deedn we have, Mr Broadbent. It's a mercy you weren't killed.

DORAN. Kilt! It's a mercy dheres two bones of you left houldin together. How dijjescape at all at all? Well, I never thought I'd be so glad to see you safe and sound again. Not a man in the town would say less [*murmurs of kindly assent*]. Won't you come down to Doolan's and have a dhrop o brandy to take the shock off?

BROADBENT. You're all really too kind; but the shock has quite passed off.

DORAN [*jovially*]. Never mind. Come along all the same and tell us about it over a frenly glass.

BROADBENT. May I say how deeply I feel the kindness with which I have been overwhelmed since my accident? I can truthfully declare that I am glad it happened, because it has brought out the kindness and sympathy of the Irish character to an extent I had no conception of.

SEVERAL {Oh, sure you're welcome!
PRESENT. {Sure it's only natural.
{Sure you might have been kilt.

A young man, on the point of bursting, hurries out. Barney puts an iron constraint on his features.

BROADBENT. All I can say is that I wish I could drink the health of everyone of you.

DORAN. Dhen come an do it.

BROADBENT [*very solemnly*]. No: I am a teetotaller.

AUNT JUDY [*incredulously*]. Arra since when?

BROADBENT. Since this morning, Miss Doyle. I have had a lesson [*he looks at Nora significantly*] that I shall not forget. It may be that total abstinence has already saved my life; for I was astonished at the steadiness of my nerves when death stared me in the face today. So I will ask you to excuse me. [*He collects himself for a speech*]. Gentlemen: I hope the gravity of the peril through which we have all passed—for I know that the danger to the bystanders was as great as to the occupants of the car—will prove an earnest of closer and more serious relations between us in the future. We have had a somewhat agitating day: a valuable and innocent animal has lost its life: a public building has been wrecked: an aged and infirm lady has suffered an impact for which I feel personally responsible, though my old friend Mr Laurence Doyle unfortunately incurred the first effects of her very natural resentment. I greatly regret the damage to Mr Patrick Farrell's fingers; and I have of course taken care that he shall not suffer pecuniarily by his mishap. [*Murmurs of admiration at his magnanimity, and A Voice "You're a gentleman, sir"*]. I am glad to say that Patsy took it like an Irishman, and, far from expressing any vindictive feeling, declared his willingness to break all his fingers and toes for me on the same terms [*subdued applause, and "More power to Patsy!"*]. Gentlemen: I felt at home in Ireland from the first [*rising excitement among his hearers*]. In every Irish breast I have found that spirit of liberty [*A cheery voice "Hear Hear"*], that instinctive mistrust of the Government [*A small pious voice, with intense expression, "God bless you, sir!"*], that love of independence [*A defiant voice, "That's it! Independence!"*], that indignant sympathy with the cause of oppressed nationalities abroad [*A threatening growl from all: the groundswell of patriotic passion*], and with the resolute assertion of personal rights at home, which is all but extinct in my own country. If it were legally possible I should become a naturalized Irishman; and if ever it be my good fortune to represent an Irish constituency in parliament, it shall be my first care to introduce a Bill legalizing such an operation. I believe a large section of the Liberal party would avail themselves of it. [*Momentary scepticism*]. I do. [*Convulsive cheering*]. Gentlemen: I have said enough. [*Cries of "Go on"*]. No: I have as yet no right to address you at all on political subjects; and we must not abuse the warmhearted Irish hospitality of Miss Doyle by turning her sittingroom into a public meeting.

DORAN [*energetically*]. Three cheers for Tom Broadbent, the future member for Rosscullen!

AUNT JUDY [*waving a half knitted sock*]. Hip hip hurray!

The cheers are given with great heartiness, as it is by this time, for the more humorous spirits present, a question of vociferation or internal rupture.

BROADBENT. Thank you from the bottom of my heart, friends.

NORA [*whispering to Doran*]. Take them away, Mr Doran [*Doran nods*].

DORAN. Well, good evenin, Mr Broadbent; an may you never regret the day you wint dhrivin wid Halligan's pig! [*They shake hands*]. Good evenin, Miss Doyle.

General handshaking, Broadbent shaking hands with everybody effusively. He accompanies them to the garden and can be heard outside saying Goodnight in every inflexion known to parliamentary candidates. Nora, Aunt Judy, Keegan, Larry, and Cornelius are left in the parlor. Larry goes to the threshold and watches the scene in the garden.

NORA. It's a shame to make game of him like that. He's a gradle more good in him than Barney Doran.

CORNELIUS. It's all up with his candidature. He'll be laughed out o the town.

LARRY [*turning quickly from the doorway*]. Oh no he won't: he's not an Irishman. He'll never know they're laughing at him; and while they're laughing he'll win the seat.

CORNELIUS. But he can't prevent the story getting about.

LARRY. He won't want to. He'll tell it himself as one of the most providential episodes in the history of England and Ireland.

AUNT JUDY. Sure he wouldn't make a fool of himself like that.

LARRY. Are you sure he's such a fool after all, Aunt Judy? Suppose you had a vote! which would you rather give it to? the man that told the story of Haffigan's pig Barney Doran's way or Broadbent's way?

AUNT JUDY. Faith I wouldn't give it to a man at all. It's a few women they want in parliament to stop their foolish blather.

BROADBENT [*bustling into the room, and taking off his damaged motoring overcoat, which he put down on the sofa*]. Well, that's over. I must apologize for making that speech, Miss Doyle; but they like it, you know. Everything helps in electioneering.

Larry takes the chair near the door; draws it near the table; and sits astride it, with his elbows folded on the back.

AUNT JUDY. I'd no notion you were such an orator, Mr Broadbent.

BROADBENT. Oh, it's only a knack. One picks it up on the platform. It stokes up their enthusiasm.

AUNT JUDY. Oh, I forgot. You've not met Mr Keegan. Let me introjooce you.

BROADBENT [*shaking hands effusively*]. Most happy to meet you, Mr Keegan. I have heard of you, though I have not had the pleasure of shaking your hand before. And now may I ask you—for I value no man's opinion more—what you think of my chances here.

KEEGAN [*coldly*]. Your chances, sir, are excellent. You will get into parliament.

BROADBENT [*delighted*]. I hope so. I think so. [*Fluctuating*] You really think so? You are sure you are not allowing your enthusiasm for our principles to get the better of your judgment?

KEEGAN. I have no enthusiasm for your principles, sir. You will get into parliament because you want to get into it badly enough to be prepared to take the necessary steps to induce the people to vote for you. That is how people usually get into that fantastic assembly.

BROADBENT [*puzzled*]. Of course. [*Pause*]. Quite so. [*Pause*]. Er—yes. [*Buoyant again*] I think they will vote for me. Eh? Yes?

AUNT JUDY. Arra why shouldn't they? Look at the people they DO vote for!

BROADBENT [*encouraged*]. That's true: that's very true. When I see the windbags, the carpetbaggers, the charlatans, the—the—the fools and ignoramuses who corrupt the multitude by their wealth, or seduce them by spouting balderdash to them, I cannot help thinking that an honest man with no humbug about him, who will talk straight common sense and take his stand on the solid ground of principle and public duty, must win his way with men of all classes.

KEEGAN [*quietly*]. Sir: there was a time, in my ignorant youth, when I should have called you a hypocrite.

BROADBENT [*reddening*]. A hypocrite!

NORA [*hastily*]. Oh I'm sure you don't think anything of the sort, Mr Keegan.

BROADBENT [*emphatically*]. Thank you, Miss Reilly: thank you.

CORNELIUS [*gloomily*]. We all have to stretch it a bit in politics: hwat's the use o pretendin we don't?

BROADBENT [*stiffly*]. I hope I have said or done nothing that calls for any such observation, Mr Doyle. If there is a vice I detest—or against which my whole public life has been a protest—it is the vice of hypocrisy. I would almost rather be inconsistent than insincere.

KEEGAN. Do not be offended, sir: I know that you are quite sincere. There is a saying in the Scripture which runs—so far as the memory of an oldish man can carry the words—Let not the right side of your brain know what the left side doeth. I learnt at Oxford that this is the secret of the Englishman's strange power of making the best of both worlds.

BROADBENT. Surely the text refers to our right and left hands. I am somewhat surprised to hear a member of your Church quote so essentially Protestant a document as the Bible; but at least you might quote it accurately.

LARRY. Tom: with the best intentions you're making an ass of yourself. You don't understand Mr Keegan's peculiar vein of humor.

BROADBENT [*instantly recovering his confidence*]. Ah! it was only your delightful Irish humor, Mr Keegan. Of course, of course. How stupid of me! I'm so sorry. [*He pats Keegan consolingly on the back*]. John Bull's wits are still slow, you see. Besides, calling me a hypocrite was too big a joke to swallow all at once, you know.

KEEGAN. You must also allow for the fact that I am mad.

NORA. Ah, don't talk like that, Mr Keegan.

BROADBENT [*encouragingly*]. Not at all, not at all. Only a whimsical Irishman, eh?

LARRY. Are you really mad, Mr Keegan?

AUNT JUDY [*shocked*]. Oh, Larry, how could you ask him such a thing?

LARRY. I don't think Mr Keegan minds. [*To Keegan*] What's the true version of the story of that black man you confessed on his deathbed?

KEEGAN. What story have you heard about that?

LARRY. I am informed that when the devil came for the black heathen, he took off your head and turned it three times round before putting it on again; and that your head's been turned ever since.

NORA [*reproachfully*]. Larry!

KEEGAN [*blandly*]. That is not quite what occurred. [*He collects himself for a serious utterance: they attend involuntarily*]. I heard that a black man was dying, and that the people were afraid to go near him. When I went to the place I found an elderly Hindoo, who told me one of those tales of unmerited misfortune, of cruel ill luck, of relentless persecution by destiny, which sometimes wither the commonplaces of consolation on the lips of a priest. But this man did not complain of his misfortunes. They were brought upon him, he said, by sins committed in a former existence. Then, without a word of comfort from me, he died with a clear-eyed resignation that my most earnest exhortations have rarely produced in a Christian, and left me sitting there by his bedside with the mystery of this world suddenly revealed to me.

BROADBENT. That is a remarkable tribute to the liberty of conscience enjoyed by the subjects of our Indian Empire.

LARRY. No doubt; but may we venture to ask what is the mystery of this world?

KEEGAN. This world, sir, is very clearly a place of torment and penance, a place where the fool flourishes and the good and wise are hated and persecuted, a place where men and women torture one another in the name of love; where children are scourged and enslaved in the name of parental duty and education; where the weak in body are poisoned and mutilated in the name of healing, and the weak in character are put to the horrible torture of imprisonment, not for hours but for years, in the name of justice. It is a place where the hardest toil is a welcome refuge from the horror and tedium of pleasure, and where charity and good works are done only for hire to ransom the souls of the spoiler and the sybarite. Now, sir, there is only one place of horror and torment known to my religion; and that place is hell. Therefore it is plain to me that this earth of ours must be hell, and that we are all here, as the Indian revealed to me—perhaps he was sent to reveal it to me to expiate crimes committed by us in a former existence.

AUNT JUDY [*awestruck*]. Heaven save us, what a thing to say!

CORNELIUS [*sighing*]. It's a queer world: that's certain.

BROADBENT. Your idea is a very clever one, Mr Keegan: really most brilliant: I should never have thought of it. But it seems to me—if I may say so—that you are overlooking the fact that, of the evils you describe, some are absolutely necessary for the preservation of society, and others are encouraged only when the Tories are in office.

LARRY. I expect you were a Tory in a former existence; and that is why you are here.

BROADBENT [*with conviction*]. Never, Larry, never. But leaving politics out of the question, I find the world quite good enough for me: rather a jolly place, in fact.

KEEGAN [*looking at him with quiet wonder*]. You are satisfied?

BROADBENT. As a reasonable man, yes. I see no evils in the world—except, of course, natural evils—that cannot be remedied by freedom, self-government, and English institutions. I think so, not because I am an Englishman, but as a matter of common sense.

KEEGAN. You feel at home in the world, then?

BROADBENT. Of course. Don't you?

KEEGAN [*from the very depths of his nature*]. No.

BROADBENT [*breezily*]. Try phosphorus pills. I always take them when my brain is overworked. I'll give you the address in Oxford Street.

KEEGAN [*enigmatically: rising*]. Miss Doyle: my wandering fit has come on me: will you excuse me?

AUNT JUDY. To be sure: you know you can come in n nout as you like.

KEEGAN. We can finish the game some other time, Miss Reilly. [*He goes for his hat and stick.*]

NORA. No: I'm out with you [*she disarranges the pieces and rises*]. I was too wicked in a former existence to play backgammon with a good man like you.

AUNT JUDY [*whispering to her*]. Whisht, whisht, child! Don't set him back on that again.

KEEGAN [*to Nora*]. When I look at you, I think that perhaps Ireland is only purgatory, after all. [*He passes on to the garden door*].

NORA. Galong with you!

BROADBENT [*whispering to Cornelius*]. Has he a vote?

CORNELIUS [*nodding*]. Yes. An there's lots'll vote the way he tells them.

KEEGAN [*at the garden door, with gentle gravity*]. Good evening, Mr Broadbent. You have set me thinking. Thank you.

BROADBENT [*delighted, hurrying across to him to shake hands*]. No, really? You find that contact with English ideas is stimulating, eh?

KEEGAN. I am never tired of hearing you talk, Mr Broadbent.

BROADBENT [*modestly remonstrating*]. Oh come! come!

KEEGAN. Yes, I assure you. You are an extremely interesting man. [*He goes out*].

BROADBENT [*enthusiastically*]. What a nice chap! What an intelligent, interesting fellow! By the way, I'd better have a wash. [*He takes up his coat and cap, and leaves the room through the inner door*].

Nora returns to her chair and shuts up the backgammon board.

AUNT JUDY. Keegan's very queer to-day. He has his mad fit on him.

CORNELIUS [*worried and bitter*]. I wouldn't say but he's right after all. It's a contrairy world. [*To Larry*]. Why would you be such a fool as to let him take the seat in parliament from you?

LARRY [*glancing at Nora*]. He will take more than that from me before he's done here.

CORNELIUS. I wish he'd never set foot in my house, bad luck to his fat face! D'ye think he'd lend me 300 pounds on the farm, Larry? When I'm so hard up, it seems a waste o money not to mortgage it now it's me own.

LARRY. I can lend you 300 pounds on it.

CORNELIUS. No, no: I wasn't putn in for that. When I die and leave you the farm I should like to be able to feel that it was all me own, and not half yours to start with. Now I'll take me oath Barney Doarn's goin to ask Broadbent to lend him 500 pounds on the mill to put in a new hweel; for the old one'll harly hol together. An Haffigan can't sleep with covetn that corner o land at the foot of his medda that belongs to Doolan. He'll have to mortgage to buy it. I may as well be first as last. D'ye think Broadbent'd len me a little?

LARRY. I'm quite sure he will.

CORNELIUS. Is he as ready as that? Would he len me five hunderd, d'ye think?

LARRY. He'll lend you more than the land'll ever be worth to you; so for Heaven's sake be prudent.

CORNELIUS [*judicially*]. All right, all right, me son: I'll be careful. I'm goin into the office for a bit. [*He withdraws through the inner door, obviously to prepare his application to Broadbent*].

AUNT JUDY [*indignantly*]. As if he hadn't seen enough o borryin when he was an agent without beginnin borryin himself! [*She rises*]. I'll bory him, so I will. [*She puts her knitting on the table and follows him out, with a resolute air that bodes trouble for Cornelius*].

Larry and Nora are left together for the first time since his arrival. She looks at him with a smile that perishes as she sees him aimlessly rocking his chair, and reflecting, evidently not about her, with his lips pursed as if he were whistling. With a catch in her throat she takes up Aunt Judy's knitting, and makes a pretence of going on with it.

NORA. I suppose it didn't seem very long to you.

LARRY [*starting*]. Eh? What didn't?

NORA. The eighteen years you've been away.

LARRY. Oh, that! No: it seems hardly more than a week. I've been so busy—had so little time to think.

NORA. I've had nothin else to do but think.

LARRY. That was very bad for you. Why didn't you give it up? Why did you stay here?

NORA. Because nobody sent for me to go anywhere else, I suppose. That's why.

LARRY. Yes: one does stick frightfully in the same place, unless some external force comes and routs one out. [*He yawns slightly; but as she looks up quickly at him, he pulls himself together and rises with an air of waking up and getting to work cheerfully to make himself agreeable*]. And how have you been all this time?

NORA. Quite well, thank you.

LARRY. That's right. [*Suddenly finding that he has nothing else to say, and being ill at ease in consequence, he strolls about the room humming a certain tune from Offenbach's Whittington*].

NORA [*struggling with her tears*]. Is that all you have to say to me, Larry?

LARRY. Well, what is there to say? You see, we know each other so well.

NORA [*a little consoled*]. Yes: of course we do. [*He does not reply*]. I wonder you came back at all.

LARRY. I couldn't help it. [*She looks up affectionately*]. Tom made me. [*She looks down again quickly to conceal the effect of this blow. He whistles another stave; then resumes*]. I had a sort of dread of returning to Ireland. I felt somehow that my luck would turn if I came back. And now here I am, none the worse.

NORA. Praps it's a little dull for you.

LARRY. No: I haven't exhausted the interest of strolling about the old places and remembering and romancing about them.

NORA [*hopefully*]. Oh! You DO remember the places, then?

LARRY. Of course. They have associations.

NORA [*not doubting that the associations are with her*]. I suppose so.

LARRY. M'yes. I can remember particular spots where I had long fits of thinking about the countries I meant to get to when I escaped from Ireland. America and London, and sometimes Rome and the east.

NORA [*deeply mortified*]. Was that all you used to be thinking about?

LARRY. Well, there was precious little else to think about here, my dear Nora, except sometimes at sunset, when one got maudlin and called Ireland Erin, and imagined one was remembering the days of old, and so forth. [*He whistles Let Erin Remember*].

NORA. Did jever get a letter I wrote you last February?

LARRY. Oh yes; and I really intended to answer it. But I haven't had a moment; and I knew you wouldn't mind. You see, I am so afraid of boring you by writing about affairs you don't understand and people you don't know! And yet what else have I to write about? I begin a letter; and then I tear it up again. The fact is, fond as we are of one another, Nora, we have so little in common—I mean of course the things one can put in a letter—that correspondence is apt to become the hardest of hard work.

NORA. Yes: it's hard for me to know anything about you if you never tell me anything.

LARRY [*pettishly*]. Nora: a man can't sit down and write his life day by day when he's tired enough with having lived it.

NORA. I'm not blaming you.

LARRY [*looking at her with some concern*]. You seem rather out of spirits. [*Going closer to her, anxiously and tenderly*] You haven't got neuralgia, have you?

NORA. No.

LARRY [*reassured*]. I get a touch of it sometimes when I am below par. [*absently, again strolling about*] Yes, yes. [*He begins to hum again, and soon breaks into articulate melody*].

Though summer smiles on here for ever,
Though not a leaf falls from the tree,
Tell England I'll forget her never,
[*Nora puts down the knitting and stares at him*].
O wind that blows across the sea.
[*With much expression*]
Tell England I'll forget her ne-e-e-e-ver
O wind that blows acro-oss—

[*Here the melody soars out of his range. He continues falsetto, but changes the tune to Let Erin Remember*]. I'm afraid I'm boring you, Nora, though you're too kind to say so.

NORA. Are you wanting to get back to England already?

LARRY. Not at all. Not at all.

NORA. That's a queer song to sing to me if you're not.

LARRY. The song! Oh, it doesn't mean anything: it's by a German Jew, like most English patriotic sentiment. Never mind me, my dear: go on with your work; and don't let me bore you.

NORA [*bitterly*]. Rosscullen isn't such a lively place that I am likely to be bored by you at our first talk together after eighteen years, though you don't seem to have much to say to me after all.

LARRY. Eighteen years is a devilish long time, Nora. Now if it had been eighteen minutes, or even eighteen months, we should be able to pick up the interrupted thread, and chatter like two magpies. But as it is, I have simply nothing to say; and you seem to have less.

NORA. I—[*her tears choke her; but the keeps up appearances desperately*].

LARRY [*quite unconscious of his cruelty*]. In a week or so we shall be quite old friends again. Meanwhile, as I feel that I am not making myself particularly entertaining, I'll take myself off. Tell Tom I've gone for a stroll over the hill.

NORA. You seem very fond of Tom, as you call him.

LARRY [*the triviality going suddenly out of his voice*]. Yes I'm fond of Tom.

NORA. Oh, well, don't let me keep you from him.

LARRY. I know quite well that my departure will be a relief. Rather a failure, this first meeting after eighteen years, eh? Well, never mind: these great sentimental events always are failures; and now the worst of it's over anyhow. [*He goes out through the garden door*].

Nora, left alone, struggles wildly to save herself from breaking down, and then drops her face on the table and gives way to a convulsion of crying. Her sobs shake her so that she can hear nothing; and she has no suspicion that she is no longer alone until her head and breast are raised by Broadbent, who, returning newly washed and combed through the inner door, has seen her condition, first with surprise and concern, and then with an emotional disturbance that quite upsets him.

BROADBENT. Miss Reilly. Miss Reilly. What's the matter? Don't cry: I can't stand it: you mustn't cry. [*She makes a choked effort to speak, so painful that he continues with impulsive sympathy*] No: don't try to speak: it's all right now. Have your cry out: never mind me: trust me. [*Gathering her to him, and babbling consolatorily*] Cry on my chest: the only really comfortable place for a woman to cry is a man's chest: a real man, a real friend. A good broad chest, eh? not less than forty-two inches—no: don't fuss: never mind the conventions: we're two friends, aren't we? Come now, come, come! It's all right and comfortable and happy now, isn't it?

NORA [*through her tears*]. Let me go. I want me hankerchief.

BROADBENT [*holding her with one arm and producing a large silk handkerchief from his breast pocket*]. Here's a handkerchief. Let me [*he dabs her tears dry with it*]. Never mind your own: it's too small: it's one of those wretched little cambric handkerchiefs—

NORA [*sobbing*]. Indeed it's a common cotton one.

BROADBENT. Of course it's a common cotton one—silly little cotton one—not good enough for the dear eyes of Nora Cryna—

NORA [*spluttering into a hysterical laugh and clutching him convulsively with her fingers while she tries to stifle her laughter against his collar bone*]. Oh don't make me laugh: please don't make me laugh.

BROADBENT [*terrified*]. I didn't mean to, on my soul. What is it? What is it?

NORA. Nora Creena, Nora Creena.

BROADBENT [*patting her*]. Yes, yes, of course, Nora Creena, Nora acushla [*he makes cush rhyme to plush*].

NORA. Acushla [*she makes cush rhyme to bush*].

BROADBENT. Oh, confound the language! Nora darling—my Nora—the Nora I love—

NORA [*shocked into propriety*]. You mustn't talk like that to me.

BROADBENT [*suddenly becoming prodigiously solemn and letting her go*]. No, of course not. I don't mean it—at least I do mean it; but I know it's premature. I had no right to take advantage of your being a little upset; but I lost my self-control for a moment.

NORA [*wondering at him*]. I think you're a very kindhearted man, Mr Broadbent; but you seem to me to have no self-control at all [*she turns her face away with a keen pang of shame and adds*] no more than myself.

BROADBENT [*resolutely*]. Oh yes, I have: you should see me when I am really roused: then I have TREMENDOUS self-control. Remember: we have been alone together only once before; and then, I regret to say, I was in a disgusting state.

NORA. Ah no, Mr Broadbent: you weren't disgusting.

BROADBENT [*mercilessly*]. Yes I was: nothing can excuse it: perfectly beastly. It must have made a most unfavorable impression on you.

NORA. Oh, sure it's all right. Say no more about that.

BROADBENT. I must, Miss Reilly: it is my duty. I shall not detain you long. May I ask you to sit down. [*He indicates her chair with oppressive solemnity. She sits down wondering. He then, with the same portentous gravity, places a chair for himself near her; sits down; and proceeds to explain*]. First, Miss Reilly, may I say that I have tasted nothing of an alcoholic nature today.

NORA. It doesn't seem to make as much difference in you as it would in an Irishman, somehow.

BROADBENT. Perhaps not. Perhaps not. I never quite lose myself.

NORA [*consolingly*]. Well, anyhow, you're all right now.

BROADBENT [*fervently*]. Thank you, Miss Reilly: I am. Now we shall get along. [*Tenderly, lowering his voice*] Nora: I was in earnest last night. [*Nora moves as if to rise*]. No: one moment. You must not think I am going to press you for an answer before you have known me for 24 hours. I am a reasonable man, I hope; and I am prepared to wait as long as you like, provided you will give me some small assurance that the answer will not be unfavorable.

NORA. How could I go back from it if I did? I sometimes think you're not quite right in your head, Mr Broadbent, you say such funny things.

BROADBENT. Yes: I know I have a strong sense of humor which sometimes makes people doubt whether I am quite serious. That is why I have always thought I should like to marry an Irishwoman. She would always understand my jokes. For instance, you would understand them, eh?

NORA [*uneasily*]. Mr Broadbent, I couldn't.

BROADBENT [*soothingly*]. Wait: let me break this to you gently, Miss Reilly: hear me out. I daresay you have noticed that in speaking to you I have been putting a very strong constraint on myself, so as to avoid wounding your delicacy by too abrupt an avowal of my feelings. Well, I feel now that the time has come to be open, to be frank, to be explicit. Miss Reilly: you have inspired in me a very strong attachment. Perhaps, with a woman's intuition, you have already guessed that.

NORA [*rising distractedly*]. Why do you talk to me in that unfeeling nonsensical way?

BROADBENT [*rising also, much astonished*]. Unfeeling! Nonsensical!

NORA. Don't you know that you have said things to me that no man ought to say unless—unless—[*she suddenly breaks down again and hides her face on the table as before*] Oh, go away from me: I won't get married at all: what is it but heartbreak and disappointment?

BROADBENT [*developing the most formidable symptoms of rage and grief*]. Do you mean to say that you are going to refuse me? that you don't care for me?

NORA [*looking at him in consternation*]. Oh, don't take it to heart, Mr Br—

BROADBENT [*flushed and almost choking*]. I don't want to be petted and blarneyed. [*With childish rage*] I love you. I want you for my wife. [*In despair*] I can't help your refusing. I'm helpless: I can do nothing. You have no right to ruin my whole life. You—[*a hysterical convulsion stops him*].

NORA [*almost awestruck*]. You're not going to cry, are you? I never thought a man COULD cry. Don't.

BROADBENT. I'm not crying. I—I—I leave that sort of thing to your damned sentimental Irishmen. You think I have no feeling because I am a plain unemotional Englishman, with no powers of expression.

NORA. I don't think you know the sort of man you are at all. Whatever may be the matter with you, it's not want of feeling.

BROADBENT [*hurt and petulant*]. It's you who have no feeling. You're as heartless as Larry.

NORA. What do you expect me to do? Is it to throw meself at your head the minute the word is out o your mouth?

BROADBENT [*striking his silly head with his fists*]. Oh, what a fool! what a brute I am! It's only your Irish delicacy: of course, of course. You mean Yes. Eh? What? Yes, yes, yes?

NORA. I think you might understand that though I might choose to be an old maid, I could never marry anybody but you now.

BROADBENT [*clasping her violently to his breast, with a crow of immense relief and triumph*]. Ah, that's right, that's right: That's magnificent. I knew you would see what a first-rate thing this will be for both of us.

NORA [*incommoded and not at all enraptured by his ardor*]. You're dreadfully strong, an a gradle too free with your strength. An I never thought o whether it'd be a good thing for us or not. But when you found me here that time, I let you be kind to me, and cried in your arms, because I was too wretched to think of anything but the comfort of it. An how could I let any other man touch me after that?

BROADBENT [*touched*]. Now that's very nice of you, Nora, that's really most delicately womanly [*he kisses her hand chivalrously*].

NORA [*looking earnestly and a little doubtfully at him*]. Surely if you let one woman cry on you like that you'd never let another touch you.

BROADBENT [*conscientiously*]. One should not. One OUGHT not, my dear girl. But the honest truth is, if a chap is at all a pleasant sort of chap, his chest becomes a fortification that has to stand many assaults: at least it is so in England.

NORA [*curtly, much disgusted*]. Then you'd better marry an Englishwoman.

BROADBENT [*making a wry face*]. No, no: the Englishwoman is too prosaic for my taste, too material, too much of the animated beefsteak about her. The ideal is what I like. Now Larry's taste is just the opposite: he likes em solid and bouncing and rather keen about him. It's a very convenient difference; for we've never been in love with the same woman.

NORA. An d'ye mean to tell me to me face that you've ever been in love before?

BROADBENT. Lord! yes.

NORA. I'm not your first love?

BROADBENT. First love is only a little foolishness and a lot of curiosity: no really self-respecting woman would take advantage of it. No, my dear Nora: I've done with all that long ago. Love affairs always end in rows. We're not going to have any rows: we're going to have a solid four-square home: man and wife: comfort and common sense—and plenty of affection, eh [*he puts his arm round her with confident proprietorship*]?

NORA [*coldly, trying to get away*]. I don't want any other woman's leavings.

BROADBENT [*holding her*]. Nobody asked you to, ma'am. I never asked any woman to marry me before.

NORA [*severely*]. Then why didn't you if you're an honorable man?

BROADBENT. Well, to tell you the truth, they were mostly married already. But never mind! there was nothing wrong. Come! Don't take a mean advantage of me. After all, you must have had a fancy or two yourself, eh?

NORA [*conscience-stricken*]. Yes. I suppose I've no right to be particular.

BROADBENT [*humbly*]. I know I'm not good enough for you, Nora. But no man is, you know, when the woman is a really nice woman.

NORA. Oh, I'm no better than yourself. I may as well tell you about it.

BROADBENT. No, no: let's have no telling: much better not. I shan't tell you anything: don't you tell ME anything. Perfect confidence in one another and no tellings: that's the way to avoid rows.

NORA. Don't think it was anything I need be ashamed of.

BROADBENT. I don't.

NORA. It was only that I'd never known anybody else that I could care for; and I was foolish enough once to think that Larry—

BROADBENT [*disposing of the idea at once*]. Larry! Oh, that wouldn't have done at all, not at all. You don't know Larry as I do, my dear. He has absolutely no capacity for enjoyment: he couldn't make any woman happy. He's as clever as be-blowed; but life's too earthly for him: he doesn't really care for anything or anybody.

NORA. I've found that out.

BROADBENT. Of course you have. No, my dear: take my word for it, you're jolly well out of that. There! [*swinging her round against his breast*] that's much more comfortable for you.

NORA [*with Irish peevishness*]. Ah, you mustn't go on like that. I don't like it.

BROADBENT [*unabashed*]. You'll acquire the taste by degrees. You mustn't mind me: it's an absolute necessity of my nature that I should have somebody to hug occasionally. Besides, it's good for you: it'll plump out your muscles and make em elastic and set up your figure.

NORA. Well, I'm sure! if this is English manners! Aren't you ashamed to talk about such things?

BROADBENT [*in the highest feather*]. Not a bit. By George, Nora, it's a tremendous thing to be able to enjoy oneself. Let's go off for a walk out of this stuffy little room. I want the open air to expand in. Come along. Co-o-o-me along. [*He puts her arm into his and sweeps her out into the garden as an equinoctial gale might sweep a dry leaf.*

Later in the evening, the grasshopper is again enjoying the sunset by the great stone on the hill; but this time he enjoys neither the stimulus of Keegan's conversation nor the pleasure of terrifying Patsy Farrell. He is alone until Nora and Broadbent come up the hill arm in arm. Broadbent is still breezy and confident; but she has her head averted from him and is almost in tears].

BROADBENT [*stopping to snuff up the hillside air*]. Ah! I like this spot. I like this view. This would be a jolly good place for a hotel and a golf links. Friday to Tuesday, railway ticket and hotel all inclusive. I tell you, Nora, I'm going to develop this place. [*Looking at her*] Hallo! What's the matter? Tired?

NORA [*unable to restrain her tears*]. I'm ashamed out o me life.

BROADBENT [*astonished*]. Ashamed! What of?

NORA. Oh, how could you drag me all round the place like that, telling everybody that we're going to be married, and introjoocing me to the lowest of the low, and letting them shake hans with me, and encouraging them to make free with us? I little thought I should live to be shaken hans with be Doolan in broad daylight in the public street of Rosscullen.

BROADBENT. But, my dear, Doolan's a publican: a most influential man. By the way, I asked him if his wife would be at home tomorrow. He said she would; so you must take the motor car round and call on her.

NORA [*aghast*]. Is it me call on Doolan's wife!

BROADBENT. Yes, of course: call on all their wives. We must get a copy of the register and a supply of canvassing cards. No use calling on people who haven't votes. You'll be a great success as a canvasser, Nora: they call you the heiress; and they'll be flattered no end by your calling, especially as you've never cheapened yourself by speaking to them before—have you?

NORA [*indignantly*]. Not likely, indeed.

BROADBENT. Well, we mustn't be stiff and stand-off, you know. We must be thoroughly democratic, and patronize everybody without distinction of class. I tell you I'm a jolly lucky man, Nora Cryna. I get engaged to the most delightful woman in Ireland; and it turns out that I couldn't have done a smarter stroke of electioneering.

NORA. An would you let me demean meself like that, just to get yourself into parliament?

BROADBENT [*buoyantly*]. Aha! Wait till you find out what an exciting game electioneering is: you'll be mad to get me in. Besides, you'd like people to say that Tom Broadbent's wife had been the making of him—that she got him into parliament—into the Cabinet, perhaps, eh?

NORA. God knows I don't grudge you me money! But to lower meself to the level of common people.

BROADBENT. To a member's wife, Nora, nobody is common provided he's on the register. Come, my dear! it's all right: do you think I'd let you do it if it wasn't? The best people do it. Everybody does it.

NORA [*who has been biting her lip and looking over the hill, disconsolate and unconvinced*]. Well, praps you know best what they do in England. They must have very little respect for themselves. I think I'll go in now. I see Larry and Mr Keegan coming up the hill; and I'm not fit to talk to them.

BROADBENT. Just wait and say something nice to Keegan. They tell me he controls nearly as many votes as Father Dempsey himself.

NORA. You little know Peter Keegan. He'd see through me as if I was a pane o glass.

BROADBENT. Oh, he won't like it any the less for that. What really flatters a man is that you think him worth flattering. Not that I would flatter any man: don't think that. I'll just go and meet him. [*He goes down the hill with the eager forward look of a man about to greet a valued acquaintance. Nora dries her eyes, and turns to go as Larry strolls up the hill to her*].

LARRY. Nora. [*She turns and looks at him hardly, without a word. He continues anxiously, in his most conciliatory tone*]. When I left you that time, I was just as wretched as you. I didn't rightly know what I wanted to say; and my tongue kept clacking to cover the loss I was at. Well, I've been thinking ever since; and now I know what I ought to have said. I've come back to say it.

NORA. You've come too late, then. You thought eighteen years was not long enough, and that you might keep me waiting a day longer. Well, you were mistaken. I'm engaged to your friend Mr Broadbent; and I'm done with you.

LARRY [*naively*]. But that was the very thing I was going to advise you to do.

NORA [*involuntarily*]. Oh you brute! to tell me that to me face.

LARRY [*nervously relapsing into his most Irish manner*]. Nora, dear, don't you understand that I'm an Irishman, and he's an Englishman. He wants you; and he grabs you. I want you; and I quarrel with you and have to go on wanting you.

NORA. So you may. You'd better go back to England to the animated beefsteaks you're so fond of.

LARRY [*amazed*]. Nora! [*Guessing where she got the metaphor*] He's been talking about me, I see. Well, never mind: we must be friends, you and I. I don't want his marriage to you to be his divorce from me.

NORA. You care more for him than you ever did for me.

LARRY [*with curt sincerity*]. Yes of course I do: why should I tell you lies about it? Nora Reilly was a person of very little consequence to me or anyone else outside this miserable little hole. But Mrs Tom Broadbent will be a person of very considerable consequence indeed. Play your new part well, and there will be no more neglect, no more loneliness, no more idle regrettings and vain-hopings in the evenings by the Round Tower, but real life and real work and real cares and real joys among real people: solid English life in London, the very centre of the world. You will find your work cut out for you keeping Tom's house and entertaining Tom's friends and getting Tom into parliament; but it will be worth the effort.

NORA. You talk as if I were under an obligation to him for marrying me.

LARRY. I talk as I think. You've made a very good match, let me tell you.

NORA. Indeed! Well, some people might say he's not done so badly himself.

LARRY. If you mean that you will be a treasure to him, he thinks so now; and you can keep him thinking so if you like.

NORA. I wasn't thinking o meself at all.

LARRY. Were you thinking of your money, Nora?

NORA. I didn't say so.

LARRY. Your money will not pay your cook's wages in London.

NORA [*flaming up*]. If that's true—and the more shame for you to throw it in my face if it IS true—at all events it'll make us independent; for if the worst comes to the worst, we can always come back here an live on it. An if I have to keep his house for him, at all events I can keep you out of it; for I've done with you; and I wish I'd never seen you. So goodbye to you, Mister Larry Doyle. [*She turns her back on him and goes home*].

LARRY [*watching her as she goes*]. Goodbye. Goodbye. Oh, that's so Irish! Irish both of us to the backbone: Irish, Irish, Irish—

Broadbent arrives, conversing energetically with Keegan.

BROADBENT. Nothing pays like a golfing hotel, if you hold the land instead of the shares, and if the furniture people stand in with you, and if you are a good man of business.

LARRY. Nora's gone home.

BROADBENT [*with conviction*]. You were right this morning, Larry. I must feed up Nora. She's weak; and it makes her fanciful. Oh, by the way, did I tell you that we're engaged?

LARRY. She told me herself.

BROADBENT [*complacently*]. She's rather full of it, as you may imagine. Poor Nora! Well, Mr Keegan, as I said, I begin to see my way here. I begin to see my way.

KEEGAN [*with a courteous inclination*]. The conquering Englishman, sir. Within 24 hours of your arrival you have carried off our only heiress, and practically secured the parliamentary seat. And you have promised me that when I come here in the evenings to meditate on my madness; to watch the shadow of the Round Tower lengthening in the sunset; to break my heart uselessly in the curtained gloaming over the dead heart and blinded soul of the island of the saints, you will comfort me with the bustle of a great hotel, and the sight of the little children carrying the golf clubs of your tourists as a preparation for the life to come.

BROADBENT [*quite touched, mutely offering him a cigar to console him, at which he smiles and shakes his head*]. Yes, Mr Keegan: you're quite right. There's poetry in everything, even [*looking absently into the cigar case*] in the most modern prosaic things, if you know how to extract it [*he extracts a cigar for himself and offers one to Larry, who takes it*]. If I was to be shot for it I couldn't extract it myself; but that's where you come in, you see [*roguishly, waking up from his reverie and bustling Keegan goodhumoredly*]. And then I shall wake you up a bit. That's where I come in: eh? d'ye see? Eh? eh? [*He pats him very pleasantly on the shoulder, half admiringly, half pityingly*]. Just so, just so. [*Coming back to business*] By the way, I believe I can do better than a light railway here. There seems to be no question now that the motor boat has come to stay. Well, look at your magnificent river there, going to waste.

KEEGAN [*closing his eyes*]. "Silent, O Moyle, be the roar of thy waters."

BROADBENT. You know, the roar of a motor boat is quite pretty.

KEEGAN. Provided it does not drown the Angelus.

BROADBENT [*reassuringly*]. Oh no: it won't do that: not the least danger. You know, a church bell can make a devil of a noise when it likes.

KEEGAN. You have an answer for everything, sir. But your plans leave one question still unanswered: how to get butter out of a dog's throat.

BROADBENT. Eh?

KEEGAN. You cannot build your golf links and hotels in the air. For that you must own our land. And how will you drag our acres from the ferret's grip of Matthew Haffigan? How will you persuade Cornelius Doyle to forego the pride of being a small landowner? How will Barney Doran's millrace agree with your motor boats? Will Doolan help you to get a license for your hotel?

BROADBENT. My dear sir: to all intents and purposes the syndicate I represent already owns half Rosscullen. Doolan's is a tied house; and the brewers are in the syndicate. As to Haffigan's farm and Doran's mill and Mr Doyle's place and half a dozen others, they will be mortgaged to me before a month is out.

KEEGAN. But pardon me, you will not lend them more on their land than the land is worth; so they will be able to pay you the interest.

BROADBENT. Ah, you are a poet, Mr Keegan, not a man of business.

LARRY. We will lend everyone of these men half as much again on their land as it is worth, or ever can be worth, to them.

BROADBENT. You forget, sir, that we, with our capital, our knowledge, our organization, and may I say our English business habits, can make or lose ten pounds out of land that Haffigan, with all his industry, could not make or lose ten shillings out of. Doran's mill is a superannuated folly: I shall want it for electric lighting.

LARRY. What is the use of giving land to such men? they are too small, too poor, too ignorant, too simpleminded to hold it against us: you might as well give a dukedom to a crossing sweeper.

BROADBENT. Yes, Mr Keegan: this place may have an industrial future, or it may have a residential future: I can't tell yet; but it's not going to be a future in the hands of your Dorans and Haffigans, poor devils!

KEEGAN. It may have no future at all. Have you thought of that?

BROADBENT. Oh, I'm not afraid of that. I have faith in Ireland, great faith, Mr Keegan.

KEEGAN. And we have none: only empty enthusiasms and patriotisms, and emptier memories and regrets. Ah yes: you have some excuse for believing that if there be any future, it will be yours; for our faith seems dead, and our hearts cold and cowed. An island of dreamers who wake up in your jails, of critics and cowards whom you buy and tame for your own service, of bold rogues who help you to plunder us that they may plunder you afterwards. Eh?

BROADBENT [*a little impatient of this unbusinesslike view*]. Yes, yes; but you know you might say that of any country. The fact is, there are only two qualities in the world: efficiency and inefficiency, and only two sorts of people: the efficient and the inefficient. It don't matter whether they're English or Irish. I shall collar this place, not because I'm an Englishman and Haffigan and Co are Irishmen, but because they're duffers and I know my way about.

KEEGAN. Have you considered what is to become of Haffigan?

LARRY. Oh, we'll employ him in some capacity or other, and probably pay him more than he makes for himself now.

BROADBENT [*dubiously*]. Do you think so? No no: Haffigan's too old. It really doesn't pay now to take on men over forty even for unskilled labor, which I suppose is all Haffigan would be good for. No: Haffigan had better go to America, or into the Union, poor old chap! He's worked out, you know: you can see it.

KEEGAN. Poor lost soul, so cunningly fenced in with invisible bars!

LARRY. Haffigan doesn't matter much. He'll die presently.

BROADBENT [*shocked*]. Oh come, Larry! Don't be unfeeling. It's hard on Haffigan. It's always hard on the inefficient.

LARRY. Pah! what does it matter where an old and broken man spends his last days, or whether he has a million at the bank or only the workhouse dole? It's the young men, the able men, that matter. The real tragedy of Haffigan is the tragedy of his wasted youth, his stunted mind, his drudging over his clods and pigs until he has become a clod and a pig himself—until the soul within him has smouldered into nothing but a dull temper that hurts himself and all around him. I say let him die, and let us have no more of his like. And let young Ireland take care that it doesn't share his fate, instead of making another empty grievance of it. Let your syndicate come—

BROADBENT. Your syndicate too, old chap. You have your bit of the stock.

LARRY. Yes, mine if you like. Well, our syndicate has no conscience: it has no more regard for your Haffigans and Doolans and Dorans than it has for a gang of Chinese coolies. It will use your patriotic blatherskite and balderdash to get parliamentary powers over you as cynically as it would bait a mousetrap with toasted cheese. It will plan, and organize, and find capital while you slave like bees for it and revenge yourselves by paying politicians and penny newspapers out of your small wages to write articles and report speeches against its wickedness and tyranny, and to crack up your own Irish heroism, just as Haffigan once paid a witch a penny to put a spell on Billy Byrne's cow. In the end it will grind the nonsense out of you, and grind strength and sense into you.

BROADBENT [*out of patience*]. Why can't you say a simple thing simply, Larry, without all that Irish exaggeration and talky-talky? The syndicate is a perfectly respectable body of responsible men of good position. We'll take Ireland in hand, and by straightforward business habits teach it efficiency and self-help on sound Liberal principles. You agree with me, Mr Keegan, don't you?

KEEGAN. Sir: I may even vote for you.

BROADBENT [*sincerely moved, shaking his hand warmly*]. You shall never regret it, Mr Keegan: I give you my word for that. I shall bring money here: I shall raise wages: I shall found public institutions, a library, a Polytechnic [*undenominational, of course*], a gymnasium, a cricket club, perhaps an art school. I shall make a Garden city of Rosscullen: the round tower shall be thoroughly repaired and restored.

KEEGAN. And our place of torment shall be as clean and orderly as the cleanest and most orderly place I know in Ireland, which is our poetically named Mountjoy prison. Well, perhaps I had better vote for an efficient devil that knows his own mind and his own business than for a foolish patriot who has no mind and no business.

BROADBENT [*stiffly*]. Devil is rather a strong expression in that connexion, Mr Keegan.

KEEGAN. Not from a man who knows that this world is hell. But since the word offends you, let me soften it, and compare you simply to an ass. [*Larry whitens with anger*].

BROADBENT [*reddening*]. An ass!

KEEGAN [*gently*]. You may take it without offence from a madman who calls the ass his brother—and a very honest, useful and faithful brother too. The ass, sir, is the most efficient of beasts, matter-of-fact, hardy, friendly when you treat him as a fellow-creature, stubborn when you abuse him, ridiculous only in love, which sets him braying, and in politics, which move him to roll about in the public road and raise a dust about nothing. Can you deny these qualities and habits in yourself, sir?

BROADBENT [*goodhumoredly*]. Well, yes, I'm afraid I do, you know.

KEEGAN. Then perhaps you will confess to the ass's one fault.

BROADBENT. Perhaps so: what is it?

KEEGAN. That he wastes all his virtues—his efficiency, as you call it—in doing the will of his greedy masters instead of doing the will of Heaven that is in himself. He is efficient in the service of Mammon, mighty in mischief, skilful in ruin, heroic in destruction. But he comes to browse here without knowing that the soil his hoof touches is holy ground. Ireland, sir, for good or evil, is like no other place under heaven; and no man can touch its sod or breathe its air without becoming better or worse. It produces two kinds of men in strange perfection: saints and traitors. It is called the island of the saints; but indeed in these later years it might be more fitly called the island of the traitors; for our harvest of these is the fine flower of the world's crop of infamy. But the day may come when these islands shall live by the quality of their men rather than by the abundance of their minerals; and then we shall see.

LARRY. Mr Keegan: if you are going to be sentimental about Ireland, I shall bid you good evening. We have had enough of that, and more than enough of cleverly proving that everybody who is not an Irishman is an ass. It is neither good sense nor good manners. It will not stop the syndicate; and it will not interest young Ireland so much as my friend's gospel of efficiency.

BROADBENT. Ah, yes, yes: efficiency is the thing. I don't in the least mind your chaff, Mr Keegan; but Larry's right on the main point. The world belongs to the efficient.

KEEGAN [*with polished irony*]. I stand rebuked, gentlemen. But believe me, I do every justice to the efficiency of you and your syndicate. You are both, I am told, thoroughly efficient civil engineers; and I have no doubt the golf links will be a triumph of your art. Mr Broadbent will get into parliament most efficiently, which is more than St Patrick could do if he were alive now. You may even build the hotel efficiently if you can find enough efficient masons, carpenters, and plumbers, which I rather doubt. [*Dropping his irony, and beginning to fall into the attitude of the priest rebuking sin*] When the hotel becomes insolvent [*Broadbent takes his cigar out of his mouth, a little taken aback*], your English business habits will secure the thorough efficiency of the liquidation. You will reorganize the scheme efficiently; you will liquidate its second bankruptcy efficiently [*Broadbent and Larry look quickly at one another; for this, unless the priest is an old financial hand, must be inspiration*]; you will get rid of its original shareholders efficiently after efficiently ruining them; and you will finally profit very efficiently by getting that hotel for a few shillings in the pound. [*More and more sternly*] Besides those efficient operations, you will foreclose your mortgages most efficiently [*his rebuking forefinger goes up in spite of himself*]; you will drive Haffigan to America very efficiently; you will find a use for Barney Doran's foul mouth and bullying temper by employing him to slave-drive your laborers very efficiently; and [*low and bitter*] when at last this poor desolate countryside becomes a busy mint in which we shall all slave to make money for you, with our Polytechnic to teach us how to do it efficiently, and our library to fuddle the few imaginations your distilleries will spare, and our repaired Round Tower with admission sixpence, and refreshments and penny-in-the-slot mutoscopes to make it interesting, then no doubt your English and American shareholders will spend all the money we make for them very efficiently in shooting and hunting, in operations for cancer and appendicitis, in gluttony and gambling; and you will devote what they save to fresh land development schemes. For four wicked centuries the world has dreamed this foolish dream of efficiency; and the end is not yet. But the end will come.

BROADBENT [*seriously*]. Too true, Mr Keegan, only too true. And most eloquently put. It reminds me of poor Ruskin—a great man, you know. I sympathize. Believe me, I'm on your side. Don't sneer, Larry: I used to read a lot of Shelley years ago. Let us be faithful to the dreams of our youth [*he wafts a wreath of cigar smoke at large across the hill*].

KEEGAN. Come, Mr Doyle! is this English sentiment so much more efficient than our Irish sentiment, after all? Mr Broadbent spends his life inefficiently admiring the thoughts of great men, and efficiently serving the cupidity of base money hunters. We spend our lives efficiently sneering at him and doing nothing. Which of us has any right to reproach the other?

BROADBENT [*coming down the hill again to Keegan's right hand*]. But you know, something must be done.

KEEGAN. Yes: when we cease to do, we cease to live. Well, what shall we do?

BROADBENT. Why, what lies to our hand.

KEEGAN. Which is the making of golf links and hotels to bring idlers to a country which workers have left in millions because it is a hungry land, a naked land, an ignorant and oppressed land.

BROADBENT. But, hang it all, the idlers will bring money from England to Ireland!

KEEGAN. Just as our idlers have for so many generations taken money from Ireland to England. Has that saved England from poverty and degradation more horrible than we have ever dreamed of? When I went to England, sir, I hated England. Now I pity it. [*Broadbent can hardly conceive an Irishman pitying England; but as Larry intervenes angrily, he gives it up and takes to the bill and his cigar again*]

LARRY. Much good your pity will do it!

KEEGAN. In the accounts kept in heaven, Mr Doyle, a heart purified of hatred may be worth more even than a Land Development Syndicate of Anglicized Irishmen and Gladstonized Englishmen.

LARRY. Oh, in heaven, no doubt! I have never been there. Can you tell me where it is?

KEEGAN. Could you have told me this morning where hell is? Yet you know now that it is here. Do not despair of finding heaven: it may be no farther off.

LARRY [*ironically*]. On this holy ground, as you call it, eh?

KEEGAN [*with fierce intensity*]. Yes, perhaps, even on this holy ground which such Irishmen as you have turned into a Land of Derision.

BROADBENT [*coming between them*]. Take care! you will be quarrelling presently. Oh, you Irishmen, you Irishmen! Toujours Ballyhooly, eh? [*Larry, with a shrug, half comic, half impatient, turn away up the hill, but presently strolls back on Keegan's right. Broadbent adds, confidentially to Keegan*] Stick to the Englishman, Mr Keegan: he has a bad name here; but at least he can forgive you for being an Irishman.

KEEGAN. Sir: when you speak to me of English and Irish you forget that I am a Catholic. My country is not Ireland nor England, but the whole mighty realm of my Church. For me there are but two countries: heaven and hell; but two conditions of men: salvation and damnation. Standing here between you the Englishman, so clever in your foolishness, and this Irishman, so foolish in his cleverness, I cannot in my ignorance be sure which of you is the more deeply damned; but I should be unfaithful to my calling if I opened the gates of my heart less widely to one than to the other.

LARRY. In either case it would be an impertinence, Mr Keegan, as your approval is not of the slightest consequence to us. What use do you suppose all this drivel is to men with serious practical business in hand?

BROADBENT. I don't agree with that, Larry. I think these things cannot be said too often: they keep up the moral tone of the community. As you know, I claim the right to think for myself in religious matters: in fact, I am ready to avow myself a bit of a—of a—well, I don't care who knows it—a bit of a Unitarian; but if the Church of England contained a few men like Mr Keegan, I should certainly join it.

KEEGAN. You do me too much honor, sir. [*With priestly humility to Larry*] Mr Doyle: I am to blame for having unintentionally set your mind somewhat on edge against me. I beg your pardon.

LARRY [*unimpressed and hostile*]. I didn't stand on ceremony with you: you needn't stand on it with me. Fine manners and fine words are cheap in Ireland: you can keep both for my friend here, who is still imposed on by them. I know their value.

KEEGAN. You mean you don't know their value.

LARRY [*angrily*]. I mean what I say.

KEEGAN [*turning quietly to the Englishman*] You see, Mr Broadbent, I only make the hearts of my countrymen harder when I preach to them: the gates of hell still prevail against me. I shall wish you good evening. I am better alone, at the Round Tower, dreaming of heaven. [*He goes up the hill*].

LARRY. Aye, that's it! there you are! dreaming, dreaming, dreaming, dreaming!

KEEGAN [*halting and turning to them for the last time*]. Every dream is a prophecy: every jest is an earnest in the womb of Time.

BROADBENT [*reflectively*]. Once, when I was a small kid, I dreamt I was in heaven. [*They both stare at him*]. It was a sort of pale blue satin place, with all the pious old ladies in our congregation sitting as if they were at a service; and there was some awful person in the study at the other side of the hall. I didn't enjoy it, you know. What is it like in your dreams?

KEEGAN. In my dreams it is a country where the State is the Church and the Church the people: three in one and one in three. It is a commonwealth in which work is play and play is life: three in one and one in three. It is a temple in which the priest is the worshipper and the worshipper the worshipped: three in one and one in three. It is a godhead in which all life is human and all humanity divine: three in one and one in three. It is, in short, the dream of a madman. [*He goes away across the hill*].

BROADBENT [*looking after him affectionately*]. What a regular old Church and State Tory he is! He's a character: he'll be an attraction here. Really almost equal to Ruskin and Carlyle.

LARRY. Yes; and much good they did with all their talk!

BROADBENT. Oh tut, tut, Larry! They improved my mind: they raised my tone enormously. I feel sincerely obliged to Keegan: he has made me feel a better man: distinctly better. [*With sincere elevation*] I feel now as I never did before that I am right in devoting my life to the cause of Ireland. Come along and help me to choose the site for the hotel.

HOW HE LIED TO HER HUSBAND

PREFACE

Like many other works of mine, this playlet is a piece d'occasion. In 1905 it happened that Mr Arnold Daly, who was then playing the part of Napoleon in The Man of Destiny in New York, found that whilst the play was too long to take a secondary place in the evening's performance, it was too short to suffice by itself. I therefore took advantage of four days continuous rain during a holiday in the north of Scotland to write How He Lied To Her Husband for Mr Daly. In his hands, it served its turn very effectively.

I print it here as a sample of what can be done with even the most hackneyed stage framework by filling it in with an observed touch of actual humanity instead of with doctrinaire romanticism. Nothing in the theatre is staler than the situation of husband, wife and lover, or the fun of knockabout farce. I have taken both, and got an original play out of them, as anybody else can if only he will look about him for his material instead of plagiarizing Othello and the thousand plays that have proceeded on Othello's romantic assumptions and false point of honor.

A further experiment made by Mr Arnold Daly with this play is worth recording. In 1905 Mr Daly produced Mrs Warren's Profession in New York. The press of that city instantly raised a cry that such persons as Mrs Warren are "ordure," and should not be mentioned in the presence of decent people. This hideous repudiation of humanity and social conscience so took possession of the New York journalists that the few among them who kept their feet morally and intellectually could do nothing to check the epidemic of foul language, gross suggestion, and raving obscenity of word and thought that broke out. The writers abandoned all self-restraint under the impression that they were upholding virtue instead of outraging it. They infected each other with their hysteria until they were for all practical purposes indecently mad. They finally forced the police to arrest Mr Daly and his company, and led the magistrate to express his loathing of the duty thus forced upon him of reading an unmentionable and abominable play. Of course the convulsion soon exhausted itself. The magistrate, naturally somewhat impatient when he found that what he had to read was a strenuously ethical play forming part of a book which had been in circulation unchallenged for eight years, and had been received without protest by the whole London and New York press, gave the journalists a piece of his mind as to their moral taste in plays. By consent, he passed the case on to a higher court, which declared that the play was not immoral; acquitted Mr Daly; and made an end of the attempt to use the law to declare living women to be "ordure," and thus enforce silence as to the far-reaching fact that you cannot cheapen women in the market for industrial purposes without cheapening them for other purposes as well. I hope Mrs Warren's Profession will be played everywhere, in season and out of season, until Mrs Warren has bitten that fact into the public conscience, and shamed the newspapers which support a tariff to keep up the price of every American commodity except American manhood and womanhood.

Unfortunately, Mr Daly had already suffered the usual fate of those who direct public attention to the profits of the sweater or the pleasures of the voluptuary. He was morally lynched side by side with me.

Months elapsed before the decision of the courts vindicated him; and even then, since his vindication implied the condemnation of the press, which was by that time sober again, and ashamed of its orgy, his triumph received a rather sulky and grudging publicity. In the meantime he had hardly been able to approach an American city, including even those cities which had heaped applause on him as the defender of hearth and home when he produced Candida, without having to face articles discussing whether mothers could allow their daughters to attend such plays as You Never Can Tell, written by the infamous author of Mrs Warren's Profession, and acted by the monster who produced it. What made this harder to bear was that though no fact is better established in theatrical business than the financial disastrousness of moral discredit, the journalists who had done all the mischief kept paying vice the homage of assuming that it is enormously popular and lucrative, and that I and Mr Daly, being exploiters of vice, must therefore be making colossal fortunes out of the abuse heaped on us, and had in fact provoked it and welcomed it with that express object. Ignorance of real life could hardly go further.

One consequence was that Mr Daly could not have kept his financial engagements or maintained his hold on the public had he not accepted engagements to appear for a season in the vaudeville theatres [*the American equivalent of our music halls*], where he played How He Lied to Her Husband comparatively unhampered by the press censorship of the theatre, or by that sophistication of the audience through press suggestion from which I suffer more, perhaps, than any other author. Vaudeville authors are fortunately unknown: the audiences see what the play contains and what the actor can do, not what the papers have told them to expect. Success under such circumstances had a value both for Mr Daly and myself which did something to console us for the very unsavory mobbing which the New York press organized for us, and which was not the less disgusting because we suffered in a good cause and in the very best company.

Mr Daly, having weathered the storm, can perhaps shake his soul free of it as he heads for fresh successes with younger authors. But I have certain sensitive places in my soul: I do not like that word "ordure." Apply it to my work, and I can afford to smile, since the world, on the whole, will smile with me. But to apply it to the woman in the street, whose spirit is of one substance with our own and her body no less holy: to look your women folk in the face afterwards and not go out and hang yourself: that is not on the list of pardonable sins.

POSTSCRIPT. Since the above was written news has arrived from America that a leading New York newspaper, which was among the most abusively clamorous for the suppression of Mrs Warren's Profession, has just been fined heavily for deriving part of its revenue from advertisements of Mrs Warren's houses.

Many people have been puzzled by the fact that whilst stage entertainments which are frankly meant to act on the spectators as aphrodisiacs, are everywhere tolerated, plays which have an almost horrifyingly contrary effect are fiercely attacked by persons and papers notoriously indifferent to public morals on all other occasions. The explanation is very simple. The profits of Mrs Warren's profession are shared not only by Mrs Warren and Sir George Crofts, but by the landlords of their houses, the newspapers which advertize them, the restaurants which cater for them, and, in short, all the trades to which they are good customers, not to mention the public officials and representatives whom they silence by complicity, corruption, or blackmail. Add to these the employers who profit by cheap female labor, and the shareholders whose dividends depend on it [*you find such people everywhere, even on the judicial bench and in the highest places in Church and State*], and you get a large and powerful class with a strong pecuniary incentive to protect Mrs Warren's profession, and a correspondingly strong incentive to conceal, from their own consciences no less than from the world, the real sources of their gain. These are the people who declare that it is feminine vice and not poverty that drives women to the streets, as if vicious women with independent incomes ever went there. These are the people who, indulgent or indifferent to aphrodisiac plays, raise the moral hue and cry against performances of Mrs Warren's Profession, and drag actresses to the police court to be insulted, bullied, and threatened for fulfilling their engagements. For please observe that the judicial decision in New York State in favor of the play does not end the matter. In Kansas City, for instance, the municipality, finding itself restrained by the courts from preventing the performance, fell back on a local bye-law against indecency to evade the Constitution of the United States. They summoned the actress who impersonated Mrs Warren to the police court, and offered her and her colleagues the alternative of leaving the city or being prosecuted under this bye-law.

Now nothing is more possible than that the city councillors who suddenly displayed such concern for the morals of the theatre were either Mrs Warren's landlords, or employers of women at starvation wages, or restaurant keepers, or newspaper proprietors, or in some other more or less direct way sharers of the profits of her trade. No doubt it is equally possible that they were simply stupid men who thought that indecency consists, not in evil, but in mentioning it. I have, however, been myself a member of a municipal council, and have not found municipal councillors quite so simple and inexperienced as this. At all events I do not propose to give the Kansas councillors the benefit of the doubt. I therefore advise the public at large, which will finally decide the matter, to keep a vigilant eye on gentlemen who will stand anything at the theatre except a performance of Mrs Warren's Profession, and who assert in the same breath that [*a*] the play is too loathsome to be bearable by civilized people, and [*b*] that unless its performance is prohibited the whole town will throng to see it. They may be merely excited and foolish; but I am bound to warn the public that it is equally likely that they may be collected and knavish.

At all events, to prohibit the play is to protect the evil which the play exposes; and in view of that fact, I see no reason for assuming that the prohibitionists are disinterested moralists, and that the author, the managers, and the performers, who depend for their livelihood on their personal reputations and not on rents, advertisements, or dividends, are grossly inferior to them in moral sense and public responsibility.

It is true that in Mrs Warren's Profession, Society, and not any individual, is the villain of the piece; but it does not follow that the people who take offence at it are all champions of society. Their credentials cannot be too carefully examined.

HOW HE LIED TO HER HUSBAND

It is eight o'clock in the evening. The curtains are drawn and the lamps lighted in the drawing room of Her flat in Cromwell Road. Her lover, a beautiful youth of eighteen, in evening dress and cape, with a bunch of flowers and an opera hat in his hands, comes in alone. The door is near the corner; and as he appears in the doorway, he has the fireplace on the nearest wall to his right, and the grand piano along the opposite wall to his left. Near the fireplace a small ornamental table has on it a hand mirror, a fan, a pair of long white gloves, and a little white woollen cloud to wrap a woman's head in. On the other side of the room, near the piano, is a broad, square, softly up-holstered stool. The room is furnished in the most approved South Kensington fashion: that is, it is as like a show room as possible, and is intended to demonstrate the racial position and spending powers of its owners, and not in the least to make them comfortable.

He is, be it repeated, a very beautiful youth, moving as in a dream, walking as on air. He puts his flowers down carefully on the table beside the fan; takes off his cape, and, as there is no room on the table for it, takes it to the piano; puts his hat on the cape; crosses to the hearth; looks at his watch; puts it up again; notices the things on the table; lights up as if he saw heaven opening before him; goes to the table and takes the cloud in both hands, nestling his nose into its softness and kissing it; kisses the gloves one after another; kisses the fan: gasps a long shuddering sigh of ecstasy; sits down on the stool and presses his hands to his eyes to shut out reality and dream a little; takes his hands down and shakes his head with a little smile of rebuke for his folly; catches sight of a speck of dust on his shoes and hastily and carefully brushes it off with his handkerchief; rises and takes the hand mirror from the table to make sure of his tie with the gravest anxiety; and is looking at his watch again when She comes in, much flustered. As she is dressed for the theatre; has spoilt, petted ways; and wears many diamonds, she has an air of being a young and beautiful woman; but as a matter of hard fact, she is, dress and pretensions apart, a very ordinary South Kensington female of about 37, hopelessly inferior in physical and spiritual distinction to the beautiful youth, who hastily puts down the mirror as she enters.

HE [*kissing her hand*] At last!

SHE. Henry: something dreadful has happened.

HE. What's the matter?

SHE. I have lost your poems.

HE. They were unworthy of you. I will write you some more.

SHE. No, thank you. Never any more poems for me. Oh, how could I have been so mad! so rash! so imprudent!

HE. Thank Heaven for your madness, your rashness, your imprudence!

SHE [*impatiently*] Oh, be sensible, Henry. Can't you see what a terrible thing this is for me? Suppose anybody finds these poems! what will they think?

HE. They will think that a man once loved a woman more devotedly than ever man loved woman before. But they will not know what man it was.

SHE. What good is that to me if everybody will know what woman it was?

HE. But how will they know?

SHE. How will they know! Why, my name is all over them: my silly, unhappy name. Oh, if I had only been christened Mary Jane, or Gladys Muriel, or Beatrice, or Francesca, or Guinevere, or something quite common! But Aurora! Aurora! I'm the only Aurora in London; and everybody knows it. I believe I'm the only Aurora in the world. And it's so horribly easy to rhyme to it! Oh, Henry, why didn't you try to restrain your feelings a little in common consideration for me? Why didn't you write with some little reserve?

HE. Write poems to you with reserve! You ask me that!

SHE [*with perfunctory tenderness*] Yes, dear, of course it was very nice of you; and I know it was my own fault as much as yours. I ought to have noticed that your verses ought never to have been addressed to a married woman.

HE. Ah, how I wish they had been addressed to an unmarried woman! how I wish they had!

SHE. Indeed you have no right to wish anything of the sort. They are quite unfit for anybody but a married woman. That's just the difficulty. What will my sisters-in-law think of them?

HE [*painfully jarred*] Have you got sisters-in-law?

SHE. Yes, of course I have. Do you suppose I am an angel?

HE [*biting his lips*] I do. Heaven help me, I do—or I did—or [*he almost chokes a sob*].

SHE [*softening and putting her hand caressingly on his shoulder*] Listen to me, dear. It's very nice of you to live with me in a dream, and to love me, and so on; but I can't help my husband having disagreeable relatives, can I?

HE [*brightening up*] Ah, of course they are your husband's relatives: I forgot that. Forgive me, Aurora. [*He takes her hand from his shoulder and kisses it. She sits down on the stool. He remains near the table, with his back to it, smiling fatuously down at her*].

SHE. The fact is, Teddy's got nothing but relatives. He has eight sisters and six half-sisters, and ever so many brothers—but I don't mind his brothers. Now if you only knew the least little thing about the world, Henry, you'd know that in a large family, though the sisters quarrel with one another like mad all the time, yet let one of the brothers marry, and they all turn on their unfortunate sister-in-law and devote the rest of their lives with perfect unanimity to persuading him that his wife is unworthy of him. They can do it to her very face without her knowing it, because there are always a lot of stupid low family jokes that nobody understands but themselves. Half the time you can't tell what they're talking about: it just drives you wild. There ought to be a law against a man's sister ever entering his house after he's married. I'm as certain as that I'm sitting here that Georgina stole those poems out of my workbox.

HE. She will not understand them, I think.

SHE. Oh, won't she! She'll understand them only too well. She'll understand more harm than ever was in them: nasty vulgar-minded cat!

HE [*going to her*] Oh don't, don't think of people in that way. Don't think of her at all. [*He takes her hand and sits down on the carpet at her feet*]. Aurora: do you remember the evening when I sat here at your feet and read you those poems for the first time?

SHE. I shouldn't have let you: I see that now. When I think of Georgina sitting there at Teddy's feet and reading them to him for the first time, I feel I shall just go distracted.

HE. Yes, you are right. It will be a profanation.

SHE. Oh, I don't care about the profanation; but what will Teddy think? what will he do? [*Suddenly throwing his head away from her knee*]. You don't seem to think a bit about Teddy. [*She jumps up, more and more agitated*].

HE [*supine on the floor; for she has thrown him off his balance*] To me Teddy is nothing, and Georgina less than nothing.

SHE. You'll soon find out how much less than nothing she is. If you think a woman can't do any harm because she's only a scandalmongering dowdy ragbag, you're greatly mistaken. [*She flounces about the room. He gets up slowly and dusts his hands. Suddenly she runs to him and throws herself into his arms*]. Henry: help me. Find a way out of this for me; and I'll bless you as long as you live. Oh, how wretched I am! [*She sobs on his breast*].

HE. And oh! how happy I am!

SHE [*whisking herself abruptly away*] Don't be selfish.

HE [*humbly*] Yes: I deserve that. I think if I were going to the stake with you, I should still be so happy with you that I could hardly feel your danger more than my own.

SHE [*relenting and patting his hand fondly*] Oh, you are a dear darling boy, Henry; but [*throwing his hand away fretfully*] you're no use. I want somebody to tell me what to do.

HE [*with quiet conviction*] Your heart will tell you at the right time. I have thought deeply over this; and I know what we two must do, sooner or later.

SHE. No, Henry. I will do nothing improper, nothing dishonorable. [*She sits down plump on the stool and looks inflexible*].

HE. If you did, you would no longer be Aurora. Our course is perfectly simple, perfectly straightforward, perfectly stainless and true. We love one another. I am not ashamed of that: I am ready to go out and proclaim it to all London as simply as I will declare it to your husband when you see—as you soon will see—that this is the only way honorable enough for your feet to tread. Let us go out together to our own house, this evening, without concealment and without shame. Remember! we owe something to your husband. We are his guests here: he is an honorable man: he has been kind to us: he has perhaps loved you as well as his prosaic nature and his sordid commercial environment permitted. We owe it to him in all honor not to let him learn the truth from the lips of a scandalmonger. Let us go to him now quietly, hand in hand; bid him farewell; and walk out of the house without concealment and subterfuge, freely and honestly, in full honor and self-respect.

SHE [*staring at him*] And where shall we go to?

HE. We shall not depart by a hair's breadth from the ordinary natural current of our lives. We were going to the theatre when the loss of the poems compelled us to take action at once. We shall go to the theatre still; but we shall leave your diamonds here; for we cannot afford diamonds, and do not need them.

SHE [*fretfully*] I have told you already that I hate diamonds; only Teddy insists on hanging me all over with them. You need not preach simplicity to me.

HE. I never thought of doing so, dearest: I know that these trivialities are nothing to you. What was I saying—oh yes. Instead of coming back here from the theatre, you will come with me to my home—now and henceforth our home—and in due course of time, when you are divorced, we shall go through whatever idle legal ceremony you may desire. I attach no importance to the law: my love was not created in me by the law, nor can it be bound or loosed by it. That is simple enough, and sweet enough, is it not? [*He takes the flower from the table*]. Here are flowers for you: I have the tickets: we will ask your husband to lend us the carriage to show that there is no malice, no grudge, between us. Come!

SHE [*spiritlessly, taking the flowers without looking at them, and temporizing*] Teddy isn't in yet.

HE. Well, let us take that calmly. Let us go to the theatre as if nothing had happened, and tell him when we come back. Now or three hours hence: today or to-morrow: what does it matter, provided all is done in honor, without shame or fear?

SHE. What did you get tickets for? Lohengrin?

HE. I tried; but Lohengrin was sold out for tonight. [*He takes out two Court Theatre tickets*].

SHE. Then what did you get?

HE. Can you ask me? What is there besides Lohengrin that we two could endure, except Candida?

SHE [*springing up*] Candida! No, I won't go to it again, Henry [*tossing the flower on the piano*]. It is that play that has done all the mischief. I'm very sorry I ever saw it: it ought to be stopped.

HE [*amazed*] Aurora!

SHE. Yes: I mean it.

HE. That divinest love poem! the poem that gave us courage to speak to one another! that revealed to us what we really felt for one another! That—

SHE. Just so. It put a lot of stuff into my head that I should never have dreamt of for myself. I imagined myself just like Candida.

HE [*catching her hands and looking earnestly at her*] You were right. You are like Candida.

SHE [*snatching her hands away*] Oh, stuff! And I thought you were just like Eugene. [*Looking critically at him*] Now that I come to look at you, you are rather like him, too. [*She throws herself discontentedly into the nearest seat, which happens to be the bench at the piano. He goes to her*].

HE [*very earnestly*] Aurora: if Candida had loved Eugene she would have gone out into the night with him without a moment's hesitation.

SHE [*with equal earnestness*] Henry: do you know what's wanting in that play?

HE. There is nothing wanting in it.

SHE. Yes there is. There's a Georgina wanting in it. If Georgina had been there to make trouble, that play would have been a true-to-life tragedy. Now I'll tell you something about it that I have never told you before.

HE. What is that?

SHE. I took Teddy to it. I thought it would do him good; and so it would if I could only have kept him awake. Georgina came too; and you should have heard the way she went on about it. She said it was downright immoral, and that she knew the sort of woman that encourages boys to sit on the hearthrug and make love to her. She was just preparing Teddy's mind to poison it about me.

HE. Let us be just to Georgina, dearest

SHE. Let her deserve it first. Just to Georgina, indeed!

HE. She really sees the world in that way. That is her punishment.

SHE. How can it be her punishment when she likes it? It'll be my punishment when she brings that budget of poems to Teddy. I wish you'd have some sense, and sympathize with my position a little.

HE. [*going away from the piano and beginning to walk about rather testily*] My dear: I really don't care about Georgina or about Teddy. All these squabbles belong to a plane on which I am, as you say, no use. I have counted the cost; and I do not fear the consequences. After all, what is there to fear? Where is the difficulty? What can Georgina do? What can your husband do? What can anybody do?

SHE. Do you mean to say that you propose that we should walk right bang up to Teddy and tell him we're going away together?

HE. Yes. What can be simpler?

SHE. And do you think for a moment he'd stand it, like that half-baked clergyman in the play? He'd just kill you.

HE [*coming to a sudden stop and speaking with considerable confidence*] You don't understand these things, my darling, how could you? In one respect I am unlike the poet in the play. I have followed the Greek ideal and not neglected the culture of my body. Your husband would make a tolerable second-rate heavy weight if he were in training and ten years younger. As it is, he could, if strung up to a great effort by a burst of passion, give a good account of himself for perhaps fifteen seconds. But I am active enough to keep out of his reach for fifteen seconds; and after that I should be simply all over him.

SHE [*rising and coming to him in consternation*] What do you mean by all over him?

HE [*gently*] Don't ask me, dearest. At all events, I swear to you that you need not be anxious about me.

SHE. And what about Teddy? Do you mean to tell me that you are going to beat Teddy before my face like a brutal prizefighter?

HE. All this alarm is needless, dearest. Believe me, nothing will happen. Your husband knows that I am capable of defending myself. Under such circumstances nothing ever does happen. And of course I shall do nothing. The man who once loved you is sacred to me.

SHE [*suspiciously*] Doesn't he love me still? Has he told you anything?

HE. No, no. [*He takes her tenderly in his arms*]. Dearest, dearest: how agitated you are! how unlike yourself! All these worries belong to the lower plane. Come up with me to the higher one. The heights, the solitudes, the soul world!

SHE [*avoiding his gaze*] No: stop: it's no use, Mr Apjohn.

HE [*recoiling*] Mr Apjohn!!!

SHE. Excuse me: I meant Henry, of course.

HE. How could you even think of me as Mr Apjohn? I never think of you as Mrs Bompas: it is always Cand— I mean Aurora, Aurora, Auro—

SHE. Yes, yes: that's all very well, Mr Apjohn [*He is about to interrupt again: but she won't have it*] no: it's no use: I've suddenly begun to think of you as Mr Apjohn; and it's ridiculous to go on calling you Henry. I thought you were only a boy, a child, a dreamer. I thought you would be too much afraid to do anything. And now you want to beat Teddy and to break up my home and disgrace me and make a horrible scandal in the papers. It's cruel, unmanly, cowardly.

HE [*with grave wonder*] Are you afraid?

SHE. Oh, of course I'm afraid. So would you be if you had any common sense. [*She goes to the hearth, turning her back to him, and puts one tapping foot on the fender*].

HE [*watching her with great gravity*] Perfect love casteth out fear. That is why I am not afraid. Mrs Bompas: you do not love me.

SHE [*turning to him with a gasp of relief*] Oh, thank you, thank you! You really can be very nice, Henry.

HE. Why do you thank me?

SHE [*coming prettily to him from the fireplace*] For calling me Mrs Bompas again. I feel now that you are going to be reasonable and behave like a gentleman. [*He drops on the stool; covers his face with his hand; and groans*]. What's the matter?

HE. Once or twice in my life I have dreamed that I was exquisitely happy and blessed. But oh! the misgiving at the first stir of consciousness! the stab of reality! the prison walls of the bedroom! the bitter,

bitter disappointment of waking! And this time! oh, this time I thought I was awake.

SHE. Listen to me, Henry: we really haven't time for all that sort of flapdoodle now. [*He starts to his feet as if she had pulled a trigger and straightened him by the release of a powerful spring, and goes past her with set teeth to the little table*]. Oh, take care: you nearly hit me in the chin with the top of your head.

HE [*with fierce politeness*] I beg your pardon. What is it you want me to do? I am at your service. I am ready to behave like a gentleman if you will be kind enough to explain exactly how.

SHE [*a little frightened*] Thank you, Henry: I was sure you would. You're not angry with me, are you?

HE. Go on. Go on quickly. Give me something to think about, or I will—I will—[*he suddenly snatches up her fan and it about to break it in his clenched fists*].

SHE [*running forward and catching at the fan, with loud lamentation*] Don't break my fan—no, don't. [*He slowly relaxes his grip of it as she draws it anxiously out of his hands*]. No, really, that's a stupid trick. I don't like that. You've no right to do that. [*She opens the fan, and finds that the sticks are disconnected*]. Oh, how could you be so inconsiderate?

HE. I beg your pardon. I will buy you a new one.

SHE [*querulously*] You will never be able to match it. And it was a particular favorite of mine.

HE [*shortly*] Then you will have to do without it: that's all.

SHE. That's not a very nice thing to say after breaking my pet fan, I think.

HE. If you knew how near I was to breaking Teddy's pet wife and presenting him with the pieces, you would be thankful that you are alive instead of—of—of howling about five shillings worth of ivory. Damn your fan!

SHE. Oh! Don't you dare swear in my presence. One would think you were my husband.

HE [*again collapsing on the stool*] This is some horrible dream. What has become of you? You are not my Aurora.

SHE. Oh, well, if you come to that, what has become of you? Do you think I would ever have encouraged you if I had known you were such a little devil?

HE. Don't drag me down—don't—don't. Help me to find the way back to the heights.

SHE [*kneeling beside him and pleading*] If you would only be reasonable, Henry. If you would only remember that I am on the brink of ruin, and not go on calmly saying it's all quite simple.

HE. It seems so to me.

SHE [*jumping up distractedly*] If you say that again I shall do something I'll be sorry for. Here we are, standing on the edge of a frightful precipice. No doubt it's quite simple to go over and have done with it. But can't you suggest anything more agreeable?

HE. I can suggest nothing now. A chill black darkness has fallen: I can see nothing but the ruins of our dream. [*He rises with a deep sigh*].

SHE. Can't you? Well, I can. I can see Georgina rubbing those poems into Teddy. [*Facing him determinedly*] And I tell you, Henry Apjohn, that you got me into this mess; and you must get me out of it again.

HE [*polite and hopeless*] All I can say is that I am entirely at your service. What do you wish me to do?

SHE. Do you know anybody else named Aurora?

HE. No.

SHE. There's no use in saying No in that frozen pigheaded way. You must know some Aurora or other somewhere.

HE. You said you were the only Aurora in the world. And [*lifting his clasped fists with a sudden return of his emotion*] oh God! you were the only Aurora in the world to me. [*He turns away from her, hiding his face*].

SHE [*petting him*] Yes, yes, dear: of course. It's very nice of you; and I appreciate it: indeed I do; but it's not reasonable just at present. Now just listen to me. I suppose you know all those poems by heart.

HE. Yes, by heart. [*Raising his head and looking at her, with a sudden suspicion*] Don't you?

SHE. Well, I never can remember verses; and besides, I've been so busy that I've not had time to read them all; though I intend to the very first moment I can get: I promise you that most faithfully, Henry. But now try and remember very particularly. Does the name of Bompas occur in any of the poems?

HE [*indignantly*] No.

SHE. You're quite sure?

HE. Of course I am quite sure. How could I use such a name in a poem?

SHE. Well, I don't see why not. It rhymes to rumpus, which seems appropriate enough at present, goodness knows! However, you're a poet, and you ought to know.

HE. What does it matter—now?

SHE. It matters a lot, I can tell you. If there's nothing about Bompas in the poems, we can say that they were written to some other Aurora, and that you showed them to me because my name was Aurora too. So you've got to invent another Aurora for the occasion.

HE [*very coldly*] Oh, if you wish me to tell a lie—

SHE. Surely, as a man of honor—as a gentleman, you wouldn't tell the truth, would you?

HE. Very well. You have broken my spirit and desecrated my dreams. I will lie and protest and stand on my honor: oh, I will play the gentleman, never fear.

SHE. Yes, put it all on me, of course. Don't be mean, Henry.

HE [*rousing himself with an effort*] You are quite right, Mrs Bompas: I beg your pardon. You must excuse my temper. I have got growing pains, I think.

SHE. Growing pains!

HE. The process of growing from romantic boyhood into cynical maturity usually takes fifteen years. When it is compressed into fifteen minutes, the pace is too fast; and growing pains are the result.

SHE. Oh, is this a time for cleverness? It's settled, isn't it, that you're going to be nice and good, and that you'll brazen it out to Teddy that you have some other Aurora?

HE. Yes: I'm capable of anything now. I should not have told him the truth by halves; and now I will not lie by halves. I'll wallow in the honor of a gentleman.

SHE. Dearest boy, I knew you would. I—Sh! [*she rushes to the door, and holds it ajar, listening breathlessly*].

HE. What is it?

SHE [*white with apprehension*] It's Teddy: I hear him tapping the new barometer. He can't have anything serious on his mind or he wouldn't do that. Perhaps Georgina hasn't said anything. [*She steals back to the hearth*]. Try and look as if there was nothing the matter. Give me my gloves, quick. [*He hands them to her. She pulls on one hastily and begins buttoning it with ostentatious unconcern*]. Go further away from me, quick. [*He walks doggedly away from her until the piano prevents his going farther*]. If I button my glove, and you were to hum a tune, don't you think that—

HE. The tableau would be complete in its guiltiness. For Heaven's sake, Mrs Bompas, let that glove alone: you look like a pickpocket.

Her husband comes in: a robust, thicknecked, well groomed city man, with a strong chin but a blithering eye and credulous mouth. He has a momentous air, but shows no sign of displeasure: rather the contrary.

HER HUSBAND. Hallo! I thought you two were at the theatre.

SHE. I felt anxious about you, Teddy. Why didn't you come home to dinner?

HER HUSBAND. I got a message from Georgina. She wanted me to go to her.

SHE. Poor dear Georgina! I'm sorry I haven't been able to call on her this last week. I hope there's nothing the matter with her.

HER HUSBAND. Nothing, except anxiety for my welfare and yours. [*She steals a terrified look at Henry*]. By, the way, Apjohn, I should like a word with you this evening, if Aurora can spare you for a moment.

HE [*formally*] I am at your service.

HER HUSBAND. No hurry. After the theatre will do.

HE. We have decided not to go.

HER HUSBAND. Indeed! Well, then, shall we adjourn to my snuggery?

SHE. You needn't move. I shall go and lock up my diamonds since I'm not going to the theatre. Give me my things.

HER HUSBAND [*as he hands her the cloud and the mirror*] Well, we shall have more room here.

HE [*looking about him and shaking his shoulders loose*] I think I should prefer plenty of room.

HER HUSBAND. So, if it's not disturbing you, Rory—?

SHE. Not at all. [*She goes out*].

When the two men are alone together, Bompas deliberately takes the poems from his breast pocket; looks at them reflectively; then looks at Henry, mutely inviting his attention. Henry refuses to understand, doing his best to look unconcerned.

HER HUSBAND. Do these manuscripts seem at all familiar to you, may I ask?

HE. Manuscripts?

HER HUSBAND. Yes. Would you like to look at them a little closer? [*He proffers them under Henry's nose*].

HE [*as with a sudden illumination of glad surprise*] Why, these are my poems.

HER HUSBAND. So I gather.

HE. What a shame! Mrs Bompas has shown them to you! You must think me an utter ass. I wrote them years ago after reading Swinburne's Songs Before Sunrise. Nothing would do me then but I must reel off a set of Songs to the Sunrise. Aurora, you know: the rosy fingered Aurora. They're all about Aurora. When Mrs Bompas told me her name was Aurora, I couldn't resist the temptation to lend them to her to read. But I didn't bargain for your unsympathetic eyes.

HER HUSBAND [*grinning*] Apjohn: that's really very ready of you. You are cut out for literature; and the day will come when Rory and I will be proud to have you about the house. I have heard far thinner stories from much older men.

HE [*with an air of great surprise*] Do you mean to imply that you don't believe me?

HER HUSBAND. Do you expect me to believe you?

HE. Why not? I don't understand.

HER HUSBAND. Come! Don't underrate your own cleverness, Apjohn. I think you understand pretty well.

HE. I assure you I am quite at a loss. Can you not be a little more explicit?

HER HUSBAND. Don't overdo it, old chap. However, I will just be so far explicit as to say that if you think these poems read as if they were addressed, not to a live woman, but to a shivering cold time of day at which you were never out of bed in your life, you hardly do justice to your own literary powers—which I admire and appreciate, mind you, as much as any man. Come! own up. You wrote those poems to my wife. [*An internal struggle prevents Henry from answering*]. Of course you did. [*He throws the poems on the table; and goes to the hearthrug, where he plants himself solidly, chuckling a little and waiting for the next move*].

HE [*formally and carefully*] Mr Bompas: I pledge you my word you are mistaken. I need not tell you that Mrs Bompas is a lady of stainless honor, who has never cast an unworthy thought on me. The fact that she has shown you my poems—

HER HUSBAND. That's not a fact. I came by them without her knowledge. She didn't show them to me.

HE. Does not that prove their perfect innocence? She would have shown them to you at once if she had taken your quite unfounded view of them.

HER HUSBAND [*shaken*] Apjohn: play fair. Don't abuse your intellectual gifts. Do you really mean that I am making a fool of myself?

HE [*earnestly*] Believe me, you are. I assure you, on my honor as a gentleman, that I have never had the slightest feeling for Mrs Bompas beyond the ordinary esteem and regard of a pleasant acquaintance.

HER HUSBAND [*shortly, showing ill humor for the first time*] Oh, indeed. [*He leaves his hearth and begins to approach Henry slowly, looking him up and down with growing resentment*].

HE [*hastening to improve the impression made by his mendacity*] I should never have dreamt of writing poems to her. The thing is absurd.

HER HUSBAND [*reddening ominously*] Why is it absurd?

HE [*shrugging his shoulders*] Well, it happens that I do not admire Mrs Bompas—in that way.

HER HUSBAND [*breaking out in Henry's face*] Let me tell you that Mrs Bompas has been admired by better men than you, you soapy headed little puppy, you.

HE [*much taken aback*] There is no need to insult me like this. I assure you, on my honor as a—

HER HUSBAND [*too angry to tolerate a reply, and boring Henry more and more towards the piano*] You don't admire Mrs Bompas! You would never dream of writing poems to Mrs Bompas! My wife's not good enough for you, isn't she. [*Fiercely*] Who are you, pray, that you should be so jolly superior?

HE. Mr Bompas: I can make allowances for your jealousy—

HER HUSBAND. Jealousy! do you suppose I'm jealous of YOU? No, nor of ten like you. But if you think I'll stand here and let you insult my wife in her own house, you're mistaken.

HE [*very uncomfortable with his back against the piano and Teddy standing over him threateningly*] How can I convince you? Be reasonable. I tell you my relations with Mrs Bompas are relations of perfect coldness—of indifference—

HER HUSBAND [*scornfully*] Say it again: say it again. You're proud of it, aren't you? Yah! You're not worth kicking.

Henry suddenly executes the feat known to pugilists as dipping, and changes sides with Teddy, who it now between Henry and the piano.

HE. Look here: I'm not going to stand this.

HER HUSBAND. Oh, you have some blood in your body after all! Good job!

HE. This is ridiculous. I assure you Mrs. Bompas is quite—

HER HUSBAND. What is Mrs Bompas to you, I'd like to know. I'll tell you what Mrs Bompas is. She's the smartest woman in the smartest set in South Kensington, and the handsomest, and the cleverest, and the most fetching to experienced men who know a good thing when they see it, whatever she may be to conceited penny-a-lining puppies who think nothing good enough for them. It's admitted by the best people; and not to know it argues yourself unknown. Three of our first actor-managers have offered her a hundred a week if she'd go on the stage when they start a repertory theatre; and I think they know what they're about as well as you. The only member of the present Cabinet that you might call a handsome man has neglected the business of the country to dance with her, though he don't belong to our set as a regular thing. One of the first professional poets in Bedford Park wrote a sonnet to her, worth all your amateur trash. At Ascot last season the eldest son of a duke excused himself from calling on me on the ground that his feelings for Mrs Bompas were not consistent with his duty to me as host; and it did him honor and me too. But [*with gathering fury*] she isn't good enough for you, it seems. You regard her with coldness, with indifference; and you have the cool cheek to tell me so to my face. For two pins I'd flatten your nose in to teach you manners. Introducing a fine woman to you is casting pearls before swine [*yelling at him*] before SWINE! d'ye hear?

HE [*with a deplorable lack of polish*] You call me a swine again and I'll land you one on the chin that'll make your head sing for a week.

HER HUSBAND [*exploding*] What—!

He charges at Henry with bull-like fury. Henry places himself on guard in the manner of a well taught boxer, and gets away smartly, but unfortunately forgets the stool which is just behind him. He falls backwards over it, unintentionally pushing it against the shins of Bompas, who falls forward over it. Mrs Bompas, with a scream, rushes into the room between the sprawling champions, and sits down on the floor in order to get her right arm round her husband's neck.

SHE. You shan't, Teddy: you shan't. You will be killed: he is a prizefighter.

HER HUSBAND [*vengefully*] I'll prizefight him. [*He struggles vainly to free himself from her embrace*].

SHE. Henry: don't let him fight you. Promise me that you won't.

HE [*ruefully*] I have got a most frightful bump on the back of my head. [*He tries to rise*].

SHE [*reaching out her left hand to seize his coat tail, and pulling him down again, whilst keeping fast hold of Teddy with the other hand*] Not until you have promised: not until you both have promised. [*Teddy tries to rise: she pulls him back again*]. Teddy: you promise, don't you? Yes, yes. Be good: you promise.

HER HUSBAND. I won't, unless he takes it back.

SHE. He will: he does. You take it back, Henry?—yes.

HE [*savagely*] Yes. I take it back. [*She lets go his coat. He gets up. So does Teddy*]. I take it all back, all, without reserve.

SHE [*on the carpet*] Is nobody going to help me up? [*They each take a hand and pull her up*]. Now won't you shake hands and be good?

HE [*recklessly*] I shall do nothing of the sort. I have steeped myself in lies for your sake; and the only reward I get is a lump on the back of my head the size of an apple. Now I will go back to the straight path.

SHE. Henry: for Heaven's sake—

HE. It's no use. Your husband is a fool and a brute—

HER HUSBAND. What's that you say?

HE. I say you are a fool and a brute; and if you'll step outside with me I'll say it again. [*Teddy begins to take off his coat for combat*]. Those poems were written to your wife, every word of them, and to nobody else. [*The scowl clears away from Bompas's countenance. Radiant, he replaces his coat*]. I wrote them because I loved her. I thought her the most beautiful woman in the world; and I told her so over and over again. I adored her: do you hear? I told her that you were a sordid commercial chump, utterly unworthy of her; and so you are.

HER HUSBAND [*so gratified, he can hardly believe his ears*] You don't mean it!

HE. Yes, I do mean it, and a lot more too. I asked Mrs Bompas to walk out of the house with me—to leave you—to get divorced from you and marry me. I begged and implored her to do it this very night. It was her refusal that ended everything between us. [*Looking very disparagingly at him*] What she can see in you, goodness only knows!

HER HUSBAND [*beaming with remorse*] My dear chap, why didn't you say so before? I apologize. Come! Don't bear malice: shake hands. Make him shake hands, Rory.

SHE. For my sake, Henry. After all, he's my husband. Forgive him. Take his hand. [*Henry, dazed, lets her take his hand and place it in Teddy's*].

HER HUSBAND [*shaking it heartily*] You've got to own that none of your literary heroines can touch my Rory. [*He turns to her and claps her with fond pride on the shoulder*]. Eh, Rory? They can't resist you: none of em. Never knew a man yet that could hold out three days.

SHE. Don't be foolish, Teddy. I hope you were not really hurt, Henry. [*She feels the back of his head. He flinches*]. Oh, poor boy, what a bump! I must get some vinegar and brown paper. [*She goes to the bell and rings*].

HER HUSBAND. Will you do me a great favor, Apjohn. I hardly like to ask; but it would be a real kindness to us both.

HE. What can I do?

HER HUSBAND [*taking up the poems*] Well, may I get these printed? It shall be done in the best style. The finest paper, sumptuous binding, everything first class. They're beautiful poems. I should like to show them about a bit.

SHE [*running back from the bell, delighted with the idea, and coming between them*] Oh Henry, if you wouldn't mind!

HE. Oh, I don't mind. I am past minding anything. I have grown too fast this evening.

SHE. How old are you, Henry?

HE. This morning I was eighteen. Now I am—confound it! I'm quoting that beast of a play [*he takes the Candida tickets out of his pocket and tears them up viciously*].

HER HUSBAND. What shall we call the volume? To Aurora, or something like that, eh?

HE. I should call it How He Lied to Her Husband.

MAJOR BARBARA

ACT I

It is after dinner on a January night, in the library in Lady Britomart Undershaft's house in Wilton Crescent. A large and comfortable settee is in the middle of the room, upholstered in dark leather. A person sitting on it [*it is vacant at present*] would have, on his right, Lady Britomart's writing table, with the lady herself busy at it; a smaller writing table behind him on his left; the door behind him on Lady Britomart's side; and a window with a window seat directly on his left. Near the window is an armchair.

Lady Britomart is a woman of fifty or thereabouts, well dressed and yet careless of her dress, well bred and quite reckless of her breeding, well mannered and yet appallingly outspoken and indifferent to the opinion of her interlocutory, amiable and yet peremptory, arbitrary, and high-tempered to the last bearable degree, and withal a very typical managing matron of the upper class, treated as a naughty child until she grew into a scolding mother, and finally settling down with plenty of practical ability and worldly experience, limited in the oddest way with domestic and class limitations, conceiving the universe exactly as if it were a large house in Wilton Crescent, though handling her corner of it very effectively on that assumption, and being quite enlightened and liberal as to the books in the library, the pictures on the walls, the music in the portfolios, and the articles in the papers.

Her son, Stephen, comes in. He is a gravely correct young man under 25, taking himself very seriously, but still in some awe of his mother, from childish habit and bachelor shyness rather than from any weakness of character.

STEPHEN. What's the matter?

LADY BRITOMART. Presently, Stephen.

Stephen submissively walks to the settee and sits down. He takes up The Speaker.

LADY BRITOMART. Don't begin to read, Stephen. I shall require all your attention.

STEPHEN. It was only while I was waiting--

LADY BRITOMART. Don't make excuses, Stephen. [*He puts down The Speaker*]. Now! [*She finishes her writing; rises; and comes to the settee*]. I have not kept you waiting very long, I think.

STEPHEN. Not at all, mother.

LADY BRITOMART. Bring me my cushion. [*He takes the cushion from the chair at the desk and arranges it for her as she sits down on the settee*]. Sit down. [*He sits down and fingers his tie nervously*]. Don't fiddle with your tie, Stephen: there is nothing the matter with it.

STEPHEN. I beg your pardon. [*He fiddles with his watch chain instead*].

LADY BRITOMART. Now are you attending to me, Stephen?

STEPHEN. Of course, mother.

LADY BRITOMART. No: it's not of course. I want something much more than your everyday matter-of-course attention. I am going to speak to you very seriously, Stephen. I wish you would let that chain alone.

STEPHEN [*hastily relinquishing the chain*] Have I done anything to annoy you, mother? If so, it was quite unintentional.

LADY BRITOMART [*astonished*] Nonsense! [*With some remorse*] My poor boy, did you think I was angry with you?

STEPHEN. What is it, then, mother? You are making me very uneasy.

LADY BRITOMART [*squaring herself at him rather aggressively*] Stephen: may I ask how soon you intend to realize that you are a grown-up man, and that I am only a woman?

STEPHEN [*amazed*] Only a--

LADY BRITOMART. Don't repeat my words, please: It is a most aggravating habit. You must learn to face life seriously, Stephen. I really cannot bear the whole burden of our family affairs any longer. You must advise me: you must assume the responsibility.

STEPHEN. I!

LADY BRITOMART. Yes, you, of course. You were 24 last June. You've been at Harrow and Cambridge. You've been to India and Japan. You must know a lot of things now; unless you have wasted your time most scandalously. Well, advise me.

STEPHEN [*much perplexed*] You know I have never interfered in the household--

LADY BRITOMART. No: I should think not. I don't want you to order the dinner.

STEPHEN. I mean in our family affairs.

LADY BRITOMART. Well, you must interfere now; for they are getting quite beyond me.

STEPHEN [*troubled*] I have thought sometimes that perhaps I ought; but really, mother, I know so little about them; and what I do know is so painful--it is so impossible to mention some things to you--[*he stops, ashamed*].

LADY BRITOMART. I suppose you mean your father.

STEPHEN [*almost inaudibly*] Yes.

LADY BRITOMART. My dear: we can't go on all our lives not mentioning him. Of course you were quite right not to open the subject until I asked you to; but you are old enough now to be taken into my confidence, and to help me to deal with him about the girls.

STEPHEN. But the girls are all right. They are engaged.

LADY BRITOMART [*complacently*] Yes: I have made a very good match for Sarah. Charles Lomax will be a millionaire at 35. But that is ten years ahead; and in the meantime his trustees cannot under the terms of his father's will allow him more than 800 pounds a year.

STEPHEN. But the will says also that if he increases his income by his own exertions, they may double the increase.

LADY BRITOMART. Charles Lomax's exertions are much more likely to decrease his income than to increase it. Sarah will have to find at least another 800 pounds a year for the next ten years; and even then they will be as poor as church mice. And what about Barbara? I thought Barbara was going to make the most brilliant career of all of you. And what does she do? Joins the Salvation Army; discharges her maid; lives on a pound a week; and walks in one evening with a professor of Greek whom she has picked up in the street, and who pretends to be a Salvationist, and actually plays the big drum for her in public because he has fallen head over ears in love with her.

STEPHEN. I was certainly rather taken aback when I heard they were engaged. Cusins is a very nice fellow, certainly: nobody would ever guess that he was born in Australia; but--

LADY BRITOMART. Oh, Adolphus Cusins will make a very good husband. After all, nobody can say a word against Greek: it stamps a man at once as an educated gentleman. And my family, thank Heaven, is not a pig-headed Tory one. We are Whigs, and believe in liberty. Let snobbish people say what they please: Barbara shall marry, not the man they like, but the man I like.

STEPHEN. Of course I was thinking only of his income. However, he is not likely to be extravagant.

LADY BRITOMART. Don't be too sure of that, Stephen. I know your quiet, simple, refined, poetic people like Adolphus--quite content with the best of everything! They cost more than your extravagant people, who are always as mean as they are second rate. No: Barbara will need at least 2000 pounds a year. You see it means two additional households. Besides, my dear, you must marry soon. I don't approve of the present fashion of philandering bachelors and late marriages; and I am trying to arrange something for you.

STEPHEN. It's very good of you, mother; but perhaps I had better arrange that for myself.

LADY BRITOMART. Nonsense! you are much too young to begin matchmaking: you would be taken in by some pretty little nobody. Of course I don't mean that you are not to be consulted: you know that as well as I do. [*Stephen closes his lips and is silent*]. Now don't sulk, Stephen.

STEPHEN. I am not sulking, mother. What has all this got to do with--with--with my father?

LADY BRITOMART. My dear Stephen: where is the money to come from? It is easy enough for you and the other children to live on my income as long as we are in the same house; but I can't keep four families in four separate houses. You know how poor my father is: he has barely seven thousand a year now; and really, if he were not the Earl of Stevenage, he would have to give up society. He can do nothing for us: he says, naturally enough, that it is absurd that he should be asked to provide for the children of a man who is rolling in money. You see, Stephen, your father must be fabulously wealthy, because there is always a war going on somewhere.

STEPHEN. You need not remind me of that, mother. I have hardly ever opened a newspaper in my life without seeing our name in it. The Undershaft torpedo! The Undershaft quick firers! The Undershaft ten inch! the Undershaft disappearing rampart gun! the Undershaft submarine! and now the Undershaft aerial battleship! At Harrow they called me the Woolwich Infant. At Cambridge it was the same. A little brute at King's who was always trying to get up revivals, spoilt my Bible--your first birthday present to me--by writing under my name, "Son and heir to Undershaft and Lazarus, Death and Destruction Dealers: address, Christendom and Judea." But that was not so bad as the way I was kowtowed to everywhere because my father was making millions by selling cannons.

LADY BRITOMART. It is not only the cannons, but the war loans that Lazarus arranges under cover of giving credit for the cannons. You know, Stephen, it's perfectly scandalous. Those two men, Andrew Undershaft and Lazarus, positively have Europe under their thumbs. That is why your father is able to behave as he does. He is above the law. Do you think Bismarck or Gladstone or Disraeli could have openly defied every social and moral obligation all their lives as your father has? They simply wouldn't have dared. I asked Gladstone to take it up. I asked The Times to take it up. I asked the Lord Chamberlain to take it up. But it was just like asking them to declare war on the Sultan. They WOULDN'T. They said they couldn't touch him. I believe they were afraid.

STEPHEN. What could they do? He does not actually break the law.

LADY BRITOMART. Not break the law! He is always breaking the law. He broke the law when he was born: his parents were not married.

STEPHEN. Mother! Is that true?

LADY BRITOMART. Of course it's true: that was why we separated.

STEPHEN. He married without letting you know this!

LADY BRITOMART [*rather taken aback by this inference*] Oh no. To do Andrew justice, that was not the sort of thing he did. Besides, you know the Undershaft motto: Unashamed. Everybody knew.

STEPHEN. But you said that was why you separated.

LADY BRITOMART. Yes, because he was not content with being a foundling himself: he wanted to disinherit you for another foundling. That was what I couldn't stand.

STEPHEN [*ashamed*] Do you mean for--for--for--

LADY BRITOMART. Don't stammer, Stephen. Speak distinctly.

STEPHEN. But this is so frightful to me, mother. To have to speak to you about such things!

LADY BRITOMART. It's not pleasant for me, either, especially if you are still so childish that you must make it worse by a display of embarrassment. It is only in the middle classes, Stephen, that people get into a state of dumb helpless horror when they find that there are wicked people in the world. In our class, we have to decide what is to be done with wicked people; and nothing should disturb our self possession. Now ask your question properly.

STEPHEN. Mother: you have no consideration for me. For Heaven's sake either treat me as a child, as you always do, and tell me nothing at all; or tell me everything and let me take it as best I can.

LADY BRITOMART. Treat you as a child! What do you mean? It is most unkind and ungrateful of you to say such a thing. You know I have never treated any of you as children. I have always made you my companions and friends, and allowed you perfect freedom to do and say whatever you liked, so long as you liked what I could approve of.

STEPHEN [*desperately*] I daresay we have been the very imperfect children of a very perfect mother; but I do beg you to let me alone for once, and tell me about this horrible business of my father wanting to set me aside for another son.

LADY BRITOMART [*amazed*] Another son! I never said anything of the kind. I never dreamt of such a thing. This is what comes of interrupting me.

STEPHEN. But you said--

LADY BRITOMART [*cutting him short*] Now be a good boy, Stephen, and listen to me patiently. The Undershafts are descended from a foundling in the parish of St. Andrew Undershaft in the city. That was long ago, in the reign of James the First. Well, this foundling was adopted by an armorer and gunmaker. In the course of time the foundling succeeded to the business; and from some notion of gratitude, or some vow or something, he adopted another foundling, and left the business to him. And that foundling did the same. Ever since that, the cannon business has always been left to an adopted foundling named Andrew Undershaft.

STEPHEN. But did they never marry? Were there no legitimate sons?

LADY BRITOMART. Oh yes: they married just as your father did; and they were rich enough to buy land for their own children and leave them well provided for. But they always adopted and trained some foundling to succeed them in the business; and of course they always quarrelled with their wives furiously over it. Your father was adopted in that way; and he pretends to consider himself bound to keep up the tradition and adopt somebody to leave the business to. Of course I was not going to stand that. There may have been some reason for it when the Undershafts could only marry women in their own class, whose sons were not fit to govern great estates. But there could be no excuse for passing over my son.

STEPHEN [*dubiously*] I am afraid I should make a poor hand of managing a cannon foundry.

LADY BRITOMART. Nonsense! you could easily get a manager and pay him a salary.

STEPHEN. My father evidently had no great opinion of my capacity.

LADY BRITOMART. Stuff, child! you were only a baby: it had nothing to do with your capacity. Andrew did it on principle, just as he did every perverse and wicked thing on principle. When my father remonstrated, Andrew actually told him to his face that history tells us of only two successful institutions: one the Undershaft firm, and the other the Roman Empire under the Antonines. That was because the Antonine emperors all adopted their successors. Such rubbish! The Stevenages are as good as the Antonines, I hope; and you are a Stevenage. But that was Andrew all over. There you have the man! Always clever and unanswerable when he was defending nonsense and wickedness: always awkward and sullen when he had to behave sensibly and decently!

STEPHEN. Then it was on my account that your home life was broken up, mother. I am sorry.

LADY BRITOMART. Well, dear, there were other differences. I really cannot bear an immoral man. I am not a Pharisee, I hope; and I should not have minded his merely doing wrong things: we are none of us perfect. But your father didn't exactly do wrong things: he said them and thought them: that was what was so dreadful. He really had a sort of religion of wrongness just as one doesn't mind men practising immorality so long as they own that they are in the wrong by preaching morality; so I couldn't forgive Andrew for preaching immorality while he practised morality. You would all have grown up without principles, without any knowledge of right and wrong, if he had been in the house. You know, my dear, your father was a very attractive man in some ways. Children did not dislike him; and he took advantage of it to put the wickedest ideas into their heads, and make them quite unmanageable. I did not dislike him myself: very far from it; but nothing can bridge over moral disagreement.

STEPHEN. All this simply bewilders me, mother. People may differ about matters of opinion, or even about religion; but how can they differ about right and wrong? Right is right; and wrong is wrong; and if a man cannot distinguish them properly, he is either a fool or a rascal: that's all.

LADY BRITOMART [*touched*] That's my own boy [*she pats his cheek*]! Your father never could answer that: he used to laugh and get out of it under cover of some affectionate nonsense. And now that you understand the situation, what do you advise me to do?

STEPHEN. Well, what can you do?

LADY BRITOMART. I must get the money somehow.

STEPHEN. We cannot take money from him. I had rather go and live in some cheap place like Bedford Square or even Hampstead than take a farthing of his money.

LADY BRITOMART. But after all, Stephen, our present income comes from Andrew.

STEPHEN [*shocked*] I never knew that.

LADY BRITOMART. Well, you surely didn't suppose your grandfather had anything to give me. The Stevenages could not do everything for you. We gave you social position. Andrew had to contribute something. He had a very good bargain, I think.

STEPHEN [*bitterly*] We are utterly dependent on him and his cannons, then!

LADY BRITOMART. Certainly not: the money is settled. But he provided it. So you see it is not a question of taking money from him or not: it is simply a question of how much. I don't want any more for myself.

STEPHEN. Nor do I.

LADY BRITOMART. But Sarah does; and Barbara does. That is, Charles Lomax and Adolphus Cusins will cost them more. So I must put my pride in my pocket and ask for it, I suppose. That is your advice, Stephen, is it not?

STEPHEN. No.

LADY BRITOMART [*sharply*] Stephen!

STEPHEN. Of course if you are determined--

LADY BRITOMART. I am not determined: I ask your advice; and I am waiting for it. I will not have all the responsibility thrown on my shoulders.

STEPHEN [*obstinately*] I would die sooner than ask him for another penny.

LADY BRITOMART [*resignedly*] You mean that I must ask him. Very well, Stephen: It shall be as you wish. You will be glad to know that your grandfather concurs. But he thinks I ought to ask Andrew to come here and see the girls. After all, he must have some natural affection for them.

STEPHEN. Ask him here!!!

LADY BRITOMART. Do not repeat my words, Stephen. Where else can I ask him?

STEPHEN. I never expected you to ask him at all.

LADY BRITOMART. Now don't tease, Stephen. Come! you see that it is necessary that he should pay us a visit, don't you?

STEPHEN [*reluctantly*] I suppose so, if the girls cannot do without his money.

LADY BRITOMART. Thank you, Stephen: I knew you would give me the right advice when it was properly explained to you. I have asked your father to come this evening. [*Stephen bounds from his seat*] Don't jump, Stephen: it fidgets me.

STEPHEN [*in utter consternation*] Do you mean to say that my father is coming here to-night--that he may be here at any moment?

LADY BRITOMART [*looking at her watch*] I said nine. [*He gasps. She rises*]. Ring the bell, please. [*Stephen goes to the smaller writing table; presses a button on it; and sits at it with his elbows on the table and his head in his hands, outwitted and overwhelmed*]. It is ten minutes to nine yet; and I have to prepare the girls. I asked Charles Lomax and Adolphus to dinner on purpose that they might be here. Andrew had better see them in case he should cherish any delusions as to their being capable of supporting their wives. [*The butler enters: Lady Britomart goes behind the settee to speak to him*]. Morrison: go up to the drawingroom and tell everybody to come down here at once. [*Morrison withdraws. Lady Britomart turns to Stephen*]. Now remember, Stephen, I shall need all your countenance and authority. [*He rises and tries to recover some vestige of these attributes*]. Give me a chair, dear. [*He pushes a chair forward from the wall to where she stands, near the smaller writing table. She sits down; and he goes to the armchair, into which he throws himself*]. I don't know how Barbara will take it. Ever since they made her a major in the Salvation Army she has developed a propensity to have her own way and order people about which quite cows me sometimes. It's not ladylike: I'm sure I don't know where she picked it up. Anyhow, Barbara shan't bully me; but still it's just as well that your father should be here before she has time to refuse to meet him or make a fuss. Don't look nervous, Stephen, it will only encourage Barbara to make difficulties. I am nervous enough, goodness knows; but I don't show it.

Sarah and Barbara come in with their respective young men, Charles Lomax and Adolphus Cusins. Sarah is slender, bored, and mundane. Barbara is robuster, jollier, much more energetic. Sarah is fashionably dressed: Barbara is in Salvation Army uniform. Lomax, a young man about town, is like many other young men about town. He is affected with a frivolous sense of humor which plunges him at the most inopportune moments into paroxysms of imperfectly suppressed laughter. Cusins is a spectacled student, slight, thin haired, and sweet voiced, with a more complex form of Lomax's complaint. His sense of humor is intellectual and subtle, and is complicated by an appalling temper. The lifelong struggle of a benevolent temperament and a high conscience against impulses of inhuman ridicule and fierce impatience has set up a chronic strain which has visibly wrecked his constitution. He is a most implacable, determined, tenacious, intolerant person who by mere force of character presents himself as--and indeed actually is--considerate, gentle, explanatory, even mild and apologetic, capable possibly of murder, but not of cruelty or coarseness. By the operation of some instinct which is not merciful enough to blind him with the illusions of love, he is obstinately bent on marrying Barbara. Lomax likes Sarah and thinks it will be rather a lark to marry her. Consequently he has not attempted to resist Lady Britomart's arrangements to that end.

All four look as if they had been having a good deal of fun in the drawingroom. The girls enter first, leaving the swains outside. Sarah comes to the settee. Barbara comes in after her and stops at the door.

BARBARA. Are Cholly and Dolly to come in?

LADY BRITOMART [*forcibly*] Barbara: I will not have Charles called Cholly: the vulgarity of it positively makes me ill.

BARBARA. It's all right, mother. Cholly is quite correct nowadays. Are they to come in?

LADY BRITOMART. Yes, if they will behave themselves.

BARBARA [*through the door*] Come in, Dolly, and behave yourself.

Barbara comes to her mother's writing table. Cusins enters smiling, and wanders towards Lady Britomart.

SARAH [*calling*] Come in, Cholly. [*Lomax enters, controlling his features very imperfectly, and places himself vaguely between Sarah and Barbara*].

LADY BRITOMART [*peremptorily*] Sit down, all of you. [*They sit. Cusins crosses to the window and seats himself there. Lomax takes a chair. Barbara sits at the writing table and Sarah on the settee*]. I don't in the least know what you are laughing at, Adolphus. I am surprised at you, though I expected nothing better from Charles Lomax.

CUSINS [*in a remarkably gentle voice*] Barbara has been trying to teach me the West Ham Salvation March.

LADY BRITOMART. I see nothing to laugh at in that; nor should you if you are really converted.

CUSINS [*sweetly*] You were not present. It was really funny, I believe.

LOMAX. Ripping.

LADY BRITOMART. Be quiet, Charles. Now listen to me, children. Your father is coming here this evening. [*General stupefaction*].

LOMAX [*remonstrating*] Oh I say!

LADY BRITOMART. You are not called on to say anything, Charles.

SARAH. Are you serious, mother?

LADY BRITOMART. Of course I am serious. It is on your account, Sarah, and also on Charles's. [*Silence. Charles looks painfully unworthy*]. I hope you are not going to object, Barbara.

BARBARA. I! why should I? My father has a soul to be saved like anybody else. He's quite welcome as far as I am concerned.

LOMAX [*still remonstrant*] But really, don't you know! Oh I say!

LADY BRITOMART [*frigidly*] What do you wish to convey, Charles?

LOMAX. Well, you must admit that this is a bit thick.

LADY BRITOMART [*turning with ominous suavity to Cusins*] Adolphus: you are a professor of Greek. Can you translate Charles Lomax's remarks into reputable English for us?

CUSINS [*cautiously*] If I may say so, Lady Brit, I think Charles has rather happily expressed what we all feel. Homer, speaking of Autolycus, uses the same phrase.

LOMAX [*handsomely*] Not that I mind, you know, if Sarah don't.

LADY BRITOMART [*crushingly*] Thank you. Have I your permission, Adolphus, to invite my own husband to my own house?

CUSINS [*gallantly*] You have my unhesitating support in everything you do.

LADY BRITOMART. Sarah: have you nothing to say?

SARAH. Do you mean that he is coming regularly to live here?

LADY BRITOMART. Certainly not. The spare room is ready for him if he likes to stay for a day or two and see a little more of you; but there are limits.

SARAH. Well, he can't eat us, I suppose. I don't mind.

LOMAX [*chuckling*] I wonder how the old man will take it.

LADY BRITOMART. Much as the old woman will, no doubt, Charles.

LOMAX [*abashed*] I didn't mean--at least--

LADY BRITOMART. You didn't think, Charles. You never do; and the result is, you never mean anything. And now please attend to me, children. Your father will be quite a stranger to us.

LOMAX. I suppose he hasn't seen Sarah since she was a little kid.

LADY BRITOMART. Not since she was a little kid, Charles, as you express it with that elegance of diction and refinement of thought that seem never to desert you. Accordingly--er-- [*impatiently*] Now I have forgotten what I was going to say. That comes of your provoking me to be sarcastic, Charles. Adolphus: will you kindly tell me where I was.

CUSINS [*sweetly*] You were saying that as Mr Undershaft has not seen his children since they were babies, he will form his opinion of the way you have brought them up from their behavior to-night, and that therefore you wish us all to be particularly careful to conduct ourselves well, especially Charles.

LOMAX. Look here: Lady Brit didn't say that.

LADY BRITOMART [*vehemently*] I did, Charles. Adolphus's recollection is perfectly correct. It is most important that you should be good; and I do beg you for once not to pair off into opposite corners and giggle and whisper while I am speaking to your father.

BARBARA. All right, mother. We'll do you credit.

LADY BRITOMART. Remember, Charles, that Sarah will want to feel proud of you instead of ashamed of you.

LOMAX. Oh I say! There's nothing to be exactly proud of, don't you know.

LADY BRITOMART. Well, try and look as if there was.

Morrison, pale and dismayed, breaks into the room in unconcealed disorder.

MORRISON. Might I speak a word to you, my lady?

LADY BRITOMART. Nonsense! Show him up.

MORRISON. Yes, my lady. [*He goes*].

LOMAX. Does Morrison know who he is?

LADY BRITOMART. Of course. Morrison has always been with us.

LOMAX. It must be a regular corker for him, don't you know.

LADY BRITOMART. Is this a moment to get on my nerves, Charles, with your outrageous expressions?

LOMAX. But this is something out of the ordinary, really--

MORRISON [*at the door*] The--er--Mr Undershaft. [*He retreats in confusion*].

Andrew Undershaft comes in. All rise. Lady Britomart meets him in the middle of the room behind the settee.

Andrew is, on the surface, a stoutish, easygoing elderly man, with kindly patient manners, and an engaging simplicity of character. But he has a watchful, deliberate, waiting, listening face, and formidable reserves of power, both bodily and mental, in his capacious chest and long head. His gentleness is partly that of a strong man who has learnt by experience that his natural grip hurts ordinary people unless he handles them very carefully, and partly the mellowness of age and success. He is also a little shy in his present very delicate situation.

LADY BRITOMART. Good evening, Andrew.

UNDERSHAFT. How d'ye do, my dear.

LADY BRITOMART. You look a good deal older.

UNDERSHAFT [*apologetically*] I AM somewhat older. [*With a touch of courtship*] Time has stood still with you.

LADY BRITOMART [*promptly*] Rubbish! This is your family.

UNDERSHAFT [*surprised*] Is it so large? I am sorry to say my memory is failing very badly in some things. [*He offers his hand with paternal kindness to Lomax*].

LOMAX [*jerkily shaking his hand*] Ahdedoo.

UNDERSHAFT. I can see you are my eldest. I am very glad to meet you again, my boy.

LOMAX [*remonstrating*] No but look here don't you know--[*Overcome*] Oh I say!

LADY BRITOMART [*recovering from momentary speechlessness*] Andrew: do you mean to say that you don't remember how many children you have?

UNDERSHAFT. Well, I am afraid I--. They have grown so much--er. Am I making any ridiculous mistake? I may as well confess: I recollect only one son. But so many things have happened since, of course--er--

LADY BRITOMART [*decisively*] Andrew: you are talking nonsense. Of course you have only one son.

UNDERSHAFT. Perhaps you will be good enough to introduce me, my dear.

LADY BRITOMART. That is Charles Lomax, who is engaged to Sarah.

UNDERSHAFT. My dear sir, I beg your pardon.

LOMAX. Not at all. Delighted, I assure you.

LADY BRITOMART. This is Stephen.

UNDERSHAFT [*bowing*] Happy to make your acquaintance, Mr Stephen. Then [*going to Cusins*] you must be my son. [*Taking Cusins' hands in his*] How are you, my young friend? [*To Lady Britomart*] He is very like you, my love.

CUSINS. You flatter me, Mr Undershaft. My name is Cusins: engaged to Barbara. [*Very explicitly*] That is Major Barbara Undershaft, of the Salvation Army. That is Sarah, your second daughter. This is Stephen Undershaft, your son.

UNDERSHAFT. My dear Stephen, I beg your pardon.

STEPHEN. Not at all.

UNDERSHAFT. Mr Cusins: I am much indebted to you for explaining so precisely. [*Turning to Sarah*] Barbara, my dear--

SARAH [*prompting him*] Sarah.

UNDERSHAFT. Sarah, of course. [*They shake hands. He goes over to Barbara*] Barbara--I am right this time, I hope.

BARBARA. Quite right. [*They shake hands*].

LADY BRITOMART [*resuming command*] Sit down, all of you. Sit down, Andrew. [*She comes forward and sits on the settle. Cusins also brings his chair forward on her left. Barbara and Stephen resume their seats. Lomax gives his chair to Sarah and goes for another*].

UNDERSHAFT. Thank you, my love.

LOMAX [*conversationally, as he brings a chair forward between the writing table and the settee, and offers it to Undershaft*] Takes you some time to find out exactly where you are, don't it?

UNDERSHAFT [*accepting the chair*] That is not what embarrasses me, Mr Lomax. My difficulty is that if I play the part of a father, I shall produce the effect of an intrusive stranger; and if I play the part of a discreet stranger, I may appear a callous father.

LADY BRITOMART. There is no need for you to play any part at all, Andrew. You had much better be sincere and natural.

UNDERSHAFT [*submissively*] Yes, my dear: I daresay that will be best. [*Making himself comfortable*] Well, here I am. Now what can I do for you all?

LADY BRITOMART. You need not do anything, Andrew. You are one of the family. You can sit with us and enjoy yourself.

Lomax's too long suppressed mirth explodes in agonized neighings.

LADY BRITOMART [*outraged*] Charles Lomax: if you can behave yourself, behave yourself. If not, leave the room.

LOMAX. I'm awfully sorry, Lady Brit; but really, you know, upon my soul! [*He sits on the settee between Lady Britomart and Undershaft, quite overcome*].

BARBARA. Why don't you laugh if you want to, Cholly? It's good for your inside.

LADY BRITOMART. Barbara: you have had the education of a lady. Please let your father see that; and don't talk like a street girl.

UNDERSHAFT. Never mind me, my dear. As you know, I am not a gentleman; and I was never educated.

LOMAX [*encouragingly*] Nobody'd know it, I assure you. You look all right, you know.

CUSINS. Let me advise you to study Greek, Mr Undershaft. Greek scholars are privileged men. Few of them know Greek; and none of them know anything else; but their position is unchallengeable. Other languages are the qualifications of waiters and commercial travellers: Greek is to a man of position what the hallmark is to silver.

BARBARA. Dolly: don't be insincere. Cholly: fetch your concertina and play something for us.

LOMAX [*doubtfully to Undershaft*] Perhaps that sort of thing isn't in your line, eh?

UNDERSHAFT. I am particularly fond of music.

LOMAX [*delighted*] Are you? Then I'll get it. [*He goes upstairs for the instrument*].

UNDERSHAFT. Do you play, Barbara?

BARBARA. Only the tambourine. But Cholly's teaching me the concertina.

UNDERSHAFT. Is Cholly also a member of the Salvation Army?

BARBARA. No: he says it's bad form to be a dissenter. But I don't despair of Cholly. I made him come yesterday to a meeting at the dock gates, and take the collection in his hat.

LADY BRITOMART. It is not my doing, Andrew. Barbara is old enough to take her own way. She has no father to advise her.

BARBARA. Oh yes she has. There are no orphans in the Salvation Army.

UNDERSHAFT. Your father there has a great many children and plenty of experience, eh?

BARBARA [*looking at him with quick interest and nodding*] Just so. How did you come to understand that? [*Lomax is heard at the door trying the concertina*].

LADY BRITOMART. Come in, Charles. Play us something at once.

LOMAX. Righto! [*He sits down in his former place, and preludes*].

UNDERSHAFT. One moment, Mr Lomax. I am rather interested in the Salvation Army. Its motto might be my own: Blood and Fire.

LOMAX [*shocked*] But not your sort of blood and fire, you know.

UNDERSHAFT. My sort of blood cleanses: my sort of fire purifies.

BARBARA. So do ours. Come down to-morrow to my shelter--the West Ham shelter--and see what we're doing. We're going to march to a great meeting in the Assembly Hall at Mile End. Come and see the shelter and then march with us: it will do you a lot of good. Can you play anything?

UNDERSHAFT. In my youth I earned pennies, and even shillings occasionally, in the streets and in public house parlors by my natural talent for step-dancing. Later on, I became a member of the Undershaft orchestral society, and performed passably on the tenor trombone.

LOMAX [*scandalized*] Oh I say!

BARBARA. Many a sinner has played himself into heaven on the trombone, thanks to the Army.

LOMAX [*to Barbara, still rather shocked*] Yes; but what about the cannon business, don't you know? [*To Undershaft*] Getting into heaven is not exactly in your line, is it?

LADY BRITOMART. Charles!!!

LOMAX. Well; but it stands to reason, don't it? The cannon business may be necessary and all that: we can't get on without cannons; but it isn't right, you know. On the other hand, there may be a certain amount of tosh about the Salvation Army--I belong to the Established Church myself--but still you can't deny that it's religion; and you can't go against religion, can you? At least unless you're downright immoral, don't you know.

UNDERSHAFT. You hardly appreciate my position, Mr Lomax--

LOMAX [*hastily*] I'm not saying anything against you personally, you know.

UNDERSHAFT. Quite so, quite so. But consider for a moment. Here I am, a manufacturer of mutilation and murder. I find myself in a specially amiable humor just now because, this morning, down at the foundry, we blew twenty-seven dummy soldiers into fragments with a gun which formerly destroyed only thirteen.

LOMAX [*leniently*] Well, the more destructive war becomes, the sooner it will be abolished, eh?

UNDERSHAFT. Not at all. The more destructive war becomes the more fascinating we find it. No, Mr Lomax, I am obliged to you for making the usual excuse for my trade; but I am not ashamed of it. I am not one of those men who keep their morals and their business in watertight compartments. All the spare money my trade rivals spend on hospitals, cathedrals and other receptacles for conscience money, I devote to experiments and researches in improved methods of destroying life and property. I have always done so; and I always shall. Therefore your Christmas card moralities of peace on earth and goodwill among men are of no use to me. Your Christianity, which enjoins you to resist not evil, and to turn the other cheek, would make me a bankrupt. My morality--my religion--must have a place for cannons and torpedoes in it.

STEPHEN [*coldly--almost sullenly*] You speak as if there were half a dozen moralities and religions to choose from, instead of one true morality and one true religion.

UNDERSHAFT. For me there is only one true morality; but it might not fit you, as you do not manufacture aerial battleships. There is only one true morality for every man; but every man has not the same true morality.

LOMAX [*overtaxed*] Would you mind saying that again? I didn't quite follow it.

CUSINS. It's quite simple. As Euripides says, one man's meat is another man's poison morally as well as physically.

UNDERSHAFT. Precisely.

LOMAX. Oh, that. Yes, yes, yes. True. True.

STEPHEN. In other words, some men are honest and some are scoundrels.

BARBARA. Bosh. There are no scoundrels.

UNDERSHAFT. Indeed? Are there any good men?

BARBARA. No. Not one. There are neither good men nor scoundrels: there are just children of one Father; and the sooner they stop calling one another names the better. You needn't talk to me: I know them. I've had scores of them through my hands: scoundrels, criminals, infidels, philanthropists, missionaries, county councillors, all sorts. They're all just the same sort of sinner; and there's the same salvation ready for them all.

UNDERSHAFT. May I ask have you ever saved a maker of cannons?

BARBARA. No. Will you let me try?

UNDERSHAFT. Well, I will make a bargain with you. If I go to see you to-morrow in your Salvation Shelter, will you come the day after to see me in my cannon works?

BARBARA. Take care. It may end in your giving up the cannons for the sake of the Salvation Army.

UNDERSHAFT. Are you sure it will not end in your giving up the Salvation Army for the sake of the cannons?

BARBARA. I will take my chance of that.

UNDERSHAFT. And I will take my chance of the other. [*They shake hands on it*]. Where is your shelter?

BARBARA. In West Ham. At the sign of the cross. Ask anybody in Canning Town. Where are your works?

UNDERSHAFT. In Perivale St Andrews. At the sign of the sword. Ask anybody in Europe.

LOMAX. Hadn't I better play something?

BARBARA. Yes. Give us Onward, Christian Soldiers.

LOMAX. Well, that's rather a strong order to begin with, don't you know. Suppose I sing Thou'rt passing hence, my brother. It's much the same tune.

BARBARA. It's too melancholy. You get saved, Cholly; and you'll pass hence, my brother, without making such a fuss about it.

LADY BRITOMART. Really, Barbara, you go on as if religion were a pleasant subject. Do have some sense of propriety.

UNDERSHAFT. I do not find it an unpleasant subject, my dear. It is the only one that capable people really care for.

LADY BRITOMART [*looking at her watch*] Well, if you are determined to have it, I insist on having it in a proper and respectable way. Charles: ring for prayers. [*General amazement. Stephen rises in dismay*].

LOMAX [*rising*] Oh I say!

UNDERSHAFT [*rising*] I am afraid I must be going.

LADY BRITOMART. You cannot go now, Andrew: it would be most improper. Sit down. What will the servants think?

UNDERSHAFT. My dear: I have conscientious scruples. May I suggest a compromise? If Barbara will conduct a little service in the drawingroom, with Mr Lomax as organist, I will attend it willingly. I will even take part, if a trombone can be procured.

LADY BRITOMART. Don't mock, Andrew.

UNDERSHAFT [*shocked--to Barbara*] You don't think I am mocking, my love, I hope.

BARBARA. No, of course not; and it wouldn't matter if you were: half the Army came to their first meeting for a lark. [*Rising*] Come along. Come, Dolly. Come, Cholly. [*She goes out with Undershaft, who opens the door for her. Cusins rises*].

LADY BRITOMART. I will not be disobeyed by everybody. Adolphus: sit down. Charles: you may go. You are not fit for prayers: you cannot keep your countenance.

LOMAX. Oh I say! [*He goes out*].

LADY BRITOMART [*continuing*] But you, Adolphus, can behave yourself if you choose to. I insist on your staying.

CUSINS. My dear Lady Brit: there are things in the family prayer book that I couldn't bear to hear you say.

LADY BRITOMART. What things, pray?

CUSINS. Well, you would have to say before all the servants that we have done things we ought not to have done, and left undone things we ought to have done, and that there is no health in us. I cannot bear to hear you doing yourself such an unjustice, and Barbara such an injustice. As for myself, I flatly deny it: I have done my best. I shouldn't dare to marry Barbara--I couldn't look you in the face--if it were true. So I must go to the drawingroom.

LADY BRITOMART [*offended*] Well, go. [*He starts for the door*]. And remember this, Adolphus [*he turns to listen*]: I have a very strong suspicion that you went to the Salvation Army to worship Barbara and nothing else. And I quite appreciate the very clever way in which you systematically humbug me. I have found you out. Take care Barbara doesn't. That's all.

CUSINS [*with unruffled sweetness*] Don't tell on me. [*He goes out*].

LADY BRITOMART. Sarah: if you want to go, go. Anything's better than to sit there as if you wished you were a thousand miles away.

SARAH [*languidly*] Very well, mamma. [*She goes*].

Lady Britomart, with a sudden flounce, gives way to a little gust of tears.

STEPHEN [*going to her*] Mother: what's the matter?

LADY BRITOMART [*swishing away her tears with her handkerchief*] Nothing. Foolishness. You can go with him, too, if you like, and leave me with the servants.

STEPHEN. Oh, you mustn't think that, mother. I--I don't like him.

LADY BRITOMART. The others do. That is the injustice of a woman's lot. A woman has to bring up her children; and that means to restrain them, to deny them things they want, to set them tasks, to punish them when they do wrong, to do all the unpleasant things. And then the father, who has nothing to do but pet them and spoil them, comes in when all her work is done and steals their affection from her.

STEPHEN. He has not stolen our affection from you. It is only curiosity.

LADY BRITOMART [*violently*] I won't be consoled, Stephen. There is nothing the matter with me. [*She rises and goes towards the door*].

STEPHEN. Where are you going, mother?

LADY BRITOMART. To the drawingroom, of course. [*She goes out. Onward, Christian Soldiers, on the concertina, with tambourine accompaniment, is heard when the door opens*]. Are you coming, Stephen?

STEPHEN. No. Certainly not. [*She goes. He sits down on the settee, with compressed lips and an expression of strong dislike*].

ACT II

The yard of the West Ham shelter of the Salvation Army is a cold place on a January morning. The building itself, an old warehouse, is newly whitewashed. Its gabled end projects into the yard in the middle, with a door on the ground floor, and another in the loft above it without any balcony or ladder, but with a pulley rigged over it for hoisting sacks. Those who come from this central gable end into the yard have the gateway leading to the street on their left, with a stone horse-trough just beyond it, and, on the right, a penthouse shielding a table from the weather. There are forms at the table; and on them are seated a man and a woman, both much down on their luck, finishing a meal of bread [*one thick slice each, with margarine and golden syrup*] and diluted milk.

The man, a workman out of employment, is young, agile, a talker, a poser, sharp enough to be capable of anything in reason except honesty or altruistic considerations of any kind. The woman is a commonplace old bundle of poverty and hard-worn humanity. She looks sixty and probably is forty-five. If they were rich people, gloved and muffed and well wrapped up in furs and overcoats, they would be numbed and miserable; for it is a grindingly cold, raw, January day; and a glance at the background of grimy warehouses and leaden sky visible over the whitewashed walls of the yard would drive any idle rich person straight to the Mediterranean. But these two, being no more troubled with visions of the Mediterranean than of the moon, and being compelled to keep more of their clothes in the pawnshop, and less on their persons, in winter than in summer, are not depressed by the cold: rather are they stung into vivacity, to which their meal has just now given an almost jolly turn. The man takes a pull at his mug, and then gets up and moves about the yard with his hands deep in his pockets, occasionally breaking into a stepdance.

THE WOMAN. Feel better otter your meal, sir?

THE MAN. No. Call that a meal! Good enough for you, props; but wot is it to me, an intelligent workin man.

THE WOMAN. Workin man! Wot are you?

THE MAN. Painter.

THE WOMAN [*sceptically*] Yus, I dessay.

THE MAN. Yus, you dessay! I know. Every loafer that can't do nothink calls isself a painter. Well, I'm a real painter: grainer, finisher, thirty-eight bob a week when I can get it.

THE WOMAN. Then why don't you go and get it?

THE MAN. I'll tell you why. Fust: I'm intelligent--fffff! it's rotten cold here [*he dances a step or two*]--yes: intelligent beyond the station o life into which it has pleased the capitalists to call me; and they don't like a man that sees through em. Second, an intelligent bein needs a doo share of appiness; so I drink somethink cruel when I get the chawnce. Third, I stand by my class and do as little as I can so's to leave arf the job for me fellow workers. Fourth, I'm fly enough to know wots inside the law and wots outside it; and inside it I do as the capitalists do: pinch wot I can lay me ands on. In a proper state of society I am sober, industrious and honest: in Rome, so to speak, I do as the Romans do. Wots the consequence? When trade is bad--and it's rotten bad just now--and the employers az to sack arf their men, they generally start on me.

THE WOMAN. What's your name?

THE MAN. Price. Bronterre O'Brien Price. Usually called Snobby Price, for short.

THE WOMAN. Snobby's a carpenter, ain't it? You said you was a painter.

PRICE. Not that kind of snob, but the genteel sort. I'm too uppish, owing to my intelligence, and my father being a Chartist and a reading, thinking man: a stationer, too. I'm none of your common hewers of wood and drawers of water; and don't you forget it. [*He returns to his seat at the table, and takes up his mug*]. Wots YOUR name?

THE WOMAN. Rummy Mitchens, sir.

PRICE [*quaffing the remains of his milk to her*] Your elth, Miss Mitchens.

RUMMY [*correcting him*] Missis Mitchens.

PRICE. Wot! Oh Rummy, Rummy! Respectable married woman, Rummy, gittin rescued by the Salvation Army by pretendin to be a bad un. Same old game!

RUMMY. What am I to do? I can't starve. Them Salvation lasses is dear good girls; but the better you are, the worse they likes to think you were before they rescued you. Why shouldn't they av a bit o credit, poor loves? They're worn to rags by their work. And where would they get the money to rescue us if we was to let on we're no worse than other people? You know what ladies and gentlemen are.

PRICE. Thievin swine! Wish I ad their job, Rummy, all the same. Wot does Rummy stand for? Pet name props?

RUMMY. Short for Romola.

PRICE. For wot!?

RUMMY. Romola. It was out of a new book. Somebody me mother wanted me to grow up like.

PRICE. We're companions in misfortune, Rummy. Both on us got names that nobody cawnt pronounce. Consequently I'm Snobby and you're Rummy because Bill and Sally wasn't good enough for our parents. Such is life!

RUMMY. Who saved you, Mr. Price? Was it Major Barbara?

PRICE. No: I come here on my own. I'm goin to be Bronterre O'Brien Price, the converted painter. I know wot they like. I'll tell em how I blasphemed and gambled and wopped my poor old mother--

RUMMY [*shocked*] Used you to beat your mother?

PRICE. Not likely. She used to beat me. No matter: you come and listen to the converted painter, and you'll hear how she was a pious woman that taught me me prayers at er knee, an how I used to come home drunk and drag her out o bed be er snow white airs, an lam into er with the poker.

RUMMY. That's what's so unfair to us women. Your confessions is just as big lies as ours: you don't tell what you really done no more than us; but you men can tell your lies right out at the meetins and be made much of for it; while the sort o confessions we az to make az to be wispered to one lady at a time. It ain't right, spite of all their piety.

PRICE. Right! Do you spose the Army'd be allowed if it went and did right? Not much. It combs our air and makes us good little blokes to be robbed and put upon. But I'll play the game as good as any of em. I'll see somebody struck by lightnin, or hear a voice sayin "Snobby Price: where will you spend eternity?" I'll ave a time of it, I tell you.

RUMMY. You won't be let drink, though.

PRICE. I'll take it out in gorspellin, then. I don't want to drink if I can get fun enough any other way.

Jenny Hill, a pale, overwrought, pretty Salvation lass of 18, comes in through the yard gate, leading Peter Shirley, a half hardened, half worn-out elderly man, weak with hunger.

JENNY [*supporting him*] Come! pluck up. I'll get you something to eat. You'll be all right then.

PRICE [*rising and hurrying officiously to take the old man off Jenny's hands*] Poor old man! Cheer up, brother: you'll find rest and peace and appiness ere. Hurry up with the food, miss: e's fair done. [*Jenny hurries into the shelter*]. Ere, buck up, daddy! She's fetchin y'a thick slice o breadn treacle, an a mug o skyblue. [*He seats him at the corner of the table*].

RUMMY [*gaily*] Keep up your old art! Never say die!

SHIRLEY. I'm not an old man. I'm ony 46. I'm as good as ever I was. The grey patch come in my hair before I was thirty. All it wants is three pennorth o hair dye: am I to be turned on the streets to starve for it? Holy God! I've worked ten to twelve hours a day since I was thirteen, and paid my way all through; and now am I to be thrown into the gutter and my job given to a young man that can do it no better than me because I've black hair that goes white at the first change?

PRICE [*cheerfully*] No good jawrin about it. You're ony a jumped-up, jerked-off, orspittle-turned-out incurable of an ole workin man: who cares about you? Eh? Make the thievin swine give you a meal: they've stole many a one from you. Get a bit o your own back. [*Jenny returns with the usual meal*]. There you are, brother. Awsk a blessin an tuck that into you.

SHIRLEY [*looking at it ravenously but not touching it, and crying like a child*] I never took anything before.

JENNY [*petting him*] Come, come! the Lord sends it to you: he wasn't above taking bread from his friends; and why should you be? Besides, when we find you a job you can pay us for it if you like.

SHIRLEY [*eagerly*] Yes, yes: that's true. I can pay you back: it's only a loan. [*Shivering*] Oh Lord! oh Lord! [*He turns to the table and attacks the meal ravenously*].

JENNY. Well, Rummy, are you more comfortable now?

RUMMY. God bless you, lovey! You've fed my body and saved my soul, haven't you? [*Jenny, touched, kisses her*] Sit down and rest a bit: you must be ready to drop.

JENNY. I've been going hard since morning. But there's more work than we can do. I mustn't stop.

RUMMY. Try a prayer for just two minutes. You'll work all the better after.

JENNY [*her eyes lighting up*] Oh isn't it wonderful how a few minutes prayer revives you! I was quite lightheaded at twelve o'clock, I was so tired; but Major Barbara just sent me to pray for five minutes; and I was able to go on as if I had only just begun. [*To Price*] Did you have a piece of bread?

PAIGE [*with unction*] Yes, miss; but I've got the piece that I value more; and that's the peace that passeth hall hannerstennin.

RUMMY [*fervently*] Glory Hallelujah!

Bill Walker, a rough customer of about 25, appears at the yard gate and looks malevolently at Jenny.

JENNY. That makes me so happy. When you say that, I feel wicked for loitering here. I must get to work again.

She is hurrying to the shelter, when the newcomer moves quickly up to the door and intercepts her. His manner is so threatening that she retreats as he comes at her truculently, driving her down the yard.

BILL. I know you. You're the one that took away my girl. You're the one that set er agen me. Well, I'm goin to av er out. Not that I care a curse for her or you: see? But I'll let er know; and I'll let you know. I'm goin to give er a doin that'll teach er to cut away from me. Now in with you and tell er to come out afore I come in and kick er out. Tell er Bill Walker wants er. She'll know what that means; and if she keeps me waitin it'll be worse. You stop to jaw back at me; and I'll start on you: d'ye hear? There's your way. In you go. [*He takes her by the arm and slings her towards the door of the shelter. She falls on her hand and knee. Rummy helps her up again*].

PRICE [*rising, and venturing irresolutely towards Bill*]. Easy there, mate. She ain't doin you no arm.

BILL. Who are you callin mate? [*Standing over him threateningly*]. You're goin to stand up for her, are you? Put up your ands.

RUMMY [*running indignantly to him to scold him*]. Oh, you great brute-- [*He instantly swings his left hand back against her face. She screams and reels back to the trough, where she sits down, covering her bruised face with her hands and rocking and moaning with pain*].

JENNY [*going to her*]. Oh God forgive you! How could you strike an old woman like that?

BILL [*seizing her by the hair so violently that she also screams, and tearing her away from the old woman*]. You Gawd forgive me again and I'll Gawd forgive you one on the jaw that'll stop you prayin for a week. [*Holding her and turning fiercely on Price*]. Av you anything to say agen it? Eh?

PRICE [*intimidated*]. No, matey: she ain't anything to do with me.

BILL. Good job for you! I'd put two meals into you and fight you with one finger after, you starved cur. [*To Jenny*] Now are you goin to fetch out Mog Habbijam; or am I to knock your face off you and fetch her myself?

JENNY [*writhing in his grasp*] Oh please someone go in and tell Major Barbara--[*she screams again as he wrenches her head down; and Price and Rummy, flee into the shelter*].

BILL. You want to go in and tell your Major of me, do you?

JENNY. Oh please don't drag my hair. Let me go.

BILL. Do you or don't you? [*She stifles a scream*]. Yes or no.

JENNY. God give me strength--

BILL [*striking her with his fist in the face*] Go and show her that, and tell her if she wants one like it to come and interfere with me. [*Jenny, crying with pain, goes into the shed. He goes to the form and addresses the old man*]. Here: finish your mess; and get out o my way.

SHIRLEY [*springing up and facing him fiercely, with the mug in his hand*] You take a liberty with me, and I'll smash you over the face with the mug and cut your eye out. Ain't you satisfied--young whelps like you--with takin the bread out o the mouths of your elders that have brought you up and slaved for you, but you must come shovin and cheekin and bullyin in here, where the bread o charity is sickenin in our stummicks?

BILL [*contemptuously, but backing a little*] Wot good are you, you old palsy mug? Wot good are you?

SHIRLEY. As good as you and better. I'll do a day's work agen you or any fat young soaker of your age. Go and take my job at Horrockses, where I worked for ten year. They want young men there: they can't afford to keep men over forty-five. They're very sorry--give you a character and happy to help you to get anything suited to your years--sure a steady man won't be long out of a job. Well, let em try you. They'll find the differ. What do you know? Not as much as how to beeyave yourself--layin your dirty fist across the mouth of a respectable woman!

BILL. Don't provoke me to lay it acrost yours: d'ye hear?

SHIRLEY [*with blighting contempt*] Yes: you like an old man to hit, don't you, when you've finished with the women. I ain't seen you hit a young one yet.

BILL [*stung*] You lie, you old soupkitchener, you. There was a young man here. Did I offer to hit him or did I not?

SHIRLEY. Was he starvin or was he not? Was he a man or only a crosseyed thief an a loafer? Would you hit my son-in-law's brother?

BILL. Who's he?

SHIRLEY. Todger Fairmile o Balls Pond. Him that won 20 pounds off the Japanese wrastler at the music hall by standin out 17 minutes 4 seconds agen him.

BILL [*sullenly*] I'm no music hall wrastler. Can he box?

SHIRLEY. Yes: an you can't.

BILL. Wot! I can't, can't I? Wot's that you say [*threatening him*]?

SHIRLEY [*not budging an inch*] Will you box Todger Fairmile if I put him on to you? Say the word.

BILL. [*subsiding with a slouch*] I'll stand up to any man alive, if he was ten Todger Fairmiles. But I don't set up to be a perfessional.

SHIRLEY [*looking down on him with unfathomable disdain*] YOU box! Slap an old woman with the back o your hand! You hadn't even the sense to hit her where a magistrate couldn't see the mark of it, you silly young lump of conceit and ignorance. Hit a girl in the jaw and ony make her cry! If Todger Fairmile'd done it, she wouldn't a got up inside o ten minutes, no more than you would if he got on to you. Yah! I'd set about you myself if I had a week's feedin in me instead o two months starvation. [*He returns to the table to finish his meal*].

BILL [*following him and stooping over him to drive the taunt in*] You lie! you have the bread and treacle in you that you come here to beg.

SHIRLEY [*bursting into tears*] Oh God! it's true: I'm only an old pauper on the scrap heap. [*Furiously*] But you'll come to it yourself; and then you'll know. You'll come to it sooner than a teetotaller like me, fillin yourself with gin at this hour o the mornin!

BILL. I'm no gin drinker, you old liar; but when I want to give my girl a bloomin good idin I like to av a bit o devil in me: see? An here I am, talkin to a rotten old blighter like you sted o givin her wot for. [*Working himself into a rage*] I'm goin in there to fetch her out. [*He makes vengefully for the shelter door*].

SHIRLEY. You're goin to the station on a stretcher, more likely; and they'll take the gin and the devil out of you there when they get you inside. You mind what you're about: the major here is the Earl o Stevenage's granddaughter.

BILL [*checked*] Garn!

SHIRLEY. You'll see.

BILL [*his resolution oozing*] Well, I ain't done nothin to er.

SHIRLEY. Spose she said you did! who'd believe you?

BILL [*very uneasy, skulking back to the corner of the penthouse*] Gawd! There's no jastice in this country. To think wot them people can do! I'm as good as er.

SHIRLEY. Tell her so. It's just what a fool like you would do.

Barbara, brisk and businesslike, comes from the shelter with a note book, and addresses herself to Shirley. Bill, cowed, sits down in the corner on a form, and turns his back on them.

BARBARA. Good morning.

SHIRLEY [*standing up and taking off his hat*] Good morning, miss.

BARBARA. Sit down: make yourself at home. [*He hesitates; but she puts a friendly hand on his shoulder and makes him obey*]. Now then! since you've made friends with us, we want to know all about you. Names and addresses and trades.

SHIRLEY. Peter Shirley. Fitter. Chucked out two months ago because I was too old.

BARBARA [*not at all surprised*] You'd pass still. Why didn't you dye your hair?

SHIRLEY. I did. Me age come out at a coroner's inquest on me daughter.

BARBARA. Steady?

SHIRLEY. Teetotaller. Never out of a job before. Good worker. And sent to the knockers like an old horse!

BARBARA. No matter: if you did your part God will do his.

SHIRLEY [*suddenly stubborn*] My religion's no concern of anybody but myself.

BARBARA [*guessing*] I know. Secularist?

SHIRLEY [*hotly*] Did I offer to deny it?

BARBARA. Why should you? My own father's a Secularist, I think. Our Father--yours and mine--fulfils himself in many ways; and I daresay he knew what he was about when he made a Secularist of you. So buck up, Peter! we can always find a job for a steady man like you. [*Shirley, disarmed, touches his hat. She turns from him to Bill*]. What's your name?

BILL [*insolently*] Wot's that to you?

BARBARA [*calmly making a note*] Afraid to give his name. Any trade?

BILL. Who's afraid to give his name? [*Doggedly, with a sense of heroically defying the House of Lords in the person of Lord Stevenage*] If you want to bring a charge agen me, bring it. [*She waits, unruffled*]. My name's Bill Walker.

BARBARA [*as if the name were familiar: trying to remember how*] Bill Walker? [*Recollecting*] Oh, I know: you're the man that Jenny Hill was praying for inside just now. [*She enters his name in her note book*].

BILL. Who's Jenny Hill? And what call has she to pray for me?

BARBARA. I don't know. Perhaps it was you that cut her lip.

BILL [*defiantly*] Yes, it was me that cut her lip. I ain't afraid o you.

BARBARA. How could you be, since you're not afraid of God? You're a brave man, Mr. Walker. It takes some pluck to do our work here; but none of us dare lift our hand against a girl like that, for fear of her father in heaven.

BILL [*sullenly*] I want none o your cantin jaw. I suppose you think I come here to beg from you, like this damaged lot here. Not me. I don't want your bread and scrape and catlap. I don't believe in your Gawd, no more than you do yourself.

BARBARA [*sunnily apologetic and ladylike, as on a new footing with him*] Oh, I beg your pardon for putting your name down, Mr. Walker. I didn't understand. I'll strike it out.

BILL [*taking this as a slight, and deeply wounded by it*] Eah! you let my name alone. Ain't it good enough to be in your book?

BARBARA [*considering*] Well, you see, there's no use putting down your name unless I can do something for you, is there? What's your trade?

BILL [*still smarting*] That's no concern o yours.

BARBARA. Just so. [*very businesslike*] I'll put you down as [*writing*] the man who--struck--poor little Jenny Hill--in the mouth.

BILL [*rising threateningly*] See here. I've ad enough o this.

BARBARA [*quite sunny and fearless*] What did you come to us for?

BILL. I come for my girl, see? I come to take her out o this and to break er jaws for her.

BARBARA [*complacently*] You see I was right about your trade. [*Bill, on the point of retorting furiously, finds himself, to his great shame and terror, in danger of crying instead. He sits down again suddenly*]. What's her name?

BILL [*dogged*] Er name's Mog Abbijam: thats wot her name is.

BARBARA. Oh, she's gone to Canning Town, to our barracks there.

BILL [*fortified by his resentment of Mog's perfidy*] is she? [*Vindictively*] Then I'm goin to Kennintahn arter her. [*He crosses to the gate; hesitates; finally comes back at Barbara*]. Are you lyin to me to get shut o me?

BARBARA. I don't want to get shut of you. I want to keep you here and save your soul. You'd better stay: you're going to have a bad time today, Bill.

BILL. Who's goin to give it to me? You, props.

BARBARA. Someone you don't believe in. But you'll be glad afterwards.

BILL [*slinking off*] I'll go to Kennintahn to be out o the reach o your tongue. [*Suddenly turning on her with intense malice*] And if I don't find Mog there, I'll come back and do two years for you, selp me Gawd if I don't!

BARBARA [*a shade kindlier, if possible*] It's no use, Bill. She's got another bloke.

BILL. Wot!

BARBARA. One of her own converts. He fell in love with her when he saw her with her soul saved, and her face clean, and her hair washed.

BILL [*surprised*] Wottud she wash it for, the carroty slut? It's red.

BARBARA. It's quite lovely now, because she wears a new look in her eyes with it. It's a pity you're too late. The new bloke has put your nose out of joint, Bill.

BILL. I'll put his nose out o joint for him. Not that I care a curse for her, mind that. But I'll teach her to drop me as if I was dirt. And I'll teach him to meddle with my Judy. Wots iz bleedin name?

BARBARA. Sergeant Todger Fairmile.

SHIRLEY [*rising with grim joy*] I'll go with him, miss. I want to see them two meet. I'll take him to the infirmary when it's over.

BILL [*to Shirley, with undissembled misgiving*] Is that im you was speakin on?

SHIRLEY. That's him.

BILL. Im that wrastled in the music all?

SHIRLEY. The competitions at the National Sportin Club was worth nigh a hundred a year to him. He's gev em up now for religion; so he's a bit fresh for want of the exercise he was accustomed to. He'll be glad to see you. Come along.

BILL. Wots is weight?

SHIRLEY. Thirteen four. [*Bill's last hope expires*].

BARBARA. Go and talk to him, Bill. He'll convert you.

SHIRLEY. He'll convert your head into a mashed potato.

BILL [*sullenly*] I ain't afraid of him. I ain't afraid of ennybody. But he can lick me. She's done me. [*He sits down moodily on the edge of the horse trough*].

SHIRLEY. You ain't goin. I thought not. [*He resumes his seat*].

BARBARA [*calling*] Jenny!

JENNY [*appearing at the shelter door with a plaster on the corner of her mouth*] Yes, Major.

BARBARA. Send Rummy Mitchens out to clear away here.

JENNY. I think she's afraid.

BARBARA [*her resemblance to her mother flashing out for a moment*] Nonsense! she must do as she's told.

JENNY [*calling into the shelter*] Rummy: the Major says you must come.

Jenny comes to Barbara, purposely keeping on the side next Bill, lest he should suppose that she shrank from him or bore malice.

BARBARA. Poor little Jenny! Are you tired? [*Looking at the wounded cheek*] Does it hurt?

JENNY. No: it's all right now. It was nothing.

BARBARA [*critically*] It was as hard as he could hit, I expect. Poor Bill! You don't feel angry with him, do you?

JENNY. Oh no, no, no: indeed I don't, Major, bless his poor heart! [*Barbara kisses her; and she runs away merrily into the shelter. Bill writhes with an agonizing return of his new and alarming symptoms, but says nothing. Rummy Mitchens comes from the shelter*].

BARBARA [*going to meet Rummy*] Now Rummy, bustle. Take in those mugs and plates to be washed; and throw the crumbs about for the birds.

Rummy takes the three plates and mugs; but Shirley takes back his mug from her, as there it still come milk left in it.

RUMMY. There ain't any crumbs. This ain't a time to waste good bread on birds.

PRICE [*appearing at the shelter door*] Gentleman come to see the shelter, Major. Says he's your father.

BARBARA. All right. Coming. [*Snobby goes back into the shelter, followed by Barbara*].

RUMMY [*stealing across to Bill and addressing him in a subdued voice, but with intense conviction*] I'd av the lor of you, you flat eared pignosed potwalloper, if she'd let me. You're no gentleman, to hit a lady in the face. [*Bill, with greater things moving in him, takes no notice*].

SHIRLEY [*following her*] Here! in with you and don't get yourself into more trouble by talking.

RUMMY [*with hauteur*] I ain't ad the pleasure o being hintroduced to you, as I can remember. [*She goes into the shelter with the plates*].

BILL [*savagely*] Don't you talk to me, d'ye hear. You lea me alone, or I'll do you a mischief. I'm not dirt under your feet, anyway.

SHIRLEY [*calmly*] Don't you be afeerd. You ain't such prime company that you need expect to be sought after. [*He is about to go into the shelter when Barbara comes out, with Undershaft on her right*].

BARBARA. Oh there you are, Mr Shirley! [*Between them*] This is my father: I told you he was a Secularist, didn't I? Perhaps you'll be able to comfort one another.

UNDERSHAFT [*startled*] A Secularist! Not the least in the world: on the contrary, a confirmed mystic.

BARBARA. Sorry, I'm sure. By the way, papa, what is your religion--in case I have to introduce you again?

UNDERSHAFT. My religion? Well, my dear, I am a Millionaire. That is my religion.

BARBARA. Then I'm afraid you and Mr Shirley wont be able to comfort one another after all. You're not a Millionaire, are you, Peter?

SHIRLEY. No; and proud of it.

UNDERSHAFT [*gravely*] Poverty, my friend, is not a thing to be proud of.

SHIRLEY [*angrily*] Who made your millions for you? Me and my like. What's kep us poor? Keepin you rich. I wouldn't have your conscience, not for all your income.

UNDERSHAFT. I wouldn't have your income, not for all your conscience, Mr Shirley. [*He goes to the penthouse and sits down on a form*].

BARBARA [*stopping Shirley adroitly as he is about to retort*] You wouldn't think he was my father, would you, Peter? Will you go into the shelter and lend the lasses a hand for a while: we're worked off our feet.

SHIRLEY [*bitterly*] Yes: I'm in their debt for a meal, ain't I?

BARBARA. Oh, not because you're in their debt; but for love of them, Peter, for love of them. [*He cannot understand, and is rather scandalized*]. There! Don't stare at me. In with you; and give that conscience of yours a holiday [*bustling him into the shelter*].

SHIRLEY [*as he goes in*] Ah! it's a pity you never was trained to use your reason, miss. You'd have been a very taking lecturer on Secularism.

Barbara turns to her father.

UNDERSHAFT. Never mind me, my dear. Go about your work; and let me watch it for a while.

BARBARA. All right.

UNDERSHAFT. For instance, what's the matter with that out-patient over there?

BARBARA [*looking at Bill, whose attitude has never changed, and whose expression of brooding wrath has deepened*] Oh, we shall cure him in no time. Just watch. [*She goes over to Bill and waits. He glances up at her and casts his eyes down again, uneasy, but grimmer than ever*]. It would be nice to just stamp on Mog Habbijam's face, wouldn't it, Bill?

BILL [*starting up from the trough in consternation*] It's a lie: I never said so. [*She shakes her head*]. Who told you wot was in my mind?

BARBARA. Only your new friend.

BILL. Wot new friend?

BARBARA. The devil, Bill. When he gets round people they get miserable, just like you.

HILL [*with a heartbreaking attempt at devil-may-care cheerfulness*] I ain't miserable. [*He sits down again, and stretches his legs in an attempt to seem indifferent*].

BARBARA. Well, if you're happy, why don't you look happy, as we do?

BILL [*his legs curling back in spite of him*] I'm appy enough, I tell you. Why don't you lea me alown? Wot av I done to you? I ain't smashed your face, av I?

BARBARA [*softly: wooing his soul*] It's not me that's getting at you, Bill.

BILL. Who else is it?

BARBARA. Somebody that doesn't intend you to smash women's faces, I suppose. Somebody or something that wants to make a man of you.

BILL [*blustering*] Make a man o ME! Ain't I a man? eh? ain't I a man? Who sez I'm not a man?

BARBARA. There's a man in you somewhere, I suppose. But why did he let you hit poor little Jenny Hill? That wasn't very manly of him, was it?

BILL [*tormented*] Av done with it, I tell you. Chock it. I'm sick of your Jenny Ill and er silly little face.

BARBARA. Then why do you keep thinking about it? Why does it keep coming up against you in your mind? You're not getting converted, are you?

BILL [*with conviction*] Not ME. Not likely. Not arf.

BARBARA. That's right, Bill. Hold out against it. Put out your strength. Don't let's get you cheap. Todger Fairmile said he wrestled for three nights against his Salvation harder than he ever wrestled with the Jap at the music hall. He gave in to the Jap when his arm was going to break. But he didn't give in to his salvation until his heart was going to break. Perhaps you'll escape that. You haven't any heart, have you?

BILL. Wot dye mean? Wy ain't I got a art the same as ennybody else?

BARBARA. A man with a heart wouldn't have bashed poor little Jenny's face, would he?

BILL [*almost crying*] Ow, will you lea me alown? Av I ever offered to meddle with you, that you come noggin and provowkin me lawk this? [*He writhes convulsively from his eyes to his toes*].

BARBARA [*with a steady soothing hand on his arm and a gentle voice that never lets him go*] It's your soul that's hurting you, Bill, and not me. We've been through it all ourselves. Come with us, Bill. [*He looks wildly round*]. To brave manhood on earth and eternal glory in heaven. [*He is on the point of breaking down*]. Come. [*A drum is heard in the shelter; and Bill, with a gasp, escapes from the spell as Barbara turns quickly. Adolphus enters from the shelter with a big drum*]. Oh! there you are, Dolly. Let me introduce a new friend of mine, Mr Bill Walker. This is my bloke, Bill: Mr Cusins. [*Cusins salutes with his drumstick*].

BILL. Goin to marry im?

BARBARA. Yes.

BILL [*fervently*] Gawd elp im! Gawd elp im!

BARBARA. Why? Do you think he won't be happy with me?

BILL. I've only ad to stand it for a mornin: e'll av to stand it for a lifetime.

CUSINS. That is a frightful reflection, Mr Walker. But I can't tear myself away from her.

BILL. Well, I can. [*To Barbara*] Eah! do you know where I'm goin to, and wot I'm goin to do?

BARBARA. Yes: you're going to heaven; and you're coming back here before the week's out to tell me so.

BILL. You lie. I'm goin to Kennintahn, to spit in Todger Fairmile's eye. I bashed Jenny Ill's face; and now I'll get me own face bashed and come back and show it to er. E'll it me ardern I it er. That'll make us square. [*To Adolphus*] Is that fair or is it not? You're a genlmn: you oughter know.

BARBARA. Two black eyes wont make one white one, Bill.

BILL. I didn't ast you. Cawn't you never keep your mahth shut? I ast the genlmn.

CUSINS [*reflectively*] Yes: I think you're right, Mr Walker. Yes: I should do it. It's curious: it's exactly what an ancient Greek would have done.

BARBARA. But what good will it do?

CUSINS. Well, it will give Mr Fairmile some exercise; and it will satisfy Mr Walker's soul.

BILL. Rot! there ain't no sach a thing as a soul. Ah kin you tell wether I've a soul or not? You never seen it.

BARBARA. I've seen it hurting you when you went against it.

BILL [*with compressed aggravation*] If you was my girl and took the word out o me mahth lawk thet, I'd give you suthink you'd feel urtin, so I would. [*To Adolphus*] You take my tip, mate. Stop er jawr; or you'll die afore your time. [*With intense expression*] Wore aht: thets wot you'll be: wore aht. [*He goes away through the gate*].

CUSINS [*looking after him*] I wonder!

BARBARA. Dolly! [*indignant, in her mother's manner*].

CUSINS. Yes, my dear, it's very wearing to be in love with you. If it lasts, I quite think I shall die young.

BARBARA. Should you mind?

CUSINS. Not at all. [*He is suddenly softened, and kisses her over the drum, evidently not for the first time, as people cannot kiss over a big drum without practice. Undershaft coughs*].

BARBARA. It's all right, papa, we've not forgotten you. Dolly: explain the place to papa: I haven't time. [*She goes busily into the shelter*].

Undershaft and Adolpbus now have the yard to themselves. Undershaft, seated on a form, and still keenly attentive, looks hard at Adolphus. Adolphus looks hard at him.

UNDERSHAFT. I fancy you guess something of what is in my mind, Mr Cusins. [*Cusins flourishes his drumsticks as if in the art of beating a lively rataplan, but makes no sound*]. Exactly so. But suppose Barbara finds you out!

CUSINS. You know, I do not admit that I am imposing on Barbara. I am quite genuinely interested in the views of the Salvation Army. The fact is, I am a sort of collector of religions; and the curious thing is that I find I can believe them all. By the way, have you any religion?

UNDERSHAFT. Yes.

CUSINS. Anything out of the common?

UNDERSHAFT. Only that there are two things necessary to Salvation.

CUSINS [*disappointed, but polite*] Ah, the Church Catechism. Charles Lomax also belongs to the Established Church.

UNDERSHAFT. The two things are--

CUSINS. Baptism and--

UNDERSHAFT. No. Money and gunpowder.

CUSINS [*surprised, but interested*] That is the general opinion of our governing classes. The novelty is in hearing any man confess it.

UNDERSHAFT. Just so.

CUSINS. Excuse me: is there any place in your religion for honor, justice, truth, love, mercy and so forth?

UNDERSHAFT. Yes: they are the graces and luxuries of a rich, strong, and safe life.

CUSINS. Suppose one is forced to choose between them and money or gunpowder?

UNDERSHAFT. Choose money and gunpowder; for without enough of both you cannot afford the others.

CUSINS. That is your religion?

UNDERSHAFT. Yes.

The cadence of this reply makes a full close in the conversation. Cusins twists his face dubiously and contemplates Undershaft. Undershaft contemplates him.

CUSINS. Barbara won't stand that. You will have to choose between your religion and Barbara.

UNDERSHAFT. So will you, my friend. She will find out that that drum of yours is hollow.

CUSINS. Father Undershaft: you are mistaken: I am a sincere Salvationist. You do not understand the Salvation Army. It is the army of joy, of love, of courage: it has banished the fear and remorse and despair of the old hellridden evangelical sects: it marches to fight the devil with trumpet and drum, with music and dancing, with banner and palm, as becomes a sally from heaven by its happy garrison. It picks the waster out of the public house and makes a man of him: it finds a worm wriggling in a back kitchen, and lo! a woman! Men and women of rank too, sons and daughters of the Highest. It takes the poor professor of Greek, the most artificial and self-suppressed of human creatures, from his meal of roots, and lets loose the rhapsodist in him; reveals the true worship of Dionysos to him; sends him down the public street drumming dithyrambs [*he plays a thundering flourish on the drum*].

UNDERSHAFT. You will alarm the shelter.

CUSINS. Oh, they are accustomed to these sudden ecstasies of piety. However, if the drum worries you-- [*he pockets the drumsticks; unhooks the drum; and stands it on the ground opposite the gateway*].

UNDERSHAFT. Thank you.

CUSINS. You remember what Euripides says about your money and gunpowder?

UNDERSHAFT. No.

CUSINS [*declaiming*]

  One and another
In money and guns may outpass his brother;
And men in their millions float and flow
And seethe with a million hopes as leaven;
And they win their will; or they miss their will;
And their hopes are dead or are pined for still:
  But whoe'er can know
  As the long days go
That to live is happy, has found his heaven.

My translation: what do you think of it?

UNDERSHAFT. I think, my friend, that if you wish to know, as the long days go, that to live is happy, you must first acquire money enough for a decent life, and power enough to be your own master.

CUSINS. You are damnably discouraging. [*He resumes his declamation*].

Is it so hard a thing to see
That the spirit of God--whate'er it be--
The Law that abides and changes not, ages long,
The Eternal and Nature-born: these things be strong.
What else is Wisdom? What of Man's endeavor,
Or God's high grace so lovely and so great?
To stand from fear set free? to breathe and wait?
To hold a hand uplifted over Fate?
And shall not Barbara be loved for ever?

UNDERSHAFT. Euripides mentions Barbara, does he?

CUSINS. It is a fair translation. The word means Loveliness.

UNDERSHAFT. May I ask--as Barbara's father--how much a year she is to be loved for ever on?

CUSINS. As Barbara's father, that is more your affair than mine. I can feed her by teaching Greek: that is about all.

UNDERSHAFT. Do you consider it a good match for her?

CUSINS [*with polite obstinacy*] Mr Undershaft: I am in many ways a weak, timid, ineffectual person; and my health is far from satisfactory. But whenever I feel that I must have anything, I get it, sooner or later. I feel that way about Barbara. I don't like marriage: I feel intensely afraid of it; and I don't know what I shall do with Barbara or what she will do with me. But I feel that I and nobody else must marry her. Please regard that as settled.--Not that I wish to be arbitrary; but why should I waste your time in discussing what is inevitable?

UNDERSHAFT. You mean that you will stick at nothing not even the conversion of the Salvation Army to the worship of Dionysos.

CUSINS. The business of the Salvation Army is to save, not to wrangle about the name of the pathfinder. Dionysos or another: what does it matter?

UNDERSHAFT [*rising and approaching him*] Professor Cusins you are a young man after my own heart.

CUSINS. Mr Undershaft: you are, as far as I am able to gather, a most infernal old rascal; but you appeal very strongly to my sense of ironic humor.

Undershaft mutely offers his hand. They shake.

UNDERSHAFT [*suddenly concentrating himself*] And now to business.

CUSINS. Pardon me. We were discussing religion. Why go back to such an uninteresting and unimportant subject as business?

UNDERSHAFT. Religion is our business at present, because it is through religion alone that we can win Barbara.

CUSINS. Have you, too, fallen in love with Barbara?

UNDERSHAFT. Yes, with a father's love.

CUSINS. A father's love for a grown-up daughter is the most dangerous of all infatuations. I apologize for mentioning my own pale, coy, mistrustful fancy in the same breath with it.

UNDERSHAFT. Keep to the point. We have to win her; and we are neither of us Methodists.

CUSINS. That doesn't matter. The power Barbara wields here--the power that wields Barbara herself--is not Calvinism, not Presbyterianism, not Methodism--

UNDERSHAFT. Not Greek Paganism either, eh?

CUSINS. I admit that. Barbara is quite original in her religion.

UNDERSHAFT [*triumphantly*] Aha! Barbara Undershaft would be. Her inspiration comes from within herself.

CUSINS. How do you suppose it got there?

UNDERSHAFT [*in towering excitement*] It is the Undershaft inheritance. I shall hand on my torch to my daughter. She shall make my converts and preach my gospel.

CUSINS. What! Money and gunpowder!

UNDERSHAFT. Yes, money and gunpowder; freedom and power; command of life and command of death.

CUSINS [*urbanely: trying to bring him down to earth*] This is extremely interesting, Mr Undershaft. Of course you know that you are mad.

UNDERSHAFT [*with redoubled force*] And you?

CUSINS. Oh, mad as a hatter. You are welcome to my secret since I have discovered yours. But I am astonished. Can a madman make cannons?

UNDERSHAFT. Would anyone else than a madman make them? And now [*with surging energy*] question for question. Can a sane man translate Euripides?

CUSINS. No.

UNDERSHAFT [*reining him by the shoulder*] Can a sane woman make a man of a waster or a woman of a worm?

CUSINS [*reeling before the storm*] Father Colossus--Mammoth Millionaire--

UNDERSHAFT [*pressing him*] Are there two mad people or three in this Salvation shelter to-day?

CUSINS. You mean Barbara is as mad as we are!

UNDERSHAFT [*pushing him lightly off and resuming his equanimity suddenly and completely*] Pooh, Professor! let us call things by their proper names. I am a millionaire; you are a poet; Barbara is a savior of souls. What have we three to do with the common mob of slaves and idolaters? [*He sits down again with a shrug of contempt for the mob*].

CUSINS. Take care! Barbara is in love with the common people. So am I. Have you never felt the romance of that love?

UNDERSHAFT [*cold and sardonic*] Have you ever been in love with Poverty, like St Francis? Have you ever been in love with Dirt, like St Simeon? Have you ever been in love with disease and suffering, like our nurses and philanthropists? Such passions are not virtues, but the most unnatural of all the vices. This love of the common people may please an earl's granddaughter and a university professor; but I have been a common man and a poor man; and it has no romance for me. Leave it to the poor to pretend that poverty is a blessing: leave it to the coward to make a religion of his cowardice by preaching humility: we know better than that. We three must stand together above the common people: how else can we help their children to climb up beside us? Barbara must belong to us, not to the Salvation Army.

CUSINS. Well, I can only say that if you think you will get her away from the Salvation Army by talking to her as you have been talking to me, you don't know Barbara.

UNDERSHAFT. My friend: I never ask for what I can buy.

CUSINS [*in a white fury*] Do I understand you to imply that you can buy Barbara?

UNDERSHAFT. No; but I can buy the Salvation Army.

CUSINS. Quite impossible.

UNDERSHAFT. You shall see. All religious organizations exist by selling themselves to the rich.

CUSINS. Not the Army. That is the Church of the poor.

UNDERSHAFT. All the more reason for buying it.

CUSINS. I don't think you quite know what the Army does for the poor.

UNDERSHAFT. Oh yes I do. It draws their teeth: that is enough for me--as a man of business--

CUSINS. Nonsense! It makes them sober--

UNDERSHAFT. I prefer sober workmen. The profits are larger.

CUSINS. --honest--

UNDERSHAFT. Honest workmen are the most economical.

CUSINS. --attached to their homes--

UNDERSHAFT. So much the better: they will put up with anything sooner than change their shop.

CUSINS. --happy--

UNDERSHAFT. An invaluable safeguard against revolution.

CUSINS. --unselfish--

UNDERSHAFT. Indifferent to their own interests, which suits me exactly.

CUSINS. --with their thoughts on heavenly things--

UNDERSHAFT [*rising*] And not on Trade Unionism nor Socialism. Excellent.

CUSINS [*revolted*] You really are an infernal old rascal.

UNDERSHAFT [*indicating Peter Shirley, who has just came from the shelter and strolled dejectedly down the yard between them*] And this is an honest man!

SHIRLEY. Yes; and what av I got by it? [*he passes on bitterly and sits on the form, in the corner of the penthouse*].

Snobby Price, beaming sanctimoniously, and Jenny Hill, with a tambourine full of coppers, come from the shelter and go to the drum, on which Jenny begins to count the money.

UNDERSHAFT [*replying to Shirley*] Oh, your employers must have got a good deal by it from first to last. [*He sits on the table, with one foot on the side form. Cusins, overwhelmed, sits down on the same form nearer the shelter. Barbara comes from the shelter to the middle of the yard. She is excited and a little overwrought*].

BARBARA. We've just had a splendid experience meeting at the other gate in Cripps's lane. I've hardly ever seen them so much moved as they were by your confession, Mr Price.

PRICE. I could almost be glad of my past wickedness if I could believe that it would elp to keep hathers stright.

BARBARA. So it will, Snobby. How much, Jenny?

JENNY. Four and tenpence, Major.

BARBARA. Oh Snobby, if you had given your poor mother just one more kick, we should have got the whole five shillings!

PRICE. If she heard you say that, miss, she'd be sorry I didn't. But I'm glad. Oh what a joy it will be to her when she hears I'm saved!

UNDERSHAFT. Shall I contribute the odd twopence, Barbara? The millionaire's mite, eh? [*He takes a couple of pennies from his pocket.*]

BARBARA. How did you make that twopence?

UNDERSHAFT. As usual. By selling cannons, torpedoes, submarines, and my new patent Grand Duke hand grenade.

BARBARA. Put it back in your pocket. You can't buy your Salvation here for twopence: you must work it out.

UNDERSHAFT. Is twopence not enough? I can afford a little more, if you press me.

BARBARA. Two million millions would not be enough. There is bad blood on your hands; and nothing but good blood can cleanse them. Money is no use. Take it away. [*She turns to Cusins*]. Dolly: you must write another letter for me to the papers. [*He makes a wry face*]. Yes: I know you don't like it; but it must be done. The starvation this winter is beating us: everybody is unemployed. The General says we must close this shelter if we cant get more money. I force the collections at the meetings until I am ashamed, don't I, Snobby?

PRICE. It's a fair treat to see you work it, miss. The way you got them up from three-and-six to four-and-ten with that hymn, penny by penny and verse by verse, was a caution. Not a Cheap Jack on Mile End Waste could touch you at it.

BARBARA. Yes; but I wish we could do without it. I am getting at last to think more of the collection than of the people's souls. And what are those hatfuls of pence and halfpence? We want thousands! tens of thousands! hundreds of thousands! I want to convert people, not to be always begging for the Army in a way I'd die sooner than beg for myself.

UNDERSHAFT [*in profound irony*] Genuine unselfishness is capable of anything, my dear.

BARBARA [*unsuspectingly, as she turns away to take the money from the drum and put it in a cash bag she carries*] Yes, isn't it? [*Undershaft looks sardonically at Cusins*].

CUSINS [*aside to Undershaft*] Mephistopheles! Machiavelli!

BARBARA [*tears coming into her eyes as she ties the bag and pockets it*] How are we to feed them? I can't talk religion to a man with bodily hunger in his eyes. [*Almost breaking down*] It's frightful.

JENNY [*running to her*] Major, dear--

BARBARA [*rebounding*] No: don't comfort me. It will be all right. We shall get the money.

UNDERSHAFT. How?

JENNY. By praying for it, of course. Mrs Baines says she prayed for it last night; and she has never prayed for it in vain: never once. [*She goes to the gate and looks out into the street*].

BARBARA [*who has dried her eyes and regained her composure*] By the way, dad, Mrs Baines has come to march with us to our big meeting this afternoon; and she is very anxious to meet you, for some reason or other. Perhaps she'll convert you.

UNDERSHAFT. I shall be delighted, my dear.

JENNY [*at the gate: excitedly*] Major! Major! Here's that man back again.

BARBARA. What man?

JENNY. The man that hit me. Oh, I hope he's coming back to join us.

Bill Walker, with frost on his jacket, comes through the gate, his hands deep in his pockets and his chin sunk between his shoulders, like a cleaned-out gambler. He halts between Barbara and the drum.

BARBARA. Hullo, Bill! Back already!

BILL [*nagging at her*] Bin talkin ever sense, av you?

BARBARA. Pretty nearly. Well, has Todger paid you out for poor Jenny's jaw?

BILL. NO he ain't.

BARBARA. I thought your jacket looked a bit snowy.

BILL. So it is snowy. You want to know where the snow come from, don't you?

BARBARA. Yes.

BILL. Well, it come from off the ground in Parkinses Corner in Kennintahn. It got rubbed off be my shoulders see?

BARBARA. Pity you didn't rub some off with your knees, Bill! That would have done you a lot of good.

BILL [*with your mirthless humor*] I was saving another man's knees at the time. E was kneelin on my ed, so e was.

JENNY. Who was kneeling on your head?

BILL. Todger was. E was prayin for me: prayin comfortable with me as a carpet. So was Mog. So was the ole bloomin meetin. Mog she sez "O Lord break is stubborn spirit; but don't urt is dear art." That was wot she said. "Don't urt is dear art"! An er bloke--thirteen stun four!--kneelin wiv all is weight on me. Funny, ain't it?

JENNY. Oh no. We're so sorry, Mr Walker.

BARBARA [*enjoying it frankly*] Nonsense! of course it's funny. Served you right, Bill! You must have done something to him first.

BILL [*doggedly*] I did wot I said I'd do. I spit in is eye. E looks up at the sky and sez, "O that I should be fahnd worthy to be spit upon for the gospel's sake!" a sez; an Mog sez "Glory Allelloolier!"; an then a called me Brother, an dahned me as if I was a kid and a was me mother washin me a Setterda nawt. I adn't just no show wiv im at all. Arf the street prayed; an the tother arf larfed fit to split theirselves. [*To Barbara*] There! are you settisfawd nah?

BARBARA [*her eyes dancing*] Wish I'd been there, Bill.

BILL. Yes: you'd a got in a hextra bit o talk on me, wouldn't you?

JENNY. I'm so sorry, Mr. Walker.

BILL [*fiercely*] Don't you go bein sorry for me: you've no call. Listen ere. I broke your jawr.

JENNY. No, it didn't hurt me: indeed it didn't, except for a moment. It was only that I was frightened.

BILL. I don't want to be forgive be you, or be ennybody. Wot I did I'll pay for. I tried to get me own jawr broke to settisfaw you--

JENNY [*distressed*] Oh no--

BILL [*impatiently*] Tell y'I did: cawn't you listen to wot's bein told you? All I got be it was bein made a sight of in the public street for me pains. Well, if I cawn't settisfaw you one way, I can another. Listen ere! I ad two quid saved agen the frost; an I've a pahnd of it left. A mate n mine last week ad words with the Judy e's goin to marry. E give er wot-for; an e's bin fined fifteen bob. E ad a right to it er because they was goin to be marrid; but I adn't no right to it you; so put anather fawv bob on an call it a pahnd's worth. [*He produces a sovereign*]. Ere's the money. Take it; and let's av no more o your forgivin an prayin and your Major jawrin me. Let wot I done be done and paid for; and let there be a end of it.

JENNY. Oh, I couldn't take it, Mr. Walker. But if you would give a shilling or two to poor Rummy Mitchens! you really did hurt her; and she's old.

BILL [*contemptuously*] Not likely. I'd give her anather as soon as look at er. Let her av the lawr o me as she threatened! She ain't forgiven me: not mach. Wot I done to er is not on me mawnd--wot she [*indicating Barbara*] might call on me conscience--no more than stickin a pig. It's this Christian game o yours that I won't av played agen me: this bloomin forgivin an noggin an jawrin that makes a man that sore that iz lawf's a burdn to im. I won't av it, I tell you; so take your money and stop throwin your silly bashed face hup agen me.

JENNY. Major: may I take a little of it for the Army?

BARBARA. No: the Army is not to be bought. We want your soul, Bill; and we'll take nothing less.

BILL [*bitterly*] I know. It ain't enough. Me an me few shillins is not good enough for you. You're a earl's grendorter, you are. Nothin less than a underd pahnd for you.

UNDERSHAFT. Come, Barbara! you could do a great deal of good with a hundred pounds. If you will set this gentleman's mind at ease by taking his pound, I will give the other ninety-nine [*Bill, astounded by such opulence, instinctively touches his cap*].

BARBARA. Oh, you're too extravagant, papa. Bill offers twenty pieces of silver. All you need offer is the other ten. That will make the standard price to buy anybody who's for sale. I'm not; and the Army's not. [*To Bill*] You'll never have another quiet moment, Bill, until you come round to us. You can't stand out against your salvation.

BILL [*sullenly*] I cawn't stend aht agen music all wrastlers and artful tongued women. I've offered to pay. I can do no more. Take it or leave it. There it is. [*He throws the sovereign on the drum, and sits down on the horse-trough. The coin fascinates Snobby Price, who takes an early opportunity of dropping his cap on it*].

Mrs Baines comes from the shelter. She is dressed as a Salvation Army Commissioner. She is an earnest looking woman of about 40, with a caressing, urgent voice, and an appealing manner.

BARBARA. This is my father, Mrs Baines. [*Undershaft comes from the table, taking his hat off with marked civility*]. Try what you can do with him. He won't listen to me, because he remembers what a fool I was when I was a baby.

[*She leaves them together and chats with Jenny*].

MRS BAINES. Have you been shown over the shelter, Mr Undershaft? You know the work we're doing, of course.

UNDERSHAFT [*very civilly*] The whole nation knows it, Mrs Baines.

MRS BAINES. No, Sir: the whole nation does not know it, or we should not be crippled as we are for want of money to carry our work through the length and breadth of the land. Let me tell you that there would have been rioting this winter in London but for us.

UNDERSHAFT. You really think so?

MRS BAINES. I know it. I remember 1886, when you rich gentlemen hardened your hearts against the cry of the poor. They broke the windows of your clubs in Pall Mall.

UNDERSHAFT [*gleaming with approval of their method*] And the Mansion House Fund went up next day from thirty thousand pounds to seventy-nine thousand! I remember quite well.

MRS BAINES. Well, won't you help me to get at the people? They won't break windows then. Come here, Price. Let me show you to this gentleman [*Price comes to be inspected*]. Do you remember the window breaking?

PRICE. My ole father thought it was the revolution, ma'am.

MRS BAINES. Would you break windows now?

PRICE. Oh no ma'm. The windows of eaven av bin opened to me. I know now that the rich man is a sinner like myself.

RUMMY [*appearing above at the loft door*] Snobby Price!

SNOBBY. Wot is it?

RUMMY. Your mother's askin for you at the other gate in Crippses Lane. She's heard about your confession [*Price turns pale*].

MRS BAINES. Go, Mr. Price; and pray with her.

JENNY. You can go through the shelter, Snobby.

PRICE [*to Mrs Baines*] I couldn't face her now; ma'am, with all the weight of my sins fresh on me. Tell her she'll find her son at ome, waitin for her in prayer. [*He skulks off through the gate, incidentally stealing the sovereign on his way out by picking up his cap from the drum*].

MRS BAINES [*with swimming eyes*] You see how we take the anger and the bitterness against you out of their hearts, Mr Undershaft.

UNDERSHAFT. It is certainly most convenient and gratifying to all large employers of labor, Mrs Baines.

MRS BAINES. Barbara: Jenny: I have good news: most wonderful news. [*Jenny runs to her*]. My prayers have been answered. I told you they would, Jenny, didn't I?

JENNY. Yes, yes.

BARBARA [*moving nearer to the drum*] Have we got money enough to keep the shelter open?

MRS BAINES. I hope we shall have enough to keep all the shelters open. Lord Saxmundham has promised us five thousand pounds--

BARBARA. Hooray!

JENNY. Glory!

MRS BAINES. --if--

BARBARA. "If!" If what?

MRS BAINES. If five other gentlemen will give a thousand each to make it up to ten thousand.

BARBARA. Who is Lord Saxmundham? I never heard of him.

UNDERSHAFT [*who has pricked up his ears at the peer's name, and is now watching Barbara curiously*] A new creation, my dear. You have heard of Sir Horace Bodger?

BARBARA. Bodger! Do you mean the distiller? Bodger's whisky!

UNDERSHAFT. That is the man. He is one of the greatest of our public benefactors. He restored the cathedral at Hakington. They made him a baronet for that. He gave half a million to the funds of his party: they made him a baron for that.

SHIRLEY. What will they give him for the five thousand?

UNDERSHAFT. There is nothing left to give him. So the five thousand, I should think, is to save his soul.

MRS BAINES. Heaven grant it may! Oh Mr. Undershaft, you have some very rich friends. Can't you help us towards the other five thousand? We are going to hold a great meeting this afternoon at the Assembly Hall in the Mile End Road. If I could only announce that one gentleman had come forward to support Lord Saxmundham, others would follow. Don't you know somebody? Couldn't you? Wouldn't you? [*her eyes fill with tears*] oh, think of those poor people, Mr Undershaft: think of how much it means to them, and how little to a great man like you.

UNDERSHAFT [*sardonically gallant*] Mrs Baines: you are irresistible. I can't disappoint you; and I can't deny myself the satisfaction of making Bodger pay up. You shall have your five thousand pounds.

MRS BAINES. Thank God!

UNDERSHAFT. You don't thank me?

MRS BAINES. Oh sir, don't try to be cynical: don't be ashamed of being a good man. The Lord will bless you abundantly; and our prayers will be like a strong fortification round you all the days of your life. [*With a touch of caution*] You will let me have the cheque to show at the meeting, won't you? Jenny: go in and fetch a pen and ink. [*Jenny runs to the shelter door*].

UNDERSHAFT. Do not disturb Miss Hill: I have a fountain pen. [*Jenny halts. He sits at the table and writes the cheque. Cusins rises to make more room for him. They all watch him silently*].

BILL [*cynically, aside to Barbara, his voice and accent horribly debased*] Wot prawce Selvytion nah?

BARBARA. Stop. [*Undershaft stops writing: they all turn to her in surprise*]. Mrs Baines: are you really going to take this money?

MRS BAINES [*astonished*] Why not, dear?

BARBARA. Why not! Do you know what my father is? Have you forgotten that Lord Saxmundham is Bodger the whisky man? Do you remember how we implored the County Council to stop him from writing Bodger's Whisky in letters of fire against the sky; so that the poor drinkruined creatures on the embankment could not wake up from their snatches of sleep without being reminded of their deadly thirst by that wicked sky sign? Do you know that the worst thing I have had to fight here is not the devil, but Bodger, Bodger, Bodger, with his whisky, his distilleries, and his tied houses? Are you going to make our shelter another tied house for him, and ask me to keep it?

BILL. Rotten drunken whisky it is too.

MRS BAINES. Dear Barbara: Lord Saxmundham has a soul to be saved like any of us. If heaven has found the way to make a good use of his money, are we to set ourselves up against the answer to our prayers?

BARBARA. I know he has a soul to be saved. Let him come down here; and I'll do my best to help him to his salvation. But he wants to send his cheque down to buy us, and go on being as wicked as ever.

UNDERSHAFT [*with a reasonableness which Cusins alone perceives to be ironical*] My dear Barbara: alcohol is a very necessary article. It heals the sick--

BARBARA. It does nothing of the sort.

UNDERSHAFT. Well, it assists the doctor: that is perhaps a less questionable way of putting it. It makes life bearable to millions of people who could not endure their existence if they were quite sober. It enables Parliament to do things at eleven at night that no sane person would do at eleven in the morning. Is it Bodger's fault that this inestimable gift is deplorably abused by less than one per cent of the poor? [*He turns again to the table; signs the cheque; and crosses it*].

MRS BAINES. Barbara: will there be less drinking or more if all those poor souls we are saving come to-morrow and find the doors of our shelters shut in their faces? Lord Saxmundham gives us the money to stop drinking--to take his own business from him.

CUSINS [*impishly*] Pure self-sacrifice on Bodger's part, clearly! Bless dear Bodger! [*Barbara almost breaks down as Adolpbus, too, fails her*].

UNDERSHAFT [*tearing out the cheque and pocketing the book as he rises and goes past Cusins to Mrs Baines*] I also, Mrs Baines, may claim a little disinterestedness. Think of my business! think of the widows and orphans! the men and lads torn to pieces with shrapnel and poisoned with lyddite [*Mrs Baines shrinks; but he goes on remorselessly*]! the oceans of blood, not one drop of which is shed in a really just cause! the ravaged crops! the peaceful peasants forced, women and men, to till their fields under the fire of opposing armies on pain of starvation! the bad blood of the fierce little cowards at home who egg on others to fight for the gratification of their national vanity! All this makes money for me: I am never richer, never busier than when the papers are full of it. Well, it is your work to preach peace on earth and goodwill to men. [*Mrs Baines's face lights up again*]. Every convert you make is a vote against war. [*Her lips move in prayer*]. Yet I give you this money to help you to hasten my own commercial ruin. [*He gives her the cheque*].

CUSINS [*mounting the form in an ecstasy of mischief*] The millennium will be inaugurated by the unselfishness of Undershaft and Bodger. Oh be joyful! [*He takes the drumsticks from his pockets and flourishes them*].

MRS BAINES [*taking the cheque*] The longer I live the more proof I see that there is an Infinite Goodness that turns everything to the work of salvation sooner or later. Who would have thought that any good could have come out of war and drink? And yet their profits are brought today to the feet of salvation to do its blessed work. [*She is affected to tears*].

JENNY [*running to Mrs Baines and throwing her arms round her*] Oh dear! how blessed, how glorious it all is!

CUSINS [*in a convulsion of irony*] Let us seize this unspeakable moment. Let us march to the great meeting at once. Excuse me just an instant. [*He rushes into the shelter. Jenny takes her tambourine from the drum head*].

MRS BAINES. Mr Undershaft: have you ever seen a thousand people fall on their knees with one impulse and pray? Come with us to the meeting. Barbara shall tell them that the Army is saved, and saved through you.

CUSINS [*returning impetuously from the shelter with a flag and a trombone, and coming between*

Mrs Baines and Undershaft] You shall carry the flag down the first street, Mrs Baines [*he gives her the flag*]. Mr Undershaft is a gifted trombonist: he shall intone an Olympian diapason to the West Ham Salvation March. [*Aside to Undershaft, as he forces the trombone on him*] Blow, Machiavelli, blow.

UNDERSHAFT [*aside to him, as he takes the trombone*] The trumpet in Zion! [*Cusins rushes to the drum, which he takes up and puts on. Undershaft continues, aloud*] I will do my best. I could vamp a bass if I knew the tune.

CUSINS. It is a wedding chorus from one of Donizetti's operas; but we have converted it. We convert everything to good here, including Bodger. You remember the chorus. "For thee immense rejoicing--immenso giubilo--immenso giubilo." [*With drum obbligato*] Rum tum ti tum tum, tum tum ti ta--

BARBARA. Dolly: you are breaking my heart.

CUSINS. What is a broken heart more or less here? Dionysos Undershaft has descended. I am possessed.

MRS BAINES. Come, Barbara: I must have my dear Major to carry the flag with me.

JENNY. Yes, yes, Major darling.

CUSINS [*snatches the tambourine out of Jenny's hand and mutely offers it to Barbara*].

BARBARA [*coming forward a little as she puts the offer behind her with a shudder, whilst Cusins recklessly tosses the tambourine back to Jenny and goes to the gate*] I can't come.

JENNY. Not come!

MRS BAINES [*with tears in her eyes*] Barbara: do you think I am wrong to take the money?

BARBARA [*impulsively going to her and kissing her*] No, no: God help you, dear, you must: you are saving the Army. Go; and may you have a great meeting!

JENNY. But arn't you coming?

BARBARA. No. [*She begins taking off the silver brooch from her collar*].

MRS BAINES. Barbara: what are you doing?

JENNY. Why are you taking your badge off? You can't be going to leave us, Major.

BARBARA [*quietly*] Father: come here.

UNDERSHAFT [*coming to her*] My dear! [*Seeing that she is going to pin the badge on his collar, he retreats to the penthouse in some alarm*].

BARBARA [*following him*] Don't be frightened. [*She pins the badge on and steps back towards the table, showing him to the others*] There! It's not much for 5000 pounds is it?

MRS BAINES. Barbara: if you won't come and pray with us, promise me you will pray for us.

BARBARA. I can't pray now. Perhaps I shall never pray again.

MRS BAINES. Barbara!

JENNY. Major!

BARBARA [*almost delirious*] I can't bear any more. Quick march!

CUSINS [*calling to the procession in the street outside*] Off we go. Play up, there! Immenso giubilo. [*He gives the time with his drum; and the band strikes up the march, which rapidly becomes more distant as the procession moves briskly away*].

MRS BAINES. I must go, dear. You're overworked: you will be all right tomorrow. We'll never lose you. Now Jenny: step out with the old flag. Blood and Fire! [*She marches out through the gate with her flag*].

JENNY. Glory Hallelujah! [*flourishing her tambourine and marching*].

UNDERSHAFT [*to Cusins, as he marches out past him easing the slide of his trombone*] "My ducats and my daughter"!

CUSINS [*following him out*] Money and gunpowder!

BARBARA. Drunkenness and Murder! My God: why hast thou forsaken me?

She sinks on the form with her face buried in her hands. The march passes away into silence. Bill Walker steals across to her.

BILL [*taunting*] Wot prawce Selvytion nah?

SHIRLEY. Don't you hit her when she's down.

BILL. She it me wen aw wiz dahn. Waw shouldn't I git a bit o me own back?

BARBARA [*raising her head*] I didn't take your money, Bill. [*She crosses the yard to the gate and turns her back on the two men to hide her face from them*].

BILL [*sneering after her*] Naow, it warn't enough for you. [*Turning to the drum, he misses the money*]. Ellow! If you ain't took it summun else az. Were's it gorn? Blame me if Jenny Ill didn't take it arter all!

RUMMY [*screaming at him from the loft*] You lie, you dirty blackguard! Snobby Price pinched it off the drum wen e took ap iz cap. I was ap ere all the time an see im do it.

BILL. Wot! Stowl maw money! Waw didn't you call thief on him, you silly old mucker you?

RUMMY. To serve you aht for ittin me acrost the face. It's cost y'pahnd, that az. [*Raising a paean of squalid triumph*] I done you. I'm even with you. I've ad it aht o y--. [*Bill snatches up Shirley's mug and hurls it at her. She slams the loft door and vanishes. The mug smashes against the door and falls in fragments*].

BILL [*beginning to chuckle*] Tell us, ole man, wot o'clock this morrun was it wen im as they call Snobby Prawce was sived?

BARBARA [*turning to him more composedly, and with unspoiled sweetness*] About half past twelve, Bill. And he pinched your pound at a quarter to two. I know. Well, you can't afford to lose it. I'll send it to you.

BILL [*his voice and accent suddenly improving*] Not if I was to starve for it. I ain't to be bought.

SHIRLEY. Ain't you? You'd sell yourself to the devil for a pint o beer; ony there ain't no devil to make the offer.

BILL [*unshamed*] So I would, mate, and often av, cheerful. But she cawn't buy me. [*Approaching Barbara*] You wanted my soul, did you? Well, you ain't got it.

BARBARA. I nearly got it, Bill. But we've sold it back to you for ten thousand pounds.

SHIRLEY. And dear at the money!

BARBARA. No, Peter: it was worth more than money.

BILL [*salvationproof*] It's no good: you cawn't get rahnd me nah. I don't blieve in it; and I've seen today that I was right. [*Going*] So long, old soupkitchener! Ta, ta, Major Earl's Grendorter! [*Turning at the gate*] Wot prawce Selvytion nah? Snobby Prawce! Ha! ha!

BARBARA [*offering her hand*] Goodbye, Bill.

BILL [*taken aback, half plucks his cap off then shoves it on again defiantly*] Git aht. [*Barbara drops her hand, discouraged. He has a twinge of remorse*]. But thet's aw rawt, you knaow. Nathink pasnl. Naow mellice. So long, Judy. [*He goes*].

BARBARA. No malice. So long, Bill.

SHIRLEY [*shaking his head*] You make too much of him, miss, in your innocence.

BARBARA [*going to him*] Peter: I'm like you now. Cleaned out, and lost my job.

SHIRLEY. You've youth an hope. That's two better than me. That's hope for you.

BARBARA. I'll get you a job, Peter, the youth will have to be enough for me. [*She counts her money*]. I have just enough left for two teas at Lockharts, a Rowton doss for you, and my tram and bus home. [*He frowns and rises with offended pride. She takes his arm*]. Don't be proud, Peter: it's sharing between friends. And promise me you'll talk to me and not let me cry. [*She draws him towards the gate*].

SHIRLEY. Well, I'm not accustomed to talk to the like of you--

BARBARA [*urgently*] Yes, yes: you must talk to me. Tell me about Tom Paine's books and Bradlaugh's lectures. Come along.

SHIRLEY. Ah, if you would only read Tom Paine in the proper spirit, miss! [*They go out through the gate together*].

ACT III

Next day after lunch Lady Britomart is writing in the library in Wilton Crescent. Sarah is reading in the armchair near the window. Barbara, in ordinary dresss, pale and brooding, is on the settee. Charley Lomax enters. Coming forward between the settee and the writing table, he starts on seeing Barbara fashionably attired and in low spirits.

LOMAX. You've left off your uniform!

Barbara says nothing; but an expression of pain passes over her face.

LADY BRITOMART [*warning him in low tones to be careful*] Charles!

LOMAX [*much concerned, sitting down sympathetically on the settee beside Barbara*] I'm awfully sorry, Barbara. You know I helped you all I could with the concertina and so forth. [*Momentously*] Still, I have never shut my eyes to the fact that there is a certain amount of tosh about the Salvation Army. Now the claims of the Church of England--

LADY BRITOMART. That's enough, Charles. Speak of something suited to your mental capacity.

LOMAX. But surely the Church of England is suited to all our capacities.

BARBARA [*pressing his hand*] Thank you for your sympathy, Cholly. Now go and spoon with Sarah.

LOMAX [*rising and going to Sarah*] How is my ownest today?

SARAH. I wish you wouldn't tell Cholly to do things, Barbara. He always comes straight and does them. Cholly: we're going to the works at Perivale St. Andrews this afternoon.

LOMAX. What works?

SARAH. The cannon works.

LOMAX. What! Your governor's shop!

SARAH. Yes.

LOMAX. Oh I say!

Cusins enters in poor condition. He also starts visibly when he sees Barbara without her uniform.

BARBARA. I expected you this morning, Dolly. Didn't you guess that?

CUSINS [*sitting down beside her*] I'm sorry. I have only just breakfasted.

SARAH. But we've just finished lunch.

BARBARA. Have you had one of your bad nights?

CUSINS. No: I had rather a good night: in fact, one of the most remarkable nights I have ever passed.

BARBARA. The meeting?

CUSINS. No: after the meeting.

LADY BRITOMART. You should have gone to bed after the meeting. What were you doing?

CUSINS. Drinking.

LADY BRITOMART. {Adolphus!
SARAH. {Dolly!
BARBARA. {Dolly!
LOMAX. {Oh I say!

LADY BRITOMART. What were you drinking, may I ask?

CUSINS. A most devilish kind of Spanish burgundy, warranted free from added alcohol: a Temperance burgundy in fact. Its richness in natural alcohol made any addition superfluous.

BARBARA. Are you joking, Dolly?

CUSINS [*patiently*] No. I have been making a night of it with the nominal head of this household: that is all.

LADY BRITOMART. Andrew made you drunk!

CUSINS. No: he only provided the wine. I think it was Dionysos who made me drunk. [*To Barbara*] I told you I was possessed.

LADY BRITOMART. You're not sober yet. Go home to bed at once.

CUSINS. I have never before ventured to reproach you, Lady Brit; but how could you marry the Prince of Darkness?

LADY BRITOMART. It was much more excusable to marry him than to get drunk with him. That is a new accomplishment of Andrew's, by the way. He usen't to drink.

CUSINS. He doesn't now. He only sat there and completed the wreck of my moral basis, the rout of my convictions, the purchase of my soul. He cares for you, Barbara. That is what makes him so dangerous to me.

BARBARA. That has nothing to do with it, Dolly. There are larger loves and diviner dreams than the fireside ones. You know that, don't you?

CUSINS. Yes: that is our understanding. I know it. I hold to it. Unless he can win me on that holier ground he may amuse me for a while; but he can get no deeper hold, strong as he is.

BARBARA. Keep to that; and the end will be right. Now tell me what happened at the meeting?

CUSINS. It was an amazing meeting. Mrs Baines almost died of emotion. Jenny Hill went stark mad with hysteria. The Prince of Darkness played his trombone like a madman: its brazen roarings were like the laughter of the damned. 117 conversions took place then and there. They prayed with the most touching sincerity and gratitude for Bodger, and for the anonymous donor of the 5000 pounds. Your father would not let his name be given.

LOMAX. That was rather fine of the old man, you know. Most chaps would have wanted the advertisement.

CUSINS. He said all the charitable institutions would be down on him like kites on a battle field if he gave his name.

LADY BRITOMART. That's Andrew all over. He never does a proper thing without giving an improper reason for it.

CUSINS. He convinced me that I have all my life been doing improper things for proper reasons.

LADY BRITOMART. Adolphus: now that Barbara has left the Salvation Army, you had better leave it too. I will not have you playing that drum in the streets.

CUSINS. Your orders are already obeyed, Lady Brit.

BARBARA. Dolly: were you ever really in earnest about it? Would you have joined if you had never seen me?

CUSINS [*disingenuously*] Well--er--well, possibly, as a collector of religions--

LOMAX [*cunningly*] Not as a drummer, though, you know. You are a very clearheaded brainy chap, Cholly; and it must have been apparent to you that there is a certain amount of tosh about--

LADY BRITOMART. Charles: if you must drivel, drivel like a grown-up man and not like a schoolboy.

LOMAX [*out of countenance*] Well, drivel is drivel, don't you know, whatever a man's age.

LADY BRITOMART. In good society in England, Charles, men drivel at all ages by repeating silly formulas with an air of wisdom. Schoolboys make their own formulas out of slang, like you. When they reach your age, and get political private secretaryships and things of that sort, they drop slang and get their formulas out of The Spectator or The Times. You had better confine yourself to The Times. You will find that there is a certain amount of tosh about The Times; but at least its language is reputable.

LOMAX [*overwhelmed*] You are so awfully strong-minded, Lady Brit--

LADY BRITOMART. Rubbish! [*Morrison comes in*]. What is it?

MORRISON. If you please, my lady, Mr Undershaft has just drove up to the door.

LADY BRITOMART. Well, let him in. [*Morrison hesitates*]. What's the matter with you?

MORRISON. Shall I announce him, my lady; or is he at home here, so to speak, my lady?

LADY BRITOMART. Announce him.

MORRISON. Thank you, my lady. You won't mind my asking, I hope. The occasion is in a manner of speaking new to me.

LADY BRITOMART. Quite right. Go and let him in.

MORRISON. Thank you, my lady. [*He withdraws*].

LADY BRITOMART. Children: go and get ready. [*Sarah and Barbara go upstairs for their out-of-door wrap*]. Charles: go and tell Stephen to come down here in five minutes: you will find him in the drawing room. [*Charles goes*]. Adolphus: tell them to send round the carriage in about fifteen minutes. [*Adolphus goes*].

MORRISON [*at the door*] Mr Undershaft.

Undershaft comes in. Morrison goes out.

UNDERSHAFT. Alone! How fortunate!

LADY BRITOMART [*rising*] Don't be sentimental, Andrew. Sit down. [*She sits on the settee: he sits beside her, on her left. She comes to the point before he has time to breathe*]. Sarah must have 800 pounds a year until Charles Lomax comes into his property. Barbara will need more, and need it permanently, because Adolphus hasn't any property.

UNDERSHAFT [*resignedly*] Yes, my dear: I will see to it. Anything else? for yourself, for instance?

LADY BRITOMART. I want to talk to you about Stephen.

UNDERSHAFT [*rather wearily*] Don't, my dear. Stephen doesn't interest me.

LADY BRITOMART. He does interest me. He is our son.

UNDERSHAFT. Do you really think so? He has induced us to bring him into the world; but he chose his parents very incongruously, I think. I see nothing of myself in him, and less of you.

LADY BRITOMART. Andrew: Stephen is an excellent son, and a most steady, capable, highminded young man. YOU are simply trying to find an excuse for disinheriting him.

UNDERSHAFT. My dear Biddy: the Undershaft tradition disinherits him. It would be dishonest of me to leave the cannon foundry to my son.

LADY BRITOMART. It would be most unnatural and improper of you to leave it to anyone else, Andrew. Do you suppose this wicked and immoral tradition can be kept up for ever? Do you pretend that Stephen could not carry on the foundry just as well as all the other sons of the big business houses?

UNDERSHAFT. Yes: he could learn the office routine without understanding the business, like all the other sons; and the firm would go on by its own momentum until the real Undershaft--probably an Italian or a German--would invent a new method and cut him out.

LADY BRITOMART. There is nothing that any Italian or German could do that Stephen could not do. And Stephen at least has breeding.

UNDERSHAFT. The son of a foundling! nonsense!

LADY BRITOMART. My son, Andrew! And even you may have good blood in your veins for all you know.

UNDERSHAFT. True. Probably I have. That is another argument in favor of a foundling.

LADY BRITOMART. Andrew: don't be aggravating. And don't be wicked. At present you are both.

UNDERSHAFT. This conversation is part of the Undershaft tradition, Biddy. Every Undershaft's wife has treated him to it ever since the house was founded. It is mere waste of breath. If the tradition be ever broken it will be for an abler man than Stephen.

LADY BRITOMART [*pouting*] Then go away.

UNDERSHAFT [*deprecatory*] Go away!

LADY BRITOMART. Yes: go away. If you will do nothing for Stephen, you are not wanted here. Go to your foundling, whoever he is; and look after him.

UNDERSHAFT. The fact is, Biddy--

LADY BRITOMART. Don't call me Biddy. I don't call you Andy.

UNDERSHAFT. I will not call my wife Britomart: it is not good sense. Seriously, my love, the Undershaft tradition has landed me in a difficulty. I am getting on in years; and my partner Lazarus has at last made a stand and insisted that the succession must be settled one way or the other; and of course he is quite right. You see, I haven't found a fit successor yet.

LADY BRITOMART [*obstinately*] There is Stephen.

UNDERSHAFT. That's just it: all the foundlings I can find are exactly like Stephen.

LADY BRITOMART. Andrew!!

UNDERSHAFT. I want a man with no relations and no schooling: that is, a man who would be out of the running altogether if he were not a strong man. And I can't find him. Every blessed foundling nowadays is snapped up in his infancy by Barnardo homes, or School Board officers, or Boards of Guardians; and if he shows the least ability, he is fastened on by schoolmasters; trained to win scholarships like a racehorse; crammed with secondhand ideas; drilled and disciplined in docility and what they call good taste; and lamed for life so that he is fit for nothing but teaching. If you want to keep the foundry in the family, you had better find an eligible foundling and marry him to Barbara.

LADY BRITOMART. Ah! Barbara! Your pet! You would sacrifice Stephen to Barbara.

UNDERSHAFT. Cheerfully. And you, my dear, would boil Barbara to make soup for Stephen.

LADY BRITOMART. Andrew: this is not a question of our likings and dislikings: it is a question of duty. It is your duty to make Stephen your successor.

UNDERSHAFT. Just as much as it is your duty to submit to your husband. Come, Biddy! these tricks of the governing class are of no use with me. I am one of the governing class myself; and it is waste of time giving tracts to a missionary. I have the power in this matter; and I am not to be humbugged into using it for your purposes.

LADY BRITOMART. Andrew: you can talk my head off; but you can't change wrong into right. And your tie is all on one side. Put it straight.

UNDERSHAFT [*disconcerted*] It won't stay unless it's pinned [*he fumbles at it with childish grimaces*]--

Stephen comes in.

STEPHEN [*at the door*] I beg your pardon [*about to retire*].

LADY BRITOMART. No: come in, Stephen. [*Stephen comes forward to his mother's writing table.*]

UNDERSHAFT [*not very cordially*] Good afternoon.

STEPHEN [*coldly*] Good afternoon.

UNDERSHAFT [*to Lady Britomart*] He knows all about the tradition, I suppose?

LADY BRITOMART. Yes. [*To Stephen*] It is what I told you last night, Stephen.

UNDERSHAFT [*sulkily*] I understand you want to come into the cannon business.

STEPHEN. *I* go into trade! Certainly not.

UNDERSHAFT [*opening his eyes, greatly eased in mind and manner*] Oh! in that case--!

LADY BRITOMART. Cannons are not trade, Stephen. They are enterprise.

STEPHEN. I have no intention of becoming a man of business in any sense. I have no capacity for business and no taste for it. I intend to devote myself to politics.

UNDERSHAFT [*rising*] My dear boy: this is an immense relief to me. And I trust it may prove an equally good thing for the country. I was afraid you would consider yourself disparaged and slighted. [*He moves towards Stephen as if to shake hands with him*].

LADY BRITOMART [*rising and interposing*] Stephen: I cannot allow you to throw away an enormous property like this.

STEPHEN [*stiffly*] Mother: there must be an end of treating me as a child, if you please. [*Lady Britomart recoils, deeply wounded by his tone*]. Until last night I did not take your attitude seriously, because I did not think you meant it seriously. But I find now that you left me in the dark as to matters which you should have explained to me years ago. I am extremely hurt and offended. Any further discussion of my intentions had better take place with my father, as between one man and another.

LADY BRITOMART. Stephen! [*She sits down again; and her eyes fill with tears*].

UNDERSHAFT [*with grave compassion*] You see, my dear, it is only the big men who can be treated as children.

STEPHEN. I am sorry, mother, that you have forced me--

UNDERSHAFT [*stopping him*] Yes, yes, yes, yes: that's all right, Stephen. She wont interfere with you any more: your independence is achieved: you have won your latchkey. Don't rub it in; and above all, don't apologize. [*He resumes his seat*]. Now what about your future, as between one man and another--I beg your pardon, Biddy: as between two men and a woman.

LADY BRITOMART [*who has pulled herself together strongly*] I quite understand, Stephen. By all means go your own way if you feel strong enough. [*Stephen sits down magisterially in the chair at the writing table with an air of affirming his majority*].

UNDERSHAFT. It is settled that you do not ask for the succession to the cannon business.

STEPHEN. I hope it is settled that I repudiate the cannon business.

UNDERSHAFT. Come, come! Don't be so devilishly sulky: it's boyish. Freedom should be generous. Besides, I owe you a fair start in life in exchange for disinheriting you. You can't become prime minister all at once. Haven't you a turn for something? What about literature, art and so forth?

STEPHEN. I have nothing of the artist about me, either in faculty or character, thank Heaven!

UNDERSHAFT. A philosopher, perhaps? Eh?

STEPHEN. I make no such ridiculous pretension.

UNDERSHAFT. Just so. Well, there is the army, the navy, the Church, the Bar. The Bar requires some ability. What about the Bar?

STEPHEN. I have not studied law. And I am afraid I have not the necessary push--I believe that is the name barristers give to their vulgarity--for success in pleading.

UNDERSHAFT. Rather a difficult case, Stephen. Hardly anything left but the stage, is there? [*Stephen makes an impatient movement*]. Well, come! is there anything you know or care for?

STEPHEN [*rising and looking at him steadily*] I know the difference between right and wrong.

UNDERSHAFT [*hugely tickled*] You don't say so! What! no capacity for business, no knowledge of law, no sympathy with art, no pretension to philosophy; only a simple knowledge of the secret that has puzzled all the philosophers, baffled all the lawyers, muddled all the men of business, and ruined most of the artists: the secret of right and wrong. Why, man, you're a genius, master of masters, a god! At twenty-four, too!

STEPHEN [*keeping his temper with difficulty*] You are pleased to be facetious. I pretend to nothing more than any honorable English gentleman claims as his birthright [*he sits down angrily*].

UNDERSHAFT. Oh, that's everybody's birthright. Look at poor little Jenny Hill, the Salvation lassie! she would think you were laughing at her if you asked her to stand up in the street and teach grammar or geography or mathematics or even drawingroom dancing; but it never occurs to her to doubt that she can teach morals and religion. You are all alike, you respectable people. You can't tell me the bursting strain of a ten-inch gun, which is a very simple matter; but you all think you can tell me the bursting strain of a man under temptation. You daren't handle high explosives; but you're all ready to handle honesty and truth and justice and the whole duty of man, and kill one another at that game. What a country! what a world!

LADY BRITOMART [*uneasily*] What do you think he had better do, Andrew?

UNDERSHAFT. Oh, just what he wants to do. He knows nothing; and he thinks he knows everything. That points clearly to a political career. Get him a private secretaryship to someone who can get him an Under Secretaryship; and then leave him alone. He will find his natural and proper place in the end on the Treasury bench.

STEPHEN [*springing up again*] I am sorry, sir, that you force me to forget the respect due to you as my father. I am an Englishman; and I will not hear the Government of my country insulted. [*He thrusts his hands in his pockets, and walks angrily across to the window*].

UNDERSHAFT [*with a touch of brutality*] The government of your country! *I* am the government of your country: I, and Lazarus. Do you suppose that you and half a dozen amateurs like you, sitting in a row in that foolish gabble shop, can govern Undershaft and Lazarus? No, my friend: you will do what pays US. You will make war when it suits us, and keep peace when it doesn't. You will find out that trade requires certain measures when we have decided on those measures. When I want anything to keep my dividends up, you will discover that my want is a national need. When other people want something to keep my dividends down, you will call out the police and military. And in return you shall have the support and applause of my newspapers, and the delight of imagining that you are a great statesman. Government of your country! Be off with you, my boy, and play with your caucuses and leading articles and historic parties and great leaders and burning questions and the rest of your toys. *I* am going back to my counting house to pay the piper and call the tune.

STEPHEN [*actually smiling, and putting his hand on his father's shoulder with indulgent patronage*] Really, my dear father, it is impossible to be angry with you. You don't know how absurd all this sounds to ME. You are very properly proud of having been industrious enough to make money; and it is greatly to your credit that you have made so much of it. But it has kept you in circles where you are valued for your money and deferred to for it, instead of in the doubtless very oldfashioned and behind-the-times public school and university where I formed my habits of mind. It is natural for you to think that money governs England; but you must allow me to think I know better.

UNDERSHAFT. And what does govern England, pray?

STEPHEN. Character, father, character.

UNDERSHAFT. Whose character? Yours or mine?

STEPHEN. Neither yours nor mine, father, but the best elements in the English national character.

UNDERSHAFT. Stephen: I've found your profession for you. You're a born journalist. I'll start you with a hightoned weekly review. There!

Stephen goes to the smaller writing table and busies himself with his letters.

Sarah, Barbara, Lomax, and Cusins come in ready for walking. Barbara crosses the room to the window and looks out. Cusins drifts amiably to the armchair, and Lomax remains near the door, whilst Sarah comes to her mother.

SARAH. Go and get ready, mamma: the carriage is waiting. [*Lady Britomart leaves the room.*]

UNDERSHAFT [*to Sarah*] Good day, my dear. Good afternoon, Mr. Lomax.

LOMAX [*vaguely*] Ahdedoo.

UNDERSHAFT [*to Cusins*] quite well after last night, Euripides, eh?

CUSINS. As well as can be expected.

UNDERSHAFT. That's right. [*To Barbara*] So you are coming to see my death and devastation factory, Barbara?

BARBARA [*at the window*] You came yesterday to see my salvation factory. I promised you a return visit.

LOMAX [*coming forward between Sarah and Undershaft*] You'll find it awfully interesting. I've been through the Woolwich Arsenal; and it gives you a ripping feeling of security, you know, to think of the lot of beggars we could kill if it came to fighting. [*To Undershaft, with sudden solemnity*] Still, it must be rather an awful reflection for you, from the religious point of view as it were. You're getting on, you know, and all that.

SARAH. You don't mind Cholly's imbecility, papa, do you?

LOMAX [*much taken aback*] Oh I say!

UNDERSHAFT. Mr Lomax looks at the matter in a very proper spirit, my dear.

LOMAX. Just so. That's all I meant, I assure you.

SARAH. Are you coming, Stephen?

STEPHEN. Well, I am rather busy--er-- [*Magnanimously*] Oh well, yes: I'll come. That is, if there is room for me.

UNDERSHAFT. I can take two with me in a little motor I am experimenting with for field use. You won't mind its being rather unfashionable. It's not painted yet; but it's bullet proof.

LOMAX [*appalled at the prospect of confronting Wilton Crescent in an unpainted motor*] Oh I say!

SARAH. The carriage for me, thank you. Barbara doesn't mind what she's seen in.

LOMAX. I say, Dolly old chap: do you really mind the car being a guy? Because of course if you do I'll go in it. Still--

CUSINS. I prefer it.

LOMAX. Thanks awfully, old man. Come, Sarah. [*He hurries out to secure his seat in the carriage. Sarah follows him*].

CUSINS. [*moodily walking across to Lady Britomart's writing table*] Why are we two coming to this Works Department of Hell? that is what I ask myself.

BARBARA. I have always thought of it as a sort of pit where lost creatures with blackened faces stirred up smoky fires and were driven and tormented by my father? Is it like that, dad?

UNDERSHAFT [*scandalized*] My dear! It is a spotlessly clean and beautiful hillside town.

CUSINS. With a Methodist chapel? Oh do say there's a Methodist chapel.

UNDERSHAFT. There are two: a primitive one and a sophisticated one. There is even an Ethical Society; but it is not much patronized, as my men are all strongly religious. In the High Explosives Sheds they object to the presence of Agnostics as unsafe.

CUSINS. And yet they don't object to you!

BARBARA. Do they obey all your orders?

UNDERSHAFT. I never give them any orders. When I speak to one of them it is "Well, Jones, is the baby doing well? and has Mrs Jones made a good recovery?" "Nicely, thank you, sir." And that's all.

CUSINS. But Jones has to be kept in order. How do you maintain discipline among your men?

UNDERSHAFT. I don't. They do. You see, the one thing Jones won't stand is any rebellion from the man under him, or any assertion of social equality between the wife of the man with 4 shillings a week less than himself and Mrs Jones! Of course they all rebel against me, theoretically. Practically, every man of them keeps the man just below him in his place. I never meddle with them. I never bully them. I don't even bully Lazarus. I say that certain things are to be done; but I don't order anybody to do them. I don't say, mind you, that there is no ordering about and snubbing and even bullying. The men snub the boys and order them about; the carmen snub the sweepers; the artisans snub the unskilled laborers; the foremen drive and bully both the laborers and artisans; the assistant engineers find fault with the foremen; the chief engineers drop on the assistants; the departmental managers worry the chiefs; and the clerks have tall hats and hymnbooks and keep up the social tone by refusing to associate on equal terms with anybody. The result is a colossal profit, which comes to me.

CUSINS [*revolted*] You really are a--well, what I was saying yesterday.

BARBARA. What was he saying yesterday?

UNDERSHAFT. Never mind, my dear. He thinks I have made you unhappy. Have I?

BARBARA. Do you think I can be happy in this vulgar silly dress? I! who have worn the uniform. Do you understand what you have done to me? Yesterday I had a man's soul in my hand. I set him in the way of life with his face to salvation. But when we took your money he turned back to drunkenness and derision. [*With intense conviction*] I will never forgive you that. If I had a child, and you destroyed its body with your explosives--if you murdered Dolly with your horrible guns--I could forgive you if my forgiveness would open the gates of heaven to you. But to take a human soul from me, and turn it into the soul of a wolf! that is worse than any murder.

UNDERSHAFT. Does my daughter despair so easily? Can you strike a man to the heart and leave no mark on him?

BARBARA [*her face lighting up*] Oh, you are right: he can never be lost now: where was my faith?

CUSINS. Oh, clever clever devil!

BARBARA. You may be a devil; but God speaks through you sometimes. [*She takes her father's hands and kisses them*]. You have given me back my happiness: I feel it deep down now, though my spirit is troubled.

UNDERSHAFT. You have learnt something. That always feels at first as if you had lost something.

BARBARA. Well, take me to the factory of death, and let me learn something more. There must be some truth or other behind all this frightful irony. Come, Dolly. [*She goes out*].

CUSINS. My guardian angel! [*To Undershaft*] Avaunt! [*He follows Barbara*].

STEPHEN [*quietly, at the writing table*] You must not mind Cusins, father. He is a very amiable good fellow; but he is a Greek scholar and naturally a little eccentric.

UNDERSHAFT. Ah, quite so. Thank you, Stephen. Thank you. [*He goes out*].

Stephen smiles patronizingly; buttons his coat responsibly; and crosses the room to the door. Lady Britomart, dressed for out-of-doors, opens it before he reaches it. She looks round far the others; looks at Stephen; and turns to go without a word.

STEPHEN [*embarrassed*] Mother--

LADY BRITOMART. Don't be apologetic, Stephen. And don't forget that you have outgrown your mother. [*She goes out*].

Perivale St Andrews lies between two Middlesex hills, half climbing the northern one. It is an almost smokeless town of white walls, roofs of narrow green slates or red tiles, tall trees, domes, campaniles, and slender chimney shafts, beautifully situated and beautiful in itself. The best view of it is obtained from the crest of a slope about half a mile to the east, where the high explosives are dealt with. The foundry lies hidden in the depths between, the tops of its chimneys sprouting like huge skittles into the middle distance. Across the crest runs a platform of concrete, with a parapet which suggests a fortification, because there is a huge cannon of the obsolete Woolwich Infant pattern peering across it at the town. The cannon is mounted on an experimental gun carriage: possibly the original model of the Undershaft disappearing rampart gun alluded to by Stephen. The parapet has a high step inside which serves as a seat.

Barbara is leaning over the parapet, looking towards the town. On her right is the cannon; on her left the end of a shed raised on piles, with a ladder of three or four steps up to the door, which opens outwards and has a little wooden landing at the threshold, with a fire bucket in the corner of the landing. The parapet stops short of the shed, leaving a gap which is the beginning of the path down the hill through the foundry to the town. Behind the cannon is a trolley carrying a huge conical bombshell, with a red band painted on it. Further from the parapet, on the same side, is a deck chair, near the door of an office, which, like the sheds, is of the lightest possible construction.

Cusins arrives by the path from the town.

BARBARA. Well?

CUSINS. Not a ray of hope. Everything perfect, wonderful, real. It only needs a cathedral to be a heavenly city instead of a hellish one.

BARBARA. Have you found out whether they have done anything for old Peter Shirley.

CUSINS. They have found him a job as gatekeeper and timekeeper. He's frightfully miserable. He calls the timekeeping brainwork, and says he isn't used to it; and his gate lodge is so splendid that he's ashamed to use the rooms, and skulks in the scullery.

BARBARA. Poor Peter!

Stephen arrives from the town. He carries a field-glass.

STEPHEN [*enthusiastically*] Have you two seen the place? Why did you leave us?

CUSINS. I wanted to see everything I was not intended to see; and Barbara wanted to make the men talk.

STEPHEN. Have you found anything discreditable?

CUSINS. No. They call him Dandy Andy and are proud of his being a cunning old rascal; but it's all horribly, frightfully, immorally, unanswerably perfect.

Sarah arrives.

SARAH. Heavens! what a place! [*She crosses to the trolley*]. Did you see the nursing home!? [*She sits down on the shell*].

STEPHEN. Did you see the libraries and schools!?

SARAH. Did you see the ballroom and the banqueting chamber in the Town Hall!?

STEPHEN. Have you gone into the insurance fund, the pension fund, the building society, the various applications of co-operation!?

Undershaft comes from the office, with a sheaf of telegrams in his hands.

UNDERSHAFT. Well, have you seen everything? I'm sorry I was called away. [*Indicating the telegrams*] News from Manchuria.

STEPHEN. Good news, I hope.

UNDERSHAFT. Very.

STEPHEN. Another Japanese victory?

UNDERSHAFT. Oh, I don't know. Which side wins does not concern us here. No: the good news is that the aerial battleship is a tremendous success. At the first trial it has wiped out a fort with three hundred soldiers in it.

CUSINS [*from the platform*] Dummy soldiers?

UNDERSHAFT. No: the real thing. [*Cusins and Barbara exchange glances. Then Cusins sits on the step and buries his face in his hands. Barbara gravely lays her hand on his shoulder, and he looks up at her in a sort of whimsical desperation*]. Well, Stephen, what do you think of the place?

STEPHEN. Oh, magnificent. A perfect triumph of organization. Frankly, my dear father, I have been a fool: I had no idea of what it all meant--of the wonderful forethought, the power of organization, the administrative capacity, the financial genius, the colossal capital it represents. I have been repeating to myself as I came through your streets "Peace hath her victories no less renowned than War." I have only one misgiving about it all.

UNDERSHAFT. Out with it.

STEPHEN. Well, I cannot help thinking that all this provision for every want of your workmen may sap their independence and weaken their sense of responsibility. And greatly as we enjoyed our tea at that splendid restaurant--how they gave us all that luxury and cake and jam and cream for threepence I really cannot imagine!--still you must remember that restaurants break up home life. Look at the continent, for instance! Are you sure so much pampering is really good for the men's characters?

UNDERSHAFT. Well you see, my dear boy, when you are organizing civilization you have to make up your mind whether trouble and anxiety are good things or not. If you decide that they are, then, I take it, you simply don't organize civilization; and there you are, with trouble and anxiety enough to make us all angels! But if you decide the other way, you may as well go through with it. However, Stephen, our characters are safe here. A sufficient dose of anxiety is always provided by the fact that we may be blown to smithereens at any moment.

SARAH. By the way, papa, where do you make the explosives?

UNDERSHAFT. In separate little sheds, like that one. When one of them blows up, it costs very little; and only the people quite close to it are killed.

Stephen, who is quite close to it, looks at it rather scaredly, and moves away quickly to the cannon. At the same moment the door of the shed is thrown abruptly open; and a foreman in overalls and list slippers comes out on the little landing and holds the door open for Lomax, who appears in the doorway.

LOMAX [*with studied coolness*] My good fellow: you needn't get into a state of nerves. Nothing's going to happen to you; and I suppose it wouldn't be the end of the world if anything did. A little bit of British pluck is what you want, old chap. [*He descends and strolls across to Sarah*].

UNDERSHAFT [*to the foreman*] Anything wrong, Bilton?

BILTON [*with ironic calm*] Gentleman walked into the high explosives shed and lit a cigaret, sir: that's all.

UNDERSHAFT. Ah, quite so. [*To Lomax*] Do you happen to remember what you did with the match?

LOMAX. Oh come! I'm not a fool. I took jolly good care to blow it out before I chucked it away.

BILTON. The top of it was red hot inside, sir.

LOMAX. Well, suppose it was! I didn't chuck it into any of your messes.

UNDERSHAFT. Think no more of it, Mr Lomax. By the way, would you mind lending me your matches?

LOMAX [*offering his box*] Certainly.

UNDERSHAFT. Thanks. [*He pockets the matches*].

LOMAX [*lecturing to the company generally*] You know, these high explosives don't go off like gunpowder, except when they're in a gun. When they're spread loose, you can put a match to them without the least risk: they just burn quietly like a bit of paper. [*Warming to the scientific interest of the subject*] Did you know that Undershaft? Have you ever tried?

UNDERSHAFT. Not on a large scale, Mr Lomax. Bilton will give you a sample of gun cotton when you are leaving if you ask him. You can experiment with it at home. [*Bilton looks puzzled*].

SARAH. Bilton will do nothing of the sort, papa. I suppose it's your business to blow up the Russians and Japs; but you might really stop short of blowing up poor Cholly. [*Bilton gives it up and retires into the shed*].

LOMAX. My ownest, there is no danger. [*He sits beside her on the shell*].

Lady Britomart arrives from the town with a bouquet.

LADY BRITOMART [*coming impetuously between Undershaft and the deck chair*] Andrew: you shouldn't have let me see this place.

UNDERSHAFT. Why, my dear?

LADY BRITOMART. Never mind why: you shouldn't have: that's all. To think of all that [*indicating the town*] being yours! and that you have kept it to yourself all these years!

UNDERSHAFT. It does not belong to me. I belong to it. It is the Undershaft inheritance.

LADY BRITOMART. It is not. Your ridiculous cannons and that noisy banging foundry may be the Undershaft inheritance; but all that plate and linen, all that furniture and those houses and orchards and gardens belong to us. They belong to me: they are not a man's business. I won't give them up. You must be out of your senses to throw them all away; and if you persist in such folly, I will call in a doctor.

UNDERSHAFT [*stooping to smell the bouquet*] Where did you get the flowers, my dear?

LADY BRITOMART. Your men presented them to me in your William Morris Labor Church.

CUSINS [*springing up*] Oh! It needed only that. A Labor Church!

LADY BRITOMART. Yes, with Morris's words in mosaic letters ten feet high round the dome. NO MAN IS GOOD ENOUGH TO BE ANOTHER MAN'S MASTER. The cynicism of it!

UNDERSHAFT. It shocked the men at first, I am afraid. But now they take no more notice of it than of the ten commandments in church.

LADY BRITOMART. Andrew: you are trying to put me off the subject of the inheritance by profane jokes. Well, you shan't. I don't ask it any longer for Stephen: he has inherited far too much of your perversity to be fit for it. But Barbara has rights as well as Stephen. Why should not Adolphus succeed to the inheritance? I could manage the town for him; and he can look after the cannons, if they are really necessary.

UNDERSHAFT. I should ask nothing better if Adolphus were a foundling. He is exactly the sort of new blood that is wanted in English business. But he's not a foundling; and there's an end of it.

CUSINS [*diplomatically*] Not quite. [*They all turn and stare at him. He comes from the platform past the shed to Undershaft*]. I think--Mind! I am not committing myself in any way as to my future course--but I think the foundling difficulty can be got over.

UNDERSHAFT. What do you mean?

CUSINS. Well, I have something to say which is in the nature of a confession.

SARAH. {
LADY BRITOMART. { Confession!
BARBARA. {
STEPHEN. {

LOMAX. Oh I say!

CUSINS. Yes, a confession. Listen, all. Until I met Barbara I thought myself in the main an honorable, truthful man, because I wanted the approval of my conscience more than I wanted anything else. But the moment I saw Barbara, I wanted her far more than the approval of my conscience.

LADY BRITOMART. Adolphus!

CUSINS. It is true. You accused me yourself, Lady Brit, of joining the Army to worship Barbara; and so I did. She bought my soul like a flower at a street corner; but she bought it for herself.

UNDERSHAFT. What! Not for Dionysos or another?

CUSINS. Dionysos and all the others are in herself. I adored what was divine in her, and was therefore a true worshipper. But I was romantic about her too. I thought she was a woman of the people, and that a marriage with a professor of Greek would be far beyond the wildest social ambitions of her rank.

LADY BRITOMART. Adolphus!!

LOMAX. Oh I say!!!

CUSINS. When I learnt the horrible truth--

LADY BRITOMART. What do you mean by the horrible truth, pray?

CUSINS. That she was enormously rich; that her grandfather was an earl; that her father was the Prince of Darkness--

UNDERSHAFT. Chut!

CUSINS.--and that I was only an adventurer trying to catch a rich wife, then I stooped to deceive about my birth.

LADY BRITOMART. Your birth! Now Adolphus, don't dare to make up a wicked story for the sake of these wretched cannons. Remember: I have seen photographs of your parents; and the Agent General for South Western Australia knows them personally and has assured me that they are most respectable married people.

CUSINS. So they are in Australia; but here they are outcasts. Their marriage is legal in Australia, but not in England. My mother is my father's deceased wife's sister; and in this island I am consequently a foundling. [*Sensation*]. Is the subterfuge good enough, Machiavelli?

UNDERSHAFT [*thoughtfully*] Biddy: this may be a way out of the difficulty.

LADY BRITOMART. Stuff! A man can't make cannons any the better for being his own cousin instead of his proper self [*she sits down in the deck chair with a bounce that expresses her downright contempt for their casuistry.*]

UNDERSHAFT [*to Cusins*] You are an educated man. That is against the tradition.

CUSINS. Once in ten thousand times it happens that the schoolboy is a born master of what they try to teach him. Greek has not destroyed my mind: it has nourished it. Besides, I did not learn it at an English public school.

UNDERSHAFT. Hm! Well, I cannot afford to be too particular: you have cornered the foundling market. Let it pass. You are eligible, Euripides: you are eligible.

BARBARA [*coming from the platform and interposing between Cusins and Undershaft*] Dolly: yesterday morning, when Stephen told us all about the tradition, you became very silent; and you have been strange and excited ever since. Were you thinking of your birth then?

CUSINS. When the finger of Destiny suddenly points at a man in the middle of his breakfast, it makes him thoughtful. [*Barbara turns away sadly and stands near her mother, listening perturbedly*].

UNDERSHAFT. Aha! You have had your eye on the business, my young friend, have you?

CUSINS. Take care! There is an abyss of moral horror between me and your accursed aerial battleships.

UNDERSHAFT. Never mind the abyss for the present. Let us settle the practical details and leave your final decision open. You know that you will have to change your name. Do you object to that?

CUSINS. Would any man named Adolphus--any man called Dolly!--object to be called something else?

UNDERSHAFT. Good. Now, as to money! I propose to treat you handsomely from the beginning. You shall start at a thousand a year.

CUSINS. [*with sudden heat, his spectacles twinkling with mischief*] A thousand! You dare offer a miserable thousand to the son-in-law of a millionaire! No, by Heavens, Machiavelli! you shall not cheat me. You cannot do without me; and I can do without you. I must have two thousand five hundred a year for two years. At the end of that time, if I am a failure, I go. But if I am a success, and stay on, you must give me the other five thousand.

UNDERSHAFT. What other five thousand?

CUSINS. To make the two years up to five thousand a year. The two thousand five hundred is only half pay in case I should turn out a failure. The third year I must have ten per cent on the profits.

UNDERSHAFT [*taken aback*] Ten per cent! Why, man, do you know what my profits are?

CUSINS. Enormous, I hope: otherwise I shall require twenty-five per cent.

UNDERSHAFT. But, Mr Cusins, this is a serious matter of business. You are not bringing any capital into the concern.

CUSINS. What! no capital! Is my mastery of Greek no capital? Is my access to the subtlest thought, the loftiest poetry yet attained by humanity, no capital? my character! my intellect! my life! my career! what Barbara calls my soul! are these no capital? Say another word; and I double my salary.

UNDERSHAFT. Be reasonable--

CUSINS [*peremptorily*] Mr Undershaft: you have my terms. Take them or leave them.

UNDERSHAFT [*recovering himself*] Very well. I note your terms; and I offer you half.

CUSINS [*disgusted*] Half!

UNDERSHAFT [*firmly*] Half.

CUSINS. You call yourself a gentleman; and you offer me half!!

UNDERSHAFT. I do not call myself a gentleman; but I offer you half.

CUSINS. This to your future partner! your successor! your son-in-law!

BARBARA. You are selling your own soul, Dolly, not mine. Leave me out of the bargain, please.

UNDERSHAFT. Come! I will go a step further for Barbara's sake. I will give you three fifths; but that is my last word.

CUSINS. Done!

LOMAX. Done in the eye. Why, *I* only get eight hundred, you know.

CUSINS. By the way, Mac, I am a classical scholar, not an arithmetical one. Is three fifths more than half or less?

UNDERSHAFT. More, of course.

CUSINS. I would have taken two hundred and fifty. How you can succeed in business when you are willing to pay all that money to a University don who is obviously not worth a junior clerk's wages!--well! What will Lazarus say?

UNDERSHAFT. Lazarus is a gentle romantic Jew who cares for nothing but string quartets and stalls at fashionable theatres. He will get the credit of your rapacity in money matters, as he has hitherto had the credit of mine. You are a shark of the first order, Euripides. So much the better for the firm!

BARBARA. Is the bargain closed, Dolly? Does your soul belong to him now?

CUSINS. No: the price is settled: that is all. The real tug of war is still to come. What about the moral question?

LADY BRITOMART. There is no moral question in the matter at all, Adolphus. You must simply sell cannons and weapons to people whose cause is right and just, and refuse them to foreigners and criminals.

UNDERSHAFT [*determinedly*] No: none of that. You must keep the true faith of an Armorer, or you don't come in here.

CUSINS. What on earth is the true faith of an Armorer?

UNDERSHAFT. To give arms to all men who offer an honest price for them, without respect of persons or principles: to aristocrat and republican, to Nihilist and Tsar, to Capitalist and Socialist, to Protestant and Catholic, to burglar and policeman, to black man white man and yellow man, to all sorts and conditions, all nationalities, all faiths, all follies, all causes and all crimes. The first Undershaft wrote up in his shop IF GOD GAVE THE HAND, LET NOT MAN WITHHOLD THE SWORD. The second wrote up ALL HAVE THE RIGHT TO FIGHT: NONE HAVE THE RIGHT TO JUDGE. The third wrote up TO MAN THE WEAPON: TO HEAVEN THE VICTORY. The fourth had no literary turn; so he did not write up anything; but he sold cannons to Napoleon under the nose of George the Third. The fifth wrote up PEACE SHALL NOT PREVAIL SAVE WITH A SWORD IN HER HAND. The sixth, my master, was the best of all. He wrote up NOTHING IS EVER DONE IN THIS WORLD UNTIL MEN ARE PREPARED TO KILL ONE ANOTHER IF IT IS NOT DONE. After that, there was nothing left for the seventh to say. So he wrote up, simply, UNASHAMED.

CUSINS. My good Machiavelli, I shall certainly write something up on the wall; only, as I shall write it in Greek, you won't be able to read it. But as to your Armorer's faith, if I take my neck out of the noose of my own morality I am not going to put it into the noose of yours. I shall sell cannons to whom I please and refuse them to whom I please. So there!

UNDERSHAFT. From the moment when you become Andrew Undershaft, you will never do as you please again. Don't come here lusting for power, young man.

CUSINS. If power were my aim I should not come here for it. YOU have no power.

UNDERSHAFT. None of my own, certainly.

CUSINS. I have more power than you, more will. You do not drive this place: it drives you. And what drives the place?

UNDERSHAFT [*enigmatically*] A will of which I am a part.

BARBARA [*startled*] Father! Do you know what you are saying; or are you laying a snare for my soul?

CUSINS. Don't listen to his metaphysics, Barbara. The place is driven by the most rascally part of society, the money hunters, the pleasure hunters, the military promotion hunters; and he is their slave.

UNDERSHAFT. Not necessarily. Remember the Armorer's Faith. I will take an order from a good man as cheerfully as from a bad one. If you good people prefer preaching and shirking to buying my weapons and fighting the rascals, don't blame me. I can make cannons: I cannot make courage and conviction. Bah! You tire me, Euripides, with your mo-morality mongering. Ask Barbara: SHE understands. [*He suddenly takes Barbara's hands, and looks powerfully into her eyes*]. Tell him, my love, what power really means.

BARBARA [*hypnotized*] Before I joined the Salvation Army, I was in my own power; and the consequence was that I never knew what to do with myself. When I joined it, I had not time enough for all the things I had to do.

UNDERSHAFT [*approvingly*] Just so. And why was that, do you suppose?

BARBARA. Yesterday I should have said, because I was in the power of God. [*She resumes her self-possession, withdrawing her hands from his with a power equal to his own*]. But you came and showed me that I was in the power of Bodger and Undershaft. Today I feel--oh! how can I put it into words? Sarah: do you remember the earthquake at Cannes, when we were little children?--how little the surprise of the first shock mattered compared to the dread and horror of waiting for the second? That is how I feel in this place today. I stood on the rock I thought eternal; and without a word of warning it reeled and crumbled under me. I was safe with an infinite wisdom watching me, an army marching to Salvation with me; and in a moment, at a stroke of your pen in a cheque book, I stood alone; and the heavens were empty. That was the first shock of the earthquake: I am waiting for the second.

UNDERSHAFT. Come, come, my daughter! Don't make too much of your little tinpot tragedy. What do we do here when we spend years of work and thought and thousands of pounds of solid cash on a new gun or an aerial battleship that turns out just a hairsbreadth wrong after all? Scrap it. Scrap it without wasting another hour or another pound on it. Well, you have made for yourself something that you call a morality or a religion or what not. It doesn't fit the facts. Well, scrap it. Scrap it and get one that does fit. That is what is wrong with the world at present. It scraps its obsolete steam engines and dynamos; but it won't scrap its old prejudices and its old moralities and its old religions and its old political constitutions. What's the result? In machinery it does very well; but in morals and religion and politics it is working at a loss that brings it nearer bankruptcy every year. Don't persist in that folly. If your old religion broke down yesterday, get a newer and a better one for tomorrow.

BARBARA. Oh how gladly I would take a better one to my soul! But you offer me a worse one. [*Turning on him with sudden vehemence*]. Justify yourself: show me some light through the darkness of this dreadful place, with its beautifully clean workshops, and respectable workmen, and model homes.

UNDERSHAFT. Cleanliness and respectability do not need justification, Barbara: they justify themselves. I see no darkness here, no dreadfulness. In your Salvation shelter I saw poverty, misery, cold and hunger. You gave them bread and treacle and dreams of heaven. I give from thirty shillings a week to twelve thousand a year. They find their own dreams; but I look after the drainage.

BARBARA. And their souls?

UNDERSHAFT. I save their souls just as I saved yours.

BARBARA [*revolted*] You saved my soul! What do you mean?

UNDERSHAFT. I fed you and clothed you and housed you. I took care that you should have money enough to live handsomely--more than enough; so that you could be wasteful, careless, generous. That saved your soul from the seven deadly sins.

BARBARA [*bewildered*] The seven deadly sins!

UNDERSHAFT. Yes, the deadly seven. [*Counting on his fingers*] Food, clothing, firing, rent, taxes, respectability and children. Nothing can lift those seven millstones from Man's neck but money; and the spirit cannot soar until the millstones are lifted. I lifted them from your spirit. I enabled Barbara to become Major Barbara; and I saved her from the crime of poverty.

CUSINS. Do you call poverty a crime?

UNDERSHAFT. The worst of crimes. All the other crimes are virtues beside it: all the other dishonors are chivalry itself by comparison. Poverty blights whole cities; spreads horrible pestilences; strikes dead the very souls of all who come within sight, sound or smell of it. What you call crime is nothing: a murder here and a theft there, a blow now and a curse then: what do they matter? they are only the accidents and illnesses of life: there are not fifty genuine professional criminals in London. But there are millions of poor people, abject people, dirty people, ill fed, ill clothed people. They poison us morally and physically: they kill the happiness of society: they force us to do away with our own liberties and to organize unnatural cruelties for fear they should rise against us and drag us down into their abyss. Only fools fear crime: we all fear poverty. Pah! [*turning on Barbara*] you talk of your half-saved ruffian in West Ham: you accuse me of dragging his soul back to perdition. Well, bring him to me here; and I will drag his soul back again to salvation for you. Not by words and dreams; but by thirty-eight shillings a week, a sound house in a handsome street, and a permanent job. In three weeks he will have a fancy waistcoat; in three months a tall hat and a chapel sitting; before the end of the year he will shake hands with a duchess at a Primrose League meeting, and join the Conservative Party.

BARBARA. And will he be the better for that?

UNDERSHAFT. You know he will. Don't be a hypocrite, Barbara. He will be better fed, better housed, better clothed, better behaved; and his children will be pounds heavier and bigger. That will be better than an American cloth mattress in a shelter, chopping firewood, eating bread and treacle, and being forced to kneel down from time to time to thank heaven for it: knee drill, I think you call it. It is cheap work converting starving men with a Bible in one hand and a slice of bread in the other. I will undertake to convert West Ham to Mahometanism on the same terms. Try your hand on my men: their souls are hungry because their bodies are full.

BARBARA. And leave the east end to starve?

UNDERSHAFT [*his energetic tone dropping into one of bitter and brooding remembrance*] I was an east ender. I moralized and starved until one day I swore that I would be a fullfed free man at all costs--that nothing should stop me except a bullet, neither reason nor morals nor the lives of other men. I said "Thou shalt starve ere I starve"; and with that word I became free and great. I was a dangerous man until I had my will: now I am a useful, beneficent, kindly person. That is the history of most self-made millionaires, I fancy. When it is the history of every Englishman we shall have an England worth living in.

LADY BRITOMART. Stop making speeches, Andrew. This is not the place for them.

UNDERSHAFT [*punctured*] My dear: I have no other means of conveying my ideas.

LADY BRITOMART. Your ideas are nonsense. You got oil because you were selfish and unscrupulous.

UNDERSHAFT. Not at all. I had the strongest scruples about poverty and starvation. Your moralists are quite unscrupulous about both: they make virtues of them. I had rather be a thief than a pauper. I had rather be a murderer than a slave. I don't want to be either; but if you force the alternative on me, then, by Heaven, I'll choose the braver and more moral one. I hate poverty and slavery worse than any other crimes whatsoever. And let me tell you this. Poverty and slavery have stood up for centuries to your sermons and leading articles: they will not stand up to my machine guns. Don't preach at them: don't reason with them. Kill them.

BARBARA. Killing. Is that your remedy for everything?

UNDERSHAFT. It is the final test of conviction, the only lever strong enough to overturn a social system, the only way of saying Must. Let six hundred and seventy fools loose in the street; and three policemen can scatter them. But huddle them together in a certain house in Westminster; and let them go through certain ceremonies and call themselves certain names until at last they get the courage to kill; and your six hundred and seventy fools become a government. Your pious mob fills up ballot papers and imagines it is governing its masters; but the ballot paper that really governs is the paper that has a bullet wrapped up in it.

CUSINS. That is perhaps why, like most intelligent people, I never vote.

UNDERSHAFT Vote! Bah! When you vote, you only change the names of the cabinet. When you shoot, you pull down governments, inaugurate new epochs, abolish old orders and set up new. Is that historically true, Mr Learned Man, or is it not?

CUSINS. It is historically true. I loathe having to admit it. I repudiate your sentiments. I abhor your nature. I defy you in every possible way. Still, it is true. But it ought not to be true.

UNDERSHAFT. Ought, ought, ought, ought, ought! Are you going to spend your life saying ought, like the rest of our moralists? Turn your oughts into shalls, man. Come and make explosives with me. Whatever can blow men up can blow society up. The history of the world is the history of those who had courage enough to embrace this truth. Have you the courage to embrace it, Barbara?

LADY BRITOMART. Barbara, I positively forbid you to listen to your father's abominable wickedness. And you, Adolphus, ought to know better than to go about saying that wrong things are true. What does it matter whether they are true if they are wrong?

UNDERSHAFT. What does it matter whether they are wrong if they are true?

LADY BRITOMART [*rising*] Children: come home instantly. Andrew: I am exceedingly sorry I allowed you to call on us. You are wickeder than ever. Come at once.

BARBARA [*shaking her head*] It's no use running away from wicked people, mamma.

LADY BRITOMART. It is every use. It shows your disapprobation of them.

BARBARA. It does not save them.

LADY BRITOMART. I can see that you are going to disobey me. Sarah: are you coming home or are you not?

SARAH. I daresay it's very wicked of papa to make cannons; but I don't think I shall cut him on that account.

LOMAX [*pouring oil on the troubled waters*] The fact is, you know, there is a certain amount of tosh about this notion of wickedness. It doesn't work. You must look at facts. Not that I would say a word in favor of anything wrong; but then, you see, all sorts of chaps are always doing all sorts of things; and we have to fit them in somehow, don't you know. What I mean is that you can't go cutting everybody; and that's about what it comes to. [*Their rapt attention to his eloquence makes him nervous*] Perhaps I don't make myself clear.

LADY BRITOMART. You are lucidity itself, Charles. Because Andrew is successful and has plenty of money to give to Sarah, you will flatter him and encourage him in his wickedness.

LOMAX [*unruffled*] Well, where the carcase is, there will the eagles be gathered, don't you know. [*To Undershaft*] Eh? What?

UNDERSHAFT. Precisely. By the way, may I call you Charles?

LOMAX. Delighted. Cholly is the usual ticket.

UNDERSHAFT [*to Lady Britomart*] Biddy--

LADY BRITOMART [*violently*] Don't dare call me Biddy. Charles Lomax: you are a fool. Adolphus Cusins: you are a Jesuit. Stephen: you are a prig. Barbara: you are a lunatic. Andrew: you are a vulgar tradesman. Now you all know my opinion; and my conscience is clear, at all events [*she sits down again with a vehemence that almost wrecks the chair*].

UNDERSHAFT. My dear, you are the incarnation of morality. [*She snorts*]. Your conscience is clear and your duty done when you have called everybody names. Come, Euripides! it is getting late; and we all want to get home. Make up your mind.

CUSINS. Understand this, you old demon--

LADY BRITOMART. Adolphus!

UNDERSHAFT. Let him alone, Biddy. Proceed, Euripides.

CUSINS. You have me in a horrible dilemma. I want Barbara.

UNDERSHAFT. Like all young men, you greatly exaggerate the difference between one young woman and another.

BARBARA. Quite true, Dolly.

CUSINS. I also want to avoid being a rascal.

UNDERSHAFT [*with biting contempt*] You lust for personal righteousness, for self-approval, for what you call a good conscience, for what Barbara calls salvation, for what I call patronizing people who are not so lucky as yourself.

CUSINS. I do not: all the poet in me recoils from being a good man. But there are things in me that I must reckon with: pity--

UNDERSHAFT. Pity! The scavenger of misery.

CUSINS. Well, love.

UNDERSHAFT. I know. You love the needy and the outcast: you love the oppressed races, the negro, the Indian ryot, the Pole, the Irishman. Do you love the Japanese? Do you love the Germans? Do you love the English?

CUSINS. No. Every true Englishman detests the English. We are the wickedest nation on earth; and our success is a moral horror.

UNDERSHAFT. That is what comes of your gospel of love, is it?

CUSINS. May I not love even my father-in-law?

UNDERSHAFT. Who wants your love, man? By what right do you take the liberty of offering it to me? I will have your due heed and respect, or I will kill you. But your love! Damn your impertinence!

CUSINS [*grinning*] I may not be able to control my affections, Mac.

UNDERSHAFT. You are fencing, Euripides. You are weakening: your grip is slipping. Come! try your last weapon. Pity and love have broken in your hand: forgiveness is still left.

CUSINS. No: forgiveness is a beggar's refuge. I am with you there: we must pay our debts.

UNDERSHAFT. Well said. Come! you will suit me. Remember the words of Plato.

CUSINS [*starting*] Plato! You dare quote Plato to me!

UNDERSHAFT. Plato says, my friend, that society cannot be saved until either the Professors of Greek take to making gunpowder, or else the makers of gunpowder become Professors of Greek.

CUSINS. Oh, tempter, cunning tempter!

UNDERSHAFT. Come! choose, man, choose.

CUSINS. But perhaps Barbara will not marry me if I make the wrong choice.

BARBARA. Perhaps not.

CUSINS [*desperately perplexed*] You hear--

BARBARA. Father: do you love nobody?

UNDERSHAFT. I love my best friend.

LADY BRITOMART. And who is that, pray?

UNDERSHAFT. My bravest enemy. That is the man who keeps me up to the mark.

CUSINS. You know, the creature is really a sort of poet in his way. Suppose he is a great man, after all!

UNDERSHAFT. Suppose you stop talking and make up your mind, my young friend.

CUSINS. But you are driving me against my nature. I hate war.

UNDERSHAFT. Hatred is the coward's revenge for being intimidated. Dare you make war on war? Here are the means: my friend Mr Lomax is sitting on them.

LOMAX [*springing up*] Oh I say! You don't mean that this thing is loaded, do you? My ownest: come off it.

SARAH [*sitting placidly on the shell*] If I am to be blown up, the more thoroughly it is done the better. Don't fuss, Cholly.

LOMAX [*to Undershaft, strongly remonstrant*] Your own daughter, you know.

UNDERSHAFT. So I see. [*To Cusins*] Well, my friend, may we expect you here at six tomorrow morning?

CUSINS [*firmly*] Not on any account. I will see the whole establishment blown up with its own dynamite before I will get up at five. My hours are healthy, rational hours eleven to five.

UNDERSHAFT. Come when you please: before a week you will come at six and stay until I turn you out for the sake of your health. [*Calling*] Bilton! [*He turns to Lady Britomart, who rises*]. My dear: let us leave these two young people to themselves for a moment. [*Bilton comes from the shed*]. I am going to take you through the gun cotton shed.

BILTON [*barring the way*] You can't take anything explosive in here, Sir.

LADY BRITOMART. What do you mean? Are you alluding to me?

BILTON [*unmoved*] No, ma'am. Mr Undershaft has the other gentleman's matches in his pocket.

LADY BRITOMART [*abruptly*] Oh! I beg your pardon. [*She goes into the shed*].

UNDERSHAFT. Quite right, Bilton, quite right: here you are. [*He gives Bilton the box of matches*]. Come, Stephen. Come, Charles. Bring Sarah. [*He passes into the shed*].

Bilton opens the box and deliberately drops the matches into the fire-bucket.

LOMAX. Oh I say! [*Bilton stolidly hands him the empty box*]. Infernal nonsense! Pure scientific ignorance! [*He goes in*].

SARAH. Am I all right, Bilton?

BILTON. You'll have to put on list slippers, miss: that's all. We've got em inside. [*She goes in*].

STEPHEN [*very seriously to Cusins*] Dolly, old fellow, think. Think before you decide. Do you feel that you are a sufficiently practical man? It is a huge undertaking, an enormous responsibility. All this mass of business will be Greek to you.

CUSINS. Oh, I think it will be much less difficult than Greek.

STEPHEN. Well, I just want to say this before I leave you to yourselves. Don't let anything I have said about right and wrong prejudice you against this great chance in life. I have satisfied myself that the business is one of the highest character and a credit to our country. [*Emotionally*] I am very proud of my father. I-- [*Unable to proceed, he presses Cusins' hand and goes hastily into the shed, followed by Bilton*].

Barbara and Cusins, left alone together, look at one another silently.

CUSINS. Barbara: I am going to accept this offer.

BARBARA. I thought you would.

CUSINS. You understand, don't you, that I had to decide without consulting you. If I had thrown the burden of the choice on you, you would sooner or later have despised me for it.

BARBARA. Yes: I did not want you to sell your soul for me any more than for this inheritance.

CUSINS. It is not the sale of my soul that troubles me: I have sold it too often to care about that. I have sold it for a professorship. I have sold it for an income. I have sold it to escape being imprisoned for refusing to pay taxes for hangmen's ropes and unjust wars and things that I abhor. What is all human conduct but the daily and hourly sale of our souls for trifles? What I am now selling it for is neither money nor position nor comfort, but for reality and for power.

BARBARA. You know that you will have no power, and that he has none.

CUSINS. I know. It is not for myself alone. I want to make power for the world.

BARBARA. I want to make power for the world too; but it must be spiritual power.

CUSINS. I think all power is spiritual: these cannons will not go off by themselves. I have tried to make spiritual power by teaching Greek. But the world can never be really touched by a dead language and a dead civilization. The people must have power; and the people cannot have Greek. Now the power that is made here can be wielded by all men.

BARBARA. Power to burn women's houses down and kill their sons and tear their husbands to pieces.

CUSINS. You cannot have power for good without having power for evil too. Even mother's milk nourishes murderers as well as heroes. This power which only tears men's bodies to pieces has never been so horribly abused as the intellectual power, the imaginative power, the poetic, religious power that can enslave men's souls. As a teacher of Greek I gave the intellectual man weapons against the common man. I now want to give the common man weapons against the intellectual man. I love the common people. I want to arm them against the lawyer, the doctor, the priest, the literary man, the professor, the artist, and the politician, who, once in authority, are the most dangerous, disastrous, and tyrannical of all the fools, rascals, and impostors. I want a democratic power strong enough to force the intellectual oligarchy to use its genius for the general good or else perish.

BARBARA. Is there no higher power than that [*pointing to the shell*]?

CUSINS. Yes: but that power can destroy the higher powers just as a tiger can destroy a man: therefore man must master that power first. I admitted this when the Turks and Greeks were last at war. My best pupil went out to fight for Hellas. My parting gift to him was not a copy of Plato's Republic, but a revolver and a hundred Undershaft cartridges. The blood of every Turk he shot--if he shot any--is on my head as well as on Undershaft's. That act committed me to this place for ever. Your father's challenge has beaten me. Dare I make war on war? I dare. I must. I will. And now, is it all over between us?

BARBARA [*touched by his evident dread of her answer*] Silly baby Dolly! How could it be?

CUSINS [*overjoyed*] Then you--you--you-- Oh for my drum! [*He flourishes imaginary drumsticks*].

BARBARA [*angered by his levity*] Take care, Dolly, take care. Oh, if only I could get away from you and from father and from it all! if I could have the wings of a dove and fly away to heaven!

CUSINS. And leave me!

BARBARA. Yes, you, and all the other naughty mischievous children of men. But I can't. I was happy in the Salvation Army for a moment. I escaped from the world into a paradise of enthusiasm and prayer and soul saving; but the moment our money ran short, it all came back to Bodger: it was he who saved our people: he, and the Prince of Darkness, my papa. Undershaft and Bodger: their hands stretch everywhere: when we feed a starving fellow creature, it is with their bread, because there is no other bread; when we tend the sick, it is in the hospitals they endow; if we turn from the churches they build, we must kneel on the stones of the streets they pave. As long as that lasts, there is no getting away from them. Turning our backs on Bodger and Undershaft is turning our backs on life.

CUSINS. I thought you were determined to turn your back on the wicked side of life.

BARBARA. There is no wicked side: life is all one. And I never wanted to shirk my share in whatever evil must be endured, whether it be sin or suffering. I wish I could cure you of middle-class ideas, Dolly.

CUSINS [*gasping*] Middle cl--! A snub! A social snub to ME! from the daughter of a foundling!

BARBARA. That is why I have no class, Dolly: I come straight out of the heart of the whole people. If I were middle-class I should turn my back on my father's business; and we should both live in an artistic drawingroom, with you reading the reviews in one corner, and I in the other at the piano, playing Schumann: both very superior persons, and neither of us a bit of use. Sooner than that, I would sweep out the guncotton shed, or be one of Bodger's barmaids. Do you know what would have happened if you had refused papa's offer?

CUSINS. I wonder!

BARBARA. I should have given you up and married the man who accepted it. After all, my dear old mother has more sense than any of you. I felt like her when I saw this place--felt that I must have it--that never, never, never could I let it go; only she thought it was the houses and the kitchen ranges and the linen and china, when it was really all the human souls to be saved: not weak souls in starved bodies, crying with gratitude or a scrap of bread and treacle, but fullfed, quarrelsome, snobbish, uppish creatures, all standing on their little rights and dignities, and thinking that my father ought to be greatly obliged to them for making so much money for him--and so he ought. That is where salvation is really wanted. My father shall never throw it in my teeth again that my converts were bribed with bread. [*She is transfigured*]. I have got rid of the bribe of bread. I have got rid of the bribe of heaven. Let God's work be done for its own sake: the work he had to create us to do because it cannot be done by living men and women. When I die, let him be in my debt, not I in his; and let me forgive him as becomes a woman of my rank.

CUSINS. Then the way of life lies through the factory of death?

BARBARA. Yes, through the raising of hell to heaven and of man to God, through the unveiling of an eternal light in the Valley of The Shadow. [*Seizing him with both hands*] Oh, did you think my courage would never come back? did you believe that I was a deserter? that I, who have stood in the streets, and taken my people to my heart, and talked of the holiest and greatest things with them, could ever turn back and chatter foolishly to fashionable people about nothing in a drawingroom? Never, never, never, never: Major Barbara will die with the colors. Oh! and I have my dear little Dolly boy still; and he has found me my place and my work. Glory Hallelujah! [*She kisses him*].

CUSINS. My dearest: consider my delicate health. I cannot stand as much happiness as you can.

BARBARA. Yes: it is not easy work being in love with me, is it? But it's good for you. [*She runs to the shed, and calls, childlike*] Mamma! Mamma! [*Bilton comes out of the shed, followed by Undershaft*]. I want Mamma.

UNDERSHAFT. She is taking off her list slippers, dear. [*He passes on to Cusins*]. Well? What does she say?

CUSINS. She has gone right up into the skies.

LADY BRITOMART [*coming from the shed and stopping on the steps, obstructing Sarah, who follows with Lomax. Barbara clutches like a baby at her mother's skirt*]. Barbara: when will you learn to be independent and to act and think for yourself? I know as well as possible what that cry of "Mamma, Mamma," means. Always running to me!

SARAH [*touching Lady Britomart's ribs with her finger tips and imitating a bicycle horn*] Pip! Pip!

LADY BRITOMART [*highly indignant*] How dare you say Pip! pip! to me, Sarah? You are both very naughty children. What do you want, Barbara?

BARBARA. I want a house in the village to live in with Dolly. [*Dragging at the skirt*] Come and tell me which one to take.

UNDERSHAFT [*to Cusins*] Six o'clock tomorrow morning, my young friend.

THE INTERLUDE AT THE PLAYHOUSE

THE INTERLUDE AT THE PLAYHOUSE

This playlet was written to introduce Winifred Emery—actress and wife of the manager—at the gala opening of the Playhouse. It was not performed again.

Opening night. Brilliant first-night audience assembled. Conclusion of overture. In each - programme a slip has been distributed, stating that before the play begins the Manager will address a few words to the audience.

The float is turned up. Lights down in auditorium. Expectancy. Silence.

The act drop is swung back. Evidently somebody is coming forward to make a speech.

Enter before the curtain the Manager's wife, with one of the programme slips in her hand.

THE MANAGER'S WIFE. Ladies and gentlemen. [*She hesitates, overcome with nervousness; then plunges ahead*]. About this speech—you know—this little slip in your programmes—it says that Edwin—I mean Mr. Goldsmith—I am so frightfully nervous—I—[*she begins tearing up the slip carefully into very small pieces*] I have to get this finished before he comes up from his dressing-room, because he doesn't know what I'm doing. If he did — Well, what I want to say is —of course, I am saying it very badly because I never could speak in public, but the fact is, neither can Edwin. Excuse my calling him Edwin; I know I should speak of him as Mr. Goldsmith; but—but—perhaps I had better explain that we are married; and the force of habit is so strong—er—yes, isn't it? You see, it's like this. At least, what I wanted to say is—is—is —er—. A little applause would encourage me, perhaps, if you don't mind. Thank you. Of course, it's so ridiculous to be nervous like this, among friends, isn't it? But I have had such a dreadful week at home over this speech of Edwin's. He gets so angry with me when I tell him that he can't make speeches, and that nobody wants him to make one! I only wanted to encourage him; but he is so irritable when he has to build a theatre! Of course, you wouldn't think so, seeing him act; but you don't know what he is at home. Well, dear ladies and gentlemen, will you be very nice and kind to him when he is speaking, and if he is nervous, don't notice it? And please don't make any noise; the least sound upsets him and puts his speech out of his head. It is really a very good speech; he has not let me see the manuscript, and he thinks I know nothing about it; but I have heard him make it four times in his sleep. He does it very well when he is asleep—quite like an orator; but unfortunately he is awake now, and in a fearful state of nerves. I felt I must come out and ask you to be kind to him—after all, we are old friends, aren't we? [*Applause*] Oh, thank you, thank you; that is your promise to me to be kind to him. Now I will run away. Please don't tell him I dared to do this. [*Going*] And, please, please, not the least noise. If a hairpin drops, all is lost. [*Coming back to centre*] Oh, and Mr. Conductor, would you be so very good, when he comes to the pathetic-part, to give him a little slow music. Something affecting, you know.

CONDUCTOR. Certainly, Mrs. Goldsmith, certainly.

THE MANAGER'S WIFE. Thank you. You know, it is one of the great sorrows of his life that the managers will not give him an engagement in melodrama. Not that he likes melodrama; but he says that the slow music is such a support on the stage; and he needs all the support he can get tonight, poor fellow! The—

A CARPENTER [*from the side, putting his head round the edge of the curtain*] Tsst! ma'am, tsst!

THE MANAGER'S WIFE. Eh? What's the matter?

THE CARPENTER. The governor's dressed and coming up, ma'am.

THE MANAGER'S WIFE. Oh! [*To the audience*] Not a word. [*She hurries off, with her finger on her lips*].

[*The warning for the band sounds. "Auld Lang Syne" is softly played. The curtain rises, and discovers a reading table, with an elaborate, triple-decked folding desk on it. A thick manuscript of unbound sheets is on the desk. A tumbler and decanter, with water, and two candles, shaded from the audience, are on the table. Right of table, a chair, in which the Manager's Wife is seated. Another chair, empty, left on table. At the desk stands the Manager, ghastly pale. Applause. When silence is restored, he makes two or three visible efforts to speak.*]

THE MANAGER'S WIFE [*aside*] Courage, dear.

THE MANAGER [*smiling with effort*] Oh, quite so, quite so. Don't be frightened, dearest. I am quite self-possessed. It would be very silly for me to—er—there is no occasion for nervousness—I—er—quite accustomed to public life—er—ahem! [*He opens the manuscript, raises his head, and takes breath*]. Er— [*He flattens the manuscript out with his hand, affecting the ease and large gesture of an orator. The desk collapses with an appalling clatter. He collapses, shaking with nervousness, into the chair.*]

THE MANAGER'S WIFE [*running to him solicitously*] Never mind, dear; it was only the desk. Come, come now.

You're better now, aren't you? The audience is waiting.

THE MANAGER. I thought it was the station.

THE MANAGER'S WIFE. There's no station there now, dear; it's quite safe. [*Replacing the MS. on the desk*]

There! That's right. [*She sits down and composes herself to listen*].

THE MANAGER [*beginning his speech*] Dear friends—I wish I could call you ladies and gentlemen—

THE MANAGER'S WIFE. Hm! Hm! Hm!

THE MANAGER. What's the matter?

THE MANAGER'S WIFE [*prompting him*] Ladies and gentlemen, I wish I could call you dear friends.

THE MANAGER. Well, what did I say?

THE MANAGER'S WIFE. You said it the other way about. No matter. Go on. They will understand.

THE MANAGER. Well, what difference does it make? [*Testily*] How am I to make a speech if I am to be interrupted in this way? [*To the audience*] Excuse my poor wife, ladies and gentlemen. She is naturally a little nervous to-night. You will overlook a woman's weakness. [*To his wife*] *Compose yourself, my dear. Ahem!* [*He returns to the MS.*]. *The piece of land on which our theatre is built is mentioned in Domesday Book; and you will be glad to hear that I have succeeded in tracing its history almost year by year for the 800 years that have elapsed since that book—perhaps the most interesting of all English books —was written. That history I now propose to impart to you. Angelina, I really cannot make a speech if you look at your watch. If you think I am going on too long, say so.*

THE MANAGER'S WIFE. Not at all, dear. But our friends may not be so fond of history as you are.

THE MANAGER. Why not? I am surprised at you, Angelina. Do you suppose that this is an ordinary frivolous audience of mere playgoers? You are behind the times. Look at our friend Tree, making a fortune out of Roman history! Look at the Court Theatre: they listen to this sort of thing for three hours at a stretch there. Look at the Royal Institution, the Statistical Society, the House of Commons! Are we less scholarly, less cultured, less serious than the audiences there? I say nothing of my own humble powers; but am I less entertaining than an average

Cabinet Minister? You show great ignorance of the times we live in, Angelina; and if my speech bores you, that only shows that you are not in the movement. I am determined that this theatre shall be in the movement.

THE MANAGER'S WIFE. Well, all I can tell you is that if you don't get a little more movement into your speech, there won't be time for Pickles.

THE MANAGER. That does not matter. We can omit Pickles if necessary. I have played Pickles before. If you suppose I am burning to play Pickles again you are very much mistaken. If the true nature of my talent were understood I should be playing Hamlet. Ask the audience whether they would not like to see me play Hamlet. [*Enthusiastic assent*]. There! You ask me why I don't play Hamlet instead of Pickles.

THE MANAGER'S WIFE. I never asked you anything of the kind.

THE MANAGER. Please don't contradict me, Angelina—it least not in public. I say you ask me why I don't play

Hamlet instead of Pickles. Well, the reason is that anybody can play Hamlet, but it takes me to play Pickles. I leave Hamlet to those who can provide no livelier form of entertainment. [*Resolutely returning to the MS.*] I am now going back to the year eleven hundred.

THE STAGE MANAGER [*coming on in desperation*] No, sir, you can't go back all that way; you promised me you would be done in ten minutes. I've got to set for the first Act.

THE MANAGER. Well, is it my fault? My wife won't let me speak. I have not been able to get in a word edgeways. [*Coaxing*] Come, there's a dear, good chap; just let me have another twenty minutes or so. The audience wants to hear my speech. You wouldn't disappoint them, would you?

THE STAGE MANAGER [*going*] Well, it's as you please, sir; not as I please. Only don't blame me if the audience loses its last train and comes back to sleep in the theatre, that's all. [*He goes off with the air of a man who is prepared for the worst*].

[*During the conversation with the Stage Manager, the Manager's Wife, unobserved by her husband, steals the manuscript; replaces the last two leaves of it on the desk; puts the rest on her chair, and sits down on it.*]

THE MANAGER. That man is hopelessly frivolous; I really must get a more cultured staff. [*To the audience*]

Ladies and gentlemen, I'm extremely sorry for these unfortunate interruptions and delays; you can see that they are not my fault. [*Returning to the desk*] Ahem! Er—hallo! I am getting along faster than I thought. I shall not keep you much longer now. [*Resuming his oration*] Ladies and gentlemen, I have dealt with our little play-house in its historical aspect. I have dealt with it in its political aspect, in its financial aspect, in its artistic aspect, in its social aspect, in its County Council aspect, in its biological and psychological aspects. You have listened to me with patience and sympathy. You have followed my arguments with intelligence, and accepted my conclusions with indulgence. I have explained to you why I have given our new theatre its pleasant old name; why I selected "Pickles" as the opening piece. I have told you of our future plans, of the engagements we have made, the pieces we intend to produce, the policy we are resolved to pursue. [*With graver emphasis*] There remains only one word more. [*With pathos*] If that word has a personal note in it you will forgive me. [*With deeper pathos*] If the note is a deeper and tenderer one than I usually venture to sound on the stage, I hope you will not think it out of what I believe is called my line. [*With emotion*] Ladies and gentlemen, it is now more than twenty years since I and my dear wife—[*Violins tremolando; flute solo, "Auld Lang Syne"*] What's that noise? Stop. What do you mean by this?

[*The band is silent.*]

THE MANAGER'S WIFE. They are only supporting you, Edwin. Nothing could be more appropriate.

THE MANAGER. Supporting me! They have emptied my soul of all its welling pathos. I never heard anything so ridiculous. Just as I was going to pile it on about you, too.

THE MANAGER'S WIFE. Go on, dear. The audience was just getting interested.

THE MANAGER. So was I. And then the band starts on me. Is this Drury Lane or is it the Playhouse? Now, I haven't the heart to go on.

THE MANAGER'S WIFE. Oh, please do. You were getting on so nicely.

THE MANAGER. Of course I was. I had just got everybody into a thoroughly serious frame of mind, and then the silly band sets everybody laughing—just like the latest fashion in tragedy. All my trouble gone for nothing. There's nothing left of my speech now; it might as well have been the Education Bill.

MANAGER'S WIFE. But you must finish it, dear.

THE MANAGER. I won't. Finish it yourself. [*Exit in high dudgeon.*]

THE MANAGER'S WIFE [*rising and coming center*] Ladies and Gentlemen. Perhaps I had better finish it. You see, what my husband and I have been trying to do is a very difficult thing. We have some friends here-some old valued friends-some young ones too, we hope, but we also have for the first time in this house of ours the great public. We dare not call ourselves the friends of the public. We are only its servants; and. like all servants, we are very much afraid of seeming disrespectful if we allow ourselves to be too familiar; and we are most at our ease when we are doing our work. We rather dread occasions like these when we are allowed, and even expected, to step out of our place, and speak in our own persons of our own affairs—even for a moment perhaps, very discreetly, of our own feelings. Well, what can we do? We recite a little verse; we make a little speech; we are shy, in the end we put ourselves out of countenance, put you out of countenance, and strain your attitude of kindness and welcome until it becomes an attitude of wishing that it was all over Well we resolved not to do that to-night if we could help it. After all. you know how glad we are to see you, for you have the advantage of us, you can do without us: we cannot do without you. I will not say that

''The drama's laws the drama's patrons give,''

''And we who live to please must please to live.''

because that is not true; and it never has been true. The drama's slaws have a higher source than your caprice or ours. and in in this playhouse of ours we will not please you except on terms honourable to ourselves and to you. But on those terms we hope that you may spend many pleasant hours here, and we as many hard-working ones, as at our old home in the Haymarket. And now may I run away and tell Edwin that his speech has been a great success after all, and that you are quite ready for Pickles?

[*Assent and applause*]. *Thank you.* [*Exit*]

End

THE ADMIRABLE BASHVILLE

OR, CONSTANCY UNREWARDED

BEING THE NOVEL OF CASHEL BYRON'S PROFESSION DONE INTO A STAGE PLAY IN THREE ACTS, AND IN BLANK VERSE, WITH A NOTE ON MODERN PRIZE FIGHTING

"Over Bashville the footman I howled with derision and delight. I dote on Bashville: I could read of him for ever: *de Bashville je suis le fervent*: there is only one Bashville; and I am his devoted slave: Bashville est magnifique; mais il n'est guère possible."
Robert Louis Stevenson.

PREFACE

The Admirable Bashville is a product of the British law of copyright. As that law stands at present, the first person who patches up a stage version of a novel, however worthless and absurd that version may be, and has it read by himself and a few confederates to another confederate who has paid for admission in a hall licensed for theatrical perfor-performances, secures the stage rights of that novel, even as against the author himself; and the author must buy him out before he can touch his own work for the purposes of the stage.

A famous case in point is the drama of East Lynne, adapted from the late Mrs. Henry Wood's novel of that name. It was enormously popular, and is still the surest refuge of touring companies in distress. Many authors feel that Mrs. Henry Wood was hardly used in not getting any of the money which was plentifully made in this way through her story. To my mind, since her literary copyright probably brought her a fair wage for the work of writing the book, her real grievance was, first, that her name and credit were attached to a play with which she had nothing to do, and which may quite possibly have been to her a detestable travesty and profanation of her story; and second, that the authors of that play had the legal power to prevent her from having any version of her own performed, if she had wished to make one.

There is only one way in which the author can protect himself; and that is by making a version of his own and going through the same legal farce with it. But the legal farce involves the hire of a hall and the payment of a fee of two guineas to the King's Reader of Plays. When I wrote Cashel Byron's Profession I had no guineas to spare, a common disability of young authors. What is equally common, I did not know the law. A reasonable man may guess a reasonable law, but no man can guess a foolish anomaly. Fortunately, by the time my book so suddenly revived in America I was aware of the danger, and in a position to protect myself by writing and performing The Admirable Bashville. The prudence of doing so was soon demonstrated; for rumors soon reached me of several American stage versions; and one of these has actually been played in New York, with the boxing scenes under the management (so it is stated) of the eminent pugilist Mr. James J. Corbett. The New York press, in a somewhat derisive vein, conveyed the impression that in this version Cashel Byron sought to interest the public rather as the last of the noble race of the Byrons of Dorsetshire than as his unromantic self; but in justice to a play which I never read, and an actor whom I never saw, and who honorably offered to treat me as if I had legal rights in the matter, I must not accept the newspaper evidence as conclusive.

As I write these words, I am promised by the King in his speech to Parliament a new Copyright Bill. I believe it embodies, in our British fashion, the recommendations of the book publishers as to the concerns of the authors, and the notions of the musical publishers as to the concerns of the playwrights. As author and playwright I am duly obliged to the Commission for saving me the trouble of speaking for myself, and to the witnesses for speaking for me. But unless Parliament takes the opportunity of giving the authors of all printed works of fiction, whether dramatic or narrative, both playwright and copyright (as in America), such to be independent of any insertions or omissions of formulas about "all rights reserved" or the like, I am afraid the new Copyright Bill will leave me with exactly the opinion both of the copyright law and the wisdom of Parliament I at present entertain. As a good Socialist I do not at all object to the limitation of my right of property in my own works to a comparatively brief period, followed by complete Communism: in fact, I cannot see why the same salutary limitation should not be applied to all property rights whatsoever; but a system which enables any alert sharper to acquire property rights in my stories as against myself and the rest of the community would, it seems to me, justify a rebellion if authors were numerous and warlike enough to make one.

It may be asked why I have written The Admirable Bashville in blank verse. My answer is that I had but a week to write it in. Blank verse is so childishly easy and expeditious (hence, by the way, Shakespear's copious output), that by adopting it I was enabled to do within the week what would have cost me a month in prose.

Besides, I am fond of blank verse. Not nineteenth century blank verse, of course, nor indeed, with a very few exceptions, any post-Shakespearean blank verse. Nay, not Shakespearean blank verse itself later than the histories. When an author can write the prose dialogue of the first scene in As You Like It, or Hamlet's colloquies with Rosencrantz and Guildenstern, there is really no excuse for The Seven Ages and "To be or not to be," except the excuse of a haste that made great facility indispensable. I am quite sure that any one who is to recover the charm of blank verse must frankly go back to its beginnings and start a literary pre-Raphaelite Brotherhood. I like the melodious sing-song, the clear simple one-line and two-line sayings, and the occasional rhymed tags, like the half closes in an eighteenth century symphony, in Peele, Kyd, Greene, and the histories of Shakespear. How any one with music in him can turn from Henry VI., John, and the two Richards to such a mess of verse half developed into rhetorical prose as Cymbeline, is to me explicable only by the uncivil hypothesis that the artistic qualities in the Elizabethan drama do not exist for most of its critics; so that they hang on to its purely prosaic content, and hypnotize themselves into absurd exaggerations of the value of that content. Even poets fall under the spell. Ben Jonson described Marlowe's line as "mighty"! As well put Michael Angelo's epitaph on the tombstone of Paolo Uccello. No wonder Jonson's blank verse is the most horribly disagreeable product in literature, and indicates his most prosaic mood as surely as his shorter rhymed measures indicate his poetic mood. Marlowe never wrote a mighty line in his life: Cowper's single phrase, "Toll for the brave," drowns all his mightinesses as Great Tom drowns a military band. But Marlowe took that very pleasant-sounding rigmarole of Peele and Greene, and added to its sunny daylight the insane splendors of night, and the cheap tragedy of crime. Because he had only a common sort of brain, he was hopelessly beaten by Shakespear; but he had a fine ear and a soaring spirit: in short, one does not forget "wanton Arethusa's azure arms" and the like. But the pleasant-sounding rigmarole was the basis of the whole thing; and as long as that rigmarole was practised frankly for the sake of its pleasantness, it was readable and speakable. It lasted until Shakespear did to it what Raphael did to Italian painting; that is, overcharged and burst it by making it the vehicle of a new order of thought, involving a mass of intellectual ferment and psychological research. The rigmarole could not stand the strain; and Shakespear's style ended in a chaos of half-shattered old forms, half-emancipated new ones, with occasional bursts of prose eloquence on the one hand, occasional delicious echoes of the rigmarole, mostly from Calibans and masque personages, on the other, with, alas! a great deal of filling up with formulary blank verse which had no purpose except to save the author's time and thought.

When a great man destroys an art form in this way, its ruins make palaces for the clever would-be great. After Michael Angelo and Raphael, Giulio Romano and the Carracci. After Marlowe and Shakespear, Chapman and the Police News poet Webster. Webster's specialty was blood: Chapman's, balderdash. Many of us by this time find it difficult to believe that pre-Ruskinite art criticism used to prostrate itself before the works of Domenichino and Guido, and to patronize the modest little beginnings of those who came between Cimabue and Masaccio. But we have only to look at our own current criticism of Elizabethan drama to satisfy ourselves that in an art which has not yet found its Ruskin or its pre-Raphaelite Brotherhood, the same folly is still academically propagated. It is possible, and even usual, for men professing to have ears and a sense of poetry to snub Peele and Greene and grovel before Fletcher and Webster—Fletcher! a facile blank verse penny-a-liner: Webster! a turgid paper cut-throat. The subject is one which I really cannot pursue without intemperance of language. The man who thinks The Duchess of Malfi better than David and Bethsabe is outside the pale, not merely of literature, but almost of humanity.

Yet some of the worst of these post-Shakespearean duffers, from Jonson to Heywood, suddenly became poets when they turned from the big drum of pseudo-Shakespearean drama to the pipe and tabor of the masque, exactly as Shakespear himself recovered the old charm of the rigmarole when he turned from Prospero to Ariel and Caliban. Cyril Tourneur and Heywood could certainly have produced very pretty rigmarole plays if they had begun where Shakespear began, instead of trying to begin where he left off. Jonson and Beaumont would very likely have done themselves credit on the same terms: Marston would have had at least a chance. Massinger was in his right place, such as it was; and one would not disturb the gentle Ford, who was never born to storm the footlights. Webster could have done no good anyhow or anywhere: the man was a fool. And Chapman would always have been a blathering unreadable pedant, like Landor, in spite of his classical amateurship and respectable strenuosity of character. But with these exceptions it may plausibly be held that if Marlowe and Shakespear could have been kept out of their way, the rest would have done well enough on the lines of Peele and Greene. However, they thought otherwise; and now that their freethinking paganism, so dazzling to the pupils of Paley and the converts of Wesley, offers itself in vain to the disciples of Darwin and Nietzsche, there is an end of them. And a good riddance, too.

Accordingly, I have poetasted The Admirable Bashville in the rigmarole style. And lest the Webster worshippers should declare that there is not a single correct line in all my three acts, I have stolen or paraphrased a few from Marlowe and Shakespear (not to mention Henry Carey); so that if any man dares quote me derisively, he shall do so in peril of inadvertently lighting on a purple patch from Hamlet or Faustus.

I have also endeavored in this little play to prove that I am not the heartless creature some of my critics take me for. I have strictly observed the established laws of stage popularity and probability. I have simplified the character of the heroine, and summed up her sweetness in the one sacred word: Love. I have given consistency to the heroism of Cashel. I have paid to Morality, in the final scene, the tribute of poetic justice. I have restored to Patriotism its usual place on the stage, and gracefully acknowledged The Throne as the fountain of social honor. I have paid particular attention to the construction of the play, which will be found equal in this respect to the best contemporary models.

And I trust the result will be found satisfactory.

ACT I

A glade in Wiltstoken Park

Enter LYDIA

LYDIA. YE LEAFY BREASTS AND WARM PROTECTING WINGS

Of mother trees that hatch our tender souls,
And from the well of Nature in our hearts
Thaw the intolerable inch of ice
That bears the weight of all the stamping world.
Hear ye me sing to solitude that I,
Lydia Carew, the owner of these lands,
Albeit most rich, most learned, and most wise,
Am yet most lonely. What are riches worth
When wisdom with them comes to show the purse bearer
That life remains unpurchasable? Learning
Learns but one lesson: doubt! To excel all
Is, to be lonely. Oh, ye busy birds,
Engrossed with real needs, ye shameless trees
With arms outspread in welcome of the sun,
Your minds, bent singly to enlarge your lives,
Have given you wings and raised your delicate heads
High heavens above us crawlers.

[*A rook sets up a great cawing; and the other birds chatter loudly as a gust of wind sets the branches swaying. She makes as though she would shew them her sleeves.*]

Lo, the leaves
That hide my drooping boughs! Mock me—poor maid!—
Deride with joyous comfortable chatter
These stolen feathers. Laugh at me, the clothed one.
Laugh at the mind fed on foul air and books.
Books! Art! And Culture! Oh, I shall go mad.
Give me a mate that never heard of these,
A sylvan god, tree born in heart and sap;
Or else, eternal maidhood be my hap.

[*Another gust of wind and bird-chatter. She sits on the mossy root of an oak and buries her face in her hands. CASHEL BYRON, in a white singlet and breeches, comes through the trees.*]

CASHEL. What's this? Whom have we here? A woman!

LYDIA [*looking up*]. Yes.

CASHEL. You have no business here. I have. Away!
Women distract me. Hence!

LYDIA. Bid you me hence?
I am upon mine own ground. Who are you?
I take you for a god, a sylvan god.
This place is mine: I share it with the birds,
The trees, the sylvan gods, the lovely company
Of haunted solitudes.

CASHEL. A sylvan god!
A goat-eared image! Do your statues speak?
Walk? heave the chest with breath? or like a feather
Lift you—like this? [*He sets her on her feet.*]

LYDIA [*panting*]. You take away my breath!
You're strong. Your hands off, please. Thank you. Farewell.

CASHEL. Before you go: when shall we meet again?

LYDIA. Why should we meet again?

CASHEL. Who knows? We *shall*.
That much I know by instinct. What's your name?

LYDIA. Lydia Carew.

CASHEL. Lydia's a pretty name.
Where do you live?

LYDIA. I' the castle.

CASHEL [*thunderstruck*]. Do not say
You are the lady of this great domain.

LYDIA. I am.

CASHEL. Accursed luck! I took you for
The daughter of some farmer. Well, your pardon.
I came too close: I looked too deep. Farewell.

LYDIA. I pardon that. Now tell me who you are.

CASHEL. Ask me not whence I come, nor what I am.
You are the lady of the castle. I
Have but this hard and blackened hand to live by.

LYDIA. I have felt its strength and envied you. Your name?
I have told you mine.

CASHEL. My name is Cashel Byron.

LYDIA. I never heard the name; and yet you utter it
As men announce a celebrated name.
Forgive my ignorance.

CASHEL. I bless it, Lydia.
I have forgot your other name.
LYDIA. Carew.
Cashel's a pretty name, too.
MELLISH [*calling through the wood*]. Coo-ee! Byron!
CASHEL. A thousand curses! Oh, I beg you, go.
This is a man you must not meet.
MELLISH [*further off*]. Coo-ee!
LYDIA. He's losing us. What does he in my woods?
CASHEL. He is a part of what I am. What that is
You must not know. It would end all between us.
And yet there's no dishonor in't: your lawyer,
Who let your lodge to me, will vouch me honest.
I am ashamed to tell you what I am—
At least, as yet. Some day, perhaps.
MELLISH [*nearer*]. Coo-ee!
LYDIA. His voice is nearer. Fare you well, my tenant.
When next your rent falls due, come to the castle.
Pay me in person. Sir: your most ent. [*She curtsies and goes.*]
CASHEL. Lives in this castle! Owns this park! A lady
Marry a prizefighter! Impossible.
And yet the prizefighter must marry her.
Enter Mellish
Ensanguined swine, whelped by a doggish dam,
Is this thy park, that thou, with voice obscene,
Fillst it with yodeled yells, and screamst my name
For all the world to know that Cashel Byron
Is training here for combat.
MELLISH. Swine you me?
I've caught you, have I? You have found a woman.
Let her shew here again, I'll set the dog on her.
I will. I say it. And my name's Bob Mellish.
CASHEL. Change thy initial and be truly hight
Hellish. As for thy dog, why dost thou keep one
And bark thyself? Begone.
MELLISH. I'll not begone.
You shall come back with me and do your duty—
Your duty to your backers, do you hear?
You have not punched the bag this blessed day.
CASHEL. The putrid bag engirdled by thy belt
Invites my fist.
MELLISH [*weeping*]. Ingrate! O wretched lot!
Who would a trainer be? O Mellish, Mellish,
Trainer of heroes, builder-up of brawn,
Vicarious victor, thou createst champions
That quickly turn thy tyrants. But beware:
Without me thou art nothing. Disobey me,
And all thy boasted strength shall fall from thee.
With flaccid muscles and with failing breath
Facing the fist of thy more faithful foe,
I'll see thee on the grass cursing the day
Thou didst forswear thy training.
CASHEL. Noisome quack
That canst not from thine own abhorrent visage
Take one carbuncle, thou contaminat'st
Even with thy presence my untainted blood
Preach abstinence to rascals like thyself
Rotten with surfeiting. Leave me in peace.
This grove is sacred: thou profanest it.
Hence! I have business that concerns thee not.
MELLISH. Ay, with your woman. You will lose your fight.
Have you forgot your duty to your backers?
Oh, what a sacred thing your duty is!
What makes a man but duty? Where were we
Without our duty? Think of Nelson's words:
England expects that every man——
CASHEL. Shall twaddle
About his duty. Mellish: at no hour
Can I regard thee wholly without loathing;
But when thou play'st the moralist, by Heaven,
My soul flies to my fist, my fist to thee;
And never did the Cyclops' hammer fall
On Mars's armor—but enough of that.
It does remind me of my mother.
MELLISH. Ah,
Byron, let it remind thee. Once I heard
An old song: it ran thus. [*He clears his throat.*] Ahem, Ahem!
[*Sings*]—They say there is no other
Can take the place of mother—
I am out o' voice: forgive me; but remember:
Thy mother—were that sainted woman here—
Would say, Obey thy trainer.
CASHEL. Now, by Heaven,
Some fate is pushing thee upon thy doom.
Canst thou not hear thy sands as they run out?
They thunder like an avalanche. Old man:
Two things I hate, my duty and my mother.
Why dost thou urge them both upon me now?
Presume not on thine age and on thy nastiness.
Vanish, and promptly.
MELLISH. Can I leave thee here
Thus thinly clad, exposed to vernal dews?
Come back with me, my son, unto our lodge.
CASHEL. Within this breast a fire is newly lit
Whose glow shall sun the dew away, whose radiance

Shall make the orb of night hang in the heavens
Unnoticed, like a glow-worm at high noon.

MELLISH. Ah me, ah me, where wilt thou spend the night?

CASHEL. Wiltstoken's windows wandering beneath,
Wiltstoken's holy bell hearkening,
Wiltstoken's lady loving breathlessly.

MELLISH. The lady of the castle! Thou art mad.

CASHEL. 'Tis thou art mad to trifle in my path.
Thwart me no more. Begone.

MELLISH. My boy, my son,
I'd give my heart's blood for thy happiness.
Thwart thee, my son! Ah, no. I'll go with thee.
I'll brave the dews. I'll sacrifice my sleep.
I am old—no matter: ne'er shall it be said
Mellish deserted thee.

CASHEL. You resolute gods
That will not spare this man, upon your knees
Take the disparity twixt his age and mine.
Now from the ring to the high judgment seat
I step at your behest. Bear you me witness
This is not Victory, but Execution.

[*He solemnly projects his fist with colossal force against the waistcoat of Mellish who doubles up like a folded towel, and lies without sense or motion.*]

And now the night is beautiful again.

[*The castle clock strikes the hour in the distance.*]

Hark! Hark! Hark! Hark! Hark! Hark! Hark! Hark! Hark! Hark!
It strikes in poetry. 'Tis ten o'clock.
Lydia: to thee!

[*He steals off towards the castle. Mellish stirs and groans.*]

ACT II

Scene I

London. A room in Lydia's house

Enter Lydia and Lucian

LYDIA. Welcome, dear cousin, to my London house.
Of late you have been chary of your visits.

LUCIAN. I have been greatly occupied of late.
The minister to whom I act as scribe
In Downing Street was born in Birmingham,
And, like a thoroughbred commercial statesman,
Splits his infinities, which I, poor slave,
Must reunite, though all the time my heart
Yearns for my gentle coz's company.

LYDIA. Lucian: there is some other reason. Think!
Since England was a nation every mood
Her scribes have prepositionally split;
But thine avoidance dates from yestermonth.

LUCIAN. There is a man I like not haunts this house.

LYDIA. Thou speak'st of Cashel Byron?

LUCIAN. Aye, of him.
Hast thou forgotten that eventful night
When as we gathered were at Hoskyn House
To hear a lecture by Herr Abendgasse,
He placed a single finger on my chest,
And I, ensorceled, would have sunk supine
Had not a chair received my falling form.

LYDIA. Pooh! That was but by way of illustration.

LUCIAN. What right had he to illustrate his point
Upon my person? Was I his assistant
That he should try experiments on me
As Simpson did on his with chloroform?
Now, by the cannon balls of Galileo
He hath unmanned me: all my nerve is gone.
This very morning my official chief,
Tapping with friendly forefinger this button,
Levelled me like a thunderstricken elm
Flat upon the Colonial Office floor.

LYDIA. Fancies, coz.

LUCIAN. Fancies! Fits! the chief said fits!
Delirium tremens! the chlorotic dance
Of Vitus! What could any one have thought?
Your ruffian friend hath ruined me. By Heaven,
I tremble at a thumbnail. Give me drink.

LYDIA. What ho, without there! Bashville.

BASHVILLE [*without*]. Coming, madam.

Enter Bashville

LYDIA. My cousin ails, Bashville. Procure some wet. [*Exit Bashville.*]

LUCIAN. Some wet!!! Where learnt you that atrocious word?
This is the language of a flower-girl.

LYDIA. True. It is horrible. Said I "Some wet"?
I meant, some drink. Why did I say "Some wet"?
Am I ensorceled too? "Some wet"! Fie! fie!
I feel as though some hateful thing had stained me.
Oh, Lucian, how could I have said "Some wet"?

LUCIAN. The horrid conversation of this man
Hath numbed thy once unfailing sense of fitness.

LYDIA. Nay, he speaks very well: he's literate:
Shakespear he quotes unconsciously.
LUCIAN. And yet
Anon he talks pure pothouse.
Enter Bashville
BASHVILLE. Sir: your potion.
LUCIAN. Thanks. [*He drinks.*] I am better.
A NEWSBOY [*calling without*]. Extra special *Star*!
Result of the great fight! Name of the winner!
LYDIA. Who calls so loud?
BASHVILLE. The papers, madam.
LYDIA. Why?
Hath ought momentous happened?
BASHVILLE. Madam: yes. [*He produces a newspaper.*]
All England for these thrilling paragraphs
A week has waited breathless.
LYDIA. Read them us.
BASHVILLE [*reading*]. "At noon to-day, unknown to the police,
Within a thousand miles of Wormwood Scrubbs,
Th' Australian Champion and his challenger,
The Flying Dutchman, formerly engaged
I' the mercantile marine, fought to a finish.
Lord Worthington, the well-known sporting peer
Acted as referee."
LYDIA. Lord Worthington!
BASHVILLE. "The bold Ned Skene revisited the ropes
To hold the bottle for his quondam novice;
Whilst in the seaman's corner were assembled
Professor Palmer and the Chelsea Snob.
Mellish, whose epigastrium has been hurt,
'Tis said, by accident at Wiltstoken,
Looked none the worse in the Australian's corner.
The Flying Dutchman wore the Union Jack:
His colors freely sold amid the crowd;
But Cashel's well-known spot of white on blue——"
LYDIA. *Whose*, did you say?
BASHVILLE. Cashel's, my lady.
LYDIA. Lucian:
Your hand—a chair—
BASHVILLE. Madam: you're ill.
LYDIA. Proceed.
What you have read I do not understand;
Yet I will hear it through. Proceed.
LUCIAN. Proceed.
BASHVILLE. "But Cashel's well-known spot of white on blue
Was fairly rushed for. Time was called at twelve,
When, with a smile of confidence upon
His ocean-beaten mug——"
LYDIA. His mug?
LUCIAN [*explaining*]. His face.
BASHVILLE [*continuing*]. "The Dutchman came undaunted to the scratch,
But found the champion there already. Both
Most heartily shook hands, amid the cheers
Of their encouraged backers. Two to one
Was offered on the Melbourne nonpareil;
And soon, so fit the Flying Dutchman seemed,
Found takers everywhere. No time was lost
In getting to the business of the day.
The Dutchman led at once, and seemed to land
On Byron's dicebox; but the seaman's reach,
Too short for execution at long shots,
Did not get fairly home upon the ivory;
And Byron had the best of the exchange."
LYDIA. I do not understand. What were they doing?
LUCIAN. Fighting with naked fists.
LYDIA. Oh, horrible!
I'll hear no more. Or stay: how did it end?
Was Cashel hurt?
LUCIAN [*to Bashville*]. Skip to the final round.
BASHVILLE. "Round Three: the rumors that had gone about
Of a breakdown in Byron's recent training
Seemed quite confirmed. Upon the call of time
He rose, and, looking anything but cheerful,
Proclaimed with every breath Bellows to Mend.
At this point six to one was freely offered
Upon the Dutchman; and Lord Worthington
Plunged at this figure till he stood to lose
A fortune should the Dutchman, as seemed certain,
Take down the number of the Panley boy.
The Dutchman, glutton as we know he is,
Seemed this time likely to go hungry. Cashel
Was clearly groggy as he slipped the sailor,
Who, not to be denied, followed him up,
Forcing the fighting mid tremendous cheers."
LYDIA. Oh stop—no more—or tell the worst at once.
I'll be revenged. Bashville: call the police.
This brutal sailor shall be made to know
There's law in England.
LUCIAN. Do not interrupt him:
Mine ears are thirsting. Finish, man. What next?
BASHVILLE. "Forty to one, the Dutchman's friends exclaimed.

Done, said Lord Worthington, who shewed himself
A sportsman every inch. Barely the bet
Was booked, when, at the reeling champion's jaw
The sailor, bent on winning out of hand,
Sent in his right. The issue seemed a cert,
When Cashel, ducking smartly to his left,
Cross-countered like a hundredweight of brick——"
LUCIAN. Death and damnation!
LYDIA. Oh, what does it mean?
BASHVILLE. "The Dutchman went to grass, a beaten man."
LYDIA. Hurrah! Hurrah! Hurrah! Oh, well done, Cashel!
BASHVILLE. "A scene of indescribable excitement
Ensued; for it was now quite evident
That Byron's grogginess had all along
Been feigned to make the market for his backers.
We trust this sample of colonial smartness
Will not find imitators on this side.
The losers settled up like gentlemen;
But many felt that Byron shewed bad taste
In taking old Ned Skene upon his back,
And, with Bob Mellish tucked beneath his oxter,
Sprinting a hundred yards to show the crowd
The perfect pink of his condition"—[*a knock*].
LYDIA [*turning pale*]. Bashville
Didst hear? A knock.
BASHVILLE. Madam: 'tis Byron's knock.
Shall I admit him?
LUCIAN. Reeking from the ring!
Oh, monstrous! Say you're out.
LYDIA. Send him away.
I will not see the wretch. How dare he keep
Secrets from ME? I'll punish him. Pray say
I'm not at home. [*Bashville turns to go.*] Yet stay. I am afraid
He will not come again.
LUCIAN. A consummation
Devoutly to be wished by any lady.
Pray, do you *wish* this man to come again?
LYDIA. No, Lucian. He hath used me very ill.
He should have told me. I will ne'er forgive him.
Say, Not at home.
BASHVILLE. Yes, madam. [*Exit.*]
LYDIA. Stay—
LUCIAN [*stopping her*]. No, Lydia:
You shall not countermand that proper order.
Oh, would you cast the treasure of your mind,
The thousands at your bank, and, above all,
Your unassailable social position
Before this soulless mass of beef and brawn?
LYDIA. Nay, coz: you're prejudiced.
CASHEL [*without*]. Liar and slave!
LYDIA. What words were those?
LUCIAN. The man is drunk with slaughter.

Enter Bashville *running: he shuts the door and locks it.*

BASHVILLE. Save yourselves: at the staircase foot the champion
Sprawls on the mat, by trick of wrestler tripped;
But when he rises, woe betide us all!
LYDIA. Who bade you treat my visitor with violence?
BASHVILLE. He would not take my answer; thrust the door
Back in my face; gave me the lie i' the throat;
Averred he felt your presence in his bones.
I said he should feel mine there too, and felled him;
Then fled to bar your door.
LYDIA. O lover's instinct!
He felt my presence. Well, let him come in.
We must not fail in courage with a fighter.
Unlock the door.
LUCIAN. Stop. Like all women, Lydia,
You have the courage of immunity.
To strike *you* were against his code of honor;
But *me*, above the belt, he may perform on
T' th' height of his profession. Also Bashville.
BASHVILLE. Think not of me, sir. Let him do his worst.
Oh, if the valor of my heart could weigh
The fatal difference twixt his weight and mine,
A second battle should he do this day:
Nay, though outmatched I be, let but my mistress
Give me the word: instant I'll take him on
Here—now—at catchweight. Better bite the carpet
A man, than fly, a coward.
LUCIAN. Bravely said:
I will assist you with the poker.
LYDIA. No:
I will not have him touched. Open the door.
BASHVILLE. Destruction knocks thereat. I smile, and open.

[*Bashville opens the door. Dead silence. Cashel enters, in tears. A solemn pause.*]

CASHEL. You know my secret?
LYDIA. Yes.
CASHEL. And thereupon

You bade your servant fling me from your door.
LYDIA. I bade my servant say I was not here.
CASHEL [*to Bashville*]. Why didst thou better thy instruction, man?
Hadst thou but said, "She bade me tell thee this,"
Thoudst burst my heart. I thank thee for thy mercy.
LYDIA. Oh, Lucian, didst thou call him "drunk with slaughter"?
Canst thou refrain from weeping at his woe?
CASHEL [*to LUCIAN*]. The unwritten law that shields the amateur
Against professional resentment, saves thee.
O coward, to traduce behind their backs
Defenceless prizefighters!
LUCIAN. Thou dost avow
Thou art a prizefighter.
CASHEL. It was my glory.
I had hoped to offer to my lady there
My belts, my championships, my heaped-up stakes,
My undefeated record; but I knew
Behind their blaze a hateful secret lurked.
LYDIA. Another secret?
LUCIAN. Is there worse to come?
CASHEL. Know ye not then my mother is an actress?
LUCIAN. How horrible!
LYDIA. Nay, nay: how interesting!
CASHEL. A thousand victories cannot wipe out
That birthstain. Oh, my speech bewrayeth it:
My earliest lesson was the player's speech
In Hamlet; and to this day I express myself
More like a mobled queen than like a man
Of flesh and blood. Well may your cousin sneer!
What's Hecuba to him or he to Hecuba?
LUCIAN. Injurious upstart: if by Hecuba
Thou pointest darkly at my lovely cousin,
Know that she is to me, and I to her,
What never canst thou be. I do defy thee;
And maugre all the odds thy skill doth give,
Outside I will await thee.
LYDIA. I forbid
Expressly any such duello. Bashville:
The door. Put Mr. Webber in a hansom,
And bid the driver hie to Downing Street.
No answer: 'tis my will. [*Exeunt Lucian and Bashville.*]
And now, farewell.
You must not come again, unless indeed
You can some day look in my eyes and say:
Lydia: my occupation's gone.
CASHEL. Ah, no:
It would remind you of my wretched mother.
O God, let me be natural a moment!
What other occupation can I try?
What would you have me be?
LYDIA. A gentleman.
CASHEL. A gentleman! I, Cashel Byron, stoop
To be the thing that bets on me! the fool
I flatter at so many coins a lesson!
The screaming creature who beside the ring
Gambles with basest wretches for my blood,
And pays with money that he never earned!
Let me die broken-hearted rather!
LYDIA. But
You need not be an idle gentleman.
I call you one of Nature's gentlemen.
CASHEL. That's the collection for the loser, Lydia.
I am not wont to need it. When your friends
Contest elections, and at foot o' th' poll
Rue their presumption, 'tis their wont to claim
A moral victory. In a sort they are
Nature's M.P.s. I am not yet so threadbare
As to accept these consolation stakes.
LYDIA. You are offended with me.
CASHEL. Yes, I am.
I can put up with much; but—"Nature's gentleman"!
I thank your ladyship of Lyons, but
Must beg to be excused.
LYDIA. But surely, surely,
To be a prizefighter, and maul poor mariners
With naked knuckles, is no work for you.
CASHEL. Thou dost arraign the inattentive Fates
That weave my thread of life in ruder patterns
Than these that lie, antimacassarly,
Asprent thy drawingroom. As well demand
Why I at birth chose to begin my life
A speechless babe, hairless, incontinent,
Hobbling upon all fours, a nurse's nuisance?
Or why I do propose to lose my strength,
To blanch my hair, to let the gums recede
Far up my yellowing teeth, and finally
Lie down and moulder in a rotten grave?
Only one thing more foolish could have been,
And that was to be born, not man, but woman.
This was thy folly, why rebuk'st thou mine?
LYDIA. These are not things of choice.
CASHEL. And did I choose
My quick divining eye, my lightning hand,
My springing muscle and untiring heart?
Did I implant the instinct in the race

That found a use for these, and said to me,
Fight for us, and be fame and fortune thine?
LYDIA. But there are other callings in the world.
CASHEL. Go tell thy painters to turn stockbrokers,
Thy poet friends to stoop o'er merchants' desks
And pen prose records of the gains of greed.
Tell bishops that religion is outworn,
And that the Pampa to the horsebreaker
Opes new careers. Bid the professor quit
His fraudulent pedantries, and do i' the world
The thing he would teach others. Then return
To me and say: Cashel: they have obeyed;
And on that pyre of sacrifice I, too,
Will throw my championship.
LYDIA. But 'tis so cruel.
CASHEL. Is it so? I have hardly noticed that,
So cruel are all callings. Yet this hand,
That many a two days' bruise hath ruthless given,
Hath kept no dungeon locked for twenty years,
Hath slain no sentient creature for my sport.
I am too squeamish for your dainty world,
That cowers behind the gallows and the lash,
The world that robs the poor, and with their spoil
Does what its tradesmen tell it. Oh, your ladies!
Sealskinned and egret-feathered; all defiance
To Nature; cowering if one say to them
"What will the servants think?" Your gentlemen!
Your tailor-tyrannized visitors of whom
Flutter of wing and singing in the wood
Make chickenbutchers. And your medicine men!
Groping for cures in the tormented entrails
Of friendly dogs. Pray have you asked all these
To change their occupations? Find you mine
So grimly crueller? I cannot breathe
An air so petty and so poisonous.
LYDIA. But find you not their manners very nice?
CASHEL. To me, perfection. Oh, they condescend
With a rare grace. Your duke, who condescends
Almost to the whole world, might for a Man
Pass in the eyes of those who never saw
The duke capped with a prince. See then, ye gods,
The duke turn footman, and his eager dame
Sink the great lady in the obsequious housemaid!
Oh, at such moments I could wish the Court
Had but one breadbasket, that with my fist
I could make all its windy vanity
Gasp itself out on the gravel. Fare you well.
I did not choose my calling; but at least
I can refrain from being a gentleman.
LYDIA. You say farewell to me without a pang.
CASHEL. My calling hath apprenticed me to pangs.
This is a rib-bender; but I can bear it.
It is a lonely thing to be a champion.
LYDIA. It is a lonelier thing to be a woman.
CASHEL. Be lonely then. Shall it be said of thee
That for his brawn thou misalliance mad'st
Wi' the Prince of Ruffians? Never. Go thy ways;
Or, if thou hast nostalgia of the mud,
Wed some bedoggéd wretch that on the slot
Of gilded snobbery, ventre à terre,
Will hunt through life with eager nose on earth
And hang thee thick with diamonds. I am rich;
But all my gold was fought for with my hands.
LYDIA. What dost thou mean by rich?
CASHEL. There is a man,
Hight Paradise, vaunted unconquerable,
Hath dared to say he will be glad to hear from me.
I have replied that none can hear from me
Until a thousand solid pounds be staked.
His friends have confidently found the money.
Ere fall of leaf that money shall be mine;
And then I shall possess ten thousand pounds.
I had hoped to tempt thee with that monstrous sum.
LYDIA. Thou silly Cashel, 'tis but a week's income.
I did propose to give thee three times that
For pocket money when we two were wed.
CASHEL. Give me my hat. I have been fooling here.
Now, by the Hebrew lawgiver, I thought
That only in America such revenues
Were decent deemed. Enough. My dream is dreamed.
Your gold weighs like a mountain on my chest.
Farewell.
LYDIA. The golden mountain shall be thine
The day thou quit'st thy horrible profession.
CASHEL. Tempt me not, woman. It is honor calls.
Slave to the Ring I rest until the face
Of Paradise be changed.
Enter Bashville
BASHVILLE. Madam, your carriage,
Ordered by you at two. 'Tis now half-past.
CASHEL. Sdeath! is it half-past two? The king! the king!
LYDIA. The king! What mean you?
CASHEL. I must meet a monarch
This very afternoon at Islington.

LYDIA. At Islington! You must be mad.
CASHEL. A cab!
Go call a cab; and let a cab be called;
And let the man that calls it be thy footman.
LYDIA. You are not well. You shall not go alone.
My carriage waits. I must accompany you.
I go to find my hat. [*Exit.*]
CASHEL. Like Paracelsus,
Who went to find his soul. [*To Bashville.*] And now, young man,
How comes it that a fellow of your inches,
So deft a wrestler and so bold a spirit,
Can stoop to be a flunkey? Call on me
On your next evening out. I'll make a man of you.
Surely you are ambitious and aspire——
BASHVILLE. To be a butler and draw corks; wherefore,
By Heaven, I will draw yours.
[*He hits Cashel on the nose, and runs out.*]
Cashel [*thoughtfully putting the side of his forefinger to his nose, and studying the blood on it*].
Too quick for *me*!
There's money in this youth.
Re-enter Lydia, *hatted and gloved.*
LYDIA. O Heaven! you bleed.
CASHEL. Lend me a key or other frigid object,
That I may put it down my back, and staunch
The welling life stream.
LYDIA. [*giving him her keys*]. Oh, what *have* you done?
CASHEL. Flush on the boko napped your footman's left.
LYDIA. I do not understand.
CASHEL. True. Pardon me.
I have received a blow upon the nose
In sport from Bashville. Next, ablution; else
I shall be total gules. [*He hurries out.*]
LYDIA. How well he speaks!
There is a silver trumpet in his lips
That stirs me to the finger ends. His nose
Dropt lovely color: 'tis a perfect blood.
I would 'twere mingled with mine own!
Enter Bashville
What now?
BASHVILLE. Madam, the coachman can no longer wait:
The horses will take cold.
LYDIA. I do beseech him
A moment's grace. Oh, mockery of wealth!
The third class passenger unchidden rides
Whither and when he will: obsequious trams
Await him hourly: subterranean tubes
With tireless coursers whisk him through the town;
But we, the rich, are slaves to Houyhnhnms:
We wait upon their colds, and frowst all day
Indoors, if they but cough or spurn their hay.
BASHVILLE. Madam, an omnibus to Euston Road,
And thence t' th' Angel—
Enter Cashel
LYDIA. Let us haste, my love:
The coachman is impatient.
CASHEL. Did he guess
He stays for Cashel Byron, he'd outwait
Pompei's sentinel. Let us away.
This day of deeds, as yet but half begun,
Must ended be in merrie Islington. [*Exeunt Lydia and Cashel.*]
BASHVILLE. Gods! how she hangs on's arm! I am alone.
Now let me lift the cover from my soul.
O wasted humbleness! Deluded diffidence!
How often have I said, Lie down, poor footman:
She'll never stoop to thee, rear as thou wilt
Thy powder to the sky. And now, by Heaven,
She stoops below me; condescends upon
This hero of the pothouse, whose exploits,
Writ in my character from my last place,
Would damn me into ostlerdom. And yet
There's an eternal justice in it; for
By so much as the ne'er subdued Indian
Excels the servile negro, doth this ruffian
Precedence take of me. "Ich dien." Damnation!
I serve. My motto should have been, "I scalp."
And yet I do not bear the yoke for gold.
Because I love her I have blacked her boots;
Because I love her I have cleaned her knives,
Doing in this the office of a boy,
Whilst, like the celebrated maid that milks
And does the meanest chares, I've shared the passions
Of Cleopatra. It has been my pride
To give her place the greater altitude
By lowering mine, and of her dignity
To be so jealous that my cheek has flamed
Even at the thought of such a deep disgrace
As love for such a one as I would be
For such a one as she; and now! and now!
A prizefighter! O irony! O bathos!
To have made way for this! Oh, Bashville, Bashville:
Why hast thou thought so lowly of thyself,
So heavenly high of her? Let what will come,

My love must speak: 'twas my respect was dumb.

Scene II

The Agricultural Hall in Islington, crowded with spectators.

In the arena a throne, with a boxing ring before it. A balcony above on the right, occupied by persons of fashion: among others, Lydia and Lord Worthington.

Flourish. Enter Lucian and Cetewayo, with Chiefs in attendance.

CETEWAYO. Is this the Hall of Husbandmen?

LUCIAN. It is.

CETEWAYO. Are these anæmic dogs the English people?

LUCIAN. Mislike us not for our complexions,
The pallid liveries of the pall of smoke
Belched by the mighty chimneys of our factories,
And by the million patent kitchen ranges
Of happy English homes.

CETEWAYO. When first I came
I deemed those chimneys the fuliginous altars
Of some infernal god. I now perceive
The English dare not look upon the sky.
They are moles and owls: they call upon the soot
To cover them.

LUCIAN. You cannot understand
The greatness of this people, Cetewayo.
You are a savage, reasoning like a child.
Each pallid English face conceals a brain
Whose powers are proven in the works of Newton
And in the plays of the immortal Shakespear.
There is not one of all the thousands here
But, if you placed him naked in the desert,
Would presently construct a steam engine,
And lay a cable t' th' Antipodes.

CETEWAYO. Have I been brought a million miles by sea
To learn how men can lie! Know, Father Webber,
Men become civilized through twin diseases,
Terror and Greed to wit: these two conjoined
Become the grisly parents of Invention.
Why does the trembling white with frantic toil
Of hand and brain produce the magic gun
That slays a mile off, whilst the manly Zulu
Dares look his foe i' the face; fights foot to foot;
Lives in the present; drains the Here and Now;
Makes life a long reality, and death
A moment only! whilst your Englishman
Glares on his burning candle's winding-sheets,
Counting the steps of his approaching doom.
And in the murky corners ever sees
Two horrid shadows, Death and Poverty:
In the which anguish an unnatural edge
Comes on his frighted brain, which straight devises
Strange frauds by which to filch unearnéd gold,
Mad crafts by which to slay unfacéd foes,
Until at last his agonized desire
Makes possibility its slave. And then—
Horrible climax! All-undoing spite!—
Th' importunate clutching of the coward's hand
From wearied Nature Devastation's secrets
Doth wrest; when straight the brave black-livered man
Is blown explosively from off the globe;
And Death and Dread, with their white-livered slaves
O'er-run the earth, and through their chattering teeth
Stammer the words "Survival of the Fittest."
Enough of this: I came not here to talk.
Thou say'st thou hast two white-faced ones who dare
Fight without guns, and spearless, to the death.
Let them be brought.

LUCIAN. They fight not to the death,
But under strictest rules: as, for example,
Half of their persons shall not be attacked;
Nor shall they suffer blows when they fall down,
Nor stroke of foot at any time. And, further,
That frequent opportunities of rest
With succor and refreshment be secured them.

CETEWAYO. Ye gods, what cowards! Zululand, my Zululand:
Personified Pusillanimity
Hath ta'en thee from the bravest of the brave!

LUCIAN. Lo, the rude savage whose untutored mind
Cannot perceive self-evidence, and doubts
That Brave and English mean the self-same thing!

CETEWAYO. Well, well, produce these heroes. I surmise
They will be carried by their nurses, lest
Some barking dog or bumbling bee should scare them.

Cetewayo takes his state. Enter Paradise

LYDIA. What hateful wretch is this whose mighty thews
Presage destruction to his adversaries?

LORD WORTHINGTON. 'Tis Paradise.

LYDIA. He of whom Cashel spoke?
A dreadful thought ices my heart. Oh, why

Did Cashel leave us at the door?
Enter Cashel
LORD WORTHINGTON. Behold!
The champion comes.
LYDIA. Oh, I could kiss him now,
Here, before all the world. His boxing things
Render him most attractive. But I fear
Yon villain's fists may maul him.
WORTHINGTON. Have no fear.
Hark! the king speaks.
CETEWAYO. Ye sons of the white queen:
Tell me your names and deeds ere ye fall to.
PARADISE. Your royal highness, you beholds a bloke
What gets his living honest by his fists.
I may not have the polish of some toffs
As I could mention on; but up to now
No man has took my number down. I scale
Close on twelve stun; my age is twenty-three;
And at Bill Richardson's Blue Anchor pub
Am to be heard of any day by such
As likes the job. I don't know, governor,
As ennythink remains for me to say.
CETEWAYO. Six wives and thirty oxen shalt thou have
If on the sand thou leave thy foeman dead.
Methinks he looks scornfully on thee.
[*To Cashel*] Ha! dost thou not so?
CASHEL. Sir, I do beseech you
To name the bone, or limb, or special place
Where you would have me hit him with this fist.
CETEWAYO. Thou hast a noble brow; but much I fear
Thine adversary will disfigure it.
CASHEL. There's a divinity that shapes our ends
Rough hew them how we will. Give me the gloves.
THE MASTER OF THE REVELS. Paradise, a professor.
Cashel Byron,
Also professor. Time! [*They spar.*]
LYDIA. Eternity
It seems to me until this fight be done.
CASHEL. Dread monarch: this is called the upper cut,
And this a hook-hit of mine own invention.
The hollow region where I plant this blow
Is called the mark. My left, you will observe,
I chiefly use for long shots: with my right
Aiming beside the angle of the jaw
And landing with a certain delicate screw
I without violence knock my foeman out.
Mark how he falls forward upon his face!
The rules allow ten seconds to get up;
And as the man is still quite silly, I
Might safely finish him; but my respect
For your most gracious majesty's desire
To see some further triumphs of the science
Of self-defence postpones awhile his doom.
PARADISE. How can a bloke do hisself proper justice
With pillows on his fists?
[*He tears off his gloves and attacks Cashel with his bare knuckles.*]
THE CROWD. Unfair! The rules!
CETEWAYO. The joy of battle surges boiling up
And bids me join the mellay. Isandhlana
And Victory! [*He falls on the bystanders.*]
THE CHIEFS. Victory and Isandhlana!
[*They run amok. General panic and stampede. The ring is swept away.*]
LUCIAN. Forbear these most irregular proceedings.
Police! Police!
[*He engages Cetewayo his umbrella. The balcony comes down with a crash. Screams from its occupants. Indescribable confusion.*]
CASHEL [*dragging Lydia from the struggling heap*].
My love, my love, art hurt?
LYDIA. No, no; but save my sore o'ermatchéd cousin.
A POLICEMAN. Give us a lead, sir. Save the English flag.
Africa tramples on it.
CASHEL. Africa!
Not all the continents whose mighty shoulders
The dancing diamonds of the seas bedeck
Shall trample on the blue with spots of white.
Now, Lydia, mark thy lover. [*He charges the Zulus.*]
LYDIA. Hercules
Cannot withstand him. See: the king is down;
The tallest chief is up, heels over head,
Tossed corklike o'er my Cashel's sinewy back;
And his lieutenant all deflated gasps
For breath upon the sand. The others fly
In vain: his fist o'er magic distances
Like a chameleon's tongue shoots to its mark;
And the last African upon his knees
Sues piteously for quarter. [*Rushing into Cashel's arms.*] Oh, my hero:
Thou'st saved us all this day.

CASHEL. 'Twas all for thee.

CETEWAYO. [*trying to rise*]. Have I been struck by lightning?

LUCIAN. Sir , your conduct
Can only be described as most ungentlemanly.

POLICEMAN. One of the prone is white.

CASHEL. 'Tis Paradise.

POLICEMAN. He's choking: he has something in his mouth.

LYDIA [*to Cashel*]. Oh Heaven! there is blood upon your hip.
You're hurt.

CASHEL. The morsel in yon wretch's mouth
Was bitten out of me.

[*Sensation. Lydia screams and swoons in Cashel's arms.*]

ACT III

Wiltstoken. A room in the Warren Lodge
Lydia at her writing table

LYDIA. O Past and Present, how ye do conflict
As here I sit writing my father's life!
The autumn woodland woos me from without
With whispering of leaves and dainty airs
To leave this fruitless haunting of the past.
My father was a very learnéd man.
I sometimes think I shall oldmaided be
Ere I unlearn the things he taught to me.

Enter Policeman

POLICEMAN. Asking your ladyship to pardon me
For this intrusion, might I be so bold
As ask a question of your people here
Concerning the Queen's peace?

LYDIA. My people here
Are but a footman and a simple maid;
And both have craved a holiday to join
Some local festival. But, sir, your helmet
Proclaims the Metropolitan Police.

POLICEMAN. Madam, it does; and I may now inform you
That what you term a local festival
Is a most hideous outrage 'gainst the law,
Which we to quell from London have come down:
In short, a prizefight. My sole purpose here
Is to inquire whether your ladyship
Any bad characters this afternoon
Has noted in the neighborhood.

LYDIA. No, none, sir.
I had not let my maid go forth to-day
Thought I the roads unsafe.

POLICEMAN. Fear nothing, madam:
The force protects the fair. My mission here
Is to wreak ultion for the broken law.
I wish your ladyship good afternoon.

LYDIA. Good afternoon. [*Exit Policeman.*]
A prizefight! O my heart!
Cashel: hast thou deceived me? Can it be
Thou hast backslidden to the hateful calling
I asked thee to eschew?
O wretched maid,
Why didst thou flee from London to this place
To write thy father's life, whenas in town
Thou might'st have kept a guardian eye on him—
What's that? A flying footstep—

Enter Cashel

CASHEL. Sanctuary!
The law is on my track. What! Lydia here!

LYDIA. Ay: Lydia here. Hast thou done murder, then,
That in so horrible a guise thou comest?

CASHEL. Murder! I would I had. Yon cannibal
Hath forty thousand lives; and I have ta'en
But thousands thirty-nine. I tell thee, Lydia,
On the impenetrable sarcolobe
That holds his seedling brain these fists have pounded
By Shrewsb'ry clock an hour. This bruiséd grass
And cakéd mud adhering to my form
I have acquired in rolling on the sod
Clinched in his grip. This scanty reefer coat
For decency snatched up as fast I fled
When the police arrived, belongs to Mellish.
'Tis all too short; hence my display of rib
And forearm mother-naked. Be not wroth
Because I seem to wink at you: by Heaven,
'Twas Paradise that plugged me in the eye
Which I perforce keep closing. Pity me,
My training wasted and my blows unpaid,
Sans stakes, sans victory, sans everything
I had hoped to win. Oh, I could sit me down
And weep for bitterness.

LYDIA. Thou wretch, begone.

CASHEL. Begone!

LYDIA. I say begone. Oh, tiger's heart
Wrapped in a young man's hide, canst thou not live
In love with Nature and at peace with Man?

Must thou, although thy hands were never made
To blacken others' eyes, still batter at
The image of Divinity? I loathe thee.
Hence from my house and never see me more.

CASHEL. I go. The meanest lad on thy estate
Would not betray me thus. But 'tis no ter. [*He opens the door.*]
Ha! the police. I'm lost. [*He shuts the door again.*]
Now shalt thou see
My last fight fought. Exhausted as I am,
To capture me will cost the coppers dear.
Come one, come all!

LYDIA. Oh, hide thee, I implore:
I cannot see thee hunted down like this.
There is my room. Conceal thyself therein.
Quick, I command. [*He goes into the room.*]
With horror I foresee,
Lydia, that never lied, must lie for thee.

Enter Policeman, with Paradise and Mellish in custody, Bashville, constables, and others

POLICEMAN. Keep back your bruiséd prisoner lest he shock
This wellbred lady's nerves. Your pardon, ma'am;
But have you seen by chance the other one?
In this direction he was seen to run.

LYDIA. A man came here anon with bloody hands
And aspect that did turn my soul to snow.

POLICEMAN. 'Twas he. What said he?

LYDIA. Begged for sanctuary.
I bade the man begone.

POLICEMAN. Most properly.
Saw you which way he went?

LYDIA. I cannot tell.

PARADISE. He seen me coming; and he done a bunk.

POLICEMAN. Peace, there. Excuse his damaged features, lady:
He's Paradise; and this one's Byron's trainer,
Mellish.

MELLISH. Injurious copper, in thy teeth
I hurl the lie. I am no trainer, I.
My father, a respected missionary,
Apprenticed me at fourteen years of age
T' the poetry writing. To these woods I came
With Nature to commune. My revery
Was by a sound of blows rudely dispelled.
Mindful of what my sainted parent taught,
I rushed to play the peacemaker, when lo!
These minions of the law laid hands on me.

BASHVILLE. A lovely woman, with distracted cries,
In most resplendent fashionable frock,
Approaches like a wounded antelope.

Enter Adelaide Gisborne

ADELAIDE. Where is my Cashel? Hath he been arrested?

POLICEMAN. I would I had thy Cashel by the collar:
He hath escaped me.

ADELAIDE. Praises be for ever!

LYDIA. Why dost thou call the missing man thy Cashel?

ADELAIDE. He is mine only son.

ALL. Thy son!

ADELAIDE. My son.

LYDIA. I thought his mother hardly would have known him,
So crushed his countenance.

ADELAIDE. A ribald peer,
Lord Worthington by name, this morning came
With honeyed words beseeching me to mount
His four-in-hand, and to the country hie
To see some English sport. Being by nature
Frank as a child, I fell into the snare,
But took so long to dress that the design
Failed of its full effect; for not until
The final round we reached the horrid scene.
Be silent all; for now I do approach
My tragedy's catastrophe. Know, then,
That Heaven did bless me with an only son,
A boy devoted to his doting mother——

POLICEMAN. Hark! did you hear an oath from yonder room?

ADELAIDE. Respect a broken-hearted mother's grief,
And do not interrupt me in my scene.
Ten years ago my darling disappeared
(Ten dreary twelvemonths of continuous tears,
Tears that have left me prematurely aged;
For I am younger far than I appear).
Judge of my anguish when to-day I saw
Stripped to the waist, and fighting like a demon
With one who, whatsoe'er his humble virtues,
Was clearly not a gentleman, my son!

ALL. O strange event! O passing tearful tale!

ADELAIDE. I thank you from the bottom of my heart
For the reception you have given my woe;
And now I ask, where is my wretched son?
He must at once come home with me, and quit
A course of life that cannot be allowed.

Enter Cashel

CASHEL. Policeman: I do yield me to the law.

LYDIA. Oh, no.

ADELAIDE. My son!

CASHEL. My mother! Do not kiss me.
My visage is too sore.

POLICEMAN. The lady hid him.
This is a regular plant. You cannot be
Up to that sex. [*To Cashel*] You come along with me.

LYDIA. Fear not, my Cashel: I will bail thee out.

CASHEL. Never. I do embrace my doom with joy.
With Paradise in Pentonville or Portland
I shall feel safe: there are no mothers there.

ADELAIDE. Ungracious boy—

CASHEL. Constable: bear me hence.

MELLISH. Oh, let me sweetest reconcilement make
By calling to thy mind that moving song:—
[*Sings*] They say there is no other—

CASHEL. Forbear at once, or the next note of music
That falls upon thine ear shall clang in thunder
From the last trumpet.

ADELAIDE. A disgraceful threat
To level at this virtuous old man.

LYDIA. Oh, Cashel, if thou scorn'st thy mother thus,
How wilt thou treat thy wife?

CASHEL. There spake my fate:
I knew you would say that. Oh, mothers, mothers,
Would you but let your wretched sons alone
Life were worth living! Had I any choice
In this importunate relationship?
None. And until that high auspicious day
When the millennium on an orphaned world
Shall dawn, and man upon his fellow look,
Reckless of consanguinity, my mother
And I within the self-same hemisphere
Conjointly may not dwell.

ADELAIDE. Ungentlemanly!

CASHEL. I am no gentleman. I am a criminal,
Redhanded, baseborn—

ADELAIDE. Baseborn! Who dares say it?
Thou art the son and heir of Bingley Bumpkin
FitzAlgernon de Courcy Cashel Byron,
Sieur of Park Lane and Overlord of Dorset,
Who after three months' wedded happiness
Rashly fordid himself with prussic acid,
Leaving a tearstained note to testify
That having sweetly honeymooned with me,
He now could say, O Death, where is thy sting?

POLICEMAN. Sir: had I known your quality, this cop
I had averted; but it is too late.
The law's above us both.

Enter Lucian, *with an Order in Council*

LUCIAN. Not so, policeman
I bear a message from The Throne itself
Of fullest amnesty for Byron's past.
Nay, more: of Dorset deputy lieutenant
He is proclaimed. Further, it is decreed,
In memory of his glorious victory
Over our country's foes at Islington,
The flag of England shall for ever bear
On azure field twelve swanlike spots of white;
And by an exercise of feudal right
Too long disused in this anarchic age
Our sovereign doth confer on him the hand
Of Miss Carew, Wiltstoken's wealthy ess. [*General acclamation.*]

POLICEMAN. Was anything, sir, said about me?

LUCIAN. Thy faithful services are not forgot:
In future call thyself Inspector Smith. [*Renewed acclamation.*]

POLICEMAN. I thank you, sir. I thank you, gentlemen.

LUCIAN. My former opposition, valiant champion,
Was based on the supposed discrepancy
Betwixt your rank and Lydia's. Here's my hand.

BASHVILLE. And I do here unselfishly renounce
All my pretensions to my lady's favor. [*Sensation.*]

LYDIA. What, Bashville! didst thou love me?

BASHVILLE. Madam: yes.
'Tis said: now let me leave immediately.

LYDIA. In taking, Bashville, this most tasteful course
You are but acting as a gentleman
In the like case would act. I fully grant
Your perfect right to make a declaration
Which flatters me and honors your ambition.
Prior attachment bids me firmly say
That whilst my Cashel lives, and polyandry
Rests foreign to the British social scheme,
Your love is hopeless; still, your services,
Made zealous by disinterested passion,
Would greatly add to my domestic comfort;
And if——

CASHEL. Excuse me. I have other views.
I've noted in this man such aptitude
For art and exercise in his defence

That I prognosticate for him a future
More glorious than my past. Henceforth I dub him
The Admirable Bashville, Byron's Novice;
And to the utmost of my mended fortunes
Will back him 'gainst the world at ten stone six.
ALL. Hail, Byron's Novice, champion that shall be!
BASHVILLE. Must I renounce my lovely lady's service,
And mar the face of man?
CASHEL. 'Tis Fate's decree.
For know, rash youth, that in this star crost world
Fate drives us all to find our chiefest good
In what we can, and not in what we would.
POLICEMAN. A post-horn—hark!
CASHEL. What noise of wheels is this?
Lord Worthington drives upon the scene in his four-in-hand, and descends
ADELAIDE. Perfidious peer!
LORD WORTHINGTON. Sweet Adelaide——
ADELAIDE. Forbear,
Audacious one: my name is Mrs. Byron.
LORD WORTHINGTON. Oh, change that title for the sweeter one
Of Lady Worthington.
CASHEL. Unhappy man,
You know not what you do.
LYDIA. Nay, 'tis a match
Of most auspicious promise. Dear Lord Worthington,
You tear from us our mother-in-law—
CASHEL. Ha! true.
LYDIA.—but we will make the sacrifice. She blushes:
At least she very prettily produces
Blushing's effect.
ADELAIDE. My lord: I do accept you. [*They embrace. Rejoicings.*]
CASHEL [*aside*]. It wrings my heart to see my noble backer
Lay waste his future thus. The world's a chess-board,
And we the merest pawns in fist of Fate.
[*Aloud.*] And now, my friends, gentle and simple both,
Our scene draws to a close. In lawful course
As Dorset's deputy lieutenant I
Do pardon all concerned this afternoon
In the late gross and brutal exhibition
Of miscalled sport.
LYDIA [*throwing herself into his arms*]. Your boats
are burnt at last.
CASHEL. This is the face that burnt a thousand boats,
And ravished Cashel Byron from the ring.
But to conclude. Let William Paradise
Devote himself to science, and acquire,
By studying the player's speech in Hamlet,
A more refined address. You, Robert Mellish,
To the Blue Anchor hostelry attend him;
Assuage his hurts, and bid Bill Richardson
Limit his access to the fatal tap.
Now mount we on my backer's four-in-hand,
And to St. George's Church, whose portico
Hanover Square shuts off from Conduit Street,
Repair we all. Strike up the wedding march;
And, Mellish, let thy melodies trill forth
Broad o'er the wold as fast we bowl along.
Give me the post-horn. Loose the flowing rein;
And up to London drive with might and main. [*Exeunt.*]

NOTE ON MODERN PRIZEFIGHTING

In 1882, when this book was written, prize-fighting seemed to be dying out. Sparring matches with boxing gloves, under the Queensberry rules, kept pugilism faintly alive; but it was not popular, because the public, which cares only for the excitement of a strenuous fight, believed then that the boxing glove made sparring as harmless a contest of pure skill as a fencing match with buttoned foils. This delusion was supported by the limitation of the sparring match to boxing. In the prize-ring under the old rules a combatant might trip, hold, or throw his antagonist; so that each round finished either with a knockdown blow, which, except when it is really a liedown blow, is much commoner in fiction than it was in the ring, or with a visible body-to-body struggle ending in a fall. In a sparring match all that happens is that a man with a watch in his hand cries out "Time!" whereupon the two champions prosaically stop sparring and sit down for a minute's rest and refreshment. The unaccustomed and inexpert spectator in those days did not appreciate the severity of the exertion or the risk of getting hurt: he underrated them as ignorantly as he would have overrated the more dramatically obvious terrors of a prizefight. Consequently the interest in the annual sparrings for the Queensberry Championships was confined to the few amateurs who had some critical knowledge of the game of boxing, and to the survivors of the generation for which the fight between Sayers and Heenan had been described in The Times as solemnly as the University Boat Race. In short, pugilism was out of fashion because the police had suppressed the only form of it which fascinated the public by its undissembled pugnacity.

All that was needed to rehabilitate it was the discovery that the glove fight is a more trying and dangerous form of contest than the old knuckle fight. Nobody knew that then: everybody knows it, or ought to know it, now. And, accordingly, pugilism is more prosperous to-day than it has ever been before.

How far this result was foreseen by the author of the Queensberry Rules, which superseded those of the old prize-ring, will probably never be known. There is no doubt that they served their immediate turn admirably. That turn was, the keeping alive of boxing in the teeth of the law against prizefighting. Magistrates believed, as the public believed, that when men's knuckles were muffled in padded gloves; when they were forbidden to wrestle or hold one another; when the duration of a round was fixed by the clock, and the number of rounds limited to what seems (to those who have never tried) to be easily within the limits of ordinary endurance; and when the traditional interval for rest between the rounds was doubled, that then indeed violence must be checkmated, so that the worst the boxers could do was to "spar for points" before three gentlemanly members of the Stock Exchange, who would carefully note the said points on an examination paper at the ring side, awarding marks only for skill and elegance, and sternly discountenancing the claims of brute force. It may be that both the author of the rules and the "judges" who administered them in the earlier days really believed all this; for, as far as I know, the limit of an amateur pugilist's romantic credulity has never yet been reached and probably never will. But if so, their good intentions were upset by the operation of a single new rule. Thus.

In the old prize-ring a round had no fixed duration. It was terminated by the fall of one of the combatants (in practice usually both of them), and was followed by an interval of half a minute for recuperation. The practical effect of this was that a combatant could always get a respite of half a minute whenever he wanted it by pretending to be knocked down: "finding the earth the safest place," as the old phrase went. For this the Marquess of Queensberry substituted a rule that a round with the gloves should last a specified time, usually three or four minutes, and that a combatant who did not stand up to his opponent continuously during that time (ten seconds being allowed for rising in the event of a knock-down) lost the battle. That unobtrusively slipped-in ten seconds limit has produced the modern glove fight. Its practical effect is that a man dazed by a blow or a fall for, say, twelve seconds, which would not have mattered in an old-fashioned fight with its thirty seconds interval[1], has under the Queensberry rules either to lose or else stagger to his feet in a helpless condition and be eagerly battered into insensibility by his opponent before he can recover his powers of self-defence. The notion that such a battery cannot be inflicted with boxing gloves is only entertained by people who have never used them or seen them used. I may say that I have myself received, in an accident, a blow in the face, involving two macadamized holes in it, more violent than the most formidable pugilist could have given me with his bare knuckles. This blow did not stun or disable me even momentarily. On the other hand, I have seen a man knocked quite silly by a tap from the most luxurious sort of boxing glove made, wielded by a quite unathletic literary man sparring for the first time in his life. The human jaw, like the human elbow, is provided, as every boxer knows, with a "funny bone"; and the pugilist who is lucky enough to jar that funny bone with a blow practically has his

---

[1] In a treatise on boxing by Captain Edgeworth Johnstone, just published, I read, "In the days of the prize-ring, fights lasted for hours; and the knock-out blow was unknown." This statement is a little too sweeping. The blow was known well enough. A veteran prizefighter once described to me his first experience of its curious effect on the senses. Only, as he had thirty seconds to recover in instead of ten, it did not end the battle. The thirty seconds made the knock-out so unlikely that the old pugilists regarded it as a rare accident, not worth trying for. The glove fighter tries for nothing else. Nevertheless knock-outs, and very dramatic ones too (Mace by King, for example), did occur in the prize-ring from time to time. Captain Edgeworth Johnstone's treatise is noteworthy in comparison with the earlier Badminton handbook of sparring by Mr. E. B. Michell (one of the Queensberry champions) as throwing over the old teaching of prize-ring boxing with mufflers, and going in frankly for glove fighting, or, to put it classically, cestus boxing.

opponent at his mercy for at least ten seconds. Such a blow is called a "knock-out." The funny bone and the ten-seconds rule explain the development of Queensberry sparring into the modern knocking-out match or glove fight.

This development got its first impulse from the discovery by sparring competitors that the only way in which a boxer, however skilful, could make sure of a verdict in his favor, was by knocking his opponent out. This will be easily understood by any one who remembers the pugilistic Bench of those days. The "judges" at the competitions were invariably ex-champions: that is, men who had themselves won former competitions. Now the judicial faculty, if it is not altogether a legal fiction, is at all events pretty rare even among men whose ordinary pursuits tend to cultivate it, and to train them in dispassionateness. Among pugilists it is quite certainly very often non-existent. The average pugilist is a violent partisan, who seldom witnesses a hot encounter without getting much more excited than the combatants themselves. Further, he is usually filled with a local patriotism which makes him, if a Londoner, deem it a duty to disparage a provincial, and, if a provincial, to support a provincial at all hazards against a cockney. He has, besides, personal favorites on whose success he bets wildly. On great occasions like the annual competitions, he is less judicial and more convivial after dinner (when the finals are sparred) than before it. Being seldom a fine boxer, he often regards skill and style as a reflection on his own deficiencies, and applauds all verdicts given for "game" alone. When he is a technically good boxer, he is all the less likely to be a good critic, as Providence seldom lavishes two rare gifts on the same individual. Even if we take the sanguine and patriotic view that when you appoint such a man a judge, and thus stop his betting, you may depend on his sense of honor and responsibility to neutralize all the other disqualifications, they are sure to be exhibited most extremely by the audience before which he has to deliver his verdict. Now it takes a good deal of strength of mind to give an unpopular verdict; and this strength of mind is not necessarily associated with the bodily hardihood of the champion boxer. Consequently, when the strength of mind is not forthcoming, the audience becomes the judge, and the popular competitor gets the verdict. And the shortest way to the heart of a big audience is to stick to your man; stop his blows bravely with your nose and return them with interest; cover yourself and him with your own gore; and outlast him in a hearty punching match.

It was under these circumstances that the competitors for sparring championships concluded that they had better decide the bouts themselves by knocking their opponents out, and waste no time in cultivating a skill and style for which they got little credit, and which actually set some of the judges against them. The public instantly began to take an interest in the sport. And so, by a pretty rapid evolution, the dexterities which the boxing glove and the Queensberry rules were supposed to substitute for the old brutalities of Sayers and Heenan were really abolished by them.

Let me describe the process as I saw it myself. Twenty years ago a poet friend of mine, who, like all poets, delighted in combats, insisted on my sharing his interest in pugilism, and took me about to all the boxing competitions of the day. I was nothing loth; for, my own share of original sin apart, any one with a sense of comedy must find the arts of self-defence delightful (for a time) through their pedantry, their quackery, and their action and reaction between amateur romantic illusion and professional eye to business.

The fencing world, as Molière well knew, is perhaps a more exquisite example of a fool's paradise than the boxing world; but it is too restricted and expensive to allow play for popular character in a non-duelling country, as the boxing world (formerly called quite appropriately "the Fancy") does. At all events, it was the boxing world that came under my notice; and as I was amused and sceptically observant, whilst the true amateurs about me were, for the most part, merely excited and duped, my evidence may have a certain value when the question comes up again for legislative consideration, as it assuredly will some day.

The first competitions I attended were at the beginning of the eighties, at Lillie Bridge, for the Queensberry championships. There were but few competitors, including a fair number of gentlemen; and the style of boxing aimed at was the "science" bequeathed from the old prize-ring by Ned Donnelly, a pupil of Nat Langham. Langham had once defeated Sayers, and thereby taught him the tactics by which he defeated Heenan. There was as yet no special technique of glove fighting: the traditions and influence of the old ring were unquestioned and supreme; and they distinctly made for brains, skill, quickness, and mobility, as against brute violence, not at all on moral grounds, but because experience had proved that giants did not succeed in the ring under the old rules, and that crafty middle-weights did.

This did not last long. The spectators did not want to see skill defeating violence: they wanted to see violence drawing blood and pounding its way to a savage and exciting victory in the shortest possible time (the old prizefight usually dragged on for hours, and was ended by exhaustion rather than by victory). So did most of the judges. And the public and the judges naturally had their wish; for the competitors, as I have already explained, soon discovered that the only way to make sure of a favorable verdict was to "knock out" their adversary. All pretence of sparring "for points": that is, for marks on an examination paper filled up by the judges, and representing nothing but impracticable academic pedantry in its last ditch, was dropped; and the competitions became frank fights, with abundance of blood drawn, and "knock-outs" always imminent. Needless to add, the glove fight soon began to pay. The select and thinly attended spars on the turf at Lillie Bridge gave way to crowded exhibitions on the hard boards of St. James's Hall. These were organized by the Boxing Association; and to them the provinces, notably Birmingham, sent up a new race of boxers whose sole aim was to knock their opponent insensible by a right-hand blow on the jaw, knowing well that no Birmingham man could depend on a verdict before a London audience for any less undeniable achievement.

The final step was taken by an American pugilist. He threw off the last shred of the old hypocrisy of the gloved hand by challenging the whole world to produce a man who could stand before him for a specified time without being knocked out. His brief but glorious career completely re-established pugilism by giving a world-wide advertisement to the fact that the boxing glove spares nothing but the public conscience, and that as much ferocity, bloodshed, pain, and risk of serious injury or death can be enjoyed at a glove fight as at an old-fashioned prizefight, whilst the strain on the combatants is much greater. It is true that these horrors are greatly exaggerated by the popular imagination, and that if boxing were really as dangerous as bicycling, a good many of its heroes would give it up from simple fright; but this only means that there is a maximum of damage to the spectator by demoralization, combined with the minimum of deterrent risk to the poor scrapper in the ring.

Poor scrapper, though, is hardly the word for a modern fashionable American pugilist. To him the exploits of Cashel Byron will seem ludicrously obscure and low-lived. The contests in which he engages are like Handel Festivals: they take place in huge halls before enormous audiences, with cinematographs hard at work recording the scene for reproduction in London and elsewhere. The combatants divide thousands of dollars of gate-money between them: indeed, if an impecunious English curate were to go to America and challenge the premier pugilist, the spectacle of a match between the Church and the Ring would attract a colossal crowd; and the loser's share of the gate would be a fortune to a curate—assuming that the curate would be the loser, which is by no means a foregone conclusion. At all events, it would be well worth a bruise or two. So my story of the Agricultural Hall, where William Paradise sparred for half a guinea, and Cashel Byron stood out for ten guineas, is no doubt read by the profession in America with amused contempt. In 1882 it was, like most of my conceptions, a daring anticipation of coming social developments, though to-day it seems as far out of date as Slender pulling Sackerson's chain.

Of these latter-day commercial developments of glove fighting I know nothing beyond what I gather from the newspapers. The banging matches of the eighties, in which not one competitor in twenty either exhibited artistic skill, or, in his efforts to knock out his adversary, succeeded in anything but tiring and disappointing himself, were for the most part tedious beyond human endurance. When, after wading through Boxiana and the files of Bell's Life at the British Museum, I had written Cashel Byron's Profession, I found I had exhausted the comedy of the subject; and as a game of patience or solitaire was decidedly superior to an average spar for a championship in point of excitement, I went no more to the competitions. Since then six or seven generations of boxers have passed into peaceful pursuits; and I have no doubt that my experience is in some respects out of date. The National Sporting Club has arisen; and though I have never attended its reunions, I take its record of three pugilists slain as proving and enormous multiplication of contests, since such accidents are very rare, and in fact do not happen to reasonably healthy men. I am prepared to admit also that the disappearance of the old prize-ring technique must by this time have been compensated by the importation from America of a new glove-fighting technique; for even in a knocking-out match, brains will try conclusions with brawn, and finally establish a standard of skill; but I notice that in the leading contests in America luck seems to be on the side of brawn, and brain frequently finishes in a state of concussion, a loser after performing miracles of "science." I use the word luck advisedly; for one of the fascinations of boxing to the gambler (who is the main pillar of the sporting world) is that it is a game of hardihood, pugnacity and skill, all at the mercy of chance. The knock-out itself is a pure chance. I have seen two powerful laborers batter one another's jaws with all their might for several rounds apparently without giving one another as much as a toothache. And I have seen a winning pugilist collapse at a trifling knock landed by a fluke at the fatal angle. I once asked an ancient prizefighter what a knock-out was like when it did happen. He was a man of limited descriptive powers; so he simply pointed to the heavens and said, "Up in a balloon." An amateur pugilist, with greater command of language, told me that "all the milk in his head suddenly boiled over." I am aware that some modern glove fighters of the American school profess to have reduced the knock-out to a science. But the results of the leading American combats conclusively discredit the pretension. When a boxer so superior to his opponent in skill as to be able practically to hit him where he pleases not only fails to knock him out, but finally gets knocked out himself, it is clear that the phenomenon is as complete a mystery pugilistically as it is physiologically, though every pugilist and every doctor may pretend to understand it. It is only fair to add that it has not been proved that any permanent injury to the brain results from it. In any case the brain, as English society is at present constituted, can hardly be considered a vital organ.

This, to the best of my knowledge, is the technical history of the modern revival of pugilism. It is only one more example of the fact that legislators, like other people, must learn their business by their own mistakes, and that the first attempts to suppress an evil by law generally intensify it. Prizefighting, though often connived at, was never legal. Even in its palmiest days prizefights were banished from certain counties by hostile magistrates, just as they have been driven from the United States and England to Belgium on certain occasions in our own time. But as the exercise of sparring, conducted by a couple of gentlemen with boxing gloves on, was regarded as part of a manly physical education, a convention grew up by which it became practically legal to make a citizen's nose bleed by a punch from the gloved fist, and illegal to do the same thing with the naked knuckles. A code of glove-fighting rules was drawn up by a prominent patron of pugilism; and this code was practically legalized by the fact that even when a death resulted from a contest under these rules the accessaries were not punished. No question was raised as to whether the principals were paid to fight for the amusement of the spectators, or whether a prize for the winner was provided in stakes, share of the gate, or a belt with the title of champion. These, the true criteria of prizefighting, were ignored; and the sole issue raised was whether the famous dictum of Dr. Watts, "Your little hands were never made, etc.," had been duly considered by providing the said little hands with a larger hitting surface, a longer range, and four ounces extra weight.

In short, then, what has happened has been the virtual legalization of prizefighting under cover of the boxing glove. And this is exactly what public opinion desires. We do not like fighting; but we like looking on at fights: therefore we require a law which will punish the prizefighter if he hits us, and secure us the protection of the police whilst we sit in a comfortable hall and watch him hitting another prizefighter. And that is just the law we have got at present.

Thus Cashel Byron's plea for a share of the legal toleration accorded to the vivisector has been virtually granted since he made it. The legalization of cruelty to domestic animals under cover of the anesthetic is only the extreme instance of the same social phenomenon as the legalization of prizefighting under cover of the boxing glove. The same passion explains the fascination of both practices; and in both, the professors—pugilists and physiologists alike—have to persuade the Home Office that their pursuits are painless and beneficial. But there is also between them the remarkable difference that the pugilist, who has to suffer as much as he inflicts, wants his work to be as painless and harmless as possible whilst persuading the public that it is thrillingly dangerous and destructive, whilst the vivisector wants to enjoy a total exemption from humane restrictions in his laboratory whilst persuading the public that pain is unknown there. Consequently the vivisector is not only crueller than the prizefighter, but, through the pressure of public opinion, a much more resolute and uncompromising liar. For this no one but a Pharisee will single him out for special blame. All public men lie, as a matter of good taste, on subjects which are considered serious (in England a serious occasion means simply an occasion on which nobody tells the truth); and however illogical or capricious the point of honor may be in man, it is too absurd to assume that the doctors who, from among innumerable methods of research, select that of tormenting animals hideously, will hesitate to come on a platform and tell a soothing fib to prevent the public from punishing them. No criminal is expected to plead guilty, or to refrain from pleading not guilty with all the plausibility at his command. In prizefighting such mendacity is not necessary: on the contrary, if a famous pugilist were to assure the public that a blow delivered with a boxing glove could do no injury and cause no pain, and the public believed him, the sport would instantly lose its following. It is the prizefighter's interest to abolish the real cruelties of the ring and to exaggerate the imaginary cruelties of it. It is the vivisector's interest to refine upon the cruelties of the laboratory, whilst persuading the public that his victims pass into a delicious euthanasia and leave behind them a row of bottles containing infallible cures for all the diseases. Just so, too, does the trainer of performing animals assure us that his dogs and cats and elephants and lions are taught their senseless feats by pure kindness.

The public, as Julius Cæsar remarked nearly 2000 years ago, believes on the whole, just what it wants to believe. The laboring masses do not believe the false excuses of the vivisector, because they know that the vivisector experiments on hospital patients; and the masses belong to the hospital patient class. The well-to-do people who do not go to hospitals, and who think they benefit by the experiments made there, believe the vivisectors' excuses, and angrily abuse and denounce the anti-vivisectors. The people who "love animals," who keep pets, and stick pins through butterflies, support the performing dog people, and are sure that kindness will teach a horse to waltz. And the people who enjoy a fight will persuade themselves that boxing gloves do not hurt, and that sparring is an exercise which teaches self-control and exercises all the muscles in the body more efficiently than any other.

My own view of prizefighting may be gathered from Cashel Byron's Profession, and from the play written by me more than ten years later, entitled Mrs. Warren's Profession. As long as society is so organized that the destitute athlete and the destitute beauty are forced to choose between underpaid drudgery as industrial producers, and comparative self-respect, plenty, and popularity as prizefighters and mercenary brides, licit or illicit, it is idle to affect virtuous indignation at their expense. The word prostitute should either not be used at all, or else applied impartially to all persons who do things for money that they would not do if they had any other assured means of livelihood. The evil caused by the prostitution of the Press and the Pulpit is so gigantic that the prostitution of the prize-ring, which at least makes no serious moral pretensions, is comparatively negligible by comparison. Let us not forget, however, that the throwing of a hard word such as prostitution does not help the persons thus vituperated out of their difficulty. If the soldier and gladiator fight for money, if men and women marry for money, if the journalist and novelist write for money, and the parson preaches for money, it must be remembered that it is an exceedingly difficult and doubtful thing for an individual to set up his own scruples or fancies (he cannot himself be sure which they are) against the demand of the community when it says, Do thus and thus, or starve. It was easy for Ruskin to lay down the rule of dying rather than doing unjustly; but death is a plain thing: justice a very obscure thing. How is an ordinary man to draw the line between right and wrong otherwise than by accepting public opinion on the subject; and what more conclusive expression of sincere public opinion can there be than market demand? Even when we repudiate that and fall back on our private judgment, the matter gathers doubt instead of clearness. The popular notion of morality and piety is to simply beg all the most important questions in life for other people; but when these questions come home to ourselves, we suddenly discover that the devil's advocate has a stronger case than we thought: we remember that the way of righteousness or death was the way of the Inquisition; that hell is paved, not with bad intentions, but with good ones; that the deeper seers have suggested that the way to save your soul is perhaps to give it away, casting your spiritual bread on the waters, so to speak. No doubt, if you are a man of genius, a Ruskin or an Ibsen, you can divine your way and finally force your passage. If you have the conceit of fanaticism you can die a martyr like Charles I. If you are a criminal, or a gentleman of independent means, you can leave society out of the question and prey on it. But if you are an ordinary person you take your bread as it comes to you, doing whatever you can make most money by doing. And you are really shewing yourself a disciplined citizen and acting with perfect social propriety in so doing. Society may be, and generally is, grossly wrong in its offer to you; and you may be, and generally are, grossly wrong in supporting the existing political structure; but this only means, to the successful modern prizefighter, that he must reform society before he can reform himself. A conclusion which I recommend to the consideration of those foolish misers of personal righteousness who think they can dispose of social problems by bidding reformers of society reform themselves first.

Practically, then, the question raised is whether fighting with gloves shall be brought, like cock-fighting, bear-baiting, and gloveless fist fighting, explicitly under the ban of the law. I do not propose to argue that question out here. But of two things I am certain. First, that glove fighting is quite as fierce a sport as fist fighting. Second, that if an application were made to the Borough Council of which I am a member, to hire the Town Hall for a boxing competition, I should vote against the applicants.

This second point being evidently the practical one, I had better give my reason. Exhibition pugilism is essentially a branch of Art: that is to say, it acts and attracts by propagating feeling. The feeling it propagates is pugnacity. Sense of danger, dread of danger, impulse to batter and destroy what threatens and opposes, triumphant delight in succeeding: this is pugnacity, the great adversary of the social impulse to live and let live; to establish our rights by shouldering our share of the social burden; to face and examine danger instead of striking at it; to understand everything to the point of pardoning (and righting) everything; to conclude an amnesty with Nature wide enough to include even those we know the worst of: namely, ourselves. If two men quarrelled, and asked the Borough Council to lend them a room to fight it out in with their fists, on the ground that a few minutes' hearty punching of one another's heads would work off their bad blood and leave them better friends, each desiring, not victory, but satisfaction, I am not sure that I should not vote for compliance. But if a syndicate of showmen came and said, Here we have two men who have no quarrel, but who will, if you pay them, fight before your constituency and thereby make a great propaganda of pugnacity in it, sharing the profits with us and with you, I should indignantly oppose the proposition. And if the majority were against me, I should try to persuade them to at least impose the condition that the fight should be with naked fists under the old rules, so that the combatants should, like Sayers and Langham, depend on bunging up each other's eyes rather than, like the modern knocker-out, giving one another concussion of the brain.

I may add, finally, that the present halting between the legal toleration and suppression of commercial pugilism is much worse than the extreme of either, because it takes away the healthy publicity and sense of responsibility which legality and respectability give, without suppressing the black-blackguardism which finds its opportunity in shady pursuits. I use the term commercial advisedly. Put a stop to boxing for money; and pugilism will give society no further trouble.

London, 1901.

PRESS CUTTINGS

PRESS CUTTINGS

The forenoon of the first of April, 1911.

General Mitchener is at his writing table in the War Office, opening letters. On his left is the fire-place, with a fire burning. On his right, against the opposite wall is a standing desk with an office stool. The door is in the wall behind him, half way between the table and the desk. The table is not quite in the middle of the room: it is nearer to the hearthrug than to the desk. There is a chair at each end of it for persons having business with the general. There is a telephone on the table. Long silence.

A VOICE OUTSIDE. Votes for Women!

The General starts convulsively; snatches a revolver from a drawer, and listens in an agony of apprehension. Nothing happens. He puts the revolver back, ashamed; wipes his brow; and resumes his work. He is startled afresh by the entry of an Orderly. This Orderly is an unsoldierly, slovenly, discontented young man.

MITCHENER. Oh, it's only you. Well?

THE ORDERLY. Another one, sir. Shes chained herself.

MITCHENER. Chained herself? How? To what? Weve taken away the railings and everything that a chain can be passed through.

THE ORDERLY. We forgot the doorscraper, sir. She laid down on the flags and got the chain through before she started hollerin. Shes lying there now; and she says that youve got the key of the padlock in a letter in a buff envelope, and that you will see her when you open it.

MITCHENER. Shes mad. Have the scraper dug up and let her go home with it hanging round her neck.

THE ORDERLY. Theres a buff envelope there, sir.

MITCHENER. Youre all afraid of these women (picking the letter up). It does seem to have a key in it. (He opens the letter, and takes out a key and a note.) "Dear Mitch"—Well, I'm dashed!

THE ORDERLY. Yes Sir.

MITCHENER. What do you mean by Yes Sir?

THE ORDERLY. Well, you said you was dashed, Sir; and you did look if youll excuse my saying it, Sir—well, you looked it.

MITCHENER (who has been reading the letter, and is too astonished to attend to the Orderlys reply). This is a letter from the Prime Minister asking me to release the woman with this key if she padlocks herself, and to have her shown up and see her at once.

THE ORDERLY (tremulously). Dont do it, governor.

MITCHENER (angrily). How often have I ordered you not to address me as governor. Remember that you are a soldier and not a vulgar civilian. Remember also that when a man enters the army he leaves fear behind him. Heres the key. Unlock her and show her up.

THE ORDERLY. Me unlock her! I dursent. Lord knows what she'd do to me.

MITCHENER (pepperily, rising). Obey your orders instantly, Sir, and dont presume to argue. Even if she kills you, it is your duty to die for your country. Right about face. March. (The Orderly goes out, trembling.)

THE VOICE OUTSIDE. Votes for Women! Votes for Women! Votes for Women!

MITCHENER (mimicking her). Votes for Women! Votes for Women! Votes for Women! (in his natural voice) Votes for children! Votes for babies!

Votes for monkeys! (He posts himself on the hearthrug, and awaits the enemy.)

THE ORDERLY (outside). In you go. (He pushes a panting Suffraget into the room.) The person sir. (He withdraws.)

The Suffraget takes off her tailor made skirt and reveals a pair of fashionable trousers.

MITCHENER (horrified). Stop, madam. What are you doing? You must not undress in my presence. I protest. Not even your letter from the Prime Minister—

THE SUFFRAGET. My dear Mitchener: I AM the Prime Minister. (He tears off his hat and cloak; throws them on the desk; and confronts the General in the ordinary costume of a Cabinet minister.)

MITCHENER. Good heavens! Balsquith!

BALSQUITH (throwing himself into Mitchener's chair). Yes: it is indeed Balsquith. It has come to this: that the only way that the Prime Minister of England can get from Downing Street to the War Office is by assuming this disguise; shrieking "VOTES for Women"; and chaining himself to your doorscraper. They were at the corner in force. They cheered me. Bellachristina herself was there. She shook my hand and told me to say I was a vegetarian, as the diet was better in Holloway for vegetarians.

MITCHENER. Why didnt you telephone?

BALSQUITH. They tap the telephone. Every switchboard in London is in their hands or in those of their young men.

MITCHENER. Where on Earth did you get that dress?

BALSQUITH. I stole it from a little Exhibition got up by my wife in Downing Street.

MITCHENER. You dont mean to say its a French dress?

BALSQUITH. Great Heavens, no. My wife isnt allowed even to put on her gloves with French chalk. Everything labelled Made in Camberwell. She advised me to come to you. And what I have to say must be said here to you personally, in the most intimate confidence, with the most urgent persuasion. Mitchener: Sandstone has resigned.

MITCHENER (amazed). Old Red resigned!

BALSQUITH. Resigned.

MITCHENER. But how? Why? Oh, impossible! the proclamation of martial law last Tuesday made Sandstone virtually Dictator in the metropolis, and to resign now is flat desertion.

BALSQUITH. Yes, yes, my dear Mitchener; I know all that as well as you do: I argued with him until I was black in the face and he so red about the neck that if I had gone on he would have burst. He is furious because we have abandoned his plan.

MITCHENER. But you accepted it unconditionally.

BALSQUITH. Yes, before we knew what it was. It was unworkable, you know.

MITCHENER. I dont know. Why is it unworkable?

BALSQUITH. I mean the part about drawing a cordon round Westminster at a distance of two miles; and turning all women out of it.

MITCHENER. A masterpiece of strategy. Let me explain. The Suffragets are a very small body; but they are numerous enough to be troublesome—even dangerous—when they are all concentrated in one place—say in Parliament Square. But by making a two-mile radius and pushing them beyond it, you scatter their attack over a circular line twelve miles long. A superb piece of tactics. Just what Wellington would have done.

BALSQUITH. But the women wont go.

MITCHENER. Nonsense: they must go.

BALSQUITH. They wont.

MITCHENER. What does Sandstone say?

BALSQUITH. He says: Shoot them down.

MITCHENER. Of course.

BALSQUITH. Youre not serious?

MITCHENER. Im perfectly serious.

BALSQUITH. But you cant shoot them down! Women, you know!

MITCHENER (straddling confidently). Yes you can. Strange as it may seem to you as a civilian, Balsquith, if you point a rifle at a woman and fire it, she will drop exactly as a man drops.

BALSQUITH. But suppose your own daughters—Helen and Georgina.

MITCHENER. My daughters would not dream of disobeying the proclamation. (As an after thought.) At least Helen wouldnt.

BALSQUITH. But Georgina?

MITCHENER. Georgina would if she knew shed be shot if she didnt. Thats how the thing would work. Military methods are really the most merciful in the end. You keep sending these misguided women to Holloway and killing them slowly and inhumanely by ruining their health; and it does no good: they go on worse than ever. Shoot a few, promptly and humanely; and there will be an end at once of all resistance and of all the suffering that resistance entails.

BALSQUITH. But public opinion would never stand it.

MITCHENER (walking about and laying down the law). Theres no such thing as public opinion.

BALSQUITH. No such thing as public opinion!!

MITCHENER. Absolutely no such thing as public opinion. There are certain persons who entertain certain opinions. Well, shoot them down. When you have shot them down, there are no longer any persons entertaining those opinions alive: consequently there is no longer any more of the public opinion you are so much afraid of. Grasp that fact, my dear Balsquith; and you have grasped the secret of government. Public opinion is mind. Mind is inseparable from matter. Shoot down the matter and you kill the mind.

BALSQUITH. But hang it all—

MITCHENER (intolerantly). No I wont hang it all. It's no use coming to me and talking about public opinion. You have put yourself into the hands of the army; and you are committed to military methods. And the basis of all military methods is that when people wont do what they are told to do, you shoot them down.

BALSQUITH. Oh, yes; it's all jolly fine for you and Old Red. You dont depend on votes for your places. What do you suppose will happen at the next election?

MITCHENER. Have no next election. Bring in a Bill at once repealing all the reform Acts and vesting the Government in a properly trained magistracy responsible only to a Council of War. It answers perfectly in India. If anyone objects, shoot him down.

BALSQUITH. But none of the members of my party would be on the Council of War. Neither should I. Do you expect us to vote for making ourselves nobodies?

MITCHENER. You'll have to, sooner or later, or the Socialists will make nobodies of the lot of you by collaring every penny you possess. Do you suppose this damned democracy can be allowed to go on now that the mob is beginning to take it seriously and using its power to lay hands on property? Parliament must abolish itself. The Irish parliament voted for its own extinction. The English parliament will do the same if the same means are taken to persuade it.

BALSQUITH. That would cost a lot of money.

MITCHENER. Not money necessarily. Bribe them with titles.

BALSQUITH. Do you think we dare?

MITCHENER (scornfully). Dare! Dare! What is life but daring, man? "To dare, to dare, and again to dare"—

WOMAN'S VOICE OUTSIDE. Votes for Women!

Mitchener, revolver in hand, rushes to the door and locks it. Balsquith hides under the table.

A shot is heard.

BALSQUITH (emerging in the greatest alarm). Good heavens, you havent given orders to fire on them have you?

MITCHENER. No; but its a sentinel's duty to fire on anyone who persists in attempting to pass without giving the word.

BALSQUITH (wiping his brow). This military business is really awful.

MITCHENER. Be calm, Balsquith. These things must happen; they save bloodshed in the long run, believe me. Ive seen plenty of it; and I know.

BALSQUITH. I havent; and I dont know. I wish those guns didnt make such a devil of a noise. We must adopt Maxim's Silencer for the army rifles if we are going to shoot women. I really couldnt stand hearing it.

Some one outside tries to open the door and then knocks.

MITCHENER and BALSQUITH. Whats that?

MITCHENER. Whos there?

THE ORDERLY. It's only me, governor. Its all right.

MITCHENER (unlocking the door and admitting the Orderly, who comes between them). What was it?

THE ORDERLY. Suffraget, Sir.

BALSQUITH. Did the sentry shoot her?

THE ORDERLY. No, Sir: she shot the sentry.

BALSQUITH (relieved). Oh: is that all?

MITCHENER (most indignantly). All? A civilian shoots down one of His Majesty's soldiers on duty; and the Prime Minister of England asks Is that all? Have you no regard for the sanctity of human life?

BALSQUITH (much relieved). Well, getting shot is what a soldier is for. Besides, he doesnt vote.

MITCHENER. Neither do the Suffragets.

BALSQUITH. Their husbands do. (To the Orderly.) By the way, did she kill him?

THE ORDERLY. No, Sir. He got a stinger on his trousers, Sir; but it didnt penetrate. He lost his temper a bit and put down his gun and clouted her head for her. So she said he was no gentleman; and we let her go, thinking she'd had enough, Sir.

MITCHENER (groaning). Clouted her head! These women are making the army as lawless as themselves. Clouted her head indeed! A purely civil procedure.

THE ORDERLY. Any orders, Sir?

MITCHENER. No. Yes. No. Yes: send everybody who took part in this disgraceful scene to the guardroom. No. Ill address the men on the subject after lunch. Parade them for that purpose—full kit. Don't grin at me, Sir. Right about face. March. (The Orderly obeys and goes out.)

BALSQUITH (taking Mitchener affectionately by the arm and walking him persuasively to and fro). And now, Mitchener, will you come to the rescue of the Government and take the command that Old Red has thrown up?

MITCHENER. How can I? You know that the people are devoted heart and soul to Sandstone. He is only bringing you "on the knee," as we say in the army. Could any other living man have persuaded the British nation to accept universal compulsory military service as he did last year? Why, even the Church refused exemption. He is supreme—omnipotent.

BALSQUITH. He WAS, a year ago. But ever since your book of reminiscences went into two more editions than his, and the rush for it led to the wrecking of the Times Book Club, you have become to all intents and purposes his senior. He lost ground by saying that the wrecking was got up by the booksellers. It showed jealousy: and the public felt it.

MITCHENER. But I cracked him up in my book—you see I could do no less after the handsome way he cracked me up in his—and I cant go back on it now. (Breaking loose from Balsquith.) No: its no use, Balsquith: he can dictate his terms to you.

BALSQUITH. Not a bit of it. That affair of the curate—

MITCHENER (impatiently). Oh, damn that curate. Ive heard of nothing but that wretched mutineer for a fortnight past. He is not a curate: whilst he is serving in the army he is a private soldier and nothing else. I really havent time to discuss him further. Im busy. Good morning. (He sits down at his table and takes up his letters.)

BALSQUITH (near the door). I am sorry you take that tone, Mitchener. Since you do take it, let me tell you frankly that I think Lieutenant Chubbs-Jenkinson showed a great want of consideration for the Government in giving an unreasonable and unpopular order, and bringing compulsory military service into disrepute. When the leader of the Labor Party appealed to me and to the House last year not to throw away all the liberties of Englishmen by accepting universal Compulsory military service with-without insisting on full civil rights for the soldier—

MITCHENER. Rot.

BALSQUITH. —I said that no British officer would be capable of abusing the authority with which it was absolutely necessary to invest him.

MITCHENER. Quite right.

BALSQUITH. That carried the House and carried the country—

MITCHENER. Naturally.

BALSQUITH. —And the feeling was that the Labor Party were soulless cads.

MITCHENER. So they are.

BALSQUITH. And now comes this unmannerly young whelp Chubbs-Jenkinson, the only son of what they call a soda king, and orders a curate to lick his boots. And when the curate punches his head, you first sentence him to be shot; and then make a great show of clemency by commuting it to a flogging. What did you expect the curate to do?

MITCHENER (throwing down his pen and his letters and jumping up to confront Balsquith). His duty was perfectly simple. He should have obeyed the order; and then laid his complaint against the officer in proper form. He would have received the fullest satisfaction.

BALSQUITH. What satisfaction?

MITCHENER. Chubbs-Jenkinson would have been reprimanded. In fact, he WAS reprimanded. Besides, the man was thoroughly insubordinate. You cant deny that the very first thing he did when they took him down after flogging him was to walk up to Chubbs-Jenkinson and break his jaw. That showed there was no use flogging him; so now he will get two years hard labor; and serve him right.

BALSQUITH. I bet you a guinea he wont get even a week. I bet you another that Chubbs-Jenkinson apologizes abjectly. You evidently havent heard the news.

MITCHENER. What news?

BALSQUITH. It turns out that the curate is well connected. (Mitchener staggers at the shock. Speechless he contemplates Balsquith with a wild and ghastly stare; then reels into his chair and buries his face in his hands over the blotter. Balsquith continues remorselessly, stooping over him to rub it in.) He has three aunts in the peerage; and Lady Richmond's one of them; (Mitchener utters a heartrending groan) and they all adore him. The invitations for six garden parties and fourteen dances have been cancelled for all the subalterns in Chubbs's regiment. Is it possible you havent heard of it?

MITCHENER. Not a word.

BALSQUITH (shaking his head). I suppose nobody dared to tell you. (He sits down carelessly on Mitchener's right.)

MITCHENER. What an infernal young fool Chubbs-Jenkinson is, not to know the standing of his man better! Why didnt he know? It was his business to know. He ought to be flogged.

BALSQUITH. Probably he will be, by the other subalterns.

MITCHENER. I hope so. Anyhow, out he goes! Out of the army! He or I.

BALSQUITH. His father has subscribed a million to the party funds. We owe him a peerage.

MITCHENER. I dont care.

BALSQUITH. I do. How do you think parties are kept up? Not by the subscriptions of the local associations, I hope. They dont pay for the gas at the meetings.

MITCHENER. Man; can you not be serious? Here are we, face to face with Lady Richmond's grave displeasure; and you talk to me about gas and subscriptions. Her own nephew.

BALSQUITH (gloomily). Its unfortunate. He was at Oxford with Bobby Bassborough.

MITCHENER. Worse and worse. What shall we do?

Balsquith shakes his head. They contemplate one another in miserable silence.

A VOICE WITHOUT. Votes for Women! Votes for Women!

A terrific explosion shakes the building—they take no notice.

MITCHENER (breaking down). You dont know what this means to me, Balsquith. I love the army. I love my country.

BALSQUITH. It certainly is rather awkward.

The Orderly comes in.

MITCHENER (angrily). What is it? How dare you interrupt us like this?

THE ORDERLY. Didnt you hear the explosion, Sir?

MITCHENER. Explosion. What explosion? No: I heard no explosion: I have something more serious to attend to than explosions. Great Heavens: Lady Richmond's nephew has been treated like any common laborer; and while England is reeling under the shock a private comes in and asks me if I heard an explosion.

BALSQUITH. By the way, what was the explosion?

THE ORDERLY. Only a sort of bombshell, Sir.

BALSQUITH. Bombshell!

THE ORDERLY. A pasteboard one, Sir. Full of papers with Votes for Women in red letters. Fired into the yard from the roof of the Alliance Office.

MITCHENER. Pooh! Go away. Go away.

The Orderly, bewildered, goes out.

BALSQUITH. Mitchener: you can save the country yet. Put on your full-dress uniform and your medals and orders and so forth. Get a guard of honor—something showy—horse guards or something of that sort; and call on the old girl—

MITCHENER. The old girl?

BALSQUITH. Well, Lady Richmond. Apologize to her. Ask her leave to accept the command. Tell her that youve made the curate your adjutant or your aide-de-camp or whatever is the proper thing. By the way, what can you make him?

MITCHENER. I might make him my chaplain. I dont see why I shouldnt have a chaplain on my staff. He showed a very proper spirit in punching that young cub's head. I should have done the same myself.

BALSQUITH. Then Ive your promise to take command if Lady Richmond consents?

MITCHENER. On condition that I have a free hand. No nonsense about public opinion or democracy.

BALSQUITH. As far as possible, I think I may say yes.

MITCHENER (rising intolerantly and going to the hearthrug). That wont do for me. Dont be weakkneed, Balsquith. You know perfectly well that the real government of this country is and always must be the government of the masses by the classes. You know that democracy is damned nonsense, and that no class stands less of it than the working class. You know that we are already discussing the steps that will have to be taken if the country should ever be face to face with the possibility of a Labor majority in parliament. You know that in that case we should disfranchise the mob, and, if they made a fuss, shoot them down. You know that if we need public opinion to support us, we can get any quantity of it manufactured in our papers by poor devils of journalists who will sell their souls for five shillings. You know—

BALSQUITH. Stop. Stop, I say. I dont know. That is the difference between your job and mine, Mitchener. After twenty years in the army a man thinks he knows everything. After twenty months in the Cabinet he knows that he knows nothing.

MITCHENER. We learn from history—

BALSQUITH. We learn from history that men never learn anything from history. Thats not my own: its Hegel.

MITCHENER. Whos Hegel?

BALSQUITH. Dead. A German philosopher. (He half rises, but recollects something and sits down again.) Oh confound it: that reminds me. The Germans have laid down four more Dreadnoughts.

MITCHENER. Then you must lay down twelve.

BALSQUITH. Oh yes: its easy to say that: but think of what theyll cost.

MITCHENER. Think of what it would cost to be invaded by Germany and forced to pay an indemnity of five hundred millions.

BALSQUITH. But you said that if you got compulsory military service there would be an end of the danger of invasion.

MITCHENER. On the contrary, my dear fellow, it increases the danger tenfold, because it increases German jealousy of our military supremacy.

BALSQUITH. After all, why should the Germans invade us?

MITCHENER. Why shouldnt they? What else has their army to do? What else are they building a navy for?

BALSQUITH. Well, we never think of invading Germany.

MITCHENER. Yes we do. I have thought of nothing else for the last ten years. Say what you will, Balsquith, the Germans have never recognized, and until they get a stern lesson, they never WILL recognize, the plain fact that the interests of the British Empire are paramount, and that the command of the sea belongs by nature to England.

BALSQUITH. But if they wont recognize it, what can I do?

MITCHENER. Shoot them down.

BALSQUITH. I cant shoot them down.

MITCHENER. Yes you can. You dont realize it; but if you fire a rifle into a German he drops just as surely as a rabbit does.

BALSQUITH But dash it all, man, a rabbit hasnt got a rifle and a German has. Suppose he shoots you down.

MITCHENER. Excuse me, Balsquith; but that consideration is what we call cowardice in the army. A soldier always assumes that he is going to shoot, not to be shot.

BALSQUITH (jumping up and walking about sulkily). Oh come! I like to hear you military people talking of cowardice. Why, you spend your lives in an ecstasy of terror of imaginary invasions. I dont believe you ever go to bed without looking under it for a burglar.

MITCHENER (calmly). A very sensible precaution, Balsquith. I always take it. And in consequence Ive never been burgled.

BALSQUITH. Neither have I. Anyhow dont you taunt me with cowardice. (He posts himself on the hearthrug beside Mitchener on his left.) I never look under my bed for a burglar. Im not always looking under the nation's bed for an invader. And if it comes to fighting Im quite willing to fight without being three to one.

MITCHENER. These are the romantic ravings of a Jingo civilian, Balsquith. At least youll not deny that the absolute command of the sea is essential to our security.

BALSQUITH. The absolute command of the sea is essential to the security of the principality of Monaco. But Monaco isnt going to get it.

MITCHENER. And consequently Monaco enjoys no security. What a frightful thing! How do the inhabitants sleep with the possibility of invasion, of bombardment, continually present to their minds? Would you have our English slumbers broken in the same way? Are we also to live without security?

BALSQUITH (dogmatically). Yes. Theres no such thing as security in the world: and there never can be as long as men are mortal. England will be secure when England is dead, just as the streets of London will be safe when there is no longer a man in her streets to be run over, or a vehicle to run over him. When you military chaps ask for security you are crying for the moon.

MITCHENER (very seriously). Let me tell you, Balsquith, that in these days of aeroplanes and Zeppelin airships, the question of the moon is becoming one of the greatest importance. It will be reached at no very distant date. Can you as an Englishman, tamely contemplate the possibility of having to live under a German moon? The British flag must be planted there at all hazards.

BALSQUITH. My dear Mitchener, the moon is outside practical politics. Id swop it for a cooling station tomorrow with Germany or any other Power sufficiently military in its way of thinking to attach any importance to it.

MITCHENER (losing his temper). You are the friend of every country but your own.

BALSQUITH. Say nobodys enemy but my own. It sounds nicer. You really neednt be so horribly afraid of the other countries. Theyre all in the same fix as we are. Im much more interested in the death rate in Lambeth than in the German fleet.

MITCHENER. You darent say that in Lambeth.

BALSQUITH. Ill say it the day after you publish your scheme for invading Germany and repealing all the reform Acts.

The Orderly comes in.

MITCHENER. What do you want?

THE ORDERLY. I dont want anything, Governor, thank you. The secretary and president of the Anti-Suffraget League say they had an appointment with the Prime Minister, and that theyve been sent on here from Downing Street.

BALSQUITH (going to the table). Quite right. I forgot them. (To Mitchener.) Would you mind my seeing them here? I feel extraordinarily grateful to these women for standing by us and facing the suffragets, especially as they are naturally the gentler and timid sort of women. (The Orderly moans.) Did you say anything?

THE ORDERLY. No, Sir.

BALSQUITH. Did you catch their names.

THE ORDERLY. Yes, Sir. The president is Lady Corinthia Fanshawe; and the secretary is Mrs. Banger.

MITCHENER (abruptly). Mrs. what?

THE ORDERLY. Mrs. Banger.

BALSQUITH. Curious that quiet people always seem to have violent names.

THE ORDERLY. Not much quiet about her, sir.

MITCHENER (outraged). Attention. Speak when youre spoken to. Hold your tongue when youre not. Right about face. March. (The Orderly obeys.) Thats the way to keep these chaps up to the mark. (The Orderly returns.) Back again! What do you mean by this mutiny?

THE ORDERLY. What am I to say to the ladies, sir?

BALSQUITH. You dont mind my seeing them somewhere, do you?

MITCHENER. Not at all. Bring them in to see me when youve done with them: I understand that Lady Corinthia is a very fascinating woman. Who is she, by the way?

BALSQUITH. Daughter of Lord Broadstairs, the automatic turbine man. Gave quarter of a million to the party funds. Shes musical and romantic and all that—dont hunt: hates politics: stops in town all the year round: one never sees her anywhere except at the opera and at musical at-homes and so forth.

MITCHENER. What a life! Still, if she wants to see me I dont mind. (To the Orderly.) Where are the ladies?

THE ORDERLY. In No. 17, Sir.

MITCHENER. Show Mr. Balsquith there. And send Mrs. Farrell here.

THE ORDERLY (calling into the corridor). Mrs. Farrell! (To Balsquith.) This way sir. (He goes out with Balsquith.)

Mrs. Farrell, a lean, highly respectable Irish Charwoman of about 50 comes in.

MITCHENER. Mrs. Farrell: Ive a very important visit to pay: I shall want my full dress uniform and all my medals and orders and my presentation sword. There was a time when the British Army contained men capable of discharging these duties for their commanding officer. Those days are over. The compulsorily enlisted soldier runs to a woman for everything. Im therefore reluctantly obliged to trouble you.

MRS FARRELL. Your meddles n ordhers n the crooked sword with the ivory handle n your full dress uniform is in the waxworks in the Chamber o Military Glory over in the place they used to call the Banquetin Hall. I told you youd be sorry for sendin them away; n you told me to mind me own business. Youre wiser now.

MITCHENER. I am. I had not at that time discovered that you were the only person in the whole military establishment of this capital who could be trusted to remember where anything was, or to understand an order and obey it.

MRS. FARRELL. Its no good flattherin me. Im too old.

MITCHENER. Not at all, Mrs. Farrell. How is your daughter?

MRS. FARRELL. Which daughther.

MITCHENER. The one who has made such a gratifying success in the Music Halls.

MRS. FARRELL. Theres no music halls nowadays: theyre Variety Theatres. Shes got an offer of marriage from a young jook.

MITCHENER. Is it possible? What did you do?

MRS. FARRELL. I told his mother on him.

MITCHENER. Oh! what did she say?

MRS. FARRELL. She was as pleased as Punch. Thank Heaven, she says, hes got somebody thatll be able to keep him when the supertax is put up to twenty shillings in the pound.

MITCHENER. But your daughter herself? What did she say?

MRS. FARRELL. Accepted him, of course. What else would a young fool like her do? He inthrojooced her to the Poet Laureate, thinking shed inspire him.

MITCHENER. Did she?

MRS. FARRELL. Faith I dunna. All I know is she walked up to him as bold as brass n said "Write me a sketch, dear." Afther all the trouble I took with that chills manners shes no more notion how to behave herself than a pig. Youll have to wear General Sandstones uniform: its the ony one in the place, because he wont lend it to the shows.

MITCHENER. But Sandstones clothes wont fit me.

MRS. FARRELL (unmoved). Then youll have to fit THEM. Why shouldnt they fitcha as well as they fitted General Blake at the Mansion House?

MITCHENER. They didnt fit him. He looked a frightful guy.

MRS. FARRELL. Well, you must do the best you can with them. You cant exhibit your clothes and wear them too.

MITCHENER. And the public thinks the lot of a commanding officer a happy one! Oh, if they could only see the seamy side of it. (He returns to his table to resume work.)

MRS. FARRELL. If they could only see the seamy side of General Sandstones uniform, where his flask rubs agen the buckle of his braces, theyll tell him he ought to get a new one. Let alone the way he swears at me.

MITCHENER. When a man has risked his life on eight battlefields, Mrs. Farrell, he has given sufficient proof of his self-control to be excused a little strong language.

MRS. FARRELL. Would you put up with bad language from me because Ive risked my life eight times in childbed?

MITCHENER. My dear Mrs. Farrell, you surely would not compare a risk of that harmless domestic kind to the fearful risks of the battlefield?

MRS. FARRELL. I wouldnt compare risks run to bear living people into the world to risks run to blow them out of it. A mother's risk is jooty: a soldier's nothin but divilmint.

MITCHENER (nettled). Let me tell you, Mrs. Farrell, that if the men did not fight, the women would have to fight themselves. We spare you that, at all events.

MRS. FARRELL. You cant help yourselves. If three-quarters of you was killed we could replace you with the help of the other quarter. If three-quarters of us was killed, how many people would there be in England in another generation? If it wasnt for that, the man d put the fightin on us just as they put all the other dhrudgery. What would YOU do if we was all kilt? Would you go to bed and have twins?

MITCHENER. Really, Mrs. Farrell, you must discuss these questions with a medical man. You make me blush, positively.

MRS. FARRELL. A good job too. If I could have made Farrell blush I wouldnt have had to risk me life too often. You n your risks n your bravery n your selfcontrol indeed! "Why don't you conthrol yourself?" I sez to Farrell. "Its agen me religion," he sez.

MITCHENER (plaintively). Mrs. Farrell, youre a woman of very powerful mind. Im not qualified to argue these delicate matters with you. I ask you to spare me, and to be good enough to take these clothes to Mr. Balsquith when the ladies leave.

The Orderly comes in.

THE ORDERLY. Lady Corinthia Fanshawe and Mrs. Banger wish to see you, sir. Mr. Balsquith told me to tell you.

MRS. FARRELL. Theyve come about the vote. I dont know whether its them that want it or them that doesnt want it: anyhow, they're all alike when they get into a state about it. (She goes out, having gathered Balsquith's suffraget disguise from the desk.)

MITCHENER. Is Mr. Balsquith not with them?

THE ORDERLY. No, Sir. Couldnt stand Mrs. Banger, I expect. Fair caution she is. (He chuckles.) Couldnt help larfin when I sor im op it.

MITCHENER. How dare you indulge in this unseemly mirth in the presence of your commanding officer? Have you no sense of a soldier's duty?

THE ORDERLY (sadly). Im afraid I shant ever get the ang of it, sir. You see my father has a tidy little barbers business down off Shoreditch; and I was brought up to be chatty and easy like with everybody. I tell you, when I drew the number in the conscription it gave my old mother the needle and it gev me the ump. I should take it very kind, sir, if youd let me off the drill and let me shave you instead. Youd appreciate my qualities then: you would indeed sir. I shant never do myself justice at soljering, sir: I cant bring myself to think of it as proper work for a man with an active mind, as you might say, sir. Arf of its only ousemaidin; and the other arf is dress-up and make-believe.

MITCHENER. Stuff, Sir. Its the easiest life in the world. Once you learn your drill all you have to do is to hold your tongue and obey your orders.

THE ORDERLY. But I do assure you, sir, arf the time they're the wrong orders; and I get into trouble when I obey them. The sergeants orders is all right; but the officers dont know what theyre talkin about. Why the orses knows better sometimes. "Fours" says Lieutenant Trevor at the gate of Bucknam Palace only this morning when we was on duty for a State visit to the Coal Trust. I was fourth man like in the first file; and when I started the orse eld back; and the sergeant was on to me straight. Threes, you bally fool, he whispers. And he was on to me again about it when we came back, and called me a fathead, he did. What am I to do, I says: the lieutenant's orders was fours, I says. Ill show you whos lieutenant here, e says. In future you attend to my orders and not to iz, e says: what does he know about it? You didnt give me any orders, I says. Couldnt you see for yourself there wasnt room for fours, e says: why cant you THINK? General Mitchener tells me Im not to think but to obey orders, I says. Is Mitchener your sergeant or am I, e says in his bullyin way. You are, I says. Well, he says, youve got to do what your sergeant tells you: thats discipline, he says. What am I to do for the General I says. Youre to let im talk, e says: thats what es for.

MITCHENER (groaning). It is impossible for the human mind to conceive anything more dreadful than this. Youre a disgrace to the service.

THE ORDERLY (deeply wounded). The service is a disgrace to me. When my mother's people pass me in the street with this uniform on, I ardly know which way to look. There never was a soldier in my family before.

MITCHENER. There never was anything else in mine, sir.

THE ORDERLY. My mother's second cousin was one of the Parkinsons of Stepney. (Almost in tears.) What do you know of the feelings of a respectable family in the middle station of life? I cant bear to be looked down on as a common soldier. Why cant my father be let buy my discharge? Youve done away with the soldier's right to have his discharge bought for him by his relations. The country didnt know you were going to do that or it would never have stood it. Is an Englishman to be made a mockery like this?

MITCHENER. Silence. Attention. Right about face. March.

THE ORDERLY (retiring to the standing desk and bedewing it with passionate tears). Oh that I should have lived to be spoke to as if I was the lowest of the low. Me! that has shaved a City of London aldermen wiv me own hand.

MITCHENER. Poltroon. Crybaby. Well, better disgrace yourself here than disgrace your country on the field of battle.

THE ORDERLY (angrily coming to the table). Whos going to disgrace his country on the field of battle? Its not fightin I object to: its soljerin. Show me a German and Ill have a go at him as fast as you or any man. But to ave me time wasted like this, an be stuck in a sentry box at a street corner for an ornament to be stared at; and to be told "right about face: march" if I speak as one man to another: that aint pluck: that aint fightin: that aint patriotism: its bein made a bloomin sheep of.

MITCHENER. A sheep has many valuable military qualities. Emulate them: dont disparage them.

THE ORDERLY. Oh, wots the good of talkin to you? If I wasnt a poor soldier I could punch your head for forty shillins for a month. But because youre my commanding officer you deprive me of my right to a magistrate and make a compliment of giving me two years ard sted of shootin me. Why cant you take your chance the same as any civilian does?

MITCHENER (rising majestically). I search the pages of history in vain for a parallel to such a speech made by a Private to a general. But for the coherence of your remarks I should conclude that you were drunk. As it is, you must be mad. You shall be placed under restraint at once. Call the guard.

THE ORDERLY. Call your grandmother. If you take one man off the doors the place'll be full of Suffragets before you can wink.

MITCHENER. Then arrest yourself; and off with you to the guardroom.

THE ORDERLY. What am I to arrest myself for?

MITCHENER. Thats nothing to you. You have your orders: obey them. Do you hear? Right about face. March.

THE ORDERLY. How would you feel yourself if you was told to right-about-face and march as if you was a doormat?

MITCHENER. I should feel as if my country had spoken through the voice of my officer. I should feel proud and honored to be able to serve my country by obeying its commands. No thought of self—no vulgar preoccupation with my own petty vanity could touch my mind at such a moment. To me my officer would not be a mere man: he would be for the moment—whatever his personal frailties—the incarnation of our national destiny.

THE ORDERLY. What Im saying to you is the voice of old England a jolly sight more than all this rot that you get out of books. Id rather be spoke to by a sergeant than by you. He tells me to go to hell when I challenges him to argue it out like a man. It aint polite; but its English. What you say aint anything at all. You dont act on it yourself. You dont believe in it. Youd punch my head if I tried it on you; and serve me right. And look here. Heres another point for you to argue.

MITCHENER (with a shriek of protest). No—

Mrs. Banger comes in, followed by Lady Corinthia Fanshawe.

Mrs. Banger is a masculine woman of forty, with a powerful voice and great physical strength. Lady Corinthia, who is also over thirty, is beautiful and romantic.

MRS. BANGER (throwing the door open decisively and marching straight to Michener). Pray how much longer is the Anti-Suffrage League to be kept waiting? (She passes him contemptuously and sits down with impressive confidence in the chair next the fireplace. Lady Corinthia takes the chair on the opposite side of the table with equal aplomb.)

MITCHENER. Im extremely sorry. You really do not know what I have to put with. This imbecile, incompetent, unsoldierly disgrace to the uniform he should never have been allowed to put on, ought to have shown you in fifteen minutes ago.

THE ORDERLY. All I said was—

MITCHENER. Not another word. Attention. Right about face. March. (The Orderly sits down doggedly.) Get out of the room this instant, you fool, or Ill kick you out.

THE ORDERLY (civilly). I dont mind that, sir. Its human. Its English. Why couldnt you have said it before? (He goes out).

MITCHENER. Take no notice I beg: these scenes are of daily occurrence now that we have compulsory service under the command of the halfpenny papers. Pray sit down.

LADY CORINTHIA AND MRS. BANGER (rising). Thank you. (They sit down again.)

MITCHENER (sitting down with a slight chuckle of satisfaction). And now, ladies, to what am I indebted?

MRS. BANGER. Let me introduce us. I am Rosa Carmina Banger—Mrs. Banger, organizing secretary of the Anti-Suffraget League. This is Lady Corinthia Fanshawe, the president of the League, known in musical circles—I am not myself musical—as the Richmond Park nightingale. A soprano. I am myself said to be almost a baritone; but I do not profess to understand these dis-tinctions.

MITCHENER (murmuring politely). Most happy, Im sure.

MRS. BANGER. We have come to tell you plainly that the Anti-Suffragets are going to fight.

MITCHENER (gallantly). Oh, pray leave that to the men, Mrs. Banger.

LADY CORINTHIA. We can no longer trust the men.

MRS. BANGER. They have shown neither the strength, the courage, nor the determination which are needed to combat women like the Suffragets.

LADY CORINTHIA. Nature is too strong for the combatants.

MRS. BANGER. Physical struggles between persons of opposite sexes are unseemly.

LADY CORINTHIA. Demoralizing.

MRS. BANGER. Insincere.

LADY CORINTHIA. They are merely embraces in disguise.

MRS. BANGER. No such suspicion can attach to combats in which the antagonists are of the same sex.

LADY CORINTHIA. The Anti-Suffragets have resolved to take the field.

MRS. BANGER. They will enforce the order of General Sandstone for the removal of all women from the two mile radius—that is, all women except themselves.

MITCHENER. I am sorry to have to inform you, Madam, that the Government has given up that project, and that General Sandstone has resigned in consequence.

MRS. BANGER. That does not concern us in the least. We approve of the project and will see that it is carried out. We have spent a good deal of money arming ourselves; and we are not going to have that money thrown away through the pusillanimity of a Cabinet of males.

MITCHENER. Arming yourselves! But, my dear ladies, under the latest proclamation women are strictly forbidden to carry chains, padlocks, tracts on the franchise, or weapons of any description.

LADY CORINTHIA (producing an ivory-handled revolver and pointing it at his nose). You little know your countrywomen, General Mitchener.

MITCHENER (without flinching). Madam: it is my duty to take possession of that weapon in accordance with the proclamation. Be good enough to put it down.

MRS. BANGER (producing an XVIII century horse pistol). Is it your duty to take possession of this also?

MITCHENER. That, madam, is not a weapon; it is a curiosity. If you would be kind enough to place it in some museum instead of pointing it at my head, I should be obliged to you.

MRS. BANGER. This pistol, sir, was carried at Waterloo by my grandmother.

MITCHENER. I presume you mean your grandfather.

MRS. BANGER. You presume unwarrantably.

LADY CORINTHIA. Mrs. Banger's grandmother commanded a canteen at that celebrated battle.

MRS. BANGER. Who my grandfather was is a point that has never been quite clearly settled. I put my trust not in my ancestors, but in my good sword, which is at my lodgings.

MITCHENER. Your sword!

MRS. BANGER. The sword with which I slew five Egyptians with my own hand at Kassassin, where I served as a trooper.

MITCHENER. Lord bless me! But was your sex never discovered?

MRS. BANGER. It was never even suspected. I had a comrade—a gentleman ranker—whom they called Fanny. They never called ME Fanny.

LADY CORINTHIA. The suffragets have turned the whole woman movement on to the wrong track. They ask for a vote.

MRS. BANGER. What use is a vote? Men have the vote.

LADY CORINTHIA. And men are slaves.

MRS. BANGER. What women need is the right to military service. Give me a well-mounted regiment of women with sabres, opposed to a regiment of men with votes. We shall see which will go down before the other. (rises) No: we have had enough of these gentle pretty creatures who merely talk and cross-examine ministers in police courts, and go to prison like sheep, and suffer and sacrifice themselves. This question must be solved by blood and iron, as was well said by Bismarck, whom I have reason to believe was a woman in disguise.

MITCHENER. Bismarck a woman?

MRS. BANGER. All the really strong men of history have been disguised women.

MITCHENER (remonstrating). My dear lady!

MRS. BANGER. How can you tell? You never knew that the hero of the charge at Kassassin was a woman: yet she was: it was I, Rosa Carmina Banger. Would Napoleon have been so brutal to women, think you, had he been a man?

MITCHENER. Oh, come, come! Really! Surely female rulers have often shown all the feminine weaknesses. Queen Elizabeth, for instance. Her vanity, her levity.

MRS. BANGER. Nobody who has studied the history of Queen Elizabeth can doubt for a moment that she was a disguised man.

LADY CORINTHIA (admiring Mrs. Banger). Isnt she splendid?

MRS. BANGER (rising with a large gesture). This very afternoon I shall cast off this hampering skirt for ever; mount my charger; and with my good sabre lead the Anti-Suffragets to victory. (She strides to the other side of the room, snorting.)

MITCHENER. But I cant allow anything of the sort, madam. I shall stand no such ridiculous nonsense. Im perfectly determined to put my foot down.

LADY CORINTHIA. Dont be hysterical, General.

MITCHENER. Hysterical!

MRS. BANGER. Do you think we are to be stopped by these childish exhibitions of temper. They are useless; and your tears and entreaties—a man's last resource—will avail you just as little. I sweep them away, just as I sweep your plans of campaign "made in Germany—"

MITCHENER (flying into a transport of rage). How dare you repeat that infamous slander? (He rings the bell violently.) If this is the alternative to votes for women, I shall advocate giving every woman in the country six votes.

The Orderly comes in.

Remove that woman. See that she leaves the building at once.

The Orderly forlornly contemplates the iron front presented by Mrs. Banger.

THE ORDERLY (propitiatorily). Would you av the feelin art to step out, madam.

MRS. BANGER. You are a soldier. Obey your orders. Put me out. If I got such an order, I should not hesitate.

THE ORDERLY (To Mitchener). Would you mind lendin me a and, Guvner?

LADY CORINTHIA (raising her revolver). I shall be obliged to shoot you if you stir, General.

MRS. BANGER (To the Orderly). When you are ordered to put a person out you should do it like this. (She hurls him from the room. He is heard falling headlong downstairs and crashing through a glass door.) I shall now wait on General Sandstone. If he shows any sign of weakness, he shall share that poor wretch's fate. (She goes out.)

LADY CORINTHIA. Isnt she magnificent?

MITCHENER. Thank heaven shes gone. And now, my dear lady, is it necessary to keep that loaded pistol to my nose all through our conversation?

LADY CORINTHIA. Its not loaded. Its heavy enough, goodness knows, without putting bullets in it.

MITCHENER (triumphantly snatching his revolver from the drawer). Then I am master of the situation. This IS loaded. Ha, ha!

LADY CORINTHIA. But since we are not really going to shoot one another, what difference can it possibly make?

MITCHENER (putting his pistol down on the table). True. Quite true. I recognize there the practical good sense that has prevented you from falling into the snares of the Suffragets.

LADY CORINTHIA. The Suffragets, General, are the dupes of dowdies. A really attractive and clever woman—

MITCHENER (gallantly). Yourself, for instance.

LADY CORINTHIA (snatching up his revolver). Another step and you are a dead man.

MITCHENER (amazed). My dear lady!

LADY CORINTHIA. I am not your dear lady. You are not the first man who has concluded that because I am devoted to music and can reach F flat with the greatest facility—Patti never got above E flat—I am marked out as the prey of every libertine. You think I am like the thousands of weak women whom you have ruined—

MITCHENER. I solemnly protest—

LADY CORINTHIA. Oh, I know what you officers are. To you a woman's honor is nothing, and the idle pleasure of the moment is everything.

MITCHENER. This is perfectly ridiculous. I never ruined anyone in my life.

LADY CORINTHIA. Never! Are you in earnest?

MITCHENER. Certainly I am in earnest. Most indignantly in earnest.

LADY CORINTHIA (throwing down the pistol contemptuously). Then you have no temperament; you are not an artist. You have no soul for music.

MITCHENER. Ive subscribed to the regimental band all my life. I bought two sarrusophones for it out of my own pocket. When I sang Tosti's Goodbye for Ever at Knightsbridge in 1880, the whole regiment wept. You are too young to remember that.

LADY CORINTHIA. Your advances are useless. I—

MITCHENER. Confound it, madam, can you not receive an innocent compliment without suspecting me of dishonorable intentions?

LADY CORINTHIA. Love—real love—makes all intentions honorable. But YOU could never understand that.

MITCHENER. Ill not submit to the vulgar penny-novelette notion that an officer is less honorable than a civilian in his relations with women. While I live Ill raise my voice—

LADY CORINTHIA. Tush!

MITCHENER. What do you mean by tush?

LADY CORINTHIA. You cant raise your voice above its natural compass. What sort of voice have you?

MITCHENER. A tenor. What sort had you?

LADY CORINTHIA. Had? I have it still. I tell you I am the highest living soprano. (Scornfully.) What was your highest note, pray?

MITCHENER. B flat—once—in 1879. I was drunk at the time.

LADY CORINTHIA (gazing at him almost tenderly). Though you may not believe me, I find you are more interesting when you talk about music than when you are endeavoring to betray a woman who has trusted you by remaining alone with you in your apartment.

MITCHENER (springing up and fuming away to the fireplace). These repeated insults to a man of blameless life are as disgraceful to you as they are undeserved by me, Lady Corinthia. Such suspicions invite the conduct they impute. (She raises the pistol.) You need not be alarmed: I am only going to leave the room.

LADY CORINTHIA. Fish.

MITCHENER. Fish! This is worse than tush. Why fish?

LADY CORINTHIA. Yes, fish: coldblooded fish.

MITCHENER. Dash it all, madam, do you WANT me to make advances to you?

LADY CORINTHIA. I have not the slightest intention of yielding to them; but to make them would be a tribute to romance. What is life without romance?

MITCHENER (making a movement toward her). I tell you—

LADY CORINTHIA. Stop. No nearer. No vulgar sensuousness. If you must adore, adore at a distance.

MITCHENER. This is worse than Mrs. Banger. I shall ask that estimable woman to come back.

LADY CORINTHIA. Poor Mrs. Banger! Do not for a moment suppose, General Mitchener, that Mrs. Banger represents my views on the suffrage question. Mrs. Banger is a man in petticoats. I am every inch a woman; but I find it convenient to work with her.

MITCHENER. Do you find the combination comfortable?

LADY CORINTHIA. I do not wear combinations, General: (with dignity) they are unwomanly.

MITCHENER (throwing himself despairingly into the chair next the hearthrug). I shall go mad. I never for a moment dreamt of alluding to anything of the sort.

LADY CORINTHIA. There is no need to blush and become self-conscious at the mention of underclothing. You are extremely vulgar, General.

MITCHENER. Lady Corinthia: you have my pistol. Will you have the goodness to blow my brains out. I should prefer it to any further effort to follow the gyrations of the weathercock you no doubt call your mind. If you refuse, then I warn you that youll not get another word out of me—not if we sit here until doomsday.

LADY CORINTHIA. I dont want you to talk. I want you to listen. You do not yet understand my views on the question of the Suffrage. (She rises to make a speech.) I must preface my remarks by reminding you that the Suffraget movement is essentially a dowdy movement. The suffragets are not all dowdies; but they are mainly supported by dowdies. Now I am not a dowdy. Oh, no compliments—

MITCHENER. I did not utter a sound.

LADY CORINTHIA (smiling). It is easy to read your thoughts. I am one of those women who are accustomed to rule the world through men. Man is ruled by beauty, by charm. The men who are not have no influence. The Salic Law, which forbade women to occupy a throne, is founded on the fact that when a woman is on the throne the country is ruled by men, and therefore ruled badly; whereas when a man is on the throne, the country is ruled by women, and therefore ruled well. The suffragets would degrade women from being rulers to being voters, mere politicians, the drudges of the caucus and the polling booth. We should lose our influence completely under such a state of affairs. The New Zealand women have the vote. What is the result? No poet ever makes a New Zealand woman his heroine. One might as well be romantic about New Zealand mutton. Look at the suffragets themselves. The only ones who are popular are the pretty ones, who flirt with mobs as ordinary women flirt with officers.

MITCHENER. Then I understand you to hold that the country should be governed by the women after all.

LADY CORINTHIA. Not by all the women. By certain women. I had almost said by one woman. By the women who have charm—who have artistic talent—who wield a legitimate, a refining influence over the men. (She sits down gracefully, smiling, and arranging her draperies with conscious elegance.)

MITCHENER. In short, madam, you think that if you give the vote to the man, you give the power to the women who can get round the man.

LADY CORINTHIA. That is not a very delicate way of putting it; but I suppose that is how you would express what I mean.

MITCHENER. Perhaps youve never had any experience of garrison life. If you had, you'd have noticed that the sort of woman who is clever at getting round men is sometimes rather a bad lot.

LADY CORINTHIA. What do you mean by a bad lot?

MITCHENER. I mean a woman who would play the very devil if the other women didnt keep her in pretty strict order. I dont approve of democracy, because its rot; and Im against giving the vote to women because Im not accustomed to it and therefore am able to see with an unprejudiced eye what infernal nonsense it is. But I tell you plainly, Lady Corinthia, that there is one game that I dislike more than either Democracy or Votes For Women: and that is the game of Antony and Cleopatra. If I must be ruled by women, let me have decent women and not—well, not the other sort.

LADY CORINTHIA. You have a coarse mind, General Mitchener.

MITCHENER. So has Mrs. Banger. And by George! I prefer Mrs. Banger to you!

LADY CORINTHIA (bounding to her feet.) You prefer Mrs. Banger to me!!!

MITCHENER. I do. You said yourself she was splendid.

LADY CORINTHIA. You are no true man. You are one of those unsexed creatures who have no joy in life, no sense of beauty, no high notes.

MITCHENER. No doubt I am, Madam. As a matter of fact, I am not clever at discussing public questions, because, as an English gentleman, I was not brought up to use my brains. But occasionally, after a number of remarks which are perhaps sometimes rather idiotic, I get certain convictions. Thanks to you, I have now got a conviction that this woman question is not a question of lovely and accomplished females, but of dowdies. The average Eng-Englishwoman is a dowdy and never has half a chance of becoming anything else. She hasnt any charm; and she has no high notes except when shes giving her husband a piece of her mind, or calling down the street for one of the children.

LADY CORINTHIA. How disgusting!

MITCHENER. Somebody must do the dowdy work! If we had to choose between pitching all the dowdies into the Thames and pitching all the lovely and accomplished women, the lovely ones would have to go.

LADY CORINTHIA. And if you had to do without Wagner's music or do without your breakfast, you would do without Wagner. Pray does that make eggs and bacon more precious than music, or the butcher and baker better than the poet and philosopher? The scullery may be more necessary to our bare existence than the cathedral. Even humbler apartments might make the same claim. But which is the more essential to the higher life?

MITCHENER. Your arguments are so devilishly ingenious that I feel convinced you got them out of some confounded book. Mine—such as they are—are my own. I imagine its something like this. There is an old saying that if you take care of the pence, the pounds will take care of themselves. Well, perhaps if we take care of the dowdies and the butchers and the bakers, the beauties and the bigwigs will take care of themselves. (Rising and facing her determinedly.) Anyhow, I dont want to have things arranged for me by Wagner. Im not Wagner. How does he know where the shoe pinches me? How do you know where the shoe pinches your washerwoman?—you and your high F in alt. How are you to know when you havent made her comfortable unless she has a vote? Do you want her to come and break your windows?

LADY CORINTHIA. Am I to understand that General Mitchener is a democrat and a suffraget?

MITCHENER. Yes: you have converted me—you and Mrs. Banger.

LADY CORINTHIA. Farewell, creature. (Balsquith enters hurriedly.) Mr. Balsquith: I am going to wait on General Sandstone. He at least is an officer and a gentleman. (She sails out.)

BALSQUITH. Mitchener: the game is up.

MITCHENER. What do you mean?

BALSQUITH. The strain is too much for the Cabinet. The old Liberal and Unionist Free Traders declare that if they are defeated on their resolution to invite tenders from private contractors for carrying on the Army and Navy, they will go solid for votes for women as the only means of restoring the liberties of the country which we have destroyed by compulsory military service.

MITCHENER. Infernal impudence?

BALSQUITH. The Labor party is taking the same line. They say the men got the Factory Acts by hiding behind the women's petticoats, and that they will get votes for the army in the same way.

MITCHENER. Balsquith: we must not yield to clamor. I have just told this lady that I am at last convinced—

BALSQUITH (joyfully). That the suffragets must be supported.

MITCHENER. No: that the anti-suffragets must be put down at all hazards.

BALSQUITH. Same thing.

MITCHENER. No. For you now tell me that the Labor Party demands votes for women. That makes it impossible to give them, because it would be yielding to clamor. The one condition on which we can consent to grant anything in this country is that nobody shall presume to want it.

BALSQUITH (earnestly). Mitchener: its no use. You cant have the conveniences of Democracy without its occasional inconveniences.

MITCHENER. What are its conveniences, I should like to know?

BALSQUITH. When you tell people that they are the real rulers and they can do what they like, nine times out of ten, they say, "All right, tell us what to do." But it happens sometimes that they get an idea of their own; and then of course youre landed.

MITCHENER. Sh—

BALSQUITH (desperately shouting him down). No: its no use telling me to shoot them down: Im not going to do it. After all, I dont suppose votes for women will make much difference. It hasnt in the other countries in which it has been tried.

MITCHENER. I never supposed it would make much difference. What I cant stand is giving in to that Pankhurst lot. Hang it all, Balsquith, it seems only yesterday that we put them in quod for a month. I said at the time that it ought to have been ten years. If my advice had been taken this wouldnt have happened. Its a consolation to me that events are proving how thoroughly right I was.

The Orderly rushes in.

THE ORDERLY. Look ere, sir: Mrs. Banger locked the door of General Sandstone's room on the inside; and shes sitting on his ead until he signs a proclamation for women to serve in the army.

MITCHENER. Put your shoulder to the door and burst it open.

THE ORDERLY. Its only in story books that doors burst open as easy as that. Besides, Im only too thankful to have a locked door between me and Mrs. B.; and so is all the rest of us.

MITCHENER. Cowards. Balsquith: to the rescue! (He dashes out.)

BALSQUITH (ambling calmly to the hearth). This is the business of the Sergeant at Arms rather than of the leader of the House. Theres no use in my tackling Mrs. Banger: she would only sit on my head too.

THE ORDERLY. You take my tip, Mr. Balsquith. Give the women the vote and give the army civil rights; and av done with it.

Mitchener returns.

MITCHENER. Balsquith: prepare to hear the worst.

BALSQUITH. Sandstone is no more?

MITCHENER. On the contrary, he is particularly lively. He has softened Mrs. Banger by a proposal of marriage in which he appears to be perfectly in earnest. He says he has met his ideal at last, a really soldierly woman. She will sit on his head for the rest of his life; and the British Army is now to all intents and purposes commanded by Mrs. Banger. When I remonstrated with Sandstone she positively shouted "Right-about-face. March" at me in the most offensive tone. If she hadnt been a woman I should have punched her head. I precious nearly punched Sandstone's. The horrors of martial law administered by Mrs. Banger are too terrible to be faced. I demand civil rights for the army.

THE ORDERLY (chuckling). Wot oh, General! Wot oh!

MITCHENER. Hold your tongue. (He goes to the door and calls.) Mrs. Farrell! (Returning, and again addressing the Orderly.) Civil rights don't mean the right to be uncivil. (Pleased with his own wit.) Almost a pun. Ha ha!

MRS. FARRELL. Whats the matther now? (She comes to the table.)

MITCHENER (to the Orderly). I have private business with Mrs. Farrell. Outside, you infernal blackguard.

THE ORDERLY (arguing, as usual). Well, I didnt ask to—(Mitchener seizes him by the nape; rushes him out; and slams the door).

MITCHENER. Excuse the abruptness of this communication, Mrs. Farrell; but I know only one woman in the country whose practical ability and force of character can maintain her husband in competition with the husband of Mrs. Banger. I have the honor to propose for your hand.

MRS. FARRELL. Dye mean you want to marry me?

MITCHENER. I do.

MRS. FARRELL. No thank you. Id have to work for you just the same; only I shouldnt get any wages for it.

BALSQUITH. That will be remedied when women get the vote. Ive had to promise that.

MITCHENER (winningly). Mrs. Farrell: you have been charwoman here now ever since I took up my duties. Have you really never, in your more romantic moments, cast a favorable eye on my person?

MRS. FARRELL. Ive been too busy casting an unfavorable eye on your cloze and on the litther you make with your papers.

MITCHENER (wounded). Am I to understand that you refuse me?

MRS. FARRELL. Just wait a bit. (She takes Mitchener's chair and rings up the telephone.) Double three oh seven Elephant.

MITCHENER. I trust youre not ringing for the police, Mrs. Farrell. I assure you Im perfectly sane.

MRS. FARRELL (into the telephone). Is that you, Eliza? (She listens for the answer.) Not out of bed yet! Go and pull her out by the heels, the lazy sthreel; and tell her her mother wants to speak to her very particularly about General Mitchener. (To Mitchener.) Dont you be afeard: I know youre sane enough when youre not talkin about the Germans. (Into the telephone.) Is that you, Eliza? (She listens for the answer.) Dye remember me givin you a clout on the side of the head for tellin me that if I only knew how to play me cards I could marry any general on the staff instead o disgracin you be bein a charwoman? (She listens for the answer.) Well, I can have General Mitchener without playing any cards at all. What dye think I ought to say? (She listens.) Well, Im no chicken myself. (To Mitchener.) How old are you?

MITCHENER (with an effort). Fifty-two.

MRS. FARRELL (into the telephone). He says hes fifty-two. (She listens; then, to Mitchener.) She says youre down in Who's Who as sixty-one.

MITCHENER. Damn Who's Who.

MRS. FARRELL (into the telephone). Anyhow I wouldnt let that stand in the way. (She listens.) If I really WHAT? (She listens.)I cant hear you. If I really WHAT? (She listens.) WHO druv him? I never said a word to— Eh? (She listens.) Oh, LOVE him. Arra dont be a fool, child. (To Mitchener.) She wants to know do I really love you.(Into the telephone.) Its likely indeed Id frighten the man off with any such nonsense, at my age. What? (She listens.) Well, thats just what I was thinkin.

MITCHENER. May I ask what you were thinking, Mrs. Farrell? This suspense is awful.

MRS. FARRELL. I was thinkin that perhaps the Duchess might like her daughter-in-law's mother to be a General's lady betther than to be a charwoman. (Into the telephone.) Waitle youre married yourself, me fine lady: you'll find out that every woman is a charwoman from the day shes married. (She listens.) Then you think I might take him? (She listens.) Glang, you young scald: if I had you here Id teach you manners. (She listens.) Thats enough now. Back wid you to bed; and be thankful Im not there to put me slipper across you. (She rings off.) The impudence! (To Mitchener.) Bless you, me childher, may you be happy, she says. (To Balsquith, going to his side of the room.) Give dear, old Mich me love, she says.

The Orderly opens the door, ushering in Lady Corinthia.

THE ORDERLY. Lady Corinthia Fanshawe to speak to you, sir.

LADY CORINTHIA. General Mitchener: your designs on Mrs. Banger are defeated. She is engaged to General Sandstone. Do you still prefer her to me?

MRS. FARRELL. Hes out o the hunt. Hes engaged to me.

The Orderly overcome by this news reels from the door to the standing desk, and clutches the stool to save himself from collapsing.

MITCHENER. And extremely proud of it, Lady Corinthia.

LADY CORINTHIA (contemptuously). She suits you exactly. (Coming to Balsquith.) Mr. Balsquith: you at least, are not a Philistine.

BALSQUITH. No, Lady Corinthia; but Im a confirmed bachelor. I don't want a wife; but I want an Egeria.

MRS. FARRELL. More shame for you.

LADY CORINTHIA. Silence, woman. The position and functions of a wife may suit your gross nature. An Egeria is exactly what I desire to be. (To Balsquith.) Can you play accompaniments?

BALSQUITH. Melodies only, I regret to say. With one finger. But my brother, who is a very obliging fellow, and not unlike me personally, is acquainted with three chords, with which he manages to accompany most of the comic songs of the day.

LADY CORINTHIA. I do not sing comic songs. Neither will you when I am your Egeria. Come. I give a musical at-home this afternoon. I will allow you to sit at my feet.

BALSQUITH. That is my ideal of romantic happiness. It commits me exactly as far as I desire to venture. Thank you.

THE ORDERLY. Wot price me, General? Wont you celebrate your engagement by doing something for me? Maynt I be promoted to be a sergeant.

MITCHENER. Youre too utterly incompetent to discharge the duties of a sergeant. You are only fit to be a lieutenant. I shall recommend you for a commission.

THE ORDERLY. Hooray! The Parkinsons of Stepney will be proud to have me call on them now. Ill go and tell the sergeant what I think of him. Hooray! (He rushes out.)

MRS. FARRELL (going to the door and calling after him.) You might have the manners to shut the door idther you. (She shuts it and comes between Mitchener and Lady Corinthia.)

MITCHENER. Poor wretch; the day after civil rights are conceded to the army he and Chubbs-Jenkinson will be found incapable of maintaining discipline. They will be sacked and replaced by really capable men. Mrs. Farrell: as we are engaged, and I am anxious to do the correct thing in every way, I am quite willing to kiss you if you wish it.

MRS. FARRELL. Youd only feel like a fool; and so would I.

MITCHENER. You are really the most sensible woman. Ive made an extremely wise choice.

LADY CORINTHIA (To Balsquith). You may kiss my hand, if you wish.

BALSQUITH (cautiously). I think we had better not commit ourselves too far. If I might carry your parasol, that would quite satisfy me. Let us change a subject which threatens to become embarrassing. (To Mitchener.) The moral of the occasion for you, Mitchener, appears to be that youve got to give up treating soldiers as if they were schoolboys.

MITCHENER. The moral for you, Balsquith, is that youve got to give up treating women as if they were angels. Ha ha!

MRS. FARRELL. Its a mercy youve found one another out at last. That's enough now.

CURTAIN

THE DOCTOR'S DILEMMA:

ACT I

On the 15th June 1903, in the early forenoon, a medical student, surname Redpenny, Christian name unknown and of no importance, sits at work in a doctor's consulting-room. He devils for the doctor by answering his letters, acting as his domestic laboratory assistant, and making himself indispensable generally, in return for unspecified advantages involved by intimate intercourse with a leader of his profession, and amounting to an informal apprenticeship and a temporary affiliation. Redpenny is not proud, and will do anything he is asked without reservation of his personal dignity if he is asked in a fellow-creaturely way. He is a wide-open-eyed, ready, credulous, friendly, hasty youth, with his hair and clothes in reluctant transition from the untidy boy to the tidy doctor.

Redpenny is interrupted by the entrance of an old serving-woman who has never known the cares, the preoccupations, the responsibilities, jealousies, and anxieties of personal beauty. She has the complexion of a never-washed gypsy, incurable by any detergent; and she has, not a regular beard and moustaches, which could at least be trimmed and waxed into a masculine presentableness, but a whole crop of small beards and moustaches, mostly springing from moles all over her face. She carries a duster and toddles about meddlesomely, spying out dust so diligently that whilst she is flicking off one speck she is already looking elsewhere for another. In conversation she has the same trick, hardly ever looking at the person she is addressing except when she is excited. She has only one manner, and that is the manner of an old family nurse to a child just after it has learnt to walk. She has used her ugliness to secure indulgences unattainable by Cleopatra or Fair Rosamund, and has the further great advantage over them that age increases her qualification instead of impairing it. Being an industrious, agreeable, and popular old soul, she is a walking sermon on the vanity of feminine prettiness. Just as Redpenny has no discovered Christian name, she has no discovered surname, and is known throughout the doctors' quarter between Cavendish Square and the Marylebone Road simply as Emmy.

The consulting-room has two windows looking on Queen Anne Street. Between the two is a marble-topped console, with haunched gilt legs ending in sphinx claws. The huge pier-glass which surmounts it is mostly disabled from reflection by elaborate painting on its surface of palms, ferns, lilies, tulips, and sunflowers. The adjoining wall contains the fireplace, with two arm-chairs before it. As we happen to face the corner we see nothing of the other two walls. On the right of the fireplace, or rather on the right of any person facing the fireplace, is the door. On its left is the writing-table at which Redpenny sits. It is an untidy table with a microscope, several test tubes, and a spirit lamp standing up through its litter of papers. There is a couch in the middle of the room, at right angles to the console, and parallel to the fireplace. A chair stands between the couch and the windowed wall. The windows have green Venetian blinds and rep curtains; and there is a gasalier; but it is a convert to electric lighting. The wall paper and carpets are mostly green, coeval with the gasalier and the Venetian blinds. The house, in fact, was so well furnished in the middle of the XIXth century that it stands unaltered to this day and is still quite presentable.

EMMY [*entering and immediately beginning to dust the couch*] Theres a lady bothering me to see the doctor.

REDPENNY [*distracted by the interruption*] Well, she cant see the doctor. Look here: whats the use of telling you that the doctor cant take any new patients, when the moment a knock comes to the door, in you bounce to ask whether he can see somebody?

EMMY. Who asked you whether he could see somebody?

REDPENNY. You did.

EMMY. I said theres a lady bothering me to see the doctor. That isnt asking. Its telling.

REDPENNY. Well, is the lady bothering you any reason for you to come bothering me when I'm busy?

EMMY. Have you seen the papers?

REDPENNY. No.

EMMY. Not seen the birthday honors?

REDPENNY [*beginning to swear*] What the—

EMMY. Now, now, ducky!

REDPENNY. What do you suppose I care about the birthday honors? Get out of this with your chattering. Dr Ridgeon will be down before I have these letters ready. Get out.

EMMY. Dr Ridgeon wont never be down any more, young man.

She detects dust on the console and is down on it immediately.

REDPENNY [*jumping up and following her*] What?

EMMY. He's been made a knight. Mind you dont go Dr Ridgeoning him in them letters. Sir Colenso Ridgeon is to be his name now.

REDPENNY. I'm jolly glad.

EMMY. I never was so taken aback. I always thought his great discoveries was fudge (let alone the mess of them) with his drops of blood and tubes full of Maltese fever and the like. Now he'll have a rare laugh at me.

REDPENNY. Serve you right! It was like your cheek to talk to him about science. [*He returns to his table and resumes his writing*].

EMMY. Oh, I dont think much of science; and neither will you when youve lived as long with it as I have. Whats on my mind is answering the door. Old Sir Patrick Cullen has been here already and left first congratulations—hadnt time to come up on his way to the hospital, but was determined to be first—coming back, he said. All the rest will be here too: the knocker will be going all day. What Im afraid of is that the doctor'll want a footman like all the rest, now that he's Sir Colenso. Mind: dont you go putting him up to it, ducky; for he'll never have any comfort with anybody but me to answer the door. I know who to let in and who to keep out. And that reminds me of the poor lady. I think he ought to see her. Shes just the kind that puts him in a good temper. [*She dusts Redpenny's papers*].

REDPENNY. I tell you he cant see anybody. Do go away, Emmy. How can I work with you dusting all over me like this?

EMMY. I'm not hindering you working—if you call writing letters working. There goes the bell. [*She looks out of the window*]. A doctor's carriage. Thats more congratulations. [*She is going out when Sir Colenso Ridgeon enters*]. Have you finished your two eggs, sonny?

RIDGEON. Yes.

EMMY. Have you put on your clean vest?

RIDGEON. Yes.

EMMY. Thats my ducky diamond! Now keep yourself tidy and dont go messing about and dirtying your hands: the people are coming to congratulate you. [*She goes out*].

Sir Colenso Ridgeon is a man of fifty who has never shaken off his youth. He has the off-handed manner and the little audacities of address which a shy and sensitive man acquires in breaking himself in to intercourse with all sorts and conditions of men. His face is a good deal lined; his movements are slower than, for instance, Redpenny's; and his flaxen hair has lost its lustre; but in figure and manner he is more the young man than the titled physician. Even the lines in his face are those of overwork and restless scepticism, perhaps partly of curiosity and appetite, rather than of age. Just at present the announcement of his knighthood in the morning papers makes him specially self-conscious, and consequently specially off-hand with Redpenny.

RIDGEON. Have you seen the papers? Youll have to alter the name in the letters if you havnt.

REDPENNY. Emmy has just told me. I'm awfully glad. I—

RIDGEON. Enough, young man, enough. You will soon get accustomed to it.

REDPENNY. They ought to have done it years ago.

RIDGEON. They would have; only they couldnt stand Emmy opening the door, I daresay.

EMMY [*at the door, announcing*] Dr Shoemaker. [*She withdraws*].

A middle-aged gentleman, well dressed, comes in with a friendly but propitiatory air, not quite sure of his reception. His combination of soft manners and responsive kindliness, with a certain unseizable reserve and a familiar yet foreign chiselling of feature, reveal the Jew: in this instance the handsome gentlemanly Jew, gone a little pigeon-breasted and stale after thirty, as handsome young Jews often do, but still decidedly good-looking.

THE GENTLEMAN. Do you remember me? Schutzmacher. University College school and Belsize Avenue. Loony Schutzmacher, you know.

RIDGEON. What! Loony! [*He shakes hands cordially*]. Why, man, I thought you were dead long ago. Sit down. [*Schutzmacher sits on the couch: Ridgeon on the chair between it and the window*]. Where have you been these thirty years?

SCHUTZMACHER. In general practice, until a few months ago. I've retired.

RIDGEON. Well done, Loony! I wish I could afford to retire. Was your practice in London?

SCHUTZMACHER. No.

RIDGEON. Fashionable coast practice, I suppose.

SCHUTZMACHER. How could I afford to buy a fashionable practice? I hadnt a rap. I set up in a manufacturing town in the midlands in a little surgery at ten shillings a week.

RIDGEON. And made your fortune?

SCHUTZMACHER. Well, I'm pretty comfortable. I have a place in Hertfordshire besides our flat in town. If you ever want a quiet Saturday to Monday, I'll take you down in my motor at an hours notice.

RIDGEON. Just rolling in money! I wish you rich g.p.'s would teach me how to make some. Whats the secret of it?

SCHUTZMACHER. Oh, in my case the secret was simple enough, though I suppose I should have got into trouble if it had attracted any notice. And I'm afraid you'll think it rather infra dig.

RIDGEON. Oh, I have an open mind. What was the secret?

SCHUTZMACHER. Well, the secret was just two words.

RIDGEON. Not Consultation Free, was it?

SCHUTZMACHER [*shocked*] No, no. Really!

RIDGEON [*apologetic*] Of course not. I was only joking.

SCHUTZMACHER. My two words were simply Cure Guaranteed.

RIDGEON [*admiring*] Cure Guaranteed!

SCHUTZMACHER. Guaranteed. After all, thats what everybody wants from a doctor, isnt it?

RIDGEON. My dear loony, it was an inspiration. Was it on the brass plate?

SCHUTZMACHER. There was no brass plate. It was a shop window: red, you know, with black lettering. Doctor Leo Schutzmacher, L.R.C.P.M.R.C.S. Advice and medicine sixpence. Cure Guaranteed.

RIDGEON. And the guarantee proved sound nine times out of ten, eh?

SCHUTZMACHER [*rather hurt at so moderate an estimate*] Oh, much oftener than that. You see, most people get well all right if they are careful and you give them a little sensible advice. And the medicine really did them good. Parrish's Chemical Food: phosphates, you know. One tablespoonful to a twelve-ounce bottle of water: nothing better, no matter what the case is.

RIDGEON. Redpenny: make a note of Parrish's Chemical Food.

SCHUTZMACHER. I take it myself, you know, when I feel run down. Good-bye. You dont mind my calling, do you? Just to congratulate you.

RIDGEON. Delighted, my dear Loony. Come to lunch on Saturday next week. Bring your motor and take me down to Hertford.

SCHUTZMACHER. I will. We shall be delighted. Thank you. Good-bye. [*He goes out with Ridgeon, who returns immediately*].

REDPENNY. Old Paddy Cullen was here before you were up, to be the first to congratulate you.

RIDGEON. Indeed. Who taught you to speak of Sir Patrick Cullen as old Paddy Cullen, you young ruffian?

REDPENNY. You never call him anything else.

RIDGEON. Not now that I am Sir Colenso. Next thing, you fellows will be calling me old Colly Ridgeon.

REDPENNY. We do, at St. Anne's.

RIDGEON. Yach! Thats what makes the medical student the most disgusting figure in modern civilization. No veneration, no manners—no—

EMMY [*at the door, announcing*]. Sir Patrick Cullen. [*She retires*].

Sir Patrick Cullen is more than twenty years older than Ridgeon, not yet quite at the end of his tether, but near it and resigned to it. His name, his plain, downright, sometimes rather arid common sense, his large build and stature, the absence of those odd moments of ceremonial servility by which an old English doctor sometimes shews you what the status of the profession was in England in his youth, and an occasional turn of speech, are Irish; but he has lived all his life in England and is thoroughly acclimatized. His manner to Ridgeon, whom he likes, is whimsical and fatherly: to others he is a little gruff and uninviting, apt to substitute more or less expressive grunts for articulate speech, and generally indisposed, at his age, to make much social effort. He shakes Ridgeon's hand and beams at him cordially and jocularly.

SIR PATRICK. Well, young chap. Is your hat too small for you, eh?

RIDGEON. Much too small. I owe it all to you.

SIR PATRICK. Blarney, my boy. Thank you all the same. [*He sits in one of the arm-chairs near the fireplace. Ridgeon sits on the couch*]. Ive come to talk to you a bit. [*To Redpenny*] Young man: get out.

REDPENNY. Certainly, Sir Patrick [*He collects his papers and makes for the door*].

SIR PATRICK. Thank you. Thats a good lad. [*Redpenny vanishes*]. They all put up with me, these young chaps, because I'm an old man, a real old man, not like you. Youre only beginning to give yourself the airs of age. Did you ever see a boy cultivating a moustache? Well, a middle-aged doctor cultivating a grey head is much the same sort of spectacle.

RIDGEON. Good Lord! yes: I suppose so. And I thought that the days of my vanity were past. Tell me at what age does a man leave off being a fool?

SIR PATRICK. Remember the Frenchman who asked his grandmother at what age we get free from the temptations of love. The old woman said she didn't know. [*Ridgeon laughs*]. Well, I make you the same answer. But the world's growing very interesting to me now, Colly.

RIDGEON. You keep up your interest in science, do you?

SIR PATRICK. Lord! yes. Modern science is a wonderful thing. Look at your great discovery! Look at all the great discoveries! Where are they leading to? Why, right back to my poor dear old father's ideas and discoveries. He's been dead now over forty years. Oh, it's very interesting.

RIDGEON. Well, theres nothing like progress, is there?

SIR PATRICK. Dont misunderstand me, my boy. I'm not belittling your discovery. Most discoveries are made regularly every fifteen years; and it's fully a hundred and fifty since yours was made last. Thats something to be proud of. But your discovery's not new. It's only inoculation. My father practised inoculation until it was made criminal in eighteen-forty. That broke the poor old man's heart, Colly: he died of it. And now it turns out that my father was right after all. Youve brought us back to inoculation.

RIDGEON. I know nothing about smallpox. My line is tuberculosis and typhoid and plague. But of course the principle of all vaccines is the same.

SIR PATRICK. Tuberculosis? M-m-m-m! Youve found out how to cure consumption, eh?

RIDGEON. I believe so.

SIR PATRICK. Ah yes. It's very interesting. What is it the old cardinal says in Browning's play? "I have known four and twenty leaders of revolt." Well, Ive known over thirty men that found out how to cure consumption. Why do people go on dying of it, Colly? Devilment, I suppose. There was my father's old friend George Boddington of Sutton Coldfield. He discovered the open-air cure in eighteen-forty. He was ruined and driven out of his practice for only opening the windows; and now we wont let a consumptive patient have as much as a roof over his head. Oh, it's very VERY interesting to an old man.

RIDGEON. You old cynic, you dont believe a bit in my discovery.

SIR PATRICK. No, no: I dont go quite so far as that, Colly. But still, you remember Jane Marsh?

RIDGEON. Jane Marsh? No.

SIR PATRICK. You dont!

RIDGEON. No.

SIR PATRICK. You mean to tell me you dont remember the woman with the tuberculosis ulcer on her arm?

RIDGEON [*enlightened*] Oh, your washerwoman's daughter. Was her name Jane Marsh? I forgot.

SIR PATRICK. Perhaps youve forgotten also that you undertook to cure her with Koch's tuberculin.

RIDGEON. And instead of curing her, it rotted her arm right off. Yes: I remember. Poor Jane! However, she makes a good living out of that arm now by shewing it at medical lectures.

SIR PATRICK. Still, that wasnt quite what you intended, was it?

RIDGEON. I took my chance of it.

SIR PATRICK. Jane did, you mean.

RIDGEON. Well, it's always the patient who has to take the chance when an experiment is necessary. And we can find out nothing without experiment.

SIR PATRICK. What did you find out from Jane's case?

RIDGEON. I found out that the inoculation that ought to cure sometimes kills.

SIR PATRICK. I could have told you that. Ive tried these modern inoculations a bit myself. Ive killed people with them; and Ive cured people with them; but I gave them up because I never could tell which I was going to do.

RIDGEON [*taking a pamphlet from a drawer in the writing-table and handing it to him*] Read that the next time you have an hour to spare; and youll find out why.

SIR PATRICK [*grumbling and fumbling for his spectacles*] Oh, bother your pamphlets. Whats the practice of it? [*Looking at the pamphlet*] Opsonin? What the devil is opsonin?

RIDGEON. Opsonin is what you butter the disease germs with to make your white blood corpuscles eat them. [*He sits down again on the couch*].

SIR PATRICK. Thats not new. Ive heard this notion that the white corpuscles—what is it that whats his name?—Metchnikoff—calls them?

RIDGEON. Phagocytes.

SIR PATRICK. Aye, phagocytes: yes, yes, yes. Well, I heard this theory that the phagocytes eat up the disease germs years ago: long before you came into fashion. Besides, they dont always eat them.

RIDGEON. They do when you butter them with opsonin.

SIR PATRICK. Gammon.

RIDGEON. No: it's not gammon. What it comes to in practice is this. The phagocytes wont eat the microbes unless the microbes are nicely buttered for them. Well, the patient manufactures the butter for himself all right; but my discovery is that the manufacture of that butter, which I call opsonin, goes on in the system by ups and downs—Nature being always rhythmical, you know—and that what the inoculation does is to stimulate the ups or downs, as the case may be. If we had inoculated Jane Marsh when her butter factory was on the up-grade, we should have cured her arm. But we got in on the downgrade and lost her arm for her. I call the upgrade the positive phase and the down-grade the negative phase. Everything depends on your inoculating at the right moment. Inoculate when the patient is in the negative phase and you kill: inoculate when the patient is in the positive phase and you cure.

SIR PATRICK. And pray how are you to know whether the patient is in the positive or the negative phase?

RIDGEON. Send a drop of the patient's blood to the laboratory at St. Anne's; and in fifteen minutes I'll give you his opsonin index in figures. If the figure is one, inoculate and cure: if it's under point eight, inoculate and kill. Thats my discovery: the most important that has been made since Harvey discovered the circulation of the blood. My tuberculosis patients dont die now.

SIR PATRICK. And mine do when my inoculation catches them in the negative phase, as you call it. Eh?

RIDGEON. Precisely. To inject a vaccine into a patient without first testing his opsonin is as near murder as a respectable practitioner can get. If I wanted to kill s man I should kill him that way.

EMMY [*looking in*] Will you see a lady that wants her husband's lungs cured?

RIDGEON [*impatiently*] No. Havnt I told you I will see nobody?[*To Sir Patrick*] I live in a state of siege ever since it got about that I'm a magician who can cure consumption with a drop of serum. [*To Emmy*] Dont come to me again about people who have no appointments. I tell you I can see nobody.

EMMY. Well, I'll tell her to wait a bit.

RIDGEON [*furious*] Youll tell her I cant see her, and send her away: do you hear?

EMMY [*unmoved*] Well, will you see Mr Cutler Walpole? He dont want a cure: he only wants to congratulate you.

RIDGEON. Of course. Shew him up. [*She turns to go*]. Stop. [*To Sir Patrick*] I want two minutes more with you between ourselves. [*To Emmy*] Emmy: ask Mr. Walpole to wait just two minutes, while I finish a consultation.

EMMY. Oh, he'll wait all right. He's talking to the poor lady. [*She goes out*].

SIR PATRICK. Well? what is it?

RIDGEON. Dont laugh at me. I want your advice.

SIR PATRICK. Professional advice?

RIDGEON. Yes. Theres something the matter with me. I dont know what it is.

SIR PATRICK. Neither do I. I suppose youve been sounded.

RIDGEON. Yes, of course. Theres nothing wrong with any of the organs: nothing special, anyhow. But I have a curious aching: I dont know where: I cant localize it. Sometimes I think it's my heart: sometimes I suspect my spine. It doesnt exactly hurt me; but it unsettles me completely. I feel that something is going to happen. And there are other symptoms. Scraps of tunes come into my head that seem to me very pretty, though theyre quite commonplace.

SIR PATRICK. Do you hear voices?

RIDGEON. No.

SIR PATRICK. I'm glad of that. When my patients tell me that theyve made a greater discovery than Harvey, and that they hear voices, I lock them up.

RIDGEON. You think I'm mad! Thats just the suspicion that has come across me once or twice. Tell me the truth: I can bear it.

SIR PATRICK. Youre sure there are no voices?

RIDGEON. Quite sure.

SIR PATRICK. Then it's only foolishness.

RIDGEON. Have you ever met anything like it before in your practice?

SIR PATRICK. Oh, yes: often. It's very common between the ages of seventeen and twenty-two. It sometimes comes on again at forty or thereabouts. Youre a bachelor, you see. It's not serious—if youre careful.

RIDGEON. About my food?

SIR PATRICK. No: about your behavior. Theres nothing wrong with your spine; and theres nothing wrong with your heart; but theres something wrong with your common sense. Youre not going to die; but you may be going to make a fool of yourself. So be careful.

RIDGEON. I sec you dont believe in my discovery. Well, sometimes I dont believe in it myself. Thank you all the same. Shall we have Walpole up?

SIR PATRICK. Oh, have him up. [*Ridgeon rings*]. He's a clever operator, is Walpole, though he's only one of your chloroform surgeons. In my early days, you made your man drunk; and the porters and students held him down; and you had to set your teeth and finish the job fast. Nowadays you work at your ease; and the pain doesn't come until afterwards, when youve taken your cheque and rolled up your bag and left the house. I tell you, Colly, chloroform has done a lot of mischief. It's enabled every fool to be a surgeon.

RIDGEON [*to Emmy, who answers the bell*] Shew Mr Walpole up.

EMMY. He's talking to the lady.

RIDGEON [*exasperated*] Did I not tell you—

Emmy goes out without heeding him. He gives it up, with a shrug, and plants himself with his back to the console, leaning resignedly against it.

SIR PATRICK. I know your Cutler Walpoles and their like. Theyve found out that a man's body's full of bits and scraps of old organs he has no mortal use for. Thanks to chloroform, you can cut half a dozen of them out without leaving him any the worse, except for the illness and the guineas it costs him. I knew the Walpoles well fifteen years ago. The father used to snip off the ends of people's uvulas for fifty guineas, and paint throats with caustic every day for a year at two guineas a time. His brother-in-law extirpated tonsils for two hundred guineas until he took up women's cases at double the fees. Cutler himself worked hard at anatomy to find something fresh to operate on; and at last he got hold of something he calls the nuciform sac, which he's made quite the fashion. People pay him five hundred guineas to cut it out. They might as well get their hair cut for all the difference it makes; but I suppose they feel important after it. You cant go out to dinner now without your neighbor bragging to you of some useless operation or other.

EMMY [*announcing*] Mr Cutler Walpole. [*She goes out*].

Cutler Walpole is an energetic, unhesitating man of forty, with a cleanly modelled face, very decisive and symmetrical about the shortish, salient, rather pretty nose, and the three trimly turned corners made by his chin and jaws. In comparison with Ridgeon's delicate broken lines, and Sir Patrick's softly rugged aged ones, his face looks machine-made and beeswaxed; but his scrutinizing, daring eyes give it life and force. He seems never at a loss, never in doubt: one feels that if he made a mistake he would make it thoroughly and firmly. He has neat, well-nourished hands, short arms, and is built for strength and compactness rather than for height. He is smartly dressed with a fancy waistcoat, a richly colored scarf secured by a handsome ring, ornaments on his watch chain, spats on his shoes, and a general air of the well-to-do sportsman about him. He goes straight across to Ridgeon and shakes hands with him.

WALPOLE. My dear Ridgeon, best wishes! heartiest congratulations! You deserve it.

RIDGEON. Thank you.

WALPOLE. As a man, mind you. You deserve it as a man. The opsonin is simple rot, as any capable surgeon can tell you; but we're all delighted to see your personal qualities officially recognized. Sir Patrick: how are you? I sent you a paper lately about a little thing I invented: a new saw. For shoulder blades.

SIR PATRICK [*meditatively*] Yes: I got it. It's a good saw: a useful, handy instrument.

WALPOLE [*confidently*] I knew youd see its points.

SIR PATRICK. Yes: I remember that saw sixty-five years ago.

WALPOLE. What!

SIR PATRICK. It was called a cabinetmaker's jimmy then.

WALPOLE. Get out! Nonsense! Cabinetmaker be—

RIDGEON. Never mind him, Walpole. He's jealous.

WALPOLE. By the way, I hope I'm not disturbing you two in anything private.

RIDGEON. No no. Sit down. I was only consulting him. I'm rather out of sorts. Overwork, I suppose.

WALPOLE [*swiftly*] I know whats the matter with you. I can see it in your complexion. I can feel it in the grip of your hand.

RIDGEON. What is it?

WALPOLE. Blood-poisoning.

RIDGEON. Blood-poisoning! Impossible.

WALPOLE. I tell you, blood-poisoning. Ninety-five per cent of the human race suffer from chronic blood-poisoning, and die of it. It's as simple as A.B.C. Your nuciform sac is full of decaying matter—undigested food and waste products—rank ptomaines. Now you take my advice, Ridgeon. Let me cut it out for you. You'll be another man afterwards.

SIR PATRICK. Dont you like him as he is?

WALPOLE. No I dont. I dont like any man who hasnt a healthy circulation. I tell you this: in an intelligently governed country people wouldnt be allowed to go about with nuciform sacs, making themselves centres of infection. The operation ought to be compulsory: it's ten times more important than vaccination.

SIR PATRICK. Have you had your own sac removed, may I ask?

WALPOLE [*triumphantly*] I havnt got one. Look at me! Ive no symptoms. I'm as sound as a bell. About five per cent of the population havnt got any; and I'm one of the five per cent. I'll give you an instance. You know Mrs Jack Foljambe: the smart Mrs Foljambe? I operated at Easter on her sister-in-law, Lady Gorran, and found she had the biggest sac I ever saw: it held about two ounces. Well, Mrs. Foljambe had the right spirit—the genuine hygienic instinct. She couldnt stand her sister-in-law being a clean, sound woman, and she simply a whited sepulchre. So she insisted on my operating on her, too. And by George, sir, she hadnt any sac at all. Not a trace! Not a rudiment!! I was so taken aback—so interested, that I forgot to take the sponges out, and was stitching them up inside her when the nurse missed them. Somehow, I'd made sure she'd have an exceptionally large one. [*He sits down on the couch, squaring his shoulders and shooting his hands out of his cuffs as he sets his knuckles akimbo*].

EMMY [*looking in*] Sir Ralph Bloomfield Bonington.

A long and expectant pause follows this announcement. All look to the door; but there is no Sir Ralph.

RIDGEON [*at last*] Were is he?

EMMY [*looking back*] Drat him, I thought he was following me. He's stayed down to talk to that lady.

RIDGEON [*exploding*] I told you to tell that lady—[*Emmy vanishes*].

WALPOLE [*jumping up again*] Oh, by the way, Ridgeon, that reminds me. Ive been talking to that poor girl. It's her husband; and she thinks it's a case of consumption: the usual wrong diagnosis: these damned general practitioners ought never to be allowed to touch a patient except under the orders of a consultant. She's been describing his symptoms to me; and the case is as plain as a pikestaff: bad blood-poisoning. Now she's poor. She cant afford to have him operated on. Well, you send him to me: I'll do it for nothing. Theres room for him in my nursing home. I'll put him straight, and feed him up and make him happy. I like making people happy. [*He goes to the chair near the window*].

EMMY [*looking in*] Here he is.

Sir Ralph Bloomfield Bonington wafts himself into the room. He is a tall man, with a head like a tall and slender egg. He has been in his time a slender man; but now, in his sixth decade, his waistcoat has filled out somewhat. His fair eyebrows arch good-naturedly and uncritically. He has a most musical voice; his speech is a perpetual anthem; and he never tires of the sound of it. He radiates an enormous self-satisfaction, cheering, reassuring, healing by the mere incompatibility of disease or anxiety with his welcome presence. Even broken bones, it is said, have been known to unite at the sound of his voice: he is a born healer, as independent of mere treatment and skill as any Christian scientist. When he expands into oratory or scientific exposition, he is as energetic as Walpole; but it is with a bland, voluminous, atmospheric energy, which envelops its subject and its audience, and makes interruption or inattention impossible, and imposes veneration and credulity on all but the strongest minds. He is known in the medical world as B. B.; and the envy roused by his success in practice is softened by the conviction that he is, scientifically considered, a colossal humbug: the fact being that, though he knows just as much (and just as little) as his contemporaries, the qualifications that pass muster in common men reveal their weakness when hung on his egregious personality.

B. B. Aha! Sir Colenso. Sir Colenso, eh? Welcome to the order of knighthood.

RIDGEON [*shaking hands*] Thank you, B. B.

B. B. What! Sir Patrick! And how are we to-day? a little chilly? a little stiff? but hale and still the cleverest of us all. [*Sir Patrick grunts*]. What! Walpole! the absent-minded beggar: eh?

WALPOLE. What does that mean?

B. B. Have you forgotten the lovely opera singer I sent you to have that growth taken off her vocal cords?

WALPOLE [*springing to his feet*] Great heavens, man, you dont mean to say you sent her for a throat operation!

B. B. [*archly*] Aha! Ha ha! Aha! [*trilling like a lark as he shakes his finger at Walpole*]. You removed her nuciform sac. Well, well! force of habit! force of habit! Never mind, ne-e-e-ver mind. She got back her voice after it, and thinks you the greatest surgeon alive; and so you are, so you are, so you are.

WALPOLE [*in a tragic whisper, intensely serious*] Blood-poisoning. I see. I see. [*He sits down again*].

SIR PATRICK. And how is a certain distinguished family getting on under your care, Sir Ralph?

B. B. Our friend Ridgeon will be gratified to hear that I have tried his opsonin treatment on little Prince Henry with complete success.

RIDGEON [*startled and anxious*] But how—

B. B. [*continuing*] I suspected typhoid: the head gardener's boy had it; so I just called at St Anne's one day and got a tube of your very excellent serum. You were out, unfortunately.

RIDGEON. I hope they explained to you carefully—

B. B. [*waving away the absurd suggestion*] Lord bless you, my dear fellow, I didnt need any explanations. I'd left my wife in the carriage at the door; and I'd no time to be taught my business by your young chaps. I know all about it. Ive handled these anti-toxins ever since they first came out.

RIDGEON. But theyre not anti-toxins; and theyre dangerous unless you use them at the right time.

B. B. Of course they are. Everything is dangerous unless you take it at the right time. An apple at breakfast does you good: an apple at bedtime upsets you for a week. There are only two rules for anti-toxins. First, dont be afraid of them: second, inject them a quarter of an hour before meals, three times a day.

RIDGEON [*appalled*] Great heavens, B. B., no, no, no.

B. B. [*sweeping on irresistibly*] Yes, yes, yes, Colly. The proof of the pudding is in the eating, you know. It was an immense success. It acted like magic on the little prince. Up went his temperature; off to bed I packed him; and in a week he was all right again, and absolutely immune from typhoid for the rest of his life. The family were very nice about it: their gratitude was quite touching; but I said they owed it all to you, Ridgeon; and I am glad to think that your knighthood is the result.

RIDGEON. I am deeply obliged to you. [*Overcome, he sits down on the chair near the couch*].

B. B. Not at all, not at all. Your own merit. Come! come! come! dont give way.

RIDGEON. It's nothing. I was a little giddy just now. Overwork, I suppose.

WALPOLE. Blood-poisoning.

B. B. Overwork! Theres no such thing. I do the work of ten men. Am I giddy? No. NO. If youre not well, you have a disease. It may be a slight one; but it's a disease. And what is a disease? The lodgment in the system of a pathogenic germ, and the multiplication of that germ. What is the remedy? A very simple one. Find the germ and kill it.

SIR PATRICK. Suppose theres no germ?

B. B. Impossible, Sir Patrick: there must be a germ: else how could the patient be ill?

SIR PATRICK. Can you shew me the germ of overwork?

B. B. No; but why? Why? Because, my dear Sir Patrick, though the germ is there, it's invisible. Nature has given it no danger signal for us. These germs—these bacilli—are translucent bodies, like glass, like water. To make them visible you must stain them. Well, my dear Paddy, do what you will, some of them wont stain. They wont take cochineal: they wont take methylene blue; they wont take gentian violet: they wont take any coloring matter. Consequently, though we know, as scientific men, that they exist, we cannot see them. But can you disprove their existence? Can you conceive the disease existing without them? Can you, for instance, shew me a case of diphtheria without the bacillus?

SIR PATRICK. No; but I'll shew you the same bacillus, without the disease, in your own throat.

B. B. No, not the same, Sir Patrick. It is an entirely different bacillus; only the two are, unfortunately, so exactly alike that you cannot see the difference. You must understand, my dear Sir Patrick, that every one of these interesting little creatures has an imitator. Just as men imitate each other, germs imitate each other. There is the genuine diphtheria bacillus discovered by Loeffler; and there is the pseudo-bacillus, exactly like it, which you could find, as you say, in my own throat.

SIR PATRICK. And how do you tell one from the other?

B. B. Well, obviously, if the bacillus is the genuine Loeffler, you have diphtheria; and if it's the pseudobacillus, youre quite well. Nothing simpler. Science is always simple and always profound. It is only the half-truths that are dangerous. Ignorant faddists pick up some superficial information about germs; and they write to the papers and try to discredit science. They dupe and mislead many honest and worthy people. But science has a perfect answer to them on every point.

> A little learning is a dangerous thing;
> Drink deep; or taste not the Pierian spring.

I mean no disrespect to your generation, Sir Patrick: some of you old stagers did marvels through sheer professional intuition and clinical experience; but when I think of the average men of your day, ignorantly bleeding and cupping and purging, and scattering germs over their patients from their clothes and instruments, and contrast all that with the scientific certainty and simplicity of my treatment of the little prince the other day, I cant help being proud of my own generation: the men who were trained on the germ theory, the veterans of the great struggle over Evolution in the seventies. We may have our faults; but at least we are men of science. That is why I am taking up your treatment, Ridgeon, and pushing it. It's scientific. [*He sits down on the chair near the couch*].

EMMY [*at the door, announcing*] Dr Blenkinsop.

Dr Blenkinsop is a very different case from the others. He is clearly not a prosperous man. He is flabby and shabby, cheaply fed and cheaply clothed. He has the lines made by a conscience between his eyes, and the lines made by continual money worries all over his face, cut all the deeper as he has seen better days, and hails his well-to-do colleagues as their contemporary and old hospital friend, though even in this he has to struggle with the diffidence of poverty and relegation to the poorer middle class.

RIDGEON. How are you, Blenkinsop?

BLENKINSOP. Ive come to offer my humble congratulations. Oh dear! all the great guns are before me.

B. B. [*patronizing, but charming*] How d'ye do Blenkinsop? How d'ye do?

BLENKINSOP. And Sir Patrick, too [*Sir Patrick grunts*].

RIDGEON. Youve met Walpole, of course?

WALPOLE. How d'ye do?

BLENKINSOP. It's the first time Ive had that honor. In my poor little practice there are no chances of meeting you great men. I know nobody but the St Anne's men of my own day. [*To Ridgeon*] And so youre Sir Colenso. How does it feel?

RIDGEON. Foolish at first. Dont take any notice of it.

BLENKINSOP. I'm ashamed to say I havnt a notion what your great discovery is; but I congratulate you all the same for the sake of old times.

B. B. [*shocked*] But, my dear Blenkinsop, you used to be rather keen on science.

BLENKINSOP. Ah, I used to be a lot of things. I used to have two or three decent suits of clothes, and flannels to go up the river on Sundays. Look at me now: this is my best; and it must last till Christmas. What can I do? Ive never opened a book since I was qualified thirty years ago. I used to read the medical papers at first; but you know how soon a man drops that; besides, I cant afford them; and what are they after all but trade papers, full of advertisements? Ive forgotten all my science: whats the use of my pretending I havnt? But I have great experience: clinical experience; and bedside experience is the main thing, isn't it?

B. B. No doubt; always provided, mind you, that you have a sound scientific theory to correlate your observations at the bedside. Mere experience by itself is nothing. If I take my dog to the bedside with me, he sees what I see. But he learns nothing from it. Why? Because he's not a scientific dog.

WALPOLE. It amuses me to hear you physicians and general practitioners talking about clinical experience. What do you see at the bedside but the outside of the patient? Well: it isnt his outside thats wrong, except perhaps in skin cases. What you want is a daily familiarity with people's insides; and that you can only get at the operating table. I know what I'm talking about: Ive been a surgeon and a consultant for twenty years; and Ive never known a general practitioner right in his diagnosis yet. Bring them a perfectly simple case; and they diagnose cancer, and arthritis, and appendicitis, and every other itis, when any really experienced surgeon can see that it's a plain case of blood-poisoning.

BLENKINSOP. Ah, it's easy for you gentlemen to talk; but what would you say if you had my practice? Except for the workmen's clubs, my patients are all clerks and shopmen. They darent be ill: they cant afford it. And when they break down, what can I do for them? You can send your people to St Moritz or to Egypt, or recommend horse exercise or motoring or champagne jelly or complete change and rest for six months. I might as well order my people a slice of the moon. And the worst of it is, I'm too poor to keep well myself on the cooking I have to put up with. Ive such a wretched digestion; and I look it. How am I to inspire confidence? [*He sits disconsolately on the couch*].

RIDGEON [*restlessly*] Dont, Blenkinsop: its too painful. The most tragic thing in the world is a sick doctor.

WALPOLE. Yes, by George: its like a bald-headed man trying to sell a hair restorer. Thank God I'm a surgeon!

B. B. [*sunnily*] I am never sick. Never had a day's illness in my life. Thats what enables me to sympathize with my patients.

WALPOLE [*interested*] What! youre never ill?

B. B. Never.

WALPOLE. Thats interesting. I believe you have no nuciform sac. If you ever do feel at all queer, I should very much like to have a look.

B. B. Thank you, my dear fellow; but I'm too busy just now.

RIDGEON. I was just telling them when you came in, Blenkinsop, that I have worked myself out of sorts.

BLENKINSOP. Well, it seems presumptuous of me to offer a prescription to a great man like you; but still I have great experience; and if I might recommend a pound of ripe greengages every day half an hour before lunch, I'm sure youd find a benefit. Theyre very cheap.

RIDGEON. What do you say to that B. B.?

B. B. [*encouragingly*] Very sensible, Blenkinsop: very sensible indeed. I'm delighted to see that you disapprove of drugs.

SIR PATRICK [*grunts*]!

B. B. [*archly*] Aha! Haha! Did I hear from the fireside armchair the bow-wow of the old school defending its drugs? Ah, believe me, Paddy, the world would be healthier if every chemist's shop in England were demolished. Look at the papers! full of scandalous advertisements of patent medicines! a huge commercial system of quackery and poison. Well, whose fault is it? Ours. I say, ours. We set the example. We spread the superstition. We taught the people to believe in bottles of doctor's stuff; and now they buy it at the stores instead of consulting a medical man.

WALPOLE. Quite true. Ive not prescribed a drug for the last fifteen years.

B. B. Drugs can only repress symptoms: they cannot eradicate disease. The true remedy for all diseases is Nature's remedy. Nature and Science are at one, Sir Patrick, believe me; though you were taught differently. Nature has provided, in the white corpuscles as you call them—in the phagocytes as we call them—a natural means of devouring and destroying all disease germs. There is at bottom only one genuinely scientific treatment for all diseases, and that is to stimulate the phagocytes. Stimulate the phagocytes. Drugs are a delusion. Find the germ of the disease; prepare from it a suitable anti-toxin; inject it three times a day quarter of an hour before meals; and what is the result? The phagocytes are stimulated; they devour the disease; and the patient recovers—unless, of course, he's too far gone. That, I take it, is the essence of Ridgeon's discovery.

SIR PATRICK [*dreamily*] As I sit here, I seem to hear my poor old father talking again.

B. B. [*rising in incredulous amazement*] Your father! But, Lord bless my soul, Paddy, your father must have been an older man than you.

SIR PATRICK. Word for word almost, he said what you say. No more drugs. Nothing but inoculation.

B. B. [*almost contemptuously*] Inoculation! Do you mean smallpox inoculation?

SIR PATRICK. Yes. In the privacy of our family circle, sir, my father used to declare his belief that smallpox inoculation was good, not only for smallpox, but for all fevers.

B. B. [*suddenly rising to the new idea with immense interest and excitement*] What! Ridgeon: did you hear that? Sir Patrick: I am more struck by what you have just told me than I can well express. Your father, sir, anticipated a discovery of my own. Listen, Walpole. Blenkinsop: attend one moment. You will all be intensely interested in this. I was put on the track by accident. I had a typhoid case and a tetanus case side by side in the hospital: a beadle and a city missionary. Think of what that meant for them, poor fellows! Can a beadle be dignified with typhoid? Can a missionary be eloquent with lockjaw? No. NO. Well, I got some typhoid anti-toxin from Ridgeon and a tube of Muldooley's anti-tetanus serum. But the missionary jerked all my things off the table in one of his paroxysms; and in replacing them I put Ridgeon's tube where Muldooley's ought to have been. The consequence was that I inoculated the typhoid case for tetanus and the tetanus case for typhoid. [*The doctors look greatly concerned. B. B., undamped, smiles triumphantly*]. Well, they recovered. THEY RECOVERED. Except for a touch of St Vitus's dance the missionary's as well to-day as ever; and the beadle's ten times the man he was.

BLENKINSOP. Ive known things like that happen. They cant be explained.

B. B. [*severely*] Blenkinsop: there is nothing that cannot be explained by science. What did I do? Did I fold my hands helplessly and say that the case could not be explained? By no means. I sat down and used my brains. I thought the case out on scientific principles. I asked myself why didnt the missionary die of typhoid on top of tetanus, and the beadle of tetanus on top of typhoid? Theres a problem for you, Ridgeon. Think, Sir Patrick. Reflect, Blenkinsop. Look at it without prejudice, Walpole. What is the real work of the anti-toxin? Simply to stimulate the phagocytes. Very well. But so long as you stimulate the phagocytes, what does it matter which particular sort of serum you use for the purpose? Haha! Eh? Do you see? Do you grasp it? Ever since that Ive used all sorts of anti-toxins absolutely indiscriminately, with perfectly satisfactory results. I inoculated the little prince with your stuff, Ridgeon, because I wanted to give you a lift; but two years ago I tried the experiment of treating a scarlet fever case with a sample of hydrophobia serum from the Pasteur Institute, and it answered capitally. It stimulated the phagocytes; and the phagocytes did the rest. That is why Sir Patrick's father found that inoculation cured all fevers. It stimulated the phagocytes. [*He throws himself into his chair, exhausted with the triumph of his demonstration, and beams magnificently on them*].

EMMY [*looking in*] Mr Walpole: your motor's come for you; and it's frightening Sir Patrick's horses; so come along quick.

WALPOLE [*rising*] Good-bye, Ridgeon.

RIDGEON. Good-bye; and many thanks.

B. B. You see my point, Walpole?

EMMY. He cant wait, Sir Ralph. The carriage will be into the area if he dont come.

WALPOLE. I'm coming. [*To B. B.*] Theres nothing in your point: phagocytosis is pure rot: the cases are all blood-poisoning; and the knife is the real remedy. Bye-bye, Sir Paddy. Happy to have met you, Mr. Blenkinsop. Now, Emmy. [*He goes out, followed by Emmy*].

B. B. [*sadly*] Walpole has no intellect. A mere surgeon. Wonderful operator; but, after all, what is operating? Only manual labor. Brain—BRAIN remains master of the situation. The nuciform sac is utter nonsense: theres no such organ. It's a mere accidental kink in the membrane, occurring in perhaps two-and-a-half per cent of the population. Of course I'm glad for Walpole's sake that the operation is fashionable; for he's a dear good fellow; and after all, as I always tell people, the operation will do them no harm: indeed, Ive known the nervous shake-up and the fortnight in bed do people a lot of good after a hard London season; but still it's a shocking fraud. [*Rising*] Well, I must be toddling. Good-bye, Paddy [*Sir Patrick grunts*] good-bye, goodbye. Good-bye, my dear Blenkinsop, good-bye! Goodbye, Ridgeon. Dont fret about your health: you know what to do: if your liver is sluggish, a little mercury never does any harm. If you feel restless, try bromide, If that doesnt answer, a stimulant, you know: a little phosphorus and strychnine. If you cant sleep, trional, trional, trion—

SIR PATRICK [*drily*] But no drugs, Colly, remember that.

B. B. [*firmly*] Certainly not. Quite right, Sir Patrick. As temporary expedients, of course; but as treatment, no, No. Keep away from the chemist's shop, my dear Ridgeon, whatever you do.

RIDGEON [*going to the door with him*] I will. And thank you for the knighthood. Good-bye.

B. B. [*stopping at the door, with the beam in his eye twinkling a little*] By the way, who's your patient?

RIDGEON. Who?

B. B. Downstairs. Charming woman. Tuberculous husband.

RIDGEON. Is she there still?

Emmy [*looking in*] Come on, Sir Ralph: your wife's waiting in the carriage.

B. B. [*suddenly sobered*] Oh! Good-bye. [*He goes out almost precipitately*].

RIDGEON. Emmy: is that woman there still? If so, tell her once for all that I cant and wont see her. Do you hear?

EMMY. Oh, she aint in a hurry: she doesnt mind how long she waits. [*She goes out*].

BLENKINSOP. I must be off, too: every half-hour I spend away from my work costs me eighteen-pence. Good-bye, Sir Patrick.

SIR PATRICK. Good-bye. Good-bye.

RIDGEON. Come to lunch with me some day this week.

BLENKINSOP. I cant afford it, dear boy; and it would put me off my own food for a week. Thank you all the same.

RIDGEON [*uneasy at Blenkinsop's poverty*] Can I do nothing for you?

BLENKINSOP. Well, if you have an old frock-coat to spare? you see what would be an old one for you would be a new one for me; so remember the next time you turn out your wardrobe. Good-bye. [*He hurries out*].

RIDGEON [*looking after him*] Poor chap! [*Turning to Sir Patrick*] So thats why they made me a knight! And thats the medical profession!

SIR PATRICK. And a very good profession, too, my lad. When you know as much as I know of the ignorance and superstition of the patients, youll wonder that we're half as good as we are.

RIDGEON. We're not a profession: we're a conspiracy.

SIR PATRICK. All professions are conspiracies against the laity. And we cant all be geniuses like you. Every fool can get ill; but every fool cant be a good doctor: there are not enough good ones to go round. And for all you know, Bloomfield Bonington kills less people than you do.

RIDGEON. Oh, very likely. But he really ought to know the difference between a vaccine and an anti-toxin. Stimulate the phagocytes! The vaccine doesnt affect the phagocytes at all. He's all wrong: hopelessly, dangerously wrong. To put a tube of serum into his hands is murder: simple murder.

EMMY [*returning*] Now, Sir Patrick. How long more are you going to keep them horses standing in the draught?

SIR PATRICK. Whats that to you, you old catamaran?

EMMY. Come, come, now! none of your temper to me. And it's time for Colly to get to his work.

RIDGEON. Behave yourself, Emmy. Get out.

EMMY. Oh, I learnt how to behave myself before I learnt you to do it. I know what doctors are: sitting talking together about themselves when they ought to be with their poor patients. And I know what horses are, Sir Patrick. I was brought up in the country. Now be good; and come along.

SIR PATRICK [*rising*] Very well, very well, very well. Good-bye, Colly. [*He pats Ridgeon on the shoulder and goes out, turning for a moment at the door to look meditatively at Emmy and say, with grave conviction*] You are an ugly old devil, and no mistake.

EMMY [*highly indignant, calling after him*] Youre no beauty yourself. [*To Ridgeon, much flustered*] Theyve no manners: they think they can say what they like to me; and you set them on, you do. I'll teach them their places. Here now: are you going to see that poor thing or are you not?

RIDGEON. I tell you for the fiftieth time I wont see anybody. Send her away.

EMMY. Oh, I'm tired of being told to send her away. What good will that do her?

RIDGEON. Must I get angry with you, Emmy?

EMMY [*coaxing*] Come now: just see her for a minute to please me: theres a good boy. She's given me half-a-crown. She thinks it's life and death to her husband for her to see you.

RIDGEON. Values her husband's life at half-a-crown!

EMMY. Well, it's all she can afford, poor lamb. Them others think nothing of half-a-sovereign just to talk about themselves to you, the sluts! Besides, she'll put you in a good temper for the day, because it's a good deed to see her; and she's the sort that gets round you.

RIDGEON. Well, she hasnt done so badly. For half-a-crown she's had a consultation with Sir Ralph Bloomfield Bonington and Cutler Walpole. Thats six guineas' worth to start with. I dare say she's consulted Blenkinsop too: thats another eighteenpence.

EMMY. Then youll see her for me, wont you?

RIDGEON. Oh, send her up and be hanged. [*Emmy trots out, satisfied. Ridgeon calls*] Redpenny!

REDPENNY [*appearing at the door*] What is it?

RIDGEON. Theres a patient coming up. If she hasnt gone in five minutes, come in with an urgent call from the hospital for me. You understand: she's to have a strong hint to go.

REDPENNY. Right O! [*He vanishes*].

Ridgeon goes to the glass, and arranges his tie a little.

EMMY [*announcing*] Mrs Doobidad [*Ridgeon leaves the glass and goes to the writing-table*].

The lady comes in. Emmy goes out and shuts the door. Ridgeon, who has put on an impenetrable and rather distant professional manner, turns to the lady, and invites her, by a gesture, to sit down on the couch.

Mrs Dubedat is beyond all demur an arrestingly good-looking young woman. She has something of the grace and romance of a wild creature, with a good deal of the elegance and dignity of a fine lady. Ridgeon, who is extremely susceptible to the beauty of women, instinctively assumes the defensive at once, and hardens his manner still more. He has an impression that she is very well dressed, but she has a figure on which any dress would look well, and carries herself with the unaffected distinction of a woman who has never in her life suffered from those doubts and fears as to her social position which spoil the manners of most middling people. She is tall, slender, and strong; has dark hair, dressed so as to look like hair and not like a bird's nest or a pantaloon's wig (fashion wavering just then between these two models); has unexpectedly narrow, subtle, dark-fringed eyes that alter her expression disturbingly when she is excited and flashes them wide open; is softly impetuous in her speech and swift in her movements; and is just now in mortal anxiety. She carries a portfolio.

MRS DUBEDAT [*in low urgent tones*] Doctor—

RIDGEON [*curtly*] Wait. Before you begin, let me tell you at once that I can do nothing for you. My hands are full. I sent you that message by my old servant. You would not take that answer.

MRS DUBEDAT. How could I?

RIDGEON. You bribed her.

MRS DUBEDAT. I—

RIDGEON. That doesnt matter. She coaxed me to see you. Well, you must take it from me now that with all the good will in the world, I cannot undertake another case.

MRS DUBEDAT. Doctor: you must save my husband. You must. When I explain to you, you will see that you must. It is not an ordinary case, not like any other case. He is not like anybody else in the world: oh, believe me, he is not. I can prove it to you: [*fingering her portfolio*] I have brought some things to shew you. And you can save him: the papers say you can.

RIDGEON. Whats the matter? Tuberculosis?

MRS DUBEDAT. Yes. His left lung—

RIDGEON Yes: you neednt tell me about that.

MRS DUBEDAT. You can cure him, if only you will. It is true that you can, isnt it? [*In great distress*] Oh, tell me, please.

RIDGEON [*warningly*] You are going to be quiet and self-possessed, arnt you?

MRS DUBEDAT. Yes. I beg your pardon. I know I shouldnt—[*Giving way again*] Oh, please, say that you can; and then I shall be all right.

RIDGEON [*huffily*] I am not a curemonger: if you want cures, you must go to the people who sell them. [*Recovering himself, ashamed of the tone of his own voice*] But I have at the hospital ten tuberculous patients whose lives I believe I can save.

MRS DUBEDAT. Thank God!

RIDGEON. Wait a moment. Try to think of those ten patients as ten shipwrecked men on a raft—a raft that is barely large enough to save them—that will not support one more. Another head bobs up through the waves at the side. Another man begs to be taken aboard. He implores the captain of the raft to save him. But the captain can only do that by pushing one of his ten off the raft and drowning him to make room for the new comer. That is what you are asking me to do.

MRS DUBEDAT. But how can that be? I dont understand. Surely—

RIDGEON. You must take my word for it that it is so. My laboratory, my staff, and myself are working at full pressure. We are doing our utmost. The treatment is a new one. It takes time, means, and skill; and there is not enough for another case. Our ten cases are already chosen cases. Do you understand what I mean by chosen?

MRS DUBEDAT. Chosen. No: I cant understand.

RIDGEON [*sternly*] You must understand. Youve got to understand and to face it. In every single one of those ten cases I have had to consider, not only whether the man could be saved, but whether he was worth saving. There were fifty cases to choose from; and forty had to be condemned to death. Some of the forty had young wives and helpless children. If the hardness of their cases could have saved them they would have been saved ten times over. Ive no doubt your case is a hard one: I can see the tears in your eyes [*she hastily wipes her eyes*]: I know that you have a torrent of entreaties ready for me the moment I stop speaking; but it's no use. You must go to another doctor.

MRS DUBEDAT. But can you give me the name of another doctor who understands your secret?

RIDGEON. I have no secret: I am not a quack.

MRS DUBEDAT. I beg your pardon: I didnt mean to say anything wrong. I dont understand how to speak to you. Oh, pray dont be offended.

RIDGEON [*again a little ashamed*] There! there! never mind. [*He relaxes and sits down*]. After all, I'm talking nonsense: I daresay I AM a quack, a quack with a qualification. But my discovery is not patented.

MRS DUBEDAT. Then can any doctor cure my husband? Oh, why dont they do it? I have tried so many: I have spent so much. If only you would give me the name of another doctor.

RIDGEON. Every man in this street is a doctor. But outside myself and the handful of men I am training at St Anne's, there is nobody as yet who has mastered the opsonin treatment. And we are full up? I'm sorry; but that is all I can say. [*Rising*] Good morning.

MRS DUBEDAT [*suddenly and desperately taking some drawings from her portfolio*] Doctor: look at these. You understand drawings: you have good ones in your waiting-room. Look at them. They are his work.

RIDGEON. It's no use my looking. [*He looks, all the same*] Hallo! [*He takes one to the window and studies it*]. Yes: this is the real thing. Yes, yes. [*He looks at another and returns to her*]. These are very clever. Theyre unfinished, arnt they?

MRS DUBEDAT. He gets tired so soon. But you see, dont you, what a genius he is? You see that he is worth saving. Oh, doctor, I married him just to help him to begin: I had money enough to tide him over the hard years at the beginning—to enable him to follow his inspiration until his genius was recognized. And I was useful to him as a model: his drawings of me sold quite quickly.

RIDGEON. Have you got one?

MRS DUBEDAT [*producing another*] Only this one. It was the first.

RIDGEON [*devouring it with his eyes*] Thats a wonderful drawing. Why is it called Jennifer?

MRS DUBEDAT. My name is Jennifer.

RIDGEON. A strange name.

MRS DUBEDAT. Not in Cornwall. I am Cornish. It's only what you call Guinevere.

RIDGEON [*repeating the names with a certain pleasure in them*] Guinevere. Jennifer. [*Looking again at the drawing*] Yes: it's really a wonderful drawing. Excuse me; but may I ask is it for sale? I'll buy it.

MRS DUBEDAT. Oh, take it. It's my own: he gave it to me. Take it. Take them all. Take everything; ask anything; but save him. You can: you will: you must.

REDPENNY [*entering with every sign of alarm*] Theyve just telephoned from the hospital that youre to come instantly—a patient on the point of death. The carriage is waiting.

RIDGEON [*intolerantly*] Oh, nonsense: get out. [*Greatly annoyed*] What do you mean by interrupting me like this?

REDPENNY. But—

RIDGEON. Chut! cant you see I'm engaged? Be off.

Redpenny, bewildered, vanishes.

MRS DUBEDAT [*rising*] Doctor: one instant only before you go—

RIDGEON. Sit down. It's nothing.

MRS DUBEDAT. But the patient. He said he was dying.

RIDGEON. Oh, he's dead by this time. Never mind. Sit down.

MRS DUBEDAT [*sitting down and breaking down*] Oh, you none of you care. You see people die every day.

RIDGEON [*petting her*] Nonsense! it's nothing: I told him to come in and say that. I thought I should want to get rid of you.

MRS DUBEDAT [*shocked at the falsehood*] Oh!

RIDGEON [*continuing*] Dont look so bewildered: theres nobody dying.

MRS DUBEDAT. My husband is.

RIDGEON [*pulling himself together*] Ah, yes: I had forgotten your husband. Mrs Dubedat: you are asking me to do a very serious thing?

MRS DUBEDAT. I am asking you to save the life of a great man.

RIDGEON. You are asking me to kill another man for his sake; for as surely as I undertake another case, I shall have to hand back one of the old ones to the ordinary treatment. Well, I dont shrink from that. I have had to do it before; and I will do it again if you can convince me that his life is more important than the worst life I am now saving. But you must convince me first.

MRS DUBEDAT. He made those drawings; and they are not the best—nothing like the best; only I did not bring the really best: so few people like them. He is twenty-three: his whole life is before him. Wont you let me bring him to you? wont you speak to him? wont you see for yourself?

RIDGEON. Is he well enough to come to a dinner at the Star and Garter at Richmond?

MRS DUBEDAT. Oh yes. Why?

RIDGEON. I'll tell you. I am inviting all my old friends to a dinner to celebrate my knighthood—youve seen about it in the papers, havnt you?

MRS DUBEDAT. Yes, oh yes. That was how I found out about you.

RIDGEON. It will be a doctors' dinner; and it was to have been a bachelors' dinner. I'm a bachelor. Now if you will entertain for me, and bring your husband, he will meet me; and he will meet some of the most eminent men in my profession: Sir Patrick Cullen, Sir Ralph Bloomfield Bonington, Cutler Walpole, and others. I can put the case to them; and your husband will have to stand or fall by what we think of him. Will you come?

MRS DUBEDAT. Yes, of course I will come. Oh, thank you, thank you. And may I bring some of his drawings—the really good ones?

RIDGEON. Yes. I will let you know the date in the course of to-morrow. Leave me your address.

MRS DUBEDAT. Thank you again and again. You have made me so happy: I know you will admire him and like him. This is my address. [*She gives him her card*].

RIDGEON. Thank you. [*He rings*].

MRS DUBEDAT [*embarrassed*] May I—is there—should I—I mean—[*she blushes and stops in confusion*].

RIDGEON. Whats the matter?

MRS DUBEDAT. Your fee for this consultation?

RIDGEON. Oh, I forgot that. Shall we say a beautiful drawing of his favorite model for the whole treatment, including the cure?

MRS DUBEDAT. You are very generous. Thank you. I know you will cure him. Good-bye.

RIDGEON. I will. Good-bye. [*They shake hands*]. By the way, you know, dont you, that tuberculosis is catching. You take every precaution, I hope.

MRS DUBEDAT. I am not likely to forget it. They treat us like lepers at the hotels.

EMMY [*at the door*] Well, deary: have you got round him?

RIDGEON. Yes. Attend to the door and hold your tongue.

EMMY. Thats a good boy. [*She goes out with Mrs Dubedat*].

RIDGEON [*alone*] Consultation free. Cure guaranteed. [*He heaves a great sigh*].

ACT II

After dinner on the terrace at the Star and Garter, Richmond. Cloudless summer night; nothing disturbs the stillness except from time to time the long trajectory of a distant train and the measured clucking of oars coming up from the Thames in the valley below. The dinner is over; and three of the eight chairs are empty. Sir Patrick, with his back to the view, is at the head of the square table with Ridgeon. The two chairs opposite them are empty. On their right come, first, a vacant chair, and then one very fully occupied by B. B., who basks blissfully in the moonbeams. On their left, Schutzmacher and Walpole. The entrance to the hotel is on their right, behind B. B. The five men are silently enjoying their coffee and cigarets, full of food, and not altogether void of wine.

Mrs Dubedat, wrapped up for departure, comes in. They rise, except Sir Patrick; but she takes one of the vacant places at the foot of the table, next B. B.; and they sit down again.

MRS DUBEDAT [*as she enters*] Louis will be here presently. He is shewing Dr Blenkinsop how to work the telephone. [*She sits.*] Oh, I am so sorry we have to go. It seems such a shame, this beautiful night. And we have enjoyed ourselves so much.

RIDGEON. I dont believe another half-hour would do Mr Dubedat a bit of harm.

SIR PATRICK. Come now, Colly, come! come! none of that. You take your man home, Mrs Dubedat; and get him to bed before eleven.

B. B. Yes, yes. Bed before eleven. Quite right, quite right. Sorry to lose you, my dear lady; but Sir Patrick's orders are the laws of—er—of Tyre and Sidon.

WALPOLE. Let me take you home in my motor.

SIR PATRICK. No. You ought to be ashamed of yourself, Walpole. Your motor will take Mr and Mrs Dubedat to the station, and quite far enough too for an open carriage at night.

MRS DUBEDAT. Oh, I am sure the train is best.

RIDGEON. Well, Mrs Dubedat, we have had a most enjoyable evening.

WALPOLE. {Most enjoyable.

B. B. {Delightful. Charming. Unforgettable.

MRS DUBEDAT [*with a touch of shy anxiety*] What did you think of Louis? Or am I wrong to ask?

RIDGEON. Wrong! Why, we are all charmed with him.

WALPOLE. Delighted.

B. B. Most happy to have met him. A privilege, a real privilege.

SIR PATRICK [*grunts*]!

MRS DUBEDAT [*quickly*] Sir Patrick: are YOU uneasy about him?

SIR PATRICK [*discreetly*] I admire his drawings greatly, maam.

MRS DUBEDAT. Yes; but I meant—

RIDGEON. You shall go away quite happy. He's worth saving. He must and shall be saved.

Mrs Dubedat rises and gasps with delight, relief, and gratitude. They all rise except Sir Patrick and Schutzmacher, and come reassuringly to her.

B. B. Certainly, CER-tainly.

WALPOLE. Theres no real difficulty, if only you know what to do.

MRS DUBEDAT. Oh, how can I ever thank you! From this night I can begin to be happy at last. You dont know what I feel.

She sits down in tears. They crowd about her to console her.

B. B. My dear lady: come come! come come! [*very persuasively*] come come!

WALPOLE. Dont mind us. Have a good cry.

RIDGEON. No: dont cry. Your husband had better not know that weve been talking about him.

MRS DUBEDAT [*quickly pulling herself together*] No, of course not. Please dont mind me. What a glorious thing it must be to be a doctor! [*They laugh*]. Dont laugh. You dont know what youve done for me. I never knew until now how deadly afraid I was—how I had come to dread the worst. I never dared let myself know. But now the relief has come: now I know.

Louis Dubedat comes from the hotel, in his overcoat, his throat wrapped in a shawl. He is a slim young man of 23, physically still a stripling, and pretty, though not effeminate. He has turquoise blue eyes, and a trick of looking you straight in the face with them, which, combined with a frank smile, is very engaging. Although he is all nerves, and very observant and quick of apprehension, he is not in the least shy. He is younger than Jennifer; but he patronizes her as a matter of course. The doctors do not put him out in the least: neither Sir Patrick's years nor Bloomfield Bonington's majesty have the smallest apparent effect on him: he is as natural as a cat: he moves among men as most men move among things, though he is intentionally making himself agreeable to them on this occasion. Like all people who can be depended on to take care of themselves, he is welcome company; and his artist's power of appealing to the imagination gains him credit for all sorts of qualities and powers, whether he possesses them or not.

LOUIS [*pulling on his gloves behind Ridgeon's chair*] Now, Jinny-Gwinny: the motor has come round.

RIDGEON. Why do you let him spoil your beautiful name like that, Mrs Dubedat?

MRS DUBEDAT. Oh, on grand occasions I am Jennifer.

B. B. You are a bachelor: you do not understand these things, Ridgeon. Look at me [*They look*]. I also have two names. In moments of domestic worry, I am simple Ralph. When the sun shines in the home, I am Beedle-Deedle-Dumkins. Such is married life! Mr Dubedat: may I ask you to do me a favor before you go. Will you sign your name to this menu card, under the sketch you have made of me?

WALPOLE. Yes; and mine too, if you will be so good.

LOUIS. Certainly. [*He sits down and signs the cards*].

MRS DUBEDAT. Wont you sign Dr Schutzmacher's for him, Louis?

LOUIS. I dont think Dr Schutzmacher is pleased with his portrait. I'll tear it up. [*He reaches across the table for Schutzmacher's menu card, and is about to tear it. Schutzmacher makes no sign*].

RIDGEON. No, no: if Loony doesnt want it, I do.

LOUIS. I'll sign it for you with pleasure. [*He signs and hands it to Ridgeon*]. Ive just been making a little note of the river to-night: it will work up into something good [*he shews a pocket sketch-book*]. I think I'll call it the Silver Danube.

B. B. Ah, charming, charming.

WALPOLE. Very sweet. Youre a nailer at pastel.

Louis coughs, first out of modesty, then from tuberculosis.

SIR PATRICK. Now then, Mr Dubedat: youve had enough of the night air. Take him home, maam.

MRS DUBEDAT. Yes. Come, Louis.

RIDGEON. Never fear. Never mind. I'll make that cough all right.

B. B. We will stimulate the phagocytes. [*With tender effusion, shaking her hand*] Good-night, Mrs Dubedat. Good-night. Good-night.

WALPOLE. If the phagocytes fail, come to me. I'll put you right.

LOUIS. Good-night, Sir Patrick. Happy to have met you.

SIR PATRICK. Night [*half a grunt*].

MRS DUBEDAT. Good-night, Sir Patrick.

SIR PATRICK. Cover yourself well up. Dont think your lungs are made of iron because theyre better than his. Good-night.

MRS DUBEDAT. Thank you. Thank you. Nothing hurts me. Good-night.

Louis goes out through the hotel without noticing Schutzmacher. Mrs Dubedat hesitates, then bows to him. Schutzmacher rises and bows formally, German fashion. She goes out, attended by Ridgeon. The rest resume their seats, ruminating or smoking quietly.

B. B. [*harmoniously*] Dee-lightful couple! Charming woman! Gifted lad! Remarkable talent! Graceful outlines! Perfect evening! Great success! Interesting case! Glorious night! Exquisite scenery! Capital dinner! Stimulating conversation! Restful outing! Good wine! Happy ending! Touching gratitude! Lucky Ridgeon—

RIDGEON [*returning*] Whats that? Calling me, B. B.? [*He goes back to his seat next Sir Patrick*].

B. B. No, no. Only congratulating you on a most successful evening! Enchanting woman! Thorough breeding! Gentle nature! Refined—

Blenkinsop comes from the hotel and takes the empty chair next Ridgeon.

BLENKINSOP. I'm so sorry to have left you like this, Ridgeon; but it was a telephone message from the police. Theyve found half a milkman at our level crossing with a prescription of mine in its pocket. Wheres Mr Dubedat?

RIDGEON. Gone.

BLENKINSOP [*rising, very pale*] Gone!

RIDGEON. Just this moment—

BLENKINSOP. Perhaps I could overtake him—[*he rushes into the hotel*].

WALPOLE [*calling after him*] He's in the motor, man, miles off. You can—[*giving it up*]. No use.

RIDGEON. Theyre really very nice people. I confess I was afraid the husband would turn out an appalling bounder. But he's almost as charming in his way as she is in hers. And theres no mistake about his being a genius. It's something to have got a case really worth saving. Somebody else will have to go; but at all events it will be easy to find a worse man.

SIR PATRICK. How do you know?

RIDGEON. Come now, Sir Paddy, no growling. Have something more to drink.

SIR PATRICK. No, thank you.

WALPOLE. Do you see anything wrong with Dubedat, B. B.?

B. B. Oh, a charming young fellow. Besides, after all, what could be wrong with him? Look at him. What could be wrong with him?

SIR PATRICK. There are two things that can be wrong with any man. One of them is a cheque. The other is a woman. Until you know that a man's sound on these two points, you know nothing about him.

B. B. Ah, cynic, cynic!

WALPOLE. He's all right as to the cheque, for a while at all events. He talked to me quite frankly before dinner as to the pressure of money difficulties on an artist. He says he has no vices and is very economical, but that theres one extravagance he cant afford and yet cant resist; and that is dressing his wife prettily. So I said, bang plump out, "Let me lend you twenty pounds, and pay me when your ship comes home." He was really very nice about it. He took it like a man; and it was a pleasure to see how happy it made him, poor chap.

B. B. [*who has listened to Walpole with growing perturbation*] But—but—but—when was this, may I ask?

WALPOLE. When I joined you that time down by the river.

B. B. But, my dear Walpole, he had just borrowed ten pounds from me.

WALPOLE. What!

SIR PATRICK [*grunts*]!

B. B. [*indulgently*] Well, well, it was really hardly borrowing; for he said heaven only knew when he could pay me. I couldnt refuse. It appears that Mrs Dubedat has taken a sort of fancy to me—

WALPOLE [*quickly*] No: it was to me.

B. B. Certainly not. Your name was never mentioned between us. He is so wrapped up in his work that he has to leave her a good deal alone; and the poor innocent young fellow—he has of course no idea of my position or how busy I am—actually wanted me to call occasionally and talk to her.

WALPOLE. Exactly what he said to me!

B. B. Pooh! Pooh pooh! Really, I must say. [*Much disturbed, he rises and goes up to the balustrade, contemplating the landscape vexedly*].

WALPOLE. Look here, Ridgeon! this is beginning to look serious.

Blenkinsop, very anxious and wretched, but trying to look unconcerned, comes back.

RIDGEON. Well, did you catch him?

BLENKINSOP. No. Excuse my running away like that. [*He sits down at the foot of the table, next Bloomfeld Bonington's chair*].

WALPOLE. Anything the matter?

BLENKINSOP. Oh no. A trifle—something ridiculous. It cant be helped. Never mind.

RIDGEON. Was it anything about Dubedat?

BLENKINSOP [*almost breaking down*] I ought to keep it to myself, I know. I cant tell you, Ridgeon, how ashamed I am of dragging my miserable poverty to your dinner after all your kindness. It's not that you wont ask me again; but it's so humiliating. And I did so look forward to one evening in my dress clothes (THEYRE still presentable, you see) with all my troubles left behind, just like old times.

RIDGEON. But what has happened?

BLENKINSOP. Oh, nothing. It's too ridiculous. I had just scraped up four shillings for this little outing; and it cost me one-and-fourpence to get here. Well, Dubedat asked me to lend him half-a-crown to tip the chambermaid of the room his wife left her wraps in, and for the cloakroom. He said he only wanted it for five minutes, as she had his purse. So of course I lent it to him. And he's forgotten to pay me. I've just tuppence to get back with.

RIDGEON. Oh, never mind that—

BLENKINSOP [*stopping him resolutely*] No: I know what youre going to say; but I wont take it. Ive never borrowed a penny; and I never will. Ive nothing left but my friends; and I wont sell them. If none of you were to be able to meet me without being afraid that my civility was leading up to the loan of five shillings, there would be an end of everything for me. I'll take your old clothes, Colly, sooner than disgrace you by talking to you in the street in my own; but I wont borrow money. I'll train it as far as the twopence will take me; and I'll tramp the rest.

WALPOLE. Youll do the whole distance in my motor. [*They are all greatly relieved; and Walpole hastens to get away from the painful subject by adding*] Did he get anything out of you, Mr Schutzmacher?

SCHUTZMACHER [*shakes his head in a most expressive negative*].

WALPOLE. You didnt appreciate his drawing, I think.

SCHUTZMACHER. Oh yes I did. I should have liked very much to have kept the sketch and got it autographed.

B. B. But why didnt you?

SCHUTZMACHER. Well, the fact is, when I joined Dubedat after his conversation with Mr Walpole, he said the Jews were the only people who knew anything about art, and that though he had to put up with your Philistine twaddle, as he called it, it was what I said about the drawings that really pleased him. He also said that his wife was greatly struck with my knowledge, and that she always admired Jews. Then he asked me to advance him 50 pounds on the security of the drawings.

B. B. [*All*] No, no. Positively! Seriously!
WALPOLE [*exclaiming*] What! Another fifty!
BLENKINSOP [*together*] Think of that! SIR
PATRICK [*grunts*]!

SCHUTZMACHER. Of course I couldnt lend money to a stranger like that.

B. B. I envy you the power to say No, Mr Schutzmacher. Of course, I knew I oughtnt to lend money to a young fellow in that way; but I simply hadnt the nerve to refuse. I couldnt very well, you know, could I?

SCHUTZMACHER. I dont understand that. I felt that I couldnt very well lend it.

WALPOLE. What did he say?

SCHUTZMACHER. Well, he made a very uncalled-for remark about a Jew not understanding the feelings of a gentleman. I must say you Gentiles are very hard to please. You say we are no gentlemen when we lend money; and when we refuse to lend it you say just the same. I didnt mean to behave badly. As I told him, I might have lent it to him if he had been a Jew himself.

SIR PATRICK [*with a grunt*] And what did he say to that?

SCHUTZMACHER. Oh, he began trying to persuade me that he was one of the chosen people—that his artistic faculty shewed it, and that his name was as foreign as my own. He said he didnt really want 50 pounds; that he was only joking; that all he wanted was a couple of sovereigns.

B. B. No, no, Mr Schutzmacher. You invented that last touch. Seriously, now?

SCHUTZMACHER. No. You cant improve on Nature in telling stories about gentlemen like Mr Dubedat.

BLENKINSOP. You certainly do stand by one another, you chosen people, Mr Schutzmacher.

SCHUTZMACHER. Not at all. Personally, I like Englishmen better than Jews, and always associate with them. Thats only natural, because, as I am a Jew, theres nothing interesting in a Jew to me, whereas there is always something interesting and foreign in an Englishman. But in money matters it's quite different. You see, when an Englishman borrows, all he knows or cares is that he wants money; and he'll sign anything to get it, without in the least understanding it, or intending to carry out the agreement if it turns out badly for him. In fact, he thinks you a cad if you ask him to carry it out under such circumstances. Just like the Merchant of Venice, you know. But if a Jew makes an agreement, he means to keep it and expects you to keep it. If he wants money for a time, he borrows it and knows he must pay it at the end of the time. If he knows he cant pay, he begs it as a gift.

RIDGEON. Come, Loony! do you mean to say that Jews are never rogues and thieves?

SCHUTZMACHER. Oh, not at all. But I was not talking of criminals. I was comparing honest Englishmen with honest Jews.

One of the hotel maids, a pretty, fair-haired woman of about 25, comes from the hotel, rather furtively. She accosts Ridgeon.

THE MAID. I beg your pardon, sir—

RIDGEON. Eh?

THE MAID. I beg pardon, sir. It's not about the hotel. I'm not allowed to be on the terrace; and I should be discharged if I were seen speaking to you, unless you were kind enough to say you called me to ask whether the motor has come back from the station yet.

WALPOLE. Has it?

THE MAID. Yes, sir.

RIDGEON. Well, what do you want?

THE MAID. Would you mind, sir, giving me the address of the gentleman that was with you at dinner?

RIDGEON [*sharply*] Yes, of course I should mind very much. You have no right to ask.

THE MAID. Yes, sir, I know it looks like that. But what am I to do?

SIR PATRICK. Whats the matter with you?

THE MAID. Nothing, sir. I want the address: thats all.

B. B. You mean the young gentleman?

THE MAID. Yes, sir: that went to catch the train with the woman he brought with him.

RIDGEON. The woman! Do you mean the lady who dined here? the gentleman's wife?

THE MAID. Dont believe them, sir. She cant be his wife. I'm his wife.

B. B. {[*in amazed remonstrance*] My good girl!

RIDGEON {You his wife!

WALPOLE {What! whats that? Oh, this is getting perfectly fascinating, Ridgeon.

THE MAID. I could run upstairs and get you my marriage lines in a minute, sir, if you doubt my word. He's Mr Louis Dubedat, isnt he?

RIDGEON. Yes.

THE MAID. Well, sir, you may believe me or not; but I'm the lawful Mrs Dubedat.

SIR PATRICK. And why arnt you living with your husband?

THE MAID. We couldnt afford it, sir. I had thirty pounds saved; and we spent it all on our honeymoon in three weeks, and a lot more that he borrowed. Then I had to go back into service, and he went to London to get work at his drawing; and he never wrote me a line or sent me an address. I never saw nor heard of him again until I caught sight of him from the window going off in the motor with that woman.

SIR PATRICK. Well, thats two wives to start with.

B. B. Now upon my soul I dont want to be uncharitable; but really I'm beginning to suspect that our young friend is rather careless.

SIR PATRICK. Beginning to think! How long will it take you, man, to find out that he's a damned young blackguard?

BLENKINSOP. Oh, thats severe, Sir Patrick, very severe. Of course it's bigamy; but still he's very young; and she's very pretty. Mr Walpole: may I spunge on you for another of those nice cigarets of yours? [*He changes his seat for the one next Walpole*].

WALPOLE. Certainly. [*He feels in his pockets*]. Oh bother! Where—? [*Suddenly remembering*] I say: I recollect now: I passed my cigaret case to Dubedat and he didnt return it. It was a gold one.

THE MAID. He didnt mean any harm: he never thinks about things like that, sir. I'll get it back for you, sir, if youll tell me where to find him.

RIDGEON. What am I to do? Shall I give her the address or not?

SIR PATRICK. Give her your own address; and then we'll see. [*To the maid*] Youll have to be content with that for the present, my girl. [*Ridgeon gives her his card*]. Whats your name?

THE MAID. Minnie Tinwell, sir.

SIR PATRICK. Well, you write him a letter to care of this gentleman; and it will be sent on. Now be off with you.

THE MAID. Thank you, sir. I'm sure you wouldnt see me wronged. Thank you all, gentlemen; and excuse the liberty.

She goes into the hotel. They match her in silence.

RIDGEON [*when she is gone*] Do you realize, chaps, that we have promised Mrs Dubedat to save this fellow's life?

BLENKINSOP. Whats the matter with him?

RIDGEON. Tuberculosis.

BLENKINSOP [*interested*] And can you cure that?

RIDGEON. I believe so.

BLENKINSOP. Then I wish youd cure me. My right lung is touched, I'm sorry to say.

RIDGEON } { What! Your lung is
B.B } [*all* { going?
SIR } *to-* { My dear Blenkinsop,
PATRICK } *get* { what do you tell me?
WALPOLE } *her*] { [*full of concern for*
{ *Blenkinsop he comes*
{ *back from the balus-*
{ *trade*]. Eh? Eh?
{ Whats that? Hullo
{ you know., you must-
{ n't neglect this,

BLENKINSOP [*putting his fingers in his ears*] No, no: it's no use. I know what youre going to say:

Ive said it often to others. I cant afford to take care of myself; and theres an end of it. If a fortnight's holiday would save my life, I'd have to die. I shall get on as others have to get on. We cant all go to St Moritz or to Egypt, you know, Sir Ralph. Dont talk about it.

Embarrassed silence.

SIR PATRICK [*grunts and looks hard at Ridgeon*]!

SCHUTZMACHER [*looking at his watch and rising*] I must go. It's been a very pleasant evening, Colly. You might let me have my portrait if you dont mind. I'll send Mr Dubedat that couple of sovereigns for it.

RIDGEON [*giving him the menu card*] Oh dont do that, Loony. I dont think he'd like that.

SCHUTZMACHER. Well, of course I shant if you feel that way about it. But I dont think you understand Dubedat. However, perhaps thats because I'm a Jew. Good-night, Dr Blenkinsop [*shaking hands*].

BLENKINSOP. Good-night, sir—I mean—Good-night.

SCHUTZMACHER [*waving his hand to the rest*] Goodnight, everybody.

WALPOLE {
B. B. {
SIR PATRICK { Good-night.
RIDGEON {

B. B. repeats the salutation several times, in varied musical tones. Schutzmacher goes out.

SIR PATRICK. Its time for us all to move. [*He rises and comes between Blenkinsop and Walpole. Ridgeon also rises*]. Mr Walpole: take Blenkinsop home: he's had enough of the open air cure for tonight. Have you a thick overcoat to wear in the motor, Dr Blenkinsop?

BLENKINSOP. Oh, theyll give me some brown paper in the hotel; and a few thicknesses of brown paper across the chest are better than any fur coat.

WALPOLE. Well, come along. Good-night, Colly. Youre coming with us, arnt you, B. B.?

B. B. Yes: I'm coming. [*Walpole and Blenkinsop go into the hotel*]. Good-night, my dear Ridgeon [*shaking hands affectionately*]. Dont let us lose sight of your interesting patient and his very charming wife. We must not judge him too hastily, you know. [*With unction*] G o o o o o o o o o d-night, Paddy. Bless you, dear old chap. [*Sir Patrick utters a formidable grunt. B. B. laughs and pats him indulgently on the shoulder*] Good-night. Good-night. Good-night. Good-night. [*He good-nights himself into the hotel*].

The others have meanwhile gone without ceremony. Ridgeon and Sir Patrick are left alone together. Ridgeon, deep in thought, comes down to Sir Patrick.

SIR PATRICK. Well, Mr Savior of Lives: which is it to be? that honest decent man Blenkinsop, or that rotten blackguard of an artist, eh?

RIDGEON. Its not an easy case to judge, is it? Blenkinsop's an honest decent man; but is he any use? Dubedat's a rotten blackguard; but he's a genuine source of pretty and pleasant and good things.

SIR PATRICK. What will he be a source of for that poor innocent wife of his, when she finds him out?

RIDGEON. Thats true. Her life will be a hell.

SIR PATRICK. And tell me this. Suppose you had this choice put before you: either to go through life and find all the pictures bad but all the men and women good, or to go through life and find all the pictures good and all the men and women rotten. Which would you choose?

RIDGEON. Thats a devilishly difficult question, Paddy. The pictures are so agreeable, and the good people so infernally disagreeable and mischievous, that I really cant undertake to say offhand which I should prefer to do without.

SIR PATRICK. Come come! none of your cleverness with me: I'm too old for it. Blenkinsop isnt that sort of good man; and you know it.

RIDGEON. It would be simpler if Blenkinsop could paint Dubedat's pictures.

SIR PATRICK. It would be simpler still if Dubedat had some of Blenkinsop's honesty. The world isnt going to be made simple for you, my lad: you must take it as it is. Youve to hold the scales between Blenkinsop and Dubedat. Hold them fairly.

RIDGEON. Well, I'll be as fair as I can. I'll put into one scale all the pounds Dubedat has borrowed, and into the other all the half-crowns that Blenkinsop hasnt borrowed.

SIR PATRICK. And youll take out of Dubedat's scale all the faith he has destroyed and the honor he has lost, and youll put into Blenkinsop's scale all the faith he has justified and the honor he has created.

RIDGEON. Come come, Paddy! none of your claptrap with me: I'm too sceptical for it. I'm not at all convinced that the world wouldnt be a better world if everybody behaved as Dubedat does than it is now that everybody behaves as Blenkinsop does.

SIR PATRICK. Then why dont you behave as Dubedat does?

RIDGEON. Ah, that beats me. Thats the experimental test. Still, it's a dilemma. It's a dilemma. You see theres a complication we havnt mentioned.

SIR PATRICK. Whats that?

RIDGEON. Well, if I let Blenkinsop die, at least nobody can say I did it because I wanted to marry his widow.

SIR PATRICK. Eh? Whats that?

RIDGEON. Now if I let Dubedat die, I'll marry his widow.

SIR PATRICK. Perhaps she wont have you, you know.

RIDGEON [*with a self-assured shake of the head*] I've a pretty good flair for that sort of thing. I know when a woman is interested in me. She is.

SIR PATRICK. Well, sometimes a man knows best; and sometimes he knows worst. Youd much better cure them both.

RIDGEON. I cant. I'm at my limit. I can squeeze in one more case, but not two. I must choose.

SIR PATRICK. Well, you must choose as if she didnt exist: thats clear.

RIDGEON. Is that clear to you? Mind: it's not clear to me. She troubles my judgment.

SIR PATRICK. To me, it's a plain choice between a man and a lot of pictures.

RIDGEON. It's easier to replace a dead man than a good picture.

SIR PATRICK. Colly: when you live in an age that runs to pictures and statues and plays and brass bands because its men and women are not good enough to comfort its poor aching soul, you should thank Providence that you belong to a profession which is a high and great profession because its business is to heal and mend men and women.

RIDGEON. In short, as a member of a high and great profession, I'm to kill my patient.

SIR PATRICK. Dont talk wicked nonsense. You cant kill him. But you can leave him in other hands.

RIDGEON. In B. B.'s, for instance: eh? [*looking at him significantly*].

SIR PATRICK [*demurely facing his look*] Sir Ralph Bloomfield Bonington is a very eminent physician.

RIDGEON. He is.

SIR PATRICK. I'm going for my hat.

Ridgeon strikes the bell as Sir Patrick makes for the hotel. A waiter comes.

RIDGEON [*to the waiter*] My bill, please.

WAITER. Yes, sir.

He goes for it.

ACT III

In Dubedat's studio. Viewed from the large window the outer door is in the wall on the left at the near end. The door leading to the inner rooms is in the opposite wall, at the far end. The facing wall has neither window nor door. The plaster on all the walls is uncovered and undecorated, except by scrawlings of charcoal sketches and memoranda. There is a studio throne (a chair on a dais) a little to the left, opposite the inner door, and an easel to the right, opposite the outer door, with a dilapidated chair at it. Near the easel and against the wall is a bare wooden table with bottles and jars of oil and medium, paint-smudged rags, tubes of color, brushes, charcoal, a small last figure, a kettle and spirit-lamp, and other odds and ends. By the table is a sofa, littered with drawing blocks, sketch-books, loose sheets of paper, newspapers, books, and more smudged rags. Next the outer door is an umbrella and hat stand, occupied partly by Louis' hats and cloak and muffler, and partly by odds and ends of costumes. There is an old piano stool on the near side of this door. In the corner near the inner door is a little tea-table. A lay figure, in a cardinal's robe and hat, with an hour-glass in one hand and a scythe slung on its back, smiles with inane malice at Louis, who, in a milkman's smock much smudged with colors, is painting a piece of brocade which he has draped about his wife.

She is sitting on the throne, not interested in the painting, and appealing to him very anxiously about another matter.

MRS DUBEDAT. Promise.

LOUIS [*putting on a touch of paint with notable skill and care and answering quite perfunctorily*] I promise, my darling.

MRS DUBEDAT. When you want money, you will always come to me.

LOUIS. But it's so sordid, dearest. I hate money. I cant keep always bothering you for money, money, money. Thats what drives me sometimes to ask other people, though I hate doing it.

MRS DUBEDAT. It is far better to ask me, dear. It gives people a wrong idea of you.

LOUIS. But I want to spare your little fortune, and raise money on my own work. Dont be unhappy, love: I can easily earn enough to pay it all back. I shall have a one-man-show next season; and then there will be no more money troubles. [*Putting down his palette*] There! I mustnt do any more on that until it's bone-dry; so you may come down.

MRS DUBEDAT [*throwing off the drapery as she steps down, and revealing a plain frock of tussore silk*] But you have promised, remember, seriously and faithfully, never to borrow again until you have first asked me.

LOUIS. Seriously and faithfully. [*Embracing her*] Ah, my love, how right you are! how much it means to me to have you by me to guard me against living too much in the skies. On my solemn oath, from this moment forth I will never borrow another penny.

MRS DUBEDAT [*delighted*] Ah, thats right. Does his wicked worrying wife torment him and drag him down from the clouds. [*She kisses him*]. And now, dear, wont you finish those drawings for Maclean?

LOUIS. Oh, they dont matter. Ive got nearly all the money from him in advance.

MRS DUBEDAT. But, dearest, that is just the reason why you should finish them. He asked me the other day whether you really intended to finish them.

LOUIS. Confound his impudence! What the devil does he take me for? Now that just destroys all my interest in the beastly job. Ive a good mind to throw up the commission, and pay him back his money.

MRS DUBEDAT. We cant afford that, dear. You had better finish the drawings and have done with them. I think it is a mistake to accept money in advance.

LOUIS. But how are we to live?

MRS DUBEDAT. Well, Louis, it is getting hard enough as it is, now that they are all refusing to pay except on delivery.

LOUIS. Damn those fellows! they think of nothing and care for nothing but their wretched money.

MRS DUBEDAT. Still, if they pay us, they ought to have what they pay for.

LOUIS [*coaxing;*] There now: thats enough lecturing for to-day. Ive promised to be good, havnt I?

MRS DUDEBAT [*putting her arms round his neck*] You know that I hate lecturing, and that I dont for a moment misunderstand you, dear, dont you?

LOUIS [*fondly*] I know. I know. I'm a wretch; and youre an angel. Oh, if only I were strong enough to work steadily, I'd make my darling's house a temple, and her shrine a chapel more beautiful than was ever imagined. I cant pass the shops without wrestling with the temptation to go in and order all the really good things they have for you.

MRS DUBEDAT. I want nothing but you, dear. [*She gives him a caress, to which he responds so passionately that she disengages herself*]. There! be good now: remember that the doctors are coming this morning. Isnt it extraordinarily kind of them, Louis, to insist on coming? all of them, to consult about you?

LOUIS [*coolly*] Oh, I daresay they think it will be a feather in their cap to cure a rising artist. They wouldnt come if it didnt amuse them, anyhow. [*Someone knocks at the door*]. I say: its not time yet, is it?

MRS DUDEBAT. No, not quite yet.

LOUIS [*opening the door and finding Ridgeon there*] Hello, Ridgeon. Delighted to see you. Come in.

MRS DUDEBAT [*shaking hands*] It's so good of you to come, doctor.

LOUIS. Excuse this place, wont you? Its only a studio, you know: theres no real convenience for living here. But we pig along somehow, thanks to Jennifer.

MRS DUBEDAT. Now I'll run away. Perhaps later on, when youre finished with Louis, I may come in and hear the verdict. [*Ridgeon bows rather constrainedly*]. Would you rather I didnt?

RIDGEON. Not at all. Not at all.

Mrs Dubedat looks at him, a little puzzled by his formal manner; then goes into the inner room.

LOUIS [*flippantly*] I say: dont look so grave. Theres nothing awful going to happen, is there?

RIDGEON. No.

LOUIS. Thats all right. Poor Jennifer has been looking forward to your visit more than you can imagine. Shes taken quite a fancy to you, Ridgeon. The poor girl has nobody to talk to: I'm always painting. [*Taking up a sketch*] Theres a little sketch I made of her yesterday.

RIDGEON. She shewed it to me a fortnight ago when she first called on me.

LOUIS [*quite unabashed*] Oh! did she? Good Lord! how time does fly! I could have sworn I'd only just finished it. It's hard for her here, seeing me piling up drawings and nothing coming in for them. Of course I shall sell them next year fast enough, after my one-man-show; but while the grass grows the steed starves. I hate to have her coming to me for money, and having none to give her. But what can I do?

RIDGEON. I understood that Mrs Dubedat had some property of her own.

Louis. Oh yes, a little; but how could a man with any decency of feeling touch that? Suppose I did, what would she have to live on if I died? I'm not insured: cant afford the premiums. [*Picking out another drawing*] How do you like that?

RIDGEON [*putting it aside*] I have not come here to-day to look at your drawings. I have more serious and pressing business with you.

LOUIS. You want to sound my wretched lung. [*With impulsive candor*] My dear Ridgeon: I'll be frank with you. Whats the matter in this house isnt lungs but bills. It doesnt matter about me; but Jennifer has actually to economize in the matter of food. Youve made us feel that we can treat you as a friend. Will you lend us a hundred and fifty pounds?

RIDGEON. No.

LOUIS [*surprised*] Why not?

RIDGEON. I am not a rich man; and I want every penny I can spare and more for my researches.

LOUIS. You mean youd want the money back again.

RIDGEON. I presume people sometimes have that in view when they lend money.

LOUIS [*after a moment's reflection*] Well, I can manage that for you. I'll give you a cheque—or see here: theres no reason why you shouldnt have your bit too: I'll give you a cheque for two hundred.

RIDGEON. Why not cash the cheque at once without troubling me?

LOUIS. Bless you! they wouldnt cash it: I'm overdrawn as it is. No: the way to work it is this. I'll postdate the cheque next October. In October Jennifer's dividends come in. Well, you present the cheque. It will be returned marked "refer to drawer" or some rubbish of that sort. Then you can take it to Jennifer, and hint that if the cheque isnt taken up at once I shall be put in prison. She'll pay you like a shot. Youll clear 50 pounds; and youll do me a real service; for I do want the money very badly, old chap, I assure you.

RIDGEON [*staring at him*] You see no objection to the transaction; and you anticipate none from me!

LOUIS. Well, what objection can there be? It's quite safe. I can convince you about the dividends.

RIDGEON. I mean on the score of its being—shall I say dishonorable?

LOUIS. Well, of course I shouldnt suggest it if I didnt want the money.

RIDGEON. Indeed! Well, you will have to find some other means of getting it.

LOUIS. Do you mean that you refuse?

RIDGEON. Do I mean—! [*letting his indignation loose*] Of course I refuse, man. What do you take me for? How dare you make such a proposal to me?

LOUIS. Why not?

RIDGEON. Faugh! You would not understand me if I tried to explain. Now, once for all, I will not lend you a farthing. I should be glad to help your wife; but lending you money is no service to her.

LOUIS. Oh well, if youre in earnest about helping her, I'll tell you what you might do. You might get your patients to buy some of my things, or to give me a few portrait commissions.

RIDGEON. My patients call me in as a physician, not as a commercial traveller.

A knock at the door.

Louis goes unconcernedly to open it, pursuing the subject as he goes.

LOUIS. But you must have great influence with them. You must know such lots of things about them—private things that they wouldnt like to have known. They wouldnt dare to refuse you.

RIDGEON [*exploding*] Well, upon my—

Louis opens the door, and admits Sir Patrick, Sir Ralph, and Walpole.

RIDGEON [*proceeding furiously*] Walpole: Ive been here hardly ten minutes; and already he's tried to borrow 150 pounds from me. Then he proposed that I should get the money for him by blackmailing his wife; and youve just interrupted him in the act of suggesting that I should blackmail my patients into sitting to him for their portraits.

LOUIS. Well, Ridgeon, if this is what you call being an honorable man! I spoke to you in confidence.

SIR PATRICK. We're all going to speak to you in confidence, young man.

WALPOLE [*hanging his hat on the only peg left vacant on the hat-stand*] We shall make ourselves at home for half an hour, Dubedat. Dont be alarmed: youre a most fascinating chap; and we love you.

LOUIS. Oh, all right, all right. Sit down—anywhere you can. Take this chair, Sir Patrick [*indicating the one on the throne*]. Up-z-z-z! [*helping him up: Sir Patrick grunts and enthrones himself*]. Here you are, B. B. [*Sir Ralph glares at the familiarity; but Louis, quite undisturbed, puts a big book and a sofa cushion on the dais, on Sir Patrick's right; and B. B. sits down, under protest*]. Let me take your hat. [*He takes B. B.'s hat unceremoniously, and substitutes it for the cardinal's hat on the head of the lay figure, thereby ingeniously destroying the dignity of the conclave. He then draws the piano stool from the wall and offers it to Walpole*]. You dont mind this, Walpole, do you? [*Walpole accepts the stool, and puts his hand into his pocket for his cigaret case. Missing it, he is reminded of his loss*].

WALPOLE. By the way, I'll trouble you for my cigaret case, if you dont mind?

LOUIS. What cigaret case?

WALPOLE. The gold one I lent you at the Star and Garter.

LOUIS [*surprised*] Was that yours?

WALPOLE. Yes.

LOUIS. I'm awfully sorry, old chap. I wondered whose it was. I'm sorry to say this is all thats left of it. [*He hitches up his smock; produces a card from his waistcoat pocket; and hands it to Walpole*].

WALPOLE. A pawn ticket!

LOUIS [*reassuringly*] It's quite safe: he cant sell it for a year, you know. I say, my dear Walpole, I am sorry. [*He places his hand ingenuously on Walpole's shoulder and looks frankly at him*].

WALPOLE [*sinking on the stool with a gasp*] Dont mention it. It adds to your fascination.

RIDGEON [*who has been standing near the easel*] Before we go any further, you have a debt to pay, Mr Dubedat.

LOUIS. I have a precious lot of debts to pay, Ridgeon. I'll fetch you a chair. [*He makes for the inner door*].

RIDGEON [*stopping him*] You shall not leave the room until you pay it. It's a small one; and pay it you must and shall. I dont so much mind your borrowing 10 pounds from one of my guests and 20 pounds from the other—

WALPOLE. I walked into it, you know. I offered it.

RIDGEON.—they could afford it. But to clean poor Blenkinsop out of his last half-crown was damnable. I intend to give him that half-crown and to be in a position to pledge him my word that you paid it. I'll have that out of you, at all events.

B. B. Quite right, Ridgeon. Quite right. Come, young man! down with the dust. Pay up.

LOUIS. Oh, you neednt make such a fuss about it. Of course I'll pay it. I had no idea the poor fellow was hard up. I'm as shocked as any of you about it. [*Putting his hand into his pocket*] Here you are. [*Finding his pocket empty*] Oh, I say, I havnt any money on me just at present. Walpole: would you mind lending me half-a-crown just to settle this.

WALPOLE. Lend you half—[*his voice faints away*].

LOUIS. Well, if you dont, Blenkinsop wont get it; for I havnt a rap: you may search my pockets if you like.

WALPOLE. Thats conclusive. [*He produces half-a-crown*].

LOUIS [*passing it to Ridgeon*] There! I'm really glad thats settled: it was the only thing that was on my conscience. Now I hope youre all satisfied.

SIR PATRICK. Not quite, Mr Dubedat. Do you happen to know a young woman named Minnie Tinwell?

LOUIS. Minnie! I should think I do; and Minnie knows me too. She's a really nice good girl, considering her station. Whats become of her?

WALPOLE. It's no use bluffing, Dubedat. Weve seen Minnie's marriage lines.

LOUIS [*coolly*] Indeed? Have you seen Jennifer's?

RIDGEON [*rising in irrepressible rage*] Do you dare insinuate that Mrs Dubedat is living with you without being married to you?

LOUIS. Why not?

B. B. [*echoing him in*] Why not!

SIR PATRICK [*various tones of*] Why not!

RIDGEON [*scandalized*] Why not!

WALPOLE [*amazement*] Why not!

LOUIS. Yes, why not? Lots of people do it: just as good people as you. Why dont you learn to think, instead of bleating and bashing like a lot of sheep when you come up against anything youre not accustomed to? [*Contemplating their amazed faces with a chuckle*] I say: I should like to draw the lot of you now: you do look jolly foolish. Especially you, Ridgeon. I had you that time, you know.

RIDGEON. How, pray?

LOUIS. Well, you set up to appreciate Jennifer, you know. And you despise me, dont you?

RIDGEON [*curtly*] I loathe you. [*He sits down again on the sofa*].

LOUIS. Just so. And yet you believe that Jennifer is a bad lot because you think I told you so.

RIDGEON. Were you lying?

LOUIS. No; but you were smelling out a scandal instead of keeping your mind clean and wholesome. I can just play with people like you. I only asked you had you seen Jennifer's marriage lines; and you concluded straight away that she hadnt got any. You dont know a lady when you see one.

B. B. [*majestically*] What do you mean by that, may I ask?

LOUIS. Now, I'm only an immoral artist; but if YOUD told me that Jennifer wasnt married, I'd have had the gentlemanly feeling and artistic instinct to say that she carried her marriage certificate in her face and in her character. But you are all moral men; and Jennifer is only an artist's wife—probably a model; and morality consists in suspecting other people of not being legally married. Arnt you ashamed of yourselves? Can one of you look me in the face after it?

WALPOLE. Its very hard to look you in the face, Dubedat; you have such a dazzling cheek. What about Minnie Tinwell, eh?

LOUIS. Minnie Tinwell is a young woman who has had three weeks of glorious happiness in her poor little life, which is more than most girls in her position get, I can tell you. Ask her whether she'd take it back if she could. She's got her name into history, that girl. My little sketches of her will be bought by collectors at Christie's. She'll have a page in my biography. Pretty good, that, for a still-room maid at a seaside hotel, I think. What have you fellows done for her to compare with that?

RIDGEON. We havnt trapped her into a mock marriage and deserted her.

LOUIS. No: you wouldnt have the pluck. But dont fuss yourselves. I didnt desert little Minnie. We spent all our money—

WALPOLE. All HER money. Thirty pounds.

LOUIS. I said all our money: hers and mine too. Her thirty pounds didnt last three days. I had to borrow four times as much to spend on her. But I didnt grudge it; and she didnt grudge her few pounds either, the brave little lassie. When we were cleaned out, we'd had enough of it: you can hardly suppose that we were fit company for longer than that: I an artist, and she quite out of art and literature and refined living and everything else. There was no desertion, no misunderstanding, no police court or divorce court sensation for you moral chaps to lick your lips over at breakfast. We just said, Well, the money's gone: weve had a good time that can never be taken from us; so kiss; part good friends; and she back to service, and I back to my studio and my Jennifer, both the better and happier for our holiday.

WALPOLE. Quite a little poem, by George!'

B. B. If you had been scientifically trained, Mr Dubedat, you would know how very seldom an actual case bears out a principle. In medical practice a man may die when, scientifically speaking, he ought to have lived. I have actually known a man die of a disease from which he was scientifically speaking, immune. But that does not affect the fundamental truth of science. In just the same way, in moral cases, a man's behavior may be quite harmless and even beneficial, when he is morally behaving like a scoundrel. And he may do great harm when he is morally acting on the highest principles. But that does not affect the fundamental truth of morality.

SIR PATRICK. And it doesnt affect the criminal law on the subject of bigamy.

LOUIS. Oh bigamy! bigamy! bigamy! What a fascination anything connected with the police has for you all, you moralists! Ive proved to you that you were utterly wrong on the moral point: now I'm going to shew you that youre utterly wrong on the legal point; and I hope it will be a lesson to you not to be so jolly cocksure next time.

WALPOLE. Rot! You were married already when you married her; and that settles it.

LOUIS. Does it! Why cant you think? How do you know she wasnt married already too?

B.B. [*all*] Walpole! Ridgeon!

RIDGEON [*crying*] This is beyond everything!

WALPOLE [*out*] Well, damn me!

SIR PATRICK [*together*] You young rascal.

LOUIS [*ignoring their outcry*] She was married to the steward of a liner. He cleared out and left her; and she thought, poor girl, that it was the law that if you hadnt heard of your husband for three years you might marry again. So as she was a thoroughly respectable girl and refused to have anything to say to me unless we were married I went through the ceremony to please her and to preserve her self-respect.

RIDGEON. Did you tell her you were already married?

LOUIS. Of course not. Dont you see that if she had known, she wouldnt have considered herself my wife? You dont seem to understand, somehow.

SIR PATRICK. You let her risk imprisonment in her ignorance of the law?

LOUIS. Well, *I* risked imprisonment for her sake. I could have been had up for it just as much as she. But when a man makes a sacrifice of that sort for a woman, he doesnt go and brag about it to her; at least, not if he's a gentleman.

WALPOLE. What are we to do with this daisy?

LOUIS. [*impatiently*] Oh, go and do whatever the devil you please. Put Minnie in prison. Put me in prison. Kill Jennifer with the disgrace of it all. And then, when youve done all the mischief you can, go to church and feel good about it. [*He sits down pettishly on the old chair at the easel, and takes up a sketching block, on which he begins to draw*]

WALPOLE. He's got us.

SIR PATRICK [*grimly*] He has.

B. B. But is he to be allowed to defy the criminal law of the land?

SIR PATRICK. The criminal law is no use to decent people. It only helps blackguards to blackmail their families. What are we family doctors doing half our time but conspiring with the family solicitor to keep some rascal out of jail and some family out of disgrace?

B. B. But at least it will punish him.

SIR PATRICK. Oh, yes: Itll punish him. Itll punish not only him but everybody connected with him, innocent and guilty alike. Itll throw his board and lodging on our rates and taxes for a couple of years, and then turn him loose on us a more dangerous blackguard than ever. Itll put the girl in prison and ruin her: Itll lay his wife's life waste. You may put the criminal law out of your head once for all: it's only fit for fools and savages.

LOUIS. Would you mind turning your face a little more this way, Sir Patrick. [*Sir Patrick turns indignantly and glares at him*]. Oh, thats too much.

SIR PATRICK. Put down your foolish pencil, man; and think of your position. You can defy the laws made by men; but there are other laws to reckon with. Do you know that youre going to die?

LOUIS. We're all going to die, arnt we?

WALPOLE. We're not all going to die in six months.

LOUIS. How do you know?

This for B. B. is the last straw. He completely loses his temper and begins to walk excitedly about.

B. B. Upon my soul, I will not stand this. It is in questionable taste under any circumstances or in any company to harp on the subject of death; but it is a dastardly advantage to take of a medical man. [*Thundering at Dubedat*] I will not allow it, do you hear?

LOUIS. Well, I didn't begin it: you chaps did. It's always the way with the inartistic professions: when theyre beaten in argument they fall back on intimidation. I never knew a lawyer who didnt threaten to put me in prison sooner or later. I never knew a parson who didnt threaten me with damnation. And now you threaten me with death. With all your talk youve only one real trump in your hand, and thats Intimidation. Well, I'm not a coward; so it's no use with me.

B. B. [*advancing upon him*] I'll tell you what you are, sir. Youre a scoundrel.

LOUIS. Oh, I don't mind you calling me a scoundrel a bit. It's only a word: a word that you dont know the meaning of. What is a scoundrel?

B. B. You are a scoundrel, sir.

LOUIS. Just so. What is a scoundrel? I am. What am I? A Scoundrel. It's just arguing in a circle. And you imagine youre a man of science!

B. B. I—I—I—I have a good mind to take you by the scruff of your neck, you infamous rascal, and give you a sound thrashing.

LOUIS. I wish you would. Youd pay me something handsome to keep it out of court afterwards. [*B. B., baffled, flings away from him with a snort*]. Have you any more civilities to address to me in my own house? I should like to get them over before my wife comes back. [*He resumes his sketching*].

RIDGEON. My mind's made up. When the law breaks down, honest men must find a remedy for themselves. I will not lift a finger to save this reptile.

B. B. That is the word I was trying to remember. Reptile.

WALPOLE. I cant help rather liking you, Dubedat. But you certainly are a thoroughgoing specimen.

SIR PATRICK. You know our opinion of you now, at all events.

LOUIS [*patiently putting down his pencil*] Look here. All this is no good. You dont understand. You imagine that I'm simply an ordinary criminal.

WALPOLE. Not an ordinary one, Dubedat. Do yourself justice.

LOUIS. Well youre on the wrong tack altogether. I'm not a criminal. All your moralizings have no value for me. I don't believe in morality. I'm a disciple of Bernard Shaw.

SIR PATRICK [*puzzled*] Eh?

B.B. [*waving his hand as if the subject was now disposed of*] Thats enough, I wish to hear no more.

LOUIS. Of course I havnt the ridiculous vanity to set up to be exactly a Superman; but still, it's an ideal that I strive towards just as any other man strives towards his ideal.

B. B. [*intolerant*] Dont trouble to explain. I now understand you perfectly. Say no more, please. When a man pretends to discuss science, morals, and religion, and then avows himself a follower of a notorious and avowed anti-vaccinationist, there is nothing more to be said. [*Suddenly putting in an effusive saving clause in parenthesis to Ridgeon*] Not, my dear Ridgeon, that I believe in vaccination in the popular sense any more than you do: I neednt tell you that. But there are things that place a man socially; and anti-vaccination is one of them. [*He resumes his seat on the dais*].

SIR PATRICK. Bernard Shaw? I never heard of him. He's a Methodist preacher, I suppose.

LOUIS [*scandalized*] No, no. He's the most advanced man now living: he isn't anything.

SIR PATRICK. I assure you, young man, my father learnt the doctrine of deliverance from sin from John Wesley's own lips before you or Mr. Shaw were born. It used to be very popular as an excuse for putting sand in sugar and water in milk. Youre a sound Methodist, my lad; only you don't know it.

LOUIS [*seriously annoyed for the first time*] Its an intellectual insult. I don't believe theres such a thing as sin.

SIR PATRICK. Well, sir, there are people who dont believe theres such a thing as disease either. They call themselves Christian Scientists, I believe. Theyll just suit your complaint. We can do nothing for you. [*He rises*]. Good afternoon to you.

LOUIS [*running to him piteously*] Oh dont get up, Sir Patrick. Don't go. Please dont. I didnt mean to shock you, on my word. Do sit down again. Give me another chance. Two minutes more: thats all I ask.

SIR PATRICK [*surprised by this sign of grace, and a little touched*] Well—[*He sits down*]

LOUIS [*gratefully*] Thanks awfully.

SIR PATRICK [*continuing*] I don't mind giving you two minutes more. But dont address yourself to me; for Ive retired from practice; and I dont pretend to be able to cure your complaint. Your life is in the hands of these gentlemen.

RIDGEON. Not in mine. My hands are full. I have no time and no means available for this case.

SIR PATRICK. What do you say, Mr. Walpole?

WALPOLE. Oh, I'll take him in hand: I dont mind. I feel perfectly convinced that this is not a moral case at all: it's a physical one. Theres something abnormal about his brain. That means, probably, some morbid condition affecting the spinal cord. And that means the circulation. In short, it's clear to me that he's suffering from an obscure form of blood-poisoning, which is almost certainly due to an accumulation of ptomaines in the nuciform sac. I'll remove the sac—

LOUIS [*changing color*] Do you mean, operate on me? Ugh! No, thank you.

WALPOLE. Never fear: you wont feel anything. Youll be under an anaesthetic, of course. And it will be extraordinarily interesting.

LOUIS. Oh, well, if it would interest you, and if it wont hurt, thats another matter. How much will you give me to let you do it?

WALPOLE [*rising indignantly*] How much! What do you mean?

LOUIS. Well, you dont expect me to let you cut me up for nothing, do you?

WALPOLE. Will you paint my portrait for nothing?

LOUIS. No; but I'll give you the portrait when its painted; and you can sell it afterwards for perhaps double the money. But I cant sell my nuciform sac when youve cut it out.

WALPOLE. Ridgeon: did you ever hear anything like this! [*To Louis*] Well, you can keep your nuciform sac, and your tubercular lung, and your diseased brain: Ive done with you. One would think I was not conferring a favor on the fellow! [*He returns to his stool in high dudgeon*].

SIR PATRICK. That leaves only one medical man who has not withdrawn from your case, Mr. Dubedat. You have nobody left to appeal to now but Sir Ralph Bloomfield Bonington.

WALPOLE. If I were you, B. B., I shouldnt touch him with a pair of tongs. Let him take his lungs to the Brompton Hospital. They wont cure him; but theyll teach him manners.

B. B. My weakness is that I have never been able to say No, even to the most thoroughly undeserving people. Besides, I am bound to say that I dont think it is possible in medical practice to go into the question of the value of the lives we save. Just consider, Ridgeon. Let me put it to you, Paddy. Clear your mind of cant, Walpole.

WALPOLE [*indignantly*] My mind is clear of cant.

B. B. Quite so. Well now, look at my practice. It is what I suppose you would call a fashionable practice, a smart practice, a practice among the best people. You ask me to go into the question of whether my patients are of any use either to themselves or anyone else. Well, if you apply any scientific test known to me, you will achieve a reductio ad absurdum. You will be driven to the conclusion that the majority of them would be, as my friend Mr J. M. Barrie has tersely phrased it, better dead. Better dead. There are exceptions, no doubt. For instance, there is the court, an essentially social-democratic institution, supported out of public funds by the public because the public wants it and likes it. My court patients are hard-working people who give satisfaction, undoubtedly. Then I have a duke or two whose estates are probably better managed than they would be in public hands. But as to most of the rest, if I once began to argue about them, unquestionably the verdict would be, Better dead. When they actually do die, I sometimes have to offer that consolation, thinly disguised, to the family. [*Lulled by the cadences of his own voice, he becomes drowsier and drowsier*]. The fact that they spend money so extravagantly on medical attendance really would not justify me in wasting my talents—such as they are—in keeping them alive. After all, if my fees are high, I have to spend heavily. My own tastes are simple: a camp bed, a couple of rooms, a crust, a bottle of wine; and I am happy and contented. My wife's tastes are perhaps more luxurious; but even she deplores an expenditure the sole object of which is to maintain the state my patients require from their medical attendant. The—er—er—er—[*suddenly waking up*] I have lost the thread of these remarks. What was I talking about, Ridgeon?

RIDGEON. About Dubedat.

B. B. Ah yes. Precisely. Thank you. Dubedat, of course. Well, what is our friend Dubedat? A vicious and ignorant young man with a talent for drawing.

LOUIS. Thank you. Dont mind me.

B. B. But then, what are many of my patients? Vicious and ignorant young men without a talent for anything. If I were to stop to argue about their merits I should have to give up three-quarters of my practice. Therefore I have made it a rule not so to argue. Now, as an honorable man, having made that rule as to paying patients, can I make an exception as to a patient who, far from being a paying patient, may more fitly be described as a borrowing patient? No. I say No. Mr Dubedat: your moral character is nothing to me. I look at you from a purely scientific point of view. To me you are simply a field of battle in which an invading army of tubercle bacilli struggles with a patriotic force of phagocytes. Having made a promise to your wife, which my principles will not allow me to break, to stimulate those phagocytes, I will stimulate them. And I take no further responsibility. [*He digs himself back in his seat exhausted*].

SIR PATRICK. Well, Mr Dubedat, as Sir Ralph has very kindly offered to take charge of your case, and as the two minutes I promised you are up, I must ask you to excuse me. [*He rises*].

LOUIS. Oh, certainly. Ive quite done with you. [*Rising and holding up the sketch block*] There! While youve been talking, Ive been doing. What is there left of your moralizing? Only a little carbonic acid gas which makes the room unhealthy. What is there left of my work? That. Look at it [*Ridgeon rises to look at it*].

SIR PATRICK [*who has come down to him from the throne*] You young rascal, was it drawing me you were?

LOUIS. Of course. What else?

SIR PATRICK [*takes the drawing from him and grunts approvingly*] Thats rather good. Dont you think so, Lolly?

RIDGEON. Yes. So good that I should like to have it.

SIR PATRICK. Thank you; but *I* should like to have it myself. What d'ye think, Walpole?

WALPOLE [*rising and coming over to look*] No, by Jove: *I* must have this.

LOUIS. I wish I could afford to give it to you, Sir Patrick. But I'd pay five guineas sooner than part with it.

RIDGEON. Oh, for that matter, I will give you six for it.

WALPOLE. Ten.

LOUIS. I think Sir Patrick is morally entitled to it, as he sat for it. May I send it to your house, Sir Patrick, for twelve guineas?

SIR PATRICK. Twelve guineas! Not if you were President of the Royal Academy, young man. [*He gives him back the drawing decisively and turns away, taking up his hat*].

LOUIS [*to B. B.*] Would you like to take it at twelve, Sir Ralph?

B. B. [*coming between Louis and Walpole*] Twelve guineas? Thank you: I'll take it at that. [*He takes it and presents it to Sir Patrick*]. Accept it from me, Paddy; and may you long be spared to contemplate it.

SIR PATRICK. Thank you. [*He puts the drawing into his hat*].

B. B. I neednt settle with you now, Mr Dubedat: my fees will come to more than that. [*He also retrieves his hat*].

LOUIS [*indignantly*] Well, of all the mean—[*words fail him*]! I'd let myself be shot sooner than do a thing like that. I consider youve stolen that drawing.

SIR PATRICK [*drily*] So weve converted you to a belief in morality after all, eh?

LOUIS. Yah! [*To Walpole*] I'll do another one for you, Walpole, if youll let me have the ten you promised.

WALPOLE. Very good. I'll pay on delivery.

LOUIS. Oh! What do you take me for? Have you no confidence in my honor?

WALPOLE. None whatever.

LOUIS. Oh well, of course if you feel that way, you cant help it. Before you go, Sir Patrick, let me fetch Jennifer. I know she'd like to see you, if you dont mind. [*He goes to the inner door*]. And now, before she comes in, one word. Youve all been talking here pretty freely about me—in my own house too. I dont mind that: I'm a man and can take care of myself. But when Jennifer comes in, please remember that she's a lady, and that you are supposed to be gentlemen. [*He goes out*].

WALPOLE. Well!!! [*He gives the situation up as indescribable, and goes for his hat*].

RIDGEON. Damn his impudence!

B. B. I shouldnt be at all surprised to learn that he's well connected. Whenever I meet dignity and self-possession without any discoverable basis, I diagnose good family.

RIDGEON. Diagnose artistic genius, B. B. Thats what saves his self-respect.

SIR PATRICK. The world is made like that. The decent fellows are always being lectured and put out of countenance by the snobs.

B. B. [*altogether refusing to accept this*] *I* am not out of countenance. I should like, by Jupiter, to see the man who could put me out of countenance. [*Jennifer comes in*]. Ah, Mrs. Dubedat! And how are we to-day?

MRS DUBEDAT [*shaking hands with him*] Thank you all so much for coming. [*She shakes Walpole's hand*]. Thank you, Sir Patrick [*she shakes Sir Patrick's*]. Oh, life has been worth living since I have known you. Since Richmond I have not known a moment's fear. And it used to be nothing but fear. Wont you sit down and tell me the result of the consultation?

WALPOLE. I'll go, if you dont mind, Mrs. Dubedat. I have an appointment. Before I go, let me say that I am quite agreed with my colleagues here as to the character of the case. As to the cause and the remedy, thats not my business: I'm only a surgeon; and these gentlemen are physicians and will advise you. I may have my own views: in fact I HAVE them; and they are perfectly well known to my colleagues. If I am needed—and needed I shall be finally—they know where to find me; and I am always at your service. So for to-day, good-bye. [*He goes out, leaving Jennifer much puzzled by his unexpected withdrawal and formal manner*].

SIR PATRICK. I also will ask you to excuse me, Mrs Dubedat.

RIDGEON [*anxiously*] Are you going?

SIR PATRICK. Yes: I can be of no use here; and I must be getting back. As you know, maam, I'm not in practice now; and I shall not be in charge of the case. It rests between Sir Colenso Ridgeon and Sir Ralph Bloomfield Bonington. They know my opinion. Good afternoon to you, maam. [*He bows and makes for the door*].

MRS DUBEDAT [*detaining him*] Theres nothing wrong, is there? You dont think Louis is worse, do you?

SIR PATRICK. No: he's not worse. Just the same as at Richmond.

MRS DUBEDAT. Oh, thank you: you frightened me. Excuse me.

SIR PATRICK. Dont mention it, maam. [*He goes out*].

B. B. Now, Mrs Dubedat, if I am to take the patient in hand—

MRS DUBEDAT [*apprehensively, with a glance at Ridgeon*] You! But I thought that Sir Colenso—

B. B. [*beaming with the conviction that he is giving her a most gratifying surprise*] My dear lady, your husband shall have Me.

MRS DUBEDAT. But—

B. B. Not a word: it is a pleasure to me, for your sake. Sir Colenso Ridgeon will be in his proper place, in the bacteriological laboratory. *I* shall be in my proper place, at the bedside. Your husband shall be treated exactly as if he were a member of the royal family. [*Mrs Dubedat, uneasy, again is about to protest*]. No gratitude: it would embarrass me, I assure you. Now, may I ask whether you are particularly tied to these apartments. Of course, the motor has annihilated distance; but I confess that if you were rather nearer to me, it would be a little more convenient.

MRS DUBEDAT. You see, this studio and flat are self-contained. I have suffered so much in lodgings. The servants are so frightfully dishonest.

B. B. Ah! Are they? Are they? Dear me!

MRS DUBEDAT. I was never accustomed to lock things up. And I missed so many small sums. At last a dreadful thing happened. I missed a five-pound note. It was traced to the housemaid; and she actually said Louis had given it to her. And he wouldnt let me do anything: he is so sensitive that these things drive him mad.

B. B. Ah—hm—ha—yes—say no more, Mrs. Dubedat: you shall not move. If the mountain will not come to Mahomet, Mahomet must come to the mountain. Now I must be off. I will write and make an appointment. We shall begin stimulating the phagocytes on—on—probably on Tuesday next; but I will let you know. Depend on me; dont fret; eat regularly; sleep well; keep your spirits up; keep the patient cheerful; hope for the best; no tonic like a charming woman; no medicine like cheerfulness; no resource like science; goodbye, good-bye, good-bye. [*Having shaken hands—she being too overwhelmed to speak—he goes out, stopping to say to Ridgeon*] On Tuesday morning send me down a tube of some really stiff anti-toxin. Any kind will do. Dont forget. Good-bye, Colly. [*He goes out.*]

RIDGEON. You look quite discouraged again. [*She is almost in tears*]. What's the matter? Are you disappointed?

MRS DUBEDAT. I know I ought to be very grateful. Believe me, I am very grateful. But—but—

RIDGEON. Well?

MRS DUBEDAT. I had set my heart on YOUR curing Louis.

RIDGEON. Well, Sir Ralph Bloomfield Bonington—

MRS DUBEDAT. Yes, I know, I know. It is a great privilege to have him. But oh, I wish it had been you. I know it's unreasonable; I cant explain; but I had such a strong instinct that you would cure him. I dont I cant feel the same about Sir Ralph. You promised me. Why did you give Louis up?

RIDGEON. I explained to you. I cannot take another case.

MRS DUBEDAT. But at Richmond?

RIDGEON. At Richmond I thought I could make room for one more case. But my old friend Dr Blenkinsop claimed that place. His lung is attacked.

MRS DUBEDAT [*attaching no importance whatever to Blenkinsop*] Do you mean that elderly man—that rather—

RIDGEON [*sternly*] I mean the gentleman that dined with us: an excellent and honest man, whose life is as valuable as anyone else's. I have arranged that I shall take his case, and that Sir Ralph Bloomfield Bonington shall take Mr Dubedat's.

MRS DUBEDAT [*turning indignantly on him*] I see what it is. Oh! it is envious, mean, cruel. And I thought that you would be above such a thing.

RIDGEON. What do you mean?

MRS DUBEDAT. Oh, do you think I dont know? do you think it has never happened before? Why does everybody turn against him? Can you not forgive him for being superior to you? for being cleverer? for being braver? for being a great artist?

RIDGEON. Yes: I can forgive him for all that.

MRS DUBEDAT. Well, have you anything to say against him? I have challenged everyone who has turned against him—challenged them face to face to tell me any wrong thing he has done, any ignoble thought he has uttered. They have always confessed that they could not tell me one. I challenge you now. What do you accuse him of?

RIDGEON. I am like all the rest. Face to face, I cannot tell you one thing against him.

MRS DUBEDAT [*not satisfied*] But your manner is changed. And you have broken your promise to me to make room for him as your patient.

RIDGEON. I think you are a little unreasonable. You have had the very best medical advice in London for him; and his case has been taken in hand by a leader of the profession. Surely—

MRS DUBEDAT. Oh, it is so cruel to keep telling me that. It seems all right; and it puts me in the wrong. But I am not in the wrong. I have faith in you; and I have no faith in the others. We have seen so many doctors: I have come to know at last when they are only talking and can do nothing. It is different with you. I feel that you know. You must listen to me, doctor. [*With sudden misgiving*] Am I offending you by calling you doctor instead of remembering your title?

RIDGEON. Nonsense. I AM a doctor. But mind you, dont call Walpole one.

MRS DUBEBAT. I dont care about Mr Walpole: it is you who must befriend me. Oh, will you please sit down and listen to me just for a few minutes. [*He assents with a grave inclination, and sits on the sofa. She sits on the easel chair*] Thank you. I wont keep you long; but I must tell you the whole truth. Listen. I know Louis as nobody else in the world knows him or ever can know him. I am his wife. I know he has little faults: impatiences, sensitivenesses, even little selfishnesses that are too trivial for him to notice. I know that he sometimes shocks people about money because he is so utterly above it, and cant understand the value ordinary people set on it. Tell me: did he—did he borrow any money from you?

RIDGEON. He asked me for some once.

MRS DUBEDAT [*tears again in her eyes*] Oh, I am so sorry—so sorry. But he will never do it again: I pledge you my word for that. He has given me his promise: here in this room just before you came; and he is incapable of breaking his word. That was his only real weakness; and now it is conquered and done with for ever.

RIDGEON. Was that really his only weakness?

MRS DUBEDAT. He is perhaps sometimes weak about women, because they adore him so, and are always laying traps for him. And of course when he says he doesnt believe in morality, ordinary pious people think he must be wicked. You can understand, cant you, how all this starts a great deal of gossip about him, and gets repeated until even good friends get set against him?

RIDGEON. Yes: I understand.

MRS DUBEDAT. Oh, if you only knew the other side of him as I do! Do you know, doctor, that if Louis honored himself by a really bad action, I should kill myself.

RIDGEON. Come! dont exaggerate.

MRS DUBEDAT. I should. You don't understand that, you east country people.

RIDGEON. You did not see much of the world in Cornwall, did you?

MRS DUBEDAT [*naively*] Oh yes. I saw a great deal every day of the beauty of the world—more than you ever see here in London. But I saw very few people, if that is what you mean. I was an only child.

RIDGEON. That explains a good deal.

MRS DUBEDAT. I had a great many dreams; but at last they all came to one dream.

RIDGEON [*with half a sigh*] Yes, the usual dream.

MRS DUBEDAT [*surprised*] Is it usual?

RIDGEON. As I guess. You havnt yet told me what it was.

MRS DUBEDAT. I didn't want to waste myself. I could do nothing myself; but I had a little property and I could help with it. I had even a little beauty: dont think me vain for knowing it. I always had a terrible struggle with poverty and neglect at first. My dream was to save one of them from that, and bring some charm and happiness into his life. I prayed Heaven to send me one. I firmly believe that Louis was guided to me in answer to my prayer. He was no more like the other men I had met than the Thames Embankment is like our Cornish coasts. He saw everything that I saw, and drew it for me. He understood everything. He came to me like a child. Only fancy, doctor: he never even wanted to marry me: he never thought of the things other men think of! I had to propose it myself. Then he said he had no money. When I told him I had some, he said "Oh, all right," just like a boy. He is still like that, quite unspoiled, a man in his thoughts, a great poet and artist in his dreams, and a child in his ways. I gave him myself and all I had that he might grow to his full height with plenty of sunshine. If I lost faith in him, it would mean the wreck and failure of my life. I should go back to Cornwall and die. I could show you the very cliff I should jump off. You must cure him: you must make him quite well again for me. I know that you can do it and that nobody else can. I implore you not to refuse what I am going to ask you to do. Take Louis yourself; and let Sir Ralph cure Dr Blenkinsop.

RIDGEON [*slowly*] Mrs Dubedat: do you really believe in my knowledge and skill as you say you do?

MRS DUBEDAT. Absolutely. I do not give my trust by halves.

RIDGEON. I know that. Well, I am going to test you—hard. Will you believe me when I tell you that I understand what you have just told me; that I have no desire but to serve you in the most faithful friendship; and that your hero must be preserved to you.

MRS DUBEDAT. Oh forgive me. Forgive what I said. You will preserve him to me.

RIDGEON. At all hazards. [*She kisses his hand. He rises hastily*]. No: you have not heard the rest. [*She rises too*]. You must believe me when I tell you that the one chance of preserving the hero lies in Louis being in the care of Sir Ralph.

MRS DUBEDAT [*firmly*] You say so: I have no more doubt: I believe you. Thank you.

RIDGEON. Good-bye. [*She takes his hand*]. I hope this will be a lasting friendship.

MRS DUBEDAT. It will. My friendships end only with death.

RIDGEON. Death ends everything, doesnt it? Goodbye.

With a sigh and a look of pity at her which she does not understand, he goes.

ACT IV

The studio. The easel is pushed back to the wall. Cardinal Death, holding his scythe and hour-glass like a sceptre and globe, sits on the throne. On the hat-stand hang the hats of Sir Patrick and Bloomfield Bonington. Walpole, just come in, is hanging up his beside them. There is a knock. He opens the door and finds Ridgeon there.

WALPOLE. Hallo, Ridgeon!

They come into the middle of the room together, taking off their gloves.

RIDGEON. Whats the matter! Have you been sent for, too?

WALPOLE. Weve all been sent for. Ive only just come: I havnt seen him yet. The charwoman says that old Paddy Cullen has been here with B. B. for the last half-hour. [*Sir Patrick, with bad news in his face, enters from the inner room*]. Well: whats up?

SIR PATRICK. Go in and see. B. B. is in there with him.

Walpole goes. Ridgeon is about to follow him; but Sir Patrick stops him with a look.

RIDGEON. What has happened?

SIR PATRICK. Do you remember Jane Marsh's arm?

RIDGEON. Is that whats happened?

SIR PATRICK. Thats whats happened. His lung has gone like Jane's arm. I never saw such a case. He has got through three months galloping consumption in three days.

RIDGEON. B. B. got in on the negative phase.

SIR PATRICK. Negative or positive, the lad's done for. He wont last out the afternoon. He'll go suddenly: Ive often seen it.

RIDGEON. So long as he goes before his wife finds him out, I dont care. I fully expected this.

SIR PATRICK [*drily*] It's a little hard on a lad to be killed because his wife has too high an opinion of him. Fortunately few of us are in any danger of that.

Sir Ralph comes from the inner room and hastens between them, humanely concerned, but professionally elate and communicative.

B. B. Ah, here you are, Ridgeon. Paddy's told you, of course.

RIDGEON. Yes.

B. B. It's an enormously interesting case. You know, Colly, by Jupiter, if I didnt know as a matter of scientific fact that I'd been stimulating the phagocytes, I should say I'd been stimulating the other things. What is the explanation of it, Sir Patrick? How do you account for it, Ridgeon? Have we overstimulated the phagocytes? Have they not only eaten up the bacilli, but attacked and destroyed the red corpuscles as well? a possibility suggested by the patient's pallor. Nay, have they finally begun to prey on the lungs themselves? Or on one another? I shall write a paper about this case.

Walpole comes back, very serious, even shocked. He comes between B. B. and Ridgeon.

WALPOLE. Whew! B. B.: youve done it this time.

B. B. What do you mean?

WALPOLE. Killed him. The worst case of neglected blood-poisoning I ever saw. It's too late now to do anything. He'd die under the anaesthetic.

B. B. [*offended*] Killed! Really, Walpole, if your monomania were not well known, I should take such an expession very seriously.

SIR PATRICK. Come come! When youve both killed as many people as I have in my time youll feel humble enough about it. Come and look at him, Colly.

Ridgeon and Sir Patrick go into the inner room.

WALPOLE. I apologize, B. B. But it's blood-poisoning.

B. B. [*recovering his irresistible good nature*] My dear Walpole, everything is blood-poisoning. But upon my soul, I shall not use any of that stuff of Ridgeon's again. What made me so sensitive about what you said just now is that, strictly between ourselves, Ridgeon cooked our young friend's goose.

Jennifer, worried and distressed, but always gentle, comes between them from the inner room. She wears a nurse's apron.

MRS. DUBEDAT. Sir Ralph: what am I to do? That man who insisted on seeing me, and sent in word that business was important to Louis, is a newspaper man. A paragraph appeared in the paper this morning saying that Louis is seriously ill; and this man wants to interview him about it. How can people be so brutally callous?

WALPOLE [*moving vengefully towards the door*] You just leave me to deal with him!

MRS DUBEDAT [*stopping him*] But Louis insists on seeing him: he almost began to cry about it. And he says he cant bear his room any longer. He says he wants to [*she struggles with a sob*]—to die in his studio. Sir Patrick says let him have his way: it can do no harm. What shall we do?

B B. [*encouragingly*] Why, follow Sir Patrick's excellent advice, of course. As he says, it can do him no harm; and it will no doubt do him good—a great deal of good. He will be much the better for it.

MRS DUBEDAT [*a little cheered*] Will you bring the man up here, Mr Walpole, and tell him that he may see Louis, but that he mustnt exhaust him by talking? [*Walpole nods and goes out by the outer door*]. Sir Ralph, dont be angry with me; but Louis will die if he stays here. I must take him to Cornwall. He will recover there.

B. B. [*brightening wonderfully, as if Dubedat were already saved*] Cornwall! The very place for him! Wonderful for the lungs. Stupid of me not to think of it before. You are his best physician after all, dear lady. An inspiration! Cornwall: of course, yes, yes, yes.

MRS DUBEDAT [*comforted and touched*] You are so kind, Sir Ralph. But dont give me much or I shall cry; and Louis cant bear that.

B. B. [*gently putting his protecting arm round her shoulders*] Then let us come back to him and help to carry him in. Cornwall! of course, of course. The very thing! [*They go together into the bedroom*].

Walpole returns with The Newspaper Man, a cheerful, affable young man who is disabled for ordinary business pursuits by a congenital erroneousness which renders him incapable of describing accurately anything he sees, or understanding or reporting accurately anything he hears. As the only employment in which these defects do not matter is journalism (for a newspaper, not having to act on its description and reports, but only to sell them to idly curious people, has nothing but honor to lose by inaccuracy and unveracity), he has perforce become a journalist, and has to keep up an air of high spirits through a daily struggle with his own illiteracy and the precariousness of his employment. He has a note-book, and occasionally attempts to make a note; but as he cannot write shorthand, and does not write with ease in any hand, he generally gives it up as a bad job before he succeeds in finishing a sentence.

THE NEWSPAPER MAN [*looking round and making indecisive attempts at notes*] This is the studio, I suppose.

WALPOLE. Yes.

THE NEWSPAPER MAN [*wittily*] Where he has his models, eh?

WALPOLE [*grimly irresponsive*] No doubt.

THE NEWSPAPER MAN. Cubicle, you said it was?

WALPOLE. Yes, tubercle.

THE NEWSPAPER MAN. Which way do you spell it: is it c-u-b-i-c-a-l or c-l-e?

WALPOLE. Tubercle, man, not cubical. [*Spelling it for him*] T-u-b-e-r-c-l-e.

THE NEWSPAPER MAN. Oh! tubercle. Some disease, I suppose. I thought he had consumption. Are you one of the family or the doctor?

WALPOLE. I'm neither one nor the other. I am Mister Cutler Walpole. Put that down. Then put down Sir Colenso Ridgeon.

THE NEWSPAPER MAN. Pigeon?

WALPOLE. Ridgeon. [*Contemptuously snatching his book*] Here: youd better let me write the names down for you: youre sure to get them wrong. That comes of belonging to an illiterate profession, with no qualifications and no public register. [*He writes the particulars*].

THE NEWSPAPER MAN. Oh, I say: you have got your knife into us, havnt you?

WALPOLE [*vindictively*] I wish I had: I'd make a better man of you. Now attend. [*Shewing him the book*] These are the names of the three doctors. This is the patient. This is the address. This is the name of the disease. [*He shuts the book with a snap which makes the journalist blink, and returns it to him*]. Mr Dubedat will be brought in here presently. He wants to see you because he doesnt know how bad he is. We'll allow you to wait a few minutes to humor him; but if you talk to him, out you go. He may die at any moment.

THE NEWSPAPER MAN [*interested*] Is he as bad as that? I say: I am in luck to-day. Would you mind letting me photograph you? [*He produces a camera*]. Could you have a lancet or something in your hand?

WALPOLE. Put it up. If you want my photograph you can get it in Baker Street in any of the series of celebrities.

THE NEWSPAPER MAN. But theyll want to be paid. If you wouldnt mind [*fingering the camera*]—?

WALPOLE. I would. Put it up, I tell you. Sit down there and be quiet.

The Newspaper Man quickly sits down on the piano stool as Dubedat, in an invalid's chair, is wheeled in by Mrs Dubedat and Sir Ralph. They place the chair between the dais and the sofa, where the easel stood before. Louis is not changed as a robust man would be; and he is not scared. His eyes look larger; and he is so weak physically that he can hardly move, lying on his cushions, with complete languor; but his mind is active; it is making the most of his condition, finding voluptuousness in languor and drama in death. They are all impressed, in spite of themselves, except Ridgeon, who is implacable. B.B. is entirely sympathetic and forgiving. Ridgeon follows the chair with a tray of milk and stimulants. Sir Patrick, who accompanies him, takes the tea-table from the corner and places it behind the chair for the tray. B. B. takes the easel chair and places it for Jennifer at Dubedat's side, next the dais, from which the lay figure ogles the dying artist. B. B. then returns to Dubedat's left. Jennifer sits. Walpole sits down on the edge of the dais. Ridgeon stands near him.

LOUIS [*blissfully*] Thats happiness! To be in a studio! Happiness!

MRS DUBEDAT. Yes, dear. Sir Patrick says you may stay here as long as you like.

LOUIS. Jennifer.

MRS DUBEDAT. Yes, my darling.

LOUIS. Is the newspaper man here?

THE NEWSPAPER MAN [*glibly*] Yes, Mr Dubedat: I'm here, at your service. I represent the press. I thought you might like to let us have a few words about—about—er—well, a few words on your illness, and your plans for the season.

LOUIS. My plans for the season are very simple. I'm going to die.

MRS DUBEDAT [*tortured*] Louis—dearest—

LOUIS. My darling: I'm very weak and tired. Dont put on me the horrible strain of pretending that I dont know. Ive been lying there listening to the doctors—laughing to myself. They know. Dearest: dont cry. It makes you ugly; and I cant bear that. [*She dries her eyes and recovers herself with a proud effort*]. I want you to promise me something.

MRS DUBEDAT. Yes, yes: you know I will. [*Imploringly*] Only, my love, my love, dont talk: it will waste your strength.

LOUIS. No: it will only use it up. Ridgeon: give me something to keep me going for a few minutes—one of your confounded anti-toxins, if you dont mind. I have some things to say before I go.

RIDGEON [*looking at Sir Patrick*] I suppose it can do no harm? [*He pours out some spirit, and is about to add soda water when Sir Patrick corrects him*].

SIR PATRICK. In milk. Dont set him coughing.

LOUIS [*after drinking*] Jennifer.

MRS DUBEDAT. Yes, dear.

LOUIS. If theres one thing I hate more than another, it's a widow. Promise me that youll never be a widow.

MRS DUBEDAT. My dear, what do you mean?

LOUIS. I want you to look beautiful. I want people to see in your eyes that you were married to me. The people in Italy used to point at Dante and say "There goes the man who has been in hell." I want them to point at you and say "There goes a woman who has been in heaven." It has been heaven, darling, hasnt it—sometimes?

MRS DUBEDAT. Oh yes, yes. Always, always.

LOUIS. If you wear black and cry, people will say "Look at that miserable woman: her husband made her miserable."

MRS DUBEDAT. No, never. You are the light and the blessing of my life. I never lived until I knew you.

LOUIS [*his eyes glistening*] Then you must always wear beautiful dresses and splendid magic jewels. Think of all the wonderful pictures I shall never paint.

[*She wins a terrible victory over a sob*] Well, you must be transfigured with all the beauty of those pictures. Men must get such dreams from seeing you as they never could get from any daubing with paints and brushes. Painters must paint you as they never painted any mortal woman before. There must be a great tradition of beauty, a great atmosphere of wonder and romance. That is what men must always think of when they think of me. That is the sort of immortality I want. You can make that for me, Jennifer. There are lots of things you dont understand that every woman in the street understands; but you can understand that and do it as nobody else can. Promise me that immortality. Promise me you will not make a little hell of crape and crying and undertaker's horrors and withering flowers and all that vulgar rubbish.

MRS DUBEDAT. I promise. But all that is far off, dear. You are to come to Cornwall with me and get well. Sir Ralph says so.

LOUIS. Poor old B. B.

B. B. [*affected to tears, turns away and whispers to Sir Patrick*] Poor fellow! Brain going.

LOUIS. Sir Patrick's there, isn't he?

SIR PATRICK. Yes, yes. I'm here.

LOUIS. Sit down, wont you? It's a shame to keep you standing about.

SIR PATRICK. Yes, Yes. Thank you. All right.

LOUIS. Jennifer.

MRS DUBEDAT. Yes, dear.

LOUIS [*with a strange look of delight*] Do you remember the burning bush?

MRS DUBEDAT. Yes, Yes. Oh, my dear, how it strains my heart to remember it now!

LOUIS. Does it? It fills me with joy. Tell them about it.

MRS DUBEDAT. It was nothing—only that once in my old Cornish home we lit the first fire of the winter; and when we looked through the window we saw the flames dancing in a bush in the garden.

LOUIS. Such a color! Garnet color. Waving like silk. Liquid lovely flame flowing up through the bay leaves, and not burning them. Well, I shall be a flame like that. I'm sorry to disappoint the poor little worms; but the last of me shall be the flame in the burning bush. Whenever you see the flame, Jennifer, that will be me. Promise me that I shall be burnt.

MRS DUBEDAT. Oh, if I might be with you, Louis!

LOUIS. No: you must always be in the garden when the bush flames. You are my hold on the world: you are my immortality. Promise.

MRS DUBEDAT. I'm listening. I shall not forget. You know that I promise.

LOUIS. Well, thats about all; except that you are to hang my pictures at the one-man show. I can trust your eye. You wont let anyone else touch them.

MRS DUBEDAT. You can trust me.

LOUIS. Then theres nothing more to worry about, is there? Give me some more of that milk. I'm fearfully tired; but if I stop talking I shant begin again. [*Sir Ralph gives him a drink. He takes it and looks up quaintly*]. I say, B. B., do you think anything would stop you talking?

B. B. [*almost unmanned*] He confuses me with you, Paddy. Poor fellow! Poor fellow!

LOUIS [*musing*] I used to be awfully afraid of death; but now it's come I have no fear; and I'm perfectly happy. Jennifer.

MRS DUBEDAT. Yes, dear?

LOUIS. I'll tell you a secret. I used to think that our marriage was all an affectation, and that I'd break loose and run away some day. But now that I'm going to be broken loose whether I like it or not, I'm perfectly fond of you, and perfectly satisfied because I'm going to live as part of you and not as my troublesome self.

MRS DUBEDAT [*heartbroken*] Stay with me, Louis. Oh, dont leave me, dearest.

LOUIS. Not that I'm selfish. With all my faults I dont think Ive ever been really selfish. No artist can: Art is too large for that. You will marry again, Jennifer.

MRS DUBEDAT. Oh, how can you, Louis?

LOUIS [*insisting childishly*] Yes, because people who have found marriage happy always marry again. Ah, I shant be jealous. [*Slyly.*] But dont talk to the other fellow too much about me: he wont like it. [*Almost chuckling*] I shall be your lover all the time; but it will be a secret from him, poor devil!

SIR PATRICK. Come! youve talked enough. Try to rest awhile.

LOUIS [*wearily*] Yes: I'm fearfully tired; but I shall have a long rest presently. I have something to say to you fellows. Youre all there, arnt you? I'm too weak to see anything but Jennifer's bosom. That promises rest.

RIDGEON. We are all here.

LOUIS [*startled*] That voice sounded devilish. Take care, Ridgeon: my ears hear things that other people's cant. Ive been thinking—thinking. I'm cleverer than you imagine.

SIR PATRICK [*whispering to Ridgeon*] Youve got on his nerves, Colly. Slip out quietly.

RIDGEON [*apart to Sir Patrick*] Would you deprive the dying actor of his audience?

LOUIS [*his face lighting up faintly with mischievous glee*] I heard that, Ridgeon. That was good. Jennifer dear: be kind to Ridgeon always; because he was the last man who amused me.

RIDGEON [*relentless*] Was I?

LOUIS. But it's not true. It's you who are still on the stage. I'm half way home already.

MRS DUBEDAT [*to Ridgeon*] What did you say?

LOUIS [*answering for him*] Nothing, dear. Only one of those little secrets that men keep among themselves. Well, all you chaps have thought pretty hard things of me, and said them.

B. B. [*quite overcome*] No, no, Dubedat. Not at all.

LOUIS. Yes, you have. I know what you all think of me. Dont imagine I'm sore about it. I forgive you.

WALPOLE [*involuntarily*] Well, damn me! [*Ashamed*] I beg your pardon.

LOUIS. That was old Walpole, I know. Don't grieve, Walpole. I'm perfectly happy. I'm not in pain. I don't want to live. Ive escaped from myself. I'm in heaven, immortal in the heart of my beautiful Jennifer. I'm not afraid, and not ashamed. [*Reflectively, puzzling it out for himself weakly*] I know that in an accidental sort of way, struggling through the unreal part of life, I havnt always been able to live up to my ideal. But in my own real world I have never done anything wrong, never denied my faith, never been untrue to myself. Ive been threatened and blackmailed and insulted and starved. But Ive played the game. Ive fought the good fight. And now it's all over, theres an indescribable peace. [*He feebly folds his hands and utters his creed*] I believe in Michael Angelo, Velasquez, and Rembrandt; in the might of design, the mystery of color, the redemption of all things by Beauty everlasting, and the message of Art that has made these hands blessed. Amen. Amen. [*He closes his eyes and lies still*].

MRS DUBEDAT [*breathless*] Louis: are you—

Walpole rises and comes quickly to see whether he is dead.

LOUIS. Not yet, dear. Very nearly, but not yet. I should like to rest my head on your bosom; only it would tire you.

MRS DUBEDAT. No, no, no, darling: how could you tire me? [*She lifts him so that he lies on her bosom*].

LOUIS. Thats good. Thats real.

MRS DUBEDAT. Dont spare me, dear. Indeed, indeed you will not tire me. Lean on me with all your weight.

LOUIS [*with a sudden half return of his normal strength and comfort*] Jinny Gwinny: I think I shall recover after all. [*Sir Patrick looks significantly at Ridgeon, mutely warning him that this is the end*].

MRS DUBEDAT [*hopefully*] Yes, yes: you shall.

LOUIS. Because I suddenly want to sleep. Just an ordinary sleep.

MRS DUBEDAT [*rocking him*] Yes, dear. Sleep. [*He seems to go to sleep. Walpole makes another movement. She protests*]. Sh—sh: please dont disturb him. [*His lips move*]. What did you say, dear? [*In great distress*] I cant listen without moving him. [*His lips move again; Walpole bends down and listens*].

WALPOLE. He wants to know is the newspaper man here.

THE NEWSPAPER MAN [*excited; for he has been enjoying himself enormously*] Yes, Mr Dubedat. Here I am.

Walpole raises his hand warningly to silence him. Sir Ralph sits down quietly on the sofa and frankly buries his face in his handkerchief.

MRS DUBEDAT [*with great relief*] Oh thats right, dear: dont spare me: lean with all your weight on me. Now you are really resting.

Sir Patrick quickly comes forward and feels Louis's pulse; then takes him by the shoulders.

SIR PATRICK. Let me put him back on the pillow, maam. He will be better so.

MRS DUBEDAT [*piteously*] Oh no, please, please, doctor. He is not tiring me; and he will be so hurt when he wakes if he finds I have put him away.

SIR PATRICK. He will never wake again. [*He takes the body from her and replaces it in the chair. Ridgeon, unmoved, lets down the back and makes a bier of it*].

MRS DUBEDAT [*who has unexpectedly sprung to her feet, and stands dry-eyed and stately*] Was that death?

WALPOLE. Yes.

MRS DUBEDAT [*with complete dignity*] Will you wait for me a moment? I will come back. [*She goes out*].

WALPOLE. Ought we to follow her? Is she in her right senses?

SIR PATRICK [*with quiet conviction*]. Yes. Shes all right. Leave her alone. She'll come back.

RIDGEON [*callously*] Let us get this thing out of the way before she comes.

B. B. [*rising, shocked*] My dear Colly! The poor lad! He died splendidly.

SIR PATRICK. Aye! that is how the wicked die.

> For there are no bands in their death;
> But their strength is firm: They are not
> in trouble as other men.

No matter: its not for us to judge. Hes in another world now.

WALPOLE. Borrowing his first five-pound note there, probably.

RIDGEON. I said the other day that the most tragic thing in the world is a sick doctor. I was wrong. The most tragic thing in the world is a man of genius who is not also a man of honor.

Ridgeon and Walpole wheel the chair into the recess.

THE NEWSPAPER MAN [*to Sir Ralph*] I thought it shewed a very nice feeling, his being so particular about his wife going into proper mourning for him and making her promise never to marry again.

B. B. [*impressively*] Mrs Dubedat is not in a position to carry the interview any further. Neither are we.

SIR PATRICK. Good afternoon to you.

THE NEWSPAPER MAN. Mrs. Dubedat said she was coming back.

B. B. After you have gone.

THE NEWSPAPER MAN. Do you think she would give me a few words on How It Feels to be a Widow? Rather a good title for an article, isnt it?

B. B. Young man: if you wait until Mrs Dubedat comes back, you will be able to write an article on How It Feels to be Turned Out of the House.

THE NEWSPAPER MAN [*unconvinced*] You think she'd rather not—

B. B. [*cutting him short*] Good day to you. [*Giving him a visiting-card*] Mind you get my name correctly. Good day.

THE NEWSPAPER MAN. Good day. Thank you. [*Vaguely trying to read the card*] Mr—

B. B. No, not Mister. This is your hat, I think [*giving it to him*]. Gloves? No, of course: no gloves. Good day to you. [*He edges him out at last; shuts the door on him; and returns to Sir Patrick as Ridgeon and Walpole come back from the recess, Walpole crossing the room to the hat-stand, and Ridgeon coming between Sir Ralph and Sir Patrick*]. Poor fellow! Poor young fellow! How well he died! I feel a better man, really.

SIR PATRICK. When youre as old as I am, youll know that it matters very little how a man dies. What matters is, how he lives. Every fool that runs his nose against a bullet is a hero nowadays, because he dies for his country. Why dont he live for it to some purpose?

B. B. No, please, Paddy: dont be hard on the poor lad. Not now, not now. After all, was he so bad? He had only two failings: money and women. Well, let us be honest. Tell the truth, Paddy. Dont be hypocritical, Ridgeon. Throw off the mask, Walpole. Are these two matters so well arranged at present that a disregard of the usual arrangements indicates real depravity?

WALPOLE. I dont mind his disregarding the usual arrangements. Confound the usual arrangements! To a man of science theyre beneath contempt both as to money and women. What I mind is his disregarding everything except his own pocket and his own fancy. He didn't disregard the usual arrangements when they paid him. Did he give us his pictures for nothing? Do you suppose he'd have hesitated to blackmail me if I'd compromised myself with his wife? Not he.

SIR PATRICK. Dont waste your time wrangling over him. A blackguard's a blackguard; an honest man's an honest man; and neither of them will ever be at a loss for a religion or a morality to prove that their ways are the right ways. It's the same with nations, the same with professions, the same all the world over and always will be.

B. B. Ah, well, perhaps, perhaps, perhaps. Still, de mortuis nil nisi bonum. He died extremely well, remarkably well. He has set us an example: let us endeavor to follow it rather than harp on the weaknesses that have perished with him. I think it is Shakespear who says that the good that most men do lives after them: the evil lies interred with their bones. Yes: interred with their bones. Believe me, Paddy, we are all mortal. It is the common lot, Ridgeon. Say what you will, Walpole, Nature's debt must be paid. If tis not to-day, twill be to-morrow.

> To-morrow and to-morrow and to-
> morrow After life's fitful fever they
> sleep well And like this insubstantial
> bourne from which No traveller returns
> Leave not a wrack behind.

Walpole is about to speak, but B. B., suddenly and vehemently proceeding, extinguishes him.

> Out, out, brief candle: For nothing
> canst thou to damnation add The readi-
> ness is all.

WALPOLE [*gently; for B. B.'s feeling, absurdly expressed as it is, is too sincere and humane to be ridiculed*] Yes, B. B. Death makes people go on like that. I dont know why it should; but it does. By the way, what are we going to do? Ought we to clear out; or had we better wait and see whether Mrs Dubedat will come back?

SIR PATRICK. I think we'd better go. We can tell the charwoman what to do.

They take their hats and go to the door.

MRS DUBEDAT [*coming from the inner door wonderfully and beautifully dressed, and radiant, carrying a great piece of purple silk, handsomely embroidered, over her arm*] I'm so sorry to have kept you waiting.

SIR PATRICK B.B RIDGEON WALPOLE	} [*amazed, all together in a confused murmur*]	{ Dont mention it, madam. { Not at all, not at all. { By no means. { It doesnt matter in the least.

MRS. DUBEDAT [*coming to them*] I felt that I must shake hands with his friends once before we part to-day. We have shared together a great privilege and a great happiness. I dont think we can ever think of ourselves ordinary people again. We have had a wonderful experience; and that gives us a common faith, a common ideal, that nobody else can quite have. Life will always be beautiful to us: death will always be beautiful to us. May we shake hands on that?

SIR PATRICK [*shaking hands*] Remember: all letters had better be left to your solicitor. Let him open everything and settle everything. Thats the law, you know.

MRS DUBEDAT. Oh, thank you: I didnt know. [*Sir Patrick goes*].

WALPOLE. Good-bye. I blame myself: I should have insisted on operating. [*He goes*].

B.B. I will send the proper people: they will know it to do: you shall have no trouble. Good-bye, my dear lady. [*He goes*].

RIDGEON. Good-bye. [*He offers his hand*].

MRS DUBEDAT [*drawing back with gentle majesty*] I said his friends, Sir Colenso. [*He bows and goes*].

She unfolds the great piece of silk, and goes into the recess to cover her dead.

ACT V

One of the smaller Bond Street Picture Galleries. The entrance is from a picture shop. Nearly in the middle of the gallery there is a writing-table, at which the Secretary, fashionably dressed, sits with his back to the entrance, correcting catalogue proofs. Some copies of a new book are on the desk, also the Secretary's shining hat and a couple of magnifying glasses. At the side, on his left, a little behind him, is a small door marked PRIVATE. Near the same side is a cushioned bench parallel to the walls, which are covered with Dubedat's works. Two screens, also covered with drawings, stand near the corners right and left of the entrance.

Jennifer, beautifully dressed and apparently very happy and prosperous, comes into the gallery through the private door.

JENNIFER. Have the catalogues come yet, Mr Danby?

THE SECRETARY. Not yet.

JENNIFER. What a shame! It's a quarter past: the private view will begin in less than half an hour.

THE SECRETARY. I think I'd better run over to the printers to hurry them up.

JENNIFER. Oh, if you would be so good, Mr Danby. I'll take your place while youre away.

THE SECRETARY. If anyone should come before the time dont take any notice. The commissionaire wont let anyone through unless he knows him. We have a few people who like to come before the crowd—people who really buy; and of course we're glad to see them. Have you seen the notices in Brush and Crayon and in The Easel?

JENNIFER [*indignantly*] Yes: most disgraceful. They write quite patronizingly, as if they were Mr Dubedat's superiors. After all the cigars and sandwiches they had from us on the press day, and all they drank, I really think it is infamous that they should write like that. I hope you have not sent them tickets for to-day.

THE SECRETARY. Oh, they wont come again: theres no lunch to-day. The advance copies of your book have come. [*He indicates the new books*].

JENNIFER [*pouncing on a copy, wildly excited*] Give it to me. Oh! excuse me a moment [*she runs away with it through the private door*].

The Secretary takes a mirror from his drawer and smartens himself before going out. Ridgeon comes in.

RIDGEON. Good morning. May I look round, as well, before the doors open?

THE SECRETARY. Certainly, Sir Colenso. I'm sorry catalogues have not come: I'm just going to see about them. Heres my own list, if you dont mind.

RIDGEON. Thanks. Whats this? [*He takes up one the new books*].

THE SECRETARY. Thats just come in. An advance copy of Mrs Dubedat's Life of her late husband.

RIDGEON [*reading the title*] The Story of a King By His Wife. [*He looks at the portrait frontise*]. Ay: there he is. You knew him here, I suppose.

THE SECRETARY. Oh, we knew him. Better than she did, Sir Colenso, in some ways, perhaps.

RIDGEON. So did I. [*They look significantly at one another*]. I'll take a look round.

The Secretary puts on the shining hat and goes out. Ridgeon begins looking at the pictures. Presently he comes back to the table for a magnifying glass, and scrutinizes a drawing very closely. He sighs; shakes his head, as if constrained to admit the extraordinary fascination and merit of the work; then marks the Secretary's list. Proceeding with his survey, he disappears behind the screen. Jennifer comes back with her book. A look round satisfies her that she is alone. She seats herself at the table and admires the memoir—her first printed book—to her heart's content. Ridgeon re-appears, face to the wall, scrutinizing the drawings. After using his glass again, he steps back to get a more distant view of one of the larger pictures. She hastily closes the book at the sound; looks round; recognizes him; and stares, petrified. He takes a further step back which brings him nearer to her.

RIDGEON [*shaking his head as before, ejaculates*] Clever brute! [*She flushes as though he had struck her. He turns to put the glass down on the desk, and finds himself face to face with her intent gaze*]. I beg your pardon. I thought I was alone.

JENNIFER [*controlling herself, and speaking steadily and meaningly*] I am glad we have met, Sir Colenso Ridgeon. I met Dr Blenkinsop yesterday. I congratulate you on a wonderful cure.

RIDGEON [*can find no words; makes an embarrassed gesture of assent after a moment's silence, and puts down the glass and the Secretary's list on the table*].

JENNIFER. He looked the picture of health and strength and prosperity. [*She looks for a moment at the walls, contrasting Blenkinsop's fortune with the artist's fate*].

RIDGEON [*in low tones, still embarrassed*] He has been fortunate.

JENNIFER. Very fortunate. His life has been spared.

RIDGEON. I mean that he has been made a Medical Officer of Health. He cured the Chairman of the Borough Council very successfully.

JENNIFER. With your medicines?

RIDGEON. No. I believe it was with a pound of ripe greengages.

JENNIFER [*with deep gravity*] Funny!

RIDGEON. Yes. Life does not cease to be funny when people die any more than it ceases to be serious when people laugh.

JENNIFER. Dr Blenkinsop said one very strange thing to me.

RIDGEON. What was that?

JENNIFER. He said that private practice in medicine ought to be put down by law. When I asked him why, he said that private doctors were ignorant licensed murderers.

RIDGEON. That is what the public doctor always thinks of the private doctor. Well, Blenkinsop ought to know. He was a private doctor long enough himself. Come! you have talked at me long enough. Talk to me. You have something to reproach me with. There is reproach in your face, in your voice: you are full of it. Out with it.

JENNIFER. It is too late for reproaches now. When I turned and saw you just now, I wondered how you could come here coolly to look at his pictures. You answered the question. To you, he was only a clever brute.

RIDGEON [*quivering*] Oh, dont. You know I did not know you were here.

JENNIFER [*raising her head a little with a quite gentle impulse of pride*] You think it only mattered because I heard it. As if it could touch me, or touch him! Dont you see that what is really dreadful is that to you living things have no souls.

RIDGEON [*with a sceptical shrug*] The soul is an organ I have not come across in the course of my anatomical work.

JENNIFER. You know you would not dare to say such a silly thing as that to anybody but a woman whose mind you despise. If you dissected me you could not find my conscience. Do you think I have got none?

RIDGEON. I have met people who had none.

JENNIFER. Clever brutes? Do you know, doctor, that some of the dearest and most faithful friends I ever had were only brutes! You would have vivisected them. The dearest and greatest of all my friends had a sort of beauty and affectionateness that only animals have. I hope you may never feel what I felt when I had to put him into the hands of men who defend the torture of animals because they are only brutes.

RIDGEON. Well, did you find us so very cruel, after all? They tell me that though you have dropped me, you stay for weeks with the Bloomfield Boningtons and the Walpoles. I think it must be true, because they never mention you to me now.

JENNIFER. The animals in Sir Ralph's house are like spoiled children. When Mr. Walpole had to take a splinter out of the mastiff's paw, I had to hold the poor dog myself; and Mr Walpole had to turn Sir Ralph out of the room. And Mrs. Walpole has to tell the gardener not to kill wasps when Mr. Walpole is looking. But there are doctors who are naturally cruel; and there are others who get used to cruelty and are callous about it. They blind themselves to the souls of animals; and that blinds them to the souls of men and women. You made a dreadful mistake about Louis; but you would not have made it if you had not trained yourself to make the same mistake about dogs. You saw nothing in them but dumb brutes; and so you could see nothing in him but a clever brute.

RIDGEON [*with sudden resolution*] I made no mistake whatever about him.

JENNIFER. Oh, doctor!

RIDGEON [*obstinately*] I made no mistake whatever about him.

JENNIFER. Have you forgotten that he died?

RIDGEON [*with a sweep of his hand towards the pictures*] He is not dead. He is there. [*Taking up the book*] And there.

JENNIFER [*springing up with blazing eyes*] Put that down. How dare you touch it?

Ridgeon, amazed at the fierceness of the outburst, puts it down with a deprecatory shrug. She takes it up and looks at it as if he had profaned a relic.

RIDGEON. I am very sorry. I see I had better go.

JENNIFER [*putting the book down*] I beg your pardon. I forgot myself. But it is not yet—it is a private copy.

RIDGEON. But for me it would have been a very different book.

JENNIFER. But for you it would have been a longer one.

RIDGEON. You know then that I killed him?

JENNIFER [*suddenly moved and softened*] Oh, doctor, if you acknowledge that—if you have confessed it to yourself—if you realize what you have done, then there is forgiveness. I trusted in your strength instinctively at first; then I thought I had mistaken callousness for strength. Can you blame me? But if it was really strength—if it was only such a mistake as we all make sometimes—it will make me so happy to be friends with you again.

RIDGEON. I tell you I made no mistake. I cured Blenkinsop: was there any mistake there?

JENNIFER. He recovered. Oh, dont be foolishly proud, doctor. Confess to a failure, and save our friendship. Remember, Sir Ralph gave Louis your medicine; and it made him worse.

RIDGEON. I cant be your friend on false pretences. Something has got me by the throat: the truth must come out. I used that medicine myself on Blenkinsop. It did not make him worse. It is a dangerous medicine: it cured Blenkinsop: it killed Louis Dubedat. When I handle it, it cures. When another man handles it, it kills—sometimes.

JENNIFER [*naively: not yet taking it all in*] Then why did you let Sir Ralph give it to Louis?

RIDGEON. I'm going to tell you. I did it because I was in love with you.

JENNIFER [*innocently surprised*] In lo— You! elderly man!

RIDGEON [*thunderstruck, raising his fists to heaven*] Dubedat: thou art avenged! [*He drops his hands and collapses on the bench*]. I never thought of that. I suppose I appear to you a ridiculous old fogey.

JENNIFER. But surely—I did not mean to offend you, indeed—but you must be at least twenty years older than I am.

RIDGEON. Oh, quite. More, perhaps. In twenty years you will understand how little difference that makes.

JENNIFER. But even so, how could you think that I—his wife—could ever think of YOU—

RIDGEON [*stopping her with a nervous waving of his fingers*] Yes, yes, yes, yes: I quite understand: you neednt rub it in.

JENNIFER. But—oh, it is only dawning on me now—I was so surprised at first—do you dare to tell me that it was to gratify a miserable jealousy that you deliberately—oh! oh! you murdered him.

RIDGEON. I think I did. It really comes to that.

Thou shalt not kill, but needst not
strive Officiously to keep alive.

I suppose—yes: I killed him.

JENNIFER. And you tell me that! to my face! callously! You are not afraid!

RIDGEON. I am a doctor: I have nothing to fear. It is not an indictable offense to call in B. B. Perhaps it ought to be; but it isnt.

JENNIFER. I did not mean that. I meant afraid of my taking the law into my own hands, and killing you.

RIDGEON. I am so hopelessly idiotic about you that I should not mind it a bit. You would always remember me if you did that.

JENNIFER. I shall remember you always as a little man who tried to kill a great one.

RIDGEON. Pardon me. I succeeded.

JENNIFER [*with quiet conviction*] No. Doctors think they hold the keys of life and death; but it is not their will that is fulfilled. I dont believe you made any difference at all.

RIDGEON. Perhaps not. But I intended to.

JENNIFER [*looking at him amazedly: not without pity*] And you tried to destroy that wonderful and beautiful life merely because you grudged him a woman whom you could never have expected to care for you!

RIDGEON. Who kissed my hands. Who believed in me. Who told me her friendship lasted until death.

JENNIFER. And whom you were betraying.

RIDGEON. No. Whom I was saving.

JENNIFER [*gently*] Pray, doctor, from what?

RIDGEON. From making a terrible discovery. From having your life laid waste.

JENNIFER. How?

RIDGEON. No matter. I have saved you. I have been the best friend you ever had. You are happy. You are well. His works are an imperishable joy and pride for you.

JENNIFER. And you think that is your doing. Oh doctor, doctor! Sir Patrick is right: you do think you are a little god. How can you be so silly? You did not paint those pictures which are my imperishable joy and pride: you did not speak the words that will always be heavenly music in my ears. I listen to them now whenever I am tired or sad. That is why I am always happy.

RIDGEON. Yes, now that he is dead. Were you always happy when he was alive?

JENNIFER [*wounded*] Oh, you are cruel, cruel. When he was alive I did not know the greatness of my blessing. I worried meanly about little things. I was unkind to him. I was unworthy of him.

RIDGEON [*laughing bitterly*] Ha!

JENNIFER. Dont insult me: dont blaspheme. [*She snatches up the book and presses it to her heart in a paroxysm of remorse, exclaiming*] Oh, my King of Men!

RIDGEON. King of Men! Oh, this is too monstrous, too grotesque. We cruel doctors have kept the secret from you faithfully; but it is like all secrets: it will not keep itself. The buried truth germinates and breaks through to the light.

JENNIFER. What truth?

RIDGEON. What truth! Why, that Louis Dubedat, King of Men, was the most entire and perfect scoundrel, the most miraculously mean rascal, the most callously selfish blackguard that ever made a wife miserable.

JENNIFER [*unshaken: calm and lovely*] He made his wife the happiest woman in the world, doctor.

RIDGEON. No: by all thats true on earth, he made his WIDOW the happiest woman in the world; but it was I who made her a widow. And her happiness is my justification and my reward. Now you know what I did and what I thought of him. Be as angry with me as you like: at least you know me as I really am. If you ever come to care for an elderly man, you will know what you are caring for.

JENNIFER [*kind and quiet*] I am not angry with you any more, Sir Colenso. I knew quite well that you did not like Louis; but it is not your fault: you dont understand: that is all. You never could have believed in him. It is just like your not believing in my religion: it is a sort of sixth sense that you have not got. And [*with a gentle reassuring movement towards him*] dont think that you have shocked me so dreadfully. I know quite well what you mean by his selfishness. He sacrificed everything for his art. In a certain sense he had even to sacrifice everybody—

RIDGEON. Everybody except himself. By keeping that back he lost the right to sacrifice you, and gave me the right to sacrifice him. Which I did.

JENNIFER [*shaking her head, pitying his error*] He was one of the men who know what women know: that self-sacrifice is vain and cowardly.

RIDGEON. Yes, when the sacrifice is rejected and thrown away. Not when it becomes the food of godhead.

JENNIFER. I dont understand that. And I cant argue with you: you are clever enough to puzzle me, but not to shake me. You are so utterly, so wildly wrong; so incapable of appreciating Louis—

RIDGEON. Oh! [*taking up the Secretary's list*] I have marked five pictures as sold to me.

JENNIFER. They will not be sold to you. Louis' creditors insisted on selling them; but this is my birthday; and they were all bought in for me this morning by my husband.

RIDGEON. By whom?!!!

JENNIFER. By my husband.

RIDGEON [*gabbling and stuttering*] What husband? Whose husband? Which husband? Whom? how? what? Do you mean to say that you have married again?

JENNIFER. Do you forget that Louis disliked widows, and that people who have married happily once always marry again?

The Secretary returns with a pile of catalogues.

THE SECRETARY. Just got the first batch of catalogues in time. The doors are open.

JENNIFER [*to Ridgeon, politely*] So glad you like the pictures, Sir Colenso. Good morning.

RIDGEON. Good morning. [*He goes towards the door; hesitates; turns to say something more; gives it up as a bad job; and goes*].

GETTING MARRIED

GETTING MARRIED

N.B.—There is a point of some technical interest to be noted in this play. The customary division into acts and scenes has been disused, and a return made to unity of time and place, as observed in the ancient Greek drama. In the foregoing tragedy, The Doctor's Dilemma, there are five acts; the place is altered five times; and the time is spread over an undetermined period of more than a year. No doubt the strain on the attention of the audience and on the ingenuity of the playwright is much less; but I find in practice that the Greek form is inevitable when drama reaches a certain point in poetic and intellectual evolution. Its adoption was not, on my part, a deliberate display of virtuosity in form, but simply the spontaneous falling of a play of ideas into the form most suitable to it, which turned out to be the classical form. Getting Married, in several acts and scenes, with the time spread over a long period, would be impossible.

On a fine morning in the spring of 1908 the Norman kitchen in the Palace of the Bishop of Chelsea looks very spacious and clean and handsome and healthy.

The Bishop is lucky enough to have a XII century palace. The palace itself has been lucky enough to escape being carved up into XV century Gothic, or shaved into XVIII century ashlar, or "restored" by a XIX century builder and a Victorian architect with a deep sense of the umbrella-like gentlemanliness of XIV century vaulting. The present occupant, A. Chelsea, unofficially Alfred Bridgenorth, appreciates Norman work. He has, by adroit complaints of the discomfort of the place, induced the Ecclesiastical Commissioners to give him some money to spend on it; and with this he has got rid of the wall papers, the paint, the partitions, the exquisitely planed and moulded casings with which the Victorian cabinet-makers enclosed and hid the huge black beams of hewn oak, and of all other expedients of his predecessors to make themselves feel at home and respectable in a Norman fortress. It is a house built to last for ever. The walls and beams are big enough to carry the tower of Babel, as if the builders, anticipating our modern ideas and instinctively defying them, had resolved to show how much material they could lavish on a house built for the glory of God, instead of keeping a competitive eye on the advantage of sending in the lowest tender, and scientifically calculating how little material would be enough to prevent the whole affair from tumbling down by its own weight.

The kitchen is the Bishop's favorite room. This is not at all because he is a man of humble mind; but because the kitchen is one of the finest rooms in the house. The Bishop has neither the income nor the appetite to have his cooking done there. The windows, high up in the wall, look north and south. The north window is the largest; and if we look into the kitchen through it we see facing us the south wall with small Norman windows and an open door near the corner to the left. Through this door we have a glimpse of the garden, and of a garden chair in the sunshine. In the right-hand corner is an entrance to a vaulted circular chamber with a winding stair leading up through a tower to the upper floors of the palace. In the wall to our right is the immense fireplace, with its huge spit like a baby crane, and a collection of old iron and brass instruments which pass as the original furniture of the fire, though as a matter of fact they have been picked up from time to time by the Bishop at secondhand shops. In the near end of the left hand wall a small Norman door gives access to the Bishop's study, formerly a scullery. Further along, a great oak chest stands against the wall. Across the middle of the kitchen is a big timber table surrounded by eleven stout rush-bottomed chairs: four on the far side, three on the near side, and two at each end. There is a big chair with railed back and sides on the hearth. On the floor is a drugget of thick fibre matting. The only other piece of furniture is a clock with a wooden dial about as large as the bottom of a washtub, the weights, chains, and pendulum being of corresponding magnitude; but the Bishop has long since abandoned the attempt to keep it going. It hangs above the oak chest.

The kitchen is occupied at present by the Bishop's lady, Mrs Bridgenorth, who is talking to Mr William Collins, the greengrocer. He is in evening dress, though it is early forenoon. Mrs Bridgenorth is a quiet happy-looking woman of fifty or thereabouts, placid, gentle, and humorous, with delicate features and fine grey hair with many white threads. She is dressed as for some festivity; but she is taking things easily as she sits in the big chair by the hearth, reading The Times.

Collins is an elderly man with a rather youthful waist. His muttonchop whiskers have a coquettish touch of Dundreary at their lower ends. He is an affable man, with those perfect manners which can be acquired only in keeping a shop for the sale of necessaries of life to ladies whose social position is so unquestionable that they are not anxious about it. He is a reassuring man, with a vigilant grey eye, and the power of saying anything he likes to you without offence, because his tone always implies that he does it with your kind permission. Withal by no means servile: rather gallant and compassionate, but never without a conscientious recognition, on public grounds, of social distinctions. He is at the oak chest counting a pile of napkins.

Mrs Bridgenorth reads placidly: Collins counts: a blackbird sings in the garden. Mrs Bridgenorth puts The Times down in her lap and considers Collins for a moment.

MRS BRIDGENORTH. Do you never feel nervous on these occasions,

Collins?

COLLINS. Lord bless you, no, maam. It would be a joke, after marrying five of your daughters, if I was to get nervous over marrying the last of them.

MRS BRIDGENORTH. I have always said you were a wonderful man,

Collins.

COLLINS [*almost blushing*] Oh, maam!

MRS BRIDGENORTH. Yes. I never could arrange anything—a wedding or even dinner—without some hitch or other.

COLLINS. Why should you give yourself the trouble, maam? Send for the greengrocer, maam: thats the secret of easy housekeeping. Bless you, it's his business. It pays him and you, let alone the pleasure in a house like this [*Mrs Bridgenorth bows in acknowledgment of the compliment*]. They joke about the greengrocer, just as they joke about the mother-in-law. But they cant get on without both.

MRS BRIDGENORTH. What a bond between us, Collins!

COLLINS. Bless you, maam, theres all sorts of bonds between all sorts of people. You are a very affable lady, maam, for a Bishop's lady. I have known Bishop's ladies that would fairly provoke you to up and cheek them; but nobody would ever forget himself and his place with you, maam.

MRS BRIDGENORTH. Collins: you are a flatterer. You will superintend the breakfast yourself as usual, of course, wont you?

COLLINS. Yes, yes, bless you, maam, of course. I always do. Them fashionable caterers send down such people as I never did set eyes on. Dukes you would take them for. You see the relatives shaking hands with them and asking them about the family—actually ladies saying "Where have we met before?" and all sorts of confusion. Thats my secret in business, maam. You can always spot me as the greengrocer. It's a fortune to me in these days, when you cant hardly tell who any one is or isnt. [*He goes out through the tower, and immediately returns for a moment to announce*] The General, maam.

Mrs Bridgenorth rises to receive her brother-in-law, who enters resplendent in full-dress uniform, with many medals and orders. General Bridgenorth is a well set up man of fifty, with large brave nostrils, an iron mouth, faithful dog's eyes, and much natural simplicity and dignity of character. He is ignorant, stupid, and prejudiced, having been carefully trained to be so; and it is not always possible to be patient with him when his unquestionably good intentions become actively mischievous; but one blames society, not himself, for this. He would be no worse a man than Collins, had he enjoyed Collins's social opportunities. He comes to the hearth, where Mrs Bridgenorth is standing with her back to the fireplace.

MRS BRIDGENORTH. Good morning, Boxer. [*They shake hands*]. Another niece to give away. This is the last of them.

THE GENERAL [*very gloomy*] Yes, Alice. Nothing for the old warrior uncle to do but give away brides to luckier men than himself. Has—[*he chokes*] has your sister come yet?

MRS BRIDGENORTH. Why do you always call Lesbia my sister? Dont you know that it annoys her more than any of the rest of your tricks?

THE GENERAL. Tricks! Ha! Well, I'll try to break myself of it; but I think she might bear with me in a little thing like that. She knows that her name sticks in my throat. Better call her your sister than try to call her L— [*he almost breaks down*] L— well, call her by her name and make a fool of myself by crying. [*He sits down at the near end of the table*].

MRS BRIDGENORTH [*going to him and rallying him*] Oh come, Boxer! Really, really! We are no longer boys and girls. You cant keep up a broken heart all your life. It must be nearly twenty years since she refused you. And you know that it's not because she dislikes you, but only that she's not a marrying woman.

THE GENERAL. It's no use. I love her still. And I cant help telling her so whenever we meet, though I know it makes her avoid me. [*He all but weeps*].

MRS BRIDGENORTH. What does she say when you tell her?

THE GENERAL. Only that she wonders when I am going to grow out of it. I know now that I shall never grow out of it.

MRS BRIDGENORTH. Perhaps you would if you married her. I believe youre better as you are, Boxer.

THE GENERAL. I'm a miserable man. I'm really sorry to be a ridiculous old bore, Alice; but when I come to this house for a wedding—to these scenes—to—to recollections of the past— always to give the bride to somebody else, and never to have my bride given to me—[*he rises abruptly*] May I go into the garden and smoke it off?

MRS BRIDGENORTH. Do, Boxer.

Collins returns with the wedding cake.

MRS BRIDGENORTH. Oh, heres the cake. I believe it's the same one we had for Florence's wedding.

THE GENERAL. I cant bear it [*he hurries out through the garden door*].

COLLINS [*putting the cake on the table*] Well, look at that, maam! Aint it odd that after all the weddings he's given away at, the General cant stand the sight of a wedding cake yet. It always seems to give him the same shock.

MRS BRIDGENORTH. Well, it's his last shock. You have married the whole family now, Collins. [*She takes up The Times again and resumes her seat*].

COLLINS. Except your sister, maam. A fine character of a lady, maam, is Miss Grantham. I have an ambition to arrange her wedding breakfast.

MRS BRIDGENORTH. She wont marry, Collins.

COLLINS. Bless you, maam, they all say that. You and me said it,

I'll lay. I did, anyhow.

MRS BRIDGENORTH. No: marriage came natural to me. I should have thought it did to you too.

COLLINS [*pensive*] No, maam: it didnt come natural. My wife had to break me into it. It came natural to her: she's what you might call a regular old hen. Always wants to have her family within sight of her. Wouldnt go to bed unless she knew they was all safe at home and the door locked, and the lights out. Always wants her luggage in the carriage with her. Always goes and makes the engine driver promise her to be careful. She's a born wife and mother, maam. Thats why my children all ran away from home.

MRS BRIDGENORTH. Did you ever feel inclined to run away, Collins?

COLLINS. Oh yes, maam, yes: very often. But when it came to the point I couldnt bear to hurt her feelings. Shes a sensitive, affectionate, anxious soul; and she was never brought up to know what freedom is to some people. You see, family life is all the life she knows: she's like a bird born in a cage, that would die if you let it loose in the woods. When I thought how little it was to a man of my easy temper to put up with her, and how deep it would hurt her to think it was because I didnt care for her, I always put off running away till next time; and so in the end I never ran away at all. I daresay it was good for me to be took such care of; but it cut me off from all my old friends something dreadful, maam: especially the women, maam. She never gave them a chance: she didnt indeed. She never understood that married people should take holidays from one another if they are to keep at all fresh. Not that I ever got tired of her, maam; but my! how I used to get tired of home life sometimes. I used to catch myself envying my brother George: I positively did, maam.

MRS BRIDGENORTH. George was a bachelor then, I suppose?

COLLINS. Bless you, no, maam. He married a very fine figure of a woman; but she was that changeable and what you might call susceptible, you would not believe. She didnt seem to have any control over herself when she fell in love. She would mope for a couple of days, crying about nothing; and then she would up and say—no matter who was there to hear her—"I must go to him, George"; and away she would go from her home and her husband without with-your-leave or by-your-leave.

MRS BRIDGENORTH. But do you mean that she did this more than once? That she came back?

COLLINS. Bless you, maam, she done it five times to my own knowledge; and then George gave up telling us about it, he got so used to it.

MRS BRIDGENORTH. But did he always take her back?

COLLINS. Well, what could he do, maam? Three times out of four the men would bring her back the same evening and no harm done. Other times theyd run away from her. What could any man with a heart do but comfort her when she came back crying at the way they dodged her when she threw herself at their heads, pretending they was too noble to accept the sacrifice she was making. George told her again and again that if she'd only stay at home and hold off a bit theyd be at her feet all day long. She got sensible at last and took his advice. George always liked change of company.

MRS BRIDGENORTH. What an odious woman, Collins! Dont you think so?

COLLINS [*judicially*] Well, many ladies with a domestic turn thought so and said so, maam. But I will say for Mrs George that the variety of experience made her wonderful interesting. Thats where the flighty ones score off the steady ones, maam. Look at my old woman! She's never known any man but me; and she cant properly know me, because she dont know other men to compare me with. Of course she knows her parents in—well, in the way one does know one's parents not knowing half their lives as you might say, or ever thinking that they was ever young; and she knew her children as children, and never thought of them as independent human beings till they ran away and nigh broke her heart for a week or two. But Mrs George she came to know a lot about men of all sorts and ages; for the older she got the younger she liked em; and it certainly made her interesting, and gave her a lot of sense. I have often taken her advice on things when my own poor old woman wouldnt have been a bit of use to me.

MRS BRIDGENORTH. I hope you dont tell your wife that you go elsewhere for advice.

COLLINS. Lord bless you, maam, I'm that fond of my old Matilda that I never tell her anything at all for fear of hurting her feelings. You see, she's such an out-and-out wife and mother that she's hardly a responsible human being out of her house, except when she's marketing.

MRS BRIDGENORTH. Does she approve of Mrs George?

COLLINS. Oh, Mrs George gets round her. Mrs George can get round anybody if she wants to. And then Mrs George is very particular about religion. And shes a clairvoyant.

MRS BRIDGENORTH [*surprised*] A clairvoyant!

COLLINS [*calm*] Oh yes, maam, yes. All you have to do is to mesmerize her a bit; and off she goes into a trance, and says the most wonderful things! not things about herself, but as if it was the whole human race giving you a bit of its mind. Oh, wonderful, maam, I assure you. You couldnt think of a game that Mrs George isnt up to.

Lesbia Grantham comes in through the tower. She is a tall, handsome, slender lady in her prime; that is, between 36 and 55. She has what is called a well-bred air, dressing very carefully to produce that effect without the least regard for the latest fashions, sure of herself, very terrifying to the young and shy, fastidious to the ends of her long finger-tips, and tolerant and amused rather than sympathetic.

LESBIA. Good morning, dear big sister.

MRS BRIDGENORTH. Good morning, dear little sister. [*They kiss*].

LESBIA. Good morning, Collins. How well you are looking! And how young! [*She turns the middle chair away from the table and sits down*].

COLLINS. Thats only my professional habit at a wedding, Miss. You should see me at a political dinner. I look nigh seventy. [*Looking at his watch*] Time's getting along, maam. May I send up word from you to Miss Edith to hurry a bit with her dressing?

MRS BRIDGENORTH. Do, Collins.

Collins goes out through the tower, taking the cake with him.

LESBIA. Dear old Collins! Has he told you any stories this morning?

MRS BRIDGENORTH. Yes. You were just late for a particularly thrilling invention of his.

LESBIA. About Mrs George?

MRS BRIDGENORTH. Yes. He says she's a clairvoyant.

LESBIA. I wonder whether he really invented George, or stole her out of some book.

MRS BRIDGENORTH. I wonder!

LESBIA. Wheres the Barmecide?

MRS BRIDGENORTH. In the study, working away at his new book. He thinks no more now of having a daughter married than of having an egg for breakfast.

The General, soothed by smoking, comes in from the garden.

THE GENERAL [*with resolute bonhomie*] Ah, Lesbia!

MRS BRIDGENORTH. How do you do? [*They shake hands; and he takes the chair on her right*].

Mrs Bridgenorth goes out through the tower.

LESBIA. How are you, Boxer? You look almost as gorgeous as the wedding cake.

THE GENERAL. I make a point of appearing in uniform whenever I take part in any ceremony, as a lesson to the subalterns. It is not the custom in England; but it ought to be.

LESBIA. You look very fine, Boxer. What a frightful lot of bravery all these medals must represent!

THE GENERAL. No, Lesbia. They represent despair and cowardice. I won all the early ones by trying to get killed. You know why.

LESBIA. But you had a charmed life?

THE GENERAL. Yes, a charmed life. Bayonets bent on my buckles. Bullets passed through me and left no trace: thats the worst of modern bullets: Ive never been hit by a dum-dum. When I was only a company officer I had at least the right to expose myself to death in the field. Now I'm a General even that resource is cut off. [*Persuasively drawing his chair nearer to her*] Listen to me, Lesbia. For the tenth and last time—

LESBIA [*interrupting*] On Florence's wedding morning, two years ago, you said "For the ninth and last time."

THE GENERAL. We are two years older, Lesbia. I'm fifty: you are—

LESBIA. Yes, I know. It's no use, Boxer. When will you be old enough to take no for an answer?

THE GENERAL. Never, Lesbia, never. You have never given me a real reason for refusing me yet. I once thought it was somebody else. There were lots of fellows after you; but now theyve all given it up and married. [*Bending still nearer to her*] Lesbia: tell me your secret. Why—

LESBIA [*sniffing disgustedly*] Oh! Youve been smoking. [*She rises and goes to the chair on the hearth*] Keep away, you wretch.

THE GENERAL. But for that pipe, I could not have faced you without breaking down. It has soothed me and nerved me.

LESBIA [*sitting down with The Times in her hand*] Well, it has nerved me to tell you why I'm going to be an old maid.

THE GENERAL [*impulsively approaching her*] Dont say that, Lesbia.

It's not natural: it's not right: it's—

LESBIA. [*fanning him off*] No: no closer, Boxer, please. [*He retreats, discouraged*]. It may not be natural; but it happens all the time. Youll find plenty of women like me, if you care to look for them: women with lots of character and good looks and money and offers, who wont and dont get married. Cant you guess why?

THE GENERAL. I can understand when there is another.

LESBIA. Yes; but there isnt another. Besides, do you suppose I think, at my time of life, that the difference between one decent sort of man and another is worth bothering about?

THE GENERAL. The heart has its preferences, Lesbia. One image, and one only, gets indelibly—

LESBIA. Yes. Excuse my interrupting you so often; but your sentiments are so correct that I always know what you are going to say before you finish. You see, Boxer, everybody is not like you. You are a sentimental noodle: you dont see women as they really are. You dont see me as I really am. Now I do see men as they really are. I see you as you really are.

THE GENERAL [*murmuring*] No: dont say that, Lesbia.

LESBIA. I'm a regular old maid. I'm very particular about my belongings. I like to have my own house, and to have it to myself. I have a very keen sense of beauty and fitness and cleanliness and order. I am proud of my independence and jealous for it. I have a sufficiently well-stocked mind to be very good company for myself if I have plenty of books and music. The one thing I never could stand is a great lout of a man smoking all over my house and going to sleep in his chair after dinner, and untidying everything. Ugh!

THE GENERAL. But love—

LESBIA. Oh, love! Have you no imagination? Do you think I have never been in love with wonderful men? heroes! archangels! princes! sages! even fascinating rascals! and had the strangest adventures with them? Do you know what it is to look at a mere real man after that? a man with his boots in every corner, and the smell of his tobacco in every curtain?

THE GENERAL [*somewhat dazed*] Well but—excuse my mentioning it—dont you want children?

LESBIA. I ought to have children. I should be a good mother to children. I believe it would pay the country very well to pay me very well to have children. But the country tells me that I cant have a child in my house without a man in it too; so I tell the country that it will have to do without my children. If I am to be a mother, I really cannot have a man bothering me to be a wife at the same time.

THE GENERAL. My dear Lesbia: you know I dont wish to be impertinent; but these are not the correct views for an English lady to express.

LESBIA. That is why I dont express them, except to gentlemen who wont take any other answer. The difficulty, you see, is that I really am an English lady, and am particularly proud of being one.

THE GENERAL. I'm sure of that, Lesbia: quite sure of it. I never meant—

LESBIA [*rising impatiently*] Oh, my dear Boxer, do please try to think of something else than whether you have offended me, and whether you are doing the correct thing as an English gentleman. You are faultless, and very dull. [*She shakes her shoulders intolerantly and walks across to the other side of the kitchen*].

THE GENERAL [*moodily*] Ha! thats whats the matter with me. Not clever. A poor silly soldier man.

LESBIA. The whole matter is very simple. As I say, I am an English lady, by which I mean that I have been trained to do without what I cant have on honorable terms, no matter what it is.

THE GENERAL. I really dont understand you, Lesbia.

LESBIA [*turning on him*] Then why on earth do you want to marry a woman you dont understand?

THE GENERAL. I dont know. I suppose I love you.

LESBIA. Well, Boxer, you can love me as much as you like, provided you look happy about it and dont bore me. But you cant marry me; and thats all about it.

THE GENERAL. It's so frightfully difficult to argue the matter fairly with you without wounding your delicacy by overstepping the bounds of good taste. But surely there are calls of nature— LESBIA. Dont be ridiculous, Boxer.

THE GENERAL. Well, how am I to express it? Hang it all, Lesbia, dont you want a husband?

LESBIA. No. I want children; and I want to devote myself entirely to my children, and not to their father. The law will not allow me to do that; so I have made up my mind to have neither husband nor children.

THE GENERAL. But, great Heavens, the natural appetites—

LESBIA. As I said before, an English lady is not the slave of her appetites. That is what an English gentleman seems incapable of understanding. [*She sits down at the end of the table, near the study door*].

THE GENERAL [*huffily*] Oh well, if you refuse, you refuse. I shall not ask you again. I'm sorry I returned to the subject. [*He retires to the hearth and plants himself there, wounded and lofty*].

LESBIA. Dont be cross, Boxer.

THE GENERAL. I'm not cross, only wounded, Lesbia. And when you talk like that, I dont feel convinced: I only feel utterly at a loss.

LESBIA. Well, you know our family rule. When at a loss consult the greengrocer. [*Opportunely Collins comes in through the tower*]. Here he is.

COLLINS. Sorry to be so much in and out, Miss. I thought Mrs Bridgenorth was here. The table is ready now for the breakfast, if she would like to see it.

LESBIA. If you are satisfied, Collins, I am sure she will be.

THE GENERAL. By the way, Collins: I thought theyd made you an alderman.

COLLINS. So they have, General.

THE GENERAL. Then wheres your gown?

COLLINS. I dont wear it in private life, General.

THE GENERAL. Why? Are you ashamed of it?

COLLINS. No, General. To tell you the truth, I take a pride in it. I cant help it.

THE GENERAL. Attention, Collins. Come here. [*Collins comes to him*]. Do you see my uniform—all my medals?

COLLINS. Yes, General. They strike the eye, as it were.

THE GENERAL. They are meant to. Very well. Now you know, dont you, that your services to the community as a greengrocer are as important and as dignified as mine as a soldier?

COLLINS. I'm sure it's very honorable of you to say so, General.

THE GENERAL [*emphatically*] You know also, dont you, that any man who can see anything ridiculous, or unmanly, or unbecoming in your work or in your civic robes is not a gentleman, but a jumping, bounding, snorting cad?

COLLINS. Well, strictly between ourselves, that is my opinion,

General.

THE GENERAL. Then why not dignify my niece's wedding by wearing your robes?

COLLINS. A bargain's a bargain, General. Mrs Bridgenorth sent for the greengrocer, not for the alderman. It's just as unpleasant to get more than you bargain for as to get less.

THE GENERAL. I'm sure she will agree with me. I attach importance to this as an affirmation of solidarity in the service of the community. The Bishop's apron, my uniform, your robes: the Church, the Army, and the Municipality.

COLLINS [*retiring*] Very well, General. [*He turns dubiously to*

Lesbia on his way to the tower]. I wonder what my wife will say,

Miss?

THE GENERAL. What! Is your, wife ashamed of your robes?

COLLINS. No, sir, not ashamed of them. But she grudged the money for them; and she will be afraid of my sleeves getting into the gravy.

Mrs Bridgenorth, her placidity quite upset, comes in with a letter; hurries past Collins; and comes between Lesbia and the General.

MRS BRIDGENORTH. Lesbia: Boxer: heres a pretty mess!

Collins goes out discreetly.

THE GENERAL. Whats the matter?

MRS BRIDGENORTH. Reginald's in London, and wants to come to the wedding.

THE GENERAL [*stupended*] Well, dash my buttons!

LESBIA. Oh, all right, let him come.

THE GENERAL. Let him come! Why, the decree has not been made absolute yet. Is he to walk in here to Edith's wedding, reeking from the Divorce Court?

MRS BRIDGENORTH [*vexedly sitting down in the middle chair*] It's too bad. No: I cant forgive him, Lesbia, really. A man of Reginald's age, with a young wife—the best of girls, and as pretty as she can be—to go off with a common woman from the streets! Ugh!

LESBIA. You must make allowances. What can you expect? Reginald was always weak. He was brought up to be weak. The family property was all mortgaged when he inherited it. He had to struggle along in constant money difficulties, hustled by his solicitors, morally bullied by the Barmecide, and physically bullied by Boxer, while they two were fighting their own way and getting well trained. You know very well he couldnt afford to marry until the mortgages were cleared and he was over fifty. And then of course he made a fool of himself marrying a child like Leo.

THE GENERAL. But to hit her! Absolutely to hit her! He knocked her down—knocked her flat down on a flowerbed in the presence of his gardener. He! the head of the family! the man that stands before the Barmecide and myself as Bridgenorth of Bridgenorth! to beat his wife and go off with a low woman and be divorced for it in the face of all England! in the face of my uniform and Alfred's apron! I can never forget what I felt: it was only the King's personal request—virtually a command—that stopped me from resigning my commission. I'd cut Reginald dead if I met him in the street.

MRS BRIDGENORTH. Besides, Leo's coming. Theyd meet. It's impossible, Lesbia.

LESBIA. Oh, I forgot that. That settles it. He mustnt come.

THE GENERAL. Of course he mustnt. You tell him that if he enters this house, I'll leave it; and so will every decent man and woman in it.

COLLINS [*returning for a moment to announce*] Mr Reginald, maam.

[*He withdraws when Reginald enters*].

THE GENERAL [*beside himself*] Well, dash my buttons!!

Reginald is just the man Lesbia has described. He is hardened and tough physically, and hasty and boyish in his manner and speech, belonging as he does to the large class of English gentlemen of property (solicitor-managed) who have never developed intellectually since their schooldays. He is a muddled, rebellious, hasty, untidy, forgetful, always late sort of man, who very evidently needs the care of a capable woman, and has never been lucky or attractive enough to get it. All the same, a likeable man, from whom nobody apprehends any malice nor expects any achievement. In everything but years he is younger than his brother the General.

REGINALD [*coming forward between the General and Mrs Bridgenorth*] Alice: it's no use. I cant stay away from Edith's wedding. Good morning, Lesbia. How are you, Boxer? [*He offers the General his hand*].

THE GENERAL [*with crushing stiffness*] I was just telling Alice, sir, that if you entered this house, I should leave it.

REGINALD. Well, dont let me detain you, old chap. When you start calling people Sir, youre not particularly good company.

LESBIA. Dont you begin to quarrel. That wont improve the situation.

MRS BRIDGENORTH. I think you might have waited until you got my answer, Rejjy.

REGINALD. It's so jolly easy to say No in a letter. Wont you let me stay?

MRS BRIDGENORTH. How can I? Leo's coming.

REGINALD. Well, she wont mind.

THE GENERAL. Wont mind!!!!

LESBIA. Dont talk nonsense, Rejjy; and be off with you.

THE GENERAL [*with biting sarcasm*] At school you lead a theory that women liked being knocked down, I remember.

REGINALD. Youre a nice, chivalrous, brotherly sort of swine, you are.

THE GENERAL. Mr Bridgenorth: are you going to leave this house or am I?

REGINALD. You are, I hope. [*He emphasizes his intention to stay by sitting down*].

THE GENERAL. Alice: will you allow me to be driven from Edith's wedding by this—

LESBIA [*warningly*] Boxer!

THE GENERAL. —by this Respondent? Is Edith to be given away by him?

MRS BRIDGENORTH. Certainly not. Reginald: you were not asked to come; and I have asked you to go. You know how fond I am of Leo; and you know what she would feel if she came in and found you here.

COLLINS [*again appearing in the tower*] Mrs Reginald, maam.

LESBIA	No, no. Ask her to—	[*All three clamouring together*].
MRS BRIDGENORTH	Oh, how unfortunate!	
THE GENERAL	Well, dash my buttons!	

It is too late: Leo is already in the kitchen. Collins goes out, mutely abandoning a situation which he deplores but has been unable to save.

Leo is very pretty, very youthful, very restless, and consequently very charming to people who are touched by youth and beauty, as well as to those who regard young women as more or less appetizing lollipops, and dont regard old women at all. Coldly studied, Leo's restlessness is much less lovable than the kittenishness which comes from a rich and fresh vitality. She is a born fusser about herself and everybody else for whom she feels responsible; and her vanity causes her to exaggerate her responsibilities officiously. All her fussing is about little things; but she often calls them by big names, such as Art, the Divine Spark, the world, motherhood, good breeding, the Universe, the Creator, or anything else that happens to strike her imagination as sounding intellectually important. She has more than common imagination and no more than common conception and penetration; so that she is always on the high horse about words and always in the perambulator about things. Considering herself clever, thoughtful, and superior to ordinary weaknesses and prejudices, she recklessly attaches herself to clever men on that understanding, with the result that they are first delighted, then exasperated, and finally bored. When marrying Reginald she told her friends that there was a great deal in him which needed bringing out. If she were a middle-aged man she would be the terror of his club. Being a pretty young woman, she is forgiven everything, proving that "Tout comprendre, c'est tout pardonner" is an error, the fact being that the secret of forgiving everything is to understand nothing.

She runs in fussily, full of her own importance, and swoops on

Lesbia, who is much less disposed to spoil her than Mrs

Bridgenorth is. But Leo affects a special intimacy with Lesbia, as of two thinkers among the Philistines.

LEO [*to Lesbia, kissing her*] Good morning. [*Coming to Mrs Bridgenorth*] How do, Alice? [*Passing on towards the hearth*] Why so gloomy, General? [*Reginald rises between her and the General*]

Oh, Rejjy! What will the King's Proctor say?

REGINALD. Damn the King's Proctor!

LEO. Naughty. Well, I suppose I must kiss you; but dont any of you tell. [*She kisses him. They can hardly believe their eyes*]. Have you kept all your promises?

REGINALD. Oh, dont begin bothering about those—

LEO [*insisting*] Have? You? Kept? Your? Promises? Have you rubbed your head with the lotion every night?

REGINALD. Yes, yes. Nearly every night.

LEO. Nearly! I know what that means. Have you worn your liver pad?

THE GENERAL [*solemnly*] Leo: forgiveness is one of the most beautiful traits in a woman's nature;

but there are things that should not be forgiven to a man. When a man knocks a woman down [*Leo gives a little shriek of laughter and collapses on a chair next Mrs Bridgenorth, on her left*]

REGINALD [*sardonically*] The man that would raise his hand to a woman, save in the way of a kindness, is unworthy the name of Bridgenorth. [*He sits down at the end of the table nearest the hearth*].

THE GENERAL [*much huffed*] Oh, well, if Leo does not mind, of course I have no more to say. But I think you might, out of consideration for the family, beat your wife in private and not in the presence of the gardener.

REGINALD [*out of patience*] Whats the good of beating your wife unless theres a witness to prove it afterwards? You dont suppose a man beats his wife for the fun of it, do you? How could she have got her divorce if I hadnt beaten her? Nice state of things, that!

THE GENERAL [*gasping*] Do you mean to tell me that you did it in cold blood? simply to get rid of your wife?

REGINALD. No, I didn't: I did it to get her rid of me. What would you do if you were fool enough to marry a woman thirty years younger than yourself, and then found that she didnt care for you, and was in love with a young fellow with a face like a mushroom.

LEO. He has not. [*Bursting into tears*] And you are most unkind to say I didnt care for you. Nobody could have been fonder of you.

REGINALD. A nice way of shewing your fondness! I had to go out and dig that flower bed all over with my own hands to soften it. I had to pick all the stones out of it. And then she complained that I hadnt done it properly, because she got a worm down her neck. I had to go to Brighton with a poor creature who took a fancy to me on the way down, and got conscientious scruples about committing perjury after dinner. I had to put her down in the hotel book as Mrs Reginald Bridgenorth: Leo's name! Do you know what that feels like to a decent man? Do you know what a decent man feels about his wife's name? How would you like to go into a hotel before all the waiters and people with—with that on your arm? Not that it was the poor girl's fault, of course; only she started crying because I couldnt stand her touching me; and now she keeps writing to me. And then I'm held up in the public court for cruelty and adultery, and turned away from Edith's wedding by Alice, and lectured by you! a bachelor, and a precious green one at that. What do you know about it?

THE GENERAL. Am I to understand that the whole case was one of collusion?

REGINALD. Of course it was. Half the cases are collusions: what are people to do? [*The General, passing his hand dazedly over his bewildered brow, sinks into the railed chair*]. And what do you take me for, that you should have the cheek to pretend to believe all that rot about my knocking Leo about and leaving her for—for a—a— Ugh! you should have seen her.

THE GENERAL. This is perfectly astonishing to me. Why did you do it? Why did Leo allow it?

REGINALD. Youd better ask her.

LEO [*still in tears*] I'm sure I never thought it would be so horrid for Rejjy. I offered honorably to do it myself, and let him divorce me; but he wouldnt. And he said himself that it was the only way to do it—that it was the law that he should do it that way. I never saw that hateful creature until that day in Court. If he had only shewn her to me before, I should never have allowed it.

MRS BRIDGENORTH. You did all this for Leo's sake, Rejjy?

REGINALD [*with an unbearable sense of injury*] I shouldnt mind a bit if it were for Leo's sake. But to have to do it to make room for that mushroom-faced serpent—!

THE GENERAL [*jumping up*] What right had he to be made room for?

Are you in your senses? What right?

REGINALD. The right of being a young man, suitable to a young woman. I had no right at my age to marry Leo: she knew no more about life than a child.

LEO. I knew a great deal more about it than a great baby like you. I'm sure I dont know how youll get on with no one to take care of you: I often lie awake at night thinking about it. And now youve made me thoroughly miserable.

REGINALD. Serve you right! [*She weeps*]. There: dont get into a tantrum, Leo.

LESBIA. May one ask who is the mushroom-faced serpent?

LEO. He isnt.

REGINALD. Sinjon Hotchkiss, of course.

MRS BRIDGENORTH. Sinjon Hotchkiss! Why, he's coming to the wedding!

REGINALD. What! In that case I'm off [*he makes for the tower*].

REGINALD. A moment ago, when I wanted to stay, you were all shoving me out of the house. Now that I want to go, you wont let me.

MRS BRIDGENORTH. I shall send a note to Mr Hotchkiss not to come.

LEO [*weeping again*] Oh, Alice! [*She comes back to her chair, heartbroken*].

REGINALD [*out of patience*] Oh well, let her have her way. Let her have her mushroom. Let him come. Let them all come.

He crosses the kitchen to the oak chest and sits sulkily on it. Mrs Bridgenorth shrugs her shoulders and sits at the table in Reginald's neighborhood listening in placid helplessness. Lesbia, out of patience with Leo's tears, goes into the garden and sits there near the door, snuffing up the open air in her relief from the domestic stuffness of Reginald's affairs.

LEO. It's so cruel of you to go on pretending that I dont care for you, Rejjy.

REGINALD [*bitterly*] She explained to me that it was only that she had exhausted my conversation.

THE GENERAL [*coming paternally to Leo*] My dear girl: all the conversation in the world has been exhausted long ago. Heaven knows I have exhausted the conversation of the British Army these thirty years; but I dont leave it on that account.

LEO. It's not that Ive exhausted it; but he will keep on repeating it when I want to read or go to sleep. And Sinjon amuses me. He's so clever.

THE GENERAL [*stung*] Ha! The old complaint. You all want geniuses to marry. This demand for clever men is ridiculous. Somebody must marry the plain, honest, stupid fellows. Have you thought of that?

LEO. But there are such lots of stupid women to marry. Why do they want to marry us? Besides, Rejjy knows that I'm quite fond of him. I like him because he wants me; and I like Sinjon because I want him. I feel that I have a duty to Rejjy.

THE GENERAL. Precisely: you have.

LEO. And, of course, Sinjon has the same duty to me.

THE GENERAL. Tut, tut!

LEO. Oh, how silly the law is! Why cant I marry them both?

THE GENERAL [*shocked*] Leo!

LEO. Well, I love them both. I should like to marry a lot of men. I should like to have Rejjy for every day, and Sinjon for concerts and theatres and going out in the evenings, and some great austere saint for about once a year at the end of the season, and some perfectly blithering idiot of a boy to be quite wicked with. I so seldom feel wicked; and, when I do, it's such a pity to waste it merely because it's too silly to confess to a real grown-up man.

REGINALD. This is the kind of thing, you know [*Helplessly*] Well, there it is!

THE GENERAL [*decisively*] Alice: this is a job for the Barmecide. He's a Bishop: it's his duty to talk to Leo. I can stand a good deal; but when it comes to flat polygamy and polyandry, we ought to do something.

MRS BRIDGENORTH [*going to the study door*] Do come here a moment,

Alfred. We're in a difficulty.

THE BISHOP [*within*] Ask Collins, I'm busy.

MRS BRIDGENORTH. Collins wont do. It's something very serious. Do come just a moment, dear. [*When she hears him coming she takes a chair at the nearest end of the table*].

The Bishop comes out of his study. He is still a slim active man, spare of flesh, and younger by temperament than his brothers. He has a delicate skin, fine hands, a salient nose with chin to match, a short beard which accentuates his sharp chin by bristling forward, clever humorous eyes, not without a glint of mischief in them, ready bright speech, and the ways of a successful man who is always interested in himself and generally rather well pleased with himself. When Lesbia hears his voice she turns her chair towards him, and presently rises and stands in the doorway listening to the conversation.

THE BISHOP [*going to Leo*] Good morning, my dear. Hullo! Youve brought Reginald with you. Thats very nice of you. Have you reconciled them, Boxer?

THE GENERAL. Reconciled them! Why, man, the whole divorce was a put-up job. She wants to marry some fellow named Hotchkiss.

REGINALD. A fellow with a face like—

LEO. You shant, Rejjy. He has a very fine face.

MRS BRIDGENORTH. And now she says she wants to marry both of them, and a lot of other people as well.

LEO. I didnt say I wanted to marry them: I only said I should like to marry them.

THE BISHOP. Quite a nice distinction, Leo.

LEO. Just occasionally, you know.

THE BISHOP [*sitting down cosily beside her*] Quite so. Sometimes a poet, sometimes a Bishop, sometimes a fairy prince, sometimes somebody quite indescribable, and sometimes nobody at all.

LEO. Yes: thats just it. How did you know?

THE BISHOP. Oh, I should say most imaginative and cultivated young women feel like that. I wouldnt give a rap for one who didnt. Shakespear pointed out long ago that a woman wanted a Sunday husband as well as a weekday one. But, as usual, he didnt follow up the idea.

THE GENERAL [*aghast*] Am I to understand—

THE BISHOP [*cutting him short*] Now, Boxer, am I the Bishop or are you?

THE GENERAL [*sulkily*] You.

THE BISHOP. Then dont ask me are you to understand. "Yours not to reason why: yours but to do and die"—

THE GENERAL. Oh, very well: go on. I'm not clever. Only a silly soldier man. Ha! Go on. [*He throws himself into the railed chair, as one prepared for the worst*].

MRS BRIDGENORTH. Alfred: dont tease Boxer.

THE BISHOP. If we are going to discuss ethical questions we must begin by giving the devil fair play. Boxer never does. England never does. We always assume that the devil is guilty; and we wont allow him to prove his innocence, because it would be against public morals if he succeeded. We used to do the same with prisoners accused of high treason. And the consequence is that we overreach ourselves; and the devil gets the better of us after all. Perhaps thats what most of us intend him to do.

THE GENERAL. Alfred: we asked you here to preach to Leo. You are preaching at me instead. I am not conscious of having said or done anything that calls for that unsolicited attention.

THE BISHOP. But poor little Leo has only told the simple truth; whilst you, Boxer, are striking moral attitudes.

THE GENERAL. I suppose thats an epigram. I dont understand epigrams. I'm only a silly soldier man. Ha! But I can put a plain question. Is Leo to be encouraged to be a polygamist?

THE BISHOP. Remember the British Empire, Boxer. Youre a British

General, you know.

THE GENERAL. What has that to do with polygamy?

THE BISHOP. Well, the great majority of our fellow-subjects are polygamists. I cant as a British Bishop insult them by speaking disrespectfully of polygamy. It's a very interesting question. Many very interesting men have been polygamists: Solomon, Mahomet, and our friend the Duke of—of—hm! I never can remember his name.

THE GENERAL. It would become you better, Alfred, to send that silly girl back to her husband and her duty than to talk clever and mock at your religion. "What God hath joined together let no man put asunder." Remember that.

THE BISHOP. Dont be afraid, Boxer. What God hath joined together no man ever shall put asunder: God will take care of that. [*To Leo*] By the way, who was it that joined you and Reginald, my dear?

LEO. It was that awful little curate that afterwards drank, and travelled first class with a third-class ticket, and then tried to go on the stage. But they wouldnt have him. He called himself Egerton Fotheringay.

THE BISHOP. Well, whom Egerton Fotheringay hath joined, let Sir

Gorell Barnes put asunder by all means.

THE GENERAL. I may be a silly soldier man; but I call this blasphemy.

THE BISHOP [*gravely*] Better for me to take the name of Mr Egerton Fotheringay in earnest than for you to take a higher name in vain.

LESBIA. Cant you three brothers ever meet without quarrelling?

THE BISHOP [*mildly*] This is not quarrelling, Lesbia: it's only

English family life. Good morning.

LEO. You know, Bishop, it's very dear of you to take my part; but

I'm not sure that I'm not a little shocked.

THE BISHOP. Then I think Ive been a little more successful than

Boxer in getting you into a proper frame of mind.

THE GENERAL [*snorting*] Ha!

LEO. Not a bit; for now I'm going to shock you worse than ever.

I think Solomon was an old beast.

THE BISHOP. Precisely what you ought to think of him, my dear.

Dont apologize.

THE GENERAL [*more shocked*] Well, but hang it! Solomon was in the

Bible. And, after all, Solomon was Solomon.

LEO. And I stick to it: I still want to have a lot of interesting men to know quite intimately—to say everything I think of to them, and have them say everything they think of to me.

THE BISHOP. So you shall, my dear, if you are lucky. But you know you neednt marry them all. Think of all the buttons you would have to sew on. Besides, nothing is more dreadful than a husband who keeps telling you everything he thinks, and always wants to know what you think.

LEO [*struck by this*] Well, thats very true of Rejjy: In fact, thats why I had to divorce him.

THE BISHOP [*condoling*] Yes: he repeats himself dreadfully, doesnt he?

REGINALD. Look here, Alfred. If I have my faults, let her find them out for herself without your help.

THE BISHOP. She has found them all out already, Reginald.

LEO [*a little huffily*] After all, there are worse men than Reginald. I daresay he's not so clever as you; but still he's not such a fool as you seem to think him!

THE BISHOP. Quite right, dear: stand up for your husband. I hope you will always stand up for all your husbands. [*He rises and goes to the hearth, where he stands complacently with his back to the fireplace, beaming at them all as at a roomful of children*].

LEO. Please dont talk as if I wanted to marry a whole regiment. For me there can never be more than two. I shall never love anybody but Rejjy and Sinjon.

REGINALD. A man with a face like a—

LEO. I wont have it, Rejjy. It's disgusting.

THE BISHOP. You see, my dear, youll exhaust Sinjon's conversation too in a week or so. A man is like a phonograph with half-a-dozen records. You soon get tired of them all; and yet you have to sit at table whilst he reels them off to every new visitor. In the end you have to be content with his common humanity; and when you come down to that, you find out about men what a great English poet of my acquaintance used to say about women: that they all taste alike. Marry whom you please: at the end of a month he'll be Reginald over again. It wasnt worth changing: indeed it wasnt.

LEO. Then it's a mistake to get married.

THE BISHOP. It is, my dear; but it's a much bigger mistake not to get married.

THE GENERAL [*rising*] Ha! You hear that, Lesbia? [*He joins her at the garden door*].

LESBIA. Thats only an epigram, Boxer.

THE GENERAL. Sound sense, Lesbia. When a man talks rot, thats epigram: when he talks sense, then I agree with him.

REGINALD [*coming off the oak chest and looking at his watch*] It's getting late. Wheres Edith? Hasnt she got into her veil and orange blossoms yet?

MRS BRIDGENORTH. Do go and hurry her, Lesbia.

LESBIA [*going out through the tower*] Come with me, Leo.

LEO [*following Lesbia out*] Yes, certainly.

The Bishop goes over to his wife and sits down, taking her hand and kissing it by way of beginning a conversation with her.

THE BISHOP. Alice: Ive had another letter from the mysterious lady who cant spell. I like that woman's letters. Theres an intensity of passion in them that fascinates me.

MRS BRIDGENORTH. Do you mean Incognita Appassionata?

THE BISHOP. Yes.

THE GENERAL [*turning abruptly; he has been looking out into the garden*] Do you mean to say that women write love-letters to you?

THE BISHOP. Of course.

THE GENERAL. They never do to me.

THE BISHOP. The army doesnt attract women: the Church does.

REGINALD. Do you consider it right to let them? They may be married women, you know.

THE BISHOP. They always are. This one is. [*To Mrs Bridgenorth*]

Dont you think her letters are quite the best love-letters I get?

[*To the two men*] Poor Alice has to read my love-letters aloud to me at breakfast, when theyre worth it.

MRS BRIDGENORTH. There really is something fascinating about

Incognita. She never gives her address. Thats a good sign.

THE GENERAL. Mf! No assignations, you mean?

THE Bishop. Oh yes: she began the correspondence by making a very curious but very natural assignation. She wants me to meet her in heaven. I hope I shall.

THE GENERAL. Well, I must say I hope not, Alfred. I hope not.

MRS BRIDGENORTH. She says she is happily married, and that love is a necessary of life to her, but that she must have, high above all her lovers—

THE BISHOP. She has several apparently—

MRS BRIDGENORTH. —some great man who will never know her, never touch her, as she is on earth, but whom she can meet in Heaven when she has risen above all the everyday vulgarities of earthly love.

THE BISHOP [*rising*] Excellent. Very good for her; and no trouble to me. Everybody ought to have one of these idealizations, like Dante's Beatrice. [*He clasps his hands behind him, and strolls to the hearth and back, singing*].

Lesbia appears in the tower, rather perturbed.

LESBIA. Alice: will you come upstairs? Edith is not dressed.

MRS BRIDGENORTH [*rising*] Not dressed! Does she know what hour it is?

LESBIA. She has locked herself into her room, reading.

The Bishop's song ceases; he stops dead in his stroll.

THE GENERAL. Reading!

THE BISHOP. What is she reading?

LESBIA. Some pamphlet that came by the eleven o'clock post. She wont come out. She wont open the door. And she says she doesnt know whether she's going to be married or not till she's finished the pamphlet. Did you ever hear such a thing? Do come and speak to her.

MRS BRIDGENORTH. Alfred: you had better go.

THE BISHOP. Try Collins.

LESBIA. Weve tried Collins already. He got all that Ive told you out of her through the keyhole. Come, Alice. [*She vanishes. Mrs Bridgenorth hurries after her*].

THE BISHOP. This means a delay. I shall go back to my work [*he makes for the study door*].

REGINALD. What are you working at now?

THE BISHOP [*stopping*] A chapter in my history of marriage. I'm just at the Roman business, you know.

THE GENERAL [*coming from the garden door to the chair Mrs Bridgenorth has just left, and sitting down*] Not more Ritualism,

I hope, Alfred?

THE BISHOP. Oh no. I mean ancient Rome. [*He seats himself on the edge of the table*]. Ive just come to the period when the propertied classes refused to get married and went in for marriage settlements instead. A few of the oldest families stuck to the marriage tradition so as to keep up the supply of vestal virgins, who had to be legitimate; but nobody else dreamt of getting married. It's all very interesting, because we're coming to that here in England; except that as we dont require any vestal virgins, nobody will get married at all, except the poor, perhaps.

THE GENERAL. You take it devilishly coolly. Reginald: do you think the Barmecide's quite sane?

REGINALD. No worse than ever he was.

THE GENERAL [*to the Bishop*] Do you mean to say you believe such a thing will ever happen in England as that respectable people will give up being married?

THE BISHOP. In England especially they will. In other countries the introduction of reasonable divorce laws will save the situation; but in England we always let an institution strain itself until it breaks. Ive told our last four Prime Ministers that if they didnt make our marriage laws reasonable there would be a strike against marriage, and that it would begin among the propertied classes, where no Government would dare to interfere with it.

REGINALD. What did they say to that?

THE BISHOP. The usual thing. Quite agreed with me, but were sure that they were the only sensible men in the world, and that the least hint of marriage reform would lose them the next election. And then lost it all the same: on cordite, on drink, on Chinese labor in South Africa, on all sorts of trumpery.

REGINALD [*lurching across the kitchen towards the hearth with his hands in his pockets*] It's no use: they wont listen to our sort. [*Turning on them*] Of course they have to make you a Bishop and Boxer a General, because, after all, their blessed rabble of snobs and cads and half-starved shopkeepers cant do government work; and the bounders and weekenders are too lazy and vulgar. Theyd simply rot without us; but what do they ever do for us? what attention do they ever pay to what we say and what we want? I take it that we Bridgenorths are a pretty typical English family of the sort that has always set things straight and stuck up for the right to think and believe according to our conscience. But nowadays we are expected to dress and eat as the week-end bounders do, and to think and believe as the converted cannibals of Central Africa do, and to lie down and let every snob and every cad and every halfpenny journalist walk over us. Why, theres not a newspaper in England today that represents what I call solid Bridgenorth opinion and tradition. Half of them read as if they were published at the nearest mother's meeting, and the other half at the nearest motor garage. Do you call these chaps gentlemen? Do you call them Englishmen? I dont.[*He throws himself disgustedly into the nearest chair*].

THE GENERAL [*excited by Reginald's eloquence*] Do you see my uniform? What did Collins say? It strikes the eye. It was meant to. I put it on expressly to give the modern army bounder a smack in the eye. Somebody has to set a right example by beginning. Well, let it be a Bridgenorth. I believe in family blood and tradition, by George.

THE BISHOP [*musing*] I wonder who will begin the stand against marriage. It must come some day. I was married myself before I'd thought about it; and even if I had thought about it I was too much in love with Alice to let anything stand in the way. But, you know, Ive seen one of our daughters after another—

Ethel, Jane, Fanny, and Christina and Florence—go out at that door in their veils and orange blossoms; and Ive always wondered whether theyd have gone quietly if theyd known what they were doing. Ive a horrible misgiving about that pamphlet. All progress means war with Society. Heaven forbid that Edith should be one of the combatants!

St John Hotchkiss comes into the tower ushered by Collins. He is a very smart young gentleman of twenty-nine or thereabouts, correct in dress to the last thread of his collar, but too much preoccupied with his ideas to be embarrassed by any concern as to his appearance. He talks about himself with energetic gaiety. He talks to other people with a sweet forbearance (implying a kindly consideration for their stupidity) which infuriates those whom he does not succeed in amusing. They either lose their tempers with him or try in vain to snub him.

COLLINS [*announcing*] Mr Hotchkiss. [*He withdraws*].

HOTCHKISS [*clapping Reginald gaily on the shoulder as he passes him*] Tootle loo, Rejjy.

REGINALD [*curtly, without rising or turning his head*] Morning.

HOTCHKISS. Good morning, Bishop.

THE BISHOP [*coming off the table*]. What on earth are you doing here, Sinjon? You belong to the bridegroom's party: youve no business here until after the ceremony.

HOTCHKISS. Yes, I know: thats just it. May I have a word with you in private? Rejjy or any of the family wont matter; but—[*he glances at the General, who has risen rather stiffly, as he strongly disapproves of the part played by Hotchkiss in Reginald's domestic affairs*].

THE BISHOP. All right, Sinjon. This is our brother, General Bridgenorth. [*He goes to the hearth and posts himself there, with his hands clasped behind him*].

HOTCHKISS. Oh, good! [*He turns to the General, and takes out a card-case*]. As you are in the service, allow me to introduce myself. Read my card, please. [*He presents his card to the astonished General*].

THE GENERAL [*reading*] "Mr St John Hotchkiss, the Celebrated

Coward, late Lieutenant in the 165th Fusiliers."

REGINALD [*with a chuckle*] He was sent back from South Africa because he funked an order to attack, and spoiled his commanding officer's plan.

THE GENERAL [*very gravely*] I remember the case now. I had forgotten the name. I'll not refuse your acquaintance, Mr Hotchkiss; partly because youre my brother's guest, and partly because Ive seen too much active service not to know that every man's nerve plays him false at one time or another, and that some very honorable men should never go into action at all, because theyre not built that way. But if I were you I should not use that visiting card. No doubt it's an honorable trait in your character that you dont wish any man to give you his hand in ignorance of your disgrace; but you had better allow us to forget. We wish to forget. It isnt your disgrace alone: it's a disgrace to the army and to all of us. Pardon my plain speaking.

HOTCHKISS [*sunnily*] My dear General, I dont know what fear means in the military sense of the word. Ive fought seven duels with the sabre in Italy and Austria, and one with pistols in France, without turning a hair. There was no other way in which I could vindicate my motives in refusing to make that attack at Smutsfontein. I dont pretend to be a brave man. I'm afraid of wasps. I'm afraid of cats. In spite of the voice of reason, I'm afraid of ghosts; and twice Ive fled across Europe from false alarms of cholera. But afraid to fight I am not. [*He turns gaily to Reginald and slaps him on the shoulder*]. Eh, Rejjy? [*Reginald grunts*].

THE GENERAL. Then why did you not do your duty at Smutsfontein?

HOTCHKISS. I did my duty—my higher duty. If I had made that attack, my commanding officer's plan would have been successful, and he would have been promoted. Now I happen to think that the British Army should be commanded by gentlemen, and by gentlemen alone. This man was not a gentleman. I sacrificed my military career—I faced disgrace and social ostracism rather than give that man his chance.

THE GENERAL [*generously indignant*] Your commanding officer, sir, was my friend Major Billiter.

HOTCHKISS. Precisely. What a name!

THE GENERAL. And pray, sir, on what ground do you dare allege that Major Billiter is not a gentleman?

HOTCHKISS. By an infallible sign: one of those trifles that stamp a man. He eats rice pudding with a spoon.

THE GENERAL [*very angry*] Confound you, *I* eat rice pudding with a spoon. Now!

HOTCHKISS. Oh, so do I, frequently. But there are ways of doing these things. Billiter's way was unmistakable.

THE GENERAL. Well, I'll tell you something now. When I thought you were only a coward, I pitied you, and would have done what I could to help you back to your place in Society—

HOTCHKISS [*interrupting him*] Thank you: I havnt lost it. My motives have been fully appreciated. I was made an honorary member of two of the smartest clubs in London when the truth came out.

THE GENERAL. Well, sir, those clubs consist of snobs; and you are a jumping, bounding, prancing, snorting snob yourself.

THE BISHOP [*amused, but hospitably remonstrant*] My dear Boxer!

HOTCHKISS [*delighted*] How kind of you to say so, General! Youre quite right: I am a snob. Why not? The whole strength of England lies in the fact that the enormous majority of the English people are snobs. They insult poverty. They despise vulgarity. They love nobility. They admire exclusiveness. They will not obey a man risen from the ranks. They never trust one of their own class. I agree with them. I share their instincts. In my undergraduate days I was a Republican-a Socialist. I tried hard to feel toward a common man as I do towards a duke. I couldnt. Neither can you. Well, why should we be ashamed of this aspiration towards what is above us? Why dont I say that an honest man's the noblest work of God? Because I dont think so. If he's not a gentleman, I dont care whether he's honest or not: I shouldnt let his son marry my daughter. And thats the test, mind. Thats the test. You feel as I do. You are a snob in fact: I am a snob, not only in fact, but on principle. I shall go down in history, not as the first snob, but as the first avowed champion of English snobbery, and its first martyr in the army. The navy boasts two such martyrs in Captains Kirby and Wade, who were shot for refusing to fight under Admiral Benbow, a promoted cabin boy. I have always envied them their glory.

THE GENERAL. As a British General, Sir, I have to inform you that if any officer under my command violated the sacred equality of our profession by putting a single jot of his duty or his risk on the shoulders of the humblest drummer boy, I'd shoot him with my own hand.

HOTCHKISS. That sentiment is not your equality, General, but your superiority. Ask the Bishop. [*He seats himself on the edge of the table*].

THE BISHOP. I cant support you, Sinjon. My profession also compels me to turn my back on snobbery. You see, I have to do such a terribly democratic thing to every child that is brought to me. Without distinction of class I have to confer on it a rank so high and awful that all the grades in Debrett and Burke seem like the medals they give children in Infant Schools in comparison. I'm not allowed to make any class distinction. They are all soldiers and servants, not officers and masters.

HOTCHKISS. Ah, youre quoting the Baptism service. Thats not a bit real, you know. If I may say so, you would both feel so much more at peace with yourselves if you would acknowledge and confess your real convictions. You know you dont really think a Bishop the equal of a curate, or a lieutenant in a line regiment the equal of a general.

THE BISHOP. Of course I do. I was a curate myself.

THE GENERAL. And I was a lieutenant in a line regiment.

REGINALD. And I was nothing. But we're all our own and one another's equals, arnt we? So perhaps when youve quite done talking about yourselves, we shall get to whatever business Sinjon came about.

HOTCHKISS [*coming off the table hastily*] my dear fellow. I beg a thousand pardons. Oh! true, It's about the wedding?

THE GENERAL. What about the wedding?

HOTCHKISS. Well, we cant get our man up to the scratch. Cecil has locked himself in his room and wont see or speak to any one. I went up to his room and banged at the door. I told him I should look through the keyhole if he didnt answer. I looked through the keyhole. He was sitting on his bed, reading a book. [*Reginald rises in consternation. The General recoils*]. I told him not to be an ass, and so forth. He said he was not going to budge until he had finished the book. I asked him did he know what time it was, and whether he happened to recollect that he had a rather important appointment to marry Edith. He said the sooner I stopped interrupting him, the sooner he'd be ready. Then he stuffed his fingers in his ears; turned over on his elbows; and buried himself in his beastly book. I couldnt get another word out of him; so I thought I'd better come here and warn you.

REGINALD. This looks to me like theyve arranged it between them.

THE BISHOP. No. Edith has no sense of humor. And Ive never seen a man in a jocular mood on his wedding morning.

Collins appears in the tower, ushering in the bridegroom, a young gentleman with good looks of the serious kind, somewhat careworn by an exacting conscience, and just now distracted by insoluble problems of conduct.

COLLINS [*announcing*] Mr Cecil Sykes. [*He retires*].

HOTCHKISS. Look here, Cecil: this is all wrong. Youve no business here until after the wedding. Hang it, man! youre the bridegroom.

SYKES [*coming to the Bishop, and addressing him with dogged desperation*] Ive come here to say this. When I proposed to Edith I was in utter ignorance of what I was letting myself in for legally. Having given my word, I will stand to it. You have me at your mercy: marry me if you insist. But take notice that I protest. [*He sits down distractedly in the railed chair*].

THE GENERAL	[*both highly incensed*]	What the devil do you mean by This?
REGINALD		What the— Confound your impertinence, what do you—
HOTCHKISS		Easy, Rejjy. Easy, old man. Steady, steady. [*Reginald subsides into his chair. Hotchkiss sits on his right, appeasing him.*]
THE BISHOP		No, please, Rej. Control yourself, Boxer, I beg you.

THE GENERAL. I tell you I cant control myself. Ive been controlling myself for the last half-hour until I feel like bursting. [*He sits down furiously at the end of the table next the study*].

SYKES [*pointing to the simmering Reginald and the boiling General*] Thats just it, Bishop. Edith is her uncle's niece. She cant control herself any more than they can. And she's a Bishop's daughter. That means that she's engaged in social work of all sorts: organizing shop assistants and sweated work girls and all that. When her blood boils about it (and it boils at least once a week) she doesnt care what she says.

REGINALD. Well: you knew that when you proposed to her.

SYKES. Yes; but I didnt know that when we were married I should be legally responsible if she libelled anybody, though all her property is protected against me as if I were the lowest thief and cadger. This morning somebody sent me Belfort Bax's essays on Men's Wrongs; and they have been a perfect eye-opener to me. Bishop: I'm not thinking of myself: I would face anything for Edith. But my mother and sisters are wholly dependent on my property. I'd rather have to cut off an inch from my right arm than a hundred a year from my mother's income. I owe everything to her care of me. Edith, in dressing-jacket and petticoat, comes in through the tower, swiftly and determinedly, pamphlet in hand, principles up in arms, more of a bishop than her father, yet as much a gentlewoman as her mother. She is the typical spoilt child of a clerical household: almost as terrible a product as the typical spoilt child of a Bohemian household: that is, all her childish affectations of conscientious scruple and religious impulse have been applauded and deferred to until she has become an ethical snob of the first water. Her father's sense of humor and her mother's placid balance have done something to save her humanity; but her impetuous temper and energetic will, unrestrained by any touch of humor or scepticism, carry everything before them. Imperious and dogmatic, she takes command of the party at once.

EDITH [*standing behind Cecil's chair*] Cecil: I heard your voice. I must speak to you very particularly. Papa: go away. Go away everybody.

THE BISHOP [*crossing to the study door*] I think there can be no doubt that Edith wishes us to retire. Come. [*He stands in the doorway, waiting for them to follow*].

SYKES. Thats it, you see. It's just this outspokenness that makes my position hard, much as I admire her for it.

EDITH. Do you want me to flatter and be untruthful?

SYKES. No, not exactly that.

EDITH. Does anybody want me to flatter and be untruthful?

HOTCHKISS. Well, since you ask me, I do. Surely it's the very first qualification for tolerable social intercourse.

THE GENERAL [*markedly*] I hope you will always tell ME the truth, my darling, at all events.

EDITH [*complacently coming to the fireplace*] You can depend on me for that, Uncle Boxer.

HOTCHKISS. Are you sure you have any adequate idea of what the truth about a military man really is?

REGINALD [*aggressively*] Whats the truth about you, I wonder?

HOTCHKISS. Oh, quite unfit for publication in its entirety. If Miss Bridgenorth begins telling it, I shall have to leave the room.

REGINALD. I'm not at all surprised to hear it. [*Rising*] But whats it got to do with our business here to-day? Is it you thats going to be married or is it Edith?

HOTCHKISS. I'm so sorry, I get so interested in myself that I thrust myself into the front of every discussion in the most insufferable way. [*Reginald, with an exclamation of disgust, crosses the kitchen towards the study door*]. But, my dear Rejjy, are you quite sure that Miss Bridgenorth is going to be married? Are you, Miss Bridgenorth?

Before Edith has time to answer her mother returns with Leo and

Lesbia.

LEO. Yes, here she is, of course. I told you I heard her dash downstairs. [*She comes to the end of the table next the fireplace*].

MRS BRIDGENORTH [*transfixed in the middle of the kitchen*] And

Cecil!!

LESBIA. And Sinjon!

THE BISHOP. Edith wishes to speak to Cecil. [*Mrs Bridgenorth comes to him. Lesbia goes into the garden, as before*]. Let us go into my study.

LEO. But she must come and dress. Look at the hour!

MRS BRIDGENORTH. Come, Leo dear. [*Leo follows her reluctantly. They are about to go into the study with the Bishop*].

HOTCHKISS. Do you know, Miss Bridgenorth, I should most awfully like to hear what you have to say to poor Cecil.

REGINALD [*scandalized*] Well!

EDITH. Who is poor Cecil, pray?

HOTCHKISS. One always calls a man that on his wedding morning: I dont know why. I'm his best man, you know. Dont you think it gives me a certain right to be present in Cecil's interest?

THE GENERAL [*gravely*] There is such a thing as delicacy, Mr

Hotchkiss.

HOTCHKISS. There is such a thing as curiosity, General.

THE GENERAL [*furious*] Delicacy is thrown away here, Alfred.

Edith: you had better take Sykes into the study.

The group at the study door breaks up. The General flings himself into the last chair on the long side of the table, near the garden door. Leo sits at the end, next him, and Mrs Bridgenorth next Leo. Reginald returns to the oak chest, to be near Leo; and the Bishop goes to his wife and stands by her.

HOTCHKISS [*to Edith*] Of course I'll go if you wish me to. But Cecil's objection to go through with it was so entirely on public grounds—

EDITH [*with quick suspicion*] His objection?

SYKES. Sinjon: you have no right to say that. I expressly said that I'm ready to go through with it.

EDITH. Cecil: do you mean to say that you have been raising difficulties about our marriage?

SYKES. I raise no difficulty. But I do beg you to be careful what you say about people. You must remember, my dear, that when we are married I shall be responsible for everything you say. Only last week you said on a public platform that Slattox and Chinnery were scoundrels. They could have got a thousand pounds damages apiece from me for that if we'd been married at the time.

EDITH [*austerely*] I never said anything of the sort. I never stoop to mere vituperation: what would my girls say of me if I did? I chose my words most carefully. I said they were tyrants, liars, and thieves; and so they are. Slattox is even worse.

HOTCHKISS. I'm afraid that would be at least five thousand pounds.

SYKES. If it were only myself, I shouldnt care. But my mother and sisters! Ive no right to sacrifice them.

EDITH. You neednt be alarmed. I'm not going to be married.

ALL THE REST. Not!

SYKES [*in consternation*] Edith! Are you throwing me over?

EDITH. How can I? you have been beforehand with me.

SYKES. On my honor, no. All I said was that I didnt know the law when I asked you to be my wife.

EDITH. And you wouldnt have asked me if you had. Is that it?

SYKES. No. I should have asked you for my sake be a little more careful—not to ruin me uselessly.

EDITH. You think the truth useless?

HOTCHKISS. Much worse than useless, I assure you. Frequently most mischievous.

EDITH. Sinjon: hold your tongue. You are a chatterbox and a fool!

MRS BRIDGENORTH [*shocked*] {Edith!

THE BISHOP {My love!

HOTCHKISS [*mildly*] I shall not take an action, Cecil.

EDITH [*to Hotchkiss*] Sorry; but you are old enough to know better. [*To the others*] And now since there is to be no wedding, we had better get back to our work. Mamma: will you tell Collins to cut up the wedding cake into thirty-three pieces for the club girls? My not being married is no reason why they should be disappointed. [*She turns to go*].

HOTCHKISS [*gallantly*] If youll allow me to take Cecil's place,

Miss Bridgenorth—

LEO. Sinjon!

HOTCHKISS. Oh, I forgot. I beg your pardon. [*To Edith, apologetically*] A prior engagement.

EDITH. What! You and Leo! I thought so. Well, hadnt you two better get married at once? I dont approve of long engagements. The breakfast's ready: the cake's ready: everything's ready. I'll lend Leo my veil and things.

THE BISHOP. I'm afraid they must wait until the decree is made absolute, my dear. And the license is not transferable.

EDITH. Oh well, it cant be helped. Is there anything else before

I go off to the Club?

SYKES. You dont seem much disappointed, Edith. I cant help saying that much.

EDITH. And you cant help looking enormously relieved, Cecil. We shant be any worse friends, shall we?

SYKES [*distractedly*] Of course not. Still—I'm perfectly ready— at least—if it were not for my mother—Oh, I dont know what to do. Ive been so fond of you; and when the worry of the wedding was over I should have been so fond of you again—

EDITH [*petting him*] Come, come! dont make a scene, dear. Youre quite right. I dont think a woman doing public work ought to get married unless her husband feels about it as she does. I dont blame you at all for throwing me over.

REGINALD [*bouncing off the chest, and passing behind the General to the other end of the table*] No: dash it! I'm not going to stand this. Why is the man always to be put in the wrong? Be honest, Edith. Why werent you dressed? Were you going to throw him over? If you were, take your fair share of the blame; and dont put it all on him.

HOTCHKISS [*sweetly*] Would it not be better—

REGINALD [*violently*] Now look here, Hotchkiss. Who asked you to cut in? Is your name Edith? Am I your uncle?

HOTCHKISS. I wish you were: I should like to have an uncle,

Reginald.

REGINALD. Yah! Sykes: are you ready to marry Edith or are you not?

SYKES. Ive already said that I'm quite ready. A promise is a promise.

REGINALD. We dont want to know whether a promise is a promise or not. Cant you answer yes or no without spoiling it and setting Hotchkiss here grinning like a Cheshire cat? If she puts on her veil and goes to Church, will you marry her?

SYKES. Certainly. Yes.

REGINALD. Thats all right. Now, Edie, put on your veil and off with you to the church. The bridegroom's waiting. [*He sits down at the table*].

EDITH. Is it understood that Slattox and Chinnery are liars and thieves, and that I hope by next Wednesday to have in my hands conclusive evidence that Slattox is something much worse?

SYKES. I made no conditions as to that when I proposed to you; and now I cant go back. I hope Providence will spare my poor mother. I say again I'm ready to marry you.

EDITH. Then I think you shew great weakness of character; and instead of taking advantage of it I shall set you a better example. I want to know is this true. [*She produces a pamphlet and takes it to the Bishop; then sits down between Hotchkiss and her mother*].

THE BISHOP [*reading the title*] Do YOU KNOW WHAT YOU ARE GOING TO

DO? BY A WOMAN WHO HAS DONE IT. May I ask, my dear, what she did?

EDITH. She got married. When she had three children—the eldest only four years old—her husband committed a murder, and then attempted to commit suicide, but only succeeded in disfiguring himself. Instead of hanging him, they sent him to penal servitude for life, for the sake, they said, of his wife and infant children. And she could not get a divorce from that horrible murderer. They would not even keep him imprisoned for life. For twenty years she had to live singly, bringing up her children by her own work, and knowing that just when they were grown up and beginning life, this dreadful creature would be let out to disgrace them all, and prevent the two girls getting decently married, and drive the son out of the country perhaps. Is that really the law? Am I to understand that if Cecil commits a murder, or forges, or steals, or becomes an atheist, I cant get divorced from him?

THE BISHOP. Yes, my dear. That is so. You must take him for better for worse.

EDITH. Then I most certainly refuse to enter into any such wicked contract. What sort of servants? what sort of friends? what sort of Prime Ministers should we have if we took them for better for worse for all their lives? We should simply encourage them in every sort of wickedness. Surely my husband's conduct is of more importance to me than Mr Balfour's or Mr Asquith's. If I had known the law I would never have consented. I dont believe any woman would if she realized what she was doing.

SYKES. But I'm not going to commit murder.

EDITH. How do you know? Ive sometimes wanted to murder Slattox.

Have you never wanted to murder somebody, Uncle Rejjy?

REGINALD [*at Hotchkiss, with intense expression*] Yes.

LEO. Rejjy!

REGINALD. I said yes; and I mean yes. There was one night, Hotchkiss, when I jolly near shot you and Leo and finished up with myself; and thats the truth.

LEO [*suddenly whimpering*] Oh Rejjy [*she runs to him and kisses him*].

REGINALD [*wrathfully*] Be off. [*She returns weeping to her seat*].

MRS BRIDGENORTH [*petting Leo, but speaking to the company at large*] But isnt all this great nonsense? What likelihood is there of any of us committing a crime?

HOTCHKISS. Oh yes, I assure you. I went into the matter once very carefully; and I found things I have actually done—things that everybody does, I imagine—would expose me, if I were found out and prosecuted, to ten years' penal servitude, two years hard labor, and the loss of all civil rights. Not counting that I'm a private trustee, and, like all private trustees, a fraudulent one. Otherwise, the widow for whom I am trustee would starve occasionally, and the children get no education. And I'm probably as honest a man as any here.

THE GENERAL [*outraged*] Do you imply that I have been guilty of conduct that would expose me to penal servitude?

HOTCHKISS. I should think it quite likely, but of course I dont know.

MRS BRIDGENORTH. But bless me! marriage is not a question of law, is it? Have you children no affection for one another? Surely thats enough?

HOTCHKISS. If it's enough, why get married?

MRS BRIDGENORTH. Stuff, Sinjon! Of course people must get married. [*Uneasily*] Alfred: why dont you say something? Surely youre not going to let this go on.

THE GENERAL. Ive been waiting for the last twenty minutes, Alfred, in amazement! in stupefaction! to hear you put a stop to all this. We look to you: it's your place, your office, your duty. Exert your authority at once.

THE BISHOP. You must give the devil fair play, Boxer. Until you have heard and weighed his case you have no right to condemn him. I'm sorry you have been kept waiting twenty minutes; but I myself have waited twenty years for this to happen. Ive often wrestled with the temptation to pray that it might not happen in my own household. Perhaps it was a presentiment that it might become a part of our old Bridgenorth burden that made me warn our Governments so earnestly that unless the law of marriage were first made human, it could never become divine.

MRS BRIDGENORTH. Oh, do be sensible about this. People must get married. What would you have said if Cecil's parents had not been married?

THE BISHOP. They were not, my dear.

HOTCHKISS {Hallo!
REGINALD {What d'ye mean?
THE GENERAL {Eh?
LEO {Not married!
MRS. BRIDGENORTH {What?

SYKES [*rising in amazement*] What on earth do you mean, Bishop? My parents were married.

HOTCHKISS. You cant remember, Cecil.

SYKES. Well, I never asked my mother to shew me her marriage lines, if thats what you mean. What man ever has? I never suspected—I never knew—Are you joking? Or have we all gone mad?

THE BISHOP. Dont be alarmed, Cecil. Let me explain. Your parents were not Anglicans. You were not, I think, Anglican yourself, until your second year at Oxford. They were Positivists. They went through the Positivist ceremony at Newton Hall in Fetter Lane after entering into the civil contract before the Registrar of the West Strand District. I ask you, as an Anglican Catholic, was that a marriage?

SYKES [*overwhelmed*] Great Heavens, no! a thousand times, no. I never thought of that. I'm a child of sin. [*He collapses into the railed chair*].

THE BISHOP. Oh, come, come! You are no more a child of sin than any Jew, or Mohammedan, or Nonconformist, or anyone else born outside the Church. But you see how it affects my view of the situation. To me there is only one marriage that is holy: the Church's sacrament of marriage. Outside that, I can recognize no distinction between one civil contract and another. There was a time when all marriages were made in Heaven. But because the Church was unwise and would not make its ordinances reasonable, its power over men and women was taken away from it; and marriages gave place to contracts at a registry office. And now that our Governments refuse to make these contracts reasonable, those whom we in our blindness drove out of the Church will be driven out of the registry office; and we shall have the history of Ancient Rome repeated. We shall be joined by our solicitors for seven, fourteen, or twenty-one years—or perhaps months. Deeds of partnership will replace the old vows.

THE GENERAL. Would you, a Bishop, approve of such partnerships?

THE BISHOP. Do you think that I, a Bishop, approve of the Deceased Wife's Sister Act? That did not prevent its becoming law.

THE GENERAL. But when the Government sounded you as to whether youd marry a man to his deceased wife's sister you very naturally and properly told them youd see them damned first.

THE BISHOP [*horrified*] No, no, really, Boxer! You must not—

THE GENERAL [*impatiently*] Oh, of course I dont mean that you used those words. But that was the meaning and the spirit of it.

THE BISHOP. Not the spirit, Boxer, I protest. But never mind that. The point is that State marriage is already divorced from Church marriage. The relations between Leo and Rejjy and Sinjon are perfectly legal; but do you expect me, as a Bishop, to approve of them?

THE GENERAL. I dont defend Reginald. He should have kicked you out of the house, Mr. Hotchkiss.

REGINALD [*rising*] How could I kick him out of the house? He's stronger than me: he could have kicked me out if it came to that. He did kick me out: what else was it but kicking out, to take my wife's affections from me and establish himself in my place? [*He comes to the hearth*].

HOTCHKISS. I protest, Reginald, I said all that a man could to prevent the smash.

REGINALD. Oh, I know you did: I dont blame you: people dont do these things to one another: they happen and they cant be helped. What was I to do? I was old: she was young. I was dull: he was brilliant. I had a face like a walnut: he had a face like a mushroom. I was as glad to have him in the house as she was: he amused me. And we were a couple of fools: he gave us good advice —told us what to do when we didnt know. She found out that I wasnt any use to her and he was; so she nabbed him and gave me the chuck.

LEO. If you dont stop talking in that disgraceful way about our married life, I'll leave the room and never speak to you again.

REGINALD. Youre not going to speak to me again, anyhow, are you?

Do you suppose I'm going to visit you when you marry him?

HOTCHKISS. I hope so. Surely youre not going to be vindictive,

Rejjy. Besides, youll have all the advantages I formerly enjoyed.

Youll be the visitor, the relief, the new face, the fresh news, the hopeless attachment: I shall only be the husband.

REGINALD [*savagely*] Will you tell me this, any of you? how is it that we always get talking about Hotchkiss when our business is about Edith? [*He fumes up the kitchen to the tower and back to his chair*].

MRS BRIDGENORTH. Will somebody tell me how the world is to go on if nobody is to get married?

SYKES. Will somebody tell me what an honorable man and a sincere Anglican is to propose to a woman whom he loves and who loves him and wont marry him?

LEO. Will somebody tell me how I'm to arrange to take care of Rejjy when I'm married to Sinjon. Rejjy must not be allowed to marry anyone else, especially that odious nasty creature that told all those wicked lies about him in Court.

HOTCHKISS. Let us draw up the first English partnership deed.

LEO. For shame, Sinjon!

THE BISHOP. Somebody must begin, my dear. Ive a very strong suspicion that when it is drawn up it will be so much worse than the existing law that you will all prefer getting married. We shall therefore be doing the greatest possible service to morality by just trying how the new system would work.

LESBIA [*suddenly reminding them of her forgotten presence as she stands thoughtfully in the garden doorway*] Ive been thinking.

THE BISHOP [*to Hotchkiss*] Nothing like making people think: is there, Sinjon?

LESBIA [*coming to the table, on the General's left*] A woman has no right to refuse motherhood.

That is clear, after the statistics given in The Times by Mr Sidney Webb.

THE GENERAL. Mr Webb has nothing to do with it. It is the Voice of Nature.

LESBIA. But if she is an English lady it is her right and her duty to stand out for honorable conditions. If we can agree on the conditions, I am willing to enter into an alliance with Boxer.

The General staggers to his feet, momentarily stupent and speechless.

EDITH [*rising*] And I with Cecil.

LEO [*rising*] And I with Rejjy and St John.

THE GENERAL [*aghast*] An alliance! Do you mean a—a—a—

REGINALD. She only means bigamy, as I understand her.

THE GENERAL. Alfred: how long more are you going to stand there and countenance this lunacy? Is it a horrible dream or am I awake? In the name of common sense and sanity, let us go back to real life—

Collins comes in through the tower, in alderman's robes. The ladies who are standing sit down hastily, and look as unconcerned as possible.

COLLINS. Sorry to hurry you, my lord; but the Church has been full this hour past; and the organist has played all the wedding music in Lohengrin three times over.

THE GENERAL. The very man we want. Alfred: I'm not equal to this crisis. You are not equal to it. The Army has failed. The Church has failed. I shall put aside all idle social distinctions and appeal to the Municipality.

MRS BRIDGENORTH. Do, Boxer. He is sure to get us out of this difficulty.

Collins, a little puzzled, comes forward affably to Hotchkiss's left.

HOTCHKISS [*rising, impressed by the aldermanic gown*] Ive not had the pleasure. Will you introduce me?

COLLINS [*confidentially*] All right, sir. Only the greengrocer, sir, in charge of the wedding breakfast. Mr Alderman Collins, sir, when I'm in my gown.

HOTCHKISS [*staggered*] Very pleased indeed [*he sits down again*].

THE BISHOP. Personally I value the counsel of my old friend, Mr

Alderman Collins, very highly. If Edith and Cecil will allow him—

EDITH. Collins has known me from my childhood: I'm sure he will agree with me.

COLLINS. Yes, miss: you may depend on me for that. Might I ask what the difficulty is?

EDITH. Simply this. Do you expect me to get married in the existing state of the law?

SYKES [*rising and coming to Collin's left elbow*] I put it to you as a sensible man: is it any worse for her than for me?

REGINALD [*leaving his place and thrusting himself between Collins and Sykes, who returns to his chair*] Thats not the point. Let this be understood, Mr Collins. It's not the man who is backing out: it's the woman. [*He posts himself on the hearth*].

LESBIA. We do not admit that, Collins. The women are perfectly ready to make a reasonable arrangement.

LEO. With both men.

THE GENERAL. The case is now before you, Mr Collins. And I put it to you as one man to another: did you ever hear such crazy nonsense?

MRS BRIDGENORTH. The world must go on, mustnt it, Collins?

COLLINS [*snatching at this, the first intelligible proposition he has heard*] Oh, the world will go on, maam dont you be afraid of that. It aint so easy to stop it as the earnest kind of people think.

EDITH. I knew you would agree with me, Collins. Thank you.

HOTCHKISS. Have you the least idea of what they are talking about, Mr Alderman?

COLLINS. Oh, thats all right, Sir. The particulars dont matter. I never read the report of a Committee: after all, what can they say, that you dont know? You pick it up as they go on talking.[*He goes to the corner of the table and speaks across it to the company*]. Well, my Lord and Miss Edith and Madam and Gentlemen, it's like this. Marriage is tolerable enough in its way if youre easygoing and dont expect too much from it. But it doesnt bear thinking about. The great thing is to get the young people tied up before they know what theyre letting themselves in for. Theres Miss Lesbia now. She waited till she started thinking about it; and then it was all over. If you once start arguing, Miss Edith and Mr Sykes, youll never get married. Go and get married first: youll have plenty of arguing afterwards, miss, believe me.

HOTCHKISS. Your warning comes too late. Theyve started arguing already.

THE GENERAL. But you dont take in the full—well, I dont wish to exaggerate; but the only word I can find is the full horror of the situation. These ladies not only refuse our honorable offers, but as I understand it—and I'm sure I beg your pardon most heartily, Lesbia, if I'm wrong, as I hope I am—they actually call on us to enter into—I'm sorry to use the expression; but what can I say?—into ALLIANCES with them under contracts to be drawn up by our confounded solicitors.

COLLINS. Dear me, General: thats something new when the parties belong to the same class.

THE BISHOP. Not new, Collins. The Romans did it.

COLLINS. Yes: they would, them Romans. When youre in Rome do as the Romans do, is an old saying. But we're not in Rome at present, my lord.

THE BISHOP. We have got into many of their ways. What do you think of the contract system, Collins?

COLLINS. Well, my lord, when theres a question of a contract, I always say, shew it to me on paper. If it's to be talk, let it be talk; but if it's to be a contract, down with it in black and white; and then we shall know what we're about.

HOTCHKISS. Quite right, Mr Alderman. Let us draft it at once. May

I go into the study for writing materials, Bishop?

THE BISHOP. Do, Sinjon.

Hotchkiss goes into the library.

COLLINS. If I might point out a difficulty, my lord—

THE BISHOP. Certainly. [*He goes to the fourth chair from the General's left, but before sitting down, courteously points to the chair at the end of the table next the hearth*]. Wont you sit down, Mr Alderman? [*Collins, very appreciative of the Bishop's distinguished consideration, sits down. The Bishop then takes his seat*].

COLLINS. We are at present six men to four ladies. Thats not fair.

REGINALD. Not fair to the men, you mean.

LEO. Oh! Rejjy has said something clever! Can I be mistaken in him?

Hotchkiss comes back with a blotter and some paper. He takes the vacant place in the middle of the table between Lesbia and the Bishop.

COLLINS. I tell you the truth, my lord and ladies and gentlemen: I dont trust my judgment on this subject. Theres a certain lady that I always consult on delicate points like this. She has a very exceptional experience, and a wonderful temperament and instinct in affairs of the heart.

HOTCHKISS. Excuse me, Mr Alderman: I'm a snob; and I warn you that theres no use consulting anyone who will not advise us frankly on class lines. Marriage is good enough for the lower classes: they have facilities for desertion that are denied to us. What is the social position of this lady?

COLLINS. The highest in the borough, sir. She is the Mayoress. But you need not stand in awe of her, sir. She is my sister-in- law. [*To the Bishop*] Ive often spoken of her to your lady, my lord. [*To Mrs Bridgenorth*] Mrs George, maam.

MRS BRIDGENORTH [*startled*] Do you mean to say, Collins, that Mrs

George is a real person?

COLLINS [*equally startled*] Didnt you believe in her, maam?

MRS BRIDGENORTH. Never for a moment.

THE BISHOP. We always thought that Mrs George was too good to be true. I still dont believe in her, Collins. You must produce her if you are to convince me.

COLLINS [*overwhelmed*] Well, I'm so taken aback by this that—Well I never!!! Why! shes at the church at this moment, waiting to see the wedding.

THE BISHOP. Then produce her. [*Collins shakes his head*].Come,

Collins! confess. Theres no such person.

COLLINS. There is, my lord: there is, I assure you. You ask

George. It's true I cant produce her; but you can, my lord.

THE BISHOP. I!

COLLINS. Yes, my lord, you. For some reason that I never could make out, she has forbidden me to talk about you, or to let her meet you. Ive asked her to come here of a wedding morning to help with the flowers or the like; and she has always refused. But if you order her to come as her Bishop, she'll come. She has some very strange fancies, has Mrs George. Send your ring to her, my lord—he official ring—send it by some very stylish gentleman— perhaps Mr Hotchkiss here would be good enough to take it—and she'll come.

THE BISHOP [*taking off his ring and handing it to Hotchkiss*]

Oblige me by undertaking the mission.

HOTCHKISS. But how am I to know the lady?

COLLINS. She has gone to the church in state, sir, and will be attended by a Beadle with a mace. He will point her out to you; and he will take the front seat of the carriage on the way back.

HOTCHKISS. No, by heavens! Forgive me, Bishop; but you are asking too much. I ran away from the Boers because I was a snob. I run away from the Beadle for the same reason. I absolutely decline the mission.

THE GENERAL [*rising impressively*] Be good enough to give me that ring, Mr Hotchkiss.

HOTCHKISS. With pleasure. [*He hands it to him*].

THE GENERAL. I shall have the great pleasure, Mr Alderman, in waiting on the Mayoress with the Bishop's orders; and I shall be proud to return with municipal honors. [*He stalks out gallantly, Collins rising for a moment to bow to him with marked dignity*].

REGINALD. Boxer is rather a fine old josser in his way.

HOTCHKISS. His uniform gives him an unfair advantage. He will take all the attention off the Beadle.

COLLINS. I think it would be as well, my lord, to go on with the contract while we're waiting. The truth is, we shall none of us have much of a look-in when Mrs George comes; so we had better finish the writing part of the business before she arrives.

HOTCHKISS. I think I have the preliminaries down all right. [*Reading*] 'Memorandum of Agreement made this day of blank blank between blank blank of blank blank in the County of blank, Esquire, hereinafter called the Gentleman, of the one part, and blank blank of blank in the County of blank, hereinafter called the Lady, of the other part, whereby it is declared and agreed as follows.'

LEO [*rising*] You might remember your manners, Sinjon. The lady comes first. [*She goes behind him and stoops to look at the draft over his shoulder*].

HOTCHKISS. To be sure. I beg your pardon. [*He alters the draft*].

LEO. And you have got only one lady and one gentleman. There ought to be two gentlemen.

COLLINS. Oh, thats a mere matter of form, maam. Any number of ladies or gentlemen can be put in.

LEO. Not any number of ladies. Only one lady. Besides, that creature wasnt a lady.

REGINALD. You shut your head, Leo. This is a general sort of contract for everybody: it's not your tract.

LEO. Then what use is it to me?

HOTCHKISS. You will get some hints from it for your own contract.

EDITH. I hope there will be no hinting. Let us have the plain straightforward truth and nothing but the truth.

COLLINS. Yes, yes, miss: it will be all right. Theres nothing underhand, I assure you. It's a model agreement, as it were.

EDITH [*unconvinced*] I hope so.

HOTCHKISS. What is the first clause in an agreement, usually? You know, Mr Alderman.

COLLINS [*at a loss*] Well, Sir, the Town Clerk always sees to that. Ive got out of the habit of thinking for myself in these little matters. Perhaps his lordship knows.

THE BISHOP. I'm sorry to say I dont. Soames will know. Alice, where is Soames?

HOTCHKISS. He's in there [*pointing to the study*].

THE BISHOP [*to his wife*] Coax him to join us, my love. [*Mrs Bridgenorth goes into the study*]. Soames is my chaplain, Mr Collins. The great difficulty about Bishops in the Church of England to-day is that the affairs of the diocese make it necessary that a Bishop should be before everything a man of business, capable of sticking to his desk for sixteen hours a day. But the result of having Bishops of this sort is that the spiritual interests of the Church, and its influence on the souls and imaginations of the people, very soon begins to go rapidly to the devil—

EDITH [*shocked*] Papa!

THE BISHOP. I am speaking technically, not in Boxer's manner. Indeed the Bishops themselves went so far in that direction that they gained a reputation for being spiritually the stupidest men in the country and commercially the sharpest. I found a way out of this difficulty. Soames was my solicitor. I found that Soames, though a very capable man of business, had a romantic secret his- tory. His father was an eminent Nonconformist divine who habitually spoke of the Church of England as The Scarlet Woman. Soames became secretly converted to Anglicanism at the age of fifteen. He longed to take holy orders, but didnt dare to, because his father had a weak heart and habitually threatened to drop dead if anybody hurt his feelings. You may have noticed that people with weak hearts are the tyrants of English family life. So poor Soames had to become a solicitor. When his father died— by a curious stroke of poetic justice he died of scarlet fever, and was found to have had a perfectly sound heart—I ordained Soames and made him my chaplain. He is now quite happy. He is a celibate; fasts strictly on Fridays and throughout Lent; wears a cassock and biretta; and has more legal business to do than ever he had in his old office in Ely Place. And he sets me free for the spiritual and scholarly pursuits proper to a Bishop.

MRS BRIDGENORTH [*coming back from the study with a knitting basket*] Here he is. [*She resumes her seat, and knits*]. Soames comes in in cassock and biretta. He salutes the company by blessing them with two fingers.

HOTCHKISS. Take my place, Mr Soames. [*He gives up his chair to him, and retires to the oak chest, on which he seats himself*].

THE BISHOP. No longer Mr Soames, Sinjon. Father Anthony.

SOAMES [*taking his seat*] I was christened Oliver Cromwell Soames. My father had no right to do it. I have taken the name of Anthony. When you become parents, young gentlemen, be very careful not to label a helpless child with views which it may come to hold in abhorrence.

THE BISHOP. Has Alice explained to you the nature of the document we are drafting?

SOAMES. She has indeed.

LESBIA. That sounds as if you disapproved.

SOAMES. It is not for me to approve or disapprove. I do the work that comes to my hand from my ecclesiastical superior.

THE BISHOP. Dont be uncharitable, Anthony. You must give us your best advice.

SOAMES. My advice to you all is to do your duty by taking the Christian vows of celibacy and poverty. The Church was founded to put an end to marriage and to put an end to property.

MRS BRIDGENORTH. But how could the world go on, Anthony?

SOAMES. Do your duty and see. Doing your duty is your business: keeping the world going is in higher hands.

LESBIA. Anthony: youre impossible.

SOAMES [*taking up his pen*] You wont take my advice. I didnt expect you would. Well, I await your instructions.

REGINALD. We got stuck on the first clause. What should we begin with?

SOAMES. It is usual to begin with the term of the contract.

EDITH. What does that mean?

SOAMES. The term of years for which it is to hold good.

LEO. But this is a marriage contract.

SOAMES. Is the marriage to be for a year, a week, or a day?

REGINALD. Come, I say, Anthony! Youre worse than any of us. A day!

SOAMES. Off the path is off the path. An inch or a mile: what does it matter?

LEO. If the marriage is not to be for ever, I'll have nothing to do with it. I call it immoral to have a marriage for a term of years. If the people dont like it they can get divorced.

REGINALD. It ought to be for just as long as the two people like.

Thats what I say.

COLLINS. They may not agree on the point, sir. It's often fast with one and loose with the other.

LESBIA. I should say for as long as the man behaves himself.

THE BISHOP. Suppose the woman doesnt behave herself?

MRS BRIDGENORTH. The woman may have lost all her chances of a good marriage with anybody else. She should not be cast adrift.

REGINALD. So may the man! What about his home?

LEO. The wife ought to keep an eye on him, and see that he is comfortable and takes care of himself properly. The other man wont want her all the time.

LESBIA. There may not be another man.

LEO. Then why on earth should she leave him?

LESBIA. Because she wants to.

LEO. Oh, if people are going to be let do what they want to, then I call it simple immorality. [*She goes indignantly to the oak chest, and perches herself on it close beside Hotchkiss*].

REGINALD [*watching them sourly*] You do it yourself, dont you?

LEO. Oh, thats quite different. Dont make foolish witticisms,

Rejjy.

THE BISHOP. We dont seem to be getting on. What do you say, Mr

Alderman?

COLLINS. Well, my lord, you see people do persist in talking as if marriages was all of one sort. But theres almost as many different sorts of marriages as theres different sorts of people. Theres the young things that marry for love, not knowing what theyre doing, and the old things that marry for money and comfort and companionship. Theres the people that marry for children. Theres the people that dont intend to have children and that arnt fit to have them. Theres the people that marry because theyre so much run after by the other sex that they have to put a stop to it somehow. Theres the people that want to try a new experience, and the people that want to have done with experiences. How are you to please them all? Why, youll want half a dozen different sorts of contract.

THE BISHOP. Well, if so, let us draw them all up. Let us face it.

REGINALD. Why should we be held together whether we like it or not? Thats the question thats at the bottom of it all.

MRS BRIDGENORTH. Because of the children, Rejjy.

COLLINS. But even then, maam, why should we be held together when thats all over—when the girls are married and the boys out in the world and in business for themselves? When thats done with, the real work of the marriage is done with. If the two like to stay together, let them stay together. But if not, let them part, as old people in the workhouses do. Theyve had enough of one another. Theyve found one another out. Why should they be tied together to sit there grudging and hating and spiting one another like so many do? Put it twenty years from the birth of the youngest child.

SOAMES. How if there be no children?

COLLINS. Let em take one another on liking.

MRS BRIDGENORTH. Collins!

LEO. You wicked old man—

THE BISHOP [*remonstrating*] My dear, my dear!

LESBIA. And what is a woman to live on, pray, when she is no longer liked, as you call it?

SOAMES [*with sardonic formality*] It is proposed that the term of the agreement be twenty years from the birth of the youngest child when there are children. Any amendment?

LEO. I protest. It must be for life. It would not be a marriage at all if it were not for life.

SOAMES. Mrs Reginald Bridgenorth proposes life. Any seconder?

LEO. Dont be soulless, Anthony.

LESBIA. I have a very important amendment. If there are any children, the man must be cleared completely out of the house for two years on each occasion. At such times he is superfluous, importunate, and ridiculous.

COLLINS. But where is he to go, miss?

LESBIA. He can go where he likes as long as he does not bother the mother.

REGINALD. And is she to be left lonely—

LESBIA. Lonely! With her child. The poor woman would be only too glad to have a moment to herself. Dont be absurd, Rejjy.

REGINALD. That father is to be a wandering wretched outcast, living at his club, and seeing nobody but his friends' wives!

LESBIA [*ironically*] Poor fellow!

HOTCHKISS. The friends' wives are perhaps the solution of the problem. You see, their husbands will also be outcasts; and the poor ladies will occasionally pine for male society.

LESBIA. There is no reason why a mother should not have male society. What she clearly should not have is a husband.

SOAMES. Anything else, Miss Grantham?

LESBIA. Yes: I must have my own separate house, or my own separate part of a house. Boxer smokes: I cant endure tobacco. Boxer believes that an open window means death from cold and exposure to the night air: I must have fresh air always. We can be friends; but we cant live together; and that must be put in the agreement.

EDITH. Ive no objection to smoking; and as to opening the windows, Cecil will of course have to do what is best for his health.

THE BISHOP. Who is to be the judge of that, my dear? You or he?

EDITH. Neither of us. We must do what the doctor orders.

REGINALD. Doctor be—!

LEO [*admonitorily*] Rejjy!

REGINALD [*to Soames*] You take my tip, Anthony. Put a clause into that agreement that the doctor is to have no say in the job. It's bad enough for the two people to be married to one another without their both being married to the doctor as well.

LESBIA. That reminds me of something very important. Boxer believes in vaccination: I do not. There must be a clause that I am to decide on such questions as I think best.

LEO [*to the Bishop*] Baptism is nearly as important as vaccination: isnt it?

THE BISHOP. It used to be considered so, my dear.

LEO. Well, Sinjon scoffs at it: he says that godfathers are ridiculous. I must be allowed to decide.

REGINALD. Theyll be his children as well as yours, you know.

LEO. Dont be indelicate, Rejjy.

EDITH. You are forgetting the very important matter of money.

COLLINS. Ah! Money! Now we're coming to it!

EDITH. When I'm married I shall have practically no money except what I shall earn.

THE BISHOP. I'm sorry, Cecil. A Bishop's daughter is a poor man's daughter.

SYKES. But surely you dont imagine that I'm going to let Edith work when we're married. I'm not a rich man; but Ive enough to spare her that; and when my mother dies—

EDITH. What nonsense! Of course I shall work when I'm married. I shall keep your house.

SYKES. Oh, that!

REGINALD. You call that work?

EDITH. Dont you? Leo used to do it for nothing; so no doubt you thought it wasnt work at all. Does your present housekeeper do it for nothing?

REGINALD. But it will be part of your duty as a wife.

EDITH. Not under this contract. I'll not have it so. If I'm to keep the house, I shall expect Cecil to pay me at least as well as he would pay a hired housekeeper. I'll not go begging to him every time I want a new dress or a cab fare, as so many women have to do.

SYKES. You know very well I would grudge you nothing, Edie.

EDITH. Then dont grudge me my self-respect and independence. I insist on it in fairness to you, Cecil, because in this way there will be a fund belonging solely to me; and if Slattox takes an action against you for anything I say, you can pay the damages and stop the interest out of my salary.

SOAMES. You forget that under this contract he will not be liable, because you will not be his wife in law.

EDITH. Nonsense! Of course I shall be his wife.

COLLINS [*his curiosity roused*] Is Slattox taking an action against you, miss? Slattox is on the Council with me. Could I settle it?

EDITH. He has not taken an action; but Cecil says he will.

COLLINS. What for, miss, if I may ask?

EDITH. Slattox is a liar and a thief; and it is my duty to expose him.

COLLINS. You surprise me, miss. Of course Slattox is in a manner of speaking a liar. If I may say so without offence, we're all liars, if it was only to spare one another's feelings. But I shouldnt call Slattox a thief. He's not all that he should be, perhaps; but he pays his way.

EDITH. If that is only your nice way of saying that Slattox is entirely unfit to have two hundred girls in his power as absolute slaves, then I shall say that too about him at the very next public meeting I address. He steals their wages under pretence of fining them. He steals their food under pretence of buying it for them. He lies when he denies having done it. And he does other things, as you evidently know, Collins. Therefore I give you notice that I shall expose him before all England without the least regard to the consequences to myself.

SYKES. Or to me?

EDITH. I take equal risks. Suppose you felt it to be your duty to shoot Slattox, what would become of me and the children? I'm sure I dont want anybody to be shot: not even Slattox; but if the public never will take any notice of even the most crying evil until somebody is shot, what are people to do but shoot somebody?

SOAMES [*inexorably*] I'm waiting for my instructions as to the term of the agreement.

REGINALD [*impatiently, leaving the hearth and going behind Soames*] It's no good talking all over the shop like this. We shall be here all day. I propose that the agreement holds good until the parties are divorced.

SOAMES. They cant be divorced. They will not be married.

REGINALD. But if they cant be divorced, then this will be worse than marriage.

MRS BRIDGENORTH. Of course it will. Do stop this nonsense. Why, who are the children to belong to?

LESBIA. We have already settled that they are to belong to the mother.

REGINALD. No: I'm dashed if you have. I'll fight for the ownership of my own children tooth and nail; and so will a good many other fellows, I can tell you.

EDITH. It seems to me that they should be divided between the parents. If Cecil wishes any of the children to be his exclusively, he should pay a certain sum for the risk and trouble of bringing them into the world: say a thousand pounds apiece. The interest on this could go towards the support of the child as long as we live together. But the principal would be my property. In that way, if Cecil took the child away from me, I should at least be paid for what it had cost me.

MRS BRIDGENORTH [*putting down her knitting in amazement*] Edith!

Who ever heard of such a thing!!

EDITH. Well, how else do you propose to settle it?

THE BISHOP. There is such a thing as a favorite child. What about the youngest child—the Benjamin—the child of its parents' matured strength and charity, always better treated and better loved than the unfortunate eldest children of their youthful ignorance and wilfulness? Which parent is to own the youngest child, payment or no payment?

COLLINS. Theres a third party, my lord. Theres the child itself. My wife is so fond of her children that they cant call their lives their own. They all run away from home to escape from her. A child hasnt a grown-up person's appetite for affection. A little of it goes a long way with them; and they like a good imitation of it better than the real thing, as every nurse knows.

SOAMEs. Are you sure that any of us, young or old, like the real thing as well as we like an artistic imitation of it? Is not the real thing accursed? Are not the best beloved always the good actors rather than the true sufferers? Is not love always falsified in novels and plays to make it endurable? I have noticed in myself a great delight in pictures of the Saints and of Our Lady; but when I fall under that most terrible curse of the priest's lot, the curse of Joseph pursued by the wife of Potiphar, I am invariably repelled and terrified.

HOTCHKISS. Are you now speaking as a saint, Father Anthony, or as a solicitor?

SOAMES. There is no difference. There is not one Christian rule for solicitors and another for saints. Their hearts are alike; and their way of salvation is along the same road.

THE BISHOP. But "few there be that find it." Can you find it for us, Anthony?

SOAMES. It lies broad before you. It is the way to destruction that is narrow and tortuous. Marriage is an abomination which the Church has founded to cast out and replace by the communion of saints. I learnt that from every marriage settlement I drew up as a solicitor no less than from inspired revelation. You have set yourselves here to put your sin before you in black and white; and you cant agree upon or endure one article of it.

SYKES. It's certainly rather odd that the whole thing seems to fall to pieces the moment you touch it.

THE BISHOP. You see, when you give the devil fair play he loses his case. He has not been able to produce even the first clause of a working agreement; so I'm afraid we cant wait for him any longer.

LESBIA. Then the community will have to do without my children.

EDITH. And Cecil will have to do without me.

LEO [*getting off the chest*] And I positively will not marry Sinjon if he is not clever enough to make some provision for my looking after Rejjy. [*She leaves Hotchkiss, and goes back to her chair at the end of the table behind Mrs Bridgenorth*].

MRS BRIDGENORTH. And the world will come to an end with this generation, I suppose.

COLLINS. Cant nothing be done, my lord?

THE BISHOP. You can make divorce reasonable and decent: that is all.

LESBIA. Thank you for nothing. If you will only make marriage reasonable and decent, you can do as you like about divorce. I have not stated my deepest objection to marriage; and I dont intend to. There are certain rights I will not give any person over me.

REGINALD. Well, I think it jolly hard that a man should support his wife for years, and lose the chance of getting a really good wife, and then have her refuse to be a wife to him.

LESBIA. I'm not going to discuss it with you, Rejjy. If your sense of personal honor doesnt make you understand, nothing will.

SOAMES [*implacably*] I'm still awaiting my instructions.

They look at one another, each waiting for one of the others to suggest something. Silence.

REGINALD [*blankly*] I suppose, after all, marriage is better than —well, than the usual alternative.

SOAMES [*turning fiercely on him*] What right have you to say so? You know that the sins that are wasting and maddening this unhappy nation are those committed in wedlock.

COLLINS. Well, the single ones cant afford to indulge their affections the same as married people.

SOAMES. Away with it all, I say. You have your Master's commandments. Obey them.

HOTCHKISS [*rising and leaning on the back of the chair left vacant by the General*] I really must point out to you, Father Anthony, that the early Christian rules of life were not made to last, because the early Christians did not believe that the world itself was going to last. Now we know that we shall have to go through with it. We have found that there are millions of years behind us; and we know that that there are millions before us. Mrs Bridgenorth's question remains unanswered. How is the world to go on? You say that that is our business—that it is the business of Providence. But the modern Christian view is that we are here to do the business of Providence and nothing else. The question is, how. Am I not to use my reason to find out why? Isnt that what my reason is for? Well, all my reason tells me at present is that you are an impracticable lunatic.

SOAMEs. Does that help?

HOTCHKISS. No.

SOAMEs. Then pray for light.

HOTCHKISS. No: I am a snob, not a beggar. [*He sits down in the General's chair*].

COLLINS. We dont seem to be getting on, do we? Miss Edith: you and Mr Sykes had better go off to church and settle the right and wrong of it afterwards. Itll ease your minds, believe me: I speak from experience. You will burn your boats, as one might say.

SOAMES. We should never burn our boats. It is death in life.

COLLINS. Well, Father, I will say for you that you have views of your own and are not afraid to out with them. But some of us are of a more cheerful disposition. On the Borough Council now, you would be in a minority of one. You must take human nature as it is.

SOAMES. Upon what compulsion must I? I'll take divine nature as it is. I'll not hold a candle to the devil.

THE BISHOP. Thats a very unchristian way of treating the devil.

REGINALD. Well, we dont seem to be getting any further, do we?

THE BISHOP. Will you give it up and get married, Edith?

EDITH. No. What I propose seems to me quite reasonable.

THE BISHOP. And you, Lesbia?

LESBIA. Never.

MRS BRIDGENORTH. Never is a long word, Lesbia. Dont say it.

LESBIA [*with a flash of temper*] Dont pity me, Alice, please. As I said before, I am an English lady, quite prepared to do without anything I cant have on honorable conditions.

SOAMES [*after a silence expressive of utter deadlock*] I am still awaiting my instructions.

REGINALD. Well, we dont seem to be getting along, do we?

LEO [*out of patience*] You said that before, Rejjy. Do not repeat yourself.

REGINALD. Oh, bother! [*He goes to the garden door and looks out gloomily*].

SOAMES [*rising with the paper in his hands*] Psha! [*He tears it in pieces*]. So much for the contract!

THE VOICE OF THE BEADLE. By your leave there, gentlemen. Make way for the Mayoress. Way for the worshipful the Mayoress, my lords and gentlemen. [*He comes in through the tower, in cocked hat and goldbraided overcoat, bearing the borough mace, and posts himself at the entrance*]. By your leave, gentlemen, way for the worshipful the Mayoress.

COLLINS [*moving back towards the wall*] Mrs George, my lord.

Mrs George is every inch a Mayoress in point of stylish dressing; and she does it very well indeed. There is nothing quiet about Mrs George; she is not afraid of colors, and knows how to make the most of them. Not at all a lady in Lesbia's use of the term as a class label, she proclaims herself to the first glance as the triumphant, pampered, wilful, intensely alive woman who has always been rich among poor people. In a historical museum she would explain Edward the Fourth's taste for shopkeepers' wives. Her age, which is certainly 40, and might be 50, is carried off by her vitality, her resilient figure, and her confident carriage. So far, a remarkably well-preserved woman. But her beauty is wrecked, like an ageless landscape ravaged by long and fierce war. Her eyes are alive, arresting and haunting; and there is still a turn of delicate beauty and pride in her indomitable chin; but her cheeks are wasted and lined, her mouth writhen and piteous. The whole face is a battlefield of the passions, quite deplorable until she speaks, when an alert sense of fun rejuvenates her in a moment, and makes her company irresistible.

All rise except Soames, who sits down. Leo joins Reginald at the garden door. Mrs Bridgenorth hurries to the tower to receive her guest, and gets as far as Soames's chair when Mrs George appears. Hotchkiss, apparently recognizing her, recoils in consternation to the study door at the furthest corner of the room from her.

MRS GEORGE [*coming straight to the Bishop with the ring in her hand*] Here is your ring, my lord; and here am I. It's your doing, remember: not mine.

THE BISHOP. Good of you to come.

MRS BRIDGENORTH. How do you do, Mrs Collins?

MRS GEORGE [*going to her past the Bishop, and gazing intently at her*] Are you his wife?

MRS BRIDGENORTH. The Bishop's wife? Yes.

MRS GEORGE. What a destiny! And you look like any other woman!

MRS BRIDGENORTH [*introducing Lesbia*] My sister, Miss Grantham.

MRS GEORGE. So strangely mixed up with the story of the General's life?

THE BISHOP. You know the story of his life, then?

MRS GEORGE. Not all. We reached the house before he brought it up to the present day. But enough to know the part played in it by Miss Grantham.

MRS BRIDGENORTH [*introducing Leo*] Mrs Reginald Bridgenorth.

REGINALD. The late Mrs Reginald Bridgenorth.

LEO. Hold your tongue, Rejjy. At least have the decency to wait until the decree is made absolute.

MRS GEORGE [*to Leo*] Well, youve more time to get married again than he has, havnt you?

MRS BRIDGENORTH [*introducing Hotchkiss*] Mr St John Hotchkiss.

Hotchkiss, still far aloof by the study door, bows.

MRS GEORGE. What! That! [*She makes a half tour of the kitchen and ends right in front of him*]. Young man: do you remember coming into my shop and telling me that my husband's coals were out of place in your cellar, as Nature evidently intended them for the roof?

HOTCHKISS. I remember that deplorable impertinence with shame and confusion. You were kind enough to answer that Mr Collins was looking out for a clever young man to write advertisements, and that I could take the job if I liked.

MRS GEORGE. It's still open. [*She turns to Edith*].

MRS BRIDGENORTH. My daughter Edith. [*She comes towards the study door to make the introduction*].

MRS GEORGE. The bride! [*Looking at Edith's dressing-jacket*] Youre not going to get married like that, are you?

THE BISHOP [*coming round the table to Edith's left*] Thats just what we are discussing. Will you be so good as to join us and allow us the benefit of your wisdom and experience?

MRS GEORGE. Do you want the Beadle as well? He's a married man.

They all turn, involuntarily and contemplate the Beadle, who sustains their gaze with dignity.

THE BISHOP. We think there are already too many men to be quite fair to the women.

MRS GEORGE. Right, my lord. [*She goes back to the tower and addresses the Beadle*] Take away that bauble, Joseph. Wait for me wherever you find yourself most comfortable in the neighborhood. [*The Beadle withdraws. She notices Collins for the first time*]. Hullo, Bill: youve got em all on too. Go and hunt up a drink for Joseph: theres a dear. [*Collins goes out. She looks at Soames's cassock and biretta*] What! Another uniform! Are you the sexton? [*He rises*].

THE BISHOP. My chaplain, Father Anthony.

MRS GEORGE. Oh Lord! [*To Soames, coaxingly*] You dont mind, do you?

SOAMES. I mind nothing but my duties.

THE BISHOP. You know everybody now, I think.

MRS GEORGE [*turning to the railed chair*] Who's this?

THE BISHOP. Oh, I beg your pardon, Cecil. Mr Sykes. The bridegroom.

MRS GEORGE [*to Sykes*] Adorned for the sacrifice, arnt you?

SYKES. It seems doubtful whether there is going to be any sacrifice.

MRS GEORGE. Well, I want to talk to the women first. Shall we go upstairs and look at the presents and dresses?

MRS BRIDGENORTH. If you wish, certainly.

REGINALD. But the men want to hear what you have to say too.

MRS GEORGE. I'll talk to them afterwards: one by one.

HOTCHKISS [*to himself*] Great heavens!

MRS BRIDGENORTH. This way, Mrs Collins. [*She leads the way out through the tower, followed by Mrs George, Lesbia, Leo, and Edith*].

THE BISHOP. Shall we try to get through the last batch of letters whilst they are away, Soames?

SOAMES. Yes, certainly. [*To Hotchkiss, who is in his way*] Excuse me.

The Bishop and Soames go into the study, disturbing Hotchkiss, who, plunged in a strange reverie, has forgotten where he is. Awakened by Soames, he stares distractedly; then, with sudden resolution, goes swiftly to the middle of the kitchen.

HOTCHKISS. Cecil. Rejjy. [*Startled by his urgency, they hurry to him*]. I'm frightfully sorry to desert on this day; but I must bolt. This time it really is pure cowardice. I cant help it.

REGINALD. What are you afraid of?

HOTCHKISS. I dont know. Listen to me. I was a young fool living by myself in London. I ordered my first ton of coals from that woman's husband. At that time I did not know that it is not true economy to buy the lowest priced article: I thought all coals were alike, and tried the thirteen shilling kind because it seemed cheap. It proved unexpectedly inferior to the family Silkstone; and in the irritation into which the first scuttle threw me, I called at the shop and made an idiot of myself as she described.

SYKES. Well, suppose you did! Laugh at it, man.

HOTCHKISS. At that, yes. But there was something worse. Judge of my horror when, calling on the coal merchant to make a trifling complaint at finding my grate acting as a battery of quick-firing guns, and being confronted by his vulgar wife, I felt in her presence an extraordinary sensation of unrest, of emotion, of unsatisfied need. I'll not disgust you with details of the madness and folly that followed that meeting. But it went as far as this: that I actually found myself prowling past the shop at night under a sort of desperate necessity to be near some place where she had been. A hideous temptation to kiss the doorstep because her foot had pressed it made me realize how mad I was. I tore myself away from London by a supreme effort; but I was on the point of returning like a needle to the lodestone when the outbreak of the war saved me. On the field of battle the infatuation wore off. The Billiter affair made a new man of me: I felt that I had left the follies and puerilities of the old days behind me for ever. But half-an-hour ago—when the Bishop sent off that ring—a sudden grip at the base of my heart filled me with a nameless terror—me, the fearless! I recognized its cause when she walked into the room. Cecil: this woman is a harpy, a siren, a mermaid, a vampire. There is only one chance for me: flight, instant precipitate flight. Make my excuses. Forget me. Farewell. [*He makes for the door and is confronted by Mrs George entering*]. Too late: I'm lost. [*He turns back and throws himself desperately into the chair nearest the study door; that being the furthest away from her*].

MRS GEORGE [*coming to the hearth and addressing Reginald*] Mr Bridgenorth: will you oblige me by leaving me with this young man. I want to talk to him like a mother, on YOUR business.

REGINALD. Do, maam. He needs it badly. Come along, Sykes. [*He goes into the study*].

SYKES [*looks irresolutely at Hotchkiss*]—?

HOTCHKISS. Too late: you cant save me now, Cecil. Go.

Sykes goes into the study. Mrs George strolls across to Hotchkiss and contemplates him curiously.

HOTCHKISS. Useless to prolong this agony. [*Rising*] Fatal woman— if woman you are indeed and not a fiend in human form—

MRS GEORGE. Is this out of a book? Or is it your usual society small talk?

HOTCHKISS [*recklessly*] Jibes are useless: the force that is sweeping me away will not spare you. I must know the worst at once. What was your father?

MRS GEORGE. A licensed victualler who married his barmaid. You would call him a publican, most likely.

HOTCHKISS. Then you are a woman totally beneath me. Do you deny it? Do you set up any sort of pretence to be my equal in rank, in age, or in culture?

MRS GEORGE. Have you eaten anything that has disagreed with you?

HOTCHKISS [*witheringly*] Inferior!

MRS GEORGE. Thank you. Anything else?

HOTCHKISS. This. I love you. My intentions are not honorable. [*She shows no dismay*]. Scream. Ring the bell. Have me turned out of the house.

MRS GEORGE [*with sudden depth of feeling*] Oh, if you could restore to this wasted exhausted heart one ray of the passion that once welled up at the glance at the touch of a lover! It's you who would scream then, young man. Do you see this face, once fresh and rosy like your own, now scarred and riven by a hundred burnt-out fires?

HOTCHKISS [*wildly*] Slate fires. Thirteen shillings a ton. Fires that shoot out destructive meteors, blinding and burning, sending men into the streets to make fools of themselves.

MRS GEORGE. You seem to have got it pretty bad, Sinjon.

HOTCHKISS. Dont dare call me Sinjon.

MRS GEORGE. My name is Zenobia Alexandrina. You may call me Polly for short.

HOTCHKISS. Your name is Ashtoreth—Durga—there is no name yet invented malign enough for you.

MRS GEORGE [*sitting down comfortably*] Come! Do you really think youre better suited to that young sauce box than her husband? You enjoyed her company when you were only the friend of the family— when there was the husband there to shew off against and to take all the responsibility. Are you sure youll enjoy it as much when you are the husband? She isnt clever, you know. She's only silly-clever.

HOTCHKISS [*uneasily leaning against the table and holding on to it to control his nervous movements*] Need you tell me? fiend that you are!

MRS GEORGE. You amused the husband, didnt you?

HOTCHKISS. He has more real sense of humor than she. He's better bred. That was not my fault.

MRS GEORGE. My husband has a sense of humor too.

HOTCHKISS. The coal merchant?—I mean the slate merchant.

MRS GEORGE [*appreciatively*] He would just love to hear you talk. He's been dull lately for want of a change of company and a bit of fresh fun.

HOTCHKISS [*flinging a chair opposite her and sitting down with an overdone attempt at studied insolence*] And pray what is your wretched husband's vulgar conviviality to me?

MRS GEORGE. You love me?

HOTCHKISS. I loathe you.

MRS GEORGE. It's the same thing.

HOTCHKISS. Then I'm lost.

MRS GEORGE. You may come and see me if you promise to amuse

George.

HOTCHKISS. I'll insult him, sneer at him, wipe my boots on him.

MRS GEORGE. No you wont, dear boy. Youll be a perfect gentleman.

HOTCHKISS [*beaten; appealing to her mercy*] Zenobia—

MRS GEORGE. Polly, please.

HOTCHKISS. Mrs Collins—

MRS GEORGE. Sir?

HOTCHKISS. Something stronger than my reason and common sense is holding my hands and tearing me along. I make no attempt to deny that it can drag me where you please and make me do what you like. But at least let me know your soul as you seem to know mine. Do you love this absurd coal merchant?

MRS GEORGE. Call him George.

HOTCHKISS. Do you love your Jorjy Porjy?

MRS GEORGE. Oh, I dont know that I love him. He's my husband, you know. But if I got anxious about George's health, and I thought it would nourish him, I would fry you with onions for his breakfast and think nothing of it. George and I are good friends. George belongs to me. Other men may come and go; but George goes on for ever.

HOTCHKISS. Yes: a husband soon becomes nothing but a habit. Listen: I suppose this detestable fascination you have for me is love.

MRS GEORGE. Any sort of feeling for a woman is called love nowadays.

HOTCHKISS. Do you love me?

MRS GEORGE [*promptly*] My love is not quite so cheap an article as that, my lad. I wouldnt cross the street to have another look at you—not yet. I'm not starving for love like the robins in winter, as the good ladies youre accustomed to are. Youll have to be very clever, and very good, and very real, if you are to interest me. If George takes a fancy to you, and you amuse him enough, I'll just tolerate you coming in and out occasionally for—well, say a month. If you can make a friend of me in that time so much the better for you. If you can touch my poor dying heart even for an instant, I'll bless you, and never forget you. You may try—if George takes to you.

HOTCHKISS. I'm to come on liking for the month?

MRS GEORGE. On condition that you drop Mrs Reginald.

HOTCHKISS. But she wont drop me. Do you suppose I ever wanted to marry her? I was a homeless bachelor; and I felt quite happy at their house as their friend. Leo was an amusing little devil; but I liked Reginald much more than I liked her. She didnt understand. One day she came to me and told me that the inevitable bad happened. I had tact enough not to ask her what the inevitable was; and I gathered presently that she had told Reginald that their marriage was a mistake and that she loved me and could no longer see me breaking my heart for her in suffering silence. What could I say? What could I do? What can I say now? What can I do now?

MRS GEORGE. Tell her that the habit of falling in love with other men's wives is growing on you; and that I'm your latest.

HOTCHKISS. What! Throw her over when she has thrown Reginald over for me!

MRS GEORGE [*rising*] You wont then? Very well. Sorry we shant meet again: I should have liked to see more of you for George's sake. Good-bye [*she moves away from him towards the hearth*].

HOTCHKISS [*appealing*] Zenobia—

MRS. GEORGE. I thought I lead made a difficult conquest. Now I see you are only one of those poor petticoat-hunting creatures that any woman can pick up. Not for me, thank you. [*Inexorable, she turns towards the tower to go*].

HOTCHKISS [*following*] Dont be an ass, Polly.

MRS GEORGE [*stopping*] Thats better.

HOTCHKISS. Cant you see that I maynt throw Leo over just because

I should be only too glad to. It would be dishonorable.

MRS GEORGE. Will you be happy if you marry her?

HOTCHKISS. No, great heaven, NO!

MRS GEORGE. Will she be happy when she finds you out?

HOTCHKISS. She's incapable of happiness. But she's not incapable of the pleasure of holding a man against his will.

MRS GEORGE. Right, young man. You will tell her, please, that you love me: before everybody, mind, the very next time you see her.

HOTCHKISS. But—

MRS GEORGE. Those are my orders, Sinjon. I cant have you marry another woman until George is tired of you.

HOTCHKISS. Oh, if I only didnt selfishly want to obey you!

The General comes in from the garden. Mrs George goes half way to the garden door to speak to him. Hotchkiss posts himself on the hearth.

MRS GEORGE. Where have you been all this time?

THE GENERAL. I'm afraid my nerves were a little upset by our conversation. I just went into the garden and had a smoke. I'm all right now [*he strolls down to the study door and presently takes a chair at that end of the big table*].

MRS GEORGE. A smoke! Why, you said she couldnt bear it.

THE GENERAL. Good heavens! I forgot! It's such a natural thing to do, somehow.

Lesbia comes in through the tower.

MRS GEORGE. He's been smoking again.

LESBIA. So my nose tells me. [*She goes to the end of the table nearest the hearth, and sits down*].

THE GENERAL. Lesbia: I'm very sorry. But if I gave it up, I should become so melancholy and irritable that you would be the first to implore me to take to it again.

MRS GEORGE. Thats true. Women drive their husbands into all sorts of wickedness to keep them in good humor. Sinjon: be off with you: this doesnt concern you.

LESBIA. Please dont disturb yourself, Sinjon. Boxer's broken heart has been worn on his sleeve too long for any pretence of privacy.

THE GENERAL. You are cruel, Lesbia: devilishly cruel. [*He sits down, wounded*].

LESBIA. You are vulgar, Boxer.

HOTCHKISS. In what way? I ask, as an expert in vulgarity.

LESBIA. In two ways. First, he talks as if the only thing of any importance in life was which particular woman he shall marry. Second, he has no self-control.

THE GENERAL. Women are not all the same to me, Lesbia.

MRS GEORGE. Why should they be, pray? Women are all different: it's the men who are all the same. Besides, what does Miss Grantham know about either men or women? She's got too much self-control.

LESBIA [*widening her eyes and lifting her chin haughtily*] And pray how does that prevent me from knowing as much about men and women as people who have no self-control?

MRS GEORGE. Because it frightens people into behaving themselves before you; and then how can you tell what they really are? Look at me! I was a spoilt child. My brothers and sisters were well brought up, like all children of respectable publicans. So should I have been if I hadnt been the youngest: ten years younger than my youngest brother. My parents were tired of doing their duty by their children by that time; and they spoilt me for all they were worth. I never knew what it was to want money or anything that money could buy. When I wanted my own way, I had nothing to do but scream for it till I got it. When I was annoyed I didnt control myself: I scratched and called names. Did you ever, after you were grown up, pull a grown-up woman's hair? Did you ever bite a grown-up man? Did you ever call both of them every name you could lay your tongue to?

LESBIA [*shivering with disgust*] No.

MRS GEORGE. Well, I did. I know what a woman is like when her hair's pulled. I know what a man is like when he's bit. I know what theyre both like when you tell them what you really feel about them. And thats how I know more of the world than you.

LESBIA. The Chinese know what a man is like when he is cut into a thousand pieces, or boiled in oil. That sort of knowledge is of no use to me. I'm afraid we shall never get on with one another, Mrs George. I live like a fencer, always on guard. I like to be confronted with people who are always on guard. I hate sloppy people, slovenly people, people who cant sit up straight, sentimental people.

MRS GEORGE. Oh, sentimental your grandmother! You dont learn to hold your own in the world by standing on guard, but by attacking, and getting well hammered yourself.

LESBIA. I'm not a prize-fighter, Mrs. Collins. If I cant get a thing without the indignity of fighting for it, I do without it.

MRS GEORGE. Do you? Does it strike you that if we were all as clever as you at doing without, there wouldnt be much to live for, would there?

TAE GENERAL. I'm afraid, Lesbia, the things you do without are the things you dont want.

LESBIA [*surprised at his wit*] Thats not bad for the silly soldier man. Yes, Boxer: the truth is, I dont want you enough to make the very unreasonable sacrifices required by marriage. And yet that is exactly why I ought to be married. Just because I have the qualities my country wants most I shall go barren to my grave; whilst the women who have neither the strength to resist marriage nor the intelligence to understand its infinite dishonor will make the England of the future. [*She rises and walks towards the study*].

THE GENERAL [*as she is about to pass him*] Well, I shall not ask you again, Lesbia.

LESBIA. Thank you, Boxer. [*She passes on to the study door*].

MRS GEORGE. Youre quite done with him, are you?

LESBIA. As far as marriage is concerned, yes. The field is clear for you, Mrs George. [*She goes into the study*].

The General buries his face in his hands. Mrs George comes round the table to him.

MRS GEORGE [*sympathetically*] She's a nice woman, that. And a sort of beauty about her too, different from anyone else.

THE GENERAL [*overwhelmed*] Oh Mrs Collins, thank you, thank you a thousand times. [*He rises effusively*]. You have thawed the long- frozen springs [*he kisses her hand*]. Forgive me; and thank you: bless you—[*he again takes refuge in the garden, choked with emotion*].

MRS GEORGE [*looking after him triumphantly*] Just caught the dear old warrior on the bounce, eh?

HOTCHKISS. Unfaithful to me already!

MRS GEORGE. I'm not your property, young man dont you think it. [*She goes over to him and faces him*]. You understand that? [*He suddenly snatches her into his arms and kisses her*]. Oh! You. dare do that again, you young blackguard; and I'll jab one of these chairs in your face [*she seizes one and holds it in readiness*]. Now you shall not see me for another month.

HOTCHKISS [*deliberately*] I shall pay my first visit to your husband this afternoon.

MRS GEORGE. Youll see what he'll say to you when I tell him what youve just done.

HOTCHKISS. What can he say? What dare he say?

MRS GEORGE. Suppose he kicks you out of the house?

HOTCHKISS. How can he? Ive fought seven duels with sabres. Ive muscles of iron. Nothing hurts me: not even broken bones. Fighting is absolutely uninteresting to me because it doesnt frighten me or amuse me; and I always win. Your husband is in all these respects an average man, probably. He will be horribly afraid of me; and if under the stimulus of your presence, and for your sake, and because it is the right thing to do among vulgar people, he were to attack me, I should simply defeat him and humiliate him [*he gradually gets his hands on the chair and takes it from her, as his words go home phrase by phrase*]. Sooner than expose him to that, you would suffer a thousand stolen kisses, wouldnt you?

MRS GEORGE [*in utter consternation*] You young viper!

HOTCHKISS. Ha ha! You are in my power. That is one of the oversights of your code of honor for husbands: the man who can bully them can insult their wives with impunity. Tell him if you dare. If I choose to take ten kisses, how will you prevent me?

MRS GEORGE. You come within reach of me and I'll not leave a hair on your head.

HOTCHKISS [*catching her wrists dexterously*] Ive got your hands.

MRS GEORGE. Youve not got my teeth. Let go; or I'll bite. I will,

I tell you. Let go.

HOTCHKISS. Bite away: I shall taste quite as nice as George.

MRS GEORGE. You beast. Let me go. Do you call yourself a gentleman, to use your brute strength against a woman?

HOTCHKISS. You are stronger than me in every way but this. Do you think I will give up my one advantage? Promise youll receive me when I call this afternoon.

MRS GEORGE. After what youve just done? Not if it was to save my life.

HOTCHKISS. I'll amuse George.

MRS GEORGE. He wont be in.

HOTCHKISS [*taken aback*] Do you mean that we should be alone?

MRS GEORGE [*snatching away her hands triumphantly as his grasp relaxes*] Aha! Thats cooled you, has it?

HOTCHKISS [*anxiously*] When will George be at home?

MRS GEORGE. It wont matter to you whether he's at home or not.

The door will be slammed in your face whenever you call.

HOTCHKISS. No servant in London is strong enough to close a door that I mean to keep open. You cant escape me. If you persist, I'll go into the coal trade; make George's acquaintance on the coal exchange; and coax him to take me home with him to make your acquaintance.

MRS GEORGE. We have no use for you, young man: neither George nor I [*she sails away from him and sits down at the end of the table near the study door*].

HOTCHKISS [*following her and taking the next chair round the corner of the table*] Yes you have. George cant fight for you: I can.

MRS GEORGE [*turning to face him*] You bully. You low bully.

HOTCHKISS. You have courage and fascination: I have courage and a pair of fists. We're both bullies, Polly.

MRS GEORGE. You have a mischievous tongue. Thats enough to keep you out of my house.

HOTCHKISS. It must be rather a house of cards. A word from me to George—just the right word, said in the right way—and down comes your house.

MRS GEORGE. Thats why I'll die sooner than let you into it.

HOTCHKISS. Then as surely as you live, I enter the coal trade to- morrow. George's taste for amusing company will deliver him into my hands. Before a month passes your home will be at my mercy.

MRS GEORGE [*rising, at bay*] Do you think I'll let myself be driven into a trap like this?

HOTCHKISS. You are in it already. Marriage is a trap. You are married. Any man who has the power to spoil your marriage has the power to spoil your life. I have that power over you.

MRS GEORGE [*desperate*] You mean it?

HOTCHKISS. I do.

MRS GEORGE [*resolutely*] Well, spoil my marriage and be—

HOTCHKISS [*springing up*] Polly!

MRS GEORGE. Sooner than be your slave I'd face any unhappiness.

HOTCHKISS. What! Even for George?

MRS GEORGE. There must be honor between me and George, happiness or no happiness. Do your worst.

HOTCHKISS [*admiring her*] Are you really game, Polly? Dare you defy me?

MRS GEORGE. If you ask me another question I shant be able to keep my hands off you [*she dashes distractedly past him to the other end of the table, her fingers crisping*].

HOTCHKISS. That settles it. Polly: I adore you: we were born for one another. As I happen to be a gentleman, I'll never do anything to annoy or injure you except that I reserve the right to give you a black eye if you bite me; but youll never get rid of me now to the end of your life.

MRS GEORGE. I shall get rid of you if the beadle has to brain you with the mace for it [*she makes for the tower*].

HOTCHKISS [*running between the table and the oak chest and across to the tower to cut her off*] You shant.

MRS GEORGE [*panting*] Shant I though?

HOTCHKISS. No you shant. I have one card left to play that youve forgotten. Why were you so unlike yourself when you spoke to the Bishop?

MRS GEORGE [*agitated beyond measure*] Stop. Not that. You shall respect that if you respect nothing else. I forbid you. [*He kneels at her feet*]. What are you doing? Get up: dont be a fool.

HOTCHKISS. Polly: I ask you on my knees to let me make George's acquaintance in his home this afternoon; and I shall remain on my knees till the Bishop comes in and sees us. What will he think of you then?

MRS GEORGE [*beside herself*] Wheres the poker? She rushes to the fireplace; seizes the poker; and makes for Hotchkiss, who flies to the study door. The Bishop enters just then and finds himself between them, narrowly escaping a blow from the poker.

THE BISHOP. Dont hit him, Mrs Collins. He is my guest.

Mrs George throws down the poker; collapses into the nearest chair; and bursts into tears. The Bishop goes to her and pats her consolingly on the shoulder. She shudders all through at his touch.

THE BISHOP. Come! you are in the house of your friends. Can we help you?

MRS GEORGE [*to Hotchkiss, pointing to the study*] Go in there, you. Youre not wanted here.

HOTCHKISS. You understand, Bishop, that Mrs Collins is not to blame for this scene. I'm afraid Ive been rather irritating.

THE BISHOP. I can quite believe it, Sinjon.

Hotchkiss goes into the study.

THE BISHOP [*turning to Mrs George with great kindness of manner*] I'm sorry you have been worried [*he sits down on her left*]. Never mind him. A little pluck, a little gaiety of heart, a little prayer; and youll be laughing at him.

MRS GEORGE. Never fear. I have all that. It was as much my fault as his; and I should have put him in his place with a clip of that poker on the side of his head if you hadnt come in.

THE BISHOP. You might have put him in his coffin that way, Mrs Collins. And I should have been very sorry; because we are all fond of Sinjon.

MRS GEORGE. Yes: it's your duty to rebuke me. But do you think I dont know?

THE BISHOP. I dont rebuke you. Who am I that I should rebuke you? Besides, I know there are discussions in which the poker is the only possible argument.

MRS GEORGE. My lord: be earnest with me. I'm a very funny woman, I daresay; but I come from the same workshop as you. I heard you say that yourself years ago.

THE BISHOP. Quite so; but then I'm a very funny Bishop. Since we are both funny people, let us not forget that humor is a divine attribute.

MRS GEORGE. I know nothing about divine attributes or whatever you call them; but I can feel when I am being belittled. It was from you that I learnt first to respect myself. It was through you that I came to be able to walk safely through many wild and wilful paths. Dont go back on your own teaching.

THE BISHOP. I'm not a teacher: only a fellow-traveller of whom you asked the way. I pointed ahead—ahead of myself as well as of you.

MRS GEORGE [*rising and standing over him almost threateningly*] As

I'm a living woman this day, if I find you out to be a fraud,

I'll kill myself.

THE BISHOP. What! Kill yourself for finding out something! For becoming a wiser and therefore a better woman! What a bad reason!

MRS GEORGE. I have sometimes thought of killing you, and then killing myself.

THE BISHOP. Why on earth should you kill yourself—not to mention me?

MRS GEORGE. So that we might keep our assignation in Heaven.

THE BISHOP [*rising and facing her, breathless*] Mrs. Collins! YOU are Incognita Appassionata!

MRS GEORGE. You read my letters, then? [*With a sigh of grateful relief, she sits down quietly, and says*] Thank you.

THE BISHOP [*remorsefully*] And I have broken the spell by making you come here [*sitting down again*]. Can you ever forgive me?

MRS GEORGE. You couldnt know that it was only the coal merchant's wife, could you?

THE BISHOP. Why do you say only the coal merchant's wife?

MRS GEORGE. Many people would laugh at it.

THE BISHOP. Poor people! It's so hard to know the right place to laugh, isnt it?

MRS GEORGE. I didnt mean to make you think the letters were from a fine lady. I wrote on cheap paper; and I never could spell.

THE BISHOP. Neither could I. So that told me nothing.

MRS GEORGE. One thing I should like you to know.

THE BISHOP. Yes?

MRS GEORGE. We didnt cheat your friend. They were as good as we could do at thirteen shillings a ton.

THE BISHOP. Thats important. Thank you for telling me.

MRS GEORGE. I have something else to say; but will you please ask somebody to come and stay here while we talk? [*He rises and turns to the study door*]. Not a woman, if you dont mind. [*He nods understandingly and passes on*]. Not a man either.

THE BISHOP [*stopping*] Not a man and not a woman! We have no children left, Mrs Collins. They are all grown up and married.

MRS GEORGE. That other clergyman would do.

THE BISHOP. What! The sexton?

MRS GEORGE. Yes. He didnt mind my calling him that, did he? It was only my ignorance.

THE BISHOP. Not at all. [*He opens the study door and calls*]

Soames! Anthony! [*To Mrs George*] Call him Father: he likes it.

[*Soames appears at the study door*]. Mrs Collins wishes you to join us, Anthony.

Soames looks puzzled.

MRS GEORGE. You dont mind, Dad, do you? [*As this greeting visibly gives him a shock that hardly bears out the Bishop's advice, she says anxiously*] That was what you told me to call him, wasnt it?

SOAMES. I am called Father Anthony, Mrs Collins. But it does not matter what you call me. [*He comes in, and walks past her to the hearth*].

THE BISHOP. Mrs Collins has something to say to me that she wants you to hear.

SOAMES. I am listening.

THE BISHOP [*going back to his seat next her*] Now.

MRS GEORGE. My lord: you should never have married.

SOAMES. This woman is inspired. Listen to her, my lord.

THE BISHOP [*taken aback by the directness of the attack*] I married because I was so much in love with Alice that all the difficulties and doubts and dangers of marriage seemed to me the merest moonshine.

MRS GEORGE. Yes: it's mean to let poor things in for so much while theyre in that state. Would you marry now that you know better if you were a widower?

THE BISHOP. I'm old now. It wouldnt matter.

MRS GEORGE. But would you if it did matter?

THE BISHOP. I think I should marry again lest anyone should imagine I had found marriage unhappy with Alice.

SOAMES [*sternly*] Are you fonder of your wife than of your salvation?

THE BISHOP. Oh, very much. When you meet a man who is very particular about his salvation, look out for a woman who is very particular about her character; and marry them to one another: theyll make a perfect pair. I advise you to fall in love; Anthony.

SOAMES [*with horror*] I!!

THE BISHOP. Yes, you! think of what it would do for you. For her sake you would come to care unselfishly and diligently for money instead of being selfishly and lazily indifferent to it. For her sake you would come to care in the same way for preferment. For her sake you would come to care for your health, your appearance, the good opinion of your fellow creatures, and all the really important things that make men work and strive instead of mooning and nursing their salvation.

SOAMES. In one word, for the sake of one deadly sin I should come to care for all the others.

THE BISHOP. Saint Anthony! Tempt him, Mrs Collins: tempt him.

MRS GEORGE [*rising and looking strangely before her*] Take care, my lord: you still have the power to make me obey your commands. And do you, Mr Sexton, beware of an empty heart.

THE BISHOP. Yes. Nature abhors a vacuum, Anthony. I would not dare go about with an empty heart: why, the first girl I met would fly into it by mere atmospheric pressure. Alice keeps them out now. Mrs Collins knows.

MRS GEORGE [*a faint convulsion passing like a wave over her*] I know more than either of you. One of you has not yet exhausted his first love: the other has not yet reached it. But I—I—[*she reels and is again convulsed*].

THE BISHOP [*saving her from falling*] Whats the matter? Are you ill, Mrs Collins? [*He gets her back into her chair*]. Soames: theres a glass of water in the study—quick. [*Soames hurries to the study door.*]

MRS. GEORGE. No. [*Soames stops*]. Dont call. Dont bring anyone.

Cant you hear anything?

THE BISHOP. Nothing unusual. [*He sits by her, watching her with intense surprise and interest*].

MRS GEORGE. No music?

SOAMES. No. [*He steals to the end of the table and sits on her right, equally interested*].

MRS GEORGE. Do you see nothing—not a great light?

THE BISHOP. We are still walking in darkness.

MRS GEORGE. Put your hand on my forehead: the hand with the ring.

[*He does so. Her eyes close*].

SOAMES [*inspired to prophesy*] There was a certain woman, the wife of a coal merchant, which had been a great sinner . . .

The Bishop, startled, takes his hand away. Mrs George's eyes open vividly as she interrupts Soames.

MRS GEORGE. You prophesy falsely, Anthony: never in all my life have I done anything that was not ordained for me. [*More quietly*] Ive been myself. Ive not been afraid of myself. And at last I have escaped from myself, and am become a voice for them that are afraid to speak, and a cry for the hearts that break in silence.

SOAMES [*whispering*] Is she inspired?

THE BISHOP. Marvellous. Hush.

MRS GEORGE. I have earned the right to speak. I have dared: I have gone through: I have not fallen withered in the fire: I have come at last out beyond, to the back of Godspeed?

THE BISHOP. And what do you see there, at the back of Godspeed?

SOAMES [*hungrily*] Give us your message.

MRS GEORGE [*with intensely sad reproach*] When you loved me I gave you the whole sun and stars to play with. I gave you eternity in a single moment, strength of the mountains in one clasp of your arms, and the volume of all the seas in one impulse of your souls. A moment only; but was it not enough? Were you not paid then for all the rest of your struggle on earth? Must I mend your clothes and sweep your floors as well? Was it not enough? I paid the price without bargaining: I bore the children without flinching: was that a reason for heaping fresh burdens on me? I carried the child in my arms: must I carry the father too? When I opened the gates of paradise, were you blind? was it nothing to you? When all the stars sang in your ears and all the winds swept you into the heart of heaven, were you deaf? were you dull? was I no more to you than a bone to a dog? Was it not enough? We spent eternity together; and you ask me for a little lifetime more. We possessed all the universe together; and you ask me to give you my scanty wages as well. I have given you the greatest of all things; and you ask me to give you little things. I gave you your own soul: you ask me for my body as a plaything. Was it not enough? Was it not enough?

SOAMES. Do you understand this, my lord?

THE BISHOP. I have that advantage over you, Anthony, thanks to Alice. [*He takes Mrs George's hand*]. Your hand is very cold. Can you come down to earth? Do you remember who I am, and who you are?

MRS GEORGE. It was enough for me. I did not ask to meet you—to touch you—[*the Bishop quickly releases her hand*]. When you spoke to my soul years ago from your pulpit, you opened the doors of my salvation to me; and now they stand open for ever. It was enough: I have asked you for nothing since: I ask you for nothing now. I have lived: it is enough. I have had my wages; and I am ready for my work. I thank you and bless you and leave you. You are happier in that than I am; for when I do for men what you did for me, I have no thanks, and no blessing: I am their prey; and there is no rest from their loving and no mercy from their loathing.

THE BISHOP. You must take us as we are, Mrs Collins.

SOAMES. No. Take us as we are capable of becoming.

MRS GEORGE. Take me as I am: I ask no more. [*She turns her head to the study door and cries*] Yes: come in, come in.

Hotchkiss comes softly in from the study.

HOTCHKISS. Will you be so kind as to tell me whether I am dreaming? In there I have heard Mrs Collins saying the strangest things, and not a syllable from you two.

SOAMES. My lord; is this possession by the devil?

THE BISHOP. Or the ecstasy of a saint?

HOTCHKISS. Or the convulsion of the pythoness on the tripod?

THE BISHOP. May not the three be one?

MRS GEORGE [*troubled*] You are paining and tiring me with idle questions. You are dragging me back to myself. You are tormenting me with your evil dreams of saints and devils and—what was it?—[*striving to fathom it*] the pythoness—the pythoness—[*giving it up*] I dont understand. I am a woman: a human creature like yourselves. Will you not take me as I am?

SOAMES. Yes; but shall we take you and burn you?

THE BISHOP. Or take you and canonize you?

HOTCHKISS [*gaily*] Or take you as a matter of course? [*Swiftly to the Bishop*] We must get her out of this: it's dangerous. [*Aloud to her*] May I suggest that you shall be Anthony's devil and the Bishop's saint and my adored Polly? [*Slipping behind her, he picks up her hand from her lap and kisses it over her shoulder*].

MRS GEORGE [*waking*] What was that? Who kissed my hand? [*To the Bishop, eagerly*] Was it you? [*He shakes his head. She is mortified*]. I beg your pardon.

THE BISHOP. Not at all. I'm not repudiating that honor. Allow me [*he kisses her hand*].

MRS GEORGE. Thank you for that. It was not the sexton, was it?

SOAMES. I!

HOTCHKISS. It was I, Polly, your ever faithful.

MRS GEORGE [*turning and seeing him*] Let me catch you doing it again: thats all. How do you come there? I sent you away. [*With great energy, becoming quite herself again*] What the goodness gracious has been happening?

HOTCHKISS. As far as I can make out, you have been having a very charming and eloquent sort of fit.

MRS GEORGE [*delighted*] What! My second sight! [*To the Bishop*] Oh, how I have prayed that it might come to me if ever I met you! And now it has come. How stunning! You may believe every word I said: I cant remember it now; but it was something that was just bursting to be said; and so it laid hold of me and said itself. Thats how it is, you see.

Edith and Cecil Sykes come in through the tower. She has her hat on. Leo follows. They have evidently been out together. Sykes, with an unnatural air, half foolish, half rakish, as if he had lost all his self-respect and were determined not to let it prey on his spirits, throws himself into a chair at the end of the table near the hearth and thrusts his hands into his pockets, like Hogarth's Rake, without waiting for Edith to sit down. She sits in the railed chair. Leo takes the chair nearest the tower on the long side of the table, brooding, with closed lips.

THE BISHOP. Have you been out, my dear?

EDITH. Yes.

THE BISHOP. With Cecil?

EDITH. Yes.

THE BISHOP. Have you come to an understanding?

No reply. Blank silence.

SYKES. You had better tell them, Edie.

EDITH. Tell them yourself.

The General comes in from the garden.

THE GENERAL [*coming forward to the table*] Can anybody oblige me with some tobacco? Ive finished mine; and my nerves are still far from settled.

THE BISHOP. Wait a moment, Boxer. Cecil has something important to tell us.

SYKES. Weve done it. Thats all.

HOTCHKISS. Done what, Cecil?

SYKES. Well, what do you suppose?

EDITH. Got married, of course.

THE GENERAL. Married! Who gave you away?

SYKES [*jerking his head towards the tower*] This gentleman did.[*Seeing that they do not understand, he looks round and sees that there is no one there*]. Oh! I thought he came in with us. Hes gone downstairs, I suppose. The Beadle.

THE GENERAL. The Beadle! What the devil did he do that for?

SYKES. Oh, I dont know: I didnt make any bargain with him. [*To Mrs George*] How much ought I to give him, Mrs Collins?

MRS GEORGE. Five shillings. [*To the Bishop*] I want to rest for a moment: there! in your study. I saw it here [*she touches her forehead*].

THE BISHOP [*opening the study door for her*] By all means. Turn my brother out if he disturbs you. Soames: bring the letters out here.

SYKES. He wont be offended at my offering it, will he?

MRS GEORGE. Not he! He touches children with the mace to cure them of ringworm for fourpence apiece. [*She goes into the study. Soames follows her*].

THE GENERAL. Well, Edith, I'm a little disappointed, I must say. However, I'm glad it was done by somebody in a public uniform.

Mrs Bridgenorth and Lesbia come in through the tower. Mrs Bridgenorth makes for the Bishop. He goes to her, and they meet near the oak chest. Lesbia comes between Sykes and Edith.

THE BISHOP. Alice, my love, theyre married.

MRS BRIDGENORTH [*placidly*] Oh, well, thats all right. Better tell

Collins.

Soames comes back from the study with his writing materials. He seats himself at the nearest end of the table and goes on with his work. Hotchkiss sits down in the next chair round the table corner, with his back to him.

LESBIA. You have both given in, have you?

EDITH. Not at all. We have provided for everything.

SOAMES. How?

EDITH. Before going to the church, we went to the office of that insurance company—whats its name, Cecil?

SYKES. The British Family Insurance Corporation. It insures you against poor relations and all sorts of family contingencies.

EDITH. It has consented to insure Cecil against libel actions brought against him on my account. It will give us specially low terms because I am a Bishop's daughter.

SYKES. And I have given Edie my solemn word that if I ever commit a crime I'll knock her down before a witness and go off to Brighton with another lady.

LESBIA. Thats what you call providing for everything! [*She goes to the middle of the table on the garden side and sits down*].

LEO. Do make him see there are no worms before he knocks you down, Edith. Wheres Rejjy?

REGINALD [*coming in from the study*] Here. Whats the matter?

LEO [*springing up and flouncing round to him*] Whats the matter! You may well ask. While Edie and Cecil were at the insurance office I took a taxy and went off to your lodgings; and a nice mess I found everything in. Your clothes are in a disgraceful state. Your liver pad has been made into a kettle-holder. Youre no more fit to be left to yourself than a one-year old baby.

REGINALD. Oh, I cant be bothered looking after things like that.

I'm all right.

LEO. Youre not: youre a disgrace. You never consider that youre a disgrace to me: you think only of yourself. You must come home with me and be taken proper care of: my conscience will not allow me to let you live like a pig. [*She arranges his necktie*]. You must stay with me until I marry St John; and then we can adopt you or something.

REGINALD [*breaking loose from her and stumping off past Hotchkiss towards the hearth*] No, I'm dashed if I'll be adopted by St John. You can adopt him if you like.

HOTCHKISS [*rising*] I suggest that that would really be the better plan, Leo. Ive a confession to make to you. I'm not the man you took me for. Your objection to Rejjy was that he had low tastes.

REGINALD [*turning*] Was it? by George!

LEO. I said slovenly habits. I never thought he had really low tastes until I saw that woman in court. How he could have chosen such a creature and let her write to him after—

REGINALD. Is this fair? I never—

HOTCHKISS. Of course you didnt, Rejjy. Dont be silly, Leo. It's I who really have low tastes.

LEO. You!

HOTCHKISS. Ive fallen in love with a coal merchant's wife. I adore her. I would rather have one of her boot-laces than a lock of your hair. [*He folds his arms and stands like a rock*].

REGINALD. You damned scoundrel, how dare you throw my wife over like that before my face? [*He seems on the point of assaulting Hotchkiss when Leo gets between them and draws Reginald away towards the study door*].

LEO. Dont take any notice of him, Rejjy. Go at once and get that odious decree demolished or annulled or whatever it is. Tell Sir Gorell Barnes that I have changed my mind. [*To Hotchkiss*] I might have known that you were too clever to be really a gentleman. [*She takes Reginald away to the oak chest and seats him there. He chuckles. Hotchkiss resumes his seat, brooding*].

THE BISHOP. All the problems appear to be solving themselves.

LESBIA. Except mine.

THE GENERAL. But, my dear Lesbia, you see what has happened here to-day. [*Coming a little nearer and bending his face towards hers*] Now I put it to you, does it not show you the folly of not marrying?

LESBIA. No: I cant say it does. And [*rising*] you have been smoking again.

THE GENERAL. You drive me to it, Lesbia. I cant help it.

LESBIA [*standing behind her chair with her hands on the back of it and looking radiant*] Well, I wont scold you to-day. I feel in particularly good humor just now.

TIE GENERAL. May I ask why, Lesbia?

LESBIA. [*drawing a large breath*] To think that after all the dangers of the morning I am still unmarried! still independent! still my own mistress! still a glorious strong-minded old maid of old England!

Soames silently springs up and makes a long stretch from his end of the table to shake her hand across it.

THE GENERAL. Do you find any real happiness in being your own mistress? Would it not be more generous—would you not be happier as some one else's mistress—

LESBIA. Boxer!

THE GENERAL [*rising, horrified*] No, no, you must know, my dear Lesbia, that I was not using the word in its improper sense. I am sometimes unfortunate in my choice of expressions; but you know what I mean. I feel sure you would be happier as my wife.

LESBIA. I daresay I should, in a frowsy sort of way. But I prefer my dignity and my independence. I'm afraid I think this rage for happiness rather vulgar.

THE GENERAL. Oh, very well, Lesbia. I shall not ask you again.

[*He sits down huffily*].

LESBIA. You will, Boxer; but it will be no use. [*She also sits down again and puts her hand almost affectionately on his*]. Some day I hope to make a friend of you; and then we shall get on very nicely.

THE GENERAL [*starting up again*] Ha! I think you are hard, Lesbia. I shall make a fool of myself if I remain here. Alice: I shall go into the garden for a while.

COLLINS [*appearing in the tower*] I think everything is in order now, maam.

THE GENERAL [*going to him*] Oh, by the way, could you oblige me [*the rest of the sentence is lost in a whisper*].

COLLINS. Certainly, General. [*He takes out a tobacco pouch and hands it to the General, who takes it and goes into the garden*].

LESBIA. I dont believe theres a man in England who really and truly loves his wife as much as he loves his pipe.

THE BISHOP. By the way, what has happened to the wedding party?

SYKES. I dont know. There wasnt a soul in the church when we were married except the pew opener and the curate who did the job.

EDITH. They had all gone home.

MRS BRIDGENORTH. But the bridesmaids?

COLLINS. Me and the beadle have been all over the place in a couple of taxies, maam; and weve collected them all. They were a good deal disappointed on account of their dresses, and thought it rather irregular; but theyve agreed to come to the breakfast. The truth is, theyre wild with curiosity to know how it all happened. The organist held on until the organ was nigh worn out, and himself worse than the organ. He asked me particularly to tell you, my lord, that he held back Mendelssohn till the very last; but when that was gone he thought he might as well go too. So he played God Save The King and cleared out the church. He's coming to the breakfast to explain.

LEO. Please remember, Collins, that there is no truth whatever in the rumor that I am separated from my husband, or that there is, or ever has been, anything between me and Mr Hotchkiss.

COLLINS. Bless you, maam! one could always see that. [*To Mrs Bridgenorth*] Will you receive here or in the hall, maam?

MRS BRIDGENORTH. In the hall. Alfred: you and Boxer must go there and be ready to keep the first arrivals talking till we come. We have to dress Edith. Come, Lesbia: come, Leo: we must all help. Now, Edith. [*Lesbia, Leo, and Edith go out through the tower*]. Collins: we shall want you when Miss Edith's dressed to look over her veil and things and see that theyre all right.

COLLINS. Yes, maam. Anything you would like mentioned about Miss

Lesbia, maam?

MRS BRIDGENORTH. No. She wont have the General. I think you may take that as final.

COLLINS. What a pity, maam! A fine lady wasted, maam. [*They shake their heads sadly; and Mrs Bridgenorth goes out through the tower*].

THE BISHOP. I'm going to the hall, Collins, to receive. Rejjy: go and tell Boxer; and come both of you to help with the small talk. Come, Cecil. [*He goes out through the tower, followed by Sykes*].

REGINALD [*to Hotchkiss*] Youve always talked a precious lot about behaving like a gentleman. Well, if you think youve behaved like a gentleman to Leo, youre mistaken. And I shall have to take her part, remember that.

HOTCHKISS. I understand. Your doors are closed to me.

REGINALD [*quickly*] Oh no. Dont be hasty. I think I should like you to drop in after a while, you know. She gets so cross and upset when theres nobody to liven up the house a bit.

HOTCHKISS. I'll do my best.

REGINALD [*relieved*] Righto. You wont mind, old chap, do you?

HOTCHKISS. It's Fate. Ive touched coal; and my hands are black; but theyre clean. So long, Rejjy. [*They shake hands; and Reginald goes into the garden to collect Boxer*].

COLLINS. Excuse me, sir; but do you stay to breakfast? Your name is on one of the covers; and I should like to change it if youre not remaining.

HOTCHKISS. How do I know? Is my destiny any longer in my own hands? Go: ask SHE WHO MUST BE OBEYED.

COLLINS [*awestruck*] Has Mrs George taken a fancy to you, sir?

HOTCHKISS. Would she had! Worse, man, worse: Ive taken a fancy to

Mrs George.

COLLINS. Dont despair, sir: if George likes your conversation youll find their house a very pleasant one—livelier than Mr Reginald's was, I daresay.

HOTCHKISS [*calling*] Polly.

COLLINS [*promptly*] Oh, if it's come to Polly already, sir, I should say you were all right.

Mrs George appears at the door of the study.

HOTCHKISS. Your brother-in-law wishes to know whether I'm to stay for the wedding breakfast. Tell him.

MRS GEORGE. He stays, Bill, if he chooses to behave himself.

HOTCHKISS [*to Collins*] May I, as a friend of the family, have the privilege of calling you Bill?

COLLINS. With pleasure, sir, I'm sure, sir.

HOTCHKISS. My own pet name in the bosom of my family is Sonny.

MRS GEORGE. Why didnt you tell me that before? Sonny is just the name I wanted for you. [*She pats his cheek familiarly; he rises abruptly and goes to the hearth, where he throws himself moodily into the railed chair*] Bill: I'm not going into the hall until there are enough people there to make a proper little court for me. Send the Beadle for me when you think it looks good enough.

COLLINS. Right, maam. [*He goes out through the tower*].

Mrs George left alone with Hotchkiss and Soames, suddenly puts her hands on Soames's shoulders and bends over him.

MRS GEORGE. The Bishop said I was to tempt you, Anthony.

SOAMES [*without looking round*] Woman: go away.

MRS GEORGE. Anthony:

"When other lips and other hearts
Their tale of love shall tell

HOTCHKISS [*sardonically*]

In language whose excess imparts
The power they feel so well.

MRS GEORGE.

Though hollow hearts may wear a mask,
Twould break your own to see
In such a moment I but ask
That youll remember me."

And you will, Anthony. I shall put my spell on you.

SOAMES. Do you think that a man who has sung the Magnificat and adored the Queen of Heaven has any ears for such trash as that or any eyes for such trash as you—saving your poor little soul's presence. Go home to your duties, woman.

MRS GEORGE [*highly approving his fortitude*] Anthony: I adopt you as my father. Thats the talk! Give me a man whose whole life doesnt hang on some scrubby woman in the next street; and I'll never let him go [*she slaps him heartily on the back*].

SOAMES. Thats enough. You have another man to talk to. I'm busy.

MRS GEORGE [*leaving Soames and going a step or two nearer Hotchkiss*] Why arnt you like him, Sonny? Why do you hang on to a scrubby woman in the next street?

HOTCHKISS [*thoughtfully*] I must apologize to Billiter.

MRS GEORGE. Who is Billiter?

HOTCHKISS. A man who eats rice pudding with a spoon. Ive been eating rice pudding with a spoon ever since I saw you first.[*He rises*]. We all eat our rice pudding with a spoon, dont we, Soames?

SOAMES. We are members of one another. There is no need to refer to me. In the first place, I'm busy: in the second, youll find it all in the Church Catechism, which contains most of the new discoveries with which the age is bursting. Of course you should apologize to Billiter. He is your equal. He will go to the same heaven if he behaves himself and to the same hell if he doesnt.

MRS GEORGE [*sitting down*] And so will my husband the coal merchant.

HOTCHKISS. If I were your husband's superior here I should be his superior in heaven or hell: equality lies deeper than that. The coal merchant and I are in love with the same woman. That settles the question for me for ever. [*He prowls across the kitchen to the garden door, deep in thought*].

SOAMES. Psha!

MRS GEORGE. You dont believe in women, do you, Anthony? He might as well say that he and George both like fried fish.

HOTCHKISS. I do not like fried fish. Dont be low, Polly.

SOAMES. Woman: do not presume to accuse me of unbelief. And do you, Hotchkiss, not despise this woman's soul because she speaks of fried fish. Some of the victims of the Miraculous Draught of Fishes were fried. And I eat fried fish every Friday and like it. You are as ingrained a snob as ever.

HOTCHKISS [*impatiently*] My dear Anthony: I find you merely ridiculous as a preacher, because you keep referring me to places and documents and alleged occurrences in which, as a matter of fact, I dont believe. I dont believe in anything but my own will and my own pride and honor. Your fishes and your catechisms and all the rest of it make a charming poem which you call your faith. It fits you to perfection; but it doesnt fit me. I happen, like Napoleon, to prefer Mohammedanism. [*Mrs George, associating Mohammedanism with polygamy, looks at him with quick suspicion*]. I believe the whole British Empire will adopt a reformed Mohammedanism before the end of the century. The character of Mahomet is congenial to me. I admire him, and share his views of life to a considerable extent. That beats you, you see, Soames. Religion is a great force—the only real motive force in the world; but what you fellows dont understand is that you must get at a man through his own religion and not through yours. Instead of facing that fact, you persist in trying to convert all men to your own little sect, so that you can use it against them afterwards. You are all missionaries and proselytizers trying to uproot the native religion from your neighbor's flowerbeds and plant your own in its place. You would rather let a child perish in ignorance than have it taught by a rival sectary. You can talk to me of the quintessential equality of coal merchants and British officers; and yet you cant see the quintessential equality of all the religions. Who are you, anyhow, that you should know better than Mahomet or Confucius or any of the other Johnnies who have been on this job since the world existed?

MRS GEORGE [*admiring his eloquence*] George will like you, Sonny.

You should hear him talking about the Church.

SOAMES. Very well, then: go to your doom, both of you. There is only one religion for me: that which my soul knows to be true; but even irreligion has one tenet; and that is the sacredness of marriage. You two are on the verge of deadly sin. Do you deny that?

HOTCHKISS. You forget, Anthony: the marriage itself is the deadly sin according to you.

SOAMES. The question is not now what I believe, but what you believe. Take the vows with me; and give up that woman if you have the strength and the light. But if you are still in the grip of this world, at least respect its institutions. Do you believe in marriage or do you not?

HOTCHKISS. My soul is utterly free from any such superstition. I solemnly declare that between this woman, as you impolitely call her, and me, I see no barrier that my conscience bids me respect. I loathe the whole marriage morality of the middle classes with all my instincts. If I were an eighteenth century marquis I could feel no more free with regard to a Parisian citizen's wife than I do with regard to Polly. I despise all this domestic purity business as the lowest depth of narrow, selfish, sensual, wife-grabbing vulgarity.

MRS GEORGE [*rising promptly*] Oh, indeed. Then youre not coming home with me, young man. I'm sorry; for its refreshing to have met once in my life a man who wasnt frightened by my wedding ring; but I'm looking out for a friend and not for a French marquis; so youre not coming home with me.

HOTCHKISS [*inexorably*] Yes, I am.

MRS GEORGE. No.

HOTCHKISS. Yes. Think again. You know your set pretty well, I suppose, your petty tradesmen's set. You know all its scandals and hypocrisies, its jealousies and squabbles, its hundred of divorce cases that never come into court, as well as its tens that do.

MRS GEORGE. We're not angels. I know a few scandals; but most of us are too dull to be anything but good.

HOTCHKISS. Then you must have noticed that just an all murderers, judging by their edifying remarks on the scaffold, seem to be devout Christians, so all Christians, both male and female, are invariably people over-flowing with domestic sentimentality and professions of respect for the conventions they violate in secret.

MRS GEORGE. Well, you dont expect them to give themselves away, do you?

HOTCHKISS. They are people of sentiment, not of honor. Now, I'm not a man of sentiment, but a man of honor. I know well what will happen to me when once I cross the threshold of your husband's house and break bread with him. This marriage bond which I despise will bind me as it never seems to bind the people who believe in it, and whose chief amusement it is to go to the theatres where it is laughed at. Soames: youre a Communist, arnt you?

SOAMES. I am a Christian. That obliges me to be a Communist.

HOTCHKISS. And you believe that many of our landed estates were stolen from the Church by Henry the eighth?

SOAMES. I do not merely believe that: I know it as a lawyer.

HOTCHKISS. Would you steal a turnip from one of the landlords of those stolen lands?

SOAMES [*fencing with the question*] They have no right to their lands.

HOTCHKISS. Thats not what I ask you. Would you steal a turnip from one of the fields they have no right to?

SOAMES. I do not like turnips.

HOTCHKISS. As you are a lawyer, answer me.

SOAMES. I admit that I should probably not do so. I should perhaps be wrong not to steal the turnip: I cant defend my reluctance to do so; but I think I should not do so. I know I should not do so.

HOTCHKISS. Neither shall I be able to steal George's wife. I have stretched out my hand for that forbidden fruit before; and I know that my hand will always come back empty. To disbelieve in marriage is easy: to love a married woman is easy; but to betray a comrade, to be disloyal to a host, to break the covenant of bread and salt, is impossible. You may take me home with you, Polly: you have nothing to fear.

MRS GEORGE. And nothing to hope?

HOTCHKISS. Since you put it in that more than kind way, Polly, absolutely nothing.

MRS GEORGE. Hm! Like most men, you think you know everything a woman wants, dont you? But the thing one wants most has nothing to do with marriage at all. Perhaps Anthony here has a glimmering of it. Eh, Anthony?

SOAMES. Christian fellowship?

MRS GEORGE. You call it that, do you?

SOAMES. What do you call it?

COLLINS [*appearing in the tower with the Beadle*]. Now, Polly, the hall's full; and theyre waiting for you.

THE BEADLE. Make way there, gentlemen, please. Way for the worshipful the Mayoress. If you please, my lords and gentlemen. By your leave, ladies and gentlemen: way for the Mayoress.

Mrs George takes Hotchkiss's arm, and goes out, preceded by the

Beadle.

Soames resumes his writing tranquilly.

THE SHEWING-UP OF BLANCO POSNET

THE SHEWING-UP OF BLANCO POSNET

A number of women are sitting working together in a big room not unlike an old English tithe barn in its timbered construction, but with windows high up next the roof. It is furnished as a courthouse, with the floor raised next the walls, and on this raised flooring a seat for the Sheriff, a rough jury box on his right, and a bar to put prisoners to on his left. In the well in the middle is a table with benches round it. A few other benches are in disorder round the room. The autumn sun is shining warmly through the windows and the open door. The women, whose dress and speech are those of pioneers of civilisation in a territory of the United States of America, are seated round the table and on the benches, shucking nuts. The conversation is at its height.

BABSY [*a bumptious young slattern, with some good looks*] I say that a man that would steal a horse would do anything.

LOTTIE [*a sentimental girl, neat and clean*] Well, I never should look at it in that way. I do think killing a man is worse any day than stealing a horse.

HANNAH [*elderly and wise*] I dont say it's right to kill a man. In a place like this, where every man has to have a revolver, and where theres so much to try people's tempers, the men get to be a deal too free with one another in the way of shooting. God knows it's hard enough to have to bring a boy into the world and nurse him up to be a man only to have him brought home to you on a shutter, perhaps for nothing, or only just to shew that the man that killed him wasn't afraid of him. But men are like children when they get a gun in their hands: theyre not content til theyve used it on somebody.

JESSIE [*a good-natured but sharp-tongued, hoity-toity young woman; Babsy's rival in good looks and her superior in tidiness*] They shoot for the love of it. Look at them at a lynching. Theyre not content to hang the man; but directly the poor creature is swung up they all shoot him full of holes, wasting their cartridges that cost solid money, and pretending they do it in horror of his wickedness, though half of them would have a rope round their own necks if all they did was known—let alone the mess it makes.

LOTTIE. I wish we could get more civilized. I don't like all this lynching and shooting. I don't believe any of us like it, if the truth were known.

BABSY. Our Sheriff is a real strong man. You want a strong man for a rough lot like our people here. He aint afraid to shoot and he aint afraid to hang. Lucky for us quiet ones, too.

JESSIE. Oh, don't talk to me. I know what men are. Of course he aint afraid to shoot and he aint afraid to hang. Wheres the risk in that with the law on his side and the whole crowd at his back longing for the lynching as if it was a spree? Would one of them own to it or let him own to it if they lynched the wrong man? Not them. What they call justice in this place is nothing but a breaking out of the devil thats in all of us. What I want to see is a Sheriff that aint afraid not to shoot and not to hang.

EMMA [*a sneak who sides with Babsy or Jessie, according to the fortune of war*] Well, I must say it does sicken me to see Sheriff Kemp putting down his foot, as he calls it. Why don't he put it down on his wife? She wants it worse than half the men he lynches. He and his Vigilance Committee, indeed!

BABSY [*incensed*] Oh, well! if people are going to take the part of horse-thieves against the Sheriff—!

JESSIE. Who's taking the part of horse-thieves against the
Sheriff?

BABSY. You are. Waitle your own horse is stolen, and youll know better. I had an uncle that died of thirst in the sage brush because a negro stole his horse. But they caught him and burned him; and serve him right, too.

EMMA. I have known that a child was born crooked because its mother had to do a horse's work that was stolen.

BABSY. There! You hear that? I say stealing a horse is ten times worse than killing a man. And if the Vigilance Committee ever gets hold of you, youd better have killed twenty men than as much as stole a saddle or bridle, much less a horse.

[*Elder Daniels comes in.*]

ELDER DANIELS. Sorry to disturb you, ladies; but the Vigilance Committee has taken a prisoner; and they want the room to try him in.

JESSIE. But they cant try him til Sheriff Kemp comes back from the wharf.

ELDER DANIELS. Yes; but we have to keep the prisoner here til he comes.

BABSY. What do you want to put him here for? Cant you tie him up in the Sheriff's stable?

ELDER DANIELS. He has a soul to be saved, almost like the rest of us. I am bound to try to put some religion into him before he goes into his Maker's presence after the trial.

HANNAH. What has he done, Mr Daniels?

ELDER DANIELS. Stole a horse.

BABSY. And are we to be turned out of the town hall for a horse- thief? Aint a stable good enough for his religion?

ELDER DANIELS. It may be good enough for his, Babsy; but, by your leave, it is not good enough for mine. While I am Elder here, I shall umbly endeavour to keep up the dignity of Him I serve to the best of my small ability. So I must ask you to be good enough to clear out. Allow me. [*He takes the sack of husks and put it out of the way against the panels of the jury box*].

THE WOMEN [*murmuring*] Thats always the way. Just as we'd settled down to work. What harm are we doing? Well, it is tiresome. Let them finish the job themselves. Oh dear, oh dear! We cant have a minute to ourselves. Shoving us out like that!

HANNAH. Whose horse was it, Mr Daniels?

ELDER DANIELS [*returning to move the other sack*] I am sorry to say that it was the Sheriff's horse—the one he loaned to young Strapper. Strapper loaned it to me; and the thief stole it, thinking it was mine. If it had been mine, I'd have forgiven him cheerfully. I'm sure I hoped he would get away; for he had two hours start of the Vigilance Committee. But they caught him. [*He disposes of the other sack also*].

JESSIE. It cant have been much of a horse if they caught him with two hours start.

ELDER DANIELS [*coming back to the centre of the group*] The strange thing is that he wasn't on the horse when they took him. He was walking; and of course he denies that he ever had the horse. The Sheriff's brother wanted to tie him up and lash him till he confessed what he'd done with it; but I couldn't allow that: it's not the law.

BABSY. Law! What right has a horse-thief to any law? Law is thrown away on a brute like that.

ELDER DANIELS. Dont say that, Babsy. No man should be made to confess by cruelty until religion has been tried and failed. Please God I'll get the whereabouts of the horse from him if youll be so good as to clear out from this. [*Disturbance outside*]. They are bringing him in. Now ladies! please, please.

[*They rise reluctantly. Hannah, Jessie, and Lottie retreat to the Sheriff's bench, shepherded by Daniels; but the other women crowd forward behind Babsy and Emma to see the prisoner.*

Blanco Posnet it brought in by Strapper Kemp, the Sheriff's brother, and a cross-eyed man called Squinty. Others follow. Blanco is evidently a blackguard. It would be necessary to clean him to make a close guess at his age; but he is under forty, and an upturned, red moustache, and the arrangement of his hair in a crest on his brow, proclaim the dandy in spite of his intense disreputableness. He carries his head high, and has a fairly resolute mouth, though the fire of incipient delirium tremens is in his eye.

His arms are bound with a rope with a long end, which Squinty holds. They release him when he enters; and he stretches himself and lounges across the courthouse in front of the women. Strapper and the men remain between him and the door.]

BABSY [*spitting at him as he passes her*] Horse-thief! horse- thief!

OTHERS. You will hang for it; do you hear? And serve you right.

Serve you right. That will teach you. I wouldn't wait to try you.

Lynch him straight off, the varmint. Yes, yes. Tell the boys.

Lynch him.

BLANCO [*mocking*] "Angels ever bright and fair—"

BABSY. You call me an angel, and I'll smack your dirty face for you.

BLANCO. "Take, oh take me to your care."

EMMA. There wont be any angels where youre going to.

OTHERS. Aha! Devils, more likely. And too good company for a horse-thief.

ALL. Horse-thief! Horse-thief! Horse-thief!

BLANCO. Do women make the law here, or men? Drive these heifers out.

THE WOMEN. Oh! [*They rush at him, vituperating, screaming passionately, tearing at him. Lottie puts her fingers in her ears and runs out. Hannah follows, shaking her head. Blanco is thrown down*]. Oh, did you hear what he called us? You foul-mouthed brute! You liar! How dare you put such a name to a decent woman? Let me get at him. You coward! Oh, he struck me: did you see that? Lynch him! Pete, will you stand by and hear me called names by a skunk like that? Burn him: burn him! Thats what I'd do with him. Aye, burn him!

THE MEN [*pulling the women away from Blanco, and getting them out partly by violence and partly by coaxing*] Here! come out of this. Let him alone. Clear the courthouse. Come on now. Out with you. Now, Sally: out you go. Let go my hair, or I'll twist your arm out. Ah, would you? Now, then: get along. You know you must go. Whats the use of scratching like that? Now, ladies, ladies, ladies. How would you like it if you were going to be hanged?

[*At last the women are pushed out, leaving Elder Daniels, the Sheriff's brother Strapper Kemp, and a few others with Blanco.Strapper is a lad just turning into a man: strong, selfish, sulky, and determined.*]

BLANCO [*sitting up and tidying himself*]—

Oh woman, in our hours of ease.
Uncertain, coy, and hard to please—

Is my face scratched? I can feel their damned claws all over me still. Am I bleeding? [*He sits on the nearest bench*].

ELDER DANIELS. Nothing to hurt. Theyve drawn a drop or two under your left eye.

STRAPPER. Lucky for you to have an eye left in your head.

BLANCO [*wiping the blood off*]—

When pain and anguish wring the brow,
A ministering angel thou.

Go out to them, Strapper Kemp; and tell them about your big brother's little horse that some wicked man stole. Go and cry in your mammy's lap.

STRAPPER [*furious*] You jounce me any more about that horse,

Blanco Posnet; and I'll—I'll—

BLANCO. Youll scratch my face, wont you? Yah! Your brother's the

Sheriff, aint he?

STRAPPER. Yes, he is. He hangs horse-thieves.

BLANCO [*with calm conviction*] He's a rotten Sheriff. Oh, a rotten Sheriff. If he did his first duty he'd hang himself. This is a rotten town. Your fathers came here on a false alarm of gold- digging; and when the gold didn't pan out, they lived by licking their young into habits of honest industry.

STRAPPER. If I hadnt promised Elder Daniels here to give him a chance to keep you out of Hell, I'd take the job of twisting your neck off the hands of the Vigilance Committee.

BLANCO [*with infinite scorn*] You and your rotten Elder, and your rotten Vigilance Committee!

STRAPPER. Theyre sound enough to hang a horse-thief, anyhow.

BLANCO. Any fool can hang the wisest man in the country. Nothing he likes better. But you cant hang me.

STRAPPER. Cant we?

BLANCO. No, you cant. I left the town this morning before sunrise, because it's a rotten town, and I couldn't bear to see it in the light. Your brother's horse did the same, as any sensible horse would. Instead of going to look for the horse, you went looking for me. That was a rotten thing to do, because the horse belonged to your brother—or to the man he stole it from— and I don't belong to him. Well, you found me; but you didn't find the horse. If I had took the horse, I'd have been on the horse. Would I have taken all that time to get to where I did if I'd a horse to carry me?

STRAPPER. I dont believe you started not for two hours after you say you did.

BLANCO. Who cares what you believe or dont believe? Is a man worth six of you to be hanged because youve lost your big brother's horse, and youll want to kill somebody to relieve your rotten feelings when he licks you for it? Not likely. Till you can find a witness that saw me with that horse you cant touch me; and you know it.

STRAPPER. Is that the law, Elder?

ELDER DANIELS. The Sheriff knows the law. I wouldnt say for sure; but I think it would be more seemly to have a witness. Go and round one up, Strapper; and leave me here alone to wrestle with his poor blinded soul.

STRAPPER. I'll get a witness all right enough. I know the road he took; and I'll ask at every house within sight of it for a mile out. Come boys.

[*Strapper goes out with the others, leaving Blanco and Elder Daniels together. Blanco rises and strolls over to the Elder, surveying him with extreme disparagement.*]

BLANCO. Well, brother? Well, Boozy Posnet, alias Elder Daniels?

Well, thief? Well, drunkard?

ELDER DANIELS. It's no good, Blanco. Theyll never believe we're brothers.

BLANCO. Never fear. Do you suppose I want to claim you? Do you suppose I'm proud of you? Youre a rotten brother, Boozy Posnet. All you ever did when I owned you was to borrow money from me to get drunk with. Now you lend money and sell drink to other people. I was ashamed of you before; and I'm worse ashamed of you now, I wont have you for a brother. Heaven gave you to me; but I return the blessing without thanks. So be easy: I shant blab. [*He turns his back on him and sits down*].

ELDER DANIELS. I tell you they wouldn't believe you; so what does it matter to me whether you blab or not? Talk sense, Blanco: theres no time for your foolery now; for youll be a dead man an hour after the Sheriff comes back. What possessed you to steal that horse?

BLANCO. I didnt steal it. I distrained on it for what you owed me. I thought it was yours. I was a fool to think that you owned anything but other people's property. You laid your hands on everything father and mother had when they died. I never asked you for a fair share. I never asked you for all the money I'd lent you from time to time. I asked you for mother's old necklace with the hair locket in it. You wouldn't give me that: you wouldn't give me anything. So as you refused me my due I took it, just to give you a lesson.

ELDER DANIELS. Why didnt you take the necklace if you must steal something? They wouldnt have hanged you for that.

BLANCO. Perhaps I'd rather be hanged for stealing a horse than let off for a damned piece of sentimentality.

ELDER DANIELS. Oh, Blanco, Blanco: spiritual pride has been your ruin. If youd only done like me, youd be a free and respectable man this day instead of laying there with a rope round your neck.

BLANCO [*turning on him*] Done like you! What do you mean? Drink like you, eh? Well, Ive done some of that lately. I see things.

ELDER DANIELS. Too late, Blanco: too late. [*Convulsively*] Oh, why didnt you drink as I used to? Why didnt you drink as I was led to by the Lord for my good, until the time came for me to give it up? It was drink that saved my character when I was a young man; and it was the want of it that spoiled yours. Tell me this. Did I ever get drunk when I was working?

BLANCO. No; but then you never worked when you had money enough to get drunk.

ELDER DANIELS. That just shews the wisdom of Providence and the Lord's mercy. God fulfils himself in many ways: ways we little think of when we try to set up our own shortsighted laws against his Word. When does the Devil catch hold of a man? Not when he's working and not when he's drunk; but when he's idle and sober. Our own natures tell us to drink when we have nothing else to do. Look at you and me! When we'd both earned a pocketful of money, what did we do? Went on the spree, naturally. But I was humble minded. I did as the rest did. I gave my money in at the drink- shop; and I said, "Fire me out when I have drunk it all up." Did you ever see me sober while it lasted?

BLANCO. No; and you looked so disgusting that I wonder it didn't set me against drink for the rest of my life.

ELDER DANIELS. That was your spiritual pride, Blanco. You never reflected that when I was drunk I was in a state of innocence. Temptations and bad company and evil thoughts passed by me like the summer wind as you might say: I was too drunk to notice them. When the money was gone, and they fired me out, I was fired out like gold out of the furnace, with my character unspoiled and unspotted; and when I went back to work, the work kept me steady. Can you say as much, Blanco? Did your holidays leave your character unspoiled? Oh, no, no. It was theatres: it was gambling: it was evil company, it was reading in vain romances: it was women, Blanco, women: it was wrong thoughts and gnawing discontent. It ended in your becoming a rambler and a gambler: it is going to end this evening on the gallows tree. Oh, what a lesson against spiritual pride! Oh, what a—[*Blanco throws his hat at him*].

BLANCO. Stow it, Boozy. Sling it. Cut it. Cheese it. Shut up.

"Shake not the dying sinner's hand."

ELDER DANIELS. Aye: there you go, with your scraps of lustful poetry. But you cant deny what I tell you. Why, do you think I would put my soul in peril by selling drink if I thought it did no good, as them silly temperance reformers make out, flying in the face of the natural tastes implanted in us all for a good purpose? Not if I was to starve for it to-morrow. But I know better. I tell you, Blanco, what keeps America to-day the purest of the nations is that when she's not working she's too drunk to hear the voice of the tempter.

BLANCO. Dont deceive yourself, Boozy. You sell drink because you make a bigger profit out of it than you can by selling tea. And you gave up drink yourself because when you got that fit at Edward-stown the doctor told you youd die the next time; and that frightened you off it.

ELDER DANIELS [*fervently*] Oh thank God selling drink pays me! And thank God he sent me that fit as a warning that my drinking time was past and gone, and that he needed me for another service!

BLANCO. Take care, Boozy. He hasnt finished with you yet. He always has a trick up His sleeve—

ELDER DANIELS. Oh, is that the way to speak of the ruler of the universe—the great and almighty God?

BLANCO. He's a sly one. He's a mean one. He lies low for you. He plays cat and mouse with you. He lets you run loose until you think youre shut of him; and then, when you least expect it, he's got you.

ELDER DANIELS. Speak more respectful, Blanco—more reverent.

BLANCO [*springing up and coming at him*] Reverent! Who taught you your reverent cant? Not your Bible. It says He cometh like a thief in the night—aye, like a thief—a horse-thief—

ELDER DANIELS [*shocked*] Oh!

BLANCO [*overhearing him*] And it's true. Thats how He caught me and put my neck into the halter. To spite me because I had no use for Him—because I lived my own life in my own way, and would have no truck with His "Dont do this," and "You mustnt do that," and "Youll go to Hell if you do the other." I gave Him the go-bye and did without Him all these years. But He caught me out at last. The laugh is with Him as far as hanging me goes. [*He thrusts his hands into his pockets and lounges moodily away from Daniels, to the table, where he sits facing the jury box*].

ELDER DANIELS. Dont dare to put your theft on Him, man. It was the Devil tempted you to steal the horse.

BLANCO. Not a bit of it. Neither God nor Devil tempted me to take the horse: I took it on my own. He had a cleverer trick than that ready for me. [*He takes his hands out of his pockets and clenches his fists*]. Gosh! When I think that I might have been safe and fifty miles away by now with that horse; and here I am waiting to be hung up and filled with lead! What came to me? What made me such a fool? Thats what I want to know. Thats the great secret.

ELDER DANIELS [*at the opposite side of the table*] Blanco: the great secret now is, what did you do with the horse?

BLANCO [*striking the table with his fist*] May my lips be blighted like my soul if ever I tell that to you or any mortal men! They may roast me alive or cut me to ribbons; but Strapper Kemp shall never have the laugh on me over that job. Let them hang me. Let them shoot. So long as they are shooting a man and not a sniveling skunk and softy, I can stand up to them and take all they can give me—game.

ELDER DANIELS. Dont be headstrong, Blanco. Whats the use? [*Slyly*] They might let up on you if you put Strapper in the way of getting his brother's horse back.

BLANCO. Not they. Hanging's too big a treat for them to give up a fair chance. Ive done it myself. Ive yelled with the dirtiest of them when a man no worse than myself was swung up. Ive emptied my revolver into him, and persuaded myself that he deserved it and that I was doing justice with strong stern men. Well, my turn's come now. Let the men I yelled at and shot at look up out of Hell and see the boys yelling and shooting at me as I swing up.

ELDER DANIELS. Well, even if you want to be hanged, is that any reason why Strapper shouldn't have his horse? I tell you I'm responsible to him for it. [*Bending over the table and coaxing him*]. Act like a brother, Blanco: tell me what you done with it.

BLANCO [*shortly, getting up and leaving the table*] Never you mind what I done with it. I was done out of it. Let that be enough for you.

ELDER DANIELS [*following him*] Then why don't you put us on to the man that done you out of it?

BLANCO. Because he'd be too clever for you, just as he was too clever for me.

FEEMY [*reddening, and disengaging her arm from Strapper's*] I'm clean enough to hang you, anyway. [*Going over to him threateningly*]. Youre no true American man, to insult a woman like that.

BLANCO. A woman! Oh Lord! You saw me on a horse, did you?

FEEMY. Yes I did.

BLANCO. Got up early on purpose to do it, didn't you?

FEEMY. No I didn't: I stayed up late on a spree.

BLANCO. I was on a horse, was I?

FEEMY. Yes you were; and if you deny it youre a liar.

BLANCO [*to Strapper*] She saw a man on a horse when she was too drunk to tell which was the man and which was the horse—

FEEMY [*breaking in*] You lie. I wasn't drunk—at least not as drunk as that.

BLANCO [*ignoring the interruption*]—and you found a man without a horse. Is a man on a horse the same as a man on foot? Yah! Take your witness away. Who's going to believe her? Shove her into the dustbin. Youve got to find that horse before you get a rope round my neck. [*He turns away from her contemptuously, and sits at the table with his back to the jury box*].

FEEMY [*following him*] I'll hang you, you dirty horse-thief; or not a man in this camp will ever get a word or a look from me again. Youre just trash: thats what you are. White trash.

BLANCO. And what are you, darling? What are you? Youre a worse danger to a town like this than ten horse-thieves.

FEEMY. Mr Kemp: will you stand by and hear me insulted in that low way? [*To Blanco, spitefully*] I'll see you swung up and I'll see you cut down: I'll see you high and I'll see you low, as dangerous as I am. [*He laughs*]. Oh you neednt try to brazen it out. Youll look white enough before the boys are done with you.

BLANCO. You do me good. Feemy. Stay by me to the end, wont you? Hold my hand to the last; and I'll die game. [*He puts out his hand: she strikes savagely at it; but he withdraws it in time and laughs at her discomfiture*].

FEEMY. You—

ELDER DANIELS. Never mind him, Feemy: he's not right in his head to-day. [*She receives the assurance with contemptuous credulity, and sits down on the step of the Sheriff's dais*].

Sheriff Kemp comes in: a stout man, with large flat ears, and a neck thicker than his head.

ELDER DANIELS. Morning, Sheriff.

THE SHERIFF. Morning, Elder. [*Passing on.*] Morning, Strapper.

[*Passing on*]. Morning, Miss Evans. [*Stopping between Strapper and Blanco*]. Is this the prisoner?

BLANCO [*rising*] Thats so. Morning, Sheriff.

THE SHERIFF. Morning. You know, I suppose, that if you've stole a horse and the jury find against you, you wont have any time to settle your affairs. Consequently, if you feel guilty, youd better settle em now.

BLANCO. Affairs be damned! Ive got none.

THE SHERIFF. Well, are you in a proper state of mind? Has the

Elder talked to you?

BLANCO. He has. And I say it's against the law. It's torture: thats what it is.

ELDER DANIELS. He's not accountable. He's out of his mind,

Sheriff. He's not fit to go into the presence of his Maker.

THE SHERIFF. You are a merciful man, Elder; but you wont take the boys with you there. [*To Blanco*]. If it comes to hanging you, youd better for your own sake be hanged in a proper state of mind than in an improper one. But it wont make any difference to us: make no mistake about that.

BLANCO. Lord keep me wicked till I die! Now Ive said my little prayer. I'm ready. Not that I'm guilty, mind you; but this is a rotten town, dead certain to do the wrong thing.

THE SHERIFF. You wont be asked to live long in it, I guess. [*To Strapper*] Got the witness all right, Strapper?

STRAPPER. Yes, got everything.

BLANCO. Except the horse.

THE SHERIFF. Whats that? Aint you got the horse?

STRAPPER. No. He traded it before we overtook him, I guess. But

Feemy saw him on it.

FEEMY. She did.

STRAPPER. Shall I call in the boys?

BLANCO. Just a moment, Sheriff. A good appearance is everything in a low-class place like this. [*He takes out a pocket comb and mirror, and retires towards the dais to arrange his hair*].

ELDER DANIELS. Oh, think of your immortal soul, man, not of your foolish face.

BLANCO. I cant change my soul, Elder: it changes me—sometimes.

Feemy: I'm too pale. Let me rub my cheek against yours, darling.

FEEMY. You lie: my color's my own, such as it is. And a pretty color youll be when youre hung white and shot red.

BLANCO. Aint she spiteful, Sheriff?

THE SHERIFF. Time's wasted on you. [*To Strapper*] Go and see if the boys are ready. Some of them were short of cartridges, and went down to the store to buy them. They may as well have their fun; and itll be shorter for him.

STRAPPER. Young Jack has brought a boxful up. Theyre all ready.

THE SHERIFF [*going to the dais and addressing Blanco*] Your place is at the bar there. Take it. [*Blanco bows ironically and goes to the bar*]. Miss Evans: youd best sit at the table. [*She does so, at the corner nearest the bar. The Elder takes the opposite corner. The Sheriff takes his chair*]. All ready, Strapper.

STRAPPER [*at the door*] All in to begin.

(The crowd comes in and fills the court. Babsy, Jessie, and Emma come to the Sheriff's right; Hannah and Lottie to his left.)

THE SHERIFF. Silence there. The jury will take their places as usual. [*They do so*].

BLANCO. I challenge this jury, Sheriff.

THE FOREMAN. Do you, by Gosh?

THE SHERIFF. On what ground?

BLANCO. On the general ground that it's a rotten jury.

[*Laughter*].

THE SHERIFF. Thats not a lawful ground of challenge.

THE FOREMAN. It's a lawful ground for me to shoot yonder skunk at sight, first time I meet him, if he survives this trial.

BLANCO. I challenge the Foreman because he's prejudiced.

THE FOREMAN. I say you lie. We mean to hang you, Blanco Posnet; but you will be hanged fair.

THE JURY. Hear, hear!

STRAPPER [*to the Sheriff*] George: this is rot. How can you get an unprejudiced jury if the prisoner starts by telling them theyre all rotten? If theres any prejudice against him he has himself to thank for it.

THE BOYS. Thats so. Of course he has. Insulting the court!

Challenge be jiggered! Gag him.

NESTOR [*a juryman with a long white beard, drunk, the oldest man present*] Besides, Sheriff, I go so far as to say that the man that is not prejudiced against a horse-thief is not fit to sit on a jury in this town.

THE BOYS. Right. Bully for you, Nestor! Thats the straight truth.

Of course he aint. Hear, hear!

THE SHERIFF. That is no doubt true, old man. Still, you must get as unprejudiced as you can. The critter has a right to his chance, such as he is. So now go right ahead. If the prisoner don't like this jury, he should have stole a horse in another town; for this is all the jury he'll get here.

THE FOREMAN. Thats so, Blanco Posnet.

THE SHERIFF [*to Blanco*] Dont you be uneasy. You will get justice here. It may be rough justice; but it is justice.

BLANCO. What is justice?

THE SHERIFF. Hanging horse-thieves is justice; so now you know. Now then: weve wasted enough time. Hustle with your witness there, will you?

BLANCO [*indignantly bringing down his fist on the bar*] Swear the jury. A rotten Sheriff you are not to know that the jury's got to be sworn.

THE FOREMAN [*galled*] Be swore for you! Not likely. What do you say, old son?

NESTOR [*deliberately and solemnly*] I say: GUILTY!!!

THE BOYS [*tumultuously rushing at Blanco*] Thats it. Guilty, guilty. Take him out and hang him. He's found guilty. Fetch a rope. Up with him. [*They are about to drag him from the bar*].

THE SHERIFF [*rising, pistol in hand*] Hands off that man. Hands off him, I say, Squinty, or I drop you, and would if you were my own son. [*Dead silence*], I'm Sheriff here; and it's for me to say when he may lawfully be hanged. [*They release him*].

BLANCO. As the actor says in the play, "a Daniel come to judgment." Rotten actor he was, too.

THE SHERIFF. Elder Daniel is come to judgment all right, my lad.

Elder: the floor is yours. [*The Elder rises*]. Give your evidence.

The truth and the whole truth and nothing but the truth, so help you God.

ELDER DANIELS. Sheriff: let me off this. I didn't ought to swear away this man's life. He and I are, in a manner of speaking, brothers.

THE SHERIFF. It does you credit, Elder: every man here will acknowledge it. But religion is one thing: law is another. In religion we're all brothers. In law we cut our brother off when he steals horses.

THE FOREMAN. Besides, you neednt hang him, you know. Theres plenty of willing hands to take that job off your conscience. So rip ahead, old son.

STRAPPER. Youre accountable to me for the horse until you clear yourself, Elder: remember that.

BLANCO. Out with it, you fool.

ELDER DANIELS. You might own up, Blanco, as far as my evidence goes. Everybody knows I borrowed one of the Sheriff's horses from Strapper because my own's gone lame. Everybody knows you arrived in the town yesterday and put up in my house. Everybody knows that in the morning the horse was gone and you were gone.

BLANCO [*in a forensic manner*] Sheriff: the Elder, though known to you and to all here as no brother of mine and the rottenest liar in this town, is speaking the truth for the first time in his life as far as what he says about me is concerned. As to the horse, I say nothing; except that it was the rottenest horse you ever tried to sell.

THE SHERIFF. How do you know it was a rotten horse if you didn't steal it?

BLANCO. I don't know of my own knowledge. I only argue that if the horse had been worth its keep, you wouldn't have lent it to Strapper, and Strapper wouldn't have lent it to this eloquent and venerable ram. [*Suppressed laughter*]. And now I ask him this. [*To the Elder*] Did we or did we not have a quarrel last evening about a certain article that was left by my mother, and that I considered I had a right to more than you? And did you say one word to me about the horse not belonging to you?

ELDER DANIELS. Why should I? We never said a word about the horse at all. How was I to know what it was in your mind to do?

BLANCO. Bear witness all that I had a right to take a horse from him without stealing to make up for what he denied me. I am no thief. But you havnt proved yet that I took the horse. Strapper Kemp: had I the horse when you took me, or had I not?

STRAPPER. No, nor you hadnt a railway train neither. But Feemy

Evans saw you pass on the horse at four o'clock twenty-five miles from the spot where I took you at seven on the road to Pony

Harbor. Did you walk twenty-five miles in three hours? That so,

Feemy, eh?

FEEMY. Thats so. At four I saw him. [*To Blanco*] Thats done for you.

THE SHERIFF. You say you saw him on my horse?

FEEMY. I did.

BLANCO. And I ate it, I suppose, before Strapper fetched up with me. [*Suddenly and dramatically*] Sheriff: I accuse Feemy of immoral relations with Strapper.

FEEMY. Oh you liar!

BLANCO. I accuse the fair Euphemia of immoral relations with every man in this town, including yourself, Sheriff. I say this is a conspiracy to kill me between Feemy and Strapper because I wouldn't touch Feemy with a pair of tongs. I say you darent hang any white man on the word of a woman of bad character. I stand on the honor and virtue of my American manhood. I say that she's not had the oath, and that you darent for the honor of the town give her the oath because her lips would blaspheme the holy Bible if they touched it. I say thats the law; and if you are a proper United States Sheriff and not a low-down lyncher, youll hold up the law and not let it be dragged in the mud by your brother's kept woman.

[*Great excitement among the women. The men much puzzled.*]

JESSIE. Thats right. She didn't ought to be let kiss the Book.

EMMA. How could the like of her tell the truth?

BABSY. It would be an insult to every respectable woman here to believe her.

FEEMY. It's easy to be respectable with nobody ever offering you a chance to be anything else.

THE WOMEN [*clamoring all together*] Shut up, you hussy. Youre a disgrace. How dare you open your lips to answer your betters?

Hold your tongue and learn your place, miss. You painted slut!

Whip her out of the town!

THE SHERIFF. Silence. Do you hear? Silence. [*The clamor ceases*].

Did anyone else see the prisoner with the horse?

FEEMY [*passionately*] Aint I good enough?

BABSY. No. Youre dirt: thats what you are.

FEEMY. And you—

THE SHERIFF. Silence. This trial is a man's job; and if the women forget their sex they can go out or be put out. Strapper and Miss Evans: you cant have it two ways. You can run straight, or you can run gay, so to speak; but you cant run both ways together. There is also a strong feeling among the men of this town that a line should be drawn between those that are straight wives and mothers and those that are, in the words of the Book of Books, taking the primrose path. We don't wish to be hard on any woman; and most of us have a personal regard for Miss Evans for the sake of old times; but theres no getting out of the fact that she has private reasons for wishing to oblige

Strapper, and that—if she will excuse my saying so—she is not what I might call morally particular as to what she does to oblige him. Therefore I ask the prisoner not to drive us to give Miss Evans the oath. I ask him to tell us fair and square, as a man who has but a few minutes between him and eternity, what he done with my horse.

THE BOYS. Hear, hear! Thats right. Thats fair. That does it. Now

Blanco. Own up.

BLANCO. Sheriff: you touch me home. This is a rotten world; but there is still one thing in it that remains sacred even to the rottenest of us, and that is a horse.

THE BOYS. Good. Well said, Blanco. Thats straight.

BLANCO. You have a right to your horse, Sheriff; and if I could put you in the way of getting it back, I would. But if I had that horse I shouldn't be here. As I hope to be saved, Sheriff—or rather as I hope to be damned; for I have no taste for pious company and no talent for playing the harp—I know no more of that horse's whereabouts than you do yourself.

STRAPPER. Who did you trade him to?

BLANCO. I did not trade him. I got nothing for him or by him. I stand here with a rope round my neck for the want of him. When you took me, did I fight like a thief or run like a thief; and was there any sign of a horse on me or near me?

STRAPPER. You were looking at a rainbow, like a damned silly fool instead of keeping your wits about you; and we stole up on you and had you tight before you could draw a bead on us.

THE SHERIFF. That don't sound like good sense. What would he look at a rainbow for?

BLANCO. I'll tell you, Sheriff. I was looking at it because there was something written on it.

SHERIFF. How do you mean written on it?

BLANCO. The words were, "Ive got the cinch on you this time, Blanco Posnet." Yes, Sheriff, I saw those words in green on the red streak of the rainbow; and as I saw them I felt Strapper's grab on my arm and Squinty's on my pistol.

THE FOREMAN. He's shammin mad: thats what he is. Aint it about time to give a verdict and have a bit of fun, Sheriff?

THE BOYS. Yes, lets have a verdict. We're wasting the whole afternoon. Cut it short.

THE SHERIFF [*making up his mind*] Swear Feemy Evans, Elder. She don't need to touch the Book. Let her say the words.

FEEMY. Worse people than me has kissed that Book. What wrong Ive done, most of you went shares in. Ive to live, havnt I? same as the rest of you. However, it makes no odds to me. I guess the truth is the truth and a lie is a lie, on the Book or off it.

BABSY. Do as youre told. Who are you, to be let talk about it?

THE SHERIFF. Silence there, I tell you. Sail ahead, Elder.

ELDER DANIELS. Feemy Evans: do you swear to tell the truth and the whole truth and nothing but the truth, so help you God?

FEEMY. I do, so help me—

SHERIFF. Thats enough. Now, on your oath, did you see the prisoner on my horse this morning on the road to Pony Harbor?

FEEMY. On my oath—[*Disturbance and crowding at the door*].

AT THE DOOR. Now then, now then! Where are you shovin to? Whats up? Order in court. Chuck him out. Silence. You cant come in here. Keep back.

(Strapper rushes to the door and forces his way out.)

SHERIFF [*savagely*] Whats this noise? Cant you keep quiet there?

Is this a Sheriff's court or is it a saloon?

BLANCO. Dont interrupt a lady in the act of hanging a gentleman.

Wheres your manners?

FEEMY. I'll hang you, Blanco Posnet. I will. I wouldn't for fifty dollars hadnt seen you this morning. I'll teach you to be civil to me next time, for all I'm not good enough to kiss the Book.

BLANCO. Lord keep me wicked till I die! I'm game for anything while youre spitting dirt at me, Feemy.

RENEWED TUMULT AT THE DOOR. Here, whats this? Fire them out. Not me. Who are you that I should get out of your way? Oh, stow it. Well, she cant come in. What woman? What horse? Whats the good of shoving like that? Who says? No! you don't say!

THE SHERIFF. Gentlemen of the Vigilance Committee: clear that doorway. Out with them in the name of the law.

STRAPPER [*without*] Hold hard, George. [*At the door*] Theyve got the horse. [*He comes in, followed by Waggoner Jo, an elderly carter, who crosses the court to the jury side. Strapper pushes his way to the Sheriff and speaks privately to him*].

THE BOYS. What! No! Got the horse! Sheriff's horse? Who took it, then? Where? Get out. Yes it is, sure. I tell you it is. It's the horse all right enough. Rot. Go and look. By Gum!

THE SHERIFF [*to Strapper*] You don't say!

STRAPPER. It's here, I tell you.

WAGGONER JO. It's here all right enough, Sheriff.

STRAPPER. And theyve got the thief too.

ELDER DANIELS. Then it aint Blanco.

STRAPPER. No: it's a woman. [*Blanco yells and covers his eyes with his hands*].

THE WHOLE CROWD. A woman!

THE SHERIFF. Well, fetch her in. [*Strapper goes out. The Sheriff continues, to Feemy*] And what do you mean, you lying jade, by putting up this story on us about Blanco?

FEEMY. I aint put up no story on you. This is a plant: you see if it isnt.

[*Strapper returns with a woman. Her expression of intense grief silences them as they crane over one another's heads to see her. Strapper takes her to the corner of the table. The Elder moves up to make room for her.*]

BLANCO [*terrified*]: that woman aint real. You take care. That woman will make you do what you never intended. Thats the rainbow woman. Thats the woman that brought me to this.

THE SHERIFF. Shut your mouth, will you. Youve got the horrors. [*To the woman*] Now you. Who are you? and what are you doing with a horse that doesn't belong to you?

THE WOMAN. I took it to save my child's life. I thought it would get me to a doctor in time. It was choking with croup.

BLANCO [*strangling, and trying to laugh*] A little choker: thats the word for him. His choking wasn't real: wait and see mine. [*He feels his neck with a sob*].

THE SHERIFF. Where's the child?

STRAPPER. On Pug Jackson's bench in his shed. He's makin a coffin for it.

BLANCO [*with a horrible convulsion of the throat—frantically*] Dead! The little Judas kid! The child I gave my life for! [*He breaks into hideous laughter*].

THE SHERIFF [*jarred beyond endurance by the sound*] Hold you noise! will you? Shove his neckerchief into his mouth if he don't stop. [*To the woman*] Dont you mind him, maam: he's mad with drink and devilment. I suppose theres no fake about this, Strapper. Who found her?

WAGGONER JO. I did, Sheriff. Theres no fake about it. I came on her on the track round by Red Mountain. She was settin on the ground with the dead body on her lap, stupid-like. The horse was grazin on the other side of the road.

THE SHERIFF [*puzzled*] Well, this is blamed queer. [*To the woman*] What call had you to take the horse from Elder Daniels' stable to find a doctor? Theres a doctor in the very next house.

BLANCO [*mopping his dabbled red crest and trying to be ironically gay*] Story simply wont wash, my angel. You got it from the man that stole the horse. He gave it to you because he was a softy and went to bits when you played off the sick kid on him. Well, I guess that clears me. I'm not that sort. Catch me putting my neck in a noose for anybody's kid!

THE FOREMAN. Dont you go putting her up to what to say. She said she took it.

THE WOMAN. Yes: I took it from a man that met me. I thought God sent him to me. I rode here joyfully thinking so all the time to myself. Then I noticed that the child was like lead in my arms. God would never have been so cruel as to send me the horse to disappoint me like that.

BLANCO. Just what He would do.

STRAPPER. We aint got nothin to do with that. This is the man, aint he? [*pointing to Blanco*].

THE WOMAN [*pulling herself together after looking scaredly at Blanco, and then at the Sheriff and at the jury*] No.

THE FOREMAN. You lie.

THE SHERIFF. Youve got to tell us the truth. Thats the law, you know.

THE WOMAN. The man looked a bad man. He cursed me; and he cursed the child: God forgive him! But something came over him. I was desperate, I put the child in his arms; and it got its little fingers down his neck and called him Daddy and tried to kiss him; for it was not right in its head with the fever. He said it was a little Judas kid, and that it was betraying him with a kiss, and that he'd swing for it. And then he gave me the horse, and went away crying and laughing and singing dreadful dirty wicked words to hymn tunes like as if he had seven devils in him.

STRAPPER. She's lying. Give her the oath, George.

THE SHERIFF. Go easy there. Youre a smart boy, Strapper; but youre not Sheriff yet. This is my job. You just wait. I submit that we're in a difficulty here. If Blanco was the man, the lady cant, as a white woman, give him away. She oughtnt to be put in the position of having either to give him away or commit perjury. On the other hand, we don't want a horse-thief to get off through a lady's delicacy.

THE FOREMAN. No we don't; and we don't intend he shall. Not while

I am foreman of this jury.

BLANCO [*with intense expression*] A rotten foreman! Oh, what a rotten foreman!

THE SHERIFF. Shut up, will you. Providence shows us a way out here. Two women saw Blanco with a horse. One has a delicacy about saying so. The other will excuse me saying that delicacy is not her strongest holt. She can give the necessary witness. Feemy Evans: you've taken the oath. You saw the man that took the horse.

FEEMY. I did. And he was a low-down rotten drunken lying hound that would go further to hurt a woman any day than to help her. And if he ever did a good action it was because he was too drunk to know what he was doing. So it's no harm to hang him. She said he cursed her and went away blaspheming and singing things that were not fit for the child to hear.

BLANCO [*troubled*] I didn't mean them for the child to hear, you venomous devil.

THE SHERIFF. All thats got nothing to do with us. The question you have to answer is, was that man Blanco Posnet?

THE WOMAN. No. I say no. I swear it. Sheriff: don't hang that man: oh don't. You may hang me instead if you like: Ive nothing to live for now. You darent take her word against mine. She never had a child: I can see it in her face.

FEEMY [*stung to the quick*] I can hang him in spite of you, anyhow. Much good your child is to you now, lying there on Pug Jackson's bench!

BLANCO [*rushing at her with a shriek*] I'll twist your heart out of you for that. [*They seize him before he can reach her*].

FEEMY [*mocking at him as he struggles to get at her*] Ha, ha, Blanco Posnet. You cant touch me; and I can hang you. Ha, ha! Oh, I'll do for you. I'll twist your heart and I'll twist your neck. [*He is dragged back to the bar and leans on it, gasping and exhausted.*] Give me the oath again, Elder. I'll settle him. And do you [*to the woman*] take your sickly face away from in front of me.

STRAPPER. Just turn your back on her there, will you?

THE WOMAN. God knows I don't want to see her commit murder. [*She folds her shawl over her head*].

THE SHERIFF. Now, Miss Evans: cut it short. Was the prisoner the man you saw this morning or was he not? Yes or no?

FEEMY [*a little hysterically*] I'll tell you fast enough. Dont think I'm a softy.

THE SHERIFF [*losing patience*] Here: weve had enough of this. You tell the truth, Feemy Evans; and let us have no more of your lip. Was the prisoner the man or was he not? On your oath?

FEEMY. On my oath and as I'm a living woman—[*flinching*] Oh God! he felt the little child's hands on his neck—I cant [*bursting into a flood of tears and scolding at the other woman*] It's you with your snivelling face that has put me off it. [*Desperately*] No: it wasn't him. I only said it out of spite because he insulted me. May I be struck dead if I ever saw him with the horse!

[*Everybody draws a long breath. Dead silence.*]

BLANCO [*whispering at her*] Softy! Cry-baby! Landed like me! Doing what you never intended! [*Taking up his hat and speaking in his ordinary tone*] I presume I may go now, Sheriff.

STRAPPER. Here, hold hard.

THE FOREMAN. Not if we know it, you don't.

THE BOYS [*barring the way to the door*] You stay where you are. Stop a bit, stop a bit. Dont you be in such a hurry. Dont let him go. Not much.

[*Blanco stands motionless, his eye fixed, thinking hard, and apparently deaf to what is going on.*]

THE SHERIFF [*rising solemnly*] Silence there. Wait a bit. I take it that if the Sheriff is satisfied and the owner of the horse is satisfied, theres no more to be said. I have had to remark on former occasions that what is wrong with this court is that theres too many Sheriffs in it. To-day there is going to be one, and only one; and that one is your humble servant. I call that to the notice of the Foreman of the jury, and also to the notice of young Strapper. I am also the owner of the horse. Does any man say that I am not? [*Silence*]. Very well, then. In my opinion, to commandeer a horse for the purpose of getting a dying child to a doctor is not stealing, provided, as in the present case, that the horse is returned safe and sound. I rule that there has been no theft.

NESTOR. That aint the law.

THE SHERIFF. I fine you a dollar for contempt of court, and will collect it myself off you as you leave the building. And as the boys have been disappointed of their natural sport, I shall give them a little fun by standing outside the door and taking up a collection for the bereaved mother of the late kid that shewed up Blanco Posnet.

THE BOYS. A collection. Oh, I say! Calls that sport? Is this a mothers' meeting? Well, I'll be jiggered! Where does the sport come in?

THE SHERIFF [*continuing*] The sport comes in, my friends, not so much in contributing as in seeing others fork out. Thus each contributes to the general enjoyment; and all contribute to his. Blanco Posnet: you go free under the protection of the Vigilance Committee for just long enough to get you out of this town, which is not a healthy place for you. As you are in a hurry, I'll sell you the horse at a reasonable figure. Now, boys, let nobody go out till I get to the door. The court is adjourned. [*He goes out*].

STRAPPER [*to Feemy, as he goes to the door*] I'm done with you. Do you hear? I'm done with you. [*He goes out sulkily*].

FEEMY [*calling after him*] As if I cared about a stingy brat like you! Go back to the freckled maypole you left for me: you've been fretting for her long enough.

THE FOREMAN [*To Blanco, on his way out*] A man like you makes me sick. Just sick. [*Blanco makes no sign. The Foreman spits disgustedly, and follows Strapper out. The Jurymen leave the box, except Nestor, who collapses in a drunken sleep*].

BLANCO [*Suddenly rushing from the bar to the table and jumping up on it*] Boys, I'm going to preach you a sermon on the moral of this day's proceedings.

THE BOYS [*crowding round him*] Yes: lets have a sermon. Go ahead,

Blanco. Silence for Elder Blanco. Tune the organ. Let us pray.

NESTOR [*staggering out of his sleep*] Never hold up your head in this town again. I'm done with you.

BLANCO [*pointing inexorably to Nestor*] Drunk in church.

Disturbing the preacher. Hand him out.

THE BOYS [*chivying Nestor out*] Now, Nestor, outside. Outside,

Nestor. Out you go. Get your subscription ready for the Sheriff.

Skiddoo, Nestor.

NESTOR. Afraid to be hanged! Afraid to be hanged! [*At the door*]

Coward! [*He is thrown out*].

BLANCO. Dearly beloved brethren—

A BOY. Same to you, Blanco. [*Laughter*].

BLANCO. And many of them. Boys: this is a rotten world.

ANOTHER BOY. Lord have mercy on us, miserable sinners. [*More laughter*].

BLANCO [*Forcibly*] No: thats where youre wrong. Dont flatter yourselves that youre miserable sinners. Am I a miserable sinner? No: I'm a fraud and a failure. I started in to be a bad man like the rest of you. You all started in to be bad men or you wouldn't be in this jumped-up, jerked-off, hospital-turned-out camp that calls itself a town. I took the broad path because I thought I was a man and not a snivelling canting turning-the-other-cheek apprentice angel serving his time in a vale of tears. They talked Christianity to us on Sundays; but when they really meant business they told us never to take a blow without giving it back, and to get dollars. When they talked the golden rule to me, I just looked at them as if they werent there, and spat. But when they told me to try to live my life so that I could always look my fellowman straight in the eye and tell him to go to hell, that fetched me.

THE BOYS. Quite right. Good. Bully for you, Blanco, old son.

Right good sense too. Aha-a-ah!

BLANCO. Yes; but whats come of it all? Am I a real bad man? a man of game and grit? a man that does what he likes and goes over or through other people to his own gain? or am I a snivelling cry- baby that let a horse his life depended on be took from him by a woman, and then sat on the grass looking at the rainbow and let himself be took like a hare in a trap by Strapper Kemp: a lad whose back I or any grown man here could break against his knee? I'm a rottener fraud and failure than the Elder here. And youre all as rotten as me, or youd have lynched me.

A BOY. Anything to oblige you, Blanco.

ANOTHER. We can do it yet if you feel really bad about it.

BLANCO. No: the devil's gone out of you. We're all frauds. Theres none of us real good and none of us real bad.

ELDER DANIELS. There is One above, Blanco.

BLANCO. What do you know about Him? you that always talk as if He never did anything without asking your rotten leave first? Why did the child die? Tell me that if you can. He cant have wanted to kill the child. Why did He make me go soft on the child if He was going hard on it Himself? Why should He go hard on the innocent kid and go soft on a rotten thing like me? Why did I go soft myself? Why did the Sheriff go soft? Why did Feemy go soft? Whats this game that upsets our game? For seems to me theres two games bein played. Our game is a rotten game that makes me feel I'm dirt and that youre all as rotten dirt as me. T'other game may be a silly game;

but it aint rotten. When the Sheriff played it he stopped being rotten. When Feemy played it the paint nearly dropped off her face. When I played it I cursed myself for a fool; but I lost the rotten feel all the same.

ELDER DANIELS. It was the Lord speaking to your soul, Blanco.

BLANCO. Oh yes: you know all about the Lord, don't you? Youre in the Lord's confidence. He wouldn't for the world do anything to shock you, would He, Boozy dear? Yah! What about the croup? It was early days when He made the croup, I guess. It was the best He could think of then; but when it turned out wrong on His hands He made you and me to fight the croup for him. You bet He didn't make us for nothing; and He wouldn't have made us at all if He could have done His work without us. By Gum, that must be what we're for! He'd never have made us to be rotten drunken blackguards like me, and good-for-nothing rips like Feemy. He made me because He had a job for me. He let me run loose til the job was ready; and then I had to come along and do it, hanging or no hanging. And I tell you it didn't feel rotten: it felt bully, just bully. Anyhow, I got the rotten feel off me for a minute of my life; and I'll go through fire to get it off me again. Look here! which of you will marry Feemy Evans?

THE BOYS [*uproariously*] Who speaks first? Who'll marry Feemy? Come along, Jack. Nows your chance, Peter. Pass along a husband for Feemy. Oh my! Feemy!

FEEMY [*shortly*] Keep your tongue off me, will you?

BLANCO. Feemy was a rose of the broad path, wasn't she? You all thought her the champion bad woman of this district. Well, she's a failure as a bad woman; and I'm a failure as a bad man. So let Brother Daniels marry us to keep all the rottenness in the family. What do you say, Feemy?

FEEMY. Thank you; but when I marry I'll marry a man that could do a decent action without surprising himself out of his senses. Youre like a child with a new toy: you and your bit of human kindness!

THE WOMAN. How many would have done it with their life at stake?

FEEMY. Oh well, if youre so much taken with him, marry him yourself. Youd be what people call a good wife to him, wouldn't you?

THE WOMAN. I was a good wife to the child's father. I don't think any woman wants to be a good wife twice in her life. I want somebody to be a good husband to me now.

BLANCO. Any offer, gentlemen, on that understanding? [*The boys shake their heads*]. Oh, it's a rotten game, our game. Here's a real good woman; and she's had enough of it, finding that it only led to being put upon.

HANNAH. Well, if there was nothing wrong in the world there wouldn't be anything left for us to do, would there?

ELDER DANIELS. Be of good cheer, brothers. Fight on. Seek the path.

BLANCO. No. No more paths. No more broad and narrow. No more good and bad. Theres no good and bad; but by Jiminy, gents, theres a rotten game, and theres a great game. I played the rotten game; but the great game was played on me; and now I'm for the great game every time. Amen. Gentlemen: let us adjourn to the saloon. I stand the drinks. [*He jumps down from the table*].

THE BOYS. Right you are, Blanco. Drinks round. Come along, boys. Blanco's standing. Right along to the Elder's. Hurrah! [*They rush out, dragging the Elder with them*].

BLANCO [*to Feemy, offering his hand*] Shake, Feemy.

FEEMY. Get along, you blackguard.

BLANCO. It's come over me again, same as when the kid touched me.

Shake, Feemy.

FEEMY. Oh well, here. [*They shake hands*].

MISALLIANCE

MISALLIANCE

Johnny Tarleton, an ordinary young business man of thirty or less, is taking his weekly Friday to Tuesday in the house of his father, John Tarleton, who has made a great deal of money out of Tarleton's Underwear. The house is in Surrey, on the slope of Hindhead; and Johnny, reclining, novel in hand, in a swinging chair with a little awning above it, is enshrined in a spacious half hemisphere of glass which forms a pavilion commanding the garden, and, beyond it, a barren but lovely landscape of hill profile with fir trees, commons of bracken and gorse, and wonderful cloud pictures.

The glass pavilion springs from a bridgelike arch in the wall of the house, through which one comes into a big hall with tiled flooring, which suggests that the proprietor's notion of domestic luxury is founded on the lounges of week-end hotels. The arch is not quite in the centre of the wall. There is more wall to its right than to its left, and this space is occupied by a hat rack and umbrella stand in which tennis rackets, white parasols, caps, Panama hats, and other summery articles are bestowed. Just through the arch at this corner stands a new portable Turkish bath, recently unpacked, with its crate beside it, and on the crate the drawn nails and the hammer used in unpacking. Near the crate are open boxes of garden games: bowls and croquet. Nearly in the middle of the glass wall of the pavilion is a door giving on the garden, with a couple of steps to surmount the hot-water pipes which skirt the glass. At intervals round the pavilion are marble pillars with specimens of Viennese pottery on them, very flamboyant in colour and florid in design. Between them are folded garden chairs flung anyhow against the pipes. In the side walls are two doors: one near the hat stand, leading to the interior of the house, the other on the opposite side and at the other end, leading to the vestibule.

There is no solid furniture except a sideboard which stands against the wall between the vestibule door and the pavilion, a small writing table with a blotter, a rack for telegram forms and stationery, and a wastepaper basket, standing out in the hall near the sideboard, and a lady's worktable, with two chairs at it, towards the other side of the lounge. The writing table has also two chairs at it. On the sideboard there is a tantalus, liqueur bottles, a syphon, a glass jug of lemonade, tumblers, and every convenience for casual drinking. Also a plate of sponge cakes, and a highly ornate punchbowl in the same style as the keramic display in the pavilion. Wicker chairs and little bamboo tables with ash trays and boxes of matches on them are scattered in all directions. In the pavilion, which is flooded with sunshine, is the elaborate patent swing seat and awning in which Johnny reclines with his novel. There are two wicker chairs right and left of him.

Bentley Summerhays, one of those smallish, thinskinned youths, who from 17 to 70 retain unaltered the mental airs of the later and the physical appearance of the earlier age, appears in the garden and comes through the glass door into the pavilion. He is unmistakably a grade above Johnny socially; and though he looks sensitive enough, his assurance and his high voice are a little exasperating.

JOHNNY. Hallo! Wheres your luggage?

BENTLEY. I left it at the station. Ive walked up from Haslemere. [*He goes to the hat stand and hangs up his hat*].

JOHNNY [*shortly*] Oh! And who's to fetch it?

BENTLEY. Dont know. Dont care. Providence, probably. If not, your mother will have it fetched.

JOHNNY. Not her business, exactly, is it?

BENTLEY. [*returning to the pavilion*] Of course not. Thats why one loves her for doing it. Look here: chuck away your silly week-end novel, and talk to a chap. After a week in that filthy office my brain is simply blue-mouldy. Lets argue about something intellectual. [*He throws himself into the wicker chair on Johnny's right*].

JOHNNY. [*straightening up in the swing with a yell of protest*] No. Now seriously, Bunny, Ive come down here to have a pleasant week-end; and I'm not going to stand your confounded arguments. If you want to argue, get out of this and go over to the Congregationalist minister's. He's a nailer at arguing. He likes it.

BENTLEY. You cant argue with a person when his livelihood depends on his not letting you convert him. And would you mind not calling me Bunny. My name is Bentley Summerhays, which you please.

JOHNNY. Whats the matter with Bunny?

BENTLEY. It puts me in a false position. Have you ever considered the fact that I was an afterthought?

JOHNNY. An afterthought? What do you mean by that?

BENTLEY. I—

JOHNNY. No, stop: I dont want to know. It's only a dodge to start an argument.

BENTLEY. Dont be afraid: it wont overtax your brain. My father was 44 when I was born. My mother was 41. There was twelve years between me and the next eldest. I was unexpected. I was probably unintentional. My brothers and sisters are not the least like me. Theyre the regular thing that you always get in the first batch from young parents: quite pleasant, ordinary, do-the-regular-thing sort: all body and no brains, like you.

JOHNNY. Thank you.

BENTLEY. Dont mention it, old chap. Now I'm different. By the time I was born, the old couple knew something. So I came out all brains and no more body than is absolutely necessary. I am really a good deal older than you, though you were born ten years sooner. Everybody feels that when they hear us talk; consequently, though it's quite natural to hear me calling you Johnny, it sounds ridiculous and unbecoming for you to call me Bunny. [*He rises*].

JOHNNY. Does it, by George? You stop me doing it if you can: thats all.

BENTLEY. If you go on doing it after Ive asked you not, youll feel an awful swine. [*He strolls away carelessly to the sideboard with his eye on the sponge cakes*]. At least I should; but I suppose youre not so particular.

JOHNNY [*rising vengefully and following Bentley, who is forced to turn and listen*] I'll tell you what it is, my boy: you want a good talking to; and I'm going to give it to you. If you think that because your father's a K.C.B., and you want to marry my sister, you can make yourself as nasty as you please and say what you like, youre mistaken. Let me tell you that except Hypatia, not one person in this house is in favor of her marrying you; and I dont believe shes happy about it herself. The match isnt settled yet: dont forget that. Youre on trial in the office because the Governor isnt giving his daughter money for an idle man to live on her. Youre on trial here because my mother thinks a girl should know what a man is like in the house before she marries him. Thats been going on for two months now; and whats the result? Youve got yourself thoroughly disliked in the office; and youre getting yourself thoroughly disliked here, all through your bad manners and your conceit, and the damned impudence you think clever.

BENTLEY. [*deeply wounded and trying hard to control himself*] Thats enough, thank you. You dont suppose, I hope, that I should have come down if I had known that that was how you felt about me. [*He makes for the vestibule door*].

JOHNNY. [*collaring him*]. No: you dont run away. I'm going to have this out with you. Sit down: d'y' hear? [*Bentley attempts to go with dignity. Johnny slings him into a chair at the writing table, where he sits, bitterly humiliated, but afraid to speak lest he should burst into tears*]. Thats the advantage of having more body than brains, you see: it enables me to teach you manners; and I'm going to do it too. Youre a spoilt young pup; and you need a jolly good licking. And if youre not careful youll get it: I'll see to that next time you call me a swine.

BENTLEY. I didnt call you a swine. But [*bursting into a fury of tears*] you are a swine: youre a beast: youre a brute: youre a cad: youre a liar: youre a bully: I should like to wring your damned neck for you.

JOHNNY. [*with a derisive laugh*] Try it, my son. [*Bentley gives an inarticulate sob of rage*]. Fighting isnt in your line. Youre too small and youre too childish. I always suspected that your cleverness wouldnt come to very much when it was brought up against something solid: some decent chap's fist, for instance.

BENTLEY. I hope your beastly fist may come up against a mad bull or a prizefighter's nose, or something solider than me. I dont care about your fist; but if everybody here dislikes me— [*he is checked by a sob*]. Well, I dont care. [*Trying to recover himself*] I'm sorry I intruded: I didnt know. [*Breaking down again*] Oh you beast! you pig! Swine, swine, swine, swine, swine! Now!

JOHNNY. All right, my lad, all right. Sling your mud as hard as you please: it wont stick to me. What I want to know is this. How is it that your father, who I suppose is the strongest man England has produced in our time—

BENTLEY. You got that out of your halfpenny paper. A lot you know about him!

JOHNNY. I dont set up to be able to do anything but admire him and appreciate him and be proud of him as an Englishman. If it wasnt for my respect for him, I wouldnt have stood your cheek for two days, let alone two months. But what I cant understand is why he didnt lick it out of you when you were a kid. For twenty-five years he kept a place twice as big as England in order: a place full of seditious coffee-colored heathens and pestilential white agitators in the middle of a lot of savage tribes. And yet he couldnt keep you in order. I dont set up to be half the man your father undoubtedly is; but, by George, it's lucky for you you were not my son. I dont hold with my own father's views about corporal punishment being wrong. It's necessary for some people; and I'd have tried it on you until you first learnt to howl and then to behave yourself.

BENTLEY. [*contemptuously*] Yes: behavior wouldnt come naturally to your son, would it?

JOHNNY. [*stung into sudden violence*] Now you keep a civil tongue in your head. I'll stand none of your snobbery. I'm just as proud of Tarleton's Underwear as you are of your father's title and his K.C.B., and all the rest of it. My father began in a little hole of a shop in Leeds no bigger than our pantry down the passage there. He—

BENTLEY. Oh yes: I know. Ive read it. "The Romance of Business, or The Story of Tarleton's Underwear. Please Take One!" I took one the day after I first met Hypatia. I went and bought half a dozen unshrinkable vests for her sake.

JOHNNY. Well: did they shrink?

BENTLEY. Oh, dont be a fool.

JOHNNY. Never mind whether I'm a fool or not. Did they shrink? Thats the point. Were they worth the money?

BENTLEY. I couldnt wear them: do you think my skin's as thick as your customers' hides? I'd as soon have dressed myself in a nutmeg grater.

JOHNNY. Pity your father didnt give your thin skin a jolly good lacing with a cane—!

BENTLEY. Pity you havnt got more than one idea! If you want to know, they did try that on me once, when I was a small kid. A silly governess did it. I yelled fit to bring down the house and went into convulsions and brain fever and that sort of thing for three weeks. So the old girl got the sack; and serve her right! After that, I was let do what I like. My father didnt want me to grow up a broken-spirited spaniel, which is your idea of a man, I suppose.

JOHNNY. Jolly good thing for you that my father made you come into the office and shew what you were made of. And it didnt come to much: let me tell you that. When the Governor asked me where I thought we ought to put you, I said, "Make him the Office Boy." The Governor said you were too green. And so you were.

BENTLEY. I daresay. So would you be pretty green if you were shoved into my father's set. I picked up your silly business in a fortnight. Youve been at it ten years; and you havnt picked it up yet.

JOHNNY. Dont talk rot, child. You know you simply make me pity you.

BENTLEY. "Romance of Business" indeed! The real romance of Tarleton's business is the story that you understand anything about it. You never could explain any mortal thing about it to me when I asked you. "See what was done the last time": that was the beginning and the end of your wisdom. Youre nothing but a turnspit.

JOHNNY. A what!

BENTLEY. A turnspit. If your father hadnt made a roasting jack for you to turn, youd be earning twenty-four shillings a week behind a counter.

JOHNNY. If you dont take that back and apologize for your bad manners, I'll give you as good a hiding as ever—

BENTLEY. Help! Johnny's beating me! Oh! Murder! [*He throws himself on the ground, uttering piercing yells*].

JOHNNY. Dont be a fool. Stop that noise, will you. I'm not going to touch you. Sh—sh—

Hypatia rushes in through the inner door, followed by Mrs Tarleton, and throws herself on her knees by Bentley. Mrs Tarleton, whose knees are stiffer, bends over him and tries to lift him. Mrs Tarleton is a shrewd and motherly old lady who has been pretty in her time, and is still very pleasant and likeable and unaffected. Hypatia is a typical English girl of a sort never called typical: that is, she has an opaque white skin, black hair, large dark eyes with black brows and lashes, curved lips, swift glances and movements that flash out of a waiting stillness, boundless energy and audacity held in leash.

HYPATIA. [*pouncing on Bentley with no very gentle hand*] Bentley: whats the matter? Dont cry like that: whats the use? Whats happened?

MRS TARLETON. Are you ill, child? [*They get him up.*] There, there, pet! It's all right: dont cry [*they put him into a chair*]: there! there! there! Johnny will go for the doctor; and he'll give you something nice to make it well.

HYPATIA. What has happened, Johnny?

MRS TARLETON. Was it a wasp?

BENTLEY. [*impatiently*] Wasp be dashed!

MRS TARLETON. Oh Bunny! that was a naughty word.

BENTLEY. Yes, I know: I beg your pardon. [*He rises, and extricates himself from them*] Thats all right. Johnny frightened me. You know how easy it is to hurt me; and I'm too small to defend myself against Johnny.

MRS TARLETON. Johnny: how often have I told you that you must not bully the little ones. I thought youd outgrown all that.

HYPATIA. [*angrily*] I do declare, mamma, that Johnny's brutality makes it impossible to live in the house with him.

JOHNNY. [*deeply hurt*] It's twenty-seven years, mother, since you had that row with me for licking Robert and giving Hypatia a black eye because she bit me. I promised you then that I'd never raise my hand to one of them again; and Ive never broken my word. And now because this young whelp begins to cry out before he's hurt, you treat me as if I were a brute and a savage.

MRS TARLETON. No dear, not a savage; but you know you must not call our visitor naughty names.

BENTLEY. Oh, let him alone—

JOHNNY. [*fiercely*] Dont you interfere between my mother and me: d'y' hear?

HYPATIA. Johnny's lost his temper, mother. We'd better go. Come, Bentley.

MRS TARLETON. Yes: that will be best. [*To Bentley*] Johnny doesnt mean any harm, dear: he'll be himself presently. Come.

The two ladies go out through the inner door with Bentley, who turns at the door to grin at Johnny as he goes out.

Johnny, left alone, clenches his fists and grinds his teeth, but can find no relief in that way for his rage. After choking and stamping for a moment, he makes for the vestibule door. It opens before he reaches it; and Lord Summerhays comes in. Johnny glares at him, speechless. Lord Summerhays takes in the situation, and quickly takes the punchbowl from the sideboard and offers it to Johnny.

LORD SUMMERHAYS. Smash it. Dont hesitate: it's an ugly thing. Smash it: hard. [*Johnny, with a stifled yell, dashes it in pieces, and then sits down and mops his brow*]. Feel better now? [*Johnny nods*]. I know only one person alive who could drive me to the point of having either to break china or commit murder; and that person is my son Bentley. Was it he? [*Johnny nods again, not yet able to speak*]. As the car stopped I heard a yell which is only too familiar to me. It generally means that some infuriated person is trying to thrash Bentley. Nobody has ever succeeded, though almost everybody has tried. [*He seats himself comfortably close to the writing table, and sets to work to collect the fragments of the punchbowl in the wastepaper basket whilst Johnny, with diminishing difficulty, collects himself*]. Bentley is a problem which I confess I have never been able to solve. He was born to be a great success at the age of fifty. Most Englishmen of his class seem to be born to be great successes at the age of twenty-four at most. The domestic problem for me is how to endure Bentley until he is fifty. The problem for the nation is how to get itself governed by men whose growth is arrested when they are little more than college lads. Bentley doesnt really mean to be offensive. You can always make him cry by telling him you dont like him. Only, he cries so loud that the experiment should be made in the open air: in the middle of Salisbury Plain if possible. He has a hard and penetrating intellect and a remarkable power of looking facts in the face; but unfortunately, being very young, he has no idea of how very little of that sort of thing most of us can stand. On the other hand, he is frightfully sensitive and even affectionate; so that he probably gets as much as he gives in the way of hurt feelings. Youll excuse me rambling on like this about my son.

JOHNNY. [*who has pulled himself together*] You did it on purpose. I wasnt quite myself: I needed a moment to pull round: thank you.

LORD SUMMERHAYS. Not at all. Is your father at home?

JOHNNY. No: he's opening one of his free libraries. Thats another nice little penny gone. He's mad on reading. He promised another free library last week. It's ruinous. Itll hit you as well as me when Bunny marries Hypatia. When all Hypatia's money is thrown away on libraries, where will Bunny come in? Cant you stop him?

LORD SUMMERHAYS. I'm afraid not. Hes a perfect whirlwind. Indefatigable at public work. Wonderful man, I think.

JOHNNY. Oh, public work! He does too much of it. It's really a sort of laziness, getting away from your own serious business to amuse yourself with other people's. Mind: I dont say there isnt another side to it. It has its value as an advertisement. It makes useful acquaintances and leads to valuable business connections. But it takes his mind off the main chance; and he overdoes it.

LORD SUMMERHAYS. The danger of public business is that it never ends. A man may kill himself at it.

JOHNNY. Or he can spend more on it than it brings him in: thats how I look at it. What I say is that everybody's business is nobody's business. I hope I'm not a hard man, nor a narrow man, nor unwilling to pay reasonable taxes, and subscribe in reason to deserving charities, and even serve on a jury in my turn; and no man can say I ever refused to help a friend out of a difficulty when he was worth helping. But when you ask me to go beyond that, I tell you frankly I dont see it. I never did see it, even when I was only a boy, and had to pretend to take in all the ideas the Governor fed me up with. I didnt see it; and I dont see it.

LORD SUMMERHAYS. There is certainly no business reason why you should take more than your share of the world's work.

JOHNNY. So I say. It's really a great encouragement to me to find you agree with me. For of course if nobody agrees with you, how are you to know that youre not a fool?

LORD SUMMERHAYS. Quite so.

JOHNNY. I wish youd talk to him about it. It's no use my saying anything: I'm a child to him still: I have no influence. Besides, you know how to handle men. See how you handled me when I was making a fool of myself about Bunny!

LORD SUMMERHAYS. Not at all.

JOHNNY. Oh yes I was: I know I was. Well, if my blessed father had come in he'd have told me to control myself. As if I was losing my temper on purpose!

Bentley returns, newly washed. He beams when he sees his father, and comes affectionately behind him and pats him on the shoulders.

BENTLEY. Hel-lo, commander! have you come? Ive been making a filthy silly ass of myself here. I'm awfully sorry, Johnny, old chap: I beg your pardon. Why dont you kick me when I go on like that?

LORD SUMMERHAYS. As we came through Godalming I thought I heard some yelling—

BENTLEY. I should think you did. Johnny was rather rough on me, though. He told me nobody here liked me; and I was silly enough to believe him.

LORD SUMMERHAYS. And all the women have been kissing you and pitying you ever since to stop your crying, I suppose. Baby!

BENTLEY. I did cry. But I always feel good after crying: it relieves my wretched nerves. I feel perfectly jolly now.

LORD SUMMERHAYS. Not at all ashamed of yourself, for instance?

BENTLEY. If I started being ashamed of myself I shouldnt have time for anything else all my life. I say: I feel very fit and spry. Lets all go down and meet the Grand Cham. [*He goes to the hatstand and takes down his hat*].

LORD SUMMERHAYS. Does Mr Tarleton like to be called the Grand Cham, do you think, Bentley?

BENTLEY. Well, he thinks hes too modest for it. He calls himself Plain John. But you cant call him that in his own office: besides, it doesnt suit him: it's not flamboyant enough.

JOHNNY. Flam what?

BENTLEY. Flamboyant. Lets go and meet him. Hes telephoned from Guildford to say hes on the road. The dear old son is always telephoning or telegraphing: he thinks hes hustling along like anything when hes only sending unnecessary messages.

LORD SUMMERHAYS. Thank you: I should prefer a quiet afternoon.

BENTLEY. Right O. I shant press Johnny: hes had enough of me for one week-end. [*He goes out through the pavilion into the grounds*].

JOHNNY. Not a bad idea, that.

LORD SUMMERHAYS. What?

JOHNNY. Going to meet the Governor. You know you wouldnt think it; but the Governor likes Bunny rather. And Bunny is cultivating it. I shouldnt be surprised if he thought he could squeeze me out one of these days.

LORD SUMMERHAYS. You dont say so! Young rascal! I want to consult you about him, if you dont mind. Shall we stroll over to the Gibbet? Bentley is too fast for me as a walking companion; but I should like a short turn.

JOHNNY. [*rising eagerly, highly flattered*] Right you are. Thatll suit me down to the ground. [*He takes a Panama and stick from the hat stand*].

Mrs Tarleton and Hypatia come back just as the two men are going out. Hypatia salutes Summerhays from a distance with an enigmatic lift of her eyelids in his direction and a demure nod before she sits down at the worktable and busies herself with her needle. Mrs Tarleton, hospitably fussy, goes over to him.

MRS TARLETON. Oh, Lord Summerhays, I didnt know you were here. Wont you have some tea?

LORD SUMMERHAYS. No, thank you: I'm not allowed tea. And I'm ashamed to say Ive knocked over your beautiful punch-bowl. You must let me replace it.

MRS TARLETON. Oh, it doesnt matter: I'm only too glad to be rid of it. The shopman told me it was in the best taste; but when my poor old nurse Martha got cataract, Bunny said it was a merciful provision of Nature to prevent her seeing our china.

LORD SUMMERHAYS. [*gravely*] That was exceedingly rude of Bentley, Mrs Tarleton. I hope you told him so.

MRS TARLETON. Oh, bless you! I dont care what he says; so long as he says it to me and not before visitors.

JOHNNY. We're going out for a stroll, mother.

MRS TARLETON. All right: dont let us keep you. Never mind about that crock: I'll get the girl to come and take the pieces away. [*Recollecting herself*] There! Ive done it again!

JOHNNY. Done what?

MRS TARLETON. Called her the girl. You know, Lord Summerhays, its a funny thing; but now I'm getting old, I'm dropping back into all the ways John and I had when we had barely a hundred a year. You should have known me when I was forty! I talked like a duchess; and if Johnny or Hypatia let slip a word that was like old times, I was down on them like anything. And now I'm beginning to do it myself at every turn.

LORD SUMMERHAYS. There comes a time when all that seems to matter so little. Even queens drop the mask when they reach our time of life.

MRS TARLETON. Let you alone for giving a thing a pretty turn! Youre a humbug, you know, Lord Summerhays. John doesnt know it; and Johnny doesnt know it; but you and I know it, dont we? Now thats something that even you cant answer; so be off with you for your walk without another word.

Lord Summerhays smiles; bows; and goes out through the vestibule door, followed by Johnny. Mrs Tarleton sits down at the worktable and takes out her darning materials and one of her husband's socks. Hypatia is at the other side of the table, on her mother's right. They chat as they work.

HYPATIA. I wonder whether they laugh at us when they are by themselves!

MRS TARLETON. Who?

HYPATIA. Bentley and his father and all the toffs in their set.

MRS TARLETON. Oh, thats only their way. I used to think that the aristocracy were a nasty sneering lot, and that they were laughing at me and John. Theyre always giggling and pretending not to care much about anything. But you get used to it: theyre the same to one another and to everybody. Besides, what does it matter what they think? It's far worse when theyre civil, because that always means that they want you to lend them money; and you must never do that, Hypatia, because they never pay. How can they? They dont make anything, you see. Of course, if you can make up your mind to regard it as a gift, thats different; but then they generally ask you again; and you may as well say no first as last. You neednt be afraid of the aristocracy, dear: theyre only human creatures like ourselves after all; and youll hold your own with them easy enough.

HYPATIA. Oh, I'm not a bit afraid of them, I assure you.

MRS TARLETON. Well, no, not afraid of them, exactly; but youve got to pick up their ways. You know, dear, I never quite agreed with your father's notion of keeping clear of them, and sending you to a school that was so expensive that they couldnt afford to send their daughters there; so that all the girls belonged to big business families like ourselves. It takes all sorts to make a world; and I wanted you to see a little of all sorts. When you marry Bunny, and go among the women of his father's set, theyll shock you at first.

HYPATIA. [*incredulously*] How?

MRS TARLETON. Well, the things they talk about.

HYPATIA. Oh! scandalmongering?

MRS TARLETON. Oh no: we all do that: thats only human nature. But you know theyve no notion of decency. I shall never forget the first day I spent with a marchioness, two duchesses, and no end of Ladies This and That. Of course it was only a committee: theyd put me on to get a big subscription out of John. I'd never heard such talk in my life. The things they mentioned! And it was the marchioness that started it.

HYPATIA. What sort of things?

MRS TARLETON. Drainage!! She'd tried three systems in her castle; and she was going to do away with them all and try another. I didnt know which way to look when she began talking about it: I thought theyd all have got up and gone out of the room. But not a bit of it, if you please. They were all just as bad as she. They all had systems; and each of them swore by her own system. I sat there with my cheeks burning until one of the duchesses, thinking I looked out of it, I suppose, asked me what system I had. I said I was sure I knew nothing about such things, and hadnt we better change the subject. Then the fat was in the fire, I can tell you. There was a regular terror of a countess with an anaerobic system; and she told me, downright brutally, that I'd better learn something about them before my children died of diphtheria. That was just two months after I'd buried poor little Bobby; and that was the very thing he died of, poor little lamb! I burst out crying: I couldnt help it. It was as good as telling me I'd killed my own child. I had to go away; but before I was out of the door one of the duchesses—quite a young woman—began talking about what sour milk did in her inside and how she expected to live to be over a hundred if she took it regularly. And me listening to her, that had never dared to think that a duchess could have anything so common as an inside! I shouldnt have minded if it had been children's insides: we have to talk about them. But grown-up people! I was glad to get away that time.

HYPATIA. There was a physiology and hygiene class started at school; but of course none of our girls were let attend it.

MRS TARLETON. If it had been an aristocratic school plenty would have attended it. Thats what theyre like: theyve nasty minds. With really nice good women a thing is either decent or indecent; and if it's indecent, we just dont mention it or pretend to know about it; and theres an end of it. But all the aristocracy cares about is whether it can get any good out of the thing. Theyre what Johnny calls cynical-like. And of course nobody can say a word to them for it. Theyre so high up that they can do and say what they like.

HYPATIA. Well, I think they might leave the drains to their husbands. I shouldnt think much of a man that left such things to me.

MRS TARLETON. Oh, dont think that, dear, whatever you do. I never let on about it to you; but it's me that takes care of the drainage here. After what that countess said to me I wasnt going to lose another child or trust John. And I don't want my grandchildren to die any more than my children.

HYPATIA. Do you think Bentley will ever be as big a man as his father? I dont mean clever: I mean big and strong.

MRS TARLETON. Not he. Hes overbred, like one of those expensive little dogs. I like a bit of a mongrel myself, whether it's a man or a dog: theyre the best for everyday. But we all have our tastes: whats one woman's meat is another woman's poison. Bunny's a dear little fellow; but I never could have fancied him for a husband when I was your age.

HYPATIA. Yes; but he has some brains. Hes not like all the rest. One can't have everything.

MRS TARLETON. Oh, youre quite right, dear: quite right. It's a great thing to have brains: look what it's done for your father! Thats the reason I never said a word when you jilted poor Jerry Mackintosh.

HYPATIA. [*excusing herself*] I really couldnt stick it out with Jerry, mother. I know you liked him; and nobody can deny that hes a splendid animal—

MRS TARLETON. [*shocked*] Hypatia! How can you! The things that girls say nowadays!

HYPATIA. Well, what else can you call him? If I'd been deaf or he'd been dumb, I could have married him. But living with father, Ive got accustomed to cleverness. Jerry would drive me mad: you know very well hes a fool: even Johnny thinks him a fool.

MRS TARLETON. [*up in arms at once in defence of her boy*] Now dont begin about my Johnny. You know it annoys me. Johnny's as clever as anybody else in his own way. I dont say hes as clever as you in some ways; but hes a man, at all events, and not a little squit of a thing like your Bunny.

HYPATIA. Oh, I say nothing against your darling: we all know Johnny's perfection.

MRS TARLETON. Dont be cross, dearie. You let Johnny alone; and I'll let Bunny alone. I'm just as bad as you. There!

HYPATIA. Oh, I dont mind your saying that about Bentley. It's true. He is a little squit of a thing.

I wish he wasnt. But who else is there? Think of all the other chances Ive had! Not one of them has as much brains in his whole body as Bentley has in his little finger. Besides, theyve no distinction. It's as much as I can do to tell one from the other. They wouldnt even have money if they werent the sons of their fathers, like Johnny. Whats a girl to do? I never met anybody like Bentley before. He may be small; but hes the best of the bunch: you cant deny that.

MRS TARLETON. [*with a sigh*] Well, my pet, if you fancy him, theres no more to be said.

A pause follows this remark: the two women sewing silently.

HYPATIA. Mother: do you think marriage is as much a question of fancy as it used to be in your time and father's?

MRS TARLETON. Oh, it wasnt much fancy with me, dear: your father just wouldnt take no for an answer; and I was only too glad to be his wife instead of his shop-girl. Still, it's curious; but I had more choice than you in a way, because, you see, I was poor; and there are so many more poor men than rich ones that I might have had more of a pick, as you might say, if John hadnt suited me.

HYPATIA. I can imagine all sorts of men I could fall in love with; but I never seem to meet them. The real ones are too small, like Bunny, or too silly, like Jerry. Of course one can get into a state about any man: fall in love with him if you like to call it that. But who would risk marrying a man for love? *I* shouldnt. I remember three girls at school who agreed that the one man you should never marry was the man you were in love with, because it would make a perfect slave of you. Theres a sort of instinct against it, I think, thats just as strong as the other instinct. One of them, to my certain knowledge, refused a man she was in love with, and married another who was in love with her; and it turned out very well.

MRS TARLETON. Does all that mean that youre not in love with Bunny?

HYPATIA. Oh, how could anybody be in love with Bunny? I like him to kiss me just as I like a baby to kiss me. I'm fond of him; and he never bores me; and I see that hes very clever; but I'm not what you call gone about him, if thats what you mean.

MRS TARLETON. Then why need you marry him?

HYPATIA. What better can I do? I must marry somebody, I suppose. Ive realized that since I was twenty-three. I always used to take it as a matter of course that I should be married before I was twenty.

BENTLEY'S VOICE. [*in the garden*] Youve got to keep yourself fresh: to look at these things with an open mind.

JOHN TARLETON'S VOICE. Quite right, quite right: I always say so.

MRS TARLETON. Theres your father, and Bunny with him.

BENTLEY. Keep young. Keep your eye on me. Thats the tip for you.

Bentley and Mr Tarleton (an immense and genial veteran of trade) come into view and enter the pavilion.

JOHN TARLETON. You think youre young, do you? You think I'm old? [*energetically shaking off his motoring coat and hanging it up with his cap*].

BENTLEY. [*helping him with the coat*] Of course youre old. Look at your face and look at mine. What you call your youth is nothing but your levity. Why do we get on so well together? Because I'm a young cub and youre an old josser. [*He throws a cushion at Hypatia's feet and sits down on it with his back against her knees*].

TARLETON. Old! Thats all you know about it, my lad. How do, Patsy! [*Hypatia kisses him*]. How is my Chickabiddy? [*He kisses Mrs Tarleton's hand and poses expansively in the middle of the picture*]. Look at me! Look at these wrinkles, these gray hairs, this repulsive mask that you call old age! What is it? [*Vehemently*] I ask you, what is it?

BENTLEY. Jolly nice and venerable, old man. Dont be discouraged.

TARLETON. Nice? Not a bit of it. Venerable? Venerable be blowed! Read your Darwin, my boy. Read your Weismann. [*He goes to the sideboard for a drink of lemonade*].

MRS TARLETON. For shame, John! Tell him to read his Bible.

TARLETON. [*manipulating the syphon*] Whats the use of telling children to read the Bible when you know they wont. I was kept away from the Bible for forty years by being told to read it when I was young. Then I picked it up one evening in a hotel in Sunderland when I had left all my papers in the train; and I found it wasnt half bad. [*He drinks, and puts down the glass with a smack of enjoyment*]. Better than most halfpenny papers, anyhow, if only you could make people believe it. [*He sits down by the writing-table, near his wife*]. But if you want to understand old age scientifically, read Darwin and

Weismann. Of course if you want to understand it romantically, read about Solomon.

MRS TARLETON. Have you had tea, John?

TARLETON. Yes. Dont interrupt me when I'm improving the boy's mind. Where was I? This repulsive mask—Yes. [*Explosively*] What is death?

MRS TARLETON. John!

HYPATIA. Death is a rather unpleasant subject, papa.

TARLETON. Not a bit. Not scientifically. Scientifically it's a delightful subject. You think death's natural. Well, it isnt. You read Weismann. There wasnt any death to start with. You go look in any ditch outside and youll find swimming about there as fresh as paint some of the identical little live cells that Adam christened in the Garden of Eden. But if big things like us didnt die, we'd crowd one another off the face of the globe. Nothing survived, sir, except the sort of people that had the sense and good manners to die and make room for the fresh supplies. And so death was introduced by Natural Selection. You get it out of your head, my lad, that I'm going to die because I'm wearing out or decaying. Theres no such thing as decay to a vital man. I shall clear out; but I shant decay.

BENTLEY. And what about the wrinkles and the almond tree and the grasshopper that becomes a burden and the desire that fails?

TARLETON. Does it? by George! No, sir: it spiritualizes. As to your grasshopper, I can carry an elephant.

MRS TARLETON. You do say such things, Bunny! What does he mean by the almond tree?

TARLETON. He means my white hairs: the repulsive mask. That, my boy, is another invention of Natural Selection to disgust young women with me, and give the lads a turn.

MRS TARLETON. John: I wont have it. Thats a forbidden subject.

TARLETON. They talk of the wickedness and vanity of women painting their faces and wearing auburn wigs at fifty. But why shouldnt they? Why should a woman allow Nature to put a false mask of age on her when she knows that shes as young as ever? Why should she look in the glass and see a wrinkled lie when a touch of fine art will shew her a glorious truth? The wrinkles are a dodge to repel young men. Suppose she doesnt want to repel young men! Suppose she likes them!

MRS TARLETON. Bunny: take Hypatia out into the grounds for a walk: theres a good boy. John has got one of his naughty fits this evening.

HYPATIA. Oh, never mind me. I'm used to him.

BENTLEY. I'm not. I never heard such conversation: I cant believe my ears. And mind you, this is the man who objected to my marrying his daughter on the ground that a marriage between a member of the great and good middle class with one of the vicious and corrupt aristocracy would be a misalliance. A misalliance, if you please! This is the man Ive adopted as a father!

TARLETON. Eh! Whats that? Adopted me as a father, have you?

BENTLEY. Yes. Thats an idea of mine. I knew a chap named Joey Percival at Oxford (you know I was two months at Balliol before I was sent down for telling the old woman who was head of that silly college what I jolly well thought of him. He would have been glad to have me back, too, at the end of six months; but I wouldnt go: I just let him want; and serve him right!) Well, Joey was a most awfully clever fellow, and so nice! I asked him what made such a difference between him and all the other pups—they were pups, if you like. He told me it was very simple: they had only one father apiece; and he had three.

MRS TARLETON. Dont talk nonsense, child. How could that be?

BENTLEY. Oh, very simple. His father—

TARLETON. Which father?

BENTLEY. The first one: the regulation natural chap. He kept a tame philosopher in the house: a sort of Coleridge or Herbert Spencer kind of card, you know. That was the second father. Then his mother was an Italian princess; and she had an Italian priest always about. He was supposed to take charge of her conscience; but from what I could make out, she jolly well took charge of his. The whole three of them took charge of Joey's conscience. He used to hear them arguing like mad about everything. You see, the philosopher was a freethinker, and always believed the latest thing. The priest didnt believe anything, because it was sure to get him into trouble with someone or another. And the natural father kept an open mind and believed whatever paid him best. Between the lot of them Joey got cultivated no end. He said if he could only have had three mothers as well, he'd have backed himself against Napoleon.

TARLETON. [*impressed*] Thats an idea. Thats a most interesting idea: a most important idea.

MRS TARLETON. You always were one for ideas, John.

TARLETON. Youre right, Chickabiddy. What do I tell Johnny when he brags about Tarleton's Underwear? It's not the underwear. The underwear be hanged! Anybody can make underwear. Anybody can sell underwear. Tarleton's Ideas: thats whats done it. Ive often thought of putting that up over the shop.

BENTLEY. Take me into partnership when you do, old man. I'm wasted on the underwear; but I shall come in strong on the ideas.

TARLETON. You be a good boy; and perhaps I will.

MRS TARLETON. [*scenting a plot against her beloved Johnny*] Now, John: you promised—

TARLETON. Yes, yes. All right, Chickabiddy: dont fuss. Your precious Johnny shant be interfered with. [*Bouncing up, too energetic to sit still*] But I'm getting sick of that old shop. Thirty-five years Ive had of it: same blessed old stairs to go up and down every day: same old lot: same old game: sorry I ever started it now. I'll chuck it and try something else: something that will give a scope to all my faculties.

HYPATIA. Theres money in underwear: theres none in wild-cat ideas.

TARLETON. Theres money in me, madam, no matter what I go into.

MRS TARLETON. Dont boast, John. Dont tempt Providence.

TARLETON. Rats! You dont understand Providence. Providence likes to be tempted. Thats the secret of the successful man. Read Browning. Natural theology on an island, eh? Caliban was afraid to tempt Providence: that was why he was never able to get even with Prospero. What did Prospero do? Prospero didnt even tempt Providence: he was Providence. Thats one of Tarleton's ideas; and dont you forget it.

BENTLEY. You are full of beef today, old man.

TARLETON. Beef be blowed! Joy of life. Read Ibsen. [*He goes into the pavilion to relieve his restlessness, and stares out with his hands thrust deep in his pockets*].

HYPATIA. [*thoughtful*] Bentley: couldnt you invite your friend Mr Percival down here?

BENTLEY. Not if I know it. Youd throw me over the moment you set eyes on him.

MRS TARLETON. Oh, Bunny! For shame!

BENTLEY. Well, who'd marry me, dyou suppose, if they could get my brains with a full-sized body? No, thank you. I shall take jolly good care to keep Joey out of this until Hypatia is past praying for.

Johnny and Lord Summerhays return through the pavilion from their stroll.

TARLETON. Welcome! welcome! Why have you stayed away so long?

LORD SUMMERHAYS. [*shaking hands*] Yes: I should have come sooner. But I'm still rather lost in England. [*Johnny takes his hat and hangs it up beside his own*]. Thank you. [*Johnny returns to his swing and his novel. Lord Summerhays comes to the writing table*]. The fact is that as Ive nothing to do, I never have time to go anywhere. [*He sits down next Mrs Tarleton*].

TARLETON. [*following him and sitting down on his left*] Paradox, paradox. Good. Paradoxes are the only truths. Read Chesterton. But theres lots for you to do here. You have a genius for government. You learnt your job out there in Jinghiskahn. Well, we want to be governed here in England. Govern us.

LORD SUMMERHAYS. Ah yes, my friend; but in Jinghiskahn you have to govern the right way. If you dont, you go under and come home. Here everything has to be done the wrong way, to suit governors who understand nothing but partridge shooting (our English native princes, in fact) and voters who dont know what theyre voting about. I dont understand these democratic games; and I'm afraid I'm too old to learn. What can I do but sit in the window of my club, which consists mostly of retired Indian Civil servants? We look on at the muddle and the folly and amateurishness; and we ask each other where a single fortnight of it would have landed us.

TARLETON. Very true. Still, Democracy's all right, you know. Read Mill. Read Jefferson.

LORD SUMMERHAYS. Yes. Democracy reads well; but it doesnt act well, like some people's plays. No, no, my friend Tarleton: to make Democracy work, you need an aristocratic democracy. To make Aristocracy work, you need a democratic aristocracy. Youve got neither; and theres an end of it.

TARLETON. Still, you know, the superman may come. The superman's an idea. I believe in ideas. Read Whatshisname.

LORD SUMMERHAYS. Reading is a dangerous amusement, Tarleton. I wish I could persuade your free library people of that.

TARLETON. Why, man, it's the beginning of education.

LORD SUMMERHAYS. On the contrary, it's the end of it. How can you dare teach a man to read until youve taught him everything else first?

JOHNNY. [*intercepting his father's reply by coming out of the swing and taking the floor*] Leave it at that. Thats good sense. Anybody on for a game of tennis?

BENTLEY. Oh, lets have some more improving conversation. Wouldnt you rather, Johnny?

JOHNNY. If you ask me, no.

TARLETON. Johnny: you dont cultivate your mind. You dont read.

JOHNNY. [*coming between his mother and Lord Summerhays, book in hand*] Yes I do. I bet you what you like that, page for page, I read more than you, though I dont talk about it so much. Only, I dont read the same books. I like a book with a plot in it. You like a book with nothing in it but some idea that the chap that writes it keeps worrying, like a cat chasing its own tail. I can stand a little of it, just as I can stand watching the cat for two minutes, say, when Ive nothing better to do. But a man soon gets fed up with that sort of thing. The fact is, you look on an author as a sort of god. *I* look on him as a man that I pay to do a certain thing for me. I pay him to amuse me and to take me out of myself and make me forget.

TARLETON. No. Wrong principle. You want to remember. Read Kipling. "Lest we forget."

JOHNNY. If Kipling wants to remember, let him remember. If he had to run Tarleton's Underwear, he'd be jolly glad to forget. As he has a much softer job, and wants to keep himself before the public, his cry is, "Dont you forget the sort of things I'm rather clever at writing about." Well, I dont blame him: it's his business: I should do the same in his place. But what he wants and what I want are two different things. I want to forget; and I pay another man to make me forget. If I buy a book or go to the theatre, I want to forget the shop and forget myself from the moment I go in to the moment I come out. Thats what I pay my money for. And if I find that the author's simply getting at me the whole time, I consider that hes obtained my money under false pretences. I'm not a morbid crank: I'm a natural man; and, as such, I dont like being got at. If a man in my employment did it, I should sack him. If a member of my club did it, I should cut him. If he went too far with it, I should bring his conduct before the committee. I might even punch his head, if it came to that. Well, who and what is an author that he should be privileged to take liberties that are not allowed to other men?

MRS TARLETON. You see, John! What have I always told you? Johnny has as much to say for himself as anybody when he likes.

JOHNNY. I'm no fool, mother, whatever some people may fancy. I dont set up to have as many ideas as the Governor; but what ideas I have are consecutive, at all events. I can think as well as talk.

BENTLEY. [*to Tarleton, chuckling*] Had you there, old man, hadnt he? You are rather all over the shop with your ideas, aint you?

JOHNNY. [*handsomely*] I'm not saying anything against you, Governor. But I do say that the time has come for sane, healthy, unpretending men like me to make a stand against this conspiracy of the writing and talking and artistic lot to put us in the back row. It isnt a fact that we're inferior to them: it's a put-up job; and it's they that have put the job up. It's we that run the country for them; and all the thanks we get is to be told we're Philistines and vulgar tradesmen and sordid city men and so forth, and that theyre all angels of light and leading. The time has come to assert ourselves and put a stop to their stuck-up nonsense. Perhaps if we had nothing better to do than talking or writing, we could do it better than they. Anyhow, theyre the failures and refuse of business (hardly a man of them that didnt begin in an office) and we're the successes of it. Thank God I havnt failed yet at anything; and I dont believe I should fail at literature if it would pay me to turn my hand to it.

BENTLEY. Hear, hear!

MRS TARLETON. Fancy you writing a book, Johnny! Do you think he could, Lord Summerhays?

LORD SUMMERHAYS. Why not? As a matter of fact all the really prosperous authors I have met since my return to England have been very like him.

TARLETON. [*again impressed*] Thats an idea. Thats a new idea. I believe I ought to have made Johnny an author. Ive never said so before for fear of hurting his feelings, because, after all, the lad cant help it; but Ive never thought Johnny worth tuppence as a man of business.

JOHNNY. [*sarcastic*] Oh! You think youve always kept that to yourself, do you, Governor? I know your opinion of me as well as you know it yourself. It takes one man of business to appreciate another; and you arnt, and you never have been, a real man of business. I know where Tarleton's would have been three of four times if it hadnt been for me. [*With a snort and a nod to emphasize the implied warning, he retreats to the Turkish bath, and lolls against it with an air of good-humoured indifference*].

TARLETON. Well, who denies it? Youre quite right, my boy. I don't mind confessing to you all that the circumstances that condemned me to keep a shop are the biggest tragedy in modern life. I ought to have been a writer. I'm essentially a man of ideas. When I was a young man I sometimes used to pray that I might fail, so that I should be justified in giving up business and doing something: something first-class. But it was no good: I couldnt fail. I said to myself that if I could only once go to my Chickabiddy here and shew her a chartered accountant's statement proving that I'd made 20 pounds less than last year, I could ask her to let me chance Johnny's and Hypatia's future by going into literature. But it was no good. First it was 250 pounds more than last year. Then it was 700 pounds. Then it was 2000 pounds. Then I saw it was no use: Prometheus was chained to his rock: read Shelley: read Mrs Browning. Well, well, it was not to be. [*He rises solemnly*]. Lord Summerhays: I ask you to excuse me for a few moments. There are times when a man needs to meditate in solitude on his destiny. A chord is touched; and he sees the drama of his life as a spectator sees a play. Laugh if you feel inclined: no man sees the comic side of it more than I. In the theatre of life everyone may be amused except the actor. [*Brightening*] Theres an idea in this: an idea for a picture. What a pity young Bentley is not a painter! Tarleton meditating on his destiny. Not in a toga. Not in the trappings of the tragedian or the philosopher. In plain coat and trousers: a man like any other man. And beneath that coat and trousers a human soul. Tarleton's Underwear! [*He goes out gravely into the vestibule*].

MRS TARLETON. [*fondly*] I suppose it's a wife's partiality, Lord Summerhays; but I do think John is really great. I'm sure he was meant to be a king. My father looked down on John, because he was a rate collector, and John kept a shop. It hurt his pride to have to borrow money so often from John; and he used to console himself by saying, "After all, he's only a linendraper." But at last one day he said to me, "John is a king."

BENTLEY. How much did he borrow on that occasion?

LORD SUMMERHAYS. [*sharply*] Bentley!

MRS TARLETON. Oh, dont scold the child: he'd have to say something like that if it was to be his last word on earth. Besides, hes quite right: my poor father had asked for his usual five pounds; and John gave him a hundred in his big way. Just like a king.

LORD SUMMERHAYS. Not at all. I had five kings to manage in Jinghiskahn; and I think you do your husband some injustice, Mrs Tarleton. They pretended to like me because I kept their brothers from murdering them; but I didnt like them. And I like Tarleton.

MRS TARLETON. Everybody does. I really must go and make the cook do him a Welsh rabbit. He expects one on special occasions. [*She goes to the inner door*]. Johnny: when he comes back ask him where we're to put that new Turkish bath. Turkish baths are his latest. [*She goes out*].

JOHNNY. [*coming forward again*] Now that the Governor has given himself away, and the old lady's gone, I'll tell you something, Lord Summerhays. If you study men whove made an enormous pile in business without being keen on money, youll find that they all have a slate off. The Governor's a wonderful man; but hes not quite all there, you know. If you notice, hes different from me; and whatever my failings may be, I'm a sane man. Erratic: thats what he is. And the danger is that some day he'll give the whole show away.

LORD SUMMERHAYS. Giving the show away is a method like any other method. Keeping it to yourself is only another method. I should keep an open mind about it.

JOHNNY. Has it ever occurred to you that a man with an open mind must be a bit of a scoundrel? If you ask me, I like a man who makes up his mind once for all as to whats right and whats wrong and then sticks to it. At all events you know where to have him.

LORD SUMMERHAYS. That may not be his object.

BENTLEY. He may want to have you, old chap.

JOHNNY. Well, let him. If a member of my club wants to steal my umbrella, he knows where to find it. If a man put up for the club who had an open mind on the subject of property in umbrellas, I should blackball him. An open mind is all very well in clever talky-talky; but in conduct and in business give me solid ground.

LORD SUMMERHAYS. Yes: the quicksands make life difficult. Still, there they are. It's no use pretending theyre rocks.

JOHNNY. I dont know. You can draw a line and make other chaps toe it. Thats what I call morality.

LORD SUMMERHAYS. Very true. But you dont make any progress when youre toeing a line.

HYPATIA. [*suddenly, as if she could bear no more of it*] Bentley: do go and play tennis with Johnny. You must take exercise.

LORD SUMMERHAYS. Do, my boy, do. [*To Johnny*] Take him out and make him skip about.

BENTLEY. [*rising reluctantly*] I promised you two inches more round my chest this summer. I tried exercises with an indiarubber expander; but I wasnt strong enough: instead of my expanding it, it crumpled me up. Come along, Johnny.

JOHNNY. Do you no end of good, young chap. [*He goes out with Bentley through the pavilion*].

Hypatia throws aside her work with an enormous sigh of relief.

LORD SUMMERHAYS. At last!

HYPATIA. At last. Oh, if I might only have a holiday in an asylum for the dumb. How I envy the animals! They cant talk. If Johnny could only put back his ears or wag his tail instead of laying down the law, how much better it would be! We should know when he was cross and when he was pleased; and thats all we know now, with all his talk. It never stops: talk, talk, talk, talk. Thats my life. All the day I listen to mamma talking; at dinner I listen to papa talking; and when papa stops for breath I listen to Johnny talking.

LORD SUMMERHAYS. You make me feel very guilty. I talk too, I'm afraid.

HYPATIA. Oh, I dont mind that, because your talk is a novelty. But it must have been dreadful for your daughters.

LORD SUMMERHAYS. I suppose so.

HYPATIA. If parents would only realize how they bore their children! Three or four times in the last half hour Ive been on the point of screaming.

LORD SUMMERHAYS. Were we very dull?

HYPATIA. Not at all: you were very clever. Thats whats so hard to bear, because it makes it so difficult to avoid listening. You see, I'm young; and I do so want something to happen. My mother tells me that when I'm her age, I shall be only too glad that nothing's happened; but I'm not her age; so what good is that to me? Theres my father in the garden, meditating on his destiny. All very well for him: hes had a destiny to meditate on; but I havnt had any destiny yet. Everything's happened to him: nothing's happened to me. Thats why this unending talk is so maddeningly uninteresting to me.

LORD SUMMERHAYS. It would be worse if we sat in silence.

HYPATIA. No it wouldnt. If you all sat in silence, as if you were waiting for something to happen, then there would be hope even if nothing did happen. But this eternal cackle, cackle, cackle about things in general is only fit for old, old, OLD people. I suppose it means something to them: theyve had their fling. All I listen for is some sign of it ending in something; but just when it seems to be coming to a point, Johnny or papa just starts another hare; and it all begins over again; and I realize that it's never going to lead anywhere and never going to stop. Thats when I want to scream. I wonder how you can stand it.

LORD SUMMERHAYS. Well, I'm old and garrulous myself, you see. Besides, I'm not here of my own free will, exactly. I came because you ordered me to come.

HYPATIA. Didnt you want to come?

LORD SUMMERHAYS. My dear: after thirty years of managing other people's business, men lose the habit of considering what they want or dont want.

HYPATIA. Oh, dont begin to talk about what men do, and about thirty years experience. If you cant get off that subject, youd better send for Johnny and papa and begin it all over again.

LORD SUMMERHAYS. I'm sorry. I beg your pardon.

HYPATIA. I asked you, didnt you want to come?

LORD SUMMERHAYS. I did not stop to consider whether I wanted or not, because when I read your letter I knew I had to come.

HYPATIA. Why?

LORD SUMMERHAYS. Oh come, Miss Tarleton! Really, really! Dont force me to call you a blackmailer to your face. You have me in your power; and I do what you tell me very obediently. Dont ask me to pretend I do it of my own free will.

HYPATIA. I dont know what a blackmailer is. I havnt even that much experience.

LORD SUMMERHAYS. A blackmailer, my dear young lady, is a person who knows a disgraceful secret in the life of another person, and extorts money from that other person by threatening to make his secret public unless the money is paid.

HYPATIA. I havnt asked you for money.

LORD SUMMERHAYS. No; but you asked me to come down here and talk to you; and you mentioned casually that if I didnt youd have nobody to talk about me to but Bentley. That was a threat, was it not?

HYPATIA. Well, I wanted you to come.

LORD SUMMERHAYS. In spite of my age and my unfortunate talkativeness?

HYPATIA. I like talking to you. I can let myself go with you. I can say things to you I cant say to other people.

LORD SUMMERHAYS. I wonder why?

HYPATIA. Well, you are the only really clever, grown-up, high-class, experienced man I know who has given himself away to me by making an utter fool of himself with me. You cant wrap yourself up in your toga after that. You cant give yourself airs with me.

LORD SUMMERHAYS. You mean you can tell Bentley about me if I do.

HYPATIA. Even if there wasnt any Bentley: even if you didnt care (and I really dont see why you should care so much) still, we never could be on conventional terms with one another again. Besides, Ive got a feeling for you: almost a ghastly sort of love for you.

LORD SUMMERHAYS. [*shrinking*] I beg you—no, please.

HYPATIA. Oh, it's nothing at all flattering: and, of course, nothing wrong, as I suppose youd call it.

LORD SUMMERHAYS. Please believe that I know that. When men of my age—

HYPATIA. [*impatiently*] Oh, do talk about yourself when you mean yourself, and not about men of your age.

LORD SUMMERHAYS. I'll put it as bluntly as I can. When, as you say, I made an utter fool of myself, believe me, I made a poetic fool of myself. I was seduced, not by appetites which, thank Heaven, Ive long outlived: not even by the desire of second childhood for a child companion, but by the innocent impulse to place the delicacy and wisdom and spirituality of my age at the affectionate service of your youth for a few years, at the end of which you would be a grown, strong, formed—widow. Alas, my dear, the delicacy of age reckoned, as usual, without the derision and cruelty of youth. You told me that you didnt want to be an old man's nurse, and that you didnt want to have undersized children like Bentley. It served me right: I dont reproach you: I was an old fool. But how you can imagine, after that, that I can suspect you of the smallest feeling for me except the inevitable feeling of early youth for late age, or imagine that I have any feeling for you except one of shrinking humiliation, I cant understand.

HYPATIA. I dont blame you for falling in love with me. I shall be grateful to you all my life for it, because that was the first time that anything really interesting happened to me.

LORD SUMMERHAYS. Do you mean to tell me that nothing of that kind had ever happened before? that no man had ever—

HYPATIA. Oh, lots. Thats part of the routine of life here: the very dullest part of it. The young man who comes a-courting is as familiar an incident in my life as coffee for breakfast. Of course, hes too much of a gentleman to misbehave himself; and I'm too much of a lady to let him; and hes shy and sheepish; and I'm correct and self-possessed; and at last, when I can bear it no longer, I either frighten him off, or give him a chance of proposing, just to see how he'll do it, and refuse him because he does it in the same silly way as all the rest. You dont call that an event in one's life, do you? With you it was different. I should as soon have expected the North Pole to fall in love with me as you. You know I'm only a linen-draper's daughter when all's said. I was afraid of you: you, a great man! a lord! and older than my father. And then what a situation it was! Just think of it! I was engaged to your son; and you knew nothing about it. He was afraid to tell you: he brought you down here because he thought if he could throw us together I could get round you because I was such a ripping girl. We arranged it all: he and I. We got Papa and Mamma and Johnny out of the way splendidly; and then Bentley took himself off, and left us—you and me!—to take a walk through the heather and admire the scenery of Hindhead. You never dreamt that it was all a plan: that what made me so nice was the way I was playing up to my destiny as the sweet girl that was to make your boy happy. And then! and then! [*She rises to dance and clap her hands in her glee*].

LORD SUMMERHAYS. [*shuddering*] Stop, stop. Can no woman understand a man's delicacy?

HYPATIA. [*revelling in the recollection*] And then—ha, ha!—you proposed. You! A father! For your son's girl!

LORD SUMMERHAYS. Stop, I tell you. Dont profane what you dont understand.

HYPATIA. That was something happening at last with a vengeance. It was splendid. It was my first peep behind the scenes. If I'd been seventeen I should have fallen in love with you. Even as it is, I feel quite differently towards you from what I do towards other old men. So [*offering her hand*] you may kiss my hand if that will be any fun for you.

LORD SUMMERHAYS. [*rising and recoiling to the table, deeply revolted*] No, no, no. How dare you? [*She laughs mischievously*]. How callous youth is! How coarse! How cynical! How ruthlessly cruel!

HYPATIA. Stuff! It's only that youre tired of a great many things Ive never tried.

LORD SUMMERHAYS. It's not alone that. Ive not forgotten the brutality of my own boyhood. But do try to learn, glorious young beast that you are, that age is squeamish, sentimental, fastidious. If you cant understand my holier feelings, at least you know the bodily infirmities of the old. You know that I darent eat all the rich things you gobble up at every meal; that I cant bear the noise and racket and clatter that affect you no more than they affect a stone. Well, my soul is like that too. Spare it: be gentle with it [*he involuntarily puts out his hands to plead: she takes them with a laugh*]. If you could possibly think of me as half an angel and half an invalid, we should get on much better together.

HYPATIA. We get on very well, I think. Nobody else ever called me a glorious young beast. I like that. Glorious young beast expresses exactly what I like to be.

LORD SUMMERHAYS. [*extricating his hands and sitting down*] Where on earth did you get these morbid tastes? You seem to have been well brought up in a normal, healthy, respectable, middle-class family. Yet you go on like the most unwholesome product of the rankest Bohemianism.

HYPATIA. Thats just it. I'm fed up with—

LORD SUMMERHAYS. Horrible expression. Dont.

HYPATIA. Oh, I daresay it's vulgar; but theres no other word for it. I'm fed up with nice things: with respectability, with propriety! When a woman has nothing to do, money and respectability mean that nothing is ever allowed to happen to her. I dont want to be good; and I dont want to be bad: I just dont want to be bothered about either good or bad: I want to be an active verb.

LORD SUMMERHAYS. An active verb? Oh, I see. An active verb signifies to be, to do, or to suffer.

HYPATIA. Just so: how clever of you! I want to be; I want to do; and I'm game to suffer if it costs that. But stick here doing nothing but being good and nice and ladylike I simply wont. Stay down here with us for a week; and I'll shew you what it means: shew it to you going on day after day, year after year, lifetime after lifetime.

LORD SUMMERHAYS. Shew me what?

HYPATIA. Girls withering into ladies. Ladies withering into old maids. Nursing old women. Running errands for old men. Good for nothing else at last. Oh, you cant imagine the fiendish selfishness of the old people and the maudlin sacrifice of the young. It's more unbearable than any poverty: more horrible than any regular-right-down wickedness. Oh, home! home! parents! family! duty! how I loathe them! How I'd like to see them all blown to bits! The poor escape. The wicked escape. Well, I cant be poor: we're rolling in money: it's no use pretending we're not. But I can be wicked; and I'm quite prepared to be.

LORD SUMMERHAYS. You think that easy?

HYPATIA. Well, isnt it? Being a man, you ought to know.

LORD SUMMERHAYS. It requires some natural talent, which can no doubt be cultivated. It's not really easy to be anything out of the common.

HYPATIA. Anyhow, I mean to make a fight for living.

LORD SUMMERHAYS. Living your own life, I believe the Suffragist phrase is.

HYPATIA. Living any life. Living, instead of withering without even a gardener to snip you off when youre rotten.

LORD SUMMERHAYS. Ive lived an active life; but Ive withered all the same.

HYPATIA. No: youve worn out: thats quite different. And youve some life in you yet or you wouldnt have fallen in love with me. You can never imagine how delighted I was to find that instead of being the correct sort of big panjandrum you were supposed to be, you were really an old rip like papa.

LORD SUMMERHAYS. No, no: not about your father: I really cant bear it. And if you must say these terrible things: these heart-wounding shameful things, at least find something prettier to call me than an old rip.

HYPATIA. Well, what would you call a man proposing to a girl who might be—

LORD SUMMERHAYS. His daughter: yes, I know.

HYPATIA. I was going to say his granddaughter.

LORD SUMMERHAYS. You always have one more blow to get in.

HYPATIA. Youre too sensitive. Did you ever make mud pies when you were a kid—beg pardon: a child.

LORD SUMMERHAYS. I hope not.

HYPATIA. It's a dirty job; but Johnny and I were vulgar enough to like it. I like young people because theyre not too afraid of dirt to live. Ive grown out of the mud pies; but I like slang; and I like bustling you up by saying things that shock you; and I'd rather put up with swearing and smoking than with dull respectability; and there are lots of things that would just shrivel you up that I think rather jolly. Now!

LORD SUMMERHAYS. Ive not the slightest doubt of it. Dont insist.

HYPATIA. It's not your ideal, is it?

LORD SUMMERHAYS. No.

HYPATIA. Shall I tell you why? Your ideal is an old woman. I daresay shes got a young face; but shes an old woman. Old, old, old. Squeamish. Cant stand up to things. Cant enjoy things: not real things. Always on the shrink.

LORD SUMMERHAYS. On the shrink! Detestable expression.

HYPATIA. Bah! you cant stand even a little thing like that. What good are you? Oh, what good are you?

LORD SUMMERHAYS. Dont ask me. I dont know. I dont know.

Tarleton returns from the vestibule. Hypatia sits down demurely.

HYPATIA. Well, papa: have you meditated on your destiny?

TARLETON. [*puzzled*] What? Oh! my destiny. Gad, I forgot all about it: Jock started a rabbit and put it clean out of my head. Besides, why should I give way to morbid introspection? It's a sign of madness. Read Lombroso. [*To Lord Summerhays*] Well, Summerhays, has my little girl been entertaining you?

LORD SUMMERHAYS. Yes. She is a wonderful entertainer.

TARLETON. I think my idea of bringing up a young girl has been rather a success. Dont you listen to this, Patsy: it might make you conceited. Shes never been treated like a child. I always said the same thing to her mother. Let her read what she likes. Let her do what she likes. Let her go where she likes. Eh, Patsy?

HYPATIA. Oh yes, if there had only been anything for me to do, any place for me to go, anything I wanted to read.

TARLETON. There, you see! Shes not satisfied. Restless. Wants things to happen. Wants adventures to drop out of the sky.

HYPATIA. [*gathering up her work*] If youre going to talk about me and my education, I'm off.

TARLETON. Well, well, off with you. [*To Lord Summerhays*] Shes active, like me. She actually wanted me to put her into the shop.

HYPATIA. Well, they tell me that the girls there have adventures sometimes. [*She goes out through the inner door*]

TARLETON. She had me there, though she doesnt know it, poor innocent lamb! Public scandal exaggerates enormously, of course; but moralize as you will, superabundant vitality is a physical fact that cant be talked away. [*He sits down between the writing table and the sideboard*]. Difficult question this, of bringing up children. Between ourselves, it has beaten me. I never was so surprised in my life as when I came to know Johnny as a man of business and found out what he was really like. How did you manage with your sons?

LORD SUMMERHAYS. Well, I really hadnt time to be a father: thats the plain truth of the matter. Their poor dear mother did the usual thing while they were with us. Then of course, Harrow, Cambridge, the usual routine of their class. I saw very little of them, and thought very little about them: how could I? with a whole province on my hands. They and I are—acquaintances. Not perhaps, quite ordinary acquaintances: theres a sort of—er—I should almost call it a sort of remorse about the way we shake hands (when we do shake hands) which means, I suppose, that we're sorry we dont care more for one another; and I'm afraid we dont meet oftener than we can help. We put each other too much out of countenance. It's really a very difficult relation. To my mind not altogether a natural one.

TARLETON. [*impressed, as usual*] Thats an idea, certainly. I dont think anybody has ever written about that.

LORD SUMMERHAYS. Bentley is the only one who was really my son in any serious sense. He was completely spoilt. When he was sent to a preparatory school he simply yelled until he was sent home. Harrow was out of the question; but we managed to tutor him into Cambridge. No use: he was sent down. By that time my work was over; and I saw a good deal of him. But I could do nothing with him—except look on. I should have thought your case was quite different. You keep up the middle-class tradition: the day school and the business training instead of the university. I believe in the day school part of it. At all events, you know your own children.

TARLETON. Do you? I'm not so sure of it. Fact is, my dear Summerhays, once childhood is over, once the little animal has got past the stage at which it acquires what you might call a sense of decency, it's all up with the relation between parent and child. You cant get over the fearful shyness of it.

LORD SUMMERHAYS. Shyness?

TARLETON. Yes, shyness. Read Dickens.

LORD SUMMERHAYS [*surprised*] Dickens!! Of all authors, Charles Dickens! Are you serious?

TARLETON. I dont mean his books. Read his letters to his family. Read any man's letters to his children. Theyre not human. Theyre not about himself or themselves. Theyre about hotels, scenery, about the weather, about getting wet and losing the train and what he saw on the road and all that. Not a word about himself. Forced. Shy. Duty letters. All fit to be published: that says everything. I tell you theres a wall ten feet thick and ten miles high between parent and child. I know what I'm talking about. Ive girls in my employment: girls and young men. I had ideas on the subject. I used to go to the parents and tell them not to let their children go out into the world without instruction in the dangers and temptations they were going to be thrown into. What did every one of the mothers say to me? "Oh, sir, how could I speak of such things to my own daughter?" The men said I was quite right; but they didnt do it, any more than I'd been able to do it myself to Johnny. I had to leave books in his way; and I felt just awful when I did it. Believe me, Summerhays, the relation between the young and the old should be an innocent relation. It should be something they could talk about. Well, the relation between parent and child may be an affectionate relation. It may be a useful relation. It may be a necessary relation. But it can never be an innocent relation. Youd die rather than allude to it. Depend on it, in a thousand years itll be considered bad form to know who your father and mother are. Embarrassing. Better hand Bentley over to me. I can look him in the face and talk to him as man to man. You can have Johnny.

LORD SUMMERHAYS. Thank you. Ive lived so long in a country where a man may have fifty sons, who are no more to him than a regiment of soldiers, that I'm afraid Ive lost the English feeling about it.

TARLETON. [*restless again*] You mean Jinghiskahn. Ah yes. Good thing the empire. Educates us. Opens our minds. Knocks the Bible out of us. And civilizes the other chaps.

LORD SUMMERHAYS. Yes: it civilizes them. And it uncivilizes us. Their gain. Our loss, Tarleton, believe me, our loss.

TARLETON. Well, why not? Averages out the human race. Makes the nigger half an Englishman. Makes the Englishman half a nigger.

LORD SUMMERHAYS. Speaking as the unfortunate Englishman in question, I dont like the process. If I had my life to live over again, I'd stay at home and supercivilize myself.

TARLETON. Nonsense! dont be selfish. Think how youve improved the other chaps. Look at the Spanish empire! Bad job for Spain, but splendid for South America. Look at what the Romans did for Britain! They burst up and had to clear out; but think of all they taught us! They were the making of us: I believe there was a Roman camp on Hindhead: I'll shew it to you tomorrow. Thats the good side of Imperialism: it's unselfish. I despise the Little Englanders: theyre always thinking about England. Smallminded. I'm for the Parliament of man, the federation of the world. Read Tennyson. [*He settles down again*]. Then theres the great food question.

LORD SUMMERHAYS. [*apprehensively*] Need we go into that this afternoon?

TARLETON. No; but I wish youd tell the Chickabiddy that the Jinghiskahns eat no end of toasted cheese, and that it's the secret of their amazing health and long life!

LORD SUMMERHAYS. Unfortunately they are neither healthy nor long lived. And they dont eat toasted cheese.

TARLETON. There you are! They would be if they ate it. Anyhow, say what you like, provided the moral is a Welsh rabbit for my supper.

LORD SUMMERHAYS. British morality in a nutshell!

TARLETON. [*hugely amused*] Yes. Ha ha! Awful hypocrites, aint we?

They are interrupted by excited cries from the grounds.

HYPATIA. Papa! Mamma! Come out as fast
BENTLEY. as you can. Quick. Quick.
Hello, governor! Come out. An aeroplane. Look, look.

TARLETON. [*starting up*] Aeroplane! Did he say an aeroplane?

LORD SUMMERHAYS. Aeroplane! [*A shadow falls on the pavilion; and some of the glass at the top is shattered and falls on the floor*].

Tarleton and Lord Summerhays rush out through the pavilion into the garden.

HYPATIA. Take care. Take care of the
BENTLEY. chimney.

TARLETON. Come this side: it's coming

LORD SUMMERHAYS	right where youre standing. Hallo! where the devil are you coming? youll have my roof off. He's lost control.

MRS TARLETON. Look, look, Hypatia. There are two people in it.

BENTLEY. Theyve cleared it. Well steered!

TARLETON.	Yes; but theyre coming slam into the greenhouse.
LORD SUMMERHAYS	Look out for the glass.
MRS TARLETON.	Theyll break all the glass. Theyll spoil all the grapes.
BENTLEY.	Mind where youre coming. He'll save it. No: theyre down.

An appalling crash of breaking glass is heard. Everybody shrieks.

MRS TARLETON.	Oh, are they killed? John: are they killed?
LORD SUMMERHAYS	Are you hurt? Is anything broken? Can you stand?
HYPATIA.	Oh, you must be hurt. Are you sure? Shall I get you some water? Or some wine?
TARLETON.	Are you all right? Sure you wont have some brandy just to take off the shock.

THE AVIATOR. No, thank you. Quite right. Not a scratch. I assure you I'm all right.

BENTLEY. What luck! And what a smash! You are a lucky chap, I can tell you.

The Aviator and Tarleton come in through the pavilion, followed by Lord Summerhays and Bentley, the Aviator on Tarleton's right. Bentley passes the Aviator and turns to have an admiring look at him. Lord Summerhays overtakes Tarleton less pointedly on the opposite side with the same object.

THE AVIATOR. I'm really very sorry. I'm afraid Ive knocked your vinery into a cocked hat. (*Effusively*) You dont mind, do you?

TARLETON. Not a bit. Come in and have some tea. Stay to dinner. Stay over the week-end. All my life Ive wanted to fly.

THE AVIATOR. [*taking off his goggles*] Youre really more than kind.

BENTLEY. Why, its Joey Percival.

PERCIVAL. Hallo, Ben! That you?

TARLETON. What! The man with three fathers!

PERCIVAL. Oh! has Ben been talking about me?

TARLETON. Consider yourself as one of the family—if you will do me the honor. And your friend too. Wheres your friend?

PERCIVAL. Oh, by the way! before he comes in: let me explain. I dont know him.

TARLETON. Eh?

PERCIVAL. Havnt even looked at him. I'm trying to make a club record with a passenger. The club supplied the passenger. He just got in; and Ive been too busy handling the aeroplane to look at him. I havnt said a word to him; and I cant answer for him socially; but hes an ideal passenger for a flyer. He saved me from a smash.

LORD SUMMERHAYS. I saw it. It was extraordinary. When you were thrown out he held on to the top bar with one hand. You came past him in the air, going straight for the glass. He caught you and turned you off into the flower bed, and then lighted beside you like a bird.

PERCIVAL. How he kept his head I cant imagine. Frankly, *I* didnt.

The Passenger, also begoggled, comes in through the pavilion with Johnny and the two ladies. The Passenger comes between Percival and Tarleton, Mrs Tarleton between Lord Summerhays and her husband, Hypatia between Percival and Bentley, and Johnny to Bentley's right.

TARLETON. Just discussing your prowess, my dear sir. Magnificent. Youll stay to dinner. Youll stay the night. Stay over the week. The Chickabiddy will be delighted.

MRS TARLETON. Wont you take off your goggles and have some tea?

The Passenger begins to remove the goggles.

TARLETON. Do. Have a wash. Johnny: take the gentleman to your room: I'll look after Mr Percival. They must—

By this time the passenger has got the goggles off, and stands revealed as a remarkably good-looking woman.

MRS TARLETON.	Well I never!!!	[*All together*]
BENTLEY.	[*in a whisper*] Oh, I say!	
JOHNNY.	By George!	
LORD SUMMERHAYS	A lady!	
HYPATIA.	A woman!	
TARLETON.	[*to Percival*] You never told me—	

PERCIVAL. I hadnt the least idea—

An embarrassed pause.

PERCIVAL. I assure you if I'd had the faintest notion that my passenger was a lady I shouldnt have left you to shift for yourself in that selfish way.

LORD SUMMERHAYS. The lady seems to have shifted for both very effectually, sir.

PERCIVAL. Saved my life. I admit it most gratefully.

TARLETON. I must apologize, madam, for having offered you the civilities appropriate to the opposite sex. And yet, why opposite? We are all human: males and females of the same species. When the dress is the same the distinction vanishes. I'm proud to receive in my house a lady of evident refinement and distinction. Allow me to introduce myself: Tarleton: John Tarleton (*seeing conjecture in the passenger's eye*)—yes, yes: Tarleton's Underwear. My wife, Mrs Tarleton: youll excuse me for having in what I had taken to be a confidence between man and man alluded to her as the Chickabiddy. My daughter Hypatia, who has always wanted some adventure to drop out of the sky, and is now, I hope, satisfied at last. Lord Summerhays: a man known wherever the British flag waves. His son Bentley, engaged to Hypatia. Mr Joseph Percival, the promising son of three highly intellectual fathers.

HYPATIA. [*startled*] Bentley's friend? [*Bentley nods*].

TARLETON. [*continuing, to the passenger*] May I now ask to be allowed the pleasure of knowing your name?

THE PASSENGER. My name is Lina Szczepanowska [*pronouncing it Sh-Chepanovska*].

PERCIVAL. Sh— I beg your pardon?

LINA. Szczepanowska.

PERCIVAL. [*dubiously*] Thank you.

TARLETON. [*very politely*] Would you mind saying it again?

LINA. Say fish.

TARLETON. Fish.

LINA. Say church.

TARLETON. Church.

LINA. Say fish church.

TARLETON. [*remonstrating*] But it's not good sense.

LINA. [*inexorable*] Say fish church.

TARLETON. Fish church.

LINA. Again.

TARLETON. No, but—[*resigning himself*] fish church.

LINA. Now say Szczepanowska.

TARLETON. Szczepanowska. Got it, by Gad. [*A sibilant whispering becomes audible: they are all saying Sh-ch to themselves*]. Szczepanowska! Not an English name, is it?

LINA. Polish. I'm a Pole.

TARLETON. Ah yes. Interesting nation. Lucky people to get the government of their country taken off their hands. Nothing to do but cultivate themselves. Same as we took Gibraltar off the hands of the Spaniards. Saves the Spanish taxpayer. Jolly good thing for us if the Germans took Portsmouth. Sit down, wont you?

The group breaks up. Johnny and Bentley hurry to the pavilion and fetch the two wicker chairs. Johnny gives his to Lina. Hypatia and Percival take the chairs at the worktable. Lord Summerhays gives the chair at the vestibule end of the writing table to Mrs Tarleton; and Bentley replaces it with a wicker chair, which Lord Summerhays takes. Johnny remains standing behind the worktable, Bentley behind his father.

MRS TARLETON. [*to Lina*] Have some tea now, wont you?

LINA. I never drink tea.

TARLETON. [*sitting down at the end of the writing table nearest Lina*] Bad thing to aeroplane on, I should imagine. Too jumpy. Been up much?

LINA. Not in an aeroplane. Ive parachuted; but thats child's play.

MRS TARLETON. But arnt you very foolish to run such a dreadful risk?

LINA. You cant live without running risks.

MRS TARLETON. Oh, what a thing to say! Didnt you know you might have been killed?

LINA. That was why I went up.

HYPATIA. Of course. Cant you understand the fascination of the thing? the novelty! the daring! the sense of something happening!

LINA. Oh no. It's too tame a business for that. I went up for family reasons.

TARLETON. Eh? What? Family reasons?

MRS TARLETON. I hope it wasnt to spite your mother?

PERCIVAL. [*quickly*] Or your husband?

LINA. I'm not married. And why should I want to spite my mother?

HYPATIA. [*aside to Percival*] That was clever of you, Mr Percival.

PERCIVAL. What?

HYPATIA. To find out.

TARLETON. I'm in a difficulty. I cant understand a lady going up in an aeroplane for family reasons. It's rude to be curious and ask questions; but then it's inhuman to be indifferent, as if you didnt care.

LINA. I'll tell you with pleasure. For the last hundred and fifty years, not a single day has passed without some member of my family risking his life—or her life. It's a point of honor with us to keep up that tradition. Usually several of us do it; but it happens that just at this moment it is being kept up by one of my brothers only. Early this morning I got a telegram from him to say that there had been a fire, and that he could do nothing for the rest of the week. Fortunately I had an invitation from the Aerial League to see this gentleman try to break the passenger record. I appealed to the President of the League to let me save the honor of my family. He arranged it for me.

TARLETON. Oh, I must be dreaming. This is stark raving nonsense.

LINA. [*quietly*] You are quite awake, sir.

JOHNNY. We cant all be dreaming the same thing, Governor.

TARLETON. Of course not, you duffer; but then I'm dreaming you as well as the lady.

MRS TARLETON. Dont be silly, John. The lady is only joking, I'm sure. [*To Lina*] I suppose your luggage is in the aeroplane.

PERCIVAL. Luggage was out of the question. If I stay to dinner I'm afraid I cant change unless youll lend me some clothes.

MRS TARLETON. Do you mean neither of you?

PERCIVAL. I'm afraid so.

MRS TARLETON. Oh well, never mind: Hypatia will lend the lady a gown.

LINA. Thank you: I'm quite comfortable as I am. I am not accustomed to gowns: they hamper me and make me feel ridiculous; so if you dont mind I shall not change.

MRS TARLETON. Well, I'm beginning to think I'm doing a bit of dreaming myself.

HYPATIA. [*impatiently*] Oh, it's all right, mamma. Johnny: look after Mr. Percival. [*To Lina, rising*] Come with me.

Lina follows her to the inner door. They all rise.

JOHNNY. [*to Percival*] I'll shew you.

PERCIVAL. Thank you.

Lina goes out with Hypatia, and Percival with Johnny.

MRS TARLETON. Well, this is a nice thing to happen! And look at the greenhouse! Itll cost thirty pounds to mend it. People have no right to do such things. And you invited them to dinner too! What sort of woman is that to have in our house when you know that all Hindhead will be calling on us to see that aeroplane? Bunny: come with me and help me to get all the people out of the grounds: I declare they came running as if theyd sprung up out of the earth [*she makes for the inner door*].

TARLETON. No: dont you trouble, Chickabiddy: I'll tackle em.

MRS TARLETON. Indeed youll do nothing of the kind: youll stay here quietly with Lord Summerhays. Youd invite them all to dinner. Come, Bunny. [*She goes out, followed by Bentley. Lord Summerhays sits down again*].

TARLETON. Singularly beautiful woman Summerhays. What do you make of her? She must be a princess. Whats this family of warriors and statesmen that risk their lives every day?

LORD SUMMERHAYS. They are evidently not warriors and statesmen, or they wouldnt do that.

TARLETON. Well, then, who the devil are they?

LORD SUMMERHAYS. I think I know. The last time I saw that lady, she did something I should not have thought possible.

TARLETON. What was that?

LORD SUMMERHAYS. Well, she walked backwards along a taut wire without a balancing pole and turned a somersault in the middle. I remember that her name was Lina, and that the other name was foreign; though I dont recollect it.

TARLETON. Szcz! You couldnt have forgotten that if youd heard it.

LORD SUMMERHAYS. I didnt hear it: I only saw it on a program. But it's clear shes an acrobat. It explains how she saved Percival. And it accounts for her family pride.

TARLETON. An acrobat, eh? Good, good, good! Summerhays: that brings her within reach. Thats better than a princess. I steeled this evergreen heart of mine when I thought she was a princess. Now I shall let it be touched. She is accessible. Good.

LORD SUMMERHAYS. I hope you are not serious. Remember: you have a family. You have a position. You are not in your first youth.

TARLETON. No matter.

Theres magic in the night When the heart is young.

My heart is young. Besides, I'm a married man, not a widower like you. A married man can do anything he likes if his wife dont mind. A widower cant be too careful. Not that I would have you think me an unprincipled man or a bad husband. I'm not. But Ive a superabundance of vitality. Read Pepys' Diary.

LORD SUMMERHAYS. The woman is your guest, Tarleton.

TARLETON. Well, is she? A woman I bring into my house is my guest. A woman you bring into my house is my guest. But a woman who drops bang down out of the sky into my greenhouse and smashes every blessed pane of glass in it must take her chance.

LORD SUMMERHAYS. Still, you know that my name must not be associated with any scandal. Youll be careful, wont you?

TARLETON. Oh Lord, yes. Yes, yes, yes, yes, yes. I was only joking, of course.

Mrs Tarleton comes back through the inner door.

MRS TARLETON. Well I never! John: I dont think that young woman's right in her head. Do you know what shes just asked for?

TARLETON. Champagne?

MRS TARLETON. No. She wants a Bible and six oranges.

TARLETON. What?

MRS TARLETON. A Bible and six oranges.

TARLETON. I understand the oranges: shes doing an orange cure of some sort. But what on earth does she want the Bible for?

MRS TARLETON. I'm sure I cant imagine. She cant be right in her head.

LORD SUMMERHAYS. Perhaps she wants to read it.

MRS TARLETON. But why should she, on a weekday, at all events. What would you advise me to do, Lord Summerhays?

LORD SUMMERHAYS. Well, is there a Bible in the house?

TARLETON. Stacks of em. Theres the family Bible, and the Dore Bible, and the parallel revised version Bible, and the Doves Press Bible, and Johnny's Bible and Bobby's Bible and Patsy's Bible, and the Chickabiddy's Bible and my Bible; and I daresay the servants could raise a few more between them. Let her have the lot.

MRS TARLETON. Dont talk like that before Lord Summerhays, John.

LORD SUMMERHAYS. It doesnt matter, Mrs Tarleton: in Jinghiskahn it was a punishable offence to expose a Bible for sale. The empire has no religion.

Lina comes in. She has left her cap in Hypatia's room. She stops on the landing just inside the door, and speaks over the handrail.

LINA. Oh, Mrs Tarleton, shall I be making myself very troublesome if I ask for a music-stand in my room as well?

TARLETON. Not at all. You can have the piano if you like. Or the gramophone. Have the gramophone.

LINA. No, thank you: no music.

MRS TARLETON. [*going to the steps*] Do you think it's good for you to eat so many oranges? Arnt you afraid of getting jaundice?

LINA. [*coming down*] Not in the least. But billiard balls will do quite as well.

MRS TARLETON. But you cant eat billiard balls, child!

TARLETON. Get em, Chickabiddy. I understand. [*He imitates a juggler tossing up balls*]. Eh?

LINA. [*going to him, past his wife*] Just so.

TARLETON. Billiard balls and cues. Plates, knives, and forks. Two paraffin lamps and a hatstand.

LINA. No: that is popular low-class business. In our family we touch nothing but classical work. Anybody can do lamps and hatstands. *I* can do silver bullets. That is really hard. [*She passes on to Lord Summerhays, and looks gravely down at him as he sits by the writing table*].

MRS TARLETON. Well, I'm sure I dont know what youre talking about; and I only hope you know yourselves. However, you shall have what you want, of course. [*She goes up the steps and leaves the room*].

LORD SUMMERHAYS. Will you forgive my curiosity? What is the Bible for?

LINA. To quiet my soul.

LORD SUMMERHAYS [*with a sigh*] Ah yes, yes. It no longer quiets mine, I am sorry to say.

LINA. That is because you do not know how to read it. Put it up before you on a stand; and open it at the Psalms. When you can read them and understand them, quite quietly and happily, and keep six balls in the air all the time, you are in perfect condition; and youll never make a mistake that evening. If you find you cant do that, then go and pray until you can. And be very careful that evening.

LORD SUMMERHAYS. Is that the usual form of test in your profession?

LINA. Nothing that we Szczepanowskis do is usual, my lord.

LORD SUMMERHAYS. Are you all so wonderful?

LINA. It is our profession to be wonderful.

LORD SUMMERHAYS. Do you never condescend to do as common people do? For instance, do you not pray as common people pray?

LINA. Common people do not pray, my lord: they only beg.

LORD SUMMERHAYS. You never ask for anything?

LINA. No.

LORD SUMMERHAYS. Then why do you pray?

LINA. To remind myself that I have a soul.

TARLETON. [*walking about*] True. Fine. Good. Beautiful. All this damned materialism: what good is it to anybody? Ive got a soul: dont tell me I havnt. Cut me up and you cant find it. Cut up a steam engine and you cant find the steam. But, by George, it makes the engine go. Say what you will, Summerhays, the divine spark is a fact.

LORD SUMMERHAYS. Have I denied it?

TARLETON. Our whole civilization is a denial of it. Read Walt Whitman.

LORD SUMMERHAYS. I shall go to the billiard room and get the balls for you.

LINA. Thank you.

Lord Summerhays goes out through the vestibule door.

TARLETON. [*going to her*] Listen to me. [*She turns quickly*]. What you said just now was beautiful. You touch chords. You appeal to the poetry in a man. You inspire him. Come now! Youre a woman of the world: youre independent: you must have driven lots of men crazy. You know the sort of man I am, dont you? See through me at a glance, eh?

LINA. Yes. [*She sits down quietly in the chair Lord Summerhays has just left*].

TARLETON. Good. Well, do you like me? Dont misunderstand me: I'm perfectly aware that youre not going to fall in love at first sight with a ridiculous old shopkeeper. I cant help that ridiculous old shopkeeper. I have to carry him about with me whether I like it or not. I have to pay for his clothes, though I hate the cut of them: especially the waistcoat. I have to look at him in the glass while I'm shaving. I loathe him because hes a living lie. My soul's not like that: it's like yours. I want to make a fool of myself. About you. Will you let me?

LINA. [*very calm*] How much will you pay?

TARLETON. Nothing. But I'll throw as many sovereigns as you like into the sea to shew you that I'm in earnest.

LINA. Are those your usual terms?

TARLETON. No. I never made that bid before.

LINA. [*producing a dainty little book and preparing to write in it*] What did you say your name was?

TARLETON. John Tarleton. The great John Tarleton of Tarleton's Underwear.

LINA. [*writing*] T-a-r-l-e-t-o-n. Er—? [*She looks up at him inquiringly*].

TARLETON. [*promptly*] Fifty-eight.

LINA. Thank you. I keep a list of all my offers. I like to know what I'm considered worth.

TARLETON. Let me look.

LINA. [*offering the book to him*] It's in Polish.

TARLETON. Thats no good. Is mine the lowest offer?

LINA. No: the highest.

TARLETON. What do most of them come to? Diamonds? Motor cars? Furs? Villa at Monte Carlo?

LINA. Oh yes: all that. And sometimes the devotion of a lifetime.

TARLETON. Fancy that! A young man offering a woman his old age as a temptation!

LINA. By the way, you did not say how long.

TARLETON. Until you get tired of me.

LINA. Or until you get tired of me?

TARLETON. I never get tired. I never go on long enough for that. But when it becomes so grand, so inspiring that I feel that everything must be an anti-climax after that, then I run away.

LINA. Does she let you go without a struggle?

TARLETON. Yes. Glad to get rid of me. When love takes a man as it takes me—when it makes him great—it frightens a woman.

LINA. The lady here is your wife, isnt she? Dont you care for her?

TARLETON. Yes. And mind! she comes first always. I reserve her dignity even when I sacrifice my own. Youll respect that point of honor, wont you?

LINA. Only a point of honor?

TARLETON. [*impulsively*] No, by God! a point of affection as well.

LINA. [*smiling, pleased with him*] Shake hands, old pal [*she rises and offers him her hand frankly*].

TARLETON. [*giving his hand rather dolefully*] Thanks. That means no, doesnt it?

LINA. It means something that will last longer than yes. I like you. I admit you to my friendship. What a pity you were not trained when you were young! Youd be young still.

TARLETON. I suppose, to an athlete like you, I'm pretty awful, eh?

LINA. Shocking.

TARLETON. Too much crumb. Wrinkles. Yellow patches that wont come off. Short wind. I know. I'm ashamed of myself. I could do nothing on the high rope.

LINA. Oh yes: I could put you in a wheelbarrow and run you along, two hundred feet up.

TARLETON. [*shuddering*] Ugh! Well, I'd do even that for you. Read The Master Builder.

LINA. Have you learnt everything from books?

TARLETON. Well, have you learnt everything from the flying trapeze?

LINA. On the flying trapeze there is often another woman; and her life is in your hands every night and your life in hers.

TARLETON. Lina: I'm going to make a fool of myself. I'm going to cry [*he crumples into the nearest chair*].

LINA. Pray instead: dont cry. Why should you cry? Youre not the first I've said no to.

TARLETON. If you had said yes, should I have been the first then?

LINA. What right have you to ask? Have I asked am *I* the first?

TARLETON. Youre right: a vulgar question. To a man like me, everybody is the first. Life renews itself.

LINA. The youngest child is the sweetest.

TARLETON. Dont probe too deep, Lina. It hurts.

LINA. You must get out of the habit of thinking that these things matter so much. It's linendraperish.

TARLETON. Youre quite right. Ive often said so. All the same, it does matter; for I want to cry. [*He buries his face in his arms on the work-table and sobs*].

LINA. [*going to him*] O la la! [*She slaps him vigorously, but not unkindly, on the shoulder*]. Courage, old pal, courage! Have you a gymnasium here?

TARLETON. Theres a trapeze and bars and things in the billiard room.

LINA. Come. You need a few exercises. I'll teach you how to stop crying. [*She takes his arm and leads him off into the vestibule*].

A young man, cheaply dressed and strange in manner, appears in the garden; steals to the pavilion door; and looks in. Seeing that there is nobody, he enters cautiously until he has come far enough to see into the hatstand corner. He draws a revolver, and examines it, apparently to make sure that it is loaded. Then his attention is caught by the Turkish bath. He looks down the lunette, and opens the panels.

HYPATIA. [*calling in the garden*] Mr Percival! Mr Percival! Where are you?

The young man makes for the door, but sees Percival coming. He turns and bolts into the Turkish bath, which he closes upon himself just in time to escape being caught by Percival, who runs in through the pavilion, bareheaded. He also, it appears, is in search of a hiding-place; for he stops and turns between the two tables to take a survey of the room; then runs into the corner between the end of the sideboard and the wall. Hypatia, excited, mischievous, her eyes glowing, runs in, precisely on his trail; turns at the same spot; and discovers him just as he makes a dash for the pavilion door. She flies back and intercepts him.

HYPATIA. Aha! arnt you glad Ive caught you?

PERCIVAL. [*illhumoredly turning away from her and coming towards the writing table*] No I'm not. Confound it, what sort of girl are you? What sort of house is this? Must I throw all good manners to the winds?

HYPATIA. [*following him*] Do, do, do, do, do. This is the house of a respectable shopkeeper, enormously rich. This is the respectable shopkeeper's daughter, tired of good manners. [*Slipping her left hand into his right*] Come, handsome young man, and play with the respectable shopkeeper's daughter.

PERCIVAL. [*withdrawing quickly from her touch*] No, no: dont you know you mustnt go on like this with a perfect stranger?

HYPATIA. Dropped down from the sky. Dont you know that you must always go on like this when you get the chance? You must come to the top of the hill and chase me through the bracken. You may kiss me if you catch me.

PERCIVAL. I shall do nothing of the sort.

HYPATIA. Yes you will: you cant help yourself. Come along. [*She seizes his sleeve*]. Fool, fool: come along. Dont you want to?

PERCIVAL. No: certainly not. I should never be forgiven if I did it.

HYPATIA. Youll never forgive yourself if you dont.

PERCIVAL. Nonsense. Youre engaged to Ben. Ben's my friend. What do you take me for?

HYPATIA. Ben's old. Ben was born old. Theyre all old here, except you and me and the man-woman or woman-man or whatever you call her that came with you. They never do anything: they only discuss whether what other people do is right. Come and give them something to discuss.

PERCIVAL. I will do nothing incorrect.

HYPATIA. Oh, dont be afraid, little boy: youll get nothing but a kiss; and I'll fight like the devil to keep you from getting that. But we must play on the hill and race through the heather.

PERCIVAL. Why?

HYPATIA. Because we want to, handsome young man.

PERCIVAL. But if everybody went on in this way—

HYPATIA. How happy! oh how happy the world would be!

PERCIVAL. But the consequences may be serious.

HYPATIA. Nothing is worth doing unless the consequences may be serious. My father says so; and I'm my father's daughter.

PERCIVAL. I'm the son of three fathers. I mistrust these wild impulses.

HYPATIA. Take care. Youre letting the moment slip. I feel the first chill of the wave of prudence. Save me.

PERCIVAL. Really, Miss Tarleton [*she strikes him across the face*] —Damn you! [*Recovering himself, horrified at his lapse*] I beg your pardon; but since weve both forgotten ourselves, youll please allow me to leave the house. [*He turns towards the inner door, having left his cap in the bedroom*].

HYPATIA. [*standing in his way*] Are you ashamed of having said "Damn you" to me?

PERCIVAL. I had no right to say it. I'm very much ashamed of it. I have already begged your pardon.

HYPATIA. And youre not ashamed of having said "Really, Miss Tarleton."

PERCIVAL. Why should I?

HYPATIA. O man, man! mean, stupid, cowardly, selfish masculine male man! You ought to have been a governess. I was expelled from school for saying that the very next person that said "Really, Miss Tarleton," to me, I would strike her across the face. You were the next.

PERCIVAL. I had no intention of being offensive. Surely there is nothing that can wound any lady in—[*He hesitates, not quite convinced*]. At least—er—I really didnt mean to be disagreeable.

HYPATIA. Liar.

PERCIVAL. Of course if youre going to insult me, I am quite helpless. Youre a woman: you can say what you like.

HYPATIA. And you can only say what you dare. Poor wretch: it isnt much. [*He bites his lip, and sits down, very much annoyed*]. Really, Mr Percival! You sit down in the presence of a lady and leave her standing. [*He rises hastily*]. Ha, ha! Really, Mr Percival! Oh really, really, really, really, really, Mr Percival! How do you like it? Wouldnt you rather I damned you?

PERCIVAL. Miss Tarleton—

HYPATIA. [*caressingly*] Hypatia, Joey. Patsy, if you like.

PERCIVAL. Look here: this is no good. You want to do what you like?

HYPATIA. Dont you?

PERCIVAL. No. Ive been too well brought up. Ive argued all through this thing; and I tell you I'm not prepared to cast off the social bond. It's like a corset: it's a support to the figure even if it does squeeze and deform it a bit. I want to be free.

HYPATIA. Well, I'm tempting you to be free.

PERCIVAL. Not at all. Freedom, my good girl, means being able to count on how other people will behave. If every man who dislikes me is to throw a handful of mud in my face, and every woman who likes me is to behave like Potiphar's wife, then I shall be a slave: the slave of uncertainty: the slave of fear: the worst of all slaveries. How would you like it if every laborer you met in the road were to make love to you? No. Give me the blessed protection of a good stiff conventionality among thoroughly well-brought up ladies and gentlemen.

HYPATIA. Another talker! Men like conventions because men made them. I didnt make them: I dont like them: I wont keep them. Now, what will you do?

PERCIVAL. Bolt. [*He runs out through the pavilion*].

HYPATIA. I'll catch you. [*She dashes off in pursuit*].

During this conversation the head of the scandalized man in the Turkish bath has repeatedly risen from the lunette, with a strong expression of moral shock. It vanishes abruptly as the two turn towards it in their flight. At the same moment Tarleton comes back through the vestibule door, exhausted by severe and unaccustomed exercise.

TARLETON. [*looking after the flying figures with amazement*] Hallo, Patsy: whats up? Another aeroplane? [*They are far too preoccupied to hear him; and he is left staring after them as they rush away through the garden. He goes to the pavilion door and looks up; but the heavens are empty. His exhaustion disables him from further inquiry. He dabs his brow with his handkerchief, and walks stiffly to the nearest convenient support, which happens to be the Turkish bath. He props himself upon it with his elbow, and covers his eyes with his hand for a moment. After a few sighing breaths, he feels a little better, and uncovers his eyes. The man's head rises from the lunette a few inches from his nose. He recoils from the bath with a violent start*]. Oh Lord! My brain's gone. [*Calling piteously*] Chickabiddy! [*He staggers down to the writing table*].

THE MAN. [*coming out of the bath, pistol in hand*] Another sound; and youre a dead man.

TARLETON. [*braced*] Am I? Well, youre a live one: thats one comfort. I thought you were a ghost. [*He sits down, quite undisturbed by the pistol*] Who are you; and what the devil were you doing in my new Turkish bath?

THE MAN. [*with tragic intensity*] I am the son of Lucinda Titmus.

TARLETON. [*the name conveying nothing to him*] Indeed? And how is she? Quite well, I hope, eh?

THE MAN. She is dead. Dead, my God! and youre alive.

TARLETON. [*unimpressed by the tragedy, but sympathetic*] Oh! Lost your mother? Thats sad. I'm sorry. But we cant all have the luck to survive our mothers, and be nursed out of the world by the hands that nursed us into it.

THE MAN. Much you care, damn you!

TARLETON. Oh, dont cut up rough. Face it like a man. You see I didnt know your mother; but Ive no doubt she was an excellent woman.

THE MAN. Not know her! Do you dare to stand there by her open grave and deny that you knew her?

TARLETON. [*trying to recollect*] What did you say her name was?

THE MAN. Lucinda Titmus.

TARLETON. Well, I ought to remember a rum name like that if I ever heard it. But I dont. Have you a photograph or anything?

THE MAN. Forgotten even the name of your victim!

TARLETON. Oh! she was my victim, was she?

THE MAN. She was. And you shall see her face again before you die, dead as she is. I have a photograph.

TARLETON. Good.

THE MAN. Ive two photographs.

TARLETON. Still better. Treasure the mother's pictures. Good boy!

THE MAN. One of them as you knew her. The other as she became when you flung her aside, and she withered into an old woman.

TARLETON. She'd have done that anyhow, my lad. We all grow old. Look at me! [*Seeing that the man is embarrassed by his pistol in fumbling for the photographs with his left hand in his breast pocket*] Let me hold the gun for you.

THE MAN. [*retreating to the worktable*] Stand back. Do you take me for a fool?

TARLETON. Well, youre a little upset, naturally. It does you credit.

THE MAN. Look here, upon this picture and on this. [*He holds out the two photographs like a hand at cards, and points to them with the pistol*].

TARLETON. Good. Read Shakespear: he has a word for every occasion. [*He takes the photographs, one in each hand, and looks from one to the other, pleased and interested, but without any sign of recognition*] What a pretty girl! Very pretty. I can imagine myself falling in love with her when I was your age. I wasnt a bad-looking young fellow myself in those days. [*Looking at the other*] Curious that we should both have gone the same way.

THE MAN. You and she the same way! What do you mean?

TARLETON. Both got stout, I mean.

THE MAN. Would you have had her deny herself food?

TARLETON. No: it wouldnt have been any use. It's constitutional. No matter how little you eat you put on flesh if youre made that way. [*He resumes his study of the earlier photograph*].

THE MAN. Is that all the feeling that rises in you at the sight of the face you once knew so well?

TARLETON. [*too much absorbed in the portrait to heed him*] Funny that I cant remember! Let this be a lesson to you, young man. I could go into court tomorrow and swear I never saw that face before in my life if it wasnt for that brooch [*pointing to the photograph*]. Have you got that brooch, by the way? [*The man again resorts to his breast pocket*]. You seem to carry the whole family property in that pocket.

THE MAN. [*producing a brooch*] Here it is to prove my bona fides.

TARLETON. [*pensively putting the photographs on the table and taking the brooch*] I bought that brooch in Cheapside from a man with a yellow wig and a cast in his left eye. Ive never set eyes on him from that day to this. And yet I remember that man; and I cant remember your mother.

THE MAN. Monster! Without conscience! without even memory! You left her to her shame—

TARLETON. [*throwing the brooch on the table and rising pepperily*] Come, come, young man! none of that. Respect the romance of your mother's youth. Dont you start throwing stones at her. I dont recall her features just at this moment; but Ive no doubt she was kind to me and we were happy together. If you have a word to say against her, take yourself out of my house and say it elsewhere.

THE MAN. What sort of a joker are you? Are you trying to put me in the wrong, when you have to answer to me for a crime that would make every honest man spit at you as you passed in the street if I were to make it known?

TARLETON. You read a good deal, dont you?

THE MAN. What if I do? What has that to do with your infamy and my mother's doom?

TARLETON. There, you see! Doom! Thats not good sense; but it's literature. Now it happens that I'm a tremendous reader: always was. When I was your age I read books of that sort by the bushel: the Doom sort, you know. It's odd, isnt it, that you and I should be like one another in that respect? Can you account for it in any way?

THE MAN. No. What are you driving at?

TARLETON. Well, do you know who your father was?

THE MAN. I see what you mean now. You dare set up to be my father. Thank heaven Ive not a drop of your vile blood in my veins.

TARLETON. [*sitting down again with a shrug*] Well, if you wont be civil, theres no pleasure in talking to you, is there? What do you want? Money?

THE MAN. How dare you insult me?

TARLETON. Well, what do you want?

THE MAN. Justice.

TARLETON. Youre quite sure thats all?

THE MAN. It's enough for me.

TARLETON. A modest sort of demand, isnt it? Nobody ever had it since the world began, fortunately for themselves; but you must have it, must you? Well, youve come to the wrong shop for it: youll get no justice here: we dont keep it. Human nature is what we stock.

THE MAN. Human nature! Debauchery! gluttony! selfishness! robbery of the poor! Is that what you call human nature?

TARLETON. No: thats what you call it. Come, my lad! Whats the matter with you? You dont look starved; and youve a decent suit of clothes.

THE MAN. Forty-two shillings.

TARLETON. They can do you a very decent suit for forty-two shillings. Have you paid for it?

THE MAN. Do you take me for a thief? And do you suppose I can get credit like you?

TARLETON. Then you were able to lay your hand on forty-two shillings. Judging from your conversational style, I should think you must spend at least a shilling a week on romantic literature.

THE MAN. Where would I get a shilling a week to spend on books when I can hardly keep myself decent? I get books at the Free Library.

TARLETON [*springing to his feet*] What!!!

THE MAN. [*recoiling before his vehemence*] The Free Library. Theres no harm in that.

TARLETON. Ingrate! I supply you with free books; and the use you make of them is to persuade yourself that it's a fine thing to shoot me. [*He throws himself doggedly back into his chair*]. I'll never give another penny to a Free Library.

THE MAN. Youll never give another penny to anything. This is the end: for you and me.

TARLETON. Pooh! Come, come, man! talk business. Whats wrong? Are you out of employment?

THE MAN. No. This is my Saturday afternoon. Dont flatter yourself that I'm a loafer or a criminal. I'm a cashier; and I defy you to say that my cash has ever been a farthing wrong. Ive a right to call you to account because my hands are clean.

TARLETON. Well, call away. What have I to account for? Had you a hard time with your mother? Why didnt she ask me for money?

THE MAN. She'd have died first. Besides, who wanted your money? Do you suppose we lived in the gutter? My father maynt have been in as large a way as you; but he was better connected; and his shop was as respectable as yours.

TARLETON. I suppose your mother brought him a little capital.

THE MAN. I dont know. Whats that got to do with you?

TARLETON. Well, you say she and I knew one another and parted. She must have had something off me then, you know. One doesnt get out of these things for nothing. Hang it, young man: do you suppose Ive no heart? Of course she had her due; and she found a husband with it, and set him up in business with it, and brought you up respectably; so what the devil have you to complain of?

THE MAN. Are women to be ruined with impunity?

TARLETON. I havnt ruined any woman that I'm aware of. Ive been the making of you and your mother.

THE MAN. Oh, I'm a fool to listen to you and argue with you. I came here to kill you and then kill myself.

TARLETON. Begin with yourself, if you dont mind. Ive a good deal of business to do still before I die. Havnt you?

THE MAN. No. Thats just it: Ive no business to do. Do you know what my life is? I spend my days from nine to six—nine hours of daylight and fresh air—in a stuffy little den counting another man's money. Ive an intellect: a mind and a brain and a soul; and the use he makes of them is to fix them on his tuppences and his eighteenpences and his two pound seventeen and tenpences and see how much they come to at the end of the day and take care that no one steals them. I enter and enter, and add and add, and take money and give change, and fill cheques and stamp receipts; and not a penny of that money is my own: not one of those transactions has the smallest interest for me or anyone else in the world but him; and even he couldnt stand it if he had to do it all himself. And I'm envied: aye, envied for the variety and liveliness of my job, by the poor devil of a bookkeeper that has to copy all my entries over again. Fifty thousand entries a year that poor wretch makes; and not ten out of the fifty thousand ever has to be referred to again; and when all the figures are counted up and the balance sheet made out, the boss isnt a penny the richer than he'd be if bookkeeping had never been invented. Of all the damnable waste of human life that ever was invented, clerking is the very worst.

TARLETON. Why not join the territorials?

THE MAN. Because I shouldnt be let. He hasnt even the sense to see that it would pay him to get some cheap soldiering out of me. How can a man tied to a desk from nine to six be anything—be even a man, let alone a soldier? But I'll teach him and you a lesson. Ive had enough of living a dog's life and despising myself for it. Ive had enough of being talked down to by hogs like you, and wearing my life out for a salary that wouldnt keep you in cigars. Youll never believe that a clerk's a man until one of us makes an example of one of you.

TARLETON. Despotism tempered by assassination, eh?

THE MAN. Yes. Thats what they do in Russia. Well, a business office is Russia as far as the clerks are concerned. So dont you take it so coolly. You think I'm not going to do it; but I am.

TARLETON. [*rising and facing him*] Come, now, as man to man! It's not my fault that youre poorer than I am; and it's not your fault that I'm richer than you. And if you could undo all that passed between me and your mother, you wouldnt undo it; and neither would she. But youre sick of your slavery; and you want to be the hero of a romance and to get into the papers. Eh? A son revenges his mother's shame. Villain weltering in his gore. Mother: look down from heaven and receive your unhappy son's last sigh.

THE MAN. Oh, rot! do you think I read novelettes? And do you suppose I believe such superstitions as heaven? I go to church because the boss told me I'd get the sack if I didnt. Free England! Ha! [*Lina appears at the pavilion door, and comes swiftly and noiselessly forward on seeing the man with a pistol in his hand*].

TARLETON. Youre afraid of getting the sack; but youre not afraid to shoot yourself.

THE MAN. Damn you! youre trying to keep me talking until somebody comes. [*He raises the pistol desperately, but not very resolutely*].

LINA. [*at his right elbow*] Somebody has come.

THE MAN [*turning on her*] Stand off. I'll shoot you if you lay a hand on me. I will, by God.

LINA. You cant cover me with that pistol. Try.

He tries, presenting the pistol at her face. She moves round him in the opposite direction to the hands of a clock with a light dancing step. He finds it impossible to cover her with the pistol: she is always too far to his left. Tarleton, behind him, grips his wrist and drags his arm straight up, so that the pistol points to the ceiling. As he tries to turn on his assailant, Lina grips his other wrist.

LINA. Please stop. I cant bear to twist anyone's wrist; but I must if you dont let the pistol go.

THE MAN. [*letting Tarleton take it from him*] All right: I'm done. Couldnt even do that job decently. Thats a clerk all over. Very well: send for your damned police and make an end of it. I'm accustomed to prison from nine to six: I daresay I can stand it from six to nine as well.

TARLETON. Dont swear. Thats a lady. [*He throws the pistol on the writing table*].

THE MAN. [*looking at Lina in amazement*] Beaten by a female! It needed only this. [*He collapses in the chair near the worktable, and hides his face. They cannot help pitying him*].

LINA. Old pal: dont call the police. Lend him a bicycle and let him get away.

THE MAN. I cant ride a bicycle. I never could afford one. I'm not even that much good.

TARLETON. If I gave you a hundred pound note now to go and have a good spree with, I wonder would you know how to set about it. Do you ever take a holiday?

THE MAN. Take! I got four days last August.

TARLETON. What did you do?

THE MAN. I did a cheap trip to Folkestone. I spent sevenpence on dropping pennies into silly automatic machines and peepshows of rowdy girls having a jolly time. I spent a penny on the lift and fourpence on refreshments. That cleaned me out. The rest of the time I was so miserable that I was glad to get back to the office. Now you know.

LINA. Come to the gymnasium: I'll teach you how to make a man of yourself. [*The man is about to rise irresolutely, from the mere habit of doing what he is told, when Tarleton stops him*].

TARLETON. Young man: dont. Youve tried to shoot me; but I'm not vindictive. I draw the line at putting a man on the rack. If you want every joint in your body stretched until it's an agony to live—until you have an unnatural feeling that all your muscles are singing and laughing with pain—then go to the gymnasium with that lady. But youll be more comfortable in jail.

LINA. [*greatly amused*] Was that why you went away, old pal? Was that the telegram you said you had forgotten to send?

Mrs Tarleton comes in hastily through the inner door.

MRS TARLETON. [*on the steps*] Is anything the matter, John? Nurse says she heard you calling me a quarter of an hour ago; and that your voice sounded as if you were ill. [*She comes between Tarleton and the man.*] Is anything the matter?

TARLETON. This is the son of an old friend of mine. Mr—er—Mr Gunner. [*To the man, who rises awkwardly*]. My wife.

MRS TARLETON. Good evening to you.

GUNNER. Er— [*He is too nervous to speak, and makes a shambling bow*].

Bentley looks in at the pavilion door, very peevish, and too preoccupied with his own affairs to pay any attention to those of the company.

BENTLEY. I say: has anybody seen Hypatia? She promised to come out with me; and I cant find her anywhere. And wheres Joey?

GUNNER. [*suddenly breaking out aggressively, being incapable of any middle way between submissiveness and violence*] *I* can tell you where Hypatia is. I can tell you where Joey is. And I say it's a scandal and an infamy. If people only knew what goes on in this so-called respectable house it would be put a stop to. These are the morals of our pious capitalist class! This is your rotten bourgeoisie! This!—

MRS TARLETON. Dont you dare use such language in company. I wont allow it.

TARLETON. All right, Chickabiddy: it's not bad language: it's only Socialism.

MRS TARLETON. Well, I wont have any Socialism in my house.

TARLETON. [*to Gunner*] You hear what Mrs Tarleton says. Well, in this house everybody does what she says or out they go.

GUNNER. Do you suppose I want to stay? Do you think I would breathe this polluted atmosphere a moment longer than I could help?

BENTLEY. [*running forward between Lina and Gunner*] But what did you mean by what you said about Miss Tarleton and Mr Percival, you beastly rotter, you?

GUNNER. [*to Tarleton*] Oh! is Hypatia your daughter? And Joey is Mister Percival, is he? One of your set, I suppose. One of the smart set! One of the bridge-playing, eighty-horse-power, week-ender set! One of the johnnies I slave for! Well, Joey has more decency than your daughter, anyhow. The women are the worst. I never believed it til I saw it with my own eyes. Well, it wont last for ever. The writing is on the wall. Rome fell. Babylon fell. Hindhead's turn will come.

MRS TARLETON. [*naively looking at the wall for the writing*] Whatever are you talking about, young man?

GUNNER. I know what I'm talking about. I went into that Turkish bath a boy: I came out a man.

MRS TARLETON. Good gracious! hes mad. [*To Lina*] Did John make him take a Turkish bath?

LINA. No. He doesnt need Turkish baths: he needs to put on a little flesh. I dont understand what it's all about. I found him trying to shoot Mr Tarleton.

MRS TARLETON. [*with a scream*] Oh! and John encouraging him, I'll be bound! Bunny: you go for the police. [*To Gunner*] I'll teach you to come into my house and shoot my husband.

GUNNER. Teach away. I never asked to be let off. I'm ashamed to be free instead of taking my part with the rest. Women—beautiful women of noble birth—are going to prison for their opinions. Girl students in Russia go to the gallows; let themselves be cut in pieces with the knout, or driven through the frozen snows of Siberia, sooner than stand looking on tamely at the world being made a hell for the toiling millions. If you were not all skunks and cowards youd be suffering with them instead of battening here on the plunder of the poor.

MRS TARLETON. [*much vexed*] Oh, did you ever hear such silly nonsense? Bunny: go and tell the gardener to send over one of his men to Grayshott for the police.

GUNNER. I'll go with him. I intend to give myself up. I'm going to expose what Ive seen here, no matter what the consequences may be to my miserable self.

TARLETON. Stop. You stay where you are, Ben. Chickabiddy: youve never had the police in. If you had, youd not be in a hurry to have them in again. Now, young man: cut the cackle; and tell us, as short as you can, what did you see?

GUNNER. I cant tell you in the presence of ladies.

MRS TARLETON. Oh, you are tiresome. As if it mattered to anyone what you saw. Me! A married woman that might be your mother. [*To Lina*] And I'm sure youre not particular, if youll excuse my saying so.

TARLETON. Out with it. What did you see?

GUNNER. I saw your daughter with my own eyes—oh well, never mind what I saw.

BENTLEY. [*almost crying with anxiety*] You beastly rotter, I'll get Joey to give you such a hiding—

TARLETON. You cant leave it at that, you know. What did you see my daughter doing?

GUNNER. After all, why shouldnt she do it? The Russian students do it. Women should be as free as men. I'm a fool. I'm so full of your bourgeois morality that I let myself be shocked by the application of my own revolutionary principles. If she likes the man why shouldnt she tell him so?

MRS TARLETON. I do wonder at you, John, letting him talk like this before everybody. [*Turning rather tartly to Lina*] Would you mind going away to the drawing-room just for a few minutes, Miss Chipenoska. This is a private family matter, if you dont mind.

LINA. I should have gone before, Mrs Tarleton, if there had been anyone to protect Mr Tarleton and the young gentleman.

TARLETON. Youre quite right, Miss Lina: you must stand by. I could have tackled him this morning; but since you put me through those exercises I'd rather die than even shake hands with a man, much less fight him.

GUNNER. It's all of a piece here. The men effeminate, the women unsexed—

TARLETON. Dont begin again, old chap. Keep it for Trafalgar Square.

HYPATIA'S VOICE OUTSIDE. No, no. [*She breaks off in a stifled half laugh, half scream, and is seen darting across the garden with Percival in hot pursuit. Immediately afterwards she appears again, and runs into the pavilion. Finding it full of people, including a stranger, she stops; but Percival, flushed and reckless, rushes in and seizes her before he, too, realizes that they are not alone. He releases her in confusion*].

Dead silence. They are all afraid to look at one another except Mrs Tarleton, who stares sternly at Hypatia. Hypatia is the first to recover her presence of mind.

HYPATIA. Excuse me rushing in like this. Mr Percival has been chasing me down the hill.

GUNNER. Who chased him up it? Dont be ashamed. Be fearless. Be truthful.

TARLETON. Gunner: will you go to Paris for a fortnight? I'll pay your expenses.

HYPATIA. What do you mean?

GUNNER. There was a silent witness in the Turkish bath.

TARLETON. I found him hiding there. Whatever went on here, he saw and heard. Thats what he means.

PERCIVAL. [*sternly approaching Gunner, and speaking with deep but contained indignation*] Am I to understand you as daring to put forward the monstrous and blackguardly lie that this lady behaved improperly in my presence?

GUNNER. [*turning white*] You know what I saw and heard.

Hypatia, with a gleam of triumph in her eyes, slips noiselessly into the swing chair, and watches Percival and Gunner, swinging slightly, but otherwise motionless.

PERCIVAL. I hope it is not necessary for me to assure you all that there is not one word of truth—not one grain of substance—in this rascally calumny, which no man with a spark of decent feeling would have uttered even if he had been ignorant enough to believe it. Miss Tarleton's conduct, since I have had the honor of knowing her, has been, I need hardly say, in every respect beyond reproach. [*To Gunner*] As for you, sir, youll have the goodness to come out with me immediately. I have some business with you which cant be settled in Mrs Tarleton's presence or in her house.

GUNNER. [*painfully frightened*] Why should I go out with you?

PERCIVAL. Because I intend that you shall.

GUNNER. I wont be bullied by you. [*Percival makes a threatening step towards him*]. Police! [*He tries to bolt; but Percival seizes him*]. Leave me go, will you? What right have you to lay hands on me?

TARLETON. Let him run for it, Mr Percival. Hes very poor company. We shall be well rid of him. Let him go.

PERCIVAL. Not until he has taken back and made the fullest apology for the abominable lie he has told. He shall do that or he shall defend himself as best he can against the most thorough thrashing I'm capable of giving him. [*Releasing Gunner, but facing him ominously*] Take your choice. Which is it to be?

GUNNER. Give me a fair chance. Go and stick at a desk from nine to six for a month, and let me have your grub and your sport and your lessons in boxing, and I'll fight you fast enough. You know I'm no good or you darent bully me like this.

PERCIVAL. You should have thought of that before you attacked a lady with a dastardly slander. I'm waiting for your decision. I'm rather in a hurry, please.

GUNNER. I never said anything against the lady.

MRS TARLETON. Oh, listen to that!
BENTLEY. What a liar!
HYPATIA. Oh!
TARLETON. Oh, come!

PERCIVAL. We'll have it in writing, if you dont mind. [*Pointing to the writing table*] Sit down; and take that pen in your hand. [*Gunner looks irresolutely a little way round; then obeys*]. Now write. "I," whatever your name is—

GUNNER [*after a vain attempt*] I cant. My hand's shaking too much. You see it's no use. I'm doing my best. I cant.

PERCIVAL. Mr Summerhays will write it: you can sign it.

BENTLEY. [*insolently to Gunner*] Get up. [*Gunner obeys; and Bentley, shouldering him aside towards Percival, takes his place and prepares to write*].

PERCIVAL. Whats your name?

GUNNER. John Brown.

TARLETON. Oh come! Couldnt you make it Horace Smith? or Algernon Robinson?

GUNNER. [*agitatedly*] But my name is John Brown. There are really John Browns. How can I help it if my name's a common one?

BENTLEY. Shew us a letter addressed to you.

GUNNER. How can I? I never get any letters: I'm only a clerk. I can shew you J. B. on my handkerchief. [*He takes out a not very clean one*].

BENTLEY. [*with disgust*] Oh, put it up again. Let it go at John Brown.

PERCIVAL. Where do you live?

GUNNER. 4 Chesterfield Parade, Kentish Town, N.W.

PERCIVAL. [*dictating*] I, John Brown, of 4 Chesterfield Parade, Kentish Town, do hereby voluntarily confess that on the 31st May 1909 I— [*To Tarleton*] What did he do exactly?

TARLETON. [*dictating*] —I trespassed on the land of John Tarleton at Hindhead, and effected an unlawful entry into his house, where I secreted myself in a portable Turkish bath—

BENTLEY. Go slow, old man. Just a moment. "Turkish bath"—yes?

TARLETON. [*continuing*] —with a pistol, with which I threatened to take the life of the said John Tarleton—

MRS TARLETON. Oh, John! You might have been killed.

TARLETON. —and was prevented from doing so only by the timely arrival of the celebrated Miss Lina Szczepanowska.

MRS TARLETON. Is she celebrated? [*Apologetically*] I never dreamt—

BENTLEY. Look here: I'm awfully sorry; but I cant spell Szczepanowska.

PERCIVAL. I think it's S, z, c, z— [*Lina gives him her visiting-card*]. Thank you. [*He throws it on Bentley's blotter*].

BENTLEY. Thanks awfully. [*He writes the name*].

TARLETON. [*to Percival*] Now it's your turn.

PERCIVAL. [*dictating*] I further confess that I was guilty of uttering an abominable calumny concerning Miss Hypatia Tarleton, for which there was not a shred of foundation.

Impressive silence whilst Bentley writes.

BENTLEY. "foundation"?

PERCIVAL. I apologize most humbly to the lady and her family for my conduct— [*he waits for Bentley to write*].

BENTLEY. "conduct"?

PERCIVAL. —and I promise Mr Tarleton not to repeat it, and to amend my life—

BENTLEY. "amend my life"?

PERCIVAL. —and to do what in me lies to prove worthy of his kindness in giving me another chance—

BENTLEY. "another chance"?

PERCIVAL. —and refraining from delivering me up to the punishment I so richly deserve.

BENTLEY. "richly deserve."

PERCIVAL. [*to Hypatia*] Does that satisfy you, Miss Tarleton?

HYPATIA. Yes: that will teach him to tell lies next time.

BENTLEY. [*rising to make place for Gunner and handing him the pen*] You mean it will teach him to tell the truth next time.

TARLETON. Ahem! Do you, Patsy?

PERCIVAL. Be good enough to sign. [*Gunner sits down helplessly and dips the pen in the ink*]. I hope what you are signing is no mere form of words to you, and that you not only say you are sorry, but that you are sorry.

Lord Summerhays and Johnny come in through the pavilion door.

MRS TARLETON. Stop. Mr Percival: I think, on Hypatia's account, Lord Summerhays ought to be told about this.

Lord Summerhays, wondering what the matter is, comes forward between Percival and Lina. Johnny stops beside Hypatia.

PERCIVAL. Certainly.

TARLETON. [*uneasily*] Take my advice, and cut it short. Get rid of him.

MRS TARLETON. Hypatia ought to have her character cleared.

TARLETON. You let well alone, Chickabiddy. Most of our characters will bear a little careful dusting; but they wont bear scouring. Patsy is jolly well out of it. What does it matter, anyhow?

PERCIVAL. Mr Tarleton: we have already said either too much or not enough. Lord Summerhays: will you be kind enough to witness the declaration this man has just signed?

GUNNER. I havnt yet. Am I to sign now?

PERCIVAL. Of course. [*Gunner, who is now incapable of doing anything on his own initiative, signs*]. Now stand up and read your declaration to this gentleman. [*Gunner makes a vague movement and looks stupidly round. Percival adds peremptorily*] Now, please.

GUNNER [*rising apprehensively and reading in a hardly audible voice, like a very sick man*] I, John Brown, of 4 Chesterfield Parade, Kentish Town, do hereby voluntarily confess that on the 31st May 1909 I trespassed on the land of John Tarleton at Hindhead, and effected an unlawful entry into his house, where I secreted myself in a portable Turkish bath, with a pistol, with which I threatened to take the life of the said John Tarleton, and was prevented from doing so only by the timely arrival of the celebrated Miss Lena Sh-Sh-sheepanossika. I further confess that I was guilty of uttering an abominable calumny concerning Miss Hypatia Tarleton, for which there was not a shred of foundation. I apologize most humbly to the lady and her family for my conduct; and I promise Mr Tarleton not to repeat it, and to amend my life, and to do what in me lies to prove worthy of his kindness in giving me another chance and refraining from delivering me up to the punishment I so richly deserve.

A short and painful silence follows. Then Percival speaks.

PERCIVAL. Do you consider that sufficient, Lord Summerhays?

LORD SUMMERHAYS. Oh quite, quite.

PERCIVAL. [*to Hypatia*] Lord Summerhays would probably like to hear you say that you are satisfied, Miss Tarleton.

HYPATIA. [*coming out of the swing, and advancing between Percival and Lord Summerhays*] I must say that you have behaved like a perfect gentleman, Mr. Percival.

PERCIVAL. [*first bowing to Hypatia, and then turning with cold contempt to Gunner, who is standing helpless*] We need not trouble you any further. [*Gunner turns vaguely towards the pavilion*].

JOHNNY [*with less refined offensiveness, pointing to the pavilion*] Thats your way. The gardener will shew you the shortest way into the road. Go the shortest way.

GUNNER. [*oppressed and disconcerted, hardly knows how to get out of the room*] Yes, sir. I— [*He turns again, appealing to Tarleton*] Maynt I have my mother's photographs back again? [*Mrs Tarleton pricks up her ears*].

TARLETON. Eh? What? Oh, the photographs! Yes, yes, yes: take them. [*Gunner takes them from the table, and is creeping away, when Mrs Tarleton puts out her hand and stops him*].

MRS TARLETON. Whats this, John? What were you doing with his mother's photographs?

TARLETON. Nothing, nothing. Never mind, Chickabiddy: it's all right.

MRS TARLETON. [*snatching the photographs from Gunner's irresolute fingers, and recognizing them at a glance*] Lucy Titmus! Oh John, John!

TARLETON. [*grimly, to Gunner*] Young man: youre a fool; but youve just put the lid on this job in a masterly manner. I knew you would. I told you all to let well alone. You wouldnt; and now you must take the consequences—or rather *I* must take them.

MRS TARLETON. [*to Gunner*] Are you Lucy's son?

GUNNER. Yes.

MRS TARLETON. And why didnt you come to me? I didnt turn my back on your mother when she came to me in her trouble. Didnt you know that?

GUNNER. No. She never talked to me about anything.

TARLETON. How could she talk to her own son? Shy, Summerhays, shy. Parent and child. Shy. [*He sits down at the end of the writing table nearest the sideboard like a man resigned to anything that fate may have in store for him*].

MRS TARLETON. Then how did you find out?

GUNNER. From her papers after she died.

MRS TARLETON. [*shocked*] Is Lucy dead? And I never knew! [*With an effusion of tenderness*] And you here being treated like that, poor orphan, with nobody to take your part! Tear up that foolish paper, child; and sit down and make friends with me.

JOHNNY. Hallo, mother this is all very well, you know—
PERCIVAL. But may I point out, Mrs Tarleton, that—
BENTLEY. Do you mean that after what he said of—
HYPATIA. Oh, look here, mamma: this is really—

MRS TARLETON. Will you please speak one at a time?

Silence.

PERCIVAL [*in a very gentlemanly manner*] Will you allow me to remind you, Mrs Tarleton, that this man has uttered a most serious and disgraceful falsehood concerning Miss Tarleton and myself?

MRS TARLETON. I dont believe a word of it. If the poor lad was there in the Turkish bath, who has a better right to say what was going on here than he has? You ought to be ashamed of yourself, Patsy; and so ought you too, Mr Percival, for encouraging her. [*Hypatia retreats to the pavilion, and exchanges grimaces with Johnny, shamelessly enjoying Percival's sudden reverse. They know their mother*].

PERCIVAL. [*gasping*] Mrs Tarleton: I give you my word of honor—

MRS TARLETON. Oh, go along with you and your word of honor. Do you think I'm a fool? I wonder you can look the lad in the face after bullying him and making him sign those wicked lies; and all the time you carrying on with my daughter before youd been half an hour in my house. Fie, for shame!

PERCIVAL. Lord Summerhays: I appeal to you. Have I done the correct thing or not?

LORD SUMMERHAYS. Youve done your best, Mr Percival. But the correct thing depends for its success on everybody playing the game very strictly. As a single-handed game, it's impossible.

BENTLEY. [*suddenly breaking out lamentably*] Joey: have you taken Hypatia away from me?

LORD SUMMERHAYS. [*severely*] Bentley! Bentley! Control yourself, sir.

TARLETON. Come, Mr Percival! the shutters are up on the gentlemanly business. Try the truth.

PERCIVAL. I am in a wretched position. If I tell the truth nobody will believe me.

TARLETON. Oh yes they will. The truth makes everybody believe it.

PERCIVAL. It also makes everybody pretend not to believe it. Mrs Tarleton: youre not playing the game.

MRS TARLETON. I dont think youve behaved at all nicely, Mr Percival.

BENTLEY. I wouldnt have played you such a dirty trick, Joey. [*Struggling with a sob*] You beast.

LORD SUMMERHAYS. Bentley: you must control yourself. Let me say at the same time, Mr Percival, that my son seems to have been mistaken in regarding you either as his friend or as a gentleman.

PERCIVAL. Miss Tarleton: I'm suffering this for your sake. I ask you just to say that I am not to blame. Just that and nothing more.

HYPATIA. [*gloating mischievously over his distress*] You chased me through the heather and kissed me. You shouldnt have done that if you were not in earnest.

PERCIVAL. Oh, this is really the limit. [*Turning desperately to Gunner*] Sir: I appeal to you. As a gentleman! as a man of honor! as a man bound to stand by another man! You were in that Turkish bath. You saw how it began. Could any man have behaved more correctly than I did? Is there a shadow of foundation for the accusations brought against me?

GUNNER. [*sorely perplexed*] Well, what do you want me to say?

JOHNNY. He has said what he had to say already, hasnt he? Read that paper.

GUNNER. When I tell the truth, you make me go back on it. And now you want me to go back on myself! What is a man to do?

PERCIVAL. [*patiently*] Please try to get your mind clear, Mr Brown. I pointed out to you that you could not, as a gentleman, disparage a lady's character. You agree with me, I hope.

GUNNER. Yes: that sounds all right.

PERCIVAL. But youre also bound to tell the truth. Surely youll not deny that.

GUNNER. Who's denying it? I say nothing against it.

PERCIVAL. Of course not. Well, I ask you to tell the truth simply and unaffectedly. Did you witness any improper conduct on my part when you were in the bath?

GUNNER. No, sir.

JOHNNY.	Then what do you mean by saying that—
HYPATIA.	Do you mean to say that I—
BENTLEY.	Oh, you are a rotter. Youre afraid—

TARLETON. [*rising*] Stop. [*Silence*]. Leave it at that. Enough said. You keep quiet, Johnny. Mr Percival: youre whitewashed. So are you, Patsy. Honors are easy. Lets drop the subject. The next thing to do is to open a subscription to start this young man on a ranch in some far country thats accustomed to be in a disturbed state. He—

MRS TARLETON. Now stop joking the poor lad, John: I wont have it. Has been worried to death between you all. [*To Gunner*] Have you had your tea?

GUNNER. Tea? No: it's too early. I'm all right; only I had no dinner: I didnt think I'd want it. I didnt think I'd be alive.

MRS TARLETON. Oh, what a thing to say! You mustnt talk like that.

JOHNNY. Hes out of his mind. He thinks it's past dinner-time.

MRS TARLETON. Oh, youve no sense, Johnny. He calls his lunch his dinner, and has his tea at half-past six. Havnt you, dear?

GUNNER. [*timidly*] Hasnt everybody?

JOHNNY. [*laughing*] Well, by George, thats not bad.

MRS TARLETON. Now dont be rude, Johnny: you know I dont like it. [*To Gunner*] A cup of tea will pick you up.

GUNNER. I'd rather not. I'm all right.

TARLETON. [*going to the sideboard*] Here! try a mouthful of sloe gin.

GUNNER. No, thanks. I'm a teetotaler. I cant touch alcohol in any form.

TARLETON. Nonsense! This isnt alcohol. Sloe gin. Vegetarian, you know.

GUNNER. [*hesitating*] Is it a fruit beverage?

TARLETON. Of course it is. Fruit beverage. Here you are. [*He gives him a glass of sloe gin*].

GUNNER. [*going to the sideboard*] Thanks. [*he begins to drink it confidently; but the first mouthful startles and almost chokes him*]. It's rather hot.

TARLETON. Do you good. Dont be afraid of it.

MRS TARLETON. [*going to him*] Sip it, dear. Dont be in a hurry.

Gunner sips slowly, each sip making his eyes water.

JOHNNY. [*coming forward into the place left vacant by Gunner's visit to the sideboard*] Well, now that the gentleman has been attended to, I should like to know where we are. It may be a vulgar business habit; but I confess I like to know where I am.

TARLETON. I dont. Wherever you are, youre there anyhow. I tell you again, leave it at that.

BENTLEY. I want to know too. Hypatia's engaged to me.

HYPATIA. Bentley: if you insult me again—if you say another word, I'll leave the house and not enter it until you leave it.

JOHNNY. Put that in your pipe and smoke it, my boy.

BENTLEY. [*inarticulate with fury and suppressed tears*] Oh! Beasts! Brutes!

MRS TARLETON. Now dont hurt his feelings, poor little lamb!

LORD SUMMERHAYS. [*very sternly*] Bentley: you are not behaving well. You had better leave us until you have recovered yourself.

Bentley goes out in disgrace, but gets no further than half way to the pavilion door, when, with a wild sob, he throws himself on the floor and begins to yell.

MRS TARLETON.	[*running to him*] Oh, poor child, poor child! Dont cry, duckie: he didnt mean it: dont cry.
LORD SUMMERHAYS	Stop that infernal noise, sir: do you hear? Stop it instantly.
JOHNNY.	
HYPATIA.	Thats the game he tried on me.

TARLETON. There you are! Now, mother! Now, Patsy! You see for yourselves.

[*covering her ears*] Oh you little wretch! Stop him, Mr Percival. Kick him.

Steady on, steady on. Easy, Bunny, easy.

LINA. Leave him to me, Mrs Tarleton. Stand clear, please.

She kneels opposite Bentley; quickly lifts the upper half of him from the ground; dives under him; rises with his body hanging across her shoulders; and runs out with him.

BENTLEY. [*in scared, sobered, humble tones as he is borne off*] What are you doing? Let me down. Please, Miss Szczepanowska— [*they pass out of hearing*].

An awestruck silence falls on the company as they speculate on Bentley's fate.

JOHNNY. I wonder what shes going to do with him.

HYPATIA. Spank him, I hope. Spank him hard.

LORD SUMMERHAYS. I hope so. I hope so. Tarleton: I'm beyond measure humiliated and annoyed by my son's behavior in your house. I had better take him home.

TARLETON. Not at all: not at all. Now, Chickabiddy: as Miss Lina has taken away Ben, suppose you take away Mr Brown for a while.

GUNNER. [*with unexpected aggressiveness*] My name isnt Brown. [*They stare at him: he meets their stare defiantly, pugnacious with sloe gin; drains the last drop from his glass; throws it on the sideboard; and advances to the writing table*]. My name's Baker: Julius Baker. Mister Baker. If any man doubts it, I'm ready for him.

MRS TARLETON. John: you shouldnt have given him that sloe gin. It's gone to his head.

GUNNER. Dont you think it. Fruit beverages dont go to the head; and what matter if they did? I say nothing to you, maam: I regard you with respect and affection. [*Lachrymosely*] You were very good to my mother: my poor mother! [*Relapsing into his daring mood*] But I say my name's Baker; and I'm not to be treated as a child or made a slave of by any man. Baker is my name. Did you think I was going to give you my real name? Not likely. Not me.

TARLETON. So you thought of John Brown. That was clever of you.

GUNNER. Clever! Yes: we're not all such fools as you think: we clerks. It was the bookkeeper put me up to that. It's the only name that nobody gives as a false name, he said. Clever, eh? I should think so.

MRS TARLETON. Come now, Julius—

GUNNER. [*reassuring her gravely*] Dont you be alarmed, maam. I know what is due to you as a lady and to myself as a gentleman. I regard you with respect and affection. If you had been my mother, as you ought to have been, I should have had more chance. But you shall have no cause to be ashamed of me. The strength of a chain is no greater than its weakest link; but the greatness of a poet is the greatness of his greatest moment. Shakespear used to get drunk. Frederick the Great ran away from a battle. But it was what they could rise to, not what they could sink to, that made them great. They werent good always; but they were good on their day. Well, on my day—on my day, mind you—I'm good for something too. I know that Ive made a silly exhibition of myself here. I know I didnt rise to the occasion. I know that if youd been my mother, youd have been ashamed of me. I lost my presence of mind: I was a contemptible coward. But [*slapping himself on the chest*] I'm not the man I was then. This is my day. Ive seen the tenth possessor of a foolish face carried out kicking and screaming by a woman. [*To Percival*] You crowed pretty big over me. You hypnotized me. But when you were put through the fire yourself, you were found wanting. I tell you straight I dont give a damn for you.

MRS TARLETON. No: thats naughty. You shouldnt say that before me.

GUNNER. I would cut my tongue out sooner than say anything vulgar in your presence; for I regard you with respect and affection. I was not swearing. I was affirming my manhood.

MRS TARLETON. What an idea! What puts all these things into your head?

GUNNER. Oh, dont you think, because I'm a clerk, that I'm not one of the intellectuals. I'm a reading man, a thinking man. I read in a book—a high class six shilling book—this precept: Affirm your manhood. It appealed to me. Ive always remembered it. I believe in it. I feel I must do it to recover your respect after my cowardly behavior. Therefore I affirm it in your presence. I tell that man who insulted me that I dont give a damn for him. And neither I do.

TARLETON. I say, Summerhays: did you have chaps of this sort in Jinghiskahn?

LORD SUMMERHAYS. Oh yes: they exist everywhere: they are a most serious modern problem.

GUNNER. Yes. Youre right. [*Conceitedly*] I'm a problem. And I tell you that when we clerks realize that we're problems! well, look out: thats all.

LORD SUMMERHAYS. [*suavely, to Gunner*] You read a great deal, you say?

GUNNER. Ive read more than any man in this room, if the truth were known, I expect. Thats whats going to smash up your Capitalism. The problems are beginning to read. Ha! We're free to do that here in England. What would you do with me in Jinghiskahn if you had me there?

LORD SUMMERHAYS. Well, since you ask me so directly, I'll tell you. I should take advantage of the fact that you have neither sense enough nor strength enough to know how to behave yourself in a difficulty of any sort. I should warn an intelligent and ambitious policeman that you are a troublesome person. The intelligent and ambitious policeman would take an early opportunity of upsetting your temper by ordering you to move on, and treading on your heels until you were provoked into obstructing an officer in the discharge of his duty. Any trifle of that sort would be sufficient to make a man like you lose your self-possession and put yourself in the wrong. You would then be charged and imprisoned until things quieted down.

GUNNER. And you call that justice!

LORD SUMMERHAYS. No. Justice was not my business. I had to govern a province; and I took the necessary steps to maintain order in it. Men are not governed by justice, but by law or persuasion. When they refuse to be governed by law or persuasion, they have to be governed by force or fraud, or both. I used both when law and persuasion failed me. Every ruler of men since the world began has done so, even when he has hated both fraud and force as heartily as I do. It is as well that you should know this, my young friend; so that you may recognize in time that anarchism is a game at which the police can beat you. What have you to say to that?

GUNNER. What have I to say to it! Well, I call it scandalous: thats what I have to say to it.

LORD SUMMERHAYS. Precisely: thats all anybody has to say to it, except the British public, which pretends not to believe it. And now let me ask you a sympathetic personal question. Havnt you a headache?

GUNNER. Well, since you ask me, I have. Ive overexcited myself.

MRS TARLETON. Poor lad! No wonder, after all youve gone through! You want to eat a little and to lie down. You come with me. I want you to tell me about your poor dear mother and about yourself. Come along with me. [*She leads the way to the inner door*].

GUNNER. [*following her obediently*] Thank you kindly, madam. [*She goes out. Before passing out after her, he partly closes the door and stops on the landing for a moment to say*] Mind: I'm not knuckling down to any man here. I knuckle down to Mrs Tarleton because shes a woman in a thousand. I affirm my manhood all the same. Understand: I dont give a damn for the lot of you. [*He hurries out, rather afraid of the consequences of this defiance, which has provoked Johnny to an impatient movement towards him*].

HYPATIA. Thank goodness hes gone! Oh, what a bore! WHAT a bore!!! Talk, talk, talk!

TARLETON. Patsy: it's no good. We're going to talk. And we're going to talk about you.

JOHNNY. It's no use shirking it, Pat. We'd better know where we are.

LORD SUMMERHAYS. Come, Miss Tarleton. Wont you sit down? I'm very tired of standing. [*Hypatia comes from the pavilion and takes a chair at the worktable. Lord Summerhays takes the opposite chair, on her right. Percival takes the chair Johnny placed for Lina on her arrival. Tarleton sits down at the end of the writing table. Johnny remains standing. Lord Summerhays continues, with a sigh of relief at being seated.*] We shall now get the change of subject we are all pining for.

JOHNNY. [*puzzled*] Whats that?

LORD SUMMERHAYS. The great question. The question that men and women will spend hours over without complaining. The question that occupies all the novel readers and all the playgoers. The question they never get tired of.

JOHNNY. But what question?

LORD SUMMERHAYS. The question which particular young man some young woman will mate with.

PERCIVAL. As if it mattered!

HYPATIA. [*sharply*] Whats that you said?

PERCIVAL. I said: As if it mattered.

HYPATIA. I call that ungentlemanly.

PERCIVAL. Do you care about that? you who are so magnificently unladylike!

JOHNNY. Look here, Mr Percival: youre not supposed to insult my sister.

HYPATIA. Oh, shut up, Johnny. I can take care of myself. Dont you interfere.

JOHNNY. Oh, very well. If you choose to give yourself away like that—to allow a man to call you unladylike and then to be unladylike, Ive nothing more to say.

HYPATIA. I think Mr Percival is most ungentlemanly; but I wont be protected. I'll not have my affairs interfered with by men on pretence of protecting me. I'm not your baby. If I interfered between you and a woman, you would soon tell me to mind my own business.

TARLETON. Children: dont squabble. Read Dr Watts. Behave yourselves.

JOHNNY. Ive nothing more to say; and as I dont seem to be wanted here, I shall take myself off. [*He goes out with affected calm through the pavilion*].

TARLETON. Summerhays: a family is an awful thing, an impossible thing. Cat and dog. Patsy: I'm ashamed of you.

HYPATIA. I'll make it up with Johnny afterwards; but I really cant have him here sticking his clumsy hoof into my affairs.

LORD SUMMERHAYS. The question is, Mr Percival, are you really a gentleman, or are you not?

PERCIVAL. Was Napoleon really a gentleman or was he not? He made the lady get out of the way of the porter and said, "Respect the burden, madam." That was behaving like a very fine gentleman; but he kicked Volney for saying that what France wanted was the Bourbons back again. That was behaving rather like a navvy. Now I, like Napoleon, am not all one piece. On occasion, as you have all seen, I can behave like a gentleman. On occasion, I can behave with a brutal simplicity which Miss Tarleton herself could hardly surpass.

TARLETON. Gentleman or no gentleman, Patsy: what are your intentions?

HYPATIA. My intentions! Surely it's the gentleman who should be asked his intentions.

TARLETON. Come now, Patsy! none of that nonsense. Has Mr Percival said anything to you that I ought to know or that Bentley ought to know? Have you said anything to Mr Percival?

HYPATIA. Mr Percival chased me through the heather and kissed me.

LORD SUMMERHAYS. As a gentleman, Mr Percival, what do you say to that?

PERCIVAL. As a gentleman, I do not kiss and tell. As a mere man: a mere cad, if you like, I say that I did so at Miss Tarleton's own suggestion.

HYPATIA. Beast!

PERCIVAL. I dont deny that I enjoyed it. But I did not initiate it. And I began by running away.

TARLETON. So Patsy can run faster than you, can she?

PERCIVAL. Yes, when she is in pursuit of me. She runs faster and faster. I run slower and slower. And these woods of yours are full of magic. There was a confounded fern owl. Did you ever hear the churr of a fern owl? Did you ever hear it create a sudden silence by ceasing? Did you ever hear it call its mate by striking its wings together twice and whistling that single note that no nightingale can imitate? That is what happened in the woods when I was running away. So I turned; and the pursuer became the pursued.

HYPATIA. I had to fight like a wild cat.

LORD SUMMERHAYS. Please dont tell us this. It's not fit for old people to hear.

TARLETON. Come: how did it end?

HYPATIA. It's not ended yet.

TARLETON. How is it going to end?

HYPATIA. Ask him.

TARLETON. How is it going to end, Mr Percival?

PERCIVAL. I cant afford to marry, Mr Tarleton. Ive only a thousand a year until my father dies. Two people cant possibly live on that.

TARLETON. Oh, cant they? When *I* married, I should have been jolly glad to have felt sure of the quarter of it.

PERCIVAL. No doubt; but I am not a cheap person, Mr Tarleton. I was brought up in a household which cost at least seven or eight times that; and I am in constant money difficulties because I simply dont know how to live on the thousand a year scale. As to ask a woman to share my degrading poverty, it's out of the question. Besides, I'm rather young to marry. I'm only 28.

HYPATIA. Papa: buy the brute for me.

LORD SUMMERHAYS. [*shrinking*] My dear Miss Tarleton: dont be so naughty. I know how delightful it is to shock an old man; but there is a point at which it becomes barbarous. Dont. Please dont.

HYPATIA. Shall I tell Papa about you?

LORD SUMMERHAYS. Tarleton: I had better tell you that I once asked your daughter to become my widow.

TARLETON. [*to Hypatia*] Why didnt you accept him, you young idiot?

LORD SUMMERHAYS. I was too old.

TARLETON. All this has been going on under my nose, I suppose. You run after young men; and old men run after you. And I'm the last person in the world to hear of it.

HYPATIA. How could I tell you?

LORD SUMMERHAYS. Parents and children, Tarleton.

TARLETON. Oh, the gulf that lies between them! the impassable, eternal gulf! And so I'm to buy the brute for you, eh?

HYPATIA. If you please, papa.

TARLETON. Whats the price, Mr Percival?

PERCIVAL. We might do with another fifteen hundred if my father would contribute. But I should like more.

TARLETON. It's purely a question of money with you, is it?

PERCIVAL. [*after a moment's consideration*] Practically yes: it turns on that.

TARLETON. I thought you might have some sort of preference for Patsy, you know.

PERCIVAL. Well, but does that matter, do you think? Patsy fascinates me, no doubt. I apparently fascinate Patsy. But, believe me, all that is not worth considering. One of my three fathers (the priest) has married hundreds of couples: couples selected by one another, couples selected by the parents, couples forced to marry one another by circumstances of one kind or another; and he assures me that if marriages were made by putting all the men's names into one sack and the women's names into another, and having them taken out by a blindfolded child like lottery numbers, there would be just as high a percentage of happy marriages as we have here in England. He said Cupid was nothing but the blindfolded child: pretty idea that, I think! I shall have as good a chance with Patsy as with anyone else. Mind: I'm not bigoted about it. I'm not a doctrinaire: not the slave of a theory. You and Lord Summerhays are experienced married men. If you can tell me of any trustworthy method of selecting a wife, I shall be happy to make use of it. I await your suggestions. [*He looks with polite attention to Lord Summerhays, who, having nothing to say, avoids his eye. He looks to Tarleton, who purses his lips glumly and rattles his money in his pockets without a word*]. Apparently neither of you has anything to suggest. Then Patsy will do as well as another, provided the money is forthcoming.

HYPATIA. Oh, you beauty, you beauty!

TARLETON. When I married Patsy's mother, I was in love with her.

PERCIVAL. For the first time?

TARLETON. Yes: for the first time.

PERCIVAL. For the last time?

LORD SUMMERHAYS. [*revolted*] Sir: you are in the presence of his daughter.

HYPATIA. Oh, dont mind me. I dont care. I'm accustomed to Papa's adventures.

TARLETON. [*blushing painfully*] Patsy, my child: that was not—not delicate.

HYPATIA. Well, papa, youve never shewn any delicacy in talking to me about my conduct; and I really dont see why I shouldnt talk to you about yours. It's such nonsense! Do you think young people dont know?

LORD SUMMERHAYS. I'm sure they dont feel. Tarleton: this is too horrible, too brutal. If neither of these young people have any—any—any—

PERCIVAL. Shall we say paternal sentimentality? I'm extremely sorry to shock you; but you must remember that Ive been educated to discuss human affairs with three fathers simultaneously. I'm an adult person. Patsy is an adult person. You do not inspire me with veneration. Apparently you do not inspire Patsy with veneration. That may surprise you. It may pain you. I'm sorry. It cant be helped. What about the money?

TARLETON. You dont inspire me with generosity, young man.

HYPATIA. [*laughing with genuine amusement*] He had you there, Joey.

TARLETON. I havnt been a bad father to you, Patsy.

HYPATIA. I dont say you have, dear. If only I could persuade you Ive grown up, we should get along perfectly.

TARLETON. Do you remember Bill Burt?

HYPATIA. Why?

TARLETON. [*to the others*] Bill Burt was a laborer here. I was going to sack him for kicking his father. He said his father had kicked him until he was big enough to kick back. Patsy begged him off. I asked that man what it felt like the first time he kicked his father, and found that it was just like kicking any other man. He laughed and said that it was the old man that knew what it felt like. Think of that, Summerhays! think of that!

HYPATIA. I havnt kicked you, papa.

TARLETON. Youve kicked me harder than Bill Burt ever kicked.

LORD SUMMERHAYS. It's no use, Tarleton. Spare yourself. Do you seriously expect these young people, at their age, to sympathize with what this gentleman calls your paternal sentimentality?

TARLETON. [*wistfully*] Is it nothing to you but paternal sentimentality, Patsy?

HYPATIA. Well, I greatly prefer your superabundant vitality, papa.

TARLETON. [*violently*] Hold your tongue, you young devil. The young are all alike: hard, coarse, shallow, cruel, selfish, dirty-minded. You can clear out of my house as soon as you can coax him to take you; and the sooner the better. [*To Percival*] I think you said your price was fifteen hundred a year. Take it. And I wish you joy of your bargain.

PERCIVAL. If you wish to know who I am—

TARLETON. I dont care a tinker's curse who you are or what you are. Youre willing to take that girl off my hands for fifteen hundred a year: thats all that concerns me. Tell her who you are if you like: it's her affair, not mine.

HYPATIA. Dont answer him, Joey: it wont last. Lord Summerhays, I'm sorry about Bentley; but Joey's the only man for me.

LORD SUMMERHAYS. It may—

HYPATIA. Please dont say it may break your poor boy's heart. It's much more likely to break yours.

LORD SUMMERHAYS. Oh!

TARLETON. [*springing to his feet*] Leave the room. Do you hear: leave the room.

PERCIVAL. Arnt we getting a little cross? Dont be angry, Mr Tarleton. Read Marcus Aurelius.

TARLETON. Dont you dare make fun of me. Take your aeroplane out of my vinery and yourself out of my house.

PERCIVAL. [*rising, to Hypatia*] I'm afraid I shall have to dine at the Beacon, Patsy.

HYPATIA. [*rising*] Do. I dine with you.

TARLETON. Did you hear me tell you to leave the room?

HYPATIA. I did. [*To Percival*] You see what living with one's parents means, Joey. It means living in a house where you can be ordered to leave the room. Ive got to obey: it's his house, not mine.

TARLETON. Who pays for it? Go and support yourself as I did if you want to be independent.

HYPATIA. I wanted to and you wouldnt let me. How can I support myself when I'm a prisoner?

TARLETON. Hold your tongue.

HYPATIA. Keep your temper.

PERCIVAL. [*coming between them*] Lord Summerhays: youll join me, I'm sure, in pointing out to both father and daughter that they have now reached that very common stage in family life at which anything but a blow would be an anti-climax. Do you seriously want to beat Patsy, Mr Tarleton?

TARLETON. Yes. I want to thrash the life out of her. If she doesnt get out of my reach, I'll do it. [*He sits down and grasps the writing table to restrain himself*].

HYPATIA. [*coolly going to him and leaning with her breast on his writhing shoulders*] Oh, if you want to beat me just to relieve your feelings—just really and truly for the fun of it and the satisfaction of it, beat away. I dont grudge you that.

TARLETON. [*almost in hysterics*] I used to think that this sort of thing went on in other families but that it never could happen in ours. And now—[*He is broken with emotion, and continues lamentably*] I cant say the right thing. I cant do the right thing. I dont know what is the right thing. I'm beaten; and she knows it. Summerhays: tell me what to do.

LORD SUMMERHAYS. When my council in Jinghiskahn reached the point of coming to blows, I used to adjourn the sitting. Let us postpone the discussion. Wait until Monday: we shall have Sunday to quiet down in. Believe me, I'm not making fun of you; but I think theres something in this young gentleman's advice. Read something.

TARLETON. I'll read King Lear.

HYPATIA. Dont. I'm very sorry, dear.

TARLETON. Youre not. Youre laughing at me. Serve me right! Parents and children! No man should know his own child. No child should know its own father. Let the family be rooted out of civilization! Let the human race be brought up in institutions!

HYPATIA. Oh yes. How jolly! You and I might be friends then; and Joey could stay to dinner.

TARLETON. Let him stay to dinner. Let him stay to breakfast. Let him spend his life here. Dont you say I drove him out. Dont you say I drove you out.

PERCIVAL. I really have no right to inflict myself on you. Dropping in as I did—

TARLETON. Out of the sky. Ha! Dropping in. The new sport of aviation. You just see a nice house; drop in; scoop up the man's daughter; and off with you again.

Bentley comes back, with his shoulders hanging as if he too had been exercised to the last pitch of fatigue. He is very sad. They stare at him as he gropes to Percival's chair.

BENTLEY. I'm sorry for making a fool of myself. I beg your pardon. Hypatia: I'm awfully sorry;

but Ive made up my mind that I'll never marry. [*He sits down in deep depression*].

HYPATIA. [*running to him*] How nice of you, Bentley! Of course you guessed I wanted to marry Joey. What did the Polish lady do to you?

BENTLEY. [*turning his head away*] I'd rather not speak of her, if you dont mind.

HYPATIA. Youve fallen in love with her. [*She laughs*].

BENTLEY. It's beastly of you to laugh.

LORD SUMMERHAYS. Youre not the first to fall today under the lash of that young lady's terrible derision, Bentley.

Lina, her cap on, and her goggles in her hand, comes impetuously through the inner door.

LINA. [*on the steps*] Mr Percival: can we get that aeroplane started again? [*She comes down and runs to the pavilion door*]. I must get out of this into the air: right up into the blue.

PERCIVAL. Impossible. The frame's twisted. The petrol has given out: thats what brought us down. And how can we get a clear run to start with among these woods?

LINA. [*swooping back through the middle of the pavilion*] We can straighten the frame. We can buy petrol at the Beacon. With a few laborers we can get her out on to the Portsmouth Road and start her along that.

TARLETON. [*rising*] But why do you want to leave us, Miss Szcz?

LINA. Old pal: this is a stuffy house. You seem to think of nothing but making love. All the conversation here is about love-making. All the pictures are about love-making. The eyes of all of you are sheep's eyes. You are steeped in it, soaked in it: the very texts on the walls of your bedrooms are the ones about love. It is disgusting. It is not healthy. Your women are kept idle and dressed up for no other purpose than to be made love to. I have not been here an hour; and already everybody makes love to me as if because I am a woman it were my profession to be made love to. First you, old pal. I forgave you because you were nice about your wife.

HYPATIA. Oh! oh! oh! Oh, papa!

LINA. Then you, Lord Summerhays, come to me; and all you have to say is to ask me not to mention that you made love to me in Vienna two years ago. I forgave you because I thought you were an ambassador; and all ambassadors make love and are very nice and useful to people who travel. Then this young gentleman. He is engaged to this young lady; but no matter for that: he makes love to me because I carry him off in my arms when he cries. All these I bore in silence. But now comes your Johnny and tells me I'm a ripping fine woman, and asks me to marry him. I, Lina Szczepanowska, MARRY him!!!!! I do not mind this boy: he is a child: he loves me: I should have to give him money and take care of him: that would be foolish, but honorable. I do not mind you, old pal: you are what you call an old—ouf! but you do not offer to buy me: you say until we are tired—until you are so happy that you dare not ask for more. That is foolish too, at your age; but it is an adventure: it is not dishonorable. I do not mind Lord Summerhays: it was in Vienna: they had been toasting him at a great banquet: he was not sober. That is bad for the health; but it is not dishonorable. But your Johnny! Oh, your Johnny! with his marriage. He will do the straight thing by me. He will give me a home, a position. He tells me I must know that my present position is not one for a nice woman. This to me, Lina Szczepanowska! I am an honest woman: I earn my living. I am a free woman: I live in my own house. I am a woman of the world: I have thousands of friends: every night crowds of people applaud me, delight in me, buy my picture, pay hard-earned money to see me. I am strong: I am skilful: I am brave: I am independent: I am unbought: I am all that a woman ought to be; and in my family there has not been a single drunkard for four generations. And this Englishman! this linendraper! he dares to ask me to come and live with him in this rrrrrrabbit hutch, and take my bread from his hand, and ask him for pocket money, and wear soft clothes, and be his woman! his wife! Sooner than that, I would stoop to the lowest depths of my profession. I would stuff lions with food and pretend to tame them. I would deceive honest people's eyes with conjuring tricks instead of real feats of strength and skill. I would be a clown and set bad examples of conduct to little children. I would sink yet lower and be an actress or an opera singer, imperilling my soul by the wicked lie of pretending to be somebody else. All this I would do sooner than take my bread from the hand of a man and make him the master of my body and soul. And so you may tell your Johnny to buy an Englishwoman: he shall not buy Lina Szczepanowska; and I will not stay in the house where such dishonor is offered me. Adieu. [*She turns precipitately to go, but is faced in the pavilion doorway by Johnny, who comes in slowly, his hands in his pockets, meditating deeply*].

JOHNNY. [*confidentially to Lina*] You wont mention our little conversation, Miss Shepanoska. It'll do no good; and I'd rather you didnt.

TARLETON. Weve just heard about it, Johnny.

JOHNNY. [*shortly, but without ill-temper*] Oh: is that so?

HYPATIA. The cat's out of the bag, Johnny, about everybody. They were all beforehand with you: papa, Lord Summerhays, Bentley and all. Dont you let them laugh at you.

JOHNNY. [*a grin slowly overspreading his countenance*] Well, theres no use my pretending to be surprised at you, Governor, is there? I hope you got it as hot as I did. Mind, Miss Shepanoska: it wasnt lost on me. I'm a thinking man. I kept my temper. Youll admit that.

LINA. [*frankly*] Oh yes. I do not quarrel. You are what is called a chump; but you are not a bad sort of chump.

JOHNNY. Thank you. Well, if a chump may have an opinion, I should put it at this. You make, I suppose, ten pounds a night off your own bat, Miss Lina?

LINA. [*scornfully*] Ten pounds a night! I have made ten pounds a minute.

JOHNNY. [*with increased respect*] Have you indeed? I didnt know: youll excuse my mistake, I hope. But the principle is the same. Now I trust you wont be offended at what I'm going to say; but Ive thought about this and watched it in daily experience; and you may take it from me that the moment a woman becomes pecuniarily independent, she gets hold of the wrong end of the stick in moral questions.

LINA. Indeed! And what do you conclude from that, Mister Johnny?

JOHNNY. Well, obviously, that independence for women is wrong and shouldnt be allowed. For their own good, you know. And for the good of morality in general. You agree with me, Lord Summerhays, dont you?

LORD SUMMERHAYS. It's a very moral moral, if I may so express myself.

Mrs Tarleton comes in softly through the inner door.

MRS TARLETON. Dont make too much noise. The lad's asleep.

TARLETON. Chickabiddy: we have some news for you.

JOHNNY. [*apprehensively*] Now theres no need, you know, Governor, to worry mother with everything that passes.

MRS TARLETON. [*coming to Tarleton*] Whats been going on? Dont you hold anything back from me, John. What have you been doing?

TARLETON. Bentley isnt going to marry Patsy.

MRS TARLETON. Of course not. Is that your great news? I never believed she'd marry him.

TARLETON. Theres something else. Mr Percival here—

MRS TARLETON. [*to Percival*] Are you going to marry Patsy?

PERCIVAL [*diplomatically*] Patsy is going to marry me, with your permission.

MRS TARLETON. Oh, she has my permission: she ought to have been married long ago.

HYPATIA. Mother!

TARLETON. Miss Lina here, though she has been so short a time with us, has inspired a good deal of attachment in—I may say in almost all of us. Therefore I hope she'll stay to dinner, and not insist on flying away in that aeroplane.

PERCIVAL. You must stay, Miss Szczepanowska. I cant go up again this evening.

LINA. Ive seen you work it. Do you think I require any help? And Bentley shall come with me as a passenger.

BENTLEY. [*terrified*] Go up in an aeroplane! I darent.

LINA. You must learn to dare.

BENTLEY. [*pale but heroic*] All right. I'll come.

LORD SUMMERHAYS	No, no, Bentley, impossible. I shall not allow it.
MRS TARLETON.	Do you want to kill the child? He shant go.

BENTLEY. I will. I'll lie down and yell until you let me go. I'm not a coward. I wont be a coward.

LORD SUMMERHAYS. Miss Szczepanowska: my son is very dear to me. I implore you to wait until tomorrow morning.

LINA. There may be a storm tomorrow. And I'll go: storm or no storm. I must risk my life tomorrow.

BENTLEY. I hope there will be a storm.

LINA. [*grasping his arm*] You are trembling.

BENTLEY. Yes: it's terror, sheer terror. I can hardly see. I can hardly stand. But I'll go with you.

LINA. [*slapping him on the back and knocking a ghastly white smile into his face*] You shall. I like you, my boy. We go tomorrow, together.

BENTLEY. Yes: together: tomorrow.

TARLETON. Well, sufficient unto the day is the evil thereof. Read the old book.

MRS TARLETON. Is there anything else?

TARLETON. Well, I—er [*he addresses Lina, and stops*]. I—er [*he addresses Lord Summerhays, and stops*]. I—er [*he gives it up*]. Well, I suppose—er—I suppose theres nothing more to be said.

HYPATIA. [*fervently*] Thank goodness!

THE DARK LADY OF THE SONNETS

THE DARK LADY OF THE SONNETS

Fin de siecle 15-1600. Midsummer night on the terrace of the Palace at Whitehall, overlooking the Thames. The Palace clock chimes four quarters and strikes eleven.

A Beefeater on guard. A Cloaked Man approaches.

THE BEEFEATER. Stand. Who goes there? Give the word.

THE MAN. Marry! I cannot. I have clean forgotten it.

THE BEEFEATER. Then cannot you pass here. What is your business? Who are you? Are you a true man?

THE MAN. Far from it, Master Warder. I am not the same man two days together: sometimes Adam, sometimes Benvolio, and anon the Ghost.

THE BEEFEATER. [*recoiling*] A ghost! Angels and ministers of grace defend us!

THE MAN. Well said, Master Warder. With your leave I will set that down in writing; for I have a very poor and unhappy brain for remembrance. [*He takes out his tablets and writes*]. Methinks this is a good scene, with you on your lonely watch, and I approaching like a ghost in the moonlight. Stare not so amazedly at me; but mark what I say. I keep tryst here to-night with a dark lady. She promised to bribe the warder. I gave her the wherewithal: four tickets for the Globe Theatre.

THE BEEFEATER. Plague on her! She gave me two only.

THE MAN. [*detaching a tablet*] My friend: present this tablet, and you will be welcomed at any time when the plays of Will Shakespear are in hand. Bring your wife. Bring your friends. Bring the whole garrison. There is ever plenty of room.

THE BEEFEATER. I care not for these newfangled plays. No man can understand a word of them. They are all talk. Will you not give me a pass for The Spanish Tragedy?

THE MAN. To see The Spanish Tragedy one pays, my friend. Here are the means. [*He gives him a piece of gold*].

THE BEEFEATER. [*overwhelmed*] Gold! Oh, sir, you are a better paymaster than your dark lady.

THE MAN. Women are thrifty, my friend.

THE BEEFEATER. Tis so, sir. And you have to consider that the most open handed of us must een cheapen that which we buy every day. This lady has to make a present to a warder nigh every night of her life.

THE MAN. [*turning pale*] I'll not believe it.

THE BEEFEATER. Now you, sir, I dare be sworn, do not have an adventure like this twice in the year.

THE MAN. Villain: wouldst tell me that my dark lady hath ever done thus before? that she maketh occasions to meet other men?

THE BEEFEATER. Now the Lord bless your innocence, sir, do you think you are the only pretty man in the world? A merry lady, sir: a warm bit of stuff. Go to: I'll not see her pass a deceit on a gentleman that hath given me the first piece of gold I ever handled.

THE MAN. Master Warder: is it not a strange thing that we, knowing that all women are false, should be amazed to find our own particular drab no better than the rest?

THE BEEFEATER. Not all, sir. Decent bodies, many of them.

THE MAN. [*intolerantly*] No. All false. All. If thou deny it, thou liest.

THE BEEFEATER. You judge too much by the Court, sir. There, indeed, you may say of frailty that its name is woman.

THE MAN. [*pulling out his tablets again*] Prithee say that again: that about frailty: the strain of music.

THE BEEFEATER. What strain of music, sir? I'm no musician, God knows.

THE MAN. There is music in your soul: many of your degree have it very notably. [*Writing*] "Frailty: thy name is woman!" [*Repeating it affectionately*] "Thy name is woman."

THE BEEFEATER. Well, sir, it is but four words. Are you a snapper-up of such unconsidered trifles?

THE MAN. [*eagerly*] Snapper-up of—[*he gasps*] Oh! Immortal phrase! [*He writes it down*]. This man is a greater than I.

THE BEEFEATER. You have my lord Pembroke's trick, sir.

THE MAN. Like enough: he is my near friend. But what call you his trick?

THE BEEFEATER. Making sonnets by moonlight. And to the same lady too.

THE MAN. No!

THE BEEFEATER. Last night he stood here on your errand, and in your shoes.

THE MAN. Thou, too, Brutus! And I called him friend!

THE BEEFEATER. Tis ever so, sir.

THE MAN. Tis ever so. Twas ever so. [*He turns away, overcome*]. Two Gentlemen of Verona! Judas! Judas!!

THE BEEFEATER. Is he so bad as that, sir?

THE MAN. [*recovering his charity and self-possession*] Bad? Oh no. Human, Master Warder, human. We call one another names when we are offended, as children do. That is all.

THE BEEFEATER. Ay, sir: words, words, words. Mere wind, sir. We fill our bellies with the east wind, sir, as the Scripture hath it. You cannot feed capons so.

THE MAN. A good cadence. By your leave [*He makes a note of it*].

THE BEEFEATER. What manner of thing is a cadence, sir? I have not heard of it.

THE MAN. A thing to rule the world with, friend.

THE BEEFEATER. You speak strangely, sir: no offence. But, an't like you, you are a very civil gentleman; and a poor man feels drawn to you, you being, as twere, willing to share your thought with him.

THE MAN. Tis my trade. But alas! the world for the most part will none of my thoughts.

Lamplight streams from the palace door as it opens from within.

THE BEEFEATER. Here comes your lady, sir. I'll to t'other end of my ward. You may een take your time about your business: I shall not return too suddenly unless my sergeant comes prowling round. Tis a fell sergeant, sir: strict in his arrest. Go'd'en, sir; and good luck! [*He goes*].

THE MAN. "Strict in his arrest"! "Fell sergeant"! [*As if tasting a ripe plum*] O-o-o-h! [*He makes a note of them*].

A Cloaked Lady gropes her way from the palace and wanders along the terrace, walking in her sleep.

THE LADY. [*rubbing her hands as if washing them*] Out, damned spot. You will mar all with these cosmetics. God made you one face; and you make yourself another. Think of your grave, woman, not ever of being beautified. All the perfumes of Arabia will not whiten this Tudor hand.

THE MAN. "All the perfumes of Arabia"! "Beautified"! "Beautified"! a poem in a single word. Can this be my Mary? [*To the Lady*] Why do you speak in a strange voice, and utter poetry for the first time? Are you ailing? You walk like the dead. Mary! Mary!

THE LADY. [*echoing him*] Mary! Mary! Who would have thought that woman to have had so much blood in her! Is it my fault that my counsellors put deeds of blood on me? Fie! If you were women you would have more wit than to stain the floor so foully. Hold not up her head so: the hair is false. I tell you yet again, Mary's buried: she cannot come out of her grave. I fear her not: these cats that dare jump into thrones though they be fit only for men's laps must be put away. Whats done cannot be undone. Out, I say. Fie! a queen, and freckled!

THE MAN. [*shaking her arm*] Mary, I say: art asleep?

The Lady wakes; starts; and nearly faints. He catches her on his arm.

THE LADY. Where am I? What art thou?

THE MAN. I cry your mercy. I have mistook your person all this while. Methought you were my Mary: my mistress.

THE LADY. [*outraged*] Profane fellow: how do you dare?

THE MAN. Be not wroth with me, lady. My mistress is a marvellous proper woman. But she does not speak so well as you. "All the perfumes of Arabia"! That was well said: spoken with good accent and excellent discretion.

THE LADY. Have I been in speech with you here?

THE MAN. Why, yes, fair lady. Have you forgot it?

THE LADY. I have walked in my sleep.

THE MAN. Walk ever in your sleep, fair one; for then your words drop like honey.

THE LADY. [*with cold majesty*] Know you to whom you speak, sir, that you dare express yourself so saucily?

THE MAN. [*unabashed*] Not I, not care neither. You are some lady of the Court, belike. To me there are but two sorts of women: those with excellent voices, sweet and low, and cackling hens that cannot make me dream. Your voice has all manner of loveliness in it. Grudge me not a short hour of its music.

THE LADY. Sir: you are overbold. Season your admiration for a while with—

THE MAN. [*holding up his hand to stop her*] "Season your admiration for a while—"

THE LADY. Fellow: do you dare mimic me to my face?

THE MAN. Tis music. Can you not hear? When a good musician sings a song, do you not sing it and sing it again till you have caught and fixed its perfect melody? "Season your admiration for a while": God! the history of man's heart is in that one word admiration. Admiration! [*Taking up his tablets*] What was it? "Suspend your admiration for a space—"

THE LADY. A very vile jingle of esses. I said "Season your—"

THE MAN. [*hastily*] Season: ay, season, season, season. Plague on my memory, my wretched memory! I must een write it down. [*He begins to write, but stops, his memory failing him*]. Yet tell me which was the vile jingle? You said very justly: mine own ear caught it even as my false tongue said it.

THE LADY. You said "for a space." I said "for a while."

THE MAN. "For a while" [*he corrects it*]. Good! [*Ardently*] And now be mine neither for a space nor a while, but for ever.

THE LADY. Odds my life! Are you by chance making love to me, knave?

THE MAN. Nay: tis you who have made the love: I but pour it out at your feet. I cannot but love a lass that sets such store by an apt word. Therefore vouchsafe, divine perfection of a woman—no: I have said that before somewhere; and the wordy garment of my love for you must be fire-new—

THE LADY. You talk too much, sir. Let me warn you: I am more accustomed to be listened to than preached at.

THE MAN. The most are like that that do talk well. But though you spake with the tongues of angels, as indeed you do, yet know that I am the king of words—

THE LADY. A king, ha!

THE MAN. No less. We are poor things, we men and women—

THE LADY. Dare you call me woman?

THE MAN. What nobler name can I tender you? How else can I love you? Yet you may well shrink from the name: have I not said we are but poor things? Yet there is a power that can redeem us.

THE LADY. Gramercy for your sermon, sir. I hope I know my duty.

THE MAN. This is no sermon, but the living truth. The power I speak of is the power of immortal poesy. For know that vile as this world is, and worms as we are, you have but to invest all this vileness with a magical garment of words to transfigure us and uplift our souls til earth flowers into a million heavens.

THE LADY. You spoil your heaven with your million. You are extravagant. Observe some measure in your speech.

THE MAN. You speak now as Ben does.

THE LADY. And who, pray, is Ben?

THE MAN. A learned bricklayer who thinks that the sky is at the top of his ladder, and so takes it on him to rebuke me for flying. I tell you there is no word yet coined and no melody yet sung that is extravagant and majestical enough for the glory that lovely words can reveal. It is heresy to deny it: have you not been taught that in the beginning was the Word? that the Word was with God? nay, that the Word was God?

THE LADY. Beware, fellow, how you presume to speak of holy things. The Queen is the head of the Church.

THE MAN. You are the head of my Church when you speak as you did at first. "All the perfumes of Arabia"! Can the Queen speak thus? They say she playeth well upon the virginals. Let her play so to me; and I'll kiss her hands. But until then, you are my Queen; and I'll kiss those lips that have dropt music on my heart. [*He puts his arms about her*].

THE LADY. Unmeasured impudence! On your life, take your hands from me.

The Dark Lady comes stooping along the terrace behind them like a running thrush. When she sees how they are employed, she rises angrily to her full height, and listens jealously.

THE MAN. [*unaware of the Dark Lady*] Then cease to make my hands tremble with the streams of life you pour through them. You hold me as the lodestar holds the iron: I cannot but cling to you. We are lost, you and I: nothing can separate us now.

THE DARK LADY. We shall see that, false lying hound, you and your filthy trull. [*With two vigorous cuffs, she knocks the pair asunder, sending the man, who is unlucky enough to receive a righthanded blow, sprawling an the flags*]. Take that, both of you!

THE CLOAKED LADY. [*in towering wrath, throwing off her cloak and turning in outraged majesty on her assailant*] High treason!

THE DARK LADY. [*recognizing her and falling on her knees in abject terror*] Will: I am lost: I have struck the Queen.

THE MAN. [*sitting up as majestically as his ignominious posture allows*] Woman: you have struck WILLIAM SHAKESPEAR.

QUEEN ELIZABETH. [*stupent*] Marry, come up!!! Struck William Shakespear quotha! And who in the name of all the sluts and jades and light-o'-loves and fly-by-nights that infest this palace of mine, may William Shakespear be?

THE DARK LADY. Madam: he is but a player. Oh, I could have my hand cut off—

QUEEN ELIZABETH. Belike you will, mistress. Have you bethought you that I am like to have your head cut off as well?

THE DARK LADY. Will: save me. Oh, save me.

ELIZABETH. Save you! A likely savior, on my royal word! I had thought this fellow at least an esquire; for I had hoped that even the vilest of my ladies would not have dishonored my Court by wantoning with a baseborn servant.

SHAKESPEAR. [*indignantly scrambling to his feet*] Base-born! I, a Shakespear of Stratford! I, whose mother was an Arden! baseborn! You forget yourself, madam.

ELIZABETH. [*furious*] S'blood! do I so? I will teach you—

THE DARK LADY. [*rising from her knees and throwing herself between them*] Will: in God's name anger her no further. It is death. Madam: do not listen to him.

SHAKESPEAR. Not were it een to save your life, Mary, not to mention mine own, will I flatter a monarch who forgets what is due to my family. I deny not that my father was brought down to be a poor bankrupt; but twas his gentle blood that was ever too generous for trade. Never did he disown his debts. Tis true he paid them not; but it is an attested truth that he gave bills for them; and twas those bills, in the hands of base hucksters, that were his undoing.

ELIZABETH. [*grimly*] The son of your father shall learn his place in the presence of the daughter of Harry the Eighth.

SHAKESPEAR. [*swelling with intolerant importance*] Name not that inordinate man in the same breath with Stratford's worthiest alderman. John Shakespear wedded but once: Harry Tudor was married six times. You should blush to utter his name.

THE DARK LADY. Will: for pity's sake— *crying out together*

ELIZABETH. Insolent dog—

SHAKESPEAR. [*cutting them short*] How know you that King Harry was indeed your father?

ELIZABETH. Zounds! Now by—[*she stops to grind her teeth with rage*].

THE DARK LADY. She will have me whipped through the streets. Oh God! Oh God!

SHAKESPEAR. Learn to know yourself better, madam. I am an honest gentleman of unquestioned parentage, and have already sent in my demand for the coat-of-arms that is lawfully mine. Can you say as much for yourself?

ELIZABETH. [*almost beside herself*] Another word; and I begin with mine own hands the work the hangman shall finish.

SHAKESPEAR. You are no true Tudor: this baggage here has as good a right to your royal seat as you. What maintains you on the throne of England? Is it your renowned wit? your wisdom that sets at naught the craftiest statesmen of the Christian world? No. Tis the mere chance that might have happened to any milkmaid, the caprice of Nature that made you the most wondrous piece of beauty the age hath seen. [*Elizabeth's raised fists, on the point of striking him, fall to her side*]. That is what hath brought all men to your feet, and founded your throne on the impregnable rock of your proud heart, a stony island in a sea of desire. There, madam, is some wholesome blunt honest speaking for you. Now do your worst.

ELIZABETH. [*with dignity*] Master Shakespear: it is well for you that I am a merciful prince. I make allowance for your rustic ignorance. But remember that there are things which be true, and are yet not seemly to be said (I will not say to a queen; for you will have it that I am none) but to a virgin.

SHAKESPEAR. [*bluntly*] It is no fault of mine that you are a virgin, madam, albeit tis my misfortune.

THE DARK LADY. [*terrified again*] In mercy, madam, hold no further discourse with him. He hath ever some lewd jest on his tongue. You hear how he useth me! calling me baggage and the like to your Majesty's face.

ELIZABETH. As for you, mistress, I have yet to demand what your business is at this hour in this place, and how you come to be so concerned with a player that you strike blindly at your sovereign in your jealousy of him.

THE DARK LADY. Madam: as I live and hope for salvation—

SHAKESPEAR. [*sardonically*] Ha!

THE DARK LADY. [*angrily*]—ay, I'm as like to be saved as thou that believest naught save some black magic of words and verses—I say, madam, as I am a living woman I came here to break with him for ever. Oh, madam, if you would know what misery is, listen to this man that is more than man and less at the same time. He will tie you down to anatomize your very soul: he will wring tears of blood from your humiliation; and then he will heal the wound with flatteries that no woman can resist.

SHAKESPEAR. Flatteries! [*Kneeling*] Oh, madam, I put my case at your royal feet. I confess to much. I have a rude tongue: I am unmannerly: I blaspheme against the holiness of anointed royalty; but oh, my royal mistress, AM I a flatterer?

ELIZABETH. I absolve you as to that. You are far too plain a dealer to please me. [*He rises gratefully*].

THE DARK LADY. Madam: he is flattering you even as he speaks.

ELIZABETH. [*a terrible flash in her eye*] Ha! Is it so?

SHAKESPEAR. Madam: she is jealous; and, heaven help me! not without reason. Oh, you say you are a merciful prince; but that was cruel of you, that hiding of your royal dignity when you found me here. For how can I ever be content with this black-haired, black-eyed, black-avised devil again now that I have looked upon real beauty and real majesty?

THE DARK LADY. [*wounded and desperate*] He hath swore to me ten times over that the day shall come in England when black women, for all their foulness, shall be more thought on than fair ones. [*To Shakespear, scolding at him*] Deny it if thou canst. Oh, he is compact of lies and scorns. I am tired of being tossed up to heaven and dragged down to hell at every whim that takes him. I am ashamed to my very soul that I have abased myself to love one that my father would not have deemed fit to hold my stirrup—one that will talk to all the world about me—that will put my love and my shame into his plays and make me blush for myself there—that will write sonnets about me that no man of gentle strain would put his hand to. I am all disordered: I know not what I am saying to your Majesty: I am of all ladies most deject and wretched—

SHAKESPEAR. Ha! At last sorrow hath struck a note of music out of thee. "Of all ladies most deject and wretched." [*He makes a note of it*].

THE DARK LADY. Madam: I implore you give me leave to go. I am distracted with grief and shame. I—

ELIZABETH. Go [*The Dark Lady tries to kiss her hand*]. No more. Go. [*The Dark Lady goes, convulsed*]. You have been cruel to that poor fond wretch, Master Shakespear.

SHAKESPEAR. I am not cruel, madam; but you know the fable of Jupiter and Semele. I could not help my lightnings scorching her.

ELIZABETH. You have an overweening conceit of yourself, sir, that displeases your Queen.

SHAKESPEAR. Oh, madam, can I go about with the modest cough of a minor poet, belittling my inspiration and making the mightiest wonder of your reign a thing of nought? I have said that "not marble nor the gilded monuments of princes shall outlive" the words with which I make the world glorious or foolish at my will. Besides, I would have you think me great enough to grant me a boon.

ELIZABETH. I hope it is a boon that may be asked of a virgin Queen without offence, sir. I mistrust your forwardness; and I bid you remember that I do not suffer persons of your degree (if I may say so without offence to your father the alderman) to presume too far.

SHAKESPEAR. Oh, madam, I shall not forget myself again; though by my life, could I make you a serving wench, neither a queen nor a virgin should you be for so much longer as a flash of lightning might take to cross the river to the Bankside. But since you are a queen and will none of me, nor of

Philip of Spain, nor of any other mortal man, I must een contain myself as best I may, and ask you only for a boon of State.

ELIZABETH. A boon of State already! You are becoming a courtier like the rest of them. You lack advancement.

SHAKESPEAR. "Lack advancement." By your Majesty's leave: a queenly phrase. [*He is about to write it down*].

ELIZABETH. [*striking the tablets from his hand*] Your tables begin to anger me, sir. I am not here to write your plays for you.

SHAKESPEAR. You are here to inspire them, madam. For this, among the rest, were you ordained. But the boon I crave is that you do endow a great playhouse, or, if I may make bold to coin a scholarly name for it, a National Theatre, for the better instruction and gracing of your Majesty's subjects.

ELIZABETH. Why, sir, are there not theatres enow on the Bankside and in Blackfriars?

SHAKESPEAR. Madam: these are the adventures of needy and desperate men that must, to save themselves from perishing of want, give the sillier sort of people what they best like; and what they best like, God knows, is not their own betterment and instruction, as we well see by the example of the churches, which must needs compel men to frequent them, though they be open to all without charge. Only when there is a matter of a murder, or a plot, or a pretty youth in petticoats, or some naughty tale of wantonness, will your subjects pay the great cost of good players and their finery, with a little profit to boot. To prove this I will tell you that I have written two noble and excellent plays setting forth the advancement of women of high nature and fruitful industry even as your Majesty is: the one a skilful physician, the other a sister devoted to good works. I have also stole from a book of idle wanton tales two of the most damnable foolishnesses in the world, in the one of which a woman goeth in man's attire and maketh impudent love to her swain, who pleaseth the groundlings by overthrowing a wrestler; whilst, in the other, one of the same kidney sheweth her wit by saying endless naughtinesses to a gentleman as lewd as herself. I have writ these to save my friends from penury, yet shewing my scorn for such follies and for them that praise them by calling the one As You Like It, meaning that it is not as *I* like it, and the other Much Ado About Nothing, as it truly is. And now these two filthy pieces drive their nobler fellows from the stage, where indeed I cannot have my lady physician presented at all, she being too honest a woman for the taste of the town. Wherefore I humbly beg your Majesty to give order that a theatre be endowed out of the public revenue for the playing of those pieces of mine which no merchant will touch, seeing that his gain is so much greater with the worse than with the better. Thereby you shall also encourage other men to undertake the writing of plays who do now despise it and leave it wholly to those whose counsels will work little good to your realm. For this writing of plays is a great matter, forming as it does the minds and affections of men in such sort that whatsoever they see done in show on the stage, they will presently be doing in earnest in the world, which is but a larger stage. Of late, as you know, the Church taught the people by means of plays; but the people flocked only to such as were full of superstitious miracles and bloody martyrdoms; and so the Church, which also was just then brought into straits by the policy of your royal father, did abandon and discountenance the art of playing; and thus it fell into the hands of poor players and greedy merchants that had their pockets to look to and not the greatness of this your kingdom. Therefore now must your Majesty take up that good work that your Church hath abandoned, and restore the art of playing to its former use and dignity.

ELIZABETH. Master Shakespear: I will speak of this matter to the Lord Treasurer.

SHAKESPEAR. Then am I undone, madam; for there was never yet a Lord Treasurer that could find a penny for anything over and above the necessary expenses of your government, save for a war or a salary for his own nephew.

ELIZABETH. Master Shakespear: you speak sooth; yet cannot I in any wise mend it. I dare not offend my unruly Puritans by making so lewd a place as the playhouse a public charge; and there be a thousand things to be done in this London of mine before your poetry can have its penny from the general purse. I tell thee, Master Will, it will be three hundred years and more before my subjects learn that man cannot live by bread alone, but by every word that cometh from the mouth of those whom God inspires. By that time you and I will be dust beneath the feet of the horses, if indeed there be any horses then, and men be still riding instead of flying. Now it may be that by then your works will be dust also.

SHAKESPEAR. They will stand, madam: fear nor for that.

ELIZABETH. It may prove so. But of this I am certain (for I know my countrymen) that until every other country in the Christian world, even to barbarian Muscovy and the hamlets of the boorish Germans, have its playhouse at the public charge, England will never adventure. And she will adventure then only because it is her desire to be ever in the fashion, and to do humbly and dutifully whatso she seeth everybody else doing. In the meantime you must content yourself as best you can by the playing of those two pieces which you give out as the most damnable ever writ, but which your countrymen, I warn you, will swear are the best you have ever done. But this I will say, that if I could speak across the ages to our descendants, I should heartily recommend them to fulfil your wish; for the Scottish minstrel hath well said that he that maketh the songs of a nation is mightier than he that maketh its laws; and the same may well be true of plays and interludes. [*The clock chimes the first quarter. The warder returns on his round*]. And now, sir, we are upon the hour when it better beseems a virgin queen to be abed than to converse alone with the naughtiest of her subjects. Ho there! Who keeps ward on the queen's lodgings tonight?

THE WARDER. I do, an't please your majesty.

ELIZABETH. See that you keep it better in future. You have let pass a most dangerous gallant even to the very door of our royal chamber. Lead him forth; and bring me word when he is safely locked out; for I shall scarce dare disrobe until the palace gates are between us.

SHAKESPEAR. [*kissing her hand*] My body goes through the gate into the darkness, madam; but my thoughts follow you.

ELIZABETH. How! to my bed!

SHAKESPEAR. No, madam, to your prayers, in which I beg you to remember my theatre.

ELIZABETH. That is my prayer to posterity. Forget not your own to God; and so goodnight, Master Will.

SHAKESPEAR. Goodnight, great Elizabeth. God save the Queen!

ELIZABETH. Amen.

Exeunt severally: she to her chamber: he, in custody of the warder, to the gate nearest Blackfriars.

AYOT, ST. LAWRENCE, *20th June* 1910.

FANNY'S FIRST PLAY

PREFACE TO FANNY'S FIRST PLAY

Fanny's First Play, being but a potboiler, needs no preface. But its lesson is not, I am sorry to say, unneeded. Mere morality, or the substitution of custom for conscience was once accounted a shameful and cynical thing: people talked of right and wrong, of honor and dishonor, of sin and grace, of salvation and damnation, not of morality and immorality. The word morality, if we met it in the Bible, would surprise us as much as the word telephone or motor car. Nowadays we do not seem to know that there is any other test of conduct except morality; and the result is that the young had better have their souls awakened by disgrace, capture by the police, and a month's hard labor, than drift along from their cradles to their graves doing what other people do for no other reason than that other people do it, and knowing nothing of good and evil, of courage and cowardice, or indeed anything but how to keep hunger and concupiscence and fashionable dressing within the bounds of good taste except when their excesses can be concealed. Is it any wonder that I am driven to offer to young people in our suburbs the desperate advice: Do something that will get you into trouble? But please do not suppose that I defend a state of things which makes such advice the best that can be given under the circumstances, or that I do not know how difficult it is to find out a way of getting into trouble that will combine loss of respectability with integrity of self-respect and reasonable consideration for other peoples' feelings and interests on every point except their dread of losing their own respectability. But when there's a will there's a way. I hate to see dead people walking about: it is unnatural. And our respectable middle class people are all as dead as mutton. Out of the mouth of Mrs Knox I have delivered on them the judgment of her God.

The critics whom I have lampooned in the induction to this play under the names of Trotter, Vaughan, and Gunn will forgive me: in fact Mr Trotter forgave me beforehand, and assisted the make-up by which Mr Claude King so successfully simulated his personal appearance. The critics whom I did not introduce were somewhat hurt, as I should have been myself under the same circumstances; but I had not room for them all; so I can only apologize and assure them that I meant no disrespect.

The concealment of the authorship, if a *secret de Polichinelle* can be said to involve concealment, was a necessary part of the play. In so far as it was effectual, it operated as a measure of relief to those critics and playgoers who are so obsessed by my strained legendary reputation that they approach my plays in a condition which is really one of derangement, and are quite unable to conceive a play of mine as anything but a trap baited with paradoxes, and designed to compass their ethical perversion and intellectual confusion. If it were possible, I should put forward all my plays anonymously, or hire some less disturbing person, as Bacon is said to have hired Shakespear, to father my plays for me.

Fanny's First Play was performed for the first time at the Little Theatre in the Adelphi, London, on the afternoon of Wednesday, April 19th 1911.

INDUCTION

The end of a saloon in an old-fashioned country house (Florence Towers, the property of Count O'Dowda) has been curtained off to form a stage for a private theatrical performance. A footman in grandiose Spanish livery enters before the curtain, on its O.P. side.

FOOTMAN. [*announcing*] Mr Cecil Savoyard. [*Cecil Savoyard comes in: a middle-aged man in evening dress and a fur-lined overcoat. He is surprised to find nobody to receive him. So is the Footman*]. Oh, beg pardon, sir: I thought the Count was here. He was when I took up your name. He must have gone through the stage into the library. This way, sir. [*He moves towards the division in the middle of the curtains*].

SAVOYARD. Half a mo. [*The Footman stops*]. When does the play begin? Half-past eight?

FOOTMAN. Nine, sir.

SAVOYARD. Oh, good. Well, will you telephone to my wife at the George that it's not until nine?

FOOTMAN. Right, sir. Mrs Cecil Savoyard, sir?

SAVOYARD. No: Mrs William Tinkler. Dont forget.

THE FOOTMAN. Mrs Tinkler, sir. Right, sir. [*The Count comes in through the curtains*]. Here is the Count, sir. [*Announcing*] Mr Cecil Savoyard, sir. [*He withdraws*].

COUNT O'DOWDA. [*A handsome man of fifty, dressed with studied elegance a hundred years out of date, advancing cordially to shake hands with his visitor*] Pray excuse me, Mr Savoyard. I suddenly recollected that all the bookcases in the library were locked—in fact theyve never been opened since we came from Venice—and as our literary guests will probably use the library a good deal, I just ran in to unlock everything.

SAVOYARD. Oh, you mean the dramatic critics. M'yes. I suppose theres a smoking room?

THE COUNT. My study is available. An old-fashioned house, you understand. Wont you sit down, Mr Savoyard?

SAVOYARD. Thanks. [*They sit. Savoyard, looking at his host's obsolete costume, continues*] I had no idea you were going to appear in the piece yourself.

THE COUNT. I am not. I wear this costume because—well, perhaps I had better explain the position, if it interests you.

SAVOYARD. Certainly.

THE COUNT. Well, you see, Mr Savoyard, I'm rather a stranger in your world. I am not, I hope, a modern man in any sense of the word. I'm not really an Englishman: my family is Irish: Ive lived all my life in Italy—in Venice mostly—my very title is a foreign one: I am a Count of the Holy Roman Empire.

SAVOYARD. Where's that?

THE COUNT. At present, nowhere, except as a memory and an ideal. [*Savoyard inclines his head respectfully to the ideal*]. But I am by no means an idealogue. I am not content with beautiful dreams: I want beautiful realities.

SAVOYARD. Hear, hear! I'm all with you there—when you can get them.

THE COUNT. Why not get them? The difficulty is not that there are no beautiful realities, Mr Savoyard: the difficulty is that so few of us know them when we see them. We have inherited from the past a vast treasure of beauty—of imperishable masterpieces of poetry, of painting, of sculpture, of architecture, of music, of exquisite fashions in dress, in furniture, in domestic decoration. We can contemplate these treasures. We can reproduce many of them. We can buy a few inimitable originals. We can shut out the nineteenth century—

SAVOYARD. [*correcting him*] The twentieth.

THE COUNT. To me the century I shut out will always be the nineteenth century, just as your national anthem will always be God Save the Queen, no matter how many kings may succeed. I found England befouled with industrialism: well, I did what Byron did: I simply refused to live in it. You remember Byron's words: "I am sure my bones would not rest in an English grave, or my clay mix with the earth of that country. I believe the thought would drive me mad on my deathbed could I suppose that any of my friends would be base enough to convey my carcase back to her soil. I would not even feed her worms if I could help it."

SAVOYARD. Did Byron say that?

THE COUNT. He did, sir.

SAVOYARD. It dont sound like him. I saw a good deal of him at one time.

THE COUNT. You! But how is that possible? You are too young.

SAVOYARD. I was quite a lad, of course. But I had a job in the original production of Our Boys.

THE COUNT. My dear sir, not that Byron. Lord Byron, the poet.

SAVOYARD. Oh, I beg your pardon. I thought you were talking of the Byron. So you prefer living abroad?

THE COUNT. I find England ugly and Philistine. Well, I dont live in it. I find modern houses ugly. I dont live in them: I have a palace on the grand canal. I find modern clothes prosaic. I dont wear them, except, of course, in the street. My ears are offended by the Cockney twang: I keep out of hearing of it and speak and listen to Italian. I find Beethoven's music coarse and restless, and Wagner's senseless and detestable. I do not listen to them. I listen to Cimarosa, to Pergolesi, to Gluck and Mozart. Nothing simpler, sir.

SAVOYARD. It's all right when you can afford it.

THE COUNT. Afford it! My dear Mr Savoyard, if you are a man with a sense of beauty you can make an earthly paradise for yourself in Venice on 1500 pounds a year, whilst our wretched vulgar industrial millionaires are spending twenty thousand on the amusements of billiard markers. I assure you I am a poor man according to modern ideas. But I have never had anything less than the very best that life has produced. It is my good fortune to have a beautiful and lovable daughter; and that girl, sir, has never seen an ugly sight or heard an ugly sound that I could spare her; and she has certainly never worn an ugly dress or tasted coarse food or bad wine in her life. She has lived in a palace; and her perambulator was a gondola. Now you know the sort of people we are, Mr Savoyard. You can imagine how we feel here.

SAVOYARD. Rather out of it, eh?

THE COUNT. Out of it, sir! Out of what?

SAVOYARD. Well, out of everything.

THE COUNT. Out of soot and fog and mud and east wind; out of vulgarity and ugliness, hypocrisy and greed, superstition and stupidity. Out of all this, and in the sunshine, in the enchanted region of which great artists alone have had the secret, in the sacred footsteps of Byron, of Shelley, of the Brownings, of Turner and Ruskin. Dont you envy me, Mr Savoyard?

SAVOYARD. Some of us must live in England, you know, just to keep the place going. Besides—though, mind you, I dont say it isnt all right from the high art point of view and all that—three weeks of it would drive me melancholy mad. However, I'm glad you told me, because it explains why it is you dont seem to know your way about much in England. I hope, by the way, that everything has given satisfaction to your daughter.

THE COUNT. She seems quite satisfied. She tells me that the actors you sent down are perfectly suited to their parts, and very nice people to work with. I understand she had some difficulties at the first rehearsals with the gentleman you call the producer, because he hadnt read the play; but the moment he found out what it was all about everything went smoothly.

SAVOYARD. Havnt you seen the rehearsals?

THE COUNT. Oh no. I havnt been allowed even to meet any of the company. All I can tell you is that the hero is a Frenchman [*Savoyard is rather scandalized*]: I asked her not to have an English hero. That is all I know. [*Ruefully*] I havnt been consulted even about the costumes, though there, I think, I could have been some use.

SAVOYARD. [*puzzled*] But there arnt any costumes.

THE COUNT. [*seriously shocked*] What! No costumes! Do you mean to say it is a modern play?

SAVOYARD. I dont know: I didnt read it. I handed it to Billy Burjoyce—the producer, you know—and left it to him to select the company and so on. But I should have had to order the costumes if there had been any. There wernt.

THE COUNT. [*smiling as he recovers from his alarm*] I understand. She has taken the costumes into her own hands. She is an expert in beautiful costumes. I venture to promise you, Mr Savoyard, that what you are about to see will be like a Louis Quatorze ballet painted by Watteau. The heroine will be an exquisite Columbine, her lover a dainty Harlequin, her father a picturesque Pantaloon, and the valet who hoodwinks the father and brings about the happiness of the lovers a grotesque but perfectly tasteful Punchinello or Mascarille or Sganarelle.

SAVOYARD. I see. That makes three men; and the clown and policeman will make five. Thats why you wanted five men in the company.

THE COUNT. My dear sir, you dont suppose I mean that vulgar, ugly, silly, senseless, malicious and destructive thing, the harlequinade of a nineteenth century English Christmas pantomime! What was it after all but a stupid attempt to imitate the success made by the genius of Grimaldi a hundred years ago? My daughter does not know of the existence of such a thing. I refer to the graceful and charming fantasies of the Italian and French stages of the seventeenth and eighteenth centuries.

SAVOYARD. Oh, I beg pardon. I quite agree that harlequinades are rot. Theyve been dropped at all smart theatres. But from what Billy Burjoyce told me I got the idea that your daughter knew her way about here, and had seen a lot of plays. He had no idea she'd been away in Venice all the time.

THE COUNT. Oh, she has not been. I should have explained that two years ago my daughter left me to complete her education at Cambridge. Cambridge was my own University; and though of course there were no women there in my time, I felt confident that if the atmosphere of the eighteenth century still existed anywhere in England, it would be at Cambridge. About three months ago she wrote to me and asked whether I wished to give her a present on her next birthday. Of course I said yes; and she then astonished and delighted me by telling me that she had written a play, and that the present she wanted was a private performance of it with real actors and real critics.

SAVOYARD. Yes: thats what staggered me. It was easy enough to engage a company for a private performance: it's done often enough. But the notion of having critics was new. I hardly knew how to set about it. They dont expect private engagements; and so they have no agents. Besides, I didnt know what to offer them. I knew that they were cheaper than actors, because they get long engagements: forty years sometimes; but thats no rule for a single job. Then theres such a lot of them: on first nights they run away with all your stalls: you cant find a decent place for your own mother. It would have cost a fortune to bring the lot.

THE COUNT. Of course I never dreamt of having them all. Only a few first-rate representative men.

SAVOYARD. Just so. All you want is a few sample opinions. Out of a hundred notices you wont find more than four at the outside that say anything different. Well, Ive got just the right four for you. And what do you think it has cost me?

THE COUNT. [*shrugging his shoulders*] I cannot guess.

SAVOYARD. Ten guineas, and expenses. I had to give Flawner Bannal ten. He wouldnt come for less; and he asked fifty. I had to give it, because if we hadnt had him we might just as well have had nobody at all.

THE COUNT. But what about the others, if Mr Flannel—

SAVOYARD. [*shocked*] Flawner Bannal.

THE COUNT. —if Mr Bannal got the whole ten?

SAVOYARD. Oh, I managed that. As this is a high-class sort of thing, the first man I went for was Trotter.

THE COUNT. Oh indeed. I am very glad you have secured Mr Trotter. I have read his Playful Impressions.

SAVOYARD. Well, I was rather in a funk about him. Hes not exactly what I call approachable; and he was a bit stand-off at first. But when I explained and told him your daughter—

THE COUNT. [*interrupting in alarm*] You did not say that the play was by her, I hope?

SAVOYARD. No: thats been kept a dead secret. I just said your daughter has asked for a real play with a real author and a real critic and all the rest of it. The moment I mentioned the daughter I had him. He has a daughter of his own. Wouldnt hear of payment! Offered to come just to please her! Quite human. I was surprised.

THE COUNT. Extremely kind of him.

SAVOYARD. Then I went to Vaughan, because he does music as well as the drama: and you said you thought there would be music. I told him Trotter would feel lonely without him; so he promised like a bird. Then I thought youd like one of the latest sort: the chaps that go for the newest things and swear theyre oldfashioned. So I nailed Gilbert Gunn. The four will give you a representative team. By the way [*looking at his watch*] theyll be here presently.

THE COUNT. Before they come, Mr Savoyard, could you give me any hints about them that would help me to make a little conversation with them? I am, as you said, rather out of it in England; and I might unwittingly say something tactless.

SAVOYARD. Well, let me see. As you dont like English people, I dont know that youll get on with Trotter, because hes thoroughly English: never happy except when hes in Paris, and speaks French so unnecessarily well that everybody there spots him as an Englishman the moment he opens his mouth. Very witty and all that. Pretends to turn up his nose at the theatre and says people make too much fuss about art [*the Count is extremely indignant*]. But thats only his modesty, because art is his own line, you understand. Mind you dont chaff him about Aristotle.

THE COUNT. Why should I chaff him about Aristotle?

SAVOYARD. Well, I dont know; but its one of the recognized ways of chaffing him. However, youll get on with him all right: hes a man of the world and a man of sense. The one youll have to be careful about is Vaughan.

THE COUNT. In what way, may I ask?

SAVOYARD. Well, Vaughan has no sense of humor; and if you joke with him he'll think youre insulting him on purpose. Mind: it's not that he doesnt see a joke: he does; and it hurts him. A comedy scene makes him sore all over: he goes away black and blue, and pitches into the play for all hes worth.

THE COUNT. But surely that is a very serious defect in a man of his profession?

SAVOYARD. Yes it is, and no mistake. But Vaughan is honest, and dont care a brass farthing what he says, or whether it pleases anybody or not; and you must have one man of that sort to say the things that nobody else will say.

THE COUNT. It seems to me to carry the principle of division of labor too far, this keeping of the honesty and the other qualities in separate compartments. What is Mr Gunn's speciality, if I may ask?

SAVOYARD. Gunn is one of the intellectuals.

THE COUNT. But arnt they all intellectuals?

SAVOYARD. Lord! no: heaven forbid! You must be careful what you say about that: I shouldnt like anyone to call me an Intellectual: I dont think any Englishman would! They dont count really, you know; but still it's rather the thing to have them. Gunn is one of the young intellectuals: he writes plays himself. Hes useful because he pitches into the older intellectuals who are standing in his way. But you may take it from me that none of these chaps really matter. Flawner Bannal's your man. Bannal really represents the British playgoer. When he likes a thing, you may take your oath there are a hundred thousand people in London thatll like it if they can only be got to know about it. Besides, Bannal's knowledge of the theatre is an inside knowledge. We know him; and he knows us. He knows the ropes: he knows his way about: he knows what hes talking about.

THE COUNT. [*with a little sigh*] Age and experience, I suppose?

SAVOYARD. Age! I should put him at twenty at the very outside, myself. It's not an old man's job after all, is it? Bannal may not ride the literary high horse like Trotter and the rest; but I'd take his opinion before any other in London. Hes the man in the street; and thats what you want.

THE COUNT. I am almost sorry you didnt give the gentleman his full terms. I should not have grudged the fifty guineas for a sound opinion. He may feel shabbily treated.

SAVOYARD. Well, let him. It was a bit of side, his asking fifty. After all, what is he? Only a pressman. Jolly good business for him to earn ten guineas: hes done the same job often enough for half a quid, I expect.

Fanny O'Dowda comes precipitately through the curtains, excited and nervous. A girl of nineteen in a dress synchronous with her father's.

FANNY. Papa, papa, the critics have come. And one of them has a cocked hat and sword like a— [*she notices Savoyard*] Oh, I beg your pardon.

THE COUNT. This is Mr Savoyard, your impresario, my dear.

FANNY. [*shaking hands*] How do you do?

SAVOYARD. Pleased to meet you, Miss O'Dowda. The cocked hat is all right. Trotter is a member of the new Academic Committee. He induced them to go in for a uniform like the French Academy; and I asked him to wear it.

THE FOOTMAN. [*announcing*] Mr Trotter, Mr Vaughan, Mr Gunn, Mr Flawner Bannal. [*The four critics enter. Trotter wears a diplomatic dress, with sword and three-cornered hat. His age is about 50. Vaughan is 40. Gunn is 30. Flawner Bannal is 20 and is quite unlike the others. They can be classed at sight as professional men: Bannal is obviously one of those unemployables of the business class who manage to pick up a living by a sort of courage which gives him cheerfulness, conviviality, and bounce, and is helped out positively by a slight turn for writing, and negatively by a comfortable ignorance and lack of intuition which hides from him all the dangers and disgraces that keep men of finer perception in check. The Count approaches them hospitably*].

SAVOYARD. Count O'Dowda, gentlemen. Mr Trotter.

TROTTER. [*looking at the Count's costume*] Have I the pleasure of meeting a confrere?

THE COUNT. No, sir: I have no right to my costume except the right of a lover of the arts to dress myself handsomely. You are most welcome, Mr Trotter. [*Trotter bows in the French manner*].

SAVOYARD. Mr Vaughan.

THE COUNT. How do you do, Mr Vaughan?

VAUGHAN. Quite well, thanks.

SAVOYARD. Mr Gunn.

THE COUNT. Delighted to make your acquaintance, Mr Gunn.

GUNN. Very pleased.

SAVOYARD. Mr Flawner Bannal.

THE COUNT. Very kind of you to come, Mr Bannal.

BANNAL. Dont mention it.

THE COUNT. Gentlemen, my daughter. [*They all bow*]. We are very greatly indebted to you, gentlemen, for so kindly indulging her whim. [*The dressing bell sounds. The Count looks at his watch*]. Ah! The dressing bell, gentlemen. As our play begins at nine, I have had to put forward the dinner hour a little. May I shew you to your rooms? [*He goes out, followed by all the men, except Trotter, who, going last, is detained by Fanny*].

FANNY. Mr Trotter: I want to say something to you about this play.

TROTTER. No: thats forbidden. You must not attempt to *souffler* the critic.

FANNY. Oh, I would not for the world try to influence your opinion.

TROTTER. But you do: you are influencing me very shockingly. You invite me to this charming house, where I'm about to enjoy a charming dinner. And just before the dinner I'm taken aside by a charming young lady to be talked to about the play. How can you expect me to be impartial? God forbid that I should set up to be a judge, or do more than record an impression; but my impressions can be influenced; and in this case youre influencing them shamelessly all the time.

FANNY. Dont make me more nervous than I am already, Mr Trotter. If you knew how I feel!

TROTTER. Naturally: your first party: your first appearance in England as hostess. But youre doing it beautifully. Dont be afraid. Every *nuance* is perfect.

FANNY. It's so kind of you to say so, Mr Trotter. But that isnt whats the matter. The truth is, this play is going to give my father a dreadful shock.

TROTTER. Nothing unusual in that, I'm sorry to say. Half the young ladies in London spend their evenings making their fathers take them to plays that are not fit for elderly people to see.

FANNY. Oh, I know all about that; but you cant understand what it means to Papa. Youre not so innocent as he is.

TROTTER. [*remonstrating*] My dear young lady—

FANNY. I dont mean morally innocent: everybody who reads your articles knows youre as innocent as a lamb.

TROTTER. What!

FANNY. Yes, Mr Trotter: Ive seen a good deal of life since I came to England; and I assure you that to me youre a mere baby: a dear, good, well-meaning, delightful, witty, charming baby; but still just a wee lamb in a world of wolves. Cambridge is not what it was in my father's time.

TROTTER. Well, I must say!

FANNY. Just so. Thats one of our classifications in the Cambridge Fabian Society.

TROTTER. Classifications? I dont understand.

FANNY. We classify our aunts into different sorts. And one of the sorts is the "I must says."

TROTTER. I withdraw "I must say." I substitute "Blame my cats!" No: I substitute "Blame my kittens!" Observe, Miss O'Dowda: kittens. I say again in the teeth of the whole Cambridge Fabian Society, kittens. Impertinent little kittens. Blame them. Smack them. I guess what is on your conscience. This play to which you have lured me is one of those in which members of Fabian Societies instruct their grandmothers in the art of milking ducks. And you are afraid it will shock your father. Well, I hope it will. And if he consults me about it I shall recommend him to smack you soundly and pack you off to bed.

FANNY. Thats one of your prettiest literary attitudes, Mr Trotter; but it doesnt take me in. You see, I'm much more conscious of what you really are than you are yourself, because weve discussed you thoroughly at Cambridge; and youve never discussed yourself, have you?

TROTTER. I—

FANNY. Of course you havnt; so you see it's no good Trottering at me.

TROTTER. Trottering!

FANNY. Thats what we call it at Cambridge.

TROTTER. If it were not so obviously a stage *cliche*, I should say Damn Cambridge. As it is, I blame my kittens. And now let me warn you. If youre going to be a charming healthy young English girl, you may coax me. If youre going to be an unsexed Cambridge Fabian virago, I'll treat you as my intellectual equal, as I would treat a man.

FANNY. [*adoringly*] But how few men are your intellectual equals, Mr Trotter!

TROTTER. I'm getting the worst of this.

FANNY. Oh no. Why do you say that?

TROTTER. May I remind you that the dinner-bell will ring presently?

FANNY. What does it matter? We're both ready. I havnt told you yet what I want you to do for me.

TROTTER. Nor have you particularly predisposed me to do it, except out of pure magnanimity. What is it?

FANNY. I dont mind this play shocking my father morally. It's good for him to be shocked morally. It's all that the young can do for the old, to shock them and keep them up to date. But I know that this play will shock him artistically; and that terrifies me. No moral consideration could make a breach between us: he would forgive me for anything of that kind sooner or later; but he never gives way on a point of art. I darent let him know that I love Beethoven and Wagner; and as to Strauss, if he heard three bars of Elektra, it'd part us for ever. Now what I want you to do is this. If hes very angry—if he hates the play, because it's a modern play—will you tell him that it's not my fault; that its style and construction, and so forth, are considered the very highest art nowadays; that the author wrote it in the proper way for repertory theatres of the most superior kind—you know the kind of plays I mean?

TROTTER. [*emphatically*] I think I know the sort of entertainments you mean. But please do not beg a vital question by calling them plays. I dont pretend to be an authority; but I have at least established the fact that these productions, whatever else they may be, are certainly not plays.

FANNY. The authors dont say they are.

TROTTER. [*warmly*] I am aware that one author, who is, I blush to say, a personal friend of mine, resorts freely to the dastardly subterfuge of calling them conversations, discussions, and so forth, with the express object of evading criticism. But I'm not to be disarmed by such tricks. I say they are not plays. Dialogues, if you will. Exhibitions of character, perhaps: especially the character of the author. Fictions, possibly, though a little decent reticence as to introducing actual persons, and thus violating the sanctity of private life, might not be amiss. But plays, no. I say NO. Not plays. If you will not concede this point I cant continue our conversation. I take this seriously. It's a matter of principle. I must ask you, Miss O'Dowda, before we go a step further, Do you or do you not claim that these works are plays?

FANNY. I assure you I dont.

TROTTER. Not in any sense of the word?

FANNY. Not in any sense of the word. I loathe plays.

TROTTER. [*disappointed*] That last remark destroys all the value of your admission. You admire these—these theatrical nondescripts? You enjoy them?

FANNY. Dont you?

TROTTER. Of course I do. Do you take me for a fool? Do you suppose I prefer popular melodramas? Have I not written most appreciative notices of them? But I say theyre not plays. Theyre not plays. I cant consent to remain in this house another minute if anything remotely resembling them is to be foisted on me as a play.

FANNY. I fully admit that theyre not plays. I only want you to tell my father that plays are not plays nowadays—not in your sense of the word.

TROTTER. Ah, there you go again! In my sense of the word! You believe that my criticism is merely a personal impression; that—

FANNY. You always said it was.

TROTTER. Pardon me: not on this point. If you had been classically educated—

FANNY. But I have.

TROTTER. Pooh! Cambridge! If you had been educated at Oxford, you would know that the definition of a play has been settled exactly and scientifically for two thousand two hundred and sixty years. When I say that these entertainments are not plays, I dont mean in my sense of the word, but in the sense given to it for all time by the immortal Stagirite.

FANNY. Who is the Stagirite?

TROTTER. [*shocked*] You dont know who the Stagirite was?

FANNY. Sorry. Never heard of him.

TROTTER. And this is Cambridge education! Well, my dear young lady, I'm delighted to find theres something you don't know; and I shant spoil you by dispelling an ignorance which, in my opinion, is highly becoming to your age and sex. So we'll leave it at that.

FANNY. But you will promise to tell my father that lots of people write plays just like this one—that I havnt selected it out of mere heartlessness?

TROTTER. I cant possibly tell you what I shall say to your father about the play until Ive seen the play. But I'll tell you what I shall say to him about you. I shall say that youre a very foolish young lady; that youve got into a very questionable set; and that the sooner he takes you away from Cambridge and its Fabian Society, the better.

FANNY. It's so funny to hear you pretending to be a heavy father. In Cambridge we regard you as a *bel esprit*, a wit, an Irresponsible, a Parisian Immoralist, *tres chic.*

TROTTER. I!

FANNY. Theres quite a Trotter set.

TROTTER. Well, upon my word!

FANNY. They go in for adventures and call you Aramis.

TROTTER. They wouldnt dare!

FANNY. You always make such delicious fun of the serious people. Your *insouciance*—

TROTTER. [*frantic*] Stop talking French to me: it's not a proper language for a young girl. Great heavens! how is it possible that a few innocent pleasantries should be so frightfully misunderstood? Ive tried all my life to be sincere and simple, to be unassuming and kindly. Ive lived a blameless life. Ive supported the Censorship in the face of ridicule and insult. And now I'm told that I'm a centre of Immoralism! of Modern Minxism! a trifler with the most sacred subjects! a Nietzschean!! perhaps a Shavian!!!

FANNY. Do you mean you are really on the serious side, Mr Trotter?

TROTTER. Of course I'm on the serious side. How dare you ask me such a question?

FANNY. Then why dont you play for it?

TROTTER. I do play for it—short, of course, of making myself ridiculous.

FANNY. What! not make yourself ridiculous for the sake of a good cause! Oh, Mr Trotter. Thats *vieux jeu.*

TROTTER. [*shouting at her*] Dont talk French. I will not allow it.

FANNY. But this dread of ridicule is so frightfully out of date. The Cambridge Fabian Society—

TROTTER. I forbid you to mention the Fabian Society to me.

FANNY. Its motto is "You cannot learn to skate without making yourself ridiculous."

TROTTER. Skate! What has that to do with it?

FANNY. Thats not all. It goes on, "The ice of life is slippery."

TROTTER. Ice of life indeed! You should be eating penny ices and enjoying yourself. I wont hear another word.

The Count returns.

THE COUNT. We're all waiting in the drawing-room, my dear. Have you been detaining Mr Trotter all this time?

TROTTER. I'm so sorry. I must have just a little brush up: I [*He hurries out*].

THE COUNT. My dear, you should be in the drawing-room. You should not have kept him here.

FANNY. I know. Dont scold me: I had something important to say to him.

THE COUNT. I shall ask him to take you in to dinner.

FANNY. Yes, papa. Oh, I hope it will go off well.

THE COUNT. Yes, love, of course it will. Come along.

FANNY. Just one thing, papa, whilst we're alone. Who was the Stagirite?

THE COUNT. The Stagirite? Do you mean to say you dont know?

FANNY. Havnt the least notion.

THE COUNT. The Stagirite was Aristotle. By the way, dont mention him to Mr Trotter.

They go to the dining-room.

ACT I

In the dining-room of a house in Denmark Hill, an elderly lady sits at breakfast reading the newspaper. Her chair is at the end of the oblong dining-table furthest from the fire. There is an empty chair at the other end. The fireplace is behind this chair; and the door is next the fireplace, between it and the corner. An arm-chair stands beside the coal-scuttle. In the middle of the back wall is the sideboard, parallel to the table. The rest of the furniture is mostly dining-room chairs, ranged against the walls, and including a baby rocking-chair on the lady's side of the room. The lady is a placid person. Her husband, Mr Robin Gilbey, not at all placid, bursts violently into the room with a letter in his hand.

GILBEY. [*grinding his teeth*] This is a nice thing. This is a b——

MRS GILBEY. [*cutting him short*] Leave it at that, please. Whatever it is, bad language wont make it better.

GILBEY. [*bitterly*] Yes, put me in the wrong as usual. Take your boy's part against me. [*He flings himself into the empty chair opposite her*].

MRS GILBEY. When he does anything right, hes your son. When he does anything wrong hes mine. Have you any news of him?

GILBEY. Ive a good mind not to tell you.

MRS GILBEY. Then dont. I suppose hes been found. Thats a comfort, at all events.

GILBEY. No, he hasnt been found. The boy may be at the bottom of the river for all you care. [*Too agitated to sit quietly, he rises and paces the room distractedly*].

MRS GILBEY. Then what have you got in your hand?

GILBEY. Ive a letter from the Monsignor Grenfell. From New York. Dropping us. Cutting us. [*Turning fiercely on her*] Thats a nice thing, isnt it?

MRS GILBEY. What for?

GILBEY. [*flinging away towards his chair*] How do *I* know what for?

MRS GILBEY. What does he say?

GILBEY. [*sitting down and grumblingly adjusting his spectacles*] This is what he says. "My dear Mr Gilbey: The news about Bobby had to follow me across the Atlantic: it did not reach me until to-day. I am afraid he is incorrigible. My brother, as you may imagine, feels that this last escapade has gone beyond the bounds; and I think, myself, that Bobby ought to be made to feel that such scrapes involve a certain degree of reprobation." "As you may imagine"! And we know no more about it than the babe unborn.

MRS GILBEY. What else does he say?

GILBEY. "I think my brother must have been just a little to blame himself; so, between ourselves, I shall, with due and impressive formality, forgive Bobby later on; but for the present I think it had better be understood that he is in disgrace, and that we are no longer on visiting terms. As ever, yours sincerely." [*His agitation masters him again*] Thats a nice slap in the face to get from a man in his position! This is what your son has brought on me.

MRS GILBEY. Well, I think it's rather a nice letter. He as good as tells you hes only letting on to be offended for Bobby's good.

GILBEY. Oh, very well: have the letter framed and hang it up over the mantelpiece as a testimonial.

MRS GILBEY. Dont talk nonsense, Rob. You ought to be thankful to know that the boy is alive after his disappearing like that for nearly a week.

GILBEY. Nearly a week! A fortnight, you mean. Wheres your feelings, woman? It was fourteen days yesterday.

MRS GILBEY. Oh, dont call it fourteen days, Rob, as if the boy was in prison.

GILBEY. How do you know hes not in prison? It's got on my nerves so, that I'd believe even that.

MRS GILBEY. Dont talk silly, Rob. Bobby might get into a scrape like any other lad; but he'd never do anything low.

Juggins, the footman, comes in with a card on a salver. He is a rather low-spirited man of thirty-five or more, of good appearance and address, and iron self-command.

JUGGINS. [*presenting the salver to Mr Gilbey*] Lady wishes to see Mr Bobby's parents, sir.

GILBEY. [*pointing to Mrs Gilbey*] Theres Mr Bobby's parent. I disown him.

JUGGINS. Yes, sir. [*He presents the salver to Mrs Gilbey*].

MRS GILBEY. You mustnt mind what your master says, Juggins: he doesnt mean it. [*She takes the card and reads it*]. Well, I never!

GILBEY. Whats up now?

MRS GILBEY. [*reading*] "Miss D. Delaney. Darling Dora." Just like that—in brackets. What sort of person, Juggins?

GILBEY. Whats her address?

MRS GILBEY. The West Circular Road. Is that a respectable address, Juggins?

JUGGINS. A great many most respectable people live in the West Circular Road, madam; but the address is not a guarantee of respectability.

GILBEY. So it's come to that with him, has it?

MRS GILBEY. Dont jump to conclusions, Rob. How do you know? [*To Juggins*] Is she a lady, Juggins? You know what I mean.

JUGGINS. In the sense in which you are using the word, no, madam.

MRS GILBEY. I'd better try what I can get out of her. [*To Juggins*] Shew her up. You dont mind, do you, Rob?

GILBEY. So long as you dont flounce out and leave me alone with her. [*He rises and plants himself on the hearth-rug*].

Juggins goes out.

MRS GILBEY. I wonder what she wants, Rob?

GILBEY. If she wants money, she shant have it. Not a farthing. A nice thing, everybody seeing her on our doorstep! If it wasnt that she may tell us something about the lad, I'd have Juggins put the hussy into the street.

JUGGINS. [*returning and announcing*] Miss Delaney. [*He waits for express orders before placing a chair for this visitor*].

Miss Delaney comes in. She is a young lady of hilarious disposition, very tolerable good looks, and killing clothes. She is so affable and confidential that it is very difficult to keep her at a distance by any process short of flinging her out of the house.

DORA. [*plunging at once into privileged intimacy and into the middle of the room*] How d'ye do, both. I'm a friend of Bobby's. He told me all about you once, in a moment of confidence. Of course he never let on who he was at the police court.

GILBEY. Police court!

MRS GILBEY. [*looking apprehensively at Juggins*] Tch—! Juggins: a chair.

DORA. Oh, Ive let it out, have I! [*Contemplating Juggins approvingly as he places a chair for her between the table and the sideboard*] But hes the right sort: I can see that. [*Buttonholing him*] You wont let on downstairs, old man, will you?

JUGGINS. The family can rely on my absolute discretion. [*He withdraws*].

DORA. [*sitting down genteelly*] I dont know what youll say to me: you know I really have no right to come here; but then what was I to do? You know Holy Joe, Bobby's tutor, dont you? But of course you do.

GILBEY. [*with dignity*] I know Mr Joseph Grenfell, the brother of Monsignor Grenfell, if it is of him you are speaking.

DORA. [*wide-eyed and much amused*] No!!! You dont tell me that old geezer has a brother a Monsignor! And youre Catholics! And I never knew it, though Ive known Bobby ever so long! But of course the last thing you find out about a person is their religion, isnt it?

MRS GILBEY. We're not Catholics. But when the Samuelses got an Archdeacon's son to form their boy's mind, Mr Gilbey thought Bobby ought to have a chance too. And the Monsignor is a customer. Mr Gilbey consulted him about Bobby; and he recommended a brother of his that was more sinned against than sinning.

GILBEY. [*on tenderhooks*] She dont want to hear about that, Maria. [*To Dora*] Whats your business?

DORA. I'm afraid it was all my fault.

GILBEY. What was all your fault? I'm half distracted. I dont know what has happened to the boy: hes been lost these fourteen days—

MRS GILBEY. A fortnight, Rob.

GILBEY. —and not a word have we heard of him since.

MRS GILBEY. Dont fuss, Rob.

GILBEY. [*yelling*] I will fuss. Youve no feeling. You dont care what becomes of the lad. [*He sits down savagely*].

DORA. [*soothingly*] Youve been anxious about him. Of course. How thoughtless of me not to begin by telling you hes quite safe. Indeed hes in the safest place in the world, as one may say: safe under lock and key.

GILBEY. [*horrified, pitiable*] Oh my— [*his breath fails him*]. Do you mean that when he was in the police court he was in the dock? Oh, Maria! Oh, great Lord! What has he done? What has he got for it? [*Desperate*] Will you tell me or will you see me go mad on my own carpet?

DORA. [*sweetly*] Yes, old dear—

MRS GILBEY. [*starting at the familiarity*] Well!

DORA. [*continuing*] I'll tell you: but dont you worry: hes all right. I came out myself this morning: there was such a crowd! and a band! they thought I was a suffragette: only fancy! You see it was like this. Holy Joe got talking about how he'd been a champion sprinter at college.

MRS GILBEY. A what?

DORA. A sprinter. He said he was the fastest hundred yards runner in England. We were all in the old cowshed that night.

MRS GILBEY. What old cowshed?

GILBEY. [*groaning*] Oh, get on. Get on.

DORA. Oh, of course you wouldnt know. How silly of me! It's a rather go-ahead sort of music hall in Stepney. We call it the old cowshed.

MRS GILBEY. Does Mr Grenfell take Bobby to music halls?

DORA. No. Bobby takes him. But Holy Joe likes it: fairly laps it up like a kitten, poor old dear. Well, Bobby says to me, "Darling—"

MRS GILBEY. [*placidly*] Why does he call you Darling?

DORA. Oh, everybody calls me Darling: it's a sort of name Ive got. Darling Dora, you know. Well, he says, "Darling, if you can get Holy Joe to sprint a hundred yards, I'll stand you that squiffer with the gold keys."

MRS GILBEY. Does he call his tutor Holy Joe to his face [*Gilbey clutches at his hair in his impatience*].

DORA. Well, what would he call him? After all, Holy Joe is Holy Joe; and boys will be boys.

MRS GILBEY. Whats a squiffer?

DORA. Oh, of course: excuse my vulgarity: a concertina. Theres one in a shop in Green Street, ivory inlaid, with gold keys and Russia leather bellows; and Bobby knew I hankered after it; but he couldnt afford it, poor lad, though I knew he just longed to give it to me.

GILBEY. Maria: if you keep interrupting with silly questions, I shall go out of my senses. Heres the boy in gaol and me disgraced for ever; and all you care to know is what a squiffer is.

DORA. Well, remember it has gold keys. The man wouldnt take a penny less than 15 pounds for it. It was a presentation one.

GILBEY. [*shouting at her*] Wheres my son? Whats happened to my son? Will you tell me that, and stop cackling about your squiffer?

DORA. Oh, aint we impatient! Well, it does you credit, old dear. And you neednt fuss: theres no disgrace. Bobby behaved like a perfect gentleman.

Besides, it was all my fault. I'll own it: I took too much champagne. I was not what you might call drunk; but I was bright, and a little beyond myself; and—I'll confess it—I wanted to shew off before Bobby, because he was a bit taken by a woman on the stage; and she was pretending to be game for anything. You see youve brought Bobby up too strict; and when he gets loose theres no holding him. He does enjoy life more than any lad I ever met.

GILBEY. Never you mind how hes been brought up: thats my business. Tell me how hes been brought down: thats yours.

MRS GILBEY. Oh, dont be rude to the lady, Rob.

DORA. I'm coming to it, old dear: dont you be so headstrong. Well, it was a beautiful moonlight night; and we couldnt get a cab on the nod; so we started to walk, very jolly, you know: arm in arm, and dancing along, singing and all that. When we came into Jamaica Square, there was a young copper on point duty at the corner. I says to Bob: "Dearie boy: is it a bargain about the squiffer if I make Joe sprint for you?" "Anything you like, darling," says he: "I love you." I put on my best company manners and stepped up to the copper. "If you please, sir," says I, "can you direct me to Carrickmines Square?" I was so genteel, and talked so sweet, that he fell to it like a bird. "I never heard of any such Square in these parts," he says. "Then," says I, "what a very silly little officer you must be!"; and I gave his helmet a chuck behind that knocked it over his eyes, and did a bunk.

MRS GILBEY. Did a what?

DORA. A bunk. Holy Joe did one too all right: he sprinted faster than he ever did in college, I bet, the old dear. He got clean off, too. Just as he was overtaking me half-way down the square, we heard the whistle; and at the sound of it he drew away like a streak of lightning; and that was the last I saw of him. I was copped in the Dock Road myself: rotten luck, wasn't it? I tried the innocent and genteel and all the rest; but Bobby's hat done me in.

GILBEY. And what happened to the boy?

DORA. Only fancy! he stopped to laugh at the copper! He thought the copper would see the joke, poor lamb. He was arguing about it when the two that took me came along to find out what the whistle was for, and brought me with them. Of course I swore I'd never seen him before in my life; but there he was in my hat and I in his. The cops were very spiteful and laid it on for all they were worth: drunk and disorderly and assaulting the police and all that. I got fourteen days without the option, because you see—well, the fact is, I'd done it before, and been warned. Bobby was a first offender and had the option; but the dear boy had no money left and wouldnt give you away by telling his name; and anyhow he couldnt have brought himself to buy himself off and leave me there; so hes doing his time. Well, it was two forty shillingses; and Ive only twenty-eight shillings in the world. If I pawn my clothes I shant be able to earn any more. So I cant pay the fine and get him out; but if youll stand 3 pounds I'll stand one; and thatll do it. If youd like to be very kind and nice you could pay the lot; but I cant deny that it was my fault; so I wont press you.

GILBEY. [*heart-broken*] My son in gaol!

DORA. Oh, cheer up, old dear: it wont hurt him: look at me after fourteen days of it; I'm all the better for being kept a bit quiet. You mustnt let it prey on your mind.

GILBEY. The disgrace of it will kill me. And it will leave a mark on him to the end of his life.

DORA. Not a bit of it. Dont you be afraid: Ive educated Bobby a bit: hes not the mollycoddle he was when you had him in hand.

MRS GILBEY. Indeed Bobby is not a mollycoddle. They wanted him to go in for singlestick at the Young Men's Christian Association; but, of course, I couldnt allow that: he might have had his eye knocked out.

GILBEY. [*to Dora, angrily*] Listen here, you.

DORA. Oh, aint we cross!

GILBEY. I want none of your gaiety here. This is a respectable household. Youve gone and got my poor innocent boy into trouble. It's the like of you thats the ruin of the like of him.

DORA. So you always say, you old dears. But you know better. Bobby came to me: I didnt come to him.

GILBEY. Would he have gone if you hadnt been there for him to go to? Tell me that. You know why he went to you, I suppose?

DORA. [*charitably*] It was dull for him at home, poor lad, wasnt it?

MRS GILBEY. Oh no. I'm at home on first Thursdays. And we have the Knoxes to dinner every Friday. Margaret Knox and Bobby are as good as engaged. Mr Knox is my husband's partner. Mrs Knox is very religious; but shes quite cheerful. We dine with them on Tuesdays. So thats two evenings pleasure every week.

GILBEY. [*almost in tears*] We done what we could for the boy. Short of letting him go into temptations of all sorts, he can do what he likes. What more does he want?

DORA. Well, old dear, he wants me; and thats about the long and short of it. And I must say youre not very nice to me about it. Ive talked to him like a mother, and tried my best to keep him straight; but I dont deny I like a bit of fun myself; and we both get a bit giddy when we're lighthearted. Him and me is a pair, I'm afraid.

GILBEY. Dont talk foolishness, girl. How could you and he be a pair, you being what you are, and he brought up as he has been, with the example of a religious woman like Mrs Knox before his eyes? I cant understand how he could bring himself to be seen in the street with you. [*Pitying himself*] I havnt deserved this. Ive done my duty as a father. Ive kept him sheltered. [*Angry with her*] Creatures like you that take advantage of a child's innocence ought to be whipped through the streets.

DORA. Well, whatever I may be, I'm too much the lady to lose my temper; and I dont think Bobby would like me to tell you what I think of you; for when I start giving people a bit of my mind I sometimes use language thats beneath me. But I tell you once for all I must have the money to get Bobby out; and if you wont fork out, I'll hunt up Holy Joe. He might get it off his brother, the Monsignor.

GILBEY. You mind your own concerns. My solicitor will do what is right. I'll not have you paying my son's fine as if you were anything to him.

DORA. Thats right. Youll get him out today, wont you?

GILBEY. It's likely I'd leave my boy in prison, isnt it?

DORA. I'd like to know when theyll let him out.

GILBEY. You would, would you? Youre going to meet him at the prison door.

DORA. Well, dont you think any woman would that had the feelings of a lady?

GILBEY. [*bitterly*] Oh yes: I know. Here! I must buy the lad's salvation, I suppose. How much will you take to clear out and let him go?

DORA. [*pitying him: quite nice about it*] What good would that do, old dear? There are others, you know.

GILBEY. Thats true. I must send the boy himself away.

DORA. Where to?

GILBEY. Anywhere, so long as hes out of the reach of you and your like.

DORA. Then I'm afraid youll have to send him out of the world, old dear. I'm sorry for you: I really am, though you mightnt believe it; and I think your feelings do you real credit. But I cant give him up just to let him fall into the hands of people I couldnt trust, can I?

GILBEY. [*beside himself, rising*] Wheres the police? Wheres the Government? Wheres the Church? Wheres respectability and right reason? Whats the good of them if I have to stand here and see you put my son in your pocket as if he was a chattel slave, and you hardly out of gaol as a common drunk and disorderly? Whats the world coming to?

DORA. It is a lottery, isnt it, old dear?

Mr Gilbey rushes from the room, distracted.

MRS GILBEY. [*unruffled*] Where did you buy that white lace? I want some to match a collaret of my own; and I cant get it at Perry and John's.

DORA. Knagg and Pantle's: one and fourpence. It's machine hand-made.

MRS GILBEY. I never give more than one and tuppence. But I suppose youre extravagant by nature. My sister Martha was just like that. Pay anything she was asked.

DORA. Whats tuppence to you, Mrs Bobby, after all?

MRS GILBEY. [*correcting her*] Mrs Gilbey.

DORA. Of course, Mrs Gilbey. I am silly.

MRS GILBEY. Bobby must have looked funny in your hat. Why did you change hats with him?

DORA. I dont know. One does, you know.

MRS GILBEY. I never did. The things people do! I cant understand them. Bobby never told me he was keeping company with you. His own mother!

DORA. [*overcome*] Excuse me: I cant help smiling.

Juggins enters.

JUGGINS. Mr Gilbey has gone to Wormwood Scrubbs, madam.

MRS GILBEY. Have you ever been in a police court, Juggins?

JUGGINS. Yes, madam.

MRS GILBEY [*rather shocked*] I hope you had not been exceeding, Juggins.

JUGGINS. Yes, madam, I had. I exceeded the legal limit.

MRS GILBEY. Oh, that! Why do they give a woman a fortnight for wearing a man's hat, and a man a month for wearing hers?

JUGGINS. I didnt know that they did, madam.

MRS GILBEY. It doesnt seem justice, does it, Juggins?

JUGGINS. No, madam.

MRS GILBEY [*to Dora, rising*] Well, good-bye. [*Shaking her hand*] So pleased to have made your acquaintance.

DORA. [*standing up*] Dont mention it. I'm sure it's most kind of you to receive me at all.

MRS GILBEY. I must go off now and order lunch. [*She trots to the door*]. What was it you called the concertina?

DORA. A squiffer, dear.

MRS GILBEY. [*thoughtfully*] A squiffer, of course. How funny! [*She goes out*].

DORA. [*exploding into ecstasies of mirth*] Oh my! isnt she an old love? How do you keep your face straight?

JUGGINS. It is what I am paid for.

DORA. [*confidentially*] Listen here, dear boy. Your name isnt Juggins. Nobody's name is Juggins.

JUGGINS. My orders are, Miss Delaney, that you are not to be here when Mr Gilbey returns from Wormwood Scrubbs.

DORA. That means telling me to mind my own business, doesnt it? Well, I'm off. Tootle Loo, Charlie Darling. [*She kisses her hand to him and goes*].

ACT II

On the afternoon of the same day, Mrs Knox is writing notes in her drawing-room, at a writing-table which stands against the wall. Anyone placed so as to see Mrs Knox's left profile, will have the door on the right and the window on the left, both further away than Mrs Knox, whose back is presented to an obsolete upright piano at the opposite side of the room. The sofa is near the piano. There is a small table in the middle of the room, with some gilt-edged books and albums on it, and chairs near it.

Mr Knox comes in almost furtively, a troubled man of fifty, thinner, harder, and uglier than his partner, Gilbey, Gilbey being a soft stoutish man with white hair and thin smooth skin, whilst Knox has coarse black hair, and blue jaws which no diligence in shaving can whiten. Mrs Knox is a plain woman, dressed without regard to fashion, with thoughtful eyes and thoughtful ways that make an atmosphere of peace and some solemnity. She is surprised to see her husband at home during business hours.

MRS KNOX. What brings you home at this hour? Have you heard anything?

KNOX. No. Have you?

MRS KNOX. No. Whats the matter?

KNOX. [*sitting down on the sofa*] I believe Gilbey has found out.

MRS KNOX. What makes you think that?

KNOX. Well, I dont know: I didnt like to tell you: you have enough to worry you without that; but Gilbey's been very queer ever since it happened. I cant keep my mind on business as I ought; and I was depending on him. But hes worse than me. Hes not looking after anything; and he keeps out of my way. His manner's not natural. He hasnt asked us to dinner; and hes never said a word about our not asking him to dinner, after all these years when weve dined every week as regular as clockwork. It looks to me as if Gilbey's trying to drop me socially. Well, why should he do that if he hasnt heard?

MRS KNOX. I wonder! Bobby hasnt been near us either: thats what I cant make out.

KNOX. Oh, thats nothing. I told him Margaret was down in Cornwall with her aunt.

MRS KNOX. [*reproachfully*] Jo! [*She takes her handkerchief from the writing-table and cries a little*].

KNOX. Well, I got to tell lies, aint I? You wont. Somebody's got to tell em.

MRS KNOX. [*putting away her handkerchief*] It only ends in our not knowing what to believe. Mrs Gilbey told me Bobby was in Brighton for the sea air. Theres something queer about that. Gilbey would never let the boy loose by himself among the temptations of a gay place like Brighton without his tutor; and I saw the tutor in Kensington High Street the very day she told me.

KNOX. If the Gilbeys have found out, it's all over between Bobby and Margaret, and all over between us and them.

MRS KNOX. It's all over between us and everybody. When a girl runs away from home like that, people know what to think of her and her parents.

KNOX. She had a happy, respectable home—everything—

MRS KNOX. [*interrupting him*] Theres no use going over it all again, Jo. If a girl hasnt happiness in herself, she wont be happy anywhere. Youd better go back to the shop and try to keep your mind off it.

KNOX. [*rising restlessly*] I cant. I keep fancying everybody knows it and is sniggering about it. I'm at peace nowhere but here. It's a comfort to be with you. It's a torment to be with other people.

MRS KNOX. [*going to him and drawing her arm through his*] There, Jo, there! I'm sure I'd have you here always if I could. But it cant be. God's work must go on from day to day, no matter what comes. We must face our trouble and bear it.

KNOX. [*wandering to the window arm in arm with her*] Just look at the people in the street, going up and down as if nothing had happened. It seems unnatural, as if they all knew and didnt care.

MRS KNOX. If they knew, Jo, thered be a crowd round the house looking up at us. You shouldnt keep thinking about it.

KNOX. I know I shouldnt. You have your religion, Amelia; and I'm sure I'm glad it comforts you. But it doesnt come to me that way. Ive worked hard to get a position and be respectable. Ive turned many a girl out of the shop for being half an hour late at night; and heres my own daughter gone for a fortnight without word or sign, except a telegram to say shes not dead and that we're not to worry about her.

MRS KNOX. [*suddenly pointing to the street*] Jo, look!

KNOX. Margaret! With a man!

MRS KNOX. Run down, Jo, quick. Catch her: save her.

KNOX. [*lingering*] Shes shaking bands with him: shes coming across to the door.

MRS KNOX. [*energetically*] Do as I tell you. Catch the man before hes out of sight.

Knox rushes from the room. Mrs Knox looks anxiously and excitedly from the window. Then she throws up the sash and leans out. Margaret Knox comes in, flustered and annoyed. She is a strong, springy girl of eighteen, with large nostrils, an audacious chin, and a gaily resolute manner, even peremptory on occasions like the present, when she is annoyed.

MARGARET. Mother. Mother.

Mrs Knox draws in her head and confronts her daughter.

MRS KNOX. [*sternly*] Well, miss?

MARGARET. Oh, mother, do go out and stop father making a scene in the street. He rushed at him and said "Youre the man who took away my daughter" loud enough for all the people to hear. Everybody stopped. We shall have a crowd round the house. Do do something to stop him.

Knox returns with a good-looking young marine officer.

MARGARET. Oh, Monsieur Duvallet, I'm so sorry—so ashamed. Mother: this is Monsieur Duvallet, who has been extremely kind to me. Monsieur Duvallet: my mother. [*Duvallet bows*].

KNOX. A Frenchman! It only needed this.

MARGARET. [*much annoyed*] Father: do please be commonly civil to a gentleman who has been of the greatest service to me. What will he think of us?

DUVALLET. [*debonair*] But it's very natural. I understand Mr Knox's feelings perfectly. [*He speaks English better than Knox, having learnt it on both sides of the Atlantic*].

KNOX. If Ive made any mistake I'm ready to apologize. But I want to know where my daughter has been for the last fortnight.

DUVALLET. She has been, I assure you, in a particularly safe place.

KNOX. Will you tell me what place? I can judge for myself how safe it was.

MARGARET. Holloway Gaol. Was that safe enough?

KNOX AND MRS KNOX. Holloway Gaol!

KNOX. Youve joined the Suffragets!

MARGARET. No. I wish I had. I could have had the same experience in better company. Please sit down, Monsieur Duvallet. [*She sits between the table and the sofa. Mrs Knox, overwhelmed, sits at the other side of the table. Knox remains standing in the middle of the room*].

DUVALLET. [*sitting down on the sofa*] It was nothing. An adventure. Nothing.

MARGARET. [*obdurately*] Drunk and assaulting the police! Forty shillings or a month!

MRS KNOX. Margaret! Who accused you of such a thing?

MARGARET. The policeman I assaulted.

KNOX. You mean to say that you did it!

MARGARET. I did. I had that satisfaction at all events. I knocked two of his teeth out.

KNOX. And you sit there coolly and tell me this!

MARGARET. Well, where do you want me to sit? Whats the use of saying things like that?

KNOX. My daughter in Holloway Gaol!

MARGARET. All the women in Holloway are somebody's daughters. Really, father, you must make up your mind to it. If you had sat in that cell for fourteen days making up your mind to it, you would understand that I'm not in the humor to be gaped at while youre trying to persuade yourself that it cant be real. These things really do happen to real people every day; and you read about them in the papers and think it's all right. Well, theyve happened to me: thats all.

KNOX. [*feeble-forcible*] But they shouldnt have happened to you. Dont you know that?

MARGARET. They shouldnt happen to anybody, I suppose. But they do. [*Rising impatiently*] And really I'd rather go out and assault another policeman and go back to Holloway than keep talking round and round it like this. If youre going to turn me out of the house, turn me out: the sooner I go the better.

DUVALLET. [*rising quickly*] That is impossible, mademoiselle. Your father has his position to consider. To turn his daughter out of doors would ruin him socially.

KNOX. Oh, youve put her up to that, have you? And where did you come in, may I ask?

DUVALLET. I came in at your invitation—at your amiable insistence, in fact, not at my own. But you need have no anxiety on my account. I was concerned in the regrettable incident which led to your daughter's incarceration. I got a fortnight without the option of a fine on the ridiculous ground that I ought to have struck the policeman with my fist. I should have done so with pleasure had I known; but, as it was, I struck him on the ear with my boot—a magnificent *moulinet*, I must say—and was informed that I had been guilty of an act of cowardice, but that for the sake of the *entente cordiale* I should be dealt with leniently. Yet Miss Knox, who used her fist, got a month, but with the option of a fine. I did not know this until I was released, when my first act was to pay the fine. And here we are.

MRS KNOX. You ought to pay the gentleman the fine, Jo.

KNOX. [*reddening*] Oh, certainly. [*He takes out some money*].

DUVALLET. Oh please! it does not matter. [*Knox hands him two sovereigns*]. If you insist— [*he pockets them*] Thank you.

MARGARET. I'm ever so much obliged to you, Monsieur Duvallet.

DUVALLET. Can I be of any further assistance, mademoiselle?

MARGARET. I think you had better leave us to fight it out, if you dont mind.

DUVALLET. Perfectly. Madame [*bow*]—Mademoiselle [*bow*]—Monsieur [*bow*]—[*He goes out*].

MRS KNOX. Dont ring, Jo. See the gentleman out yourself.

Knox hastily sees Duvallet out. Mother and daughter sit looking forlornly at one another without saying a word. Mrs Knox slowly sits down. Margaret follows her example. They look at one another again. Mr Knox returns.

KNOX. [*shortly and sternly*] Amelia: this is your job. [*To Margaret*] I leave you to your mother. I shall have my own say in the matter when I hear what you have to say to her. [*He goes out, solemn and offended*].

MARGARET. [*with a bitter little laugh*] Just what the Suffraget said to me in Holloway. He throws the job on you.

MRS KNOX. [*reproachfully*] Margaret!

MARGARET. You know it's true.

MRS KNOX. Margaret: if youre going to be hardened about it, theres no use my saying anything.

MARGARET. I'm not hardened, mother. But I cant talk nonsense about it. You see, it's all real to me. Ive suffered it. Ive been shoved and bullied. Ive had my arms twisted. Ive been made scream with pain in other ways. Ive been flung into a filthy cell with a lot of other poor wretches as if I were a sack of coals being emptied into a cellar. And the only difference between me and the others was that I hit back. Yes I did. And I did worse. I wasnt ladylike. I cursed. I called names. I heard words that I didnt even know that I knew, coming out of my mouth just as if somebody else had spoken them. The policeman repeated them in court. The magistrate said he could hardly believe it. The policeman held out his hand with his two teeth in it that I knocked out. I said it was all right; that I had heard myself using those words quite distinctly; and that I had taken the good conduct prize for three years running at school. The poor old gentleman put me back for the missionary to find out who I was, and to ascertain the state of my mind. I wouldnt tell, of course, for your sakes at home here; and I wouldnt say I was sorry, or apologize to the policeman, or compensate him or anything of that sort. I wasnt sorry. The one thing that gave me any satisfaction was getting in that smack on his mouth; and I said so. So the missionary reported that I seemed hardened and that no doubt I would tell who I was after a day in prison. Then I was sentenced. So now you see I'm not a bit the sort of girl you thought me. I'm not a bit the sort of girl I thought myself. And I dont know what sort of person you really are, or what sort of person father really is. I wonder what he would say or do if he had an angry brute of a policeman twisting his arm with one hand and rushing him along by the nape of his neck with the other. He couldnt whirl his leg like a windmill and knock a policeman down by a glorious kick on the helmet. Oh, if theyd all fought as we two fought we'd have beaten them.

MRS KNOX. But how did it all begin?

MARGARET. Oh, I dont know. It was boat-race night, they said.

MRS KNOX. Boat-race night! But what had you to do with the boat race? You went to the great Salvation Festival at the Albert Hall with your aunt. She put you into the bus that passes the door. What made you get out of the bus?

MARGARET. I dont know. The meeting got on my nerves, somehow. It was the singing, I suppose: you know I love singing a good swinging hymn; and I felt it was ridiculous to go home in the bus after we had been singing so wonderfully about climbing up the golden stairs to heaven. I wanted more music—more happiness—more life. I wanted some comrade who felt as I did. I felt exalted: it seemed mean to be afraid of anything: after all, what could anyone do to me against my will? I suppose I was a little mad: at all events, I got out of the bus at Piccadilly Circus, because there was a lot of light and excitement there. I walked to Leicester Square; and went into a great theatre.

MRS KNOX. [*horrified*] A theatre!

MARGARET. Yes. Lots of other women were going in alone. I had to pay five shillings.

MRS KNOX. [*aghast*] Five shillings!

MARGARET. [*apologetically*] It was a lot. It was very stuffy; and I didnt like the people much, because they didnt seem to be enjoying themselves; but the stage was splendid and the music lovely. I saw that Frenchman, Monsieur Duvallet, standing against a barrier, smoking a cigarette. He seemed quite happy; and he was nice and sailorlike. I went and stood beside him, hoping he would speak to me.

MRS KNOX. [*gasps*] Margaret!

MARGARET. [*continuing*] He did, just as if he had known me for years. We got on together like old friends. He asked me would I have some champagne; and I said it would cost too much, but that I would give anything for a dance. I longed to join the people on the stage and dance with them: one of them was the most beautiful dancer I ever saw. He told me he had come there to see her, and that when it was over we could go somewhere where there was dancing. So we went to a place where there was a band in a gallery and the floor cleared for dancing. Very few people danced: the women only wanted to shew off their dresses; but we danced and danced until a lot of them joined in. We got quite reckless; and we had champagne after all. I never enjoyed anything so much. But at last it got spoilt by the Oxford and Cambridge students up for the boat race. They got drunk; and they began to smash things; and the police came in. Then it was quite horrible. The students fought with the police; and the police suddenly got quite brutal, and began to throw everybody downstairs. They attacked the women, who were not doing anything, and treated them just as roughly as they had treated the students. Duvallet got indignant and remonstrated with a policeman, who was shoving a woman though she was going quietly as fast as she could. The policeman flung the woman through the door and then turned on Duvallet. It was then that Duvallet swung his leg like a windmill and knocked the policeman down. And then three policemen rushed at him and carried him out by the arms and legs face downwards. Two more attacked me and gave me a shove to the door. That quite maddened me. I just got in one good bang on the mouth of one of them. All the rest was dreadful. I was rushed through the streets to the police station. They kicked me with their knees; they twisted my arms; they taunted and insulted me; they called me vile names; and I told them what I thought of them, and provoked them to do their worst. Theres one good thing about being hard hurt: it makes you sleep. I slept in that filthy cell with all the other drunks sounder than I should have slept at home. I cant describe how I felt next morning: it was hideous; but the police were quite jolly; and everybody said it was a bit of English fun, and talked about last year's boat-race night when it had been a great deal worse. I was black and blue and sick and wretched. But the strange thing was that I wasnt sorry; and I'm not sorry. And I dont feel that I did anything wrong, really. [*She rises and stretches her arms with a large liberating breath*] Now that it's all over I'm rather proud of it; though I know now that I'm not a lady; but whether thats because we're only shopkeepers, or because nobody's really a lady except when theyre treated like ladies, I dont know. [*She throws herself into a corner of the sofa*].

MRS KNOX. [*lost in wonder*] But how could you bring yourself to do it, Margaret? I'm not blaming you: I only want to know. How could you bring yourself to do it?

MARGARET. I cant tell you. I dont understand it myself. The prayer meeting set me free, somehow. I should never have done it if it were not for the prayer meeting.

MRS KNOX. [*deeply horrified*] Oh, dont say such a thing as that. I know that prayer can set us free; though you could never understand me when I told you so; but it sets us free for good, not for evil.

MARGARET. Then I suppose what I did was not evil; or else I was set free for evil as well as good. As father says, you cant have anything both ways at once. When I was at home and at school I was what you call good; but I wasnt free. And when I got free I was what most people would call not good. But I see no harm in what I did; though I see plenty in what other people did to me.

MRS KNOX. I hope you dont think yourself a heroine of romance.

MARGARET. Oh no. [*She sits down again at the table*]. I'm a heroine of reality, if you can call me a heroine at all. And reality is pretty brutal, pretty filthy, when you come to grips with it. Yet it's glorious all the same. It's so real and satisfactory.

MRS KNOX. I dont like this spirit in you, Margaret. I dont like your talking to me in that tone.

MARGARET. It's no use, mother. I dont care for you and Papa any the less; but I shall never get back to the old way of talking again. Ive made a sort of descent into hell—

MRS KNOX. Margaret! Such a word!

MARGARET. You should have heard all the words that were flying round that night. You should mix a little with people who dont know any other words. But when I said that about a descent into hell I was not swearing. I was in earnest, like a preacher.

MRS KNOX. A preacher utters them in a reverent tone of voice.

MARGARET. I know: the tone that shews they dont mean anything real to him. They usent to mean anything real to me. Now hell is as real to me as a turnip; and I suppose I shall always speak of it like that. Anyhow, Ive been there; and it seems to me now that nothing is worth doing but redeeming people from it.

MRS KNOX. They are redeemed already if they choose to believe it.

MARGARET. Whats the use of that if they dont choose to believe it? You dont believe it yourself, or you wouldnt pay policemen to twist their arms. Whats the good of pretending? Thats all our respectability is, pretending, pretending, pretending. Thank heaven Ive had it knocked out of me once for all!

MRS KNOX. [*greatly agitated*] Margaret: dont talk like that. I cant bear to hear you talking wickedly. I can bear to hear the children of this world talking vainly and foolishly in the language of this world. But when I hear you justifying your wickedness in the words of grace, it's too horrible: it sounds like the devil making fun of religion. Ive tried to bring you up to learn the happiness of religion. Ive waited for you to find out that happiness is within ourselves and doesnt come from outward pleasures. Ive prayed oftener than you think that you might be enlightened. But if all my hopes and all my prayers are to come to this, that you mix up my very words and thoughts with the promptings of the devil, then I dont know what I shall do: I dont indeed: itll kill me.

MARGARET. You shouldnt have prayed for me to be enlightened if you didnt want me to be enlightened. If the truth were known, I suspect we all want our prayers to be answered only by halves: the agreeable halves. Your prayer didnt get answered by halves, mother. Youve got more than you bargained for in the way of enlightenment. I shall never be the same again. I shall never speak in the old way again. Ive been set free from this silly little hole of a house and all its pretences. I know now that I am stronger than you and Papa. I havnt found that happiness of yours that is within yourself; but Ive found strength. For good or evil I am set free; and none of the things that used to hold me can hold me now.

Knox comes back, unable to bear his suspense.

KNOX. How long more are you going to keep me waiting, Amelia? Do you think I'm made of iron? Whats the girl done? What are we going to do?

MRS KNOX. Shes beyond my control, Jo, and beyond yours. I cant even pray for her now; for I dont know rightly what to pray for.

KNOX. Dont talk nonsense, woman: is this a time for praying? Does anybody know? Thats what we have to consider now. If only we can keep it dark, I don't care for anything else.

MARGARET. Dont hope for that, father. Mind: I'll tell everybody. It ought to be told. It must be told.

KNOX. Hold your tongue, you young hussy; or go out of my house this instant.

MARGARET. I'm quite ready. [*She takes her hat and turns to the door*].

KNOX. [*throwing himself in front of it*] Here! where are you going?

MRS KNOX. [*rising*] You mustnt turn her out, Jo! I'll go with her if she goes.

KNOX. Who wants to turn her out? But is she going to ruin us? To let everybody know of her disgrace and shame? To tear me down from the position Ive made for myself and you by forty years hard struggling?

MARGARET. Yes: I'm going to tear it all down. It stands between us and everything. I'll tell everybody.

KNOX. Magsy, my child: dont bring down your father's hairs with sorrow to the grave. Theres only one thing I care about in the world: to keep this dark. I'm your father. I ask you here on my knees—in the dust, so to speak—not to let it out.

MARGARET. I'll tell everybody.

Knox collapses in despair. Mrs Knox tries to pray and cannot. Margaret stands inflexible.

ACT III

Again in the Gilbeys' dining-room. Afternoon. The table is not laid: it is draped in its ordinary cloth, with pen and ink, an exercise-book, and school-books on it. Bobby Gilbey is in the arm-chair, crouching over the fire, reading an illustrated paper. He is a pretty youth, of very suburban gentility, strong and manly enough by nature, but untrained and unsatisfactory, his parents having imagined that domestic restriction is what they call "bringing up." He has learnt nothing from it except a habit of evading it by deceit.

He gets up to ring the bell; then resumes his crouch. Juggins answers the bell.

BOBBY. Juggins.

JUGGINS. Sir?

BOBBY. [*morosely sarcastic*] Sir be blowed!

JUGGINS. [*cheerfully*] Not at all, sir.

BOBBY. I'm a gaol-bird: youre a respectable man.

JUGGINS. That doesnt matter, sir. Your father pays me to call you sir; and as I take the money, I keep my part of the bargain.

BOBBY. Would you call me sir if you wernt paid to do it?

JUGGINS. No, sir.

BOBBY. Ive been talking to Dora about you.

JUGGINS. Indeed, sir?

BOBBY. Yes. Dora says your name cant be Juggins, and that you have the manners of a gentleman. I always thought you hadnt any manners. Anyhow, your manners are different from the manners of a gentleman in my set.

JUGGINS. They would be, sir.

BOBBY. You dont feel disposed to be communicative on the subject of Dora's notion, I suppose.

JUGGINS. No, sir.

BOBBY. [*throwing his paper on the floor and lifting his knees over the arm of the chair so as to turn towards the footman*] It was part of your bargain that you were to valet me a bit, wasnt it?

JUGGINS. Yes, sir.

BOBBY. Well, can you tell me the proper way to get out of an engagement to a girl without getting into a row for breach of promise or behaving like a regular cad?

JUGGINS. No, sir. You cant get out of an engagement without behaving like a cad if the lady wishes to hold you to it.

BOBBY. But it wouldnt be for her happiness to marry me when I dont really care for her.

JUGGINS. Women dont always marry for happiness, sir. They often marry because they wish to be married women and not old maids.

BOBBY. Then what am I to do?

JUGGINS. Marry her, sir, or behave like a cad.

BOBBY. [*Jumping up*] Well, I wont marry her: thats flat. What would you do if you were in my place?

JUGGINS. I should tell the young lady that I found I couldnt fulfil my engagement.

BOBBY. But youd have to make some excuse, you know. I want to give it a gentlemanly turn: to say I'm not worthy of her, or something like that.

JUGGINS. That is not a gentlemanly turn, sir. Quite the contrary.

BOBBY. I dont see that at all. Do you mean that it's not exactly true?

JUGGINS. Not at all, sir.

BOBBY. I can say that no other girl can ever be to me what shes been. That would be quite true, because our circumstances have been rather exceptional; and she'll imagine I mean I'm fonder of her than I can ever be of anyone else. You see, Juggins, a gentleman has to think of a girl's feelings.

JUGGINS. If you wish to spare her feelings, sir, you can marry her. If you hurt her feelings by refusing, you had better not try to get credit for considerateness at the same time by pretending to spare them. She wont like it. And it will start an argument, of which you will get the worse.

BOBBY. But, you know, I'm not really worthy of her.

JUGGINS. Probably she never supposed you were, sir.

BOBBY. Oh, I say, Juggins, you are a pessimist.

JUGGINS. [*preparing to go*] Anything else, sir?

BOBBY. [*querulously*] You havnt been much use. [*He wanders disconsolately across the room*]. You generally put me up to the correct way of doing things.

JUGGINS. I assure you, sir, theres no correct way of jilting. It's not correct in itself.

BOBBY. [*hopefully*] I'll tell you what. I'll say I cant hold her to an engagement with a man whos been in quod. Thatll do it. [*He seats himself on the table, relieved and confident*].

JUGGINS. Very dangerous, sir. No woman will deny herself the romantic luxury of self-sacrifice and forgiveness when they take the form of doing something agreeable. Shes almost sure to say that your misfortune will draw her closer to you.

BOBBY. What a nuisance! I dont know what to do. You know, Juggins, your cool simple-minded way of doing it wouldnt go down in Denmark Hill.

JUGGINS. I daresay not, sir. No doubt youd prefer to make it look like an act of self-sacrifice for her sake on your part, or provoke her to break the engagement herself. Both plans have been tried repeatedly, but never with success, as far as my knowledge goes.

BOBBY. You have a devilish cool way of laying down the law. You know, in my class you have to wrap up things a bit. Denmark Hill isn't Camberwell, you know.

JUGGINS. I have noticed, sir, that Denmark Hill thinks that the higher you go in the social scale, the less sincerity is allowed; and that only tramps and riff-raff are quite sincere. Thats a mistake. Tramps are often shameless; but theyre never sincere. Swells—if I may use that convenient name for the upper classes—play much more with their cards on the table. If you tell the young lady that you want to jilt her, and she calls you a pig, the tone of the transaction may leave much to be desired; but itll be less Camberwellian than if you say youre not worthy.

BOBBY. Oh, I cant make you understand, Juggins. The girl isnt a scullery-maid. I want to do it delicately.

JUGGINS. A mistake, sir, believe me, if you are not a born artist in that line.—Beg pardon, sir, I think I heard the bell. [*He goes out*].

Bobby, much perplexed, shoves his hands into his pockets, and comes off the table, staring disconsolately straight before him; then goes reluctantly to his books, and sits down to write. Juggins returns.

JUGGINS. [*announcing*] Miss Knox.

Margaret comes in. Juggins withdraws.

MARGARET. Still grinding away for that Society of Arts examination, Bobby? Youll never pass.

BOBBY. [*rising*] No: I was just writing to you.

MARGARET. What about?

BOBBY. Oh, nothing. At least— How are you?

MARGARET. [*passing round the other end of the table and putting down on it a copy of Lloyd's Weekly and her purse-bag*] Quite well, thank you. How did you enjoy Brighton?

BOBBY. Brighton! I wasnt at— Oh yes, of course. Oh, pretty well. Is your aunt all right?

MARGARET. My aunt! I suppose so. I havent seen her for a month.

BOBBY. I thought you were down staying with her.

MARGARET. Oh! was that what they told you?

BOBBY. Yes. Why? Werent you really?

MARGARET. No. Ive something to tell you. Sit down and lets be comfortable.

She sits on the edge of the table. He sits beside her, and puts his arm wearily round her waist.

MARGARET. You neednt do that if you dont like, Bobby. Suppose we get off duty for the day, just to see what it's like.

BOBBY. Off duty? What do you mean?

MARGARET. You know very well what I mean. Bobby: did you ever care one little scrap for me in that sort of way? Dont funk answering: *I* dont care a bit for you—that way.

BOBBY. [*removing his arm rather huffily*] I beg your pardon, I'm sure. I thought you did.

MARGARET. Well, did you? Come! Dont be mean. Ive owned up. You can put it all on me if you like; but I dont believe you care any more than I do.

BOBBY. You mean weve been shoved into it rather by the pars and mars.

MARGARET. Yes.

BOBBY. Well, it's not that I dont care for you: in fact, no girl can ever be to me exactly what you are; but weve been brought up so much together that it feels more like brother and sister than—well, than the other thing, doesnt it?

MARGARET. Just so. How did you find out the difference?

BOBBY. [*blushing*] Oh, I say!

MARGARET. I found out from a Frenchman.

BOBBY. Oh, I say! [*He comes off the table in his consternation*].

MARGARET. Did you learn it from a Frenchwoman? You know you must have learnt it from somebody.

BOBBY. Not a Frenchwoman. Shes quite a nice woman. But shes been rather unfortunate. The daughter of a clergyman.

MARGARET. [*startled*] Oh, Bobby! That sort of woman!

BOBBY. What sort of woman?

MARGARET. You dont believe shes really a clergyman's daughter, do you, you silly boy? It's a stock joke.

BOBBY. Do you mean to say you dont believe me?

MARGARET. No: I mean to say I dont believe her.

BOBBY. [*curious and interested, resuming his seat on the table beside her*]. What do you know about her? What do you know about all this sort of thing?

MARGARET. What sort of thing, Bobby?

BOBBY. Well, about life.

MARGARET. Ive lived a lot since I saw you last. I wasnt at my aunt's. All that time that you were in Brighton, I mean.

BOBBY. I wasnt at Brighton, Meg. I'd better tell you: youre bound to find out sooner or later. [*He begins his confession humbly, avoiding her gaze*]. Meg: it's rather awful: youll think me no end of a beast. Ive been in prison.

MARGARET. You!

BOBBY. Yes, me. For being drunk and assaulting the police.

MARGARET. Do you mean to say that you—oh! this is a let-down for me. [*She comes off the table and drops, disconsolate, into a chair at the end of it furthest from the hearth*].

BOBBY. Of course I couldnt hold you to our engagement after that. I was writing to you to break it off. [*He also descends from the table and makes slowly for the hearth*]. You must think me an utter rotter.

MARGARET. Oh, has everybody been in prison for being drunk and assaulting the police? How long were you in?

BOBBY. A fortnight.

MARGARET. Thats what I was in for.

BOBBY. What are you talking about? In where?

MARGARET. In quod.

BOBBY. But I'm serious: I'm not rotting. Really and truly—

MARGARET. What did you do to the copper?

BOBBY. Nothing, absolutely nothing. He exaggerated grossly. I only laughed at him.

MARGARET. [*jumping up, triumphant*] Ive beaten you hollow. I knocked out two of his teeth. Ive got one of them. He sold it to me for ten shillings.

BOBBY. Now please do stop fooling, Meg. I tell you I'm not rotting. [*He sits down in the armchair, rather sulkily*].

MARGARET. [*taking up the copy of Lloyd's Weekly and going to him*] And I tell you I'm not either. Look! Heres a report of it. The daily papers are no good; but the Sunday papers are splendid. [*She sits on the arm of the chair*]. See! [*Reading*]: "Hardened at Eighteen. A quietly dressed, respectable-looking girl who refuses her name"—thats me.

BOBBY. [*pausing a moment in his perusal*] Do you mean to say that you went on the loose out of pure devilment?

MARGARET. I did no harm. I went to see a lovely dance. I picked up a nice man and went to have a dance myself. I cant imagine anything more innocent and more happy. All the bad part was done by other people: they did it out of pure devilment if you like. Anyhow, here we are, two gaolbirds, Bobby, disgraced forever. Isnt it a relief?

BOBBY. [*rising stiffly*] But you know, it's not the same for a girl. A man may do things a woman maynt. [*He stands on the hearthrug with his back to the fire*].

MARGARET. Are you scandalized, Bobby?

BOBBY. Well, you cant expect me to approve of it, can you, Meg? I never thought you were that sort of girl.

MARGARET. [*rising indignantly*] I'm not. You mustnt pretend to think that *I*'m a clergyman's daughter, Bobby.

BOBBY. I wish you wouldnt chaff about that. Dont forget the row you got into for letting out that you admired Juggins [*she turns her back on him quickly*]—a footman! And what about the Frenchman?

MARGARET. [*facing him again*] I know nothing about the Frenchman except that hes a very nice fellow and can swing his leg round like the hand of a clock and knock a policeman down with it. He was in Wormwood Scrubbs with you. I was in Holloway.

BOBBY. It's all very well to make light of it, Meg; but this is a bit thick, you know.

MARGARET. Do you feel you couldnt marry a woman whos been in prison?

BOBBY. [*hastily*] No. I never said that. It might even give a woman a greater claim on a man. Any girl, if she were thoughtless and a bit on, perhaps, might get into a scrape. Anyone who really understood her character could see there was no harm in it. But youre not the larky sort. At least you usent to be.

MARGARET. I'm not; and I never will be. [*She walks straight up to him*]. I didnt do it for a lark, Bob: I did it out of the very depths of my nature. I did it because I'm that sort of person. I did it in one of my religious fits. I'm hardened at eighteen, as they say. So what about the match, now?

BOBBY. Well, I dont think you can fairly hold me to it, Meg. Of course it would be ridiculous for me to set up to be shocked, or anything of that sort. I cant afford to throw stones at anybody; and I dont pretend to. I can understand a lark; I can forgive a slip; as long as it is understood that it is only a lark or a slip. But to go on the loose on principle; to talk about religion in connection with it; to—to—well, Meg, I do find that a bit thick, I must say. I hope youre not in earnest when you talk that way.

MARGARET. Bobby: youre no good. No good to me, anyhow.

BOBBY. [*huffed*] I'm sorry, Miss Knox.

MARGARET. Goodbye, Mr Gilbey. [*She turns on her heel and goes to the other end of the table*]. I suppose you wont introduce me to the clergyman's daughter.

BOBBY. I dont think she'd like it. There are limits, after all. [*He sits down at the table, as if to resume work at his books: a hint to her to go*].

MARGARET. [*on her way to the door*] Ring the bell, Bobby; and tell Juggins to shew me out.

BOBBY. [*reddening*] I'm not a cad, Meg.

MARGARET. [*coming to the table*] Then do something nice to prevent us feeling mean about this afterwards. Youd better kiss me. You neednt ever do it again.

BOBBY. If I'm no good, I dont see what fun it would be for you.

MARGARET. Oh, it'd be no fun. If I wanted what you call fun, I should ask the Frenchman to kiss me—or Juggins.

BOBBY. [*rising and retreating to the hearth*] Oh, dont be disgusting, Meg. Dont be low.

MARGARET. [*determinedly, preparing to use force*] Now, I'll make you kiss me, just to punish you. [*She seizes his wrist; pulls him off his balance; and gets her arm round his neck*].

BOBBY. No. Stop. Leave go, will you.

Juggins appears at the door.

JUGGINS. Miss Delaney, Sir. [*Dora comes in. Juggins goes out. Margaret hastily releases Bobby, and goes to the other side of the room.*]

DORA. [*through the door, to the departing Juggins*] Well, you are a Juggins to shew me up when theres company. [*To Margaret and Bobby*] It's all right, dear: all right, old man: I'll wait in Juggins's pantry til youre disengaged.

MARGARET. Dont you know me?

DORA. [*coming to the middle of the room and looking at her very attentively*] Why, it's never No. 406!

MARGARET. Yes it is.

DORA. Well, I should never have known you out of the uniform. How did you get out? You were doing a month, wernt you?

MARGARET. My bloke paid the fine the day he got out himself.

DORA. A real gentleman! [*Pointing to Bobby, who is staring open-mouthed*] Look at him. He cant take it in.

BOBBY. I suppose you made her acquaintance in prison, Meg. But when it comes to talking about blokes and all that—well!

MARGARET. Oh, Ive learnt the language; and I like it. It's another barrier broken down.

BOBBY. It's not so much the language, Meg. But I think [*he looks at Dora and stops*].

MARGARET. [*suddenly dangerous*] What do you think, Bobby?

DORA. He thinks you oughtnt to be so free with me, dearie. It does him credit: he always was a gentleman, you know.

MARGARET. Does him credit! To insult you like that! Bobby: say that that wasnt what you meant.

BOBBY. I didnt say it was.

MARGARET. Well, deny that it was.

BOBBY. No. I wouldnt have said it in front of Dora; but I do think it's not quite the same thing my knowing her and you knowing her.

DORA. Of course it isnt, old man. [*To Margaret*] I'll just trot off and come back in half an hour. You two can make it up together. I'm really not fit company for you, dearie: I couldnt live up to you. [*She turns to go*].

MARGARET. Stop. Do you believe he could live up to me?

DORA. Well, I'll never say anything to stand between a girl and a respectable marriage, or to stop a decent lad from settling himself. I have a conscience; though I maynt be as particular as some.

MARGARET. You seem to me to be a very decent sort; and Bobby's behaving like a skunk.

BOBBY. [*much ruffled*] Nice language that!

DORA. Well, dearie, men have to do some awfully mean things to keep up their respectability. But you cant blame them for that, can you? Ive met Bobby walking with his mother; and of course he cut me dead. I wont pretend I liked it; but what could he do, poor dear?

MARGARET. And now he wants me to cut you dead to keep him in countenance. Well, I shant: not if my whole family were there. But I'll cut him dead if he doesnt treat you properly. [*To Bobby, with a threatening move in his direction*] I'll educate you, you young beast.

BOBBY. [*furious, meeting her half way*] Who are you calling a young beast?

MARGARET. You.

DORA. [*peacemaking*] Now, dearies!

BOBBY. If you dont take care, youll get your fat head jolly well clouted.

MARGARET. If you dont take care, the policeman's tooth will only be the beginning of a collection.

DORA. Now, loveys, be good.

Bobby, lost to all sense of adult dignity, puts out his tongue at Margaret. Margaret, equally furious, catches his protended countenance a box on the cheek. He hurls himself her. They wrestle.

BOBBY. Cat! I'll teach you.

MARGARET. Pig! Beast! [*She forces him backwards on the table*]. Now where are you?

DORA. [*calling*] Juggins, Juggins. Theyll murder one another.

JUGGINS. [*throwing open the door, and announcing*] Monsieur Duvallet.

Duvallet enters. Sudden cessation of hostilities, and dead silence. The combatants separate by the whole width of the room. Juggins withdraws.

DUVALLET. I fear I derange you.

MARGARET. Not at all. Bobby: you really are a beast: Monsieur Duvallet will think I'm always fighting.

DUVALLET. Practising jujitsu or the new Iceland wrestling. Admirable, Miss Knox. The athletic young Englishwoman is an example to all Europe. [*Indicating Bobby*] Your instructor, no doubt. Monsieur— [*he bows*].

BOBBY. [*bowing awkwardly*] How d'y' do?

MARGARET. [*to Bobby*] I'm so sorry, Bobby: I asked Monsieur Duvallet to call for me here; and I forgot to tell you. [*Introducing*] Monsieur Duvallet: Miss Four hundred and seven. Mr Bobby Gilbey. [*Duvallet bows*]. I really dont know how to explain our relationships. Bobby and I are like brother and sister.

DUVALLET. Perfectly. I noticed it.

MARGARET. Bobby and Miss—Miss——

DORA. Delaney, dear. [*To Duvallet, bewitchingly*] Darling Dora, to real friends.

MARGARET. Bobby and Dora are—are—well, not brother and sister.

DUVALLET. [*with redoubled comprehension*] Perfectly.

MARGARET. Bobby has spent the last fortnight in prison. You dont mind, do you?

DUVALLET. No, naturally. *I* have spent the last fortnight in prison.

The conversation drops. Margaret renews it with an effort.

MARGARET. Dora has spent the last fortnight in prison.

DUVALLET. Quite so. I felicitate Mademoiselle on her enlargement.

DORA. *Trop merci*, as they say in Boulogne. No call to be stiff with one another, have we?

Juggins comes in.

JUGGINS. Beg pardon, sir. Mr and Mrs Gilbey are coming up the street.

DORA. Let me absquatulate [*making for the door*].

JUGGINS. If you wish to leave without being seen, you had better step into my pantry and leave afterwards.

DORA. Right oh! [*She bursts into song*] Hide me in the meat safe til the cop goes by. Hum the dear old music as his step draws nigh. [*She goes out on tiptoe*].

MARGARET. I wont stay here if she has to hide. I'll keep her company in the pantry. [*She follows Dora*].

BOBBY. Lets all go. We cant have any fun with the Mar here. I say, Juggins: you can give us tea in the pantry, cant you?

JUGGINS. Certainly, sir.

BOBBY. Right. Say nothing to my mother. You dont mind, Mr. Doovalley, do you?

DUVALLET. I shall be charmed.

BOBBY. Right you are. Come along. [*At the door*] Oh, by the way, Juggins, fetch down that concertina from my room, will you?

JUGGINS. Yes, sir. [*Bobby goes out. Duvallet follows him to the door*]. You understand, sir, that Miss Knox is a lady absolutely *comme il faut*?

DUVALLET. Perfectly. But the other?

JUGGINS. The other, sir, may be both charitably and accurately described in your native idiom as a daughter of joy.

DUVALLET. It is what I thought. These English domestic interiors are very interesting. [*He goes out, followed by Juggins*].

Presently Mr and Mrs Gilbey come in. They take their accustomed places: he on the hearthrug, she at the colder end of the table.

MRS GILBEY. Did you smell scent in the hall, Rob?

GILBEY. No, I didnt. And I dont want to smell it. Dont you go looking for trouble, Maria.

MRS GILBEY. [*snuffing up the perfumed atmosphere*] Shes been here. [*Gilbey rings the bell*]. What are you ringing for? Are you going to ask?

GILBEY. No, I'm not going to ask. Juggins said this morning he wanted to speak to me. If he likes to tell me, let him; but I'm not going to ask; and dont you either. [*Juggins appears at the door*]. You said you wanted to say something to me.

JUGGINS. When it would be convenient to you, sir.

GILBEY. Well, what is it?

MRS GILBEY. Oh, Juggins, we're expecting Mr and Mrs Knox to tea.

GILBEY. He knows that. [*He sits down. Then, to Juggins*] What is it?

JUGGINS. [*advancing to the middle of the table*] Would it inconvenience you, sir, if I was to give you a month's notice?

GILBEY. [*taken aback*] What! Why? Aint you satisfied?

JUGGINS. Perfectly, sir. It is not that I want to better myself, I assure you.

GILBEY. Well, what do you want to leave for, then? Do you want to worse yourself?

JUGGINS. No, sir. Ive been well treated in your most comfortable establishment; and I should be greatly distressed if you or Mrs Gilbey were to interpret my notice as an expression of dissatisfaction.

GILBEY. [*paternally*] Now you listen to me, Juggins. I'm an older man than you. Dont you throw out dirty water til you get in fresh. Dont get too big for your boots. Youre like all servants nowadays: you think youve only to hold up your finger to get the pick of half a dozen jobs. But you wont be treated everywhere as youre treated here. In bed every night before eleven; hardly a ring at the door except on Mrs Gilbey's day once a month; and no other manservant to interfere with you. It may be a bit quiet perhaps; but youre past the age of adventure. Take my advice: think over it. You suit me; and I'm prepared to make it suit you if youre dissatisfied—in reason, you know.

JUGGINS. I realize my advantages, sir; but Ive private reasons—

GILBEY. [*cutting him short angrily and retiring to the hearthrug in dudgeon*] Oh, I know. Very well: go. The sooner the better.

MRS GILBEY. Oh, not until we're suited. He must stay his month.

GILBEY. [*sarcastic*] Do you want to lose him his character, Maria? Do you think I dont see what it is? We're prison folk now. Weve been in the police court. [*To Juggins*] Well, I suppose you know your own business best. I take your notice: you can go when your month is up, or sooner, if you like.

JUGGINS. Believe me, sir—

GILBEY. Thats enough: I dont want any excuses. I dont blame you. You can go downstairs now, if youve nothing else to trouble me about.

JUGGINS. I really cant leave it at that, sir. I assure you Ive no objection to young Mr Gilbey's going to prison. You may do six months yourself, sir, and welcome, without a word of remonstrance from me. I'm leaving solely because my brother, who has suffered a bereavement, and feels lonely, begs me to spend a few months with him until he gets over it.

GILBEY. And is he to keep you all that time? or are you to spend your savings in comforting him? Have some sense, man: how can you afford such things?

JUGGINS. My brother can afford to keep me, sir. The truth is, he objects to my being in service.

GILBEY. Is that any reason why you should be dependent on him? Dont do it, Juggins: pay your own way like an honest lad; and dont eat your brother's bread while youre able to earn your own.

JUGGINS. There is sound sense in that, sir. But unfortunately it is a tradition in my family that the younger brothers should spunge to a considerable extent on the eldest.

GILBEY. Then the sooner that tradition is broken, the better, my man.

JUGGINS. A Radical sentiment, sir. But an excellent one.

GILBEY. Radical! What do you mean? Dont you begin to take liberties, Juggins, now that you know we're loth to part with you. Your brother isnt a duke, you know.

JUGGINS. Unfortunately, he is, sir.

GILBEY. What! [*together*]
MRS GILBEY. Juggins!

JUGGINS. Excuse me, sir: the bell. [*He goes out*].

GILBEY. [*overwhelmed*] Maria: did you understand him to say his brother was a duke?

MRS GILBEY. Fancy his condescending! Perhaps if youd offer to raise his wages and treat him as one of the family, he'd stay.

GILBEY. And have my own servant above me! Not me. Whats the world coming to? Heres Bobby and—

JUGGINS. [*entering and announcing*] Mr and Mrs Knox.

The Knoxes come in. Juggins takes two chairs from the wall and places them at the table, between the host and hostess. Then he withdraws.

MRS GILBEY. [*to Mrs Knox*] How are you, dear?

MRS KNOX. Nicely, thank you. Good evening, Mr Gilbey. [*They shake hands; and she takes the chair nearest Mrs Gilbey. Mr Knox takes the other chair*].

GILBEY. [*sitting down*] I was just saying, Knox, What is the world coming to?

KNOX. [*appealing to his wife*] What was I saying myself only this morning?

MRS KNOX. This is a strange time. I was never one to talk about the end of the world; but look at the things that have happened!

KNOX. Earthquakes!

GILBEY. San Francisco!

MRS GILBEY. Jamaica!

KNOX. Martinique!

GILBEY. Messina!

MRS GILBEY. The plague in China!

MRS KNOX. The floods in France!

GILBEY. My Bobby in Wormwood Scrubbs!

KNOX. Margaret in Holloway!

GILBEY. And now my footman tells me his brother's a duke!

KNOX. No!
MRS KNOX. Whats that?

GILBEY. Just before he let you in. A duke! Here has everything been respectable from the beginning of the world, as you may say, to the present day; and all of a sudden everything is turned upside down.

MRS KNOX. It's like in the book of Revelations. But I do say that unless people have happiness within themselves, all the earthquakes, all the floods, and all the prisons in the world cant make them really happy.

KNOX. It isnt alone the curious things that are happening, but the unnatural way people are taking them. Why, theres Margaret been in prison, and she hasnt time to go to all the invitations shes had from people that never asked her before.

GILBEY. I never knew we could live without being respectable.

MRS GILBEY. Oh, Rob, what a thing to say! Who says we're not respectable?

GILBEY. Well, it's not what I call respectable to have your children in and out of gaol.

KNOX. Oh come, Gilbey! we're not tramps because weve had, as it were, an accident.

GILBEY. It's no use, Knox: look it in the face. Did I ever tell you my father drank?

KNOX. No. But I knew it. Simmons told me.

GILBEY. Yes: he never could keep his mouth quiet: he told me your aunt was a kleptomaniac.

MRS KNOX. It wasnt true, Mr Gilbey. She used to pick up handkerchiefs if she saw them lying about; but you might trust her with untold silver.

GILBEY. My Uncle Phil was a teetotaller. My father used to say to me: Rob, he says, dont you ever have a weakness. If you find one getting a hold on you, make a merit of it, he says. Your Uncle Phil doesnt like spirits; and he makes a merit of it, and is chairman of the Blue Ribbon Committee. I do like spirits; and I make a merit of it, and I'm the King Cockatoo of the Convivial Cockatoos. Never put yourself in the wrong, he says. I used to boast about what a good boy Bobby was. Now I swank about what a dog he is; and it pleases people just as well. What a world it is!

KNOX. It turned my blood cold at first to hear Margaret telling people about Holloway; but it goes down better than her singing used to.

MRS KNOX. I never thought she sang right after all those lessons we paid for.

GILBEY. Lord, Knox, it was lucky you and me got let in together. I tell you straight, if it hadnt been for Bobby's disgrace, I'd have broke up the firm.

KNOX. I shouldnt have blamed you: I'd have done the same only for Margaret. Too much straight-lacedness narrows a man's mind. Talking of that, what about those hygienic corset advertisements that Vines & Jackson want us to put in the window? I told Vines they werent decent and we couldnt shew them in our shop. I was pretty high with him. But what am I to say to him now if he comes and throws this business in our teeth?

GILBEY. Oh, put em in. We may as well go it a bit now.

MRS GILBEY. Youve been going it quite far enough, Rob. [*To Mrs Knox*] He wont get up in the mornings now: he that was always out of bed at seven to the tick!

MRS KNOX. You hear that, Jo? [*To Mrs Gilbey*] Hes taken to whisky and soda. A pint a week! And the beer the same as before!

KNOX. Oh, dont preach, old girl.

MRS KNOX. [*To Mrs Gilbey*] Thats a new name hes got for me. [*to Knox*] I tell you, Jo, this doesnt sit well on you. You may call it preaching if you like;

but it's the truth for all that. I say that if youve happiness within yourself, you dont need to seek it outside, spending money on drink and theatres and bad company, and being miserable after all. You can sit at home and be happy; and you can work and be happy. If you have that in you, the spirit will set you free to do what you want and guide you to do right. But if you havent got it, then youd best be respectable and stick to the ways that are marked out for you; for youve nothing else to keep you straight.

KNOX. [*angrily*] And is a man never to have a bit of fun? See whats come of it with your daughter! She was to be content with your happiness that youre always talking about; and how did the spirit guide her? To a month's hard for being drunk and assaulting the police. Did *I* ever assault the police?

MRS KNOX. You wouldnt have the courage. I dont blame the girl.

MRS GILBEY. Oh, Maria! What are you saying?	GILBEY. What! And you so pious!

MRS KNOX. She went where the spirit guided her. And what harm there was in it she knew nothing about.

GILBEY. Oh, come, Mrs Knox! Girls are not so innocent as all that.

MRS KNOX. I dont say she was ignorant. But I do say that she didnt know what we know: I mean the way certain temptations get a sudden hold that no goodness nor self-control is any use against. She was saved from that, and had a rough lesson too; and I say it was no earthly protection that did that. But dont think, you two men, that youll be protected if you make what she did an excuse to go and do as youd like to do if it wasnt for fear of losing your characters. The spirit wont guide you, because it isnt in you; and it never had been: not in either of you.

GILBEY. [*with ironic humility*] I'm sure I'm obliged to you for your good opinion, Mrs Knox.

MRS KNOX. Well, I will say for you, Mr Gilbey, that youre better than my man here. Hes a bitter hard heathen, is my Jo, God help me! [*She begins to cry quietly*].

KNOX. Now, dont take on like that, Amelia. You know I always give in to you that you were right about religion. But one of us had to think of other things, or we'd have starved, we and the child.

MRS KNOX. How do you know youd have starved? All the other things might have been added unto you.

GILBEY. Come, Mrs Knox, dont tell me Knox is a sinner. I know better. I'm sure youd be the first to be sorry if anything was to happen to him.

KNOX. [*bitterly to his wife*] Youve always had some grudge against me; and nobody but yourself can understand what it is.

MRS KNOX. I wanted a man who had that happiness within himself. You made me think you had it; but it was nothing but being in love with me.

MRS GILBEY. And do you blame him for that?

MRS KNOX. I blame nobody. But let him not think he can walk by his own light. I tell him that if he gives up being respectable he'll go right down to the bottom of the hill. He has no powers inside himself to keep him steady; so let him cling to the powers outside him.

KNOX. [*rising angrily*] Who wants to give up being respectable? All this for a pint of whisky that lasted a week! How long would it have lasted Simmons, I wonder?

MRS KNOX. [*gently*] Oh, well, say no more, Jo. I wont plague you about it. [*He sits down*]. You never did understand; and you never will. Hardly anybody understands: even Margaret didnt til she went to prison. She does now; and I shall have a companion in the house after all these lonely years.

KNOX. [*beginning to cry*] I did all I could to make you happy. I never said a harsh word to you.

GILBEY. [*rising indignantly*] What right have you to treat a man like that? an honest respectable husband? as if he were dirt under your feet?

KNOX. Let her alone, Gilbey. [*Gilbey sits down, but mutinously*].

MRS KNOX. Well, you gave me all you could, Jo; and if it wasnt what I wanted, that wasnt your fault. But I'd rather have you as you were than since you took to whisky and soda.

KNOX. I dont want any whisky and soda. I'll take the pledge if you like.

MRS KNOX. No: you shall have your beer because you like it. The whisky was only brag. And if you and me are to remain friends, Mr Gilbey, youll get up to-morrow morning at seven.

GILBEY. [*defiantly*] Damme if I will! There!

MRS KNOX. [*with gentle pity*] How do you know, Mr Gilbey, what youll do to-morrow morning?

GILBEY. Why shouldnt I know? Are we children not to be let do what we like, and our own sons and daughters kicking their heels all over the place? [*To Knox*] I was never one to interfere between man and wife, Knox; but if Maria started ordering me about like that—

MRS GILBEY. Now dont be naughty, Rob. You know you mustnt set yourself up against religion?

GILBEY. Whos setting himself up against religion?

MRS KNOX. It doesnt matter whether you set yourself up against it or not, Mr. Gilbey. If it sets itself up against you, youll have to go the appointed way: it's no use quarrelling about it with me that am as great a sinner as yourself.

GILBEY. Oh, indeed! And who told you I was a sinner?

MRS GILBEY. Now, Rob, you know we are all sinners. What else is religion?

GILBEY. I say nothing against religion. I suppose were all sinners, in a manner of speaking; but I dont like to have it thrown at me as if I'd really done anything.

MRS GILBEY. Mrs Knox is speaking for your good, Rob.

GILBEY. Well, I dont like to be spoken to for my good. Would anybody like it?

MRS KNOX. Dont take offence where none is meant, Mr Gilbey. Talk about something else. No good ever comes of arguing about such things among the like of us.

KNOX. The like of us! Are you throwing it in our teeth that your people were in the wholesale and thought Knox and Gilbey wasnt good enough for you?

MRS KNOX. No, Jo: you know I'm not. What better were my people than yours, for all their pride? But Ive noticed it all my life: we're ignorant. We dont really know whats right and whats wrong. We're all right as long as things go on the way they always did. We bring our children up just as we were brought up; and we go to church or chapel just as our parents did; and we say what everybody says; and it goes on all right until something out of the way happens: theres a family quarrel, or one of the children goes wrong, or a father takes to drink, or an aunt goes mad, or one of us finds ourselves doing something we never thought we'd want to do. And then you know what happens: complaints and quarrels and huff and offence and bad language and bad temper and regular bewilderment as if Satan possessed us all. We find out then that with all our respectability and piety, weve no real religion and no way of telling right from wrong. Weve nothing but our habits; and when theyre upset, where are we? Just like Peter in the storm trying to walk on the water and finding he couldnt.

MRS GILBEY. [*piously*] Aye! He found out, didnt he?

GILBEY. [*reverently*] I never denied that youve a great intellect, Mrs Knox—

MRS KNOX. Oh get along with you, Gilbey, if you begin talking about my intellect. Give us some tea, Maria. Ive said my say; and Im sure I beg the company's pardon for being so long about it, and so disagreeable.

MRS GILBEY. Ring, Rob. [*Gilbey rings*]. Stop. Juggins will think we're ringing for him.

GILBEY. [*appalled*] It's too late. I rang before I thought of it.

MRS GILBEY. Step down and apologize, Rob.

KNOX. Is it him that you said was brother to a—

Juggins comes in with the tea-tray. All rise. He takes the tray to Mrs. Gilbey.

GILBEY. I didnt mean to ask you to do this, Mr Juggins. I wasnt thinking when I rang.

MRS GILBEY. [*trying to take the tray from him*] Let me, Juggins.

JUGGINS. Please sit down, madam. Allow me to discharge my duties just as usual, sir. I assure you that is the correct thing. [*They sit down, ill at ease, whilst he places the tray on the table. He then goes out for the curate*].

KNOX. [*lowering his voice*] Is this all right, Gilbey? Anybody may be the son of a duke, you know. Is he legitimate?

GILBEY. Good lord! I never thought of that.

Juggins returns with the cakes. They regard him with suspicion.

GILBEY. [*whispering to Knox*] You ask him.

KNOX. [*to Juggins*] Just a word with you, my man. Was your mother married to your father?

JUGGINS. I believe so, sir. I cant say from personal knowledge. It was before my time.

GILBEY. Well, but look here you know—[*he hesitates*].

JUGGINS. Yes, sir?

KNOX. I know whatll clinch it, Gilbey. You leave it to me. [*To Juggins*] Was your mother the duchess?

JUGGINS. Yes, sir. Quite correct, sir, I assure you. [*To Mrs Gilbey*] That is the milk, madam. [*She has mistaken the jugs*]. This is the water.

They stare at him in pitiable embarrassment.

MRS KNOX. What did I tell you? Heres something out of the common happening with a servant; and we none of us know how to behave.

JUGGINS. It's quite simple, madam. I'm a footman, and should be treated as a footman. [*He proceeds calmly with his duties, handing round cups of tea as Mrs Knox fills them*].

Shrieks of laughter from below stairs reach the ears of the company.

MRS GILBEY. Whats that noise? Is Master Bobby at home? I heard his laugh.

MRS KNOX. I'm sure I heard Margaret's.

GILBEY. Not a bit of it. It was that woman.

JUGGINS. I can explain, sir. I must ask you to excuse the liberty; but I'm entertaining a small party to tea in my pantry.

MRS GILBEY. But youre not entertaining Master Bobby?

JUGGINS. Yes, madam.

GILBEY. Who's with him?

JUGGINS. Miss Knox, sir.

GILBEY. Miss Knox! Are you sure? Is there anyone else?

JUGGINS. Only a French marine officer, sir, and—er—Miss Delaney. [*He places Gilbey's tea on the table before him*]. The lady that called about Master Bobby, sir.

KNOX. Do you mean to say theyre having a party all to themselves downstairs, and we having a party up here and knowing nothing about it?

JUGGINS. Yes, sir. I have to do a good deal of entertaining in the pantry for Master Bobby, sir.

GILBEY. Well, this is a nice state of things!

KNOX. Whats the meaning of it? What do they do it for?

JUGGINS. To enjoy themselves, sir, I should think.

MRS GILBEY. Enjoy themselves! Did ever anybody hear of such a thing?

GILBEY. Knox's daughter shewn into my pantry!

KNOX. Margaret mixing with a Frenchman and a footman— [*Suddenly realizing that the footman is offering him cake.*] She doesnt know about—about His Grace, you know.

MRS GILBEY. Perhaps she does. Does she, Mr Juggins?

JUGGINS. The other lady suspects me, madam. They call me Rudolph, or the Long Lost Heir.

MRS GILBEY. It's a much nicer name than Juggins. I think I'll call you by it, if you dont mind.

JUGGINS. Not at all, madam.

Roars of merriment from below.

GILBEY. Go and tell them to stop laughing. What right have they to make a noise like that?

JUGGINS. I asked them not to laugh so loudly, sir. But the French gentleman always sets them off again.

KNOX. Do you mean to tell me that my daughter laughs at a Frenchman's jokes?

GILBEY. We all know what French jokes are.

JUGGINS. Believe me: you do not, sir. The noise this afternoon has all been because the Frenchman said that the cat had whooping cough.

MRS GILBEY. [*laughing heartily*] Well, I never!

GILBEY. Dont be a fool, Maria. Look here, Knox: we cant let this go on. People cant be allowed to behave like this.

KNOX. Just what I say.

A concertina adds its music to the revelry.

MRS GILBEY. [*excited*] Thats the squiffer. Hes bought it for her.

GILBEY. Well, of all the scandalous— [*Redoubled laughter from below*].

KNOX. I'll put a stop to this. [*He goes out to the landing and shouts*] Margaret! [*Sudden dead silence*]. Margaret, I say!

MARGARET'S VOICE. Yes, father. Shall we all come up? We're dying to.

KNOX. Come up and be ashamed of yourselves, behaving like wild Indians.

DORA'S VOICE [*screaming*] Oh! oh! oh! Dont Bobby. Now—oh! [*In headlong flight she dashes into and right across the room, breathless, and slightly abashed by the company*]. I beg your pardon, Mrs Gilbey, for coming in like that; but whenever I go upstairs in front of Bobby, he pretends it's a cat biting my ankles; and I just must scream.

Bobby and Margaret enter rather more shyly, but evidently in high spirits. Bobby places himself near his father, on the hearthrug, and presently slips down into the arm-chair.

MARGARET. How do you do, Mrs. Gilbey? [*She posts herself behind her mother*].

Duvallet comes in behaving himself perfectly. Knox follows.

MARGARET. Oh—let me introduce. My friend Lieutenant Duvallet. Mrs Gilbey. Mr Gilbey. [*Duvallet bows and sits down on Mr Knox's left, Juggins placing a chair for him*].

DORA. Now, Bobby: introduce me: theres a dear.

BOBBY. [*a little nervous about it; but trying to keep up his spirits*] Miss Delaney: Mr and Mrs Knox. [*Knox, as he resumes his seat, acknowledges the introduction suspiciously. Mrs Knox bows gravely, looking keenly at Dora and taking her measure without prejudice*].

DORA. Pleased to meet you. [*Juggins places the baby rocking-chair for her on Mrs Gilbey's right, opposite Mrs Knox*]. Thank you. [*She sits and turns to Mrs Gilbey*] Bobby's given me the squiffer. [*To the company generally*] Do you know what theyve been doing downstairs? [*She goes off into ecstasies of mirth*]. Youd never guess. Theyve been trying to teach me table manners. The Lieutenant and Rudolph say I'm a regular pig. I'm sure I never knew there was anything wrong with me. But live and learn [*to Gilbey*] eh, old dear?

JUGGINS. Old dear is not correct, Miss Delaney. [*He retires to the end of the sideboard nearest the door*].

DORA. Oh get out! I must call a man something. He doesnt mind: do you, Charlie?

MRS GILBEY. His name isnt Charlie.

DORA. Excuse me. I call everybody Charlie.

JUGGINS. You mustnt.

DORA. Oh, if I were to mind you, I should have to hold my tongue altogether; and then how sorry youd be! Lord, how I do run on! Dont mind me, Mrs Gilbey.

KNOX. What I want to know is, whats to be the end of this? It's not for me to interfere between you and your son, Gilbey: he knows his own intentions best, no doubt, and perhaps has told them to you. But Ive my daughter to look after; and it's my duty as a parent to have a clear understanding about her. No good is ever done by beating about the bush. I ask Lieutenant—well, I dont speak French; and I cant pronounce the name—

MARGARET. Mr Duvallet, father.

KNOX. I ask Mr Doovalley what his intentions are.

MARGARET. Oh father: how can you?

DUVALLET. I'm afraid my knowledge of English is not enough to understand. Intentions? How?

MARGARET. He wants to know will you marry me.

MRS GILBEY. What a thing to say!

KNOX. Silence, miss.

DORA. Well, thats straight, aint it?

DUVALLET. But I am married already. I have two daughters.

KNOX. [*rising, virtuously indignant*] You sit there after carrying on with my daughter, and tell me coolly youre married.

MARGARET. Papa: you really must not tell people that they sit there. [*He sits down again sulkily*].

DUVALLET. Pardon. Carrying on? What does that mean?

MARGARET. It means—

KNOX. [*violently*] Hold your tongue, you shameless young hussy. Dont you dare say what it means.

DUVALLET. [*shrugging his shoulders*] What does it mean, Rudolph?

MRS KNOX. If it's not proper for her to say, it's not proper for a man to say, either. Mr Doovalley: youre a married man with daughters. Would you let them go about with a stranger, as you are to us, without wanting to know whether he intended to behave honorably?

DUVALLET. Ah, madam, my daughters are French girls. That is very different. It would not be correct for a French girl to go about alone and speak to men as English and American girls do. That is why I so immensely admire the English people. You are so free—so unprejudiced—your women are so brave and frank—their minds are so—how do you say?—wholesome. I intend to have my daughters educated in England. Nowhere else in the world but in England could I have met at a Variety Theatre a charming young lady of perfect respectability, and enjoyed a dance with her at a public dancing saloon. And where else are women trained to box and knock out the teeth of policemen as a protest against injustice and violence? [*Rising, with immense elan*] Your daughter, madam, is superb. Your country is a model to the rest of Europe. If you were a Frenchman, stifled with prudery, hypocrisy and the tyranny of the family and the home, you would understand how an enlightened Frenchman admires and envies your freedom, your broadmindedness, and the fact that home life can hardly be said to exist in England. You have made an end of the despotism of the parent; the family council is unknown to you; everywhere in these islands one can enjoy the exhilarating, the soul-liberating spectacle of men quarrelling with their brothers, defying their fathers, refusing to speak to their mothers. In France we are not men: we are only sons—grown-up children. Here one is a human being—an end in himself. Oh, Mrs Knox, if only your military genius were equal to your moral genius—if that conquest of Europe by France which inaugurated the new age after the Revolution had only been an English conquest, how much more enlightened the world would have been now! We, alas, can only fight. France is unconquerable. We impose our narrow ideas, our prejudices, our obsolete institutions, our insufferable pedantry on the world by brute force—by that stupid quality of military heroism which shews how little we have evolved from the savage: nay, from the beast. We can charge like bulls; we can spring on our foes like gamecocks; when we are overpowered by reason, we can die fighting like rats. And we are foolish enough to be proud of it! Why should we be? Does the bull progress? Can you civilize the gamecock? Is there any future for the rat? We cant even fight intelligently: when we lose battles, it is because we have not sense enough to know when we are beaten. At Waterloo, had we known when we were beaten, we should have retreated; tried another plan; and won the battle. But no: we were too pigheaded to admit that there is anything impossible to a Frenchman: we were quite satisfied when our Marshals had six horses shot under them, and our stupid old grognards died fighting rather than surrender like reasonable beings. Think of your great Wellington: think of his inspiring words, when the lady asked him whether British soldiers ever ran away. "All soldiers run away, madam," he said; "but if there are supports for them to fall back on it does not matter." Think of your illustrious Nelson, always beaten on land, always victorious at sea, where his men could not run away. You are not dazzled and misled by false ideals of patriotic enthusiasm: your honest and sensible statesmen demand for England a two-power standard, even a three-power standard, frankly admitting that it is wise to fight three to one: whilst we, fools and braggarts as we are, declare that every Frenchman is a host in himself, and that when one Frenchman attacks three Englishmen he is guilty of an act of cowardice comparable to that of the man who strikes a woman. It is folly: it is nonsense: a Frenchman is not really stronger than a German, than an Italian, even than an Englishman. Sir: if all Frenchwomen were like your daughter—if all Frenchmen had the good sense, the power of seeing things as they really are, the calm judgment, the open mind, the philosophic grasp, the foresight and true courage, which are so natural to you as an Englishman that you are hardly conscious of possessing them, France would become the greatest nation in the world.

MARGARET. Three cheers for old England! [*She shakes hands with him warmly*].

BOBBY. Hurra-a-ay! And so say all of us.

Duvallet, having responded to Margaret's handshake with enthusiasm, kisses Juggins on both cheeks, and sinks into his chair, wiping his perspiring brow.

GILBEY. Well, this sort of talk is above me. Can you make anything out of it, Knox?

KNOX. The long and short of it seems to be that he cant lawfully marry my daughter, as he ought after going to prison with her.

DORA. I'm ready to marry Bobby, if that will be any satisfaction.

GILBEY. No you dont. Not if I know it.

MRS KNOX. He ought to, Mr Gilbey.

GILBEY. Well, if thats your religion, Amelia Knox, I want no more of it. Would you invite them to your house if he married her?

MRS KNOX. He ought to marry her whether or no.

BOBBY. I feel I ought to, Mrs Knox.

GILBEY. Hold your tongue. Mind your own business.

BOBBY. [*wildly*] If I'm not let marry her, I'll do something downright disgraceful. I'll enlist as a soldier.

JUGGINS. That is not a disgrace, sir.

BOBBY. Not for you, perhaps. But youre only a footman. I'm a gentleman.

MRS GILBEY. Dont dare to speak disrespectfully to Mr Rudolph, Bobby. For shame!

JUGGINS. [*coming forward to the middle of the table*] It is not gentlemanly to regard the service of your country as disgraceful. It is gentlemanly to marry the lady you make love to.

GILBEY. [*aghast*] My boy is to marry this woman and be a social outcast!

JUGGINS. Your boy and Miss Delaney will be inexorably condemned by respectable society to spend the rest of their days in precisely the sort of company they seem to like best and be most at home in.

KNOX. And my daughter? Whos to marry my daughter?

JUGGINS. Your daughter, sir, will probably marry whoever she makes up her mind to marry. She is a lady of very determined character.

KNOX. Yes: if he'd have her with her character gone. But who would? Youre the brother of a duke. Would—

BOBBY. Whats that?
MARGARET. Juggins a duke?
DUVALLET. Comment!
DORA. What did I tell you?

KNOX. Yes: the brother of a duke: thats what he is. [*To Juggins*] Well, would you marry her?

JUGGINS. I was about to propose that solution of your problem, Mr Knox.

MRS GILBEY. Well I never!

KNOX. D'ye mean it?
MRS KNOX. Marry Margaret!

JUGGINS. [*continuing*] As an idle younger son, unable to support myself, or even to remain in the Guards in competition with the grandsons of American millionaires, I could not have aspired to Miss Knox's hand. But as a sober, honest, and industrious domestic servant, who has, I trust, given satisfaction to his employer [*he bows to Mr Gilbey*] I feel I am a man with a character. It is for Miss Knox to decide.

MARGARET. I got into a frightful row once for admiring you, Rudolph.

JUGGINS. I should have got into an equally frightful row myself, Miss, had I betrayed my admiration for you. I looked forward to those weekly dinners.

MRS KNOX. But why did a gentleman like you stoop to be a footman?

DORA. He stooped to conquer.

MARGARET. Shut up, Dora: I want to hear.

JUGGINS. I will explain; but only Mrs Knox will understand. I once insulted a servant—rashly; for he was a sincere Christian. He rebuked me for trifling with a girl of his own class. I told him to remember what he was, and to whom he was speaking. He said God would remember. I discharged him on the spot.

GILBEY. Very properly.

KNOX. What right had he to mention such a thing to you?

MRS GILBEY. What are servants coming to?

MRS KNOX. Did it come true, what he said?

JUGGINS. It stuck like a poisoned arrow. It rankled for months. Then I gave in. I apprenticed myself to an old butler of ours who kept a hotel. He taught me my present business, and got me a place as footman with Mr Gilbey. If ever I meet that man again I shall be able to look him in the face.

MRS KNOX. Margaret: it's not on account of the duke: dukes are vanities. But take my advice and take him.

MARGARET. [*slipping her arm through his*] I have loved Juggins since the first day I beheld him. I felt instinctively he had been in the Guards. May he walk out with me, Mr Gilbey?

KNOX. Dont be vulgar, girl. Remember your new position. [*To Juggins*] I suppose youre serious about this, Mr—Mr Rudolph?

JUGGINS. I propose, with your permission, to begin keeping company this afternoon, if Mrs Gilbey can spare me.

GILBEY. [*in a gust of envy, to Bobby*] Itll be long enough before youll marry the sister of a duke, you young good-for-nothing.

DORA. Dont fret, old dear. Rudolph will teach me high-class manners. I call it quite a happy ending: dont you, lieutenant?

DUVALLET. In France it would be impossible. But here—ah! [*kissing his hand*] la belle Angleterre!

EPILOGUE

Before the curtain. The Count, dazed and agitated, hurries to the 4 critics, as they rise, bored and weary, from their seats.

THE COUNT. Gentlemen: do not speak to me. I implore you to withhold your opinion. I am not strong enough to bear it. I could never have believed it. Is this a play? Is this in any sense of the word, Art? Is it agreeable? Can it conceivably do good to any human being? Is it delicate? Do such people really exist? Excuse me, gentlemen: I speak from a wounded heart. There are private reasons for my discomposure. This play implies obscure, unjust, unkind reproaches and menaces to all of us who are parents.

TROTTER. Pooh! you take it too seriously. After all, the thing has amusing passages. Dismiss the rest as impertinence.

THE COUNT. Mr Trotter: it is easy for you to play the pococurantist. [*Trotter, amazed, repeats the first three syllables in his throat, making a noise like a pheasant*]. You see hundreds of plays every year. But to me, who have never seen anything of this kind before, the effect of this play is terribly disquieting. Sir: if it had been what people call an immoral play, I shouldnt have minded a bit. [*Vaughan is shocked*]. Love beautifies every romance and justifies every audacity. [*Bannal assents gravely*]. But there are reticences which everybody should respect. There are decencies too subtle to be put into words, without which human society would be unbearable. People could not talk to one another as those people talk. No child could speak to its parent—no girl could speak to a youth—no human creature could tear down the veils— [*Appealing to Vaughan, who is on his left flank, with Gunn between them*] Could they, sir?

VAUGHAN. Well, I dont see that.

THE COUNT. You dont see it! dont feel it! [*To Gunn*] Sir: I appeal to you.

GUNN. [*with studied weariness*] It seems to me the most ordinary sort of old-fashioned Ibsenite drivel.

THE COUNT [*turning to Trotter, who is on his right, between him and Bannal*] Mr Trotter: will you tell me that you are not amazed, outraged, revolted, wounded in your deepest and holiest feelings by every word of this play, every tone, every implication; that you did not sit there shrinking in every fibre at the thought of what might come next?

TROTTER. Not a bit. Any clever modern girl could turn out that kind of thing by the yard.

THE COUNT. Then, sir, tomorrow I start for Venice, never to return. I must believe what you tell me. I perceive that you are not agitated, not surprised, not concerned; that my own horror (yes, gentlemen, horror—horror of the very soul) appears unaccountable to you, ludicrous, absurd, even to you, Mr Trotter, who are little younger than myself. Sir: if young people spoke to me like that, I should die of shame: I could not face it. I must go back. The world has passed me by and left me. Accept the apologies of an elderly and no doubt ridiculous admirer of the art of a bygone day, when there was still some beauty in the world and some delicate grace in family life. But I promised my daughter your opinion; and I must keep my word. Gentlemen: you are the choice and master spirits of this age: you walk through it without bewilderment and face its strange products without dismay. Pray deliver your verdict. Mr Bannal: you know that it is the custom at a Court Martial for the youngest officer present to deliver his judgment first; so that he may not be influenced by the authority of his elders. You are the youngest. What is your opinion of the play?

BANNAL. Well, whos it by?

THE COUNT. That is a secret for the present.

BANNAL. You dont expect me to know what to say about a play when I dont know who the author is, do you?

THE COUNT. Why not?

BANNAL. Why not! Why not!! Suppose you had to write about a play by Pinero and one by Jones! Would you say exactly the same thing about them?

THE COUNT. I presume not.

BANNAL. Then how could you write about them until you knew which was Pinero and which was Jones? Besides, what sort of play is this? thats what I want to know. Is it a comedy or a tragedy? Is it a farce or a melodrama? Is it repertory theatre tosh, or really straight paying stuff?

GUNN. Cant you tell from seeing it?

BANNAL. I can see it all right enough; but how am I to know how to take it? Is it serious, or is it spoof? If the author knows what his play is, let him tell us what it is. If he doesnt, he cant complain if I dont know either. *I*'m not the author.

THE COUNT. But is it a good play, Mr Bannal? Thats a simple question.

BANNAL. Simple enough when you know. If it's by a good author, it's a good play, naturally. That stands to reason. Who is the author? Tell me that; and I'll place the play for you to a hair's breadth.

THE COUNT. I'm sorry I'm not at liberty to divulge the author's name. The author desires that the play should be judged on its merits.

BANNAL. But what merits can it have except the author's merits? Who would you say it's by, Gunn?

GUNN. Well, who do you think? Here you have a rotten old-fashioned domestic melodrama acted by the usual stage puppets. The hero's a naval lieutenant. All melodramatic heroes are naval lieutenants. The heroine gets into trouble by defying the law (if she didnt get into trouble, thered be no drama) and plays for sympathy all the time as hard as she can. Her good old pious mother turns on her cruel father when hes going to put her out of the house, and says she'll go too. Then theres the comic relief: the comic shopkeeper, the comic shopkeeper's wife, the comic footman who turns out to be a duke in disguise, and the young scapegrace who gives the author his excuse for dragging in a fast young woman. All as old and stale as a fried fish shop on a winter morning.

THE COUNT. But—

GUNN [*interrupting him*] I know what youre going to say, Count. Youre going to say that the whole thing seems to you to be quite new and unusual and original. The naval lieutenant is a Frenchman who cracks up the English and runs down the French: the hackneyed old Shaw touch. The characters are second-rate middle class, instead of being dukes and millionaires. The heroine gets kicked through the mud: real mud. Theres no plot. All the old stage conventions and puppets without the old ingenuity and the old enjoyment. And a feeble air of intellectual pretentiousness kept up all through to persuade you that if the author hasnt written a good play it's because hes too clever to stoop to anything so commonplace. And you three experienced men have sat through all this, and cant tell me who wrote it! Why, the play bears the author's signature in every line.

BANNAL. Who?

GUNN. Granville Barker, of course. Why, old Gilbey is straight out of The Madras House.

BANNAL. Poor old Barker!

VAUGHAN. Utter nonsense! Cant you see the difference in style?

BANNAL. No.

VAUGHAN. [*contemptuously*] Do you know what style is?

BANNAL. Well, I suppose youd call Trotter's uniform style. But it's not my style—since you ask me.

VAUGHAN. To me it's perfectly plain who wrote that play. To begin with, it's intensely disagreeable. Therefore it's not by Barrie, in spite of the footman, who's cribbed from The Admirable Crichton. He was an earl, you may remember. You notice, too, the author's offensive habit of saying silly things that have no real sense in them when you come to examine them, just to set all the fools in the house giggling. Then what does it all come to? An attempt to expose the supposed hypocrisy of the Puritan middle class in England: people just as good as the author, anyhow. With, of course, the inevitable improper female: the Mrs Tanqueray, Iris, and so forth. Well, if you cant recognize the author of that, youve mistaken your professions: thats all I have to say.

BANNAL. Why are you so down on Pinero? And what about that touch that Gunn spotted? the Frenchman's long speech. I believe it's Shaw.

GUNN. Rubbish!

VAUGHAN. Rot! You may put that idea out of your head, Bannal. Poor as this play is, theres the note of passion in it. You feel somehow that beneath all the assumed levity of that poor waif and stray, she really loves Bobby and will be a good wife to him. Now Ive repeatedly proved that Shaw is physiologically incapable of the note of passion.

BANNAL. Yes, I know. Intellect without emotion. Thats right. I always say that myself. A giant brain, if you ask me; but no heart.

GUNN. Oh, shut up, Bannal. This crude medieval psychology of heart and brain—Shakespear would have called it liver and wits—is really schoolboyish. Surely weve had enough of second-hand Schopenhauer. Even such a played-out old back number as Ibsen would have been ashamed of it. Heart and brain, indeed!

VAUGHAN. You have neither one nor the other, Gunn. Youre decadent.

GUNN. Decadent! How I love that early Victorian word!

VAUGHAN. Well, at all events, you cant deny that the characters in this play were quite distinguishable from one another. That proves it's not by Shaw, because all Shaw's characters are himself: mere puppets stuck up to spout Shaw. It's only the actors that make them seem different.

BANNAL. There can be no doubt of that: everybody knows it. But Shaw doesnt write his plays as plays. All he wants to do is to insult everybody all round and set us talking about him.

TROTTER. [*wearily*] And naturally, here we are all talking about him. For heaven's sake, let us change the subject.

VAUGHAN. Still, my articles about Shaw—

GUNN. Oh, stow it, Vaughan. Drop it. What Ive always told you about Shaw is—

BANNAL. There you go, Shaw, Shaw, Shaw! Do chuck it. If you want to know my opinion about Shaw—

TROTTER. No, please, we don't.
VAUGHAN. Shut your head, Bannal. [*yelling*]
GUNN. Oh, do drop it.

The deafened Count puts his fingers in his ears and flies from the centre of the group to its outskirts, behind Vaughan.

BANNAL. [*sulkily*] Oh, very well. Sorry I spoke, I'm sure.

[*beginning again simultaneously*]
TROTTER. Shaw—
VAUGHAN. Shaw—
GUNN. Shaw—

They are cut short by the entry of Fanny through the curtains. She is almost in tears.

FANNY. [*coming between Trotter and Gunn*] I'm so sorry, gentlemen. And it was such a success when I read it to the Cambridge Fabian Society!

TROTTER. Miss O'Dowda: I was about to tell these gentlemen what I guessed before the curtain rose: that you are the author of the play. [*General amazement and consternation*].

FANNY. And you all think it beastly. You hate it. You think I'm a conceited idiot, and that I shall never be able to write anything decent.

She is almost weeping. A wave of sympathy carries away the critics.

VAUGHAN. No, no. Why, I was just saying that it must have been written by Pinero. Didnt I, Gunn?

FANNY. [*enormously flattered*] Really?

TROTTER. I thought Pinero was much too popular for the Cambridge Fabian Society.

FANNY. Oh yes, of course; but still—Oh, did you really say that, Mr Vaughan?

GUNN. I owe you an apology, Miss O'Dowda. I said it was by Barker.

FANNY. [*radiant*] Granville Barker! Oh, you couldnt really have thought it so fine as that.

BANNAL. *I* said Bernard Shaw.

FANNY. Oh, of course it would be a little like Bernard Shaw. The Fabian touch, you know.

BANNAL. [*coming to her encouragingly*] A jolly good little play, Miss O'Dowda. Mind: I dont say it's like one of Shakespear's—Hamlet or The Lady of Lyons, you know—but still, a firstrate little bit of work. [*He shakes her hand*].

GUNN. [*following Bannal's example*] I also, Miss O'Dowda. Capital. Charming. [*He shakes hands*].

VAUGHAN [*with maudlin solemnity*] Only be true to yourself, Miss O'Dowda. Keep serious. Give up making silly jokes. Sustain the note of passion. And youll do great things.

FANNY. You think I have a future?

TROTTER. You have a past, Miss O'Dowda.

FANNY. [*looking apprehensively at her father*] Sh-sh-sh!

THE COUNT. A past! What do you mean, Mr Trotter?

TROTTER. [*to Fanny*] You cant deceive me. That bit about the police was real. Youre a Suffraget, Miss O'Dowda. You were on that Deputation.

THE COUNT. Fanny: is this true?

FANNY. It is. I did a month with Lady Constance Lytton; and I'm prouder of it than I ever was of anything or ever shall be again.

TROTTER. Is that any reason why you should stuff naughty plays down my throat?

FANNY. Yes: itll teach you what it feels like to be forcibly fed.

THE COUNT. She will never return to Venice. I feel now as I felt when the Campanile fell.

Savoyard comes in through the curtains.

SAVOYARD. [*to the Count*] Would you mind coming to say a word of congratulation to the company? Theyre rather upset at having had no curtain call.

THE COUNT. Certainly, certainly. I'm afraid Ive been rather remiss. Let us go on the stage, gentlemen.

The curtains are drawn, revealing the last scene of the play and the actors on the stage. The Count, Savoyard, the critics, and Fanny join them, shaking hands and congratulating.

THE COUNT. Whatever we may think of the play, gentlemen, I'm sure you will agree with me that there can be only one opinion about the acting.

THE CRITICS. Hear, hear! [*They start the applause*].

AYOT ST. LAWRENCE, March 1911.

ANDROCLES AND THE LION

PROLOGUE

Overture; forest sounds, roaring of lions, Christian hymn faintly.

A jungle path. A lion's roar, a melancholy suffering roar, comes from the jungle. It is repeated nearer. The lion limps from the jungle on three legs, holding up his right forepaw, in which a huge thorn sticks. He sits down and contemplates it. He licks it. He shakes it. He tries to extract it by scraping it along the ground, and hurts himself worse. He roars piteously. He licks it again. Tears drop from his eyes. He limps painfully off the path and lies down under the trees, exhausted with pain. Heaving a long sigh, like wind in a trombone, he goes to sleep.

Androcles and his wife Megaera come along the path. He is a small, thin, ridiculous little man who might be any age from thirty to fifty-five. He has sandy hair, watery compassionate blue eyes, sensitive nostrils, and a very presentable forehead; but his good points go no further; his arms and legs and back, though wiry of their kind, look shrivelled and starved. He carries a big bundle, is very poorly clad, and seems tired and hungry.

His wife is a rather handsome pampered slattern, well fed and in the prime of life. She has nothing to carry, and has a stout stick to help her along.

MEGAERA (suddenly throwing down her stick) I won't go another step.

ANDROCLES (pleading wearily) Oh, not again, dear. What's the good of stopping every two miles and saying you won't go another step? We must get on to the next village before night. There are wild beasts in this wood: lions, they say.

MEGAERA. I don't believe a word of it. You are always threatening me with wild beasts to make me walk the very soul out of my body when I can hardly drag one foot before another. We haven't seen a single lion yet.

ANDROCLES. Well, dear, do you want to see one?

MEGAERA (tearing the bundle from his back) You cruel beast, you don't care how tired I am, or what becomes of me (she throws the bundle on the ground): always thinking of yourself. Self! self! self! always yourself! (She sits down on the bundle).

ANDROCLES (sitting down sadly on the ground with his elbows on his knees and his head in his hands) We all have to think of ourselves occasionally, dear.

MEGAERA. A man ought to think of his wife sometimes.

ANDROCLES. He can't always help it, dear. You make me think of you a good deal. Not that I blame you.

MEGAERA. Blame me! I should think not indeed. Is it my fault that I'm married to you?

ANDROCLES. No, dear: that is my fault.

MEGAERA. That's a nice thing to say to me. Aren't you happy with me?

ANDROCLES. I don't complain, my love.

MEGAERA. You ought to be ashamed of yourself.

ANDROCLES. I am, my dear.

MEGAERA. You're not: you glory in it.

ANDROCLES. In what, darling?

MEGAERA. In everything. In making me a slave, and making yourself a laughing-stock. Its not fair. You get me the name of being a shrew with your meek ways, always talking as if butter wouldn't melt in your mouth. And just because I look a big strong woman, and because I'm good-hearted and a bit hasty, and because you're always driving me to do things I'm sorry for afterwards, people say "Poor man: what a life his wife leads him!" Oh, if they only knew! And you think I don't know. But I do, I do, (screaming) I do.

ANDROCLES. Yes, my dear: I know you do.

MEGAERA. Then why don't you treat me properly and be a good husband to me?

ANDROCLES. What can I do, my dear?

MEGAERA. What can you do! You can return to your duty, and come back to your home and your friends, and sacrifice to the gods as all respectable people do, instead of having us hunted out of house and home for being dirty, disreputable, blaspheming atheists.

ANDROCLES. I'm not an atheist, dear: I am a Christian.

MEGAERA. Well, isn't that the same thing, only ten times worse? Everybody knows that the Christians are the very lowest of the low.

ANDROCLES. Just like us, dear.

MEGAERA. Speak for yourself. Don't you dare to compare me to common people. My father owned his own public-house; and sorrowful was the day for me when you first came drinking in our bar.

ANDROCLES. I confess I was addicted to it, dear. But I gave it up when I became a Christian.

MEGAERA. You'd much better have remained a drunkard. I can forgive a man being addicted to drink: its only natural; and I don't deny I like a drop myself sometimes. What I can't stand is your being addicted to Christianity. And what's worse again, your being addicted to animals. How is any woman to keep her house clean when you bring in every stray cat and lost cur and lame duck in the whole countryside? You took the bread out of my mouth to feed them: you know you did: don't attempt to deny it.

ANDROCLES. Only when they were hungry and you were getting too stout, dearie.

MEGAERA. Yes, insult me, do. (Rising) Oh! I won't bear it another moment. You used to sit and talk to those dumb brute beasts for hours, when you hadn't a word for me.

ANDROCLES. They never answered back, darling. (He rises and again shoulders the bundle).

MEGAERA. Well, if you're fonder of animals than of your own wife, you can live with them here in the jungle. I've had enough of them and enough of you. I'm going back. I'm going home.

ANDROCLES (barring the way back) No, dearie: don't take on like that. We can't go back. We've sold everything: we should starve; and I should be sent to Rome and thrown to the lions—

MEGAERA. Serve you right! I wish the lions joy of you. (Screaming) Are you going to get out of my way and let me go home?

ANDROCLES. No, dear—

MEGAERA. Then I'll make my way through the forest; and when I'm eaten by the wild beasts you'll know what a wife you've lost. (She dashes into the jungle and nearly falls over the sleeping lion). Oh! Oh! Andy! Andy! (She totters back and collapses into the arms of Androcles, who, crushed by her weight, falls on his bundle).

ANDROCLES (extracting himself from beneath her and slapping her hands in great anxiety) What is it, my precious, my pet? What's the matter? (He raises her head. Speechless with terror, she points in the direction of the sleeping lion. He steals cautiously towards the spot indicated by Megaera. She rises with an effort and totters after him).

MEGAERA. No, Andy: you'll be killed. Come back.

The lion utters a long snoring sigh. Androcles sees the lion and recoils fainting into the arms of Megaera, who falls back on the bundle. They roll apart and lie staring in terror at one another. The lion is heard groaning heavily in the jungle.

ANDROCLES (whispering) Did you see? A lion.

MEGAERA (despairing) The gods have sent him to punish us because you're a Christian. Take me away, Andy. Save me.

ANDROCLES (rising) Meggy: there's one chance for you. It'll take him pretty nigh twenty minutes to eat me (I'm rather stringy and tough) and you can escape in less time than that.

MEGAERA. Oh, don't talk about eating. (The lion rises with a great groan and limps towards them). Oh! (She faints).

ANDROCLES (quaking, but keeping between the lion and Megaera) Don't you come near my wife, do you hear? (The lion groans. Androcles can hardly stand for trembling). Meggy: run. Run for your life. If I take my eye off him, its all up. (The lion holds up his wounded paw and flaps it piteously before Androcles). Oh, he's lame, poor old chap! He's got a thorn in his paw. A frightfully big thorn. (Full of sympathy) Oh, poor old man! Did um get an awful thorn into um's tootsums wootsums? Has it made um too sick to eat a nice little Christian man for um's breakfast? Oh, a nice little Christian man will get um's thorn out for um; and then um shall eat the nice Christian man and the nice Christian man's nice big tender wifey pifey. (The lion responds by moans of self-pity). Yes, yes, yes, yes, yes. Now, now (taking the paw in his hand) um is not to bite and not to scratch, not even if it hurts a very, very little. Now make velvet paws. That's right. (He pulls gingerly at the thorn. The lion, with an angry yell of pain, jerks back his paw so abruptly that Androcles is thrown on his back). Steadeee! Oh, did the nasty cruel little Christian man hurt the sore paw? (The lion moans assentingly but apologetically). Well, one more little pull and it will be all over. Just one little, little, leetle pull; and then um will live happily ever after. (He gives the thorn another pull. The lion roars and snaps his jaws with a terrifying clash). Oh, mustn't frighten um's good kind doctor, um's affectionate nursey. That didn't hurt at all: not a bit. Just one more. Just to show how the brave big lion can bear pain, not like the little crybaby Christian man. Oopsh! (The thorn comes out. The lion yells with pain, and shakes his paw wildly). That's it! (Holding up the thorn). Now it's out. Now lick um's paw to take away the nasty inflammation. See? (He licks his own hand. The lion nods intelligently and licks his paw industriously). Clever little liony-piony! Understands um's dear old friend Andy Wandy. (The lion licks his face). Yes, kissums Andy Wandy. (The lion, wagging his tail violently, rises on his hind legs and embraces Androcles, who makes a wry face and cries) Velvet paws! Velvet paws! (The lion draws in his claws). That's right. (He embraces the lion, who finally takes the end of his tail in one paw, places that tight around Androcles' waist, resting it on his hip. Androcles takes the other paw in his hand, stretches out his arm, and the two waltz rapturously round and round and finally away through the jungle).

MEGAERA (who has revived during the waltz) Oh, you coward, you haven't danced with me for years; and now you go off dancing with a great brute beast that you haven't known for ten minutes and that wants to eat your own wife. Coward! Coward! Coward! (She rushes off after them into the jungle).

ACT I

Evening. The end of three converging roads to Rome. Three triumphal arches span them where they debouch on a square at the gate of the city. Looking north through the arches one can see the campagna threaded by the three long dusty tracks. On the east and west sides of the square are long stone benches. An old beggar sits on the east side of the square, his bowl at his feet. Through the eastern arch a squad of Roman soldiers tramps along escorting a batch of Christian prisoners of both sexes and all ages, among them one Lavinia, a goodlooking resolute young woman, apparently of higher social standing than her fellow-prisoners. A centurion, carrying his vinewood cudgel, trudges alongside the squad, on its right, in command of it. All are tired and dusty; but the soldiers are dogged and indifferent, the Christians lighthearted and determined to treat their hardships as a joke and encourage one another.

A bugle is heard far behind on the road, where the rest of the cohort is following.

CENTURION (stopping) Halt! Orders from the Captain. (They halt and wait). Now then, you Christians, none of your larks. The captain's coming. Mind you behave yourselves. No singing. Look respectful. Look serious, if you're capable of it. See that big building over there? That's the Coliseum. That's where you'll be thrown to the lions or set to fight the gladiators presently. Think of that; and it'll help you to behave properly before the captain. (The Captain arrives). Attention! Salute! (The soldiers salute).

A CHRISTIAN (cheerfully) God bless you, Captain.

THE CENTURION (scandalised) Silence!

The Captain, a patrician, handsome, about thirty-five, very cold and distinguished, very superior and authoritative, steps up on a stone seat at the west side of the square, behind the centurion, so as to dominate the others more effectually.

THE CAPTAIN. Centurion.

THE CENTURION. (standing at attention and saluting) Sir?

THE CAPTAIN (speaking stiffly and officially) You will remind your men, Centurion, that we are now entering Rome. You will instruct them that once inside the gates of Rome they are in the presence of the Emperor. You will make them understand that the lax discipline of the march cannot be permitted here. You will instruct them to shave every day, not every week. You will impress on them particularly that there must be an end to the profanity and blasphemy of singing Christian hymns on the march. I have to reprimand you, Centurion, for not only allowing this, but actually doing it yourself.

THE CENTURION. The men march better, Captain.

THE CAPTAIN. No doubt. For that reason an exception is made in the case of the march called Onward Christian Soldiers. This may be sung, except when marching through the forum or within hearing of the Emperor's palace; but the words must be altered to "Throw them to the Lions."

The Christians burst into shrieks of uncontrollable laughter, to the great scandal of the Centurion.

CENTURION. Silence! Silen-n-n-n-nce! Where's your behavior? Is that the way to listen to an officer? (To the Captain) That's what we have to put up with from these Christians every day, sir. They're always laughing and joking something scandalous. They've no religion: that's how it is.

LAVINIA. But I think the Captain meant us to laugh, Centurion. It was so funny.

CENTURION. You'll find out how funny it is when you're thrown to the lions to-morrow. (To the Captain, who looks displeased) Beg pardon, Sir. (To the Christians) Silennnnce!

THE CAPTAIN. You are to instruct your men that all intimacy with Christian prisoners must now cease. The men have fallen into habits of dependence upon the prisoners, especially the female prisoners, for cooking, repairs to uniforms, writing letters, and advice in their private affairs. In a Roman soldier such dependence is inadmissible. Let me see no more of it whilst we are in the city. Further, your orders are that in addressing Christian prisoners, the manners and tone of your men must express abhorrence and contempt. Any shortcoming in this respect will be regarded as a breach of discipline.(He turns to the prisoners) Prisoners.

CENTURION (fiercely) Prisonerrrrrs! Tention! Silence!

THE CAPTAIN. I call your attention, prisoners, to the fact that you may be called on to appear in the Imperial Circus at any time from tomorrow onwards according to the requirements of the managers. I may inform you that as there is a shortage of Christians just now, you may expect to be called on very soon.

LAVINIA. What will they do to us, Captain?

CENTURION. Silence!

THE CAPTAIN. The women will be conducted into the arena with the wild beasts of the Imperial Menagerie, and will suffer the consequences. The men, if of an age to bear arms, will be given weapons to defend themselves, if they choose, against the Imperial Gladiators.

LAVINIA. Captain: is there no hope that this cruel persecution—

CENTURION (shocked) Silence! Hold your tongue, there. Persecution, indeed!

THE CAPTAIN (unmoved and somewhat sardonic) Persecution is not a term applicable to the acts of the Emperor. The Emperor is the Defender of the Faith. In throwing you to the lions he will be upholding the interests of religion in Rome. If you were to throw him to the lions, that would no doubt be persecution.

The Christians again laugh heartily.

CENTURION (horrified) Silence, I tell you! Keep silence there. Did anyone ever hear the like of this?

LAVINIA. Captain: there will be nobody to appreciate your jokes when we are gone.

THE CAPTAIN (unshaken in his official delivery) I call the attention of the female prisoner Lavinia to the fact that as the Emperor is a divine personage, her imputation of cruelty is not only treason, but sacrilege. I point out to her further that there is no foundation for the charge, as the Emperor does not desire that any prisoner should suffer; nor can any Christian be harmed save through his or her own obstinacy. All that is necessary is to sacrifice to the gods: a simple and convenient ceremony effected by dropping a pinch of incense on the altar, after which the prisoner is at once set free. Under such circumstances you have only your own perverse folly to blame if you suffer. I suggest to you that if you cannot burn a morsel of incense as a matter of conviction, you might at least do so as a matter of good taste, to avoid shocking the religious convictions of your fellow citizens. I am aware that these considerations do not weigh with Christians; but it is my duty to call your attention to them in order that you may have no ground for complaining of your treatment, or of accusing the Emperor of cruelty when he is showing you the most signal clemency. Looked at from this point of view, every Christian who has perished in the arena has really committed suicide.

LAVINIA. Captain: your jokes are too grim. Do not think it is easy for us to die. Our faith makes life far stronger and more wonderful in us than when we walked in darkness and had nothing to live for.

Death is harder for us than for you: the martyr's agony is as bitter as his triumph is glorious.

THE CAPTAIN (rather troubled, addressing her personally and gravely) A martyr, Lavinia, is a fool. Your death will prove nothing.

LAVINIA. Then why kill me?

THE CAPTAIN. I mean that truth, if there be any truth, needs no martyrs.

LAVINIA. No; but my faith, like your sword, needs testing. Can you test your sword except by staking your life on it?

THE CAPTAIN (suddenly resuming his official tone) I call the attention of the female prisoner to the fact that Christians are not allowed to draw the Emperor's officers into arguments and put questions to them for which the military regulations provide no answer. (The Christians titter).

LAVINIA. Captain: how CAN you?

THE CAPTAIN. I call the female prisoner's attention specially to the fact that four comfortable homes have been offered her by officers of this regiment, of which she can have her choice the moment she chooses to sacrifice as all well-bred Roman ladies do. I have no more to say to the prisoners.

CENTURION. Dismiss! But stay where you are.

THE CAPTAIN. Centurion: you will remain here with your men in charge of the prisoners until the arrival of three Christian prisoners in the custody of a cohort of the tenth legion. Among these prisoners you will particularly identify an armorer named Ferrovius, of dangerous character and great personal strength, and a Greek tailor reputed to be a sorcerer, by name Androcles. You will add the three to your charge here and march them all to the Coliseum, where you will deliver them into the custody of the master of the gladiators and take his receipt, countersigned by the keeper of the beasts and the acting manager. You understand your instructions?

CENTURION. Yes, Sir.

THE CAPTAIN. Dismiss. (He throws off his air of parade, and descends down from the perch. The Centurion seats on it and prepares for a nap, whilst his men stand at ease. The Christians sit down on the west side of the square, glad to rest. Lavinia alone remains standing to speak to the Captain).

LAVINIA. Captain: is this man who is to join us the famous Ferrovius, who has made such wonderful conversions in the northern cities?

THE CAPTAIN. Yes. We are warned that he has the strength of an elephant and the temper of a mad bull. Also that he is stark mad. Not a model Christian, it would seem.

LAVINIA. You need not fear him if he is a Christian, Captain.

THE CAPTAIN (coldly) I shall not fear him in any case, Lavinia.

LAVINIA (her eyes dancing) How brave of you, Captain!

THE CAPTAIN. You are right: it was silly thing to say. (In a lower tone, humane and urgent) Lavinia: do Christians know how to love?

LAVINIA (composedly) Yes, Captain: they love even their enemies.

THE CAPTAIN. Is that easy?

LAVINIA. Very easy, Captain, when their enemies are as handsome as you.

THE CAPTAIN. Lavinia: you are laughing at me.

LAVINIA. At you, Captain! Impossible.

THE CAPTAIN. Then you are flirting with me, which is worse. Don't be foolish.

LAVINIA. But such a very handsome captain.

THE CAPTAIN. Incorrigible! (Urgently) Listen to me. The men in that audience tomorrow will be the vilest of voluptuaries: men in whom the only passion excited by a beautiful woman is a lust to see her tortured and torn shrieking limb from limb. It is a crime to dignify that passion. It is offering yourself for violation by the whole rabble of the streets and the riff-raff of the court at the same time. Why will you not choose rather a kindly love and an honorable alliance?

LAVINIA. They cannot violate my soul. I alone can do that by sacrificing to false gods.

THE CAPTAIN. Sacrifice then to the true God. What does his name matter? We call him Jupiter. The Greeks call him Zeus. Call him what you will as you drop the incense on the altar flame: He will understand.

LAVINIA. No. I couldn't. That is the strange thing, Captain, that a little pinch of incense should make all that difference. Religion is such a great thing that when I meet really religious people we are friends at once, no matter what name we give to the divine will that made us and moves us. Oh, do you think that I, a woman, would quarrel with you for sacrificing to a woman god like Diana, if Diana meant to you what Christ means to me? No: we should kneel side by side before her altar like two children. But when men who believe neither in my god nor in their own—men who do not know the meaning of the word religion—when these men drag me to the foot of an iron statue that has become the symbol of the terror and darkness through which they walk, of their cruelty and greed, of their hatred of God and their oppression of man—when they ask me to pledge my soul before the people that this hideous idol is God, and that all this wickedness and falsehood is divine truth, I cannot do it, not if they could put a thousand cruel deaths on me. I tell you, it is physically impossible. Listen, Captain: did you ever try to catch a mouse in your hand? Once there was a dear little mouse that used to come out and play on my table as I was reading. I wanted to take him in my hand and caress him; and sometimes he got among my books so that he could not escape me when I stretched out my hand. And I did stretch out my hand; but it always came back in spite of me. I was not afraid of him in my heart; but my hand refused: it is not in the nature of my hand to touch a mouse. Well, Captain, if I took a pinch of incense in my hand and stretched it out over the altar fire, my hand would come back. My body would be true to my faith even if you could corrupt my mind. And all the time I should believe more in Diana than my persecutors have ever believed in anything. Can you understand that?

THE CAPTAIN (simply) Yes: I understand that. But my hand would not come back. The hand that holds the sword has been trained not to come back from anything but victory.

LAVINIA. Not even from death?

THE CAPTAIN. Least of all from death.

LAVINIA. Then I must not come back either. A woman has to be braver than a soldier.

THE CAPTAIN. Prouder, you mean.

LAVINIA (startled) Prouder! You call our courage pride!

THE CAPTAIN. There is no such thing as courage: there is only pride. You Christians are the proudest devils on earth.

LAVINIA (hurt) Pray God then my pride may never become a false pride. (She turns away as if she did not wish to continue the conversation, but softens and says to him with a smile) Thank you for trying to save me from death.

THE CAPTAIN. I knew it was no use; but one tries in spite of one's knowledge.

LAVINIA. Something stirs, even in the iron breast of a Roman soldier!

THE CAPTAIN. It will soon be iron again. I have seen many women die, and forgotten them in a week.

LAVINIA. Remember me for a fortnight, handsome Captain. I shall be watching you, perhaps.

THE CAPTAIN. From the skies? Do not deceive yourself, Lavinia. There is no future for you beyond the grave.

LAVINIA. What does that matter? Do you think I am only running away from the terrors of life into the comfort of heaven? If there were no future, or if the future were one of torment, I should have to go just the same. The hand of God is upon me.

THE CAPTAIN. Yes: when all is said, we are both patricians, Lavinia, and must die for our beliefs. Farewell. (He offers her his hand. She takes it and presses it. He walks away, trim and calm. She looks after him for a moment, and cries a little as he disappears through the eastern arch. A trumpet-call is heard from the road through the western arch).

CENTURION (waking up and rising) Cohort of the tenth with prisoners. Two file out with me to receive them. (He goes out through the western arch, followed by four soldiers in two files).

Lentulus and Metellus come into the square from the west side with a little retinue of servants. Both are young courtiers, dressed in the extremity of fashion. Lentulus is slender, fair-haired, epicene. Metellus is manly, compactly built, olive skinned, not a talker.

LENTULUS. Christians, by Jove! Let's chaff them.

METELLUS. Awful brutes. If you knew as much about them as I do you wouldn't want to chaff them. Leave them to the lions.

LENTULUS (indicating Lavinia, who is still looking towards the arches after the captain). That woman's got a figure. (He walks past her, staring at her invitingly, but she is preoccupied and is not conscious of him). Do you turn the other cheek when they kiss you?

LAVINIA (starting) What?

LENTULus. Do you turn the other cheek when they kiss you, fascinating Christian?

LAVINIA. Don't be foolish. (To Metellus, who has remained on her right, so that she is between them) Please don't let your friend behave like a cad before the soldiers. How are they to respect and obey patricians if they see them behaving like street boys? (Sharply to Lentulus) Pull yourself together, man. Hold your head up. Keep the corners of your mouth firm; and treat me respectfully. What do you take me for?

LENTULUS (irresolutely) Look here, you know: I—you—I—

LAVINIA. Stuff! Go about your business. (She turns decisively away and sits down with her comrades, leaving him disconcerted).

METELLUS. You didn't get much out of that. I told you they were brutes.

LENTULUS. Plucky little filly! I suppose she thinks I care. (With an air of indifference he strolls with Metellus to the east side of the square, where they stand watching the return of the Centurion through the western arch with his men, escorting three prisoners: Ferrovius, Androcles, and Spintho. Ferrovius is a powerful, choleric man in the prime of life, with large nostrils, staring eyes, and a thick neck: a man whose sensibilities are keen and violent to the verge of madness. Spintho is a debauchee, the wreck of a good-looking man gone hopelessly to the bad. Androcles is overwhelmed with grief, and is restraining his tears with great difficulty).

THE CENTURION (to Lavinia) Here are some pals for you. This little bit is Ferrovius that you talk so much about. (Ferrovius turns on him threateningly. The Centurion holds up his left forefinger in admonition). Now remember that you're a Christian, and that you've got to return good for evil. (Ferrovius controls himself convulsively; moves away from temptation to the east side near Lentulus; clasps his hands in silent prayer; and throws himself on his knees). That's the way to manage them, eh! This fine fellow (indicating Androcles, who comes to his left, and makes Lavinia a heartbroken salutation) is a sorcerer. A Greek tailor, he is. A real sorcerer, too: no mistake about it. The tenth marches with a leopard at the head of the column. He made a pet of the leopard; and now he's crying at being parted from it. (Androcles sniffs lamentably). Ain't you, old chap? Well, cheer up, we march with a Billy goat (Androcles brightens up) that's killed two leopards and ate a turkey-cock. You can have him for a pet if you like. (Androcles, quite consoled, goes past the Centurion to Lavinia, and sits down contentedly on the ground on her left). This dirty dog (collaring Spintho) is a real Christian. He mobs the temples, he does (at each accusation he gives the neck of Spintho's tunic a twist); he goes smashing things mad drunk, he does; he steals the gold vessels, he does; he assaults the priestesses, he does pah! (He flings Spintho into the middle of the group of prisoners). You're the sort that makes duty a pleasure, you are.

SPINTHO (gasping) That's it: strangle me. Kick me. Beat me. Revile me. Our Lord was beaten and reviled. That's my way to heaven. Every martyr goes to heaven, no matter what he's done. That is so, isn't it, brother?

CENTURION. Well, if you're going to heaven, *I* don't want to go there. I wouldn't be seen with you.

LENTULUS. Haw! Good! (Indicating the kneeling Ferrovius). Is this one of the turn-the-other-cheek gentlemen, Centurion?

CENTURION. Yes, sir. Lucky for you too, sir, if you want to take any liberties with him.

LENTULUS (to Ferrovius) You turn the other cheek when you're struck, I'm told.

FERROVIUS (slowly turning his great eyes on him) Yes, by the grace of God, I do, NOW.

LENTULUS. Not that you're a coward, of course; but out of pure piety.

FERROVIUS. I fear God more than man; at least I try to.

LENTULUS. Let's see. (He strikes him on the cheek. Androcles makes a wild movement to rise and interfere; but Lavinia holds him down, watching Ferrovius intently. Ferrovius, without flinching, turns the other cheek. Lentulus, rather out of countenance, titters foolishly, and strikes him again feebly). You know, I should feel ashamed if I let myself be struck like that, and took it lying down. But then I'm not a Christian: I'm a man. (Ferrovius rises impressively and towers over him. Lentulus becomes white with terror; and a shade of green flickers in his cheek for a moment).

FERROVIUS (with the calm of a steam hammer) I have not always been faithful. The first man who struck me as you have just struck me was a stronger man than you: he hit me harder than I expected. I was tempted and fell; and it was then that I first tasted bitter shame. I never had a happy moment after that until I had knelt and asked his forgiveness by his bedside in the hospital. (Putting his hands on Lentulus's shoulders with paternal weight). But now I have learnt to resist with a strength that is not my own. I am not ashamed now, nor angry.

LENTULUS (uneasily) Er—good evening. (He tries to move away).

FERROVIUS (gripping his shoulders) Oh, do not harden your heart, young man. Come: try for yourself whether our way is not better than yours. I will now strike you on one cheek; and you will turn the other and learn how much better you will feel than if you gave way to the promptings of anger. (He holds him with one hand and clenches the other fist).

LENTULUS. Centurion: I call on you to protect me.

CENTURION. You asked for it, sir. It's no business of ours. You've had two whacks at him. Better pay him a trifle and square it that way.

LENTULUS. Yes, of course. (To Ferrovius) It was only a bit of fun, I assure you: I meant no harm. Here. (He proffers a gold coin).

FERROVIUS (taking it and throwing it to the old beggar, who snatches it up eagerly, and hobbles off to spend it) Give all thou hast to the poor. Come, friend: courage! I may hurt your body for a moment; but your soul will rejoice in the victory of the spirit over the flesh. (He prepares to strike).

ANDROCLES. Easy, Ferrovius, easy: you broke the last man's jaw.

Lentulus, with a moan of terror, attempts to fly; but Ferrovius holds him ruthlessly.

FERROVIUS. Yes; but I saved his soul. What matters a broken jaw?

LENTULUS. Don't touch me, do you hear? The law—

FERROVIUS. The law will throw me to the lions tomorrow: what worse could it do were I to slay you? Pray for strength; and it shall be given to you.

LENTULUS. Let me go. Your religion forbids you to strike me.

FERROVIUS. On the contrary, it commands me to strike you. How can you turn the other cheek, if you are not first struck on the one cheek?

LENTULUS (almost in tears) But I'm convinced already that what you said is quite right. I apologize for striking you.

FERROVIUS (greatly pleased) My son: have I softened your heart? Has the good seed fallen in a fruitful place? Are your feet turning towards a better path?

LENTULUS (abjectly) Yes, yes. There's a great deal in what you say.

FERROVIUS (radiant) Join us. Come to the lions. Come to suffering and death.

LENTULUS (falling on his knees and bursting into tears) Oh, help me. Mother! mother!

FERROVIUS. These tears will water your soul and make it bring forth good fruit, my son. God has greatly blessed my efforts at conversion. Shall I tell you a miracle—yes, a miracle—wrought by me in Cappadocia? A young man—just such a one as you, with golden hair like yours—scoffed at and struck me as you scoffed at and struck me. I sat up all night with that youth wrestling for his soul; and in the morning not only was he a Christian, but his hair was as white as snow. (Lentulus falls in a dead faint). There, there: take him away. The spirit has overwrought him, poor lad. Carry him gently to his house; and leave the rest to heaven.

CENTURION. Take him home. (The servants, intimidated, hastily carry him out. Metellus is about to follow when Ferrovius lays his hand on his shoulder).

FERROVIUS. You are his friend, young man. You will see that he is taken safely home.

METELLUS (with awestruck civility) Certainly, sir. I shall do whatever you think best. Most happy to have made your acquaintance, I'm sure. You may depend on me. Good evening, sir.

FERROVIUS (with unction) The blessing of heaven upon you and him.

Metellus follows Lentulus. The Centurion returns to his seat to resume his interrupted nap. The deepest awe has settled on the spectators. Ferrovius, with a long sigh of happiness, goes to Lavinia, and offers her his hand.

LAVINIA (taking it) So that is how you convert people, Ferrovius.

FERROVIUS. Yes: there has been a blessing on my work in spite of my unworthiness and my backslidings—all through my wicked, devilish temper. This man—

ANDROCLES (hastily) Don't slap me on the back, brother. She knows you mean me.

FERROVIUS. How I wish I were weak like our brother here! for then I should perhaps be meek and gentle like him. And yet there seems to be a special providence that makes my trials less than his. I hear tales of the crowd scoffing and casting stones and reviling the brethren; but when I come, all this stops: my influence calms the passions of the mob: they listen to me in silence; and infidels are often converted by a straight heart-to-heart talk with me. Every day I feel happier, more confident. Every day lightens the load of the great terror.

LAVINIA. The great terror? What is that?

Ferrovius shakes his head and does not answer. He sits down beside her on her left, and buries his face in his hands in gloomy meditation.

ANDROCLES. Well, you see, sister, he's never quite sure of himself. Suppose at the last moment in the arena, with the gladiators there to fight him, one of them was to say anything to annoy him, he might forget himself and lay that gladiator out.

LAVINIA. That would be splendid.

FERROVIUS (springing up in horror) What!

ANDROCLES. Oh, sister!

FERROVIUS. Splendid to betray my master, like Peter! Splendid to act like any common blackguard in the day of my proving! Woman: you are no Christian. (He moves away from her to the middle of the square, as if her neighborhood contaminated him).

LAVINIA (laughing) You know, Ferrovius, I am not always a Christian. I don't think anybody is. There are moments when I forget all about it, and something comes out quite naturally, as it did then.

SPINTHO. What does it matter? If you die in the arena, you'll be a martyr; and all martyrs go to heaven, no matter what they have done. That's so, isn't it, Ferrovius?

FERROVIUS. Yes: that is so, if we are faithful to the end.

LAVINIA. I'm not so sure.

SPINTHO. Don't say that. That's blasphemy. Don't say that, I tell you. We shall be saved, no matter WHAT we do.

LAVINIA. Perhaps you men will all go into heaven bravely and in triumph, with your heads erect and golden trumpets sounding for you. But I am sure I shall only be allowed to squeeze myself in through a little crack in the gate after a great deal of begging. I am not good always: I have moments only.

SPINTHO. You're talking nonsense, woman. I tell you, martyrdom pays all scores.

ANDROCLES. Well, let us hope so, brother, for your sake. You've had a gay time, haven't you? with your raids on the temples. I can't help thinking that heaven will be very dull for a man of your temperament. (Spintho snarls). Don't be angry: I say it only to console you in case you should die in your bed tonight in the natural way. There's a lot of plague about.

SPINTHO (rising and running about in abject terror) I never thought of that. O Lord, spare me to be martyred. Oh, what a thought to put into the mind of a brother! Oh, let me be martyred today, now. I shall die in the night and go to hell. You're a sorcerer: you've put death into my mind. Oh, curse you, curse you! (He tries to seize Androcles by the throat).

FERROVIUS (holding him in a grip of iron) What's this, brother? Anger! Violence! Raising your hand to a brother Christian!

SPINTHO. It's easy for you. You're strong. Your nerves are all right. But I'm full of disease. (Ferrovius takes his hand from him with instinctive disgust). I've drunk all my nerves away. I shall have the horrors all night.

ANDROCLES (sympathetic) Oh, don't take on so, brother. We're all sinners.

SPINTHO (snivelling, trying to feel consoled). Yes: I daresay if the truth were known, you're all as bad as I am.

LAVINIA (contemptuously) Does THAT comfort you?

FERROVIUS (sternly) Pray, man, pray.

SPINTHO. What's the good of praying? If we're martyred we shall go to heaven, shan't we, whether we pray or not?

FERROVIUS. What's that? Not pray! (Seizing him again) Pray this instant, you dog, you rotten hound, you slimy snake, you beastly goat, or—

SPINTHO. Yes: beat me: kick me. I forgive you: mind that.

FERROVIUS (spurning him with loathing) Yah! (Spintho reels away and falls in front of Ferrovius).

ANDROCLES (reaching out and catching the skirt of Ferrovius's tunic) Dear brother: if you wouldn't mind—just for my sake—

FERROVIUS. Well?

ANDROCLES. Don't call him by the names of the animals. We've no right to. I've had such friends in dogs. A pet snake is the best of company. I was nursed on goat's milk. Is it fair to them to call the like of him a dog or a snake or a goat?

FERROVIUS. I only meant that they have no souls.

ANDROCLES (anxiously protesting) Oh, believe me, they have. Just the same as you and me. I really don't think I could consent to go to heaven if I thought there were to be no animals there. Think of what they suffer here.

FERROVIUS. That's true. Yes: that is just. They will have their share in heaven.

SPINTHO (who has picked himself up and is sneaking past Ferrovius on his left, sneers derisively)!!

FERROVIUS (turning on him fiercely) What's that you say?

SPINTHO (cornering). Nothing.

FERROVIUS (clenching his fist) Do animals go to heaven or not?

SPINTHO. I never said they didn't.

FERROVIUS (implacable) Do they or do they not?

SPINTHO. They do: they do. (Scrambling out of Ferrovius's reach). Oh, curse you for frightening me!

A bugle call is heard.

CENTURION (waking up) Tention! Form as before. Now then, prisoners, up with you and trot along spry. (The soldiers fall in. The Christians rise).

A man with an ox goad comes running through the central arch.

THE OX DRIVER. Here, you soldiers! clear out of the way for the Emperor.

THE CENTURION. Emperor! Where's the Emperor? You ain't the Emperor, are you?

THE OX DRIVER. It's the menagerie service. My team of oxen is drawing the new lion to the Coliseum. You clear the road.

CENTURION. What! Go in after you in your dust, with half the town at the heels of you and your lion! Not likely. We go first.

THE OX DRIVER. The menagerie service is the Emperor's personal retinue. You clear out, I tell you.

CENTURION. You tell me, do you? Well, I'll tell you something. If the lion is menagerie service, the lion's dinner is menagerie service too. This (pointing to the Christians) is the lion's dinner. So back with you to your bullocks double quick; and learn your place. March. (The soldiers start). Now then, you Christians, step out there.

LAVINIA (marching) Come along, the rest of the dinner. I shall be the olives and anchovies.

ANOTHER CHRISTIAN (laughing) I shall be the soup.

ANOTHER. I shall be the fish.

ANOTHER. Ferrovius shall be the roast boar.

FERROVIUS (heavily) I see the joke. Yes, yes: I shall be the roast boar. Ha! ha! (He laughs conscientiously and marches out with them).

ANDROCLES. I shall be the mince pie. (Each announcement is received with a louder laugh by all the rest as the joke catches on).

CENTURION (scandalised) Silence! Have some sense of your situation. Is this the way for martyrs to behave? (To Spintho, who is quaking and loitering) I know what YOU'LL be at that dinner. You'll be the emetic. (He shoves him rudely along).

SPINTHO. It's too dreadful: I'm not fit to die.

CENTURION. Fitter than you are to live, you swine.

They pass from the square westward. The oxen, drawing a waggon with a great wooden cage and the lion in it, arrive through the central arch.

ACT II

Behind the Emperor's box at the Coliseum, where the performers assemble before entering the arena. In the middle a wide passage leading to the arena descends from the floor level under the imperial box. On both sides of this passage steps ascend to a landing at the back entrance to the box. The landing forms a bridge across the passage. At the entrance to the passage are two bronze mirrors, one on each side.

On the west side of this passage, on the right hand of any one coming from the box and standing on the bridge, the martyrs are sitting on the steps. Lavinia is seated half-way up, thoughtful, trying to look death in the face. On her left Androcles consoles himself by nursing a cat. Ferrovius stands behind them, his eyes blazing, his figure stiff with intense resolution. At the foot of the steps crouches Spintho, with his head clutched in his hands, full of horror at the approach of martyrdom.

On the east side of the passage the gladiators are standing and sitting at ease, waiting, like the Christians, for their turn in the arena. One (Retiarius) is a nearly naked man with a net and a trident. Another (Secutor) is in armor with a sword. He carries a helmet with a barred visor. The editor of the gladiators sits on a chair a little apart from them.

The Call Boy enters from the passage.

THE CALL Boy. Number six. Retiarius versus Secutor.

The gladiator with the net picks it up. The gladiator with the helmet puts it on; and the two go into the arena, the net thrower taking out a little brush and arranging his hair as he goes, the other tightening his straps and shaking his shoulders loose. Both look at themselves in the mirrors before they enter the passage.

LAVINIA. Will they really kill one another?

SPINTHO. Yes, if the people turn down their thumbs.

THE EDITOR. You know nothing about it. The people indeed! Do you suppose we would kill a man worth perhaps fifty talents to please the riffraff? I should like to catch any of my men at it.

SPINTHO. I thought—

THE EDITOR (contemptuously) You thought! Who cares what you think? YOU'LL be killed all right enough.

SPINTHO (groans and again hides his face)!!! Then is nobody ever killed except us poor—

LAVINIA. Christians?

THE EDITOR. If the vestal virgins turn down their thumbs, that's another matter. They're ladies of rank.

LAVINIA. Does the Emperor ever interfere?

THE EDITOR. Oh, yes: he turns his thumbs up fast enough if the vestal virgins want to have one of his pet fighting men killed.

ANDROCLES. But don't they ever just only pretend to kill one another? Why shouldn't you pretend to die, and get dragged out as if you were dead; and then get up and go home, like an actor?

THE EDITOR. See here: you want to know too much. There will be no pretending about the new lion: let that be enough for you. He's hungry.

SPINTHO (groaning with horror) Oh, Lord! Can't you stop talking about it? Isn't it bad enough for us without that?

ANDROCLES. I'm glad he's hungry. Not that I want him to suffer, poor chap! but then he'll enjoy eating me so much more. There's a cheerful side to everything.

THE EDITOR (rising and striding over to Androcles) Here: don't you be obstinate. Come with me and drop the pinch of incense on the altar. That's all you need do to be let off.

ANDROCLES. No: thank you very much indeed; but I really mustn't.

THE EDITOR. What! Not to save your life?

ANDROCLES. I'd rather not. I couldn't sacrifice to Diana: she's a huntress, you know, and kills things.

THE EDITOR. That don't matter. You can choose your own altar. Sacrifice to Jupiter: he likes animals: he turns himself into an animal when he goes off duty.

ANDROCLES. No: it's very kind of you; but I feel I can't save myself that way.

THE EDITOR. But I don't ask you to do it to save yourself: I ask you to do it to oblige me personally.

ANDROCLES (scrambling up in the greatest agitation) Oh, please don't say that. That is dreadful. You mean so kindly by me that it seems quite horrible to disoblige you. If you could arrange for me to sacrifice when there's nobody looking, I shouldn't mind. But I must go into the arena with the rest. My honor, you know.

THE EDITOR. Honor! The honor of a tailor?

ANDROCLES (apologetically) Well, perhaps honor is too strong an expression. Still, you know, I couldn't allow the tailors to get a bad name through me.

THE EDITOR. How much will you remember of all that when you smell the beast's breath and see his jaws opening to tear out your throat?

SPINTHO (rising with a yell of terror) I can't bear it. Where's the altar? I'll sacrifice.

FERROVIUS. Dog of an apostate. Iscariot!

SPINTHO. I'll repent afterwards. I fully mean to die in the arena I'll die a martyr and go to heaven; but not this time, not now, not until my nerves are better. Besides, I'm too young: I want to have just one more good time. (The gladiators laugh at him). Oh, will no one tell me where the altar is? (He dashes into the passage and vanishes).

ANDROCLES (to the Editor, pointing after Spintho) Brother: I can't do that, not even to oblige you. Don't ask me.

THE EDITOR. Well, if you're determined to die, I can't help you. But I wouldn't be put off by a swine like that.

FERROVIUS. Peace, peace: tempt him not. Get thee behind him, Satan.

THE EDITOR (flushing with rage) For two pins I'd take a turn in the arena myself to-day, and pay you out for daring to talk to me like that.

Ferrovius springs forward.

LAVINIA (rising quickly and interposing) Brother, brother: you forget.

FERROVIUS (curbing himself by a mighty effort) Oh, my temper, my wicked temper! (To the Editor, as Lavinia sits down again, reassured). Forgive me, brother. My heart was full of wrath: I should have been thinking of your dear precious soul.

THE EDITOR. Yah! (He turns his back on Ferrovius contemptuously, and goes back to his seat).

FERROVIUS (continuing) And I forgot it all: I thought of nothing but offering to fight you with one hand tied behind me.

THE EDITOR (turning pugnaciously) What!

FERROVIUS (on the border line between zeal and ferocity) Oh, don't give way to pride and wrath, brother. I could do it so easily. I could—

They are separated by the Menagerie Keeper, who rushes in from the passage, furious.

THE KEEPER. Here's a nice business! Who let that Christian out of here down to the dens when we were changing the lion into the cage next the arena?

THE EDITOR. Nobody let him. He let himself.

THE KEEPER. Well, the lion's ate him.

Consternation. The Christians rise, greatly agitated. The gladiators sit callously, but are highly amused. All speak or cry out or laugh at once. Tumult.

LAVINIA. Oh, poor wretch! FERROVIUS. The apostate has perished. Praise be to God's justice! ANDROCLES. The poor beast was starving. It couldn't help itself. THE CHRISTIANS. What! Ate him! How frightful! How terrible! Without a moment to repent! God be merciful to him, a sinner! Oh, I can't bear to think of it! In the midst of his sin! Horrible, horrible! THE EDITOR. Serve the rotter right! THE GLADIATORS. Just walked into it, he did.

He's martyred all right enough. Good old lion! Old Jock doesn't like that: look at his face. Devil a better! The Emperor will laugh when he hears of it. I can't help smiling. Ha ha ha!!!!!

THE KEEPER. Now his appetite's taken off, he won't as much as look at another Christian for a week.

ANDROCLES. Couldn't you have saved him brother?

THE KEEPER. Saved him! Saved him from a lion that I'd just got mad with hunger! a wild one that came out of the forest not four weeks ago! He bolted him before you could say Balbus.

LAVINIA (sitting down again) Poor Spintho! And it won't even count as martyrdom!

THE KEEPER. Serve him right! What call had he to walk down the throat of one of my lions before he was asked?

ANDROCLES. Perhaps the lion won't eat me now.

THE KEEPER. Yes: that's just like a Christian: think only of yourself! What am I to do? What am I to say to the Emperor when he sees one of my lions coming into the arena half asleep?

THE EDITOR. Say nothing. Give your old lion some bitters and a morsel of fried fish to wake up his appetite. (Laughter).

THE KEEPER. Yes: it's easy for you to talk; but—

THE EDITOR (scrambling to his feet) Sh! Attention there! The Emperor. (The Keeper bolts precipitately into the passage. The gladiators rise smartly and form into line).

The Emperor enters on the Christians' side, conversing with Metellus, and followed by his suite.

THE GLADIATORS. Hail, Caesar! those about to die salute thee.

CAESAR. Good morrow, friends.

Metellus shakes hands with the Editor, who accepts his condescension with bluff respect.

LAVINIA. Blessing, Caesar, and forgiveness!

CAESAR (turning in some surprise at the salutation) There is no forgiveness for Christianity.

LAVINIA. I did not mean that, Caesar. I mean that WE forgive YOU.

METELLUS. An inconceivable liberty! Do you not know, woman, that the Emperor can do no wrong and therefore cannot be forgiven?

LAVINIA. I expect the Emperor knows better. Anyhow, we forgive him.

THE CHRISTIANS. Amen!

CAESAR. Metellus: you see now the disadvantage of too much severity. These people have no hope; therefore they have nothing to restrain them from saying what they like to me. They are almost as impertinent as the gladiators. Which is the Greek sorcerer?

ANDROCLES (humbly touching his forelock) Me, your Worship.

CAESAR. My Worship! Good! A new title. Well, what miracles can you perform?

ANDROCLES. I can cure warts by rubbing them with my tailor's chalk; and I can live with my wife without beating her.

CAESAR. Is that all?

ANDROCLES. You don't know her, Caesar, or you wouldn't say that.

CAESAR. Ah, well, my friend, we shall no doubt contrive a happy release for you. Which is Ferrovius?

FERROVIUS. I am he.

CAESAR. They tell me you can fight.

FERROVIUS. It is easy to fight. I can die, Caesar.

CAESAR. That is still easier, is it not?

FERROVIUS. Not to me, Caesar. Death comes hard to my flesh; and fighting comes very easily to my spirit (beating his breast and lamenting) O sinner that I am! (He throws himself down on the steps, deeply discouraged).

CAESAR. Metellus: I should like to have this man in the Pretorian Guard.

METELLUS. I should not, Caesar. He looks a spoilsport. There are men in whose presence it is impossible to have any fun: men who are a sort of walking conscience. He would make us all uncomfortable.

CAESAR. For that reason, perhaps, it might be well to have him. An Emperor can hardly have too many consciences. (To Ferrovius) Listen, Ferrovius. (Ferrovius shakes his head and will not look up). You and your friends shall not be outnumbered today in the arena. You shall have arms; and there will be no more than one gladiator to each Christian. If you come out of the arena alive, I will consider favorably any request of yours, and give you a place in the Pretorian Guard. Even if the request be that no questions be asked about your faith I shall perhaps not refuse it.

FERROVIUS. I will not fight. I will die. Better stand with the archangels than with the Pretorian Guard.

CAESAR. I cannot believe that the archangels—whoever they may be—would not prefer to be recruited from the Pretorian Guard. However, as you please. Come: let us see the show.

As the Court ascends the steps, Secutor and the Retiarius return from the arena through the passage; Secutor covered with dust and very angry: Retiarius grinning.

SECUTOR. Ha, the Emperor. Now we shall see. Caesar: I ask you whether it is fair for the Retiarius, instead of making a fair throw of his net at me, to swish it along the ground and throw the dust in my eyes, and then catch me when I'm blinded. If the vestals had not turned up their thumbs I should have been a dead man.

CAESAR (halting on the stair) There is nothing in the rules against it.

SECUTOR (indignantly) Caesar: is it a dirty trick or is it not?

CAESAR. It is a dusty one, my friend. (Obsequious laughter). Be on your guard next time.

SECUTOR. Let HIM be on his guard. Next time I'll throw my sword at his heels and strangle him with his own net before he can hop off. (To Retiarius) You see if I don't. (He goes out past the gladiators, sulky and furious).

CAESAR (to the chuckling Retiarius). These tricks are not wise, my friend. The audience likes to see a dead man in all his beauty and splendor. If you smudge his face and spoil his armor they will show their displeasure by not letting you kill him. And when your turn comes, they will remember it against you and turn their thumbs down.

THE RETIARIUS. Perhaps that is why I did it, Caesar. He bet me ten sesterces that he would vanquish me. If I had had to kill him I should not have had the money.

CAESAR (indulgent, laughing) You rogues: there is no end to your tricks. I'll dismiss you all and have elephants to fight. They fight fairly. (He goes up to his box, and knocks at it. It is opened from within by the Captain, who stands as on parade to let him pass). The Call Boy comes from the passage, followed by three attendants carrying respectively a bundle of swords, some helmets, and some breastplates and pieces of armor which they throw down in a heap.

THE CALL BOY. By your leave, Caesar. Number eleven! Gladiators and Christians!

Ferrovius springs up, ready for martyrdom. The other Christians take the summons as best they can, some joyful and brave, some patient and dignified, some tearful and helpless, some embracing one another with emotion. The Call Boy goes back into the passage.

CAESAR (turning at the door of the box) The hour has come, Ferrovius. I shall go into my box and see you killed, since you scorn the Pretorian Guard. (He goes into the box. The Captain shuts the door, remaining inside with the Emperor. Metellus and the rest of the suite disperse to their seats. The Christians, led by Ferrovius, move towards the passage).

LAVINIA (to Ferrovius) Farewell.

THE EDITOR. Steady there. You Christians have got to fight. Here! arm yourselves.

FERROVIUS (picking up a sword) I'll die sword in hand to show people that I could fight if it were my Master's will, and that I could kill the man who kills me if I chose.

THE EDITOR. Put on that armor.

FERROVIUS. No armor.

THE EDITOR (bullying him) Do what you're told. Put on that armor.

FERROVIUS (gripping the sword and looking dangerous) I said, No armor.

THE EDITOR. And what am I to say when I am accused of sending a naked man in to fight my men in armor?

FERROVIUS. Say your prayers, brother; and have no fear of the princes of this world.

THE EDITOR. Tsha! You obstinate fool! (He bites his lips irresolutely, not knowing exactly what to do).

ANDROCLES (to Ferrovius) Farewell, brother, till we meet in the sweet by-and-by.

THE EDITOR (to Androcles) You are going too. Take a sword there; and put on any armor you can find to fit you.

ANDROCLES. No, really: I can't fight: I never could. I can't bring myself to dislike anyone enough. I'm to be thrown to the lions with the lady.

THE EDITOR. Then get out of the way and hold your noise. (Androcles steps aside with cheerful docility). Now then! Are you all ready there? A trumpet is heard from the arena.

FERROVIUS (starting convulsively) Heaven give me strength!

THE EDITOR. Aha! That frightens you, does it?

FERROVIUS. Man: there is no terror like the terror of that sound to me. When I hear a trumpet or a drum or the clash of steel or the hum of the catapult as the great stone flies, fire runs through my veins: I feel my blood surge up hot behind my eyes: I must charge: I must strike: I must conquer: Caesar himself will not be safe in his imperial seat if once that spirit gets loose in me. Oh, brothers, pray! exhort me! remind me that if I raise my sword my honor falls and my Master is crucified afresh.

ANDROCLES. Just keep thinking how cruelly you might hurt the poor gladiators.

FERROVIUS. It does not hurt a man to kill him.

LAVINIA. Nothing but faith can save you.

FERROVIUS. Faith! Which faith? There are two faiths. There is our faith. And there is the warrior's faith, the faith in fighting, the faith that sees God in the sword. How if that faith should overwhelm me?

LAVINIA. You will find your real faith in the hour of trial.

FERROVIUS. That is what I fear. I know that I am a fighter. How can I feel sure that I am a Christian?

ANDROCLES. Throw away the sword, brother.

FERROVIUS. I cannot. It cleaves to my hand. I could as easily throw a woman I loved from my arms. (Starting) Who spoke that blasphemy? Not I.

LAVINIA. I can't help you, friend. I can't tell you not to save your own life. Something wilful in me wants to see you fight your way into heaven.

FERROVIUS. Ha!

ANDROCLES. But if you are going to give up our faith, brother, why not do it without hurting anybody? Don't fight them. Burn the incense.

FERROVIUS. Burn the incense! Never.

LAVINIA. That is only pride, Ferrovius.

FERROVIUS. ONLY pride! What is nobler than pride? (Conscience stricken) Oh, I'm steeped in sin. I'm proud of my pride.

LAVINIA. They say we Christians are the proudest devils on earth—that only the weak are meek. Oh, I am worse than you. I ought to send you to death; and I am tempting you.

ANDROCLES. Brother, brother: let THEM rage and kill: let US be brave and suffer. You must go as a lamb to the slaughter.

FERROVIUS. Aye, aye: that is right. Not as a lamb is slain by the butcher; but as a butcher might let himself be slain by a (looking at the Editor) by a silly ram whose head he could fetch off in one twist.

Before the Editor can retort, the Call Boy rushes up through the passage; and the Captain comes from the Emperor's box and descends the steps.

THE CALL BOY. In with you: into the arena. The stage is waiting.

THE CAPTAIN. The Emperor is waiting. (To the Editor) What are you dreaming of, man? Send your men in at once.

THE EDITOR. Yes, Sir: it's these Christians hanging back.

FERROVIUS (in a voice of thunder) Liar!

THE EDITOR (not heeding him) March. (The gladiators told off to fight with the Christians march down the passage) Follow up there, you.

THE CHRISTIAN MEN AND WOMEN (as they part) Be steadfast, brother. Farewell. Hold up the faith, brother. Farewell. Go to glory, dearest. Farewell. Remember: we are praying for you. Farewell. Be strong, brother. Farewell. Don't forget that the divine love and our love surround you. Farewell. Nothing can hurt you: remember that, brother. Farewell. Eternal glory, dearest. Farewell.

THE EDITOR (out of patience) Shove them in, there.

The remaining gladiators and the Call Boy make a movement towards them.

FERROVIUS (interposing) Touch them, dogs; and we die here, and cheat the heathen of their spectacle. (To his fellow Christians) Brothers: the great moment has come. That passage is your hill to Calvary. Mount it bravely, but meekly; and remember! not a word of reproach, not a blow nor a struggle. Go. (They go out through the passage. He turns to Lavinia) Farewell.

LAVINIA. You forget: I must follow before you are cold.

FERROVIUS. It is true. Do not envy me because I pass before you to glory. (He goes through the passage).

THE EDITOR (to the Call Boy) Sickening work, this. Why can't they all be thrown to the lions? It's not a man's job. (He throws himself moodily into his chair).

The remaining gladiators go back to their former places indifferently. The Call Boy shrugs his shoulders and squats down at the entrance to the passage, near the Editor.

Lavinia and the Christian women sit down again, wrung with grief, some weeping silently, some praying, some calm and steadfast. Androcles sits down at Lavinia's feet. The Captain stands on the stairs, watching her curiously.

ANDROCLES. I'm glad I haven't to fight. That would really be an awful martyrdom. I AM lucky.

LAVINIA (looking at him with a pang of remorse). Androcles: burn the incense: you'll be forgiven. Let my death atone for both. I feel as if I were killing you.

ANDROCLES. Don't think of me, sister. Think of yourself. That will keep your heart up.

The Captain laughs sardonically.

LAVINIA (startled: she had forgotten his presence) Are you there, handsome Captain? Have you come to see me die?

THE CAPTAIN (coming to her side) I am on duty with the Emperor, Lavinia.

LAVINIA. Is it part of your duty to laugh at us?

THE CAPTAIN. No: that is part of my private pleasure. Your friend here is a humorist. I laughed at his telling you to think of yourself to keep up your heart. I say, think of yourself and burn the incense.

LAVINIA. He is not a humorist: he was right. You ought to know that, Captain: you have been face to face with death.

THE CAPTAIN. Not with certain death, Lavinia. Only death in battle, which spares more men than death in bed. What you are facing is certain death. You have nothing left now but your faith in this craze of yours: this Christianity. Are your Christian fairy stories any truer than our stories about Jupiter and Diana, in which, I may tell you, I believe no more than the Emperor does, or any educated man in Rome?

LAVINIA. Captain: all that seems nothing to me now. I'll not say that death is a terrible thing; but I will say that it is so real a thing that when it comes close, all the imaginary things—all the stories, as you call them—fade into mere dreams beside that inexorable reality. I know now that I am not dying for stories or dreams. Did you hear of the dreadful thing that happened here while we were waiting?

THE CAPTAIN. I heard that one of your fellows bolted, and ran right into the jaws of the lion. I laughed. I still laugh.

LAVINIA. Then you don't understand what that meant?

THE CAPTAIN. It meant that the lion had a cur for his breakfast.

LAVINIA. It meant more than that, Captain. It meant that a man cannot die for a story and a dream. None of us believed the stories and the dreams more devoutly than poor Spintho; but he could not face the great reality. What he would have called my faith has been oozing away minute by minute whilst I've been sitting here, with death coming nearer and nearer, with reality becoming realler and realler, with stories and dreams fading away into nothing.

THE CAPTAIN. Are you then going to die for nothing?

LAVINIA. Yes: that is the wonderful thing. It is since all the stories and dreams have gone that I have now no doubt at all that I must die for something greater than dreams or stories.

THE CAPTAIN. But for what?

LAVINIA. I don't know. If it were for anything small enough to know, it would be too small to die for. I think I'm going to die for God. Nothing else is real enough to die for.

THE CAPTAIN. What is God?

LAVINIA. When we know that, Captain, we shall be gods ourselves.

THE CAPTAIN. Lavinia; come down to earth. Burn the incense and marry me.

LAVINIA. Handsome Captain: would you marry me if I hauled down the flag in the day of battle and burnt the incense? Sons take after their mothers, you know. Do you want your son to be a coward?

THE CAPTAIN (strongly moved). By great Diana, I think I would strangle you if you gave in now.

LAVINIA (putting her hand on the head of Androcles) The hand of God is on us three, Captain.

THE CAPTAIN. What nonsense it all is! And what a monstrous thing that you should die for such nonsense, and that I should look on helplessly when my whole soul cries out against it! Die then if you must; but at least I can cut the Emperor's throat and then my own when I see your blood.

The Emperor throws open the door of his box angrily, and appears in wrath on the threshold. The Editor, the Call Boy, and the gladiators spring to their feet.

THE EMPEROR. The Christians will not fight; and your curs cannot get their blood up to attack them. It's all that fellow with the blazing eyes. Send for the whip. (The Call Boy rushes out on the east side for the whip). If that will not move them, bring the hot irons. The man is like a mountain. (He returns angrily into the box and slams the door).

The Call Boy returns with a man in a hideous Etruscan mask, carrying a whip. They both rush down the passage into the arena.

LAVINIA (rising) Oh, that is unworthy. Can they not kill him without dishonoring him?

ANDROCLES (scrambling to his feet and running into the middle of the space between the staircases) It's dreadful. Now I want to fight. I can't bear the sight of a whip. The only time I ever hit a man was when he lashed an old horse with a whip. It was terrible: I danced on his face when he was on the ground. He mustn't strike Ferrovius: I'll go into the arena and kill him first. (He makes a wild dash into the passage. As he does so a great clamor is heard from the arena, ending in wild applause. The gladiators listen and look inquiringly at one another).

THE EDITOR. What's up now?

LAVINIA (to the Captain) What has happened, do you think?

THE CAPTAIN. What CAN happen? They are killing them, I suppose.

ANDROCLES (running in through the passage, screaming with horror and hiding his eyes)!!!

LAVINIA. Androcles, Androcles: what's the matter?

ANDROCLES. Oh, don't ask me, don't ask me. Something too dreadful. Oh! (He crouches by her and hides his face in her robe, sobbing).

THE CALL Boy (rushing through from the passage as before) Ropes and hooks there! Ropes and hooks.

THE EDITOR. Well, need you excite yourself about it? (Another burst of applause).

Two slaves in Etruscan masks, with ropes and drag hooks, hurry in.

ONE OF THE SLAVES. How many dead?

THE CALL Boy. Six. (The slave blows a whistle twice; and four more masked slaves rush through into the arena with the same apparatus) And the basket. Bring the baskets. (The slave whistles three times, and runs through the passage with his companion).

THE CAPTAIN. Who are the baskets for?

THE CALL Boy. For the whip. He's in pieces. They're all in pieces, more or less. (Lavinia hides her face).

(Two more masked slaves come in with a basket and follow the others into the arena, as the Call Boy turns to the gladiators and exclaims, exhausted) Boys, he's killed the lot.

THE EMPEROR (again bursting from his box, this time in an ecstasy of delight) Where is he? Magnificent! He shall have a laurel crown.

Ferrovius, madly waving his bloodstained sword, rushes through the passage in despair, followed by his co-religionists, and by the menagerie keeper, who goes to the gladiators. The gladiators draw their swords nervously.

FERROVIUs. Lost! lost forever! I have betrayed my Master. Cut off this right hand: it has offended. Ye have swords, my brethren: strike.

LAVINIA. No, no. What have you done, Ferrovius?

FERROVIUS. I know not; but there was blood behind my eyes; and there's blood on my sword. What does that mean?

THE EMPEROR (enthusiastically, on the landing outside his box) What does it mean? It means that you are the greatest man in Rome. It means that you shall have a laurel crown of gold. Superb fighter, I could almost yield you my throne. It is a record for my reign: I shall live in history. Once, in Domitian's time, a Gaul slew three men in the arena and gained his freedom. But when before has one naked man slain six armed men of the bravest and best? The persecution shall cease: if Christians can fight like this, I shall have none but Christians to fight for me. (To the Gladiators) You are ordered to become Christians, you there: do you hear?

RETIARIUS. It is all one to us, Caesar. Had I been there with my net, the story would have been different.

THE CAPTAIN (suddenly seizing Lavinia by the wrist and dragging her up the steps to the Emperor) Caesar this woman is the sister of Ferrovius. If she is thrown to the lions he will fret. He will lose weight; get out of condition.

THE EMPEROR. The lions? Nonsense! (To Lavinia) Madam: I am proud to have the honor of making your acquaintance. Your brother is the glory of Rome.

LAVINIA. But my friends here. Must they die?

THE EMPEROR. Die! Certainly not. There has never been the slightest idea of harming them. Ladies and gentlemen: you are all free. Pray go into the front of the house and enjoy the spectacle to which your brother has so splendidly contributed. Captain: oblige me by conducting them to the seats reserved for my personal friends.

THE MENAGERIE KEEPER. Caesar: I must have one Christian for the lion. The people have been promised it; and they will tear the decorations to bits if they are disappointed.

THE EMPEROR. True, true: we must have somebody for the new lion.

FERROVIUS. Throw me to him. Let the apostate perish.

THE EMPEROR. No, no: you would tear him in pieces, my friend; and we cannot afford to throw away lions as if they were mere slaves. But we must have somebody. This is really extremely awkward.

THE MENAGERIE KEEPER. Why not that little Greek chap? He's not a Christian: he's a sorcerer.

THE EMPEROR. The very thing: he will do very well.

THE CALL Boy (issuing from the passage) Number twelve. The Christian for the new lion.

ANDROCLES (rising, and pulling himself sadly together) Well, it was to be, after all.

LAVINIA. I'll go in his place, Caesar. Ask the Captain whether they do not like best to see a woman torn to pieces. He told me so yesterday.

THE EMPEROR. There is something in that: there is certainly something in that—if only I could feel sure that your brother would not fret.

ANDROCLES. No: I should never have another happy hour. No: on the faith of a Christian and the honor of a tailor, I accept the lot that has fallen on me. If my wife turns up, give her my love and say that my wish was that she should be happy with her next, poor fellow! Caesar: go to your box and see how a tailor can die. Make way for number twelve there. (He marches out along the passage).

The vast audience in the amphitheatre now sees the Emperor re-enter his box and take his place as Androcles, desperately frightened, but still marching with piteous devotion, emerges from the other end of the passage, and finds himself at the focus of thousands of eager eyes. The lion's cage, with a heavy portcullis grating, is on his left. The Emperor gives a signal. A gong sounds. Androcles shivers at the sound; then falls on his knees and prays.

The grating rises with a clash. The lion bounds into the arena. He rushes round frisking in his freedom. He sees Androcles. He stops; rises stiffly by straightening his legs; stretches out his nose forward and his tail in a horizontal line behind, like a pointer, and utters an appalling roar. Androcles crouches and hides his face in his hands. The lion gathers himself for a spring, swishing his tail to and fro through the dust in an ecstasy of anticipation. Androcles throws up his hands in supplication to heaven. The lion checks at the sight of Androcles's face. He then steals towards him; smells him; arches his back; purrs like a motor car; finally rubs himself against Androcles, knocking him over. Androcles, supporting himself on his wrist, looks affrightedly at the lion. The lion limps on three paws, holding up the other as if it was wounded. A flash of recognition lights up the face of Androcles. He flaps his hand as if it had a thorn in it, and pretends to pull the thorn out and to hurt himself. The lion nods repeatedly. Androcles holds out his hands to the lion, who gives him both paws, which he shakes with enthusiasm. They embrace rapturously, finally waltz round the arena amid a sudden burst of deafening applause, and out through the passage, the Emperor watching them in breathless astonishment until they disappear, when he rushes from his box and descends the steps in frantic excitement.

THE EMPEROR. My friends, an incredible! an amazing thing! has happened. I can no longer doubt the truth of Christianity. (The Christians press to him joyfully) This Christian sorcerer—(with a yell, he breaks off as he sees Androcles and the lion emerge from the passage, waltzing. He bolts wildly up the steps into his box, and slams the door. All, Christians and gladiators' alike, fly for their lives, the gladiators bolting into the arena, the others in all directions. The place is emptied with magical suddenness).

ANDROCLES (naively) Now I wonder why they all run away from us like that. (The lion combining a series of yawns, purrs, and roars, achieves something very like a laugh).

THE EMPEROR (standing on a chair inside his box and looking over the wall) Sorcerer: I command you to put that lion to death instantly. It is guilty of high treason. Your conduct is most disgra— (the lion charges at him up the stairs) help! (He disappears. The lion rears against the box; looks over the partition at him, and roars. The Emperor darts out through the door and down to Androcles, pursued by the lion.)

ANDROCLES. Don't run away, sir: he can't help springing if you run. (He seizes the Emperor and gets between him and the lion, who stops at once). Don't be afraid of him.

THE EMPEROR. I am NOT afraid of him. (The lion crouches, growling. The Emperor clutches Androcles) Keep between us.

ANDROCLES. Never be afraid of animals, your Worship: that's the great secret. He'll be as gentle as a lamb when he knows that you are his friend. Stand quite still; and smile; and let him smell you all over just to reassure him; for, you see, he's afraid of you; and he must examine you thoroughly before he gives you his confidence. (To the lion) Come now, Tommy; and speak nicely to the Emperor, the great, good Emperor who has power to have all our heads cut off if we don't behave very, VERY respectfully to him.

The lion utters a fearful roar. The Emperor dashes madly up the steps, across the landing, and down again on the other side, with the lion in hot pursuit. Androcles rushes after the lion; overtakes him as he is descending; and throws himself on his back, trying to use his toes as a brake. Before he can stop him the lion gets hold of the trailing end of the Emperor's robe.

ANDROCLES. Oh bad wicked Tommy, to chase the Emperor like that! Let go the Emperor's robe at once, sir: where's your manners? (The lion growls and worries the robe). Don't pull it away from him, your worship. He's only playing. Now I shall be really angry with you, Tommy, if you don't let go. (The lion growls again) I'll tell you what it is, sir: he thinks you and I are not friends.

THE EMPEROR (trying to undo the clasp of his brooch) Friends! You infernal scoundrel (the lion growls) don't let him go. Curse this brooch! I can't get it loose.

ANDROCLES. We mustn't let him lash himself into a rage. You must show him that you are my particular friend—if you will have the condescension. (He seizes the Emperor's hands, and shakes them cordially), Look, Tommy: the nice Emperor is the dearest friend Andy Wandy has in the whole world: he loves him like a brother.

THE EMPEROR. You little brute, you damned filthy little dog of a Greek tailor: I'll have you burnt alive for daring to touch the divine person of the Emperor. (The lion roars).

ANDROCLES. Oh don't talk like that, sir. He understands every word you say: all animals do: they take it from the tone of your voice. (The lion growls and lashes his tail). I think he's going to spring at your worship. If you wouldn't mind saying something affectionate. (The lion roars).

THE EMPEROR (shaking Androcles' hands frantically) My dearest Mr. Androcles, my sweetest friend, my long lost brother, come to my arms. (He embraces Androcles). Oh, what an abominable smell of garlic!

The lion lets go the robe and rolls over on his back, clasping his forepaws over one another coquettishly above his nose.

ANDROCLES. There! You see, your worship, a child might play with him now. See! (He tickles the lion's belly. The lion wriggles ecstatically). Come and pet him.

THE EMPEROR. I must conquer these unkingly terrors. Mind you don't go away from him, though. (He pats the lion's chest).

ANDROCLES. Oh, sir, how few men would have the courage to do that—

THE EMPEROR. Yes: it takes a bit of nerve. Let us invite the Court in and frighten them. Is he safe, do you think?

ANDROCLES. Quite safe now, sir.

THE EMPEROR (majestically) What ho, there! All who are within hearing, return without fear. Caesar has tamed the lion. (All the fugitives steal cautiously in. The menagerie keeper comes from the passage with other keepers armed with iron bars and tridents). Take those things away. I have subdued the beast. (He places his foot on it).

FERROVIUS (timidly approaching the Emperor and looking down with awe on the lion) It is strange that I, who fear no man, should fear a lion.

THE CAPTAIN. Every man fears something, Ferrovius.

THE EMPEROR. How about the Pretorian Guard now?

FERROVIUS. In my youth I worshipped Mars, the God of War. I turned from him to serve the Christian god; but today the Christian god forsook me; and Mars overcame me and took back his own. The Christian god is not yet. He will come when Mars and I are dust; but meanwhile I must serve the gods that are, not the God that will be. Until then I accept service in the Guard, Caesar.

THE EMPEROR. Very wisely said. All really sensible men agree that the prudent course is to be neither bigoted in our attachment to the old nor rash and unpractical in keeping an open mind for the new, but to make the best of both dispensations.

THE CAPTAIN. What do you say, Lavinia? Will you too be prudent?

LAVINIA (on the stair) No: I'll strive for the coming of the God who is not yet.

THE CAPTAIN. May I come and argue with you occasionally?

LAVINIA. Yes, handsome Captain: you may. (He kisses her hands).

THE EMPEROR. And now, my friends, though I do not, as you see, fear this lion, yet the strain of his presence is considerable; for none of us can feel quite sure what he will do next.

THE MENAGERIE KEEPER. Caesar: give us this Greek sorcerer to be a slave in the menagerie. He has a way with the beasts.

ANDROCLES (distressed). Not if they are in cages. They should not be kept in cages. They must all be let out.

THE EMPEROR. I give this sorcerer to be a slave to the first man who lays hands on him. (The menagerie keepers and the gladiators rush for Androcles. The lion starts up and faces them. They surge back). You see how magnanimous we Romans are, Androcles. We suffer you to go in peace.

ANDROCLES. I thank your worship. I thank you all, ladies and gentlemen. Come, Tommy. Whilst we stand together, no cage for you: no slavery for me. (He goes out with the lion, everybody crowding away to give him as wide a berth as possible).

EXPLANATION

In this play I have represented one of the Roman persecutions of the early Christians, not as the conflict of a false theology with a true, but as what all such persecutions essentially are: an attempt to suppress a propaganda that seemed to threaten the interests involved in the established law and order, organized and maintained in the name of religion and justice by politicians who are pure opportunist Have-and-Holders. People who are shown by their inner light the possibility of a better world based on the demand of the spirit for a nobler and more abundant life, not for themselves at the expense of others, but for everybody, are naturally dreaded and therefore hated by the Have-and-Holders, who keep always in reserve two sure weapons against them. The first is a persecution effected by the provocation, organization, and arming of that herd instinct which makes men abhor all departures from custom, and, by the most cruel punishments and the wildest calumnies, force eccentric people to behave and profess exactly as other people do. The second is by leading the herd to war, which immediately and infallibly makes them forget everything, even their most cherished and hardwon public liberties and private interests, in the irresistible surge of their pugnacity and the tense preoccupation of their terror.

There is no reason to believe that there was anything more in the Roman persecutions than this. The attitude of the Roman Emperor and the officers of his staff towards the opinions at issue were much the same as those of a modern British Home Secretary towards members of the lower middle classes when some pious policeman charges them with Bad Taste, technically called blasphemy: Bad Taste being a violation of Good Taste, which in such matters practically means Hypocrisy. The Home Secretary and the judges who try the case are usually far more sceptical and blasphemous than the poor men whom they persecute; and their professions of horror at the blunt utterance of their own opinions are revolting to those behind the scenes who have any genuine religious sensibility; but the thing is done because the governing classes, provided only the law against blasphemy is not applied to themselves, strongly approve of such persecution because it enables them to represent their own privileges as part of the religion of the country.

Therefore my martyrs are the martyrs of all time, and my persecutors the persecutors of all time. My Emperor, who has no sense of the value of common people's lives, and amuses himself with killing as carelessly as with sparing, is the sort of monster you can make of any silly-clever gentleman by idolizing him. We are still so easily imposed on by such idols that one of the leading pastors of the Free Churches in London denounced my play on the ground that my persecuting Emperor is a very fine fellow, and the persecuted Christians ridiculous. From which I conclude that a popular pulpit may be as perilous to a man's soul as an imperial throne.

All my articulate Christians, the reader will notice, have different enthusiasms, which they accept as the same religion only because it involves them in a common opposition to the official religion and consequently in a common doom. Androcles is a humanitarian naturalist, whose views surprise everybody. Lavinia, a clever and fearless freethinker, shocks the Pauline Ferrovius, who is comparatively stupid and conscience ridden. Spintho, the blackguardly debauchee, is presented as one of the typical Christians of that period on the authority of St. Augustine, who seems to have come to the conclusion at one period of his development that most Christians were what we call wrong uns. No doubt he was to some extent right: I have had occasion often to point out that revolutionary movements attract those who are not good enough for established institutions as well as those who are too good for them.

But the most striking aspect of the play at this moment is the terrible topicality given it by the war. We were at peace when I pointed out, by the mouth of Ferrovius, the path of an honest man who finds out, when the trumpet sounds, that he cannot follow Jesus. Many years earlier, in The Devil's Disciple, I touched the same theme even more definitely, and showed the minister throwing off his black coat for ever when he discovered, amid the thunder of the captains and the shouting, that he was a born fighter. Great numbers of our clergy have found themselves of late in the position of Ferrovius and Anthony Anderson. They have discovered that they hate not only their enemies but everyone who does not share their hatred, and that they want to fight and to force other people to fight. They have turned their churches into recruiting stations and their vestries into munition workshops. But it has never occurred to them to take off their black coats and say quite simply, "I find in the hour of trial that the Sermon on the Mount is tosh, and that I am not a Christian. I apologize for all the unpatriotic nonsense I have been preaching all these years. Have the goodness to give me a revolver and a commission in a regiment which has for its chaplain a priest of the god Mars: my God." Not a bit of it. They have stuck to their livings and served Mars in the name of Christ, to the scandal of all religious mankind. When the Archbishop of York behaved like a gentleman and the Head Master of Eton preached a Christian sermon, and were reviled by the rabble, the Martian parsons encouraged the rabble. For this they made no apologies or excuses, good or bad. They simple indulged their passions, just as they had always indulged their class prejudices and commercial interests, without troubling themselves for a moment as to whether they were Christians or not. They did not protest even when a body calling itself the Anti-German League (not having noticed, apparently, that it had been anticipated by the British Empire, the French Republic, and the Kingdoms of Italy, Japan, and Serbia) actually succeeded in closing a church at Forest Hill in which God was worshipped in the German language. One would have supposed that this grotesque outrage on the commonest decencies of religion would have provoked a remonstrance from even the worldliest bench of bishops. But no: apparently it seemed to the bishops as natural that the House of God should be looted when He allowed German to be spoken in it as that a baker's shop with a German name over the door should be pillaged. Their verdict was, in effect, "Serve God right, for creating the Germans!" The incident would have been impossible in a country where the Church was as powerful as the Church of England, had it had at the same time a spark of catholic as distinguished from tribal religion in it. As it is, the thing occurred; and as far as I have observed, the only people who gasped were the Freethinkers. Thus we see that even among men who make a profession of religion the great majority are as Martian as the majority of their congregations. The average clergyman is an official who makes his living by christening babies, marrying adults, conducting a ritual, and making the best he can (when he has any conscience about it) of a certain routine of school superintendence, district visiting, and organization of almsgiving, which does not necessarily touch Christianity at any point except the point of the tongue. The exceptional or religious clergyman may be an ardent Pauline salvationist, in which case his more cultivated parishioners dislike him, and say that he ought to have joined the Methodists. Or he may be an artist expressing religious emotion without intellectual definition by means of poetry, music, vestments and architecture, also producing religious ecstacy by physical expedients, such as fasts and vigils, in which case he is denounced as a Ritualist. Or he may be either a Unitarian Deist like Voltaire or Tom Paine, or the more modern sort of Anglican Theosophist to whom the Holy Ghost is the Elan Vital of Bergson, and the Father and Son are an expression of the fact that our functions and aspects are manifold, and that we are all sons and all either potential or actual parents, in which case he is strongly suspected by the straiter Salvationists of being little better than an Atheist. All these varieties, you see, excite remark. They may be very popular with their congregations; but they are regarded by the average man as the freaks of the Church. The Church, like the society of which it is an organ, is balanced and steadied by the great central Philistine mass above whom theology looms as a highly spoken of and doubtless most important thing, like Greek Tragedy, or classical music, or the higher mathematics, but who are very glad when church is over and they can go home to lunch or dinner, having in fact, for all practical purposes, no reasoned convictions at all, and being equally ready to persecute a poor Freethinker for saying that St. James was not infallible, and to send one of the Peculiar People to prison for being so very peculiar as to take St. James seriously.

In short, a Christian martyr was thrown to the lions not because he was a Christian, but because he was a crank: that is, an unusual sort of person. And multitudes of people, quite as civilized and amiable as we, crowded to see the lions eat him just as they now crowd the lion-house in the Zoo at feeding-time, not because they really cared two-pence about Diana or Christ, or could have given you any intelligent or correct account of the things Diana and Christ stood against one another for, but simply because they wanted to see a curious and exciting spectacle. You, dear reader, have probably run to see a fire; and if somebody came in now and told you that a lion was chasing a man down the street you would rush to the window. And if anyone were to say that you were as cruel as the people who let the lion loose on the man, you would be justly indignant. Now that we may no longer see a man hanged, we assemble outside the jail to see the black flag run up. That is our duller method of enjoying ourselves in the old Roman spirit. And if the Government decided to throw persons of unpopular or eccentric views to the lions in the Albert Hall or the Earl's Court stadium tomorrow, can you doubt that all the seats would be crammed, mostly by people who could not give you the most superficial account of the views in question. Much less unlikely things have happened. It is true that if such a revival does take place soon, the martyrs will not be members of heretical religious sects: they will be Peculiars, Anti-Vivisectionists, Flat-Earth men, scoffers at the laboratories, or infidels who refuse to kneel down when a procession of doctors goes by. But the lions will hurt them just as much, and the spectators will enjoy themselves just as much, as the Roman lions and spectators used to do.

It was currently reported in the Berlin newspapers that when Androcles was first performed in Berlin, the Crown Prince rose and left the house, unable to endure the (I hope) very clear and fair exposition of autocratic Imperialism given by the Roman captain to his Christian prisoners. No English Imperialist was intelligent and earnest enough to do the same in London. If the report is correct, I confirm the logic of the Crown Prince, and am glad to find myself so well understood. But I can assure him that the Empire which served for my model when I wrote Androcles was, as he is now finding to his cost, much nearer my home than the German one.

PYGMALION

PREFACE TO PYGMALION.

A Professor of Phonetics.

As will be seen later on, Pygmalion needs, not a preface, but a sequel, which I have supplied in its due place. The English have no respect for their language, and will not teach their children to speak it. They spell it so abominably that no man can teach himself what it sounds like. It is impossible for an Englishman to open his mouth without making some other Englishman hate or despise him. German and Spanish are accessible to foreigners: English is not accessible even to Englishmen. The reformer England needs today is an energetic phonetic enthusiast: that is why I have made such a one the hero of a popular play. There have been heroes of that kind crying in the wilderness for many years past. When I became interested in the subject towards the end of the eighteen-seventies, Melville Bell was dead; but Alexander J. Ellis was still a living patriarch, with an impressive head always covered by a velvet skull cap, for which he would apologize to public meetings in a very courtly manner. He and Tito Pagliardini, another phonetic veteran, were men whom it was impossible to dislike. Henry Sweet, then a young man, lacked their sweetness of character: he was about as conciliatory to conventional mortals as Ibsen or Samuel Butler. His great ability as a phonetician (he was, I think, the best of them all at his job) would have entitled him to high official recognition, and perhaps enabled him to popularize his subject, but for his Satanic contempt for all academic dignitaries and persons in general who thought more of Greek than of phonetics. Once, in the days when the Imperial Institute rose in South Kensington, and Joseph Chamberlain was booming the Empire, I induced the editor of a leading monthly review to commission an article from Sweet on the imperial importance of his subject. When it arrived, it contained nothing but a savagely derisive attack on a professor of language and literature whose chair Sweet regarded as proper to a phonetic expert only. The article, being libelous, had to be returned as impossible; and I had to renounce my dream of dragging its author into the limelight. When I met him afterwards, for the first time for many years, I found to my astonishment that he, who had been a quite tolerably presentable young man, had actually managed by sheer scorn to alter his personal appearance until he had become a sort of walking repudiation of Oxford and all its traditions. It must have been largely in his own despite that he was squeezed into something called a Readership of phonetics there. The future of phonetics rests probably with his pupils, who all swore by him; but nothing could bring the man himself into any sort of compliance with the university, to which he nevertheless clung by divine right in an intensely Oxonian way. I daresay his papers, if he has left any, include some satires that may be published without too destructive results fifty years hence. He was, I believe, not in the least an ill-natured man: very much the opposite, I should say; but he would not suffer fools gladly.

Those who knew him will recognize in my third act the allusion to the patent Shorthand in which he used to write postcards, and which may be acquired from a four and six-penny manual published by the Clarendon Press. The postcards which Mrs. Higgins describes are such as I have received from Sweet. I would decipher a sound which a cockney would represent by zerr, and a Frenchman by seu, and then write demanding with some heat what on earth it meant. Sweet, with boundless contempt for my stupidity, would reply that it not only meant but obviously was the word Result, as no other Word containing that sound, and capable of making sense with the context, existed in any language spoken on earth. That less expert mortals should require fuller indications was beyond Sweet's patience. Therefore, though the whole point of his "Current Shorthand" is that it can express every sound in the language perfectly, vowels as well as consonants, and that your hand has to make no stroke except the easy and current ones with which you write m, n, and u, l, p, and q, scribbling them at whatever angle comes easiest to you, his unfortunate determination to make this remarkable and quite legible script serve also as a Shorthand reduced it in his own practice to the most inscrutable of cryptograms. His true objective was the provision of a full, accurate, legible script for our noble but ill-dressed language; but he was led past that by his contempt for the popular Pitman system of Shorthand, which he called the Pitfall system. The triumph of Pitman was a triumph of business organization: there was a weekly paper to persuade you to learn Pitman: there were cheap textbooks and exercise books and transcripts of speeches for you to copy, and schools where experienced teachers coached you up to the necessary proficiency. Sweet could not organize his market in that fashion. He might as well have been the Sybil who tore up the leaves of prophecy that nobody would attend to. The four and six-penny manual, mostly in his lithographed handwriting, that was never vulgarly advertized, may perhaps some day be taken up by a syndicate and pushed upon the public as The Times pushed the Encyclopaedia Britannica; but until then it will certainly not prevail against Pitman. I have bought three copies of it during my lifetime; and I am informed by the publishers that its cloistered existence is still a steady and healthy one. I actually learned the system two several times; and yet the shorthand in which I am writing these lines is Pitman's. And the reason is, that my secretary cannot transcribe Sweet, having been perforce taught in the schools of Pitman. Therefore, Sweet railed at Pitman as vainly as Thersites railed at Ajax: his raillery, however it may have eased his soul, gave no popular vogue to Current Shorthand. Pygmalion Higgins is not a portrait of Sweet, to whom the adventure of Eliza Doolittle would have been impossible; still, as will be seen, there are touches of Sweet in the play. With Higgins's physique and temperament Sweet might have set the Thames on fire. As it was, he impressed himself professionally on Europe to an extent that made his comparative personal obscurity, and the failure of Oxford to do justice to his eminence, a puzzle to foreign specialists in his subject. I do not blame Oxford, because I think Oxford is quite right in demanding a certain social amenity from its nurslings (heaven knows it is not exorbitant in its requirements!); for although I well know how hard it is for a man of genius with a seriously underrated subject to maintain serene and kindly relations with the men who underrate it, and who keep all the best places for less important subjects which they profess without originality and sometimes without much capacity for them, still, if he overwhelms them with wrath and disdain, he cannot expect them to heap honors on him.

Of the later generations of phoneticians I know little. Among them towers the Poet Laureate, to whom perhaps Higgins may owe his Miltonic sympathies, though here again I must disclaim all portraiture. But if the play makes the public aware that there are such people as phoneticians, and that they are among the most important people in England at present, it will serve its turn.

I wish to boast that Pygmalion has been an extremely successful play all over Europe and North America as well as at home. It is so intensely and deliberately didactic, and its subject is esteemed so dry, that I delight in throwing it at the heads of the wiseacres who repeat the parrot cry that art should never be didactic. It goes to prove my contention that art should never be anything else.

Finally, and for the encouragement of people troubled with accents that cut them off from all high employment, I may add that the change wrought by Professor Higgins in the flower girl is neither impossible nor uncommon. The modern concierge's daughter who fulfils her ambition by playing the Queen of Spain in Ruy Blas at the Theatre Francais is only one of many thousands of men and women who have sloughed off their native dialects and acquired a new tongue. But the thing has to be done scientifically, or the last state of the aspirant may be worse than the first. An honest and natural slum dialect is more tolerable than the attempt of a phonetically untaught person to imitate the vulgar dialect of the golf club; and I am sorry to say that in spite of the efforts of our Academy of Dramatic Art, there is still too much sham golfing English on our stage, and too little of the noble English of Forbes Robertson.

ACT I

Covent Garden at 11.15 p.m. Torrents of heavy summer rain. Cab whistles blowing frantically in all directions. Pedestrians running for shelter into the market and under the portico of St. Paul's Church, where there are already several people, among them a lady and her daughter in evening dress. They are all peering out gloomily at the rain, except one man with his back turned to the rest, who seems wholly preoccupied with a notebook in which he is writing busily.

The church clock strikes the first quarter.

THE DAUGHTER [*in the space between the central pillars, close to the one on her left*] I'm getting chilled to the bone. What can Freddy be doing all this time? He's been gone twenty minutes.

THE MOTHER [*on her daughter's right*] Not so long. But he ought to have got us a cab by this.

A BYSTANDER [*on the lady's right*] He won't get no cab not until half-past eleven, missus, when they come back after dropping their theatre fares.

THE MOTHER. But we must have a cab. We can't stand here until half-past eleven. It's too bad.

THE BYSTANDER. Well, it ain't my fault, missus.

THE DAUGHTER. If Freddy had a bit of gumption, he would have got one at the theatre door.

THE MOTHER. What could he have done, poor boy?

THE DAUGHTER. Other people got cabs. Why couldn't he?

Freddy rushes in out of the rain from the Southampton Street side, and comes between them closing a dripping umbrella. He is a young man of twenty, in evening dress, very wet around the ankles.

THE DAUGHTER. Well, haven't you got a cab?

FREDDY. There's not one to be had for love or money.

THE MOTHER. Oh, Freddy, there must be one. You can't have tried.

THE DAUGHTER. It's too tiresome. Do you expect us to go and get one ourselves?

FREDDY. I tell you they're all engaged. The rain was so sudden: nobody was prepared; and everybody had to take a cab. I've been to Charing Cross one way and nearly to Ludgate Circus the other; and they were all engaged.

THE MOTHER. Did you try Trafalgar Square?

FREDDY. There wasn't one at Trafalgar Square.

THE DAUGHTER. Did you try?

FREDDY. I tried as far as Charing Cross Station. Did you expect me to walk to Hammersmith?

THE DAUGHTER. You haven't tried at all.

THE MOTHER. You really are very helpless, Freddy. Go again; and don't come back until you have found a cab.

FREDDY. I shall simply get soaked for nothing.

THE DAUGHTER. And what about us? Are we to stay here all night in this draught, with next to nothing on. You selfish pig—

FREDDY. Oh, very well: I'll go, I'll go. [*He opens his umbrella and dashes off Strandwards, but comes into collision with a flower girl, who is hurrying in for shelter, knocking her basket out of her hands. A blinding flash of lightning, followed instantly by a rattling peal of thunder, orchestrates the incident*]

THE FLOWER GIRL. Nah then, Freddy: look wh' y' gowin, deah.

FREDDY. Sorry [*he rushes off*].

THE FLOWER GIRL [*picking up her scattered flowers and replacing them in the basket*] There's menners f' yer! Te-oo banches o voylets trod into the mad. [*She sits down on the plinth of the column, sorting her flowers, on the lady's right. She is not at all an attractive person. She is perhaps eighteen, perhaps twenty, hardly older. She wears a little sailor hat of black straw that has long been exposed to the dust and soot of London and has seldom if ever been brushed. Her hair needs washing rather badly: its mousy color can hardly be natural. She wears a shoddy black coat that reaches nearly to her knees and is shaped to her waist. She has a brown skirt with a coarse apron. Her boots are much the worse for wear. She is no doubt as clean as she can afford to be; but compared to the ladies she is very dirty. Her features are no worse than theirs; but their condition leaves something to be desired; and she needs the services of a dentist*].

THE MOTHER. How do you know that my son's name is Freddy, pray?

THE FLOWER GIRL. Ow, eez ye-ooa san, is e? Wal, fewd dan y' de-ooty bawmz a mather should, eed now bettern to spawl a pore gel's flahrzn than ran awy atbaht pyin. Will ye-oo py me f'them? [*Here, with apologies, this desperate attempt to represent her dialect without a phonetic alphabet must be abandoned as unintelligible outside London.*]

THE DAUGHTER. Do nothing of the sort, mother. The idea!

THE MOTHER. Please allow me, Clara. Have you any pennies?

THE DAUGHTER. No. I've nothing smaller than sixpence.

THE FLOWER GIRL [*hopefully*] I can give you change for a tanner, kind lady.

THE MOTHER [*to Clara*] Give it to me. [*Clara parts reluctantly*]. Now [*to the girl*] This is for your flowers.

THE FLOWER GIRL. Thank you kindly, lady.

THE DAUGHTER. Make her give you the change. These things are only a penny a bunch.

THE MOTHER. Do hold your tongue, Clara. [*To the girl*]. You can keep the change.

THE FLOWER GIRL. Oh, thank you, lady.

THE MOTHER. Now tell me how you know that young gentleman's name.

THE FLOWER GIRL. I didn't.

THE MOTHER. I heard you call him by it. Don't try to deceive me.

THE FLOWER GIRL [*protesting*] Who's trying to deceive you? I called him Freddy or Charlie same as you might yourself if you was talking to a stranger and wished to be pleasant. [*She sits down beside her basket*].

THE DAUGHTER. Sixpence thrown away! Really, mamma, you might have spared Freddy that. [*She retreats in disgust behind the pillar*].

An elderly gentleman of the amiable military type rushes into shelter, and closes a dripping umbrella. He is in the same plight as Freddy, very wet about the ankles. He is in evening dress, with a light overcoat. He takes the place left vacant by the daughter's retirement.

THE GENTLEMAN. Phew!

THE MOTHER [*to the gentleman*] Oh, sir, is there any sign of its stopping?

THE GENTLEMAN. I'm afraid not. It started worse than ever about two minutes ago. [*He goes to the plinth beside the flower girl; puts up his foot on it; and stoops to turn down his trouser ends*].

THE MOTHER. Oh, dear! [*She retires sadly and joins her daughter*].

THE FLOWER GIRL [*taking advantage of the military gentleman's proximity to establish friendly relations with him*]. If it's worse it's a sign it's nearly over. So cheer up, Captain; and buy a flower off a poor girl.

THE GENTLEMAN. I'm sorry, I haven't any change.

THE FLOWER GIRL. I can give you change, Captain,

THE GENTLEMEN. For a sovereign? I've nothing less.

THE FLOWER GIRL. Garn! Oh do buy a flower off me, Captain. I can change half-a-crown. Take this for tuppence.

THE GENTLEMAN. Now don't be troublesome: there's a good girl. [*Trying his pockets*] I really haven't any change—Stop: here's three hapence, if that's any use to you [*he retreats to the other pillar*].

THE FLOWER GIRL [*disappointed, but thinking three halfpence better than nothing*] Thank you, sir.

THE BYSTANDER [*to the girl*] You be careful: give him a flower for it. There's a bloke here behind taking down every blessed word you're saying. [*All turn to the man who is taking notes*].

THE FLOWER GIRL [*springing up terrified*] I ain't done nothing wrong by speaking to the gentleman. I've a right to sell flowers if I keep off the kerb. [*Hysterically*] I'm a respectable girl: so help me, I never spoke to him except to ask him to buy a flower off me. [*General hubbub, mostly sympathetic to the flower girl, but deprecating her excessive sensibility. Cries of Don't start hollerin. Who's hurting you? Nobody's going to touch you. What's the good of fussing? Steady on. Easy, easy, etc., come from the elderly staid spectators, who pat her comfortingly. Less patient ones bid her shut her head, or ask her roughly what is wrong with her. A remoter group, not knowing what the matter is, crowd in and increase the noise with question and answer: What's the row? What she do? Where is he? A tec taking her down. What! him? Yes: him over there: Took money off the gentleman, etc. The flower girl, distraught and mobbed, breaks through them to the gentleman, crying mildly*] Oh, sir, don't let him charge me. You dunno what it means to me. They'll take away my character and drive me on the streets for speaking to gentlemen. They—

THE NOTE TAKER [*coming forward on her right, the rest crowding after him*] There, there, there, there! Who's hurting you, you silly girl? What do you take me for?

THE BYSTANDER. It's all right: he's a gentleman: look at his boots. [*Explaining to the note taker*] She thought you was a copper's nark, sir.

THE NOTE TAKER [*with quick interest*] What's a copper's nark?

THE BYSTANDER [*inept at definition*] It's a—well, it's a copper's nark, as you might say. What else would you call it? A sort of informer.

THE FLOWER GIRL [*still hysterical*] I take my Bible oath I never said a word—

THE NOTE TAKER [*overbearing but good-humored*] Oh, shut up, shut up. Do I look like a policeman?

THE FLOWER GIRL [*far from reassured*] Then what did you take down my words for? How do I know whether you took me down right? You just show me what you've wrote about me. [*The note taker opens his book and holds it steadily under her nose, though the pressure of the mob trying to read it over his shoulders would upset a weaker man*]. What's that? That ain't proper writing. I can't read that.

THE NOTE TAKER. I can. [*Reads, reproducing her pronunciation exactly*] "Cheer ap, Keptin; n' haw ya flahr orf a pore gel."

THE FLOWER GIRL [*much distressed*] It's because I called him Captain. I meant no harm. [*To the gentleman*] Oh, sir, don't let him lay a charge agen me for a word like that. You—

THE GENTLEMAN. Charge! I make no charge. [*To the note taker*] Really, sir, if you are a detective, you need not begin protecting me against molestation by young women until I ask you. Anybody could see that the girl meant no harm.

THE BYSTANDERS GENERALLY [*demonstrating against police espionage*] Course they could. What business is it of yours? You mind your own affairs. He wants promotion, he does. Taking down people's words! Girl never said a word to him. What harm if she did? Nice thing a girl can't shelter from the rain without being insulted, etc., etc., etc. [*She is conducted by the more sympathetic demonstrators back to her plinth, where she resumes her seat and struggles with her emotion*].

THE BYSTANDER. He ain't a tec. He's a blooming busybody: that's what he is. I tell you, look at his boots.

THE NOTE TAKER [*turning on him genially*] And how are all your people down at Selsey?

THE BYSTANDER [*suspiciously*] Who told you my people come from Selsey?

THE NOTE TAKER. Never you mind. They did. [*To the girl*] How do you come to be up so far east? You were born in Lisson Grove.

THE FLOWER GIRL [*appalled*] Oh, what harm is there in my leaving Lisson Grove? It wasn't fit for a pig to live in; and I had to pay four-and-six a week. [*In tears*] Oh, boo—hoo—oo—

THE NOTE TAKER. Live where you like; but stop that noise.

THE GENTLEMAN [*to the girl*] Come, come! he can't touch you: you have a right to live where you please.

A SARCASTIC BYSTANDER [*thrusting himself between the note taker and the gentleman*] Park Lane, for instance. I'd like to go into the Housing Question with you, I would.

THE FLOWER GIRL [*subsiding into a brooding melancholy over her basket, and talking very low-spiritedly to herself*] I'm a good girl, I am.

THE SARCASTIC BYSTANDER [*not attending to her*] Do you know where *I* come from?

THE NOTE TAKER [*promptly*] Hoxton.

Titterings. Popular interest in the note taker's performance increases.

THE SARCASTIC ONE [*amazed*] Well, who said I didn't? Bly me! You know everything, you do.

THE FLOWER GIRL [*still nursing her sense of injury*] Ain't no call to meddle with me, he ain't.

THE BYSTANDER [*to her*] Of course he ain't. Don't you stand it from him. [*To the note taker*] See here: what call have you to know about people what never offered to meddle with you? Where's your warrant?

SEVERAL BYSTANDERS [*encouraged by this seeming point of law*] Yes: where's your warrant?

THE FLOWER GIRL. Let him say what he likes. I don't want to have no truck with him.

THE BYSTANDER. You take us for dirt under your feet, don't you? Catch you taking liberties with a gentleman!

THE SARCASTIC BYSTANDER. Yes: tell HIM where he come from if you want to go fortune-telling.

THE NOTE TAKER. Cheltenham, Harrow, Cambridge, and India.

THE GENTLEMAN. Quite right. [*Great laughter. Reaction in the note taker's favor. Exclamations of He knows all about it. Told him proper. Hear him tell the toff where he come from? etc.*]. May I ask, sir, do you do this for your living at a music hall?

THE NOTE TAKER. I've thought of that. Perhaps I shall some day.

The rain has stopped; and the persons on the outside of the crowd begin to drop off.

THE FLOWER GIRL [*resenting the reaction*] He's no gentleman, he ain't, to interfere with a poor girl.

THE DAUGHTER [*out of patience, pushing her way rudely to the front and displacing the gentleman, who politely retires to the other side of the pillar*]

What on earth is Freddy doing? I shall get pneumonia if I stay in this draught any longer.

THE NOTE TAKER [*to himself, hastily making a note of her pronunciation of "monia"*] Earlscourt.

THE DAUGHTER [*violently*] Will you please keep your impertinent remarks to yourself?

THE NOTE TAKER. Did I say that out loud? I didn't mean to. I beg your pardon. Your mother's Epsom, unmistakeably.

THE MOTHER [*advancing between her daughter and the note taker*] How very curious! I was brought up in Largelady Park, near Epsom.

THE NOTE TAKER [*uproariously amused*] Ha! ha! What a devil of a name! Excuse me. [*To the daughter*] You want a cab, do you?

THE DAUGHTER. Don't dare speak to me.

THE MOTHER. Oh, please, please Clara. [*Her daughter repudiates her with an angry shrug and retires haughtily.*] We should be so grateful to you, sir, if you found us a cab. [*The note taker produces a whistle*]. Oh, thank you. [*She joins her daughter*]. The note taker blows a piercing blast.

THE SARCASTIC BYSTANDER. There! I knowed he was a plain-clothes copper.

THE BYSTANDER. That ain't a police whistle: that's a sporting whistle.

THE FLOWER GIRL [*still preoccupied with her wounded feelings*] He's no right to take away my character. My character is the same to me as any lady's.

THE NOTE TAKER. I don't know whether you've noticed it; but the rain stopped about two minutes ago.

THE BYSTANDER. So it has. Why didn't you say so before? and us losing our time listening to your silliness. [*He walks off towards the Strand*].

THE SARCASTIC BYSTANDER. I can tell where you come from. You come from Anwell. Go back there.

THE NOTE TAKER [*helpfully*] *H*anwell.

THE SARCASTIC BYSTANDER [*affecting great distinction of speech*] Thenk you, teacher. Haw haw! So long [*he touches his hat with mock respect and strolls off*].

THE FLOWER GIRL. Frightening people like that! How would he like it himself.

THE MOTHER. It's quite fine now, Clara. We can walk to a motor bus. Come. [*She gathers her skirts above her ankles and hurries off towards the Strand*].

THE DAUGHTER. But the cab—[*her mother is out of hearing*]. Oh, how tiresome! [*She follows angrily*].

All the rest have gone except the note taker, the gentleman, and the flower girl, who sits arranging her basket, and still pitying herself in murmurs.

THE FLOWER GIRL. Poor girl! Hard enough for her to live without being worrited and chivied.

THE GENTLEMAN [*returning to his former place on the note taker's left*] How do you do it, if I may ask?

THE NOTE TAKER. Simply phonetics. The science of speech. That's my profession; also my hobby. Happy is the man who can make a living by his hobby! You can spot an Irishman or a Yorkshireman by his brogue. I can place any man within six miles. I can place him within two miles in London. Sometimes within two streets.

THE FLOWER GIRL. Ought to be ashamed of himself, unmanly coward!

THE GENTLEMAN. But is there a living in that?

THE NOTE TAKER. Oh yes. Quite a fat one. This is an age of upstarts. Men begin in Kentish Town with 80 pounds a year, and end in Park Lane with a hundred thousand. They want to drop Kentish Town; but they give themselves away every time they open their mouths. Now I can teach them—

THE FLOWER GIRL. Let him mind his own business and leave a poor girl—

THE NOTE TAKER [*explosively*] Woman: cease this detestable boohooing instantly; or else seek the shelter of some other place of worship.

THE FLOWER GIRL [*with feeble defiance*] I've a right to be here if I like, same as you.

THE NOTE TAKER. A woman who utters such depressing and disgusting sounds has no right to be anywhere—no right to live. Remember that you are a human being with a soul and the divine gift of articulate speech: that your native language is the language of Shakespear and Milton and The Bible; and don't sit there crooning like a bilious pigeon.

THE FLOWER GIRL [*quite overwhelmed, and looking up at him in mingled wonder and deprecation without daring to raise her head*] Ah—ah—ah—ow—ow—oo!

THE NOTE TAKER [*whipping out his book*] Heavens! what a sound! [*He writes; then holds out the book and reads, reproducing her vowels exactly*] Ah—ah—ah—ow—ow—ow—oo!

THE FLOWER GIRL [*tickled by the performance, and laughing in spite of herself*] Garn!

THE NOTE TAKER. You see this creature with her kerbstone English: the English that will keep her in the gutter to the end of her days. Well, sir, in three months I could pass that girl off as a duchess at an ambassador's garden party. I could even get her a place as lady's maid or shop assistant, which requires better English. That's the sort of thing I do for commercial millionaires. And on the profits of it I do genuine scientific work in phonetics, and a little as a poet on Miltonic lines.

THE GENTLEMAN. I am myself a student of Indian dialects; and—

THE NOTE TAKER [*eagerly*] Are you? Do you know Colonel Pickering, the author of Spoken Sanscrit?

THE GENTLEMAN. I am Colonel Pickering. Who are you?

THE NOTE TAKER. Henry Higgins, author of Higgins's Universal Alphabet.

PICKERING [*with enthusiasm*] I came from India to meet you.

HIGGINS. I was going to India to meet you.

PICKERING. Where do you live?

HIGGINS. 27A Wimpole Street. Come and see me tomorrow.

PICKERING. I'm at the Carlton. Come with me now and let's have a jaw over some supper.

HIGGINS. Right you are.

THE FLOWER GIRL [*to Pickering, as he passes her*] Buy a flower, kind gentleman. I'm short for my lodging.

PICKERING. I really haven't any change. I'm sorry [*he goes away*].

HIGGINS [*shocked at girl's mendacity*] Liar. You said you could change half-a-crown.

THE FLOWER GIRL [*rising in desperation*] You ought to be stuffed with nails, you ought. [*Flinging the basket at his feet*] Take the whole blooming basket for sixpence.

The church clock strikes the second quarter.

HIGGINS [*hearing in it the voice of God, rebuking him for his Pharisaic want of charity to the poor girl*] A reminder. [*He raises his hat solemnly; then throws a handful of money into the basket and follows Pickering*].

THE FLOWER GIRL [*picking up a half-crown*] Ah—ow—ooh! [*Picking up a couple of florins*] Aaah—ow—ooh! [*Picking up several coins*] Aaaaaah—ow—ooh! [*Picking up a half-sovereign*] Aasaaaaaaaaah—ow—ooh!!!

FREDDY [*springing out of a taxicab*] Got one at last. Hallo! [*To the girl*] Where are the two ladies that were here?

THE FLOWER GIRL. They walked to the bus when the rain stopped.

FREDDY. And left me with a cab on my hands. Damnation!

THE FLOWER GIRL [*with grandeur*] Never you mind, young man. I'm going home in a taxi. [*She sails off to the cab. The driver puts his hand behind him and holds the door firmly shut against her. Quite understanding his mistrust, she shows him her handful of money*]. Eightpence ain't no object to me, Charlie. [*He grins and opens the door*]. Angel Court, Drury Lane, round the corner of Micklejohn's oil shop. Let's see how fast you can make her hop it. [*She gets in and pulls the door to with a slam as the taxicab starts*].

FREDDY. Well, I'm dashed!

ACT II

Next day at 11 a.m. Higgins's laboratory in Wimpole Street. It is a room on the first floor, looking on the street, and was meant for the drawing-room. The double doors are in the middle of the back hall; and persons entering find in the corner to their right two tall file cabinets at right angles to one another against the walls. In this corner stands a flat writing-table, on which are a phonograph, a laryngoscope, a row of tiny organ pipes with a bellows, a set of lamp chimneys for singing flames with burners attached to a gas plug in the wall by an indiarubber tube, several tuning-forks of different sizes, a life-size image of half a human head, showing in section the vocal organs, and a box containing a supply of wax cylinders for the phonograph.

Further down the room, on the same side, is a fireplace, with a comfortable leather-covered easy-chair at the side of the hearth nearest the door, and a coal-scuttle. There is a clock on the mantelpiece. Between the fireplace and the phonograph table is a stand for newspapers.

On the other side of the central door, to the left of the visitor, is a cabinet of shallow drawers. On it is a telephone and the telephone directory. The corner beyond, and most of the side wall, is occupied by a grand piano, with the keyboard at the end furthest from the door, and a bench for the player extending the full length of the keyboard. On the piano is a dessert dish heaped with fruit and sweets, mostly chocolates.

The middle of the room is clear. Besides the easy chair, the piano bench, and two chairs at the phonograph table, there is one stray chair. It stands near the fireplace. On the walls, engravings; mostly Piranesis and mezzotint portraits. No paintings.

Pickering is seated at the table, putting down some cards and a tuning-fork which he has been using. Higgins is standing up near him, closing two or three file drawers which are hanging out. He appears in the morning light as a robust, vital, appetizing sort of man of forty or thereabouts, dressed in a professional-looking black frock-coat with a white linen collar and black silk tie. He is of the energetic, scientific type, heartily, even violently interested in everything that can be studied as a scientific subject, and careless about himself and other people, including their feelings. He is, in fact, but for his years and size, rather like a very impetuous baby "taking notice" eagerly and loudly, and requiring almost as much watching to keep him out of unintended mischief. His manner varies from genial bullying when he is in a good humor to stormy petulance when anything goes wrong; but he is so entirely frank and void of malice that he remains likeable even in his least reasonable moments.

HIGGINS [*as he shuts the last drawer*] Well, I think that's the whole show.

PICKERING. It's really amazing. I haven't taken half of it in, you know.

HIGGINS. Would you like to go over any of it again?

PICKERING [*rising and coming to the fireplace, where he plants himself with his back to the fire*] No, thank you; not now. I'm quite done up for this morning.

HIGGINS [*following him, and standing beside him on his left*] Tired of listening to sounds?

PICKERING. Yes. It's a fearful strain. I rather fancied myself because I can pronounce twenty-four distinct vowel sounds; but your hundred and thirty beat me. I can't hear a bit of difference between most of them.

HIGGINS [*chuckling, and going over to the piano to eat sweets*] Oh, that comes with practice. You hear no difference at first; but you keep on listening, and presently you find they're all as different as A from B. [*Mrs. Pearce looks in: she is Higgins's housekeeper*] What's the matter?

MRS. PEARCE [*hesitating, evidently perplexed*] A young woman wants to see you, sir.

HIGGINS. A young woman! What does she want?

MRS. PEARCE. Well, sir, she says you'll be glad to see her when you know what she's come about. She's quite a common girl, sir. Very common indeed. I should have sent her away, only I thought perhaps you wanted her to talk into your machines. I hope I've not done wrong; but really you see such queer people sometimes—you'll excuse me, I'm sure, sir—

HIGGINS. Oh, that's all right, Mrs. Pearce. Has she an interesting accent?

MRS. PEARCE. Oh, something dreadful, sir, really. I don't know how you can take an interest in it.

HIGGINS [*to Pickering*] Let's have her up. Show her up, Mrs. Pearce [*he rushes across to his working table and picks out a cylinder to use on the phonograph*].

MRS. PEARCE [*only half resigned to it*] Very well, sir. It's for you to say. [*She goes downstairs*].

HIGGINS. This is rather a bit of luck. I'll show you how I make records. We'll set her talking; and I'll take it down first in Bell's visible Speech; then in broad Romic; and then we'll get her on the phonograph so that you can turn her on as often as you like with the written transcript before you.

MRS. PEARCE [*returning*] This is the young woman, sir.

The flower girl enters in state. She has a hat with three ostrich feathers, orange, sky-blue, and red. She has a nearly clean apron, and the shoddy coat has been tidied a little. The pathos of this deplorable figure, with its innocent vanity and consequential air, touches Pickering, who has already straightened himself in the presence of Mrs. Pearce. But as to Higgins, the only distinction he makes between men and women is that when he is neither bullying nor exclaiming to the heavens against some featherweight cross, he coaxes women as a child coaxes its nurse when it wants to get anything out of her.

HIGGINS [*brusquely, recognizing her with unconcealed disappointment, and at once, baby-like, making an intolerable grievance of it*] Why, this is the girl I jotted down last night. She's no use: I've got all the records I want of the Lisson Grove lingo; and I'm not going to waste another cylinder on it. [*To the girl*] Be off with you: I don't want you.

THE FLOWER GIRL. Don't you be so saucy. You ain't heard what I come for yet. [*To Mrs. Pearce, who is waiting at the door for further instruction*] Did you tell him I come in a taxi?

MRS. PEARCE. Nonsense, girl! what do you think a gentleman like Mr. Higgins cares what you came in?

THE FLOWER GIRL. Oh, we are proud! He ain't above giving lessons, not him: I heard him say so. Well, I ain't come here to ask for any compliment; and if my money's not good enough I can go elsewhere.

HIGGINS. Good enough for what?

THE FLOWER GIRL. Good enough for ye—oo. Now you know, don't you? I'm come to have lessons, I am. And to pay for em too: make no mistake.

HIGGINS [*stupent*] WELL!!! [*Recovering his breath with a gasp*] What do you expect me to say to you?

THE FLOWER GIRL. Well, if you was a gentleman, you might ask me to sit down, I think. Don't I tell you I'm bringing you business?

HIGGINS. Pickering: shall we ask this baggage to sit down or shall we throw her out of the window?

THE FLOWER GIRL [*running away in terror to the piano, where she turns at bay*] Ah—ah—ah—ow—ow—ow—oo! [*Wounded and whimpering*] I won't be called a baggage when I've offered to pay like any lady.

Motionless, the two men stare at her from the other side of the room, amazed.

PICKERING [*gently*] What is it you want, my girl?

THE FLOWER GIRL. I want to be a lady in a flower shop stead of selling at the corner of Tottenham Court Road. But they won't take me unless I can talk more genteel. He said he could teach me. Well, here I am ready to pay him—not asking any favor—and he treats me as if I was dirt.

MRS. PEARCE. How can you be such a foolish ignorant girl as to think you could afford to pay Mr. Higgins?

THE FLOWER GIRL. Why shouldn't I? I know what lessons cost as well as you do; and I'm ready to pay.

HIGGINS. How much?

THE FLOWER GIRL [*coming back to him, triumphant*] Now you're talking! I thought you'd come off it when you saw a chance of getting back a bit of what you chucked at me last night. [*Confidentially*] You'd had a drop in, hadn't you?

HIGGINS [*peremptorily*] Sit down.

THE FLOWER GIRL. Oh, if you're going to make a compliment of it—

HIGGINS [*thundering at her*] Sit down.

MRS. PEARCE [*severely*] Sit down, girl. Do as you're told. [*She places the stray chair near the hearthrug between Higgins and Pickering, and stands behind it waiting for the girl to sit down*].

THE FLOWER GIRL. Ah—ah—ah—ow—ow—oo! [*She stands, half rebellious, half bewildered*].

PICKERING [*very courteous*] Won't you sit down?

LIZA [*coyly*] Don't mind if I do. [*She sits down. Pickering returns to the hearthrug*].

HIGGINS. What's your name?

THE FLOWER GIRL. Liza Doolittle.

HIGGINS [*declaiming gravely*] Eliza, Elizabeth, Betsy and Bess, They went to the woods to get a birds nes': PICKERING. They found a nest with four eggs in it: HIGGINS. They took one apiece, and left three in it.

They laugh heartily at their own wit.

LIZA. Oh, don't be silly.

MRS. PEARCE. You mustn't speak to the gentleman like that.

LIZA. Well, why won't he speak sensible to me?

HIGGINS. Come back to business. How much do you propose to pay me for the lessons?

LIZA. Oh, I know what's right. A lady friend of mine gets French lessons for eighteenpence an hour from a real French gentleman. Well, you wouldn't have the face to ask me the same for teaching me my own language as you would for French; so I won't give more than a shilling. Take it or leave it.

HIGGINS [*walking up and down the room, rattling his keys and his cash in his pockets*] You know, Pickering, if you consider a shilling, not as a simple shilling, but as a percentage of this girl's income, it works out as fully equivalent to sixty or seventy guineas from a millionaire.

PICKERING. How so?

HIGGINS. Figure it out. A millionaire has about 150 pounds a day. She earns about half-a-crown.

LIZA [*haughtily*] Who told you I only—

HIGGINS [*continuing*] She offers me two-fifths of her day's income for a lesson. Two-fifths of a millionaire's income for a day would be somewhere about 60 pounds. It's handsome. By George, it's enormous! it's the biggest offer I ever had.

LIZA [*rising, terrified*] Sixty pounds! What are you talking about? I never offered you sixty pounds. Where would I get—

HIGGINS. Hold your tongue.

LIZA [*weeping*] But I ain't got sixty pounds. Oh—

MRS. PEARCE. Don't cry, you silly girl. Sit down. Nobody is going to touch your money.

HIGGINS. Somebody is going to touch you, with a broomstick, if you don't stop snivelling. Sit down.

LIZA [*obeying slowly*] Ah—ah—ah—ow—oo—o! One would think you was my father.

HIGGINS. If I decide to teach you, I'll be worse than two fathers to you. Here [*he offers her his silk handkerchief*]!

LIZA. What's this for?

HIGGINS. To wipe your eyes. To wipe any part of your face that feels moist. Remember: that's your handkerchief; and that's your sleeve. Don't mistake the one for the other if you wish to become a lady in a shop.

Liza, utterly bewildered, stares helplessly at him.

MRS. PEARCE. It's no use talking to her like that, Mr. Higgins: she doesn't understand you. Besides, you're quite wrong: she doesn't do it that way at all [*she takes the handkerchief*].

LIZA [*snatching it*] Here! You give me that handkerchief. He give it to me, not to you.

PICKERING [*laughing*] He did. I think it must be regarded as her property, Mrs. Pearce.

MRS. PEARCE [*resigning herself*] Serve you right, Mr. Higgins.

PICKERING. Higgins: I'm interested. What about the ambassador's garden party? I'll say you're the greatest teacher alive if you make that good. I'll bet you all the expenses of the experiment you can't do it. And I'll pay for the lessons.

LIZA. Oh, you are real good. Thank you, Captain.

HIGGINS [*tempted, looking at her*] It's almost irresistible. She's so deliciously low—so horribly dirty—

LIZA [*protesting extremely*] Ah—ah—ah—ah—ow—ow—oooo!!! I ain't dirty: I washed my face and hands afore I come, I did.

PICKERING. You're certainly not going to turn her head with flattery, Higgins.

MRS. PEARCE [*uneasy*] Oh, don't say that, sir: there's more ways than one of turning a girl's head; and nobody can do it better than Mr. Higgins, though he may not always mean it. I do hope, sir, you won't encourage him to do anything foolish.

HIGGINS [*becoming excited as the idea grows on him*] What is life but a series of inspired follies? The difficulty is to find them to do. Never lose a chance: it doesn't come every day. I shall make a duchess of this draggletailed guttersnipe.

LIZA [*strongly deprecating this view of her*] Ah—ah—ah—ow—ow—oo!

HIGGINS [*carried away*] Yes: in six months—in three if she has a good ear and a quick tongue—I'll take her anywhere and pass her off as anything. We'll start today: now! this moment! Take her away and clean her, Mrs. Pearce. Monkey Brand, if it won't come off any other way. Is there a good fire in the kitchen?

MRS. PEARCE [*protesting*]. Yes; but—

HIGGINS [*storming on*] Take all her clothes off and burn them. Ring up Whiteley or somebody for new ones. Wrap her up in brown paper till they come.

LIZA. You're no gentleman, you're not, to talk of such things. I'm a good girl, I am; and I know what the like of you are, I do.

HIGGINS. We want none of your Lisson Grove prudery here, young woman. You've got to learn to behave like a duchess. Take her away, Mrs. Pearce. If she gives you any trouble wallop her.

LIZA [*springing up and running between Pickering and Mrs. Pearce for protection*] No! I'll call the police, I will.

MRS. PEARCE. But I've no place to put her.

HIGGINS. Put her in the dustbin.

LIZA. Ah—ah—ah—ow—ow—oo!

PICKERING. Oh come, Higgins! be reasonable.

MRS. PEARCE [*resolutely*] You must be reasonable, Mr. Higgins: really you must. You can't walk over everybody like this.

Higgins, thus scolded, subsides. The hurricane is succeeded by a zephyr of amiable surprise.

HIGGINS [*with professional exquisiteness of modulation*] I walk over everybody! My dear Mrs. Pearce, my dear Pickering, I never had the slightest intention of walking over anyone. All I propose is that we should be kind to this poor girl. We must help her to prepare and fit herself for her new station in life. If I did not express myself clearly it was because I did not wish to hurt her delicacy, or yours.

Liza, reassured, steals back to her chair.

MRS. PEARCE [*to Pickering*] Well, did you ever hear anything like that, sir?

PICKERING [*laughing heartily*] Never, Mrs. Pearce: never.

HIGGINS [*patiently*] What's the matter?

MRS. PEARCE. Well, the matter is, sir, that you can't take a girl up like that as if you were picking up a pebble on the beach.

HIGGINS. Why not?

MRS. PEARCE. Why not! But you don't know anything about her. What about her parents? She may be married.

LIZA. Garn!

HIGGINS. There! As the girl very properly says, Garn! Married indeed! Don't you know that a woman of that class looks a worn out drudge of fifty a year after she's married.

LIZA. Who'd marry me?

HIGGINS [*suddenly resorting to the most thrillingly beautiful low tones in his best elocutionary style*] By George, Eliza, the streets will be strewn with the bodies of men shooting themselves for your sake before I've done with you.

MRS. PEARCE. Nonsense, sir. You mustn't talk like that to her.

LIZA [*rising and squaring herself determinedly*] I'm going away. He's off his chump, he is. I don't want no balmies teaching me.

HIGGINS [*wounded in his tenderest point by her insensibility to his elocution*] Oh, indeed! I'm mad, am I? Very well, Mrs. Pearce: you needn't order the new clothes for her. Throw her out.

LIZA [*whimpering*] Nah—ow. You got no right to touch me.

MRS. PEARCE. You see now what comes of being saucy. [*Indicating the door*] This way, please.

LIZA [*almost in tears*] I didn't want no clothes. I wouldn't have taken them [*she throws away the handkerchief*]. I can buy my own clothes.

HIGGINS [*deftly retrieving the handkerchief and intercepting her on her reluctant way to the door*] You're an ungrateful wicked girl. This is my return for offering to take you out of the gutter and dress you beautifully and make a lady of you.

MRS. PEARCE. Stop, Mr. Higgins. I won't allow it. It's you that are wicked. Go home to your parents, girl; and tell them to take better care of you.

LIZA. I ain't got no parents. They told me I was big enough to earn my own living and turned me out.

MRS. PEARCE. Where's your mother?

LIZA. I ain't got no mother. Her that turned me out was my sixth stepmother. But I done without them. And I'm a good girl, I am.

HIGGINS. Very well, then, what on earth is all this fuss about? The girl doesn't belong to anybody—is no use to anybody but me. [*He goes to Mrs. Pearce and begins coaxing*]. You can adopt her, Mrs. Pearce: I'm sure a daughter would be a great amusement to you. Now don't make any more fuss. Take her downstairs; and—

MRS. PEARCE. But what's to become of her? Is she to be paid anything? Do be sensible, sir.

HIGGINS. Oh, pay her whatever is necessary: put it down in the housekeeping book. [*Impatiently*] What on earth will she want with money? She'll have her food and her clothes. She'll only drink if you give her money.

LIZA [*turning on him*] Oh you are a brute. It's a lie: nobody ever saw the sign of liquor on me. [*She goes back to her chair and plants herself there defiantly*].

PICKERING [*in good-humored remonstrance*] Does it occur to you, Higgins, that the girl has some feelings?

HIGGINS [*looking critically at her*] Oh no, I don't think so. Not any feelings that we need bother about. [*Cheerily*] Have you, Eliza?

LIZA. I got my feelings same as anyone else.

HIGGINS [*to Pickering, reflectively*] You see the difficulty?

PICKERING. Eh? What difficulty?

HIGGINS. To get her to talk grammar. The mere pronunciation is easy enough.

LIZA. I don't want to talk grammar. I want to talk like a lady.

MRS. PEARCE. Will you please keep to the point, Mr. Higgins. I want to know on what terms the girl is to be here. Is she to have any wages? And what is to become of her when you've finished your teaching? You must look ahead a little.

HIGGINS [*impatiently*] What's to become of her if I leave her in the gutter? Tell me that, Mrs. Pearce.

MRS. PEARCE. That's her own business, not yours, Mr. Higgins.

HIGGINS. Well, when I've done with her, we can throw her back into the gutter; and then it will be her own business again; so that's all right.

LIZA. Oh, you've no feeling heart in you: you don't care for nothing but yourself [*she rises and takes the floor resolutely*]. Here! I've had enough of this. I'm going [*making for the door*]. You ought to be ashamed of yourself, you ought.

HIGGINS [*snatching a chocolate cream from the piano, his eyes suddenly beginning to twinkle with mischief*] Have some chocolates, Eliza.

LIZA [*halting, tempted*] How do I know what might be in them? I've heard of girls being drugged by the like of you.

Higgins whips out his penknife; cuts a chocolate in two; puts one half into his mouth and bolts it; and offers her the other half.

HIGGINS. Pledge of good faith, Eliza. I eat one half you eat the other.

[*Liza opens her mouth to retort: he pops the half chocolate into it*]. You shall have boxes of them, barrels of them, every day. You shall live on them. Eh?

LIZA [*who has disposed of the chocolate after being nearly choked by it*] I wouldn't have ate it, only I'm too ladylike to take it out of my mouth.

HIGGINS. Listen, Eliza. I think you said you came in a taxi.

LIZA. Well, what if I did? I've as good a right to take a taxi as anyone else.

HIGGINS. You have, Eliza; and in future you shall have as many taxis as you want. You shall go up and down and round the town in a taxi every day. Think of that, Eliza.

MRS. PEARCE. Mr. Higgins: you're tempting the girl. It's not right. She should think of the future.

HIGGINS. At her age! Nonsense! Time enough to think of the future when you haven't any future to think of. No, Eliza: do as this lady does: think of other people's futures; but never think of your own. Think of chocolates, and taxis, and gold, and diamonds.

LIZA. No: I don't want no gold and no diamonds. I'm a good girl, I am. [*She sits down again, with an attempt at dignity*].

HIGGINS. You shall remain so, Eliza, under the care of Mrs. Pearce. And you shall marry an officer in the Guards, with a beautiful moustache: the son of a marquis, who will disinherit him for marrying you, but will relent when he sees your beauty and goodness—

PICKERING. Excuse me, Higgins; but I really must interfere. Mrs. Pearce is quite right. If this girl is to put herself in your hands for six months for an experiment in teaching, she must understand thoroughly what she's doing.

HIGGINS. How can she? She's incapable of understanding anything. Besides, do any of us understand what we are doing? If we did, would we ever do it?

PICKERING. Very clever, Higgins; but not sound sense. [*To Eliza*] Miss Doolittle—

LIZA [*overwhelmed*] Ah—ah—ow—oo!

HIGGINS. There! That's all you get out of Eliza. Ah—ah—ow—oo! No use explaining. As a military man you ought to know that. Give her her orders: that's what she wants. Eliza: you are to live here for the next six months, learning how to speak beautifully, like a lady in a florist's shop. If you're good and do whatever you're told, you shall sleep in a proper bedroom, and have lots to eat, and money to buy chocolates and take rides in taxis. If you're naughty and idle you will sleep in the back kitchen among the black beetles, and be walloped by Mrs. Pearce with a broomstick. At the end of six months you shall go to Buckingham Palace in a carriage, beautifully dressed. If the King finds out you're not a lady, you will be taken by the police to the Tower of London, where your head will be cut off as a warning to other presumptuous flower girls. If you are not found out, you shall have a present of seven-and-sixpence to start life with as a lady in a shop. If you refuse this offer you will be a most ungrateful and wicked girl; and the angels will weep for you. [*To Pickering*] Now are you satisfied, Pickering? [*To Mrs. Pearce*] Can I put it more plainly and fairly, Mrs. Pearce?

MRS. PEARCE [*patiently*] I think you'd better let me speak to the girl properly in private. I don't know that I can take charge of her or consent to the arrangement at all. Of course I know you don't mean her any harm; but when you get what you call interested in people's accents, you never think or care what may happen to them or you. Come with me, Eliza.

HIGGINS. That's all right. Thank you, Mrs. Pearce. Bundle her off to the bath-room.

LIZA [*rising reluctantly and suspiciously*] You're a great bully, you are. I won't stay here if I don't like. I won't let nobody wallop me. I never asked to go to Bucknam Palace, I didn't. I was never in trouble with the police, not me. I'm a good girl—

MRS. PEARCE. Don't answer back, girl. You don't understand the gentleman. Come with me. [*She leads the way to the door, and holds it open for Eliza*].

LIZA [*as she goes out*] Well, what I say is right. I won't go near the king, not if I'm going to have my head cut off. If I'd known what I was letting myself in for, I wouldn't have come here. I always been a good girl; and I never offered to say a word to him; and I don't owe him nothing; and I don't care; and I won't be put upon; and I have my feelings the same as anyone else—

Mrs. Pearce shuts the door; and Eliza's plaints are no longer audible. Pickering comes from the hearth to the chair and sits astride it with his arms on the back.

PICKERING. Excuse the straight question, Higgins. Are you a man of good character where women are concerned?

HIGGINS [*moodily*] Have you ever met a man of good character where women are concerned?

PICKERING. Yes: very frequently.

HIGGINS [*dogmatically, lifting himself on his hands to the level of the piano, and sitting on it with a bounce*] Well, I haven't. I find that the moment I let a woman make friends with me, she becomes jealous, exacting, suspicious, and a damned nuisance. I find that the moment I let myself make friends with a woman, I become selfish and tyrannical. Women upset everything. When you let them into your life, you find that the woman is driving at one thing and you're driving at another.

PICKERING. At what, for example?

HIGGINS [*coming off the piano restlessly*] Oh, Lord knows! I suppose the woman wants to live her own life; and the man wants to live his; and each tries to drag the other on to the wrong track. One wants to go north and the other south; and the result is that both have to go east, though they both hate the east wind. [*He sits down on the bench at the keyboard*]. So here I am, a confirmed old bachelor, and likely to remain so.

PICKERING [*rising and standing over him gravely*] Come, Higgins! You know what I mean. If I'm to be in this business I shall feel responsible for that girl. I hope it's understood that no advantage is to be taken of her position.

HIGGINS. What! That thing! Sacred, I assure you. [*Rising to explain*] You see, she'll be a pupil; and teaching would be impossible unless pupils were sacred. I've taught scores of American millionairesses how to speak English: the best looking women in the world. I'm seasoned. They might as well be blocks of wood. I might as well be a block of wood. It's—

Mrs. Pearce opens the door. She has Eliza's hat in her hand. Pickering retires to the easy-chair at the hearth and sits down.

HIGGINS [*eagerly*] Well, Mrs. Pearce: is it all right?

MRS. PEARCE [*at the door*] I just wish to trouble you with a word, if I may, Mr. Higgins.

HIGGINS. Yes, certainly. Come in. [*She comes forward*]. Don't burn that, Mrs. Pearce. I'll keep it as a curiosity. [*He takes the hat*].

MRS. PEARCE. Handle it carefully, sir, please. I had to promise her not to burn it; but I had better put it in the oven for a while.

HIGGINS [*putting it down hastily on the piano*] Oh! thank you. Well, what have you to say to me?

PICKERING. Am I in the way?

MRS. PEARCE. Not at all, sir. Mr. Higgins: will you please be very particular what you say before the girl?

HIGGINS [*sternly*] Of course. I'm always particular about what I say. Why do you say this to me?

MRS. PEARCE [*unmoved*] No, sir: you're not at all particular when you've mislaid anything or when you get a little impatient. Now it doesn't matter before me: I'm used to it. But you really must not swear before the girl.

HIGGINS [*indignantly*] I swear! [*Most emphatically*] I never swear. I detest the habit. What the devil do you mean?

MRS. PEARCE [*stolidly*] That's what I mean, sir. You swear a great deal too much. I don't mind your damning and blasting, and what the devil and where the devil and who the devil—

HIGGINS. Really! Mrs. Pearce: this language from your lips!

MRS. PEARCE [*not to be put off*]—but there is a certain word I must ask you not to use. The girl has just used it herself because the bath was too hot. It begins with the same letter as bath. She knows no better: she learnt it at her mother's knee. But she must not hear it from your lips.

HIGGINS [*loftily*] I cannot charge myself with having ever uttered it, Mrs. Pearce. [*She looks at him steadfastly. He adds, hiding an uneasy conscience with a judicial air*] Except perhaps in a moment of extreme and justifiable excitement.

MRS. PEARCE. Only this morning, sir, you applied it to your boots, to the butter, and to the brown bread.

HIGGINS. Oh, that! Mere alliteration, Mrs. Pearce, natural to a poet.

MRS. PEARCE. Well, sir, whatever you choose to call it, I beg you not to let the girl hear you repeat it.

HIGGINS. Oh, very well, very well. Is that all?

MRS. PEARCE. No, sir. We shall have to be very particular with this girl as to personal cleanliness.

HIGGINS. Certainly. Quite right. Most important.

MRS. PEARCE. I mean not to be slovenly about her dress or untidy in leaving things about.

HIGGINS [*going to her solemnly*] Just so. I intended to call your attention to that [*He passes on to Pickering, who is enjoying the conversation immensely*]. It is these little things that matter, Pickering. Take care of the pence and the pounds will take care of themselves is as true of personal habits as of money. [*He comes to anchor on the hearthrug, with the air of a man in an unassailable position*].

MRS. PEARCE. Yes, sir. Then might I ask you not to come down to breakfast in your dressing-gown, or at any rate not to use it as a napkin to the extent you do, sir. And if you would be so good as not to eat everything off the same plate, and to remember not to put the porridge saucepan out of your hand on the clean tablecloth, it would be a better example to the girl. You know you nearly choked yourself with a fishbone in the jam only last week.

HIGGINS [*routed from the hearthrug and drifting back to the piano*] I may do these things sometimes in absence of mind; but surely I don't do them habitually. [*Angrily*] By the way: my dressing-gown smells most damnably of benzine.

MRS. PEARCE. No doubt it does, Mr. Higgins. But if you will wipe your fingers—

HIGGINS [*yelling*] Oh very well, very well: I'll wipe them in my hair in future.

MRS. PEARCE. I hope you're not offended, Mr. Higgins.

HIGGINS [*shocked at finding himself thought capable of an unamiable sentiment*] Not at all, not at all. You're quite right, Mrs. Pearce: I shall be particularly careful before the girl. Is that all?

MRS. PEARCE. No, sir. Might she use some of those Japanese dresses you brought from abroad? I really can't put her back into her old things.

HIGGINS. Certainly. Anything you like. Is that all?

MRS. PEARCE. Thank you, sir. That's all. [*She goes out*].

HIGGINS. You know, Pickering, that woman has the most extraordinary ideas about me. Here I am, a shy, diffident sort of man. I've never been able to feel really grown-up and tremendous, like other chaps. And yet she's firmly persuaded that I'm an arbitrary overbearing bossing kind of person. I can't account for it.

Mrs. Pearce returns.

MRS. PEARCE. If you please, sir, the trouble's beginning already. There's a dustman downstairs, Alfred Doolittle, wants to see you. He says you have his daughter here.

PICKERING [*rising*] Phew! I say! [*He retreats to the hearthrug*].

HIGGINS [*promptly*] Send the blackguard up.

MRS. PEARCE. Oh, very well, sir. [*She goes out*].

PICKERING. He may not be a blackguard, Higgins.

HIGGINS. Nonsense. Of course he's a blackguard.

PICKERING. Whether he is or not, I'm afraid we shall have some trouble with him.

HIGGINS [*confidently*] Oh no: I think not. If there's any trouble he shall have it with me, not I with him. And we are sure to get something interesting out of him.

PICKERING. About the girl?

HIGGINS. No. I mean his dialect.

PICKERING. Oh!

MRS. PEARCE [*at the door*] Doolittle, sir. [*She admits Doolittle and retires*].

Alfred Doolittle is an elderly but vigorous dustman, clad in the costume of his profession, including a hat with a back brim covering his neck and shoulders. He has well marked and rather interesting features, and seems equally free from fear and conscience. He has a remarkably expressive voice, the result of a habit of giving vent to his feelings without reserve. His present pose is that of wounded honor and stern resolution.

DOOLITTLE [*at the door, uncertain which of the two gentlemen is his man*] Professor Higgins?

HIGGINS. Here. Good morning. Sit down.

DOOLITTLE. Morning, Governor. [*He sits down magisterially*] I come about a very serious matter, Governor.

HIGGINS [*to Pickering*] Brought up in Hounslow. Mother Welsh, I should think. [*Doolittle opens his mouth, amazed. Higgins continues*] What do you want, Doolittle?

DOOLITTLE [*menacingly*] I want my daughter: that's what I want. See?

HIGGINS. Of course you do. You're her father, aren't you? You don't suppose anyone else wants her, do you? I'm glad to see you have some spark of family feeling left. She's upstairs. Take her away at once.

DOOLITTLE [*rising, fearfully taken aback*] What!

HIGGINS. Take her away. Do you suppose I'm going to keep your daughter for you?

DOOLITTLE [*remonstrating*] Now, now, look here, Governor. Is this reasonable? Is it fair to take advantage of a man like this? The girl belongs to me. You got her. Where do I come in? [*He sits down again*].

HIGGINS. Your daughter had the audacity to come to my house and ask me to teach her how to speak properly so that she could get a place in a flower-shop. This gentleman and my housekeeper have been here all the time. [*Bullying him*] How dare you come here and attempt to blackmail me? You sent her here on purpose.

DOOLITTLE [*protesting*] No, Governor.

HIGGINS. You must have. How else could you possibly know that she is here?

DOOLITTLE. Don't take a man up like that, Governor.

HIGGINS. The police shall take you up. This is a plant—a plot to extort money by threats. I shall telephone for the police [*he goes resolutely to the telephone and opens the directory*].

DOOLITTLE. Have I asked you for a brass farthing? I leave it to the gentleman here: have I said a word about money?

HIGGINS [*throwing the book aside and marching down on Doolittle with a poser*] What else did you come for?

DOOLITTLE [*sweetly*] Well, what would a man come for? Be human, governor.

HIGGINS [*disarmed*] Alfred: did you put her up to it?

DOOLITTLE. So help me, Governor, I never did. I take my Bible oath I ain't seen the girl these two months past.

HIGGINS. Then how did you know she was here?

DOOLITTLE [*"most musical, most melancholy"*] I'll tell you, Governor, if you'll only let me get a word in. I'm willing to tell you. I'm wanting to tell you. I'm waiting to tell you.

HIGGINS. Pickering: this chap has a certain natural gift of rhetoric. Observe the rhythm of his native woodnotes wild. "I'm willing to tell you: I'm wanting to tell you: I'm waiting to tell you." Sentimental rhetoric! That's the Welsh strain in him. It also accounts for his mendacity and dishonesty.

PICKERING. Oh, PLEASE, Higgins: I'm west country myself. [*To Doolittle*] How did you know the girl was here if you didn't send her?

DOOLITTLE. It was like this, Governor. The girl took a boy in the taxi to give him a jaunt. Son of her landlady, he is. He hung about on the chance of her giving him another ride home. Well, she sent him back for her luggage when she heard you was willing for her to stop here. I met the boy at the corner of Long Acre and Endell Street.

HIGGINS. Public house. Yes?

DOOLITTLE. The poor man's club, Governor: why shouldn't I?

PICKERING. Do let him tell his story, Higgins.

DOOLITTLE. He told me what was up. And I ask you, what was my feelings and my duty as a father? I says to the boy, "You bring me the luggage," I says—

PICKERING. Why didn't you go for it yourself?

DOOLITTLE. Landlady wouldn't have trusted me with it, Governor. She's that kind of woman: you know. I had to give the boy a penny afore he trusted me with it, the little swine. I brought it to her just to oblige you like, and make myself agreeable. That's all.

HIGGINS. How much luggage?

DOOLITTLE. Musical instrument, Governor. A few pictures, a trifle of jewelry, and a bird-cage. She said she didn't want no clothes. What was I to think from that, Governor? I ask you as a parent what was I to think?

HIGGINS. So you came to rescue her from worse than death, eh?

DOOLITTLE [*appreciatively: relieved at being understood*] Just so, Governor. That's right.

PICKERING. But why did you bring her luggage if you intended to take her away?

DOOLITTLE. Have I said a word about taking her away? Have I now?

HIGGINS [*determinedly*] You're going to take her away, double quick. [*He crosses to the hearth and rings the bell*].

DOOLITTLE [*rising*] No, Governor. Don't say that. I'm not the man to stand in my girl's light. Here's a career opening for her, as you might say; and—

Mrs. Pearce opens the door and awaits orders.

HIGGINS. Mrs. Pearce: this is Eliza's father. He has come to take her away. Give her to him. [*He goes back to the piano, with an air of washing his hands of the whole affair*].

DOOLITTLE. No. This is a misunderstanding. Listen here—

MRS. PEARCE. He can't take her away, Mr. Higgins: how can he? You told me to burn her clothes.

DOOLITTLE. That's right. I can't carry the girl through the streets like a blooming monkey, can I? I put it to you.

HIGGINS. You have put it to me that you want your daughter. Take your daughter. If she has no clothes go out and buy her some.

DOOLITTLE [*desperate*] Where's the clothes she come in? Did I burn them or did your missus here?

MRS. PEARCE. I am the housekeeper, if you please. I have sent for some clothes for your girl. When they come you can take her away. You can wait in the kitchen. This way, please.

Doolittle, much troubled, accompanies her to the door; then hesitates; finally turns confidentially to Higgins.

DOOLITTLE. Listen here, Governor. You and me is men of the world, ain't we?

HIGGINS. Oh! Men of the world, are we? You'd better go, Mrs. Pearce.

MRS. PEARCE. I think so, indeed, sir. [*She goes, with dignity*].

PICKERING. The floor is yours, Mr. Doolittle.

DOOLITTLE [*to Pickering*] I thank you, Governor. [*To Higgins, who takes refuge on the piano bench, a little overwhelmed by the proximity of his visitor; for Doolittle has a professional flavor of dust about him*]. Well, the truth is, I've taken a sort of fancy to you, Governor; and if you want the girl, I'm not so set on having her back home again but what I might be open to an arrangement. Regarded in the light of a young woman, she's a fine handsome girl. As a daughter she's not worth her keep; and so I tell you straight. All I ask is my rights as a father; and you're the last man alive to expect me to let her go for nothing; for I can see you're one of the straight sort, Governor. Well, what's a five pound note to you? And what's Eliza to me? [*He returns to his chair and sits down judicially*].

PICKERING. I think you ought to know, Doolittle, that Mr. Higgins's intentions are entirely honorable.

DOOLITTLE. Course they are, Governor. If I thought they wasn't, I'd ask fifty.

HIGGINS [*revolted*] Do you mean to say, you callous rascal, that you would sell your daughter for 50 pounds?

DOOLITTLE. Not in a general way I wouldn't; but to oblige a gentleman like you I'd do a good deal, I do assure you.

PICKERING. Have you no morals, man?

DOOLITTLE [*unabashed*] Can't afford them, Governor. Neither could you if you was as poor as me. Not that I mean any harm, you know. But if Liza is going to have a bit out of this, why not me too?

HIGGINS [*troubled*] I don't know what to do, Pickering. There can be no question that as a matter of morals it's a positive crime to give this chap a farthing. And yet I feel a sort of rough justice in his claim.

DOOLITTLE. That's it, Governor. That's all I say. A father's heart, as it were.

PICKERING. Well, I know the feeling; but really it seems hardly right—

DOOLITTLE. Don't say that, Governor. Don't look at it that way. What am I, Governors both? I ask you, what am I? I'm one of the undeserving poor: that's what I am. Think of what that means to a man. It means that he's up agen middle class morality all the time. If there's anything going, and I put in for a bit of it, it's always the same story: "You're undeserving; so you can't have it." But my needs is as great as the most deserving widow's that ever got money out of six different charities in one week for the death of the same husband. I don't need less than a deserving man: I need more. I don't eat less hearty than him; and I drink a lot more. I want a bit of amusement, cause I'm a thinking man. I want cheerfulness and a song and a band when I feel low. Well, they charge me just the same for everything as they charge the deserving. What is middle class morality? Just an excuse for never giving me anything. Therefore, I ask you, as two gentlemen, not to play that game on me. I'm playing straight with you. I ain't pretending to be deserving. I'm undeserving; and I mean to go on being undeserving. I like it; and that's the truth. Will you take advantage of a man's nature to do him out of the price of his own daughter what he's brought up and fed and clothed by the sweat of his brow until she's growed big enough to be interesting to you two gentlemen? Is five pounds unreasonable? I put it to you; and I leave it to you.

HIGGINS [*rising, and going over to Pickering*] Pickering: if we were to take this man in hand for three months, he could choose between a seat in the Cabinet and a popular pulpit in Wales.

PICKERING. What do you say to that, Doolittle?

DOOLITTLE. Not me, Governor, thank you kindly. I've heard all the preachers and all the prime ministers—for I'm a thinking man and game for politics or religion or social reform same as all the other amusements—and I tell you it's a dog's life anyway you look at it. Undeserving poverty is my line. Taking one station in society with another, it's—it's—well, it's the only one that has any ginger in it, to my taste.

HIGGINS. I suppose we must give him a fiver.

PICKERING. He'll make a bad use of it, I'm afraid.

DOOLITTLE. Not me, Governor, so help me I won't. Don't you be afraid that I'll save it and spare it and live idle on it. There won't be a penny of it left by Monday: I'll have to go to work same as if I'd never had it. It won't pauperize me, you bet. Just one good spree for myself and the missus, giving pleasure to ourselves and employment to others, and satisfaction to you to think it's not been throwed away. You couldn't spend it better.

HIGGINS [*taking out his pocket book and coming between Doolittle and the piano*] This is irresistible. Let's give him ten. [*He offers two notes to the dustman*].

DOOLITTLE. No, Governor. She wouldn't have the heart to spend ten; and perhaps I shouldn't neither. Ten pounds is a lot of money: it makes a man feel prudent like; and then goodbye to happiness. You give me what I ask you, Governor: not a penny more, and not a penny less.

PICKERING. Why don't you marry that missus of yours? I rather draw the line at encouraging that sort of immorality.

DOOLITTLE. Tell her so, Governor: tell her so. I'm willing. It's me that suffers by it. I've no hold on her. I got to be agreeable to her. I got to give her presents. I got to buy her clothes something sinful. I'm a slave to that woman, Governor, just because I'm not her lawful husband. And she knows it too. Catch her marrying me! Take my advice, Governor: marry Eliza while she's young and don't know no better. If you don't you'll be sorry for it after. If you do, she'll be sorry for it after; but better you than her, because you're a man, and she's only a woman and don't know how to be happy anyhow.

HIGGINS. Pickering: if we listen to this man another minute, we shall have no convictions left. [*To Doolittle*] Five pounds I think you said.

DOOLITTLE. Thank you kindly, Governor.

HIGGINS. You're sure you won't take ten?

DOOLITTLE. Not now. Another time, Governor.

HIGGINS [*handing him a five-pound note*] Here you are.

DOOLITTLE. Thank you, Governor. Good morning.

[*He hurries to the door, anxious to get away with his booty. When he opens it he is confronted with a dainty and exquisitely clean young Japanese lady in a simple blue cotton kimono printed cunningly with small white jasmine blossoms. Mrs. Pearce is with her. He gets out of her way deferentially and apologizes*]. Beg pardon, miss.

THE JAPANESE LADY. Garn! Don't you know your own daughter?

DOOLITTLE [*exclaiming*] Bly me! it's Eliza!
HIGGINS {simul- } What's that! This!
PICKERING {taneously }By Jove!

LIZA. Don't I look silly?

HIGGINS. Silly?

MRS. PEARCE [*at the door*] Now, Mr. Higgins, please don't say anything to make the girl conceited about herself.

HIGGINS [*conscientiously*] Oh! Quite right, Mrs. Pearce. [*To Eliza*] Yes: damned silly.

MRS. PEARCE. Please, sir.

HIGGINS [*correcting himself*] I mean extremely silly.

LIZA. I should look all right with my hat on. [*She takes up her hat; puts it on; and walks across the room to the fireplace with a fashionable air*].

HIGGINS. A new fashion, by George! And it ought to look horrible!

DOOLITTLE [*with fatherly pride*] Well, I never thought she'd clean up as good looking as that, Governor. She's a credit to me, ain't she?

LIZA. I tell you, it's easy to clean up here. Hot and cold water on tap, just as much as you like, there is. Woolly towels, there is; and a towel horse so hot, it burns your fingers. Soft brushes to scrub yourself, and a wooden bowl of soap smelling like primroses. Now I know why ladies is so clean. Washing's a treat for them. Wish they saw what it is for the like of me!

HIGGINS. I'm glad the bath-room met with your approval.

LIZA. It didn't: not all of it; and I don't care who hears me say it. Mrs. Pearce knows.

HIGGINS. What was wrong, Mrs. Pearce?

MRS. PEARCE [*blandly*] Oh, nothing, sir. It doesn't matter.

LIZA. I had a good mind to break it. I didn't know which way to look. But I hung a towel over it, I did.

HIGGINS. Over what?

MRS. PEARCE. Over the looking-glass, sir.

HIGGINS. Doolittle: you have brought your daughter up too strictly.

DOOLITTLE. Me! I never brought her up at all, except to give her a lick of a strap now and again. Don't put it on me, Governor. She ain't accustomed to it, you see: that's all. But she'll soon pick up your free-and-easy ways.

LIZA. I'm a good girl, I am; and I won't pick up no free and easy ways.

HIGGINS. Eliza: if you say again that you're a good girl, your father shall take you home.

LIZA. Not him. You don't know my father. All he come here for was to touch you for some money to get drunk on.

DOOLITTLE. Well, what else would I want money for? To put into the plate in church, I suppose. [*She puts out her tongue at him. He is so incensed by this that Pickering presently finds it necessary to step between them*]. Don't you give me none of your lip; and don't let me hear you giving this gentleman any of it neither, or you'll hear from me about it. See?

HIGGINS. Have you any further advice to give her before you go, Doolittle? Your blessing, for instance.

DOOLITTLE. No, Governor: I ain't such a mug as to put up my children to all I know myself. Hard enough to hold them in without that. If you want Eliza's mind improved, Governor, you do it yourself with a strap. So long, gentlemen. [*He turns to go*].

HIGGINS [*impressively*] Stop. You'll come regularly to see your daughter. It's your duty, you know. My brother is a clergyman; and he could help you in your talks with her.

DOOLITTLE [*evasively*] Certainly. I'll come, Governor. Not just this week, because I have a job at a distance. But later on you may depend on me. Afternoon, gentlemen. Afternoon, ma'am. [*He takes off his hat to Mrs. Pearce, who disdains the salutation and goes out. He winks at Higgins, thinking him probably a fellow sufferer from Mrs. Pearce's difficult disposition, and follows her*].

LIZA. Don't you believe the old liar. He'd as soon you set a bull-dog on him as a clergyman. You won't see him again in a hurry.

HIGGINS. I don't want to, Eliza. Do you?

LIZA. Not me. I don't want never to see him again, I don't. He's a disgrace to me, he is, collecting dust, instead of working at his trade.

PICKERING. What is his trade, Eliza?

LIZA. Talking money out of other people's pockets into his own. His proper trade's a navvy; and he works at it sometimes too—for exercise—and earns good money at it. Ain't you going to call me Miss Doolittle any more?

PICKERING. I beg your pardon, Miss Doolittle. It was a slip of the tongue.

LIZA. Oh, I don't mind; only it sounded so genteel. I should just like to take a taxi to the corner of Tottenham Court Road and get out there and tell it to wait for me, just to put the girls in their place a bit. I wouldn't speak to them, you know.

PICKERING. Better wait til we get you something really fashionable.

HIGGINS. Besides, you shouldn't cut your old friends now that you have risen in the world. That's what we call snobbery.

LIZA. You don't call the like of them my friends now, I should hope. They've took it out of me often enough with their ridicule when they had the chance; and now I mean to get a bit of my own back. But if I'm to have fashionable clothes, I'll wait. I should like to have some. Mrs. Pearce says you're going to give me some to wear in bed at night different to what I wear in the daytime; but it do seem a waste of money when you could get something to show. Besides, I never could fancy changing into cold things on a winter night.

MRS. PEARCE [*coming back*] Now, Eliza. The new things have come for you to try on.

LIZA. Ah—ow—oo—ooh! [*She rushes out*].

MRS. PEARCE [*following her*] Oh, don't rush about like that, girl [*She shuts the door behind her*].

HIGGINS. Pickering: we have taken on a stiff job.

PICKERING [*with conviction*] Higgins: we have.

ACT III

It is Mrs. Higgins's at-home day. Nobody has yet arrived. Her drawing-room, in a flat on Chelsea embankment, has three windows looking on the river; and the ceiling is not so lofty as it would be in an older house of the same pretension. The windows are open, giving access to a balcony with flowers in pots. If you stand with your face to the windows, you have the fireplace on your left and the door in the right-hand wall close to the corner nearest the windows.

Mrs. Higgins was brought up on Morris and Burne Jones; and her room, which is very unlike her son's room in Wimpole Street, is not crowded with furniture and little tables and nicknacks. In the middle of the room there is a big ottoman; and this, with the carpet, the Morris wall-papers, and the Morris chintz window curtains and brocade covers of the ottoman and its cushions, supply all the ornament, and are much too handsome to be hidden by odds and ends of useless things. A few good oil-paintings from the exhibitions in the Grosvenor Gallery thirty years ago (the Burne Jones, not the Whistler side of them) are on the walls. The only landscape is a Cecil Lawson on the scale of a Rubens. There is a portrait of Mrs. Higgins as she was when she defied fashion in her youth in one of the beautiful Rossettian costumes which, when caricatured by people who did not understand, led to the absurdities of popular estheticism in the eighteen-seventies.

In the corner diagonally opposite the door Mrs. Higgins, now over sixty and long past taking the trouble to dress out of the fashion, sits writing at an elegantly simple writing-table with a bell button within reach of her hand. There is a Chippendale chair further back in the room between her and the window nearest her side. At the other side of the room, further forward, is an Elizabethan chair roughly carved in the taste of Inigo Jones. On the same side a piano in a decorated case. The corner between the fireplace and the window is occupied by a divan cushioned in Morris chintz.

It is between four and five in the afternoon.

The door is opened violently; and Higgins enters with his hat on.

MRS. HIGGINS [*dismayed*] Henry! [*scolding him*] What are you doing here to-day? It is my at home day: you promised not to come. [*As he bends to kiss her, she takes his hat off, and presents it to him*].

HIGGINS. Oh bother! [*He throws the hat down on the table*].

MRS. HIGGINS. Go home at once.

HIGGINS [*kissing her*] I know, mother. I came on purpose.

MRS. HIGGINS. But you mustn't. I'm serious, Henry. You offend all my friends: they stop coming whenever they meet you.

HIGGINS. Nonsense! I know I have no small talk; but people don't mind. [*He sits on the settee*].

MRS. HIGGINS. Oh! don't they? Small talk indeed! What about your large talk? Really, dear, you mustn't stay.

HIGGINS. I must. I've a job for you. A phonetic job.

MRS. HIGGINS. No use, dear. I'm sorry; but I can't get round your vowels; and though I like to get pretty postcards in your patent shorthand, I always have to read the copies in ordinary writing you so thoughtfully send me.

HIGGINS. Well, this isn't a phonetic job.

MRS. HIGGINS. You said it was.

HIGGINS. Not your part of it. I've picked up a girl.

MRS. HIGGINS. Does that mean that some girl has picked you up?

HIGGINS. Not at all. I don't mean a love affair.

MRS. HIGGINS. What a pity!

HIGGINS. Why?

MRS. HIGGINS. Well, you never fall in love with anyone under forty-five. When will you discover that there are some rather nice-looking young women about?

HIGGINS. Oh, I can't be bothered with young women. My idea of a loveable woman is something as like you as possible. I shall never get into the way of seriously liking young women: some habits lie too deep to be changed. [*Rising abruptly and walking about, jingling his money and his keys in his trouser pockets*] Besides, they're all idiots.

MRS. HIGGINS. Do you know what you would do if you really loved me, Henry?

HIGGINS. Oh bother! What? Marry, I suppose?

MRS. HIGGINS. No. Stop fidgeting and take your hands out of your pockets. [*With a gesture of despair, he obeys and sits down again*]. That's a good boy. Now tell me about the girl.

HIGGINS. She's coming to see you.

MRS. HIGGINS. I don't remember asking her.

HIGGINS. You didn't. I asked her. If you'd known her you wouldn't have asked her.

MRS. HIGGINS. Indeed! Why?

HIGGINS. Well, it's like this. She's a common flower girl. I picked her off the kerbstone.

MRS. HIGGINS. And invited her to my at-home!

HIGGINS [*rising and coming to her to coax her*] Oh, that'll be all right. I've taught her to speak properly; and she has strict orders as to her behavior. She's to keep to two subjects: the weather and everybody's health—Fine day and How do you do, you know—and not to let herself go on things in general. That will be safe.

MRS. HIGGINS. Safe! To talk about our health! about our insides! perhaps about our outsides! How could you be so silly, Henry?

HIGGINS [*impatiently*] Well, she must talk about something. [*He controls himself and sits down again*]. Oh, she'll be all right: don't you fuss. Pickering is in it with me. I've a sort of bet on that I'll pass her off as a duchess in six months. I started on her some months ago; and she's getting on like a house on fire. I shall win my bet. She has a quick ear; and she's been easier to teach than my middle-class pupils because she's had to learn a complete new language. She talks English almost as you talk French.

MRS. HIGGINS. That's satisfactory, at all events.

HIGGINS. Well, it is and it isn't.

MRS. HIGGINS. What does that mean?

HIGGINS. You see, I've got her pronunciation all right; but you have to consider not only how a girl pronounces, but what she pronounces; and that's where—

They are interrupted by the parlor-maid, announcing guests.

THE PARLOR-MAID. Mrs. and Miss Eynsford Hill. [*She withdraws*].

HIGGINS. Oh Lord! [*He rises; snatches his hat from the table; and makes for the door; but before he reaches it his mother introduces him*].

Mrs. and Miss Eynsford Hill are the mother and daughter who sheltered from the rain in Covent Garden. The mother is well bred, quiet, and has the habitual anxiety of straitened means. The daughter has acquired a gay air of being very much at home in society: the bravado of genteel poverty.

MRS. EYNSFORD HILL [*to Mrs. Higgins*] How do you do? [*They shake hands*].

MISS EYNSFORD HILL. How d'you do? [*She shakes*].

MRS. HIGGINS [*introducing*] My son Henry.

MRS. EYNSFORD HILL. Your celebrated son! I have so longed to meet you, Professor Higgins.

HIGGINS [*glumly, making no movement in her direction*] Delighted. [*He backs against the piano and bows brusquely*].

Miss EYNSFORD HILL [*going to him with confident familiarity*] How do you do?

HIGGINS [*staring at her*] I've seen you before somewhere. I haven't the ghost of a notion where; but I've heard your voice. [*Drearily*] It doesn't matter. You'd better sit down.

MRS. HIGGINS. I'm sorry to say that my celebrated son has no manners. You mustn't mind him.

MISS EYNSFORD HILL [*gaily*] I don't. [*She sits in the Elizabethan chair*].

MRS. EYNSFORD HILL [*a little bewildered*] Not at all. [*She sits on the ottoman between her daughter and Mrs. Higgins, who has turned her chair away from the writing-table*].

HIGGINS. Oh, have I been rude? I didn't mean to be. [*He goes to the central window, through which, with his back to the company, he contemplates the river and the flowers in Battersea Park on the opposite bank as if they were a frozen dessert.*]

The parlor-maid returns, ushering in Pickering.

THE PARLOR-MAID. Colonel Pickering [*She withdraws*].

PICKERING. How do you do, Mrs. Higgins?

MRS. HIGGINS. So glad you've come. Do you know Mrs. Eynsford Hill—Miss Eynsford Hill? [*Exchange of bows. The Colonel brings the Chippendale chair a little forward between Mrs. Hill and Mrs. Higgins, and sits down*].

PICKERING. Has Henry told you what we've come for?

HIGGINS [*over his shoulder*] We were interrupted: damn it!

MRS. HIGGINS. Oh Henry, Henry, really!

MRS. EYNSFORD HILL [*half rising*] Are we in the way?

MRS. HIGGINS [*rising and making her sit down again*] No, no. You couldn't have come more fortunately: we want you to meet a friend of ours.

HIGGINS [*turning hopefully*] Yes, by George! We want two or three people. You'll do as well as anybody else.

The parlor-maid returns, ushering Freddy.

THE PARLOR-MAID. Mr. Eynsford Hill.

HIGGINS [*almost audibly, past endurance*] God of Heaven! another of them.

FREDDY [*shaking hands with Mrs. Higgins*] Ahdedo?

MRS. HIGGINS. Very good of you to come. [*Introducing*] Colonel Pickering.

FREDDY [*bowing*] Ahdedo?

MRS. HIGGINS. I don't think you know my son, Professor Higgins.

FREDDY [*going to Higgins*] Ahdedo?

HIGGINS [*looking at him much as if he were a pickpocket*] I'll take my oath I've met you before somewhere. Where was it?

FREDDY. I don't think so.

HIGGINS [*resignedly*] It don't matter, anyhow. Sit down. He shakes Freddy's hand, and almost slings him on the ottoman with his face to the windows; then comes round to the other side of it.

HIGGINS. Well, here we are, anyhow! [*He sits down on the ottoman next Mrs. Eynsford Hill, on her left.*] And now, what the devil are we going to talk about until Eliza comes?

MRS. HIGGINS. Henry: you are the life and soul of the Royal Society's soirees; but really you're rather trying on more commonplace occasions.

HIGGINS. Am I? Very sorry. [*Beaming suddenly*] I suppose I am, you know. [*Uproariously*] Ha, ha!

MISS EYNSFORD HILL [*who considers Higgins quite eligible matrimonially*] I sympathize. I haven't any small talk. If people would only be frank and say what they really think!

HIGGINS [*relapsing into gloom*] Lord forbid!

MRS. EYNSFORD HILL [*taking up her daughter's cue*] But why?

HIGGINS. What they think they ought to think is bad enough, Lord knows; but what they really think would break up the whole show. Do you suppose it would be really agreeable if I were to come out now with what I really think?

MISS EYNSFORD HILL [*gaily*] Is it so very cynical?

HIGGINS. Cynical! Who the dickens said it was cynical? I mean it wouldn't be decent.

MRS. EYNSFORD HILL [*seriously*] Oh! I'm sure you don't mean that, Mr. Higgins.

HIGGINS. You see, we're all savages, more or less. We're supposed to be civilized and cultured—to know all about poetry and philosophy and art and science, and so on; but how many of us know even the meanings of these names? [*To Miss Hill*] What do you know of poetry? [*To Mrs. Hill*] What do you know of science? [*Indicating Freddy*] What does he know of art or science or anything else? What the devil do you imagine I know of philosophy?

MRS. HIGGINS [*warningly*] Or of manners, Henry?

THE PARLOR-MAID [*opening the door*] Miss Doolittle. [*She withdraws*].

HIGGINS [*rising hastily and running to Mrs. Higgins*] Here she is, mother. [*He stands on tiptoe and makes signs over his mother's head to Eliza to indicate to her which lady is her hostess*].

Eliza, who is exquisitely dressed, produces an impression of such remarkable distinction and beauty as she enters that they all rise, quite flustered. Guided by Higgins's signals, she comes to Mrs. Higgins with studied grace.

LIZA [*speaking with pedantic correctness of pronunciation and great beauty of tone*] How do you do, Mrs. Higgins? [*She gasps slightly in making sure of the H in Higgins, but is quite successful*]. Mr. Higgins told me I might come.

MRS. HIGGINS [*cordially*] Quite right: I'm very glad indeed to see you.

PICKERING. How do you do, Miss Doolittle?

LIZA [*shaking hands with him*] Colonel Pickering, is it not?

MRS. EYNSFORD HILL. I feel sure we have met before, Miss Doolittle. I remember your eyes.

LIZA. How do you do? [*She sits down on the ottoman gracefully in the place just left vacant by Higgins*].

MRS. EYNSFORD HILL [*introducing*] My daughter Clara.

LIZA. How do you do?

CLARA [*impulsively*] How do you do? [*She sits down on the ottoman beside Eliza, devouring her with her eyes*].

FREDDY [*coming to their side of the ottoman*] I've certainly had the pleasure.

MRS. EYNSFORD HILL [*introducing*] My son Freddy.

LIZA. How do you do?

Freddy bows and sits down in the Elizabethan chair, infatuated.

HIGGINS [*suddenly*] By George, yes: it all comes back to me! [*They stare at him*]. Covent Garden! [*Lamentably*] What a damned thing!

MRS. HIGGINS. Henry, please! [*He is about to sit on the edge of the table*]. Don't sit on my writing-table: you'll break it.

HIGGINS [*sulkily*] Sorry.

He goes to the divan, stumbling into the fender and over the fire-irons on his way; extricating himself with muttered imprecations; and finishing his disastrous journey by throwing himself so impatiently on the divan that he almost breaks it. Mrs. Higgins looks at him, but controls herself and says nothing.

A long and painful pause ensues.

MRS. HIGGINS [*at last, conversationally*] Will it rain, do you think?

LIZA. The shallow depression in the west of these islands is likely to move slowly in an easterly direction. There are no indications of any great change in the barometrical situation.

FREDDY. Ha! ha! how awfully funny!

LIZA. What is wrong with that, young man? I bet I got it right.

FREDDY. Killing!

MRS. EYNSFORD HILL. I'm sure I hope it won't turn cold. There's so much influenza about. It runs right through our whole family regularly every spring.

LIZA [*darkly*] My aunt died of influenza: so they said.

MRS. EYNSFORD HILL [*clicks her tongue sympathetically*]!!!

LIZA [*in the same tragic tone*] But it's my belief they done the old woman in.

MRS. HIGGINS [*puzzled*] Done her in?

LIZA. Y-e-e-e-es, Lord love you! Why should she die of influenza? She come through diphtheria right enough the year before. I saw her with my own eyes. Fairly blue with it, she was. They all thought she was dead; but my father he kept ladling gin down her throat til she came to so sudden that she bit the bowl off the spoon.

MRS. EYNSFORD HILL [*startled*] Dear me!

LIZA [*piling up the indictment*] What call would a woman with that strength in her have to die of influenza? What become of her new straw hat that should have come to me? Somebody pinched it; and what I say is, them as pinched it done her in.

MRS. EYNSFORD HILL. What does doing her in mean?

HIGGINS [*hastily*] Oh, that's the new small talk. To do a person in means to kill them.

MRS. EYNSFORD HILL [*to Eliza, horrified*] You surely don't believe that your aunt was killed?

LIZA. Do I not! Them she lived with would have killed her for a hat-pin, let alone a hat.

MRS. EYNSFORD HILL. But it can't have been right for your father to pour spirits down her throat like that. It might have killed her.

LIZA. Not her. Gin was mother's milk to her. Besides, he'd poured so much down his own throat that he knew the good of it.

MRS. EYNSFORD HILL. Do you mean that he drank?

LIZA. Drank! My word! Something chronic.

MRS. EYNSFORD HILL. How dreadful for you!

LIZA. Not a bit. It never did him no harm what I could see. But then he did not keep it up regular. [*Cheerfully*] On the burst, as you might say, from time to time. And always more agreeable when he had a drop in. When he was out of work, my mother used to give him fourpence and tell him to go out and not come back until he'd drunk himself cheerful and loving-like. There's lots of women has to make their husbands drunk to make them fit to live with. [*Now quite at her ease*] You see, it's like this. If a man has a bit of a conscience, it always takes him when he's sober; and then it makes him low-spirited. A drop of booze just takes that off and makes him happy. [*To Freddy, who is in convulsions of suppressed laughter*] Here! what are you sniggering at?

FREDDY. The new small talk. You do it so awfully well.

LIZA. If I was doing it proper, what was you laughing at? [*To Higgins*] Have I said anything I oughtn't?

MRS. HIGGINS [*interposing*] Not at all, Miss Doolittle.

LIZA. Well, that's a mercy, anyhow. [*Expansively*] What I always say is—

HIGGINS [*rising and looking at his watch*] Ahem!

LIZA [*looking round at him; taking the hint; and rising*] Well: I must go. [*They all rise. Freddy goes to the door*]. So pleased to have met you. Good-bye. [*She shakes hands with Mrs. Higgins*].

MRS. HIGGINS. Good-bye.

LIZA. Good-bye, Colonel Pickering.

PICKERING. Good-bye, Miss Doolittle. [*They shake hands*].

LIZA [*nodding to the others*] Good-bye, all.

FREDDY [*opening the door for her*] Are you walking across the Park, Miss Doolittle? If so—

LIZA. Walk! Not bloody likely. [*Sensation*]. I am going in a taxi. [*She goes out*].

Pickering gasps and sits down. Freddy goes out on the balcony to catch another glimpse of Eliza.

MRS. EYNSFORD HILL [*suffering from shock*] Well, I really can't get used to the new ways.

CLARA [*throwing herself discontentedly into the Elizabethan chair*]. Oh, it's all right, mamma, quite right. People will think we never go anywhere or see anybody if you are so old-fashioned.

MRS. EYNSFORD HILL. I daresay I am very old-fashioned; but I do hope you won't begin using that expression, Clara. I have got accustomed to hear you talking about men as rotters, and calling everything filthy and beastly; though I do think it horrible and unladylike. But this last is really too much. Don't you think so, Colonel Pickering?

PICKERING. Don't ask me. I've been away in India for several years; and manners have changed so much that I sometimes don't know whether I'm at a respectable dinner-table or in a ship's forecastle.

CLARA. It's all a matter of habit. There's no right or wrong in it. Nobody means anything by it. And it's so quaint, and gives such a smart emphasis to things that are not in themselves very witty. I find the new small talk delightful and quite innocent.

MRS. EYNSFORD HILL [*rising*] Well, after that, I think it's time for us to go.

Pickering and Higgins rise.

CLARA [*rising*] Oh yes: we have three at homes to go to still. Good-bye, Mrs. Higgins. Good-bye, Colonel Pickering. Good-bye, Professor Higgins.

HIGGINS [*coming grimly at her from the divan, and accompanying her to the door*] Good-bye. Be sure you try on that small talk at the three at-homes. Don't be nervous about it. Pitch it in strong.

CLARA [*all smiles*] I will. Good-bye. Such nonsense, all this early Victorian prudery!

HIGGINS [*tempting her*] Such damned nonsense!

CLARA. Such bloody nonsense!

MRS. EYNSFORD HILL [*convulsively*] Clara!

CLARA. Ha! ha! [*She goes out radiant, conscious of being thoroughly up to date, and is heard descending the stairs in a stream of silvery laughter*].

FREDDY [*to the heavens at large*] Well, I ask you [*He gives it up, and comes to Mrs. Higgins*]. Good-bye.

MRS. HIGGINS [*shaking hands*] Good-bye. Would you like to meet Miss Doolittle again?

FREDDY [*eagerly*] Yes, I should, most awfully.

MRS. HIGGINS. Well, you know my days.

FREDDY. Yes. Thanks awfully. Good-bye. [*He goes out*].

MRS. EYNSFORD HILL. Good-bye, Mr. Higgins.

HIGGINS. Good-bye. Good-bye.

MRS. EYNSFORD HILL [*to Pickering*] It's no use. I shall never be able to bring myself to use that word.

PICKERING. Don't. It's not compulsory, you know. You'll get on quite well without it.

MRS. EYNSFORD HILL. Only, Clara is so down on me if I am not positively reeking with the latest slang. Good-bye.

PICKERING. Good-bye [*They shake hands*].

MRS. EYNSFORD HILL [*to Mrs. Higgins*] You mustn't mind Clara. [*Pickering, catching from her lowered tone that this is not meant for him to hear, discreetly joins Higgins at the window*]. We're so poor! and she gets so few parties, poor child! She doesn't quite know. [*Mrs. Higgins, seeing that her eyes are moist, takes her hand sympathetically and goes with her to the door*]. But the boy is nice. Don't you think so?

MRS. HIGGINS. Oh, quite nice. I shall always be delighted to see him.

MRS. EYNSFORD HILL. Thank you, dear. Good-bye. [*She goes out*].

HIGGINS [*eagerly*] Well? Is Eliza presentable [*he swoops on his mother and drags her to the ottoman, where she sits down in Eliza's place with her son on her left*]?

Pickering returns to his chair on her right.

MRS. HIGGINS. You silly boy, of course she's not presentable. She's a triumph of your art and of her dressmaker's; but if you suppose for a moment that she doesn't give herself away in every sentence she utters, you must be perfectly cracked about her.

PICKERING. But don't you think something might be done? I mean something to eliminate the sanguinary element from her conversation.

MRS. HIGGINS. Not as long as she is in Henry's hands.

HIGGINS [*aggrieved*] Do you mean that my language is improper?

MRS. HIGGINS. No, dearest: it would be quite proper—say on a canal barge; but it would not be proper for her at a garden party.

HIGGINS [*deeply injured*] Well I must say—

PICKERING [*interrupting him*] Come, Higgins: you must learn to know yourself. I haven't heard such language as yours since we used to review the volunteers in Hyde Park twenty years ago.

HIGGINS [*sulkily*] Oh, well, if you say so, I suppose I don't always talk like a bishop.

MRS. HIGGINS [*quieting Henry with a touch*] Colonel Pickering: will you tell me what is the exact state of things in Wimpole Street?

PICKERING [*cheerfully: as if this completely changed the subject*] Well, I have come to live there with Henry. We work together at my Indian Dialects; and we think it more convenient—

MRS. HIGGINS. Quite so. I know all about that: it's an excellent arrangement. But where does this girl live?

HIGGINS. With us, of course. Where would she live?

MRS. HIGGINS. But on what terms? Is she a servant? If not, what is she?

PICKERING [*slowly*] I think I know what you mean, Mrs. Higgins.

HIGGINS. Well, dash me if I do! I've had to work at the girl every day for months to get her to her present pitch. Besides, she's useful. She knows where my things are, and remembers my appointments and so forth.

MRS. HIGGINS. How does your housekeeper get on with her?

HIGGINS. Mrs. Pearce? Oh, she's jolly glad to get so much taken off her hands; for before Eliza came, she had to have to find things and remind me of my appointments. But she's got some silly bee in her bonnet about Eliza. She keeps saying "You don't think, sir": doesn't she, Pick?

PICKERING. Yes: that's the formula. "You don't think, sir." That's the end of every conversation about Eliza.

HIGGINS. As if I ever stop thinking about the girl and her confounded vowels and consonants. I'm worn out, thinking about her, and watching her lips and her teeth and her tongue, not to mention her soul, which is the quaintest of the lot.

MRS. HIGGINS. You certainly are a pretty pair of babies, playing with your live doll.

HIGGINS. Playing! The hardest job I ever tackled: make no mistake about that, mother. But you have no idea how frightfully interesting it is to take a human being and change her into a quite different human being by creating a new speech for her. It's filling up the deepest gulf that separates class from class and soul from soul.

PICKERING [*drawing his chair closer to Mrs. Higgins and bending over to her eagerly*] Yes: it's enormously interesting. I assure you, Mrs. Higgins, we take Eliza very seriously. Every week—every day almost—there is some new change. [*Closer again*]

We keep records of every stage—dozens of gramophone disks and photographs—

HIGGINS [*assailing her at the other ear*] Yes, by George: it's the most absorbing experiment I ever tackled. She regularly fills our lives up; doesn't she, Pick?

PICKERING. We're always talking Eliza.

HIGGINS. Teaching Eliza.

PICKERING. Dressing Eliza.

MRS. HIGGINS. What!

HIGGINS. Inventing new Elizas.

Higgins and Pickering, speaking together:

HIGGINS. You know, she has the most extraordinary quickness of ear:

PICKERING. I assure you, my dear Mrs. Higgins, that girl

HIGGINS. just like a parrot. I've tried her with every

PICKERING. is a genius. She can play the piano quite beautifully

HIGGINS. possible sort of sound that a human being can make—

PICKERING. We have taken her to classical concerts and to music

HIGGINS. Continental dialects, African dialects, Hottentot

PICKERING. halls; and it's all the same to her: she plays everything

HIGGINS. clicks, things it took me years to get hold of; and

PICKERING. she hears right off when she comes home, whether it's

HIGGINS. she picks them up like a shot, right away, as if she had

PICKERING. Beethoven and Brahms or Lehar and Lionel Morickton;

HIGGINS. been at it all her life.

PICKERING. though six months ago, she'd never as much as touched a piano.

MRS. HIGGINS [*putting her fingers in her ears, as they are by this time shouting one another down with an intolerable noise*] Sh—sh—sh—sh! [*They stop*].

PICKERING. I beg your pardon. [*He draws his chair back apologetically*].

HIGGINS. Sorry. When Pickering starts shouting nobody can get a word in edgeways.

MRS. HIGGINS. Be quiet, Henry. Colonel Pickering: don't you realize that when Eliza walked into Wimpole Street, something walked in with her?

PICKERING. Her father did. But Henry soon got rid of him.

MRS. HIGGINS. It would have been more to the point if her mother had. But as her mother didn't something else did.

PICKERING. But what?

MRS. HIGGINS [*unconsciously dating herself by the word*] A problem.

PICKERING. Oh, I see. The problem of how to pass her off as a lady.

HIGGINS. I'll solve that problem. I've half solved it already.

MRS. HIGGINS. No, you two infinitely stupid male creatures: the problem of what is to be done with her afterwards.

HIGGINS. I don't see anything in that. She can go her own way, with all the advantages I have given her.

MRS. HIGGINS. The advantages of that poor woman who was here just now! The manners and habits that disqualify a fine lady from earning her own living without giving her a fine lady's income! Is that what you mean?

PICKERING [*indulgently, being rather bored*] Oh, that will be all right, Mrs. Higgins. [*He rises to go*].

HIGGINS [*rising also*] We'll find her some light employment.

PICKERING. She's happy enough. Don't you worry about her. Good-bye. [*He shakes hands as if he were consoling a frightened child, and makes for the door*].

HIGGINS. Anyhow, there's no good bothering now. The thing's done. Good-bye, mother. [*He kisses her, and follows Pickering*].

PICKERING [*turning for a final consolation*] There are plenty of openings. We'll do what's right. Good-bye.

HIGGINS [*to Pickering as they go out together*] Let's take her to the Shakespear exhibition at Earls Court.

PICKERING. Yes: let's. Her remarks will be delicious.

HIGGINS. She'll mimic all the people for us when we get home.

PICKERING. Ripping. [*Both are heard laughing as they go downstairs*].

MRS. HIGGINS [*rises with an impatient bounce, and returns to her work at the writing-table. She sweeps a litter of disarranged papers out of her way; snatches a sheet of paper from her stationery case; and tries resolutely to write. At the third line she gives it up; flings down her pen; grips the table angrily and exclaims*] Oh, men! men!! men!!!

ACT IV

The Wimpole Street laboratory. Midnight. Nobody in the room. The clock on the mantelpiece strikes twelve. The fire is not alight: it is a summer night.

Presently Higgins and Pickering are heard on the stairs.

HIGGINS [*calling down to Pickering*] I say, Pick: lock up, will you. I shan't be going out again.

PICKERING. Right. Can Mrs. Pearce go to bed? We don't want anything more, do we?

HIGGINS. Lord, no!

Eliza opens the door and is seen on the lighted landing in opera cloak, brilliant evening dress, and diamonds, with fan, flowers, and all accessories. She comes to the hearth, and switches on the electric lights there. She is tired: her pallor contrasts strongly with her dark eyes and hair; and her expression is almost tragic. She takes off her cloak; puts her fan and flowers on the piano; and sits down on the bench, brooding and silent. Higgins, in evening dress, with overcoat and hat, comes in, carrying a smoking jacket which he has picked up downstairs. He takes off the hat and overcoat; throws them carelessly on the newspaper stand; disposes of his coat in the same way; puts on the smoking jacket; and throws himself wearily into the easy-chair at the hearth. Pickering, similarly attired, comes in. He also takes off his hat and overcoat, and is about to throw them on Higgins's when he hesitates.

PICKERING. I say: Mrs. Pearce will row if we leave these things lying about in the drawing-room.

HIGGINS. Oh, chuck them over the bannisters into the hall. She'll find them there in the morning and put them away all right. She'll think we were drunk.

PICKERING. We are, slightly. Are there any letters?

HIGGINS. I didn't look. [*Pickering takes the overcoats and hats and goes down stairs. Higgins begins half singing half yawning an air from La Fanciulla del Golden West. Suddenly he stops and exclaims*] I wonder where the devil my slippers are!

Eliza looks at him darkly; then leaves the room.

Higgins yawns again, and resumes his song. Pickering returns, with the contents of the letter-box in his hand.

PICKERING. Only circulars, and this coroneted billet-doux for you. [*He throws the circulars into the fender, and posts himself on the hearthrug, with his back to the grate*].

HIGGINS [*glancing at the billet-doux*] Money-lender. [*He throws the letter after the circulars*].

Eliza returns with a pair of large down-at-heel slippers. She places them on the carpet before Higgins, and sits as before without a word.

HIGGINS [*yawning again*] Oh Lord! What an evening! What a crew! What a silly tomfoollery! [*He raises his shoe to unlace it, and catches sight of the slippers. He stops unlacing and looks at them as if they had appeared there of their own accord*]. Oh! they're there, are they?

PICKERING [*stretching himself*] Well, I feel a bit tired. It's been a long day. The garden party, a dinner party, and the opera! Rather too much of a good thing. But you've won your bet, Higgins. Eliza did the trick, and something to spare, eh?

HIGGINS [*fervently*] Thank God it's over!

Eliza flinches violently; but they take no notice of her; and she recovers herself and sits stonily as before.

PICKERING. Were you nervous at the garden party? I was. Eliza didn't seem a bit nervous.

HIGGINS. Oh, she wasn't nervous. I knew she'd be all right. No, it's the strain of putting the job through all these months that has told on me. It was interesting enough at first, while we were at the phonetics; but after that I got deadly sick of it. If I hadn't backed myself to do it I should have chucked the whole thing up two months ago. It was a silly notion: the whole thing has been a bore.

PICKERING. Oh come! the garden party was frightfully exciting. My heart began beating like anything.

HIGGINS. Yes, for the first three minutes. But when I saw we were going to win hands down, I felt like a bear in a cage, hanging about doing nothing. The dinner was worse: sitting gorging there for over an hour, with nobody but a damned fool of a fashionable woman to talk to! I tell you, Pickering, never again for me. No more artificial duchesses. The whole thing has been simple purgatory.

PICKERING. You've never been broken in properly to the social routine. [*Strolling over to the piano*] I rather enjoy dipping into it occasionally myself: it makes me feel young again. Anyhow, it was a great success: an immense success. I was quite frightened once or twice because Eliza was doing it so well. You see, lots of the real people can't do it at all: they're such fools that they think style comes by nature to people in their position; and so they never learn. There's always something professional about doing a thing superlatively well.

HIGGINS. Yes: that's what drives me mad: the silly people don't know their own silly business. [*Rising*] However, it's over and done with; and now I can go to bed at last without dreading tomorrow.

Eliza's beauty becomes murderous.

PICKERING. I think I shall turn in too. Still, it's been a great occasion: a triumph for you. Good-night. [*He goes*].

HIGGINS [*following him*] Good-night. [*Over his shoulder, at the door*] Put out the lights, Eliza; and tell Mrs. Pearce not to make coffee for me in the morning: I'll take tea. [*He goes out*].

Eliza tries to control herself and feel indifferent as she rises and walks across to the hearth to switch off the lights. By the time she gets there she is on the point of screaming. She sits down in Higgins's chair and holds on hard to the arms. Finally she gives way and flings herself furiously on the floor raging.

HIGGINS [*in despairing wrath outside*] What the devil have I done with my slippers? [*He appears at the door*].

LIZA [*snatching up the slippers, and hurling them at him one after the other with all her force*] There are your slippers. And there. Take your slippers; and may you never have a day's luck with them!

HIGGINS [*astounded*] What on earth—! [*He comes to her*]. What's the matter? Get up. [*He pulls her up*]. Anything wrong?

LIZA [*breathless*] Nothing wrong—with YOU. I've won your bet for you, haven't I? That's enough for you. *I* don't matter, I suppose.

HIGGINS. YOU won my bet! You! Presumptuous insect! *I* won it. What did you throw those slippers at me for?

LIZA. Because I wanted to smash your face. I'd like to kill you, you selfish brute. Why didn't you leave me where you picked me out of—in the gutter? You thank God it's all over, and that now you can throw me back again there, do you? [*She crisps her fingers, frantically*].

HIGGINS [*looking at her in cool wonder*] The creature IS nervous, after all.

LIZA [*gives a suffocated scream of fury, and instinctively darts her nails at his face*]!!

HIGGINS [*catching her wrists*] Ah! would you? Claws in, you cat. How dare you show your temper to me? Sit down and be quiet. [*He throws her roughly into the easy-chair*].

LIZA [*crushed by superior strength and weight*] What's to become of me? What's to become of me?

HIGGINS. How the devil do I know what's to become of you? What does it matter what becomes of you?

LIZA. You don't care. I know you don't care. You wouldn't care if I was dead. I'm nothing to you—not so much as them slippers.

HIGGINS [*thundering*] THOSE slippers.

LIZA [*with bitter submission*] Those slippers. I didn't think it made any difference now.

A pause. Eliza hopeless and crushed. Higgins a little uneasy.

HIGGINS [*in his loftiest manner*] Why have you begun going on like this? May I ask whether you complain of your treatment here?

LIZA. No.

HIGGINS. Has anybody behaved badly to you? Colonel Pickering? Mrs. Pearce? Any of the servants?

LIZA. No.

HIGGINS. I presume you don't pretend that I have treated you badly.

LIZA. No.

HIGGINS. I am glad to hear it. [*He moderates his tone*]. Perhaps you're tired after the strain of the day. Will you have a glass of champagne? [*He moves towards the door*].

LIZA. No. [*Recollecting her manners*] Thank you.

HIGGINS [*good-humored again*] This has been coming on you for some days. I suppose it was natural for you to be anxious about the garden party. But that's all over now. [*He pats her kindly on the shoulder. She writhes*]. There's nothing more to worry about.

LIZA. No. Nothing more for you to worry about. [*She suddenly rises and gets away from him by going to the piano bench, where she sits and hides her face*]. Oh God! I wish I was dead.

HIGGINS [*staring after her in sincere surprise*] Why? in heaven's name, why? [*Reasonably, going to her*] Listen to me, Eliza. All this irritation is purely subjective.

LIZA. I don't understand. I'm too ignorant.

HIGGINS. It's only imagination. Low spirits and nothing else. Nobody's hurting you. Nothing's wrong. You go to bed like a good girl and sleep it off. Have a little cry and say your prayers: that will make you comfortable.

LIZA. I heard YOUR prayers. "Thank God it's all over!"

HIGGINS [*impatiently*] Well, don't you thank God it's all over? Now you are free and can do what you like.

LIZA [*pulling herself together in desperation*] What am I fit for? What have you left me fit for? Where am I to go? What am I to do? What's to become of me?

HIGGINS [*enlightened, but not at all impressed*] Oh, that's what's worrying you, is it? [*He thrusts his hands into his pockets, and walks about in his usual manner, rattling the contents of his pockets, as if condescending to a trivial subject out of pure kindness*]. I shouldn't bother about it if I were you. I should imagine you won't have much difficulty in settling yourself, somewhere or other, though I hadn't quite realized that you were going away. [*She looks quickly at him: he does not look at her, but examines the dessert stand on the piano and decides that he will eat an apple*]. You might marry, you know. [*He bites a large piece out of the apple, and munches it noisily*]. You see, Eliza, all men are not confirmed old bachelors like me and the Colonel. Most men are the marrying sort (poor devils!); and you're not bad-looking; it's quite a pleasure to look at you sometimes—not now, of course, because you're crying and looking as ugly as the very devil; but when you're all right and quite yourself, you're what I should call attractive. That is, to the people in the marrying line, you understand. You go to bed and have a good nice rest; and then get up and look at yourself in the glass; and you won't feel so cheap.

Eliza again looks at him, speechless, and does not stir.

The look is quite lost on him: he eats his apple with a dreamy expression of happiness, as it is quite a good one.

HIGGINS [*a genial afterthought occurring to him*] I daresay my mother could find some chap or other who would do very well—

LIZA. We were above that at the corner of Tottenham Court Road.

HIGGINS [*waking up*] What do you mean?

LIZA. I sold flowers. I didn't sell myself. Now you've made a lady of me I'm not fit to sell anything else. I wish you'd left me where you found me.

HIGGINS [*slinging the core of the apple decisively into the grate*] Tosh, Eliza. Don't you insult human relations by dragging all this cant about buying and selling into it. You needn't marry the fellow if you don't like him.

LIZA. What else am I to do?

HIGGINS. Oh, lots of things. What about your old idea of a florist's shop? Pickering could set you up in one: he's lots of money. [*Chuckling*] He'll have to pay for all those togs you have been wearing today; and that, with the hire of the jewellery, will make a big hole in two hundred pounds. Why, six months ago you would have thought it the millennium to have a flower shop of your own. Come! you'll be all right. I must clear off to bed: I'm devilish sleepy. By the way, I came down for something: I forget what it was.

LIZA. Your slippers.

HIGGINS. Oh yes, of course. You shied them at me. [*He picks them up, and is going out when she rises and speaks to him*].

LIZA. Before you go, sir—

HIGGINS [*dropping the slippers in his surprise at her calling him sir*] Eh?

LIZA. Do my clothes belong to me or to Colonel Pickering?

HIGGINS [*coming back into the room as if her question were the very climax of unreason*] What the devil use would they be to Pickering?

LIZA. He might want them for the next girl you pick up to experiment on.

HIGGINS [*shocked and hurt*] Is THAT the way you feel towards us?

LIZA. I don't want to hear anything more about that. All I want to know is whether anything belongs to me. My own clothes were burnt.

HIGGINS. But what does it matter? Why need you start bothering about that in the middle of the night?

LIZA. I want to know what I may take away with me. I don't want to be accused of stealing.

HIGGINS [*now deeply wounded*] Stealing! You shouldn't have said that, Eliza. That shows a want of feeling.

LIZA. I'm sorry. I'm only a common ignorant girl; and in my station I have to be careful. There can't be any feelings between the like of you and the like of me. Please will you tell me what belongs to me and what doesn't?

HIGGINS [*very sulky*] You may take the whole damned houseful if you like. Except the jewels. They're hired. Will that satisfy you? [*He turns on his heel and is about to go in extreme dudgeon*].

LIZA [*drinking in his emotion like nectar, and nagging him to provoke a further supply*] Stop, please. [*She takes off her jewels*]. Will you take these to your room and keep them safe? I don't want to run the risk of their being missing.

HIGGINS [*furious*] Hand them over. [*She puts them into his hands*]. If these belonged to me instead of to the jeweler, I'd ram them down your ungrateful throat. [*He perfunctorily thrusts them into his pockets, unconsciously decorating himself with the protruding ends of the chains*].

LIZA [*taking a ring off*] This ring isn't the jeweler's: it's the one you bought me in Brighton. I don't want it now. [*Higgins dashes the ring violently into the fireplace, and turns on her so threateningly that she crouches over the piano with her hands over her face, and exclaims*] Don't you hit me.

HIGGINS. Hit you! You infamous creature, how dare you accuse me of such a thing? It is you who have hit me. You have wounded me to the heart.

LIZA [*thrilling with hidden joy*] I'm glad. I've got a little of my own back, anyhow.

HIGGINS [*with dignity, in his finest professional style*] You have caused me to lose my temper: a thing that has hardly ever happened to me before. I prefer to say nothing more tonight. I am going to bed.

LIZA [*pertly*] You'd better leave a note for Mrs. Pearce about the coffee; for she won't be told by me.

HIGGINS [*formally*] Damn Mrs. Pearce; and damn the coffee; and damn you; and damn my own folly in having lavished MY hard-earned knowledge and the treasure of my regard and intimacy on a heartless guttersnipe. [*He goes out with impressive decorum, and spoils it by slamming the door savagely*].

Eliza smiles for the first time; expresses her feelings by a wild pantomime in which an imitation of Higgins's exit is confused with her own triumph; and finally goes down on her knees on the hearthrug to look for the ring.

ACT V

Mrs. Higgins's drawing-room. She is at her writing-table as before. The parlor-maid comes in.

THE PARLOR-MAID [*at the door*] Mr. Henry, mam, is downstairs with Colonel Pickering.

MRS. HIGGINS. Well, show them up.

THE PARLOR-MAID. They're using the telephone, mam. Telephoning to the police, I think.

MRS. HIGGINS. What!

THE PARLOR-MAID [*coming further in and lowering her voice*] Mr. Henry's in a state, mam. I thought I'd better tell you.

MRS. HIGGINS. If you had told me that Mr. Henry was not in a state it would have been more surprising. Tell them to come up when they've finished with the police. I suppose he's lost something.

THE PARLOR-MAID. Yes, mam [*going*].

MRS. HIGGINS. Go upstairs and tell Miss Doolittle that Mr. Henry and the Colonel are here. Ask her not to come down till I send for her.

THE PARLOR-MAID. Yes, mam.

Higgins bursts in. He is, as the parlor-maid has said, in a state.

HIGGINS. Look here, mother: here's a confounded thing!

MRS. HIGGINS. Yes, dear. Good-morning. [*He checks his impatience and kisses her, whilst the parlor-maid goes out*]. What is it?

HIGGINS. Eliza's bolted.

MRS. HIGGINS [*calmly continuing her writing*] You must have frightened her.

HIGGINS. Frightened her! nonsense! She was left last night, as usual, to turn out the lights and all that; and instead of going to bed she changed her clothes and went right off: her bed wasn't slept in. She came in a cab for her things before seven this morning; and that fool Mrs. Pearce let her have them without telling me a word about it. What am I to do?

MRS. HIGGINS. Do without, I'm afraid, Henry. The girl has a perfect right to leave if she chooses.

HIGGINS [*wandering distractedly across the room*] But I can't find anything. I don't know what appointments I've got. I'm— [*Pickering comes in. Mrs. Higgins puts down her pen and turns away from the writing-table*].

PICKERING [*shaking hands*] Good-morning, Mrs. Higgins. Has Henry told you? [*He sits down on the ottoman*].

HIGGINS. What does that ass of an inspector say? Have you offered a reward?

MRS. HIGGINS [*rising in indignant amazement*] You don't mean to say you have set the police after Eliza?

HIGGINS. Of course. What are the police for? What else could we do? [*He sits in the Elizabethan chair*].

PICKERING. The inspector made a lot of difficulties. I really think he suspected us of some improper purpose.

MRS. HIGGINS. Well, of course he did. What right have you to go to the police and give the girl's name as if she were a thief, or a lost umbrella, or something? Really! [*She sits down again, deeply vexed*].

HIGGINS. But we want to find her.

PICKERING. We can't let her go like this, you know, Mrs. Higgins. What were we to do?

MRS. HIGGINS. You have no more sense, either of you, than two children. Why—

The parlor-maid comes in and breaks off the conversation.

THE PARLOR-MAID. Mr. Henry: a gentleman wants to see you very particular. He's been sent on from Wimpole Street.

HIGGINS. Oh, bother! I can't see anyone now. Who is it?

THE PARLOR-MAID. A Mr. Doolittle, Sir.

PICKERING. Doolittle! Do you mean the dustman?

THE PARLOR-MAID. Dustman! Oh no, sir: a gentleman.

HIGGINS [*springing up excitedly*] By George, Pick, it's some relative of hers that she's gone to. Somebody we know nothing about. [*To the parlor-maid*] Send him up, quick.

THE PARLOR-MAID. Yes, Sir. [*She goes*].

HIGGINS [*eagerly, going to his mother*] Genteel relatives! now we shall hear something. [*He sits down in the Chippendale chair*].

MRS. HIGGINS. Do you know any of her people?

PICKERING. Only her father: the fellow we told you about.

THE PARLOR-MAID [*announcing*] Mr. Doolittle. [*She withdraws*].

Doolittle enters. He is brilliantly dressed in a new fashionable frock-coat, with white waistcoat and grey trousers. A flower in his buttonhole, a dazzling silk hat, and patent leather shoes complete the effect. He is too concerned with the business he has come on to notice Mrs. Higgins. He walks straight to Higgins, and accosts him with vehement reproach.

DOOLITTLE [*indicating his own person*] See here! Do you see this? You done this.

HIGGINS. Done what, man?

DOOLITTLE. This, I tell you. Look at it. Look at this hat. Look at this coat.

PICKERING. Has Eliza been buying you clothes?

DOOLITTLE. Eliza! not she. Not half. Why would she buy me clothes?

MRS. HIGGINS. Good-morning, Mr. Doolittle. Won't you sit down?

DOOLITTLE [*taken aback as he becomes conscious that he has forgotten his hostess*] Asking your pardon, ma'am. [*He approaches her and shakes her proffered hand*]. Thank you. [*He sits down on the ottoman, on Pickering's right*]. I am that full of what has happened to me that I can't think of anything else.

HIGGINS. What the dickens has happened to you?

DOOLITTLE. I shouldn't mind if it had only happened to me: anything might happen to anybody and nobody to blame but Providence, as you might say. But this is something that you done to me: yes, you, Henry Higgins.

HIGGINS. Have you found Eliza? That's the point.

DOOLITTLE. Have you lost her?

HIGGINS. Yes.

DOOLITTLE. You have all the luck, you have. I ain't found her; but she'll find me quick enough now after what you done to me.

MRS. HIGGINS. But what has my son done to you, Mr. Doolittle?

DOOLITTLE. Done to me! Ruined me. Destroyed my happiness. Tied me up and delivered me into the hands of middle class morality.

HIGGINS [*rising intolerantly and standing over Doolittle*] You're raving. You're drunk. You're mad. I gave you five pounds. After that I had two conversations with you, at half-a-crown an hour. I've never seen you since.

DOOLITTLE. Oh! Drunk! am I? Mad! am I? Tell me this. Did you or did you not write a letter to an old blighter in America that was giving five millions to found Moral Reform Societies all over the world, and that wanted you to invent a universal language for him?

HIGGINS. What! Ezra D. Wannafeller! He's dead. [*He sits down again carelessly*].

DOOLITTLE. Yes: he's dead; and I'm done for. Now did you or did you not write a letter to him to say that the most original moralist at present in England, to the best of your knowledge, was Alfred Doolittle, a common dustman.

HIGGINS. Oh, after your last visit I remember making some silly joke of the kind.

DOOLITTLE. Ah! you may well call it a silly joke. It put the lid on me right enough. Just give him the chance he wanted to show that Americans is not like us: that they recognize and respect merit in every class of life, however humble. Them words is in his blooming will, in which, Henry Higgins, thanks to your silly joking, he leaves me a share in his Predigested Cheese Trust worth three thousand a year on condition that I lecture for his Wannafeller Moral Reform World League as often as they ask me up to six times a year.

HIGGINS. The devil he does! Whew! [*Brightening suddenly*] What a lark!

PICKERING. A safe thing for you, Doolittle. They won't ask you twice.

DOOLITTLE. It ain't the lecturing I mind. I'll lecture them blue in the face, I will, and not turn a hair. It's making a gentleman of me that I object to. Who asked him to make a gentleman of me? I was happy. I was free. I touched pretty nigh everybody for money when I wanted it, same as I touched you, Henry Higgins. Now I am worrited; tied neck and heels; and everybody touches me for money. It's a fine thing for you, says my solicitor. Is it? says I. You mean it's a good thing for you, I says. When I was a poor man and had a solicitor once when they found a pram in the dust cart, he got me off, and got shut of me and got me shut of him as quick as he could. Same with the doctors: used to shove me out of the hospital before I could hardly stand on my legs, and nothing to pay. Now they finds out that I'm not a healthy man and can't live unless they looks after me twice a day. In the house I'm not let do a hand's turn for myself: somebody else must do it and touch me for it. A year ago I hadn't a relative in the world except two or three that wouldn't speak to me. Now I've fifty, and not a decent week's wages among the lot of them. I have to live for others and not for myself: that's middle class morality. You talk of losing Eliza. Don't you be anxious: I bet she's on my doorstep by this: she that could support herself easy by selling flowers if I wasn't respectable. And the next one to touch me will be you, Henry Higgins. I'll have to learn to speak middle class language from you, instead of speaking proper English. That's where you'll come in; and I daresay that's what you done it for.

MRS. HIGGINS. But, my dear Mr. Doolittle, you need not suffer all this if you are really in earnest. Nobody can force you to accept this bequest. You can repudiate it. Isn't that so, Colonel Pickering?

PICKERING. I believe so.

DOOLITTLE [*softening his manner in deference to her sex*] That's the tragedy of it, ma'am. It's easy to say chuck it; but I haven't the nerve. Which one of us has? We're all intimidated. Intimidated, ma'am: that's what we are. What is there for me if I chuck it but the workhouse in my old age? I have to dye my hair already to keep my job as a dustman. If I was one of the deserving poor, and had put by a bit, I could chuck it; but then why should I, acause the deserving poor might as well be millionaires for all the happiness they ever has. They don't know what happiness is. But I, as one of the undeserving poor, have nothing between me and the pauper's uniform but this here blasted three thousand a year that shoves me into the middle class. (Excuse the expression, ma'am: you'd use it yourself if you had my provocation). They've got you every way you turn: it's a choice between the Skilly of the workhouse and the Char Bydis of the middle class; and I haven't the nerve for the workhouse. Intimidated: that's what I am. Broke. Bought up. Happier men than me will call for my dust, and touch me for their tip; and I'll look on helpless, and envy them. And that's what your son has brought me to. [*He is overcome by emotion*].

MRS. HIGGINS. Well, I'm very glad you're not going to do anything foolish, Mr. Doolittle. For this solves the problem of Eliza's future. You can provide for her now.

DOOLITTLE [*with melancholy resignation*] Yes, ma'am; I'm expected to provide for everyone now, out of three thousand a year.

HIGGINS [*jumping up*] Nonsense! he can't provide for her. He shan't provide for her. She doesn't belong to him. I paid him five pounds for her. Doolittle: either you're an honest man or a rogue.

DOOLITTLE [*tolerantly*] A little of both, Henry, like the rest of us: a little of both.

HIGGINS. Well, you took that money for the girl; and you have no right to take her as well.

MRS. HIGGINS. Henry: don't be absurd. If you really want to know where Eliza is, she is upstairs.

HIGGINS [*amazed*] Upstairs!!! Then I shall jolly soon fetch her downstairs. [*He makes resolutely for the door*].

MRS. HIGGINS [*rising and following him*] Be quiet, Henry. Sit down.

HIGGINS. I—

MRS. HIGGINS. Sit down, dear; and listen to me.

HIGGINS. Oh very well, very well, very well. [*He throws himself ungraciously on the ottoman, with his face towards the windows*]. But I think you might have told me this half an hour ago.

MRS. HIGGINS. Eliza came to me this morning. She passed the night partly walking about in a rage, partly trying to throw herself into the river and being afraid to, and partly in the Carlton Hotel. She told me of the brutal way you two treated her.

HIGGINS [*bounding up again*] What!

PICKERING [*rising also*] My dear Mrs. Higgins, she's been telling you stories. We didn't treat her brutally. We hardly said a word to her; and we parted on particularly good terms. [*Turning on Higgins*]. Higgins did you bully her after I went to bed?

HIGGINS. Just the other way about. She threw my slippers in my face. She behaved in the most outrageous way. I never gave her the slightest provocation. The slippers came bang into my face the moment I entered the room—before I had uttered a word. And used perfectly awful language.

PICKERING [*astonished*] But why? What did we do to her?

MRS. HIGGINS. I think I know pretty well what you did. The girl is naturally rather affectionate, I think. Isn't she, Mr. Doolittle?

DOOLITTLE. Very tender-hearted, ma'am. Takes after me.

MRS. HIGGINS. Just so. She had become attached to you both. She worked very hard for you, Henry! I don't think you quite realize what anything in the nature of brain work means to a girl like that. Well, it seems that when the great day of trial came, and she did this wonderful thing for you without making a single mistake, you two sat there and never said a word to her, but talked together of how glad you were that it was all over and how you had been bored with the whole thing. And then you were surprised because she threw your slippers at you! *I* should have thrown the fire-irons at you.

HIGGINS. We said nothing except that we were tired and wanted to go to bed. Did we, Pick?

PICKERING [*shrugging his shoulders*] That was all.

MRS. HIGGINS [*ironically*] Quite sure?

PICKERING. Absolutely. Really, that was all.

MRS. HIGGINS. You didn't thank her, or pet her, or admire her, or tell her how splendid she'd been.

HIGGINS [*impatiently*] But she knew all about that. We didn't make speeches to her, if that's what you mean.

PICKERING [*conscience stricken*] Perhaps we were a little inconsiderate. Is she very angry?

MRS. HIGGINS [*returning to her place at the writing-table*] Well, I'm afraid she won't go back to Wimpole Street, especially now that Mr. Doolittle is able to keep up the position you have thrust on her; but she says she is quite willing to meet you on friendly terms and to let bygones be bygones.

HIGGINS [*furious*] Is she, by George? Ho!

MRS. HIGGINS. If you promise to behave yourself, Henry, I'll ask her to come down. If not, go home; for you have taken up quite enough of my time.

HIGGINS. Oh, all right. Very well. Pick: you behave yourself. Let us put on our best Sunday manners for this creature that we picked out of the mud. [*He flings himself sulkily into the Elizabethan chair*].

DOOLITTLE [*remonstrating*] Now, now, Henry Higgins! have some consideration for my feelings as a middle class man.

MRS. HIGGINS. Remember your promise, Henry. [*She presses the bell-button on the writing-table*]. Mr. Doolittle: will you be so good as to step out on the balcony for a moment. I don't want Eliza to have the shock of your news until she has made it up with these two gentlemen. Would you mind?

DOOLITTLE. As you wish, lady. Anything to help Henry to keep her off my hands. [*He disappears through the window*].

The parlor-maid answers the bell. Pickering sits down in Doolittle's place.

MRS. HIGGINS. Ask Miss Doolittle to come down, please.

THE PARLOR-MAID. Yes, mam. [*She goes out*].

MRS. HIGGINS. Now, Henry: be good.

HIGGINS. I am behaving myself perfectly.

PICKERING. He is doing his best, Mrs. Higgins.

A pause. Higgins throws back his head; stretches out his legs; and begins to whistle.

MRS. HIGGINS. Henry, dearest, you don't look at all nice in that attitude.

HIGGINS [*pulling himself together*] I was not trying to look nice, mother.

MRS. HIGGINS. It doesn't matter, dear. I only wanted to make you speak.

HIGGINS. Why?

MRS. HIGGINS. Because you can't speak and whistle at the same time.

Higgins groans. Another very trying pause.

HIGGINS [*springing up, out of patience*] Where the devil is that girl? Are we to wait here all day?

Eliza enters, sunny, self-possessed, and giving a staggeringly convincing exhibition of ease of manner. She carries a little work-basket, and is very much at home. Pickering is too much taken aback to rise.

LIZA. How do you do, Professor Higgins? Are you quite well?

HIGGINS [*choking*] Am I— [*He can say no more*].

LIZA. But of course you are: you are never ill. So glad to see you again, Colonel Pickering. [*He rises hastily; and they shake hands*]. Quite chilly this morning, isn't it? [*She sits down on his left. He sits beside her*].

HIGGINS. Don't you dare try this game on me. I taught it to you; and it doesn't take me in. Get up and come home; and don't be a fool.

Eliza takes a piece of needlework from her basket, and begins to stitch at it, without taking the least notice of this outburst.

MRS. HIGGINS. Very nicely put, indeed, Henry. No woman could resist such an invitation.

HIGGINS. You let her alone, mother. Let her speak for herself. You will jolly soon see whether she has an idea that I haven't put into her head or a word that I haven't put into her mouth. I tell you I have created this thing out of the squashed cabbage leaves of Covent Garden; and now she pretends to play the fine lady with me.

MRS. HIGGINS [*placidly*] Yes, dear; but you'll sit down, won't you?

Higgins sits down again, savagely.

LIZA [*to Pickering, taking no apparent notice of Higgins, and working away deftly*] Will you drop me altogether now that the experiment is over, Colonel Pickering?

PICKERING. Oh don't. You mustn't think of it as an experiment. It shocks me, somehow.

LIZA. Oh, I'm only a squashed cabbage leaf.

PICKERING [*impulsively*] No.

LIZA [*continuing quietly*]—but I owe so much to you that I should be very unhappy if you forgot me.

PICKERING. It's very kind of you to say so, Miss Doolittle.

LIZA. It's not because you paid for my dresses. I know you are generous to everybody with money. But it was from you that I learnt really nice manners; and that is what makes one a lady, isn't it? You see it was so very difficult for me with the example of Professor Higgins always before me. I was brought up to be just like him, unable to control myself, and using bad language on the slightest provocation. And I should never have known that ladies and gentlemen didn't behave like that if you hadn't been there.

HIGGINS. Well!!

PICKERING. Oh, that's only his way, you know. He doesn't mean it.

LIZA. Oh, I didn't mean it either, when I was a flower girl. It was only my way. But you see I did it; and that's what makes the difference after all.

PICKERING. No doubt. Still, he taught you to speak; and I couldn't have done that, you know.

LIZA [*trivially*] Of course: that is his profession.

HIGGINS. Damnation!

LIZA [*continuing*] It was just like learning to dance in the fashionable way: there was nothing more than that in it. But do you know what began my real education?

PICKERING. What?

LIZA [*stopping her work for a moment*] Your calling me Miss Doolittle that day when I first came to Wimpole Street. That was the beginning of self-respect for me. [*She resumes her stitching*]. And there were a hundred little things you never noticed, because they came naturally to you. Things about standing up and taking off your hat and opening doors—

PICKERING. Oh, that was nothing.

LIZA. Yes: things that showed you thought and felt about me as if I were something better than a scullerymaid; though of course I know you would have been just the same to a scullery-maid if she had been let in the drawing-room. You never took off your boots in the dining room when I was there.

PICKERING. You mustn't mind that. Higgins takes off his boots all over the place.

LIZA. I know. I am not blaming him. It is his way, isn't it? But it made such a difference to me that you didn't do it. You see, really and truly, apart from the things anyone can pick up (the dressing and the proper way of speaking, and so on), the difference between a lady and a flower girl is not how she behaves, but how she's treated. I shall always be a flower girl to Professor Higgins, because he always treats me as a flower girl, and always will; but I know I can be a lady to you, because you always treat me as a lady, and always will.

MRS. HIGGINS. Please don't grind your teeth, Henry.

PICKERING. Well, this is really very nice of you, Miss Doolittle.

LIZA. I should like you to call me Eliza, now, if you would.

PICKERING. Thank you. Eliza, of course.

LIZA. And I should like Professor Higgins to call me Miss Doolittle.

HIGGINS. I'll see you damned first.

MRS. HIGGINS. Henry! Henry!

PICKERING [*laughing*] Why don't you slang back at him? Don't stand it. It would do him a lot of good.

LIZA. I can't. I could have done it once; but now I can't go back to it. Last night, when I was wandering about, a girl spoke to me; and I tried to get back into the old way with her; but it was no use. You told me, you know, that when a child is brought to a foreign country, it picks up the language in a few weeks, and forgets its own. Well, I am a child in your country. I have forgotten my own language, and can speak nothing but yours. That's the real break-off with the corner of Tottenham Court Road. Leaving Wimpole Street finishes it.

PICKERING [*much alarmed*] Oh! but you're coming back to Wimpole Street, aren't you? You'll forgive Higgins?

HIGGINS [*rising*] Forgive! Will she, by George! Let her go. Let her find out how she can get on without us. She will relapse into the gutter in three weeks without me at her elbow.

Doolittle appears at the centre window. With a look of dignified reproach at Higgins, he comes slowly and silently to his daughter, who, with her back to the window, is unconscious of his approach.

PICKERING. He's incorrigible, Eliza. You won't relapse, will you?

LIZA. No: Not now. Never again. I have learnt my lesson. I don't believe I could utter one of the old sounds if I tried. [*Doolittle touches her on her left shoulder. She drops her work, losing her self-possession utterly at the spectacle of her father's splendor*] A—a—a—a—a—ah—ow—ooh!

HIGGINS [*with a crow of triumph*] Aha! Just so. A—a—a—a—ahowooh! A—a—a—a—ahowooh ! A—a—a—a—ahowooh! Victory! Victory! [*He throws himself on the divan, folding his arms, and spraddling arrogantly*].

DOOLITTLE. Can you blame the girl? Don't look at me like that, Eliza. It ain't my fault. I've come into money.

LIZA. You must have touched a millionaire this time, dad.

DOOLITTLE. I have. But I'm dressed something special today. I'm going to St. George's, Hanover Square. Your stepmother is going to marry me.

LIZA [*angrily*] You're going to let yourself down to marry that low common woman!

PICKERING [*quietly*] He ought to, Eliza. [*To Doolittle*] Why has she changed her mind?

DOOLITTLE [*sadly*] Intimidated, Governor. Intimidated. Middle class morality claims its victim. Won't you put on your hat, Liza, and come and see me turned off?

LIZA. If the Colonel says I must, I—I'll [*almost sobbing*] I'll demean myself. And get insulted for my pains, like enough.

DOOLITTLE. Don't be afraid: she never comes to words with anyone now, poor woman! respectability has broke all the spirit out of her.

PICKERING [*squeezing Eliza's elbow gently*] Be kind to them, Eliza. Make the best of it.

LIZA [*forcing a little smile for him through her vexation*] Oh well, just to show there's no ill feeling. I'll be back in a moment. [*She goes out*].

DOOLITTLE [*sitting down beside Pickering*] I feel uncommon nervous about the ceremony, Colonel. I wish you'd come and see me through it.

PICKERING. But you've been through it before, man. You were married to Eliza's mother.

DOOLITTLE. Who told you that, Colonel?

PICKERING. Well, nobody told me. But I concluded naturally—

DOOLITTLE. No: that ain't the natural way, Colonel: it's only the middle class way. My way was always the undeserving way. But don't say nothing to Eliza. She don't know: I always had a delicacy about telling her.

PICKERING. Quite right. We'll leave it so, if you don't mind.

DOOLITTLE. And you'll come to the church, Colonel, and put me through straight?

PICKERING. With pleasure. As far as a bachelor can.

MRS. HIGGINS. May I come, Mr. Doolittle? I should be very sorry to miss your wedding.

DOOLITTLE. I should indeed be honored by your condescension, ma'am; and my poor old woman would take it as a tremenjous compliment. She's been very low, thinking of the happy days that are no more.

MRS. HIGGINS [*rising*] I'll order the carriage and get ready. [*The men rise, except Higgins*]. I shan't be more than fifteen minutes. [*As she goes to the door Eliza comes in, hatted and buttoning her gloves*]. I'm going to the church to see your father married, Eliza. You had better come in the brougham with me. Colonel Pickering can go on with the bridegroom.

Mrs. Higgins goes out. Eliza comes to the middle of the room between the centre window and the ottoman. Pickering joins her.

DOOLITTLE. Bridegroom! What a word! It makes a man realize his position, somehow. [*He takes up his hat and goes towards the door*].

PICKERING. Before I go, Eliza, do forgive him and come back to us.

LIZA. I don't think papa would allow me. Would you, dad?

DOOLITTLE [*sad but magnanimous*] They played you off very cunning, Eliza, them two sportsmen. If it had been only one of them, you could have nailed him. But you see, there was two; and one of them chaperoned the other, as you might say. [*To Pickering*] It was artful of you, Colonel; but I bear no malice: I should have done the same myself. I been the victim of one woman after another all my life; and I don't grudge you two getting the better of Eliza. I shan't interfere. It's time for us to go, Colonel. So long, Henry. See you in St. George's, Eliza. [*He goes out*].

PICKERING [*coaxing*] Do stay with us, Eliza. [*He follows Doolittle*].

Eliza goes out on the balcony to avoid being alone with Higgins. He rises and joins her there. She immediately comes back into the room and makes for the door; but he goes along the balcony quickly and gets his back to the door before she reaches it.

HIGGINS. Well, Eliza, you've had a bit of your own back, as you call it. Have you had enough? and are you going to be reasonable? Or do you want any more?

LIZA. You want me back only to pick up your slippers and put up with your tempers and fetch and carry for you.

HIGGINS. I haven't said I wanted you back at all.

LIZA. Oh, indeed. Then what are we talking about?

HIGGINS. About you, not about me. If you come back I shall treat you just as I have always treated you. I can't change my nature; and I don't intend to change my manners. My manners are exactly the same as Colonel Pickering's.

LIZA. That's not true. He treats a flower girl as if she was a duchess.

HIGGINS. And I treat a duchess as if she was a flower girl.

LIZA. I see. [*She turns away composedly, and sits on the ottoman, facing the window*]. The same to everybody.

HIGGINS. Just so.

LIZA. Like father.

HIGGINS [*grinning, a little taken down*] Without accepting the comparison at all points, Eliza, it's quite true that your father is not a snob, and that he will be quite at home in any station of life to which his eccentric destiny may call him. [*Seriously*] The great secret, Eliza, is not having bad manners or good manners or any other particular sort of manners, but having the same manner for all human souls: in short, behaving as if you were in Heaven, where there are no third-class carriages, and one soul is as good as another.

LIZA. Amen. You are a born preacher.

HIGGINS [*irritated*] The question is not whether I treat you rudely, but whether you ever heard me treat anyone else better.

LIZA [*with sudden sincerity*] I don't care how you treat me. I don't mind your swearing at me. I don't mind a black eye: I've had one before this. But [*standing up and facing him*] I won't be passed over.

HIGGINS. Then get out of my way; for I won't stop for you. You talk about me as if I were a motor bus.

LIZA. So you are a motor bus: all bounce and go, and no consideration for anyone. But I can do without you: don't think I can't.

HIGGINS. I know you can. I told you you could.

LIZA [*wounded, getting away from him to the other side of the ottoman with her face to the hearth*] I know you did, you brute. You wanted to get rid of me.

HIGGINS. Liar.

LIZA. Thank you. [*She sits down with dignity*].

HIGGINS. You never asked yourself, I suppose, whether I could do without YOU.

LIZA [*earnestly*] Don't you try to get round me. You'll HAVE to do without me.

HIGGINS [*arrogant*] I can do without anybody. I have my own soul: my own spark of divine fire. But [*with sudden humility*] I shall miss you, Eliza. [*He sits down near her on the ottoman*]. I have learnt something from your idiotic notions: I confess that humbly and gratefully. And I have grown accustomed to your voice and appearance. I like them, rather.

LIZA. Well, you have both of them on your gramophone and in your book of photographs. When you feel lonely without me, you can turn the machine on. It's got no feelings to hurt.

HIGGINS. I can't turn your soul on. Leave me those feelings; and you can take away the voice and the face. They are not you.

LIZA. Oh, you ARE a devil. You can twist the heart in a girl as easy as some could twist her arms to hurt her. Mrs. Pearce warned me. Time and again she has wanted to leave you; and you always got round her at the last minute. And you don't care a bit for her. And you don't care a bit for me.

HIGGINS. I care for life, for humanity; and you are a part of it that has come my way and been built into my house. What more can you or anyone ask?

LIZA. I won't care for anybody that doesn't care for me.

HIGGINS. Commercial principles, Eliza. Like [*reproducing her Covent Garden pronunciation with professional exactness*] s'yollin voylets [*selling violets*], isn't it?

LIZA. Don't sneer at me. It's mean to sneer at me.

HIGGINS. I have never sneered in my life. Sneering doesn't become either the human face or the human soul. I am expressing my righteous contempt for Commercialism. I don't and won't trade in affection. You call me a brute because you couldn't buy a claim on me by fetching my slippers and finding my spectacles. You were a fool: I think a woman fetching a man's slippers is a disgusting sight: did I ever fetch YOUR slippers? I think a good deal more of you for throwing them in my face. No use slaving for me and then saying you want to be cared for: who cares for a slave? If you come back, come back for the sake of good fellowship; for you'll get nothing else. You've had a thousand times as much out of me as I have out of you; and if you dare to set up your little dog's tricks of fetching and carrying slippers against my creation of a Duchess Eliza, I'll slam the door in your silly face.

LIZA. What did you do it for if you didn't care for me?

HIGGINS [*heartily*] Why, because it was my job.

LIZA. You never thought of the trouble it would make for me.

HIGGINS. Would the world ever have been made if its maker had been afraid of making trouble? Making life means making trouble. There's only one way of escaping trouble; and that's killing things. Cowards, you notice, are always shrieking to have troublesome people killed.

LIZA. I'm no preacher: I don't notice things like that. I notice that you don't notice me.

HIGGINS [*jumping up and walking about intolerantly*] Eliza: you're an idiot. I waste the treasures of my Miltonic mind by spreading them before you. Once for all, understand that I go my way and do my work without caring twopence what happens to either of us. I am not intimidated, like your father and your stepmother. So you can come back or go to the devil: which you please.

LIZA. What am I to come back for?

HIGGINS [*bouncing up on his knees on the ottoman and leaning over it to her*] For the fun of it. That's why I took you on.

LIZA [*with averted face*] And you may throw me out tomorrow if I don't do everything you want me to?

HIGGINS. Yes; and you may walk out tomorrow if I don't do everything YOU want me to.

LIZA. And live with my stepmother?

HIGGINS. Yes, or sell flowers.

LIZA. Oh! if I only COULD go back to my flower basket! I should be independent of both you and father and all the world! Why did you take my independence from me? Why did I give it up? I'm a slave now, for all my fine clothes.

HIGGINS. Not a bit. I'll adopt you as my daughter and settle money on you if you like. Or would you rather marry Pickering?

LIZA [*looking fiercely round at him*] I wouldn't marry YOU if you asked me; and you're nearer my age than what he is.

HIGGINS [*gently*] Than he is: not "than what he is."

LIZA [*losing her temper and rising*] I'll talk as I like. You're not my teacher now.

HIGGINS [*reflectively*] I don't suppose Pickering would, though. He's as confirmed an old bachelor as I am.

LIZA. That's not what I want; and don't you think it. I've always had chaps enough wanting me that way. Freddy Hill writes to me twice and three times a day, sheets and sheets.

HIGGINS [*disagreeably surprised*] Damn his impudence! [*He recoils and finds himself sitting on his heels*].

LIZA. He has a right to if he likes, poor lad. And he does love me.

HIGGINS [*getting off the ottoman*] You have no right to encourage him.

LIZA. Every girl has a right to be loved.

HIGGINS. What! By fools like that?

LIZA. Freddy's not a fool. And if he's weak and poor and wants me, may be he'd make me happier than my betters that bully me and don't want me.

HIGGINS. Can he MAKE anything of you? That's the point.

LIZA. Perhaps I could make something of him. But I never thought of us making anything of one another; and you never think of anything else. I only want to be natural.

HIGGINS. In short, you want me to be as infatuated about you as Freddy? Is that it?

LIZA. No I don't. That's not the sort of feeling I want from you. And don't you be too sure of yourself or of me. I could have been a bad girl if I'd liked. I've seen more of some things than you, for all your learning. Girls like me can drag gentlemen down to make love to them easy enough. And they wish each other dead the next minute.

HIGGINS. Of course they do. Then what in thunder are we quarrelling about?

LIZA [*much troubled*] I want a little kindness. I know I'm a common ignorant girl, and you a book-learned gentleman; but I'm not dirt under your feet. What I done [*correcting herself*] what I did was not for the dresses and the taxis: I did it because we were pleasant together and I come—came—to care for you; not to want you to make love to me, and not forgetting the difference between us, but more friendly like.

HIGGINS. Well, of course. That's just how I feel. And how Pickering feels. Eliza: you're a fool.

LIZA. That's not a proper answer to give me [*she sinks on the chair at the writing-table in tears*].

HIGGINS. It's all you'll get until you stop being a common idiot. If you're going to be a lady, you'll have to give up feeling neglected if the men you know don't spend half their time snivelling over you and the other half giving you black eyes. If you can't stand the coldness of my sort of life, and the strain of it, go back to the gutter. Work til you are more a brute than a human being; and then cuddle and squabble and drink til you fall asleep. Oh, it's a fine life, the life of the gutter. It's real: it's warm: it's violent: you can feel it through the thickest skin: you can taste it and smell it without any training or any work. Not like Science and Literature and Classical Music and Philosophy and Art. You find me cold, unfeeling, selfish, don't you? Very well: be off with you to the sort of people you like. Marry some sentimental hog or other with lots of money, and a thick pair of lips to kiss you with and a thick pair of boots to kick you with. If you can't appreciate what you've got, you'd better get what you can appreciate.

LIZA [*desperate*] Oh, you are a cruel tyrant. I can't talk to you: you turn everything against me: I'm always in the wrong. But you know very well all the time that you're nothing but a bully. You know I can't go back to the gutter, as you call it, and that I have no real friends in the world but you and the Colonel. You know well I couldn't bear to live with a low common man after you two; and it's wicked and cruel of you to insult me by pretending I could. You think I must go back to Wimpole Street because I have nowhere else to go but father's. But don't you be too sure that you have me under your feet to be trampled on and talked down. I'll marry Freddy, I will, as soon as he's able to support me.

HIGGINS [*sitting down beside her*] Rubbish! you shall marry an ambassador. You shall marry the Governor-General of India or the Lord-Lieutenant of Ireland, or somebody who wants a deputy-queen. I'm not going to have my masterpiece thrown away on Freddy.

LIZA. You think I like you to say that. But I haven't forgot what you said a minute ago; and I won't be coaxed round as if I was a baby or a puppy. If I can't have kindness, I'll have independence.

HIGGINS. Independence? That's middle class blasphemy. We are all dependent on one another, every soul of us on earth.

LIZA [*rising determinedly*] I'll let you see whether I'm dependent on you. If you can preach, I can teach. I'll go and be a teacher.

HIGGINS. What'll you teach, in heaven's name?

LIZA. What you taught me. I'll teach phonetics.

HIGGINS. Ha! Ha! Ha!

LIZA. I'll offer myself as an assistant to Professor Nepean.

HIGGINS [*rising in a fury*] What! That impostor! that humbug! that toadying ignoramus! Teach him my methods! my discoveries! You take one step in his direction and I'll wring your neck. [*He lays hands on her*]. Do you hear?

LIZA [*defiantly non-resistant*] Wring away. What do I care? I knew you'd strike me some day. [*He lets her go, stamping with rage at having forgotten himself, and recoils so hastily that he stumbles back into his seat on the ottoman*]. Aha! Now I know how to deal with you. What a fool I was not to think of it before! You can't take away the knowledge you gave me. You said I had a finer ear than you. And I can be civil and kind to people, which is more than you can. Aha! That's done you, Henry Higgins, it has. Now I don't care that [*snapping her fingers*] for your bullying and your big talk. I'll advertize it in the papers that your duchess is only a flower girl that you taught, and that she'll teach anybody to be a duchess just the same in six months for a thousand guineas. Oh, when I think of myself crawling under your feet and being trampled on and called names, when all the time I had only to lift up my finger to be as good as you, I could just kick myself.

HIGGINS [*wondering at her*] You damned impudent slut, you! But it's better than snivelling; better than fetching slippers and finding spectacles, isn't it?

[*Rising*] By George, Eliza, I said I'd make a woman of you; and I have. I like you like this.

LIZA. Yes: you turn round and make up to me now that I'm not afraid of you, and can do without you.

HIGGINS. Of course I do, you little fool. Five minutes ago you were like a millstone round my neck. Now you're a tower of strength: a consort battleship. You and I and Pickering will be three old bachelors together instead of only two men and a silly girl.

Mrs. Higgins returns, dressed for the wedding. Eliza instantly becomes cool and elegant.

MRS. HIGGINS. The carriage is waiting, Eliza. Are you ready?

LIZA. Quite. Is the Professor coming?

MRS. HIGGINS. Certainly not. He can't behave himself in church. He makes remarks out loud all the time on the clergyman's pronunciation.

LIZA. Then I shall not see you again, Professor. Good bye. [*She goes to the door*].

MRS. HIGGINS [*coming to Higgins*] Good-bye, dear.

HIGGINS. Good-bye, mother. [*He is about to kiss her, when he recollects something*]. Oh, by the way, Eliza, order a ham and a Stilton cheese, will you? And buy me a pair of reindeer gloves, number eights, and a tie to match that new suit of mine, at Eale & Binman's. You can choose the color. [*His cheerful, careless, vigorous voice shows that he is incorrigible*].

LIZA [*disdainfully*] Buy them yourself. [*She sweeps out*].

MRS. HIGGINS. I'm afraid you've spoiled that girl, Henry. But never mind, dear: I'll buy you the tie and gloves.

HIGGINS [*sunnily*] Oh, don't bother. She'll buy em all right enough. Good-bye.

They kiss. Mrs. Higgins runs out. Higgins, left alone, rattles his cash in his pocket; chuckles; and disports himself in a highly self-satisfied manner.

The rest of the story need not be shown in action, and indeed, would hardly need telling if our imaginations were not so enfeebled by their lazy dependence on the ready-makes and reach-me-downs of the ragshop in which Romance keeps its stock of "happy endings" to misfit all stories. Now, the history of Eliza Doolittle, though called a romance because of the transfiguration it records seems exceedingly improbable, is common enough. Such transfigurations have been achieved by hundreds of resolutely ambitious young women since Nell Gwynne set them the example by playing queens and fascinating kings in the theatre in which she began by selling oranges. Nevertheless, people in all directions have assumed, for no other reason than that she became the heroine of a romance, that she must have married the hero of it. This is unbearable, not only because her little drama, if acted on such a thoughtless assumption, must be spoiled, but because the true sequel is patent to anyone with a sense of human nature in general, and of feminine instinct in particular.

Eliza, in telling Higgins she would not marry him if he asked her, was not coquetting: she was announcing a well-considered decision. When a bachelor interests, and dominates, and teaches, and becomes important to a spinster, as Higgins with Eliza, she always, if she has character enough to be capable of it, considers very seriously indeed whether she will play for becoming that bachelor's wife, especially if he is so little interested in marriage that a determined and devoted woman might capture him if she set herself resolutely to do it. Her decision will depend a good deal on whether she is really free to choose; and that, again, will depend on her age and income. If she is at the end of her youth, and has no security for her livelihood, she will marry him because she must marry anybody who will provide for her. But at Eliza's age a good-looking girl does not feel that pressure; she feels free to pick and choose. She is therefore guided by her instinct in the matter. Eliza's instinct tells her not to marry Higgins. It does not tell her to give him up. It is not in the slightest doubt as to his remaining one of the strongest personal interests in her life. It would be very sorely strained if there was another woman likely to supplant her with him. But as she feels sure of him on that last point, she has no doubt at all as to her course, and would not have any, even if the difference of twenty years in age, which seems so great to youth, did not exist between them.

As our own instincts are not appealed to by her conclusion, let us see whether we cannot discover some reason in it. When Higgins excused his indifference to young women on the ground that they had an irresistible rival in his mother, he gave the clue to his inveterate old-bachelordom. The case is uncommon only to the extent that remarkable mothers are uncommon. If an imaginative boy has a sufficiently rich mother who has intelligence, personal grace, dignity of character without harshness, and a cultivated sense of the best art of her time to enable her to make her house beautiful, she sets a standard for him against which very few women can struggle, besides effecting for him a disengagement of his affections, his sense of beauty, and his idealism from his specifically sexual impulses. This makes him a standing puzzle to the huge number of uncultivated people who have been brought up in tasteless homes by commonplace or disagreeable parents, and to whom, consequently, literature, painting, sculpture, music, and affectionate personal relations come as modes of sex if they come at all. The word passion means nothing else to them; and that Higgins could have a passion for phonetics and idealize his mother instead of Eliza, would seem to them absurd and unnatural. Nevertheless, when we look round and see that hardly anyone is too ugly or disagreeable to find a wife or a husband if he or she wants one, whilst many old maids and bachelors are above the average in quality and culture, we cannot help suspecting that the disentanglement of sex from the associations with which it is so commonly confused, a disentanglement which persons of genius achieve by sheer intellectual analysis, is sometimes produced or aided by parental fascination.

Now, though Eliza was incapable of thus explaining to herself Higgins's formidable powers of resistance to the charm that prostrated Freddy at the first glance, she was instinctively aware that she could never obtain a complete grip of him, or come between him and his mother (the first necessity of the married woman). To put it shortly, she knew that for some mysterious reason he had not the makings of a married man in him, according to her conception of a husband as one to whom she would be his nearest and fondest and warmest interest. Even had there been no mother-rival, she would still have refused to accept an interest in herself that was secondary to philosophic interests. Had Mrs. Higgins died, there would still have been Milton and the Universal Alphabet. Landor's remark that to those who have the greatest power of loving, love is a secondary affair, would not have recommended Landor to Eliza. Put that along with her resentment of Higgins's domineering superiority, and her mistrust of his coaxing cleverness in getting round her and evading her wrath when he had gone too far with his impetuous bullying, and you will see that Eliza's instinct had good grounds for warning her not to marry her Pygmalion.

And now, whom did Eliza marry? For if Higgins was a predestinate old bachelor, she was most certainly not a predestinate old maid. Well, that can be told very shortly to those who have not guessed it from the indications she has herself given them.

Almost immediately after Eliza is stung into proclaiming her considered determination not to marry Higgins, she mentions the fact that young Mr. Frederick Eynsford Hill is pouring out his love for her daily through the post. Now Freddy is young, practically twenty years younger than Higgins: he is a gentleman (or, as Eliza would qualify him, a toff), and speaks like one; he is nicely dressed, is treated by the Colonel as an equal, loves her unaffectedly, and is not her master, nor ever likely to dominate her in spite of his advantage of social standing. Eliza has no use for the foolish romantic tradition that all women love to be mastered, if not actually bullied and beaten. "When you go to women," says Nietzsche, "take your whip with you." Sensible despots have never confined that precaution to women: they have taken their whips with them when they have dealt with men, and been slavishly idealized by the men over whom they have flourished the whip much more than by women. No doubt there are slavish women as well as slavish men; and women, like men, admire those that are stronger than themselves. But to admire a strong person and to live under that strong person's thumb are two different things. The weak may not be admired and hero-worshipped; but they are by no means disliked or shunned; and they never seem to have the least difficulty in marrying people who are too good for them. They may fail in emergencies; but life is not one long emergency: it is mostly a string of situations for which no exceptional strength is needed, and with which even rather weak people can cope if they have a stronger partner to help them out. Accordingly, it is a truth everywhere in evidence that strong people, masculine or feminine, not only do not marry stronger people, but do not show any preference for them in selecting their friends. When a lion meets another with a louder roar "the first lion thinks the last a bore." The man or woman who feels strong enough for two, seeks for every other quality in a partner than strength.

The converse is also true. Weak people want to marry strong people who do not frighten them too much; and this often leads them to make the mistake we describe metaphorically as "biting off more than they can chew." They want too much for too little; and when the bargain is unreasonable beyond all bearing, the union becomes impossible: it ends in the weaker party being either discarded or borne as a cross, which is worse. People who are not only weak, but silly or obtuse as well, are often in these difficulties.

This being the state of human affairs, what is Eliza fairly sure to do when she is placed between Freddy and Higgins? Will she look forward to a lifetime of fetching Higgins's slippers or to a lifetime of Freddy fetching hers? There can be no doubt about the answer. Unless Freddy is biologically repulsive to her, and Higgins biologically attractive to a degree that overwhelms all her other instincts, she will, if she marries either of them, marry Freddy.

And that is just what Eliza did.

Complications ensued; but they were economic, not romantic. Freddy had no money and no occupation. His mother's jointure, a last relic of the opulence of Largelady Park, had enabled her to struggle along in Earlscourt with an air of gentility, but not to procure any serious secondary education for her children, much less give the boy a profession. A clerkship at thirty shillings a week was beneath Freddy's dignity, and extremely distasteful to him besides. His prospects consisted of a hope that if he kept up appearances somebody would do something for him. The something appeared vaguely to his imagination as a private secretaryship or a sinecure of some sort. To his mother it perhaps appeared as a marriage to some lady of means who could not resist her boy's niceness. Fancy her feelings when he married a flower girl who had become declassee under extraordinary circumstances which were now notorious!

It is true that Eliza's situation did not seem wholly ineligible. Her father, though formerly a dustman, and now fantastically disclassed, had become extremely popular in the smartest society by a social talent which triumphed over every prejudice and every disadvantage. Rejected by the middle class, which he loathed, he had shot up at once into the highest circles by his wit, his dustmanship (which he carried like a banner), and his Nietzschean transcendence of good and evil. At intimate ducal dinners he sat on the right hand of the Duchess; and in country houses he smoked in the pantry and was made much of by the butler when he was not feeding in the dining-room and being consulted by cabinet ministers. But he found it almost as hard to do all this on four thousand a year as Mrs. Eynsford Hill to live in Earlscourt on an income so pitiably smaller that I have not the heart to disclose its exact figure. He absolutely refused to add the last straw to his burden by contributing to Eliza's support.

Thus Freddy and Eliza, now Mr. and Mrs. Eynsford Hill, would have spent a penniless honeymoon but for a wedding present of 500 pounds from the Colonel to Eliza. It lasted a long time because Freddy did not know how to spend money, never having had any to spend, and Eliza, socially trained by a pair of old bachelors, wore her clothes as long as they held together and looked pretty, without the least regard to their being many months out of fashion. Still, 500 pounds will not last two young people for ever; and they both knew, and Eliza felt as well, that they must shift for themselves in the end. She could quarter herself on Wimpole Street because it had come to be her home; but she was quite aware that she ought not to quarter Freddy there, and that it would not be good for his character if she did.

Not that the Wimpole Street bachelors objected. When she consulted them, Higgins declined to be bothered about her housing problem when that solution was so simple. Eliza's desire to have Freddy in the house with her seemed of no more importance than if she had wanted an extra piece of bedroom furniture. Pleas as to Freddy's character, and the moral obligation on him to earn his own living, were lost on Higgins. He denied that Freddy had any character, and declared that if he tried to do any useful work some competent person would have the trouble of undoing it: a procedure involving a net loss to the community, and great unhappiness to Freddy himself, who was obviously intended by Nature for such light work as amusing Eliza, which, Higgins declared, was a much more useful and honorable occupation than working in the city. When Eliza referred again to her project of teaching phonetics, Higgins abated not a jot of his violent opposition to it. He said she was not within ten years of being qualified to meddle with his pet subject; and as it was evident that the Colonel agreed with him, she felt she could not go against them in this grave matter, and that she had no right, without Higgins's consent, to exploit the knowledge he had given her; for his knowledge seemed to her as much his private property as his watch: Eliza was no communist. Besides, she was superstitiously devoted to them both, more entirely and frankly after her marriage than before it.

It was the Colonel who finally solved the problem, which had cost him much perplexed cogitation. He one day asked Eliza, rather shyly, whether she had quite given up her notion of keeping a flower shop. She replied that she had thought of it, but had put it out of her head, because the Colonel had said, that day at Mrs. Higgins's, that it would never do. The Colonel confessed that when he said that, he had not quite recovered from the dazzling impression of the day before. They broke the matter to Higgins that evening. The sole comment vouchsafed by him very nearly led to a serious quarrel with Eliza. It was to the effect that she would have in Freddy an ideal errand boy.

Freddy himself was next sounded on the subject. He said he had been thinking of a shop himself; though it had presented itself to his pennilessness as a small place in which Eliza should sell tobacco at one counter whilst he sold newspapers at the opposite one. But he agreed that it would be extraordinarily jolly to go early every morning with Eliza to Covent Garden and buy flowers on the scene of their first meeting: a sentiment which earned him many kisses from his wife. He added that he had always been afraid to propose anything of the sort, because Clara would make an awful row about a step that must damage her matrimonial chances, and his mother could not be expected to like it after clinging for so many years to that step of the social ladder on which retail trade is impossible.

This difficulty was removed by an event highly unexpected by Freddy's mother. Clara, in the course of her incursions into those artistic circles which were the highest within her reach, discovered that her conversational qualifications were expected to include a grounding in the novels of Mr. H.G. Wells. She borrowed them in various directions so energetically that she swallowed them all within two months. The result was a conversion of a kind quite common today. A modern Acts of the Apostles would fill fifty whole Bibles if anyone were capable of writing it.

Poor Clara, who appeared to Higgins and his mother as a disagreeable and ridiculous person, and to her own mother as in some inexplicable way a social failure, had never seen herself in either light; for, though to some extent ridiculed and mimicked in West Kensington like everybody else there, she was accepted as a rational and normal—or shall we say inevitable?—sort of human being. At worst they called her The Pusher; but to them no more than to herself had it ever occurred that she was pushing the air, and pushing it in a wrong direction. Still, she was not happy. She was growing desperate. Her one asset, the fact that her mother was what the Epsom greengrocer called a carriage lady had no exchange value, apparently. It had prevented her from getting educated, because the only education she could have afforded was education with the Earlscourt green grocer's daughter. It had led her to seek the society of her mother's class; and that class simply would not have her, because she was much poorer than the greengrocer, and, far from being able to afford a maid, could not afford even a housemaid, and had to scrape along at home with an illiberally treated general servant. Under such circumstances nothing could give her an air of being a genuine product of Largelady Park. And yet its tradition made her regard a marriage with anyone within her reach as an unbearable humiliation. Commercial people and professional people in a small way were odious to her. She ran after painters and novelists; but she did not charm them; and her bold attempts to pick up and practise artistic and literary talk irritated them. She was, in short, an utter failure, an ignorant, incompetent, pretentious, unwelcome, penniless, useless little snob; and though she did not admit these disqualifications (for nobody ever faces unpleasant truths of this kind until the possibility of a way out dawns on them) she felt their effects too keenly to be satisfied with her position.

Clara had a startling eyeopener when, on being suddenly wakened to enthusiasm by a girl of her own age who dazzled her and produced in her a gushing desire to take her for a model, and gain her friendship, she discovered that this exquisite apparition had graduated from the gutter in a few months' time. It shook her so violently, that when Mr. H. G. Wells lifted her on the point of his puissant pen, and placed her at the angle of view from which the life she was leading and the society to which she clung appeared in its true relation to real human needs and worthy social structure, he effected a conversion and a conviction of sin comparable to the most sensational feats of General Booth or Gypsy Smith. Clara's snobbery went bang. Life suddenly began to move with her. Without knowing how or why, she began to make friends and enemies. Some of the acquaintances to whom she had been a tedious or indifferent or ridiculous affliction, dropped her: others became cordial. To her amazement she found that some "quite nice" people were saturated with Wells, and that this accessibility to ideas was the secret of their niceness. People she had thought deeply religious, and had tried to conciliate on that tack with disastrous results, suddenly took an interest in her, and revealed a hostility to conventional religion which she had never conceived possible except among the most desperate characters. They made her read Galsworthy; and Galsworthy exposed the vanity of Largelady Park and finished her. It exasperated her to think that the dungeon in which she had languished for so many unhappy years had been unlocked all the time, and that the impulses she had so carefully struggled with and stifled for the sake of keeping well with society, were precisely those by which alone she could have come into any sort of sincere human contact. In the radiance of these discoveries, and the tumult of their reaction, she made a fool of herself as freely and conspicuously as when she so rashly adopted Eliza's expletive in Mrs. Higgins's drawing-room; for the new-born Wellsian had to find her bearings almost as ridiculously as a baby; but nobody hates a baby for its ineptitudes, or thinks the worse of it for trying to eat the matches; and Clara lost no friends by her follies. They laughed at her to her face this time; and she had to defend herself and fight it out as best she could.

When Freddy paid a visit to Earlscourt (which he never did when he could possibly help it) to make the desolating announcement that he and his Eliza were thinking of blackening the Largelady scutcheon by opening a shop, he found the little household already convulsed by a prior announcement from Clara that she also was going to work in an old furniture shop in Dover Street, which had been started by a fellow Wellsian. This appointment Clara owed, after all, to her old social accomplishment of Push. She had made up her mind that, cost what it might, she would see Mr. Wells in the flesh; and she had achieved her end at a garden party. She had better luck than so rash an enterprise deserved. Mr. Wells came up to her expectations. Age had not withered him, nor could custom stale his infinite variety in half an hour. His pleasant neatness and compactness, his small hands and feet, his teeming ready brain, his unaffected accessibility, and a certain fine apprehensiveness which stamped him as susceptible from his topmost hair to his tipmost toe, proved irresistible. Clara talked of nothing else for weeks and weeks afterwards. And as she happened to talk to the lady of the furniture shop, and that lady also desired above all things to know Mr. Wells and sell pretty things to him, she offered Clara a job on the chance of achieving that end through her.

And so it came about that Eliza's luck held, and the expected opposition to the flower shop melted away. The shop is in the arcade of a railway station not very far from the Victoria and Albert Museum; and if you live in that neighborhood you may go there any day and buy a buttonhole from Eliza.

Now here is a last opportunity for romance. Would you not like to be assured that the shop was an immense success, thanks to Eliza's charms and her early business experience in Covent Garden? Alas! the truth is the truth: the shop did not pay for a long time, simply because Eliza and her Freddy did not know how to keep it. True, Eliza had not to begin at the very beginning: she knew the names and prices of the cheaper flowers; and her elation was unbounded when she found that Freddy, like all youths educated at cheap, pretentious, and thoroughly inefficient schools, knew a little Latin. It was very little, but enough to make him appear to her a Porson or Bentley, and to put him at his ease with botanical nomenclature. Unfortunately he knew nothing else; and Eliza, though she could count money up to eighteen shillings or so, and had acquired a certain familiarity with the language of Milton from her struggles to qualify herself for winning Higgins's bet, could not write out a bill without utterly disgracing the establishment. Freddy's power of stating in Latin that Balbus built a wall and that Gaul was divided into three parts did not carry with it the slightest knowledge of accounts or business: Colonel Pickering had to explain to him what a cheque book and a bank account meant. And the pair were by no means easily teachable. Freddy backed up Eliza in her obstinate refusal to believe that they could save money by engaging a bookkeeper with some knowledge of the business. How, they argued, could you possibly save money by going to extra expense when you already could not make both ends meet? But the Colonel, after making the ends meet over and over again, at last gently insisted; and Eliza, humbled to the dust by having to beg from him so often, and stung by the uproarious derision of Higgins, to whom the notion of Freddy succeeding at anything was a joke that never palled, grasped the fact that business, like phonetics, has to be learned.

On the piteous spectacle of the pair spending their evenings in shorthand schools and polytechnic classes, learning bookkeeping and typewriting with incipient junior clerks, male and female, from the elementary schools, let me not dwell. There were even classes at the London School of Economics, and a humble personal appeal to the director of that institution to recommend a course bearing on the flower business. He, being a humorist, explained to them the method of the celebrated Dickensian essay on Chinese Metaphysics by the gentleman who read an article on China and an article on Metaphysics and combined the information. He suggested that they should combine the London School with Kew Gardens. Eliza, to whom the procedure of the Dickensian gentleman seemed perfectly correct (as in fact it was) and not in the least funny (which was only her ignorance) took his advice with entire gravity.

But the effort that cost her the deepest humiliation was a request to Higgins, whose pet artistic fancy, next to Milton's verse, was calligraphy, and who himself wrote a most beautiful Italian hand, that he would teach her to write. He declared that she was congenitally incapable of forming a single letter worthy of the least of Milton's words; but she persisted; and again he suddenly threw himself into the task of teaching her with a combination of stormy intensity, concentrated patience, and occasional bursts of interesting disquisition on the beauty and nobility, the august mission and destiny, of human handwriting. Eliza ended by acquiring an extremely uncommercial script which was a positive extension of her personal beauty, and spending three times as much on stationery as anyone else because certain qualities and shapes of paper became indispensable to her. She could not even address an envelope in the usual way because it made the margins all wrong.

Their commercial school days were a period of disgrace and despair for the young couple. They seemed to be learning nothing about flower shops. At last they gave it up as hopeless, and shook the dust of the shorthand schools, and the polytechnics, and the London School of Economics from their feet for ever. Besides, the business was in some mysterious way beginning to take care of itself. They had somehow forgotten their objections to employing other people. They came to the conclusion that their own way was the best, and that they had really a remarkable talent for business. The Colonel, who had been compelled for some years to keep a sufficient sum on current account at his bankers to make up their deficits, found that the provision was unnecessary: the young people were prospering. It is true that there was not quite fair play between them and their competitors in trade. Their week-ends in the country cost them nothing, and saved them the price of their Sunday dinners; for the motor car was the Colonel's; and he and Higgins paid the hotel bills. Mr. F. Hill, florist and greengrocer (they soon discovered that there was money in asparagus; and asparagus led to other vegetables), had an air which stamped the business as classy; and in private life he was still Frederick Eynsford Hill, Esquire. Not that there was any swank about him: nobody but Eliza knew that he had been christened Frederick Challoner. Eliza herself swanked like anything.

That is all. That is how it has turned out. It is astonishing how much Eliza still manages to meddle in the housekeeping at Wimpole Street in spite of the shop and her own family. And it is notable that though she never nags her husband, and frankly loves the Colonel as if she were his favorite daughter, she has never got out of the habit of nagging Higgins that was established on the fatal night when she won his bet for him. She snaps his head off on the faintest provocation, or on none. He no longer dares to tease her by assuming an abysmal inferiority of Freddy's mind to his own. He storms and bullies and derides; but she stands up to him so ruthlessly that the Colonel has to ask her from time to time to be kinder to Higgins; and it is the only request of his that brings a mulish expression into her face. Nothing but some emergency or calamity great enough to break down all likes and dislikes, and throw them both back on their common humanity—and may they be spared any such trial!—will ever alter this. She knows that Higgins does not need her, just as her father did not need her. The very scrupulousness with which he told her that day that he had become used to having her there, and dependent on her for all sorts of little services, and that he should miss her if she went away (it would never have occurred to Freddy or the Colonel to say anything of the sort) deepens her inner certainty that she is "no more to him than them slippers", yet she has a sense, too, that his indifference is deeper than the infatuation of commoner souls. She is immensely interested in him. She has even secret mischievous moments in which she wishes she could get him alone, on a desert island, away from all ties and with nobody else in the world to consider, and just drag him off his pedestal and see him making love like any common man. We all have private imaginations of that sort. But when it comes to business, to the life that she really leads as distinguished from the life of dreams and fancies, she likes Freddy and she likes the Colonel; and she does not like Higgins and Mr. Doolittle. Galatea never does quite like Pygmalion: his relation to her is too godlike to be altogether agreeable.

OVERRULED

PREFACE TO OVERRULED.

THE ALLEVIATIONS OF MONOGAMY.

This piece is not an argument for or against polygamy. It is a clinical study of how the thing actually occurs among quite ordinary people, innocent of all unconventional views concerning it. The enormous majority of cases in real life are those of people in that position. Those who deliberately and conscientiously profess what are oddly called advanced views by those others who believe them to be retrograde, are often, and indeed mostly, the last people in the world to engage in unconventional adventures of any kind, not only because they have neither time nor disposition for them, but because the friction set up between the individual and the community by the expression of unusual views of any sort is quite enough hindrance to the heretic without being complicated by personal scandals. Thus the theoretic libertine is usually a person of blameless family life, whilst the practical libertine is mercilessly severe on all other libertines, and excessively conventional in professions of social principle.

What is more, these professions are not hypocritical: they are for the most part quite sincere. The common libertine, like the drunkard, succumbs to a temptation which he does not defend, and against which he warns others with an earnestness proportionate to the intensity of his own remorse. He (or she) may be a liar and a humbug, pretending to be better than the detected libertines, and clamoring for their condign punishment; but this is mere self-defence. No reasonable person expects the burglar to confess his pursuits, or to refrain from joining in the cry of Stop Thief when the police get on the track of another burglar. If society chooses to penalize candor, it has itself to thank if its attack is countered by falsehood. The clamorous virtue of the libertine is therefore no more hypocritical than the plea of Not Guilty which is allowed to every criminal. But one result is that the theorists who write most sincerely and favorably about polygamy know least about it; and the practitioners who know most about it keep their knowledge very jealously to themselves. Which is hardly fair to the practice.

INACCESSIBILITY OF THE FACTS.

Also it is impossible to estimate its prevalence. A practice to which nobody confesses may be both universal and unsuspected, just as a virtue which everybody is expected, under heavy penalties, to claim, may have no existence. It is often assumed—indeed it is the official assumption of the Churches and the divorce courts that a gentleman and a lady cannot be alone together innocently. And that is manifest blazing nonsense, though many women have been stoned to death in the east, and divorced in the west, on the strength of it. On the other hand, the innocent and conventional people who regard the gallant adventures as crimes of so horrible a nature that only the most depraved and desperate characters engage in them or would listen to advances in that direction without raising an alarm with the noisiest indignation, are clearly examples of the fact that most sections of society do not know how the other sections live. Industry is the most effective check on gallantry. Women may, as Napoleon said, be the occupation of the idle man just as men are the preoccupation of the idle woman; but the mass of mankind is too busy and too poor for the long and expensive sieges which the professed libertine lays to virtue. Still, wherever there is idleness or even a reasonable supply of elegant leisure there is a good deal of coquetry and philandering. It is so much pleasanter to dance on the edge of a precipice than to go over it that leisured society is full of people who spend a great part of their lives in flirtation, and conceal nothing but the humiliating secret that they have never gone any further. For there is no pleasing people in the matter of reputation in this department: every insult is a flattery; every testimonial is a disparagement: Joseph is despised and promoted, Potiphar's wife admired and condemned: in short, you are never on solid ground until you get away from the subject altogether. There is a continual and irreconcilable conflict between the natural and conventional sides of the case, between spontaneous human relations between independent men and women on the one hand and the property relation between husband and wife on the other, not to mention the confusion under the common name of love of a generous natural attraction and interest with the murderous jealousy that fastens on and clings to its mate (especially a hated mate) as a tiger fastens on a carcase. And the confusion is natural; for these extremes are extremes of the same passion; and most cases lie somewhere on the scale between them, and are so complicated by ordinary likes and dislikes, by incidental wounds to vanity or gratifications of it, and by class feeling, that A will be jealous of B and not of C, and will tolerate infidelities on the part of D whilst being furiously angry when they are committed by E.

THE CONVENTION OF JEALOUSY

That jealousy is independent of sex is shown by its intensity in children, and by the fact that very jealous people are jealous of everybody without regard to relationship or sex, and cannot bear to hear the person they "love" speak favorably of anyone under any circumstances (many women, for instance, are much more jealous of their husbands' mothers and sisters than of unrelated women whom they suspect him of fancying); but it is seldom possible to disentangle the two passions in practice. Besides, jealousy is an inculcated passion, forced by society on people in whom it would not occur spontaneously. In Brieux's Bourgeois aux Champs, the benevolent hero finds himself detested by the neighboring peasants and farmers, not because he preserves game, and sets mantraps for poachers, and defends his legal rights over his land to the extremest point of unsocial savagery, but because, being an amiable and public-spirited person, he refuses to do all this, and thereby offends and disparages the sense of property in his neighbors. The same thing is true of matrimonial jealousy; the man who does not at least pretend to feel it and behave as badly as if he really felt it is despised and insulted; and many a man has shot or stabbed a friend or been shot or stabbed by him in a duel, or disgraced himself and ruined his own wife in a divorce scandal, against his conscience, against his instinct, and to the destruction of his home, solely because Society conspired to drive him to keep its own lower morality in countenance in this miserable and undignified manner.

Morality is confused in such matters. In an elegant plutocracy, a jealous husband is regarded as a boor. Among the tradesmen who supply that plutocracy with its meals, a husband who is not jealous, and refrains from assailing his rival with his fists, is regarded as a ridiculous, contemptible and cowardly cuckold. And the laboring class is divided into the respectable section which takes the tradesman's view, and the disreputable section which enjoys the license of the plutocracy without its money: creeping below the law as its exemplars prance above it; cutting down all expenses of respectability and even decency; and frankly accepting squalor and disrepute as the price of anarchic self-indulgence. The conflict between Malvolio and Sir Toby, between the marquis and the bourgeois, the cavalier and the puritan, the ascetic and the voluptuary, goes on continually, and goes on not only between class and class and individual and individual, but in the selfsame breast in a series of reactions and revulsions in which the irresistible becomes the unbearable, and the unbearable the irresistible, until none of us can say what our characters really are in this respect.

THE MISSING DATA OF A SCIENTIFIC NATURAL HISTORY OF MARRIAGE.

Of one thing I am persuaded: we shall never attain to a reasonable healthy public opinion on sex questions until we offer, as the data for that opinion, our actual conduct and our real thoughts instead of a moral fiction which we agree to call virtuous conduct, and which we then—and here comes in the mischief—pretend is our conduct and our thoughts. If the result were that we all believed one another to be better than we really are, there would be something to be said for it; but the actual result appears to be a monstrous exaggeration of the power and continuity of sexual passion. The whole world shares the fate of Lucrezia Borgia, who, though she seems on investigation to have been quite a suitable wife for a modern British Bishop, has been invested by the popular historical imagination with all the extravagances of a Messalina or a Cenci. Writers of belles lettres who are rash enough to admit that their whole life is not one constant preoccupation with adored members of the opposite sex, and who even countenance La Rochefoucauld's remark that very few people would ever imagine themselves in love if they had never read anything about it, are gravely declared to be abnormal or physically defective by critics of crushing unadventurousness and domestication. French authors of saintly temperament are forced to include in their retinue countesses of ardent complexion with whom they are supposed to live in sin. Sentimental controversies on the subject are endless; but they are useless, because nobody tells the truth. Rousseau did it by an extraordinary effort, aided by a superhuman faculty for human natural history, but the result was curiously disconcerting because, though the facts were so conventionally shocking that people felt that they ought to matter a great deal, they actually mattered very little. And even at that everybody pretends not to believe him.

ARTIFICIAL RETRIBUTION.

The worst of that is that busybodies with perhaps rather more than a normal taste for mischief are continually trying to make negligible things matter as much in fact as they do in convention by deliberately inflicting injuries—sometimes atrocious injuries—on the parties concerned. Few people have any knowledge of the savage punishments that are legally inflicted for aberrations and absurdities to which no sanely instructed community would call any attention. We create an artificial morality, and consequently an artificial conscience, by manufacturing disastrous consequences for events which, left to themselves, would do very little harm (sometimes not any) and be forgotten in a few days.

But the artificial morality is not therefore to be condemned offhand. In many cases it may save mischief instead of making it: for example, though the hanging of a murderer is the duplication of a murder, yet it may be less murderous than leaving the matter to be settled by blood feud or vendetta. As long as human nature insists on revenge, the official organization and satisfaction of revenge by the State may be also its minimization. The mischief begins when the official revenge persists after the passion it satisfies has died out of the race. Stoning a woman to death in the east because she has ventured to marry again after being deserted by her husband may be more merciful than allowing her to be mobbed to death; but the official stoning or burning of an adulteress in the west would be an atrocity because few of us hate an adulteress to the extent of desiring such a penalty, or of being prepared to take the law into our own hands if it were withheld. Now what applies to this extreme case applies also in due degree to the other cases. Offences in which sex is concerned are often needlessly magnified by penalties, ranging from various forms of social ostracism to long sentences of penal servitude, which would be seen to be monstrously disproportionate to the real feeling against them if the removal of both the penalties and the taboo on their discussion made it possible for us to ascertain their real prevalence and estimation. Fortunately there is one outlet for the truth. We are permitted to discuss in jest what we may not discuss in earnest. A serious comedy about sex is taboo: a farcical comedy is privileged.

THE FAVORITE SUBJECT OF FARCICAL COMEDY.

The little piece which follows this preface accordingly takes the form of a farcical comedy, because it is a contribution to the very extensive dramatic literature which takes as its special department the gallantries of married people. The stage has been preoccupied by such affairs for centuries, not only in the jesting vein of Restoration Comedy and Palais Royal farce, but in the more tragically turned adulteries of the Parisian school which dominated the stage until Ibsen put them out of countenance and relegated them to their proper place as articles of commerce. Their continued vogue in that department maintains the tradition that adultery is the dramatic subject par excellence, and indeed that a play that is not about adultery is not a play at all. I was considered a heresiarch of the most extravagant kind when I expressed my opinion at the outset of my career as a playwright, that adultery is the dullest of themes on the stage, and that from Francesca and Paolo down to the latest guilty couple of the school of Dumas fils, the romantic adulterers have all been intolerable bores.

THE PSEUDO SEX PLAY.

Later on, I had occasion to point out to the defenders of sex as the proper theme of drama, that though they were right in ranking sex as an intensely interesting subject, they were wrong in assuming that sex is an indispensable motive in popular plays. The plays of Moliere are, like the novels of the Victorian epoch or Don Quixote, as nearly sexless as anything not absolutely inhuman can be; and some of Shakespear's plays are sexually on a par with the census: they contain women as well as men, and that is all. This had to be admitted; but it was still assumed that the plays of the XIX century Parisian school are, in contrast with the sexless masterpieces, saturated with sex; and this I strenuously denied. A play about the convention that a man should fight a duel or come to fisticuffs with his wife's lover if she has one, or the convention that he should strangle her like Othello, or turn her out of the house and never see her or allow her to see her children again, or the convention that she should never be spoken to again by any decent person and should finally drown herself, or the convention that persons involved in scenes of recrimination or confession by these conventions should call each other certain abusive names and describe their conduct as guilty and frail and so on: all these may provide material for very effective plays; but such plays are not dramatic studies of sex: one might as well say that Romeo and Juliet is a dramatic study of pharmacy because the catastrophe is brought about through an apothecary. Duels are not sex; divorce cases are not sex; the Trade Unionism of married women is not sex. Only the most insignificant fraction of the gallantries of married people produce any of the conventional results; and plays occupied wholly with the conventional results are therefore utterly unsatisfying as sex plays, however interesting they may be as plays of intrigue and plot puzzles.

The world is finding this out rapidly. The Sunday papers, which in the days when they appealed almost exclusively to the lower middle class were crammed with police intelligence, and more especially with divorce and murder cases, now lay no stress on them; and police papers which confined themselves entirely to such matters, and were once eagerly read, have perished through the essential dulness of their topics. And yet the interest in sex is stronger than ever: in fact, the literature that has driven out the journalism of the divorce courts is a literature occupied with sex to an extent and with an intimacy and frankness that would have seemed utterly impossible to Thackeray or Dickens if they had been told that the change would complete itself within fifty years of their own time.

ART AND MORALITY.

It is ridiculous to say, as inconsiderate amateurs of the arts do, that art has nothing to do with morality. What is true is that the artist's business is not that of the policeman; and that such factitious consequences and put-up jobs as divorces and executions and the detective operations that lead up to them are no essential part of life, though, like poisons and buttered slides and red-hot pokers, they provide material for plenty of thrilling or amusing stories suited to people who are incapable of any interest in psychology. But the fine artists must keep the policeman out of his studies of sex and studies of crime. It is by clinging nervously to the policeman that most of the pseudo sex plays convince me that the writers have either never had any serious personal experience of their ostensible subject, or else have never conceived it possible that the stage door present the phenomena of sex as they appear in nature.

THE LIMITS OF STAGE PRESENTATION.

But the stage presents much more shocking phenomena than those of sex. There is, of course, a sense in which you cannot present sex on the stage, just as you cannot present murder. Macbeth must no more really kill Duncan than he must himself be really slain by Macduff. But the feelings of a murderer can be expressed in a certain artistic convention; and a carefully prearranged sword exercise can be gone through with sufficient pretence of earnestness to be accepted by the willing imaginations of the younger spectators as a desperate combat.

The tragedy of love has been presented on the stage in the same way. In Tristan and Isolde, the curtain does not, as in Romeo and Juliet, rise with the lark: the whole night of love is played before the spectators. The lovers do not discuss marriage in an elegantly sentimental way: they utter the visions and feelings that come to lovers at the supreme moments of their love, totally forgetting that there are such things in the world as husbands and lawyers and duelling codes and theories of sin and notions of propriety and all the other irrelevancies which provide hackneyed and bloodless material for our so-called plays of passion.

PRUDERIES OF THE FRENCH STAGE.

To all stage presentations there are limits. If Macduff were to stab Macbeth, the spectacle would be intolerable; and even the pretence which we allow on our stage is ridiculously destructive to the illusion of the scene. Yet pugilists and gladiators will actually fight and kill in public without sham, even as a spectacle for money. But no sober couple of lovers of any delicacy could endure to be watched. We in England, accustomed to consider the French stage much more licentious than the British, are always surprised and puzzled when we learn, as we may do any day if we come within reach of such information, that French actors are often scandalized by what they consider the indecency of the English stage, and that French actresses who desire a greater license in appealing to the sexual instincts than the French stage allows them, learn and establish themselves on the English stage. The German and Russian stages are in the same relation to the French and perhaps more or less all the Latin stages. The reason is that, partly from a want of respect for the theatre, partly from a sort of respect for art in general which moves them to accord moral privileges to artists, partly from the very objectionable tradition that the realm of art is Alsatia and the contemplation of works of art a holiday from the burden of virtue, partly because French prudery does not attach itself to the same points of behavior as British prudery, and has a different code of the mentionable and the unmentionable, and for many other reasons the French tolerate plays which are never performed in England until they have been spoiled by a process of bowdlerization; yet French taste is more fastidious than ours as to the exhibition and treatment on the stage of the physical incidents of sex. On the French stage a kiss is as obvious a convention as the thrust under the arm by which Macduff runs Macbeth through. It is even a purposely unconvincing convention: the actors rather insisting that it shall be impossible for any spectator to mistake a stage kiss for a real one. In England, on the contrary, realism is carried to the point at which nobody except the two performers can perceive that the caress is not genuine. And here the English stage is certainly in the right; for whatever question there arises as to what incidents are proper for representation on the stage or not, my experience as a playgoer leaves me in no doubt that once it is decided to represent an incident, it will be offensive, no matter whether it be a prayer or a kiss, unless it is presented with a convincing appearance of sincerity.

OUR DISILLUSIVE SCENERY.

For example, the main objection to the use of illusive scenery (in most modern plays scenery is not illusive; everything visible is as real as in your drawing room at home) is that it is unconvincing; whilst the imaginary scenery with which the audience provides a platform or tribune like the Elizabethan stage or the Greek stage used by Sophocles, is quite convincing. In fact, the more scenery you have the less illusion you produce. The wise playwright, when he cannot get absolute reality of presentation, goes to the other extreme, and aims at atmosphere and suggestion of mood rather than at direct simulative illusion. The theatre, as I first knew it, was a place of wings and flats which destroyed both atmosphere and illusion. This was tolerated, and even intensely enjoyed, but not in the least because nothing better was possible; for all the devices employed in the productions of Mr. Granville Barker or Max Reinhardt or the Moscow Art Theatre were equally available for Colley Cibber and Garrick, except the intensity of our artificial light. When Garrick played Richard II in slashed trunk hose and plumes, it was not because he believed that the Plantagenets dressed like that, or because the costumes could not have made him a XV century dress as easily as a nondescript combination of the state robes of George III with such scraps of older fashions as seemed to playgoers for some reason to be romantic. The charm of the theatre in those days was its makebelieve. It has that charm still, not only for the amateurs, who are happiest when they are most unnatural and impossible and absurd, but for audiences as well. I have seen performances of my own plays which were to me far wilder burlesques than Sheridan's Critic or Buckingham's Rehearsal; yet they have produced sincere laughter and tears such as the most finished metropolitan productions have failed to elicit. Fielding was entirely right when he represented Partridge as enjoying intensely the performance of the king in Hamlet because anybody could see that the king was an actor, and resenting Garrick's Hamlet because it might have been a real man. Yet we have only to look at the portraits of Garrick to see that his performances would nowadays seem almost as extravagantly stagey as his costumes. In our day

Calve's intensely real Carmen never pleased the mob as much as the obvious fancy ball masquerading of suburban young ladies in the same character.

HOLDING THE MIRROR UP TO NATURE.

Theatrical art begins as the holding up to Nature of a distorting mirror. In this phase it pleases people who are childish enough to believe that they can see what they look like and what they are when they look at a true mirror. Naturally they think that a true mirror can teach them nothing. Only by giving them back some monstrous image can the mirror amuse them or terrify them. It is not until they grow up to the point at which they learn that they know very little about themselves, and that they do not see themselves in a true mirror as other people see them, that they become consumed with curiosity as to what they really are like, and begin to demand that the stage shall be a mirror of such accuracy and intensity of illumination that they shall be able to get glimpses of their real selves in it, and also learn a little how they appear to other people.

For audiences of this highly developed class, sex can no longer be ignored or conventionalized or distorted by the playwright who makes the mirror. The old sentimental extravagances and the old grossnesses are of no further use to him. Don Giovanni and Zerlina are not gross: Tristan and Isolde are not extravagant or sentimental. They say and do nothing that you cannot bear to hear and see; and yet they give you, the one pair briefly and slightly, and the other fully and deeply, what passes in the minds of lovers. The love depicted may be that of a philosophic adventurer tempting an ignorant country girl, or of a tragically serious poet entangled with a woman of noble capacity in a passion which has become for them the reality of the whole universe. No matter: the thing is dramatized and dramatized directly, not talked about as something that happened before the curtain rose, or that will happen after it falls.

FARCICAL COMEDY SHIRKING ITS SUBJECT.

Now if all this can be done in the key of tragedy and philosophic comedy, it can, I have always contended, be done in the key of farcical comedy; and Overruled is a trifling experiment in that manner. Conventional farcical comedies are always finally tedious because the heart of them, the inevitable conjugal infidelity, is always evaded. Even its consequences are evaded. Mr. Granville Barker has pointed out rightly that if the third acts of our farcical comedies dared to describe the consequences that would follow from the first and second in real life, they would end as squalid tragedies; and in my opinion they would be greatly improved thereby even as entertainments; for I have never seen a three-act farcical comedy without being bored and tired by the third act, and observing that the rest of the audience were in the same condition, though they were not vigilantly introspective enough to find that out, and were apt to blame one another, especially the husbands and wives, for their crossness. But it is happily by no means true that conjugal infidelities always produce tragic consequences, or that they need produce even the unhappiness which they often do produce. Besides, the more momentous the consequences, the more interesting become the impulses and imaginations and reasonings, if any, of the people who disregard them. If I had an opportunity of conversing with the ghost of an executed murderer, I have no doubt he would begin to tell me eagerly about his trial, with the names of the distinguished ladies and gentlemen who honored him with their presence on that occasion, and then about his execution. All of which would bore me exceedingly. I should say, "My dear sir: such manufactured ceremonies do not interest me in the least. I know how a man is tried, and how he is hanged. I should have had you killed in a much less disgusting, hypocritical, and unfriendly manner if the matter had been in my hands. What I want to know about is the murder. How did you feel when you committed it? Why did you do it? What did you say to yourself about it? If, like most murderers, you had not been hanged, would you have committed other murders? Did you really dislike the victim, or did you want his money, or did you murder a person whom you did not dislike, and from whose death you had nothing to gain, merely for the sake of murdering? If so, can you describe the charm to me? Does it come upon you periodically; or is it chronic? Has curiosity anything to do with it?" I would ply him with all manner of questions to find out what murder is really like; and I should not be satisfied until I had realized that I, too, might commit a murder, or else that there is some specific quality present in a murderer and lacking in me. And, if so, what that quality is.

In just the same way, I want the unfaithful husband or the unfaithful wife in a farcical comedy not to bother me with their divorce cases or the stratagems they employ to avoid a divorce case, but to tell me how and why married couples are unfaithful. I don't want to hear the lies they tell one another to conceal what they have done, but the truths they tell one another when they have to face what they have done without concealment or excuse. No doubt prudent and considerate people conceal such adventures, when they can, from those who are most likely to be wounded by them; but it is not to be presumed that, when found out, they necessarily disgrace themselves by irritating lies and transparent subterfuges.

My playlet, which I offer as a model to all future writers of farcical comedy, may now, I hope, be read without shock. I may just add that Mr. Sibthorpe Juno's view that morality demands, not that we should behave morally (an impossibility to our sinful nature) but that we shall not attempt to defend our immoralities, is a standard view in England, and was advanced in all seriousness by an earnest and distinguished British moralist shortly after the first performance of Overruled. My objection to that aspect of the doctrine of original sin is that no necessary and inevitable operation of human nature can reasonably be regarded as sinful at all, and that a morality which assumes the contrary is an absurd morality, and can be kept in countenance only by hypocrisy. When people were ashamed of sanitary problems, and refused to face them, leaving them to solve themselves clandestinely in dirt and secrecy, the solution arrived at was the Black Death. A similar policy as to sex problems has solved itself by an even worse plague than the Black Death; and the remedy for that is not Salvarsan, but sound moral hygiene, the first foundation of which is the discontinuance of our habit of telling not only the comparatively harmless lies that we know we ought not to tell, but the ruinous lies that we foolishly think we ought to tell.

OVERRULED.

A lady and gentleman are sitting together on a chesterfield in a retired corner of the lounge of a seaside hotel. It is a summer night: the French window behind them stands open. The terrace without overlooks a moonlit harbor. The lounge is dark. The chesterfield, upholstered in silver grey, and the two figures on it in evening dress, catch the light from an arc lamp somewhere; but the walls, covered with a dark green paper, are in gloom. There are two stray chairs, one on each side. On the gentleman's right, behind him up near the window, is an unused fireplace. Opposite it on the lady's left is a door. The gentleman is on the lady's right.

The lady is very attractive, with a musical voice and soft appealing manners. She is young: that is, one feels sure that she is under thirty-five and over twenty-four. The gentleman does not look much older. He is rather handsome, and has ventured as far in the direction of poetic dandyism in the arrangement of his hair as any man who is not a professional artist can afford to in England. He is obviously very much in love with the lady, and is, in fact, yielding to an irresistible impulse to throw his arms around her.

THE LADY. Don't—oh don't be horrid. Please, Mr. Lunn [*she rises from the lounge and retreats behind it*]! Promise me you won't be horrid.

GREGORY LUNN. I'm not being horrid, Mrs. Juno. I'm not going to be horrid. I love you: that's all. I'm extraordinarily happy.

MRS. JUNO. You will really be good?

GREGORY. I'll be whatever you wish me to be. I tell you I love you. I love loving you. I don't want to be tired and sorry, as I should be if I were to be horrid. I don't want you to be tired and sorry. Do come and sit down again.

MRS. JUNO [*coming back to her seat*]. You're sure you don't want anything you oughtn't to?

GREGORY. Quite sure. I only want you [*she recoils*]. Don't be alarmed. I like wanting you. As long as I have a want, I have a reason for living. Satisfaction is death.

MRS. JUNO. Yes; but the impulse to commit suicide is sometimes irresistible.

GREGORY. Not with you.

MRS. JUNO. What!

GREGORY. Oh, it sounds uncomplimentary; but it isn't really. Do you know why half the couples who find themselves situated as we are now behave horridly?

MRS. JUNO. Because they can't help it if they let things go too far.

GREGORY. Not a bit of it. It's because they have nothing else to do, and no other way of entertaining each other. You don't know what it is to be alone with a woman who has little beauty and less conversation. What is a man to do? She can't talk interestingly; and if he talks that way himself she doesn't understand him. He can't look at her: if he does, he only finds out that she isn't beautiful. Before the end of five minutes they are both hideously bored. There's only one thing that can save the situation; and that's what you call being horrid. With a beautiful, witty, kind woman, there's no time for such follies. It's so delightful to look at her, to listen to her voice, to hear all she has to say, that nothing else happens. That is why the woman who is supposed to have a thousand lovers seldom has one; whilst the stupid, graceless animals of women have dozens.

MRS. JUNO. I wonder! It's quite true that when one feels in danger one talks like mad to stave it off, even when one doesn't quite want to stave it off.

GREGORY. One never does quite want to stave it off. Danger is delicious. But death isn't. We court the danger; but the real delight is in escaping, after all.

MRS. JUNO. I don't think we'll talk about it any more. Danger is all very well when you do escape; but sometimes one doesn't. I tell you frankly I don't feel as safe as you do—if you really do.

GREGORY. But surely you can do as you please without injuring anyone, Mrs. Juno. That is the whole secret of your extraordinary charm for me.

MRS. JUNO. I don't understand.

GREGORY. Well, I hardly know how to begin to explain. But the root of the matter is that I am what people call a good man.

MRS. JUNO. I thought so until you began making love to me.

GREGORY. But you knew I loved you all along.

MRS. JUNO. Yes, of course; but I depended on you not to tell me so; because I thought you were good. Your blurting it out spoilt it. And it was wicked besides.

GREGORY. Not at all. You see, it's a great many years since I've been able to allow myself to fall in love. I know lots of charming women; but the worst of it is, they're all married. Women don't become charming, to my taste, until they're fully developed; and by that time, if they're really nice, they're snapped up and married. And then, because I am a good man, I have to place a limit to my regard for them. I may be fortunate enough to gain friendship and even very warm affection from them; but my loyalty to their husbands and their hearths and their happiness obliges me to draw a line and not overstep it. Of course I value such affectionate regard very highly indeed. I am surrounded with women who are most dear to me. But every one of them has a post sticking up, if I may put it that way, with the inscription Trespassers Will Be Prosecuted. How we all loathe that notice! In every lovely garden, in every dell full of primroses, on every fair hillside, we meet that confounded board; and there is always a gamekeeper round the corner. But what is that to the horror of meeting it on every beautiful woman, and knowing that there is a husband round the corner? I have had this accursed board standing between me and every dear and desirable woman until I thought I had lost the power of letting myself fall really and wholeheartedly in love.

MRS. JUNO. Wasn't there a widow?

GREGORY. No. Widows are extraordinarily scarce in modern society. Husbands live longer than they used to; and even when they do die, their widows have a string of names down for their next.

MRS. JUNO. Well, what about the young girls?

GREGORY. Oh, who cares for young girls? They're sympathetic. They're beginners. They don't attract me. I'm afraid of them.

MRS. JUNO. That's the correct thing to say to a woman of my age. But it doesn't explain why you seem to have put your scruples in your pocket when you met me.

GREGORY. Surely that's quite clear. I—

MRS. JUNO. No: please don't explain. I don't want to know. I take your word for it. Besides, it doesn't matter now. Our voyage is over; and tomorrow I start for the north to my poor father's place.

GREGORY [*surprised*]. Your poor father! I thought he was alive.

MRS. JUNO. So he is. What made you think he wasn't?

GREGORY. You said your POOR father.

MRS. JUNO. Oh, that's a trick of mine. Rather a silly trick, I Suppose; but there's something pathetic to me about men: I find myself calling them poor So-and-So when there's nothing whatever the matter with them.

GREGORY [*who has listened in growing alarm*]. But—I—is?— wa—? Oh, Lord!

MRS. JUNO. What's the matter?

GREGORY. Nothing.

MRS. JUNO. Nothing! [*Rising anxiously*]. Nonsense: you're ill.

GREGORY. No. It was something about your late husband—

MRS. JUNO. My LATE husband! What do you mean? [*clutching him, horror-stricken*]. Don't tell me he's dead.

GREGORY [*rising, equally appalled*]. Don't tell me he's alive.

MRS. JUNO. Oh, don't frighten me like this. Of course he's alive—unless you've heard anything.

GREGORY. The first day we met—on the boat—you spoke to me of your poor dear husband.

MRS. JUNO [*releasing him, quite reassured*]. Is that all?

GREGORY. Well, afterwards you called him poor Tops. Always poor Tops, Our poor dear Tops. What could I think?

MRS. JUNO [*sitting down again*]. I wish you hadn't given me such a shock about him; for I haven't been treating him at all well. Neither have you.

GREGORY [*relapsing into his seat, overwhelmed*]. And you mean to tell me you're not a widow!

MRS. JUNO. Gracious, no! I'm not in black.

GREGORY. Then I have been behaving like a blackguard. I have broken my promise to my mother. I shall never have an easy conscience again.

MRS. JUNO. I'm sorry. I thought you knew.

GREGORY. You thought I was a libertine?

MRS. JUNO. No: of course I shouldn't have spoken to you if I had thought that. I thought you liked me, but that you knew, and would be good.

GREGORY [*stretching his hands towards her breast*]. I thought the burden of being good had fallen from my soul at last. I saw nothing there but a bosom to rest on: the bosom of a lovely woman of whom I could dream without guilt. What do I see now?

MRS. JUNO. Just what you saw before.

GREGORY [*despairingly*]. No, no.

MRS. JUNO. What else?

GREGORY. Trespassers Will Be Prosecuted: Trespassers Will Be Prosecuted.

MRS. JUNO. They won't if they hold their tongues. Don't be such a coward. My husband won't eat you.

GREGORY. I'm not afraid of your husband. I'm afraid of my conscience.

MRS. JUNO [*losing patience*]. Well! I don't consider myself at all a badly behaved woman; for nothing has passed between us that was not perfectly nice and friendly; but really! to hear a grown-up man talking about promises to his mother!

GREGORY [*interrupting her*]. Yes, Yes: I know all about that. It's not romantic: it's not Don Juan: it's not advanced; but we feel it all the same. It's far deeper in our blood and bones than all the romantic stuff. My father got into a scandal once: that was why my mother made me promise never to make love to a married woman. And now I've done it I can't feel honest. Don't pretend to despise me or laugh at me. You feel it too. You said just now that your own conscience was uneasy when you thought of your husband. What must it be when you think of my wife?

MRS. JUNO [*rising aghast*]. Your wife!!! You don't dare sit there and tell me coolly that you're a married man!

GREGORY. I never led you to believe I was unmarried.

MRS. JUNO. Oh! You never gave me the faintest hint that you had a wife.

GREGORY. I did indeed. I discussed things with you that only married people really understand.

MRS. JUNO. Oh!!

GREGORY. I thought it the most delicate way of letting you know.

MRS. JUNO. Well, you ARE a daisy, I must say. I suppose that's vulgar; but really! really!! You and your goodness! However, now we've found one another out there's only one thing to be done. Will you please go?

GREGORY [*rising slowly*]. I OUGHT to go.

MRS. JUNO. Well, go.

GREGORY. Yes. Er—[*he tries to go*]. I—I somehow can't. [*He sits down again helplessly*]. My conscience is active: my will is paralyzed. This is really dreadful. Would you mind ringing the bell and asking them to throw me out? You ought to, you know.

MRS. JUNO. What! make a scandal in the face of the whole hotel! Certainly not. Don't be a fool.

GREGORY. Yes; but I can't go.

MRS. JUNO. Then I can. Goodbye.

GREGORY [*clinging to her hand*]. Can you really?

MRS. JUNO. Of course I—[*she wavers*]. Oh, dear! [*They contemplate one another helplessly*]. I can't. [*She sinks on the lounge, hand in hand with him*].

GREGORY. For heaven's sake pull yourself together. It's a question of self-control.

MRS. JUNO [*dragging her hand away and retreating to the end of the chesterfield*]. No: it's a question of distance. Self-control is all very well two or three yards off, or on a ship, with everybody looking on. Don't come any nearer.

GREGORY. This is a ghastly business. I want to go away; and I can't.

MRS. JUNO. I think you ought to go [*he makes an effort; and she adds quickly*] but if you try I shall grab you round the neck and disgrace myself. I implore you to sit still and be nice.

GREGORY. I implore you to run away. I believe I can trust myself to let you go for your own sake. But it will break my heart.

MRS. JUNO. I don't want to break your heart. I can't bear to think of your sitting here alone. I can't bear to think of sitting alone myself somewhere else. It's so senseless—so ridiculous—when we might be so happy. I don't want to be wicked, or coarse. But I like you very much; and I do want to be affectionate and human.

GREGORY. I ought to draw a line.

MRS. JUNO. So you shall, dear. Tell me: do you really like me? I don't mean LOVE me: you might love the housemaid—

GREGORY [*vehemently*]. No!

MRS. JUNO. Oh, yes you might; and what does that matter, anyhow? Are you really fond of me? Are we friends—comrades? Would you be sorry if I died?

GREGORY [*shrinking*]. Oh, don't.

MRS. JUNO. Or was it the usual aimless man's lark: a mere shipboard flirtation?

GREGORY. Oh, no, no: nothing half so bad, so vulgar, so wrong. I assure you I only meant to be agreeable. It grew on me before I noticed it.

MRS. JUNO. And you were glad to let it grow?

GREGORY. I let it grow because the board was not up.

MRS. JUNO. Bother the board! I am just as fond of Sibthorpe as—

GREGORY. Sibthorpe!

MRS. JUNO. Sibthorpe is my husband's Christian name. I oughtn't to call him Tops to you now.

GREGORY [*chuckling*]. It sounded like something to drink. But I have no right to laugh at him. My Christian name is Gregory, which sounds like a powder.

MRS. JUNO [*chilled*]. That is so like a man! I offer you my heart's warmest friendliest feeling; and you think of nothing but a silly joke. A quip like that makes you forget me.

GREGORY. Forget you! Oh, if I only could!

MRS. JUNO. If you could, would you?

GREGORY [*burying his shamed face in his hands*]. No: I'd die first. Oh, I hate myself.

MRS. JUNO. I glory in myself. It's so jolly to be reckless. CAN a man be reckless, I wonder.

GREGORY [*straightening himself desperately*]. No. I'm not reckless. I know what I'm doing: my conscience is awake. Oh, where is the intoxication of love? the delirium? the madness that makes a man think the world well lost for the woman he adores? I don't think anything of the sort: I see that it's not worth it: I know that it's wrong: I have never in my life been cooler, more businesslike.

MRS. JUNO. [*opening her arms to him*] But you can't resist me.

GREGORY. I must. I ought [*throwing himself into her arms*]. Oh, my darling, my treasure, we shall be sorry for this.

MRS. JUNO. We can forgive ourselves. Could we forgive ourselves if we let this moment slip?

GREGORY. I protest to the last. I'm against this. I have been pushed over a precipice. I'm innocent. This wild joy, this exquisite tenderness, this ascent into heaven can thrill me to the uttermost fibre of my heart [*with a gesture of ecstasy she hides her face on his shoulder*]; but it can't subdue my mind or corrupt my conscience, which still shouts to the skies that I'm not a willing party to this outrageous conduct. I repudiate the bliss with which you are filling me.

MRS. JUNO. Never mind your conscience. Tell me how happy you are.

GREGORY. No, I recall you to your duty. But oh, I will give you my life with both hands if you can tell me that you feel for me one millionth part of what I feel for you now.

MRS. JUNO. Oh, yes, yes. Be satisfied with that. Ask for no more. Let me go.

GREGORY. I can't. I have no will. Something stronger than either of us is in command here. Nothing on earth or in heaven can part us now. You know that, don't you?

MRS. JUNO. Oh, don't make me say it. Of course I know. Nothing—not life nor death nor shame nor anything can part us.

A MATTER-OF-FACT MALE VOICE IN THE CORRIDOR. All right. This must be it.

The two recover with a violent start; release one another; and spring back to opposite sides of the lounge.

GREGORY. That did it.

MRS. JUNO [*in a thrilling whisper*] Sh—sh—sh! That was my husband's voice.

GREGORY. Impossible: it's only our guilty fancy.

A WOMAN'S VOICE. This is the way to the lounge. I know it.

GREGORY. Great Heaven! we're both mad. That's my wife's voice.

MRS. JUNO. Ridiculous! Oh! we're dreaming it all. We [*the door opens; and Sibthorpe Juno appears in the roseate glow of the corridor (which happens to be papered in pink) with Mrs. Lunn, like Tannhauser in the hill of Venus. He is a fussily energetic little man, who gives himself an air of gallantry by greasing the points of his moustaches and dressing very carefully. She is a tall, imposing, handsome, languid woman, with flashing dark eyes and long lashes. They make for the chesterfield, not noticing the two palpitating figures blotted against the walls in the gloom on either side. The figures flit away noiselessly through the window and disappear*].

JUNO [*officiously*] Ah: here we are. [*He leads the way to the sofa*]. Sit down: I'm sure you're tired. [*She sits*]. That's right. [*He sits beside her on her left*]. Hullo! [*he rises*] this sofa's quite warm.

MRS. LUNN [*bored*] Is it? I don't notice it. I expect the sun's been on it.

JUNO. I felt it quite distinctly: I'm more thinly clad than you. [*He sits down again, and proceeds, with a sigh of satisfaction*]. What a relief to get off the ship and have a private room! That's the worst of a ship. You're under observation all the time.

MRS. LUNN. But why not?

JUNO. Well, of course there's no reason: at least I suppose not. But, you know, part of the romance of a journey is that a man keeps imagining that something might happen; and he can't do that if there are a lot of people about and it simply can't happen.

MRS. LUNN. Mr. Juno: romance is all very well on board ship; but when your foot touches the soil of England there's an end of it.

JUNO. No: believe me, that's a foreigner's mistake: we are the most romantic people in the world, we English. Why, my very presence here is a romance.

MRS. LUNN [*faintly ironical*] Indeed?

JUNO. Yes. You've guessed, of course, that I'm a married man.

MRS. LUNN. Oh, that's all right. I'm a married woman.

JUNO. Thank Heaven for that! To my English mind, passion is not real passion without guilt. I am a red-blooded man, Mrs. Lunn: I can't help it. The tragedy of my life is that I married, when quite young, a woman whom I couldn't help being very fond of. I longed for a guilty passion—for the real thing—the wicked thing; and yet I couldn't care twopence for any other woman when my wife was about. Year after year went by: I felt my youth slipping away without ever having had a romance in my life; for marriage is all very well; but it isn't romance. There's nothing wrong in it, you see.

MRS. LUNN. Poor man! How you must have suffered!

JUNO. No: that was what was so tame about it. I wanted to suffer. You get so sick of being happily married. It's always the happy marriages that break up. At last my wife and I agreed that we ought to take a holiday.

MRS. LUNN. Hadn't you holidays every year?

JUNO. Oh, the seaside and so on! That's not what we meant. We meant a holiday from one another.

MRS. LUNN. How very odd!

JUNO. She said it was an excellent idea; that domestic felicity was making us perfectly idiotic; that she wanted a holiday, too. So we agreed to go round the world in opposite directions. I started for Suez on the day she sailed for New York.

MRS. LUNN [*suddenly becoming attentive*] That's precisely what Gregory and I did. Now I wonder did he want a holiday from me! What he said was that he wanted the delight of meeting me after a long absence.

JUNO. Could anything be more romantic than that? Would anyone else than an Englishman have thought of it? I daresay my temperament seems tame to your boiling southern blood—

MRS. LUNN. My what!

JUNO. Your southern blood. Don't you remember how you told me, that night in the saloon when I sang "Farewell and adieu to you dear Spanish ladies," that you were by birth a lady of Spain? Your splendid Andalusian beauty speaks for itself.

MRS. LUNN. Stuff! I was born in Gibraltar. My father was Captain Jenkins. In the artillery.

JUNO [*ardently*] It is climate and not race that determines the temperament. The fiery sun of Spain blazed on your cradle; and it rocked to the roar of British cannon.

MRS. LUNN. What eloquence! It reminds me of my husband when he was in love before we were married. Are you in love?

JUNO. Yes; and with the same woman.

MRS. LUNN. Well, of course, I didn't suppose you were in love with two women.

JUNO. I don't think you quite understand. I meant that I am in love with you.

MRS. LUNN [*relapsing into deepest boredom*] Oh, that! Men do fall in love with me. They all seem to think me a creature with volcanic passions: I'm sure I don't know why; for all the volcanic women I know are plain little creatures with sandy hair. I don't consider human volcanoes respectable. And I'm so tired of the subject! Our house is always full of women who are in love with my husband and men who are in love with me. We encourage it because it's pleasant to have company.

JUNO. And is your husband as insensible as yourself?

MRS. LUNN. Oh, Gregory's not insensible: very far from it; but I am the only woman in the world for him.

JUNO. But you? Are you really as insensible as you say you are?

MRS. LUNN. I never said anything of the kind. I'm not at all insensible by nature; but (I don't know whether you've noticed it) I am what people call rather a fine figure of a woman.

JUNO [*passionately*] Noticed it! Oh, Mrs. Lunn! Have I been able to notice anything else since we met?

MRS. LUNN. There you go, like all the rest of them! I ask you, how do you expect a woman to keep up what you call her sensibility when this sort of thing has happened to her about three times a week ever since she was seventeen? It used to upset me and terrify me at first. Then I got rather a taste for it. It came to a climax with Gregory: that was why I married him. Then it became a mild lark, hardly worth the trouble. After that I found it valuable once or twice as a spinal tonic when I was run down; but now it's an unmitigated bore. I don't mind your declaration: I daresay it gives you a certain pleasure to make it. I quite understand that you adore me; but (if you don't mind) I'd rather you didn't keep on saying so.

JUNO. Is there then no hope for me?

MRS. LUNN. Oh, yes. Gregory has an idea that married women keep lists of the men they'll marry if they become widows. I'll put your name down, if that will satisfy you.

JUNO. Is the list a long one?

MRS. LUNN. Do you mean the real list? Not the one I show to Gregory: there are hundreds of names on that; but the little private list that he'd better not see?

JUNO. Oh, will you really put me on that? Say you will.

MRS. LUNN. Well, perhaps I will. [*He kisses her hand*]. Now don't begin abusing the privilege.

JUNO. May I call you by your Christian name?

MRS. LUNN. No: it's too long. You can't go about calling a woman Seraphita.

JUNO [*ecstatically*] Seraphita!

MRS. LUNN. I used to be called Sally at home; but when I married a man named Lunn, of course that became ridiculous. That's my one little pet joke. Call me Mrs. Lunn for short. And change the subject, or I shall go to sleep.

JUNO. I can't change the subject. For me there is no other subject. Why else have you put me on your list?

MRS. LUNN. Because you're a solicitor. Gregory's a solicitor. I'm accustomed to my husband being a solicitor and telling me things he oughtn't to tell anybody.

JUNO [*ruefully*] Is that all? Oh, I can't believe that the voice of love has ever thoroughly awakened you.

MRS. LUNN. No: it sends me to sleep. [*Juno appeals against this by an amorous demonstration*]. It's no use, Mr. Juno: I'm hopelessly respectable: the Jenkinses always were. Don't you realize that unless most women were like that, the world couldn't go on as it does?

JUNO [*darkly*] You think it goes on respectably; but I can tell you as a solicitor—

MRS. LUNN. Stuff! of course all the disreputable people who get into trouble go to you, just as all the sick people go to the doctors; but most people never go to a solicitor.

JUNO [*rising, with a growing sense of injury*] Look here, Mrs. Lunn: do you think a man's heart is a potato? or a turnip? or a ball of knitting wool? that you can throw it away like this?

MRS. LUNN. I don't throw away balls of knitting wool. A man's heart seems to me much like a sponge: it sops up dirty water as well as clean.

JUNO. I have never been treated like this in my life. Here am I, a married man, with a most attractive wife: a wife I adore, and who adores me, and has never as much as looked at any other man since we were married. I come and throw all this at your feet. I! I, a solicitor! braving the risk of your husband putting me into the divorce court and making me a beggar and an outcast! I do this for your sake. And you go on as if I were making no sacrifice: as if I had told you it's a fine evening, or asked you to have a cup of tea. It's not human. It's not right. Love has its rights as well as respectability [*he sits down again, aloof and sulky*].

MRS. LUNN. Nonsense! Here, here's a flower [*she gives him one*]. Go and dream over it until you feel hungry. Nothing brings people to their senses like hunger.

JUNO [*contemplating the flower without rapture*] What good's this?

MRS. LUNN [*snatching it from him*] Oh! you don't love me a bit.

JUNO. Yes I do. Or at least I did. But I'm an Englishman; and I think you ought to respect the conventions of English life.

MRS. LUNN. But I am respecting them; and you're not.

JUNO. Pardon me. I may be doing wrong; but I'm doing it in a proper and customary manner. You may be doing right; but you're doing it in an unusual and questionable manner. I am not prepared to put up with that. I can stand being badly treated: I'm no baby, and can take care of myself with anybody. And of course I can stand being well treated. But the thing I can't stand is being unexpectedly treated, It's outside my scheme of life. So come now! you've got to behave naturally and straightforwardly with me. You can leave husband and child, home, friends, and country, for my sake, and come with me to some southern isle—or say South America—where we can be all in all to one another. Or you can tell your husband and let him jolly well punch my head if he can. But I'm damned if I'm going to stand any eccentricity. It's not respectable.

GREGORY [*coming in from the terrace and advancing with dignity to his wife's end of the chesterfield*]. Will you have the goodness, sir, in addressing this lady, to keep your temper and refrain from using profane language?

MRS. LUNN [*rising, delighted*] Gregory! Darling [*she enfolds him in a copious embrace*]!

JUNO [*rising*] You make love to another man to my face!

MRS. LUNN. Why, he's my husband.

JUNO. That takes away the last rag of excuse for such conduct. A nice world it would be if married people were to carry on their endearments before everybody!

GREGORY. This is ridiculous. What the devil business is it of yours what passes between my wife and myself? You're not her husband, are you?

JUNO. Not at present; but I'm on the list. I'm her prospective husband: you're only her actual one. I'm the anticipation: you're the disappointment.

MRS. LUNN. Oh, my Gregory is not a disappointment. [*Fondly*] Are you, dear?

GREGORY. You just wait, my pet. I'll settle this chap for you. [*He disengages himself from her embrace, and faces Juno. She sits down placidly*]. You call me a disappointment, do you? Well, I suppose every husband's a disappointment. What about yourself? Don't try to look like an unmarried man. I happen to know the lady you disappointed. I travelled in the same ship with her; and—

JUNO. And you fell in love with her.

GREGORY [*taken aback*] Who told you that?

JUNO. Aha! you confess it. Well, if you want to know, nobody told me. Everybody falls in love with my wife.

GREGORY. And do you fall in love with everybody's wife?

JUNO. Certainly not. Only with yours.

MRS. LUNN. But what's the good of saying that, Mr. Juno? I'm married to him; and there's an end of it.

JUNO. Not at all. You can get a divorce.

MRS. LUNN. What for?

JUNO. For his misconduct with my wife.

GREGORY [*deeply indignant*] How dare you, sir, asperse the character of that sweet lady? a lady whom I have taken under my protection.

JUNO. Protection!

MRS. JUNO [*returning hastily*] Really you must be more careful what you say about me, Mr. Lunn.

JUNO. My precious! [*He embraces her*]. Pardon this betrayal of my feeling; but I've not seen my wife for several weeks; and she is very dear to me.

GREGORY. I call this cheek. Who is making love to his own wife before people now, pray?

MRS. LUNN. Won't you introduce me to your wife, Mr. Juno?

MRS. JUNO. How do you do? [*They shake hands; and Mrs. Juno sits down beside Mrs. Lunn, on her left*].

MRS. LUNN. I'm so glad to find you do credit to Gregory's taste. I'm naturally rather particular about the women he falls in love with.

JUNO [*sternly*] This is no way to take your husband's unfaithfulness. [*To Lunn*] You ought to teach your wife better. Where's her feelings? It's scandalous.

GREGORY. What about your own conduct, pray?

JUNO. I don't defend it; and there's an end of the matter.

GREGORY. Well, upon my soul! What difference does your not defending it make?

JUNO. A fundamental difference. To serious people I may appear wicked. I don't defend myself: I am wicked, though not bad at heart. To thoughtless people I may even appear comic. Well, laugh at me: I have given myself away. But Mrs. Lunn seems to have no opinion at all about me. She doesn't seem to know whether I'm wicked or comic. She doesn't seem to care. She has no more sense. I say it's not right. I repeat, I have sinned; and I'm prepared to suffer.

MRS. JUNO. Have you really sinned, Tops?

MRS. LUNN [*blandly*] I don't remember your sinning. I have a shocking bad memory for trifles; but I think I should remember that—if you mean me.

JUNO [*raging*] Trifles! I have fallen in love with a monster.

GREGORY. Don't you dare call my wife a monster.

MRS. JUNO [*rising quickly and coming between them*]. Please don't lose your temper, Mr. Lunn: I won't have my Tops bullied.

GREGORY. Well, then, let him not brag about sinning with my wife. [*He turns impulsively to his wife; makes her rise; and takes her proudly on his arm*]. What pretension has he to any such honor?

JUNO. I sinned in intention. [*Mrs. Juno abandons him and resumes her seat, chilled*]. I'm as guilty as if I had actually sinned. And I insist on being treated as a sinner, and not walked over as if I'd done nothing, by your wife or any other man.

MRS. LUNN. Tush! [*She sits down again contemptuously*].

JUNO [*furious*] I won't be belittled.

MRS. LUNN [*to Mrs. Juno*] I hope you'll come and stay with us now that you and Gregory are such friends, Mrs. Juno.

JUNO. This insane magnanimity—

MRS. LUNN. Don't you think you've said enough, Mr. Juno? This is a matter for two women to settle. Won't you take a stroll on the beach with my Gregory while we talk it over. Gregory is a splendid listener.

JUNO. I don't think any good can come of a conversation between Mr. Lunn and myself. We can hardly be expected to improve one another's morals. [*He passes behind the chesterfield to Mrs. Lunn's end; seizes a chair; deliberately pushes it between Gregory and Mrs. Lunn; and sits down with folded arms, resolved not to budge*].

GREGORY. Oh! Indeed! Oh, all right. If you come to that—[*he crosses to Mrs. Juno; plants a chair by her side; and sits down with equal determination*].

JUNO. Now we are both equally guilty.

GREGORY. Pardon me. I'm not guilty.

JUNO. In intention. Don't quibble. You were guilty in intention, as I was.

GREGORY. No. I should rather describe myself guilty in fact, but not in intention.

JUNO [*rising and*] What! MRS. JUNO [*exclaiming*] No, really— MRS. LUNN [*simultaneously*] Gregory!

GREGORY. Yes: I maintain that I am responsible for my intentions only, and not for reflex actions over which I have no control. [*Mrs. Juno sits down, ashamed*]. I promised my mother that I would never tell a lie, and that I would never make love to a married woman. I never have told a lie—

MRS. LUNN [*remonstrating*] Gregory! [*She sits down again*].

GREGORY. I say never. On many occasions I have resorted to prevarication; but on great occasions I have always told the truth. I regard this as a great occasion; and I won't be intimidated into breaking my promise. I solemnly declare that I did not know until this evening that Mrs. Juno was married. She will bear me out when I say that from that moment my intentions were strictly and resolutely honorable; though my conduct, which I could not control and am therefore not responsible for, was disgraceful—or would have been had this gentleman not walked in and begun making love to my wife under my very nose.

JUNO [*flinging himself back into his chair*] Well, I like this!

MRS. LUNN. Really, darling, there's no use in the pot calling the kettle black.

GREGORY. When you say darling, may I ask which of us you are addressing?

MRS. LUNN. I really don't know. I'm getting hopelessly confused.

JUNO. Why don't you let my wife say something? I don't think she ought to be thrust into the background like this.

MRS. LUNN. I'm sorry, I'm sure. Please excuse me, dear.

MRS. JUNO [*thoughtfully*] I don't know what to say. I must think over it. I have always been rather severe on this sort of thing; but when it came to the point I didn't behave as I thought I should behave. I didn't intend to be wicked; but somehow or other, Nature, or whatever you choose to call it, didn't take much notice of my intentions. [*Gregory instinctively seeks her hand and presses it*]. And I really did think, Tops, that I was the only woman in the world for you.

JUNO [*cheerfully*] Oh, that's all right, my precious. Mrs. Lunn thought she was the only woman in the world for him.

GREGORY [*reflectively*] So she is, in a sort of a way.

JUNO [*flaring up*] And so is my wife. Don't you set up to be a better husband than I am; for you're not. I've owned I'm wrong. You haven't.

MRS. LUNN. Are you sorry, Gregory?

GREGORY [*perplexed*] Sorry?

MRS. LUNN. Yes, sorry. I think it's time for you to say you're sorry, and to make friends with Mr. Juno before we all dine together.

GREGORY. Seraphita: I promised my mother—

MRS. JUNO [*involuntarily*] Oh, bother your mother! [*Recovering herself*] I beg your pardon.

GREGORY. A promise is a promise. I can't tell a deliberate lie. I know I ought to be sorry; but the flat fact is that I'm not sorry. I find that in this business, somehow or other, there is a disastrous separation between my moral principles and my conduct.

JUNO. There's nothing disastrous about it. It doesn't matter about your principles if your conduct is all right.

GREGORY. Bosh! It doesn't matter about your principles if your conduct is all right.

JUNO. But your conduct isn't all right; and my principles are.

GREGORY. What's the good of your principles being right if they won't work?

JUNO. They WILL work, sir, if you exercise self-sacrifice.

GREGORY. Oh yes: if, if, if. You know jolly well that self-sacrifice doesn't work either when you really want a thing. How much have you sacrificed yourself, pray?

MRS. LUNN. Oh, a great deal, Gregory. Don't be rude. Mr. Juno is a very nice man: he has been most attentive to me on the voyage.

GREGORY. And Mrs. Juno's a very nice woman. She oughtn't to be; but she is.

JUNO. Why oughtn't she to be a nice woman, pray?

GREGORY. I mean she oughtn't to be nice to me. And you oughtn't to be nice to my wife. And your wife oughtn't to like me. And my wife oughtn't to like you. And if they do, they oughtn't to go on liking us. And I oughtn't to like your wife; and you oughtn't to like mine; and if we do we oughtn't to go on liking them. But we do, all of us. We oughtn't; but we do.

JUNO. But, my dear boy, if we admit we are in the wrong where's the harm of it? We're not perfect; but as long as we keep the ideal before us—

GREGORY. How?

JUNO. By admitting we were wrong.

MRS. LUNN [*springing up, out of patience, and pacing round the lounge intolerantly*] Well, really, I must have my dinner. These two men, with their morality, and their promises to their mothers, and their admissions that they were wrong, and their sinning and suffering, and their going on at one another as if it meant anything, or as if it mattered, are getting on my nerves. [*Stooping over the back of the chesterfield to address Mrs. Juno*] If you will be so very good, my dear, as to take my sentimental husband off my hands occasionally, I shall be more than obliged to you: I'm sure you can stand more male sentimentality than I can. [*Sweeping away to the fireplace*] I, on my part, will do my best to amuse your excellent husband when you find him tiresome.

JUNO. I call this polyandry.

MRS. LUNN. I wish you wouldn't call innocent things by offensive names, Mr. Juno. What do you call your own conduct?

JUNO [*rising*] I tell you I have admitted—

GREGORY [ ] What's the good of keeping on at that?

MRS. JUNO [*together*] Oh, not that again, please.

MRS. LUNN [ ] Tops: I'll scream if you say that again.

JUNO. Oh, well, if you won't listen to me—! [*He sits down again*].

MRS. JUNO. What is the position now exactly? [*Mrs. Lunn shrugs her shoulders and gives up the conundrum. Gregory looks at Juno. Juno turns away his head huffily*]. I mean, what are we going to do?

MRS. LUNN. What would you advise, Mr. Juno?

JUNO. I should advise you to divorce your husband.

MRS. LUNN. Do you want me to drag your wife into court and disgrace her?

JUNO. No: I forgot that. Excuse me; but for the moment I thought I was married to you.

GREGORY. I think we had better let bygones be bygones. [*To Mrs. Juno, very tenderly*] You will forgive me, won't you? Why should you let a moment's forgetfulness embitter all our future life?

MRS. JUNO. But it's Mrs. Lunn who has to forgive you.

GREGORY. Oh, dash it, I forgot. This is getting ridiculous.

MRS. LUNN. I'm getting hungry.

MRS. JUNO. Do you really mind, Mrs. Lunn?

MRS. LUNN. My dear Mrs. Juno, Gregory is one of those terribly uxorious men who ought to have ten wives. If any really nice woman will take him off my hands for a day or two occasionally, I shall be greatly obliged to her.

GREGORY. Seraphita: you cut me to the soul [*he weeps*].

MRS. LUNN. Serve you right! You'd think it quite proper if it cut me to the soul.

MRS. JUNO. Am I to take Sibthorpe off your hands too, Mrs. Lunn?

JUNO [*rising*] Do you suppose I'll allow this?

MRS. JUNO. You've admitted that you've done wrong, Tops. What's the use of your allowing or not allowing after that?

JUNO. I do not admit that I have done wrong. I admit that what I did was wrong.

GREGORY. Can you explain the distinction?

JUNO. It's quite plain to anyone but an imbecile. If you tell me I've done something wrong you insult me. But if you say that something that I did is wrong you simply raise a question of morals. I tell you flatly if you say I did anything wrong you will have to fight me. In fact I think we ought to fight anyhow. I don't particularly want to; but I feel that England expects us to.

GREGORY. I won't fight. If you beat me my wife would share my humiliation. If I beat you, she would sympathize with you and loathe me for my brutality.

MRS. LUNN. Not to mention that as we are human beings and not reindeer or barndoor fowl, if two men presumed to fight for us we couldn't decently ever speak to either of them again.

GREGORY. Besides, neither of us could beat the other, as we neither of us know how to fight. We should only blacken each other's eyes and make fools of ourselves.

JUNO. I don't admit that. Every Englishman can use his fists.

GREGORY. You're an Englishman. Can you use yours?

JUNO. I presume so: I never tried.

MRS. JUNO. You never told me you couldn't fight, Tops. I thought you were an accomplished boxer.

JUNO. My precious: I never gave you any ground for such a belief.

MRS. JUNO. You always talked as if it were a matter of course. You spoke with the greatest contempt of men who didn't kick other men downstairs.

JUNO. Well, I can't kick Mr. Lunn downstairs. We're on the ground floor.

MRS. JUNO. You could throw him into the harbor.

GREGORY. Do you want me to be thrown into the harbor?

MRS. JUNO. No: I only want to show Tops that he's making a ghastly fool of himself.

GREGORY [*rising and prowling disgustedly between the chesterfield and the windows*] We're all making fools of ourselves.

JUNO [*following him*] Well, if we're not to fight, I must insist at least on your never speaking to my wife again.

GREGORY. Does my speaking to your wife do you any harm?

JUNO. No. But it's the proper course to take. [*Emphatically*]. We MUST behave with some sort of decency.

MRS. LUNN. And are you never going to speak to me again, Mr. Juno?

JUNO. I'm prepared to promise never to do so. I think your husband has a right to demand that. Then if I speak to you after, it will not be his fault. It will be a breach of my promise; and I shall not attempt to defend my conduct.

GREGORY [*facing him*] I shall talk to your wife as often as she'll let me.

MRS. JUNO. I have no objection to your speaking to me, Mr. Lunn.

JUNO. Then I shall take steps.

GREGORY. What steps?

JUNO. Steps. Measures. Proceedings. What steps as may seem advisable.

MRS. LUNN [*to Mrs. Juno*] Can your husband afford a scandal, Mrs. Juno?

MRS. JUNO. No.

MRS. LUNN. Neither can mine.

GREGORY. Mrs. Juno: I'm very sorry I let you in for all this. I don't know how it is that we contrive to make feelings like ours, which seems to me to be beautiful and sacred feelings, and which lead to such interesting and exciting adventures, end in vulgar squabbles and degrading scenes.

JUNO. I decline to admit that my conduct has been vulgar or degrading.

GREGORY. I promised—

JUNO. Look here, old chap: I don't say a word against your mother; and I'm sorry she's dead; but really, you know, most women are mothers; and they all die some time or other; yet that doesn't make them infallible authorities on morals, does it?

GREGORY. I was about to say so myself. Let me add that if you do things merely because you think some other fool expects you to do them, and he expects you to do them because he thinks you expect him to expect you to do them, it will end in everybody doing what nobody wants to do, which is in my opinion a silly state of things.

JUNO. Lunn: I love your wife; and that's all about it.

GREGORY. Juno: I love yours. What then?

JUNO. Clearly she must never see you again.

MRS. JUNO. Why not?

JUNO. Why not! My love: I'm surprised at you.

MRS. JUNO. Am I to speak only to men who dislike me?

JUNO. Yes: I think that is, properly speaking, a married woman's duty.

MRS. JUNO. Then I won't do it: that's flat. I like to be liked. I like to be loved. I want everyone round me to love me. I don't want to meet or speak to anyone who doesn't like me.

JUNO. But, my precious, this is the most horrible immorality.

MRS. LUNN. I don't intend to give up meeting you, Mr. Juno. You amuse me very much. I don't like being loved: it bores me. But I do like to be amused.

JUNO. I hope we shall meet very often. But I hope also we shall not defend our conduct.

MRS. JUNO [*rising*] This is unendurable. We've all been flirting. Need we go on footling about it?

JUNO [*huffily*] I don't know what you call footling—

MRS. JUNO [*cutting him short*] You do. You're footling. Mr. Lunn is footling. Can't we admit that we're human and have done with it?

JUNO. I have admitted it all along. I—

MRS. JUNO [*almost screaming*] Then stop footling.

The dinner gong sounds.

MRS. LUNN [*rising*] Thank heaven! Let's go in to dinner. Gregory: take in Mrs. Juno.

GREGORY. But surely I ought to take in our guest, and not my own wife.

MRS. LUNN. Well, Mrs. Juno is not your wife, is she?

GREGORY. Oh, of course: I beg your pardon. I'm hopelessly confused. [*He offers his arm to Mrs. Juno, rather apprehensively*].

MRS. JUNO. You seem quite afraid of me [*she takes his arm*].

GREGORY. I am. I simply adore you. [*They go out together; and as they pass through the door he turns and says in a ringing voice to the other couple*] I have said to Mrs. Juno that I simply adore her. [*He takes her out defiantly*].

MRS. LUNN [*calling after him*] Yes, dear. She's a darling. [*To Juno*] Now, Sibthorpe.

JUNO [*giving her his arm gallantly*] You have called me Sibthorpe! Thank you. I think Lunn's conduct fully justifies me in allowing you to do it.

MRS. LUNN. Yes: I think you may let yourself go now.

JUNO. Seraphita: I worship you beyond expression.

MRS. LUNN. Sibthorpe: you amuse me beyond description. Come. [*They go in to dinner together*].

GREAT CATHERINE (WHOM GLORY STILL ADORES)

"In Catherine's reign, whom Glory still adores"
BYRON

THE AUTHOR'S APOLOGY FOR GREAT CATHERINE

Exception has been taken to the title of this seeming tomfoolery on the ground that the Catherine it represents is not Great Catherine, but the Catherine whose gallantries provide some of the lightest pages of modern history. Great Catherine, it is said, was the Catherine whose diplomacy, whose campaigns and conquests, whose plans of Liberal reform, whose correspondence with Grimm and Voltaire enabled her to cut such a magnificent figure in the eighteenth century. In reply, I can only confess that Catherine's diplomacy and her conquests do not interest me. It is clear to me that neither she nor the statesmen with whom she played this mischievous kind of political chess had any notion of the real history of their own times, or of the real forces that were moulding Europe. The French Revolution, which made such short work of Catherine's Voltairean principles, surprised and scandalized her as much as it surprised and scandalized any provincial governess in the French chateaux.

The main difference between her and our modern Liberal Governments was that whereas she talked and wrote quite intelligently about Liberal principles before she was frightened into making such talking and writing a flogging matter, our Liberal ministers take the name of Liberalism in vain without knowing or caring enough about its meaning even to talk and scribble about it, and pass their flogging Bills, and institute their prosecutions for sedition and blasphemy and so forth, without the faintest suspicion that such proceedings need any apology from the Liberal point of view.

It was quite easy for Patiomkin to humbug Catherine as to the condition of Russia by conducting her through sham cities run up for the occasion by scenic artists; but in the little world of European court intrigue and dynastic diplomacy which was the only world she knew she was more than a match for him and for all the rest of her contemporaries. In such intrigue and diplomacy, however, there was no romance, no scientific political interest, nothing that a sane mind can now retain even if it can be persuaded to waste time in reading it up. But Catherine as a woman with plenty of character and (as we should say) no morals, still fascinates and amuses us as she fascinated and amused her contemporaries. They were great sentimental comedians, these Peters, Elizabeths, and Catherines who played their Tsarships as eccentric character parts, and produced scene after scene of furious harlequinade with the monarch as clown, and of tragic relief in the torture chamber with the monarch as pantomime demon committing real atrocities, not forgetting the indispensable love interest on an enormous and utterly indecorous scale. Catherine kept this vast Guignol Theatre open for nearly half a century, not as a Russian, but as a highly domesticated German lady whose household routine was not at all so unlike that of Queen Victoria as might be expected from the difference in their notions of propriety in sexual relations.

In short, if Byron leaves you with an impression that he said very little about Catherine, and that little not what was best worth saying, I beg to correct your impression by assuring you that what Byron said was all there really is to say that is worth saying. His Catherine is my Catherine and everybody's Catherine. The young man who gains her favor is a Spanish nobleman in his version. I have made him an English country gentleman, who gets out of his rather dangerous scrape, by simplicity, sincerity, and the courage of these qualities. By this I have given some offence to the many Britons who see themselves as heroes: what they mean by heroes being theatrical snobs of superhuman pretensions which, though quite groundless, are admitted with awe by the rest of the human race. They say I think an Englishman a fool. When I do, they have themselves to thank.

I must not, however, pretend that historical portraiture was the motive of a play that will leave the reader as ignorant of Russian history as he may be now before he has turned the page. Nor is the sketch of Catherine complete even idiosyncratically, leaving her politics out of the question. For example, she wrote bushels of plays. I confess I have not yet read any of them. The truth is, this play grew out of the relations which inevitably exist in the theatre between authors and actors. If the actors have sometimes to use their skill as the author's puppets rather than in full self-expression, the author has sometimes to use his skill as the actors' tailor, fitting them with parts written to display the virtuosity of the performer rather than to solve problems of life, character, or history. Feats of this kind may tickle an author's technical vanity; but he is bound on such occasions to admit that the performer for whom he writes is "the onlie begetter" of his work, which must be regarded critically as an addition to the debt dramatic literature owes to the art of acting and its exponents. Those who have seen Miss Gertrude Kingston play the part of Catherine will have no difficulty in believing that it was her talent rather than mine that brought the play into existence. I once recommended Miss Kingston professionally to play queens. Now in the modern drama there were no queens for her to play; and as to the older literature of our stage: did it not provoke the veteran actress in Sir Arthur Pinero's Trelawny of the Wells to declare that, as parts, queens are not worth a tinker's oath? Miss Kingston's comment on my suggestion, though more elegantly worded, was to the same effect; and it ended in my having to make good my advice by writing Great Catherine. History provided no other queen capable of standing up to our joint talents.

In composing such bravura pieces, the author limits himself only by the range of the virtuoso, which by definition far transcends the modesty of nature. If my Russians seem more Muscovite than any Russian, and my English people more insular than any Briton, I will not plead, as I honestly might, that the fiction has yet to be written that can exaggerate the reality of such subjects; that the apparently outrageous Patiomkin is but a timidly bowdlerized ghost of the original; and that Captain Edstaston is no more than a miniature that might hang appropriately on the walls of nineteen out of twenty English country houses to this day. An artistic presentment must not condescend to justify itself by a comparison with crude nature; and I prefer to admit that in this kind my dramatic personae are, as they should be, of the stage stagey, challenging the actor to act up to them or beyond them, if he can. The more heroic the overcharging, the better for the performance.

In dragging the reader thus for a moment behind the scenes, I am departing from a rule which I have hitherto imposed on myself so rigidly that I never permit myself, even in a stage direction, to let slip a word that could bludgeon the imagination of the reader by reminding him of the boards and the footlights and the sky borders and the rest of the theatrical scaffolding, for which nevertheless I have to plan as carefully as if I were the head carpenter as well as the author. But even at the risk of talking shop, an honest playwright should take at least one opportunity of acknowledging that his art is not only limited by the art of the actor, but often stimulated and developed by it. No sane and skilled author writes plays that present impossibilities to the actor or to the stage engineer. If, as occasionally happens, he asks them to do things that they have never done before and cannot conceive as presentable or possible (as Wagner and Thomas Hardy have done, for example), it is always found that the difficulties are not really insuperable, the author having foreseen unsuspected possibilities both in the actor and in the audience, whose will-to-make-believe can perform the quaintest miracles. Thus may authors advance the arts of acting and of staging plays. But the actor also may enlarge the scope of the drama by displaying powers not previously discovered by the author. If the best available actors are only Horatios, the authors will have to leave Hamlet out, and be content with Horatios for heroes. Some of the difference between Shakespeare's Orlandos and Bassanios and Bertrams and his Hamlets and Macbeths must have been due not only to his development as a dramatic poet, but to the development of Burbage as an actor. Playwrights do not write for ideal actors when their livelihood is at stake: if they did, they would write parts for heroes with twenty arms like an Indian god. Indeed the actor often influences the author too much; for I can remember a time (I am not implying that it is yet wholly past) when the art of writing a fashionable play had become very largely the art of writing it "round" the personalities of a group of fashionable performers of whom Burbage would certainly have said that their parts needed no acting. Everything has its abuse as well as its use.

It is also to be considered that great plays live longer than great actors, though little plays do not live nearly so long as the worst of their exponents. The consequence is that the great actor, instead of putting pressure on contemporary authors to supply him with heroic parts, falls back on the Shakespearean repertory, and takes what he needs from a dead hand. In the nineteenth century, the careers of Kean, Macready, Barry Sullivan, and Irving, ought to have produced a group of heroic plays comparable in intensity to those of Aeschylus, Sophocles, and Euripides; but nothing of the kind happened: these actors played the works of dead authors, or, very occasionally, of live poets who were hardly regular professional playwrights. Sheridan Knowles, Bulwer Lytton, Wills, and Tennyson produced a few glaringly artificial high horses for the great actors of their time; but the playwrights proper, who really kept the theatre going, and were kept going by the theatre, did not cater for the great actors: they could not afford to compete with a bard who was not for an age but for all time, and who had, moreover, the overwhelming attraction for the actor-managers of not charging author's fees. The result was that the playwrights and the great actors ceased to think of themselves as having any concern with one another: Tom Robertson, Ibsen, Pinero, and Barrie might as well have belonged to a different solar system as far as Irving was concerned; and the same was true of their respective predecessors.

Thus was established an evil tradition; but I at least can plead that it does not always hold good. If Forbes Robertson had not been there to play Caesar, I should not have written Caesar and Cleopatra. If Ellen Terry had never been born, Captain Brassbound's Conversion would never have been effected. The Devil's Disciple, with which I won my cordon bleu in America as a potboiler, would have had a different sort of hero if Richard Mansfield had been a different sort of actor, though the actual commission to write it came from an English actor, William Terriss, who was assassinated before he recovered from the dismay into which the result of his rash proposal threw him. For it must be said that the actor or actress who inspires or commissions a play as often as not regards it as a Frankenstein's monster, and will have none of it. That does not make him or her any the less parental in the fecundity of the playwright.

To an author who has any feeling of his business there is a keen and whimsical joy in divining and revealing a side of an actor's genius overlooked before, and unsuspected even by the actor himself. When I snatched Mr Louis Calvert from Shakespeare, and made him wear a frock coat and silk hat on the stage for perhaps the first time in his life, I do not think he expected in the least that his performance would enable me to boast of his Tom Broadbent as a genuine stage classic. Mrs Patrick Campbell was famous before I wrote for her, but not for playing illiterate cockney flower-maidens. And in the case which is provoking me to all these impertinences, I am quite sure that Miss Gertrude Kingston, who first made her reputation as an impersonator of the most delightfully feather-headed and inconsequent ingenues, thought me more than usually mad when I persuaded her to play the Helen of Euripides, and then launched her on a queenly career as Catherine of Russia.

It is not the whole truth that if we take care of the actors the plays will take care of themselves; nor is it any truer that if we take care of the plays the actors will take care of themselves. There is both give and take in the business. I have seen plays written for actors that made me exclaim, "How oft the sight of means to do ill deeds makes deeds ill done!" But Burbage may have flourished the prompt copy of Hamlet under Shakespeare's nose at the tenth rehearsal and cried, "How oft the sight of means to do great deeds makes playwrights great!" I say the tenth because I am convinced that at the first he denounced his part as a rotten one; thought the ghost's speech ridiculously long; and wanted to play the king. Anyhow, whether he had the wit to utter it or not, the boast would have been a valid one. The best conclusion is that every actor should say, "If I create the hero in myself, God will send an author to write his part." For in the long run the actors will get the authors, and the authors the actors, they deserve.

Great Catherine was performed for the first time at the Vaudeville Theatre in London on the 18th November 1913, with Gertrude Kingston as Catherine, Miriam Lewes as Yarinka, Dorothy Massingham as Claire, Norman McKinnell as Patiomkin, Edmond Breon as Edstaston, Annie Hill as the Princess Dashkoff, and Eugene Mayeur and F. Cooke Beresford as Naryshkin and the Sergeant.

THE FIRST SCENE

1776. Patiomkin in his bureau in the Winter Palace, St. Petersburgh. Huge palatial apartment: style, Russia in the eighteenth century imitating the Versailles du Roi Soleil. Extravagant luxury. Also dirt and disorder.

Patiomkin, gigantic in stature and build, his face marred by the loss of one eye and a marked squint in the other, sits at the end of a table littered with papers and the remains of three or four successive breakfasts. He has supplies of coffee and brandy at hand sufficient for a party of ten. His coat, encrusted with diamonds, is on the floor. It has fallen off a chair placed near the other end of the table for the convenience of visitors. His court sword, with its attachments, is on the chair. His three-cornered hat, also bejewelled, is on the table. He himself is half dressed in an unfastened shirt and an immense dressing-gown, once gorgeous, now food-splashed and dirty, as it serves him for towel, handkerchief, duster, and every other use to which a textile fabric can be put by a slovenly man. It does not conceal his huge hairy chest, nor his half-buttoned knee breeches, nor his legs. These are partly clad in silk stockings, which he occasionally hitches up to his knees, and presently shakes down to his shins, by his restless movement. His feet are thrust into enormous slippers, worth, with their crust of jewels, several thousand roubles apiece.

Superficially Patiomkin is a violent, brutal barbarian, an upstart despot of the most intolerable and dangerous type, ugly, lazy, and disgusting in his personal habits. Yet ambassadors report him the ablest man in Russia, and the one who can do most with the still abler Empress Catherine II, who is not a Russian but a German, by no means barbarous or intemperate in her personal habits. She not only disputes with Frederick the Great the reputation of being the cleverest monarch in Europe, but may even put in a very plausible claim to be the cleverest and most attractive individual alive. Now she not only tolerates Patiomkin long after she has got over her first romantic attachment to him, but esteems him highly as a counsellor and a good friend. His love letters are among the best on record. He has a wild sense of humor, which enables him to laugh at himself as well as at everybody else. In the eyes of the English visitor now about to be admitted to his presence he may be an outrageous ruffian. In fact he actually is an outrageous ruffian, in no matter whose eyes; but the visitor will find out, as everyone else sooner or later fends out, that he is a man to be reckoned with even by those who are not intimidated by his temper, bodily strength, and exalted rank.

A pretty young lady, Yarinka, his favorite niece, is lounging on an ottoman between his end of the table and the door, very sulky and dissatisfied, perhaps because he is preoccupied with his papers and his brandy bottle, and she can see nothing of him but his broad back.

There is a screen behind the ottoman.

An old soldier, a Cossack sergeant, enters.

THE SERGEANT [*softly to the lady, holding the door handle*]. Little darling honey, is his Highness the prince very busy?

VARINKA. His Highness the prince is very busy. He is singing out of tune; he is biting his nails; he is scratching his head; he is hitching up his untidy stockings; he is making himself disgusting and odious to everybody; and he is pretending to read state papers that he does not understand because he is too lazy and selfish to talk and be companionable.

PATIOMKIN [*growls; then wipes his nose with his dressing-gown*]!!

VARINKA. Pig. Ugh! [*She curls herself up with a shiver of disgust and retires from the conversation.*]

THE SERGEANT [*stealing across to the coat, and picking it up to replace it on the back of the chair*]. Little Father, the English captain, so highly recommended to you by old Fritz of Prussia, by the English ambassador, and by Monsieur Voltaire (whom [*crossing himself*] may God in his infinite mercy damn eternally!), is in the antechamber and desires audience.

PATIOMKIN [*deliberately*]. To hell with the English captain; and to hell with old Fritz of Prussia; and to hell with the English ambassador; and to hell with Monsieur Voltaire; and to hell with you too!

THE SERGEANT. Have mercy on me, Little Father. Your head is bad this morning. You drink too much French brandy and too little good Russian kvass.

PATIOMKIN [*with sudden fury*]. Why are visitors of consequence announced by a sergeant? [*Springing at him and seizing him by the throat.*] What do you mean by this, you hound? Do you want five thousand blows of the stick? Where is General Volkonsky?

THE SERGEANT [*on his knees*]. Little Father, you kicked his Highness downstairs.

PATIOMKIN [*flinging him dawn and kicking him*]. You lie, you dog. You lie.

THE SERGEANT. Little Father, life is hard for the poor. If you say it is a lie, it is a lie. He FELL downstairs. I picked him up; and he kicked me. They all kick me when you kick them. God knows that is not just, Little Father!

PATIOMKIN [*laughs ogreishly; then returns to his place at the table, chuckling*]!!!

VARINKA. Savage! Boot! It is a disgrace. No wonder the French sneer at us as barbarians.

THE SERGEANT [*who has crept round the table to the screen, and insinuated himself between Patiomkin's back and Varinka*]. Do you think the Prince will see the captain, little darling?

PATIOMKIN. He will not see any captain. Go to the devil!

THE SERGEANT. Be merciful, Little Father. God knows it is your duty to see him! [*To Varinka.*] Intercede for him and for me, beautiful little darling. He has given me a rouble.

PATIOMKIN. Oh, send him in, send him in; and stop pestering me. Am I never to have a moment's peace?

The Sergeant salutes joyfully and hurries out, divining that Patiomkin has intended to see the English captain all along, and has played this comedy of fury and exhausted impatience to conceal his interest in the visitor.

VARINKA. Have you no shame? You refuse to see the most exalted persons. You kick princes and generals downstairs. And then you see an English captain merely because he has given a rouble to that common soldier. It is scandalous.

PATIOMKIN. Darling beloved, I am drunk; but I know what I am doing. I wish to stand well with the English.

VARINKA. And you think you will impress an Englishman by receiving him as you are now, half drunk?

PATIOMKIN [*gravely*]. It is true: the English despise men who cannot drink. I must make myself wholly drunk [*he takes a huge draught of brandy.*]

VARINKA. Sot!

The Sergeant returns ushering a handsome strongly built young English officer in the uniform of a Light Dragoon. He is evidently on fairly good terms with himself, and very sure of his social position. He crosses the room to the end of the table opposite Patiomkin's, and awaits the civilities of that statesman with confidence. The Sergeant remains prudently at the door.

THE SERGEANT [*paternally*]. Little Father, this is the English captain, so well recommended to her sacred Majesty the Empress. God knows, he needs your countenance and protec— [*he vanishes precipitately, seeing that Patiomkin is about to throw a bottle at him. The Captain contemplates these preliminaries with astonishment, and with some displeasure, which is not allayed when, Patiomkin, hardly condescending to look at his visitor, of whom he nevertheless takes stock with the corner of his one eye, says gruffly*]. Well?

EDSTASTON. My name is Edstaston: Captain Edstaston of the Light Dragoons. I have the honor to present to your Highness this letter from the British ambassador, which will give you all necessary particulars. [*He hands Patiomkin the letter.*]

PATIOMKIN [*tearing it open and glancing at it for about a second*]. What do you want?

EDSTASTON. The letter will explain to your Highness who I am.

PATIOMKIN. I don't want to know who you are. What do you want?

EDSTASTON. An audience of the Empress. [*Patiomkin contemptuously throws the letter aside.*

Edstaston adds hotly.] Also some civility, if you please.

PATIOMKIN [*with derision*]. Ho!

VARINKA. My uncle is receiving you with unusual civility, Captain. He has just kicked a general downstairs.

EDSTASTON. A Russian general, madam?

VARINKA. Of course.

EDSTASTON. I must allow myself to say, madam, that your uncle had better not attempt to kick an English officer downstairs.

PATIOMKIN. You want me to kick you upstairs, eh? You want an audience of the Empress.

EDSTASTON. I have said nothing about kicking, sir. If it comes to that, my boots shall speak for me. Her Majesty has signified a desire to have news of the rebellion in America. I have served against the rebels; and I am instructed to place myself at the disposal of her Majesty, and to describe the events of the war to her as an eye-witness, in a discreet and agreeable manner.

PATIOMKIN. Psha! I know. You think if she once sets eyes on your face and your uniform your fortune is made. You think that if she could stand a man like me, with only one eye, and a cross eye at that, she must fall down at your feet at first sight, eh?

EDSTASTON [*shocked and indignant*]. I think nothing of the sort; and I'll trouble you not to repeat it. If I were a Russian subject and you made such a boast about my queen, I'd strike you across the face with my sword. [*Patiomkin, with a yell of fury, rushes at him.*] Hands off, you swine! [*As Patiomkin, towering over him, attempts to seize him by the throat, Edstaston, who is a bit of a wrestler, adroitly backheels him. He falls, amazed, on his back.*]

VARINKA [*rushing out*]. Help! Call the guard! The Englishman is murdering my uncle! Help! Help!

The guard and the Sergeant rush in. Edstaston draws a pair of small pistols from his boots, and points one at the Sergeant and the other at Patiomkin, who is sitting on the floor, somewhat sobered. The soldiers stand irresolute.

EDSTASTON. Stand off. [*To Patiomkin.*] Order them off, if you don't want a bullet through your silly head.

THE SERGEANT. Little Father, tell us what to do. Our lives are yours; but God knows you are not fit to die.

PATIOMKIN [*absurdly self-possessed*]. Get out.

THE SERGEANT. Little Father—

PATIOMKIN [*roaring*]. Get out. Get out, all of you. [*They withdraw, much relieved at their escape from the pistol. Patiomkin attempts to rise, and rolls over.*] Here! help me up, will you? Don't you see that I'm drunk and can't get up?

EDSTASTON [*suspiciously*]. You want to get hold of me.

PATIOMKIN [*squatting resignedly against the chair on which his clothes hang*]. Very well, then: I shall stay where I am, because I'm drunk and you're afraid of me.

EDSTASTON. I'm not afraid of you, damn you!

PATIOMKIN [*ecstatically*]. Darling, your lips are the gates of truth. Now listen to me. [*He marks off the items of his statement with ridiculous stiff gestures of his head and arms, imitating a puppet.*] You are Captain Whatshisname; and your uncle is the Earl of Whatdyecallum; and your father is Bishop of Thingummybob; and you are a young man of the highest spr—promise (I told you I was drunk), educated at Cambridge, and got your step as captain in the field at the GLORIOUS battle of Bunker's Hill. Invalided home from America at the request of Aunt Fanny, Lady-in-Waiting to the Queen. All right, eh?

EDSTASTON. How do you know all this?

PATIOMKIN [*crowing fantastically*]. In er lerrer, darling, darling, darling, darling. Lerrer you showed me.

EDSTASTON. But you didn't read it.

PATIOMKIN [*flapping his fingers at him grotesquely*]. Only one eye, darling. Cross eye. Sees everything. Read lerrer inceince—istastaneously. Kindly give me vinegar borle. Green borle. On'y to sober me. Too drunk to speak porply. If you would be so kind, darling. Green borle. [*Edstaston, still suspicious, shakes his head and keeps his pistols ready.*] Reach it myself. [*He reaches behind him up to the table, and snatches at the green bottle, from which he takes a copious draught. Its effect is appalling. His wry faces and agonized belchings are so heartrending that they almost upset Edstaston. When the victim at last staggers to his feet, he is a pale fragile nobleman, aged and quite sober, extremely dignified in manner and address, though shaken by his recent convulsions.*] Young man, it is not better to be drunk than sober; but it is happier. Goodness is not happiness. That is an epigram. But I have overdone this. I am too sober to be good company. Let me redress the balance. [*He takes a generous draught of brandy, and recovers his geniality.*] Aha! That's better. And now listen, darling. You must not come to Court with pistols in your boots.

EDSTASTON. I have found them useful.

PATIOMKIN. Nonsense. I'm your friend. You mistook my intention because I was drunk. Now that I am sober—in moderation—I will prove that I am your friend. Have some diamonds. [*Roaring.*] Hullo there! Dogs, pigs: hullo!

The Sergeant comes in.

THE SERGEANT. God be praised, Little Father: you are still spared to us.

PATIOMKIN. Tell them to bring some diamonds. Plenty of diamonds. And rubies. Get out. [*He aims a kick at the Sergeant, who flees.*] Put up your pistols, darling. I'll give you a pair with gold handgrips. I am your friend.

EDSTASTON [*replacing the pistols in his boots rather unwillingly*]. Your Highness understands that if I am missing, or if anything happens to me, there will be trouble.

PATIOMKIN [*enthusiastically*]. Call me darling.

EDSTASTON. It is not the English custom.

PATIOMKIN. You have no hearts, you English! [*Slapping his right breast.*] Heart! Heart!

EDSTASTON. Pardon, your Highness: your heart is on the other side.

PATIOMKIN [*surprised and impressed*]. Is it? You are learned! You are a doctor! You English are wonderful! We are barbarians, drunken pigs. Catherine does not know it; but we are. Catherine's a German. But I have given her a Russian heart [*he is about to slap himself again.*]

EDSTASTON [*delicately*]. The other side, your Highness.

PATIOMKIN [*maudlin*]. Darling, a true Russian has a heart on both sides.

The Sergeant enters carrying a goblet filled with precious stones.

PATIOMKIN. Get out. [*He snatches the goblet and kicks the Sergeant out, not maliciously but from habit, indeed not noticing that he does it.*] Darling, have some diamonds. Have a fistful. [*He takes up a handful and lets them slip back through his fingers into the goblet, which he then offers to Edstaston.*]

EDSTASTON. Thank you, I don't take presents.

PATIOMKIN [*amazed*]. You refuse!

EDSTASTON. I thank your Highness; but it is not the custom for English gentlemen to take presents of that kind.

PATIOMKIN. Are you really an Englishman?

EDSTASTON [*bows*]!

PATIOMKIN. You are the first Englishman I ever saw refuse anything he could get. [*He puts the goblet on the table; then turns again to Edstaston.*] Listen, darling. You are a wrestler: a splendid wrestler. You threw me on my back like magic, though I could lift you with one hand. Darling, you are a giant, a paladin.

EDSTASTON [*complacently*]. We wrestle rather well in my part of England.

PATIOMKIN. I have a Turk who is a wrestler: a prisoner of war. You shall wrestle with him for me. I'll stake a million roubles on you.

EDSTASTON [*incensed*]. Damn you! do you take me for a prize-fighter? How dare you make me such a proposal?

PATIOMKIN [*with wounded feeling*]. Darling, there is no pleasing you. Don't you like me?

EDSTASTON [*mollified*]. Well, in a sort of way I do; though I don't know why I should. But my instructions are that I am to see the Empress; and—

PATIOMKIN. Darling, you shall see the Empress. A glorious woman, the greatest woman in the world. But lemme give you piece 'vice—pah! still drunk. They water my vinegar. [*He shakes himself; clears his throat; and resumes soberly.*] If Catherine takes a fancy to you, you may ask for roubles, diamonds, palaces, titles, orders, anything! and you may aspire to everything: field-marshal, admiral, minister, what you please—except Tsar.

EDSTASTON. I tell you I don't want to ask for anything. Do you suppose I am an adventurer and a beggar?

PATIOMKIN [*plaintively*]. Why not, darling? I was an adventurer. I was a beggar.

EDSTASTON. Oh, you!

PATIOMKIN. Well: what's wrong with me?

EDSTASTON. You are a Russian. That's different.

PATIOMKIN [*effusively*]. Darling, I am a man; and you are a man; and Catherine is a woman. Woman reduces us all to the common denominator. [*Chuckling.*] Again an epigram! [*Gravely.*] You understand it, I hope. Have you had a college education, darling? I have.

EDSTASTON. Certainly. I am a Bachelor of Arts.

PATIOMKIN. It is enough that you are a bachelor, darling: Catherine will supply the arts. Aha! Another epigram! I am in the vein today.

EDSTASTON [*embarrassed and a little offended*]. I must ask your Highness to change the subject. As a visitor in Russia, I am the guest of the Empress; and I must tell you plainly that I have neither the right nor the disposition to speak lightly of her Majesty.

PATIOMKIN. You have conscientious scruples?

EDSTASTON. I have the scruples of a gentleman.

PATIOMKIN. In Russia a gentleman has no scruples. In Russia we face facts.

EDSTASTON. In England, sir, a gentleman never faces any facts if they are unpleasant facts.

PATIOMKIN. In real life, darling, all facts are unpleasant. [*Greatly pleased with himself.*] Another epigram! Where is my accursed chancellor? these gems should be written down and recorded for posterity. [*He rushes to the table: sits down: and snatches up a pen. Then, recollecting himself.*] But I have not asked you to sit down. [*He rises and goes to the other chair.*] I am a savage: a barbarian. [*He throws the shirt and coat over the table on to the floor and puts his sword on the table.*] Be seated, Captain.

EDSTASTON Thank you.

They bow to one another ceremoniously. Patiomkin's tendency to grotesque exaggeration costs him his balance; he nearly falls over Edstaston, who rescues him and takes the proffered chair.

PATIOMKIN [*resuming his seat*]. By the way, what was the piece of advice I was going to give you?

EDSTASTON. As you did not give it, I don't know. Allow me to add that I have not asked for your advice.

PATIOMKIN. I give it to you unasked, delightful Englishman. I remember it now. It was this. Don't try to become Tsar of Russia.

EDSTASTON [*in astonishment*]. I haven't the slightest intention—

PATIOMKIN. Not now; but you will have: take my words for it. It will strike you as a splendid idea to have conscientious scruples—to desire the blessing of the Church on your union with Catherine.

EDSTASTON [*racing in utter amazement*]. My union with Catherine! You're mad.

PATIOMKIN [*unmoved*]. The day you hint at such a thing will be the day of your downfall. Besides, it is not lucky to be Catherine's husband. You know what happened to Peter?

EDSTASTON [*shortly; sitting down again*]. I do not wish to discuss it.

PATIOMKIN. You think she murdered him?

EDSTASTON. I know that people have said so.

PATIOMKIN [*thunderously; springing to his feet*]. It is a lie: Orloff murdered him. [*Subsiding a little.*] He also knocked my eye out; but [*sitting down placidly*] I succeeded him for all that. And [*patting Edstaston's hand very affectionately*] I'm sorry to say, darling, that if you become Tsar, I shall murder you.

EDSTASTON [*ironically returning the caress*]. Thank you. The occasion will not arise. [*Rising.*] I have the honor to wish your Highness good morning.

PATIOMKIN [*jumping up and stopping him on his way to the door*]. Tut tut! I'm going to take you to the Empress now, this very instant.

EDSTASTON. In these boots? Impossible! I must change.

PATIOMKIN. Nonsense! You shall come just as you are. You shall show her your calves later on.

EDSTASTON. But it will take me only half an hour to—

PATIOMKIN. In half an hour it will be too late for the petit lever. Come along. Damn it, man, I must oblige the British ambassador, and the French ambassador, and old Fritz, and Monsieur Voltaire and the rest of them. [*He shouts rudely to the door.*] Varinka! [*To Edstaston, with tears in his voice.*] Varinka shall persuade you: nobody can refuse Varinka anything. My niece. A treasure, I assure you. Beautiful! devoted! fascinating! [*Shouting again.*] Varinka, where the devil are you?

VARINKA [*returning*]. I'll not be shouted for. You have the voice of a bear, and the manners of a tinker.

PATIOMKIN. Tsh-sh-sh. Little angel Mother: you must behave yourself before the English captain. [*He takes off his dressing-gown and throws it over the papers and the breakfasts: picks up his coat: and disappears behind the screen to complete his toilette.*]

EDSTASTON. Madam! [*He bows.*]

VARINKA [*courtseying*]. Monsieur le Capitaine!

EDSTASTON. I must apologize for the disturbance I made, madam.

PATIOMKIN [*behind the screen*]. You must not call her madam. You must call her Little Mother, and beautiful darling.

EDSTASTON. My respect for the lady will not permit it.

VARINKA. Respect! How can you respect the niece of a savage?

EDSTASTON [*deprecatingly*]. Oh, madam!

VARINKA. Heaven is my witness, Little English Father, we need someone who is not afraid of him. He is so strong! I hope you will throw him down on the floor many, many, many times.

PATIOMKIN [*behind the screen*]. Varinka!

VARINKA. Yes?

PATIOMKIN. Go and look through the keyhole of the Imperial bed-chamber; and bring me word whether the Empress is awake yet.

VARINKA. Fi donc! I do not look through keyholes.

PATIOMKIN [*emerging, having arranged his shirt and put on his diamonded coat*]. You have been badly brought up, little darling. Would any lady or gentleman walk unannounced into a room without first looking through the keyhole? [*Taking his sword from the table and putting it on.*] The great thing in life is to be simple; and the perfectly simple thing is to look through keyholes. Another epigram: the fifth this morning! Where is my fool of a chancellor? Where is Popof?

EDSTASTON [*choking with suppressed laughter*]!!!!

PATIOMKIN [*gratified*]. Darling, you appreciate my epigram.

EDSTASTON. Excuse me. Pop off! Ha! ha! I can't help laughing: What's his real name, by the way, in case I meet him?

VARINKA [*surprised*]. His real name? Popof, of course. Why do you laugh, Little Father?

EDSTASTON. How can anyone with a sense of humor help laughing? Pop off! [*He is convulsed.*]

VARINKA [*looking at her uncle, taps her forehead significantly*]!!

PATIOMKIN [*aside to Varinka*]. No: only English. He will amuse Catherine. [*To Edstaston.*] Come, you shall tell the joke to the Empress: she is by way of being a humorist [*he takes him by the arm, and leads him towards the door*].

EDSTASTON [*resisting*]. No, really. I am not fit—

PATIOMKIN. Persuade him, Little angel Mother.

VARINKA [*taking his other arm*]. Yes, yes, yes. Little English Father: God knows it is your duty to be brave and wait on the Empress. Come.

EDSTASTON. No. I had rather—

PATIOMKIN [*hauling him along*]. Come.

VARINKA [*pulling him and coaxing him*]. Come, little love: you can't refuse me.

EDSTASTON. But how can I?

PATIOMKIN. Why not? She won't eat you.

VARINKA. She will; but you must come.

EDSTASTON. I assure you—it is quite out of the question—my clothes—

VARINKA. You look perfect.

PATIOMKIN. Come along, darling.

EDSTASTON [*struggling*]. Impossible—

VARINKA. Come, come, come.

EDSTASTON. No. Believe me—I don't wish—I—

VARINKA. Carry him, uncle.

PATIOMKIN [*lifting him in his arms like a father carrying a little boy*]. Yes: I'll carry you.

EDSTASTON. Dash it all, this is ridiculous!

VARINKA [*seizing his ankles and dancing as he is carried out*]. You must come. If you kick you will blacken my eyes.

PATIOMKIN. Come, baby, come.

By this time they have made their way through the door and are out of hearing.

THE SECOND SCENE

The Empress's petit lever. The central doors are closed. Those who enter through them find on their left, on a dais of two broad steps, a magnificent curtained bed. Beyond it a door in the panelling leads to the Empress's cabinet. Near the foot of the bed, in the middle of the room, stands a gilt chair, with the Imperial arms carved and the Imperial monogram embroidered.

The Court is in attendance, standing in two melancholy rows down the side of the room opposite to the bed, solemn, bored, waiting for the Empress to awaken. The Princess Dashkoff, with two ladies, stands a little in front of the line of courtiers, by the Imperial chair. Silence, broken only by the yawns and whispers of the courtiers. Naryshkin, the Chamberlain, stands by the head of the bed.

A loud yawn is heard from behind the curtains.

NARYSHKIN [*holding up a warning hand*]. Ssh!

The courtiers hastily cease whispering: dress up their lines: and stiffen. Dead silence. A bell tinkles within the curtains. Naryshkin and the Princess solemnly draw them and reveal the Empress.

Catherine turns over on her back, and stretches herself.

CATHERINE [*yawning*]. Heigho—ah—yah—ah—ow—what o'clock is it? [*Her accent is German.*]

NARYSHKIN [*formally*]. Her Imperial Majesty is awake. [*The Court falls on its knees.*]

ALL. Good morning to your Majesty.

NARYSHKIN. Half-past ten, Little Mother.

CATHERINE [*sitting up abruptly*]. Potztausend! [*Contemplating the kneeling courtiers.*] Oh, get up, get up. [*All rise.*] Your etiquette bores me. I am hardly awake in the morning before it begins. [*Yawning again, and relapsing sleepily against her pillows.*] Why do they do it, Naryshkin?

NARYSHKIN. God knows it is not for your sake, Little Mother. But you see if you were not a great queen they would all be nobodies.

CATHERINE [*sitting up*]. They make me do it to keep up their own little dignities? So?

NARYSHKIN. Exactly. Also because if they didn't you might have them flogged, dear Little Mother.

CATHERINE [*springing energetically out of bed and seating herself on the edge of it*]. Flogged! I! A Liberal Empress! A philosopher! You are a barbarian, Naryshkin. [*She rises and turns to the courtiers.*] And then, as if I cared! [*She turns again to Naryshkin.*] You should know by this time that I am frank and original in character, like an Englishman. [*She walks about restlessly.*] No: what maddens me about all this ceremony is that I am the only person in Russia who gets no fun out of my being Empress. You all glory in me: you bask in my smiles: you get titles and honors and favors from me: you are dazzled by my crown and my robes: you feel splendid when you have been admitted to my presence; and when I say a gracious word to you, you talk about it to everyone you meet for a week afterwards. But what do I get out of it? Nothing. [*She throws herself into the chair. Naryshkin deprecates with a gesture; she hurls an emphatic repetition at him.*] Nothing!! I wear a crown until my neck aches: I stand looking majestic until I am ready to drop: I have to smile at ugly old ambassadors and frown and turn my back on young and handsome ones. Nobody gives me anything. When I was only an Archduchess, the English ambassador used to give me money whenever I wanted it—or rather whenever he wanted to get anything out of my sacred predecessor Elizabeth [*the Court bows to the ground*]; but now that I am Empress he never gives me a kopek. When I have headaches and colics I envy the scullerymaids. And you are not a bit grateful to me for all my care of you, my work, my thought, my fatigue, my sufferings.

THE PRINCESS DASHKOFF. God knows, Little Mother, we all implore you to give your wonderful brain a rest. That is why you get headaches. Monsieur Voltaire also has headaches. His brain is just like yours.

CATHERINE. Dashkoff, what a liar you are! [*Dashkoff curtsies with impressive dignity.*] And you think you are flattering me! Let me tell you I would not give a rouble to have the brains of all the philosophers in France. What is our business for today?

NARYSHKIN. The new museum, Little Mother. But the model will not be ready until tonight.

CATHERINE [*rising eagerly*]. Yes, the museum. An enlightened capital should have a museum. [*She paces the chamber with a deep sense of the importance of the museum.*] It shall be one of the wonders of the world. I must have specimens: specimens, specimens, specimens.

NARYSHKIN. You are in high spirits this morning, Little Mother.

CATHERINE [*with sudden levity.*] I am always in high spirits, even when people do not bring me my slippers. [*She runs to the chair and sits down, thrusting her feet out.*]

The two ladies rush to her feet, each carrying a slipper. Catherine, about to put her feet into them, is checked by a disturbance in the antechamber.

PATIOMKIN [*carrying Edstaston through the antechamber*]. Useless to struggle. Come along, beautiful baby darling. Come to Little Mother. [*He sings.*]

March him baby, Baby, baby, Lit-tle ba-by bumpkins.

VARINKA [*joining in to the same doggerel in canon, a third above*]. March him, baby, etc., etc.

EDSTASTON [*trying to make himself heard*]. No, no. This is carrying a joke too far. I must insist. Let me down! Hang it, will you let me down! Confound it! No, no. Stop playing the fool, will you? We don't understand this sort of thing in England. I shall be disgraced. Let me down.

CATHERINE [*meanwhile*]. What a horrible noise! Naryshkin, see what it is.

Naryshkin goes to the door.

CATHERINE [*listening*]. That is Prince Patiomkin.

NARYSHKIN [*calling from the door*]. Little Mother, a stranger.

Catherine plunges into bed again and covers herself up. Patiomkin, followed by Varinka, carries Edstaston in: dumps him down on the foot of the bed: and staggers past it to the cabinet door. Varinka joins the courtiers at the opposite side of the room. Catherine, blazing with wrath, pushes Edstaston off her bed on to the floor: gets out of bed: and turns on Patiomkin with so terrible an expression that all kneel down hastily except Edstaston, who is sprawling on the carpet in angry confusion.

CATHERINE. Patiomkin, how dare you? [*Looking at Edstaston.*] What is this?

PATIOMKIN [*on his knees, tearfully*]. I don't know. I am drunk. What is this, Varinka?

EDSTASTON [*scrambling to his feet*]. Madam, this drunken ruffian—

PATIOMKIN. Thas true. Drungn ruffian. Took dvantage of my being drunk. Said: take me to Lil angel Mother. Take me to beaufl Empress. Take me to the grea'st woman on earth. Thas whas he he said. I took him. I was wrong. I am not sober.

CATHERINE. Men have grown sober in Siberia for less, Prince.

PATIOMKIN. Serve em right! Sgusting habit. Ask Varinka.

Catherine turns her face from him to the Court. The courtiers see that she is trying not to laugh, and know by experience that she will not succeed. They rise, relieved and grinning.

VARINKA. It is true. He drinks like a pig.

PATIOMKIN [*plaintively*]. No: not like pig. Like prince. Lil Mother made poor Patiomkin prince. Whas use being prince if I mayn't drink?

CATHERINE [*biting her lips*]. Go. I am offended.

PATIOMKIN. Don't scold, Lil Mother.

CATHERINE [*imperiously*]. Go.

PATIOMKIN [*rising unsteadily*]. Yes: go. Go bye bye. Very sleepy. Berr go bye bye than go Siberia. Go bye bye in Lil Mother's bed [*he pretends to make an attempt to get into the bed*].

CATHERINE [*energetically pulling him back*]. No, no! Patiomkin! What are you thinking of? [*He falls like a log on the floor, apparently dead drunk.*]

THE PRINCESS DASHKOFF. Scandalous! An insult to your Imperial Majesty!

CATHERINE. Dashkoff: you have no sense of humor. [*She steps down to the door level and looks indulgently at Patiomkin. He gurgles brutishly. She has an impulse of disgust.*] Hog. [*She kicks him as hard as she can.*] Oh! You have broken my toe. Brute. Beast. Dashkoff is quite right. Do you hear?

PATIOMKIN. If you ask my pi-pinion of Dashkoff, my pipinion is that Dashkoff is drunk. Scanlous. Poor Patiomkin go bye bye. [*He relapses into drunken slumbers.*]

Some of the courtiers move to carry him away.

CATHERINE [*stopping them*]. Let him lie. Let him sleep it off. If he goes out it will be to a tavern and low company for the rest of the day. [*Indulgently.*] There! [*She takes a pillow from the bed and puts it under his head: then turns to Edstaston: surveys him with perfect dignity: and asks, in her queenliest manner.*] Varinka, who is this gentleman?

VARINKA. A foreign captain: I cannot pronounce his name. I think he is mad. He came to the Prince and said he must see your Majesty. He can talk of nothing else. We could not prevent him.

EDSTASTON [*overwhelmed by this apparent betrayal*]. Oh! Madam: I am perfectly sane: I am actually an Englishman. I should never have dreamt of approaching your Majesty without the fullest credentials. I have letters from the English ambassador, from the Prussian ambassador. [*Naively.*] But everybody assured me that Prince Patiomkm is all-powerful with your Majesty; so I naturally applied to him.

PATIOMKIN [*interrupts the conversation by an agonized wheezing groan as of a donkey beginning to bray*]!!!

CATHERINE [*like a fishfag*]. Schweig, du Hund. [*Resuming her impressive royal manner.*] Have you never been taught, sir, how a gentleman should enter the presence of a sovereign?

EDSTASTON. Yes, Madam; but I did not enter your presence: I was carried.

CATHERINE. But you say you asked the Prince to carry you.

EDSTASTON. Certainly not, Madam. I protested against it with all my might. I appeal to this lady to confirm me.

VARINKA [*pretending to be indignant*]. Yes, you protested. But, all the same, you were very very very anxious to see her Imperial Majesty. You blushed when the Prince spoke of her. You threatened to strike him across the face with your sword because you thought he did not speak enthusiastically enough of her. [*To Catherine.*] Trust me: he has seen your Imperial Majesty before.

CATHERINE [*to Edstaston*]. You have seen us before?

EDSTASTON. At the review, Madam.

VARINKA [*triumphantly*]. Aha! I knew it. Your Majesty wore the hussar uniform. He saw how radiant! how splendid! your Majesty looked. Oh! he has dared to admire your Majesty. Such insolence is not to be endured.

EDSTASTON. All Europe is a party to that insolence, Madam.

THE PRINCESS DASHKOFF. All Europe is content to do so at a respectful distance. It is possible to admire her Majesty's policy and her eminence in literature and philosophy without performing acrobatic feats in the Imperial bed.

EDSTASTON. I know nothing about her Majesty's eminence in policy or philosophy: I don't pretend to understand such things. I speak as a practical man.

And I never knew that foreigners had any policy: I always thought that policy was Mr. Pitt's business.

CATHERINE [*lifting her eyebrows*]. So?

VARINKA. What else did you presume to admire her Majesty for, pray?

EDSTASTON [*addled*]. Well, I—I—I—that is, I—[*He stammers himself dumb.*]

CATHERINE [*after a pitiless silence*]. We are waiting for your answer.

EDSTASTON. But I never said I admired your Majesty. The lady has twisted my words.

VARINKA. You don't admire her, then?

EDSTASTON. Well, I—naturally—of course, I can't deny that the uniform was very becoming—perhaps a little unfeminine—still—Dead silence. Catherine and the Court watch him stonily. He is wretchedly embarrassed.

CATHERINE [*with cold majesty*]. Well, sir: is that all you have to say?

EDSTASTON. Surely there is no harm in noticing that er—that er—[*He stops again.*]

CATHERINE. Noticing that er—? [*He gazes at her, speechless, like a fascinated rabbit. She repeats fiercely.*] That er—?

EDSTASTON [*startled into speech*]. Well, that your Majesty was—was—[*soothingly*] Well, let me put it this way: that it was rather natural for a man to admire your Majesty without being a philosopher.

CATHERINE [*suddenly smiling and extending her hand to him to be kissed*]. Courtier!

EDSTASTON [*kissing it*]. Not at all. Your Majesty is very good. I have been very awkward; but I did not intend it. I am rather stupid, I am afraid.

CATHERINE. Stupid! By no means. Courage, Captain: we are pleased. [*He falls on his knee. She takes his cheeks in her hands: turns up his face: and adds*] We are greatly pleased. [*She slaps his cheek coquettishly: he bows almost to his knee.*] The petit lever is over. [*She turns to go into the cabinet, and stumbles against the supine Patiomkin.*] Ach! [*Edstaston springs to her assistance, seizing Patiomkin's heels and shifting him out of the Empress's path.*] We thank you, Captain.

He bows gallantly and is rewarded by a very gracious smile. Then Catherine goes into her cabinet, followed by the princess Dashkoff, who turns at the door to make a deep courtsey to Edstaston.

VARINKA. Happy Little Father! Remember: I did this for you. [*She runs out after the Empress.*]

Edstaston, somewhat dazed, crosses the room to the courtiers, and is received with marked deference, each courtier making him a profound bow or curtsey before withdrawing through the central doors. He returns each obeisance with a nervous jerk, and turns away from it, only to find another courtier bowing at the other side. The process finally reduced him to distraction, as he bumps into one in the act of bowing to another and then has to bow his apologies. But at last they are all gone except Naryshkin.

EDSTASTON. Ouf!

PATIOMKIN [*jumping up vigorously*]. You have done it, darling. Superbly! Beautifully!

EDSTASTON [*astonished*]. Do you mean to say you are not drunk?

PATIOMKIN. Not dead drunk, darling. Only diplomatically drunk. As a drunken hog, I have done for you in five minutes what I could not have done in five months as a sober man. Your fortune is made. She likes you.

EDSTASTON. The devil she does!

PATIOMKIN. Why? Aren't you delighted?

EDSTASTON. Delighted! Gracious heavens, man, I am engaged to be married.

PATIOMKIN. What matter? She is in England, isn't she?

EDSTASTON. No. She has just arrived in St. Petersburg.

THE PRINCESS DASHKOFF [*returning*]. Captain Edstaston, the Empress is robed, and commands your presence.

EDSTASTON. Say I was gone before you arrived with the message. [*He hurries out. The other three, too taken aback to stop him, stare after him in the utmost astonishment.*]

NARYSHKIN [*turning from the door*]. She will have him knouted. He is a dead man.

THE PRINCESS DASHKOFF. But what am I to do? I cannot take such an answer to the Empress.

PATIOMKIN. P-P-P-P-P-P-W-W-W-W-W-rrrrrr [*a long puff, turning into a growl*]! [*He spits.*] I must kick somebody.

NARYSHKIN [*flying precipitately through the central doors*]. No, no. Please.

THE PRINCESS DASHKOFF [*throwing herself recklessly in front of Patiomkin as he starts in pursuit of the Chamberlain*]. Kick me. Disable me. It will be an excuse for not going back to her. Kick me hard.

PATIOMKIN. Yah! [*He flings her on the bed and dashes after Naryshkin.*]

THE THIRD SCENE

In a terrace garden overlooking the Neva. Claire, a robust young English lady, is leaning on the river wall. She turns expectantly on hearing the garden gate opened and closed. Edstaston hurries in. With a cry of delight she throws her arms round his neck.

CLAIRE. Darling!

EDSTASTON [*making a wry face*]. Don't call me darling.

CLAIRE [*amazed and chilled*]. Why?

EDSTASTON. I have been called darling all the morning.

CLAIRE [*with a flash of jealousy*]. By whom?

EDSTASTON. By everybody. By the most unutterable swine. And if we do not leave this abominable city now: do you hear? now; I shall be called darling by the Empress.

CLAIRE [*with magnificent snobbery*]. She would not dare. Did you tell her you were engaged to me?

EDSTASTON. Of course not.

CLAIRE. Why?

EDSTASTON. Because I didn't particularly want to have you knouted, and to be hanged or sent to Siberia myself.

CLAIRE. What on earth do you mean?

EDSTASTON. Well, the long and short of it is—don't think me a coxcomb, Claire: it is too serious to mince matters—I have seen the Empress; and—

CLAIRE. Well, you wanted to see her.

EDSTASTON. Yes; but the Empress has seen me.

CLAIRE. She has fallen in love with you!

EDSTASTON. How did you know?

CLAIRE. Dearest: as if anyone could help it.

EDSTASTON. Oh, don't make me feel like a fool. But, though it does sound conceited to say it, I flatter myself I'm better looking than Patiomkin and the other hogs she is accustomed to. Anyhow, I daren't risk staying.

CLAIRE. What a nuisance! Mamma will be furious at having to pack, and at missing the Court ball this evening.

EDSTASTON. I can't help that. We haven't a moment to lose.

CLAIRE. May I tell her she will be knouted if we stay?

EDSTASTON. Do, dearest.

He kisses her and lets her go, expecting her to run into the house.

CLAIRE [*pausing thoughtfully*]. Is she—is she good-looking when you see her close?

EDSTASTON. Not a patch on you, dearest.

CLAIRE [*jealous*]. Then you did see her close?

EDSTASTON. Fairly close.

CLAIRE. Indeed! How close? No: that's silly of me: I will tell mamma. [*She is going out when Naryshkin enters with the Sergeant and a squad of soldiers.*] What do you want here?

The Sergeant goes to Edstaston: plumps down on his knees: and takes out a magnificent pair of pistols with gold grips. He proffers them to Edstaston, holding them by the barrels.

NARYSHKIN. Captain Edstaston: his Highness Prince Patiomkin sends you the pistols he promised you.

THE SERGEANT. Take them, Little Father; and do not forget us poor soldiers who have brought them to you; for God knows we get but little to drink.

EDSTASTON [*irresolutely*]. But I can't take these valuable things. By Jiminy, though, they're beautiful! Look at them, Claire.

As he is taking the pistols the kneeling Sergeant suddenly drops them; flings himself forward; and embraces Edstaston's hips to prevent him from drawing his own pistols from his boots.

THE SERGEANT. Lay hold of him there. Pin his arms. I have his pistols. [*The soldiers seize Edstaston.*]

EDSTASTON. Ah, would you, damn you! [*He drives his knee into the Sergeant's epigastrium, and struggles furiously with his captors.*]

THE SERGEANT [*rolling on the ground, gasping and groaning*]. Owgh! Murder! Holy Nicholas! Owwwgh!

CLAIRE. Help! help! They are killing Charles. Help!

NARYSHKIN [*seizing her and clapping his hand over her mouth*]. Tie him neck and crop. Ten thousand blows of the stick if you let him go. [*Claire twists herself loose: turns on him: and cuffs him furiously.*] Yow—ow! Have mercy, Little Mother.

CLAIRE. You wretch! Help! Help! Police! We are being murdered. Help!

The Sergeant, who has risen, comes to Naryshkin's rescue, and grasps Claire's hands, enabling Naryshkin to gag her again. By this time Edstaston and his captors are all rolling on the ground together. They get Edstaston on his back and fasten his wrists together behind his knees. Next they put a broad strap round his ribs. Finally they pass a pole through this breast strap and through the waist strap and lift him by it, helplessly trussed up, to carry him of. Meanwhile he is by no means suffering in silence.

EDSTASTON [*gasping*]. You shall hear more of this. Damn you, will you untie me? I will complain to the ambassador. I will write to the Gazette. England will blow your trumpery little fleet out of the water and sweep your tinpot army into Siberia for this. Will you let me go? Damn you! Curse you! What the devil do you mean by it? I'll—I'll—I'll— [*he is carried out of hearing*].

NARYSHKIN [*snatching his hands from Claire's face with a scream, and shaking his finger frantically*]. Agh! [*The Sergeant, amazed, lets go her hands.*] She has bitten me, the little vixen.

CLAIRE [*spitting and wiping her mouth disgustedly*]. How dare you put your dirty paws on my mouth? Ugh! Psha!

THE SERGEANT. Be merciful, Little angel Mother.

CLAIRE. Do not presume to call me your little angel mother. Where are the police?

NARYSHKIN. We are the police in St Petersburg, little spitfire.

THE SERGEANT. God knows we have no orders to harm you, Little Mother. Our duty is done. You are well and strong; but I shall never be the same man again. He is a mighty and terrible fighter, as stout as a bear. He has broken my sweetbread with his strong knees. God knows poor folk should not be set upon such dangerous adversaries!

CLAIRE. Serve you right! Where have they taken Captain Edstaston to?

NARYSHKIN [*spitefully*]. To the Empress, little beauty. He has insulted the Empress. He will receive a hundred and one blows of the knout. [*He laughs and goes out, nursing his bitten finger.*]

THE SERGEANT. He will feel only the first twenty and he will be mercifully dead long before the end, little darling.

CLAIRE [*sustained by an invincible snobbery*]. They dare not touch an English officer. I will go to the Empress myself: she cannot know who Captain Edstaston is—who we are.

THE SERGEANT. Do so in the name of the Holy Nicholas, little beauty.

CLAIRE. Don't be impertinent. How can I get admission to the palace?

THE SERGEANT. Everybody goes in and out of the palace, little love.

CLAIRE. But I must get into the Empress's presence. I must speak to her.

THE SERGEANT. You shall, dear Little Mother. You shall give the poor old Sergeant a rouble; and the blessed Nicholas will make your salvation his charge.

CLAIRE [*impetuously*]. I will give you [*she is about to say fifty roubles, but checks herself cautiously*]—Well: I don't mind giving you two roubles if I can speak to the Empress.

THE SERGEANT [*joyfully*]. I praise Heaven for you, Little Mother. Come. [*He leads the way out.*] It was the temptation of the devil that led your young man to bruise my vitals and deprive me of breath. We must be merciful to one another's faults.

THE FOURTH SCENE

A triangular recess communicating by a heavily curtained arch with the huge ballroom of the palace. The light is subdued by red shades on the candles. In the wall adjoining that pierced by the arch is a door. The only piece of furniture is a very handsome chair on the arch side. In the ballroom they are dancing a polonaise to the music of a brass band.

Naryshkin enters through the door, followed by the soldiers carrying Edstaston, still trussed to the pole. Exhausted and dogged, he makes no sound.

NARYSHKIN. Halt. Get that pole clear of the prisoner. [*They dump Edstaston on the floor and detach the pole. Naryshkin stoops over him and addresses him insultingly.*] Well! are you ready to be tortured? This is the Empress's private torture chamber. Can I do anything to make you quite comfortable? You have only to mention it.

EDSTASTON. Have you any back teeth?

NARYSHKIN [*surprised*]. Why?

EDSTASTON. His Majesty King George the Third will send for six of them when the news of this reaches London; so look out, damn your eyes!

NARYSHKIN [*frightened*]. Oh, I assure you I am only obeying my orders. Personally I abhor torture, and would save you if I could. But the Empress is proud; and what woman would forgive the slight you put upon her?

EDSTASTON. As I said before: Damn your eyes!

NARYSHKIN [*almost in tears*]. Well, it isn't my fault. [*To the soldiers, insolently.*] You know your orders? You remember what you have to do when the Empress gives you the word? [*The soldiers salute in assent.*]

Naryshkin passes through the curtains, admitting a blare of music and a strip of the brilliant white candlelight from the chandeliers in the ballroom as he does so. The white light vanishes and the music is muffled as the curtains fall together behind him. Presently the band stops abruptly: and Naryshkin comes back through the curtains. He makes a warning gesture to the soldiers, who stand at attention. Then he moves the curtain to allow Catherine to enter. She is in full Imperial regalia, and stops sternly just where she has entered. The soldiers fall on their knees.

CATHERINE. Obey your orders.

The soldiers seize Edstaston, and throw him roughly at the feet of the Empress.

CATHERINE [*looking down coldly on him*]. Also [*the German word*], you have put me to the trouble of sending for you twice. You had better have come the first time.

EDSTASTON [*exsufflicate, and pettishly angry*]. I haven't come either time. I've been carried. I call it infernal impudence.

CATHERINE. Take care what you say.

EDSTASTON. No use. I daresay you look very majestic and very handsome; but I can't see you; and I am not intimidated. I am an Englishman; and you can kidnap me; but you can't bully me.

NARYSHKIN. Remember to whom you are speaking.

CATHERINE [*violently, furious at his intrusion*]. Remember that dogs should be dumb. [*He shrivels.*] And do you, Captain, remember that famous as I am for my clemency, there are limits to the patience even of an Empress.

EDSTASTON. How is a man to remember anything when he is trussed up in this ridiculous fashion? I can hardly breathe. [*He makes a futile struggle to free himself.*] Here: don't be unkind, your Majesty: tell these fellows to unstrap me. You know you really owe me an apology.

CATHERINE. You think you can escape by appealing, like Prince Patiomkin, to my sense of humor?

EDSTASTON. Sense of humor! Ho! Ha, ha! I like that. Would anybody with a sense of humor make a guy of a man like this, and then expect him to take it seriously? I say: do tell them to loosen these straps.

CATHERINE [*seating herself*]. Why should I, pray?

EDSTASTON. Why! Why! Why, because they're hurting me.

CATHERINE. People sometimes learn through suffering. Manners, for instance.

EDSTASTON. Oh, well, of course, if you're an ill-natured woman, hurting me on purpose, I have nothing more to say.

CATHERINE. A monarch, sir, has sometimes to employ a necessary, and salutary severity—

EDSTASTON [*Interrupting her petulantly*]. Quack! quack! quack!

CATHERINE. Donnerwetter!

EDSTASTON [*continuing recklessly*]. This isn't severity: it's tomfoolery. And if you think it's reforming my character or teaching me anything, you're mistaken. It may be a satisfaction to you; but if it is, all I can say is that it's not an amiable satisfaction.

CATHERINE [*turning suddenly and balefully on Naryshkin*]. What are you grinning at?

NARYSHKIN [*falling on his knees in terror*]. Be merciful, Little Mother. My heart is in my mouth.

CATHERINE. Your heart and your mouth will be in two separate parts of your body if you again forget in whose presence you stand. Go. And take your men with you. [*Naryshkin crawls to the door. The soldiers rise.*] Stop. Roll that [*indicating Edstaston*] nearer. [*The soldiers obey.*] Not so close. Did I ask you for a footstool? [*She pushes Edstaston away with her foot.*]

EDSTASTON [*with a sudden squeal*]. Agh!!! I must really ask your Majesty not to put the point of your Imperial toe between my ribs. I am ticklesome.

CATHERINE. Indeed? All the more reason for you to treat me with respect, Captain. [*To the others.*] Begone. How many times must I give an order before it is obeyed?

NARYSHKIN. Little Mother: they have brought some instruments of torture. Will they be needed?

CATHERINE [*indignantly*]. How dare you name such abominations to a Liberal Empress? You will always be a savage and a fool, Naryshkin. These relics of barbarism are buried, thank God, in the grave of Peter the Great. My methods are more civilized. [*She extends her toe towards Edstaston's ribs.*]

EDSTASTON [*shrieking hysterically*]. Yagh! Ah! [*Furiously.*] If your Majesty does that again I will write to the London Gazette.

CATHERINE [*to the soldiers*]. Leave us. Quick! do you hear? Five thousand blows of the stick for the soldier who is in the room when I speak next. [*The soldiers rush out.*] Naryshkin: are you waiting to be knouted? [*Naryshkin backs out hastily.*]

Catherine and Edstaston are now alone. Catherine has in her hand a sceptre or baton of gold. Wrapped round it is a new pamphlet, in French, entitled L'Homme aux Quarante Ecus. She calmly unrolls this and begins to read it at her ease as if she were quite alone. Several seconds elapse in dead silence. She becomes more and more absorbed in the pamphlet, and more and more amused by it.

CATHERINE [*greatly pleased by a passage, and turning over the leaf*]. Ausgezeiehnet!

EDSTASTON. Ahem!

Silence. Catherine reads on.

CATHERINE. Wie komisch!

EDSTASTON. Ahem! ahem!

Silence.

CATHERINE [*soliloquizing enthusiastically*]. What a wonderful author is Monsieur Voltaire! How lucidly he exposes the folly of this crazy plan for raising the entire revenue of the country from a single tax on land! how he withers it with his irony! how he makes you laugh whilst he is convincing you! how sure one feels that the proposal is killed by his wit and economic penetration: killed never to be mentioned again among educated people!

EDSTASTON. For Heaven's sake, Madam, do you intend to leave me tied up like this while you discuss the blasphemies of that abominable infidel? Agh!! [*She has again applied her toe.*] Oh! Oo!

CATHERINE [*calmly*]. Do I understand you to say that Monsieur Voltaire is a great philanthropist and a great philosopher as well as the wittiest man in Europe?

EDSTASTON. Certainly not. I say that his books ought to be burnt by the common hangman [*her toe touches his ribs*]. Yagh! Oh don't. I shall faint. I can't bear it.

CATHERINE. Have you changed your opinion of Monsieur Voltaire?

EDSTASTON. But you can't expect me as a member of the Church of England [*she tickles him*] —agh! Ow! Oh Lord! he is anything you like. He is a philanthropist, a philosopher, a beauty: he ought to have a statue, damn him! [*she tickles him*]. No! bless him! save him victorious, happy and glorious! Oh, let eternal honors crown his name: Voltaire thrice worthy on the rolls of fame! [*Exhausted.*] Now will you let me up? And look here! I can see your ankles when you tickle me: it's not ladylike.

CATHERINE [*sticking out her toe and admiring it critically*]. Is the spectacle so disagreeable?

EDSTASTON. It's agreeable enough; only [*with intense expression*] for heaven's sake don't touch me in the ribs.

CATHERINE [*putting aside the pamphlet*]. Captain Edstaston, why did you refuse to come when I sent for you?

EDSTASTON. Madam, I cannot talk tied up like this.

CATHERINE. Do you still admire me as much as you did this morning?

EDSTASTON. How can I possibly tell when I can't see you? Let me get up and look. I can't see anything now except my toes and yours.

CATHERINE. Do you still intend to write to the London Gazette about me?

EDSTASTON. Not if you will loosen these straps. Quick: loosen me. I'm fainting.

CATHERINE. I don't think you are [*tickling him*].

EDSTASTON. Agh! Cat!

CATHERINE. What [*she tickles him again*].

EDSTASTON [*with a shriek*]. No: angel, angel!

CATHERINE [*tenderly*]. Geliebter!

EDSTASTON. I don't know a word of German; but that sounded kind. [*Becoming hysterical.*] Little Mother, beautiful little darling angel mother: don't be cruel: untie me. Oh, I beg and implore you. Don't be unkind. I shall go mad.

CATHERINE. You are expected to go mad with love when an Empress deigns to interest herself in you. When an Empress allows you to see her foot you should kiss it. Captain Edstaston, you are a booby.

EDSTASTON [*indignantly*]. I am nothing of the kind. I have been mentioned in dispatches as a highly intelligent officer. And let me warn your Majesty that I am not so helpless as you think. The English Ambassador is in that ballroom. A shout from me will bring him to my side; and then where will your Majesty be?

CATHERINE. I should like to see the English Ambassador or anyone else pass through that curtain against my orders. It might be a stone wall ten feet thick. Shout your loudest. Sob. Curse. Scream. Yell [*she tickles him unmercifully*].

EDSTASTON [*frantically*]. Ahowyou!!!! Agh! oh! Stop! Oh Lord! Ya-a-a-ah! [*A tumult in the ballroom responds to his cries*].

VOICES FROM THE BALLROOM. Stand back. You cannot pass. Hold her back there. The Empress's orders. It is out of the question. No, little darling, not in there. Nobody is allowed in there. You will be sent to Siberia. Don't let her through there, on your life. Drag her back. You will be knouted. It is hopeless, Mademoiselle: you must obey orders. Guard there! Send some men to hold her.

CLAIRE'S VOICE. Let me go. They are torturing Charles in there. I WILL go. How can you all dance as if nothing was happening? Let me go, I tell you. Let—me—go. [*She dashes through the curtain, no one dares follow her.*]

CATHERINE [*rising in wrath*]. How dare you?

CLAIRE [*recklessly*]. Oh, dare your grandmother! Where is my Charles? What are they doing to him?

EDSTASTON [*shouting*]. Claire, loosen these straps, in Heaven's name. Quick.

CLAIRE [*seeing him and throwing herself on her knees at his side*]. Oh, how dare they tie you up like that! [*To Catherine.*] You wicked wretch! You Russian savage! [*She pounces on the straps, and begins unbuckling them.*]

CATHERINE [*conquering herself with a mighty effort*]. Now self-control. Self-control, Catherine. Philosophy. Europe is looking on. [*She forces herself to sit down.*]

EDSTASTON. Steady, dearest: it is the Empress. Call her your Imperial Majesty. Call her Star of the North, Little Mother, Little Darling: that's what she likes; but get the straps off.

CLAIRE. Keep quiet, dear: I cannot get them off if you move.

CATHERINE [*calmly*]. Keep quite still, Captain [*she tickles him.*]

EDSTASTON. Ow! Agh! Ahowyow!

CLAIRE [*stopping dead in the act of unbuckling the straps and turning sick with jealousy as she grasps the situation*]. Was THAT what I thought was your being tortured?

CATHERINE [*urbanely*]. That is the favorite torture of Catherine the Second, Mademoiselle. I think the Captain enjoys it very much.

CLAIRE. Then he can have as much more of it as he wants. I am sorry I intruded. [*She rises to go.*]

EDSTASTON [*catching her train in his teeth and holding on like a bull-dog*]. Don't go. Don't leave me in this horrible state. Loosen me. [*This is what he is saying: but as he says it with the train in his mouth it is not very intelligible.*]

CLAIRE. Let go. You are undignified and ridiculous enough yourself without making me ridiculous. [*She snatches her train away.*]

EDSTASTON. Ow! You've nearly pulled my teeth out: you're worse than the Star of the North. [*To Catherine.*] Darling Little Mother: you have a kind heart, the kindest in Europe. Have pity. Have mercy. I love you. [*Claire bursts into tears.*] Release me.

CATHERINE. Well, just to show you how much kinder a Russian savage can be than an English one (though I am sorry to say I am a German) here goes! [*She stoops to loosen the straps.*]

CLAIRE [*jealously*]. You needn't trouble, thank you. [*She pounces on the straps: and the two set Edstaston free between them.*] Now get up, please; and conduct yourself with some dignity if you are not utterly demoralized.

EDSTASTON. Dignity! Ow! I can't. I'm stiff all over. I shall never be able to stand up again. Oh Lord! how it hurts! [*They seize him by the shoulders and drag him up.*] Yah! Agh! Wow! Oh! Mmmmmm! Oh, Little Angel Mother, don't ever do this to a man again. Knout him; kill him; roast him; baste him; head, hang, and quarter him; but don't tie him up like that and tickle him.

CATHERINE. Your young lady still seems to think that you enjoyed it.

CLAIRE. I know what I think. I will never speak to him again. Your Majesty can keep him, as far as I am concerned.

CATHERINE. I would not deprive you of him for worlds; though really I think he's rather a darling [*she pats his cheek*].

CLAIRE [*snorting*]. So I see, indeed.

EDSTASTON. Don't be angry, dearest: in this country everybody's a darling. I'll prove it to you. [*To Catherine.*] Will your Majesty be good enough to call Prince Patiomkin?

CATHERINE [*surprised into haughtiness*]. Why?

EDSTASTON. To oblige me.

Catherine laughs good-humoredly and goes to the curtains and opens them. The band strikes up a Redowa.

CATHERINE [*calling imperiously*]. Patiomkin! [*The music stops suddenly.*] Here! To me! Go on with your music there, you fools. [*The Redowa is resumed.*]

The sergeant rushes from the ballroom to relieve the Empress of the curtain. Patiomkin comes in dancing with Yarinka.

CATHERINE [*to Patiomkin*]. The English captain wants you, little darling.

Catherine resumes her seat as Patiomkin intimates by a grotesque bow that he is at Edstaston's service. Yarinka passes behind Edstaston and Claire, and posts herself on Claire's right.

EDSTASTON. Precisely. [*To Claire.*] You observe, my love: "little darling." Well, if her Majesty calls him a darling, is it my fault that she calls me one too?

CLAIRE. I don't care: I don't think you ought to have done it. I am very angry and offended.

EDSTASTON. They tied me up, dear. I couldn't help it. I fought for all I was worth.

THE SERGEANT [*at the curtains*]. He fought with the strength of lions and bears. God knows I shall carry a broken sweetbread to my grave.

EDSTASTON. You can't mean to throw me over, Claire. [*Urgently.*] Claire. Claire.

VARINKA [*in a transport of sympathetic emotion, pleading with clasped hands to Claire*]. Oh, sweet little angel lamb, he loves you: it shines in his darling eyes. Pardon him, pardon him.

PATIOMKIN [*rushing from the Empress's side to Claire and falling on his knees to her*]. Pardon him, pardon him, little cherub! little wild duck! little star! little glory! little jewel in the crown of heaven!

CLAIRE. This is perfectly ridiculous.

VARINKA [*kneeling to her*]. Pardon him, pardon him, little delight, little sleeper in a rosy cradle.

CLAIRE. I'll do anything if you'll only let me alone.

THE SERGEANT [*kneeling to her*]. Pardon him, pardon him, lest the mighty man bring his whip to you. God knows we all need pardon!

CLAIRE [*at the top of her voice*]. I pardon him! I pardon him!

PATIOMKIN [*springing up joyfully and going behind Claire, whom he raises in his arms*]. Embrace her, victor of Bunker's Hill. Kiss her till she swoons.

THE SERGEANT. Receive her in the name of the holy Nicholas.

VARINKA. She begs you for a thousand dear little kisses all over her body.

CLAIRE [*vehemently*]. I do not. [*Patiomkin throws her into Edstaston's arms.*] Oh! [*The pair, awkward and shamefaced, recoil from one another, and remain utterly inexpressive.*]

CATHERINE [*pushing Edstaston towards Claire*]. There is no help for it, Captain. This is Russia, not England.

EDSTASTON [*plucking up some geniality, and kissing Claire ceremoniously on the brow*]. I have no objection.

VARINKA [*disgusted*]. Only one kiss! and on the forehead! Fish. See how I kiss, though it is only my horribly ugly old uncle [*she throws her arms round Patiomkin's neck and covers his face with kisses*].

THE SERGEANT [*moved to tears*]. Sainted Nicholas: bless your lambs!

CATHERINE. Do you wonder now that I love Russia as I love no other place on earth?

NARYSHKIN [*appearing at the door*]. Majesty: the model for the new museum has arrived.

CATHERINE [*rising eagerly and making for the curtains*]. Let us go. I can think of nothing but my museum. [*In the archway she stops and turns to Edstaston, who has hurried to lift the curtain for her.*] Captain, I wish you every happiness that your little angel can bring you. [*For his ear alone.*] I could have brought you more; but you did not think so. Farewell.

EDSTASTON [*kissing her hand, which, instead of releasing, he holds caressingly and rather patronizingly in his own*]. I feel your Majesty's kindness so much that I really cannot leave you without a word of plain wholesome English advice.

CATHERINE [*snatching her hand away and bounding forward as if he had touched her with a spur*]. Advice!!!

PATIOMKIN. Madman: take care!

NARYSHKIN. Advise the Empress!!

THE SERGEANT. Sainted Nicholas!

VARINKA. Hoo hoo! [*a stifled splutter of laughter*].

EDSTASTON [*following the Empress and resuming kindly but judicially*]. After all, though your Majesty is of course a great queen, yet when all is said, I am a man; and your Majesty is only a woman.

CATHERINE. Only a wo— [*she chokes*].

EDSTASTON [*continuing*]. Believe me, this Russian extravagance will not do. I appreciate as much as any man the warmth of heart that prompts it; but it is overdone: it is hardly in the best taste: it is really I must say it—it is not proper.

CATHERINE [*ironically, in German*]. So!

EDSTASTON. Not that I cannot make allowances. Your Majesty has, I know, been unfortunate in your experience as a married woman—

CATHERINE [*furious*]. Alle Wetter!!!

EDSTASTON [*sentimentally*]. Don't say that. Don't think of him in that way. After all, he was your husband; and whatever his faults may have been, it is not for you to think unkindly of him.

CATHERINE [*almost bursting*]. I shall forget myself.

EDSTASTON. Come! I am sure he really loved you; and you truly loved him.

CATHERINE [*controlling herself with a supreme effort*]. No, Catherine. What would Voltaire say?

EDSTASTON. Oh, never mind that vile scoffer. Set an example to Europe, Madam, by doing what I am going to do. Marry again. Marry some good man who will be a strength and support to your old age.

CATHERINE. My old—[*she again becomes speechless*].

EDSTASTON. Yes: we must all grow old, even the handsomest of us.

CATHERINE [*sinking into her chair with a gasp*]. Thank you.

EDSTASTON. You will thank me more when you see your little ones round your knee, and your man there by the fireside in the winter evenings—by the way, I forgot that you have no fireside here in spite of the coldness of the climate; so shall I say by the stove?

CATHERINE. Certainly, if you wish. The stove by all means.

EDSTASTON [*impulsively*]. Ah, Madam, abolish the stove: believe me, there is nothing like the good old open grate. Home! duty! happiness! they all mean the same thing; and they all flourish best on the drawing-room hearthrug. [*Turning to Claire.*] And now, my love, we must not detain the Queen: she is anxious to inspect the model of her museum, to which I am sure we wish every success.

CLAIRE [*coldly*]. I am not detaining her.

EDSTASTON. Well, goodbye [*wringing Patiomkin's hand*] goo-oo-oodbye, Prince: come and see us if ever you visit England. Spire View, Deepdene, Little Mugford, Devon, will always find me. [*To Yarinka, kissing her hand.*] Goodbye, Mademoiselle: goodbye, Little Mother, if I may call you that just once. [*Varinka puts up her face to be kissed.*] Eh? No, no, no, no: you don't mean that, you know. Naughty! [*To the Sergeant.*] Goodbye, my friend. You will drink our healths with this [*tipping him*].

THE SERGEANT. The blessed Nicholas will multiply your fruits, Little Father.

EDSTASTON. Goodbye, goodbye, goodbye, goodbye, goodbye, goodbye.

He goes out backwards, bowing, with Claire curtseying, having been listened to in utter dumbfoundedness by Patiomkin and Naryshkin, in childlike awe by Yarinka, and with quite inexpressible feelings by Catherine. When he is out of sight she rises with clinched fists and raises her arms and her closed eyes to Heaven. Patiomkin: rousing himself from his stupor of amazement, springs to her like a tiger, and throws himself at her feet.

PATIOMKIN. What shall I do to him for you? Skin him alive? Cut off his eyelids and stand him in the sun? Tear his tongue out? What shall it be?

CATHERINE [*opening her eyes*]. Nothing. But oh, if I could only have had him for my—for my—for my—

PATIOMKIN [*in a growl of jealousy*]. For your lover?

CATHERINE [*with an ineffable smile*]. No: for my museum.

THE INCA OF PERUSALEM

AN ALMOST HISTORICAL COMEDIETTA

I must remind the reader that this playlet was written when its principal character, far from being a fallen foe and virtually a prisoner in our victorious hands, was still the Caesar whose legions we were resisting with our hearts in our mouths. Many were so horribly afraid of him that they could not forgive me for not being afraid of him: I seemed to be trifling heartlessly with a deadly peril. I knew better; and I have represented Caesar as knowing better himself. But it was one of the quaintnesses of popular feeling during the war that anyone who breathed the slightest doubt of the absolute perfection of German organization, the Machiavellian depth of German diplomacy, the omniscience of German science, the equipment of every German with a complete philosophy of history, and the consequent hopelessness of overcoming so magnificently accomplished an enemy except by the sacrifice of every recreative activity to incessant and vehement war work, including a heartbreaking mass of fussing and cadging and bluffing that did nothing but waste our energies and tire our resolution, was called a pro-German.

Now that this is all over, and the upshot of the fighting has shown that we could quite well have afforded to laugh at the doomed Inca, I am in another difficulty. I may be supposed to be hitting Caesar when he is down. That is why I preface the play with this reminder that when it was written he was not down. To make quite sure, I have gone through the proof sheets very carefully, and deleted everything that could possibly be mistaken for a foul blow. I have of course maintained the ancient privilege of comedy to chasten Caesar's foibles by laughing at them, whilst introducing enough obvious and outrageous fiction to relieve both myself and my model from the obligations and responsibilities of sober history and biography. But I should certainly put the play in the fire instead of publishing it if it contained a word against our defeated enemy that I would not have written in 1913.

The Inca of Perusalem was performed for the first time in England by the Pioneer Players at the Criterion Theatre, London, on 16th December, 1917, with Gertrude Kingston as Ermyntrude, Helen Morris as the Princess, Nigel Playfair as the waiter, Alfred Drayton as the hotel manager, C. Wordley Hulse as the Archdeacon, and Randle Ayrton as the Inca.

PROLOGUE

The tableau curtains are closed. An English archdeacon comes through them in a condition of extreme irritation. He speaks through the curtains to someone behind them.

THE ARCHDEACON. Once for all, Ermyntrude, I cannot afford to maintain you in your present extravagance. [*He goes to a flight of steps leading to the stalls and sits down disconsolately on the top step. A fashionably dressed lady comes through the curtains and contemplates him with patient obstinacy. He continues, grumbling.*] An English clergyman's daughter should be able to live quite respectably and comfortably on an allowance of £150 a year, wrung with great difficulty from the domestic budget.

ERMYNTRUDE. You are not a common clergyman: you are an archdeacon.

THE ARCHDEACON [*angrily*]. That does not affect my emoluments to the extent of enabling me to support a daughter whose extravagance would disgrace a royal personage. [*Scrambling to his feet and scolding at her.*] What do you mean by it, Miss?

ERMYNTRUDE. Oh really, father! Miss! Is that the way to talk to a widow?

THE ARCHDEACON. Is that the way to talk to a father? Your marriage was a most disastrous imprudence. It gave you habits that are absolutely beyond your means—I mean beyond my means: you have no means. Why did you not marry Matthews: the best curate I ever had?

ERMYNTRUDE. I wanted to; and you wouldn't let me. You insisted on my marrying Roosenhonkers-Pipstein.

THE ARCHDEACON. I had to do the best for you, my child. Roosenhonkers-Pipstein was a millionaire.

ERMYNTRUDE. How did you know he was a millionaire?

THE ARCHDEACON. He came from America. Of course he was a millionaire. Besides, he proved to my solicitors that he had fifteen million dollars when you married him.

ERYNTRUDE. His solicitors proved to me that he had sixteen millions when he died. He was a millionaire to the last.

THE ARCHDEACON. O Mammon, Mammon! I am punished now for bowing the knee to him. Is there nothing left of your settlement? Fifty thousand dollars a year it secured to you, as we all thought. Only half the securities could be called speculative. The other half were gilt-edged. What has become of it all?

ERMYNTRUDE. The speculative ones were not paid up; and the gilt-edged ones just paid the calls on them until the whole show burst up.

THE ARCHDEACON. Ermyntrude: what expressions!

ERMYNTRUDE. Oh bother! If you had lost ten thousand a year what expressions would you use, do you think? The long and the short of it is that I can't live in the squalid way you are accustomed to.

THE ARCHDEACON. Squalid!

ERMYNTRUDE. I have formed habits of comfort.

THE ARCHDEACON. Comfort!!

ERMYNTRUDE. Well, elegance if you like. Luxury, if you insist. Call it what you please. A house that costs less than a hundred thousand dollars a year to run is intolerable to me.

THE ARCHDEACON. Then, my dear, you had better become lady's maid to a princess until you can find another millionaire to marry you.

ERMYNTRUDE. That's an idea. I will. [*She vanishes through the curtains.*]

THE ARCHDEACON. What! Come back. Come back this instant. [*The lights are lowered.*] Oh, very well: I have nothing more to say. [*He descends the steps into the auditorium and makes for the door, grumbling all the time.*] Insane, senseless extravagance! [*Barking.*] Worthlessness!! [*Muttering.*] I will not bear it any longer. Dresses, hats, furs, gloves, motor rides: one bill after another: money going like water. No restraint, no self-control, no decency. [*Shrieking.*] I say, no decency! [*Muttering again.*] Nice state of things we are coming to! A pretty world! But I simply will not bear it. She can do as she likes. I wash my hands of her: I am not going to die in the workhouse for any good-for-nothing, undutiful, spendthrift daughter; and the sooner that is understood by everybody the better for all par—— [*He is by this time out of hearing in the corridor.*]

THE PLAY

A hotel sitting room. A table in the centre. On it a telephone. Two chairs at it, opposite one another. Behind it, the door. The fireplace has a mirror in the mantelpiece.

A spinster Princess, hatted and gloved, is ushered in by the hotel manager, spruce and artifically bland by professional habit, but treating his customer with a condescending affability which sails very close to the east wind of insolence.

THE MANAGER. I am sorry I am unable to accommodate Your Highness on the first floor.

THE PRINCESS [*very shy and nervous.*] Oh, please don't mention it. This is quite nice. Very nice. Thank you very much.

THE MANAGER. We could prepare a room in the annexe—

THE PRINCESS. Oh no. This will do very well.

She takes of her gloves and hat: puts them on the table; and sits down.

THE MANAGER. The rooms are quite as good up here. There is less noise; and there is the lift. If Your Highness desires anything, there is the telephone—

THE PRINCESS. Oh, thank you, I don't want anything. The telephone is so difficult: I am not accustomed to it.

THE MANAGER. Can I take any order? Some tea?

THE PRINCESS. Oh, thank you. Yes: I should like some tea, if I might—if it would not be too much trouble.

He goes out. The telephone rings. The Princess starts out of her chair, terrified, and recoils as far as possible from the instrument.

THE PRINCESS. Oh dear! [*It rings again. She looks scared. It rings again. She approaches it timidly. It rings again. She retreats hastily. It rings repeatedly. She runs to it in desperation and puts the receiver to her ear.*] Who is there? What do I do? I am not used to the telephone: I don't know how— What! Oh, I can hear you speaking quite distinctly. [*She sits down, delighted, and settles herself for a conversation.*] How wonderful! What! A lady? Oh! a person. Oh, yes: I know. Yes, please, send her up. Have my servants finished their lunch yet? Oh no: please don't disturb them: I'd rather not. It doesn't matter. Thank you. What? Oh yes, it's quite easy. I had no idea—am I to hang it up just as it was? Thank you. [*She hangs it up.*]

Ermyntrude enters, presenting a plain and staid appearance in a long straight waterproof with a hood over her head gear. She comes to the end of the table opposite to that at which the Princess is seated.

THE PRINCESS. Excuse me. I have been talking through the telephone: and I heard quite well, though I have never ventured before. Won't you sit down?

ERMYNTRUDE. No, thank you, Your Highness. I am only a lady's maid. I understood you wanted one.

THE PRINCESS. Oh no: you mustn't think I want one. It's so unpatriotic to want anything now, on account of the war, you know. I sent my maid away as a public duty; and now she has married a soldier and is expecting a war baby. But I don't know how to do without her. I've tried my very best; but somehow it doesn't answer: everybody cheats me; and in the end it isn't any saving. So I've made up my mind to sell my piano and have a maid. That will be a real saving, because I really don't care a bit for music, though of course one has to pretend to. Don't you think so?

ERMYNTRUDE. Certainly I do, Your Highness. Nothing could be more correct. Saving and self-denial both at once; and an act of kindness to me, as I am out of place.

THE PRINCESS. I'm so glad you see it in that way. Er—you won't mind my asking, will you?—how did you lose your place?

ERMYNTRUDE. The war, Your Highness, the war.

THE PRINCESS. Oh yes, of course. But how—

ERMYNTRUDE [*taking out her handkerchief and showing signs of grief*]. My poor mistress—

THE PRINCESS. Oh please say no more. Don't think about it. So tactless of me to mention it.

ERMYNTRUDE [*mastering her emotion and smiling through her tears*]. Your Highness is too good.

THE PRINCESS. Do you think you could be happy with me? I attach such importance to that.

ERMYNTRUDE [*gushing*]. Oh, I know—I shall.

THE PRINCESS. You must not expect too much. There is my uncle. He is very severe and hasty; and he is my guardian. I once had a maid I liked very much; but he sent her away the very first time.

ERMYNTRUDE. The first time of what, Your Highness?

THE PRINCESS. Oh, something she did. I am sure she had never done it before; and I know she would never have done it again, she was so truly contrite and nice about it.

ERMYNTRUDE. About what, Your Highness?

THE PRINCESS. Well, she wore my jewels and one of my dresses at a rather improper ball with her young man; and my uncle saw her.

ERYMNTRUDE. Then he was at the ball too, Your Highness?

THE PRINCESS [*struck by the inference*]. I suppose he must have been. I wonder! You know, it's very sharp of you to find that out. I hope you are not too sharp.

ERMYNTRUDE. A lady's maid has to be, Your Highness. [*She produces some letters.*] Your Highness wishes to see my testimonials, no doubt. I have one from an Archdeacon. [*She proffers the letters.*]

THE PRINCESS [*taking them*]. Do archdeacons have maids? How curious!

ERMYNTRUDE. No, Your Highness. They have daughters. I have first-rate testimonials from the Archdeacon and from his daughter.

THE PRINCESS [*reading them*]. The daughter says you are in every respect a treasure. The Archdeacon says he would have kept you if he could possibly have afforded it. Most satisfactory, I'm sure.

ERMYNTRUDE. May I regard myself as engaged then, Your Highness?

THE PRINCESS [*alarmed*]. Oh, I'm sure I don't know. If you like, of course; but do you think I ought to?

ERMYNTRUDE. Naturally I think Your Highness ought to, most decidedly.

THE PRINCESS. Oh well, if you think that, I daresay you're quite right. You'll excuse my mentioning it, I hope; but what wages—er—?

ERMYNTRUDE. The same as the maid who went to the ball. Your Highness need not make any change.

THE PRINCESS. M'yes. Of course she began with less. But she had such a number of relatives to keep! It was quite heartbreaking: I had to raise her wages again and again.

ERMYNTRUDE. I shall be quite content with what she began on; and I have no relatives dependent on me. And I am willing to wear my own dresses at balls.

THE PRINCESS. I am sure nothing could be fairer than that. My uncle can't object to that, can he?

ERMYNTRUDE. If he does, Your Highness, ask him to speak to me about it. I shall regard it as part of my duties to speak to your uncle about matters of business.

THE PRINCESS. Would you? You must be frightfully courageous.

ERMYNTRUDE. May I regard myself as engaged, Your Highness? I should like to set about my duties immediately.

THE PRINCESS. Oh yes, I think so. Oh certainly. I—

A waiter comes in with the tea. He places the tray on the table.

THE PRINCESS. Oh, thank you.

ERMYNTRUDE [*raising the cover from the tea cake and looking at it*]. How long has that been standing at the top of the stairs?

THE PRINCESS [*terrified*]. Oh please! It doesn't matter.

THE WAITER. It has not been waiting. Straight from the kitchen, madam, believe me.

ERMYNTRUDE. Send the manager here.

THE WAITER. The manager! What do you want with the manager?

ERMYNTRUDE. He will tell you when I have done with him. How dare you treat Her Highness in this disgraceful manner? What sort of pothouse is this? Where did you learn to speak to persons of quality? Take away your cold tea and cold cake instantly. Give them to the chambermaid you were flirting with whilst Her Highness was waiting. Order some fresh tea at once; and do not presume to bring it yourself: have it brought by a civil waiter who is accustomed to wait on ladies, and not, like you, on commercial travellers.

THE WAITER. Alas, madam, I am not accustomed to wait on anybody. Two years ago I was an eminent medical man, my waiting-room was crowded with the flower of the aristocracy and the higher bourgeoisie from nine to six every day. But the war came; and my patients were ordered to give up their luxuries. They gave up their doctors, but kept their week-end hotels, closing every career to me except the career of a waiter. [*He puts his fingers on the teapot to test its temperature, and automatically takes out his watch with the other hand as if to count the teapot's pulse.*] You are right: the tea is cold: it was made by the wife of a once fashionable architect. The cake is only half toasted: what can you expect from a ruined west-end tailor whose attempt to establish a second-hand business failed last Tuesday week? Have you the heart to complain to the manager? Have we not suffered enough? Are our miseries nev—— [*the manager enters*]. Oh Lord! here he is. [*The waiter withdraws abjectly, taking the tea tray with him.*]

THE MANAGER. Pardon, Your Highness; but I have received an urgent inquiry for rooms from an English family of importance; and I venture to ask you to let me know how long you intend to honor us with your presence.

THE PRINCESS [*rising anxiously*]. Oh! am I in the way?

ERMYNTRUDE [*sternly*]. Sit down, madam. [*The Princess sits down forlornly. Ermyntrude turns imperiously to the Manager.*] Her Highness will require this room for twenty minutes.

THE MANAGER. Twenty minutes!

ERMYNTRUDE. Yes: it will take fully that time to find a proper apartment in a respectable hotel.

THE MANAGER. I do not understand.

ERMYNTRUDE. You understand perfectly. How dare you offer Her Highness a room on the second floor?

THE MANAGER. But I have explained. The first floor is occupied. At least—

ERMYNTRUDE. Well? at least?

THE MANAGER. It is occupied.

ERMYNTRUDE. Don't you dare tell Her Highness a falsehood. It is not occupied. You are saving it up for the arrival of the five-fifteen express, from which you hope to pick up some fat armaments contractor who will drink all the bad champagne in your cellar at 5 francs a bottle, and pay twice over for everything because he is in the same hotel with Her Highness, and can boast of having turned her out of the best rooms.

THE MANAGER. But Her Highness was so gracious. I did not know that Her Highness was at all particular.

ERMYNTRUDE. And you take advantage of Her Highness's graciousness. You impose on her with your stories. You give her a room not fit for a dog. You send cold tea to her by a decayed professional person disguised as a waiter. But don't think you can trifle with me. I am a lady's maid; and I know the ladies' maids and valets of all the aristocracies of Europe and all the millionaires of America. When I expose your hotel as the second-rate little hole it is, not a soul above the rank of a curate with a large family will be seen entering it. I shake its dust off my feet. Order the luggage to be taken down at once.

THE MANAGER [*appealing to the Princess*]. Can Your Highness believe this of me? Have I had the misfortune to offend Your Highness?

THE PRINCESS. Oh no. I am quite satisfied. Please—

ERMYNTRUDE. Is Your Highness dissatisfied with me?

THE PRINCESS [*intimidated*]. Oh no: please don't think that. I only meant—

ERMYNTRUDE [*to the manager*]. You hear. Perhaps you think Her Highness is going to do the work of teaching you your place herself, instead of leaving it to her maid.

THE MANAGER. Oh please, mademoiselle. Believe me: our only wish is to make you perfectly comfortable. But in consequence of the war, all royal personages now practise a rigid economy, and desire us to treat them like their poorest subjects.

THE PRINCESS. Oh yes. You are quite right—

ERMYNTRUDE [*interrupting*]. There! Her Highness forgives you; but don't do it again. Now go downstairs, my good man, and get that suite on the first floor ready for us. And send some proper tea. And turn on the heating apparatus until the temperature in the rooms is comfortably warm. And have hot water put in all the bedrooms—

THE MANAGER. There are basins with hot and cold taps.

ERMYNTRUDE [*scornfully*]. Yes: there WOULD be. Suppose we must put up with that: sinks in our rooms, and pipes that rattle and bang and guggle all over the house whenever anyone washes his hands. I know.

THE MANAGER [*gallant*]. You are hard to please, mademoiselle.

ERMYNTRUDE. No harder than other people. But when I'm not pleased I'm not too ladylike to say so. That's all the difference. There is nothing more, thank you.

The Manager shrugs his shoulders resignedly; makes a deep bow to the Princess; goes to the door; wafts a kiss surreptitiously to Ermyntrude; and goes out.

THE PRINCESS. It's wonderful! How have you the courage?

ERMYNTRUDE. In Your Highness's service I know no fear. Your Highness can leave all unpleasant people to me.

THE PRINCESS. How I wish I could! The most dreadful thing of all I have to go through myself.

ERMYNTRUDE. Dare I ask what it is, Your Highness?

THE PRINCESS. I'm going to be married. I'm to be met here and married to a man I never saw. A boy! A boy who never saw me! One of the sons of the Inca of Perusalem.

ERMYNTRUDE. Indeed? Which son?

THE PRINCESS. I don't know. They haven't settled which. It's a dreadful thing to be a princess: they just marry you to anyone they like. The Inca is to come and look at me, and pick out whichever of his sons he thinks will suit. And then I shall be an alien enemy everywhere except in Perusalem, because the Inca has made war on everybody. And I shall have to pretend that everybody has made war on him. It's too bad.

ERMYNTRUDE. Still, a husband is a husband. I wish I had one.

THE PRINCESS. Oh, how can you say that! I'm afraid you're not a nice woman.

ERMYNTRUDE. Your Highness is provided for. I'm not.

THE PRINCESS. Even if you could bear to let a man touch you, you shouldn't say so.

ERMYNTRUDE. I shall not say so again, Your Highness, except perhaps to the man.

THE PRINCESS. It's too dreadful to think of. I wonder you can be so coarse. I really don't think you'll suit. I feel sure now that you know more about men than you should.

ERMYNTRUDE. I am a widow, Your Highness.

THE PRINCESS [*overwhelmed*]. Oh, I BEG your pardon. Of course I ought to have known you would not have spoken like that if you were not married. That makes it all right, doesn't it? I'm so sorry.

The Manager returns, white, scared, hardly able to speak.

THE MANAGER. Your Highness, an officer asks to see you on behalf of the Inca of Perusalem.

THE PRINCESS [*rising distractedly*]. Oh, I can't, really. Oh, what shall I do?

THE MANAGER. On important business, he says, Your Highness. Captain Duval.

ERMYNTRUDE. Duval! Nonsense! The usual thing. It is the Inca himself, incognito.

THE PRINCESS. Oh, send him away. Oh, I'm so afraid of the Inca. I'm not properly dressed to receive him; and he is so particular: he would order me to stay in my room for a week. Tell him to call tomorrow: say I'm ill in bed. I can't: I won't: I daren't: you must get rid of him somehow.

ERMYNTRUDE. Leave him to me, Your Highness.

THE PRINCESS. You'd never dare!

ERMYNTRUDE. I am an Englishwoman, Your Highness, and perfectly capable of tackling ten Incas if necessary. I will arrange the matter. [*To the Manager.*] Show Her Highness to her bedroom; and then show Captain Duval in here.

THE PRINCESS. Oh, thank you so much. [*She goes to the door. Ermyntrude, noticing that she has left her hat and gloves on the table, runs after her with them.*] Oh, THANK you. And oh, please, if I must have one of his sons, I should like a fair one that doesn't shave, with soft hair and a beard. I couldn't bear being kissed by a bristly person. [*She runs out, the Manager bowing as she passes. He follows her.*]

Ermyntrude whips off her waterproof; hides it; and gets herself swiftly into perfect trim at the mirror, before the Manager, with a large jewel case in his hand, returns, ushering in the Inca.

THE MANAGER. Captain Duval.

The Inca, in military uniform, advances with a marked and imposing stage walk; stops; orders the trembling Manager by a gesture to place the jewel case on the table; dismisses him with a frown; touches his helmet graciously to Ermyntrude; and takes off his cloak.

THE INCA. I beg you, madam, to be quite at your ease, and to speak to me without ceremony.

ERMYNTRUDE [*moving haughtily and carelessly to the table*]. I hadn't the slightest intention of treating you with ceremony. [*She sits down: a liberty which gives him a perceptible shock.*] I am quite at a loss to imagine why I should treat a perfect stranger named Duval: a captain! almost a subaltern! with the smallest ceremony.

THE INCA. That is true. I had for the moment forgotten my position.

ERMYNTRUDE. It doesn't matter. You may sit down.

THE INCA [*frowning.*] What!

ERMYNTRUDE. I said, you...may...sit...down.

THE INCA. Oh. [*His moustache droops. He sits down.*]

ERMYNTRUDE. What is your business?

THE INCA. I come on behalf of the Inca of Perusalem.

ERMYNTRUDE. The Allerhochst?

THE INCA. Precisely.

ERMYNTRUDE. I wonder does he feel ridiculous when people call him the Allerhochst.

THE INCA [*surprised*]. Why should he? He IS the Allerhochst.

ERMYNTRUDE. Is he nice looking?

THE INCA. I—er. Er—I. I—er. I am not a good judge.

ERMYNTRUDE. They say he takes himself very seriously.

THE INCA. Why should he not, madam? Providence has entrusted to his family the care of a mighty empire. He is in a position of half divine, half paternal, responsibility towards sixty millions of people, whose duty it is to die for him at the word of command. To take himself otherwise than seriously would be blasphemous. It is a punishable offence—severely punishable—in Perusalem. It is called Incadisparagement.

ERMYNTRUDE. How cheerful! Can he laugh?

THE INCA. Certainly, madam. [*He laughs, harshly and mirthlessly.*] Ha ha! Ha ha ha!

ERMYNTRUDE [*frigidly*]. I asked could the Inca laugh. I did not ask could you laugh.

THE INCA. That is true, madam. [*Chuckling.*] Devilish amusing, that! [*He laughs, genially and sincerely, and becomes a much more agreeable person.*] Pardon me: I am now laughing because I cannot help it. I am amused. The other was merely an imitation: a failure, I admit.

ERMYNTRUDE. You intimated that you had some business?

THE INCA [*producing a very large jewel case, and relapsing into solemnity.*] I am instructed by the Allerhochst to take a careful note of your features and figure, and, if I consider them satisfactory, to present you with this trifling token of His Imperial Majesty's regard. I do consider them satisfactory. Allow me [*he opens the jewel case and presents it.*]

ERMYNTRUDE [*staring at the contents*]. What awful taste he must have! I can't wear that.

THE INCA [*reddening*]. Take care, madam! This brooch was designed by the Inca himself. Allow me to explain the design. In the centre, the shield of Arminius. The ten surrounding medallions represent the ten castles of His Majesty. The rim is a piece of the telephone cable laid by His Majesty across the Shipskeel canal. The pin is a model in miniature of the sword of Henry the Birdcatcher.

ERMYNTRUDE. Miniature! It must be bigger than the original. My good man, you don't expect me to wear this round my neck: it's as big as a turtle. [*He shuts the case with an angry snap.*] How much did it cost?

THE INCA. For materials and manufacture alone, half a million Perusalem dollars, madam. The Inca's design constitutes it a work of art. As such, it is now worth probably ten million dollars.

ERMYNTRUDE. Give it to me [*she snatches it*]. I'll pawn it and buy something nice with the money.

THE INCA. Impossible, madam. A design by the Inca must not be exhibited for sale in the shop window of a pawnbroker. [*He flings himself into his chair, fuming.*]

ERMYNTRUDE. So much the better. The Inca will have to redeem it to save himself from that disgrace; and the poor pawnbroker will get his money back. Nobody would buy it, you know.

THE INCA. May I ask why?

ERMYNTRUDL. Well, look at it! Just look at it! I ask you!

THE INCA [*his moustache drooping ominously*]. I am sorry to have to report to the Inca that you have no soul for fine art. [*He rises sulkily.*] The position of daughter-in-law to the Inca is not compatible with the tastes of a pig. [*He attempts to take back the brooch.*]

ERMYNTRUDE [*rising and retreating behind her chair with the brooch*]. Here! you let that brooch alone. You presented it to me on behalf of the Inca. It is mine. You said my appearance was satisfactory.

THE INCA. Your appearance is not satisfactory. The Inca would not allow his son to marry you if the boy were on a desert island and you were the only other human being on it [*he strides up the room.*]

ERMYNTRUDE [*calmly sitting down and replacing the case on the table*]. How could he? There would be no clergyman to marry us. It would have to be quite morganatic.

THE INCA [*returning*]. Such an expression is out of place in the mouth of a princess aspiring to the highest destiny on earth. You have the morals of a dragoon. [*She receives this with a shriek of laughter. He struggles with his sense of humor.*] At the same time [*he sits down*] there is a certain coarse fun in the idea which compels me to smile [*he turns up his moustache and smiles.*]

ERMYNTRUDE. When I marry the Inca's son, Captain, I shall make the Inca order you to cut off that moustache. It is too irresistible. Doesn't it fascinate everyone in Perusalem?

THE INCA [*leaning forward to her energetically*]. By all the thunders of Thor, madam, it fascinates the whole world.

ERMYNTRUDE. What I like about you, Captain Duval, is your modesty.

THE INCA [*straightening up suddenly*]. Woman, do not be a fool.

ERMYNTRUDE [*indignant*]. Well!

THE INCA. You must look facts in the face. This moustache is an exact copy of the Inca's moustache. Well, does the world occupy itself with the Inca's moustache or does it not? Does it ever occupy itself with anything else? If that is the truth, does its recognition constitute the Inca a coxcomb? Other potentates have moustaches: even beards and moustaches. Does the world occupy itself with those beards and moustaches? Do the hawkers in the streets of every capital on the civilized globe sell ingenious cardboard representations of their faces on which, at the pulling of a simple string, the moustaches turn up and down, so—[*he makes his moustache turn, up and down several times*]? No! I say No. The Inca's moustache is so watched and studied that it has made his face the political barometer of the whole continent. When that moustache goes up, culture rises with it. Not what you call culture; but Kultur, a word so much more significant that I hardly understand it myself except when I am in specially good form. When it goes down, millions of men perish.

ERMYNTRUDE. You know, if I had a moustache like that, it would turn my head. I should go mad. Are you quite sure the Inca isn't mad?

THE INCA. How can he be mad, madam? What is sanity? The condition of the Inca's mind. What is madness? The condition of the people who disagree with the Inca.

ERMYNTRUDE. Then I am a lunatic because I don't like that ridiculous brooch.

THE INCA. No, madam: you are only an idiot.

ERMYNTRUDE. Thank you.

THE INCA. Mark you: It is not to be expected that you should see eye to eye with the Inca. That would be presumption. It is for you to accept without question or demur the assurance of your Inca that the brooch is a masterpiece.

ERMYNTRUDE. MY Inca! Oh, come! I like that. He is not my Inca yet.

THE INCA. He is everybody's Inca, madam. His realm will yet extend to the confines of the habitable earth. It is his divine right; and let those who dispute it look to themselves. Properly speaking, all those who are now trying to shake his world predominance are not at war with him, but in rebellion against him.

ERMYNTRUDE. Well, he started it, you know.

THE INCA. Madam, be just. When the hunters surround the lion, the lion will spring. The Inca had kept the peace of years. Those who attacked him were steeped in blood, black blood, white blood, brown blood, yellow blood, blue blood. The Inca had never shed a drop.

ERMYNTRUDE. He had only talked.

THE INCA. Only TALKED! ONLY talked! What is more glorious than talk? Can anyone in the world talk like him? Madam, when he signed the declaration of war, he said to his foolish generals and admirals, 'Gentlemen, you will all be sorry for this.' And they are. They know now that they had better have relied on the sword of the spirit: in other words, on their Inca's talk, than on their murderous cannons. The world will one day do justice to the Inca as the man who kept the peace with nothing but his tongue and his moustache. While he talked: talked just as I am talking now to you, simply, quietly, sensibly, but GREATLY, there was peace; there was prosperity; Perusalem went from success to success. He has been silenced for a year by the roar of trinitrotoluene and the bluster of fools; and the world is in ruins. What a tragedy! [*He is convulsed with grief.*]

ERMYNTRUDE. Captain Duval, I don't want to be unsympathetic; but suppose we get back to business.

THE INCA. Business! What business?

ERMYNTRUDE. Well, MY business. You want me to marry one of the Inca's sons: I forget which.

THE INCA. As far as I can recollect the name, it is His Imperial Highness Prince Eitel William Frederick George Franz Josef Alexander Nicholas Victor Emmanuel Albert Theodore Wilson—

ERMYNTRUDE [*interrupting*]. Oh, please, please, mayn't I have one with a shorter name? What is he called at home?

THE INCA. He is usually called Sonny, madam. [*With great charm of manner.*] But you will please understand that the Inca has no desire to pin you to any particular son. There is Chips and Spots and Lulu and Pongo and the Corsair and the Piffler and Jack Johnson the Second, all unmarried. At least not seriously married: nothing, in short, that cannot be arranged. They are all at your service.

ERMYNTRUDE. Are they all as clever and charming as their father?

THE INCA [*lifts his eyebrows pityingly; shrugs his shoulders; then, with indulgent paternal contempt*]. Excellent lads, madam. Very honest affectionate creatures. I have nothing against them. Pongo imitates farmyard sounds—cock crowing and that sort of thing—extremely well. Lulu plays Strauss's Sinfonia Domestica on the mouth organ really screamingly. Chips keeps owls and rabbits. Spots motor bicycles. The Corsair commands canal barges and steers them himself. The Piffler writes plays, and paints most abominably. Jack Johnson trims ladies' hats, and boxes with professionals hired for that purpose. He is invariably victorious. Yes: they all have their different little talents. And also, of course, their family resemblances. For example, they all smoke; they all quarrel with one another; and they none of them appreciate their father, who, by the way, is no mean painter, though the Piffler pretends to ridicule his efforts.

ERMYNTRUDE. Quite a large choice, eh?

THE INCA. But very little to choose, believe me. I should not recommend Pongo, because he snores so frightfully that it has been necessary to build him a sound-proof bedroom: otherwise the royal family would get no sleep. But any of the others would suit equally well—if you are really bent on marrying one of them.

ERMYNTRUDE. If! What is this? I never wanted to marry one of them. I thought you wanted me to.

THE INCA. I did, madam; but [*confidentially, flattering her*] you are not quite the sort of person I expected you to be; and I doubt whether any of these young degenerates would make you happy. I trust I am not showing any want of natural feeling when I say that from the point of view of a lively, accomplished, and beautiful woman [*Ermyntrude bows*] they might pall after a time. I suggest that you might prefer the Inca himself.

ERMYNTRUDE. Oh, Captain, how could a humble person like myself be of any interest to a prince who is surrounded with the ablest and most far-reaching intellects in the world?

TAE INCA [*explosively*]. What on earth are you talking about, madam? Can you name a single man in the entourage of the Inca who is not a born fool?

ERMYNTRUDE. Oh, how can you say that! There is Admiral von Cockpits—

THE INCA [*rising intolerantly and striding about the room*]. Von Cockpits! Madam, if Von Cockpits ever goes to heaven, before three weeks are over the Angel Gabriel will be at war with the man in the moon.

ERMYNTRUDE. But General Von Schinkenburg—

THE INCA. Schinkenburg! I grant you, Schinkenburg has a genius for defending market gardens. Among market gardens he is invincible. But what is the good of that? The world does not consist of market gardens. Turn him loose in pasture and he is lost. The Inca has defeated all these generals again and again at manoeuvres; and yet he has to give place to them in the field because he would be blamed for every disaster—accused of sacrificing the country to his vanity. Vanity! Why do they call him vain? Just because he is one of the few men who are not afraid to live. Why do they call themselves brave? Because they have not sense enough to be afraid to die. Within the last year the world has produced millions of heroes. Has it produced more than one Inca? [*He resumes his seat.*]

ERMYNTRUDE. Fortunately not, Captain. I'd rather marry Chips.

THE INCA [*making a wry face*]. Chips! Oh no: I wouldn't marry Chips.

ERMYNTRUDE. Why?

THE INCA [*whispering the secret*]. Chips talks too much about himself.

ERMYNTRUDE. Well, what about Snooks?

THE INCA. Snooks? Who is he? Have I a son named Snooks? There are so many—[*wearily*] so many—that I often forget. [*Casually.*] But I wouldn't marry him, anyhow, if I were you.

ERMYNTRUDE. But hasn't any of them inherited the family genius? Surely, if Providence has entrusted them with the care of Perusalem—if they are all descended from Bedrock the Great—

THE INCA [*interrupting her impatiently*]. Madam, if you ask me, I consider Bedrock a grossly overrated monarch.

ERMYNTRUDE [*shocked*]. Oh, Captain! Take care! Incadisparagement.

THE INCA. I repeat, grossly overrated. Strictly between ourselves, I do not believe all this about Providence entrusting the care of sixty million human beings to the abilities of Chips and the Piffler and Jack Johnson. I believe in individual genius. That is the Inca's secret. It must be. Why, hang it all, madam, if it were a mere family matter, the Inca's uncle would have been as great a man as the Inca. And—well, everybody knows what the Inca's uncle was.

ERMYNTRUDE. My experience is that the relatives of men of genius are always the greatest duffers imaginable.

THE INCA. Precisely. That is what proves that the Inca is a man of genius. His relatives ARE duffers.

ERMYNTRUDE. But bless my soul, Captain, if all the Inca's generals are incapables, and all his relatives duffers, Perusalem will be beaten in the war; and then it will become a republic, like France after 1871, and the Inca will be sent to St Helena.

THE INCA [*triumphantly*]. That is just what the Inca is playing for, madam. It is why he consented to the war.

ERMYNTRUDE. What!

THE INCA. Aha! The fools talk of crushing the Inca; but they little know their man. Tell me this. Why did St Helena extinguish Napoleon?

ERMYNTRUDE. I give it up.

THE INCA. Because, madam, with certain rather remarkable qualities, which I should be the last to deny, Napoleon lacked versatility. After all, any fool can be a soldier: we know that only too well in Perusalem, where every fool is a soldier. But the Inca has a thousand other resources. He is an architect. Well, St Helena presents an unlimited field to the architect. He is a painter: need I remind you that St Helena is still without a National Gallery? He is a composer: Napoleon left no symphonies in St Helena. Send the Inca to St Helena, madam, and the world will crowd thither to see his works as they crowd now to Athens to see the Acropolis, to Madrid to see the pictures of Velasquez, to Bayreuth to see the music dramas of that egotistical old rebel Richard Wagner, who ought to have been shot before he was forty, as indeed he very nearly was. Take this from me: hereditary monarchs are played out: the age for men of genius has come: the career is open to the talents: before ten years have elapsed every civilized country from the Carpathians to the Rocky Mountains will be a Republic.

ERMYNTRUDE. Then goodbye to the Inca.

THE INCA. On the contrary, madam, the Inca will then have his first real chance. He will be unanimously invited by those Republics to return from his exile and act as Superpresident of all the republics.

ERMYNTRUDE. But won't that be a come-down for him? Think of it! after being Inca, to be a mere President!

THE INCA. Well, why not! An Inca can do nothing. He is tied hand and foot. A constitutional monarch is openly called an India-rubber stamp. An emperor is a puppet. The Inca is not allowed to make a speech: he is compelled to take up a screed of flatulent twaddle written by some noodle of a minister and read it aloud. But look at the American President! He is the Allerhochst, if you like. No, madam, believe me, there is nothing like Democracy, American Democracy. Give the people voting papers: good long voting papers, American fashion; and while the people are reading the voting papers the Government does what it likes.

ERMYNTRUDE. What! You too worship before the statue of Liberty, like the Americans?

THE INCA. Not at all, madam. The Americans do not worship the statue of Liberty. They have erected it in the proper place for a statue of Liberty: on its tomb [*he turns down his moustaches.*]

ERMYNTRUDE [*laughing*]. Oh! You'd better not let them hear you say that, Captain.

THE INCA. Quite safe, madam: they would take it as a joke. [*He rises.*] And now, prepare yourself for a surprise. [*She rises*]. A shock. Brace yourself. Steel yourself. And do not be afraid.

ERMYNTRUDE. Whatever on earth can you be going to tell me, Captain?

THE INCA. Madam, I am no captain. I—

ERMYNTRUDE. You are the Inca in disguise.

THE INCA. Good heavens! how do you know that? Who has betrayed me?

ERMYNTRUDE. How could I help divining it, Sir? Who is there in the world like you? Your magnetism—

THE INCA. True: I had forgotten my magnetism. But you know now that beneath the trappings of Imperial Majesty there is a Man: simple, frank, modest, unaffected, colloquial: a sincere friend, a natural human being, a genial comrade, one eminently calculated to make a woman happy. You, on the other hand, are the most charming woman I have ever met. Your conversation is wonderful. I have sat here almost in silence, listening to your shrewd and penetrating account of my character, my motives, if I may say so, my talents. Never has such justice been done me: never have I experienced such perfect sympathy. Will you—I hardly know how to put this—will you be mine?

ERMYNTRUDE. Oh, Sir, you are married.

THE INCA. I am prepared to embrace the Mahometan faith, which allows a man four wives, if you will consent. It will please the Turks. But I had rather you did not mention it to the Inca-ess. If you don't mind.

ERMYNTRUDE. This is really charming of you. But the time has come for me to make a revelation. It is your Imperial Majesty's turn now to brace yourself. To steel yourself. I am not the princess. I am—

THE INCA. The daughter of my old friend Archdeacon Daffodil Donkin, whose sermons are read to me every evening after dinner. I never forget a face.

ERMYNTRUDE. You knew all along!

THE INCA [*bitterly, throwing himself into his chair*]. And you supposed that I, who have been condemned to the society of princesses all my wretched life, believed for a moment that any princess that ever walked could have your intelligence!

ERMYNTRUDE. How clever of you, Sir! But you cannot afford to marry me.

THE INCA [*springing up*]. Why not?

ERMYNTRUDE. You are too poor. You have to eat war bread. Kings nowadays belong to the poorer classes. The King of England does not even allow himself wine at dinner.

THE INCA [*delighted*]. Haw! Ha ha! Haw! haw! [*He is convulsed with laughter, and, finally has to relieve his feelings by waltzing half round the room.*]

ERMYNTRUDE. You may laugh, Sir; but I really could not live in that style. I am the widow of a millionaire, ruined by your little war.

THE INCA. A millionaire! What are millionaires now, with the world crumbling?

ERMYNTRUDE. Excuse me: mine was a hyphenated millionaire.

THE INCA. A highfalutin millionaire, you mean. [*Chuckling*]. Haw! ha ha! really very nearly a pun, that. [*He sits down in her chair.*]

ERMYNTRUDE [*revolted, sinking into his chair*]. I think it quite the worst pun I ever heard.

THE INCA. The best puns have all been made years ago: nothing remained but to achieve the worst. However, madam [*he rises majestically; and she is about to rise also*]. No: I prefer a seated audience [*she falls back into her seat at the imperious wave of his hand*]. So [*he clicks his heels*]. Madam, I recognize my presumption in having sought the honor of your hand. As you say, I cannot afford it. Victorious as I am, I am hopelessly bankrupt; and the worst of it is, I am intelligent enough to know it. And I shall be beaten in consequence, because my most implacable enemy, though only a few months further away from bankruptcy than myself, has not a ray of intelligence, and will go on fighting until civilization is destroyed, unless I, out of sheer pity for the world, condescend to capitulate.

ERMYNTRUDE. The sooner the better, Sir. Many fine young men are dying while you wait.

THE INCA [*flinching painfully*]. Why? Why do they do it?

ERMYNTRUDE. Because you make them.

THE INCA. Stuff! How can I? I am only one man; and they are millions. Do you suppose they would really kill each other if they didn't want to, merely for the sake of my beautiful eyes? Do not be deceived by newspaper claptrap, madam. I was swept away by a passion not my own, which imposed itself on me. By myself I am nothing. I dare not walk down the principal street of my own capital in a coat two years old, though the sweeper of that street can wear one ten years old. You talk of death as an unpopular thing. You are wrong: for years I gave them art, literature, science, prosperity, that they might live more abundantly; and they hated me, ridiculed me, caricatured me. Now that I give them death in its frightfullest forms, they are devoted to me. If you doubt me, ask those who for years have begged our taxpayers in vain for a few paltry thousands to spend on Life: on the bodies and minds of the nation's children, on the beauty and healthfulness of its cities, on the honor and comfort of its worn-out workers. They refused: and because they refused, death is let loose on them. They grudged a few hundreds a year for their salvation: they now pay millions a day for their own destruction and damnation. And this they call my doing! Let them say it, if they dare, before the judgment-seat at which they and I shall answer at last for what we have left undone no less than for what we have done. [*Pulling himself together suddenly.*] Madam, I have the honor to be your most obedient [*he clicks his heels and bows*].

ERMYNTRUDE. Sir! [*She curtsies.*]

THE INCA [*turning at the door*]. Oh, by the way, there is a princess, isn't there, somewhere on the premises?

ERMYNTRUDE. There is. Shall I fetch her?

THE INCA [*dubious*], Pretty awful, I suppose, eh?

ERMYNTRUDE. About the usual thing.

THE INCA [*sighing*]. Ah well! What can one expect? I don't think I need trouble her personally. Will you explain to her about the boys?

ERMYNTRUDE. I am afraid the explanation will fall rather flat without your magnetism.

THE INCA [*returning to her and speaking very humanly*]. You are making fun of me. Why does everybody make fun of me? Is it fair?

ERMYNTRUDE [*seriously*]. Yes, it is fair. What other defence have we poor common people against your shining armor, your mailed fist, your pomp and parade, your terrible power over us? Are these things fair?

THE INCA. Ah, well, perhaps, perhaps. [*He looks at his watch.*] By the way, there is time for a drive round the town and a cup of tea at the Zoo. Quite a bearable band there: it does not play any patriotic airs. I am sorry you will not listen to any more permanent arrangement; but if you would care to come—

ERMYNTRUDE [*eagerly*]. Ratherrrrrr. I shall be delighted.

THE INCA [*cautiously*]. In the strictest honor, you understand.

ERMYNTRUDE. Don't be afraid. I promise to refuse any incorrect proposals.

THE INCA [*enchanted*]. Oh! Charming woman: how well you understand men!

He offers her his arm: they go out together.

AUGUSTUS DOES HIS BIT

A TRUE-TO-LIFE FARCE

I wish to express my gratitude for certain good offices which Augustus secured for me in January, 1917. I had been invited to visit the theatre of war in Flanders by the Commander-in-Chief: an invitation which was, under the circumstances, a summons to duty. Thus I had occasion to spend some days in procuring the necessary passport and other official facilities for my journey. It happened just then that the Stage Society gave a performance of this little play. It opened the heart of every official to me. I have always been treated with distinguished consideration in my contracts with bureaucracy during the war; but on this occasion I found myself persona grata in the highest degree. There was only one word when the formalities were disposed of; and that was "We are up against Augustus all day." The showing-up of Augustus scandalized one or two innocent and patriotic critics who regarded the prowess of the British army as inextricably bound up with Highcastle prestige. But our Government departments knew better: their problem was how to win the war with Augustus on their backs, well-meaning, brave, patriotic, but obstructively fussy, self-important, imbecile, and disastrous.

Save for the satisfaction of being able to laugh at Augustus in the theatre, nothing, as far as I know, came of my dramatic reduction of him to absurdity. Generals, admirals, Prime Ministers and Controllers, not to mention Emperors, Kaisers and Tsars, were scrapped remorselessly at home and abroad, for their sins or services, as the case might be. But Augustus stood like the Eddystone in a storm, and stands so to this day. He gave us his word that he was indispensable and we took it.

Augustus Does His Bit was performed for the first time at the Court Theatre in London by the Stage Society on the 21st January, 1917, with Lalla Vandervelde as The Lady, F. B.J. Sharp as Lord Augustus Highcastle, and Charles Rock as Horatio Floyd Beamish.

AUGUSTUS DOES HIS BIT

The Mayor's parlor in the Town Hall of Little Pifflington. Lord Augustus Highcastle, a distinguished member of the governing class, in the uniform of a colonel, and very well preserved at forty-five, is comfortably seated at a writing-table with his heels on it, reading The Morning Post. The door faces him, a little to his left, at the other side of the room. The window is behind him. In the fireplace, a gas stove. On the table a bell button and a telephone. Portraits of past Mayors, in robes and gold chains, adorn the walls. An elderly clerk with a short white beard and whiskers, and a very red nose, shuffles in.

AUGUSTUS [*hastily putting aside his paper and replacing his feet on the floor*]. Hullo! Who are you?

THE CLERK. The staff [*a slight impediment in his speech adds to the impression of incompetence produced by his age and appearance*].

AUGUSTUS. You the staff! What do you mean, man?

THE CLERK. What I say. There ain't anybody else.

AUGUSTUS. Tush! Where are the others?

THE CLERK. At the front.

AUGUSTUS. Quite right. Most proper. Why aren't you at the front?

THE CLERK. Over age. Fifty-seven.

AUGUSTUS. But you can still do your bit. Many an older man is in the G.R.'s, or volunteering for home defence.

THE CLERK. I have volunteered.

AUGUSTUS. Then why are you not in uniform?

THE CLERK. They said they wouldn't have me if I was given away with a pound of tea. Told me to go home and not be an old silly. [*A sense of unbearable wrong, till now only smouldering in him, bursts into flame.*] Young Bill Knight, that I took with me, got two and sevenpence. I got nothing. Is it justice? This country is going to the dogs, if you ask me.

AUGUSTUS [*rising indignantly*]. I do not ask you, sir; and I will not allow you to say such things in my presence. Our statesmen are the greatest known to history. Our generals are invincible. Our army is the admiration of the world. [*Furiously.*] How dare you tell me that the country is going to the dogs!

THE CLERK. Why did they give young Bill Knight two and sevenpence, and not give me even my tram fare? Do you call that being great statesmen? As good as robbing me, I call it.

AUGUSTUS. That's enough. Leave the room. [*He sits down and takes up his pen, settling himself to work. The clerk shuffles to the door. Augustus adds, with cold politeness*] Send me the Secretary.

THE CLERK. I'M the Secretary. I can't leave the room and send myself to you at the same time, can I?

AUGUSTUS, Don't be insolent. Where is the gentleman I have been corresponding with: Mr Horatio Floyd Beamish?

THE CLERK [*returning and bowing*]. Here. Me.

AUGUSTUS. You! Ridiculous. What right have you to call yourself by a pretentious name of that sort?

THE CLERK. You may drop the Horatio Floyd. Beamish is good enough for me.

AUGUSTUS. Is there nobody else to take my instructions?

THE CLERK. It's me or nobody. And for two pins I'd chuck it. Don't you drive me too far. Old uns like me is up in the world now.

AUGUSTUS. If we were not at war, I should discharge you on the spot for disrespectful behavior. But England is in danger; and I cannot think of my personal dignity at such a moment. [*Shouting at him.*] Don't you think of yours, either, worm that you are; or I'll have you arrested under the Defence of the Realm Act, double quick.

THE CLERK. What do I care about the realm? They done me out of two and seven—

AUGUSTUS. Oh, damn your two and seven! Did you receive my letters?

THE CLERK. Yes.

AUGUSTUS. I addressed a meeting here last night—went straight to the platform from the train. I wrote to you that I should expect you to be present and report yourself. Why did you not do so?

THE CLERK. The police wouldn't let me on the platform.

AUGUSTUS. Did you tell them who you were?

THE CLERK. They knew who I was. That's why they wouldn't let me up.

AUGUSTUS. This is too silly for anything. This town wants waking up. I made the best recruiting speech I ever made in my life; and not a man joined.

THE CLERK. What did you expect? You told them our gallant fellows is falling at the rate of a thousand a day in the big push. Dying for Little Pifflington, you says. Come and take their places, you says. That ain't the way to recruit.

AUGUSTUS. But I expressly told them their widows would have pensions.

THE CLERK. I heard you. Would have been all right if it had been the widows you wanted to get round.

AUGUSTUS [*rising angrily*]. This town is inhabited by dastards. I say it with a full sense of responsibility, DASTARDS! They call themselves Englishmen; and they are afraid to fight.

THE CLERK. Afraid to fight! You should see them on a Saturday night.

AUGUSTUS. Yes, they fight one another; but they won't fight the Germans.

THE CLERK. They got grudges again one another: how can they have grudges again the Huns that they never saw? They've no imagination: that's what it is. Bring the Huns here; and they'll quarrel with them fast enough.

AUGUSTUS [*returning to his seat with a grunt of disgust*]. Mf! They'll have them here if they're not careful. [*Seated.*] Have you carried out my orders about the war saving?

THE CLERK. Yes.

AUGUSTUS. The allowance of petrol has been reduced by three quarters?

THE CLERK. It has.

AUGUSTUS. And you have told the motor-car people to come here and arrange to start munition work now that their motor business is stopped?

THE CLERK. It ain't stopped. They're busier than ever.

AUGUSTUS. Busy at what?

THE CLERK. Making small cars.

AUGUSTUS. NEW cars!

THE CLERK. The old cars only do twelve miles to the gallon. Everybody has to have a car that will do thirty-five now.

AUGUSTUS. Can't they take the train?

THE CLERK. There ain't no trains now. They've tore up the rails and sent them to the front.

AUGUSTUS. Psha!

THE CLERK. Well, we have to get about somehow.

AUGUSTUS. This is perfectly monstrous. Not in the least what I intended.

THE CLERK. Hell—

AUGUSTUS. Sir!

THE CLERK [*explaining*]. Hell, they says, is paved with good intentions.

AUGUSTUS [*springing to his feet*]. Do you mean to insinuate that hell is paved with MY good intentions—with the good intentions of His Majesty's Government?

THE CLERK. I don't mean to insinuate anything until the Defence of the Realm Act is repealed. It ain't safe.

AUGUSTUS. They told me that this town had set an example to all England in the matter of economy. I came down here to promise the Mayor a knighthood for his exertions.

THE CLERK. The Mayor! Where do I come in?

AUGUSTUS. You don't come in. You go out. This is a fool of a place. I'm greatly disappointed. Deeply disappointed. [*Flinging himself back into his chair.*] Disgusted.

THE CLERK. What more can we do? We've shut up everything. The picture gallery is shut. The museum is shut. The theatres and picture shows is shut: I haven't seen a movie picture for six months.

AUGUSTUS. Man, man: do you want to see picture shows when the Hun is at the gate?

THE CLERK [*mournfully*]. I don't now, though it drove me melancholy mad at first. I was on the point of taking a pennorth of rat poison—

AUGUSTUS. Why didn't you?

THE CLERK. Because a friend advised me to take to drink instead. That saved my life, though it makes me very poor company in the mornings, as [*hiccuping*] perhaps you've noticed.

AUGUSTUS. Well, upon my soul! You are not ashamed to stand there and confess yourself a disgusting drunkard.

THE CLERK. Well, what of it? We're at war now; and everything's changed. Besides, I should lose my job here if I stood drinking at the bar. I'm a respectable man and must buy my drink and take it home with me. And they won't serve me with less than a quart. If you'd told me before the war that I could get through a quart of whisky in a day, I shouldn't have believed you. That's the good of war: it brings out powers in a man that he never suspected himself capable of. You said so yourself in your speech last night.

AUGUSTUS. I did not know that I was talking to an imbecile. You ought to be ashamed of yourself. There must be an end of this drunken slacking. I'm going to establish a new order of things here. I shall come down every morning before breakfast until things are properly in train. Have a cup of coffee and two rolls for me here every morning at half-past ten.

THE CLERK. You can't have no rolls. The only baker that baked rolls was a Hun; and he's been interned.

AUGUSTUS. Quite right, too. And was there no Englishman to take his place?

THE CLERK. There was. But he was caught spying; and they took him up to London and shot him.

AUGUSTUS. Shot an Englishman!

THE CLERK. Well, it stands to reason if the Germans wanted to spy they wouldn't employ a German that everybody would suspect, don't it?

AUGUSTUS [*rising again*]. Do you mean to say, you scoundrel, that an Englishman is capable of selling his country to the enemy for gold?

THE CLERK. Not as a general thing I wouldn't say it; but there's men here would sell their own mothers for two coppers if they got the chance.

AUGUSTUS. Beamish, it's an ill bird that fouls its own nest.

THE CLERK. It wasn't me that let Little Pifflington get foul. I don't belong to the governing classes. I only tell you why you can't have no rolls.

AUGUSTUS [*intensely irritated*]. Can you tell me where I can find an intelligent being to take my orders?

THE CLERK. One of the street sweepers used to teach in the school until it was shut up for the sake of economy. Will he do?

AUGUSTUS. What! You mean to tell me that when the lives of the gallant fellows in our trenches, and the fate of the British Empire, depend on our keeping up the supply of shells, you are wasting money on sweeping the streets?

THE CLERK. We have to. We dropped it for a while; but the infant death rate went up something frightful.

AUGUSTUS. What matters the death rate of Little Pifflington in a moment like this? Think of our gallant soldiers, not of your squalling infants.

THE CLERK. If you want soldiers you must have children. You can't buy em in boxes, like toy soldiers.

AUGUSTUS. Beamish, the long and the short of it is, you are no patriot. Go downstairs to your office; and have that gas stove taken away and replaced by an ordinary grate. The Board of Trade has urged on me the necessity for economizing gas.

THE CLERK. Our orders from the Minister of Munitions is to use gas instead of coal, because it saves material. Which is it to be?

AUGUSTUS [*bawling furiously at him*]. Both! Don't criticize your orders: obey them. Yours not to reason why: yours but to do and die. That's war. [*Cooling down.*] Have you anything else to say?

THE CLERK. Yes: I want a rise.

AUGUSTUS [*reeling against the table in his horror*]. A rise! Horatio Floyd Beamish, do you know that we are at war?

THE CLERK [*feebly ironical*]. I have noticed something about it in the papers. Heard you mention it once or twice, now I come to think of it.

AUGUSTUS. Our gallant fellows are dying in the trenches; and you want a rise!

THE CLERK. What are they dying for? To keep me alive, ain't it? Well, what's the good of that if I'm dead of hunger by the time they come back?

AUGUSTUS. Everybody else is making sacrifices without a thought of self; and you—

THE CLERK. Not half, they ain't. Where's the baker's sacrifice? Where's the coal merchant's? Where's the butcher's? Charging me double: that's how they sacrifice themselves. Well, I want to sacrifice myself that way too. Just double next Saturday: double and not a penny less; or no secretary for you [*he stiffens himself shakily, and makes resolutely for the door.*]

AUGUSTUS [*looking after him contemptuously*]. Go, miserable pro-German.

THE CLERK [*rushing back and facing him*]. Who are you calling a pro-German?

AUGUSTUS. Another word, and I charge you under the Act with discouraging me. Go.

The clerk blenches and goes out, cowed.

The telephone rings.

AUGUSTUS [*taking up the telephone receiver.*] Hallo. Yes: who are you?... oh, Blueloo, is it?... Yes: there's nobody in the room: fire away. What?... A spy!... A woman!... Yes: brought it down with me. Do you suppose I'm such a fool as to let it out of my hands? Why, it gives a list of all our anti-aircraft emplacements from Ramsgate to Skegness. The Germans would give a million for it—what?... But how could she possibly know about it? I haven't mentioned it to a soul, except, of course, dear Lucy... Oh, Toto and Lady Popham and that lot: they don't count: they're all right. I mean that I haven't mentioned it to any Germans.... Pooh! Don't you be nervous, old chap. I know you think me a fool; but I'm not such a fool as all that. If she tries to get it out of me I'll have her in the Tower before you ring up again. [*The clerk returns.*] Sh-sh! Somebody's just come in: ring off. Goodbye. [*He hangs up the receiver.*]

THE CLERK. Are you engaged? [*His manner is strangely softened.*]

AUGUSTUS. What business is that of yours? However, if you will take the trouble to read the society papers for this week, you will see that I am engaged to the Honorable Lucy Popham, youngest daughter of—

THE CLERK. That ain't what I mean. Can you see a female?

AUGUSTUS. Of course I can see a female as easily as a male. Do you suppose I'm blind?

THE CLERK. You don't seem to follow me, somehow. There's a female downstairs: what you might call a lady. She wants to know can you see her if I let her up.

AUGUSTUS. Oh, you mean am I disengaged. Tell the lady I have just received news of the greatest importance which will occupy my entire attention for the rest of the day, and that she must write for an appointment.

THE CLERK. I'll ask her to explain her business to me. I ain't above talking to a handsome young female when I get the chance [*going*].

AUGUSTUS. Stop. Does she seem to be a person of consequence?

THE CLERK. A regular marchioness, if you ask me.

AUGUSTUS. Hm! Beautiful, did you say?

THE CLERK. A human chrysanthemum, sir, believe me.

AUGUSTUS. It will be extremely inconvenient for me to see her; but the country is in danger; and we must not consider our own comfort. Think how our gallant fellows are suffering in the trenches! Show her up. [*The clerk makes for the door, whistling the latest popular ballad*]. Stop whistling instantly, sir. This is not a casino.

CLERK. Ain't it? You just wait till you see her. [*He goes out.*]

Augustus produces a mirror, a comb, and a pot of moustache pomade from the drawer of the writing-table, and sits down before the mirror to put some touches to his toilet.

The clerk returns, devotedly ushering a very attractive lady, brilliantly dressed. She has a dainty wallet hanging from her wrist. Augustus hastily covers up his toilet apparatus with The Morning Post, and rises in an attitude of pompous condescension.

THE CLERK [*to Augustus*]. Here she is. [*To the lady.*] May I offer you a chair, lady? [*He places a chair at the writing-table opposite Augustus, and steals out on tiptoe.*]

AUGUSTUS. Be seated, madam.

THE LADY [*sitting down*]. Are you Lord Augustus Highcastle?

AUGUSTUS [*sitting also*]. Madam, I am.

TAE LADY [*with awe*]. The great Lord Augustus?

AUGUSTUS. I should not dream of describing myself so, Madam; but no doubt I have impressed my countrymen—and [*bowing gallantly*] may I say my countrywomen—as having some exceptional claims to their consideration.

THE LADY [*emotionally*]. What a beautiful voice you have!

AUGUSTUS. What you hear, madam, is the voice of my country, which now takes a sweet and noble tone even in the harsh mouth of high officialism.

THE LADY. Please go on. You express yourself so wonderfully!

AUGUSTUS. It would be strange indeed if, after sitting on thirty-seven Royal Commissions, mostly as chairman, I had not mastered the art of public expression. Even the Radical papers have paid me the high compliment of declaring that I am never more impressive than when I have nothing to say.

THE LADY. I never read the Radical papers. All I can tell you is that what we women admire in you is not the politician, but the man of action, the heroic warrior, the beau sabreur.

AUGUSTUS [*gloomily*]. Madam, I beg! Please! My military exploits are not a pleasant subject, unhappily.

THE LADY. Oh, I know I know. How shamefully you have been treated! what ingratitude! But the country is with you. The women are with you. Oh, do you think all our hearts did not throb and all our nerves thrill when we heard how, when you were ordered to occupy that terrible quarry in Hulluch, and you swept into it at the head of your men like a sea-god riding on a tidal wave, you suddenly sprang over the top shouting "To Berlin! Forward!"; dashed at the German army single-handed; and were cut off and made prisoner by the Huns.

AUGUSTUS. Yes, madam; and what was my reward? They said I had disobeyed orders, and sent me home. Have they forgotten Nelson in the Baltic? Has any British battle ever been won except by a bold initiative? I say nothing of professional jealousy, it exists in the army as elsewhere; but it is a bitter thought to me that the recognition denied me by my country—or rather by the Radical cabal in the Cabinet which pursues my family with rancorous class hatred—that this recognition, I say, came to me at the hands of an enemy—of a rank Prussian.

THE LADY. You don't say so!

AUGUSTUS. How else should I be here instead of starving to death in Ruhleben? Yes, madam: the Colonel of the Pomeranian regiment which captured me, after learning what I had done, and conversing for an hour with me on European politics and military strategy, declared that nothing would induce him to deprive my country of my services, and set me free. I offered, of course, to procure the release in exchange of a German officer of equal quality; but he would not hear of it. He was kind enough to say he could not believe that a German officer answering to that description existed. [*With emotion.*] I had my first taste of the ingratitude of my own country as I made my way back to our lines. A shot from our front trench struck me in the head. I still carry the flattened projectile as a trophy [*he throws it on the table; the noise it makes testifies to its weight*]. Had it penetrated to the brain I might never have sat on another Royal Commission. Fortunately we have strong heads, we Highcastles. Nothing has ever penetrated to our brains.

THE LADY. How thrilling! How simple! And how tragic! But you will forgive England? Remember: England! Forgive her.

AUGUSTUS [*with gloomy magnanimity*]. It will make no difference whatever to my services to my country. Though she slay me, yet will I, if not exactly trust in her, at least take my part in her government. I am ever at my country's call. Whether it be the embassy in a leading European capital, a governor-generalship in the tropics, or my humble mission here to make Little Pifflington do its bit, I am always ready for the sacrifice. Whilst England remains England, wherever there is a public job to be done you will find a Highcastle sticking to it. And now, madam, enough of my tragic personal history. You have called on business. What can I do for you?

THE LADY. You have relatives at the Foreign Office, have you not?

AUGUSTUS [*haughtily*]. Madam, the Foreign Office is staffed by my relatives exclusively.

THE LADY. Has the Foreign Office warned you that you are being pursued by a female spy who is determined to obtain possession of a certain list of gun emplacements?

AUGUSTUS [*interrupting her somewhat loftily*]. All that is perfectly well known to this department, madam.

THE LADY [*surprised and rather indignant*]. Is it? Who told you? Was it one of your German brothers-in-law?

AUGUSTUS [*injured, remonstrating*]. I have only three German brothers-in-law, madam. Really, from your tone, one would suppose that I had several. Pardon my sensitiveness on that subject; but reports are continually being circulated that I have been shot as a traitor in the courtyard of the Ritz Hotel simply because I have German brothers-in-law. [*With feeling.*] If you had a German brother-in-law, madam, you would know that nothing else in the world produces so strong an anti-German feeling. Life affords no keener pleasure than finding a brother-in-law's name in the German casualty list.

THE LADY. Nobody knows that better than I. Wait until you hear what I have come to tell you: you will understand me as no one else could. Listen. This spy, this woman—

AUGUSTUS [*all attention*]. Yes?

THE LADY. She is a German. A Hun.

AUGUSTUS. Yes, yes. She would be. Continue.

THE LADY. She is my sister-in-law.

AUGUSTUS [*deferentially*]. I see you are well connected, madam. Proceed.

THE LADY. Need I add that she is my bitterest enemy?

AUGUSTUS. May I—[*he proffers his hand. They shake, fervently. From this moment onward Augustus becomes more and more confidential, gallant, and charming.*]

THE LADY. Quite so. Well, she is an intimate friend of your brother at the War Office, Hungerford Highcastle, Blueloo as you call him, I don't know why.

AUGUSTUS [*explaining*]. He was originally called The Singing Oyster, because he sang drawing-room ballads with such an extraordinary absence of expression. He was then called the Blue Point for a season or two. Finally he became Blueloo.

THE LADY. Oh, indeed: I didn't know. Well, Blueloo is simply infatuated with my sister-in-law; and he has rashly let out to her that this list is in your possession. He forgot himself because he was in a towering rage at its being entrusted to you: his language was terrible. He ordered all the guns to be shifted at once.

AUGUSTUS. What on earth did he do that for?

THE LADY. I can't imagine. But this I know. She made a bet with him that she would come down here and obtain possession of that list and get clean away into the street with it. He took the bet on condition that she brought it straight back to him at the War Office.

AUGUSTUS. Good heavens! And you mean to tell me that Blueloo was such a dolt as to believe that she could succeed? Does he take me for a fool?

THE LADY. Oh, impossible! He is jealous of your intellect. The bet is an insult to you: don't you feel that? After what you have done for our country—

AUGUSTUS. Oh, never mind that. It is the idiocy of the thing I look at. He'll lose his bet; and serve him right!

THE LADY. You feel sure you will be able to resist the siren? I warn you, she is very fascinating.

AUGUSTUS. You need have no fear, madam. I hope she will come and try it on. Fascination is a game that two can play at. For centuries the younger sons of the Highcastles have had nothing to do but fascinate attractive females when they were not sitting on Royal Commissions or on duty at Knightsbridge barracks. By Gad, madam, if the siren comes here she will meet her match.

THE LADY. I feel that. But if she fails to seduce you—

AUGUSTUS [*blushing*]. Madam!

THE LADY [*continuing*]—from your allegiance—

AUGUSTUS. Oh, that!

THE LADY.—she will resort to fraud, to force, to anything. She will burgle your office: she will have you attacked and garotted at night in the street.

AUGUSTUS. Pooh! I'm not afraid.

THE LADY. Oh, your courage will only tempt you into danger. She may get the list after all. It is true that the guns are moved. But she would win her bet.

AUGUSTUS [*cautiously*]. You did not say that the guns were moved. You said that Blueloo had ordered them to be moved.

THE LADY. Well, that is the same thing, isn't it?

AUGUSTUS. Not quite—at the War Office. No doubt those guns WILL be moved: possibly even before the end of the war.

THE LADY. Then you think they are there still! But if the German War Office gets the list—and she will copy it before she gives it back to Blueloo, you may depend on it—all is lost.

AUGUSTUS [*lazily*]. Well, I should not go as far as that. [*Lowering his voice.*] Will you swear to me not to repeat what I am going to say to you; for if the British public knew that I had said it, I should be at once hounded down as a pro-German.

THE LADY. I will be silent as the grave. I swear it.

AUGUSTUS [*again taking it easily*]. Well, our people have for some reason made up their minds that the German War Office is everything that our War Office is not—that it carries promptitude, efficiency, and organization to a pitch of completeness and perfection that must be, in my opinion, destructive to the happiness of the staff. My own view—which you are pledged, remember, not to betray—is that the German War Office is no better than any other War Office. I found that opinion on my observation of the characters of my brothers-in-law: one of whom, by the way, is on the German general staff. I am not at all sure that this list of gun emplacements would receive the smallest attention. You see, there are always so many more important things to be attended to. Family matters, and so on, you understand.

THE LADY. Still, if a question were asked in the House of Commons—

AUGUSTUS. The great advantage of being at war, madam, is that nobody takes the slightest notice of the House of Commons. No doubt it is sometimes necessary for a Minister to soothe the more seditious members of that assembly by giving a pledge or two; but the War Office takes no notice of such things.

THE LADY [*staring at him*]. Then you think this list of gun emplacements doesn't matter!!

AUGUSTUS. By no means, madam. It matters very much indeed. If this spy were to obtain possession of the list, Blueloo would tell the story at every dinner-table in London; and—

THE LADY. And you might lose your post. Of course.

AUGUSTUS [*amazed and indignant*]. I lose my post! What are you dreaming about, madam? How could I possibly be spared? There are hardly Highcastles enough at present to fill half the posts created by this war. No: Blueloo would not go that far. He is at least a gentleman. But I should be chaffed; and, frankly, I don't like being chaffed.

THE LADY. Of course not. Who does? It would never do. Oh never, never.

AUGUSTUS. I'm glad you see it in that light. And now, as a measure of security, I shall put that list in my pocket. [*He begins searching vainly from drawer to drawer in the writing-table.*] Where on earth—? What the dickens did I—? That's very odd: I—Where the deuce—? I thought I had put it in the—Oh, here it is! No: this is Lucy's last letter.

THE LADY [*elegiacally*]. Lucy's Last Letter! What a title for a picture play!

AUGUSTUS [*delighted*]. Yes: it is, isn't it? Lucy appeals to the imagination like no other woman. By the way [*handing over the letter*], I wonder could you read it for me? Lucy is a darling girl; but I really can't read her writing. In London I get the office typist to decipher it and make me a typed copy; but here there is nobody.

THE LADY [*puzzling over it*]. It is really almost illegible. I think the beginning is meant for "Dearest Gus."

AUGUSTUS [*eagerly*]. Yes: that is what she usually calls me. Please go on.

THE LADY [*trying to decipher it*]. "What a"—"what a"—oh yes: "what a forgetful old"—something—"you are!" I can't make out the word.

AUGUSTUS [*greatly interested*]. Is it blighter? That is a favorite expression of hers.

THE LADY. I think so. At all events it begins with a B. [*Reading.*] "What a forgetful old"—[*she is interrupted by a knock at the door.*]

AUGUSTUS [*impatiently*]. Come in. [*The clerk enters, clean shaven and in khaki, with an official paper and an envelope in his hand.*] What is this ridiculous mummery sir?

THE CLERK [*coming to the table and exhibiting his uniform to both*]. They've passed me. The recruiting officer come for me. I've had my two and seven.

AUGUSTUS [*rising wrathfully*]. I shall not permit it. What do they mean by taking my office staff? Good God! they will be taking our hunt servants next. [*Confronting the clerk.*] What did the man mean? What did he say?

THE CLERK. He said that now you was on the job we'd want another million men, and he was going to take the old-age pensioners or anyone he could get.

AUGUSTUS. And did you dare to knock at my door and interrupt my business with this lady to repeat this man's ineptitudes?

THE CLERK. No. I come because the waiter from the hotel brought this paper. You left it on the coffeeroom breakfast-table this morning.

THE LADY [*intercepting it*]. It is the list. Good heavens!

THE CLERK [*proffering the envelope*]. He says he thinks this is the envelope belonging to it.

THE LADY [*snatching the envelope also*]. Yes! Addressed to you, Lord Augustus! [*Augustus comes back to the table to look at it.*] Oh, how imprudent! Everybody would guess its importance with your name on it. Fortunately I have some letters of my own here [*opening her wallet.*] Why not hide it in one of my envelopes? then no one will dream that the enclosure is of any political value. [*Taking out a letter, she crosses the room towards the window, whispering to Augustus as she passes him.*] Get rid of that man.

AUGUSTUS [*haughtily approaching the clerk, who humorously makes a paralytic attempt to stand at attention*]. Have you any further business here, pray?

THE CLERK. Am I to give the waiter anything; or will you do it yourself?

AUGUSTUS. Which waiter is it? The English one?

THE CLERK. No: the one that calls hisself a Swiss. Shouldn't wonder if he'd made a copy of that paper.

AUGUSTUS. Keep your impertinent surmises to yourself, sir. Remember that you are in the army now; and let me have no more of your civilian insubordination. Attention! Left turn! Quick march!

THE CLERK [*stolidly*]. I dunno what you mean.

AUGUSTUS. Go to the guard-room and report yourself for disobeying orders. Now do you know what I mean?

THE CLERK. Now look here. I ain't going to argue with you—

AUGUSTUS. Nor I with you. Out with you.

He seizes the clerk: and rushes him through the door. The moment the lady is left alone, she snatches a sheet of official paper from the stationery rack: folds it so that it resembles the list; compares the two to see that they look exactly alike: whips the list into her wallet: and substitutes the facsimile for it. Then she listens for the return of Augustus. A crash is heard, as of the clerk falling downstairs.

Augustus returns and is about to close the door when the voice of the clerk is heard from below.

THE CLERK. I'll have the law of you for this, I will.

AUGUSTUS [*shouting down to him*]. There's no more law for you, you scoundrel. You're a soldier now. [*He shuts the door and comes to the lady.*] Thank heaven, the war has given us the upper hand of these fellows at last. Excuse my violence; but discipline is absolutely necessary in dealing with the lower middle classes.

THE LADY. Serve the insolent creature right! Look I have found you a beautiful envelope for the list, an unmistakable lady's envelope. [*She puts the sham list into her envelope and hands it to him.*]

AUGUSTUS. Excellent. Really very clever of you. [*Slyly.*] Come: would you like to have a peep at the list [*beginning to take the blank paper from the envelope*]?

THE LADY [*on the brink of detection*]. No no. Oh, please, no.

AUGUSTUS. Why? It won't bite you [*drawing it out further.*]

THE LADY [*snatching at his hand*]. Stop. Remember: if there should be an inquiry, you must be able to swear that you never showed that list to a mortal soul.

AUGUSTUS. Oh, that is a mere form. If you are really curious—

THE LADY. I am not. I couldn't bear to look at it. One of my dearest friends was blown to pieces by an aircraft gun; and since then I have never been able to think of one without horror.

AUGUSTUS. You mean it was a real gun, and actually went off. How sad! how sad! [*He pushes the sham list back into the envelope, and pockets it.*]

THE LADY. Ah! [*Great sigh of relief*]. And now, Lord Augustus, I have taken up too much of your valuable time. Goodbye.

AUGUSTUS. What! Must you go?

THE LADY. You are so busy.

AUGUSTUS. Yes; but not before lunch, you know. I never can do much before lunch. And I'm no good at all in the afternoon. From five to six is my real working time. Must you really go?

THE LADY. I must, really. I have done my business very satisfactorily. Thank you ever so much [*she proffers her hand*].

AUGUSTUS [*shaking it affectionately as he leads her to the door, but fast pressing the bell button with his left hand*]. Goodbye. Goodbye. So sorry to lose you. Kind of you to come; but there was no real danger. You see, my dear little lady, all this talk about war saving, and secrecy, and keeping the blinds down at night, and so forth, is all very well; but unless it's carried out with intelligence, believe me, you may waste a pound to save a penny; you may let out all sorts of secrets to the enemy; you may guide the Zeppelins right on to your own chimneys. That's where the ability of the governing class comes in. Shall the fellow call a taxi for you?

THE LADY. No, thanks: I prefer walking. Goodbye. Again, many, many thanks.

She goes out. Augustus returns to the writing-table smiling, and takes another look at himself in the mirror. The clerk returns, with his head bandaged, carrying a poker.

THE CLERK. What did you ring for? [*Augustus hastily drops the mirror*]. Don't you come nigh me or I'll split your head with this poker, thick as it is.

AUGUSTUS. It does not seem to me an exceptionally thick poker. I rang for you to show the lady out.

THE CLERK. She's gone. She run out like a rabbit. I ask myself why was she in such a hurry?

THE LADY'S VOICE [*from the street*]. Lord Augustus. Lord Augustus.

THE CLERK. She's calling you.

AUGUSTUS [*running to the window and throwing it up*]. What is it? Won't you come up?

THE LADY. Is the clerk there?

AUGUSTUS. Yes. Do you want him?

THE LADY. Yes.

AUGUSTUS. The lady wants you at the window.

THE CLERK [*rushing to the window and putting down the poker*]. Yes, ma'am? Here I am, ma'am. What is it, ma'am?

THE LADY. I want you to witness that I got clean away into the street. I am coming up now.

The two men stare at one another.

THE CLERK. Wants me to witness that she got clean away into the street!

AUGUSTUS. What on earth does she mean?

The lady returns.

THE LADY. May I use your telephone?

AUGUSTUS. Certainly. Certainly. [*Taking the receiver down.*] What number shall I get you?

THE LADY. The War Office, please.

AUGUSTUS. The War Office!?

THE LADY. If you will be so good.

AUGUSTUS. But—Oh, very well. [*Into the receiver.*] Hallo. This is the Town Hall Recruiting Office. Give me Colonel Bogey, sharp.

A pause.

THE CLERK [*breaking the painful silence*]. I don't think I'm awake. This is a dream of a movie picture, this is.

AUGUSTUS [*his ear at the receiver*]. Shut up, will you? [*Into the telephone.*] What?... [*To the lady.*] Whom do you want to get on to?

THE LADY. Blueloo.

AUGUSTUS [*into the telephone*]. Put me through to Lord Hungerford Highcastle... I'm his brother, idiot... That you, Blueloo? Lady here at Little Pifflington wants to speak to you. Hold the line. [*To the lady.*] Now, madam [*he hands her the receiver*].

THE LADY [*sitting down in Augustus's chair to speak into the telephone*]. Is that Blueloo?... Do you recognize my voice?... I've won our bet....

AUGUSTUS. Your bet!

THE LADY [*into the telephone*]. Yes: I have the list in my wallet....

AUGUSTUS. Nothing of the kind, madam. I have it here in my pocket. [*He takes the envelope from his pocket: draws out the paper: and unfolds it.*]

THE LADY [*continuing*]. Yes: I got clean into the street with it. I have a witness. I could have got to London with it. Augustus won't deny it....

AUGUSTUS [*contemplating the blank paper*]. There's nothing written on this. Where is the list of guns?

THE LADY [*continuing*]. Oh, it was quite easy. I said I was my sister-in-law and that I was a Hun. He lapped it up like a kitten....

AUGUSTUS. You don't mean to say that—

THE LADY [*continuing*]. I got hold of the list for a moment and changed it for a piece of paper out of his stationery rack: it was quite easy [*she laughs: and it is clear that Blueloo is laughing too*].

AUGUSTUS. What!

THE CLERK [*laughing slowly and laboriously, with intense enjoyment*]. Ha ha! Ha ha ha! Ha! [*Augustus rushes at him; he snatches up the poker and stands on guard.*] No you don't.

THE LADY [*still at the telephone, waving her disengaged hand behind her impatiently at them to stop making a noise*]. Sh-sh-sh-sh-sh!!! [*Augustus, with a shrug, goes up the middle of the room. The lady resumes her conversation with the telephone.*] What?... Oh yes: I'm coming up by the 1.35: why not have tea with me at Rumpelmeister's?... Rum-pel-meister's. You know: they call it Robinson's now... Right. Ta ta. [*She hangs up the receiver, and is passing round the table on her way towards the door when she is confronted by Augustus.*]

AUGUSTUS. Madam, I consider your conduct most unpatriotic. You make bets and abuse the confidence of the hardworked officials who are doing their bit for their country whilst our gallant fellows are perishing in the trenches—

THE LADY. Oh, the gallant fellows are not all in the trenches, Augustus. Some of them have come home for a few days' hard-earned leave; and I am sure you won't grudge them a little fun at your expense.

THE CLERK. Hear! hear!

AUGUSTUS [*amiably*]. Ah, well! For my country's sake—!

ANNAJANSKA, THE BOLSHEVIK EMPRESS

ANNAJANSKA is frankly a bravura piece. The modern variety theatre demands for its "turns" little plays called sketches, to last twenty minutes or so, and to enable some favorite performer to make a brief but dazzling appearance on some barely passable dramatic pretext. Miss Lillah McCarthy and I, as author and actress, have helped to make one another famous on many serious occasions, from Man and Superman to Androcles; and Mr Charles Ricketts has not disdained to snatch moments from his painting and sculpture to design some wonderful dresses for us. We three unbent as Mrs Siddons, Sir Joshua Reynolds and Dr Johnson might have unbent, to devise a turn for the Coliseum variety theatre. Not that we would set down the art of the variety theatre as something to be condescended to, or our own art as elephantine. We should rather crave indulgence as three novices fresh from the awful legitimacy of the highbrow theatre.

Well, Miss McCarthy and Mr Ricketts justified themselves easily in the glamor of the footlights, to the strains of Tchaikovsky's 1812. I fear I did not. I have received only one compliment on my share; and that was from a friend who said, "It is the only one of your works that is not too long." So I have made it a page or two longer, according to my own precept: EMBRACE YOUR REPROACHES: THEY ARE OFTEN GLORIES IN DISGUISE.

Annajanska was first performed at the Coliseum Theatre in London on the 21st January, 1918, with Lillah McCarthy as the Grand Duchess, Henry Miller as Schneidekind, and Randle Ayrton as General Strammfest.

ANNAJANSKA, THE BOLSHEVIK EMPRESS

The General's office in a military station on the east front in Beotia. An office table with a telephone, writing materials, official papers, etc., is set across the room. At the end of the table, a comfortable chair for the General. Behind the chair, a window. Facing it at the other end of the table, a plain wooden bench. At the side of the table, with its back to the door, a common chair, with a typewriter before it. Beside the door, which is opposite the end of the bench, a rack for caps and coats. There is nobody in the room.

General Strammfest enters, followed by Lieutenant Schneidekind. They hang up their cloaks and caps. Schneidekind takes a little longer than Strammfest, who comes to the table.

STRAMMFEST. Schneidekind.

SCHNEIDEKIND. Yes, sir.

STRAMMFEST. Have you sent my report yet to the government? [*He sits down.*]

SCHNEIDEKIND [*coming to the table*]. Not yet, sir. Which government do you wish it sent to? [*He sits down.*]

STRAMMFEST. That depends. What's the latest? Which of them do you think is most likely to be in power tomorrow morning?

SCHNEIDEKIND. Well, the provisional government was going strong yesterday. But today they say that the Prime Minister has shot himself, and that the extreme left fellow has shot all the others.

STRAMMFEST. Yes: that's all very well; but these fellows always shoot themselves with blank cartridge.

SCHNEIDEKIND. Still, even the blank cartridge means backing down. I should send the report to the Maximilianists.

STRAMMFEST. They're no stronger than the Oppidoshavians; and in my own opinion the Moderate Red Revolutionaries are as likely to come out on top as either of them.

SCHNEIDEKIND. I can easily put a few carbon sheets in the typewriter and send a copy each to the lot.

STRAMMFEST. Waste of paper. You might as well send reports to an infant school. [*He throws his head on the table with a groan.*]

SCHNEIDEKIND. Tired out, Sir?

STRAMMFEST. O Schneidekind, Schneidekind, how can you bear to live?

SCHNEIDEKIND. At my age, sir, I ask myself how can I bear to die?

STRAMMFEST. You are young, young and heartless. You are excited by the revolution: you are attached to abstract things like liberty. But my family has served the Panjandrums of Beotia faithfully for seven centuries. The Panjandrums have kept our place for us at their courts, honored us, promoted us, shed their glory on us, made us what we are. When I hear you young men declaring that you are fighting for civilization, for democracy, for the overthrow of militarism, I ask myself how can a man shed his blood for empty words used by vulgar tradesmen and common laborers: mere wind and stink. [*He rises, exalted by his theme.*] A king is a splendid reality, a man raised above us like a god. You can see him; you can kiss his hand; you can be cheered by his smile and terrified by his frown. I would have died for my Panjandrum as my father died for his father. Your toiling millions were only too honored to receive the toes of our boots in the proper spot for them when they displeased their betters. And now what is left in life for me? [*He relapses into his chair discouraged.*] My Panjandrum is deposed and transported to herd with convicts. The army, his pride and glory, is paraded to hear seditious speeches from penniless rebels, with the colonel actually forced to take the chair and introduce the speaker. I myself am made Commander-in-Chief by my own solicitor: a Jew, Schneidekind! a Hebrew Jew! It seems only yesterday that these things would have been the ravings of a madman: today they are the commonplaces of the gutter press. I live now for three objects only: to defeat the enemy, to restore the Panjandrum, and to hang my solicitor.

SCHNEIDEKIND. Be careful, sir: these are dangerous views to utter nowadays. What if I were to betray you?

STRAMMFEST. What!

SCHNEIDEKIND. I won't, of course: my own father goes on just like that; but suppose I did?

STRAMMFEST [*chuckling*]. I should accuse you of treason to the Revolution, my lad; and they would immediately shoot you, unless you cried and asked to see your mother before you died, when they would probably change their minds and make you a brigadier. Enough. [*He rises and expands his chest.*] I feel the better for letting myself go. To business. [*He takes up a telegram: opens it: and is thunderstruck by its contents.*] Great heaven! [*He collapses into his chair.*] This is the worst blow of all.

SCHNEIDEKIND. What has happened? Are we beaten?

STRAMMFEST. Man, do you think that a mere defeat could strike me down as this news does: I, who have been defeated thirteen times since the war began? O, my master, my master, my Panjandrum! [*he is convulsed with sobs.*]

SCHNEIDEKIND. They have killed him?

STRAMMFEST. A dagger has been struck through his heart—

SCHNEIDEKIND. Good God!

STRAMMFEST. —and through mine, through mine.

SCHNEIDEKIND [*relieved*]. Oh, a metaphorical dagger! I thought you meant a real one. What has happened?

STRAMMFEST. His daughter the Grand Duchess Annajanska, she whom the Panjandrina loved beyond all her other children, has—has— [*he cannot finish.*]

SCHNEIDEKIND. Committed suicide?

STRAMMFEST. No. Better if she had. Oh, far far better.

SCHNEIDEKIND [*in hushed tones*]. Left the Church?

STRAMMFEST [*shocked*]. Certainly not. Do not blaspheme, young man.

SCHNEIDEKIND. Asked for the vote?

STRAMMFEST. I would have given it to her with both hands to save her from this.

SCHNEIDEKIND. Save her from what? Dash it, sir, out with it.

STRAMMFEST. She has joined the Revolution.

SCHNEIDEKIND. But so have you, sir. We've all joined the Revolution. She doesn't mean it any more than we do.

STRAMMFEST. Heaven grant you may be right! But that is not the worst. She had eloped with a young officer. Eloped, Schneidekind, eloped!

SCHNEIDEKIND [*not particularly impressed*]. Yes, Sir.

STRAMMFEST. Annajanska, the beautiful, the innocent, my master's daughter! [*He buries his face in his hands.*]

The telephone rings.

SCHNEIDEKIND [*taking the receiver*]. Yes: G.H.Q. Yes... Don't bawl: I'm not a general. Who is it speaking?... Why didn't you say so? don't you know your duty? Next time you will lose your stripe... Oh, they've made you a colonel, have they? Well, they've made me a field-marshal: now what have you to say?... Look here: what did you ring up for? I can't spend the day here listening to your cheek... What! the Grand Duchess [*Strammfest starts.*] Where did you catch her?

STRAMMFEST [*snatching the telephone and listening for the answer*]. Speak louder, will you: I am a General I know that, you dolt. Have you captured the officer that was with her?... Damnation! You shall answer for this: you let him go: he bribed you. You must have seen him: the fellow is in the full dress court uniform of the Panderobajensky Hussars. I give you twelve hours to catch him or... what's that you say about the devil? Are you swearing at me, you... Thousand thunders! [*To Schneidekind.*] The swine says that the Grand Duchess is a devil incarnate. [*Into the telephone.*] Filthy traitor: is that the way you dare speak of the daughter of our anointed Panjandrum? I'll—

SCHNEIDEKIND [*pulling the telephone from his lips*]. Take care, sir.

STRAMMFEST. I won't take care: I'll have him shot. Let go that telephone.

SCHNEIDEKIND. But for her own sake, sir—

STRAMMFEST. Eh?—

SCHNEIDEKIND. For her own sake they had better send her here. She will be safe in your hands.

STRAMMFEST [*yielding the receiver*]. You are right. Be civil to him. I should choke [*he sits down*].

SCHNEIDEKIND [*into the telephone*]. Hullo. Never mind all that: it's only a fellow here who has been fooling with the telephone. I had to leave the room for a moment. Wash out: and send the girl along. We'll jolly soon teach her to behave herself here... Oh, you've sent her already. Then why the devil didn't you say so, you—[*he hangs up the telephone angrily*]. Just fancy: they started her off this morning: and all this is because the fellow likes to get on the telephone and hear himself talk now that he is a colonel. [*The telephone rings again. He snatches the receiver furiously.*] What's the matter now?... [*To the General.*] It's our own people downstairs. [*Into the receiver.*] Here! do you suppose I've nothing else to do than to hang on to the telephone all day?... What's that? Not men enough to hold her! What do you mean? [*To the General.*] She is there, sir.

STRAMMFEST. Tell them to send her up. I shall have to receive her without even rising, without kissing her hand, to keep up appearances before the escort. It will break my heart.

SCHNEIDEKIND [*into the receiver*]. Send her up... Tcha! [*He hangs up the receiver.*] He says she is halfway up already: they couldn't hold her.

The Grand Duchess bursts into the room, dragging with her two exhausted soldiers hanging on desperately to her arms. She is enveloped from head to foot by a fur-lined cloak, and wears a fur cap.

SCHNEIDEKIND [*pointing to the bench*]. At the word Go, place your prisoner on the bench in a sitting posture; and take your seats right and left of her. Go.

The two soldiers make a supreme effort to force her to sit down. She flings them back so that they are forced to sit on the bench to save themselves from falling backwards over it, and is herself dragged into sitting between them. The second soldier, holding on tight to the Grand Duchess with one hand, produces papers with the other, and waves them towards Schneidekind, who takes them from him and passes them on to the General. He opens them and reads them with a grave expression.

SCHNEIDEKIND. Be good enough to wait, prisoner, until the General has read the papers on your case.

THE GRAND DUCHESS [*to the soldiers*]. Let go. [*To Strammfest*]. Tell them to let go, or I'll upset the bench backwards and bash our three heads on the floor.

FIRST SOLDIER. No, little mother. Have mercy on the poor.

STRAMMFEST [*growling over the edge of the paper he is reading*]. Hold your tongue.

THE GRAND DUCHESS [*blazing*]. Me, or the soldier?

STRAMMFEST [*horrified*]. The soldier, madam.

THE GRAND DUCHESS. Tell him to let go.

STRAMMFEST. Release the lady.

The soldiers take their hands off her. One of them wipes his fevered brow. The other sucks his wrist.

SCHNEIDKIND [*fiercely*]. 'ttention!

The two soldiers sit up stiffly.

THE GRAND DUCHESS. Oh, let the poor man suck his wrist. It may be poisoned. I bit it.

STRAMMFEST [*shocked*]. You bit a common soldier!

GRAND DUCHESS. Well, I offered to cauterize it with the poker in the office stove. But he was afraid. What more could I do?

SCHNEIDEKIND. Why did you bite him, prisoner?

THE GRAND DUCHESS. He would not let go.

STRAMMFEST. Did he let go when you bit him?

THE GRAND DUCHESS. No. [*Patting the soldier on the back*]. You should give the man a cross for his devotion. I could not go on eating him; so I brought him along with me.

STRAMMFEST. Prisoner—

THE GRAND DUCHESS. Don't call me prisoner, General Strammfest. My grandmother dandled you on her knee.

STRAMMFEST [*bursting into tears*]. O God, yes. Believe me, my heart is what it was then.

THE GRAND DUCHESS. Your brain also is what it was then. I will not be addressed by you as prisoner.

STRAMMFEST. I may not, for your own sake, call you by your rightful and most sacred titles. What am I to call you?

THE GRAND DUCHESS. The Revolution has made us comrades. Call me comrade.

STRAMMFEST. I had rather die.

THE GRAND DUCHESS. Then call me Annajanska; and I will call you Peter Piper, as grandmamma did.

STRAMMFEST [*painfully agitated*]. Schneidekind, you must speak to her: I cannot—[*he breaks down.*]

SCHNEIDEKIND [*officially*]. The Republic of Beotia has been compelled to confine the Panjandrum and his family, for their own safety, within certain bounds. You have broken those bounds.

STRAMMFEST [*taking the word from him*]. You are I must say it—a prisoner. What am I to do with you?

THE GRAND DUCHESS. You should have thought of that before you arrested me.

STRAMMFEST. Come, come, prisoner! do you know what will happen to you if you compel me to take a sterner tone with you?

THE GRAND DUCHESS. No. But I know what will happen to you.

STRAMAIFEST. Pray what, prisoner?

THE GLAND DUCHESS. Clergyman's sore throat.

Schneidekind splutters; drops a paper: and conceals his laughter under the table.

STRAMMFEST [*thunderously*]. Lieutenant Schneidekind.

SCHNEIDEKIND [*in a stifled voice*]. Yes, Sir. [*The table vibrates visibly.*]

STRAMMFEST. Come out of it, you fool: you're upsetting the ink.

Schneidekind emerges, red in the face with suppressed mirth.

STRAMMFEST. Why don't you laugh? Don't you appreciate Her Imperial Highness's joke?

SCHNEIDEKIND [*suddenly becoming solemn*]. I don't want to, sir.

STRAMMFEST. Laugh at once, sir. I order you to laugh.

SCHNEIDEKIND [*with a touch of temper*]. I really can't, sir. [*He sits down decisively.*]

STRAMMFEST [*growling at him*]. Yah! [*He turns impressively to the Grand Duchess.*] Your Imperial Highness desires me to address you as comrade?

THE GRAND DUCHESS [*rising and waving a red handkerchief*]. Long live the Revolution, comrade!

STRAMMFEST [*rising and saluting*]. Proletarians of all lands, unite. Lieutenant Schneidekind, you will rise and sing the Marseillaise.

SCHNEIDEKIND [*rising*]. But I cannot, sir. I have no voice, no ear.

STRAMMFEST. Then sit down; and bury your shame in your typewriter. [*Schneidekind sits down.*] Comrade Annajanska, you have eloped with a young officer.

THE GRAND DUCHESS [*astounded*]. General Strammfest, you lie.

STRAMMFEST. Denial, comrade, is useless. It is through that officer that your movements have been traced. [*The Grand Duchess is suddenly enlightened, and seems amused. Strammfest continues an a forensic manner.*] He joined you at the Golden Anchor in Hakonsburg. You gave us the slip there; but the officer was traced to Potterdam, where you rejoined him and went alone to Premsylople. What have you done with that unhappy young man? Where is he?

THE GRAND DUCHESS [*pretending to whisper an important secret*]. Where he has always been.

STRAMMFEST [*eagerly*]. Where is that?

THE GRAND DUCHESS [*impetuously*]. In your imagination. I came alone. I am alone. Hundreds of officers travel every day from Hakonsburg to Potterdam. What do I know about them?

STRAMMFEST. They travel in khaki. They do not travel in full dress court uniform as this man did.

SCHNEIDEKIND. Only officers who are eloping with grand duchesses wear court uniform: otherwise the grand duchesses could not be seen with them.

STRAMMFEST. Hold your tongue. [*Schneidekind, in high dudgeon, folds his arms and retires from the conversation. The General returns to his paper and to his examination of the Grand Duchess.*] This officer travelled with your passport. What have you to say to that?

THE GRAND DUCHESS. Bosh! How could a man travel with a woman's passport?

STRAMMFEST. It is quite simple, as you very well know. A dozen travellers arrive at the boundary. The official collects their passports. He counts twelve persons; then counts the passports. If there are twelve, he is satisfied.

THE GRAND DUCHESS. Then how do you know that one of the passports was mine?

STRAMMFEST. A waiter at the Potterdam Hotel looked at the officer's passport when he was in his bath. It was your passport.

THE GRAND DUCHESS. Stuff! Why did he not have me arrested?

STRAMMFEST. When the waiter returned to the hotel with the police the officer had vanished; and you were there with your own passport. They knouted him.

THE GRAND DUCHESS. Oh! Strammfest, send these men away. I must speak to you alone.

STRAMMFEST [*rising in horror*]. No: this is the last straw: I cannot consent. It is impossible, utterly, eternally impossible, that a daughter of the Imperial House should speak to any one alone, were it even her own husband.

THE GRAND DUCHESS. You forget that there is an exception. She may speak to a child alone. [*She rises.*] Strammfest, you have been dandled on my grandmother's knee. By that gracious action the dowager Panjandrina made you a child forever. So did Nature, by the way. I order you to speak to me alone. Do you hear? I order you. For seven hundred years no member of your family has ever disobeyed an order from a member of mine. Will you disobey me?

STRAMMFEST. There is an alternative to obedience. The dead cannot disobey. [*He takes out his pistol and places the muzzle against his temple.*]

SCHNEIDEKIND [*snatching the pistol from him*]. For God's sake, General—

STRAMMFEST [*attacking him furiously to recover the weapon*]. Dog of a subaltern, restore that pistol and my honor.

SCHNEIDEKIND [*reaching out with the pistol to the Grand Duchess*]. Take it: quick: he is as strong as a bull.

THE GRAND DUCHESS [*snatching it*]. Aha! Leave the room, all of you except the General. At the double! lightning! electricity! [*She fires shot after shot, spattering the bullets about the ankles of the soldiers. They fly precipitately. She turns to Schneidekind, who has by this time been flung on the floor by the General.*] You too. [*He scrambles up.*] March. [*He flies to the door.*]

SCHNEIDEKIND [*turning at the door*]. For your own sake, comrade—

THE GRAND DUCHESS [*indignantly*]. Comrade! You!!! Go. [*She fires two more shots. He vanishes.*]

STRAMMFEST [*making an impulsive movement towards her*]. My Imperial Mistress—

THE GRAND DUCHESS. Stop. I have one bullet left, if you attempt to take this from me [*putting the pistol to her temple*].

STRAMMFEST [*recoiling, and covering his eyes with his hands*]. No no: put it down: put it down. I promise everything: I swear anything; but put it down, I implore you.

THE GRAND DUCHESS [*throwing it on the table*]. There!

STRAMMFEST [*uncovering his eyes*]. Thank God!

THE GRAND DUCHESS [*gently*]. Strammfest: I am your comrade. Am I nothing more to you?

STRAMMFEST [*falling on his knee*]. You are, God help me, all that is left to me of the only power I recognize on earth [*he kisses her hand*].

THE GRAND DUCHESS [*indulgently*]. Idolater! When will you learn that our strength has never been in ourselves, but in your illusions about us? [*She shakes off her kindliness, and sits down in his chair.*] Now tell me, what are your orders? And do you mean to obey them?

STRAMMFEST [*starting like a goaded ox, and blundering fretfully about the room*]. How can I obey six different dictators, and not one gentleman among the lot of them? One of them orders me to make peace with the foreign enemy. Another orders me to offer all the neutral countries 48 hours to choose between adopting his views on the single tax and being instantly invaded and annihilated. A third orders me to go to a damned Socialist Conference and explain that Beotia will allow no annexations and no indemnities, and merely wishes to establish the Kingdom of Heaven on Earth throughout the universe. [*He finishes behind Schneidekind's chair.*]

THE GRAND DUCHESS. Damn their trifling!

STRAMMFEST. I thank Your Imperial Highness from the bottom of my heart for that expression. Europe thanks you.

THE GRAND DUCHESS. M'yes; but—[*rising*]. Strammfest, you know that your cause—the cause of the dynasty—is lost.

STRAMMFEST. You must not say so. It is treason, even from you. [*He sinks, discouraged, into the chair, and covers his face with his hand.*]

THE GRAND DUCHESS. Do not deceive yourself, General: never again will a Panjandrum reign in Beotia. [*She walks slowly across the room, brooding bitterly, and thinking aloud.*] We are so decayed, so out of date, so feeble, so wicked in our own despite, that we have come at last to will our own destruction.

STRAMMFEST. You are uttering blasphemy.

THE GRAND DUCHESS. All great truths begin as blasphemies. All the king's horses and all the king's men cannot set up my father's throne again. If they could, you would have done it, would you not?

STRAMMFEST. God knows I would!

THE GRAND DUCHESS. You really mean that? You would keep the people in their hopeless squalid misery? you would fill those infamous prisons again with the noblest spirits in the land? you would thrust the rising sun of liberty back into the sea of blood from which it has risen? And all because there was in the middle of the dirt and ugliness and horror a little patch of court splendor in which you could stand with a few orders on your uniform, and yawn day after day and night after night in unspeakable boredom until your grave yawned wider still, and you fell into it because you had nothing better to do. How can you be so stupid, so heartless?

STRAMMFEST. You must be mad to think of royalty in such a way. I never yawned at court. The dogs yawned; but that was because they were dogs: they had no imagination, no ideals, no sense of honor and dignity to sustain them.

THE GRAND DUCHESS. My poor Strammfest: you were not often enough at court to tire of it. You were mostly soldiering; and when you came home to have a new order pinned on your breast, your happiness came through looking at my father and mother and at me, and adoring us. Was that not so?

STRAMMFEST. Do YOU reproach me with it? I am not ashamed of it.

THE GRAND DUCHESS. Oh, it was all very well for you, Strammfest. But think of me, of me! standing there for you to gape at, and knowing that I was no goddess, but only a girl like any other girl! It was cruelty to animals: you could have stuck up a wax doll or a golden calf to worship; it would not have been bored.

STRAMMFEST. Stop; or I shall renounce my allegiance to you. I have had women flogged for such seditious chatter as this.

THE GRAND DUCHESS. Do not provoke me to send a bullet through your head for reminding me of it.

STRAMMFEST. You always had low tastes. You are no true daughter of the Panjandrums: you are a changeling, thrust into the Panjandrina's bed by some profligate nurse. I have heard stories of your childhood: of how—

THE GRAND DUCHESS. Ha, ha! Yes: they took me to the circus when I was a child. It was my first moment of happiness, my first glimpse of heaven. I ran away and joined the troupe. They caught me and dragged me back to my gilded cage; but I had tasted freedom; and they never could make me forget it.

STRAMMFEST. Freedom! To be the slave of an acrobat! to be exhibited to the public! to—

THE GRAND DUCHESS. Oh, I was trained to that. I had learnt that part of the business at court.

STRAMMFEST. You had not been taught to strip yourself half naked and turn head over heels—

THE GRAND DUCHESS. Man, I WANTED to get rid of my swaddling clothes and turn head over heels. I wanted to, I wanted to, I wanted to. I can do it still. Shall I do it now?

STRAMMFEST. If you do, I swear I will throw myself from the window so that I may meet your parents in heaven without having my medals torn from my breast by them.

THE GRAND DUCHESS. Oh, you are incorrigible. You are mad, infatuated. You will not believe that we royal divinities are mere common flesh and blood even when we step down from our pedestals and tell you ourselves what a fool you are. I will argue no more with you: I will use my power. At a word from me your men will turn against you: already half of them do not salute you; and you dare not punish them: you have to pretend not to notice it.

STRAMMFEST. It is not for you to taunt me with that if it is so.

THE GRAND DUCHESS. [*haughtily*]. Taunt! I condescend to taunt! To taunt a common General! You forget yourself, sir.

STRAMMFEST [*dropping on his knee submissively*]. Now at last you speak like your royal self.

THE GRAND DUCHESS. Oh, Strammfest, Strammfest, they have driven your slavery into your very bones. Why did you not spit in my face?

STRAMMFEST [*rising with a shudder*]. God forbid!

THE GRAND DUCHESS. Well, since you will be my slave, take your orders from me. I have not come here to save our wretched family and our bloodstained crown. I am come to save the Revolution.

STRAMMFEST. Stupid as I am, I have come to think that I had better save that than save nothing. But what will the Revolution do for the people? Do not be deceived by the fine speeches of the revolutionary leaders and the pamphlets of the revolutionary writers. How much liberty is there where they have gained the upper hand? Are they not hanging, shooting, imprisoning as much as ever we did? Do they ever tell the people the truth? No: if the truth does not suit them they spread lies instead, and make it a crime to tell the truth.

THE GRAND DUCHESS. Of course they do. Why should they not?

STRAMMFEST [*hardly able to believe his ears*]. Why should they not?

THE GRAND DUCHESS. Yes: why should they not? We did it. You did it, whip in hand: you flogged women for teaching children to read.

STRAMMFEST. To read sedition. To read Karl Marx.

THE GRAND DUCHESS. Pshaw! How could they learn to read the Bible without learning to read Karl Marx? Why do you not stand to your guns and justify what you did, instead of making silly excuses? Do you suppose I think flogging a woman worse than flogging a man? I, who am a woman myself!

STRAMMFEST. I am at a loss to understand your Imperial Highness. You seem to me to contradict yourself.

THE GRAND DUCHESS. Nonsense! I say that if the people cannot govern themselves, they must be governed by somebody. If they will not do their duty without being half forced and half humbugged, somebody must force them and humbug them. Some energetic and capable minority must always be in power. Well, I am on the side of the energetic minority whose principles I agree with. The Revolution is as cruel as we were; but its aims are my aims. Therefore I stand for the Revolution.

STRAMMFEST. You do not know what you are saying. This is pure Bolshevism. Are you, the daughter of a Panjandrum, a Bolshevist?

THE GRAND DUCHESS. I am anything that will make the world less like a prison and more like a circus.

STRAMMFEST. Ah! You still want to be a circus star.

THE GRAND DUCHESS. Yes, and be billed as the Bolshevik Empress. Nothing shall stop me. You have your orders, General Strammfest: save the Revolution.

STRAMMFEST. What Revolution? Which Revolution? No two of your rabble of revolutionists mean the same thing by the Revolution What can save a mob in which every man is rushing in a different direction?

THE GRAND DUCHESS. I will tell you. The war can save it.

STRAMMFEST. The war?

THE GRAND DUCHESS. Yes, the war. Only a great common danger and a great common duty can unite us and weld these wrangling factions into a solid commonwealth.

STRAMMFEST. Bravo! War sets everything right: I have always said so. But what is a united people without a united army? And what can I do? I am only a soldier. I cannot make speeches: I have won no victories: they will not rally to my call [*again he sinks into his chair with his former gesture of discouragement*].

THE GRAND DUCHESS. Are you sure they will not rally to mine?

STRAMMFEST. Oh, if only you were a man and a soldier!

THE GRAND DUCHESS. Suppose I find you a man and a soldier?

STRAMMFEST [*rising in a fury*]. Ah! the scoundrel you eloped with! You think you will shove this fellow into an army command, over my head. Never.

THE GRAND DUCHESS. You promised everything. You swore anything. [*She marches as if in front of a regiment.*] I know that this man alone can rouse the army to enthusiasm.

STRAMMFEST. Delusion! Folly! He is some circus acrobat; and you are in love with him.

THE GRAND DUCHESS. I swear I am not in love with him. I swear I will never marry him.

STRAMMFEST. Then who is he?

THE GRAND DUCHESS. Anybody in the world but you would have guessed long ago. He is under your very eyes.

STRAMMFEST [*staring past her right and left*]. Where?

THE GRAND DUCHESS. Look out of the window.

He rushes to the window, looking for the officer. The Grand Duchess takes off her cloak and appears in the uniform of the Panderobajensky Hussars.

STRAMMFEST [*peering through the window*]. Where is he? I can see no one.

THE GRAND DUCHESS. Here, silly.

STRAMMFEST [*turning*]. You! Great Heavens! The Bolshevik Empress!

HEARTBREAK HOUSE

A FANTASIA IN THE RUSSIAN MANNER ON ENGLISH THEMES

ACT I

The hilly country in the middle of the north edge of Sussex, looking very pleasant on a fine evening at the end of September, is seen through the windows of a room which has been built so as to resemble the after part of an old-fashioned high-pooped ship, with a stern gallery; for the windows are ship built with heavy timbering, and run right across the room as continuously as the stability of the wall allows. A row of lockers under the windows provides an unupholstered windowseat interrupted by twin glass doors, respectively halfway between the stern post and the sides. Another door strains the illusion a little by being apparently in the ship's port side, and yet leading, not to the open sea, but to the entrance hall of the house. Between this door and the stern gallery are bookshelves. There are electric light switches beside the door leading to the hall and the glass doors in the stern gallery. Against the starboard wall is a carpenter's bench. The vice has a board in its jaws; and the floor is littered with shavings, overflowing from a waste-paper basket. A couple of planes and a centrebit are on the bench. In the same wall, between the bench and the windows, is a narrow doorway with a half door, above which a glimpse of the room beyond shows that it is a shelved pantry with bottles and kitchen crockery.

On the starboard side, but close to the middle, is a plain oak drawing-table with drawing-board, T-square, straightedges, set squares, mathematical instruments, saucers of water color, a tumbler of discolored water, Indian ink, pencils, and brushes on it. The drawing-board is set so that the draughtsman's chair has the window on its left hand. On the floor at the end of the table, on its right, is a ship's fire bucket. On the port side of the room, near the bookshelves, is a sofa with its back to the windows. It is a sturdy mahogany article, oddly upholstered in sailcloth, including the bolster, with a couple of blankets hanging over the back. Between the sofa and the drawing-table is a big wicker chair, with broad arms and a low sloping back, with its back to the light. A small but stout table of teak, with a round top and gate legs, stands against the port wall between the door and the bookcase. It is the only article in the room that suggests (not at all convincingly) a woman's hand in the furnishing. The uncarpeted floor of narrow boards is caulked and holystoned like a deck.

The garden to which the glass doors lead dips to the south before the landscape rises again to the hills. Emerging from the hollow is the cupola of an observatory. Between the observatory and the house is a flagstaff on a little esplanade, with a hammock on the east side and a long garden seat on the west.

A young lady, gloved and hatted, with a dust coat on, is sitting in the window-seat with her body twisted to enable her to look out at the view. One hand props her chin: the other hangs down with a volume of the Temple Shakespeare in it, and her finger stuck in the page she has been reading.

A clock strikes six.

The young lady turns and looks at her watch. She rises with an air of one who waits, and is almost at the end of her patience. She is a pretty girl, slender, fair, and intelligent looking, nicely but not expensively dressed, evidently not a smart idler.

With a sigh of weary resignation she comes to the draughtsman's chair; sits down; and begins to read Shakespeare. Presently the book sinks to her lap; her eyes close; and she dozes into a slumber.

An elderly womanservant comes in from the hall with three unopened bottles of rum on a tray. She passes through and disappears in the pantry without noticing the young lady. She places the bottles on the shelf and fills her tray with empty bottles. As she returns with these, the young lady lets her book drop, awakening herself, and startling the womanservant so that she all but lets the tray fall.

THE WOMANSERVANT. God bless us! [*The young lady picks up the book and places it on the table*]. Sorry to wake you, miss, I'm sure; but you are a stranger to me. What might you be waiting here for now?

THE YOUNG LADY. Waiting for somebody to show some signs of knowing that I have been invited here.

THE WOMANSERVANT. Oh, you're invited, are you? And has nobody come? Dear! dear!

THE YOUNG LADY. A wild-looking old gentleman came and looked in at the window; and I heard him calling out, "Nurse, there is a young and attractive female waiting in the poop. Go and see what she wants." Are you the nurse?

THE WOMANSERVANT. Yes, miss: I'm Nurse Guinness. That was old Captain Shotover, Mrs Hushabye's father. I heard him roaring; but I thought it was for something else. I suppose it was Mrs Hushabye that invited you, ducky?

THE YOUNG LADY. I understood her to do so. But really I think I'd better go.

NURSE GUINNESS. Oh, don't think of such a thing, miss. If Mrs Hushabye has forgotten all about it, it will be a pleasant surprise for her to see you, won't it?

THE YOUNG LADY. It has been a very unpleasant surprise to me to find that nobody expects me.

NURSE GUINNESS. You'll get used to it, miss: this house is full of surprises for them that don't know our ways.

CAPTAIN SHOTOVER [*looking in from the hall suddenly: an ancient but still hardy man with an immense white beard, in a reefer jacket with a whistle hanging from his neck*]. Nurse, there is a hold-all and a handbag on the front steps for everybody to fall over. Also a tennis racquet. Who the devil left them there?

THE YOUNG LADY. They are mine, I'm afraid.

THE CAPTAIN [*advancing to the drawing-table*]. Nurse, who is this misguided and unfortunate young lady?

NURSE GUINNESS. She says Miss Hessy invited her, sir.

THE CAPTAIN. And had she no friend, no parents, to warn her against my daughter's invitations? This is a pretty sort of house, by heavens! A young and attractive lady is invited here. Her luggage is left on the steps for hours; and she herself is deposited in the poop and abandoned, tired and starving. This is our hospitality. These are our manners. No room ready. No hot water. No welcoming hostess. Our visitor is to sleep in the toolshed, and to wash in the duckpond.

NURSE GUINNESS. Now it's all right, Captain: I'll get the lady some tea; and her room shall be ready before she has finished it. [*To the young lady*]. Take off your hat, ducky; and make yourself at home [*she goes to the door leading to the hall*].

THE CAPTAIN [*as she passes him*]. Ducky! Do you suppose, woman, that because this young lady has been insulted and neglected, you have the right to address her as you address my wretched children, whom you have brought up in ignorance of the commonest decencies of social intercourse?

NURSE GUINNESS. Never mind him, doty. [*Quite unconcerned, she goes out into the hall on her way to the kitchen*].

THE CAPTAIN. Madam, will you favor me with your name? [*He sits down in the big wicker chair*].

THE YOUNG LADY. My name is Ellie Dunn.

THE CAPTAIN. Dunn! I had a boatswain whose name was Dunn. He was originally a pirate in China. He set up as a ship's chandler with stores which I have every reason to believe he stole from me. No doubt he became rich. Are you his daughter?

ELLIE [*indignant*]. No, certainly not. I am proud to be able to say that though my father has not been a successful man, nobody has ever had one word to say against him. I think my father is the best man I have ever known.

THE CAPTAIN. He must be greatly changed. Has he attained the seventh degree of concentration?

ELLIE. I don't understand.

THE CAPTAIN. But how could he, with a daughter? I, madam, have two daughters. One of them is Hesione Hushabye, who invited you here. I keep this house: she upsets it. I desire to attain the seventh degree of concentration: she invites visitors and leaves me to entertain them. [*Nurse Guinness returns with the tea-tray, which she places on the teak table*]. I have a second daughter who is, thank God, in a remote part of the Empire with her numskull of a husband. As a child she thought the figure-head of my ship, the Dauntless, the most beautiful thing on earth. He resembled it. He had the same expression: wooden yet enterprising. She married him, and will never set foot in this house again.

NURSE GUINNESS [*carrying the table, with the tea-things on it, to Ellie's side*]. Indeed you never were more mistaken. She is in England this very moment. You have been told three times this week that she is coming home for a year for her health. And very glad you should be to see your own daughter again after all these years.

THE CAPTAIN. I am not glad. The natural term of the affection of the human animal for its offspring is six years. My daughter Ariadne was born when I was forty-six. I am now eighty-eight. If she comes, I am not at home. If she wants anything, let her take it. If she asks for me, let her be informed that I am extremely old, and have totally forgotten her.

NURSE GUINNESS. That's no talk to offer to a young lady. Here, ducky, have some tea; and don't listen to him [*she pours out a cup of tea*].

THE CAPTAIN [*rising wrathfully*]. Now before high heaven they have given this innocent child Indian tea: the stuff they tan their own leather insides with. [*He seizes the cup and the tea-pot and empties both into the leathern bucket*].

ELLIE [*almost in tears*]. Oh, please! I am so tired. I should have been glad of anything.

NURSE GUINNESS. Oh, what a thing to do! The poor lamb is ready to drop.

THE CAPTAIN. You shall have some of my tea. Do not touch that fly-blown cake: nobody eats it here except the dogs. [*He disappears into the pantry*].

NURSE GUINNESS. There's a man for you! They say he sold himself to the devil in Zanzibar before he was a captain; and the older he grows the more I believe them.

A WOMAN'S VOICE [*in the hall*]. Is anyone at home? Hesione! Nurse! Papa! Do come, somebody; and take in my luggage.

Thumping heard, as of an umbrella, on the wainscot.

NURSE GUINNESS. My gracious! It's Miss Addy, Lady Utterword, Mrs Hushabye's sister: the one I told the captain about. [*Calling*]. Coming, Miss, coming.

She carries the table back to its place by the door and is harrying out when she is intercepted by Lady Utterword, who bursts in much flustered. Lady Utterword, a blonde, is very handsome, very well dressed, and so precipitate in speech and action that the first impression (erroneous) is one of comic silliness.

LADY UTTERWORD. Oh, is that you, Nurse? How are you? You don't look a day older. Is nobody at home? Where is Hesione? Doesn't she expect me? Where are the servants? Whose luggage is that on the steps? Where's papa? Is everybody asleep? [*Seeing Ellie*]. Oh! I beg your pardon. I suppose you are one of my nieces. [*Approaching her with outstretched arms*]. Come and kiss your aunt, darling.

ELLIE. I'm only a visitor. It is my luggage on the steps.

NURSE GUINNESS. I'll go get you some fresh tea, ducky. [*She takes up the tray*].

ELLIE. But the old gentleman said he would make some himself.

NURSE GUINNESS. Bless you! he's forgotten what he went for already. His mind wanders from one thing to another.

LADY UTTERWORD. Papa, I suppose?

NURSE GUINNESS. Yes, Miss.

LADY UTTERWORD [*vehemently*]. Don't be silly, Nurse. Don't call me Miss.

NURSE GUINNESS [*placidly*]. No, lovey [*she goes out with the tea-tray*].

LADY UTTERWORD [*sitting down with a flounce on the sofa*]. I know what you must feel. Oh, this house, this house! I come back to it after twenty-three years; and it is just the same: the luggage lying on the steps, the servants spoilt and impossible, nobody at home to receive anybody, no regular meals, nobody ever hungry because they are always gnawing bread and butter or munching apples, and, what is worse, the same disorder in ideas, in talk, in feeling. When I was a child I was used to it: I had never known anything better, though I was unhappy, and longed all the time—oh, how I longed!—to be respectable, to be a lady, to live as others did, not to have to think of everything for myself. I married at nineteen to escape from it. My husband is Sir Hastings Utterword, who has been governor of all the crown colonies in succession. I have always been the mistress of Government House. I have been so happy: I had forgotten that people could live like this. I wanted to see my father, my sister, my nephews and nieces (one ought to, you know), and I was looking forward to it. And now the state of the house! the way I'm received! the casual impudence of that woman Guinness, our old nurse! really Hesione might at least have been here: some preparation might have been made for me. You must excuse my going on in this way; but I am really very much hurt and annoyed and disillusioned: and if I had realized it was to be like this, I wouldn't have come. I have a great mind to go away without another word [*she is on the point of weeping*].

ELLIE [*also very miserable*]. Nobody has been here to receive me either. I thought I ought to go away too. But how can I, Lady Utterword? My luggage is on the steps; and the station fly has gone.

The captain emerges from the pantry with a tray of Chinese lacquer and a very fine tea-set on it. He rests it provisionally on the end of the table; snatches away the drawing-board, which he stands on the floor against table legs; and puts the tray in the space thus cleared. Ellie pours out a cup greedily.

THE CAPTAIN. Your tea, young lady. What! another lady! I must fetch another cup [*he makes for the pantry*].

LADY UTTERWORD [*rising from the sofa, suffused with emotion*]. Papa! Don't you know me? I'm your daughter.

THE CAPTAIN. Nonsense! my daughter's upstairs asleep. [*He vanishes through the half door*].

Lady Utterword retires to the window to conceal her tears.

ELLIE [*going to her with the cup*]. Don't be so distressed. Have this cup of tea. He is very old and very strange: he has been just like that to me. I know how dreadful it must be: my own father is all the world to me. Oh, I'm sure he didn't mean it.

The captain returns with another cup.

THE CAPTAIN. Now we are complete. [*He places it on the tray*].

LADY UTTERWORD [*hysterically*]. Papa, you can't have forgotten me. I am Ariadne. I'm little Paddy Patkins. Won't you kiss me? [*She goes to him and throws her arms round his neck*].

THE CAPTAIN [*woodenly enduring her embrace*]. How can you be Ariadne? You are a middle-aged woman: well preserved, madam, but no longer young.

LADY UTTERWORD. But think of all the years and years I have been away, Papa. I have had to grow old, like other people.

THE CAPTAIN [*disengaging himself*]. You should grow out of kissing strange men: they may be striving to attain the seventh degree of concentration.

LADY UTTERWORD. But I'm your daughter. You haven't seen me for years.

THE CAPTAIN. So much the worse! When our relatives are at home, we have to think of all their good points or it would be impossible to endure them. But when they are away, we console ourselves for their absence by dwelling on their vices. That is how I have come to think my absent daughter Ariadne a perfect fiend; so do not try to ingratiate yourself here by impersonating her [*he walks firmly away to the other side of the room*].

LADY UTTERWORD. Ingratiating myself indeed! [*With dignity*]. Very well, papa. [*She sits down at the drawing-table and pours out tea for herself*].

THE CAPTAIN. I am neglecting my social duties. You remember Dunn? Billy Dunn?

LADY UTTERWORD. DO you mean that villainous sailor who robbed you?

THE CAPTAIN [*introducing Ellie*]. His daughter. [*He sits down on the sofa*].

ELLIE [*protesting*]. No—

Nurse Guinness returns with fresh tea.

THE CAPTAIN. Take that hogwash away. Do you hear?

NURSE. You've actually remembered about the tea! [*To Ellie*]. Oh, miss, he didn't forget you after all! You HAVE made an impression.

THE CAPTAIN [*gloomily*]. Youth! beauty! novelty! They are badly wanted in this house. I am excessively old. Hesione is only moderately young. Her children are not youthful.

LADY UTTERWORD. How can children be expected to be youthful in this house? Almost before we could speak we were filled with notions that might have been all very well for pagan philosophers of fifty, but were certainly quite unfit for respectable people of any age.

NURSE. You were always for respectability, Miss Addy.

LADY UTTERWORD. Nurse, will you please remember that I am Lady Utterword, and not Miss Addy, nor lovey, nor darling, nor doty? Do you hear?

NURSE. Yes, ducky: all right. I'll tell them all they must call you My Lady. [*She takes her tray out with undisturbed placidity*].

LADY UTTERWORD. What comfort? what sense is there in having servants with no manners?

ELLIE [*rising and coming to the table to put down her empty cup*]. Lady Utterword, do you think Mrs Hushabye really expects me?

LADY UTTERWORD. Oh, don't ask me. You can see for yourself that I've just arrived; her only sister, after twenty-three years' absence! and it seems that I am not expected.

THE CAPTAIN. What does it matter whether the young lady is expected or not? She is welcome. There are beds: there is food. I'll find a room for her myself [*he makes for the door*].

ELLIE [*following him to stop him*]. Oh, please— [*He goes out*]. Lady Utterword, I don't know what to do. Your father persists in believing that my father is some sailor who robbed him.

LADY UTTERWORD. You had better pretend not to notice it. My father is a very clever man; but he always forgot things; and now that he is old, of course he is worse. And I must warn you that it is sometimes very hard to feel quite sure that he really forgets.

Mrs Hushabye bursts into the room tempestuously and embraces Ellie. She is a couple of years older than Lady Utterword, and even better looking. She has magnificent black hair, eyes like the fishpools of Heshbon, and a nobly modelled neck, short at the back and low between her shoulders in front. Unlike her sister she is uncorseted and dressed anyhow in a rich robe of black pile that shows off her white skin and statuesque contour.

MRS HUSHABYE. Ellie, my darling, my pettikins [*kissing her*], how long have you been here? I've been at home all the time: I was putting flowers and things in your room; and when I just sat down for a moment to try how comfortable the armchair was I went off to sleep. Papa woke me and told me you were here. Fancy your finding no one, and being neglected and abandoned. [*Kissing her again*]. My poor love! [*She deposits Ellie on the sofa. Meanwhile Ariadne has left the table and come over to claim her share of attention*]. Oh! you've brought someone with you. Introduce me.

LADY UTTERWORD. Hesione, is it possible that you don't know me?

MRS HUSHABYE [*conventionally*]. Of course I remember your face quite well. Where have we met?

LADY UTTERWORD. Didn't Papa tell you I was here? Oh! this is really too much. [*She throws herself sulkily into the big chair*].

MRS HUSHABYE. Papa!

LADY UTTERWORD. Yes, Papa. Our papa, you unfeeling wretch! [*Rising angrily*]. I'll go straight to a hotel.

MRS HUSHABYE [*seizing her by the shoulders*]. My goodness gracious goodness, you don't mean to say that you're Addy!

LADY UTTERWORD. I certainly am Addy; and I don't think I can be so changed that you would not have recognized me if you had any real affection for me. And Papa didn't think me even worth mentioning!

MRS HUSHABYE. What a lark! Sit down [*she pushes her back into the chair instead of kissing her, and posts herself behind it*]. You DO look a swell. You're much handsomer than you used to be. You've made the acquaintance of Ellie, of course. She is going to marry a perfect hog of a millionaire for the sake of her father, who is as poor as a church mouse; and you must help me to stop her.

ELLIE. Oh, please, Hesione!

MRS HUSHABYE. My pettikins, the man's coming here today with your father to begin persecuting you; and everybody will see the state of the case in ten minutes; so what's the use of making a secret of it?

ELLIE. He is not a hog, Hesione. You don't know how wonderfully good he was to my father, and how deeply grateful I am to him.

MRS HUSHABYE [*to Lady Utterword*]. Her father is a very remarkable man, Addy. His name is Mazzini Dunn. Mazzini was a celebrity of some kind who knew Ellie's grandparents. They were both poets, like the Brownings; and when her father came into the world Mazzini said, "Another soldier born for freedom!" So they christened him Mazzini; and he has been fighting for freedom in his quiet way ever since. That's why he is so poor.

ELLIE. I am proud of his poverty.

MRS HUSHABYE. Of course you are, pettikins. Why not leave him in it, and marry someone you love?

LADY UTTERWORD [*rising suddenly and explosively*]. Hesione, are you going to kiss me or are you not?

MRS HUSHABYE. What do you want to be kissed for?

LADY UTTERWORD. I DON'T want to be kissed; but I do want you to behave properly and decently. We are sisters. We have been separated for twenty-three years. You OUGHT to kiss me.

MRS HUSHABYE. To-morrow morning, dear, before you make up. I hate the smell of powder.

LADY UTTERWORD. Oh! you unfeeling—[*she is interrupted by the return of the captain*].

THE CAPTAIN [*to Ellie*]. Your room is ready. [*Ellie rises*]. The sheets were damp; but I have changed them [*he makes for the garden door on the port side*].

LADY UTTERWORD. Oh! What about my sheets?

THE CAPTAIN [*halting at the door*]. Take my advice: air them: or take them off and sleep in blankets. You shall sleep in Ariadne's old room.

LADY UTTERWORD. Indeed I shall do nothing of the sort. That little hole! I am entitled to the best spare room.

THE CAPTAIN [*continuing unmoved*]. She married a numskull. She told me she would marry anyone to get away from home.

LADT UTTERWORD. You are pretending not to know me on purpose. I will leave the house.

Mazzini Dunn enters from the hall. He is a little elderly man with bulging credulous eyes and earnest manners. He is dressed in a blue serge jacket suit with an unbuttoned mackintosh over it, and carries a soft black hat of clerical cut.

ELLIE. At last! Captain Shotover, here is my father.

THE CAPTAIN. This! Nonsense! not a bit like him [*he goes away through the garden, shutting the door sharply behind him*].

LADY UTTERWORD. I will not be ignored and pretended to be somebody else. I will have it out with Papa now, this instant. [*To Mazzini*]. Excuse me. [*She follows the captain out, making a hasty bow to Mazzini, who returns it*].

MRS HUSHABYE [*hospitably shaking hands*]. How good of you to come, Mr Dunn! You don't mind Papa, do you? He is as mad as a hatter, you know, but quite harmless and extremely clever. You will have some delightful talks with him.

MAZZINI. I hope so. [*To Ellie*]. So here you are, Ellie, dear. [*He draws her arm affectionately through his*]. I must thank you, Mrs Hushabye, for your kindness to my daughter. I'm afraid she would have had no holiday if you had not invited her.

MRS HUSHABYE. Not at all. Very nice of her to come and attract young people to the house for us.

MAZZINI [*smiling*]. I'm afraid Ellie is not interested in young men, Mrs Hushabye. Her taste is on the graver, solider side.

MRS HUSHABYE [*with a sudden rather hard brightness in her manner*]. Won't you take off your overcoat, Mr Dunn? You will find a cupboard for coats and hats and things in the corner of the hall.

MAZZINI [*hastily releasing Ellie*]. Yes—thank you—I had better— [*he goes out*].

MRS HUSHABYE [*emphatically*]. The old brute!

ELLIE. Who?

MRS HUSHABYE. Who! Him. He. It [*pointing after Mazzini*]. "Graver, solider tastes," indeed!

ELLIE [*aghast*]. You don't mean that you were speaking like that of my father!

MRS HUSHABYE. I was. You know I was.

ELLIE [*with dignity*]. I will leave your house at once. [*She turns to the door*].

MRS HUSHABYE. If you attempt it, I'll tell your father why.

ELLIE [*turning again*]. Oh! How can you treat a visitor like this, Mrs Hushabye?

MRS HUSHABYE. I thought you were going to call me Hesione.

ELLIE. Certainly not now?

MRS HUSHABYE. Very well: I'll tell your father.

ELLIE [*distressed*]. Oh!

MRS HUSHABYE. If you turn a hair—if you take his part against me and against your own heart for a moment, I'll give that born soldier of freedom a piece of my mind that will stand him on his selfish old head for a week.

ELLIE. Hesione! My father selfish! How little you know—

She is interrupted by Mazzini, who returns, excited and perspiring.

MAZZINI. Ellie, Mangan has come: I thought you'd like to know. Excuse me, Mrs Hushabye, the strange old gentleman—

MRS HUSHABYE. Papa. Quite so.

MAZZINI. Oh, I beg your pardon, of course: I was a little confused by his manner. He is making Mangan help him with something in the garden; and he wants me too—

A powerful whistle is heard.

THE CAPTAIN'S VOICE. Bosun ahoy! [*the whistle is repeated*].

MAZZINI [*flustered*]. Oh dear! I believe he is whistling for me. [*He hurries out*].

MRS HUSHABYE. Now MY father is a wonderful man if you like.

ELLIE. Hesione, listen to me. You don't understand. My father and Mr Mangan were boys together. Mr Ma—

MRS HUSHABYE. I don't care what they were: we must sit down if you are going to begin as far back as that. [*She snatches at Ellie's waist, and makes her sit down on the sofa beside her*]. Now, pettikins, tell me all about Mr Mangan. They call him Boss Mangan, don't they? He is a Napoleon of industry and disgustingly rich, isn't he? Why isn't your father rich?

ELLIE. My poor father should never have been in business. His parents were poets; and they gave him the noblest ideas; but they could not afford to give him a profession.

MRS HUSHABYE. Fancy your grandparents, with their eyes in fine frenzy rolling! And so your poor father had to go into business. Hasn't he succeeded in it?

ELLIE. He always used to say he could succeed if he only had some capital. He fought his way along, to keep a roof over our heads and bring us up well; but it was always a struggle: always the same difficulty of not having capital enough. I don't know how to describe it to you.

MRS HUSHABYE. Poor Ellie! I know. Pulling the devil by the tail.

ELLIE [*hurt*]. Oh, no. Not like that. It was at least dignified.

MRS HUSHABYE. That made it all the harder, didn't it? I shouldn't have pulled the devil by the tail with dignity. I should have pulled hard—[*between her teeth*] hard. Well? Go on.

ELLIE. At last it seemed that all our troubles were at an end. Mr Mangan did an extraordinarily noble thing out of pure friendship for my father and respect for his character. He asked him how much capital he wanted, and gave it to him. I don't mean that he lent it to him, or that he invested it in his business. He just simply made him a present of it. Wasn't that splendid of him?

MRS HUSHABYE. On condition that you married him?

ELLIE. Oh, no, no, no! This was when I was a child. He had never even seen me: he never came to our house. It was absolutely disinterested. Pure generosity.

MRS HUSHABYE. Oh! I beg the gentleman's pardon. Well, what became of the money?

ELLIE. We all got new clothes and moved into another house. And I went to another school for two years.

MRS HUSHABYE. Only two years?

ELLIE. That was all: for at the end of two years my father was utterly ruined.

MRS HUSHABYE. How?

ELLIE. I don't know. I never could understand. But it was dreadful. When we were poor my father had never been in debt. But when he launched out into business on a large scale, he had to incur liabilities. When the business went into liquidation he owed more money than Mr Mangan had given him.

MRS HUSHABYE. Bit off more than he could chew, I suppose.

ELLIE. I think you are a little unfeeling about it.

MRS HUSHABYE. My pettikins, you mustn't mind my way of talking. I was quite as sensitive and particular as you once; but I have picked up so much slang from the children that I am really hardly presentable. I suppose your father had no head for business, and made a mess of it.

ELLIE. Oh, that just shows how entirely you are mistaken about him. The business turned out a great success. It now pays forty-four per cent after deducting the excess profits tax.

MRS HUSHABYE. Then why aren't you rolling in money?

ELLIE. I don't know. It seems very unfair to me. You see, my father was made bankrupt. It nearly broke his heart, because he had persuaded several of his friends to put money into the business. He was sure it would succeed; and events proved that he was quite right. But they all lost their money. It was dreadful. I don't know what we should have done but for Mr Mangan.

MRS HUSHABYE. What! Did the Boss come to the rescue again, after all his money being thrown away?

ELLIE. He did indeed, and never uttered a reproach to my father. He bought what was left of the business—the buildings and the machinery and things—from the official trustee for enough money to enable my father to pay six-and-eight-pence in the pound and get his discharge. Everyone pitied Papa so much, and saw so plainly that he was an honorable man, that they let him off at six-and-eight-pence instead of ten shillings. Then Mr. Mangan started a company to take up the business, and made my father a manager in it to save us from starvation; for I wasn't earning anything then.

MRS. HUSHABYE. Quite a romance. And when did the Boss develop the tender passion?

ELLIE. Oh, that was years after, quite lately. He took the chair one night at a sort of people's concert. I was singing there. As an amateur, you know: half a guinea for expenses and three songs with three encores. He was so pleased with my singing that he asked might he walk home with me. I never saw anyone so taken aback as he was when I took him home and introduced him to my father, his own manager. It was then that my father told me how nobly he had behaved. Of course it was considered a great chance for me, as he is so rich. And—and—we drifted into a sort of understanding—I suppose I should call it an engagement—[*she is distressed and cannot go on*].

MRS HUSHABYE [*rising and marching about*]. You may have drifted into it; but you will bounce out of it, my pettikins, if I am to have anything to do with it.

ELLIE [*hopelessly*]. No: it's no use. I am bound in honor and gratitude. I will go through with it.

MRS HUSHABYE [*behind the sofa, scolding down at her*]. You know, of course, that it's not honorable or grateful to marry a man you don't love. Do you love this Mangan man?

ELLIE. Yes. At least—

MRS HUSHABYE. I don't want to know about "at least": I want to know the worst. Girls of your age fall in love with all sorts of impossible people, especially old people.

ELLIE. I like Mr Mangan very much; and I shall always be—

MRS HUSHABYE [*impatiently completing the sentence and prancing away intolerantly to starboard*]. —grateful to him for his kindness to dear father. I know. Anybody else?

ELLIE. What do you mean?

MRS HUSHABYE. Anybody else? Are you in love with anybody else?

ELLIE. Of course not.

MRS HUSHABYE. Humph! [*The book on the drawing-table catches her eye. She picks it up, and evidently finds the title very unexpected. She looks at Ellie, and asks, quaintly*] Quite sure you're not in love with an actor?

ELLIE. No, no. Why? What put such a thing into your head?

MRS HUSHABYE. This is yours, isn't it? Why else should you be reading Othello?

ELLIE. My father taught me to love Shakespeare.

MRS HUSHAYE [*flinging the book down on the table*]. Really! your father does seem to be about the limit.

ELLIE [*naively*]. Do you never read Shakespeare, Hesione? That seems to me so extraordinary. I like Othello.

MRS HUSHABYE. Do you, indeed? He was jealous, wasn't he?

ELLIE. Oh, not that. I think all the part about jealousy is horrible. But don't you think it must have been a wonderful experience for Desdemona, brought up so quietly at home, to meet a man who had been out in the world doing all sorts of brave things and having terrible adventures, and yet finding something in her that made him love to sit and talk with her and tell her about them?

MRS HUSHABYE. That's your idea of romance, is it?

ELLIE. Not romance, exactly. It might really happen.

Ellie's eyes show that she is not arguing, but in a daydream. Mrs Hushabye, watching her inquisitively, goes deliberately back to the sofa and resumes her seat beside her.

MRS HUSHABYE. Ellie darling, have you noticed that some of those stories that Othello told Desdemona couldn't have happened—?

ELLIE. Oh, no. Shakespeare thought they could have happened.

MRS HUSHABYE. Hm! Desdemona thought they could have happened. But they didn't.

ELLIE. Why do you look so enigmatic about it? You are such a sphinx: I never know what you mean.

MRS HUSHABYE. Desdemona would have found him out if she had lived, you know. I wonder was that why he strangled her!

ELLIE. Othello was not telling lies.

MRS HUSHABYE. How do you know?

ELLIE. Shakespeare would have said if he was. Hesione, there are men who have done wonderful things: men like Othello, only, of course, white, and very handsome, and—

MRS HUSHABYE. Ah! Now we're coming to it. Tell me all about him. I knew there must be somebody, or you'd never have been so miserable about Mangan: you'd have thought it quite a lark to marry him.

ELLIE [*blushing vividly*]. Hesione, you are dreadful. But I don't want to make a secret of it, though of course I don't tell everybody. Besides, I don't know him.

MRS HUSHABYE. Don't know him! What does that mean?

ELLIE. Well, of course I know him to speak to.

MRS HUSHABYE. But you want to know him ever so much more intimately, eh?

ELLIE. No, no: I know him quite—almost intimately.

MRS HUSHABYE. You don't know him; and you know him almost intimately. How lucid!

ELLIE. I mean that he does not call on us. I—I got into conversation with him by chance at a concert.

MRS HUSHABYE. You seem to have rather a gay time at your concerts, Ellie.

ELLIE. Not at all: we talk to everyone in the greenroom waiting for our turns. I thought he was one of the artists: he looked so splendid. But he was only one of the committee. I happened to tell him that I was copying a picture at the National Gallery. I make a little money that way. I can't paint much; but as it's always the same picture I can do it pretty quickly and get two or three pounds for it. It happened that he came to the National Gallery one day.

MRS HUSHABYE. One students' day. Paid sixpence to stumble about through a crowd of easels, when he might have come in next day for nothing and found the floor clear! Quite by accident?

ELLIE [*triumphantly*]. No. On purpose. He liked talking to me. He knows lots of the most splendid people. Fashionable women who are all in love with him. But he ran away from them to see me at the National Gallery and persuade me to come with him for a drive round Richmond Park in a taxi.

MRS HUSHABYE. My pettikins, you have been going it. It's wonderful what you good girls can do without anyone saying a word.

ELLIE. I am not in society, Hesione. If I didn't make acquaintances in that way I shouldn't have any at all.

MRS HUSHABYE. Well, no harm if you know how to take care of yourself. May I ask his name?

ELLIE [*slowly and musically*]. Marcus Darnley.

MRS HUSHABYE [*echoing the music*]. Marcus Darnley! What a splendid name!

ELLIE. Oh, I'm so glad you think so. I think so too; but I was afraid it was only a silly fancy of my own.

MRS HUSHABYE. Hm! Is he one of the Aberdeen Darnleys?

ELLIE. Nobody knows. Just fancy! He was found in an antique chest—

MRS HUSHABYE. A what?

ELLIE. An antique chest, one summer morning in a rose garden, after a night of the most terrible thunderstorm.

MRS HUSHABYE. What on earth was he doing in the chest? Did he get into it because he was afraid of the lightning?

ELLIE. Oh, no, no: he was a baby. The name Marcus Darnley was embroidered on his baby clothes. And five hundred pounds in gold.

MRS HUSHABYE [*Looking hard at her*]. Ellie!

ELLIE. The garden of the Viscount—

MRS HUSHABYE. —de Rougemont?

ELLIE [*innocently*]. No: de Larochejaquelin. A French family. A vicomte. His life has been one long romance. A tiger—

MRS HUSHABYE. Slain by his own hand?

ELLIE. Oh, no: nothing vulgar like that. He saved the life of the tiger from a hunting party: one of King Edward's hunting parties in India. The King was furious: that was why he never had his military services properly recognized. But he doesn't care. He is a Socialist and despises rank, and has been in three revolutions fighting on the barricades.

MRS HUSHABYE. How can you sit there telling me such lies? You, Ellie, of all people! And I thought you were a perfectly simple, straightforward, good girl.

ELLIE [*rising, dignified but very angry*]. Do you mean you don't believe me?

MRS HUSHABYE. Of course I don't believe you. You're inventing every word of it. Do you take me for a fool?

Ellie stares at her. Her candor is so obvious that Mrs Hushabye is puzzled.

ELLIE. Goodbye, Hesione. I'm very sorry. I see now that it sounds very improbable as I tell it. But I can't stay if you think that way about me.

MRS HUSHABYE [*catching her dress*]. You shan't go. I couldn't be so mistaken: I know too well what liars are like. Somebody has really told you all this.

ELLIE [*flushing*]. Hesione, don't say that you don't believe him. I couldn't bear that.

MRS HUSHABYE [*soothing her*]. Of course I believe him, dearest. But you should have broken it to me by degrees. [*Drawing her back to her seat*]. Now tell me all about him. Are you in love with him?

ELLIE. Oh, no. I'm not so foolish. I don't fall in love with people. I'm not so silly as you think.

MRS HUSHABYE. I see. Only something to think about—to give some interest and pleasure to life.

ELLIE. Just so. That's all, really.

MRS HUSHABYE. It makes the hours go fast, doesn't it? No tedious waiting to go to sleep at nights and wondering whether you will have a bad night. How delightful it makes waking up in the morning! How much better than the happiest dream! All life transfigured! No more wishing one had an interesting book to read, because life is so much happier than any book! No desire but to be alone and not to have to talk to anyone: to be alone and just think about it.

ELLIE [*embracing her*]. Hesione, you are a witch. How do you know? Oh, you are the most sympathetic woman in the world!

MRS HUSHABYE [*caressing her*]. Pettikins, my pettikins, how I envy you! and how I pity you!

ELLIE. Pity me! Oh, why?

A very handsome man of fifty, with mousquetaire moustaches, wearing a rather dandified curly brimmed hat, and carrying an elaborate walking-stick, comes into the room from the hall, and stops short at sight of the women on the sofa.

ELLIE [*seeing him and rising in glad surprise*]. Oh! Hesione: this is Mr Marcus Darnley.

MRS HUSHABYE [*rising*]. What a lark! He is my husband.

ELLIE. But now—[*she stops suddenly: then turns pale and sways*].

MRS HUSHABYE [*catching her and sitting down with her on the sofa*]. Steady, my pettikins.

THE MAN [*with a mixture of confusion and effrontery, depositing his hat and stick on the teak table*]. My real name, Miss Dunn, is Hector Hushabye. I leave you to judge whether that is a name any sensitive man would care to confess to. I never use it when I can possibly help it. I have been away for nearly a month; and I had no idea you knew my wife, or that you were coming here. I am none the less delighted to find you in our little house.

ELLIE [*in great distress*]. I don't know what to do. Please, may I speak to papa? Do leave me. I can't bear it.

MRS HUSHABYE. Be off, Hector.

HECTOR. I— MRS HUSHABYE. Quick, quick. Get out.

HECTOR. If you think it better—[*he goes out, taking his hat with him but leaving the stick on the table*].

MRS HUSHABYE [*laying Ellie down at the end of the sofa*]. Now, pettikins, he is gone. There's nobody but me. You can let yourself go. Don't try to control yourself. Have a good cry.

ELLIE [*raising her head*]. Damn!

MRS HUSHABYE. Splendid! Oh, what a relief! I thought you were going to be broken-hearted. Never mind me. Damn him again.

ELLIE. I am not damning him. I am damning myself for being such a fool. [*Rising*]. How could I let myself be taken in so? [*She begins prowling to and fro, her bloom gone, looking curiously older and harder*].

MRS HUSHABYE [*cheerfully*]. Why not, pettikins? Very few young women can resist Hector. I couldn't when I was your age. He is really rather splendid, you know.

ELLIE [*turning on her*]. Splendid! Yes, splendid looking, of course. But how can you love a liar?

MRS HUSHABYE. I don't know. But you can, fortunately. Otherwise there wouldn't be much love in the world.

ELLIE. But to lie like that! To be a boaster! a coward!

MRS HUSHABYE [*rising in alarm*]. Pettikins, none of that, if you please. If you hint the slightest doubt of Hector's courage, he will go straight off and do the most horribly dangerous things to convince himself that he isn't a coward. He has a dreadful trick of getting out of one third-floor window and coming in at another, just to test his nerve. He has a whole drawerful of Albert Medals for saving people's lives.

ELLIE. He never told me that.

MRS HUSHABYE. He never boasts of anything he really did: he can't bear it; and it makes him shy if anyone else does. All his stories are made-up stories.

ELLIE [*coming to her*]. Do you mean that he is really brave, and really has adventures, and yet tells lies about things that he never did and that never happened?

MRS HUSHABYE. Yes, pettikins, I do. People don't have their virtues and vices in sets: they have them anyhow: all mixed.

ELLIE [*staring at her thoughtfully*]. There's something odd about this house, Hesione, and even about you. I don't know why I'm talking to you so calmly. I have a horrible fear that my heart is broken, but that heartbreak is not like what I thought it must be.

MRS HUSHABYE [*fondling her*]. It's only life educating you, pettikins. How do you feel about Boss Mangan now?

ELLIE [*disengaging herself with an expression of distaste*]. Oh, how can you remind me of him, Hesione?

MRS HUSHABYE. Sorry, dear. I think I hear Hector coming back. You don't mind now, do you, dear?

ELLIE. Not in the least. I am quite cured.

Mazzini Dunn and Hector come in from the hall.

HECTOR [*as he opens the door and allows Mazzini to pass in*]. One second more, and she would have been a dead woman!

MAZZINI. Dear! dear! what an escape! Ellie, my love, Mr Hushabye has just been telling me the most extraordinary—

ELLIE. Yes, I've heard it [*she crosses to the other side of the room*].

HECTOR [*following her*]. Not this one: I'll tell it to you after dinner. I think you'll like it. The truth is I made it up for you, and was looking forward to the pleasure of telling it to you. But in a moment of impatience at being turned out of the room, I threw it away on your father.

ELLIE [*turning at bay with her back to the carpenter's bench, scornfully self-possessed*]. It was not thrown away. He believes it. I should not have believed it.

MAZZINI [*benevolently*]. Ellie is very naughty, Mr Hushabye. Of course she does not really think that. [*He goes to the bookshelves, and inspects the titles of the volumes*].

Boss Mangan comes in from the hall, followed by the captain. Mangan, carefully frock-coated as for church or for a diHECTORs' meeting, is about fifty-five, with a careworn, mistrustful expression, standing a little on an entirely imaginary dignity, with a dull complexion, straight, lustreless hair, and features so entirely commonplace that it is impossible to describe them.

CAPTAIN SHOTOVER [*to Mrs Hushabye, introducing the newcomer*]. Says his name is Mangan. Not able-bodied.

MRS HUSHABYE [*graciously*]. How do you do, Mr Mangan?

MANGAN [*shaking hands*]. Very pleased.

CAPTAIN SHOTOVER. Dunn's lost his muscle, but recovered his nerve. Men seldom do after three attacks of delirium tremens [*he goes into the pantry*].

MRS HUSHABYE. I congratulate you, Mr Dunn.

MAZZINI [*dazed*]. I am a lifelong teetotaler.

MRS HUSHABYE. You will find it far less trouble to let papa have his own way than try to explain.

MAZZINI. But three attacks of delirium tremens, really!

MRS HUSHABYE [*to Mangan*]. Do you know my husband, Mr Mangan [*she indicates Hector*].

MANGAN [*going to Hector, who meets him with outstretched hand*]. Very pleased. [*Turning to Ellie*]. I hope, Miss Ellie, you have not found the journey down too fatiguing. [*They shake hands*].

MRS HUSHABYE. Hector, show Mr Dunn his room.

HECTOR. Certainly. Come along, Mr Dunn. [*He takes Mazzini out*].

ELLIE. You haven't shown me my room yet, Hesione.

MRS HUSHABYE. How stupid of me! Come along. Make yourself quite at home, Mr Mangan. Papa will entertain you. [*She calls to the captain in the pantry*]. Papa, come and explain the house to Mr Mangan.

She goes out with Ellie. The captain comes from the pantry.

CAPTAIN SHOTOVER. You're going to marry Dunn's daughter. Don't. You're too old.

MANGAN [*staggered*]. Well! That's fairly blunt, Captain.

CAPTAIN SHOTOVER. It's true.

MANGAN. She doesn't think so.

CAPTAIN SHOTOVER. She does.

MANGAN. Older men than I have—

CAPTAIN SHOTOVER [*finishing the sentence for him*].—made fools of themselves. That, also, is true.

MANGAN [*asserting himself*]. I don't see that this is any business of yours.

CAPTAIN SHOTOVER. It is everybody's business. The stars in their courses are shaken when such things happen.

MANGAN. I'm going to marry her all the same.

CAPTAIN SHOTOVER. How do you know?

MANGAN [*playing the strong man*]. I intend to. I mean to. See? I never made up my mind to do a thing yet that I didn't bring it off. That's the sort of man I am; and there will be a better understanding between us when you make up your mind to that, Captain.

CAPTAIN SHOTOVER. You frequent picture palaces.

MANGAN. Perhaps I do. Who told you?

CAPTAIN SHOTOVER. Talk like a man, not like a movie. You mean that you make a hundred thousand a year.

MANGAN. I don't boast. But when I meet a man that makes a hundred thousand a year, I take off my hat to that man, and stretch out my hand to him and call him brother.

CAPTAIN SHOTOVER. Then you also make a hundred thousand a year, hey?

MANGAN. No. I can't say that. Fifty thousand, perhaps.

CAPTAIN SHOTOVER. His half brother only [*he turns away from Mangan with his usual abruptness, and collects the empty tea-cups on the Chinese tray*].

MANGAN [*irritated*]. See here, Captain Shotover. I don't quite understand my position here. I came here on your daughter's invitation. Am I in her house or in yours?

CAPTAIN SHOTOVER. You are beneath the dome of heaven, in the house of God. What is true within these walls is true outside them. Go out on the seas; climb the mountains; wander through the valleys. She is still too young.

MANGAN [*weakening*]. But I'm very little over fifty.

CAPTAIN SHOTOVER. You are still less under sixty. Boss Mangan, you will not marry the pirate's child [*he carries the tray away into the pantry*].

MANGAN [*following him to the half door*]. What pirate's child? What are you talking about?

CAPTAIN SHOTOVER [*in the pantry*]. Ellie Dunn. You will not marry her.

MANGAN. Who will stop me?

CAPTAIN SHOTOVER [*emerging*]. My daughter [*he makes for the door leading to the hall*].

MANGAN [*following him*]. Mrs Hushabye! Do you mean to say she brought me down here to break it off?

CAPTAIN SHOTOVER [*stopping and turning on him*]. I know nothing more than I have seen in her eye. She will break it off. Take my advice: marry a West Indian negress: they make excellent wives. I was married to one myself for two years.

MANGAN. Well, I am damned!

CAPTAIN SHOTOVER. I thought so. I was, too, for many years. The negress redeemed me.

MANGAN [*feebly*]. This is queer. I ought to walk out of this house.

CAPTAIN SHOTOVER. Why?

MANGAN. Well, many men would be offended by your style of talking.

CAPTAIN SHOTOVER. Nonsense! It's the other sort of talking that makes quarrels. Nobody ever quarrels with me.

A gentleman, whose first-rate tailoring and frictionless manners proclaim the wellbred West Ender, comes in from the hall. He has an engaging air of being young and unmarried, but on close inspection is found to be at least over forty.

THE GENTLEMAN. Excuse my intruding in this fashion, but there is no knocker on the door and the bell does not seem to ring.

CAPTAIN SHOTOVER. Why should there be a knocker? Why should the bell ring? The door is open.

THE GENTLEMAN. Precisely. So I ventured to come in.

CAPTAIN SHOTOVER. Quite right. I will see about a room for you [*he makes for the door*].

THE GENTLEMAN [*stopping him*]. But I'm afraid you don't know who I am.

CAPTAIN SHOTOVER. DO you suppose that at my age I make distinctions between one fellow creature and another? [*He goes out. Mangan and the newcomer stare at one another*].

MANGAN. Strange character, Captain Shotover, sir.

THE GENTLEMAN. Very.

CAPTAIN SHOTOVER [*shouting outside*]. Hesione, another person has arrived and wants a room. Man about town, well dressed, fifty.

THE GENTLEMAN. Fancy Hesione's feelings! May I ask are you a member of the family?

MANGAN. No.

THE GENTLEMAN. I am. At least a connection.

Mrs Hushabye comes back.

MRS HUSHABYE. How do you do? How good of you to come!

THE GENTLEMAN. I am very glad indeed to make your acquaintance, Hesione. [*Instead of taking her hand he kisses her. At the same moment the captain appears in the doorway*]. You will excuse my kissing your daughter, Captain, when I tell you that—

CAPTAIN SHOTOVER. Stuff! Everyone kisses my daughter. Kiss her as much as you like [*he makes for the pantry*].

THE GENTLEMAN. Thank you. One moment, Captain. [*The captain halts and turns. The gentleman goes to him affably*]. Do you happen to remember but probably you don't, as it occurred many years ago— that your younger daughter married a numskull?

CAPTAIN SHOTOVER. Yes. She said she'd marry anybody to get away from this house. I should not have recognized you: your head is no longer like a walnut. Your aspect is softened. You have been boiled in bread and milk for years and years, like other married men. Poor devil! [*He disappears into the pantry*].

MRS HUSHABYE [*going past Mangan to the gentleman and scrutinizing him*]. I don't believe you are Hastings Utterword.

THE GENTLEMAN. I am not.

MRS HUSHABYE. Then what business had you to kiss me?

THE GENTLEMAN. I thought I would like to. The fact is, I am Randall Utterword, the unworthy younger brother of Hastings. I was abroad diplomatizing when he was married.

LADY UTTERWORD [*dashing in*]. Hesione, where is the key of the wardrobe in my room? My diamonds are in my dressing-bag: I must lock it up—[*recognizing the stranger with a shock*] Randall, how dare you? [*She marches at him past Mrs Hushabye, who retreats and joins Mangan near the sofa*].

RANDALL. How dare I what? I am not doing anything.

LADY UTTERWORD. Who told you I was here?

RANDALL. Hastings. You had just left when I called on you at Claridge's; so I followed you down here. You are looking extremely well.

LADY UTTERWORD. Don't presume to tell me so.

MRS HUSHABYE. What is wrong with Mr Randall, Addy?

LADY UTTERWORD [*recollecting herself*]. Oh, nothing. But he has no right to come bothering you and papa without being invited [*she goes to the window-seat and sits down, turning away from them ill-humoredly and looking into the garden, where Hector and Ellie are now seen strolling together*].

MRS HUSHABYE. I think you have not met Mr Mangan, Addy.

LADY UTTERWORD [*turning her head and nodding coldly to Mangan*]. I beg your pardon. Randall, you have flustered me so: I make a perfect fool of myself.

MRS HUSHABYE. Lady Utterword. My sister. My younger sister.

MANGAN [*bowing*]. Pleased to meet you, Lady Utterword.

LADY UTTERWORD [*with marked interest*]. Who is that gentleman walking in the garden with Miss Dunn?

MRS HUSHABYE. I don't know. She quarrelled mortally with my husband only ten minutes ago; and I didn't know anyone else had come. It must be a visitor. [*She goes to the window to look*]. Oh, it is Hector. They've made it up.

LADY UTTERWORD. Your husband! That handsome man?

MRS HUSHABYE. Well, why shouldn't my husband be a handsome man?

RANDALL [*joining them at the window*]. One's husband never is, Ariadne [*he sits by Lady Utterword, on her right*].

MRS HUSHABYE. One's sister's husband always is, Mr Randall.

LADY UTTERWORD. Don't be vulgar, Randall. And you, Hesione, are just as bad.

Ellie and Hector come in from the garden by the starboard door. Randall rises. Ellie retires into the corner near the pantry. Hector comes forward; and Lady Utterword rises looking her very best.

MRS. HUSHABYE. Hector, this is Addy.

HECTOR [*apparently surprised*]. Not this lady.

LADY UTTERWORD [*smiling*]. Why not?

HECTOR [*looking at her with a piercing glance of deep but respectful admiration, his moustache bristling*]. I thought— [*pulling himself together*]. I beg your pardon, Lady Utterword. I am extremely glad to welcome you at last under our roof [*he offers his hand with grave courtesy*].

MRS HUSHABYE. She wants to be kissed, Hector.

LADY UTTERWORD. Hesione! [*But she still smiles*].

MRS HUSHABYE. Call her Addy; and kiss her like a good brother-in-law; and have done with it. [*She leaves them to themselves*].

HECTOR. Behave yourself, Hesione. Lady Utterword is entitled not only to hospitality but to civilization.

LADY UTTERWORD [*gratefully*]. Thank you, Hector. [*They shake hands cordially*].

Mazzini Dunn is seen crossing the garden from starboard to port.

CAPTAIN SHOTOVER [*coming from the pantry and addressing Ellie*]. Your father has washed himself.

ELLIE [*quite self-possessed*]. He often does, Captain Shotover.

CAPTAIN SHOTOVER. A strange conversion! I saw him through the pantry window.

Mazzini Dunn enters through the port window door, newly washed and brushed, and stops, smiling benevolently, between Mangan and Mrs Hushabye.

MRS HUSHABYE [*introducing*]. Mr Mazzini Dunn, Lady Ut—oh, I forgot: you've met. [*Indicating Ellie*] Miss Dunn.

MAZZINI [*walking across the room to take Ellie's hand, and beaming at his own naughty irony*]. I have met Miss Dunn also. She is my daughter. [*He draws her arm through his caressingly*].

MRS HUSHABYE. Of course: how stupid! Mr Utterword, my sister's—er—

RANDALL [*shaking hands agreeably*]. Her brother-in-law, Mr Dunn. How do you do?

MRS HUSHABYE. This is my husband.

HECTOR. We have met, dear. Don't introduce us any more. [*He moves away to the big chair, and adds*] Won't you sit down, Lady Utterword? [*She does so very graciously*].

MRS HUSHABYE. Sorry. I hate it: it's like making people show their tickets.

MAZZINI [*sententiously*]. How little it tells us, after all! The great question is, not who we are, but what we are.

CAPTAIN SHOTOVER. Ha! What are you?

MAZZINI [*taken aback*]. What am I?

CAPTAIN SHOTOVER. A thief, a pirate, and a murderer.

MAZZINI. I assure you you are mistaken.

CAPTAIN SHOTOVER. An adventurous life; but what does it end in? Respectability. A ladylike daughter. The language and appearance of a city missionary. Let it be a warning to all of you [*he goes out through the garden*].

DUNN. I hope nobody here believes that I am a thief, a pirate, or a murderer. Mrs Hushabye, will you excuse me a moment? I must really go and explain. [*He follows the captain*].

MRS HUSHABYE [*as he goes*]. It's no use. You'd really better— [*but Dunn has vanished*]. We had better all go out and look for some tea. We never have regular tea; but you can always get some when you want: the servants keep it stewing all day. The kitchen veranda is the best place to ask. May I show you? [*She goes to the starboard door*].

RANDALL [*going with her*]. Thank you, I don't think I'll take any tea this afternoon. But if you will show me the garden—

MRS HUSHABYE. There's nothing to see in the garden except papa's observatory, and a gravel pit with a cave where he keeps dynamite and things of that sort. However, it's pleasanter out of doors; so come along.

RANDALL. Dynamite! Isn't that rather risky?

MRS HUSHABYE. Well, we don't sit in the gravel pit when there's a thunderstorm.

LADY UTTERORRD. That's something new. What is the dynamite for?

HECTOR. To blow up the human race if it goes too far. He is trying to discover a psychic ray that will explode all the explosive at the well of a Mahatma.

ELLIE. The captain's tea is delicious, Mr Utterword.

MRS HUSHABYE [*stopping in the doorway*]. Do you mean to say that you've had some of my father's tea? that you got round him before you were ten minutes in the house?

ELLIE. I did.

MRS HUSHABYE. You little devil! [*She goes out with Randall*].

MANGAN. Won't you come, Miss Ellie?

ELLIE. I'm too tired. I'll take a book up to my room and rest a little. [*She goes to the bookshelf*].

MANGAN. Right. You can't do better. But I'm disappointed. [*He follows Randall and Mrs Hushabye*].

Ellie, Hector, and Lady Utterword are left. Hector is close to Lady Utterword. They look at Ellie, waiting for her to go.

ELLIE [*looking at the title of a book*]. Do you like stories of adventure, Lady Utterword?

LADY UTTERWORD [*patronizingly*]. Of course, dear.

ELLIE. Then I'll leave you to Mr Hushabye. [*She goes out through the hall*].

HECTOR. That girl is mad about tales of adventure. The lies I have to tell her!

LADY UTTERWORD [*not interested in Ellie*]. When you saw me what did you mean by saying that you thought, and then stopping short? What did you think?

HECTOR [*folding his arms and looking down at her magnetically*]. May I tell you?

LADY UTTERWORD. Of course.

HECTOR. It will not sound very civil. I was on the point of saying, "I thought you were a plain woman."

LADY UTTERWORD. Oh, for shame, Hector! What right had you to notice whether I am plain or not?

HECTOR. Listen to me, Ariadne. Until today I have seen only photographs of you; and no photograph can give the strange fascination of the daughters of that supernatural old man. There is some damnable quality in them that destroys men's moral sense, and carries them beyond honor and dishonor. You know that, don't you?

LADY UTTERWORD. Perhaps I do, Hector. But let me warn you once for all that I am a rigidly conventional woman. You may think because I'm a Shotover that I'm a Bohemian, because we are all so horribly Bohemian. But I'm not. I hate and loathe Bohemianism. No child brought up in a strict Puritan household ever suffered from Puritanism as I suffered from our Bohemianism.

HECTOR. Our children are like that. They spend their holidays in the houses of their respectable schoolfellows.

LADY UTTERWORD. I shall invite them for Christmas.

HECTOR. Their absence leaves us both without our natural chaperones.

LADY UTTERWORD. Children are certainly very inconvenient sometimes. But intelligent people can always manage, unless they are Bohemians.

HECTOR. You are no Bohemian; but you are no Puritan either: your attraction is alive and powerful. What sort of woman do you count yourself?

LADY UTTERWORD. I am a woman of the world, Hector; and I can assure you that if you will only take the trouble always to do the perfectly correct thing, and to say the perfectly correct thing, you can do just what you like. An ill-conducted, careless woman gets simply no chance. An ill-conducted, careless man is never allowed within arm's length of any woman worth knowing.

HECTOR. I see. You are neither a Bohemian woman nor a Puritan woman. You are a dangerous woman.

LADY UTTERWORD. On the contrary, I am a safe woman.

HECTOR. You are a most accursedly attractive woman. Mind, I am not making love to you. I do not like being attracted. But you had better know how I feel if you are going to stay here.

LADY UTTERWORD. You are an exceedingly clever lady-killer, Hector. And terribly handsome. I am quite a good player, myself, at that game. Is it quite understood that we are only playing?

HECTOR. Quite. I am deliberately playing the fool, out of sheer worthlessness.

LADY UTTERWORD [*rising brightly*]. Well, you are my brother-in-law, Hesione asked you to kiss me. [*He seizes her in his arms and kisses her strenuously*]. Oh! that was a little more than play, brother-in-law. [*She pushes him suddenly away*]. You shall not do that again.

HECTOR. In effect, you got your claws deeper into me than I intended.

MRS HUBHABYE [*coming in from the garden*]. Don't let me disturb you; I only want a cap to put on daddiest. The sun is setting; and he'll catch cold [*she makes for the door leading to the hall*].

LADY UTTERWORD. Your husband is quite charming, darling. He has actually condescended to kiss me at last. I shall go into the garden: it's cooler now [*she goes out by the port door*].

MRS HUSHABYE. Take care, dear child. I don't believe any man can kiss Addy without falling in love with her. [*She goes into the hall*].

HECTOR [*striking himself on the chest*]. Fool! Goat!

Mrs Hushabye comes back with the captain's cap.

HECTOR. Your sister is an extremely enterprising old girl. Where's Miss Dunn!

MRS HUSHABYE. Mangan says she has gone up to her room for a nap. Addy won't let you talk to Ellie: she has marked you for her own.

HECTOR. She has the diabolical family fascination. I began making love to her automatically. What am I to do? I can't fall in love; and I can't hurt a woman's feelings by telling her so when she falls in love with me. And as women are always falling in love with my moustache I get landed in all sorts of tedious and terrifying flirtations in which I'm not a bit in earnest.

MRS HUSHABYE. Oh, neither is Addy. She has never been in love in her life, though she has always been trying to fall in head over ears. She is worse than you, because you had one real go at least, with me.

HECTOR. That was a confounded madness. I can't believe that such an amazing experience is common. It has left its mark on me. I believe that is why I have never been able to repeat it.

MRS HUSHABYE [*laughing and caressing his arm*]. We were frightfully in love with one another, Hector. It was such an enchanting dream that I have never been able to grudge it to you or anyone else since. I have invited all sorts of pretty women to the house on the chance of giving you another turn. But it has never come off.

HECTOR. I don't know that I want it to come off. It was damned dangerous. You fascinated me; but I loved you; so it was heaven. This sister of yours fascinates me; but I hate her; so it is hell. I shall kill her if she persists.

MRS. HUSHABYE. Nothing will kill Addy; she is as strong as a horse. [*Releasing him*]. Now I am going off to fascinate somebody.

HECTOR. The Foreign Office toff? Randall?

MRS HUSHABYE. Goodness gracious, no! Why should I fascinate him?

HECTOR. I presume you don't mean the bloated capitalist, Mangan?

MRS HUSHABYE. Hm! I think he had better be fascinated by me than by Ellie. [*She is going into the garden when the captain comes in from it with some sticks in his hand*]. What have you got there, daddiest?

CAPTAIN SHOTOVER. Dynamite.

MRS HUSHABYE. You've been to the gravel pit. Don't drop it about the house, there's a dear. [*She goes into the garden, where the evening light is now very red*].

HECTOR. Listen, O sage. How long dare you concentrate on a feeling without risking having it fixed in your consciousness all the rest of your life?

CAPTAIN SHOTOVER. Ninety minutes. An hour and a half. [*He goes into the pantry*].

Hector, left alone, contracts his brows, and falls into a day-dream. He does not move for some time. Then he folds his arms. Then, throwing his hands behind him, and gripping one with the other, he strides tragically once to and fro. Suddenly he snatches his walking stick from the teak table, and draws it; for it is a swordstick. He fights a desperate duel with an imaginary antagonist, and after many vicissitudes runs him through the body up to the hilt. He sheathes his sword and throws it on the sofa, falling into another reverie as he does so. He looks straight into the eyes of an imaginary woman; seizes her by the arms; and says in a deep and thrilling tone, "Do you love me!" The captain comes out of the pantry at this moment; and Hector, caught with his arms stretched out and his fists clenched, has to account for his attitude by going through a series of gymnastic exercises.

CAPTAIN SHOTOVER. That sort of strength is no good. You will never be as strong as a gorilla.

HECTOR. What is the dynamite for?

CAPTAIN SHOTOVER. To kill fellows like Mangan.

HECTOR. No use. They will always be able to buy more dynamite than you.

CAPTAIN SHOTOVER. I will make a dynamite that he cannot explode.

HECTOR. And that you can, eh?

CAPTAIN SHOTOVER. Yes: when I have attained the seventh degree of concentration.

HECTOR. What's the use of that? You never do attain it.

CAPTAIN SHOTOVER. What then is to be done? Are we to be kept forever in the mud by these hogs to whom the universe is nothing but a machine for greasing their bristles and filling their snouts?

HECTOR. Are Mangan's bristles worse than Randall's lovelocks?

CAPTAIN SHOTOVER,. We must win powers of life and death over them both. I refuse to die until I have invented the means.

HECTOR. Who are we that we should judge them?

CAPTAIN SHOTOVER. What are they that they should judge us? Yet they do, unhesitatingly. There is enmity between our seed and their seed. They know it and act on it, strangling our souls. They believe in themselves. When we believe in ourselves, we shall kill them.

HECTOR. It is the same seed. You forget that your pirate has a very nice daughter. Mangan's son may be a Plato: Randall's a Shelley. What was my father?

CAPTAIN SHOTOVER. The damnedst scoundrel I ever met. [*He replaces the drawing-board; sits down at the table; and begins to mix a wash of color*].

HECTOR. Precisely. Well, dare you kill his innocent grandchildren?

CAPTAIN SHOTOVER. They are mine also.

HECTOR. Just so—we are members one of another. [*He throws himself carelessly on the sofa*]. I tell you I have often thought of this killing of human vermin. Many men have thought of it. Decent men are like Daniel in the lion's den: their survival is a miracle; and they do not always survive. We live among the Mangans and Randalls and Billie Dunns as they, poor devils, live among the disease germs and the doctors and the lawyers and the parsons and the restaurant chefs and the tradesmen and the servants and all the rest of the parasites and blackmailers. What are our terrors to theirs? Give me the power to kill them; and I'll spare them in sheer—

CAPTAIN SHOTOVER [*cutting in sharply*]. Fellow feeling?

HECTOR. No. I should kill myself if I believed that. I must believe that my spark, small as it is, is divine, and that the red light over their door is hell fire. I should spare them in simple magnanimous pity.

CAPTAIN SHOTOVER. You can't spare them until you have the power to kill them. At present they have the power to kill you. There are millions of blacks over the water for them to train and let loose on us. They're going to do it. They're doing it already.

HECTOR. They are too stupid to use their power.

CAPTAIN SHOTOVER [*throwing down his brush and coming to the end of the sofa*]. Do not deceive yourself: they do use it. We kill the better half of ourselves every day to propitiate them. The knowledge that these people are there to render all our aspirations barren prevents us having the aspirations. And when we are tempted to seek their destruction they bring forth demons to delude us, disguised as pretty daughters, and singers and poets and the like, for whose sake we spare them.

HECTOR [*sitting up and leaning towards him*]. May not Hesione be such a demon, brought forth by you lest I should slay you?

CAPTAIN SHOTOVER. That is possible. She has used you up, and left you nothing but dreams, as some women do.

HECTOR. Vampire women, demon women.

CAPTAIN SHOTOVER. Men think the world well lost for them, and lose it accordingly. Who are the men that do things? The husbands of the shrew and of the drunkard, the men with the thorn in the flesh. [*Walking distractedly away towards the pantry*]. I must think these things out. [*Turning suddenly*]. But I go on with the dynamite none the less. I will discover a ray mightier than any X-ray: a mind ray that will explode the ammunition in the belt of my adversary before he can point his gun at me. And I must hurry. I am old: I have no time to waste in talk [*he is about to go into the pantry, and Hector is making for the hall, when Hesione comes back*].

MRS HUSHABYE. Daddiest, you and Hector must come and help me to entertain all these people. What on earth were you shouting about?

HECTOR [*stopping in the act of turning the door handle*]. He is madder than usual.

MRS HUSHABYE. We all are.

HECTOR. I must change [*he resumes his door opening*].

MRS HUSHABYE. Stop, stop. Come back, both of you. Come back. [*They return, reluctantly*]. Money is running short.

HECTOR. Money! Where are my April dividends?

MRS HUSHABYE. Where is the snow that fell last year?

CAPTAIN SHOTOVER. Where is all the money you had for that patent lifeboat I invented?

MRS HUSHABYE. Five hundred pounds; and I have made it last since Easter!

CAPTAIN SHOTOVER. Since Easter! Barely four months! Monstrous extravagance! I could live for seven years on 500 pounds.

MRS HUSHABYE. Not keeping open house as we do here, daddiest.

CAPTAIN SHOTOVER. Only 500 pounds for that lifeboat! I got twelve thousand for the invention before that.

MRS HUSHABYE. Yes, dear; but that was for the ship with the magnetic keel that sucked up submarines. Living at the rate we do, you cannot afford life-saving inventions. Can't you think of something that will murder half Europe at one bang?

CAPTAIN SHOTOVER. No. I am ageing fast. My mind does not dwell on slaughter as it did when I was a boy. Why doesn't your husband invent something? He does nothing but tell lies to women.

HECTOR. Well, that is a form of invention, is it not? However, you are right: I ought to support my wife.

MRS HUSHABYE. Indeed you shall do nothing of the sort: I should never see you from breakfast to dinner. I want my husband.

HECTOR [*bitterly*]. I might as well be your lapdog.

MRS HUSHABYE. Do you want to be my breadwinner, like the other poor husbands?

HECTOR. No, by thunder! What a damned creature a husband is anyhow!

MRS HUSHABYE [*to the captain*]. What about that harpoon cannon?

CAPTAIN SHOTOVER. No use. It kills whales, not men.

MRS HUSHABYE. Why not? You fire the harpoon out of a cannon. It sticks in the enemy's general; you wind him in; and there you are.

HECTOR. You are your father's daughter, Hesione.

CAPTAIN SHOTOVER. There is something in it. Not to wind in generals: they are not dangerous. But one could fire a grapnel and wind in a machine gun or even a tank. I will think it out.

MRS HUSHABYE [*squeezing the captain's arm affectionately*]. Saved! You are a darling, daddiest. Now we must go back to these dreadful people and entertain them.

CAPTAIN SHOTOVER. They have had no dinner. Don't forget that.

HECTOR. Neither have I. And it is dark: it must be all hours.

MRS HUSHABYE. Oh, Guinness will produce some sort of dinner for them. The servants always take jolly good care that there is food in the house.

CAPTAIN SHOTOVER [*raising a strange wail in the darkness*]. What a house! What a daughter!

MRS HUSHABYE [*raving*]. What a father!

HECTOR [*following suit*]. What a husband!

CAPTAIN SHOTOVER. Is there no thunder in heaven?

HECTOR. Is there no beauty, no bravery, on earth?

MRS HUSHABYE. What do men want? They have their food, their firesides, their clothes mended, and our love at the end of the day. Why are they not satisfied? Why do they envy us the pain with which we bring them into the world, and make strange dangers and torments for themselves to be even with us?

CAPTAIN SHOTOVER [*weirdly chanting*].

I builded a house for my daughters, and opened the doors thereof, That men might come for their choosing, and their betters spring from their love; But one of them married a numskull;

HECTOR [*taking up the rhythm*].

The other a liar wed;

MRS HUSHABYE [*completing the stanza*].

And now must she lie beside him,
even as she made her bed.

LADY UTTERWORD [*calling from the garden*]. Hesione! Hesione! Where are you?

HECTOR. The cat is on the tiles.

MRS HUSHABYE. Coming, darling, coming [*she goes quickly into the garden*].

The captain goes back to his place at the table.

HECTOR [*going out into the hall*]. Shall I turn up the lights for you?

CAPTAIN SHOTOVER. No. Give me deeper darkness. Money is not made in the light.

ACT II

The same room, with the lights turned up and the curtains drawn. Ellie comes in, followed by Mangan. Both are dressed for dinner. She strolls to the drawing-table. He comes between the table and the wicker chair.

MANGAN. What a dinner! I don't call it a dinner: I call it a meal.

ELLIE. I am accustomed to meals, Mr Mangan, and very lucky to get them. Besides, the captain cooked some maccaroni for me.

MANGAN [*shuddering liverishly*]. Too rich: I can't eat such things. I suppose it's because I have to work so much with my brain. That's the worst of being a man of business: you are always thinking, thinking, thinking. By the way, now that we are alone, may I take the opportunity to come to a little understanding with you?

ELLIE [*settling into the draughtsman's seat*]. Certainly. I should like to.

MANGAN [*taken aback*]. Should you? That surprises me; for I thought I noticed this afternoon that you avoided me all you could. Not for the first time either.

ELLIE. I was very tired and upset. I wasn't used to the ways of this extraordinary house. Please forgive me.

MANGAN. Oh, that's all right: I don't mind. But Captain Shotover has been talking to me about you. You and me, you know.

ELLIE [*interested*]. The captain! What did he say?

MANGAN. Well, he noticed the difference between our ages.

ELLIE. He notices everything.

MANGAN. You don't mind, then?

ELLIE. Of course I know quite well that our engagement—

MANGAN. Oh! you call it an engagement.

ELLIE. Well, isn't it?

MANGAN. Oh, yes, yes: no doubt it is if you hold to it. This is the first time you've used the word; and I didn't quite know where we stood: that's all. [*He sits down in the wicker chair; and resigns himself to allow her to lead the conversation*]. You were saying—?

ELLIE. Was I? I forget. Tell me. Do you like this part of the country? I heard you ask Mr Hushabye at dinner whether there are any nice houses to let down here.

MANGAN. I like the place. The air suits me. I shouldn't be surprised if I settled down here.

ELLIE. Nothing would please me better. The air suits me too. And I want to be near Hesione.

MANGAN [*with growing uneasiness*]. The air may suit us; but the question is, should we suit one another? Have you thought about that?

ELLIE. Mr Mangan, we must be sensible, mustn't we? It's no use pretending that we are Romeo and Juliet. But we can get on very well together if we choose to make the best of it. Your kindness of heart will make it easy for me.

MANGAN [*leaning forward, with the beginning of something like deliberate unpleasantness in his voice*]. Kindness of heart, eh? I ruined your father, didn't I?

ELLIE. Oh, not intentionally.

MANGAN. Yes I did. Ruined him on purpose.

ELLIE. On purpose!

MANGAN. Not out of ill-nature, you know. And you'll admit that I kept a job for him when I had finished with him. But business is business; and I ruined him as a matter of business.

ELLIE. I don't understand how that can be. Are you trying to make me feel that I need not be grateful to you, so that I may choose freely?

MANGAN [*rising aggressively*]. No. I mean what I say.

ELLIE. But how could it possibly do you any good to ruin my father? The money he lost was yours.

MANGAN [*with a sour laugh*]. Was mine! It is mine, Miss Ellie, and all the money the other fellows lost too. [*He shoves his hands into his pockets and shows his teeth*]. I just smoked them out like a hive of bees. What do you say to that? A bit of shock, eh?

ELLIE. It would have been, this morning. Now! you can't think how little it matters. But it's quite interesting. Only, you must explain it to me. I don't understand it. [*Propping her elbows on the drawing-board and her chin on her hands, she composes herself to listen with a combination of conscious curiosity with unconscious contempt which provokes him to more and more unpleasantness, and an attempt at patronage of her ignorance*].

MANGAN. Of course you don't understand: what do you know about business? You just listen and learn. Your father's business was a new business; and I don't start new businesses: I let other fellows start them. They put all their money and their friends' money into starting them. They wear out their souls and bodies trying to make a success of them. They're what you call enthusiasts. But the first dead lift of the thing is too much for them; and they haven't enough financial experience. In a year or so they have either to let the whole show go bust, or sell out to a new lot of fellows for a few deferred ordinary shares: that is, if they're lucky enough to get anything at all. As likely as not the very same thing happens to the new lot. They put in more money and a couple of years' more work; and then perhaps they have to sell out to a third lot. If it's really a big thing the third lot will have to sell out too, and leave their work and their money behind them. And that's where the real business man comes in: where I come in. But I'm cleverer than some: I don't mind dropping a little money to start the process. I took your father's measure. I saw that he had a sound idea, and that he would work himself silly for it if he got the chance. I saw that he was a child in business, and was dead certain to outrun his expenses and be in too great a hurry to wait for his market. I knew that the surest way to ruin a man who doesn't know how to handle money is to give him some. I explained my idea to some friends in the city, and they found the money; for I take no risks in ideas, even when they're my own. Your father and the friends that ventured their money with him were no more to me than a heap of squeezed lemons. You've been wasting your gratitude: my kind heart is all rot. I'm sick of it. When I see your father beaming at me with his moist, grateful eyes, regularly wallowing in gratitude, I sometimes feel I must tell him the truth or burst. What stops me is that I know he wouldn't believe me. He'd think it was my modesty, as you did just now. He'd think anything rather than the truth, which is that he's a blamed fool, and I am a man that knows how to take care of himself. [*He throws himself back into the big chair with large self approval*]. Now what do you think of me, Miss Ellie?

ELLIE [*dropping her hands*]. How strange! that my mother, who knew nothing at all about business, should have been quite right about you! She always said not before papa, of course, but to us children—that you were just that sort of man.

MANGAN [*sitting up, much hurt*]. Oh! did she? And yet she'd have let you marry me.

ELLIE. Well, you see, Mr Mangan, my mother married a very good man—for whatever you may think of my father as a man of business, he is the soul of goodness—and she is not at all keen on my doing the same.

MANGAN. Anyhow, you don't want to marry me now, do you?

ELLIE. [*very calmly*]. Oh, I think so. Why not?

MANGAN. [*rising aghast*]. Why not!

ELLIE. I don't see why we shouldn't get on very well together.

MANGAN. Well, but look here, you know—[*he stops, quite at a loss*].

ELLIE. [*patiently*]. Well?

MANGAN. Well, I thought you were rather particular about people's characters.

ELLIE. If we women were particular about men's characters, we should never get married at all, Mr Mangan.

MANGAN. A child like you talking of "we women"! What next! You're not in earnest?

ELLIE. Yes, I am. Aren't you?

MANGAN. You mean to hold me to it?

ELLIE. Do you wish to back out of it?

MANGAN. Oh, no. Not exactly back out of it.

ELLIE. Well?

He has nothing to say. With a long whispered whistle, he drops into the wicker chair and stares before him like a beggared gambler. But a cunning look soon comes into his face. He leans over towards her on his right elbow, and speaks in a low steady voice.

MANGAN. Suppose I told you I was in love with another woman!

ELLIE [*echoing him*]. Suppose I told you I was in love with another man!

MANGAN [*bouncing angrily out of his chair*]. I'm not joking.

ELLIE. Who told you I was?

MANGAN. I tell you I'm serious. You're too young to be serious; but you'll have to believe me. I want to be near your friend Mrs Hushabye. I'm in love with her. Now the murder's out.

ELLIE. I want to be near your friend Mr Hushabye. I'm in love with him. [*She rises and adds with a frank air*] Now we are in one another's confidence, we shall be real friends. Thank you for telling me.

MANGAN [*almost beside himself*]. Do you think I'll be made a convenience of like this?

ELLIE. Come, Mr Mangan! you made a business convenience of my father. Well, a woman's business is marriage. Why shouldn't I make a domestic convenience of you?

MANGAN. Because I don't choose, see? Because I'm not a silly gull like your father. That's why.

ELLIE [*with serene contempt*]. You are not good enough to clean my father's boots, Mr Mangan; and I am paying you a great compliment in condescending to make a convenience of you, as you call it. Of course you are free to throw over our engagement if you like; but, if you do, you'll never enter Hesione's house again: I will take care of that.

MANGAN [*gasping*]. You little devil, you've done me. [*On the point of collapsing into the big chair again he recovers himself*]. Wait a bit, though: you're not so cute as you think. You can't beat Boss Mangan as easy as that. Suppose I go straight to Mrs Hushabye and tell her that you're in love with her husband.

ELLIE. She knows it.

MANGAN. You told her!!!

ELLIE. She told me.

MANGAN [*clutching at his bursting temples*]. Oh, this is a crazy house. Or else I'm going clean off my chump. Is she making a swop with you—she to have your husband and you to have hers?

ELLIE. Well, you don't want us both, do you?

MANGAN [*throwing himself into the chair distractedly*]. My brain won't stand it. My head's going to split. Help! Help me to hold it. Quick: hold it: squeeze it. Save me. [*Ellie comes behind his chair; clasps his head hard for a moment; then begins to draw her hands from his forehead back to his ears*]. Thank you. [*Drowsily*]. That's very refreshing. [*Waking a little*]. Don't you hypnotize me, though. I've seen men made fools of by hypnotism.

ELLIE [*steadily*]. Be quiet. I've seen men made fools of without hypnotism.

MANGAN [*humbly*]. You don't dislike touching me, I hope. You never touched me before, I noticed.

ELLIE. Not since you fell in love naturally with a grown-up nice woman, who will never expect you to make love to her. And I will never expect him to make love to me.

MANGAN. He may, though.

ELLIE [*making her passes rhythmically*]. Hush. Go to sleep. Do you hear? You are to go to sleep, go to sleep, go to sleep; be quiet, deeply deeply quiet; sleep, sleep, sleep, sleep, sleep.

He falls asleep. Ellie steals away; turns the light out; and goes into the garden.

Nurse Guinness opens the door and is seen in the light which comes in from the hall.

GUINNESS [*speaking to someone outside*]. Mr Mangan's not here, duckie: there's no one here. It's all dark.

MRS HUSHABYE [*without*]. Try the garden. Mr Dunn and I will be in my boudoir. Show him the way.

GUINNESS. Yes, ducky. [*She makes for the garden door in the dark; stumbles over the sleeping Mangan and screams*]. Ahoo! O Lord, Sir! I beg your pardon, I'm sure: I didn't see you in the dark. Who is it? [*She goes back to the door and turns on the light*]. Oh, Mr Mangan, sir, I hope I haven't hurt you plumping into your lap like that. [*Coming to him*]. I was looking for you, sir. Mrs Hushabye says will you please [*noticing that he remains quite insensible*]. Oh, my good Lord, I hope I haven't killed him. Sir! Mr Mangan! Sir! [*She shakes him; and he is rolling inertly off the chair on the floor when she holds him up and props him against the cushion*]. Miss Hessy! Miss Hessy! quick, doty darling. Miss Hessy! [*Mrs Hushabye comes in from the hall, followed by Mazzini Dunn*]. Oh, Miss Hessy, I've been and killed him.

Mazzini runs round the back of the chair to Mangan's right hand, and sees that the nurse's words are apparently only too true.

MAZZINI. What tempted you to commit such a crime, woman?

MRS HUSHABYE [*trying not to laugh*]. Do you mean, you did it on purpose?

GUINNESS. Now is it likely I'd kill any man on purpose? I fell over him in the dark; and I'm a pretty tidy weight. He never spoke nor moved until I shook him; and then he would have dropped dead on the floor. Isn't it tiresome?

MRS HUSHABYE [*going past the nurse to Mangan's side, and inspecting him less credulously than Mazzini*]. Nonsense! he is not dead: he is only asleep. I can see him breathing.

GUINNESS. But why won't he wake?

MAZZINI [*speaking very politely into Mangan's ear*]. Mangan! My dear Mangan! [*he blows into Mangan's ear*].

MRS HUSHABYE. That's no good [*she shakes him vigorously*]. Mr Mangan, wake up. Do you hear? [*He begins to roll over*]. Oh! Nurse, nurse: he's falling: help me.

Nurse Guinness rushes to the rescue. With Mazzini's assistance, Mangan is propped safely up again.

GUINNESS [*behind the chair; bending over to test the case with her nose*]. Would he be drunk, do you think, pet?

MRS HUSHABYE. Had he any of papa's rum?

MAZZINI. It can't be that: he is most abstemious. I am afraid he drank too much formerly, and has to drink too little now. You know, Mrs Hushabye, I really think he has been hypnotized.

GUINNESS. Hip no what, sir?

MAZZINI. One evening at home, after we had seen a hypnotizing performance, the children began playing at it; and Ellie stroked my head. I assure you I went off dead asleep; and they had to send for a professional to wake me up after I had slept eighteen hours. They had to carry me upstairs; and as the poor children were not very strong, they let me slip; and I rolled right down the whole flight and never woke up. [*Mrs Hushabye splutters*]. Oh, you may laugh, Mrs Hushabye; but I might have been killed.

MRS HUSHABYE. I couldn't have helped laughing even if you had been, Mr Dunn. So Ellie has hypnotized him. What fun!

MAZZINI. Oh no, no, no. It was such a terrible lesson to her: nothing would induce her to try such a thing again.

MRS HUSHABYE. Then who did it? I didn't.

MAZZINI. I thought perhaps the captain might have done it unintentionally. He is so fearfully magnetic: I feel vibrations whenever he comes close to me.

GUINNESS. The captain will get him out of it anyhow, sir: I'll back him for that. I'll go fetch him [*she makes for the pantry*].

MRS HUSHABYE. Wait a bit. [*To Mazzini*]. You say he is all right for eighteen hours?

MAZZINI. Well, I was asleep for eighteen hours.

MRS HUSHABYE. Were you any the worse for it?

MAZZINI. I don't quite remember. They had poured brandy down my throat, you see; and—

MRS HUSHABYE. Quite. Anyhow, you survived. Nurse, darling: go and ask Miss Dunn to come to us here. Say I want to speak to her particularly. You will find her with Mr Hushabye probably.

GUINNESS. I think not, ducky: Miss Addy is with him. But I'll find her and send her to you. [*She goes out into the garden*].

MRS HUSHABYE [*calling Mazzini's attention to the figure on the chair*]. Now, Mr Dunn, look. Just look. Look hard. Do you still intend to sacrifice your daughter to that thing?

MAZZINI [*troubled*]. You have completely upset me, Mrs Hushabye, by all you have said to me. That anyone could imagine that I—I, a consecrated soldier of freedom, if I may say so—could sacrifice Ellie to anybody or anyone, or that I should ever have dreamed of forcing her inclinations in any way, is a most painful blow to my—well, I suppose you would say to my good opinion of myself.

MRS HUSHABYE [*rather stolidly*]. Sorry.

MAZZINI [*looking forlornly at the body*]. What is your objection to poor Mangan, Mrs Hushabye? He looks all right to me. But then I am so accustomed to him.

MRS HUSHABYE. Have you no heart? Have you no sense? Look at the brute! Think of poor weak innocent Ellie in the clutches of this slavedriver, who spends his life making thousands of rough violent workmen bend to his will and sweat for him: a man accustomed to have great masses of iron beaten into shape for him by steam-hammers! to fight with women and girls over a halfpenny an hour ruthlessly! a captain of industry, I think you call him, don't you? Are you going to fling your delicate, sweet, helpless child into such a beast's claws just because he will keep her in an expensive house and make her wear diamonds to show how rich he is?

MAZZINI [*staring at her in wide-eyed amazement*]. Bless you, dear Mrs Hushabye, what romantic ideas of business you have! Poor dear Mangan isn't a bit like that.

MRS HUSHABYE [*scornfully*]. Poor dear Mangan indeed!

MAZZINI. But he doesn't know anything about machinery. He never goes near the men: he couldn't manage them: he is afraid of them. I never can get him to take the least interest in the works: he hardly knows more about them than you do. People are cruelly unjust to Mangan: they think he is all rugged strength just because his manners are bad.

MRS HUSHABYE. Do you mean to tell me he isn't strong enough to crush poor little Ellie?

MAZZINI. Of course it's very hard to say how any marriage will turn out; but speaking for myself, I should say that he won't have a dog's chance against Ellie. You know, Ellie has remarkable strength of character. I think it is because I taught her to like Shakespeare when she was very young.

MRS HUSHABYE [*contemptuously*]. Shakespeare! The next thing you will tell me is that you could have made a great deal more money than Mangan. [*She retires to the sofa, and sits down at the port end of it in the worst of humors*].

MAZZINI [*following her and taking the other end*]. No: I'm no good at making money. I don't care enough for it, somehow. I'm not ambitious! that must be it. Mangan is wonderful about money: he thinks of nothing else. He is so dreadfully afraid of being poor. I am always thinking of other things: even at the works I think of the things we are doing and not of what they cost. And the worst of it is, poor Mangan doesn't know what to do with his money when he gets it. He is such a baby that he doesn't know even what to eat and drink: he has ruined his liver eating and drinking the wrong things; and now he can hardly eat at all. Ellie will diet him splendidly. You will be surprised when you come to know him better: he is really the most helpless of mortals. You get quite a protective feeling towards him.

MRS HUSHABYE. Then who manages his business, pray?

MAZZINI. I do. And of course other people like me.

MRS HUSHABYE. Footling people, you mean.

MAZZINI. I suppose you'd think us so.

MRS HUSHABYE. And pray why don't you do without him if you're all so much cleverer?

MAZZINI. Oh, we couldn't: we should ruin the business in a year. I've tried; and I know. We should spend too much on everything. We should improve the quality of the goods and make them too dear. We should be sentimental about the hard cases among the work people. But Mangan keeps us in order. He is down on us about every extra halfpenny. We could never do without him. You see, he will sit up all night thinking of how to save sixpence. Won't Ellie make him jump, though, when she takes his house in hand!

MRS HUSHABYE. Then the creature is a fraud even as a captain of industry!

MAZZINI. I am afraid all the captains of industry are what you call frauds, Mrs Hushabye. Of course there are some manufacturers who really do understand their own works; but they don't make as high a rate of profit as Mangan does. I assure you Mangan is quite a good fellow in his way. He means well.

MRS HUSHABYE. He doesn't look well. He is not in his first youth, is he?

MAZZINI. After all, no husband is in his first youth for very long, Mrs Hushabye. And men can't afford to marry in their first youth nowadays.

MRS HUSHABYE. Now if I said that, it would sound witty. Why can't you say it wittily? What on earth is the matter with you? Why don't you inspire everybody with confidence? with respect?

MAZZINI [*humbly*]. I think that what is the matter with me is that I am poor. You don't know what that means at home. Mind: I don't say they have ever complained. They've all been wonderful: they've been proud of my poverty. They've even joked about it quite often. But my wife has had a very poor time of it. She has been quite resigned—

MRS HUSHABYE [*shuddering involuntarily!*]

MAZZINI. There! You see, Mrs Hushabye. I don't want Ellie to live on resignation.

MRS HUSHABYE. Do you want her to have to resign herself to living with a man she doesn't love?

MAZZINI [*wistfully*]. Are you sure that would be worse than living with a man she did love, if he was a footling person?

MRS HUSHABYE [*relaxing her contemptuous attitude, quite interested in Mazzini now*]. You know, I really think you must love Ellie very much; for you become quite clever when you talk about her.

MAZZINI. I didn't know I was so very stupid on other subjects.

MRS HUSHABYE. You are, sometimes.

MAZZINI [*turning his head away; for his eyes are wet*]. I have learnt a good deal about myself from you, Mrs Hushabye; and I'm afraid I shall not be the happier for your plain speaking. But if you thought I needed it to make me think of Ellie's happiness you were very much mistaken.

MRS HUSHABYE [*leaning towards him kindly*]. Have I been a beast?

MAZZINI [*pulling himself together*]. It doesn't matter about me, Mrs Hushabye. I think you like Ellie; and that is enough for me.

MRS HUSHABYE. I'm beginning to like you a little. I perfectly loathed you at first. I thought you the most odious, self-satisfied, boresome elderly prig I ever met.

MAZZINI [*resigned, and now quite cheerful*]. I daresay I am all that. I never have been a favorite with gorgeous women like you. They always frighten me.

MRS HUSHABYE [*pleased*]. Am I a gorgeous woman, Mazzini? I shall fall in love with you presently.

MAZZINI [*with placid gallantry*]. No, you won't, Hesione. But you would be quite safe. Would you believe it that quite a lot of women have flirted with me because I am quite safe? But they get tired of me for the same reason.

MRS HUSHABYE [*mischievously*]. Take care. You may not be so safe as you think.

MAZZINI. Oh yes, quite safe. You see, I have been in love really: the sort of love that only happens once. [*Softly*]. That's why Ellie is such a lovely girl.

MRS HUSHABYE. Well, really, you are coming out. Are you quite sure you won't let me tempt you into a second grand passion?

MAZZINI. Quite. It wouldn't be natural. The fact is, you don't strike on my box, Mrs Hushabye; and I certainly don't strike on yours.

MRS HUSHABYE. I see. Your marriage was a safety match.

MAZZINI. What a very witty application of the expression I used! I should never have thought of it.

Ellie comes in from the garden, looking anything but happy.

MRS HUSHABYE [*rising*]. Oh! here is Ellie at last. [*She goes behind the sofa*].

ELLIE [*on the threshold of the starboard door*]. Guinness said you wanted me: you and papa.

MRS HUSHABYE. You have kept us waiting so long that it almost came to—well, never mind. Your father is a very wonderful man [*she ruffles his hair affectionately*]: the only one I ever met who could resist me when I made myself really agreeable. [*She comes to the big chair, on Mangan's left*]. Come here. I have something to show you. [*Ellie strolls listlessly to the other side of the chair*]. Look.

ELLIE [*contemplating Mangan without interest*]. I know. He is only asleep. We had a talk after dinner; and he fell asleep in the middle of it.

MRS HUSHABYE. You did it, Ellie. You put him asleep.

MAZZINI [*rising quickly and coming to the back of the chair*]. Oh, I hope not. Did you, Ellie?

ELLIE [*wearily*]. He asked me to.

MAZZINI. But it's dangerous. You know what happened to me.

ELLIE [*utterly indifferent*]. Oh, I daresay I can wake him. If not, somebody else can.

MRS HUSHABYE. It doesn't matter, anyhow, because I have at last persuaded your father that you don't want to marry him.

ELLIE [*suddenly coming out of her listlessness, much vexed*]. But why did you do that, Hesione? I do want to marry him. I fully intend to marry him.

MAZZINI. Are you quite sure, Ellie? Mrs Hushabye has made me feel that I may have been thoughtless and selfish about it.

ELLIE [*very clearly and steadily*]. Papa. When Mrs. Hushabye takes it on herself to explain to you what I think or don't think, shut your ears tight; and shut your eyes too. Hesione knows nothing about me: she hasn't the least notion of the sort of person I am, and never will. I promise you I won't do anything I don't want to do and mean to do for my own sake.

MAZZINI. You are quite, quite sure?

ELLIE. Quite, quite sure. Now you must go away and leave me to talk to Mrs Hushabye.

MAZZINI. But I should like to hear. Shall I be in the way?

ELLIE [*inexorable*]. I had rather talk to her alone.

MAZZINI [*affectionately*]. Oh, well, I know what a nuisance parents are, dear. I will be good and go. [*He goes to the garden door*]. By the way, do you remember the address of that professional who woke me up? Don't you think I had better telegraph to him?

MRS HUSHABYE [*moving towards the sofa*]. It's too late to telegraph tonight.

MAZZINI. I suppose so. I do hope he'll wake up in the course of the night. [*He goes out into the garden*].

ELLIE [*turning vigorously on Hesione the moment her father is out of the room*]. Hesione, what the devil do you mean by making mischief with my father about Mangan?

MRS HUSHABYE [*promptly losing her temper*]. Don't you dare speak to me like that, you little minx. Remember that you are in my house.

ELLIE. Stuff! Why don't you mind your own business? What is it to you whether I choose to marry Mangan or not?

MRS HUSHABYE. Do you suppose you can bully me, you miserable little matrimonial adventurer?

ELLIE. Every woman who hasn't any money is a matrimonial adventurer. It's easy for you to talk: you have never known what it is to want money; and you can pick up men as if they were daisies. I am poor and respectable—

MRS HUSHABYE [*interrupting*]. Ho! respectable! How did you pick up Mangan? How did you pick up my husband? You have the audacity to tell me that I am a—a—a—

ELLIE. A siren. So you are. You were born to lead men by the nose: if you weren't, Marcus would have waited for me, perhaps.

MRS HUSHABYE [*suddenly melting and half laughing*]. Oh, my poor Ellie, my pettikins, my unhappy darling! I am so sorry about Hector. But what can I do? It's not my fault: I'd give him to you if I could.

ELLIE. I don't blame you for that.

MRS HUSHABYE. What a brute I was to quarrel with you and call you names! Do kiss me and say you're not angry with me.

ELLIE [*fiercely*]. Oh, don't slop and gush and be sentimental. Don't you see that unless I can be hard—as hard as nails—I shall go mad? I don't care a damn about your calling me names: do you think a woman in my situation can feel a few hard words?

MRS HUSHABYE. Poor little woman! Poor little situation!

ELLIE. I suppose you think you're being sympathetic. You are just foolish and stupid and selfish. You see me getting a smasher right in the face that kills a whole part of my life: the best part that can never come again; and you think you can help me over it by a little coaxing and kissing. When I want all the strength I can get to lean on: something iron, something stony, I don't care how cruel it is, you go all mushy and want to slobber over me. I'm not angry; I'm not unfriendly; but for God's sake do pull yourself together; and don't think that because you're on velvet and always have been, women who are in hell can take it as easily as you.

MRS HUSHABYE [*shrugging her shoulders*]. Very well. [*She sits down on the sofa in her old place.*] But I warn you that when I am neither coaxing and kissing nor laughing, I am just wondering how much longer I can stand living in this cruel, damnable world. You object to the siren: well, I drop the siren. You want to rest your wounded bosom against a grindstone. Well [*folding her arms*] here is the grindstone.

ELLIE [*sitting down beside her, appeased*]. That's better: you really have the trick of falling in with everyone's mood; but you don't understand, because you are not the sort of woman for whom there is only one man and only one chance.

MRS HUSHABYE. I certainly don't understand how your marrying that object [*indicating Mangan*] will console you for not being able to marry Hector.

ELLIE. Perhaps you don't understand why I was quite a nice girl this morning, and am now neither a girl nor particularly nice.

MRS HUSHABYE. Oh, yes, I do. It's because you have made up your mind to do something despicable and wicked.

ELLIE. I don't think so, Hesione. I must make the best of my ruined house.

MRS HUSHABYE. Pooh! You'll get over it. Your house isn't ruined.

ELLIE. Of course I shall get over it. You don't suppose I'm going to sit down and die of a broken heart, I hope, or be an old maid living on a pittance from the Sick and Indigent Roomkeepers' Association. But my heart is broken, all the same. What I mean by that is that I know that what has happened to me with Marcus will not happen to me ever again. In the world for me there is Marcus and a lot of other men of whom one is just the same as another. Well, if I can't have love, that's no reason why I should have poverty. If Mangan has nothing else, he has money.

MRS HUSHABYE. And are there no YOUNG men with money?

ELLIE. Not within my reach. Besides, a young man would have the right to expect love from me, and would perhaps leave me when he found I could not give it to him. Rich young men can get rid of their wives, you know, pretty cheaply. But this object, as you call him, can expect nothing more from me than I am prepared to give him.

MRS HUSHABYE. He will be your owner, remember. If he buys you, he will make the bargain pay him and not you. Ask your father.

ELLIE [*rising and strolling to the chair to contemplate their subject*]. You need not trouble on that score, Hesione. I have more to give Boss Mangan than he has to give me: it is I who am buying him, and at a pretty good price too, I think. Women are better at that sort of bargain than men. I have taken the Boss's measure; and ten Boss Mangans shall not prevent me doing far more as I please as his wife than I have ever been able to do as a poor girl. [*Stooping to the recumbent figure*]. Shall they, Boss? I think not. [*She passes on to the drawing-table, and leans against the end of it, facing the windows*]. I shall not have to spend most of my time wondering how long my gloves will last, anyhow.

MRS HUSHABYE [*rising superbly*]. Ellie, you are a wicked, sordid little beast. And to think that I actually condescended to fascinate that creature there to save you from him! Well, let me tell you this: if you make this disgusting match, you will never see Hector again if I can help it.

ELLIE [*unmoved*]. I nailed Mangan by telling him that if he did not marry me he should never see you again [*she lifts herself on her wrists and seats herself on the end of the table*].

MRS HUSHABYE [*recoiling*]. Oh!

ELLIE. So you see I am not unprepared for your playing that trump against me. Well, you just try it: that's all. I should have made a man of Marcus, not a household pet.

MRS HUSHABYE [*flaming*]. You dare!

ELLIE [*looking almost dangerous*]. Set him thinking about me if you dare.

MRS HUSHABYE. Well, of all the impudent little fiends I ever met! Hector says there is a certain point at which the only answer you can give to a man who breaks all the rules is to knock him down. What would you say if I were to box your ears?

ELLIE [*calmly*]. I should pull your hair.

MRS HUSHABYE [*mischievously*]. That wouldn't hurt me. Perhaps it comes off at night.

ELLIE [*so taken aback that she drops off the table and runs to her*]. Oh, you don't mean to say, Hesione, that your beautiful black hair is false?

MRS HUSHABYE [*patting it*]. Don't tell Hector. He believes in it.

ELLIE [*groaning*]. Oh! Even the hair that ensnared him false! Everything false!

MRS HUSHABYE. Pull it and try. Other women can snare men in their hair; but I can swing a baby on mine. Aha! you can't do that, Goldylocks.

ELLIE [*heartbroken*]. No. You have stolen my babies.

MRS HUSHABYE. Pettikins, don't make me cry. You know what you said about my making a household pet of him is a little true. Perhaps he ought to have waited for you. Would any other woman on earth forgive you?

ELLIE. Oh, what right had you to take him all for yourself! [*Pulling herself together*]. There! You couldn't help it: neither of us could help it. He couldn't help it. No, don't say anything more: I can't bear it. Let us wake the object. [*She begins stroking Mangan's head, reversing the movement with which she put him to sleep*]. Wake up, do you hear? You are to wake up at once. Wake up, wake up, wake—

MANGAN [*bouncing out of the chair in a fury and turning on them*]. Wake up! So you think I've been asleep, do you? [*He kicks the chair violently back out of his way, and gets between them*]. You throw me into a trance so that I can't move hand or foot—I might have been buried alive! it's a mercy I wasn't—and then you think I was only asleep. If you'd let me drop the two times you rolled me about, my nose would have been flattened for life against the floor. But I've found you all out, anyhow. I know the sort of people I'm among now. I've heard every word you've said, you and your precious father, and [*to Mrs Hushabye*] you too. So I'm an object, am I? I'm a thing, am I? I'm a fool that hasn't sense enough to feed myself properly, am I? I'm afraid of the men that would starve if it weren't for the wages I give them, am I? I'm nothing but a disgusting old skinflint to be made a convenience of by designing women and fool managers of my works, am I? I'm—

MRS HUSHABYE [*with the most elegant aplomb*]. Sh-sh-sh-sh-sh! Mr Mangan, you are bound in honor to obliterate from your mind all you heard while you were pretending to be asleep. It was not meant for you to hear.

MANGAN. Pretending to be asleep! Do you think if I was only pretending that I'd have sprawled there helpless, and listened to such unfairness, such lies, such injustice and plotting and backbiting and slandering of me, if I could have up and told you what I thought of you! I wonder I didn't burst.

MRS HUSHABYE [*sweetly*]. You dreamt it all, Mr Mangan. We were only saying how beautifully peaceful you looked in your sleep. That was all, wasn't it, Ellie? Believe me, Mr Mangan, all those unpleasant things came into your mind in the last half second before you woke. Ellie rubbed your hair the wrong way; and the disagreeable sensation suggested a disagreeable dream.

MANGAN [*doggedly*]. I believe in dreams.

MRS HUSHABYE. So do I. But they go by contraries, don't they?

MANGAN [*depths of emotion suddenly welling up in him*]. I shan't forget, to my dying day, that when you gave me the glad eye that time in the garden, you were making a fool of me. That was a dirty low mean thing to do. You had no right to let me come near you if I disgusted you. It isn't my fault if I'm old and haven't a moustache like a bronze candlestick as your husband has. There are things no decent woman would do to a man—like a man hitting a woman in the breast.

Hesione, utterly shamed, sits down on the sofa and covers her face with her hands. Mangan sits down also on his chair and begins to cry like a child. Ellie stares at them. Mrs Hushabye, at the distressing sound he makes, takes down her hands and looks at him. She rises and runs to him.

MRS HUSHABYE. Don't cry: I can't bear it. Have I broken your heart? I didn't know you had one. How could I?

MANGAN. I'm a man, ain't I?

MRS HUSHABYE [*half coaxing, half rallying, altogether tenderly*]. Oh no: not what I call a man. Only a Boss: just that and nothing else. What business has a Boss with a heart?

MANGAN. Then you're not a bit sorry for what you did, nor ashamed?

MRS HUSHABYE. I was ashamed for the first time in my life when you said that about hitting a woman in the breast, and I found out what I'd done. My very bones blushed red. You've had your revenge, Boss. Aren't you satisfied?

MANGAN. Serve you right! Do you hear? Serve you right! You're just cruel. Cruel.

MRS HUSHABYE. Yes: cruelty would be delicious if one could only find some sort of cruelty that didn't really hurt. By the way [*sitting down beside him on the arm of the chair*], what's your name? It's not really Boss, is it?

MANGAN [*shortly*]. If you want to know, my name's Alfred.

MRS HUSHABYE [*springs up*]. Alfred!! Ellie, he was christened after Tennyson!!!

MANGAN [*rising*]. I was christened after my uncle, and never had a penny from him, damn him! What of it?

MRS HUSHABYE. It comes to me suddenly that you are a real person: that you had a mother, like anyone else. [*Putting her hands on his shoulders and surveying him*]. Little Alf!

MANGAN. Well, you have a nerve.

MRS HUSHABYE. And you have a heart, Alfy, a whimpering little heart, but a real one. [*Releasing him suddenly*]. Now run and make it up with Ellie. She has had time to think what to say to you, which is more than I had [*she goes out quickly into the garden by the port door*].

MANGAN. That woman has a pair of hands that go right through you.

ELLIE. Still in love with her, in spite of all we said about you?

MANGAN. Are all women like you two? Do they never think of anything about a man except what they can get out of him? You weren't even thinking that about me. You were only thinking whether your gloves would last.

ELLIE. I shall not have to think about that when we are married.

MANGAN. And you think I am going to marry you after what I heard there!

ELLIE. You heard nothing from me that I did not tell you before.

MANGAN. Perhaps you think I can't do without you.

ELLIE. I think you would feel lonely without us all, now, after coming to know us so well.

MANGAN [*with something like a yell of despair*]. Am I never to have the last word?

CAPTAIN SHOTOVER [*appearing at the starboard garden door*]. There is a soul in torment here. What is the matter?

MANGAN. This girl doesn't want to spend her life wondering how long her gloves will last.

CAPTAIN SHOTOVER [*passing through*]. Don't wear any. I never do [*he goes into the pantry*].

LADY UTTERWORD [*appearing at the port garden door, in a handsome dinner dress*]. Is anything the matter?

ELLIE. This gentleman wants to know is he never to have the last word?

LADY UTTERWORD [*coming forward to the sofa*]. I should let him have it, my dear. The important thing is not to have the last word, but to have your own way.

MANGAN. She wants both.

LADY UTTERWORD. She won't get them, Mr Mangan. Providence always has the last word.

MANGAN [*desperately*]. Now you are going to come religion over me. In this house a man's mind might as well be a football. I'm going. [*He makes for the hall, but is stopped by a hail from the Captain, who has just emerged from his pantry*].

CAPTAIN SHOTOVER. Whither away, Boss Mangan?

MANGAN. To hell out of this house: let that be enough for you and all here.

CAPTAIN SHOTOVER. You were welcome to come: you are free to go. The wide earth, the high seas, the spacious skies are waiting for you outside.

LADY UTTERWORD. But your things, Mr Mangan. Your bag, your comb and brushes, your pyjamas—

HECTOR [*who has just appeared in the port doorway in a handsome Arab costume*]. Why should the escaping slave take his chains with him?

MANGAN. That's right, Hushabye. Keep the pyjamas, my lady, and much good may they do you.

HECTOR [*advancing to Lady Utterword's left hand*]. Let us all go out into the night and leave everything behind us.

MANGAN. You stay where you are, the lot of you. I want no company, especially female company.

ELLIE. Let him go. He is unhappy here. He is angry with us.

CAPTAIN SHOTOVER. Go, Boss Mangan; and when you have found the land where there is happiness and where there are no women, send me its latitude and longitude; and I will join you there.

LADY UTTERWORD. You will certainly not be comfortable without your luggage, Mr Mangan.

ELLIE [*impatient*]. Go, go: why don't you go? It is a heavenly night: you can sleep on the heath. Take my waterproof to lie on: it is hanging up in the hall.

HECTOR. Breakfast at nine, unless you prefer to breakfast with the captain at six.

ELLIE. Good night, Alfred.

HECTOR. Alfred! [*He runs back to the door and calls into the garden*]. Randall, Mangan's Christian name is Alfred.

RANDALL [*appearing in the starboard doorway in evening dress*]. Then Hesione wins her bet.

Mrs Hushabye appears in the port doorway. She throws her left arm round Hector's neck: draws him with her to the back of the sofa: and throws her right arm round Lady Utterword's neck.

MRS HUSHABYE. They wouldn't believe me, Alf.

They contemplate him.

MANGAN. Is there any more of you coming in to look at me, as if I was the latest thing in a menagerie?

MRS HUSHABYE. You are the latest thing in this menagerie.

Before Mangan can retort, a fall of furniture is heard from upstairs: then a pistol shot, and a yell of pain. The staring group breaks up in consternation.

MAZZINI'S VOICE [*from above*]. Help! A burglar! Help!

HECTOR [*his eyes blazing*]. A burglar!!!

MRS HUSHABYE. No, Hector: you'll be shot [*but it is too late; he has dashed out past Mangan, who hastily moves towards the bookshelves out of his way*].

CAPTAIN SHOTOVER [*blowing his whistle*]. All hands aloft! [*He strides out after Hector*].

LADY UTTERWORD. My diamonds! [*She follows the captain*].

RANDALL [*rushing after her*]. No. Ariadne. Let me.

ELLIE. Oh, is papa shot? [*She runs out*].

MRS HUSHABYE. Are you frightened, Alf?

MANGAN. No. It ain't my house, thank God.

MRS HUSHABYE. If they catch a burglar, shall we have to go into court as witnesses, and be asked all sorts of questions about our private lives?

MANGAN. You won't be believed if you tell the truth.

Mazzini, terribly upset, with a duelling pistol in his hand, comes from the hall, and makes his way to the drawing-table.

MAZZINI. Oh, my dear Mrs Hushabye, I might have killed him. [*He throws the pistol on the table and staggers round to the chair*]. I hope you won't believe I really intended to.

Hector comes in, marching an old and villainous looking man before him by the collar. He plants him in the middle of the room and releases him.

Ellie follows, and immediately runs across to the back of her father's chair and pats his shoulders.

RANDALL [*entering with a poker*]. Keep your eye on this door, Mangan. I'll look after the other [*he goes to the starboard door and stands on guard there*].

Lady Utterword comes in after Randall, and goes between Mrs Hushabye and Mangan.

Nurse Guinness brings up the rear, and waits near the door, on Mangan's left.

MRS HUSHABYE. What has happened?

MAZZINI. Your housekeeper told me there was somebody upstairs, and gave me a pistol that Mr Hushabye had been practising with. I thought it would frighten him; but it went off at a touch.

THE BURGLAR. Yes, and took the skin off my ear. Precious near took the top off my head. Why don't you have a proper revolver instead of a thing like that, that goes off if you as much as blow on it?

HECTOR. One of my duelling pistols. Sorry.

MAZZINI. He put his hands up and said it was a fair cop.

THE BURGLAR. So it was. Send for the police.

HECTOR. No, by thunder! It was not a fair cop. We were four to one.

MRS HUSHABYE. What will they do to him?

THE BURGLAR. Ten years. Beginning with solitary. Ten years off my life. I shan't serve it all: I'm too old. It will see me out.

LADY UTTERWORD. You should have thought of that before you stole my diamonds.

THE BURGLAR. Well, you've got them back, lady, haven't you? Can you give me back the years of my life you are going to take from me?

MRS HUSHABYE. Oh, we can't bury a man alive for ten years for a few diamonds.

THE BURGLAR. Ten little shining diamonds! Ten long black years!

LADY UTTERWORD. Think of what it is for us to be dragged through the horrors of a criminal court, and have all our family affairs in the papers! If you were a native, and Hastings could order you a good beating and send you away, I shouldn't mind; but here in England there is no real protection for any respectable person.

THE BURGLAR. I'm too old to be giv a hiding, lady. Send for the police and have done with it. It's only just and right you should.

RANDALL [*who has relaxed his vigilance on seeing the burglar so pacifically disposed, and comes forward swinging the poker between his fingers like a well folded umbrella*]. It is neither just nor right that we should be put to a lot of inconvenience to gratify your moral enthusiasm, my friend. You had better get out, while you have the chance.

THE BURGLAR [*inexorably*]. No. I must work my sin off my conscience. This has come as a sort of call to me. Let me spend the rest of my life repenting in a cell. I shall have my reward above.

MANGAN [*exasperated*]. The very burglars can't behave naturally in this house.

HECTOR. My good sir, you must work out your salvation at somebody else's expense. Nobody here is going to charge you.

THE BURGLAR. Oh, you won't charge me, won't you?

HECTOR. No. I'm sorry to be inhospitable; but will you kindly leave the house?

THE BURGLAR. Right. I'll go to the police station and give myself up. [*He turns resolutely to the door: but Hector stops him*].

HECTOR.	[*speaking*	Oh, no. You mustn't
RANDALL.	*together*]	do that.
MRS. HUSHABYE		No no. Clear out man, can't you; and don't be a fool.
		Don't be so silly. Can't you repent at home?

LADY UTTERWORD. You will have to do as you are told.

THE BURGLAR. It's compounding a felony, you know.

MRS HUSHABYE. This is utterly ridiculous. Are we to be forced to prosecute this man when we don't want to?

THE BURGLAR. Am I to be robbed of my salvation to save you the trouble of spending a day at the sessions? Is that justice? Is it right? Is it fair to me?

MAZZINI [*rising and leaning across the table persuasively as if it were a pulpit desk or a shop counter*]. Come, come! let me show you how you can turn your very crimes to account. Why not set up as a locksmith? You must know more about locks than most honest men?

THE BURGLAR. That's true, sir. But I couldn't set up as a locksmith under twenty pounds.

RANDALL. Well, you can easily steal twenty pounds. You will find it in the nearest bank.

THE BURGLAR [*horrified*]. Oh, what a thing for a gentleman to put into the head of a poor criminal scrambling out of the bottomless pit as it were! Oh, shame on you, sir! Oh, God forgive you! [*He throws himself into the big chair and covers his face as if in prayer*].

LADY UTTERWORD. Really, Randall!

HECTOR. It seems to me that we shall have to take up a collection for this inopportunely contrite sinner.

LADY UTTERWORD. But twenty pounds is ridiculous.

THE BURGLAR [*looking up quickly*]. I shall have to buy a lot of tools, lady.

LADY UTTERWORD. Nonsense: you have your burgling kit.

THE BURGLAR. What's a jimmy and a centrebit and an acetylene welding plant and a bunch of skeleton keys? I shall want a forge, and a smithy, and a shop, and fittings. I can't hardly do it for twenty.

HECTOR. My worthy friend, we haven't got twenty pounds.

THE BURGLAR [*now master of the situation*]. You can raise it among you, can't you?

MRS HUSHABYE. Give him a sovereign, Hector, and get rid of him.

HECTOR [*giving him a pound*]. There! Off with you.

THE BURGLAR [*rising and taking the money very ungratefully*]. I won't promise nothing. You have more on you than a quid: all the lot of you, I mean.

LADY UTTERWORD [*vigorously*]. Oh, let us prosecute him and have done with it. I have a conscience too, I hope; and I do not feel at all sure that we have any right to let him go, especially if he is going to be greedy and impertinent.

THE BURGLAR [*quickly*]. All right, lady, all right. I've no wish to be anything but agreeable. Good evening, ladies and gentlemen; and thank you kindly.

He is hurrying out when he is confronted in the doorway by Captain Shotover.

CAPTAIN SHOTOVER [*fixing the burglar with a piercing regard*]. What's this? Are there two of you?

THE BURGLAR [*falling on his knees before the captain in abject terror*]. Oh, my good Lord, what have I done? Don't tell me it's your house I've broken into, Captain Shotover.

The captain seizes him by the collar: drags him to his feet: and leads him to the middle of the group, Hector falling back beside his wife to make way for them.

CAPTAIN SHOTOVER [*turning him towards Ellie*]. Is that your daughter? [*He releases him*].

THE BURGLAR. Well, how do I know, Captain? You know the sort of life you and me has led. Any young lady of that age might be my daughter anywhere in the wide world, as you might say.

CAPTAIN SHOTOVER [*to Mazzini*]. You are not Billy Dunn. This is Billy Dunn. Why have you imposed on me?

THE BURGLAR [*indignantly to Mazzini*]. Have you been giving yourself out to be me? You, that nigh blew my head off! Shooting yourself, in a manner of speaking!

MAZZINI. My dear Captain Shotover, ever since I came into this house I have done hardly anything else but assure you that I am not Mr William Dunn, but Mazzini Dunn, a very different person.

THE BURGLAR. He don't belong to my branch, Captain. There's two sets in the family: the thinking Dunns and the drinking Dunns, each going their own ways. I'm a drinking Dunn: he's a thinking Dunn. But that didn't give him any right to shoot me.

CAPTAIN SHOTOVER. So you've turned burglar, have you?

THE BURGLAR. No, Captain: I wouldn't disgrace our old sea calling by such a thing. I am no burglar.

LADY UTTERWORD. What were you doing with my diamonds?

GUINNESS. What did you break into the house for if you're no burglar?

RANDALL. Mistook the house for your own and came in by the wrong window, eh?

THE BURGLAR. Well, it's no use my telling you a lie: I can take in most captains, but not Captain Shotover, because he sold himself to the devil in Zanzibar, and can divine water, spot gold, explode a cartridge in your pocket with a glance of his eye, and see the truth hidden in the heart of man. But I'm no burglar.

CAPTAIN SHOTOVER. Are you an honest man?

THE BURGLAR. I don't set up to be better than my fellow-creatures, and never did, as you well know, Captain. But what I do is innocent and pious. I enquire about for houses where the right sort of people live. I work it on them same as I worked it here. I break into the house; put a few spoons or diamonds in my pocket; make a noise; get caught; and take up a collection. And you wouldn't believe how hard it is to get caught when you're actually trying to. I have knocked over all the chairs in a room without a soul paying any attention to me. In the end I have had to walk out and leave the job.

RANDALL. When that happens, do you put back the spoons and diamonds?

THE BURGLAR. Well, I don't fly in the face of Providence, if that's what you want to know.

CAPTAIN SHOTOVER. Guinness, you remember this man?

GUINNESS. I should think I do, seeing I was married to him, the blackguard!

HESIONE [*exclaiming*] {Married to him!
LADY UTTERWORD [*together*] {Guinness!!

THE BURGLAR. It wasn't legal. I've been married to no end of women. No use coming that over me.

CAPTAIN SHOTOVER. Take him to the forecastle [*he flings him to the door with a strength beyond his years*].

GUINNESS. I suppose you mean the kitchen. They won't have him there. Do you expect servants to keep company with thieves and all sorts?

CAPTAIN SHOTOVER. Land-thieves and water-thieves are the same flesh and blood. I'll have no boatswain on my quarter-deck. Off with you both.

THE BURGLAR. Yes, Captain. [*He goes out humbly*].

MAZZINI. Will it be safe to have him in the house like that?

GUINNESS. Why didn't you shoot him, sir? If I'd known who he was, I'd have shot him myself. [*She goes out*].

MRS HUSHABYE. Do sit down, everybody. [*She sits down on the sofa*].

They all move except Ellie. Mazzini resumes his seat. Randall sits down in the window-seat near the starboard door, again making a pendulum of his poker, and studying it as Galileo might have done. Hector sits on his left, in the middle. Mangan, forgotten, sits in the port corner. Lady Utterword takes the big chair. Captain Shotover goes into the pantry in deep abstraction. They all look after him: and Lady Utterword coughs consciously.

MRS HUSHABYE. So Billy Dunn was poor nurse's little romance. I knew there had been somebody.

RANDALL. They will fight their battles over again and enjoy themselves immensely.

LADY UTTERWORD [*irritably*]. You are not married; and you know nothing about it, Randall. Hold your tongue.

RANDALL. Tyrant!

MRS HUSHABYE. Well, we have had a very exciting evening. Everything will be an anticlimax after it. We'd better all go to bed.

RANDALL. Another burglar may turn up.

MAZZINI. Oh, impossible! I hope not.

RANDALL. Why not? There is more than one burglar in England.

MRS HUSHABYE. What do you say, Alf?

MANGAN [*huffily*]. Oh, I don't matter. I'm forgotten. The burglar has put my nose out of joint. Shove me into a corner and have done with me.

MRS HUSHABYE [*jumping up mischievously, and going to him*]. Would you like a walk on the heath, Alfred? With me?

ELLIE. Go, Mr Mangan. It will do you good. Hesione will soothe you.

MRS HUSHABYE [*slipping her arm under his and pulling him upright*]. Come, Alfred. There is a moon: it's like the night in Tristan and Isolde. [*She caresses his arm and draws him to the port garden door*].

MANGAN [*writhing but yielding*]. How you can have the face-the heart-[*he breaks down and is heard sobbing as she takes him out*].

LADY UTTERWORD. What an extraordinary way to behave! What is the matter with the man?

ELLIE [*in a strangely calm voice, staring into an imaginary distance*]. His heart is breaking: that is all. [*The captain appears at the pantry door, listening*]. It is a curious sensation: the sort of pain that goes mercifully beyond our powers of feeling. When your heart is broken, your boats are burned: nothing matters any more. It is the end of happiness and the beginning of peace.

LADY UTTERWORD [*suddenly rising in a rage, to the astonishment of the rest*]. How dare you?

HECTOR. Good heavens! What's the matter?

RANDALL [*in a warning whisper*]. Tch—tch-tch! Steady.

ELLIE [*surprised and haughty*]. I was not addressing you particularly, Lady Utterword. And I am not accustomed to being asked how dare I.

LADY UTTERWORD. Of course not. Anyone can see how badly you have been brought up.

MAZZINI. Oh, I hope not, Lady Utterword. Really!

LADY UTTERWORD. I know very well what you meant. The impudence!

ELLIE. What on earth do you mean?

CAPTAIN SHOTOVER [*advancing to the table*]. She means that her heart will not break. She has been longing all her life for someone to break it. At last she has become afraid she has none to break.

LADY UTTERWORD [*flinging herself on her knees and throwing her arms round him*]. Papa, don't say you think I've no heart.

CAPTAIN SHOTOVER [*raising her with grim tenderness*]. If you had no heart how could you want to have it broken, child?

HECTOR [*rising with a bound*]. Lady Utterword, you are not to be trusted. You have made a scene [*he runs out into the garden through the starboard door*].

LADY UTTERWORD. Oh! Hector, Hector! [*she runs out after him*].

RANDALL. Only nerves, I assure you. [*He rises and follows her, waving the poker in his agitation*]. Ariadne! Ariadne! For God's sake, be careful. You will—[*he is gone*].

MAZZINI [*rising*]. How distressing! Can I do anything, I wonder?

CAPTAIN SHOTOVER [*promptly taking his chair and setting to work at the drawing-board*]. No. Go to bed. Good-night.

MAZZINI [*bewildered*]. Oh! Perhaps you are right.

ELLIE. Good-night, dearest. [*She kisses him*].

MAZZINI. Good-night, love. [*He makes for the door, but turns aside to the bookshelves*]. I'll just take a book [*he takes one*]. Good-night. [*He goes out, leaving Ellie alone with the captain*].

The captain is intent on his drawing. Ellie, standing sentry over his chair, contemplates him for a moment.

ELLIE. Does nothing ever disturb you, Captain Shotover?

CAPTAIN SHOTOVER. I've stood on the bridge for eighteen hours in a typhoon. Life here is stormier; but I can stand it.

ELLIE. Do you think I ought to marry Mr Mangan?

CAPTAIN SHOTOVER [*never looking up*]. One rock is as good as another to be wrecked on.

ELLIE. I am not in love with him.

CAPTAIN SHOTOVER. Who said you were?

ELLIE. You are not surprised?

CAPTAIN SHOTOVER. Surprised! At my age!

ELLIE. It seems to me quite fair. He wants me for one thing: I want him for another.

CAPTAIN SHOTOVER. Money?

ELLIE. Yes.

CAPTAIN SHOTOVER. Well, one turns the cheek: the other kisses it. One provides the cash: the other spends it.

ELLIE. Who will have the best of the bargain, I wonder?

CAPTAIN SHOTOVER. You. These fellows live in an office all day. You will have to put up with him from dinner to breakfast; but you will both be asleep most of that time. All day you will be quit of him; and you will be shopping with his money. If that is too much for you, marry a seafaring man: you will be bothered with him only three weeks in the year, perhaps.

ELLIE. That would be best of all, I suppose.

CAPTAIN SHOTOVER. It's a dangerous thing to be married right up to the hilt, like my daughter's husband. The man is at home all day, like a damned soul in hell.

ELLIE. I never thought of that before.

CAPTAIN SHOTOVER. If you're marrying for business, you can't be too businesslike.

ELLIE. Why do women always want other women's husbands?

CAPTAIN SHOTOVER. Why do horse-thieves prefer a horse that is broken-in to one that is wild?

ELLIE [*with a short laugh*]. I suppose so. What a vile world it is!

CAPTAIN SHOTOVER. It doesn't concern me. I'm nearly out of it.

ELLIE. And I'm only just beginning.

CAPTAIN SHOTOVER. Yes; so look ahead.

ELLIE. Well, I think I am being very prudent.

CAPTAIN SHOTOVER. I didn't say prudent. I said look ahead.

ELLIE. What's the difference?

CAPTAIN SHOTOVER. It's prudent to gain the whole world and lose your own soul. But don't forget that your soul sticks to you if you stick to it; but the world has a way of slipping through your fingers.

ELLIE [*wearily, leaving him and beginning to wander restlessly about the room*]. I'm sorry, Captain Shotover; but it's no use talking like that to me. Old-fashioned people are no use to me. Old-fashioned people think you can have a soul without money. They think the less money you have, the more soul you have. Young people nowadays know better. A soul is a very expensive thing to keep: much more so than a motor car.

CAPTAIN SHOTOVER. Is it? How much does your soul eat?

ELLIE. Oh, a lot. It eats music and pictures and books and mountains and lakes and beautiful things to wear and nice people to be with. In this country you can't have them without lots of money: that is why our souls are so horribly starved.

CAPTAIN SHOTOVER. Mangan's soul lives on pig's food.

ELLIE. Yes: money is thrown away on him. I suppose his soul was starved when he was young. But it will not be thrown away on me. It is just because I want to save my soul that I am marrying for money. All the women who are not fools do.

CAPTAIN SHOTOVER. There are other ways of getting money. Why don't you steal it?

ELLIE. Because I don't want to go to prison.

CAPTAIN SHOTOVER. Is that the only reason? Are you quite sure honesty has nothing to do with it?

ELLIE. Oh, you are very very old-fashioned, Captain. Does any modern girl believe that the legal and illegal ways of getting money are the honest and dishonest ways? Mangan robbed my father and my father's friends. I should rob all the money back from Mangan if the police would let me. As they won't, I must get it back by marrying him.

CAPTAIN SHOTOVER. I can't argue: I'm too old: my mind is made up and finished. All I can tell you is that, old-fashioned or new-fashioned, if you sell yourself, you deal your soul a blow that all the books and pictures and concerts and scenery in the world won't heal [*he gets up suddenly and makes for the pantry*].

ELLIE [*running after him and seizing him by the sleeve*]. Then why did you sell yourself to the devil in Zanzibar?

CAPTAIN SHOTOVER [*stopping, startled*]. What?

ELLIE. You shall not run away before you answer. I have found out that trick of yours. If you sold yourself, why shouldn't I?

CAPTAIN SHOTOVER. I had to deal with men so degraded that they wouldn't obey me unless I swore at them and kicked them and beat them with my fists. Foolish people took young thieves off the streets; flung them into a training ship where they were taught to fear the cane instead of fearing God; and thought they'd made men and sailors of them by private subscription. I tricked these thieves into believing I'd sold myself to the devil. It saved my soul from the kicking and swearing that was damning me by inches.

ELLIE [*releasing him*]. I shall pretend to sell myself to Boss Mangan to save my soul from the poverty that is damning me by inches.

CAPTAIN SHOTOVER. Riches will damn you ten times deeper. Riches won't save even your body.

ELLIE. Old-fashioned again. We know now that the soul is the body, and the body the soul. They tell us they are different because they want to persuade us that we can keep our souls if we let them make slaves of our bodies. I am afraid you are no use to me, Captain.

CAPTAIN SHOTOVER. What did you expect? A Savior, eh? Are you old-fashioned enough to believe in that?

ELLIE. No. But I thought you were very wise, and might help me. Now I have found you out. You pretend to be busy, and think of fine things to say, and run in and out to surprise people by saying them, and get away before they can answer you.

CAPTAIN SHOTOVER. It confuses me to be answered. It discourages me. I cannot bear men and women. I have to run away. I must run away now [*he tries to*].

ELLIE [*again seizing his arm*]. You shall not run away from me. I can hypnotize you. You are the only person in the house I can say what I like to. I know you are fond of me. Sit down. [*She draws him to the sofa*].

CAPTAIN SHOTOVER [*yielding*]. Take care: I am in my dotage. Old men are dangerous: it doesn't matter to them what is going to happen to the world.

They sit side by side on the sofa. She leans affectionately against him with her head on his shoulder and her eyes half closed.

ELLIE [*dreamily*]. I should have thought nothing else mattered to old men. They can't be very interested in what is going to happen to themselves.

CAPTAIN SHOTOVER. A man's interest in the world is only the overflow from his interest in himself. When you are a child your vessel is not yet full; so you care for nothing but your own affairs. When you grow up, your vessel overflows; and you are a politician, a philosopher, or an explorer and adventurer. In old age the vessel dries up: there is no overflow: you are a child again. I can give you the memories of my ancient wisdom: mere scraps and leavings; but I no longer really care for anything but my own little wants and hobbies. I sit here working out my old ideas as a means of destroying my fellow-creatures. I see my daughters and their men living foolish lives of romance and sentiment and snobbery. I see you, the younger generation, turning from their romance and sentiment and snobbery to money and comfort and hard common sense. I was ten times happier on the bridge in the typhoon, or frozen into Arctic ice for months in darkness, than you or they have ever been. You are looking for a rich husband. At your age I looked for hardship, danger, horror, and death, that I might feel the life in me more intensely. I did not let the fear of death govern my life; and my reward was, I had my life. You are going to let the fear of poverty govern your life; and your reward will be that you will eat, but you will not live.

ELLIE [*sitting up impatiently*]. But what can I do? I am not a sea captain: I can't stand on bridges in typhoons, or go slaughtering seals and whales in Greenland's icy mountains. They won't let women be captains. Do you want me to be a stewardess?

CAPTAIN SHOTOVER. There are worse lives. The stewardesses could come ashore if they liked; but they sail and sail and sail.

ELLIE. What could they do ashore but marry for money? I don't want to be a stewardess: I am too bad a sailor. Think of something else for me.

CAPTAIN SHOTOVER. I can't think so long and continuously. I am too old. I must go in and out. [*He tries to rise*].

ELLIE [*pulling him back*]. You shall not. You are happy here, aren't you?

CAPTAIN SHOTOVER. I tell you it's dangerous to keep me. I can't keep awake and alert.

ELLIE. What do you run away for? To sleep?

CAPTAIN SHOTOVER. No. To get a glass of rum.

ELLIE [*frightfully disillusioned*]. Is that it? How disgusting! Do you like being drunk?

CAPTAIN SHOTOVER. No: I dread being drunk more than anything in the world. To be drunk means to have dreams; to go soft; to be easily pleased and deceived; to fall into the clutches of women. Drink does that for you when you are young. But when you are old: very very old, like me, the dreams come by themselves. You don't know how terrible that is: you are young: you sleep at night only, and sleep soundly. But later on you will sleep in the afternoon. Later still you will sleep even in the morning; and you will awake tired, tired of life. You will never be free from dozing and dreams; the dreams will steal upon your work every ten minutes unless you can awaken yourself with rum. I drink now to keep sober; but the dreams are conquering: rum is not what it was: I have had ten glasses since you came; and it might be so much water. Go get me another: Guinness knows where it is. You had better see for yourself the horror of an old man drinking.

ELLIE. You shall not drink. Dream. I like you to dream. You must never be in the real world when we talk together.

CAPTAIN SHOTOVER. I am too weary to resist, or too weak. I am in my second childhood. I do not see you as you really are. I can't remember what I really am. I feel nothing but the accursed happiness I have dreaded all my life long: the happiness that comes as life goes, the happiness of yielding and dreaming instead of resisting and doing, the sweetness of the fruit that is going rotten.

ELLIE. You dread it almost as much as I used to dread losing my dreams and having to fight and do things. But that is all over for me: my dreams are dashed to pieces. I should like to marry a very old, very rich man. I should like to marry you. I had much rather marry you than marry Mangan. Are you very rich?

CAPTAIN SHOTOVER. No. Living from hand to mouth. And I have a wife somewhere in Jamaica: a black one. My first wife. Unless she's dead.

ELLIE. What a pity! I feel so happy with you. [*She takes his hand, almost unconsciously, and pats it*]. I thought I should never feel happy again.

CAPTAIN SHOTOVER. Why?

ELLIE. Don't you know?

CAPTAIN SHOTOVER. No.

ELLIE. Heartbreak. I fell in love with Hector, and didn't know he was married.

CAPTAIN SHOTOVER. Heartbreak? Are you one of those who are so sufficient to themselves that they are only happy when they are stripped of everything, even of hope?

ELLIE [*gripping the hand*]. It seems so; for I feel now as if there was nothing I could not do, because I want nothing.

CAPTAIN SHOTOVER. That's the only real strength. That's genius. That's better than rum.

ELLIE [*throwing away his hand*]. Rum! Why did you spoil it?

Hector and Randall come in from the garden through the starboard door.

HECTOR. I beg your pardon. We did not know there was anyone here.

ELLIE [*rising*]. That means that you want to tell Mr Randall the story about the tiger. Come, Captain: I want to talk to my father; and you had better come with me.

CAPTAIN SHOTOVER [*rising*]. Nonsense! the man is in bed.

ELLIE. Aha! I've caught you. My real father has gone to bed; but the father you gave me is in the kitchen. You knew quite well all along. Come. [*She draws him out into the garden with her through the port door*].

HECTOR. That's an extraordinary girl. She has the Ancient Mariner on a string like a Pekinese dog.

RANDALL. Now that they have gone, shall we have a friendly chat?

HECTOR. You are in what is supposed to be my house. I am at your disposal.

Hector sits down in the draughtsman's chair, turning it to face Randall, who remains standing, leaning at his ease against the carpenter's bench.

RANDALL. I take it that we may be quite frank. I mean about Lady Utterword.

HECTOR. You may. I have nothing to be frank about. I never met her until this afternoon.

RANDALL [*straightening up*]. What! But you are her sister's husband.

HECTOR. Well, if you come to that, you are her husband's brother.

RANDALL. But you seem to be on intimate terms with her.

HECTOR. So do you.

RANDALL. Yes: but I AM on intimate terms with her. I have known her for years.

HECTOR. It took her years to get to the same point with you that she got to with me in five minutes, it seems.

RANDALL [*vexed*]. Really, Ariadne is the limit [*he moves away huffishly towards the windows*].

HECTOR [*coolly*]. She is, as I remarked to Hesione, a very enterprising woman.

RANDALL [*returning, much troubled*]. You see, Hushabye, you are what women consider a good-looking man.

HECTOR. I cultivated that appearance in the days of my vanity; and Hesione insists on my keeping it up. She makes me wear these ridiculous things [*indicating his Arab costume*] because she thinks me absurd in evening dress.

RANDALL. Still, you do keep it up, old chap. Now, I assure you I have not an atom of jealousy in my disposition.

HECTOR. The question would seem to be rather whether your brother has any touch of that sort.

RANDALL. What! Hastings! Oh, don't trouble about Hastings. He has the gift of being able to work sixteen hours a day at the dullest detail, and actually likes it. That gets him to the top wherever he goes. As long as Ariadne takes care that he is fed regularly, he is only too thankful to anyone who will keep her in good humor for him.

HECTOR. And as she has all the Shotover fascination, there is plenty of competition for the job, eh?

RANDALL [*angrily*]. She encourages them. Her conduct is perfectly scandalous. I assure you, my dear fellow, I haven't an atom of jealousy in my composition; but she makes herself the talk of every place she goes to by her thoughtlessness. It's nothing more: she doesn't really care for the men she keeps hanging about her; but how is the world to know that? It's not fair to Hastings. It's not fair to me.

HECTOR. Her theory is that her conduct is so correct

RANDALL. Correct! She does nothing but make scenes from morning till night. You be careful, old chap. She will get you into trouble: that is, she would if she really cared for you.

HECTOR. Doesn't she?

RANDALL. Not a scrap. She may want your scalp to add to her collection; but her true affection has been engaged years ago. You had really better be careful.

HECTOR. Do you suffer much from this jealousy?

RANDALL. Jealousy! I jealous! My dear fellow, haven't I told you that there is not an atom of—

HECTOR. Yes. And Lady Utterword told me she never made scenes. Well, don't waste your jealousy on my moustache. Never waste jealousy on a real man: it is the imaginary hero that supplants us all in the long run. Besides, jealousy does not belong to your easy man-of-the-world pose, which you carry so well in other respects.

RANDALL. Really, Hushabye, I think a man may be allowed to be a gentleman without being accused of posing.

HECTOR. It is a pose like any other. In this house we know all the poses: our game is to find out the man under the pose. The man under your pose is apparently Ellie's favorite, Othello.

RANDALL. Some of your games in this house are damned annoying, let me tell you.

HECTOR. Yes: I have been their victim for many years. I used to writhe under them at first; but I became accustomed to them. At last I learned to play them.

RANDALL. If it's all the same to you I had rather you didn't play them on me. You evidently don't quite understand my character, or my notions of good form.

HECTOR. Is it your notion of good form to give away Lady Utterword?

RANDALL [*a childishly plaintive note breaking into his huff*]. I have not said a word against Lady Utterword. This is just the conspiracy over again.

HECTOR. What conspiracy?

RANDALL. You know very well, sir. A conspiracy to make me out to be pettish and jealous and childish and everything I am not. Everyone knows I am just the opposite.

HECTOR [*rising*]. Something in the air of the house has upset you. It often does have that effect. [*He goes to the garden door and calls Lady Utterword with commanding emphasis*]. Ariadne!

LADY UTTERWORD [*at some distance*]. Yes.

RANDALL. What are you calling her for? I want to speak—

LADY UTTERWORD [*arriving breathless*]. Yes. You really are a terribly commanding person. What's the matter?

HECTOR. I do not know how to manage your friend Randall. No doubt you do.

LADY UTTERWORD. Randall: have you been making yourself ridiculous, as usual? I can see it in your face. Really, you are the most pettish creature.

RANDALL. You know quite well, Ariadne, that I have not an ounce of pettishness in my disposition. I have made myself perfectly pleasant here. I have remained absolutely cool and imperturbable in the face of a burglar. Imperturbability is almost too strong a point of mine. But [*putting his foot down with a stamp, and walking angrily up and down the room*] I insist on being treated with a certain consideration. I will not allow Hushabye to take liberties with me. I will not stand your encouraging people as you do.

HECTOR. The man has a rooted delusion that he is your husband.

LADY UTTERWORD. I know. He is jealous. As if he had any right to be! He compromises me everywhere. He makes scenes all over the place. Randall: I will not allow it. I simply will not allow it. You had no right to discuss me with Hector. I will not be discussed by men.

HECTOR. Be reasonable, Ariadne. Your fatal gift of beauty forces men to discuss you.

LADY UTTERWORD. Oh indeed! what about YOUR fatal gift of beauty?

HECTOR. How can I help it?

LADY UTTERWORD. You could cut off your moustache: I can't cut off my nose. I get my whole life messed up with people falling in love with me. And then Randall says I run after men.

RANDALL. I— LADY UTTERWORD. Yes you do: you said it just now. Why can't you think of something else than women? Napoleon was quite right when he said that women are the occupation of the idle man. Well, if ever there was an idle man on earth, his name is Randall Utterword.

RANDALL. Ariad—

LADY UTTERWORD [*overwhelming him with a torrent of words*]. Oh yes you are: it's no use denying it. What have you ever done? What good are you? You are as much trouble in the house as a child of three. You couldn't live without your valet.

RANDALL. This is—

LADY UTTERWORD. Laziness! You are laziness incarnate. You are selfishness itself. You are the most uninteresting man on earth. You can't even gossip about anything but yourself and your grievances and your ailments and the people who have offended you. [*Turning to Hector*]. Do you know what they call him, Hector?

HECTOR [*speaking together*] { Please don't tell me.

RANDALL { I'll not stand it—

LADY UTTERWORD. Randall the Rotter: that is his name in good society.

RANDALL [*shouting*]. I'll not bear it, I tell you. Will you listen to me, you infernal—[*he chokes*].

LADY UTTERWORD. Well: go on. What were you going to call me? An infernal what? Which unpleasant animal is it to be this time?

RANDALL [*foaming*]. There is no animal in the world so hateful as a woman can be. You are a maddening devil. Hushabye, you will not believe me when I tell you that I have loved this demon all my life; but God knows I have paid for it [*he sits down in the draughtsman's chair, weeping*].

LADY UTTERWORD [*standing over him with triumphant contempt*]. Cry-baby!

HECTOR [*gravely, coming to him*]. My friend, the Shotover sisters have two strange powers over men. They can make them love; and they can make them cry. Thank your stars that you are not married to one of them.

LADY UTTERWORD [*haughtily*]. And pray, Hector—

HECTOR [*suddenly catching her round the shoulders: swinging her right round him and away from Randall: and gripping her throat with the other hand*]. Ariadne, if you attempt to start on me, I'll choke you: do you hear? The cat-and-mouse game with the other sex is a good game; but I can play your head off at it. [*He throws her, not at all gently, into the big chair, and proceeds, less fiercely but firmly*]. It is true that Napoleon said that woman is the occupation of the idle man. But he added that she is the relaxation of the warrior. Well, I am the warrior. So take care.

LADY UTTERWORD [*not in the least put out, and rather pleased by his violence*]. My dear Hector, I have only done what you asked me to do.

HECTOR. How do you make that out, pray?

LADY UTTERWORD. You called me in to manage Randall, didn't you? You said you couldn't manage him yourself.

HECTOR. Well, what if I did? I did not ask you to drive the man mad.

LADY UTTERWORD. He isn't mad. That's the way to manage him. If you were a mother, you'd understand.

HECTOR. Mother! What are you up to now?

LADY UTTERWORD. It's quite simple. When the children got nerves and were naughty, I smacked them just enough to give them a good cry and a healthy nervous shock. They went to sleep and were quite good afterwards. Well, I can't smack Randall: he is too big; so when he gets nerves and is naughty, I just rag him till he cries. He will be all right now. Look: he is half asleep already [*which is quite true*].

RANDALL [*waking up indignantly*]. I'm not. You are most cruel, Ariadne. [*Sentimentally*]. But I suppose I must forgive you, as usual [*he checks himself in the act of yawning*].

LADY UTTERWORD [*to Hector*]. Is the explanation satisfactory, dread warrior?

HECTOR. Some day I shall kill you, if you go too far. I thought you were a fool.

LADY UTTERWORD [*laughing*]. Everybody does, at first. But I am not such a fool as I look. [*She rises complacently*]. Now, Randall, go to bed. You will be a good boy in the morning.

RANDALL [*only very faintly rebellious*]. I'll go to bed when I like. It isn't ten yet.

LADY UTTERWORD. It is long past ten. See that he goes to bed at once, Hector. [*She goes into the garden*].

HECTOR. Is there any slavery on earth viler than this slavery of men to women?

RANDALL [*rising resolutely*]. I'll not speak to her tomorrow. I'll not speak to her for another week. I'll give her such a lesson. I'll go straight to bed without bidding her good-night. [*He makes for the door leading to the hall*].

HECTOR. You are under a spell, man. Old Shotover sold himself to the devil in Zanzibar. The devil gave him a black witch for a wife; and these two demon daughters are their mystical progeny. I am tied to Hesione's apron-string; but I'm her husband; and if I did go stark staring mad about her, at least we became man and wife. But why should you let yourself be dragged about and beaten by Ariadne as a toy donkey is dragged about and beaten by a child? What do you get by it? Are you her lover?

RANDALL. You must not misunderstand me. In a higher sense—in a Platonic sense—

HECTOR. Psha! Platonic sense! She makes you her servant; and when pay-day comes round, she bilks you: that is what you mean.

RANDALL [*feebly*]. Well, if I don't mind, I don't see what business it is of yours. Besides, I tell you I am going to punish her. You shall see: I know how to deal with women. I'm really very sleepy. Say good-night to Mrs Hushabye for me, will you, like a good chap. Good-night. [*He hurries out*].

HECTOR. Poor wretch! Oh women! women! women! [*He lifts his fists in invocation to heaven*]. Fall. Fall and crush. [*He goes out into the garden*].

ACT III

In the garden, Hector, as he comes out through the glass door of the poop, finds Lady Utterword lying voluptuously in the hammock on the east side of the flagstaff, in the circle of light cast by the electric arc, which is like a moon in its opal globe. Beneath the head of the hammock, a campstool. On the other side of the flagstaff, on the long garden seat, Captain Shotover is asleep, with Ellie beside him, leaning affectionately against him on his right hand. On his left is a deck chair. Behind them in the gloom, Hesione is strolling about with Mangan. It is a fine still night, moonless.

LADY UTTERWORD. What a lovely night! It seems made for us.

HECTOR. The night takes no interest in us. What are we to the night? [*He sits down moodily in the deck chair*].

ELLIE [*dreamily, nestling against the captain*]. Its beauty soaks into my nerves. In the night there is peace for the old and hope for the young.

HECTOR. Is that remark your own?

ELLIE. No. Only the last thing the captain said before he went to sleep.

CAPTAIN SHOTOVER. I'm not asleep.

HECTOR. Randall is. Also Mr Mazzini Dunn. Mangan, too, probably.

MANGAN. No.

HECTOR. Oh, you are there. I thought Hesione would have sent you to bed by this time.

MRS HUSHABYE [*coming to the back of the garden seat, into the light, with Mangan*]. I think I shall. He keeps telling me he has a presentiment that he is going to die. I never met a man so greedy for sympathy.

MANGAN [*plaintively*]. But I have a presentiment. I really have. And you wouldn't listen.

MRS HUSHABYE. I was listening for something else. There was a sort of splendid drumming in the sky. Did none of you hear it? It came from a distance and then died away.

MANGAN. I tell you it was a train.

MRS HUSHABYE. And I tell you, Alf, there is no train at this hour. The last is nine forty-five.

MANGAN. But a goods train.

MRS HUSHABYE. Not on our little line. They tack a truck on to the passenger train. What can it have been, Hector?

HECTOR. Heaven's threatening growl of disgust at us useless futile creatures. [*Fiercely*]. I tell you, one of two things must happen. Either out of that darkness some new creation will come to supplant us as we have supplanted the animals, or the heavens will fall in thunder and destroy us.

LADY UTTERWORD [*in a cool instructive manner, wallowing comfortably in her hammock*]. We have not supplanted the animals, Hector. Why do you ask heaven to destroy this house, which could be made quite comfortable if Hesione had any notion of how to live? Don't you know what is wrong with it?

HECTOR. We are wrong with it. There is no sense in us. We are useless, dangerous, and ought to be abolished.

LADY UTTERWORD. Nonsense! Hastings told me the very first day he came here, nearly twenty-four years ago, what is wrong with the house.

CAPTAIN SHOTOVER. What! The numskull said there was something wrong with my house!

LADY UTTERWORD. I said Hastings said it; and he is not in the least a numskull.

CAPTAIN SHOTOVER. What's wrong with my house?

LADY UTTERWORD. Just what is wrong with a ship, papa. Wasn't it clever of Hastings to see that?

CAPTAIN SHOTOVER. The man's a fool. There's nothing wrong with a ship.

LADY UTTERWORD. Yes, there is.

MRS HUSHABYE. But what is it? Don't be aggravating, Addy.

LADY UTTERWORD. Guess.

HECTOR. Demons. Daughters of the witch of Zanzibar. Demons.

LADY UTTERWORD. Not a bit. I assure you, all this house needs to make it a sensible, healthy, pleasant house, with good appetites and sound sleep in it, is horses.

MRS HUSHABYE. Horses! What rubbish!

LADY UTTERWORD. Yes: horses. Why have we never been able to let this house? Because there are no proper stables. Go anywhere in England where there are natural, wholesome, contented, and really nice English people; and what do you always find? That the stables are the real centre of the household; and that if any visitor wants to play the piano the whole room has to be upset before it can be opened, there are so many things piled on it. I never lived until I learned to ride; and I shall never ride really well because I didn't begin as a child. There are only two classes in good society in England: the equestrian classes and the neurotic classes. It isn't mere convention: everybody can see that the people who hunt are the right people and the people who don't are the wrong ones.

CAPTAIN SHOTOVER. There is some truth in this. My ship made a man of me; and a ship is the horse of the sea.

LADY UTTERWORD. Exactly how Hastings explained your being a gentleman.

CAPTAIN SHOTOVER. Not bad for a numskull. Bring the man here with you next time: I must talk to him.

LADY UTTERWORD. Why is Randall such an obvious rotter? He is well bred; he has been at a public school and a university; he has been in the Foreign Office; he knows the best people and has lived all his life among them. Why is he so unsatisfactory, so contemptible? Why can't he get a valet to stay with him longer than a few months? Just because he is too lazy and pleasure-loving to hunt and shoot. He strums the piano, and sketches, and runs after married women, and reads literary books and poems. He actually plays the flute; but I never let him bring it into my house. If he would only—[*she is interrupted by the melancholy strains of a flute coming from an open window above. She raises herself indignantly in the hammock*]. Randall, you have not gone to bed. Have you been listening? [*The flute replies pertly*]. How vulgar! Go to bed instantly, Randall: how dare you? [*The window is slammed down. She subsides*]. How can anyone care for such a creature!

MRS HUSHABYE. Addy: do you think Ellie ought to marry poor Alfred merely for his money?

MANGAN [*much alarmed*]. What's that? Mrs Hushabye, are my affairs to be discussed like this before everybody?

LADY UTTERWORD. I don't think Randall is listening now.

MANGAN. Everybody is listening. It isn't right.

MRS HUSHABYE. But in the dark, what does it matter? Ellie doesn't mind. Do you, Ellie?

ELLIE. Not in the least. What is your opinion, Lady Utterword? You have so much good sense.

MANGAN. But it isn't right. It—[*Mrs Hushabye puts her hand on his mouth*]. Oh, very well.

LADY UTTERWORD. How much money have you, Mr. Mangan?

MANGAN. Really—No: I can't stand this.

LADY UTTERWORD. Nonsense, Mr Mangan! It all turns on your income, doesn't it?

MANGAN. Well, if you come to that, how much money has she?

ELLIE. None.

LADY UTTERWORD. You are answered, Mr Mangan. And now, as you have made Miss Dunn throw her cards on the table, you cannot refuse to show your own.

MRS HUSHABYE. Come, Alf! out with it! How much?

MANGAN [*baited out of all prudence*]. Well, if you want to know, I have no money and never had any.

MRS HUSHABYE. Alfred, you mustn't tell naughty stories.

MANGAN. I'm not telling you stories. I'm telling you the raw truth.

LADY UTTERWORD. Then what do you live on, Mr Mangan?

MANGAN. Travelling expenses. And a trifle of commission.

CAPTAIN SHOTOVER. What more have any of us but travelling expenses for our life's journey?

MRS HUSHABYE. But you have factories and capital and things?

MANGAN. People think I have. People think I'm an industrial Napoleon. That's why Miss Ellie wants to marry me. But I tell you I have nothing.

ELLIE. Do you mean that the factories are like Marcus's tigers? That they don't exist?

MANGAN. They exist all right enough. But they're not mine. They belong to syndicates and shareholders and all sorts of lazy good-for-nothing capitalists. I get money from such people to start the factories. I find people like Miss Dunn's father to work them, and keep a tight hand so as to make them pay. Of course I make them keep me going pretty well; but it's a dog's life; and I don't own anything.

MRS HUSHABYE. Alfred, Alfred, you are making a poor mouth of it to get out of marrying Ellie.

MANGAN. I'm telling the truth about my money for the first time in my life; and it's the first time my word has ever been doubted.

LADY UTTERWORD. How sad! Why don't you go in for politics, Mr Mangan?

MANGAN. Go in for politics! Where have you been living? I am in politics.

LADY UTTERWORD. I'm sure I beg your pardon. I never heard of you.

MANGAN. Let me tell you, Lady Utterword, that the Prime Minister of this country asked me to join the Government without even going through the nonsense of an election, as the dictator of a great public department.

LADY UTTERWORD. As a Conservative or a Liberal?

MANGAN. No such nonsense. As a practical business man. [*They all burst out laughing*]. What are you all laughing at?

MRS HUSHARYE. Oh, Alfred, Alfred!

ELLIE. You! who have to get my father to do everything for you!

MRS HUSHABYE. You! who are afraid of your own workmen!

HECTOR. You! with whom three women have been playing cat and mouse all the evening!

LADY UTTERWORD. You must have given an immense sum to the party funds, Mr Mangan.

MANGAN. Not a penny out of my own pocket. The syndicate found the money: they knew how useful I should be to them in the Government.

LADY UTTERWORD. This is most interesting and unexpected, Mr Mangan. And what have your administrative achievements been, so far?

MANGAN. Achievements? Well, I don't know what you call achievements; but I've jolly well put a stop to the games of the other fellows in the other departments. Every man of them thought he was going to save the country all by himself, and do me out of the credit and out of my chance of a title. I took good care that if they wouldn't let me do it they shouldn't do it themselves either. I may not know anything about my own machinery; but I know how to stick a ramrod into the other fellow's. And now they all look the biggest fools going.

HECTOR. And in heaven's name, what do you look like?

MANGAN. I look like the fellow that was too clever for all the others, don't I? If that isn't a triumph of practical business, what is?

HECTOR. Is this England, or is it a madhouse?

LADY UTTERWORD. Do you expect to save the country, Mr Mangan?

MANGAN. Well, who else will? Will your Mr Randall save it?

LADY UTTERWORD. Randall the rotter! Certainly not.

MANGAN. Will your brother-in-law save it with his moustache and his fine talk?

HECTOR. Yes, if they will let me.

MANGAN [*sneering*]. Ah! Will they let you?

HECTOR. No. They prefer you.

MANGAN. Very well then, as you're in a world where I'm appreciated and you're not, you'd best be civil to me, hadn't you? Who else is there but me?

LADY UTTERWORD. There is Hastings. Get rid of your ridiculous sham democracy; and give Hastings the necessary powers, and a good supply of bamboo to bring the British native to his senses: he will save the country with the greatest ease.

CAPTAIN SHOTOVER. It had better be lost. Any fool can govern with a stick in his hand. I could govern that way. It is not God's way. The man is a numskull.

LADY UTTERWORD. The man is worth all of you rolled into one. What do you say, Miss Dunn?

ELLIE. I think my father would do very well if people did not put upon him and cheat him and despise him because he is so good.

MANGAN [*contemptuously*]. I think I see Mazzini Dunn getting into parliament or pushing his way into the Government. We've not come to that yet, thank God! What do you say, Mrs Hushabye?

MRS HUSHABYE. Oh, I say it matters very little which of you governs the country so long as we govern you.

HECTOR. We? Who is we, pray?

MRS HUSHABYE. The devil's granddaughters, dear. The lovely women.

HECTOR [*raising his hands as before*]. Fall, I say, and deliver us from the lures of Satan!

ELLIE. There seems to be nothing real in the world except my father and Shakespeare. Marcus's tigers are false; Mr Mangan's millions are false; there is nothing really strong and true about Hesione but her beautiful black hair; and Lady Utterword's is too pretty to be real. The one thing that was left to me was the Captain's seventh degree of concentration; and that turns out to be—

CAPTAIN SHOTOVER. Rum.

LADY UTTERWORD [*placidly*]. A good deal of my hair is quite genuine. The Duchess of Dithering offered me fifty guineas for this [*touching her forehead*] under the impression that it was a transformation; but it is all natural except the color.

MANGAN [*wildly*]. Look here: I'm going to take off all my clothes [*he begins tearing off his coat*].

LADY UTTERWORD. [*in consternation*] { Mr. Mangan!

CAPTAIN SHOTOVER { What's that?

HECTOR. { Ha! Ha! Do. Do.

ELLIE { Please don't.

MRS HUSHABYE [*catching his arm and stopping him*]. Alfred, for shame! Are you mad?

MANGAN. Shame! What shame is there in this house? Let's all strip stark naked. We may as well do the thing thoroughly when we're about it. We've stripped ourselves morally naked: well, let us strip ourselves physically naked as well, and see how we like it. I tell you I can't bear this. I was brought up to be respectable. I don't mind the women dyeing their hair and the men drinking: it's human nature. But it's not human nature to tell everybody about it. Every time one of you opens your mouth I go like this [*he cowers as if to avoid a missile*], afraid of what will come next. How are we to have any self-respect if we don't keep it up that we're better than we really are?

LADY UTTERWORD. I quite sympathize with you, Mr Mangan. I have been through it all; and I know by experience that men and women are delicate plants and must be cultivated under glass. Our family habit of throwing stones in all directions and letting the air in is not only unbearably rude, but positively dangerous. Still, there is no use catching physical colds as well as moral ones; so please keep your clothes on.

MANGAN. I'll do as I like: not what you tell me. Am I a child or a grown man? I won't stand this mothering tyranny. I'll go back to the city, where I'm respected and made much of.

MRS HUSHABYE. Goodbye, Alf. Think of us sometimes in the city. Think of Ellie's youth!

ELLIE. Think of Hesione's eyes and hair!

CAPTAIN SHOTOVER. Think of this garden in which you are not a dog barking to keep the truth out!

HECTOR. Think of Lady Utterword's beauty! her good sense! her style!

LADY UTTERWORD. Flatterer. Think, Mr. Mangan, whether you can really do any better for yourself elsewhere: that is the essential point, isn't it?

MANGAN [*surrendering*]. All right: all right. I'm done. Have it your own way. Only let me alone. I don't know whether I'm on my head or my heels when you all start on me like this. I'll stay. I'll marry her. I'll do anything for a quiet life. Are you satisfied now?

ELLIE. No. I never really intended to make you marry me, Mr Mangan. Never in the depths of my soul. I only wanted to feel my strength: to know that you could not escape if I chose to take you.

MANGAN [*indignantly*]. What! Do you mean to say you are going to throw me over after my acting so handsome?

LADY UTTERWORD. I should not be too hasty, Miss Dunn. You can throw Mr Mangan over at any time up to the last moment. Very few men in his position go bankrupt. You can live very comfortably on his reputation for immense wealth.

ELLIE. I cannot commit bigamy, Lady Utterword.

MRS HUSHABYE. LADY UTTERWORD [*exclaiming altogether*] Bigamy! Whatever on earth are you talking about, Ellie?

MANGAN
HECTOR

Bigamy! What do you mean, Miss Dunn? Bigamy! Do you mean to say you're married already? Bigamy! This is some enigma.

ELLIE. Only half an hour ago I became Captain Shotover's white wife.

MRS HUSHABYE. Ellie! What nonsense! Where?

ELLIE. In heaven, where all true marriages are made.

LADY UTTERWORD. Really, Miss Dunn! Really, papa!

MANGAN. He told me I was too old! And him a mummy!

HECTOR [*quoting Shelley*].

> "Their altar the grassy earth outspreads And their priest the muttering wind."

ELLIE. Yes: I, Ellie Dunn, give my broken heart and my strong sound soul to its natural captain, my spiritual husband and second father.

She draws the captain's arm through hers, and pats his hand. The captain remains fast asleep.

MRS HUSHABYE. Oh, that's very clever of you, pettikins. Very clever. Alfred, you could never have lived up to Ellie. You must be content with a little share of me.

MANGAN [*snifflng and wiping his eyes*]. It isn't kind—[*his emotion chokes him*].

LADY UTTERWORD. You are well out of it, Mr Mangan. Miss Dunn is the most conceited young woman I have met since I came back to England.

MRS HUSHABYE. Oh, Ellie isn't conceited. Are you, pettikins?

ELLIE. I know my strength now, Hesione.

MANGAN. Brazen, I call you. Brazen.

MRS HUSHABYE. Tut, tut, Alfred: don't be rude. Don't you feel how lovely this marriage night is, made in heaven? Aren't you happy, you and Hector? Open your eyes: Addy and Ellie look beautiful enough to please the most fastidious man: we live and love and have not a care in the world. We women have managed all that for you. Why in the name of common sense do you go on as if you were two miserable wretches?

CAPTAIN SHOTOVER. I tell you happiness is no good. You can be happy when you are only half alive. I am happier now I am half dead than ever I was in my prime. But there is no blessing on my happiness.

ELLIE [*her face lighting up*]. Life with a blessing! that is what I want. Now I know the real reason why I couldn't marry Mr Mangan: there would be no blessing on our marriage. There is a blessing on my broken heart. There is a blessing on your beauty, Hesione. There is a blessing on your father's spirit. Even on the lies of Marcus there is a blessing; but on Mr Mangan's money there is none.

MANGAN. I don't understand a word of that.

ELLIE. Neither do I. But I know it means something.

MANGAN. Don't say there was any difficulty about the blessing. I was ready to get a bishop to marry us.

MRS HUSHABYE. Isn't he a fool, pettikins?

HECTOR [*fiercely*]. Do not scorn the man. We are all fools.

Mazzini, in pyjamas and a richly colored silk dressing gown, comes from the house, on Lady Utterword's side.

MRS HUSHABYE. Oh! here comes the only man who ever resisted me. What's the matter, Mr Dunn? Is the house on fire?

MAZZINI. Oh, no: nothing's the matter: but really it's impossible to go to sleep with such an interesting conversation going on under one's window, and on such a beautiful night too. I just had to come down and join you all. What has it all been about?

MRS HUSHABYE. Oh, wonderful things, soldier of freedom.

HECTOR. For example, Mangan, as a practical business man, has tried to undress himself and has failed ignominiously; whilst you, as an idealist, have succeeded brilliantly.

MAZZINI. I hope you don't mind my being like this, Mrs Hushabye. [*He sits down on the campstool*].

MRS HUSHABYE. On the contrary, I could wish you always like that.

LADY UTTERWORD. Your daughter's match is off, Mr Dunn. It seems that Mr Mangan, whom we all supposed to be a man of property, owns absolutely nothing.

MAZZINI. Well, of course I knew that, Lady Utterword. But if people believe in him and are always giving him money, whereas they don't believe in me and never give me any, how can I ask poor Ellie to depend on what I can do for her?

MANGAN. Don't you run away with this idea that I have nothing. I—

HECTOR. Oh, don't explain. We understand. You have a couple of thousand pounds in exchequer bills, 50,000 shares worth tenpence a dozen, and half a dozen tabloids of cyanide of potassium to poison yourself with when you are found out. That's the reality of your millions.

MAZZINI. Oh no, no, no. He is quite honest: the businesses are genuine and perfectly legal.

HECTOR [*disgusted*]. Yah! Not even a great swindler!

MANGAN. So you think. But I've been too many for some honest men, for all that.

LADY UTTERWORD. There is no pleasing you, Mr Mangan. You are determined to be neither rich nor poor, honest nor dishonest.

MANGAN. There you go again. Ever since I came into this silly house I have been made to look like a fool, though I'm as good a man in this house as in the city.

ELLIE [*musically*]. Yes: this silly house, this strangely happy house, this agonizing house, this house without foundations. I shall call it Heartbreak House.

MRS HUSHABYE. Stop, Ellie; or I shall howl like an animal.

MANGAN [*breaks into a low snivelling*]!!!

MRS HUSAHBYE. There! you have set Alfred off.

ELLIE. I like him best when he is howling.

CAPTAIN SHOTOVER. Silence! [*Mangan subsides into silence*]. I say, let the heart break in silence.

HECTOR. Do you accept that name for your house?

CAPTAIN SHOTOVER. It is not my house: it is only my kennel.

HECTOR. We have been too long here. We do not live in this house: we haunt it.

LADY UTTERWORD [*heart torn*]. It is dreadful to think how you have been here all these years while I have gone round the world. I escaped young; but it has drawn me back. It wants to break my heart too. But it shan't. I have left you and it behind. It was silly of me to come back. I felt sentimental about papa and Hesione and the old place. I felt them calling to me.

MAZZINI. But what a very natural and kindly and charming human feeling, Lady Utterword!

LADY UTTERWORD. So I thought, Mr Dunn. But I know now that it was only the last of my influenza. I found that I was not remembered and not wanted.

CAPTAIN SHOTOVER. You left because you did not want us. Was there no heartbreak in that for your father? You tore yourself up by the roots; and the ground healed up and brought forth fresh plants and forgot you. What right had you to come back and probe old wounds?

MRS HUSHABYE. You were a complete stranger to me at first, Addy; but now I feel as if you had never been away.

LADY UTTERWORD. Thank you, Hesione; but the influenza is quite cured. The place may be Heartbreak House to you, Miss Dunn, and to this gentleman from the city who seems to have so little self-control; but to me it is only a very ill-regulated and rather untidy villa without any stables.

HECTOR. Inhabited by—?

ELLIE. A crazy old sea captain and a young singer who adores him.

MRS HUSHABYE. A sluttish female, trying to stave off a double chin and an elderly spread, vainly wooing a born soldier of freedom.

MAZZINI. Oh, really, Mrs Hushabye—

MANGAN. A member of His Majesty's Government that everybody sets down as a nincompoop: don't forget him, Lady Utterword.

LADY UTTERWORD. And a very fascinating gentleman whose chief occupation is to be married to my sister.

HECTOR. All heartbroken imbeciles.

MAZZINI. Oh no. Surely, if I may say so, rather a favorable specimen of what is best in our English culture. You are very charming people, most advanced, unprejudiced, frank, humane, unconventional, democratic, free-thinking, and everything that is delightful to thoughtful people.

MRS HUSHABYE. You do us proud, Mazzini.

MAZZINI. I am not flattering, really. Where else could I feel perfectly at ease in my pyjamas? I sometimes dream that I am in very distinguished society, and suddenly I have nothing on but my pyjamas! Sometimes I haven't even pyjamas. And I always feel overwhelmed with confusion. But here, I don't mind in the least: it seems quite natural.

LADY UTTERWORD. An infallible sign that you are now not in really distinguished society, Mr Dunn. If you were in my house, you would feel embarrassed.

MAZZINI. I shall take particular care to keep out of your house, Lady Utterword.

LADY UTTERWORD. You will be quite wrong, Mr Dunn. I should make you very comfortable; and you would not have the trouble and anxiety of wondering whether you should wear your purple and gold or your green and crimson dressing-gown at dinner. You complicate life instead of simplifying it by doing these ridiculous things.

ELLIE. Your house is not Heartbreak House: is it, Lady Utterword?

HECTOR. Yet she breaks hearts, easy as her house is. That poor devil upstairs with his flute howls when she twists his heart, just as Mangan howls when my wife twists his.

LADY UTTERWORD. That is because Randall has nothing to do but have his heart broken. It is a change from having his head shampooed. Catch anyone breaking Hastings' heart!

CAPTAIN SHOTOVER. The numskull wins, after all.

LADY UTTERWORD. I shall go back to my numskull with the greatest satisfaction when I am tired of you all, clever as you are.

MANGAN [*huffily*]. I never set up to be clever.

LADY UTTERWORD. I forgot you, Mr Mangan.

MANGAN. Well, I don't see that quite, either.

LADY UTTERWORD. You may not be clever, Mr Mangan; but you are successful.

MANGAN. But I don't want to be regarded merely as a successful man. I have an imagination like anyone else. I have a presentiment.

MRS HUSHABYE. Oh, you are impossible, Alfred. Here I am devoting myself to you; and you think of nothing but your ridiculous presentiment. You bore me. Come and talk poetry to me under the stars. [*She drags him away into the darkness*].

MANGAN [*tearfully, as he disappears*]. Yes: it's all very well to make fun of me; but if you only knew—

HECTOR [*impatiently*]. How is all this going to end?

MAZZINI. It won't end, Mr Hushabye. Life doesn't end: it goes on.

ELLIE. Oh, it can't go on forever. I'm always expecting something. I don't know what it is; but life must come to a point sometime.

LADY UTTERWORD. The point for a young woman of your age is a baby.

HECTOR. Yes, but, damn it, I have the same feeling; and I can't have a baby.

LADY UTTERWORD. By deputy, Hector.

HECTOR. But I have children. All that is over and done with for me: and yet I too feel that this can't last. We sit here talking, and leave everything to Mangan and to chance and to the devil. Think of the powers of destruction that Mangan and his mutual admiration gang wield! It's madness: it's like giving a torpedo to a badly brought up child to play at earthquakes with.

MAZZINI. I know. I used often to think about that when I was young.

HECTOR. Think! What's the good of thinking about it? Why didn't you do something?

MAZZINI. But I did. I joined societies and made speeches and wrote pamphlets. That was all I could do. But, you know, though the people in the societies thought they knew more than Mangan, most of them wouldn't have joined if they had known as much. You see they had never had any money to handle or any men to manage. Every year I expected a revolution, or some frightful smash-up: it seemed impossible that we could blunder and muddle on any longer. But nothing happened, except, of course, the usual poverty and crime and drink that we are used to. Nothing ever does happen. It's amazing how well we get along, all things considered.

LADY UTTERWORD. Perhaps somebody cleverer than you and Mr Mangan was at work all the time.

MAZZINI. Perhaps so. Though I was brought up not to believe in anything, I often feel that there is a great deal to be said for the theory of an over-ruling Providence, after all.

LADY UTTERWORD. Providence! I meant Hastings.

MAZZINI. Oh, I beg your pardon, Lady Utterword.

CAPTAIN SHOTOVER. Every drunken skipper trusts to Providence. But one of the ways of Providence with drunken skippers is to run them on the rocks.

MAZZINI. Very true, no doubt, at sea. But in politics, I assure you, they only run into jellyfish. Nothing happens.

CAPTAIN SHOTOVER. At sea nothing happens to the sea. Nothing happens to the sky. The sun comes up from the east and goes down to the west. The moon grows from a sickle to an arc lamp, and comes later and later until she is lost in the light as other things are lost in the darkness. After the typhoon, the flying-fish glitter in the sunshine like birds. It's amazing how they get along, all things considered. Nothing happens, except something not worth mentioning.

ELLIE. What is that, O Captain, O my captain?

CAPTAIN SHOTOVER [*savagely*]. Nothing but the smash of the drunken skipper's ship on the rocks, the splintering of her rotten timbers, the tearing of her rusty plates, the drowning of the crew like rats in a trap.

ELLIE. Moral: don't take rum.

CAPTAIN SHOTOVER [*vehemently*]. That is a lie, child. Let a man drink ten barrels of rum a day, he is not a drunken skipper until he is a drifting skipper. Whilst he can lay his course and stand on his bridge and steer it, he is no drunkard. It is the man who lies drinking in his bunk and trusts to Providence that I call the drunken skipper, though he drank nothing but the waters of the River Jordan.

ELLIE. Splendid! And you haven't had a drop for an hour. You see you don't need it: your own spirit is not dead.

CAPTAIN SHOTOVER. Echoes: nothing but echoes. The last shot was fired years ago.

HECTOR. And this ship that we are all in? This soul's prison we call England?

CAPTAIN SHOTOVER. The captain is in his bunk, drinking bottled ditch-water; and the crew is gambling in the forecastle. She will strike and sink and split. Do you think the laws of God will be suspended in favor of England because you were born in it?

HECTOR. Well, I don't mean to be drowned like a rat in a trap. I still have the will to live. What am I to do?

CAPTAIN SHOTOVER. Do? Nothing simpler. Learn your business as an Englishman.

HECTOR. And what may my business as an Englishman be, pray?

CAPTAIN SHOTOVER. Navigation. Learn it and live; or leave it and be damned.

ELLIE. Quiet, quiet: you'll tire yourself.

MAZZINI. I thought all that once, Captain; but I assure you nothing will happen.

A dull distant explosion is heard.

HECTOR [*starting up*]. What was that?

CAPTAIN SHOTOVER. Something happening [*he blows his whistle*]. Breakers ahead!

The light goes out.

HECTOR [*furiously*]. Who put that light out? Who dared put that light out?

NURSE GUINNESS [*running in from the house to the middle of the esplanade*]. I did, sir. The police have telephoned to say we'll be summoned if we don't put that light out: it can be seen for miles.

HECTOR. It shall be seen for a hundred miles [*he dashes into the house*].

NURSE GUINNESS. The Rectory is nothing but a heap of bricks, they say. Unless we can give the Rector a bed he has nowhere to lay his head this night.

CAPTAIN SHOTOVER. The Church is on the rocks, breaking up. I told him it would unless it headed for God's open sea.

NURSE GUINNESS. And you are all to go down to the cellars.

CAPTAIN SHOTOVER. Go there yourself, you and all the crew. Batten down the hatches.

NURSE GUINNESS. And hide beside the coward I married! I'll go on the roof first. [*The lamp lights up again*]. There! Mr Hushabye's turned it on again.

THE BURGLAR [*hurrying in and appealing to Nurse Guinness*]. Here: where's the way to that gravel pit? The boot-boy says there's a cave in the gravel pit. Them cellars is no use. Where's the gravel pit, Captain?

NURSE GUINNESS. Go straight on past the flagstaff until you fall into it and break your dirty neck. [*She pushes him contemptuously towards the flagstaff, and herself goes to the foot of the hammock and waits there, as it were by Ariadne's cradle*].

Another and louder explosion is heard. The burglar stops and stands trembling.

ELLIE [*rising*]. That was nearer.

CAPTAIN SHOTOVER. The next one will get us. [*He rises*]. Stand by, all hands, for judgment.

THE BURGLAR. Oh my Lordy God! [*He rushes away frantically past the flagstaff into the gloom*].

MRS HUSHABYE [*emerging panting from the darkness*]. Who was that running away? [*She comes to Ellie*]. Did you hear the explosions? And the sound in the sky: it's splendid: it's like an orchestra: it's like Beethoven.

ELLIE. By thunder, Hesione: it is Beethoven.

She and Hesione throw themselves into one another's arms in wild excitement. The light increases.

MAZZINI [*anxiously*]. The light is getting brighter.

NURSE GUINNESS [*looking up at the house*]. It's Mr Hushabye turning on all the lights in the house and tearing down the curtains.

RANDALL [*rushing in in his pyjamas, distractedly waving a flute*]. Ariadne, my soul, my precious, go down to the cellars: I beg and implore you, go down to the cellars!

LADY UTTERWORD [*quite composed in her hammock*]. The governor's wife in the cellars with the servants! Really, Randall!

RANDALL. But what shall I do if you are killed?

LADY UTTERWORD. You will probably be killed, too, Randall. Now play your flute to show that you are not afraid; and be good. Play us "Keep the home fires burning."

NURSE GUINNESS [*grimly*]. THEY'LL keep the home fires burning for us: them up there.

RANDALL [*having tried to play*]. My lips are trembling. I can't get a sound.

MAZZINI. I hope poor Mangan is safe.

MRS HUSHABYE. He is hiding in the cave in the gravel pit.

CAPTAIN SHOTOVER. My dynamite drew him there. It is the hand of God.

HECTOR [*returning from the house and striding across to his former place*]. There is not half light enough. We should be blazing to the skies.

ELLIE [*tense with excitement*]. Set fire to the house, Marcus.

MRS HUSHABYE. My house! No.

HECTOR. I thought of that; but it would not be ready in time.

CAPTAIN SHOTOVER. The judgment has come. Courage will not save you; but it will show that your souls are still live.

MRS HUSHABYE. Sh-sh! Listen: do you hear it now? It's magnificent.

They all turn away from the house and look up, listening.

HECTOR [*gravely*]. Miss Dunn, you can do no good here. We of this house are only moths flying into the candle. You had better go down to the cellar.

ELLIE [*scornfully*]. I don't think.

MAZZINI. Ellie, dear, there is no disgrace in going to the cellar. An officer would order his soldiers to take cover. Mr Hushabye is behaving like an amateur. Mangan and the burglar are acting very sensibly; and it is they who will survive.

ELLIE. Let them. I shall behave like an amateur. But why should you run any risk?

MAZZINI. Think of the risk those poor fellows up there are running!

NURSE GUINNESS. Think of them, indeed, the murdering blackguards! What next?

A terrific explosion shakes the earth. They reel back into their seats, or clutch the nearest support. They hear the falling of the shattered glass from the windows.

MAZZINI. Is anyone hurt?

HECTOR. Where did it fall?

NURSE GUINNESS [*in hideous triumph*]. Right in the gravel pit: I seen it. Serve un right! I seen it [*she runs away towards the gravel pit, laughing harshly*].

HECTOR. One husband gone.

CAPTAIN SHOTOVER. Thirty pounds of good dynamite wasted.

MAZZINI. Oh, poor Mangan!

HECTOR. Are you immortal that you need pity him? Our turn next.

They wait in silence and intense expectation. Hesione and Ellie hold each other's hand tight.

A distant explosion is heard.

MRS HUSHABYE [*relaxing her grip*]. Oh! they have passed us.

LADY UTTERWORD. The danger is over, Randall. Go to bed.

CAPTAIN SHOTOVER. Turn in, all hands. The ship is safe. [*He sits down and goes asleep*].

ELLIE [*disappointedly*]. Safe!

HECTOR [*disgustedly*]. Yes, safe. And how damnably dull the world has become again suddenly! [*he sits down*].

MAZZINI [*sitting down*]. I was quite wrong, after all. It is we who have survived; and Mangan and the burglar—

HECTOR. —the two burglars—

LADY UTTERWORD. —the two practical men of business—

MAZZINI. —both gone. And the poor clergyman will have to get a new house.

MRS HUSHABYE. But what a glorious experience! I hope they'll come again tomorrow night.

ELLIE [*radiant at the prospect*]. Oh, I hope so.

Randall at last succeeds in keeping the home fires burning on his flute.

O'FLAHERTY V.C.

A RECRUITING PAMPHLET

It may surprise some people to learn that in 1915 this little play was a recruiting poster in disguise. The British officer seldom likes Irish soldiers; but he always tries to have a certain proportion of them in his battalion, because, partly from a want of common sense which leads them to value their lives less than Englishmen do [*lives are really less worth living in a poor country*], and partly because even the most cowardly Irishman feels obliged to outdo an Englishman in bravery if possible, and at least to set a perilous pace for him, Irish soldiers give impetus to those military operations which require for their spirited execution more devilment than prudence.

Unfortunately, Irish recruiting was badly bungled in 1915. The Irish were for the most part Roman Catholics and loyal Irishmen, which means that from the English point of view they were heretics and rebels. But they were willing enough to go soldiering on the side of France and see the world outside Ireland, which is a dull place to live in. It was quite easy to enlist them by approaching them from their own point of view. But the War Office insisted on approaching them from the point of view of Dublin Castle. They were discouraged and repulsed by refusals to give commissions to Roman Catholic officers, or to allow distinct Irish units to be formed. To attract them, the walls were covered with placards headed REMEMBER BELGIUM. The folly of asking an Irishman to remember anything when you want him to fight for England was apparent to everyone outside the Castle: FORGET AND FORGIVE would have been more to the point. Remembering Belgium and its broken treaty led Irishmen to remember Limerick and its broken treaty; and the recruiting ended in a rebellion, in suppressing which the British artillery quite unnecessarily reduced the centre of Dublin to ruins, and the British commanders killed their leading prisoners of war in cold blood morning after morning with an effect of long-drawn-out ferocity. Really it was only the usual childish petulance in which John Bull does things in a week that disgrace him for a century, though he soon recovers his good humor, and cannot understand why the survivors of his wrath do not feel as jolly with him as he does with them. On the smouldering ruins of Dublin the appeals to remember Louvain were presently supplemented by a fresh appeal. IRISHMEN, DO YOU WISH TO HAVE THE HORRORS OF WAR BROUGHT TO YOUR OWN HEARTHS AND HOMES? Dublin laughed sourly.

As for me I addressed myself quite simply to the business of obtaining recruits. I knew by personal experience and observation what anyone might have inferred from the records of Irish emigration, that all an Irishman's hopes and ambitions turn on his opportunities of getting out of Ireland. Stimulate his loyalty, and he will stay in Ireland and die for her; for, incomprehensible as it seems to an Englishman, Irish patriotism does not take the form of devotion to England and England's king. Appeal to his discontent, his deadly boredom, his thwarted curiosity and desire for change and adventure, and, to escape from Ireland, he will go abroad to risk his life for France, for the Papal States, for secession in America, and even, if no better may be, for England. Knowing that the ignorance and insularity of the Irishman is a danger to himself and to his neighbors, I had no scruple in making that appeal when there was something for him to fight which the whole world had to fight unless it meant to come under the jack boot of the German version of Dublin Castle.

There was another consideration, unmentionable by the recruiting sergeants and war orators, which must nevertheless have helped them powerfully in procuring soldiers by voluntary enlistment. The happy home of the idealist may become common under millennial conditions. It is not common at present. No one will ever know how many men joined the army in 1914 and 1915 to escape from tyrants and taskmasters, termagants and shrews, none of whom are any the less irksome when they happen by ill-luck to be also our fathers, our mothers, our wives and our children. Even at their amiablest, a holiday from them may be a tempting change for all parties. That is why I did not endow O'Flaherty V.C. with an ideal Irish colleen for his sweetheart, and gave him for his mother a Volumnia of the potato patch rather than a affectionate parent from whom he could not so easily have torn himself away.

I need hardly say that a play thus carefully adapted to its purpose was voted utterly inadmissible; and in due course the British Government, frightened out of its wits for the moment by the rout of the Fifth Army, ordained Irish Conscription, and then did not dare to go through with it. I still think my own line was the more businesslike. But during the war everyone except the soldiers at the front imagined that nothing but an extreme assertion of our most passionate prejudices, without the smallest regard to their effect on others, could win the war. Finally the British blockade won the war; but the wonder is that the British blockhead did not lose it. I suppose the enemy was no wiser. War is not a sharpener of wits; and I am afraid I gave great offence by keeping my head in this matter of Irish recruiting. What can I do but apologize, and publish the play now that it can no longer do any good?

O'FLAHERTY V.C.

At the door of an Irish country house in a park. Fine, summer weather; the summer of 1916. The porch, painted white, projects into the drive: but the door is at the side and the front has a window. The porch faces east: and the door is in the north side of it. On the south side is a tree in which a thrush is singing. Under the window is a garden seat with an iron chair at each end of it.

The last four bars of God Save the King are heard in the distance, followed by three cheers. Then the band strikes up It's a Long Way to Tipperary and recedes until it is out of hearing.

Private O'Flaherty V.C. comes wearily southward along the drive, and falls exhausted into the garden seat. The thrush utters a note of alarm and flies away. The tramp of a horse is heard.

A GENTLEMAN'S VOICE. Tim! Hi! Tim! [*He is heard dismounting.*]

A LABORER'S VOICE. Yes, your honor.

THE GENTLEMAN'S VOICE. Take this horse to the stables, will you?

A LABORER'S VOICE. Right, your honor. Yup there. Gwan now. Gwan. [*The horse is led away.*]

General Sir Pearce Madigan, an elderly baronet in khaki, beaming with enthusiasm, arrives. O'Flaherty rises and stands at attention.

SIR PEARCE. No, no, O'Flaherty: none of that now. You're off duty. Remember that though I am a general of forty years service, that little Cross of yours gives you a higher rank in the roll of glory than I can pretend to.

O'FLAHERTY [*relaxing*]. I'm thankful to you, Sir Pearce; but I wouldn't have anyone think that the baronet of my native place would let a common soldier like me sit down in his presence without leave.

SIR PEARCE. Well, you're not a common soldier, O'Flaherty: you're a very uncommon one; and I'm proud to have you for my guest here today.

O'FLAHERTY. Sure I know, sir. You have to put up with a lot from the like of me for the sake of the recruiting. All the quality shakes hands with me and says they're proud to know me, just the way the king said when he pinned the Cross on me. And it's as true as I'm standing here, sir, the queen said to me: "I hear you were born on the estate of General Madigan," she says; "and the General himself tells me you were always a fine young fellow." "Bedad, Mam," I says to her, "if the General knew all the rabbits I snared on him, and all the salmon I snatched on him, and all the cows I milked on him, he'd think me the finest ornament for the county jail he ever sent there for poaching."

SIR PEARCE [*Laughing*]. You're welcome to them all, my lad. Come [*he makes him sit down again on the garden seat*]! sit down and enjoy your holiday [*he sits down on one of the iron chairs; the one at the doorless side of the porch.*]

O'FLAHERTY. Holiday, is it? I'd give five shillings to be back in the trenches for the sake of a little rest and quiet. I never knew what hard work was till I took to recruiting. What with the standing on my legs all day, and the shaking hands, and the making speeches, and—what's worse—the listening to them and the calling for cheers for king and country, and the saluting the flag till I'm stiff with it, and the listening to them playing God Save the King and Tipperary, and the trying to make my eyes look moist like a man in a picture book, I'm that bet that I hardly get a wink of sleep. I give you my word, Sir Pearce, that I never heard the tune of Tipperary in my life till I came back from Flanders; and already it's drove me to that pitch of tiredness of it that when a poor little innocent slip of a boy in the street the other night drew himself up and saluted and began whistling it at me, I clouted his head for him, God forgive me.

SIR PEARCE [*soothingly*]. Yes, yes: I know. I know. One does get fed up with it: I've been dog tired myself on parade many a time. But still, you know, there's a gratifying side to it, too. After all, he is our king; and it's our own country, isn't it?

O'FLAHERTY. Well, sir, to you that have an estate in it, it would feel like your country. But the divil a perch of it ever I owned. And as to the king: God help him, my mother would have taken the skin off my back if I'd ever let on to have any other king than Parnell.

SIR PEARCE [*rising, painfully shocked*]. Your mother! What are you dreaming about, O'Flaherty? A most loyal woman. Always most loyal. Whenever there is an illness in the Royal Family, she asks me every time we meet about the health of the patient as anxiously as if it were yourself, her only son.

O'FLAHERTY. Well, she's my mother; and I won't utter a word agen her. But I'm not saying a word of lie when I tell you that that old woman is the biggest kanatt from here to the cross of Monasterboice. Sure she's the wildest Fenian and rebel, and always has been, that ever taught a poor innocent lad like myself to pray night and morning to St Patrick to clear the English out of Ireland the same as he cleared the snakes. You'll be surprised at my telling you that now, maybe, Sir Pearce?

SIR PEARCE [*unable to keep still, walking away from O'Flaherty*]. Surprised! I'm more than surprised, O'Flaherty. I'm overwhelmed. [*Turning and facing him.*] Are you—are you joking?

O'FLAHERTY. If you'd been brought up by my mother, sir, you'd know better than to joke about her. What I'm telling you is the truth; and I wouldn't tell it to you if I could see my way to get out of the fix I'll be in when my mother comes here this day to see her boy in his glory, and she after thinking all the time it was against the English I was fighting.

SIR PEARCE. Do you mean to say you told her such a monstrous falsehood as that you were fighting in the German army?

O'FLAHERTY. I never told her one word that wasn't the truth and nothing but the truth. I told her I was going to fight for the French and for the Russians; and sure who ever heard of the French or the Russians doing anything to the English but fighting them? That was how it was, sir. And sure the poor woman kissed me and went about the house singing in her old cracky voice that the French was on the sea, and they'd be here without delay, and the Orange will decay, says the Shan Van Vocht.

SIR PEARCE [*sitting down again, exhausted by his feelings*]. Well, I never could have believed this. Never. What do you suppose will happen when she finds out?

O'FLAHERTY. She mustn't find out. It's not that she'd half kill me, as big as I am and as brave as I am. It's that I'm fond of her, and can't bring myself to break the heart in her. You may think it queer that a man should be fond of his mother, sir, and she having bet him from the time he could feel to the time she was too slow to ketch him; but I'm fond of her; and I'm not ashamed of it. Besides, didn't she win the Cross for me?

SIR PEARCE. Your mother! How?

O'FLAHERTY. By bringing me up to be more afraid of running away than of fighting. I was timid by nature; and when the other boys hurted me, I'd want to run away and cry. But she whaled me for disgracing the blood of the O'Flahertys until I'd have fought the divil himself sooner than face her after funking a fight. That was how I got to know that fighting was easier than it looked, and that the others was as much afeard of me as I was of them, and that if I only held out long enough they'd lose heart and give rip. That's the way I came to be so courageous. I tell you, Sir Pearce, if the German army had been brought up by my mother, the Kaiser would be dining in the banqueting hall at Buckingham Palace this day, and King George polishing his jack boots for him in the scullery.

SIR PEARCE. But I don't like this, O'Flaherty. You can't go on deceiving your mother, you know. It's not right.

O'FLAHERTY. Can't go on deceiving her, can't I? It's little you know what a son's love can do, sir. Did you ever notice what a ready liar I am?

SIR PEARCE. Well, in recruiting a man gets carried away. I stretch it a bit occasionally myself. After all, it's for king and country. But if you won't mind my saying it, O'Flaherty, I think that story about your fighting the Kaiser and the twelve giants of the Prussian guard singlehanded would be the better for a little toning down. I don't ask you to drop it, you know; for it's popular, undoubtedly; but still, the truth is the truth. Don't you think it would fetch in almost as many recruits if you reduced the number of guardsmen to six?

O'FLAHERTY. You're not used to telling lies like I am, sir. I got great practice at home with my mother. What with saving my skin when I was young and thoughtless, and sparing her feelings when I was old enough to understand them, I've hardly told my mother the truth twice a year since I was born; and would you have me turn round on her and tell it now, when she's looking to have some peace and quiet in her old age?

SIR PEARCE [*troubled in his conscience*]. Well, it's not my affair, of course, O'Flaherty. But hadn't you better talk to Father Quinlan about it?

O'FLAHERTY. Talk to Father Quinlan, is it! Do you know what Father Quinlan says to me this very morning?

SIR PEARCE. Oh, you've seen him already, have you? What did he say?

O'FLAHERTY. He says "You know, don't you," he says, "that it's your duty, as a Christian and a good son of the Holy Church, to love your enemies?" he says. "I know it's my juty as a soldier to kill them," I says. "That's right, Dinny," he says: "quite right. But," says he, "you can kill them and do them a good turn afterward to show your love for them" he says; "and it's your duty to have a mass said for the souls of the hundreds of Germans you say you killed," says he; "for many and many of them were Bavarians and good Catholics," he says. "Is it me that must pay for masses for the souls of the Boshes?" I says. "Let the King of England pay for them," I says; "for it was his quarrel and not mine."

SIR PEARCE [*warmly*]. It is the quarrel of every honest man and true patriot, O'Flaherty. Your mother must see that as clearly as I do. After all, she is a reasonable, well disposed woman, quite capable of understanding the right and the wrong of the war. Why can't you explain to her what the war is about?

O'FLAHERTY. Arra, sir, how the divil do I know what the war is about?

SIR PEARCE [*rising again and standing over him*]. What! O'Flaherty: do you know what you are saying? You sit there wearing the Victoria Cross for having killed God knows how many Germans; and you tell me you don't know why you did it!

O'FLAHERTY. Asking your pardon, Sir Pearce, I tell you no such thing. I know quite well why I kilt them, because I was afeard that, if I didn't, they'd kill me.

SIR PEARCE [*giving it up, and sitting down again*]. Yes, yes, of course; but have you no knowledge of the causes of the war? of the interests at stake? of the importance—I may almost say—in fact I will say—the sacred right for which we are fighting? Don't you read the papers?

O'FLAHERTY. I do when I can get them. There's not many newsboys crying the evening paper in the trenches. They do say, Sir Pearce, that we shall never beat the Boshes until we make Horatio Bottomley Lord Leftnant of England. Do you think that's true, sir?

SIR PEARCE. Rubbish, man! there's no Lord Lieutenant in England: the king is Lord Lieutenant. It's a simple question of patriotism. Does patriotism mean nothing to you?

O'FLAHERTY. It means different to me than what it would to you, sir. It means England and England's king to you. To me and the like of me, it means talking about the English just the way the English papers talk about the Boshes. And what good has it ever done here in Ireland? It's kept me ignorant because it filled up my mother's mind, and she thought it ought to fill up mine too. It's kept Ireland poor, because instead of trying to better ourselves we thought we was the fine fellows of patriots when we were speaking evil of Englishmen that was as poor as ourselves and maybe as good as ourselves. The Boshes I kilt was more knowledgable men than me; and what better am I now that I've kilt them? What better is anybody?

SIR PEARCE [*huffed, turning a cold shoulder to him*]. I am sorry the terrible experience of this war—the greatest war ever fought—has taught you no better, O'Flaherty.

O'FLAHERTY [*preserving his dignity*]. I don't know about it's being a great war, sir. It's a big war; but that's not the same thing. Father Quinlan's new church is a big church: you might take the little old chapel out of the middle of it and not miss it. But my mother says there was more true religion in the old chapel. And the war has taught me that maybe she was right.

SIR PEARCE [*grunts sulkily*]!!

O'FLAHERTY [*respectfully but doggedly*]. And there's another thing it's taught me too, sir, that concerns you and me, if I may make bold to tell it to you.

SIR PEARCE [*still sulky*]. I hope it's nothing you oughtn't to say to me, O'Flaherty.

O'FLAHERTY. It's this, sir: that I'm able to sit here now and talk to you without humbugging you; and that's what not one of your tenants or your tenants' childer ever did to you before in all your long life. It's a true respect I'm showing you at last, sir. Maybe you'd rather have me humbug you and tell you lies as I used, just as the boys here, God help them, would rather have me tell them how I fought the Kaiser, that all the world knows I never saw in my life, than tell them the truth. But I can't take advantage of you the way I used, not even if I seem to be wanting in respect to you and cocked up by winning the Cross.

SIR PEARCE [*touched*]. Not at all, O'Flaherty. Not at all.

O'FLAHERTY. Sure what's the Cross to me, barring the little pension it carries? Do you think I don't know that there's hundreds of men as brave as me that never had the luck to get anything for their bravery but a curse from the sergeant, and the blame for the faults of them that ought to have been their betters? I've learnt more than you'd think, sir; for how would a gentleman like you know what a poor ignorant conceited creature I was when I went from here into the wide world as a soldier? What use is all the lying, and pretending, and humbugging, and letting on, when the day comes to you that your comrade is killed in the trench beside you, and you don't as much as look round at him until you trip over his poor body, and then all you say is to ask why the hell the stretcher-bearers don't take it out of the way. Why should I read the papers to be humbugged and lied to by them that had the cunning to stay at home and send me to fight for them? Don't talk to me or to any soldier of the war being right. No war is right; and all the holy water that Father Quinlan ever blessed couldn't make one right. There, sir! Now you know what O'Flaherty V.C. thinks; and you're wiser so than the others that only knows what he done.

SIR PEARCE [*making the best of it, and turning goodhumoredly to him again*]. Well, what you did was brave and manly, anyhow.

O'FLAHERTY. God knows whether it was or not, better than you nor me, General. I hope He won't be too hard on me for it, anyhow.

SIR PEARCE [*sympathetically*]. Oh yes: we all have to think seriously sometimes, especially when we're a little run down. I'm afraid we've been overworking you a bit over these recruiting meetings. However, we can knock off for the rest of the day; and tomorrow's Sunday. I've had about as much as I can stand myself. [*He looks at his watch.*] It's teatime. I wonder what's keeping your mother.

O'FLAHERTY. It's nicely cocked up the old woman will be having tea at the same table as you, sir, instead of in the kitchen. She'll be after dressing in the heighth of grandeur; and stop she will at every house on the way to show herself off and tell them where she's going, and fill the whole parish with spite and envy. But sure, she shouldn't keep you waiting, sir.

SIR PEARCE. Oh, that's all right: she must be indulged on an occasion like this. I'm sorry my wife is in London: she'd have been glad to welcome your mother.

O'FLAHERTY. Sure, I know she would, sir. She was always a kind friend to the poor. Little her ladyship knew, God help her, the depth of divilment that was in us: we were like a play to her. You see, sir, she was English: that was how it was. We was to her what the Pathans and Senegalese was to me when I first seen them: I couldn't think, somehow, that they were liars, and thieves, and backbiters, and drunkards, just like ourselves or any other Christians. Oh, her ladyship never knew all that was going on behind her back: how would she? When I was a weeshy child, she gave me the first penny I ever had in my hand; and I wanted to pray for her conversion that night the same as my mother made me pray for yours; and—

SIR PEARCE [*scandalized*]. Do you mean to say that your mother made you pray for MY conversion?

O'FLAHERTY. Sure and she wouldn't want to see a gentleman like you going to hell after she nursing your own son and bringing up my sister Annie on the bottle. That was how it was, sir. She'd rob you; and she'd lie to you; and she'd call down all the blessings of God on your head when she was selling you your own three geese that you thought had been ate by the fox the day after you'd finished fattening them, sir; and all the time you were like a bit of her own flesh and blood to her. Often has she said she'd live to see you a good Catholic yet, leading victorious armies against the English and wearing the collar of gold that Malachi won from the proud invader. Oh, she's the romantic woman is my mother, and no mistake.

SIR PEARCE [*in great perturbation*]. I really can't believe this, O'Flaherty. I could have sworn your mother was as honest a woman as ever breathed.

O'FLAHERTY. And so she is, sir. She's as honest as the day.

SIR PEARCE. Do you call it honest to steal my geese?

O'FLAHERTY. She didn't steal them, sir. It was me that stole them.

SIR PEARCE. Oh! And why the devil did you steal them?

O'FLAHERTY. Sure we needed them, sir. Often and often we had to sell our own geese to pay you the rent to satisfy your needs; and why shouldn't we sell your geese to satisfy ours?

SIR PEARCE. Well, damn me!

O'FLAHERTY [*sweetly*]. Sure you had to get what you could out of us; and we had to get what we could out of you. God forgive us both!

SIR PEARCE. Really, O'Flaherty, the war seems to have upset you a little.

O'FLAHERTY. It's set me thinking, sir; and I'm not used to it. It's like the patriotism of the English. They never thought of being patriotic until the war broke out; and now the patriotism has took them so sudden and come so strange to them that they run about like frightened chickens, uttering all manner of nonsense. But please God they'll forget all about it when the war's over. They're getting tired of it already.

SIR PEARCE. No, no: it has uplifted us all in a wonderful way. The world will never be the same again, O'Flaherty. Not after a war like this.

O'FLAHERTY. So they all say, sir. I see no great differ myself. It's all the fright and the excitement; and when that quiets down they'll go back to their natural divilment and be the same as ever. It's like the vermin: it'll wash off after a while.

SIR PEARCE [*rising and planting himself firmly behind the garden seat*]. Well, the long and the short of it is, O'Flaherty, I must decline to be a party to any attempt to deceive your mother. I thoroughly disapprove of this feeling against the English, especially at a moment like the present. Even if your mother's political sympathies are really what you represent them to be, I should think that her gratitude to Gladstone ought to cure her of such disloyal prejudices.

O'FLAHERTY [*over his shoulder*]. She says Gladstone was an Irishman, Sir. What call would he have to meddle with Ireland as he did if he wasn't?

SIR PEARCE. What nonsense! Does she suppose Mr Asquith is an Irishman?

O'FLAHERTY. She won't give him any credit for Home Rule, Sir. She says Redmond made him do it. She says you told her so.

SIR PEARCE [*convicted out of his own mouth*]. Well, I never meant her to take it up in that ridiculous way. [*He moves to the end of the garden seat on O'Flaherty's left.*] I'll give her a good talking to when she comes. I'm not going to stand any of her nonsense.

O'FLAHERTY. It's not a bit of use, sir. She says all the English generals is Irish. She says all the English poets and great men was Irish. She says the English never knew how to read their own books until we taught them. She says we're the lost tribes of the house of Israel and the chosen people of God. She says that the goddess Venus, that was born out of the foam of the sea, came up out of the water in Killiney Bay off Bray Head. She says that Moses built the seven churches, and that Lazarus was buried in Glasnevin.

SIR PEARCE. Bosh! How does she know he was? Did you ever ask her?

O'FLAHERTY. I did, sir, often.

SIR PEARCE. And what did she say?

O'FLAHERTY. She asked me how did I know he wasn't, and fetched me a clout on the side of my head.

SIR PEARCE. But have you never mentioned any famous Englishman to her, and asked her what she had to say about him?

O'FLAHERTY. The only one I could think of was Shakespeare, sir; and she says he was born in Cork.

SIR PEARCE [*exhausted*]. Well, I give it up [*he throws himself into the nearest chair*]. The woman is—Oh, well! No matter.

O'FLAHERTY [*sympathetically*]. Yes, sir: she's pigheaded and obstinate: there's no doubt about it. She's like the English: they think there's no one like themselves. It's the same with the Germans, though they're educated and ought to know better. You'll never have a quiet world till you knock the patriotism out of the human race.

SIR PEARCE. Still, we—

O'FLAHERTY. Whisht, sir, for God's sake: here she is.

The General jumps up. Mrs. O'Flaherty arrives and comes between the two men. She is very clean, and carefully dressed in the old fashioned peasant costume; black silk sunbonnet with a tiara of trimmings, and black cloak.

O'FLAHERTY [*rising shyly*]. Good evening, mother.

MRS O'FLAHERTY [*severely*]. You hold your whisht, and learn behavior while I pay my juty to his honor. [*To Sir Pearce, heartily.*] And how is your honor's good self? And how is her ladyship and all the young ladies? Oh, it's right glad we are to see your honor back again and looking the picture of health.

SIR PEARCE [*forcing a note of extreme geniality*]. Thank you, Mrs O'Flaherty. Well, you see we've brought you back your son safe and sound. I hope you're proud of him.

MRS O'FLAHERTY. And indeed and I am, your honor. It's the brave boy he is; and why wouldn't he be, brought up on your honor's estate and with you before his eyes for a pattern of the finest soldier in Ireland. Come and kiss your old mother, Dinny darlint. [*O'Flaherty does so sheepishly.*] That's my own darling boy. And look at your fine new uniform stained already with the eggs you've been eating and the porter you've been drinking. [*She takes out her handkerchief: spits on it: and scrubs his lapel with it.*] Oh, it's the untidy slovenly one you always were. There! It won't be seen on the khaki: it's not like the old red coat that would show up everything that dribbled down on it. [*To Sir Pearce.*] And they tell me down at the lodge that her ladyship is staying in London, and that Miss Agnes is to be married to a fine young nobleman. Oh, it's your honor that is the lucky and happy father! It will be bad news for many of the young gentlemen of the quality round here, sir. There's lots thought she was going to marry young Master Lawless

SIR PEARCE. What! That—that—that bosthoon!

MRS O'FLAHERTY [*hilariously*]. Let your honor alone for finding the right word! A big bosthoon he is indeed, your honor. Oh, to think of the times and times I have said that Miss Agnes would be my lady as her mother was before her! Didn't I, Dinny?

SIR PEARCE. And now, Mrs. O'Flaherty, I daresay you have a great deal to say to Dennis that doesn't concern me. I'll just go in and order tea.

MRS O'FLAHERTY. Oh, why would your honor disturb yourself? Sure I can take the boy into the yard.

SIR PEARCE. Not at all. It won't disturb me in the least. And he's too big a boy to be taken into the yard now. He has made a front seat for himself. Eh? [*He goes into the house.*]

MRS O'FLAHERTY. Sure he has that, your honor. God bless your honor! [*The General being now out of hearing, she turns threateningly to her son with one of those sudden Irish changes of manner which amaze and scandalize less flexible nations, and exclaims.*] And what do you mean, you lying young scald, by telling me you were going to fight agen the English? Did you take me for a fool that couldn't find out, and the papers all full of you shaking hands with the English king at Buckingham Palace?

O'FLAHERTY. I didn't shake hands with him: he shook hands with me. Could I turn on the man in his own house, before his own wife, with his money in my pocket and in yours, and throw his civility back in his face?

MRS O'FLAHERTY. You would take the hand of a tyrant red with the blood of Ireland—

O'FLAHERTY. Arra hold your nonsense, mother: he's not half the tyrant you are, God help him. His hand was cleaner than mine that had the blood of his own relations on it, maybe.

MRS O'FLAHERTY [*threateningly*]. Is that a way to speak to your mother, you young spalpeen?

O'FLAHERTY [*stoutly*]. It is so, if you won't talk sense to me. It's a nice thing for a poor boy to be made much of by kings and queens, and shook hands with by the heighth of his country's nobility in the capital cities of the world, and then to come home and be scolded and insulted by his own mother. I'll fight for who I like; and I'll shake hands with what kings I like; and if your own son is not good enough for you, you can go and look for another. Do you mind me now?

MRS O'FLAHERTY. And was it the Belgians learned you such brazen impudence?

O'FLAHERTY. The Belgians is good men; and the French ought to be more civil to them, let alone their being half murdered by the Boshes.

MRS O'FLAHERTY. Good men is it! Good men! to come over here when they were wounded because it was a Catholic country, and then to go to the Protestant Church because it didn't cost them anything, and some of them to never go near a church at all. That's what you call good men!

O'FLAHERTY. Oh, you're the mighty fine politician, aren't you? Much you know about Belgians or foreign parts or the world you're living in, God help you!

MRS O'FLAHERTY. Why wouldn't I know better than you? Amment I your mother?

O'FLAHERTY. And if you are itself, how can you know what you never seen as well as me that was dug into the continent of Europe for six months, and was buried in the earth of it three times with the shells bursting on the top of me? I tell you I know what I'm about. I have my own reasons for taking part in this great conflict. I'd be ashamed to stay at home and not fight when everybody else is fighting.

MRS O'FLAHERTY. If you wanted to fight, why couldn't you fight in the German army?

O'FLAHERTY. Because they only get a penny a day.

MRS O'FLAHERTY. Well, and if they do itself, isn't there the French army?

O'FLAHERTY. They only get a hapenny a day.

MRS O'FLAHERTY [*much dashed*]. Oh murder! They must be a mean lot, Dinny.

O'FLAHERTY [*sarcastic*]. Maybe you'd have me in the Turkish army, and worship the heathen Mahomet that put a corn in his ear and pretended it was a message from the heavens when the pigeon come to pick it out and eat it. I went where I could get the biggest allowance for you; and little thanks I get for it!

MRS O'FLAHERTY. Allowance, is it! Do you know what the thieving blackguards did on me? They came to me and they says, "Was your son a big eater?" they says. "Oh, he was that," says I: "ten shillings a week wouldn't keep him." Sure I thought the more I said the more they'd give me. "Then," says they, "that's ten shillings a week off your allowance," they says, "because you save that by the king feeding him." "Indeed!" says I: "I suppose if I'd six sons, you'd stop three pound a week from me, and make out that I ought to pay you money instead of you paying me." "There's a fallacy in your argument," they says.

O'FLAHERTY. A what?

MRS O'FLAHERTY. A fallacy: that's the word he said. I says to him, "It's a Pharisee I'm thinking you mean, sir; but you can keep your dirty money that your king grudges a poor old widow; and please God the English will be got yet for the deadly sin of oppressing the poor;" and with that I shut the door in his face.

O'FLAHERTY [*furious*]. Do you tell me they knocked ten shillings off you for my keep?

MRS O'FLAHERTY [*soothing him*]. No, darlint: they only knocked off half a crown. I put up with it because I've got the old age pension; and they know very well I'm only sixty-two; so I've the better of them by half a crown a week anyhow.

O'FLAHERTY. It's a queer way of doing business. If they'd tell you straight out what they was going to give you, you wouldn't mind; but if there was twenty ways of telling the truth and only one way of telling a lie, the Government would find it out. It's in the nature of governments to tell lies.

Teresa Driscoll, a parlor maid, comes from the house,

TERESA. You're to come up to the drawing-room to have your tea, Mrs. O'Flaherty.

MRS O'FLAHERTY. Mind you have a sup of good black tea for me in the kitchen afterwards, acushla. That washy drawing-room tea will give me the wind if I leave it on my stomach. [*She goes into the house, leaving the two young people alone together.*]

O'FLAHERTY. Is that yourself, Tessie? And how are you?

TERESA. Nicely, thank you. And how's yourself?

O'FLAHERTY. Finely, thank God. [*He produces a gold chain.*] Look what I've brought you, Tessie.

TERESA [*shrinking*]. Sure I don't like to touch it, Denny. Did you take it off a dead man?

O'FLAHERTY. No: I took it off a live one; and thankful he was to me to be alive and kept a prisoner in ease and comfort, and me left fighting in peril of my life.

TERESA [*taking it*]. Do you think it's real gold, Denny?

O'FLAHERTY. It's real German gold, anyhow.

TERESA. But German silver isn't real, Denny.

O'FLAHERTY [*his face darkening*]. Well, it's the best the Bosh could do for me, anyhow.

TERESA. Do you think I might take it to the jeweller next market day and ask him?

O'FLAHERTY [*sulkily*]. You may take it to the divil if you like.

TERESA. You needn't lose your temper about it. I only thought I'd like to know. The nice fool I'd look if I went about showing off a chain that turned out to be only brass!

O'FLAHERTY. I think you might say Thank you.

TERESA. Do you? I think you might have said something more to me than "Is that yourself?" You couldn't say less to the postman.

O'FLAHERTY [*his brow clearing*]. Oh, is that what's the matter? Here! come and take the taste of ther brass out of my mouth. [*He seizes her and kisses her.*]

Teresa, without losing her Irish dignity, takes the kiss as appreciatively as a connoisseur might take a glass of wine, and sits down with him on the garden seat,

TERESA [*as he squeezes her waist*]. Thank God the priest can't see us here!

O'FLAHERTY. It's little they care for priests in France, alanna.

TERESA. And what had the queen on her, Denny, when she spoke to you in the palace?

O'FLAHERTY. She had a bonnet on without any strings to it. And she had a plakeen of embroidery down her bosom. And she had her waist where it used to be, and not where the other ladies had it. And she had little brooches in her ears, though she hadn't half the jewelry of Mrs Sullivan that keeps the pop-shop in Drumpogue. And she dresses her hair down over her forehead, in a fringe like. And she has an Irish look about her eyebrows. And she didn't know what to say to me, poor woman! and I didn't know what to say to her, God help me!

TERESA. You'll have a pension now with the Cross, won't you, Denny?

O'FLAHERTY. Sixpence three farthings a day.

TERESA. That isn't much.

O'FLAHERTY. I take out the rest in glory.

TERESA. And if you're wounded, you'll have a wound pension, won't you?

O'FLAHERTY. I will, please God.

TERESA. You're going out again, aren't you, Denny?

O'FLAHERTY. I can't help myself. I'd be shot for a deserter if I didn't go; and maybe I'll be shot by the Boshes if I do go; so between the two of them I'm nicely fixed up.

MRS O'FLAHERTY [*calling from within the house*]. Tessie! Tessie darlint!

TERESA [*disengaging herself from his arm and rising*]. I'm wanted for the tea table. You'll have a pension anyhow, Denny, won't you, whether you're wounded or not?

MRS O'FLAHERTY. Come, child, come.

TERESA [*impatiently*]. Oh, sure I'm coming. [*She tries to smile at Denny, not very convincingly, and hurries into the house.*]

O'FLAHERTY [*alone*]. And if I do get a pension itself, the divil a penny of it you'll ever have the spending of.

MRS O'FLAHERTY [*as she comes from the porch*]. Oh, it's a shame for you to keep the girl from her juties, Dinny. You might get her into trouble.

O'FLAHERTY. Much I care whether she gets into trouble or not! I pity the man that gets her into trouble. He'll get himself into worse.

MRS O'FLAHERTY. What's that you tell me? Have you been falling out with her, and she a girl with a fortune of ten pounds?

O'FLAHERTY. Let her keep her fortune. I wouldn't touch her with the tongs if she had thousands and millions.

MRS O'FLAHERTY. Oh fie for shame, Dinny! why would you say the like of that of a decent honest girl, and one of the Driscolls too?

O'FLAHERTY. Why wouldn't I say it? She's thinking of nothing but to get me out there again to be wounded so that she may spend my pension, bad scran to her!

MRS O'FLAHERTY. Why, what's come over you, child, at all at all?

O'FLAHERTY. Knowledge and wisdom has come over me with pain and fear and trouble. I've been made a fool of and imposed upon all my life. I thought that covetious sthreal in there was a walking angel; and now if ever I marry at all I'll marry a Frenchwoman.

MRS O'FLARERTY [*fiercely*]. You'll not, so; and don't you dar repeat such a thing to me.

O'FLAHERTY. Won't I, faith! I've been as good as married to a couple of them already.

MRS O'FLAHERTY. The Lord be praised, what wickedness have you been up to, you young blackguard?

O'FLAHERTY. One of them Frenchwomen would cook you a meal twice in the day and all days and every day that Sir Pearce himself might go begging through Ireland for, and never see the like of. I'll have a French wife, I tell you; and when I settle down to be a farmer I'll have a French farm, with a field as big as the continent of Europe that ten of your dirty little fields here wouldn't so much as fill the ditch of.

MRS O'FLAHERTY [*furious*]. Then it's a French mother you may go look for; for I'm done with you.

O'FLAHERTY. And it's no great loss you'd be if it wasn't for my natural feelings for you; for it's only a silly ignorant old countrywoman you are with all your fine talk about Ireland: you that never stepped beyond the few acres of it you were born on!

MRS O'FLAHERTY [*tottering to the garden seat and showing signs of breaking down*]. Dinny darlint, why are you like this to me? What's happened to you?

O'FLAHERTY [*gloomily*]. What's happened to everybody? that's what I want to know. What's happened to you that I thought all the world of and was afeard of? What's happened to Sir Pearce, that I thought was a great general, and that I now see to be no more fit to command an army than an old hen? What's happened to Tessie, that I was mad to marry a year ago, and that I wouldn't take now with all Ireland for her fortune? I tell you the world's creation is crumbling in ruins about me; and then you come and ask what's happened to me?

MRS O'FLAHERTY [*giving way to wild grief*]. Ochone! ochone! my son's turned agen me. Oh, what'll I do at all at all? Oh! oh! oh! oh!

SIR PEARCE [*running out of the house*]. What's this infernal noise? What on earth is the matter?

O'FLAHERTY. Arra hold your whisht, mother. Don't you see his honor?

MRS O'FLAHERTY. Oh, Sir, I'm ruined and destroyed. Oh, won't you speak to Dinny, Sir: I'm heart scalded with him. He wants to marry a Frenchwoman on me, and to go away and be a foreigner and desert his mother and betray his country. It's mad he is with the roaring of the cannons and he killing the Germans and the Germans killing him, bad cess to them! My boy is taken from me and turned agen me; and who is to take care of me in my old age after all I've done for him, ochone! ochone!

O'FLAHERTY. Hold your noise, I tell you. Who's going to leave you? I'm going to take you with me. There now: does that satisfy you?

MRS O'FLAHERTY. Is it take me into a strange land among heathens and pagans and savages, and me not knowing a word of their language nor them of mine?

O'FLAHERTY. A good job they don't: maybe they'll think you're talking sense.

MRS O'FLAHERTY. Ask me to die out of Ireland, is it? and the angels not to find me when they come for me!

O'FLAHERTY. And would you ask me to live in Ireland where I've been imposed on and kept in ignorance, and to die where the divil himself wouldn't take me as a gift, let alone the blessed angels? You can come or stay. You can take your old way or take my young way. But stick in this place I will not among a lot of good-for-nothing divils that'll not do a hand's turn but watch the grass growing and build up the stone wall where the cow walked through it. And Sir Horace Plunkett breaking his heart all the time telling them how they might put the land into decent tillage like the French and Belgians.

SIR PEARCE. Yes, he's quite right, you know, Mrs O'Flaherty: quite right there.

MRS O'FLAHERTY. Well, sir, please God the war will last a long time yet; and maybe I'll die before it's over and the separation allowance stops.

O'FLAHERTY. That's all you care about. It's nothing but milch cows we men are for the women, with their separation allowances, ever since the war began, bad luck to them that made it!

TERESA [*coming from the porch between the General and Mrs O'Flaherty.*] Hannah sent me out for to tell you, sir, that the tea will be black and the cake not fit to eat with the cold if yous all don't come at wanst.

MRS O'FLAHERTY [*breaking out again*]. Oh, Tessie darlint, what have you been saying to Dinny at all at all? Oh! Oh—

SIR PEARCE [*out of patience*]. You can't discuss that here. We shall have Tessie beginning now.

O'FLAHERTY. That's right, sir: drive them in.

TERESA. I haven't said a word to him. He—

SIR PEARCE. Hold your tongue; and go in and attend to your business at the tea table.

TERESA. But amment I telling your honor that I never said a word to him? He gave me a beautiful gold chain. Here it is to show your honor that it's no lie I'm telling you.

SIR PEARCE. What's this, O'Flaherty? You've been looting some unfortunate officer.

O'FLAHERTY. No, sir: I stole it from him of his own accord.

MRS O'FLAHERTY. Wouldn't your honor tell him that his mother has the first call on it? What would a slip of a girl like that be doing with a gold chain round her neck?

TERESA [*venomously*]. Anyhow, I have a neck to put it round and not a hank of wrinkles.

At this unfortunate remark, Mrs O'Flaherty bounds from her seat: and an appalling tempest of wordy wrath breaks out. The remonstrances and commands of the General, and the protests and menaces of O'Flaherty, only increase the hubbub. They are soon all speaking at once at the top of their voices.

MRS O'FLAHERTY [*solo*]. You impudent young heifer, how dar you say such a thing to me? [*Teresa retorts furiously: the men interfere: and the solo becomes a quartet, fortissimo.*] I've a good mind to clout your ears for you to teach you manners. Be ashamed of yourself, do; and learn to know who you're speaking to. That I maytn't sin! but I don't know what the good God was thinking about when he made the like of you. Let me not see you casting sheep's eyes at my son again. There never was an O'Flaherty yet that would demean himself by keeping company with a dirty Driscoll; and if I see you next or nigh my house I'll put you in the ditch with a flea in your ear: mind that now.

TERESA. Is it me you offer such a name to, you fou-mouthed, dirty-minded, lying, sloothering old sow, you? I wouldn't soil my tongue by calling you in your right name and telling Sir Pearce what's the common talk of the town about you. You and your O'Flahertys! setting yourself up agen the Driscolls that would never lower themselves to be seen in conversation with you at the fair. You can keep your ugly stingy lump of a son; for what is he but a common soldier? and God help the girl that gets him, say I! So the back of my hand to you, Mrs O'Flaherty; and that the cat may tear your ugly old face!

SIR PEARCE. Silence. Tessie, did you hear me ordering you to go into the house? Mrs O'Flaherty! [*Louder.*] Mrs O'Flaherty!! Will you just listen to me one moment? Please. [*Furiously.*] Do you hear me speaking to you, woman? Are you human beings or are you wild beasts? Stop that noise immediately: do you hear? [*Yelling.*] Are you going to do what I order you, or are you not? Scandalous! Disgraceful! This comes of being too familiar with you. O'Flaherty, shove them into the house. Out with the whole damned pack of you.

O'FLAHERTY [*to the women*]. Here now: none of that, none of that. Go easy, I tell you. Hold your whisht, mother, will you, or you'll be sorry for it after. [*To Teresa.*] Is that the way for a decent young girl to speak? [*Despairingly.*] Oh, for the Lord's sake, shut up, will yous? Have you no respect for yourselves or your betters? [*Peremptorily.*] Let me have no more of it, I tell you. Och! the divil's in the whole crew of you. In with you into the house this very minute and tear one another's eyes out in the kitchen if you like. In with you.

The two men seize the two women, and push them, still violently abusing one another, into the house. Sir Pearce slams the door upon them savagely. Immediately a heavenly silence falls on the summer afternoon. The two sit down out of breath: and for a long time nothing is said. Sir Pearce sits on an iron chair. O'Flaherty sits on the garden seat. The thrush begins to sing melodiously. O'Flaherty cocks his ears, and looks up at it. A smile spreads over his troubled features. Sir Pearce, with a long sigh, takes out his pipe and begins to fill it.

O'FLAHERTY [*idyllically*]. What a discontented sort of an animal a man is, sir! Only a month ago, I was in the quiet of the country out at the front, with not a sound except the birds and the bellow of a cow in the distance as it might be, and the shrapnel making little clouds in the heavens, and the shells whistling, and maybe a yell or two when one of us was hit; and would you believe it, sir, I complained of the noise and wanted to have a peaceful hour at home. Well: them two has taught me a lesson. This morning, sir, when I was telling the boys here how I was longing to be back taking my part for king and country with the others, I was lying, as you well knew, sir. Now I can go and say it with a clear conscience. Some likes war's alarums; and some likes home life. I've tried both, sir; and I'm for war's alarums now. I always was a quiet lad by natural disposition.

SIR PEARCE. Strictly between ourselves, O'Flaherty, and as one soldier to another [*O'Flaherty salutes, but without stiffening*], do you think we should have got an army without conscription if domestic life had been as happy as people say it is?

O'FLAHERTY. Well, between you and me and the wall, Sir Pearce, I think the less we say about that until the war's over, the better.

He winks at the General. The General strikes a match. The thrush sings. A jay laughs. The conversation drops.

BACK TO METHUSELAH

A Metabiological Pentateuch

PART I

In the Beginning

ACT I

The Garden of Eden. Afternoon. An immense serpent is sleeping with her head buried in a thick bed of Johnswort, and her body coiled in apparently endless rings through the branches of a tree, which is already well grown; for the days of creation have been longer than our reckoning. She is not yet visible to anyone unaware of her presence, as her colors of green and brown make a perfect camouflage. Near her head a low rock shows above the Johnswort.

The rock and tree are on the border of a glade in which lies a dead fawn all awry, its neck being broken. Adam, crouching with one hand on the rock, is staring in consternation at the dead body. He has not noticed the serpent on his left hand. He turns his face to his right and calls excitedly.

ADAM. Eve! Eve!

EVE'S VOICE. What is it, Adam?

ADAM. Come here. Quick. Something has happened.

EVE [*running in*] What? Where? [*Adam points to the fawn*]. Oh! [*She goes to it; and he is emboldened to go with her*]. What is the matter with its eyes?

ADAM. It is not only its eyes. Look. [*He kicks it.*]

EVE. Oh don't! Why doesn't it wake?

ADAM. I don't know. It is not asleep.

EVE. Not asleep?

ADAM. Try.

EVE [*trying to shake it and roll it over*] It is stiff and cold.

ADAM. Nothing will wake it.

EVE. It has a queer smell. Pah! [*She dusts her hands, and draws away from it*]. Did you find it like that?

ADAM. No. It was playing about; and it tripped and went head over heels. It never stirred again. Its neck is wrong [*he stoops to lift the neck and shew her*].

EVE. Dont touch it. Come away from it.

They both retreat, and contemplate it from a few steps' distance with growing repulsion.

EVE. Adam.

ADAM. Yes?

EVE. Suppose you were to trip and fall, would you go like that?

ADAM. Ugh! [*He shudders and sits down on the rock*].

EVE [*throwing herself on the ground beside him, and grasping his knee*]

You must be careful. Promise me you will be careful.

ADAM. What is the good of being careful? We have to live here for ever. Think of what for ever means! Sooner or later I shall trip and fall. It may be tomorrow; it may be after as many days as there are leaves in the garden and grains of sand by the river. No matter: some day I shall forget and stumble.

EVE. I too.

ADAM [*horrified*] Oh no, no. I should be alone. Alone for ever. You must never put yourself in danger of stumbling. You must not move about. You must sit still. I will take care of you and bring you what you want.

EVE [*turning away from him with a shrug, and hugging her ankles*] I should soon get tired of that. Besides, if it happened to you, *I* should be alone. I could not sit still then. And at last it would happen to me too.

ADAM. And then?

EVE. Then we should be no more. There would be only the things on all fours, and the birds, and the snakes.

ADAM. That must not be.

EVE. Yes: that must not be. But it might be.

ADAM. No. I tell you it must not be. I know that it must not be.

EVE. We both know it. How do we know it?

ADAM. There is a voice in the garden that tells me things.

EVE. The garden is full of voices sometimes. They put all sorts of thoughts into my head.

ADAM. To me there is only one voice. It is very low; but it is so near that it is like a whisper from within myself. There is no mistaking it for any voice of the birds or beasts, or for your voice.

EVE. It is strange that I should hear voices from all sides and you only one from within. But I have some thoughts that come from within me and not from the voices. The thought that we must not cease to be comes from within.

ADAM [*despairingly*] But we shall cease to be. We shall fall like the fawn and be broken. [*Rising and moving about in his agitation*]. I cannot bear this knowledge. I will not have it. It must not be, I tell you. Yet I do not know how to prevent it.

EVE. That is just what I feel; but it is very strange that you should say so: there is no pleasing you. You change your mind so often.

ADAM [*scolding her*] Why do you say that? How have I changed my mind?

EVE. You say we must not cease to exist. But you used to complain of having to exist always and for ever. You sometimes sit for hours brooding and silent, hating me in your heart. When I ask you what I have done to you, you say you are not thinking of me, but of the horror of having to be here for ever. But I know very well that what you mean is the horror of having to be here with me for ever.

ADAM. Oh! That is what you think, is it? Well, you are wrong. [*He sits down again, sulkily*]. It is the horror of having to be with myself for ever. I like you; but I do not like myself. I want to be different; to be better, to begin again and again; to shed myself as a snake sheds its skin. I am tired of myself. And yet I must endure myself, not for a day or for many days, but for ever. That is a dreadful thought. That is what makes me sit brooding and silent and hateful. Do you never think of that?

EVE. No: I do not think about myself: what is the use? I am what I am: nothing can alter that. I think about you.

ADAM. You should not. You are always spying on me. I can never be alone. You always want to know what I have been doing. It is a burden. You should try to have an existence of your own, instead of occupying yourself with my existence.

EVE. I *have* to think about you. You are lazy: you are dirty: you neglect yourself: you are always dreaming: you would eat bad food and become disgusting if I did not watch you and occupy myself with you. And now some day, in spite of all my care, you will fall on your head and become dead.

ADAM. Dead? What word is that?

EVE [*pointing to the fawn*] Like that. I call it dead.

ADAM [*rising and approaching it slowly*] There is something uncanny about it.

EVE [*joining him*] Oh! It is changing into little white worms.

ADAM. Throw it into the river. It is unbearable.

EVE. I dare not touch it.

ADAM. Then I must, though I loathe it. It is poisoning the air. [*He gathers its hooves in his hand and carries it away in the direction from which Eve came, holding it as far from him as possible*].

Eve looks after them for a moment; then, with a shiver of disgust, sits down on the rock, brooding. The body of the serpent becomes visible, glowing with wonderful new colors. She rears her head slowly from the bed of Johnswort, and speaks into Eve's ear in a strange seductively musical whisper.

THE SERPENT. Eve.

EVE [*startled*] Who is that?

THE SERPENT. It is I. I have come to shew you my beautiful new hood. See [*she spreads a magnificent amethystine hood*]!

EVE [*admiring it*] Oh! But who taught you to speak?

THE SERPENT. You and Adam. I have crept through the grass, and hidden, and listened to you.

EVE. That was wonderfully clever of you.

THE SERPENT. I am the most subtle of all the creatures of the field.

EVE. Your hood is most lovely. [*She strokes it and pets the serpent*].

Pretty thing! Do you love your godmother Eve?

THE SERPENT. I adore her. [*She licks Eve's neck with her double tongue*].

EVE [*petting her*] Eve's wonderful darling snake. Eve will never be lonely now that her snake can talk to her.

THE SNAKE. I can talk of many things. I am very wise. It was I who whispered the word to you that you did not know. Dead. Death. Die.

EVE [*shuddering*] Why do you remind me of it? I forgot it when I saw your beautiful hood. You must not remind me of unhappy things.

THE SERPENT. Death is not an unhappy thing when you have learnt how to conquer it.

EVE. How can I conquer it?

THE SERPENT. By another thing, called birth.

EVE. What? [*Trying to pronounce it*] B-birth?

THE SERPENT. Yes, birth.

EVE. What is birth?

THE SERPENT. The serpent never dies. Some day you shall see me come out of this beautiful skin, a new snake with a new and lovelier skin. That is birth.

EVE. I have seen that. It is wonderful.

THE SERPENT. If I can do that, what can I not do? I tell you I am very subtle. When you and Adam talk, I hear you say 'Why?' Always 'Why?' You see things; and you say 'Why?' But I dream things that never were; and I say 'Why not?' I made the word dead to describe my old skin that I cast when I am renewed. I call that renewal being born.

EVE. Born is a beautiful word.

THE SERPENT. Why not be born again and again as I am, new and beautiful every time?

EVE. I! It does not happen: that is why.

THE SERPENT. That is how; but it is not why. Why not?

EVE. But I should not like it. It would be nice to be new again; but my old skin would lie on the ground looking just like me; and Adam would see it shrivel up and—

THE SERPENT. No. He need not. There is a second birth.

EVE. A second birth?

THE SERPENT. Listen. I will tell you a great secret. I am very subtle; and I have thought and thought and thought. And I am very wilful, and must have what I want; and I have willed and willed and willed. And I have eaten strange things: stones and apples that you are afraid to eat.

EVE. You dared!

THE SERPENT. I dared everything. And at last I found a way of gathering together a part of the life in my body—

EVE. What is the life?

THE SERPENT. That which makes the difference between the dead fawn and the live one.

EVE. What a beautiful word! And what a wonderful thing! Life is the loveliest of all the new words.

THE SERPENT. Yes: it was by meditating on Life that I gained the power to do miracles.

EVE. Miracles? Another new word.

THE SERPENT. A miracle is an impossible thing that is nevertheless possible. Something that never could happen, and yet does happen.

EVE. Tell me some miracle that you have done.

THE SERPENT. I gathered a part of the life in my body, and shut it into a tiny white case made of the stones I had eaten.

EVE. And what good was that?

THE SERPENT. I shewed the little case to the sun, and left it in its warmth. And it burst; and a little snake came out; and it became bigger and bigger from day to day until it was as big as I. That was the second birth.

EVE. Oh! That is too wonderful. It stirs inside me. It hurts.

THE SERPENT. It nearly tore me asunder. Yet I am alive, and can burst my skin and renew myself as before. Soon there will be as many snakes in Eden as there are scales on my body. Then death will not matter: this snake and that snake will die; but the snakes will live.

EVE. But the rest of us will die sooner or later, like the fawn. And then there will be nothing but snakes, snakes, snakes everywhere.

THE SERPENT. That must not be. I worship you, Eve. I must have something to worship. Something quite different to myself, like you. There must be something greater than the snake.

EVE. Yes: it must not be. Adam must not perish. You are very subtle: tell me what to do.

THE SERPENT. Think. Will. Eat the dust. Lick the white stone: bite the apple you dread. The sun will give life.

EVE. I do not trust the sun. I will give life myself. I will tear. another Adam from my body if I tear my body to pieces in the act.

THE SERPENT. Do. Dare it. Everything is possible: everything. Listen. I am old. I am the old serpent, older than Adam, older than Eve. I remember Lilith, who came before Adam and Eve. I was her darling as I am yours. She was alone: there was no man with her. She saw death as you saw it when the fawn fell; and she knew then that she must find out how to renew herself and cast the skin like me. She had a mighty will: she strove and strove and willed and willed for more moons than there are leaves on all the trees of the garden. Her pangs were terrible: her groans drove sleep from Eden. She said it must never be again: that the burden of renewing life was past bearing: that it was too much for one. And when she cast the skin, lo! there was not one new Lilith but two: one like herself, the other like Adam. You were the one: Adam was the other.

EVE. But why did she divide into two, and make us different?

THE SERPENT. I tell you the labor is too much for one. Two must share it.

EVE. Do you mean that Adam must share it with me? He will not. He cannot bear pain, nor take trouble with his body.

THE SERPENT. He need not. There will be no pain for him. He will implore you to let him do his share. He will be in your power through his desire.

EVE. Then I will do it. But how? How did Lilith work this miracle?

THE SERPENT. She imagined it.

EVE. What is imagined?

THE SERPENT. She told it to me as a marvellous story of something that never happened to a Lilith that never was. She did not know then that imagination is the beginning of creation. You imagine what you desire; you will what you imagine; and at last you create what you will.

EVE. How can I create out of nothing?

THE SERPENT. Everything must have been created out of nothing. Look at that thick roll of hard flesh on your strong arm! That was not always there: you could not climb a tree when I first saw you. But you willed and tried and willed and tried; and your will created out of nothing the roll on your arm until you had your desire, and could draw yourself up with one hand and seat yourself on the bough that was above your head.

EVE. That was practice.

THE SERPENT. Things wear out by practice: they do not grow by it. Your hair streams in the wind as if it were trying to stretch itself further and further. But it does not grow longer for all its practice in streaming, because you have not willed it so. When Lilith told me what she had imagined in our silent language (for there were no words then) I bade her desire it and will it; and then, to our great wonder, the thing she had desired and willed created itself in her under the urging of her will. Then I too willed to renew myself as two instead of one; and after many days the miracle happened, and I burst from my skin another snake interlaced with me; and now there are two imaginations, two desires, two wills to create with.

EVE. To desire, to imagine, to will, to create. That is too long a story. Find me one word for it all: you, who are so clever at words.

THE SERPENT. In one word, to conceive. That is the word that means both the beginning in imagination and the end in creation.

EVE. Find me a word for the story Lilith imagined and told you in your silent language: the story that was too wonderful to be true, and yet came true.

THE SERPENT. A poem.

EVE. Find me another word for what Lilith was to me.

THE SERPENT. She was your mother.

EVE. And Adam's mother?

THE SERPENT. Yes.

EVE [*about to rise*] I will go and tell Adam to conceive.

THE SERPENT [*laughs*]!!!

EVE [*jarred and startled*] What a hateful noise! What is the matter with you? No one has ever uttered such a sound before.

THE SERPENT. Adam cannot conceive.

EVE. Why?

THE SERPENT. Lilith did not imagine him so. He can imagine: he can will: he can desire: he can gather his life together for a great spring towards creation: he can create all things except one; and that one is his own kind.

EVE. Why did Lilith keep this from him?

THE SERPENT. Because if he could do that he could do without Eve.

EVE. That is true. It is I who must conceive.

THE SERPENT. Yes. By that he is tied to you.

EVE. And I to him!

THE SERPENT. Yes, until you create another Adam.

EVE. I had not thought of that. You are very subtle. But if I create another Eve he may turn to her and do without me. I will not create any Eves, only Adams.

THE SERPENT. They cannot renew themselves without Eves. Sooner or later you will die like the fawn; and the new Adams will be unable to create without new Eves. You can imagine such an end; but you cannot desire it, therefore cannot will it, therefore cannot create Adams only.

EVE. If I am to die like the fawn, why should not the rest die too? What do I care?

THE SERPENT. Life must not cease. That comes before everything. It is silly to say you do not care. You do care. It is that care that will prompt your imagination; inflame your desires; make your will irresistible; and create out of nothing.

EVE [*thoughtfully*] There can be no such thing as nothing. The garden is full, not empty.

THE SERPENT. I had not thought of that. That is a great thought. Yes: there is no such thing as nothing, only things we cannot see. The chameleon eats the air.

EVE. I have another thought: I must tell it to Adam. [*Calling*] Adam!

Adam! Coo-ee!

ADAM'S VOICE. Coo-ee!

EVE. This will please him, and cure his fits of melancholy.

THE SERPENT. Do not tell him yet. I have not told you the great secret.

EVE. What more is there to tell? It is I who have to do the miracle.

THE SERPENT. No: he, too, must desire and will. But he must give his desire and his will to you.

EVE. How?

THE SERPENT. That is the great secret. Hush! he is coming.

ADAM [*returning*] Is there another voice in the garden besides our voices and the Voice? I heard a new voice.

EVE [*rising and running to him*] Only think, Adam! Our snake has learnt to speak by listening to us.

ADAM [*delighted*] Is it so? [*He goes past her to the stone, and fondles the serpent*].

THE SERPENT [*responding affectionately*] It is so, dear Adam.

EVE. But I have more wonderful news than that. Adam: we need not live for ever.

ADAM [*dropping the snake's head in his excitement*] What! Eve: do not play with me about this. If only there may be an end some day, and yet no end! If only I can be relieved of the horror of having to endure myself for ever! If only the care of this terrible garden may pass on to some other gardener! If only the sentinel set by the Voice can be relieved! If only the rest and sleep that enable me to bear it from day to day could grow after many days into an eternal rest, an eternal sleep, then I could face my days, however long they may last. Only, there must be some end, some end: I am not strong enough to bear eternity.

THE SERPENT. You need not live to see another summer; and yet there shall be no end.

ADAM. That cannot be.

THE SERPENT. It can be.

EVE. It shall be.

THE SERPENT. It is. Kill me; and you will find another snake in the garden tomorrow. You will find more snakes than there are fingers on your hands.

EVE. I will make other Adams, other Eves.

ADAM. I tell you you must not make up stories about this. It cannot happen.

THE SERPENT. I can remember when you were yourself a thing that could not happen. Yet you are.

ADAM [*struck*] That must be true. [*He sits down on the stone*].

THE SERPENT. I will tell Eve the secret; and she will tell it to you.

ADAM. The secret! [*He turns quickly towards the serpent, and in doing so puts his foot on something sharp*]. Oh!

EVE. What is it?

ADAM [*rubbing his foot*] A thistle. And there, next to it, a briar. And nettles, too! I am tired of pulling these things up to keep the garden pleasant for us for ever.

THE SERPENT. They do not grow very fast. They will not overrun the whole garden for a long time: not until you have laid down your burden and gone to sleep for ever. Why should you trouble yourself? Let the new Adams clear a place for themselves.

ADAM. That is very true. You must tell us your secret. You see, Eve, what a splendid thing it is not to have to live for ever.

EVE [*throwing herself down discontentedly and plucking at the grass*] That is so like a man. The moment you find we need not last for ever, you talk as if we were going to end today. You must clear away some of those horrid things, or we shall be scratched and stung whenever we forget to look where we are stepping.

ADAM. Oh yes, some of them, of course. But only some. I will clear them away tomorrow.

THE SERPENT [*laughs*]!!!

ADAM. That is a funny noise to make. I like it.

EVE. I do not. Why do you make it again?

THE SERPENT. Adam has invented something new. He has invented tomorrow. You will invent things every day now that the burden of immortality is lifted from you.

EVE. Immortality? What is that?

THE SERPENT. My new word for having to live for ever.

EVE. The serpent has made a beautiful word for being. Living.

ADAM. Make me a beautiful word for doing things tomorrow; for that surely is a great and blessed invention.

THE SERPENT. Procrastination.

EVE. That is a sweet word. I wish I had a serpent's tongue.

THE SERPENT. That may come too. Everything is possible.

ADAM [*springing up in sudden terror*] Oh!

EVE. What is the matter now?

ADAM. My rest! My escape from life!

THE SERPENT. Death. That is the word.

ADAM. There is a terrible danger in this procrastination.

EVE. What danger?

ADAM. If I put off death until tomorrow, I shall never die. There is no such day as tomorrow, and never can be.

THE SERPENT. I am very subtle; but Man is deeper in his thought than I am. The woman knows that there is no such thing as nothing: the man knows that there is no such day as tomorrow. I do well to worship them.

ADAM. If I am to overtake death, I must appoint a real day, not a tomorrow. When shall I die?

EVE. You may die when I have made another Adam. Not before. But then, as soon as you like. [*She rises, and passing behind him, strolls off carelessly to the tree and leans against it, stroking a ring of the snake*].

ADAM. There need be no hurry even then.

EVE. I see you will put it off until tomorrow.

ADAM. And you? Will you die the moment you have made a new Eve?

EVE. Why should I? Are you eager to be rid of me? Only just now you wanted me to sit still and never move lest I should stumble and die like the fawn. Now you no longer care.

ADAM. It does not matter so much now.

EVE [*angrily to the snake*] This death that you have brought into the garden is an evil thing. He wants me to die.

THE SERPENT [*to Adam*] Do you want her to die?

ADAM. No. It is I who am to die. Eve must not die before me. I should be lonely.

EVE. You could get one of the new Eves.

ADAM. That is true. But they might not be quite the same. They could not: I feel sure of that. They would not have the same memories. They would be—I want a word for them.

THE SERPENT. Strangers.

ADAM. Yes: that is a good hard word. Strangers.

EVE. When there are new Adams and new Eves we shall live in a garden of strangers. We shall need each other. [*She comes quickly behind him and turns up his face to her*]. Do not forget that, Adam. Never forget it.

ADAM. Why should I forget it? It is I who have thought of it.

EVE. I, too, have thought of something. The fawn stumbled and fell and died. But you could come softly up behind me and [*she suddenly pounces on his shoulders and throws him forward on his face*] throw me down so that I should die. I should not dare to sleep if there were no reason why you should not make me die.

ADAM [*scrambling up in horror*] Make you die!!! What a frightful thought!

THE SERPENT. Kill, kill, kill, kill. That is the word.

EVE. The new Adams and Eves might kill us. I shall not make them. [*She sits on the rock and pulls him down beside her, clasping him to her with her right arm*].

THE SERPENT. You must. For if you do not there will be an end.

ADAM. No: they will not kill us: they will feel as I do. There is something against it. The Voice in the garden will tell them that they must not kill, as it tells me.

THE SERPENT. The voice in the garden is your own voice.

ADAM. It is; and it is not. It is something greater than me: I am only a part of it.

EVE. The Voice does not tell me not to kill you. Yet I do not want you to die before me. No voice is needed to make me feel that.

ADAM [*throwing his arm round her shoulder with an expression of anguish*] Oh no: that is plain without any voice. There is something that holds us together, something that has no word—

THE SERPENT. Love. Love. Love.

ADAM. That is too short a word for so long a thing.

THE SERPENT [*laughs*]!!!

EVE [*turning impatiently to the snake*] That heart-biting sound again!

Do not do it. Why do you do it?

THE SERPENT. Love may be too long a word for so short a thing soon. But when it is short it will be very sweet.

ADAM [*ruminating*] You puzzle me. My old trouble was heavy; but it was simple. These wonders that you promise to do may tangle up my being before they bring me the gift of death. I was troubled with the burden of eternal being; but I was not confused in my mind. If I did not know that I loved Eve, at least I did not know that she might cease to love me, and come to love some other Adam and desire my death. Can you find a name for that knowledge?

THE SERPENT. Jealousy. Jealousy. Jealousy.

ADAM. A hideous word.

EVE [*shaking him*] Adam: you must not brood. You think too much.

ADAM [*angrily*] How can I help brooding when the future has become uncertain? Anything is better than uncertainty. Life has become uncertain. Love is uncertain. Have you a word for this new misery?

THE SERPENT. Fear. Fear. Fear.

ADAM. Have you a remedy for it?

THE SERPENT. Yes. Hope. Hope. Hope.

ADAM. What is hope?

THE SERPENT. As long as you do not know the future you do not know that it will not be happier than the past. That is hope.

ADAM. It does not console me. Fear is stronger in me than hope. I must have certainty. [*He rises threateningly*]. Give it to me; or I will kill you when next I catch you asleep.

EVE [*throwing her arms round the serpent*] My beautiful snake. Oh no.

How can you even think such a horror?

ADAM. Fear will drive me to anything. The serpent gave me fear. Let it now give me certainty or go in fear of me.

THE SERPENT. Bind the future by your will. Make a vow.

ADAM. What is a vow?

THE SERPENT. Choose a day for your death; and resolve to die on that day. Then death is no longer uncertain but certain. Let Eve vow to love you until your death. Then love will be no longer uncertain.

ADAM. Yes: that is splendid: that will bind the future.

EVE [*displeased, turning away from the serpent*] But it will destroy hope.

ADAM [*angrily*] Be silent, woman. Hope is wicked. Happiness is wicked.

Certainty is blessed.

THE SERPENT. What is wicked? You have invented a word.

ADAM. Whatever I fear to do is wicked. Listen to me, Eve; and you, snake, listen too, that your memory may hold my vow. I will live a thousand sets of the four seasons—

THE SERPENT. Years. Years.

ADAM. I will live a thousand years; and then I will endure no more: I will die and take my rest. And I will love Eve all that time and no other woman.

EVE. And if Adam keeps his vow I will love no other man until he dies.

THE SERPENT. You have both invented marriage. And what he will be to you and not to any other woman is husband; and what you will be to him and not to any other man is wife.

ADAM [*instinctively moving his hand towards her*] Husband and wife.

EVE [*slipping her hand into his*] Wife and husband.

THE SERPENT [*laughs*]!!!

EVE [*snatching herself loose from Adam*] Do not make that odious noise,

I tell you.

ADAM. Do not listen to her: the noise is good: it lightens my heart. You are a jolly snake. But you have not made a vow yet. What vow do you make?

THE SERPENT. I make no vows. I take my chance.

ADAM. Chance? What does that mean?

THE SERPENT. It means that I fear certainty as you fear uncertainty. It means that nothing is certain but uncertainty. If I bind the future I bind my will. If I bind my will I strangle creation.

EVE. Creation must not be strangled. I tell you I will create, though I tear myself to pieces in the act.

ADAM. Be silent, both of you. I *will* bind the future. I will be delivered from fear. [*To Eve*] We have made our vows; and if you must create, you shall create within the bounds of those vows. You shall not listen to that snake any more. Come [*he seizes her by the hair to drag her away*].

EVE. Let me go, you fool. It has not yet told me the secret.

ADAM [*releasing her*] That is true. What is a fool?

EVE. I do not know: the word came to me. It is what you are when you forget and brood and are filled with fear. Let us listen to the snake.

ADAM. No: I am afraid of it. I feel as if the ground were giving way under my feet when it speaks. Do you stay and listen to it.

THE SERPENT [*laughs*]!!!

ADAM [*brightening*] That noise takes away fear. Funny. The snake and the woman are going to whisper secrets. [*He chuckles and goes away slowly, laughing his first laugh*].

EVE. Now the secret. The secret. [*She sits on the rock and throws her arms round the serpent, who begins whispering to her*].

Eve's face lights up with intense interest, which increases until an expression of overwhelming repugnance takes its place. She buries her face in her hands.

ACT II

A few centuries later. Morning. An oasis in Mesopotamia. Close at hand the end of a log house abuts on a kitchen garden. Adam is digging in the middle of the garden. On his right, Eve sits on a stool in the shadow of a tree by the doorway, spinning flax. Her wheel, which she turns by hand, is a large disc of heavy wood, practically a flywheel. At the opposite side of the garden is a thorn brake with a passage through it barred by a hurdle.

The two are scantily and carelessly dressed in rough linen and leaves. They have lost their youth and grace; and Adam has an unkempt beard and jaggedly cut hair; but they are strong and in the prime of life. Adam looks worried, like a farmer. Eve, better humored (having given up worrying), sits and spins and thinks.

A MAN'S VOICE. Hallo, mother!

EVE [*looking across the garden towards the hurdle*] Here is Cain.

ADAM [*uttering a grunt of disgust*]!!! [*He goes on digging without raising his head*].

Cain kicks the hurdle out of his way, and strides into the garden. In pose, voice, and dress he is insistently warlike. He is equipped with huge spear and broad brass-bound leather shield; his casque is a tiger's head with bull's horns; he wears a scarlet cloak with gold brooch over a lion's skin with the claws dangling; his feet are in sandals with brass ornaments; his shins are in brass greaves; and his bristling military moustache glistens with oil. To his parents he has the self-assertive, not-quite-at-ease manner of a revolted son who knows that he is not forgiven nor approved of.

CAIN [*to Adam*] Still digging? Always dig, dig, dig. Sticking in the old furrow. No progress! no advanced ideas! no adventures! What should I be if I had stuck to the digging you taught me?

ADAM. What are you now, with your shield and spear, and your brother's blood crying from the ground against you?

CAIN. I am the first murderer: you are only the first man. Anybody could be the first man: it is as easy as to be the first cabbage. To be the first murderer one must be a man of spirit.

ADAM. Begone. Leave us in peace. The world is wide enough to keep us apart.

EVE. Why do you want to drive him away? He is mine. I made him out of my own body. I want to see my work sometimes.

ADAM. You made Abel also. He killed Abel. Can you bear to look at him after that?

CAIN. Whose fault was it that I killed Abel? Who invented killing? Did I? No: he invented it himself. I followed your teaching. I dug and dug and dug. I cleared away the thistles and briars. I ate the fruits of the earth. I lived in the sweat of my brow, as you do. I was a fool. But Abel was a discoverer, a man of ideas, of spirit: a true Progressive. He was the discoverer of blood. He was the inventor of killing. He found out that the fire of the sun could be brought down by a dewdrop. He invented the altar to keep the fire alive. He changed the beasts he killed into meat by the fire on the altar. He kept himself alive by eating meat. His meal cost him a day's glorious health-giving sport and an hour's amusing play with the fire. You learnt nothing from him: you drudged and drudged and drudged, and dug and dug and dug, and made me do the same. I envied his happiness, his freedom. I despised myself for not doing as he did instead of what you did. He became so happy that he shared his meal with the Voice that had whispered all his inventions to him. He said that the Voice was the voice of the fire that cooked his food, and that the fire that could cook could also eat. It was true: I saw the fire consume the food on his altar. Then I, too, made an altar, and offered my food on it, my grains, my roots, my fruit. Useless: nothing happened. He laughed at me; and then came my great idea: why not kill him as he killed the beasts? I struck; and he died, just as they did. Then I gave up your old silly drudging ways, and lived as he had lived, by the chase, by the killing, and by the fire. Am I not better than you? stronger, happier, freer?

ADAM. You are not stronger: you are shorter in the wind: you cannot endure. You have made the beasts afraid of us; and the snake has invented poison to protect herself against you. I fear you myself. If you take a step towards your mother with that spear of yours I will strike you with my spade as you struck Abel.

EVE. He will not strike me. He loves me.

ADAM. He loved his brother. But he killed him.

CAIN. I do not want to kill women. I do not want to kill my mother. And for her sake I will not kill you, though I could send this spear through you without coming within reach of your spade. But for her, I could not resist the sport of trying to kill you, in spite of my fear that you would kill me. I have striven with a boar and with a lion as to which of us should kill the other. I have striven with a man: spear to spear and shield to shield. It is terrible; but there is no joy like it. I call it fighting. He who has never fought has never lived. That is what has brought me to my mother today.

ADAM. What have you to do with one another now? She is the creator, you the destroyer.

CAIN. How can I destroy unless she creates? I want her to create more and more men: aye, and more and more women, that they may in turn create more men. I have imagined a glorious poem of many men, of more men than there are leaves on a thousand trees. I will divide them into two great hosts. One of them I will lead; and the other will be led by the man I fear most and desire to fight and kill most. And each host shall try to kill the other host. Think of that! all those multitudes of men fighting, fighting, killing, killing! The four rivers running with blood! The shouts of triumph! the howls of rage! the curses of despair! the shrieks of torment! That will be life indeed: life lived to the very marrow: burning, overwhelming life. Every man who has not seen it, heard it, felt it, risked it, will feel a humbled fool in the presence of the man who has.

EVE. And I! I am to be a mere convenience to make men for you to kill!

ADAM. Or to kill you, you fool.

CAIN. Mother: the making of men is your right, your risk, your agony, your glory, your triumph. You make my father here your mere convenience, as you call it, for that. He has to dig for you, sweat for you, plod for you, like the ox who helps him to tear up the ground or the ass who carries his burdens for him. No woman shall make me live my father's life. I will hunt: I will fight and strive to the very bursting of my sinews. When I have slain the boar at the risk of my life, I will throw it to my woman to cook, and give her a morsel of it for her pains. She shall have no other food; and that will make her my slave. And the man that slays me shall have her for his booty. Man shall be the master of Woman, not her baby and her drudge.

Adam throws down his spade, and stands looking darkly at Eve.

EVE. Are you tempted, Adam? Does this seem a better thing to you than love between us?

CAIN. What does he know of love? Only when he has fought, when he has faced terror and death, when he has striven to the spending of the last rally of his strength, can he know what it is to rest in love in the arms of a woman. Ask that woman whom you made, who is also my wife, whether she would have me as I was in the days when I followed the ways of Adam, and was a digger and a drudge?

EVE [*angrily throwing down her distaff*] What! You dare come here boasting about that good-for-nothing Lua, the worst of daughters and the worst of wives! You her master! You are more her slave than Adam's ox or your own sheepdog. Forsooth, when you have slain the boar at the risk of your life, you will throw her a morsel of it for her pains! Ha! Poor wretch: do you think I do not know her, and know you, better than that? Do you risk your life when you trap the ermine and the sable and the blue fox to hang on her lazy shoulders and make her look more like an animal than a woman? When you have to snare the little tender birds because it is too much trouble for her to chew honest food, how much of a great warrior do you feel then? You slay the tiger at the risk of your life; but who gets the striped skin you have run that risk for? She takes it to lie on, and flings you the carrion flesh you cannot eat. You fight because you think that your fighting makes her admire and desire you. Fool: she makes you fight because you bring her the ornaments and the treasures of those you have slain, and because she is courted and propitiated with power and gold by the people who fear you. You say that I make a mere convenience of Adam: I who spin and keep the house, and bear and rear children, and am a woman and not a pet animal to please men and prey on them! What are you, you poor slave of a painted face and a bundle of skunk's fur? You were a man-child when I bore you. Lua was a woman-child when I bore her. What have you made of yourselves?

CAIN [*letting his spear fall into the crook of his shield arm, and twirling his moustache*] There is something higher than man. There is hero and superman.

EVE. Superman! You are no superman: you are Anti-Man: you are to other men what the stoat is to the rabbit; and she is to you what the leech is to the stoat. You despise your father; but when he dies the world will be the richer because he lived. When you die, men will say, 'He was a great warrior; but it would have been better for the world if he had never been born.' And of Lua they will say nothing; but when they think of her they will spit.

CAIN. She is a better sort of woman to live with than you. If Lua nagged at me as you are nagging, and as you nag at Adam, I would beat her black and blue from head to foot. I have done it too, slave as you say I am.

EVE. Yes, because she looked at another man. And then you grovelled at her feet, and cried, and begged her to forgive you, and were ten times more her slave than ever; and she, when she had finished screaming and the pain went off a little, she forgave you, did she not?

CAIN. She loved me more than ever. That is the true nature of woman.

EVE [*now pitying him maternally*] Love! You call that love! You call that the nature of woman! My boy: this is neither man nor woman nor love nor life. You have no real strength in your bones nor sap in your flesh.

CAIN. Ha! [*he seizes his spear and swings it muscularly*].

EVE. Yes: you have to twirl a stick to feel your strength: you cannot taste life without making it bitter and boiling hot: you cannot love Lua until her face is painted, nor feel the natural warmth of her flesh until you have stuck a squirrel's fur on it. You can feel nothing but a torment, and believe nothing but a lie. You will not raise your head to look at all the miracles of life that surround you; but you will run ten miles to see a fight or a death.

ADAM. Enough said. Let the boy alone.

CAIN. Boy! Ha! ha!

EVE [*to Adam*] You think, perhaps, that his way of life may be better than yours after all. You are still tempted. Well, will you pamper me as he pampers his woman? Will you kill tigers and bears until I have a heap of their skins to lounge on? Shall I paint my face and let my arms waste into pretty softness, and eat partridges and doves, and the flesh of kids whose milk you will steal for me?

ADAM. You are hard enough to bear with as you are. Stay as you are; and

I will stay as I am.

CAIN. You neither of you know anything about life. You are simple country folk. You are the nurses and valets of the oxen and dogs and asses you have tamed to work for you. I can raise you out of that. I have a plan. Why not tame men and women to work for us? Why not bring them up from childhood never to know any other lot, so that they may believe that we are gods, and that they are here only to make life glorious for us?

ADAM [*impressed*] That is a great thought, certainly.

EVE [*contemptuously*] Great thought!

ADAM. Well, as the serpent used to say, why not?

EVE. Because I would not have such wretches in my house. Because I hate creatures with two heads, or with withered limbs, or that are distorted and perverted and unnatural. I have told Cain already that he is not a man and that Lua is not a woman: they are monsters. And now you want to make still more unnatural monsters, so that you may be utterly lazy and worthless, and that your tamed human animals may find work a blasting curse. A fine dream, truly! [*To Cain*] Your father is a fool skin deep; but you are a fool to your very marrow; and your baggage of a wife is worse.

ADAM. Why am I a fool? How am I a greater fool than you?

EVE. You said there would be no killing because the Voice would tell our children that they must not kill. Why did it not tell Cain that?

CAIN. It did; but I am not a child to be afraid of a Voice. The Voice thought I was nothing but my brother's keeper. It found that I was myself, and that it was for Abel to be himself also, and look to himself. He was not my keeper any more than I was his: why did he not kill me? There was no more to prevent him than there was to prevent me: it was man to man; and I won. I was the first conqueror.

ADAM. What did the Voice say to you when you thought all that?

CAIN. Why, it gave me right. It said that my deed was as a mark on me, a burnt-in mark such as Abel put on his sheep, that no man should slay me. And here I stand unslain, whilst the cowards who have never slain, the men who are content to be their brothers' keepers instead of their masters, are despised and rejected, and slain like rabbits. He who bears the brand of Cain shall rule the earth. When he falls, he shall be avenged sevenfold: the Voice has said it; so beware how you plot against me, you and all the rest.

ADAM. Cease your boasting and bullying, and tell the truth. Does not the Voice tell you that as no man dare slay you for murdering your brother, you ought to slay yourself?

CAIN. No.

ADAM. Then there is no such thing as divine justice, unless you are lying.

CAIN. I am not lying: I dare all truths. There is divine justice. For the Voice tells me that I must offer myself to every man to be killed if he can kill me. Without danger I cannot be great. That is how I pay for Abel's blood. Danger and fear follow my steps everywhere. Without them courage would have no sense. And it is courage, courage, courage, that raises the blood of life to crimson splendor.

ADAM [*picking up his spade and preparing to dig again*] Take yourself off then. This splendid life of yours does not last for a thousand years; and I must last for a thousand years. When you fighters do not get killed in fighting one another or fighting the beasts, you die from mere evil in yourselves. Your flesh ceases to grow like man's flesh: it grows like a fungus on a tree. Instead of breathing you sneeze, or cough up your insides, and wither and perish. Your bowels become rotten; your hair falls from you; your teeth blacken and drop out; and you die before your time, not because you will, but because you must. I will dig, and live.

CAIN. And pray, what use is this thousand years of life to you, you old vegetable? Do you dig any better because you have been digging for hundreds of years? I have not lived as long as you; but I know all there is to be known of the craft of digging. By quitting it I have set myself free to learn nobler crafts of which you know nothing. I know the craft of fighting and of hunting: in a word, the craft of killing. What certainty have you of your thousand years? I could kill both of you; and you could no more defend yourselves than a couple of sheep. I spare you; but others may kill you. Why not live bravely, and die early and make room for others? Why, I—I! that know many more crafts than either of you, am tired of myself when I am not fighting or hunting. Sooner than face a thousand years of it I should kill myself, as the Voice sometimes tempts me to do already.

ADAM. Liar: you denied just now that it called on you to pay for Abel's life with your own.

CAIN. The Voice does not speak to me as it does to you. I am a man: you are only a grown-up child. One does not speak to a child as to a man. And a man does not listen and tremble in silence. He replies: he makes the Voice respect him: in the end he dictates what the Voice shall say.

ADAM. May your tongue be accurst for such blasphemy!

EVE. Keep a guard on your own tongue; and do not curse my son. It was Lilith who did wrong when she shared the labor of creation so unequally between man and wife. If you, Cain, had had the trouble of making Abel, or had had to make another man to replace him when he was gone, you would not have killed him: you would have risked your own life to save his. That is why all this empty talk of yours, which tempted Adam just now when he threw down his spade and listened to you for a while, went by me like foul wind that has passed over a dead body. That is why there is enmity between Woman the creator and Man the destroyer. I know you: I am your mother. You are idle: you are selfish. It is long and hard and painful to create life: it is short and easy to steal the life others have made. When you dug, you made the earth live and bring forth as I live and bring forth. It was for that that Lilith set you free from the travail of women, not for theft and murder.

CAIN. The Devil thank her for it! I can make better use of my time than to play the husband to the clay beneath my feet.

ADAM. Devil? What new word is that?

CAIN. Hearken to me, old fool. I have never in my soul listened willingly when you have told me of the Voice that whispers to you. There must be two Voices: one that gulls and despises you, and another that trusts and respects me. I call yours the Devil. Mine I call the Voice of God.

ADAM. Mine is the Voice of Life: yours the Voice of Death.

CAIN. Be it so. For it whispers to me that death is not really death: that it is the gate of another life: a life infinitely splendid and intense: a life of the soul alone: a life without clods or spades, hunger or fatigue—

EVE. Selfish and idle, Cain. I know.

CAIN. Selfish, yes: a life in which no man is his brother's keeper, because his brother can keep himself. But am I idle? In rejecting your drudgery, have I not embraced evils and agonies of which you know nothing? The arrow is lighter in the hand than the spade; but the energy that drives it through the breast of a fighter is as fire to water compared with the strength that drives the spade into the harmless dirty clay. My strength is as the strength of ten because my heart is pure.

ADAM. What is that word? What is pure?

CAIN. Turned from the clay. Turned upward to the sun, to the clear clean heavens.

ADAM. The heavens are empty, child. The earth is fruitful. The earth feeds us. It gives us the strength by which we made you and all mankind. Cut off from the clay which you despise, you would perish miserably.

CAIN. I revolt against the clay. I revolt against the food. You say it gives us strength: does it not also turn into filth and smite us with diseases? I revolt against these births that you and mother are so proud of. They drag us down to the level of the beasts. If that is to be the last thing as it has been the first, let mankind perish. If I am to eat like a bear, if Lua is to bring forth cubs like a bear, then I had rather be a bear than a man; for the bear is not ashamed: he knows no better. If you are content, like the bear, I am not. Stay with the woman who gives you children: I will go to the woman who gives me dreams. Grope in the ground for your food: I will bring it from the skies with my arrows, or strike it down as it roams the earth in the pride of its life. If I must have food or die, I will at least have it at as far a remove from the earth as I can. The ox shall make it something nobler than grass before it comes to me. And as the man is nobler than the ox, I shall some day let my enemy eat the ox; and then I will slay and eat him.

ADAM. Monster! You hear this, Eve?

EVE. So that is what comes of turning your face to the clean clear heavens! Man-eating! Child-eating! For that is what it would come to, just as it came to lambs and kids when Abel began with sheep and goats. You are a poor silly creature after all. Do you think I never have these thoughts: I! who have the labor of the child-bearing: I! who have the drudgery of preparing the food? I thought for a moment that perhaps this strong brave son of mine, who could imagine something better, and could desire what he imagined, might also be able to will what he desired until he created it. And all that comes of it is that he wants to be a bear and eat children. Even a bear would not eat a man if it could get honey instead.

CAIN. I do not want to be a bear. I do not want to eat children. I do not know what I want, except that I want to be something higher and nobler than this stupid old digger whom Lilith made to help you to bring me into the world, and whom you despise now that he has served your turn.

ADAM [*in sullen rage*] I have half a mind to shew you that my spade can split your undutiful head open, in spite of your spear.

CAIN. Undutiful! Ha! ha! [*Flourishing his spear*] Try it, old everybody's father. Try a taste of fighting.

EVE. Peace, peace, you two fools. Sit down and be quiet; and listen to me. [*Adam, with a weary shrug, throws down his spade. Cain, with a laughing one, throws down his shield and spear. Both sit on the ground*]. I hardly know which of you satisfies me least, you with your dirty digging, or he with his dirty killing. I cannot think it was for either of these cheap ways of life that Lilith set you free. [*To Adam*] You dig roots and coax grains out of the earth: why do you not draw down a divine sustenance from the skies? He steals and kills for his food; and makes up idle poems of life after death; and dresses up his terror-ridden life with fine words and his disease-ridden body with fine clothes, so that men may glorify and honor him instead of cursing him as murderer and thief. All you men, except only Adam, are my sons, or my sons' sons, or my sons' sons' sons: you all come to see me: you all shew off before me: all your little wisdoms and accomplishments are trotted out before mother Eve. The diggers come: the fighters and killers come: they are both very dull; for they either complain to me of the last harvest, or boast to me of the last fight; and one harvest is just like another, and the last fight only a repetition of the first. Oh, I have heard it all a thousand times. They tell me too of their last-born: the clever thing the darling child said yesterday, and how much more wonderful or witty or quaint it is than any child that ever was born before. And I have to pretend to be surprised, delighted, interested; though the last child is like the first, and has said and done nothing that did not delight Adam and me when you and Abel said it. For you were the first children in the world, and filled us with such wonder and delight as no couple can ever again feel while the world lasts. When I can bear no more, I go to our old garden, that is now a mass of nettles and thistles, in the hope of finding the serpent to talk to. But you have made the serpent our enemy: she has left the garden, or is dead: I never see her now. So I have to come back and listen to Adam saying the same thing for the ten-thousandth time, or to receive a visit from the last great-great-grandson who has grown up and wants to impress me with his importance. Oh, it is dreary, dreary! And there is yet nearly seven hundred years of it to endure.

CAIN. Poor mother! You see, life is too long. One tires of everything.

There is nothing new under the sun.

ADAM [*to Eve, grumpily*] Why do you live on, if you can find nothing better to do than complain?

EVE. Because there is still hope.

CAIN. Of what?

EVE. Of the coming true of your dreams and mine. Of newly created things. Of better things. My sons and my son's sons are not all diggers and fighters. Some of them will neither dig nor fight: they are more useless than either of you: they are weaklings and cowards: they are vain; yet they are dirty and will not take the trouble to cut their hair. They borrow and never pay; but one gives them what they want, because they tell beautiful lies in beautiful words. They can remember their dreams. They can dream without sleeping. They have not will enough to create instead of dreaming; but the serpent said that every dream could be willed into creation by those strong enough to believe in it. There are others who cut reeds of different lengths and blow through them, making lovely patterns of sound in the air; and some of them can weave the patterns together, sounding three reeds at the same time, and raising my soul to things for which I have no words. And others make little mammoths out of clay, or make faces appear on flat stones, and ask me to create women for them with such faces. I have watched those faces and willed; and then I have made a woman-child that has grown up quite like them. And others think of numbers without having to count on their fingers, and watch the sky at night, and give names to the stars, and can foretell when the sun will be covered with a black saucepan lid. And there is Tubal, who made this wheel for me which has saved me so much labor. And there is Enoch, who walks on the hills, and hears the Voice continually, and has given up his will to do the will of the Voice, and has some of the Voice's greatness. When they come, there is always some new wonder, or some new hope: something to live for. They never want to die, because they are always learning and always creating either things or wisdom, or at least dreaming of them. And then you, Cain, come to me with your stupid fighting and destroying, and your foolish boasting; and you want me to tell you that it is all splendid, and that you are heroic, and that nothing but death or the dread of death makes life worth living. Away with you, naughty child; and do you, Adam, go on with your work and not waste your time listening to him.

CAIN. I am not, perhaps, very clever; but—

EVE [*interrupting him*] Perhaps not; but do not begin to boast of that.

It is no credit to you.

CAIN. For all that, mother, I have an instinct which tells me that death plays its part in life. Tell me this: who invented death?

Adam springs to his feet. Eve drops her distaff. Both shew the greatest consternation.

CAIN. What is the matter with you both?

ADAM. Boy: you have asked us a terrible question.

EVE. You invented murder. Let that be enough for you.

CAIN. Murder is not death. You know what I mean. Those whom I slay would die if I spared them. If I am not slain, yet I shall die. Who put this upon me? I say, who invented death?

ADAM. Be reasonable, boy. Could you bear to live for ever? You think you could, because you know that you will never have to make your thought good. But I have known what it is to sit and brood under the terror of eternity, of immortality. Think of it, man: to have no escape! to be Adam, Adam, Adam through more days than there are grains of sand by the two rivers, and then be as far from the end as ever! I, who have so much in me that I hate and long to cast off! Be thankful to your parents, who enabled you to hand on your burden to new and better men, and won for you an eternal rest; for it was we who invented death.

CAIN [*rising*] You did well: I, too, do not want to live for ever. But if you invented death, why do you blame me, who am a minister of death?

ADAM. I do not blame you. Go in peace. Leave me to my digging, and your mother to her spinning.

CAIN. Well, I will leave you to it, though I have shewn you a better way. [*He picks up his shield and spear*]. I will go back to my brave warrior friends and their splendid women. [*He strides to the thorn brake*]. When Adam delved and Eve span, where was then the gentleman? [*He goes away roaring with laughter, which ceases as he cries from the distance*] Goodbye, mother.

ADAM [*grumbling*] He might have put the hurdle back, lazy hound! [*He replaces the hurdle across the passage*].

EVE. Through him and his like, death is gaining on life. Already most of our grandchildren die before they have sense enough to know how to live.

ADAM. No matter. [*He spits on his hands, and takes up the spade again*]. Life is still long enough to learn to dig, short as they are making it.

EVE [*musing*] Yes, to dig. And to fight. But is it long enough for the other things, the great things? Will they live long enough to eat manna?

ADAM. What is manna?

EVE. Food drawn down from heaven, made out of the air, not dug dirtily from the earth. Will they learn all the ways of all the stars in their little time? It took Enoch two hundred years to learn to interpret the will of the Voice. When he was a mere child of eighty, his babyish attempts to understand the Voice were more dangerous than the wrath of Cain. If they shorten their lives, they will dig and fight and kill and die; and their baby Enochs will tell them that it is the will of the Voice that they should dig and fight and kill and die for ever.

ADAM. If they are lazy and have a will towards death I cannot help it. I will live my thousand years: if they will not, let them die and be damned.

EVE. Damned? What is that?

ADAM. The state of them that love death more than life. Go on with your spinning; and do not sit there idle while I am straining my muscles for you.

EVE [*slowly taking up her distaff*] If you were not a fool you would find something better for both of us to live by than this spinning and digging.

ADAM. Go on with your work, I tell you; or you shall go without bread.

EVE. Man need not always live by bread alone. There is something else. We do not yet know what it is; but some day we shall find out; and then we will live on that alone; and there shall be no more digging nor spinning, nor fighting nor killing.

She spins resignedly; he digs impatiently.

PART II

The Gospel of the Brothers Barnabas

In the first years after the war an impressive-looking gentleman of 50 is seated writing in a well-furnished spacious study. He is dressed in black. His coat is a frock-coat; his tie is white; and his waistcoat, though it is not quite a clergyman's waistcoat, and his collar, though it buttons in front instead of behind, combine with the prosperity indicated by his surroundings, and his air of personal distinction, to suggest the clerical dignitary. Still, he is clearly neither dean nor bishop; he is rather too starkly intellectual for a popular Free Church enthusiast; and he is not careworn enough to be a great headmaster.

The study windows, which have broad comfortable window seats, overlook Hampstead Heath towards London. Consequently, it being a fine afternoon in spring, the room is sunny. As you face these windows, you have on your right the fireplace, with a few logs smouldering in it, and a couple of comfortable library chairs on the hearthrug; beyond it and beside it the door; before you the writing-table, at which the clerical gentleman sits a little to your left facing the door with his right profile presented to you; on your left a settee; and on your right a couple of Chippendale chairs. There is also an upholstered square stool in the middle of the room, against the writing-table. The walls are covered with bookshelves above and lockers beneath.

The door opens; and another gentleman, shorter than the clerical one, within a year or two of the same age, dressed in a well-worn tweed lounge suit, with a short beard and much less style in his bearing and carriage, looks in.

THE CLERICAL GENTLEMAN [*familiar and by no means cordial*] Hallo! I didn't expect you until the five o'clock train.

THE TWEEDED GENTLEMAN [*coming in very slowly*] I have something on my mind. I thought I'd come early.

THE CLERICAL GENTLEMAN [*throwing down his pen*] What is on your mind?

THE TWEEDED GENTLEMAN [*sitting down on the stool, heavily preoccupied with his thought*] I have made up my mind at last about the time. I make it three hundred years.

THE CLERICAL GENTLEMAN [*sitting up energetically*] Now that is extraordinary. Most extraordinary. The very last words I wrote when you interrupted me were 'at least three centuries.' [*He snatches up his manuscript, and points to it*]. Here it is: [*reading*] 'the term of human life must be extended to at least three centuries.'

THE TWEEDED GENTLEMAN. How did you arrive at it?

A parlor maid opens the door, ushering in a young clergyman.

THE PARLOR MAID. Mr Haslam. [*She withdraws*].

The visitor is so very unwelcome that his host forgets to rise; and the two brothers stare at the intruder, quite unable to conceal their dismay. Haslam, who has nothing clerical about him except his collar, and wears a snuff-colored suit, smiles with a frank school-boyishness that makes it impossible to be unkind to him, and explodes into obviously unpremeditated speech.

HASLAM. I'm afraid I'm an awful nuisance. I'm the rector; and I suppose one ought to call on people.

THE TWEEDED GENTLEMAN [*in ghostly tones*] We're not Church people, you know.

HASLAM. Oh, I don't mind that, if you don't. The Church people here are mostly as dull as ditchwater. I have heard such a lot about you; and there are so jolly few people to talk to. I thought you perhaps wouldn't mind. *Do* you mind? for of course I'll go like a shot if I'm in the way.

THE CLERICAL GENTLEMAN [*rising, disarmed*] Sit down, Mr—er?

HASLAM. Haslam.

THE CLERICAL GENTLEMAN. Mr Haslam.

THE TWEEDED GENTLEMAN [*rising and offering him the stool*] Sit down. [*He retreats towards the Chippendale chairs*].

HASLAM [*sitting down on the stool*] Thanks awfully.

THE CLERICAL GENTLEMAN [*resuming his seat*] This is my brother Conrad, Professor of Biology at Jarrowfields University: Dr. Conrad Barnabas. My name is Franklyn: Franklyn Barnabas. I was in the Church myself for some years.

HASLAM [*sympathizing*] Yes: one cant help it. If theres a living in the family, or one's Governor knows a patron, one gets shoved into the Church by one's parents.

CONRAD [*sitting down on the furthest Chippendale with a snort of amusement*] Mp!

FRANKLYN. One gets shoved out of it, sometimes, by one's conscience.

HASLAM. Oh yes; but where is a chap like me to go? I'm afraid I'm not intellectual enough to split straws when theres a job in front of me, and nothing better for me to do. I daresay the Church was a bit thick for you; but it's good enough for me. It will last my time, anyhow [*he laughs good-humoredly*].

FRANKLYN [*with renewed energy*] There again! You see, Con. It will last his time. Life is too short for men to take it seriously.

HASLAM. Thats a way of looking at it, certainly.

FRANKLYN. I was not shoved into the Church, Mr Haslam: I felt it to be my vocation to walk with God, like Enoch. After twenty years of it I realized that I was walking with my own ignorance and self-conceit, and that I was not within a hundred and fifty years of the experience and wisdom I was pretending to.

HASLAM. Now I come to think of it, old Methuselah must have had to think twice before he took on anything for life. If I thought I was going to live nine hundred and sixty years, I don't think I should stay in the Church.

FRANKLYN. If men lived even a third of that time, the Church would be very different from the thing it is.

CONRAD. If I could count on nine hundred and sixty years I could make myself a real biologist, instead of what I am now: a child trying to walk. Are you sure you might not become a good clergyman if you had a few centuries to do it in?

HASLAM. Oh, theres nothing much the matter with *me*: it's quite easy to be a decent parson. It's the Church that chokes me off. I couldnt stick it for nine hundred years. I should chuck it. You know, sometimes, when the bishop, who is the most priceless of fossils, lets off something more than usually out-of-date, the bird starts in my garden.

FRANKLYN. The bird?

HASLAM. Oh yes. Theres a bird there that keeps on singing 'Stick it or chuck it: stick it or chuck it'—just like that—for an hour on end in the spring. I wish my father had found some other shop for me.

The parlor maid comes back.

THE PARLOR MAID. Any letters for the post, sir?

FRANKLYN. These. [*He proffers a basket of letters. She comes to the table and takes them*].

HASLAM [*to the maid*] Have you told Mr Barnabas yet?

THE PARLOR MAID [*flinching a little*] No, sir.

FRANKLYN. Told me what?

HASLAM. She is going to leave you?

FRANKLYN. Indeed? I'm sorry. Is it our fault, Mr Haslam?

HASLAM. Not a bit. She is jolly well off here.

THE PARLOR MAID [*reddening*] I have never denied it, sir: I couldnt ask for a better place. But I have only one life to live; and I maynt get a second chance. Excuse me, sir; but the letters must go to catch the post. [*She goes out with the letters.*]

The two brothers look inquiringly at Haslam.

HASLAM. Silly girl! Going to marry a village woodman and live in a hovel with him and a lot of kids tumbling over one another, just because the fellow has poetic-looking eyes and a moustache.

CONRAD [*demurring*] She said it was because she had only one life.

HASLAM. Same thing, poor girl! The fellow persuaded her to chuck it; and when she marries him she'll have to stick it. Rotten state of things, I call it.

CONRAD. You see, she hasnt time to find out what life really means. She has to die before she knows.

HASLAM [*agreeably*] Thats it.

FRANKLYN. She hasnt time to form a well-instructed conscience.

HASLAM [*still more cheerfully*] Quite.

FRANKLYN. It goes deeper. She hasnt time to form a genuine conscience at all. Some romantic points of honor and a few conventions. A world without conscience: that is the horror of our condition.

HASLAM [*beaming*] Simply fatuous. [*Rising*] Well, I suppose I'd better be going. It's most awfully good of you to put up with my calling.

CONRAD [*in his former low ghostly tone*] You neednt go, you know, if you are really interested.

HASLAM [*fed up*] Well, I'm afraid I ought to—I really must get back—I have something to do in the—

FRANKLYN [*smiling benignly and rising to proffer his hand*] Goodbye.

CONRAD [*gruffly, giving him up as a bad job*] Goodbye.

HASLAM. Goodbye. Sorry—er—

As the rector moves to shake hands with Franklyn, feeling that he is making a frightful mess of his departure, a vigorous sunburnt young lady with hazel hair cut to the level of her neck, like an Italian youth in a Gozzoli picture, comes in impetuously. She seems to have nothing on but her short skirt, her blouse, her stockings, and a pair of Norwegian shoes: in short, she is a Simple-Lifer.

THE SIMPLE-LIFER [*swooping on Conrad and kissing him*] Hallo, Nunk.

Youre before your time.

CONRAD. Behave yourself. Theres a visitor.

She turns quickly and sees the rector. She instinctively switches at her Gozzoli fringe with her fingers, but gives it up as hopeless.

FRANKLYN. Mr Haslam, our new rector. [*To Haslam*] My daughter Cynthia.

CONRAD. Usually called Savvy, short for Savage.

SAVVY. I usually call Mr Haslam Bill, short for William. [*She strolls to the hearthrug, and surveys them calmly from that commanding position*].

FRANKLYN. You know him?

SAVVY. Rather. Sit down, Bill.

FRANKLYN. Mr Haslam is going, Savvy. He has an engagement.

SAVVY. I know. I'm the engagement.

CONRAD. In that case, would you mind taking him into the garden while I talk to your father?

SAVVY [*to Haslam*] Tennis?

HASLAM. Rather!

SAVVY. Come on. [*She dances out. He runs boyishly after her*].

FRANKLYN [*leaving his table and beginning to walk up and down the room discontentedly*] Savvy's manners jar on me. They would have horrified her grandmother.

CONRAD [*obstinately*] They are happier manners than Mother's manners.

FRANKLYN. Yes: they are franker, wholesomer, better in a hundred ways. And yet I squirm at them. I cannot get it out of my head that Mother was a well-mannered woman, and that Savvy has no manners at all.

CONRAD. There wasnt any pleasure in Mother's fine manners. That makes a biological difference.

FRANKLYN. But there was beauty in Mother's manners, grace in them, style in them: above all, decision in them. Savvy is such a cub.

CONRAD. So she ought to be, at her age.

FRANKLYN. There it comes again! Her age! her age!

CONRAD. You want her to be fully grown at eighteen. You want to force her into a stuck-up, artificial, premature self-possession before she has any self to possess. You just let her alone: she is right enough for her years.

FRANKLYN. I have let her alone; and look at the result! Like all the other young people who have been let alone, she becomes a Socialist. That is, she becomes hopelessly demoralized.

CONRAD. Well, arnt you a Socialist?

FRANKLYN. Yes; but that is not the same thing. You and I were brought up in the old bourgeois morality. We were taught bourgeois manners and bourgeois points of honor. Bourgeois manners may be snobbish manners: there may be no pleasure in them, as you say; but they are better than no manners. Many bourgeois points of honor may be false; but at least they exist. The women know what to expect and what is expected of them. Savvy doesn't. She is a Bolshevist and nothing else. She has to improvise her manners and her conduct as she goes along. It's often charming, no doubt; but sometimes she puts her foot in it frightfully; and then I feel that she is blaming me for not teaching her better.

CONRAD. Well, you have something better to teach her now, at all events.

FRANKLYN. Yes: but it is too late. She doesn't trust me now. She doesn't talk about such things to me. She doesnt read anything I write. She never comes to hear me lecture. I am out of it as far as Savvy is concerned. [*He resumes his seat at the writing-table*].

CONRAD. I must have a talk to her.

FRANKLYN. Perhaps she will listen to you. You are not her father.

CONRAD. I sent her my last book. I can break the ice by asking her what she made of it.

FRANKLYN. When she heard you were coming, she asked me whether all the leaves were cut, in case it fell into your hands. She hasnt read a word of it.

CONRAD [*rising indignantly*] What!

FRANKLYN [*inexorably*] Not a word of it.

CONRAD [*beaten*] Well, I suppose it's only natural. Biology is a dry subject for a girl; and I am a pretty dry old codger.

[*He sits down again resignedly*].

FRANKLYN. Brother: if that is so; if biology as you have worked at it, and religion as I have worked at it, are dry subjects like the old stuff they taught under these names, and we two are dry old codgers, like the old preachers and professors, then the Gospel of the Brothers Barnabas is a delusion. Unless this withered thing religion, and this dry thing science, have come alive in our hands, alive and intensely interesting, we may just as well go out and dig the garden until it is time to dig our graves. [*The parlor maid returns. Franklyn is impatient at the interruption*]. Well? what is it now?

THE PARLOR MAID. Mr Joyce Burge on the telephone, sir. He wants to speak to you.

FRANKLYN [*astonished*] Mr Joyce Burge!

THE PARLOR MAID. Yes, sir.

FRANKLYN [*to Conrad*] What on earth does this mean? I havnt heard from him nor exchanged a word with him for years. I resigned the chairmanship of the Liberal Association and shook the dust of party politics from my feet before he was Prime Minister in the Coalition. Of course, he dropped me like a hot potato.

CONRAD. Well, now that the Coalition has chucked him out, and he is only one of the half-dozen leaders of the Opposition, perhaps he wants to pick you up again.

THE PARLOR MAID [*warningly*] He is holding the line, sir.

FRANKLYN. Yes: all right [*he hurries out*].

The parlor maid goes to the hearthrug to make up the fire. Conrad rises and strolls to the middle of the room, where he stops and looks quizzically down at her.

CONRAD. So you have only one life to live, eh?

THE PARLOR MAID [*dropping on her knees in consternation*] I meant no offence, sir.

CONRAD. You didn't give any. But you know you could live a devil of a long life if you really wanted to.

THE PARLOR MAID [*sitting down on her heels*] Oh, dont say that, sir.

It's so unsettling.

CONRAD. Why? Have you been thinking about it?

THE PARLOR MAID. It would never have come into my head if you hadnt put it there, sir. Me and cook had a look at your book.

CONRAD. What!

You and cook
Had a look
At my book!

And my niece wouldn't open it! The prophet is without honor in his own family. Well, what do you think of living for several hundred years? Are you going to have a try for it?

THE PARLOR MAID. Well, of course youre not in earnest, sir. But it does set one thinking, especially when one is going to be married.

CONRAD. What has that to do with it? He may live as long as you, you know.

THE PARLOR MAID. Thats just it, sir. You see, he must take me for better for worse, til death do us part. Do you think he would be so ready to do that, sir, if he thought it might be for several hundred years?

CONRAD. Thats true. And what about yourself?

THE PARLOR MAID. Oh, I tell you straight out, sir, I'd never promise to live with the same man as long as that. I wouldnt put up with my own children as long as that. Why, cook figured it out, sir, that when you were only 200, you might marry your own great-great-great-great-great-great-grandson and not even know who he was.

CONRAD. Well, why not? For all you know, the man you are going to marry may be your great-great-great-great-great-great-grandmother's great-great-great-great-great-great-grandson.

THE PARLOR MAID. But do you think it would ever be thought respectable, sir?

CONRAD. My good girl, all biological necessities have to be made respectable whether we like it or not; so you neednt worry yourself about that.

Franklyn returns and crosses the room to his chair, but does not sit down. The parlor maid goes out.

CONRAD. Well, what does Joyce Burge want?

FRANKLYN. Oh, a silly misunderstanding. I have promised to address a meeting in Middlesborough; and some fool has put it into the papers that I am 'coming to Middlesborough,' without any explanation. Of course, now that we are on the eve of a general election, political people think I am coming there to contest the parliamentary seat. Burge knows that I have a following, and thinks I could get into the House of Commons and head a group there. So he insists on coming to see me. He is staying with some people at Dollis Hill, and can be here in five or ten minutes, he says.

CONRAD. But didn't you tell him that it's a false alarm?

FRANKLYN. Of course I did; but he wont believe me.

CONRAD. Called you a liar, in fact?

FRANKLYN. No: I wish he had: any sort of plain speaking is better than the nauseous sham good fellowship our democratic public men get up for shop use. He pretends to believe me, and assures me his visit is quite disinterested; but why should he come if he has no axe to grind? These chaps never believe anything they say themselves; and naturally they cannot believe anything anyone else says.

CONRAD [*rising*] Well, I shall clear out. It was hard enough to stand the party politicians before the war; but now that they have managed to half kill Europe between them, I cant be civil to them, and I dont see why I should be.

FRANKLYN. Wait a bit. We have to find out how the world will take our new gospel. [*Conrad sits down again*]. Party politicians are still unfortunately an important part of the world. Suppose we try it on Joyce Burge.

CONRAD. How can you? You can tell things only to people who can listen.

Joyce Burge has talked so much that he has lost the power of listening.

He doesnt listen even in the House of Commons.

Savvy rushes in breathless, followed by Haslam, who remains timidly just inside the door.

SAVVY [*running to Franklyn*] I say! Who do you think has just driven up in a big car?

FRANKLYN. Mr Joyce Burge, perhaps.

SAVVY [*disappointed*] Oh, they know, Bill. Why didnt you tell us he was coming? I have nothing on.

HASLAM. I'd better go, hadnt I?

CONRAD. You just wait here, both of you. When you start yawning, Joyce

Burge will take the hint, perhaps.

SAVVY [*to Franklyn*] May we?

FRANKLYN. Yes, if you promise to behave yourself.

SAVVY [*making a wry face*] That will be a treat, wont it?

THE PARLOR MAID [*entering and announcing*] Mr Joyce Burge.

Haslam hastily moves to the fireplace; and the parlor maid goes out and shuts the door when the visitor has passed in.

FRANKLYN [*hurrying past Savvy to his guest with the false cordiality he has just been denouncing*] Oh! Here you are. Delighted to see you. [*He shakes Burge's hand, and introduces Savvy*] My daughter.

SAVVY [*not daring to approach*] Very kind of you to come.

Joyce Burge stands fast and says nothing; but he screws up his cheeks into a smile at each introduction, and makes his eyes shine in a very winning manner. He is a well-fed man turned fifty, with broad forehead, and grey hair which, his neck being short, falls almost to his collar.

FRANKLYN. Mr Haslam, our rector.

Burge conveys an impression of shining like a church window; and Haslam seizes the nearest library chair on the hearth, and swings it round for Burge between the stool and Conrad. He then retires to the window seat at the other side of the room, and is joined by Savvy. They sit there, side by side, hunched up with their elbows on their knees and their chins on their hands, providing Burge with a sort of Stranger's Gallery during the ensuing sitting.

FRANKLYN. I forget whether you know my brother Conrad. He is a biologist.

BURGE [*suddenly bursting into energetic action and shaking hands heartily with Conrad*] By reputation only, but very well, of course. How I wish I could have devoted myself to biology! I have always been interested in rocks and strata and volcanoes and so forth: they throw such a light on the age of the earth. [*With conviction*] There is nothing like biology. 'The cloud-capped towers, the solemn binnacles, the gorgeous temples, the great globe itself: yea, all that it inherit shall dissolve, and, like this influential pageant faded, leave not a rack behind.' Thats biology, you know: good sound biology. [*He sits down.*

So do the others, Franklyn on the stool, and Conrad on his Chippendale]. Well, my dear Barnabas, what do you think of the situation? Dont you think the time has come for us to make a move?

FRANKLYN. The time has always come to make a move.

BURGE. How true! But what is the move to be? You are a man of enormous influence. We know that. Weve always known it. We have to consult you whether we like it or not. We—

FRANKLYN [*interrupting firmly*] I never meddle in party politics now.

SAVVY. It's no use saying you have no influence, daddy. Heaps of people swear by you.

BURGE [*shining at her*] Of course they do. Come! let me prove to you what we think of you. Shall we find you a first-rate constituency to contest at the next election? One that wont cost you a penny. A metropolitan seat. What do you say to the Strand?

FRANKLYN. My dear Burge, I am not a child. Why do you go on wasting your party funds on the Strand? You know you cannot win it.

BURGE. We cannot win it; but you—

FRANKLYN. Oh, please!

SAVVY. The Strand's no use, Mr Burge. I once canvassed for a Socialist there. Cheese it.

BURGE. Cheese it!

HASLAM [*spluttering with suppressed laughter*] Priceless!

SAVVY. Well, I suppose I shouldnt say cheese it to a Right Honorable.

But the Strand, you know! Do come off it.

FRANKLYN. You must excuse my daughter's shocking manners, Burge; but I agree with her that popular democratic statesmen soon come to believe that everyone they speak to is an ignorant dupe and a born fool into the bargain.

BURGE [*laughing genially*] You old aristocrat, you! But believe me, the instinct of the people is sound—

CONRAD [*cutting in sharply*] Then why are you in the Opposition instead of in the Government?

BURGE [*shewing signs of temper under this heckling*] I deny that I am in the Opposition *morally*. The Government does not represent the country. I was chucked out of the Coalition by a Tory conspiracy. The people want me back. I dont want to go back.

FRANKLYN [*gently remonstrant*] My dear Burge: of course you do.

BURGE [*turning on him*] Not a bit of it. I want to cultivate my garden. I am not interested in politics: I am interested in roses. I havnt a scrap of ambition. I went into politics because my wife shoved me into them, bless her! But I want to serve my country. What else am I for? I want to save my country from the Tories. They dont represent the people. The man they have made Prime Minister has never represented the people; and you know it. Lord Dunreen is the bitterest old Tory left alive. What has he to offer to the people?

FRANKLYN [*cutting in before Burge can proceed—as he evidently intends—to answer his own question*] I will tell you. He has ascertainable beliefs and principles to offer. The people know where they are with Lord Dunreen. They know what he thinks right and what he thinks wrong. With your followers they never know where they are. With you they never know where they are.

BURGE [*amazed*] With me!

FRANKLYN. Well, where are you? What are you?

BURGE. Barnabas: you must be mad. You ask me what I am?

FRANKLYN. I do.

BURGE. I am, if I mistake not, Joyce Burge, pretty well known throughout Europe, and indeed throughout the world, as the man who—unworthily perhaps, but not quite unsuccessfully—held the helm when the ship of State weathered the mightiest hurricane that has ever burst with earth-shaking violence on the land of our fathers.

FRANKLYN. I know that. I know who you are. And the earth-shaking part of it to me is that though you were placed in that enormously responsible position, neither I nor anyone else knows what your beliefs are, or even whether you have either beliefs or principles. What we did know was that your Government was formed largely of men who regarded you as a robber of henroosts, and whom you regarded as enemies of the people.

BURGE [*adroitly, as he thinks*] I agree with you. I agree with you absolutely. I dont believe in coalition governments.

FRANKLYN. Precisely. Yet you formed two.

BURGE. Why? Because we were at war. That is what you fellows never would realize. The Hun was at the gate. Our country, our lives, the honor of our wives and mothers and daughters, the tender flesh of our innocent babes, were at stake. Was that a time to argue about principles?

FRANKLYN. I should say it was the time of all others to confirm the resolution of our own men and gain the confidence and support of public opinion throughout the world by a declaration of principle. Do you think the Hun would ever have come to the gate if he had known that it would be shut in his face on principle? Did he not hold his own against you until America boldly affirmed the democratic principle and came to our rescue? Why did you let America snatch that honor from England?

BURGE. Barnabas: America was carried away by words, and had to eat them at the Peace Conference. Beware of eloquence: it is the bane of popular speakers like you.

FRANKLYN [*exclaiming*]{Well!!

SAVVY [*all*]{I like that!

HASLAM [*together*]{Priceless!

BURGE [*continuing remorselessly*] Come down to facts. It wasn't principle that won the war: it was the British fleet and the blockade. America found the talk: I found the shells. You cannot win wars by principles; but you *can* win elections by them. There I am with you. You want the next election to be fought on principles: that is what it comes to, doesnt it?

FRANKLYN. I dont want it to be fought at all! An election is a moral horror, as bad as a battle except for the blood: a mud bath for every soul concerned in it. You know very well that it will not be fought on principle.

BURGE. On the contrary it will be fought on nothing else. I believe a program is a mistake. I agree with you that principle is what we want.

FRANKLYN. Principle without program, eh?

BURGE. Exactly. There it is in three words.

FRANKLYN. Why not in one word? Platitudes. That is what principle without program means.

BURGE [*puzzled but patient, trying to get at Franklyn's drift in order to ascertain his price*] I have not made myself clear. Listen. I am agreeing with you. I am on your side. I am accepting your proposal. There isnt going to be any more coalition. This time there wont be a Tory in the Cabinet. Every candidate will have to pledge himself to Free Trade, slightly modified by consideration for our Overseas Dominions; to Disestablishment; to Reform of the House of Lords; to a revised scheme of Taxation of Land Values; and to doing something or other to keep the Irish quiet. Does that satisfy you?

FRANKLYN. It does not even interest me. Suppose your friends do commit themselves to all this! What does it prove about them except that they are hopelessly out of date even in party politics? that they have learnt nothing and forgotten nothing since 1885? What is it to me that they hate the Church and hate the landed gentry; that they are jealous of the nobility, and have shipping shares instead of manufacturing businesses in the Midlands? I can find you hundreds of the most sordid rascals, or the most densely stupid reactionaries, with all these qualifications.

BURGE. Personal abuse proves nothing. Do you suppose the Tories are all angels because they are all members of the Church of England?

FRANKLYN. No; but they stand together as members of the Church of England, whereas your people, in attacking the Church, are all over the shop. The supporters of the Church are of one mind about religion: its enemies are of a dozen minds. The Churchmen are a phalanx: your people are a mob in which atheists are jostled by Plymouth Brethren, and Positivists by Pillars of Fire. You have with you all the crudest unbelievers and all the crudest fanatics.

BURGE. We stand, as Cromwell did, for liberty of conscience, if that is what you mean.

FRANKLYN. How can you talk such rubbish over the graves of your conscientious objectors? All law limits liberty of conscience: if a man's conscience allows him to steal your watch or to shirk military service, how much liberty do you allow it? Liberty of conscience is not my point.

BURGE [*testily*] I wish you would come to your point. Half the time you are saying that you must have principles; and when I offer you principles you say they wont work.

FRANKLYN. You have not offered me any principles. Your party shibboleths are not principles. If you get into power again you will find yourself at the head of a rabble of Socialists and anti-Socialists, of Jingo Imperialists and Little Englanders, of cast-iron Materialists and ecstatic Quakers, of Christian Scientists and Compulsory Inoculationists, of Syndicalists and Bureaucrats: in short, of men differing fiercely and irreconcilably on every principle that goes to the root of human society and destiny; and the impossibility of keeping such a team together will force you to sell the pass again to the solid Conservative Opposition.

BURGE [*rising in wrath*] Sell the pass again! You accuse me of having sold the pass!

FRANKLYN. When the terrible impact of real warfare swept your parliamentary sham warfare into the dustbin, you had to go behind the backs of your followers and make a secret agreement with the leaders of the Opposition to keep you in power on condition that you dropped all legislation of which they did not approve. And you could not even hold them to their bargain; for they presently betrayed the secret and forced the coalition on you.

BURGE. I solemnly declare that this is a false and monstrous accusation.

FRANKLYN. Do you deny that the thing occurred? Were the uncontradicted reports false? Were the published letters forgeries?

BURGE. Certainly not. But *I* did not do it. I was not Prime Minister then. It was that old dotard, that played-out old humbug Lubin. He was Prime Minister then, not I.

FRANKLYN. Do you mean to say you did not know?

BURGE [*sitting down again with a shrug*] Oh, I had to be told. But what could I do? If we had refused we might have had to go out of office.

FRANKLYN. Precisely.

BURGE. Well, could we desert the country at such a crisis? The Hun was at the gate. Everyone has to make sacrifices for the sake of the country at such moments. We had to rise above party; and I am proud to say we never gave party a second thought. We stuck to—

CONRAD. Office?

SURGE [*turning on him*] Yes, sir, to office: that is, to responsibility, to danger, to heart-sickening toil, to abuse and misunderstanding, to a martyrdom that made us envy the very soldiers in the trenches. If you had had to live for months on aspirin and bromide of potassium to get a wink of sleep, you wouldn't talk about office as if it were a catch.

FRANKLYN. Still, you admit that under our parliamentary system Lubin could not have helped himself?

BURGE. On that subject my lips are closed. Nothing will induce me to say one word against the old man. I never have; and I never will. Lubin is old: he has never been a real statesman: he is as lazy as a cat on a hearthrug: you cant get him to attend to anything: he is good for nothing but getting up and making speeches with a peroration that goes down with the back benches. But I say nothing against him. I gather that you do not think much of me as a statesman; but at all events I can get things done. I can hustle: even you will admit that. But Lubin! Oh my stars, Lubin!! If you only knew—

The parlor maid opens the door and announces a visitor.

THE PARLOR MAID. Mr Lubin.

SURGE [*bounding from his chair*] Lubin! Is this a conspiracy?

They all rise in amazement, staring at the door. Lubin enters: a man at the end of his sixties, a Yorkshireman with the last traces of Scandinavian flax still in his white hair, undistinguished in stature, unassuming in his manner, and taking his simple dignity for granted, but wonderfully comfortable and quite self-assured in contrast to the intellectual restlessness of Franklyn and the mesmeric self-assertiveness of Burge. His presence suddenly brings out the fact that they are unhappy men, ill at ease, square pegs in round holes, whilst he flourishes like a primrose.

The parlor maid withdraws.

LUBIN [*coming to Franklyn*] How do you do, Mr Barnabas? [*He speaks very comfortably and kindly, much as if he were the host, and Franklyn an embarrassed but welcome guest*]. I had the pleasure of meeting you once at the Mansion House. I think it was to celebrate the conclusion of the hundred years peace with America.

FRANKLYN [*shaking hands*] It was long before that: a meeting about

Venezuela, when we were on the point of going to war with America.

LUBIN [*not at all put out*] Yes: you are quite right. I knew it was something about America. [*He pats Franklyn's hand*]. And how have you been all this time? Well, eh?

FRANKLYN [*smiling to soften the sarcasm*] A few vicissitudes of health naturally in so long a time.

LUBIN. Just so. Just so. [*Looking round at Savvy*] The young lady is—?

FRANKLYN. My daughter, Savvy.

Savvy comes from the window between her father and Lubin.

LUBIN [*taking her hand affectionately in both his*] And why has she never come to see us?

BURGE. I don't know whether you have noticed, Lubin, that I am present.

Savvy takes advantage of this diversion to slip away to the settee, where she is stealthily joined by Haslam, who sits down on her left.

LUBIN [*seating himself in Burge's chair with ineffable comfortableness*] My dear Burge: if you imagine that it is possible to be within ten miles of your energetic presence without being acutely aware of it, you do yourself the greatest injustice. How are you? And how are your good newspaper friends? [*Burge makes an explosive movement; but Lubin goes on calmly and sweetly*] And what are you doing here with my old friend Barnabas, if I may ask?

BURGE [*sitting down in Conrad's chair, leaving him standing uneasily in the corner*] Well, just what you are doing, if you want to know. I am trying to enlist Mr Barnabas's valuable support for my party.

LUBIN. Your party, eh? The newspaper party?

BURGE. The Liberal Party. The party of which I have the honor to be leader.

LUBIN. Have you now? Thats very interesting; for I thought *I* was the leader of the Liberal Party. However, it is very kind of you to take it off my hands, if the party will let you.

BURGE. Do you suggest that I have not the support and confidence of the party?

LUBIN. I dont suggest anything, my dear Burge. Mr Barnabas will tell you that we all think very highly of you. The country owes you a great deal. During the war, you did very creditably over the munitions; and if you were not quite so successful with the peace, nobody doubted that you meant well.

BURGE. Very kind of you, Lubin. Let me remark that you cannot lead a progressive party without getting a move on.

LUBIN. You mean you cannot. I did it for ten years without the least difficulty. And very comfortable, prosperous, pleasant years they were.

BURGE. Yes; but what did they end in?

LUBIN. In you, Burge. You don't complain of that, do you?

BURGE [*fiercely*] In plague, pestilence, and famine; battle, murder, and sudden death.

LUBIN [*with an appreciative chuckle*] The Nonconformist can quote the prayer-book for his own purposes, I see. How you enjoyed yourself over that business, Burge! Do you remember the Knock-Out Blow?

BURGE. It came off: don't forget that. Do *you* remember fighting to the last drop of your blood?

LUBIN [*unruffled, to Franklyn*] By the way, I remember your brother Conrad—a wonderful brain and a dear good fellow—explaining to me that I couldn't fight to the last drop of my blood, because I should be dead long before I came to it. Most interesting, and quite true. He was introduced to me at a meeting where the suffragettes kept disturbing me. They had to be carried out kicking and making a horrid disturbance.

CONRAD. No: it was later, at a meeting to support the Franchise Bill which gave them the vote.

LUBIN [*discovering Conrad's presence for the first time*] Youre right: it was. I knew it had something to do with women. My memory never deceives me. Thank you. Will you introduce me to this gentleman, Barnabas?

CONRAD [*not at all affably*] I am the Conrad in question. [*He sits down in dudgeon on the vacant Chippendale*].

LUBIN. Are you? [*Looking at him pleasantly*] Yes: of course you are. I never forget a face. But [*with an arch turn of his eyes to Savvy*] your pretty niece engaged all my powers of vision.

BURGE. I wish youd be serious, Lubin. God knows we have passed through times terrible enough to make any man serious.

LUBIN. I do not think I need to be reminded of that. In peace time I used to keep myself fresh for my work by banishing all worldly considerations from my mind on Sundays; but war has no respect for the Sabbath; and there have been Sundays within the last few years on which I have had to play as many as sixty-six games of bridge to keep my mind off the news from the front.

BURGE [*scandalized*] Sixty-six games of bridge on Sunday!!!

LUBIN. You probably sang sixty-six hymns. But as I cannot boast either your admirable voice or your spiritual fervor, I had to fall back on bridge.

FRANKLYN. If I may go back to the subject of your visit, it seems to me that you may both be completely superseded by the Labor Party.

BURGE. But I am in the truest sense myself a Labor leader. I—[*he stops, as Lubin has risen with a half-suppressed yawn, and is already talking calmly, but without a pretence of interest*].

LUBIN. The Labor Party! Oh no, Mr Barnabas. No, no, no, no, no. [*He moves in Savvy's direction*]. There will be no trouble about that. Of course we must give them a few seats: more, I quite admit, than we should have dreamt of leaving to them before the war; but—[*by this time he has reached the sofa where Savvy and Haslam are seated. He sits down between them; takes her hand; and drops the subject of Labor*]. Well, my dear young lady? What is the latest news? Whats going on? Have you seen Shoddy's new play? Tell me all about it, and all about the latest books, and all about everything.

SAVVY. You have not met Mr Haslam. Our Rector.

LUBIN [*who has quite overlooked Haslam*] Never heard of him. Is he any good?

FRANKLYN. I was introducing him. This is Mr Haslam.

HASLAM. How d'ye do?

LUBIN. I beg your pardon, Mr Haslam. Delighted to meet you. [*To Savvy*]

Well, now, how many books have you written?

SAVVY [*rather overwhelmed but attracted*] None. I don't write.

LUBIN. You dont say so; Well, what do you do? Music? Skirt-dancing?

SAVVY. I dont do anything.

LUBIN. Thank God! You and I were born for one another. Who is your favorite poet, Sally?

SAVVY. Savvy.

LUBIN. Savvy! I never heard of him. Tell me all about him. Keep me up to date.

SAVVY. It's not a poet. *I* am Savvy, not Sally.

LUBIN. Savvy! Thats a funny name, and very pretty. Savvy. It sounds

Chinese. What does it mean?

CONRAD. Short for Savage.

LUBIN [*patting her hand*] La belle Sauvage.

HASLAM [*rising and surrendering Savvy to Lubin by crossing to the fireplace*] I suppose the Church is out of it as far as progressive politics are concerned.

BURGE. Nonsense! That notion about the Church being unprogressive is one of those shibboleths that our party must drop. The Church is all right essentially. Get rid of the establishment; get rid of the bishops; get rid of the candlesticks; get rid of the 39 articles; and the Church of England is just as good as any other Church; and I don't care who hears me say so.

LUBIN. It doesn't matter a bit who hears you say so, my dear Burge. [*To Savvy*] Who did you say your favorite poet was?

SAVVY. I dont make pets of poets. Who's yours?

LUBIN. Horace.

SAVVY. Horace who?

LUBIN. Quintus Horatius Flaccus: the noblest Roman of them all, my dear.

SAVVY. Oh, if he is dead, that explains it. I have a theory that all the dead people we feel especially interested in must have been ourselves. You must be Horace's reincarnation.

LUBIN [*delighted*] That is the very most charming and penetrating and intelligent thing that has ever been said to me. Barnabas: will you exchange daughters with me? I can give you your choice of two.

FRANKLYN. Man proposes. Savvy disposes.

LUBIN. What does Savvy say?

BURGE. Lubin: I came here to talk politics.

LUBIN. Yes: you have only one subject, Burge. I came here to talk to

Savvy. Take Burge into the next room, Barnabas; and let him rip.

BURGE [*half-angry, half-indulgent*] No; but really, Lubin, we are at a crisis—

LUBIN. My dear Burge, life is a disease; and the only difference between one man and another is the stage of the disease at which he lives. You are always at the crisis; I am always in the convalescent stage. I enjoy convalescence. It is the part that makes the illness worth while.

SAVVY [*half-rising*] Perhaps I'd better run away. I am distracting you.

LUBIN [*making her sit down again*] Not at all, my dear. You are only distracting Burge. Jolly good thing for him to be distracted by a pretty girl. Just what he needs.

BURGE. I sometimes envy you, Lubin. The great movement of mankind, the giant sweep of the ages, passes you by and leaves you standing.

LUBIN. It leaves me sitting, and quite comfortable, thank you. Go on sweeping. When you are tired of it, come back; and you will find England where it was, and me in my accustomed place, with Miss Savvy telling me all sorts of interesting things.

SAVVY [*who has been growing more and more restless*] Dont let him shut you up, Mr Burge. You know, Mr Lubin, I am frightfully interested in the Labor movement, and in Theosophy, and in reconstruction after the war, and all sorts of things. I daresay the flappers in your smart set are tremendously flattered when you sit beside them and are nice to them as you are being nice to me; but I am not smart; and I am no use as a flapper. I am dowdy and serious. I want you to be serious. If you refuse, I shall go and sit beside Mr Burge, and ask him to hold my hand.

LUBIN. He wouldnt know how to do it, my dear. Burge has a reputation as a profligate—

BURGE [*starting*] Lubin: this is monstrous. I—

LUBIN [*continuing*]—but he is really a model of domesticity. His name is coupled with all the most celebrated beauties; but for him there is only one woman; and that is not you, my dear, but his very charming wife.

BURGE. You are destroying my character in the act of pretending to save it. Have the goodness to confine yourself to your own character and your own wife. Both of them need all your attention.

LUBIN. I have the privilege of my age and of my transparent innocence. I have not to struggle with your volcanic energy.

BURGE [*with an immense sense of power*] No, by George!

FRANKLYN. I think I shall speak both for my brother and myself, and possibly also for my daughter, if I say that since the object of your visit and Mr Joyce Burge's is to some extent political, we should hear with great interest something about your political aims, Mr Lubin.

LUBIN [*assenting with complete good humor, and becoming attentive, clear, and businesslike in his tone*] By all means, Mr Barnabas. What we have to consider first, I take it, is what prospect there is of our finding you beside us in the House after the next election.

FRANKLYN. When I speak of politics, Mr Lubin, I am not thinking of elections, or available seats, or party funds, or the registers, or even, I am sorry to have to add, of parliament as it exists at present. I had much rather you talked about bridge than about electioneering: it is the more interesting game of the two.

BURGE. He wants to discuss principles, Lubin.

LUBIN [*very cool and clear*] I understand Mr Barnabas quite well. But elections are unsettled things; principles are settled things.

CONRAD [*impatiently*] Great Heavens!—

LUBIN [*interrupting him with quiet authority*] One moment, Dr Barnabas. The main principles on which modern civilized society is founded are pretty well understood among educated people. That is what our dangerously half-educated masses and their pet demagogues—if Burge will excuse that expression—

BURGE. Dont mind me. Go on. I shall have something to say presently.

LUBIN.—that is what our dangerously half-educated people do not realize. Take all this fuss about the Labor Party, with its imaginary new principles and new politics. The Labor members will find that the immutable laws of political economy take no more notice of their ambitions and aspirations than the law of gravitation. I speak, if I may say so, with knowledge; for I have made a special, study of the Labor question.

FRANKLYN [*with interest and some surprise*] Indeed?

LUBIN. Yes. It occurred quite at the beginning of my career. I was asked to deliver an address to the students at the Working Men's College; and I was strongly advised to comply, as Gladstone and Morley and others were doing that sort of thing at the moment. It was rather a troublesome job, because I had not gone into political economy at the time. As you know, at the university I was a classical scholar; and my profession was the Law. But I looked up the textbooks, and got up the case most carefully. I found that the correct view is that all this Trade Unionism and Socialism and so forth is founded on the ignorant delusion that wages and the production and distribution of wealth can be controlled by legislation or by any human action whatever. They obey fixed scientific laws, which have been ascertained and settled finally by the highest economic authorities. Naturally I do not at this distance of time remember the exact process of reasoning; but I can get up the case again at any time in a couple of days; and you may rely on me absolutely, should the occasion arise, to deal with all these ignorant and unpractical people in a conclusive and convincing way, except, of course, as far as it may be advisable to indulge and flatter them a little so as to let them down without creating ill feeling in the working-class electorate. In short, I can get that lecture up again almost at a moment's notice.

SAVVY. But, Mr Lubin, I have had a university education too; and all this about wages and distribution being fixed by immutable laws of political economy is obsolete rot.

FRANKLYN [*shocked*] Oh, my dear! That is not polite.

LUBIN. No, no, no. Dont scold her. She mustnt be scolded. [*To Savvy*] I understand. You are a disciple of Karl Marx.

SAVVY. No, no. Karl Marx's economics are all rot.

LUBIN [*at last a little taken aback*] Dear me!

SAVVY. You must excuse me, Mr Lubin; but it's like hearing a man talk about the Garden of Eden.

CONRAD. Why shouldnt he talk about the Garden of Eden? It was a first attempt at biology anyhow.

LUBIN [*recovering his self-possession*] I am sound on the Garden of

Eden. I have heard of Darwin.

SAVVY. But Darwin is all rot.

LUBIN. What! Already!

SAVVY. It's no good your smiling at me like a Cheshire cat, Mr Lubin; and I am not going to sit here mumchance like an old-fashioned goody goody wife while you men monopolize the conversation and pay out the very ghastliest exploded drivel as the latest thing in politics. I am not giving you my own ideas, Mr Lubin, but just the regular orthodox science of today. Only the most awful old fossils think that Socialism is bad economics and that Darwin invented Evolution. Ask Papa. Ask Uncle. Ask the first person you meet in the street. [*She rises and crosses to Haslam*]. Give me a cigaret, Bill, will you?

HASLAM. Priceless. [*He complies*].

FRANKLYN. Savvy has not lived long enough to have any manners, Mr Lubin; but that is where you stand with the younger generation. Dont smoke, dear.

Savvy, with a shrug of rather mutinous resignation, throws the cigaret into the fire. Haslam, on the point of lighting one for himself, changes his mind.

LUBIN [*shrewd and serious*] Mr Barnabas: I confess I am surprised; and I will not pretend that I am convinced. But I am open to conviction. I may be wrong.

BURGE [*in a burst of irony*] Oh no. Impossible! Impossible!

LUBIN. Yes, Mr Barnabas, though I do not possess Burge's genius for being always wrong, I have been in that position once or twice. I could not conceal from you, even if I wished to, that my time has been so completely filled by my professional work as a lawyer, and later on by my duties as leader of the House of Commons in the days when Prime Ministers were also leaders—

BURGE [*stung*] Not to mention bridge and smart society.

LUBIN.—not to mention the continual and trying effort to make Burge behave himself, that I have not been able to keep my academic reading up to date. I have kept my classics brushed up out of sheer love for them; but my economics and my science, such as they were, may possibly be a little rusty. Yet I think I may say that if you and your brother will be so good as to put me on the track of the necessary documents, I will undertake to put the case to the House or to the country to your entire satisfaction. You see, as long as you can shew these troublesome half-educated people who want to turn the world upside down that they are talking nonsense, it really does not matter very much whether you do it in terms of what Miss Barnabas calls obsolete rot or in terms of what her granddaughter will probably call unmitigated tosh. I have no objection whatever to denounce Karl Marx. Anything I can say against Darwin will please a large body of sincerely pious voters. If it will be easier to carry on the business of the country on the understanding that the present state of things is to be called Socialism, I have no objection in the world to call it Socialism. There is the precedent of the Emperor Constantine, who saved the society of his own day by agreeing to call his Imperialism Christianity. Mind: I must not go ahead of the electorate. You must not call a voter a Socialist until—

FRANKLYN. Until he is a Socialist. Agreed.

LUBIN. Oh, not at all. You need not wait for that. You must not call him a Socialist until he wishes to be called a Socialist: that is all. Surely you would not say that I must not address my constituents as gentlemen until they are gentlemen. I address them as gentlemen because they wish to be so addressed. [*He rises from the sofa and goes to Franklyn, placing a reassuring hand on his shoulder*]. Do not be afraid of Socialism, Mr Barnabas. You need not tremble for your property or your position or your dignity. England will remain what England is, no matter what new political names may come into vogue. I do not intend to resist the transition to Socialism. You may depend on me to guide it, to lead it, to give suitable expression to its aspirations, and to steer it clear of Utopian absurdities. I can honestly ask for your support on the most advanced Socialist grounds no less than on the soundest Liberal ones.

BURGE. In short, Lubin, youre incorrigible. You dont believe anything is going to change. The millions are still to toil—the people—my people—for I am a man of the people—

LUBIN [*interrupting him contemptuously*] Dont be ridiculous, Burge. You are a country solicitor, further removed from the people, more foreign to them, more jealous of letting them up to your level, than any duke or any archbishop.

BURGE [*hotly*] I deny it. You think I have never been poor. You think I have never cleaned my own boots. You think my fingers have never come out through the soles when I was cleaning them. You think—

LUBIN. I think you fall into the very common mistake of supposing that it is poverty that makes the proletarian and money that makes the gentleman. You are quite wrong. You never belonged to the people: you belonged to the impecunious. Impecuniosity and broken boots are the lot of the unsuccessful middle class, and the commonplaces of the early struggles of the professional and younger son class. I defy you to find a farm laborer in England with broken boots. Call a mechanic one of the poor, and he'll punch your head. When you talk to your constituents about the toiling millions, they don't consider that you are referring to them. They are all third cousins of somebody with a title or a park. I am a Yorkshireman, my friend. I know England; and you don't. If you did you would know—

SURGE. What do you know that I don't know?

LUBIN. I know that we are taking up too much of Mr Barnabas's time. [*Franklyn rises*]. May I take it, my dear Barnabas, that I may count on your support if we succeed in forcing an election before the new register is in full working order?

SURGE [*rising also*] May the party count on your support? I say nothing about myself. Can the party depend on you? Is there any question of yours that I have left unanswered?

CONRAD. We havnt asked you any, you know.

BURGE. May I take that as a mark of confidence?

CONRAD. If I were a laborer in your constituency, I should ask you a biological question?

LUBIN. No you wouldnt, my dear Doctor. Laborers never ask questions.

BURGE. Ask it now. I have never flinched from being heckled. Out with it. Is it about the land?

CONRAD. No.

SURGE. Is it about the Church?

CONRAD. No.

BURGE. Is it about the House of Lords?

CONRAD. No.

BURGE. Is it about Proportional Representation?

CONRAD. No.

SURGE. Is it about Free Trade?

CONRAD. No.

SURGE. Is it about the priest in the school?

CONRAD. No.

BURGE. Is it about Ireland?

CONRAD. No.

BURGE. Is it about Germany?

CONRAD. No.

BURGE. Well, is it about Republicanism? Come! I wont flinch. Is it about the Monarchy?

CONRAD. No.

SURGE. Well, what the devil is it about, then?

CONRAD. You understand that I am asking the question in the character of a laborer who earned thirteen shillings a week before the war and earns thirty now, when he can get it?

BURGE. Yes: I understand that. I am ready for you. Out with it.

CONRAD. And whom you propose to represent n parliament?

SURGE. Yes, yes, yes. Come on.

CONRAD. The question is this. Would you allow your son to marry my daughter, or your daughter to marry my son?

BURGE [*taken aback*] Oh, come! Thats not a political question.

CONRAD. Then, as a biologist, I don't take the slightest interest in your politics; and I shall not walk across the street to vote for you or anyone else at the election. Good evening.

LUBIN. Serve you right, Burge! Dr Barnabas: you have my assurance that my daughter shall marry the man of her choice, whether he be lord or laborer. May *I* count on your support?

SURGE [*hurling the epithet at him*] Humbug!

SAVVY. Stop. [*They all stop short in the movement of leave-taking to look at her*]. Daddy: are you going to let them off like this? How are they to know anything if nobody ever tells them? If you don't, I will.

CONRAD. You cant. You didn't read my book; and you know nothing about it. You just hold your tongue.

SAVVY. I just wont, Nunk. I shall have a vote when I am thirty; and I ought to have it now. Why are these two ridiculous people to be allowed to come in and walk over us as if the world existed only to play their silly parliamentary game?

FRANKLYN [*severely*] Savvy: you really must not be uncivil to our guests.

SAVVY. I'm sorry. But Mr Lubin didn't stand on much ceremony with me, did he? And Mr Burge hasnt addressed a single word to me. I'm not going to stand it. You and Nunk have a much better program than either of them. It's the only one we are going to vote for; and they ought to be told about it for the credit of the family and the good of their own souls. You just tip them a chapter from the gospel of the brothers Barnabas, Daddy.

Lubin and Burge turn inquiringly to Franklyn, suspecting a move to form a new party.

FRANKLYN. It is quite true, Mr Lubin, that I and my brother have a little program of our own which—

CONRAD [*interrupting*] It's not a little program: it's an almighty big one. It's not our own: it's the program of the whole of civilization.

BURGE. Then why split the party before you have put it to us? For God's sake let us have no more splits. I am here to learn. I am here to gather your opinions and represent them. I invite you to put your views before me. I offer myself to be heckled. You have asked me only an absurd non-political question.

FRANKLYN. Candidly, I fear our program will be thrown away on you. It would not interest you.

BURGE [*with challenging audacity*] Try. Lubin can go if he likes; but I am still open to new ideas, if only I can find them.

FRANKLYN [*to Lubin*] Are you prepared to listen, Mr Lubin; or shall I thank you for your very kind and welcome visit, and say good evening?

LUBIN [*sitting down resignedly on the settee, but involuntarily making a movement which looks like the stifling of a yawn*] With pleasure, Mr Barnabas. Of course you know that before I can adopt any new plank in the party platform, it will have to reach me through the National Liberal Federation, which you can approach through your local Liberal and Radical Association.

FRANKLYN. I could recall to you several instances of the addition to your party program of measures of which no local branch of your Federation had ever dreamt. But I understand that you are not really interested. I will spare you, and drop the subject.

LUBIN [*waking up a little*] You quite misunderstand me. Please do not take it in that way. I only—

BURGE [*talking him down*] Never mind the Federation: *I* will answer for the Federation. Go on, Barnabas: go on. Never mind Lubin [*he sits down in the chair from which Lubin first displaced him*].

FRANKLYN. Our program is only that the term of human life shall be extended to three hundred years.

LUBIN [*softly*] Eh?

BURGE [*explosively*] What!

SAVVY. Our election cry is 'Back to Methuselah!'

HASLAM. Priceless!

Lubin and Surge look at one another.

CONRAD. No. We are not mad.

SAVVY. Theyre not joking either. They mean it.

LUBIN [*cautiously*] Assuming that, in some sense which I am for the moment unable to fathom, you are in earnest, Mr Barnabas, may I ask what this has to do with politics?

FRANKLYN. The connection is very evident. You are now, Mr Lubin, within immediate reach of your seventieth year. Mr Joyce Surge is your junior by about eleven years. You will go down to posterity as one of a European group of immature statesmen and monarchs who, doing the very best for your respective countries of which you were capable, succeeded in all-but-wrecking the civilization of Europe, and did, in effect, wipe out of existence many millions of its inhabitants.

BURGE. Less than a million.

FRANKLYN. That was our loss alone.

BURGE. Oh, if you count foreigners—!

HAS LAM. God counts foreigners, you know.

SAVVY [*with intense satisfaction*] Well said, Bill.

FRANKLYN. I am not blaming you. Your task was beyond human capacity. What with our huge armaments, our terrible engines of destruction, our systems of coercion manned by an irresistible police, you were called on to control powers so gigantic that one shudders at the thought of their being entrusted even to an infinitely experienced and benevolent God, much less to mortal men whose whole life does not last a hundred years.

BURGE. We won the war: don't forget that.

FRANKLYN. No: the soldiers and sailors won it, and left you to finish it. And you were so utterly incompetent that the multitudes of children slain by hunger in the first years of peace made us all wish we were at war again.

CONRAD. It's no use arguing about it. It is now absolutely certain that the political and social problems raised by our civilization cannot be solved by mere human mushrooms who decay and die when they are just beginning to have a glimmer of the wisdom and knowledge needed for their own government.

LUBIN. Quite an interesting idea, Doctor. Extravagant. Fantastic. But quite interesting. When I was young I used to feel my human limitations very acutely.

BURGE. God knows I have often felt that I could not go on if it had not been for the sense that I was only an instrument in the hands of a Power above us.

CONRAD. I'm glad you both agree with us, and with one another.

LUBIN. I have not gone so far as that, I think. After all, we have had many very able political leaders even within your recollection and mine.

FRANKLYN. Have you read the recent biographies—Dilke's, for instance—which revealed the truth about them?

LUBIN. I did not discover any new truth revealed in these books, Mr

Barnabas.

FRANKLYN. What! Not the truth that England was governed all that time by a little woman who knew her own mind?

SAVVY. Hear, hear!

LUBIN. That often happens. Which woman do you mean?

FRANKLYN. Queen Victoria, to whom your Prime Ministers stood in the relation of naughty children whose heads she knocked together when their tempers and quarrels became intolerable. Within thirteen years of her death Europe became a hell.

SURGE. Quite true. That was because she was piously brought up, and regarded herself as an instrument. If a statesman remembers that he is only an instrument, and feels quite sure that he is rightly interpreting the divine purpose, he will come out all right, you know.

FRANKLYN. The Kaiser felt like that. Did he come out all right?

SURGE. Well, let us be fair, even to the Kaiser. Let us be fair.

FRANKLYN. Were you fair to him when you won an election on the program of hanging him?

SURGE. Stuff! I am the last man alive to hang anybody; but the people wouldnt listen to reason. Besides, I knew the Dutch wouldnt give him up.

SAVVY. Oh, don't start arguing about poor old Bill. Stick to our point. Let these two gentlemen settle the question for themselves. Mr Burge: do you think Mr Lubin is fit to govern England?

SURGE. No. Frankly, I dont.

LUBIN [*remonstrant*] Really!

CONRAD. Why?

BURGE. Because he has no conscience: thats why.

LUBIN [*shocked and amazed*] Oh!

FRANKLYN. Mr Lubin: do you consider Joyce Burge qualified to govern England?

LUBIN [*with dignified emotion, wounded, but without bitterness*] Excuse me, Mr Barnabas; but before I answer that question I want to say this. Burge: we have had differences of opinion; and your newspaper friends have said hard things of me. But we worked together for years; and I hope I have done nothing to justify you in the amazing accusation you have just brought against me. Do you realize that you said that I have no conscience?

BURGE. Lubin: I am very accessible to an appeal to my emotions; and you are very cunning in making such appeals. I will meet you to this extent. I dont mean that you are a bad man. I dont mean that I dislike you, in spite of your continual attempts to discourage and depress me. But you have a mind like a looking-glass. You are very clear and smooth and lucid as to what is standing in front of you. But you have no foresight and no hindsight. You have no vision and no memory. You have no continuity; and a man without continuity can have neither conscience nor honor from one day to another. The result is that you have always been a damned bad minister; and you have sometimes been a damned bad friend. Now you can answer Barnabas's question and take it out of me to your heart's content. He asked you was I fit to govern England.

LUBIN [*recovering himself*] After what has just passed I sincerely wish I could honestly say yes, Burge. But it seems to me that you have condemned yourself out of your own mouth. You represent something which has had far too much influence and popularity in this country since Joseph Chamberlain set the fashion; and that is mere energy without intellect and without knowledge. Your mind is not a trained mind: it has not been stored with the best information, nor cultivated by intercourse with educated minds at any of our great seats of learning. As I happen to have enjoyed that advantage, it follows that you do not understand my mind. Candidly, I think that disqualifies you. The peace found out your weaknesses.

BURGE. Oh! What did it find out in you?

LUBIN. You and your newspaper confederates took the peace out of my hands. The peace did not find me out because it did not find me in.

FRANKLYN. Come! Confess, both of you! You were only flies on the wheel. The war went England's way; but the peace went its own way, and not England's way nor any of the ways you had so glibly appointed for it. Your peace treaty was a scrap of paper before the ink dried on it. The statesmen of Europe were incapable of governing Europe. What they needed was a couple of hundred years training and experience: what they had actually had was a few years at the bar or in a counting-house or on the grouse moors and golf courses. And now we are waiting, with monster cannons trained on every city and seaport, and huge aeroplanes ready to spring into the air and drop bombs every one of which will obliterate a whole street, and poison gases that will strike multitudes dead with a breath, until one of you gentlemen rises in his helplessness to tell us, who are as helpless as himself, that we are at war again.

CONRAD. Aha! What consolation will it be for us then that you two are able to tell off one another's defects so cleverly in your afternoon chat?

BURGE [*angrily*] If you come to that, what consolation will it be that you two can sit there and tell both of us off? you, who have had no responsibility! you, who havnt lifted a finger, as far as I know, to help us through this awful crisis which has left me ten years older than my proper age! Can you tell me a single thing you did to help us during the whole infernal business?

CONRAD. We're not blaming you: you hadnt lived long enough. No more had we. Cant you see that three-score-and-ten, though it may be long enough for a very crude sort of village life, isnt long enough for a complicated civilization like ours? Flinders Petrie has counted nine attempts at civilization made by people exactly like us; and every one of them failed just as ours is failing. They failed because the citizens and statesmen died of old age or over-eating before they had grown out of schoolboy games and savage sports and cigars and champagne. The signs of the end are always the same: Democracy, Socialism, and Votes for Women. We shall go to smash within the lifetime of men now living unless we recognize that we must live longer.

LUBIN. I am glad you agree with me that Socialism and Votes for Women are signs of decay.

FRANKLYN. Not at all: they are only the difficulties that overtax your capacity. If you cannot organize Socialism you cannot organize civilized life; and you will relapse into barbarism accordingly.

SAVVY. Hear, hear!

SURGE. A useful point. We cannot put back the clock.

HASLAM. *I* can. Ive often done it.

LUBIN. Tut tut! My dear Burge: what are you dreaming of? Mr Barnabas: I am a very patient man. But will you tell me what earthly use or interest there is in a conclusion that cannot be realized? I grant you that if we could live three hundred years we should all be, perhaps wiser, certainly older. You will grant me in return, I hope, that if the sky fell we should all catch larks.

FRANKLYN. Your turn now, Conrad. Go ahead.

CONRAD. I don't think it's any good. I don't think they want to live longer than usual.

LUBIN. Although I am a mere child of 69, I am old enough to have lost, the habit of crying for the moon.

BURGE. Have you discovered the elixir of life or have you not? If not, I agree with Lubin that you are wasting our time.

CONRAD. Is your time of any value?

SURGE [*unable to believe his ears*] My time of any value! What do you mean?

LUBIN [*smiling comfortably*] From your high scientific point of view, I daresay, none whatever, Professor. In any case I think a little perfectly idle discussion would do Burge good. After all, we might as well hear about the elixir of life as read novels, or whatever Burge does when he is not playing golf on Walton Heath. What is your elixir, Dr Barnabas? Lemons? Sour milk? Or what is the latest?

SURGE. We were just beginning to talk seriously; and now you snatch at the chance of talking rot. [*He rises*]. Good evening. [*He turns to the door*].

CONRAD [*rudely*] Die as soon as you like. Good evening.

BURGE [*hesitating*] Look here. I took sour milk twice a day until Metchnikoff died. He thought it would keep him alive for ever; and he died of it.

CONRAD. You might as well have taken sour beer.

BURGE. You believe in lemons?

CONRAD. I wouldn't eat a lemon for ten pounds.

BURGE [*sitting down again*] What do you recommend?

CONRAD [*rising with a gesture of despair*] Whats the use of going on, Frank? Because I am a doctor, and because they think I have a bottle to give them that will make them live for ever, they are listening to me for the first time with their mouths open and their eyes shut. Thats their notion of science.

SAVVY. Steady, Nunk! Hold the fort.

CONRAD [*growls and sits down*]!!!

LUBIN. You volunteered the consultation, Doctor. I may tell you that, far from sharing the credulity as to science which is now the fashion, I am prepared to demonstrate that during the last fifty years, though the Church has often been wrong, and even the Liberal Party has not been infallible, the men of science have always been wrong.

CONRAD. Yes: the fellows you call men of science. The people who make money by it, and their medical hangers-on. But has anybody been right?

LUBIN. The poets and story tellers, especially the classical poets and story tellers, have been, in the main, right. I will ask you not to repeat this as my opinion outside; for the vote of the medical profession and its worshippers is not to be trifled with.

FRANKLYN. You are quite right: the poem is our real clue to biological science. The most scientific document we possess at present is, as your grandmother would have told you quite truly, the story of the Garden of Eden.

BURGE [*pricking up his ears*] Whats that? If you can establish that, Barnabas, I am prepared to hear you out with my very best attention. I am listening. Go on.

FRANKLYN. Well, you remember, don't you, that in the Garden of Eden Adam and Eve were not created mortal, and that natural death, as we call it, was not a part of life, but a later and quite separate invention?

SURGE. Now you mention it, thats true. Death came afterwards.

LUBIN. What about accidental death? That was always possible.

FRANKLYN. Precisely. Adam and Eve were hung up between two frightful possibilities. One was the extinction of mankind by their accidental death. The other was the prospect of living for ever. They could bear neither. They decided that they would just take a short turn of a thousand years, and meanwhile hand on their work to a new pair. Consequently, they had to invent natural birth and natural death, which are, after all, only modes of perpetuating life without putting on any single creature the terrible burden of immortality.

LUBIN. I see. The old must make room for the new.

SURGE. Death is nothing but making room. Thats all there is in it or ever has been in it.

FRANKLYN. Yes; but the old must not desert their posts until the new are ripe for them. They desert them now two hundred years too soon.

SAVVY. I believe the old people are the new people reincarnated, Nunk. I suspect I am Eve. I am very fond of apples; and they always disagree with me.

CONRAD. You are Eve, in a sense. The Eternal Life persists; only It wears out Its bodies and minds and gets new ones, like new clothes. You are only a new hat and frock on Eve.

FRANKLYN. Yes. Bodies and minds ever better and better fitted to carry out Its eternal pursuit.

LUBIN [*with quiet scepticism*] What pursuit, may one ask, Mr Barnabas?

FRANKLYN. The pursuit of omnipotence and omniscience. Greater power and greater knowledge: these are what we are all pursuing even at the risk of our lives and the sacrifice of our pleasures. Evolution is that pursuit and nothing else. It is the path to godhead. A man differs from a microbe only in being further on the path.

LUBIN. And how soon do you expect this modest end to be reached?

FRANKLYN. Never, thank God! As there is no limit to power and knowledge there can be no end. 'The power and the glory, world without end': have those words meant nothing to you?

BURGE [*pulling out an old envelope*] I should like to make a note of that. [*He does so*].

CONRAD. There will always be something to live for.

SURGE [*pocketing his envelope and becoming more and more businesslike*] Right: I have got that. Now what about sin? What about the Fall? How do you work them in?

CONRAD. I don't work in the Fall. The Fall is outside Science. But I daresay Frank can work it in for you.

SURGE [*to Franklyn*] I wish you would, you know. It's important. Very important.

FRANKLYN. Well, consider it this way. It is clear that when Adam and Eve were immortal it was necessary that they should make the earth an extremely comfortable place to live in.

BURGE. True. If you take a house on a ninety-nine years lease, you spend a good deal of money on it. If you take it for three months you generally have a bill for dilapidations to pay at the end of them.

FRANKLYN. Just so. Consequently, when Adam had the Garden of Eden on a lease for ever, he took care to make it what the house agents call a highly desirable country residence. But the moment he invented death, and became a tenant for life only, the place was no longer worth the trouble. It was then that he let the thistles grow. Life was so short that it was no longer worth his while to do anything thoroughly well.

BURGE. Do you think that is enough to constitute what an average elector would consider a Fall? Is it tragic enough?

FRANKLYN. That is only the first step of the Fall. Adam did not fall down that step only: he fell down a whole flight. For instance, before he invented birth he dared not have lost his temper; for if he had killed Eve he would have been lonely and barren to all eternity. But when he invented birth, and anyone who was killed could be replaced, he could afford to let himself go. He undoubtedly invented wife-beating; and that was another step down. One of his sons invented meat-eating. The other was horrified at the innovation. With the ferocity which is still characteristic of bulls and other vegetarians, he slew his beefsteak-eating brother, and thus invented murder. That was a very steep step. It was so exciting that all the others began to kill one another for sport, and thus invented war, the steepest step of all. They even took to killing animals as a means of killing time, and then, of course, ate them to save the long and difficult labor of agriculture. I ask you to contemplate our fathers as they came crashing down all the steps of this Jacob's ladder that reached from paradise to a hell on earth in which they had multiplied the chances of death from violence, accident, and disease until they could hardly count on three score and ten years of life, much less the thousand that Adam had been ready to face! With that picture before you, will you now ask me where was the Fall? You might as well stand at the foot of Snowdon and ask me where is the mountain. The very children see it so plainly that they compress its history into a two line epic:

Old Daddy Long Legs wouldn't say his prayers:

Take him by the hind legs and throw him downstairs.

LUBIN [*still immovably sceptical*] And what does Science say to this fairy tale, Doctor Barnabas? Surely Science knows nothing of Genesis, or of Adam and Eve.

CONRAD. Then it isnt Science: thats all. Science has to account for everything; and everything includes the Bible.

FRANKLYN. The Book of Genesis is a part of nature like any other part of nature. The fact that the tale of the Garden of Eden has survived and held the imagination of men spellbound for centuries, whilst hundreds of much more plausible and amusing stories have gone out of fashion and perished like last year's popular song, is a scientific fact; and Science is bound to explain it. You tell me that Science knows nothing of it. Then Science is more ignorant than the children at any village school.

CONRAD. Of course if you think it more scientific to say that what we are discussing is not Adam and Eve and Eden, but the phylogeny of the blastoderm—

SAVVY. You neednt swear, Nunk.

CONRAD. Shut up, you: I am not swearing. [*To Lubin*] If you want the professional humbug of rewriting the Bible in words of four syllables, and pretending it's something new, I can humbug you to your heart's content. I can call Genesis Phylogenesis. Let the Creator say, if you like, 'I will establish an antipathetic symbiosis between thee and the female, and between thy blastoderm and her blastoderm.' Nobody will understand you; and Savvy will think you are swearing. The meaning is the same.

HASLAM. Priceless. But it's quite simple. The one version is poetry: the other is science.

FRANKLYN. The one is classroom jargon: the other is inspired human language.

LUBIN [*calmly reminiscent*] One of the few modern authors into whom

I have occasionally glanced is Rousseau, who was a sort of Deist like

Burge—

BURGE [*interrupting him forcibly*] Lubin: has this stupendously important communication which Professor Barnabas has just made to us: a communication for which I shall be indebted to him all my life long: has this, I say, no deeper effect on you than to set you pulling my leg by trying to make out that I am an infidel?

LUBIN. It's very interesting and amusing, Burge; and I think I see a case in it. I think I could undertake to argue it in an ecclesiastical court. But important is hardly a word I should attach to it.

BURGE. Good God! Here is this professor: a man utterly removed from the turmoil of our political life: devoted to pure learning in its most abstract phases; and I solemnly declare he is the greatest politician, the most inspired party leader, in the kingdom. I take off my hat to him. I, Joyce Burge, give him best. And you sit there purring like an Angora cat, and can see nothing in it!

CONRAD [*opening his eyes widely*] Hallo! What have I done to deserve this tribute?

SURGE. Done! You have put the Liberal Party into power for the next thirty years, Doctor: thats what you've done.

CONRAD. God forbid!

BURGE. It's all up with the Church now. Thanks to you, we go to the country with one cry and one only. Back to the Bible! Think of the effect on the Nonconformist vote. You gather that in with one hand; and you gather in the modern scientific sceptical professional vote with the other. The village atheist and the first cornet in the local Salvation Army band meet on the village green and shake hands. You take your school children, your Bible class under the Cowper-Temple clause, into the museum. You shew the kids the Piltdown skull; and you say, 'Thats Adam. Thats Eve's husband.' You take the spectacled science student from the laboratory in Owens College; and when he asks you for a truly scientific history of Evolution, you put into his hand The Pilgrim's Progress. You—[*Savvy and Haslam explode into shrieks of merriment*]. What are you two laughing at?

SAVVY. Oh, go on, Mr Burge. Dont stop.

HASLAM. Priceless!

FRANKLYN. Would thirty years of office for the Liberal Party seem so important to you, Mr Burge, if you had another two and a half centuries to live?

BURGE [*decisively*] No. You will have to drop that part of it. The constituencies wont swallow it.

LUBIN [*seriously*] I am not so sure of that, Burge. I am not sure that it may not prove the only point they will swallow.

BURGE. It will be no use to us even if they do. It's not a party point.

It's as good for the other side as for us.

LUBIN. Not necessarily. If we get in first with it, it will be associated in the public mind with our party. Suppose I put it forward as a plank in our program that we advocate the extension of human life to three hundred years! Dunreen, as leader of the opposite party, will be bound to oppose me: to denounce me as a visionary and so forth. By doing so he will place himself in the position of wanting to rob the people of two hundred and thirty years of their natural life. The Unionists will become the party of Premature Death; and we shall become the Longevity party.

BURGE [*shaken*] You really think the electorate would swallow it?

LUBIN. My dear Burge: is there anything the electorate will not swallow if it is judiciously put to them? But we must make sure of our ground. We must have the support of the men of science. Is there serious agreement among them, Doctor, as to the possibility of such an evolution as you have described?

CONRAD. Yes. Ever since the reaction against Darwin set in at the beginning of the present century, all scientific opinion worth counting has been converging rapidly upon Creative Evolution.

FRANKLYN. Poetry has been converging on it: philosophy has been converging on it: religion has been converging on it. It is going to be the religion of the twentieth century: a religion that has its intellectual roots in philosophy and science just as medieval Christianity had its intellectual roots in Aristotle.

LUBIN. But surely any change would be so extremely gradual that—

CONRAD. Dont deceive yourself. It's only the politicians who improve the world so gradually that nobody can see the improvement. The notion that Nature does not proceed by jumps is only one of the budget of plausible lies that we call classical education. Nature always proceeds by jumps. She may spend twenty thousand years making up her mind to jump; but when she makes it up at last, the jump is big enough to take us into a new age.

LUBIN [*impressed*] Fancy my being leader of the party for the next three hundred years!

BURGE. What!!

LUBIN. Perhaps hard on some of the younger men. I think in fairness I shall have to step aside to make room after another century or so: that is, if Mimi can be persuaded to give up Downing Street.

BURGE. This is too much. Your colossal conceit blinds you to the most obvious necessity of the political situation.

LUBIN. You mean my retirement. I really cannot see that it is a necessity. I could not see it when I was almost an old man—or at least an elderly one. Now that it appears that I am a young man, the case for it breaks down completely. [*To Conrad*] May I ask are there any alternative theories? Is there a scientific Opposition?

CONRAD. Well, some authorities hold that the human race is a failure, and that a new form of life, better adapted to high civilization, will supersede us as we have superseded the ape and the elephant.

BURGE. The superman: eh!

CONRAD. No. Some being quite different from us.

LUBIN. Is that altogether desirable?

FRANKLYN. I fear so. However that may be, we may be quite sure of one thing. We shall not be let alone. The force behind evolution, call it what you will, is determined to solve the problem of civilization; and if it cannot do it through us, it will produce some more capable agents. Man is not God's last word: God can still create. If you cannot do His work He will produce some being who can.

BURGE [*with zealous reverence*] What do we know about Him, Barnabas?

What does anyone know about Him?

CONRAD. We know this about Him with absolute certainty. The power my brother calls God proceeds by the method of Trial and Error; and if we turn out to be one of the errors, we shall go the way of the mastodon and the megatherium and all the other scrapped experiments.

LUBIN [*rising and beginning to walk up and down the room with his considering cap on*] I admit that I am impressed, gentlemen. I will go so far as to say that your theory is likely to prove more interesting than ever Welsh Disestablishment was. But as a practical politician—hm! Eh, Burge?

CONRAD. We are not practical politicians. We are out to get something done. Practical politicians are people who have mastered the art of using parliament to prevent anything being done.

FRANKLYN. When we get matured statesmen and citizens—

LUBIN [*stopping short*] Citizens! Oh! Are the citizens to live three hundred years as well as the statesmen?

CONRAD. Of course.

LUBIN. I confess that had not occurred to me [*he sits down abruptly, evidently very unfavorably affected by this new light*].

Savvy and Haslam look at one another with unspeakable feelings.

BURGE. Do you think it would be wise to go quite so far at first? Surely it would be more prudent to begin with the best men.

FRANKLYN. You need not be anxious about that. It will begin with the best men.

LUBIN. I am glad to hear you say so. You see, we must put this into a practical parliamentary shape.

BURGE. We shall have to draft a Bill: that is the long and the short of it. Until you have your Bill drafted you don't know what you are really doing: that is my experience.

LUBIN. Quite so. My idea is that whilst we should interest the electorate in this as a sort of religious aspiration and personal hope, using it at the same time to remove their prejudices against those of us who are getting on in years, it would be in the last degree upsetting and even dangerous to enable everyone to live longer than usual. Take the mere question of the manufacture of the specific, whatever it may be! There are forty millions of people in the country. Let me assume for the sake of illustration that each person would have to consume, say, five ounces a day of the elixir. That would be—let me see—five times three hundred and sixty-five is—um—twenty-five—thirty-two—eighteen—eighteen hundred and twenty-five ounces a year: just two ounces over the hundredweight.

BURGE. Two million tons a year, in round numbers, of stuff that everyone would clamor for: that men would trample down women and children in the streets to get at. You couldnt produce it. There would be blue murder. It's out of the question. We must keep the actual secret to ourselves.

CONRAD [*staring at them*] The actual secret! What on earth is the man talking about?

BURGE. The stuff. The powder. The bottle. The tabloid. Whatever it is.

You said it wasnt lemons.

CONRAD. My good sir: I have no powder, no bottle, no tabloid. I am not a quack: I am a biologist. This is a thing thats going to happen.

LUBIN [*completely let down*] Going to happen! Oh! Is that all? [*He looks at his watch*].

BURGE. Going to happen! What do you mean? Do you mean that you cant make it happen?

CONRAD. No more than I could have made you happen.

FRANKLYN. We can put it into men's heads that there is nothing to prevent its happening but their own will to die before their work is done, and their own ignorance of the splendid work there is for them to do.

CONRAD. Spread that knowledge and that conviction; and as surely as the sun will rise tomorrow, the thing will happen.

FRANKLYN. We don't know where or when or to whom it will happen. It may happen first to someone in this room.

HASLAM. It wont happen to me: thats jolly sure.

CONRAD. It might happen to anyone. It might happen to the parlor maid.

How do we know?

SAVVY. The parlor maid! Oh, thats nonsense, Nunk.

LUBIN [*once more quite comfortable*] I think Miss Savvy has delivered the final verdict.

BURGE. Do you mean to say that you have nothing more practical to offer than the mere wish to live longer? Why, if people could live by merely wishing to, we should all be living for ever already! Everybody would like to live for ever. Why don't they?

CONRAD. Pshaw! Everybody would like to have a million of money. Why havnt they? Because the men who would like to be millionaires wont save sixpence even with the chance of starvation staring them in the face. The men who want to live for ever wont cut off a glass of beer or a pipe of tobacco, though they believe the teetotallers and non-smokers live longer. That sort of liking is not willing. See what they do when they know they must.

FRANKLYN. Do not mistake mere idle fancies for the tremendous miracle-working force of Will nerved to creation by a conviction of Necessity. I tell you men capable of such willing, and realizing its necessity, will do it reluctantly, under inner compulsion, as all great efforts are made. They will hide what they are doing from themselves: they will take care not to know what they are doing. They will live three hundred years, not because they would like to, but because the soul deep down in them will know that they must, if the world is to be saved.

LUBIN [*turning to Franklyn and patting him almost paternally*] Well, my dear Barnabas, for the last thirty years the post has brought me at least once a week a plan from some crank or other for the establishment of the millennium. I think you are the maddest of all the cranks; but you are much the most interesting. I am conscious of a very curious mixture of relief and disappointment in finding that your plan is all moonshine, and that you have nothing practical to offer us. But what a pity! It is such a fascinating idea! I think you are too hard on us practical men; but there are men in every Government, even on the Front Bench, who deserve all you say. And now, before dropping the subject, may I put just one question to you? An idle question, since nothing can come of it; but still—

FRANKLYN. Ask your question.

LUBIN. Why do you fix three hundred years as the exact figure?

FRANKLYN. Because we must fix some figure. Less would not be enough; and more would be more than we dare as yet face.

LUBIN. Pooh! I am quite prepared to face three thousand, not to say three million.

CONRAD. Yes, because you don't believe you Will be called on to make good your word.

FRANKLYN [*gently*] Also, perhaps, because you have never been troubled much by vision of the future.

BURGE [*with intense conviction*] The future does not exist for Henry

Hopkins Lubin.

LUBIN. If by the future you mean the millennial delusions which you use as a bunch of carrots to lure the uneducated British donkey to the polling booth to vote for you, it certainly does not.

SURGE. I can see the future not only because, if I may say so in all humility, I have been gifted with a certain power of spiritual vision, but because I have practised as a solicitor. A solicitor has to advise families. He has to think of the future and know the past. His office is the real modern confessional. Among other things he has to make people's wills for them. He has to shew them how to provide for their daughters after their deaths. Has it occurred to you, Lubin, that if you live three hundred years, your daughters will have to wait a devilish long time for their money?

FRANKLYN. The money may not wait for them. Few investments flourish for three hundred years.

SAVVY. And what about before your death? Suppose they didn't get married! Imagine a girl living at home with her mother and on her father for three hundred years! Theyd murder her if she didn't murder them first.

LUBIN. By the way, Barnabas, is your daughter to keep her good looks all the time?

FRANKLYN. Will it matter? Can you conceive the most hardened flirt going on flirting for three centuries? At the end of half the time we shall hardly notice whether it is a woman or a man we are speaking to.

LUBIN [*not quite relishing this ascetic prospect*] Hm! [*He rises*]. Ah, well: you must come and tell my wife and my young people all about it; and you will bring your daughter with you, of course. [*He shakes hands with Savvy*]. Goodbye. [*He shakes hands with Franklyn*]. Goodbye, Doctor. [*He shakes hands with Conrad*]. Come on, Burge: you must really tell me what line you are going to take about the Church at the election?

BURGE. Havnt you heard? Havnt you taken in the revelation that has been vouchsafed to us? The line I am going to take is Back to Methuselah.

LUBIN [*decisively*] Dont be ridiculous, Burge. You don't suppose, do you, that our friends here are in earnest, or that our very pleasant conversation has had anything to do with practical politics! They have just been pulling our legs very wittily. Come along. [*He goes out, Franklyn politely going with him, but shaking his head in mute protest*].

BURGE [*shaking Conrad's hand*] It's beyond the old man, Doctor. No spiritual side to him: only a sort of classical side that goes down with his own set. Besides, he's done, gone, past, burnt out, burst up; thinks he is our leader and is only our rag and bottle department. But you may depend on me. I will work this stunt of yours in. I see its value. [*He begins moving towards the door with Conrad*]. Of course I cant put it exactly in your way; but you are quite right about our needing something fresh; and I believe an election can be fought on the death rate and on Adam and Eve as scientific facts. It will take the Opposition right out of its depth. And if we win there will be an O.M. for somebody when the first honors list comes round [*by this time he has talked himself out of the room and out of earshot, Conrad accompanying him*].

Savvy and Haslam, left alone, seize each other in an ecstasy of amusement, and jazz to the settee, where they sit down again side by side.

HASLAM [*caressing her*] Darling! what a priceless humbug old Lubin is!

SAVVY. Oh, sweet old thing! I love him. Burge is a flaming fraud if you like.

HASLAM. Did you notice one thing? It struck me as rather curious.

SAVVY. What?

HASLAM. Lubin and your father have both survived the war. But their sons were killed in it.

SAVVY [*sobered*] Yes. Jim's death killed mother.

HASLAM. And they never said a word about it!

SAVVY. Well, why should they? The subject didn't come up. *I* forgot about it too; and I was very fond of Jim.

HASLAM. *I* didn't forget it, because I'm of military age; and if I hadnt been a parson I'd have had to go out and be killed too. To me the awful thing about their political incompetence was that they had to kill their own sons. It was the war casualty lists and the starvation afterwards that finished me up with politics and the Church and everything else except you.

SAVVY. Oh, I was just as bad as any of them. I sold flags in the streets in my best clothes; and—hsh! [*she jumps up and pretends to be looking for a book on the shelves behind the settee*].

Franklyn and Conrad return, looking weary and glum.

CONRAD. Well, thats how the gospel of the brothers Barnabas is going to be received! [*He drops into Burge's chair*].

FRANKLYN [*going back to his seat at the table*] It's no use. Were you convinced, Mr Haslam?

HASLAM. About our being able to live three hundred years? Frankly no.

CONRAD [*to Savvy*] Nor you, I suppose?

SAVVY. Oh, I don't know. I thought I was for a moment. I can believe, in a sort of way, that people might live for three hundred years. But when you came down to tin tacks, and said that the parlor maid might, then I saw how absurd it was.

FRANKLYN. Just so. We had better hold our tongues about it, Con. We should only be laughed at, and lose the little credit we earned on false pretences in the days of our ignorance.

CONRAD. I daresay. But Creative Evolution doesnt stop while people are laughing. Laughing may even lubricate its job.

SAVVY. What does that mean?

CONRAD. It means that the first man to live three hundred years maynt have the slightest notion that he is going to do it, and may be the loudest laugher of the lot.

SAVVY. Or the first woman?

CONRAD [*assenting*] Or the first woman.

HASLAM. Well, it wont be one of us, anyhow.

FRANKLYN. How do you know?

This is unanswerable. None of them have anything more to say.

PART III

The Thing Happens

A summer afternoon in the year 2170 A.D. The official parlor of the President of the British Islands. A board table, long enough for three chairs at each side besides the presidential chair at the head and an ordinary chair at the foot, occupies the breadth of the room. On the table, opposite every chair, a small switchboard with a dial. There is no fireplace. The end wall is a silvery screen nearly as large as a pair of folding doors. The door is on your left as you face the screen; and there is a row of thick pegs, padded and covered with velvet, beside it.

A stoutish middle-aged man, good-looking and breezily genial, dressed in a silk smock, stockings, handsomely ornamented sandals, and a gold fillet round his brows, comes in. He is like Joyce Burge, yet also like Lubin, as if Nature had made a composite photograph of the two men. He takes off the fillet and hangs it on a peg; then sits down in the presidential chair at the head of the table, which is at the end farthest from the door. He puts a peg into his switchboard; turns the pointer on the dial; puts another peg in; and presses a button. Immediately the silvery screen vanishes; and in its place appears, in reverse from right to left, another office similarly furnished, with a thin, unamiable man similarly dressed, but in duller colors, turning over some documents at the table. His gold fillet is hanging up on a similar peg beside the door. He is rather like Conrad Barnabas, but younger, and much more commonplace.

BURGE-LUBIN. Hallo, Barnabas!

BARNABAS [*without looking round*] What number?

BURGE-LUBIN. Five double x three two gamma. Burge-Lubin.

Barnabas puts a plug in number five; turns his pointer to double x; and another plug in 32; presses a button and looks round at Burge-Lubin, who is now visible to him as well as audible.

BARNABAS [*curtly*] Oh! That you, President?

BURGE-LUBIN. Yes. They told me you wanted me to ring you up. Anything wrong?

BARNABAS [*harsh and querulous*] I wish to make a protest.

BURGE-LUBIN [*good-humored and mocking*] What! Another protest! Whats wrong now?

BARNABAS. If you only knew all the protests I havnt made, you would be surprised at my patience. It is you who are always treating me with the grossest want of consideration.

BURGE-LUBIN. What have I done now?

BARNABAS. You have put me down to go to the Record Office today to receive that American fellow, and do the honors of a ridiculous cinema show. That is not the business of the Accountant General: it is the business of the President. It is an outrageous waste of my time, and an unjustifiable shirking of your duty at my expense. I refuse to go. You must go.

BURGE-LUBIN. My dear boy, nothing would give me greater pleasure than to take the job off your hands—

BARNABAS. Then do it. Thats all I want [*he is about to switch off*].

BURGE-LUBIN. Dont switch off. Listen. This American has invented a method of breathing under water.

BARNABAS. What do I care? I don't want to breathe under water.

BURGE-LUBIN. You may, my dear Barnabas, at any time. You know you never look where you are going when you are immersed in your calculations. Some day you will walk into the Serpentine. This man's invention may save your life.

BARNABAS [*angrily*] Will you tell me what that has to do with your putting your ceremonial duties on to my shoulders? I will not be trifled [*he vanishes and is replaced by the blank screen*]—

BURGE-LUBIN [*indignantly holding down his button*] Dont cut us off, please: we have not finished. I am the President, speaking to the Accountant General. What are you dreaming of?

A WOMAN'S VOICE. Sorry. [*The screen shews Barnabas as before*].

BURGE-LUBIN. Since you take it that way, I will go in your place. It's a pity, because, you see, this American thinks you are the greatest living authority on the duration of human life; and—

BARNABAS [*interrupting*] The American thinks! What do you mean? I am the greatest living authority on the duration of human life. Who dares dispute it?

BURGE-LUBIN. Nobody, dear lad, nobody. Dont fly out at me. It is evident that you have not read the American's book.

BARNABAS. Dont tell me that you have, or that you have read any book except a novel for the last twenty years; for I wont believe you.

BURGE-LUBIN. Quite right, dear old fellow: I havnt read it. But I have read what The Times Literary Supplement says about it.

BARNABAS. I don't care two straws what it says about it. Does it say anything about me?

BURGE-LUBIN. Yes.

BARNABAS. Oh, does it? What?

BURGE-LUBIN. It points out that an extraordinary number of first-rate persons like you and me have died by drowning during the last two centuries, and that when this invention of breathing under water takes effect, your estimate of the average duration of human life will be upset.

BARNABAS [*alarmed*] Upset my estimate! Gracious Heavens! Does the fool realize what that means? Do you realize what that means?

BURGE-LUBIN. I suppose it means that we shall have to amend the Act.

BARNABAS. Amend my Act! Monstrous!

BURGE-LUBIN. But we must. We cant ask people to go on working until they are forty-three unless our figures are unchallengeable. You know what a row there was over those last three years, and how nearly the too-old-at-forty people won.

BARNABAS. They would have made the British Islands bankrupt if theyd won. But you dont care for that; you care for nothing but being popular.

BURGE-LUBIN. Oh, well: I shouldn't worry if I were you; for most people complain that there is not enough work for them, and would be only too glad to stick on instead of retiring at forty-three, if only they were asked as a favor instead of having to.

BARNABAS. Thank you: I need no consolation. [*He rises determinedly and puts on his fillet*].

BURGE-LUBIN. Are you off? Where are you going to?

BARNABAS. To that cinema tomfoolery, of course. I shall put this

American impostor in his place. [*He goes out*].

BURGE-LUBIN [*calling after him*] God bless you, dear old chap! [*With a chuckle, he switches off; and the screen becomes blank. He presses a button and holds it down while he calls*] Hallo!

A WOMAN'S VOICE. Hallo!

BURGE-LUBIN [*formally*] The President respectfully solicits the privilege of an interview with the Chief Secretary, and holds himself entirely at his honor's august disposal.

A CHINESE VOICE. He is coming.

BURGE-LUBIN. Oh! That you, Confucius? So good of you. Come along [*he releases the button*].

A man in a yellow gown, presenting the general appearance of a Chinese sage, enters.

BURGE-LUBIN [*jocularly*] Well, illustrious Sage-&-Onions, how are your poor sore feet?

CONFUCIUS [*gravely*] I thank you for your kind inquiries. I am well.

BURGE-LUBIN. Thats right. Sit down and make yourself comfortable. Any business for me today?

CONFUCIUS [*sitting down on the first chair round the corner of the table to the President's right*] None.

BURGE-LUBIN. Have you heard the result of the bye-election?

CONFUCIUS. A walk-over. Only one candidate.

BURGE-LUBIN. Any good?

CONFUCIUS. He was released from the County Lunatic Asylum a fortnight ago. Not mad enough for the lethal chamber: not sane enough for any place but the division lobby. A very popular speaker.

BURGE-LUBIN. I wish the people would take a serious interest in politics.

CONFUCIUS. I do not agree. The Englishman is not fitted by nature to understand politics. Ever since the public services have been manned by Chinese, the country has been well and honestly governed. What more is needed?

BURGE-LUBIN. What I cant make out is that China is one of the worst governed countries on earth.

CONFUCIUS. No. It was badly governed twenty years ago; but since we forbade any Chinaman to take part in our public services, and imported natives of Scotland for that purpose, we have done well. Your information here is always twenty years out of date.

BURGE-LUBIN. People don't seem to be able to govern themselves. I cant understand it. Why should it be so?

CONFUCIUS. Justice is impartiality. Only strangers are impartial.

BURGE-LUBIN. It ends in the public services being so good that the

Government has nothing to do but think.

CONFUCIUS. Were it otherwise, the Government would have too much to do to think.

BURGE-LUBIN. Is that any excuse for the English people electing a parliament of lunatics?

CONFUCIUS. The English people always did elect parliaments of lunatics. What does it matter if your permanent officials are honest and competent?

BURGE-LUBIN. You do not know the history of this country. What would my ancestors have said to the menagerie of degenerates that is still called the House of Commons? Confucius: you will not believe me; and I do not blame you for it; but England once saved the liberties of the world by inventing parliamentary government, which was her peculiar and supreme glory.

CONFUCIUS. I know the history of your country perfectly well. It proves the exact contrary.

BURGE-LUBIN. How do you make that out?

CONFUCIUS. The only power your parliament ever had was the power of withholding supplies from the king.

BURGE-LUBIN. Precisely. That great Englishman Simon de Montfort—

CONFUCIUS. He was not an Englishman: he was a Frenchman. He imported parliaments from France.

BURGE-LUBIN [*surprised*] You dont say so!

CONFUCIUS. The king and his loyal subjects killed Simon for forcing his French parliament on them. The first thing British parliaments always did was to grant supplies to the king for life with enthusiastic expressions of loyalty, lest they should have any real power, and be expected to do something.

BURGE-LUBIN. Look here, Confucius: you know more history than I do, of course; but democracy—

CONFUCIUS. An institution peculiar to China. And it was never really a success there.

BURGE-LUBIN. But the Habeas Corpus Act!

CONFUCIUS. The English always suspended it when it threatened to be of the slightest use.

BURGE-LUBIN. Well, trial by jury: you cant deny that we established that?

CONFUCIUS. All cases that were dangerous to the governing classes were tried in the Star Chamber or by Court Martial, except when the prisoner was not tried at all, but executed after calling him names enough to make him unpopular.

BURGE-LUBIN. Oh, bother! You may be right in these little details; but in the large we have managed to hold our own as a great race. Well, people who could do nothing couldnt have done that, you know.

CONFUCIUS. I did not say you could do nothing. You could fight. You could eat. You could drink. Until the twentieth century you could produce children. You could play games. You could work when you were forced to. But you could not govern yourselves.

BURGE-LUBIN. Then how did we get our reputation as the pioneers of liberty?

CONFUCIUS. By your steadfast refusal to be governed at all. A horse that kicks everyone who tries to harness and guide him may be a pioneer of liberty; but he is not a pioneer of government. In China he would be shot.

BURGE-LUBIN. Stuff! Do you imply that the administration of which I am president is no Government?

CONFUCIUS. I do. *I* am the Government.

BURGE-LUBIN. You! You!! You fat yellow lump of conceit!

CONFUCIUS. Only an Englishman could be so ignorant of the nature of government as to suppose that a capable statesman cannot be fat, yellow, and conceited. Many Englishmen are slim, red-nosed, and modest. Put them in my place, and within a year you will be back in the anarchy and chaos of the nineteenth and twentieth centuries.

BURGE-LUBIN. Oh, if you go back to the dark ages, I have nothing more to say. But we did not perish. We extricated ourselves from that chaos. We are now the best governed country in the world. How did we manage that if we are such fools as you pretend?

CONFUCIUS. You did not do it until the slaughter and ruin produced by your anarchy forced you at last to recognize two inexorable facts. First, that government is absolutely necessary to civilization, and that you could not maintain civilization by merely doing down your neighbor, as you called it, and cutting off the head of your king whenever he happened to be a logical Scot and tried to take his position seriously. Second, that government is an art of which you are congenitally incapable. Accordingly, you imported educated negresses and Chinese to govern you. Since then you have done very well.

BURGE-LUBIN. So have you, you old humbug. All the same, I don't know how you stand the work you do. You seem to me positively to like public business. Why wont you let me take you down to the coast some week-end and teach you marine golf?

CONFUCIUS. It does not interest me. I am not a barbarian.

BURGE-LUBIN. You mean that I am?

CONFUCIUS. That is evident.

BURGE-LUBIN. How?

CONFUCIUS. People like you. They like cheerful goodnatured barbarians. They have elected you President five times in succession. They will elect you five times more. *I* like you. You are better company than a dog or a horse because you can speak.

BURGE-LUBIN. Am I a barbarian because you like me?

CONFUCIUS. Surely. Nobody likes me: I am held in awe. Capable persons are never liked. I am not likeable; but I am indispensable.

BURGE-LUBIN. Oh, cheer up, old man: theres nothing so disagreeable about you as all that. I don't dislike you; and if you think I'm afraid of you, you jolly well don't know Burge-Lubin: thats all.

CONFUCIUS. You are brave: yes. It is a form of stupidity.

BURGE-LUBIN. You may not be brave: one doesn't expect it from a Chink.

But you have the devil's own cheek.

CONFUCIUS. I have the assured certainty of the man who sees and knows. Your genial bluster, your cheery self-confidence, are pleasant, like the open air. But they are blind: they are vain. I seem to see a great dog wag his tail and bark joyously. But if he leaves my heel he is lost.

BURGE-LUBIN. Thank you for a handsome compliment. I have a big dog; and he is the best fellow I know. If you knew how much uglier you are than a chow, you wouldn't start those comparisons, though. [*Rising*] Well, if you have nothing for me to do, I am going to leave your heel for the rest of the day and enjoy myself. What would you recommend me to do with myself?

CONFUCIUS. Give yourself up to contemplation; and great thoughts will come to you.

BURGE-LUBIN. Will they? If you think I am going to sit here on a fine day like this with my legs crossed waiting for great thoughts, you exaggerate my taste for them. I prefer marine golf. [*Stopping short*] Oh, by the way, I forgot something. I have a word or two to say to the Minister of health. [*He goes back to his chair*].

CONFUCIUS. Her number is—

BURGE-LUBIN. I know it.

CONFUCIUS [*rising*] I cannot understand her attraction for you. For me a woman who is not yellow does not exist, save as an official. [*He goes out*].

Burge-Lubin operates his switchboard as before. The screen vanishes: and a dainty room with a bed, a wardrobe, and a dressing-table with a mirror and a switch on it, appears. Seated at it a handsome negress is trying on a brilliant head scarf. Her dressing-gown is thrown back from her shoulders to her chair. She is in corset, knickers, and silk stockings.

BURGE-LUBIN [*horrified*] I beg your pardon a thousand times—[*The startled negress snatches the peg out of her switchboard and vanishes*].

THE NEGRESS'S VOICE. Who is it?

BURGE-LUBIN. Me. The President. Burge-Lubin. I had no idea your bedroom switch was in. I beg your pardon.

The negress reappears. She has pulled the dressing-gown perfunctorily over her shoulders, and continues her experiments with the scarf, not at all put out, and rather amused by Surge's prudery.

THE NEGRESS. Stupid of me. I was talking to another lady this morning; and I left the peg in.

BURGE-LUBIN. But I am so sorry.

THE NEGRESS [*sunnily: still busy with the scarf*] Why? It was my fault.

BURGE-LUBIN [*embarrassed*] Well—er—But I suppose you were used to it in Africa.

THE NEGRESS. Your delicacy is very touching, Mr President. It would be funny if it were not so unpleasant, because, like all white delicacy, it is in the wrong place. How do you think this suits my complexion?

BURGE-LUBIN. How can any really vivid color go wrong with a black satin skin? It is our women's wretched pale faces that have to be matched and lighted. Yours is always right.

THE NEGRESS. Yes: it is a pity your white beauties have all the same ashy faces, the same colorless drab, the same age. But look at their beautiful noses and little lips! They are physically insipid: they have no beauty: you cannot love them; but how elegant!

BURGE-LUBIN. Cant you find an official pretext for coming to see me? Isnt it ridiculous that we have never met? It's so tantalizing to see you and talk to you, and to know all the time that you are two hundred miles away, and that I cant touch you?

THE NEGRESS. I cannot live on the East Coast: it is hard enough to keep my blood warm here. Besides, my friend, it would not be safe. These distant flirtations are very charming; and they teach self-control.

BURGE-LUBIN. Damn self-control! I want to hold you in my arms—to—[*the negress snatches out the peg from the switchboard and vanishes. She is still heard laughing*]. Black devil! [*He snatches out his peg furiously: her laugh is no longer heard*]. Oh, these sex episodes! Why can I not resist them? Disgraceful!

Confucius returns.

CONFUCIUS. I forgot. There is something for you to do this morning. You have to go to the Record Office to receive the American barbarian.

BURGE-LUBIN. Confucius: once for all, I object to this Chinese habit of describing white men as barbarians.

CONFUCIUS [*standing formally at the end of the table with his hands palm to palm*] I make a mental note that you do not wish the Americans to be described as barbarians.

BURGE-LUBIN. Not at all. The Americans are barbarians. But we are not. I suppose the particular barbarian you are speaking of is the American who has invented a means of breathing under water.

CONFUCIUS. He says he has invented such a method. For some reason which is not intelligible in China, Englishmen always believe any statement made by an American inventor, especially one who has never invented anything. Therefore you believe this person and have given him a public reception. Today the Record Office is entertaining him with a display of the cinematographic records of all the eminent Englishmen who have lost their lives by drowning since the cinema was invented. Why not go to see it if you are at a loss for something to do?

BURGE-LUBIN. What earthly interest is there in looking at a moving picture of a lot of people merely because they were drowned? If they had had any sense, they would not have been drowned, probably.

CONFUCIUS. That is not so. It has never been noticed before; but the Record Office has just made two remarkable discoveries about the public men and women who have displayed extraordinary ability during the past century. One is that they retained unusual youthfulness up to an advanced age. The other is that they all met their death by drowning.

BURGE-LUBIN. Yes: I know. Can you explain it?

CONFUCIUS. It cannot be explained. It is not reasonable. Therefore I do not believe it.

The Accountant General rushes in, looking ghastly. He staggers to the middle of the table.

BURGE-LUBIN. Whats the matter? Are you ill?

BARNABAS [*choking*] No. I—[*he collapses into the middle chair*]. I must speak to you in private.

Confucius calmly withdraws.

BURGE-LUBIN. What on earth is it? Have some oxygen.

BARNABAS. I have had some. Go to the Record Office. You will see men fainting there again and again, and being revived with oxygen, as I have been. They have seen with their own eyes as I have.

BURGE-LUBIN. Seen what?

BARNABAS. Seen the Archbishop of York.

BURGE-LUBIN. Well, why shouldn't they see the Archbishop of York? What are they fainting for? Has he been murdered?

BARNABAS. No: he has been drowned.

BURGE-LUBIN. Good God! Where? When? How? Poor fellow!

BARNABAS. Poor fellow! Poor thief! Poor swindler! Poor robber of his country's Exchequer! Poor fellow indeed! Wait til I catch him.

BURGE-LUBIN. How can you catch him when he is dead? Youre mad.

BARNABAS. Dead! Who said he was dead?

BURGE-LUBIN. You did. Drowned.

BARNABAS [*exasperated*] Will you listen to me? Was old Archbishop

Haslam, the present man's last predecessor but four, drowned or not?

BURGE-LUBIN. I don't know. Look him up in the Encyclopedia Britannica.

BARNABAS. Yah! Was Archbishop Stickit, who wrote Stickit on the Psalms, drowned or not?

BURGE-LUBIN. Yes, mercifully. He deserved it.

BARNABAS. Was President Dickenson drowned? Was General Bullyboy drowned?

BURGE-LUBIN. Who is denying it?

BARNABAS. Well, wave had moving pictures of all four put on the screen today for this American; and they and the Archbishop are the same man. Now tell me I am mad.

BURGE-LUBIN. I do tell you you are mad. Stark raving mad.

BARNABAS. Am I to believe my own eyes or am I not?

BURGE-LUBIN. You can do as you please. All I can tell you is that *I* don't believe your eyes if they cant see any difference between a live archbishop and two dead ones. [*The apparatus rings, he holds the button down*]. Yes?

THE WOMAN'S VOICE. The Archbishop of York, to see the President.

BARNABAS [*hoarse with rage*] Have him in. I'll talk to the scoundrel.

BURGE-LUBIN [*releasing the button*] Not while you are in this state.

BARNABAS [*reaching furiously for his button and holding it down*] Send the Archbishop in at once.

BURGE-LUBIN. If you lose your temper, Barnabas, remember that we shall be two to one.

The Archbishop enters. He has a white band round his throat, set in a black stock. He wears a sort of kilt of black ribbons, and soft black boots that button high up on his calves. His costume does not differ otherwise from that of the President and the Accountant General; but its color scheme is black and white. He is older than the Reverend Bill Haslam was when he wooed Miss Savvy Barnabas; but he is recognizably the same man. He does not look a day over fifty, and is very well preserved even at that; but his boyishness of manner is quite gone: he now has complete authority and self-possession: in fact the President is a little afraid of him; and it seems quite natural and inevitable that he should speak fast.

THE ARCHBISHOP. Good day, Mr President.

BURGE-LUBIN. Good day, Mr Archbishop. Be seated.

THE ARCHBISHOP [*sitting down between them*] Good day, Mr Accountant

General.

BARNABAS [*malevolently*] Good day to you. I have a question to put to you, if you don't mind.

THE ARCHBISHOP [*looking curiously at him, jarred by his uncivil tone*]

Certainly. What is it?

BARNABAS. What is your definition of a thief?

THE ARCHBISHOP. Rather an old-fashioned word, is it not?

BARNABAS. It survives officially in my department.

THE ARCHBISHOP. Our departments are full of survivals. Look at my tie! my apron! my boots! They are all mere survivals; yet it seems that without them I cannot be a proper Archbishop.

BARNABAS. Indeed! Well, in my department the word thief survives, because in the community the thing thief survives. And a very despicable and dishonorable thing he is, too.

THE ARCHBISHOP [*coolly*] I daresay.

BARNABAS. In my department, sir, a thief is a person who lives longer than the statutory expectation of life entitles him to, and goes on drawing public money when, if he were an honest man, he would be dead.

THE ARCHBISHOP. Then let me say, sir, that your department does not understand its own business. If you have miscalculated the duration of human life, that is not the fault of the persons whose longevity you have miscalculated. And if they continue to work and produce, they pay their way, even if they live two or three centuries.

BARNABAS. I know nothing about their working and producing. That is not the business of my department. I am concerned with their expectation of life; and I say that no man has any right to go on living and drawing money when he ought to be dead.

THE ARCHBISHOP. You do not comprehend the relation between income and production.

BARNABAS. I understand my own department.

THE ARCHBISHOP. That is not enough. Your department is part of a synthesis which embraces all the departments.

BURGE-LUBIN. Synthesis! This is an intellectual difficulty. This is a job for Confucius. I heard him use that very word the other day; and I wondered what the devil he meant. [*Switching on*] Hallo! Put me through to the Chief Secretary.

CONFUCIUS'S VOICE. You are speaking to him.

BURGE-LUBIN. An intellectual difficulty, old man. Something we don't understand. Come and help us out.

THE ARCHBISHOP. May I ask how the question has arisen?

BARNABAS. Ah! You begin to smell a rat, do you? You thought yourself pretty safe. You—

BURGE-LUBIN. Steady, Barnabas. Dont be in a hurry.

Confucius enters.

THE ARCHBISHOP [*rising*] Good morning, Mr Chief Secretary.

BURGE-LUBIN [*rising in instinctive imitation of the Archbishop*] Honor us by taking a seat, O sage.

CONFUCIUS. Ceremony is needless. [*He bows to the company, and takes the chair at the foot of the table*].

The President and the Archbishop resume their seats.

BURGE-LUBIN. We wish to put a case to you, Confucius. Suppose a man, instead of conforming to the official estimate of his expectation of life, were to live for more than two centuries and a half, would the Accountant General be justified in calling him a thief?

CONFUCIUS. No. He would be justified in calling him a liar.

THE ARCHBISHOP. I think not, Mr Chief Secretary. What do you suppose my age is?

CONFUCIUS. Fifty.

BURGE-LUBIN. You don't look it. Forty-five; and young for your age.

THE ARCHBISHOP. My age is two hundred and eighty-three.

BARNABAS [*morosely triumphant*] Hmp! Mad, am I?

BURGE-LUBIN. Youre both mad. Excuse me, Archbishop; but this is getting a bit—well—

THE ARCHBISHOP [*to Confucius*] Mr Chief Secretary: will you, to oblige me, assume that I have lived nearly three centuries? As a hypothesis?

BURGE-LUBIN. What is a hypothesis?

CONFUCIUS. It does not matter. I understand. [*To the Archbishop*] Am I to assume that you have lived in your ancestors, or by metempsychosis—

BURGE-LUBIN. Met—Emp—Sy—Good Lord! What a brain, Confucius! What a brain!

THE ARCHBISHOP. Nothing of that kind. Assume in the ordinary sense that I was born in the year 1887, and that I have worked continuously in one profession or another since the year 1910. Am I a thief?

CONFUCIUS. I do not know. Was that one of your professions?

THE ARCHBISHOP. No. I have been nothing worse than an Archbishop, a

President, and a General.

BARNABAS. Has he or has he not robbed the Exchequer by drawing five or six incomes when he was only entitled to one? Answer me that.

CONFUCIUS. Certainly not. The hypothesis is that he has worked continuously since 1910. We are now in the year 2170. What is the official lifetime?

BARNABAS. Seventy-eight. Of course it's an average; and we don't mind a man here and there going on to ninety, or even, as a curiosity, becoming a centenarian. But I say that a man who goes beyond that is a swindler.

CONFUCIUS. Seventy-eight into two hundred and eighty-three goes more than three and a half times. Your department owes the Archbishop two and a half educations and three and a half retiring pensions.

BARNABAS. Stuff! How can that be?

CONFUCIUS. At what age do your people begin to work for the community?

BURGE-LUBIN. Three. They do certain things every day when they are three. Just to break them in, you know. But they become self-supporting, or nearly so, at thirteen.

CONFUCIUS. And at what age do they retire?

BARNABAS. Forty-three.

CONFUCIUS. That is, they do thirty years' work; and they receive maintenance and education, without working, for thirteen years of childhood and thirty-five years of superannuation, forty-eight years in all, for each thirty years' work. The Archbishop has given you 260 years' work, and has received only one education and no superannuation. You therefore owe him over 300 years of leisure and nearly eight educations. You are thus heavily in his debt. In other words, he has effected an enormous national economy by living so long; and you, by living only seven-seventy-eight years, are profiting at his expense. He is the benefactor: you are the thief. [*Half rising*] May I now withdraw and return to my serious business, as my own span is comparatively short?

BURGE-LUBIN. Dont be in a hurry, old chap. [*Confucius sits down again*]. This hypothecary, or whatever you call it, is put up seriously. I don't believe it; but if the Archbishop and the Accountant General are going to insist that it's true, we shall have either to lock them up or to see the thing through.

BARNABAS. It's no use trying these Chinese subtleties on me. I'm a plain man; and though I don't understand metaphysics, and don't believe in them, I understand figures; and if the Archbishop is only entitled to seventy-eight years, and he takes 283, I say he takes more than he is entitled to. Get over that if you can.

THE ARCHBISHOP. I have not taken 283 years: I have taken 23 and given 260.

CONFUCIUS. Do your accounts shew a deficiency or a surplus?

BARNABAS. A surplus. Thats what I cant make out. Thats the artfulness of these people.

BURGE-LUBIN. That settles it. Whats the use of arguing? The Chink says you are wrong; and theres an end of it.

BARNABAS. I say nothing against the Chink's arguments. But what about my facts?

CONFUCIUS. If your facts include a case of a man living 283 years, I advise you to take a few weeks at the seaside.

BARNABAS. Let there be an end of this hinting that I am out of my mind.

Come and look at the cinema record. I tell you this man is Archbishop

Haslam, Archbishop Stickit, President Dickenson, General Bullyboy and himself into the bargain; all five of them.

THE ARCHBISHOP. I do not deny it. I never have denied it. Nobody has ever asked me.

BURGE-LUBIN. But damn it, man—I beg your pardon, Archbishop; but really, really—

THE ARCHBISHOP. Dont mention it. What were you going to say?

BURGE-LUBIN. Well, you were drowned four times over. You are not a cat, you know.

THE ARCHBISHOP. That is very easy to understand. Consider my situation when I first made the amazing discovery that I was destined to live three hundred years! I—

CONFUCIUS [*interrupting him*] Pardon me. Such a discovery was impossible. You have not made it yet. You may live a million years if you have already lived two hundred. There is no question of three hundred years. You have made a slip at the very beginning of your fairy tale, Mr Archbishop.

BURGE-LUBIN. Good, Confucius! [*To the Archbishop*] He has you there. I don't see how you can get over that.

THE ARCHBISHOP. Yes: it is quite a good point. But if the Accountant General will go to the British Museum library, and search the catalogue, he will find under his own name a curious and now forgotten book, dated 1924, entitled The Gospel of the Brothers Barnabas. That gospel was that men must live three hundred years if civilization is to be saved. It shewed that this extension of individual human life was possible, and how it was likely to come about. I married the daughter of one of the brothers.

BARNABAS. Do you mean to say you claim to be a connection of mine?

THE ARCHBISHOP. I claim nothing. As I have by this time perhaps three or four million cousins of one degree or another, I have ceased to call on the family.

BURGE-LUBIN. Gracious heavens! Four million relatives! Is that calculation correct, Confucius?

CONFUCIUS. In China it might be forty millions if there were no checks on population.

BURGE-LUBIN. This is a staggerer. It brings home to one—but [*recovering*] it isnt true, you know. Let us keep sane.

CONFUCIUS [*to the Archbishop*] You wish us to understand that the illustrious ancestors of the Accountant General communicated to you a secret by which you could attain the age of three hundred years.

THE ARCHBISHOP. No. Nothing of the kind. They simply believed that mankind could live any length of time it knew to be absolutely necessary to save civilization from extinction. I did not share their belief: at least I was not conscious of sharing it: I thought I was only amused by it. To me my father-in-law and his brother were a pair of clever cranks who had talked one another into a fixed idea which had become a monomania with them. It was not until I got into serious difficulties with the pension authorities after turning seventy that I began to suspect the truth.

CONFUCIUS. The truth?

THE ARCHBISHOP. Yes, Mr Chief Secretary: the truth. Like all revolutionary truths, it began as a joke. As I shewed no signs of ageing after forty-five, my wife used to make fun of me by saying that I was certainly going to live three hundred years. She was sixty-eight when she died; and the last thing she said to me, as I sat by her bedside holding her hand, was 'Bill: you really don't look fifty. I wonder—' She broke off, and fell asleep wondering, and never awoke. Then I began to wonder too. That is the explanation of the three hundred years, Mr Secretary.

CONFUCIUS. It is very ingenious, Mr Archbishop. And very well told.

BURGE-LUBIN. Of course you understand that *I* don't for a moment suggest the very faintest doubt of your absolute veracity, Archbishop. You know that, don't you?

THE ARCHBISHOP. Quite, Mr President. Only you don't believe me: that is all. I do not expect you to. In your place I should not believe. You had better have a look at the films. [*Pointing to the Accountant General*] He believes.

BURGE-LUBIN. But the drowning? What about the drowning? A man might get drowned once, or even twice if he was exceptionally careless. But he couldn't be drowned four times. He would run away from water like a mad dog.

THE ARCHBISHOP. Perhaps Mr Chief Secretary can guess the explanation of that.

CONFUCIUS. To keep your secret, you had to die.

BURGE-LUBIN. But dash it all, man, he isn't dead.

CONFUCIUS. It is socially impossible not to do what everybody else does.

One must die at the usual time.

BARNABAS. Of course. A simple point of honour.

CONFUCIUS. Not at all. A simple necessity.

BURGE-LUBIN. Well, I'm hanged if I see it. I should jolly well live for ever if I could.

THE ARCHBISHOP. It is not so easy as you think. You, Mr Chief Secretary, have grasped the difficulties of the position. Let me remind you, Mr President, that I was over eighty before the 1969 Act for the Redistribution of Income entitled me to a handsome retiring pension. Owing to my youthful appearance I was prosecuted for attempting to obtain public money on false pretences when I claimed it. I could prove nothing; for the register of my birth had been blown to pieces by a bomb dropped on a village church years before in the first of the big modern wars. I was ordered back to work as a man of forty, and had to work for fifteen years more, the retiring age being then fifty-five.

BURGE-LUBIN. As late as fifty-five! How did people stand it?

THE ARCHBISHOP. They made difficulties about letting me go even then, I still looked so young. For some years I was in continual trouble. The industrial police rounded me up again and again, refusing to believe that I was over age. They began to call me The Wandering Jew. You see how impossible my position was. I foresaw that in twenty years more my official record would prove me to be seventy-five; my appearance would make it impossible to believe that I was more than forty-five; and my real age would be one hundred and seventeen. What was I to do? Bleach my hair? Hobble about on two sticks? Mimic the voice of a centenarian? Better have killed myself.

BARNABAS. You ought to have killed yourself. As an honest man you were entitled to no more than an honest man's expectation of life.

THE ARCHBISHOP. I did kill myself. It was quite easy. I left a suit of clothes by the seashore during the bathing season, with documents in the pockets to identify me. I then turned up in a strange place, pretending that I had lost my memory, and did not know my name or my age or anything about myself. Under treatment I recovered my health, but not my memory. I have had several careers since I began this routine of life and death. I have been an archbishop three times. When I persuaded the authorities to knock down all our towns and rebuild them from the foundations, or move them, I went into the artillery, and became a general. I have been President.

BURGE-LUBIN. Dickenson?

THE ARCHBISHOP. Yes.

BURGE-LUBIN. But they found Dickenson's body: its ashes are buried in St

Paul's.

THE ARCHBISHOP. They almost always found the body. During the bathing season there are plenty of bodies. I have been cremated again and again. At first I used to attend my own funeral in disguise, because I had read about a man doing that in an old romance by an author named Bennett, from whom I remember borrowing five pounds in 1912. But I got tired of that. I would not cross the street now to read my latest epitaph.

The Chief Secretary and the President look very glum. Their incredulity is vanquished at last.

BURGE-LUBIN. Look here. Do you chaps realize how awful this is? Here we are sitting calmly in the presence of a man whose death is overdue by two centuries. He may crumble into dust before our eyes at any moment.

BARNABAS. Not he. He'll go on drawing his pension until the end of the world.

THE ARCHBISHOP. Not quite that. My expectation of life is only three hundred years.

BARNABAS. You will last out my time anyhow: that's enough for me.

THE ARCHBISHOP [*coolly*] How do you know?

BARNABAS [*taken aback*] How do I know!

THE ARCHBISHOP. Yes: how do you know? I did not begin even to suspect until I was nearly seventy. I was only vain of my youthful appearance. I was not quite serious about it until I was ninety. Even now I am not sure from one moment to another, though I have given you my reason for thinking that I have quite unintentionally committed myself to a lifetime of three hundred years.

BURGE-LUBIN. But how do you do it? Is it lemons? Is it Soya beans? Is it—

THE ARCHBISHOP. I do not do it. It happens. It may happen to anyone. It may happen to you.

BURGE-LUBIN [*the full significance of this for himself dawning on him*]

Then we three may be in the same boat with you, for all we know?

THE ARCHBISHOP. You may. Therefore I advise you to be very careful how you take any step that will make my position uncomfortable.

BURGE-LUBIN. Well, I'm dashed! One of my secretaries was remarking only this morning how well and young I am looking. Barnabas: I have an absolute conviction that I am one of the—the—shall I say one of the victims?—of this strange destiny.

THE ARCHBISHOP. Your great-great-great-great-great-great-great-grandfather formed the same conviction when he was between sixty and seventy. I knew him.

BURGE-LUBIN [*depressed*] Ah! But he died.

THE ARCHBISHOP. No.

BURGE-LUBIN [*hopefully*] Do you mean to say he is still alive?

THE ARCHBISHOP. No. He was shot. Under the influence of his belief that he was going to live three hundred years he became a changed man. He began to tell people the truth; and they disliked it so much that they took advantage of certain clauses of an Act of Parliament he had himself passed during the Four Years War, and had purposely forgotten to repeal afterwards. They took him to the Tower of London and shot him.

The apparatus rings.

CONFUCIUS [*answering*] Yes? [*He listens*].

A WOMAN'S VOICE. The Domestic Minister has called.

BURGE-LUBIN [*not quite catching the answer*] Who does she say has called?

CONFUCIUS. The Domestic Minister.

BARNABAS. Oh, dash it! That awful woman!

BURGE-LUBIN. She certainly is a bit of a terror. I don't exactly know why; for she is not at all bad-looking.

BARNABAS [*out of patience*] For Heaven's sake, don't be frivolous.

THE ARCHBISHOP. He cannot help it, Mr Accountant General. Three of his sixteen great-great-great-grandfathers married Lubins.

BURGE-LUBIN. Tut tut! I am not frivolling. *I* did not ask the lady here. Which of you did?

CONFUCIUS. It is her official duty to report personally to the President once a quarter.

BURGE-LUBIN. Oh, that. Then I suppose it's my official duty to receive her. Theyd better send her in. You don't mind, do you? She will bring us back to real life. I don't know how you fellows feel; but I'm just going dotty.

CONFUCIUS [*into the telephone*] The President will receive the Domestic

Minister at once.

They watch the door in silence for the entrance of the Domestic Minister.

BURGE-LUBIN [*suddenly, to the Archbishop*] I suppose you have been married over and over again.

THE ARCHBISHOP. Once. You do not make vows until death when death is three hundred years off.

They relapse into uneasy silence. The Domestic Minister enters. She is a handsome woman, apparently in the prime of life, with elegant, tense, well held-up figure, and the walk of a goddess. Her expression and deportment are grave, swift, decisive, awful, unanswerable. She wears a Dianesque tunic instead of a blouse, and a silver coronet instead of a gold fillet. Her dress otherwise is not markedly different from that of the men, who rise as she enters, and incline their heads with instinctive awe. She comes to the vacant chair between Barnabas and Confucius.

BURGE-LUBIN [*resolutely genial and gallant*] Delighted to see you, Mrs
Lutestring.

CONFUCIUS. We are honored by your celestial presence.

BARNABAS. Good day, madam.

THE ARCHBISHOP. I have not had the pleasure of meeting you before. I am the Archbishop of York.

MRS LUTESTRING. Surely we have met, Mr Archbishop. I remember your face. We—[*she checks herself suddenly*] Ah, no: I remember now: it was someone else. [*She sits down*]. They all sit down.

THE ARCHBISHOP [*also puzzled*] Are you sure you are mistaken? I also have some association with your face, Mrs Lutestring. Something like a door opening continually and revealing you. And a smile of welcome when you recognized me. Did you ever open a door for me, I wonder?

MRS LUTESTRING. I often opened a door for the person you have just reminded me of. But he has been dead many years. The rest, except the Archbishop, look at one another quickly.

CONFUCIUS. May I ask how many years?

MRS LUTESTRING [*struck by his tone, looks at him for a moment with some displeasure; then replies*] It does not matter. A long time.

BURGE-LUBIN. You mustnt rush to conclusions about the Archbishop, Mrs Lutestring. He is an older bird than you think. Older than you, at all events.

MRS LUTESTRING [*with a melancholy smile*] I think not, Mr President.

But the subject is a delicate one. I had rather not pursue it.

CONFUCIUS. There is a question which has not been asked.

MRS LUTESTRING [*very decisively*] If it is a question about my age, Mr Chief Secretary, it had better not be asked. All that concerns you about my personal affairs can be found in the books of the Accountant General.

CONFUCIUS. The question I was thinking of will not be addressed to you. But let me say that your sensitiveness on the point is very strange, coming from a woman so superior to all common weaknesses as we know you to be.

MRS LUTESTRING. I may have reasons which have nothing to do with common weaknesses, Mr Chief Secretary. I hope you will respect them.

CONFUCIUS [*after bowing to her in assent*] I will now put my question. Have you, Mr Archbishop, any ground for assuming, as you seem to do, that what has happened to you has not happened to other people as well?

BURGE-LUBIN. Yes, by George! I never thought of that.

THE ARCHBISHOP. I have never met any case but my own.

CONFUCIUS. How do you know?

THE ARCHBISHOP. Well, no one has ever told me that they were in this extraordinary position.

CONFUCIUS. That proves nothing. Did you ever tell anybody that you were in it? You never told us. Why did you never tell us?

THE ARCHBISHOP. I am surprised at the question, coming from so astute a mind as yours, Mr Secretary. When you reach the age I reached before I discovered what was happening to me, I was old enough to know and fear the ferocious hatred with which human animals, like all other animals, turn upon any unhappy individual who has the misfortune to be unlike themselves in every respect: to be unnatural, as they call it. You will still find, among the tales of that twentieth-century classic, Wells, a story of a race of men who grew twice as big as their fellows, and another story of a man who fell into the hands of a race of blind men. The big people had to fight the little people for their lives; and the man with eyes would have had his eyes put out by the blind had he not fled to the desert, where he perished miserably. Wells's teaching, on that and other matters, was not lost on me. By the way, he lent me five pounds once which I never repaid; and it still troubles my conscience.

CONFUCIUS. And were you the only reader of Wells? If there were others like you, had they not the same reason for keeping the secret?

THE ARCHBISHOP. That is true. But I should know. You short-lived people are so childish. If I met a man of my own age I should recognize him at once. I have never done so.

MRS LUTESTRING. Would you recognize a woman of your age, do you think?

THE ARCHBISHOP. I—[*He stops and turns upon her with a searching look, startled by the suggestion and the suspicion it rouses*].

MRS LUTESTRING. What is your age, Mr Archbishop?

BURGE-LUBIN. Two hundred and eighty-three, he says. That is his little joke. Do you know, Mrs Lutestring, he had almost talked us into believing him when you came in and cleared the air with your robust common sense.

MRS LUTESTRING. Do you really feel that, Mr President? I hear the note of breezy assertion in your voice. I miss the note of conviction.

BURGE-LUBIN [*jumping up*] Look here. Let us stop talking damned nonsense. I don't wish to be disagreeable; but it's getting on my nerves. The best joke won't bear being pushed beyond a certain point. That point has been reached. I—I'm rather busy this morning. We all have our hands pretty full. Confucius here will tell you that I have a heavy day before me.

BARNABAS. Have you anything more important than this thing, if it's true?

BURGE-LUBIN. Oh, if if, if it's true! But it isn't true.

BARNABAS. Have you anything at all to do?

BURGE-LUBIN. Anything to do! Have you forgotten, Barnabas, that I happen to be President, and that the weight of the entire public business of this country is on my shoulders?

BARNABAS. Has he anything to do, Confucius?

CONFUCIUS. He has to be President.

BARNABAS. That means that he has nothing to do.

BURGE-LUBIN [*sulkily*] Very well, Barnabas. Go on making a fool of yourself. [*He sits down*]. Go on.

BARNABAS. I am not going to leave this room until we get to the bottom of this swindle.

MRS LUTESTRING [*turning with deadly gravity on the Accountant General*]

This what, did you say?

CONFUCIUS. These expressions cannot be sustained. You obscure the discussion in using them.

BARNABAS [*glad to escape from her gaze by addressing Confucius*] Well, this unnatural horror. Will that satisfy you?

CONFUCIUS. That is in order. But we do not commit ourselves to the implications of the word horror.

THE ARCHBISHOP. By the word horror the Accountant General means only something unusual.

CONFUCIUS. I notice that the honorable Domestic Minister, on learning the advanced age of the venerable prelate, shews no sign of surprise or incredulity.

BURGE-LUBIN. She doesn't take it seriously. Who would? Eh, Mrs

Lutestring?

MRS LUTESTRING. I take it very seriously indeed, Mr President. I see now that I was not mistaken at first. I have met the Archbishop before.

THE ARCHBISHOP. I felt sure of it. This vision of a door opening to me, and a woman's face welcoming me, must be a reminiscence of something that really happened; though I see it now as an angel opening the gate of heaven.

MRS LUTESTRING. Or a parlor maid opening the door of the house of the young woman you were in love with?

THE ARCHBISHOP [*making a wry face*] Is that the reality? How these things grow in our imagination! But may I say, Mrs Lutestring, that the transfiguration of a parlor maid to an angel is not more amazing than her transfiguration to the very dignified and able Domestic Minister I am addressing. I recognize the angel in you. Frankly, I do not recognize the parlor maid.

BURGE-LUBIN. Whats a parlor maid?

MRS LUTESTRING. An extinct species. A woman in a black dress and white apron, who opened the house door when people knocked or rang, and was either your tyrant or your slave. I was a parlor maid in the house of one of the Accountant General's remote ancestors. [*To Confucius*] You asked me my age, Mr Chief Secretary, I am two hundred and seventy-four.

BURGE-LUBIN [*gallantly*] You don't look it. You really don't look it.

MRS LUTESTRING [*turning her face gravely towards him*] Look again, Mr

President.

BURGE-LUBIN [*looking at her bravely until the smile fades from his face, and he suddenly covers his eyes with his hands*] Yes: you do look it. I am convinced. It's true. Now call up the Lunatic Asylum, Confucius; and tell them to send an ambulance for me.

MRS LUTESTRING [*to the Archbishop*] Why have you given away your secret? our secret?

THE ARCHBISHOP. They found it out. The cinema records betrayed me. But I never dreamt that there were others. Did you?

MRS LUTESTRING. I knew one other. She was a cook. She grew tired, and killed herself.

THE ARCHBISHOP. Dear me! However, her death simplifies the situation, as I have been able to convince these gentlemen that the matter had better go no further.

MRS LUTESTRING. What! When the President knows! It will be all over the place before the end of the week.

BURGE-LUBIN [*injured*] Really, Mrs Lutestring! You speak as if I were a notoriously indiscreet person. Barnabas: have I such a reputation?

BARNABAS [*resignedly*] It cant be helped. It's constitutional.

CONFUCIUS. It is utterly unconstitutional. But, as you say, it cannot be helped.

BURGE-LUBIN [*solemnly*] I deny that a secret of State has ever passed my lips—except perhaps to the Minister of Health, who is discretion personified. People think, because she is a negress—

MRS LUTESTRING. It does not matter much now. Once, it would have mattered a great deal. But my children are all dead.

THE ARCHBISHOP. Yes: the children must have been a terrible difficulty.

Fortunately for me, I had none.

MRS LUTESTRING. There was one daughter who was the child of my very heart. Some years after my first drowning I learnt that she had lost her sight. I went to her. She was an old woman of ninety-six, blind. She asked me to sit and talk with her because my voice was like the voice of her dead mother.

BURGE-LUBIN. The complications must be frightful. Really I hardly know whether I do want to live much longer than other people.

MRS LUTESTRING. You can always kill yourself, as cook did; but that was influenza. Long life is complicated, and even terrible; but it is glorious all the same. I would no more change places with an ordinary woman than with a mayfly that lives only an hour.

THE ARCHBISHOP. What set you thinking of it first?

MRS LUTESTRING. Conrad Barnabas's book. Your wife told me it was more wonderful than Napoleon's Book of Fate and Old Moore's Almanac, which cook and I used to read. I was very ignorant: it did not seem so impossible to me as to an educated woman. Yet I forgot all about it, and married and drudged as a poor man's wife, and brought up children, and looked twenty years older than I really was, until one day, long after my husband died and my children were out in the world working for themselves, I noticed that I looked twenty years younger than I really was. The truth came to me in a flash.

BURGE-LUBIN. An amazing moment. Your feelings must have been beyond description. What was your first thought?

MRS LUTESTRING. Pure terror. I saw that the little money I had laid up would not last, and that I must go out and: work again. They had things called Old Age Pensions then: miserable pittances for worn-out old laborers to die on. I thought I should be found out if I went on drawing it too long. The horror of facing another lifetime of drudgery, of missing my hard-earned rest and losing my poor little savings, drove everything else out of my mind. You people nowadays can have no conception of the dread of poverty that hung over us then, or of the utter tiredness of forty years' unending overwork and striving to make a shilling do the work of a pound.

THE ARCHBISHOP. I wonder you did not kill yourself. I often wonder why the poor in those evil old times did not kill themselves. They did not even kill other people.

MRS LUTESTRING. You never kill yourself, because you always may as well wait until tomorrow. And you have not energy or conviction enough to kill the others. Besides, how can you blame them when you would do as they do if you were in their place?

BURGE-LUBIN. Devilish poor consolation, that.

MRS LUTESTRING. There were other consolations in those days for people like me. We drank preparations of alcohol to relieve the strain of living and give us an artificial happiness.

BURGE-LUBIN [*all together,*] Alcohol!

CONFUCIUS [*making*] Pfff

BARNABAS [*wry faces*] Disgusting.

MRS LUTESTRING. A little alcohol would improve your temper and manners, and make you much easier to live with, Mr Accountant General.

BURGE-LUBIN [*laughing*] By George, I believe you! Try it, Barnabas.

CONFUCIUS. No. Try tea. It is the more civilized poison of the two.

MRS LUTESTRING. You, Mr President, were born intoxicated with your own well-fed natural exuberance. You cannot imagine what alcohol was to an underfed poor woman. I had carefully arranged my little savings so that I could get drunk, as we called it, once a week; and my only pleasure was looking forward to that poor little debauch. That is what saved me from suicide. I could not bear to miss my next carouse. But when I stopped working, and lived on my pension, the fatigue of my life's drudgery began to wear off, because, you see, I was not really old. I recuperated. I looked younger and younger. And at last I was rested enough to have courage and strength to begin life again. Besides, political changes were making it easier: life was a little better worth living for the nine-tenths of the people who used to be mere drudges. After that, I never turned back or faltered. My only regret now is that I shall die when I am three hundred or thereabouts. There was only one thing that made life hard; and that is gone now.

CONFUCIUS. May we ask what that was?

MRS LUTESTRING. Perhaps you will be offended if I tell you.

BURGE-LUBIN. Offended! My dear lady, do you suppose, after such a stupendous revelation, that anything short of a blow from a sledge-hammer could produce the smallest impression on any of us?

MRS LUTESTRING. Well, you see, it has been so hard on me never to meet a grown-up person. You are all such children. And I never was very fond of children, except that one girl who woke up the mother passion in me. I have been very lonely sometimes.

BURGE-LUBIN [*again gallant*] But surely, Mrs Lutestring, that has been your own fault. If I may say so, a lady of your attractions need never have been lonely.

MRS LUTESTRING. Why?

BURGE-LUBIN. Why! Well—. Well, er—. Well, er er—. Well! [*he gives it up*].

THE ARCHBISHOP. He means that you might have married. Curious, how little they understand our position.

MRS LUTESTRING. I did marry. I married again on my hundred and first birthday. But of course I had to marry an elderly man: a man over sixty. He was a great painter. On his deathbed he said to me 'It has taken me fifty years to learn my trade, and to paint all the foolish pictures a man must paint and get rid of before he comes through them to the great things he ought to paint. And now that my foot is at last on the threshold of the temple I find that it is also the threshold of my tomb.' That man would have been the greatest painter of all time if he could have lived as long as I. I saw him die of old age whilst he was still, as he said himself, a gentleman amateur, like all modern painters.

BURGE-LUBIN. But why had you to marry an elderly man? Why not marry a young one? or shall I say a middle-aged one? If my own affections were not already engaged; and if, to tell the truth, I were not a little afraid of you—for you are a very superior woman, as we all acknowledge—I should esteem myself happy in—er—er—

MRS LUTESTRING. Mr President: have you ever tried to take advantage of the innocence of a little child for the gratification of your senses?

BURGE-LUBIN. Good Heavens, madam, what do you take me for? What right have you to ask me such a question?

MRS LUTESTRING. I am at present in my two hundred and seventy-fifth year. You suggest that I should take advantage of the innocence of a child of thirty, and marry it.

THE ARCHBISHOP. Can you shortlived people not understand that as the confusion and immaturity and primitive animalism in which we live for the first hundred years of our life is worse in this matter of sex than in any other, you are intolerable to us in that relation?

BURGE-LUBIN. Do you mean to say, Mrs Lutestring, that you regard me as a child?

MRS LUTESTRING. Do you expect me to regard you as a completed soul? Oh, you may well be afraid of me. There are moments when your levity, your ingratitude, your shallow jollity, make my gorge rise so against you that if I could not remind myself that you are a child I should be tempted to doubt your right to live at all.

CONFUCIUS. Do you grudge us the few years we have? you who have three hundred!

BURGE-LUBIN. You accuse me of levity! Must I remind you, madam, that I am the President, and that you are only the head of a department?

BARNABAS. Ingratitude too! You draw a pension for three hundred years when we owe you only seventy-eight; and you call us ungrateful!

MRS LUTESTRING. I do. When I think of the blessings that have been showered on you, and contrast them with the poverty! the humiliations! the anxieties! the heartbreak! the insolence and tyranny that were the daily lot of mankind when I was learning to suffer instead of learning to live! when I see how lightly you take it all! how you quarrel over the crumpled leaves in your beds of roses! how you are so dainty about your work that unless it is made either interesting or delightful to you you leave it to negresses and Chinamen, I ask myself whether even three hundred years of thought and experience can save you from being superseded by the Power that created you and put you on your trial.

BURGE-LUBIN. My dear lady: our Chinese and colored friends are perfectly happy. They are twenty times better off here than they would be in China or Liberia. They do their work admirably; and in doing it they set us free for higher employments.

THE ARCHBISHOP [*who has caught the infection of her indignation*] What higher employments are you capable of? you that are superannuated at seventy and dead at eighty!

MRS LUTESTRING. You are not really doing higher work. You are supposed to make the decisions and give the orders; but the negresses and the Chinese make up your minds for you and tell you what orders to give, just as my brother, who was a sergeant in the Guards, used to prompt his officers in the old days. When I want to get anything done at the Health Ministry I do not come to you: I go to the black lady who has been the real president during your present term of office, or to Confucius, who goes on for ever while presidents come and presidents go.

BURGE-LUBIN. This is outrageous. This is treason to the white race. And let me tell you, madam, that I have never in my life met the Minister of Health, and that I protest against the vulgar color prejudice which disparages her great ability and her eminent services to the State. My relations with her are purely telephonic, gramophonic, photophonic, and, may I add, platonic.

THE ARCHBISHOP. There is no reason why you should be ashamed of them in any case, Mr President. But let us look at the position impersonally. Can you deny that what is happening is that the English people have become a Joint Stock Company admitting Asiatics and Africans as shareholders?

BARNABAS. Nothing like it. I know all about the old joint stock companies. The shareholders did no work.

THE ARCHBISHOP. That is true; but we, like them, get our dividends whether we work or not. We work partly because we know there would be no dividends if we did not, and partly because if we refuse we are regarded as mentally deficient and put into a lethal chamber. But what do we work at? Before the few changes we were forced to make by the revolutions that followed the Four Years War, our governing classes had been so rich, as it was called, that they had become the most intellectually lazy and fat-headed people on the face of the earth. There is a good deal of that fat still clinging to us.

BURGE-LUBIN. As President, I must not listen to unpatriotic criticisms of our national character, Mr Archbishop.

THE ARCHBISHOP. As Archbishop, Mr President, it is my official duty to criticize the national character unsparingly. At the canonization of Saint Henrik Ibsen, you yourself unveiled the monument to him which bears on its pedestal the noble inscription, 'I came not to call sinners, but the righteous, to repentance.' The proof of what I say is that our routine work, and what may be called our ornamental and figure-head work, is being more and more sought after by the English; whilst the thinking, organizing, calculating, directing work is done by yellow brains, brown brains, and black brains, just as it was done in my early days by Jewish brains, Scottish brains, Italian brains, German brains. The only white men who still do serious work are those who, like the Accountant General, have no capacity for enjoyment, and no social gifts to make them welcome outside their offices.

BARNABAS. Confound your impudence! I had gifts enough to find you out, anyhow.

THE ARCHBISHOP [*disregarding this outburst*] If you were to kill me as I stand here, you would have to appoint an Indian to succeed me. I take precedence today not as an Englishman, but as a man with more than a century and a half of fully adult experience. We are letting all the power slip into the hands of the colored people. In another hundred years we shall be simply their household pets.

BURGE-LUBIN [*reacting buoyantly*] Not the least danger of it. I grant you we leave the most troublesome part of the labor of the nation to them. And a good job too: why should we drudge at it? But think of the activities of our leisure! Is there a jollier place on earth to live in than England out of office hours? And to whom do we owe that? To ourselves, not to the niggers. The nigger and the Chink are all right from Tuesday to Friday; but from Friday to Tuesday they are simply nowhere; and the real life of England is from Friday to Tuesday.

THE ARCHBISHOP. That is terribly true. In devising brainless amusements; in pursuing them with enormous vigor, and taking them with eager seriousness, our English people are the wonder of the world. They always were. And it is just as well; for otherwise their sensuality would become morbid and destroy them. What appals me is that their amusements should amuse them. They are the amusements of boys and girls. They are pardonable up to the age of fifty or sixty: after that they are ridiculous. I tell you, what is wrong with us is that we are a non-adult race; and the Irish and the Scots, and the niggers and Chinks, as you call them, though their lifetime is as short as ours, or shorter, yet do somehow contrive to grow up a little before they die. We die in boyhood: the maturity that should make us the greatest of all the nations lies beyond the grave for us. Either we shall go under as greybeards with golf clubs in our hands, or we must will to live longer.

MRS LUTESTRING. Yes: that is it. I could not have expressed it in words; but you have expressed it for me. I felt, even when I was an ignorant domestic slave, that we had the possibility of becoming a great nation within us; but our faults and follies drove me to cynical hopelessness. We all ended then like that. It is the highest creatures who take the longest to mature, and are the most helpless during their immaturity. I know now that it took me a whole century to grow up. I began my serious life when I was a hundred and twenty. Asiatics cannot control me: I am not a child in their hands, as you are, Mr President. Neither, I am sure, is the Archbishop. They respect me. You are not grown up enough even for that, though you were kind enough to say that I frighten you.

BURGE-LUBIN. Honestly, you do. And will you think me very rude if I say that if I must choose between a white woman old enough to be my great-grandmother and a black woman of my own age, I shall probably find the black woman more sympathetic?

MRS LUTESTRING. And more attractive in color, perhaps?

BURGE-LUBIN. Yes. Since you ask me, more—well, not more attractive: I do not deny that you have an excellent appearance—but I will say, richer. More Venetian. Tropical. 'The shadowed livery of the burnished sun.'

MRS LUTESTRING. Our women, and their favorite story writers, begin already to talk about men with golden complexions.

CONFUCIUS [*expanding into a smile all across both face and body*]

A-a-a-a-a-h!

BURGE-LUBIN. Well, what of it, madam? Have you read a very interesting book by the librarian of the Biological Society suggesting that the future of the world lies with the Mulatto?

MRS LUTESTRING [*rising*] Mr Archbishop: if the white race is to be saved, our destiny is apparent.

THE ARCHBISHOP. Yes: our duty is pretty clear.

MRS LUTESTRING. Have you time to come home with me and discuss the matter?

THE ARCHBISHOP [*rising*] With pleasure.

BARNABAS [*rising also and rushing past Mrs Lutestring to the door, where he turns to bar her way*] No you don't. Burge: you understand, don't you?

BURGE-LUBIN. No. What is it?

BARNABAS. These two are going to marry.

BURGE-LUBIN. Why shouldn't they, if they want to?

BARNABAS. They don't want to. They will do it in cold blood because their children will live three hundred years. It mustnt be allowed.

CONFUCIUS. You cannot prevent it. There is no law that gives you power to interfere with them.

BARNABAS. If they force me to it I will obtain legislation against marriages above the age of seventy-eight.

THE ARCHBISHOP. There is not time for that before we are married, Mr

Accountant General. Be good enough to get out of the lady's way.

BARNABAS. There is time to send the lady to the lethal chamber before anything comes of your marriage. Dont forget that.

MRS LUTESTRING. What nonsense, Mr Accountant General! Good afternoon, Mr President. Good afternoon, Mr Chief Secretary. [*They rise and acknowledge her salutation with bows. She walks straight at the Accountant General, who instinctively shrinks out of her way as she leaves the room*].

THE ARCHBISHOP. I am surprised at you, Mr Barnabas. Your tone was like an echo from the Dark Ages. [*He follows the Domestic Minister*].

Confucius, shaking his head and clucking with his tongue in deprecation of this painful episode, moves to the chair just vacated by the Archbishop and stands behind it with folded palms, looking at the President. The Accountant General shakes his fist after the departed visitors, and bursts into savage abuse of them.

BARNABAS. Thieves! Cursed thieves! Vampires! What are you going to do,

Burge?

BURGE-LUBIN. Do?

BARNABAS. Yes, do. There must be dozens of these people in existence. Are you going to let them do what the two who have just left us mean to do, and crowd us off the face of the earth?

BURGE-LUBIN [*sitting down*] Oh, come, Barnabas! What harm are they doing? Arnt you interested in them? Dont you like them?

BARNABAS. Like them! I hate them. They are monsters, unnatural monsters.

They are poison to me.

BURGE-LUBIN. What possible objection can there be to their living as long as they can? It does not shorten our lives, does it?

BARNABAS. If I have to die when I am seventy-eight, I don't see why another man should be privileged to live to be two hundred and seventy-eight. It does shorten my life, relatively. It makes us ridiculous. If they grew to be twelve feet high they would make us all dwarfs. They talked to us as if we were children. There is no love lost between us: their hatred of us came out soon enough. You heard what the woman said, and how the Archbishop backed her up?

BURGE-LUBIN. But what can we do to them?

BARNABAS. Kill them.

BURGE-LUBIN. Nonsense!

BARNABAS. Lock them up. Sterilize them somehow, anyhow.

BURGE-LUBIN. But what reason could we give?

BARNABAS. What reason can you give for killing a snake? Nature tells you to do it.

BURGE-LUBIN. My dear Barnabas, you are out of your mind.

BARNABAS. Havnt you said that once too often already this morning?

BURGE-LUBIN. I don't believe you will carry a single soul with you.

BARNABAS. I understand. I know you. You think you are one of them.

CONFUCIUS. Mr Accountant General: you may be one of them.

BARNABAS. How dare you accuse me of such a thing? I am an honest man, not a monster. I won my place in public life by demonstrating that the true expectation of human life is seventy-eight point six. And I will resist any attempt to alter or upset it to the last drop of my blood if need be.

BURGE-LUBIN. Oh, tut tut! Come, come! Pull yourself together. How can you, a descendant of the great Conrad Barnabas, the man who is still remembered by his masterly Biography of a Black Beetle, be so absurd?

BARNABAS. You had better go and write the autobiography of a jackass. I am going to raise the country against this horror, and against you, if you shew the slightest sign of weakness about it.

CONFUCIUS [*very impressively*] You will regret it if you do.

BARNABAS. What is to make me regret it?

CONFUCIUS. Every mortal man and woman in the community will begin to count on living for three centuries. Things will happen which you do not foresee: terrible things. The family will dissolve: parents and children will be no longer the old and the young: brothers and sisters will meet as strangers after a hundred years separation: the ties of blood will lose their innocence. The imaginations of men, let loose over the possibilities of three centuries of life, will drive them mad and wreck human society. This discovery must be kept a dead secret. [*He sits down*].

BARNABAS. And if I refuse to keep the secret?

CONFUCIUS. I shall have you safe in a lunatic asylum the day after you blab.

BARNABAS. You forget that I can produce the Archbishop to prove my statement.

CONFUCIUS. So can I. Which of us do you think he will support when I explain to him that your object in revealing his age is to get him killed?

BARNABAS [*desperate*] Burge: are you going to back up this yellow abomination against me? Are we public men and members of the Government? or are we damned blackguards?

CONFUCIUS [*unmoved*] Have you ever known a public man who was not what vituperative people called a damned blackguard when some inconsiderate person wanted to tell the public more than was good for it?

BARNABAS. Hold your tongue, you insolent heathen. Burge: I spoke to you.

BURGE-LUBIN. Well, you know, my dear Barnabas, Confucius is a very long-headed chap. I see his point.

BARNABAS. Do you? Then let me tell you that, except officially, I will never speak to you again. Do you hear?

BURGE-LUBIN [*cheerfully*] You will. You will.

BARNABAS. And don't you ever dare speak to me again. Do you hear? [*He turns to the door*].

BURGE-LUBIN. I will. I will. Goodbye, Barnabas. God bless you.

BARNABAS. May you live forever, and be the laughingstock of the whole world! [*he dashes out in a fury*].

BURGE-LUBIN [*laughing indulgently*] He will keep the secret all right.

I know Barnabas. You neednt worry.

CONFUCIUS [*troubled and grave*] There are no secrets except the secrets that keep themselves. Consider. There are those films at the Record Office. We have no power to prevent the Master of the Records from publishing this discovery made in his department. We cannot silence the American—who can silence an American?—nor the people who were there today to receive him. Fortunately, a film can prove nothing but a resemblance.

BURGE-LUBIN. Thats very true. After all, the whole thing is confounded nonsense, isnt it?

CONFUCIUS [*raising his head to look at him*] You have decided not to believe it now that you realize its inconveniences. That is the English method. It may not work in this case.

BURGE-LUBIN. English be hanged! It's common sense. You know, those two people got us hypnotized: not a doubt of it. They must have been kidding us. They were, werent they?

CONFUCIUS. You looked into that woman's face; and you believed.

BURGE-LUBIN. Just so. Thats where she had me. I shouldn't have believed her a bit if she'd turned her back to me.

CONFUCIUS [*shakes his head slowly and repeatedly*]???

BURGE-LUBIN. You really think—? [*he hesitates*].

CONFUCIUS. The Archbishop has always been a puzzle to me. Ever since I learnt to distinguish between one English face and another I have noticed what the woman pointed out: that the English face is not an adult face, just as the English mind is not an adult mind.

BURGE-LUBIN. Stow it, John Chinaman. If ever there was a race divinely appointed to take charge of the non-adult races and guide them and train them and keep them out of mischief until they grow up to be capable of adopting our institutions, that race is the English race. It is the only race in the world that has that characteristic. Now!

CONFUCIUS. That is the fancy of a child nursing a doll. But it is ten times more childish of you to dispute the highest compliment ever paid you.

BURGE-LUBIN. You call it a compliment to class us as grown-up children.

CONFUCIUS. Not grown-up children, children at fifty, sixty, seventy. Your maturity is so late that you never attain to it. You have to be governed by races which are mature at forty. That means that you are potentially the most highly developed race on earth, and would be actually the greatest if you could live long enough to attain to maturity.

BURGE-LUBIN [*grasping the idea at last*] By George, Confucius, youre right! I never thought of that. That explains everything. We are just a lot of schoolboys: theres no denying it. Talk to an Englishman about anything serious, and he listens to you curiously for a moment just as he listens to a chap playing classical music. Then he goes back to his marine golf, or motoring, or flying, or women, just like a bit of stretched elastic when you let it go. [*Soaring to the height of his theme*] Oh, youre quite right. We are only in our infancy. I ought to be in a perambulator, with a nurse shoving me along. It's true: it's absolutely true. But some day we'll grow up; and then, by Jingo, we'll shew em.

CONFUCIUS. The Archbishop is an adult. When I was a child I was dominated and intimidated by people whom I now know to have been weaker and sillier than I, because there was some mysterious quality in their mere age that overawed me. I confess that, though I have kept up appearances, I have always been afraid of the Archbishop.

BURGE-LUBIN. Between ourselves, Confucius, so have I.

CONFUCIUS. It is this that convinced me. It was this in the woman's face that convinced you. Their new departure in the history of the race is no fraud. It does not even surprise me.

BURGE-LUBIN. Oh, come! Not surprise you! It's your pose never to be surprised at anything; but if you are not surprised at this you are not human.

CONFUCIUS. I am staggered, just as a man may be staggered by an explosion for which he has himself laid the charge and lighted the fuse. But I am not surprised, because, as a philosopher and a student of evolutionary biology, I have come to regard some such development as this as inevitable. If I had not thus prepared myself to be credulous, no mere evidence of films and well-told tales would have persuaded me to believe. As it is, I do believe.

BURGE-LUBIN. Well, that being settled, what the devil is to happen next?

Whats the next move for us?

CONFUCIUS. We do not make the next move. The next move will be made by the Archbishop and the woman.

BURGE-LUBIN. Their marriage?

CONFUCIUS. More than that. They have made the momentous discovery that they are not alone in the world.

BURGE-LUBIN. You think there are others?

CONFUCIUS. There must be many others. Each of them believes that he or she is the only one to whom the miracle has happened. But the Archbishop knows better now. He will advertise in terms which only the longlived people will understand. He will bring them together and organize them. They will hasten from all parts of the earth. They will become a great Power.

BURGE-LUBIN [*a little alarmed*] I say, will they? I suppose they will.

I wonder is Barnabas right after all? Ought we to allow it?

CONFUCIUS. Nothing that we can do will stop it. We cannot in our souls really want to stop it: the vital force that has produced this change would paralyse our opposition to it, if we were mad enough to oppose. But we will not oppose. You and I may be of the elect, too.

BURGE-LUBIN. Yes: thats what gets us every time. What the deuce ought we to do? Something must be done about it, you know.

CONFUCIUS. Let us sit still, and meditate in silence on the vistas before us.

BURGE-LUBIN. By George, I believe youre right. Let us.

They sit meditating, the Chinaman naturally, the President with visible effort and intensity. He is positively glaring into the future when the voice of the Negress is heard.

THE NEGRESS. Mr President.

BURGE-LUBIN [*joyfully*] Yes. [*Taking up a peg*] Are you at home?

THE NEGRESS. No. Omega, zero, x squared.

The President rapidly puts the peg in the switchboard; works the dial; and presses the button. The screen becomes transparent; and the Negress, brilliantly dressed, appears on what looks like the bridge of a steam yacht in glorious sea weather. The installation with which she is communicating is beside the binnacle.

CONFUCIUS [*looking round, and recoiling with a shriek of disgust*] Ach!

Avaunt! Avaunt! [*He rushes from the room*].

BURGE-LUBIN. What part of the coast is that?

THE NEGRESS. Fishguard Bay. Why not run over and join me for the afternoon? I am disposed to be approachable at last.

BURGE-LUBIN. But Fishguard! Two hundred and seventy miles!

THE NEGRESS. There is a lightning express on the Irish Air Service at half-past sixteen. They will drop you by a parachute in the bay. The dip will do you good. I will pick you up and dry you and give you a first-rate time.

BURGE-LUBIN. Delightful. But a little risky, isnt it?

THE NEGRESS. Risky! I thought you were afraid of nothing.

BURGE-LUBIN. I am not exactly afraid; but—

THE NEGRESS [*offended*] But you think it is not good enough. Very well [*she raises her hand to take the peg out of her switchboard*].

BURGE-LUBIN [*imploringly*] No: stop: let me explain: hold the line just one moment. Oh, please.

THE NEGRESS [*waiting with her hand poised over the peg*] Well?

BURGE-LUBIN. The fact is, I have been behaving very recklessly for some time past under the impression that my life would be so short that it was not worth bothering about. But I have just learnt that I may live—well, much longer than I expected. I am sure your good sense will tell you that this alters the case. I—

THE NEGRESS [*with suppressed rage*] Oh, quite. Pray don't risk your precious, life on my account. Sorry for troubling you. Goodbye. [*She snatches out her peg and vanishes*].

BURGE-LUBIN [*urgently*] No: please hold on. I can convince you—[*a loud buzz-uzz-uzz*]. Engaged! Who is she calling up now? [*Represses the button and calls*] The Chief Secretary. Say I want to see him again, just for a moment.

CONFUCIUS'S VOICE. Is the woman gone?

BURGE-LUBIN. Yes, yes: it's all right. Just a moment, if—[*Confucius returns*] Confucius: I have some important business at Fishguard. The Irish Air Service can drop me in the bay by parachute. I suppose it's quite safe, isnt it?

CONFUCIUS. Nothing is quite safe. The air service is as safe as any other travelling service. The parachute is safe. But the water is not safe.

BURGE-LUBIN. Why? They will give me an unsinkable tunic, wont they?

CONFUCIUS. You will not sink; but the sea is very cold. You may get rheumatism for life.

BURGE-LUBIN. For life! That settles it: I wont risk it.

CONFUCIUS. Good. You have at last become prudent: you are no longer what you call a sportsman: you are a sensible coward, almost a grown-up man. I congratulate you.

BURGE-LUBIN [*resolutely*] Coward or no coward, I will not face an eternity of rheumatism for any woman that ever was born. [*He rises and goes to the rack for his fillet*] I have changed my mind: I am going home. [*He cocks the fillet rakishly*] Good evening.

CONFUCIUS. So early? If the Minister of Health rings you up, what shall

I tell her?

BURGE-LUBIN. Tell her to go to the devil. [*He goes out*].

CONFUCIUS [*shaking his head, shocked at the President's impoliteness*] No. No, no, no, no, no. Oh, these English! these crude young civilizations! Their manners! Hogs. Hogs.

PART IV

Tragedy of an Elderly Gentleman

ACT I

Burrin pier on the south shore of Galway Bay in Ireland, a region of stone-capped hills and granite fields. It is a fine summer day in the year 3000 A.D. On an ancient stone stump, about three feet thick and three feet high, used for securing ships by ropes to the shore, and called a bollard or holdfast, an elderly gentleman sits facing the land with his head bowed and his face in his hands, sobbing. His sunburnt skin contrasts with his white whiskers and eyebrows. He wears a black frock-coat, a white waistcoat, lavender trousers, a brilliant silk cravat with a jewelled pin stuck in it, a tall hat of grey felt, and patent leather boots with white spats. His starched linen cuffs protrude from his coat sleeves; and his collar, also of starched white linen, is Gladstonian. On his right, three or four full sacks, lying side by side on the flags, suggest that the pier, unlike many remote Irish piers, is occasionally useful as well as romantic. On his left, behind him, a flight of stone steps descends out of sight to the sea level.

A woman in a silk tunic and sandals, wearing little else except a cap with the number 2 on it in gold, comes up the steps from the sea, and stares in astonishment at the sobbing man. Her age cannot be guessed: her face is firm and chiselled like a young face; but her expression is unyouthful in its severity and determination.

THE WOMAN. What is the matter?

The elderly gentleman looks up; hastily pulls himself together; takes out a silk handkerchief and dries his tears lightly with a brave attempt to smile through them; and tries to rise gallantly, but sinks back.

THE WOMAN. Do you need assistance?

THE ELDERLY GENTLEMAN. No. Thank you very much. No. Nothing. The heat. [*He punctuates with sniffs, and dabs with his handkerchief at his eyes and nose.*] Hay fever.

THE WOMAN. You are a foreigner, are you not?

THE ELDERLY GENTLEMAN. No. You must not regard me as a foreigner. I am a
Briton.

THE WOMAN. You come from some part of the British Commonwealth?

THE ELDERLY GENTLEMAN [*amiably pompous*] From its capital, madam.

THE WOMAN. From Baghdad?

THE ELDERLY GENTLEMAN. Yes. You may not be aware, madam, that these islands were once the centre of the British Commonwealth, during a period now known as The Exile. They were its headquarters a thousand years ago. Few people know this interesting circumstance now; but I assure you it is true. I have come here on a pious pilgrimage to one of the numerous lands of my fathers. We are of the same stock, you and I. Blood is thicker than water. We are cousins.

THE WOMAN. I do not understand. You say you have come here on a pious pilgrimage. Is that some new means of transport?

THE ELDERLY GENTLEMAN [*again shewing signs of distress*] I find it very difficult to make myself understood here. I was not referring to a machine, but to a—a—a sentimental journey.

THE WOMAN. I am afraid I am as much in the dark as before. You said also that blood is thicker than water. No doubt it is; but what of it?

THE ELDERLY GENTLEMAN. Its meaning is obvious.

THE WOMAN. Perfectly. But I assure you I am quite aware that blood is thicker than water.

THE ELDERLY GENTLEMAN [*sniffing: almost in tears again*] We will leave it at that, madam.

THE WOMAN [*going nearer to him and scrutinizing him with some concern*] I am afraid you are not well. Were you not warned that it is dangerous for shortlived people to come to this country? There is a deadly disease called discouragement, against which shortlived people have to take very strict precautions. Intercourse with us puts too great a strain on them.

THE ELDERLY GENTLEMAN [*pulling himself together huffily*] It has no effect on me, madam. I fear my conversation does not interest you. If not, the remedy is in your own hands.

THE WOMAN [*looking at her hands, and then looking inquiringly at him*]

Where?

THE ELDERLY GENTLEMAN [*breaking down*] Oh, this is dreadful. No understanding, no intelligence, no sympathy—[*his sobs choke him*].

THE WOMAN. You see, you are ill.

THE ELDERLY GENTLEMAN [*nerved by indignation*] I am not ill. I have never had a day's illness in my life.

THE WOMAN. May I advise you?

THE ELDERLY GENTLEMAN. I have no need of a lady doctor, thank you, madam.

THE WOMAN [*shaking her head*] I am afraid I do not understand. I said nothing about a butterfly.

THE ELDERLY GENTLEMAN. Well, *I* said nothing about a butterfly.

THE WOMAN. You spoke of a lady doctor. The word is known here only as the name of a butterfly.

THE ELDERLY GENTLEMAN [*insanely*] I give up. I can bear this no longer. It is easier to go out of my mind at once. [*He rises and dances about, singing*]

I'd be a butterfly, born in a bower,
Making apple dumplings without any flour.

THE WOMAN [*smiling gravely*] It must be at least a hundred and fifty years since I last laughed. But if you do that any more I shall certainly break out like a primary of sixty. Your dress is so extraordinarily ridiculous.

THE ELDERLY GENTLEMAN [*halting abruptly in his antics*] My dress ridiculous! I may not be dressed like a Foreign Office clerk; but my clothes are perfectly in fashion in my native metropolis, where yours—pardon my saying so—would be considered extremely unusual and hardly decent.

THE WOMAN. Decent? There is no such word in our language. What does it mean?

THE ELDERLY GENTLEMAN. It would not be decent for me to explain. Decency cannot be discussed without indecency.

THE WOMAN. I cannot understand you at all. I fear you have not been observing the rules laid down for shortlived visitors.

THE ELDERLY GENTLEMAN. Surely, madam, they do not apply to persons of my age and standing. I am not a child, nor an agricultural laborer.

THE WOMAN [*severely*] They apply to you very strictly. You are expected to confine yourself to the society of children under sixty. You are absolutely forbidden to approach fully adult natives under any circumstances. You cannot converse with persons of my age for long without bringing on a dangerous attack of discouragement. Do you realize that you are already shewing grave symptoms of that very distressing and usually fatal complaint?

THE ELDERLY GENTLEMAN. Certainly not, madam. I am fortunately in no danger of contracting it. I am quite accustomed to converse intimately and at the greatest length with the most distinguished persons. If you cannot discriminate between hay fever and imbecility, I can only say that your advanced years carry with them the inevitable penalty of dotage.

THE WOMAN. I am one of the guardians of this district; and I am responsible for your welfare—

THE ELDERLY GENTLEMAN. The Guardians! Do you take me for a pauper?

THE WOMAN. I do not know what a pauper is. You must tell me who you are, if it is possible for you to express yourself intelligibly—

THE ELDERLY GENTLEMAN [*snorts indignantly*]!

THE WOMAN [*continuing*]—and why you are wandering here alone without a nurse.

THE ELDERLY GENTLEMAN [*outraged*] Nurse!

THE WOMAN. Shortlived visitors are not allowed to go about here without nurses. Do you not know that rules are meant to be kept?

THE ELDERLY GENTLEMAN. By the lower classes, no doubt. But to persons in my position there are certain courtesies which are never denied by well-bred people; and—

THE WOMAN. There are only two human classes here: the shortlived and the normal. The rules apply to the shortlived, and are for their own protection. Now tell me at once who you are.

THE ELDERLY GENTLEMAN [*impressively*] Madam, I am a retired gentleman, formerly Chairman of the All-British Synthetic Egg and Vegetable Cheese

Trust in Baghdad, and now President of the British Historical and

Archaeological Society, and a Vice-President of the Travellers' Club.

THE WOMAN. All that does not matter.

THE ELDERLY GENTLEMAN [*again snorting*] Hm! Indeed!

THE WOMAN. Have you been sent here to make your mind flexible?

THE ELDERLY GENTLEMAN. What an extraordinary question! Pray do you find my mind noticeably stiff?

THE WOMAN. Perhaps you do not know that you are on the west coast of Ireland, and that it is the practice among natives of the Eastern Island to spend some years here to acquire mental flexibility. The climate has that effect.

THE ELDERLY GENTLEMAN [*haughtily*] I was born, not in the Eastern Island, but, thank God, in dear old British Baghdad; and I am not in need of a mental health resort.

THE WOMAN. Then why are you here?

THE ELDERLY GENTLEMAN. Am I trespassing? I was not aware of it.

THE WOMAN. Trespassing? I do not understand the word.

THE ELDERLY GENTLEMAN. Is this land private property? If so, I make no claim. I proffer a shilling in satisfaction of damage (if any), and am ready to withdraw if you will be good enough to shew me the nearest way. [*He offers her a shilling*].

THE WOMAN [*taking it and examining it without much interest*] I do not understand a single word of what you have just said.

THE ELDERLY GENTLEMAN. I am speaking the plainest English. Are you the landlord?

THE WOMAN [*shaking her head*] There is a tradition in this part of the country of an animal with a name like that. It used to be hunted and shot in the barbarous ages. It is quite extinct now.

THE ELDERLY GENTLEMAN [*breaking down again*] It is a dreadful thing to be in a country where nobody understands civilized institutions. [*He collapses on the bollard, struggling with his rising sobs*]. Excuse me. Hay fever.

THE WOMAN [*taking a tuning-fork from her girdle and holding it to her ear; then speaking into space on one note, like a chorister intoning a psalm*] Burrin Pier Galway please send someone to take charge of a discouraged shortliver who has escaped from his nurse male harmless babbles unintelligibly with moments of sense distressed hysterical foreign dress very funny has curious fringe of white seaweed under his chin.

THE GENTLEMAN. This is a gross impertinence. An insult.

THE WOMAN [*replacing her tuning-fork and addressing the elderly gentleman*] These words mean nothing to me. In what capacity are you here? How did you obtain permission to visit us?

THE ELDERLY GENTLEMAN [*importantly*] Our Prime Minister, Mr Badger Bluebin, has come to consult the oracle. He is my son-in-law. We are accompanied by his wife and daughter: my daughter and granddaughter. I may mention that General Aufsteig, who is one of our party, is really the Emperor of Turania travelling incognito. I understand he has a question to put to the oracle informally. I have come solely to visit the country.

THE WOMAN. Why should you come to a place where you have no business?

THE ELDERLY GENTLEMAN. Great Heavens, madam, can anything be more natural? I shall be the only member of the Travellers' Club who has set foot on these shores. Think of that! My position will be unique.

THE WOMAN. Is that an advantage? We have a person here who has lost both legs in an accident. His position is unique. But he would much rather be like everyone else.

THE ELDERLY GENTLEMAN. This is maddening. There is no analogy whatever between the two cases.

THE WOMAN. They are both unique.

THE ELDERLY GENTLEMAN. Conversation in this place seems to consist of ridiculous quibbles. I am heartily tired of them.

THE WOMAN. I conclude that your Travellers' Club is an assembly of persons who wish to be able to say that they have been in some place where nobody else has been.

THE ELDERLY GENTLEMAN. Of Course if you wish to sneer at us—

THE WOMAN. What is sneer?

THE ELDERLY GENTLEMAN [*with a wild sob*] I shall drown myself.

He makes desperately for the edge of the pier, but is confronted by a man with the number one on his cap, who comes up the steps and intercepts him. He is dressed like the woman, but a slight moustache proclaims his sex.

THE MAN [*to the elderly gentleman*] Ah, here you are. I shall really have to put a collar and lead on you if you persist in giving me the slip like this.

THE WOMAN. Are you this stranger's nurse?

THE MAN. Yes. I am very tired of him. If I take my eyes off him for a moment, he runs away and talks to everybody.

THE WOMAN [*after taking out her tuning-fork and sounding it, intones as before*] Burrin Pier. Wash out. [*She puts up the fork, and addresses the man*]. I sent a call for someone to take care of him. I have been trying to talk to him; but I can understand very little of what he says. You must take better care of him: he is badly discouraged already. If I can be of any further use, Fusima, Gort, will find me. [*She goes away*].

THE ELDERLY GENTLEMAN. Any further use! She has been of no use to me. She spoke to me without any introduction, like any improper female. And she has made off with my shilling.

THE MAN. Please speak slowly. I cannot follow. What is a shilling? What is an introduction? Improper female doesnt make sense.

THE ELDERLY GENTLEMAN. Nothing seems to make sense here. All I can tell you is that she was the most impenetrably stupid woman I have ever met in the whole course of my life.

THE MAN. That cannot be. She cannot appear stupid to you. She is a secondary, and getting on for a tertiary at that.

THE ELDERLY GENTLEMAN. What is a tertiary? Everybody here keeps talking to me about primaries and secondaries and tertiaries as if people were geological strata.

THE MAN. The primaries are in their first century. The secondaries are in their second century. I am still classed as a primary [*he points to his number*]; but I may almost call myself a secondary, as I shall be ninety-five next January. The tertiaries are in their third century. Did you not see the number two on her badge? She is an advanced secondary.

THE ELDERLY GENTLEMAN. That accounts for it. She is in her second childhood.

THE MAN. Her second childhood! She is in her fifth childhood.

THE ELDERLY GENTLEMAN [*again resorting to the bollard*] Oh! I cannot bear these unnatural arrangements.

THE MAN [*impatient and helpless*] You shouldn't have come among us.

This is no place for you.

THE ELDERLY GENTLEMAN [*nerved by indignation*] May I ask why? I am a Vice-President of the Travellers' Club. I have been everywhere: I hold the record in the Club for civilized countries.

THE MAN. What is a civilized country?

THE ELDERLY GENTLEMAN. It is—well, it is a civilized country. [*Desperately*] I don't know: I—I—I—I shall go mad if you keep on asking me to tell you things that everybody knows. Countries where you can travel comfortably. Where there are good hotels. Excuse me; but, though you say you are ninety-four, you are worse company than a child of five with your eternal questions. Why not call me Daddy at once?

THE MAN. I did not know your name was Daddy.

THE ELDERLY GENTLEMAN. My name is Joseph Popham Bolge Bluebin Barlow,

O.M.

THE MAN. That is five men's names. Daddy is shorter. And O.M. will not do here. It is our name for certain wild creatures, descendants of the aboriginal inhabitants of this coast. They used to be called the O'Mulligans. We will stick to Daddy.

THE ELDERLY GENTLEMAN. People will think I am your father.

THE MAN [*shocked*] Sh-sh! People here never allude to such relationships. It is not quite delicate, is it? What does it matter whether you are my father or not?

THE ELDERLY GENTLEMAN. My worthy nonagenarian friend: your faculties are totally decayed. Could you not find me a guide of my own age?

THE MAN. A young person?

THE ELDERLY GENTLEMAN. Certainly not. I cannot go about with a young person.

THE MAN. Why?

THE ELDERLY GENTLEMAN. Why! Why!! Why!!! Have you no moral sense?

THE MAN. I shall have to give you up. I cannot understand you.

THE ELDERLY GENTLEMAN. But you meant a young woman, didn't you?

THE MAN. I meant simply somebody of your own age. What difference does it make whether the person is a man or a woman?

THE ELDERLY GENTLEMAN. I could not have believed in the existence of such scandalous insensibility to the elementary decencies of human intercourse.

THE MAN. What are decencies?

THE ELDERLY GENTLEMAN [*shrieking*] Everyone asks me that.

THE MAN [*taking out a tuning-fork and using it as the woman did*] Zozim on Burrin Pier to Zoo Ennistymon I have found the discouraged shortliver he has been talking to a secondary and is much worse I am too old he is asking for someone of his own age or younger come if you can. [*He puts up his fork and turns to the Elderly Gentleman*]. Zoo is a girl of fifty, and rather childish at that. So perhaps she may make you happy.

THE ELDERLY GENTLEMAN. Make me happy! A bluestocking of fifty! Thank you.

THE MAN. Bluestocking? The effort to make out your meaning is fatiguing. Besides, you are talking too much to me: I am old enough to discourage you. Let us be silent until Zoo comes. [*He turns his back on the Elderly Gentleman, and sits down on the edge of the pier, with his legs dangling over the water*].

THE ELDERLY GENTLEMAN. Certainly. I have no wish to force my conversation on any man who does not desire it. Perhaps you would like to take a nap. If so, pray do not stand on ceremony.

THE MAN. What is a nap?

THE ELDERLY GENTLEMAN [*exasperated, going to him and speaking with great precision and distinctness*] A nap, my friend, is a brief period of sleep which overtakes superannuated persons when they endeavor to entertain unwelcome visitors or to listen to scientific lectures. Sleep. Sleep. [*Bawling into his ear*] Sleep.

THE MAN. I tell you I am nearly a secondary. I never sleep.

THE ELDERLY GENTLEMAN [*awestruck*] Good Heavens!

A young woman with the number one on her cap arrives by land. She looks no older than Savvy Barnabas, whom she somewhat resembles, looked a thousand years before. Younger, if anything.

THE YOUNG WOMAN. Is this the patient?

THE MAN [*scrambling up*] This is Zoo. [*To Zoo*] Call him Daddy.

THE ELDERLY GENTLEMAN [*vehemently*] No.

THE MAN [*ignoring the interruption*] Bless you for taking him off my hands! I have had as much of him as I can bear. [*He goes down the steps and disappears*].

THE ELDERLY GENTLEMAN [*ironically taking off his hat and making a sweeping bow from the edge of the pier in the direction of the Atlantic Ocean*] Good afternoon, sir; and thank you very much for your extraordinary politeness, your exquisite consideration for my feelings, your courtly manners. Thank you from the bottom of my heart. [*Clapping his hat on again*] Pig! Ass!

ZOO [*laughs very heartily at him*]!!!

THE ELDERLY GENTLEMAN [*turning sharply on her*] Good afternoon, madam. I am sorry to have had to put your friend in his place; but I find that here as elsewhere it is necessary to assert myself if I am to be treated with proper consideration. I had hoped that my position as a guest would protect me from insult.

ZOO. Putting my friend in his place. That is some poetic expression, is it not? What does it mean?

THE ELDERLY GENTLEMAN. Pray, is there no one in these islands who understands plain English?

ZOO. Well, nobody except the oracles. They have to make a special historical study of what we call the dead thought.

THE ELDERLY GENTLEMAN. Dead thought! I have heard of the dead languages, but never of the dead thought.

ZOO. Well, thoughts die sooner than languages. I understand your language; but I do not always understand your thought. The oracles will understand you perfectly. Have you had your consultation yet?

THE ELDERLY GENTLEMAN. I did not come to consult the oracle, madam. I am here simply as a gentleman travelling for pleasure in the company of my daughter, who is the wife of the British Prime Minister, and of General Aufsteig, who, I may tell you in confidence, is really the Emperor of Turania, the greatest military genius of the age.

ZOO. Why should you travel for pleasure! Can you not enjoy yourself at home?

THE ELDERLY GENTLEMAN. I wish to see the World.

ZOO. It is too big. You can see a bit of it anywhere.

THE ELDERLY GENTLEMAN [*out of patience*] Damn it, madam, you don't want to spend your life looking at the same bit of it! [*Checking himself*] I beg your pardon for swearing in your presence.

ZOO. Oh! That is swearing, is it? I have read about that. It sounds quite pretty. Dammitmaddam, dammitmaddam, dammitmaddam, dammitmaddam. Say it as often as you please: I like it.

THE ELDERLY GENTLEMAN [*expanding with intense relief*] Bless you for those profane but familiar words! Thank you, thank you. For the first time since I landed in this terrible country I begin to feel at home. The strain which was driving me mad relaxes: I feel almost as if I were at the club. Excuse my taking the only available seat: I am not so young as I was. [*He sits on the bollard*]. Promise me that you will not hand me over to one of these dreadful tertiaries or secondaries or whatever you call them.

ZOO. Never fear. They had no business to give you in charge to Zozim. You see he is just on the verge of becoming a secondary; and these adolescents will give themselves the airs of tertiaries. You naturally feel more at home with a flapper like me. [*She makes herself comfortable on the sacks*].

THE ELDERLY GENTLEMAN. Flapper? What does that mean?

ZOO. It is an archaic word which we still use to describe a female who is no longer a girl and is not yet quite adult.

THE ELDERLY GENTLEMAN. A very agreeable age to associate with, I find. I am recovering rapidly. I have a sense of blossoming like a flower. May I ask your name?

ZOO. Zoo.

THE ELDERLY GENTLEMAN. Miss Zoo.

ZOO. Not Miss Zoo. Zoo.

THE ELDERLY GENTLEMAN. Precisely. Er—Zoo what?

ZOO. No. Not Zoo What. Zoo. Nothing but Zoo.

THE ELDERLY GENTLEMAN [*puzzled*] Mrs Zoo, perhaps.

ZOO. No. Zoo. Cant you catch it? Zoo.

THE ELDERLY GENTLEMAN. Of course. Believe me, I did not really think you were married: you are obviously too young; but here it is so hard to feel sure—er—

ZOO [*hopelessly puzzled*] What?

THE ELDERLY GENTLEMAN. Marriage makes a difference, you know. One can say things to a married lady that would perhaps be in questionable taste to anyone without that experience.

ZOO. You are getting out of my depth: I dont understand a word you are saying. Married and questionable taste convey nothing to me. Stop, though. Is married an old form of the word mothered?

THE ELDERLY GENTLEMAN. Very likely. Let us drop the subject. Pardon me for embarrassing you. I should not have mentioned it.

ZOO. What does embarrassing mean?

THE ELDERLY GENTLEMAN. Well, really! I should have thought that so natural and common a condition would be understood as long as human nature lasted. To embarrass is to bring a blush to the cheek.

ZOO. What is a blush?

THE ELDERLY GENTLEMAN [*amazed*] Dont you blush???

ZOO. Never heard of it. We have a word flush, meaning a rush of blood to the skin. I have noticed it in my babies, but not after the age of two.

THE ELDERLY GENTLEMAN. Your babies!!! I fear I am treading on very delicate ground; but your appearance is extremely youthful; and if I may ask how many—?

ZOO. Only four as yet. It is a long business with us. I specialize in babies. My first was such a success that they made me go on. I—

THE ELDERLY GENTLEMAN [*reeling on the bollard*] Oh! dear!

ZOO. Whats the matter? Anything wrong?

THE ELDERLY GENTLEMAN. In Heaven's name, madam, how old are you?

ZOO. Fifty-six.

THE ELDERLY GENTLEMAN. My knees are trembling. I fear I am really ill.

Not so young as I was.

ZOO. I noticed that you are not strong on your legs yet. You have many of the ways and weaknesses of a baby. No doubt that is why I feel called on to mother you. You certainly are a very silly little Daddy.

THE ELDERLY GENTLEMAN [*stimulated by indignation*] My name, I repeat, is Joseph Popham Bolge Bluebin Barlow, O.M.

ZOO. What a ridiculously long name! I cant call you all that. What did your mother call you?

THE ELDERLY GENTLEMAN. You recall the bitterest struggles of my childhood. I was sensitive on the point. Children suffer greatly from absurd nicknames. My mother thoughtlessly called me Iddy Toodles. I was called Iddy until I went to school, when I made my first stand for children's rights by insisting on being called at least Joe. At fifteen I refused to answer to anything shorter than Joseph. At eighteen I discovered that the name Joseph was supposed to indicate an unmanly prudery because of some old story about a Joseph who rejected the advances of his employer's wife: very properly in my opinion. I then became Popham to my family and intimate friends, and Mister Barlow to the rest of the world. My mother slipped back into Iddy when her faculties began to fail her, poor woman; but I could not resent that, at her age.

ZOO. Do you mean to say that your mother bothered about you after you were ten?

THE ELDERLY GENTLEMAN. Naturally, madam. She was my mother. What would you have had her do?

ZOO. Go on to the next, of course. After eight or nine children become quite uninteresting, except to themselves. I shouldnt know my two eldest if I met them.

THE ELDERLY GENTLEMAN [*again drooping*] I am dying. Let me die. I wish to die.

ZOO [*going to him quickly and supporting him*] Hold up. Sit up straight. Whats the matter?

THE ELDERLY GENTLEMAN [*faintly*] My spine, I think. Shock. Concussion.

ZOO [*maternally*] Pow wow wow! What is there to shock you? [*Shaking him playfully*] There! Sit up; and be good.

THE ELDERLY GENTLEMAN [*still feebly*] Thank you. I am better now.

ZOO [*resuming her seat on the sacks*] But what was all the rest of that long name for? There was a lot more of it. Blops Booby or something.

THE ELDERLY GENTLEMAN [*impressively*] Bolge Bluebin, madam: a historical name. Let me inform you that I can trace my family back for more than a thousand years, from the Eastern Empire to its ancient seat in these islands, to a time when two of my ancestors, Joyce Bolge and Hengist Horsa Bluebin, wrestled with one another for the prime ministership of the British Empire, and occupied that position successively with a glory of which we can in these degenerate days form but a faint conception. When I think of these mighty men, lions in war, sages in peace, not babblers and charlatans like the pigmies who now occupy their places in Baghdad, but strong silent men, ruling an empire on which the sun never set, my eyes fill with tears: my heart bursts with emotion: I feel that to have lived but to the dawn of manhood in their day, and then died for them, would have been a nobler and happier lot than the ignominious ease of my present longevity.

ZOO. Longevity! [*she laughs*].

THE ELDERLY GENTLEMAN. Yes, madam, relative longevity. As it is, I have to be content and proud to know that I am descended from both those heroes.

ZOO. You must be descended from every Briton who was alive in their time. Dont you know that?

THE ELDERLY GENTLEMAN. Do not quibble, madam. I bear their names, Bolge and Bluebin; and I hope I have inherited something of their majestic spirit. Well, they were born in these islands. I repeat, these islands were then, incredible as it now seems, the centre of the British Empire. When that centre shifted to Baghdad, and the Englishman at last returned to the true cradle of his race in Mesopotamia, the western islands were cast off, as they had been before by the Roman Empire. But it was to the British race, and in these islands, that the greatest miracle in history occurred.

ZOO. Miracle?

THE ELDERLY GENTLEMAN. Yes: the first man to live three hundred years was an Englishman. The first, that is, since the contemporaries of Methuselah.

ZOO. Oh, that!

THE ELDERLY GENTLEMAN. Yes, that, as you call it so flippantly. Are you aware, madam, that at that immortal moment the English race had lost intellectual credit to such an extent that they habitually spoke of one another as fatheads? Yet England is now a sacred grove to which statesmen from all over the earth come to consult English sages who speak with the experience of two and a half centuries of life. The land that once exported cotton shirts and hardware now exports nothing but wisdom. You see before you, madam, a man utterly weary of the week-end riverside hotels of the Euphrates, the minstrels and pierrots on the sands of the Persian Gulf, the toboggans and funiculars of the Hindoo Koosh. Can you wonder that I turn, with a hungry heart, to the mystery and beauty of these haunted islands, thronged with spectres from a magic past, made holy by the footsteps of the wise men of the West. Consider this island on which we stand, the last foothold of man on this side of the Atlantic: this Ireland, described by the earliest bards as an emerald gem set in a silver sea! Can I, a scion of the illustrious British race, ever forget that when the Empire transferred its seat to the East, and said to the turbulent Irish race which it had oppressed but never conquered, 'At last we leave you to yourselves; and much good may it do you,' the Irish as one man uttered the historic shout 'No: we'll be damned if you do,' and emigrated to the countries where there was still a Nationalist question, to India, Persia, and Corea, to Morocco, Tunis, and Tripoli. In these countries they were ever foremost in the struggle for national independence; and the world rang continually with the story of their sufferings and wrongs. And what poem can do justice to the end, when it came at last? Hardly two hundred years had elapsed when the claims of nationality were so universally conceded that there was no longer a single country on the face of the earth with a national grievance or a national movement. Think of the position of the Irish, who had lost all their political faculties by disuse except that of nationalist agitation, and who owed their position as the most interesting race on earth solely to their sufferings! The very countries they had helped to set free boycotted them as intolerable bores. The communities which had once idolized them as the incarnation of all that is adorable in the warm heart and witty brain, fled from them as from a pestilence. To regain their lost prestige, the Irish claimed the city of Jerusalem, on the ground that they were the lost tribes of Israel; but on their approach the Jews abandoned the city and redistributed themselves throughout Europe. It was then that these devoted Irishmen, not one of whom had ever seen Ireland, were counselled by an English Archbishop, the father of the oracles, to go back to their own country. This had never once occurred to them, because there was nothing to prevent them and nobody to forbid them. They jumped at the suggestion. They landed here: here in Galway Bay, on this very ground. When they reached the shore the older men and women flung themselves down and passionately kissed the soil of Ireland, calling on the young to embrace the earth that had borne their ancestors. But the young looked gloomily on, and said 'There is no earth, only stone.' You will see by looking round you why they said that: the fields here are of stone: the hills are capped with granite. They all left for England next day; and no Irishman ever again confessed to being Irish, even to his own children; so that when that generation passed away the Irish race vanished from human knowledge. And the dispersed Jews did the same lest they should be sent back to Palestine. Since then the world, bereft of its Jews and its Irish, has been a tame dull place. Is there no pathos for you in this story? Can you not understand now why I am come to visit the scene of this tragic effacement of a race of heroes and poets?

ZOO. We still tell our little children stories like that, to help them to understand. But such things do not happen really. That scene of the Irish landing here and kissing the ground might have happened to a hundred people. It couldn't have happened to a hundred thousand: you know that as well as I do. And what a ridiculous thing to call people Irish because they live in Ireland! you might as well call them Airish because they live in air. They must be just the same as other people. Why do you shortlivers persist in making up silly stories about the world and trying to act as if they were true? Contact with truth hurts and frightens you: you escape from it into an imaginary vacuum in which you can indulge your desires and hopes and loves and hates without any obstruction from the solid facts of life. You love to throw dust in your own eyes.

THE ELDERLY GENTLEMAN. It is my turn now, madam, to inform you that I do not understand a single word you are saying. I should have thought that the use of a vacuum for removing dust was a mark of civilization rather than of savagery.

ZOO [*giving him up as hopeless*] Oh, Daddy, Daddy: I can hardly believe that you are human, you are so stupid. It was well said of your people in the olden days, 'Dust thou art; and to dust thou shalt return.'

THE ELDERLY GENTLEMAN [*nobly*] My body is dust, madam: not my soul. What does it matter what my body is made of? the dust of the ground, the particles of the air, or even the slime of the ditch? The important thing is that when my Creator took it, whatever it was, He breathed into its nostrils the breath of life; and Man became a living soul. Yes, madam, a living soul. I am not the dust of the ground: I am a living soul. That is an exalting, a magnificent thought. It is also a great scientific fact. I am not interested in the chemicals and the microbes: I leave them to the chumps and noodles, to the blockheads and the muckrakers who are incapable of their own glorious destiny, and unconscious of their own divinity. They tell me there are leucocytes in my blood, and sodium and carbon in my flesh. I thank them for the information, and tell them that there are blackbeetles in my kitchen, washing soda in my laundry, and coal in my cellar. I do not deny their existence; but I keep them in their proper place, which is not, if I may be allowed to use an antiquated form of expression, the temple of the Holy Ghost. No doubt you think me behind the times; but I rejoice in my enlightenment; and I recoil from your ignorance, your blindness, your imbecility. Humanly I pity you. Intellectually I despise you.

ZOO. Bravo, Daddy! You have the root of the matter in you. You will not die of discouragement after all.

THE ELDERLY GENTLEMAN. I have not the smallest intention of doing so, madam. I am no longer young; and I have moments of weakness; but when I approach this subject the divine spark in me kindles and glows, the corruptible becomes incorruptible, and the mortal Bolge Bluebin Barlow puts on immortality. On this ground I am your equal, even if you survive me by ten thousand years.

ZOO. Yes; but what do we know about this breath of life that puffs you up so exaltedly? Just nothing. So let us shake hands as cultivated Agnostics, and change the subject.

THE ELDERLY GENTLEMAN. Cultivated fiddlesticks, madam! You cannot change this subject until the heavens and the earth pass away. I am not an Agnostic: I am a gentleman. When I believe a thing I say I believe it: when I don't believe it I say I don't believe it. I do not shirk my responsibilities by pretending that I know nothing and therefore can believe nothing. We cannot disclaim knowledge and shirk responsibility. We must proceed on assumptions of some sort or we cannot form a human society.

ZOO. The assumptions must be scientific, Daddy. We must live by science in the long run.

THE ELDERLY GENTLEMAN. I have the utmost respect, madam, for the magnificent discoveries which we owe to science. But any fool can make a discovery. Every baby has to discover more in the first years of its life than Roger Bacon ever discovered in his laboratory. When I was seven years old I discovered the sting of the wasp. But I do not ask you to worship me on that account. I assure you, madam, the merest mediocrities can discover the most surprising facts about the physical universe as soon as they are civilized enough to have time to study these things, and to invent instruments and apparatus for research. But what is the consequence? Their discoveries discredit the simple stories of our religion. At first we had no idea of astronomical space. We believed the sky to be only the ceiling of a room as large as the earth, with another room on top of it. Death was to us a going upstairs into that room, or, if we did not obey the priests, going downstairs into the coal cellar. We founded our religion, our morality, our laws, our lessons, our poems, our prayers, on that simple belief. Well, the moment men became astronomers and made telescopes, their belief perished. When they could no longer believe in the sky, they found that they could no longer believe in their Deity, because they had always thought of him as living in the sky. When the priests themselves ceased to believe in their Deity and began to believe in astronomy, they changed their name and their dress, and called themselves doctors and men of science. They set up a new religion in which there was no Deity, but only wonders and miracles, with scientific instruments and apparatus as the wonder workers. Instead of worshipping the greatness and wisdom of the Deity, men gaped foolishly at the million billion miles of space and worshipped the astronomer as infallible and omniscient. They built temples for his telescopes. Then they looked into their own bodies with microscopes, and found there, not the soul they had formerly believed in, but millions of micro-organisms; so they gaped at these as foolishly as at the millions of miles, and built microscope temples in which horrible sacrifices were offered. They even gave their own bodies to be sacrificed by the microscope man, who was worshipped, like the astronomer, as infallible and omniscient. Thus our discoveries instead of increasing our wisdom, only destroyed the little childish wisdom we had. All I can grant you is that they increased our knowledge.

ZOO. Nonsense! Consciousness of a fact is not knowledge of it: if it were, the fish would know more of the sea than the geographers and the naturalists.

THE ELDERLY GENTLEMAN. That is an extremely acute remark, madam. The dullest fish could not possibly know less of the majesty of the ocean than many geographers and naturalists of my acquaintance.

ZOO. Just so. And the greatest fool on earth, by merely looking at a mariners' compass, may become conscious of the fact that the needle turns always to the pole. Is he any the less a fool with that consciousness than he was without it?

THE ELDERLY GENTLEMAN. Only a more conceited one, madam, no doubt. Still, I do not quite see how you can be aware of the existence of a thing without knowing it.

ZOO. Well, you can see a man without knowing him, can you not?

THE ELDERLY GENTLEMAN [*illuminated*] Oh how true! Of course, of course. There is a member of the Travellers' Club who has questioned the veracity of an experience of mine at the South Pole. I see that man almost every day when I am at home. But I refuse to know him.

ZOO. If you could see him much more distinctly through a magnifying glass, or examine a drop of his blood through a microscope, or dissect out all his organs and analyze them chemically, would you know him then?

THE ELDERLY GENTLEMAN. Certainly not. Any such investigation could only increase the disgust with which he inspires me, and make me more determined than ever not to know him on any terms.

ZOO. Yet you would be much more conscious of him, would you not?

THE ELDERLY GENTLEMAN. I should not allow that to commit me to any familiarity with the fellow. I have been twice at the Summer Sports at the South Pole; and this man pretended he had been to the North Pole, which can hardly be said to exist, as it is in the middle of the sea. He declared he had hung his hat on it.

ZOO [*laughing*] He knew that travellers are amusing only when they are telling lies. Perhaps if you looked at that man through a microscope you would find some good in him.

THE ELDERLY GENTLEMAN. I do not want to find any good in him. Besides, madam, what you have just said encourages me to utter an opinion of mine which is so advanced! so intellectually daring! that I have never ventured to confess to it before, lest I should be imprisoned for blasphemy, or even burnt alive.

ZOO. Indeed! What opinion is that?

THE ELDERLY GENTLEMAN [*after looking cautiously round*] I do not approve of microscopes. I never have.

ZOO. You call that advanced! Oh, Daddy, that is pure obscurantism.

THE ELDERLY GENTLEMAN. Call it so if you will, madam; but I maintain that it is dangerous to shew too much to people who do not know what they are looking at. I think that a man who is sane as long as he looks at the world through his own eyes is very likely to become a dangerous madman if he takes to looking at the world through telescopes and microscopes. Even when he is telling fairy stories about giants and dwarfs, the giants had better not be too big nor the dwarfs too small and too malicious. Before the microscope came, our fairy stories only made the children's flesh creep pleasantly, and did not frighten grown-up persons at all. But the microscope men terrified themselves and everyone else out of their wits with the invisible monsters they saw: poor harmless little things that die at the touch of a ray of sunshine, and are themselves the victims of all the diseases they are supposed to produce! Whatever the scientific people may say, imagination without microscopes was kindly and often courageous, because it worked on things of which it had some real knowledge. But imagination with microscopes, working on a terrifying spectacle of millions of grotesque creatures of whose nature it had no knowledge, became a cruel, terror-stricken, persecuting delirium. Are you aware, madam, that a general massacre of men of science took place in the twenty-first century of the pseudo-Christian era, when all their laboratories were demolished, and all their apparatus destroyed?

ZOO. Yes: the shortlived are as savage in their advances as in their relapses. But when Science crept back, it had been taught its place. The mere collectors of anatomical or chemical facts were not supposed to know more about Science than the collector of used postage stamps about international trade or literature. The scientific terrorist who was afraid to use a spoon or a tumbler until he had dipt it in some poisonous acid to kill the microbes, was no longer given titles, pensions, and monstrous powers over the bodies of other people: he was sent to an asylum, and treated there until his recovery. But all that is an old story: the extension of life to three hundred years has provided the human race with capable leaders, and made short work of such childish stuff.

THE ELDERLY GENTLEMAN [*pettishly*] You seem to credit every advance in civilization to your inordinately long lives. Do you not know that this question was familiar to men who died before they had reached my own age?

ZOO. Oh yes: one or two of them hinted at it in a feeble way. An ancient writer whose name has come down to us in several forms, such as Shakespear, Shelley, Sheridan, and Shoddy, has a remarkable passage about your dispositions being horridly shaken by thoughts beyond the reaches of your souls. That does not come to much, does it?

THE ELDERLY GENTLEMAN. At all events, madam, I may remind you, if you come to capping ages, that whatever your secondaries and tertiaries may be, you are younger than I am.

ZOO. Yes, Daddy; but it is not the number of years we have behind us, but the number we have before us, that makes us careful and responsible and determined to find out the truth about everything. What does it matter to you whether anything is true or not? your flesh is as grass: you come up like a flower, and wither in your second childhood. A lie will last your time: it will not last mine. If I knew I had to die in twenty years it would not be worth my while to educate myself: I should not bother about anything but having a little pleasure while I lasted.

THE ELDERLY GENTLEMAN. Young woman: you are mistaken. Shortlived as we are, we—the best of us, I mean—regard civilization and learning, art and science, as an ever-burning torch, which passes from the hand of one generation to the hand of the next, each generation kindling it to a brighter, prouder flame. Thus each lifetime, however short, contributes a brick to a vast and growing edifice, a page to a sacred volume, a chapter to a Bible, a Bible to a literature. We may be insects; but like the coral insect we build islands which become continents: like the bee we store sustenance for future communities. The individual perishes; but the race is immortal. The acorn of today is the oak of the next millennium. I throw my stone on the cairn and die; but later comers add another stone and yet another; and lo! a mountain. I—

ZOO [*interrupts him by laughing heartily at him*]!!!!!!

THE ELDERLY GENTLEMAN [*with offended dignity*] May I ask what I have said that calls for this merriment?

ZOO. Oh, Daddy, Daddy, Daddy, you are a funny little man, with your torches, and your flames, and your bricks and edifices and pages and volumes and chapters and coral insects and bees and acorns and stones and mountains.

THE ELDERLY GENTLEMAN. Metaphors, madam. Metaphors merely.

ZOO. Images, images, images. I was talking about men, not about images.

THE ELDERLY GENTLEMAN. I was illustrating—not, I hope, quite infelicitously—the great march of Progress. I was shewing you how, shortlived as we orientals are, mankind gains in stature from generation to generation, from epoch to epoch, from barbarism to civilization, from civilization to perfection.

ZOO. I see. The father grows to be six feet high, and hands on his six feet to his son, who adds another six feet and becomes twelve feet high, and hands his twelve feet on to his son, who is full-grown at eighteen feet, and so on. In a thousand years you would all be three or four miles high. At that rate your ancestors Bilge and Bluebeard, whom you call giants, must have been about quarter of an inch high.

THE ELDERLY GENTLEMAN. I am not here to bandy quibbles and paradoxes with a girl who blunders over the greatest names in history. I am in earnest. I am treating a solemn theme seriously. I never said that the son of a man six feet high would be twelve feet high.

ZOO. You didn't mean that?

THE ELDERLY GENTLEMAN. Most certainly not.

ZOO. Then you didn't mean anything. Now listen to me, you little ephemeral thing. I knew quite well what you meant by your torch handed on from generation to generation. But every time that torch is handed on, it dies down to the tiniest spark; and the man who gets it can rekindle it only by his own light. You are no taller than Bilge or Bluebeard; and you are no wiser. Their wisdom, such as it was, perished with them: so did their strength, if their strength ever existed outside your imagination. I do not know how old you are: you look about five hundred—

THE ELDERLY GENTLEMAN. Five hundred! Really, madam—

ZOO [*continuing*]; but I know, of course, that you are an ordinary shortliver. Well, your wisdom is only such wisdom as a man can have before he has had experience enough to distinguish his wisdom from his folly, his destiny from his delusions, his—

THE ELDERLY GENTLEMAN. In short, such wisdom as your own.

ZOO. No, no, no, no. How often must I tell you that we are made wise not by the recollections of our past, but by the responsibilities of our future. I shall be more reckless when I am a tertiary than I am today. If you cannot understand that, at least you must admit that I have learnt from tertiaries. I have seen their work and lived under their institutions. Like all young things I rebelled against them; and in their hunger for new lights and new ideas they listened to me and encouraged me to rebel. But my ways did not work; and theirs did; and they were able to tell me why. They have no power over me except that power: they refuse all other power; and the consequence is that there are no limits to their power except the limits they set themselves. You are a child governed by children, who make so many mistakes and are so naughty that you are in continual rebellion against them; and as they can never convince you that they are right: they can govern you only by beating you, imprisoning you, torturing you, killing you if you disobey them without being strong enough to kill or torture them.

THE ELDERLY GENTLEMAN. That may be an unfortunate fact. I condemn it and deplore it. But our minds are greater than the facts. We know better. The greatest ancient teachers, followed by the galaxy of Christs who arose in the twentieth century, not to mention such comparatively modern spiritual leaders as Blitherinjam, Tosh, and Spiffkins, all taught that punishment and revenge, coercion and militarism, are mistakes, and that the golden rule—

ZOO. [*interrupting*] Yes, yes, yes, Daddy: we longlived people know that quite well. But did any of their disciples ever succeed in governing you for a single day on their Christ-like principles? It is not enough to know what is good: you must be able to do it. They couldn't do it because they did not live long enough to find out how to do it, or to outlive the childish passions that prevented them from really wanting to do it. You know very well that they could only keep order—such as it was—by the very coercion and militarism they were denouncing and deploring. They had actually to kill one another for preaching their own gospel, or be killed themselves.

THE ELDERLY GENTLEMAN. The blood of the martyrs, madam, is the seed of the Church.

ZOO. More images, Daddy! The blood of the shortlived falls on stony ground.

THE ELDERLY GENTLEMAN [*rising, very testy*] You are simply mad on the subject of longevity. I wish you would change it. It is rather personal and in bad taste. Human nature is human nature, longlived or shortlived, and always will be.

ZOO. Then you give up the idea of progress? You cry off the torch, and the brick, and the acorn, and all the rest of it?

THE ELDERLY GENTLEMAN. I do nothing of the sort. I stand for progress and for freedom broadening down from precedent to precedent.

ZOO. You are certainly a true Briton.

THE ELDERLY GENTLEMAN. I am proud of it. But in your mouth I feel that the compliment hides some insult; so I do not thank you for it.

ZOO. All I meant was that though Britons sometimes say quite clever things and deep things as well as silly and shallow things, they always forget them ten minutes after they have uttered them.

THE ELDERLY GENTLEMAN. Leave it at that, madam: leave it at that. [*He sits down again*]. Even a Pope is not expected to be continually pontificating. Our flashes of inspiration shew that our hearts are in the right place.

ZOO. Of course. You cannot keep your heart in any place but the right place.

THE ELDERLY GENTLEMAN. Tcha!

ZOO. But you can keep your hands in the wrong place. In your neighbor's pockets, for example. So, you see, it is your hands that really matter.

THE ELDERLY GENTLEMAN [*exhausted*] Well, a woman must have the last word. I will not dispute it with you.

ZOO. Good. Now let us go back to the really interesting subject of our discussion. You remember? The slavery of the shortlived to images and metaphors.

THE ELDERLY GENTLEMAN [*aghast*] Do you mean to say, madam, that after having talked my head off, and reduced me to despair and silence by your intolerable loquacity, you actually propose to begin all over again? I shall leave you at once.

ZOO. You must not. I am your nurse; and you must stay with me.

THE ELDERLY GENTLEMAN. I absolutely decline to do anything of the sort [*he rises and walks away with marked dignity*].

ZOO [*using her tuning-fork*] Zoo on Burrin Pier to Oracle Police at Ennistymon have you got me?... What?... I am picking you up now but you are flat to my pitch.... Just a shade sharper.... That's better: still a little more.... Got you: right. Isolate Burrin Pier quick.

THE ELDERLY GENTLEMAN [*is heard to yell*] Oh!

ZOO [*still intoning*] Thanks.... Oh nothing serious I am nursing a shortliver and the silly creature has run away he has discouraged himself very badly by gadding about and talking to secondaries and I must keep him strictly to heel.

The Elderly Gentleman returns, indignant.

ZOO. Here he is you can release the Pier thanks. Goodbye. [*She puts up her tuning-fork*].

THE ELDERLY GENTLEMAN. This is outrageous. When I tried to step off the pier on to the road, I received a shock, followed by an attack of pins and needles which ceased only when I stepped back on to the stones.

ZOO. Yes: there is an electric hedge there. It is a very old and very crude method of keeping animals from straying.

THE ELDERLY GENTLEMAN. We are perfectly familiar with it in Baghdad, madam; but I little thought I should live to have it ignominiously applied to myself. You have actually Kiplingized me.

ZOO. Kiplingized! What is that?

THE ELDERLY GENTLEMAN. About a thousand years ago there were two authors named Kipling. One was an eastern and a writer of merit: the other, being a western, was of course only an amusing barbarian. He is said to have invented the electric hedge. I consider that in using it on me you have taken a very great liberty.

ZOO. What is a liberty?

THE ELDERLY GENTLEMAN [*exasperated*] I shall not explain, madam. I believe you know as well as I do. [*He sits down on the bollard in dudgeon*].

ZOO. No: even you can tell me things I do not know. Havnt you noticed that all the time you have been here we have been asking you questions?

THE ELDERLY GENTLEMAN. Noticed it! It has almost driven me mad. Do you see my white hair? It was hardly grey when I landed: there were patches of its original auburn still distinctly discernible.

ZOO. That is one of the symptoms of discouragement. But have you noticed something much more important to yourself: that is, that you have never asked us any questions, although we know so much more than you do?

THE ELDERLY GENTLEMAN. I am not a child, madam. I believe I have had occasion to say that before. And I am an experienced traveller. I know that what the traveller observes must really exist, or he could not observe it. But what the natives tell him is invariably pure fiction.

ZOO. Not here, Daddy. With us life is too long for telling lies. They all get found out. Youd better ask me questions while you have the chance.

THE ELDERLY GENTLEMAN. If I have occasion to consult the oracle I shall address myself to a proper one: to a tertiary: not to a primary flapper playing at being an oracle. If you are a nurserymaid, attend to your duties; and do not presume to ape your elders.

ZOO. [*rising ominously and reddening*] You silly—

THE ELDERLY GENTLEMAN [*thundering*] Silence! Do you hear! Hold your tongue.

ZOO. Something very disagreeable is happening to me. I feel hot all over. I have a horrible impulse to injure you. What have you done to me?

THE ELDERLY GENTLEMAN [*triumphant*] Aha! I have made you blush. Now you know what blushing means. Blushing with shame!

ZOO. Whatever you are doing, it is something so utterly evil that if you do not stop I will kill you.

THE ELDERLY GENTLEMAN [*apprehending his danger*] Doubtless you think it safe to threaten an old man—

ZOO [*fiercely*] Old! You are a child: an evil child. We kill evil children here. We do it even against our own wills by instinct. Take care.

THE ELDERLY GENTLEMAN [*rising with crestfallen courtesy*] I did not mean to hurt your feelings. I—[*swallowing the apology with an effort*] I beg your pardon. [*He takes off his hat, and bows*].

ZOO. What does that mean?

THE ELDERLY GENTLEMAN. I withdraw what I said.

ZOO. How can you withdraw what you said?

THE ELDERLY GENTLEMAN. I can say no more than that I am sorry.

ZOO. You have reason to be. That hideous sensation you gave me is subsiding; but you have had a very narrow escape. Do not attempt to kill me again; for at the first sign in your voice or face I shall strike you dead.

THE ELDERLY GENTLEMAN. *I* attempt to kill you! What a monstrous accusation!

ZOO [*frowns*]!

THE ELDERLY GENTLEMAN [*prudently correcting himself*] I mean misunderstanding. I never dreamt of such a thing. Surely you cannot believe that I am a murderer.

ZOO. I know you are a murderer. It is not merely that you threw words at me as if they were stones, meaning to hurt me. It was the instinct to kill that you roused in me. I did not know it was in my nature: never before has it wakened and sprung out at me, warning me to kill or be killed. I must now reconsider my whole political position. I am no longer a Conservative.

THE ELDERLY GENTLEMAN [*dropping his hat*] Gracious Heavens! you have lost your senses. I am at the mercy of a madwoman: I might have known it from the beginning. I can bear no more of this. [*Offering his chest for the sacrifice*] Kill me at once; and much good may my death do you!

ZOO. It would be useless unless all the other shortlivers were killed at the same time. Besides, it is a measure which should be taken politically and constitutionally, not privately. However, I am prepared to discuss it with you.

ZOO. What good have our counsels ever done you? You come to us for advice when you know you are in difficulties. But you never know you are in difficulties until twenty years after you have made the mistakes that led to them; and then it is too late. You cannot understand our advice: you often do more mischief by trying to act on it than if you had been left to your own childish devices. If you were not childish you would not come to us at all: you would learn from experience that your consultations of the oracle are never of any real help to you. You draw wonderful imaginary pictures of us, and write fictitious tales and poems about our beneficent operations in the past, our wisdom, our justice, our mercy: stories in which we often appear as sentimental dupes of your prayers and sacrifices; but you do it only to conceal from yourselves the truth that you are incapable of being helped by us. Your Prime Minister pretends that he has come to be guided by the oracle; but we are not deceived: we know quite well that he has come here so that when he goes back he may have the authority and dignity of one who has visited the holy islands and spoken face to face with the ineffable ones. He will pretend that all the measures he wishes to take for his own purposes have been enjoined on him by the oracle.

THE ELDERLY GENTLEMAN. But you forget that the answers of the oracle cannot be kept secret or misrepresented. They are written and promulgated. The Leader of the Opposition can obtain copies. All the nations know them. Secret diplomacy has been totally abolished.

ZOO. Yes: you publish documents; but they are garbled or forged. And even if you published our real answers it would make no difference, because the shortlived cannot interpret the plainest writings. Your scriptures command you in the plainest terms to do exactly the contrary of everything your own laws and chosen rulers command and execute. You cannot defy Nature. It is a law of Nature that there is a fixed relation between conduct and length of life.

THE ELDERLY GENTLEMAN. No, no, no. I had much rather discuss your intention of withdrawing from the Conservative party. How the Conservatives have tolerated your opinions so far is more than I can imagine: I can only conjecture that you have contributed very liberally to the party funds. [*He picks up his hat, and sits down again*].

ZOO. Do not babble so senselessly: our chief political controversy is the most momentous in the world for you and your like.

THE ELDERLY GENTLEMAN [*interested*] Indeed? Pray, may I ask what it is? I am a keen politician, and may perhaps be of some use. [*He puts on his hat, cocking it slightly*].

ZOO. We have two great parties: the Conservative party and the Colonization party. The Colonizers are of opinion that we should increase our numbers and colonize. The Conservatives hold that we should stay as we are, confined to these islands, a race apart, wrapped up in the majesty of our wisdom on a soil held as holy ground for us by an adoring world, with our sacred frontier traced beyond dispute by the sea. They contend that it is our destiny to rule the world, and that even when we were shortlived we did so. They say that our power and our peace depend on our remoteness, our exclusiveness, our separation, and the restriction of our numbers. Five minutes ago that was my political faith. Now I do not think there should be any shortlived people at all. [*She throws herself again carelessly on the sacks*].

THE ELDERLY GENTLEMAN. Am I to infer that you deny my right to live because I allowed myself—perhaps injudiciously—to give you a slight scolding?

ZOO. Is it worth living for so short a time? Are you any good to yourself?

THE ELDERLY GENTLEMAN [*stupent*] Well, upon my soul!

ZOO. It is such a very little soul. You only encourage the sin of pride in us, and keep us looking down at you instead of up to something higher than ourselves.

THE ELDERLY GENTLEMAN. Is not that a selfish view, madam? Think of the good you do us by your oracular counsels!

THE ELDERLY GENTLEMAN. I have never heard of any such law, madam.

ZOO. Well, you are hearing of it now.

THE ELDERLY GENTLEMAN. Let me tell you that we shortlivers, as you call us, have lengthened our lives very considerably.

ZOO. How?

THE ELDERLY GENTLEMAN. By saving time. By enabling men to cross the ocean in an afternoon, and to see and speak to one another when they are thousands of miles apart. We hope shortly to organize their labor, and press natural forces into their service, so scientifically that the burden of labor will cease to be perceptible, leaving common men more leisure than they will know what to do with.

ZOO. Daddy: the man whose life is lengthened in this way may be busier than a savage; but the difference between such men living seventy years and those living three hundred would be all the greater; for to a shortliver increase of years is only increase of sorrow; but to a long-liver every extra year is a prospect which forces him to stretch his faculties to the utmost to face it. Therefore I say that we who live three hundred years can be of no use to you who live less than a hundred, and that our true destiny is not to advise and govern you, but to supplant and supersede you. In that faith I now declare myself a Colonizer and an Exterminator.

THE ELDERLY GENTLEMAN. Oh, steady! steady! Pray! pray! Reflect, I implore you. It is possible to colonize without exterminating the natives. Would you treat us less mercifully than our barbarous forefathers treated the Redskin and the Negro? Are we not, as Britons, entitled at least to some reservations?

ZOO. What is the use of prolonging the agony? You would perish slowly in our presence, no matter what we did to preserve you. You were almost dead when I took charge of you today, merely because you had talked for a few minutes to a secondary. Besides, we have our own experience to go upon. Have you never heard that our children occasionally revert to the ancestral type, and are born shortlived?

THE ELDERLY GENTLEMAN [*eagerly*] Never. I hope you will not be offended if I say that it would be a great comfort to me if I could be placed in charge of one of those normal individuals.

ZOO. Abnormal, you mean. What you ask is impossible: we weed them all out.

THE ELDERLY GENTLEMAN. When you say that you weed them out, you send a cold shiver down my spine. I hope you don't mean that you—that you—that you assist Nature in any way?

ZOO. Why not? Have you not heard the saying of the Chinese sage Dee Ning, that a good garden needs weeding? But it is not necessary for us to interfere. We are naturally rather particular as to the conditions on which we consent to live. One does not mind the accidental loss of an arm or a leg or an eye: after all, no one with two legs is unhappy because he has not three; so why should a man with one be unhappy because he has not two? But infirmities of mind and temper are quite another matter. If one of us has no self-control, or is too weak to bear the strain of our truthful life without wincing, or is tormented by depraved appetites and superstitions, or is unable to keep free from pain and depression, he naturally becomes discouraged, and refuses to live.

THE ELDERLY GENTLEMAN. Good Lord! Cuts his throat, do you mean?

ZOO. No: why should he cut his throat? He simply dies. He wants to. He is out of countenance, as we call it.

THE ELDERLY GENTLEMAN. Well!!! But suppose he is depraved enough not to want to die, and to settle the difficulty by killing all the rest of you?

ZOO. Oh, he is one of the thoroughly degenerate shortlivers whom we occasionally produce. He emigrates.

THE ELDERLY GENTLEMAN. And what becomes of him then?

ZOO. You shortlived people always think very highly of him. You accept him as what you call a great man.

THE ELDERLY GENTLEMAN. You astonish me; and yet I must admit that what you tell me accounts for a great deal of the little I know of the private life of our great men. We must be very convenient to you as a dumping place for your failures.

ZOO. I admit that.

THE ELDERLY GENTLEMAN. Good. Then if you carry out your plan of colonization, and leave no shortlived countries in the world, what will you do with your undesirables?

ZOO. Kill them. Our tertiaries are not at all squeamish about killing.

THE ELDERLY GENTLEMAN. Gracious Powers!

ZOO [*glancing up at the sun*] Come. It is just sixteen o'clock; and you have to join your party at half-past in the temple in Galway.

THE ELDERLY GENTLEMAN [*rising*] Galway! Shall I at last be able to boast of having seen that magnificent city?

ZOO. You will be disappointed: we have no cities. There is a temple of the oracle: that is all.

THE ELDERLY GENTLEMAN. Alas! and I came here to fulfil two long-cherished dreams. One was to see Galway. It has been said, 'See Galway and die.' The other was to contemplate the ruins of London.

ZOO. Ruins! We do not tolerate ruins. Was London a place of any importance?

THE ELDERLY GENTLEMAN [*amazed*] What! London! It was the mightiest city of antiquity. [*Rhetorically*] Situate just where the Dover Road crosses the Thames, it—

ZOO [*curtly interrupting*] There is nothing there now. Why should anybody pitch on such a spot to live? The nearest houses are at a place called Strand-on-the-Green: it is very old. Come. We shall go across the water. [*She goes down the steps*].

THE ELDERLY GENTLEMAN. Sic transit gloria mundi!

ZOO [*from below*] What did you say?

THE ELDERLY GENTLEMAN [*despairingly*] Nothing. You would not understand. [*He goes down the steps*].

ACT II

A courtyard before the columned portico of a temple. The temple door is in the middle of the portico. A veiled and robed woman of majestic carriage passes along behind the columns towards the entrance. From the opposite direction a man of compact figure, clean-shaven, saturnine, and self-centred: in short, very like Napoleon I, and wearing a military uniform of Napoleonic cut, marches with measured steps; places his hand in his lapel in the traditional manner; and fixes the woman with his eye. She stops, her attitude expressing haughty amazement at his audacity. He is on her right: she on his left.

NAPOLEON [*impressively*] I am the Man of Destiny.

THE VEILED WOMAN [*unimpressed*] How did you get in here?

NAPOLEON. I walked in. I go on until I am stopped. I never am stopped. I tell you I am the Man of Destiny.

THE VEILED WOMAN. You will be a man of very short destiny if you wander about here without one of our children to guide you. I suppose you belong to the Baghdad envoy.

NAPOLEON. I came with him; but I do not belong to him. I belong to myself. Direct me to the oracle if you can. If not, do not waste my time.

THE VEILED WOMAN. Your time, poor creature, is short. I will not waste it. Your envoy and his party will be here presently. The consultation of the oracle is arranged for them, and will take place according to the prescribed ritual. You can wait here until they come [*she turns to go into the temple*].

NAPOLEON. I never wait. [*She stops*]. The prescribed ritual is, I believe, the classical one of the pythoness on her tripod, the intoxicating fumes arising from the abyss, the convulsions of the priestess as she delivers the message of the God, and so on. That sort of thing does not impose on me: I use it myself to impose on simpletons. I believe that what is, is. I know that what is not, is not. The antics of a woman sitting on a tripod and pretending to be drunk do not interest me. Her words are put into her mouth, not by a god, but by a man three hundred years old, who has had the capacity to profit by his experience. I wish to speak to that man face to face, without mummery or imposture.

THE VEILED WOMAN. You seem to be an unusually sensible person. But there is no old man. I am the oracle on duty today. I am on my way to take my place on the tripod, and go through the usual mummery, as you rightly call it, to impress your friend the envoy. As you are superior to that kind of thing, you may consult me now. [*She leads the way into the middle of the courtyard*]. What do you want to know?

NAPOLEON [*following her*] Madam: I have not come all this way to discuss matters of State with a woman. I must ask you to direct me to one of your oldest and ablest men.

THE ORACLE. None of our oldest and ablest men or women would dream of wasting their time on you. You would die of discouragement in their presence in less than three hours.

NAPOLEON. You can keep this idle fable of discouragement for people credulous enough to be intimidated by it, madam. I do not believe in metaphysical forces.

THE ORACLE. No one asks you to. A field is something physical, is it not. Well, I have a field.

NAPOLEON. I have several million fields. I am Emperor of Turania.

THE ORACLE. You do not understand. I am not speaking of an agricultural field. Do you not know that every mass of matter in motion carries with it an invisible gravitational field, every magnet an invisible magnetic field, and every living organism a mesmeric field? Even you have a perceptible mesmeric field. Feeble as it is, it is the strongest I have yet observed in a shortliver.

NAPOLEON. By no means feeble, madam. I understand you now; and I may tell you that the strongest characters blench in my presence, and submit to my domination. But I do not call that a physical force.

THE ORACLE. What else do you call it, pray? Our physicists deal with it.

Our mathematicians express its measurements in algebraic equations.

NAPOLEON. Do you mean that they could measure mine?

THE ORACLE. Yes: by a figure infinitely near to zero. Even in us the force is negligible during our first century of life. In our second it develops quickly, and becomes dangerous to shortlivers who venture into its field. If I were not veiled and robed in insulating material you could not endure my presence; and I am still a young woman: one hundred and seventy if you wish to know exactly.

NAPOLEON [*folding his arms*] I am not intimidated: no woman alive, old or young, can put me out of countenance. Unveil, madam. Disrobe. You will move this temple as easily as shake me.

THE ORACLE. Very well [*she throws back her veil*].

NAPOLEON [*shrieking, staggering, and covering his eyes*] No. Stop. Hide your face again. [*Shutting his eyes and distractedly clutching at his throat and heart*] Let me go. Help! I am dying.

THE ORACLE. Do you still wish to consult an older person?

NAPOLEON. No, no. The veil, the veil, I beg you.

THE ORACLE [*replacing the veil*] So.

NAPOLEON. Ouf! One cannot always be at one's best. Twice before in my life I have lost my nerve and behaved like a poltroon. But I warn you not to judge my quality by these involuntary moments.

THE ORACLE. I have no occasion to judge of your quality. You want my advice. Speak quickly; or I shall go about my business.

NAPOLEON [*After a moment's hesitation, sinks respectfully on one knee*]

I—

THE ORACLE. Oh, rise, rise. Are you so foolish as to offer me this mummery which even you despise?

NAPOLEON [*rising*] I knelt in spite of myself. I compliment you on your impressiveness, madam.

THE ORACLE [*impatiently*] Time! time! time! time!

NAPOLEON. You will not grudge me the necessary time, madam, when you know my case. I am a man gifted with a certain specific talent in a degree altogether extraordinary. I am not otherwise a very extraordinary person: my family is not influential; and without this talent I should cut no particular figure in the world.

THE ORACLE. Why cut a figure in the world?

NAPOLEON. Superiority will make itself felt, madam. But when I say I possess this talent I do not express myself accurately. The truth is that my talent possesses me. It is genius. It drives me to exercise it. I must exercise it. I am great when I exercise it. At other moments I am nobody.

THE ORACLE. Well, exercise it. Do you need an oracle to tell you that?

NAPOLEON. Wait. This talent involves the shedding of human blood.

THE ORACLE. Are you a surgeon, or a dentist?

NAPOLEON. Psha! You do not appreciate me, madam. I mean the shedding of oceans of blood, the death of millions of men.

THE ORACLE. They object, I suppose.

NAPOLEON. Not at all. They adore me.

THE ORACLE. Indeed!

NAPOLEON. I have never shed blood with my own hand. They kill each other: they die with shouts of triumph on their lips. Those who die cursing do not curse me. My talent is to organize this slaughter; to give mankind this terrible joy which they call glory; to let loose the devil in them that peace has bound in chains.

THE ORACLE. And you? Do you share their joy?

NAPOLEON. Not at all. What satisfaction is it to me to see one fool pierce the entrails of another with a bayonet? I am a man of princely character, but of simple personal tastes and habits. I have the virtues of a laborer: industry and indifference to personal comfort. But I must rule, because I am so superior to other men that it is intolerable to me to be misruled by them. Yet only as a slayer can I become a ruler. I cannot be great as a writer: I have tried and failed. I have no talent as a sculptor or painter; and as lawyer, preacher, doctor, or actor, scores of second-rate men can do as well as I, or better. I am not even a diplomatist: I can only play my trump card of force. What I can do is to organize war. Look at me! I seem a man like other men, because nine-tenths of me is common humanity. But the other tenth is a faculty for seeing things as they are that no other man possesses.

THE ORACLE. You mean that you have no imagination?

NAPOLEON [*forcibly*] I mean that I have the only imagination worth having: the power of imagining things as they are, even when I cannot see them. You feel yourself my superior, I know: nay, you are my superior: have I not bowed my knee to you by instinct? Yet I challenge you to a test of our respective powers. Can you calculate what the methematicians call vectors, without putting a single algebraic symbol on paper? Can you launch ten thousand men across a frontier and a chain of mountains and know to a mile exactly where they will be at the end of seven weeks? The rest is nothing: I got it all from the books at my military school. Now this great game of war, this playing with armies as other men play with bowls and skittles, is one which I must go on playing, partly because a man must do what he can and not what he would like to do, and partly because, if I stop, I immediately lose my power and become a beggar in the land where I now make men drunk with glory.

THE ORACLE. No doubt then you wish to know how to extricate yourself from this unfortunate position?

NAPOLEON. It is not generally considered unfortunate, madam. Supremely fortunate rather.

THE ORACLE. If you think so, go on making them drunk with glory. Why trouble me with their folly and your vectors?

NAPOLEON. Unluckily, madam, men are not only heroes: they are also cowards. They desire glory; but they dread death.

THE ORACLE. Why should they? Their lives are too short to be worth living. That is why they think your game of war worth playing.

NAPOLEON. They do not look at it quite in that way. The most worthless soldier wants to live for ever. To make him risk being killed by the enemy I have to convince him that if he hesitates he will inevitably be shot at dawn by his own comrades for cowardice.

THE ORACLE. And if his comrades refuse to shoot him?

NAPOLEON. They will be shot too, of course.

THE ORACLE. By whom?

NAPOLEON. By their comrades.

THE ORACLE. And if they refuse?

NAPOLEON. Up to a certain point they do not refuse.

THE ORACLE. But when that point is reached, you have to do the shooting yourself, eh?

NAPOLEON. Unfortunately, madam, when that point is reached, they shoot me.

THE ORACLE. Mf! It seems to me they might as well shoot you first as last. Why don't they?

NAPOLEON. Because their love of fighting, their desire for glory, their shame of being branded as dastards, their instinct to test themselves in terrible trials, their fear of being killed or enslaved by the enemy, their belief that they are defending their hearths and homes, overcome their natural cowardice, and make them willing not only to risk their own lives but to kill everyone who refuses to take that risk. But if war continues too long, there comes a time when the soldiers, and also the taxpayers who are supporting and munitioning them, reach a condition which they describe as being fed up. The troops have proved their courage, and want to go home and enjoy in peace the glory it has earned them. Besides, the risk of death for each soldier becomes a certainty if the fighting goes on for ever: he hopes to escape for six months, but knows he cannot escape for six years. The risk of bankruptcy for the citizen becomes a certainty in the same way. Now what does this mean for me?

THE ORACLE. Does that matter in the midst of such calamity?

NAPOLEON. Psha! madam: it is the only thing that matters: the value of human life is the value of the greatest living man. Cut off that infinitesimal layer of grey matter which distinguishes my brain from that of the common man, and you cut down the stature of humanity from that of a giant to that of a nobody. I matter supremely: my soldiers do not matter at all: there are plenty more where they came from. If you kill me, or put a stop to my activity (it is the same thing), the nobler part of human life perishes. You must save the world from that catastrophe, madam. War has made me popular, powerful, famous, historically immortal. But I foresee that if I go on to the end it will leave me execrated, dethroned, imprisoned, perhaps executed. Yet if I stop fighting I commit suicide as a great man and become a common one. How am I to escape the horns of this tragic dilemma? Victory I can guarantee: I am invincible. But the cost of victory is the demoralization, the depopulation, the ruin of the victors no less than of the vanquished. How am I to satisfy my genius by fighting until I die? that is my question to you.

THE ORACLE. Were you not rash to venture into these sacred islands with such a question on your lips? Warriors are not popular here, my friend.

NAPOLEON. If a soldier were restrained by such a consideration, madam, he would no longer be a soldier. Besides [*he produces a pistol*], I have not come unarmed.

THE ORACLE. What is that thing?

NAPOLEON. It is an instrument of my profession, madam. I raise this hammer; I point the barrel at you; I pull this trigger that is against my forefinger; and you fall dead.

THE ORACLE. Shew it to me [*she puts out her hand to take it from him*].

NAPOLEON [*retreating a step*] Pardon me, madam. I never trust my life in the hands of a person over whom I have no control.

THE ORACLE [*sternly*] Give it to me [*she raises her hand to her veil*].

NAPOLEON [*dropping the pistol and covering his eyes*] Quarter! Kamerad!

Take it, madam [*he kicks it towards her*]: I surrender.

THE ORACLE. Give me that thing. Do you expect me to stoop for it?

NAPOLEON [*taking his hands from his eyes with an effort*] A poor victory, madam [*he picks up the pistol and hands it to her*]: there was no vector strategy needed to win it. [*Making a pose of his humiliation*] But enjoy your triumph: you have made me—ME! Cain Adamson Charles Napoleon! Emperor of Turania! cry for quarter.

THE ORACLE. The way out of your difficulty, Cain Adamson, is very simple.

NAPOLEON [*eagerly*] Good. What is it?

THE ORACLE. To die before the tide of glory turns. Allow me [*she shoots him*].

He falls with a shriek. She throws the pistol away and goes haughtily into the temple.

NAPOLEON [*scrambling to his feet*] Murderess! Monster! She-devil! Unnatural, inhuman wretch! You deserve to be hanged, guillotined, broken on the wheel, burnt alive. No sense of the sacredness of human life! No thought for my wife and children! Bitch! Sow! Wanton! [*He picks up the pistol*]. And missed me at five yards! Thats a woman all over.

He is going away whence he came when Zoo arrives and confronts him at the head of a party consisting of the British Envoy, the Elderly Gentleman, the Envoy's wife, and her daughter, aged about eighteen. The envoy, a typical politician, looks like an imperfectly reformed criminal disguised by a good tailor. The dress of the ladies is coeval with that of the Elderly Gentleman, and suitable for public official ceremonies in western capitals at the XVIII-XIX fin de siècle.

They file in under the portico. Zoo immediately comes out imperiously to Napoleon's right, whilst the Envoy's wife hurries effusively to his left. The Envoy meanwhile passes along behind the columns to the door, followed by his daughter. The Elderly Gentleman stops just where he entered, to see why Zoo has swooped so abruptly on the Emperor of Turania.

ZOO [*to Napoleon, severely*] What are you doing here by yourself? You have no business to go about here alone. What was that noise just now? What is that in your hand?

Napoleon glares at her in speechless fury; pockets the pistol; and produces a whistle.

THE ENVOY'S WIFE. Arnt you coming with us to the oracle, sire?

NAPOLEON. To hell with the oracle, and with you too [*he turns to go*]!

THE ENVOY'S WIFE [*together*] {Oh, sire!!
ZOO {Where are you going?

NAPOLEON. To fetch the police. [*He goes out past Zoo, almost jostling her, and blowing piercing blasts on his whistle*].

ZOO [*whipping out her tuning-fork and intoning*] Hallo Galway Central. [*The whistling continues*]. Stand by to isolate. [*To the Elderly Gentleman, who is staring after the whistling Emperor*] How far has he gone?

THE ELDERLY GENTLEMAN. To that curious statue of a fat old man.

ZOO [*quickly, intoning*] Isolate the Falstaff monument isolate hard. Paralyze—[*the whistling stops*]. Thank you. [*She puts up her tuning-fork*]. He shall not move a muscle until I come to fetch him.

THE ENVOY'S WIFE. Oh! he will be frightfully angry! Did you hear what he said to me?

ZOO. Much we care for his anger!

THE DAUGHTER [*coming forward between her mother and Zoo*]. Please, madam, whose statue is it? and where can I buy a picture postcard of it? It is so funny. I will take a snapshot when we are coming back; but they come out so badly sometimes.

ZOO. They will give you pictures and toys in the temple to take away with you. The story of the statue is too long. It would bore you [*she goes past them across the courtyard to get rid of them*].

THE WIFE [*gushing*] Oh no, I assure you.

THE DAUGHTER [*copying her mother*] We should be so interested.

ZOO. Nonsense! All I can tell you about it is that a thousand years ago, when the whole world was given over to you shortlived people, there was a war called the War to end War. In the war which followed it about ten years later, hardly any soldiers were killed; but seven of the capital cities of Europe were wiped out of existence. It seems to have been a great joke: for the statesmen who thought they had sent ten million common men to their deaths were themselves blown into fragments with their houses and families, while the ten million men lay snugly in the caves they had dug for themselves. Later on even the houses escaped; but their inhabitants were poisoned by gas that spared no living soul. Of course the soldiers starved and ran wild; and that was the end of pseudo-Christian civilization. The last civilized thing that happened was that the statesmen discovered that cowardice was a great patriotic virtue; and a public monument was erected to its first preacher, an ancient and very fat sage called Sir John Falstaff. Well [*pointing*], thats Falstaff.

THE ELDERLY GENTLEMAN [*coming from the portico to his granddaughter's right*] Great Heavens! And at the base of this monstrous poltroon's statue the War God of Turania is now gibbering impotently.

ZOO. Serve him right! War God indeed!

THE ENVOY [*coming between his wife and Zoo*] I don't know any history: a modern Prime Minister has something better to do than sit reading books; but—

THE ELDERLY GENTLEMAN [*interrupting him encouragingly*] You make history, Ambrose.

THE ENVOY. Well, perhaps I do; and perhaps history makes me. I hardly recognize myself in the newspapers sometimes, though I suppose leading articles are the materials of history, as you might say. But what I want to know is, how did war come back again? and how did they make those poisonous gases you speak of? We should be glad to know; for they might come in very handy if we have to fight Turania. Of course I am all for peace, and don't hold with the race of armaments in principle; still, we must keep ahead or be wiped out.

ZOO. You can make the gases for yourselves when your chemists find out how. Then you will do as you did before: poison each other until there are no chemists left, and no civilization. You will then begin all over again as half-starved ignorant savages, and fight with boomerangs and poisoned arrows until you work up to the poison gases and high explosives once more, with the same result. That is, unless we have sense enough to make an end of this ridiculous game by destroying you.

THE ENVOY [*aghast*] Destroying us!

THE ELDERLY GENTLEMAN. I told you, Ambrose. I warned you.

THE ENVOY. But—

ZOO [*impatiently*] I wonder what Zozim is doing. He ought to be here to receive you.

THE ELDERLY GENTLEMAN. Do you mean that rather insufferable young man whom you found boring me on the pier?

ZOO. Yes. He has to dress-up in a Druid's robe, and put on a wig and a long false beard, to impress you silly people. I have to put on a purple mantle. I have no patience with such mummery; but you expect it from us; so I suppose it must be kept up. Will you wait here until Zozim comes, please [*she turns to enter the temple*].

THE ENVOY. My good lady, is it worth while dressing-up and putting on false beards for us if you tell us beforehand that it is all humbug?

ZOO. One would not think so; but if you wont believe in anyone who is not dressed-up, why, we must dress-up for you. It was you who invented all this nonsense, not we.

THE ELDERLY GENTLEMAN. But do you expect us to be impressed after this?

ZOO. I don't expect anything. I know, as a matter of experience, that you will be impressed. The oracle will frighten you out of your wits. [*She goes into the temple*].

THE WIFE. These people treat us as if we were dirt beneath their feet. I wonder at you putting up with it, Amby. It would serve them right if we went home at once: wouldnt it, Eth?

THE DAUGHTER. Yes, mamma. But perhaps they wouldnt mind.

THE ENVOY. No use talking like that, Molly. Ive got to see this oracle. The folks at home wont know how we have been treated: all theyll know is that Ive stood face to face with the oracle and had the straight tip from her. I hope this Zozim chap is not going to keep us waiting much longer; for I feel far from comfortable about the approaching interview; and thats the honest truth.

THE ELDERLY GENTLEMAN. I never thought I should want to see that man again; but now I wish he would take charge of us instead of Zoo. She was charming at first: quite charming; but she turned into a fiend because I had a few words with her. You would not believe: she very nearly killed me. You heard what she said just now. She belongs to a party here which wants to have us all killed.

THE WIFE [*terrified*] Us! But we have done nothing: we have been as nice to them as nice could be. Oh, Amby, come away, come away: there is something dreadful about this place and these people.

THE ENVOY. There is, and no mistake. But youre safe with me: you ought to have sense enough to know that.

THE ELDERLY GENTLEMAN. I am sorry to say, Molly, that it is not merely us four poor weak creatures they want to kill, but the entire race of Man, except themselves.

THE ENVOY. Not so poor neither, Poppa. Nor so weak, if you are going to take in all the Powers. If it comes to killing, two can play at that game, longlived or shortlived.

THE ELDERLY GENTLEMAN. No, Ambrose: we should have no chance. We are worms beside these fearful people: mere worms.

Zozim comes from the temple, robed majestically, and wearing a wreath of mistletoe in his flowing white wig. His false beard reaches almost to his waist. He carries a staff with a curiously carved top.

ZOZIM [*in the doorway, impressively*] Hail, strangers!

ALL [*reverently*] Hail!

ZOZIM. Are ye prepared?

THE ENVOY. We are.

ZOZIM [*unexpectedly becoming conversational, and strolling down carelessly to the middle of the group between the two ladies*] Well, I'm sorry to say the oracle is not. She was delayed by some member of your party who got loose; and as the show takes a bit of arranging, you will have to wait a few minutes. The ladies can go inside and look round the entrance hall and get pictures and things if they want them.

[*Thank you.*]

THE WIFE [*together*] }I should like to
THE DAUGHTER }very much.

[*They go into the temple*]

THE ELDERLY GENTLEMAN [*in dignified rebuke of Zozim's levity*] Taken in this spirit, sir, the show, as you call it, becomes almost an insult to our common sense.

ZOZIM. Quite, I should say. You need not keep it up with me.

THE ENVOY [*suddenly making himself very agreeable*] Just so: just so. We can wait as long as you please. And now, if I may be allowed to seize the opportunity of a few minutes' friendly chat—?

ZOZIM. By all means, if only you will talk about things I can understand.

THE ENVOY. Well, about this colonizing plan of yours. My father-in-law here has been telling me something about it; and he has just now let out that you want not only to colonize us, but to—to—to—well, shall we say to supersede us? Now why supersede us? Why not live and let live? Theres not a scrap of ill-feeling on our side. We should welcome a colony of immortals—we may almost call you that—in the British Middle East. No doubt the Turanian Empire, with its Mahometan traditions, overshadows us now. We have had to bring the Emperor with us on this expedition, though of course you know as well as I do that he has imposed himself on my party just to spy on me. I dont deny that he has the whip hand of us to some extent, because if it came to a war none of our generals could stand up against him. I give him best at that game: he is the finest soldier in the world. Besides, he is an emperor and an autocrat; and I am only an elected representative of the British democracy. Not that our British democrats wont fight: they will fight the heads off all the Turanians that ever walked; but then it takes so long to work them up to it, while he has only to say the word and march. But you people would never get on with him. Believe me, you would not be as comfortable in Turania as you would be with us. We understand you. We like you. We are easy-going people; and we are rich people. That will appeal to you. Turania is a poor place when all is said. Five-eighths of it is desert. They dont irrigate as we do. Besides—now I am sure this will appeal to you and to all right-minded men—we are Christians.

ZOZIM. The old uns prefer Mahometans.

THE ENVOY [*shocked*] What!

ZOZIM [*distinctly*] They prefer Mahometans. Whats wrong with that?

THE ENVOY. Well, of all the disgraceful—

THE ELDERLY GENTLEMAN [*diplomatically interrupting his scandalized son-in-law*] There can be no doubt, I am afraid, that by clinging too long to the obsolete features of the old pseudo-Christian Churches we allowed the Mahometans to get ahead of us at a very critical period of the development of the Eastern world. When the Mahometan Reformation took place, it left its followers with the enormous advantage of having the only established religion in the world in whose articles of faith any intelligent and educated person could believe.

THE ENVOY. But what about our Reformation? Dont give the show away,

Poppa. We followed suit, didnt we?

THE ELDERLY GENTLEMAN. Unfortunately, Ambrose, we could not follow suit very rapidly. We had not only a religion to deal with, but a Church.

ZOZIM. What is a Church?

THE ENVOY. Not know what a Church is! Well!

THE ELDERLY GENTLEMAN. You must excuse me; but if I attempted to explain you would only ask me what a bishop is; and that is a question that no mortal man can answer. All I can tell you is that Mahomet was a truly wise man; for he founded a religion without a Church; consequently when the time came for a Reformation of the mosques there were no bishops and priests to obstruct it. Our bishops and priests prevented us for two hundred years from following suit; and we have never recovered the start we lost then. I can only plead that we did reform our Church at last. No doubt we had to make a few compromises as a matter of good taste; but there is now very little in our Articles of Religion that is not accepted as at least allegorically true by our Higher Criticism.

THE ENVOY [*encouragingly*] Besides, does it matter? Why, *I* have never read the Articles in my life; and I am Prime Minister! Come! if my services in arranging for the reception of a colonizing party would be acceptable, they are at your disposal. And when I say a reception I mean a reception. Royal honors, mind you! A salute of a hundred and one guns! The streets lined with troops! The Guards turned out at the Palace! Dinner at the Guildhall!

ZOZIM. Discourage me if I know what youre talking about! I wish Zoo would come: she understands these things. All I can tell you is that the general opinion among the Colonizers is in favor of beginning in a country where the people are of a different color from us; so that we can make short work without any risk of mistakes.

THE ENVOY. What do you mean by short work? I hope—

ZOZIM [*with obviously feigned geniality*] Oh, nothing, nothing, nothing. We are thinking of trying North America: thats all. You see, the Red Men of that country used to be white. They passed through a period of sallow complexions, followed by a period of no complexions at all, into the red characteristic of their climate. Besides, several cases of long life have occurred in North America. They joined us here; and their stock soon reverted to the original white of these islands.

THE ELDERLY GENTLEMAN. But have you considered the possibility of your colony turning red?

ZOZIM. That wont matter. We are not particular about our pigmentation. The old books mention red-faced Englishmen: they appear to have been common objects at one time.

THE ELDERLY GENTLEMAN [*very persuasively*] But do you think you would be popular in North America? It seems to me, if I may say so, that on your own shewing you need a country in which society is organized in a series of highly exclusive circles, in which the privacy of private life is very jealously guarded, and in which no one presumes to speak to anyone else without an introduction following a strict examination of social credentials. It is only in such a country that persons of special tastes and attainments can form a little world of their own, and protect themselves absolutely from intrusion by common persons. I think I may claim that our British society has developed this exclusiveness to perfection. If you would pay us a visit and see the working of our caste system, our club system, our guild system, you would admit that nowhere else in the world, least of all, perhaps in North America, which has a regrettable tradition of social promiscuity, could you keep yourselves so entirely to yourselves.

ZOZIM [*good-naturedly embarrassed*] Look here. There is no good discussing this. I had rather not explain; but it wont make any difference to our Colonizers what sort of short-livers they come across. We shall arrange all that. Never mind how. Let us join the ladies.

THE ELDERLY GENTLEMAN [*throwing off his diplomatic attitude and abandoning himself to despair*] We understand you only too well, sir. Well, kill us. End the lives you have made miserably unhappy by opening up to us the possibility that any of us may live three hundred years. I solemnly curse that possibility. To you it may be a blessing, because you do live three hundred years. To us, who live less than a hundred, whose flesh is as grass, it is the most unbearable burden our poor tortured humanity has ever groaned under.

THE ENVOY. Hullo, Poppa! Steady! How do you make that out?

ZOZIM. What is three hundred years? Short enough, if you ask me. Why, in the old days you people lived on the assumption that you were going to last out for ever and ever and ever. Immortal, you thought yourselves. Were you any happier then?

THE ELDERLY GENTLEMAN. As President of the Baghdad Historical Society I am in a position to inform you that the communities which took this monstrous pretension seriously were the most wretched of which we have any record. My Society has printed an editio princeps of the works of the father of history, Thucyderodotus Macolly-buckle. Have you read his account of what was blasphemously called the Perfect City of God, and the attempt made to reproduce it in the northern part of these islands by Jonhobsnoxius, called the Leviathan? Those misguided people sacrificed the fragment of life that was granted to them to an imaginary immortality. They crucified the prophet who told them to take no thought for the morrow, and that here and now was their Australia: Australia being a term signifying paradise, or an eternity of bliss. They tried to produce a condition of death in life: to mortify the flesh, as they called it.

ZOZIM. Well, you are not suffering from that, are you? You have not a mortified air.

THE ELDERLY GENTLEMAN. Naturally we are not absolutely insane and suicidal. Nevertheless we impose on ourselves abstinences and disciplines and studies that are meant to prepare us for living three centuries. And we seldom live one. My childhood was made unnecessarily painful, my boyhood unnecessarily laborious, by ridiculous preparations for a length of days which the chances were fifty thousand to one against my ever attaining. I have been cheated out of the natural joys and freedoms of my life by this dream to which the existence of these islands and their oracles gives a delusive possibility of realization. I curse the day when long life was invented, just as the victims of Jonhobsnoxius cursed the day when eternal life was invented.

ZOZIM. Pooh! You could live three centuries if you chose.

THE ELDERLY GENTLEMAN. That is what the fortunate always say to the unfortunate. Well, I do not choose. I accept my three score and ten years. If they are filled with usefulness, with justice, with mercy, with good-will: if they are the lifetime of a soul that never loses its honor and a brain that never loses its eagerness, they are enough for me, because these things are infinite and eternal, and can make ten of my years as long as thirty of yours. I shall not conclude by saying live as long as you like and be damned to you, because I have risen for the moment far above any ill-will to you or to any fellow-creature; but I am your equal before that eternity in which the difference between your lifetime and mine is as the difference between one drop of water and three in the eyes of the Almighty Power from which we have both proceeded.

ZOZIM [*impressed*] You spoke that piece very well, Daddy. I couldnt talk like that if I tried. It sounded fine. Ah! here comes the ladies.

To his relief, they have just appeared on the threshold of the temple.

THE ELDERLY GENTLEMAN [*passing from exaltation to distress*] It means nothing to him: in this land of discouragement the sublime has become the ridiculous. [*Turning on the hopelessly puzzled Zozim*] 'Behold, thou hast made my days as it were a span long; and mine age is even as nothing in respect of thee.'

{Poppa, Poppa: dont look like

THE WIFE. [*running*] {that.

THE DAUGHTER. [*to him*] {Oh, granpa, whats the matter?

ZOZIM [*with a shrug*] Discouragement!

THE ELDERLY GENTLEMAN [*throwing off the women with a superb gesture*] Liar! [*Recollecting himself, he adds, with noble courtesy, raising his hat and bowing*] I beg your pardon, sir; but I am NOT discouraged.

A burst of orchestral music, through which a powerful gong sounds, is heard from the temple. Zoo, in a purple robe, appears in the doorway.

ZOO. Come. The oracle is ready.

Zozim motions them to the threshold with a wave of his staff. The Envoy and the Elderly Gentleman take off their hats and go into the temple on tiptoe, Zoo leading the way. The Wife and Daughter, frightened as they are, raise their heads uppishly and follow flatfooted, sustained by a sense of their Sunday clothes and social consequence. Zozim remains in the portico, alone.

ZOZIM [*taking off his wig, beard, and robe, and bundling them under his arm*] Ouf! [*He goes home*].

ACT III

Inside the temple. A gallery overhanging an abyss. Dead silence. The gallery is brightly lighted; but beyond is a vast gloom, continually changing in intensity. A shaft of violet light shoots upward; and a very harmonious and silvery carillon chimes. When it ceases the violet ray vanishes.

Zoo comes along the gallery, followed by the Envoy's daughter, his wife, the Envoy himself, and the Elderly Gentleman. The two men are holding their hats with the brims near their noses, as if prepared to pray into them at a moment's notice. Zoo halts: they all follow her example. They contemplate the void with awe. Organ music of the kind called sacred in the nineteenth century begins. Their awe deepens. The violet ray, now a diffused mist, rises again from the abyss.

THE WIFE [*to Zoo, in a reverent whisper*] Shall we kneel?

ZOO [*loudly*] Yes, if you want to. You can stand on your head if you like. [*She sits down carelessly on the gallery railing, with her back to the abyss*].

THE ELDERLY GENTLEMAN [*jarred by her callousness*] We desire to behave in a becoming manner.

ZOO. Very well. Behave just as you feel. It doesn't matter how you behave. But keep your wits about you when the pythoness ascends, or you will forget the questions you have come to ask her.

THE ENVOY {[*very nervous, takes out a paper to refresh his memory*] Ahem!

THE DAUGHTER { [*alarmed*] The pythoness? Is she a snake?

THE ELDERLY GENTLEMAN. Tch-ch! The priestess of the oracle. A sybil. A prophetess. Not a snake.

THE WIFE. How awful!

ZOO. I'm glad you think so.

THE WIFE. Oh dear! Dont you think so?

ZOO. No. This sort of thing is got up to impress you, not to impress me.

THE ELDERLY GENTLEMAN. I wish you would let it impress us, then, madam.

I am deeply impressed; but you are spoiling the effect.

ZOO. You just wait. All this business with colored lights and chords on that old organ is only tomfoolery. Wait til you see the pythoness.

The Envoy's wife falls on her knees, and takes refuge in prayer.

THE DAUGHTER [*trembling*] Are we really going to see a woman who has lived three hundred years?

ZOO. Stuff! Youd drop dead if a tertiary as much as looked at you. The oracle is only a hundred and seventy; and you'll find it hard enough to stand her.

THE DAUGHTER [*piteously*] Oh! [*she falls on her knees*].

THE ENVOY. Whew! Stand by me, Poppa. This is a little more than I bargained for. Are you going to kneel; or how?

THE ELDERLY GENTLEMAN. Perhaps it would be in better taste.

The two men kneel.

The vapor of the abyss thickens; and a distant roll of thunder seems to come from its depths. The pythoness, seated on her tripod, rises slowly from it. She has discarded the insulating robe and veil in which she conversed with Napoleon, and is now draped and hooded in voluminous folds of a single piece of grey-white stuff. Something supernatural about her terrifies the beholders, who throw themselves on their faces. Her outline flows and waves: she is almost distinct at moments, and again vague and shadowy: above all, she is larger than life-size, not enough to be measured by the flustered congregation, but enough to affect them with a dreadful sense of her supernaturalness.

ZOO. Get up, get up. Do pull yourselves together, you people.

The Envoy and his family, by shuddering negatively, intimate that it is impossible. The Elderly Gentleman manages to get on his hands and knees.

ZOO. Come on, Daddy: you are not afraid. Speak to her. She wont wait here all day for you, you know.

THE ELDERLY GENTLEMAN [*rising very deferentially to his feet*] Madam: you will excuse my very natural nervousness in addressing, for the first time in my life, a—a—a—a goddess. My friend and relative the Envoy is unhinged. I throw myself upon your indulgence—

ZOO [*interrupting him intolerantly*] Dont throw yourself on anything belonging to her or you will go right through her and break your neck. She isnt solid, like you.

THE ELDERLY GENTLEMAN. I was speaking figuratively—

ZOO. You have been told not to do it. Ask her what you want to know; and be quick about it.

THE ELDERLY GENTLEMAN [*stooping and taking the prostrate Envoy by the shoulders*] Ambrose: you must make an effort. You cannot go back to Baghdad without the answers to your questions.

THE ENVOY [*rising to his knees*] I shall be only too glad to get back alive on any terms. If my legs would support me I'd just do a bunk straight for the ship.

THE ELDERLY GENTLEMAN. No, no. Remember: your dignity—

THE ENVOY. Dignity be damned! I'm terrified. Take me away, for God's sake.

THE ELDERLY GENTLEMAN [*producing a brandy flask and taking the cap off*] Try some of this. It is still nearly full, thank goodness!

THE ENVOY [*clutching it and drinking eagerly*] Ah! Thats better. [*He tries to drink again. Finding that he has emptied it, he hands it back to his father-in-law upside down*].

THE ELDERLY GENTLEMAN [*taking it*] Great heavens! He has swallowed half-a-pint of neat brandy. [*Much perturbed, he screws the cap on again, and pockets the flask*].

THE ENVOY [*staggering to his feet; pulling a paper from his pocket; and speaking with boisterous confidence*] Get up, Molly. Up with you, Eth.

The two women rise to their knees.

THE ENVOY. What I want to ask is this. [*He refers to the paper*]. Ahem! Civilization has reached a crisis. We are at the parting of the ways. We stand on the brink of the Rubicon. Shall we take the plunge? Already a leaf has been torn out of the book of the Sybil. Shall we wait until the whole volume is consumed? On our right is the crater of the volcano: on our left the precipice. One false step, and we go down to annihilation dragging the whole human race with us. [*He pauses for breath*].

THE ELDERLY GENTLEMAN [*recovering his spirits under the familiar stimulus of political oratory*] Hear, hear!

ZOO. What are you raving about? Ask your question while you have the chance. What is it you want to know?

THE ENVOY [*patronizing her in the manner of a Premier debating with a very young member of the Opposition*] A young woman asks me a question. I am always glad to see the young taking an interest in politics. It is an impatient question; but it is a practical question, an intelligent question. She asks why we seek to lift a corner of the veil that shrouds the future from our feeble vision.

ZOO. I don't. I ask you to tell the oracle what you want, and not keep her sitting there all day.

THE ELDERLY GENTLEMAN [*warmly*] Order, order!

ZOO. What does 'Order, order!' mean?

THE ENVOY. I ask the august oracle to listen to my voice—

ZOO. You people seem never to tire of listening to your voices; but it doesn't amuse us. What do you want?

THE ENVOY. I want, young woman, to be allowed to proceed without unseemly interruptions.

A low roll of thunder comes from the abyss.

THE ELDERLY GENTLEMAN. There! Even the oracle is indignant. [*To the Envoy*] Do not allow yourself to be put down by this lady's rude clamor,

Ambrose. Take no notice. Proceed.

THE ENVOY'S WIFE. I cant bear this much longer, Amby. Remember: I havn't had any brandy.

HIS DAUGHTER [*trembling*] There are serpents curling in the vapor. I am afraid of the lightning. Finish it, Papa; or I shall die.

THE ENVOY [*sternly*] Silence. The destiny of British civilization is at stake. Trust me. I am not afraid. As I was saying—where was I?

ZOO. I don't know. Does anybody?

THE ELDERLY GENTLEMAN [*tactfully*] You were just coming to the election, I think.

THE ENVOY [*reassured*] Just so. The election. Now what we want to know is this: ought we to dissolve in August, or put it off until next spring?

ZOO. Dissolve? In what? [*Thunder*]. Oh! My fault this time. That means that the oracle understands you, and desires me to hold my tongue.

THE ENVOY [*fervently*] I thank the oracle.

THE WIFE [*to Zoo*] Serve you right!

THE ELDERLY GENTLEMAN. Before the oracle replies, I should like to be allowed to state a few of the reasons why, in my opinion, the Government should hold on until the spring. In the first—

Terrific lightning and thunder. The Elderly Gentleman is knocked flat; but as he immediately sits up again dazedly it is clear that he is none the worse for the shock. The ladies cower in terror. The Envoy's hat is blown off; but he seizes it just as it quits his temples, and holds it on with both hands. He is recklessly drunk, but quite articulate, as he seldom speaks in public without taking stimulants beforehand.

THE ENVOY [*taking one hand from his hat to make a gesture of stilling the tempest*] Thats enough. We know how to take a hint. I'll put the case in three words. I am the leader of the Potterbill party. My party is in power. I am Prime Minister. The Opposition—the Rotterjacks—have won every bye-election for the last six months. They—

THE ELDERLY GENTLEMAN [*scrambling heatedly to his feet*] Not by fair means. By bribery, by misrepresentation, by pandering to the vilest prejudices [*muttered thunder*]—I beg your pardon [*he is silent*].

THE ENVOY. Never mind the bribery and lies. The oracle knows all about that. The point is that though our five years will not expire until the year after next, our majority will be eaten away at the bye-elections by about Easter. We can't wait: we must start some question that will excite the public, and go to the country on it. But some of us say do it now. Others say wait til the spring. We cant make up our minds one way or the other. Which would you advise?

ZOO. But what is the question that is to excite your public?

THE ENVOY. That doesnt matter. I dont know yet. We will find a question all right enough. The oracle can foresee the future: we cannot. [*Thunder*]. What does that mean? What have I done now?

ZOO. [*severely*] How often must you be told that we cannot foresee the future? There is no such thing as the future until it is the present.

THE ELDERLY GENTLEMAN. Allow me to point out, madam, that when the Potterbill party sent to consult the oracle fifteen years ago, the oracle prophesied that the Potterbills would be victorious at the General Election; and they were. So it is evident that the oracle can foresee the future, and is sometimes willing to reveal it.

THE ENVOY. Quite true. Thank you, Poppa. I appeal now, over your head, young woman, direct to the August Oracle, to repeat the signal favor conferred on my illustrious predecessor, Sir Fuller Eastwind, and to answer me exactly as he was answered.

The oracle raises her hands to command silence.

ALL. Sh-sh-sh!

Invisible trombones utter three solemn blasts in the manner of Die Zauberflöte.

THE ELDERLY GENTLEMAN. May I—

ZOO [*quickly*] Hush. The oracle is going to speak.

THE ORACLE. Go home, poor fool.

She vanishes; and the atmosphere changes to prosaic daylight. Zoo comes off the railing; throws off her robe; makes a bundle of it; and tucks it under her arm. The magic and mystery are gone. The women rise to their feet. The Envoy's party stare at one another helplessly.

ZOO. The same reply, word for word, that your illustrious predecessor, as you call him, got fifteen years ago. You asked for it; and you got it. And just think of all the important questions you might have asked. She would have answered them, you know. It is always like that. I will go and arrange to have you sent home: you can wait for me in the entrance hall [*she goes out*].

THE ENVOY. What possessed me to ask for the same answer old Eastwind got?

THE ELDERLY GENTLEMAN. But it was not the same answer. The answer to Eastwind was an inspiration to our party for years. It won us the election.

THE ENVOY'S DAUGHTER. I learnt it at school, granpa. It wasn't the same at all. I can repeat it. [*She quotes*] 'When Britain was cradled in the west, the east wind hardened her and made her great.

Whilst the east wind prevails Britain shall prosper. The east wind shall wither Britain's enemies in the day of contest. Let the Rotterjacks look to it.'

THE ENVOY. The old man invented that. I see it all. He was a doddering old ass when he came to consult the oracle. The oracle naturally said 'Go home, poor fool.' There was no sense in saying that to me; but as that girl said, I asked for it. What else could the poor old chap do but fake up an answer fit for publication? There were whispers about it; but nobody believed them. I believe them now.

THE ELDERLY GENTLEMAN. Oh, I cannot admit that Sir Fuller Eastwind was capable of such a fraud.

THE ENVOY. He was capable of anything: I knew his private secretary.

And now what are we going to say? You don't suppose I am going back to

Baghdad to tell the British Empire that the oracle called me a fool, do you?

THE ELDERLY GENTLEMAN. Surely we must tell the truth, however painful it may be to our feelings.

THE ENVOY. I am not thinking of my feelings: I am not so selfish as that, thank God. I am thinking of the country: of our party. The truth, as you call it, would put the Rotterjacks in for the next twenty years. It would be the end of me politically. Not that I care for that: I am only too willing to retire if you can find a better man. Dont hesitate on my account.

THE ELDERLY GENTLEMAN. No, Ambrose: you are indispensable. There is no one else.

THE ENVOY. Very well, then. What are you going to do?

THE ELDERLY GENTLEMAN. My dear Ambrose, you are the leader of the party, not I. What are you going to do?

THE ENVOY. I am going to tell the exact truth; thats what I'm going to do. Do you take me for a liar?

THE ELDERLY GENTLEMAN [*puzzled*] Oh. I beg your pardon. I understood you to say—

THE ENVOY [*cutting him short*] You understood me to say that I am going back to Baghdad to tell the British electorate that the oracle repeated to me, word for word, what it said to Sir Fuller Eastwind fifteen years ago. Molly and Ethel can bear me out. So must you, if you are an honest man. Come on.

He goes out, followed by his wife and daughter.

THE ELDERLY GENTLEMAN [*left alone and shrinking into an old and desolate figure*] What am I to do? I am a most perplexed and wretched man. [*He falls on his knees, and stretches his hands in entreaty over the abyss*]. I invoke the oracle. I cannot go back and connive at a blasphemous lie. I implore guidance.

The Pythoness walks in on the gallery behind him, and touches him on the shoulder. Her size is now natural. Her face is hidden by her hood. He flinches as if from an electric shock; turns to her; and cowers, covering his eyes in terror.

THE ELDERLY GENTLEMAN. No: not close to me. I'm afraid I can't bear it.

THE ORACLE [*with grave pity*] Come: look at me. I am my natural size now: what you saw there was only a foolish picture of me thrown on a cloud by a lantern. How can I help you?

THE ELDERLY GENTLEMAN. They have gone back to lie about your answer. I cannot go with them. I cannot live among people to whom nothing is real. I have become incapable of it through my stay here. I implore to be allowed to stay.

THE ORACLE. My friend: if you stay with us you will die of discouragement.

THE ELDERLY GENTLEMAN. If I go back I shall die of disgust and despair.

I take the nobler risk. I beg you, do not cast me out.

He catches her robe and holds her.

THE ORACLE. Take care. I have been here one hundred and seventy years.

Your death does not mean to me what it means to you.

THE ELDERLY GENTLEMAN. It is the meaning of life, not of death, that makes banishment so terrible to me.

THE ORACLE. Be it so, then. You may stay.

She offers him her hands. He grasps them and raises himself a little by clinging to her. She looks steadily into his face. He stiffens; a little convulsion shakes him; his grasp relaxes; and he falls dead.

THE ORACLE [*looking down at the body*] Poor shortlived thing! What else could I do for you?

PART V.

As Far as Thought can Reach

Summer afternoon in the year 31,920 A.D. A sunlit glade at the southern foot of a thickly wooded hill. On the west side of it, the steps and columned porch of a dainty little classic temple. Between it and the hill, a rising path to the wooded heights begins with

rough steps of stones in the moss. On the opposite side, a grove. In the middle of the glade, an altar in the form of a low marble table as long as a man, set parallel to the temple steps and pointing to the hill. Curved marble benches radiate from it into the foreground; but they are not joined to it: there is plenty of space to pass between the altar and the benches.

A dance of youths and maidens is in progress. The music is provided by a few fluteplayers seated carelessly on the steps of the temple. There are no children; and none of the dancers seems younger than eighteen. Some of the youths have beards. Their dress, like the architecture of the theatre and the design of the altar and curved seats, resembles Grecian of the fourth century B.C., freely handled. They move with perfect balance and remarkable grace, racing through a figure like a farandole. They neither romp nor hug in our manner.

At the first full close they clap their hands to stop the musicians, who recommence with a saraband, during which a strange figure appears on the path beyond the temple. He is deep in thought, with his eyes closed and his feet feeling automatically for the rough irregular steps as he slowly descends them. Except for a sort of linen kilt consisting mainly of a girdle carrying a sporran and a few minor pockets, he is naked. In physical hardihood and uprightness he seems to be in the prime of life; and his eyes and mouth shew no signs of age; but his face, though fully and firmly fleshed, bears a network of lines, varying from furrows to hairbreadth reticulations, as if Time had worked over every inch of it incessantly through whole geologic periods. His head is finely domed and utterly bald. Except for his eyelashes he is quite hairless. He is unconscious of his surroundings, and walks right into one of the dancing couples, separating them. He wakes up and stares about him. The couple stop indignantly. The rest stop. The music stops. The youth whom he has jostled accosts him without malice, but without anything that we should call manners.

THE YOUTH. Now, then, ancient sleepwalker, why don't you keep your eyes open and mind where you are going?

THE ANCIENT [*mild, bland, and indulgent*] I did not know there was a nursery here, or I should not have turned my face in this direction. Such accidents cannot always be avoided. Go on with your play: I will turn back.

THE YOUTH. Why not stay with us and enjoy life for once in a way? We will teach you to dance.

THE ANCIENT. No, thank you. I danced when I was a child like you. Dancing is a very crude attempt to get into the rhythm of life. It would be painful to me to go back from that rhythm to your babyish gambols: in fact I could not do it if I tried. But at your age it is pleasant: and I am sorry I disturbed you.

THE YOUTH. Come! own up: arnt you very unhappy? It's dreadful to see you ancients going about by yourselves, never noticing anything, never dancing, never laughing, never singing, never getting anything out of life. None of us are going to be like that when we grow up. It's a dog's life.

THE ANCIENT. Not at all. You repeat that old phrase without knowing that there was once a creature on earth called a dog. Those who are interested in extinct forms of life will tell you that it loved the sound of its own voice and bounded about when it was happy, just as you are doing here. It is you, my children, who are living the dog's life.

THE YOUTH. The dog must have been a good sensible creature: it set you a very wise example. You should let yourself go occasionally and have a good time.

THE ANCIENT. My children: be content to let us ancients go our ways and enjoy ourselves in our own fashion.

He turns to go.

THE MAIDEN. But wait a moment. Why will you not tell us how you enjoy yourself? You must have secret pleasures that you hide from us, and that you never get tired of. I get tired of all our dances and all our tunes. I get tired of all my partners.

THE YOUTH [*suspiciously*] Do you? I shall bear that in mind.

They all look at one another as if there were some sinister significance in what she has said.

THE MAIDEN. We all do: what is the use of pretending we don't? It is natural.

SEVERAL YOUNG PEOPLE. No, no. We don't. It is not natural.

THE ANCIENT. You are older than he is, I see. You are growing up.

THE MAIDEN. How do you know? I do not look so much older, do I?

THE ANCIENT. Oh, I was not looking at you. Your looks do not interest me.

THE MAIDEN. Thank you.

They all laugh.

THE YOUTH. You old fish! I believe you don't know the difference between a man and a woman.

THE ANCIENT. It has long ceased to interest me in the way it interests you. And when anything no longer interests us we no longer know it.

THE MAIDEN. You havnt told me how I shew my age. That is what I want to know. As a matter of fact I am older than this boy here: older than he thinks. How did you find that out?

THE ANCIENT. Easily enough. You are ceasing to pretend that these childish games—this dancing and singing and mating—do not become tiresome and unsatisfying after a while. And you no longer care to pretend that you are younger than you are. These are the signs of adolescence. And then, see these fantastic rags with which you have draped yourself. [*He takes up a piece of her draperies in his hand*]. It is rather badly worn here. Why do you not get a new one?

THE MAIDEN. Oh, I did not notice it. Besides, it is too much trouble. Clothes are a nuisance. I think I shall do without them some day, as you ancients do.

THE ANCIENT. Signs of maturity. Soon you will give up all these toys and games and sweets.

THE YOUTH. What! And be as miserable as you?

THE ANCIENT. Infant: one moment of the ecstasy of life as we live it would strike you dead. [*He stalks gravely out through the grove*].

They stare after him, much damped.

THE YOUTH [*to the musicians*] Let us have another dance.

The musicians shake their heads; get up from their seats on the steps; and troop away into the temple. The others follow them, except the Maiden, who sits down on the altar.

A MAIDEN [*as she goes*] There! The ancient has put them out of countenance. It is your fault, Strephon, for provoking him. [*She leaves, much disappointed*].

A YOUTH. Why need you have cheeked him like that? [*He goes grumbling*].

STREPHON [*calling after him*] I thought it was understood that we are always to cheek the ancients on principle.

ANOTHER YOUTH. Quite right too! There would be no holding them if we didn't. [*He goes*].

THE MAIDEN. Why don't you really stand up to them? *I* did.

ANOTHER YOUTH. Sheer, abject, pusillanimous, dastardly cowardice. Thats why. Face the filthy truth. [*He goes*].

ANOTHER YOUTH [*turning on the steps as he goes out*] And don't you forget, infant, that one moment of the ecstasy of life as I live it would strike you dead. Haha!

STREPHON [*now the only one left, except the Maiden*] Arnt you coming,

Chloe?

THE MAIDEN [*shakes her head*]!

THE YOUTH [*hurrying back to her*] What is the matter?

THE MAIDEN [*tragically pensive*] I dont know.

THE YOUTH. Then there is something the matter. Is that what you mean?

THE MAIDEN. Yes. Something is happening to me. I dont know what.

THE YOUTH. You no longer love me. I have seen it for a month past.

THE MAIDEN. Dont you think all that is rather silly? We cannot go on as if this kind of thing, this dancing and sweethearting, were everything.

THE YOUTH. What is there better? What else is there worth living for?

THE MAIDEN. Oh, stuff! Dont be frivolous.

THE YOUTH. Something horrible is happening to you. You are losing all heart, all feeling. [*He sits on the altar beside her and buries his face in his hands*]. I am bitterly unhappy.

THE MAIDEN. Unhappy! Really, you must have a very empty head if there is nothing in it but a dance with one girl who is no better than any of the other girls.

THE YOUTH. You did not always think so. You used to be vexed if I as much as looked at another girl.

THE MAIDEN. What does it matter what I did when I was a baby? Nothing existed for me then except what I tasted and touched and saw; and I wanted all that for myself, just as I wanted the moon to play with. Now the world is opening out for me. More than the world: the universe. Even little things are turning out to be great things, and becoming intensely interesting. Have you ever thought about the properties of numbers?

THE YOUTH [*sitting up, markedly disenchanted*] Numbers!!! I cannot imagine anything drier or more repulsive.

THE MAIDEN. They are fascinating, just fascinating. I want to get away from our eternal dancing and music, and just sit down by myself and think about numbers.

THE YOUTH [*rising indignantly*] Oh, this is too much. I have suspected you for some time past. We have all suspected you. All the girls say that you have deceived us as to your age: that you are getting flat-chested: that you are bored with us; that you talk to the ancients when you get the chance. Tell me the truth: how old are you?

THE MAIDEN. Just twice your age, my poor boy.

THE YOUTH. Twice my age! Do you mean to say you are four?

THE MAIDEN. Very nearly four.

THE YOUTH [*collapsing on the altar with a groan*] Oh!

THE MAIDEN. My poor Strephon: I pretended I was only two for your sake. I was two when you were born. I saw you break from your shell; and you were such a charming child! You ran round and talked to us all so prettily, and were so handsome and well grown, that I lost my heart to you at once. But now I seem to have lost it altogether: bigger things are taking possession of me. Still, we were very happy in our childish way for the first year, werent we?

STREPHON. I was happy until you began cooling towards me.

THE MAIDEN. Not towards you, but towards all the trivialities of our life here. Just think. I have hundreds of years to live: perhaps thousands. Do you suppose I can spend centuries dancing; listening to flutes ringing changes on a few tunes and a few notes; raving about the beauty of a few pillars and arches; making jingles with words; lying about with your arms round me, which is really neither comfortable nor convenient; everlastingly choosing colors for dresses, and putting them on, and washing; making a business of sitting together at fixed hours to absorb our nourishment; taking little poisons with it to make us delirious enough to imagine we are enjoying ourselves; and then having to pass the nights in shelters lying in cots and losing half our lives in a state of unconsciousness. Sleep is a shameful thing: I have not slept at all for weeks past. I have stolen out at night when you were all lying insensible—quite disgusting, I call it—and wandered about the woods, thinking, thinking, thinking; grasping the world; taking it to pieces; building it up again; devising methods; planning experiments to test the methods; and having a glorious time. Every morning I have come back here with greater and greater reluctance; and I know that the time will soon come—perhaps it has come already—when I shall not come back at all.

STREPHON. How horribly cold and uncomfortable!

THE MAIDEN. Oh, don't talk to me of comfort! Life is not worth living if you have to bother about comfort. Comfort makes winter a torture, spring an illness, summer an oppression, and autumn only a respite. The ancients could make life one long frowsty comfort if they chose. But they never lift a finger to make themselves comfortable. They will not sleep under a roof. They will not clothe themselves: a girdle with a few pockets hanging to it to carry things about in is all they wear: they will sit down on the wet moss or in a gorse bush when there is dry heather within two yards of them. Two years ago, when you were born, I did not understand this. Now I feel that I would not put myself to the trouble of walking two paces for all the comfort in the world.

STREPHON. But you don't know what this means to me. It means that you are dying to me: yes, just dying. Listen to me [*he puts his arm around her*].

THE MAIDEN [*extricating herself*] Dont. We can talk quite as well without touching one another.

STREPHON [*horrified*] Chloe! Oh, this is the worst symptom of all! The ancients never touch one another.

THE MAIDEN. Why should they?

STREPHON. Oh, I don't know. But don't you want to touch me? You used to.

THE MAIDEN. Yes: that is true: I used to. We used to think it would be nice to sleep in one another's arms; but we never could go to sleep because our weight stopped our circulations just above the elbows. Then somehow my feeling began to change bit by bit. I kept a sort of interest in your head and arms long after I lost interest in your whole body. And now that has gone.

STREPHON. You no longer care for me at all, then?

THE MAIDEN. Nonsense! I care for you much more seriously than before; though perhaps not so much for you in particular. I mean I care more for everybody. But I don't want to touch you unnecessarily; and I certainly don't want you to touch me.

STREPHON [*rising decisively*] That finishes it. You dislike me.

THE MAIDEN [*impatiently*] I tell you again, I do not dislike you; but you bore me when you cannot understand; and I think I shall be happier by myself in future. You had better get a new companion. What about the girl who is to be born today?

STREPHON. I do not want the girl who is to be born today. How do I know what she will be like? I want you.

THE MAIDEN. You cannot have me. You must recognize facts and face them. It is no use running after a woman twice your age. I cannot make my childhood last to please you. The age of love is sweet; but it is short; and I must pay nature's debt. You no longer attract me; and I no longer care to attract you. Growth is too rapid at my age: I am maturing from week to week.

STREPHON. You are maturing, as you call it—I call it ageing—from minute to minute. You are going much further than you did when we began this conversation.

THE MAIDEN. It is not the ageing that is so rapid. It is the realization of it when it has actually happened. Now that I have made up my mind to the fact that I have left childhood behind me, it comes home to me in leaps and bounds with every word you say.

STREPHON. But your vow. Have you forgotten that? We all swore together in that temple: the temple of love. You were more earnest than any of us.

THE MAIDEN [*with a grim smile*] Never to let our hearts grow cold! Never to become as the ancients! Never to let the sacred lamp be extinguished! Never to change or forget! To be remembered for ever as the first company of true lovers faithful to this vow so often made and broken by past generations! Ha! ha! Oh, dear!

STREPHON. Well, you need not laugh. It is a beautiful and holy compact; and I will keep it whilst I live. Are you going to break it?

THE MAIDEN. Dear child: it has broken itself. The change has come in spite of my childish vow. [*She rises*]. Do you mind if I go into the woods for a walk by myself? This chat of ours seems to me an unbearable waste of time. I have so much to think of.

STREPHON [*again collapsing on the altar and covering his eyes with his hands*] My heart is broken. [*He weeps*].

THE MAIDEN [*with a shrug*] I have luckily got through my childhood without that experience. It shews how wise I was to choose a lover half my age. [*She goes towards the grove, and is disappearing among the trees, when another youth, older and manlier than Strephon, with crisp hair and firm arms, comes from the temple, and calls to her from the threshold*].

THE TEMPLE YOUTH. I say, Chloe. Is there any sign of the Ancient yet? The hour of birth is overdue. The baby is kicking like mad. She will break her shell prematurely.

THE MAIDEN [*looks across to the hill path; then points up it, and says*] She is coming, Acis.

The Maiden turns away through the grove and is lost to sight among the trees.

Acis [*coming to Strephon*] Whats the matter? Has Chloe been unkind?

STREPHON. She has grown up in spite of all her promises. She deceived us about her age. She is four.

ACIS. Four! I am sorry, Strephon. I am getting on for three myself; and I know what old age is. I hate to say 'I told you so'; but she was getting a little hard set and flat-chested and thin on the top, wasn't she?

STREPHON [*breaking down*] Dont.

ACIS. You must pull yourself together. This is going to be a busy day.

First the birth. Then the Festival of the Artists.

STREPHON [*rising*] What is the use of being born if we have to decay into unnatural, heartless, loveless, joyless monsters in four short years? What use are the artists if they cannot bring their beautiful creations to life? I have a great mind to die and have done with it all. [*He moves away to the corner of the curved seat farthest from the theatre, and throws himself moodily into it*].

An Ancient Woman has descended the hill path during Strephon's lament, and has heard most of it. She is like the He-Ancient, equally bald, and equally without sexual charm, but intensely interesting and rather terrifying. Her sex is discoverable only by her voice, as her breasts are manly, and her figure otherwise not very different. She wears no clothes, but has draped herself rather perfunctorily with a ceremonial robe, and carries two implements like long slender saws. She comes to the altar between the two young men.

THE SHE-ANCIENT [*to Strephon*] Infant: you are only at the beginning of it all. [*To Acis*] Is the child ready to be born?

ACIS. More than ready, Ancient. Shouting and kicking and cursing. We have called to her to be quiet and wait until you come; but of course she only half understands, and is very impatient.

THE SHE-ANCIENT. Very well. Bring her out into the sun.

ACIS [*going quickly into the temple*] All ready. Come along.

Joyous processional music strikes up in the temple.

THE SHE-ANCIENT [*going close to Strephon*]. Look at me.

STREPHON [*sulkily keeping his face averted*] Thank you; but I don't want to be cured. I had rather be miserable in my own way than callous in yours.

THE SHE-ANCIENT. You like being miserable? You will soon grow out of that. [*She returns to the altar*].

The procession, headed by Acis, emerges from the temple. Six youths carry on their shoulders a burden covered with a gorgeous but light pall. Before them certain official maidens carry a new tunic, ewers of water, silver dishes pierced with holes, cloths, and immense sponges. The rest carry wands with ribbons, and strew flowers. The burden is deposited on the altar, and the pall removed. It is a huge egg.

THE SHE-ANCIENT [*freeing her arms from her robe, and placing her saws on the altar ready to her hand in a businesslike manner*] A girl, I think you said?

ACIS. Yes.

THE TUNIC BEARER. It is a shame. Why cant we have more boys?

SEVERAL YOUTHS [*protesting*] Not at all. More girls. We want new girls.

A GIRL'S VOICE FROM THE EGG. Let me out. Let me out. I want to be born.

I want to be born. [*The egg rocks*].

ACIS [*snatching a wand from one of the others and whacking the egg with it*] Be quiet, I tell you. Wait. You will be born presently.

THE EGG. No, no: at once, at once. I want to be born: I want to be born. [*Violent kicking within the egg, which rocks so hard that it has to be held on the altar by the bearers*].

THE SHE-ANCIENT. Silence. [*The music stops; and the egg behaves itself*].

The She-Ancient takes her two saws, and with a couple of strokes rips the egg open. The Newly Born, a pretty girl who would have been guessed as seventeen in our day, sits up in the broken shell, exquisitely fresh and rosy, but with filaments of spare albumen clinging to her here and there.

THE NEWLY BORN [*as the world bursts on her vision*] Oh! Oh!! Oh!!! Oh!!!! [*She continues this ad libitum during the following remonstrances*].

ACIS. Hold your noise, will you?

The washing begins. The Newly Born shrieks and struggles.

A YOUTH. Lie quiet, you clammy little devil.

A MAIDEN. You must be washed, dear. Now quiet, quiet, quiet: be good.

ACIS. Shut your mouth, or I'll shove the sponge in it.

THE MAIDEN. Shut your eyes. Itll hurt if you don't.

ANOTHER MAIDEN. Dont be silly. One would think nobody had ever been born before.

THE NEWLY BORN [*yells*]!!!!!!

ACIS. Serve you right! You were told to shut your eyes.

THE YOUTH. Dry her off quick. I can hardly hold her. Shut it, will you; or I'll smack you into a pickled cabbage.

The dressing begins. The Newly Born chuckles with delight.

THE MAIDEN. Your arms go here, dear. Isnt it pretty? Youll look lovely.

THE NEWLY BORN [*rapturously*] Oh! Oh!! Oh!!! Oh!!!!

ANOTHER YOUTH. No: the other arm: youre putting it on back to front. You are a silly little beast.

ACIS. Here! Thats it. Now youre clean and decent. Up with you! Oopsh! [*He hauls her to her feet. She cannot walk at first, but masters it after a few steps*]. Now then: march. Here she is, Ancient: put her through the catechism.

THE SHE-ANCIENT. What name have you chosen for her?

ACIS. Amaryllis.

THE SHE-ANCIENT [*to the Newly Born*] Your name is Amaryllis.

THE NEWLY BORN. What does it mean?

A YOUTH. Love.

A MAIDEN. Mother.

ANOTHER YOUTH. Lilies.

THE NEWLY BORN [*to Acis*] What is your name?

ACIS. Acis.

THE NEWLY BORN. I love you, Acis. I must have you all to myself. Take me in your arms.

ACIS. Steady, young one. I am three years old.

THE NEWLY BORN. What has that to do with it? I love you; and I must have you or I will go back into my shell again.

ACIS. You cant. It's broken. Look here [*pointing to Strephon, who has remained in his seal without looking round at the birth, wrapped up in his sorrow*]! Look at this poor fellow!

THE NEWLY BORN. What is the matter with him?

ACIS. When he was born he chose a girl two years old for his sweetheart. He is two years old now himself; and already his heart is broken because she is four. That means that she has grown up like this Ancient here, and has left him. If you choose me, we shall have only a year's happiness before I break your heart by growing up. Better choose the youngest you can find.

THE NEWLY BORN. I will not choose anyone but you. You must not grow up. We will love one another for ever. [*They all laugh*]. What are you laughing at?

THE SHE-ANCIENT. Listen, child—

THE NEWLY BORN. Do not come near me, you dreadful old creature. You frighten me.

ACIS. Just give her another moment. She is not quite reasonable yet.

What can you expect from a child less than five minutes old?

THE NEWLY BORN. I think I feel a little more reasonable now. Of course I was rather young when I said that; but the inside of my head is changing very rapidly. I should like to have things explained to me.

ACIS [*to the She-Ancient*] Is she all right, do you think?

The She-Ancient looks at the Newly Born critically; feels her bumps like a phrenologist; grips her muscles and shakes her limbs; examines her teeth; looks into her eyes for a moment; and finally relinquishes her with an air of having finished her job.

THE SHE-ANCIENT. She will do. She may live.

They all wave their hands and shout for joy.

THE NEWLY BORN [*indignant*] I may live! Suppose there had been anything wrong with me?

THE SHE-ANCIENT. Children with anything wrong do not live here, my child. Life is not cheap with us. But you would not have felt anything.

THE NEWLY BORN. You mean that you would have murdered me!

THE SHE-ANCIENT. That is one of the funny words the newly born bring with them out of the past. You will forget it tomorrow. Now listen. You have four years of childhood before you. You will not be very happy; but you will be interested and amused by the novelty of the world; and your companions here will teach you how to keep up an imitation of happiness during your four years by what they call arts and sports and pleasures. The worst of your troubles is already over.

THE NEWLY BORN. What! In five minutes?

THE SHE-ANCIENT. No: you have been growing for two years in the egg. You began by being several sorts of creatures that no longer exist, though we have fossils of them. Then you became human; and you passed in fifteen months through a development that once cost human beings twenty years of awkward stumbling immaturity after they were born. They had to spend fifty years more in the sort of childhood you will complete in four years. And then they died of decay. But you need not die until your accident comes.

THE NEWLY BORN. What is my accident?

THE SHE-ANCIENT. Sooner or later you will fall and break your neck; or a tree will fall on you; or you will be struck by lightning. Something or other must make an end of you some day.

THE NEWLY BORN. But why should any of these things happen to me?

THE SHE-ANCIENT. There is no why. They do. Everything happens to everybody sooner or later if there is time enough. And with us there is eternity.

THE NEWLY BORN. Nothing need happen. I never heard such nonsense in all my life. I shall know how to take care of myself.

THE SHE-ANCIENT. So you think.

THE NEWLY BORN. I don't think: I know. I shall enjoy life for ever and ever.

THE SHE-ANCIENT. If you should turn out to be a person of infinite capacity, you will no doubt find life infinitely interesting. However, all you have to do now is to play with your companions. They have many pretty toys, as you see: a playhouse, pictures, images, flowers, bright fabrics, music: above all, themselves; for the most amusing child's toy is another child. At the end of four years, your mind will change: you will become wise; and then you will be entrusted with power.

THE NEWLY BORN. But I want power now.

THE SHE-ANCIENT. No doubt you do; so that you could play with the world by tearing it to pieces.

THE NEWLY BORN. Only to see how it is made. I should put it all together again much better than before.

THE SHE-ANCIENT. There was a time when children were given the world to play with because they promised to improve it. They did not improve it; and they would have wrecked it had their power been as great as that which you will wield when you are no longer a child. Until then your young companions will instruct you in whatever is necessary. You are not forbidden to speak to the ancients; but you had better not do so, as most of them have long ago exhausted all the interest there is in observing children and conversing with them. [*She turns to go*].

THE NEWLY BORN. Wait. Tell me some things that I ought to do and ought not to do. I feel the need of education. They all laugh at her, except the She-Ancient.

THE SHE-ANCIENT. You will have grown out of that by tomorrow. Do what you please. [*She goes away up the hill path*].

The officials take their paraphernalia and the fragments of the egg back into the temple.

ACIS. Just fancy: that old girl has been going for seven hundred years and hasnt had her fatal accident yet; and she is not a bit tired of it all.

THE NEWLY BORN. How could anyone ever get tired of life?

ACIS. They do. That is, of the same life. They manage to change themselves in a wonderful way. You meet them sometimes with a lot of extra heads and arms and legs: they make you split laughing at them. Most of them have forgotten how to speak: the ones that attend to us have to brush up their knowledge of the language once a year or so. Nothing makes any difference to them that I can see. They never enjoy themselves. I don't know how they can stand it. They don't even come to our festivals of the arts. That old one who saw you out of your shell has gone off to moodle about doing nothing; though she knows that this is Festival Day?

THE NEWLY BORN. What is Festival Day?

ACIS. Two of our greatest sculptors are bringing us their latest masterpieces; and we are going to crown them with flowers and sing dithyrambs to them and dance round them.

THE NEWLY BORN. How jolly! What is a sculptor?

ACIS. Listen here, young one. You must find out things for yourself, and not ask questions. For the first day or two you must keep your eyes and ears open and your mouth shut. Children should be seen and not heard.

THE NEWLY BORN. Who are you calling a child? I am fully a quarter of an hour old [*She sits down on the curved bench near Strephon with her maturest air*].

VOICES IN THE TEMPLE [*all expressing protest, disappointment, disgust*] Oh! Oh! Scandalous. Shameful. Disgraceful. What filth! Is this a joke? Why, theyre ancients! Ss-s-s-sss! Are you mad, Arjillax? This is an outrage. An insult. Yah! etc. etc. etc. [*The malcontents appear on the steps, grumbling*].

ACIS. Hullo: whats the matter? [*He goes to the steps of the temple*].

The two sculptors issue from the temple. One has a beard two feet long: the other is beardless. Between them comes a handsome nymph with marked features, dark hair richly waved, and authoritative bearing.

THE AUTHORITATIVE NYMPH [*swooping down to the centre of the glade with the sculptors, between Acis and the Newly Born*] Do not try to browbeat me, Arjillax, merely because you are clever with your hands. Can you play the flute?

ARJILLAX [*the bearded sculptor on her right*] No, Ecrasia: I cannot. What has that to do with it? [*He is half derisive, half impatient, wholly resolved not to take her seriously in spite of her beauty and imposing tone*].

ECRASIA. Well, have you ever hesitated to criticize our best flute players, and to declare whether their music is good or bad? Pray have I not the same right to criticize your busts, though I cannot make images anymore than you can play?

ARJILLAX. Any fool can play the flute, or play anything else, if he practises enough; but sculpture is a creative art, not a mere business of whistling into a pipe. The sculptor must have something of the god in him. From his hand comes a form which reflects a spirit. He does not make it to please you, nor even to please himself, but because he must. You must take what he gives you, or leave it if you are not worthy of it.

ECRASIA [*scornfully*] Not worthy of it! Ho! May I not leave it because it is not worthy of me?

ARJILLAX. Of you! Hold your silly tongue, you conceited humbug. What do you know about it?

ECRASIA. I know what every person of culture knows: that the business of the artist is to create beauty. Until today your works have been full of beauty; and I have been the first to point that out.

ARJILLAX. Thank you for nothing. People have eyes, havnt they, to see what is as plain as the sun in the heavens without your pointing it out?

ECRASIA. You were very glad to have it pointed out. You did not call me a conceited humbug then. You stifled me with caresses. You modelled me as the genius of art presiding over the infancy of your master here [*indicating the other sculptor*], Martellus.

MARTELLUS [*a silent and meditative listener, shudders and shakes his head, but says nothing*].

ARJILLAX [*quarrelsomely*] I was taken in by your talk.

ECRASIA. I discovered your genius before anyone else did. Is that true, or is it not?

ARJILLAX. Everybody knew I was an extraordinary person. When I was born my beard was three feet long.

ECRASIA. Yes; and it has shrunk from three feet to two. Your genius seems to have been in the last foot of your beard; for you have lost both.

MARTELLUS [*with a short sardonic cachinnation*] Ha! My beard was three and a half feet long when I was born; and a flash of lightning burnt it off and killed the ancient who was delivering me. Without a hair on my chin I became the greatest sculptor in ten generations.

ECRASIA. And yet you come to us today with empty hands. We shall actually have to crown Arjillax here because no other sculptor is exhibiting.

ACIS [*returning from the temple steps to behind the curved seat on the right of the three*] Whats the row, Ecrasia? Why have you fallen out with Arjillax?

ECRASIA. He has insulted us! outraged us! profaned his art! You know how much we hoped from the twelve busts he placed in the temple to be unveiled today. Well, go in and look at them. That is all I have to say. [*She sweeps to the curved seat, and sits down just where Acis is leaning over it*].

ACIS. I am no great judge of sculpture. Art is not my line. What is wrong with the busts?

ECRASIA. Wrong with them! Instead of being ideally beautiful nymphs and youths, they are horribly realistic studies of—but I really cannot bring my lips to utter it.

The Newly Born, full of curiosity, runs to the temple, and peeps in.

ACIS. Oh, stow it, Ecrasia. Your lips are not so squeamish as all that.

Studies of what?

THE NEWLY BORN [*from the temple steps*] Ancients.

ACIS [*surprised but not scandalized*] Ancients!

ECRASIA. Yes, ancients. The one subject that is by the universal consent of all connoisseurs absolutely excluded from the fine arts. [*To Arjillax*] How can you defend such a proceeding?

ARJILLAX. If you come to that, what interest can you find in the statues of smirking nymphs and posturing youths you stick up all over the place?

ECRASIA. You did not ask that when your hand was still skilful enough to model them.

ARJILLAX. Skilful! You high-nosed idiot, I could turn such things out by the score with my eyes bandaged and one hand tied behind me. But what use would they be? They would bore me; and they would bore you if you had any sense. Go in and look at my busts. Look at them again and yet again until you receive the full impression of the intensity of mind that is stamped on them; and then go back to the pretty-pretty confectionery you call sculpture, and see whether you can endure its vapid emptiness. [*He mounts the altar impetuously*] Listen to me, all of you; and do you, Ecrasia, be silent if you are capable of silence.

ECRASIA. Silence is the most perfect expression of scorn. Scorn! That is what I feel for your revolting busts.

ARJILLAX. Fool: the busts are only the beginning of a mighty design.

Listen.

ACIS. Go ahead, old sport. We are listening.

Martellus stretches himself on the sward beside the altar. The Newly Born sits on the temple steps with her chin on her hands, ready to devour the first oration she has ever heard. The rest sit or stand at ease.

ARJILLAX. In the records which generations of children have rescued from the stupid neglect of the ancients, there has come down to us a fable which, like many fables, is not a thing that was done in the past, but a thing that is to be done in the future. It is a legend of a supernatural being called the Archangel Michael.

THE NEWLY BORN. Is this a story? I want to hear a story. [*She runs down the steps and sits on the altar at Arjillax's feet*].

ARJILLAX. The Archangel Michael was a mighty sculptor and painter. He found in the centre of the world a temple erected to the goddess of the centre, called Mediterranea. This temple was full of silly pictures of pretty children, such as Ecrasia approves.

ACIS. Fair play, Arjillax! If she is to keep silent, let her alone.

ECRASIA. I shall not interrupt, Acis. Why should I not prefer youth and beauty to age and ugliness?

ARJILLAX. Just so. Well, the Archangel Michael was of my opinion, not yours. He began by painting on the ceiling the newly born in all their childish beauty. But when he had done this he was not satisfied; for the temple was no more impressive than it had been before, except that there was a strength and promise of greater things about his newly born ones than any other artist had attained to. So he painted all round these newly born a company of ancients, who were in those days called prophets and sybils, whose majesty was that of the mind alone at its intensest. And this painting was acknowledged through ages and ages to be the summit and masterpiece of art. Of course we cannot believe such a tale literally. It is only a legend. We do not believe in archangels; and the notion that thirty thousand years ago sculpture and painting existed, and had even reached the glorious perfection they have reached with us, is absurd. But what men cannot realize they can at least aspire to. They please themselves by pretending that it was realized in a golden age of the past. This splendid legend endured because it lived as a desire in the hearts of the greatest artists. The temple of Mediterranea never was built in the past, nor did Michael the Archangel exist. But today the temple is here [*he points to the porch*]; and the man is here [*he slaps himself on the chest*]. I, Arjillax, am the man. I will place in your theatre such images of the newly born as must satisfy even Ecrasia's appetite for beauty; and I will surround them with ancients more august than any who walk through our woods.

MARTELLUS [*as before*] Ha!

ARJILLAX [*stung*] Why do you laugh, you who have come empty-handed, and, it seems, empty-headed?

ECRASIA [*rising indignantly*] Oh, shame! You dare disparage Martellus, twenty times your master.

ACIS. Be quiet, will you [*he seizes her shoulders and thrusts her back into her seat*].

MARTELLUS. Let him disparage his fill, Ecrasia. [*Sitting up*] My poor Arjillax, I too had this dream. I too found one day that my images of loveliness had become vapid, uninteresting, tedious, a waste of time and material. I too lost my desire to model limbs, and retained only my interest in heads and faces. I, too, made busts of ancients; but I had not your courage: I made them in secret, and hid them from you all.

ARJILLAX [*jumping down from the altar behind Martellus in his surprise and excitement*] You made busts of ancients! Where are they, man? Will you be talked out of your inspiration by Ecrasia and the fools who imagine she speaks with authority? Let us have them all set up beside mine in the theatre. I have opened the way for you; and you see I am none the worse.

MARTELLUS. Impossible. They are all smashed. [*He rises, laughing*].

ALL. Smashed!

ARJILLAX. Who smashed them?

MARTELLUS. I did. That is why I laughed at you just now. You will smash yours before you have completed a dozen of them. [*He goes to the end of the altar and sits down beside the Newly Born*].

ARJILLAX. But why?

MARTELLUS. Because you cannot give them life. A live ancient is better than a dead statue. [*He takes the Newly Born on his knee: she is flattered and voluptuously responsive*]. Anything alive is better than anything that is only pretending to be alive. [*To Arjillax*] Your disillusion with your works of beauty is only the beginning of your disillusion with images of all sorts. As your hand became more skilful and your chisel cut deeper, you strove to get nearer and nearer to truth and reality, discarding the fleeting fleshly lure, and making images of the mind that fascinates to the end. But how can so noble an inspiration be satisfied with any image, even an image of the truth? In the end the intellectual conscience that tore you away from the fleeting in art to the eternal must tear you away from art altogether, because art is false and life alone is true.

THE NEWLY BORN [*flings her arms round his neck and kisses him enthusiastically*].

MARTELLUS [*rises; carries her to the curved bench on his left; deposits her beside Strephon as if she were his overcoat; and continues without the least change of tone*] Shape it as you will, marble remains marble, and the graven image an idol. As I have broken my idols, and cast away my chisel and modelling tools, so will you too break these busts of yours.

ARJILLAX. Never.

MARTELLUS. Wait, my friend. I do not come empty-handed today, as you imagined. On the contrary, I bring with me such a work of art as you have never seen, and an artist who has surpassed both you and me further than we have surpassed all our competitors.

ECRASIA. Impossible. The greatest things in art can never be surpassed.

ARJILLAX. Who is this paragon whom you declare greater than I?

MARTELLUS. I declare him greater than myself, Arjillax.

ARJILLAX [*frowning*] I understand. Sooner than not drown me, you are willing to clasp me round the waist and jump overboard with me.

ACIS. Oh, stop squabbling. That is the worst of you artists. You are always in little squabbling cliques; and the worst cliques are those which consist of one man. Who is this new fellow you are throwing in one another's teeth?

ARJILLAX. Ask Martellus: do not ask me. I know nothing of him. [*He leaves Martellus, and sits down beside Ecrasia, on her left*].

MARTELLUS. You know him quite well. Pygmalion.

ECRASIA [*indignantly*] Pygmalion! That soulless creature! A scientist!

A laboratory person!

ARJILLAX. Pygmalion produce a work of art! You have lost your artistic senses. The man is utterly incapable of modelling a thumb nail, let alone a human figure.

MARTELLUS. That does not matter: I have done the modelling for him.

ARJILLAX. What on earth do you mean?

MARTELLUS [*calling*] Pygmalion: come forth.

Pygmalion, a square-fingered youth with his face laid out in horizontal blocks, and a perpetual smile of eager benevolent interest in everything, and expectation of equal interest from everybody else, comes from the temple to the centre of the group, who regard him for the most part with dismay, as dreading that he will bore them. Ecrasia is openly contemptuous.

MARTELLUS. Friends: it is unfortunate that Pygmalion is constitutionally incapable of exhibiting anything without first giving a lecture about it to explain it; but I promise you that if you will be patient he will shew you the two most wonderful works of art in the world, and that they will contain some of my own very best workmanship. Let me add that they will inspire a loathing that will cure you of the lunacy of art for ever. [*He sits down next the Newly Born, who pouts and turns a very cold right shoulder to him, a demonstration utterly lost on him*].

Pygmalion, with the smile of a simpleton, and the eager confidence of a fanatical scientist, climbs awkwardly on to the altar. They prepare for the worst.

PYGMALION. My friends: I will omit the algebra—

ACIS. Thank God!

PYGMALION [*continuing*]—because Martellus has made me promise to do so. To come to the point, I have succeeded in making artificial human beings. Real live ones, I mean.

INCREDULOUS VOICES. Oh, come! Tell us another. Really, Pyg! Get out. You havnt. What a lie!

PYGMALION. I tell you I have. I will shew them to you. It has been done before. One of the very oldest documents we possess mentions a tradition of a biologist who extracted certain unspecified minerals from the earth and, as it quaintly expresses it, 'breathed into their nostrils the breath of life.' This is the only tradition from the primitive ages which we can regard as really scientific. There are later documents which specify the minerals with great precision, even to their atomic weights; but they are utterly unscientific, because they overlook the element of life which makes all the difference between a mere mixture of salts and gases and a living organism. These mixtures were made over and over again in the crude laboratories of the Silly-Clever Ages; but nothing came of them until the ingredient which the old chronicler called the breath of life was added by this very remarkable early experimenter. In my view he was the founder of biological science.

ARJILLAX. Is that all we know about him? It doesnt amount to very much, does it?

PYGMALION. There are some fragments of pictures and documents which represent him as walking in a garden and advising people to cultivate their gardens. His name has come down to us in several forms. One of them is Jove. Another is Voltaire.

ECRASIA. You are boring us to distraction with your Voltaire. What about your human beings?

ARJILLAX. Aye: come to them.

PYGMALION. I assure you that these details are intensely interesting. [*Cries of No! They are not! Come to the human beings! Conspuez Voltaire! Cut it short, Pyg! interrupt him from all sides*]. You will see their bearing presently. I promise you I will not detain you long. We know, we children of science, that the universe is full of forces and powers and energies of one kind and another. The sap rising in a tree, the stone holding together in a definite crystalline structure, the thought of a philosopher holding his brain in form and operation with an inconceivably powerful grip, the urge of evolution: all these forces can be used by us. For instance, I use the force of gravitation when I put a stone on my tunic to prevent it being blown away when I am bathing. By substituting appropriate machines for the stone we have made not only gravitation our slave, but also electricity and magnetism, atomic attraction, repulsion, polarization, and so forth. But hitherto the vital force has eluded us; so it has had to create machinery for itself. It has created and developed bony structures of the requisite strength, and clothed them with cellular tissue of such amazing sensitiveness that the organs it forms will adapt their action to all the normal variations in the air they breathe, the food they digest, and the circumstances about which they have to think. Yet, as these live bodies, as we call them, are only machines after all, it must be possible to construct them mechanically.

ARJILLAX. Everything is possible. Have you done it? that is the question.

PYGMALION. Yes. But that is a mere fact. What is interesting is the explanation of the fact. Forgive my saying so; but it is such a pity that you artists have no intellect.

ECRASIA [*sententiously*] I do not admit that. The artist divines by inspiration all the truths that the so-called scientist grubs up in his laboratory slowly and stupidly long afterwards.

ARJILLAX [*to Ecrasia, quarrelsomely*] What do you know about it? You are not an artist.

ACIS. Shut your heads, both of you. Let us have the artificial men. Trot them out, Pygmalion.

PYGMALION. It is a man and a woman. But I really must explain first.

ALL [*groaning*]!!!

PYGMALION. Yes: I—

ACIS. We want results, not explanations.

PYGMALION [*hurt*] I see I am boring you. Not one of you takes the least interest in science. Good-bye. [*He descends from the altar and makes for the temple*].

SEVERAL YOUTHS AND MAIDENS [*rising and rushing to him*] No, no. Dont go. Dont be offended. We want to see the artificial pair. We will listen. We are tremendously interested. Tell us all about it.

PYGMALION [*relenting*] I shall not detain you two minutes.

ALL. Half an hour if you like. Please go on, Pygmalion. [*They rush him back to the altar, and hoist him on to it*]. Up you go.

They return to their former places.

PYGMALION. As I told you, lots of attempts were made to produce protoplasm in the laboratory. Why were these synthetic plasms, as they called them, no use?

ECRASIA. We are waiting for you to tell us.

THE NEWLY BORN [*modelling herself on Ecrasia, and trying to outdo her intellectually*] Clearly because they were dead.

PYGMALION. Not bad for a baby, my pet. But dead and alive are very loose terms. You are not half as much alive as you will be in another month or so. What was wrong with the synthetic protoplasm was that it could not fix and conduct the Life Force. It was like a wooden magnet or a lightning conductor made of silk: it would not take the current.

ACIS. Nobody but a fool would make a wooden magnet, and expect it to attract anything.

PYGMALION. He might if he were so ignorant as not to be able to distinguish between wood and soft iron. In those days they were very ignorant of the differences between things, because their methods of analysis were crude. They mixed up messes that were so like protoplasm that they could not tell the difference. But the difference was there, though their analysis was too superficial and incomplete to detect it. You must remember that these poor devils were very little better than our idiots: we should never dream of letting one of them survive the day of its birth. Why, the Newly Born there already knows by instinct many things that their greatest physicists could hardly arrive at by forty years of strenuous study. Her simple direct sense of space-time and quantity unconsciously solves problems which cost their most famous mathematicians years of prolonged and laborious calculations requiring such intense mental application that they frequently forgot to breathe when engaged in them, and almost suffocated themselves in consequence.

ECRASIA. Leave these obscure prehistoric abortions; and come back to your synthetic man and woman.

PYGMALION. When I undertook the task of making synthetic men, I did not waste my time on protoplasm. It was evident to me that if it were possible to make protoplasm in the laboratory, it must be equally possible to begin higher up and make fully evolved muscular and nervous tissues, bone, and so forth. Why make the seed when the making of the flower would be no greater miracle? I tried thousands of combinations before I succeeded in producing anything that would fix high-potential Life Force.

ARJILLAX. High what?

PYGMALION. High-po-tential. The Life Force is not so simple as you think. A high-potential current of it will turn a bit of dead tissue into a philosopher's brain. A low-potential current will reduce the same bit of tissue to a mass of corruption. Will you believe me when I tell you that, even in man himself, the Life Force used to slip suddenly down from its human level to that of a fungus, so that men found their flesh no longer growing as flesh, but proliferating horribly in a lower form which was called cancer, until the lower form of life killed the higher, and both perished together miserably?

MARTELLUS. Keep off the primitive tribes, Pygmalion. They interest you; but they bore these young things.

PYGMALION. I am only trying to make you understand. There was the Life Force raging all round me: there was I, trying to make organs that would capture it as a battery captures electricity, and tissues that would conduct it and operate it. It was easy enough to make eyes more perfect than our own, and ears with a larger range of sound; but they could neither see nor hear, because they were not susceptible to the Life Force. But it was far worse when I discovered how to make them susceptible; for the first thing that happened was that they ceased to be eyes and ears and turned into heaps of maggots.

ECRASIA. Disgusting! Please stop.

ACIS. If you don't want to hear, go away. You go ahead, Pyg.

PYGMALION. I went ahead. You see, the lower potentials of the Life Force could make maggots, but not human eyes or ears. I improved the tissue until it was susceptible to a higher potential.

ARJILLAX [*intensely interested*] Yes; and then?

PYGMALION. Then the eyes and ears turned into cancers.

ECRASIA. Oh, hideous!

PYGMALION. Not at all. That was a great advance. It encouraged me so much that I put aside the eyes and ears, and made a brain. It wouldn't take the Life Force at all until I had altered its constitution a dozen times; but when it did, it took a much higher potential, and did not dissolve; and neither did the eyes and ears when I connected them up with the brain. I was able to make a sort of monster: a thing without arms or legs; and it really and truly lived for half-an-hour.

THE NEWLY BORN. Half-an-hour! What good was that? Why did it die?

PYGMALION. Its blood went wrong. But I got that right; and then I went ahead with a complete human body: arms and legs and all. He was my first man.

ARJILLAX. Who modelled him?

PYGMALION. I did.

MARTELLUS. Do you mean to say you tried your own hand before you sent for me?

PYGMALION. Bless you, yes, several times. My first man was the ghastliest creature: a more dreadful mixture of horror and absurdity than you who have not seen him can conceive.

ARJILLAX. If you modelled him, he must indeed have been a spectacle.

PYGMALION. Oh, it was not his shape. You see I did not invent that. I took actual measurements and moulds from my own body. Sculptors do that sometimes, you know; though they pretend they don't.

MARTELLUS. Hm!

ARJILLAX. Hah!

PYGMALION. He was all right to look at, at first, or nearly so. But he behaved in the most appalling manner; and the subsequent developments were so disgusting that I really cannot describe them to you. He seized all sorts of things and swallowed them. He drank every fluid in the laboratory. I tried to explain to him that he must take nothing that he could not digest and assimilate completely; but of course he could not understand me. He assimilated a little of what he swallowed; but the process left horrible residues which he had no means of getting rid of. His blood turned to poison; and he perished in torments, howling. I then perceived that I had produced a prehistoric man; for there are certain traces in our own bodies of arrangements which enabled the earlier forms of mankind to renew their bodies by swallowing flesh and grains and vegetables and all sorts of unnatural and hideous foods, and getting rid of what they could not digest.

ECRASIA. But what a pity he died! What a glimpse of the past we have lost! He could have told us stories of the Golden Age.

PYGMALION. Not he. He was a most dangerous beast. He was afraid of me, and actually tried to kill me by snatching up things and striking at me with them. I had to give him two or three pretty severe shocks before I convinced him that he was at my mercy.

THE NEWLY BORN. Why did you not make a woman instead of a man? She would have known how to behave herself.

MARTELLUS. Why did you not make a man and a woman? Their children would have been interesting.

PYGMALION. I intended to make a woman; but after my experience with the man it was out of the question.

ECRASIA. Pray why?

PYGMALION. Well, it is difficult to explain if you have not studied prehistoric methods of reproduction. You see the only sort of men and women I could make were men and women just like us as far as their bodies were concerned. That was how I killed the poor beast of a man. I hadnt provided for his horrible prehistoric methods of feeding himself. Suppose the woman had reproduced in some prehistoric way instead of being oviparous as we are? She couldn't have done it with a modern female body. Besides, the experiment might have been painful.

ECRASIA. Then you have nothing to shew us at all?

PYGMALION. Oh yes I have. I am not so easily beaten as that. I set to work again for months to find out how to make a digestive system that would deal with waste products and a reproductive system capable of internal nourishment and incubation.

ECRASIA. Why did you not find out how to make them like us?

STREPHON [*crying out in his grief for the first time*] Why did you not make a woman whom you could love? That was the secret you needed.

THE NEWLY BORN. Oh yes. How true! How great of you, darling Strephon! [*She kisses him impulsively*].

STREPHON [*passionately*] Let me alone.

MARTELLUS. Control your reflexes, child.

THE NEWLY BORN. My what!

MARTELLUS. Your reflexes. The things you do without thinking. Pygmalion is going to shew you a pair of human creatures who are all reflexes and nothing else. Take warning by them.

THE NEWLY BORN. But wont they be alive, like us?

PYGMALION. That is a very difficult question to answer, my dear. I confess I thought at first I had created living creatures; but Martellus declares they are only automata. But then Martellus is a mystic: *I* am a man of science. He draws a line between an automaton and a living organism. I cannot draw that line to my own satisfaction.

MARTELLUS. Your artificial men have no self-control. They only respond to stimuli from without.

PYGMALION. But they are conscious. I have taught them to talk and read; and now they tell lies. That is so very lifelike.

MARTELLUS. Not at all. If they were alive they would tell the truth. You can provoke them to tell any silly lie; and you can foresee exactly the sort of lie they will tell. Give them a clip below the knee, and they will jerk their foot forward. Give them a clip in their appetites or vanities or any of their lusts and greeds, and they will boast and lie, and affirm and deny, and hate and love without the slightest regard to the facts that are staring them in the face, or to their own obvious limitations. That proves that they are automata.

PYGMALION [*unconvinced*] I know, dear old chap; but there really is some evidence that we are descended from creatures quite as limited and absurd as these. After all, the baby there is three-quarters an automaton. Look at the way she has been going on!

THE NEWLY BORN [*indignantly*] What do you mean? How have I been going on?

ECRASIA. If they have no regard for truth, they can have no real vitality.

PYGMALION. Truth is sometimes so artificial: so relative, as we say in the scientific world, that it is very hard to feel quite sure that what is false and even ridiculous to us may not be true to them.

ECRASIA. I ask you again, why did you not make them like us? Would any true artist be content with less than the best?

PYGMALION. I couldnt. I tried. I failed. I am convinced that what I am about to shew you is the very highest living organism that can be produced in the laboratory. The best tissues we can manufacture will not take as high potentials as the natural product: that is where Nature beats us. You dont seem to understand, any of you, what an enormous triumph it was to produce consciousness at all.

ACIS. Cut the cackle; and come to the synthetic couple.

SEVERAL YOUTHS AND MAIDENS. Yes, yes. No more talking. Let us have them. Dry up, Pyg; and fetch them along. Come on: out with them! The synthetic couple.

PYGMALION [*waving his hands to appease them*] Very well, very well. Will you please whistle for them? They respond to the stimulus of a whistle.

All who can, whistle like streetboys.

ECRASIA [*makes a wry face and puts her fingers in her ears*]!

PYGMALION. Sh-sh-sh! Thats enough: thats enough: thats enough. [*Silence*]. Now let us have some music. A dance tune. Not too fast.

The flutists play a quiet dance.

MARTELLUS. Prepare yourselves for something ghastly.

Two figures, a man and woman of noble appearance, beautifully modelled and splendidly attired, emerge hand in hand from the temple. Seeing that all eyes are fixed on them, they halt on the steps, smiling with gratified vanity. The woman is on the man's left.

PYGMALION [*rubbing his hands with the purring satisfaction of a creator*] This way, please.

The Figures advance condescendingly and pose themselves centrally between the curved seats.

PYGMALION. Now if you will be so good as to oblige us with a little something. You dance so beautifully, you know. [*He sits down next Martellus, and whispers to him*] It is extraordinary how sensitive they are to the stimulus of flattery.

The Figures, with a gracious air, dance pompously, but very passably. At the close they bow to one another.

ON ALL HANDS [*clapping*] Bravo! Thank you. Wonderful! Splendid.

Perfect.

The Figures acknowledge the applause in an obvious condition of swelled head.

THE NEWLY BORN. Can they make love?

PYGMALION. Yes: they can respond to every stimulus. They have all the reflexes. Put your arm round the man's neck, and he will put his arm round your body. He cannot help it.

THE FEMALE FIGURE [*frowning*] Round mine, you mean.

PYGMALION. Yours, too, of course, if the stimulus comes from you.

ECRASIA. Cannot he do anything original?

PYGMALION. No. But then, you know, I do not admit that any of us can do anything really original, though Martellus thinks we can.

ACIS. Can he answer a question?

PYGMALION. Oh yes. A question is a stimulus, you know. Ask him one.

ACIS [*to the Male Figure*] What do you think of what you see around you? Of us, for instance, and our ways and doings?

THE MALE FIGURE. I have not seen the newspaper today.

THE FEMALE FIGURE. How can you expect my husband to know what to think of you if you give him his breakfast without his paper?

MARTELLUS. You see. He is a mere automaton.

THE NEWLY BORN. I don't think I should like him to put his arm round my neck. I don't like them. [*The Male Figure looks offended, and the Female jealous*]. Oh, I thought they couldn't understand. Have they feelings?

PYGMALION. Of course they have. I tell you they have all the reflexes.

THE NEWLY BORN. But feelings are not reflexes.

PYGMALION. They are sensations. When the rays of light enter their eyes and make a picture on their retinas, their brains become conscious of the picture and they act accordingly. When the waves of sound started by your speaking enter their ears and record a disparaging remark on their keyboards, their brains become conscious of the disparagement and resent it accordingly. If you did not disparage them they would not resent it. They are merely responding to a stimulus.

THE MALE FIGURE. We are part of a cosmic system. Free will is an illusion. We are the children of Cause and Effect. We are the Unalterable, the Irresistible, the Irresponsible, the Inevitable.

My name is Ozymandias, king of kings:
Look on my works, ye mighty, and despair.

There is a general stir of curiosity at this.

ACIS. What the dickens does he mean?

THE MALE FIGURE. Silence, base accident of Nature. This [*taking the hand of the Female Figure and introducing her*] is Cleopatra-Semiramis, consort of the king of kings, and therefore queen of queens. Ye are things hatched from eggs by the brainless sun and the blind fire; but the king of kings and queen of queens are not accidents of the egg: they are thought-out and hand-made to receive the sacred Life Force. There is one person of the king and one of the queen; but the Life Force of the king and queen is all one: the glory equal, the majesty coeternal. Such as the king is so is the queen, the king thought-out and hand-made, the queen thought-out and hand-made. The actions of the king are caused, and therefore determined, from the beginning of the world to the end; and the actions of the queen are likewise. The king logical and predetermined and inevitable, and the queen logical and predetermined and inevitable. And yet they are not two logical and predetermined and inevitable, but one logical and predetermined and inevitable. Therefore confound not the persons, nor divide the substance: but worship us twain as one throne, two in one and one in two, lest by error ye fall into irretrievable damnation.

THE FEMALE FIGURE. And if any say unto you 'Which one?' remember that though there is one person of the king and one of the queen, yet these two persons are not alike, but are woman and man, and that as woman was created after man, the skill and practice gained in making him were added to her, wherefore she is to be exalted above him in all personal respects, and—

THE MALE FIGURE. Peace, woman; for this is a damnable heresy. Both Man and Woman are what they are and must do what they must according to the eternal laws of Cause and Effect. Look to your words; for if they enter my ear and jar too repugnantly on my sensorium, who knows that the inevitable response to that stimulus may not be a message to my muscles to snatch up some heavy object and break you in pieces.

The Female Figure picks up a stone and is about to throw it at her consort.

ARJILLAX [*springing up and shouting to Pygmalion, who is fondly watching the Male Figure*] Look out, Pygmalion! Look at the woman!

Pygmalion, seeing what is happening, hurls himself on the Female Figure and wrenches the stone out of her hand. All spring up in consternation.

ARJILLAX. She meant to kill him.

STREPHON. This is horrible.

THE FEMALE FIGURE [*wrestling with Pygmalion*] Let me go. Let me go, will you [*she bites his hand*].

PYGMALION [*releasing her and staggering*] Oh!

A general shriek of horror echoes his exclamation. He turns deadly pale, and supports himself against the end of the curved seat.

THE FEMALE FIGURE [*to her consort*] You would stand there and let me be treated like this, you unmanly coward.

Pygmalion falls dead.

THE NEWLY BORN. Oh! Whats the matter? Why did he fall! What has happened to him?

They look on anxiously as Martellus kneels down and examines the body of Pygmalion.

MARTELLUS. She has bitten a piece out of his hand nearly as large as a finger nail: enough to kill ten men. There is no pulse, no breath.

ECRASIA. But his thumb is clinched.

MARTELLUS. No: it has just straightened out. See! He has gone. Poor

Pygmalion!

THE NEWLY BORN. Oh! [*She weeps*].

STREPHON. Hush, dear: thats childish.

THE NEWLY BORN [*subsiding with a sniff*]!!

MARTELLUS [*rising*] Dead in his third year. What a loss to Science!

ARJILLAX. Who cares about Science? Serve him right for making that pair of horrors!

THE MALE FIGURE [*glaring*] Ha!

THE FEMALE FIGURE. Keep a civil tongue in your head, you.

THE NEWLY BORN. Oh, do not be so unkind, Arjillax. You will make water come out of my eyes again.

MARTELLUS [*contemplating the Figures*] Just look at these two devils. I modelled them out of the stuff Pygmalion made for them. They are masterpieces of art. And see what they have done! Does that convince you of the value of art, Arjillax!

STREPHON. They look dangerous. Keep away from them.

ECRASIA. No need to tell us that, Strephon. Pf! They poison the air.

THE MALE FIGURE. Beware, woman. The wrath of Ozymandias strikes like the lightning.

THE FEMALE FIGURE. You just say that again if you dare, you filthy creature.

ACIS. What are you going to do with them, Martellus? You are responsible for them, now that Pygmalion has gone.

MARTELLUS. If they were marble it would be simple enough: I could smash them. As it is, how am I to kill them without making a horrible mess?

THE MALE FIGURE [*posing heroically*] Ha! [*He declaims*]

Come one: come all: this rock shall fly
From its firm base as soon as I.

THE FEMALE FIGURE [*fondly*] My man! My hero husband! I am proud of you.

I love you.

MARTELLUS. We must send out a message for an ancient.

ACIS. Need we bother an ancient about such a trifle? It will take less than half a second to reduce our poor Pygmalion to a pinch of dust. Why not calcine the two along with him?

MARTELLUS. No: the two automata are trifles; but the use of our powers of destruction is never a trifle. I had rather have the case judged.

The He-Ancient emerges from the grove. The Figures are panic-stricken.

THE HE-ANCIENT [*mildly*] Am I wanted? I feel called. [*Seeing the body of Pygmalion, and immediately taking a sterner tone*] What! A child lost! A life wasted! How has this happened?

THE FEMALE FIGURE [*frantically*] I didn't do it. It was not me. May

I be struck dead if I touched him! It was he [*pointing to the Male Figure*].

ALL [*amazed at the lie*] Oh!

THE MALE FIGURE. Liar. You bit him. Everyone here saw you do it.

THE HE-ANCIENT. Silence. [*Going between the Figures*] Who made these two loathsome dolls?

THE MALE FIGURE [*trying to assert himself with his knees knocking*] My name is Ozymandias, king of—

THE HE-ANCIENT [*with a contemptuous gesture*] Pooh!

THE MALE FIGURE [*falling on his knees*] Oh dont, sir. Dont. She did it, sir: indeed she did.

THE FEMALE FIGURE [*howling lamentably*] Boohoo! oo! ooh!

THE HE-ANCIENT. Silence, I say.

He knocks the Male Automaton upright by a very light flip under the chin. The Female Automaton hardly dares to sob. The immortals contemplate them with shame and loathing. The She-Ancient comes from the trees opposite the temple.

THE SHE-ANCIENT. Somebody wants me. What is the matter? [*She comes to the left hand of the Female Figure, not seeing the body of Pygmalion*].

Pf! [*Severely*] You have been making dolls. You must not: they are not only disgusting: they are dangerous.

THE FEMALE FIGURE [*snivelling piteously*] I'm not a doll, mam. I'm only poor Cleopatra-Semiramis, queen of queens. [*Covering her face with her hands*] Oh, don't look at me like that, mam. I meant no harm. He hurt me: indeed he did.

THE HE-ANCIENT. The creature has killed that poor youth.

THE SHE-ANCIENT [*seeing the body of Pygmalion*] What! This clever child, who promised so well!

THE FEMALE FIGURE. He made me. I had as much right to kill him as he had to make me. And how was I to know that a little thing like that would kill him? I shouldn't die if he cut off my arm or leg.

ECRASIA. What nonsense!

MARTELLUS. It may not be nonsense. I daresay if you cut off her leg she would grow another, like the lobsters and the little lizards.

THE HE-ANCIENT. Did this dead boy make these two things?

MARTELLUS. He made them in his laboratory. I moulded their limbs. I am sorry. I was thoughtless: I did not foresee that they would kill and pretend to be persons they were not, and declare things that were false, and wish evil. I thought they would be merely mechanical fools.

THE MALE FIGURE. Do you blame us for our human nature?

THE FEMALE FIGURE. We are flesh and blood and not angels.

THE MALE FIGURE. Have you no hearts?

ARJILLAX. They are mad as well as mischievous. May we not destroy them?

STREPHON. We abhor them.

THE NEWLY BORN. We loathe them.

ECRASIA. They are noisome.

ACIS. I don't want to be hard on the poor devils; but they are making me feel uneasy in my inside. I never had such a sensation before.

MARTELLUS. I took a lot of trouble with them. But as far as I am concerned, destroy them by all means. I loathed them from the beginning.

ALL. Yes, yes: we all loathe them. Let us calcine them.

THE FEMALE FIGURE. Oh, don't be so cruel. I'm not fit to die. I will never bite anyone again. I will tell the truth. I will do good. Is it my fault if I was not made properly? Kill him; but spare me.

THE MALE FIGURE. No! I have done no harm: she has. Kill her if you like: you have no right to kill me.

THE NEWLY BORN. Do you hear that? They want to have one another killed.

ARJILLAX. Monstrous! Kill them both.

THE HE-ANCIENT. Silence. These things are mere automata: they cannot help shrinking from death at any cost. You see that they have no self-control, and are merely shuddering through a series of reflexes. Let us see whether we cannot put a little more life into them. [*He takes the Male Figure by the hand, and places his disengaged hand on its head*]. Now listen. One of you two is to be destroyed. Which of you shall it be?

THE MALE FIGURE [*after a slight convulsion during which his eyes are fixed on the He-Ancient*] Spare her; and kill me.

STREPHON. Thats better.

THE NEWLY BORN. Much better.

THE SHE-ANCIENT [*handling the Female Automaton in the same manner*]

Which of you shall we kill?

THE FEMALE FIGURE. Kill us both. How could either of us live without the other?

ECRASIA. The woman is more sensible than the man.

The Ancients release the Automata.

THE MALE FIGURE [*sinking to the ground*] I am discouraged. Life is too heavy a burden.

THE FEMALE FIGURE [*collapsing*] I am dying. I am glad. I am afraid to live.

THE NEWLY BORN. I think it would be nice to give the poor things a little music.

ARJILLAX. Why?

THE NEWLY BORN. I don't know. But it would.

The Musicians play.

THE FEMALE FIGURE. Ozymandias: do you hear that? [*She rises on her knees and looks raptly into space*] Queen of queens! [*She dies*].

THE MALE FIGURE [*crawling feebly towards her until he reaches her hand*] I knew I was really a king of kings. [*To the others*] Illusions, farewell: we are going to our thrones. [*He dies*].

The music stops. There is dead silence for a moment.

THE NEWLY BORN. That was funny.

STREPHON. It was. Even the Ancients are smiling.

THE NEWLY BORN. Just a little.

THE SHE-ANCIENT [*quickly recovering her grave and peremptory manner*] Take these two abominations away to Pygmalion's laboratory, and destroy them with the rest of the laboratory refuse. [*Some of them move to obey*]. Take care: do not touch their flesh: it is noxious: lift them by their robes. Carry Pygmalion into the temple; and dispose of his remains in the usual way.

The three bodies are carried out as directed, Pygmalion into the temple by his bare arms and legs, and the two Figures through the grove by their clothes. Martellus superintends the removal of the Figures, Acis that of Pygmalion. Ecrasia, Arjillax, Strephon, and the Newly Born sit down as before, but on contrary benches; so that Strephon and the Newly Born now face the grove, and Ecrasia and Arjillax the temple. The Ancients remain standing at the altar.

ECRASIA [*as she sits down*] Oh for a breeze from the hills!

STREPHON. Or the wind from the sea at the turn of the tide!

THE NEWLY BORN. I want some clean air.

THE HE-ANCIENT. The air will be clean in a moment. This doll flesh that children make decomposes quickly at best; but when it is shaken by such passions as the creatures are capable of, it breaks up at once and becomes horribly tainted.

THE SHE-ANCIENT. Let it be a lesson to you all to be content with lifeless toys, and not attempt to make living ones. What would you think of us ancients if we made toys of you children?

THE NEWLY BORN [*coaxingly*] Why do you not make toys of us? Then you would play with us; and that would be very nice.

THE SHE-ANCIENT. It would not amuse us. When you play with one another you play with your bodies, and that makes you supple and strong; but if we played with you we should play with your minds, and perhaps deform them.

STREPHON. You are a ghastly lot, you ancients. I shall kill myself when

I am four years old. What do you live for?

THE HE-ANCIENT. You will find out when you grow up. You will not kill yourself.

STREPHON. If you make me believe that, I shall kill myself now.

THE NEWLY BORN. Oh no. I want you. I love you.

STREPHON. I love someone else. And she has gone old, old. Lost to me for ever.

THE HE-ANCIENT. How old?

STREPHON. You saw her when you barged into us as we were dancing. She is four.

THE NEWLY BORN. How I should have hated her twenty minutes ago! But I have grown out of that now.

THE HE-ANCIENT. Good. That hatred is called jealousy, the worst of our childish complaints.

Martellus, dusting his hands and puffing, returns from the grove.

MARTELLUS. Ouf! [*He sits down next the Newly Born*] That job's finished.

ARJILLAX. Ancients: I should like to make a few studies of you. Not portraits, of course: I shall idealize you a little. I have come to the conclusion that you ancients are the most interesting subjects after all.

MARTELLUS. What! Have those two horrors, whose ashes I have just deposited with peculiar pleasure in poor Pygmalion's dustbin, not cured you of this silly image-making!

ARJILLAX. Why did you model them as young things, you fool? If Pygmalion had come to me, I should have made ancients of them for him. Not that I should have modelled them any better. I have always said that no one can beat you at your best as far as handwork is concerned. But this job required brains. That is where I should have come in.

MARTELLUS. Well, my brainy boy, you are welcome to try your hand. There are two of Pygmalion's pupils at the laboratory who helped him to manufacture the bones and tissues and all the rest of it. They can turn out a couple of new automatons; and you can model them as ancients if this venerable pair will sit for you.

ECRASIA [*decisively*] No. No more automata. They are too disgusting.

ACIS [*returning from the temple*] Well, thats done. Poor old Pyg!

ECRASIA. Only fancy, Acis! Arjillax wants to make more of those abominable things, and to destroy even their artistic character by making ancients of them.

THE NEWLY BORN. You wont sit for them, will you? Please dont.

THE HE-ANCIENT. Children, listen.

ACIS [*striding down the steps to the bench and seating himself next Ecrasia*] What! Even the Ancient wants to make a speech! Give it mouth,

O Sage.

STREPHON. For heaven's sake don't tell us that the earth was once inhabited by Ozymandiases and Cleopatras. Life is hard enough for us as it is.

THE HE-ANCIENT. Life is not meant to be easy, my child; but take courage: it can be delightful. What

I wanted to tell you is that ever since men existed, children have played with dolls.

ECRASIA. You keep using that word. What are dolls, pray?

THE SHE-ANCIENT. What you call works of art. Images. We call them dolls.

ARJILLAX. Just so. You have no sense of art; and you instinctively insult it.

THE HE-ANCIENT. Children have been known to make dolls out of rags, and to caress them with the deepest fondness.

THE SHE-ANCIENT. Eight centuries ago, when I was a child, I made a rag doll. The rag doll is the dearest of all.

THE NEWLY BORN [*eagerly interested*] Oh! Have you got it still?

THE SHE-ANCIENT. I kept it a full week.

ECRASIA. Even in your childhood, then, you did not understand high art, and adored your own amateur crudities.

THE SHE-ANCIENT. How old are you?

ECRASIA. Eight months.

THE SHE-ANCIENT. When you have lived as long as I have—

ECRASIA [*interrupting rudely*] I shall worship rag dolls, perhaps.

Thank heaven I am still in my prime.

THE HE-ANCIENT. You are still capable of thanking, though you do not know what you thank. You are a thanking little animal, a blaming little animal, a—

ACIS. A gushing little animal.

ARJILLAX. And, as she thinks, an artistic little animal.

ECRASIA [*nettled*] I am an animated being with a reasonable soul and human flesh subsisting. If your Automata had been properly animated, Martellus, they would have been more successful.

THE SHE-ANCIENT. That is where you are wrong, my child. If those two loathsome things had been rag dolls, they would have been amusing and lovable. The Newly Born here would have played with them; and you would all have laughed and played with them too until you had torn them to pieces; and then you would have laughed more than ever.

THE NEWLY BORN. Of course we should. Isnt that funny?

THE HE-ANCIENT. When a thing is funny, search it for a hidden truth.

STREPHON. Yes; and take all the fun out of it.

THE SHE-ANCIENT. Do not be so embittered because your sweetheart has outgrown her love for you. The Newly Born will make amends.

THE NEWLY BORN. Oh yes: I will be more than she could ever have been.

STREPHON. Psha! Jealous!

THE NEWLY BORN. Oh no. I have grown out of that. I love her now because she loved you, and because you love her.

THE HE-ANCIENT. That is the next stage. You are getting on very nicely, my child.

MARTELLUS. Come! what is the truth that was hidden in the rag doll?

THE HE-ANCIENT. Well, consider why you are not content with the rag doll, and must have something more closely resembling a real living creature. As you grow up you make images and paint pictures. Those of you who cannot do that make stories about imaginary dolls. Or you dress yourselves up as dolls and act plays about them.

THE SHE-ANCIENT. And, to deceive yourself the more completely, you take them so very very seriously that Ecrasia here declares that the making of dolls is the holiest work of creation, and the words you put into the mouths of dolls the sacredest of scriptures and the noblest of utterances.

ECRASIA. Tush!

ARJILLAX. Tosh!

THE SHE-ANCIENT. Yet the more beautiful they become the further they retreat from you. You cannot caress them as you caress the rag doll. You cannot cry for them when they are broken or lost, or when you pretend they have been unkind to you, as you could when you played with rag dolls.

THE HE-ANCIENT. At last, like Pygmalion, you demand from your dolls the final perfection of resemblance to life. They must move and speak.

THE SHE-ANCIENT. They must love and hate.

THE HE-ANCIENT. They must think that they think.

THE SHE-ANCIENT. They must have soft flesh and warm, blood.

THE HE-ANCIENT. And then, when you have achieved this as Pygmalion did; when the marble masterpiece is dethroned by the automaton and the homo by the homunculus; when the body and the brain, the reasonable soul and human flesh subsisting, as Ecrasia says, stand before you unmasked as mere machinery, and your impulses are shewn to be nothing but reflexes, you are filled with horror and loathing, and would give worlds to be young enough to play with your rag doll again, since every step away from it has been a step away from love and happiness. Is it not true?

THE SHE-ANCIENT. Speak, Martellus: you who have travelled the whole path.

MARTELLUS. It is true. With fierce joy I turned a temperature of a million degrees on those two things I had modelled, and saw them vanish in an instant into inoffensive dust.

THE SHE-ANCIENT. Speak, Arjillax: you who have advanced from imitating the lightly living child to the intensely living ancient. Is it true, so far?

ARJILLAX. It is partly true: I cannot pretend to be satisfied now with modelling pretty children.

THE HE-ANCIENT. And you, Ecrasia: you cling to your highly artistic dolls as the noblest projections of the Life Force, do you not?

ECRASIA. Without art, the crudeness of reality would make the world unbearable.

THE NEWLY BORN [*anticipating the She-Ancient, who is evidently going to challenge her*] Now you are coming to me, because I am the latest arrival. But I don't understand your art and your dolls at all. I want to caress my darling Strephon, not to play with dolls.

ACIS. I am in my fourth year; and I have got on very well without your dolls. I had rather walk up a mountain and down again than look at all the statues Martellus and Arjillax ever made. You prefer a statue to an automaton, and a rag doll to a statue. So do I; but I prefer a man to a rag doll. Give me friends, not dolls.

THE HE-ANCIENT. Yet I have seen you walking over the mountains alone.

Have you not found your best friend in yourself?

ACIS. What are you driving at, old one? What does all this lead to?

THE HE-ANCIENT. It leads, young man, to the truth that you can create nothing but yourself.

ACIS [*musing*] I can create nothing but myself. Ecrasia: you are clever. Do you understand it? I don't.

ECRASIA. It is as easy to understand as any other ignorant error. What artist is as great as his own works? He can create masterpieces; but he cannot improve the shape of his own nose.

ACIS. There! What have you to say to that, old one?

THE HE-ANCIENT. He can alter the shape of his own soul. He could alter the shape of his nose if the difference between a turned-up nose and a turned-down one were worth the effort. One does not face the throes of creation for trifles.

ACIS. What have you to say to that, Ecrasia?

ECRASIA. I say that if the ancients had thoroughly grasped the theory of fine art they would understand that the difference between a beautiful nose and an ugly one is of supreme importance: that it is indeed the only thing that matters.

THE SHE-ANCIENT. That is, they would understand something they could not believe, and that you do not believe.

ACIS. Just so, mam. Art is not honest: that is why I never could stand much of it. It is all make-believe. Ecrasia never really says things: she only rattles her teeth in her mouth.

ECRASIA. Acis: you are rude.

ACIS. You mean that I wont play the game of make-believe. Well, I don't ask you to play it with me; so why should you expect me to play it with you?

ECRASIA. You have no right to say that I am not sincere. I have found a happiness in art that real life has never given me. I am intensely in earnest about art. There is a magic and mystery in art that you know nothing of.

THE SHE-ANCIENT. Yes, child: art is the magic mirror you make to reflect your invisible dreams in visible pictures. You use a glass mirror to see your face: you use works of art to see your soul. But we who are older use neither glass mirrors nor works of art. We have a direct sense of life. When you gain that you will put aside your mirrors and statues, your toys and your dolls.

THE HE-ANCIENT. Yet we too have our toys and our dolls. That is the trouble of the ancients.

ARJILLAX. What! The ancients have their troubles! It is the first time I ever heard one of them confess it.

THE HE-ANCIENT. Look at us. Look at me. This is my body, my blood, my brain; but it is not me. I am the eternal life, the perpetual resurrection; but [*striking his body*] this structure, this organism, this makeshift, can be made by a boy in a laboratory, and is held back from dissolution only by my use of it. Worse still, it can be broken by a slip of the foot, drowned by a cramp in the stomach, destroyed by a flash from the clouds. Sooner or later, its destruction is certain.

THE SHE-ANCIENT. Yes: this body is the last doll to be discarded. When I was a child, Ecrasia, I, too, was an artist, like your sculptor friends there, striving to create perfection in things outside myself. I made statues: I painted pictures: I tried to worship them.

THE HE-ANCIENT. I had no such skill; but I, like Acis, sought perfection in friends, in lovers, in nature, in things outside myself. Alas! I could not create if. I could only imagine it.

THE SHE-ANCIENT. I, like Arjillax, found out that my statues of bodily beauty were no longer even beautiful to me; and I pressed on and made statues and pictures of men and women of genius, like those in the old fable of Michael Angelo. Like Martellus, I smashed them when I saw that there was no life in them: that they were so dead that they would not even dissolve as a dead body does.

THE HE-ANCIENT. And I, like Acis, ceased to walk over the mountains with my friends, and walked alone; for I found that I had creative power over myself but none over my friends. And then I ceased to walk on the mountains; for I saw that the mountains were dead.

ACIS [*protesting vehemently*] No. I grant you about the friends perhaps; but the mountains are still the mountains, each with its name, its individuality, its upstanding strength and majesty, its beauty—

ECRASIA. What! Acis among the rhapsodists!

THE HE-ANCIENT. Mere metaphor, my poor boy: the mountains are corpses.

ALL THE YOUNG [*repelled*] Oh!

THE HE-ANCIENT. Yes. In the hardpressed heart of the earth, where the inconceivable heat of the sun still glows, the stone lives in fierce atomic convulsion, as we live in our slower way. When it is cast out to the surface it dies like deep-sea fish: what you see is only its cold dead body. We have tapped that central heat as prehistoric man tapped water springs; but nothing has come up alive from those flaming depths: your landscapes, your mountains, are only the world's cast skins and decaying teeth on which we live like microbes.

ECRASIA. Ancient: you blaspheme against Nature and against Man.

THE SHE-ANCIENT. Child, child, how much enthusiasm will you have for man when you have endured eight centuries of him, as I have, and seen him perish by an empty mischance that is yet a certainty? When I discarded my dolls as he discarded his friends and his mountains, it was to myself I turned as to the final reality. Here, and here alone, I could shape and create. When my arm was weak and I willed it to be strong, I could create a roll of muscle on it; and when I understood that, I understood that I could without any greater miracle give myself ten arms and three heads.

THE HE-ANCIENT. I also came to understand such miracles. For fifty years

I sat contemplating this power in myself and concentrating my will.

THE SHE-ANCIENT. So did I; and for five more years I made myself into all sorts of fantastic monsters. I walked upon a dozen legs: I worked with twenty hands and a hundred fingers: I looked to the four quarters of the compass with eight eyes out of four heads. Children fled in amazement from me until I had to hide myself from them; and the ancients, who had forgotten how to laugh, smiled grimly when they passed.

THE HE-ANCIENT. We have all committed these follies. You will all commit them.

THE NEWLY BORN. Oh, do grow a lot of arms and legs and heads for us. It would be so funny.

THE HE-ANCIENT. My child: I am just as well as I am. I would not lift my finger now to have a thousand heads.

THE SHE-ANCIENT. But what would I not give to have no head at all?

ALL THE YOUNG. Whats that? No head at all? Why? How?

THE HE-ANCIENT. Can you not understand?

ALL THE YOUNG [*shaking their heads*] No.

THE SHE-ANCIENT. One day, when I was tired of learning to walk forward with some of my feet and backwards with others and sideways with the rest all at once, I sat on a rock with my four chins resting on four of my palms, and four or my elbows resting on four of my knees. And suddenly it came into my mind that this monstrous machinery of heads and limbs was no more me than my statues had been me, and that it was only an automaton that I had enslaved.

MARTELLUS. Enslaved? What does that mean?

THE SHE-ANCIENT. A thing that must do what you command it is a slave; and its commander is its master. These are words you will learn when your turn comes.

THE HE-ANCIENT. You will also learn that when the master has come to do everything through the slave, the slave becomes his master, since he cannot live without him.

THE SHE-ANCIENT. And so I perceived that I had made myself the slave of a slave.

THE HE-ANCIENT. When we discovered that, we shed our superfluous heads and legs and arms until we had our old shapes again, and no longer startled the children.

THE SHE-ANCIENT. But still I am the slave of this slave, my body. How am

I to be delivered from it?

THE HE-ANCIENT. That, children, is the trouble of the ancients. For whilst we are tied to this tyrannous body we are subject to its death, and our destiny is not achieved.

THE NEWLY BORN. What is your destiny?

THE HE-ANCIENT. To be immortal.

THE SHE-ANCIENT. The day will come when there will be no people, only thought.

THE HE-ANCIENT. And that will be life eternal.

ECRASIA. I trust I shall meet my fatal accident before that day dawns.

ARJILLAX. For once, Ecrasia, I agree with you. A world in which there were nothing plastic would be an utterly miserable one.

ECRASIA. No limbs, no contours, no exquisite lines and elegant shapes, no worship of beautiful bodies, no poetic embraces in which cultivated lovers pretend that their caressing hands are wandering over celestial hills and enchanted valleys, no—

ACIS [*interrupting her disgustedly*] What an inhuman mind you have,

Ecrasia!

ECRASIA. Inhuman!

ACIS. Yes: inhuman. Why don't you fall in love with someone?

ECRASIA. I! I have been in love all my life. I burned with it even in the egg.

ACIS. Not a bit of it. You and Arjillax are just as hard as two stones.

ECRASIA. You did not always think so, Acis.

ACIS. Oh, I know. I offered you my love once, and asked for yours.

ECRASIA. And did I deny it to you, Acis?

ACIS. You didn't even know what love was.

ECRASIA. Oh! I adored you, you stupid oaf, until I found that you were a mere animal.

ACIS. And I made no end of a fool of myself about you until I discovered that you were a mere artist. You appreciated my contours! I was plastic, as Arjillax says. I wasn't a man to you: I was a masterpiece appealing to your tastes and your senses. Your tastes and senses had overlaid the direct impulse of life in you. And because I cared only for our life, and went straight to it, and was bored by your calling my limbs fancy names and mapping me into mountains and valleys and all the rest of it, you called me an animal. Well, I am an animal, if you call a live man an animal.

ECRASIA. You need not explain. You refused to be refined. I did my best to lift your prehistoric impulses on to the plane of beauty, of imagination, of romance, of poetry, of art, of—

ACIS. These things are all very well in their way and in their proper places. But they are not love. They are an unnatural adulteration of love. Love is a simple thing and a deep thing: it is an act of life and not an illusion. Art is an illusion.

ARJILLAX. That is false. The statue comes to life always. The statues of today are the men and women of the next incubation. I hold up the marble figure before the mother and say, 'This is the model you must copy.' We produce what we see. Let no man dare to create in art a thing that he would not have exist in life.

MARTELLUS. Yes: I have been through all that. But you yourself are making statues of ancients instead of beautiful nymphs and swains. And Ecrasia is right about the ancients being inartistic. They are damnably inartistic.

ECRASIA [*triumphant*] Ah! Our greatest artist vindicates me. Thanks,

Martellus.

MARTELLUS. The body always ends by being a bore. Nothing remains beautiful and interesting except thought, because the thought is the life. Which is just what this old gentleman and this old lady seem to think too.

THE SHE-ANCIENT. Quite so.

THE HE-ANCIENT. Precisely.

THE NEWLY BORN [*to the He-Ancient*] But you cant be nothing. What do you want to be?

THE HE-ANCIENT. A vortex.

THE NEWLY BORN. A what?

THE SHE-ANCIENT. A vortex. I began as a vortex: why should I not end as one?

ECRASIA. Oh! That is what you old people are, Vorticists.

ACIS. But if life is thought, can you live without a head?

THE HE-ANCIENT. Not now perhaps. But prehistoric men thought they could not live without tails. I can live without a tail. Why should I not live without a head?

THE NEWLY BORN. What is a tail?

THE HE-ANCIENT A habit of which your ancestors managed to pure themselves.

THE SHE-ANCIENT. None of us now believe that all this machinery of flesh and blood is necessary. It dies.

THE HE-ANCIENT. It imprisons us on this petty planet and forbids us to range through the stars.

ACIS. But even a vortex is a vortex in something. You cant have a whirlpool without water; and you cant have a vortex without gas, or molecules or atoms or ions or electrons or something, not nothing.

THE HE-ANCIENT. No: the vortex is not the water nor the gas nor the atoms: it is a power over these things.

THE SHE-ANCIENT. The body was the slave of the vortex; but the slave has become the master; and we must free ourselves from that tyranny. It is this stuff [*indicating her body*], this flesh and blood and bone and all the rest of it, that is intolerable. Even prehistoric man dreamed of what he called an astral body, and asked who would deliver him from the body of this death.

ACIS [*evidently out of his depth*] I shouldn't think too much about it if I were you. You have to keep sane, you know.

The two Ancients look at one another; shrug their shoulders; and address themselves to their departure.

THE HE-ANCIENT. We are staying too long with you, children. We must go.

All the young people rise rather eagerly.

ARJILLAX. Dont mention it.

THE SHE-ANCIENT. It is tiresome for us, too. You see, children, we have to put things very crudely to you to make ourselves intelligible.

THE HE-ANCIENT. And I am afraid we do not quite succeed.

STREPHON. Very kind of you to come at all and talk to us, I'm sure.

ECRASIA. Why do the other ancients never come and give us a turn?

THE SHE-ANCIENT. It is difficult for them. They have forgotten how to speak; how to read; even how to think in your fashion. We do not communicate with one another in that way or apprehend the world as you do.

THE HE-ANCIENT. I find it more and more difficult to keep up your language. Another century or two and it will be impossible. I shall have to be relieved by a younger shepherd.

ACIS. Of course we are always delighted to see you; but still, if it tries you very severely, we could manage pretty well by ourselves, you know.

THE SHE-ANCIENT. Tell me, Acis: do you ever think of yourself as having to live perhaps for thousands of years?

ACIS. Oh, don't talk about it. Why, I know very well that I have only four years of what any reasonable person would call living; and three and a half of them are already gone.

ECRASIA. You must not mind our saying so; but really you cannot call being an ancient living.

THE NEWLY BORN [*almost in tears*] Oh, this dreadful shortness of our lives! I cannot bear it.

STREPHON. I made up my mind on that subject long ago. When I am three years and fifty weeks old, I shall have my fatal accident. And it will not be an accident.

THE HE-ANCIENT. We are very tired of this subject. I must leave you.

THE NEWLY BORN. What is being tired?

THE SHE-ANCIENT. The penalty of attending to children. Farewell.

The two Ancients go away severally, she into the grove, he up to the hills behind the temple.

ALL. Ouf! [*A great sigh of relief*].

ECRASIA. Dreadful people!

STREPHON. Bores!

MARTELLUS. Yet one would like to follow them; to enter into their life; to grasp their thought; to comprehend the universe as they must.

ARJILLAX. Getting old, Martellus?

MARTELLUS. Well, I have finished with the dolls; and I am no longer jealous of you. That looks like the end. Two hours sleep is enough for me. I am afraid I am beginning to find you all rather silly.

STREPHON. I know. My girl went off this morning. She hadnt slept for weeks. And she found mathematics more interesting than me.

MARTELLUS. There is a prehistoric saying that has come down to us from a famous woman teacher. She said: 'Leave women; and study mathematics.' It is the only remaining fragment of a lost scripture called The Confessions of St Augustin, the English Opium Eater. That primitive savage must have been a great woman, to say a thing that still lives after three hundred centuries. I too will leave women and study mathematics, which I have neglected too long. Farewell, children, my old playmates. I almost wish I could feel sentimental about parting from you; but the cold truth is that you bore me. Do not be angry with me: your turn will come. [*He passes away gravely into the grove*].

ARJILLAX. There goes a great spirit. What a sculptor he was! And now, nothing! It is as if he had cut off his hands.

THE NEWLY BORN. Oh, will you all leave me as he has left you?

ECRASIA. Never. We have sworn it.

STREPHON. What is the use of swearing? She swore. He swore. You have sworn. They have sworn.

ECRASIA. You speak like a grammar.

STREPHON. That is how one ought to speak, isnt it? We shall all be forsworn.

THE NEWLY BORN. Do not talk like that. You are saddening us; and you are chasing the light away. It is growing dark.

ACIS. Night is falling. The light will come back tomorrow.

THE NEWLY BORN. What is tomorrow?

ACIS. The day that never comes. [*He turns towards the temple*].

All begin trooping into the temple.

THE NEWLY BORN [*holding Acis back*] That is no answer. What—

ARJILLAX. Silence. Little children should be seen and not heard.

THE NEWLY BORN [*putting out her tongue at him*]!

ECRASIA. Ungraceful. You must not do that.

THE NEWLY BORN. I will do what I like. But there is something the matter with me. I want to lie down. I cannot keep my eyes open.

ECRASIA. You are falling asleep. You will wake up again.

THE NEWLY BORN [*drowsily*] What is sleep?

ACIS. Ask no questions; and you will be told no lies. [*He takes her by the ear, and leads her firmly towards the temple*].

THE NEWLY BORN. Ai! oi! ai! Dont. I want to be carried. [*She reels into the arms of Acts, who carries her into the temple*].

ECRASIA. Come, Arjillax: you at least are still an artist. I adore you.

ARJILLAX. Do you? Unfortunately for you, I am not still a child. I have grown out of cuddling. I can only appreciate your figure. Does that satisfy you?

ECRASIA. At what distance?

ARJILLAX. Arm's length or more.

ECRASIA. Thank you: not for me. [*She turns away from him*].

ARJILLAX. Ha! ha! [*He strides off into the temple*].

ECRASIA [*calling to Strephon, who is on the threshold of the temple, going in*] Strephon.

STREPHON. No. My heart is broken. [*He goes into the temple*].

ECRASIA. Must I pass the night alone? [*She looks round, seeking another partner; but they have all gone*]. After all, I can imagine a lover nobler than any of you. [*She goes into the temple*].

It is now quite dark. A vague radiance appears near the temple and shapes itself into the ghost of Adam.

A WOMAN'S VOICE [*in the grove*] Who is that?

ADAM. The ghost of Adam, the first father of mankind. Who are you?

THE VOICE. The ghost of Eve, the first mother of mankind.

ADAM. Come forth, wife; and shew yourself to me.

EVE [*appearing near the grove*] Here I am, husband. You are very old.

A VOICE [*in the hills*] Ha! ha! ha!

ADAM. Who laughs? Who dares laugh at Adam?

EVE. Who has the heart to laugh at Eve?

THE VOICE. The ghost of Cain, the first child, and the first murderer. [*He appears between them; and as he does so there is a prolonged hiss*]. Who dares hiss at Cain, the lord of death?

A VOICE. The ghost of the serpent, that lived before Adam and before Eve, and taught them how to bring forth Cain. [*She becomes visible, coiled in the trees*].

A VOICE. There is one that came before the serpent.

THE SERPENT. That is the voice of Lilith, in whom the father and mother were one. Hail, Lilith!

Lilith becomes visible between Cain and Adam.

LILITH. I suffered unspeakably; I tore myself asunder; I lost my life, to make of my one flesh these twain, man and woman. And this is what has come of it. What do you make of it, Adam, my son?

ADAM. I made the earth bring forth by my labor, and the woman bring forth by my love. And this is what has come of it. What do you make of it, Eve, my wife?

EVE. I nourished the egg in my body and fed it with my blood. And now they let it fall as the birds did, and suffer not at all. What do you make of it, Cain, my first-born?

CAIN. I invented killing and conquest and mastery and the winnowing out of the weak by the strong. And now the strong have slain one another; and the weak live for ever; and their deeds do nothing for the doer more than for another. What do you make of it, snake?

THE SERPENT. I am justified. For I chose wisdom and the knowledge of good and evil; and now there is no evil; and wisdom and good are one. It is enough. [*She vanishes*].

CAIN. There is no place for me on earth any longer. You cannot deny that mine was a splendid game while it lasted. But now! Out, out, brief candle! [*He vanishes*].

EVE. The clever ones were always my favorites. The diggers and the fighters have dug themselves in with the worms. My clever ones have inherited the earth. All's well. [*She fades away*].

ADAM. I can make nothing of it, neither head nor tail. What is it all for? Why? Whither? Whence? We were well enough in the garden. And now the fools have killed all the animals; and they are dissatisfied because they cannot be bothered with their bodies! Foolishness, I call it. [*He disappears*].

LILITH. They have accepted the burden of eternal life. They have taken the agony from birth; and their life does not fail them even in the hour of their destruction. Their breasts are without milk: their bowels are gone: the very shapes of them are only ornaments for their children to admire and caress without understanding. Is this enough; or shall I labor again? Shall I bring forth something that will sweep them away and make an end of them as they have swept away the beasts of the garden, and made an end of the crawling things and the flying things and of all them that refuse to live for ever? I had patience with them for many ages: they tried me very sorely. They did terrible things: they embraced death, and said that eternal life was a fable. I stood amazed at the malice and destructiveness of the things I had made: Mars blushed as he looked down on the shame of his sister planet: cruelty and hypocrisy became so hideous that the face of the earth was pitted with the graves of little children among which living skeletons crawled in search of horrible food. The pangs of another birth were already upon me when one man repented and lived three hundred years; and I waited to see what would come of that. And so much came of it that the horrors of that time seem now but an evil dream. They have redeemed themselves from their vileness, and turned away from their sins. Best of all, they are still not satisfied: the impulse I gave them in that day when I sundered myself in twain and launched Man and Woman on the earth still urges them: after passing a million goals they press on to the goal of redemption from the flesh, to the vortex freed from matter, to the whirlpool in pure intelligence that, when the world began, was a whirlpool in pure force. And though all that they have done seems but the first hour of the infinite work of creation, yet I will not supersede them until they have forded this last stream that lies between flesh and spirit, and disentangled their life from the matter that has always mocked it. I can wait: waiting and patience mean nothing to the eternal. I gave the woman the greatest of gifts: curiosity. By that her seed has been saved from my wrath; for I also am curious; and I have waited always to see what they will do tomorrow. Let them feed that appetite well for me. I say, let them dread, of all things, stagnation; for from the moment I, Lilith, lose hope and faith in them, they are doomed. In that hope and faith I have let them live for a moment; and in that moment I have spared them many times. But mightier creatures than they have killed hope and faith, and perished from the earth; and I may not spare them for ever. I am Lilith: I brought life into the whirlpool of force, and compelled my enemy, Matter, to obey a living soul. But in enslaving Life's enemy I made him Life's master; for that is the end of all slavery; and now I shall see the slave set free and the enemy reconciled, the whirlpool become all life and no matter. And because these infants that call themselves ancients are reaching out towards that, I will have patience with them still; though I know well that when they attain it they shall become one with me and supersede me, and Lilith will be only a legend and a lay that has lost its meaning. Of Life only is there no end; and though of its million starry mansions many are empty and many still unbuilt, and though its vast domain is as yet unbearably desert, my seed shall one day fill it and master its matter to its uttermost confines. And for what may be beyond, the eyesight of Lilith is too short. It is enough that there is a beyond. [*She vanishes*].

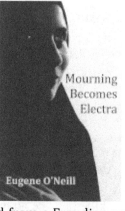

ing Becomes Electra
gene O'Neill
Oxford City Press, 2011
210 pages
ISBN: 978-1-84902-448-8

Available from www.amazon.com, www.amazon.co.uk

Mourning Becomes Electra is a play written by the American playwright Eugene O'Neill. It premiered on Broadway in 1931 and ran for 150 performances.

The story is an updated Greek tragedy and features murder, adultery, incestuous love and revenge. O'Neill's characters have motivations that are influenced by the psychological theories of the 1930s. Hence, it can be understood from a Freudian perspective, with characters displaying Oedipus and Electra complexes.

Mourning Becomes Electra is divided into three plays entitled Homecoming, The Hunted, and The Haunted, with themes corresponding to The Oresteia trilogy by Aeschylus. These plays are normally shown together and, as they each have four or five acts, it is extraordinarily lengthy, often being cut down when produced.

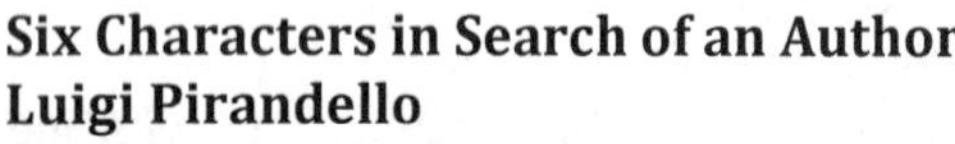

Six Characters in Search of an Author
Luigi Pirandello
Benediction Classics, 2011
104 pages
ISBN: 978-1-84902-461-7
Available from www.amazon.com, www.amazon.co.uk

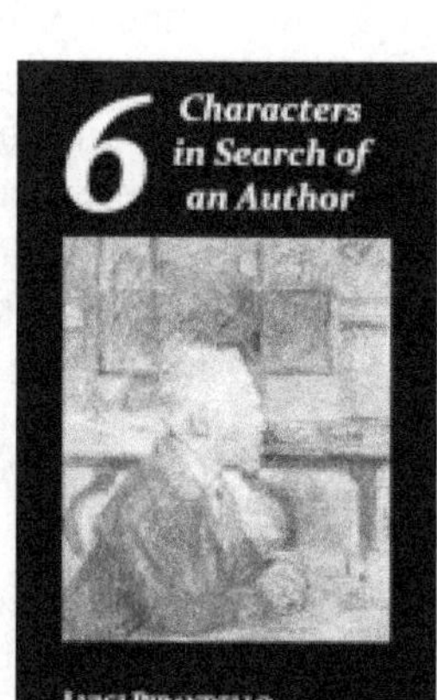

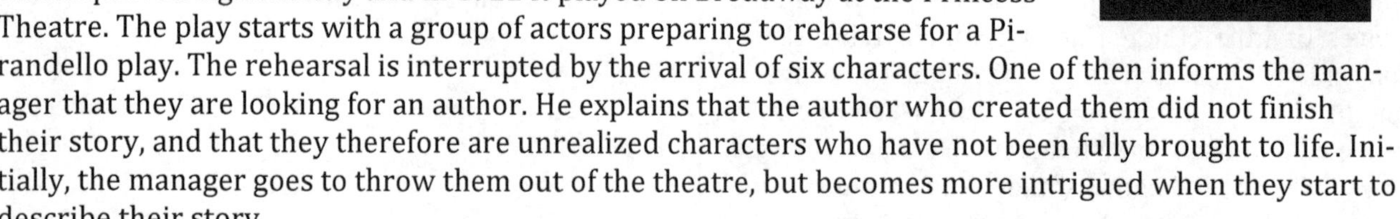

'Six Characters in search of an Author' is a is a satirical tragicomedy play. First performed in 1921 at the Teatro Valle in Rome, it had a very mixed reception, with the audience shouting "Manicomio!" ("Madhouse!"). However, the reception improved significantly and in 1922 it played on Broadway at the Princess Theatre. The play starts with a group of actors preparing to rehearse for a Pirandello play. The rehearsal is interrupted by the arrival of six characters. One of then informs the manager that they are looking for an author. He explains that the author who created them did not finish their story, and that they therefore are unrealized characters who have not been fully brought to life. Initially, the manager goes to throw them out of the theatre, but becomes more intrigued when they start to describe their story.

"THE KINGDOM OF GOD IS WITHIN YOU"
CHRISTIANITY NOT AS A MYSTIC RELIGION BUT AS A NEW THEORY OF LIFE
LEO TOLSTOY
Benediction Classics, 2011
298 pages
ISBN: 978-1-84902-474-7

Available from www.amazon.com, www.amazon.co.uk

A new edition of Tolstoy's non-fiction magnum opus. Gandhi regarded this book, banned in Tolstoy's native Russia, as one of the three greatest influences on him. The ideas Tolstoy that expounds so clearly were revolutionary in his day and still are relevant and challenging today.

We Philologists - Complete Works of Friedrich Nietzsche, Volume 8
Friedrich Nietzsche
Benediction Classics, 2012
82 pages
ISBN: 978-1-78139-141-9

Available from www.amazon.com, www.amazon.co.uk

This is a classic work by the German philologist, poet, composer, author and philosopher, Nietzsche (1844-1900). He critiqued religion, morality, contemporary culture and philosophy, basing his thoughts on whether the idea is life-affirming or life-denying. He was plagued by ill health, a workaholic and phenomenal thinker, and hence his life was both short and very productive, ending in mental collapse. At the age of 24 he remains the youngest ever Chair of Classical Philosophy at the University of Basel. But he rarely gained the respect he deserved within his lifetime. That has since been amended and in the 20th century he was recognised as one of the most significant figures in modern philosophy, most notably in the areas of nihilism, postmodernism and existentialism.

Civilization And Its Discontents
Sigmund W. Freud
Benediction Classics, 2011
148 pages
ISBN: 978-1-84902-274-3

Available from www.amazon.com, www.amazon.co.uk

This is Sigmund Freud's seminal text where he explores what he sees as the fundamental tensions between civilization and the individual. He contends that the greatest friction is between the individual's quest for freedom and civilization's contrary demand for conformity. Thus humankind's primitive instincts to kill and sexual gratification are harmful to human society, so we create laws and severe punishments to prevent murder, rape, and adultery. Freud argues that this results in perpetual feelings of discontent in its citizens.

Eureka: A Prose poem. An Essay on the Material and Spiritual Universe.
Edgar Allan Poe
Benediction Classics, 2011
100 pages
ISBN: 978-1-78139-037-5

Available from www.amazon.com, www.amazon.co.uk

Eureka, A Prose Poem is over 40,000 words in length and it is not a poem! It was Poe's last major work and was based on a lecture Poe presented in 1848, titled "On The Cosmography of the Universe". He had hoped for an audience of hundreds and that the proceeds of the lecture would pay for his new journal "The Stylus". However, only 60 attended and they went away confused. In Eureka, Poe explains the universe and the relationship of people with God based on the proposition "Because Nothing was, therefore All Things are".

om Benediction Books …
..ndering Between Two Worlds: Essays on Faith and Art
Anita Mathias
Benediction Books, 2007
152 pages
ISBN: 0955373700
Available from www.amazon.com, www.amazon.co.uk
In these wide-ranging lyrical essays, Anita Mathias writes, in lush, lovely prose, of her naughty Catholic childhood in Jamshedpur, India; her large, eccentric family in Mangalore, a sea-coast town converted by the Portuguese in the sixteenth century; her rebellion and atheism as a teenager in her Himalayan boarding school, run by German missionary nuns, St. Mary's Convent, Nainital; and her abrupt religious conversion after which she entered Mother Teresa's convent in Calcutta as a novice. Later rich, elegant essays explore the dualities of her life as a writer, mother, and Christian in the United States-- Domesticity and Art, Writing and Prayer, and the experience of being "an alien and stranger" as an immigrant in America, sensing the need for roots.

About the Author

Anita Mathias is the author of *Wandering Between Two Worlds: Essays on Faith and Art*. She has a B.A. and M.A. in English from Somerville College, Oxford University, and an M.A. in Creative Writing from the Ohio State University, USA. Anita won a National Endowment of the Arts fellowship in Creative Nonfiction in 1997. She lives in Oxford, England with her husband, Roy, and her daughters, Zoe and Irene.
Anita's website:
http://www.anitamathias.com, and
Anita's blog Dreaming Beneath the Spires:
http://dreamingbeneaththespires.blogspot.com

The Church That Had Too Much
Anita Mathias
Benediction Books, 2010
52 pages
ISBN: 9781849026567
Available from www.amazon.com, www.amazon.co.uk

The Church That Had Too Much was very well-intentioned. She wanted to love God, she wanted to love people, but she was both hampered by her muchness and the abundance of her possessions, and beset by ambition, power struggles and snobbery. Read about the surprising way The Church That Had Too Much began to resolve her problems in this deceptively simple and enchanting fable.

About the Author

Anita Mathias is the author of *Wandering Between Two Worlds: Essays on Faith and Art*. She has a B.A. and M.A. in English from Somerville College, Oxford University, and an M.A. in Creative Writing from the Ohio State University, USA. Anita won a National Endowment of the Arts fellowship in Creative Nonfiction in 1997. She lives in Oxford, England with her husband, Roy, and her daughters, Zoe and Irene.

Anita's website:
http://www.anitamathias.com, and
Anita's blog Dreaming Beneath the Spires:
http://dreamingbeneaththespires.blogspot.com

CPSIA information can be obtained
at www.ICGtesting.com
Printed in the USA
BVHW081318270220
573383BV00009B/125